KU-023-765

CHARLES DICKENS

The Greatest Novels

So true are these avowals at the present day, that I can now only take the reader into one

confidence more. Of all my books, I like this the best. It will be easily believed that

I am a fond parent to every child of my fancy, and that no one can ever love

that family as dearly as I love them. But, like many fond parents,

I have in my heart of hearts a favourite child.

And his name is David Copperfield.

CHARLES DICKENS

1867

CHARLES DICKENS

The Greatest Novels

Great Expectations, David Copperfield,
Oliver Twist, A Christmas Carol

with illustrations by
F. W. PAILTHORPE, PHIZ,
GEORGE CRUICKSHANK
AND JOHN LEECH

Collector's Library Editions

This edition first published in 2008 by CRW Publishing Limited
69 Gloucester Crescent, London NW1 7EG
under the *Collector's Library Editions* imprint

ISBN   978 1 905716 47 0

Text copyright © CRW Publishing Limited 2008

All rights reserved.
This publication or any part thereof may not be reproduced, stored
in a retrieval system or transmitted in any form or by any means,
electronic, mechanical, photocopying, recording or otherwise,
without prior permission in writing from the publishers.

2 4 6 8 10 9 7 5 3 1

Typeset in Great Britain by Antony Gray
Printed and bound in China by Imago

CONTENTS

Great Expectations

My father's family name being Pirrip, and my christian name Philip, my infant tongue could make of both names nothing longer or more explicit than Pip. So I called myself Pip, and came to be called Pip.

I give Pirrip as my father's family name, on the authority of his tombstone and my sister – Mrs Joe Gargery, who married the blacksmith. As I never saw my father or my mother, and never saw any likeness of either of them (for their days were long before the days of photographs), my first fancies regarding what they were like, were unreasonably derived from their tombstones. The shape of the letters on my father's, gave me an odd idea that he was a square, stout, dark man, with curly black hair. From the character and turn of the inscription, '*Also Georgiana Wife of the Above*', I drew a childish conclusion that my mother was freckled and sickly. To five little stone lozenges, each about a foot and a half long, which were arranged in a neat row beside their grave, and were sacred to the memory of five little brothers of mine – who gave up trying to get a living exceedingly early in that universal struggle – I am indebted for a belief I religiously entertained that they had all been born on their backs with their hands in their trousers-pockets, and had never taken them out in this state of existence.

Ours was the marsh country, down by the river, within, as the river wound, twenty miles of the sea. My first most vivid and broad impression of the identity of things, seems to me to have been gained on a memorable raw afternoon towards evening. At such a time I found out for certain, that this bleak place overgrown with nettles was the churchyard; and that Philip Pirrip, late of this parish, and also Georgiana wife of the above, were dead and buried; and that Alexander, Bartholomew, Abraham, Tobias, and Roger, infant children of the aforesaid, were also dead and buried; and that the dark flat wilderness beyond the churchyard, intersected with dykes and mounds and gates, with scattered cattle feeding on it, was the marshes; and that the low leaden line beyond was the river; and that the distant savage lair from which the wind was rushing, was the sea; and that the small bundle of shivers growing afraid of it all and beginning to cry, was Pip.

'Hold your noise!' cried a terrible voice, as a man started up from among the graves at the side of the church porch. 'Keep still, you little devil, or I'll cut your throat!'

A fearful man, all in coarse grey, with a great iron on his leg. A man with no hat, and with broken shoes, and with an old rag tied round his head. A man who had been soaked in water, and smothered in mud, and lamed by stones, and cut by flints, and stung by nettles, and torn by briars; who limped and shivered, and glared and growled; and whose teeth chattered in his head as he seized me by the chin.

'O! Don't cut my throat, sir,' I pleaded in terror. 'Pray don't do it, sir.'

'Tell us your name!' said the man. 'Quick!'

'Pip, sir.'

'Once more,' said the man, staring at me. 'Give it mouth!'

'Pip. Pip, sir.'

'Show us where you live,' said the man. 'Pint out the place!'

I pointed to where our village lay, on the flat inshore among the alder trees and pollards, a mile or more from the church.

The man, after looking at me for a moment, turned me upside down, and emptied my pockets. There was nothing in them but a piece of bread. When the church came to itself – for he was so sudden and strong that he made it go head over heels before me, and I saw the steeple under my feet – when the church came to itself, I say, I was seated on a high tombstone, trembling, while he ate the bread ravenously.

'You young dog,' said the man, licking his lips, 'what fat cheeks you ha' got.'

I believe they were fat, though I was at that time undersized, for my years, and not strong.

'Darn me if I couldn't eat 'em,' said the man, with a threatening shake of his head, 'and if I han't half a mind to't!'

I earnestly expressed my hope that he wouldn't, and held tighter to the tombstone on which he had put me; partly, to keep myself upon it; partly, to keep myself from crying.

The terrible stranger in the churchyard

'Now lookee here!' said the man. 'Where's your mother?'

'There, sir!' said I.

He started, made a short run, and stopped and looked over his shoulder.

'There, sir!' I timidly explained. 'Also Georgiana. That's my mother.'

' Oh!' said he, coming back. 'And is that your father alonger your mother?'

'Yes, sir,' said I; 'him too; late of this parish.'

'Ha!' he muttered then, considering. 'Who d'ye live with – supposin' you're kindly let to live, which I han't made up my mind about?'

'My sister, sir – Mrs Joe Gargery – wife of Joe Gargery, the blacksmith, sir.'

'Blacksmith, eh?' said he. And looked down at his leg.

After darkly looking at his leg and at me several times, he came closer to my tombstone, took me by both arms, and tilted me back as far as he could hold me; so that his eyes looked most powerfully down into mine, and mine looked most helplessly up into his.

'Now lookee here,' he said, 'the question being whether you're to be let to live. You know what a file is?'

'Yes, sir.'

'And you know what wittles is?'

'Yes, sir.'

After each question he tilted me over a little more, so as to give me a greater sense of helplessness and danger.

'You get me a file.' He tilted me again. 'And you get me wittles.' He tilted me again. 'You bring 'em both to me.' He tilted me again. 'Or I'll have your heart and liver out.' He tilted me again.

I was dreadfully frightened, and so giddy that I clung to him with both hands, and said, 'If you would kindly please to let me keep upright, sir, perhaps I shouldn't be sick, and perhaps I could attend more.'

He gave me a most tremendous dip and roll, so that the church jumped over its own weathercock. Then, he held me by the arms in an upright position on the top of the stone, and went on in these fearful terms: 'You bring me, tomorrow morning early, that file and them wittles. You bring the lot to me, at that old battery over yonder. You do it, and you never dare to say a word or dare to make a sign concerning your having seen such a person as me, or any person sum-ever, and you shall be let to live. You fail, or you go from my words in any partickler, no matter how small it is, and your heart and your liver shall be tore out, roasted and ate. Now, I ain't alone, as you may think I am. There's a young man hid with me, in comparison with which young man I am a angel. That young man hears the words I speak. That young man has a secret way pecooliar to himself, of getting at a boy, and at his heart, and at his liver. It is in wain for a boy to attempt to hide himself from that young man. A boy may lock his door, may be warm in bed, may tuck himself up, may draw the clothes over his head, may think himself comfortable and safe, but that young man will softly creep and creep his way to him and tear him open. I am a keeping that young man from harming

of you at the present moment, with great difficulty. I find it wery hard to hold that young man off of your inside. Now, what do you say?'

I said that I would get him the file, and I would get him what broken bits of food I could, and I would come to him at the battery, early in the morning.

'Say, Lord strike you dead if you don't!' said the man.

I said so and he took me down.

'Now,' he pursued, 'you remember what you've undertook, and you remember that young man, and you get home!'

'Goo–good-night, sir,' I faltered.

'Much of that!' said he, glancing about him over the cold wet flat. 'I wish I was a frog. Or a eel!'

At the same time, he hugged his shuddering body in both his arms – clasping himself, as if to hold himself together – and limped towards the low church wall. As I saw him go, picking his way among the nettles, and among the brambles that bound the green mounds, he looked in my young eyes as if he were eluding the hands of the dead people, stretching up cautiously out of their graves, to get a twist upon his ankle and pull him in.

When he came to the low church wall, he got over it, like a man whose legs were numbed and stiff, and then turned round to look for me. When I saw him turning, I set my face towards home, and made the best use of my legs. But presently I looked over my shoulder, and saw him going on again towards the river, still hugging himself in both arms, and picking his way with his sore feet among the great stones dropped into the marshes here and there, for stepping-places when the rains were heavy, or the tide was in.

The marshes were just a long black horizontal line then, as I stopped to look after him; and the river was just another horizontal line, not nearly so broad nor yet so black; and the sky was just a row of long angry red lines and dense black lines intermixed. On the edge of the river I could faintly make out the only two black things in all the prospect that seemed to be standing upright; one of these was the beacon by which the sailors steered – like an unhooped cask upon a pole – an ugly thing when you were near it; the other a gibbet, with some chains hanging to it which had once held a pirate. The man was limping on towards this latter, as if he were the pirate come to life, and come down, and going back to hook himself up again. It gave me a terrible turn when I thought so; and as I saw the cattle lifting their heads to gaze after him, I wondered whether they thought so too. I looked all round for the horrible young man, and could see no signs of him. But now I was frightened again, and ran home without stopping.

Chapter 2

My sister, Mrs Joe Gargery, was more than twenty years older than I, and had established a great reputation with herself and the neighbours because she had brought me up 'by hand'. Having at that time to find out for myself what the expression meant, and knowing her to have a hard and heavy hand, and to be much in the habit of laying it upon her husband as well as upon me, I supposed that Joe Gargery and I were both brought up by hand.

She was not a good-looking woman, my sister; and I had a general impression that she must have made Joe Gargery marry her by hand. Joe was a fair man, with curls of flaxen hair on each side of his smooth face, and with eyes of such a very undecided blue that they seemed to have somehow got mixed with their own whites. He was a mild, good-natured, sweet-tempered, easy-going, foolish, dear fellow – a sort of Hercules in strength, and also in weakness.

My sister, Mrs Joe, with black hair and eyes, had such a prevailing redness of skin, that I sometimes used to wonder whether it was possible she washed herself with a nutmeg-grater instead of soap. She was tall and bony, and almost always wore a coarse apron, fastened over her figure behind with two loops, and having a square impregnable bib in front, that was stuck full of pins and needles. She made it a powerful merit in herself, and a strong reproach against Joe, that she wore this apron so much. Though I really see no reason why she should have worn it at all: or why, if she did wear it at all, she should not have taken it off every day of her life.

Joe's forge adjoined our house, which was a wooden house, as many of the dwellings in our country were – most of them, at that time. When I ran home from the churchyard, the forge was shut up, and Joe was sitting alone in the kitchen. Joe and I being fellow-sufferers, and having confidences as such, Joe imparted a confidence to me, the moment I raised the latch of the door and peeped in at him opposite to it, sitting in the chimney corner.

'Mrs Joe has been out a dozen times, looking for you, Pip. And she's out now, making it a baker's dozen.'

'Is she?'

'Yes, Pip,' said Joe; 'and what's worse, she's got Tickler with her.'

At this dismal intelligence, I twisted the only button on my waistcoat round and round, and looked in great depression at the fire. Tickler was a wax-ended piece of cane, worn smooth by collision with my tickled frame.

'She sot down,' said Joe, 'and she got up, and she made a grab at Tickler, and she rampaged out. That's what she did,' said Joe, slowly clearing the fire between the lower bars with the poker, and looking at it: 'she rampaged out, Pip.'

'Has she been gone long, Joe?' I always treated him as a larger species of child, and as no more than my equal.

'Well,' said Joe, glancing up at the Dutch clock, 'she's been on the rampage, this last spell, about five minutes, Pip. She's a-coming! Get behind the door, old chap, and have the jack-towel betwixt you.'

I took the advice. My sister, Mrs Joe, throwing the door wide open, and finding an obstruction behind it, immediately divined the cause, and applied Tickler to its further investigation. She concluded by throwing me – I often served as a connubial missile – at Joe, who, glad to get hold of me on any terms, passed me on into the chimney and quietly fenced me up there with his great leg.

'Where have you been, you young monkey?' said Mrs Joe, stamping her foot. 'Tell me directly what you've been doing to wear me away with fret and fright and worrit, or I'd have you out of that corner if you was fifty Pips, and he was five hundred Gargerys.'

'I have only been to the churchyard,' said I, from my stool, crying and rubbing myself.

'Churchyard!' repeated my sister. 'If it warn't for me you'd have been to the churchyard long ago, and stayed there. Who brought you up by hand?'

'You did,' said I.

'And why did I do it, I should like to know?' exclaimed my sister.

I whimpered, 'I don't know.'

'*I* don't!' said my sister. 'I'd never do it again! I know that. I may truly say I've never had this apron of mine off, since born you were. It's bad enough to be a blacksmith's wife (and him a Gargery), without being your mother.'

My thoughts strayed from that question as I looked disconsolately at the fire. For, the fugitive out on the marshes with the ironed leg, the mysterious young man, the file, the food, and the dreadful pledge I was under to commit a larceny on those sheltering premises, rose before me in the avenging coals.

'Hah!' said Mrs Joe, restoring Tickler to his station. 'Church-yard, indeed! You may well say churchyard, you two.' One of us, by the by, had not said it at all. 'You'll drive *me* to the churchyard betwixt you, one of these days, and oh, a pr–r–recious pair you'd be without me!'

As she applied herself to set the tea-things, Joe peeped down at me over his leg, as if he were mentally casting me and himself up, and calculating what kind of pair we practically should make, under the grievous circumstances foreshadowed. After that, he sat feeling his right-side flaxen curls and whisker, and following Mrs Joe about with his blue eyes, as his manner always was at squally times.

My sister had a trenchant way of cutting our bread and butter for us, that never varied. First, with her left hand she jammed the loaf hard and fast against her bib – where it sometimes got a pin into it, and sometimes a needle, which we afterwards got into our mouths. Then she took some butter (not too much) on a knife and spread it on the loaf, in an apothecary kind of way, as if she were making a plaster – using both sides of the knife with a slapping dexterity, and trimming and moulding the butter off round the crust. Then, she gave the knife a final smart wipe on the edge of the plaster, and then sawed a very thick round off the loaf: which she finally, before separating from the loaf, hewed into two halves, of which Joe got one, and I the other.

On the present occasion, though I was hungry, I dared not eat my slice. I felt that I must have something in reserve for my dreadful acquaintance, and his ally the still more dreadful young man. I knew Mrs Joe's housekeeping to be of the strictest kind, and that my larcenous researches might find nothing available in the safe. Therefore I resolved to put my hunk of bread and butter down the leg of my trousers.

The effort of resolution necessary to the achievement of this purpose, I found to be quite awful. It was as if I had to make up my mind to leap from the top of a high house, or plunge into a great depth of water. And it was made the more difficult by the unconscious Joe. In our already-mentioned freemasonry as fellow-sufferers, and in his good-natured companionship with me, it was our evening habit to compare the way we bit through our slices, by silently holding them up to each other's admiration now and then – which stimulated us to new exertions. Tonight, Joe several times invited me, by the display of his fast-diminishing slice, to enter upon our usual friendly competition; but he found me, each time, with my yellow mug of tea on one knee, and my untouched bread and butter on the other. At last, I desperately considered that the thing I contemplated must be done, and that it had best be done in the least improbable manner consistent with the circumstances. I took advantage of a moment when Joe had just looked at me, and got my bread and butter down my leg.

Joe was evidently made uncomfortable by what he supposed to be my loss of appetite, and took a thoughtful bite out of his slice, which he didn't seem to enjoy. He turned it about in his mouth much longer than usual, pondering over it a good deal, and after all gulped it down like a pill. He was about to take another bite, and had just got his head on one side for a good purchase on it, when his eye fell on me, and he saw that my bread and butter was gone.

The wonder and consternation with which Joe stopped on the threshold of his bite and stared at me, were too evident to escape my sister's observation.

'What's the matter now?' said she, smartly, as she put down her cup.

'I say, you know!' muttered Joe, shaking his head at me in a very serious remonstrance. 'Pip, old chap! You'll do yourself a mischief. It'll stick somewhere. You can't have chawed it, Pip.'

'What's the matter *now*?' repeated my sister, more sharply than before.

'If you can cough any trifle on it up, Pip, I'd recommend you to do it,' said Joe, all aghast. 'Manners is manners, but still your elth's your elth.'

By this time, my sister was quite desperate, so she pounced on Joe, and, taking him by the two whiskers, knocked his head for a little while against the wall behind him: while I sat in the corner, looking guiltily on.

'Now, perhaps you'll mention what's the matter,' said my sister, out of breath, 'you staring great stuck pig.'

Joe looked at her in a helpless way; then took a helpless bite, and looked at me again.

'You know, Pip,' said Joe, solemnly, with his last bite in his cheek, and speaking in a confidential voice, as if we two were quite alone, 'you and me is always friends, and I'd be the last to tell upon you, any time. But such a' – he moved his chair, and looked about the floor between us, and then again at me – 'such a most uncommon bolt as that!'

'Been bolting his food, has he?' cried my sister.

'You know, old chap,' said Joe, looking at me, and not at Mrs Joe, with his bite still in his cheek, 'I bolted, myself, when I was your age – frequent – and as a boy I've been among a many bolters; but I never see your bolting equal yet, Pip, and it's a mercy you ain't bolted dead.'

My sister made a dive at me, and fished me up by the hair; saying nothing more than the awful words, 'You come along and be dosed.'

Some medical beast had revived tar-water in those days as a fine medicine, and Mrs Joe always kept a supply of it in the cupboard; having a belief in its virtues correspondent to its nastiness. At the best of times, so much of this elixir was administered to me as a choice restorative, that I was conscious of going about, smelling like a new fence. On this particular evening, the urgency of my case demanded a pint of this mixture, which was poured down my throat, for my greater comfort, while Mrs Joe held my head under her arm, as a boot would be held in a boot-jack. Joe got off with half a pint; but was made to swallow that (much to his disturbance, as he sat slowly munching and meditating before the fire), 'because he had had a turn.' Judging from myself, I should say he certainly had a turn afterwards, if he had had none before.

Conscience is a dreadful thing when it accuses man or boy; but when, in the case of a boy, that secret burden co-operates with another secret burden down the leg of his trousers, it is (as I can testify) a great punishment. The guilty knowledge that I was going to rob Mrs Joe – I never thought I was going to rob Joe, for I never thought of any of the housekeeping property as his – united to the necessity of always keeping one hand on my bread and butter as I sat, or when I was ordered about the kitchen on any small errand, almost drove me out of my mind. Then, as the marsh winds made the fire glow and flare, I thought I heard the voice outside, of the man with the iron on his leg who had sworn me to secrecy, declaring that he couldn't and wouldn't starve until tomorrow, but must be fed now. At other times, I thought, 'What if the young man who was with so much difficulty restrained from imbruing his hands in me, should yield to a constitutional impatience, or should mistake the time, and should think himself accredited to my heart and liver tonight, instead of tomorrow!' If ever anybody's hair stood on end with terror, mine must have done so then. But, perhaps, nobody's ever did?

It was Christmas Eve, and I had to stir the pudding for next day, with a copper-stick, from seven to eight by the Dutch clock. I tried it with the load upon my leg (and that made me think afresh of the man with the load on *his* leg), and found the tendency of exercise to bring the bread and butter out at my ankle, quite unmanageable. Happily I slipped away, and deposited that part of my conscience in my garret bedroom.

'Hark!' said I, when I had done my stirring, and was taking a final warm in the chimney corner before being sent up to bed; 'was that great guns, Joe?'

'Ah!' said Joe. 'There's another conwict off.'

'What does that mean, Joe?' said I.

Mrs Joe, who always took explanations upon herself, said snappishly, 'Escaped. Escaped.' Administering the definition like tar-water.

While Mrs Joe sat with her head bending over her needlework, I put my mouth into the forms of saying to Joe, 'What's a convict?' Joe put *his* mouth into the forms of returning such a highly elaborate answer, that I could make out nothing of it but the single word, 'Pip'.

'There was a conwict off last night,' said Joe, aloud, 'after sunset-gun. And they fired warning of him. And now it appears they're firing warning of another.'

'*Who's* firing?' said I.

'Drat that boy,' interposed my sister, frowning at me over her work, 'what a questioner he is. Ask no questions, and you'll be told no lies.'

It was not very polite to herself, I thought, to imply that I should be told lies by her, even if I did ask questions. But she never was polite, unless there was company.

At this point, Joe greatly augmented my curiosity by taking the utmost pains to open his mouth very wide, and to put it into the form of a word that looked to me like 'sulks'. Therefore, I naturally pointed to Mrs Joe, and put my mouth into the form of saying 'her?' But Joe wouldn't hear of that at all, and again opened his mouth very wide, and shook the form of a most emphatic word out of it. But I could make nothing of the word.

'Mrs Joe,' said I, as a last resort, 'I should like to know – if you wouldn't much mind – where the firing comes from?'

'Lord bless the boy!' exclaimed my sister, as if she didn't quite mean that, but rather the contrary. 'From the Hulks!'

'Oh–h!' said I, looking at Joe. 'Hulks!'

Joe gave a reproachful cough, as much as to say, 'Well, I told you so.'

'And please what's hulks?' said I.

'That's the way with this boy!' exclaimed my sister, pointing me out with her needle and thread, and shaking her head at me. 'Answer him one question, and he'll ask you a dozen directly. Hulks are prison-ships, right 'cross th' meshes.' We always used that name for marshes in our country.

'I wonder who's put into prison-ships, and why they're put there?' said I, in a general way, and with quiet desperation.

It was too much for Mrs Joe, who immediately rose. 'I tell you what, young fellow,' said she, 'I didn't bring you up by hand to badger people's lives out. It would be blame to me, and not praise, if I had. People are put in the hulks because they murder, and because they rob, and forge, and do all sorts of bad; and they always begin by asking questions. Now, you get along to bed!'

I was never allowed a candle to light me to bed, and, as I went upstairs in the dark, with my head tingling – from Mrs Joe's thimble having played the tambourine upon it, to accompany her last words – I felt fearfully sensible of the great convenience that the hulks were handy for me. I was clearly on my way there. I had begun by asking questions, and I was going to rob Mrs Joe.

Since that time, which is far enough away now, I have often thought that few people know what secrecy there is in the young, under terror. No matter how unreasonable the terror, so that it be terror. I was in mortal terror of the young man who wanted my heart and liver; I was in mortal terror of my interlocutor with the iron leg; I was in mortal terror of myself, from whom an awful promise had been extracted; I had no hope of deliverance through my all-powerful sister, who repulsed me at every turn; I am afraid to think of what I might have done on requirement, in the secrecy of my terror.

If I slept at all that night, it was only to imagine myself drifting down the river on a strong spring-tide, to the hulks; a ghostly pirate calling out to me through a speaking-trumpet, as I passed the gibbet-station, that I had better come ashore and be hanged there at once, and not put it off. I was afraid to sleep, even if I had been inclined, for I knew that at the first faint dawn of morning I must rob the pantry. There was no doing it in the night, for there was no getting a light by easy friction then; to have got one, I must have struck it out of flint and steel, and have made a noise like the very pirate himself rattling his chains.

As soon as the great black velvet pall outside my little window was shot with grey, I got up and went downstairs; every board upon the way, and every crack in every board, calling after me, 'Stop thief!' and 'Get up, Mrs Joe!' In the pantry, which was far more abundantly supplied than usual, owing to the season, I was very much alarmed, by a hare hanging up by the heels, whom I rather thought I caught, when my back was half turned, winking. I had no time for verification, no time for selection, no time for anything, for I had no time to spare. I stole some bread, some rind of cheese, about half a jar of mincemeat (which I tied up in my pocket-handkerchief with my last night's slice), some brandy from a stone bottle (which I decanted into a glass bottle I had secretly used for making that intoxicating fluid, Spanish liquorice-water, up in my room; diluting the stone bottle from a jug in the kitchen cupboard), a meat bone with very little on it, and a beautiful round compact pork pie. I was nearly going away without the pie, but I was tempted to mount upon a shelf, to look what it was that was put away so carefully in a covered earthenware dish in a corner, and I found it was the pie, and I took it, in the hope that it was not intended for early use, and would not be missed for some time.

There was a door in the kitchen communicating with the forge; I unlocked and unbolted that door, and got a file from among Joe's tools. Then I put the fastenings as I had found them, opened the door at which I had entered when I ran home last night, shut it, and ran for the misty marshes.

Chapter 3

It was a rimy morning, and very damp. I had seen the damp lying on the outside of my little window, as if some goblin had been crying there all night, and using the window for a pocket-handkerchief. Now I saw the damp lying on the bare hedges and spare grass, like a coarser sort of spiders' webs; hanging itself from twig to twig and blade to blade. On every rail and gate, wet lay clammy, and the marsh-mist was so thick, that the wooden finger on the post directing people to our village – a direction which they never accepted, for they never came there – was invisible to me until I was quite close under it. Then, as I looked up at it, while it dripped, it seemed to my oppressed conscience like a phantom devoting me to the Hulks.

The mist was heavier yet when I got out upon the marshes, so that instead of my running at everything, everything seemed to run at me. This was very disagreeable to a guilty mind. The gates and dykes and banks came bursting at me through the mist, as if they cried as plainly as could be, 'A boy with Somebody else's pork pie! Stop him!' The cattle came upon me with like suddenness, staring out of their eyes, and steaming out of their nostrils, 'Halloa, young thief!' One black ox, with a white cravat on – who even had to my awakened conscience something of a clerical air – fixed me so obstinately with his eyes, and moved his blunt head round in such an accusatory manner as I moved round, that I blubbered out to him, 'I couldn't help it, sir! It wasn't for myself I took it!' Upon which he put down his head, blew a cloud of smoke out of his nose, and vanished with a kick-up of his hind legs, and a flourish of his tail.

All this time I was getting on towards the river; but however fast I went, I couldn't warm my feet, to which the damp cold seemed riveted, as the iron was riveted to the leg of the man I was running to meet. I knew my way to the battery, pretty straight, for I had been down there on a Sunday with Joe, and Joe, sitting on an old gun, had told me that when I was 'prentice to him, regularly bound, we would have such larks there! However, in the confusion of the mist, I found myself at last too far to the right, and consequently had to try back along the riverside, on the bank of loose stones above the mud and the stakes that staked the tide out. Making my way along here with all despatch, I had just crossed a ditch which I knew to be very near the battery, and had just scrambled up the mound beyond the ditch, when I saw the man sitting before me. His back was towards me, and he had his arms folded, and was nodding forward, heavy with sleep.

I thought he would be more glad if I came upon him with his breakfast, in that unexpected manner, so I went forward softly and touched him on the shoulder. He instantly jumped up, and it was not the same man, but another man!

And yet this man was dressed in coarse grey, too, and had a great iron on his leg, and was lame, and hoarse, and cold, and was everything that the other man was; except that he had not the same face, and had a flat, broad-brimmed, low-crowned felt hat on. All this I saw in a moment, for I had only a moment to see it in: he swore an oath at me, made a hit at me – it was a round, weak blow that missed me and almost knocked himself down, for it made him stumble – and then he ran into the mist, stumbling twice as he went, and I lost him.

'It's the young man!' I thought, feeling my heart shoot as I identified him. I dare say I should have felt a pain in my liver, too, if I had known where it was.

I was soon at the battery, after that, and there was the right man – hugging himself and limping to and fro, as if he had never all night left off hugging and limping – waiting for me. He was awfully cold, to be sure. I half expected to see him drop down before my face and die of deadly cold. His eyes looked so awfully hungry, too, that when I handed him the file and he laid it down on the grass, it occurred to me he would have tried to eat it, if he had not seen my bundle. He did not turn me upside down, this time, to get at what I had, but left me right side

upwards while I opened the bundle and emptied my pockets.

'What's in the bottle, boy?' said he.

'Brandy,' said I.

He was already handing mincemeat down his throat in the most curious manner – more like a man who was putting it away somewhere in a violent hurry, than a man who was eating it – but he left off to take some of the liquor. He shivered all the while so violently, that it was quite as much as he could do to keep the neck of the bottle between his teeth, without biting it off.

'I think you have got the ague,' said I.

'I'm much of your opinion, boy,' said he.

'It's bad about here,' I told him. 'You've been lying out on the meshes, and they're dreadful aguish. Rheumatic too.'

'I'll eat my breakfast afore they're the death of me,' said he. 'I'd do that if I was going to be strung up to that there gallows as there is over there, directly arterwards. I'll beat the shivers so far, I'll bet you.'

He was gobbling mincemeat, meat bone, bread, cheese, and pork pie, all at once: staring distrustfully while he did so at the mist all round us, and often stopping – even stopping his jaws – to listen. Some real or fancied sound, some clink upon the river or breathing of beast upon the marsh, now gave him a start, and he said, suddenly: 'You're not a deceiving imp? You brought no one with you?'

'No, sir! No!'

'Nor giv' no one the office to follow you?'

'No!'

'Well,' said he, 'I believe you. You'd be but a fierce young hound indeed, if at your time of life you could help to hunt a wretched warmint, hunted as near death and dunghill as this poor wretched warmint is!'

Something clicked in his throat as if he had works in him like a clock, and was going to strike. And he smeared his ragged rough sleeve over his eyes.

Pitying his desolation, and watching him as he gradually settled down upon the pie, I made bold to say, 'I am glad you enjoy it.'

'Did you speak?'

'I said, I was glad you enjoyed it.'

'Thankee, my boy. I do.'

I had often watched a large dog of ours eating his food; and I now noticed a decided similarity between the dog's way of eating, and the man's. The man took strong sharp sudden bites, just like the dog. He swallowed, or rather snapped up, every mouthful, too soon and too fast; and he looked sideways here and there while he ate, as if he thought there was danger in every direction of somebody's coming to take the pie away. He was altogether too unsettled in his mind over it, to appreciate it comfortably, I thought, or to have anybody to dine with him, without making a chop with his jaws at the visitor. In all of which particulars he was very like the dog.

'I am afraid you won't leave any of it for him,' said I, timidly; after a silence during which I had hesitated as to the politeness of making the remark. 'There's no more to be got where that came from.' It was the certainty of this fact that impelled me to offer the hint.

'Leave any for him? Who's him?' said my friend, stopping in his crunching of pie-crust.

'The young man. That you spoke of. That was hid with you.'

'Oh ah!' he returned, with something like a gruff laugh. 'Him? Yes, yes! *He* don't want no wittles.'

'I thought he looked as if he did,' said I.

The man stopped eating, and regarded me with the keenest scrutiny and the greatest surprise.

'Looked? When?'

'Just now.'

'Where?'

'Yonder,' said I, pointing; 'over there, where I found him nodding asleep, and thought it was you.'

He held me by the collar and stared at me so, that I began to think his first idea about cutting my throat had revived.

'Dressed like you, you know, only with a hat,' I explained, trembling; 'and – and' – I was very anxious to put this delicately – 'and with – the same reason for wanting to borrow a file. Didn't you hear the cannon last night?'

'Then, there *was* firing!' he said to himself.

'I wonder you shouldn't have been sure of that,' I returned, 'for we heard it up at home, and that's further away, and we were shut in besides.'

'Why, see now!' said he. 'When a man's alone on these flats, with a light head and a light stomach, perishing of cold and want, he hears nothin' all night, but guns firing, and voices calling. Hears? He sees the soldiers, with their red coats lighted up by the torches carried afore, closing in round him. Hears his number called, hears himself challenged, hears the rattle of the muskets, hears the orders, 'Make ready! Present! Cover him steady, men!' and is laid hands on – and there's nothin'! Why, if I see one pursuing party last night – coming up in order, damn 'em, with their tramp, tramp – I see a hundred. And as to firing! Why, I see the mist shake with the cannon, arter it was broad day – but this man;' he had said all the rest as if he had forgotten my being there; 'did you notice anything in him?'

'He had a badly bruised face,' said I, recalling what I hardly knew I knew.

'Not here?' exclaimed the man, striking his left cheek mercilessly, with the flat of his hand.

'Yes, there!'

'Where is he?' He crammed what little food was left, into the breast of his grey jacket. 'Show me the way he went. I'll pull him down, like a bloodhound. Curse this iron on my sore leg! Give us hold of the file, boy.'

I indicated in what direction the mist had shrouded the other man, and he looked up at it for an instant. But he was down on the rank wet grass, filing at his iron like a madman, and not minding me or minding his own leg, which had an old chafe upon it and was bloody, but which he handled as roughly as if it had no more feeling in it than the file. I was very much afraid of him again, now that he had worked himself into this fierce hurry, and I was likewise very much afraid of keeping away from home any longer. I told him I must go, but he took no notice, so I thought the best thing I could do was to slip off. The last I saw of him, his head was bent over his knee and

he was working hard at his fetter, muttering impatient imprecations at it and his leg. The last I heard of him, I stopped in the mist to listen, and the file was still going.

Chapter 4

I fully expected to find a constable in the kitchen, waiting to take me up. But not only was there no constable there, but no discovery had yet been made of the robbery. Mrs Joe was prodigiously busy in getting the house ready for the festivities of the day, and Joe had been put upon the kitchen doorstep to keep him out of the dustpan – an article into which his destiny always led him, sooner or later, when my sister was vigorously reaping the floors of her establishment.

'And where the deuce ha' *you* been?' was Mrs Joe's Christmas salutation, when I and my conscience showed ourselves.

I said I had been down to hear the carols. 'Ah, well!' observed Mrs Joe. 'You might ha' done worse.' Not a doubt of that, I thought.

'Perhaps if I warn't a blacksmith's wife, and (what's the same thing) a slave with her apron never off, *I* should have been to hear the carols,' said Mrs Joe. 'I'm rather partial to carols myself, and that's the best of reasons for my never hearing any.'

Joe, who had ventured into the kitchen after me as the dustpan had retired before us, drew the back of his hand across his nose with a conciliatory air, when Mrs Joe darted a look at him, and, when her eyes were withdrawn, secretly crossed his two forefingers, and exhibited them to me, as our token that Mrs Joe was in a cross temper. This was so much her normal state, that Joe and I would often, for weeks together, be, as to our fingers, like monumental crusaders as to their legs.

We were to have a superb dinner, consisting of a leg of pickled pork and greens, and a pair of roast stuffed fowls. A handsome mince-pie had been made yesterday morning (which accounted for the mincemeat not being missed), and the pudding was already on the boil. These extensive arrangements occasioned us to be cut off unceremoniously in respect of breakfast; 'for I ain't,' said Mrs Joe, 'I ain't a going to have no formal cramming and busting and washing up now, with what I've got before me, I promise you!'

So, we had our slices served out, as if we were two thousand troops on a forced march instead of a man and boy at home; and we took gulps of milk and water, with apologetic countenances, from a jug on the dresser. In the meantime, Mrs Joe put clean white curtains up, and tacked a new flowered-flounce across the wide chimney to replace the old one, and uncovered the little state parlour across the passage, which was never uncovered at any other time, but passed the rest of the year in a cool haze of silver paper, which even extended to the four little white crockery poodles on the mantel-shelf, each with a black nose and a basket of flowers in his mouth, and each the counterpart of the other. Mrs Joe was a very clean housekeeper, but had an exquisite art of making her cleanliness more uncomfortable and unacceptable than dirt itself. Cleanliness is next to godliness, and some people do the same by their religion.

My sister having so much to do, was going to church vicariously; that is to say, Joe and I were going. In his working clothes, Joe was a well-knit characteristic-looking blacksmith; in his holiday clothes, he was more like a scarecrow in good circumstances, than anything else. Nothing that he wore then, fitted him or seemed to belong to him; and everything that he wore then, grazed him. On the present festive occasion he emerged from his room, when the blithe bells were going, the picture of misery, in a full suit of Sunday penitentials. As to me, I think my sister must have had some general idea that I was a young offender whom an *accoucheur* policeman had taken up (on my birthday) and delivered over to her, to be dealt with according to the outraged majesty of the law. I was always treated as if I had insisted on being born in opposition to the dictates of reason, religion, and morality, and against the dissuading arguments of my best friends. Even when I was taken to have a new suit of clothes, the tailor had orders to make them like a kind of reformatory, and on no account to let me have the free use of my limbs.

Joe and I going to church, therefore, must have been a moving spectacle for compassionate minds. Yet, what I suffered outside, was nothing to what I underwent within. The terrors that had assailed me whenever Mrs Joe had gone near the pantry, or out of the room, were only to be equalled by the remorse with which my mind dwelt on what my hands had done. Under the weight of my wicked secret, I pondered whether the Church would be powerful enough to shield me from the vengeance of the terrible young man, if I divulged to that establishment. I conceived the idea that the time when the banns were read and when the clergyman said, 'Ye are now to declare it!' would be the time for me to rise and propose a private conference in the vestry. I am far from being sure that I might not have astonished our small congregation by resorting to this extreme measure, but for its being Christmas Day and no Sunday.

Mr Wopsle, the clerk at church, was to dine with us; and Mr Hubble, the wheelwright, and Mrs Hubble; and Uncle Pumblechook (Joe's uncle, but Mrs Joe appropriated him), who was a well-to-do corn-chandler in the nearest town, and drove his own chaise-cart. The dinner hour was half-past one. When Joe and I got home, we found the table laid, and Mrs Joe dressed, and the dinner dressing, and the front door unlocked (it never was at any other time) for the company to enter by, and everything most splendid. And still, not a word of the robbery.

The time came, without bringing with it any relief to my feelings, and the company came. Mr Wopsle, united to a Roman nose and a large shining bald forehead, had a deep voice which he was uncommonly proud of; indeed it was understood among his acquaintance that if you could only give him his head, he would read the clergyman into fits; he himself confessed that if the Church was 'thrown open', meaning to competition, he would not despair of making his mark in it. The Church not being 'thrown open', he was, as I have said, our clerk. But he punished the 'amens' tremendously; and when he gave out the psalm – always giving the whole verse – he looked all round the congregation first, as much as to say, 'You have heard our friend overhead; oblige me with your opinion of this style!'

I opened the door to the company – making believe that it was a habit of ours to open that door – and I opened it first to Mr Wopsle, next to Mr and Mrs Hubble, and last of all to Uncle Pumblechook. N.B. *I* was not allowed to call him uncle, under the severest penalties.

'Mrs Joe,' said Uncle Pumblechook; a large hard-breathing middle-aged slow man, with a mouth like a fish, dull staring eyes, and sandy hair standing upright on his head, so that he looked as if he had just been all but choked, and had that moment come to; 'I have brought you as the compliments of the season – I have brought you, mum, a bottle of sherry wine – and I have brought you, mum, a bottle of port wine.'

Every Christmas Day he presented himself, as a profound novelty, with exactly the same words, and carrying the two bottles like dumbbells. Every Christmas Day, Mrs Joe replied, as she now replied, 'Oh, Un–cle Pum–ble–chook! This is kind!' Every Christmas Day, he retorted, as he now retorted, 'It's no more than your merits. And now are you all bobbish, and how's sixpennorth of halfpence?' meaning me.

We dined on these occasions in the kitchen, and adjourned, for the nuts and oranges and apples, to the parlour; which was a change very like Joe's change from his working clothes to his Sunday dress. My sister was uncommonly lively on the present occasion, and indeed was generally more gracious in the society of Mrs Hubble than in other company. I remember Mrs Hubble as a little curly sharp-edged person in sky-blue, who held a conventionally juvenile position, because she had married Mr Hubble – I don't know at what remote period – when she was much younger than he. I remember Mr Hubble as a tough high-shouldered stooping old man, of a sawdusty fragrance, with his legs extraordinarily wide apart: so that in my short days I always saw some miles of open country between them when I met him coming up the lane.

Among this good company I should have felt myself, even if I hadn't robbed the pantry, in a false position. Not because I was squeezed in at an acute angle of the tablecloth, with the table in my chest, and the Pumblechookian elbow in my eye, nor because I was not allowed to speak (I didn't want to speak), nor because I was regaled with the scaly tips of the drumsticks of the fowls, and with those obscure corners of pork of which the pig, when living, had had the least reason to be vain. No; I should not have minded that if they would only have left me alone. But they wouldn't leave me alone. They seemed to think the opportunity lost, if they failed to point the conversation at me, every now and then, and stick the point into me. I might have been an unfortunate little bull in a Spanish arena, I got so smartingly touched up by these moral goads.

It began the moment we sat down to dinner. Mr Wopsle said grace with theatrical declamation – as it now appears to me, something like a religious cross of the ghost in *Hamlet* with Richard III – and ended with the very proper aspiration that we might be truly grateful. Upon which my sister fixed me with her eye, and said, in a low reproachful voice, 'Do you hear that? Be grateful.'

'Especially,' said Mr Pumblechook, 'be grateful, boy, to them which brought you up by hand.'

Mrs Hubble shook her head, and contemplating me with a mournful presentiment that I should come to no good, asked, 'Why is it that the young are never grateful?' This moral mystery seemed too much for the company until Mr Hubble tersely solved it by saying, 'Naterally wicious.' Everybody then murmured 'True!' and looked at me in a particularly unpleasant and personal manner.

Joe's station and influence were something feebler (if possible) when there was company, than when there was none. But he always aided and comforted me when he could, in some way of his own, and he always did so at dinner-time by giving me gravy, if there were any. There being plenty of gravy today, Joe spooned into my plate, at this point, about half a pint.

A little later on in the dinner, Mr Wopsle reviewed the sermon with some severity, and intimated – in the usual hypothetical case of the Church being 'thrown open' – what kind of a sermon *he* would have given them. After favouring them with some heads of that discourse, he remarked that he considered the subject of the day's homily, ill-chosen; which was the less excusable, he added, when there were so many subjects 'going about'.

'True again,' said Uncle Pumblechook. 'You've hit it, sir! Plenty of subjects going about, for them that know how to put salt upon their tails. That's what's wanted. A man needn't go far to find a subject, if he's ready with his salt-box.' Mr Pumblechook added, after a short interval of reflection, 'Look at pork alone. There's a subject! If you want a subject, look at pork!'

'True, sir. Many a moral for the young,' returned Mr Wopsle; and I knew he was going to lug me in, before he said it; 'might be deduced from that text.'

('You listen to this,' said my sister to me, in a severe parenthesis.)

Joe gave me some more gravy.

'Swine,' pursued Mr Wopsle, in his deepest voice, and pointing his fork at my blushes, as if he were mentioning my christian name; 'Swine were the companions of the prodigal. The gluttony of swine is put before us, as an example to the young.' (I thought this pretty well in him who had been praising up the pork for being so plump and juicy.) 'What is detestable in a pig, is more detestable in a boy.'

'Or girl,' suggested Mr Hubble.

'Of course, or girl, Mr Hubble,' assented Mr Wopsle, rather irritably, 'but there is no girl present.'

'Besides,' said Mr Pumblechook, turning sharp on me, 'think what you've got to be grateful for. If you'd been born a squeaker – '

'He *was*, if ever a child was,' said my sister, most emphatically.

Joe gave me some more gravy.

'Well, but I mean a four-footed squeaker,' said Mr Pumblechook. 'If you had been born such, would you have been here now? Not you – '

'Unless in that form,' said Mr Wopsle, nodding towards the dish.

'But I don't mean in that form, sir,' returned Mr Pumblechook, who had an objection to being interrupted; 'I mean,

enjoying himself with his elders and betters, and improving himself with their conversation, and rolling in the lap of luxury. Would he have been doing that? No, he wouldn't. And what would have been your destination?' turning on me again. 'You would have been disposed of for so many shillings according to the market price of the article, and Dunstable the butcher would have come up to you as you lay in your straw, and he would have whipped you under his left arm, and with his right he would have tucked up his frock to get a penknife from out of his waistcoat-pocket, and he would have shed your blood and had your life. No bringing up by hand then. Not a bit of it!'

Joe offered me more gravy, which I was afraid to take.

'He was a world of trouble to you, ma'am,' said Mrs Hubble, commiserating my sister.

'Trouble?' echoed my sister, 'trouble?' And then entered on a fearful catalogue of all the illnesses I had been guilty of, and all the acts of sleeplessness I had committed, and all the high places I had tumbled from, and all the low places I had tumbled into, and all the injuries I had done myself, and all the times she had wished me in my grave, and I had contumaciously refused to go there.

I think the Romans must have aggravated one another very much, with their noses. Perhaps, they became the restless people they were, in consequence. Anyhow Mr Wopsle's Roman nose so aggravated me, during the recital of my misdemeanours, that I should have liked to pull it until he howled. But all I had endured up to this time, was nothing in comparison with the awful feelings that took possession of me when the pause was broken which ensued upon my sister's recital, and in which pause everybody had looked at me (as I felt painfully conscious) with indignation and abhorrence.

'Yet,' said Mr Pumblechook, leading the company gently back to the theme from which they had strayed, 'Pork – regarded as biled – is rich, too; ain't it?'

'Have a little brandy, uncle,' said my sister.

O heavens, it had come at last! He would find it was weak, he would say it was weak, and I was lost! I held tight to the leg of the table, under the cloth, with both hands, and awaited my fate.

My sister went for the stone bottle, came back with the stone bottle, and poured his brandy out: no one else taking any. The wretched man trifled with his glass – took it up, looked at it through the light, put it down – prolonged my misery. All this time Mrs Joe and Joe were briskly clearing the table for the pie and pudding.

I couldn't keep my eyes off him. Always holding tight by the leg of the table with my hands and feet, I saw the miserable creature finger his glass playfully, take it up, smile, throw his head back, and drink the brandy off. Instantly afterwards, the company were seized with unspeakable consternation, owing to his springing to his feet, turning round several times in an appalling spasmodic whooping-cough dance, and rushing out at the door; he then became visible through the window, violently plunging and expectorating, making the most hideous faces, and apparently out of his mind.

I held on tight, while Mrs Joe and Joe ran to him. I didn't know how I had done it, but I had no doubt I had murdered him somehow. In my dreadful situation, it was a relief when he was brought back, and, surveying the company all round as if *they* had disagreed with him, sank down into his chair with the one significant gasp, 'Tar!'

I had filled up the bottle from the tar-water jug. I knew he would be worse by and by. I moved the table, like a medium of the present day, by the vigour of my unseen hold upon it.

'Tar!' cried my sister, in amazement. 'Why, how ever could tar come there?'

But Uncle Pumblechook, who was omnipotent in that kitchen, wouldn't hear the word, wouldn't hear of the subject, imperiously waved it all away with his hand, and asked for hot gin and water. My sister, who had begun to be alarmingly meditative, had to employ herself actively in getting the gin, the hot water, the sugar, and the lemon-peel, and mixing them. For the time at least, I was saved. I still held on to the leg of the table, but clutched it now with the fervour of gratitude.

By degrees, I became calm enough to release my grasp, and partake of pudding. Mr Pumblechook par- took of pudding. All partook of pudding. The course terminated, and Mr Pumble- chook had begun to beam under the genial influence of gin and water. I began to think I should get over the day, when my sister said to Joe, 'Clean plates – cold.'

I clutched the leg of the table again immediately, and pressed it to my bosom as if it had been the companion of my youth and friend of my soul. I foresaw what was coming, and I felt that this time I really was gone.

'You must taste,' said my sister, addressing the guests with her best grace, 'you must taste, to finish with, such a delightful and delicious present of Uncle Pumblechook's!'

Must they! Let them not hope to taste it!

'You must know,' said my sister, rising, 'it's a pie: a savoury pork pie.'

The company murmured their compliments. Uncle Pumble- chook, sensible of having deserved well of his fellow-creatures, said – quite vivaciously, all things considered – 'Well, Mrs Joe, we'll do our best endeavours; let us have a cut at this same pie.'

My sister went out to get it. I heard her steps proceed to the pantry. I saw Mr Pumblechook balance his knife. I saw re- awakening appetite in the Roman nostrils of Mr Wopsle. I heard Mr Hubble remark that 'a bit of savoury pork pie would lay atop of anything you could mention, and do no harm,' and I heard Joe say, 'You shall have some, Pip.' I have never been absolutely certain whether I uttered a shrill yell of terror, merely in spirit, or in the bodily hearing of the company. I felt that I could bear no more, and that I must run away. I released the leg of the table, and ran for my life.

But I ran no further than the house door, for there I ran head foremost into a party of soldiers with their muskets: one of whom held out a pair of handcuffs to me, saying, 'Here you are, look sharp, come on!'

Chapter 5

The apparition of a file of soldiers ringing down the butt-ends of their loaded muskets on our doorstep, caused the dinner-party to rise from table in confusion, and caused Mrs Joe, re-entering the kitchen empty-handed, to stop short and stare, in her wondering lament of 'Gracious goodness gracious me, what's gone – with the – pie!'

The sergeant and I were in the kitchen when Mrs Joe stood staring; at which crisis I partially recovered the use of my senses. It was the sergeant who had spoken to me, and he was now looking round at the company, with his handcuffs in-vitingly extended towards them in his right hand, and his left on my shoulder.

'Excuse me, ladies and gentlemen,' said the sergeant, 'but as I have mentioned at the door to this smart young shaver' (which he hadn't), 'I am on a chase in the name of the king, and I want the blacksmith.'

'And pray what might you want with *him?*' retorted my sister, quick to resent his being wanted at all.

'Missis,' returned the gallant sergeant, 'speaking for myself, I should reply, the honour and pleasure of his fine wife's acquaintance; speaking for the king, I answer, a little job done.'

This was received as rather neat in the sergeant; insomuch that Mr Pumblechook cried audibly, 'Good again!'

'You see, blacksmith,' said the sergeant, who had by this time picked out Joe with his eye, 'we have had an accident with these, and I find the lock of one of 'em goes wrong, and the coupling don't act pretty. As they are wanted for immediate service, will you throw your eye over them?'

Joe threw his eye over them, and pronounced that the job would necessitate the lighting of his forge fire, and would take nearer two hours than one. 'Will it? Then will you set about it at once, blacksmith?' said the offhand sergeant, 'as it's on his Majesty's service. And if my men can bear a hand anywhere, they'll make themselves useful.' With that he called to his men, who came trooping into the kitchen one after another, and piled their arms in a corner. And then they stood about, as soldiers do; now, with their hands loosely clasped before them; now, resting a knee or a shoulder; now, easing a belt or a pouch; now, opening the door to spit stiffly over their high-stocks, out into the yard.

All these things I saw without then knowing that I saw them, for I was in an agony of apprehension. But, beginning to per-ceive that the handcuffs were not for me, and that the military had so far got the better of the pie as to put it in the back-ground, I collected a little more of my scattered wits.

'Would you give me the time?' said the sergeant, addressing himself to Mr Pumblechook, as to a man whose appreciative powers justified the inference that he was equal to the time.

'It's just gone half-past two.'

'That's not so bad,' said the sergeant, reflecting; 'even if I was forced to halt here nigh two hours, that'll do. How far might you call yourselves from the marshes, hereabouts? Not above a mile, I reckon?'

'Just a mile,' said Mrs Joe.

'That'll do. We begin to close in upon 'em about dusk. A little before dusk, my orders are. That'll do.'

'Convicts, sergeant?' asked Mr Wopsle, in a matter-of-course way.

'Ay!' returned the sergeant, 'two. They're pretty well known to be out on the marshes still, and they won't try to get clear of 'em before dusk. Anybody here seen anything of any such game?'

Everybody, myself excepted, said no, with confidence. Nobody thought of me.

'Well,' said the sergeant, 'they'll find themselves trapped in a circle. I expect, sooner than they count on. Now, blacksmith! If you're ready, his Majesty the King is.'

Joe had got his coat and waistcoat and cravat off, and his leather apron on, and passed into the forge. One of the soldiers opened its wooden windows, another lighted the fire, another turned to at the bellows, the rest stood round the blaze, which was soon roaring. Then Joe began to hammer and clink, hammer and clink, and we all looked on.

The interest of the impending pursuit not only absorbed the general attention, but even made my sister liberal. She drew a pitcher of beer from the cask, for the soldiers, and invited the sergeant to take a glass of brandy. But Mr Pumblechook said sharply, 'Give him wine, Mum. I'll engage there's no tar in that:' so, the sergeant thanked him and said that, as he preferred his drink without tar, he would take wine, if it was equally convenient. When it was given him, he drank his Majesty's health and compliments of the season, and took it all at a mouthful and smacked his lips.

'Good stuff, eh, sergeant?' said Mr Pumblechook.

'I'll tell you something,' returned the sergeant; 'I suspect that stuff's of *your* providing.'

Mr Pumblechook, with a fat sort of laugh, said, 'Ay, ay? Why?'

'Because,' returned the sergeant, clapping him on the shoulder, 'you're a man that knows what's what.'

'D'ye think so?' said Mr Pumblechook, with his former laugh. 'Have another glass!'

'With you. Hob and nob,' returned the sergeant. 'The top of mine to the foot of yours – the foot of yours to the top of mine – ring once, ring twice – the best tune on the Musical Glasses! Your health. May you live a thousand years, and never be a worse judge of the right sort than you are at the present moment of your life!'

The sergeant tossed off his glass again and seemed quite ready for another glass. I noticed that Mr Pumblechook in his hospitality appeared to forget that he had made a present of the wine, but took the bottle from Mrs Joe and had all the credit of handing it about in a gush of joviality. Even I got some. And he was so very free of the wine that he even called for the other bottle, and handed that about with the same liberality, when the first was gone.

As I watched them while they all stood clustering about the forge, enjoying themselves so much, I thought what terrible good sauce for a dinner my fugitive friend on the marshes was. They had not enjoyed themselves a quarter so much, before

the entertainment was brightened with the excitement he furnished. And now, when they were all in lively anticipation of 'the two villains' being taken, and when the bellows seemed to roar for the fugitives, the fire to flare for them, the smoke to hurry away in pursuit of them, Joe to hammer and clink for them, and all the murky shadows on the wall to shake at them in menace as the blaze rose and sank and the red-hot sparks dropped and died, the pale afternoon outside almost seemed in my pitying young fancy to have turned pale on their account, poor wretches.

At last, Joe's job was done, and the ringing and roaring stopped. As Joe got on his coat, he mustered courage to propose that some of us should go down with the soldiers and see what came of the hunt. Mr Pumblechook and Mr Hubble declined, on the plea of a pipe and ladies' society; but Mr Wopsle said he would go, if Joe would. Joe said he was agreeable, and would take me, if Mrs Joe approved. We never should have got leave to go, I am sure, but for Mrs Joe's curiosity to know all about it and how it ended. As it was, she merely stipulated, 'If you bring the boy back with his head blown to bits by a musket, don't look to me to put it together again.'

The sergeant took a polite leave of the ladies, and parted from Mr Pumblechook as from a comrade; though I doubt if he were quite as fully sensible of that gentleman's merits under and conditions, as when something moist was going. His men resumed their muskets and fell in. Mr Wopsle, Joe, and I, received strict charge to keep in the rear, and to speak no word after we reached the marshes. When we were all out in the raw air and were steadily moving towards our business, I treasonably whispered to Joe, 'I hope, Joe, we shan't find them.' And Joe whispered to me, 'I'd give a shilling if they had cut and run, Pip.'

We were joined by no stragglers from the village, for the weather was cold and threatening, the way dreary, the footing bad, darkness coming on, and the people had good fires indoors and were keeping the day. A few faces hurried to glowing windows and looked after us, but none came out. We passed the finger-post, and held straight on to the churchyard. There, we were stopped a few minutes by a signal from the sergeant's hand, while two or three of his men dispersed themselves among the graves, and also examined the porch. They came in again without finding anything, and then we struck out on the open marshes, through the gate at the side of the churchyard. A bitter sleet came rattling against us here on the east wind, and Joe took me on his back.

Now that we were out upon the dismal wilderness where they little thought I had been within eight or nine hours, and had seen both men hiding, I considered for the first time, with great dread, if we should come upon them, would my particular convict suppose that it was I who had brought the soldiers there? He had asked me if I was a deceiving imp, and he said I should be a fierce young hound if I joined the hunt against him. Would he believe that I was both imp and hound in treacherous earnest, and had betrayed him?

It was of no use asking myself this question now. There I was, on Joe's back, and there was Joe beneath me, charging at the ditches like a hunter, and stimulating Mr Wopsle not to tumble on his Roman nose, and to keep up with us. The soldiers were in front of us, extending into a pretty wide line with an interval between man and man. We were taking the course I had begun with, and from which I had diverged into the mist. Either the mist was not out again yet, or the wind had dispelled it. Under the low red glare of sunset, the beacon, and the gibbet, and the mound of the battery, and the opposite shore of the river, were plain, though all of a watery lead colour.

With my heart thumping like a blacksmith at Joe's broad shoulder, I looked all about for any sign of the convicts. I could see none, I could hear none. Mr Wopsle had greatly alarmed me more than once, by his blowing and hard breathing; but I knew the sounds by this time, and could dissociate them from the object of pursuit. I got a dreadful start, when I thought I heard the file still going; but it was only a sheep bell. The sheep stopped in their eating and looked timidly at us; and the cattle, their heads turned from the wind and sleet, stared angrily as if they held us responsible for both annoyances; but, except these things, and the shudder of the dying day in every blade of grass, there was no break in the bleak stillness of the marshes.

The soldiers were moving on in the direction of the old battery, and we were moving on a little way behind them, when, all of a sudden, we all stopped. For, there had reached us, on the wings of the wind and rain, a long shout. It was repeated. It was at a distance towards the east, but it was long and loud. Nay, there seemed to be two or more shouts raised together – if one might judge from a confusion in the sound.

To this effect the sergeant and the nearest men were speaking under their breath, when Joe and I came up. After another moment's listening, Joe (who was a good judge) agreed, and Mr Wopsle (who was a bad judge) agreed. The sergeant, a decisive man, ordered that the sound should not be answered, but that the course should be changed, and that his men should make towards it 'at the double'. So we started to the right (where the East was), and Joe pounded away so wonderfully, that I had to hold on tight to keep my seat.

It was a run indeed now, and what Joe called, in the only two words he spoke all the time, 'a winder'. Down banks and up banks, and over gates, and splashing into dykes, and breaking among coarse rushes: no man cared where he went. As we came nearer to the shouting, it became more and more apparent that it was made by more than one voice. Sometimes, it seemed to stop altogether, and then the soldiers stopped. When it broke out again, the soldiers made for it at a greater rate than ever, and we after them. After a while, we had so run it down, that we could hear one voice calling 'Murder!' and another voice, 'Convicts! Runaways! Guard! This way for the runaway convicts!' Then both voices would seem to be stifled in a struggle, and then would break out again. And when it had come to this, the soldiers ran like deer, and Joe too.

The sergeant ran in first, when we had run the noise quite down, and two of his men ran in close upon him. Their pieces were cocked and levelled when we all ran in.

'Here are both men!' panted the sergeant, struggling at the bottom of a ditch. 'Surrender, you two, and confound you for two wild beasts! Come asunder!'

Water was splashing, and mud was flying, and oaths were being sworn, and blows were being struck, when some more men went down into the ditch to help the sergeant, and dragged out, separately, my convict and the other one. Both were bleeding and panting and execrating and struggling; but of course I knew them both directly.

'Mind!' said my convict, wiping blood from his face with his ragged sleeves, and shaking torn hair from his fingers; '*I* took him! *I* give him up to you! Mind that!'

'It's not much to be particular about,' said the sergeant; 'it'll do you small good, my man, being in the same plight yourself. Handcuffs there!'

'I don't expect it to do me any good. I don't want it to do me more good than it does now,' said my convict, with a greedy laugh. 'I took him. He knows it. That's enough for me.'

The other convict was livid to look at, and, in addition to the old bruised left side of his face, seemed to be bruised and torn all over. He could not so much as get his breath to speak, until they were both separately handcuffed, but leaned upon a soldier to keep himself from falling.

'Take notice, guard – he tried to murder me,' were his first words.

'Tried to murder him?' said my convict, disdainfully. 'Try, and not do it? I took him, and giv' him up; that's what I done. I not only prevented him getting off the marshes, but I dragged him here – dragged him this far on his way back. He's a gentleman, if you please, this villain. Now, the hulks has got its gentleman again, through me. Murder him? Worth my while, too, to murder him, when I could do worse and drag him back!'

The other one still gasped, 'He tried – he tried – to – murder me. Bear – bear witness.'

'Lookee here!' said my convict to the sergeant. 'Single-handed I got clear of the prison-ship; I made a dash and I done it. I could ha' got clear of these death-cold flats likewise – look at my leg: you won't find much iron on it – if I hadn't made discovery that *he* was here. Let *him* go free? Let *him* profit by the means as I found out? Let *him* make a tool of me afresh and again? Once more? No, no, no. If I had died at the bottom there;' and he made an emphatic swing at the ditch with his manacled hands; 'I'd have held to him with that grip, that you should have been safe to find him in my hold.'

The other fugitive, who was evidently in extreme horror of his companion, repeated, 'He tried to murder me. I should have been a dead man if you had not come up.'

'He lies!' said my convict, with fierce energy. 'He's a liar born, and he'll die a liar. Look at his face; ain't it written there? Let him turn those eyes of his on me. I defy him to do it.'

The other, with an effort at a scornful smile – which could not, however, collect the nervous working of his mouth into any set expression, looked at the soldiers, and looked about at the marshes and at the sky, but certainly did not look at the speaker.

'Do you see him?' pursued my convict. 'Do you see what a villain he is? Do you see those grovelling and wandering eyes?

That's how he looked when we were tried together. He never looked at me.'

The other, always working and working his dry lips and turning his eyes restlessly about him far and near, did at last turn them for a moment on the speaker, with the words, 'You are not much to look at,' and with a half-taunting glance at the bound hands. At that point, my convict became so frantically exasperated, that he would have rushed upon him but for the interposition of the soldiers. 'Didn't I tell you,' said the other convict then, 'that he would murder me, if he could?' And anyone could see that he shook with fear, and that there broke out upon his lips curious white flakes, like thin snow.

'Enough of this parley,' said the sergeant. 'Light those torches.'

As one of the soldiers, who carried a basket in lieu of a gun, went down on his knee to open it, my convict looked round him for the first time, and saw me. I had alighted from Joe's back on the brink of the ditch when we came up, and had not moved since. I looked at him eagerly when he looked at me, and slightly moved my hands and shook my head. I had been waiting for him to see me, that I might try to assure him of my innocence. It was not at all expressed to me that he even comprehended my intention, for he gave me a look that I did not understand, and it all passed in a moment. But if he had looked at me for an hour or for a day, I could not have remembered his face ever afterwards, as having been more attentive.

The soldier with the basket soon got a light, and lighted three or four torches, and took one himself and distributed the others. It had been almost dark before, but now it seemed quite dark, and soon afterwards very dark. Before we departed from that spot, four soldiers standing in a ring, fired twice into the air. Presently we saw other torches kindled at some distance behind us, and others on the marshes on the opposite bank of the river. 'All right,' said the sergeant. 'March.'

We had not gone far when three cannon were fired ahead of us with a sound that seemed to burst something inside my ear. 'You are expected on board,' said the sergeant to my convict; 'they know you are coming. Don't straggle, my man. Close up here.'

The two were kept apart, and each walked surrounded by a separate guard. I had hold of Joe's hand now, and Joe carried one of the torches. Mr Wopsle had been for going back, but Joe was resolved to see it out, so we went on with the party. There was a reasonably good path now, mostly on the edge of the river, with a divergence here and there where a dyke came, with a miniature windmill on it and a muddy sluicegate. When I looked round, I could see the other lights coming in after us. The torches we carried, dropped great blotches of fire upon the track, and I could see those, too, lying smoking and flaring. I could see nothing else but black darkness. Our lights warmed the air about us with their pitchy blaze, and the two prisoners seemed rather to like that, as they limped along in the midst of the muskets. We could not go fast, because of their lameness; and they were so spent, that two or three times we had to halt while they rested.

After an hour or so of this travelling, we came to a rough wooden hut and a landing-place. There was a guard in the hut, and they challenged, and the sergeant answered. Then, we went into the hut, where there was a smell of tobacco and whitewash, and a bright fire, and a lamp, and a stand of muskets, and a drum, and a low wooden bedstead, like an overgrown mangle without the machinery, capable of holding about a dozen soldiers all at once. Three or four soldiers who lay upon it in their greatcoats, were not much interested in us, but just lifted their heads and took a sleepy stare, and then lay down again. The sergeant made some kind of report, and some entry in a book, and then the convict whom I call the other convict was drafted off with his guard, to go on board first.

My convict never looked at me, except that once. While we stood in the hut, he stood before the fire looking thoughtfully at it, or putting up his feet by turns upon the hob, and looking thoughtfully at them as if he pitied them for their recent adventures.

Suddenly, he turned to the sergeant, and remarked: 'I wish to say something respecting this escape. It may prevent some persons laying under suspicion alonger me.'

'You can say what you like,' returned the sergeant, standing coolly looking at him with his arms folded, 'but you have no call to say it here. You'll have opportunity enough to say about it, and hear about it, before it's done with, you know.'

'I know, but this is another pint, a separate matter. A man can't starve; at least *I* can't. I took some wittles, up at the willage over yonder – where the church stands a'most out on the marshes.'

'You mean stole,' said the sergeant.

'And I'll tell you where from. From the blacksmith's.'

'Halloa!' said the sergeant, staring at Joe.

'Halloa, Pip!' said Joe, staring at me.

'It was some broken wittles – that's what it was – and a dram of liquor, and a pie.'

'Have you happened to miss such an article as a pie, blacksmith?' asked the sergeant, confidentially.

'My wife did, at the very moment when you came in. Don't you know, Pip?'

'So,' said my convict, turning his eyes on Joe in a moody manner, and without the least glance at me; 'so you're the blacksmith, are you? Then I'm sorry to say, I've eat your pie.'

'God knows you're welcome to it – so far as it was ever mine,' returned Joe, with a saving remembrance of Mrs Joe. 'We don't know what you have done, but we wouldn't have you starved to death for it, poor miserable fellow-creature – would us, Pip?'

The something that I had noticed before, clicked in the man's throat again, and he turned his back. The boat had returned, and his guard were ready, so we followed him to the landing-place made of rough stakes and stones, and saw him put into the boat, which was rowed by a crew of convicts like himself. No one seemed surprised to see him, or interested in seeing him, or glad to see him, or sorry to see him, or spoke a word, except that somebody in the boat growled as if to dogs, 'Give way, you!' which was the signal for the dip of the oars. By the light of the torches, we saw the black hulk lying out a little way from the mud of the shore, like a wicked Noah's ark. Cribbed and barred and moored by massive rusty chains, the prison-ship seemed in my young eyes to be ironed like the prisoners. We saw the boat go alongside, and we saw him taken up the side and disappear. Then, the ends of the torches were flung hissing into the water, and went out, as if it were all over with him.

Chapter 6

My state of mind regarding the pilfering from which I had been so unexpectedly exonerated, did not impel me to frank disclosure; but I hope it had some dregs of good at the bottom of it.

I do not recall that I felt any tenderness of conscience in reference to Mrs Joe, when the fear of being found out was lifted off me. But I loved Joe – perhaps for no better reason in those early days than because the dear fellow let me love him – and, as to him, my inner self was not so easily composed. It was much upon my mind (particularly when I first saw him looking about for his file) that I ought to tell Joe the whole truth. Yet I did not, and for the reason that I mistrusted that if I did, he would think me worse than I was. The fear of losing Joe's confidence, and of thenceforth sitting in the chimney-corner at night staring drearily at my for ever lost companion and friend, tied up my tongue. I morbidly represented to myself that if Joe knew it, I never afterwards could see him at the fireside feeling his fair whisker, without thinking that he was meditating on it. That, if Joe knew it, I never afterwards could see him glance, however casually, at yesterday's meat or pudding when it came on today's table, without thinking that he was debating whether I had been in the pantry. That, if Joe knew it, and at any subsequent period of our joint domestic life remarked that his beer was flat or thick, the conviction that he suspected tar in it, would bring a rush of blood to my face. In a word, I was too cowardly to do what I knew to be right, as I had been too cowardly to avoid doing what I knew to be wrong. I had had no intercourse with the world at that time, and I imitated none of its many inhabitants who act in this manner. Quite an untaught genius, I made the discovery of the line of action for myself.

As I was sleepy before we were far away from the prison-ship, Joe took me on his back again and carried me home. He must have had a tiresome journey of it, for Mr Wopsle, being knocked up, was in such a very bad temper that if the Church had been thrown open, he would probably have excommunicated the whole expedition, beginning with Joe and myself. In his lay capacity, he persisted in sitting down in the damp to such an insane extent, that when his coat was taken off to be dried at the kitchen fire, the circumstantial evidence on his trousers would have hanged him if it had been a capital offence.

By that time, I was staggering on the kitchen floor like a little drunkard, through having been newly set upon my feet, and through having been fast asleep, and through waking in the heat and lights and noise of tongues. As I came to myself (with the aid of a heavy thump between the shoulders, and the restorative exclamation 'Yah! Was there ever such a boy as this!' from my sister), I found Joe telling them about the convict's confession, and all the visitors suggesting different ways by which he had got into the pantry. Mr Pumblechook made out, after carefully surveying the premises, that he had first got upon the roof of the forge, and had then got upon the roof of the house, and had then let himself down the kitchen chimney by a rope made of his bedding cut into strips; and as Mr Pumblechook was very positive and drove his own chaise-cart – over everybody – it was agreed that it must be so. Mr Wopsle, indeed, wildly cried out 'No!' with the feeble malice of a tired man; but, as he had no theory, and no coat on, he was unanimously set at nought – not to mention his smoking hard behind, as he stood with his back to the kitchen fire to draw the damp out: which was not calculated to inspire confidence.

This was all I heard that night before my sister clutched me, as a slumberous offence to the company's eyesight, and assisted me up to bed with such a strong hand that I seemed to have fifty boots on, and to be dangling them all against the edges of the stairs. My state of mind, as I have described it, began before I was up in the morning, and lasted long after the subject had died out, and had ceased to be mentioned saving on exceptional occasions.

Chapter 7

At the time when I stood in the churchyard, reading the family tombstones, I had just enough learning to be able to spell them out. My construction even of their simple meaning was not very correct, for I read 'wife of the above' as a complimentary reference to my father's exaltation to a better world; and if any one of my deceased relations had been referred to as 'below', I have no doubt I should have formed the worst opinions of that member of the family. Neither were my notions of the theological positions to which my catechism bound me, at all accurate; for I have a lively remembrance that I supposed my declaration that I was to 'walk in the same all the days of my life', laid me under an obligation always to go through the village from our house in one particular direction, and never to vary it by turning down by the wheelwright's or up by the mill

When I was old enough, I was to be apprenticed to Joe, and until I could assume that dignity I was not to be what Mrs Joe called 'pompeyed' or (as I render it) pampered. Therefore, I was not only odd-boy about the forge, but if any neighbour happened to want an extra boy to frighten birds, or pick up stones, or do any such job, I was favoured with the employment. In order, however, that our superior position might not be compromised thereby, a money-box was kept on the kitchen mantel-shelf, into which it was publicly made known that all my earnings were dropped. I have an impression that they were to be contributed eventually towards the liquidation of the National Debt, but I know I had no hope of any personal participation in the treasure.

Mr Wopsle's great-aunt kept an evening school in the village; that is to say, she was a ridiculous old woman of limited means and unlimited infirmity, who used to go to sleep from six to seven every evening, in the society of youth who paid twopence per week each, for the improving opportunity of seeing her do it. She rented a small cottage, and Mr Wopsle had the room upstairs, where we students used to overhear him reading aloud in a most dignified and terrific manner, and occasionally bumping on the ceiling. There was a fiction that Mr Wopsle 'examined' the scholars, once a quarter. What he did on those occasions was to turn up his cuffs, stick up his hair, and give us Mark Antony's oration over the body of Caesar. This was always followed by Collins's 'Ode on the Passions', wherein I particularly venerated Mr Wopsle as Revenge, throwing his blood-stained sword in thunder down, and taking the war-denouncing trumpet with a withering look. It was not with me then, as it was in later life, when I fell into the society of the Passions, and compared them with Collins and Wopsle, rather to the disadvantage of both gentlemen.

Mr Wopsle's great-aunt, besides keeping this educational in-stitution, kept in the same room – a little general shop. She had no idea what stock she had, or what the price of anything in it was; but there was a little greasy memorandum-book kept in a drawer, which served as a catalogue of prices, and by this oracle Biddy arranged all the shop transactions. Biddy was Mr Wopsle's great-aunt's granddaughter; I confess myself quite unequal to the working out of the problem, what relation she was to Mr Wopsle. She was an orphan like myself; like me, too, had been brought up by hand. She was most noticeable, I thought, in respect of her extremities; for her hair always wanted brushing, her hands always wanted washing, and her shoes always wanted mending and pulling up at heel. This description must be re-ceived with a weekday limitation. On Sundays she went to church elaborated.

Much of my unassisted self, and more by the help of Biddy than of Mr Wopsle's great-aunt, I struggled through the alphabet as if it had been a bramble bush; getting considerably worried and scratched by every letter. After that, I fell among those thieves, the nine figures, who seemed every evening to do something new to disguise themselves and baffle recognition. But, at last I began, in a purblind groping way, to read, write, and cipher, on the very smallest scale.

One night, I was sitting in the chimney-corner with my slate, expending great efforts on the production of a letter to Joe. I think it must have been a full year after our hunt upon the marshes, for it was a long time after, and it was winter and a hard frost. With an alphabet on the hearth at my feet for reference, I contrived in an hour or two to print and smear this epistle:

mI deEr JO i opE U r krWitE wEll i opE i shAl soN B haBelL 4 2 teeDge U JO aN theN wE shOrl b sO glOdd aN wEn i M preNgtD 2 u JO woT larX an blEvE ME in F xn PiP.

There was no indispensable necessity for my communicating with Joe by letter, inasmuch as he sat beside me and we were alone. But, I delivered this written communication (slate and all) with my own hand, and Joe received it, as a miracle of erudition.

'I say, Pip, old chap!' cried Joe, opening his blue eyes wide, 'what a scholar you are! Ain't you?'

'I should like to be,' said I, glancing at the slate as he held it: with a misgiving that the writing was rather hilly.

'Why, here's a J,' said Joe, 'and an O equal to anythink! Here's a J and an O, Pip, and a J–O, Joe.'

I had never heard Joe read aloud to any greater extent than this monosyllable, and I had observed at church last Sunday, when I accidentally held our Prayer-book upside down, that it seemed to suit his convenience quite as well as if it had been all right. Wishing to embrace the present occasion of finding out whether in teaching Joe, I should have to begin quite at the beginning, I said, 'Ah! But read the rest, Joe.'

'The rest, eh, Pip?' said Joe, looking at it with a slowly searching eye. 'One, two, three. Why, here's three Js, and three Os, and three J–Os, Joes, in it, Pip!'

I leaned over Joe, and, with the aid of my forefinger, read him the whole letter.

'Astonishing!' said Joe, when I had finished. 'You *are* a scholar.'

'How do you spell Gargery, Joe?' I asked him, with a modest patronage.

'I don't spell it at all,' said Joe.

'But supposing you did?'

'It *can't* be supposed,' said Joe. 'Tho' I'm oncommon fond of reading, too.'

'Are you, Joe?'

'Oncommon. Give me,' said Joe, 'a good book, or a good newspaper, and sit me down afore a good fire, and I ask no better. Lord!' he continued, after rubbing his knees a little, 'when you *do* come to a J and a O, and says you, "Here, at last, is a J–O, Joe," how interesting reading is!'

I derived from this last, that Joe's education, like Steam, was yet in its infancy. Pursuing the subject, I enquired: 'Didn't you ever go to school, Joe, when you were as little as me?'

'No, Pip.'

'Why didn't you ever go to school, Joe, when you were as little as me?'

'Well, Pip,' said Joe, taking up the poker, and settling himself to his usual occupation when he was thoughtful, of slowly raking the fire between the lower bars: 'I'll tell you. My father, Pip, he were given to drink, and when he were overtook with drink, he hammered away at my mother most onmerciful. It were a'most the only hammering he did, indeed, 'xcepting at myself. And he hammered at me with a wigour only to be equalled by the wigour with which he didn't hammer at his anwil – you're a-listening and understanding, Pip?'

'Yes, Joe.'

' 'Consequence, my mother and me we ran away from my father several times; and then my mother she'd go out to work, and she'd say, "Joe," she'd say, "now, please God, you shall have some schooling, child," and she'd put me to school. But my father were that good in his hart that he couldn't abear to be without us. So, he'd come with a most tremenjous crowd and make such a row at the doors of the houses where we was, that they used to be obligated to have no more to do with us and to give us up to him. And then he took us home and hammered us. Which, you see, Pip,' said Joe, pausing in his meditative raking of the fire, and looking at me, 'were a drawback on my learning.'

'Certainly, poor Joe!'

'Though mind you, Pip,' said Joe, with a judicial touch or two of the poker on the top bar, 'rendering unto all their doo, and maintaining equal justice betwixt man and man, my father were that good in his hart, don't you see?'

I didn't see; but I didn't say so.

'Well!' Joe pursued, 'somebody must keep the pot a-biling, Pip, or the pot won't bile, don't you know?'

I saw that, and said so.

' 'Consequence, my father didn't make objections to my going to work; so I went to work at my present calling, which were his too, if he would have followed it, and I worked tolerable hard, I assure *you*, Pip. In time I were able to keep him, and I kep him till he went off in a purple leptic fit. And it were my intentions to have had put upon his tombstone that Whatsume'er the failings on his part, remember reader he were that good in his hart.'

Joe recited this couplet with such manifest pride and careful perspicuity, that I asked him if he had made it himself.

'I made it,' said Joe, 'my own self. I made it in a moment. It was like striking out a horseshoe complete, in a single blow. I never was so much surprised in all my life – couldn't credit my own 'ed – to tell you the truth, hardly believed it *were* my own 'ed. As I was saying, Pip, it were my intentions to have had it cut over him; but poetry costs money, cut it how you will, small or large, and it were not done. Not to mention bearers, all the money that could be spared were wanted for my mother. She were in poor elth, and quite broke. She weren't long of following, poor soul, and her share of peace come round at last.'

Joe's blue eyes turned a little watery; he rubbed, first one of them, and then the other, in a most uncongenial and uncomfortable manner, with the round knob on the top of the poker.

'It were but lonesome then,' said Joe, 'living here alone, and I got acquainted with your sister. Now, Pip;' Joe looked firmly at me, as if he knew I was not going to agree with him; 'your sister is a fine figure of a woman.'

I could not help looking at the fire, in an obvious state of doubt.

'Whatever family opinions, or whatever the world's opinions, on that subject may be, Pip, your sister is,' Joe tapped the top bar with the poker after every word following, 'a – fine – figure – of – a – woman!'

I could think of nothing better to say than 'I am glad you think so, Joe.'

'So am I,' returned Joe, catching me up. '*I* am glad I think so, Pip. A little redness, or a little matter of bone, here or there, what does it signify to me?'

I sagaciously observed, if it didn't signify to him, to whom did it signify?

'Certainly!' assented Joe. 'That's it. You're right, old chap! When I got acquainted with your sister, it were the talk how she was bringing you up by hand. Very kind of her too, all the folks

said, and I said, along with all the folks. As to you,' Joe pursued, with a countenance expressive of seeing something very nasty indeed: 'if you could have been aware how small and flabby and mean you was, dear me, you'd have formed the most contemptible opinions of yourself!'

Not exactly relishing this, I said, 'Never mind me, Joe.'

'But I did mind you, Pip,' he returned, with tender simplicity. 'When I offered to your sister to keep company, and to be asked in church, at such times as she was willing and ready to come to the forge, I said to her, "And bring the poor little child. God bless the poor little child,' I said to your sister, 'there's room for *him* at the forge! " '

I broke out crying and begging pardon, and hugged Joe round the neck: who dropped the poker to hug me, and to say, 'Ever the best of friends; ain't us, Pip? Don't cry, old chap!'

When this little interruption was over, Joe resumed: 'Well, you see, Pip, and here we are! That's about where it lights; here we are! Now, when you take me in hand in my learning, Pip (and I tell you beforehand I am awful dull, most awful dull), Mrs Joe mustn't see too much of what we're up to. It must be done, as I may say, on the sly. And why on the sly? I'll tell you why, Pip.'

He had taken up the poker again; without which, I doubt if he could have proceeded in his demonstration.

'Your sister is given to government.'

'Given to government, Joe?' I was startled, for I had some shadowy idea (and I am afraid I must add, hope) that Joe had divorced her in favour of the Lords of the Admiralty, or Treasury.

'Given to government,' said Joe. 'Which I meanter say the government of you and myself.'

'Oh!'

'And she ain't over partial to having scholars on the premises,' Joe continued, 'and in partickler would not be over partial to my being a scholar, for fear as I might rise. Like a sort of rebel, don't you see?'

I was going to retort with an enquiry, and had got as far as 'Why – ' when Joe stopped me.

'Stay a bit. I know what you're a-going to say, Pip; stay a bit! I don't deny that your sister comes the Mogul over us, now and again. I don't deny that she do throw us back-falls, and that she do drop down upon us heavy. At such times as when your sister is on the rampage, Pip,' Joe sank his voice to a whisper and glanced at the door, 'candour compels fur to admit that she is a buster.'

Joe pronounced this word as if it began with at least twelve capital Bs.

'Why don't I rise? That were your observation when I broke it off, Pip?'

'Yes, Joe.'

'Well,' said Joe, passing the poker into his left hand, that he might feel his whisker; and I had no hope of him whenever he took to that placid occupation; 'your sister's a mastermind. A mastermind.'

'What's that?' I asked, in some hope of bringing him to a stand. But Joe was readier with his definition than I had expected, and completely stopped me by arguing circularly, and answering with a fixed look, 'Her.'

'And I ain't a mastermind,' Joe resumed, when he had un-fixed his look, and got back to his whisker. 'And last of all, Pip – and this I want to say very serous to you, old chap – I see so much in my poor mother, of a woman drudging and slaving and breaking her honest hart and never getting no peace in her mortal days, that I'm dead afeerd of going wrong in the way of not doing what's right by a woman, and I'd fur rather of the two go wrong the t'other way, and be a little ill-conwenienced myself. I wish it was only me that got put out, Pip; I wish there warn't no Tickler for you, old chap; I wish I could take it all on myself; but this is the up-and-down-and-straight on it, Pip, and I hope you'll overlook shortcomings.'

Young as I was, I believe that I dated a new admiration of Joe from that night. We were equals afterwards, as we had been before; but, afterwards at quiet times when I sat looking at Joe and thinking about him, I had a new sensation of feeling conscious that I was looking up to Joe in my heart.

'However,' said Joe, rising to replenish the fire; 'here's the Dutch clock a-working himself up to being equal to strike Eight of 'em, and she's not come home yet! I hope Uncle Pumblechook's mare mayn't have set a forefoot on a piece o' ice, and gone down.'

Mrs Joe made occasional trips with Uncle Pumblechook on market-days, to assist him in buying such household stuffs and goods as required a woman's judgement; Uncle Pumblechook being a bachelor and reposing no confidences in his domestic servant. This was market-day, and Mrs Joe was out on one of these expeditions.

Joe made the fire and swept the hearth, and then we went to the door to listen for the chaise-cart. It was a dry cold night, and the wind blew keenly, and the frost was white and hard. A man would die tonight of lying out on the marshes, I thought. And then I looked at the stars, and considered how awful it would be for a man to turn his face up to them as he froze to death, and see no help or pity in all the glittering multitude.

'Here comes the mare,' said Joe, 'ringing like a peal of bells!'

The sound of her iron shoes upon the hard road was quite musical, as she came along at a much brisker trot than usual. We got a chair out, ready for Mrs Joe's alighting, and stirred up the fire that they might see a bright window, and took a final survey of the kitchen that nothing might be out of its place. When we had completed these preparations, they drove up, wrapped to the eyes. Mrs Joe was soon landed, and Uncle Pumblechook was soon down too, covering the mare with a cloth, and we were soon all in the kitchen, carrying so much cold air with us that it seemed to drive all the heat out of the fire.

'Now,' said Mrs Joe, unwrapping herself with haste and excitement, and throwing her bonnet back on her shoulders where it hung by the strings: 'if this boy ain't grateful this night, he never will be!'

I looked as grateful as any boy possibly could, who was wholly uninformed why he ought to assume that expression.

'It's only to be hoped,' said my sister, 'that he won't be Pompeyed. But I have my fears.'

'She ain't in that line, Mum,' said Mr Pumblechook. 'She knows better.'

She? I looked at Joe, making the motion with my lips and eyebrows, 'She?' Joe looked at me, making the motion with *his* lips and eyebrows, 'She?' My sister catching him in the act, he drew the back of his hand across his nose with his usual conciliatory air on such occasions, and looked at her.

'Well?' said my sister, in her snappish way. 'What are you staring at? Is the house a-fire?'

' – Which some individual,' Joe politely hinted, 'mentioned she.'

'And she is a she, I suppose?' said my sister. 'Unless you call Miss Havisham a he. And I doubt if even you'll go so far as that.'

'Miss Havisham up town?' said Joe.

'Is there any Miss Havisham down town?' returned my sister. 'She wants this boy to go and play there. And of course he's going. And he had better play there,' said my sister, shaking her head at me as an encouragement to be extremely light and sportive, 'or I'll work him.'

I held heard of Miss Havisham up town – everybody for miles round, had heard of Miss Havisham up town – as an immensely rich and grim lady who lived in a large and dismal house barricaded against robbers, and who led a life of seclusion.

'Well, to be sure!' said Joe, astounded. 'I wonder how she comes to know Pip!'

Mrs Joe returning from an expedition

'Noodle!' cried my sister. 'Who said she knew him?'

' – Which some individual,' Joe again politely hinted, 'mentioned that she wanted him to go and play there.'

'And couldn't she ask Uncle Pumblechook if he knew of a boy to go and play there? Isn't it just barely possible that Uncle Pumblechook may be a tenant of hers, and that he may sometimes – we won't say quarterly or half-yearly, for that would be requiring too much of you – but sometimes – go there to pay his rent? And couldn't she then ask Uncle Pumblechook if he knew of a boy to go and play there? And couldn't Uncle Pumblechook, being always considerate and thoughtful for us – though you may not think it, Joseph,' in a tone of the deepest reproach, as if he were the most callous of nephews, 'then mention this boy, standing prancing here' – which I solemnly declare I was not doing – 'that I have for ever been a willing slave to?'

'Good again!' cried Uncle Pumblechook. 'Well put! Prettily pointed! Good indeed! Now, Joseph, you know the case.'

'No, Joseph,' said my sister, still in a reproachful manner, while Joe apologetically drew the back of his hand across and across his nose, 'you do not yet – though you may not think it – know the case. You may consider that you do, but you do *not*, Joseph. For you do not know that Uncle Pumblechook, being sensible that for anything we can tell, this boy's fortune may be made by his going to Miss Havisham's, has offered to take him into town tonight in his own chaise-cart, and to keep him to-night, and to take him with his own hands to Miss Havisham's tomorrow morning. And Lor-a-mussy-me!' cried my sister, casting off her bonnet in sudden desperation, 'here I stand talking to mere mooncalfs, with Uncle Pumblechook waiting, and the mare catching cold at the door, and the boy grimed with crock and dirt from the hair of his head to the sole of his foot!'

With that, she pounced on me like an eagle on a lamb, and my face was squeezed into wooden bowls in sinks, and my head was put under taps of water-butts, and I was soaped, and kneaded, and towelled, and thumped, and harrowed, and rasped, until I really was quite beside myself. (I may here remark that I suppose myself to be better acquainted than any living authority, with the ridgy effect of a wedding-ring, passing unsympathetically over the human countenance.)

When my ablutions were completed, I was put into clean linen of the stiffest character, like a young penitent into sackcloth, and was trussed up in my tightest and fearfullest suit. I was then delivered over to Mr Pumblechook, who formally received me as if he were the sheriff, and who let off upon me the speech that I knew he had been dying to make all along: 'Boy, be for ever grateful to all friends, but especially unto them which brought you up by hand!'

'Goodbye, Joe!'

'God bless you, Pip, old chap!'

I had never parted from him before, and what with my feelings and what with soapsuds, I could at first see no stars from the chaise-cart. But they twinkled out one by one, without throwing any light on the questions why on earth I was going to play at Miss Havisham's, and what on earth I was expected to play at.

Chapter 8

Mr Pumblechook's premises in the High Street of the market town, were of a peppercorny and farinaceous character, as the premises of a corn-chandler and seedsman should be. It appeared to me that he must be a very happy man indeed, to have so many little drawers in his shop: and I wondered when I peeped into one or two on the lower tiers, and saw the tied-up brown paper packets inside, whether the flower-seeds and bulbs ever wanted of a fine day to break out of those jails, and bloom.

It was in the early morning after my arrival that I entertained this speculation. On the previous night, I had been sent straight to bed in an attic with a sloping roof, which was so low in the corner where the bedstead was, that I calculated the tiles as being within a foot of my eyebrows. In the same early morning, I discovered a singular affinity between seeds and corduroys. Mr Pumblechook wore corduroys, and so did his shopman; and somehow, there was a general air and flavour about the corduroys, so much in the nature of seeds, and a general air and flavour about the seeds, so much in the nature of corduroys, that I hardly knew which was which. The same opportunity served me for noticing that Mr Pumblechook appeared to conduct his business by looking across the street at the saddler, who appeared to transact *his* business by keeping his eye on the coachmaker, who appeared to get on in life by putting his hands in his pockets and contemplating the baker, who in his turn folded his arms and stared at the grocer, who stood at his door and yawned at the chemist. The watchmaker, always poring over a little desk with a magnifying glass at his eye, and always inspected by a group in smock-frocks poring over him through the glass of his shop-window, seemed to be about the only person in the High Street whose trade engaged his attention.

Mr Pumblechook and I breakfasted at eight o'clock in the parlour behind the shop, while the shopman took his mug of tea and hunch of bread and butter on a sack of peas in the front premises. I considered Mr Pumblechook wretched company. Besides being possessed by my sister's idea that a mortifying and penitential character ought to be imparted to my diet – besides giving me as much crumb as possible in combination with as little butter, and putting such a quantity of warm water into my milk that it would have been more candid to have left the milk out altogether – his conversation consisted of nothing but arithmetic. On my politely bidding him good-morning, he said, pompously, 'Seven times nine, boy?' And how should *I* be able to answer, dodged in that way, in a strange place, on an empty stomach! I was hungry, but before I had swallowed a morsel, he began a running sum that lasted all through the breakfast. 'Seven?' 'And four?' 'And eight?' 'And six?' 'And two?' 'And ten?' And so on. And after each figure was disposed of, it was as much as I could do to get a bite or a sup, before the next came; while he sat at his ease guessing nothing, and eating bacon and hot roll, in (if I may be allowed the expression) a gorging and gormandising manner.

For such reasons I was very glad when ten o'clock came and we started for Miss Havisham's; though I was not at all at my ease regarding the manner in which I should acquit myself under that lady's roof. Within a quarter of an hour we came to Miss Havisham's house, which was of old brick, and dismal, and had a great many iron bars to it. Some of the windows had been walled up; of those that remained, all the lower were rustily barred. There was a courtyard in front, and that was barred; so, we had to wait, after ringing the bell, until someone should come to open it. While we waited at the gate, I peeped in (even then Mr Pumblechook said, 'And fourteen?' but I pretended not to hear him), and saw that at the side of the house there was a large brewery. No brewing was going on in it, and none seemed to have gone on for a long time.

A window was raised, and a clear voice demanded 'What name?' To which my conductor replied, 'Pumblechook.' The voice returned, 'Quite right,' and the window was shut again, and a young lady came across the courtyard, with keys in her hand.

'This,' said Mr Pumblechook, 'is Pip.'

'This is Pip, is it?' returned the young lady, who was very pretty and seemed very proud; 'come in, Pip.'

Mr Pumblechook was coming in also, when she stopped him with the gate.

'Oh!' she said. 'Did you wish to see Miss Havisham?'

'If Miss Havisham wished to see me,' returned Mr Pumblechook, discomfited.

'Ah!' said the girl; 'but you see she don't.'

She said it so finally, and in such an undiscussible way, that Mr Pumblechook, though in a condition of ruffled dignity, could not protest. But he eyed me severely – as if *I* had done anything to him! – and departed with the words reproachfully delivered: 'Boy! Let your behaviour here be a credit unto them which brought you up by hand!' I was not free from apprehension that he would come back to propound through the gate, 'And sixteen?' But he didn't.

My young conductress locked the gate, and we went across the courtyard. It was paved and clean, but grass was growing in every crevice. The brewery buildings had a little lane of communication with it; and the wooden gates of that lane stood open, and all the brewery beyond stood open, away to the high enclosing wall; and all was empty and disused. The cold wind seemed to blow colder there, than outside the gate; and it made a shrill noise in howling in and out at the open sides of the brewery, like the noise of wind in the rigging of a ship at sea.

She saw me looking at it, and she said, 'You could drink without hurt all the strong beer that's brewed there now, boy.'

'I should think I could, miss,' said I, in a shy way.

'Better not try to brew beer there now, or it would turn out sour, boy; don't you think so?'

'It looks like it, miss.'

'Not that anybody means to try,' she added, 'for that's all done with, and the place will stand as idle as it is, till it falls. As to strong beer, there's enough of it in the cellars already, to drown the Manor House.'

'Is that the name of this house, miss?'

'One of its names, boy.'

'It has more than one, then, miss?'

'One more. Its other name was Satis; which is Greek, or Latin, or Hebrew, or all three – or all one to me – for enough.'

'Enough House!' said I: 'that's a curious name, miss.'

'Yes,' she replied; 'but it meant more than it said. It meant, when it was given, that whoever had this house, could want nothing else. They must have been easily satisfied in those days, I should think. But don't loiter, boy.'

Though she called me 'boy' so often, and with a carelessness that was far from complimentary, she was of about my own age. She seemed much older than I, of course, being a girl, and beautiful and self-possessed; and she was as scornful of me as if she had been one-and-twenty, and a queen.

We went into the house by a side door – the great front entrance had two chains across it outside – and the first thing I noticed was, that the passages were all dark, and that she had left a candle burning there. She took it up, and we went through more passages and up a staircase, and still it was all dark, and only the candle lighted us.

At last we came to the door of a room, and she said, 'Go in.'

I answered, more in shyness than politeness, 'After you, miss.'

To this, she returned: 'Don't be ridiculous, boy; I am not going in.' And scornfully walked away, and – what was worse – took the candle with her.

This was very uncomfortable, and I was half afraid. However, the only thing to be done being to knock at the door, I knocked, and was told from within to enter. I entered, therefore, and found myself in a pretty large room, well lighted with wax candles. No glimpse of daylight was to be seen in it. It was a dressing-room, as I supposed from the furniture, though much of it was of forms and uses then quite unknown to me. But prominent in it was a draped table with a gilded looking-glass, and that I made out at first sight to be a fine lady's dressing-table.

Whether I should have made out this object so soon, if there had been no fine lady sitting at it, I cannot say. In an armchair, with an elbow resting on the table and her head leaning on that hand, sat the strangest lady I have ever seen, or shall ever see.

She was dressed in rich materials – satins, and lace and silks – all of white. Her shoes were white. And she had a long white veil dependent from her hair, and she had bridal flowers in her hair, but her hair was white. Some bright jewels sparkled on her neck and on her hands, and some other jewels lay sparkling on the table. Dresses, less splendid than the dress she wore, and half-packed trunks, were scattered about. She had not quite finished dressing, for she had but one shoe on – the other was on the table near her hand – her veil was but half arranged, her watch and chain were not put on, and some lace for her bosom lay with those trinkets, and with her handkerchief, and gloves, and some flowers, and a prayer-book, all confusedly heaped about the looking-glass.

It was not in the first few moments that I saw all these things, though I saw more of them in the first moments than might be supposed. But, I saw that everything within my view which ought to be white, had been white long ago, and had lost its lustre, and was faded and yellow. I saw that the bride within the bridal dress had withered like the dress, and like the flowers, and had no brightness left but the brightness of her sunken eyes. I saw that the dress had been put upon the rounded figure of a young woman, and that the figure upon which it now hung loose, had shrunk to skin and bone. Once, I had been taken to see some ghastly waxwork at the fair, representing I know not what impossible personage lying in state. Once, I had been taken to one of our old marsh churches to see a skeleton in the ashes of a rich dress, that had been dug out of a vault under the church pavement. Now, waxwork and skeleton seemed to have dark eyes that moved and looked at me. I should have cried out, if I could.

'Who is it?' said the lady at the table.

'Pip, ma'am.'

'Pip?'

'Mr Pumblechook's boy, ma'am. Come – to play.'

'Come nearer; let me look at you. Come close.'

It was when I stood before her, avoiding her eyes, that I took note of the surrounding objects in detail, and saw that her watch had stopped at twenty minutes to nine, and that a clock in the room had stopped at twenty minutes to nine.

'Look at me,' said Miss Havisham. 'You are not afraid of a woman who has never seen the sun since you were born?'

I regret to state that I was not afraid of telling the enormous lie comprehended in the answer 'No.'

'Do you know what I touch here?' she said, laying her hands, one upon the other, on her left side.

'Yes, ma'am.' (It made me think of the young man.)

'What do I touch?'

'Your heart.

'Broken!'

She uttered the word with an eager look, and with strong emphasis, and with a weird smile that had a kind of boast in it. Afterwards, she kept her hands there for a little while, and slowly took them away as if they were heavy.

'I am tired,' said Miss Havisham. 'I want diversion, and I have done with men and women. Play.'

I think it will be conceded by my most disputatious reader, that she could hardly have directed an unfortunate boy to do anything in the wide world more difficult to be done under the circumstances.

'I sometimes have sick fancies,' she went on, 'and I have a sick fancy that I want to see some play. There, there!' with an impatient movement of the fingers of her right hand; 'play, play, play!'

For a moment, with the fear of my sister's working me before my eyes, I had a desperate idea of starting round the room in the assumed character of Mr Pumblechook's chaise-cart. But, I felt myself so unequal to the performance that I gave it up, and stood looking at Miss Havisham in what I suppose she took for a dogged manner, inasmuch as she said, when we had taken a good look at each other: 'Are you sullen and obstinate?'

'No, ma'am, I am very sorry for you, and very sorry I can't play just now. If you complain of me I shall get into trouble with my sister, so I would do it if I could; but it's so new here, and so

strange, and so fine – and melancholy – ' I stopped, fearing I might say too much, or had already said it, and we took another look at each other.

Before she spoke again, she turned her eyes from me, and looked at the dress she wore, and at the dressing-table, and finally at herself in the looking-glass.

'So new to him,' she muttered, 'so old to me; so strange to him, so familiar to me; so melancholy to both of us! Call Estella.'

As she was still looking at the reflection of herself, I thought she was still talking to herself, and kept quiet.

'Call Estella,' she repeated, flashing a look at me. 'You can do that. Call Estella. At the door.'

To stand in the dark in a mysterious passage of an unknown house, bawling Estella to a scornful young lady neither visible nor responsive, and feeling it a dreadful liberty so to roar out her name, was almost as bad as playing to order. But, she answered at last, and her light came along the dark passage like a star.

Miss Havisham beckoned her to come close, and took up a jewel from the table, and tried its effect upon her fair young bosom and against her pretty brown hair. 'Your own, one day, my dear, and you will use it well. Let me see you play cards with this boy.'

'With this boy! Why, he is a common labouring-boy!'

I thought I overheard Miss Havisham answer – only it seemed so unlikely – 'Well? You can break his heart.'

'What do you play, boy?' asked Estella of myself, with the greatest disdain.

'Nothing but beggar my neighbour, Miss.'

'Beggar him,' said Miss Havisham to Estella. So we sat down to cards.

It was then I began to understand that everything in the room had stopped, like the watch and the clock, a long time ago. I noticed that Miss Havisham put down the jewel exactly on the spot from which she had taken it up. As Estella dealt the cards, I glanced at the dressing-table again, and saw that the shoe upon it, once white, now yellow, had never been worn. I glanced down at the foot from which the shoe was absent, and saw that the silk stocking on it, once white, now yellow, had been trodden ragged. Without this arrest of everything, this standing still of all the pale decayed objects, not even the withered bridal dress on the collapsed form could have looked so like grave-clothes, or the long veil so like a shroud.

So she sat, corpse-like, as we played at cards; the frillings and trimmings on her bridal dress, looking like earthy paper. I knew nothing then of the discoveries that are occasionally made of bodies buried in ancient times, which fall to powder in the moment of being distinctly seen; but, I have often thought since, that she must have looked as if the admission of the natural light of day would have struck her to dust.

'He calls the knaves jacks, this boy!' said Estella with disdain, before our first game was out. 'And what coarse hands he has! And what thick boots!'

I had never thought of being ashamed of my hands before; but I began to consider them a very indifferent pair. Her contempt for me was so strong, that it became infectious, and I caught it.

She won the game, and I dealt. I misdealt, as was only natural, when I knew she was lying in wait for me to do wrong; and she denounced me for a stupid, clumsy labouring-boy.

'You say nothing of her,' remarked Miss Havisham to me, as she looked on. 'She says many hard things of you, yet you say nothing of her. What do you think of her?'

'I don't like to say,' I stammered.

'Tell me in my ear,' said Miss Havisham, bending down.

'I think she is very proud,' I replied, in a whisper.

'Anything else?'

'I think she is very pretty.'

'Anything else?'

'I think she is very insulting.' (She was looking at me then with a look of supreme aversion.)

'Anything else?'

'I think I should like to go home.'

'And never see her again, though she is so pretty?'

'I am not sure that I shouldn't like to see her again, but I should like to go home now.'

'You shall go soon,' said Miss Havisham aloud. 'Play the game out.'

Saving for the one weird smile at first, I should have felt almost sure that Miss Havisham's face could not smile. It had dropped into a watchful and brooding expression – most likely when all the things about her had become transfixed – and it looked as if nothing could ever lift it up again. Her chest had dropped, so that she stooped; and her voice had dropped, so that she spoke low, and with a dead lull upon her; altogether, she had the appearance of having dropped, body and soul, within and without, under the weight of a crushing blow.

I played the game to an end with Estella, and she beggared me. She threw the cards down on the table when she had won them all, as if she despised them for having been won of me.

'When shall I have you here again?' said Miss Havisham. 'Let me think.'

I was beginning to remind her that today was Wednesday, when she checked me with her former impatient movement of the fingers of her right hand.

'There! There! I know nothing of days of the week; I know nothing of weeks of the year. Come again after six days. You hear?'

'Yes, ma'am.'

'Estella, take him down. Let him have something to eat, and let him roam and look about him while he eats. Go, Pip.'

I followed the candle down, as I had followed the candle up, and she stood it in the place where we had found it. Until she opened the side entrance, I had fancied, without thinking about it, that it must necessarily be night-time. The rush of the daylight quite confounded me, and made me feel as if I had been in the candlelight of the strange room many hours.

'You are to wait here, you boy,' said Estella; and disappeared and closed the door.

I took the opportunity of being alone in the courtyard, to look at my coarse hands and my common boots. My opinion of those accessories was not favourable. They had never troubled

me before, but they troubled me now, as vulgar appendages. I determined to ask Joe why he had ever taught me to call those picture-cards, jacks, which ought to be called knaves. I wished Joe had been rather more genteelly brought up, and then I should have been so too.

She came back, with some bread and meat and a little mug of beer. She put the mug down on the stones of the yard, and gave me the bread and meat without looking at me, as insolently as if I were a dog in disgrace. I was so humiliated, hurt, spurned, offended, angry, sorry – I cannot hit upon the right name for the smart – God knows what its name was – that tears started to my eyes. The moment they sprang there, the girl looked at me with a quick delight in having been the cause of them. This gave me power to keep them back and to look at her: so, she gave a contemptuous toss – but with a sense, I thought, of having made too sure that I was so wounded – and left me.

But, when she was gone, I looked about me for a place to hide my face in, and got behind one of the gates in the brewery-lane, and leaned my sleeve against the wall there, and leaned my forehead on it and cried. As I cried, I kicked the wall, and took a hard twist at my hair; so bitter were my feelings, and so sharp was the smart without a name, that needed counteraction.

My sister's bringing up had made me sensitive. In the little world in which children have their existence, whosoever brings them up, there is nothing so finely perceived and so finely felt, as injustice. It may be only small injustice that the child can be exposed to; but the child is small, and its world is small, and its rocking-horse stands as many hands high, according to scale, as a big-boned Irish hunter. Within myself, I had sustained, from my babyhood, a perpetual conflict with injustice. I had known, from the time when I could speak, that my sister, in her capricious and violent coercion, was unjust to me. I had cherished a profound conviction that her bringing me up by hand, gave her no right to bring me up by jerks. Through all my punishments, disgraces, fasts and vigils, and other penitential performances, I had nursed this assurance; and to my communing so much with it, in a solitary and unprotected way, I in great part refer the fact that I was morally timid and very sensitive.

I got rid of my injured feelings for the time, by kicking them into the brewery-wall, and twisting them out of my hair, and then I smoothed my face with my sleeve, and came from behind the gate. The bread and meat were acceptable, and the beer was warming and tingling, and I was soon in spirits to look about me.

To be sure, it was a deserted place, down to the pigeon-house in the brewery-yard, which had been blown crooked on its pole by some high wind, and would have made the pigeons think themselves at sea, if there had been any pigeons there to be rocked by it. But, there were no pigeons in the dovecot, no horses in the stable, no pigs in the sty, no malt in the storehouse, no smells of grains and beer in the copper or the vat. All the uses and scents of the brewery might have evaporated with its last reek of smoke. In a by-yard, there was a wilderness of empty casks, which had a certain sour remembrance of better days lingering about them; but it was too sour to be accepted as a sample of the beer that was gone – and in this respect I remember those recluses as being like most others.

Behind the furthest end of the brewery, was a rank garden with an old wall: not so high but that I could struggle up and hold on long enough to look over it, and see that the rank garden was the garden of the house, and that it was overgrown with tangled weeds, but that there was a track upon the green and yellow paths, as if someone sometimes walked there, and that Estella was walking away from me even then. But she seemed to be everywhere. For, when I yielded to the temptation presented by the casks, and began to walk on them, I saw *her* walking on them at the end of the yard of casks. She had her back towards me, and held her pretty brown hair spread out in her two hands, and never looked round, and passed out of my view directly. So, in the brewery itself – by which I mean the large paved lofty place in which they used to make the beer, and where the brewing utensils still were. When I first went into it, and, rather oppressed by its gloom, stood near the door looking about me, I saw her pass among the extinguished fires, and ascend some light iron stairs, and go out by a gallery high overhead, as if she were going out into the sky.

It was in this place, and at this moment, that a strange thing happened to my fancy. I thought it a strange thing then, and I thought it a stranger thing long afterwards. I turned my eyes – a little dimmed by looking up at the frosty light – towards a great wooden beam in a low nook of the building near me on my right hand, and I saw a figure hanging there by the neck. A figure all in yellow white, with but one shoe to the feet; and it hung so, that I could see that the faded trimmings of the dress were like earthy paper, and that the face was Miss Havisham's, with a movement going over the whole countenance as if she were trying to call to me. In the terror of seeing the figure, and in the terror of being certain that it had not been there a moment before, I at first ran from it, and then ran towards it. And my terror was greatest of all when I found no figure there.

Nothing less than the frosty light of the cheerful sky, the sight of people passing beyond the bars of the courtyard gate, and the reviving influence of the rest of the bread and meat and beer, could have brought me round. Even with those aids, I might not have come to myself as soon as I did, but that I saw Estella approaching with the keys, to let me out. She would have some fair reason for looking down upon me, I thought, if she saw me frightened; and she should have no fair reason.

She gave me a triumphant glance in passing me, as if she rejoiced that my hands were so coarse and my boots were so thick, and she opened the gate, and stood holding it. I was passing out without looking at her, when she touched me with a taunting hand.

'Why don't you cry?'

'Because I don't want to.'

'You do,' said she. 'You have been crying till you are half blind, and you are near crying again now.'

She laughed contemptuously, pushed me out, and locked the gate upon me. I went straight to Mr Pumblechook's, and was immensely relieved to find him not at home. So, leaving word with the shopman on what day I was wanted at Miss Havisham's

again, I set off on the four-mile walk to our forge; pondering, as I went along, on all I had seen, and deeply revolving that I was a common labouring-boy; that my hands were coarse; that my boots were thick; that I had fallen into a despicable habit of calling knaves jacks; that I was much more ignorant than I had considered myself last night, and generally that I was in a low-lived bad way.

Chapter 9

When I reached home, my sister was very curious to know all about Miss Havisham's, and asked a number of questions. And I soon found myself getting heavily bumped from behind in the nape of the neck and the small of the back, and having my face ignominiously shoved against the kitchen wall, because I did not answer those questions at sufficient length.

If a dread of not being understood be hidden in the breasts of other young people to anything like the extent to which it used to be hidden in mine – which I consider probable, as I have no particular reason to suspect myself of having been a monstrosity – it is the key to many reservations. I felt convinced that if I described Miss Havisham's as my eyes had seen it, I should not be understood. Not only that, but I felt convinced that Miss Havisham too would not be understood; and although she was perfectly incomprehensible to me, I entertained an impression that there would be something coarse and treacherous in my dragging her as she really was (to say nothing of Miss Estella) before the contemplation of Mrs Joe. Consequently, I said as little as I could, and had my face shoved against the kitchen wall.

The worst of it was that that bullying old Pumblechook, preyed upon by a devouring curiosity to be informed of all I had seen and heard, came gaping over in his chaise-cart at teatime, to have the details divulged to him. And the mere sight of the torment, with his fishy eyes and mouth open, his sandy hair inquisitively on end, and his waistcoat heaving with windy arithmetic, made me vicious in my reticence.

'Well, boy,' Uncle Pumblechook began, as soon as he was seated in the chair of honour by the fire. 'How did you get on up town?'

I answered, 'Pretty well, sir,' and my sister shook her fist at me.

'Pretty well?' Mr Pumblechook repeated. 'Pretty well is no answer. Tell us what you mean by pretty well, boy?'

Whitewash on the forehead hardens the brain into a state of obstinacy perhaps. Anyhow, with whitewash from the wall on my forehead, my obstinacy was adamantine. I reflected for some time, and then answered as if I had discovered a new idea, 'I mean pretty well.'

My sister with an exclamation of impatience was going to fly at me – I had no shadow of defence, for Joe was busy in the forge – when Mr Pumblechook interposed with 'No! Don't lose your temper. Leave this lad to me, ma'am; leave this lad to me.' Mr Pumblechook then turned me towards him, as if he were going to cut my hair, and said: 'First (to get our thoughts in order): Forty-three pence?'

I calculated the consequences of replying 'Four Hundred Pound,' and finding them against me, went as near the answer as I could – which was somewhere about eightpence off. Mr Pumblechook then put me through my pence-table from 'twelve pence make one shilling, up to 'forty pence make three and fourpence,' and then triumphantly demanded, as if he had done for me, '*Now!* How much is forty-three pence?' To which I replied, after a long interval of reflection, 'I don't know.' And I was so aggravated that I almost doubt if I did know.

Mr Pumblechook worked his head like a screw to screw it out of me, and said, 'Is forty-three pence seven and sixpence three fardens, for instance?'

'Yes!' said I. And although my sister instantly boxed my ears, it was highly gratifying to me to see that the answer spoilt his joke, and brought him to a dead stop.

'Boy! What like is Miss Havisham?' Mr Pumblechook began again when he had recovered; folding his arms tight on his chest and applying the screw.

'Very tall and dark,' I told him.

'Is she, uncle?' asked my sister.

Mr Pumblechook winked assent; from which I at once inferred that he had never seen Miss Havisham, for she was nothing of the kind.

'Good!' said Mr Pumblechook, conceitedly. ('This is the way to have him! We are beginning to hold our own, I think, Mum?')

'I am sure, uncle,' returned Mrs Joe, 'I wish you had him always: you know so well how to deal with him.'

'Now, boy! What was she a doing of, when you went in to-day?' asked Mr Pumblechook.

'She was sitting,' I answered, 'in a black velvet coach.'

Mr Pumblechook and Mrs Joe stared at one another – as they well might – and both repeated, 'In a black velvet coach?'

'Yes,' said I. 'And Miss Estella – that's her niece, I think – handed her in cake and wine at the coach-window, on a gold plate. And we all had cake and wine on gold plates. And I got up behind the coach to eat mine, because she told me to.'

'Was anybody else there?' asked Mr Pumblechook.

'Four dogs,' said I.

'Large or small?'

'Immense,' said I. 'And they fought for veal-cutlets out of a silver basket.'

Mr Pumblechook and Mrs Joe stared at one another again, in utter amazement. I was perfectly frantic – a reckless witness under the torture – and would have told them anything.

'Where *was* this coach, in the name of gracious?' asked my sister.

'In Miss Havisham's room.' They stared again. 'But there weren't any horses to it.' I added this saving clause, in the moment of rejecting four richly caparisoned coursers, which I had had wild thoughts of harnessing.

'Can this be possible, uncle?' asked Mrs Joe. 'What can the boy mean?'

'I'll tell you, Mum,' said Mr Pumblechook. 'My opinion is, it's a sedan-chair. She's flighty, you know – very flighty – quite flighty enough to pass her days in a sedan-chair.'

'Did you ever see her in it, uncle?' asked Mrs Joe.

'How could I,' he returned, forced to the admission, 'when I never see her in my life? Never clapped eyes upon her!'

'Goodness, uncle! And yet you have spoken to her?'

'Why, don't you know,' said Mr Pumblechook, testily, 'that when I have been there, I have been took up to the outside of her door, and the door has stood ajar, and she has spoken to me that way. Don't say you don't know *that*, mum. Howsever, the boy went there to play. What did you play at, boy?'

'We played with flags,' I said. (I beg to observe that I think of myself with amazement, when I recall the lies I told on this occasion.)

'Flags!' echoed my sister.

'Yes,' said I. 'Estella waved a blue flag, and I waved a red one, and Miss Havisham waved one sprinkled all over with little gold stars, out at the coach-window. And then we all waved our swords and hurrahed.'

'Swords!' repeated my sister. 'Where did you get swords from?'

'Out of a cupboard,' said I. 'And I saw pistols in it – and jam – and pills. And there was no daylight in the room, but it was all lighted up with candles.'

'That's true, mum,' said Mr Pumblechook, with a grave nod. 'That's the state of the case, for that much I've seen myself.' And then they both stared at me, and I, with an obtrusive show of artlessness on my countenance, stared at them, and plaited the right leg of my trousers with my right hand.

If they had asked me any more questions I should undoubtedly have betrayed myself, for I was even then on the point of mentioning that there was a balloon in the yard, and should have hazarded the statement but for my invention being divided between that phenomenon and a bear in the brewery. They were so much occupied, however, in discussing the marvels I had already presented for their consideration, that I escaped. The subject still held them when Joe came in from his work to have a cup of tea. To whom my sister, more for the relief of her own mind than for the gratification of his, related my pretended experiences.

Now, when I saw Joe open his blue eyes and roll them all round the kitchen in helpless amazement, I was overtaken by penitence; but only as regarded him – not in the least as regarded the other two. Towards Joe, and Joe only, I considered myself a young monster, while they sat debating what results would come to me from Miss Havisham's acquaintance and favour. They had no doubt that Miss Havisham would 'do something' for me; their doubts related to the form that something would take. My sister stood out for 'property'. Mr Pumblechook was in favour of a handsome premium for binding me apprentice to some genteel trade – say, the corn and seed trade, for instance. Joe fell into the deepest disgrace with both, for offering the bright suggestion that I might only be presented with one of the dogs who had fought for the veal-cutlets. 'If a fool's head can't express better opinions than that,' said my sister, 'and you have got any work to do, you had better go and do it.' So he went.

After Mr Pumblechook had driven off, and when my sister

was washing up, I stole into the forge to Joe, and remained by him until he had done for the night. Then I said, 'Before the fire goes out, Joe, I should like to tell you something.'

'Should you, Pip?' said Joe, drawing his shoeing-stool near the forge. 'Then tell us. What is it, Pip?'

'Joe,' said I, taking hold of his rolled-up shirt sleeve, and twisting it between my finger and thumb, 'you remember all that about Miss Havisham's?'

'Remember?' said Joe; 'I believe you! Wonderful!'

'It's a terrible thing, Joe; it ain't true.'

'What are you telling of, Pip?' cried Joe, falling back in the greatest amazement. 'You don't mean to say it's – '

'Yes, I do; it's lies, Joe.'

'But not all of it? Why sure you don't mean to say, Pip, that there was no black welwet coach?' For I stood shaking my head. 'But at least there was dogs, Pip? Come, Pip,' said Joe, persuasively, 'if there warn't no weal-cutlets, at least there was dogs?'

'No, Joe.'

'A dog?' said Joe. 'A puppy? Come!'

'No, Joe, there was nothing at all of the kind.'

As I fixed my eyes hopelessly on Joe, Joe contemplated me in dismay. 'Pip, old chap! This won't do, old fellow! I say! Where do you expect to go to?'

'It's terrible, Joe; ain't it?'

'Terrible?' cried Joe. 'Awful! What possessed you?'

'I don't know what possessed me, Joe,' I replied, letting his shirt sleeve go, and sitting down in the ashes at his feet, hanging my head; 'but I wish you hadn't taught me to call knaves at cards, jacks; and I wish my boots weren't so thick nor my hands so coarse.'

And then I told Joe that I felt very miserable, and that I hadn't been able to explain myself to Mrs Joe and Pumblechook, who were so rude to me, and that there had been a beautiful young lady at Miss Havisham's who was dreadfully proud, and that she had said I was common, and that I knew I was common, and that I wished I was not common, and that the lies had come of it somehow, though I didn't know how.

This was a case of metaphysics, at least as difficult for Joe to deal with, as for me. But Joe took the case altogether out of the region of metaphysics, and by that means vanquished it.

'There's one thing you may be sure of, Pip,' said Joe, after some rumination, 'namely, that lies is lies. Howsever they come, they didn't ought to come, and they come from the father of lies, and work round to the same. Don't you tell no more of 'em, Pip. *That* ain't the way to get out of being common, old chap. And as to being common, I don't make it out at all clear. You are oncommon in some things. You're oncommon small. Likewise you're a oncommon scholar.'

'No, I am ignorant and backward, Joe.'

'Why, see what a letter you wrote last night! Wrote in print even! I've seen letters – ah! and from gentlefolks! – that I'll swear weren't wrote in print,' said Joe.

'I have learnt next to nothing, Joe. You think much of me. It's only that.'

'Well, Pip,' said Joe, 'be it so, or be it son't, you must be a common scholar afore you can be a oncommon one, I should hope! The king upon his throne, with his crown upon his 'ed, can't sit and write his acts of Parliament in print, without having begun, when he were a unpromoted prince, with the alphabet – Ah!' added Joe, with a shake of the head that was full of meaning, 'and begun at A too, and worked his way to Z. And *I* know what that is to do, though I can't say I've exactly done it.'

There was some hope in this piece of wisdom, and it rather encouraged me.

'Whether common ones as to callings and earnings,' pursued Joe, reflectively, 'mightn't be the better of continuing for to keep company with common ones, instead of going out to play with oncommon ones – which reminds me to hope that there were a flag, perhaps?'

'No, Joe.'

'(I'm sorry there weren't a flag, Pip.) Whether that might be, or mightn't be, is a thing as can't be looked into now, without putting your sister on the rampage; and that's a thing not to be thought of, as being done intentional. Lookee here, Pip, at what is said to you by a true friend. Which this to you the true friend say. If you can't get to be oncommon through going straight, you'll never get to do it through going crooked. So don't tell no more on 'em, Pip, and live well and die happy.'

'You are not angry with me, Joe?'

'No, old chap. But bearing in mind that them were which I meantersay of a stunning and outdacious sort – alluding to them which bordered on weal-cutlets and dog-fighting – a sincere well-wisher would adwise, Pip, their being dropped into your meditations, when you go upstairs to bed. That's all, old chap, and don't never do it no more.'

When I got up to my little room and said my prayers, I did not forget Joe's recommendation, and yet my young mind was in that disturbed and unthankful state, that I thought long after I laid me down, how common Estella would consider Joe, a mere blacksmith: how thick his boots, and how coarse his hands. I thought how Joe and my sister were then sitting in the kitchen, and how I had come up to bed from the kitchen, and how Miss Havisham and Estella never sat in a kitchen, but were far above the level of such common doings. I fell asleep recalling what I 'used to do' when I was at Miss Havisham's; as though I had been there weeks or months, instead of hours: and as though it were quite an old subject of remembrance, instead of one that had risen only that day.

That was a memorable day to me, for it made great changes in me. But it is the same with any life. Imagine one selected day struck out of it, and think how different its course would have been. Pause you who read this, and think for a moment of the long chain of iron or gold, of thorns or flowers, that would never have bound you, but for the formation of the first link on one memorable day.

Chapter 10

The felicitous idea occurred to me a morning or two later when I woke, that the best step I could take towards making myself uncommon was to get out of Biddy everything she knew. In pursuance of this luminous conception, I mentioned to Biddy when I went to Mr Wopsle's great-aunt's at night, that I had a particular reason for wishing to get on in life, and that I should feel very much obliged to her if she would impart all her learning to me. Biddy, who was the most obliging of girls, immediately said she would, and indeed began to carry out her promise within five minutes.

The educational scheme or course established by Mr Wopsle's great-aunt may be resolved into the following synopsis. The pupils ate apples and put straws down one another's backs, until Mr Wopsle's great-aunt collected her energies, and made an indiscriminate totter at them with a birch-rod. After receiving the charge with every mark of derision, the pupils formed in line and buzzingly passed a ragged book from hand to hand. The book had an alphabet in it, some figures and tables, and a little spelling – that is to say, it had had once. As soon as this volume began to circulate, Mr Wopsle's great-aunt fell into a state of coma; arising either from sleep or a rheumatic paroxysm. The pupils then entered among themselves upon a competitive examination on the subject of boots, with the view of ascertaining who could tread the hardest upon whose toes. This mental exercise lasted until Biddy made a rush at them and distributed three defaced Bibles (shaped as if they had been unskilfully cut off the chump-end of something), more illegibly printed at the best than any curiosities of literature I have since met with, speckled all over with iron-mould, and having various specimens of the insect world smashed between their leaves. This part of the course was usually lightened by several single combats between Biddy and refractory students. When the fights were over, Biddy gave out the number of a page, and then we all read aloud what we could – or what we couldn't – in a frightful chorus; Biddy leading with a high shrill monotonous voice, and none of us having the least notion of, or reverence for, what we were reading about. When this horrible din had lasted a certain time, it mechanically awoke Mr Wopsle's great-aunt, who staggered at a boy fortuitously, and pulled his ears. This was understood to terminate the course for the evening, and we emerged into the air with shrieks of intellectual victory. It is fair to remark that there was no prohibition against any pupil's entertaining himself with a slate or even with the ink (when there was any), but that it was not easy to pursue that branch of study in the winter season, on account of the little general shop in which the classes were holden – and which was also Mr Wopsle's great-aunt's sitting-room and bedchamber – being but faintly illuminated through the agency of one low-spirited dip-candle and no snuffers.

It appeared to me that it would take time to become uncommon under these circumstances: nevertheless, I resolved to try it, and that very evening Biddy entered on our special agreement, by imparting some information from her little catalogue of prices, under the head of moist sugar, and lending me, to copy at home, a large old English D which she had imitated from the heading of some newspaper, and which I supposed, until she told me what it was, to be a design for a buckle.

Of course there was a public house in the village, and of course Joe liked sometimes to smoke his pipe there. I had received strict orders from my sister to call for him at the Three Jolly Bargemen, that evening, on my way from school, and bring him home at my peril. To the Three Jolly Bargemen, therefore, I directed my steps.

There was a bar at the Jolly Bargemen, with some alarmingly long chalk scores in it on the wall at the side of the door, which seemed to me to be never paid off. They had been there ever since I could remember, and had grown more than I had. But there was a quantity of chalk about our country, and perhaps the people neglected no opportunity of turning it to account.

It being Saturday night, I found the landlord looking rather grimly at these records, but as my business was with Joe and not with him, I merely wished him good-evening, and passed into the common room at the end of the passage, where there was a bright large kitchen fire, and where Joe was smoking his pipe in company with Mr Wopsle and a stranger. Joe greeted me as usual with 'Halloa, Pip, old chap!' and the moment he said that, the stranger turned his head and looked at me.

He was a secret-looking man whom I had never seen before. His head was all on one side, and one of his eyes was half shut up, as if he were taking aim at something with an invisible gun. He had a pipe in his mouth, and he took it out, and, after slowly blowing all his smoke away and looking hard at me all the time, nodded. So I nodded, and then he nodded again, and made room on the settle beside him that I might sit down there.

But, as I was used to sit beside Joe whenever I entered that place of resort, I said 'No, thank you, sir,' and fell into the space Joe made for me on the opposite settle. The strange man, after glancing at Joe, and seeing that his attention was otherwise engaged, nodded to me again when I had taken my seat, and then rubbed his leg – in a very odd way, as it struck me.

'You was saying,' said the strange man, turning to Joe, 'that you was a blacksmith.'

'Yes. I said it, you know,' said Joe.

'What'll you drink, Mr – ? You didn't mention your name, by the by.'

Joe mentioned it now, and the strange man called him by it.

'What'll you drink, Mr Gargery? At my expense? To top up with?'

'Well,' said Joe, 'to tell you the truth, I ain't much in the habit of drinking at anybody's expense but my own.'

'Habit? No,' returned the stranger, 'but once and away, and on a Saturday night too. Come! Put a name to it, Mr Gargery.'

'I wouldn't wish to be stiff company,' said Joe. 'Rum.'

'Rum,' repeated the stranger. 'And will the other gentleman originate a sentiment?'

'Rum,' said Mr Wopsle.

'Three rums!' cried the stranger, calling to the landlord. 'Glasses round!'

'This other gentleman,' observed Joe, by way of introducing Mr Wopsle, 'is a gentleman that you would like to hear give it out. Our clerk at church.'

'Aha!' said the stranger, quickly, and cocking his eye at me. 'The lonely church, right out on the marshes, with the graves round it!'

'That's it,' said Joe.

The stranger, with a comfortable kind of grunt over his pipe, put his legs up on the settle that he had to himself. He wore a flapping broad-brimmed traveller's hat, and under it a handkerchief tied over his head in the manner of a cap: so that he showed no hair. As he looked at the fire, I thought I saw a cunning expression, followed by a half-laugh, come into his face.

'I am not acquainted with this country, gentlemen, but it seems a solitary country towards the river.'

'Most marshes is solitary,' said Joe.

'No doubt, no doubt. Do you find any gypsies, now, or tramps, or vagrants of any sort, out there?'

'No,' said Joe; 'none but a runaway convict now and then. And we don't find *them*, easy. Eh, Mr Wopsle?'

Mr Wopsle, with a majestic remembrance of old discomfiture, assented; but not warmly.

'Seems you have been out after such?' asked the stranger.

'Once,' returned Joe. 'Not that we wanted to take them, you understand; we went out as lookers on; me and Mr Wopsle, and Pip. Didn't us, Pip?'

'Yes, Joe.'

A stranger at the Three Jolly Bargemen

The stranger looked at me again – still cocking eye, as if he were expressly taking aim at me with his invisible gun – and said, 'He's a likely young parcel of bones that. What is it you call him?'

'Pip,' said Joe.

'Christened Pip?'

'No, not christened Pip.'

'Surname Pip?'

'No,' said Joe; 'it's a kind of a family name what he gave himself when a infant, and is called by.'

'Son of yours?'

'Well,' said Joe, meditatively – not, of course, that it could be in anywise necessary to consider about it, but because it was the way at the Jolly Bargemen to seem to consider deeply about everything that was discussed over pipes; 'well – no. No, he ain't.'

'Nevvy?' said the strange man.

'Well,' said Joe, with the same appearance of profound cogitation, 'he is not – no, not to deceive you, he is *not* – my nevvy.'

'What the blue blazes is he?' asked the stranger. Which appeared to me to be an enquiry of unnecessary strength.

Mr Wopsle struck in upon that; as one who knew all about relationships, having professional occasion to bear in mind what female relations a man might not marry; and expounded the ties between me and Joe. Having his hand in, Mr Wopsle finished off with a most terrifically snarling passage from Richard the Third, and seemed to think he had done quite enough to account for it when he added – 'as the poet says.'

And here I may remark that when Mr Wopsle referred to me, he considered it a necessary part of such reference to rumple my hair and poke it into my eyes. I cannot conceive why everybody of his standing who visited at our house should always have put me through the same inflammatory process under similar circumstances. Yet I do not call to mind that I was ever in my earlier youth the subject of remark in our social family circle, but some large-handed person took some such ophthalmic steps to patronise me.

All this while, the strange man looked at nobody but me, and looked at me as if he were determined to have a shot at me at last, and bring me down. But he said nothing after offering his blue blazes observation, until the glasses of rum and water were brought: and then he made his shot, and a most extraordinary shot it was.

It was not a verbal remark, but a proceeding in dumb show, and was pointedly addressed to me. He stirred his rum and water pointedly at me, and he tasted his rum and water pointedly at me. And he stirred it and he tasted it: not with a spoon that was brought to him, but *with a file*.

He did this so that nobody but I saw the file; and when he had done it, he wiped the file and put it in a breast-pocket. I knew it to be Joe's file, and I knew that he knew my convict, the moment I saw the instrument. I sat gazing at him, spellbound. But he now reclined on his settle, taking very little notice of me, and talking principally about turnips.

There was a delicious sense of cleaning-up and making a quiet pause before going on in life afresh, in our village on

Saturday nights, which stimulated Joe to dare to stay out half an hour longer on Saturdays than at other times. The half-hour and the rum and water running out together, Joe got up to go, and took me by the hand.

'Stop half a moment, Mr Gargery,' said the strange man. 'I think I've got a bright new shilling somewhere in my pocket, and if I have, the boy shall have it.'

He looked it out from a handful of small change, folded it in some crumpled paper, and gave it to me. 'Yours!' said he. 'Mind! Your own.'

I thanked him, staring at him far beyond the bounds of good manners, and holding tight to Joe. He gave Joe good-night, and he gave Mr Wopsle good-night (who went out with us), and he gave me only a look with his aiming eye – no, not a look, for he shut it up, but wonders may be done with an eye by hiding it.

On the way home, if I had been in a humour for talking, the talk must have been all on my side, for Mr Wopsle parted from us at the door of the Jolly Bargemen, and Joe went all the way home with his mouth wide open, to rinse the rum out with as much air as possible. But I was in a manner stupefied by this turning up of my old misdeed and old acquaintance, and could think of nothing else.

My sister was not in a very bad temper when we presented ourselves in the kitchen, and Joe was encouraged by that unusual circumstance to tell her about the bright shilling. 'A bad un, I'll be bound,' said Mrs Joe, triumphantly, 'or he wouldn't have given it to the boy! Let's look at it.'

I took it out of the paper, and it proved to be a good one. 'But what's this?' said Mrs Joe, throwing down the shilling and catching up the paper. 'Two one-pound notes?'

Nothing less than two fat sweltering one-pound notes that seemed to have been on terms of the warmest intimacy with all the cattle markets in the county. Joe caught up his hat again, and ran with them to the Jolly Bargemen to restore them to their owner. While he was gone I sat down on my usual stool and looked vacantly at my sister, feeling pretty sure that the man would not be there.

Presently Joe came back, saying that the man was gone, but that he, Joe, had left word at the Three Jolly Bargemen concerning the notes. Then my sister sealed them up in a piece of paper, and put them under some dried rose-leaves in an ornamental teapot on the top of a press in the state parlour. There they remained a nightmare to me many and many a night and day.

I had sadly broken sleep when I got to bed, through thinking of the strange man taking aim at me with his invisible gun, and of the guiltily coarse and common thing it was, to be on secret terms of conspiracy with convicts – a feature in my low career that I had previously forgotten. I was haunted by the file too. A dread possessed me that when I least expected it, the file would reappear. I coaxed myself to sleep by thinking of Miss Havisham's next Wednesday; and in my sleep I saw the file coming at me out of a door, without seeing who held it, and I screamed myself awake.

Chapter 11

At the appointed time I returned to Miss Havisham's, and my hesitating ring at the gate brought out Estella. She locked it after admitting me, as she had done before, and again preceded me into the dark passage where her candle stood. She took no notice of me until she had the candle in her hand, when she looked over her shoulder, superciliously saying, 'You are to come this way today,' and took me to quite another part of the house.

The passage was a long one, and seemed to pervade the whole square basement of the Manor House. We traversed but one side of the square, however, and at the end of it she stopped and put her candle down and opened a door. Here, the daylight reappeared, and I found myself in a small paved courtyard, the opposite side of which was formed by a detached dwelling-house, that looked as if it had once belonged to the manager or head clerk of the extinct brewery. There was a clock in the outer wall of this house. Like the clock in Miss Havisham's room, and like Miss Havisham's watch, it had stopped at twenty minutes to nine.

We went in at the door, which stood open, and into a gloomy room with a low ceiling, on the ground floor at the back. There was some company in the room, and Estella said to me as she joined it, 'You are to go and stand there, boy, till you are wanted.' 'There' being the window, I crossed to it, and stood 'there', in a very uncomfortable state of mind, looking out.

It opened to the ground, and looked into a most miserable corner of the neglected garden, upon a rank ruin of cabbage-stalks, and one box tree that had been clipped round long ago, like a pudding, and had a new growth at the top of it, out of shape and of a different colour, as if that part of the pudding had stuck to the saucepan and got burnt. This was my homely thought, as I contemplated the box tree. There had been some light snow, overnight, and it lay nowhere else to my knowledge; but it had not quite melted from the cold shadow of this bit of garden, and the wind caught it up in little eddies and threw it at the window, as if it pelted me for coming there.

I divined that my coming had stopped conversation in the room, and that its other occupants were looking at me. I could see nothing of the room except the shining of the fire in the window glass, but I stiffened in all my joints with the consciousness that I was under close inspection.

There were three ladies in the room and one gentleman. Before I had been standing at the window five minutes, they somehow conveyed to me that they were all toadies and humbugs, but that each of them pretended not to know that the others were toadies and humbugs: because the admission that he or she did know it, would have made him or her out to be a toady and humbug.

They all had a listless and dreary air of waiting somebody's pleasure, and the most talkative of the ladies had to speak quite rigidly to suppress a yawn. This lady, whose name was Camilla, very much reminded me of my sister, with the difference that she was older, and (as I found when I caught sight of her) of a blunter cast of features. Indeed, when I knew her better I began to think it was a mercy she had any features at all, so very blank and high was the dead wall of her face.

'Poor dear soul!' said this lady, with an abruptness of manner quite my sister's. 'Nobody's enemy but his own!'

'It would be much more commendable to be somebody else's enemy,' said the gentleman; 'far more natural.'

'Cousin Raymond,' observed another lady, 'we are to love our neighbour.'

'Sarah Pocket,' returned Cousin Raymond, 'if a man is not his own neighbour, who is?'

Miss Pocket laughed, and Camilla laughed and said (checking a yawn), 'The idea!' But I thought they seemed to think it rather a good idea too. The other lady, who had not spoken yet, said gravely and emphatically, '*Very* true!'

'Poor soul!' Camilla presently went on (I knew they had all been looking at me in the mean time), 'he is so very strange! Would anyone believe that when Tom's wife died, he actually could not be induced to see the importance of the children's having the deepest of trimmings to their mourning? "Good Lord!" says he, "Camilla, what can it signify so long as the poor bereaved little things are in black?" So like Matthew! The idea!'

'Good points in him, good points in him,' said Cousin Raymond; 'Heaven forbid I should deny good points in him; but he never had, and he never will have, any sense of the proprieties.'

'You know I was obliged,' said Camilla, 'I was obliged to be firm. I said, "It *will not do*, for the credit of the family." I told him that, without deep trimmings, the family was disgraced. I cried about it from breakfast till dinner. I injured my digestion. And at last he flung out in his violent way, and said, with a D, "Then do as you like." Thank goodness it will always be a consolation to me to know that I instantly went out in a pouring rain and bought the things.'

'*He* paid for them, did he not?' asked Estella.

'It's not the question, my dear child, who paid for them,' returned Camilla. '*I* bought them. And I shall often think of that with peace, when I wake up in the night.'

The ringing of a distant bell, combined with the echoing of some cry or call along the passage by which I had come, interrupted the conversation and caused Estella to say to me, 'Now, boy!' On my turning round, they all looked at me with the utmost contempt, and, as I went out, I heard Sarah Pocket say, 'Well, I am sure! What next!' and Camilla add, with indignation, 'Was there ever such a fancy! The i–de–a!'

As we were going with our candle along the dark passage, Estella stopped all of a sudden, and, facing round, said in her taunting manner, with her face quite close to mine: 'Well?'

'Well, miss,' I answered, almost falling over her and checking myself.

She stood looking at me, and of course I stood looking at her.

'Am I pretty?'

'Yes; I think you are very pretty.'

'Am I insulting?'

'Not so much so as you were last time,' said I.

'Not so much so?'

'No.'

She fired when she asked the last question, and she slapped my face with such force as she had, when I answered it.

'Now?' said she. 'You little coarse monster, what do you think of me now?'

'I shall not tell you.'

'Because you are going to tell upstairs. Is that it?'

'No,' said I, 'that's not it.'

'Why don't you cry again, you little wretch?'

'Because I'll never cry for you again,' said I. Which was, I suppose, as false a declaration as ever was made; for I was inwardly crying for her then, and I know what I know of the pain she cost me afterwards.

We went on our way upstairs after this episode; and, as we were going up, we met a gentleman groping his way down.

'Whom have we here?' asked the gentleman, stopping and looking at me.

'A boy,' said Estella.

He was a burly man of an exceedingly dark complexion, with an exceedingly large head and a corresponding large hand. He took my chin in his large hand and turned up my face to have a look at me by the light of the candle. He was prematurely bald on the top of his head, and had bushy black eyebrows that wouldn't lie down, but stood up bristling. His eyes were set very deep in his head, and were disagreeably sharp and suspicious. He had a large watch-chain, and strong black dots where his beard and whiskers would have been if he had let them. He was nothing to me, and I could have had no foresight then, that he ever would be anything to me, but it happened that I had this opportunity of observing him well.

'Boy of the neighbourhood? Hey?' said he.

'Yes, sir,' said I.

'How do *you* come here?'

'Miss Havisham sent for me, sir,' I explained.

'Well! Behave yourself. I have a pretty large experience of boys, and you're a bad set of fellows. Now mind!' said he, biting the side of his great forefinger as he frowned at me, 'you behave yourself!'

With these words he released me – which I was glad of, for his hand smelt of scented soap – and went his way downstairs. I wondered whether he could be a doctor; but no, I thought; he couldn't be a doctor, or he would have a quieter and more persuasive manner. There was not much time to consider the subject, for we were soon in Miss Havisham's room, where she and everything else were just as I had left them. Estella left me standing near the door, and I stood there until Miss Havisham cast her eyes upon me from the dressing-table.

'So!' she said, without being startled or surprised; 'the days have worn away, have they?'

'Yes, ma'am. Today is – '

'There, there, there!' with the impatient movement of her fingers. 'I don't want to know. Are you ready to play?'

I was obliged to answer in some confusion, 'I don't think I am, ma'am.'

'Not at cards again?' she demanded with a searching look.

'Yes, ma'am; I could do that, if I was wanted.'

'Since this house strikes you old and grave, boy,' said Miss Havisham, impatiently, 'and you are unwilling to play, are you willing to work?'

I could answer this enquiry with a better heart than I had been able to find for the other question, and I said I was quite willing.

'Then go into that opposite room,' said she, pointing at the door behind me with her withered hand, 'and wait there till I come.'

I crossed the staircase landing, and entered the room she indicated. From that room, too, the daylight was completely excluded, and it had an airless smell that was oppressive. A fire had been lately kindled in the damp old-fashioned grate, and it was more disposed to go out than to burn up, and the reluctant smoke which hung in the room seemed colder than the clearer air – like our own marsh mist. Certain wintry branches of candles on the high chimney-piece faintly lighted the chamber; or, it would be more expressive to say, faintly troubled its darkness. It was spacious, and I dare say had once been handsome, but every discernible thing in it was covered with dust and mould, and dropping to pieces. The most prominent object was a long table with a tablecloth spread on it, as if a feast had been in preparation when the house and the clocks all stopped together. An epergne or centrepiece of some kind was in the middle of this cloth; it was so heavily overhung with cobwebs that its form was quite indistinguishable; and, as I looked along the yellow expanse out of which I remember its seeming to grow, like a black fungus, I saw speckled-legged spiders with blotchy bodies running home to it, and running out from it, as if some circumstance of the greatest public importance had just transpired in the spider community.

I heard the mice too, rattling behind the panels, as if the same occurrence were important to their interests. But the black beetles took no notice of the agitation, and groped about the hearth in a ponderous elderly way, as if they were short-sighted and hard of hearing, and not on terms with one another.

These crawling things had fascinated my attention, and I was watching them from a distance, when Miss Havisham laid a hand upon my shoulder. In her other hand she had a crutch-headed stick on which she leaned, and she looked like the witch of the place.

'This,' said she, pointing to the long table with her stick, 'is where I will be laid when I am dead. They shall come and look at me here.

'With some vague misgiving that she might get upon the table then and there and die at once, the complete realisation of the ghastly waxwork at the fair, I shrank under her touch.

'What do you think that is?' she asked me, again pointing with her stick; 'that, where those cobwebs are?'

'I can't guess what it is, ma'am.'

'It's a great cake. A bride-cake. Mine!'

She looked all round the room in a glaring manner, and then said, leaning on me while her hand twitched my shoulder, 'Come, come, come! Walk me, walk me!'

I made out from this, that the work I had to do, was to walk Miss Havisham round and round the room. Accordingly, I started at once, and she leaned upon my shoulder, and we went away at a pace that might have been an imitation (founded on my first impulse under that roof) of Mr Pumblechook's chaise-cart.

She was not physically strong, and after a little time said, 'Slower!' Still, we went at an impatient fitful speed, and as we went, she twitched the hand upon my shoulder, and worked her mouth, and led me to believe that we were going fast because her thoughts went fast. After a while she said, 'Call Estella!' so I went out on the landing and roared that name as I had done on the previous occasion. When her light appeared, I returned to Miss Havisham, and we started away again round and round the room.

If only Estella had come to be a spectator of our proceedings, I should have felt sufficiently discontented; but, as she brought with her the three ladies and the gentleman whom I had seen below, I didn't know what to do. In my politeness I would have stopped; but, Miss Havisham twitched my shoulder, and we posted on – with a shamefaced consciousness on my part that they would think it was all my doing.

'Dear Miss Havisham,' said Miss Sarah Pocket. 'How well you look!'

'I do not,' returned Miss Havisham. 'I am yellow skin and bone.'

Camilla brightened when Miss Pocket met with this rebuff; and she murmured, as she plaintively contemplated Miss Havisham, 'Poor dear soul! Certainly not to be expected to look well, poor thing. The idea!'

'And how are *you*?' said Miss Havisham to Camilla. As we were close to Camilla then, I would have stopped as a matter of course, only Miss Havisham wouldn't stop. We swept on, and I felt that I was highly obnoxious to Camilla.

'Thank you, Miss Havisham,' she returned, 'I am as well as can be expected.'

'Why, what's the matter with you?' asked Miss Havisham, with exceeding sharpness.

'Nothing worth mentioning,' replied Camilla. 'I don't wish to make a display of my feelings, but I have habitually thought of you more in the night than I am quite equal to.'

'Then don't think of me,' retorted Miss Havisham.

'Very easily said!' remarked Camilla, amiably repressing a sob, while a hitch came into her upper lip, and her tears overflowed. 'Raymond is a witness what ginger and sal volatile I am obliged to take in the night. Raymond is a witness what nervous jerkings I have in my legs. Chokings and nervous jerkings, however, are nothing new to me when I think with anxiety of those I love. If I could be less affectionate and sensitive, I should have a better digestion and an iron set of nerves. I am sure I wish it could be so. But as to not thinking of you in the night – the idea!' Here, a burst of tears.

The Raymond referred to, I understood to be the gentleman present, and him I understood to be Mr Camilla. He came to the rescue at this point, and said in a consolatory and complimentary voice, 'Camilla, my dear, it is well known that your family feelings are gradually undermining you to the extent of making one of your legs shorter than the other.'

'I am not aware,' observed the grave lady whose voice I had heard but once, 'that to think of any person is to make a great claim upon that person, my dear.'

Miss Sarah Pocket, whom I now saw to be a little dry brown corrugated old woman, with a small face that might have been made of walnut shells, and a large mouth like a cat's without the whiskers, supported this position by saying, 'No, indeed, my dear. Hem!'

'Thinking is easy enough,' said the grave lady.

'What is easier, you know?' assented Miss Sarah Pocket.

'Oh, yes, yes!' cried Camilla, whose fermenting feelings appeared to rise from her legs to her bosom. 'It's all very true! It's a weakness to be so affectionate, but I can't help it. No doubt my health would be much better if it was otherwise, still I wouldn't change my disposition if I could. It's the cause of much suffering, but it's a consolation to know I possess it, when I wake up in the night.' Here another burst of feeling.

Miss Havisham and I had never stopped all this time, but kept going round and round the room: now, brushing against the skirts of the visitors: now, giving them the whole length of the dismal chambers.

'There's Matthew!' said Camilla. 'Never mixing with any natural ties, never coming here to see how Miss Havisham is! I have taken to the sofa with my stay-lace cut, and have lain there hours, insensible, with my head over the side, and my hair all down, and my feet I don't know where – '

('Much higher than your head, my love,' said Mr Camilla.)

'I have gone off into that state, hours and hours, on account of Matthew's strange and inexplicable conduct, and nobody has thanked me.'

'Really I must say I should think not!' interposed the grave lady.

'You see, my dear,' added Miss Sarah Pocket (a blandly vicious personage), 'the question to put to yourself is, who did you expect to thank you, my love?'

'Without expecting any thanks, or anything of the sort,' resumed Camilla, 'I have remained in that state hours and hours, and Raymond is a witness of the extent to which I have choked, and what the total inefficacy of ginger has been, and I have been heard at the pianoforte tuner's across the street, where the poor mistaken children have even supposed it to be pigeons cooing at a distance – and now to be told – ' Here Camilla put her hand to her throat, and began to be quite chemical as to the formation of new combinations there.

When this same Matthew was mentioned, Miss Havisham stopped me and herself, and stood looking at the speaker. This change had a great influence in bringing Camilla's chemistry to a sudden end.

'Matthew will come and see me at last,' said Miss Havisham, sternly, 'when I am laid on that table. That will be his place – there,' striking the table with her stick, 'at my head! And yours will be there! And your husband's there! And Sarah Pocket's there! And Georgiana's there! Now you all know where to take your stations when you come to feast upon me. And now go!'

At the mention of each name, she had struck the table with her stick in a new place. She now said, 'Walk me, walk me!' and we went on again.

'I suppose there's nothing to be done,' exclaimed Camilla, 'but comply and depart. It's something to have seen the object of one's love and duty, even for so short a time. I shall think of it with a melancholy satisfaction when I wake up in the night. I wish Matthew could have that comfort, but he sets it at defiance. I am determined not to make a display of my feelings, but it's very hard to be told one wants to feast on one's relations – as if one was a giant – and to be told to go. The bare idea!'

Mr Camilla interposing, as Mrs Camilla laid her hand upon her heaving bosom, that lady assumed an unnatural fortitude of manner which I supposed to be expressive of an intention to drop and choke when out of view, and kissing her hand to Miss Havisham, was escorted forth. Sarah Pocket and Georgiana contended who should remain last; but, Sarah was too knowing to be outdone, and ambled round Georgiana with that artful slipperiness, that the latter was obliged to take precedence. Sarah Pocket then made her separate effect of departing with 'Bless you, Miss Havisham dear!' and with a smile of forgiving pity on her walnut-shell countenance for the weaknesses of the rest.

While Estella was away lighting them down, Miss Havisham still walked with her hand on my shoulder, but more and more slowly. At last she stopped before the fire, and said, after muttering and looking at it some seconds: 'This is my birthday, Pip.'

I was going to wish her many happy returns, when she lifted her stick.

'I don't suffer it to be spoken of. I don't suffer those who were here just now, or anyone, to speak of it. They come here on the day, but they dare not refer to it.'

Of course I made no further effort to refer to it.

'On this day of the year, long before you were born, this heap of decay,' stabbing with her crutched stick at the pile of cobwebs on the table but not touching it, 'was brought here. It and I have worn away together. The mice have gnawed at it, and sharper teeth than teeth of mice have gnawed at me.'

She held the head of her stick against her heart as she stood looking at the table; she in her once white dress, all yellow and withered; the once white cloth all yellow and withered; everything around, in a state to crumble under a touch.

'When the ruin is complete,' said she, with a ghastly look, 'and when they lay me dead, in my bride's dress on the bride's table – which shall be done, and which will be the finished curse upon him – so much the better if it is done on this day!'

She stood looking at the table as if she stood looking at her own figure lying there. I remained quiet. Estella returned, and she too remained quiet. It seemed to me that we continued thus a long time. In the heavy air of the room, and the heavy darkness that brooded in its remoter corners, I even had an alarming fancy that Estella and I might presently begin to decay.

At length, not coming out of her distraught state by degrees, but in an instant, Miss Havisham said, 'Let me see you two play at cards; why have you not begun?' With that, we returned to her room, and sat down as before; I was beggared, as before; and again, as before, Miss Havisham watched us all the time, directed my attention to Estella's beauty, and made me notice it the more by trying her jewels on Estella's breast and hair.

Estella, for her part, likewise treated me as before; except that she did not condescend to speak. When we had played some half-dozen games, a day was appointed for my return, and I was taken down into the yard to be fed in the former dog-like manner. There, too, I was again left to wander about as I liked.

It is not much to the purpose whether a gate in that garden wall which I had scrambled up to peep over on the last occasion was, on that last occasion, open or shut. Enough that I saw no gate then, and that I saw one now. As it stood open, and as I knew that Estella had let the visitors out – for, she had returned with the keys in her hand – I strolled into the garden, and strolled all over it. It was quite a wilderness, and there were old melon-frames and cucumber-frames in it, which seemed in their decline to have produced a spontaneous growth of weak attempts at pieces of old hats and boots, with now and then a weedy offshoot into the likeness of a battered saucepan.

When I had exhausted the garden and a greenhouse with nothing in it but a fallen-down grape-vine and some bottles, I found myself in the dismal corner upon which I had looked out of window. Never questioning for a moment that the house was now empty, I looked in at another window, and found myself, to my great surprise, exchanging a broad stare with a pale young gentleman with red eyelids and light hair.

This pale young gentleman quickly disappeared, and re-appeared beside me. He had been at his books when I had found myself staring at him, and I now saw that he was inky.

'Halloa!' said he, 'young fellow!'

Halloa being a general observation which I had usually observed to be best answered by itself, *I* said 'Halloa!' politely omitting young fellow.

'Who let *you* in?' said he.

'Miss Estella.'

'Who gave you leave to prowl about?'

'Miss Estella.'

'Come and fight,' said the pale young gentleman.

What could I do but follow him? I have often asked myself the question since: but what else could I do? His manner was so final and I was so astonished, that I followed where he led, as if I had been under a spell.

'Stop a minute, though,' he said, wheeling round before we had gone many paces. 'I ought to give you a reason for fighting, too. There it is!' In a most irritating manner he instantly slapped his hands against one another, daintily flung one of his legs up behind him, pulled my hair, slapped his hands again, dipped his head, and butted it into my stomach.

The bull-like proceeding last mentioned, besides that it was unquestionably to be regarded in the light of a liberty, was particularly disagreeable just after bread and meat. I therefore hit out at him, and was going to hit out again, when he said, 'Aha! Would you?' and began dancing backwards and forwards in a manner quite unparalleled within my limited experience.

'Laws of the game!' said he. Here, he skipped from his left leg on to his right. 'Regular rules!' Here, he skipped from his right leg on to his left. 'Come to the ground, and go through the preliminaries!' Here, he dodged backwards and forwards, and did all sorts of things while I looked helplessly at him.

I was secretly afraid of him when I saw him so dexterous; but I felt morally and physically convinced that his light head of hair could have had no business in the pit of my stomach, and that I had a right to consider it irrelevant when so obtruded on my attention. Therefore, I followed him without a word, to a retired nook of the garden, formed by the junction of two walls and screened by some rubbish. On his asking me if I was satisfied with the ground, and on my replying yes, he begged my leave to absent himself for a moment, and quickly returned with a bottle of water and a sponge dipped in vinegar. 'Available for both,' he said, placing these against the wall. And then fell to pulling off, not only his jacket and waistcoat, but his shirt too, in a manner at once light-hearted, businesslike, and bloodthirsty.

Although he did not look very healthy – having pimples on his face, and a breaking out on his mouth – these dreadful preparations quite appalled me. I judged him to be about my own age, but he was much taller, and he had a way of spinning himself about that was full of appearance. For the rest, he was a young gentleman in a grey suit (when not denuded for battle), with his elbows, knees, wrists, and heels considerably in advance of the rest of him as to development.

My heart failed me when I saw him squaring at me with every demonstration of mechanical nicety, and eyeing my anatomy as if he were minutely choosing his bone. I never have been so surprised in my life, as I was when I let out the first blow, and saw him lying on his back, looking up at me with a bloody nose and his face exceedingly foreshortened.

But he was on his feet directly, and after sponging himself with a great show of dexterity began squaring again. The second greatest surprise I have ever had in my life was seeing him on his back again, looking up at me out of a black eye.

His spirit inspired me with great respect. He seemed to have no strength, and he never once hit me hard, and he was always knocked down; but he would be up again in a moment, sponging himself or drinking out of the water-bottle, with the greatest satisfaction in seconding himself according to form, and then came at me with an air and a show that made me believe he really was going to do for me at last. He got heavily bruised, for I am sorry to record that the more I hit him, the harder I hit him; but he came up again and again and again, until at last he got a bad fall with the back of his head against the wall. Even after that crisis in our affairs, he got up and turned round and round confusedly a few times, not knowing where I was; but finally went on his knees to his sponge and threw it up: at the same time panting out, 'That means you have won.'

He seemed so brave and innocent, that although I had not proposed the contest, I felt but a gloomy satisfaction in my victory. Indeed, I go so far as to hope that I regarded myself while dressing, as a species of savage young wolf, or other wild beast. However, I got dressed, darkly wiping my sanguinary face at intervals, and I said, 'Can I help you?' and he said, 'No thankee,' and I said, 'Good-afternoon,' and *he* said, 'Same to you.'

When I got into the courtyard, I found Estella waiting with the keys. But she neither asked me where I had been, nor why I had kept her waiting; and there was a bright flush upon her face, as though something had happened to delight her. Instead of going straight to the gate, too, she stepped back into the passage, and beckoned me.

'Come here! You may kiss me if you like.'

I kissed her cheek as she turned it to me. I think I would have gone through a great deal to kiss her cheek. But I felt that the kiss was given to the coarse common boy as a piece of money might have been, and that it was worth nothing.

What with the birthday visitors, and what with the cards, and what with the fight, my stay had lasted so long, that when I neared home the light on the spit of sand off the point on the marshes was gleaming against a black night-sky, and Joe's furnace was flinging a path of fire across the road.

Chapter 12

My mind grew very uneasy on the subject of the pale young gentleman. The more I thought of the fight, and recalled the pale young gentleman on his back in various stages of puffy and incrimsoned countenance, the more certain it appeared that something would be done to me. I felt that the pale young gentleman's blood was on my head, and that the law would avenge it. Without having any definite idea of the penalties I had incurred, it was clear to me that village boys could not go stalking about the country, ravaging the houses of gentlefolks and pitching into the studious youth of England, without laying themselves open to severe punishment. For some days, I even kept close at home, and looked out at the kitchen door with the greatest caution and trepidation before going on an errand, lest the officers of the county jail should pounce upon me. The pale young gentleman's nose had stained my trousers, and I tried to wash out that evidence of my guilt in the dead of night. I had cut my knuckles against the pale young gentleman's teeth, and I twisted my imagination into a thousand tangles, as I devised incredible ways of accounting for that damnatory circumstance when I should be haled before the judges.

When the day came round for my return to the scene of the deed of violence, my terrors reached their height. Whether myrmidons of justice, specially sent down from London, would be lying in ambush behind the gate? Whether Miss Havisham, preferring to take personal vengeance for an outrage done to her house, might rise in those grave-clothes of hers, draw a pistol, and shoot me dead? Whether suborned boys – a numerous band of mercenaries – might be engaged to fall upon me in the brewery, and cuff me until I was no more? It was high testimony to my confidence in the spirit of the pale young gentleman, that I never imagined *him* accessory to these retaliations; they always came into my mind as the acts of injudicious relatives of his, goaded on by the state of his visage and an indignant sympathy with the family features.

However, go to Miss Havisham's I must, and go I did. And behold! nothing came of the late struggle. It was not alluded to

in any way, and no pale young gentleman was to be discovered on the premises. I found the same gate open, and I explored the garden, and even looked in at the windows of the detached house; but, my view was suddenly stopped by the closed shutters within, and all was lifeless. Only in the corner where the combat had taken place, could I detect any evidence of the young gentleman's existence. There were traces of his gore in that spot, and I covered them with garden-mould from the eye of man.

On the broad landing between Miss Havisham's own room and that other room in which the long table was laid out, I saw a garden-chair – a light chair on wheels, that you pushed from behind. It had been placed there since my last visit, and I entered, that same day, on a regular occupation of pushing Miss Havisham in this chair (when she was tired of walking with her hand upon my shoulder) round her own room, and across the landing, and round the other room. Over and over and over again, we would make these journeys, and sometimes they would last as long as three hours at a stretch. I insensibly fall into a general mention of these journeys as numerous, be-cause it was at once settled that I should return every alternate day at noon for these purposes, and because I am now going to sum up a period of at least eight or ten months.

As we began to be more used to one another, Miss Havisham talked more to me, and asked me such questions as what had I learnt and what was I going to be? I told her I was going to be apprenticed to Joe, I believed; and I enlarged upon my knowing nothing and wanting to know everything, in the hope that she might offer some help towards that desirable end. But she did not; on the contrary, she seemed to prefer my being ignorant. Neither did she ever give me any money or anything but my daily dinner – nor even stipulate that I should be paid for my services.

Estella was always about, and always let me in and out, but never told me I might kiss her again. Sometimes, she would coldly tolerate me; sometimes, she would condescend to me; sometimes, she would be quite familiar with me; sometimes, she would tell me energetically that she hated me. Miss Havi-sham would often ask me in a whisper, or when we were alone, 'Does she grow prettier and prettier, Pip?' And when I said yes (for indeed she did), would seem to enjoy it greedily. Also, when we played at cards Miss Havisham would look on, with a miserly relish of Estella's moods, whatever they were. And sometimes, when her moods were so many and so contra-dictory of one another that I was puzzled what to say or do, Miss Havisham would embrace her with lavish fondness, mur-muring something in her ear that sounded like 'Break their hearts, my pride and hope, break their hearts and have no mercy!'

There was a song Joe used to hum fragments of at the forge, of which the burden was Old Clem. This was not a very ceremo-nious way of rendering homage to a patron saint; but I believe Old Clem stood in that relation towards smiths. It was a song that imitated the measure of beating upon iron, and was a mere lyrical excuse for the introduction of Old Clem's respected name. Thus, you were to hammer boys round – Old Clem!

With a thump and a sound – Old Clem! Beat it out, beat it out – Old Clem! With a clink for the stout – Old Clem! Blow the fire, blow the fire – Old Clem! Roaring dryer, soaring higher – Old Clem! One day soon after the appearance of the chair, Miss Havisham suddenly saying to me, with the impatient movement of her fingers, 'There, there, there! Sing!', I was surprised into crooning this ditty as I pushed her over the floor. It happened so to catch her fancy that she took it up in a low brooding voice as if she were singing in her sleep. After that, it became customary with us to have it as we moved about, and Estella would often join in; though the whole strain was so subdued, even when there were three of us, that it made less noise in the grim old house than the lightest breath of wind.

What could I become with these surroundings? How could my character fail to be influenced by them? Is it to be wondered at if my thoughts were dazed, as my eyes were, when I came out into the natural light from the misty yellow rooms?

Perhaps I might have told Joe about the pale young gentleman, if I had not previously been betrayed into those enormous inventions to which I had confessed. Under the circumstances, I felt that Joe could hardly fail to discern in the pale young gentleman, an appropriate passenger to be put into the black velvet coach; therefore I said nothing of him. Besides: that shrinking from having Miss Havisham and Estella discussed, which had come upon me in the beginning, grew much more potent as time went on. I reposed complete confidence in no one but Biddy; but I told poor Biddy everything. Why it came natural for me to do so, and why Biddy had a deep concern in everything I told her, I did not know then, though I think I know now.

Meanwhile, councils went on in the kitchen at home, fraught with almost insupportable aggravation to my exasperated spirit. That ass, Pumblechook, used often to come over of a night for the purpose of discussing my prospects with my sister; and I really do believe (to this hour with less penitence than I ought to feel), that if these hands could have taken a linchpin out of his chaise-cart, they would have done it. The miserable man was a man of that confined stolidity of mind, that he could not discuss my prospects without having me before him – as it were, to operate upon – and he would drag me up from my stool (usually by the collar) where I was quiet in a corner, and, putting me before the fire as if I were going to be cooked, would begin by saying, 'Now, Mum, here is this boy! Here is this boy which you brought up by hand. Hold up your head, boy, and be for ever grateful unto them which so did do. Now, Mum, with respections to this boy!' And then he would rumple my hair the wrong way – which from my earliest remembrance, as already hinted, I have in my soul denied the right of any fellow-creature to do – and would hold me before him by the sleeve: a spectacle of imbecility only to be equalled by himself.

Then he and my sister would pair off in such nonsensical speculations about Miss Havisham, and about what she would do with me and for me, that I used to want – quite painfully – to burst into spiteful tears, fly at Pumblechook, and pummel him all over. In these dialogues, my sister spoke to me as if she were morally wrenching one of my teeth out at every reference;

while Pumblechook himself, self-constituted my patron, would sit supervising me with a depreciatory eye, like the architect of my fortunes who thought himself engaged in a very unremunerative job.

In these discussions, Joe bore no part. But he was often talked at, while they were in progress, by reason of Mrs Joe's perceiving that he was not favourable to my being taken from the forge. I was fully old enough now, to be apprenticed to Joe; and when Joe sat with the poker on his knees thoughtfully raking out the ashes between the lower bars, my sister would so distinctly construe that innocent action into opposition on his part, that she would dive at him, take the poker out of his hands, shake him, and put it away. There was a most irritating end to every one of these debates. All in a moment, with nothing to lead up to it, my sister would stop herself in a yawn, and catching sight of me as it were incidentally, would swoop upon me with 'Come! There's enough of *you*! *You* get along to bed; *you*'ve given trouble enough for one night, I hope!' As if I had besought them as a favour to bother my life out.

We went on in this way for a long time, and it seemed likely that we should continue to go on in this way for a long time, when, one day, Miss Havisham stopped short as she and I were walking, she leaning on my shoulder; and said with some displeasure: 'You are growing tall, Pip!'

I thought it best to hint, through the medium of a meditative look, that this might be occasioned by circumstances over which I had no control.

She said no more at the time; but, she presently stopped and looked at me again; and presently again; and after that, looked frowning and moody. On the next day of my attendance, when our usual exercise was over, and I had landed her at her dressing-table, she stayed me with a movement of her impatient fingers: 'Tell me the name again of that blacksmith of yours.'

'Joe Gargery, ma'am.'

'Meaning the master you were to be apprenticed to?'

'Yes, Miss Havisham.'

'You had better be apprenticed at once. Would Gargery come here with you, and bring your indentures, do you think?'

I signified that I had no doubt he would take it as an honour to be asked.

'Then let him come.'

'At any particular time, Miss Havisham?'

'There, there! I know nothing about times. Let him come soon, and come along with you.'

When I got home at night, and delivered this message for Joe, my sister 'went on the rampage', in a more alarming degree than at any previous period. She asked me and Joe whether we supposed she was doormats under our feet, and how we dared to use her so, and what company we graciously thought she *was* fit for? When she had exhausted a torrent of such enquiries, she threw a candlestick at Joe, burst into a loud sobbing, got out the dustpan – which was always a very bad sign – put on her coarse apron, and began cleaning up to a terrible extent. Not satisfied with a dry cleaning, she took to a pail and scrubbing-brush, and cleaned us out of house and home, so that we stood shivering in the back-yard. It was ten o'clock at night before we ventured to creep in again, and then she asked Joe why he had not married a negress slave at once? Joe offered no answer, poor fellow, but stood feeling his whiskers and looking dejectedly at me, as if he thought it really might have been a better speculation.

Chapter 13

It was a trial to my feelings, on the next day but one, to see Joe arraying himself in his Sunday clothes to accompany me to Miss Havisham's. However, as he thought his court-suit necessary to the occasion, it was not for me to tell him that he looked far better in his working dress; the rather, because I knew he made himself so dreadfully uncomfortable, entirely on my account, and that it was for me he pulled up his shirt-collar so very high behind, that it made the hair on the crown of his head stand up like a tuft of feathers.

At breakfast-time, my sister declared her intention of going to town with us, and being left at Uncle Pumblechook's, and called for 'when we had done with our fine ladies' – a way of putting the case, from which Joe appeared inclined to augur the worst. The forge was shut up for the day, and Joe inscribed in chalk upon the door (as it was his custom to do on the very rare occasions when he was not at work) the monosyllable hout, accompanied by a sketch of an arrow supposed to be flying in the direction he had taken.

We walked to town, my sister leading the way in a very large beaver bonnet, and carrying a basket like the Great Seal of England in plaited straw, a pair of pattens, a spare shawl, and an umbrella, though it was a fine bright day. I am not quite clear whether these articles were carried penitent ally or ostentatiously; but I rather think they were displayed as articles of property – much as Cleopatra or any other sovereign lady on the rampage might exhibit her wealth in a pageant or procession.

When we came to Pumblechook's, my sister bounced in and left us. As it was almost noon, Joe and I held straight on to Miss Havisham's house. Estella opened the gate as usual, and, the moment she appeared, Joe took his hat off and stood weighing it by the brim in both his hands: as if he had some urgent reason in his mind for being particular to half a quarter of an ounce.

Estella took no notice of either of us, but led us the way that I knew so well. I followed next to her, and Joe came last. When I looked back at Joe in the long passage, he was still weighing his hat with the greatest care, and was coming after us in long strides on the tips of his toes.

Estella told me we were both to go in, so I took Joe by the coat-cuff and conducted him into Miss Havisham's presence. She was seated at her dressing-table, and looked round at us immediately.

'Oh!' said she to Joe. 'You are the husband of the sister of this boy?'

I could hardly have imagined dear old Joe looking so unlike himself or so like some extraordinary bird; standing, as he did, speechless, with his tuft of feathers ruffled, and his mouth open as if he wanted a worm.

'You are the husband,' repeated Miss Havisham, 'of the sister of this boy?'

It was very aggravating; but, throughout the interview, Joe persisted in addressing me instead of Miss Havisham.

'Which I meantersay, Pip,' Joe now observed, in a manner that was at once expressive of forcible argumentation, strict confidence, and great politeness, 'as I hup and married your sister, and I were at the time what you might call (if you was any ways inclined) a single man.'

'Well!' said Miss Havisham. 'And you have reared the boy, with the intention of taking him for your apprentice; is that so, Mr Gargery?'

'You know, Pip,' replied Joe, 'as you and me were ever friends, and it were looked for'ard to betwixt us, as being calc'lated to lead to larks. Not but what, Pip, if you had ever made objections to the business – such as its being open to black and sut, or suchlike – not but what they would have been attended to, don't you see?'

'Has the boy,' said Miss Havisham, 'ever made any objection? Does he like the trade?'

'Which it is well beknown to yourself, Pip,' returned Joe, strengthening his former mixture of argumentation, confidence, and politeness, 'that it were the wish of your own hart.' (I saw the idea suddenly break upon him that he would adapt his epitaph to the occasion, before he went on to say) 'And there

I present Joe to Miss Haversham

weren't no objection on your part, and Pip it were the great wish of your hart!'

It was quite in vain for me to endeavour to make him sensible that he ought to speak to Miss Havisham. The more I made faces and gestures to him to do it, the more confidential, argumentative, and polite, he persisted in being to me.

'Have you brought his indentures with you?' asked Miss Havisham.

'Well, Pip, you know,' replied Joe, as if that were a little unreasonable, 'you yourself see me put 'em in my 'at, and therefore you know as they are here.' With which he took them out, and gave them, not to Miss Havisham, but to me. I am afraid I was ashamed of the dear good fellow – I *know* I was ashamed of him – when I saw that Estella stood at the back of Miss Havisham's chair, and that her eyes laughed mischievously. I took the indentures out of his hand and gave them to Miss Havisham.

'You expected,' said Miss Havisham, as she looked them over, 'no premium with the boy?'

'Joe!' I remonstrated; for he made no reply at all. 'Why don't you answer – '

'Pip,' returned Joe, cutting me short as if he were hurt, 'which I meantersay that were not a question requiring a answer betwixt yourself and me, and which you know the answer to be full well no. You know it to be no, Pip, and wherefore should I say it?'

Miss Havisham glanced at him as if she understood what he really was, better than I had thought possible, seeing what he was there; and took up a little bag from the table beside her.

'Pip has earned a premium here,' she said, 'and here it is. There are five-and-twenty guineas in this bag. Give it to your master, Pip!'

As if he were absolutely out of his mind with the wonder awakened in him by her strange figure and the strange room, Joe, even at this pass, persisted in addressing me.

'This is very liberal on your part, Pip,' said Joe, 'and it is as such received and grateful welcome, though never looked for, far nor near nor nowheres. And now, old chap,' said Joe, conveying to me a sensation, first of burning and then of freezing, for I felt as if that familiar expression were applied to Miss Havisham; 'and now, old chap, may we do our duty! May you and me do our duty, both on us by one and another, and by them which your liberal present – have – conweyed – to be – for the satisfaction of mind – of – them as never – ' here Joe showed that he felt he had fallen into frightful difficulties, until he triumphantly rescued himself with the words, 'and from myself far be it!' These words had such a round and convincing sound for him that he said them twice.

'Goodbye, Pip!' said Miss Havisham. 'Let them out, Estella.'

'Am I to come again, Miss Havisham?' I asked.

'No. Gargery is your master now. Gargery! One word!'

Thus calling him back as I went out of the door, I heard her say to Joe, in a distinct emphatic voice, 'The boy has been a good boy here, and that is his reward. Of course, as an honest man, you will expect no other and no more.'

How Joe got out of the room, I have never been able to determine; but I know that when he did get out he was steadily proceeding upstears instead of coming down, and was deaf to all remonstrances until I went after him and laid hold of him. In another minute we were outside the gate, and it was locked, and Estella was gone. When we stood in the daylight alone again, Joe backed up against a wall, and said to me, 'Astonishing!' And there he remained so long, saying 'Astonishing' at intervals, so often, that I began to think his senses were never coming back. At length, he prolonged his remark into 'Pip, I do assure *you* this is as–ton–ishing!' and so, by degrees, became conversational and able to walk away.

I have reason to think that Joe's intellects were brightened by the encounter they had passed through, and that on our way to Pumblechook's, he invented a subtle and deep design. My reason is to be found in what took place in Mr Pumblechook's parlour: where, on our presenting ourselves, my sister sat in conference with that detested seedsman.

'Well!' cried my sister, addressing us both at once. 'And what's happened to *you*? I wonder you condescend to come back to such poor society as this, I am sure I do!'

'Miss Havisham,' said Joe, with a fixed look at me, like an effort of remembrance, 'made it wery partick'-ler that we should give her – were it compliments or respects, Pip?'

'Compliments,' I said.

'Which that were my own belief,' answered Joe – 'her compliments to Mrs J. Gargery – '

'Much good they'll do me!' observed my sister: but rather gratified too.

'And wishing,' pursued Joe, with another fixed look at me, like another effort of remembrance, 'that the state of Miss Havisham's elth were sitch as would have – allowed, were it, Pip?'

'Of her having the pleasure,' I added.

'Of ladies' company,' said Joe. And drew a long breath.

'Well!' cried my sister, with a mollified glance at Mr Pumblechook. 'She might have had the politeness to send that message at first, but it's better late than never. And what did she give young Rantipole here?'

'She giv' him,' said Joe, 'nothing.'

Mrs Joe was going to break out, but Joe went on.

'What she giv',' said Joe, 'she giv' to his friends. "And by his friends," were her explanation, "I mean into the hands of his sister, Mrs J. Gargery." Them were her words; "Mrs J. Gargery." She mayn't have know'd,' added Joe, with an appearance of reflection, 'whether it were Joe or Jorge.'

My sister looked at Pumblechook: who smoothed the elbows of his wooden armchair, and nodded at her and at the fire, as if he had known all about it beforehand.

'And how much have you got?' asked my sister, laughing. Positively, laughing!

'What would present company say to ten pound?' demanded Joe.

'They'd say,' returned my sister curtly, 'pretty well. Not too much, but pretty well.'

'It's more than that, then,' said Joe.

That fearful impostor, Pumblechook, immediately nodded, and said, as he rubbed the arms of his chair: 'It's more than that, mum.'

'Why, you don't mean to say – ' began my sister.

'Yes, I do, mum,' said Pumblechook; 'but wait a bit. Go on, Joseph. Good in you! Go on!'

'What would present company say,' proceeded Joe, 'to twenty pound?'

'Handsome would be the word,' returned my sister.

'Well then,' said Joe, 'it's more than twenty pound.'

That abject hypocrite, Pumblechook, nodded again, and said with a patronising laugh, 'It's more than that, mum. Good again! Follow her up, Joseph!'

'Then to make an end of it,' said Joe, delightedly, handing the bag to my sister; 'it's five-and-twenty pound.'

'It's five-and-twenty pound, mum,' echoed that basest of swindlers, Pumblechook, rising to shake hands with her: 'and it's no more than your merits (as I said when my opinion was asked), and I wish you joy of the money!'

If the villain had stopped here, his case would have been sufficiently awful, but he blackened his guilt by proceeding to take me into custody, with a right of patronage that left all his former criminality far behind.

'Now you see, Joseph and wife,' said Mr Pumblechook, as he took me by the arm above the elbow, 'I am one of them that always go right through with what they've begun. This boy must be bound out of hand. That's *my* way. Bound out of hand.'

'Goodness knows, Uncle Pumblechook,' said my sister (grasping the money), 'we're deeply beholden to you.'

'Never mind me, mum,' returned that diabolical corn-chandler. 'A pleasure's a pleasure all the world over. But this boy, you know; we must have him bound. I said I'd see to it – to tell you the truth.'

The justices were sitting in the town hall near at hand, and we at once went over to have me bound apprentice to Joe in the magisterial presence. I say, we went over, but I was pushed over by Pumblechook, exactly as if I had that moment picked a pocket or fired a rick; indeed, it was the general impression in court that I had been taken red-handed; for, as Pumblechook shoved me before him through the crowd, I heard some people say, 'What's he done?' and others, 'He's a young 'un, too, but looks bad, don't he ?' One person of mild and benevolent aspect even gave me a tract ornamented with a woodcut of a malevolent young man fitted up with a perfect sausage-shop of fetters, and entitled, To be read in my Cell.

The hall was a queer place, I thought, with higher pews in it than a church – and with people hanging over the pews looking on – and with mighty justices (one with a powdered head) leaning back in chairs, with folded arms, or taking snuff, or going to sleep, or writing, or reading the newspapers – and with some shining black portraits on the walls, which my unartistic eye regarded as a composition of hard-bake and sticking-plaster. Here, in a corner, my indentures were duly signed and attested, and I was 'bound'; Mr Pumblechook holding me all the while as if we had looked in on our way to the scaffold, to have those little preliminaries disposed of.

When we had come out again, and had got rid of the boys who had been put into great spirits by the expectation of seeing me publicly tortured, and who were much disappointed to find that my friends were merely rallying round me, we went back to Pumblechook's. And there my sister became so excited by the twenty-five guineas, that nothing would serve her but we must have a dinner out of that windfall, at the Blue Boar, and that Mr Pumblechook must go over in his chaise-cart, and bring the Hubbles and Mr Wopsle.

It was agreed to be done; and a most melancholy day I passed. For it inscrutably appeared to stand to reason, in the minds of the whole company, that I was an excrescence on the entertainment. And to make it worse, they all asked me from time to time – in short, whenever they had nothing else to do – why I didn't enjoy myself? And what could I possibly do then, but say that I *was* enjoying myself – when I wasn't!

However, they were grown up and had their own way, and made the most of it. That swindling Pumblechook, exalted into the beneficent contriver of the whole occasion, actually took the top of the table; and, when he addressed them on the subject of my being bound, and had fiendishly congratulated them on my being liable to imprisonment if I played at cards, drank strong liquors, kept late hours or bad company, or indulged in other vagaries which the form of my indentures appeared to contemplate as next to inevitable, he placed me standing on a chair beside him to illustrate his remarks.

My only other remembrances of the great festival are, That they wouldn't let me go to sleep, but whenever they saw me dropping off, woke me up and told me to enjoy myself. That, rather late in the evening, Mr Wopsle gave us Collins's ode, and threw his blood-stain'd sword in thunder down, with such effect that a waiter came in and said, 'The Commercials underneath sent up their compliments, and it wasn't the Tumblers' Arms.' That, they were all in excellent spirits on the road home, and sang O Lady Fair! Mr Wopsle taking the bass, and asserting with a tremendously strong voice (in reply to the inquisitive bore who leads that piece of music in a most impertinent manner, by wanting to know all about everybody's private affairs) that *he* was the man with his white locks flowing, and that he was upon the whole the weakest pilgrim going.

Finally, I remember that when I got into my little bedroom, I was truly wretched, and had a strong conviction on me that I should never like Joe's trade. I had liked it once, but once was not now.

Chapter 14

It is a most miserable thing to feel ashamed of home. There may be black ingratitude in the thing, and the punishment may be retributive and well deserved; but, that it is a miserable thing, I can testify.

Home had never been a very pleasant place to me, because of my sister's temper. But, Joe had sanctified it, and I believed in it. I had believed in the best parlour as a most elegant saloon; I had believed in the front door, as a mysterious portal of the temple of state whose solemn opening was attended with a sacrifice of roast fowls; I had believed in the kitchen as a chaste though not magnificent apartment; I had believed in the forge as the glowing road to manhood and independence. Within a single year all this was changed. Now, it was all coarse and common, and I would not have had Miss Havisham and Estella see it on any account.

How much of my ungracious condition of mind may have been my own fault, how much Miss Havisham's, how much my sister's, is now of no moment to me or to anyone. The change was made in me; the thing was done. Well or ill done, excusably or inexcusably, it was done.

Once, it had seemed to me that when I should at last roll up my shirtsleeves and go into the forge, Joe's 'prentice, I should be distinguished and happy. Now the reality was in my hold, I only felt that I was dusty with the dust of the small coal, and that I had a weight upon my daily remembrance to which the anvil was a feather. There have been occasions in my later life (I suppose as in most lives) when I have felt for a time as if a thick curtain had fallen on all its interest and romance, to shut me out from anything save dull endurance any more. Never has that curtain dropped so heavy and blank, as when my way in life lay stretched out straight before me through the newly-entered road of apprenticeship to Joe.

I remember that at a later period of my 'time', I used to stand about the churchyard on Sunday evenings, when night was falling, comparing my own perspective with the windy marsh view, and making out some likeness between them by thinking how flat and low both were, and how on both there came an unknown way and a dark mist and then the sea. I was quite as dejected on the first working-day of my apprenticeship as in that after-time; but I am glad to know that I never breathed a murmur to Joe while my indentures lasted. It is about the only thing I *am* glad to know of myself in that connection.

For, though it includes what I proceed to add, all the merit of what I proceed to add was Joe's. It was not because I was faithful, but because Joe was faithful, that I never ran away and went for a soldier or a sailor. It was not because I had a strong sense of the virtue of industry, but because Joe had a strong sense of the virtue of industry, that I worked with tolerable zeal against the grain. It is not possible to know how far the influence of any amiable honest-hearted duty-doing man flies out into the world; but it is very possible to know how it has touched one's self in going by, and I know right well that any good that intermixed itself with my apprenticeship came of plain contented Joe, and not of restless aspiring discontented me.

What I wanted, who can say? How can *I* say, when I never knew? What I dreaded was, that in some unlucky hour I, being at my grimiest and commonest, should lift up my eyes and see Estella looking in at one of the wooden windows of the forge. I was haunted by the fear that she would, sooner or later, find me out, with a black face and hands, doing the coarsest part of my work, and would exult over me and despise me. Often after dark, when I was pulling the bellows for Joe, and we were singing Old Clem, and when the thought how we used to sing it at Miss Havisham's would seem to show me Estella's face in the fire, with her pretty hair fluttering in the wind and her eyes scorning me – often at such a time I would look towards those panels of black night in the wall which the wooden windows then were, and would fancy that I saw her just drawing her face away, and would believe that she had come at last.

After that, when we went in to supper, the place and the meal would have a more homely look than ever, and I would feel more ashamed of home than ever, in my own ungracious breast.

Chapter 15

As I was getting too big for Mr Wopsle's great-aunt's room, my education under that preposterous female terminated. Not, however, until Biddy had imparted to me everything she knew, from the little catalogue of prices, to a comic song she had once bought for a halfpenny. Although the only coherent part of the latter piece of literature were the opening lines,

> When I went to Lunnon town, sirs,
> > Too rul loo rul!
> > Too rul loo rul!
> Wasn't I done very brown, sirs?
> > Too rul loo rul!
> > Too rul loo rul!

– still, in my desire to be wiser, I got this composition by heart with the utmost gravity; nor do I recollect that I questioned its merit, except that I thought (as I still do) the amount of Too rul somewhat in excess of the poetry. In my hunger for information, I made proposals to Mr Wopsle to bestow some intellectual crumbs upon me; with which he kindly complied. As it turned out, however, that he only wanted me for a dramatic lay-figure, to be contradicted and embraced and wept over and bullied and clutched and stabbed and knocked about in a variety of ways, I soon declined that course of instruction; though not until Mr Wopsle in his poetic fury had severely mauled me.

Whatever I acquired, I tried to impart to Joe. This statement sounds so well, that I cannot in my conscience let it pass unexplained. I wanted to make Joe less ignorant and common, that he might be worthier of my society and less open to Estella's reproach.

The old battery out on the marshes was our place of study, and a broken slate and a short piece of slate pencil were our educational implements: to which Joe always added a pipe of tobacco. I never knew Joe to remember anything from one Sunday to another, or to acquire, under my tuition, any piece of information whatever. Yet he would smoke his pipe at the battery with a far more sagacious air than anywhere else – even with a learned air – as if he considered himself to be advancing immensely. Dear fellow, I hope he did.

It was pleasant and quiet, out there with the sails on the river passing beyond the earthwork, and sometimes, when the tide was low, looking as if they belonged to sunken ships that were still sailing on at the bottom of the water. Whenever I watched the vessels standing out to sea with their white sails spread, I somehow thought of Miss Havisham and Estella; and whenever the light struck aslant, afar off, upon a cloud or sail or green hillside or water-line, it was just the same – Miss Havisham and Estella and the strange house and the strange life appeared to have something to do with everything that was picturesque.

One Sunday when Joe, greatly enjoying his pipe, had so plumed himself on being 'most awful dull', that I had given him up for the day, I lay on the earthwork for some time with my chin on my hand, descrying traces of Miss Havisham and Estella all over the prospect, in the sky and in the water, until at last I resolved to mention a thought concerning them that had been much in my head.

'Joe,' said I; 'don't you think I ought to pay Miss Havisham a visit?'

'Well, Pip,' returned Joe, slowly considering. 'What for?'

'What for, Joe? What is any visit made for?'

'There is some wisits p'r'aps,' said Joe, 'as for ever remains open to the question, Pip. But in regard of wisiting Miss Havisham. She might think you wanted something – expected something of her.'

'Don't you think I might say that I did not, Joe?'

'You might, old chap,' said Joe. 'And she might credit it. Similarly, she mightn't.'

Joe felt, as I did, that he had made a point there, and he pulled hard at his pipe to keep himself from weakening it by repetition.

'You see, Pip,' Joe pursued, as soon as he was past that danger, 'Miss Havisham done the handsome thing by you. When Miss Havisham done the handsome thing by you, she called me back to say to me as that were all.'

'Yes, Joe. I heard her.'

'*All*,' Joe repeated, very emphatically.

'Yes, Joe. I tell you, I heard her.'

'Which I meantersay, Pip, it might be that her meaning were – make an end on it! – as you was! – me to the North, and you to the South! – keep in sunders!'

I had thought of that too, and it was very far from comforting to me to find that he had thought of it; for it seemed to render it more probable.

'But, Joe.'

'Yes, old chap.'

'Here am I, getting on in the first year of my time, and, since the day of my being bound I have never thanked Miss Havisham, or asked after her, or shown that I remember her.'

'That's true, Pip; and unless you was to turn her out a set of shoes all four round – and which I meantersay as even a set of shoes all four round might not act acceptable as a present in a total wacancy of hoofs – '

'I don't mean that sort of remembrance, Joe; I don't mean a present.'

But Joe had got the idea of a present in his head and must harp upon it. 'Or even,' said he, 'if you was helped to knocking her up a new chain for the front door – or say a gross or two of shark-headed screws for general use – or some light fancy article, such as a toasting-fork when she took her muffins – or a gridiron when she took a sprat or suchlike – '

'I don't mean any present at all, Joe,' I interposed.

'Well,' said Joe, still harping on it as though I had particularly pressed it, 'if I was yourself, Pip, I wouldn't. No, I would *not*. For what's a door-chain when she's got one always up? And shark-headers is open to misrepresentations. And if it was a toasting-fork, you'd go into brass and do yourself no credit. And the on-commonest workman can't show himself on-common in a gridiron – for a gridiron *is* a gridiron,' said Joe, steadfastly impressing it upon me, as if he were endeavouring to rouse me from a fixed delusion, 'and you may haim at what you like, but a gridiron it will come out, either by your leave or again your leave, and you can't help yourself – '

'My dear Joe,' I cried in desperation, taking hold of his coat, 'don't go on in that way. I never thought of making Miss Havisham any present.'

'No, Pip,' Joe assented, as if he had been contending for that all along; 'and what I say to you is, you are right, Pip.'

'Yes, Joe; but what I wanted to say, was, that as we are rather slack just now, if you would give me a half-holiday tomorrow, I think I would go uptown and make a call on Miss Est – Havisham.'

'Which her name,' said Joe, gravely, 'ain't Est-avisham, Pip, unless she have been rechris'ened.'

'I know, Joe, I know. It was a slip of mine. What do you think of it, Joe?'

In brief, Joe thought that if I thought well of it, he thought well of it. But he was particular in stipulating that if I were not received with cordiality, or if I were not encouraged to repeat my visit as a visit which had no ulterior object, but was simply one of gratitude for a favour received, then this experimental trip should have no successor. By these conditions I promised to abide.

Now, Joe kept a journeyman at weekly wages whose name was Orlick. He pretended that his christian name was Dolge – a clear impossibility – but he was a fellow of that obstinate disposition that I believe him to have been the prey of no delusion in this particular, but wilfully to have imposed that name upon the village as an affront to its understanding. He was a broad-shouldered loose-limbed swarthy fellow of great strength, never in a hurry, and always slouching. He never even seemed to come to his work on purpose, but would slouch in as if by mere accident; and when he went to the Jolly Bargemen to eat his dinner, or went away at night, he would slouch out, like Cain or the Wandering Jew, as if he had no idea where he was going, and no intention of ever coming back. He lodged at a sluice-keeper's out on the marshes, and on working days would come slouching from his hermitage, with his hands in his pockets and his dinner loosely tied in a bundle round his neck and dangling on his back. On Sundays he mostly lay all day on sluicegates, or stood against ricks and barns. He always slouched, locomotively, with his eyes on the ground; and, when accosted or otherwise required to raise them, he looked up in a half resentful, half puzzled way, as though the only thought he ever had, was, that it was rather an odd and injurious fact that he should never be thinking.

This morose journeyman had no liking for me. When I was very small and timid, he gave me to understand that the devil lived in a black corner of the forge, and that he knew the fiend very well: also that it was necessary to make up the fire, once in seven years, with a live boy, and that I might consider myself fuel. When I became Joe's 'prentice, Orlick was perhaps confirmed in some suspicion that I should displace him; howbeit, he liked me still less. Not that he ever said anything, or did anything, openly importing hostility; I only noticed that he always beat his sparks in my direction, and that whenever I sang Old Clem, he came in out of time.

Dolge Orlick was at work and present, next day, when I reminded Joe of my half-holiday. He said nothing at the moment, for he and Joe had just got a piece of hot iron between them, and I was at the bellows; but by and by he said, leaning on his hammer: 'Now, master! Sure you're not a going to favour only one of us? If Young Pip has a half-holiday, do as much for Old Orlick.' I suppose he was about five-and-twenty, but he usually spoke of himself as an ancient person.

'Why, what'll you do with a half-holiday, if you get it?' said Joe.

'What'll *I* do with it? What'll *he* do with it? I'll do as much with it as *him*,' said Orlick.

'As to Pip, he's going uptown,' said Joe.

'Well then, as to Old Orlick, *he's* a going uptown,' retorted that worthy. 'Two can go uptown. 'Tain't only one wot can go uptown.'

'Don't lose your temper,' said Joe.

'Shall if I like,' growled Orlick. 'Some and their uptowning! Now, master! Come. No favouring in this shop. Be a man!'

The master refusing to entertain the subject until the journeyman was in a better temper, Orlick plunged at the furnace, drew out a red-hot bar, made at me with it as if he were going to run it through my body, whisked it round my head, laid it on the anvil, hammered it out – as if it were I, I thought, and the sparks were my spirting blood – and finally said, when he had hammered himself hot and the iron cold, and he again leaned on his hammer: 'Now, master!'

'Are you all right now?' demanded Joe.

'Ah! I am all right,' said gruff Old Orlick.

'Then, as in general you stick to your work as well as most men,' said Joe, 'let it be a half-holiday for all.'

My sister had been standing silent in the yard, within hearing – she was a most unscrupulous spy and listener – and she instantly looked in at one of the windows.

'Like you, you fool!' said she to Joe, 'giving holidays to great idle hulkers like that. You are a rich man, upon my life, to waste wages in that way. I wish *I* was his master!'

'You'd be everybody's master if you durst,' retorted Orlick, with an ill-favoured grin.

('Let her alone,' said Joe.)

'I'd be a match for all noodles and all rogues,' returned my sister, beginning to work herself into a mighty rage. 'And I couldn't be a match for the noodles, without being a match for your master, who's the dunderheaded king of the noodles. And I couldn't be a match for the rogues, without being a match for you, who are the blackest-looking and the worst rogue between this and France. Now!'

'You're a foul shrew, Mother Gargery,' growled the journeyman. 'If that makes a judge of rogues, you ought to be a good 'un.'

('Let her alone, will you?' said Joe.)

'What did you say?' cried my sister, beginning to scream. 'What did you say? What did that fellow Orlick say to me, Pip? What did he call me, with my husband standing by? O! O! O!' Each of these exclamations was a shriek; and I must remark of my sister, what is equally true of all the violent women I have ever seen, that passion was no excuse for her, because it is undeniable that instead of lapsing into passion, she consciously and deliberately took extraordinary pains to force herself into it, and became blindly furious by regular stages; 'what was the name that he gave me before the base man who swore to defend me? O! Hold me! O!'

'Ah–h–h!' growled the journeyman, between his teeth, 'I'd hold you, if you was my wife. I'd hold you under the pump, and choke it out of you.'

('I tell you, let her alone,' said Joe.)

'Oh! To hear him!' cried my sister, with a clap of her hands and a scream together – which was her next stage. 'To hear the names he's giving me! That Orlick! In my own house! Me, a married woman! With my husband standing by! O! O!' Here my sister, after a fit of clappings and screamings, beat her hands upon her bosom and upon her knees, and threw her cap off, and pulled her hair down – which were the last stages on her road to frenzy. Being by this time a perfect fury and a complete success, she made a dash at the door, which I had fortunately locked.

What could the wretched Joe do now, after his disregarded parenthetical interruptions, but stand up to his journeyman, and ask him what he meant by interfering betwixt himself and Mrs Joe; and further whether he was man enough to come on? Old Orlick felt that the situation admitted of nothing less than coming on, and was on his defence straightway; so, without so much as pulling off their singed and burnt aprons, they went at one another, like two giants. But, if any man in that neighbourhood could stand up long against Joe, I never saw the man. Orlick, as if he had been of no more account than the pale young gentleman, was very soon among the coal-dust, and in no hurry to come out of it. Then Joe unlocked the door and picked up my sister, who had dropped insensible at the window (but who had seen the fight first, I think), and who was carried into the house and laid down, and who was recommended to revive, and would do nothing but struggle and clench her hands in Joe's hair. Then came that singular calm and silence which succeed all uproars; and then with the vague sensation which I have always connected with such a lull – namely, that it was Sunday, and somebody was dead – I went upstairs to dress myself.

When I came down again, I found Joe and Orlick sweeping up, without any other traces of discomposure than a slit in one of Orlick's nostrils, which was neither expressive nor ornamental. A pot of beer had appeared from the Jolly Bargemen, and they were sharing it by turns in a peaceable manner. The lull had a sedative and philosophical influence on Joe, who followed me out into the road to say, as a parting observation that might do me good, 'On the rampage, Pip, and off the rampage, Pip – such is life!'

With what absurd emotions (for, we think the feelings that are very serious in a man quite comical in a boy) I found myself again going to Miss Havisham's, matters little here. Nor, how I passed and repassed the gate many times before I could make up my mind to ring. Nor, how I debated whether I should go away without ringing; nor, how I should undoubtedly have gone, if my time had been my own, to come back.

Miss Sarah Pocket came to the gate. No Estella.

'How, then? You here again?' said Miss Pocket. 'What do you want?'

When I said that I only came to see how Miss Havisham was, Sarah evidently deliberated whether or no she should send me about my business. But, unwilling to hazard the responsibility, she let me in, and presently brought the sharp message that I was to 'come up'.

Everything was unchanged, and Miss Havisham was alone.

'Well!' said she, fixing her eyes upon me. 'I hope you want nothing? You'll get nothing.'

'No indeed, Miss Havisham. I only wanted you to know that I am doing very well in my apprenticeship, and am always much obliged to you.'

'There, there!' with the old restless fingers. 'Come now and then; come on your birthday – ay!' she cried suddenly, turning herself and her chair towards me. 'You are looking round for Estella? Hey?'

I had been looking round – in fact, for Estella – and I stammered that I hoped she was well.

'Abroad,' said Miss Havisham; 'educating for a lady; far out of reach; prettier than ever; admired by all who see her. Do you feel that you have lost her?'

There was such a malignant enjoyment in her utterance of the last words, and she broke into such a disagreeable laugh, that I was at a loss what to say. She spared me the trouble of considering, by dismissing me. When the gate was closed upon me by Sarah of the walnut-shell countenance, I felt more than ever dissatisfied with my home and with my trade and with everything; and that was all I took by *that* motion.

As I was loitering along the High Street, looking in disconsolately at the shop windows, and thinking what I would buy if I were a gentleman, who should come out of the bookshop but Mr Wopsle. Mr Wopsle had in his hand the affecting tragedy of George Barnwell, in which he had that moment invested sixpence, with the view of heaping every word of it on the head of Pumblechook, with whom he was going to drink tea. No sooner did he see me, than he appeared to consider that a special providence had put a 'prentice in his way to be read at; and he laid hold of me, and insisted on my accompanying him to the Pumblechookian parlour. As I knew it would be miserable at home, and as the nights were dark and the way was dreary, and almost any companionship on the road was better than none, I made no great resistance; consequently, we turned into Pumblechook's just as the street and the shops were lighting up.

As I never assisted at any other representation of George Barnwell, I don't know how long it may usually take; but I know very well that it took until half-past nine o'clock that night, and that when Mr Wopsle got into Newgate, I thought he never would go to the scaffold, he became so much slower than at any former period of his disgraceful career. I thought it a little too much that he should complain of being cut short in his flower after all, as if he had not been running to seed, leaf after leaf, ever since his course began. This, however, was a mere question of length and wearisomeness. What stung me, was the identification of the whole affair with my unoffending self. When Barnwell began to go wrong, I declare I felt positively apologetic, Pumblechook's indignant stare so taxed me with it. Wopsle, too, took pains to present me in the worst light. At once ferocious and maudlin, I was made to murder my uncle with no extenuating circumstances whatever; Millwood put me down in argument, on every occasion; it became sheer monomania in my master's daughter to care a button for me; and all I can say for my gasping and procrastinating conduct on the fatal morning, is, that it was worthy of the general feebleness of my character. Even after I was happily hanged and Wopsle had closed the book, Pumblechook sat staring at me, and shaking his head, and saying, 'Take warning, boy, take warning!' as if it were a well-known fact that I contemplated murdering a near relation, provided I could only induce one to have the weakness to become my benefactor.

It was a very dark night when it was all over, and when I set out with Mr Wopsle on the walk home. Beyond town, we found a heavy mist out, and it fell wet and thick. The turnpike lamp was a blur, quite out of the lamp's usual place apparently, and its rays looked solid substance on the fog. We were noticing this, and saying how that the mist rose with a change of wind from a certain quarter of our marshes, when we came upon a man, slouching under the lee of the turnpike house.

'Halloa!' we said, stopping. 'Orlick there?'

'Ah!' he answered, slouching out. 'I was standing by, a minute, on the chance of company.'

'You are late,' I remarked.

Orlick not unnaturally answered, 'Well? And *you*'re late.'

'We have been,' said Mr Wopsle, exalted with his late performance, 'we have been indulging, Mr Orlick, in an intellectual evening.'

Old Orlick growled, as if he had nothing to say about that, and we all went on together. I asked him presently whether he had been spending his half-holiday up and down town?

'Yes,' said he, 'all of it. I come in behind yourself. I didn't see you, but I must have been pretty close behind you. By the by, the guns is going again.'

'At the hulks?' said I.

'Ay! There's some of the birds flown from the cages. The guns have been going since dark, about. You'll hear one presently.'

In effect, we had not walked many yards further, when the well-remembered boom came towards us, deadened by the mist, and heavily rolled away along the low grounds by the river, as if it were pursuing and threatening the fugitives.

'A good-night for cutting off in,' said Orlick. 'We'd be puzzled how to bring down a jailbird on the wing, tonight.'

The subject was a suggestive one to me, and I thought about it in silence. Mr Wopsle, as the ill-requited uncle of the evening's tragedy, fell to meditating aloud in his garden at Camberwell. Orlick, with his hands in his pockets, slouched heavily at my side. It was very dark, very wet, very muddy, and so we splashed along. Now and then, the sound of the signal cannon broke upon us again, and again rolled sulkily along the course of the river. I kept myself to myself and my thoughts. Mr Wopsle died amiably at Camberwell, and exceedingly game on Bosworth Field, and in the greatest agonies at Glastonbury. Orlick sometimes growled, 'Beat it out, beat it out – Old Clem! With a clink for the stout – Old Clem!' I thought he had been drinking, but he was not drunk.

Thus we came to the village. The way by which we approached it took us past the Three Jolly Bargemen, which we were surprised to find – it being eleven o'clock – in a state of commotion, with the door wide open, and unwonted lights that had been hastily caught up and put down, scattered about. Mr Wopsle dropped in to ask what was the matter (surmising that a convict had been taken), but came running out in a great hurry.

'There's something wrong,' said he, without stopping, 'up at your place, Pip. Run all!'

'What is it?' I asked, keeping up with him. So did Orlick, at my side.

'I can't quite understand. The house seems to have been violently entered when Joe Gargery was out. Supposed by convicts. Somebody has been attacked and hurt.'

We were running too fast to admit of more being said, and we made no stop until we got into our kitchen. It was full of people; the whole village was there, or in the yard; and there was a surgeon, and there was Joe, and there was a group of women, all on the floor in the midst of the kitchen. The unemployed bystanders drew back when they saw me, and so I became aware of my sister – lying without sense or movement on the bare boards where she had been knocked down by a tremendous blow on the back of the head, dealt by some unknown hand when her face was turned towards the fire – destined never to be on the rampage again, while she was the wife of Joe.

Chapter 16

With my head full of George Barnwell, I was at first disposed to believe that *I* must have had some hand in the attack upon my sister, or at all events that as her near relation, popularly known to be under obligations to her, I was a more legitimate object of suspicion than anyone else. But when, in the clearer light of next morning, I began to reconsider the matter and to hear it discussed around me on all sides, I took another view of the case, which was more reasonable.

Joe had been at the Three Jolly Bargemen, smoking his pipe, from a quarter after eight o'clock to a quarter before ten. While he was there, my sister had been standing at the kitchen door and had exchanged good-night with a farm-labourer going home. The man could not be more particular as to the time at which he saw her (he got into dense confusion when he tried to be) than that it must have been before nine. When Joe went home at five minutes before ten, he found her struck down on the floor, and promptly called in assistance. The fire had not then burnt unusually low, nor was the snuff of the candle very long; the candle, however, had been blown out.

Nothing had been taken away from any part of the house. Neither, beyond the blowing out of the candle – which stood on a table between the door and my sister, and was behind her when she stood facing the fire and was struck – was there any disarrangement of the kitchen, excepting such as she herself had made, in falling and bleeding. But there was one remarkable piece of evidence on the spot. She had been struck with something blunt and heavy, on the head and spine; after the blows were dealt, something heavy had been thrown down at her with considerable violence, as she lay on her face. And on the ground beside her, when Joe picked her up, was a convict's leg-iron which had been filed asunder.

Now, Joe, examining this iron with a smith's eye, declared it to have been filed asunder some time ago. The hue and cry going off to the hulks, and people coming thence to examine the iron, Joe's opinion was corroborated. They did not undertake to say when it had left the prison-ships to which it undoubtedly had once belonged; but they claimed to know for certain that that particular manacle had not been worn by either of two convicts who had escaped last night. Further, one of those two was already retaken, and had not freed himself of his iron.

Knowing what I knew, I set up an inference of my own here. I believed the iron to be my convict's iron – the iron I had seen and heard him filing at, on the marshes – but my mind did not accuse him of having put it to its latest use. For I believed one of two other persons to have become possessed of it, and to have turned it to this cruel account. Either Orlick, or the strange man who had shown me the file.

Now, as to Orlick; he had gone to town exactly as he told us when we picked him up at the turnpike, he had been seen about town all the evening, he had been in divers companies in several public houses, and he had come back with myself and Mr Wopsle. There was nothing against him, save the quarrel; and my sister had quarrelled with him, and with everybody else about her, ten thousand times. As to the strange man; if he had come back for his two bank-notes there could have been no dispute about them, because my sister was fully prepared to restore them. Besides, there had been no altercation; the assailant had come in so silently and suddenly, that she had been felled before she could look round.

It was horrible to think that I had provided the weapon, however undesignedly, but I could hardly think otherwise. I suffered unspeakable trouble while I considered and reconsidered whether I should at last dissolve that spell of my childhood and tell Joe all the story. For months afterwards, I every day settled the question finally in the negative, and reopened and re-argued it next morning. The contention came, after all, to this – the secret was such an old one now, had so grown into me and become a part of myself, that I could not tear it away. In addition to the dread that, having led up to so much mischief, it would be now more likely than ever to alienate Joe from me if he believed it, I had a further restraining dread that he would not believe it, but would assert it with the fabulous dogs and veal-cutlets as a monstrous invention. However, I temporised with myself, of course – for was I not wavering between right and wrong, when the thing is always done? – and resolved to make a full disclosure if I should see any such new occasion as a new chance of helping in the discovery of the assailant.

The constables, and the Bow Street men from London – for this happened in the days of the extinct red-waistcoated police – were about the house for a week or two, and did pretty much what I have heard and read of like authorities doing in other such cases. They took up several obviously wrong people, and they ran their heads very hard against wrong ideas, and persisted in trying to fit the circumstances to the ideas, instead of trying to extract ideas from the circumstances. Also, they stood about the door of the Jolly Bargemen, with knowing and reserved looks that filled the whole neighbourhood with admiration; and they had a mysterious manner of taking their drink, that was almost as good as taking the culprit. But not quite, for they never did it.

Long after these constitutional powers had dispersed, my sister lay very ill in bed. Her sight was disturbed, so that she saw objects multiplied, and grasped at visionary teacups and wineglasses instead of the realities; her hearing was greatly impaired; her memory also; and her speech was unintelligible. When, at last, she came round so far as to be helped downstairs, it was still necessary to keep my slate always by her, that she might indicate in writing what she could not indicate in speech. As she was (very bad handwriting apart) a more than indifferent speller, and as Joe was a more than indifferent reader, extraordinary complications arose between them, which I was always called in to solve. The administration of mutton instead of medicine, the substitution of tea for Joe, and the baker for bacon, were among the mildest of my own mistakes.

However, her temper was greatly improved, and she was patient. A tremulous uncertainty of the action of all her limbs soon became a part of her regular state, and afterwards, at intervals of two or three months, she would often put her hands to her head, and would then remain for about a week at a time in some gloomy aberration of mind. We were at a loss to find a suitable attendant for her, until a circumstance happened conveniently to relieve us. Mr Wopsle's great-aunt conquered a confirmed habit of living into which she had fallen, and Biddy became a part of our establishment.

It may have been about a month after my sister's reappearance in the kitchen, when Biddy came to us with a small speckled box containing the whole of her worldly effects, and became a blessing to the household. Above all she was a blessing to Joe, for the dear old fellow was sadly cut up by the constant contemplation of the wreck of his wife, and had been accustomed, while attending on her of an evening, to turn to me every now and then and say, with his blue eyes moistened, 'Such a fine figure of a woman as she once were, Pip!' Biddy

instantly taking the cleverest charge of her as though she had studied her from infancy, Joe became able in some sort to appreciate the greater quiet of his life, and to get down to the Jolly Bargemen now and then for a change that did him good. It was characteristic of the police people that they had all more or less suspected poor Joe (though he never knew it), and that they had to a man concurred in regarding him as one of the deepest spirits they had ever encountered.

Biddy's first triumph in her new office, was to solve a difficulty that had completely vanquished me. I had tried hard at it, but had made nothing of it.

Thus it was: again and again and again, my sister had traced upon the slate, a character that looked like a curious T, and then with the utmost eagerness had called our attention to it as something she particularly wanted. I had in vain tried everything producible that began with a T, from tar to toast and tub. At length it had come into my head that the sign looked like a hammer, and on my lustily calling that word in my sister's ear, she had begun to hammer on the table and had expressed a qualified assent. Thereupon, I had brought in all our hammers, one after another, but without avail. Then I bethought me of a crutch, the shape being much the same, and I borrowed one in the village, and displayed it to my sister with considerable confidence. But she shook her head to that extent when she was shown it, that we were terrified lest in her weak and shattered state she should dislocate her neck.

When my sister found that Biddy was very quick to understand her, this mysterious sign reappeared on the slate. Biddy looked thoughtfully at it, heard my explanation, looked thoughtfully at my sister, looked thoughtfully at Joe (who was always represented on the slate by his initial letter), and ran into the forge, followed by Joe and me.

'Why, of course!' cried Biddy, with an exultant face. 'Don't you see? It's *him!*'

Orlick, without a doubt! She had lost his name, and could only signify him by his hammer. We told him why we wanted him to come into the kitchen, and he slowly laid down his hammer, wiped his brow with his arm, took another wipe at it with his apron, and came slouching out, with a curious loose vagabond bend in the knees that strongly distinguished him.

I confess that I expected to see my sister denounce him, and that I was disappointed by the different result. She manifested the greatest anxiety to be on good terms with him, was evidently much pleased by his being at length produced, and motioned that she would have him given something to drink. She watched his countenance as if she were particularly wishful to be assured that he took kindly to his reception, she showed every possible desire to conciliate him, and there was an air of humble propitiation in all she did, such as I have seen pervade the bearing of a child towards a hard master. After that day, a day rarely passed without her drawing the hammer on her slate, and without Orlick's slouching in and standing doggedly before her, as if he knew no more than I did what to make of it.

Chapter 17

I now fell into a regular routine of apprenticeship life, which was varied, beyond the limits of the village and the marshes, by no more remarkable circumstance than the arrival of my birthday and my paying another visit to Miss Havisham. I found Miss Sarah Pocket still on duty at the gate, I found Miss Havisham just as I had left her, and she spoke of Estella in the very same way, if not in the very same words. The interview lasted but a few minutes, and she gave me a guinea when I was going, and told me to come again on my next birthday. I may mention at once that this became an annual custom. I tried to decline taking the guinea on the first occasion, but with no better effect than causing her to ask me very angrily, if I expected more? Then, and after that, I took it.

So unchanging was the dull old house, the yellow light in the darkened room, the faded spectre in the chair by the dressing-table glass, that I felt as if the stopping of the clocks had stopped time in that mysterious place, and, while I and everything else outside it grew older, it stood still. Daylight never entered the house, as to my thoughts and remembrances of it, any more than as to the actual fact. It bewildered me, and under its influence I continued at heart to hate my trade and to be ashamed of home.

Imperceptibly I became conscious of a change in Biddy, however. Her shoes came up at the heel, her hair grew bright and neat, her hands were always clean. She was not beautiful – she was common, and could not be like Estella – but she was pleasant and wholesome and sweet-tempered. She had not been with us more than a year (I remember her being newly out of mourning at the time it struck me), when I observed to myself one evening that she had curiously thoughtful and attentive eyes; eyes that were very pretty and very good.

It came of my lifting up my own eyes from a task I was poring at – writing some passages from a book, to improve myself in two ways at once by a sort of stratagem – and seeing Biddy observant of what I was about. I laid down my pen, and Biddy stopped in her needlework without laying it down.

'Biddy,' said I, 'how do you manage it? Either I am very stupid, or you are very clever.'

'What is it that I manage? I don't know,' returned Biddy, smiling.

She managed her whole domestic life, and wonderfully too; but I did not mean that, though that made what I did mean more surprising.

'How do you manage, Biddy,' said I, 'to learn everything that I learn, and always to keep up with me?' I was beginning to be rather vain of my knowledge, for I spent my birthday guineas on it, and set aside the greater part of my pocket-money for similar investment; though I have no doubt, now, that the little I knew was extremely dear at the price.

'I might as well ask you,' said Biddy, 'how *you* manage?'

'No; because when I come in from the forge of a night, anyone can see me turning to at it. But you never turn to at it, Biddy.'

'I suppose I must catch it – like a cough,' said Biddy, quietly; and went on with her sewing.

Pursuing my idea as I leaned back in my wooden chair and looked at Biddy sewing away with her head on one side, I began to think her rather an extraordinary girl. For, I called to mind now, that she was equally accomplished in the terms of our trade, and the names of our different sorts of work, and our various tools. In short, whatever I knew, Biddy knew. Theoretically, she was already as good a blacksmith as I, or better.

'You are one of those, Biddy,' said I, 'who make the most of every chance. You never had a chance before you came here, and see how improved you are!'

Biddy looked at me for an instant, and went on with her sewing. 'I was your first teacher, though; wasn't I?' said she, as she sewed.

'Biddy!' I exclaimed, in amazement. 'Why, you are crying!'

'No, I am not,' said Biddy, looking up and laughing. 'What put that in your head?'

What could have put it in my head, but the glistening of a tear as it dropped on her work? I sat silent, recalling what a drudge she had been until Mr Wopsle's great-aunt successfully overcame that bad habit of living, so highly desirable to be got rid of by some people. I recalled the hopeless circumstances by which she had been surrounded in the miserable little shop and the miserable little noisy evening school, with that miserable old bundle of incompetence always to be dragged and shouldered. I reflected that even in those untoward times there must have been latent in Biddy what was now developing, for in my first uneasiness and discontent I had turned to her for help, as a matter of course. Biddy sat quietly sewing, shedding no more tears, and while I looked at her and thought about it all, it occurred to me that perhaps I had not been sufficiently grateful to Biddy. I might have been too reserved, and should have patronised her more (though I did not use that precise word in my meditations), with my confidence.

'Yes, Biddy,' I observed, when I had done turning it over, 'you were my first teacher, and that at a time when we little thought of ever being together like this, in this kitchen.'

'Ah, poor thing!' replied Biddy. It was like her self-forget-fulness, to transfer the remark to my sister, and to get up and be busy about her, making her more comfortable: 'that's sadly true!'

'Well!' said I, 'we must talk together a little more, as we used to do. And I must consult you a little more, as I used to do. Let us have a quiet walk on the marshes next Sunday, Biddy, and a long chat.'

My sister was never left alone now; and Joe more than readily undertook the care of her on that Sunday afternoon, and Biddy and I went out together. It was summertime and lovely weather. When we had passed the village and the church and the church-yard, and were out on the marshes, and began to see the sails of the ships as they sailed on, I began to combine Miss Havisham and Estella with the prospect, in my usual way. When we came to the riverside and sat down on the bank, with the water rippling at our feet, making it all more quiet than it would have been without that sound, I resolved that it was a good time and place for the admission of Biddy into my inner confidence.

'Biddy,' said I, after binding her to secrecy, 'I want to be a gentleman.'

'Oh, I wouldn't, if I was you!' she returned. 'I don't think it would answer.'

'Biddy,' said I, with some severity, 'I have particular reasons for wanting to be a gentleman.'

'You know best, Pip; but don't you think you are happier as you are?'

'Biddy,' I exclaimed, impatiently, 'I am not at all happy as I am. I am disgusted with my calling and with my life. I have never taken to either since I was bound. Don't be absurd.'

'Was I absurd?' said Biddy, quietly raising her eyebrows; 'I am sorry for that; I didn't mean to be. I only want you to do well, and be comfortable.'

'Well, then, understand once for all that I never shall or can be comfortable – or anything but miserable – there, Biddy! – unless I can lead a very different sort of life from the life I lead now.'

'That's a pity!' said Biddy, shaking her head with a sorrowful air.

Now, I too had so often thought it a pity, that, in the singular kind of quarrel with myself which I was always carrying on, I was half inclined to shed tears of vexation and distress when Biddy gave utterance to her sentiment and my own. I told her she was right, and I knew it was much to be regretted, but still it was not to be helped.

'If I could have settled down,' I said to Biddy, plucking up the short grass within reach, much as I had once upon a time pulled my feelings out of my hair and kicked them into the brewery wall: 'if I could have settled down and been but half as fond of the forge as I was when I was little, I know it would have been much better for me. You and I and Joe would have wanted nothing then, and Joe and I would perhaps have gone partners when I was out of my time, and I might even have grown up to keep company with you, and we might have sat on this very bank on a fine Sunday, quite different people. I should have been good enough for *you*; shouldn't I, Biddy?'

Biddy sighed as she looked at the ships sailing on, and returned for answer, 'Yes; I am not over-particular.' It scarcely sounded flattering, but I knew she meant well.

'Instead of that,' said I, plucking up more grass and chewing a blade or two, 'see how I am going on. Dissatisfied, and uncomfortable, and – what would it signify to me, being coarse and common, if nobody had told me so!'

Biddy turned her face suddenly towards mine, and looked far more attentively at me than she had looked at the sailing ships.

'It was neither a very true nor a very polite thing to say,' she remarked, directing her eyes to the ships again. 'Who said it?'

I was disconcerted, for I had broken away without quite seeing where I was going to. It was not to be shuffled off, now, however, and I answered, 'The beautiful young lady at Miss Havisham's, and she's more beautiful than anybody ever was, and I admire her dreadfully, and I want to be a gentleman on her account.' Having made this lunatic confession, I began to throw my torn-up grass into the river, as if I had some thoughts of following it.

'Do you want to be a gentleman, to spite her or to gain her over?' Biddy quietly asked me, after a pause.

'I don't know,' I moodily answered.

'Because, if it is to spite her,' Biddy pursued, 'I should think – but you know best – that might be better and more independently done by caring nothing for her words. And if it is to gain her over, I should think – but you know best – she was not worth gaining over.'

Exactly what I myself had thought, many times. Exactly what was perfectly manifest to me at the moment. But how could I, a poor dazed village lad, avoid that wonderful inconsistency into which the best and wisest of men fall every day?

'It may be all quite true,' said I to Biddy, 'but I admire her dreadfully.'

In short, I turned over on my face when I came to that, and got a good grasp on the hair, on each side of my head, and wrenched it well. All the while knowing the madness of my heart to be so very mad and misplaced, that I was quite conscious it would have served my face right, if I had lifted it up by my hair, and knocked it against the pebbles as a punishment for belonging to such an idiot.

Biddy was the wisest of girls, and she tried to reason no more with me. She put her hand, which was a comfortable hand though roughened by work, upon my hands, one after another, and gently took them out of my hair. Then she softly patted my shoulder in a soothing way, while with my face upon my sleeve I cried a little – exactly as I had done in the brewery yard – and felt vaguely convinced that I was very much ill-used by somebody, or by everybody; I can't say which.

'I am glad of one thing,' said Biddy, 'and that is, that you have felt you could give me your confidence, Pip. And I am glad of another thing, and that is, that of course you know you may depend upon my keeping it and always so far deserving it. If your first teacher (dear! such a poor one, and so much in need of being taught herself!) had been your teacher at the present time, she thinks she knows what lesson she would set. But it would be a hard one to learn, and you have got beyond her, and it's of no use now.' So, with a quiet sigh for me, Biddy rose from the bank, and said, with a fresh and pleasant change of voice, 'Shall we walk a little further, or go home?'

'Biddy,' I cried, getting up, putting my arm around her neck, and giving her a kiss, 'I shall always tell you everything.'

'Till you're a gentleman,' said Biddy.

'You know I never shall be, so that's always. Not that I have any occasion to tell you anything, for you know everything I know – as I told you at home the other night.'

'Ah!' said Biddy, quite in a whisper, as she looked away at the ships. And then repeated, with her former pleasant change, 'Shall we walk a little further, or go home?'

I said to Biddy we would walk a little further, and we did so, and the summer afternoon toned down into the summer evening, and it was very beautiful. I began to consider whether I was not more naturally and wholesomely situated, after all, in these circumstances, than playing beggar my neighbour by candlelight in the room with the stopped clocks, and being despised by Estella. I thought it would be very good for me if I could get her out of my head with all the rest of those remembrances and fancies, and could go to work determined to relish what I had to do, and stick to it, and make the best of it. I asked myself the question whether I did not surely know that if Estella were beside me at that moment instead of Biddy, she would make me miserable? I was obliged to admit that I did know it for a certainty, and I said to myself, 'Pip, what a fool you are!'

We talked a good deal as we walked, and all that Biddy said seemed right. Biddy was never insulting, or capricious, or Biddy today and somebody else tomorrow; she would have derived only pain, and no pleasure, from giving me pain; she would far rather have wounded her own breast than mine. How could it be, then, that I did not like her much the better of the two?

'Biddy,' said I, when we were walking homeward, 'I wish you could put me right.'

'I wish I could!' said Biddy.

'If I could only get myself to fall in love with you – you don't mind my speaking so openly to such an old acquaintance?'

'Oh dear, not at all!' said Biddy. 'Don't mind me.'

'If I could only get myself to do it, *that* would be the thing for me.'

'But you never will, you see,' said Biddy.

It did not appear quite so unlikely to me that evening, as it would have done if we had discussed it a few hours before. I therefore observed I was not quite sure of that. But Biddy said she *was*, and she said it decisively. In my heart I believed her to

Ill used

be right; and yet I took it rather ill, too, that she should be so positive on the point.

When we came near the churchyard, we had to cross an embankment, and get over a stile near a sluice gate. There started up, from the gate, or from the rushes, or from the ooze (which was quite in his stagnant way), Old Orlick.

'Halloa!' he growled, 'where are you two going?'

'Where should we be going, but home?'

'Well, then,' said he, 'I'm jiggered if I don't see you home!'

This penalty of being jiggered was a favourite supposititious case of his. He attached no definite meaning to the word that I am aware of, but used it, like his own pretended christian name, to affront mankind, and convey an idea of something savagely damaging. When I was younger, I had had a general belief that if he had jiggered me personally, he would have done it with a sharp and twisted hook.

Biddy was much against his going with us, and said to me in a whisper, 'Don't let him come; I don't like him.' As I did not like him either, I took the liberty of saying that we thanked him, but we didn't want seeing home. He received that piece of information with a yell of laughter, and dropped back, but came slouching after us at a little distance.

Curious to know whether Biddy suspected him of having had a hand in that murderous attack of which my sister had never been able to give any account, I asked her why she did not like him.

'Oh!' she replied, glancing over her shoulder as he slouched after us, 'because I – I am afraid he likes me.'

'Did he ever tell you he liked you?' I asked indignantly.

'No,' said Biddy, glancing over her shoulder again, 'he never told me so; but he dances at me, whenever he can catch my eye.'

However novel and peculiar this testimony of attachment, I did not doubt the accuracy of the interpretation. I was very hot indeed upon Old Orlick's daring to admire her; as hot as if it were an outrage on myself.

'But it makes no difference to you, you know,' said Biddy, calmly.

'No, Biddy, it makes no difference to me; only I don't like it; I don't approve of it.

'Nor I neither,' said Biddy. 'Though *that* makes no difference to you.'

'Exactly,' said I; 'but I must tell you I should have no opinion of you, Biddy, if he danced at you with your own consent.'

I kept an eye on Orlick after that night, and whenever circumstances were favourable to his dancing at Biddy, got before him, to obscure that demonstration. He had struck root in Joe's establishment, by reason of my sister's sudden fancy for him, or I should have tried to get him dismissed. He quite understood and reciprocated my good intentions, as I had reason to know thereafter.

And now, because my mind was not confused enough before, I complicated its confusion fifty thousandfold, by having states and seasons when I was clear that Biddy was immeasurably better than Estella, and that the plain honest working life to which I was born had nothing in it to be ashamed of, but offered me sufficient means of self-respect and happiness. At those times, I would decide conclusively that my disaffection to dear old Joe and the forge, was gone, and that I was growing up in a fair way to be partners with Joe and to keep company with Biddy – when all in a moment some confounding re-membrance of the Havisham days would fall upon me, like a destructive missile, and scatter my wits again. Scattered wits take a long time picking up; and often, before I had got them well together, they would be dispersed in all directions by one stray thought, that perhaps after all Miss Havisham was going to make my fortune when my time was out.

If my time had run out, it would have left me still at the height of my perplexities, I dare say. It never did run out, however, but was brought to a premature end, as I proceed to relate.

Chapter 18

It was in the fourth year of my apprenticeship to Joe, and it was a Saturday night. There was a group assembled round the fire at the Three Jolly Bargemen, attentive to Mr Wopsle as he read the newspaper aloud. Of that group I was one.

A highly popular murder had been committed, and Mr Wopsle was imbrued in blood to the eyebrows. He gloated over every abhorrent adjective in the description, and identified himself with every witness at the inquest. He faintly moaned, 'I am done for,' as the victim, and he barbarously bellowed, 'I'll serve you out,' as the murderer. He gave the medical testimony, in pointed imitation of our local practitioner; and he piped and shook, as the aged turnpike-keeper who had heard blows, to an extent so very paralytic as to suggest a doubt regarding the mental competency of that witness. The coroner, in Mr Wopsle's hands, became Timon of Athens; the beadle, Coriolanus. He en-joyed himself thoroughly, and we all enjoyed ourselves, and were delightfully comfortable. In this cosy state of mind we came to the verdict of 'wilful murder'.

Then, and not sooner, I became aware of a strange gentleman leaning over the back of the settle opposite me, looking on. There was an expression of contempt on his face, and he bit the side of a great forefinger as he watched the group of faces.

'Well!' said the stranger to Mr Wopsle, when the reading was done, 'you have settled it all to your own satisfaction, I have no doubt?'

Everybody started and looked up, as if it were the murderer. He looked at everybody coldly and sarcastically.

'Guilty, of course?' said he. 'Out with it. Come!'

'Sir,' returned Mr Wopsle, 'without having the honour of your acquaintance, I do say "guilty".' Upon this we all took courage to unite in a confirmatory murmur.

'I know you do,' said the stranger; 'I knew you would. I told you so. But now I'll ask you a question. Do you know, or do you not know, that the law of England supposes every man to be innocent, until he is proved – proved – to be guilty?'

'Sir.' Mr Wopsle began to reply, 'as an Englishman myself, I – '

'Come!' said the stranger, biting his forefinger at him. 'Don't evade the question. Either you know it, or you don't know it. Which is it to be?'

He stood with his head on one side and himself on one side, in a bullying interrogative manner, and he threw his forefinger at Mr Wopsle – as it were to mark him out – before biting it again.

'Now!' said he. 'Do you know it, or don't you know it?'

'Certainly I know it,' replied Mr Wopsle.

'Certainly you know it. Then why didn't you say so at first? Now, I'll ask you another question;' taking possession of Mr Wopsle, as if he had a right to him. '*Do* you know that none of these witnesses have yet been cross-examined?'

Mr Wopsle was beginning, 'I can only say – ' when the stranger stopped him.

'What? You won't answer the question, yes or no? Now, I'll try you again.' Throwing his finger at him again. 'Attend to me. Are you aware, or are you not aware, that none of these wit-nesses have yet been cross-examined? Come, I only want one word from you. Yes, or no?'

Mr Wopsle hesitated, and we all began to conceive rather a poor opinion of him.

'Come!' said the stranger, 'I'll help you. You don't deserve help, but I'll help you. Look at that paper you hold in your hand. What is it?'

'What is it?' repeated Mr Wopsle, eyeing it much at a loss.

'Is it,' pursued the stranger in his most sarcastic and sus-picious manner, 'the printed paper you have just been reading from?'

'Undoubtedly.'

'Undoubtedly. Now, turn to that paper, and tell me whether it distinctly states that the prisoner expressly said that his legal advisers instructed him altogether to reserve his defence?'

'I read that just now,' Mr Wopsle pleaded.

'Never mind what you read just now, sir; I don't ask you what you read just now. You may read the Lord's Prayer backwards, if you like – and, perhaps, have done it before today. Turn to the paper. No, no, no, my friend; not to the top of the column; you know better than that; to the bottom, to the bottom.' (We all began to think Mr Wopsle full of subterfuge.) 'Well? Have you found it?'

'Here it is,' said Mr Wopsle.

'Now, follow that passage with your eye, and tell me whether it distinctly states that the prisoner expressly said that he was instructed by his legal advisers wholly to reserve his defence? Come! Do you make that of it?'

Mr Wopsle answered, 'Those are not the exact words.'

'Not the exact words!' repeated the gentleman, bitterly. 'Is that the exact substance?'

'Yes,' said Mr Wopsle.

'Yes,' repeated the stranger, looking round at the rest of the company with his right hand extended towards the witness, Wopsle. 'And now I ask you what you say to the conscience of that man who, with that passage before his eyes, can lay his head upon his pillow after having pronounced a fellow-creature guilty, unheard?'

We all began to suspect that Mr Wopsle was not the man we

had thought him, and that he was beginning to be found out.

'And that same man, remember,' pursued the gentleman, throwing his finger at Mr Wopsle heavily; 'that same man might be summoned as a juryman upon this very trial, and having thus deeply committed himself, might return to the bosom of his family and lay his head upon his pillow, after deliberately swearing that he would well and truly try the issue joined between Our Sovereign Lord the King and the prisoner at the bar, and would a true verdict give according to the evidence, so help him God!'

We were all deeply persuaded that the unfortunate Wopsle had gone too far, and had better stop in his reckless career while there was yet time.

The strange gentleman, with an air of authority not to be disputed, and with a manner expressive of knowing something secret about every one of us that would effectually do for each individual if he chose to disclose it, left the back of the settle, and came into the space between the two settles, in front of the fire, where he remained standing: his left hand in his pocket, and he biting the forefinger of his right.

'From information I have received,' said he, looking round at us as we all quailed before him, 'I have reason to believe there is a blacksmith among you, by name Joseph – or Joe – Gargery. Which is the man?'

'Here is the man,' said Joe.

The strange gentleman beckoned him out of his place, and Joe went.

'You have an apprentice,' pursued the stranger, 'commonly known as Pip? Is he here?'

'I am here!' I cried.

The stranger did not recognise me, but I recognised him as the gentleman I had met on the stairs, on the occasion of my second visit to Miss Havisham. I had known him the moment I saw him looking over the settle, and now that I stood confronting him with his hand upon my shoulder, I checked off again in detail, his large head, his dark complexion, his deep-set eyes, his bushy black eyebrows, his large watch-chain, his strong black dots of beard and whisker, and even the smell of scented soap on his great hand.

'I wish to have a private conference with you two,' said he, when he had surveyed me at his leisure. 'It will take a little time. Perhaps we had better go to your place of residence. I prefer not to anticipate my communication here; you will impart as much or as little of it as you please to your friends afterwards; I have nothing to do with that.'

Amidst a wondering silence, we three walked out of the Jolly Bargemen, and in a wondering silence walked home. While going along, the strange gentleman occasionally looked at me, and occasionally bit the side of his finger. As we neared home, Joe vaguely acknowledging the occasion as an impressive and ceremonious one, went on ahead to open the front door. Our conference was held in the state parlour, which was feebly lighted by one candle.

It began with the strange gentleman's sitting down at the table, drawing the candle to him, and looking over some entries in his pocketbook. He then put up the pocketbook and set the candle a little aside, after peering round it into the darkness at Joe and me, to ascertain which was which.

'My name,' he said, 'is Jaggers, and I am a lawyer in London. I am pretty well known. I have unusual business to transact with you, and I commence by explaining that it is not of my originating. If my advice had been asked, I should not have been here. It was not asked, and you see me here. What I have to do as the confidential agent of another, I do. No less, no more.'

Finding that he could not see us very well from where he sat, he got up, and threw one leg over the back of a chair and leaned upon it; thus having one foot on the seat of a chair, and one foot on the ground.

'Now, Joseph Gargery, I am the bearer of an offer to relieve you of this young fellow, your apprentice. You would not object to cancel his indentures at his request and for his good? You would want nothing for so doing?'

'Lord forbid that I should want anything for not standing in Pip's way,' said Joe, staring.

'Lord forbidding is pious, but not to the purpose,' returned Mr Jaggers. 'The question is, Would you want anything? Do you want anything?'

'The answer is,' returned Joe, sternly, 'No.'

I thought Mr Jaggers glanced at Joe, as if he considered him a fool for his disinterestedness. But I was too much bewildered between breathless curiosity and surprise, to be sure of it.

'Very well,' said Mr Jaggers. 'Recollect the admission you have made, and don't try to go from it presently.'

'Who's a-going to try?' retorted Joe.

'I don't say anybody is. Do you keep a dog?'

'Yes, I do keep a dog.'

'Bear in mind then, that Brag is a good dog, but that Holdfast is a better. Bear that in mind, will you?' repeated Mr Jaggers, shutting his eyes and nodding his head at Joe, as if he were forgiving him some- thing. 'Now, I return to this young fellow. And the communication I have got to make is, that he has great expectations.'

Joe and I gasped, and looked at one another.

'I am instructed to communicate to him,' said Mr Jaggers, throwing his finger at me sideways, 'that he will come into a handsome property. Further, that it is the desire of the present possessor of that property, that he be immediately removed from his present sphere of life and from this place, and be brought up as a gentleman – in a word, as a young fellow of great expectations.'

My dream was out; my wild fancy was surpassed by sober reality; Miss Havisham was going to make my fortune on a grand scale.

'Now, Mr Pip,' pursued the lawyer, 'I address the rest of what I have to say, to you. You are to understand, first, that it is the request of the person from whom I take my instructions, that you always bear the name of Pip. You will have no objection, I dare say, to your great expectations being encumbered with that easy condition. But if you have any objection, this is the time to mention it.'

My heart was beating so fast, and there was such a singing

in my ears, that I could scarcely stammer I had no objection.

'I should think not! Now you are to understand, secondly, Mr Pip, that the name of the person who is your liberal benefactor remains a profound secret, until the person chooses to reveal it. I am empowered to mention that it is the intention of the person to reveal it at first hand by word of mouth to yourself. When or where that intention may be carried out, I cannot say; no one can say. It may be years hence. Now, you are distinctly to understand that you are most positively prohibited from making any enquiry on this head, or any allusion or reference, however distant, to any individual whomsoever as *the* individual, in all the communications you have with me. If you have a suspicion in your own breast, keep that suspicion in your own breast. It is not the least to the purpose what the reasons of this prohibition are; they may be the strongest and gravest reasons, or they may be a mere whim. This is not for you to enquire into. The condition is laid down. Your acceptance of it, and your observance of it as binding, is the only remaining condition that I am charged with, by the person from whom I take my instructions, and for whom I am not otherwise responsible. That person is the person from whom you derive your expectations, and the secret is solely held by that person and by me. Again, not a very difficult condition with which to encumber such a rise in fortune; but if you have any objection to it, this is the time to mention it. Speak out.'

Once more, I stammered with difficulty that I had no objection.

'I should think not! Now, Mr Pip, I have done with stipulations.' Though he called me Mr Pip, and began rather to make up to me, he still could not get rid of a certain air of bullying suspicion; and even now he occasionally shut his eyes and threw his finger at me while he spoke, as much as to express that he knew all kinds of things to my disparagement, if he only chose to mention them. 'We come next, to mere details of arrangement. You must know that although I use the term "expectations" more than once, you are not endowed with expectations only. There is already lodged in my hands, a sum of money amply sufficient for your suitable education and maintenance. You will please consider me your guardian. Oh!' for I was going to thank him, 'I tell you at once, I am paid for my services, or I shouldn't render them. It is considered that you must be better educated, in accordance with your altered position, and that you will be alive to the importance and necessity of at once entering on that advantage.'

I said I had always longed for it.

'Never mind what you have always longed for, Mr Pip,' he retorted, 'keep to the record. If you long for it now, that's enough. Am I answered that you are ready to be placed at once, under some proper tutor? Is that it?'

I stammered yes, that was it.

'Good. Now, your inclinations are to be consulted. I don't think that wise, mind, but it's my trust. Have you ever heard of any tutor whom you would prefer to another?'

I had never heard of any tutor but Biddy, and Mr Wopsle's great-aunt; so, I replied in the negative.

'There is a certain tutor, of whom I have some knowledge, who I think might suit the purpose,' said Mr Jaggers. 'I don't recommend him, observe; because I never recommend anybody. The gentleman I speak of is one Mr Matthew Pocket.'

Ah! I caught at the name directly. Miss Havisham's relation. The Matthew whom Mr and Mrs Camilla had spoken of. The Matthew whose place was to be at Miss Havisham's head, when she lay dead, in her bride's dress on the bride's table.

'You know the name?' said Mr Jaggers, looking shrewdly at me, and then shutting up his eyes while he waited for my answer.

My answer was, that I had heard of the name.

'Oh!' said he. 'You have heard of the name! But the question is, what do you say of it?'

I said, or tried to say, that I was much obliged to him for his recommendation – 'No, my young friend!' he interrupted, shaking his great head very slowly. 'Recollect yourself!'

Not recollecting myself, I began again that I was much obliged to him for his recommendation – 'No, my young friend,' he interrupted, shaking his head and frowning and smiling both at once; 'no, no, no; it's very well done, but it won't do; you are too young to fix me with it. Recommendation is not the word, Mr Pip. Try another.'

Correcting myself, I said that I was much obliged to him for his mention of Mr Matthew Pocket – '*That's* more like it!' cried Mr Jaggers.

And (I added) I would gladly try that gentleman.

'Good. You had better try him in his own house. The way shall be prepared for you, and you can see his son first, who is in London. When will you come to London?'

I said (glancing at Joe, who stood looking on, motionless), that I supposed I could come directly.

'First,' said Mr Jaggers, 'you should have some new clothes to come in, and they should not be working clothes. Say this day week. You'll want some money. Shall I leave you twenty guineas?'

He produced a long purse with the greatest coolness, and counted them out on the table and pushed them over to me. This was the first time he had taken his leg from the chair. He sat astride of the chair when he had pushed the money over, and sat swinging his purse and eyeing Joe.

'Well, Joseph Gargery? You look dumbfoundered?'

'I *am*!' said Joe, in a very decided manner.

'It was understood that you wanted nothing for yourself, remember?'

'It were understood,' said Joe. 'And it are understood. And it ever will be similar according.'

'But what,' said Mr Jaggers, swinging his purse, 'what if it was in my instructions to make you a present, as compensation?'

'As compensation what for?' Joe demanded.

'For the loss of his services.'

Joe laid his hand upon my shoulder with the touch of a woman. I have often thought him since, like the steam-hammer, that can crush a man or pat an eggshell, in his combination of strength with gentleness. 'Pip is that hearty welcome,' said Joe, 'to go free with his services, to honour and fortun', as no words can tell him. But if you think as Money can make compensation to me for the loss of the little child – what come to the forge – and ever the best of friends! – '

O dear good Joe, whom I was so ready to leave and so unthankful to, I see you again, with your muscular blacksmith's arm before your eyes, and your broad chest heaving, and your voice dying away. O dear good faithful tender Joe, I feel the loving tremble of your hand upon my arm, as solemnly this day as if it had been the rustle of an angel's wing!

But I encouraged Joe at the time. I was lost in the mazes of my future fortunes, and could not retrace the by-paths we had trodden together. I begged Joe to be comforted, for (as he said) we had ever been the best of friends, and (as I said) we ever would be so. Joe scooped his eyes with his disengaged wrist, as if he were bent on gouging himself, but said not another word.

Mr Jaggers had looked on at this, as one who recognised in Joe the village idiot, and in me his keeper. When it was over, he said, weighing in his hand the purse he had ceased to swing: 'Now, Joseph Gargery, I warn you this is your last chance. No half measures with me. If you mean to take a present that I have it in charge to make you, speak out, and you shall have it. If on the contrary you mean to say – ' Here, to his great amazement, he was stopped by Joe's suddenly working round him with every demonstration of a fell pugilistic purpose.

'Which I meantersay,' cried Joe, 'that if you come into my place bull-baiting and badgering me, come out! Which I meantersay as sech if you're a man, come on! Which I meantersay that what I say, I meantersay and stand or fall by!'

I drew Joe away, and he immediately became placable: merely stating to me, in an obliging manner and as a polite expostulatory notice to anyone whom it might happen to concern, that he were not a-going to be bull-baited and badgered in his own place. Mr Jaggers had risen when Joe demonstrated, and had backed near the door. Without evincing any inclination to come in again, he there delivered his valedictory remarks.

They were these: 'Well, Mr Pip, I think the sooner you leave here – as you are to be a gentleman – the better. Let it stand for this day week, and you shall receive my printed address in the meantime. You can take a hackney-coach at the stagecoach office in London, and come straight to me. Understand that I express no opinion, one way or other, on the trust I undertake. I am paid for undertaking it, and I do so. Now, understand that finally. Understand that!'

He was throwing his finger at both of us, and I think would have gone on, but for his seeming to think Joe dangerous, and going off.

Something came into my head which induced me to run after him as he was going down to the Jolly Bargemen, where he had left a hired carriage.

'I beg your pardon, Mr Jaggers.'

'Holloa!' said he, facing round, 'what's the matter?'

'I wish to be quite right, Mr Jaggers, and to keep to your directions; so I thought I had better ask. Would there be any objection to my taking leave of anyone I know, about here, before I go away?'

'No,' said he, looking as if he hardly understood me.

'I don't mean the village only, but up town?'

'No,' said he. 'No objection.'

I thanked him and ran home again, and there I found that Joe had already locked the front door and vacated the state parlour, and was seated by the kitchen fire with a hand on each knee, gazing intently at the burning coals. I too sat down before the fire and gazed at the coals, and nothing was said for a long time.

My sister was in her cushioned chair in her corner, and Biddy sat at her needlework before the fire, and Joe sat next Biddy, and I sat next Joe in the corner opposite my sister. The more I looked into the glowing coals, the more incapable I became of looking at Joe; the longer the silence lasted, the more unable I felt to speak.

At length I got out, 'Joe, have you told Biddy?'

'No, Pip,' returned Joe, still looking at the fire, and holding his knees tight, as if he had private information that they intended to make off somewhere, 'which I left it to yourself, Pip.'

'I would rather you told, Joe.'

'Pip's a gentleman of fortun' then,' said Joe, 'and God bless him in it!'

Biddy dropped her work, and looked at me. Joe held his knees and looked at me. I looked at both of them. After a pause they both heartily congratulated me; but there was a certain touch of sadness in their congratulations that I rather resented.

I took it upon myself to impress Biddy (and through Biddy, Joe) with the grave obligation I considered my friends under, to know nothing and to say nothing about the maker of my fortune. It would all come out in good time, I observed, and in the meanwhile nothing was to be said, save that I had come into great expectations from a mysterious patron. Biddy nodded her head thoughtfully at the fire as she took up her work again, and said she would be very particular; and Joe, still detaining his knees, said, 'Ay, ay, I'll be ekervally partickler, Pip;' and then they congratulated me again, and went on to express so much wonder at the notion of my being a gentleman, that I didn't half like it.

Infinite pains were then taken by Biddy to convey to my sister some idea of what had happened. To the best of my belief, those efforts entirely failed. She laughed and nodded her head a great many times, and even repeated after Biddy, the words 'Pip' and 'Property'. But I doubt if they had more meaning in them than an election cry, and I cannot suggest a darker picture of her state of mind.

I never could have believed it without experience, but as Joe and Biddy became more at their cheerful ease again, I became quite gloomy. Dissatisfied with my fortune, of course I could not be; but it is possible that I may have been, without quite knowing it, dissatisfied with myself.

Anyhow, I sat with my elbow on my knee and my face upon my hand, looking into the fire, as those two talked about my going away, and about what they should do without me, and all that. And whenever I caught one of them looking at me, though never so pleasantly (and they often looked at me – particularly Biddy), I felt offended: as if they were expressing some mistrust in me. Though heaven knows they never did by word or sign.

At those times I would get up and look out at the door; for our kitchen door opened at once upon the night, and stood open on summer evenings to air the room. The very stars to which I then raised my eyes, I am afraid I took to be but poor and humble stars for glittering on the rustic objects among which I had passed my life.

'Saturday night,' said I, when we sat at our supper of bread and cheese and beer. 'Five more days, and then the day before *the* day! They'll soon go.'

'Yes, Pip,' observed Joe, whose voice sounded hollow in his beer mug. 'They'll soon go.'

'Soon, soon go,' said Biddy.

'I have been thinking, Joe, that when I go down town on Monday, and order my new clothes, I shall tell the tailor that I'll come and put them on there, or that I'll have them sent to Mr Pumblechook's. It would be very disagreeable to be stared at by all the people here.'

'Mr and Mrs Hubble might like to see you in your new genteel figure too, Pip,' said Joe, industriously cutting his bread with his cheese on it, in the palm of his left hand, and glancing at my untasted supper as if he thought of the time when we used to compare slices. 'So might Wopsle. And the Jolly Bargemen might take it as a compliment.'

'That's just what I don't want, Joe. They would make such a business of it – such a coarse and common business – that I couldn't bear myself.'

'Ah, that indeed, Pip!' said Joe. 'If you couldn't abear your-self –'

Biddy asked me here, as she sat holding my sister's plate, 'Have you thought about when you'll show yourself to Mr Gargery, and your sister, and me? You will show yourself to us; won't you?'

'Biddy,' I returned with some resentment, 'you are so exceedingly quick that it's difficult to keep up with you.'

('She always were quick,' observed Joe.)

'If you had waited another moment, Biddy, you would have heard me say that I shall bring my clothes here in a bundle one evening – most likely on the evening before I go away.'

Biddy said no more. Handsomely forgiving her, I soon exchanged an affectionate good-night with her and Joe, and went up to bed. When I got into my little room, I sat down and took a long look at it, as a mean little room that I should soon be parted from and raised above, for ever. It was furnished with fresh young remembrances too, and even at the same moment I fell into much the same confused division of mind between it and the better rooms to which I was going, as I had been in so often between the forge and Miss Havisham's, and Biddy and Estella.

The sun had been shining brightly all day on the roof of my attic, and the room was warm. As I put the window open and stood looking out, I saw Joe come slowly forth at the dark door below, and take a turn or two in the air; and then I saw Biddy come, and bring him a pipe and light it for him. He never smoked so late, and it seemed to hint to me that he wanted comforting, for some reason or other.

He presently stood at the door immediately beneath me, smoking his pipe, and Biddy stood there too, quietly talking to him, and I knew that they talked of me, for I heard my name mentioned in an endearing tone by both of them more than once. I would not have listened for more, if I could have heard more: so, I drew away from the window, and sat down in my one chair by the bedside, feeling it very sorrowful and strange that this first night of my bright fortunes should be the loneliest I had ever known.

Looking towards the open window, I saw light wreaths from Joe's pipe floating there, and I fancied it was like a blessing from Joe – not obtruded on me or paraded before me, but pervading the air we shared together. I put my light out, and crept into bed; and it was an uneasy bed now, and I never slept the old sound sleep in it any more.

Chapter 19

Morning made a considerable difference in my general prospect of life, and brightened it so much that it scarcely seemed the same. What lay heaviest on my mind, was, the consideration that six days intervened between me and the day of departure; for, I could not divest myself of a misgiving that something might happen to London in the meanwhile, and that, when I got there, it might be either greatly deteriorated or clean gone.

Joe and Biddy were very sympathetic and pleasant when I spoke of our approaching separation; but they only referred to it when I did. After breakfast, Joe brought out my indentures from the press in the best parlour, and we put them in the fire, and I felt that I was free. With all the novelty of my emancipation on me, I went to church with Joe, and thought, perhaps the clergyman wouldn't have read that about the rich man and the kingdom of heaven, if he had known all.

After our early dinner, I strolled out alone, proposing to finish off the marshes at once, and get them done with. As I passed the church, I felt (as I had felt during service in the morning) a sublime compassion for the poor creatures who were destined to go there, Sunday after Sunday, all their lives through, and to lie obscurely at last among the low green mounds. I promised myself that I would do something for them one of these days, and formed a plan in outline for bestowing a dinner of roast-beef and plum-pudding, a pint of ale, and a gallon of condescension, upon everybody in the village.

If I had often thought before, with something allied to shame, of my companionship with the fugitive whom I had once seen limping among those graves, what were my thoughts on this Sunday, when the place recalled the wretch, ragged and shivering, with his felon iron and badge! My comfort was, that it happened a long time ago, and that he had doubtless been transported a long way off, and that he was dead to me, and might be veritably dead into the bargain.

No more low wet grounds, no more dykes and sluices, no more of these grazing cattle – though they seemed, in their dull manner, to wear a more respectful air now, and to face round, in order that they might stare as long as possible at the possessor of such great expectations – farewell, monotonous acquaintances of my childhood, henceforth I was for London and greatness: not for smith's work in general and for you! I made my exultant way to the old battery, and, lying down there to consider the question whether Miss Havisham intended me for Estella, fell asleep.

When I awoke, I was much surprised to find Joe sitting beside me, smoking his pipe. He greeted me with a cheerful smile on my opening my eyes, and said: 'As being the last time, Pip, I thought I'd foller.'

'And, Joe, I am very glad you did so.'

'Thankee, Pip.'

'You may be sure, dear Joe,' I went on, after we had shaken hands, 'that I shall never forget you.'

'No, no, Pip!' said Joe, in a comfortable tone, '*I'm* sure of that. Ay, ay, old chap! Bless you, it were only necessary to get it well round in a man's mind, to be certain on it. But it took a bit of time to get it well round, the change come so oncommon plump; didn't it?'

Somehow, I was not best pleased with Joe's being so mightily secure of me. I should have liked him to have betrayed emotion, or to have said, 'It does you credit, Pip,' or something of that sort. Therefore, I made no remark on Joe's first head: merely saying as to his second, that the tidings had indeed come suddenly, but that I had always wanted to be a gentleman, and had often and often speculated on what I would do, if I were one.

'Have you though?' said Joe. 'Astonishing!'

'It's a pity now, Joe,' said I, 'that you did not get on a little more, when we had our lessons here; isn't it?'

'Well, I don't know,' returned Joe. 'I'm so awful dull. I'm only master of my own trade. It were always a pity as I was so awful dull; but it's no more of a pity now, than it was – this day twelvemonth – don't you see!'

What I had meant was, that when I came into my property and was able to do something for Joe, it would have been much more agreeable if he had been better qualified for a rise in station. He was so perfectly innocent of my meaning, however, that I thought I would mention it to Biddy in preference.

So, when we had walked home and had had tea, I took Biddy into our little garden by the side of the lane, and, after throwing out in a general way for the elevation of her spirits, that I should never forget her, said I had a favour to ask of her.

'And it is, Biddy,' said I, 'that you will not omit any opportunity of helping Joe on, a little.'

'How helping him on?' asked Biddy, with a steady sort of glance.

'Well! Joe is a dear good fellow – in fact, I think he is the dearest fellow that ever lived – but he is rather backward in some things. For instance, Biddy, in his learning and his manners.'

Although I was looking at Biddy as I spoke, and although she opened her eyes very wide when I had spoken, she did not look at me.

'Oh, his manners! Won't his manners do, then?' asked Biddy, plucking a blackcurrant leaf.

'My dear Biddy, they do very well here –'

'Oh! They *do* very well here?' interrupted Biddy, looking closely at the leaf in her hand.

'Hear me out – but if I were to remove Joe into a higher sphere, as I shall hope to remove him when I fully come into my property, they would hardly do him justice.'

'And don't you think he knows that?' asked Biddy.

It was such a provoking question (for it had never in the most distant manner occurred to me), that I said, snappishly, 'Biddy, what do you mean?'

Biddy having rubbed the leaf to pieces between her hands – and the smell of a blackcurrant bush has ever since recalled to me that evening in the little garden by the side of the lane – said, 'Have you never considered that he may be proud?'

'Proud?' I repeated, with disdainful emphasis.

'Oh! There are many kinds of pride,' said Biddy, looking full at me and shaking her head; 'pride is not all of one kind –'

'Well? What are you stopping for?' said I.

'Not all of one kind,' resumed Biddy. 'He may be too proud to let anyone take him out of a place that he is competent to fill, and fills well and with respect. To tell you the truth, I think he is: though it sounds bold in me to say so, for you must know him far better than I do.'

'Now, Biddy,' said I, 'I am very sorry to see this in you. I did not expect to see this in you. You are envious, Biddy, and grudging. You are dissatisfied on account of my rise in fortune, and you can't help showing it.'

'If you have the heart to think so,' returned Biddy, 'say so. Say so over and over again, if you have the heart to think so.'

'If you have the heart to be so, you mean, Biddy,' said I, in a virtuous and superior tone; 'don't put it off upon me. I am very sorry to see it, and it's a – it's a bad side of human nature. I did intend to ask you to use any little opportunities you might have after I was gone, of improving dear Joe. But after this, I ask you nothing. I am extremely sorry to see this in you, Biddy,' I repeated. 'It's a – it's a bad side of human nature.'

'Whether you scold me or approve of me,' returned poor Biddy, 'you may equally depend upon my trying to do all that lies in my power, here, at all times. And whatever opinion you take away of me, shall make no difference in my remembrance of you. Yet a gentleman should not be unjust neither,' said Biddy, turning away her head.

I again warmly repeated that it was a bad side of human nature (in which sentiment, waiving its application, I have since seen reason to think I was right), and I walked down the little path away from Biddy, and Biddy went into the house, and I went out at the garden gate and took a dejected stroll until supper-time; again feeling it very sorrowful and strange that this, the second night of my bright fortunes, should be as lonely and unsatisfactory as the first.

But, morning once more brightened my view, and I extended my clemency to Biddy, and we dropped the subject. Putting on the best clothes I had, I went into town as early as I could hope to find the shops open, and presented myself before Mr Trabb, the tailor; who was having his breakfast in the parlour behind his shop, and who did not think it worth his while to come out to me, but called me in to him.

'Well!' said Mr Trabb, in a hail-fellow-well-met kind of way. 'How are you, and what can I do for you?'

Mr Trabb had sliced his hot rolls into three feather beds, and was slipping butter in between the blankets, and covering it up. He was a prosperous old bachelor, and his open window looked into a prosperous little garden and orchard, and there was a prosperous iron safe let into the wall at the side of his fireplace, and I did not doubt that heaps of his prosperity were put away in it in bags.

'Mr Trabb,' said I, 'it's an unpleasant thing to have to mention, because it looks like boasting; but I have come into a handsome property.'

A change passed over Mr Trabb. He forgot the butter in bed, got up from the bedside, and wiped his fingers on the table-cloth, exclaiming, 'Lord bless my soul!'

'I am going up to my guardian in London,' said I, casually drawing some guineas out of my pocket and looking at them; 'and I want a fashionable suit of clothes to go in. I wish to pay for them,' I added – otherwise I thought he might only pretend to make them – 'with ready money.'

'My dear sir,' said Mr Trabb, as he respectfully bent his body, opened his arms, and took the liberty of touching me on the outside of each elbow, 'don't hurt me by mentioning that. May I venture to congratulate you? Would you do me the favour of stepping into the shop?'

Mr Trabb's boy was the most audacious boy in all that countryside. When I had entered he was sweeping the shop, and he had sweetened his labours by sweeping over me. He was still sweeping when I came out into the shop with Mr Trabb, and he knocked the broom against all possible corners and obstacles, to express (as I understood it) equality with any blacksmith, alive or dead.

'Hold that noise,' said Mr Trabb, with the greatest sternness, 'or I'll knock your head off! Do me the favour to be seated, sir. Now, this,' said Mr Trabb, taking down a roll of cloth, and tiding it out in a flowing manner over the counter, preparatory to getting his hand under it to show the gloss, 'is a very sweet article. I can recommend it for your purpose, sir, because it really is extra super. But you shall see some others. Give me number four, you!' (To the boy, and with a dreadfully severe stare; foreseeing the danger of that miscreant's brushing me with it, or making some other sign of familiarity.)

Mr Trabb never removed his stern eye from the boy until he had deposited number four on the counter and was at a safe distance again. Then, he commanded him to bring number five, and number eight. 'And let me have none of your tricks here,' said Mr Trabb, 'or you shall repent it, you young scoundrel, the longest day you have to live.'

Mr Trabb then bent over number four, and in a sort of deferential confidence recommended it to me as a light article for summer wear, an article much in vogue among the nobility and gentry, an article that it would ever be an honour to him to reflect upon a distinguished fellow-townsman's (if he might claim me for a fellow-townsman) having worn. 'Are you bringing numbers five and eight, you vagabond,' said Mr Trabb to the boy after that, 'or shall I kick you out of the shop and bring them myself?'

I selected the materials for a suit, with the assistance of Mr Trabb's judgement, and re-entered the parlour to be measured. For, although Mr Trabb had my measure already, and had previously been quite contented with it, he said apologetically that it 'wouldn't do under existing circumstances, sir – wouldn't do at all.' So, Mr Trabb measured and calculated me in the parlour, as if I were an estate and he the finest species of surveyor, and gave himself such a world of trouble that I felt that no suit of clothes could possibly remunerate him for his pains. When he had at last done and had appointed to send the articles to Mr Pumblechook's on the Thursday evening, he said, with his hand upon the parlour lock, 'I know, sir, that London gentlemen cannot be expected to patronise local work, as a rule; but if you would give me a turn now and then in the quality of a towns-man, I should greatly esteem it. Good-morning, sir, much obliged – door!'

The last word was flung at the boy, who had not the least notion what it meant. But I saw him collapse as his master rubbed me out with his hands, and my first decided experience of the stupendous power of money, was, that it had morally laid upon his back, Trabb's boy.

After this memorable event, I went to the hatter's, and the bootmaker's, and the hosier's, and felt rather like Mother Hubbard's dog whose outfit required the services of so many trades. I also went to the coach-office and took my place for seven o'clock on Saturday morning. It was not necessary to explain everywhere that I had come into a handsome property; but whenever I said anything to that effect, it followed that the officiating tradesman ceased to have his attention diverted through the window by the high street, and concentrated his mind upon me. When I had ordered everything I wanted, I directed my steps towards Pumblechook's, and, as I approached that gentleman's place of business, I saw him standing at his door.

He was waiting for me with great impatience. He had been out early with the chaise-cart, and had called at the forge and heard the news. He had prepared a collation for me in the Barnwell parlour, and he too ordered his shopman to 'come out of the gangway' as my sacred person passed.

'My dear friend,' said Mr Pumblechook, taking me by both hands, when he and I and the collation were alone, 'I give you joy of your good fortune. Well deserved, well deserved!'

This was coming to the point, and I thought it a sensible way of expressing himself.

'To think,' said Mr Pumblechook, after snorting admiration at me for some moments, 'that I should have been the humble instrument of leading up to this, is a proud reward.'

I begged Mr Pumblechook to remember that nothing was to be ever said or hinted, on that point.

'My dear young friend,' said Mr Pumblechook; 'if you will allow me to call you so –'

I murmured 'Certainly', and Mr Pumblechook took me by both hands again, and communicated a movement to his waistcoat, which had an emotional appearance, though it was rather low down. 'My dear young friend, rely upon my doing my little all in your absence, by keeping the fact before the mind of Joseph – Joseph!' said Mr Pumblechook, in the way of a compassionate adjuration. 'Joseph!! Joseph!!!!' Thereupon he shook his head and tapped it, expressing his sense of deficiency in Joseph.

'But, my dear young friend,' said Mr Pumblechook, 'you must be hungry, you must be exhausted. Be seated. Here is a chicken had round from the Boar, here is a tongue had round from the Boar, here's one or two little things had round from the Boar, that I hope you may not despise. But do I,' said Mr Pumblechook, getting up again the moment after he had sat down, 'see afore me, him as I ever sported with in his times of happy infancy? And may I – *may* I – ?'

This may I, meant might he shake hands? I consented, and he was fervent, and then sat down again.

'Here is wine,' said Mr Pumblechook. 'Let us drink, Thanks to fortune, and may she ever pick out her favourites with equal judgement! And yet I cannot,' said Mr Pumblechook, getting up again, 'see afore me one – and likewise drink to one – without again expressing – may I – *may* I – ?'

I said he might, and he shook hands with me again, and emptied his glass and turned it upside down. I did the same; and if I had turned myself upside down before drinking, the wine could not have gone more direct to my head.

Mr Pumblechook helped me to the liver wing, and to the best slice of tongue (none of those out-of-the-way No Thoroughfares of pork now), and took, comparatively speaking, no care of himself at all. 'Ah! poultry, poultry! You little thought,' said Mr Pumblechook, apostrophising the fowl in the dish, 'when you was a young fledgling, what was in store for you. You little thought you was to be refreshment beneath this humble roof for one as – call it a weakness, if you will,' said Mr Pumblechook, getting up again, 'but may I? *May* I – ?'

It began to be unnecessary to repeat the form of saying he might, so he did it at once. How he ever did it so often without wounding himself with my knife, I don't know.

'And your sister,' he resumed, after a little steady eating, 'which had the honour of bringing you up by hand! It's a sad picter, to reflect that she's no longer equal to fully understanding the honour. May – '

I saw he was about to come at me again, and I stopped him.

'We'll drink her health,' said I.

'Ah!' cried Mr Pumblechook, leaning back in his chair, quite flaccid with admiration, 'that's the way you know 'em, sir!' (I don't know who Sir was, but he certainly was not I, and there was no third person present); 'that's the way you know the noble-minded, sir! Ever forgiving and ever affable. It might,' said the servile Pumblechook, putting down his untasted glass in a hurry and getting up again, 'to a common person, have the appearance of repeating – but *may* I – ?'

When he had done it, he resumed his seat and drank to my sister. 'Let us never be blind,' said Mr Pumblechook, 'to her faults of temper, but it is to be hoped she meant well.'

At about this time, I began to observe that he was getting flushed in the face; as to myself, I felt all face, steeped in wine and smarting.

I mentioned to Mr Pumblechook that I wished to have my new clothes sent to his house, and he was ecstatic on my so distinguishing him. I mentioned my reason for desiring to avoid observation in the village, and he lauded it to the skies. There was nobody but himself, he intimated, worthy of my confidence, and – in short, might he? Then he asked me tenderly if I remembered our boyish games at sums, and how we had gone together to have me bound apprentice, and, in effect, how he had ever been my favourite fancy and my chosen friend? If I had taken ten times as many glasses of wine as I had, I should have known that he never had stood in that relation towards me, and should in my heart of hearts have repudiated the idea. Yet for all that, I remember feeling convinced that I had been much mistaken in him, and that he was a sensible practical good-hearted prime fellow.

By degrees he fell to reposing such great confidence in me, as to ask my advice in reference to his own affairs. He mentioned that there was an opportunity for a great amalgamation and monopoly of the corn and seed trade on those premises, if enlarged, such as had never occurred before in that, or any other neighbourhood. What alone was wanting to the realisation of a vast fortune, he considered to be more capital. Those were the two little words, more capital. Now it appeared to him (Pumblechook) that if that capital were got into the business, through a sleeping partner, sir – which sleeping partner would have nothing to do but walk in, by self or deputy, whenever he pleased, and examine the books – and walk in twice a year and take his profits away in his pocket, to the tune of fifty per cent – it appeared to him that that might be an opening for a young gentleman of spirit combined with property, which would be worthy of his attention. But what did I think? He had great

'*May I? May I* – ?'

confidence in my opinion, and what did I think? I gave it as my opinion, 'Wait a bit!' The united vastness and distinctness of this view so struck him, that he no longer asked me if he might shake hands with me, but said he really must – and did.

We drank all the wine, and Mr Pumblechook pledged himself over and over again to keep Joseph up to the mark (I don't know what mark), and to render me efficient and constant service (I don't know what service). He also made known to me for the first time in my life, and certainly after having kept his secret wonderfully well, that he had always said of me, 'That boy is no common boy, and mark me, his fortun' will be no common fortun'.' He said with a tearful smile that it was a singular thing to think of now, and I said so too. Finally, I went out into the air, with a dim perception that there was something unwonted in the conduct of the sunshine, and found that I had slumberously got to the turnpike without having taken any account of the road.

There, I was roused by Mr Pumblechook's hailing me. He was a long way down the sunny street, and was making expressive gestures for me to stop. I stopped, and he came up breathless.

'No, my dear friend,' said he, when he had recovered wind for speech. 'Not if I can help it. This occasion shall not entirely pass without that affability on your part – may I, as an old friend and well-wisher? *May* I?'

We shook hands for the hundredth time at least, and he ordered a young carter out of my way with the greatest indignation. Then, he blessed me, and stood waving his hand to me until I had passed the crook in the road; and then I turned into a field and had a long nap under a hedge before I pursued my way home.

I had scant luggage to take with me to London, for little of the little I possessed was adapted to my new station. But I began packing that same afternoon, and wildly packed up things that I knew I should want next morning, in a fiction that there was not a moment to be lost.

So, Tuesday, Wednesday, and Thursday passed; and on Friday morning I went to Mr Pumblechook's, to put on my new clothes and pay my visit to Miss Havisham. Mr Pumblechook's own room was given up to me to dress in, and was decorated with clean towels expressly for the event. My clothes were rather a disappointment, of course. Probably every new and eagerly expected garment ever put on since clothes came in, fell a trifle short of the wearer's expectation. But after I had had my new suit on, some half an hour, and had gone through an immensity of posturing with Mr Pumblechook's very limited dressing-glass, in the futile endeavour to see my legs, it seemed to fit me better. It being market morning at a neighbouring town some ten miles off, Mr Pumblechook was not at home. I had not told him exactly when I meant to leave, and was not likely to shake hands with him again before departing. This was all as it should be, and I went out in my new array: fearfully ashamed of having to pass the shopman, and suspicious after all that I was at a personal disadvantage, something like Joe in his Sunday suit.

I went circuitously to Miss Havisham's by all the back ways, and rang at the bell constrainedly, on account of the stiff long fingers of my gloves. Sarah Pocket came to the gate, and positively reeled back when she saw me so changed; her walnut-shell countenance likewise turned from brown to green and yellow.

'You?' said she. 'You? Good gracious! What do you want?'

'I am going to London, Miss Pocket,' said I, 'and want to say goodbye to Miss Havisham.'

I was not expected, for she left me locked in the yard, while she went to ask if I were to be admitted. After a very short delay, she returned and took me up, staring at me all the way.

Miss Havisham was taking exercise in the room with the long spread table, leaning on her crutch stick. The room was lighted as of yore, and at the sound of her entrance she stopped and turned. She was then just abreast of the rotted bride-cake.

'Don't go, Sarah,' she said. 'Well, Pip?'

'I start for London, Miss Havisham, tomorrow,' I was exceedingly careful what I said, 'and I thought you would kindly not mind my taking leave of you.'

'This is a gay figure, Pip,' said she, making her crutch stick play round me, as if she, the fairy godmother who had changed me, were bestowing the finishing gift.

'I have come into such good fortune since I saw you last, Miss Havisham,' I murmured. 'And I am so grateful for it, Miss Havisham!'

'Ay, ay!' said she, looking at the discomfited and envious Sarah, with delight. 'I have seen Mr Jaggers. *I* have heard about it, Pip. So you go tomorrow?'

'Yes, Miss Havisham.'

'And you are adopted by a rich person?'

'Yes, Miss Havisham.'

'Not named?'

'No, Miss Havisham.'

'And Mr Jaggers is made your guardian?'

'Yes, Miss Havisham.'

She quite gloated on these questions and answers, so keen was her enjoyment of Sarah Pocket's jealous dismay. 'Well!' she went on; 'you have a promising career before you. Be good – deserve it – and abide by Mr Jaggers's instructions.' She looked at me, and looked at Sarah, and Sarah's countenance wrung out of her watchful face a cruel smile. 'Goodbye, Pip! – you will always keep the name of Pip, you know.'

'Yes, Miss Havisham.'

'Goodbye, Pip!'

She stretched out her hand, and I went down on my knee and put it to my lips. I had not considered how I should take leave of her; it came naturally to me at the moment, to do this. She looked at Sarah Pocket with triumph in her weird eyes, and so I left my fairy godmother, with both her hands on her crutch stick, standing in the midst of the dimly lighted room beside the rotten bride-cake that was hidden in cobwebs.

Sarah Pocket conducted me down, as if I were a ghost who must be seen out. She could not get over my appearance, and was in the last degree confounded. I said 'Goodbye, Miss Pocket;' but she merely stared, and did not seem collected enough to know that I had spoken. Clear of the house, I made the best of my way back to Pumblechook's, took off my new clothes, made them into a bundle, and went back home in my older dress, carrying it – to speak the truth – much more at my ease too, though I had the bundle to carry.

And now, those six days which were to have run out so slowly, had run out fast and were gone, and tomorrow looked me in the face more steadily than I could look at it. As the six evenings had dwindled away to five, to four, to three, to two, I had become more and more appreciative of the society of Joe and Biddy. On this last evening, I dressed myself out in my new clothes, for their delight, and sat in my splendour until bedtime. We had a hot supper on the occasion, graced by the inevitable roast fowl, and we had some flip to finish with. We were all very low, and none the higher for pretending to be in spirits.

I was to leave our village at five in the morning, carrying my little hand-portmanteau, and I had told Joe that I wished to walk away all alone. I am afraid – sore afraid – that this purpose originated in my sense of the contrast there would be between me and Joe, if we went to the coach together. I had pretended with myself that there was nothing of this taint in the arrangement; but when I went up to my little room on this last night, I felt compelled to admit that it might be done so, and had an impulse upon me to go down again and entreat Joe to walk with me in the morning. I did not.

All night there were coaches in my broken sleep, going to wrong places instead of to London, and having in the traces, now dogs, now cats, now pigs, now men – never horses. Fantastic failures of journeys occupied me until the day dawned and the birds were singing. Then, I got up and partly dressed, and sat at the window to take a last look out, and in taking it fell asleep.

Biddy was astir so early to get my breakfast, that, although I did not sleep at the window an hour, I smelt the smoke of the kitchen fire when I started up with a terrible idea that it must be late in the afternoon. But long after that, and long after I heard the clinking of the teacups and was quite ready, I wanted the resolution to go downstairs. After all, I remained up there, repeatedly unlocking and unstrapping my small portmanteau and locking and strapping it up again, until Biddy called to me that I was late.

It was a hurried breakfast with no taste in it. I got up from the meal, saying with a sort of briskness, as if it had only just occurred to me, 'Well! I suppose I must be off!' and then I kissed my sister, who was laughing, and nodding and shaking in her usual chair, and kissed Biddy, and threw my arms around Joe's neck. Then I took up my little portmanteau and walked out. The last I saw of them was, when I presently heard a scuffle behind me, and looking back, saw Joe throwing an old shoe after me and Biddy throwing another old shoe. I stopped then, to wave my hat, and dear old Joe waved his strong right arm above his head, crying huskily, 'Hooroar'! and Biddy put her apron to her face.

I walked away at a good pace, thinking it was easier to go than I had supposed it would be, and reflecting that it would never have done to have an old shoe thrown after the coach, in sight of all the High Street. I whistled and made nothing of going. But the village was very peaceful and quiet, and the light mists were solemnly rising, as if to show me the world, and I had been

so innocent and little there, and all beyond was so unknown and great, that in a moment with a strong heave and sob I broke into tears. It was by the fingerpost at the end of the village, and I laid my hand upon it, and said, 'Goodbye, O my dear, dear friend!'

Heaven knows we need never be ashamed of our tears, for they are rain upon the blinding dust of earth, overlying our hard hearts. I was better after I had cried, than before – more sorry, more aware of my own ingratitude, more gentle. If I had cried before, I should have had Joe with me then.

So subdued I was by those tears, and by their breaking out again in the course of the quiet walk, that when I was on the coach, and it was clear of the town, I deliberated with an aching heart whether I would not get down when we changed horses and walk back, and have another evening at home, and a better parting. We changed, and I had not made up my mind, and still reflected for my comfort that it would be quite practicable to get down and walk back, when we changed again. And while I was occupied with those deliberations, I would fancy an exact resemblance to Joe in some man coming along the road towards us, and my heart would beat high – as if he could possibly be there!

We changed again, and yet again, and it was now too late and too far to go back, and I went on. And the mists had all solemnly risen now, and the world lay spread before me.

This is the end of the first stage of Pip's expectations

Pip leaves the village

Chapter 20

The journey from our town to the metropolis was a journey of about five hours. It was a little past midday when the four-horse stagecoach by which I was a passenger, got into the ravel of traffic frayed out about the Cross Keys, Wood Street, Cheapside, London.

We Britons had at that time particularly settled that it was treasonable to doubt our having and our being the best of everything: otherwise, while I was scared by the immensity of London, I think I might have had some faint doubts whether it was not rather ugly, crooked, narrow, and dirty.

Mr Jaggers had duly sent me his address; it was Little Britain, and he had written after it on his card, 'just out of Smithfield, and close by the coach-office.' Nevertheless, a hackney-coachman, who seemed to have as many capes to his greasy greatcoat as he was years old, packed me up in his coach and hemmed me in with a folding and jingling barrier of steps, as if he were going to take me fifty miles. His getting on his box, which I remember to have been decorated with an old weather-stained pea-green hammer-cloth, moth-eaten into rags, was quite a work of time. It was a wonderful equipage, with six great coronets outside, and ragged things behind for I don't know how many footmen to hold on by, and a harrow below them, to prevent amateur footmen from yielding to the temptation.

I had scarcely had time to enjoy the coach and to think how like a straw-yard it was, and yet how like a rag-shop, and to wonder why the horses' nosebags were kept inside, when I observed the coachman beginning to get down, as if we were going to stop presently. And stop we presently did, in a gloomy street, at certain offices with an open door, whereon was painted 'Mr Jaggers'.

'How much?' I asked the coachman.

The coachman answered, 'A shilling – unless you wish to make it more.'

I naturally said I had no wish to make it more.

'Then it must be a shilling,' observed the coachman. 'I don't want to get into trouble. I know *him!*' He darkly closed an eye at Mr Jaggers's name, and shook his head.

When he had got his shilling, and had in course of time completed the ascent to his box, and had got away (which appeared to relieve his mind), I went into the front office with my little portmanteau in my hand, and asked, was Mr Jaggers at home?

'He is not,' returned the clerk. 'He is in Court at present. Am I addressing Mr Pip?'

I signified that he was addressing Mr Pip.

'Mr Jaggers left word would you wait in his room? He couldn't say how long he might be, having a case on. But it stands to reason, his time being valuable, that he won't be longer than he can help.'

With those words, the clerk opened a door, and ushered me into an inner chamber at the back. Here we found a gentleman with one eye, in a velveteen suit and knee-breeches, who wiped his nose with his sleeve on being interrupted in the perusal of the newspaper.

'Go and wait outside, Mike,' said the clerk.

I began to say that I hoped I was not interrupting – when the clerk shoved this gentleman out with as little ceremony as I ever saw used, and tossing his fur cap out after him, left me alone.

Mr Jaggers's room was lighted by a skylight only, and was a most dismal place; the skylight, eccentrically patched like a broken head, and the distorted adjoining houses looking as if they had twisted themselves to peep down at me through it. There were not so many papers about, as I should have expected to see; and there were some odd objects about, that I should not have expected to see – such as an old rusty pistol, a sword in a scabbard, several strange-looking boxes and packages, and two dreadful casts on a shelf, of faces peculiarly swollen, and twitchy about the nose. Mr Jaggers's own high-backed chair was of deadly black horsehair, with rows of brass nails round it, like a coffin; and I fancied I could see how he leaned back in it, and bit his forefinger at the clients. The room was but small, and the clients seemed to have had a habit of backing up against the wall: the wall, especially opposite to Mr Jaggers's chair, being greasy with shoulders. I recalled, too, that the one-eyed gentleman had shuffled forth against the wall when I was the innocent cause of his being turned out.

I sat down in the cliental chair placed over against Mr Jaggers's chair, and became fascinated by the dismal atmosphere of the place. I called to mind that the clerk had the same air of knowing something to everybody else's disadvantage, as his master had. I wondered how many other clerks there were upstairs, and whether they all claimed to have the same detrimental mastery of their fellow-creatures. I wondered what was the history of all the odd litter about the room, and how it came there. I wondered whether the two swollen faces were of Mr Jaggers's family, and, if he were so unfortunate as to have had a pair of such ill-looking relations, why he stuck them on that dusty perch for the blacks and flies to settle on, instead of giving them a place at home. Of course I had no experience of a London summer day, and my spirits may have been oppressed by the hot exhausted air, and by the dust and grit that lay thick on everything. But I sat wondering and waiting in Mr Jaggers's close room, until I really could not bear the two casts on the shelf above Mr Jaggers's chair, and got up and went out.

When I told the clerk that I would take a turn in the air while I waited, he advised me to go round the corner and I should come into Smithfield. So, I came into Smithfield; and the shameful place, being all a-smear with filth and fat and blood and foam, seemed to stick to me. So I rubbed it off with all possible speed by turning into a street where I saw the great black dome of Saint Paul's bulging at me from behind a grim stone building which a bystander said was Newgate Prison. Following the wall of the jail, I found the roadway covered with straw to deaden the noise of passing vehicles; and from this, and from the quantity of people standing about, smelling strongly of spirits and beer, I inferred that the trials were on.

While I looked about me here, an exceedingly dirty and

partially drunk minister of justice asked me if I would like to step in and hear a trial or so: informing me that he could give me a front place for half a crown, whence I should command a full view of the Lord Chief Justice in his wig and robes – mentioning that awful personage like waxwork, and presently offering him at the reduced price of eighteen pence. As I declined the proposal on the plea of an appointment, he was so good as to take me into a yard and show me where the gallows was kept, and also where people were publicly whipped, and then he showed me the debtors' door, out of which culprits came to be hanged; heightening the interest of that dreadful portal by giving me to understand that 'four on 'em' would come out at that door the day after tomorrow at eight in the morning to be killed in a row. This was horrible, and gave me a sickening idea of London: the more so as the Lord Chief Justice's proprietor wore (from his hat down to his boots and up again to his pocket-handkerchief inclusive) mildewed clothes, which had evidently not belonged to him originally, and which, I took it into my head, he had bought cheap of the executioner. Under these circumstances I thought myself well rid of him for a shilling.

I dropped into the office to ask if Mr Jaggers had come in yet, and I found he had not, and I strolled out again. This time, I made the tour of Little Britain, and turned into Bartholomew Close; and now I became aware that other people were waiting about for Mr Jaggers, as well as I. There were two men of secret appearance lounging in Bartholomew Close, and thoughtfully fitting their feet into the cracks of the pavement as they talked together, one of whom said to the other when they first passed me, that 'Jaggers would do it if it was to be done.' There was a knot of three men and two women standing at a corner, and one of the women was crying on her dirty shawl, and the other comforted her by saying, as she pulled her own shawl over her shoulders, 'Jaggers is for him, 'Melia, and what more *could* you have?' There was a red-eyed little Jew who came into the Close while I was loitering there, in company with a second little Jew whom he sent upon an errand; and while the messenger was gone, I remarked this Jew, who was of a highly excitable temperament, performing a jig of anxiety under a lamppost, and accompanying himself, in a kind of frenzy, with the words, 'Oh Jaggerth, Jaggerth, Jaggerth! All otherth ith Cag-Maggerth, give me Jaggerth!' These testimonies to the popularity of my guardian made a deep impression on me, and I admired and wondered more than ever.

At length, as I was looking out at the iron gate of Bartholomew Close into Little Britain, I saw Mr Jaggers coming across the road towards me. All the others who were waiting, saw him at the same time, and there was quite a rush at him. Mr Jaggers, putting a hand on my shoulder and walking me on at his side without saying anything to me, addressed himself to his followers.

First, he took the two secret men.

'Now, I have nothing to say to *you*,' said Mr Jaggers, throwing his finger at them. 'I want to know no more than I know. As to the result, it's a toss-up. I told you from the first it was a toss-up. Have you paid Wemmick?'

'We made the money up this morning, sir,' said one of the men, submissively, while the other perused Mr Jaggers's face.

'I don't ask you when you made it up, or where, or whether you made it up at all. Has Wemmick got it?'

'Yes, sir,' said both the men together.

'Very well; then you may go. Now, I won't have it!' said Mr Jaggers, waving his hand at them to put them behind him. 'If you say a word to me, I'll throw up the case.'

'We thought, Mr Jaggers – ' one of the men began, pulling off his hat.

'That's what I told you not to do,' said Mr Jaggers. '*You* thought! I think for you; that's enough for you. If I want you, I know where to find you; I don't want you to find me. Now I won't have it. I won't hear a word.'

The two men looked at one another as Mr Jaggers waved them behind again, and humbly fell back and were heard no more.

'And now *you*!' said Mr Jaggers, suddenly stopping, and turning on the two women with the shawls, from whom the three men had meekly separated – 'Oh! Amelia, is it?'

'Yes, Mr Jaggers.'

'And do you remember,' retorted Mr Jaggers, 'that but for me you wouldn't be here and couldn't be here?'

'Oh yes, sir!' exclaimed both women together. 'Lord bless you, sir, well we knows that!'

'Then why,' said Mr Jaggers, 'do you come here?'

'My Bill, sir?' the crying woman pleaded.

'Now, I tell you what!' said Mr Jaggers. 'Once for all. If you don't know that your Bill's in good hands, I know it. And if you come here, bothering about your Bill, I'll make an example of both your Bill and you, and let him slip through my fingers. Have you paid Wemmick?'

'Oh yes, sir! Every farden.'

'Very well. Then you have done all you have got to do. Say another word – one single word – and Wemmick shall give you your money back.'

This terrible threat caused the two women to fall off immediately. No one remained now but the excitable Jew, who had already raised the skirts of Mr Jaggers's coat to his lips several times.

'I don't know this man!' said Mr Jaggers, in the most devastating strain. 'What does this fellow want?'

'Ma thear Mithter Jaggerth. Hown brother to Habraham Latharuth!'

'Who's he?' said Mr Jaggers. 'Let go of my coat.'

The suitor, kissing the hem of the garment again before relinquishing it, replied, 'Habraham Latharuth, on thuthpithion of plate.'

'You're too late,' said Mr Jaggers. 'I am over the way.'

'Holy father, Mithter Jaggerth!' cried my excitable acquaintance, turning white, 'don't thay you're again Habraham Latharuth!'

'I am,' said Mr Jaggers, 'and there's an end of it. Get out of the way.'

'Mithter Jaggerth! Half a moment! My hown cuthen'th gone to Mithter Wemmick at thith prethenth minute to hoffer him hany termth. Mithter Jaggerth! Half a quarter of a moment! If you'd have the condethenthun to be bought off from the t'other thide – at any thuperior prithe – money no object – Mithter Jaggerth – Mithter – !'

My guardian threw his supplicant off with supreme indifference, and left him dancing on the pavement as if it were redhot. Without further interruption, we reached the front office, where we found the clerk and the man in velveteen with the fur cap.

'Here's Mike,' said the clerk, getting down from his stool, and approaching Mr Jaggers confidentially.

'Oh!' said Mr Jaggers, turning to the man who was pulling a lock of hair in the middle of his forehead, like the Bull in Cock Robin pulling at the bell-rope; 'your man comes on this afternoon. Well?'

'Well, Mas'r Jaggers,' returned Mike, in the voice of a sufferer from a constitutional cold; 'arter a deal o' trouble, I've found one, sir, as might do.'

'What is he prepared to swear?'

'Well, Mas'r Jaggers,' said Mike, wiping his nose on his fur cap this time; 'in a general way, anythink.'

Mr Jaggers suddenly became most irate. 'Now, I warned you before,' said he, throwing his forefinger at the terrified client, 'that if ever you presumed to talk in that way here, I'd make an example of you. You infernal scoundrel, how dare you tell *me* that?'

The client looked scared, but bewildered too, as if he were unconscious what he had done.

Mr Jaggers and his clients

'Spooney!' said the clerk, in a low voice, giving him a stir with his elbow. 'Soft Head! Need you say it face to face?'

'Now, I ask you, you blundering booby,' said my guardian, very sternly, 'once more and for the last time, what the man you have brought here is prepared to swear?'

Mike looked hard at my guardian, as if he were trying to learn a lesson from his face, and slowly replied, 'Ayther to character, or to having been in his company and never left him all the night in question.'

'Now, be careful. In what station of life is this man?'

Mike looked at his cap, and looked at the floor, and looked at the ceiling, and looked at the clerk, and even looked at me, before beginning to reply in a nervous manner, 'We've dressed him up like – ' when my guardian blustered out: 'What? You *will*, will you?'

('Spooney!' added the clerk again, with another stir.)

After some helpless casting about, Mike brightened and began again: 'He is dressed like a 'spectable pieman. A sort of a pastry-cook.'

'Is he here?' asked my guardian.

'I left him,' said Mike, 'a setting on some doorsteps round the corner.'

'Take him past that window, and let me see him.'

The window indicated was the office window. We all three went to it, behind the wire blind, and presently saw the client go by in an accidental manner, with a murderous-looking tall individual, in a short suit of white linen and a paper cap. This guileless confectioner was not by any means sober, and had a black eye in the green stage of recovery, which was painted over.

'Tell him to take his witness away directly,' said my guardian to the clerk, in extreme disgust, 'and ask him what he means by bringing such a fellow as that.'

My guardian then took me into his own room, and while he lunched, standing, from a sandwich-box and a pocket flask of sherry (he seemed to bully his very sandwich as he ate it), informed me what arrangements he had made for me. I was to go to 'Barnard's Inn', to young Mr Pocket's rooms, where a bed had been sent in for my accommodation; I was to remain with young Mr Pocket until Monday; on Monday I was to go with him to his father's house on a visit, that I might try how I liked it. Also, I was told what my allowance was to be – it was a very liberal one – and had handed to me from one of my guardian's drawers, the cards of certain tradesmen with whom I was to deal for all kinds of clothes, and such other things as I could in reason want. 'You will find your credit good, Mr Pip,' said my guardian, whose flask of sherry smelt like a whole cask-full, as he hastily refreshed himself, 'but I shall by this means be able to check your bills, and to pull you up if I find you outrunning the constable. Of course you'll go wrong somehow, but that's no fault of mine.'

After I had pondered a little over this encouraging sentiment, I asked Mr Jaggers if I could send for a coach? He said it was not worth while, I was so near my destination; Wemmick should walk round with me, if I pleased.

I then found that Wemmick was the clerk in the next room. Another clerk was rung down from upstairs to take his place while he was out, and I accompanied him into the street, after shaking hands with my guardian. We found a new set of people lingering outside, but Wemmick made a way among them by saying coolly yet decisively, 'I tell you it's no use; he won't have a word to say to one of you;' and we soon got clear of them, and went on side by side.

Chapter 21

Casting my eyes on Mr Wemmick as we went along, to see what he was like in the light of day, I found him to be a dry man, rather short in stature, with a square wooden face, whose expression seemed to have been imperfectly chipped out with a dull-edged chisel. There were some marks in it that might have been dimples, if the material had been softer and the instrument finer, but which, as it was, were only dints. The chisel had made three or four of these attempts at embellishment over his nose, but had given them up without an effort to smooth them off. I judged him to be a bachelor from the frayed condition of his linen, and he appeared to have sustained a good many bereavements; for he wore at least four mourning rings, besides a brooch representing a lady and a weeping willow at a tomb with an urn on it. I noticed, too, that several rings and seals hung at his watch-chain, as if he were quite laden with remembrances of departed friends. He had glittering eyes – small, keen, and black – and thin wide mottled lips. He had had them, to the best of my belief, from forty to fifty years.

'So you were never in London before?' said Mr Wemmick to me.

The guileless confectioner

'No,' said I.

'*I* was new here once,' said Mr Wemmick. 'Rum to think of now!'

'You are well acquainted with it now?'

'Why, yes,' said Mr Wemmick. 'I know the moves of it.'

'Is it a very wicked place?' I asked, more for the sake of saying something than for information.

'You may get cheated, robbed, and murdered, in London. But there are plenty of people anywhere, who'll do that for you.'

'If there is bad blood between you and them,' said I, to soften it off a little.

'Oh! I don't know about bad blood,' returned Mr Wemmick. 'There's not much bad blood about. They'll do it, if there's anything to be got by it.'

'That makes it worse.'

'You think so?' returned Mr Wemmick. 'Much about the same, I should say.'

He wore his hat on the back of his head, and looked straight before him: walking in a self-contained way as if there were nothing in the streets to claim his attention. His mouth was such a post office of a mouth that he had a mechanical appearance of smiling. We had got to the top of Holborn Hill before I knew that it was merely a mechanical appearance, and that he was not smiling at all.

'Do you know where Mr Matthew Pocket lives?' I asked Mr Wemmick.

'Yes,' said he, nodding in the direction. 'At Hammer- smith, west of London.'

'Is that far?'

'Well! Say five miles.'

'Do you know him?'

'Why, you are a regular cross-examiner!' said Mr Wemmick, looking at me with an approving air. 'Yes, I know him. *I* know him!'

There was an air of toleration or depreciation about his utterance of these words, that rather depressed me; and I was still looking sideways at his block of a face in search of any encouraging note to the text, when he said here we were at Barnard's Inn. My depression was not alleviated by the announcement, for I had supposed that establishment to be an hotel kept by Mr Barnard, to which the Blue Boar in our town was a mere public house. Whereas I now found Barnard to be a disembodied spirit, or a fiction, and his inn the dingiest collection of shabby buildings ever squeezed together in a rank corner as a club for tom-cats.

We entered this haven through a wicket-gate, and were dis- gorged by an introductory passage into a melancholy little square that looked to me like a flat burying-ground. I thought it had the most dismal trees in it, and the most dismal sparrows, and the most dismal cats, and the most dismal houses (in number half a dozen or so), that I had ever seen. I thought the windows of the sets of chambers into which those houses were divided, were in every stage of dilapidated blind and curtain, crippled flowerpot, cracked glass, dusty decay and miserable makeshift; while To Let To Let To Let glared at me from empty rooms, as if no new wretches ever came there, and the vengeance of the soul of Barnard were being slowly appeased by the gradual suicide of the present occupants and their unholy interment under the gravel. A frouzy mourning of soot and smoke attired this forlorn creation of Barnard, and it had strewed ashes on its head, and was undergoing penance and humiliation as a mere dust-hole. Thus far my sense of sight; while dry rot and wet rot and all the silent rots that rot in neglected roof and cellar – rot of rat and mouse and bug and coaching-stables near at hand besides – addressed themselves faintly to my sense of smell, and moaned, 'Try Barnard's Mixture'.

So imperfect was this realisation of the first of my great expectations, that I looked in dismay at Mr Wemmick. 'Ah!' said he, mistaking me; 'the retirement reminds you of the country. So it does me.'

He led me into a corner and conducted me up a flight of stairs – which appeared to me to be slowly collapsing into sawdust, so that one of those days the upper lodgers would look out at their doors and find themselves without the means of coming down – to a set of chambers on the top floor. Mr Pocket, Jun., was painted on the door, and there was a label on the letter-box, 'Return shortly'.

'He hardly thought you'd come so soon,' Mr Wemmick explained. 'You don't want me any more?'

'No, thank you,' said I.

'As I keep the cash,' Mr Wemmick observed, 'we shall most likely meet pretty often. Good-day.'

'Good-day.'

I put out my hand, and Mr Wemmick at first looked at it as if he thought I wanted something. Then he looked at me, and said, correcting himself,

'To be sure! Yes. You're in the habit of shaking hands?'

I was rather confused, thinking it must be out of the London fashion, but said yes.

'I have got so out of it!' said Mr Wemmick – 'except at last. Very glad, I'm sure, to make your acquaintance. Good-day!'

When we had shaken hands and he was gone, I opened the staircase window and had nearly beheaded myself, for the lines had rotted away, and it came down like the guillotine. Happily it was so quick that I had not put my head out. After this escape, I was content to take a foggy view of the Inn through the window's encrusting dirt, and to stand dolefully looking out, saying to myself that London was decidedly overrated.

Mr Pocket, Junior's idea of shortly was not mine, for I had nearly maddened myself with looking out for half an hour, and had written my name with my finger several times in the dirt of every pane in the window, before I heard footsteps on the stairs. Gradually there arose before me the hat, head, neckcloth, waistcoat, trousers, boots, of a member of society of about my own standing. He had a paper-bag under each arm and a pottle of strawberries in one hand, and was out of breath.

'Mr Pip?' said he.

'Mr Pocket?' said I.

'Dear me!' he exclaimed. 'I am extremely sorry; but I knew there was a coach from your part of the country at midday, and I thought you would come by that one. The fact is, I have been out on your account – not that that is any excuse – for I thought, coming from the country, you might like a little fruit after dinner, and I went to Covent Garden Market to get it good.'

For a reason that I had, I felt as if my eyes would start out of my head. I acknowledged his attention incoherently, and began to think this was a dream.

'Dear me!' said Mr Pocket, Junior. 'This door sticks so!'

As he was fast making jam of his fruit by wrestling with the door while the paper-bags were under his arms, I begged him to allow me to hold them. He relinquished them with an agreeable smile, and combated with the door as if it were a wild beast. It yielded so suddenly at last, that he staggered back upon me, and I staggered back upon the opposite door, and we both laughed. But still I felt as if my eyes must start out of my head, and as if this must be a dream.

'Pray come in,' said Mr Pocket, Junior. 'Allow me to lead the way. I am rather bare here, but I hope you'll be able to make out tolerably well till Monday. My father thought you would get on more agreeably through tomorrow with me than with him, and might like to take a walk about London. I am sure I shall be very happy to show London to you. As to our table, you won't find that bad, I hope, for it will be supplied from our coffee-house here, and (it is only right I should add) at your expense, such being Mr Jaggers's directions. As to our lodging, it's not by any means splendid, because I have my own bread to earn, and my father hasn't anything to give me, and I shouldn't be willing to take it, if he had. This is our sitting-room – just such chairs and tables and carpet and so forth, you see, as they could spare from home. You mustn't give me credit for the tablecloth and spoons and castors, because they come for you from the coffee-house. This is my little bedroom; rather musty, but Barnard's *is* musty. This is your bedroom; the furniture's hired for the occasion, but I trust it will answer the purpose; if you should want anything, I'll go and fetch it. The chambers are retired, and we shall be alone together, but we shan't fight, I dare say. But, dear me, I beg your pardon, you're holding the fruit all this time. Pray let me take these bags from you. I am quite ashamed.'

As I stood opposite to Mr Pocket, Junior, delivering him the bags, one, two, I saw the starting appearance come into his own eyes that I knew to be in mine, and he said, falling back: 'Lord bless me, you're the prowling boy!'

'And you,' said I, 'are the pale young gentleman!'

Chapter 22

The pale young gentleman and I stood contemplating one another in Barnard's Inn, until we both burst out laughing. 'The idea of its being you!' said he. 'The idea of its being *you*!' said I. And then we contemplated one another afresh, and laughed again. 'Well!' said the pale young gentleman, reaching out his hand good-humouredly, 'it's all over now, I hope, and it will be magnanimous in you if you'll forgive me for having knocked you about so.'

I derived from this speech that Mr Herbert Pocket (for Herbert was the pale young gentleman's name) still rather confounded his intention with his execution. But I made a modest reply, and we shook hands warmly.

'You hadn't come into your good fortune at that time?' said Herbert Pocket.

'No,' said I.

'No,' he acquiesced: 'I heard it had happened very lately. *I* was rather on the look-out for good-fortune then.'

'Indeed?'

'Yes. Miss Havisham had sent for me, to see if she could take a fancy to me. But she couldn't – at all events, she didn't.'

I thought it polite to remark that I was surprised to hear that.

'Bad taste,' said Herbert, laughing, 'but a fact. Yes, she had sent for me on a trial visit, and if I had come out of it successfully, I suppose I should have been provided for; perhaps I should have been what-you-may-called it to Estella.'

'What's that?' I asked, with sudden gravity.

He was arranging his fruit in plates while we talked, which divided his attention, and was the cause of his having made this lapse of a word. 'Affianced,' he explained, still busy with the fruit. 'Betrothed. Engaged. What's-his-named. Any word of that sort.'

'How did you bear your disappointment?' I asked.

'Pooh!' said he, 'I didn't care much for it. *She*'s a Tartar.'

'Miss Havisham?'

'I don't say no to that, but I meant Estella. That girl's hard and haughty and capricious to the last degree, and has been brought up by Miss Havisham to wreak revenge on all the male sex.'

'What relation is she to Miss Havisham?'

'None,' said he. 'Only adopted.'

'Why should she wreak revenge on all the male sex? What revenge?'

'Lord, Mr Pip!' said he. 'Don't you know?'

'No,' said I.

'Dear me! It's quite a story, and shall be saved till dinner-time. And now let me take the liberty of asking you a question. How did you come there, that day?'

I told him, and he was attentive until I had finished, and then burst out laughing again, and asked me if I was sore afterwards? I didn't ask him if *he* was, for my conviction on that point was perfectly established.

'Mr Jaggers is your guardian, I understand?' he went on.

'Yes.'

'You know he is Miss Havisham's man of business and solicitor, and has her confidence when nobody else has?'

This was bringing me (I felt) towards dangerous ground. I answered with a constraint I made no attempt to disguise, that I had seen Mr Jaggers in Miss Havisham's house on the very day of our combat, but never at any other time, and that I believed he had no recollection of having ever seen me there.

'He was so obliging as to suggest my father for your tutor, and he called on my father to propose it. Of course he knew about my father from his connection with Miss Havisham. My father is Miss Havisham's cousin; not that that implies familiar intercourse between them, for he is a bad courtier and will not propitiate her.'

Herbert Pocket had a frank and easy way with him that was very taking. I had never seen anyone then, and I have never seen anyone since, who more strongly expressed to me, in every look and tone, a natural incapacity to do anything secret and mean. There was something wonderfully hopeful about his general air, and something that at the same time whispered to me he would never be successful or rich. I don't know how this was. I became imbued with the notion on that first occasion before we sat down to dinner, but I cannot define by what means.

He was still a pale young gentleman, and had a certain conquered languor about him in the midst of his spirits and briskness, that did not seem indicative of natural strength. He had not a handsome face, but it was better than handsome: being extremely amiable and cheerful. His figure was a little ungainly, as in the days when my knuckles had taken such liberties with it, but it looked as if it would always be light and young. Whether Mr Trabb's local work would have sat more gracefully on him than on me, may be a question; but I am conscious that he carried off his rather old clothes, much better than I carried off my new suit.

As he was so communicative, I felt that reserve on my part would be a bad return unsuited to our years. I therefore told him my small story, and laid stress on my being forbidden to enquire who my benefactor was. I further mentioned that as I had been brought up a blacksmith in a country place, and knew very little of the ways of politeness, I would take it as a great kindness in him if he would give me a hint whenever he saw me at a loss or going wrong.

'With pleasure,' said he, 'though I venture to prophesy that you'll want very few hints. I dare say we shall be often together, and I should like to banish any needless restraint between us. Will you do me the favour to begin at once to call me by my christian name, Herbert?'

I thanked him, and said I would. I informed him in exchange that my christian name was Philip.

'I don't take to Philip,' said he, smiling, 'for it sounds like a moral boy out of the spelling-book, who was so lazy that he fell into a pond, or so fat that he couldn't see out of his eyes, or so avaricious that he locked up his cake till the mice ate it, or so determined to go a bird's-nesting that he got himself eaten by bears who lived handy in the neighbourhood. I tell you what I should like. We are so harmonious, and you have been a blacksmith – would you mind it?'

'I shouldn't mind anything that you propose,' I answered, 'but I don't understand you.'

'Would you mind Handel for a familiar name? There's a charming piece of music, by Handel, called the "Harmonious Blacksmith".'

'I should like it very much.'

'Then, my dear Handel,' said he, turning round as the door opened, 'here is the dinner, and I must beg of you to take the top of the table, because the dinner is of your providing.'

This I would not hear of, so he took the top, and I faced him.

It was a nice little dinner – seemed to me then, a very Lord Mayor's Feast – and it acquired additional relish from being eaten under those independent circumstances, with no old people by, and with London all around us. This again was heightened by a certain gypsy character that set the banquet off; for, while the table was, as Mr Pumblechook might have said, the lap of luxury – being entirely furnished forth from the coffee-house – the circumjacent region of sitting-room was of a comparatively pastureless and shifty character: imposing on the waiter the wandering habits of putting the covers on the floor (where he fell over them), the melted butter in the arm-chair, the bread on the bookshelves, the cheese in the coal-scuttle, and the boiled fowl into my bed in the next room – where I found much of its parsley and butter in a state of congelation when I retired for the night. All this made the feast delightful, and when the waiter was not there to watch me, my pleasure was without alloy.

We had made some progress in the dinner, when I reminded Herbert of his promise to tell me about Miss Havisham.

'True,' he replied. 'I'll redeem it at once. Let me introduce the topic, Handel, by mentioning that in London it is not the custom to put the knife in the mouth – for fear of accidents – and that while the fork is reserved for that use, it is not put further in than necessary. It is scarcely worth mentioning, only it's as well to do as other people do. Also, the spoon is not generally used overhand, but under. This has two advantages. You get at your mouth better (which after all is the object), and you save a good deal of the attitude of opening oysters, on the part of the right elbow.'

He offered these friendly suggestions in such a lively way, that we both laughed and I scarcely blushed.

'Now,' he pursued, 'concerning Miss Havisham. Miss Havisham, you must know, was a spoilt child. Her mother died when she was a baby, and her father denied her nothing. Her father was a country gentleman down in your part of the world, and was a brewer. I don't know why it should be a crack thing to be a brewer; but it is indisputable that while you cannot possibly be genteel and bake, you may be as genteel as never was and brew. You see it every day.'

'Yet a gentleman may not keep a public house; may he?' said I.

'Not on any account,' returned Herbert; 'but a public house may keep a gentleman. Well! Mr Havisham was very rich and very proud. So was his daughter.'

'Miss Havisham was an only child?' I hazarded.

'Stop a moment, I am coming to that. No, she was not an only child; she had a half-brother. Her father privately married again – his cook, I rather think.'

'I thought he was proud,' said I.

'My good Handel, so he was. He married his second wife privately, because he was proud, and in course of time *she* died. When she was dead, I apprehend he first told his daughter what he had done, and then the son became a part of the family, residing in the house you are acquainted with. As the son grew a young man, he turned out riotous, extravagant, undutiful – altogether bad. At last his father disinherited him;

but he softened when he was dying, and left him well off, though not nearly so well off as Miss Havisham – Take another glass of wine, and excuse my mentioning that society as a body does not expect one to be so strictly conscientious in emptying one's glass, as to turn it bottom upwards with the rim on one's nose.'

I had been doing this, in an excess of attention to his recital. I thanked him, and apologised. He said, 'Not at all,' and resumed.

'Miss Havisham was now an heiress, and you may suppose was looked after as a great match. Her half-brother had now ample means again, but what with debts and what with new madness wasted them most fearfully again. There were stronger differences between him and her, than there had been between him and his father, and it is suspected that he cherished a deep and mortal grudge against her as having influenced the father's anger. Now, I come to the cruel part of the story – merely breaking off, my dear Handel, to remark that a dinner-napkin will not go into a tumbler.'

Why I was trying to pack mine into my tumbler, I am wholly unable to say. I only know that I found myself, with a perseverance worthy of a much better cause, making the most strenuous exertions to compress it within those limits. Again I thanked him and apologised, and again he said in the cheerfullest manner, 'Not at all, I am sure!' and resumed.

'There appeared upon the scene – say at the races, or the public balls, or anywhere else you like – a certain man, who made love to Miss Havisham. I never saw him (for this happened five-and-twenty years ago, before you and I were, Handel), but I have heard my father mention that he was a showy man, and the kind of man for the purpose. But that he was not to be, without ignorance or prejudice, mistaken for a gentleman, my father most strongly asseverates; because it is a principle of his that no man who was not a true gentleman at heart, ever was, since the world began, a true gentleman in manner. He says, no varnish can hide the grain of the wood; and that the more varnish you put on, the more the grain will express itself. Well! This man pursued Miss Havisham closely, and professed to be devoted to her. I believe she had not shown much susceptibility up to that time; but all the susceptibility she possessed, certainly came out then, and she passionately loved him. There is no doubt that she perfectly idolised him. He practised on her affection in that systematic way, that he got great sums of money from her, and he induced her to buy her brother out of a share in the brewery (which had been weakly left him by his father) at an immense price, on the plea that when he was her husband he must hold and manage it all. Your guardian was not at that time in Miss Havisham's councils, and she was too haughty and too much in love, to be advised by anyone. Her relations were poor and scheming, with the exception of my father; he was poor enough, but not time serving or jealous. The only independent one among them, he warned her that she was doing too much for this man, and was placing herself too unreservedly in his power. She took the first opportunity of angrily ordering my father out of the house, in his presence, and my father has never seen her since.'

I thought of her having said, 'Matthew will come and see me at last when I am laid dead upon that table;' and I asked Herbert whether his father was so inveterate against her?

'It's not that,' said he, 'but she charged him, in the presence of her intended husband, with being disappointed in the hope of fawning upon her for his own advancement, and, if he were to go to her now, it would look true – even to him – and even to her. To return to the man and make an end of him. The marriage day was fixed, the wedding dresses were bought, the wedding tour was planned out, the wedding guests were invited. The day came, but not the bridegroom. He wrote a letter –'

'Which she received,' I struck in, 'when she was dressing for her marriage? At twenty minutes to nine?'

'At the hour and minute,' said Herbert, nodding, 'at which she afterwards stopped all the clocks. What was in it, further than that it most heartlessly broke the marriage off, I can't tell you, because I don't know. When she recovered from a bad illness that she had, she laid the whole place waste, as you have seen it, and she has never since looked upon the light of day.'

'Is that all the story?' I asked, after considering it.

'All I know of it; and indeed I only know so much, through piecing it out for myself; for my father always avoids it, and, even when Miss Havisham invited me to go there, told me no more of it than it was absolutely requisite I should understand. But I have forgotten one thing. It has been supposed that the man to whom she gave her misplaced confidence acted throughout in concert with her half-brother; that it was a conspiracy between them; and that they shared the profits.'

'I wonder he didn't marry her and get all the property,' said I.

'He may have been married already, and her cruel mortification may have been a part of her half-brother's scheme,' said Herbert. 'Mind! I don't know that.'

'What became of the two men?' I asked, after again considering the subject.

'They fell into deeper shame and degradation – if there can be deeper – and ruin.'

'Are they alive now?'

'I don't know.'

'You said just now that Estella was not related to Miss Havisham, but adopted. When adopted?'

Herbert shrugged his shoulders. 'There has always been an Estella, since I have heard of a Miss Havisham. I know no more. And now, Handel,' said he, finally throwing off the story as it were,' there is a perfectly open understanding between us. All I know about Miss Havisham, you know.'

'And all I know,' I retorted, 'you know.'

'I fully believe it. So there can be no competition or perplexity between you and me. And as to the condition on which you hold your advancement in life – namely, that you are not to enquire or discuss to whom you owe it – you may be very sure that it will never be encroached upon, or even approached, by me, or by anyone belonging to me.'

In truth, he said this with so much delicacy, that I felt the subject done with, even though I should be under his father's roof for years and years to come. Yet he said it with so much meaning, too, that I felt he as perfectly understood Miss Havisham to be my benefactress, as I understood the fact myself.

It had not occurred to me before, that he had led up to the theme for the purpose of clearing it out of our way; but we were so much the lighter and easier for having broached it, that I now perceived this to be the case. We were very gay and sociable, and I asked him, in the course of conversation, what he was? He replied, 'A capitalist – an insurer of ships.' I suppose he saw me glancing about the room in search of some tokens of shipping, or capital, for he added, 'In the City.'

I had grand ideas of the wealth and importance of insurers of ships in the City, and I began to think with awe, of having laid a young Insurer on his back, blackened his enterprising eye, and cut his responsible head open. But, again, there came upon me, for my relief, that odd impression that Herbert Pocket would never be very successful or rich.

'I shall not rest satisfied with merely employing my capital in insuring ships. I shall buy up some good life assurance shares, and cut into the direction. I shall also do a little in the mining way. None of these things will interfere with my chartering a few thousand tons on my own account. I think I shall trade,' said he, leaning back in his chair, 'to the East Indies, for silks, shawls, spices, dyes, drugs, and precious woods. It's an interesting trade.'

'And the profits are large?' said I.

'Tremendous!' said he.

I wavered again, and began to think here were greater expectations than my own.

'I think I shall trade, also,' said he, putting his thumbs in his waistcoat pockets, 'to the West Indies, for sugar, tobacco, and rum. Also to Ceylon, especially for elephants' tusks.'

'You will want a good many ships,' said I.

'A perfect fleet,' said he.

Quite overpowered by the magnificence of these transactions, I asked him where the ships he insured mostly traded to at present?

'I haven't begun insuring yet,' he replied. 'I am looking about me.'

Somehow, that pursuit seemed more in keeping with Barnard's Inn. I said (in a tone of conviction), 'Ah–h!'

'Yes. I am in a counting-house, and looking about me.'

'Is a counting-house profitable?' I asked.

'To – do you mean to the young fellow who's in it?' he asked, in reply.

'Yes; to you.'

'Why, n–no; not to me.' He said this with the air of one carefully reckoning up and striking a balance. 'Not directly profitable. That is, it doesn't pay me anything, and I have to – keep myself.'

This certainly had not a profitable appearance, and I shook my head as if I would imply that it would be difficult to lay by much accumulative capital from such a source of income.

'But the thing is,' said Herbert Pocket, 'that you look about you. *That's* the grand thing. You are in a counting-house, you know, and you look about you.'

It struck me as a singular implication that you couldn't be

out of a counting-house, you know, and look about you; but I silently deferred to his experience.

'Then the time comes,' said Herbert, 'when you see your opening. And you go in, and you swoop upon it and you make your capital, and then there you are! When you have once made your capital, you have nothing to do but employ it.'

This was very like his way of conducting that encounter in the garden; very like. His manner of bearing his poverty, too, exactly corresponded to his manner of bearing that defeat. It seemed to me that he took all blows and buffets now, with just the same air as he had taken mine then. It was evident that he had nothing around him but the simplest necessaries, for everything that I remarked upon turned out to have been sent in on my account from the coffee-house or somewhere else.

Yet, having already made his fortune in his own mind, he was so unassuming with it that I felt quite grateful to him for not being puffed up. It was a pleasant addition to his naturally pleasant ways, and we got on famously. In the evening we went out for a walk in the streets, and went half-price to the theatre; and next day we went to church at Westminster Abbey, and in the afternoon we walked in the parks; and I wondered who shod all the horses there, and wished Joe did.

On a moderate computation, it was many months, that Sunday, since I had left Joe and Biddy. The space interposed between myself and them, partook of that expansion, and our marshes were any distance off. That I could have been at our old church in my old church-going clothes, on the very last Sunday that ever was, seemed a combination of impossibilities, geographical and social, solar and lunar. Yet in the London streets, so crowded with people and so brilliantly lighted in the dusk of evening, there were depressing hints of reproaches for that I had put the poor old kitchen at home so far away; and in the dead of night, the footsteps of some incapable impostor of a porter mooning about Barnard's Inn, under pretence of watching it, fell hollow on my heart.

On the Monday morning at a quarter before nine, Herbert went to the counting-house to report himself – to look about him, too, I suppose – and I bore him company. He was to come away in an hour or two to attend me to Hammersmith, and I was to wait about for him. It appeared to me that the eggs from which young insurers were hatched, were incubated in dust and heat, like the eggs of ostriches, judging from the places to which those incipient giants repaired on a Monday morning. Nor did the counting-house where Herbert assisted, show in my eyes as at all a good observatory; being a back second floor up a yard, of a grimy presence in all particulars, and with a look into another back second floor, rather than a look out.

I waited about until it was noon, and I went upon 'Change, and I saw fluey men sitting there under the bills about shipping, whom I took to be great merchants, though I couldn't understand why they should all be out of spirits. When Herbert came, we went and had lunch at a celebrated house which I then quite venerated, but now believe to have been the most abject superstition in Europe, and where I could not help noticing, even then, that there was much more gravy on the tablecloths and knives and waiters' clothes, than in the steaks. This collation

disposed of at a moderate price (considering the grease, which was not charged for), we went back to Barnard's Inn and got my little portmanteau, and then took coach for Hammersmith. We arrived there at two or three o'clock in the afternoon, and had very little way to walk to Mr Pocket's house. Lifting the latch of a gate, we passed direct into a little garden overlooking the river, where Mr Pocket's children were playing about. And, unless I deceive myself on a point where my interests or prepossessions are certainly not concerned, I saw that Mr and Mrs Pocket's children were not growing up or being brought up, but were tumbling up.

Mrs Pocket was sitting on a garden chair under a tree, reading, with her legs upon another garden chair; and Mrs Pocket's two nursemaids were looking about them while the children played. 'Mamma,' said Herbert, 'this is young Mr Pip.' Upon which Mrs Pocket received me with an appearance of amiable dignity.

'Master Alick and Miss Jane,' cried one of the nurses to two of the children, 'if you go a-bouncing up against them bushes you'll fall over into the river and be drownded, and what'll your pa say then?'

At the same time this nurse picked up Mrs Pocket's handkerchief, and said, 'If that don't make six times you've dropped it, Mum!' Upon which Mrs Pocket laughed and said, 'Thank you, Flopson,' and settling herself in one chair only, resumed her book. Her countenance immediately assumed a knitted and intent expression as if she had been reading for a week, but before she could have read half a dozen lines, she fixed her eyes upon me, and said, 'I hope your mamma is quite well?' This unexpected enquiry put me into such a difficulty that I began saying in the absurdest way that if there had been any such person I had no doubt she would have been quite well and would have been very much obliged and would have sent her compliments, when the nurse came to my rescue.

'Well!' she cried, picking up the pocket handkerchief, 'if that don't make seven times! What *are* you a-doing of this afternoon, Mum!' Mrs Pocket received her property, at first with a look of unutterable surprise as if she had never seen it before, and then with a laugh of recognition, and said, 'Thank you, Flopson,' and forgot me, and went on reading.

I found, now I had leisure to count them, that there were no fewer than six little Pockets present, in various stages of tumbling up. I had scarcely arrived at the total when a seventh was heard, as in the region of air, wailing dolefully.

'If there ain't baby!' said Flopson, appearing to think it most surprising. 'Make haste up, Millers!'

Millers, who was the other nurse, retired into the house, and by degrees the child's wailing was hushed and stopped, as if it were a young ventriloquist with something in its mouth. Mrs Pocket read all the time, and I was curious to know what the book could be.

We were waiting, I suppose, for Mr Pocket to come out to us; at any rate we waited there, and so I had an opportunity of observing the remarkable family phenomenon that whenever any of the children strayed near Mrs Pocket in their play, they always tripped themselves up and tumbled over her – always very much to her momentary astonishment, and their own more enduring lamentation. I was at a loss to account for this surprising circumstance, and could not help giving my mind to speculations about it, until by and by Millers came down with the baby, which Baby was handed to Flopson, which Flopson was handing it to Mrs Pocket, when she too went fairly head foremost over Mrs Pocket, baby and all, and was caught by Herbert and myself.

'Gracious me, Flopson!' said Mrs Pocket, looking off her book for a moment, 'everybody's tumbling!'

'Gracious you, indeed, Mum!' returned Flopson, very red in the face; 'what have you got there?'

'*I* got here, Flopson?' asked Mrs Pocket.

'Why, if it ain't your footstool!' cried Flopson. 'And if you keep it under your skirts like that, who's to help tumbling? Here! Take the baby, Mum, and give me your book.'

Mrs Pocket acted on the advice, and inexpertly danced the infant a little in her lap, while the other children played about it. This had lasted but a very short time, when Mrs Pocket issued summary orders that they were all to be taken into the house for a nap. Thus I made the second discovery on that first occasion, that the nurture of the little Pockets consisted of alternately tumbling up and lying down.

Under these circumstances, when Flopson and Millers had got the children into the house, like a little flock of sheep, and Mr Pocket came out of it to make my acquaintance, I was not much surprised to find that Mr Pocket was a gentleman with a rather perplexed expression of face, and with his very grey hair disordered on his head, as if he didn't quite see his way to putting anything straight.

Chapter 23

Mr Pocket said he was glad to see me, and he hoped I was not sorry to see him. 'For I really am not,' he added, with his son's smile, 'an alarming personage.' He was a young-looking man, in spite of his perplexities and his very grey hair, and his manner seemed quite natural. I use the word natural, in the sense of its being unaffected; there was something comic in his distraught way, as though it would have been downright ludicrous but for his own perception that it was very near being so. When he had talked with me a little, he said to Mrs Pocket, with a rather anxious contraction of his eyebrows, which were black and handsome, 'Belinda, I hope you have welcomed Mr Pip?' And she looked up from her book, and said, 'Yes.' She then smiled upon me in an absent state of mind, and asked me if I liked the taste of orange-flower water? As the question had no bearing, near or remote, on any foregone or subsequent transactions, I considered it to have been thrown out, like her previous approaches, in general conversational condescension.

I found out within a few hours, and may mention at once, that Mrs Pocket was the only daughter of a certain quite accidental deceased knight, who had invented for himself a conviction that his deceased father would have been made a baronet but for somebody's determined opposition arising out of entirely personal motives – I forget whose, if I ever knew – the Sovereign's, the Prime Minister's, the Lord Chancellor's, the Archbishop of Canterbury's, anybody's – and had tacked himself on to the nobles of the earth in right of this quite supposititious fact. I believe he had been knighted himself for storming the English grammar at the point of the pen, in a desperate address engrossed on vellum, on the occasion of the laying of the first stone of some building or other, and for handing some Royal Personage either the trowel or the mortar. Be that as it may, he had directed Mrs Pocket to be brought up from her cradle as one who in the nature of things must marry a title, and who was to be guarded from the acquisition of plebeian domestic knowledge.

So successful a watch and ward had been established over the young lady by this judicious parent, that she had grown up highly ornamental, but perfectly helpless and useless. With her character thus happily formed, in the first bloom of her youth she had encountered Mr Pocket: who was also in the first bloom of youth, and not quite decided whether to mount to the woolsack, or to roof himself in with a mitre. As his doing the one or the other was a mere question of time, he and Mrs Pocket had taken time by the forelock (when, to judge from its length, it would seem to have wanted cutting), and had married without the knowledge of the judicious parent. The judicious parent, having nothing to bestow or withhold but his blessing, had handsomely settled that dower upon them after a short struggle, and had informed Mr Pocket that his wife was 'a treasure for a Prince'. Mr Pocket had invested the Prince's treasure in the ways of the world ever since, and it was supposed to have brought him in but indifferent interest. Still, Mrs Pocket was in general the object of a queer sort of respectful pity, because she had not married a title; while Mr Pocket was the object of a queer sort of forgiving reproach, because he had never got one.

Mr Pocket took me into the house and showed me my room; which was a pleasant one, and so furnished as that I could use it with comfort for my own private sitting-room. He then knocked at the doors of two other similar rooms and introduced me to their occupants, by name Drummle and Startop. Drummle, an old-looking young man of a heavy order of architecture, was whistling. Startop, younger in years and appearance, was reading and holding his head, as if he thought himself in danger of exploding it with too strong a charge of knowledge.

Both Mr and Mrs Pocket had such a noticeable air of being in somebody else's hands, that I wondered who really was in possession of the house and let them live there, until I found this unknown power to be the servants. It was a smooth way of going on, perhaps, in respect of saving trouble; but it had the appearance of being expensive, for the servants felt it a duty they owed to themselves to be nice in their eating and drinking, and to keep a deal of company downstairs. They allowed a very liberal table to Mr and Mrs Pocket, yet it always appeared to me that by far the best part of the house to have boarded in, would have been the kitchen – always supposing the boarder capable of self-defence, for, before I had been there a week, a neighbouring lady with whom the family were personally unacquainted, wrote in to say that she had seen Millers slapping the baby. This greatly distressed Mrs Pocket, who burst into tears on receiving the note, and said that it was an extraordinary thing that the neighbours couldn't mind their own business.

By degrees I learnt, and chiefly from Herbert, that Mr Pocket had been educated at Harrow and at Cambridge, where he had distinguished himself; but that when he had had the happiness of marrying Mrs Pocket very early in life, he had impaired his prospects and taken up the calling of a Grinder. After grinding a number of dull blades – of whom it was remarkable that their fathers, when influential, were always going to help him to preferment, but always forgot to do it when the blades had left the Grindstone – he had wearied of that poor work and had come to London. Here, after gradually failing in loftier hopes, he had 'read' with divers who had lacked opportunities or neglected them, and had refurbished divers others for special occasions, and had turned his acquirements to the account of literary compilation and correction, and on such means, added to some very moderate private resources, still maintained the house I saw.

Mr and Mrs Pocket had a today neighbour; a widow lady of that highly sympathetic nature that she agreed with everybody, blessed everybody, and shed smiles and tears on everybody, according to circumstances. This lady's name was Mrs Coiler, and I had the honour of taking her down to dinner on the day of my installation. She gave me to understand on the stairs, that it was a blow to dear Mrs Pocket that dear Mr Pocket should be under the necessity of receiving gentlemen to read with him. That did not extend to me, she told me in a gush of love and confidence (at that time, I had known her something less than five minutes); if they were all like me, it would be quite another thing.

'But dear Mrs Pocket,' said Mrs Coiler, 'after her early disappointment (not that dear Mr Pocket was to blame in that), requires so much luxury and elegance – '

'Yes, ma'am,' I said, to stop her, for I was afraid she was going to cry.

'And she is of so aristocratic a disposition – '

'Yes, ma'am,' I said again, with the same object as before.

' – that it is hard,' said Mrs Coiler, 'to have dear Mr Pocket's time and attention diverted from dear Mrs Pocket.'

I could not help thinking that it might be harder if the butcher's time and attention were diverted from dear Mrs Pocket; but I said nothing, and indeed had enough to do in keeping a bashful watch upon my company-manners.

It came to my knowledge, through what passed between Mrs Pocket and Drummle, while I was attentive to my knife and fork, spoon, glasses, and other instruments of self-destruction, that Drummle, whose christian name was Bentley, was actually the next heir but one to a baronetcy. It further appeared that the book I had seen Mrs Pocket reading in the garden, was all about titles, and that she knew the exact date at which her grandpapa would have come into the book, if he ever had come at all. Drummle didn't say much, but in his limited way (he struck me as a sulky kind of fellow) he spoke as one of the elect, and recognised Mrs Pocket as a woman and a sister. No one but

themselves and Mrs Coiler the toady neighbour showed any interest in this part of the conversation, and it appeared to me that it was painful to Herbert; but it promised to last a long time, when the page came in with the announcement of a domestic affliction. It was, in effect, that the cook had mislaid the beef. To my unutterable amazement, I now, for the first time, saw Mr Pocket relieve his mind by going through a performance that struck me as very extraordinary, but which made no impression on anybody else, and with which I soon became as familiar as the rest. He laid down the carving-knife and fork – being engaged in carving at the moment – put his two hands into his disturbed hair, and appeared to make an extraordinary effort to lift himself up by it. When he had done this, and had not lifted himself up at all, he quietly went on with what he was about.

Mrs Coiler then changed the subject and began to flatter me. I liked it for a few moments, but she flattered me so very grossly that the pleasure was soon over. She had a serpentine way of coming close at me when she pretended to be vitally interested in the friends and localities I had left, which was altogether snaky and fork-tongued; and when she made an occasional bounce upon Startop (who said very little to her), or upon Drummle (who said less), I rather envied them for being on the opposite side of the table.

After dinner the children were introduced, and Mrs Coiler made admiring comments on their eyes, noses, and legs – a sagacious way of improving their minds. There were four little girls, and two little boys, besides the baby who might have been either, and the baby's next successor who was as yet neither. They were brought in by Flopson and Millers, much as though those two non-commissioned officers had been recruiting somewhere for children and had enlisted these: while Mrs Pocket looked at the young nobles that ought to have been, as if she rather thought she had had the pleasure of inspecting them before, but didn't quite know what to make of them.

'Here! Give me your fork, Mum, and take the baby,' said Flopson. 'Don't take it that way, or you'll get its head under the table.'

Thus advised, Mrs Pocket took it the other way, and got its head upon the table; which was announced to all present by a prodigious concussion.

'Dear, dear! give it me back, Mum,' said Flopson; 'and, Miss Jane, come and dance the baby, do!'

One of the little girls, a mere mite who seemed to have prematurely taken upon herself some charge of the others, stepped out of her place by me, and danced to and from the baby until it left off crying, and laughed. Then all the children laughed, and Mr Pocket (who in the meantime had twice endeavoured to lift himself up by the hair) laughed, and we all laughed and were glad.

Flopson, by dint of doubling the baby at the joints like a Dutch doll, then got it safely into Mrs Pocket's lap, and gave it the nutcrackers to play with: at the same time recommending Mrs Pocket to take notice that the handles of that instrument were not likely to agree with its eyes, and sharply charging Miss Jane to look after the same. Then, the two nurses left the room, and had a lively scuffle on the staircase with a dissipated page who had waited at dinner, and who had clearly lost half his buttons at the gaming-table.

I was made very uneasy in my mind by Mrs Pocket's falling into a discussion with Drummle respecting two baronetcies while she ate a sliced orange steeped in sugar and wine, and forgetting all about the baby on her lap: who did most appalling things with the nutcrackers. At length little Jane perceived its young brains to be imperilled, softly left her place, and with many small artifices coaxed the dangerous weapon away. Mrs Pocket finishing her orange at about the same time, and not approving of this, said to Jane: 'You naughty child, how dare you? Go and sit down this instant!'

'Mamma, dear,' lisped the little girl, 'baby ood have put hith eyeth out.'

'How dare you tell me so!' retorted Mrs Pocket. 'Go and sit down in your chair this moment!'

Mrs Pocket's dignity was so crushing, that I felt quite abashed: as if I myself had done something to rouse it.

'Belinda,' remonstrated Mr Pocket, from the other end of the table, 'how can you be so unreasonable? Jane only interfered for the protection of baby.'

'I will not allow anybody to interfere,' said Mrs Pocket. 'I am surprised, Matthew, that you should expose me to the affront of interference.'

'Good God!' cried Mr Pocket, in an outbreak of desolate desperation. 'Are infants to be nutcrackered into their tombs, and is nobody to save them?'

'I will not be interfered with by Jane,' said Mrs Pocket, with a majestic glance at that innocent little offender. 'I hope I know my poor grandpapa's position. Jane indeed!'

Mr Pocket got his hands in his hair again, and this time really did lift himself some inches out of his chair. 'Hear this!' he helplessly exclaimed to the elements. 'Babies are to be nut-crackered dead, for people's poor grandpapa's positions!' Then he let himself down again, and became silent.

We all looked awkwardly at the tablecloth while this was going on. A pause succeeded, during which the honest and irrepressible baby made a series of leaps and crows at little Jane, who appeared to me to be the only member of the family (irrespective of the servants) with whom it had any decided acquaintance.

'Mr Drummle,' said Mrs Pocket, 'will you ring for Flopson? Jane, you undutiful little thing, go and lie down. Now, baby darling, come with ma!'

The baby was the soul of honour, and protested with all its might. It doubled itself up the wrong way over Mrs Pocket's arm, exhibited a pair of knitted shoes and dimpled ankles to the company in lieu of its soft face, and was carried out in the highest state of mutiny. And it gained its point after all, for I saw it through the window within a few minutes, being nursed by little Jane.

It happened that the other five children were left behind at the dinner-table, through Flopson's having some private en-gagement, and their not being anybody else's business. I thus became aware of the mutual relations between them and Mr Pocket, which were exemplified in the following manner. Mr Pocket, with the normal perplexity of his face heightened, and his hair rumpled, looked at them for some minutes, as if he couldn't make out how they came to be boarding and lodging in that establishment, and why they hadn't been billeted by Nature on somebody else. Then, in a distant, missionary way he asked them certain questions – as why little Joe had that hole in his frill: who said, pa, Flopson was going to mend it when she had time – and how little Fanny came by that whitlow: who said, pa, Millers was going to poultice it when she didn't forget. Then he melted into parental tenderness, and gave them a shilling apiece and told them to go and play; and then as they went out, with one very strong effort to lift himself up by the hair, he dismissed the hopeless subject.

In the evening there was rowing on the river. As Drummle and Startop had each a boat, I resolved to set up mine, and to cut them both out. I was pretty good at most exercises in which country-boys are adepts, but, as I was conscious of wanting elegance of style for the Thames – not to say for other waters – I at once engaged to place myself under the tuition of the winner of a prize-wherry who plied at our stairs, and to whom I was introduced by my new allies. This practical authority confused me very much, by saying I had the arm of a black-smith. If he could have known how nearly the compliment had lost him his pupil, I doubt if he would have paid it.

There was a supper-tray after we got home at night, and I think we should all have enjoyed ourselves, but for a rather disagreeable domestic occurrence. Mr Pocket was in good spirits, when a housemaid came in, and said, 'If you please, sir, I should wish to speak to you.'

'Speak to your master?' said Mrs Pocket, whose dignity was roused again. 'How can you think of such a thing? Go and speak to Flopson. Or speak to me – at some other time.'

'Begging your pardon, ma'am,' returned the housemaid, 'I should wish to speak at once, and to speak to master.'

Hereupon Mr Pocket went out of the room, and we made the best of ourselves until he came back.

'This is a pretty thing, Belinda!' said Mr Pocket, returning with a countenance expressive of grief and despair. 'Here's the cook lying insensibly drunk on the kitchen floor, with a large bundle of fresh butter made up in the cupboard ready to sell for grease!'

Mrs Pocket instantly showed much amiable emotion, and said, 'This is that odious Sophia's doing!'

'What do you mean, Belinda?' demanded Mr Pocket.

'Sophia has told you,' said Mrs Pocket. 'Did I not see her, with my own eyes, and hear her with my own ears, come into the room just now and ask to speak to you?'

'But has she not taken me downstairs, Belinda,' returned Mr Pocket, 'and shown me the woman, and the bundle too?'

'And do you defend her, Matthew,' said Mrs Pocket, 'for making mischief?'

Mr Pocket uttered a dismal groan.

'Am I, grandpapa's granddaughter, to be nothing in the house?' said Mrs Pocket. 'Besides, the cook has always been a very nice respectful woman, and said in the most natural manner when she came to look after the situation, that she felt I was born to be a duchess.'

There was a sofa where Mr Pocket stood, and he dropped upon it in the attitude of a dying gladiator. Still in that attitude he said, with a hollow voice, 'Good-night, Mr Pip,' when I deemed it advisable to go to bed and leave him.

Chapter 24

After two or three days, when I had established myself in my room and had gone backwards and forwards to London several times, and had ordered all I wanted of my tradesmen, Mr Pocket and I had a long talk together. He knew more of my intended career than I knew myself, for he referred to his having been told by Mr Jaggers that I was not designed for any profession, and that I should be well enough educated for my destiny if I could 'hold my own' with the average of young men in prosperous circumstances. I acquiesced, of course, knowing nothing to the contrary.

He advised my attending certain places in London, for the acquisition of such mere rudiments as I wanted, and my investing him with the functions of explainer and director of all my studies. He hoped that with intelligent assistance I should meet with little to discourage me, and should soon be able to dispense with any aid but his. Through his way of saying this, and much more to similar purpose, he placed himself on confidential terms with me in an admirable manner: and I may state at once that he was always so zealous and honourable in fulfilling his compact with me, that he made me zealous and honourable in fulfilling mine with him. If he had shown indifference as a master, I have no doubt I should have returned the compliment as a pupil; he gave me no such excuse, and each of us did the other justice. Nor did I ever regard him as having anything ludicrous about him – or anything but what was serious, honest, and good – in his tutor communication with me.

When these points were settled, and so far carried out as that I had begun to work in earnest, it occurred to me that if I could retain my bedroom in Barnard's Inn, my life would be agreeably varied, while my manners would be none the worse for Herbert's society. Mr Pocket did not object to this arrangement, but urged that before any step could possibly be taken in it, it must be submitted to my guardian. I felt that his delicacy arose out of the consideration that the plan would save Herbert some expense, so I went off to Little Britain and imparted my wish to Mr Jaggers.

'If I could buy the furniture now hired for me,' said I, 'and one or two other little things, I should be quite at home there.'

'Go it!' said Mr Jaggers, with a short laugh. 'I told you you'd get on. Well! How much do you want?'

I said I didn't know how much.

'Come!' retorted Mr Jaggers. 'How much? Fifty pounds?'

'Oh, not nearly so much.'

'Five pounds?' said Mr Jaggers.

This was such a great fall, that I said in discomfiture, 'Oh! More than that.'

'More than that, eh!' retorted Mr Jaggers, lying in wait for me, with his hands in his pockets, his head on one side, and his eyes on the wall behind me; 'how much more?'

'It is so difficult to fix a sum,' said I, hesitating.

'Come!' said Mr Jaggers. 'Let's get at it. Twice five; will that do? Three times five; will that do? Four times five; will that do?'

I said I thought that would do handsomely.

'Four times five will do handsomely, will it?' said Mr Jaggers, knitting his brows. 'Now, what do you make of four times five?'

'What do I make of it!'

'Ah!' said Mr Jaggers; 'how much?'

'I suppose you make it twenty pounds,' said I, smiling.

'Never mind what *I* make it, my friend,' observed Mr Jaggers, with a knowing and contradictory toss of the head. 'I want to know what *you* make it?'

'Twenty pounds, of course.'

'Wemmick!' said Mr Jaggers, opening his office door. 'Take Mr Pip's written order, and pay him twenty pounds.'

This strongly marked way of doing business made a strongly marked impression on me, and that not of an agreeable kind. Mr Jaggers never laughed; but he wore great bright creaking boots; and, in poising himself on those boots, with his large head bent down and his eyebrows joined together, awaiting an answer, he sometimes caused the boots to creak, as if *they* laughed in a dry and suspicious way. As he happened to go out now, and as Wemmick was brisk and talkative, I said to Wemmick that I hardly knew what to make of Mr Jaggers's manner.

'Tell him that, and he'll take it as a compliment,' answered Wemmick; 'he don't mean that you *should* know what to make of it – oh!' for I looked surprised, 'it's not personal; it's professional: only professional.'

Wemmick was at his desk, lunching – and crunching – on a dry hard biscuit; pieces of which he threw from time to time into his slit of a mouth, as if he were posting them.

'Always seems to me,' said Wemmick, 'as if he had set a mantrap and was watching it. Suddenly – click – you're caught!'

Without remarking that mantraps were not among the amenities of life, I said I supposed he was very skilful?

'Deep,' said Wemmick, 'as Australia.' Pointing with his pen at the office floor, to express that Australia was understood, for the purposes of the figure, to be symmetrically on the opposite spot of the globe. 'If there was anything deeper,' added Wemmick, bringing his pen to paper, 'he'd be it.'

Then, I said I supposed he had a fine business, and Wemmick said, 'Ca–pi–tal!' Then I asked if there were many clerks? To which he replied: 'We don't run much into clerks, because there's only one Jaggers, and people won't have him at second hand. There are only four of us. Would you like to see 'em? You are one of us, as I may say.'

I accepted the offer. When Mr Wemmick had put all the biscuit into the post, and had paid me my money from a cash-box in a safe, the key of which safe he kept somewhere down his back, and produced from his coat-collar like an iron pigtail, we went upstairs. The house was dark and shabby, and the greasy shoulders that had left their mark in Mr Jaggers's room seemed to have been shuffling up and down the staircase for years. In the front first floor, a clerk who looked something between a publican and a rat-catcher – a large pale puffed swollen man – was attentively engaged with three or four people of shabby appearance, whom he treated as unceremoniously as everybody seemed to be treated who contributed to Mr Jaggers's coffers. 'Getting evidence together,' said Mr Wemmick, as we came out, 'for the Bailey.' In the room over that, a little flabby terrier of a clerk with dangling hair (his cropping seemed to have been forgotten when he was a puppy) was similarly engaged with a man with weak eyes, whom Mr Wemmick presented to me as a smelter who kept his pot always boiling, and who would melt me anything I pleased – and who was in an excessive white-perspiration, as if he had been trying his art on himself. In a back room, a high-shouldered man with a face-ache tied up in dirty flannel, who was dressed in old black clothes that bore the appearance of having been waxed, was stooping over his work of making fair copies of the notes of the other two gentlemen, for Mr Jaggers's own use.

This was all the establishment. When we went downstairs again, Wemmick led me into my guardian's room, and said, 'This you've seen already.'

'Pray, said I, as the two odious casts with the twitchy leer upon them caught my sight again, 'whose likenesses are those?'

'These?' said Wemmick, getting upon a chair, and blowing the dust off the horrible heads before bringing them down. 'These are two celebrated ones. Famous clients of ours that got us a world of credit. This chap (why you must have come down in the night and been peeping into the inkstand, to get this blot upon your eyebrow, you old rascal!) murdered his master, and, considering that he wasn't brought up to evidence, didn't plan it badly.'

'Is it like him?' I asked, recoiling from the brute, as Wemmick spat upon his eyebrow, and gave it a rub with his sleeve.

'Like him? It's himself, you know. The cast was made in Newgate, directly after he was taken down. You had a particular fancy for me, hadn't you, Old Artful?' said Wemmick. He then explained this affectionate apostrophe, by touching his brooch representing the lady and the weeping willow at the tomb with the urn upon it, and said, 'Had it made for me express!'

'Is the lady anybody?' said I.

'No,' returned Wemmick. 'Only his game. (You liked your bit of game, didn't you?) No; deuce a bit of a lady in the case, Mr Pip, except one – and she wasn't of this slender ladylike sort, and you wouldn't have caught *her* looking after this urn – unless there was something to drink in it.' Wemmick's attention being thus directed to his brooch, he put down the cast, and polished the brooch with his pocket-handkerchief.

'Did that other creature come to the same end?' I asked. 'He has the same look.'

'You're right,' said Wemmick; 'it's the genuine look. Much as if one nostril was caught up with a horsehair and a little fish-hook. Yes, he came to the same end; quite the natural end here, I assure you. He forged wills, this blade did, if he didn't also put the supposed testators to sleep too. You were a gentlemanly cove, though' (Mr Wemmick was again apostrophising), 'and you said you could write Greek. Yah, Bounceable! What a liar

you were! I never met such a liar as you!' Before putting his late friend on his shelf again, Wemmick touched the largest of his mourning rings, and said, 'Sent out to buy it for me, only the day before.'

While he was putting up the other cast and coming down from the chair, the thought crossed my mind that all his personal jewellery was derived from like sources. As he had shown no diffidence on the subject, I ventured on the liberty of asking him the question, when he stood before me, dusting his hands.

'Oh yes,' he returned, 'these are all gifts of that kind. One brings another, you see; that's the way of it. I always take 'em. They're curiosities. And they're property. They may not be worth much, but, after all, they're property and portable. It don't signify to you with your brilliant look-out, but as to myself, my guiding-star always is, get hold of portable property.'

When I had rendered homage to this light, he went on to say in a friendly manner: 'If at any odd time when you have nothing better to do, you wouldn't mind coming over to see me at Walworth, I could offer you a bed, and I should consider it an honour. I have not much to show you; but such two or three curiosities as I have got, you might like to look over; and I am fond of a bit of garden and a summerhouse.'

I said I should be delighted to accept his hospitality.

'Thankee,' said he: 'then we'll consider that it's to come off, when convenient to you. Have you dined with Mr Jaggers yet?'

'Not yet.'

'Well,' said Wemmick, 'he'll give you wine, and good wine. I'll give you punch, and not bad punch. And now I'll tell you something. When you go to dine with Mr Jaggers, look at his housekeeper.'

'Shall I see something very uncommon?'

'Well,' said Wemmick, 'you'll see a wild beast tamed. Not so very uncommon, you'll tell me. I reply, that depends on the original wildness of the beast, and the amount of taming. It won't lower your opinion of Mr Jaggers's powers. Keep your eye on it.'

I told him I would do so, with all the interest and curiosity that his preparation awakened. As I was taking my departure, he asked me if I would like to devote five minutes to seeing Mr Jaggers 'at it?'

For several reasons, and not least because I didn't clearly know what Mr Jaggers would be found to be 'at', I replied in the affirmative. We dived into the City, and came up in a crowded police-court, where a blood-relation (in the murderous sense) of the deceased with the fanciful taste in brooches, was standing at the bar, uncomfortably chewing something; while my guardian had a woman under examination or cross-examination – I don't know which – and was striking her, and the bench, and everybody with awe. If anybody, of whatsoever degree, said a word that he didn't approve of, he instantly required to have it 'taken down'. If anybody wouldn't make an admission, he said, 'I'll have it out of you!' and if anybody made an admission, he said, 'Now I have got you!' The magistrates shivered under a single bite of his finger. Thieves and thief-takers hung in dread rapture on his words, and shrank when a hair of his eyebrows turned in their direction. Which side he was on I couldn't make out, for he seemed to me to be grinding the whole place in a mill; I only know that when I stole out on tiptoe he was not on the side of the bench; for he was making the legs of the old gentleman who presided quite convulsive under the table, by his denunciations of his conduct as the representative of British law and justice in that chair that day.

Chapter 25

Bentley Drummle, who was so sulky a fellow that he even took up a book as if its writer had done him an injury, did not take up an acquaintance in a more agreeable spirit. Heavy in figure, movement, and comprehension – in the sluggish complexion of his face, and in the large awkward tongue that seemed to loll about in his mouth as he himself lolled about in a room – he was idle, proud, niggardly, reserved, and suspicious. He came of rich people down in Somersetshire, who had nursed this combination of qualities until they made the discovery that it was just of age and a blockhead. Thus, Bentley Drummle had come to Mr Pocket when he was a head taller than that gentleman, and half a dozen heads thicker than most gentlemen.

Startop had been spoiled by a weak mother, and kept at home when he ought to have been at school, but he was devotedly attached to her, and admired her beyond measure. He had a woman's delicacy of feature, and was – 'as you may see, though you never saw her,' said Herbert to me – 'exactly like his mother.' It was but natural that I should take to him much more kindly than to Drummle, and that, even in the earliest evenings of our boating, he and I should pull homeward abreast of one another, conversing from boat to boat, while Bentley Drummle came up in our wake alone, under the overhanging banks and among the rushes. He would always creep inshore like some uncomfortable amphibious creature, even when the tide would have sent him fast upon his way; and I always think of him as coming after us in the dark or by the backwater, when our own two boats were breaking the sunset or the moonlight in midstream.

Herbert was my intimate companion and friend. I presented him with a half-share in my boat, which was the occasion of his often coming down to Hammersmith; and my possession of a half-share in his chambers often took me up to London. We used to walk between the two places at all hours. I have an affection for the road yet (though it is not so pleasant a road as it was then), formed in the impressibility of untried youth and hope.

When I had been in Mr Pocket's family a month or two, Mr and Mrs Camilla turned up. Camilla was Mr Pocket's sister. Georgiana, whom I had seen at Miss Havisham's on the same occasion, also turned up. She was a cousin – an indigestive single woman, who called her rigidity religion, and her liver love. These people hated me with the hatred of cupidity and disappointment. As a matter of course, they fawned upon me in my prosperity with the basest meanness. Towards Mr Pocket, as a grown-up infant with no notion of his own interests, they showed the complacent forbearance I had heard them express. Mrs Pocket they held in contempt; but they allowed the poor

soul to have been heavily disappointed in life, because that shed a feeble reflected light upon themselves.

These were the surroundings among which I settled down, and applied myself to my education. I soon contracted expensive habits, and began to spend an amount of money that within a few short months I should have thought almost fabulous; but through good and evil I stuck to my books. There was no other merit in this, than my having sense enough to feel my deficiencies. Between Mr Pocket and Herbert I got on fast; and, with one or the other always at my elbow to give me the start I wanted, and clear obstructions out of my road, I must have been as great a dolt as Drummle if I had done less.

I had not seen Mr Wemmick for some weeks, when I thought I would write him a note and propose to go home with him on a certain evening. He replied that it would give him much pleasure, and that he would expect me at the office at six o'clock. Thither I went, and there I found him, putting the key of his safe down his back as the clock struck.

'Did you think of walking down to Walworth?' said he.

'Certainly,' said I, 'if you approve.'

'Very much,' was Wemmick's reply, 'for I have had my legs under the desk all day, and shall be glad to stretch them. Now I'll tell you what I've got for supper, Mr Pip. I have got a stewed steak – which is of home preparation – and a cold roast fowl – which is from the cook's-shop. I think it's tender, because the master of the shop was a juryman in some cases of ours the other day, and we let him down easy. I reminded him of it when I bought the fowl, and I said, "Pick us out a good one, old Briton, because if we had chosen to keep you in the box another day or two, we could have done it." He said to that, "Let me make you a present of the best fowl in the shop." I let him, of course. As far as it goes, it's property and portable. You don't object to an aged parent, I hope?'

I really thought he was still speaking of the fowl, until he added, 'Because I have got an aged parent at my place.' I then said what politeness required.

'So you haven't dined with Mr Jaggers yet?' he pursued, as we walked along.

'Not yet.'

'He told me so this afternoon when he heard you were coming. I expect you'll have an invitation tomorrow. He's going to ask your pals, too. Three of 'em; ain't there?'

Although I was not in the habit of counting Drummle as one of my intimate associates, I answered, 'Yes'.

'Well, he's going to ask the whole gang;' I hardly felt complimented by the word; 'and whatever he gives you, he'll give you good. Don't look forward to variety, but you'll have excellence. And there's another rum thing in his house,' proceeded Wemmick after a moment's pause, as if the remark followed on the housekeeper understood; 'he never lets a door or window be fastened at night.'

'Is he never robbed?'

'That's it!' returned Wemmick. 'He says, and gives it out publicly, "I want to see the man who'll rob *me*." Lord bless you, I have heard him, a hundred times if I have heard him once, say to regular cracksmen in our front office, "You know where I live; now no bolt is ever drawn there; why don't you do a stroke of business with me? Come; can't I tempt you?" Not a man of them, sir, would be bold enough to try it on, for love or money.'

'They dread him so much?' said I.

'Dread him!' said Wemmick. 'I believe you, they dread him. Not but what he's artful, even in his defiance of them. No silver, sir. Britannia metal, every spoon.'

'So they wouldn't have much,' I observed, 'even if they – '

'Ah! But *he* would have much,' said Wemmick, cutting me short, 'and they know it. He'd have their lives, and the lives of scores of 'em. He'd have all he could get. And its impossible to say what he couldn't get, if he gave his mind to it.'

I was falling into meditation on my guardian's greatness, when Wemmick remarked: 'As to the absence of plate, that's only his natural depth, you know. A river's its natural depth, and he's his natural depth. Look at his watch-chain. That's real enough.'

'It's very massive,' said I.

'Massive?' repeated Wemmick. 'I think so. And his watch is a gold repeater, and worth a hundred pound if it's worth a penny. Mr Pip, there are about seven hundred thieves in this town who know all about that watch; there's not a man, a woman, or a child, among them, who wouldn't identify the smallest link in that chain, and drop it as if it was red-hot, if inveigled into touching it.'

At first with such discourse, and afterwards with conversation of a more general nature, did Mr Wemmick and I beguile the time and the road, until he gave me to understand that we had arrived in the district of Walworth.

It appeared to be a collection of black lanes, ditches, and little gardens, and to present the aspect of a rather dull retirement. Wemmick's house was a little wooden cottage in the midst of plots of garden, and the top of it was cut out and painted like a battery mounted with guns.

'My own doing,' said Wemmick. 'Looks pretty; don't it?'

I highly commended it. I think it was the smallest house I ever saw: with the queerest gothic windows (by far the greater part of them sham), and a gothic door, almost too small to get in at.

'That's a real flagstaff, you see,' said Wemmick, 'and on Sundays I run up a real flag. Then look here. After I have crossed this bridge, I hoist it up – so – and cut off the communication.'

The bridge was a plank, and it crossed a chasm about four feet wide and two deep. But it was very pleasant to see the pride with which he hoisted it up, and made it fast; smiling as he did so, with a relish, and not merely mechanically.

'At nine o'clock every night, Greenwich time,' said Wemmick, 'the gun fires. There he is, you see! And when you hear him go, I think you'll say he's a stinger.'

The piece of ordnance referred to was mounted in a separate fortress, constructed of lattice work. It was protected from the weather by an ingenious little tarpaulin contrivance in the nature of an umbrella.

'Then, at the back,' said Wemmick, 'out of sight, so as not to impede the idea of fortifications – for it's a principle with me, if you have an idea, carry it out and keep it up – I don't know whether that's your opinion – ' I said, decidedly.

' – At the back, there's a pig, and there are fowls and rabbits; then I knock together my own little frame, you see, and grow cucumbers; and you'll judge at supper what sort of a salad I can raise. So, sir,' said Wemmick, smiling again, but seriously, too, as he shook his head, 'if you can suppose the little place besieged, it would hold out a devil of a time in point of provisions.'

Then, he conducted me to a bower about a dozen yards off, but which was approached by such ingenious twists of path that it took quite a long time to get at; and in this retreat our glasses were already set forth. Our punch was cooling in an ornamental lake, on whose margin the bower was raised. This piece of water (with an island in the middle which might have been the salad for supper) was of a circular form, and he had constructed a fountain in it, which, when you set a little mill going and took a cork out of a pipe, played to that powerful extent that it made the back of your hand quite wet.

'I am my own engineer, and my own carpenter, and my own plumber, and my own gardener, and my own jack of all trades,' said Wemmick, in acknowledging my compliments. 'Well, it's a good thing, you know. It brushes the Newgate cobwebs away, and pleases the Aged. You wouldn't mind being at once introduced to the Aged, would you? It wouldn't put you out?'

I expressed the readiness I felt, and we went into the Castle. There, we found, sitting by a fire, a very old man in a flannel coat: clean, cheerful, comfortable, and well cared for, but intensely deaf.

'Well, aged parent,' said Wemmick, shaking hands with him in a cordial and jocose way, 'how am you?'

'All right, John; all right!' replied the old man.

'Here's Mr Pip, aged parent,' said Wemmick, 'and I wish you could hear his name. Nod away at him, Mr Pip; that's what he likes. Nod away at him, if you please, like winking!'

'This is a fine place of my son's, sir,' cried the old man, while I nodded as hard as I possibly could. 'This is a pretty pleasure-ground, sir. This spot and these beautiful works upon it ought to be kept together by the nation, after my son's time, for the people's enjoyment.'

'You're as proud of it as punch; ain't you, Aged?' said Wemmick, contemplating the old man, with his hard face really softened; '*there's* a nod for you;' giving him a tremendous one: '*there's* another for you;' giving him a still more tremendous one; 'you like that, don't you? If you're not tired, Mr Pip – though I know it's tiring to strangers – will you tip him one more? You can't think how it pleases him.'

I tipped him several more, and he was in great spirits. We left him bestirring himself to feed the fowls, and we sat down to our punch in the arbour; where Wemmick told me as he smoked a pipe, that it had taken him a good many years to bring the property up to its present pitch of perfection.

'Is it your own, Mr Wemmick?'

'O yes,' said Wemmick. 'I have got hold of it, a bit at a time. It's a freehold, by George!'

'Is it, indeed? I hope Mr Jaggers admires it?'

'Never seen it,' said Wemmick. 'Never heard of it. Never seen the Aged. Never heard of him. No; the office is one thing, and private life is another. When I go into the office, I leave the

Castle behind me, and when I come into the Castle, I leave the office behind me. If it's not in any way disagreeable to you, you'll oblige me by doing the same. I don't wish it professionally spoken about.'

Of course I felt my good faith involved in the observance of his request. The punch being very nice, we sat there drinking it and talking, until it was almost nine o'clock. 'Getting near gunfire,' said Wemmick then, as he laid down his pipe; 'it's the Aged's treat.'

Proceeding into the Castle again, we found the Aged heating the poker, with expectant eyes, as a preliminary to the performance of this great nightly ceremony. Wemmick stood with his watch in his hand until the moment was come for him to take the red-hot poker from the Aged, and repair to the battery. He took it, and went out, and presently the stinger went off with a bang that shook the crazy little box of a cottage as if it must fall to pieces, and made every glass and teacup in it ring. Upon this the Aged – who I believe would have been blown out of his armchair but for holding on by the elbows – cried out exultingly, 'He's fired! I heerd him!' and I nodded at the old gentleman until it is no figure of speech to declare that I absolutely could not see him.

The interval between that time and supper, Wemmick devoted to showing me his collection of curiosities. They were mostly of a felonious character; comprising the pen with which a celebrated forgery had been committed, a distinguished razor or two, some locks of hair, and several manuscript confessions

'Here's Mr Pip, aged parent,' said Wemmick

written under condemnation – upon which Mr Wemmick set particular value as being, to use his own words, 'every one of 'em lies, sir.' These were agreeably dispersed among small specimens of china and glass, various neat trifles made by the proprietor of the museum, and some tobacco-stoppers carved by the Aged. They were all displayed in that chamber of the Castle into which I had been first inducted, and which served, not only as the general sitting-room, but as the kitchen too, if I might judge from a saucepan on the hob, and a brazen *bijou* over the fireplace designed for the suspension of a roasting-jack.

There was a neat little girl in attendance, who looked after the Aged in the day. When she had laid the supper-cloth, the bridge was lowered to give her the means of egress, and she withdrew for the night. The supper was excellent; and though the Castle was rather subject to dry-rot, insomuch that it tasted like a bad nut, and though the pig might have been farther off, I was heartily pleased with my whole entertainment. Nor was there any drawback on my little turret bedroom, beyond there being such a very thin ceiling between me and the flagstaff, that when I lay down on my back in bed, it seemed as if I had to balance that pole on my forehead all night.

Wemmick was up early in the morning, and I am afraid I heard him cleaning my boots. After that, he fell to gardening, and I saw him from my gothic window pretending to employ the Aged, and nodding at him in a most devoted manner. Our breakfast was as good as the supper, and at half-past eight precisely we started for Little Britain. By degrees, Wemmick got dryer and harder as we went along, and his mouth tightened into a post office again. At last, when we got to his place of business and he pulled out his key from his coat-collar, he looked as unconscious of his Walworth property as if the Castle and the drawbridge and the arbour and the lake and the fountain and the Aged, had all been blown into space together by the last discharge of the stinger.

Chapter 26

It fell out as Wemmick had told me it would, that I had an early opportunity of comparing my guardian's establishment with that of his cashier and clerk. My guardian was in his room, washing his hands with his scented soap, when I went into the office from Walworth; and he called me to him, and gave me the invitation for myself and friends which Wemmick had prepared me to receive. 'No ceremony,' he stipulated, 'and no dinner dress, and say tomorrow.' I asked him where we should come to (for I had no idea where he lived), and I believe it was in his general objection to make anything like an admission, that he replied, 'Come here, and I'll take you home with me.' I embrace this opportunity of remarking that he washed his clients off, as if it were a surgeon or a dentist. He had a closet in his room, fitted up for the purpose, which smelt of the scented soap like a perfumer's shop. It had an unusually large jack-towel on a roller inside the door, and he would wash his hands, and wipe them and dry them all over this towel, whenever he came in from a police-court or dismissed a client from his room. When I and my friends repaired to him at six o'clock next day, he seemed to have been engaged on a case of a darker complexion than usual, for we found him with his head butted into this closet, not only washing his hands, but laving his face and gargling his throat. And even when he had done all that, and had gone all round the jack-towel, he took out his penknife and scraped the case out of his nails before he put his coat on.

There were some people slinking about as usual when we passed out into the street, who were evidently anxious to speak with him; but there was something so conclusive in the halo of scented soap which encircled his presence, that they gave it up for that day. As we walked along westward, he was recognised ever and again by some face in the crowd of the streets, and whenever that happened he talked louder to me; but he never otherwise recognised anybody, or took notice that anybody recognised him.

He conducted us to Gerrard Street, Soho, to a house on the south side of that street, rather a stately house of its kind, but dolefully in want of painting, and with dirty windows. He took out his key and opened the door, and we all went into a stone hall, bare, gloomy, and little used. So, up a dark-brown staircase into a series of three dark brown rooms on the first floor. There were carved garlands on the panelled walls, and as he stood among them giving us welcome, I know what kind of loops I thought they looked like.

Dinner was laid in the best of these rooms; the second was his dressing-room; the third, his bedroom. He told us that he held the whole house, but rarely used more of it than we saw. The table was comfortably laid – no silver in the service, of course – and at the side of his chair was a capacious dumb-waiter, with a variety of bottles and decanters on it, and four dishes of fruit for dessert. I noticed throughout, that he kept everything under his own hand, and distributed everything himself.

There was a bookcase in the room; I saw from the backs of the books, that they were about evidence, criminal law, criminal biography, trials, acts of parliament, and such things. The furniture was all very solid and good, like his watch-chain. It had an official look, however, and there was nothing merely ornamental to be seen. In a corner was a little table of papers with a shaded lamp; so that he seemed to bring the office home with him in that respect too, and to wheel it out of an evening and fall to work.

As he had scarcely seen my three companions until now – for he and I had walked together – he stood on the hearth-rug, after ringing the bell, and took a searching look at them. To my surprise, he seemed at once to be principally, if not solely, interested in Drummle.

'Pip,' said he, putting his large hand on my shoulder and moving me to the window, 'I don't know one from the other. Who's the Spider?'

'The Spider?' said I.

'The blotchy, sprawly, sulky fellow.'

'That's Bentley Drummle,' I replied; 'the one with the delicate face is Startop.'

Not making the least account of 'the one with the delicate face,' he returned, 'Bentley Drummle is his name, is it? I like the look of that fellow.'

He immediately began to talk to Drummle: not at all deterred by his replying in his heavy reticent way, but apparently led on by it to screw discourse out of him. I was looking at the two, when there came between me and them, the housekeeper, with the first dish for the table.

She was a woman of about forty, I supposed – but I may have thought her younger than she was. Rather tall, of a lithe nimble figure, extremely pale, with large faded eyes, and a quantity of streaming hair. I cannot say whether any diseased affection of the heart caused her lips to be parted as if she were panting, and her face to bear a curious expression of suddenness and flutter; but I know that I had been to see *Macbeth* at the theatre, a night or two before, and that her face looked to me as if it were all disturbed by fiery air, like the faces I had seen rise out of the witches' caldron.

She set the dish on, touched my guardian quietly on the arm with a finger to notify that dinner was ready, and vanished. We took our seats at the round table, and my guardian kept Drummle on one side of him, while Startop sat on the other. It was a noble dish of fish that the housekeeper had put on table, and we had a joint of equally choice mutton afterwards, and then an equally choice bird. Sauces, wines, all the accessories we wanted, and all of the best, were given out by our host from his dumb-waiter; and when they had made the circuit of the table, he always put them back again. Similarly, he dealt us clean plates and knives and forks, for each course, and dropped those just disused into two baskets on the ground by his chair. No other attendant than the housekeeper appeared. She set on every dish; and I always saw in her face, a face rising out of the caldron. Years afterwards, I made a dreadful likeness of that woman, by causing a face that had no other natural resemblance to it than it derived from flowing hair, to pass behind a bowl of flaming spirits in a dark room.

Induced to take particular notice of the housekeeper, both by her own striking appearance and by Wemmick's preparation, I observed that whenever she was in the room, she kept her eyes attentively on my guardian, and that she would remove her hands from any dish she put before him, hesitatingly, as if she dreaded his calling her back, and wanted him to speak when she was nigh, if he had anything to say. I fancied that I could detect in his manner a consciousness of this, and a purpose of always holding her in suspense.

Dinner went off gaily, and, although my guardian seemed to follow rather than originate subjects, I knew that he wrenched the weakest part of our dispositions out of us. For myself, I found that I was expressing my tendency to lavish expenditure, and to patronise Herbert, and to boast of my great prospects, before I quite knew that I had opened my lips. It was so with all of us, but with no one more than Drummle: the development of whose inclination to gird in a grudging and suspicious way at the rest, was screwed out of him before the fish was taken off.

It was not then, but when we had got to the cheese, that our conversation turned upon our rowing feats, and that Drummle was rallied for coming up behind of a night in that slow amphibious way of his. Drummle upon this, informed our host that he much preferred our room to our company, and that as to skill he was more than our master, and that as to strength he could scatter us like chaff. By some invisible agency, my guardian wound him up to a pitch little short of ferocity about this trifle; and he fell to baring and spanning his arm to show how muscular it was, and we all fell to baring and spanning our arms in a ridiculous manner.

Now, the housekeeper was at that time clearing the table; my guardian, taking no heed of her, but with the side of his face turned from her, was leaning back in his chair biting the side of his forefinger, and showing an interest in Drummle, that, to me, was quite inexplicable. Suddenly, he clapped his large hand on the housekeeper's, like a trap, as she stretched it across the table. So suddenly and smartly did he do this, that we all stopped in our foolish contention.

'If you talk of strength,' said Mr Jaggers, '*I'*ll show you a wrist. Molly, let them see your wrist.'

Her entrapped hand was on the table, but she had already put her other hand behind her waist. 'Master,' she said, in a low voice, with her eyes attentively and entreatingly fixed upon him, 'Don't.'

'*I'*ll show you a wrist,' repeated Mr Jaggers, with an immovable determination to show it. 'Molly, let them see your wrist.'

'Master,' she again murmured. 'Please!'

'Molly,' said Mr Jaggers, not looking at her, but obstinately looking at the opposite side of the room, 'let them see *both* your wrists. Show them. Come!'

He took his hand from hers, and turned that wrist up on the table. She brought her other hand from behind her, and held the two out side by side. The last wrist was much disfigured – deeply scarred and scarred across and across. When she held her hands out, she took her eyes from Mr Jaggers, and turned them watchfully on every one of the rest of us in succession.

'There's power here,' said Mr Jaggers, coolly tracing out the sinews with his forefinger. 'Very few men have the power of wrist that this woman has. It's remarkable what mere force of grip there is in these hands. I have had occasion to notice many hands; but I never saw stronger in that respect, man's or woman's, than these.'

While he said these words in a leisurely critical style, she continued to look at every one of us in regular succession as we sat. The moment he ceased, she looked at him again. 'That'll do, Molly,' said Mr Jaggers, giving her a slight nod; 'you have been admired, and can go.' She withdrew her hands and went out of the room, and Mr Jaggers, putting the decanters on from his dumb-waiter, filled his glass and passed round the wine.

'At half-past nine, gentlemen,' said he, 'we must break up. Pray make the best use of your time. I am glad to see you all. Mr Drummle, I drink to you.'

If his object in singling out Drummle were to bring him out still more, it perfectly succeeded. In a sulky triumph, Drummle showed his morose depreciation of the rest of us, in a more and more offensive degree, until he became downright intolerable. Through all his stages, Mr Jaggers followed him with the same strange interest. He actually seemed to serve as a zest to Mr Jaggers's wine.

In our boyish want of discretion I dare say we took too much to drink, and I know we talked too much. We became particularly hot upon some boorish sneer of Drummle's, to the effect that we were too free with our money. It led to my remarking, with more zeal than discretion, that it came with a bad grace from him, to whom Startop had lent money in my presence but a week or so before.

'Well,' retorted Drummle, 'he'll be paid.'

'I don't mean to imply that he won't,' said I, 'but it might make you hold your tongue about us and our money, I should think.'

'*You* should think!' retorted Drummle. 'Oh Lord!'

'I dare say,' I went on, meaning to be very severe, 'that you wouldn't lend money to any of us if we wanted it.'

'You are right,' said Drummle. 'I wouldn't lend one of you a sixpence. I wouldn't lend anybody a sixpence.'

'Rather mean to borrow under those circumstances, I should say.'

'*You* should say,' repeated Drummle. 'Oh Lord!'

This was so very aggravating – the more especially as I found myself making no way against his surly obtuseness – that I said, disregarding Herbert's efforts to check me: 'Come, Mr Drummle, since we are on the subject, I'll tell you what passed between Herbert here and me, when you borrowed that money.'

'*I* don't want to know what passed between Herbert there and you,' growled Drummle. And I think he added in a lower growl, that we might both go to the devil and shake ourselves.

'I'll tell you, however,' said I, 'whether you want to know or not. We said that as you put it into your pocket very glad to get it, you seemed to be immensely amused at his being so weak as to lend it.'

Drummle laughed outright, and sat laughing in our faces, with his hands in his pockets and his round shoulders raised; plainly signifying that it was quite true, and that he despised us as asses all.

Hereupon Startop took him in hand, though with a much better grace than I had shown, and exhorted him to be a little more agreeable. Startop, being a lively bright young fellow, and Drummle being the exact opposite, the latter was always disposed to resent him as a direct personal affront. He now retorted in a coarse lumpish way, and Startop tried to turn the discussion aside with some small pleasantry that made us all laugh. Resenting this little success more than anything, Drummle, without any threat or warning, pulled his hands out of his pockets, dropped his round shoulders, swore, took up a large glass, and would have flung it at his adversary's head, but for our entertainer's dexterously seizing it at the instant when it was raised for that purpose.

'Gentlemen,' said Mr Jaggers, deliberately putting down the glass, and hauling out his gold repeater by its massive chain, 'I am exceedingly sorry to announce that it's half-past nine.'

On this hint we all rose to depart. Before we got to the street door, Startop was cheerily calling Drummle 'old boy', as if nothing had happened. But the old boy was so far from responding, that he would not even walk to Hammersmith on the same side of the way; so, Herbert and I, who remained in town, saw them going down the street on opposite sides; Startop leading, and Drummle lagging behind in the shadow of the houses, much as he was wont to follow in his boat.

As the door was not yet shut, I thought I would leave Herbert there for a moment, and run upstairs again to say a word to my guardian. I found him in his dressing-room surrounded by his stock of boots, already hard at it, washing his hands of us.

I told him I had come up again to say how sorry I was that anything disagreeable should have occurred, and that I hoped he would not blame me much.

'Pooh!' said he, sluicing his face, and speaking through the water-drops; 'it's nothing, Pip. I like that Spider though.'

He had turned towards me now, and was shaking his head, and blowing, and towelling himself.

'I am glad you like him, sir,' said I – 'but I don't.'

'No, no,' my guardian assented; 'don't have too much to do with him. Keep as clear of him as you can. But I like the fellow, Pip; he is one of the true sort. Why, if I was a fortune-teller – '

Looking out of the towel, he caught my eye.

'But I am not a fortune-teller,' he said, letting his head drop into a festoon of towel, and towelling away at his two ears. 'You know what I am, don't you? Good-night, Pip.'

'Good-night, sir.'

In about a month after that, the Spider's time with Mr Pocket was up for good, and, to the great relief of all the house but Mrs Pocket, he went home to the family hole.

Chapter 27

MY DEAR MR PIP – I write this by request of Mr Gargery, for to let you know that he is going to London in company with Mr Wopsle and would be glad if agreeable to be allowed to see you. He would call at Barnard's Hotel Tuesday morning at nine o'clock, when if not agreeable please leave word. Your poor sister is much the same as when you left. We talk of you in the kitchen every night, and wonder what you are saying and doing. If now considered in the light of a liberty, excuse it for the love of poor old days. No more, dear Mr Pip, from

Your ever obliged, and affectionate servant,

BIDDY

P. S. He wishes me most particular to write *what larks*. He says you will understand. I hope and do not doubt it will be agreeable to see him even though a gentleman, for you had ever a good heart, and he is a worthy worthy man. I have read him all excepting only the last little sentence, and he wishes me most particular to write again *what larks*.

I received this letter by post on Monday morning, and therefore its appointment was for next day. Let me confess exactly, with what feelings I looked forward to Joe's coming.

Not with pleasure, though I was bound to him by so many ties; no; with considerable disturbance, some mortification, and a keen sense of incongruity. If I could have kept him away by paying money, I certainly would have paid money. My greatest reassurance was, that he was coming to Barnard's Inn, not to Hammersmith, and consequently would not fall in Bentley Drummle's way. I had little objection to his being seen by Herbert or his father, for both of whom I had a respect; but I had the sharpest sensitiveness as to his being seen by Drummle, whom I held in contempt. So, throughout life, our worst weaknesses and meannesses are usually committed for the sake of the people whom we most despise.

I had begun to be always decorating the chambers in some quite unnecessary and inappropriate way or other, and very expensive those wrestles with Barnard proved to be. By this time, the rooms were vastly different from what I had found them, and I enjoyed the honour of occupying a few prominent pages in the books of a neighbouring upholsterer. I had got on so fast of late, that I had even started a boy in boots – top boots – in bondage and slavery to whom I might be said to pass my days. For, after I had made this monster (out of the refuse of my washerwoman's family) and had clothed him with a blue coat, canary waistcoat, white cravat, creamy breeches, and the boots already mentioned, I had to find him a little to do and a great deal to eat; and with both of these horrible requirements he haunted my existence.

This avenging phantom was ordered to be on duty at eight on Tuesday morning in the hall (it was two feet square, as charged for floorcloth), and Herbert suggested certain things for breakfast that he thought Joe would like. While I felt sincerely obliged to him for being so interested and considerate, I had an odd half-provoked sense of suspicion upon me, that if Joe had been coming to see *him*, he wouldn't have been quite so brisk about it.

However, I came into town on the Monday night to be ready for Joe, and I got up early in the morning, and caused the sitting-room and breakfast-table to assume their most splendid appearance. Unfortunately the morning was drizzly, and an angel could not have concealed the fact that Barnard was shedding sooty tears outside the window, like some weak giant of a sweep.

As the time approached I should have liked to run away, but the Avenger pursuant to orders was in the hall, and presently I heard Joe, on the staircase. I knew it was Joe, by his clumsy manner of coming upstairs – his state boots being always too big for him – and by the time it took him to read the names on the other floors in the course of his ascent. When at last he stopped outside our door, I could hear his finger tracing over the painted letters of my name, and I afterwards distinctly heard him breathing in at the keyhole. Finally he gave a faint single rap, and Pepper – such was the compromising name of the avenging boy – announced 'Mr Gargery!' I thought he never would have done wiping his feet, and that I must have gone out to lift him off the mat, but at last he came in.

'Joe, how are you, Joe?'

'Pip, how *air* you, Pip?'

With his good honest face all glowing and shining, and his

hat put down on the floor between us, he caught both my hands and worked them straight up and down, as if I had been the last-patented pump.

'I am glad to see you, Joe. Give me your hat.'

But Joe, taking it up carefully with both hands, like a bird's-nest with eggs in it, wouldn't hear of parting with that piece of property, and persisted in standing talking over it in a most uncomfortable way.

'Which you have that growed,' said Joe, 'and that swelled, and that gentle-folked;' Joe considered a little before he discovered this word; 'as, to be sure, you are a honour to your king and country.'

'And you, Joe, look wonderfully well.'

'Thank God,' said Joe, 'I'm ekerval to most. And your sister, she's no worse than she were. And Biddy, she's ever right and ready. And all friends is no back-erder, if not no forarder. 'Ceptin' Wopsle: he's had a drop.'

All this time (still with both hands taking great care of the bird's-nest), Joe was rolling his eyes round and round the room, and round and round the flowered pattern of my dressing-gown.

'Had a drop, Joe?'

'Why, yes,' said Joe, lowering his voice, 'he's left the Church and went into the play acting. Which the play acting have likewise brought him to London along with me. And his wish were,' said Joe, getting the bird's-nest under his left arm for the moment, and groping in it for an egg with his right; 'if no offence, as I would 'and you that.'

I took what Joe gave me, and found it to be the crumpled playbill of a small metropolitan theatre, announcing the first appearance, in that very week, of 'the celebrated Provincial Amateur of Roscian renown, whose unique performance in the highest tragic walk of our National Bard has lately occasioned so great a sensation in local dramatic circles.'

'Were you at his performance, Joe?' I enquired.

'I *were*,' said Joe, with emphasis and solemnity.

'Was there a great sensation?'

'Why,' said Joe, 'yes, there certainly were a peck of orange-peel. Partickler when he see the ghost. Though I put it to yourself, sir, whether it were calc'lated to keep a man up to his work with a good hart, to be continiwally cutting in betwixt him and the Ghost with "Amen!" A man may have had a misfortun' and been in the Church,' said Joe, lowering his voice to an argumentative and feeling tone, 'but that is no reason why you should put him out at such a time. Which I meantersay, if the ghost of a man's own father cannot be allowed to claim his attention, what can, Sir? Still more, when his mourning 'at is unfortunately made so small as that the weight of the black feathers brings it off, try to keep it on how you may.'

A ghost-seeing effect in Joe's own countenance informed me that Herbert had entered the room. So I presented Joe to Herbert, who held out his hand; but Joe backed from it, and held on by the bird's-nest.

'Your servant, Sir,' said Joe, 'which I hope as you and Pip' – here his eye fell on the Avenger, who was putting some toast on table, and so plainly denoted an intention to make that young

gentleman one of the family, that I frowned it down and confused him more – 'I meantersay, you two gentlemen – which I hope as you gets your elths in this close spot? For the present may be a wery good inn, according to London opinions,' said Joe, confidentially, 'and I believe it's character do stand i; but I wouldn't keep a pig in it myself – not in the case that I wished him to fatten wholesome and to eat with a meller flavour on him.'

Having borne this flattering testimony to the merits of our dwelling-place, and having incidentally shown this tendency to call me 'sir', Joe, being invited to sit down to table, looked all round the room for a suitable spot on which to deposit his hat – as if it were only on some few very rare substances in nature that it could find a resting-place – and ultimately stood it on an extreme corner of the chimney-piece, from which it ever afterwards fell off at intervals.

'Do you take tea, or coffee, Mr Gargery?' asked Herbert, who always presided of a morning.

'Thankee, Sir,' said Joe, stiff from head to foot, 'I'll take whichever is most agreeable to yourself.'

'What do you say to coffee?'

'Thankee, Sir,' returned Joe, evidently dispirited by the proposal, 'since you *are* so kind as make chice of coffee. I will not run contrairy to your own opinions. But don't you never find it a little 'eating?'

'Say tea, then,' said Herbert, pouring it out.

Here Joe's hat tumbled off the mantelpiece, and he started out of his chair and picked it up, and fitted it to the same exact spot. As if it were an absolute point of good breeding that it should tumble off again soon.

'When did you come to town, Mr Gargery?'

'Were it yesterday afternoon?' said Joe, after coughing behind his hand as if he had had time to catch the whooping-cough since he came. 'No it were not. Yes it were. Yes. It were yesterday afternoon' (with an appearance of mingled wisdom, relief, and strict impartiality).

'Have you seen anything of London, yet?'

'Why, yes, Sir,' said Joe, 'me and Wopsle went off straight to look at the blacking ware'us. But we didn't find that it come up to its likeness in the red bills at the shop doors: which I meantersay,' added Joe, in an explanatory manner, 'as it is there drawd too architectooralooral.'

I really believe Joe would have prolonged this word (mightily expressive to my mind of some architecture that I know) into a perfect chorus, but for his attention being providentially attracted by his hat, which was toppling. Indeed, it demanded from him a constant attention, and a quickness of eye and hand, very like that exacted by wicket-keeping. He made extraordinary play with it, and showed the greatest skill; now, rushing at it and catching it neatly as it dropped; now, merely stopping it midway, beating it up, and humouring it in various parts of the room and against a good deal of the pattern of the paper on the wall, before he felt it safe to close with it; finally splashing it into the slop-basin, where I took the liberty of laying hands upon it.

As to his shirt-collar, and his coat-collar, they were perplexing to reflect upon – insoluble mysteries both. Why should a man scrape himself to that extent, before he could consider himself full dressed? Why should he suppose it necessary to be purified by suffering for his holiday clothes? Then he fell into such unaccountable fits of meditation, with his fork midway between his plate and his mouth; had his eyes attracted in such strange directions; was afflicted with such remarkable coughs; sat so far from the table, and dropped so much more than he ate, and pretended that he hadn't dropped it; that I was heartily glad when Herbert left us for the city.

I had neither the good sense nor the good feeling to know that this was all my fault, and that if I had been easier with Joe, Joe would have been easier with me. I felt impatient of him and out of temper with him; in which condition he heaped coals of fire on my head.

'Us two being now alone, Sir' – began Joe.

'Joe,' I interrupted, pettishly, 'how can you call me Sir?'

Joe looked at me for a single instant with something faintly like reproach. Utterly preposterous as his cravat was, and as his collars were, I was conscious of a sort of dignity in the look.

'Us two being now alone,' resumed Joe, 'and me having the intentions and abilities to stay not many minutes more, I will now conclude – leastways begin – to mention what have led to my having had the present honour. For was it not,' said Joe, with his old air of lucid exposition, 'that my only wish were to be useful to you, I should not have had the honour of breaking wittles in the company and abode of gentlemen.'

I was so unwilling to see the look again, that I made no remonstrance against this tone.

'Well, Sir,' pursued Joe, 'this is how it were. I were at the Bargemen t'other night, Pip;' whenever he subsided into affection, he called me Pip, and whenever he relapsed into politeness he called me Sir; 'when there come up in his shay-cart Pumblechook. Which that same identical,' said Joe, going down a new track, 'do comb my 'air the wrong way sometimes, awful, by giving out up and down town as it were him which ever had your infant companionation and were looked upon as a play-fellow by yourself.'

'Nonsense. It was you, Joe.'

'Which I fully believed it were, Pip,' said Joe, slightly tossing his head, 'though it signify little now, Sir. Well, Pip; this same identical, which his manners is given to blusterous, come to me at the Bargemen (wot a pipe and a pint of beer do give refreshment to the working-man, Sir, and do not over stimulate), and his word were, "Joseph, Miss Havisham she wish to speak to you." '

'Miss Havisham, Joe?'

' "She wished," were Pumblechook's word, "to speak to you." ' Joe sat and rolled his eyes at the ceiling.

'Yes, Joe? Go on, please.'

'Next day, Sir,' said Joe, looking at me as if I were a long way off, 'having cleaned myself, I go and I see Miss A.'

'Miss A., Joe? Miss Havisham?'

'Which I say, Sir,' replied Joe, with an air of legal formality, as if he were making his will, 'Miss A., or otherways Havisham. Her expression air then as follering: "Mr Gargery. You air in correspondence with Mr Pip?" Having had a letter from you, I

were able to say "I am." (When I married your sister, Sir, I said, "I will;" and when I answered your friend, Pip, I said, "I am.") "Would you tell him, then," said she, "that which Estella has come home, and would be glad to see him." '

I felt my face fire up as I looked at Joe. I hope one remote cause of its firing, may have been my consciousness that if I had known his errand, I should have given him more encouragement.

'Biddy,' pursued Joe, 'when I got home and asked her fur to write the message to you, a little hung back. Biddy says, "I know he will be very glad to have it by word of mouth, it is holiday-time, you want to see him, go!" I have now concluded, Sir,' said Joe, rising from his chair, 'and, Pip, I wish you ever well and ever prospering to a greater and greater height.'

'But you are not going now, Joe?'

'Yes I am,' said Joe.

'But you are coming back to dinner, Joe?'

'No I am not,' said Joe.

Our eyes met, and all the 'Sir' melted out of that manly heart as he gave me his hand.

'Pip, dear old chap, life is made of ever so many partings welded together, as I may say, and one man's a blacksmith, and one's a whitesmith, and one's a goldsmith, and one's a copper-smith. Diwisions among such must come, and must be met as they come. If there's been any fault at all today, it's mine. You and me is not two figures to be together in London; nor yet anywheres else but what is private, and beknown, and under-stood among friends. It ain't that I am proud, but that I want to be right, as you shall never see me no more in these clothes. I'm wrong in these clothes. I'm wrong out of the forge, the kitchen, or off th' meshes. You won't find half so much fault in me if you think of me in my forge dress, with my hammer in my hand, or even my pipe. You won't find half so much fault in me if, supposing as you should ever wish to see me, you come and put your head in at the forge window and see Joe the blacksmith, there, at the old anvil, in the old burnt apron, sticking to the old work. I'm awful dull, but I hope I've beat out something nigh the rights of this at last. And so God bless you, dear old Pip, old chap, God bless you!'

I had not been mistaken in my fancy that there was a simple dignity in him. The fashion of his dress could no more come in its way when he spoke these words, than it could come in its way in Heaven. He touched me gently on the forehead, and went out. As soon as I could recover myself sufficiently, I hurried out after him and looked for him in the neighbouring streets; but he was gone.

Chapter 28

It was clear that I must repair to our town next day, and in the first flow of my repentance it was equally clear that I must stay at Joe's. But, when I had secured my box-place by tomorrow's coach, and had been down to Mr Pocket's and back, I was not by any means convinced on the last point, and began to invent reasons and make excuses for putting up at the Blue Boar. I should be an inconvenience at Joe's; I was not expected, and my bed would not be ready; I should be too far from Miss Havisham's, and she was exacting and mightn't like it. All other swindlers upon earth are nothing to the self-swindlers, and with such pretences did I cheat myself. Surely a curious thing. That I should innocently take a bad half-crown of somebody else's manufacture, is reasonable enough; but that I should knowingly reckon the spurious coin of my own make, as good money! An obliging stranger, under pretence of compactly folding up my bank-notes for security's sake, abstracts the notes and gives me nutshells; but what is his sleight of hand to mine, when I fold up my own nutshells and pass them on myself as notes!

Having settled that I must go to the Blue Boar, my mind was much disturbed by indecision whether or no to take the Avenger. It was tempting to think of that expensive mercenary publicly airing his boots in the archway of the Blue Boar's posting-yard: it was almost solemn to imagine him casually produced in the tailor's shop and confounding the disrespectful senses of Trabb's boy. On the other hand, Trabb's boy might worm himself into his intimacy and tell him things; or, reckless and desperate wretch as I knew he could be, might hoot him in the High Street. My patroness, too, might hear of him, and not approve. On the whole, I resolved to leave the Avenger behind.

It was the afternoon coach by which I had taken my place, and, as winter had now come round, I should not arrive at my destination until two or three hours after dark. Our time of starting from the Cross Keys was two o'clock. I arrived on the ground with a quarter of an hour to spare, attended by the Avenger – if I may connect that expression with one who never attended on me if he could possibly help it.

At that time it was customary to carry convicts down to the dockyards by stagecoach. As I had often heard of them in the capacity of outside passengers, and had more than once seen them on the high road dangling their ironed legs over the coach roof, I had no cause to be surprised when Herbert, meeting me in the yard, came up and told me there were two convicts going down with me. But I had a reason that was an old reason now, for constitutionally faltering whenever I heard the word convict.

'You don't mind them, Handel?' said Herbert.

'Oh no!'

'I thought you seemed as if you didn't like them?'

'I can't pretend that I do like them, and I suppose you don't particularly. But I don't mind them.'

'See! There they are,' said Herbert, 'coming out of the Tap. What a degraded and vile sight it is!'

They had been treating their guard, I suppose, for they had a gaoler with them, and all three came out wiping their mouths on their hands. The two convicts were handcuffed together, and had irons on their legs – iron of a pattern that I knew well. They wore the dress that I likewise knew well. Their keeper had a brace of pistols, and carried a thick-knobbed bludgeon under his arm; but he was on terms of good understanding with them, and stood, with them beside him, looking on at the putting-to of the horses, rather with an air as if the convicts

were an interesting exhibition not formally open at the moment, and he the curator. One was a taller and stouter man than the other, and appeared as a matter of course, according to the mysterious ways of the world both convict and free, to have had allotted to him the smaller suit of clothes. His arms and legs were like great pincushions of those shapes, and his attire disguised him absurdly; but I knew his half-closed eye at one glance. There stood the man whom I had seen on the settle at the Three Jolly Bargemen on a Saturday night, and who had brought me down with his invisible gun!

It was easy to make sure that as yet he knew me no more than if he had never seen me in his life. He looked across at me, and his eye appraised my watch-chain, and then he incidentally spat and said something to the other convict, and they laughed and slued themselves round with a clink of their coupling manacle, and looked at something else. The great numbers on their backs, as if they were street doors; their coarse mangy ungainly outer surface, as if they were lower animals; their ironed legs, apologetically garlanded with pocket-handkerchiefs; and the way in which all present looked at them and kept from them; made them (as Herbert had said) a most disagreeable and degraded spectacle.

But this was not the worst of it. It came out that the whole of the back of the coach had been taken by a family removing from London, and that there were no places for the two prisoners but on the seat in front, behind the coachman. Hereupon, a choleric gentleman, who had taken the fourth place on that seat, flew into a most violent passion, and said that it was a breach of contract to mix him up with such villainous company, and that it was poisonous and pernicious and infamous and shameful, and I don't know what else. At this time the coach was ready and the coachman impatient, and we were all preparing to get up, and the prisoners had come over with their keeper – bringing with them that curious flavour of bread-poultice, baize, rope-yarn, and hearthstone, which attends the convict presence.

'Don't take it so much amiss, sir,' pleaded the keeper to the angry passenger; 'I'll sit next you myself. I'll put 'em on the outside of the row. They won't interfere with you, sir. You needn't know they're there.'

'And don't blame *me*,' growled the convict I had recognised. '*I* don't want to go. *I* am quite ready to stay behind. As far as I am concerned anyone's welcome to *my* place.'

'Or mine,' said the other, gruffly. '*I* wouldn't have incommoded none of you, if I'd a had *my* way.' Then, they both laughed, and began cracking nuts, and spitting the shells about – as I really think I should have liked to do myself, if I had been in their place and so despised.

At length, it was voted that there was no help for the angry gentleman, and that he must either go in his chance company or remain behind. So he got into his place, still making complaints, and the keeper got into the place next him, and the convicts hauled themselves up as well as they could, and the convict I had recognised sat behind me with his breath on the hair of my head.

'Goodbye, Handel!' Herbert called out as we started. I thought what a blessed fortune it was, that he had found another name for me than Pip.

It is impossible to express with what acuteness I felt the convict's breathing, not only on the back of my head, but all along my spine. The sensation was like being touched in the marrow with some pungent and searching acid, and it set my very teeth on edge. He seemed to have more breathing business to do than another man, and to make more noise in doing it; and I was conscious of growing high-shouldered on one side, in my shrinking endeavours to fend him off.

The weather was miserably raw, and the two cursed the cold. It made us all lethargic before we had gone far, and when we had left the halfway house behind, we habitually dozed and shivered and were silent. I dozed off, myself, in considering the question whether I ought to restore a couple of pounds sterling to this creature before losing sight of him, and how it could best be done. In the act of dipping forward as if I were going to bathe among the horses, I woke in a fright and took the question up again.

But I must have lost it longer than I had thought, since, although I could recognise nothing in the darkness and the fitful lights and shadows of our lamps, I traced marsh country in the cold damp wind that blew at us. Cowering forward for warmth and to make me a screen against the wind, the convicts were closer to me than before. The very first words I heard them interchange as I became conscious, were the words of my own thought, 'Two One-Pound notes.'

'How did he get 'em?' said the convict I had never seen.

'How should I know?' returned the other. 'He had 'em stowed away somehows. Giv him by friends, I expect.'

'I wish,' said the other, with a bitter curse upon the cold, 'that I had 'em here.'

'Two one-pound notes, or friends?'

'Two one-pound notes. I'd sell all the friends I ever had, for one, and think it a blessed good bargain. Well! So he says – ?'

'So he says,' resumed the convict I had recognised – 'it was all said and done in half a minute, behind a pile of timber in the Dockyard – "You're a going to be discharged!" Yes, I was. Would I find out that boy that had fed him and kep his secret, and give him them two one-pound notes? Yes, I would. And I did.'

'More fool you,' growled the other. 'I'd have spent 'em on a man, in wittles and drink. He must have been a green one. Mean to say he knowed nothing of you?'

"Not a ha'porth. Different gangs and different ships. He was tried again for prison-breaking, and got made a lifer.'

'And was that – honour! – the only time you worked out, in this part of the country?'

'The only time.'

'What might have been your opinion of the place?'

'A most beastly place. Mudbank, mist, swamp, and work: work, swamp, mist, and mudbank.'

They both execrated the place in very strong language, and gradually growled themselves out, and had nothing left to say.

After overhearing this dialogue, I should assuredly have got down and been left in the solitude and darkness of the highway, but for feeling certain that the man had no suspicion of my identity. Indeed, I was not only so changed in the course of nature, but so differently dressed and so differently circumstanced, that it was not at all likely he could have known me without accidental help. Still, the coincidence of our being together on the coach, was sufficiently strange to fill me with a dread that some other coincidence might at any moment connect me, in his hearing, with my name. For this reason, I resolved to alight as soon as we touched the town, and put myself out of his hearing. This device I executed successfully. My little portmanteau was in the boot under my feet; I had but to turn a hinge to get it out; I threw it down before me, got down after it, and was left at the first lamp on the first stones of the town pavement. As to the convicts, they went their way with the coach, and I knew at what point they would be spirited off to the river. In my fancy, I saw the boat with its convict crew waiting for them at the slime-washed stairs – again heard the gruff 'Give way, you!' like an order to dogs – again saw the wicked Noah's Ark lying out on the black water.

I could not have said what I was afraid of, for my fear was altogether undefined and vague, but there was great fear upon me. As I walked on to the hotel, I felt that a dread, much exceeding the mere apprehension of a painful or disagreeable recognition, made me tremble. I am confident that it took no distinctness of shape, and that it was the revival for a few minutes of the terror of childhood.

The coffee-room at the Blue Boar was empty, and I had not only ordered my dinner there, but had sat down to it, before the waiter knew me. As soon as he had apologised for the remissness of his memory, he asked me if he should send boots for Mr Pumblechook?

'No,' said I, 'certainly not.'

The waiter (it was he who had brought up the Great Remonstrance from the Commercials on the day when I was bound) appeared surprised, and took the earliest opportunity of putting a dirty old copy of a local newspaper so directly in my way, that I took it up and read this paragraph:

Our readers will learn, not altogether without interest, in reference to the recent romantic rise in fortune of a young artificer in iron of this neighbourhood (what a theme, by the way, for the magic pen of our as yet not universally acknowledged townsman Tooby, the poet of our columns!) that the youth's earliest patron, companion, and friend, was a highly-respected individual not entirely unconnected with the corn and seed trade, and whose eminently convenient and commodious business premises are situate within a hundred miles of the High Street. It is not wholly irrespective of our personal feelings that we record Him as the mentor of our young Telemachus, for it is good to know that our town produced the founder of the latter's fortunes.

Does the thought-contracted brow of the local Sage or the lustrous eye of local Beauty enquire whose fortunes? We believe that Quintin Matsys was the Blacksmith of Antwerp. Verb. Sap.

I entertain a conviction, based upon large experience, that if in the days of my prosperity I had gone to the North Pole, I should have met somebody there, wandering Esquimaux or civilised man, who would have told me that Pumblechook was my earliest patron and the founder of my fortunes.

Chapter 29

Betimes in the morning I was up and out. It was too early yet to go to Miss Havisham's, so I loitered into the country on Miss Havisham's side of town – which was not Joe's side; I could go there tomorrow – thinking about my patroness, and painting brilliant pictures of her plans for me.

She had adopted Estella, she had as good as adopted me, and it could not fail to be her intention to bring us together. She reserved it for me to restore the desolate house, admit the sunshine into the dark rooms, set the clocks a going and the cold hearths a blazing, tear down the cobwebs, destroy the vermin – in short, do all the shining deeds of the young knight of romance, and marry the princess. I had stopped to look at the house as I passed; and its seared red brick walls, blocked windows, and strong green ivy clasping even the stacks of chimneys with its twigs and tendons, as if with sinewy old arms, had made up a rich attractive mystery, of which I was the hero. Estella was the inspiration of it, and the heart of it, of course. But, though she had taken such strong possession of me, though my fancy and my hope were so set upon her, though her influence on my boyish life and character had been all-powerful, I did not, even that romantic morning, invest her with any attributes save those she possessed. I mention this in this place, of a fixed purpose, because it is the clue by which I am to be followed into my poor labyrinth. According to my experience, the conventional notion of a lover cannot be always true. The unqualified truth is, that when I loved Estella with the love of a man, I loved her simply because I found her irresistible. Once for all; I knew to my sorrow, often and often, if not always, that I loved her against reason, against promise, against peace, against hope, against happiness, against all discouragement that could be. Once for all; I loved her none the less because I knew it, and it had no more influence in restraining me, than if I had devoutly believed her to be human perfection.

I so shaped out my walk as to arrive at the gate at my old time. When I had rung at the bell with an unsteady hand, I turned my back upon the gate, while I tried to get my breath and keep the beating of my heart moderately quiet. I heard the side door open, and steps come across the courtyard; but I pretended not to hear, even when the gate swung on its rusty hinges.

Being at last touched on the shoulder, I started and turned. I started much more naturally then, to find myself confronted by a man in a sober grey dress. The last man I should have expected to see in that place of porter at Miss Havisham's door.

'Orlick!'

'Ah, young master, there's more changes than yours. But come in, come in. It's opposed to my orders to hold the gate open.'

I entered and he swung it, and locked it, and took the key out.

'Yes!' said he, facing round, after doggedly preceding me a few steps towards the house. 'Here I am!'

'How did you come here?'

'I come here,' he retorted, 'on my legs. I had my box brought alongside me in a barrow.'

'Are you here for good?'

'I ain't here for harm, young master, I suppose.'

I was not so sure of that. I had leisure to entertain the retort in my mind, while he slowly lifted his heavy glance from the pavement, up my legs and arms, to my face.

'Then you have left the forge?' I said.

'Do this look like a forge?' replied Orlick, sending his glance all round him with an air of injury. 'Now, do it look like it?'

I asked him how long he had left Gargery's forge?

'One day is so like another here,' he replied, 'that I don't know without casting it up. However, I come here some time since you left.'

'I could have told you that, Orlick.'

'Ah!' said he, drily. 'But then you've got to be a scholar.'

By this time we had come to the house, where I found his room to be one just within the side door, with a little window in it looking on the courtyard. In its small proportions, it was not unlike the kind of place usually assigned to a gate-porter in Paris. Certain keys were hanging on the wall, to which he now added the gate-key; and his patchwork-covered bed was in a little inner division or recess. The whole had a slovenly, confined and sleepy look, like a cage for a human dormouse: while he, looming dark and heavy in the shadow of a corner by the window, looked like the human dormouse for whom it was fitted up – as indeed he was.

'I never saw this room before,' I remarked; 'but there used to be no porter here.'

'No,' said he; 'not till it got about that there was no protection on the premises, and it come to be considered dangerous, with convicts and Tag and Rag and Bobtail going up and down. And then I was recommended to the place as a man who could give another man as good as he brought, and I took it. It's easier than bellowsing and hammering – that's loaded, that is.'

My eye had been caught by a gun with a brass-bound stock over the chimney-piece, and his eye had followed mine.

'Well,' said I, not desirous of more conversation, 'shall I go up to Miss Havisham?'

'Burn me, if I know!' he retorted, first stretching himself and then shaking himself;' my orders ends here, young master. I give this here bell a rap with this here hammer, and you go on along the passage till you meet somebody.'

'I am expected, I believe?'

'Burn me twice over, if I can say!' said he.

Upon that I turned down the long passage which I had first trodden in my thick boots, and he made his bell sound. At the end of the passage, while the bell was still reverberating, I found Sarah Pocket: who appeared to have now become constitutionally green and yellow by reason of me.

'Oh!' said she. 'You, is it, Mr Pip?'

'It is, Miss Pocket. I am glad to tell you that Mr Pocket and family are all well.'

'Are they any wiser?' said Sarah, with a dismal shake of the head; 'they had better be wiser than well. Ah, Matthew, Matthew! You know your way, sir?'

Tolerably, for I had gone up the staircase in the dark, many a time. I ascended it now, in lighter boots than of yore, and tapped in my old way at the door of Miss Havisham's room. 'Pip's rap,' I heard her say, immediately; 'come in, Pip.'

She was in her chair near the old table, in the old dress, with her two hands crossed on her stick, her chin resting on them, and her eyes on the fire. Sitting near her, with the white shoe, that had never been worn, in her hand, and her head bent as she looked at it, was an elegant lady whom I had never seen.

'Come in, Pip,' Miss Havisham continued to mutter, without looking round or up; 'come in. Pip; how do you do, Pip? so you kiss my hand as if I were a queen, eh? – Well?'

She looked up at me suddenly, only moving her eyes, and repeated in a grimly playful manner,

'Well?'

'I heard, Miss Havisham,' said I, rather at a loss, 'that you were so kind as to wish me to come and see you, and I came directly.'

'Well?'

The lady, whom I had never seen before, lifted up her eyes and looked archly at me, and then I saw that the eyes were Estella's eyes. But she was so much changed, was so much more beautiful, so much more womanly, in all things winning admiration, had made such wonderful advance, that I seemed to have made none. I fancied, as I looked at her, that I slipped hopelessly back into the coarse and common boy again. O the sense of distance and disparity that came upon me, and the inaccessibility that came about her!

She gave me her hand. I stammered something about the pleasure I felt in seeing her again, and about my having looked forward to it for a long, long time.

'Do you find her much changed, Pip?' asked Miss Havisham, with her greedy look, and striking her stick upon a chair that stood between them, as a sign to me to sit down there.

'When I came in, Miss Havisham, I thought there was nothing of Estella in the face or figure; but now it all settles down so curiously into the old – '

'What? You are not going to say into the old Estella?' Miss Havisham interrupted. 'She was proud and insulting, and you wanted to go away from her. Don't you remember?'

I said confusedly that that was long ago, and that I knew no better then, and the like. Estella smiled with perfect composure, and said she had no doubt of my having been quite right, and of her having been very disagreeable.

'Is *he* changed?' Miss Havisham asked her.

'Very much,' said Estella, looking at me.

'Less coarse and common?' said Miss Havisham, playing with Estella's hair.

Estella laughed, and looked at the shoe in her hand, and laughed again, and looked at me, and put the shoe down. She treated me as a boy still, but she lured me on.

We sat in the dreamy room among the old strange influences which had so wrought upon me, and I learnt that she had but just come home from France, and that she was going to London. Proud and wilful as of old, she had brought those qualities into such subjection to her beauty that it was impossible and out of nature – or I thought so – to separate them from her beauty. Truly it was impossible to dissociate her presence from all those wretched hankerings after money and gentility that had disturbed my boyhood – from all those ill-regulated aspirations that had first made me ashamed of home and Joe – from all those visions that had raised her face in the glowing fire, struck it out of the iron on the anvil, extracted it from the darkness of night to look in at the wooden window of the forge and flit away. In a word, it was impossible for me to separate her, in the past or in the present, from the innermost life of my life.

It was settled that I should stay there all the rest of the day, and return to the hotel at night, and to London tomorrow. When we had conversed for a while, Miss Havisham sent us two out to walk in the neglected garden: on our coming in by and by, she said I should wheel her about a little, as in times of yore.

So, Estella and I went out into the garden by the gate through which I had strayed to my encounter with the pale young gentleman, now Herbert; I, trembling in spirit and worshipping the very hem of her dress; she, quite composed and most decidedly not worshipping the hem of mine. As we drew near to the place of encounter, she stopped and said: 'I must have been a singular little creature to hide and see that fight that day: but I did, and I enjoyed it very much.'

'You rewarded me very much.'

'Did I?' she replied, in an incidental and forgetful way. 'I remember I entertained a great objection to your adversary, because I took it ill that he should be brought here to pester me with his company.'

'He and I are great friends now.'

'Are you? I think I recollect though, that you read with his father?'

'Yes.'

I made the admission with reluctance, for it seemed to have a boyish look, and she already treated me more than enough like a boy.

'Since your change of fortune and prospects, you have changed your companions,' said Estella.

'Naturally,' said I.

'And necessarily,' she added, in a haughty tone; 'what was fit company for you once, would be quite unfit company for you now.'

In my conscience, I doubt very much whether I had any lingering intention left of going to see Joe; but if I had, this observation put it to flight.

'You had no idea of your impending good fortune, in those times?' said Estella, with a slight wave of her hand, signifying the fighting times.

'Not the least.'

The air of completeness and superiority with which she walked at my side, and the air of youthfulness and submission with which I walked at hers, made a contrast that I strongly felt. It would have rankled in me more than it did, if I had not regarded myself as eliciting it by being so set apart for her and assigned to her.

The garden was too overgrown and rank for walking in with ease, and after we had made the round of it twice or thrice, we came out again into the brewery yard. I showed her to a nicety where I had seen her walking on the casks, that first old day, and she said with a cold and careless look in that direction, 'Did I?' I reminded her where she had come out of the house and given me my meat and drink, and she said, 'I don't remember.' 'Not remember that you made me cry?' said I. 'No,' said she, and shook her head and looked about her. I verily believe that her not remembering and not minding in the least, made me cry again, inwardly – and that is the sharpest crying of all.

'You must know,' said Estella, condescending to me as a brilliant and beautiful woman might, 'that I have no heart – if that has anything to do with my memory.'

I got through some jargon to the effect that I took the liberty of doubting that. That I knew better. That there could be no such beauty without it.

'Oh! I have a heart to be stabbed in or shot in, I have no doubt,' said Estella, 'and, of course, if it ceased to beat I should cease to be. But you know what I mean. I have no softness there, no – sympathy – sentiment – nonsense.'

What *was* it that was borne in upon my mind when she stood still and looked attentively at me? Anything that I had seen in Miss Havisham? No. In some of her looks and gestures there was that tinge of resemblance to Miss Havisham which may often be noticed to have been acquired by children, from grown persons with whom they have been much associated and secluded, and which, when childhood is passed, will produce a remarkable occasional likeness of expression between faces that are otherwise quite different. And yet I could not trace this to Miss Havisham. I looked again, and though she was still looking at me, the suggestion was gone.

What *was* it?

'I am serious,' said Estella, not so much with a frown (for her brow was smooth) as with a darkening of her face; 'if we are to be thrown much together, you had better believe it at once. No!' imperiously stopping me as I opened my lips. 'I have not bestowed my tenderness anywhere. I have never had any such thing.'

In another moment we were in the brewery so long disused, and she pointed to the high gallery where I had seen her going out on that same first day, and told me she remembered to have been up there, and to have seen me standing scared below. As my eyes followed her white hand, again the same dim suggestion that I could not possibly grasp, crossed me. My involuntary start occasioned her to lay her hand upon my arm. Instantly the ghost passed once more and was gone.

What *was* it?

'What is the matter?' asked Estella. 'Are you scared again?'

'I should be if I believed what you said just now,' I replied, to turn it off.

'Then you don't? Very well. It is said, at any rate. Miss Havisham will soon be expecting you at your old post, though

I think that might be laid aside now, with other old belongings. Let us make one more round of the garden, and then go in. Come! You shall not shed tears for my cruelty today; you shall be my page, and give me your shoulder.'

Her handsome dress had trailed upon the ground. She held it in one hand now, and with the other lightly touched my shoulder as we walked. We walked round the ruined garden twice or thrice more, and it was all in bloom for me. If the green and yellow growth of weed in the chinks of the old wall had been the most precious flowers that ever blew, it could not have been more cherished in my remembrance.

There was no discrepancy of years between us, to remove her far from me; we were of nearly the same age, though of course the age told for more in her case than in mine; but the air of inaccessibility which her beauty and her manner gave her, tormented me in the midst of my delight, and at the height of the assurance I felt that our patroness had chosen us for one another. Wretched boy!

At last we went back into the house, and there I heard, with surprise, that my guardian had come down to see Miss Havisham on business, and would come back to dinner. The old wintry branches of chandeliers in the room where the mouldering table was spread, had been lighted while we were out, and Miss Havisham was in her chair and waiting for me.

It was like pushing the chair itself back into the past, when we began the old slow circuit round about the ashes of the bridal feast. But, in the funereal room, with that figure of the grave fallen back in the chair fixing its eyes upon her, Estella looked more bright and beautiful than before, and I was under stronger enchantment.

The time so melted away, that our early dinner-hour drew close at hand, and Estella left us to prepare herself. We had stopped near the centre of the long table, and Miss Havisham, with one of her withered arms stretched out of the chair, rested that clenched hand upon the yellow cloth. As Estella looked back over her shoulder before going out at the door, Miss Havisham kissed that hand to her, with a ravenous intensity that was of its kind quite dreadful.

Then, Estella being gone and we two left alone, she turned to me and said in a whisper: 'Is she beautiful, graceful, well-grown? Do you admire her?'

'Everybody must who sees her, Miss Havisham.'

She drew an arm round my neck, and drew my head close down to hers as she sat in the chair. 'Love her, love her, love her! How does she use you?'

Before I could answer (if I could have answered so difficult a question at all), she repeated, 'Love her, love her, love her! If she favours you, love her. If she wounds you, love her. If she tears your heart to pieces – and as it gets older and stronger it will tear deeper – love her, love her, love her!'

Never had I seen such passionate eagerness as was joined to her utterance of these words. I could feel the muscles of the thin arm round my neck, swell with the vehemence that possessed her.

'Hear me, Pip! I adopted her to be loved. I bred her and educated her, to be loved. I developed her into what she is, that she might be loved. Love her!'

She said the word often enough, and there could be no doubt that she meant to say it; but if the often repeated word had been hate instead of love – despair – revenge – dire death – it could not have sounded from her lips more like a curse.

'I'll tell you,' said she, in the same hurried passionate whisper, 'what real love is. It is blind devotion, unquestioning self-humiliation, utter submission, trust and belief against yourself and against the whole world, giving up your whole heart and soul to the smiter – as I did!'

When she came to that, and to a wild cry that followed that, I caught her round the waist. For she rose up in the chair, in her shroud of a dress, and struck at the air as if she would as soon have struck herself against the wall and fallen dead.

All this passed in a few seconds. As I drew her down into her chair, I was conscious of a scent that I knew, and turning, saw my guardian in the room.

He always carried (I have not yet mentioned it, I think) a pocket-handkerchief of rich silk and of imposing proportions, which was of great value to him in his profession. I have seen him so terrify a client or a witness by ceremoniously unfolding this pocket-handkerchief as if he were immediately going to blow his nose, and then pausing, as if he knew he should not have time to do it, before such client or witness committed himself, that the self-committal has followed directly, quite as a matter of course. When I saw him in the room he had this expressive pocket-handkerchief in both hands, and was looking at us. On meeting my eye, he said plainly, by a momentary and silent pause in that attitude, 'Indeed? Singular!' and then put the handkerchief to its right use with wonderful effect.

Miss Havisham had seen him as soon as I, and was (like everybody else) afraid of him. She made a strong attempt to compose herself, and stammered that he was as punctual as ever.

'As punctual as ever,' he repeated, coming up to us. '(How do you do, Pip? Shall I give you a ride, Miss Havisham? Once round?) And so you are here, Pip?'

I told him when I had arrived, and how Miss Havisham wished me to come and see Estella. To which he replied, 'Ah! Very fine young lady!' Then he pushed Miss Havisham in her chair before him, with one of his large hands, and put the other in his trousers-pocket as if the pocket were full of secrets.

'Well, Pip! How often have you seen Miss Estella before?' said he, when he came to a stop.

'How often?'

'Ah! How many times? Ten thousand times?'

'Oh! Certainly not so many.'

'Twice?'

'Jaggers,' interposed Miss Havisham, much to my relief; 'leave my Pip alone, and go with him to your dinner.'

He complied, and we groped our way down the dark stairs together. While we were still on our way to those detached apartments across the paved yard at the back, he asked me how often I had seen Miss Havisham eat and drink; offering me a breadth of choice, as usual, between a hundred times and once.

I considered, and said, 'Never.'

'And never will, Pip,' he retorted, with a frowning smile. 'She

has never allowed herself to be seen doing either, since she lived this present life of hers. She wanders about in the night, and then lays hands on such food as she takes.'

'Pray, sir,' said I, 'may I ask you a question?'

'You may,' said he, 'and I may decline to answer it. Put your question.'

'Estella's name, is it Havisham or – ?' I had nothing to add.

'Or what?' said he.

'Is it Havisham?'

'It is Havisham.'

This brought us to the dinner-table, where she and Sarah Pocket awaited us. Mr Jaggers presided, Estella sat opposite to him, I faced my green and yellow friend. We dined very well, and were waited on by a maidservant whom I had never seen in all my comings and goings, but who, for anything I know, had been in that mysterious house the whole time. After dinner a bottle of choice old port was placed before my guardian (he was evidently well acquainted with the vintage), and the two ladies left us.

Anything to equal the determined reticence of Mr Jaggers under that roof I never saw elsewhere, even in him. He kept his very looks to himself, and scarcely directed his eyes to Estella's face once during dinner. When she spoke to him, he listened, and in due course, answered, but never looked at her that I could see. On the other hand, she often looked at him, with interest and curiosity, if not distrust, but his face never showed the least consciousness. Throughout dinner he took a dry delight in making Sarah Pocket greener and yellower, by often referring in conversation with me to my expectations: but here, again, he showed no consciousness, and even made it appear that he extorted – and even did extort, though I don't know how – those references out of my innocent self.

And when he and I were left alone together, he sat with an air upon him of general lying by in consequence of information he possessed, that really was too much for me. He cross-examined his very wine when he had nothing else in hand. He held it between himself and the candle, tasted the port, rolled it in his mouth, swallowed it, looked at his glass again, smelt the port, tried it, drank it, filled again, and cross-examined the glass again, until I was as nervous as if I had known the wine to be telling him something to my disadvantage. Three or four times I feebly thought I would start conversation; but whenever he saw me going to ask him anything, he looked at me with his glass in his hand, and rolling his wine about in his mouth, as if requesting me to take notice that it was of no use, for he couldn't answer.

I think Miss Pocket was conscious that the sight of me involved her in the danger of being goaded to madness, and perhaps tearing off her cap – which was a very hideous one, in the nature of a muslin mop – and strewing the ground with her hair – which assuredly had never grown on *her* head. She did not appear when we afterwards went up to Miss Havisham's room, and we four played at whist. In the interval, Miss Havisham, in a fantastic way, had put some of the most beautiful jewels from her dressing-table into Estella's hair, and about her bosom and arms; and I saw even my guardian look at her from under his thick eyebrows, and raise them a little when her loveliness was before him, with those rich flushes of glitter and colour in it.

Of the manner and extent to which he took our trumps into custody, and came out with mean little cards at the ends of hands, before which the glory of our kings and queens was utterly abased, I say nothing; nor, of the feeling that I had, respecting his looking upon us personally in the light of three very obvious and poor riddles that he had found out long ago. What I suffered from, was the incompatibility between his cold presence and my feelings towards Estella. It was not that I knew I could never bear to speak to him about her, that I knew I could never bear to hear him creak his boots at her, that I knew I could never bear to see him wash his hands of her; it was, that my admiration should be within a foot or two of him – it was, that my feelings should be in the same place with him – *that* was the agonising circumstance.

We played until nine o'clock, and then it was arranged that when Estella came to London I should be forewarned of her coming and should meet her at the coach; and then I took leave of her, and touched her and left her.

My guardian lay at the Boar in the next room to mine. Far into the night, Miss Havisham's words, 'Love her, love her, love her!' sounded in my ears. I adapted them for my own repetition, and said to my pillow, 'I love her, I love her, I love her!' hundreds of times. Then, a burst of gratitude came upon me, that she should be destined for me, once the blacksmith's boy. Then, I thought if she were, as I feared, by no means rapturously grateful for that destiny yet, when would she begin to be interested in me? When should I awaken the heart within her, that was mute and sleeping now?

Ah me! I thought those were high and great emotions. But I never thought there was anything low and small in my keeping away from Joe, because I knew she would be contemptuous of him. It was but a day gone, and Joe had brought the tears into my eyes; they had soon dried, God forgive me! soon dried.

Chapter 30

After well considering the matter while I was dressing at the Blue Boar in the morning, I resolved to tell my guardian that I doubted Orlick's being the right sort of man to fill a post of trust at Miss Havisham's. 'Why, of course he is not the right sort of man, Pip,' said my guardian, comfortably satisfied beforehand on the general head, 'because the man who fills the post of trust never is the right sort of man.' It seemed quite to put him in spirits, to find that this particular post was not exceptionally held by the right sort of man, and he listened in a satisfied manner while I told him what knowledge I had of Orlick. 'Very good, Pip,' he observed, when I had concluded, 'I'll go round presently, and pay our friend off.' Rather alarmed by this summary action, I was for a little delay, and even hinted that our friend himself might be difficult to deal with. 'Oh no, he won't,' said my guardian, making his pocket-handkerchief-point, with perfect confidence; 'I should like to see him argue the question with *me*.'

As we were going back together to London by the midday coach, and as I breakfasted under such terrors of Pumblechook that I could scarcely hold my cup, this gave me an opportunity of saying that I wanted a walk, and that I would go on along the London road while Mr Jaggers was occupied, if he would let the coachman know that I would get into my place when overtaken. I was thus enabled to fly from the Blue Boar immediately after breakfast. By then making a loop of about a couple of miles into the open country at the back of Pumblechook's premises, I got round into the High Street again, a little beyond that pitfall, and felt myself in comparative security.

It was interesting to be in the quiet old town once more, and it was not disagreeable to be here and there suddenly recognised and stared after. One or two of the tradespeople even darted out of their shops, and went a little way down the street before me, that they might turn, as if they had forgotten something, and pass me face to face – on which occasions I don't know whether they or I made the worse pretence; they of not doing it, or I of not seeing it. Still my position was a distinguished one, and I was not at all dissatisfied with it, until fate threw me in the way of that unlimited miscreant, Trabb's boy.

Casting my eyes along the street at a certain point of my progress, I beheld Trabb's boy approaching, lashing himself with an empty blue bag. Deeming that a serene and unconscious contemplation of him would best beseem me, and would be most likely to quell his evil mind, I advanced with that expression of countenance, and was rather congratulating myself on my success, when suddenly the knees of Trabb's boy smote together, his hair uprose, his cap fell off, he trembled violently in every limb, staggered out into the road, and crying to the populace, 'Hold me! I'm so frightened!' feigned to be in a paroxysm of terror and contrition, occasioned by the dignity of my appearance. As I passed him, his teeth loudly chattered in his head, and with every mark of extreme humiliation, he prostrated himself in the dust.

This was a hard thing to bear, but this was nothing. I had not advanced another two hundred yards, when, to my inexpressible terror, amazement, and indignation, I again beheld Trabb's boy approaching. He was coming round a narrow corner. His blue bag was slung over his shoulder, honest industry beamed in his eyes, a determination to proceed to Trabb's with cheerful briskness was indicated in his gait. With a shock he became aware of me, and was severely visited as before; but this time his motion was rotatory, and he staggered round and round me with knees more afflicted, and with uplifted hands as if beseeching for mercy. His sufferings were hailed with the greatest joy by a knot of spectators, and I felt utterly confounded.

I had not got as much further down the street as the post office, when I again beheld Trabb's boy shooting round by a back way. This time, he was entirely changed. He wore the blue bag in the manner of my greatcoat, and was strutting along the pavement towards me on the opposite side of the street, attended by a company of delighted young friends to whom he from time to time exclaimed, with a wave of his hand, 'Don't know yah!' Words cannot state the amount of aggravation and injury wreaked upon me by Trabb's boy, when, passing abreast of me, he pulled up his shirt-collar, twined his side-hair, stuck an arm akimbo, and smirked extravagantly by, wriggling his elbows and body, and drawling to his attendants, 'Don't know yah, don't know yah, 'pon my soul don't know yah!' The disgrace attendant on his immediately afterwards taking to crowing and pursuing me across the bridge with crows, as from an exceedingly dejected fowl who had known me when I was a blacksmith, culminated the disgrace with which I left the town, and was, so to speak, ejected by it into the open country.

But unless I had taken the life of Trabb's boy on that occasion, I really do not even now see what I could have done save endure. To have struggled with him in the street, or to have exacted any lower recompense from him than his heart's best blood, would have been futile and degrading. Moreover, he was a boy whom no man could hurt; an invulnerable and dodging serpent who, when chased into a corner, flew out again between his captor's legs, scornfully yelping. I wrote, however, to Mr Trabb by next day's post, to say that Mr Pip must decline to deal further with one who could so far forget what he owed to the best interests of society, as to employ a boy who excited loathing in every respectable mind.

The coach, with Mr Jaggers inside, came up in due time, and I took my box-seat again, and arrived in London safe – but not sound, for my heart was gone. As soon as I arrived, I sent a penitential codfish and barrel of oysters to Joe (as reparation for not having gone myself), and then went on to Barnard's Inn.

I found Herbert dining on cold meat, and delighted to welcome me back. Having despatched the Avenger to the coffee-house for an addition to the dinner, I felt that I must open my breast that very evening to my friend and chum. As confidence was out of the question with the Avenger in the hall, which could merely be regarded in the light of an antechamber to the keyhole, I sent him to the play. A better proof of the severity of my bondage to that taskmaster could scarcely be afforded, than the degrading shifts to which I was constantly driven to find him employment. So mean is extremity, that I sometimes sent him to Hyde Park Corner to see what o'clock it was.

Dinner done and we sitting with our feet upon the fender, I said to Herbert, 'My dear Herbert, I have something very particular to tell you.'

'My dear Handel,' he returned, 'I shall esteem and respect your confidence.'

'It concerns myself, Herbert,' said I, 'and one other person.'

Herbert crossed his feet, looked at the fire with his head on one side, and having looked at it in vain for some time, looked at me because I didn't go on.

'Herbert,' said I, laying my hand upon his knee, 'I love – I adore – Estella.'

Instead of being transfixed, Herbert replied in an easy matter-of-course way, 'Exactly. Well?'

'Well, Herbert. Is that all you say? Well?'

'What next, I mean?' said Herbert. 'Of course I know *that*.'

'How do you know it?' said I.

'How do I know it, Handel? Why, from you.'

'I never told you.'

'Told me! You have never told me when you have got your hair cut, but I have had senses to perceive it. You have always adored her, ever since I have known you. You brought your adoration and your portmanteau here, together. Told me! Why, you have always told me all day long. When you told me your own story, you told me plainly that you began adoring her the first time you saw her, when you were very young indeed.'

'Very well, then,' said I, to whom this was a new and not unwelcome light, 'I have never left off adoring her. And she has come back, a most beautiful and most elegant creature. And I saw her yesterday. And if I adored her before, I now doubly adore her.'

'Lucky for you then, Handel,' said Herbert, 'that you are picked out for her and allotted to her. Without encroaching on forbidden ground, we may venture to say, that there can be no doubt between ourselves of that fact. Have you any idea yet, of Estella's views on the adoration question?'

I shook my head gloomily. 'Oh! She is thousands of miles away, from me,' said I.

'Patience, my dear Handel: time enough, time enough. But you have something more to say?'

'I am ashamed to say it,' I returned, 'and yet it's no worse to say it than to think it. You call me a lucky fellow. Of course, I am. I was a blacksmith's boy but yesterday; I am – what shall I say I am – today?'

'Say, a good fellow, if you want a phrase,' returned Herbert, smiling, and clapping his hands on the back of mine: 'a good fellow, with impetuosity and hesitation, boldness and diffidence, action and dreaming, curiously mixed in him.'

Trabb's boy

I stopped for a moment to consider whether there really was this mixture in my character. On the whole, I by no means recognised the analysis, but thought it not worth disputing.

'When I ask what I am to call myself today, Herbert,' I went on, 'I suggest what I have in my thoughts. You say I am lucky. I know I have done nothing to raise myself in life, and that fortune alone has raised me; that is being very lucky. And yet, when I think of Estella –'

('And when don't you, you know!' Herbert threw in, with his eyes on the fire; which I thought kind and sympathetic of him.)

' – Then, my dear Herbert, I cannot tell you how dependent and uncertain I feel, and how exposed to hundreds of chances. Avoiding forbidden ground, as you did just now, I may still say that on the constancy of one person (naming no person) all my expectations depend. And at the best, how indefinite and un-satisfactory, only to know so vaguely what they are!' In saying this, I relieved my mind of what had always been there, more or less, though no doubt most since yesterday.

'Now, Handel,' Herbert replied, in his gay hopeful way, 'it seems to me that in the despondency of the tender passion, we are looking into our gift-horse's mouth with a magnifying-glass. Likewise, it seems to me that, concentrating our attention on the examination, we altogether overlook one of the best points of the animal. Didn't you tell me that your guardian, Mr Jaggers, told you in the beginning, that you were not endowed with expectations only? And even if he had not told you so – though that is a very large If, I grant – could you believe that of all men in London, Mr Jaggers is the man to hold his present relations towards you unless he were sure of his ground?'

I said I could not deny that this was a strong point. I said it (people often do so in such cases) like a rather reluctant con-cession to truth and justice – as if I wanted to deny it!

'I should think it *was* a strong point,' said Herbert, 'and I should think you would be puzzled to imagine a stronger; as to the rest, you must bide your guardian's time, and he must bide his client's time. You'll be one-and-twenty before you know where you are, and then perhaps you'll get some further en-lightenment. At all events, you'll be nearer getting it, for it must come at last.'

'What a hopeful disposition you have!' said I, gratefully ad-miring his cheery ways.

'I ought to have,' said Herbert, 'for I have not much else. I must acknowledge, by the by, that the good sense of what I have just said is not my own, but my father's. The only remark I ever heard him make on your story was the final one: "The thing is settled and done, or Mr Jaggers would not be in it." And now, before I say anything more about my father, or my father's son, and repay confidence with confidence, I want to make myself seriously disagreeable to you for a moment – positively repulsive.'

'You won't succeed,' said I.

'Oh yes, I shall!' said he. 'One, two, three, and now I am in for it. Handel, my good fellow:' though he spoke in this light tone, he was very much in earnest: 'I have been thinking since we have been talking with our feet on this fender, that Estella cannot surely be a condition of your inheritance, if she was never referred to by your guardian. Am I right in so under-standing what you have told me, as that he never referred to her, directly or indirectly, in any way? Never even hinted, for instance, that your patron might have views as to your marriage ultimately?'

'Never.'

'Now, Handel, I am quite free from the flavour of sour grapes, upon my soul and honour! Not being bound to her, can you not detach yourself from her? – I told you I should be disagreeable.'

I turned my head aside, for, with a rush and a sweep, like the old marsh winds coming up from the sea, a feeling like that which had subdued me on the morning when I left the forge, when the mists were solemnly rising, and when I laid my hand upon the village fingerpost, smote upon my heart again. There was silence between us for a little while.

'Yes; but, my dear Handel,' Herbert went on, as if we had been talking instead of silent, 'its having been so strongly rooted in the breast of a boy whom nature and circumstances made so romantic, renders it very serious. Think of her bringing-up, and think of Miss Havisham. Think of what she is herself (now I am repulsive and you abominate me). This may lead to miserable things.'

'I know it, Herbert,' said I, with my head still turned away, 'but I can't help it.'

'You can't detach yourself?'

'No. Impossible!'

'You can't try, Handel?'

'No. Impossible!'

'Well!' said Herbert, getting up with a lively shake as if he had been asleep, and stirring the fire; 'now I'll endeavour to make myself agreeable again!'

So, he went round the room and shook the curtains out, put the chairs in their places, tidied the books and so forth that were lying about, looked into the hall, peeped into the letter-box, shut the door, and came back to his chair by the fire; when he sat down, nursing his left leg in both arms.

'I was going to say a word or two, Handel, concerning my father and my father's son. I am afraid it is scarcely necessary for my father's son to remark that my father's establishment is not particularly brilliant in its housekeeping.'

'There is always plenty, Herbert,' said I, to say something encouraging.

'Oh yes! and so the dustman says, I believe, with the strongest approval, and so does the marine-store shop in the back street. Gravely, Handel, for the subject is grave enough, you know how it is, as well as I do. I suppose there was a time once, when my father had not given matters up; but if ever there was, the time is gone. May I ask you if you have ever had an opportunity of remarking, down in your part of the country, that the children of not exactly suitable marriages, are always most particularly anxious to be married?'

This was such a singular question, that I asked him, in return, 'Is it so?'

'I don't know,' said Herbert; 'that's what I want to know. Because it is decidedly the case with us. My poor sister Charlotte, who was next me and died before she was fourteen, was a striking example. Little Jane is the same. In her desire to be matrimonially established, you might suppose her to have passed her short existence in the perpetual contemplation of domestic bliss. Little Alick in a frock has already made arrangements for his union with a suitable young person at Kew. And, indeed, I think we are all engaged, except the baby.'

'Then you are?' said I.

'I am,' said Herbert; 'but it's a secret.'

I assured him of my keeping the secret, and begged to be favoured with further particulars. He had spoken so sensibly and feelingly of my weakness, that I wanted to know something about his strength.

'May I ask the name?' I said.

'Name of Clara,' said Herbert.

'Live in London?'

'Yes. Perhaps I ought to mention,' said Herbert, who had become curiously crestfallen and meek, since we entered on the interesting theme, 'that she is rather below my mother's non-sensical family notions. Her father had to do with the victualling of passenger-ships. I think he was a species of purser.'

'What is he now?' said I.

'He's an invalid now,' replied Herbert.

'Living on – ?'

'On the first floor,' said Herbert. Which was not at all what I meant, for I had intended my question to apply to his means. 'I have never seen him, for he has always kept his room overhead, since I have known Clara. But I have heard him constantly. He makes tremendous rows – roars, and pegs at the floor with some frightful instrument.' In looking at me and then laughing heartily, Herbert for the time recovered his usual lively manner.

'Don't you expect to see him?' said I.

'Oh yes, I constantly expect to see him,' returned Herbert, 'because I never hear him, without expecting him to come tumbling through the ceiling. But I don't know how long the rafters may hold.'

When he had once more laughed heartily, he became meek again, and told me that the moment he began to realise capital, it was his intention to marry this young lady. He added as a self-evident proposition, engendering low spirits, 'But you *can't* marry, you know, while you're looking about you.'

As we contemplated the fire, and as I thought what a difficult vision to realise this same capital sometimes was, I put my hands in my pockets. A folded piece of paper in one of them attracting my attention, I opened it and found it to be the playbill I had received from Joe, relative to the celebrated provincial amateur of Roscian renown. 'And bless my heart,' I involuntarily added aloud, 'it's tonight!'

This changed the subject in an instant, and made us hurriedly resolve to go to the play. So, when I had pledged myself to comfort and abet Herbert in the affair of his heart by all practicable and impracticable means, and when Herbert had told me that his affianced already knew me by reputation, and that I should be presented to her, and when we had warmly shaken hands upon our mutual confidence, we blew out our candles, made up our fire, locked our door, and issued forth in quest of Mr Wopsle and Denmark.

Chapter 31

On our arrival in Denmark, we found the king and queen of that country elevated in two armchairs on a kitchen-table, holding a Court. The whole of the Danish nobility were in attendance; consisting of a noble boy in the wash-leather boots of a gigantic ancestor, a venerable peer with a dirty face, who seemed to have risen from the people late in life, and the Danish chivalry with a comb in its hair and a pair of white silk legs, and presenting on the whole a feminine appearance. My gifted townsman stood gloomily apart, with folded arms, and I could have wished that his curls and forehead had been more probable.

Several curious little circumstances transpired as the action proceeded. The late king of the country not only appeared to have been troubled with a cough at the time of his decease, but to have taken it with him to the tomb, and to have brought it back. The royal phantom also carried a ghostly manuscript round its truncheon, to which it had the appearance of occasionally referring, and that, too, with an air of anxiety and a tendency to lose the place of reference which were suggestive of a state of mortality. It was this, I conceive, which led to the shade's being advised by the gallery to 'turn over!' – a recommendation which it took extremely ill. It was likewise to be noted of this majestic spirit that whereas it always appeared with an air of having been out a long time and walked an immense distance, it perceptibly came from a closely-contiguous wall. This occasioned its terrors to be received derisively. The Queen of Denmark, a very buxom lady, though no doubt historically brazen, was considered by the public to have too much brass about her; her chin being attached to her diadem by a broad band of that metal (as if she had a gorgeous toothache), her waist being encircled by another, and each of her arms by another, so that she was openly mentioned as 'the kettledrum'. The noble boy in the ancestral boots, was inconsistent; representing himself, as it were in one breath, as an able seaman, a strolling actor, a grave digger, a clergyman, and a person of the utmost importance at a court fencing-match, on the authority of whose practised eye and nice discrimination the finest strokes were judged. This gradually led to a want of toleration for him, and even – on his being detected in holy orders, and declining to perform the funeral service – to the general indignation taking the form of nuts. Lastly, Ophelia was a prey to such slow musical madness, that when, in course of time, she had taken off her white muslin scarf, folded it up, and buried it, a sulky man who had been long cooling his impatient nose against an iron bar in the front row of the gallery, growled, 'Now the baby's put to bed, let's have supper!' Which, to say the least of it, was out of keeping.

Upon my unfortunate townsman all these incidents accumulated with playful effect. Whenever that undecided prince had to ask a question or state a doubt, the public helped him out with it. As for example; on the question whether 'twas nobler in the mind to suffer, some roared yes, and some no, and some inclining to both opinions said 'toss up for it'; and quite a debating society arose. When he asked what should such fellows as he do crawling between earth and heaven, he was encouraged with loud cries of 'Hear, hear!' When he appeared with his stocking disordered (its disorder expressed, according to usage, by one very neat fold in the top, which I suppose to be always got up with a flat iron), a conversation took place in the gallery respecting the paleness of his leg, and whether it was occasioned by the turn the ghost had given him. On his taking the recorders – very like a little black flute that had just been played in the orchestra and handed out at the door – he was called upon unanimously for Rule Britannia. When he recommended the player not to saw the air thus, the sulky man said, 'And don't *you* do it, neither; you're a deal worse than *him!*' And I grieve to add that peals of laughter greeted Mr Wopsle on every one of these occasions.

But his greatest trials were in the churchyard: which had the appearance of a primeval forest, with a kind of small ecclesiastical wash-house on one side, and a turn- pike gate on the other. Mr Wopsle, in a comprehensive black cloak, being descried entering at the turnpike, the grave digger was admonished in a friendly way, 'Look out! Here's the undertaker a coming, to see how you're getting on with your work!' I believe it is well known in a constitutional country that Mr Wopsle could not possibly have returned the skull, after moralising over it, without dusting his fingers on a white napkin taken from his breast; but even that innocent and indispensable action did not pass without the comment 'Wai–ter!' The arrival of the body for interment (in an empty black box with the lid tumbling open), was the signal for a general joy which was much enhanced by the discovery, among the bearers, of an individual obnoxious to identification. The joy attended Mr Wopsle through his struggle with Laertes on the brink of the orchestra and the grave, and slackened no more until he had tumbled the king off the kitchen-table, and had died by inches from the ankles upward.

We had made some pale efforts in the beginning to applaud Mr Wopsle; but they were too hopeless to be persisted in. Therefore we had sat, feeling keenly for him, but laughing, nevertheless, from ear to ear. I laughed in spite of myself all the time, the whole thing was so droll; and yet I had a latent impression that there was something decidedly fine in Mr Wopsle's elocution – not for old associations' sake, I am afraid, but because it was very slow, very dreary, very uphill and downhill, and very unlike any way in which any man in any natural circumstances of life or death ever expressed himself about anything. When the tragedy was over, and he had been called for and hooted, I said to Herbert, 'Let us go at once, or perhaps we shall meet him.'

We made all the haste we could downstairs, but we were not quick enough either. Standing at the door was a Jewish man with an unnatural heavy smear of eyebrow, who caught my eyes as we advanced, and said, when we came up with him: 'Mr Pip and friend?'

Identity of Mr Pip and friend confessed.

'Mr Waldengarver,' said the man, 'would be glad to have the honour.'

'Waldengarver?' I repeated – when Herbert murmured in my ear, 'Probably Wopsle.'

'Oh!' said I. 'Yes. Shall we follow you?'

'A few steps, please.' When we were in a side alley, he turned and asked, 'How do you think he looked? – *I* dressed him.'

I don't know what he had looked like, except a funeral; with the addition of a large Danish sun or star hanging round his neck by a blue ribbon, that had given him the appearance of being insured in some extraordinary Fire Office. But I said he had looked very nice.

'When he come to the grave,' said our conductor, 'he showed his cloak beautiful. But, judging from the wing, it looked to me that when he see the ghost in the queen's apartment, he might have made more of his stockings.'

I modestly assented, and we all fell through a little dirty swing door, into a sort of hot packing-case immediately behind it. Here Mr Wopsle was divesting himself of his Danish garments, and here there was just room for us to look at him over one another's shoulders, by keeping the packing-case door, or lid, wide open.

'Gentlemen,' said Mr Wopsle, 'I am proud to see you. I hope, Mr Pip, you will excuse my sending round. I had the happiness to know you in former times, and the drama has ever had a claim which has ever been acknowledged, on the noble and the affluent.'

Meanwhile, Mr Waldengarver, in a frightful perspiration, was trying to get himself out of his princely sables.

'Skin the stockings off, Mr Waldengarver,' said the owner of that property, 'or you'll bust 'em. Bust 'em, and you'll bust five-and-thirty shillings. Shakespeare never was complimented with a finer pair. Keep quiet in your chair now, and leave 'em to me.'

With that, he went upon his knees, and began to flay his victim; who, on the first stocking coming off, would certainly have fallen over backward with his chair, but for there being no room to fall anyhow.

I had been afraid until then to say a word about the play. But then, Mr Waldengarver looked up at us complacently, and said: 'Gentlemen, how did it seem to you to go, in front?'

Herbert said from behind (at the same time poking me), 'capitally.' So I said 'capitally.'

'How did you like my reading of the character, gentlemen?' said Mr Waldengarver, almost, if not quite, with patronage.

Herbert said from behind (again poking me), 'massive and concrete.' So I said boldly, as if I had originated it, and must beg to insist upon it, 'massive and concrete.'

'I am glad to have your approbation, gentlemen,' said Mr Waldengarver, with an air of dignity, in spite of his being ground against the wall at the time, and holding on by the seat of the chair.

'But I'll tell you one thing, Mr Waldengarver,' said the man who was on his knees, 'in which you're out in your reading. Now mind! I don't care who says contrary; I tell you so. You're out in your reading of Hamlet when you get your legs in profile. The last Hamlet as I dressed, made the same mistakes in his reading at rehearsal, till I got him to put a large red wafer on each of his shins, and then at that rehearsal (which was the last) I went in front, sir, to the back of the pit, and whenever his reading brought him into profile, I called out, 'I don't see no wafers!' And at night his reading was lovely.'

Mr Waldengarver smiled at me, as much as to say 'a faithful dependent – I overlook his folly;' and then said aloud, 'My view is a little too classic and thoughtful for them here; but they will improve, they will improve.'

Herbert and I said together, Oh, no doubt they would improve.

'Did you observe, gentlemen,' said Mr Waldengarver, 'that there was a man in the gallery who endeavoured to cast derision on the service – I mean, the representation?'

We basely replied that we rather thought we had noticed such a man. I added, 'He was drunk, no doubt.'

'Oh dear no, sir,' said Mr Wopsle, 'not drunk. His employer would see to that, sir. His employer would not allow him to be drunk.'

'You know his employer?' said I.

Mr Wopsle shut his eyes, and opened them again; performing both ceremonies very slowly. 'You must have observed, gentlemen,' said he, 'an ignorant and a blatant ass, with a rasping throat and a countenance expressive of low malignity, who went through – I will not say sustained – the role (if I may use a French expression) of Claudius King of Denmark. That is his employer, gentlemen. Such is the profession!'

The flaying of Hamlet

Without distinctly knowing whether I should have been more sorry for Mr Wopsle if he had been in despair, I was so sorry for him as it was, that I took the opportunity of his turning round to have his braces put on – which jostled us out at the doorway – to ask Herbert what he thought of having him home to supper? Herbert said he thought it would be kind to do so; therefore I invited him, and he went to Barnard's with us, wrapped up to the eyes, and we did our best for him, and he sat until two o'clock in the morning, reviewing his success and developing his plans. I forget in detail what they were, but I have a general recollection that he was to begin with reviving the drama, and to end with crushing it; inasmuch as his decease would leave it utterly bereft and without a chance or hope.

Miserably I went to bed after all, and miserably thought of Estella, and miserably dreamed that my expectations were all cancelled, and that I had to give my hand in marriage to Herbert's Clara, or play Hamlet to Miss Havisham's Ghost, before twenty thousand people, without knowing twenty words of it.

Chapter 32

One day when I was busy with my books and Mr Pocket, I received a note by the post, the mere outside of which threw me into a great flutter; for, though I had never seen the handwriting in which it was addressed, I divined whose hand it was. It had no set beginning, as Dear Mr Pip, or Dear Pip, or Dear Sir, or Dear Anything, but ran thus:

> I am to come to London the day after tomorrow by the midday coach. I believe it was settled you should meet me? At all events Miss Havisham has that impression, and I write in obedience to it. She sends you her regard.
>
> Yours, Estella.

If there had been time, I should probably have ordered several suits of clothes for this occasion; but as there was not, I was fain to be content with those I had. My appetite vanished instantly, and I knew no peace or rest until the day arrived. Not that its arrival brought me either; for, then I was worse than ever, and began haunting the coach-office in Wood Street, Cheapside, before the coach had left the Blue Boar in our town. For all that I knew this perfectly well, I still felt as if it were not safe to let the coach-office be out of my sight longer than five minutes at a time; and in this condition of unreason I had performed the first half-hour of a watch of four or five hours, when Wemmick ran against me.

'Halloa, Mr Pip,' said he, 'how do you do? I should hardly have thought this was *your* beat.'

I explained that I was waiting to meet somebody who was coming up by coach, and I enquired after the Castle and the Aged.

'Both flourishing, thankye,' said Wemmick, 'and particularly the Aged. He's in wonderful feather. He'll be eighty-two next birthday. I have a notion of firing eighty-two times, if the neighbourhood shouldn't complain, and that cannon of mine should prove equal to the pressure. However, this is not London talk. Where do you think I am going to?'

'To the office,' said I, for he was tending in that direction.

'Next thing to it,' returned Wemmick, 'I am going to Newgate. We are in a banker's-parcel case just at present, and I have been down the road taking a squint at the scene of action, and thereupon must have a word or two with our client.'

'Did your client commit the robbery?' I asked.

'Bless your soul and body, no,' answered Wemmick, very drily. 'But he is accused of it. So might you or I be. Either of us might be accused of it, you know.'

'Only neither of us is,' I remarked.

'Yah!' said Wemmick, touching me on the breast with his forefinger; 'you're a deep one, Mr Pip! Would you like to have a look at Newgate? Have you time to spare?'

I had so much time to spare that the proposal came as a relief, notwithstanding its irreconcilability with my latent desire to keep my eye on the coach-office. Muttering that I would make the enquiry whether I had time to walk with him, I went into the office, and ascertained from the clerk with the nicest precision and much to the trying of his temper, the earliest moment at which the coach could be expected – which I knew beforehand, quite as well as he. I then rejoined Mr Wemmick, and affecting to consult my watch and to be surprised by the information I had received, accepted his offer.

We were at Newgate in a few minutes, and we passed through the lodge where some fetters were hanging up on the bare walls among the prison rules, into the interior of the jail. At that time, jails were much neglected, and the period of exaggerated reaction consequent on all public wrongdoing – and which is always its heaviest and longest punishment – was still far off. So, felons were not lodged and fed better than soldiers (to say nothing of paupers), and seldom set fire to their prisons with the excusable object of improving the flavour of their soup. It was visiting time when Wemmick took me in; and a potman was going his rounds with beer; and the prisoners, behind bars in yards, were buying beer, and talking to friends; and a frouzy, ugly, disorderly, depressing scene it was.

It struck me that Wemmick walked among the prisoners, much as a gardener might walk among his plants. This was first put into my head by his seeing a shoot that had come up in the night, and saying, 'What, Captain Tom? Are *you* there? Ah, indeed?' and also, 'Is that Black Bill behind the cistern? Why I didn't look for you these two months; how do you find yourself?' Equally in his stopping at the bars and attending to anxious whisperers – always singly – Wemmick, with his post office in an immovable state, looked at them while in conference, as if he were taking particular notice of the advance they had made, since last observed, towards coming out in full blow at their trial.

He was highly popular, and I found that he took the familiar department of Mr Jaggers's business: though something of the state of Mr Jaggers hung about him too, forbidding approach beyond certain limits. His personal recognition of each successive client was comprised in a nod, and in his settling his hat a little easier on his head with both hands, and then tightening

the post office, and putting his hands in his pockets. In one or two instances, there was a difficulty respecting the raising of fees, and then Mr Wemmick, backing as far as possible from the insufficient money produced, said, 'It's no use, my boy. I am only a subordinate. I can't take it. Don't go on in that way with a subordinate. If you are unable to make up your quantum, my boy, you had better address yourself to a principal; there are plenty of principals in the profession, you know, and what is not worth the while of one, may be worth the while of another; that's my recommendation to you, speaking as a subordinate. Don't try on useless measures. Why should you? Now who's next?'

Thus, we walked through Wemmick's greenhouse, until he turned to me and said, 'Notice the man I shall shake hands with.' I should have done so, without the preparation, as he had shaken hands with no one yet.

Almost as soon as he had spoken, a portly upright man (whom I can see now, as I write) in a well-worn olive-coloured frock-coat, with a peculiar pallor overspreading the red in his complexion, and eyes that went wandering about when he tried to fix them, came up to a corner of the bars, and put his hand to his hat – which had a greasy and fatty surface like cold broth – with a half-serious and half-jocose military salute.

'Colonel, to you!' said Wemmick; 'how are you, colonel?'

'All right, Mr Wemmick.'

'Everything was done that could be done, but the evidence was too strong for us, colonel.'

'Yes, it was too strong, sir – but *I* don't care.'

'No, no,' said Wemmick, coolly, '*you* don't care.' Then, turning to me, 'Served His Majesty, this man. Was a soldier in the line and bought his discharge.'

I said, 'Indeed?' and the man's eyes looked at me, and then looked over my head, and then looked all round me, and then he drew his hand across his lips and laughed.

'I think I shall be out of this on Monday, sir,' he said to Wemmick.

'Perhaps,' returned my friend, 'but there's no knowing.'

'I am glad to have the chance of bidding you goodbye, Mr Wemmick,' said the man, stretching out his hand between two bars.

'Thankye,' said Wemmick, shaking hands with him. 'Same to you, colonel.'

'If what I had upon me when taken, had been real, Mr Wemmick,' said the man, unwilling to let his hand go, 'I should have asked the favour of your wearing another ring – in acknowledgment of your attentions.'

'I'll accept the will for the deed,' said Wemmick. 'By the by; you were quite a pigeon-fancier.' The man looked up at the sky. 'I am told you had a remarkable breed of tumblers. *Could* you commission any friend of yours to bring me a pair, if you've no further use for 'em?'

'It shall be done, sir.'

'All right,' said Wemmick, 'they shall be taken care of. Goodafternoon, colonel. Goodbye!' They shook hands again, and as we walked away Wemmick said to me, 'A coiner, a very good workman. The recorder's report is made today, and he is sure to be executed on Monday. Still you see, as far as it goes, a pair of pigeons are portable property, all the same.' With that he looked back, and nodded at his dead plant, and then cast his eyes about him in walking out of the yard, as if he were considering what other pot would go best in its place.

As we came out of the prison through the lodge, I found that the great importance of my guardian was appreciated by the turnkeys, no less than by those whom they held in charge. 'Well, Mr Wemmick,' said the turnkey, who kept us between the two studded and spiked lodge gates, and who carefully locked one before he unlocked the other, 'what's Mr Jaggers going to do with that Waterside murder? Is he going to make it manslaughter, or what is he going to make of it?'

'Why don't you ask him?' returned Wemmick.

'Oh, yes, I dare say!' said the turnkey.

'Now, that's the way with them here, Mr Pip,' remarked Wemmick, turning to me with his post office elongated. 'They don't mind what they ask of me, the subordinate; but you'll never catch 'em asking any questions of my principal.'

'Is this young gentleman one of the 'prentices or articled ones of your office?' asked the turnkey, with a grin at Mr Wemmick's humour.

'There he goes again, you see!' cried Wemmick, 'I told you so! Asks another question of the subordinate before the first is dry! Well, supposing Mr Pip is one of them?'

'Why then,' said the turnkey, grinning again, 'he knows what Mr Jaggers is.'

'Yah!' cried Wemmick, suddenly hitting out at the turnkey in a facetious way, 'you're as dumb as one of your own keys when you have to do with my principal, you know you are. Let us out, you old fox, or I'll get him to bring an action against you for false imprisonment.'

The turnkey laughed, and gave us good-day, and stood laughing at us over the spikes of the wicket when we descended the steps into the street.

'Mind you, Mr Pip,' said Wemmick, gravely in my ear, as he took my arm to be more confidential; 'I don't know that Mr Jaggers does a better thing than the way in which he keeps himself so high. He's always so high. His constant height is of a piece with his immense abilities. That colonel durst no more take leave of *him*, than that turnkey durst ask him his intentions respecting a case. Then, between his height and them, he slips in his subordinate – don't you see? – and so he has 'em, soul and body.'

I was very much impressed, and not for the first time, by my guardian's subtlety. To confess the truth, I very heartily wished, and not for the first time, that I had had some other guardian of minor abilities.

Mr Wemmick and I parted at the office in Little Britain, where suppliants for Mr Jaggers's notice were lingering about as usual, and I returned to my watch in the street of the coach-office, with some three hours on hand. I consumed the whole time in thinking how strange it was that I should be encompassed by all this taint of prison and crime; that, in my childhood out on our lonely marshes on a winter evening I should have first encountered it; that, it should have reappeared on two occasions, starting out like a stain that was faded but not gone; that, it should in this new way pervade my fortune and advancement. While my mind was thus engaged, I thought of the beautiful young Estella, proud and refined, coming towards me, and I thought with absolute abhorrence of the contrast between the jail and her. I wished that Wemmick had not met me, or that I had not yielded to him and gone with him, so that, of all days in the year on this day, I might not have had Newgate in my breath and on my clothes. I beat the prison dust off my feet as I sauntered to and fro, and I shook it out of my dress, and I exhaled its air from my lungs. So contaminated did I feel, remembering who was coming, that the coach came quickly after all, and I was not yet free from the soiling consciousness of Mr Wemmick's conservatory, when I saw her face at the coach window and her hand waving to me.

What *was* the nameless shadow which again in that one instant had passed?

Chapter 33

In her furred travelling-dress, Estella seemed more delicately beautiful than she had ever seemed yet, even in my eyes. Her manner was more winning than she had cared to let it be to me before, and I thought I saw Miss Havisham's influence in the change.

We stood in the Inn Yard while she pointed out her luggage to me, and when it was all collected I remembered – having forgotten everything but herself in the meanwhile – that I knew nothing of her destination.

'I am going to Richmond,' she told me. 'Our lesson is, that there are two Richmonds, one in Surrey and one in Yorkshire, and that mine is the Surrey Richmond. The distance is ten miles. I am to have a carriage, and you are to take me. This is my purse, and you are to pay my charges out of it. Oh, you must take the purse! We have no choice, you and I, but to obey our instructions. We are not free to follow our own devices, you and I.'

As she looked at me in giving me the purse, I hoped there was an inner meaning in her words. She said them slightingly, but not with displeasure.

'A carriage will have to be sent for, Estella. Will you rest here a little?'

'Yes, I am to rest here a little, and I am to drink some tea, and you are to take care of me the while.'

She drew her arm through mine, as if it must be done, and I requested a waiter who had been staring at the coach like a man who had never seen such a thing in his life, to show us a private sitting-room. Upon that, he pulled out a napkin, as if it were a magic clue without which he couldn't find the way upstairs, and led us to the black hole of the establishment: fitted up with a diminishing mirror (quite a superfluous article considering the hole's proportions), an anchovy sauce-cruet, and somebody's pattens. On my objecting to this retreat, he took us into another room with a dinner-table for thirty, and in the grate a scorched leaf of a copybook under a bushel of coal-dust.

Having looked at this extinct conflagration and shaken his head, he took my order: which, proving to be merely 'Some tea for the lady,' sent him out of the room in a very low state of mind.

I was, and I am, sensible that the air of this chamber, in its strong combination of stable with soup-stock, might have led one to infer that the coaching department was not doing well, and that the enterprising proprietor was boiling down the horses for the refreshment department. Yet the room was all in all to me, Estella being in it. I thought that with her I could have been happy there for life. (I was not at all happy there at the time, observe, and I knew it well.)

'Where are you going to, at Richmond?' I asked Estella.

'I am going to live,' said she, 'at a great expense, with a lady there, who has the power – or says she has – of taking me about, and introducing me, and showing people to me and showing me to people.'

'I suppose you will be glad of variety and admiration?'

'Yes, I suppose so.'

She answered so carelessly, that I said, 'You speak of yourself as if you were someone else.'

'Where did you learn how I speak of others? Come, come,' said Estella, smiling delightfully, 'you must not expect me to go to school to *you*; I must talk in my own way. How do you thrive with Mr Pocket?'

'I live quite pleasantly there; at least – ' It appeared to me that I was losing a chance.

'At least?' repeated Estella.

'As pleasantly as I could anywhere, away from you.'

'You silly boy,' said Estella, quite composedly, 'how can you talk such nonsense? Your friend Mr Matthew, I believe, is superior to the rest of his family?'

'Very superior indeed. He is nobody's enemy – '

' – Don't add but his own,' interposed Estella, 'for I hate that class of man. But he really is disinterested, and above small jealousy and spite, I have heard?'

'I am sure I have every reason to say so.'

'You have not every reason to say so of the rest of his people,' said Estella, nodding at me with an expression of face that was at once grave and rallying, 'for they beset Miss Havisham with reports and insinuations to your disadvantage. They watch you, misrepresent you, write letters about you (anonymous sometimes), and you are the torment and occupation of their lives. You can scarcely realise to yourself the hatred those people feel for you.'

'They do me no harm, I hope?'

Instead of answering, Estella burst out laughing. This was very singular to me, and I looked at her in considerable perplexity. When she left off – and she had not laughed languidly, but with real enjoyment – I said, in my diffident way with her: 'I hope I may suppose that you would not be amused if they did me any harm?'

'No, no, you may be sure of that,' said Estella. 'You may be certain that I laugh because they fail. Oh, those people with Miss Havisham, and the tortures they undergo!' She laughed again, and even now, when she had told me why, her laughter was very singular to me, for I could not doubt its being genuine,

and yet it seemed too much for the occasion. I thought there must really be something more here than I knew; she saw the thought in my mind and answered it.

'It is not easy for even you,' said Estella, 'to know what satisfaction it gives me to see those people thwarted, or what an enjoyable sense of the ridiculous I have when they are made ridiculous. For you were not brought up in that strange house from a mere baby – I was. You had not your little wits sharpened by their intriguing against you, suppressed and defenceless, under the mask of sympathy and pity and what not, that is soft and soothing – I had. You did not gradually open your round childish eyes wider and wider to the discovery of that impostor of a woman who calculates her stores of peace of mind for when she wakes up in the night – I did.'

It was no laughing matter with Estella now, nor was she summoning these remembrances from any shallow place. I would not have been the cause of that look of hers, for all my expectations in a heap.

'Two things I can tell you,' said Estella. 'First, notwithstanding the proverb, that constant dropping will wear away a stone, you may set your mind at rest that these people never will – never would in a hundred years – impair your ground with Miss Havisham, in any particular, great or small. Second, I am beholden to you as the cause of their being so busy and so mean in vain, and there is my hand upon it.'

As she gave it me playfully – for her darker mood had been but momentary – I held it and put it to my lips. 'You ridiculous boy,' said Estella, 'will you never take warning? Or do you kiss my hand in the same spirit in which I once let you kiss my cheek?'

'What spirit was that?' said I.

'I must think a moment. A spirit of contempt for the fawners and plotters.'

'If I say yes, may I kiss the cheek again?'

'You should have asked before you touched the hand. But, yes, if you like.'

I leaned down, and her calm face was like a statue's. 'Now,' said Estella, gliding away the instant I touched her cheek, 'you are to take care that I have some tea, and you are to take me to Richmond.'

Her reverting to this tone, as if our association were forced upon us and we were mere puppets, gave me pain; but everything in our intercourse did give me pain. Whatever her tone with me happened to be, I could put no trust in it, and build no hope on it; and yet I went on against trust and against hope. Why repeat it a thousand times? So it always was.

I rang for the tea, and the waiter, reappearing with his magic clue, brought in by degrees some fifty adjuncts to that refreshment, but of tea not a glimpse. A tea-board, cups and saucers, plates, knives and forks (including carvers), spoons (various), saltcellars, a meek little muffin confined with the utmost precaution under a strong iron cover, Moses in the bulrushes typified by a soft bit of butter in a quantity of parsley, a pale loaf with a powdered head, two proof impressions of the bars of the kitchen fireplace on triangular bits of bread, and ultimately a fat family urn: which the waiter staggered in with, expressing in his countenance burden and suffering. After a prolonged absence at this stage of the entertainment, he at length came back with a casket of precious appearance containing twigs. These I steeped in hot water, and so from the whole of these appliances extracted one cup of I don't know what, for Estella.

The bill paid, and the waiter remembered, and the ostler not forgotten, and the chambermaid taken into consideration – in a word, the whole house bribed into a state of contempt and animosity, and Estella's purse much lightened – we got into our post-coach and drove away. Turning into Cheapside and rattling up Newgate Street, we were soon under the walls of which I was so ashamed.

'What place is that?' Estella asked me.

I made a foolish pretence of not at first recognising it, and then told her. As she looked at it, and drew in her head again, murmuring 'Wretches!' I would not have confessed to my visit for any consideration.

'Mr Jaggers,' said I, by way of putting it neatly on somebody else, 'has the reputation of being more in the secrets of that dismal place than any man in London.'

'He is more in the secrets of every place, I think,' said Estella, in a low voice.

'You have been accustomed to see him often, I suppose?'

'I have been accustomed to see him at uncertain intervals, ever since I can remember. But I know him no better now, than I did before I could speak plainly. What is your own experience of him? Do you advance with him?'

'Once habituated to his distrustful manner,' said I, 'I have done very well.'

'Are you intimate?'

'I have dined with him at his private house.'

'I fancy,' said Estella, shrinking, 'that must be a curious place.'

'It is a curious place.'

I should have been chary of discussing my guardian too freely even with her; but I should have gone on with the subject so far as to describe the dinner in Gerrard Street, if we had not then come into a sudden glare of gas. It seemed, while it lasted, to be all alight and alive with that inexplicable feeling I had had before; and when we were out of it, I was as much dazed for a few moments as if I had been in lightning.

So, we fell into other talk, and it was principally about the way by which we were travelling, and about what parts of London lay on this side of it, and what on that. The great city was almost new to her, she told me, for she had never left Miss Havisham's neighbourhood until she had gone to France, and she had merely passed through London then in going and returning. I asked her if my guardian had any charge of her while she remained here? To that she emphatically said, 'God forbid!' and no more.

It was impossible for me to avoid seeing that she cared to attract me; that she made herself winning; and would have won me even if the task had needed pains. Yet this made me none the happier, for, even if she had not taken that tone of our being disposed of by others, I should have felt that she held my heart in her hand because she wilfully chose to do it, and not because

it would have wrung any tenderness in her, to crush it and throw it away.

When we passed through Hammersmith, I showed her where Mr Matthew Pocket lived, and said it was no great way from Richmond, and that I hoped I should see her sometimes.

'Oh yes, you are to see me; you are to come when you think proper; you are to be mentioned to the family; indeed you are already mentioned.'

I enquired was it a large household she was going to be a member of?

'No; there are only two; mother and daughter. The mother is a lady of some station, though not averse to increasing her income.'

'I wonder Miss Havisham could part with you again so soon.'

'It is a part of Miss Havisham's plans for me, Pip,' said Estella, with a sigh, as if she were tired; 'I am to write to her constantly and see her regularly, and report how I go on – I and the jewels – for they are nearly all mine now.'

It was the first time she had ever called me by my name. Of course she did so purposely, and knew that I should treasure it up.

We came to Richmond all too soon, and our destination there was a house by the Green: a staid old house, where hoops and powder and patches, embroidered coats, rolled stockings, ruffles, and swords, had had their court days many a time. Some ancient trees before the house were still cut into fashions as formal and unnatural as the hoops and wigs and stiff skirts; but their own allotted places in the great procession of the dead were not far off, and they would soon drop into them and go the silent way of the rest.

A bell with an old voice – which I dare say in its time had often said to the house, Here is the green farthingale, Here is the diamond-hilted sword, Here are the shoes with red heels and the blue solitaire – sounded gravely in the moonlight, and two cherry-coloured maids came fluttering out to receive Estella. The doorway soon absorbed her boxes, and she gave me her hand and a smile, and said good-night, and was absorbed likewise. And still I stood looking at the house, thinking how happy I should be if I lived there with her, and knowing that I never was happy with her, but always miserable.

I got into the carriage to be taken back to Hammersmith, and I got in with a bad heartache, and I got out with a worse heartache. At our own door I found little Jane Pocket coming home from a little party, escorted by her little lover; and I envied her little lover, in spite of his being subject to Flopson.

Mr Pocket was out lecturing; for he was a most delightful lecturer on domestic economy, and his treatises on the management of children and servants were considered the very best textbooks on those themes. But Mrs Pocket was at home, and was in a little difficulty, on account of the baby's having been accommodated with a needle-case to keep him quiet during the unaccountable absence (with a relative in the Foot Guards) of Millers. And more needles were missing than it could be regarded as quite wholesome for a patient of such tender years either to apply externally or to take as a tonic.

Mr Pocket being justly celebrated for giving most excellent

practical advice, and for having a clear and sound perception of things and a highly judicious mind, I had some notion in my heartache of begging him to accept my confidence. But happening to look up at Mrs Pocket as she sat reading her book of dignities after prescribing bed as a sovereign remedy for baby, I thought – well – No, I wouldn't.

Chapter 34

As I had grown accustomed to my expectations, I had insensibly begun to notice their effect upon myself and those around me. Their influence on my own character I disguised from my recognition as much as possible, but I knew very well that it was not all good. I lived in a state of chronic uneasiness respecting my behaviour to Joe. My conscience was not by any means comfortable about Biddy. When I woke up in the night – like Camilla – I used to think, with a weariness in my spirits, that I should have been happier and better if I had never seen Miss Havisham's face, and had risen to manhood content to be partners with Joe in the honest old forge. Many a time of an evening, when I sat alone looking at the fire, I thought, after all, there was no fire like the forge fire and the kitchen fire at home.

Yet Estella was so inseparable from all my restlessness and disquiet of mind, that I really fell into confusion as to the limits of my own part in its production. That is to say, supposing I had had no expectations, and yet had had Estella to think of, I could not make out to my satisfaction that I should have done much better. Now, concerning the influence of my position on others, I was in no such difficulty, and so I perceived – though dimly enough perhaps – that it was not beneficial to anybody, and, above all, that it was not beneficial to Herbert. My lavish habits led his easy nature into expenses that he could not afford, corrupted the simplicity of his life, and disturbed his peace with anxieties and regrets. I was not at all remorseful for having unwittingly set those other branches of the Pocket family to the poor arts they practised: because such littlenesses were their natural bent, and would have been evoked by anybody else, if I had left them slumbering. But Herbert's was a very different case, and it often caused me a twinge to think that I had done him evil service in crowding his sparsely-furnished chambers with incongruous upholstery work, and placing the canary-breasted Avenger at his disposal.

So now, as an infallible way of making little ease great ease, I began to contract a quantity of debt. I could hardly begin but Herbert must begin too, so he soon followed. At Startop's suggestion, we put ourselves down for election into a club called the Finches of the Grove: the object of which institution I have never divined, if it were not that the members should dine expensively once a fortnight, to quarrel among themselves as much as possible after dinner, and to cause six waiters to get drunk on the stairs. I know that these gratifying social ends were so invariably accomplished, that Herbert and I understood nothing else to be referred to in the first standing toast of the society: which ran, 'Gentlemen, may the present promotion of good feeling ever reign predominant among the Finches of the Grove.'

The Finches spent their money foolishly (the Hotel we dined at was in Covent Garden), and the first Finch I saw when I had the honour of joining the Grove was Bentley Drummle: at that time floundering about town in a cab of his own, and doing a great deal of damage to the posts at the street corners. Occasionally, he shot himself out of his equipage head-foremost over the apron; and I saw him on one occasion deliver himself at the door of the Grove in this unintentional way – like coals. But here I anticipate a little, for I was not a Finch, and could not be, according to the sacred laws of the society, until I came of age.

In my confidence in my own resources, I would willingly have taken Herbert's expenses on myself; but Herbert was proud, and I could make no such proposal to him. So, he got into difficulties in every direction, and continued to look about him. When we gradually fell into keeping late hours and late company, I noticed that he looked about him with a desponding eye at breakfast-time; that he began to look about him more hopefully about midday; that he drooped when he came into dinner; that he seemed to descry capital in the distance, rather clearly, after dinner; that he all but realised capital towards midnight; and that about two o'clock in the morning, he became so deeply despondent again as to talk of buying a rifle and going to America, with a general purpose of compelling buffaloes to make his fortune.

I was usually at Hammersmith about half the week, and when I was at Hammersmith I haunted Richmond: whereof separately by and by. Herbert would often come to Hammersmith when I was there, and I think at those seasons his father would occasionally have some passing perception that the opening he was looking for had not appeared yet. But in the general tumbling up of the family, his tumbling out in life somewhere was a thing to transact itself somehow. In the meantime Mr Pocket grew greyer, and tried oftener to lift himself out of his perplexities by the hair. While Mrs Pocket tripped up the family with her footstool, read her book of dignities, lost her pocket-handkerchief, told us about her grandpapa, and taught the young idea how to shoot, by shooting it into bed whenever it attracted her notice.

As I am now generalising a period of my life with the object of clearing my way before me, I can scarcely do so better than by at once completing the description of our usual manners and customs at Barnard's Inn.

We spent as much money as we could, and got as little for it as people could make up their minds to give us. We were always more or less miserable, and most of our acquaintance were in the same condition. There was a gay fiction among us that we were constantly enjoying ourselves, and a skeleton truth that we never did. To the best of my belief, our case was in the last aspect a rather common one.

Every morning, with an air ever new, Herbert went into the City to look about him. I often paid him a visit in the dark back-room in which he consorted with an ink-jar, a hat-peg, a coal-box, a string-box, an almanac, a desk and stool, and a ruler; and I do not remember that I ever saw him do anything else but look about him. If we all did what we undertake to do, as faithfully as Herbert did, we might live in a republic of the virtues. He had nothing else to do, poor fellow, except at a certain hour of every afternoon to 'go to Lloyd's' – in observance of a ceremony of seeing his principal, I think. He never did anything else in connection with Lloyd's that I could find out, except come back again. When he felt his case unusually serious, and that he positively must find an opening, he would go on 'Change at a busy time, and walk in and out, in a kind of gloomy country dance figure, among the assembled magnates. 'For,' says Herbert to me, coming home to dinner on one of those special occasions, 'I find the truth to be, Handel, that an opening won't come to one, but one must go to it – so I have been.'

If we had been less attached to one another, I think we must have hated one another regularly every morning. I detested the chambers beyond expression at that period of repentance, and could not endure the sight of the Avenger's livery: which had a more expensive and a less remunerative appearance then, than at any other time in the four-and-twenty hours. As we got more and more into debt, breakfast became a hollower and hollower form, and being on one occasion at breakfast-time threatened (by letter) with legal proceedings, 'not unwholly unconnected', as my local paper might put it, 'with jewellery', I went so far as to seize the Avenger by his blue collar and shake him off his feet – so that he was actually in the air, like a booted Cupid – for presuming to suppose that we wanted a roll.

At certain times – meaning at uncertain times, for they depended on our humour – I would say to Herbert, as if it were a remarkable discovery: 'My dear Herbert, we are getting on badly.'

'My dear Handel,' Herbert would say to me, in all sincerity, 'if you will believe me, those very words were on my lips, by a strange coincidence.'

'Then, Herbert,' I would respond, 'let us look into our affairs.'

We always derived profound satisfaction from making an appointment for this purpose. I always thought this was business, this was the way to confront the thing, this was the way to take the foe by the throat. And I know Herbert thought so too.

We ordered something rather special for dinner, with a bottle of something similarly out of the common way, in order that our minds might be fortified for the occasion, and we might come well up to the mark. Dinner over, we produced a bundle of pens, a copious supply of ink, and a goodly show of writing and blotting paper. For there was something very comfortable in having plenty of stationery.

I would then take a sheet of paper, and write across the top of it, in a neat hand, the heading, 'Memorandum of Pip's debts;' with Barnard's Inn and the date very carefully added. Herbert would also take a sheet of paper, and write across it with similar formalities, 'Memorandum of Herbert's debts.'

Each of us would then refer to a confused heap of papers at his side, which had been thrown into drawers, worn into holes in pockets, half-burnt in lighting candles, stuck for weeks into the looking-glass, and otherwise damaged. The sound of our pens going refreshed us exceedingly, insomuch that I sometimes found it difficult to distinguish between this edifying

business proceeding and actually paying the money. In point of meritorious character, the two things seemed about equal.

When we had written a little while, I would ask Herbert how he got on? Herbert would probably have been scratching his head in a most rueful manner at the sight of his accumulating figures.

'They are mounting up, Handel,' Herbert would say; 'upon my life they are mounting up.'

'Be firm, Herbert,' I would retort, plying my own pen with great assiduity. 'Look the thing in the face. Look into your affairs. Stare them out of countenance.'

'So I would, Handel, only they are staring *me* out of countenance.'

However, my determined manner would have its effect, and Herbert would fall to work again. After a time he would give up once more, on the plea that he had not got Cobbs's bill, or Lobbs's, or Nobbs's, as the case might be.

'Then, Herbert, estimate; estimate it in round numbers, and put it down.'

'What a fellow of resource you are!' my friend would reply, with admiration. 'Really your business powers are very remarkable.'

I thought so too. I established with myself, on these occasions, the reputation of a first-rate man of business – prompt, decisive, energetic, clear, cool headed. When I had got all my responsibilities down upon my list, I compared each with the bill, and ticked it off. My self-approval when I ticked an entry was quite a luxurious sensation. When I had no more ticks to make, I folded all my bills up uniformly, docketed each on the back, and tied the whole into a symmetrical bundle. Then I did the same for Herbert (who modestly said he had not my administrative genius), and felt that I had brought his affairs into a focus for him.

My business habits had one other bright feature, which I called 'leaving a margin'. For example: supposing Herbert's debts to be one hundred and sixty-four pounds four-and-two-pence, I would say, 'Leave a margin, and put them down at two hundred.' Or, supposing my own to be four times as much, I would leave a margin, and put them down at seven hundred. I had the highest opinion of the wisdom of this same margin, but I am bound to acknowledge that, on looking back, I deem it to have been an expensive device. For we always ran into new debt immediately, to the full extent of the margin, and sometimes, in the sense of freedom and solvency it imparted, got pretty far on into another margin.

But there was a calm, a rest, a virtuous hush, consequent on these examinations of our affairs, that gave me, for the time, an admirable opinion of myself. Soothed by my exertions, my method, and Herbert's compliments, I would sit with his symmetrical bundle and my own on the table before me among the stationery, and feel like a bank of some sort, rather than a private individual.

We shut our outer door on these solemn occasions in order that we might not be interrupted. I had fallen into my serene state one evening, when we heard a letter dropped through the slit in the said door, and fall on the ground. 'It's for you,

Handel,' said Herbert, going out and coming back with it, 'and I hope there is nothing the matter.' This was in allusion to its heavy black seal and border.

The letter was signed Trabb & Co., and its contents were simply, that I was an honoured sir, and that they begged to inform me that Mrs J. Gargery had departed this life on Monday last at twenty minutes past six in the evening, and that my attendance was requested at the interment on Monday next at three o'clock in the afternoon.

Chapter 35

It was the first time that a grave had opened in my road of life, and the gap it made in the smooth ground was wonderful. The figure of my sister in her chair by the kitchen fire haunted me night and day. That the place could possibly be, without her, was something my mind seemed unable to compass; and whereas she had seldom or never been in my thoughts of late, I had now the strangest idea that she was coming towards me in the street, or that she would presently knock at the door. In my rooms too, with which she had never been at all associated, there was at once the blankness of death and a perpetual suggestion of the sound of her voice or the turn of her face or figure, as if she were still alive and had been often there.

Whatever my fortunes might have been, I could scarcely have recalled my sister with much tenderness. But I suppose there is a shock of regret which may exist without much tenderness. Under its influence (and perhaps to make up for the want of the softer feeling) I was seized with a violent indignation against the assailant from whom she had suffered so much; and I felt that on sufficient proof I could have revengefully pursued Orlick, or anyone else, to the last extremity.

Having written to Joe, to offer him consolation, and to assure him that I would come to the funeral, I passed the intermediate days in the curious state of mind I have glanced at. I went down early in the morning, and alighted at the Blue Boar, in good time to walk over to the forge.

It was fine summer weather again, and, as I walked along, the times when I was a little helpless creature, and my sister did not spare me, vividly returned. But they returned with a gentle tone upon them, that softened even the edge of Tickler. For now, the very breath of the beans and clover whispered to my heart that the day must come when it would be well for my memory that others walking in the sunshine should be softened as they thought of me.

At last I came within sight of the house, and saw that Trabb and Co. had put in a funereal execution and taken possession. Two dismally absurd persons, each ostentatiously exhibiting a crutch done up in a black bandage – as if that instrument could possibly communicate any comfort to anybody – were posted at the front door; and in one of them I recognised a postboy discharged from the Boar for turning a young couple into a saw pit on their bridal morning, in consequence of intoxication rendering it necessary for him to ride his horse clasped round the neck with both arms. All the children of the village, and

most of the women, were admiring these sable warders and the closed windows of the house and forge; and as I came up, one of the two warders (the postboy) knocked at the door – implying that I was far too much exhausted by grief, to have strength remaining to knock for myself.

Another sable warder (a carpenter, who had once eaten two geese for a wager) opened the door, and showed me into the best parlour. Here, Mr Trabb had taken unto himself the best table, and had got all the leaves up, and was holding a kind of black bazaar, with the aid of a quantity of black pins. At the moment of my arrival, he had just finished putting somebody's hat into black long-clothes, like an African baby; so he held out his hand for mine. But I, misled by the action, and confused by the occasion, shook hands with him with every testimony of warm affection.

Poor dear Joe, entangled in a little black cloak tied in a large bow under his chin, was seated apart at the upper end of the room; where, as chief mourner, he had evidently been stationed by Trabb. When I bent down and said to him, 'Dear Joe, how are you?' he said, 'Pip, old chap, you know'd her when she were a fine figure of a – ' and clasped my hand and said no more.

Biddy, looking very neat and modest in her black dress, went quietly here and there, and was very helpful. When I had spoken to Biddy, as I thought it not a time for talking, I went and sat down near Joe, and there began to wonder in what part of the house it – she – my sister – was. The air of the parlour being faint with the smell of sweet cake, I looked about for the table of refreshments; it was scarcely visible until one had got accustomed to the gloom, but there was a cut-up plum-cake upon it, and there were cut-up oranges, and sandwiches, and biscuits, and two decanters that I knew very well as ornaments, but had never seen used in all my life: one full of port, and one of sherry. Standing at this table, I became conscious of the servile Pumblechook in a black cloak and several yards of hatband, who was alternately stuffing himself, and making obsequious movements to catch my attention. The moment he succeeded, he came over to me (breathing sherry and crumbs), and said in a subdued voice, 'May I, dear sir?' and did. I then descried Mr and Mrs Hubble; the last-named in a decent speechless paroxysm in a corner. We were all going to 'follow', and were all in course of being tied up separately (by Trabb) into ridiculous bundles.

'Which I meantersay, Pip,' Joe whispered me, as we were being what Mr Trabb called 'formed' in the parlour, two and two – arid it was dreadfully like a preparation for some grim kind of dance; 'which I meantersay, sir, as I would in preference have carried her to the church myself, along with three or four friendly ones wot come to it with willing harts and arms, but it were considered wot the neighbours would look down on such and would be of opinions as it were wanting in respect.'

'Pocket-handkerchiefs out, all!' cried Mr Trabb at this point, in a depressed businesslike voice – 'Pocket-handkerchiefs out! We are ready!'

So, we all put our pocket-handkerchiefs to our faces, as if our noses were bleeding, and filed out two and two; Joe and I; Biddy and Pumblechook; Mr and Mrs Hubble. The remains of my poor sister had been brought round by the kitchen door, and, it being a point of undertaking ceremony that the six bearers must be stifled and blinded under a horrible black velvet housing with a white border, the whole looked like a blind monster with twelve human legs, shuffling and blundering along under the guidance of two keepers – the postboy and his comrade.

The neighbourhood, however, highly approved of these arrangements, and we were much admired as we went through the village; the more youthful and vigorous part of the community making dashes now and then to cut us off, and lying in wait to intercept us at points of vantage. At such times the more exuberant among them called out in an excited manner on our emergence round some corner of expectancy, '*Here* they come!' '*Here* they are!' and we were all but cheered. In this progress I was much annoyed by the abject Pumblechook, who, being behind me, persisted all the way, as a delicate attention, in arranging my streaming hatband, and smoothing my cloak. My thoughts were further distracted by the excessive pride of Mr and Mrs Hubble, who were surpassingly conceited and vainglorious in being members of so distinguished a procession.

And now the range of marshes lay clear before us, with the sails of the ships on the river growing out of it; and we went into the churchyard, close to the graves of my unknown parents, Philip Pirrip, late of this parish, and Also Georgiana, Wife of the Above. And there, my sister was laid quietly in the earth while the larks sang high above it, and the light wind strewed it with beautiful shadows of clouds and trees.

Of the conduct of the worldly-minded Pumblechook while this was doing, I desire to say no more than it was all addressed to me; and that even when those noble passages were read which reminded humanity how it brought nothing into the world and can take nothing out, and how it fleeth like a shadow and never continueth long in one stay, I heard him cough a reservation of the case of a young gentleman who came unexpectedly into a large property. When we got back, he had the hardihood to tell me that he wished my sister could have known I had done her so much honour, and to hint that she would have considered it reasonably purchased at the price of her death. After that, he drank all the rest of the sherry, and Mr Hubble drank the port, and the two talked (which I have since observed to be customary in such cases) as if they were of quite another race from the deceased, and were notoriously immortal. Finally, he went away with Mr and Mrs Hubble – to make an evening of it, I felt sure, and to tell the Jolly Bargemen that he was the founder of my fortunes and my earliest benefactor.

When they were all gone, and when Trabb and his men – but not his boy: I looked for him – had crammed their mummery into bags, and were gone too, the house felt wholesomer. Soon afterwards, Biddy, Joe, and I, had a cold dinner together; but we dined in the best parlour, not in the old kitchen, and Joe was so exceedingly particular what he did with his knife and fork and the saltcellar and what not, that there was great restraint upon us. But after dinner, when I made him take his pipe, and when I had loitered with him about the forge, and when we sat

down together on the great block of stone outside it, we got on better. I noticed that after the funeral Joe changed his clothes so far, as to make a compromise between his Sunday dress and working dress: in which the dear fellow looked natural, and like the man he was.

He was very much pleased by my asking if I might sleep in my own little room, and I was pleased too; for I felt that I had done rather a great thing in making the request. When the shadows of evening were closing in, I took an opportunity of getting into the garden with Biddy for a little talk.

'Biddy,' said I, 'I think you might have written to me about these sad matters.'

'Do you, Mr Pip?' said Biddy. 'I should have written if I had thought that.'

'Don't suppose that I mean to be unkind, Biddy, when I say I consider that you ought to have thought that.'

'Do you, Mr Pip?'

She was so quiet, and had such an orderly, good, and pretty way with her, that I did not like the thought of making her cry again. After looking a little at her downcast eyes as she walked beside me, I gave up that point.

'I suppose it will be difficult for you to remain here now, Biddy, dear?'

'Oh! I can't do so, Mr Pip,' said Biddy, in a tone of regret, but still of quiet conviction. 'I have been speaking to Mrs Hubble, and I am going to her tomorrow. I hope we shall be able to take some care of Mr Gargery, together, until he settles down.'

'How are you going to live, Biddy? If you want any mo –'

'How am I going to live?' repeated Biddy, striking in, with a momentary flush upon her face. 'I'll tell you, Mr Pip. I am going to try to get the place of mistress in the new school nearly finished here. I can be well recommended by all the neighbours, and I hope I can be industrious and patient, and teach myself while I teach others. You know, Mr Pip,' pursued Biddy, with a smile, as she raised her eyes to my face, 'the new schools are not like the old, but I learnt a good deal from you after that time, and have had time since then to improve.'

'I think you would always improve, Biddy, under any circumstances.'

'Ah! Except in my bad side of human nature,' murmured Biddy.

It was not so much a reproach, as an irresistible thinking aloud. Well! I thought I would give up that point too. So, I walked a little further with Biddy, looking silently at her downcast eyes.

'I have not heard the particulars of my sister's death, Biddy.'

'They are very slight, poor thing. She had been in one of her bad states – though they had got better of late, rather than worse – for four days, when she came out of it in the evening, just at teatime, and said quite plainly, "Joe". As she had never said any word for a long while, I ran and fetched in Mr Gargery from the forge. She made signs to me that she wanted him to sit down close to her, and wanted me to put her arms round his neck. So I put them round his neck, and she laid her head down on his shoulder quite content and satisfied. And so she presently said "Joe" again, and once "Pardon", and once "Pip".

And so she never lifted her head up any more, and it was just an hour later when we laid it down on her own bed, because we found she was gone.'

Biddy cried; the darkening garden, and the lane, and the stars that were coming out, were blurred in my own sight.

'Nothing was ever discovered, Biddy?'

'Nothing.'

'Do you know what is become of Orlick?'

'I should think from the colour of his clothes that he is working in the quarries.'

'Of course you have seen him then? – Why are you looking at that dark tree in the lane?'

'I saw him there, on the night she died.'

'That was not the last time either, Biddy?'

'No; I have seen him there since we have been walking here – It is of no use,' said Biddy, laying her hand upon my arm, as I was for running out, 'you know I would not deceive you; he was not there a minute, and he is gone.'

It revived my utmost indignation to find that she was still pursued by this fellow, and I felt inveterate against him. I told her so, and told her that I would spend any money or take any pains to drive him out of that country. By degrees she led me into more temperate talk, and she told me how Joe loved me, and how Joe never complained of anything – she didn't say, of me; she had no need; I knew what she meant – but ever did his duty in his way of life, with a strong hand, a quiet tongue, and a gentle heart.

'Indeed, it would be hard to say too much for him,' said I; 'and, Biddy, we must often speak of these things, for of course I shall be often down here now. I am not going to leave poor Joe alone.'

Biddy said never a single word.

'Biddy, don't you hear me?'

'Yes, Mr Pip.'

'Not to mention your calling me Mr Pip – which appears to me to be in bad taste, Biddy – what do you mean?'

'What do I mean?' asked Biddy, timidly.

'Biddy,' said I, in a virtuously self-asserting manner, 'I must request to know what you mean by this?'

'By this?' said Biddy.

'No, don't echo,' I retorted. 'You used not to echo, Biddy.'

'Used not!' said Biddy. 'O Mr Pip! Used!'

Well! I rather thought I would give up that point too. After another silent turn in the garden, I fell back on the main position.

'Biddy,' said I, 'I made a remark respecting my coming down here often, to see Joe, which you received with a marked silence. Have the goodness, Biddy, to tell me why.'

'Are you quite sure, then, that you *will* come to see him often?' asked Biddy, stopping in the narrow garden walk, and looking at me under the stars, with a clear and honest eye.

'Oh dear me!' said I, as I found myself compelled to give up Biddy in despair. 'This really is a very bad side of human nature! Don't say any more, if you please, Biddy. This shocks me very much.'

For which cogent reason I kept Biddy at a distance during supper, and when I went up to my own old little room, took as stately a leave of her as I could, in my murmuring soul, deem reconcilable with the churchyard and the event of the day. As often as I was restless in the night, and that was every quarter of an hour, I reflected what an unkindness, what an injury, what an injustice, Biddy had done me.

Early in the morning, I was to go. Early in the morning, I was out, and looking in, unseen, at one of the wooden windows of the forge. There I stood, for minutes, looking at Joe, already at work with a glow of health and strength upon his face that made it show as if the bright sun of the life in store for him were shining on it.

'Goodbye, dear Joe! – No, don't wipe it off – for God's sake, give me your blackened hand! – I shall be down soon and often.'

'Never too soon, sir,' said Joe, 'and never too often, Pip!'

Biddy was waiting for me at the kitchen door, with a mug of new milk and a crust of bread. 'Biddy,' said I, when I gave her my hand at parting, 'I am not angry, but I am hurt.'

'No, don't be hurt,' she pleaded quite pathetically; 'let only me be hurt, if I have been ungenerous.'

Once more, the mists were rising as I walked away. If they disclosed to me as I suspect they did, that I should *not* come back, and that Biddy was quite right, all I can say is – they were quite right too.

Chapter 36

Herbert and I went on from bad to worse, in the way of increasing our debts, looking into our affairs, leaving margins, and the like exemplary transactions; and time went on, whether or no, as he has a way of doing; and I came of age – in fulfilment of Herbert's prediction, that I should do so before I knew where I was.

Herbert himself had come of age, eight months before me. As he had nothing else than his majority to come into, the event did not make a profound sensation in Barnard's Inn. But we had looked forward to my one-and-twentieth birthday, with a crowd of speculations and anticipations, for we had both considered that my guardian could hardly help saying something definite on that occasion.

I had taken care to have it well understood in Little Britain when my birthday was. On the day before it, I received an official note from Wemmick, informing me that Mr Jaggers would be glad if I would call upon him at five in the afternoon of the auspicious day. This convinced us that something great was to happen, and threw me into an unusual flutter when I repaired to my guardian's office, a model of punctuality.

In the outer office Wemmick offered me his congratulations, and incidentally rubbed the side of his nose with a folded piece of tissue-paper that I liked the look of. But he said nothing respecting it, and motioned me with a nod into my guardian's room. It was November, and my guardian was standing before his fire leaning his back against the chimney-piece, with his hands under his coat-tails.

'Well, Pip,' said he, 'I must call you Mr Pip today. Congratulations, Mr Pip.'

We shook hands – he was always a remarkably short shaker – and I thanked him.

'Take a chair, Mr Pip,' said my guardian.

As I sat down, and he preserved his attitude and bent his brows at his boots, I felt at a disadvantage, which reminded me of that old time when I had been put upon a tombstone. The two ghastly casts on the shelf were not far from him, and their expression was as if they were making a stupid apoplectic attempt to attend to the conversation.

'Now, my young friend,' my guardian began, as if I were a witness in the box, 'I am going to have a word or two with you.'

'If you please, sir.'

'What do you suppose,' said Mr Jaggers, bending forward to look at the ground, and then throwing his head back to look at the ceiling, 'what do you suppose you are living at the rate of?'

'At the rate of, sir?'

'At,' repeated Mr Jaggers, still looking at the ceiling, 'the – rate – of?' And then looked all round the room, and paused with his pocket-handkerchief in his hand, halfway to his nose.

I had looked into my affairs so often, that I had thoroughly destroyed any slight notion I might ever have had of their bearings. Reluctantly, I confessed myself quite unable to answer the question. This reply seemed agreeable to Mr Jaggers, who said, 'I thought so!' and blew his nose with an air of satisfaction.

'Now, I have asked *you* a question, my friend,' said Mr Jaggers. 'Have you anything to ask *me*?'

'Of course it would be a great relief to me to ask you several questions, sir; but I remember your prohibition.'

'Ask one,' said Mr Jaggers.

'Is my benefactor to be made known to me today?'

'No. Ask another.'

'Is that confidence to be imparted to me soon?'

'Waive that, a moment,' said Mr Jaggers, 'and ask another.'

I looked about me, but there appeared to be now no possible escape from the enquiry, 'Have – I – anything to receive, sir?' On that, Mr Jaggers said, triumphantly, 'I thought we should come to it!' and called to Wemmick to give him that piece of paper. Wemmick appeared, handed it in, and disappeared.

'Now, Mr Pip,' said Mr Jaggers, 'attend if you please. You have been drawing pretty freely here; your name occurs pretty often in Wemmick's cash-book: but you are in debt, of course?'

'I am afraid I must say yes, sir.'

'You know you must say yes; don't you?' said Mr Jaggers.

'Yes, sir.'

'I don't ask you what you owe, because you don't know; and if you did know, you wouldn't tell me; you would say less. Yes, yes, my friend,' cried Mr Jaggers, waving his forefinger to stop me, as I made a show of protesting: 'it's likely enough that you think you wouldn't, but you would. You'll excuse me, but I know better than you. Now, take this piece of paper in your hand. You have got it? Very good. Now, unfold it and tell me what it is.'

'This is a bank-note,' said I, 'for five hundred pounds.'

'That is a bank-note,' repeated Mr Jaggers, 'for five hundred pounds. And a very handsome sum of money too, I think. You consider it so?'

'How could I do otherwise!'

'Ah! But answer the question,' said Mr Jaggers.

'Undoubtedly.'

'You consider it, undoubtedly, a handsome sum of money. Now, that handsome sum of money, Pip, is your own. It is a present to you on this day, in earnest of your expectations. And at the rate of that handsome sum of money per annum, and at no higher rate, you are to live until the donor of the whole appears. That is to say, you will now take your money affairs entirely into your own hands, and you will draw from Wemmick one hundred and twenty-five pounds per quarter, until you are in communication with the fountainhead, and no longer with the mere agent. As I have told you before, I am the mere agent. I execute my instructions, and I am paid for doing so. I think them injudicious, but I am not paid for giving any opinion on their merits.'

I was beginning to express my gratitude to my benefactor for the great liberality with which I was treated, when Mr Jaggers stopped me. 'I am not paid, Pip,' said he, coolly, 'to carry your words to anyone;' and then gathered up his coat-tails, as he had gathered up the subject, and stood frowning at his boots as if he suspected them of designs against him.

After a pause, I hinted: 'There was a question just now, Mr Jaggers, which you desired me to waive for a moment. I hope I am doing nothing wrong in asking it again?'

'What is it?' said he.

I might have known that he would never help me out; but it took me aback to have to shape the question afresh, as if it were quite new. 'Is it likely,' I said, after hesitating, 'that my patron, the fountainhead you have spoken of, Mr Jaggers, will soon – ' there I delicately stopped.

'Will soon what?' asked Mr Jaggers. 'That's no question as it stands, you know.'

'Will soon come to London,' said I, after casting about for a precise form of words, 'or summon me anywhere else?'

'Now here,' replied Mr Jaggers, fixing me for the first time with his dark deep-set eyes, 'we must revert to the evening when we first encountered one another in your village. What did I tell you then, Pip?'

'You told me, Mr Jaggers, that it might be years hence when that person appeared.'

'Just so,' said Mr Jaggers, 'that's my answer.'

As we looked full at one another, I felt my breath come quicker in my strong desire to get something out of him. And as I felt that it came quicker, and as I felt that he saw that it came quicker, I felt that I had less chance than ever of getting anything out of him.

'Do you suppose it will still be years hence, Mr Jaggers?'

Mr Jaggers shook his head – not in negativing the question, but in altogether negativing the notion that he could anyhow be got to answer it – and the two horrible casts of the twitched faces looked, when my eyes strayed up to them, as if they had come to a crisis in their suspended attention, and were going to sneeze.

'Come!' said Mr Jaggers, warming the backs of his legs with the backs of his warmed hands, 'I'll be plain with you, my friend Pip. That's a question I must not be asked. You'll understand that, better, when I tell you it's a question that might compromise *me*. Come! I'll go a little further with you; I'll say something more.'

He bent down so low to frown at his boots, that he was able to rub the calves of his legs in the pause he made.

'When that person discloses,' said Mr Jaggers, straightening himself, 'you and that person will settle your own affairs. When that person discloses, my part in this business will cease and determine. When that person discloses, it will not be necessary for me to know anything about it. And that's all I have got to say.'

We looked at one another until I withdrew my eyes, and looked thoughtfully at the floor. From this last speech I derived the notion that Miss Havisham, for some reason or no reason, had not taken him into her confidence as to her designing me for Estella; that he resented this, and felt a jealousy about it; or that he really did object to that scheme, and would have nothing to do with it. When I raised my eyes again, I found that he had been shrewdly looking at me all the time, and was doing so still.

'If that is all you have to say, sir,' I remarked, 'there can be nothing left for me to say.'

He nodded assent, and pulled out his thief-dreaded watch, and asked me where I was going to dine? I replied at my own chambers, with Herbert. As a necessary sequence, I asked him if he would favour us with his company, and he promptly accepted the invitation. But he insisted on walking home with me, in order that I might make no extra preparation for him, and first he had a letter or two to write, and (of course) had his hands to wash. So I said I would go into the outer office and talk to Wemmick.

The fact was, that when the five hundred pounds had come into my pocket, a thought had come into my head which had been often there before; and it appeared to me that Wemmick was a good person to advise with, concerning such thought.

He had already locked up his safe, and made preparations for going home. He had left his desk, brought out his two greasy office candlesticks and stood them in line with the snuffers on a slab near the door, ready to be extinguished; he had raked his fire low, put his hat and greatcoat ready, and was beating himself all over the chest with his safe-key as an athletic exercise after business.

'Mr Wemmick,' said I, 'I want to ask your opinion. I am very desirous to serve a friend.'

Wemmick tightened his post office and shook his head, as if his opinion were dead against any fatal weakness of that sort.

'This friend,' I pursued, 'is trying to get on in commercial life, but has no money, and finds it difficult and disheartening to make a beginning. Now, I want somehow to help him to a beginning.'

'With money down?' said Wemmick, in a tone drier than any sawdust.

'With *some* money down,' I replied, for an uneasy remembrance shot across me of that symmetrical bundle of papers at home; 'with *some* money down, and perhaps some anticipation of my expectations.'

'Mr Pip,' said Wemmick, 'I should like just to run over with you on my fingers, if you please, the names of the various bridges up as high as Chelsea Reach. Let's see; there's London, one; Southwark, two; Blackfriars, three; Waterloo, four; Westminster, five; Vauxhall, six.' He had checked off each bridge in its turn, with the handle of his safe-key on the palm of his hand. 'There's as many as six, you see, to choose from.'

'I don't understand you,' said I.

'Choose your bridge, Mr Pip,' returned Wemmick, 'and take a walk upon your bridge, and pitch your money into the Thames over the centre arch of your bridge, and you know the end of it. Serve a friend with it, and you may know the end of it too – but it's a less pleasant and profitable end.'

I could have posted a newspaper in his mouth, he made it so wide after saying this.

'This is very discouraging,' said I.

'Meant to be so,' said Wemmick.

'Then is it your opinion,' I enquired, with some little indignation, 'that a man should never – '

' – Invest portable property in a friend?' said Wemmick. 'Certainly he should not. Unless he wants to get rid of the friend – and then it becomes a question how much portable property it may be worth to get rid of him.'

'And that,' said I, 'is your deliberate opinion, Mr Wemmick?'

'That,' he returned, 'is my deliberate opinion in this office.'

'Ah!' said I, pressing him, for I thought I saw him near a loophole here; 'but would that be your opinion at Walworth?'

'Mr Pip,' he replied with gravity, 'Walworth is one place, and this office is another. Much as the Aged is one person, and Mr Jaggers is another. They must not be confounded together. My Walworth sentiments must be taken at Walworth; none but my official sentiments can be taken in this office.'

'Very well,' said I, much relieved, 'then I shall look you up at Walworth, you may depend upon it.'

'Mr Pip,' he returned, 'you will be welcome there, in a private and personal capacity.'

We had held this conversation in a low voice, well knowing my guardian's ears to be the sharpest of the sharp. As he now appeared in his doorway, towelling his hands, Wemmick got on his greatcoat and stood by to snuff out the candles. We all three went into the street together, and from the doorstep Wemmick turned his way, and Mr Jaggers and I turned ours.

I could not help wishing more than once that evening that Mr Jaggers had had an Aged in Gerrard Street, or a Stinger, or a Something, or a Somebody, to unbend his brows a little. It was an uncomfortable consideration on a twenty-first birthday, that coming of age at all seemed hardly worth while in such a guarded and suspicious world as he made of it. He was a thousand times better informed and cleverer than Wemmick, and yet I would a thousand times rather have had Wemmick to dinner. And Mr Jaggers made not me alone intensely melancholy, because, after he was gone, Herbert said of himself, with his eyes fixed on the fire, that he thought he must have committed a felony and forgotten the details of it, he felt so dejected and guilty.

Chapter 37

Deeming Sunday the best day for taking Mr Wemmick's Walworth sentiments, I devoted the next ensuing Sunday afternoon to a pilgrimage to the Castle. On arriving before the battlements, I found the Union Jack flying and the drawbridge up, but undeterred by this show of defiance and resistance, I rang at the gate, and was admitted in a most pacific manner by the Aged.

'My son, sir,' said the old man, after securing the drawbridge, 'rather had it in his mind that you might happen to drop in, and he left word that he would soon be home from his afternoon's walk. He is very regular in his walks, is my son. Very regular in everything, is my son.'

I nodded at the old gentleman as Wemmick himself might have nodded, and we went in and sat down by the fireside.

'You made acquaintance with my son, sir,' said the old man, in his chirping way, while he warmed his hands at the blaze, 'at his office, I expect?' I nodded. 'Hah! I have heerd that my son is a wonderful hand at his business, sir?' I nodded hard. 'Yes; so they tell me. His business is the law?' I nodded harder. 'Which makes it more surprising in my son,' said the old man, 'for he was not brought up to the law, but to the wine-coopering.'

Curious to know how the old gentleman stood informed concerning the reputation of Mr Jaggers, I roared that name at him. He threw me into the greatest confusion by laughing heartily and replying in a very sprightly manner, 'No, to be sure; you're right.' And to this hour I have not the faintest notion of what he meant, or what joke he thought I had made.

As I could not sit there nodding at him perpetually, without making some other attempt to interest him, I shouted an enquiry whether his own calling in life had been 'the wine-coopering'. By dint of straining that term out of myself several times and tapping the old gentleman on the chest to associate it with him, I at last succeeded in making my meaning understood.

'No,' said the old gentleman; 'the warehousing, the warehousing. First, over yonder;' he appeared to mean up the chimney, but I believe he intended to refer me to Liverpool; 'and then in the City of London here. However, having an infirmity – for I am hard of hearing, sir – '

I expressed in pantomime the greatest astonishment. ' – Yes, hard of hearing; having that infirmity coming upon me, my son he went into the Law, and he took charge of me, and he by little and little made out this elegant and beautiful property. But returning to what you said, you know,' pursued the old man, again laughing heartily, 'what I say is, no, to be sure; you're right.'

I was modestly wondering whether my utmost ingenuity would have enabled me to say anything that would have amused him half as much as this imaginary pleasantry, when I was startled by a sudden click in the wall on one side of the chimney, and the ghostly tumbling open of a little wooden flap with 'John' upon it. The old man, following my eyes, cried with great triumph, 'My son's come home!' and we both went out to the drawbridge.

It was worth any money to see Wemmick waving a salute to me from the other side of the moat, when we might have shaken hands across it with the greatest ease. The Aged was so delighted to work the drawbridge, that I made no offer to assist him, but stood quiet until Wemmick had come across, and had presented me to Miss Skiffins: a lady by whom he was accompanied.

Miss Skiffins was of a wooden appearance, and was, like her escort, in the post office branch of the service. She might have been some two or three years younger than Wemmick, and I judged her to stand possessed of portable property. The cut of her dress from the waist upward, both before and behind, made her figure very like a boy's kite; and I might have pronounced her gown a little too decidedly orange, and her gloves a little too intensely green. But she seemed to be a good sort of fellow, and showed a high regard for the Aged. I was not long in discovering that she was a frequent visitor at the Castle; for, on our going in, and my complimenting Wemmick on his ingenious contrivance for announcing himself to the Aged, he begged me to give my attention for a moment to the other side of the chimney, and disappeared. Presently another click came, and another little door tumbled open with 'Miss Skiffins' on it; then Miss Skiffins shut up and John tumbled open; then Miss Skiffins and John both tumbled open together, and finally |shut up together. On Wemmick's return from working these mechanical appliances, I expressed the great admiration with which I regarded them, and he said, 'Well, you know, they're both pleasant and useful to the Aged. And by George, sir, it's a thing worth mentioning, that of all the people who come to this gate, the secret of those pulls is only known to the Aged, Miss Skiffins, and me!'

'And Mr Wemmick made them,' added Miss Skiffins, 'with his own hands out of his own head.'

While Miss Skiffins was taking off her bonnet (she retained her green gloves during the evening as an outward and visible sign that there was company), Wemmick invited me to take a walk with him round the property, and see how the island looked in wintertime. Thinking that he did this to give me an opportunity of taking his Walworth sentiments, I seized the opportunity as soon as we were out of the Castle.

Having thought of the matter with care, I approached my subject as if I had never hinted at it before. I informed Wemmick that I was anxious in behalf of Herbert Pocket, and I told him how we had first met, and how we had fought. I glanced at Herbert's home, and at his character, and at his having no means but such as he was dependent on his father for: those, uncertain and unpunctual. I alluded to the advantages I had derived in my first rawness and ignorance from his society, and I confessed that I feared I had but ill repaid them, and that he might have done better without me and my expectations. Keeping Miss Havisham in the background at a great distance, I still hinted at the possibility of my having competed with him in his prospects, and at the certainty of his possessing a generous soul, and being far above any mean distrusts, retaliations, or designs. For all these reasons (I told Wemmick), and because he was my young companion and friend, and I had a great affection for him, I wished my own good fortune to reflect some rays upon him, and therefore I sought advice from Wemmick's experience and knowledge of men and affairs, how I could best try with my resources to help Herbert to some present income – say of a hundred a year, to keep him in good hope and heart – and gradually to buy him on to some small partnership. I begged Wemmick, in conclusion, to understand that my help must always be rendered without Herbert's knowledge or suspicion, and that there was no one else in the world with whom I could advise. I wound up by laying my hand upon his shoulder, and saying 'I can't help confiding in you, though I know it must be troublesome to you; but that is your fault, in having ever brought me here.'

Wemmick was silent for a little while, and then said with a kind of start, 'Well, you know, Mr Pip, I must tell you one thing. This is devilish good of you.'

'Say you'll help me to be good then,' said I.

'Ecod,' replied Wemmick, shaking his head, 'that's not my trade.'

'Nor is this your trading-place,' said I.

'You are right,' he returned. 'You hit the nail on the head. Mr Pip, I'll put on my considering cap, and I think all you want to do may be done by degrees. Skiffins (that's her brother) is an accountant and agent. I'll look him up and go to work for you.'

'I thank you ten thousand times.'

'On the contrary,' said he, 'I thank you, for though we are strictly in our private and personal capacity, still it may be mentioned that there *are* Newgate cobwebs about, and it brushes them away.'

After a little further conversation to the same effect, we returned into the Castle, where we found Miss Skiffins preparing tea. The responsible duty of making the toast was delegated to the Aged, and that excellent old gentleman was so intent upon it that he seemed to be in some danger of melting his eyes. It was no nominal meal that we were going to make, but a vigorous reality. The Aged prepared such a haystack of buttered toast, that I could scarcely see him over it as it simmered on an iron stand hooked on to the top-bar; while Miss Skiffins brewed such a jorum of tea, that the pig in the back premises became strongly excited, and repeatedly expressed his desire to participate in the entertainment.

The flag had been struck, and the gun had been fired, at the right moment of time, and I felt as snugly cut off from the rest of Walworth as if the moat were thirty feet wide by as many deep. Nothing disturbed the tranquillity of the Castle, but the occasional tumbling open of John and Miss Skiffins: which little doors were a prey to some spasmodic infirmity that made me sympathetically uncomfortable until I got used to it. I inferred from the methodical nature of Miss Skiffins's arrangements that she made tea there every Sunday night; and I rather suspected that a classic brooch she wore, representing the profile of an undesirable female with a very straight nose and a very new moon, was a piece of portable property that had been given her by Wemmick.

We ate the whole of the toast, and drank tea in proportion, and it was delightful to see how warm and greasy we all got after it. The Aged especially, might have passed for some clean old chief of a savage tribe, just oiled. After a short pause of repose – Miss Skiffins, in the absence of the little servant, who, it seemed, retired to the bosom of her family on Sunday afternoons – washed up the tea-things, in a trifling ladylike amateur manner that compromised none of us. Then, she put on her gloves again, and we drew round the fire, and Wemmick said, 'Now, Aged Parent, tip us the paper.'

Wemmick explained to me while the Aged got his spectacles out, that this was according to custom, and that it gave the old gentleman infinite satisfaction to read the news aloud. 'I won't offer an apology,' said Wemmick, 'for he isn't capable of many pleasures – are you, Aged P?'

'All right, John, all right,' returned the old man, seeing himself spoken to.

'Only tip him a nod every now and then when he looks off his paper,' said Wemmick, 'and he'll be as happy as a king. We are all attention, Aged One.'

'All right, John, all right!' returned the cheerful old man: so busy and so pleased, that it really was quite charming.

The Aged's reading reminded me of the classes at Mr Wopsle's great-aunt's, with the pleasanter peculiarity that it seemed to come through a keyhole. As he wanted the candles close to him, and as he was always on the verge of putting either his head or the newspaper into them, he required as much watching as a powder-mill. But Wemmick was equally untiring and gentle in his vigilance, and the Aged read on, quite unconscious of his many rescues. Whenever he looked at us, we all expressed the greatest interest and amazement, and nodded until he resumed again.

As Wemmick and Miss Skiffins sat side by side, and as I sat in a shadowy corner, I observed a slow and gradual elongation of Mr Wemmick's mouth, powerfully suggestive of his slowly and gradually stealing his arm round Miss Skiffins's waist. In course of time I saw his hand appear on the other side of Miss Skiffins; but at that moment Miss Skiffins neatly stopped him with the green glove, unwound his arm again as if it were an article of dress, and with the greatest deliberation laid it on the table before her. Miss Skiffins's composure while she did this was one of the most remarkable sights I have ever seen, and if I could have thought the act consistent with abstraction of mind, I should have deemed that Miss Skiffins performed it mechanically.

By and by, I noticed Wemmick's arm beginning to disappear again, and gradually fading out of view. Shortly afterwards, his mouth began to widen again. After an interval of suspense on my part that was quite enthralling and almost painful, I saw his hand appear on the other side of Miss Skiffins. Instantly, Miss Skiffins stopped it with the neatness of a placid boxer, took off that girdle or cestus as before, and laid it on the table. Taking the table to represent the path of virtue, I am justified in stating that during the whole time of the Aged's reading, Wemmick's arm was straying from the path of virtue and being recalled to it by Miss Skiffins.

At last the Aged read himself into a light slumber. This was the time for Wemmick to produce a little kettle, a tray of glasses, and a black bottle with a porcelain-topped cork, representing some clerical dignitary of a rubicund and social aspect. With the aid of these appliances we all had something warm to drink: including the Aged, who was soon awake again. Miss Skiffins mixed, and I observed that she and Wemmick drank out of one glass. Of course I knew better than to offer to see Miss Skiffins home, and under the circumstances I thought I had best go first: which I did, taking a cordial leave of the Aged, and having passed a pleasant evening.

Before a week was out, I received a note from Wemmick, dated Walworth, stating that he hoped he had made some advance in that matter appertaining to our private and personal capacities, and that he would be glad if I could come and see him again upon it. So I went out to Walworth again, and yet again, and yet again, and I saw him by appointment in the City several times, but never held any communication with him on the subject in or near Little Britain. The upshot was, that we found a worthy young merchant or shipping-broker, not long established in business, who wanted intelligent help, and who wanted capital, and who in due course of time and receipt would want a partner. Between him and me, secret articles were signed of which Herbert was the subject, and I paid him half of my five hundred pounds down, and engaged for sundry other payments; some, to fall due at certain dates out of my income: some contingent on my coming into my property. Miss Skiffins's brother conducted the negotiation. Wemmick pervaded it throughout, but never appeared in it.

The whole business was so cleverly managed, that Herbert had not the least suspicion of my hand being in it. I never shall forget the radiant face with which he came home one afternoon, and told me as a mighty piece of news, of his having fallen in with one Clarriker (the young merchant's name), and of Clarriker's having shown an extraordinary inclination towards him, and of his belief that the opening had come at last. Day by day as his hopes grew stronger and his face brighter, he must have thought me a more and more affectionate friend, for I had the greatest difficulty in restraining my tears of triumph when I saw him so happy.

At length, the thing being done, and he having that day entered Clarriker's House, and he having talked to me for a whole evening in a flush of pleasure and success, I did really cry in good earnest when I went to bed, to think that my expectations had done some good to somebody.

A great event in my life, the turning-point of my life, now opens on my view. But, before I proceed to narrate it, and before I pass on to all the changes it involved, I must give one chapter to Estella. It is not much to give to the theme that so long filled my heart.

Chapter 38

If that staid old house near the Green at Richmond should ever come to be haunted when I am dead, it will be haunted, surely, by my ghost. O the many, many nights and days through which the unquiet spirit within me haunted that house when Estella lived there! Let my body be where it would, my spirit was always wandering, wandering, wandering about that house.

The lady with whom Estella was placed, Mrs Brandley by name, was a widow, with one daughter several years older than Estella. The mother looked young and the daughter looked old; the mother's complexion was pink, and the daughter's was yellow; the mother set up for frivolity, and the daughter for theology. They were in what is called a good position, and visited, and were visited by, numbers of people. Little, if any, community of feeling subsisted between them and Estella, but the understanding was established that they were necessary to her, and that she was necessary to them. Mrs Brandley had been a friend of Miss Havisham's before the time of her seclusion.

In Mrs Brandley's house and out of Mrs Brandley's house, I suffered every kind and degree of torture that Estella could cause me. The nature of my relations with her, which placed me on terms of familiarity without placing me on terms of favour, conduced to my distraction. She made use of me to tease other admirers, and she turned the very familiarity between herself and me, to the account of putting a constant slight on my devotion to her. If I had been her secretary, steward, half-brother, poor relation – if I had been a younger brother of her appointed husband – I could not have seemed to

'Now, *Aged Parent, tip us the paper.*'

myself further from my hopes when I was nearest to her. The privilege of calling her by her name and hearing her call me by mine, became under the circumstances an aggravation of my trials; and while I think it likely that it almost maddened her other lovers, I knew too certainly that it almost maddened me.

She had admirers without end. No doubt my jealousy made an admirer of everyone who went near her; but there were more than enough of them without that.

I saw her often at Richmond, I heard of her often in town, and I used often to take her and the Brandleys on the water; there were picnics, fête days, plays, operas, concerts, parties, all sorts of pleasures, through which I pursued her – and they were all miseries to me. I never had one hour's happiness in her society, and yet my mind all round the four-and-twenty hours was harping on the happiness of having her with me unto death.

Throughout this part of our intercourse – and it lasted, as will presently be seen, for what I then thought a long time – she habitually reverted to that tone which expressed that our association was forced upon us. There were other times when she would come to a sudden check in this tone and in all her many tones, and would seem to pity me.

'Pip, Pip,' she said one evening, coming to such a check, when we sat apart at a darkening window of the house in Richmond; 'will you never take warning?'

'Of what?'

'Of me.'

'Warning not to be attracted by you, do you mean, Estella?'

'Do I mean! If you don't know what I mean, you are blind.'

I should have replied that love was commonly reputed blind, but for the reason that I always was restrained – and this was not the least of my miseries – by a feeling that it was ungenerous to press myself upon her, when she knew that she could not choose but obey Miss Havisham. My dread always was, that this knowledge on her part laid me under a heavy disadvantage with her pride, and made me the subject of a rebellious struggle in her bosom.

'At any rate,' said I, 'I have no warning given me just now, for you wrote to me to come to you, this time.'

'That's true,' said Estella, with a cold careless smile that always chilled me.

After looking at the twilight without, for a little while, she went on to say: 'The time has come round when Miss Havisham wishes to have me for a day at Satis. You are to take me there, and bring me back, if you will. She would rather I did not travel alone, and objects to receiving my maid, for she has a sensitive horror of being talked of by such people. Can you take me?'

'Can I take you, Estella!'

'You can then? The day after tomorrow, if you please. You are to pay all charges out of my purse. You hear the condition of your going?'

'And must obey,' said I.

This was all the preparation I received for that visit, or for others like it: Miss Havisham never wrote to me, nor had I ever so much as seen her handwriting. We went down on the next day but one, and we found her in the room where I had first beheld her, and it is needless to add that there was no change in Satis House.

She was even more dreadfully fond of Estella than she had been when I last saw them together; I repeat the word advisedly, for there was something positively dreadful in the energy of her looks and embraces. She hung upon Estella's beauty, hung upon her words, hung upon her gestures, and sat mumbling her own trembling fingers while she looked at her, as though she were devouring the beautiful creature she had reared.

From Estella she looked at me, with a searching glance that seemed to pry into my heart and probe its wounds. 'How does she use you, Pip, how does she use you?' she asked me again, with her witch-like eagerness even in Estella's hearing. But when we sat by her flickering fire at night, she was most weird; for then, keeping Estella's hand drawn through her arm and clutched in her own hand, she extorted from her by dint of referring back to what Estella had told her in her regular letters, the names and conditions of the men whom she had fascinated; and as Miss Havisham dwelt upon this roll, with the intensity of a mind mortally hurt and diseased, she sat with her other hand on her crutch stick, and her chin on that, and her wan bright eyes glaring at me, a very spectre.

I saw in this, wretched though it made me, and bitter the sense of dependence, even of degradation, that it awakened – I saw in this, that Estella was set to wreak Miss Havisham's revenge on men, and that she was not to be given to me until she had gratified it for a term. I saw in this, a reason for her being beforehand assigned to me. Sending her out to attract and torment and do mischief, Miss Havisham sent her with the malicious assurance that she was beyond the reach of all admirers, and that all who staked upon that cast were secured to lose. I saw in this, that I, too, was tormented by a perversion of ingenuity, even while the prize was reserved for me. I saw in this, the reason for my being staved off so long, and the reason for my late guardian's declining to commit himself to the formal knowledge of such a scheme. In a word, I saw in this, Miss Havisham as I had her then and there before my eyes, and always had had her before my eyes; and I saw in this, the distinct shadow of the darkened and unhealthy house in which her life was hidden from the sun.

The candles that lighted that room of hers were placed in sconces on the wall. They were high from the ground, and they burnt with the steady dulness of artificial light in air that is seldom renewed. As I looked round at them, and at the pale gloom they made, and at the stopped clock, and at the withered articles of bridal dress upon the table and the ground, and at her own awful figure with its ghostly reflection thrown large by the fire upon the ceiling and the wall, I saw in everything the construction that my mind had come to, repeated and thrown back to me. My thoughts passed into the great room across the landing where the table was spread, and I saw it written, as it were, in the falls of the cobwebs from the centrepiece, in the crawlings of the spiders on the cloth, in the tracks of the mice as they betook their little quickened hearts behind the panels, and in the gropings and pausings of the beetles on the floor.

It happened on the occasion of this visit that some sharp words arose between Estella and Miss Havisham. It was the first time I had ever seen them opposed.

We were seated by the fire, as just now described, and Miss Havisham still had Estella's arm drawn through her own, and still clutched Estella's hand in hers, when Estella gradually began to detach herself. She had shown a proud impatience more than once before, and had rather endured that fierce affection than accepted or returned it.

'What!' said Miss Havisham, flashing her eyes upon her, 'are you tired of me?'

'Only a little tired of myself,' replied Estella, disengaging her arm, and moving to the great chimney-piece, where she stood looking down at the fire.

'Speak the truth, you ingrate!' cried Miss Havisham, passionately striking her stick upon the floor; 'you are tired of me.'

Estella looked at her with perfect composure, and again looked down at the fire. Her graceful figure and her beautiful face expressed a self-possessed indifference to the wild heat of the other, that was almost cruel.

'You stock and stone!' exclaimed Miss Havisham. 'You cold, cold heart!'

'What!' said Estella, preserving her attitude of indifference as she leaned against the great chimney-piece and only moving her eyes; 'do you reproach me for being cold? You?'

'Are you not?' was the fierce retort.

'You should know,' said Estella. 'I am what you have made me. Take all the praise, take all the blame; take all the success, take all the failure; in short, take me.'

'O, look at her, look at her!' cried Miss Havisham, bitterly. 'Look at her, so hard and thankless, on the hearth where she was reared! Where I took her into this wretched breast when it was first bleeding from its stabs, and where I have lavished years of tenderness upon her!'

'At least I was no party to the compact,' said Estella, 'for if I could walk and speak, when it was made, it was as much as I could do. But what would you have? You have been very good to me, and I owe everything to you. What would you have?'

'Love,' replied the other.

'You have it.'

'I have not,' said Miss Havisham.

'Mother by adoption,' retorted Estella, never departing from the easy grace of her attitude, never raising her voice as the other did, never yielding either to anger or tenderness, 'Mother by adoption, I have said that I owe everything to you. All I possess is freely yours. All that you have given me is at your command to have again. Beyond that, I have nothing. And if you ask me to give you what you never gave me, my gratitude and duty cannot do impossibilities.'

'Did I never give her love!' cried Miss Havisham, turning wildly to me. 'Did I never give her a burning love, inseparable from jealousy at all times, and from sharp pain, while she speaks thus to me! Let her call me mad, let her call me mad!'

'Why should I call you mad,' returned Estella, 'I, of all people? Does anyone live, who knows what set purposes you

have, half as well as I do? Does anyone live, who knows what a steady memory you have, half as well as I do? I who have sat on this same hearth on the little stool that is even now beside you there, learning your lessons and looking up into your face, when your face was strange and frightened me!'

'Soon forgotten!' moaned Miss Havisham. 'Times soon forgotten!'

'No, not forgotten,' retorted Estella. 'Not forgotten, but treasured up in my memory. When have you found me false to your teaching? When have you found me unmindful of your lessons? When have you found me giving admission here,' she touched her bosom with her hand, 'to anything that you excluded? Be just to me.'

'So proud, so proud!' moaned Miss Havisham, pushing away her grey hair with both her hands.

'Who taught me to be proud?' returned Estella. 'Who praised me when I learnt my lesson?'

'So hard, so hard!' moaned Miss Havisham, with her former action.

'Who taught me to be hard?' returned Estella. 'Who praised me when I learnt my lesson?'

'But to be proud and hard to *me!*' Miss Havisham quite shrieked, as she stretched out her arms. 'Estella, Estella, Estella, to be proud and hard to *me!*'

Estella looked at her for a moment with a kind of calm wonder, but was not otherwise disturbed; when the moment was passed, she looked down at the fire again.

'I cannot think,' said Estella, raising her eyes after a silence, 'why you should be so unreasonable when I come to see you after a separation. I have never forgotten your wrongs and their causes. I have never been unfaithful to you or your schooling. I have never shown any weakness that I can charge myself with.'

'Would it be weakness to return my love?' exclaimed Miss Havisham. 'But yes, yes, she would call it so!'

'I begin to think,' said Estella, in a musing way, after another moment of calm wonder, 'that I almost understand how this comes about. If you had brought up your adopted daughter wholly in the dark confinement of these rooms, and had never let her know that there was such a thing as the daylight by which she has never once seen your face – if you had done that, and then, for a purpose, had wanted her to understand the daylight and know all about it, you would have been disappointed and angry?'

Miss Havisham, with her head in her hands, sat making a low moaning, and swaying herself on her chair, but gave no answer.

'Or,' said Estella, ' – which is a nearer case – if you had taught her, from the dawn of her intelligence, with your utmost energy and might, that there was such a thing as daylight, but that it was made to be her enemy and destroyer, and she must always turn against it, for it had blighted you and would else blight her – if you had done this, and then, for a purpose, had wanted her to take naturally to the daylight and she could not do it, you would have been disappointed and angry?'

Miss Havisham sat listening (or it seemed so, for I could not see her face), but still made no answer.

'So,' said Estella, 'I must be taken as I have been made. The success is not mine, the failure is not mine, but the two together make me.'

Miss Havisham had settled down, I hardly knew how, upon the floor, among the faded bridal relics with which it was strewn. I took advantage of the moment – I had sought one from the first – to leave the room, after beseeching Estella's attention to her with a movement of my hand. When I left, Estella was yet standing by the great chimney-piece, just as she had stood throughout. Miss Havisham's grey hair was all adrift upon the ground, among the other bridal wrecks, and was a miserable sight to see.

It was with a depressed heart that I walked in the starlight for an hour and more, about the courtyard, and about the brewery, and about the ruined garden. When I at last took courage to return to the room, I found Estella sitting at Miss Havisham's knee, taking up some stitches in one of those old articles of dress that were dropping to pieces, and of which I have often been reminded since by the faded tatters of old banners that I have seen hanging up in cathedrals. Afterwards, Estella and I played at cards, as of yore – only we were skilful now, and played French games – and so the evening wore away, and I went to bed.

I lay in that separate building across the courtyard. It was the first time I had ever lain down to rest in Satis House, and sleep refused to come near me. A thousand Miss Havishams haunted me. She was on this side of my pillow, on that, at the head of the bed, at the foot, behind the half-opened door of the dressing-room, in the dressing-room, in the room overhead, in the room beneath – everywhere. At last, when the night was slow to creep on towards two o'clock, I felt that I absolutely could no longer bear the place as a place to lie down in, and that I must get up. I therefore got up and put on my clothes, and went out across the yard into the long stone passage, designing to gain the outer courtyard and walk there for the relief of my mind. But I was no sooner in the passage than I extinguished my candle; for I saw Miss Havisham going along it in a ghostly manner, making a low cry. I followed her at a distance, and saw her go up the staircase. She carried a bare candle in her hand, which she had probably taken from one of the sconces in her own room, and was a most unearthly object by its light. Standing at the bottom of the staircase, I felt the mildewed air of the feast-chamber, without seeing her open the door, and I heard her walking there, and so across into her own room, and so across again into that, never ceasing the low cry. After a time, I tried in the dark both to get out and to go back, but I could do neither until some streaks of day strayed in and showed me where to lay my hands. During the whole interval, whenever I went to the bottom of the staircase, I heard her footstep, saw her candle pass above, and heard her ceaseless low cry.

Before we left next day, there was no revival of the difference between her and Estella, nor was it ever revived on any similar occasion; and there were four similar occasions, to the best of my remembrance. Nor did Miss Havisham's manner towards Estella in anywise change, except that I believed it to have something like fear infused among its former characteristics.

It is impossible to turn this leaf of my life without putting Bentley Drummle's name upon it; or I would, very gladly.

On a certain occasion when the Finches were assembled in force, and when good feeling was being promoted in the usual manner by nobody's agreeing with anybody else, the presiding Finch called the Grove to order, forasmuch as Mr Drummle had not yet toasted a lady; which, according to the solemn constitution of the society, it was the brute's turn to do that day. I thought I saw him leer in an ugly way at me while the decanters were going round, but as there was no love lost between us, that might easily be. What was my indignant surprise when he called upon the company to pledge him to 'Estella!'

'Estella who?' said I.

'Never you mind,' retorted Drummle.

'Estella of where?' said I. 'You are bound to say of where.' Which he was, as a Finch.

'Of Richmond, gentlemen,' said Drummle, putting me out of the question, 'and a peerless beauty.'

Much he knew about peerless beauties, a mean miserable idiot! I whispered Herbert.

'I know that lady,' said Herbert, across the table, when the toast had been honoured.

'*Do* you?' said Drummle.

'And so do I,' I added with a scarlet face.

'*Do* you?' said Drummle. '*Oh*, Lord!'

This was the only retort – except glass or crockery – that the heavy creature was capable of making; but, I became as highly incensed by it as if it had been barbed with wit, and I immediately rose in my place and said that I could not but regard it as being like the honourable Finch's impudence to come down to that Grove – we always talked about coming down to that Grove, as a neat Parliamentary turn of expression – down to that Grove, proposing a lady of whom he knew nothing. Mr Drummle upon this, starting up, demanded what I meant by that? Whereupon I made him the extreme reply that I believed he knew where I was to be found.

Whether it was possible in a Christian country to get on without blood, after this, was a question on which the Finches were divided. The debate upon it grew so lively, indeed, that at least six more honourable members told six more, during the discussion, that they believed *they* knew where *they* were to be found. However, it was decided at last (the Grove being a court of honour) that if Mr Drummle would bring never so slight a certificate from the lady, importing that he had the honour of her acquaintance, Mr Pip must express his regret, as a gentleman and a Finch, for 'having been betrayed into a warmth which'. Next day was appointed for the production (lest our honour should take cold from delay), and next day Drummle appeared with a polite little avowal in Estella's hand, that she had had the honour of dancing with him several times. This left me no course but to regret that I had been 'betrayed into a warmth which', and on the whole to repudiate, as untenable, the idea that I was to be found anywhere. Drummle and I then sat snorting at one another for an hour, while the Grove engaged in indiscriminate contradiction, and finally the promotion of good feeling was declared to have gone ahead at an amazing rate.

I tell this lightly, but it was no light thing to me. For I cannot adequately express what pain it gave me to think that Estella should show any favour to a contemptible, clumsy, sulky booby, so very far below the average. To the present moment, I believe it to have been referable to some pure fire of generosity and disinterestedness in my love for her, that I could not endure the thought of her stooping to that hound. No doubt I should have been miserable whomsoever she had favoured; but a worthier object would have caused me a different kind and degree of distress.

It was easy for me to find out, and I did soon find out, that Drummle had begun to follow her closely, and that she allowed him to do it. A little while, and he was always in pursuit of her, and he and I crossed one another every day. He held on, in a dull persistent way, and Estella held him on; now with encouragement, now with discouragement, now almost flattering him, now openly despising him, now knowing him very well, now scarcely remembering who he was.

The Spider, as Mr Jaggers had called him, was used to lying in wait, however, and had the patience of his tribe. Added to that, he had a blockhead confidence in his money and in his family greatness, which sometimes did him good service – almost taking the place of concentration and determined purpose. So, the Spider, doggedly watching Estella, out watched many brighter insects, and would often uncoil himself and drop at the right nick of time.

At a certain assembly ball at Richmond (there used to be assembly balls at most places then), where Estella had outshone all other beauties, this blundering Drummle so hung about her, and with so much toleration on her part, that I resolved to speak to her concerning him. I took the next opportunity: which was when she was waiting for Mrs Brandley to take her home, and was sitting apart among some flowers, ready to go. I was with her, for I almost always accompanied them to and from such places.

'Are you tired, Estella?'

'Rather, Pip.'

'You should be.'

'Say, rather, I should not be; for I have my letter to Satis House to write, before I go to sleep.'

'Recounting tonight's triumph?' said I. 'Surely a very poor one, Estella.'

'What do you mean? I didn't know there had been any.'

'Estella,' said I, 'do look at that fellow in the corner yonder, who is looking over here at us.'

'Why should I look at him?' returned Estella, with her eyes on me instead. 'What is there in that fellow in the corner yonder – to use your words – that I need look at?'

'Indeed, that is the very question I want to ask you,' said I. 'For he has been hovering about you all night.'

'Moths, and all sorts of ugly creatures,' replied Estella, with a glance towards him, 'hover about a lighted candle. Can the candle help it?'

'No,' I returned: 'but cannot the Estella help it?'

'Well!' said she, laughing after a moment, 'perhaps. Yes. Anything you like.'

'But, Estella, do hear me speak. It makes me wretched that you should encourage a man so generally despised as Drummle. You know he is despised.'

'Well?' said she.

'You know he is as ungainly within as without. A deficient, ill tempered, lowering, stupid fellow.'

'Well?' said she.

'You know he has nothing to recommend him but money, and a ridiculous roll of addle-headed predecessors; now, don't you?'

'Well?' said she again; and each time she said it, she opened her lovely eyes the wider.

To overcome the difficulty of getting past that monosyllable, I took it from her, and said, repeating it with emphasis, 'Well! Then, that is why it makes me wretched.'

Now, if I could have believed that she favoured Drummle with any idea of making me – me – wretched, I should have been in better heart about it; but in that habitual way of hers, she put me so entirely out of the question, that I could believe nothing of the kind.

'Pip,' said Estella, casting her glance over the room, 'don't be foolish about its effect on you. It may have its effect on others, and may be meant to have. It's not worth discussing.'

'Yes it is,' said I, 'because I cannot bear that people should say, "she throws away her graces and attractions on a mere boor, the lowest in the crowd." '

'I can bear it,' said Estella.

'Oh! don't be so proud, Estella, and so inflexible.'

'Calls me proud and inflexible in this breath!' said Estella, opening her hands. 'And in his last breath reproached me for stooping to a boor!'

'There is no doubt you do,' said I, something hurriedly, 'for I have seen you give him looks and smiles this very night, such as you never give to – me.'

'Do you want me then,' said Estella, turning suddenly with a fixed and serious, if not angry look, 'to deceive and entrap you?'

'Do you deceive and entrap him, Estella?'

'Yes, and many others – all of them but you. Here is Mrs Brandley. I'll say no more.'

And now that I have given the one chapter to the theme that so filled my heart, and so often made it ache and ache again, I pass on, unhindered, to the event that had impended over me longer yet; the event that had begun to be prepared for, before I knew that the world held Estella, and in the days when her baby intelligence was receiving its first distortions from Miss Havisham's wasting hands.

In the Eastern story, the heavy slab that was to fall on the bed of state in the flush of conquest was slowly wrought out of the quarry, the tunnel for the rope to hold it in its place was slowly carried through the leagues of rock, the slab was slowly raised and fitted in the roof, the rope was rove to it and slowly taken through the miles of hollow to the great iron ring. All being made ready with much labour, and the hour come, the sultan was aroused in the dead of the night, and the sharpened axe that was to sever the rope from the great iron ring was put into his hand, and he struck with it, and the rope parted and rushed away, and the ceiling fell. So in my case; all the work, near and afar, that tended to the end, had been accomplished; and in an instant the blow was struck, and the roof of my stronghold dropped upon me.

Chapter 39

I was three-and-twenty years of age. Not another word had I heard to enlighten me on the subject of my expectations, and my twenty-third birthday was a week gone. We had left Barnard's Inn more than a year, and lived in the Temple. Our chambers were in Garden Court, down by the river.

Mr Pocket and I had for some time parted company as to our original relations, though we continued on the best terms. Notwithstanding my inability to settle to anything – which I hope arose out of the restless and incomplete tenure on which I held my means – I had a taste for reading, and read regularly so many hours a day. That matter of Herbert's was still progressing, and everything with me was as I have brought it down to the close of the last preceding chapter.

Business had taken Herbert on a journey to Marseilles. I was alone, and had a dull sense of being alone. Dispirited and anxious, long hoping that tomorrow or next week would clear my way, and long disappointed, I sadly missed the cheerful face and ready response of my friend.

It was wretched weather; stormy and wet, stormy and wet; mud, mud, mud, deep in all the streets. Day after day, a vast heavy veil had been driving over London from the East, and it drove still, as if in the East there were an eternity of cloud and wind. So furious had been the gusts, that high buildings in town had had the lead stripped off their roofs; and in the country, trees had been torn up, and sails of windmills carried away; and gloomy accounts had come in from the coast, of shipwreck and death. Violent blasts of rain had accompanied these rages of wind, and the day just closed as I sat down to read had been the worst of all.

Alterations have been made in that part of the Temple since that time, and it has not now so lonely a character as it had then, nor is it so exposed to the river. We lived at the top of the last house, and the wind rushing up the river shook the house that night, like discharges of cannon, or breakings of a sea. When the rain came with it and dashed against the windows, I thought, raising my eyes to them as they rocked, that I might have fancied myself in a storm-beaten lighthouse. Occasionally, the smoke came rolling down the chimney as though it could not bear to go out into such a night; and when I set the doors open and looked down the staircase, the staircase lamps were blown out; and when I shaded my face with my hands and looked through the black windows (opening them, ever so little, was out of the question in the teeth of such wind and rain) I saw that the lamps in the court were blown out, and that the lamps on the bridges and the shore were shuddering, and that the coal fires in barges on the river were being carried away before the wind like red-hot splashes in the rain.

I read with my watch upon the table, purposing to close my book at eleven o'clock. As I shut it, Saint Paul's, and all the many church-clocks in the City – some leading, some accompanying, some following – struck that hour. The sound was curiously flawed by the wind; and I was listening, and thinking how the wind assailed and tore it, when I heard a footstep on the stair.

What nervous folly made me start, and awfully connect it with the footstep of my dead sister, matters not. It was past in a moment and I listened again, and heard the footstep stumble in coming on. Remembering then that the staircase lights were blown out, I took up my reading-lamp and went out to the stairhead. Whoever was below had stopped on seeing my lamp, for all was quiet.

'There is someone down there, is there not?' I called out, looking down.

'Yes,' said a voice from the darkness beneath.

'What floor do you want?'

'The top. Mr Pip?'

'That is my name – There is nothing the matter?'

'Nothing the matter,' returned the voice. And the man came on.

I stood with my lamp held out over the stair-rail, and he came slowly within its light. It was a shaded lamp, to shine

I took up my reading-lamp and went out to the stairhead

upon a book, and its circle of light was very contracted; so that he was in it for a mere instant, and then out of it. In the instant I had seen a face that was strange to me, looking up with an incomprehensible air of being touched and pleased by the sight of me.

Moving the lamp as the man moved, I made out that he was substantially dressed, but roughly; like a voyager by sea. That he had long iron-grey hair. That his age was about sixty. That he was a muscular man, strong on his legs, and that he was browned and hardened by exposure to weather. As he ascended the last stair or two, and the light of my lamp included us both, I saw, with a stupid kind of amazement, that he was holding out both his hands to me.

'Pray what is your business?' I asked him.

'My business?' he repeated, pausing. 'Ah! Yes. I will explain my business, by your leave.'

'Do you wish to come in?'

'Yes,' he replied; 'I wish to come in, master.'

I had asked him the question inhospitably enough, for I resented the sort of bright and gratified recognition that still shone in his face. I resented it, because it seemed to imply that he expected me to respond to it. But I took him into the room I had just left, and, having set the lamp on the table, asked him as civilly as I could to explain himself.

He looked about him with the strangest air – an air of wondering pleasure, as if he had some part in the things he admired – and he pulled off a rough outer coat, and his hat. Then I saw that his head was furrowed and bald, and that the long iron-grey hair grew only on its sides. But I saw nothing that in the least explained him. On the contrary, I saw him next moment once more holding out both his hands to me.

'What do you mean?' said I, half suspecting him to be mad.

He stopped in his looking at me, and slowly rubbed his right hand over his head. 'It's disappointing to a man,' he said, in a coarse broken voice, 'arter having looked for'ard so distant, and come so fur; but you're not to blame for that – neither on us is to blame for that. I'll speak in half a minute. Give me half a minute, please.'

He sat down on a chair that stood before the fire, and covered his forehead with his large brown veinous hands. I looked at him attentively then, and recoiled a little from him; but I did not know him.

'There's no one nigh,' said he, looking over his shoulder; 'is there?'

'Why do you, a stranger coming into my rooms at this time of the night, ask that question?' said I.

'You're a game one,' he returned, shaking his head at me with a deliberate affection, at once most unintelligible and most exasperating; 'I'm glad you've grow'd up a game one! But don't catch hold of me. You'd be sorry arterwards to have done it.'

I relinquished the intention he had detected, for I knew him! Even yet I could not recall a single feature, but I knew him! If the wind and the rain had driven away the intervening years, had scattered all the intervening objects, had swept us to the churchyard where we first stood face to face on such different levels, I could not have known my convict more distinctly than

I knew him now, as he sat in the chair before the fire. No need to take a file from his pocket and show it to me; no need to take the handkerchief from his neck and twist it round his head; no need to hug himself with both his arms, and take a shivering turn across the room, looking back at me for recognition. I knew him before he gave me one of those aids, though, a moment before, I had not been conscious of remotely suspecting his identity.

He came back to where I stood, and again held out both his hands. Not knowing what to do – for, in my astonishment I had lost my self-possession – I reluctantly gave him my hands. He grasped them heartily, raised them to his lips, kissed them, and still held them.

'You acted nobly, my boy,' said he. 'Noble Pip! And I have never forgot it!'

At a change in his manner as if he were even going to embrace me, I laid a hand upon his breast and put him away.

'Stay!' said I. 'Keep off! If you are grateful to me for what I did when I was a little child, I hope you have shown your gratitude by mending your way of life. If you have come here to thank me, it was not necessary. Still, however, you have found me out, there must be something good in the feeling that has brought you here, and I will not repulse you; but surely you must understand – I – '

My attention was so attracted by the singularity of his fixed look at me, that the words died away on my tongue.

'You was a saying,' he observed, when we had confronted one another in silence, 'that surely I must understand. What, surely must I understand?'

'That I cannot wish to renew that chance intercourse with you of long ago, under these different circumstances. I am glad to believe you have repented and recovered yourself. I am glad to tell you so. I am glad that, thinking I deserve to be thanked, you have come to thank me. But our ways are different ways, none the less. You are wet, and you look weary. Will you drink something before you go?'

He had replaced his neckerchief loosely, and had stood, keenly observant of me, biting a long end of it. 'I think,' he answered, still with the end at his mouth and still observant of me, 'that I *will* drink (I thank you) afore I go.'

There was a tray ready on a side-table. I brought it to the table near the fire, and asked him what he would have? He touched one of the bottles without looking at it or speaking, and I made him some hot rum and water. I tried to keep my hand steady while I did so, but his look at me as he leaned back in his chair with the long draggled end of his neckerchief between his teeth – evidently forgotten – made my hand very difficult to master. When at last I put the glass to him, I saw with amazement that his eyes were full of tears.

Up to this time I had remained standing, not to disguise that I wished him gone. But I was softened by the softened aspect of the man, and felt a touch of reproach. 'I hope,' said I, hurriedly putting something into a glass for myself, and drawing a chair to the table, 'that you will not think I spoke harshly to you just now. I had no intention of doing it, and I am sorry for it if I did. I wish you well, and happy!'

As I put my glass to my lips, he glanced with surprise at the end of his neckerchief, dropping from his mouth when he opened it, and stretched out his hand. I gave him mine, and then he drank, and drew his sleeve across his eyes and forehead.

'How are you living?' I asked him.

'I've been a sheep-farmer, stockbreeder, other trades besides, away in the new world,' said he: 'many a thousand mile of stormy water off from this.'

'I hope you have done well?'

'I've done wonderful well. There's others went out alonger me as has done well too, but no man has done nigh as well as me. I'm famous for it.'

'I am glad to hear it.'

'I hope to hear you say so, my dear boy.'

Without stopping to try to understand those words or the tone in which they were spoken, I turned off to a point that had just come into my mind.

'Have you ever seen a messenger you once sent to me,' I enquired, 'since he undertook that trust?'

'Never set eyes upon him. I warn't likely to it.'

'He came faithfully, and he brought me the two one-pound notes. I was a poor boy then, as you know, and to a poor boy they were a little fortune. But, like you, I have done well since, and you must let me pay them back. You can put them to some other poor boy's use.' I took out my purse.

He watched me as I laid my purse upon the table and opened it, and he watched me as I separated two one-pound notes from its contents. They were clean and new, and I spread them out and handed them over to him. Still watching me, he laid them one upon the other, folded them longwise, gave them a twist, set fire to them at the lamp, and dropped the ashes into the tray.

'May I make so bold,' he said then, with a smile that was like a frown, and with a frown that was like a smile, 'as ask you *how* you have done well, since you and me was out on them lone shivering marshes?'

'How?'

'Ah!'

He emptied his glass, got up, and stood at the side of the fire, with his heavy brown hand on the mantelshelf. He put a foot up to the bars, to dry and warm it, and the wet boot began to steam; but, he neither looked at it, nor at the fire, but steadily looked at me. It was only now that I began to tremble.

When my lips had parted, and had shaped some words that were without sound, I forced myself to tell him (though I could not do it distinctly), that I had been chosen to succeed to some property.

'Might a mere warmint ask what property?' said he. I faltered, 'I don't know.'

'Might a mere warmint ask whose property?' said he. I faltered again. 'I don't know.'

'Could I make a guess, I wonder,' said the convict, 'at your income since you come of age! As to the first figure, now. Five?'

With my heart beating like a heavy hammer of disordered action, I rose out of my chair, and stood with my hand upon the back of it, looking wildly at him.

'Concerning a guardian,' he went on. 'There ought to have been some guardian or suchlike, whiles you was a minor. Some lawyer, maybe. As to the first letter of that lawyer's name, now. Would it be J?'

All the truth of my position came flashing on me; and its disappointments, dangers, disgraces, consequences of all kinds, rushed in in such a multitude that I was borne down by them and had to struggle for every breath I drew. 'Put it,' he resumed, 'as the employer of that lawyer whose name begun with a J, and might be Jaggers – put it as he had come over sea to Portsmouth, and had landed there, and had wanted to come on to you. "However, you have found me out," you says just now. Well! however did I find you out? Why, I wrote from Portsmouth to a person in London, for particulars of your address. That person's name? Why, Wemmick.'

I could not have spoken one word, though it had been to save my life. I stood, with a hand on the chair-back and a hand on my breast, where I seemed to be suffocating – I stood so, looking wildly at him, until I grasped at the chair, when the room begun to surge and turn. He caught me drew me to the sofa, put me up against the cushions, and bent on one knee before me: bringing the face that I now well remembered, and that I shuddered at, very near to mine.

'Yes, Pip, dear boy, I've made a gentleman on you! It's me wot has done it! I swore that time, sure as ever I earned a guinea, that guinea should go to you. I swore arterwards, sure as ever I spec'lated and got rich, you should get rich. I lived rough, that you should live smooth; I worked hard that you should be above work. What odds, dear boy? Do I tell it fur you to feel a obligation? Not a bit. I tell it, fur you to know as that there hunted dunghill dog wot you kep life in, got his head so high that he could make a gentleman – and, Pip, you're him!'

The abhorrence in which I held the man, the dread I had of him, the repugnance with which I shrank from him, could not have been exceeded if he had been some terrible beast.

'Look'ee here, Pip. I'm your second father. You're my son – more to me nor any son. I've put away money, only for you to spend. When I was a hired-out shepherd in a solitary hut, not seeing no faces but faces of sheep till I half forgot wot men's and women's faces wos like, I see yourn. I drops my knife many a time in that hut when I was a eating my dinner or my supper, and I says, "Here's the boy again, a looking at me whiles I eats and drinks!" I see you there a many times as plain as ever I see you on them misty marshes. "Lord strike me dead!" I says each time – and I goes out in the open air to say it under the open heavens – "but wot, if I gets liberty and money, I'll make that boy a gentleman!" And I done it. Why, look at you, dear boy! Look at these here lodgings of yourn, fit for a lord! A lord? Ah! You shall show money with lords for wagers, and beat 'em!'

In his heat and triumph, and in his knowledge that I had been nearly fainting, he did not remark on my reception of all this. It was the one grain of relief I had.

'Look'ee here!' he went on, taking my watch out of my pocket, and turning towards him a ring on my finger, while I recoiled from his touch as if he had been a snake, 'a gold 'un and a beauty: *that's* a gentleman's, I hope! A diamond all set round with rubies; *that's* a gentleman's, I hope! Look at your linen; fine and beautiful! Look at your clothes; better ain't to be got! And your books too,' turning his eyes round the room, 'mounting up, on their shelves, by hundreds! And you read 'em; don't you? I see you'd been a reading of 'em when I come in. Ha, ha, ha! You shall read 'em to me, dear boy! And if they're in foreign languages wot I don't understand, I shall be just as proud as if I did.'

Again he took both my hands and put them to his lips, while my blood ran cold within me.

'Don't you mind talking, Pip,' said he, after again drawing his sleeve over his eyes and forehead, as the click came in his throat which I well remembered – and he was all the more horrible to me that he was so much in earnest; 'you can't do better nor keep quiet, dear boy. You ain't looked slowly forward to this as I have; you wosn't prepared for this, as I wos. But didn't you never think it might be me?'

'O no, no, no,' I returned. 'Never, never!'

'Well, you see it *wos* me, and single-handed. Never a soul in it but my own self and Mr Jaggers.'

'Was there no one else?' I asked.

'No,' said he, with a glance of surprise: 'who else should there be? And, dear boy, how good-looking you have growed! There's bright eyes somewheres – eh? Isn't there bright eyes somewheres, wot you love the thoughts on?'

O Estella, Estella!

'They shall be yourn, dear boy, if money can buy 'em. Not that a gentleman like you, so well set up as you, can't win 'em off of his own game; but money shall back you! Let me finish wot I was a telling you, dear boy. From that there hut and that there hiring-out, I got money left me by my master (which died, and had been the same as me), and got my liberty and went for myself. In every single thing I went for, I went for you. "Lord strike a blight upon it," I says, wotever it was I went for, "if it ain't for him!" It all prospered wonderful. As I giv' you to understand just now, I'm famous for it. It was the money left me, and the gains of the first few year, wot I sent home to Mr Jaggers – all for you – when he first come arter you, agreeable to my letter.'

O, that he had never come! That he had left me at the forge – far from contented, yet, by comparison, happy!

'And then, dear boy, it was a recompense to me, look'ee here, to know in secret that I was making a gentleman. The blood horses of them colonists might fling up the dust over me as I was walking; what do I say? I says to myself, "I'm making a better gentleman nor ever *you*'ll be!" When one of 'em says to one another, "He was a convict, a few years ago, and is a ignorant common fellow now, for all he's lucky," what do I say? I says to myself, "If I ain't a gentleman, nor yet ain't got no learning, I'm the owner of such. All on you owns stock and land; which on you owns a brought-up London gentleman?" This way I kep myself a going. And this way I held steady afore my mind that I would for certain come one day and see my boy, and make myself known to him, on his own ground.'

He laid his hand on my shoulder. I shuddered at the thought that for anything I knew, his hand might be stained with blood.

'It warn't easy, Pip, for me to leave them parts, nor yet it warn't safe. But I held to it, and the harder it was, the stronger I held, for I was determined, and my mind firm made up. At last I done it. Dear boy, I done it!'

I tried to collect my thoughts, but I was stunned. Throughout, I had seemed to myself to attend more to the wind and the rain than to him; even now, I could not separate his voice from those voices, though those were loud and his was silent.

'Where will you put me?' he asked, presently. 'I must be put somewheres, dear boy.'

'To sleep?' said I.

'Yes. And to sleep long and sound,' he answered; 'for I've been sea-tossed and sea-washed, months and months.'

'My friend and companion,' said I, rising from the sofa, 'is absent; you must have his room.'

'He won't come back tomorrow; will he?'

'No,' said I, answering almost mechanically, in spite of my utmost efforts; 'not tomorrow.'

'Because, look'ee here, dear boy,' he said, dropping his voice, and laying a long finger on my breast in an impressive manner, 'caution is necessary'.

'How do you mean? Caution?'

'By God, it's death!'

'What's death?'

'I was sent for life. It's death to come back. There's been overmuch coming back of late years, and I should of a certainty be hanged if took.'

Nothing was needed but this; the wretched man, after loading me with his wretched gold and silver chains for years, had risked his life to come to me, and I held it there in my keeping! If I had loved him instead of abhorring him; if I had been attracted to him by the strongest admiration and affection, instead of shrinking from him with the strongest repugnance; it could have been no worse. On the contrary, it would have been better, for his preservation would then have naturally and tenderly addressed my heart.

My first care was to close the shutters, so that no light might be seen from without, and then to close and make fast the doors. While I did so, he stood at the table drinking rum and eating biscuit; and when I saw him thus engaged, I saw my convict on the marshes at his meal again. It almost seemed to me as if he must stoop down presently, to file at his leg.

When I had gone into Herbert's room, and had shut off any other communication between it and the staircase than through the room in which our conversation had been held, I asked him if he would go to bed? He said yes, but asked me for some of my 'gentleman's linen' to put on in the morning. I brought it out, and laid it ready for him, and my blood again ran cold when he again took me by both hands to give me good-night.

I got away from him, without knowing how I did it, and mended the fire in the room where we had been together, and sat down by it, afraid to go to bed. For an hour or more, I remained too stunned to think; and it was not until I began to think, that I began fully to know how wrecked I was, and how the ship in which I had sailed was gone to pieces.

Miss Havisham's intentions towards me, all a mere dream; Estella not designed for me; I only suffered in Satis House as a convenience, a sting for the greedy relations, a model with a mechanical heart to practise on when no other practice was at hand; those were the first smarts I had. But, sharpest and deepest pain of all – it was for the convict, guilty of I knew not what crimes, and liable to be taken out of those rooms where I sat thinking, and hanged at the Old Bailey door, that I had deserted Joe.

I would not have gone back to Joe now, I would not have gone back to Biddy now, for any consideration: simply, I suppose, because my sense of my own worthless conduct to them was greater than every consideration. No wisdom on earth could have given me the comfort that I should have derived from their simplicity and fidelity; but I could never, never, never, undo what I had done.

In every rage of wind and rush of rain, I heard pursuers. Twice, I could have sworn there was a knocking and whispering at the outer door. With these fears upon me, I began either to imagine or recall that I had had mysterious warnings of this man's approach. That, for weeks gone by, I had passed faces in the streets which I had thought like his. That, these likenesses had grown more numerous, as he, coming over the sea, had drawn nearer. That, his wicked spirit had somehow sent these messengers to mine, and that now on this stormy night he was as good as his word, and with me.

Crowding up with these reflections came the reflection that I had seen him with my childish eyes to be a desperately violent man; that I had heard that other convict reiterate that he had tried to murder him; that I had seen him down in the ditch, tearing and fighting like a wild beast. Out of such remembrances I brought into the light of the fire, a half-formed terror that it might not be safe to be shut up there with him in the dead of the wild solitary night. This dilated until it filled the room, and impelled me to take a candle and go in and look at my dreadful burden.

He had rolled a handkerchief round his head, and his face was set and lowering in his sleep. But he was asleep, and quietly too, though he had a pistol lying on the pillow. Assured of this, I softly removed the key to the outside of his door, and turned it on him before I again sat down by the fire. Gradually I slipped from the chair and lay on the floor. When I awoke without having parted in my sleep with the perception of my wretchedness, the clocks of the Eastward churches were striking five, the candles were wasted out, the fire was dead, and the wind and rain intensified the thick black darkness.

This is the end of the second stage of Pip's expectations

Chapter 40

It was fortunate for me that I had to take precautions to insure (so far as I could) the safety of my dreaded visitor; for, this thought pressing on me when I awoke, held other thoughts in a confused concourse at a distance.

The impossibility of keeping him concealed in the chambers was self-evident. It could not be done, and the attempt to do it would inevitably engender suspicion. True, I had no Avenger in my service now, but I was looked after by an inflammatory old female, assisted by an animated rag-bag whom she called her niece; and to keep a room secret from them would be to invite curiosity and exaggeration. They both had weak eyes, which I had long attributed to their chronically looking in at keyholes, and they were always at hand when not wanted; indeed that was their only reliable quality besides larceny. Not to get up a mystery with these people, I resolved to announce in the morning that my uncle had unexpectedly come from the country.

This course I decided on while I was yet groping about in the darkness for the means of getting a light. Not stumbling on the means after all, I was fain to go out to the adjacent lodge and get the watchman there to come with his lantern. Now, in groping my way down the black staircase I fell over something, and that something was a man crouching in a corner.

As the man made no answer when I asked him what he did there, but eluded my touch in silence, I ran to the lodge and urged the watchman to come quickly: telling him of the incident on the way back. The wind being as fierce as ever, we did not care to endanger the light in the lantern by rekindling the extinguished lamps on the staircase, but we examined the staircase from the bottom to the top and found no one there. It then occurred to me as possible that the man might have slipped into my rooms; so, lighting my candle at the watchman's, and leaving him standing at the door, I examined them carefully, including the room in which my dreaded guest lay asleep. All was quiet, and assuredly no other man was in those chambers.

It troubled me that there should have been a lurker on the stairs, on that night of all nights in the year, and I asked the watchman, on the chance of eliciting some hopeful explanation as I handed him a dram at the door, whether he had admitted at his gate any gentleman who had perceptibly been dining out? Yes, he said; at different times of the night, three. One lived in Fountain Court, and the other two lived in the lane, and he had seen them all go home. Again, the only other man who dwelt in the house of which my chambers formed a part, had been in the country for some weeks; and he certainly had not returned in the night, because we had seen his door with his seal on it as we came upstairs.

'The night being so bad, sir,' said the watchman, as he gave me back my glass, 'uncommon few have come in at my gate. Besides them three gentlemen that I have named, I don't call to mind another since about eleven o'clock, when a stranger asked for you.'

'My uncle,' I muttered. 'Yes.'

'You saw him, sir?'

'Yes. Oh yes.'

'Likewise the person with him?'

'Person with him!' I repeated.

'I judged the person to be with him,' returned the watchman. 'The person stopped, when he stopped to make enquiry of me, and the person took this way when he took this way.'

'What sort of person?'

The watchman had not particularly noticed; he should say a working person; to the best of his belief, he had a dust-coloured kind of clothes on, under a dark coat. The watchman made more light of the matter than I did, and naturally; not having my reason for attaching weight to it.

When I had got rid of him, which I thought it well to do without prolonging explanations, my mind was much troubled by these two circumstances taken together. Whereas they were easy of innocent solution apart – as, for instance, some diner-out or diner-at-home, who had not gone near this watchman's gate, might have strayed to my staircase and dropped asleep there – and my nameless visitor might have brought someone with him to show him the way – till, joined, they had an ugly look to one as prone to distrust and fear as the changes of a few hours had made me.

I lighted my fire, which burnt with a raw pale flare at that time of the morning, and fell into a doze before it. I seemed to have been dozing a whole night when the clocks struck six. As there was full an hour and a half between me and daylight, I dozed again; now, waking up uneasily, with prolix conversations about nothing, in my ears; now, making thunder of the wind in the chimney; at length, falling off into a profound sleep from which the daylight woke me with a start.

All this time I had never been able to consider my own situation, nor could I do so yet. I had not the power to attend to it. I was greatly dejected and distressed, but in an incoherent wholesale sort of way. As to forming any plan for the future, I could as soon have formed an elephant. When I opened the shutters and looked out at the wet wild morning, all of a leaden hue; when I walked from room to room; when I sat down again shivering, before the fire, waiting for my laundress to appear; I thought how miserable I was, but hardly knew why, or how long I had been so, or on what day of the week I made the reflection, or even who I was that made it.

At last the old woman and the niece came in – the latter with a head not easily distinguishable from her dusty broom – and testified surprise at sight of me and the fire. To whom I imparted how my uncle had come in the night and was then asleep, and how the breakfast preparations were to be modified accordingly. Then, I washed and dressed while they knocked the furniture about and made a dust; and so, in a sort of dream or sleepwalking, I found myself sitting by the fire again, waiting for – him – to come to breakfast.

By and by, his door opened and he came out. I could not bring myself to bear the sight of him, and I thought he had a worse look by daylight.

'I do not even know,' said I, speaking low as he took his seat at the table, 'by what name to call you. I have given out that you are my uncle.'

'That's it, dear boy! Call me uncle.'

'You assumed some name, I suppose, on board ship?'

'Yes, dear boy. I took the name of Provis.'

'Do you mean to keep that name?'

'Why, yes, dear boy, it's as good as another – unless you'd like another.'

'What is your real name?' I asked him in a whisper.

'Magwitch,' he answered, in the same tone; 'chrisen'd Abel.'

'What were you brought up to be?'

'A warmint, dear boy.'

He answered quite seriously, and used the word as if it denoted some profession.

'When you came into the Temple last night –' said I, pausing to wonder whether that could really have been last night, which seemed so long ago.

'Yes, dear boy?'

'When you came in at the gate and asked the watchman the way here, had you anyone with you?'

'With me? No, dear boy.'

'But there was someone there?'

'I didn't take particular notice,' he said, dubiously, 'not knowing the ways of the place. But I think there *was* a person, too, come in alonger me.'

'Are you known in London?'

'I hope not!' said he, giving his neck a jerk with his forefinger that made me turn hot and sick.

'Were you known in London, once?'

'Not over and above, dear boy. I was in the provinces mostly.'

'Were you – tried – in London?'

'Which time?' said he, with a sharp look.

'The last time.'

He nodded. 'First knowed Mr Jaggers that way. Jaggers was for me.'

It was on my lips to ask him what he was tried for, but he took up a knife, gave it a flourish, and with the words, 'And what I done is worked out and paid for!' fell to at his breakfast.

He ate in a ravenous way that was very disagreeable, and all his actions were uncouth, noisy, and greedy. Some of his teeth had failed him since I saw him eat on the marshes, and as he turned his food in his mouth, and turned his head sideways to bring his strongest fangs to bear upon it, he looked terribly like a hungry old dog.

If I had begun with any appetite, he would have taken it away, and I should have sat much as I did – repelled from him by an insurmountable aversion, and gloomily looking at the cloth.

'I'm a heavy grubber, dear boy,' he said, as a polite kind of apology when he had made an end of his meal, 'but I always was. If it had been in my constitution to be a lighter grubber, I might ha' got into lighter trouble. Similarly, I must have my smoke. When I was first hired out as shepherd t'other side the world, it's my belief I should ha' turned into a molloneolly-mad sheep myself, if I hadn't a had my smoke.'

As he said so he got up from table, and putting his hand into the breast of the pea-coat he wore, brought out a short black pipe, and a handful of loose tobacco of the kind that is called negro-head. Having filled his pipe, he put the surplus tobacco back again, as if his pocket were a drawer. Then, he took a live coal from the fire with the tongs, and lighted his pipe at it, and then turned round on the hearth-rug with his back to the fire, and went through his favourite action of holding out both his hands for mine.

'And this,' said he, dandling my hands up and down in his, as he puffed at his pipe; 'and this is the gentleman what I made! The real genuine one! It does me good fur to look at you, Pip. All I stip'late is, to stand by and look at you, dear boy!'

I released my hands as soon as I could, and found that I was beginning slowly to settle down to the contemplation of my condition. What I was chained to, and how heavily, became intelligible to me, as I heard his hoarse voice, and sat looking up at his furrowed bald head with its iron-grey hair at the sides.

'I mustn't see my gentleman a footing it in the mire of the streets; there mustn't be no mud on *his* boots. My gentleman must have horses, Pip! Horses to ride, and horses to drive, and horses for his servant to ride and drive as well. Shall colonists have their horses (and blood-'uns, if you please, good Lord!) and not my London gentleman? No, no. We'll show 'em another pair of shoes than that, Pip; won't us?'

He took out of his pocket a great thick pocketbook, bursting with papers, and tossed it on the table.

'There's something worth spending in that there book, dear boy. It's yourn. All I've got ain't mine; it's yourn. Don't you be afeerd on it. There's more where that come from. I've come to the old country fur to see my gentleman spend his money *like* a gentleman. That'll be *my* pleasure. *My* pleasure 'ull be fur to see him do it. And blast you all!' he wound up, looking round the room and snapping his fingers once with a loud snap, 'blast you everyone, from the judge in his wig, to the colonist a stirring up the dust, I'll show a better gentleman than the whole kit on you put together!'

'Stop!' said I, almost in a frenzy of fear and dislike, 'I want to speak to you. I want to know what is to be done. I want to know how you are to be kept out of danger, how long you are going to stay, what projects you have.'

'Look'ee here, Pip,' said he, laying his hand on my arm in a suddenly altered and subdued manner; 'first of all, look'ee here. I forgot myself half a minute ago. What I said was low; that's what it was; low. Look'ee here. Pip. Look over it. I ain't a going to be low.'

'First,' I resumed, half-groaning, 'what precautions can be taken against your being recognised and seized?'

'No, dear boy,' he said, in the same tone as before, 'that don't go first. Lowness goes first. I ain't took so many year to make a gentleman, not without knowing what's due to him. Look'ee here, Pip. I was low; that's what I was; low. Look over it, dear boy.'

Some sense of the grimly-ludicrous moved me to a fretful laugh, as I replied, 'I *have* looked over it. In heaven's name, don't harp upon it!'

'Yes, but look'ee here,' he persisted. 'Dear boy, I ain't come so fur, not fur to be low. Now, go on, dear boy. You was a saying –'

'How are you to be guarded from the danger you have incurred?'

'Well, dear boy, the danger ain't so great. Without I was informed agen, the danger ain't so much to signify. There's Jaggers, and there's Wemmick, and there's you. Who else is there to inform?'

'Is there no chance person who might identify you in the street?' said I.

'Well,' he returned, 'there ain't many. Nor yet I don't intend to advertise myself in the newspapers by the name of A. M. come back from Botany Bay; and years have rolled away, and who's to gain by it? Still, look'ee here, Pip. If the danger had been fifty times as great, I should ha' come to see you, mind you, just the same.'

'And how long do you remain?'

'How long?' said he, taking his black pipe from his mouth, and dropping his jaw as he stared at me. 'I'm not a going back. I've come for good.'

'Where are you to live?' said I. 'What is to be done with you? Where will you be safe?'

'Dear boy,' he returned, 'there's disguising wigs can be bought for money, and there's hair powder, and spectacles, and black clothes – shorts and what not. Others has done it safe afore, and what others has done afore, others can do agen. As to the where and how of living, dear boy, give me your own opinions on it.'

'You take it smoothly now,' said I, 'but you were very serious last night, when you swore it was death.'

'And so I swear it is death,' said he, putting his pipe back in his mouth, 'and death by the rope, in the open street not fur from this, and it's serious that you should fully understand it to be so. What then, when that's once done? Here I am. To go back now, 'ud be as bad as to stand ground – worse. Besides, Pip, I'm here, because I've meant it by you, years and years. As to what I dare, I'm a old bird now, as has dared all manner of traps since first he was fledged, and I'm not afeerd to perch upon a scarecrow. If there's death hid inside of it, there is, and let him come out, and I'll face him, and then I'll believe in him and not afore. And now let me have a look at my gentleman agen.'

Once more he took me by both hands and surveyed me with an air of admiring proprietorship, smoking with great complacency all the while.

It appeared to me that I could do no better than secure him some quiet lodging hard by, of which he might take possession when Herbert returned: whom I expected in two or three days. That the secret must be confided to Herbert as a matter of unavoidable necessity, even if I could have put the immense relief I should derive from sharing it with him out of the question, was plain to me. But it was by no means so plain to Mr Provis (I resolved to call him by that name), who reserved his consent to Herbert's participation until he should have seen him and formed a favourable judgement of his physiognomy. 'And even then, dear boy,' said he, pulling a greasy little clasped black Testament out of his pocket, 'we'll have him on his oath.'

To state that my terrible patron carried this little black book about the world solely to swear people on in cases of emergency, would be to state what I never quite established – but this I can say, that I never knew him put it to any other use. The book itself had the appearance of having been stolen from some court of justice, and perhaps his knowledge of its antecedents, combined with his own experience in that wise, gave him a reliance on its powers as a sort of legal spell or charm. On this first occasion of his producing it, I recalled how he had made me swear fidelity in the churchyard long ago, and how he had described himself last night as always swearing to his resolutions in his solitude.

As he was at present dressed in a seafaring slop suit, in which he looked as if he had some parrots and cigars to dispose of, I next discussed with him what dress he should wear. He cherished an extraordinary belief in the virtues of 'shorts' as a disguise, and had in his own mind sketched a dress for himself that would have made him something between a dean and a dentist. It was with considerable difficulty that I won him over to the assumption of a dress more like a prosperous farmer's; and we arranged that he should cut his hair close, and wear a little powder. Lastly, as he had not yet been seen by the laundress or her niece, he was to keep himself out of their view until his change of dress was made.

It would seem a simple matter to decide on these precautions; but in my dazed, not to say distracted, state, it took so long, that I did not get out to further them until two or three in the afternoon. He was to remain shut up in the chambers while I was gone, and was on no account to open the door.

There being to my knowledge a respectable lodging-house in Essex Street, the back of which looked into the Temple, and was almost within hail of my windows, I first of all repaired to that house, and was so fortunate as to secure the second floor for my uncle, Mr Provis. I then went from shop to shop, making such purchases as were necessary to the change in his appearance. This business transacted, I turned my face, on my own account, to Little Britain. Mr Jaggers was at his desk, but, seeing me enter, got up immediately and stood before his fire.

'Now, Pip,' said he, 'be careful.'

'I will, sir,' I returned. For, coming along I had thought well of what I was going to say.

'Don't commit yourself,' said Mr Jaggers, 'and don't commit anyone. You understand – anyone. Don't tell me anything: I don't want to know anything: I am not curious.'

Of course I saw that he knew the man was come.

'I merely want, Mr Jaggers,' said I, 'to assure myself what I have been told is true. I have no hope of its being untrue, but at least I may verify it.'

Mr Jaggers nodded. 'But did you say "told" or "informed"?' he asked me, with his head on one side, and not looking at me, but looking in a listening way at the floor. 'Told would seem to imply verbal communication. You can't have verbal communication with a man in New South Wales, you know.'

'I will say, informed, Mr Jaggers.'

'Good.'

'I have been informed by a person named Abel Magwitch, that he is the benefactor so long unknown to me.'

'That is the man,' said Mr Jaggers, ' – in New South Wales.'

'And only he?' said I.

'And only he,' said Mr Jaggers.

'I am not so unreasonable, sir, as to think you at all responsible for my mistakes and wrong conclusions; but I always supposed it was Miss Havisham.'

'As you say, Pip,' returned Mr Jaggers, turning his eyes upon me coolly, and taking a bite at his forefinger, 'I am not at all responsible for that.'

'And yet it looked so like it, sir,' I pleaded with a downcast heart.

'Not a particle of evidence, Pip,' said Mr Jaggers, shaking his head and gathering up his skirts. 'Take nothing on its looks; take everything on evidence. There's no better rule.'

'I have no more to say,' said I, with a sigh, after standing silent for a little while. 'I have verified my information, and there's an end.'

'And Magwitch – in New South Wales – having at last disclosed himself,' said Mr Jaggers, 'you will comprehend, Pip, how rigidly throughout my communication with you I have always adhered to the strict line of fact. There has never been the least departure from the strict line of fact. You are quite aware of that?'

'Quite, sir.'

'I communicated to Magwitch – in New South Wales – when he first wrote to me – from New South Wales – the caution that he must not expect me ever to deviate from the strict line of fact. I also communicated to him another caution. He appeared to me to have obscurely hinted in his letter at some distant idea of seeing you in England here. I cautioned him that I must hear no more of that; that he was not at all likely to obtain a pardon; that he was expatriated for the term of his natural life; and that his presenting him in this country would be an act of felony, rendering him liable to the extreme penalty of the law. I gave Magwitch that caution,' said Mr Jaggers, looking hard at me; 'I wrote it to New South Wales. He guided himself by it, no doubt.'

'No doubt,' said I.

'I have been informed by Wemmick,' pursued Mr Jaggers, still looking hard at me, 'that he has received a letter, under date Portsmouth, from a colonist of the name of Purvis, or – '

'Or Provis,' I suggested.

'Or Provis – thank you, Pip. Perhaps it *is* Provis? Perhaps you know it's Provis?'

'Yes,' said I.

'You know it's Provis. A letter, under date Portsmouth, from a colonist of the name of Provis, asking for the particulars of your address, on behalf of Magwitch. Wemmick sent him the particulars, I understand, by return of post. Probably it is through Provis that you have received the explanation of Magwitch – in New South Wales?'

'It came through Provis,' I replied.

'Good-day, Pip,' said Mr Jaggers, offering his hand; 'glad to have seen you. In writing by post to Magwitch – in New South Wales – or in communicating with him through Provis, have the goodness to mention that the particulars and vouchers of our long account shall be sent to you, together with the balance; for there is still a balance remaining. Good-day, Pip!'

We shook hands, and he looked hard at me as long as he could see me. I turned at the door, and he was still looking hard at me, while the two vile casts on the shelf seemed to be trying to get their eyelids open, and to force out of their swollen throats, 'O, what a man he is!'

Wemmick was out, and though he had been at his desk he could have done nothing for me. I went straight back to the Temple, where I found the terrible Provis drinking rum and water and smoking negro-head, in safety.

Next day the clothes I had ordered all came home, and he put them on. Whatever he put on, became him less (it dismally seemed to me) than what he had worn before. To my thinking there was something in him that made it hopeless to attempt to disguise him. The more I dressed him, and the better I dressed him, the more he looked like the slouching fugitive on the marshes. This effect on my anxious fancy was partly referable, no doubt, to his old face and manner growing more familiar to me: but I believed too that he dragged one of his legs as if there were still a weight of iron on it, and that from head to foot there was convict in the very grain of the man.

The influences of his solitary hut-life were upon him besides, and gave him a savage air that no dress could tame; added to these were the influences of his subsequent branded life among men, and, crowning all, his consciousness that he was dodging and hiding now. In all his ways of sitting and standing, and eating and drinking – of brooding about, in a high-shouldered reluctant style – of taking out his great horn-handled jack-knife and wiping it on his legs and cutting his food – of lifting light glasses and cups to his lips, as if they were clumsy pannikins – of chopping a wedge off his bread, and soaking up with it the last fragments of gravy round and round his plate, as if to make the most of an allowance, and then drying his fingers on it, and then swallowing it – in these ways and a thousand other small nameless instances arising every minute in the day, there was prisoner, felon, bondsman, plain as plain could be.

It had been his own idea to wear that touch of powder, and I conceded the powder after overcoming the shorts. But I can compare the effect of it, when on, to nothing but the probable effect of rouge upon the dead; so awful was the manner in which everything in him, that it was most desirable to repress, started through that thin layer of pretence, and seemed to come blazing out at the crown of his head. It was abandoned as soon as tried, and he wore his grizzled hair cut short.

Words cannot tell what a sense I had, at the same time, of the dreadful mystery that he was to me. When he fell asleep of an evening, with his knotted hands clenching the sides of the easy-chair, and his bald head tattooed with deep wrinkles falling forward on his breast, I would sit and look at him, wondering what he had done, and loading him with all the crimes in the calendar, until the impulse was powerful on me to start up and fly from him. Every hour so increased my abhorrence of him, that I even think I might have yielded to this impulse in the first agonies of being so haunted, notwithstanding all he had done for me and the risk he ran, but for the knowledge that Herbert must soon come back. Once, I actually did start out of bed in the night, and begin to dress myself in my worst clothes, hurriedly intending to leave him there with everything else I possessed, and enlist for India as a private soldier.

I doubt if a ghost could have been more terrible to me, up in those lonely rooms in the long evenings and long nights, with the wind and the rain always rushing by. A ghost could not have been taken and hanged on my account, and the consideration that he could be, and the dread that he would be, were no small addition to my horrors. When he was not asleep, or playing a complicated kind of patience with a ragged pack of cards of his own – a game that I never saw before or since, and in which he recorded his winnings by sticking his jack-knife into the table – when he was not engaged in either of these pursuits, he would ask me to read to him – 'Foreign language, dear boy!' While I complied, he, not comprehending a single word, would stand before the fire surveying me with the air of an exhibitor, and I would see him, between the fingers of the hand with which I shaded my face, appealing in dumb show to the furniture to take notice of my proficiency. The imaginary student pursued by the misshapen creature he had impiously made, was not more wretched than I, pursued by the creature who had made me, and recoiling from him with a stronger repulsion, the more he admired me and the fonder he was of me.

This is written of, I am sensible, as if it had lasted a year. It lasted about five days. Expecting Herbert all the time, I dared not go out, except when I took Provis for an airing after dark. At length, one evening when dinner was over and I had dropped into a slumber quite worn out – for my nights had been agitated and my rest broken by fearful dreams – I was roused by the welcome footstep on the staircase. Provis, who had been asleep too, staggered up at the noise I made, and in an instant I saw his jack-knife shining in his hand.

'Quiet! It's Herbert!' I said; and Herbert came bursting in, with the airy freshness of six hundred miles of France upon him.

'Handel, my dear fellow, how are you, and again how are you, and again how are you? I seem to have been gone a twelve-month! Why, so I must have been, for you have grown quite thin and pale! Handel, my – halloa! I beg your pardon.'

He was stopped in his running on and in his shaking hands with me, by seeing Provis. Provis, regarding him with a fixed attention, was slowly putting up his jack-knife, and groping in another pocket for something else.

'Herbert, my dear friend,' said I, shutting the double doors, while Herbert stood staring and wondering, 'something very strange has happened. This is – a visitor of mine.'

'It's all right, dear boy!' said Provis, coming forward, with his little clasped black book, and then addressing himself to Herbert. 'Take it in your right hand. Lord strike you dead on the spot, if ever you split in any way sumever. Kiss it!'

'Do so, as he wishes it,' I said to Herbert. So Herbert, looking at me with a friendly uneasiness and amazement, complied, and Provis immediately shaking hands with him, said, 'Now, you're on your oath, you know. And never believe me on mine, if Pip shan't make a gentleman on you!'

Chapter 41

In vain should I attempt to describe the astonishment and disquiet of Herbert, when he and I and Provis sat down before the fire, and I recounted the whole of the secret. Enough that I saw my own feelings reflected in Herbert's face, and, not least among them, my repugnance towards the man who had done so much for me.

What would alone have set a division between that man and us, if there had been no other dividing circumstance, was his triumph in my story. Saving his troublesome sense of having been 'low' on one occasion since his return – on which point he began to hold forth to Herbert, the moment my revelation was finished – he had no perception of the possibility of my finding any fault with my good fortune. His boast that he had made me a gentleman, and that he had come to see me support the character on his ample resources, was made for me quite as much as for himself. And that it was a highly agreeable boast to both of us, and that we must both be very proud of it, was a conclusion quite established in his own mind.

'Though, look'ee here, Pip's comrade,' he said to Herbert, after having discoursed for some time, 'I know very well that once since I come back – for half a minute – I've been low. I said to Pip, I knowed as I had been low. But don't you fret yourself on that score. I ain't made Pip a gentleman, and Pip ain't a-goin' to make you a gentleman, not fur me not to know what's due to ye both. Dear boy, and Pip's comrade, you two may count upon me always having a genteel muzzle on. Muzzled I have been since that half a minute when I was betrayed into lowness, muzzled I am at the present time, muzzled I ever will be.'

Herbert said, 'Certainly,' but looked as if there were no specific consolation in this, and remained perplexed and dismayed. We were anxious for the time when he would go to his lodging, and leave us together, but he was evidently jealous of leaving us together, and sat late. It was midnight before I took him round to Essex Street, and saw him safely in at his own dark door. When it closed upon him, I experienced the first moment of relief I had known since the night of his arrival.

Never quite free from an uneasy remembrance of the man on the stairs, I had always looked about me in taking my guest out after dark, and in bringing him back; and I looked about me now. Difficult as it is in a large city to avoid the suspicion of being watched when the mind is conscious of danger in that regard, I could not persuade myself that any of the people within sight cared about my movements. The few who were passing, passed on their several ways, and the street was empty when I turned back into the Temple. Nobody had come out at the gate with us, nobody went in at the gate with me. As I crossed by the fountain, I saw his lighted back windows looking bright and quiet, and, when I stood for a few moments in the doorway of the building where I lived, before going up the stairs, Garden Court was as still and lifeless as the staircase was when I ascended it.

Herbert received me with open arms, and I had never felt before so blessedly what it is to have a friend. When he had spoken some sound words of sympathy and encouragement, we sat down to consider the question, what was to be done?

The chair that Provis had occupied still remaining where it had stood – for he had a barrack way with him of hanging about one spot, in one unsettled manner, and going through one round of observances with his pipe and his negro-head and his jack-knife and his pack of cards, and what not, as if it were all put down for him on a slate – I say, his chair remaining where it had stood, Herbert unconsciously took it, but next moment started out of it, pushed it away, and took another. He had no occasion to say, after that, that he had conceived an aversion for my patron, neither had I occasion to confess my own. We interchanged that confidence without shaping a syllable.

'What,' said I to Herbert, when he was safe in another chair, 'what is to be done?'

'My poor dear Handel,' he replied, holding his head, 'I am too stunned to think.'

'So was I, Herbert, when the blow first fell. Still, something must be done. He is intent upon various new expenses – horses, and carriages, and lavish appearances of all kinds. He must be stopped somehow.'

'You mean that you can't accept – '

'How can I?' I interposed, as Herbert paused. 'Think of him! Look at him!'

An involuntary shudder passed over both of us.

'Yet I am afraid the dreadful truth is, Herbert, that he is attached to me, strongly attached to me. Was there ever such a fate!'

'My poor dear Handel,' Herbert repeated.

'Then,' said I, 'after all, stopping short here, never taking another penny from him, think what I owe him already! Then again: I am heavily in debt – very heavily for me, who have now no expectations – and I have been bred to no calling, and I am fit for nothing.'

'Well, well, well!' Herbert remonstrated. 'Don't say fit for nothing.'

'What am I fit for? I know only one thing that I am fit for, and that is, to go for a soldier. And I might have gone, my dear Herbert, but for the prospect of taking counsel with your friendship and affection.'

Of course I broke down there; and of course Herbert, beyond seizing a warm grip of my hand, pretended not to know it.

'Anyhow, my dear Handel,' said he presently, 'soldiering won't do. If you were to renounce this patronage and these favours, I suppose you would do so with some faint hope of one day repaying what you have already had. Not very strong, that hope, if you went soldiering. Besides, it's absurd. You would be infinitely better in Clarriker's house, small as it is. I am working up towards a partnership, you know.'

Poor fellow! He little suspected with whose money.

'But there is another question,' said Herbert. 'This is an ignorant determined man, who has long had one fixed idea. More than that, he seems to me (I may misjudge him) to be a man of a desperate and fierce character.'

'I know he is,' I returned. 'Let me tell you what evidence I have seen of it.' And I told him what I had not mentioned in my narrative; of that encounter with the other convict.

'See, then,' said Herbert; 'think of this! He comes here at the peril of his life, for the realisation of his fixed idea. In the moment of realisation, after all his toil and waiting, you cut the ground from under his feet, destroy his idea, and make his gains worthless to him. Do you see nothing that he might do under the disappointment?'

'I have seen it, Herbert, and dreamed of it ever since the fatal night of his arrival. Nothing has been in my thoughts so distinctly as his putting himself in the way of being taken.'

'Then you may rely upon it,' said Herbert, 'that there would be great danger of his doing it. That is his power over you as long as he remains in England, and that would be his reckless course if you forsook him.'

I was so struck by the horror of this idea, which had weighed upon me from the first, and the working out of which would make me regard myself, in some sort, as his murderer, that I could not rest in my chair, but began pacing to and fro. I said to Herbert, meanwhile, that even if Provis were recognised and taken, in spite of himself, I should be wretched as the cause, however innocently. Yes; even though I was so wretched in having him at large and near me, and even though I would far rather have worked at the forge all the days of my life than I would ever have come to this!

But there was no raving off the question, What was to be done?

'The first and the main thing to be done,' said Herbert, 'is to get him out of England. You will have to go with him, and then he may be induced to go.'

'But get him where I will, could I prevent his coming back?'

'My good Handel, is it not obvious that with Newgate in the next street, there must be far greater hazard in your breaking your mind to him and making him reckless, here, than elsewhere? If a pretext to get him away could be made out of that other convict, or out of anything else in his life, now.'

'There again!' said I, stopping before Herbert, with my open hands held out, as if they contained the desperation of the case. 'I know nothing of his life. It has almost made me mad to sit here of a night and see him before me, so bound up with my fortunes and misfortunes, and yet so unknown to me, except as the miserable wretch who terrified me two days in my childhood!'

Herbert got up, and linked his arm in mine, and we slowly walked to and fro together, studying the carpet.

'Handel,' said Herbert, stopping, 'you feel convinced that you can take no further benefits from him; do you?'

'Fully. Surely you would, too, if you were in my place?'

'And you feel convinced that you must break with him?'

'Herbert, can you ask me?'

'And you have, and are bound to have, that tenderness for the life he has risked on your account, that you must save him, if possible, from throwing it away. Then you must get him out of England before you stir a finger to extricate yourself. That done, extricate yourself, in Heaven's name, and we'll see it out together, dear old boy.'

It was a comfort to shake hands upon it, and walk up and down again, with only that done.

'Now, Herbert,' said I, 'with reference to gaining some knowledge of his history. There is but one way that I know of. I must ask him point-blank.'

'Yes. Ask him,' said Herbert, 'when we sit at breakfast in the morning.' For, he had said, on taking leave of Herbert, that he would come to breakfast with us.

With this project formed, we went to bed. I had the wildest dreams concerning him, and woke unrefreshed; I woke, too, to recover the fear which I had lost in the night, of his being found out as a returned transport. Waking, I never lost that fear.

He came round at the appointed time, took out his jack-knife, and sat down to his meal. He was full of plans 'for his gentleman's coming out strong, and like a gentleman,' and urged me to begin speedily upon the pocketbook, which he had left in my possession. He considered the chambers and his own lodging as temporary residences, and advised me to look out at once for a 'fashionable crib' near Hyde Park, in which he could have 'a shakedown'. When he had made an end of his breakfast, and was wiping his knife on his leg, I said to him, without a word of preface: 'After you were gone last night, I told my friend of the struggle that the soldiers found you engaged in on the marshes, when we came up. You remember?'

'Remember!' said he. 'I think so!'

'We want to know something about that man – and about you. It is strange to know no more about either, and particularly you, than I was able to tell last night. Is not this as good a time as another for our knowing more?'

'Well!' he said, after consideration. 'You're on your oath, you know, Pip's comrade?'

'Assuredly,' replied Herbert.

'As to anything I say, you know,' he insisted. 'The oath applies to all.'

'I understand it to do so.'

'And look'ee here! Wotever I done, is worked out and paid for,' he insisted again.

'So be it.'

He took out his black pipe and was going to fill it with negro-head, when, looking at the tangle of tobacco in his hand, he seemed to think it might perplex the thread of his narrative. He put it back again, stuck his pipe in a buttonhole of his coat, spread a hand on each knee, and, after turning an angry eye on the fire for a few silent moments, looked around at us and said what follows.

Chapter 42

'Dear boy and Pip's comrade. I am not a going fur to tell you my life, like a song or a storybook. But to give it you short and handy, I'll put it at once into a mouthful of English. In jail and out of jail, in jail and out of jail, in jail and out of jail. There, you've got it. That's *my* life pretty much, down to such times as I got shipped off, arter Pip stood my friend.

'I've been done everything to, pretty well – except hanged.

I've been locked up, as much as a silver tea-kittle. I've been carted here and carted there, and put out of this town and put out of that town, and stuck in the stocks, and whipped and worried and drove. I've no more notion where I was born than you have – if so much. I first become aware of myself, down in Essex, a thieving turnips for my living. Summun had run away from me – a man – a tinker – and he'd took the fire with him, and left me very cold.

'I know'd my name to be Magwitch, chrisen'd Abel. How did I know it? Much as I know'd the birds' names in the hedges to be chaffinch, sparrer, thrush. I might have thought it was all lies together, only as the birds' names come out true, I supposed mine did.

'So fur as I could find, there warn't a soul that see young Abel Magwitch, with as little on him as in him, but wot caught fright at him, and either drove him off, or took him up. I was took up, took up, took up, to that extent that I reg'larly grow'd up took up.

'This is the way it was, that when I was a ragged little creetur as much to be pitied as ever I see (not that I looked in the glass, for there warn't many insides of furnished houses known to me), I got the name of being hardened. "This is a terrible hardened one," they says to prison wisitors, picking out me. "May be said to live in jails, this boy." Then they looked at me, and I looked at them, and they measured my head, some on 'em – they had better a measured my stomach – and others on 'em giv me tracts what I couldn't read, and made me speeches what I couldn't unnerstand. They always went on agen me about the devil. But what the devil was I to do? I must put something into my stomach, mustn't I? – Howsomever, I'm a getting low, and I know what's due. Dear boy and Pip's comrade, don't you be afeerd of me being low.

'Tramping, begging, thieving, working sometimes when I could – though that warn't as often as you may think, till you put the question whether you would ha' been overready to give me work yourselves – a bit of a poacher, a bit of a labourer, a bit of a waggoner, a bit of a haymaker, a bit of a hawker, a bit of most things that don't pay and lead to trouble, I got to be a man. A deserting soldier in a Traveller's Rest, what lay hid up to the chin under a lot of taturs, learnt me to read; and a travelling giant what signed his name at a penny a time learnt me to write. I warn't locked up as often now as formerly, but I wore out my good share of key-metal still.

'At Epsom races, a matter of over twenty year ago, I got acquainted wi' a man whose skull I'd crack wi' this poker, like the claw of a lobster, if I'd got it on this hob. His right name was Compeyson; and that's the man, dear boy, what you see me a pounding in the ditch, according to what you truly told your comrade arter I was gone last night.

'He set up fur a gentleman, this Compeyson, and he'd been to a public boarding-school and had learning. He was a smooth one to talk, and was a dab at the ways of gentlefolks. He was good-looking too. It was the night afore the great race, when I found him on the heath, in a booth that I know'd on. Him and some more was a sitting among the tables when I went in, and the landlord (which had a knowledge of me, and was a sporting one) called him out, and said, "I think this is a man that might suit you" – meaning I was.

'Compeyson, he looks at me very noticing, and I look at him. He has a watch and a chain and a ring and a breast pin and a handsome suit of clothes.

' "To judge from appearances, you're out of luck," says Compeyson to me.

' "Yes, master, and I've never been in it much." (I had come out of Kingston Jail last on a vagrancy committal. Not but what it might have been for something else; but it warn't.)

' "Luck changes," says Compeyson; "perhaps yours is going to change."

'I says, "I hope it may be so. There's room."

' "What can you do?" says Compeyson.

' "Eat and drink," I says; "if you'll find the materials."

'Compeyson laughed, looked at me again very noticing, giv me five shillings, and appointed me for next night. Same place.

'I went to Compeyson next night, same place, and Compeyson took me on to be his man and pardner. And what was Compeyson's business in which we was to go pardners? Compeyson's business was the swindling, handwriting forging, stolen bank-note passing, and suchlike. All sorts of traps as Compeyson could set with his head, and keep his own legs out of and get the profits from and let another man in for, was Compeyson's business. He'd no more heart than a iron file, he was as cold as death, and he had the head of the devil afore mentioned.

'There was another in with Compeyson, as was called Arthur – not as being so chrisen'd, but as a surname. He was in a decline, and was a shadow to look at. Him and Compeyson had been in a bad thing with a rich lady some years afore, and they'd made a pot of money by it; but Compeyson betted and gamed, and he'd have run through the king's taxes. So, Arthur was a dying and a dying poor and with the horrors on him, and Compeyson's wife (which Compeyson kicked mostly) was a having pity on him when she could, and Compeyson was a having pity on nothing and nobody.

'I might a took warning by Arthur, but I didn't; and I won't pretend I was partick'ler – for where 'ud be the good on it, dear boy and comrade? So I begun wi' Compeyson, and a poor tool I was in his hands. Arthur lived at the top of Compeyson's house (over nigh Brentford it was), and Compeyson kept a careful account agen him for board and lodging, in case he should ever get better to work it out. But Arthur soon settled the account. The second or third time as ever I see him, he come a tearing down into Compeyson's parlour late at night, in only a flannel gown, with his hair all in a sweat, and he says to Compeyson's wife, "Sally, she really is upstairs alonger me, now, and I can't get rid of her. She's all in white," he says, "wi' white flowers in her hair, and she's awful mad, an she's got a shroud hanging over her arm, and she says she'll put it on me at five in the morning.'

'Says Compeyson: "Why, you fool, don't you know she's got a living body? And how should she be up there, without coming through the door, or in at the window, and up the stairs?"

' "I don't know how she's there," says Arthur, shivering dreadful with the horrors, "but she's standing in the corner at the foot of the bed, awful mad. And over where her heart's broke – *you* broke it! – there's drops of blood."

'Compeyson spoke hardy, but he was always a coward. "Go up alonger this drivelling sick man," he says to his wife, "and, Magwitch, lend her a hand, will you?" But he never come nigh himself.

'Compeyson's wife and me took him up to bed agen, and he raved most dreadful. "Why look at her!" he cries out. "She's a shaking the shroud at me! Don't you see her? Look at her eyes! Ain't it awful to see her so mad?" Next, he cries, "She'll put it on me, and then I'm done for! Take it away from her, take it away!" And then he catched hold of us, and kep on a talking to her, and answering of her, till I half believed I see her myself.

'Compeyson's wife, being used to him, give him some liquor to get the horrors off, and by and by he quieted. "Oh, she's gone! Has her keeper been for her?" he says. "Yes," says Compeyson's wife. "Did you tell him to lock and bar her in?" "Yes." "And to take that ugly thing away from her?" "Yes, yes, all right." "You're a good creetur," he says, "don't leave me, whatever you do, and thank you!"

'He rested pretty quiet till it might want a few minutes of five, and then he starts up with a scream, and screams out, "Here she is! She's got the shroud again. She's unfolding it. She's coming out of the corner. She's coming to the bed. Hold me, both on you – one of each side – don't let her touch me with it. Hah! She missed me that time. Don't let her throw it over my shoulders. Don't let her lift me up to get it round me. She's lifting me up. Keep me down!" Then he lifted himself up hard, and was dead.

'Compeyson took it easy as a good riddance for both sides. Him and me was soon busy, and first he swore me (being ever artful) on my own book – this here little black book, dear boy, what I swore your comrade on.

'Not to go into the things that Compeyson planned, and I done – which 'ud take a week – I'll simply say to you, dear boy, and Pip's comrade, that that man got me into such nets as made me his black slave. I was always in debt to him, always under his thumb, always a working, always a getting into danger. He was younger than me, but he'd got craft, and he'd got learning, and he overmatched me five hundred times told and no mercy. My missis as I had the hard time wi' – Stop though! I ain't brought *her* in – '

He looked about him in a confused way, as if he had lost his place in the book of his remembrance; and he turned his face to the fire, and spread his hands broader on his knees, and lifted them off and put them on again.

'There ain't no need to go into it,' he said, looking round once more. 'The time wi' Compeyson was a'most as hard a time as ever I had; that said, all's said. Did I tell you as I was tried, alone, for misdemeanour, while with Compeyson?'

I answered, No.

'Well!' he said, 'I *was*, and got convicted. As to took up on suspicion, that was twice or three times in the four or five year that it lasted; but evidence was wanting. At last, me and Com-

peyson was both committed for felony – on a charge of putting stolen notes in circulation – and there was other charges behind. Compeyson says to me, "Separate defences, no communication," and that was all. And I was so miserable poor, that I sold all the clothes I had, except what hung on my back, afore I could get Jaggers.

'When we was put in the dock, I noticed first of all what a gentleman Compeyson looked, wi' his curly hair and his black clothes and his white pocket-handkercher, and what a common sort of a wretch I looked. When the prosecution opened and the evidence was put short, aforehand, I noticed how heavy it all bore on me, and how light on him. When the evidence was giv in the box, I noticed how it was always me that had come for'ard, and could be swore to, how it was always me that the money had been paid to, how it was always me that had seemed to work the thing and get the profit. But, when the defence come on, then I see the plan plainer; for, says the counsellor for Compeyson, "My lord and gentlemen, here you has afore you, side by side, two persons as your eyes can separate wide; one, the younger, well brought up, who will be spoke to as such; one, the elder, ill brought up, who will be spoke to as such; one, the younger, seldom if ever seen in these here transactions, and only suspected; t'other, the elder, always seen in 'em and always wi' his guilt brought home. Can you doubt, if there is but one in it, which is the one, and if there is two in it, which is much the worst one?" And suchlike. And when it come to character, warn't it Compeyson as had been to school, and warn't it his schoolfellows as was in this position and in that, and warn't it him as had been know'd by witnesses in such clubs and societies, and nowt to his disadvantage? And warn't it me as had been tried afore, and as had been know'd up hill and down dale in bridewells and lock-ups? And when it come to speech-making, warn't it Compeyson as could speak to 'em wi' his face dropping every now and then into his white pocket-handker-cher – ah! and wi' verses in his speech, too – and warn't it me as could only say, "Gentlemen, this man at my side is a most precious rascal"? And when the verdict come, warn't it Compeyson as was recommended to mercy on account of good character and bad company, and giving up all the information he could agen me, and warn't it me as got never a word but guilty? And when I says to Compeyson, "Once out of this court, I'll smash that face of yourn!" ain't it Compeyson as prays the judge to be protected, and gets two turnkeys stood betwixt us? And when we're sentenced, ain't it him as gets seven year, and me fourteen, and ain't it him as the judge is sorry for, because he might a done so well, and ain't it me as the judge perceives to be a old offender of wiolent passion, likely to come to worse?'

He had worked himself into a state of great excitement, but he checked it, took two or three short breaths, swallowed as often, and stretching out his hand towards me, said, in a reassuring manner, 'I ain't a going to be low, dear boy!'

He had so heated himself that he took out his handkerchief and wiped his face and head and neck and hands, before he could go on.

'I had said to Compeyson that I'd smash that face of his, and

I swore Lord smash mine! to do it. We was in the same prison-ship, but I couldn't get at him for long, though I tried. At last I come behind him and hit him on the cheek to turn him round and get a smashing one at him, when I was seen and seized. The black-hole of that ship warn't a strong one, to a judge of black-holes that could swim and dive. I escaped to the shore, and I was a hiding among the graves there, envying them as was in 'em and all over, when I first see my boy!'

He regarded me with a look of affection that made him almost abhorrent to me again, though I had felt great pity for him.

'By my boy, I was giv to understand as Compeyson was out on them marshes too. Upon my soul, I half believe he escaped in his terror, to get quit of me, not knowing it was me as had got ashore. I hunted him down. I smashed his face. "And now," says I, "as the worst thing I can do, caring nothing for myself, I'll drag you back." And I'd have swum off, towing him by the hair, if it had come to that, and I'd a got him aboard without the soldiers.

'Of course he'd much the best of it to the last – his character was so good. He had escaped when he was made half-wild by me and my murderous intentions; and his punishment was light. I was put in irons, brought to trial again, and sent for life. I didn't stop for life, dear boy and Pip's comrade, being here.'

He wiped himself again, as he had done before, and then slowly took his tangle of tobacco from his pocket, and plucked his pipe from his buttonhole, and slowly filled it, and began to smoke.

'Is he dead?' I asked after a silence.

'Is who dead, dear boy?'

'Compeyson.'

'He hopes *I* am, if he's alive, you may be sure,' with a fierce look. 'I never heard no more of him.'

Herbert had been writing with his pencil in the cover of a book. He softly pushed the book over to me, as Provis stood smoking with his eyes on the fire, and I read in it: 'Young Havisham's name was Arthur. Compeyson is the man who professed to be Miss Havisham's lover.'

I shut the book and nodded slightly to Herbert, and put the book by; but we neither of us said anything, and both looked at Provis as he stood smoking by the fire.

Chapter 43

Why should I pause to ask how much of my shrinking from Provis might be traced to Estella? Why should I loiter on my road, to compare the state of mind in which I had tried to rid myself of the stain of the prison before meeting her at the coach-office, with the state of mind in which I now reflected on the abyss between Estella in her pride and beauty, and the returned transport whom I harboured? The road would be none the smoother for it, the end would be none the better for it; he would not be helped, nor I extenuated.

A new fear had been engendered in my mind by his narrative; or rather, his narrative had given form and purpose to the fear that was already there. If Compeyson were alive and should discover his return, I could hardly doubt the consequence. That Compeyson stood in mortal fear of him, neither of the two could know much better than I; and that any such man as that man had been described to be, would hesitate to release himself for good from a dreaded enemy by the safe means of becoming an informer, was scarcely to be imagined.

Never had I breathed, and never would I breathe – or so I resolved – a word of Estella to Provis. But, I said to Herbert that before I could go abroad, I must see both Estella and Miss Havisham. This was when we were left alone on the night of the day when Provis told us his story. I resolved to go out to Richmond next day, and I went.

On my presenting myself at Mrs Brandley's, Estella's maid was called to tell me that Estella had gone into the country. Where? To Satis House, as usual. Not as usual, I said, for she had never yet gone there without me; when was she coming back? There was an air of reservation in the answer which increased my perplexity, and the answer was that her maid believed she was only coming back at all for a little while. I could make nothing of this, except that it was meant that I should make nothing of it, and I went home again in complete discomfiture.

Another night-consultation with Herbert after Provis was gone home (I always took him home, and always looked well about me), led us to the conclusion that nothing should be said about going abroad until I came back from Miss Havisham's. In the meantime Herbert and I were to consider separately what it would be best to say; whether we should devise any pretence of being afraid that he was under suspicious obser-vation; or whether I, who had never yet been abroad, should propose an expedition. We both knew that I had but to propose anything, and he would consent. We agreed that his remaining many days in his present hazard was not to be thought of.

Next day, I had the meanness to feign that I was under a binding promise to go down to Joe; but I was capable of almost any meanness towards Joe or his name. Provis was to be strictly careful while I was gone, and Herbert was to take the charge of him that I had taken. I was to be absent only one night, and, on my return, the gratification of his impatience for my starting as a gentleman on a greater scale was to be begun. It occurred to me then, and as I afterwards found to Herbert also, that he might be best got away across the water, on that pretence – as, to make purchases, or the like.

Having thus cleared the way for my expedition to Miss Havi-sham's, I set off by the early morning coach before it was yet light, and was out in the open country-road when the day came creeping on, halting and whimpering and shivering, and wrapped in patches of cloud and rags of mist, like a beggar. When we drove up to the Blue Boar after a drizzly ride, whom should I see come out under the gateway, toothpick in hand, to look at the coach, but Bentley Drummle!

As he pretended not to see me, I pretended not to see him. It was a very lame pretence on both sides; the lamer, because we both went into the coffee-room, where he had just finished his breakfast, and where I had ordered mine. It was poisonous to me to see him in the town, for I very well knew why he had come there.

Pretending to read a smeary newspaper long out of date, which had nothing half so legible in its local news, as the foreign matter of coffee, pickles, fish-sauces, gravy, melted butter, and wine, with which it was sprinkled all over, as if it had taken the measles in a highly irregular form, I sat at my table while he stood before the fire. By degrees it became an enormous injury to me that he stood before the fire. And I got up, determined to have my share of it. I had to put my hands behind his legs for the poker when I went up to the fireplace to stir the fire, but still pretended not to know him.

'Is this a cut?' said Mr Drummle.

'Oh?' said I, poker in hand; 'it's you, is it? How do you do? I was wondering who it was, who kept the fire off.'

With that I poked tremendously, and having done so, planted myself side by side with Mr Drummle, my shoulders squared, and my back to the fire.

'You have just come down?' said Mr Drummle, edging me a little away with his shoulder.

'Yes,' said I, edging *him* a little away with *my* shoulder.

'Beastly place,' said Drummle – 'Your part of the country, I think?'

'Yes,' I assented. 'I am told it's very like your Shropshire.'

'Not in the least like it,' said Drummle.

Here Mr Drummle looked at his boots and I looked at mine, and then Mr Drummle looked at my boots and I looked at his.

'Have you been here long?' I asked, determined not to yield an inch of the fire.

'Long enough to be tired of it,' returned Drummle, pretending to yawn, but equally determined.

'Do you stay here long?'

'Can't say,' answered Mr Drummle. 'Do you?'

'Can't say,' said I.

I felt here, through a tingling in my blood, that if Mr Drummle's shoulder had claimed another hair's breadth of room, I should have jerked him into the window; equally, that if my shoulder had urged a similar claim, Mr Drummle would have jerked me into the nearest box. He whistled a little. So did I.

'Large tract of marshes about here, I believe?' said Drummle.

'Yes. What of that?' said I.

Mr Drummle looked at me, and then at my boots, and then said, 'Oh!' and laughed.

'Are you amused, Mr Drummle?'

'No,' said he, 'not particularly. I am going out for a ride in the saddle. I mean to explore those marshes for amusement. Out-of-the-way villages there, they tell me. Curious little public houses – and smithies – and that. Waiter!'

'Yes, sir.'

'Is that horse of mine ready?'

'Brought round to the door, sir.'

'I say. Look here, you sir. The lady won't ride today; the weather won't do.'

'Very good, sir.'

'And I don't dine, because I am going to dine at the lady's.'

'Very good, sir.'

Then, Drummle glanced at me, with an insolent triumph on his great-jowled face that cut me to the heart, dull as he was,

and so exasperated me, that I felt inclined to take him in my arms (as the robber in the storybook is said to have taken the old lady) and seat him on the fire.

One thing was manifest to both of us, and that was, that until relief came, neither of us could relinquish the fire. There we stood, well squared up before it, shoulder to shoulder and foot to foot, with our hands behind us, not budging an inch. The horse was visible outside in the drizzle at the door, my breakfast was put on table, Drummle's was cleared away, the waiter invited me to begin, I nodded, we both stood our ground.

'Have you been to the Grove since?' said Drummle.

'No,' said I, 'I had quite enough of the Finches the last time I was there.'

'Was that when we had a difference of opinion?'

'Yes,' I replied, very shortly.

'Come, come! they let you off easily enough,' sneered Drummle. 'You shouldn't have lost your temper.'

'Mr Drummle,' said I, 'you are not competent to give advice on that subject. When I lose my temper (not that I admit having done so on that occasion), I don't throw glasses.'

'I do,' said Drummle.

After glancing at him once or twice, in an increased state of smouldering ferocity, I said: 'Mr Drummle, I did not seek this conversation, and I don't think it's an agreeable one.'

Shoulder to shoulder

'I am sure it's not,' said he, superciliously over his shoulder, 'I don't think anything about it.'

'And therefore,' I went on, 'with your leave, I will suggest that we hold no kind of communication in future.'

'Quite my opinion,' said Drummle, 'and what I should have suggested myself, or done – more likely – without suggesting. But don't lose your temper. Haven't you lost enough without that?'

'What do you mean, sir?'

'Waiter,' said Drummle, by way of answering me.

The waiter reappeared.

'Look here, you sir. You quite understand that the young lady don't ride today, and that I dine at the young lady's?'

'Quite so, sir!'

When the waiter had felt my fast-cooling teapot with the palm of his hand, and had looked imploringly at me, and had gone out, Drummle, careful not to move the shoulder next me, took a cigar from his pocket and bit the end off, but showed no sign of stirring. Choking and boiling as I was, I felt that we could not go a word further, without introducing Estella's name, which I could not endure to hear him utter; and therefore I looked stonily at the opposite wall, as if there were no one present, and forced myself to silence. How long we might have remained in this ridiculous position it is impossible to say, but for the incursion of three thriving farmers – laid on by the waiter, I think – who came into the coffee-room unbuttoning their greatcoats and rubbing their hands, and before whom, as they charged at the fire, we were obliged to give way.

I saw him through the window, seizing his horse's mane, and mounting in his blundering brutal manner, and sidling and backing away. I thought he was gone, when he came back, calling for a light for the cigar in his mouth, which he had forgotten. A man in a dust-coloured dress appeared with what was wanted – I could not have said from where: whether from the inn yard, or the street, or where not – and as Drummle leaned down from the saddle and lighted his cigar and laughed, with a jerk of his head towards the coffee-room windows, the slouching shoulders and ragged hair of this man, whose back was towards me, reminded me of Orlick.

Too heavily out of sorts to care much at the time whether it were he or no, or after all to touch the breakfast, I washed the weather and the journey from my face and hands, and went out to the memorable old house that it would have been so much the better for me never to have entered, never to have seen.

Chapter 44

In the room where the dressing-table stood, and where the wax candles burnt on the wall, I found Miss Havisham and Estella; Miss Havisham seated on a settee near the fire, and Estella on a cushion at her feet. Estella was knitting, and Miss Havisham was looking on. They both raised their eyes as I went in, and both saw an alteration in me. I derived that from the look they interchanged.

'And what wind,' said Miss Havisham, 'blows you here, Pip?'

Though she looked steadily at me, I saw that she was rather confused. Estella, pausing a moment in her knitting with her eyes upon me, and then going on, I fancied that I read in the action of her fingers, as plainly as if she had told me in the dumb alphabet, that she perceived I had discovered my real benefactor.

'Miss Havisham,' said I, 'I went to Richmond yesterday, to speak to Estella; and finding that some wind had blown *her* here, I followed.'

Miss Havisham motioning to me for the third or fourth time to sit down, I took the chair by the dressing-table, which I had often seen her occupy. With all that ruin at my feet and about me, it seemed a natural place for me, that day.

'What I had to say to Estella, Miss Havisham, I will say before you, presently – in a few moments. It will not surprise you, it will not displease you. I am as unhappy as you can ever have meant me to be.'

Miss Havisham continued to look steadily at me. I could see in the action of Estella's fingers as they worked, that she attended to what I said: but she did not look up.

'I have found out who my patron is. It is not a fortunate discovery, and is not likely ever to enrich me in reputation, station, fortune, anything. There are reasons why I must say no more of that. It is not my secret, but another's.'

As I was silent for a while, looking at Estella and considering how to go on, Miss Havisham repeated, 'It is not your secret, but another's. Well?'

'When you first caused me to be brought here, Miss Havisham; when I belonged to the village over yonder, that I wish I had never left; I suppose I did really come here, as any other chance boy might have come – as a kind of servant, to gratify a want or a whim, and to be paid for it?'

'Ay, Pip,' replied Miss Havisham, steadily nodding her head; 'you did.'

'And that Mr Jaggers –'

'Mr Jaggers,' said Miss Havisham, taking me up in a firm tone, 'had nothing to do with it, and knew nothing of it. His being my lawyer, and his being the lawyer of your patron, is a coincidence. He holds the same relation towards numbers of people, and it might easily arise. Be that as it may, it did arise, and was not brought about by anyone.'

Anyone might have seen in her haggard face that there was no suppression or evasion so far.

'But when I fell into the mistake I have so long remained in, at least you led me on?' said I.

'Yes,' she returned, again nodding steadily, 'I let you go on.'

'Was that kind?'

'Who am I,' cried Miss Havisham, striking her stick upon the floor and flashing into wrath so suddenly that Estella glanced up at her in surprise, 'who am I, for God's sake, that I should be kind?'

It was a weak complaint to have made, and I had not meant to make it. I told her so, as she sat brooding over this outburst.

'Well, well, well!' she said. 'What else?'

'I was liberally paid for my old attendance here,' I said, to soothe her, 'in being apprenticed, and I have asked these questions only for my own information. What follows has another (and I hope more disinterested) purpose. In humouring my mistake, Miss Havisham, you punished – practised on – perhaps you will supply whatever term expresses your intention, without offence – your self-seeking relations?'

'I did. Why, they would have it so! So would you. What has been my history, that I should be at the pains of entreating either them or you not to have it so! You made your own snares. *I* never made them.'

Waiting until she was quiet again – for this, too, flashed out of her in a wild and sudden way – I went on.

'I have been thrown among one family of your relations, Miss Havisham, and have been constantly among them since I went to London. I know them to have been as honestly under my delusion as I myself. And I should be false and base if I did not tell you, whether it is acceptable to you or no, and whether you are inclined to give credence to it or no, that you deeply wrong both Mr Matthew Pocket and his son Herbert, if you suppose them to be otherwise than generous, upright, open, and incapable of anything designing or mean.'

'They are your friends,' said Miss Havisham.

'They made themselves my friends,' said I, 'when they supposed me to have superseded them; and when Sarah Pocket, Miss Georgiana, and Mistress Camilla were not my friends, I think.'

This contrasting of them with the rest seemed, I was glad to see, to do them good with her. She looked at me keenly for a little while, and then said quietly: 'What do you want for them?'

'Only,' said I, 'that you would not confound them with the others. They may be of the same blood, but, believe me, they are not of the same nature.'

Still looking at me keenly, Miss Havisham repeated: 'What do you want for them?'

'I am not so cunning, you see,' I said in answer, conscious that I reddened a little, 'as that I could hide from you, even if I desired, that I do want something. Miss Havisham, if you could spare the money to do my friend Herbert a lasting service in life, but which from the nature of the case must be done without his knowledge, I could show you how.'

'Why must it be done without his knowledge?' she asked, settling her hands upon her stick, that she might regard me the more attentively.

'Because,' said I, 'I began the service myself, more than two years ago, without his knowledge, and I don't want to be betrayed. Why I fail in my ability to finish it, I cannot explain. It is a part of the secret which is another person's and not mine.'

She gradually withdrew her eyes from me, and turned them on the fire. After watching it for what appeared in the silence and by the light of the slowly wasting candles to be a long time, she was roused by the collapse of some of the red coals, and looked towards me again – at first, vacantly – then, with a gradually concentrating attention. All this time, Estella knitted on. When Miss Havisham had fixed her attention on me, she said, speaking as if there had been no lapse in our dialogue: 'What else?'

'Estella,' said I, turning to her now, and trying to command my trembling voice, 'you know I love you. You know that I have loved you long and dearly.'

She raised her eyes to my face, on being thus addressed, and her fingers plied their work, and she looked at me with an unmoved countenance. I saw that Miss Havisham glanced from me to her, and from her to me.

'I should have said this sooner, but for my long mistake. It induced me to hope that Miss Havisham meant us for one another. While I thought you could not help yourself, as it were, I refrained from saying it. But I must say it now.'

Preserving her unmoved countenance, and with her fingers still going, Estella shook her head.

'I know,' said I, in answer to that action; 'I know. I have no hope that I shall ever call you mine, Estella. I am ignorant what may become of me very soon, how poor I may be, or where I may go. Still, I love you. I have loved you ever since I first saw you in this house.'

Looking at me perfectly unmoved and with her fingers busy, she shook her head again.

'It would have been cruel in Miss Havisham, horribly cruel, to practise on the susceptibility of a poor boy, and to torture me through all these years with a vain hope and an idle pursuit, if she had reflected on the gravity of what she did. But I think she did not. I think that in the endurance of her own trial, she forgot mine, Estella.'

I saw Miss Havisham put her hand to her heart and hold it there, as she sat looking by turns at Estella and at me.

'It seems,' said Estella, very calmly, 'that there are sentiments, fancies – I don't know how to call them – which I am not able to comprehend. When you say you love me, I know what you mean, as a form of words; but nothing more. You address nothing in my breast, you touch nothing there. I don't care for what you say at all. I have tried to warn you of this; now, have I not?'

I said in a miserable manner, 'Yes.'

'Yes. But you would not be warned, for you thought I did not mean it. Now, did you not think so?'

'I thought and hoped you could not mean it. You, so young, untried, and beautiful, Estella! Surely it is not in nature.'

'It is in *my* nature,' she returned. And then she added, with a stress upon the words, 'It is in the nature formed within me. I make a great difference between you and all other people when I say so much. I can do no more.'

'Is it not true,' said I, 'that Bentley Drummle is in town here, and pursuing you?'

'It is quite true,' she replied, referring to him with the indifference of utter contempt.

'That you encourage him, and ride out with him, and that he dines with you this very day?'

She seemed a little surprised that I should know it, but again replied, 'Quite true.'

'You cannot love him, Estella?'

Her fingers stopped for the first time, as she retorted rather angrily, 'What have I told you? Do you still think, in spite of it, that I do not mean what I say?'

'You would never marry him, Estella?'

She looked towards Miss Havisham, and considered for a moment with her work in her hands. Then she said, 'Why not tell you the truth? I am going to be married to him.'

I dropped my face into my hands, but was able to control myself better than I could have expected, considering what agony it gave me to hear her say those words. When I raised my face again, there was such a ghastly look upon Miss Havisham's that it impressed me, even in my passionate hurry and grief.

'Estella, dearest, dearest Estella, do not let Miss Havisham lead you into this fatal step. Put me aside for ever – you have done so, I well know – but bestow yourself on some worthier person than Drummle. Miss Havisham gives you to him, as the greatest slight and injury that could be done to the many far better men who admire you, and to the few who truly love you. Among those few, there may be one who loves you even as dearly, though he has not loved you as long, as I. Take him, and I can bear it better for your sake!'

My earnestness awoke a wonder in her that seemed as if it would have been touched with compassion, if she could have rendered me at all intelligible to her own mind.

'I am going,' she said again, in a gentler voice, 'to be married to him. The preparations for my marriage are making, and I shall be married soon. Why do you injuriously introduce the name of my mother by adoption? It is my own act.'

'Your own act, Estella, to fling yourself away upon a brute?'

'On whom should I fling myself away?' she retorted, with a smile. 'Should I fling myself away upon the man who would the soonest feel (if people do feel such things) that I took nothing to him? There! It is done. I shall do well enough, and so will my husband. As to leading me into what you call this fatal step, Miss Havisham would have had me wait, and not marry yet; but I am tired of the life I have led, which has very few charms for me, and I am willing enough to change it. Say no more. We shall never understand each other.'

'Such a mean brute, such a stupid brute!' I urged in despair.

'Don't be afraid of my being a blessing to him,' said Estella; 'I shall not be that. Come! Here is my hand. Do we part on this, you visionary boy – or man?'

'O Estella!' I answered, as my bitter tears fell fast on her hand, do what I would to restrain them; 'even if I remained in England and could hold my head up with the rest, how could I see you Drummle's wife?'

'Nonsense,' she returned, 'nonsense. This will pass in no time.'

'Never, Estella!'

'You will get me out of your thoughts in a week.'

'Out of my thoughts! You are part of my existence, part of myself. You have been in every line I have ever read, since I first came here, the rough common boy whose poor heart you wounded even then. You have been in every prospect I have ever seen since – on the river, on the sails of the ships, on the marshes, in the clouds, in the light, in the darkness, in the wind, in the woods, in the sea, in the streets. You have been the embodiment of every graceful fancy that my mind has ever become acquainted with. The stones of which the strongest London buildings are made, are not more real, or more impossible to be displaced by your hands, than your presence and influence have been to me, there and everywhere, and will be. Estella, to the last hour of my life, you cannot choose but remain part of my character, part of the little good in me, part of the evil. But, in this separation I associate you only with the good, and I will faithfully hold you to that always, for you must have done me far more good than harm, let me feel now what sharp distress I may. O God bless you, God forgive you!'

In what ecstasy of unhappiness I got these broken words out of myself, I don't know. The rhapsody welled up within me, like blood from an inward wound, and gushed out. I held her hand to my lips some lingering moments, and so I left her. But ever afterwards, I remembered – and soon afterwards with stronger reason – that while Estella looked at me merely with incredulous wonder, the spectral figure of Miss Havisham, her hand still covering her heart, seemed all resolved into a ghastly stare of pity and remorse.

All done, all gone! So much was done and gone, that when I went out at the gate, the light of day seemed of a darker colour than when I went in. For a while, I hid myself among some lanes and by-paths, and then struck off to walk all the way to London. For, I had by that time come to myself so far, as to consider that I could not go back to the inn and see Drummle there; that I could not bear to sit upon the coach and be spoken to; that I could do nothing half so good for myself as tire myself out.

It was past midnight when I crossed London Bridge. Pursuing the narrow intricacies of the streets which at that time tended westward near the Middlesex shore of the river, my readiest access to the Temple was close by the riverside, through Whitefriars. I was not expected till tomorrow, but I had my keys, and, if Herbert were gone to bed, could get to bed myself without disturbing him.

As it seldom happened that I came in at that Whitefriars gate after the Temple was closed, and as I was very muddy and weary, I did not take it ill that the night-porter examined me with much attention as he held the gate a little way open for me to pass in. To help his memory I mentioned my name.

'I was not quite sure, sir, but I thought so. Here's a note, sir. The messenger that brought it said, would you be so good as read it by my lantern?'

Much surprised by the request, I took the note. It was directed to Philip Pip, Esquire, and on the top of the superscription were the words, 'Please read this here.' I opened it, the watchman holding up his light, and read inside, in Wemmick's writing: 'Don't go home'.

Chapter 45

Turning from the Temple gate as soon as I had read the warning, I made the best of my way to Fleet Street, and there got a late hackney chariot and drove to the Hummums in Covent Garden. In those times a bed was always to be got there at any hour of the night, and the chamberlain, letting me in at his ready wicket, lighted the candle next in order on his shelf, and showed me straight into the bedroom next in order on his list. It was a sort of vault on the ground floor at the back, with a despotic monster of a fourpost bedstead in it, straddling over the whole place, putting one of his arbitrary legs into the fireplace, and another into the doorway, and squeezing the wretched little washing-stand in quite a divinely righteous manner.

As I had asked for a night-light, the chamberlain had brought me in, before he left me, the good old constitutional rush-light of those virtuous days – an object like the ghost of a walking-cane, which instantly broke its back if it were touched, which nothing could ever be lighted at, and which was placed in solitary confinement at the bottom of a high tin tower, perforated with round holes that made a staringly wide-awake pattern on the walls. When I had got into bed, and lay there, footsore, weary, and wretched, I found that I could no more close my own eyes than I could close the eyes of this foolish Argus. And thus, in the gloom and death of the night, we stared at one another.

What a doleful night! How anxious, how dismal, how long! There was an inhospitable smell in the room, of cold soot and hot dust; and, as I looked up into the corners of the tester over my head, I thought what a number of bluebottle flies from the butcher's, and earwigs from the market, and grubs from the country, must be holding on up there, lying by for next summer. This led me to speculate whether any of them ever tumbled down, and then I fancied that I felt light falls on my face – a disagreeable turn of thought, suggesting other and more objectionable approaches up my back. When I had lain awake a little while, those extraordinary voices with which silence teems, began to make themselves audible. The closet whispered, the fireplace sighed, the little washing-stand ticked, and one guitar-string played occasionally in the chest of drawers. At about the same time, the eyes on the wall acquired a new expression, and in every one of those staring rounds I saw written, Don't go home.

Whatever night-fancies and night-noises crowded on me, they never warded off this Don't go home. It plaited itself into whatever I thought of, as a bodily pain would have done. Not long before, I had read in the newspapers how a gentleman unknown had come to the Hummums in the night, and had gone to bed, and had destroyed himself, and had been found in the morning weltering in blood. It came into my head that he must have occupied this very vault of mine, and I got out of bed to assure myself that there were no red marks about; then opened the door to look out into the passages, and cheer myself with the companionship of a distant light, near which I knew

the chamberlain to be dozing. But all this time, why I was not to go home, and what had happened at home, and when I should go home, and whether Provis was safe at home, were questions occupying my mind so busily, that one might have supposed there could be no more room in it for any other theme. Even when I thought of Estella, and how we had parted that day for ever, and when I recalled all the circumstances of our parting, and all her looks and tones, and the action of her fingers while she knitted – even then I was pursuing, here and there and everywhere, the caution don't go home. When at last I dozed, in sheer exhaustion of mind and body, it became a vast shadowy verb which I had to conjugate, Imperative mood, present tense: do not thou go home, let him not go home, let us not go home, do not ye or you go home, let not them go home. Then, potentially: I may not and I cannot go home; and I might not, could not, would not, and should not go home; until I felt that I was going distracted, and rolled over on the pillow, and looked at the staring rounds upon the wall again.

I had left directions that I was to be called at seven; for it was plain that I must see Wemmick before seeing anyone else, and equally plain that this was a case in which his Walworth sentiments, only, could be taken. It was a relief to get out of the room where the night had been so miserable, and I needed no second knocking at the door to startle me from my uneasy bed.

The Castle battlements arose upon my view at eight o'clock. The little servant happening to be entering the fortress with two hot rolls, I passed through the postern and crossed the drawbridge, in her company, and so came without announcement into the presence of Wemmick as he was making tea for himself and the Aged. An open door afforded a perspective view of the Aged in bed.

'Halloa, Mr Pip!' said Wemmick. 'You did come home, then?'

'Yes,' I returned; 'but I didn't go home.'

'That's all right,' said he, rubbing his hands. 'I left a note for you at each of the Temple gates, on the chance. Which gate did you come to?'

I told him.

'I'll go round to the others in the course of the day and destroy the notes,' said Wemmick; 'it's a good rule never to leave documentary evidence if you can help it, because you don't know when it may be put in. I'm going to take a liberty with you – *would* you mind toasting this sausage for the Aged P?'

I said I should be delighted to do it.

'Then you can go about your work, Mary Anne,' said Wemmick to the little servant; 'which leaves us to ourselves, don't you see, Mr Pip?' he added, winking, as she disappeared.

I thanked him for his friendship and caution, and our discourse proceeded in a low tone, while I toasted the Aged's sausage and he buttered the crumb of the Aged's roll.

'Now, Mr Pip, you know,' said Wemmick, 'you and I understand one another. We are in our private and personal capacities, and we have been engaged in a confidential transaction before today. Official sentiments are one thing. We are extra-official.'

I cordially assented. I was so very nervous, that I had already lighted the Aged's sausage like a torch, and been obliged to blow it out.

'I accidentally heard, yesterday morning,' said Wemmick, 'being in a certain place where I once took you – even between you and me, it's as well not to mention names when avoidable – '

'Much better not,' said I. 'I understand you.'

'I heard there by chance, yesterday morning,' said Wemmick, 'that a certain person not altogether of un-colonial pursuits, and not unpossessed of portable property – I don't know who it may really be – we won't name this person – '

'Not necessary,' said I.

' – had made some little stir in a certain part of the world where a good many people go, not always in gratification of their own inclinations, and not quite irrespective of the government expense – '

In watching his face, I made quite a firework of the Aged's sausage, and greatly discomposed both my own attention and Wemmick's; for which I apologised.

' – by disappearing from such place, and being no more heard of thereabouts. From which,' said Wemmick, 'conjectures had been raised and theories formed. I also heard that you at your chambers in Garden Court, Temple, had been watched, and might be watched again.'

'By whom?' said I.

'I wouldn't go into that,' said Wemmick, evasively, 'it might clash with official responsibilities. I heard it, as I have in my time heard other curious things in the same place. I don't tell it you on information received. I heard it.'

He took the toasting-fork and sausage from me as he spoke, and set forth the Aged's breakfast neatly on a little tray. Previous to placing it before him, he went into the Aged's room with a clean white cloth, and tied the same under the old gentleman's chin, and propped him up, and put his nightcap on one side, and gave him quite a rakish air. Then, he placed his breakfast before him with great care, and said, 'All right, ain't you, Aged P?' To which the cheerful Aged replied, 'All right, John, my boy, all right!' As there seemed to be a tacit understanding that the Aged was not in a presentable state, and was therefore to be considered invisible, I made a pretence of being in complete ignorance of these proceedings.

'This watching of me at my chambers (which I have once had reason to suspect),' I said to Wemmick when he came back, 'is inseparable from the person to whom you have adverted; is it?'

Wemmick looked very serious. 'I couldn't undertake to say that, of my own knowledge. I mean, I couldn't undertake to say it was at first. But it either is, or it will be, or it's in great danger of being.'

As I saw that he was restrained by fealty to Little Britain from saying as much as he could, and as I knew with thankfulness to him how far out of his way he went to say what he did, I could not press him. But I told him, after a little meditation over the fire, that I would like to ask him a question, subject to his answering or not answering, as he deemed right, and sure that his course would be right. He paused in his breakfast, and crossing his arms, and pinching his shirtsleeves (his notion of indoor comfort was to sit without any coat), he nodded to me once, to put my question.

'You have heard of a man of bad character, whose true name is Compeyson?'

He answered with one other nod.

'Is he living?'

One other nod.

'Is he in London?'

He gave me one other nod, compressed the post office exceedingly, gave me one last nod, and went on with his breakfast.

'Now,' said Wemmick, 'questioning being over;' which he emphasised and repeated for my guidance; 'I come to what I did, after hearing what I heard. I went to Garden Court to find you; not finding you, I went to Clarriker's to find Mr Herbert.'

'And him you found?' said I, with great anxiety.

'And him I found. Without mentioning any names or going into any details, I gave him to understand that if he was aware of anybody – Tom, Jack, or Richard – being about the chambers, or about the immediate neighbourhood, he had better get Tom, Jack, or Richard, out of the way while you were out of the way.'

'He would be greatly puzzled what to do?'

'He *was* puzzled what to do; not the less, because I gave him my opinion that it was not safe to try to get Tom, Jack, or Richard, too far out of the way at present. Mr Pip, I'll tell you something. Under existing circumstances there is no place like a great city when you are once in it. Don't break cover too soon. Lie close. Wait till things slacken, before you try the open, even for foreign air.'

I thanked him for his valuable advice, and asked him what Herbert had done?

'Mr Herbert,' said Wemmick, 'after being all of a heap for half an hour, struck out a plan. He mentioned to me as a secret that he is courting a young lady who has, as no doubt you are aware, a bedridden pa. Which pa, having been in the purser line of life, lies a-bed in a bow-window where he can see the ships sail up and down the river. You are acquainted with the young lady, most probably?'

'Not personally,' said I.

The truth was, that she had objected to me as an expensive companion who did Herbert no good, and that, when Herbert had first proposed to present me to her, she had received the proposal with such very moderate warmth, that Herbert had felt himself obliged to confide the state of the case to me, with a view to the lapse of a little time before I made her acquaintance. When I had begun to advance Herbert's prospects by stealth, I had been able to bear this with cheerful philosophy; he and his affianced, for their part, had naturally not been very anxious to introduce a third person into their interviews; and thus, although I was assured that I had risen in Clara's esteem, and although the young lady and I had long regularly interchanged messages and remembrances by Herbert, I had never seen her. However, I did not trouble Wemmick with those particulars.

'The house with the bow-window,' said Wemmick, 'being by the riverside, down the Pool there between Limehouse and Greenwich, and being kept, it seems, by a very respectable widow, who has a furnished upper floor to let, Mr Herbert put it to me, what did I think of that as a temporary tenement for Tom, Jack, or Richard? Now, I thought very well of it, for three reasons I'll give you. That is to say. Firstly. It's altogether out of all your beats, and is well away from the usual heap of streets great and small. Secondly. Without going near it yourself, you could always hear of the safety of Tom, Jack, or Richard, through Mr Herbert. Thirdly. After a while and when it might be prudent, if you should want to slip Tom, Jack, or Richard, on board a foreign packet-boat, there he is – ready.'

Much comforted by these considerations, I thanked Wemmick again and again, and begged him to proceed.

'Well, sir! Mr Herbert threw himself into the business with a will, and by nine o'clock last night he housed Tom, Jack, or Richard – whichever it may be – you and I don't want to know – quite successfully. At the old lodgings it was understood that he was summoned to Dover, and in fact he was taken down the Dover road and cornered out of it. Now, another great advantage of all this is, that it was done without you, and when, if anyone was concerning himself about your movements, you must be known to be ever so many miles off, and quite otherwise engaged. This diverts suspicion and confuses it; and for the same reason I recommended that even if you came back last night, you should not go home. It brings in more confusion, and you want confusion.'

Wemmick, having finished his breakfast, here looked at his watch, and began to get his coat on.

'And now, Mr Pip,' said he, with his hands still in the sleeves, 'I have probably done the most I can do; but if I can ever do more – from a Walworth point of view, and in a strictly private and personal capacity – I shall be glad to do it. Here's the address. There can be no harm in your going here tonight and seeing for yourself that all is well with Tom, Jack, or Richard, before you go home – which is another reason for your not going home last night. But after you have gone home, don't go back here. You are very welcome, I am sure, Mr Pip;' his hands were now out of his sleeves, and I was shaking them; 'and let me finally impress one important point upon you.' He laid his hands upon my shoulders, and added in a solemn whisper: 'Avail yourself of this evening to lay hold of his portable property. You don't know what may happen to him. Don't let anything happen to the portable property.'

Quite despairing of making my mind clear to Wemmick on this point, I forbore to try.

'Time's up,' said Wemmick, 'and I must be off. If you had nothing more pressing to do than to keep here till dark, that's what I should advise. You look very much worried, and it would do you good to have a perfectly quiet day with the Aged – he'll be up presently – and a little bit of – you remember the pig?'

'Of course,' said I.

'Well; and a little bit of *him*. That sausage you toasted was his, and he was in all respects a first-rater. Do try him, if it is only for old acquaintance sake. Goodbye. Aged Parent!' in a cheery shout.

'All right, John; all right, my boy!' piped the old man from within.

I soon fell asleep before Wemmick's fire, and the Aged and I enjoyed one another's society by falling asleep before it more or less all day. We had loin of pork for dinner, and greens grown on the estate, and I nodded at the Aged with a good intention whenever I failed to do it drowsily. When it was quite dark, I left the Aged preparing the fire for toast; and I inferred from the number of teacups, as well as from his glances at the two little doors in the wall, that Miss Skiffins was expected.

Chapter 46

Eight o'clock had struck before I got into the air that was scented, not disagreeably, by the chips and shavings of the long-shore boat-builders, and mast, oar, and block makers. All that waterside region of the upper and lower Pool below Bridge, was unknown ground to me, and when I struck down by the river, I found that the spot I wanted was not where I had supposed it to be, and was anything but easy to find. It was called Mill Pond Bank, Chinks's Basin; and I had no other guide to Chinks's Basin than the Old Green Copper Rope-Walk.

It matters not what stranded ships repairing in dry docks I lost myself among, what old hulls of ships in course of being knocked to pieces, what ooze and slime and other dregs of tide, what yards of shipbuilders and ship-breakers, what rusty anchors blindly biting into the ground though for years off duty, what mountainous country of accumulated casks and timber, how many rope-walks that were not the Old Green Copper. After several times falling short of my destination and as often overshooting it, I came unexpectedly round a corner, upon Mill Pond Bank. It was a fresh kind of place, all circumstances considered, where the wind from the river had room to turn itself round; and there were two or three trees in it, and there was a stump of a ruined windmill, and there was the Old Green Copper Rope-Walk – whose long and narrow vista I could trace in the moonlight, along a series of wooden frames set in the ground, that looked like superannuated haymaking-rakes which had grown old and lost most of their teeth.

Selecting from the few queer houses upon Mill Pond Bank, a house with a wooden front and three stories of bow-window (not bay-window, which is another thing), I looked at the plate upon the door, and read there Mrs Whimple. That being the name I wanted, I knocked, and an elderly woman of a pleasant and thriving appearance responded. She was immediately deposed, however, by Herbert, who silently led me into the parlour and shut the door. It was an odd sensation to see his very familiar face established quite at home in that very unfamiliar room and region; and I found myself looking at him, much as I looked at the corner cupboard with the glass and china, the shells upon the chimney-piece, and the coloured engravings on the wall, representing the death of Captain Cook, a ship-launch, and his Majesty King George the Third in a state coachman's wig, leather breeches, and top-boots, on the terrace at Windsor.

'All is well, Handel,' said Herbert, 'and he is quite satisfied, though eager to see you. My dear girl is with her father; and if you'll wait till she comes down, I'll make you known to her, and then we'll go upstairs – *That's* her father.'

I had become aware of an alarming growling overhead, and had probably expressed the fact in my countenance.

'I am afraid he is a sad old rascal,' said Herbert, smiling, 'but I have never seen him. Don't you smell rum? He is always at it.'

'At rum?' said I.

'Yes,' returned Herbert, 'and you may suppose how mild it makes his gout. He persists, too, in keeping all the provisions upstairs in his room, and serving them out. He keeps them on shelves over his head, and *will* weigh them all. His room must be like a chandler's shop.'

While he thus spoke, the growling noise became a prolonged roar, and then died away.

'What else can be the consequence,' said Herbert, in explanation, 'if he *will* cut the cheese? A man with the gout in his right hand – and everywhere else – can't expect to get through a Double Gloucester without hurting himself.'

He seemed to have hurt himself very much, for he gave another furious roar.

'To have Provis for an upper lodger is quite a godsend to Mrs Whimple,' said Herbert, 'for of course people in general won't stand that noise. A curious place, Handel; isn't it?'

It was a curious place, indeed; but remarkably well kept and clean.

'Mrs Whimple,' said Herbert, when I told him so, 'is the best of housewives, and I really do not know what my Clara would do without her motherly help. For Clara has no mother of her own, Handel, and no relation in the world but old Gruff-andgrim.'

'Surely that's not his name, Herbert?'

'No, no,' said Herbert, 'that's my name for him. His name is Mr Barley. But what a blessing it is for the son of my father and mother to love a girl who has no relations, and who can never bother herself, or anybody else, about her family!'

Herbert had told me on former occasions, and now reminded me, that he first knew Miss Clara Barley when she was completing her education at an establishment at Hammersmith, and that on her being recalled home to nurse her father, he and she had confided their affection to the motherly Mrs Whimple, by whom it had been fostered and regulated with equal kindness and discretion ever since. It was understood that nothing of a tender nature could possibly be confided to Old Barley, by reason of his being totally unequal to the consideration of any subject more psychological than Gout, Rum, and Purser's stores.

As we were thus conversing in a low tone while Old Barley's sustained growl vibrated in the beam that crossed the ceiling, the room door opened, and a very pretty, slight, dark-eyed girl of twenty or so, came in with a basket in her hand: whom Herbert tenderly relieved of the basket, and presented blushing, as 'Clara'. She really was a most charming girl, and might have passed for a captive fairy, whom that truculent ogre, Old Barley, had pressed into his service.

'Look here,' said Herbert, showing me the basket, with a compassionate and tender smile after we had talked a little;

'here's poor Clara's supper, served out every night. Here's her allowance of bread, and here's her slice of cheese, and here's her rum – which I drink. This is Mr Barley's breakfast for tomorrow, served out to be cooked. Two mutton chops, three potatoes, some split peas, a little flour, two ounces of butter, a pinch of salt, and all this black pepper. It's stewed up together, and taken hot, and it's a nice thing for the gout, I should think!'

There was something so natural and winning in Clara's resigned way of looking at these stores in detail, as Herbert pointed them out – and something so confiding, loving and innocent, in her modest manner of yielding herself to Herbert's embracing arm – and something so gentle in her, so much needing protection on Mill Pond Bank, by Chinks's Basin, and the Old Green Copper Rope-Walk, with Old Barley growling in the beam – that I would not have undone the engagement between her and Herbert for all the money in the pocketbook I had never opened.

I was looking at her with pleasure and admiration, when suddenly the growl swelled into a roar again, and a frightful bumping noise was heard above, as if a giant with a wooden leg were trying to bore it through the ceiling to come at us. Upon this Clara said to Herbert, 'Papa wants me, darling!' and ran away.

'There is an unconscionable old shark for you!' said Herbert. 'What do you suppose he wants now, Handel?'

'I don't know,' said I. 'Something to drink?'

'That's it!' cried Herbert, as if I had made a guess of extraordinary merit. 'He keeps his grog ready-mixed in a little tub on the table. Wait a moment, and you'll hear Clara lift him up to take some – there he goes!' Another roar, with a prolonged shake at the end. 'Now,' said Herbert, as it was succeeded by silence, 'he's drinking. Now,' said Herbert, as the growl resounded in the beam once more, "He's down again on his back!'

Clara returned soon afterwards, and Herbert accompanied me upstairs to see our charge. As we passed Mr Barley's door, he was heard hoarsely muttering within, in a strain that rose and fell like wind, the following Refrain; in which I substitute good wishes for something quite the reverse.

'Ahoy! Bless your eyes, here's old Bill Barley. Here's old Bill Barley, bless your eyes. Here's old Bill Barley on the flat of his back, by the Lord. Lying on the flat of his back, like a drifting old dead flounder, here's your old Bill Barley, bless your eyes. Ahoy! Bless you.'

In this strain of consolation, Herbert informed me the invisible Barley would commune with himself by the day and night together; often while it was light, having, at the same time, one eye at a telescope which was fitted on his bed for the convenience of sweeping the river.

In his two cabin rooms at the top of the house, which were fresh and airy, and in which Mr Barley was less audible than below, I found Provis comfortably settled. He expressed no alarm, and seemed to feel none that was worth mentioning; but it struck me that he was softened – indefinably, for I could not have said how, and could never afterwards recall how when I tried; but certainly.

The opportunity that the day's rest had given me for reflection had resulted in my fully determining to say nothing to him respecting Compeyson. For anything I knew, his animosity towards the man might otherwise lead to his seeking him out and rushing on his own destruction. Therefore, when Herbert and I sat down with him by his fire, I asked him first of all whether he relied on Wemmick's judgement and sources of information?

'Ay, ay, dear boy!' he answered, with a grave nod, 'Jaggers knows.'

'Then, I have talked with Wemmick,' said I, 'and have come to tell you what caution he gave me and what advice.'

This I did accurately, with the reservation just mentioned; and I told him how Wemmick had heard, in Newgate prison (whether from officers or prisoners I could not say), that he was under some suspicion, and that my chambers had been watched; how Wemmick had recommended his keeping close for a time, and my keeping away from him; and what Wemmick had said about getting him abroad. I added, that of course, when the time came, I should go with him, or should follow close upon him, as might be safest in Wemmick's judgement. What was to follow that, I did not touch upon; neither indeed was I at all clear or comfortable about it in my own mind, now that I saw him in that softer condition, and in declared peril for my sake. As to altering my way of living, by enlarging my expenses, I put it to him whether in our present unsettled and

'*Here's old Bill Barley, bless your eyes.*'

difficult circumstances, it would not be simply ridiculous, if it were no worse?

He could not deny this, and indeed was very reasonable throughout. His coming back was a venture, he said, and he had always known it to be a venture. He would do nothing to make it a desperate venture, and he had very little fear of his safety with such good help.

Herbert, who had been looking at the fire and pondering, here said that something had come into his thoughts arising out of Wemmick's suggestion, which it might be worth while to pursue. 'We are both good watermen, Handel, and could take him down the river ourselves when the right time comes. No boat would then be hired for the purpose, and no boatmen; that would save at least a chance of suspicion, and any chance is worth saving. Never mind the season; don't you think it might be a good thing if you began at once to keep a boat at the Temple stairs, and were in the habit of rowing up and down the river? You fall into that habit, and then who notices or minds? Do it twenty or fifty times, and there is nothing special in your doing it the twenty-first or fifty-first.'

I liked this scheme, and Provis was quite elated by it. We agreed that it should be carried into execution, and that Provis should never recognise us if we came below bridge and rowed past Mill Pond Bank. But, we further agreed that he should pull down the blind in that part of his window which gave upon the east, whenever he saw us, and all was right.

Our conference being now ended, and everything arranged, I rose to go; remarking to Herbert that he and I had better not go home together, and that I would take half an hour's start of him. 'I don't like to leave you here,' I said to Provis, 'though I cannot doubt your being safer here than near me. Goodbye!'

'Dear boy,' he answered, clasping my hands, 'I don't know when we may meet again, and I don't like goodbye. Say good-night!'

'Good-night! Herbert will go regularly between us, and when the time comes you may be certain I shall be ready. Good-night, good-night!'

We thought it best that he should stay in his own rooms, and we left him on the landing outside his door, holding a light over the stair-rail to light us downstairs. Looking back at him, I thought of the first night of his return when our positions were reversed, and when I little supposed my heart could ever be as heavy and anxious at parting from him as it was now.

Old Barley was growling and swearing when we repassed his door, with no appearance of having ceased or of meaning to cease. When we got to the foot of the stairs, I asked Herbert whether he had preserved the name of Provis? He replied, certainly not, and that the lodger was Mr Campbell. He also explained that the utmost known of Mr Campbell there, was that he (Herbert) had Mr Campbell consigned to him, and felt a strong personal interest in his being well cared for and living a secluded life. So, when we went into the parlour where Mrs Whimple and Clara were seated at work, I said nothing of my own interest in Mr Campbell, but kept it to myself.

When I had taken leave of the pretty gentle dark-eyed girl, and of the motherly woman who had not outlived her honest sympathy with a little affair of true love, I felt as if the Old Green Copper Rope-Walk had grown quite a different place. Old Barley might be as old as the hills, and might swear like a whole field of troopers, but there were redeeming youth and trust and hope enough in Chinks's Basin to fill it to over-flowing. And then I thought of Estella, and of our parting, and went home very sadly.

All things were as quiet in the Temple as ever I had seen them. The windows of the rooms of that side, lately occupied by Provis were dark and still, and there was no lounger in Garden Court. I walked past the fountain twice or thrice before I descended the steps that were between me and my rooms, but I was quite alone. Herbert coming to my bedside when he came in – for I went straight to bed, dispirited and fatigued – made the same report. Opening one of the windows after that, he looked out into the moonlight, and told me that the pavement was as solemnly empty as the pavement of any cathedral at that same hour.

Next day, I set myself to get the boat. It was soon done, and the boat was brought round to the Temple stairs, and lay where I could reach her within a minute or two. Then, I began to go out as for training and practice: sometimes alone, sometimes with Herbert. I was often out in cold, rain, and sleet, but no-body took much note of me after I had been out a few times. At first, I kept above Blackfriars Bridge; but as the hours of the tide changed, I took towards London Bridge. It was Old London Bridge in those days, and at certain states of the tide there was a race and a fall of water there which gave it a bad reputation. But I knew well enough how to 'shoot' the bridge after seeing it done, and so began to row about among the shipping in the Pool, and down to Erith. The first time I passed Mill Pond Bank, Herbert and I were pulling a pair of oars; and, both in going and returning, we saw the blind towards the east come down. Herbert was rarely there less frequently than three times in a week, and he never brought me a single word of intelligence that was at all alarming. Still, I knew that there was cause for alarm, and I could not get rid of the notion of being watched. Once received, it is a haunting idea; how many un-designing persons I suspected of watching me, it would be hard to calculate.

In short, I was always full of fears for the rash man who was in hiding. Herbert had sometimes said to me that he found it pleasant to stand at one of our windows after dark, when the tide was running down, and to think that it was flowing, with everything it bore, towards Clara. But I thought with dread that it was flowing towards Magwitch, and that any black mark on its surface might be his pursuers, going swiftly, silently and surely, to take him.

Chapter 47

Some weeks passed without bringing any change. We waited for Wemmick, and he made no sign. If I had never known him out of Little Britain, and had never enjoyed the privilege of being on a familiar footing at the Castle, I might have doubted him; not so for a moment, knowing him as I did.

My worldly affairs began to wear a gloomy appearance and I was pressed for money by more than one creditor. Even I myself began to know the want of money (I mean of ready money in my own pocket), and to relieve it by converting some easily spared articles of jewellery into cash. But I had quite determined that it would be a heartless fraud to take more money from my patron in the existing state of my uncertain thoughts and plans. Therefore, I had sent him the unopened pocketbook by Herbert, to hold in his own keeping, and I felt a kind of satisfaction – whether it was a false kind or a true, I hardly know – in not having profited by his generosity since his revelation of himself.

As the time wore on, an impression settled heavily upon me that Estella was married. Fearful of having it confirmed, though it was all but a conviction, I avoided the newspapers, and begged Herbert (to whom I had confided the circumstances of our last interview) never to speak of her to me. Why I hoarded up this last wretched little rag of the robe of hope that was rent and given to the winds, how do I know! Why did you who read this, commit that not dissimilar inconsistency of your own, last year, last month, last week?

It was an unhappy life that I lived, and its one dominant anxiety, towering over all its other anxieties like a high mountain above a range of mountains, never disappeared from my view. Still, no new cause for fear arose. Let me start from my bed as I would, with the terror fresh upon me that he was discovered; let me sit listening as I would, with dread for Herbert's returning step at night, lest it should be fleeter than ordinary, and winged with evil news; for all that, and much more to like purpose, the round of things went on. Condemned to inaction and a state of constant restlessness and suspense, I rowed about in my boat, and waited, waited, waited, as I best could.

There were states of the tide when, having been down the river, I could not get back through the eddy-chafed arches and starlings of Old London Bridge; then, I left my boat at a wharf near the Custom House, to be brought up afterwards to the Temple stairs. I was not averse to doing this, as it served to make me and my boat a commoner incident among the water-side people there. From this slight occasion sprang two meetings that I have now to tell of.

One afternoon, late in the month of February, I came ashore at the wharf at dusk. I had pulled down as far as Greenwich with the ebb tide, and had turned with the tide. It had been a fine bright day, but had become foggy as the sun dropped, and I had had to feel my way back among the shipping pretty carefully. Both in going and returning, I had seen the signal in his window, all well.

As it was a raw evening and I was cold, I thought I would comfort myself with dinner at once; and as I had hours of dejection and solitude before me if I went home to the Temple, I thought I would afterwards go to the play. The theatre where Mr Wopsle had achieved his questionable triumph was in that waterside neighbourhood (it is nowhere now), and to that theatre I resolved to go. I was aware that Mr Wopsle had not succeeded in reviving the drama, but, on the contrary, had rather partaken of its decline. He had been ominously heard of, through the playbills, as a faithful black, in connection with a little girl of noble birth, and a monkey. And Herbert had seen him as a predatory Tartar of comic propensities, with a face like a red brick, and an outrageous hat all over bells.

I dined at what Herbert and I used to call a geographical chop-house – where there were maps of the world in porter-pot rims on every half-yard of the tablecloths, and charts of gravy on every one of the knives – to this day there is scarcely a single chop-house within the Lord Mayor's dominions which is not geographical – and wore out the time in dozing over crumbs, staring at gas, and baking in a hot blast of dinners. By and by, I roused myself and went to the play.

There, I found a virtuous boatswain in his Majesty's service – a most excellent man, though I could have wished his trousers not quite so tight in some places and not quite so loose in others – who knocked all the little men's hats over their eyes, though he was very generous and brave, and who wouldn't hear of anybody's paying taxes, though he was very patriotic. He had a bag of money in his pocket, like a pudding in the cloth, and on that property married a young person in bed-furniture, with great rejoicings; the whole population of Portsmouth (nine in number at the last census) turning out on the beach, to rub their own hands and shake everybody else's, and sing, 'Fill, fill!' A certain dark-complexioned Swab, however, who wouldn't fill, or do anything else that was proposed to him, and whose heart was openly stated (by the boatswain) to be as black as his figurehead, proposed to two other Swabs to get all mankind into difficulties; which was so effectually done (the Swab family having considerable political influence) that it took half the evening to set things right, and then it was only brought about through an honest little grocer with a white hat, black gaiters, and red nose, getting into a clock, with a grid-iron, and listening, and coming out, and knocking everybody down from behind with the gridiron whom he couldn't confute with what he had overheard. This led to Mr Wopsle's (who had never been heard of before) coming in with a star and garter on, as a plenipotentiary of great power direct from the Admiralty, to say that the Swabs were all to go to prison on the spot, and that he had brought the boatswain down the Union Jack, as a slight acknowledgment of his public services. The boatswain, unmanned for the first time, respectfully dried his eyes on the Jack, and then cheering up and addressing Mr Wopsle as Your Honour, solicited permission to take him by the fin. Mr Wopsle conceding his fin with a gracious dignity, was immediately shoved into a dusty corner while everybody danced a hornpipe; and from that corner, surveying the public with a discontented eye, became aware of me.

The second piece was the last new grand comic Christmas pantomime, in the first scene of which it pained me to suspect that I detected Mr Wopsle, with red worsted legs under a highly magnified phosphoric countenance and a shock of red curtain-fringe for his hair, engaged in the manufacture of thunderbolts in a mine, and displaying great cowardice when his gigantic master came home (very hoarse) to dinner. But he presently presented himself under worthier circumstances; for, the genius of youthful love being in want of assistance – on account of

the parental brutality of an ignorant farmer who opposed the choice of his daughter's heart, by purposely falling upon the object in a flour sack out of the first-floor window – summoned a sententious enchanter; and he, coming up from the antipodes rather unsteadily, after an apparently violent journey, proved to be Mr Wopsle in a high-crowned hat, with a necromantic work in one volume under his arm. The business of this enchanter on earth, being principally to be talked at, sung at, butted at, danced at, and flashed at with fires of various colours, he had a good deal of time on his hands. And I observed, with great surprise, that he devoted it to staring in my direction as if he were lost in amazement.

There was something so remarkable in the increasing glare of Mr Wopsle's eye, and he seemed to be turning so many things over in his mind and to grow so confused, that I could not make it out. I sat thinking of it, long after he had ascended to the clouds in a large watchcase, and still I could not make it out. I was still thinking of it when I came out of the theatre an hour afterwards, and found him waiting for me near the door.

'How do you do?' said I, shaking hands with him as we turned down the street together. 'I saw that you saw me.'

'Saw you, Mr Pip!' he returned. 'Yes, of course I saw you. But who else was there?'

'Who else?'

'It is the strangest thing,' said Mr Wopsle, drifting into his lost look again; 'and yet I could swear to him.'

Becoming alarmed, I entreated Mr Wopsle to explain his meaning.

'Whether I should have noticed him at first but for your being there,' said Mr Wopsle, going on in the same lost way, 'I can't be positive; yet I think I should.'

Involuntarily I looked round me, as I was accustomed to look round me when I went home; for these mysterious words gave me a chill.

'Oh! He can't be in sight,' said Mr Wopsle. 'He went out, before I went off; I saw him go.'

Having the reason that I had for being suspicious, I even suspected this poor actor. I mistrusted a design to entrap me into some admission. Therefore, I glanced at him as we walked on together, but said nothing.

'I had a ridiculous fancy that he must be with you, Mr Pip, till I saw that you were quite unconscious of him, sitting behind you there like a ghost.'

My former chill crept over me again, but I was resolved not to speak yet, for it was quite consistent with his words that he might be set on to induce me to connect these references with Provis. Of course, I was perfectly sure and safe that Provis had not been there.

'I dare say you wonder at me, Mr Pip; indeed, I see you do. But it is so very strange! You'll hardly believe what I am going to tell you. I could hardly believe it myself, if you told me.'

'Indeed?' said I.

'No, indeed. Mr Pip, you remember in old times a certain Christmas Day, when you were quite a child, and I dined at Gargery's, and some soldiers came to the door to get a pair of handcuffs mended?'

'I remember it very well.'

'And you remember that there was a chase after two convicts, and that we joined in it, and that Gargery took you on his back, and that I took the lead and you kept up with me as well as you could?'

'I remember it all very well.' Better than he thought – except the last clause.

'And you remember that we came up with the two in a ditch, and that there was a scuffle between them, and that one of them had been severely handled and much mauled about the face by the other?'

'I see it all before me.'

'And that the soldiers lighted torches, and put the two in the centre, and that we went on to see the last of them, over the black marshes, with the torchlight shining on their faces – I am particular about that; with the torchlight shining on their faces, when there was an outer ring of dark night all about us?'

'Yes,' said I. 'I remember all that.'

'Then, Mr Pip, one of those two prisoners sat behind you tonight. I saw him over your shoulder.'

'Steady!' I thought. I asked him then, 'Which of the two do you suppose you saw?'

'The one who had been mauled,' he answered readily, 'and I'll swear I saw him! The more I think of him, the more certain I am of him.'

'This is very curious!' said I, with the best assumption I could put on, of its being nothing more to me. 'Very curious indeed!'

I cannot exaggerate the enhanced disquiet into which this conversation threw me, or the special and peculiar terror I felt at Compeyson's having been behind me 'like a ghost'. For if he had ever been out of my thoughts for a few moments together since the hiding had begun, it was in those very moments when he was closest to me; and to think that I should be so unconscious and off my guard after all my care, was as if I had shut an avenue of a hundred doors to keep him out, and then had found him at my elbow. I could not doubt either that he was there, because I was there, and that however slight an appearance of danger there might be about us, danger was always near and active.

I put such questions to Mr Wopsle as, when did the man come in? He could not tell me that; he saw me, and over my shoulder he saw the man. It was not until he had seen him for some time that he began to identify him; but he had from the first vaguely associated him with me, and known him as somehow belonging to me in the old village time. How was he dressed? Prosperously, but not noticeably otherwise; he thought, in black. Was his face at all disfigured? No, he believed not. I believed not, too, for although in my brooding state I had taken no especial notice of the people behind me, I thought it likely that a face at all disfigured would have attracted my attention.

When Mr Wopsle had imparted to me all that he could recall or I extract, and when I had treated him to a little appropriate refreshment after the fatigues of the evening, we parted. It was between twelve and one o'clock when I reached the Temple, and the gates were shut. No one was near me when I went in and went home.

Herbert had come in, and we held a very serious council by the fire. But there was nothing to be done, saving to communicate to Wemmick what I had that night found out, and to remind him that we waited for his hint. As I thought that I might compromise him if I went too often to the Castle, I made this communication by letter. I wrote it before I went to bed and went out and posted it; and again no one was near me. Herbert and I agreed that we could do nothing else but be very cautious. And we were very cautious indeed – more cautious than before, if that were possible – and I for my part never went near Chinks's Basin, except when I rowed by, and then I only looked at Mill Pond Bank as I looked at anything else.

Chapter 48

The second of the two meetings referred to in the last chapter occurred about a week after the first. I had again left my boat at the wharf below Bridge; the time was an hour earlier in the afternoon; and, undecided where to dine, I had strolled up into Cheapside, and was strolling along it, surely the most unsettled person in all the busy concourse, when a large hand was laid upon my shoulder by someone overtaking me. It was Mr Jaggers's hand, and he passed it through my arm.

'As we are going in the same direction, Pip, we may walk together. Where are you bound for?'

'For the Temple, I think,' said I.

'Don't you know?' said Mr Jaggers.

'Well,' I returned, glad for once to get the better of him in cross-examination, 'I do *not* know, for I have not made up my mind.'

'You are going to dine?' said Mr Jaggers. 'You don't mind admitting that, I suppose?'

'No,' I returned, 'I don't mind admitting that.'

'And are not engaged?'

'I don't mind admitting, also, that I am not engaged.'

'Then,' said Mr Jaggers, 'come and dine with me.'

I was going to excuse myself, when he added, 'Wemmick's coming.' So I changed my excuse into an acceptance – the few words I had uttered serving for the beginning of either – and we went along Cheapside and slanted off to Little Britain, while the lights were springing up brilliantly in the shop windows, and the street lamp-lighters, scarcely finding ground enough to plant their ladders on in the midst of the afternoon's bustle, were skipping up and down and running in and out, opening more red eyes in the gathering fog than my rushlight tower at the Hummums had opened white eyes in the ghostly wall.

At the office in Little Britain there was the usual letter-writing, hand-washing, candle-snuffing, and safe-locking, that closed the business of the day. As I stood idle by Mr Jaggers's fire, its rising and falling flame made the two casts on the shelf look as if they were playing a diabolical game at bo-peep with me; while the pair of coarse fat office-candles that dimly lighted Mr Jaggers as he wrote in a corner, were decorated with dirty winding-sheets, as if in remembrance of a host of hanged clients.

We went to Gerrard Street, all three together, in a hackney-coach: and as soon as we got there, dinner was served. Although I should not have thought of making, in that place, the most distant reference by so much as a look to Wemmick's Walworth sentiments, yet I should have had no objection to catching his eye now and then in a friendly way. But it was not to be done. He turned his eyes on Mr Jaggers whenever he raised them from the table, and was as dry and distant to me as if there were twin Wemmicks and this was the wrong one.

'Did you send that note of Miss Havisham's to Mr Pip, Wemmick?' Mr Jaggers asked, soon after we began dinner.

'No, sir,' returned Wemmick; 'it was going by post, when you brought Mr Pip into the office. Here it is.' He handed it to his principal, instead of to me.

'It's a note of two lines, Pip,' said Mr Jaggers, handing it on, 'sent up to me by Miss Havisham, on account of her not being sure of your address. She tells me that she wants to see you on a little matter of business you mentioned to her. You'll go down?'

'Yes,' said I, casting my eyes over the note, which was exactly in those terms.

'When do you think of going down?'

'I have an impending engagement,' said I, glancing at Wemmick, who was putting fish into the post office, 'that renders me rather uncertain of my time. At once, I think.'

'If Mr Pip has the intention of going at once,' said Wemmick to Mr Jaggers, 'he needn't write an answer, you know.'

Receiving this as an intimation that it was best not to delay, I settled that I would go tomorrow, and said so. Wemmick drank a glass of wine and looked with a grimly satisfied air at Mr Jaggers, but not at me.

'So Pip! Our friend the Spider,' said Mr Jaggers, 'has played his cards. He has won the pool.'

It was as much as I could do to assent.

'Hah! He is a promising fellow – in his way – but he may not have it all his own way. The stronger will win in the end, but the stronger has to be found out first. If he should turn to and beat her – '

'Surely,' I interrupted, with a burning face and heart, 'you do not seriously think that he is scoundrel enough for that, Mr Jaggers?'

'I didn't say so, Pip. I am putting a case. If he should turn to and beat her, he may possibly get the strength on his side; if it should be a question of intellect, he certainly will not. It would be chance work to give an opinion how a fellow of that sort will turn out in such circumstances, because it's a toss-up between two results.'

'May I ask what they are?'

'A fellow like our friend the Spider,' answered Mr Jaggers, 'either beats or cringes. He may cringe and growl, or cringe and not growl; but he either beats or cringes. Ask Wemmick *his* opinion.'

'Either beats or cringes,' said Wemmick, not at all addressing himself to me.

'So, here's to Mrs Bentley Drummle,' said Mr Jaggers, taking a decanter of choicer wine from his dumb-waiter, and filling for each of us and for himself, 'and may the question of supremacy be settled to the lady's satisfaction! To the satisfaction of the lady *and* the gentleman, it never will be. Now, Molly, Molly, Molly, Molly, how slow you are today!'

She was at his elbow when he addressed her, putting a dish upon the table. As she withdrew her hands from it, she fell back a step or two, nervously muttering some excuse. And a certain action of her fingers as she spoke arrested my attention.

'What's the matter?' said Mr Jaggers.

'Nothing. Only the subject we were speaking of,' said I, 'was rather painful to me.'

The action of her fingers was like the action of knitting. She stood looking at her master, not understanding whether she was free to go, or whether he had more to say to her and would call her back if she did go. Her look was very intent. Surely, I had seen exactly such eyes and such hands, on a memorable occasion very lately!

He dismissed her, and she glided out of the room. But she remained before me, as plainly as if she were still there. I looked at those hands, I looked at those eyes, I looked at that flowing hair; and I compared them with other hands, other eyes, other hair, that I knew of, and with what those might be after twenty years of a brutal husband and a stormy life. I looked again at those hands and eyes of the housekeeper, and thought of the inexplicable feeling that had come over me when I last walked – not alone – in the ruined garden, and through the deserted brewery. I thought how the same feeling had come back when I saw a face looking at me, and a hand waving to me, from a stagecoach window; and how it had come back again and had flashed about me like lightning, when I had passed in a carriage – not alone – through a sudden glare of light in a dark street. I thought how one link of association had helped that identification in the theatre, and how such a link, wanting before, had been riveted for me now, when I had passed by a chance swift from Estella's name to the fingers with their knitting action, and the attentive eyes. And I felt absolutely certain that this woman was Estella's mother.

Mr Jaggers had seen me with Estella, and was not likely to have missed the sentiments I had been at no pains to conceal. He nodded when I said the subject was painful to me, clapped me on the back, put round the wine again, and went on with his dinner.

Only twice more did the housekeeper reappear, and then her stay in the room was very short, and Mr Jaggers was sharp with her. But her hands were Estella's hands, and her eyes were Estella's eyes, and if she had reappeared a hundred times I could have been neither more sure nor less sure that my conviction was the truth.

It was a dull evening, for Wemmick drew his wine when it came round, quite as a matter of business – just as he might have drawn his salary when that came round – and with his eyes on his chief, sat in a state of perpetual readiness for cross-examination. As to the quantity of wine, his post office was as indifferent and ready as any other post office for its quantity of letters. From my point of view, he was the wrong twin all the time, and only externally like the Wemmick of Walworth.

We took our leave early, and left together. Even when we were groping among Mr Jaggers's stock of boots for our hats, I felt that the right twin was on his way back; and we had not gone half a dozen yards down Gerrard Street in the Walworth direction before I found that I was walking arm-in-arm with the right twin, and that the wrong twin had evaporated into the evening air. 'Well!' said Wemmick, 'that's over! He's a wonderful man, without his living likeness; but I feel that I have to screw myself up when I dine with him – and I dine more comfortably unscrewed.'

I felt that this was a good statement of the case, and told him so.

'Wouldn't say it to anybody but yourself,' he answered. 'I know that what is said between you and me goes no further.'

I asked him if he had ever seen Miss Havisham's adopted daughter, Mrs Bentley Drummle? He said no. To avoid being too abrupt, I then spoke of the Aged, and of Miss Skiffins. He looked rather sly when I mentioned Miss Skiffins, and stopped in the street to blow his nose, with a roll of the head and a flourish not quite free from latent boastfulness.

'Wemmick,' said I, 'do you remember telling me, before I first went to Mr Jaggers's private house, to notice that house-keeper?'

'Did I?' he replied. 'Ah, I dare say I did. Deuce take me,' he added sullenly, 'I know I did. I find I am not quite unscrewed yet.'

'A wild beast tamed, you called her?'

'And what did *you* call her?'

'The same. How did Mr Jaggers tame her, Wemmick?'

'That's his secret. She has been with him many a long year.'

'I wish you would tell me her story. I feel a particular interest in being acquainted with it. You know that what is said between you and me goes no further.'

'Well!' Wemmick replied, 'I don't know her story – that is, I don't know all of it. But what I do know, I'll tell you. We are in our private and personal capacities, of course.'

'Of course.'

'A score or so of years ago, that woman was tried at the Old Bailey for murder and was acquitted. She was a very hand-some young woman, and I believe had some gypsy blood in her. Anyhow, it was hot enough when it was up, as you may suppose.'

'But she was acquitted.'

'Mr Jaggers was for her,' pursued Wemmick, with a look full of meaning, 'and worked the case in a way quite astonishing. It was a desperate case, and it was comparatively early days with him then, and he worked it to general admiration; in fact, it may almost be said to have made him. He worked it himself at the police-office, day after day for many days, contending against even a committal; and at the trial where he couldn't work it himself, sat under counsel, and – everyone knew – put in all the salt and pepper. The murdered person was a woman; a woman, a good ten years older, very much larger, and very much stronger. It was a case of jealousy. They both led tramping lives, and this woman in Gerrard Street here had been married

very young, over the broomstick (as we say), to a tramping man, and was a perfect fury in point of jealousy. The murdered woman – more a match for the man, certainly, in point of years – was found dead in a barn near Hounslow Heath. There had been a violent struggle, perhaps a fight. She was bruised and scratched and torn, and had been held by the throat at last and choked. Now, there was no reasonable evidence to implicate any person but this woman, and, on the improbabilities of her having been able to do it, Mr Jaggers principally rested his case. You may be sure,' said Wemmick, touching me on the sleeve, 'that he never dwelt upon the strength of her hands then, though he sometimes does now.'

I had told Wemmick of his showing us her wrists, that day of the dinner party.

'Well, sir!' Wemmick went on; 'it happened – happened, don't you see? – that this woman was so very artfully dressed from the time of her apprehension, that she looked much slighter than she really was; in particular, her sleeves are always remembered to have been so skilfully contrived that her arms had quite a delicate look. She had only a bruise or two about her – nothing for a tramp – but the backs of her hands were lacerated, and the question was, was it with fingernails? Now, Mr Jaggers showed that she had struggled through a great lot of brambles which were not as high as her face; but which she could not have got through and kept her hands out of; and bits of those brambles were actually found in her skin and put in evidence, as well as the fact that the brambles in question were found on examination to have been broken through, and to have little shreds of her dress and little spots of blood upon them here and there. But the boldest point he made was this. It was attempted to be set up in proof of her jealousy, that she was under strong suspicion of having, at about the time of the murder, frantically destroyed her child by this man – some three years old – to revenge herself upon him. Mr Jaggers worked that in this way. "We say these are not marks of finger-nails, but marks of brambles, and we show you the brambles. You say they are marks of fingernails, and you set up the hypothesis that she destroyed her child. You must accept all consequences of that hypothesis. For anything we know, she may have destroyed her child, and the child in clinging to her may have scratched her hands. What then? You are not trying her for the murder of her child; why don't you? As to this case, if you *will* have scratches, we say that, for anything we know, you may have accounted for them, assuming for the sake of argument that you have not invented them?" To sum up, sir,' said Wemmick, 'Mr Jaggers was altogether too many for the jury, and they gave in.'

'Has she been in his service ever since?'

'Yes; but not only that,' said Wemmick, 'she went into his service immediately after her acquittal, tamed as she is now. She has since been taught one thing and another in the way of her duties, but she was tamed from the beginning.'

'Do you remember the sex of the child?'

'Said to have been a girl.'

'You have nothing more to say to me tonight?'

'Nothing. I got your letter and destroyed it. Nothing.'

We exchanged a cordial good-night, and I went home, with new matter for my thoughts, though with no relief from the old.

Chapter 49

Putting Miss Havisham's note in my pocket, that it might serve as my credentials for so soon reappearing at Satis House, in case her waywardness should lead her to express any surprise at seeing me, I went down again by the coach next day. But I alighted at the Halfway House, and breakfasted there, and walked the rest of the distance; for I sought to get into the town quietly by the unfrequented ways, and to leave it in the same manner.

The best light of the day was gone when I passed along the quiet echoing courts behind the High Street. The nooks of ruin where the old monks had once had their refectories and gardens, and where the strong walls were now pressed into the service of humble sheds and stables, were almost as silent as the old monks in their graves. The cathedral chimes had at once a sadder and a more remote sound to me, as I hurried on avoiding observation, than they had ever had before; so, the swell of the old organ was borne to my ears like funeral music; and the rooks, as they hovered about the grey tower and swung in the bare high trees of the priory garden, seemed to call to me that the place was changed, and that Estella was gone out of it for ever.

An elderly woman, whom I had seen before as one of the servants who lived in the supplementary house across the back courtyard, opened the gate. The lighted candle stood in the dark passage within, as of old, and I took it up and ascended the staircase alone. Miss Havisham was not in her own room, but was in the larger room across the landing. Looking in at the door, after knocking in vain, I saw her sitting on the hearth in a ragged chair, close before, and lost in the contemplation of, the ashy fire.

Doing as I had often done, I went in and stood, touching the old chimney-piece, where she could see me when she raised her eyes. There was an air of utter loneliness upon her, that would have moved me to pity though she had wilfully done me a deeper injury than I could charge her with. As I stood compassionating her, and thinking how in the progress of time I too had come to be a part of the wrecked fortunes of that house, her eyes rested on me. She stared, and said in a low voice, 'Is it real?'

'It is I, Pip. Mr Jaggers gave me your note yesterday, and I have lost no time.'

'Thank you. Thank you.'

As I brought another of the ragged chairs to the hearth, and sat down, I remarked a new expression on her face, as if she were afraid of me.

'I want,' she said, 'to pursue that subject you mentioned to me when you were last here, and to show you that I am not all stone. But perhaps you can never believe, now, that there is anything human in my heart?'

When I said some reassuring words, she stretched out her tremulous right hand, as though she was going to touch me; but she recalled it again before I understood the action, or knew how to receive it.

'You said, speaking for your friend, that you could tell me how to do something useful and good. Something that you would like done, is it not?'

'Something that I would like done very very much.'

'What is it?'

I began explaining to her that secret history of the partnership. I had not got far into it, when I judged from her looks that she was thinking in a discursive way of me, rather than of what I said. It seemed to be so, for, when I stopped speaking, many moments passed before she showed that she was conscious of the fact.

'Do you break off,' she asked then, with her former air of being afraid of me, 'because you hate me too much to bear to speak to me?'

'No, no,' I answered, 'how can you think so, Miss Havisham! I stopped because I thought you were not following what I said.'

'Perhaps I was not,' she answered, putting a hand to her head. 'Begin again, and let me look at something else. Stay! Now tell me.'

She set her hand upon her stick, in the resolute way that sometimes was habitual to her, and looked at the fire with a strong expression of forcing herself to attend. I went on with my explanation, and told her how I had hoped to complete the transaction out of my means, but how in this I was disappointed. That part of the subject (I reminded her) involved matters which could form no part of my explanation, for they were the weighty secrets of another.

'So!' said she, assenting with her head, but not looking at me. 'And how much money is wanting to complete the purchase?'

I was rather afraid of stating it, for it sounded a large sum. 'Nine hundred pounds.'

'If I give you the money for this purpose, will you keep my secret as you have kept your own?'

'Quite as faithfully.'

'And your mind will be more at rest?'

'Much more at rest.'

'Are you very unhappy now?'

She asked this question, still without looking at me, but in an unwonted tone of sympathy. I could not reply at the moment, for my voice failed me. She put her left arm across the head of her stick, and softly laid her forehead on it.

'I am far from happy, Miss Havisham; but I have other causes of disquiet than any you know of. They are the secrets I have mentioned.'

After a little while she raised her head, and looked at the fire again.

' 'Tis noble in you to tell me that you have other causes of unhappiness. Is it true?'

'Too true.'

'Can I only serve you, Pip, by serving your friend? Regarding that as done, is there nothing I can do for you yourself?'

'Nothing. I thank you for the question. I thank you even more for the tone of the question. But, there is nothing.'

She presently rose from her seat, and looked about the blighted room for the means of writing. There were none there, and she took from her pocket a yellow set of ivory tablets, mounted in tarnished gold, and wrote upon them with a pencil in a case of tarnished gold that hung from her neck.

'You are still on friendly terms with Mr Jaggers?'

'Quite. I dined with him yesterday.'

'This is an authority to him to pay you that money, to lay out at your irresponsible discretion for your friend. I keep no money here; but if you would rather Mr Jaggers knew nothing of the matter, I will send it to you.'

'Thank you, Miss Havisham; I have not the least objection to receiving it from him.'

She read me what she had written, and it was direct and clear, and evidently intended to absolve me from any suspicion of profiting by the receipt of the money. I took the tablets from her hand, and it trembled again, and it trembled more as she took off the chain to which the pencil was attached, and put it in mine. All this she did without looking at me.

'My name is on the first leaf. If you can ever write under my name, "I forgive her", though ever so long after my broken heart is dust – pray do it!'

'O Miss Havisham,' said I, 'I can do it now. There have been sore mistakes; and my life has been a blind and thankless one; and I want forgiveness and direction far too much, to be bitter with you.'

She turned her face to me for the first time since she had averted it, and to my amazement, I may even add to my terror, dropped on her knees at my feet; with her folded hands raised to me in the manner in which, when her poor heart was young and fresh and whole, they must often have been raised to heaven from her mother's side.

To see her with her white hair and her worn face, kneeling at my feet, gave me a shock through all my frame. I entreated her to rise, and got my arms about her to help her up; but she only pressed that hand of mine which was nearest to her grasp, and hung her head over it and wept. I had never seen her shed a tear before, and in the hope that the relief might do her good, I bent over her without speaking. She was not kneeling now, but was down upon the ground.

'O!' she cried, despairingly. 'What have I done! What have I done!'

'If you mean, Miss Havisham, what have you done to injure me, let me answer. Very little. I should have loved her under any circumstances – is she married?'

'Yes!'

It was a needless question, for a new desolation in the desolate house had told me so.

'What have I done! What have I done!' She wrung her hands, and crushed her white hair, and returned to this cry over and over again. 'What have I done!'

I knew not how to answer or how to comfort her. That she had done a grievous thing in taking an impressionable child to mould into the form that her wild resentment, spurned affec-

tion, and wounded pride found vengeance in, I knew full well. But that, in shutting out the light of day, she had shut out infinitely more; that, in seclusion, she had secluded herself from a thousand natural and healing influences; that her mind, brooding solitary, had grown diseased, as all minds do and must and will that reverse the appointed order of their maker, I knew equally well. And could I look upon her without compassion, seeing her punishment in the ruin she was, in her profound unfitness for this earth on which she was placed, in the vanity of sorrow which had become a master mania, like the vanity of penitence, the vanity of remorse, the vanity of unworthiness, and other monstrous vanities that have been curses in this world?

'Until you spoke to her the other day, and until I saw in you a looking-glass that showed me what I once felt myself, I did not know what I had done. What have I done! What have I done!' And so again, twenty, fifty times over, what had she done!

'Miss Havisham,' I said, when her cry had died away, 'you may dismiss me from your mind and conscience. But Estella is a different case, and if you can ever undo any scrap of what you have done amiss in keeping a part of her right nature away from her, it will be better to do that, than to bemoan the past through a hundred years.'

'Yes, yes, I know it. But, Pip – my dear!' There was an earnest womanly compassion for me in her new affection. 'My dear! Believe this: when she first came to me, I meant to save her from misery like my own. At first I meant no more.'

'Well, well!' said I. 'I hope so.'

'But as she grew, and promised to be very beautiful, I gradually did worse, and with my praises, and with my jewels, and with my teachings, and with this figure of myself always before her, a warning to back and point my lessons, I stole her heart away and put ice in its place.'

'Better,' I could not help saying, 'to have left her a natural heart, even to be bruised or broken.'

With that, Miss Havisham looked distractedly at me for a while, and then burst out again, What had she done!

'If you knew all my story,' she pleaded, 'you would have some compassion for me and a better understanding of me.'

'Miss Havisham,' I answered, as delicately as I could, 'I believe I may say that I do know your story, and have known it ever since I first left this neighbourhood. It has inspired me with great commiseration, and I hope I understand it and its influences. Does what has passed between us give me any excuse for asking you a question relative to Estella? Not as she is, but as she was when she first came here?'

She was seated on the ground, with her arms on the ragged chair, and her head leaning on them. She looked full at me when I said this, and replied, 'Go on.'

'Whose child was Estella!'

She shook her head.

'You don't know?'

She shook her head again.

'But Mr Jaggers brought her here, or sent her here?'

'Brought her here.'

'Will you tell me how that came about?'

She answered in a low whisper and with caution: 'I had been shut up in these rooms a long time (I don't know how long; you know what time the clocks keep here), when I told him that I wanted a little girl to rear and love, and save from my fate. I had first seen him when I sent for him to lay this place waste for me; having read of him in the newspapers before I and the world parted. He told me that he would look about him for such an orphan child. One night he brought her here asleep, and I called her Estella.'

'Might I ask her age then?'

'Two or three. She herself knows nothing, but that she was left an orphan and I adopted her.'

So convinced I was of that woman's being her mother, that I wanted no evidence to establish the fact in my mind. But to my mind, I thought, the connection here was clear and straight.

What more could I hope to do by prolonging the interview? I had succeeded on behalf of Herbert, Miss Havisham had told me all she knew of Estella, I had said and done what I could to ease her mind. No matter with what other words we parted; we parted.

Twilight was closing in when I went downstairs into the natural air. I called to the woman who had opened the gate when I entered, that I would not trouble her just yet, but would walk round the place before leaving. For, I had a presentiment that I should never be there again, and I felt that the dying light was suited to my last view of it.

By the wilderness of casks that I had walked on long ago, and on which the rain of years had fallen since, rotting them in many places, and leaving miniature swamps and pools of water upon those that stood on end, I made my way to the ruined garden. I went all round it; round by the corner where Herbert and I had fought our battle; round by the paths where Estella and I had walked. So cold, so lonely, so dreary all!

Taking the brewery on my way back, I raised the rusty latch of a little door at the garden end of it, and walked through. I was going out at the opposite door – not easy to open now, for the damp wood had started and swelled, and the hinges were yielding, and the threshold was encumbered with a growth of fungus – when I turned my head to look back. A childish association revived with wonderful force in the moment of the slight action, and I fancied that I saw Miss Havisham hanging to the beam. So strong was the impression, that I stood under the beam shuddering from head to foot before I knew it was a fancy – though to be sure I was there in an instant.

The mournfulness of the place and time, and the great terror of this illusion, though it was but momentary, caused me to feel an indescribable awe as I came out between the open wooden gates where I had once wrung my hair after Estella had wrung my heart. Passing on into the front courtyard, I hesitated whether to call the woman to let me out at the locked gate, of which she had the key, or first to go upstairs and assure myself that Miss Havisham was as safe and well as I had left her. I took the latter course and went up.

I looked into the room where I had left her, and I saw her seated in the ragged chair upon the hearth close to the fire, with her back towards me. In the moment when I was withdrawing my head to go quietly away, I saw a great flaming light spring up. In the same moment I saw her running at me, shrieking, with a whirl of fire blazing all about her, and soaring at least as many feet above her head as she was high.

I had a double-caped greatcoat on, and over my arm another thick coat. That I got them off, closed with her, threw her down, and got them over her; that I dragged the great cloth from the table for the same purpose, and with it dragged down the heap of rottenness in the midst, and all the ugly things that sheltered there; that we were on the ground struggling like desperate enemies, and that the closer I covered her, the more wildly she shrieked and tried to free herself; that this occurred I knew through the result, but not through anything I felt, or thought, or knew I did. I knew nothing until I knew that we were on the floor by the great table, and that patches of tinder yet alight were floating in the smoky air, which a moment ago had been her faded bridal dress.

Then, I looked round and saw the disturbed beetles and spiders running away over the floor, and the servants coming in with breathless cries at the door. I still held her forcibly down with all my strength, like a prisoner who might escape; and I doubt if I even knew who she was, or why we had struggled, or that she had been in flames, or that the flames were out, until I saw the patches of tinder that had been her garments, no longer alight, but falling in a black shower around us.

She was insensible, and I was afraid to have her moved, or even touched. Assistance was sent for, and I held her until it came, as if I unreasonably fancied (I think I did) that if I let her go, the fire would break out again and consume her. When I got up, on the surgeon's coming to her with other aid, I was astonished to see that both my hands were burnt; for I had no knowledge of it through the sense of feeling.

On examination it was pronounced that she had received serious hurts, but that they of themselves were far from hopeless; the danger lay mainly in the nervous shock. By the surgeon's directions, her bed was carried into that room and laid upon the great table, which happened to be well suited to the dressing of her injuries. When I saw her again, an hour afterwards, she lay indeed where I had seen her strike her stick, and had heard her say she would lie one day.

Though every vestige of her dress was burnt, as they told me, she still had something of her old ghastly bridal appearance; for, they had covered her to the throat with white-cotton wool, and as she lay with a white sheet loosely overlying that, the phantom air of something that had been and was changed was still upon her.

I found, on questioning the servants, that Estella was in Paris, and I got a promise from the surgeon that he would write by the next post. Miss Havisham's family I took upon myself; intending to communicate with Matthew Pocket only, and leave him to do as he liked about informing the rest. This I did next day, through Herbert, as soon as I returned to town.

There was a stage, that evening, when she spoke collectedly of what had happened, though with a certain terrible vivacity. Towards midnight she began to wander in her speech, and after that it gradually set in that she said innumerable times in a low solemn voice, 'What have I done!' And then, 'When she first came, I meant to save her from misery like mine.' And then, 'Take the pencil and write under my name, "I forgive her!"' She never changed the order of these three sentences, but she sometimes left out a word in one or other of them; never putting in another word, but always leaving a blank and going on to the next word.

As I could do no service there, and as I had, nearer home, that pressing reason for anxiety and fear which even her wanderings could not drive out of my mind, I decided in the course of the night that I would return by the early morning coach: walking on a mile or so, and being taken up clear of the town. At about six o'clock of the morning, therefore, I leaned over her and touched her lips with mine, just as they said, not stopping for being touched, 'Take the pencil and write under my name, "I forgive her".'

Chapter 50

My hands had been dressed twice or thrice in the night, and again in the morning. My left arm was a good deal burned to the elbow, and, less severely, as high as the shoulder; it was very painful, but the flames had set in that direction, and I felt thankful it was no worse. My right hand was not so badly burnt but that I could move the fingers. It was bandaged, of course, but much less inconveniently than my left hand and arm; those I carried in a sling; and I could only wear my coat like a cloak, loose over my shoulders and fastened at the neck. My hair had been caught by the fire, but not my head or face.

When Herbert had been down to Hammersmith and had seen his father, he came back to me at our chambers, and devoted the day to attending on me. He was the kindest of nurses, and at stated times took off the bandages, and steeped them in the cooling liquid that was kept ready, and put them on again, with a patient tenderness that I was deeply grateful for.

At first, as I lay quiet on the sofa, I found it painfully difficult, I might say impossible, to get rid of the impression of the glare of the flames, their hurry and noise, and the fierce burning smell. If I dozed for a minute, I was awakened by Miss Havisham's cries, and by her running at me with all that height of fire above her head. This pain of the mind was much harder to strive against than any bodily pain I suffered; and Herbert, seeing that, did his utmost to hold my attention engaged.

Neither of us spoke of the boat, but we both thought of it. That was made apparent by our avoidance of the subject, and by our agreeing – without agreement – to make my recovery of the use of my hands a question of so many hours, not of so many weeks.

My first question when I saw Herbert had been, of course, whether all was well down the river? As he replied in the affirmative, with perfect confidence and cheerfulness, we did not resume the subject until the day was wearing away. But then, as Herbert changed the bandages, more by the light of the fire than by the outer light, he went back to it spontaneously.

'I sat with Provis last night, Handel, two good hours.'

'Where was Clara?'

'Dear little thing!' said Herbert. 'She was up and down with Gruffandgrim all the evening. He was perpetually pegging at the floor, the moment she left his sight. I doubt if he can hold out long though. What with rum and pepper – and pepper and rum – I should think his pegging must be nearly over.'

'And then you will be married, Herbert?'

'How can I take care of the dear child otherwise? – lay your arm out upon the back of the sofa, my dear boy, and I'll sit down here, and get the bandage off so gradually that you shall not know when it comes. I was speaking of Provis. Do you know, Handel, he improves?'

'I said to you I thought he was softened when I last saw him.'

'So you did. And so he is. He was very communicative last night, and told me more of his life. You remember his breaking off here about some woman that he had had great trouble with – did I hurt you?'

I had started, but not under his touch. His words had given me a start.

'I had forgotten that, Herbert, but I remember it now you speak of it.'

'Well! He went into that part of his life, and a dark wild part it is. Shall I tell you? Or would it worry you just now?'

'Tell me by all means. Every word.'

Herbert bent forward to look at me more nearly, as if my reply had been rather more hurried or more eager than he could quite account for. 'Your head is cool?' he said, touching it.

'Quite,' said I. 'Tell me what Provis said, my dear Herbert.'

'It seems,' said Herbert, ' – there's a bandage off most charmingly, and now comes the cool one – makes you shrink at first, my poor dear fellow, don't it? but it will be comfortable presently – it seems that the woman was a young woman, and a jealous woman, and a revengeful woman; revengeful, Handel, to the last degree.'

'To what last degree?'

'Murder – does it strike too cold on that sensitive place?'

'I don't feel it. How did she murder? Whom did she murder?'

'Why, the deed may not have merited quite so terrible a name,' said Herbert, 'but she was tried for it, and Mr Jaggers defended her, and the reputation of that defence first made his name known to Provis. It was another and a stronger woman who was the victim, and there had been a struggle – in a barn. Who began it, or how fair it was, or how unfair, may be doubtful; but how it ended is certainly not doubtful, for the victim was found throttled.'

'Was the woman brought in guilty?'

'No; she was acquitted – my poor Handel, I hurt you!'

'It is impossible to be gentler, Herbert. Yes? What else?'

'This acquitted young woman and Provis had a little child: a little child of whom Provis was exceedingly fond. On the evening of the very night when the object of her jealousy was strangled as I tell you, the young woman presented herself before Provis for one moment, and swore that she would destroy the child (which was in her possession), and he should never see it again; then, she vanished – there's the worst arm comfortably in the sling once more, and now there remains but the right hand, which is a far easier job. I can do it better by this light than by a stronger, for my hand is steadiest when I don't see the poor blistered patches too distinctly – you don't think your breathing is affected, my dear boy? You seem to breathe quickly.'

'Perhaps I do, Herbert. Did the woman keep her oath?'

'There comes the darkest part of Provis's life. She did.'

'That is, he says she did.'

'Why, of course, my dear boy,' returned Herbert, in a tone of surprise, and again bending forward to get a nearer look at me. 'He says it all. I have no other information.'

'No, to be sure.'

'Now, whether,' pursued Herbert, 'he had used the child's mother ill, or whether he had used the child's mother well, Provis doesn't say; but, she had shared some four or five years of the wretched life he described to us at this fireside, and he seems to have felt pity for her, and forbearance towards her. Therefore, fearing he should be called upon to depose about this destroyed child, and so be the cause of her death, he hid himself (much as he grieved for the child), kept himself dark, as he says, out of the way and out of the trial, and was only vaguely talked of as a certain man called Abel, out of whom the jealousy arose. After the acquittal she disappeared, and thus he lost the child and the child's mother.'

'I want to ask –'

'A moment, my dear boy, and I have done. That evil genius, Compeyson, the worst of scoundrels among many scoundrels, knowing of his keeping out of the way at that time, and of his reasons for doing so, of course afterwards held the knowledge over his head as a means of keeping him poorer, and working him harder. It was clear last night that this barbed the point of Provis's animosity.'

'I want to know,' said I, 'and particularly, Herbert, whether he told you when this happened?'

'Particularly? Let us remember, then, what he said as to that. His expression was, "a round score o' year ago, and a'most directly after I took up wi' Compeyson". How old were you when you came upon him in the little churchyard?'

'I think in my seventh year.'

'Ay. It had happened some three or four years then, he said, and you brought into his mind the little girl so tragically lost, who would have been about your age.'

'Herbert,' said I, after a short silence, in a hurried way, 'can you see me best by the light of the window, or the light of the fire?'

'By the firelight,' answered Herbert, coming close again.

'Look at me.'

'I do look at you, my dear boy.'

'Touch me.'

'I do touch you, my dear boy.'

'You are not afraid that I am in any fever, or that my head is much disordered by the accident of last night?'

'N–no, my dear boy,' said Herbert, after taking time to examine me. 'You are rather excited, but you are quite yourself.'

'I know I am quite myself. And the man we have in hiding down the river is Estella's father.'

Chapter 51

What purpose I had in view when I was hot on tracing out and proving Estella's parentage, I cannot say. It will presently be seen that the question was not before me in a distinct shape, until it was put before me by a wiser head than my own.

But, when Herbert and I had held our momentous conversation, I was seized with a feverish conviction that I ought to hunt the matter down – that I ought not to let it rest, but that I ought to see Mr Jaggers, and come at the bare truth. I really do not know whether I felt that I did this for Estella's sake, or whether I was glad to transfer to the man, in whose preservation I was so much concerned, some rays of the romantic interest that had so long surrounded me. Perhaps the latter possibility may be the nearer to the truth.

Anyway, I could scarcely be withheld from going out to Gerrard Street that night. Herbert's representations that if I did I should probably be laid up and stricken useless, when our fugitive's safety would depend upon me, alone restrained my impatience. On the understanding, again and again reiterated that come what would I was to go to Mr Jaggers tomorrow, I at length submitted to keep quiet, and to have my hurts looked after, and to stay at home. Early next morning we went out together, and at the corner of Giltspur Street by Smithfield, I left Herbert to go his way into the City, and took my way to Little Britain.

There were periodical occasions when Mr Jaggers and Mr Wemmick went over the office accounts, and checked off the vouchers, and put all things straight. On these occasions Wemmick took his books and papers into Mr Jaggers's room, and one of the upstairs clerks came down into the outer office. Finding such clerk on Wemmick's post that morning, I knew what was going on; but I was not sorry to have Mr Jaggers and Wemmick together, as Wemmick would then hear for himself that I said nothing to compromise him.

My appearance, with my arm bandaged and my coat loose over my shoulders, favoured my object. Although I had sent Mr Jaggers a brief account of the accident as soon as I had arrived in town, yet I had to give him all the details now; and the specialty of the occasion caused our talk to be less dry and hard, and less strictly regulated by the rules of evidence, than it had been before. While I described the disaster, Mr Jaggers stood, according to his wont, before the fire. Wemmick leaned back in his chair, staring at me, with his hands in the pockets of his trousers, and his pen put horizontally into the post. The two brutal casts, always inseparable in my mind from the official proceedings, seemed to be congestively considering whether they didn't smell fire at the present moment.

My narrative finished, and their questions exhausted, I then produced Miss Havisham's authority to receive the nine hundred pounds for Herbert. Mr Jaggers's eyes retired a little deeper into his head when I handed him the tablets, but he presently handed them over to Wemmick, with instructions to draw the cheque for his signature. While that was in course of being done, I looked on at Wemmick as he wrote, and Mr Jaggers, poising and swaying himself on his well-polished boots, looked on at me. 'I am sorry, Pip,' said he, as I put the cheque in my pocket, when he had signed it, 'that we do nothing for *you*.'

'Miss Havisham was good enough to ask me,' I returned, 'whether she could do nothing for me, and I told her no.'

'Everybody should know his own business,' said Mr Jaggers. And I saw Wemmick's lips form the words 'portable property'.

'I should *not* have told her no, if I had been you,' said Mr Jaggers; 'but every man ought to know his own business best.'

'Every man's business,' said Wemmick, rather reproachfully towards me, 'is "portable property".'

As I thought the time was now come for pursuing the theme I had at heart, I said, turning on Mr Jaggers: 'I did ask something of Miss Havisham, however, sir. I asked her to give me some information relative to her adopted daughter, and she gave me all she possessed.'

'Did she?' said Mr Jaggers, bending forward to look at his boots and then straightening himself. 'Hah! I don't think I should have done so, if I had been Miss Havisham. But *she* ought to know her own business best.'

'I know more of the history of Miss Havisham's adopted child than Miss Havisham herself does, sir. I know her mother.'

Mr Jaggers looked at me enquiringly, and repeated 'Mother?'

'I have seen her mother within these three days.'

'Yes?' said Mr Jaggers.

'And so have you, sir. And you have seen her still more recently.'

'Yes?' said Mr Jaggers.

'Perhaps I know more of Estella's history than even you do,' said I. 'I know her father, too.'

A certain stop that Mr Jaggers came to in his manner – he was too self-possessed to change his manner, but he could not help its being brought to an indefinably attentive stop – assured me that he did not know who her father was. This I had strongly suspected from Provis's account (as Herbert had repeated it) of his having kept himself dark; which I pieced on to the fact that he himself was not Mr Jaggers's client until some four years later, and when he could have no reason for claiming his identity. But, I could not be sure of this unconsciousness on Mr Jaggers's part before, though I was quite sure of it now.

'So! You know the young lady's father, Pip?' said Mr Jaggers.

'Yes,' I replied, 'and his name is Provis – from New South Wales.'

Even Mr Jaggers started when I said those words. It was the slightest start that could escape a man, the most carefully repressed and the sooner checked, but he did start, though he made it a part of the action of taking out his pocket-handkerchief. How Wemmick received the announcement I am unable to say, for I was afraid to look at him just then, lest Mr Jaggers's sharpness should detect that there had been some communication unknown to him between us.

'And on what evidence, Pip,' asked Mr Jaggers, very coolly, as he paused with his handkerchief halfway to his nose, 'does Provis make this claim?'

'He does not make it,' said I, 'and has never made it, and

has no knowledge or belief that his daughter is in existence.'

For once, the powerful pocket-handkerchief failed. My reply was so unexpected that Mr Jaggers put the handkerchief back into his pocket without completing the usual performance, folded his arms, and looked with stern attention at me, though with an immovable face.

Then I told him all I knew, and how I knew it; with one reservation that I left him to infer that I knew from Miss Havisham what I in fact knew from Wemmick. I was very careful indeed as to that. Nor did I look towards Wemmick until I had finished all I had to tell, and had been for some time silently meeting Mr Jaggers's look. When I did at last turn my eyes in Wemmick's direction, I found that he had unposted his pen, and was intent upon the table before him.

'Hah!' said Mr Jaggers at last, as he moved towards the papers on the table. ' – what item was it you were at, Wemmick, when Mr Pip came in?'

But I could not submit to be thrown off in that way, and I made a passionate, almost an indignant appeal to him to be more frank and manly with me. I reminded him of the false hopes into which I had lapsed, the length of time they had lasted, and the discovery I had made: and I hinted at the danger that weighed upon my spirits. I represented myself as being surely worthy of some little confidence from him, in return for

Confidential with Mr Jaggers

the confidence I had just now imparted. I said that I did not blame him, or suspect him, or mistrust him, but I wanted assurance of the truth from him. And if he asked me why I wanted it and why I thought I had any right to it, I would tell him, little as he cared for such poor dreams, that I loved Estella dearly and long, and that, although I had lost her and must live a bereaved life, whatever concerned her was still nearer and dearer to me than anything else in the world. And seeing that Mr Jaggers stood quite still and silent, and apparently quite obdurate, under this appeal, I turned to Wemmick, and said, 'Wemmick, I know you to be a man with a gentle heart. I have seen your pleasant home, and your old father, and all the innocent cheerful playful ways with which you refresh your business life. And I entreat you to say a word for me to Mr Jaggers, and to represent to him that, all circumstances considered, he ought to be more open with me!'

I have never seen two men look more oddly at one another than Mr Jaggers and Wemmick did after this apostrophe. At first, a misgiving crossed me that Wemmick would be instantly dismissed from his employment; but, it melted as I saw Mr Jaggers relax into something like a smile, and Wemmick become bolder.

'What's all this?' said Mr Jaggers. 'You with an old father, and you with pleasant and playful ways?'

'Well!' returned Wemmick. 'If I don't bring 'em here, what does it matter?'

'Pip,' said Mr Jaggers, laying his hand upon my arm, and smiling openly, 'this man must be the most cunning impostor in all London.'

'Not a bit of it,' returned Wemmick, growing bolder and bolder. 'I think you're another.'

Again they exchanged their former odd looks, each apparently still distrustful that the other was taking him in.

'*You* with a pleasant home?' said Mr Jaggers.

'Since it don't interfere with business,' returned Wemmick, 'let it be so. Now, I look at you, sir, I shouldn't wonder if *you* might be planning and contriving to have a pleasant home of your own, one of these days, when you're tired of all this work.'

Mr Jaggers nodded his head retrospectively two or three times, and actually drew a sigh. 'Pip,' said he, 'we won't talk about "poor dreams"; you know more about such things than I, having much fresher experience of that kind. But now, about this other matter. I'll put a case to you. Mind! I admit nothing.'

He waited for me to declare that I quite understood that he expressly said that he admitted nothing.

'Now, Pip,' said Mr Jaggers, 'put this case. Put the case that a woman, under such circumstances as you have mentioned, held her child concealed, and was obliged to communicate the fact to her legal adviser, on his representing to her that he must know, with an eye to the latitude of his defence, how the fact stood about that child. Put the case that at the same time he held a trust to find a child for an eccentric rich lady to adopt and bring up.'

'I follow you, sir.'

'Put the case that he lived in an atmosphere of evil, and that all he saw of children was, their being generated in great num-

bers for certain destruction. Put the case that he often saw children solemnly tried at a criminal bar, where they were held up to be seen; put the case that he habitually knew of their being imprisoned, whipped, transported, neglected, cast out, qualified in all ways for the hangman, and growing up to be hanged. Put the case that pretty nigh all the children he saw in his daily business life, he had reason to look upon as so much spawn, to develop into the fish that were to come to his net – to be prosecuted, defended, forsworn, made orphans, bedevilled somehow.'

'I follow you, sir.'

'Put the case, Pip, that here was one pretty little child out of the heap who could be saved; whom the father believed dead, and dared make no stir about; as to whom, over the mother, the legal adviser had this power: "I know what you did, and how you did it. You came so and so, you did such and such things to divert suspicion. I have tracked you through it all, and I tell it you all. Part with the child, unless it should be necessary to produce it to clear you, and then it shall be produced. Give the child into my hands, and I will do my best to bring you off. If you are saved, your child will be saved too; if you are lost, your child is still saved." Put the case that this was done, and that the woman was cleared.'

'I understand you perfectly.'

'But that I make no admissions?'

'That you make no admissions.' And Wemmick repeated, 'No admissions.'

'Put the case, Pip, that passion and the terror of death had a little shaken the woman's intellects, and that when she was set at liberty, she was scared out of the ways of the world and went to him to be sheltered. Put the case that he took her in, and that he kept down the old wild violent nature, whenever he saw an inkling of its breaking out, by asserting his power over her in the old way. Do you comprehend the imaginary case?'

'Quite.'

'Put the case that the child grew up, and was married for money. That the mother was still living. That the father was still living. That the mother and father, unknown to one another, were dwelling within so many miles, furlongs, yards if you like, of one another. That the secret was still a secret, except that you had got wind of it. Put that last case to yourself very carefully.'

'I do.'

'I ask Wemmick to put it to *himself* very carefully.'

And Wemmick said, 'I do.'

'For whose sake would you reveal the secret? For the father's? I think he would not be much the better for the mother. For the mother's? I think if she had done such a deed she would be safer where she was. For the daughter's? I think it would hardly serve her, to establish her parentage for the information of her husband, and to drag her back to disgrace, after an escape of twenty years, pretty secure to last for life. But, add the case that you had loved her, Pip, and had made her the subject of those "poor dreams" which have, at one time or another, been in the heads of more men than you think likely, then I tell you that you had better – and would much sooner when you had thought well of it – chop off that bandaged left hand of yours with your bandaged right hand, and then pass the chopper on to Wemmick there, to cut *that* off too.'

I looked at Wemmick, whose face was very grave. He gravely touched his lips with his forefinger. I did the same. Mr Jaggers did the same. 'Now, Wemmick,' said the latter then, resuming his usual manner, 'what item was it you were at, when Mr Pip came in?'

Standing by for a little, while they were at work, I observed that the odd looks they had cast at one another were repeated several times: with this difference now, that each of them seemed suspicious, not to say conscious, of having shown himself in a weak and unprofessional light to the other. For this reason, I suppose, they were now inflexible with one another; Mr Jaggers being highly dictatorial, and Wemmick obstinately justifying himself whenever there was the smallest point in abeyance for a moment. I had never seen them on such ill terms; for generally they got on very well indeed together.

But, they were both happily relieved by the opportune appearance of Mike, the client with the fur cap, and the habit of wiping his nose on his sleeve, whom I had seen on the very first day of my appearance within those walls. This individual, who, either in his own person or in that of some member of his family, seemed to be always in trouble (which in that place meant Newgate), called to announce that his eldest daughter was taken up on suspicion of shoplifting. As he imparted this melancholy circumstance to Wemmick, Mr Jaggers standing magisterially before the fire and taking no share in the proceedings, Mike's eye happened to twinkle with a tear.

'What are you about?' demanded Wemmick, with the utmost indignation. 'What do you come snivelling here for?'

'I didn't go to do it, Mr Wemmick.'

'You did,' said Wemmick. 'How dare you? You're not in a fit state to come here, if you can't come here without spluttering like a bad pen. What do you mean by it?'

'A man can't help his feelings, Mr Wemmick,' pleaded Mike.

'His what?' demanded Wemmick, quite savagely. 'Say that again!'

'Now look here, my man,' said Mr Jaggers, advancing a step, and pointing to the door. 'Get out of this office. I'll have no feelings here. Get out.'

'It serves you right,' said Wemmick. 'Get out.'

So the unfortunate Mike very humbly withdrew, and Mr Jaggers and Wemmick appeared to have re-established their good understanding, and went to work again with an air of refreshment upon them as if they had just had lunch.

Chapter 52

From Little Britain I went, with my cheque in my pocket, to Miss Skiffins's brother, the accountant; and Miss Skiffins's brother, the accountant, going straight to Clarriker's and bringing Clarriker to me, I had the great satisfaction of concluding that arrangement. It was the only good thing I had done, and the only completed thing I had done, since I was first apprised of my great expectations.

Clarriker informing me on that occasion that the affairs of the house were steadily progressing, that he would now be able to establish a small branch-house in the East which was much wanted for the extension of the business, and that Herbert in his new partnership capacity would go out and take charge of it, I found that I must have prepared for a separation from my friend, even though my own affairs had been more settled. And now indeed I felt as if my last anchor were loosening its hold, and I should soon be driving with the winds and waves.

But there was recompense in the joy with which Herbert would come home of a night and tell me of these changes, little imagining that he told me no news, and would sketch airy pictures of himself conducting Clara Barley to the land of the Arabian Nights, and of me going out to join them (with a caravan of camels, I believe), and of our all going up the Nile and seeing wonders. Without being sanguine as to my own part in those bright plans, I felt that Herbert's way was clearing fast, and that old Bill Barley had but to stick to his pepper and rum, and his daughter would soon be happily provided for.

We had now got into the month of March. My left arm, though it presented no bad symptoms, took in the natural course so long to heal that I was still unable to get a coat on. My right arm was tolerably restored – disfigured, but fairly serviceable.

On a Monday morning, when Herbert and I were at breakfast, I received the following letter from Wemmick by the post.

Walworth. Burn this as soon as read. Early in the week, or say Wednesday, you might do what you know of, if you felt disposed to try it. Now burn.

When I had shown this to Herbert and had put it in the fire – but not before we had both got it by heart – we considered what to do. For, of course, my being disabled could now be no longer kept out of view.

'I have thought it over, again and again,' said Herbert, 'and I think I know a better course than taking a Thames waterman. Take Startop. A good fellow, a skilled hand, fond of us, and enthusiastic and honourable.'

I had thought of him more than once.

'But how much would you tell him, Herbert?'

'It is necessary to tell him very little. Let him suppose it a mere freak, but a secret one, until the morning comes: then let him know that there is urgent reason for your getting Provis aboard and away. You go with him?'

'No doubt.'

'Where?'

It had seemed to me, in the many anxious considerations I had given the point, almost indifferent what port we made for – Hamburg, Rotterdam, Antwerp – the place signified little, so that he was out of England. Any foreign steamer that fell in our way and would take us up would do. I had always proposed to myself to get him well down the river in the boat; certainly well beyond Gravesend, which was a critical place for search or enquiry if suspicion were afoot. As foreign steamers would leave London at about the time of high-water, our plan would be to get down the river by a previous ebb-tide, and lie by in some quiet spot until we could pull off to one. The time when one would be due where we lay, wherever that might be, could be calculated pretty nearly, if we made enquiries beforehand.

Herbert assented to all this, and we went out immediately after breakfast to pursue our investigations. We found that a steamer for Hamburg was likely to suit our purpose best, and we directed our thoughts chiefly to that vessel. But we noted down what other foreign steamers would leave London with the same tide, and satisfied ourselves that we knew the build and colour of each. We then separated for a few hours; I to get at once such passports as were necessary; Herbert, to see Star-top at his lodgings. We both did what we had to do without any hindrance, and when we met again at one o'clock reported it done. I, for my part, was prepared with passports; Herbert had seen Startop, and he was more than ready to join.

Those two would pull a pair of oars, we settled, and I would steer: our charge would be sitter, and keep quiet; as speed was not our object, we should make way enough. We arranged that Herbert should not come home to dinner before going to Mill Pond Bank that evening; that he should not go there at all tomorrow evening, Tuesday; that he should prepare Provis to come down to some stairs hard by the house, on Wednesday, when he saw us approach, and not sooner; that all the arrangements with him should be concluded that Monday night; and that he should be communicated with no more in any way, until we took him on board.

These precautions well understood by both of us, I went home.

On opening the outer door of our chambers with my key, I found a letter in the box, directed to me; a very dirty letter, though not ill-written. It had been delivered by hand (of course since I left home), and its contents were these:

> If you are not afraid to come to the old marshes tonight or tomorrow night at nine, and to come to the little sluice-house by the limekiln, you had better come. If you want information regarding *your Uncle Provis*, you had better come and tell no one and lose no time. *You must come alone*. Bring this with you.

I had had load enough upon my mind before the receipt of this strange letter. What to do now, I could not tell. And the worst was, that I must decide quickly, or I should miss the afternoon coach, which would take me down in time for to-night. Tomorrow night I could not think of going, for it would be too close upon the time of flight. And again, for anything I knew, the proffered information might have some important bearing on the flight itself.

If I had had ample time for consideration, I believe I should still have gone. Having hardly any time for consideration – my watch showing me that the coach started within half an hour – I resolved to go. I should certainly not have gone, but for the reference to my Uncle Provis. That, coming on Wemmick's letter and the morning's busy preparation, turned the scale.

It is so difficult to become clearly possessed of the contents of almost any letter, in a violent hurry, that I had to read this mysterious epistle again, twice, before its injunction to me to be secret got mechanically into my mind. Yielding to it in the same mechanical kind of way, I left a note in pencil for Herbert, telling him that as I should be so soon going away, I knew not for how long, I had decided to hurry down and back, to ascertain for myself how Miss Havisham was faring. I had then barely time to get my greatcoat, lock up the chambers, and make for the coach-office by the short byways. If I had taken a hackney-chariot and gone by the streets, I should have missed my aim; going as I did, I caught the coach just as it came out of the yard. I was the only inside passenger, jolting away knee-deep in straw, when I came to myself.

For I really had not been myself since the receipt of the letter; it had so bewildered me, ensuing on the hurry of the morning. The morning hurry and flutter had been great, for, long and anxiously as I had waited for Wemmick, his hint had come like a surprise at last. And now, I began to wonder at myself for being in the coach, and to doubt whether I had sufficient reason for being there, and to consider whether I should get out presently and go back, and to argue against ever heeding an anonymous communication, and, in short, to pass through all those phases of contradiction and indecision to which I suppose very few hurried people are strangers. Still, the reference to Provis by name mastered everything. I reasoned as I had reasoned already without knowing it – if that be reasoning – in case any harm should befall him through my not going, how could I ever forgive myself!

It was dark before we got down, and the journey seemed long and dreary to me who could see little of it inside, and who could not go outside in my disabled state. Avoiding the Blue Boar, I put up at an inn of minor reputation down the town, and ordered some dinner. While it was preparing, I went to Satis House and enquired for Miss Havisham; she was still very ill, though considered something better.

My inn had once been a part of an ancient ecclesiastical house, and I dined in a little octagonal commonroom, like a font. As I was not able to cut my dinner, the old landlord with a shining bald head did it for me. This bringing us into conversation, he was so good as to entertain me with my own story – of course with the popular feature that Pumblechook was my earliest benefactor and the founder of my fortunes.

'Do you know the young man?' said I.

'Know him?' repeated the landlord. 'Ever since he was – no height at all.'

'Does he ever come back to this neighbourhood?'

'Ay, he comes back,' said the landlord, 'to his great friends, now and again, and gives the cold shoulder to the man that made him.'

'What man is that?'

'Him that I speak of,' said the landlord. 'Mr Pumblechook.'

'Is he ungrateful to no one else?'

'No doubt he would be, if he could,' returned the landlord, 'but he can't. And why? Because Pumblechook done everything for him.'

'Does Pumblechook say so?'

'Say so!' replied the landlord. 'He han't no call to say so.'

'But does he say so?'

'It would turn a man's blood to white wine winegar, to hear him tell of it, sir,' said the landlord.

I thought, 'Yet Joe, dear Joe, *you* never tell of it. Long-suffering and loving Joe, *you* never complain. Nor you, sweet-tempered Biddy!'

'Your appetite's been touched like, by your accident,' said the landlord, glancing at the bandaged arm under my coat. 'Try a tenderer bit.'

'No thank you,' I replied, turning from the table to brood over the fire. 'I can eat no more. Please take it away.'

I had never been struck at so keenly, for my thanklessness to Joe, as through the brazen impostor Pumblechook. The falser he, the truer Joe; the meaner he, the nobler Joe.

My heart was deeply and most deservedly humbled as I mused over the fire for an hour or more. The striking of the clock aroused me, but not from my dejection or remorse, and I got up and had my coat fastened round my neck, and went out. I had previously sought in my pockets for the letter, that I might refer to it again, but I could not find it, and was uneasy to think that it must have been dropped in the straw of the coach. I knew very well, however, that the appointed place was the little sluice-house by the limekiln on the marshes, and the hour nine. Towards the marshes I now went straight, having no time to spare.

Chapter 53

It was a dark night, though the full moon rose as I left the enclosed lands, and passed out upon the marshes. Beyond their dark line there was a ribbon of clear sky, hardly broad enough to hold the red large moon. In a few minutes she had ascended out of that clear field, in among the piled mountains of cloud.

There was a melancholy wind, and the marshes were very dismal. A stranger would have found them insupportable, and even to me they were so oppressive that I hesitated, half inclined to go back. But I knew them, and could have found my way on a far darker night, and had no excuse for returning, being there. So, having come there against my inclination, I went on against it.

The direction that I took was not that in which my old home lay, nor that in which we had pursued the convicts. My back was turned towards the distant hulks as I walked on, and, though I could see the old lights away on the spits of sand, I saw them over my shoulder. I knew the limekiln as well as I knew the old battery, but they were miles apart; so that if a light had been burning at each point that night, there would have been a long strip of the blank horizon between the two bright specks.

At first I had to shut some gates after me, and now and then to stand still while the cattle that were lying in the banked-up pathway arose and blundered down among the grass and reeds. But after a little while, I seemed to have the whole flats to myself.

It was another half-hour before I drew near to the kiln. The lime was burning with a sluggish stifling smell, but the fires were made up and left, and no workmen were visible. Hard by was a small stone quarry. It lay directly in my way, and had been worked that day, as I saw by the tools and barrows that were lying about.

Coming up again to the marsh level out of this excavation – for the rude path lay through it – I saw a light in the old sluice-house. I quickened my pace, and knocked at the door with my hand. Waiting for some reply, I looked about me, noticing how the sluice was abandoned and broken, and how the house – of wood with a tiled roof – would not be proof against the weather much longer, if it were so even now, and how the mud and ooze were coated with lime, and how the choking vapour of the kiln crept in a ghostly way towards me. Still there was no answer, and I knocked again. No answer still, and I tried the latch.

It rose under my hand, and the door yielded. Looking in, I saw a lighted candle on a table, a bench, and a mattress on a truckle bedstead. As there was a loft above, I called, 'Is there anyone here?' but no voice answered. Then, I looked at my watch, and, finding that it was past nine, called again, 'Is there anyone here?' There being still no answer, I went out at the door, irresolute what to do.

It was beginning to rain fast. Seeing nothing save what I had seen already, I turned back into the house, and stood just within the shelter of the doorway, looking out into the night. While I was considering that someone must have been there lately and must soon be coming back, or the candle would not be burning, it came into my head to look if the wick were long. I turned round to do so, and had taken up the candle in my hand, when it was extinguished by some violent shock, and the next thing I comprehended was, that I had been caught in a strong running noose, thrown over my head from behind.

'Now,' said a suppressed voice with an oath, 'I've got you!'

'What is this?' I cried, struggling. 'Who is it? Help, help, help!'

Not only were my arms pulled close to my sides, but the pressure on my bad arm caused me exquisite pain. Sometimes a strong man's hand, sometimes a strong man's breast, was set against my mouth to deaden my cries, and with a hot breath always close to me, I struggled ineffectually in the dark, while I was fastened tight to the wall. 'And now,' said the suppressed voice with another oath, 'call out again, and I'll make short work of you!'

Faint and sick with the pain of my injured arm, bewildered by the surprise, and yet conscious how easily this threat could be put in execution, I desisted, and tried to ease my arm were it ever so little. But it was bound too tight for that. I felt as if, having been burnt before, it were now being boiled.

The sudden exclusion of the night and the substitution of black darkness in its place warned me that the man had closed a shutter. After groping about for a little, he found the flint and steel he wanted, and began to strike a light. I strained my sight upon the sparks that fell among the tinder, and upon which he breathed and breathed, match in hand, but I could only see his lips, and the blue point of the match; even those but fitfully. The tinder was damp – no wonder there – and one after another the sparks died out.

The man was in no hurry, and struck again with the flint and steel. As the sparks fell thick and bright about him, I could see his hands and touches of his face, and could make out that he was seated and bending over the table; but nothing more. Presently I saw his blue lips again, breathing on the tinder, and then a flare of light flashed up, and showed me Orlick.

Whom I had looked for, I don't know. I had not looked for him. Seeing him, I felt that I was in a dangerous strait indeed, and I kept my eyes upon him.

He lighted the candle from the flaring match with great deliberation, and dropped the match, and trod it out. Then, he put the candle away from him on the table, so that he could see me, and sat with his arms folded on the table and looked at me. I made out that I was fastened to a stout perpendicular ladder a few inches from the wall – a fixture there – the means of ascent to the loft above.

'Now,' said he, when we had surveyed one another for some time, 'I've got you.'

'Unbind me. Let me go!'

'Ah!' he returned, 'I'll let you go. I'll let you go to the moon, I'll let you go to the stars. All in good time.'

'Why have you lured me here?'

'Don't you know?' said he, with a deadly look.

'Why have you set upon me in the dark?'

'Because I mean to do it all myself. One keeps a secret better than two. Oh you enemy, you enemy!'

His enjoyment of the spectacle I furnished, as he sat with his arms folded on the table, shaking his head at me and hugging himself, had a malignity in it that made me tremble. As I watched him in silence, he put his hand into the corner at his side, and took up a gun with a brass-bound stock.

'Do you know this?' said he, making as if he would take aim at me. 'Do you know where you saw it afore? Speak, wolf!'

'Yes,' I answered.

'You cost me that place. You did. Speak!'

'What else could I do?'

'You did that, and that would be enough, without more. How dared you come betwixt me and a young woman I liked?'

'When did I?'

'When didn't you? It was you as always give Old Orlick a bad name to her.'

'You gave it to yourself; you gained it for yourself. I could have done you no harm, if you had done yourself none.'

'You're a liar. And you'll take any pains, and spend any money, to drive me out of this country, will you?' said he, repeating my words to Biddy, in the last interview I had with her. 'Now, I'll tell you a piece of information. It was never so worth your while to get me out of this country, as it is tonight. Ah! If it was all your money twenty times told, to the last brass farden!' As he shook his heavy hand at me, with his mouth snarling like a tiger's, I felt that it was true.

'What are you going to do to me?'

'I'm a going,' said he, bringing his fist down upon the table with a heavy blow, and rising as the blow fell, to give it greater force, 'I'm a going to have your life!'

He leaned forward staring at me, slowly unclenched his hand and drew it across his mouth as if his mouth watered for me, and sat down again.

'You was always in Old Orlick's way since ever you was a child. You goes out of his way this present night. He'll have no more on you. You're dead.'

I felt that I had come to the brink of my grave. For a moment I looked wildly round my trap for any chance of escape; but there was none.

'More than that,' said he, folding his arms on the table again, 'I won't have a rag of you, I won't have a bone of you, left on earth. I'll put your body in the kiln – I'd carry two such to it, on my shoulders – and, let people suppose what they may of you, they shall never know nothing.'

My mind, with inconceivable rapidity, followed out all the consequences of such a death. Estella's father would believe I had deserted him, would be taken, would die accusing me; even Herbert would doubt me, when he compared the letter I had left for him with the fact that I had called at Miss Havisham's gate for only a moment; Joe and Biddy would never know how sorry I had been that night, none would ever know what I had suffered, how true I had meant to be, what an agony I had passed through. The death close before me was terrible, but far more terrible than death was the dread of being misremembered after death. And so quick were my thoughts, that I saw myself despised by unborn generations – Estella's children, and their children – while the wretch's words were yet on his lips.

'Now, wolf,' said he, 'afore I kill you like any other beast – which is wot I mean to do and wot I have tied you up for – I'll have a good look at you and a good goad at you. Oh, you enemy.'

It had passed through my thoughts to cry out for help again; though few could know better than I, the solitary nature of the spot, and the hopelessness of aid. But as he sat gloating over me, I was supported by a scornful detestation of him that sealed my lips. Above all things, I resolved that I would not entreat him, and that I would die making some last poor resistance to him. Softened as my thoughts of all the rest of men were in that dire extremity; humbly beseeching pardon, as I did, of heaven; melted at heart, as I was, by the thought that I had taken no farewell, and never now could take farewell, of those who were dear to me, or could explain myself to them, or ask for their compassion on my miserable errors; still, if I could have killed him, even in dying, I would have done it.

He had been drinking, and his eyes were red and bloodshot. Around his neck was slung a tin bottle, as I had often seen his meat and drink slung about him in other days. He brought the bottle to his lips, and took a fiery drink from it; and I smelt the strong spirits that I saw flash into his face.

'Wolf!' said he, folding his arms again, 'Old Orlick's a going to tell you somethink. It was you as did for your shrew sister.'

Again my mind, with its former inconceivable rapidity had exhausted the whole subject of the attack upon my sister, her illness, and her death, before his slow and hesitating speech had formed those words.

'It was you, villain,' said I.

'I tell you it was your doing – I tell you it was done through you,' he retorted, catching up the gun, and making a blow with the stock at the vacant air between us. 'I come upon her from behind, as I come upon you tonight. I giv' it her! I left her for dead, and, if there had been a limekiln as nigh her as there is now nigh you, she shouldn't have come to life again. But it warn't Old Orlick as did it; it was you. You was favoured, and he was bullied and beat. Old Orlick bullied and beat, eh? Now you pays for it. You done it; now you pays for it.'

He drank again, and became more ferocious. I saw by his tilting of the bottle that there was no great quantity left in it. I distinctly understood that he was working himself up with its contents, to make an end of me. I knew that every drop it held was a drop of my life. I knew that when I was changed into a part of the vapour that had crept towards me but a little while before, like my own warning ghost, he would do as he had done in my sister's case – make all haste to the town, and be seen slouching about there, drinking at the alehouses. My rapid mind pursued him to the town, made a picture of the street with him in it, and contrasted its lights and life with the lonely marsh and the white vapour creeping over it, into which I should have dissolved.

It was not only that I could have summed up years and years and years while he said a dozen words, but that what he did say presented pictures to me, and not mere words. In the excited and exalted state of my brain, I could not think of a place without seeing it, or of persons without seeing them. It is impossible to overstate the vividness of these images, and yet I was so intent, all the time, upon him himself – who would not be intent on the tiger crouching to spring! – that I knew of the slightest action of his fingers.

When he had drunk this second time, he rose from the bench on which he sat, and pushed the table aside. Then, he took up the candle, and shading it with his murderous hand so as to throw its light on me, stood before me, looking at me and enjoying the sight.

'Wolf, I'll tell you something more. It was Old Orlick as you tumbled over on your stairs that night.'

I saw the staircase with its extinguished lamps. I saw the shadows of the heavy stair-rails, thrown by the watchman's lantern on the wall. I saw the rooms that I was never to see again; here, a door half open, there, a door closed; all the articles of furniture around.

'And why was Old Orlick there? I'll tell you something more, wolf. You and her *have* pretty well hunted me out of this country, so far as getting a easy living in it goes, and I've took up with new companions and new masters. Some of 'em writes my letters when I wants 'em wrote – do you mind? – writes my letters, wolf! They writes fifty hands; they're not like sneaking you, as writes but one. I've had a firm mind and a firm will to have your life, since you was down here at your sister's burying. I han't seen a way to get you safe, and I've looked arter you to know your ins and outs. For, says Old Orlick to himself, "Somehow or another I'll have him!" What! When I looks for you, I finds your Uncle Provis, eh?'

Mill Pond Bank, and Chinks's Basin, and the Old Green Copper Rope-Walk, all so clear and plain! Provis in his rooms, the signal whose use was over, pretty Clara, the good motherly woman, old Billy Barley on his back, all drifting by, as on the swift stream of my life fast running out to sea!

'*You* with a uncle too! Why, I knowed you at Gargery's when you was so small a wolf that I could have took your weazen betwixt this finger and thumb and chucked you away dead (as I'd thought o' doing, odd times, when I saw you a loitering among the pollards on a Sunday), and you hadn't found no uncles then. No, not you! But when Old Orlick come for to hear that your Uncle Provis had mostlike wore the leg-iron wot Old Orlick had picked up, filed asunder, on these meshes ever so many year ago, and wot he kep by him till he dropped your sister with it, like a bullock, as he means to drop you – hey – when he come for to hear that – hey –'

In his savage taunting, he flared the candle so close at me, that I turned my face aside to save it from the flame.

'Ah!' he cried, laughing, after doing it again, 'the burnt child dreads the fire! Old Orlick knowed you was burnt, Old Orlick knowed you was a smuggling your Uncle Provis away, Old Orlick's a match for you and know'd you'd come tonight! Now I'll tell you something more, wolf, and this ends it. There's them that's as good a match for your Uncle Provis as Old Orlick has been for you. Let him 'ware them when he's lost his nevvy. Let him 'ware them when no man can't find a rag of his dear relation's clothes, nor yet a bone of his body. There's them that can't and that won't have Magwitch – yes, *I* know the name – alive in the same land with them, and that's had such sure information of him when he was alive in another land, as that he couldn't and shouldn't leave it unbeknown and put them in danger. P'raps it's them that writes fifty hands, and that's not like sneaking you as writes but one. 'Ware Compeyson, Magwitch, and the gallows!'

He flared the candle at me again, smoking my face and hair, and for an instant blinding me, and turned his powerful back as he replaced the light on the table. I had thought a prayer, and had been with Joe and Biddy and Herbert, before he turned towards me again.

There was a clear space of a few feet between the table and the opposite wall. Within this space, he now slouched backwards and forwards. His great strength seemed to sit stronger upon him than ever before, as he did this with his hands hanging loose and heavy at his sides, and with his eyes scowling at me. I had no grain of hope left. Wild as my inward hurry was, and wonderful the force of the pictures that rushed by me instead of thoughts, I could yet clearly understand that unless he had resolved that I was within a few moments of surely perishing out of all human knowledge, he would never have told me what he had told.

Of a sudden, he stopped, took the cork out of his bottle, and tossed it away. Light as it was, I heard it fall like a plummet. He swallowed slowly, tilting up the bottle by little and little, and now he looked at me no more. The last few drops of liquor he poured into the palm of his hand, and licked up. Then with a sudden hurry of violence and swearing horribly, he threw the bottle from him, and stooped; and I saw in his hand a stone-hammer with a long heavy handle.

The resolution I had made did not desert me, for, without uttering one vain word of appeal to him, I shouted out with all my might, and struggled with all my might. It was only my head and my legs that I could move, but to that extent I struggled with all the force, until then unknown, that was within me. In the same instant I heard responsive shouts, saw figures and a gleam of light dash in at the door, heard voices and tumult, and saw Orlick emerge from a struggle of men, as if it were tumbling water, clear the table at a leap, and fly out into the night!

After a blank, I found that I was lying unbound, on the floor, in the same place, with my head on someone's knee. My eyes were fixed on the ladder against the wall, when I came to myself – had opened on it before my mind saw it – and thus as I recovered consciousness, I knew that I was in the place where I had lost it.

Too indifferent at first, even to look round and ascertain who supported me, I was lying looking at the ladder, when there came between me and it, a face. The face of Trabb's boy!

'I think he's all right!' said Trabb's boy, in a sober voice; 'but ain't he just pale though!'

At these words, the face of him who supported me looked over into mine, and I saw my supporter to be – 'Herbert! Great Heaven!'

'Softly,' said Herbert. 'Gently, Handel. Don't be too eager.'

'And our old comrade, Startop!' I cried, as he too bent over me.

'Remember what he is going to assist us in,' said Herbert, 'and be calm.'

The allusion made me spring up; though I dropped again from the pain in my arm. 'The time has not gone by, Herbert, has it? What night is tonight? How long have I been here?' For I had a strange and strong misgiving that I had been lying there a long time – a day and a night – two days and nights – more.

'The time has not gone by. It is still Monday night.'

'Thank God!'

'And you have all tomorrow, Tuesday, to rest in,' said Herbert. 'But you can't help groaning, my dear Handel. What hurt have you got? Can you stand?'

'Yes, yes,' said I, 'I can walk. I have no hurt but in this throbbing arm.'

They laid it bare, and did what they could. It was violently swollen and inflamed, and I could scarcely endure to have it touched. But they tore up their handkerchiefs to make fresh bandages, and carefully replaced it in the sling, until we could get to the town and obtain some cooling lotion to put upon it. In a little while we had shut the door of the dark and empty sluice-house, and were passing through the quarry on our way back. Trabb's boy – Trabb's overgrown young man now – went before us with a lantern, which was the light I had seen come in at the door. But the moon was a good two hours higher than when I had last seen the sky, and the night though rainy was much lighter. The white vapour of the kiln was passing from us as we went by, and, as I had thought a prayer before, I thought a thanksgiving now.

Entreating Herbert to tell me how he had come to my rescue

– which at first he had flatly refused to do, but had insisted on my remaining quiet – I learnt that I had in my hurry dropped the letter, open, in our chambers, where he, coming home to bring with him Startop, whom he had met in the street on his way to me, found it, very soon after I was gone. Its tone made him uneasy, and the more so because of the inconsistency between it and the hasty letter I had left for him. His uneasiness increasing instead of subsiding after a quarter of an hour's consideration, he set off for the coach-office, with Startop, who volunteered his company, to make enquiry when the next coach went down. Finding that the afternoon coach was gone, and finding that his uneasiness grew into positive alarm, as obstacles came in his way, he resolved to follow in a post-chaise. So, he and Startop arrived at the Blue Boar, fully expecting there to find me, or tidings of me; but, finding neither, went on to Miss Havisham's, where they lost me. Hereupon they went back to the hotel (doubtless at about the time when I was hearing the popular local version of my own story) to refresh themselves, and to get someone to guide them out upon the marshes. Among the loungers under the Boar's archway happened to be Trabb's boy – true to his ancient habit of happening to be everywhere where he had no business – and Trabb's boy had seen me passing from Miss Havisham's, in the direction of my dining-place. Thus Trabb's boy became their guide, and with him they went out to the sluice-house: though

Old Orlick means murder

by the town way to the marshes, which I had avoided. Now, as they went along, Herbert reflected that I might, after all, have been brought there on some genuine and serviceable errand tending to Provis's safety, and bethinking himself that in that case interruption might be mischievous, left his guide and Startop on the edge of the quarry, and went on by himself, and stole round the house two or three times, endeavouring to ascertain whether all was right within. As he could hear nothing but indistinct sounds of one deep rough voice (this was while my mind was so busy), he even at last began to doubt whether I was there, when suddenly I cried out loudly, and he answered the cries, and rushed in, closely followed by the other two.

When I told Herbert what had passed within the house, he was for our immediately going before a magistrate in the town, late at night as it was, and getting out a warrant. But I had already considered that such a course, by detaining us there, or binding us to come back, might be fatal to Provis. There was no gainsaying this difficulty, and we relinquished all thoughts of pursuing Orlick at that time. For the present, under the circumstances, we deemed it prudent to make rather light of the matter to Trabb's boy; who I am convinced would have been much affected by disappointment, if he had known that his intervention saved me from the limekiln. Not that Trabb's boy was of a malignant nature, but that he had too much spare vivacity, and that it was in his constitution to want variety and excitement at anybody's expense. When we parted, I presented him with two guineas (which seemed to meet his views), and told him that I was sorry ever to have had an ill opinion of him (which made no impression on him at all).

Wednesday being so close upon us, we determined to go back to London that night, three in the post-chaise; the rather, as we should then be clear away, before the night's adventure began to be talked of. Herbert got a large bottle of stuff for my arm, and by dint of having this stuff dropped over it all the night through, I was just able to bear its pain on the journey. It was daylight when we reached the Temple, and I went at once to bed, and lay in bed all day.

My terror, as I lay there, of falling ill and being unfitted for tomorrow, was so besetting, that I wonder it did not disable me of itself. It would have done so, pretty surely, in conjunction with the mental wear and tear I had suffered, but for the unnatural strain upon me that tomorrow was. So anxiously looked forward to, charged with such consequences, its results so impenetrably hidden though so near.

No precaution could have been more obvious than our refraining from communication with him that day; yet this again increased my restlessness. I started at every footstep and every sound, believing that he was discovered and taken, and this was the messenger to tell me so. I persuaded myself that I knew he was taken; that there was something more upon my mind than a fear or a presentiment; that the fact had occurred, and I had a mysterious knowledge of it. As the day wore on and no ill news came, as the day closed in and darkness fell, my overshadowing dread of being disabled by illness before tomorrow morning, altogether mastered me. My burning arm throbbed, and my burning head throbbed, and I fancied I was

beginning to wander. I counted up to high numbers, to make sure of myself, and repeated passages that I knew in prose and verse. It happened sometimes that in the mere escape of a fatigued mind, I dozed for some moments or forgot; then I would say to myself with a start, 'Now it has come, and I am turning delirious!'

They kept me very quiet all day, and kept my arm constantly dressed, and gave me cooling drinks. Whenever I fell asleep, I awoke with the notion I had had in the sluice-house, that a long time had elapsed and the opportunity to save him was gone. About midnight I got out of bed and went to Herbert, with the conviction that I had been asleep for four-and-twenty hours, and that Wednesday was past. It was the last self-exhausting effort of my fretfulness, for after that I slept soundly.

Wednesday morning was dawning when I looked out of window. The winking lights upon the bridges were already pale, the coming sun was like a marsh of fire on the horizon. The river, still dark and mysterious, was spanned by bridges that were turning coldly grey, with here and there at top a warm touch from the burning in the sky. As I looked along the clustered roofs, with church towers and spires shooting into the unusually clear air, the sun rose up, and a veil seemed to be drawn from the river, and millions of sparkles burst out upon its waters. From me, too, a veil seemed to be drawn, and I felt strong and well.

Herbert lay asleep in his bed, and our old fellow-student lay asleep on the sofa. I could not dress myself without help, but I made up the fire, which was still burning, and got some coffee ready for them. In good time they too started up strong and well, and we admitted the sharp morning air at the windows, and looked at the tide that was still flowing towards us.

'When it turns at nine o'clock,' said Herbert, cheerfully, 'look out for us, and stand ready, you over there at Mill Pond Bank!'

Chapter 54

It was one of those March days when the sun shines hot and the wind blows cold: when it is summer in the light, and winter in the shade. We had our pea-coats with us, and I took a bag. Of all my worldly possessions I took no more than the few necessaries that filled the bag. Where I might go, what I might do, or when I might return, were questions utterly unknown to me; nor did I vex my mind with them, for it was wholly set on Provis's safety. I only wondered for the passing moment, as I stopped at the door and looked back, under what altered circumstances I should next see those rooms, if ever.

We loitered down to the Temple stairs, and stood loitering there, as if we were not quite decided to go upon the water at all. Of course I had taken care that the boat should be ready, and everything in order. After a little show of indecision, which there were none to see but the two or three amphibious creatures belonging to our Temple stairs, we went on board and cast off; Herbert in the bow, I steering. It was then about high-water – half-past eight.

Our plan was this. The tide, beginning to run down at nine,

and being with us until three, we intended still to creep on after it had turned, and row against it until dark. We should then be well in those long reaches below Gravesend, between Kent and Essex, where the river is broad and solitary, where the water-side inhabitants are very few, and where lone public houses are scattered here and there, of which we could choose one for a resting-place. There, we meant to lie by, all night. The steamer for Hamburg, and the steamer for Rotterdam, would start from London at about nine on Thursday morning. We should know at what time to expect them, according to where we were, and would hail the first; so that if by any accident we were not taken aboard, we should have another chance. We knew the distinguishing marks of each vessel.

The relief of being at last engaged in the execution of the purpose, was so great to me that I felt it difficult to realise the condition in which I had been in a few hours before. The crisp air, the sunlight, the movement on the river, and the moving river itself – the road that ran with us, seeming to sympathise with us, animate us, and encourage us on – freshened me with new hope. I felt mortified to be of so little use in the boat; but there were few better oarsmen than my two friends, and they rowed with a steady stroke that was to last all day.

At that time, the steam-traffic on the Thames was far below its present extent, and watermen's boats were far more numerous. Of barges, sailing colliers, and coasting traders, there were perhaps as many as now; but of steamships, great and small, not a tithe or a twentieth part so many. Early as it was, there were plenty of scullers going here and there that morning, and plenty of barges dropping down with the tide; the navigation of the river between bridges, in an open boat, was a much easier and commoner matter in those days than it is in these; and we went ahead among many skiffs and wherries, briskly.

Old London Bridge was soon passed, and old Billingsgate market with its oyster-boats and Dutchmen, and the White Tower and Traitor's Gate, and we were in among the tiers of shipping. Here, were the Leith, Aberdeen, and Glasgow steamers, loading and unloading goods, and looking immensely high out of the water as we passed alongside; here, were colliers by the score and score, with the coal-whippers plunging off stages on deck, as counterweights to measures of coal swinging up, which were then rattled over the side into barges; here, at her moorings, was tomorrow's steamer for Rotterdam, of which we took good notice; and here tomorrow's for Hamburg, under whose bowsprit we crossed. And now I, sitting in the stern, could see with a faster beating heart, Mill Pond Bank and Mill Pond stairs.

'Is he there?' said Herbert.

'Not yet.'

'Right! He was not to come down till he saw us. Can you see his signal?'

'Not well from here; but I think I see it – now I see him! Pull both. Easy, Herbert. Oars.'

We touched the stairs lightly for a single moment, and he was on board and we were off again. He had a boat-cloak with him, and a black canvas bag, and he looked as like a river-pilot as my heart could have wished.

'Dear boy!' he said, putting his arm on my shoulder, as he took his seat. 'Faithful dear boy, well done. Thankye, thankye!'

Again among the tiers of shipping, in and out, avoiding rusty chain-cables, frayed hempen hawsers, and bobbing buoys, sinking for the moment floating broken baskets, scattering floating chips of wood and shaving, cleaving floating scum of coal, in and out, under the figurehead of the John of Sunderland making a speech to the winds (as is done by many Johns), and the Betsy of Yarmouth with a firm formality of bosom and her knobby eyes starting two inches out of her head; in and out, hammers going in shipbuilders' yards, saws going at timber, clashing engines going at things unknown, pumps going in leaky ships, capstans going, ships going out to sea, and unintelligible sea-creatures roaring curses over the bulwarks at respondent lightermen; in and out – out at last upon the clearer river, where the ships' boys might take their fenders in, no longer fishing in troubled waters with them over the side, and where the festooned sails might fly out to the wind.

At the stairs where we had taken him aboard, and ever since, I had looked warily for any token of our being suspected. I had seen none. We certainly had not been, and at that time as certainly we were not, either attended or followed by any boat. If we had been waited on by any boat, I should have run in to shore, and have obliged her to go on, or to make her purpose evident. But we held our own, without any appearance of molestation.

He had his boat-cloak on him, and looked, as I have said, a natural part of the scene. It was remarkable (but perhaps the wretched life he had led accounted for it), that he was the least anxious of any of us. He was not indifferent, for he told me that he hoped to live to see his gentleman one of the best of gentlemen in a foreign country; he was not disposed to be passive or resigned, as I understood it; but he had no notion of meeting danger halfway. When it came upon him, he confronted it, but it must come before he troubled himself.

'If you knowed, dear boy,' he said to me, 'what it is to sit here alonger my dear boy and have my smoke, arter having been day by day betwixt four walls, you'd envy me. But you don't know what it is.'

'I think I know the delights of freedom,' I answered.

'Ah,' said he, shaking his head gravely. 'But you don't know it equal to me. You must have been under lock and key, dear boy, to know it equal to me – but I ain't a going to be low.'

It occurred to me as inconsistent, that for any mastering idea he should have endangered his freedom and even his life. But I reflected that perhaps freedom without danger was too much apart from all the habit of his existence to be to him what it would be to another man.

I was not far out, since he said, after smoking a little: 'You see, dear boy, when I was over yonder, t'other side the world, I was always a looking to this side; and it come flat to be there, for all I was a growing rich. Everybody knowed Magwitch, and Magwitch could come, and Magwitch could go, and nobody's head would be troubled about him. They ain't so easy concerning me here, dear boy – wouldn't be, leastwise, if they knowed where I was.'

'If all goes well,' said I, 'you will be perfectly free and safe again, within a few hours.'

'Well,' he returned, drawing a long breath, 'I hope so.'

'And think so?'

He dipped his hand in the water over the boat's gunwale, and said, smiling with that softened air upon him which was not new to me: 'Ay, I s'pose I think so, dear boy. We'd be puzzled to be more quiet and easy-going than we are at present. But – it's a flowing so soft and pleasant through the water, p'raps, as makes me think it – I was a thinking through my smoke just then, that we can no more see to the bottom of the next few hours, than we can see to the bottom of this river what I catches hold of. Nor yet we can't no more hold their tide than I can hold this. And it's run through my fingers and gone, you see!' holding up his dripping hand.

'But for your face, I should think you were a little depondent,' said I.

'Not a bit on it, dear boy! It comes of flowing on so quiet, and of that there rippling at the boat's head making a sort of a Sunday tune. Maybe I'm a growing a trifle old besides.'

He put his pipe back in his mouth with an undisturbed expression of face, and sat as composed and contented as if we were already out of England. Yet he was as submissive to a word of advice as if he had been in constant terror, for when we ran ashore to get some bottles of beer into the boat, and he was stepping out, I hinted that I thought he would be safest where he was, and he said, 'Do you, dear boy?' and quietly sat down again.

The air felt cold upon the river, but it was a bright day, and the sunshine was very cheering. The tide ran strong, I took care to lose none of it, and our steady stroke carried us on thoroughly well. By imperceptible degrees, as the tide ran out, we lost more and more of the nearer woods and hills, and dropped lower and lower between the muddy banks, but the tide was yet with us when we were off Gravesend. As our charge was wrapped in his cloak, I purposely passed within a boat or two's length of the floating custom house, and so out to catch the stream, alongside of two emigrant ships, and under the bows of a large transport with troops on the forecastle looking down at us. And soon the tide began to slacken, and the craft lying at anchor to swing, and presently they had all swung round, and the ships that were taking advantage of the new tide to get up to the Pool, began to crowd upon us in a fleet, and we kept under the shore, as much out of the strength of the tide now as we could, standing carefully off from low shallows and mud-banks.

Our oarsmen were so fresh, by dint of having occasionally let her drive with the tide for a minute or two, that a quarter of an hour's rest proved full as much as they wanted. We got ashore among some slippery stones while we ate and drank what we had with us, and looked about. It was like my own marsh country, flat and monotonous, and with a dim horizon; while the winding river turned and turned, and the great floating buoys upon it turned and turned, and everything else seemed stranded and still. For now the last of the fleet of ships was round the last low point we had headed; and the last green barge, straw-laden, with a brown sail, had followed; and some ballast-lighters, shaped like a child's first rude imitation of a boat, lay low in the mud; and a little squat shoal-lighthouse on open piles, stood crippled in the mud on stilts and crutches; and slimy stakes stuck out of the mud, and slimy stones stuck out of the mud, and red landmarks and tidemarks stuck out of the mud, and an old landing-stage and an old roofless building slipped into the mud, and all about us was stagnation and mud.

We pushed off again, and made what way we could. It was much harder work now, but Herbert and Star-top persevered, and rowed, and rowed, and rowed, until the sun went down. By that time the river had lifted us a little, so that we could see above the bank. There was the red sun, on the low level of the shore, in a purple haze, fast deepening into black; and there was the solitary flat marsh; and far away there were the rising grounds, between which and us there seemed to be no life, save here and there in the foreground a melancholy gull.

As the night was fast falling, and as the moon, being past the full, would not rise early, we held a little council: a short one, for clearly our course was to lie by at the first lonely tavern we could find. So they plied their oars once more, and I looked out for anything like a house. Thus we held on, speaking little, for four or five dull miles. It was very cold, and a collier coming by us, with her galley-fire smoking and flaring, looked like a comfortable home. The night was dark by this time as it would be until morning; what light we had, seemed to come more from the river than the sky, as the oars in their dipping struck at a few reflected stars.

At this dismal time we were evidently all possessed by the idea that we were followed. As the tide made, it flapped heavily at irregular intervals against the shore; and whenever such a sound came, one or other of us was sure to start and look in that direction. Here and there, the set of the current had worn down the bank into a little creek, and we were all suspicious of such places, and eyed them nervously. Sometimes, 'What was that ripple?' one of us would say in a low voice. Or another, 'Is that a boat yonder?' And afterwards, we would fall into a dead silence, and I would sit impatiently thinking with what an unusual amount of noise the oars worked in the thowels.

At length we descried a light and a roof, and presently afterwards ran alongside a little causeway made of stones that had been picked up hard by. Leaving the rest in the boat, I stepped ashore, and found the light to be in the window of a public house. It was a dirty place enough, and I dare say not unknown to smuggling adventurers; but there was a good fire in the kitchen, and there were eggs and bacon to eat, and various liquors to drink. Also, there were two double-bedded rooms – 'such as they were', the landlord said. No other company was in the house than the landlord, his wife, and a grizzled male creature, the 'Jack' of the little causeway, who was as slimy and smeary as if he had been low watermark too.

With this assistant, I went down to the boat again, and we all came ashore, and brought out the oars, and rudder, and boat hook, and all else, and hauled her up for the night. We made a very good meal by the kitchen fire, and then apportioned the bedrooms: Herbert and Startop were to occupy one; I and our charge the other. We found the air as carefully excluded from both as if air were fatal to life; and there were more dirty clothes and band boxes under the beds, than I should have thought the family possessed. But we considered ourselves well off, notwithstanding, for a more solitary place we could not have found.

While we were comforting ourselves by the fire after our meal, the Jack – who was sitting in a corner, and who had a bloated pair of shoes on, which he had exhibited while we were eating our eggs and bacon, as interesting relics that he had taken a few days ago from the feet of a drowned seaman washed ashore – asked me if we had seen a four-oared galley going up with the tide? When I told him no, he said she must have gone down then, and yet she 'took up too', when she left there.

'They must ha' thought better on't for some reason or another,' said the Jack, 'and gone down.'

'A four-oared galley, did you say?' said I.

'A four,' said the Jack, 'and two sitters.'

'Did they come ashore here?'

'They put in with a stone two-gallon jar, for some beer. I'd ha' been glad to pison the beer myself,' said the Jack, 'or put some rattling physic in it.'

'Why?'

'*I* know why,' said the Jack. He spoke in a slushy voice, as if much mud had washed into his throat.

'He thinks,' said the landlord: a weakly meditative man with a pale eye, who seemed to rely greatly on his Jack: 'he thinks they was, what they wasn't.'

'*I* knows what I thinks,' observed the Jack.

'*You* thinks custom 'us, Jack?' said the landlord.

'I do,' said the Jack.

'Then you're wrong, Jack.'

'*Am* I!'

In the infinite meaning of his reply and his boundless confidence in his views, the Jack took one of his bloated shoes off, looked into it, knocked a few stones out of it on the kitchen floor, and put it on again. He did this with the air of a Jack who was so right that he could afford to do anything.

'Why, what do you make out that they done with their buttons, then, Jack?' asked the landlord, vacillating weakly.

'Done with their buttons?' returned the Jack. 'Chucked 'em overboard. Swallered 'em. Sowed 'em, to come up small salad. Done with their buttons.'

'Don't be cheeky, Jack,' remonstrated the landlord, in a melancholy and pathetic way.

'A custom 'us officer knows what to do with his buttons,' said the Jack, repeating the obnoxious word with the greatest contempt, 'when they comes betwixt him and his own light. A four and two sitters don't go hanging and hovering, up with one tide and down with another, and both with and against another, without there being custom 'us at the bottom of it.' Saying which he went out in disdain; and the landlord, having no one to rely upon, found it impracticable to pursue the subject.

This dialogue made us all uneasy, and me very uneasy. The dismal wind was muttering round the house, the tide was flapping at the shore, and I had a feeling that we were caged and

threatened. A four-oared galley hovering about in so unusual a way as to attract this notice, was an ugly circumstance that I could not get rid of. When I had induced Provis to go up to bed, I went outside with my two companions (Startop by this time knew the state of the case), and held another council. Whether we should remain at the house until near the steamer's time, which would be about one in the afternoon; or whether we should put off early in the morning; was the question we discussed. On the whole we deemed it the better course to lie where we were, until within an hour or so of the steamer's time, and then to get out in her track, and drift easily with the tide. Having settled to do this, we returned into the house and went to bed.

I lay down with the greater part of my clothes on, and slept well for a few hours. When I awoke, the wind had risen, and the sign of the house (the ship) was creaking and banging about, with noises that startled me. Rising softly, for my charge lay fast asleep, I looked out of the window. It commanded the causeway where we had hauled up our boat, and, as my eyes adapted themselves to the light of the clouded moon, I saw two men looking into her. They passed by under the window, looking at nothing else, and they did not go down to the landing-place which I could discern to be empty, but struck across the marsh in the direction of the Nore.

My first impulse was to call up Herbert, and show him the two men going away. But, reflecting before I got into his room,

Boundless confidence

which was at the back of the house and adjoined mine, that he and Startop had had a harder day than I, and were fatigued, I forbore. Going back to my window I could see the two men moving over the marsh. In that light, however, I soon lost them, and feeling very cold, lay down to think of the matter, and fell asleep again.

We were up early. As we walked to and fro, all four together, before breakfast, I deemed it right to recount what I had seen. Again our charge was the least anxious of the party. It was very likely that the men belonged to the custom house, he said quietly, and that they had no thought of us. I tried to persuade myself that it was so – as, indeed, it might easily be. However, I proposed that he and I should walk away together to a distant point we could see, and that the boat should take us aboard there, or as near there as might prove feasible, at about noon. This being considered a good precaution, soon after breakfast he and I set forth, without saying anything at the tavern.

He smoked his pipe as we went along, and sometimes stopped to clap me on the shoulder. One would have supposed that it was I who was in danger, not he, and that he was reassuring me. We spoke very little. As we approached the point, I begged him to remain in a sheltered place, while I went on to reconnoitre; for it was towards it that the men had passed in the night. He complied, and I went on alone. There was no boat off the point, nor any boat drawn up anywhere near it, nor were there any signs of the men having embarked there. But, to be sure, the tide was high, and there might have been some footprints under water.

When he looked out from his shelter in the distance, and saw that I waved my hat to him to come up, he rejoined me, and there we waited; sometimes lying on the bank wrapped in our coats, and sometimes moving about to warm ourselves: until we saw our boat coming round. We got aboard easily, and rowed out into the track of the steamer. By that time it wanted but ten minutes of one o'clock, and we began to look out for her smoke.

But it was half-past one before we saw her smoke, and soon after we saw behind it the smoke of another steamer. As they were coming on at full speed, we got the two bags ready, and took that opportunity of saying goodbye to Herbert and Startop. We had all shaken hands cordially, and neither Herbert's eyes nor mine were quite dry, when I saw a four-oared galley shoot out from under the bank but a little way ahead of us, and row out into the same track.

A stretch of shore had been as yet between us and the steamer's smoke, by reason of the bend and wind of the river; but now she was visible coming head on. I called to Herbert and Startop to keep before the tide, that she might see us lying by for her, and adjured Provis to sit quite still, wrapped in his cloak. He answered cheerily, 'Trust to me, dear boy,' and sat like a statue. Meanwhile the galley, which was skilfully handled, had crossed us, let us come up with her, and fallen alongside. Leaving just room enough for the play of the oars, she kept alongside, drifting when we drifted, and pulling a stroke or two when we pulled. Of the two sitters, one held the rudder lines, and looked at us attentively – as did all the rowers, the other sitter was wrapped up, much as Provis was, and seemed to shrink, and

whisper some instruction to the steerer as he looked at us. Not a word was spoken in either boat.

Startop could make out, after a few minutes, which steamer was first, and gave me the word 'Hamburg,' in a low voice as we sat face to face. She was nearing us very fast, and the beating of her paddles grew louder and louder. I felt as if her shadow were absolutely upon us, when the galley hailed us. I answered.

'You have a returned transport there,' said the man who held the lines. 'That's the man, wrapped in the cloak. His name is Abel Magwitch, otherwise Provis. I apprehend that man, and call upon him to surrender, and you to assist.'

At the same moment, without giving any audible direction to his crew, he ran the galley aboard of us. They had pulled one sudden stroke ahead, had got their oars in, had run athwart us, and were holding on to our gunwale, before we knew what they were doing. This caused great confusion on board of the steamer, and I heard them calling to us, and heard the order given to stop the paddles, and heard them stop, but felt her driving down upon us irresistibly. In the same moment, I saw the steersman of the galley lay his hand on his prisoner's shoulder, and saw that both boats were swinging round with the force of the tide, and saw that all hands on board the steamer were running forward quite frantically. Still in the same moment, I saw the prisoner start up, lean across his captor, and pull the cloak from the neck of the shrinking sitter in the galley. Still in the same moment, I saw that the face disclosed was the face of the other convict of long ago. Still in the same moment, I saw the face tilt backward with a white terror on it that I shall never forget, and heard a great cry on board the steamer and a loud splash in the water, and felt the boat sink from under me.

It was but for an instant that I seemed to struggle with a thousand mill-weirs and a thousand flashes of light; that instant past, I was taken on board the galley. Herbert was there, and Startop was there; but our boat was gone, and the two convicts were gone.

What with the cries aboard the steamer, and the furious blowing off of her steam, and her driving on, and our driving on, I could not at first distinguish sky from water or shore from shore; but the crew of the galley righted her with great speed, and, pulling certain swift strong strokes ahead, lay upon their oars, every man looking silently and eagerly at the water astern. Presently a dark object was seen in it, bearing towards us on the tide. No man spoke, but the steersman held up his hand, and all softly backed water, and kept the boat straight and true before it. As it came nearer, I saw it to be Magwitch, swimming, but not swimming freely. He was taken on board, and instantly manacled at the wrists and ankles.

The galley was kept steady, and the silent eager lookout at the water was resumed. But the Rotterdam steamer now came up, and apparently not understanding what had happened, came on at speed. By the time she had been hailed and stopped, both steamers were drifting away from us, and we were rising and falling in a troubled wake of water. The look-out was kept, long after all was still again and the two steamers were gone; but everybody knew that it was hopeless now.

At length we gave it up, and pulled under the shore towards the tavern we had lately left, where we were received with no little surprise. Here I was able to get some comforts for Magwitch – Provis no longer – who had received some very severe injury in the chest and a deep cut in the head.

He told me that he believed himself to have gone under the keel of the steamer, and to have been struck on the head in rising. The injury to his chest (which rendered his breathing extremely painful) he thought he had received against the side of the galley. He added that he did not pretend to say what he might or might not have done to Compeyson, but that in the moment of his laying his hand on his cloak to identify him, that villain had staggered up and staggered back, and they had both gone overboard together; when the sudden wrenching of him (Magwitch) out of our boat, and the endeavour of his captor to keep him in it, had capsized us. He told me in a whisper that they had gone down, fiercely locked in each other's arms, and that there had been a struggle under water, and that he had disengaged himself, struck out, and swam away.

I never had any reason to doubt the exact truth of what he had told me. The officer who steered the galley gave the same account of their going overboard.

When I asked this officer's permission to change the prisoner's wet clothes by purchasing any spare garments I could get at the public house, he gave it readily: merely observing that he must take charge of everything his prisoner had about him. So the pocketbook which had once been in my hands, passed into the officer's. He further gave me leave to accompany the prisoner to London; but declined to accord that grace to my two friends.

The Jack at the ship was instructed where the drowned man had gone down, and undertook to search for the body in the places where it was likeliest to come ashore. His interest in its recovery seemed to me to be much heightened when he heard that it had stockings on. Probably it took about a dozen drowned men to fit him out completely; and that may have been the reason why the different articles of his dress were in various stages of decay.

We remained at the public house until the tide turned, and then Magwitch was carried down to the galley and put on board. Herbert and Startop were to get to London by land, as soon as they could. We had a doleful parting, and when I took my place by Magwitch's side, I felt that that was my place henceforth while he lived.

For now my repugnance to him had all melted away, and in the hunted wounded shackled creature who held my hand in his, I only saw a man who had meant to be my benefactor, and who had felt affectionately, gratefully, and generously, towards me with great constancy through a series of years. I only saw in him a much better man than I had been to Joe.

His breathing became more difficult and painful as the night drew on, and often he could not repress a groan. I tried to rest him on the arm I could use, in any easy position; but it was dreadful to think that I could not be sorry at heart for his being badly hurt, since it was unquestionably best that he should die. That there were, still living, people enough who were able and willing to identify him, I could not doubt. That he would be

leniently treated, I could not hope. He who had been presented in the worst light at his trial, who had since broken prison and been tried again, who had returned from transportation under a life sentence, and who had occasioned the death of the man who was the cause of his arrest.

As we returned towards the setting sun we had yesterday left behind us, and as the stream of our hopes seemed all running back, I told him how grieved I was to think he had come home for my sake.

'Dear boy,' he answered, 'I'm quite content to take my chance. I've seen my boy, and he can be a gentle- man without me.'

No. I had thought about that while we had been there side by side. No. Apart from any inclinations of my own, I understand Wemmick's hint now. I foresaw that, being convicted, his possessions would be forfeited to the Crown.

'Lookee here, dear boy,' said he. 'It's best as a gentleman should not be knowed to belong to me now. Only come to see me as if you come by chance alonger Wemmick. Sit where I can see you when I am swore to, for the last o' many times, and I don't ask no more.'

'I will never stir from your side,' said I, 'when I am suffered to be near you. Please God, I will be as true to you as you have been to me!'

I felt his hand tremble as it held mine, and he turned his face away as he lay in the bottom of the boat, and I heard that old sound in his throat – softened now, like all the rest of him. It was a good thing that he had touched this point, for it put into my mind what I might not otherwise have thought of until too late: that he need never know how his hopes of enriching me had perished.

Chapter 55

He was taken to the police court next day, and would have been immediately committed for trial, but that it was necessary to send down for an old officer of the prison-ship from which he had once escaped, to speak to his identity. Nobody doubted it; but Compeyson, who had meant to depose to it, was tumbling on the tides, dead, and it happened that there was not at that time any prison officer in London who could give the required evidence. I had gone direct to Mr Jaggers at his private house, on my arrival overnight, to retain his assistance, and Mr Jaggers on the prisoner's behalf would admit nothing. It was the sole resource, for he told me that the case must be over in five minutes when the witness was there, and that no power on earth could prevent its going against us.

I imparted to Mr Jaggers my design of keeping him in ignorance of the fate of his wealth. Mr Jaggers was querulous and angry with me for having 'let it slip through my fingers', and said we must memorialise by and by, and try at all events for some of it. But he did not conceal from me that although there might be many cases in which forfeiture would not be exacted, there were no circumstances in this case to make it one of them. I understood that very well. I was not related to the outlaw, or connected with him by any recognisable tie; he had put his hand to no writing or settlement in my favour before his apprehension, and to do so now would be idle. I had no claim, and I finally resolved, and ever afterwards abided by the resolution, that my heart should never be sickened with the hopeless task of attempting to establish one.

There appeared to be reason for supposing that the drowned informer had hoped for a reward out of this forfeiture, and had obtained some accurate knowledge of Magwitch's affairs. When his body was found, many miles from the scene of his death, and so horribly disfigured that he was only recognisable by the contents of his pockets, notes were still legible, folded in a case he carried. Among these were the name of a banking-house in New South Wales where a sum of money was, and the designation of certain lands of considerable value. Both those heads of information were in a list that Magwitch, while in prison, gave to Mr Jaggers, of the possessions he supposed I should inherit. His ignorance, poor fellow, at last served him; he never mistrusted but that my inheritance was quite safe, with Mr Jaggers's aid.

After three days' delay, during which the crown prosecution stood over for the production of the witness from the prison-ship, the witness came, and completed the easy case. He was committed to take his trial at the next session, which would come on in a month.

It was at this dark time of my life that Herbert returned home one evening, a good deal cast down, and said: 'My dear Handel, I fear I shall soon have to leave you.'

His partner having prepared me for that, I was less surprised than he thought.

'We shall lose a fine opportunity if I put off going to Cairo, and I am very much afraid I must go, Handel, when you most need me.'

'Herbert, I shall always need you, because I shall always love you; but my need is no greater now, than at another time.'

'You will be so lonely.'

'I have not leisure to think of that,' said I. 'You know that I am always with him to the full extent of the time allowed, and that I should be with him all day long, if I could. And when I come away from him, you know that my thoughts are with him.'

The dreadful condition to which he was brought, was so appalling to both of us, that we could not refer to it in plainer words.

'My dear fellow,' said Herbert, 'let the near prospect of our separation – for it is very near – be my justification for troubling you about yourself. Have you thought of your future?'

'No, for I have been afraid to think of any future.'

'But yours cannot be dismissed; indeed, my dear, dear Handel, it must not be dismissed. I wish you would enter on it now, as far as a few friendly words go, with me.'

'I will,' said I.

'In this branch house of ours, Handel, we must have a –'

I saw that his delicacy was avoiding the right word, so I said, 'A clerk.'

'A clerk. And I hope it is not at all unlikely that he may expand (as a clerk of your acquaintance has expanded) into a partner. Now, Handel – in short, my dear boy, will you come to me?'

There was something charmingly cordial and engaging in the manner in which after saying, 'Now, Handel,' as if it were the grave beginning of a portentous business exordium, he had suddenly given up that tone, stretched out his honest hand, and spoken like a schoolboy.

'Clara and I have talked about it again and again,' Herbert pursued, 'and the dear little thing begged me only this evening, with tears in her eyes, to say to you that if you will live with us when we come together, she will do her best to make you happy, and to convince her husband's friend that he is her friend too. We should get on so well, Handel!'

I thanked her heartily, and I thanked him heartily, but said I could not yet make sure of joining him as he so kindly offered. Firstly, my mind was too preoccupied to be able to take in the subject clearly. Secondly – yes, secondly, there was a vague something lingering in my thoughts that will come out very near the end of this slight narrative.

'But if you thought, Herbert, that you could, without doing any injury to your business, leave the question open for a little while –'

'For any while,' cried Herbert. 'Six months, a year!'

'Not so long as that,' said I. 'Two or three months at most.'

Herbert was highly delighted when we shook hands on this arrangement, and said he could now take courage to tell me that he believed he must go away at the end of the week.

'And Clara?' said I.

'The dear little thing,' returned Herbert, 'holds dutifully to her father as long as he lasts; but he won't last long, Mrs Whimple confides to me that he is certainly going.'

'Not to say an unfeeling thing,' said I, 'he cannot do better than go.'

'I am afraid that must be admitted,' said Herbert; 'and then I shall come back for the dear little thing, and the dear little thing and I will walk quietly into the nearest church. Remember! The blessed darling comes of no family, my dear Handel, and never looked into the red book, and hasn't a notion about her grandpapa. What a fortune for the son of my mother!'

On the Saturday in that same week, I took my leave of Herbert – full of bright hope, but sad and sorry to leave me – as he sat on one of the seaport mail coaches. I went into a coffee-house to write a little note to Clara, telling her he had gone off, sending his love to her over and over again, and then went to my lonely home – if it deserved the name, for it was now no home to me, and I had no home anywhere.

On the stairs I encountered Wemmick, who was coming down, after an unsuccessful application of his knuckles to my door. I had not seen him alone, since the disastrous issue of the attempted flight; and he had come, in his private and personal capacity, to say a few words of explanation in reference to that failure.

'The late Compeyson,' said Wemmick, 'had by little and little got at the bottom of half of the regular business now transacted, and it was from the talk of some of his people in trouble (some of his people being always in trouble) that I heard what I did. I kept my ears open, seeming to have them shut, until I heard that he was absent, and I thought that would be the best time for making the attempt. I can only suppose now, that it was a part of his policy, as a very clever man, habitually to deceive his own instruments. You don't blame me, I hope, Mr Pip? I'm sure I tried to serve you, with all my heart.'

'I am as sure of that, Wemmick, as you can be, and I thank you most earnestly for all your interest and friendship.'

'Thank you, thank you very much. It's a bad job,' said Wemmick, scratching his head, 'and I assure you I haven't been so cut up for a long time. What I look at is, the sacrifice of so much portable property. Dear me!'

'What *I* think of, Wemmick, is the poor owner of the property.'

'Yes, to be sure,' said Wemmick. 'Of course there can be no objection to your being sorry for him, and I'd put down a five-pound note myself to get him out of it. But what I look at, is this. The late Compeyson having been beforehand with him in intelligence of his return, and being so determined to bring him to book, I do not think he could have been saved. Whereas, the portable property certainly could have been saved. That's the difference between the property and the owner, don't you see?'

I invited Wemmick to come upstairs, and refresh himself with a glass of grog before walking to Walworth. He accepted the invitation. While he was drinking his moderate allowance, he said, with nothing to lead up to it, and after having appeared rather fidgety: 'What do you think of my meaning to take a holiday on Monday, Mr Pip?'

'Why, I suppose you have not done such a thing these twelve months.'

'These twelve years, more likely,' said Wemmick. 'Yes. I'm going to take a holiday. More than that; I'm going to take a walk. More than that; I'm going to ask you to take a walk with me.'

I was about to excuse myself, as being but a bad companion just then, when Wemmick anticipated me.

'I know your engagements,' said he, 'and I know you are out of sorts, Mr Pip. But if you *could* oblige me, I should take it as a kindness. It ain't a long walk, and it's an early one. Say it might occupy you (including breakfast on the walk) from eight to twelve. Couldn't you stretch a point and manage it?'

He had done so much for me at various times, that this was very little to do for him. I said I could manage it – would manage it – and he was so very much pleased by my acquiescence, that I was pleased too. At his particular request, I appointed to call for him at the Castle at half-past eight on Monday morning, and so we parted for the time.

Punctual to my appointment, I rang at the Castle gate on the Monday morning, and was received by Wemmick himself: who struck me as looking tighter than usual, and having a sleeker hat on. Within, there were two glasses of rum and milk prepared, and two biscuits. The Aged must have been stirring with the lark, for, glancing into the perspective of his bedroom, I observed that his bed was empty.

When we had fortified ourselves with the rum and milk and biscuits, and were going out for the walk with that training preparation on us, I was considerably surprised to see Wemmick take up a fishing-rod, and put it over his shoulder. 'Why, we are not going fishing!' said I. 'No,' returned Wemmick, 'but I like to walk with one.'

I thought this odd; however, I said nothing, and we set off. We went towards Camberwell Green, and when we were thereabouts, Wemmick said suddenly: 'Halloa! Here's a church!'

There was nothing very surprising in that; but again, I was rather surprised, when he said, as if he were animated by a brilliant idea: 'Let's go in!'

We went in, Wemmick leaving his fishing-rod in the porch, and looked all round. In the mean time, Wemmick was diving into his coat-pockets, and getting something out of paper there.

'Halloa!' said he. 'Here's a couple of pair of gloves! Let's put 'em on!'

As the gloves were white kid gloves, and as the post office was widened to its utmost extent, I now began to have my strong suspicions. They were strengthened into certainty when I beheld the Aged enter at a side door, escorting a lady.

'Halloa!' said Wemmick. 'Here's Miss Skiffins! Let's have a wedding.'

That discreet damsel was attired as usual, except that she was now engaged in substituting for her green kid gloves, a pair of white. The Aged was likewise occupied in preparing a similar sacrifice for the altar of Hymen. The old gentleman, however, experienced so much difficulty in getting his gloves on, that Wemmick found it necessary to put him with his back against a pillar, and then to get behind the pillar himself and pull away at them, while I for my part held the old gentleman round the waist, that he might present an equal and safe resistance. By dint of this ingenious scheme, his gloves were got on to perfection.

The clerk and clergyman then appearing, we were ranged in order at those fatal rails. True to his notion of seeming to do it all without preparation, I heard Wemmick say to himself as he took something out of his waistcoat-pocket before the service began, 'Halloa! Here's a ring!'

I acted in the capacity of backer, or best-man, to the bridegroom; while a little limp pew-opener in a soft bonnet like a baby's, made a feint of being the bosom friend of Miss Skiffins. The responsibility of giving the lady away, devolved upon the Aged, which led to the clergyman's being unintentionally scandalised, and it happened thus. When he said, 'Who giveth this woman to be married to this man?' the old gentleman, not in the least knowing what point of the ceremony we had arrived at, stood most amiably beaming at the ten commandments. Upon which, the clergyman said again, 'Who giveth this woman to be married to this man?' The old gentleman being still in a state of most estimable unconsciousness, the bridegroom cried out in his accustomed voice, 'Now, Aged P, you know; who giveth?' To which the Aged replied with great briskness, before saying that *he* gave, 'All right, John, all right, my boy!' And the clergyman came to so gloomy a pause upon it, that I had doubts for the moment whether we should get completely married that day.

It was completely done, however, and when we were going out of church, Wemmick took the cover off the font, and put his white gloves in it, and put the cover on again. Mrs Wemmick, more heedful of the future, put her white gloves in her pocket and assumed her green. '*Now*, Mr Pip,' said Wemmick, triumphantly shouldering the fishing-rod as we came out, 'let me ask you whether anybody would suppose this to be a wedding-party!'

Breakfast had been ordered at a pleasant little tavern, a mile or so away upon the rising ground beyond the green; and there was a bagatelle board in the room, in case we should desire to unbend our minds after the solemnity. It was pleasant to observe that Mrs Wemmick no longer unwound Wemmick's arm when it adapted itself to her figure, but sat in a high-backed chair against the wall, like a violoncello in its case, and submitted to be embraced as that melodious instrument might have done.

We had an excellent breakfast, and when anyone declined anything on table, Wemmick said, 'Provided by contract, you know; don't be afraid of it!' I drank to the new couple, drank to the Aged, drank to the Castle, saluted the bride at parting, and made myself as agreeable as I could.

Wemmick came down to the door with me, and I again shook hands with him, and wished him joy.

'Thankee!' said Wemmick, rubbing his hands. 'She's such a manager of fowls, you have no idea. You shall have some eggs and judge for yourself. I say, Mr Pip!' calling me back and speaking low. 'This is altogether a Walworth sentiment, please.'

'I understand. Not to be mentioned in Little Britain,' said I.

Wemmick nodded. 'After what you let out the other day, Mr Jaggers may as well not know of it. He might think my brain was softening, or something of the kind.'

Chapter 56

He lay in prison very ill, during the whole interval between his committal for trial, and the coming round of the sessions. He had broken two ribs, they had wounded one of his lungs, and he breathed with great pain and difficulty, which increased daily. It was a consequence of his hurt that he spoke so low as to be scarcely audible; therefore he spoke very little. But he was ever ready to listen to me, and it became the first duty of my life to say to him, and read to him, what I knew he ought to hear.

Being far too ill to remain in the common prison, he was removed, after the first day or so, into the infirmary. This gave me opportunities of being with him that I could not otherwise have had. And but for his illness he would have been put in irons, for he was regarded as a determined prison-breaker, and I know not what else.

Although I saw him every day, it was for only a short time; hence the regularly recurring spaces of our separation were long enough to record on his face any slight changes that occurred in his physical state. I do not recollect that I once saw any change in it for the better; he wasted, and became slowly weaker and worse, day by day from the day when the prison door closed upon him.

The kind of submission or resignation that he showed, was that of a man who was tired out. I sometimes derived an impression, from his manner or from a whispered word or two which escaped him, that he pondered over the question whether he might have been a better man under better circumstances. But he never justified himself by a hint tending that way, or tried to bend the past out of its eternal shape.

It happened on two or three occasions in my presence, that his desperate reputation was alluded to by one or other of the people in attendance on him. A smile crossed his face then, and he turned his eyes on me with a trustful look, as if he were confident that I had seen some small redeeming touch in him, even so long ago as when I was a little child. As to all the rest, he was humble and contrite, and I never knew him complain.

When the sessions came round, Mr Jaggers caused an application to be made for the postponement of his trial until the following sessions. It was obviously made with the assurance that he could not live so long, and was refused. The trial came on at once, and when he was put to the bar, he was seated in a chair. No objection was made to my getting close to the dock, on the outside of it, and holding the hand that he stretched forth to me.

The trial was very short and very clear. Such things as could be said for him, were said – how he had taken to industrious habits, and had thriven lawfully and reputably. But nothing could unsay the fact that he had returned, and was there in presence of the judge and jury. It was impossible to try him for that, and do otherwise than find him guilty.

At that time it was the custom (as I learnt from my terrible experience of that sessions) to devote a concluding day to the passing of sentences, and to make a finishing effect with the sentence of death. But for the indelible picture that my remembrance now holds before me, I could scarcely believe, even as I write these words, that I saw two-and-thirty men and women put before the judge to receive that sentence together. Foremost among the two-and-thirty was he; seated, that he might get breath enough to keep life in him.

The whole scene starts out again in the vivid colours of the moment, down to the drops of April rain on the windows of the court, glittering in the rays of April sun. Penned in the dock, as I again stood outside it at the corner with his hand in mine, were the two-and-thirty men and women; some defiant, some stricken with terror, some sobbing and weeping, some covering their faces, some staring gloomily about. There had been shrieks from among the women convicts, but they had been stilled, and a hush had succeeded. The sheriffs with their great chains and nosegays, other civic gewgaws and monsters, criers, ushers, a great gallery full of people – a large theatrical audience – looked on, as the two-and-thirty and the judge were solemnly confronted. Then the judge addressed them. Among the wretched creatures before him whom he must single out for special address, was one who almost from his infancy had been an offender against the laws; who, after repeated imprisonments and punishments, had been at length sentenced to exile for a term of years; and who, under circumstances of great violence and daring, had made his escape and been re-sentenced to exile for life. That miserable man would seem for a time to have become convinced of his errors, when far removed from the scenes of his old offences, and to have lived a peaceable and honest life. But in a fatal moment, yielding to those propensities and passions, the indulgence of which had so long rendered him a scourge to society, he had quitted his haven of rest and repentance, and had come back to the country where he was proscribed. Being here presently denounced, he had for a time succeeded in evading the officers of justice, but being at length seized while in the act of flight, he had resisted them, and had – he best knew whether by express design, or in the blindness of his hardihood – caused the death of his denouncer, to whom his whole career was known. The appointed punishment for his return to the land that had cast him out being death, and his case being this aggravated case, he must prepare himself to die.

The sun was striking in at the great windows of the court, through the glittering drops of rain upon the glass, and it made a broad shaft of light between the two-and-thirty and the judge, linking both together, and perhaps reminding some among the audience, how both were passing on, with absolute equality, to the greater Judgement that knoweth all things and cannot err. Rising for a moment, a distinct speck of face in this way of light, the prisoner said, 'My Lord, I have received my sentence of death from the Almighty, but I bow to yours,' and sat down again. There was some hushing, and the judge went on with what he had to say to the rest. Then, they were all formally doomed, and some of them were supported out, and some of them sauntered out with a haggard look of bravery, and a few nodded to the gallery, and two or three shook hands, and others went out chewing the fragments of herb they had taken from the sweet herbs lying about. He went last of all, because of having to be helped from his chair and to go very slowly; and he held my hand while all the others were removed, and while the audience got up (putting their dresses right, as they might at church or elsewhere) and pointed down at this criminal or at that, and most of all at him and me.

I earnestly hoped and prayed that he might die before the recorder's report was made, but, in the dread of his lingering on, I began that night to write out a petition to the Home Secretary of State, setting forth my knowledge of him, and how it was that he had come back for my sake. I wrote it as fervently and pathetically as I could, and when I had finished it and sent it in, I wrote out other petitions to such men in authority as I hoped were the most merciful, and drew up one to the Crown itself. For several days and nights after he was sentenced I took no rest, except when I fell asleep in my chair, but was wholly absorbed in these appeals. And after I had sent them in, I could not keep away from the places where they were, but felt as if they were more hopeful and less desperate when I was near them. In this unreasonable restlessness and pain of mind, I would roam the streets of an evening, wandering by those offices and houses where I had left the petitions. To the present hour, the weary western streets of London on a cold dusty spring night, with their ranges of stern shut-up mansions and their long rows of lamps, are melancholy to me from this association.

The daily visits I could make him were shortened now, and he was more strictly kept. Seeing, or fancying, that I was suspected of an intention of carrying poison to him, I asked to be searched before I sat down at his bedside, and told the officer who was always there, that I was willing to do anything that would assure him of the singleness of my designs. Nobody was hard with him or with me. There was duty to be done, and it was done, but not harshly. The officer always gave me the assurance that he was worse, and some other sick prisoners in the room, and some other prisoners who attended on them as sick nurses (malefactors, but not incapable of kindness, *God* be thanked!) always joined in the same report.

As the days went on, I noticed more and more that he would lie placidly looking at the white ceiling, with an absence of light in his face, until some word of mine brightened it for an instant, and then it would subside again. Sometimes he was almost, or quite, unable to speak; then, he would answer me with slight pressures on my hand, and I grew to understand his meaning very well.

The number of the days had risen to ten, when I saw a greater change in him than I had seen yet. His eyes were turned towards the door, and lighted up as I entered.

'Dear boy,' he said, as I sat down by his bed: 'I thought you was late. But I knowed you couldn't be that.'

'It is just the time,' said I. 'I waited for it at the gate.'

'You always waits at the gate; don't you, dear boy?'

'Yes. Not to lose a moment of the time.'

'Thank'ee, dear boy, thank'ee. God bless you! You've never deserted me, dear boy.'

I pressed his hand in silence, for I could not forget that I had once meant to desert him.

'And what's the best of all,' he said, 'you've been more comfortable alonger me, since I was under a dark cloud, than when the sun shone. That's best of all.'

He lay on his back, breathing with great difficulty. Do what he would, and love me though he did, the light left his face ever and again, and a film came over the placid look at the white ceiling.

'Are you in much pain today?'

'I don't complain of none, dear boy.'

'You never do complain.'

He had spoken his last words. He smiled, and I understood his touch to mean that he wished to lift my hand, and lay it on his breast. I laid it there, and he smiled again, and put both his hands upon it.

The allotted time ran out, while we were thus; but, looking round, I found the governor of the prison standing near me, and he whispered, 'You needn't go yet.' I thanked him gratefully, and asked, 'Might I speak to him, if he can hear me?'

The governor stepped aside, and beckoned the officer away. The change, though it was made without noise, drew back the film from the placid look at the white ceiling, and he looked most affectionately at me.

'Dear Magwitch, I must tell you, now at last. You understand what I say?'

A gentle pressure on my hand.

'You had a child once, whom you loved and lost.'

A stronger pressure on my hand.

'She lived and found powerful friends. She is living now. She is a lady and very beautiful. And I love her!'

With a last faint effort, which would have been powerless but for my yielding to it, and assisting it, he raised my hand to his lips. Then he gently let it sink upon his breast again, with his own hands lying on it. The placid look at the white ceiling came back, and passed away, and his head dropped quietly on his breast.

Mindful, then, of what we had read together, I thought of the two men who went up into the Temple to pray, and I knew there were no better words that I could say beside his bed, than 'O Lord, be merciful to him a sinner!'

Chapter 57

Now that I was left wholly to myself I gave notice of my intention to quit the chambers in the Temple as soon as my tenancy could legally determine, and in the meanwhile to under-let them. At once I put bills up in the windows; for I was in debt, and had scarcely any money, and began to be seriously alarmed by the state of my affairs. I ought rather to write that I should have been alarmed if I had had energy and concentration enough to help me to the clear perception of any truth beyond the fact that I was falling very ill. The late stress upon me had enabled me to put off illness, but not to put it away; I knew that it was coming on me now, and I knew very little else, and was even careless as to that.

For a day or two, I lay on the sofa, or on the floor – anywhere, according as I happened to sink down – with a heavy head and aching limbs, and no purpose, and no power. Then there came one night which appeared of great duration, and which teemed with anxiety and horror; and when in the morning I tried to sit up in my bed and think of it, I found I could not do so.

Whether I really had been down in Garden Court in the dead of the night, groping about for the boat that I supposed to be there; whether I had two or three times come to myself on the staircase with great terror, not knowing how I had got out of bed; whether I had found myself lighting the lamp, possessed by the idea that he was coming up the stairs, and that the lights were blown out; whether I had been inexpressibly harassed by the distracted talking, laughing, and groaning, of someone, and had half suspected those sounds to be of my own making; whether there had been a closed iron furnace in a dark corner of the room, and a voice had called out over and over again that Miss Havisham was consuming within it; these were things that I tried to settle with myself and get into some order, as I lay that morning on my bed. But the vapour of a limekiln would come between me and them, disordering them all, and it was through the vapour at last that I saw two men looking at me.

'What do you want?' I asked, starting; 'I don't know you.'

'Well, sir,' returned one of them, bending down and touching me on the shoulder, 'this is a matter that you'll soon arrange, I dare say, but you're arrested.'

'What is the debt?'

'Hundred and twenty-three pound, fifteen, six. Jeweller's account, I think.'

'What is to be done?'

'You had better come to my house,' said the man. 'I keep a very nice house.'

I made some attempt to get up and dress myself. When I next attended to them, they were standing a little off from the bed, looking at me. I still lay there.

'You see my state,' said I. 'I would come with you if I could; but indeed I am quite unable. If you take me from here, I think I shall die by the way.'

Perhaps they replied, or argued the point, or tried to encourage me to believe that I was better than I thought. Forasmuch as they hang in my memory by only this one slender thread, I don't know what they did, except that they forbore to remove me.

That I had a fever and was avoided, that I suffered greatly, that I often lost my reason, that the time seemed interminable, that I confounded impossible existences with my own identity; that I was a brick in the house wall, and yet entreating to be released from the giddy place where the builders had set me; that I was a steel beam of a vast engine, clashing and whirling over a gulf, and yet that I implored in my own person to have the engine stopped, and my part in it hammered off; that I

The arrest

passed through these phases of disease, I know of my own remembrance, and did in some sort know at the time. That I sometimes struggled with real people, in the belief that they were murderers, and that I would all at once comprehend that they meant to do me good, and would then sink exhausted in their arms, and suffer them to lay me down, I also knew at the time. But, above all, I knew that there was a constant tendency in all these people – who, when I was very ill, would present all kinds of extraordinary transformations of the human face, and would be much dilated in size – above all, I say, I knew that there was an extraordinary tendency in all these people, sooner or later, to settle down into the likeness of Joe.

After I had turned the worst point of my illness, I began to notice that while all its other features changed, this one consistent feature did not change. Whoever came about me, still settled down into Joe. I opened my eyes in the night, and I saw in the great chair at the bedside, Joe. I opened my eyes in the day, and, sitting on the window-seat, smoking his pipe in the shaded open window, still I saw Joe. I asked for cooling drink, and the dear hand that gave it me was Joe's. I sank back on my pillow after drinking, and the face that looked so hopefully and tenderly upon me was the face of Joe.

At last, one day, I took courage, and said, '*Is* it Joe?'

And the dear old home-voice answered, 'Which it air, old chap.'

'O Joe, you break my heart! Look angry at me, Joe. Strike me, Joe. Tell me of my ingratitude. Don't be so good to me!'

For Joe had actually laid his head down on the pillow at my side, and put his arm round my neck, in his joy that I knew him.

'Which dear old Pip, old chap,' said Joe, 'you and me was ever friends. And when you're well enough to go out for a ride – what larks!'

After which, Joe withdrew to the window, and stood with his back towards me, wiping his eyes. And as my extreme weakness prevented me from getting up and going to him, I lay there, penitently whispering, 'O God bless him! O God bless this gentle Christian man!'

Joe's eyes were red when I next found him beside me; but I was holding his hand and we both felt happy.

'How long, dear Joe?'

'Which you meantersay, Pip, how long have your illness lasted, dear old chap?'

'Yes, Joe.'

'It's the end of May, Pip. Tomorrow is the first of June.'

'And have you been here all the time, dear Joe?'

'Pretty nigh, old chap. For, as I says to Biddy when the news of your being ill were brought by letter, which it were brought by the post, and being formerly single he is now married though underpaid for a deal of walking and shoe-leather, but wealth were not a object on his part, and marriage were the great wish of his hart –'

'It is so delightful to hear you, Joe! But I interrupt you in what you said to Biddy.'

'Which it were,' said Joe, 'that how you might be amongst strangers, and that how you and me having been ever friends, a wisit at such a moment might not prove unacceptabobble. And

Biddy, her word were, "Go to him, without loss of time." That,' said Joe, summing up with his judicial air, 'were the word of Biddy. "Go to him," Biddy say, "without loss of time." In short, I shouldn't greatly deceive you,' Joe added, after a little grave reflection, 'if I represented to you that the word of that young woman were, "without a minute's loss of time." '

There Joe cut himself short, and informed me that I was to be talked to in great moderation, and that I was to take a little nourishment at stated frequent times, whether I felt inclined for it or not, and that I was to submit myself to all his orders. So, I kissed his hand, and lay quiet, while he proceeded to indite a note to Biddy, with my love in it.

Evidently Biddy had taught Joe to write. As I lay in bed looking at him, it made me, in my weak state, cry again with pleasure to see the pride with which he set about his letter. My bedstead, divested of its curtains, had been removed, with me upon it, into the sitting-room, as the airiest and largest, and the carpet had been taken away, and the room kept always fresh and wholesome night and day. At my own writing-table, pushed into a corner and cumbered with little bottles, Joe now sat down to his great work, first choosing a pen from the pen-tray as if it were a chest of large tools, and tucking up his sleeves as if he were going to wield a crowbar or sledgehammer. It was necessary for Joe to hold on heavily to the table with his left elbow, and to get his right leg well out behind him, before he could begin, and when he did begin he made every downstroke so slowly that it might have been six feet long, while at every upstroke I could hear his pen spluttering extensively. He had a curious idea that the inkstand was on the side of him where it was not, and constantly dipped his pen into space, and seemed quite satisfied with the result. Occasionally, he was tripped up by some orthographical stumbling-block, but on the whole he got on very well indeed, and when he had signed his name, and had removed a finishing blot from the paper to the crown of his head with his two forefingers, he got up and hovered about the table, trying the effect of his performance from various points of view as it lay there, with unbounded satisfaction.

Not to make Joe uneasy by talking too much, even if I had been able to talk much, I deferred asking him about Miss Havisham until next day. He shook his head when I then asked him if she had recovered?

'Is she dead, Joe?'

'Why, you see, old chap,' said Joe, in a tone of remonstrance, and by way of getting at it by degrees, 'I wouldn't go so far as to say that, for that's a deal to say; but she ain't – '

'Living, Joe?'

'That's nigher where it is,' said Joe; 'she ain't living.'

'Did she linger long, Joe?'

'Arter you was took ill, pretty much about what you might call (if you was put to it) a week,' said Joe; still determined, on my account, to come at everything by degrees.

'Dear Joe, have you heard what becomes of her property?'

'Well, old chap,' said Joe, 'it do appear that she had settled the most of it, which I meantersay tied it up, on Miss Estella. But she had wrote out a little coddleshell in her own hand a day or two afore the accident, leaving a cool four thousand to Mr Matthew Pocket. And why, do you suppose, above all things, Pip, she left that cool four thousand unto him? "Because of Pip's account of him the said Matthew." I am told by Biddy, that air the writing,' said Joe, repeating the legal turn as if it did him infinite good, ' "account of him the said Matthew". And a cool four thousand, Pip!'

I never discovered from whom Joe derived the conventional temperature of the four thousand pounds, but it appeared to make the sum of money more to him, and he had a manifest relish in insisting on its being cool.

This account gave me great joy, as it perfected the only good thing I had done. I asked Joe whether he had heard if any of the other relations had any legacies?

'Miss Sarah,' said Joe, 'she have twenty-five pound per-annium fur to buy pills, on account of being bilious. Miss Georgiana, she have twenty pound down. Mrs – what's the name of them wild beasts with humps, old chap?'

'Camels?' said I, wondering why he could possibly want to know.

Joe nodded. 'Mrs Camels,' by which I presently understood he meant Camilla, 'she have five pound fur to buy rushlights to put her in spirits when she wake up in the night.'

The accuracy of these recitals was sufficiently obvious to me, to give me great confidence in Joe's information. 'And now,' said Joe, 'you ain't that strong yet, old chap, that you can take in more nor one additional shovel-full today. Old Orlick he's been a bustin' open a dwellingouse.'

'Whose?' said I.

'Not, I grant you, but what his manners is given to blus-terous,' said Joe, apologetically; 'still, a Englishman's ouse is his Castle, and castles must not be busted 'cept when done in war time. And wotsume'er the failings on his part, he were a corn and seedsman in his hart.'

'Is it Pumblechook's house that has been broken into, then?'

'That's it, Pip,' said Joe; 'and they took his till, and they took his cashbox, and they drinked his wine, and they partook of his wittles, and they slapped his face, and they pulled his nose, and they tied him up to his bedpust, and they giv' him a dozen, and they stuffed his mouth full of flowering annuals to perwent his crying out. But he knowed Orlick, and Orlick's in the county jail.'

By these approaches we arrived at unrestricted conversation. I was slow to gain strength, but I did slowly and surely become less weak, and Joe stayed with me, and I fancied I was little Pip again.

For the tenderness of Joe was so beautifully proportioned to my need, that I was like a child in his hands. He would sit and talk to me in the old confidence, and with the old simplicity, and in the old unassertive protecting way, so that I would half believe that all my life since the days of the old kitchen was one of the mental troubles of the fever that was gone. He did everything for me except the household work, for which he had engaged a very decent woman, after paying off the laundress on his first arrival. 'Which I do assure you, Pip,' he would often say, in explanation of that liberty; 'I found her a tapping the spare bed, like a cask of beer, and drawing off the feathers in a bucket, for sale. Which she would have tapped yourn next, and draw'd it off with you a laying on it, and was then a carrying away the coals gradivally in the soup-tureen and wegetable dishes, and the wine and spirits in your wellington boots.'

We looked forward to the day when I should go out for a ride, as we had once looked forward to the day of my apprenticeship. And when the day came, and an open carriage was got into the lane, Joe wrapped me up, took me in his arms, carried me down to it, and put me in, as if I were still the small helpless creature to whom he had so abundantly given of the wealth of his great nature.

And Joe got in beside me, and we drove away together into the country, where the rich summer growth was already on the trees and on the grass, and sweet summer scents filled all the air. The day happened to be Sunday, and when I looked on the loveliness around me, and thought how it had grown and changed, and how the little wild flowers had been forming, and the voices of the birds had been strengthening, by day and by night, under the sun and under the stars, while poor I lay burning and tossing on my bed, the mere remembrance of having burned and tossed there, came like a check upon my peace. But, when I heard the Sunday bells, and looked around a little more upon the outspread beauty, I felt that I was not nearly thankful enough – that I was too weak yet, to be even that – and I laid my head on Joe's shoulder, as I had laid it long ago when he had taken me to the fair or where not, and it was too much for my young senses.

More composure came to me after a while, and we talked as we used to talk, lying on the grass at the old battery. There was no change whatever in Joe. Exactly what he had been in my eyes then, he was in my eyes still; just as simply faithful, just as simply right.

When we got back again and he lifted me out, and carried me – so easily – across the court and up the stairs, I thought of that eventful Christmas Day when he had carried me over the marshes. We had not yet made any allusion to my change of fortune, nor did I know how much of my late history he was acquainted with. I was so doubtful of myself now, and put so much trust in him, that I could not satisfy myself whether I ought to refer to it when he did not.

'Have you heard, Joe,' I asked him that evening, upon further consideration, as he smoked his pipe at the window, 'who my patron was?'

'I heerd,' returned Joe, 'as it were not Miss Havisham, old chap.'

'Did you hear who it was, Joe?'

'Well! I heerd as it were a person what sent the person what giv' you the bank-notes at the Jolly Bargemen, Pip.'

'So it was.'

'Astonishing!' said Joe, in the placidest way.

'Did you hear that he was dead, Joe?' I presently asked, with increasing diffidence.

'Which?' Him as sent the bank-notes, Pip?'

'Yes.'

'I think,' said Joe, after meditating a long time, and looking rather evasively at the window-seat, 'as I *did* hear tell that how he were something or another in a general way in that direction.'

'Did you hear anything of his circumstances, Joe?'

'Not partickler, Pip.'

'If you would like to hear, Joe – ' I was beginning, when Joe got up and came to my sofa.

'Lookee here, old chap,' said Joe, bending over me. 'Ever the best of friends; ain't us, Pip?'

I was ashamed to answer him.

'Werry good, then,' said Joe, as if I *had* answered; 'that's all right; that's agreed upon. Then why go into subjects, old chap, which as betwixt two sech must be for ever onnecessary? There's subjects enough as betwixt two sech, without onnecessary ones. Lord! To think of your poor sister and her rampages! And don't you remember Tickler?'

'I do indeed, Joe.'

'Lookee here, old chap,' said Joe. 'I done what I could to keep you and Tickler in sunders, but my power were not always fully equal to my inclinations. For when your poor sister had a mind to drop into you, it were not so much,' said Joe, in his favourite argumentative way, 'that she dropped into me too, if I put myself in opposition to her, but that she dropped into you always heavier for it. I noticed that. It ain't a grab at a man's whisker, nor yet a shake or two of a man (to which your sister was quite welcome), that 'ud put a man off from getting a little child out of punishment. But when that little child is dropped into, heavier, for that grab of whisker or shaking, then that man naterally up and says to himself, "Where, is the good as you are a doing? I grant you I see the 'arm," says the man, "but I don't see the good. I call upon you, sir, therefore, to pint out the good."'

'The man says?' I observed, as Joe waited for me to speak.

'The man says,' Joe assented. 'Is he right, that man?'

'Dear Joe, he is always right.'

'Well, old chap,' said Joe, 'then abide by your words. If he's always right (which in general he's more likely wrong), he's right when he says this: supposing ever you kep any little matter to yourself, when you was a little child, you kep it mostly because you know'd as J. Gargery's power to part you and Tickler in sunders, were not fully equal to his inclinations. Therefore, think no more of it as betwixt two sech, and do not let us pass remarks upon onnecessary subjects. Biddy giv' her-self a deal o' trouble with me afore I left (for I am most awful dull), as I should view it in this light, and, viewing it in this light, as I should ser put it. Both of which,' said Joe, quite charmed with his logical arrangement, 'being done, now this to you a true friend, say. Namely. You mustn't go a overdoing on it, but you must have your supper and your wine and water, and you must be put betwixt the sheets.'

The delicacy with which Joe dismissed this theme, and the sweet tact and kindness with which Biddy – who with her woman's wit had found me out so soon – had prepared him for it, made a deep impression on my mind. But whether Joe knew how poor I was, and how my great expectations had all dissol-ved, like our own marsh mists before the sun, I could not understand.

Another thing in Joe that I could not understand when it first began to develop itself, but which I soon arrived at a sorrowful comprehension of, was this: as I became stronger and better, Joe became a little less easy with me. In my weakness and entire dependence on him, the dear fellow had fallen into the old tone, and called me by the old names, the dear 'old Pip, old chap', that now were music in my ears. I too had fallen into the old ways, only happy and thankful that he let me. But, imperceptibly, though I held by them fast, Joe's hold upon them began to slacken; and whereas I wondered at this, at first, I soon began to understand that the cause of it was in me, and that the fault of it was all mine.

Ah! Had I given Joe no reason to doubt my constancy, and to think that in prosperity I should grow cold to him and cast him off? Had I given Joe's innocent heart no cause to feel instinctively that as I got stronger, his hold upon me would be weaker, and that he had better loosen it in time and let me go, before I plucked myself away?

It was on the third or fourth occasion of my going out walking in the Temple Gardens, leaning on Joe's arm, that I saw this change in him very plainly. We had been sitting in the bright warm sunlight, looking at the river, and I chanced to say as we got up: 'See, Joe! I can walk quite strongly. Now, you shall see me walk back by myself.'

'Which do not overdo it, Pip,' said Joe; 'but I shall be happy fur to see you able, sir.'

The last word grated on me; but how could I remonstrate! I walked no further than the gate of the gardens, and then pretended to be weaker than I was, and asked Joe for his arm. Joe gave it me, but was thoughtful.

I, for my part, was thoughtful too; for how best to check this growing change in Joe was a great perplexity to my remorseful thoughts. That I was ashamed to tell him exactly how I was placed, and what I had come down to, I do not seek to conceal; but I hope my reluctance was not quite an unworthy one. He would want to help me out of his little savings, I knew, and I knew that he ought not to help me, and that I must not suffer him to do it.

It was a thoughtful evening with both of us. But, before we went to bed, I had resolved that I would wait over tomorrow, tomorrow being Sunday, and would begin my new course with the new week. On Monday morning I would speak to Joe about this change, I would lay aside this last vestige of reserve, I would tell him what I had in my thoughts (that secondly, not yet arrived at), and why I had not decided to go out to Herbert, and then the change would be conquered for ever. As I cleared, Joe cleared, and it seemed as though he had sympathetically arrived at a resolution too.

We had a quiet day on the Sunday, and we rode out into the country, and then walked in the fields.

'I feel thankful that I have been ill, Joe,' I said.

'Dear old Pip, old chap, you're a'most come round, sir.'

'It has been a memorable time for me, Joe.'

'Likeways for myself, sir,' Joe returned.

'We have had a time together, Joe, that I can never forget. There were days once, I know, that I did for a while forget; but I never shall forget these.'

'Pip,' said Joe, appearing a little hurried and troubled, 'there has been larks. And, dear sir, what have been betwixt us – have been.'

At night, when I had gone to bed, Joe came into my room, as he had done all through my recovery. He asked me if I felt sure that I was as well as in the morning?

'Yes, dear Joe, quite.'

'And are always a getting stronger, old chap?'

'Yes, dear Joe, steadily.'

Joe patted the coverlet on my shoulder with his great good hand, and said, in what I thought a husky voice, 'Good-night!'

When I got up in the morning, refreshed and stronger yet, I was full of my resolution to tell Joe all, without delay. I would tell him before breakfast. I would dress at once and go to his room and surprise him; for it was the first day I had been up early. I went to his room, and he was not there. Not only was he not there, but his box was gone.

I hurried then to the breakfast-table, and on it found a letter. These were its brief contents.

Not wishful to intrude I have departured fur you are well again dear Pip and will do better without. Jo.

PS Ever the best of friends.

Enclosed in the letter was a receipt for the debt and costs on which I had been arrested. Down to that moment I had vainly supposed that my creditor had withdrawn or suspended proceedings until I should be quite recovered. I had never dreamed of Joe's having paid the money; but Joe had paid it, and the receipt was in his name.

What remained for me now, but to follow him to the dear old forge, and there to have out my disclosure to him, and my penitent remonstrance with him, and there to relieve my mind and heart of that reserved Secondly, which had begun as a vague something lingering in my thoughts, and had formed into a settled purpose?

The purpose was, that I would go to Biddy, that I would show her how humbled and repentant I came back, that I would tell her how I had lost all I once hoped for, that I would remind her of our old confidences in my first unhappy time. Then I would say to her, 'Biddy, I think you once liked me very well, when my errant heart, even while it strayed away from you, was quieter and better with you than it ever has been since. If you can like me only half as well once more, if you can take me with all my faults and disappointments on my head, if you can receive me like a forgiven child (and indeed I am as sorry, Biddy, and have as much need of a hushing voice and a soothing hand), I hope I am a little worthier of you than I was – not much, but a little. And, Biddy, it shall rest with you to say whether I shall work at the forge with Joe, or whether I shall try for any different occupation down in this country, or whether we shall go away to a distant place where an opportunity awaits me which I set aside when it was offered, until I knew your answer. And now, dear Biddy, if you can tell me that you will go through the world with me, you will surely make it a better world for me, and me a better man for it, and I will try hard to make it a better world for you.'

Such was my purpose. After three days more of recovery, I went down to the old place, to put it in execution. And how I sped in it, is all I have left to tell.

Chapter 58

The tidings of my high fortunes having had a heavy fall, had got down to my native place and its neighbourhood, before I got there. I found the Blue Boar in possession of the intelligence, and I found that it made a great change in the Boar's demeanour. Whereas the Boar had cultivated my good opinion with warm assiduity when I was coming into property, the Boar was exceedingly cool on the subject now that I was going out of property.

It was evening when I arrived, much fatigued by the journey I had so often made so easily. The Boar could not put me into my usual bedroom, which was engaged (probably by someone who had expectations), and could only assign me a very indifferent chamber among the pigeons and post-chaises up the yard. But I had as sound a sleep in that lodging as in the most superior accommodation the Boar could have given me, and the quality of my dreams was about the same as in the best bedroom.

Early in the morning while my breakfast was getting ready, I strolled round by Satis House. There were printed bills on the gate and on bits of carpet hanging out of the windows, announcing a sale by auction of the household furniture and effects, next week. The house itself was to be sold as old building materials, and pulled down. Lot 1 was marked in whitewashed knock-knee letters on the brew-house; Lot 2 on that part of the main building which had been so long shut up. Other lots were marked off on other parts of the structure, and the ivy had been torn down to make room for the inscriptions, and much of it trailed low in the dust and was withered already. Stepping in for a moment at the open gate and looking around me with the uncomfortable air of a stranger who had no business there, I saw the auctioneer's clerk walking on the casks and telling them off for the information of a catalogue compiler, pen in hand, who made a temporary desk of the wheeled chair I had so often pushed along to the tune of Old Clem.

When I got back to my breakfast in the Boar's coffee-room, I found Mr Pumblechook conversing with the landlord. Mr Pumblechook (not improved in appearance by his late nocturnal adventure) was waiting for me, and addressed me in the following terms.

'Young man, I am sorry to see you brought low. But what else could be expected! What else could be expected!'

As he extended his hand with a magnificently forgiving air, and as I was broken by illness and unfit to quarrel, I took it.

'William,' said Mr Pumblechook to the waiter, 'put a muffin on table. And has it come to this! Has it come to this!'

I frowningly sat down to my breakfast. Mr Pumblechook stood over me and poured out my tea – before I could touch the teapot – with the air of a benefactor who was resolved to be true to the last.

'William,' said Mr Pumblechook, mournfully, 'put the salt on. In happier times,' addressing me, 'I think you took sugar? And did you take milk? You did. Sugar and milk. William, bring a watercress.'

'Thank you,' said I, shortly, 'but I don't eat watercresses.'

'You don't eat 'em,' returned Mr Pumblechook, sighing and nodding his head several times, as if he might have expected that, and as if abstinence from watercresses were consistent with my downfall. 'True. The simple fruits of the earth. No. You needn't bring any, William.'

I went on with my breakfast, and Mr Pumblechook continued to stand over me, staring fishily and breathing noisily, as he always did.

'Little more than skin and bone!' mused Mr Pumblechook, aloud. 'And yet when he went away from here (I may say with my blessing), and I spread afore him my humble store, like the bee, he was as plump as a peach!'

This reminded me of the wonderful difference between the servile manner in which he had offered his hand in my new prosperity, saying, 'May I?' and the ostentatious clemency with which he had just now exhibited the same fat five fingers.

'Hah!' he went on, handing me the bread and butter. 'And air you a going to Joseph?'

'In heaven's name,' said I, firing in spite of myself, 'what does it matter to you where I am going? Leave that teapot alone.'

It was the worst course I could have taken, because it gave Pumblechook the opportunity he wanted.

'Yes, young man,' said he, releasing the handle of the article in question, retiring a step or two from my table, and speaking for the behoof of the landlord and waiter at the door, 'I *will* leave that teapot alone. You are right, young man. For once, you are right. I forgit myself when I take such an interest in your breakfast, as to wish your frame, exhausted by the debilitating effects of prodigygality, to be stimulated by the 'olesome nourishment of your forefathers. And yet,' said Pumblechook, turning to the landlord and waiter, and pointing me out at arm's length, 'this is him as I ever sported with in his days of happy infancy! Tell me not it cannot be; I tell you this is him!'

A low murmur from the two replied. The waiter appeared to be particularly affected.

'This is him,' said Pumblechook, 'as I have rode in my shay-cart. This is him as I have seen brought up by hand. This is him unto the sister of which I was uncle by marriage, as her name was Georgiana M'ria from her own mother, let him deny it if he can!'

The waiter seemed convinced that I could not deny it, and that it gave the case a black look.

'Young man,' said Pumblechook, screwing his head at me in the old fashion, 'you air a going to Joseph. What does it matter to me, you ask me, where you air a going? I say to you, sir, you air a going to Joseph.'

The waiter coughed, as if he modestly invited me to get over that.

'Now,' said Pumblechook, and all this with a most exasperating air of saying in the cause of virtue what was perfectly convincing and conclusive. 'I will tell you what to say to Joseph. Here is squires of the Boar present, known and respected in this town, and here is William, which his father's name was Potkins if I do not deceive myself.'

'You do not, sir,' said William.

'In their presence,' pursued Pumblechook, 'I will tell you, young man, what to say to Joseph. Says you, "Joseph, I have this day seen my earliest benefactor and the founder of my fortun's. I will name no names, Joseph, but so they are pleased to call him uptown, and I have seen that man." '

'I swear I don't see him here,' said I.

'Say that likewise,' retorted Pumblechook. 'Say you said that, and even Joseph will probably betray surprise.'

'There you quite mistake him,' said I. 'I know better.'

'Says you,' Pumblechook went on, ' "Joseph, I have seen that man, and that man bears you no malice and bears me no malice. He knows your character, Joseph, and is well acquainted with your pig-headedness and ignorance; and he knows my character, Joseph, and he knows my want of gratitoode. Yes, Joseph," says you,' here Pumblechook shook his head and hand at me, ' "He knows my total deficiency of common human gratitoode. *He* knows it, Joseph, as none can. *You* do not know it, Joseph, having no call to know it, but that man do." '

Windy donkey as he was, it really amazed me that he could have the face to talk thus to mine.

'Says you, "Joseph, he gave me a little message, which I will now repeat. It was, that in my being brought low, he saw the finger of providence. He knowed that finger when he saw it, Joseph, and he saw it plain. It pinted out this writing, Joseph. *Reward of ingratitoode to earliest benefactor, and founder of fortun's.* But that man said that he did not repent of what he had done, Joseph. Not at all. It was right to do it, it was kind to do it, it was benevolent to do it, and he would do it again." '

'It's a pity,' said I, scornfully, as I finished my interrupted breakfast, 'that the man did not say what he had done and would do again.'

'Squires of the Boar!' Pumblechook was now addressing the landlord, 'and William! I have no objections to your mentioning, either uptown or downtown, if such should be your wishes, that it was right to do it, kind to do it, benevolent to do it, and that I would do it again.'

With those words the impostor shook them both by the hand, with an air, and left the house; leaving me much more astonished than delighted by the virtues of that same indefinite 'it'. I was not long after him in leaving the house too, and when I went down the High Street I saw him holding forth (no doubt to the same effect) at his shop door to a select group, who honoured me with very unfavourable glances as I passed on the opposite side of the way.

But it was only the pleasanter to turn to Biddy and to Joe, whose great forbearance shone more brightly than before, if that could be, contrasted with this brazen pretender. I went towards them slowly, for my limbs were weak, but with a sense of increasing relief as I drew nearer to them, and a sense of leaving arrogance and untruthfulness further and further behind.

The June weather was delicious. The sky was blue, the larks

were soaring high over the green corn, I thought all that countryside more beautiful and peaceful by far than I had ever known it to be yet. Many pleasant pictures of the life that I would lead there, and of the change for the better that would come over my character when I had a guiding spirit at my side whose simple faith and clear home-wisdom I had proved, beguiled my way. They awakened a tender emotion in me; for my heart was softened by my return, and such a change had come to pass, that I felt like one who was toiling home barefoot from distant travel, and whose wanderings had lasted many years.

The schoolhouse where Biddy was mistress, I had never seen; but the little roundabout lane, by which I entered the village for quietness' sake, took me past it. I was disappointed to find that the day was a holiday; no children were there, and Biddy's house was closed. Some hopeful notion of seeing her, busily engaged in her daily duties, before she saw me, had been in my mind and was defeated.

But the forge was a very short distance off, and I went towards it under the sweet green limes, listening for the clink of Joe's hammer. Long after I ought to have heard it, and long after I had fancied I heard it and found it but a fancy, all was still. The limes were there, and the white thorns were there, and the chestnut trees were there, and their leaves rustled harmoniously when I stopped to listen; but the clink of Joe's hammer was not in the midsummer wind.

Almost fearing, without knowing why, to come in view of the forge, I saw it at last, and saw that it was closed. No gleam of fire, no glittering shower of sparks, no roar of bellows; all shut up, and still.

But the house was not deserted, and the best parlour seemed to be in use, for there were white curtains fluttering in its window, and the window was open and gay with flowers. I went softly towards it, meaning to peep over the flowers, when Joe and Biddy stood before me, arm in arm.

At first Biddy gave a cry, as if she thought it was my apparition, but in another moment she was in my embrace. I wept to see her, and she wept to see me; I, because she looked so fresh and pleasant; she, because I looked so worn and white.

'But, dear Biddy, how smart you are!'

'Yes, dear Pip.'

'And Joe, how smart *you* are!'

'Yes, dear old Pip, old chap.'

I looked at both of them, from one to the other, and then – 'It's my wedding-day,' cried Biddy, in a burst of happiness, 'and I am married to Joe!'

They had taken me into the kitchen, and I had laid my head down on the old deal table. Biddy held one of my hands to her lips, and Joe's restoring touch was on my shoulder. 'Which he warn't strong enough, my dear, fur to be surprised,' said Joe. And Biddy said, 'I ought to have thought of it, dear Joe, but I was too happy.' They were both so overjoyed to see me, so proud to see me, so touched by my coming to them, so delighted that I should have come by accident to make their day complete!

My first thought was one of great thankfulness that I had never breathed this last baffled hope to Joe. How often, while he was with me in my illness, had it risen to my lips. How irrevocable would have been his knowledge of it, if he had remained with me but another hour!

'Dear Biddy,' said I, 'you have the best husband in the whole world, and if you could have seen him by my bed you would have – but no, you couldn't love him better than you do.'

'No, I couldn't indeed,' said Biddy.

'And, dear Joe, you have the best wife in the whole world, and she will make you as happy as even you deserve to be, you dear, good, noble Joe!'

Joe looked at me with a quivering lip, and fairly put his sleeve before his eyes.

'And Joe and Biddy both, as you have been to church today and are in charity and love with all mankind, receive my humble thanks for all you have done for me, and all I have so ill repaid! And when I say that I am going away within the hour, for I am soon going abroad, and that I shall never rest until I have worked for the money with which you have kept me out of prison, and have sent it to you, don't think, dear Joe and Biddy, that if I could repay it a thousand times over, I suppose I could cancel a farthing of the debt I owe you, or that I would do so if I could!'

They were both melted by these words, and both entreated me to say no more.

'But I must say more. Dear Joe, I hope you will have children to love, and that some little fellow will sit in this chimney corner of a winter night, who may remind you of another little fellow gone out of it for ever. Don't tell him, Joe, that I was thankless; don't tell him, Biddy, that I was ungenerous and unjust; only tell him that I honoured you both, because you were both so good and true, and that, as your child, I said it would be natural to him to grow up a much better man than I did.'

'I ain't a going,' said Joe, from behind his sleeve, 'to tell him nothink o' that natur, Pip. Nor Biddy ain't. Nor yet no one ain't.'

'And now, though I know you have already done it in your own kind hearts, pray tell me, both, that you forgive me! Pray let me hear you say the words, that I may carry the sound of them away with me, and then I shall be able to believe that you can trust me, and think better of me, in the time to come!'

'O dear old Pip, old chap,' said Joe. 'God knows as I forgive you, if I have anythink to forgive!'

'Amen! And God knows I do!' echoed Biddy.

'Now let me go up and look at my old little room, and rest there a few minutes by myself. And then when I have eaten and drunk with you, go with me as far as the finger-posts, dear Joe and Biddy, before we say goodbye!'

I sold all I had, and put aside as much as I could, for a composition with my creditors – who gave me ample time to pay them in full – and I went out and joined Herbert. Within a month I had quitted England, and within two months I was clerk to Clarriker and Co., and within four months I assumed my first undivided responsibility. For the beam across the parlour ceiling at Mill Pond Bank had then ceased to tremble under old Bill Barley's growls and was at peace, and Herbert had gone away to marry Clara, and I was left in sole charge of the Eastern Branch until he brought her back.

Many a year went round before I was a partner in the House; but I lived happily with Herbert and his wife, and lived frugally, and paid my debts, and maintained a constant correspondence with Biddy and Joe. It was not until I became third in the firm, that Clarriker betrayed me to Herbert; but he then declared that the secret of Herbert's partnership had been long enough upon his conscience, and he must tell it. So he told it, and Herbert was as much moved as amazed, and the dear fellow and I were not the worse friends for the long concealment. I must not leave it to be supposed that we were ever a great House, or that we made mints of money. We were not in a grand way of business, but we had a good name, and worked for our profits, and did very well. We owed so much to Herbert's ever cheerful industry and readiness, that I often wondered how I had conceived that old idea of his inaptitude, until I was one day enlightened by the reflection, that perhaps the inaptitude had never been in him at all, but had been in me.

Chapter 59

For eleven years I had not seen Joe nor Biddy with my bodily eyes – though they had both been often before my fancy in the East – when, upon an evening in December, an hour or two after dark, I laid my hand softly on the latch of the old kitchen door. I touched it so softly that I was not heard, and I looked in unseen. There, smoking his pipe in the old place by the kitchen firelight, as hale and as strong as ever, though a little grey, sat Joe; and there, fenced into the corner with Joe's leg, and sitting on my own little stool looking at the fire, was – I again!

'We giv' him the name of Pip for your sake, dear old chap,' said Joe, delighted when I took another stool by the child's side (but I did *not* rumple his hair), 'and we hoped he might grow a little bit like you, and we think he do.'

I thought so too, and I took him out for a walk next morning, and we talked immensely, understanding one another to perfection. And I took him down to the churchyard, and set him on a certain tombstone there, and he showed me from that elevation which stone was sacred to the memory of Philip Pirrip, late of this Parish, and Also Georgiana, Wife of the Above.

'Biddy,' said I, when I talked with her after dinner, as her little girl lay sleeping in her lap, 'you must give Pip to me, one of these days; or lend him, at all events.'

'No, no,' said Biddy, gently. 'You must marry.'

'So Herbert and Clara say, but I don't think I shall, Biddy. I have so settled down in their home, that it's not at all likely. I am already quite an old bachelor.'

Biddy looked down at her child, and put its little hand to her lips, and then put the good matronly hand with which she had touched it, into mine. There was something in the action and in the light pressure of Biddy's wedding-ring, that had a very pretty eloquence in it.

'Dear Pip,' said Biddy, 'you are sure you don't fret for her?'

'O no – I think not, Biddy.'

'Tell me as an old friend. Have you quite forgotten her?'

'My dear Biddy, I have forgotten nothing in my life that ever had a foremost place there, and little that ever had any place there. But that poor dream, as I once used to call it, has all gone by, Biddy, all gone by!'

Nevertheless, I knew while I said those words, that I secretly intended to revisit the site of the old house that evening, alone, for her sake. Yes, even so. For Estella's sake.

I had heard of her as leading a most unhappy life, and as being separated from her husband, who had used her with great cruelty, and who had become quite renowned as a compound of pride, avarice, brutality, and meanness. And I had heard of the death of her husband, from an accident consequent on his ill-treatment of a horse. This release had befallen her some two years before; for anything I knew, she was married again.

The early dinner-hour at Joe's left me abundance of time, without hurrying my talk with Biddy, to walk over to the old spot before dark. But, what with loitering on the way, to look at old objects and to think of old times, the day had quite declined when I came to the place.

There was no house now, no brewery, no building whatever left, but the wall of the old garden. The cleared space had been

The old place by the kitchen firelight

enclosed with a rough fence, and looking over it, I saw that some of the old ivy had struck root anew, and was growing green on low quiet mounds of ruin. A gate in the fence standing ajar, I pushed it open and went in.

A cold silvery mist had veiled the afternoon, and the moon was not yet up to scatter it. But the stars were shining beyond the mist, and the moon was coming, and the evening was not dark. I could trace out where every part of the old house had been, and where the brewery had been, and where the gates, and where the casks. I had done so, and was looking along the desolate garden-walk, when I beheld a solitary figure in it.

The figure showed itself aware of me as I advanced. It had been moving towards me, but it stood still. As I drew nearer, I saw it to be the figure of a woman. As I drew nearer yet, it was about to turn away, when it stopped, and let me come up with it. Then, it faltered as if much surprised, and uttered my name, and I cried out: 'Estella!'

'I am greatly changed. I wonder you know me.'

The freshness of her beauty was indeed gone, but its indescribable majesty and its indescribable charm remained. Those attractions in it I had seen before; what I had never seen before was the saddened softened light of the once proud eyes; what I had never felt before was the friendly touch of the once insensible hand.

We sat down on a bench that was near, and I said, 'After so many years, it is strange that we should thus meet again, Estella, here where our first meeting was! Do you often come back?'

'I have never been here since.'

'Nor I.'

The moon began to rise, and I thought of the placid look at the white ceiling, which had passed away. The moon began to rise, and I thought of the pressure on my hand when I had spoken the last words he had heard on earth.

Estella was the next to break the silence that ensued between us.

'I have very often hoped and intended to come back, but have been prevented by many circumstances. Poor, poor old place!'

The silvery mist was touched with the first rays of the moonlight, and the same rays touched the tears that dropped from her eyes. Not knowing that I saw them, and setting herself to get the better of them, she said quietly: 'Were you wondering, as you walked along, how it came to be left in this condition?'

'Yes, Estella.'

'The ground belongs to me. It is the only possession I have not relinquished. Everything else has gone from me, little by little, but I have kept this. It was the subject of the only determined resistance I made in all the wretched years.'

'Is it to be built on?'

'At last it is. I came here to take leave of it before its change. And you,' she said, in a voice of touching interest to a wanderer, 'you live abroad still.'

'Still.'

'And do well, I am sure?'

'I work pretty hard for a sufficient living, and therefore – yes, I do well!'

'I have often thought of you,' said Estella.

'Have you?'

'Of late, very often. There was a long hard time when I kept far from me the remembrance of what I had thrown away when I was quite ignorant of its worth. But, since my duty has not been incompatible with the admission of that remembrance, I have given it a place in my heart.'

'You have always held your place in *my* heart,' I answered.

And we were silent again until she spoke.

'I little thought,' said Estella, 'that I should take leave of you in taking leave of this spot. I am very glad to do so.'

'Glad to part again, Estella? To me parting is a painful thing. To me, the remembrance of our last parting has been ever mournful and painful.'

'But you said to me,' returned Estella, very earnestly, ' "God bless you, God forgive you!" And if you could say that to me then, you will not hesitate to say that to me now – now, when suffering has been stronger than all other teaching, and has taught me to understand what your heart used to be. I have been bent and broken, but – I hope – into a better shape. Be as considerate and good to me as you were, and tell me we are friends.'

'We are friends,' said I, rising and bending over her, as she rose from the bench.

'And will continue friends apart,' said Estella.

I took her hand in mine, and we went out of the ruined place; and, as the morning mists had risen long ago when I first left the forge, so, the evening mists were rising now, and in all the broad expanse of tranquil light they showed to me, I saw no shadow of another parting from her.

David Copperfield

CHAPTER I

I Am Born

Whether I shall turn out to be the hero of my own life, or whether that station will be held by anybody else, these pages must show. To begin my life with the beginning of my life, I record that I was born (as I have been informed and believe) on a Friday, at twelve o'clock at night. It was remarked that the clock began to strike, and I began to cry, simultaneously.

In consideration of the day and hour of my birth, it was declared by the nurse, and by some sage women in the neighbourhood who had taken a lively interest in me several months before there was any possibility of our becoming personally acquainted, first, that I was destined to be unlucky in life; and secondly, that I was privileged to see ghosts and spirits; both these gifts inevitably attaching, as they believed, to all unlucky infants of either gender, born towards the small hours on a Friday night.

I need say nothing here, on the first head, because nothing can show better than my history whether that prediction was verified or falsified by the result. On the second branch of the question, I will only remark, that unless I ran through that part of my inheritance while I was still a baby, I have not come into it yet. But I do not at all complain of having been kept out of this property; and if anybody else should be in the present enjoyment of it, he is heartily welcome to keep it.

I was born with a caul, which was advertised for sale, in the newspapers, at the low price of fifteen guineas. Whether sea-going people were short of money about that time, or were short of faith and preferred cork-jackets, I don't know; all I know is that there was but one solitary bidding, and that was from an attorney connected with the bill-broking business, who offered two pounds in cash and the balance in sherry, but declined to be guaranteed from drowning on any higher bargain. Consequently the advertisement was withdrawn at a dead loss – for as to sherry, my poor dear mother's own sherry was in the market then – and ten years afterwards the caul was put up in a raffle down in our part of the country, to fifty members at half a crown a head, the winner to spend five shillings. I was present myself, and I remember to have felt quite uncomfortable and confused, at a part of myself being disposed of in that way. The caul was won, I recollect, by an old lady with a hand-basket, who, very reluctantly, produced from it the stipulated five shillings, all in halfpence, and twopence halfpenny short – as it took an immense time and a great waste of arithmetic to endeavour without any effect to prove to her. It is a fact which will be long remembered as remarkable down there, that she was never drowned, but died triumphantly in bed, at ninety-two. I have understood that it was, to the last, her proudest boast, that she never had been on the water in her life, except upon a bridge; and that over her tea (to which she was extremely partial) she, to the last, expressed her indignation at the impiety of mariners and others, who had the presumption to go 'meandering' about the world. It was in vain to represent to her that some conveniences, tea perhaps included, resulted from this objectionable practice. She always returned, with greater emphasis and with an instinctive knowledge of the strength of her objection, 'Let us have no meandering.'

Not to meander myself, at present, I will go back to my birth.

I was born at Blunderstone, in Suffolk, or 'thereby,' as they say in Scotland. I was a posthumous child. My father's eyes had closed upon the light of this world six months, when mine opened on it. There is something strange to me, even now, in the reflection that he never saw me; and something stranger yet in the shadowy remembrance that I have of my first childish associations with his white gravestone in the churchyard, and of the indefinable compassion I used to feel for it lying out alone there in the dark night, when our little parlour was warm and bright with fire and candle, and the doors of our house were – almost cruelly, it seemed to me sometimes – bolted and locked against it.

An aunt of my father's, and consequently a great-aunt of mine, of whom I shall have more to relate by and by, was the principal magnate of our family. Miss Trotwood, or Miss Betsey, as my poor mother always called her, when she sufficiently overcame her dread of this formidable personage to mention her at all (which was seldom), had been married to a husband younger than herself, who was very handsome, except in the sense of the homely adage, 'Handsome is that handsome does' – for he was strongly suspected of having beaten Miss Betsey, and even of having once, on a disputed question of supplies, made some hasty but determined arrangements to throw her out of a two pair of stairs' window. These evidences of an incompatibility of temper induced Miss Betsey to pay him off, and effect a separation by mutual consent. He went to India with his capital, and there, according to a wild legend in our family, he was once seen riding on an elephant, in company with a Baboon; but I think it must have been a Baboo – or a Begum. Anyhow, from India, tidings of his death reached home, within ten years. How they affected my aunt, nobody knew; for immediately upon the separation, she took her maiden name again, bought a cottage in a hamlet on the sea-coast a long way off, established herself there as a single woman with one servant, and was understood to live secluded, ever afterwards, in an inflexible retirement.

My father had once been a favourite of hers, I believe; but she was mortally affronted by his marriage, on the ground that my mother was 'a wax doll.' She had never seen my mother, but she knew her to be not yet twenty. My father and Miss Betsey never met again. He was double my mother's age when he married, and of but a delicate constitution. He died a year afterwards, and, as I have said, six months before I came into the world.

This was the state of matters, on the afternoon of, what *I* may be excused for calling, that eventful and important Friday. I can make no claim therefore to have known, at that time, how matters stood; or to have any remembrance, founded on the evidence of my own senses, of what follows.

My mother was sitting by the fire, but poorly in health, and very low in spirits, looking at it through her tears, and desponding heavily about herself and the fatherless little stranger, who was already welcomed by some grosses of prophetic pins, in a drawer upstairs, to a world not at all excited on the subject of his arrival; my mother, I say, was sitting by the fire, that bright, windy March afternoon, very timid and sad, and very doubtful of ever coming alive out of the trial that was before her, when, lifting her eyes as she dried them to the window opposite, she saw a strange lady coming up the garden.

My mother had a sure foreboding at the second glance, that it was Miss Betsey. The setting sun was glowing on the strange lady, over the garden fence, and she came walking up to the door with a fell rigidity of figure and composure of countenance that could have belonged to nobody else.

When she reached the house, she gave another proof of her identity. My father had often hinted that she seldom conducted herself like any ordinary Christian; and now, instead of ringing the bell, she came and looked in at that identical window, pressing the end of her nose against the glass to that extent, that my poor dear mother used to say it became perfectly flat and white in a moment.

She gave my mother such a turn, that I have always been convinced I am indebted to Miss Betsey for having been born on a Friday.

My mother had left her chair in her agitation, and gone behind it in the corner. Miss Betsey, looking round the room, slowly and enquiringly, began on the other side, and carried her eyes on, like a Saracen's Head in a Dutch clock, until they reached my mother. Then she made a frown and a gesture to my mother, like one who was accustomed to be obeyed, to come and open the door. My mother went.

'Mrs David Copperfield, I *think*,' said Miss Betsey; the emphasis referring, perhaps, to my mother's mourning weeds, and her condition.

'Yes,' said my mother faintly.

'Miss Trotwood,' said the visitor. 'You have heard of her, I dare say?'

My mother answered she had had that pleasure. And she had a disagreeable consciousness of not appearing to imply that it had been an overpowering pleasure.

'Now you see her,' said Miss Betsey. My mother bent her head, and begged her to walk in.

They went into the parlour my mother had come from, the fire in the best room on the other side of the passage not being lighted – not having been lighted, indeed, since my father's funeral; and when they were both seated, and Miss Betsey said nothing, my mother, after vainly trying to restrain herself, began to cry.

'Oh, tut, tut, tut!' said Miss Betsey, in a hurry. 'Don't do that! Come, come!'

My mother couldn't help it notwithstanding, so she cried until she had had her cry out.

'Take off your cap, child,' said Miss Betsey, 'and let me see you.'

My mother was too much afraid of her to refuse compliance with this odd request, if she had any disposition to do so. Therefore she did as she was told, and did it with such nervous hands that her hair (which was luxuriant and beautiful) fell all about her face.

'Why, bless my heart!' exclaimed Miss Betsey. 'You are a very Baby!'

My mother was, no doubt, unusually youthful in appearance even for her years; she hung her head, as if it were her fault, poor thing, and said, sobbing, that indeed she was afraid she was but a childish widow, and would be but a childish mother if she lived. In a short pause which ensued, she had a fancy that she felt Miss Betsey touch her hair, and that with no ungentle hand; but, looking at her, in her timid hope, she found that lady sitting with the skirt of her dress tucked up, her hands folded on one knee, and her feet upon the fender, frowning at the fire.

'In the name of Heaven,' said Miss Betsey suddenly, 'why Rookery?'

'Do you mean the house, ma'am?' asked my mother.

A stranger calls to see me

'Why Rookery?' said Miss Betsey. 'Cookery would have been more to the purpose, if you had had any practical ideas of life, either of you.'

'The name was Mr Copperfield's choice,' returned my mother. 'When he bought the house, he liked to think that there were rooks about it.'

The evening wind made such a disturbance just now, among some tall old elm trees at the bottom of the garden, that neither my mother nor Miss Betsey could forbear glancing that way. As the elms bent to one another, like giants who were whispering secrets, and after a few seconds of such repose fell into a violent flurry, tossing their wild arms about, as if their late confidences were really too wicked for their peace of mind, some weather-beaten, ragged old rooks' nests, burdening their higher branches, swung like wrecks upon a stormy sea.

'Where are the birds?' asked Miss Betsey.

'The – ?' My mother had been thinking of something else.

'The rooks – what has become of them?' asked Miss Betsey.

'There have not been any since we have lived here,' said my mother. 'We thought – Mr Copperfield thought – it was quite a large rookery; but the nests were very old ones, and the birds have deserted them a long while.'

'David Copperfield all over!' cried Miss Betsey. 'David Copperfield from head to foot! Calls a house a rookery when there's not a rook near it, and takes the birds on trust, because he sees the nests!'

'Mr Copperfield,' returned my mother, 'is dead, and if you dare to speak unkindly of him to me –'

My poor dear mother, I suppose, had some momentary intention of committing an assault and battery upon my aunt, who could easily have settled her with one hand, even if my mother had been in far better training for such an encounter than she was that evening. But it passed with the action of rising from her chair; and she sat down again very meekly, and fainted.

When she came to herself, or when Miss Betsey had restored her, whichever it was, she found the latter standing at the window. The twilight was by this time shading down into darkness; and dimly as they saw each other, they could not have done that without the aid of the fire.

'Well?' said Miss Betsey, coming back to her chair, as if she had only been taking a casual look at the prospect; 'and when do you expect –'

'I am all in a tremble,' faltered my mother. 'I don't know what's the matter. I shall die, I am sure!'

'No, no, no,' said Miss Betsey. 'Have some tea.'

'Oh, dear me, dear me, do you think it will do me any good?' cried my mother, in a helpless manner.

'Of course it will,' said Miss Betsey. 'It's nothing but fancy. What do you call your girl?'

'I don't know that it will be a girl, yet, ma'am,' said my mother innocently.

'Bless the Baby!' exclaimed Miss Betsey, unconsciously quoting the second sentiment of the pincushion in the drawer upstairs, but applying it to my mother instead of me. 'I don't mean that. I mean your servant.'

'Peggotty,' said my mother.

'Peggotty!' repeated Miss Betsey, with some indignation. 'Do you mean to say, child, that any human being has gone into a Christian church, and got herself named Peggotty?'

'It's her surname,' said my mother faintly. 'Mr Copperfield called her by it, because her Christian name was the same as mine.'

'Here! Peggotty!' cried Miss Betsey, opening the parlour door. 'Tea. Your mistress is a little unwell. Don't dawdle.'

Having issued this mandate with as much potentiality as if she had been a recognised authority in the house ever since it had been a house, and having looked out to confront the amazed Peggotty coming along the passage with a candle at the sound of a strange voice, Miss Betsey shut the door again, and sat down as before, with her feet on the fender, the skirt of her dress tucked up, and her hands folded on one knee.

'You were speaking about its being a girl,' said Miss Betsey. 'I have no doubt it will be a girl. I have a presentiment that it must be a girl. Now, child, from the moment of the birth of this girl –'

'Perhaps boy,' my mother took the liberty of putting in.

'I tell you I have a presentiment that it must be a girl,' returned Miss Betsey. 'Don't contradict. From the moment of this girl's birth, child, I intend to be her friend. I intend to be her godmother, and I beg you'll call her Betsey Trotwood Copperfield. There must be no mistakes in life with *this* Betsey Trotwood. There must be no trifling with *her* affections, poor dear. She must be well brought up, and well guarded from reposing any foolish confidences where they are not deserved. I must make that *my* care.'

There was a twitch of Miss Betsey's head, after each of these sentences, as if her own old wrongs were working within her, and she repressed any plainer reference to them by strong constraint. So my mother suspected, at least, as she observed her by the low glimmer of the fire, too much scared by Miss Betsey, too uneasy in herself, and too subdued and bewildered altogether, to observe anything very clearly, or to know what to say.

'And was David good to you, child?' asked Miss Betsey, when she had been silent for a little while, and these motions of her head had gradually ceased. 'Were you comfortable together?'

'We were very happy,' said my mother. 'Mr Copperfield was only too good to me.'

'What, he spoilt you, I suppose?' returned Miss Betsey.

'For being quite alone and dependent on myself in this rough world again, yes, I fear he did indeed,' sobbed my mother.

'Well! Don't cry!' said Miss Betsey. 'You were not equally matched, child – if any two people *can* be equally matched – and so I asked the question. You were an orphan, weren't you?'

'Yes.'

'And a governess?'

'I was a nursery governess in a family where Mr Copperfield came to visit. Mr Copperfield was very kind to me, and took a great deal of notice of me, and paid me a good deal of attention, and at last proposed to me. And I accepted him. And so we were married,' said my mother simply.

'Ha! Poor Baby!' mused Miss Betsey, with her frown still bent upon the fire. 'Do you know anything?'

'I beg your pardon, ma'am,' faltered my mother.

'About keeping house, for instance,' said Miss Betsey.

'Not much, I fear,' returned my mother. 'Not so much as I could wish. But Mr Copperfield was teaching me – '

('Much he knew about it himself!') said Miss Betsey, in a parenthesis.

'And I hope I should have improved, being very anxious to learn, and he very patient to teach, if the great misfortune of his death' – my mother broke down again here, and could get no further.

'Well, well!' said Miss Betsey.

'I kept my housekeeping book regularly, and balanced it with Mr Copperfield every night,' cried my mother in another burst of distress, and breaking down again.

'Well, well!' said Miss Betsey. 'Don't cry any more.'

'And I am sure we never had a word of difference respecting it, except when Mr Copperfield objected to my threes and fives being too much like each other, or to my putting curly tails to my sevens and nines,' resumed my mother in another burst, and breaking down again.

'You'll make yourself ill,' said Miss Betsey, 'and you know that will not be good either for you or for my god-daughter. Come! You mustn't do it!'

This argument had some share in quieting my mother, though her increasing indisposition perhaps had a larger one. There was an interval of silence, only broken by Miss Betsey's occasionally ejaculating 'Ha!' as she sat with her feet upon the fender.

'David had bought an annuity for himself with his money, I know,' said she, by and by. 'What did he do for you?'

'Mr Copperfield,' said my mother, answering with some difficulty, 'was so considerate and good as to secure the reversion of a part of it to me.'

'How much?' asked Miss Betsey.

'A hundred and five pounds a year,' said my mother.

'He might have done worse,' said my aunt.

The word was appropriate to the moment. My mother was so much worse that Peggotty, coming in with the tea-board and candles, and seeing at a glance how ill she was – as Miss Betsey might have done sooner if there had been light enough – conveyed her upstairs to her own room with all speed, and immediately despatched Ham Peggotty, her nephew, who had been for some days past secreted in the house, unknown to my mother, as a special messenger, in case of emergency, to fetch the nurse and doctor.

Those allied powers were considerably astonished, when they arrived within a few minutes of each other, to find an unknown lady of portentous appearance sitting before the fire, with her bonnet tied over her left arm, stopping her ears with jewellers' cotton. Peggotty knowing nothing about her, and my mother saying nothing about her, she was quite a mystery in the parlour; and the fact of her having a magazine of jewellers' cotton in her pocket, and sticking the article in her ears in that way, did not detract from the solemnity of her presence.

The doctor having been upstairs and come down again, and

having satisfied himself, I suppose, that there was a probability of this unknown lady and himself having to sit there, face to face, for some hours, laid himself out to be polite and social. He was the meekest of his sex, the mildest of little men. He sidled in and out of a room, to take up the less space. He walked as softly as the Ghost in *Hamlet*, and more slowly. He carried his head on one side, partly in modest depreciation of himself, partly in modest propitiation of everybody else. It is nothing to say, that he hadn't a word to throw at a dog. He couldn't have *thrown* a word at a mad dog. He might have offered him one gently, or half a one, or a fragment of one; for he spoke as slowly as he walked; but he wouldn't have been rude to him, and he couldn't have been quick with him, for any earthly consideration.

Mr Chillip, looking mildly at my aunt, with his head on one side, and making her a little bow, said, in allusion to the jewellers' cotton, as he softly touched his left ear: 'Some local irritation, ma'am?'

'What!' replied my aunt, pulling the cotton out of one ear like a cork.

Mr Chillip was so alarmed by her abruptness – as he told my mother afterwards – that it was a mercy he didn't lose his presence of mind. But he repeated, sweetly: 'Some local irritation, ma'am?'

'Nonsense!' replied my aunt, and corked herself again, at one blow.

Mr Chillip could do nothing after this but sit and look at her feebly, as she sat and looked at the fire, until he was called upstairs again. After some quarter of an hour's absence, he returned.

'Well?' said my aunt, taking the cotton out of the ear nearest to him.

'Well, ma'am,' returned Mr Chillip, 'we are – we are progressing slowly, ma'am.'

'Ba–a–ah!' said my aunt, with a perfect shake on the contemptuous interjection. And corked herself as before.

Really – really – as Mr Chillip told my mother, he was almost shocked; speaking in a professional point of view alone he was almost shocked. But he sat and looked at her, notwithstanding, for nearly two hours, as she sat looking at the fire, until he was again called out. After another absence, he again returned.

'Well?' said my aunt, taking out the cotton on that side again.

'Well, ma'am,' returned Mr Chillip, 'we are – we are progressing slowly, ma'am.'

'Ya–a–ah!' said my aunt. With such a snarl at him, that Mr Chillip absolutely could not bear it. It was really calculated to break his spirit, he said afterwards. He preferred to go and sit upon the stairs, in the dark and a strong draught, until he was again sent for.

Ham Peggotty, who went to the national school, and was a very dragon at his catechism, and who may therefore be regarded as a credible witness, reported next day, that happening to peep in at the parlour door an hour after this, he was instantly descried by Miss Betsey, then walking to and fro in a state of agitation, and pounced upon before he could make his escape. That there were now occasional sounds of feet and voices overhead which he inferred the cotton did not exclude, from the circumstance of his evidently being clutched by the lady as a victim on whom to expend her superabundant agitation when the sounds were loudest. That, marching him constantly up and down by the collar (as if he had been taking too much laudanum), she, at those times, shook him, rumpled his hair, made light of his linen, stopped *his* ears as if she confounded them with her own, and otherwise tousled and maltreated him. This was in part confirmed by his aunt, who saw him at half-past twelve o'clock, soon after his release, and affirmed that he was then as red as I was.

The mild Mr Chillip could not possibly bear malice at such a time, if at any time. He sidled into the parlour as soon as he was at liberty, and said to my aunt in his meekest manner: 'Well, ma'am, I am happy to congratulate you.'

'What upon?' said my aunt sharply.

Mr Chillip was fluttered again, by the extreme severity of my aunt's manner; so he made her a little bow, and gave her a little smile, to mollify her.

'Mercy on the man, what's he doing!' cried my aunt impatiently. 'Can't he speak?'

'Be calm, dear ma'am,' said Mr Chillip, in his softest accents. 'There is no longer any occasion for uneasiness, ma'am. Be calm.'

It has since been considered almost a miracle that my aunt didn't shake him, and shake what he had to say out of him. She only shook her own head at him, but in a way that made him quail.

'Well, ma'am,' resumed Mr Chillip, as soon as he had courage, 'I am happy to congratulate you. All is now over, ma'am, and well over.'

During the five minutes or so that Mr Chillip devoted to the delivery of this oration my aunt eyed him narrowly.

'How is she?' said my aunt, folding her arms with her bonnet still tied on one of them.

'Well, ma'am, she will soon be quite comfortable, I hope,' returned Mr Chillip. 'Quite as comfortable as we can expect a young mother to be, under these melancholy domestic circumstances. There cannot be any objection to your seeing her presently, ma'am. It may do her good.'

'And *she*? How is *she*?' said my aunt sharply.

Mr Chillip laid his head a little more on one side, and looked at my aunt like an amiable bird.

'The baby,' said my aunt. 'How is she?'

'Ma'am,' returned Mr Chillip, 'I apprehended you had known. It's a boy.'

My aunt said never a word, but took her bonnet by the strings, in the manner of a sling, aimed a blow at Mr Chillip's head with it, put it on bent, walked out, and never came back. She vanished like a discontented fairy, or like one of those supernatural beings whom it was popularly supposed I was entitled to see, and never came back any more.

No. I lay in my basket, and my mother lay in her bed; but Betsey Trotwood Copperfield was for ever in the land of dreams and shadows, the tremendous region whence I had so lately travelled; and the light upon the window of our room shone out upon the earthly bourne of all such travellers, and the mound above the ashes and the dust that once was he, without whom I had never been.

CHAPTER 2

I Observe

The first objects that assume a distinct presence before me, as I look far back, into the blank of my infancy, are my mother with her pretty hair and youthful shape, and Peggotty with no shape at all, and eyes so dark that they seemed to darken their whole neighbourhood in her face, and cheeks and arms so hard and red that I wondered the birds didn't peck her in preference to apples.

I believe I can remember these two at a little distance apart, dwarfed to my sight by stooping down or kneeling on the floor, and I going unsteadily from the one to the other. I have an impression on my mind, which I cannot distinguish from actual remembrance, of the touch of Peggotty's forefinger as she used to hold it out to me, and of its being roughened by needlework, like a pocket nutmeg-grater.

This may be fancy, though I think the memory of most of us can go further back into such times than many of us suppose; just as I believe the power of observation in numbers of very young children to be quite wonderful for its closeness and accuracy. Indeed, I think that most grown men who are remarkable in this respect may with greater propriety be said not to have lost the faculty than to have acquired it; the rather, as I generally observe such men to retain a certain freshness, and gentleness, and capacity of being pleased, which are also an inheritance they have preserved from their childhood.

I might have a misgiving that I am 'meandering' in stopping to say this, but that it brings me to remark that I build these conclusions, in part upon my own experience of myself; and if it should appear from anything I may set down in this narrative that I was a child of close observation, or that as a man I have a strong memory of my childhood, I undoubtedly lay claim to both of these characteristics.

Looking back, as I was saying, into the blank of my infancy, the first objects I can remember as standing out by themselves from a confusion of things are my mother and Peggotty. What else do I remember? Let me see.

There comes out of the cloud, our house – not new to me, but quite familiar, in its earliest remembrance. On the ground-floor is Peggotty's kitchen, opening into a back yard; with a pigeon-house on a pole, in the centre, without any pigeons in it; a great dog-kennel in a corner, without any dog; and a quantity of fowls that look terribly tall to me, walking about, in a menacing and ferocious manner. There is one cock who gets upon a post to crow, and seems to take particular notice of me as I look at him through the kitchen window, who makes me shiver, he is so fierce. Of the geese outside the side gate who come waddling after me with their long necks stretched out when I go that way, I dream at night, as a man environed by wild beasts might dream of lions.

Here is a long passage – what an enormous perspective I make of it! – leading from Peggotty's kitchen to the front door. A dark storeroom opens out of it, and that is a place to be run past at night; for I don't know what may be among those tubs and jars and old tea-chests, when there is nobody in there with a dimly burning light, letting a mouldy air come out at the door, in which there is the smell of soap, pickles, pepper, candles, and coffee, all at one whiff. Then there are the two parlours; the parlour in which we sit of an evening, my mother and I and Peggotty – for Peggotty is quite our companion, when her work is done and we are alone – and the best parlour where we sit on a Sunday; grandly, but not so comfortably. There is something of a doleful air about that room to me, for Peggotty has told me – I don't know when, but apparently ages ago – about my father's funeral, and the company having their black cloaks put on. One Sunday night my mother reads to Peggotty and me in there, how Lazarus was raised up from the dead. And I am so frightened that they are afterwards obliged to take me out of bed, and show me the quiet churchyard out of the bedroom window, with the dead all lying in their graves at rest, below the solemn moon.

There is nothing half so green that I know anywhere as the grass of that churchyard; nothing half so shady as its trees; nothing half so quiet as its tombstones. The sheep are feeding there, when I kneel, early in the morning, in my little bed in a closet within my mother's room, to look out at it; and I see the red light shining on the sundial, and think within myself, 'Is the sundial glad, I wonder, that it can tell the time again?'

Here is our pew in the church. What a high-backed pew! With a window near it, out of which our house can be seen, and *is* seen many times during the morning's service, by Peggotty, who likes to make herself as sure as she can that it's not being robbed, or is not in flames. But though Peggotty's eye wanders, she is much offended if mine does, and frowns to me, as I stand upon the seat, that I am to look at the clergyman. But I can't always look at him – I know him without that white thing on, and I am afraid of his wondering why I stare so, and perhaps stopping the service to enquire – and what am I to do? It's a dreadful thing to gape, but I must do something. I look at my mother, but *she* pretends not to see me. I look at a boy in the aisle, and *he* makes faces at me. I look at the sunlight coming in at the open door through the porch, and there I see a stray sheep – I don't mean a sinner, but mutton – half making up his mind to come into the church. I feel that, if I looked at him any longer, I might be tempted to say something out loud; and what would become of me then! I look up at the monumental tablets on the wall, and try to think of Mr Bodgers, late of this parish, and what the feelings of Mrs Bodgers must have been, when affliction sore, long time Mr Bodgers bore, and physicians were in vain. I wonder whether they called in Mr Chillip, and he was in vain; and if so, how he likes to be reminded of it once a week. I look from Mr Chillip, in his Sunday neckcloth, to the pulpit; and think what a good place it would be to play in, and what a castle it would make, with another boy coming up the stairs to attack it, and having the velvet cushion with the tassels thrown down on his head. In time my eyes gradually shut up;

and from seeming to hear the clergyman singing a drowsy song in the heat, I hear nothing, until I fall off the seat with a crash, and am taken out, more dead than alive, by Peggotty.

And now I see the outside of our house, with the latticed bedroom windows standing open to let in the sweet-smelling air, and the ragged old rooks' nests still dangling in the elm trees at the bottom of the front garden. Now I am in the garden at the back, beyond the yard where the empty pigeon-house and dog-kennel are – a very preserve of butterflies, as I remember it, with a high fence, and a gate and padlock; where the fruit clusters on the trees, riper and richer than fruit has ever been since, in any other garden, and where my mother gathers some in a basket, while I stand by, bolting furtive gooseberries, and trying to look unmoved. A great wind rises, and the summer is gone in a moment. We are playing in the winter twilight, dancing about the parlour. When my mother is out of breath and rests herself in an elbow-chair, I watch her winding her bright curls round her fingers and straightening her waist, and nobody knows better than I do that she likes to look so well, and is proud of being so pretty.

That is among my very earliest impressions. That, and a sense that we were both a little afraid of Peggotty, and submitted ourselves in most things to her direction, were among the first opinions – if they may be so called – that I ever derived from what I saw.

Peggotty and I were sitting one night by the parlour fire, alone. I had been reading to Peggotty about crocodiles. I must have read very perspicuously, or the poor soul must have been

Our pew at church

deeply interested, for I remember she had a cloudy impression, after I had done, that they were a sort of vegetable. I was tired of reading and dead sleepy; but having leave, as a high treat, to sit up until my mother came home from spending the evening at a neighbour's, I would rather have died upon my post (of course) than have gone to bed. I had reached that stage of sleepiness when Peggotty seemed to swell and grow immensely large. I propped my eyelids open with my two forefingers, and looked perseveringly at her as she sat at work; at the little bit of wax-candle she kept for her thread – how old it looked, being so wrinkled in all directions! – at the little house with a thatched roof, where the yard-measure lived; at her work-box with a sliding lid, with a view of St Paul's Cathedral (with a pink dome) painted on the top; at the brass thimble on her finger; at herself, whom I thought lovely. I felt so sleepy that I knew if I lost sight of anything, for a moment, I was gone.

'Peggotty,' says I, suddenly, 'were you ever married?'

'Lord, Master Davy!' replied Peggotty. 'What's put marriage in your head?'

She answered with such a start that it quite awoke me. And then she stopped in her work, and looked at me, with her needle drawn out to its thread's length.

'But *were* you ever married, Peggotty?' says I. 'You are a very handsome woman, an't you?'

I thought her in a different style from my mother, certainly, but of another school of beauty, I considered her a perfect example. There was a red velvet footstool in the best parlour, on which my mother had painted a nosegay. The groundwork of that stool, and Peggotty's complexion appeared to me to be one and the same thing. The stool was smooth, and Peggotty was rough, but that made no difference.

'Me handsome, Davy!' said Peggotty. 'Lawk, no, my dear! But what put marriage in your head?'

'I don't know! – You mustn't marry more than one person at a time, may you, Peggotty?'

'Certainly not,' says Peggotty, with the promptest decision.

'But if you marry a person, and the person dies, why then you may marry another person, mayn't you, Peggotty?'

'You may,' says Peggotty, 'if you choose, my dear. That's a matter of opinion.'

'But what is your opinion, Peggotty?' said I.

I asked her and looked curiously at her, because she looked so curiously at me.

'My opinion is,' said Peggotty, taking her eyes from me, after a little indecision, and going on with her work, 'that I never was married myself, Master Davy, and that I don't expect to be. That's all I know about the subject.'

'You an't cross, I suppose, Peggotty, are you?' said I, after sitting quiet for a minute.

I really thought she was, she had been so short with me; but I was quite mistaken, for she laid aside her work (which was a stocking of her own) and, opening her arms wide, took my curly head within them, and gave it a good squeeze. I know it was a good squeeze, because, being very plump, whenever she made any little exertion after she was dressed, some of the buttons on the back of her gown flew off. And I recollect two

bursting to the opposite side of the parlour, while she was hugging me.

'Now, let me hear some more about the Crorkindills,' said Peggotty, who was not quite right in the name yet, 'for I ain't heard half enough.'

I couldn't quite understand why Peggotty looked so queer, or why she was so ready to go back to the crocodiles. However, we returned to those monsters, with fresh wakefulness on my part, and we left their eggs in the sand for the sun to hatch; and we ran away from them, and baffled them by constantly turning, which they were unable to do quickly, on account of their unwieldy make; and we went into the water after them, as natives, and put sharp pieces of timber down their throats; and in short we ran the whole crocodile gauntlet. *I* did, at least; but I had my doubts of Peggotty, who was thoughtfully sticking her needle into various parts of her face and arms, all the time.

We had exhausted the crocodiles, and begun with the alligators, when the garden-bell rang. We went out to the door; and there was my mother, looking unusually pretty, I thought, and with her a gentleman with beautiful black hair and whiskers, who had walked home with us from church last Sunday.

As my mother stooped down on the threshold to take me in her arms and kiss me, the gentleman said I was a more highly privileged little fellow than a monarch – or something like that; for my later understanding comes, I am sensible, to my aid here.

'What does that mean?' I asked him, over her shoulder.

He patted me on the head; but somehow, I didn't like him or his deep voice, and I was jealous that his hand should touch my mother's in touching me – which it did. I put it away as well as I could.

'Oh, Davy!' remonstrated my mother.

'Dear boy!' said the gentleman. 'I cannot wonder at his devotion!'

I never saw such a beautiful colour on my mother's face before. She gently chid me for being rude; and keeping me close to her shawl, turned to thank the gentleman for taking so much trouble as to bring her home. She put out her hand to him as she spoke, and, as he met it with his own, she glanced, I thought, at me.

'Let us say "good-night," my fine boy,' said the gentleman, when he had bent his head – I saw him! – over my mother's little glove.

'Good-night!' said I.

'Come! Let us be the best friends in the world!' said the gentleman, laughing. 'Shake hands!'

My right hand was in my mother's left, so I gave him the other.

'Why, that's the wrong hand, Davy!' laughed the gentleman.

My mother drew my right hand forward, but I was resolved, for my former reason, not to give it him, and I did not. I gave him the other, and he shook it heartily, and said I was a brave fellow, and went away.

At this minute I see him turn round in the garden, and give us a last look with his ill-omened black eyes, before the door was shut.

Peggotty, who had not said a word or moved a finger, secured the fastenings instantly, and we all went into the parlour. My mother, contrary to her usual habit, instead of coming to the elbow-chair by the fire, remained at the other end of the room, and sat singing to herself.

'Hope you have had a pleasant evening, ma'am,' said Peggotty, standing as stiff as a barrel in the centre of the room, with a candlestick in her hand.

'Much obliged to you, Peggotty,' returned my mother in a cheerful voice. 'I have had a *very* pleasant evening.'

'A stranger or so makes an agreeable change,' suggested Peggotty.

'A very agreeable change, indeed,' returned my mother.

Peggotty continuing to stand motionless in the middle of the room, and my mother resuming her singing, I fell asleep, though I was not so sound asleep but that I could hear voices, without hearing what they said. When I half awoke from this uncomfortable doze, I found Peggotty and my mother both in tears, and both talking.

'Not such a one as this, Mr Copperfield wouldn't have liked,' said Peggotty. 'That I say, and that I swear!'

'Good Heavens!' cried my mother, 'you'll drive me mad! Was ever any poor girl so ill-used by her servants as I am! Why do I do myself the injustice of calling myself a girl? Have I never been married, Peggotty?'

'God knows you have, ma'am,' returned Peggotty.

'Then, how can you dare,' said my mother – 'you know I don't mean how can you dare, Peggotty, but how can you have the heart – to make me so uncomfortable and say such bitter things to me, when you are well aware that I haven't, out of this place, a single friend to turn to?'

'The more's the reason,' returned Peggotty, 'for saying that it won't do. No! That it won't do. No! No price could make it do. No!' – I thought Peggotty would have thrown the candlestick away, she was so emphatic with it.

'How can you be so aggravating,' said my mother, shedding more tears than before, 'as to talk in such an unjust manner! How can you go on as if it was all settled and arranged, Peggotty, when I tell you over and over again, you cruel thing, that beyond the commonest civilities nothing has passed! You talk of admiration. What am I to do? If people are so silly as to indulge the sentiment, is it my fault? What am I to do, I ask you? Would you wish me to shave my head and black my face, or disfigure myself with a burn, or a scald, or something of that sort? I dare say you would, Peggotty. I dare say you'd quite enjoy it.'

Peggotty seemed to take this aspersion very much to heart, I thought.

'And my dear boy,' cried my mother, coming to the elbow-chair in which I was, and caressing me, 'my own little Davy! Is it to be hinted to me that I am wanting in affection for my precious treasure, the dearest little fellow that ever was!'

'Nobody never went and hinted no such a thing,' said Peggotty.

'You did, Peggotty!' returned my mother. 'You know you did. What else was it possible to infer from what you said, you unkind creature, when you know, as well as I do, that on his account only last quarter I wouldn't buy myself a new parasol, though that old green one is frayed the whole way up, and the fringe is perfectly mangy. You know it is, Peggotty. You can't deny it.' Then, turning affectionately to me, with her cheek against mine, 'Am I a naughty mama to you, Davy? Am I a nasty, cruel, selfish, bad mama? Say I am, my child; say "yes," dear boy, and Peggoty will love you, and Peggotty's love is a great deal better than mine, Davy. *I* don't love you at all, do I?'

At this, we all fell a-crying together. I think I was the loudest of the party, but I am sure we were all sincere about it. I was quite heartbroken myself, and am afraid that in the first transports of wounded tenderness I called Peggotty a 'Beast.' That honest creature was in deep affliction, I remember, and must have become quite buttonless on the occasion; for a little volley of those explosives went off, when, after having made it up with my mother, she kneeled down by the elbow-chair, and made it up with me.

We went to bed greatly dejected. My sobs kept waking me, for a long time; and when one very strong sob quite hoisted me up in bed, I found my mother sitting on the coverlet, and leaning over me. I fell asleep in her arms, after that, and slept soundly.

Whether it was the following Sunday when I saw the gentleman again, or whether there was any greater lapse of time before he reappeared, I cannot recall. I don't profess to be clear about dates. But there he was, in church, and he walked home with us afterwards. He came in, too, to look at a famous geranium we had, in the parlour window. It did not appear to me that he took much notice of it, but before he went he asked my mother to give him a bit of the blossom. She begged him to choose it for himself, but he refused to do that – I could not understand why – so she plucked it for him, and gave it into his hand. He said he would never, never, part with it any more; and I thought he must be quite a fool not to know that it would fall to pieces in a day or two.

Peggotty began to be less with us, of an evening, than she had always been. My mother deferred to her very much – more than usual, it occurred to me – and we were all three excellent friends; still we were different from what we used to be, and were not so comfortable among ourselves. Sometimes I fancied that Peggotty perhaps objected to my mother's wearing all the pretty dresses she had in her drawers, or to her going so often to visit at that neighbour's; but I couldn't, to my satisfaction, make out how it was.

Gradually, I became used to seeing the gentleman with the black whiskers. I liked him no better than at first, and had the same uneasy jealousy of him; but if I had any reason for it beyond a child's instinctive dislike, and a general idea that Peggotty and I could make much of my mother without any help, it certainly was not *the* reason that I might have found if I had been older. No such thing came into my mind, or near it. I could observe, in little pieces, as it were; but as to making a net of a number of these pieces, and catching anybody in it, that was, as yet, beyond me.

One autumn morning I was with my mother in the front

garden, when Mr Murdstone – I knew him by that name now – came by, on horseback. He reined up his horse to salute my mother, and said he was going to Lowestoft to see some friends who were there with a yacht, and merrily proposed to take me on the saddle before him if I would like the ride.

The air was so clear and pleasant, and the horse seemed to like the idea of the ride so much himself, as he stood snorting and pawing at the garden gate, that I had a great desire to go. So I was sent upstairs to Peggotty to be made spruce; and in the mean time Mr Murdstone dismounted, and, with his horse's bridle drawn over his arm, walked slowly up and down on the outer side of the sweetbriar fence, while my mother walked slowly up and down on the inner to keep him company. I recollect Peggotty and I peeping out at them from my little window; I recollect how closely they appeared to be examining the sweetbriar between them, as they strolled along; and how, from being in a perfectly angelic temper, Peggotty turned cross in a moment, and brushed my hair the wrong way, excessively hard.

Mr Murdstone and I were soon off, and trotting along on the green turf by the side of the road. He held me quite easily with one arm, and I don't think I was restless usually; but I could not make up my mind to sit in front of him without turning my head sometimes, and looking up in his face. He had that kind of shallow black eye – I want a better word to express an eye that has no depth in it to be looked into – which, when it is abstracted, seems from some peculiarity of light to be disfigured, for a moment at a time, by a cast. Several times when I glanced at him, I observed that appearance with a sort of awe, and wondered what he was thinking about so closely. His hair and whiskers were blacker and thicker, looked at so near, than even I had given them credit for being. A squareness about the lower part of his face, and the dotted indication of the strong black beard he shaved close every day, reminded me of the waxwork that had travelled into our neighbourhood some half a year before. This, his regular eyebrows, and the rich white, and black, and brown of his complexion – confound his complexion, and his memory! – made me think him, in spite of my misgivings, a very handsome man. I have no doubt that my poor dear mother thought him so, too.

We went to an hotel by the sea, where two gentlemen were smoking cigars in a room by themselves. Each of them was lying on at least four chairs, and had a large rough jacket on. In a corner was a heap of coats and boat-cloaks, and a flag, all bundled up together.

They both rolled on to their feet in an untidy sort of manner when we came in, and said 'Halloa, Murdstone! We thought you were dead!'

'Not yet,' said Mr Murdstone.

'And who's this shaver?' said one of the gentlemen, taking hold of me.

'That's Davy,' returned Mr Murdstone.

'Davy who?' said the gentleman. 'Jones?'

'Copperfield,' said Mr Murdstone.

'What! Bewitching Mrs Copperfield's encumbrance?' cried the gentleman. 'The pretty little widow?'

'Quinion,' said Mr Murdstone, 'take care, if you please. Somebody's sharp.'

'Who is?' asked the gentleman, laughing.

I looked up quickly; being curious to know.

'Only Brooks of Sheffield,' said Mr Murdstone.

I was quite relieved to find it was only Brooks of Sheffield, for, at first, I really thought it was I.

There seemed to be something very comical in the reputation of Mr Brooks of Sheffield, for both the gentlemen laughed heartily when he was mentioned, and Mr Murdstone was a good deal amused also. After some laughing, the gentleman whom he had called Quinion said: 'And what is the opinion of Brooks of Sheffield, in reference to the projected business?'

'Why, I don't know that Brooks understands much about it at present,' replied Mr Murdstone; 'but he is not generally favourable, I believe.'

There was more laughter at this, and Mr Quinion said he would ring the bell for some sherry in which to drink to Brooks. This he did; and when the wine came, he made me have a little, with a biscuit, and, before I drank it, stand up and say 'Confusion to Brooks of Sheffield!' The toast was received with great applause, and such hearty laughter that it made me laugh too; at which they laughed the more. In short, we quite enjoyed ourselves.

We walked about on the cliff after that, and sat on the grass, and looked at things through a telescope – I could make out nothing myself when it was put to my eye, but I pretended I could – and then we came back to the hotel to an early dinner. All the time we were out, the two gentlemen smoked incessantly – which, I thought, if I might judge from the smell of their rough coats, they must have been doing ever since the coats had first come home from the tailor's. I must not forget that we went on board the yacht, where they all three descended into the cabin, and were busy with some papers. I saw them quite hard at work, when I looked down through the open skylight. They left me, during this time, with a very nice man with a very large head of red hair and a very small shiny hat upon it, who had got a cross-barred shirt or waistcoat on, with 'Skylark' in capital letters across the chest. I thought it was his name; and that as he lived on board ship and hadn't a street door to put his name on, he put it there instead; but when I called him Mr Skylark, he said it meant the vessel.

I observed all day that Mr Murdstone was graver and steadier than the two gentlemen. They were very gay and careless. They joked freely with one another, but seldom with him. It appeared to me that he was more clever and cold than they were, and that they regarded him with something of my own feeling. I remarked that once or twice, when Mr Quinion was talking, he looked at Mr Murdstone sideways, as if to make sure of his not being displeased; and that once, when Mr Passnidge (the other gentleman) was in high spirits, he trod upon his foot, and gave him a secret caution with his eyes to observe Mr Murdstone, who was sitting stern and silent. Nor do I recollect that Mr Murdstone laughed at all that day, except at the Sheffield joke – and that, by the by, was his own.

We went home early in the evening. It was a very fine evening, and my mother and he had another stroll by the sweetbriar, while I was sent in to get my tea. When he was gone, my mother asked me all about the day I had had, and what they had said and done. I mentioned what they had said about her, and she laughed, and told me they were impudent fellows who talked nonsense – but I knew it pleased her. I knew it quite as well as I know it now. I took the opportunity of asking if she was at all acquainted with Mr Brooks of Sheffield, but she answered No, only she supposed he must be a manufacturer in the knife and fork way.

Can I say of her face – altered as I have reason to remember it, perished as I know it is – that it is gone, when here it comes before me at this instant, as distinct as any face that I may choose to look on in a crowded street? Can I say of her innocent and girlish beauty that it faded, and was no more, when its breath falls on my cheek now, as it fell that night? Can I say she ever changed, when my remembrance brings her back to life, thus only; and, truer to its loving youth than I have been, or man ever is, still holds fast what it cherished then?

I write of her just as she was when I had gone to bed after this talk, and she came to bid me good-night. She kneeled down playfully by the side of the bed, and laying her chin upon her hands, and laughing, said: 'What was it they said, Davy? Tell me again. I can't believe it.'

' "Bewitching – " ' I began.

My mother put her hands upon my lips to stop me.

'It was never bewitching,' she said, laughing. 'It never could have been bewitching, Davy. Now I know it wasn't!'

'Yes it was. "Bewitching Mrs Copperfield," ' I repeated stoutly. 'And "pretty." '

'No, no, it was never pretty; not pretty,' interposed my mother, laying her fingers on my lips again.

'Yes it was. "Pretty little widow." '

'What foolish, impudent creatures!' cried my mother, laughing and covering her face. 'What ridiculous men! An't they? Davy, dear –'

'Well, Ma.'

'Don't tell Peggotty; she might be angry with them. I am dreadfully angry with them myself; but I would rather Peggotty didn't know.'

I promised, of course; and we kissed one another over and over again, and I soon fell fast asleep.

It seems to me, at this distance of time, as if it were the next day when Peggotty broached the striking and adventurous proposition I am about to mention; but it was probably about two months afterwards.

We were sitting as before, one evening (when my mother was out as before), in company with the stocking and the yard-measure, and the bit of wax, and the box with St Paul's on the lid, and the crocodile book, when Peggotty, after looking at me several times, and opening her mouth as if she were going to speak, without doing it – which I thought was merely gaping, or I should have been rather alarmed – said coaxingly: 'Master Davy, how should you like to go along with me and spend a fortnight at my brother's at Yarmouth? Wouldn't *that* be a treat?'

'Is your brother an agreeable man, Peggotty?' I enquired, provisionally.

'Oh, what an agreeable man he is!' cried Peggotty, holding up her hands. 'Then there's the sea; and the boats and ships; and the fishermen; and the beach; and Am to play with – '

Peggotty meant her nephew Ham, mentioned in my first chapter; but she spoke of him as a morsel of English Grammar.

I was flushed by her summary of delights, and replied that it would indeed be a treat, but what would my mother say?

'Why then I'll as good as bet a guinea,' said Peggotty, intent upon my face, 'that she'll let us go. I'll ask her, if you like, as soon as ever she comes home. There now!'

'But what's she to do while we're away?' said I, putting my small elbows on the table to argue the point. 'She can't live by herself.'

If Peggotty were looking for a hole, all of a sudden, in the heel of that stocking, it must have been a very little one indeed, and not worth darning.

'I say! Peggotty! She can't live by herself, you know.'

'Oh, bless you!' said Peggotty, looking at me again at last. 'Don't you know? She's going to stay for a fortnight with Mrs Grayper. Mrs Grayper's going to have a lot of company.'

Oh! If that was it, I was quite ready to go. I waited, in the utmost impatience, until my mother came home from Mrs Grayper's (for it was that identical neighbour), to ascertain if we could get leave to carry out this great idea. Without being nearly so much surprised as I had expected, my mother entered into it readily; and it was all arranged that night, and my board and lodging during the visit were to be paid for.

The day soon came for our going. It was such an early day that it came soon, even to me, who was in a fever of expectation and half afraid that an earthquake or a fiery mountain, or some other great convulsion of nature, might interpose to stop the expedition. We were to go in a carrier's cart, which departed in the morning after breakfast. I would have given any money to have been allowed to wrap myself up overnight, and sleep in my hat and boots.

It touches me nearly now, although I tell it lightly, to recollect how eager I was to leave my happy home; to think how little I suspected what I did leave for ever.

I am glad to recollect that when the carrier's cart was at the gate, and my mother stood there kissing me, a grateful fondness for her and for the old place I had never turned my back upon before, made me cry. I am glad to know that my mother cried, too, and that I felt her heart beat against mine.

I am glad to recollect that, when the carrier began to move, my mother ran out at the gate, and called to him to stop, that she might kiss me once more. I am glad to dwell upon the earnestness and love with which she lifted up her face to mine, and did so.

As we left her standing in the road, Mr Murdstone came up to where she was, and seemed to expostulate with her for being so moved. I was looking back round the awning of the cart, and wondered what business it was of his. Peggotty, who was also looking back on the other side, seemed anything but satisfied; as the face she brought back into the cart denoted.

I sat looking at Peggotty for some time, in a reverie on this supposititious case; whether, if she were employed to lose me like the boy in the fairy tale, I should be able to track my way home again by the buttons she would shed.

CHAPTER 3

I Have a Change

The carrier's horse was the laziest horse in the world, I should hope, and shuffled along, with his head down, as if he liked to keep the people waiting to whom the packages were directed. I fancied, indeed, that he sometimes chuckled audibly over this reflection, but the carrier said he was only troubled with a cough.

The carrier had a way of keeping his head down, like his horse, and of drooping sleepily forward as he drove, with one of his arms on each of his knees. I say 'drove,' but it struck me that the cart would have gone to Yarmouth quite as well without him, for the horse did all that; and as to conversation, he had no idea of it but whistling.

Peggotty had a basket of refreshments on her knee, which would have lasted us out handsomely, if we had been going to London by the same conveyance. We ate a good deal, and slept a good deal. Peggotty always went to sleep with her chin upon the handle of the basket, her hold of which never relaxed; and I could not have believed, unless I had heard her do it, that one defenceless woman could have snored so much.

We made so many deviations up and down lanes, and were such a long time delivering a bedstead at a public-house, and calling at other places, that I was quite tired, and very glad, when we saw Yarmouth. It looked rather spongy and soppy, I thought, as I carried my eye over the great dull waste that lay across the river; and I could not help wondering, if the world were really as round as my geography book said, how any part of it came to be so flat. But I reflected that Yarmouth might be situated at one of the poles; which would account for it.

As we drew a little nearer, and saw the whole adjacent prospect lying a straight low line under the sky, I hinted to Peggotty that a mound or so might have improved it; and also that if the land had been a little more separated from the sea, and the town and the tide had not been quite so much mixed up, like toast and water, it would have been nicer. But Peggotty said, with greater emphasis than usual, that we must take things as we found them, and that for her part, she was proud to call herself a Yarmouth Bloater.

When we got into the street (which was strange enough to me), and smelt the fish, and pitch, and oakum, and tar, and saw the sailors walking about, and the carts jingling up and down over the stones, I felt that I had done so busy a place an injustice; and said as much to Peggotty, who heard my expressions of delight with great complacency, and told me it was well known (I suppose to those who had the good fortune to be born Bloaters) that Yarmouth was, upon the whole, the finest place in the universe.

'Here's my Am!' screamed Peggotty, 'growed out of knowledge!'

He was waiting for us, in fact, at the public-house; and asked me how I found myself, like an old acquaintance. I did not feel, at first, that I knew him as well as he knew me, because he had never come to our house since the night I was born, and naturally he had the advantage of me. But our intimacy was much advanced by his taking me on his back to carry me home. He was, now, a huge, strong fellow of six feet high, broad in proportion, and round-shouldered; but with a simpering boy's face and curly light hair that gave him quite a sheepish look. He was dressed in a canvas jacket, and a pair of such very stiff trousers that they would have stood quite as well alone, without any legs in them. And you couldn't so properly have said he wore a hat, as that he was covered in a-top, like an old building, with something pitchy.

Ham carrying me on his back and a small box of ours under his arm, and Peggotty carrying another small box of ours, we turned down lanes bestrewn with bits of chips and little hillocks of sand, and went past gasworks, rope-walks, boat-builders' yards, shipwrights' yards, ship-breakers' yards, caulkers' yards, riggers' lofts, smiths' forges, and a great litter of such places, until we came out upon the dull waste I had already seen at a distance, when Ham said: 'Yon's our house, Mas'r Davy!'

I looked in all directions, as far as I could stare over the wilderness, and away at the sea, and away at the river, but no house could *I* make out. There was a black barge, or some other kind of superannuated boat, not far off, high and dry on the ground, with an iron funnel sticking out of it for a chimney and smoking very cosily; but nothing else in the way of a habitation that was visible to *me*.

'That's not it?' said I. 'That ship-looking thing?'

'That's it, Mas'r Davy,' returned Ham.

If it had been Aladdin's palace, roc's egg and all, I suppose I could not have been more charmed with the romantic idea of living in it. There was a delightful door cut in the side, and it was roofed in, and there were little windows in it; but the wonderful charm of it was, that it was a real boat which had no doubt been upon the water hundreds of times, and which had never been intended to be lived in, on dry land. That was the captivation of it to me. If it had ever been meant to be lived in, I might have thought it small, or inconvenient, or lonely; but never having been designed for any such use, it became a perfect abode.

It was beautifully clean inside, and as tidy as possible. There was a table, and a Dutch clock, and a chest of drawers, and on the chest of drawers there was a tea-tray with a painting on it of a lady with a parasol, taking a walk with a military-looking child who was trundling a hoop. The tray was kept from tumbling down by a Bible; and the tray, if it had tumbled down, would have smashed a quantity of cups and saucers and a teapot, that were grouped around the book. On the walls there were some common coloured pictures, framed and glazed, of Scripture subjects; such as I have never seen since in the hands of pedlars, without seeing the whole interior of Peggotty's brother's house again, at one view. Abraham in red going to sacrifice Isaac in blue, and Daniel in yellow cast into a den of green lions, were the most prominent of these. Over the little mantelshelf was a picture of the *Sarah Jane* lugger, built at Sunderland, with a real little wooden stern stuck on to it; a work of art, combining composition with carpentry, which I considered to be one of the most enviable possessions that the world could afford. There were some hooks in the beams of the ceiling, the use of which I did not divine then; and some lockers and boxes and conveniences of that sort, which served for seats and eked out the chairs.

All this I saw in the first glance after I crossed the threshold – childlike, according to my theory – and then Peggotty opened a little door and showed me my bedroom. It was the completest and most desirable bedroom ever seen – in the stern of the vessel; with a little window, where the rudder used to go through; a little looking-glass, just the right height for me, nailed against the wall, and framed with oyster-shells; a little bed, which there was just room enough to get into; and a nosegay of seaweed in a blue mug on the table. The walls were whitewashed as white as milk, and the patchwork counterpane made my eyes quite ache with its brightness. One thing I particularly noticed in this delightful house was the smell of fish; which was so searching, that when I took out my pocket-handkerchief to wipe my nose, I found it smelt exactly as if it had wrapped up a lobster. On my imparting this discovery in confidence to Peggotty, she informed me that her brother dealt in lobsters, crabs, and crawfish; and I afterwards found that a heap of these creatures, in a state of wonderful conglomeration with one another, and never leaving off pinching whatever they laid hold of, were usually to be found in a little wooden outhouse where the pots and kettles were kept.

We were welcomed by a very civil woman in a white apron, whom I had seen curtseying at the door when I was on Ham's back, about a quarter of a mile off. Likewise by a most beautiful little girl (or I thought her so) with a necklace of blue beads on, who wouldn't let me kiss her when I offered to, but ran away and hid herself. By and by, when we had dined in a sumptuous manner off boiled dabs, melted butter, and potatoes, with a chop for me, a hairy man with a very good-natured face came home. As he called Peggotty 'Lass,' and gave her a hearty smack on the cheek, I had no doubt, from the general propriety of her conduct, that he was her brother; and so he turned out – being presently introduced to me as Mr Peggotty, the master of the house.

'Glad to see you, sir,' said Mr Peggotty. 'You'll find us rough, sir, but you'll find us ready.'

I thanked him and replied that I was sure I should be happy in such a delightful place.

'How's your ma, sir?' said Mr Peggotty. 'Did you leave her pretty jolly?'

I gave Mr Peggotty to understand that she was as jolly as I could wish, and that she desired her compliments – which was a polite fiction on my part.

'I'm much obleeged to her, I'm sure,' said Mr Peggotty. 'Well, sir, if you can make out here, for a fortnut, 'long wi' her,' nodding at his sister, 'and Ham, and little Em'ly, we shall be proud of your company.'

Having done the honours of his house in this hospitable manner, Mr Peggotty went out to wash himself in a kettleful of hot water, remarking that 'cold would never get *his* muck off.' He soon returned, greatly improved in appearance; but so rubicund, that I couldn't help thinking his face had this in common with the lobsters, crabs, and crawfish – that it went into the hot water very black, and came out very red.

After tea, when the door was shut and all was made snug

I am hospitably received by Mr Peggotty

(the nights being cold and misty now), it seemed to me the most delicious retreat that the imagination of man could conceive. To hear the wind getting up out at sea, to know that the fog was creeping over the desolate flat outside, and to look at the fire, and think that there was no house near but this one, and this one a boat, was like enchantment. Little Em'ly had overcome her shyness, and was sitting by my side upon the lowest and least of the lockers, which was just large enough for us two, and just fitted into the chimney corner. Mrs Peggotty, with the white apron, was knitting on the opposite side of the fire. Peggotty at her needlework was as much at home with Saint Paul's and the bit of wax candle, as if they had never known any other roof. Ham, who had been giving me my first lesson in all-fours, was trying to recollect a scheme of telling fortunes with the dirty cards, and was printing off fishy impressions of his thumb on all the cards he turned. Mr Peggotty was smoking his pipe. I felt it was a time for conversation and confidence.

'Mr Peggotty!' says I.

'Sir,' says he.

'Did you give your son the name of Ham, because you lived in a sort of ark?'

Mr Peggotty seemed to think it a deep idea, but answered: 'No, sir. I never giv him no name.'

'Who gave him that name, then?' said I, putting question number two of the catechism to Mr Peggotty.

'Why, sir, his father giv it him,' said Mr Peggotty.

'I thought you were his father!'

'My brother Joe was *his* father,' said Mr Peggotty.

'Dead, Mr Peggotty?' I hinted, after a respectful pause.

'Drowndead,' said Mr Peggotty.

I was very much surprised that Mr Peggotty was not Ham's father, and began to wonder whether I was mistaken about his relationship to anybody else there. I was so curious to know, that I made up my mind to have it out with Mr Peggotty.

'Little Em'ly,' I said, glancing at her. 'She is your daughter, isn't she, Mr Peggotty?'

'No, sir. My brother-in-law, Tom, was *her* father.'

I couldn't help it. 'Dead, Mr Peggotty?' I hinted, after another respectful silence.

'Drowndead,' said Mr Peggotty.

I felt the difficulty of resuming the subject, but had not got to the bottom of it yet, and must get to the bottom somehow. So I said: 'Haven't you *any* children, Mr Peggotty?'

'No, master,' he answered, with a short laugh. 'I'm a bacheldore.'

'A bachelor!' I said astonished. 'Why, who's that, Mr Peggotty?' Pointing to the person in the apron who was knitting.

'That's Missis Gummidge,' said Mr Peggotty.

'Gummidge, Mr Peggotty?'

But at this point Peggotty – I mean my own peculiar Peggotty – made such impressive motions to me not to ask any more questions, that I could only sit and look at all the silent company, until it was time to go to bed. Then, in the privacy of my own little cabin, she informed me that Ham and Em'ly were an orphan nephew and niece, whom my host had at different times adopted in their childhood, when they were left destitute; and that Mrs Gummidge was the widow of his partner in a boat, who had died very poor. He was but a poor man himself, said Peggotty, but as good as gold and as true as steel – those were her similes. The only subject, she informed me, on which he ever showed a violent temper or swore an oath, was this generosity of his; and if it were ever referred to, by any one of them, he struck the table a heavy blow with his right hand (had split it on one such occasion), and swore a dreadful oath that he would be 'Gormed' if he didn't cut and run for good, if it was ever mentioned again. It appeared, in answer to my enquiries, that nobody had the least idea of the etymology of this terrible verb passive to be gormed; but they all regarded it as constituting a most solemn imprecation.

I was very sensible of my entertainer's goodness, and listened to the women's going to bed in another little crib like mine at the opposite end of the boat, and to him and Ham hanging up two hammocks for themselves on the hooks I had noticed in the roof, in a very luxurious state of mind, enhanced by my being sleepy. As slumber gradually stole upon me, I heard the wind howling out at sea and coming on across the flat so fiercely, that I had a lazy apprehension of the great deep rising in the night. But I bethought myself that I was in a boat, after all; and that a man like Mr Peggotty was not a bad person to have on board if anything did happen.

Nothing happened, however, worse than morning. Almost as soon as it shone upon the oyster-shell frame of my mirror I was out of bed, and out with little Em'ly, picking up stones upon the beach.

'You're quite a sailor, I suppose?' I said to Em'ly. I don't know that I supposed anything of the kind, but I felt it an act of gallantry to say something; and a shining sail close to us made such a pretty little image of itself, at the moment, in her bright eye, that it came into my head to say this.

'No,' replied Em'ly, shaking her head, 'I'm afraid of the sea.'

'Afraid!' I said, with a becoming air of boldness, and looking very big at the mighty ocean. '*I* ain't!'

'Ah! but it's cruel,' said Em'ly. 'I have seen it very cruel to some of our men. I have seen it tear a boat as big as our house all to pieces.'

'I hope it wasn't the boat that – '

'That father was drownded in?' said Em'ly. 'No. Not that one; I never see that boat.'

'Nor him?' I asked her.

Little Em'ly shook her head. 'Not to remember!'

Here was a coincidence! I immediately went into an explanation how I had never seen my own father; and how my mother and I had always lived by ourselves in the happiest state imaginable, and lived so then, and always meant to live so; and how my father's grave was in the churchyard near our house, and shaded by a tree, beneath the boughs of which I had walked and heard the birds sing many a pleasant morning. But there were some differences between Em'ly's orphanhood and mine, it appeared. She had lost her mother before her father; and where her father's grave was no one knew, except that it was somewhere in the depths of the sea.

'Besides,' said Em'ly, as she looked about for shells and pebbles, 'your father was a gentleman and your mother is a lady; and my father was a fisherman and my mother was a fisherman's daughter, and my Uncle Dan is a fisherman.'

'Dan is Mr Peggotty, is he?' said I.

'Uncle Dan – yonder,' answered Em'ly, nodding at the boat-house.

'Yes. I mean him. He must be very good, I should think?'

'Good?' said Em'ly. 'If I was ever to be a lady, I'd give him a sky-blue coat with diamond buttons, nankeen trousers, a red velvet waistcoat, a cocked hat, a large gold watch, a silver pipe, and a box of money.'

I said I had no doubt that Mr Peggotty well deserved these treasures. I must acknowledge that I felt it difficult to picture him quite at his ease in the raiment proposed for him by his grateful little niece, and that I was particularly doubtful of the policy of the cocked hat; but I kept these sentiments to myself.

Little Em'ly had stopped and looked up at the sky in her enumeration of these articles, as if they were a glorious vision. We went on again, picking up shells and pebbles.

'You would like to be a lady?' I said.

Em'ly looked at me and laughed, and nodded 'Yes.'

'I should like it very much. We would all be gentlefolks together, then. Me, and uncle, and Ham, and Mrs Gummidge. We wouldn't mind then, when there come stormy weather. Not for our own sakes, I mean. We would for the poor fishermen's, to be sure, and we'd help 'em with money when they come to any hurt.'

This seemed to be a very satisfactory and therefore not at all improbable picture. I expressed my pleasure in the contemplation of it, and little Em'ly was emboldened to say, shyly: 'Don't you think you are afraid of the sea, now?'

It was quiet enough to reassure me, but I have no doubt if I had seen a moderately large wave come tumbling in, I should have taken to my heels, with an awful recollection of her drowned relations. However, I said, 'No,' and I added, 'You don't seem to be, either, though you say you are;' for she was walking much too near the brink of a sort of old jetty or wooden causeway we had strolled upon, and I was afraid of her falling over.

'I'm not afraid in this way,' said little Em'ly. 'But I wake when it blows, and tremble to think of Uncle Dan and Ham, and believe I hear 'em crying out for help. That's why I should like so much to be a lady. But I'm not afraid in this way. Not a bit. Look here!'

She started from my side, and ran along a jagged timber which protruded from the place we stood upon, and overhung the deep water at some height, without the least defence. The incident is so impressed on my remembrance, that if I were a draughtsman I could draw its form here, I dare say, accurately as it was that day, and little Em'ly springing forward to her destruction (as it appeared to me), with a look that I have never forgotten, directed far out to sea.

The light, bold, fluttering little figure turned and came back safe to me, and I soon laughed at my fears, and at the cry I had uttered; fruitlessly in any case, for there was no one near. But there have been times since, in my manhood, many times there have been, when I have thought, Is it possible, among the possibilities of hidden things, that in the sudden rashness of the child and her wild look so far off there was any merciful attraction of her into danger, any tempting her towards him permitted on the part of her dead father, that her life might have a chance of ending that day? There has been a time since when I have wondered whether, if the life before her could have been revealed to me at a glance, and so revealed as that a child could fully comprehend it, and if her preservation could have depended on a motion of my hand, I ought to have held it up to save her. There has been a time since – I do not say it lasted long, but it has been – when I have asked myself the question, Would it have been better for little Em'ly to have had the waters close above her head that morning in my sight? and when I have answered, Yes, it would have been.

This may be premature. I have set it down too soon, perhaps. But let it stand.

We strolled a long way, and loaded ourselves with things that we thought curious, and put some stranded starfish carefully back into the water – I hardly know enough of the race at this moment to be quite certain whether they had reason to feel obliged to us for doing so, or the reverse – and then made our way home to Mr Peggotty's dwelling. We stopped under the lee of the lobster-outhouse to exchange an innocent kiss, and went into breakfast glowing with health and pleasure.

'Like two young mavishes,' Mr Peggotty said. I knew this meant, in our local dialect, like two young thrushes, and received it as a compliment.

Of course I was in love with little Em'ly. I am sure I loved that baby quite as truly, quite as tenderly, with greater purity and more disinterestedness, than can enter into the best love of a later time of life, high and ennobling as it is. I am sure my fancy raised up something round that blue-eyed mite of a child, which etherealised, and made a very angel of her. If, any sunny forenoon, she had spread a little pair of wings and flown away before my eyes, I don't think I should have regarded it as much more than I had reason to expect.

We used to walk about that dim old flat at Yarmouth in a loving manner, hours and hours. The days sported by us, as if Time had not grown up himself yet, but were a child too, and always at play. I told Em'ly I adored her, and that unless she confessed she adored me I should be reduced to the necessity of killing myself with a sword. She said she did, and I have no doubt she did.

As to any sense of inequality, or youthfulness, or other difficulty in our way, little Em'ly and I had no such trouble, because we had no future. We made no more provision for growing older than we did for growing younger. We were the admiration of Mrs Gummidge and Peggotty, who used to whisper of an evening when we sat, lovingly, on our little locker side by side, 'Lor! wasn't it beautiful!' Mr Peggotty smiled at us from behind his pipe, and Ham grinned all the evening and did nothing else. They had something of the sort of pleasure in us, I suppose, they might have had in a pretty toy, or a pocket model of the Colosseum.

I soon found out that Mrs Gummidge did not always make herself so agreeable as she might have been expected to do, under the circumstances of her residence with Mr Peggotty. Mrs Gummidge's was rather a fretful disposition, and she whimpered more sometimes than was comfortable for other parties in so small an establishment. I was very sorry for her; but there were moments when it would have been more agreeable, I thought, if Mrs Gummidge had had a convenient apartment of her own to retire to, and had stopped there until her spirits revived.

Mr Peggotty went occasionally to a public-house called 'The Willing Mind.' I discovered this by his being out on the second or third evening of our visit, and by Mrs Gummidge's looking up at the Dutch clock, between eight and nine, and saying he was there, and that, what was more, she had known in the morning he would go there.

Mrs Gummidge had been in a low state all day, and had burst into tears in the forenoon, when the fire smoked. 'I am a lone lorn creetur,' were Mrs Gummidge's words, when that unpleasant occurrence took place, 'and everythink goes contrairy with me.'

'Oh, it'll soon leave off,' said Peggotty – I again mean our Peggotty – 'and besides, you know, it's not more disagreeable to you than to us.'

'I feel it more,' said Mrs Gummidge.

It was a very cold day, with cutting blasts of wind. Mrs Gummidge's peculiar corner of the fireside seemed to me to be the warmest and snuggest in the place, as her chair was certainly the easiest, but it didn't suit her that day at all. She was constantly complaining of the cold, and of its occasioning a visitation in her back which she called 'the creeps.' At last she shed tears on that subject, and said again that she was 'a lone lorn creetur, and everythink went contrairy with her.'

'It is certainly very cold,' said Peggotty. 'Everybody must feel it so.'

'I feel it more than other people,' said Mrs Gummidge.

So at dinner, when Mrs Gummidge was always helped immediately after me, to whom the preference was given as a visitor of distinction. The fish were small and bony, and the potatoes were a little burnt. We all acknowledged that we felt this something of a disappointment; but Mrs Gummidge said she felt it more than we did, and shed tears again, and made that former declaration with great bitterness.

Accordingly, when Mr Peggotty came home about nine o'clock, this unfortunate Mrs Gummidge was knitting in her corner in a very wretched and miserable condition. Peggotty had been working cheerfully. Ham had been patching up a great pair of water-boots; and I, with little Em'ly by my side, had been reading to them. Mrs Gummidge had never made any other remark than a forlorn sigh, and had never raised her eyes since tea.

'Well, Mates,' said Mr Peggotty, taking his seat, 'and how are you?'

We all said something, or looked something, to welcome him, except Mrs Gummidge, who only shook her head over her knitting.

'What's amiss?' said Mr Peggotty, with a clap of his hands. 'Cheer up, old Mawther!' (Mr Peggotty meant old girl.)

Mrs Gummidge did not appear to be able to cheer up. She took out an old black silk handkerchief and wiped her eyes; but instead of putting it in her pocket, kept it out, and wiped them again, and still kept it out, ready for use.

'What's amiss, dame?' said Mr Peggotty.

'Nothing,' returned Mrs Gummidge. 'You've come from "The Willing Mind", Dan'l?'

'Why yes, I've took a short spell at "The Willing Mind" tonight,' said Mr Peggotty.

'I'm sorry I should drive you there,' said Mrs Gummidge.

'Drive! I don't want no driving,' returned Mr Peggotty, with an honest laugh. 'I only go too ready.'

'Very ready,' said Mrs Gummidge, shaking her head, and wiping her eyes. 'Yes, yes, very ready. I am sorry it should be along of me that you're so ready.'

'Along o' you? It an't along o' you!' said Mr Peggotty. 'Don't ye believe a bit on it.'

'Yes, yes, it is,' cried Mrs Gummidge. 'I know what I am. I know that I am a lone, lorn creetur, and not only that everythink goes contrairy with me, but that I go contrairy with everybody. Yes, yes. I feel more than other people do, and I show it more. It's my misfortun'.'

I really couldn't help thinking, as I sat taking in all this, that the misfortune extended to some other members of that family besides Mrs Gummidge. But Mr Peggotty made no such retort, only answering with another entreaty to Mrs Gummidge to cheer up.

'I an't what I could wish myself to be,' said Mrs Gummidge. 'I am far from it. I know what I am. My troubles has made me contrairy. I feel my troubles, and they make me contrairy. I wish I didn't feel 'em, but I do. I wish I could be hardened to 'em, but I an't. I make the house uncomfortable. I don't wonder at it. I've made your sister so all day, and Master Davy.'

Here I was suddenly melted, and roared out, 'No, you haven't, Mrs Gummidge,' in great mental distress.

'It's far from right that I should do it,' said Mrs Gummidge. 'It an't a fit return. I had better go into the house and die. I am a lone, lorn creetur, and had much better not make myself contrairy here. If things must go contrairy with me, and I must go contrairy myself, let me go contrairy in my parish. Dan'l, I'd better go into the house, and die and be a riddance!'

Mrs Gummidge retired with these words, and betook herself to bed. When she was gone, Mr Peggotty, who had not exhibited a trace of any feeling but the profoundest sympathy, looked round upon us, and nodding his head with a lively expression of that sentiment still animating his face, said in a whisper: 'She's been thinking of the old 'un!'

I did not quite understand what old one Mrs Gummidge was supposed to have fixed her mind upon, until Peggotty, on seeing me to bed, explained that it was the late Mr Gummidge; and that her brother always took that for a received truth on such occasions, and that it always had a moving effect upon him. Some time after he was in his hammock that night, I heard him myself repeat to Ham, 'Poor thing! She's been thinking of the old 'un!' And whenever Mrs Gummidge was overcome in a similar manner during the remainder of our stay (which happened some few times), he always said the same thing in extenuation of the circumstance, and always with the tenderest commiseration.

So the fortnight slipped away, varied by nothing but the variation of the tide, which altered Mr Peggotty's times of going out and coming in, and altered Ham's engagements also. When the latter was unemployed, he sometimes walked with us to show us the boats and ships, and once or twice he took us for a row. I don't know why one slight set of impressions should be more particularly associated with a place than another, though I believe this obtains with most people, in reference especially to the associations of their childhood. I never hear the name, or read the name, of Yarmouth, but I am reminded of a certain Sunday morning on the beach, the bells ringing for church, little Em'ly leaning on my shoulder, Ham lazily dropping stones into the water, and the sun, away at sea, just breaking through the heavy mist, and showing us the ships, like their own shadows.

At last the day came for going home. I bore up against the separation from Mr Peggotty and Mrs Gummidge, but my agony of mind at leaving little Em'ly was piercing. We went arm in arm to the public-house where the carrier put up, and I promised, on the road, to write to her. (I redeemed that promise afterwards, in characters larger than those in which apartments are usually announced in manuscript, as being to let.) We were greatly overcome at parting; and if ever, in my life, I have had a void made in my heart, I had one made that day.

Now, all the time I had been on my visit, I had been ungrateful to my home again, and had thought little or nothing about it. But I was no sooner turned towards it than my reproachful young conscience seemed to point that way with a steady finger; and I felt, all the more for the sinking of my spirits, that it was my nest, and that my mother was my comforter and friend.

This gained upon me as we went along; so that the nearer we drew, and the more familiar the objects became that we passed, the more excited I was to get there, and to run into her arms. But Peggotty, instead of sharing in these transports, tried to check them (though very kindly), and looked confused and out of sorts.

Blunderstone Rookery would come, however, in spite of her, when the carrier's horse pleased – and did. How well I recollect it, on a cold grey afternoon, with a dull sky, threatening rain!

The door opened, and I looked, half laughing and half crying in my pleasant agitation, for my mother. It was not she, but a strange servant.

'Why, Peggotty!' I said ruefully, 'isn't she come home?'

'Yes, yes, Master Davy,' said Peggotty. 'She's come home. Wait a bit, Master Davy, and I'll – I'll tell you something.'

Between her agitation and her natural awkwardness in getting out of the cart, Peggotty was making a most extraordinary festoon of herself, but I felt too blank and strange to tell her so. When she had got down, she took me by the hand, led me, wondering, into the kitchen, and shut the door.

'Peggotty!' said I, quite frightened. 'What's the matter?'

'Nothing's the matter, bless you, Master Davy, dear!' she answered, assuming an air of sprightliness.

'Something's the matter, I'm sure. Where's mama?'

'Where's mama, Master Davy?' repeated Peggotty.

'Yes. Why hasn't she come out to the gate, and what have we come in here for? Oh, Peggotty!' My eyes were full, and I felt as if I were going to tumble down.

'Bless the precious boy!' cried Peggotty, taking hold of me. 'What is it? Speak, my pet!'

'Not dead, too! Oh, she's not dead, Peggotty?'

Peggotty cried out No! with an astonishing volume of voice; and then sat down, and began to pant, and said I had given her a turn.

I gave her a hug to take away the turn, or to give her another turn in the right direction, and then stood before her, looking at her in anxious enquiry.

'You see, dear, I should have told you before now,' said Peggotty, 'but I hadn't an opportunity. I ought to have made it, perhaps, but I couldn't azackly' – that was always the substitute for exactly, in Peggotty's militia of words – 'bring my mind to it.'

'Go on, Peggotty,' said I, more frightened than before.

'Master Davy,' said Peggotty, untying her bonnet with a shaking hand, and speaking in a breathless sort of way. 'What do you think? You have got a Pa!'

I trembled, and turned white. Something – I don't know what, or how – connected with the grave in the churchyard, and the raising of the dead, seemed to strike me like an unwholesome wind.

'A new one,' said Peggotty.

'A new one?' I repeated.

Peggotty gave a gasp, as if she were swallowing something that was very hard, and, putting out her hand, said: 'Come and see him.'

'I don't want to see him.'

'And your mama,' said Peggotty.

I ceased to draw back, and we went straight to the best parlour, where she left me. On one side of the fire sat my mother; on the other, Mr Murdstone. My mother dropped her work, and arose hurriedly, but timidly, I thought.

'Now, Clara, my dear,' said Mr Murdstone. 'Recollect! control yourself, always control yourself! Davy boy, how do you do?'

I gave him my hand. After a moment of suspense, I went and kissed my mother; she kissed me, patted me gently on the shoulder, and sat down again to her work. I could not look at her, I could not look at him, I knew quite well that he was looking at us both; and I turned to the window and looked out there, at some shrubs that were drooping their heads in the cold.

As soon as I could creep away, I crept upstairs. My old dear bedroom was changed, and I was to lie a long way off. I rambled downstairs to find anything that was like itself, so altered it all seemed; and roamed into the yard. I very soon started back from there, for the empty dog-kennel was filled up with a great dog – deep mouthed and black-haired like Him – and he was very angry at the sight of me, and sprang out to get at me.

CHAPTER 4

I Fall into Disgrace

If the room to which my bed was removed were a sentient thing that could give evidence, I might appeal to it at this day – who sleeps there now, I wonder – to bear witness for me what a heavy heart I carried to it. I went up there, hearing the dog in the yard bark after me all the way while I climbed the stairs; and, looking as blank and strange upon the room as the room looked upon me, sat down with my small hands crossed, and thought.

I thought of the oddest things. Of the shape of the room, of the cracks in the ceiling, of the paper on the wall, of the flaws in the window-glass making ripples and dimples on the prospect, of the washing-stand being rickety on its three legs, and having a discontented something about it, which reminded me of Mrs Gummidge under the influence of the old one. I was crying all the time, but, except that I was conscious of being cold and dejected, I am sure I never thought why I cried. At last in my desolation I began to consider that I was dreadfully in love with little Em'ly, and had been torn away from her to come here, where no one seemed to want me, or to care about me, half so much as she did. This made such a very miserable piece of business of it that I rolled myself up in a corner of the counterpane, and cried myself to sleep.

I was awakened by somebody saying 'Here he is!' and uncovering my hot head. My mother and Peggotty had come to look for me, and it was one of them who had done it.

'Davy,' said my mother. 'What's the matter?'

I thought it very strange that she should ask me, and answered, 'Nothing.' I turned over on my face, I recollect, to hide my trembling lip, which answered her with greater truth.

'Davy,' said my mother. 'Davy, my child!'

I dare say no words she could have uttered would have affected me so much, then, as her calling me her child. I hid my tears in the bedclothes, and pressed her from me with my hand, when she would have raised me up.

'This is your doing, Peggotty, you cruel thing!' said my mother. 'I have no doubt at all about it. How can you reconcile it to your conscience, I wonder, to prejudice my own boy against me, or against anybody who is dear to me? What do you mean by it, Peggotty?'

Poor Peggotty lifted up her hands and eyes, and only answered, in a sort of paraphrase of the grace I usually repeated after dinner, 'Lord forgive you, Mrs Copperfield; and for what you have said this minute, may you never be truly sorry!'

'It's enough to distract me,' cried my mother. 'In my honey-moon, too, when my most inveterate enemy might relent, one would think, and not envy me a little peace of mind and happiness. Davy, you naughty boy! Peggotty, you savage creature! Oh, dear me!' cried my mother, turning from one of us to the other, in her pettish, wilful manner, 'what a troublesome world this is, when one has the most right to expect it to be as agreeable as possible!'

I felt the touch of a hand that I knew was neither hers nor Peggotty's, and slipped to my feet at the bedside. It was Mr Murdstone's hand, and he kept it on my arm as he said: 'What's this? Clara, my love, have you forgotten? – Firmness, my dear!'

'I am very sorry, Edward,' said my mother. 'I meant to be very good, but I am so uncomfortable.'

'Indeed!' he answered. 'That's a bad hearing, so soon, Clara.'

'I say it's very hard I should be made so now,' returned my mother, pouting; 'and it is – very hard – isn't it?'

He drew her to him, whispered in her ear, and kissed her. I knew as well, when I saw my mother's head lean down upon his shoulder, and her arm touch his neck – I knew as well that he could mould her pliant nature into any form he chose, as I know, now, that he did it.

'Go you below, my love,' said Mr Murdstone. 'David and I will come down, together. My friend – ' turning a darkening face on Peggotty, when he had watched my mother out, and dismissed her with a nod and a smile – 'do you know your mistress's name?'

'She has been my mistress a long time, sir,' answered Peggotty. 'I ought to know it.'

'That's true,' he answered. 'But I thought I heard you, as I came upstairs, address her by a name that is not hers. She has taken mine, you know. Will you remember that?'

Peggotty, with some uneasy glances at me, curtseyed herself out of the room without replying; seeing, I suppose, that she was expected to go, and had no excuse for remaining. When we two were left alone, he shut the door, and sitting on a chair, and holding me standing before him, looked steadily into my eyes. I felt my own attracted, no less steadily, to his. As I recall our being opposed thus, face to face, I seem again to hear my heart beat fast and high.

'David,' he said, making his lips thin, by pressing them together, 'if I have an obstinate horse or dog to deal with, what do you think I do?'

'I don't know.'

'I beat him.'

I had answered in a kind of breathless whisper, but I felt, in my silence, that my breath was shorter now.

'I make him wince and smart. I say to myself, "I'll conquer that fellow;" and if it were to cost him all the blood he had, I should do it. What is that upon your face?'

'Dirt,' I said.

He knew it was the mark of tears as well as I. But if he had asked the question twenty times, each time with twenty blows, I believe my baby heart would have burst before I would have told him so.

'You have a good deal of intelligence for a little fellow,' he said, with a grave smile that belonged to him, 'and you understood me very well, I see. Wash that face, sir, and come down with me.'

He pointed to the washing-stand, which I had made out to be like Mrs Gummidge, and motioned me with his head to obey him directly. I had little doubt then, and I have less doubt now, that he would have knocked me down without the least compunction, if I had hesitated.

'Clara, my dear,' he said, when I had done his bidding and he walked me into the parlour, with his hand still on my arm, 'you will not be made uncomfortable any more, I hope. We shall soon improve our youthful humours.'

God help me, I might have been improved for my whole life, I might have been made another creature perhaps for life, by a kind word at that season. A word of encouragement and explanation, of pity for my childish ignorance, of welcome home, of reassurance to me that it *was* home, might have made me dutiful to him in my heart henceforth, instead of in my hypocritical outside, and might have made me respect instead of hate him. I thought my mother was sorry to see me standing in the room so scared and strange, and that, presently, when I stole to a chair, she followed me with her eyes more sorrowfully still – missing, perhaps, some freedom in my childish tread – but the word was not spoken, and the time for it was gone.

We dined alone, we three together. He seemed to be very fond of my mother – I am afraid I liked him none the better for that – and she was very fond of him. I gathered from what they said, that an elder sister of his was coming to stay with them, and that she was expected that evening. I am not certain whether I found out then or afterwards, that, without being actively concerned in any business, he had some share in, or some annual charge upon the profits of, a wine-merchant's house in London, with which his family had been connected from his great-grandfather's time, and in which his sister had a similar interest; but I may mention it in this place, whether or no.

After dinner, when we were sitting by the fire, and I was meditating an escape to Peggotty without having the hardihood to slip away, lest it should offend the master of the house, a coach drove up to the garden gate, and he went out to receive the visitor. My mother followed him. I was timidly following her, when she turned round at the parlour door, in the dusk, and taking me in her embrace as she had been used to do, whispered me to love my new father and be obedient to him. She did this hurriedly and secretly, as if it were wrong, but tenderly; and, putting out her hand behind her, held mine in it, until we came near to where he was standing in the garden, where she let mine go, and drew hers through his arm.

It was Miss Murdstone who was arrived, and a gloomy-looking lady she was; dark, like her brother, whom she greatly resembled in face and voice; and with very heavy eyebrows, nearly meeting over her large nose, as if, being disabled by the wrongs of her sex from wearing whiskers, she had carried them to that account. She brought with her two uncompromising hard black boxes, with her initials on the lids in hard brass nails. When she paid the coachman she took her money out of a hard steel purse, and she kept the purse in a very jail of a bag which hung upon her arm by a heavy chain, and shut up like a bite. I had never, at that time, seen such a metallic lady altogether as Miss Murdstone was.

She was brought into the parlour with many tokens of welcome, and there formally recognised my mother as a new and near relation. Then she looked at me, and said: 'Is that your boy, sister-in-law?'

My mother acknowledged me.

'Generally speaking,' said Miss Murdstone, 'I don't like boys. How d' ye do, boy?'

Under these encouraging circumstances, I replied that I was very well, and that I hoped she was the same; with such an indifferent grace, that Miss Murdstone disposed of me in two words: 'Wants manner!'

Having uttered which with great distinctness, she begged the favour of being shown to her room, which became to me from that time forth a place of awe and dread, wherein the two black boxes were never seen open or known to be left unlocked, and where (for I peeped in once or twice when she was out) numerous little steel fetters and rivets, with which Miss Murdstone embellished herself when she was dressed, generally hung upon the looking-glass in formidable array.

As well as I could make out, she had come for good, and had no intention of ever going again. She began to 'help' my mother next morning, and was in and out of the store-closet all day, putting things to rights, and making havoc in the old arrangements. Almost the first remarkable thing I observed in Miss Murdstone was, her being constantly haunted by a suspicion that the servants had a man secreted somewhere on the premises. Under the influence of this delusion, she dived into the coal-cellar at the most untimely hours, and scarcely ever opened the door of a dark cupboard, without clapping it to again, in the belief that she had got him.

Though there was nothing very airy about Miss Murdstone, she was a perfect Lark in point of getting up. She was up (and, as I believe to this hour, looking for that man) before anybody in the house was stirring. Peggotty gave it as her opinion that she even slept with one eye open; but I could not concur in this idea, for I tried it myself after hearing the suggestion thrown out, and found it couldn't be done.

On the very first morning after her arrival she was up and ringing her bell at cock-crow. When my mother came down to breakfast and was going to make the tea, Miss Murdstone gave her a kind of peck on the cheek, which was her nearest approach to a kiss, and said: 'Now, Clara, my dear, I am come here, you know, to relieve you of all the trouble I can. You're much too pretty and thoughtless' – my mother blushed but laughed, and seemed not to dislike this character – 'to have any duties imposed upon you that can be undertaken by me. If you'll be so good as give me your keys, my dear, I'll attend to all this sort of thing in future.'

From that time, Miss Murdstone kept the keys in her own little jail all day, and under her pillow all night, and my mother had no more to do with them than I had.

My mother did not suffer her authority to pass from her without a shadow of protest. One night when Miss Murdstone had been developing certain household plans to her brother, of which he signified his approbation, my mother suddenly began to cry, and said she thought she might have been consulted.

'Clara!' said Mr Murdstone sternly. 'Clara! I wonder at you.'

'Oh, it's very well to say you wonder, Edward!' cried my mother, 'and it's very well for you to talk about firmness, but you wouldn't like it yourself.'

Firmness, I may observe, was the grand quality on which

both Mr and Miss Murdstone took their stand. However I might have expressed my comprehension of it at that time, if I had been called upon, I nevertheless did clearly comprehend in my own way, that it was another name for tyranny; and for a certain gloomy, arrogant, devil's humour, that was in them both. The creed, as I should state it now, was this. Mr Murdstone was firm; nobody in his world was to be so firm as Mr Murdstone, nobody else in his world was to be firm at all, for everybody was to be bent to his firmness. Miss Murdstone was an exception. She might be firm, but only by relationship, and in an inferior and tributary degree. My mother was another exception. She might be firm, and must be; but only in bearing their firmness, and firmly believing there was no other firmness upon earth.

'It's very hard,' said my mother, 'that in my own house – '

'*My* own house?' repeated Mr Murdstone. 'Clara!'

'*Our* own house, I mean,' faltered my mother, evidently frightened; 'I hope you must know what I mean, Edward – it's very hard that in *your* own house I may not have a word to say about domestic matters. I am sure I managed very well before we were married. There's evidence,' said my mother, sobbing; 'ask Peggotty if I didn't do very well when I wasn't interfered with!'

'Edward,' said Miss Murdstone, 'let there be an end of this. I go tomorrow.'

'Jane Murdstone,' said her brother, 'be silent! How dare you to insinuate that you don't know my character better than your words imply?'

'I am sure,' my poor mother went on, at a grievous disadvantage, and with many tears, 'I don't want anybody to go. I should be very miserable and unhappy if anybody was to go. I don't ask much. I am not unreasonable. I only want to be consulted sometimes. I am very much obliged to anybody who assists me, and I only want to be consulted as a mere form, sometimes. I thought you were pleased, once, with my being a little inexperienced and girlish, Edward – I am sure you said so – but you seem to hate me for it now, you are so severe.'

'Edward,' said Miss Murdstone, again, 'let there be an end of this. I go tomorrow.'

'Jane Murdstone,' thundered Mr Murdstone. 'Will you be silent? How dare you?'

Miss Murdstone made a jail-delivery of her pocket-handkerchief, and held it before her eyes.

'Clara,' he continued, looking at my mother, 'you surprise me! You astound me! Yes, I had a satisfaction in the thought of marrying an inexperienced and artless person, and forming her character, and infusing into it some amount of that firmness and decision of which it stood in need. But when Jane Murdstone is kind enough to come to my assistance in this endeavour, and to assume, for my sake, a condition something like a housekeeper's, and when she meets with a base return – '

'Oh, pray, pray, Edward,' cried my mother, 'don't accuse me of being ungrateful. I am sure I am not ungrateful. No one ever said I was before. I have many faults, but not that. Oh, don't, my dear!'

'When Jane Murdstone meets, I say,' he went on, after waiting until my mother was silent, 'with a base return, that feeling of mine is chilled and altered.'

'Don't, my love, say that!' implored my mother very piteously. 'Oh, don't, Edward! I can't bear to hear it. Whatever I am, I am affectionate. I know I am affectionate. I wouldn't say it, if I wasn't certain that I am. Ask Peggotty. I am sure she'll tell you I'm affectionate.'

'There is no extent of mere weakness, Clara,' said Mr Murdstone in reply, 'that can have the least weight with me. You lose breath.'

'Pray let us be friends,' said my mother. 'I couldn't live under coldness or unkindness. I am so sorry. I have a great many defects, I know, and it's very good of you, Edward, with your strength of mind, to endeavour to correct them for me. Jane, I don't object to anything. I should be quite broken-hearted if you thought of leaving – ' My mother was too much overcome to go on.

'Jane Murdstone,' said Mr Murdstone to his sister, 'any harsh words between us are, I hope, uncommon. It is not my fault that so unusual an occurrence has taken place tonight. I was betrayed into it by another. Nor is it your fault. You were betrayed into it by another. Let us both try to forget it. And as this,' he added, after these magnanimous words, 'is not a fit scene for the boy – David, go to bed!'

I could hardly find the door, through the tears that stood in my eyes. I was so sorry for my mother's distress; but I groped my way out, and groped my way up to my room in the dark, without even having the heart to say good-night to Peggotty, or to get a candle from her. When her coming up to look for me, an hour or so afterwards, awoke me, she said that my mother had gone to bed poorly, and that Mr and Miss Murdstone were sitting alone.

Going down next morning rather earlier than usual, I paused outside the parlour door, on hearing my mother's voice. She was very earnestly and humbly entreating Miss Murdstone's pardon, which that lady granted, and a perfect reconciliation took place. I never knew my mother afterwards to give an opinion on any matter, without first appealing to Miss Murdstone, or without having first ascertained by some sure means what Miss Murdstone's opinion was; and I never saw Miss Murdstone, when out of temper (she was infirm that way), move her hand towards her bag as if she were going to take out the keys and offer to resign them to my mother, without seeing that my mother was in a terrible fright.

The gloomy taint that was in the Murdstone blood darkened the Murdstone religion, which was austere and wrathful. I have thought, since, that its assuming that character was a necessary consequence of Mr Murdstone's firmness, which wouldn't allow him to let anybody off from the utmost weight of the severest penalties he could find any excuse for. Be this as it may, I well remember the tremendous visages with which we used to go to church, and the changed air of the place. Again the dreaded Sunday comes round, and I file into the old pew first, like a guarded captive brought to a condemned service. Again, Miss Murdstone, in a black velvet gown, that looks as if it had been made out of a pall, follows close upon me; then my mother; then her husband. There is no Peggotty now, as in the old time. Again, I listen to Miss Murdstone mumbling the responses, and emphasising all the dread words with a cruel relish. Again, I see her dark eyes roll round the church when she says, 'miserable sinners,' as if she were calling all the congregation names. Again, I catch rare glimpses of my mother, moving her lips timidly between the two, with one of them muttering at each ear like low thunder. Again, I wonder with a sudden fear, whether it is likely that our good old clergyman can be wrong, and Mr and Miss Murdstone right, and that all the angels in Heaven can be destroying angels. Again, if I move a finger or relax a muscle of my face, Miss Murdstone pokes me with her prayer-book, and makes my side ache.

Yes, and again, as we walk home, I note some neighbours looking at my mother, and at me, and whispering. Again, as the three go on, arm in arm, and I linger behind alone, I follow some of those looks, and wonder if my mother's step be really not so light as I have seen it, and if the gaiety of her beauty be really almost worried away. Again, I wonder whether any of the neighbours call to mind, as I do, how we used to walk home together, she and I; and I wonder stupidly about that all the dreary dismal day.

There had been some talk on occasions of my going to boarding-school. Mr and Miss Murdstone had originated it, and my mother had of course agreed with them. Nothing, however, was concluded on the subject yet. In the mean time I learnt lessons at home.

Shall I ever forget those lessons! They were presided over nominally by my mother, but really by Mr Murdstone and his sister, who were always present, and found them a favourable occasion for giving my mother lessons in that miscalled firmness, which was the bane of both our lives. I believe I was kept at home for that purpose. I had been apt enough to learn, and willing enough, when my mother and I had lived alone together. I can faintly remember learning the alphabet at her knee. To this day, when I look upon the fat black letters in the primer, the puzzling novelty of their shapes and the easy good-nature of O and Q and S seem to present themselves again before me as they used to do. But they recall no feeling of disgust or reluctance. On the contrary, I seem to have walked along a path of flowers as far as the crocodile-book, and to have been cheered by the gentleness of my mother's voice and manner all the way. But these solemn lessons which succeeded those, I remember as the death-blow at my peace, and a grievous daily drudgery and misery. They were very long, very numerous, very hard – perfectly unintelligible, some of them, to me – and I was generally as much bewildered by them as I believe my poor mother was herself.

Let me remember how it used to be, and bring one morning back again.

I come into the second-best parlour after breakfast, with my books, and an exercise-book, and a slate. My mother is ready for me at her writing-desk, but not half so ready as Mr Murdstone in his easy-chair by the window (though he pretends to be reading a book), or as Miss Murdstone, sitting near my mother stringing steel beads. The very sight of these two has such an influence over me, that I begin to feel the words I have been at infinite pains to get into my head, all sliding away, and going I don't know where. I wonder where they *do* go, by the by?

I hand the first book to my mother. Perhaps it is a grammar, perhaps a history, or geography. I take a last drowning look at the page as I give it into her hand, and start off aloud at a racing pace while I have got it fresh. I trip over a word. Mr Murdstone looks up. I trip over another word. Miss Murdstone looks up. I redden, tumble over half a dozen words, and stop. I think my mother would show me the book if she dared, but she does not dare, and she says softly: 'Oh, Davy, Davy!'

'Now, Clara,' says Mr Murdstone, 'be firm with the boy. Don't say "Oh, Davy, Davy!" That's childish. He knows his lesson, or he does not know it.'

'He does *not* know it,' Miss Murdstone interposes awfully.

'I am really afraid he does not,' says my mother.

'Then you see, Clara,' returns Miss Murdstone, 'you should just give him the book back, and make him know it.'

'Yes, certainly,' says my mother; 'that is what I intend to do, my dear Jane. Now, Davy, try once more, and don't be stupid.'

I obey the first clause of the injunction by trying once more, but am not so successful with the second, for I am very stupid. I tumble down before I get to the old place, at a point where I was all right before, and stop to think. But I can't think about the lesson. I think of the number of yards of net in Miss Murdstone's cap, or of the price of Mr Murdstone's dressing-gown, or any such ridiculous problem that I have no business with, and don't want to have anything at all to do with. Mr Murdstone makes a movement of impatience which I have been expecting for a long time. Miss Murdstone does the same. My mother glances submissively at them, shuts the book, and lays it by as an arrear to be worked out when my other tasks are done.

There is a pile of these arrears very soon, and it swells like a rolling snowball. The bigger it gets, the more stupid *I* get. The case is so hopeless, and I feel that I am wallowing in such a bog of nonsense, that I give up all idea of getting out, and abandon myself to my fate. The despairing way in which my mother and I look at each other, as I blunder on, is truly melancholy. But the greatest effect in these miserable lessons is when my mother (thinking nobody is observing her) tries to give me the cue by the motion of her lips. At that instant, Miss Murdstone, who has been lying in wait for nothing else all along, says in a deep warning voice: 'Clara!'

My mother starts, colours, and smiles faintly. Mr Murdstone comes out of his chair, takes the book, throws it at me, or boxes my ears with it, and turns me out of the room by the shoulders.

Even when the lessons are done, the worst is yet to happen, in the shape of an appalling sum. This is invented for me, and delivered to me orally by Mr Murdstone, and begins, 'If I go into a cheesemonger's shop, and buy five thousand double-Gloucester cheeses at fourpence-halfpenny each, present payment' – at which I see Miss Murdstone secretly overjoyed. I pore over these cheeses without any result or enlightenment until dinner-time; when, having made a Mulatto of myself by getting the dirt of the slate into the pores of my skin, I have a slice of bread to help me out with the cheeses, and am considered in disgrace for the rest of the evening.

It seems to me, at this distance of time, as if my unfortunate studies generally took this course. I could have done very well if I had been without the Murdstones; but the influence of the Murdstones upon me was like the fascination of two snakes on a wretched young bird. Even when I did get through the morning with tolerable credit, there was not much gained but dinner; for Miss Murdstone never could endure to see me untasked, and if I rashly made any show of being unemployed, called her brother's attention to me by saying, 'Clara, my dear, there's nothing like work – give your boy an exercise;' which caused me to be clapped down to some new labour there and then. As to any recreation with other children of my age, I had very little of that; for the gloomy theology of the Murdstones made all children out to be a swarm of little vipers (though there *was* a child once set in the midst of the Disciples), and held that they contaminated one another.

The natural result of this treatment, continued, I suppose, for some six months or more, was to make me sullen, dull, and dogged. I was not made the less so, by my sense of being daily more and more shut out and alienated from my mother. I believe I should have been almost stupefied but for one circumstance.

It was this. My father had left a small collection of books in a little room upstairs, to which I had access (for it adjoined my own), and which nobody else in our house ever troubled. From that blessed little room, *Roderick Random, Peregrine Pickle, Humphrey Clinker, Tom Jones, The Vicar of Wakefield, Don Quixote, Gil Blas,* and *Robinson Crusoe,* came out, a glorious host, to keep me company. They kept alive my fancy, and my hope of something beyond that place and time – they, and the *Arabian Nights,* and the *Tales of the Genii* – and did me no harm; for whatever harm was in some of them was not there for me; *I* knew nothing of it. It is astonishing to me now, how I found time, in the midst of my porings and blunderings over heavier themes, to read those books as I did. It is curious to me how I could ever have consoled myself under my small troubles (which were great troubles to me), by impersonating my favourite characters in them – as I did – and by putting Mr and Miss Murdstone into all the bad ones – which I did too. I have been Tom Jones (a child's Tom Jones, a harmless creature) for a week together. I have sustained my own idea of Roderick Random for a month at a stretch, I verily believe. I had a greedy relish for a few volumes of Voyages and Travels – I forget what, now – that were on those shelves; and for days and days I can remember to have gone about my region of our house, armed with the centre-piece out of an old set of boot-trees – the perfect realisation of Captain Somebody, of the Royal British Navy, in danger of being beset by savages, and resolved to sell his life at a great price. The Captain never lost dignity, from having his ears boxed with the Latin Grammar. I did; but the Captain was a Captain and a hero, in despite of all the grammars of all the languages in the world, dead or alive.

This was my only and my constant comfort. When I think of it, the picture always rises in my mind, of a summer evening, the boys at play in the churchyard, and I sitting on my bed, reading as if for life. Every barn in the neighbourhood, every stone in the church, and every foot of the churchyard, had some association of its own, in my mind, connected with these books, and stood for some locality made famous in them. I have seen Tom Pipes go climbing up the church-steeple; I have watched Strap, with the knapsack on his back, stopping to rest himself upon the wicket gate; and I *know* that Commodore Trunnion held that Club with Mr Pickle, in the parlour of our little village alehouse.

The reader now understands as well as I do, what I was when I came to that point of my youthful history to which I am now coming again.

One morning when I went into the parlour with my books, I found my mother looking anxious, Miss Murdstone looking firm, and Mr Murdstone binding something round the bottom of a cane – a lithe and limber cane, which he left off binding when I came in, and poised and switched in the air.

'I tell you, Clara,' said Mr Murdstone, 'I have been often flogged myself.'

'To be sure; of course,' said Miss Murdstone.

'Certainly, my dear Jane,' faltered my mother meekly. 'But – but do you think it did Edward good?'

'Do you think it did Edward harm, Clara?' asked Mr Murdstone gravely.

'That's the point!' said his sister.

To this my mother returned, 'Certainly, my dear Jane,' and said no more.

I felt apprehensive that I was personally interested in this dialogue, and sought Mr Murdstone's eye as it lighted on mine.

'Now, David,' he said – and I saw that cast again, as he said it – 'you must be far more careful today than usual.' He gave the cane another poise, and another switch; and having finished his preparation of it, laid it down beside him, with an expressive look, and took up his book.

This was a good freshener to my presence of mind, as a beginning. I felt the words of my lessons slipping off, not one by one, or line by line, but by the entire page. I tried to lay hold of them; but they seemed, if I may so express it, to have put skates on, and to skim away from me with a smoothness there was no checking.

We began badly, and went on worse. I had come in, with an idea of distinguishing myself rather, conceiving that I was very well prepared; but it turned out to be quite a mistake. Book after book was added to the heap of failures, Miss Murdstone being firmly watchful of us all the time. And when we came at last to the five thousand cheeses (canes he made it that day, I remember), my mother burst out crying.

'Clara!' said Miss Murdstone, in her warning voice.

'I am not quite well, my dear Jane, I think,' said my mother.

I saw him wink, solemnly, at his sister, as he rose and said, taking up the cane: 'Why, Jane, we can hardly expect Clara to bear, with perfect firmness, the worry and torment that David has occasioned her today. That would be stoical. Clara is greatly strengthened and improved, but we can hardly expect so much from her. David, you and I will go upstairs, boy.'

As he took me out at the door, my mother ran towards us. Miss Murdstone said, 'Clara! are you a perfect fool?' and interfered. I saw my mother stop her ears then, and I heard her crying.

He walked me up to my room slowly and gravely – I am certain he had a delight in that formal parade of executing justice – and when we got there, suddenly twisted my head under his arm.

'Mr Murdstone! Sir!' I cried to him. 'Don't! Pray don't beat me! I have tried to learn, sir, but I can't learn while you and Miss Murdstone are by. I can't, indeed!'

'Can't you, indeed, David?' he said. 'We'll try that.'

He had my head as in a vice, but I twined round him somehow, and stopped him for a moment, entreating him not to beat me. It was only for a moment that I stopped him, for he cut me heavily an instant afterwards, and in the same instant I caught the hand with which he held me in my mouth, between my teeth, and bit it through. It sets my teeth on edge to think of it.

He beat me then, as if he would have beaten me to death. Above all the noise we made, I heard them running up the stairs, and crying out – I heard my mother crying out – and Peggotty. Then he was gone; and the door was locked outside; and I was lying, fevered and hot, and torn, and sore, and raging in my puny way, upon the floor.

How well I recollect, when I became quiet, what an unnatural stillness seemed to reign through the whole house! How well I remember, when my smart and passion began to cool, how wicked I began to feel!

I sat listening for a long while, but there was not a sound. I crawled up from the floor, and saw my face in the glass, so swollen, red, and ugly that it almost frightened me. My stripes were sore and stiff, and made me cry afresh, when I moved; but they were nothing to the guilt I felt. It lay heavier on my breast than if I had been a most atrocious criminal, I dare say.

It had begun to grow dark, and I had shut the window (I had been lying, for the most part, with my head upon the sill, by turns crying, dozing, and looking listlessly out), when the key was turned, and Miss Murdstone came in with some bread and meat, and milk. These she put down upon the table without a word, glaring at me the while with exemplary firmness, and then retired, locking the door after her.

Long after it was dark I sat there, wondering whether anybody else would come. When this appeared improbable for that night, I undressed, and went to bed; and, there, I began to wonder fearfully what would be done to me. Whether it was a criminal act that I had committed? Whether I should be taken into custody, and sent to prison? Whether I was at all in danger of being hanged?

I never shall forget the waking, next morning; the being cheerful and fresh for the first moment, and then the being weighed down by the stale and dismal oppression of remembrance. Miss Murdstone reappeared before I was out of bed; told me, in so many words, that I was free to walk in the garden for half an hour and no longer; and retired, leaving the door open, that I might avail myself of that permission.

I did so, and did so every morning of my imprisonment, which lasted five days. If I could have seen my mother alone, I should have gone down on my knees to her and besought her forgiveness; but I saw no one, Miss Murdstone excepted, during the whole time – except at evening prayers in the parlour; to which I was escorted by Miss Murdstone after everybody else was placed; where I was stationed, a young outlaw, all alone by myself near the door; and whence I was solemnly conducted by my jailer, before anyone arose from the devotional posture. I only observed that my mother was as far off from me as she could be, and kept her face another way so that I never saw it; and that Mr Murdstone's hand was bound up in a large linen wrapper.

The length of those five days I can convey no idea of to anyone. They occupy the place of years in my remembrance. The way in which I listened to all the incidents of the house that made themselves audible to me; the ringing of bells, the opening and shutting of doors, the murmuring of voices, the footsteps on the stairs; to any laughing, whistling, or singing, outside, which seemed more dismal than anything else to me in my solitude and disgrace – the uncertain pace of the hours, especially at night, when I would wake thinking it was morning, and find that the family were not yet gone to bed, and that all the length of night had yet to come – the depressed dreams and nightmares I had – the return of day, noon, afternoon, evening, when the boys played in the churchyard, and I watched them from a distance within the room, being ashamed to show myself at the window lest they should know I was a prisoner – the strange sensation of never hearing myself speak – the fleeting intervals of something like cheerfulness, which came with eating and drinking, and went away with it – the setting in of rain one evening, with a fresh smell, and its coming down faster and faster between me and the church, until it and gathering night seemed to quench me in gloom, and fear, and remorse – all this appears to have gone round and round for years instead of days, it is so vividly and strongly stamped on my remembrance.

On the last night of my restraint, I was awakened by hearing my own name spoken in a whisper. I started up in bed, and, putting out my arms in the dark, said: 'Is that you, Peggotty?'

There was no immediate answer, but presently I heard my name again, in a tone so very mysterious and awful that I think I should have gone into a fit, if it had not occurred to me that it must have come through the keyhole.

I groped my way to the door, and, putting my own lips to the keyhole, whispered: 'Is that you, Peggotty, dear?'

'Yes, my own precious Davy,' she replied. 'Be as soft as a mouse, or the Cat'll hear us.'

I understood this to mean Miss Murdstone, and was sensible of the urgency of the case; her room being close by.

'How's mama, dear Peggotty? Is she very angry with me?'

I could hear Peggotty crying softly on her side of the keyhole, as I was doing on mine, before she answered. 'No. Not very.'

'What is going to be done with me, Peggotty, dear? Do you know?'

'School. Near London,' was Peggotty's answer. I was obliged to get her to repeat it, for she spoke it the first time quite down my throat, in consequence of my having forgotten to take my mouth away from the keyhole and put my ear there; and though her words tickled me a good deal, I didn't hear them.

'When, Peggotty?'

'Tomorrow.'

'Is that the reason why Miss Murdstone took the clothes out of my drawers?' which she had done, though I have forgotten to mention it.

'Yes,' said Peggotty. 'Box.'

'Sha'n't I see mama?'

'Yes,' said Peggotty. 'Morning.'

Then Peggotty fitted her mouth close to the keyhole, and delivered these words through it with as much feeling and earnestness as a keyhole has ever been the medium of communicating, I will venture to assert, shooting in each broken little sentence in a convulsive little burst of its own.

'Davy, dear. If I ain't ben azackly as intimate with you, lately, as I used to be. It ain't because I don't love you. Just as well and more, my pretty poppet. It's because I thought it better for you. And for someone else besides. Davy, my darling, are you listening? Can you hear?'

'Ye – ye – ye – yes, Peggotty!' I sobbed.

'My own!' said Peggotty, with infinite compassion. 'What I want to say, is. That you must never forget me. For I'll never forget you. And I'll take as much care of your mama, Davy. As ever I took of you. And I won't leave her. The day may come when she'll be glad to lay her poor head on her stupid, cross old Peggotty's arm again. And I'll write to you, my dear. Though I ain't no scholar. And I'll – I'll – ' Peggotty fell to kissing the keyhole, as she couldn't kiss me.

'Thank you, dear Peggotty!' said I. 'Oh, thank you! Thank you! Will you promise me one thing, Peggotty? Will you write and tell Mr Peggotty and little Em'ly and Mrs Gummidge and Ham, that I am not so bad as they might suppose, and that I sent 'em all my love – especially to little Em'ly? Will you, if you please, Peggotty?'

The kind soul promised, and we both of us kissed the keyhole with the greatest affection – I patted it with my hand, I recollect, as if it had been her honest face – and parted. From that night there grew up in my breast a feeling for Peggotty which I cannot very well define. She did not replace my mother; no one could do that; but she came into a vacancy in my heart, which closed upon her, and I felt towards her something I have never felt for any other human being. It was a sort of comical affection, too; and yet if she had died, I cannot think what I should have done, or how I should have acted out the tragedy it would have been to me.

In the morning Miss Murdstone appeared as usual, and told me I was going to school; which was not altogether such news to me as she supposed. She also informed me that, when I was dressed, I was to come downstairs into the parlour, and have my breakfast. There, I found my mother, very pale and with red eyes; into whose arms I ran, and begged her pardon from my suffering soul.

'Oh, Davy!' she said. 'That you could hurt anyone I love! Try to be better, pray to be better! I forgive you; but I am so grieved, Davy, that you should have such bad passions in your heart.'

They had persuaded her that I was a wicked fellow, and she was more sorry for that than for my going away. I felt it sorely. I tried to eat my parting breakfast, but my tears dropped upon my bread and butter, and trickled into my tea. I saw my mother look at me sometimes, and then glance at the watchful Miss Murdstone, and then look down, or look away.

'Master Copperfield's box there?' said Miss Murdstone, when wheels were heard at the gate.

I looked for Peggotty, but it was not she; neither she nor Mr Murdstone appeared. My former acquaintance, the carrier, was at the door; the box taken out to his cart, and lifted in.

'Clara!' said Miss Murdstone, in her warning note.

'Ready, my dear Jane,' returned my mother. 'Goodbye, Davy. You are going for your own good. Goodbye, my child. You will come home in the holidays, and be a better boy.'

'Clara!' Miss Murdstone repeated.

'Certainly, my dear Jane,' replied my mother, who was holding me. 'I forgive you, my dear boy. God bless you!'

'Clara!' Miss Murdstone repeated.

Miss Murdstone was good enough to take me out to the cart, and to say on the way that she hoped I would repent, before I came to a bad end; and then I got into the cart, and the lazy horse walked off with it.

CHAPTER 5

I Am Sent Away from Home

We might have gone about half a mile, and my pocket-handkerchief was quite wet through, when the carrier stopped short.

Looking out to ascertain for what, I saw, to my amazement, Peggotty burst from a hedge and climb into the cart. She took me in both her arms, and squeezed me to her stays until the pressure on my nose was extremely painful, though I never thought of that till afterwards when I found it very tender. Not a single word did Peggotty speak. Releasing one of her arms, she put it down in her pocket to the elbow, and brought out some paper bags of cakes which she crammed into my pockets, and a purse which she put into my hand, but not one word did she say. After another and a final squeeze with both arms, she got down from the cart, and ran away; and my belief is, and has always been, without a solitary button on her gown. I picked up one, of several that were rolling about, and treasured it as a keepsake for a long time.

The carrier looked at me, as if to enquire if she were coming back. I shook my head, and said I thought not. 'Then come up,' said the carrier to the lazy horse, who came up accordingly.

Having by this time cried as much as I possibly could, I began to think it was of no use crying any more, especially as neither Roderick Random, nor that Captain in the Royal British Navy had ever cried, that I could remember, in trying situations. The carrier, seeing me in this resolution, proposed that my pocket-handkerchief should be spread upon the horse's back to dry. I thanked him and assented; and particularly small it looked, under those circumstances.

I had now leisure to examine the purse. It was a stiff leather purse, with a snap, and had three bright shillings in it, which Peggotty had evidently polished up with whitening, for my greater delight. But its most precious contents were two half-crowns folded together in a bit of paper, on which was written, in my mother's hand, 'For Davy. With my love.' I was so overcome by this that I asked the carrier to be so good as reach me my pocket-handkerchief again, but he said he thought I had better do without it; and I thought I really had; so I wiped my eyes on my sleeve and stopped myself.

For good, too; though, in consequence of my previous emotions, I was still occasionally seized with a stormy sob. After we had jogged on for some little time, I asked the carrier if he was going all the way.

'All the way where?' enquired the carrier.

'There,' I said.

'Where's there?' enquired the carrier.

'Near London,' I said.

'Why that horse,' said the carrier, jerking the rein to point him out, 'would be deader than pork afore he got over half the ground.'

'Are you only going to Yarmouth, then?' I asked.

'That's about it,' said the carrier. 'And there I shall take you to the stage-cutch, and the stage-cutch that'll take you to – wherever it is.'

As this was a great deal for the carrier (whose name was Mr Barkis) to say – he being, as I observed in a former chapter, of a phlegmatic temperament, and not at all conversational – I offered him a cake as a mark of attention, which he ate at one gulp, exactly like an elephant, and which made no more impression on his big face than it would have done on an elephant's.

'Did *she* make 'em, now?' said Mr Barkis, always leaning forward, in his slouching way, on the footboard of the cart with an arm on each knee.

'Peggotty, do you mean, sir?'

'Ah!' said Mr Barkis. 'Her.'

'Yes. She makes all our pastry and does all our cooking.'

'Do she, though?' said Mr Barkis.

He made up his mouth as if to whistle, but he didn't whistle. He sat looking at the horse's ears, as if he saw something new there; and sat so, for a considerable time. By and by, he said: 'No sweethearts, I b'lieve?'

'Sweetmeats did you say, Mr Barkis?' For I thought he wanted something else to eat, and had pointedly alluded to that description of refreshment.

'Hearts,' said Mr Barkis. 'Sweethearts; no person walks with her!'

'With Peggotty?'

'Ah!' he said. 'Her.'

'Oh, no. She never had a sweetheart.'

'Didn't she, though!' said Mr Barkis.

Again he made up his mouth to whistle, and again he didn't whistle, but sat looking at the horse's ears.

'So she makes,' said Mr Barkis, after a long interval of reflection, 'all the apple parsties, and doos all the cooking, do she?'

I replied that such was the fact.

'Well, I'll tell you what,' said Mr Barkis. 'P'raps you might be writin' to her?'

'I shall certainly write to her,' I rejoined.

'Ah!' he said, slowly turning his eyes towards me. 'Well! If you was writin' to her, p'raps you'd recollect to say that Barkis was willin'; would you?'

'That Barkis was willing,' I repeated innocently. 'Is that all the message?'

'Ye–es,' he said, considering. 'Ye–es. Barkis is willin'.'

'But you will be at Blunderstone again tomorrow, Mr Barkis,' I said, faltering a little at the idea of my being far away from it then, 'and could give your own message so much better.'

As he repudiated this suggestion, however, with a jerk of his head, and once more confirmed his previous request by saying with profound gravity, 'Barkis is willin'. That's the message,' I readily undertook its transmission. While I was waiting for the coach in the hotel at Yarmouth that very afternoon, I procured a sheet of paper and an inkstand, and wrote a note to Peggotty which ran thus: 'My dear Peggotty. I have come here safe. Barkis is willing. My love to mama. Yours affectionately. P. S. He says he particularly wants you to know – *Barkis is willing.*'

When I had taken this commission on myself prospectively, Mr Barkis relapsed into perfect silence; and I, feeling quite worn out by all that had happened lately, lay down on a sack in the cart and fell asleep. I slept soundly until we got to Yarmouth; which was so entirely new and strange to me in the innyard to which we drove, that I at once abandoned a latent hope I had had of meeting with some of Mr Peggotty's family there, perhaps even with little Em'ly herself.

The coach was in the yard, shining very much all over, but without any horses to it as yet; and it looked in that state as if nothing was more unlikely than its ever going to London. I was thinking this, and wondering what would ultimately become of my box, which Mr Barkis had put down on the yard pavement by the pole (he having driven up the yard to turn his cart), and also what would ultimately become of me, when a lady looked out of a bow-window where some fowls and joints of meat were hanging up, and said: 'Is that the little gentleman from Blunderstone?'

'Yes, ma'am,' I said.

'What name?' enquired the lady.

'Copperfield, ma'am,' I said.

'That won't do,' returned the lady. 'Nobody's dinner is paid for here, in that name.'

'Is it Murdstone, ma'am?' I said.

'If you're Master Murdstone,' said the lady, 'why do you go and give another name, first?'

I explained to the lady how it was, who then rang a bell, and called out, 'William! show the coffee-room!' upon which a waiter came running out of a kitchen on the opposite side of the yard to show it, and seemed a good deal surprised when he found he was only to show it to me.

It was a large long room with some large maps in it. I doubt if I could have felt much stranger if the maps had been real foreign countries, and I cast away in the middle of them. I felt it was taking a liberty to sit down, with my cap in my hand, on the corner of the chair nearest the door; and when the waiter laid a cloth on purpose for me, and put a set of castors on it, I think I must have turned red all over with modesty.

He brought me some chops and vegetables, and took the covers off in such a bouncing manner that I was afraid I must have given him some offence. But he greatly relieved my mind by putting a chair for me at the table, and saying, very affably, 'Now, six-foot! come on!'

I thanked him, and took my seat at the board; but found it extremely difficult to handle my knife and fork with anything like dexterity, or to avoid splashing myself with the gravy, while he was standing opposite, staring so hard, and making me blush in the most dreadful manner every time I caught his eye. After watching me into the second chop, he said: 'There's half a pint of ale for you. Will you have it now?'

I thanked him and said 'Yes.' Upon which he poured it out of a jug into a large tumbler, and held it up against the light, and made it look beautiful.

'My eye!' he said. 'It seems a good deal, don't it?'

'It does seem a good deal,' I answered with a smile. For it was quite delightful to me to find him so pleasant. He was a twinkling-eyed, pimple-faced man, with his hair standing upright all over his head; and as he stood with one arm akimbo, holding up the glass to the light with the other hand, he looked quite friendly.

'There was a gentleman here yesterday,' he said – 'a stout gentleman, by the name of Topsawyer – perhaps you know him?'

'No,' I said, 'I don't think –'

'In breeches and gaiters, broad-brimmed hat, grey coat, speckled choker,' said the waiter.

'No,' I said bashfully, 'I haven't the pleasure –'

'He came in here,' said the waiter, looking at the light through the tumbler, 'ordered a glass of this ale – *would* order it – I told him not – drank it, and fell dead. It was too old for him. It oughtn't to be drawn; that's the fact.'

I was very much shocked to hear of this melancholy accident, and said I thought I had better have some water.

'Why, you see,' said the waiter, still looking at the light through the tumbler, with one of his eyes shut up, 'our people don't like things being ordered and left. It offends 'em. But *I'll* drink it, if you like. I'm used to it, and use is everything. I don't think it'll hurt me, if I throw my head back, and take it off quick. Shall I?'

I replied that he would much oblige me by drinking it, if he thought he could do it safely, but by no means otherwise. When he did throw his head back, and take it off quick, I had a horrible fear, I confess, of seeing him meet the fate of the lamented Mr Topsawyer, and fall lifeless on the carpet. But it didn't hurt him. On the contrary, I thought he seemed the fresher for it.

'What have we got here?' he said, putting a fork into my dish. 'Not chops?'

'Chops,' I said.

'Lord bless my soul!' he exclaimed, 'I didn't know they were chops. Why a chop's the very thing to take off the bad effects of that beer! Ain't it lucky?'

So he took a chop by the bone in one hand, and a potato in the other, and ate away with a very good appetite, to my extreme satisfaction. He afterwards took another chop, and another potato; and after that another chop and another potato. When we had done, he brought me a pudding, and, having set it before me, seemed to ruminate, and to become absent in his mind for some moments.

'How's the pie?' he said, rousing himself.

'It's a pudding,' I made answer.

'Pudding!' he exclaimed. 'Why, bless me, so it is! What!' looking at it nearer. 'You don't mean to say it's a batter-pudding!'

'Yes, it is, indeed.'

'Why, a batter-pudding,' he said, taking up a tablespoon, 'is my favourite pudding! Ain't that lucky? Come on, little 'un, and let's see who'll get most.'

The waiter certainly got most. He entreated me more than once to come in and win, but what with his tablespoon to my teaspoon, his despatch to my despatch, and his appetite to my appetite, I was left far behind at the first mouthful, and had no chance with him. I never saw anyone enjoy a pudding so much, I think; and he laughed when it was all gone, as if his enjoyment of it lasted still.

Finding him so very friendly and companionable, it was then that I asked for the pen and ink and paper, to write to Peggotty. He not only brought it immediately, but was good enough to

The friendly waiter and I

look over me while I wrote the letter. When I had finished it, he asked me where I was going to school.

I said, 'Near London,' which was all I knew.

'Oh, my eye!' he said, looking very low-spirited, 'I am sorry for that.'

'Why?' I asked him.

'Oh, Lord!' he said, shaking his head, 'that's` the school where they broke the boy's ribs – two ribs – a little boy he was. I should say he was – let me see – how old are you, about?'

I told him between eight and nine.

'That's just his age,' he said. 'He was eight years and six months old when they broke his first rib; eight years and eight months old when they broke his second, and did for him.'

I could not disguise from myself, or from the waiter, that this was an uncomfortable coincidence, and enquired how it was done. His answer was not cheering to my spirits, for it consisted of two dismal words, 'With whopping.'

The blowing of the coach-horn in the yard was a seasonable diversion, which made me get up and hesitatingly enquire, in the mingled pride and diffidence of having a purse (which I took out of my pocket), if there was anything to pay.

'There's a sheet of letter-paper,' he returned. 'Did you ever buy a sheet of letter-paper?'

I could not remember that I ever had.

'It's dear,' he said, 'on account of the duty. Threepence. That's the way we are taxed in this country. There's nothing else, except the waiter. Never mind the ink. *I* lose by that.'

'What should you – what should I – how much ought I to – what would it be right to pay the waiter, if you please?' I stammered, blushing.

'If I hadn't a family, and that family hadn't the cowpock,' said the waiter, 'I wouldn't take a sixpence. If I didn't support a aged pairint, and a lovely sister' – here the waiter was greatly agitated – 'I wouldn't take a farthing. If I had a good place, and was treated well here, I should beg acceptance of a trifle, instead of taking it. But I live on broken wittles – and I sleep on the coals' – here the waiter burst into tears.

I was very much concerned for his misfortunes, and felt that any recognition short of ninepence would be mere brutality and hardness of heart. Therefore I gave him one of my three bright shillings, which he received with much humility and veneration, and spun up with his thumb, directly afterwards, to try the goodness of.

It was a little disconcerting to me, to find, when I was being helped up behind the coach, that I was supposed to have eaten all the dinner without any assistance. I discovered this, from overhearing the lady in the bow-window say to the guard, 'Take care of that child, George, or he'll burst!' and from observing that the women-servants who were about the place came out to look and giggle at me as a young phenomenon. My unfortunate friend the waiter, who had quite recovered his spirits, did not appear to be disturbed by this, but joined in the general admiration without being at all confused. If I had any doubt of him, I suppose this half awakened it; but I am inclined to believe that with the simple confidence of a child, and the natural reliance of a child upon superior years (qualities I am

very sorry any children should prematurely change for worldly wisdom), I had no serious mistrust of him, on the whole, even then.

I felt it rather hard, I must own, to be made, without deserving it, the subject of jokes between the coachman and guard as to the coach drawing heavy behind, on account of my sitting there, and as to the greater expediency of my travelling by wagon. The story of my supposed appetite getting wind among the outside passengers, they were merry upon it likewise, and asked me whether I was going to be paid for, at school, as two brothers or three, and whether I was contracted for, or went upon the regular terms; with other pleasant questions. But the worst of it was that I knew I should be ashamed to eat anything, when an opportunity offered, and that, after a rather light dinner, I should remain hungry all night – for I had left my cakes behind, at the hotel, in my hurry. My apprehensions were realised. When we stopped for supper I couldn't muster courage to take any, though I should have liked it very much, but sat by the fire and said I didn't want anything. This did not save me from more jokes, either; for a husky-voiced gentleman with a rough face, who had been eating out of a sandwich-box nearly all the way, except when he had been drinking out of a bottle, said I was like a boa-constrictor who took enough at one meal to last him a long time; after which he actually brought a rash out upon himself with boiled beef.

We had started from Yarmouth at three o'clock in the afternoon, and we were due in London about eight next morning. It was midsummer weather, and the evening was very pleasant. When we passed through a village, I pictured to myself what the insides of the houses were like, and what the inhabitants were about; and when boys came running after us, and got up behind and swung there for a little way, I wondered whether their fathers were alive, and whether they were happy at home. I had plenty to think of, therefore, besides my mind running continually on the kind of place I was going to – which was an awful speculation. Sometimes, I remember, I resigned myself to thoughts of home and Peggotty; and to endeavouring, in a confused, blind way, to recall how I had felt, and what sort of boy I used to be, before I bit Mr Murdstone; which I couldn't satisfy myself about by any means, I seemed to have bitten him in such a remote antiquity.

The night was not so pleasant as the evening, for it got chilly; and being put between two gentlemen (the rough-faced one and another) to prevent my tumbling off the coach, I was nearly smothered by their falling asleep, and completely blocking me up. They squeezed me so hard sometimes that I could not help crying out 'Oh, if you please!' – which they didn't like at all, because it woke them. Opposite me was an elderly lady in a great fur cloak, who looked in the dark more like a haystack than a lady, she was wrapped up to such a degree. This lady had a basket with her, and she hadn't known what to do with it for a long time, until she found that on account of my legs being short, it could go underneath me. It cramped and hurt me so that it made me perfectly miserable; but if I moved in the least, and made a glass that was in the basket rattle against something else (as it was sure to do), she gave me the cruellest poke with her foot, and said, 'Come, don't *you* fidget. *Your* bones are young enough, *I*'m sure!'

At last the sun rose, and then my companions seemed to sleep easier. The difficulties under which they had laboured all night, and which had found utterance in the most terrific gasps and snorts, are not to be conceived. As the sun got higher, their sleep became lighter, and so they gradually one by one awoke. I recollect being very much surprised by the feint everybody made, then, of not having been to sleep at all, and by the uncommon indignation with which everyone repelled the charge. I labour under the same kind of astonishment to this day, having invariably observed that, of all human weaknesses, the one to which our common nature is the least disposed to confess (I cannot imagine why) is the weakness of having gone to sleep in a coach.

What an amazing place London was to me when I saw it in the distance, and how I believed all the adventures of all my favourite heroes to be constantly enacting and re-enacting there, and how I vaguely made it out in my own mind to be fuller of wonders and wickedness than all the cities of the earth, I need not stop here to relate. We approached it by degrees, and got, in due time, to the inn in the Whitechapel district, for which we were bound. I forget whether it was the Blue Bull, or the Blue Boar; but I know it was the Blue Something, and that its likeness was painted upon the back of the coach.

The guard's eye lighted on me as he was getting down, and he said at the booking-office door: 'Is there anybody here for a yoongster booked in the name of Murdstone, from Bloonderstone, Sooffolk, to be left till called for?'

Nobody answered.

'Try Copperfield, if you please, sir,' said I, looking helplessly down.

'Is there anybody here for a yoongster, booked in the name of Murdstone, from Bloonderstone, Sooffolk, but owning to the name of Copperfield, to be left till called for?' said the guard. 'Come! *Is* there anybody?'

No. There was nobody. I looked anxiously around; but the enquiry made no impression on any of the bystanders, if I except a man in gaiters, with one eye, who suggested that they had better put a brass collar round my neck, and tie me up in the stable.

A ladder was brought, and I got down after the lady, who was like a haystack; not daring to stir until her basket was removed. The coach was clear of passengers by that time, the luggage was very soon cleared out, the horses had been taken out before the luggage, and now the coach itself was wheeled and backed off by some hostlers, out of the way. Still, nobody appeared, to claim the dusty youngster from Blunderstone, Suffolk.

More solitary than Robinson Crusoe, who had nobody to look at him, and see that he was solitary, I went into the booking-office, and, by invitation of the clerk on duty, passed behind the counter, and sat down on the scale at which they weighed the luggage. Here, as I sat looking at the parcels, packages, and books, and inhaling the smell of stables (ever since associated with that morning), a procession of most tremendous considerations began to march through my mind. Supposing nobody should ever fetch me, how long would they consent to keep me there? Would they keep me long enough to spend seven shillings? Should I sleep at night in one of those wooden bins, with the other luggage, and wash myself at the pump in the yard in the morning; or should I be turned out every night, and expected to come again to be left till called for, when the office opened next day? Supposing there was no mistake in the case, and Mr Murdstone had devised this plan to get rid of me, what should I do? If they allowed me to remain there until my seven shillings were spent, I couldn't hope to remain there when I began to starve. That would obviously be inconvenient and unpleasant to the customers, besides entailing on the Blue Whatever-it-was, the risk of funeral expenses. If I started off at once, and tried to walk back home, how could I ever find my way, how could I ever hope to walk so far, how could I make sure of anyone but Peggotty, even if I got back? If I found out the nearest proper authorities, and offered myself to go for a soldier, or a sailor, I was such a little fellow that it was most likely they wouldn't take me in. These thoughts and a hundred other such thoughts turned me burning hot, and made me giddy with apprehension and dismay. I was in the height of my fever when a man entered and whispered to the clerk, who presently slanted me off the scale, and pushed me over to him, as if I were weighed, bought, delivered, and paid for.

As I went out of the office, hand in hand with this new acquaintance, I stole a look at him. He was a gaunt, sallow young man, with hollow cheeks, and a chin almost as black as Mr Murdstone's; but there the likeness ended, for his whiskers were shaved off, and his hair, instead of being glossy, was rusty and dry. He was dressed in a suit of black clothes which were rather rusty and dry too, and rather short in the sleeves and legs; and he had a white neckerchief on, that was not over-clean. I did not, and do not, suppose that this neckerchief was all the linen he wore, but it was all he showed or gave any hint of.

'You're the new boy?' he said.

'Yes, sir,' I said.

I supposed I was. I didn't know.

'I'm one of the masters at Salem House,' *he* said.

I made him a bow and felt very much overawed. I was so ashamed to allude to a commonplace thing like my box, to a scholar and a master at Salem House, that we had gone some little distance from the yard before I had the hardihood to mention it. We turned back on my humbly insinuating that it might be useful to me hereafter; and he told the clerk that the carrier had instructions to call for it at noon.

'If you please, sir,' I said, when we had accomplished about the same distance as before, 'is it far?'

'It's down by Blackheath,' he said.

'Is *that* far, sir?' I diffidently asked.

'It's a good step,' he said. 'We shall go by the stage-coach. It's about six miles.'

I was so faint and tired that the idea of holding out for six miles more was too much for me. I took heart to tell him that I had had nothing all night, and that, if he would allow me to buy something to eat, I should be very much obliged to him. He appeared surprised at this – I see him stop and look at me now – and, after considering for a few moments, said he wanted to call on an old person who lived not far off, and that the best way would be for me to buy some bread, or whatever I liked best that was wholesome, and make my breakfast at her house, where we could get some milk.

Accordingly we looked in at a baker's window, and after I had made a series of proposals to buy everything that was bilious in the shop, and he had rejected them one by one, we decided in favour of a nice little loaf of brown bread, which cost me threepence. Then, at a grocer's shop, we bought an egg and a slice of streaky bacon; which still left what I thought a good deal of change, out of the second of the bright shillings, and made me consider London a very cheap place. These provisions laid in, we went on through a great noise and uproar that confused my weary head beyond description, and over a bridge which, no doubt, was London Bridge (indeed I think he told me so, but I was half asleep), until we came to the poor person's house, which was a part of some almshouses, as I knew by their look, and by an inscription on a stone over the gate, which said they were established for twenty-five poor women.

The Master at Salem House lifted the latch of one of a number of little black doors that were all alike, and had each a little diamond-paned window on one side, and another little diamond-paned window above; and we went into the little house of one of these poor old women, who was blowing a fire to make a little saucepan boil. On seeing the master enter, the old woman stopped with the bellows on her knee, and said something that I thought sounded like 'My Charley!' but on seeing me come in too, she got up, and rubbing her hands made a confused sort of half curtsey.

'Can you cook this young gentleman's breakfast for him, if you please?' said the Master at Salem House.

'Can I?' said the old woman. 'Yes, can I, sure!'

'How's Mrs Fibbitson today?' said the master, looking at another old woman in a large chair by the fire, who was such a bundle of clothes that I feel grateful to this hour for not having sat upon her by mistake.

'Ah, she's poorly,' said the first old woman. 'It's one of her bad days. If the fire was to go out, through any accident, I verily believe she'd go out too, and never come to life again.'

As they looked at her, I looked at her also. Although it was a warm day, she seemed to think of nothing but the fire. I fancied she was jealous even of the saucepan on it; and I have reason to know that she took its impressment into the service of boiling my egg and broiling my bacon, in dudgeon; for I saw her, with my own discomfited eyes, shake her fist at me once, when those culinary operations were going on, and no one else was looking. The sun streamed in at the little window, but she sat with her own back and the back of the large chair towards it, screening the fire as if she were sedulously keeping it warm, instead of it keeping her warm, and watching it in a most distrustful manner. The completion of the preparations for my breakfast, by relieving the fire, gave her such extreme joy that she laughed aloud – and a very unmelodious laugh she had, I must say.

I sat down to my brown loaf, my egg, and my rasher of bacon, with a basin of milk besides, and made a most delicious meal. While I was yet in the full enjoyment of it, the old woman of the house said to the Master: 'Have you got your flute with you?'

'Yes,' he returned.

'Have a blow at it,' said the old woman coaxingly. 'Do!'

The Master, upon this, put his hand underneath the skirt of his coat, and brought out his flute in three pieces, which he screwed together, and began immediately to play. My impression is, after many years of consideration, that there never can have been anybody in the world who played worse. He made the most dismal sounds I have ever heard produced by any means, natural or artificial. I don't know what the tunes were – if there were such things in the performance at all, which I doubt – but the influence of the strain upon me was, first, to make me think of all my sorrows until I could hardly keep my tears back; then to take away my appetite; and lastly to make me so sleepy that I couldn't keep my eyes open. They begin to close again, and I begin to nod, as the recollection rises fresh upon me. Once more the little room with its open corner cupboard, and its square-backed chairs, and its angular little staircase leading to the room above, and its three peacock's feathers displayed over the mantelpiece – I remember wondering, when I first went in, what that peacock would have thought if he had known what his finery was doomed to come to – fades from before me, and I nod, and sleep. The flute becomes inaudible, the wheels of the coach are heard instead, and I am on my journey. The coach jolts, I wake with a start, and the flute has come back again, and the Master at Salem House is sitting with his legs crossed, playing it dolefully, while the old woman of the house looks on delighted. She fades in her turn, and he fades, and all fades, and there is no flute, no Master, no Salem House, no David Copperfield, no anything but heavy sleep.

I dreamed, I thought, that once while he was blowing into this dismal flute, the old woman of the house, who had gone nearer and nearer to him in her ecstatic admiration, leaned over the back of his chair and gave him an affectionate squeeze round the neck, which stopped his playing for a moment. I was in the middle state between sleeping and waking, either then or immediately afterwards; for, as he resumed – it was a real fact that he had stopped playing – I saw and heard the same old woman ask Mrs Fibbitson if it wasn't delicious (meaning the flute), to which Mrs Fibbitson replied, 'Aye, aye! Yes!' and nodded at the fire; to which, I am persuaded, she gave the credit of the whole performance.

When I seemed to have been dozing a long while, the Master at Salem House unscrewed his flute into the three pieces, put them up as before, and took me away. We found the coach very near at hand, and got upon the roof; but I was so dead sleepy that, when we stopped on the road to take up somebody else, they put me inside where there were no passengers, and where I slept profoundly, until I found the coach going at a footpace up a steep hill among green leaves. Presently, it stopped, and had come to its destination.

A short walk brought us – I mean the Master and me – to Salem House, which was enclosed with a high brick wall, and looked very dull. Over a door in this wall was a board with

Salem House upon it; and through a grating in this door we were surveyed, when we rang the bell, by a surly face, which I found, on the door being opened, belonged to a stout man with a bull-neck, a wooden leg, overhanging temples, and his hair cut close all round his head.

'The new boy,' said the master.

The man with the wooden leg eyed me all over (it didn't take long, for there was not much of me) and locked the gate behind us, and took out the key. We were going up to the house, among some dark heavy trees, when he called after my conductor.

'Hallo!'

We looked back, and he was standing at the door of a little lodge, where he lived, with a pair of boots in his hand.

'Here! The cobbler's been,' he said, 'since you've been out, Mr Mell, and he says he can't mend 'em any more. He says there ain't a bit of the original boot left, and he wonders you expect it.'

With these words he threw the boots towards Mr Mell, who went back a few paces to pick them up, and looked at them (very disconsolately, I was afraid) as we went on together. I observed then, for the first time, that the boots he had on were a good deal the worse for wear, and that his stocking was just breaking out in one place, like a bud.

Salem House was a square brick building with wings; of a bare and unfurnished appearance. All about it was so very quiet that I said to Mr Mell I supposed the boys were out; but he seemed surprised at my not knowing that it was holiday-time. That all the boys were at their several homes. That Mr Creakle, the proprietor, was down by the seaside with Mrs and Miss Creakle. And that I was sent in holiday-time as a punishment for my misdoing. All of which he explained to me as we went along.

My musical breakfast

I gazed upon the schoolroom into which he took me, as the most forlorn and desolate place I had ever seen. I see it now. A long room, with three long rows of desks, and six of forms, and bristling all round with pegs for hats and slates. Scraps of old copy-books and exercises litter the dirty floor. Some silkworms' houses, made of the same materials, are scattered over the desks. Two miserable little white mice, left behind by their owner, are running up and down in a fusty castle made of pasteboard and wire, looking in all the corners with their red eyes for anything to eat. A bird, in a cage, very little bigger than himself, makes a mournful rattle now and then in hopping on his perch, two inches high, or dropping from it; but neither sings nor chirps. There is a strange unwholesome smell upon the room, like mildewed corduroys, sweet apples wanting air, and rotten books. There could not well be more ink splashed about it, if it had been roofless from its first construction, and the skies had rained, snowed, hailed, and blown ink through the varying seasons of the year.

Mr Mell having left me while he took his irreparable boots upstairs, I went softly to the upper end of the room, observing all this as I crept along. Suddenly I came upon a pasteboard placard, beautifully written, which was lying on the desk, and bore these words: '*Take care of him. He bites.*'

I got upon the desk immediately, apprehensive of at least a great dog underneath. But, though I looked all round with anxious eyes, I could see nothing of him. I was still engaged in peering about, when Mr Mell came back, and asked me what I did up there.

'I beg your pardon, sir,' says I, 'if you please, I'm looking for the dog.'

'Dog?' says he; 'what dog?'

'Isn't it a dog, sir?'

'Isn't what a dog?'

'That's to be taken care of, sir; that bites?'

'No, Copperfield,' says he gravely. 'That's not a dog. That's a boy. My instructions are, Copperfield, to put this placard on your back. I am sorry to make such a beginning with you, but I must do it.'

With that, he took me down, and tied the placard, which was neatly constructed for the purpose, on my shoulders like a knapsack; and wherever I went, afterwards, I had the consolation of carrying it.

What I suffered from that placard, nobody can imagine. Whether it was possible for people to see me or not, I always fancied that somebody was reading it. It was no relief to turn round and find nobody; for wherever my back was, there I imagined somebody always to be. That cruel man with the wooden leg aggravated my sufferings. He was in authority; and if he ever saw me leaning against a tree, or a wall, or the house, he roared out from his lodge door in a stupendous voice, 'Hallo, you sir! You Copperfield! Show that badge conspicuous, or I'll report you!' The playground was a bare gravelled yard, open to all the back of the house and the offices; and I knew that the servants read it, and the butcher read it, and the baker read it; that everybody, in a word, who came backwards and forwards to the house, of a morning when I was ordered to walk there, read that I was to be taken care of, for I bit. I recollect that I positively began to have a dread of myself, as a kind of wild boy who did bite.

There was an old door in this playground, on which the boys had a custom of carving their names. It was completely covered with such inscriptions. In my dread of the end of the vacation and their coming back, I could not read a boy's name, without enquiring in what tone and with what emphasis *he* would read, 'Take care of him. He bites.' There was one boy – a certain J. Steerforth – who cut his name very deep and very often, who, I conceived, would read it in a rather strong voice, and afterwards pull my hair. There was another boy, one Tommy Traddles, who I dreaded would make game of it, and pretend to be dreadfully frightened of me. There was a third, George Demple, who I fancied would sing it. I have looked, a little shrinking creature, at that door, until the owners of all the names – there were five-and-forty of them in the school then, Mr Mell said – seemed to send me to Coventry by general acclamation, and to cry out, each in his own way, 'Take care of him. He bites!'

It was the same with the places at the desks and forms. It was the same with the groves of deserted bedsteads I peeped at, on my way to, and when I was in, my own bed. I remember dreaming night after night, of being with my mother as she used to be, or of going to a party at Mr Peggotty's, or of travelling outside the stage-coach, or of dining again with my unfortunate friend the waiter, and in all these circumstances making people scream and stare, by the unhappy disclosure that I had nothing on but my little night-shirt and that placard.

In the monotony of my life, and in my constant apprehension of the reopening of the school, it was such an insupportable affliction! I had long tasks every day to do with Mr Mell; but I did them, there being no Mr and Miss Murdstone here, and got through them without disgrace. Before and after them I walked about – supervised, as I have mentioned, by the man with the wooden leg. How vividly I call to mind the damp about the house, the green cracked flagstones in the court, an old leaky water-butt, and the discoloured trunks of some of the grim trees, which seemed to have dripped more in the rain than other trees, and to have blown less in the sun! At one we dined, Mr Mell and I, at the upper end of a long, bare dining-room, full of deal tables, and smelling of fat. Then, we had more tasks until tea, which Mr Mell drank out of a blue teacup, and I out of a tin pot. All day long, and until seven or eight in the evening, Mr Mell, at his own detached desk in the schoolroom, worked hard with pen, ink, ruler, books, and writing-paper, making out the bills (as I found) for last half year. When he had put up his things for the night he took out his flute, and blew at it, until I almost thought he would gradually blow his whole being into the large hole at the top, and ooze away at the keys.

I picture my small self in the dimly lighted rooms, sitting with my head upon my hand, listening to the doleful performance of Mr Mell, and conning tomorrow's lessons. I picture myself with my books shut up, still listening to the doleful performance of Mr Mell, and listening through it to what used to be at home, and to the blowing of the wind on Yarmouth flats, and feeling very sad and solitary. I picture myself going up to bed, among the unused rooms, and sitting on my bedside crying for a comfortable word from Peggotty. I picture myself coming downstairs in the morning, and looking through a long ghastly gash of a staircase window at the school-bell hanging on the top of an outhouse, with a weathercock above it; and dreading the time when it shall ring J. Steerforth and the rest to work, which is only second, in my foreboding apprehensions, to the time when the man with the wooden leg shall unlock the rusty gate to give admission to the awful Mr Creakle. I cannot think I was a very dangerous character in any of these aspects, but in all of them I carried the same warning on my back.

Mr Mell never said much to me, but he was never harsh to me. I suppose we were company to each other, without talking. I forgot to mention that he would talk to himself sometimes, and grin, and clench his fist, and grind his teeth, and pull his hair in an unaccountable manner. But he had these peculiarities, and at first they frightened me, though I soon got used to them.

CHAPTER 6

I Enlarge My Circle of Acquaintance

I had led this life about a month, when the man with the wooden leg began to stump about with a mop and a bucket of water, from which I inferred that preparations were making to receive Mr Creakle and the boys. I was not mistaken; for the mop came into the schoolroom before long, and turned out Mr Mell and me, who lived where we could, and got on how we could, for some days, during which we were always in the way of two or three young women, who had rarely shown themselves before, and were so continually in the midst of dust that I sneezed almost as much as if Salem House had been a great snuff-box.

One day I was informed by Mr Mell that Mr Creakle would be home that evening. In the evening, after tea, I heard that he was come. Before bedtime, I was fetched by the man with the wooden leg to appear before him.

Mr Creakle's part of the house was a good deal more comfortable than ours, and he had a snug bit of garden that looked pleasant after the dusty playground, which was such a desert in miniature, that I thought no one but a camel, or a dromedary, could have felt at home in it. It seemed to me a bold thing even to take notice that the passage looked comfortable, as I went on my way, trembling, to Mr Creakle's presence, which so abashed me, when I was ushered into it, that I hardly saw Mrs Creakle or Miss Creakle (who were both there in the parlour), or anything but Mr Creakle, a stout gentleman with a bunch of watch-chain and seals, in an armchair, with a tumbler and bottle beside him.

'So!' said Mr Creakle. 'This is the young gentleman whose teeth are to be filed! Turn him round.'

The wooden-legged man turned me about so as to exhibit the placard; and having afforded time for a full survey of it, turned me about again, with my face to Mr Creakle, and posted himself at Mr Creakle's side. Mr Creakle's face was fiery, and his eyes were small, and deep in his head; he had thick veins in his forehead, a little nose, and a large chin. He was bald on the top of his head, and had some thin wet-looking hair that was just turning grey, brushed across each temple, so that the two sides interlaced on his forehead. But the circumstance about him which impressed me most was, that he had no voice, but spoke in a whisper. The exertion this cost him, or the consciousness of talking in that feeble way, made his angry face so much more angry, and his thick veins so much thicker, when he spoke, that I am not surprised, on looking back, at this peculiarity striking me as his chief one.

'Now,' said Mr Creakle, 'what's the report of this boy?'

'There's nothing against him yet,' returned the man with the wooden leg. 'There has been no opportunity.'

I thought Mr Creakle was disappointed. I thought Mrs and Miss Creakle (at whom I now glanced for the first time, and who were, both, thin and quiet) were not disappointed.

'Come here, sir!' said Mr Creakle, beckoning to me.

'Come here!' said the man with the wooden leg, repeating the gesture.

'I have the happiness of knowing your father-in-law,' whispered Mr Creakle, taking me by the ear; 'and a worthy man he is, and a man of strong character. He knows me, and I know him. Do *you* know me? Hey?' said Mr Creakle, pinching my ear with ferocious playfulness.

'Not yet, sir,' I said, flinching with the pain.

'Not yet? Hey?' repeated Mr Creakle. 'But you will soon. Hey?'

'You will soon. Hey?' repeated the man with the wooden leg. I afterwards found that he generally acted, with his strong voice, as Mr Creakle's interpreter to the boys.

I was very much frightened, and said, I hoped so, if he pleased. I felt, all this while, as if my ear were blazing; he pinched it so hard.

'I'll tell you what I am,' whispered Mr Creakle, letting it go at last, with a screw at parting that brought the water into my eyes. 'I'm a Tartar.'

'A Tartar,' said the man with the wooden leg.

'When I say I'll do a thing, I do it,' said Mr Creakle; 'and when I say I will have a thing done, I will have it done.'

' – Will have a thing done, I will have it done,' repeated the man with the wooden leg.

'I am a determined character,' said Mr Creakle. 'That's what I am. I do my duty. That's what I do. My flesh and blood,' he looked at Mrs Creakle as he said this, 'when it rises against me, is not my flesh and blood. I discard it. Has that fellow,' to the man with the wooden leg, 'been here again?'

'No,' was the answer.

'No,' said Mr Creakle. 'He knows better. He knows me. Let him keep away. I say let him keep away,' said Mr Creakle, striking his hand upon the table, and looking at Mrs Creakle, 'for he knows me. Now you have begun to know me too, my young friend, and you may go. Take him away.'

I was very glad to be ordered away, for Mrs and Miss Creakle were both wiping their eyes, and I felt as uncomfortable for them as I did for myself. But I had a petition on my mind which concerned me so nearly, that I couldn't help saying, though I wondered at my own courage: 'If you please, sir – '

Mr Creakle whispered, 'Hah? What's this?' and bent his eyes upon me, as if he would have burnt me up with them.

'If you please, sir,' I faltered, 'if I might be allowed (I am very sorry indeed, sir, for what I did) to take this writing off, before the boys come back – '

Whether Mr Creakle was in earnest, or whether he only did it to frighten me, I don't know, but he made a burst out of his chair, before which I precipitately retreated, without waiting for the escort of the man with the wooden leg, and never once stopped until I reached my own bedroom, where, finding I was not pursued, I went to bed, as it was time, and lay quaking, for a couple of hours.

Next morning Mr Sharp came back. Mr Sharp was the first master, and superior to Mr Mell. Mr Mell took his meals with the boys, but Mr Sharp dined and supped at Mr Creakle's table. He was a limp, delicate-looking gentleman, I thought, with a good deal of nose, and a way of carrying his head on one side, as if it were a little too heavy for him. His hair was very smooth and wavy; but I was informed by the very first boy who came back that it was a wig (a second-hand one *he* said), and that Mr Sharp went out every Saturday afternoon to get it curled.

It was no other than Tommy Traddles who gave me this piece of intelligence. He was the first boy who returned. He introduced himself by informing me that I should find his name on the right-hand corner of the gate, over the top bolt; upon that I said, 'Traddles?' to which he replied, 'The same,' and then he asked me for a full account of myself and family.

It was a happy circumstance for me that Traddles came back first. He enjoyed my placard so much, that he saved me from the embarrassment of either disclosure or concealment, by presenting me to every other boy who came back, great or small, immediately on his arrival, in this form of introduction, 'Look here! Here's a game!' Happily, too, the greater part of the boys came back low-spirited, and were not so boisterous at my expense as I had expected. Some of them certainly did dance about me like wild Indians, and the greater part could not resist the temptation of pretending that I was a dog, and patting me and smoothing me lest I should bite, and saying, 'Lie down, sir!' and calling me Towser. This was naturally confusing, among so many strangers, and cost me some tears, but on the whole it was much better than I had anticipated.

I was not considered as being formally received into the school, however, until J. Steerforth arrived. Before this boy, who was reputed to be a great scholar, and was very good-looking, and at least half a dozen years my senior, I was carried as before a magistrate. He enquired, under a shed in the playground, into the particulars of my punishment, and was pleased to express his opinion that it was 'a jolly shame'; for which I became bound to him ever afterwards.

'What money have you got, Copperfield?' he said, walking aside with me when he had disposed of my affair in these terms.

I told him seven shillings.

'You had better give it to me to take care of,' he said. 'At least, you can if you like. You needn't if you don't like.'

I hastened to comply with his friendly suggestion, and opening Peggotty's purse, turned it upside down into his hand.

'Do you want to spend anything now?' he asked me.

'No, I thank you,' I replied.

'You can, if you like, you know,' said Steerforth. 'Say the word.'

'No, thank you, sir,' I repeated.

'Perhaps you'd like to spend a couple of shillings, or so, in a bottle of currant wine by and by, up in the bedroom?' said Steerforth. 'You belong to my bedroom, I find.'

It certainly had not occurred to me before, but I said: 'Yes, I should like that.'

'Very good,' said Steerforth. 'You'll be glad to spend another shilling or so in almond cakes, I dare say?'

I said: 'Yes, I should like that, too.'

'And another shilling or so in biscuits, and another in fruit, eh?' said Steerforth. 'I say, young Copperfield, you're going it!'

I smiled because he smiled, but I was a little troubled in my mind, too.

'Well!' said Steerforth. 'We must make it stretch as far as we can; that's all. I'll do the best in my power for you. I can go out when I like, and I'll smuggle the prog in.' With these words he put the money in his pocket, and kindly told me not to make myself uneasy; he would take care it should be all right.

He was as good as his word, if that were all right which I had a secret misgiving was nearly all wrong – for I feared it was a waste of my mother's two half-crowns – though I had preserved the piece of paper they were wrapped in, which was a precious saving. When we went upstairs to bed, he produced the whole seven shillings' worth, and laid it out on my bed in the moonlight, saying: 'There you are, young Copperfield, and a royal spread you've got!'

I couldn't think of doing the honours of the feast, at my time of life, while he was by; my hand shook at the very thought of it. I begged him to do me the favour of presiding; and my request being seconded by the other boys who were in that room, he acceded to it, and sat upon my pillow, handing round the viands – with perfect fairness, I must say – and dispensing the currant wine in a little glass without a foot, which was his own property. As to me, I sat on his left hand, and the rest were grouped about us, on the nearest beds and on the floor.

How well I recollect our sitting there, talking in whispers; or their talking, and my respectfully listening, I ought rather to say; the moonlight falling a little way into the room, through the window, painting a pale window on the floor, and the greater part of us in shadow, except when Steerforth dipped a match into a phosphorus-box, when he wanted to look for anything on the board, and shed a blue glare over us that was gone directly! A certain mysterious feeling, consequent on the darkness, the secrecy of the revel, and the whisper in which everything was said, steals over me again, and I listen to all they tell me, with a vague feeling of solemnity and awe, which makes me glad that they are all so near, and frightens me

(though I feign to laugh) when Traddles pretends to see a ghost in the corner.

I heard all kinds of things about the school and all belonging to it. I heard that Mr Creakle had not proferred his claim to being a Tartar without reason; that he was the sternest and most severe of masters; that he laid about him, right and left, every day of his life, charging in among the boys like a trooper, and slashing away, unmercifully. That he knew nothing himself, but the art of slashing, being more ignorant (J. Steerforth said) than the lowest boy in the school; that he had been, a good many years ago, a small hop-dealer in the Borough, and had taken to the schooling business after being bankrupt in hops, and making away with Mrs Creakle's money. With a good deal more of that sort, which I wondered how they knew.

I heard that the man with the wooden leg, whose name was Tungay, was an obstinate barbarian who had formerly assisted in the hop business, but had come into the scholastic line with Mr Creakle, in consequence, as was supposed among the boys, of his having broken his leg in Mr Creakle's service, and having done a deal of dishonest work for him, and knowing his secrets. I heard that with the single exception of Mr Creakle, Tungay considered the whole establishment, masters and boys, as his natural enemies, and that the only delight of his life was to be sour and malicious. I heard that Mr Creakle had a son, who had not been Tungay's friend, and who, assisting in the school, had once held some remonstrance with his father on an occasion when its discipline was very cruelly exercised, and was supposed, besides, to have protested against his father's usage of his mother. I heard that Mr Creakle had turned him out of doors, in consequence; and that Mrs and Miss Creakle had been in a sad way, ever since.

But the greatest wonder that I heard of Mr Creakle was there being one boy in the school on whom he never ventured to lay a hand, and that boy being J. Steerforth. Steerforth himself confirmed this when it was stated, and said that he should like to begin to see him do it. On being asked by a mild boy (not me) how he would proceed if he did begin to see him do it, he dipped a match into his phosphorus-box on purpose to shed a glare over his reply, and said he would commence with knocking him down with a blow on the forehead from the seven and sixpenny ink-bottle that was always on the mantelpiece. We sat in the dark for some time, breathless.

I heard that Mr Sharp and Mr Mell were both supposed to be wretchedly paid; and that when there was hot and cold meat for dinner at Mr Creakle's table, Mr Sharp was always expected to say he preferred cold; which was again corroborated by J. Steerforth, the only parlour-boarder. I heard that Mr Sharp's wig didn't fit him; and that he needn't be so 'bounceable' – somebody else said 'bumptious' – about it, because his own red hair was very plainly to be seen behind.

I heard that one boy, who was a coal-merchant's son, came as a set-off against the coal-bill, and was called on that account 'Exchange or Barter' – a name selected from the arithmetic-book as expressing this arrangement. I heard that the table-beer was a robbery of parents, and the pudding an imposition. I heard that Miss Creakle was regarded by the school in general as being in love with Steerforth; and I am sure, as I sat in the dark, thinking of his nice voice, and his fine face, and his easy manner, and his curling hair, I thought it very likely. I heard that Mr Mell was not a bad sort of fellow, but hadn't a sixpence to bless himself with; and that there was no doubt that old Mrs Mell, his mother, was as poor as Job. I thought of my breakfast then, and what had sounded like 'My Charley!' but I was, I am glad to remember, as mute as a mouse about it.

The hearing of all this, and a good deal more, outlasted the banquet some time. The greater part of the guests had gone to bed as soon as the eating and drinking were over; and we, who had remained whispering and listening half undressed, at last betook ourselves to bed, too.

'Good-night, young Copperfield,' said Steerforth, 'I'll take care of you.'

'You're very kind,' I gratefully returned. 'I am very much obliged to you.'

'You haven't got a sister, have you?' said Steerforth, yawning. 'No,' I answered.

'That's a pity,' said Steerforth. 'If you had had one, I should think she would have been a pretty, timid, little, bright-eyed sort of girl. I should have liked to know her. Good-night, young Copperfield.'

'Good-night, sir,' I replied.

I thought of him very much after I went to bed, and raised myself, I recollect, to look at him where he lay in the moonlight, with his handsome face turned up, and his head reclining easily on his arm. He was a person of great power in my eyes; that was of course the reason of my mind running on him. No veiled future dimly glanced upon him in the moonbeams. There was no shadowy picture of his footsteps in the garden that I dreamed of walking in all night.

CHAPTER 7

My 'First Half' at Salem House

School began in earnest next day. A profound impression was made upon me, I remember, by the roar of voices in the schoolroom suddenly becoming hushed as death when Mr Creakle entered after breakfast, and stood in the doorway looking round upon us like a giant in a story-book surveying his captives.

Tungay stood at Mr Creakle's elbow. He had no occasion, I thought, to cry out 'Silence!' so ferociously, for the boys were all struck speechless and motionless.

Mr Creakle was seen to speak, and Tungay was heard, to this effect.

'Now, boys, this is a new half. Take care what you're about, in this new half. Come fresh up to the lessons, I advise you, for I come fresh up to the punishment. I won't flinch. It will be of no use your rubbing yourselves; you won't rub the marks out that I shall give you. Now get to work, every boy!'

When this dreadful exordium was over, and Tungay had stumped out again, Mr Creakle came to where I sat, and told

me that, if I were famous for biting, he was famous for biting, too. He then showed me the cane, and asked me what I thought of *that*, for a tooth? Was it a sharp tooth, hey? Was it a double tooth, hey? Had it a deep prong, hey? Did it bite, hey? Did it bite? At every question he gave me a fleshy cut with it that made me writhe; so I was very soon made free of Salem House (as Steerforth said), and very soon in tears also.

Not that I mean to say these were special marks of distinction, which only I received. On the contrary, a large majority of the boys (especially the smaller ones) were visited with similar instances of notice, as Mr Creakle made the round of the schoolroom. Half the establishment was writhing and crying, before the day's work began; and how much of it had writhed and cried before the day's work was over, I am really afraid to recollect, lest I should seem to exaggerate.

I should think there never can have been a man who enjoyed his profession more than Mr Creakle did. He had a delight in cutting at the boys, which was like the satisfaction of a craving appetite. I am confident that he couldn't resist a chubby boy, especially; that there was a fascination in such a subject, which made him restless in his mind, until he had scored and marked him for the day. I was chubby myself, and ought to know. I am sure when I think of the fellow now, my blood rises against him with the disinterested indignation I should feel if I could have known all about him without having ever been in his power; but it rises hotly, because I know him to have been an incapable brute, who had no more right to be possessed of the great trust he held than to be Lord High Admiral, or Commander-in-Chief; in either of which capacities, it is probable that he would have done infinitely less mischief.

Miserable little propitiators of a remorseless Idol, how abject we were to him! What a launch in life I think it now, on looking back, to be so mean and servile to a man of such parts and pretensions!

Here I sit at the desk again, watching his eye – humbly watching his eye, as he rules a ciphering book for another victim whose hands have just been flattened by that identical ruler, and who is trying to wipe the sting out with a pocket-handkerchief. I have plenty to do. I don't watch his eye in idleness, but because I am morbidly attracted to it, in a dread desire to know what he will do next, and whether it will be my turn to suffer, or somebody else's. A lane of small boys beyond me, with the same interest in his eye, watch it too. I think he knows it, though he pretends he doesn't. He makes dreadful mouths as he rules the ciphering book; and now he throws his eye sideways down our lane, and we all droop over our books and tremble. A moment afterwards we are again eyeing him. An unhappy culprit, found guilty of imperfect exercise, approaches at his command. The culprit falters excuses, and professes a determination to do better tomorrow. Mr Creakle cuts a joke before he beats him, and we laugh at it – miserable little dogs, we laugh, with our visages as white as ashes, and our hearts sinking into our boots.

Here I sit at the desk again, on a drowsy summer afternoon. A buzz and hum go up around me, as if the boys were so many bluebottles. A cloggy sensation of the lukewarm fat of meat is upon me (we dined an hour or two ago), and my head is as heavy as so much lead. I would give the world to go to sleep. I sit with my eye on Mr Creakle, blinking at him like a young owl; when sleep overpowers me for a minute, he still looms through my slumber, ruling those ciphering books; until he softly comes behind me and wakes me to plainer perception of him, with a red ridge across my back.

Here I am in the playground, with my eye still fascinated by him, though I can't see him. The window at a little distance, from which I know he is having his dinner, stands for him, and I eye that instead. If he shows his face near it, mine assumes an imploring and submissive expression. If he looks out through the glass, the boldest boy (Steerforth excepted) stops in the middle of a shout or yell, and becomes contemplative. One day Traddles (the most unfortunate boy in the world) breaks that window accidentally with a ball. I shudder at this moment with the tremendous sensation of seeing it done, and feeling that the ball has bounded on to Mr Creakle's sacred head.

Poor Traddles! In a tight sky-blue suit that made his arms and legs like German sausages, or roly-poly puddings, he was the merriest and most miserable of all the boys. He was always being caned – I think he was caned every day that half year, except one holiday Monday when he was only rulered on both hands – and was always going to write to his uncle about it, and never did. After laying his head on the desk for a little while, he would cheer up somehow, begin to laugh again, and draw skeletons all over his slate, before his eyes were dry. I used at first to wonder what comfort Traddles found in drawing skeletons; and for some time looked upon him as a sort of hermit, who reminded himself by those symbols of mortality that caning couldn't last for ever. But I believe he only did it because they were easy, and didn't want any features.

He was very honourable, Traddles was, and held it as a solemn duty in the boys to stand by one another. He suffered for this on several occasions; and particularly once, when Steerforth laughed in church, and the Beadle thought it was Traddles, and took him out. I see him now, going away in custody, despised by the congregation. He never said who was the real offender, though he smarted for it next day, and was imprisoned so many hours that he came forth with a whole churchyardful of skeletons swarming all over his Latin dictionary. But he had his reward. Steerforth said there was nothing of the sneak in Traddles, and we all felt that to be the highest praise. For my part, I could have gone through a good deal (though I was much less brave than Traddles, and nothing like so old) to have won such a recompense.

To see Steerforth walk to church before us, arm in arm with Miss Creakle, was one of the great sights of my life. I didn't think Miss Creakle equal to little Em'ly in point of beauty, and I didn't love her (I didn't dare); but I thought her a young lady of extraordinary attractions, and in point of gentility not to be surpassed. When Steerforth, in white trousers, carried her parasol for her, I felt proud to know him; and believed that she could not choose but adore him with all her heart. Mr Sharp and Mr Mell were both notable personages in my eyes; but Steerforth was to them what the sun was to two stars.

Steerforth continued his protection of me, and proved a very useful friend; since nobody dared to annoy one whom he honoured with his countenance. He couldn't – or at all events he didn't – defend me from Mr Creakle, who was very severe with me; but whenever I had been treated worse than usual, he always told me that I wanted a little of his pluck, and that he wouldn't have stood it himself; which I felt he intended for encouragement, and considered to be very kind of him. There was one advantage, and only one that I know of, in Mr Creakle's severity. He found my placard in his way when he came up or down behind the form on which I sat, and wanted to make a cut at me in passing; for this reason it was soon taken off, and I saw it no more.

An accidental circumstance cemented the intimacy between Steerforth and me, in a manner that inspired me with great pride and satisfaction, though it sometimes led to inconvenience. It happened on one occasion, when he was doing me the honour of talking to me in the playground, that I hazarded the observation that something or somebody – I forget what now – was like something or somebody in *Peregrine Pickle*. He said nothing at the time; but when I was going to bed at night, asked me if I had got that book.

I told him no, and explained how it was that I had read it, and all those other books of which I have made mention.

'And do you recollect them?' Steerforth said.

Oh, yes, I replied; I had a good memory, and I believed I recollected them very well.

'Then I tell you what, young Copperfield,' said Steerforth, 'you shall tell 'em to me. I can't get to sleep very early at night, and I generally wake rather early in the morning. We'll go over 'em one after another. We'll make some regular Arabian Nights of it.'

I felt extremely flattered by this arrangement, and we commenced carrying it into execution that very evening. What ravages I committed on my favourite authors in the course of my interpretation of them, I am not in a condition to say, and should be very unwilling to know; but I had a profound faith in them, and I had, to the best of my belief, a simple, earnest manner of narrating what I did narrate; and these qualities went a long way.

The drawback was that I was often sleepy at night, or out of spirits and indisposed to resume the story; and then it was rather hard work, and it must be done; for to disappoint or displease Steerforth was of course out of the question. In the morning, too, when I felt weary, and should have enjoyed another hour's repose very much, it was a tiresome thing to be roused, like the Sultana Scheherezade, and forced into a long story before the getting-up bell rang; but Steerforth was resolute; and as he explained to me, in return, my sums and exercises, and anything in my tasks that was too hard for me, I was no loser by the transaction. Let me do myself justice, however. I was moved by no interested or selfish motive, nor was I moved by fear of him. I admired and loved him, and his approval was return enough. It was so precious to me that I look back on these trifles, now, with an aching heart.

Steerforth was considerate, too; and showed his consideration, in one particular instance, in an unflinching manner that was a little tantalising, I suspect, to poor Traddles and the rest. Peggotty's promised letter – what a comfortable letter it was! – arrived before 'the half' was many weeks old; and with it a cake in a perfect nest of oranges, and two bottles of cowslip wine. This treasure, as in duty bound, I laid at the feet of Steerforth, and begged him to dispense.

'Now, I'll tell you what, young Copperfield,' said he; 'the wine shall be kept to wet your whistle when you are story-telling.'

I blushed at the idea, and begged him, in my modesty, not to think of it. But he said he had observed I was sometimes hoarse – a little roopy was his exact expression – and it should be, every drop, devoted to the purpose he had mentioned. Accordingly, it was locked up in his box, and drawn off by himself in a phial, and administered to me through a piece of quill in the cork, when I was supposed to be in want of a restorative. Sometimes, to make it a more sovereign specific, he was so kind as to squeeze orange juice into it, or to stir it up with ginger, or dissolve a peppermint drop in it; and although I cannot assert that the flavour was improved by these experiments, or that it was exactly the compound one would have chosen for a stomachic, the last thing at night and the first thing in the morning, I drank it gratefully, and was very sensible of his attention.

We seem to me to have been months over *Peregrine*, and months more over the other stories. The institution never flagged for want of a story, I am certain; and the wine lasted out almost as well as the matter. Poor Traddles – I never think of that boy but with a strange disposition to laugh, and with tears in my eyes – was a sort of chorus, in general; and affected to be convulsed with mirth at the comic parts, and to be overcome with fear when there was any passage of an alarming character in the narrative. This rather put me out, very often. It was a great jest of his, I recollect, to pretend that he couldn't keep his teeth from chattering, whenever mention was made of an Alguazil in connection with the adventures of Gil Blas; and I remember when Gil Blas met the captain of the robbers in Madrid, this unlucky joker counterfeited such an ague of terror that he was overheard by Mr Creakle, who was prowling about the passage, and handsomely flogged for disorderly conduct in the bedroom.

Whatever I had within me that was romantic and dreamy was encouraged by so much story-telling in the dark; and in that respect the pursuit may not have been very profitable to me. But the being cherished as a kind of plaything in my room, and the consciousness that this accomplishment of mine was bruited about among the boys, and attracted a good deal of notice to me, though I was the youngest there, stimulated me to exertion. In a school carried on by sheer cruelty, whether it is presided over by a dunce or not, there is not likely to be much learned. I believe our boys were, generally, as ignorant a set as any schoolboys in existence; they were too much troubled and knocked about to learn; they could no more do that to advantage than anyone can do anything to advantage in a life of constant misfortune, torment, and worry. But my little vanity, and Steerforth's help, urged me on somehow; and without

saving me from much, if anything, in the way of punishment, made me, for the time I was there, an exception to the general body, insomuch that I did steadily pick up some crumbs of knowledge.

In this I was much assisted by Mr Mell, who had a liking for me that I am grateful to remember. It always gave me pain to observe that Steerforth treated him with systematic disparagement, and seldom lost an occasion of wounding his feelings, or inducing others to do so. This troubled me the more for a long time, because I had soon told Steerforth, from whom I could no more keep such a secret than I could keep a cake or any other tangible possession, about the two old women Mr Mell had taken me to see; and I was always afraid that Steerforth would let it out, and twit him with it.

We little thought, any one of us, I dare say, when I ate my breakfast that first morning, and went to sleep under the shadow of the peacock's feathers to the sound of the flute, what consequences would come of the introduction into those almshouses of my insignificant person. But the visit had its unforeseen consequences; and of a serious sort, too, in their way.

One day when Mr Creakle kept the house from indisposition, which naturally diffused a lively joy through the school, there was a good deal of noise in the course of the morning's work. The great relief and satisfaction experienced by the boys made them difficult to manage; and though the dreaded Tungay brought his wooden leg in twice or thrice, and took notes of the principal offenders' names, no great impression was made by it, as they were pretty sure of getting into trouble tomorrow, do what they would, and thought it wise, no doubt, to enjoy themselves today.

It was, properly, a half-holiday, being Saturday. But as the noise in the playground would have disturbed Mr Creakle, and the weather was not favourable for going out walking, we were ordered into school in the afternoon, and set some lighter tasks than usual, which were made for the occasion. It was the day of the week on which Mr Sharp went out to get his wig curled; so Mr Mell, who always did the drudgery, whatever it was, kept school by himself.

If I could associate the idea of a bull or a bear with anyone so mild as Mr Mell, I should think of him, in connection with that afternoon when the uproar was at its height, as of one of those animals, baited by a thousand dogs. I recall him bending his aching head, supported on his bony hand, over the book on his desk, and wretchedly endeavouring to get on with his tiresome work, amidst an uproar that might have made the Speaker of the House of Commons giddy. Boys started in and out of their places, playing at puss-in-the-corner with other boys; there were laughing boys, singing boys, talking boys, dancing boys, howling boys; boys shuffled with their feet, boys whirled about him, grinning, making faces, mimicking him behind his back and before his eyes; mimicking his poverty, his boots, his coat, his mother, everything belonging to him that they should have had consideration for.

'Silence!' cried Mr Mell, suddenly rising up, and striking his desk with the book. 'What does this mean! It's impossible to bear it. It's maddening. How can you do it to me, boys?'

It was my book that he struck his desk with; and as I stood beside him, following his eye as it glanced round the room, I saw the boys all stop, some suddenly surprised, some half afraid, and some sorry, perhaps.

Steerforth's place was at the bottom of the school, at the opposite end of the long room. He was lounging with his back against the wall, and his hands in his pockets, and looked at Mr Mell with his mouth shut up as if he were whistling, when Mr Mell looked at him.

'Silence, Mr Steerforth!' said Mr Mell.

'Silence yourself,' said Steerforth, turning red. 'Whom are you talking to?'

'Sit down,' said Mr Mell.

'Sit down yourself,' said Steerforth, 'and mind your business.'

There was a titter and some applause; but Mr Mell was so white that silence immediately succeeded; and one boy, who had darted out behind him to imitate his mother again, changed his mind, and pretended to want a pen mended.

'If you think, Steerforth,' said Mr Mell, 'that I am not acquainted with the power you can establish over any mind here' – he laid his hand, without considering what he did (as I supposed), upon my head – 'or that I have not observed you, within a few minutes, urging your juniors on to every sort of outrage against me, you are mistaken.'

'I don't give myself the trouble of thinking at all about you,' said Steerforth coolly; 'so I'm not mistaken, as it happens.'

'And when you make use of your position of favouritism here, sir,' pursued Mr Mell, with his lip trembling very much, 'to insult a gentleman –'

'A what? – where is he?' said Steerforth.

Here somebody cried out, 'Shame, J. Steerforth! Too bad!' It was Traddles; whom Mr Mell instantly discomfited by bidding him hold his tongue.

'To insult one who is not fortunate in life, sir, and who never gave you the least offence, and the many reasons for not insulting whom you are old enough and wise enough to understand,' said Mr Mell, with his lip trembling more and more, 'you commit a mean and base action. You can sit down or stand up as you please, sir. Copperfield, go on.'

'Young Copperfield,' said Steerforth, coming forward up the room, 'stop a bit. I tell you what, Mr Mell, once for all. When you take the liberty of calling me mean or base, or anything of that sort, you are an impudent beggar. You are always a beggar, you know; but when you do that, you are an impudent beggar.'

I am not clear whether he was going to strike Mr Mell, or Mr Mell was going to strike him, or there was any such intention on either side. I saw a rigidity come upon the whole school as if they had been turned into stone, and found Mr Creakle in the midst of us, with Tungay at his side, and Mrs and Miss Creakle looking in at the door as if they were frightened. Mr Mell, with his elbows on his desk and his face in his hands, sat, for some moments, quite still.

'Mr Mell,' said Mr Creakle, shaking him by the arm; and his whisper was so audible now that Tungay felt it unnecessary to repeat his words; 'you have not forgotten yourself, I hope?'

'No, sir, no,' returned the master, showing his face, and shaking his head, and rubbing his hands in great agitation. 'No, sir, no. I have remembered myself, I – no, Mr Creakle, I have not forgotten myself, I – I have remembered myself, sir. I – I – could wish you had remembered me a little sooner, Mr Creakle. It – it – would have been more kind, sir, more just, sir. It would have saved me something, sir.'

Mr Creakle, looking hard at Mr Mell, put his hand on

Steerforth and Mr Mells

Tungay's shoulder, and got his feet upon the form close by, and sat upon the desk. After still looking hard at Mr Mell from this throne, as he shook his head, and rubbed his hands, and remained in the same state of agitation, Mr Creakle turned to Steerforth, and said: 'Now, sir, as he don't condescend to tell me, what *is* this?'

Steerforth evaded the question for a little while; looking in scorn and anger on his opponent, and remaining silent. I could not help thinking even in that interval, I remember, what a noble fellow he was in appearance, and how homely and plain Mr Mell looked opposed to him.

'What did he mean by talking about favourites, then!' said Steerforth at length.

'Favourites?' repeated Mr Creakle, with the veins in his forehead swelling quickly. 'Who talked about favourites?'

'He did,' said Steerforth.

'And pray, what did you mean by that, sir?' demanded Mr Creakle, turning angrily on his assistant.

'I meant, Mr Creakle,' he returned in a low voice, 'as I said; that no pupil had a right to avail himself of his position of favouritism to degrade me.'

'To degrade *you*?' said Mr Creakle. 'My stars! But give me leave to ask you, Mr What's-your-name'; and here Mr Creakle folded his arms, cane and all, upon his chest, and made such a knot of his brows that his little eyes were hardly visible below them; 'whether, when you talk about favourites, you show proper respect to me? To me, sir,' said Mr Creakle, darting his head at him suddenly, and drawing it back again, 'the principal of this establishment, and your employer.'

'It was not judicious, sir, I am willing to admit,' said Mr Mell. 'I should not have done so, if I had been cool.'

Here Steerforth struck in.

'Then he said I was mean, and then he said I was base, and then I called him a beggar. If *I* had been cool, perhaps I shouldn't have called him a beggar. But I did, and I am ready to take the consequences of it.'

Without considering, perhaps, whether there were any consequences to be taken, I felt quite in a glow at this gallant speech. It made an impression on the boys, too, for there was a low stir among them, though no one spoke a word.

'I am surprised, Steerforth – although your candour does you honour,' said Mr Creakle, 'does you honour, certainly – I am surprised, Steerforth, I must say, that you should attach such an epithet to any person employed and paid in Salem House, sir.'

Steerforth gave a short laugh.

'That's not an answer, sir,' said Mr Creakle, 'to my remark. I expect more than that from you, Steerforth.'

If Mr Mell looked homely, in my eyes, before the handsome boy, it would be quite impossible to say how homely Mr Creakle looked.

'Let him deny it,' said Steerforth.

'Deny that he is a beggar, Steerforth?' cried Mr Creakle. 'Why, where does he go a-begging?'

'If he is not a beggar himself, his near relation's one,' said Steerforth. 'It's all the same.'

He glanced at me, and Mr Mell's hand gently patted me upon the shoulder. I looked up with a flush upon my face and remorse in my heart, but Mr Mell's eyes were fixed on Steerforth. He continued to pat me kindly on the shoulder, but he looked at him.

'Since you expect me, Mr Creakle, to justify myself,' said Steerforth, 'and to say what I mean – what I have to say is, that his mother lives on charity in an alms-house.'

Mr Mell still looked at him, and still patted me kindly on the shoulder, and said to himself, in a whisper, if I heard right: 'Yes, I thought so.'

Mr Creakle turned to his assistant, with a severe frown and laboured politeness: 'Now, you hear what this gentleman says, Mr Mell. Have the goodness, if you please, to set him right before the assembled school.'

'He is right, sir, without correction,' returned Mr Mell, in the midst of a dead silence; 'what he has said is true.'

'Be so good, then, as declare publicly, will you,' said Mr Creakle, putting his head on one side, and rolling his eyes round the school, 'whether it ever came to my knowledge until this moment?'

'I believe not directly,' he returned.

'Why, you know not,' said Mr Creakle. 'Don't you, man?'

'I apprehend you never supposed my worldly circumstances to be very good,' replied the assistant. 'You know what my position is, and always has been here.'

'I apprehend, if you come to that,' said Mr Creakle, with his veins swelling again bigger than ever, 'that you've been in a wrong position altogether, and mistook this for a charity school. Mr Mell, we'll part, if you please. The sooner the better.'

'There is no time,' answered Mr Mell, rising, 'like the present.'

'Sir, to you!' said Mr Creakle.

'I take my leave of you, Mr Creakle, and of all of you,' said Mr Mell, glancing round the room, and again patting me gently on the shoulder. 'James Steerforth, the best wish I can leave you is that you may come to be ashamed of what you have done today. At present I would prefer to see you anything rather than a friend to me, or to anyone in whom I feel an interest.'

Once more he laid his hand upon my shoulder; and then taking his flute and a few books from his desk, and leaving the key in it for his successor, he went out of the school, with his property under his arm. Mr Creakle then made a speech, through Tungay, in which he thanked Steerforth for asserting (though perhaps too warmly) the independence and respectability of Salem House; and which he wound up by shaking hands with Steerforth, while we gave three cheers – I did not quite know what for, but I supposed for Steerforth, and so joined in them ardently, though I felt miserable. Mr Creakle then caned Tommy Traddles for being discovered in tears, instead of cheers, on account of Mr Mell's departure; and went back to his sofa or his bed, or wherever he had come from.

We were left to ourselves now, and looked very blank, I recollect, on one another. For myself, I felt so much self-reproach and contrition for my part in what had happened that nothing would have enabled me to keep back my tears but the fear that Steerforth, who often looked at me, I saw, might think it unfriendly – or, I should rather say, considering our relative ages, and the feeling with which I regarded him, undutiful – if I showed the emotion which distressed me. He was very angry with Traddles, and said he was glad he had caught it.

Poor Traddles, who had passed the stage of lying with his head upon the desk, and was relieving himself as usual with a burst of skeletons, said he didn't care. Mr Mell was ill-used.

'Who has ill-used him, you girl?' said Steerforth.

'Why, you have,' returned Traddles.

'What have I done?' said Steerforth.

'What have you done?' retorted Traddles. 'Hurt his feelings and lost him his situation.'

'His feelings!' repeated Steerforth disdainfully. 'His feelings will soon get the better of it, I'll be bound. His feelings are not like yours, Miss Traddles. As to his situation – which was a precious one, wasn't it? – do you suppose I am not going to write home, and take care that he gets some money? Polly!'

We thought this intention very noble in Steerforth, whose mother was a widow, and rich, and would do almost anything, it was said, that he asked her. We were all extremely glad to s ee Traddles so put down, and exalted Steerforth to the skies; especially when he told us, as he condescended to do, that what he had done had been done expressly for us, and for our cause; and that he had conferred a great boon upon us by unselfishly doing it.

But I must say that when I was going on with a story in the dark that night, Mr Mell's old flute seemed more than once to sound mournfully in my ears; and that when at last Steerforth was tired, and I lay down in my bed, I fancied it playing so sorrowfully somewhere that I was quite wretched.

I soon forgot him in the contemplation of Steerforth, who, in an easy amateur way, and without any book (he seemed to me to know everything by heart), took some of his classes until a new master was found. The new master came from a grammar-school; and before he entered on his duties, dined in the parlour one day to be introduced to Steerforth. Steerforth approved of him highly, and told us he was a Brick. Without exactly understanding what learned distinction was meant by this, I respected him greatly for it, and had no doubt whatever of his superior knowledge; though he never took the pains with me – not that *I* was anybody – that Mr Mell had taken.

There was only one other event in this half-year, out of the daily school-life, that made an impression on me which still survives. It survives for many reasons.

One afternoon, when we were all harassed into a state of dire confusion, and Mr Creakle was laying about him dreadfully, Tungay came in, and called out in his usual strong way, 'Visitors for Copperfield!'

A few words were interchanged between him and Mr Creakle, as, who the visitors were, and what room they were to be shown into; and then I, who had, according to custom, stood up on the announcement being made, and felt quite faint with astonishment, was told to go by the back stairs and get a clean frill on, before I repaired to the dining-room. These orders I obeyed, in such a flutter and hurry of my young spirits as I had never known before; and when I got to the parlour door, and the thought came into my head that it might be my mother – I had only thought of Mr or Miss Murdstone until then – I drew back my hand from the lock, and stopped to have a sob before I went in.

At first I saw nobody; but feeling a pressure against the door, I looked round it, and there, to my amazement, were Mr Peggotty and Ham, ducking at me with their hats, and squeezing one another against the wall. I could not help laughing; but it was much more in the pleasure of seeing them, than at the appearance they made. We shook hands in a very cordial way; and I laughed and laughed, until I pulled out my pocket-handkerchief and wiped my eyes.

Mr Peggotty (who never shut his mouth once, I remember, during the visit) showed great concern when he saw me do this, and nudged Ham to say something.

'Cheer up, Mas'r Davy bor'!' said Ham, in his simpering way. 'Why, how you have growed!'

'Am I grown?' I said, drying my eyes. I was not crying at anything particular that I know of; but somehow it made me cry to see old friends.

'Growed, Mas'r Davy bor'? Ain't he growed!' said Ham.

'Ain't he growed!' said Mr Peggotty.

They made me laugh again by laughing at each other, and then we all three laughed until I was in danger of crying again.

'Do you know how mama is, Mr Peggotty?' I said. 'And how my dear, dear, old Peggotty is?'

'Oncommon,' said Mr Peggotty.

'And little Em'ly and Mrs Gummidge?'

'On–common,' said Mr Peggotty.

There was a silence. Mr Peggotty, to relieve it, took two prodigious lobsters, and an enormous crab, and a large canvas bag of shrimps, out of his pockets, and piled them up in Ham's arms.

'You see,' said Mr Peggotty, 'knowing as you was partial to a little relish with your wittles when you was along with us, we took the liberty. The old Mawther biled 'em, she did. Mrs Gummidge biled 'em. Yes,' said Mr Peggotty, slowly, who I thought appeared to stick to the subject on account of having no other subject ready, 'Mrs Gummidge, I do assure you, she biled 'em.'

I expressed my thanks; and Mr Peggotty, after looking at Ham, who stood smiling sheepishly over the shellfish, without making any attempt to help him, said: 'We come, you see, the wind and tide making in our favour, in one of our Yarmouth lugs to Gravesen'. My sister she wrote to me the name of this here place, and wrote to me as if ever I chanced to come to Gravesen', I was to come over and enquire for Mas'r Davy, and give her dooty, humbly wishing him well, and reporting of the fam'ly as they was oncommon toe-be-sure. Little Em'ly, you see, she'll write to my sister when I go back, as I see you, and as you was similarly oncommon, and so we make it quite a merry-go-rounder.'

I was obliged to consider a little before I understood what Mr Peggotty meant by this figure, expressive of a complete circle of intelligence. I then thanked him heartily; and said, with a consciousness of reddening, that I supposed little Em'ly was altered too, since we used to pick up shells and pebbles on the beach.

'She's getting to be a woman, that's wot she's getting to be,' said Mr Peggotty. 'Ask him.'

He meant Ham, who beamed with delight and assent over the bag of shrimps.

'Her pretty face!' said Mr Peggotty, with his own shining like a light.

'Her learning!' said Ham.

'Her writing!' said Mr Peggotty. 'Why, it's as black as jet! And so large it is, you might see it anywheres.'

It was perfectly delightful to behold with what enthusiasm Mr Peggotty became inspired when he thought of his little favourite. He stands before me again, his bluff hairy face irradiating with a joyful love and pride, for which I can find no description. His honest eyes fire up, and sparkle, as if their depths were stirred by something bright. His broad chest heaves with pleasure. His strong loose hands clench themselves, in his earnestness; and he emphasises what he says with a right arm that shows, in my pigmy view, like a sledgehammer.

Ham was quite as earnest as he. I dare say they would have said much more about her, if they had not been abashed by the unexpected coming in of Steerforth, who seeing me in a corner speaking with two strangers, stopped in a song he was singing, and said: 'I didn't know you were here, young Copperfield!' (for it was not the usual visiting-room), and crossed by us on his way out.

I am not sure whether it was in the pride of having such a friend as Steerforth, or in the desire to explain to him how I came to have such a friend as Mr Peggotty, that I called to him as he was going away. But I said, modestly – Good Heaven, how it all comes back to me this long time afterwards!

'Don't go, Steerforth, if you please. These are two Yarmouth boatmen – very kind, good people – who are relations of my nurse, and have come from Gravesend to see me.'

'Aye, aye?' said Steerforth, returning. 'I am glad to see them. How are you both?'

There was an ease in his manner – a gay and light manner it was, but not swaggering – which I still believe to have borne a kind of enchantment with it. I still believe him, in virtue of this carriage, his animal spirits, his delightful voice, his handsome face and figure, and, for aught I know, of some inborn power of attraction besides (which I think a few people possess), to have carried a spell with him to which it was a natural weakness to yield, and which not many persons could withstand. I could not but see how pleased they were with him, and how they seemed to open their hearts to him in a moment.

'You must let them know at home, if you please, Mr Peggotty,' I said, 'when that letter is sent, that Mr Steerforth is very kind to me, and that I don't know what I should ever do here without him.'

'Nonsense!' said Steerforth, laughing. 'You mustn't tell them anything of the sort.'

'And if Mr Steerforth ever comes into Norfolk, or Suffolk, Mr Peggotty,' I said, 'while I am there, you may depend upon it I shall bring him to Yarmouth, if he will let me, to see your house. You never saw such a good house, Steerforth. It's made out of a boat!'

'Made out of a boat, is it?' said Steerforth. 'It's the right sort of house for such a thorough-built boatman.'

'So 'tis, sir, so 'tis, sir,' said Ham, grinning. 'You're right, young gen'lm'n. Mas'r Davy, bor', gen'lm'n's right. A thorough-built boatman! Hor, hor! That's what he is, too!'

Mr Peggotty was no less pleased than his nephew, though his modesty forbade him to claim a personal compliment so vociferously.

'Well, sir,' he said, bowing and chuckling, and tucking in the ends of his neckerchief at his breast, 'I thankee, sir, I thankee! I do my endeavours in my line of life, sir.'

'The best of men can do no more, Mr Peggotty,' said Steerforth. He had got his name already.

'I'll pound it it's wot you do yourself, sir,' said Mr Peggotty, shaking his head, 'and wot you do well – right well! I thankee, sir. I'm obleeged to you, sir, for your welcoming manner of me. I'm rough, sir, but I'm ready – least ways, I *hope* I'm ready, you understand. My house ain't much for to see, sir, but it's hearty at your service, if ever you should come along with Mas'r Davy to see it. I'm a reg'lar Dodman, I am,' said Mr Peggotty, by which he meant snail, and this was in allusion to his being slow to go, for he had attempted to go after every sentence, and had somehow or other come back again; 'but I wish you both well, and I wish you happy!'

Ham echoed this sentiment, and we parted with them in the heartiest manner. I was almost tempted that evening to tell Steerforth about pretty little Em'ly, but I was too timid of mentioning her name, and too much afraid of his laughing at me. I remember that I thought a good deal, and in an uneasy sort of way, about Mr Peggotty having said that she was getting on to be a woman; but I decided that was nonsense.

We transported the shellfish, or the 'relish,' as Mr Peggotty had modestly called it, up into our room unobserved, and made a great supper that evening. But Traddles couldn't get happily out of it. He was too unfortunate even to come through a supper like anybody else. He was taken ill in the night – quite prostrate he was – in consequence of Crab; and after being drugged with black draughts and blue pills, to an extent which Demple (whose father was a doctor) said was enough to undermine a horse's constitution, received a caning and six chapters of Greek Testament for refusing to confess.

The rest of the half year is a jumble in my recollection of the daily strife and struggle of our lives; of the waning summer and the changing season; of the frosty mornings when we were rung out of bed, and the cold, cold smell of the dark nights when we were rung into bed again; of the evening schoolroom dimly lighted and indifferently warmed, and the morning schoolroom which was nothing but a great shivering machine; of the alternation of boiled beef with roast beef, and boiled mutton with roast mutton; of clods of bread and butter, dog's-eared lesson-books, cracked slates, tear-blotted copy-books, canings, rulerings, hair-cuttings, rainy Sundays, suet-puddings, and a dirty atmosphere of ink surrounding all.

I well remember though, how the distant idea of the holidays, after seeming for an immense time to be a stationary speck, began to come towards us, and to grow and grow. How from counting months, we came to weeks, and then to days; and how I then began to be afraid that I should not be sent for, and when I learnt from Steerforth that I *had* been sent for and was certainly to go home, had dim forebodings that I might break my leg first. How the breaking-up day changed its place fast, at last, from the week after next to next week, this week, the day after tomorrow, tomorrow, today, tonight – when I was inside the Yarmouth mail, and going home.

I had many a broken sleep inside the Yarmouth mail, and many an incoherent dream of all these things. But when I awoke at intervals, the ground outside the window was not the playground of Salem House, and the sound in my ears was not the sound of Mr Creakle giving it to Traddles, but the sound of the coachman touching up the horses.

CHAPTER 8

My Holidays: Especially One Happy Afternoon

When we arrived before day at the inn where the mail stopped, which was not the inn where my friend the waiter lived, I was shown up to a nice little bedroom, with Dolphin painted on the door. Very cold I was, I know, notwithstanding the hot tea they had given me before a large fire downstairs; and very glad I was to turn into the Dolphin's bed, pull the Dolphin's blankets round my head, and go to sleep.

Mr Barkis the carrier was to call for me in the morning at nine o'clock. I got up at eight, a little giddy from the shortness of my night's rest, and was ready for him before the appointed time. He received me exactly as if not five minutes had elapsed since we were last together, and I had only been into the hotel to get change for sixpence, or something of that sort.

As soon as I and my box were in the cart, and the carrier seated, the lazy horse walked away with us all at his accustomed pace.

'You look very well, Mr Barkis,' I said, thinking he would like to know it.

Mr Barkis rubbed his cheek with his cuff, and then looked at his cuff as if he expected to find some of the bloom upon it, but made no other acknowledgment of the compliment.

'I gave your message, Mr Barkis,' I said; 'I wrote to Peggotty.'

'Ah!' said Mr Barkis.

Mr Barkis seemed gruff, and answered drily.

'Wasn't it right, Mr Barkis?' I asked, after a little hesitation.

'Why no,' said Mr Barkis.

'Not the message?'

'The message was right enough, perhaps,' said Mr Barkis, 'but it come to an end there.'

Not understanding what he meant, I repeated inquisitively:

'Came to an end, Mr Barkis?'

'Nothing come of it,' he explained, looking at me sideways. 'No answer.'

'There was an answer expected, was there, Mr Barkis?' said I, opening my eyes. For this was a new light to me.

'When a man says he's willin',' said Mr Barkis, turning his glance slowly on me again, 'it's as much as to say, that man's a waitin' for a answer.'

'Well, Mr Barkis?'

'Well,' said Mr Barkis, carrying his eyes back to his horse's ears, 'that man's been waitin' for a answer ever since.'

'Have you told her so, Mr Barkis?'

'N–no,' growled Mr Barkis, reflecting about it. 'I ain't got no call to go and tell her so. I never said six words to her myself. *I* ain't a goin' to tell her so.'

'Would you like me to do it, Mr Barkis?' said I doubtfully.

'You might tell her, if you would,' said Mr Barkis, with another slow look at me, 'that Barkis was a waitin' for a answer. Says you – what name is it?'

'Her name?'

'Ah!' said Mr Barkis, with a nod of his head.

'Peggotty.'

'Chrisen name? Or nat'ral name?' said Mr Barkis.

'Oh, it's not her Christian name. Her Christian name is Clara.'

'Is it though?' said Mr Barkis.

He seemed to find an immense fund of reflection in this circumstance, and sat pondering and inwardly whistling for some time.

'Well!' he resumed at length. 'Says you, "Peggotty! Barkis is a waitin' for a answer." Says she, perhaps, "Answer to what?" Says you, "To what I told you." "What is that?" says she. "Barkis is willin'," says you.'

This extremely artful suggestion, Mr Barkis accompanied with a nudge of his elbow that gave me quite a stitch in my side. After that, he slouched over his horse in his usual manner; and made no other reference to the subject except, half an hour afterwards, taking a piece of chalk from his pocket, and writing up, inside the tilt of the cart, 'Clara Peggotty' – apparently as a private memorandum.

Ah, what a strange feeling it was to be going home when it was not home, and to find that every object I looked at reminded me of the happy old home, which was like a dream I could never dream again! The days when my mother and I and Peggotty were all in all to one another, and there was no one to come between us, rose up before me so sorrowfully on the road, that I am not sure I was glad to be there – not sure but that I would rather have remained away, and forgotten it in Steerforth's company. But there I was; and soon I was at our house, where the bare old elm trees wrung their many hands in the bleak wintry air, and shreds of the old rooks' nests drifted away upon the wind.

The carrier put my box down at the garden gate, and left me. I walked along the path towards the house, glancing at the windows, and fearing at every step to see Mr Murdstone or Miss Murdstone lowering out of one of them. No face appeared, however, and being come to the house, and knowing how to open the door, before dark, without knocking, I went in with a quiet, timid step.

God knows how infantine the memory may have been, that was awakened within me by the sound of my mother's voice in the old parlour, when I set foot in the hall. She was singing in a low tone. I think I must have lain in her arms, and heard her singing so to me when I was but a baby. The strain was new to me, and yet it was so old that it filled my heart brimful, like a friend come back from a long absence.

I believed, from the solitary and thoughtful way in which my mother murmured her song, that she was alone. And I went softly into the room. She was sitting by the fire, suckling an infant, whose tiny hand she held against her neck. Her eyes were looking down upon its face, and she sat singing to it. I was so far right, that she had no other companion.

I spoke to her, and she started, and cried out. But seeing me, she called me her dear Davy, her own boy! and coming half across the room to meet me, kneeled down upon the ground and kissed me, and laid my head down on her bosom near the little creature that was nestling there, and put its hand up to my lips.

I wish I had died. I wish I had died then, with that feeling in my heart! I should have been more fit for Heaven than I ever have been since.

'He is your brother,' said my mother, fondling me. 'Davy, my pretty boy! My poor child!' Then she kissed me more and more, and clasped me round the neck. This she was doing when Peggotty came running in, and bounced down on the ground beside us, and went mad about us both for a quarter of an hour.

It seemed that I had not been expected so soon, the carrier being much before his usual time. It seemed, too, that Mr and Miss Murdstone had gone out upon a visit in the neighbourhood, and would not return before night. I had never hoped for this. I had never thought it possible that we three could be together undisturbed, once more; and I felt, for the time, as if the old days were come back.

We dined together by the fireside. Peggotty was in attendance to wait upon us, but my mother wouldn't let her do it, and made her dine with us. I had my own old plate, with a brown view of a man-of-war in full sail upon it, which Peggotty had hoarded somewhere all the time I had been away, and would not have had broken, she said, for a hundred pounds. I had my own old mug with David on it, and my own old little knife and fork that wouldn't cut.

While we were at table, I thought it a favourable occasion to tell Peggotty about Mr Barkis, who, before I had finished what I had to tell her, began to laugh, and throw her apron over her face.

'Peggotty,' said my mother. 'What's the matter?'

Peggotty only laughed the more, and held her apron tight over her face when my mother tried to pull it away, and sat as if her head were in a bag.

'What are you doing, you stupid creature?' said my mother, laughing.

'Oh, drat the man!' cried Peggotty. 'He wants to marry me.'

'It would be a very good match for you, wouldn't it?' said my mother.

'Oh! I don't know,' said Peggotty. 'Don't ask me. I wouldn't have him if he was made of gold. Nor I wouldn't have anybody.'

'Then, why don't you tell him so, you ridiculous thing?' said my mother.

'Tell him so,' retorted Peggotty, looking out of her apron. 'He has never said a word to me about it. He knows better. If he was to make so bold as to say a word to me, I should slap his face.'

Her own was as red as ever I saw it, or any other face I think; but she only covered it again, for a few moments at a time, when she was taken with a violent fit of laughter; and after two or three of those attacks, went on with her dinner.

I remarked that my mother, though she smiled when Peggotty looked at her, became more serious and thoughtful. I had seen at first that she was changed. Her face was very pretty still, but it looked careworn, and too delicate; and her hand was so thin and white that it seemed to me to be almost transparent. But the change to which I now refer was super-added to this: it was in her manner, which became anxious and fluttered. At last she said, putting out her hand, and laying it affectionately on the hand of her old servant: 'Peggotty, dear, you are not going to be married?'

'Me, ma'am?' returned Peggotty, staring. 'Lord bless you, no!'

'Not just yet?' said my mother tenderly.

Changes at home

'Never!' cried Peggotty.

My mother took her hand, and said: 'Don't leave me, Peggotty. Stay with me. It will not be for long, perhaps. What should I ever do without you!'

'Me leave you, my precious!' cried Peggotty. 'Not for all the world and his wife. Why, what's put that in your silly little head?' For Peggotty had been used of old to talk to my mother sometimes like a child.

But my mother made no answer, except to thank her, and Peggotty went running on in her own fashion.

'Me leave you? I think I see myself. Peggotty go away from you? I should like to catch her at it! No, no, no,' said Peggotty, shaking her head, and folding her arms; 'not she, my dear. It isn't that there ain't some Cats that would be well enough pleased if she did, but they sha'n't be pleased. They shall be aggravated. I'll stay with you till I am a cross, cranky old woman. And when I'm too deaf, and too lame, and too blind, and too mumbly for want of teeth, to be of any use at all, even to be found fault with, then I shall go to my Davy, and ask him to take me in.'

'And Peggotty,' says I, 'I shall be glad to see you, and I'll make you as welcome as a queen.'

'Bless your dear heart!' cried Peggotty. 'I know you will!' And she kissed me beforehand, in grateful acknowledgment of my hospitality. After that, she covered her head up with her apron again, and had another laugh about Mr Barkis. After that, she took the baby out of its little cradle, and nursed it. After that, she cleared the dinner-table; after that, came in with another cap on, and her work-box, and the yard-measure, and the bit of wax candle, all just the same as ever. We sat round the fire, and talked delightfully. I told them what a hard master Mr Creakle was, and they pitied me very much. I told them what a fine fellow Steerforth was, and what a patron of mine, and Peggotty said she would walk a score of miles to see him. I took the little baby in my arms when it was awake, and nursed it lovingly. When it was asleep again, I crept close to my mother's side, according to my old custom, broken now a long time, and sat with my arms embracing her waist, and my little red cheek on her shoulder, and once more felt her beautiful hair drooping over me – like an angel's wing as I used to think, I recollect – and was very happy indeed.

While I sat thus, looking at the fire, and seeing pictures in the red-hot coals, I almost believed that I had never been away; that Mr and Miss Murdstone were such pictures, and would vanish when the fire got low; and that there was nothing real in all that I remembered, save my mother, Peggotty, and I.

Peggotty darned away at a stocking as long as she could see, and then sat with it drawn on her left hand like a glove, and her needle in her right, ready to take another stitch whenever there was a blaze. I cannot conceive whose stockings they can have been that Peggotty was always darning, or where such an unfailing supply of stockings in want of darning can have come from. From my earliest infancy she seems to have been always employed in that class of needlework, and never by any chance in any other.

'I wonder,' said Peggotty, who was sometimes seized with a fit of wondering on some most unexpected topic, 'what's become of Davy's great-aunt?'

'Lor', Peggotty!' observed my mother, rousing herself from a reverie, 'what nonsense you talk!'

'Well, but I really do wonder, ma'am,' said Peggotty.

'What can have put such a person in your head?' enquired my mother. 'Is there nobody else in the world to come there?'

'I don't know how it is,' said Peggotty, 'unless it's on account of being stupid, but my head never can pick and choose its people. They come and they go, and they don't come and they don't go, just as they like. I wonder what's become of her?'

'How absurd you are, Peggotty,' returned my mother. 'One would suppose you wanted a second visit from her.'

'Lord forbid!' cried Peggotty.

'Well, then, don't talk about such uncomfortable things, there's a good soul,' said my mother. 'Miss Betsey is shut up in her cottage by the sea, no doubt, and will remain there. At all events, she is not likely ever to trouble us again.'

'No!' mused Peggotty. 'No, that ain't likely at all. I wonder, if she was to die, whether she'd leave Davy anything?'

'Good gracious me, Peggotty,' returned my mother, 'what a nonsensical woman you are! when you know that she took offence at the poor dear boy's ever being born at all!'

'I suppose she wouldn't be inclined to forgive him now,' hinted Peggotty.

'Why should she be inclined to forgive him now?' said my mother, rather sharply.

'Now that he's got a brother, I mean,' said Peggotty.

My mother immediately began to cry, and wondered how Peggotty dared to say such a thing.

'As if this poor little innocent in its cradle had ever done any harm to you or anybody else, you jealous thing!' said she. 'You had much better go and marry Mr Barkis, the carrier. Why don't you?'

'I should make Miss Murdstone happy, if I was to,' said Peggotty.

'What a bad disposition you have, Peggotty!' returned my mother. 'You are as jealous of Miss Murdstone as it is possible for a ridiculous creature to be. You want to keep the keys your-self, and give out all the things, I suppose? I shouldn't be surprised if you did. When you know that she only does it out of kindness and the best intentions! You know she does, Peggotty – you know it well.'

Peggotty muttered something to the effect of 'Bother the best intentions!' and something else to the effect that there was a little too much of the best intentions going on.

'I know what you mean, you cross thing,' said my mother. 'I understand you, Peggotty, perfectly. You know I do, and I wonder you don't colour up like fire. But one point at a time. Miss Murdstone is the point now, Peggotty, and you sha'n't escape from it. Haven't you heard her say, over and over again, that she thinks I am too thoughtless and too – a – a –'

'Pretty,' suggested Peggotty.

'Well,' returned my mother, half laughing, 'and if she is so silly as to say so, can I be blamed for it?'

'No one says you can,' said Peggotty.

'No, I should hope not, indeed!' returned my mother. 'Haven't you heard her say, over and over again, that on this account she wishes to spare me a great deal of trouble, which she thinks I am not suited for, and which I really don't know myself that I *am* suited for; and isn't she up early and late, and going to and fro continually – and doesn't she do all sorts of things, and grope into all sorts of places, coal-holes and pantries and I don't know where, that can't be very agreeable – and do you mean to insinuate that there is not a sort of devotion in that?'

'I don't insinuate at all,' said Peggotty.

'You do, Peggotty,' returned my mother. 'You never do anything else, except your work. You are always insinuating. You revel in it. And when you talk of Mr Murdstone's good intentions –'

'I never talked of 'em,' said Peggotty.

'No, Peggotty,' returned my mother, 'but you insinuated. That's what I told you just now. That's the worst of you. You *will* insinuate. I said, at the moment, that I understood you, and you see I did. When you talk of Mr Murdstone's good intentions, and pretend to slight them (for I don't believe you really do, in your heart, Peggotty), you must be as well convinced as I am how good they are, and how they actuate him in everything. If he seems to have been at all stern with a certain person, Peggotty – you understand, and so I am sure does Davy, that I am not alluding to anybody present – it is solely because he is satisfied that it is for a certain person's benefit. He naturally loves a certain person on my account; and acts solely for a certain person's good. He is better able to judge of it than I am; for I very well know that I am a weak, light, girlish creature, and that he is a firm, grave, serious man. And he takes,' said my mother, with the tears which were engendered in her affectionate nature stealing down her face, 'he takes great pains with me; and I ought to be very thankful to him, and very submissive to him even in my thoughts; and when I am not, Peggotty, I worry and condemn myself, and feel doubtful of my own heart, and don't know what to do.'

Peggotty sat with her chin on the foot of the stocking, looking silently at the fire.

'There, Peggotty,' said my mother, changing her tone, 'don't let us fall out with one another, for I couldn't bear it. You are my true friend, I know, if I have any in the world. When I call you a ridiculous creature, or a vexatious thing, or anything of that sort, Peggotty, I only mean that you are my true friend, and always have been, ever since the night when Mr Copperfield first brought me home here, and you came out to the gate to meet me.'

Peggotty was not slow to respond, and ratify the treaty of friendship by giving me one of her best hugs. I think I had some glimpses of the real character of this conversation at the time; but I am sure, now, that the good creature originated it, and took her part in it, merely that my mother might comfort herself with the little contradictory summary in which she had indulged. The design was efficacious, for I remember that my mother seemed more at ease during the rest of the evening, and that Peggotty observed her less.

When we had had our tea, and the ashes were thrown up, and the candles snuffed, I read Peggotty a chapter out of the Crocodile Book, in remembrance of old times – she took it out of her pocket: I don't know whether she had kept it there ever since – and then we talked about Salem House, which brought me round again to Steerforth, who was my great subject. We were very happy; and that evening, as the last of its race, and destined evermore to close that volume of my life, will never pass out of my memory.

It was almost ten o'clock before we heard the sound of wheels. We all got up then; and my mother said hurriedly that, as it was so late, and Mr and Miss Murdstone approved of early hours for young people, perhaps I had better go to bed. I kissed her, and went upstairs with my candle directly, before they came in. It appeared to my childish fancy, as I ascended to the bedroom where I had been imprisoned, that they brought a cold blast of air into the house which blew away the old familiar feeling like a feather.

I felt uncomfortable about going down to breakfast in the morning, as I had never set eyes on Mr Murdstone since the day when I committed my memorable offence. However, as it must be done, I went down, after two or three false starts halfway, and as many runs back on tiptoe to my own room, and presented myself in the parlour.

He was standing before the fire with his back to it, while Miss Murdstone made the tea. He looked at me steadily as I entered, but made no sign of recognition whatever.

I went up to him, after a moment of confusion, and said: 'I beg your pardon, sir. I am very sorry for what I did, and I hope you will forgive me.'

'I am glad to hear you are sorry, David,' he replied.

The hand he gave me was the hand I had bitten. I could not restrain my eye from resting for an instant on a red spot upon it; but it was not so red as I turned, when I met that sinister expression in his face.

'How do you do, ma'am,' I said to Miss Murdstone.

'Ah, dear me!' sighed Miss Murdstone, giving me the tea-caddy scoop instead of her fingers. 'How long are the holidays?'

'A month, ma'am.'

'Counting from when?'

'From today, ma'am.'

'Oh!' said Miss Murdstone. 'Then here's *one* day off.'

She kept a calendar of the holidays in this way, and every morning checked a day off in exactly the same manner. She did it gloomily until she came to ten, but when she got into two figures she became more hopeful, and, as the time advanced, even jocular.

It was on this very first day that I had the misfortune to throw her, though she was not subject to such weakness in general, into a state of violent consternation. I came into the room where she and my mother were sitting; and the baby (who was only a few weeks old) being on my mother's lap, I took it very carefully in my arms. Suddenly Miss Murdstone gave such a scream that I all but dropped it.

'My dear Jane!' cried my mother.

'Good heavens, Clara, do you see?' exclaimed Miss Murdstone.

'See what, my dear Jane?' said my mother; 'where?'

'He's got it!' cried Miss Murdstone. 'The boy has got the baby!'

She was limp with horror; but stiffened herself to make a dart at me, and take it out of my arms. Then, she turned faint; and was so very ill, that they were obliged to give her cherry-brandy. I was solemnly interdicted by her, on her recovery, from touching my brother any more on any pretence whatever; and my poor mother, who, I could see, wished otherwise, meekly confirmed the interdict by saying, 'No doubt you are right, my dear Jane.'

On another occasion, when we three were together, this same dear baby – it was truly dear to me, for our mother's sake – was the innocent occasion of Miss Murdstone's going into a passion. My mother, who had been looking at its eyes as it lay upon her lap, said: 'Davy! come here!' and looked at mine.

I saw Miss Murdstone lay her beads down.

'I declare,' said my mother gently, 'they are exactly alike. I suppose they are mine. I think they are the colour of mine. But they are wonderfully alike.'

'What are you talking about, Clara?' said Miss Murdstone.

'My dear Jane,' faltered my mother, a little abashed by the harsh tone of this enquiry, 'I find that the baby's eyes and Davy's are exactly alike.'

'Clara!' said Miss Murdstone, rising angrily, 'you are a positive fool sometimes.'

'My dear Jane,' remonstrated my mother.

'A positive fool,' said Miss Murdstone. 'Who else could compare my brother's baby with your boy? They are not at all alike. They are exactly unlike. They are utterly dissimilar in all respects. I hope they will ever remain so. I will not sit here and hear such comparisons made.' With that she stalked out, and made the door bang after her.

In short, I was not a favourite with Miss Murdstone. In short, I was not a favourite there with anybody, not even with myself; for those who did like me could not show it, and those who did not showed it so plainly that I had a sensitive consciousness of always appearing constrained, boorish, and dull.

I felt that I made them as uncomfortable as they made me. If I came into the room where they were, and they were talking together and my mother seemed cheerful, an anxious cloud would steal over her face from the moment of my entrance. If Mr Murdstone were in his best humour, I checked him. If Miss Murdstone were in her worst, I intensified it. I had perception enough to know that my mother was the victim always; that she was afraid to speak to me, or be kind to me, lest she should give them some offence by her manner of doing so, and receive a lecture afterwards; that she was not only ceaselessly afraid of her own offending, but of my offending, and uneasily watched their looks if I only moved. Therefore I resolved to keep myself as much out of their way as I could; and many a wintry hour did I hear the church clock strike, when I was sitting in my cheerless bedroom, wrapped in my little greatcoat, poring over a book.

In the evening, sometimes, I went and sat with Peggotty in the kitchen. There I was comfortable, and not afraid of being myself. But neither of these resources was approved of in the parlour. The tormenting humour which was dominant there stopped them both. I was still held to be necessary to my poor mother's training, and, as one of her trials, could not be suffered to absent myself.

'David,' said Mr Murdstone, one day after dinner when I was going to leave the room as usual; 'I am sorry to observe that you are of a sullen disposition.'

'As sulky as a bear!' said Miss Murdstone.

I stood still, and hung my head.

'Now, David,' said Mr Murdstone, 'a sullen obdurate disposition is, of all tempers, the worst.'

'And the boy's is, of all such dispositions that ever I have seen,' remarked his sister, 'the most confirmed and stubborn. I think, my dear Clara, even you must observe it?'

'I beg your pardon, my dear Jane,' said my mother, 'but are you quite sure – I am certain you'll excuse me, my dear Jane – that you understand Davy?'

'I should be somewhat ashamed of myself, Clara,' returned Miss Murdstone, 'if I could not understand the boy, or any boy. I don't profess to be profound; but I do lay claim to common sense.'

'No doubt, my dear Jane,' returned my mother, 'your understanding is very vigorous.'

'Oh, dear, no! Pray don't say that, Clara,' interposed Miss Murdstone angrily.

'But I am sure it is,' resumed my mother; 'and everybody knows it is. I profit so much by it myself, in many ways – at least I ought to – that no one can be more convinced of it than myself; and therefore I speak with great diffidence, my dear Jane, I assure you.'

'We'll say I don't understand the boy, Clara,' returned Miss Murdstone, arranging the little fetters on her wrists. 'We'll agree, if you please, that I don't understand him at all. He is much too deep for me. But perhaps my brother's penetration may enable him to have some insight into his character. And I believe my brother was speaking on the subject when we – not very decently – interrupted him.'

'I think, Clara,' said Mr Murdstone, in a low grave voice, 'that there may be better and more dispassionate judges of such a question than you.'

'Edward,' replied my mother timidly, 'you are a far better judge of all questions than I pretend to be. Both you and Jane are. I only said – '

'You only said something weak and inconsiderate,' he replied. 'Try not to do it again, my dear Clara, and keep a watch upon yourself.'

My mother's lips moved, as if she answered, 'Yes, my dear Edward,' but she said nothing aloud.

'I was sorry, David, I remarked,' said Mr Murdstone, turning his head and his eyes stiffly towards me, 'to observe that you are of a sullen disposition. This is not a character that I can suffer to develop itself beneath my eyes without an effort at improvement. You must endeavour, sir, to change it. We must endeavour to change it for you.'

'I beg your pardon, sir,' I faltered. 'I have never meant to be sullen since I came back.'

'Don't take refuge in a lie, sir!' he returned so fiercely, that I saw my mother involuntarily put out her trembling hand as if to interpose between us. 'You have withdrawn yourself in your sullenness to your own room. You have kept your own room when you ought to have been here. You know now, once for all, that I require you to be here, and not there. Further, that I require you to bring obedience here. You know me, David, I will have it done.'

Miss Murdstone gave a hoarse chuckle.

'I will have a respectful, prompt, and ready bearing towards myself,' he continued, 'and towards Jane Murdstone, and towards your mother. I will not have this room shunned as if it were infected, at the pleasure of a child. Sit down.'

He ordered me like a dog, and I obeyed like a dog.

'One thing more,' he said. 'I observe that you have an attachment to low and common company. You are not to associate with servants. The kitchen will not improve you, in the many respects in which you need improvement. Of the woman who abets you, I say nothing – since you, Clara,' addressing my mother in a lower voice, 'from old associations and long-established fancies, have a weakness respecting her which is not yet overcome.'

'A most unaccountable delusion it is!' cried Miss Murdstone.

'I only say,' he resumed, addressing me, 'that I disapprove of your preferring such company as Mistress Peggotty, and that it is to be abandoned. Now, David, you understand me, and you know what will be the consequence if you fail to obey me to the letter.'

I knew well – better perhaps than he thought, as far as my poor mother was concerned – and I obeyed him to the letter. I retreated to my own room no more; I took refuge with Peggotty no more; but sat wearily in the parlour day after day, looking forward to night and bedtime.

What irksome constraint I underwent, sitting in the same attitude hours upon hours, afraid to move an arm or a leg lest Miss Murdstone should complain (as she did on the least pretence) of my restlessness, and afraid to move an eye lest it should light on some look of dislike or scrutiny that would find new cause for complaint in mine! What intolerable dullness to sit listening to the ticking of the clock; and watching Miss Murdstone's little shiny steel beads as she strung them; and wondering whether she would ever be married, and if so, to what sort of unhappy man; and counting the divisions in the moulding on the chimney-piece; and wandering away, with my eyes, to the ceiling, among the curls and corkscrews in the paper on the wall!

What walks I took alone, down muddy lanes, in the bad winter weather, carrying that parlour, and Mr and Miss Murdstone in it, everywhere; a monstrous load that I was obliged to bear, a daymare that there was no possibility of breaking in, a weight that brooded on my wits and blunted them!

What meals I had in silence and embarrassment, always feeling that there were a knife and fork too many, and those mine; an appetite too many, and that mine; a plate and chair too many, and those mine; a somebody too many, and that I!

What evenings, when the candles came, and I was expected to employ myself, but not daring to read an entertaining book, pored over some hard-headed, harder-hearted treatise on arithmetic; when the tables of weights and measures set themselves to tunes, as *Rule Britannia*, or *Away with Melancholy*; and wouldn't stand still to be learnt, but would go threading my grandmother's needle through my unfortunate head, in at one ear and out at the other!

What yawns and dozes I lapsed into, in spite of all my care; what starts I came out of concealed sleeps with; what answers I never got, to little observations that I rarely made; what a blank space I seemed, which everybody overlooked, and yet I was in everybody's way; what a heavy relief it was to hear Miss Murdstone hail the first stroke of nine at night, and order me to bed!

Thus the holidays lagged away, until the morning came when Miss Murdstone said: 'Here's the last day off!' and gave me the closing cup of tea of the vacation.

I was not sorry to go. I had lapsed into a stupid state; but I was recovering a little and looking forward to Steerforth, albeit Mr Creakle loomed behind him. Again Mr Barkis appeared at the gate, and again Miss Murdstone in her warning voice said, 'Clara!' when my mother bent over me, to bid me farewell.

I kissed her, and my baby brother, and was very sorry then; but not sorry to go away, for the gulf between us was there, and the parting was there, every day. And it is not so much the embrace she gave me, that lives in my mind, though it was as fervent as could be, as what followed the embrace.

I was in the carrier's cart when I heard her calling to me. I looked out, and she stood at the garden gate alone, holding her baby up in her arms for me to see. It was cold still weather; and not a hair of her head, or a fold of her dress, was stirred, as she looked intently at me, holding up her child.

So I lost her. So I saw her afterwards, in my sleep at school – a silent presence near my bed – looking at me with the same intent face – holding up her baby in her arms.

CHAPTER 9

I Have a Memorable Birthday

I pass over all that happened at school, until the anniversary of my birthday came round in March. Except that Steerforth was more to be admired than ever, I remember nothing. He was going away at the end of the half year, if not sooner, and was more spirited and independent than before in my eyes, and therefore more engaging than before; but beyond this I remember nothing. The great remembrance by which that time is marked in my mind seems to have swallowed up all lesser recollections, and to exist alone.

It is even difficult for me to believe that there was a gap of full two months between my return to Salem House and the arrival of that birthday. I can only understand that the fact was so, because I know it must have been so; otherwise I should feel convinced that there was no interval, and that the one occasion trod upon the other's heels.

How well I recollect the kind of day it was! I smell the fog that hung about the place; I see the hoar frost, ghostly, through it; I feel my rimy hair fall clammy on my cheek; I look along the dim perspective of the schoolroom, with a sputtering candle here and there to light up the foggy morning, and the breath of the boys wreathing and smoking in the raw cold as they blow upon their fingers, and tap their feet upon the floor.

It was after breakfast, and we had been summoned in from the playground, when Mr Sharp entered and said: 'David Copperfield is to go into the parlour.'

I expected a hamper from Peggotty, and brightened at the order. Some of the boys about me put in their claim not to be forgotten in the distribution of the good things, as I got out of my seat with great alacrity.

'Don't hurry, David,' said Mr Sharp. 'There's time enough, my boy, don't hurry.'

I might have been surprised by the feeling tone in which he spoke, if I had given it a thought; but I gave it none until afterwards. I hurried away to the parlour; and there I found Mr Creakle sitting at his breakfast with the cane and a newspaper before him, and Mrs Creakle with an opened letter in her hand. But no hamper.

'David Copperfield,' said Mrs Creakle, leading me to a sofa, and sitting down beside me, 'I want to speak to you very particularly. I have something to tell you, my child.'

Mr Creakle, at whom of course I looked, shook his head without looking at me, and stopped up a sigh with a very large piece of buttered toast.

'You are too young to know how the world changes every day,' said Mrs Creakle, 'and how the people in it pass away. But we all have to learn it, David; some of us when we are young, some of us when we are old, some of us at all times of our lives.'

I looked at her earnestly.

'When you came away from home at the end of the vacation,' said Mrs Creakle, after a pause, 'were they all well?' After another pause, 'Was your mama well?'

I trembled without distinctly knowing why, and still looked at her earnestly, making no attempt to answer.

'Because,' said she, 'I grieve to tell you that I hear this morning your mama is very ill.'

A mist arose between Mrs Creakle and me, and her figure seemed to move in it for an instant. Then I felt the burning tears run down my face, and it was steady again.

'She is very dangerously ill,' she added.

I knew all now.

'She is dead.'

There was no need to tell me so. I had already broken out into a desolate cry, and felt an orphan in the wide world.

She was very kind to me. She kept me there all day, and left me alone sometimes; and I cried, and wore myself to sleep, and awoke and cried again. When I could cry no more, I began to think; and then the oppression on my breast was heaviest, and my grief a dull pain that there was no ease for.

And yet my thoughts were idle; not intent on the calamity that weighed upon my heart, but idly loitering near it. I thought of our house shut up and hushed. I thought of the little baby, who, Mrs Creakle said, had been pining away for some time, and who, they believed, would die too. I thought of my father's grave in the churchyard, by our house, and of my mother lying there beneath the tree I knew so well. I stood upon a chair when I was left alone, and looked into the glass to see how red my eyes were, and how sorrowful my face was. I considered, after some hours were gone, if my tears were really hard to flow now, as they seemed to be, what, in connection with my loss, it would affect me most to think of when I drew near home – for I was going home to the funeral. I am sensible of having felt that a dignity attached to me among the rest of the boys, and that I was important in my affliction.

If ever child were stricken with sincere grief, I was. But I remember that this importance was a kind of satisfaction to me, when I walked in the playground that afternoon while the boys were in school. When I saw them glancing at me out of the windows, as they went up to their classes, I felt distinguished, and looked more melancholy, and walked slower. When school was over, and they came out and spoke to me, I felt it rather good in myself not to be proud to any of them, and to take exactly the same notice of them all, as before.

I was to go home next night; not by the mail, but by the heavy night-coach, which was called the Farmer, and was principally used by country people travelling short intermediate distances upon the road. We had no story-telling that evening, and Traddles insisted on lending me his pillow. I don't know what good he thought it would do me, for I had one of my own; but it was all he had to lend, poor fellow, except a sheet of letter-paper full of skeletons, and that he gave me at parting, as a soother of my sorrows and a contribution to my peace of mind.

I left Salem House upon the morrow afternoon. I little thought then that I left it never to return. We travelled very slowly all night, and did not get into Yarmouth before nine or ten o'clock in the morning. I looked out for Mr Barkis, but he was not there; and instead of him a fat, short-winded, merry-looking, little old man in black, with rusty little bunches of ribbons at the knees of his breeches, black stockings, and a broad-brimmed hat, came puffing up to the coach window, and said: 'Master Copperfield?'

'Yes, sir.'

'Will you come with me, young sir, if you please,' he said, opening the door, 'and I shall have the pleasure of taking you home.'

I put my hand in his, wondering who he was, and we walked away to a shop in a narrow street, on which was written Omer, Draper, Tailor, Haberdasher, Funeral Furnisher, &c. It was a close and stifling little shop; full of all sorts of clothing, made and unmade, including one window full of beaver hats and bonnets. We went into a little back parlour behind the shop, where we found three young women at work on a quantity of black materials, which were heaped upon the table, and little bits and cuttings of which were littered all over the floor. There was a good fire in the room, and a breathless smell of warm black crape – I did not know what the smell was then, but I know now.

The three young women, who appeared to be very industrious and comfortable, raised their heads to look at me, and then went on with their work. Stitch, stitch, stitch. At the same time there came from a workshop across a little yard outside the window, a regular sound of hammering that kept a kind of tune: 'Rat – tat-tat, rat – tat-tat, rat – tat-tat,' without any variation.

'Well,' said my conductor to one of the three young women, 'how do you get on, Minnie?'

'We shall be ready by the trying-on time,' she replied gaily, without looking up. 'Don't you be afraid, father.'

Mr Omer took off his broad-brimmed hat, and sat down and panted. He was so fat that he was obliged to pant some time before he could say: 'That's right.'

'Father!' said Minnie playfully. 'What a porpoise you do grow!'

'Well, I don't know how it is, my dear,' he replied, considering about it. 'I *am* rather so.'

'You are such a comfortable man, you see,' said Minnie. 'You take things so easy.'

'No use taking 'em otherwise, my dear,' said Mr Omer.

'No, indeed,' returned his daughter. 'We are all pretty gay here, thank Heaven! Ain't we, father?'

'I hope so, my dear,' said Mr Omer. 'As I have got my breath now, I think I'll measure this young scholar. Would you walk into the shop, Master Copperfield?'

I preceded Mr Omer, in compliance with his request; and after showing me a roll of cloth which he said was extra super, and too good mourning for anything short of parents, he took my various dimensions, and put them down in a book. While he was recording them he called my attention to his stock in trade, and to certain fashions which he said had 'just come up,' and to certain other fashions which he said had 'just gone out.'

'And by that sort of thing we very often lose a little mint of money,' said Mr Omer. 'But fashions are like human beings. They come in, nobody knows when, why, or how; and they go out, nobody knows when, why, or how. Everything is like life, in my opinion, if you look at it in that point of view.'

I was too sorrowful to discuss the question, which would possibly have been beyond me under any circumstances; and Mr Omer took me back into the parlour, breathing with some difficulty on the way.

He then called down a little breakneck range of steps behind a door: 'Bring up that tea and bread and butter!' which, after some time, during which I sat looking about me and thinking, and listening to the stitching in the room and the tune that was being hammered across the yard, appeared on a tray, and turned out to be for me.

'I have been acquainted with you,' said Mr Omer, after watching me for some minutes, during which I had not made much impression on the breakfast, for the black things destroyed my appetite, 'I have been acquainted with you a long time, my young friend.'

'Have you, sir?'

'All your life,' said Mr Omer. 'I may say before it. I knew your father before you. He was five foot nine and a half, and he lays in five and twen-ty foot of ground.'

'Rat – tat-tat, rat – tat-tat, rat – tat-tat,' across the yard.

'He lays in five and twen-ty foot of ground, if he lays in a fraction,' said Mr Omer pleasantly. 'It was either his request or her direction, I forget which.'

'Do you know how my little brother is, sir?' I enquired.

Mr Omer shook his head.

'Rat–tat-tat, rat–tat-tat, rat–tat-tat.'

'He is in his mother's arms,' said he.

'Oh, poor little fellow! Is he dead?'

'Don't mind it more than you can help,' said Mr Omer. 'Yes. The baby's dead.'

My wounds broke out afresh at this intelligence. I left the scarcely tasted breakfast, and went and rested my head on another table in a corner of the little room, which Minnie hastily cleared, lest I should spot the mourning that was lying there with my tears. She was a pretty, good-natured girl, and put my hair away from my eyes with a soft kind touch; but she was very cheerful at having nearly finished her work and being in good time, and was so different from me!

Presently the tune left off, and a good-looking young fellow came across the yard into the room. He had a hammer in his hand, and his mouth was full of little nails, which he was obliged to take out before he could speak.

'Well, Joram!' said Mr Omer. 'How do *you* get on?'

'All right,' said Joram. 'Done, sir.'

Minnie coloured a little, and the other two girls smiled at one another.

'What! you were at it by candlelight last night, when I was at the club, then? Were you?' said Mr Omer, shutting up one eye.

'Yes,' said Joram. 'As you said we could make a little trip of it, and go over together, if it was done, Minnie and me – and you.'

'Oh! I thought you were going to leave me out altogether,' said Mr Omer, laughing till he coughed.

' – As you was so good as to say that,' resumed the young man, 'why, I turned to with a will, you see. Will you give me your opinion of it?'

'I will,' said Mr Omer, rising. 'My dear,' and he stopped and turned to me, 'would you like to see your – '

'No, father,' Minnie interposed.

'I thought it might be agreeable, my dear,' said Mr Omer. 'But perhaps you're right.'

I can't say how I knew it was my dear, dear mother's coffin that they went to look at. I had never heard one making; I had never seen one that I know of; but it came into my mind what the noise was, while it was going on; and when the young man entered, I am sure I knew what he had been doing.

The work being now finished, the two girls, whose names I had not heard, brushed the shreds and threads from their dresses, and went into the shop to put that to rights, and wait for customers. Minnie stayed behind to fold up what they had made, and pack it in two baskets. This she did upon her knees, humming a lively little tune the while. Joram, who I had no doubt was her lover, came in and stole a kiss from her while she was busy (he didn't appear to mind me, at all), and said her father was gone for the chaise, and he must make haste and get himself ready. Then he went out again; and then she put her thimble and scissors in her pocket, and stuck a needle threaded with black thread neatly in the bosom of her gown, and put on her outer clothing smartly, at a little glass behind the door, in which I saw the reflection of her pleased face.

All this I observed, sitting at the table in the corner with my head leaning on my hand, and my thoughts running on very different things. The chaise soon came round to the front of the shop, and the baskets being put in first, I was put in next, and those three followed. I remember it as a kind of half chaise-cart, half pianoforte van, painted of a sombre colour, and drawn by a black horse with a long tail. There was plenty of room for us all.

I do not think I have ever experienced so strange a feeling in my life (I am wiser now, perhaps) as that of being with them, remembering how they had been employed, and seeing them enjoy the ride. I was not angry with them; I was more afraid of them, as if I were cast away among creatures with whom I had no community of nature. They were very cheerful. The old man sat in front to drive, and the two young people sat behind him, and whenever he spoke to them leaned forward, the one on one side of his chubby face and the other on the other, and made a great deal of him. They would have talked to me too, but I held back, and moped in my corner; scared by their love-making and hilarity, though it was far from boisterous, and almost wondering that no judgement came upon them for their hardness of heart.

So, when they stopped to bait the horse, and ate and drank and enjoyed themselves, I could touch nothing that they touched, but kept my fast unbroken. So, when we reached home, I dropped out of the chaise behind, as quickly as possible, that I might not be in their company before those solemn windows, looking blindly on me like closed eyes once bright. And oh, how little need I had had to think what would move me to tears when I came back – seeing the window of my mother's room, and next it that which, in the better time, was mine!

I was in Peggotty's arms before I got to the door, and she took me into the house. Her grief burst out when she first saw me; but she controlled it soon, and spoke in whispers, and walked softly, as if the dead could be disturbed. She had not been in bed, I found, for a long time. She sat up at night still, and watched. As long as her poor dear pretty was above the ground, she said, she would never desert her.

Mr Murdstone took no heed of me when I went into the parlour where he was, but sat by the fireside, weeping silently, and pondering in his elbow-chair. Miss Murdstone, who was busy at her writing-desk, which was covered with letters and papers, gave me her cold finger-nails, and asked me, in an iron whisper, if I had been measured for my mourning.

I said, 'Yes.'

'And your shirts,' said Miss Murdstone; 'have you brought 'em home?'

'Yes, ma'am. I have brought home all my clothes.'

This was all the consolation that her firmness administered to me. I do not doubt that she had a choice pleasure in exhibiting what she called her self-command, and her firmness, and her strength of mind, and her common sense, and the whole diabolical catalogue of her unamiable qualities, on such an occasion. She was particularly proud of her turn for business; and she showed it now in reducing everything to pen and ink, and being moved by nothing. All the rest of that day, and from morning to night afterwards, she sat at that desk; scratching composedly with a hard pen, speaking in the same imperturbable whisper to everybody; never relaxing a muscle of her face, or softening the tone of her voice, or appearing with an atom of her dress astray.

Her brother took a book sometimes, but never read it that I saw. He would open it and look at it as if he were reading, but would remain for a whole hour without turning the leaf, and then put it down and walk to and fro in the room. I used to sit with folded hands watching him, and counting his footsteps, hour after hour. He very seldom spoke to her and never to me. He seemed to be the only restless thing, except the clocks, in the whole motionless house.

In these days before the funeral I saw but little of Peggotty, except that, in passing up or down stairs, I always found her close to the room where my mother and her baby lay, and except that she came to me every night, and sat by my bed's head while I went to sleep. A day or two before the burial – I think it was a day or two before, but I am conscious of confusion in my mind about that heavy time, with nothing to mark its progress – she took me into the room. I only recollect that underneath some white covering on the bed, with a beautiful cleanliness and freshness all around it, there seemed to me to lie embodied the solemn stillness that was in the house; and that when she would have turned the cover gently back, I cried: 'Oh no! Oh no!' and held her hand.

If the funeral had been yesterday, I could not recollect it better. The very air of the best parlour, when I went in at the door, the bright condition of the fire, the shining of the wine in the decanters, the patterns of the glasses and plates, the faint, sweet smell of cake, the odour of Miss Murdstone's dress, and our black clothes. Mr Chillip is in the room, and comes to speak to me.

'And how is Master David?' he says, kindly.

I cannot tell him very well. I give him my hand, which he holds in his.

'Dear me!' says Mr Chillip, meekly smiling, with something shining in his eye. 'Our little friends grow up around us. They grow out of our knowledge, ma'am!'

This is to Miss Murdstone, who makes no reply.

'There is a great improvement here, ma'am,' says Mr Chillip.

Miss Murdstone merely answers with a frown and a formal bend; Mr Chillip, discomfited, goes into a corner, keeping me with him, and opens his mouth no more.

I remark this, because I remark everything that happens, not because I care about myself, or have done since I came home. And now the bell begins to sound, and Mr Omer and another come to make us ready. As Peggotty was wont to tell me, long ago, the followers of my father to the same grave were made ready in the same room.

There are Mr Murdstone, our neighbour Mr Grayper, Mr Chillip, and I. When we go out to the door, the Bearers and their load are in the garden; and they move before us down the path, and past the elms, and through the gate, and into the churchyard, where I have so often heard the birds sing on a summer morning.

We stand around the grave. The day seems different to me from every other day, and the light not of the same colour – of a sadder colour. Now there is a solemn hush, which we have brought from home with what is resting in the mould; and while we stand bareheaded, I hear the voice of the clergyman, sounding remote in the open air, and yet distinct and plain, saying: 'I am the Resurrection and the Life, saith the Lord!' Then I hear sobs; and standing apart among the lookers-on, I see that good and faithful servant, whom of all the people upon earth I love the best, and unto whom my childish heart is certain that the Lord will one day say: 'Well done.'

There are many faces that I know, among the little crowd; faces that I knew in church, when mine was always wondering there; faces that first saw my mother, when she came to the village in her youthful bloom. I do not mind them – I mind nothing but my grief – and yet I see and know them all; and even in the background, far away, see Minnie looking on, and her eye glancing on her sweetheart, who is near me.

It is over, and the earth is filled in, and we turn to come away. Before us stands our house, so pretty and unchanged, so linked in my mind with the young idea of what is gone, that all my sorrow has been nothing to the sorrow it calls forth. But they take me on; and Mr Chillip talks to me, and when we get home, puts some water to my lips; and when I ask his leave to go up to my room, dismisses me with the gentleness of a woman.

All this, I say, is yesterday's event. Events of later date have floated from me to the shore where all forgotten things will reappear, but this stands like a high rock in the ocean.

I knew that Peggotty would come to me in my room. The Sabbath stillness of the time (the day was so like Sunday! I have forgotten that) was suited to us both. She sat down by my side upon my little bed; and holding my hand, and sometimes putting it to her lips, and sometimes smoothing it with hers, as she might have comforted my little brother, told me, in her way, all that she had to tell concerning what had happened.

'She was never well,' said Peggotty, 'for a long time. She was uncertain in her mind, and not happy. When her baby was born, I thought at first she would get better, but she was more delicate, and sunk a little every day. She used to like to sit alone before her baby came, and then she cried; but afterwards she used to sing to it – so soft, that I once thought, when I heard her, it was like a voice up in the air, that was rising away.

'I think she got to be more timid and more frightened-like, of late; and that a hard word was like a blow to her. But she was always the same to me. She never changed to her foolish Peggotty, didn't my sweet girl.'

Here Peggotty stopped, and softly beat upon my hand a little while.

'The last time that I saw her like her own old self was the night when you came home, my dear. The day you went away, she said to me, "I never shall see my pretty darling again. Something tells me so, that tells the truth, I know."

'She tried to hold up after that; and many a time, when they told her she was thoughtless and light-hearted, made believe to be so; but it was all a bygone then. She never told her husband what she had told me – she was afraid of saying it to anybody else – till one night, a little more than a week before it happened, when she said to him: "My dear, I think I am dying."

' "It's off my mind now, Peggotty," she told me, when I laid her in her bed that night. "He will believe it more and more, poor fellow, every day for a few days to come; and then it will be passed. I am very tired. If this is sleep, sit by me while I sleep; don't leave me. God bless both my children! God protect and keep my fatherless boy!"

'I never left her afterwards,' said Peggotty. 'She often talked to them two downstairs – for she loved them; she couldn't bear not to love anyone who was about her – but when they went away from her bedside, she always turned to me, as if there was rest where Peggotty was, and never fell asleep in any other way.

'On the last night, in the evening, she kissed me, and said: "If my baby should die, too, Peggotty, please let them lay him in my arms, and bury us together." (It was done; for the poor lamb lived but a day beyond her.) "Let my dearest boy go with us to our resting-place," she said, "and tell him that his mother, when she lay here, blessed him, not once, but a thousand times." '

Another silence followed this, and another gentle beating on my hand.

'It was pretty far in the night,' said Peggotty, 'when she asked me for some drink; and when she had taken it, gave me such a patient smile, the dear! – so beautiful!

'Daybreak had come, and the sun was rising, when she said to me, how kind and considerate Mr Copperfield had always been to her, and how he had borne with her, and had told her, when she doubted herself, that a loving heart was better and stronger than wisdom, and that he was a happy man in hers. "Peggotty, my dear," she said then, "put me nearer to you," for she was very weak. "Lay your good arm underneath my neck," she said, "and turn me to you, for your face is going far off, and I want it to be near." I put it as she asked; and oh, Davy! the time had come when my first parting words to you were true – when she was glad to lay her poor head on her stupid cross old Peggotty's arm – and she died like a child that had gone to sleep!'

Thus ended Peggotty's narration. From the moment of my knowing of the death of my mother, the idea of her as she had been of late had vanished from me. I remembered her, from that instant, only as the young mother of my earliest impressions, who had been used to wind her bright curls round and round her finger, and to dance with me at twilight in the parlour. What Peggotty had told me now was so far from bringing me back to the later period that it rooted the earlier image in my mind. It may be curious, but it is true. In her death she winged her way back to her calm untroubled youth, and cancelled all the rest.

The mother who lay in the grave was the mother of my infancy; the little creature in her arms was myself, as I had once been, hushed for ever on her bosom.

CHAPTER 10

I Become Neglected, and Am Provided For

The first act of business Miss Murdstone performed when the day of the solemnity was over, and light was freely admitted into the house, was to give Peggotty a month's warning. Much as Peggotty would have disliked such a service, I believe she would have retained it, for my sake, in preference to the best upon earth. She told me we must part, and told me why; and we condoled with one another, in all sincerity.

As to me or my future, not a word was said, or a step taken. Happy they would have been, I dare say, if they could have dismissed me at a month's warning too. I mustered courage once, to ask Miss Murdstone when I was going back to school; and she answered drily, she believed I was not going back at all. I was told nothing more. I was very anxious to know what was going to be done with me, and so was Peggotty; but neither she nor I could pick up any information on the subject.

There was one change in my condition, which, while it relieved me of a great deal of present uneasiness, might have made me, if I had been capable of considering it closely, yet more uncomfortable about the future. It was this. The constraint that had been put upon me was quite abandoned. I was so far from being required to keep my dull post in the parlour that on several occasions, when I took my seat there, Miss Murdstone frowned to me to go away. I was so far from being warned off from Peggotty's society that, provided I was not in Mr Murdstone's, I was never sought out or enquired for. At first I was in daily dread of his taking my education in hand again, or of Miss Murdstone's devoting herself to it; but I soon began to think that such fears were groundless, and that all I had to anticipate was neglect.

I do not conceive that this discovery gave me much pain then. I was still giddy with the shock of my mother's death, and in a kind of stunned state as to all tributary things. I can recollect, indeed, to have speculated, at odd times, on the possibility of my not being taught any more, or cared for any more; and growing up to be a shabby, moody man, lounging an idle life away, about the village; as well as on the feasibility of my getting rid of this picture by going away somewhere, like the hero in a story, to seek my fortune; but these were transient visions, day-dreams I sat looking at sometimes, as if they were faintly painted or written on the wall of my room, and which, as they melted away, left the wall blank again.

'Peggotty,' I said in a thoughtful whisper, one evening, when I was warming my hands at the kitchen fire, 'Mr Murdstone likes me less than he used to. He never liked me much, Peggotty; but he would rather not even see me now if he can help it.'

'Perhaps it's his sorrow,' said Peggotty, stroking my hair.

'I am sure, Peggotty, I am sorry too. If I believed it was his sorrow, I should not think of it at all. But it's not that; oh, no, it's not that.'

'How do you know it's not that?' said Peggotty, after a silence.

'Oh, his sorrow is another and quite a different thing. He is sorry at this moment, sitting by the fireside with Miss Murdstone; but if I was to go in, Peggotty, he would be something besides.'

'What would he be?' said Peggotty.

'Angry,' I answered, with an involuntary imitation of his dark frown. 'If he was only sorry, he wouldn't look at me as he does. I am only sorry, and it makes me feel kinder.'

Peggotty said nothing for a little while; and I warmed my hands as silent as she.

'Davy,' she said at length.

'Yes, Peggotty?'

'I have tried, my dear, all ways I could think of – all the ways there are, and all the ways there ain't, in short – to get a suitable service here, in Blunderstone; but there's no such a thing, my love.'

'And what do you mean to do, Peggotty?' said I wistfully. 'Do you mean to go and seek your fortune?'

'I expect I shall be forced to go to Yarmouth,' replied Peggotty, 'and live there.'

'You might have gone farther off,' I said, brightening a little, 'and been as bad as lost. I shall see you, sometimes, my dear old Peggotty, there. You won't be quite at the other end of the world, will you?'

'Contrary ways, please God!' cried Peggotty, with great animation. 'As long as you are here, my pet, I shall come over every week of my life to see you; one day every week of my life!'

I felt a great weight taken off my mind by this promise; but even this was not all, for Peggotty went on to say: 'I'm a going, Davy, you see, to my brother's first, for another fortnight's visit – just till I have had time to look about me, and get to be something like myself again. Now, I have been thinking, that, perhaps, as they don't want you here at present, you might be let to go along with me.'

If anything, short of being in a different relation to everyone about me, Peggotty excepted, could have given me a sense of pleasure at that time, it would have been this project of all others. The idea of being again surrounded by those honest faces, shining welcome on me; of renewing the peacefulness of the sweet Sunday morning, when the bells were ringing, the stones dropping in the water, and the shadowy ships breaking through the mist; of roaming up and down with little Em'ly, telling her my troubles, and finding charms against them in the shells and pebbles on the beach, made a calm in my heart. It was ruffled next moment, to be sure, by a doubt of Miss Murdstone's giving her consent; but even that was set at rest soon, for she came out to take an evening grope in the store-closet while we were yet in conversation, and Peggotty, with a boldness that amazed me, broached the topic on the spot.

'The boy will be idle there,' said Miss Murdstone, looking into a pickle-jar, 'and idleness is the root of all evil. But to be sure, he would be idle here – or anywhere, in my opinion.'

Peggotty had an angry answer ready, I could see; but she swallowed it for my sake, and remained silent.

'Humph!' said Miss Murdstone, still keeping her eye on the pickles; 'it is of more importance than anything else – it is of paramount importance – that my brother should not be disturbed or made uncomfortable. I suppose I had better say yes.'

I thanked her, without making any demonstration of joy, lest it should induce her to withdraw her assent. Nor could I help thinking this a prudent course, when she looked at me out of the pickle-jar with as great an access of sourness as if her black eyes had absorbed its contents. However the permission was given, and was never retracted; for when the month was out, Peggotty and I were ready to depart.

Mr Barkis came into the house for Peggotty's boxes. I had never known him to pass the garden gate before, but on this occasion he came into the house. And he gave me a look as he shouldered the largest box and went out, which I thought had meaning in it, if meaning could ever be said to find its way into Mr Barkis's visage.

Peggotty was naturally in low spirits at leaving what had been her home so many years, and where the two strong attachments of her life – for my mother and myself – had been formed. She had been walking in the churchyard, too, very early; and she got into the cart, and sat in it with her handkerchief at her eyes.

So long as she remained in this condition, Mr Barkis gave no sign of life whatever. He sat in his usual place and attitude, like a great stuffed figure. But when she began to look about her, and to speak to me, he nodded his head and grinned several times. I have not the least notion at whom, or what he meant by it.

'It's a beautiful day, Mr Barkis!' I said, as an act of politeness.

'It ain't bad,' said Mr Barkis, who generally qualified his speech, and rarely committed himself.

'Peggotty is quite comfortable now, Mr Barkis,' I remarked, for his satisfaction.

'Is she, though?' said Mr Barkis.

After reflecting about it, with a sagacious air, Mr Barkis eyed her, and said: '*Are* you pretty comfortable?'

Peggotty laughed, and answered in the affirmative.

'But really and truly, you know; are you?' growled Mr Barkis, sliding nearer to her on the seat, and nudging her with his elbow. 'Are you? Really and truly pretty comfortable? Are you? Eh?' At each of these enquiries Mr Barkis shuffled nearer to her, and gave her another nudge; so that at last we were all crowded together in the left-hand corner of the cart, and I was so squeezed that I could hardly bear it.

Peggotty calling his attention to my sufferings, Mr Barkis gave me a little more room at once, and got away by degrees. But I could not help observing that he seemed to think he had hit upon a wonderful expedient for expressing himself in a neat, agreeable, and pointed manner, without the inconvenience of inventing conversation. He manifestly chuckled over it for some time. By and by he turned to Peggotty again, and, repeating, 'Are you pretty comfortable, though?' bore down upon us as before, until the breath was nearly wedged out of my body. By and by he made another descent upon us with the same enquiry, and the same result. At length, I got up whenever I saw him coming, and, standing on the footboard, pretended to look at the prospect; after which I did very well.

He was so polite as to stop at a public-house expressly on our

account, and entertain us with broiled mutton and beer. Even when Peggotty was in the act of drinking, he was seized with one of those approaches, and almost choked her. But as we drew nearer to the end of our journey, he had more to do and less time for gallantry; and when we got on Yarmouth pavement, we were all too much shaken and jolted, I apprehend, to have any leisure for anything else.

Mr Peggotty and Ham waited for us at the old place. They received me and Peggotty in an affectionate manner, and shook hands with Mr Barkis, who, with his hat on the very back of his head, and a shamefaced leer upon his countenance, and pervading his very legs, presented but a vacant appearance, I thought. They each took one of Peggotty's trunks, and we were going away, when Mr Barkis solemnly made a sign to me with his forefinger to come under an archway.

'I say,' growled Mr Barkis, 'it was all right.'

I looked up into his face, and answered, with an attempt to be very profound, 'Oh!'

'It didn't come to a end there,' said Mr Barkis, nodding confidentially. 'It was all right.'

Again I answered, 'Oh!'

'You know who was willin',' said my friend. 'It was Barkis, and Barkis only.'

I nodded assent.

'It's all right,' said Mr Barkis, shaking hands; 'I'm a friend of yourn. You made it all right, first. It's all right.'

In his attempts to be particularly lucid, Mr Barkis was so extremely mysterious that I might have stood looking in his face for an hour, and most assuredly should have got as much information out of it as out of the face of a clock that had stopped, but for Peggotty's calling me away. As we were going along, she asked me what he had said; and I told her he had said it was all right.

'Like his impudence,' said Peggotty, 'but I don't mind that! Davy, dear, what should you think if I was to think of being married?'

'Why – I suppose you would like me as much then, Peggotty, as you do now?' I returned, after a little consideration.

Greatly to the astonishment of the passengers in the street, as well as of her relations going on before, the good soul was obliged to stop and embrace me on the spot, with many protestations of her unalterable love.

'Tell me what should you say, darling?' she asked again, when this was over, and we were walking on.

'If you were thinking of being married – to Mr Barkis, Peggotty?'

'Yes,' said Peggotty.

'I should think it would be a very good thing. For then, you know, Peggotty, you would always have the horse and cart to bring you over to see me, and could come for nothing, and be sure of coming.'

'The sense of the dear!' cried Peggotty. 'What I have been thinking of this month back! Yes, my precious; and I think I should be more independent altogether, you see; let alone my working with a better heart in my own house than I could in anybody else's now. I don't know what I might be fit for now as a servant to a stranger. And I shall be always near my pretty's resting-place,' said Peggotty, musing, 'and be able to see it when I like; and when *I* lie down to rest, I may be laid not far off from my darling girl!'

We neither of us said anything for a little while.

'But I wouldn't so much as give it another thought,' said Peggotty cheerily, 'if my Davy was anyways against it – not if I had been asked in church thirty times three times over, and was wearing out the ring in my pocket.'

'Look at me, Peggotty,' I replied; 'and see if I am not really glad, and don't truly wish it!' As indeed I did, with all my heart.

'Well, my life,' said Peggotty, giving me a squeeze, 'I have thought of it night and day, every way I can, and I hope the right way; but I'll think of it again, and speak to my brother about it, and in the mean time we'll keep it to ourselves, Davy, you and me. Barkis is a good plain creetur,' said Peggotty, 'and if I tried to do my duty by him, I think it would be my fault if I wasn't – if I wasn't pretty comfortable,' said Peggotty, laughing heartily.

This quotation from Mr Barkis was so appropriate, and tickled us both so much, that we laughed again and again, and were quite in a pleasant humour when we came in view of Mr Peggotty's cottage.

It looked just the same, except that it may, perhaps, have shrunk a little in my eyes; and Mrs Gummidge was waiting at the door as if she had stood there ever since. All within was the same, down to the seaweed in the blue mug in my bedroom. I went into the outhouse to look about me; and the very same lobsters, crabs, and crawfish possessed by the same desire to pinch the world in general, appeared to be in the same state of conglomeration in the same old corner. But there was no little Em'ly to be seen, so I asked Mr Peggotty where she was.

'She's at school, sir,' said Mr Peggotty, wiping the heat consequent on the porterage of Peggotty's box from his forehead; 'she'll be home,' looking at the Dutch clock, 'in from twenty minutes to half an hour's time. We all on us feel the loss of her, bless ye!'

Mrs Gummidge moaned.

'Cheer up, Mawther!' cried Mr Peggotty.

'I feel it more than anybody else,' said Mrs Gummidge; 'I'm a lone lorn creetur, and she used to be a'most the only think that didn't go contrairy with me.'

Mrs Gummidge, whimpering and shaking her head, applied herself to blowing the fire. Mr Peggotty, looking round upon us while she was so engaged, said in a low voice, which he shaded with his hand: 'The old 'un!' From this I rightly conjectured that no improvement had taken place since my last visit in the state of Mrs Gummidge's spirits.

Now, the whole place was, or it should have been, quite as delightful a place as ever; and yet it did not impress me in the same way. I felt rather disappointed with it. Perhaps it was because little Em'ly was not at home. I knew the way by which she would come, and presently found myself strolling along the path to meet her.

A figure appeared in the distance before long, and I soon knew it to be Em'ly, who was a little creature still in stature, though she was grown. But when she drew nearer, and I saw her blue eyes looking bluer, and her dimpled face looking brighter, and her own self prettier and gayer, a curious feeling came over me that made me pretend not to know her, and pass by as if I were looking at something a long way off. I have done such a thing since in later life, or I am mistaken.

Little Em'ly didn't care a bit. She saw me well enough; but instead of turning round and calling after me, ran away laughing. This obliged me to run after her, and she ran so fast that we were very near the cottage before I caught her.

'Oh, it's you, is it?' said little Em'ly.

'Why, you knew who it was, Em'ly,' said I.

'And didn't *you* know who it was?' said Em'ly. I was going to kiss her, but she covered her cherry lips with her hands, and said she wasn't a baby now, and ran away, laughing more than ever, into the house.

She seemed to delight in teasing me, which was a change in her I wondered at very much. The tea table was ready, and our little locker was put out in its old place; but, instead of coming to sit by me, she went and bestowed her company upon that grumbling Mrs Gummidge; and on Mr Peggotty's enquiring why, rumpled her hair all over her face to hide it, and would do nothing but laugh.

'A little puss it is!' said Mr Peggotty, patting her with his great hand.

'So sh' is! so sh' is!' cried Ham; 'Mas'r Davy, bor, so sh' is!' and he sat and chuckled at her for some time, in a state of mingled admiration and delight, that made his face a burning red.

Little Em'ly was spoiled by them all in fact; and by no one more than Mr Peggotty himself, whom she could have coaxed into anything by only going and laying her cheek against his rough whisker. That was my opinion, at least, when I saw her do it; and I held Mr Peggotty to be thoroughly in the right. But she was so affectionate and sweet-natured, and had such a pleasant manner of being both sly and shy at once, that she captivated me more than ever.

She was tender-hearted, too; for when, as we sat round the fire after tea, an allusion was made by Mr Peggotty over his pipe to the loss I had sustained, the tears stood in her eyes, and she looked at me so kindly across the table that I felt quite thankful to her.

'Ah!' said Mr Peggotty, taking up her curls, and running them over his hand like water, 'here's another orphan, you see, sir. And here,' said Mr Peggotty, giving Ham a backhanded knock in the chest, 'is another of 'em, though he don't look much like it.'

'If I had you for my guardian, Mr Peggotty,' said I, shaking my head, 'I don't think I should *feel* much like it.'

'Well said, Mas'r Davy, bor!' cried Ham in an ecstasy. 'Hoorah! Well said! Nor more you wouldn't! Hor! Hor!' – here he returned Mr Peggotty's backhander, and little Em'ly got up and kissed Mr Peggotty.

'And how's your friend, sir?' said Mr Peggotty to me.

'Steerforth?' said I.

'That's the name!' cried Mr Peggotty, turning to Ham. 'I knowed it was something in our way.'

'You said it was Rudderford,' observed Ham, laughing.

'Well?' retorted Mr Peggotty. 'And ye steer with a rudder, don't ye? It ain't fur off. How is he, sir?'

'He was very well, indeed, when I came away, Mr Peggotty.'

'There's a friend!' said Mr Peggotty, stretching out his pipe. 'There's a friend, if you talk of friends! Why, Lord love my heart alive, if it ain't a treat to look at him!'

'He is very handsome, is he not?' said I, my heart warming with this praise.

'Handsome!' cried Mr Peggotty. 'He stands up to you like – like a – why I don't know what he *don't* stand up to you like. He's so bold!'

'Yes! That's just his character,' said I. 'He's as brave as a lion, and you can't think how frank he is, Mr Peggotty.'

'And I do suppose, now,' said Mr Peggotty, looking at me through the smoke of his pipe, 'that in the way of book-larning he'd take the wind out of almost anything.'

'Yes,' said I, delighted; 'he knows everything. He is astonishingly clever.'

'There's a friend!' murmured Mr Peggotty, with a grave toss of his head.

'Nothing seems to cost him any trouble,' said I. 'He knows a task if he only looks at it. He is the best cricketer you ever saw. He will give you almost as many men as you like at draughts, and beat you easily.'

Mr Peggotty gave his head another toss, as much as to say, 'Of course he will.'

'He is such a speaker,' I pursued, 'that he can win anybody over; and I don't know what you'd say if you were to hear him sing, Mr Peggotty.'

Mr Peggotty gave his head another toss, as much as to say, 'I have no doubt of it.'

'Then, he's such a generous, fine, noble fellow,' said I, quite carried away by my favourite theme, 'that it's hardly possible to give him as much praise as he deserves. I am sure I can never feel thankful enough for the generosity with which he has protected me, so much younger and lower in the school than himself.'

I was running on, very fast indeed, when my eyes rested on little Em'ly's face, which was bent forward over the table, listening with the deepest attention, her breath held, her blue eyes sparkling like jewels, and the colour mantling in her cheeks. She looked so extraordinarily earnest and pretty that I stopped in a sort of wonder; and they all observed her at the same time, for, as I stopped, they laughed and looked at her.

'Em'ly is like me,' said Peggotty, 'and would like to see him.'

Em'ly was confused by our all observing her, and hung down her head, and her face was covered with blushes. Glancing up presently through her stray curls, and seeing that we were all looking at her still (I am sure I, for one, could have looked at her for hours), she ran away, and kept away until it was nearly bedtime.

I lay down in the old little bed in the stern of the boat, and the wind came moaning on across the flat as it had done before. But I could not help fancying, now, that it moaned of those who were gone; and instead of thinking that the sea might rise in the night and float the boat away, I thought of the sea that had risen, since I last heard those sounds, and drowned my happy home. I recollect, as the wind and water began to sound fainter in my ears, putting a short clause into my prayers, petitioning that I might grow up to marry little Em'ly, and so dropping lovingly asleep.

The days passed pretty much as they had passed before, except – it was a great exception – that little Em'ly and I seldom wandered on the beach now. She had tasks to learn, and needlework to do; and was absent during a great part of each day. But I felt that we should not have had these old wanderings, even if it had been otherwise. Wild and full of childish whims as Em'ly was, she was more of a little woman than I had supposed. She seemed to have got a great distance away from me, in little more than a year. She liked me, but she laughed at me, and tormented me; and when I went to meet her, stole home another way, and was laughing at the door when I came back, disappointed. The best times were when she sat quietly at work in the doorway, and I sat on the wooden step at her feet, reading to her. It seems to me at this hour that I have never seen such sunlight as on those bright April afternoons; that I have never seen such a sunny little figure as I used to see sitting in the doorway of the old boat; that I have never beheld such sky, such water, such glorified ships sailing away into golden air.

On the very first evening after our arrival, Mr Barkis appeared in an exceedingly vacant and awkward condition, and with a bundle of oranges tied up in a handkerchief. As he made no allusion of any kind to this property, he was supposed to have left it behind him by accident when he went away; until Ham, running after him to restore it, came back with the information that it was intended for Peggotty. After that occasion he appeared every evening at exactly the same hour, and always with a little bundle, to which he never alluded, and which he regularly put behind the door, and left there. These offerings of affection were of a most various and eccentric description. Among them I remember a double set of pigs' trotters, a huge pincushion, half a bushel or so of apples, a pair of jet earrings, some Spanish onions, a box of dominoes, a canary bird and cage, and a leg of pickled pork.

Mr Barkis's wooing, as I remember it, was altogether of a peculiar kind. He very seldom said anything; but would sit by the fire in much the same attitude as he sat in his cart, and stare heavily at Peggotty, who was opposite. One night, being, as I suppose, inspired by love, he made a dart at the bit of wax candle she kept for her thread, and put it in his waistcoat pocket and carried it off. After that, his great delight was to produce it when it was wanted, sticking to the lining of his pocket, in a partially melted state, and pocket it again when it was done with. He seemed to enjoy himself very much, and not to feel at all called upon to talk. Even when he took Peggotty out for a walk on the flats, he had no uneasiness on that head, I believe; contenting himself with now and then asking her if she was pretty comfortable; and I remember that sometimes, after he was gone, Peggotty would throw her apron over her face, and laugh for half an hour. Indeed, we were all more or less amused, except that miserable Mrs Gummidge, whose courtship would appear to have been of an exactly parallel nature, she was so continually reminded by these transactions of the old one.

At length, when the term of my visit was nearly expired, it was given out that Peggotty and Mr Barkis were going to make a day's holiday together, and that little Em'ly and I were to accompany them. I had but a broken sleep the night before, in anticipation of the pleasure of a whole day with Em'ly. We were all astir betimes in the morning; and while we were yet at breakfast, Mr Barkis appeared in the distance, driving a chaise-cart towards the object of his affections.

Peggotty was dressed as usual, in her neat and quiet mourning; but Mr Barkis bloomed in a new blue coat, of which the tailor had given him such good measure that the cuffs would have rendered gloves unnecessary in the coldest weather, while the collar was so high that it pushed his hair up on end on the top of his head. His bright buttons, too, were of the largest size. Rendered complete by drab pantaloons and a buff waistcoat, I thought Mr Barkis a phenomenon of respectability.

When we were all in a bustle outside the door, I found that Mr Peggotty was prepared with an old shoe, which was to be thrown after us for luck, and which he offered to Mrs Gummidge for that purpose.

'No. It had better be done by somebody else, Dan'l,' said Mrs Gummidge. 'I'm a lone, lorn creetur myself, and everythink that reminds me of creeturs that ain't lone and lorn goes contrary with me.'

'Come, old gal!' cried Mr Peggotty. 'Take and heave it!'

'No, Dan'l,' returned Mrs Gummidge, whimpering and shaking her head. 'If I felt less I could do more. You don't feel like me, Dan'l; thinks don't go contrary with you, nor you with them; you had better do it yourself.'

But here Peggotty, who had been going about from one to another in a hurried way, kissing everybody, called out from the cart, in which we all were by this time (Em'ly and I on two little chairs, side by side), that Mrs Gummidge must do it. So Mrs Gummidge did it; and I am sorry to relate, cast a damp upon the festive character of our departure, by immediately bursting into tears, and sinking subdued into the arms of Ham, with the declaration that she knowed she was a burden, and had better be carried to the house at once; which I really thought was a sensible idea, that Ham might have acted on.

Away we went, however, on our holiday excursion; and the first thing we did was to stop at a church, where Mr Barkis tied the horse to some rails, and went in with Peggotty, leaving little Em'ly and me alone in the chaise. I took that occasion to put my arm round Em'ly's waist, and propose that as I was going away so very soon now we should determine to be very affectionate to one another, and very happy, all day. Little Em'ly consenting, and allowing me to kiss her, I became desperate; informing her, I recollect, that I never could love another, and that I was prepared to shed the blood of anybody who should aspire to her affections.

How merry little Em'ly made herself about it! With what a demure assumption of being immensely older and wiser than I,

the fairy little woman said I was 'a silly boy'; and then laughed so charmingly that I forgot the pain of being called by that disparaging name, in the pleasure of looking at her.

Mr Barkis and Peggotty were a good while in the church, but came out at last, and then we drove away into the country. As we were going along, Mr Barkis turned to me, and said, with a wink – by the by, I should hardly have thought, before, that he *could* wink: 'What name was it as I wrote up in the cart?'

'Clara Peggotty,' I answered.

'What name would it be as I should write up now, if there was a tilt here?'

'Clara Peggotty, again?' I suggested.

'Clara Peggotty Barkis!' he returned, and burst into a roar of laughter that shook the chaise.

In a word, they were married, and had gone into the church for no other purpose. Peggotty was resolved that it should be quietly done; and the clerk had given her away, and there had been no witnesses of the ceremony. She was a little confused when Mr Barkis made this abrupt announcement of their union, and could not hug me enough in token of her unimpaired affection; but she soon became herself again, and said she was very glad it was over.

We drove to a little inn in a by-road, where we were expected, and where we had a very comfortable dinner, and passed the day with great satisfaction. If Peggotty had been married every day for the last ten years, she could hardly have been more at her ease about it; it made no sort of difference in her; she was just the same as ever, and went out for a stroll with little Em'ly and me before tea, while Mr Barkis philosophically smoked his pipe, and enjoyed himself, I suppose, with the contemplation of his happiness. If so, it sharpened his appetite; for I distinctly call to mind that, although he had eaten a good deal of pork and greens at dinner, and had finished off with a fowl or two, he was obliged to have cold boiled bacon for tea, and disposed of a large quantity without any emotion.

I have often thought, since, what an odd, innocent, out-of-the-way kind of wedding it must have been! We got into the chaise again soon after dark, and drove cosily back, looking up at the stars, and talking about them. I was their chief exponent, and opened Mr Barkis's mind to an amazing extent. I told him all I knew, but he would have believed anything I might have taken it into my head to impart to him; for he had a profound veneration for my abilities, and informed his wife in my hearing, on that very occasion, that I was 'a young Roeshus' – by which I think he meant, prodigy.

When we had exhausted the subject of the stars, or rather when I had exhausted the mental faculties of Mr Barkis, little Em'ly and I made a cloak of an old wrapper, and sat under it for the rest of the journey. Ah, how I loved her! What happiness (I thought) if *we* were married, and were going away anywhere to live among the trees and in the fields, never growing older, never growing wiser, children ever, rambling hand in hand through sunshine and among flowery meadows, laying down our heads on moss at night, in a sweet sleep of purity and peace, and buried by the birds when we were dead! Some such picture, with no real world in it, bright with the light of our innocence, and vague as the stars afar off, was in my mind all the way. I am glad to think there were two such guileless hearts at Peggotty's marriage as little Em'ly's and mine. I am glad to think the Loves and Graces took such airy forms in its homely procession.

Well, we came to the old boat again in good time at night; and there Mr and Mrs Barkis bade us goodbye, and drove away snugly to their own home. I felt then, for the first time, that I had lost Peggotty. I should have gone to bed with a sore heart indeed under any other roof but that which sheltered little Em'ly's head.

Mr Peggotty and Ham knew what was in my thoughts as well as I did, and were ready with some supper and their hospitable faces to drive it away. Little Em'ly came and sat beside me on the locker for the only time in all that visit; and it was altogether a wonderful close to a wonderful day.

It was a night tide; and soon after we went to bed, Mr Peggotty and Ham went out to fish. I felt very brave at being left alone in the solitary house, the protector of Em'ly and Mrs Gummidge, and only wished that a lion or a serpent, or any ill-disposed monster, would make an attack upon us, that I might destroy him, and cover myself with glory. But as nothing of the sort happened to be walking about on Yarmouth flats that night, I provided the best substitute I could by dreaming of dragons until morning.

With morning came Peggotty; who called to me, as usual, under my window as if Mr Barkis the carrier had been from first to last a dream too. After breakfast she took me to her own home, and a beautiful little home it was. Of all the movables in it, I must have been most impressed by a certain old bureau of some dark wood in the parlour (the tile-floored kitchen was the general sitting-room), with a retreating top which opened, let down, and became a desk, within which was a large quarto edition of *Foxe's Book of Martyrs*. This precious volume, of which I do not recollect one word, I immediately discovered and immediately applied myself to; and I never visited the house afterwards, but I kneeled on a chair, opened the casket where this gem was enshrined, spread my arms over the desk, and fell to devouring the book afresh. I was chiefly edified, I am afraid, by the pictures, which were numerous, and represented all kinds of dismal horrors; but the *Martyrs* and Peggotty's house have been inseparable in my mind ever since, and are now.

I took leave of Mr Peggotty, and Ham, and Mrs Gummidge, and little Em'ly, that day; and passed the night at Peggotty's, in a little room in the roof (with the Crocodile Book on a shelf by the bed's head), which was to be always mine, Peggotty said, and should always be kept for me in exactly the same state.

'Young or old, Davy dear, as long as I am alive and have this house over my head,' said Peggotty, 'you shall find it as if I expected you here directly every minute. I shall keep it every day, as I used to keep your old little room, my darling; and if you was to go to China, you might think of it as being kept just the same, all the time you were away.'

I felt the truth and constancy of my dear old nurse, with all my heart, and thanked her as well as I could. That was not very well, for she spoke to me thus, with her arms round my neck, in the morning, and I was going home in the morning, and I went home in the morning, with herself and Mr Barkis in the cart. They left me at the gate, not easily or lightly; and it was a

Mrs Gummidge casts a damp on our departure

strange sight to me to see the cart go on, taking Peggotty away, and leaving me under the old elm trees looking at the house in which there was no face to look on mine with love or liking any more.

And now I fell into a state of neglect, which I cannot look back upon without compassion. I fell at once into a solitary condition – apart from all friendly notice, apart from the society of all other boys of my own age, apart from all companionship but my own spiritless thoughts – which seems to cast its gloom upon this paper as I write.

What would I have given, to have been sent to the hardest school that ever was kept! – to have been taught something, anyhow, anywhere! No such hope dawned upon me. They disliked me, and they sullenly, sternly, steadily overlooked me. I think Mr Murdstone's means were straitened at about this time; but it is little to the purpose. He could not bear me; and in putting me from him he tried, as I believe, to put away the notion that I had any claim upon him – and succeeded.

I was not actively ill-used. I was not beaten, or starved; but the wrong that was done to me had no intervals of relenting, and was done in a systematic, passionless manner. Day after day, week after week, month after month, I was coldly neglected. I wonder sometimes, when I think of it, what they would have done if I had been taken with an illness; whether I should have lain down in my lonely room, and languished through it in my usual solitary way, or whether anybody would have helped me out.

When Mr and Miss Murdstone were at home, I took my meals with them; in their absence, I ate and drank by myself. At all times I lounged about the house and neighbourhood quite disregarded, except that they were jealous of my making any friends, thinking, perhaps, that if I did, I might complain to someone. For this reason, though Mr Chillip often asked me to go and see him (he was a widower, having, some years before that, lost a little, small, light-haired wife, whom I can just remember connecting in my own thoughts with a pale tortoiseshell cat), it was but seldom that I enjoyed the happiness of passing an afternoon in his closet of a surgery; reading some book that was new to me, with the smell of the whole pharmacopoeia coming up my nose, or pounding something in a mortar under his mild directions.

For the same reason, added no doubt to the old dislike of her, I was seldom allowed to visit Peggotty. Faithful to her promise, she either came to see me, or met me somewhere near, once every week, and never empty-handed; but many and bitter were the disappointments I had, in being refused permission to pay a visit to her at her house. Some few times, however, at long intervals, I was allowed to go there; and then I found out that Mr Barkis was something of a miser, or as Peggotty dutifully expressed it, was 'a little near,' and kept a heap of money in a box under his bed, which he pretended was only full of coats and trousers. In this coffer, his riches hid themselves with such a tenacious modesty, that the smallest instalments could only be tempted out by artifice; so that Peggotty had to prepare a long and elaborate scheme, a very Gunpowder Plot, for every Saturday's expenses.

All this time I was so conscious of the waste of any promise I had given, and of my being utterly neglected, that I should have been perfectly miserable, I have no doubt, but for the old books. They were my only comfort; and I was as true to them as they were to me, and read them over and over I don't know how many times more.

I now approach a period of my life, which I can never lose the remembrance of, while I remember anything; and the recollection of which has often, without my invocation, come before me like a ghost, and haunted happier times.

I had been out, one day, loitering somewhere, in the listless, meditative manner that my way of life engendered, when, turning the corner of a lane near our house, I came upon Mr Murdstone walking with a gentleman. I was confused, and was going by them, when the gentleman cried: 'What! Brooks!'

'No, sir, David Copperfield,' I said.

'Don't tell me. You are Brooks,' said the gentleman. 'You are Brooks of Sheffield. That's your name.'

At these words, I observed the gentleman more attentively. His laugh coming to my remembrance too, I knew him to be Mr Quinion, whom I had gone over to Lowestoft with Mr Murdstone to see, before – it is no matter – I need not recall when.

'And how do you get on, and where are you being educated, Brooks?' said Mr Quinion.

He had put his hand upon my shoulder, and turned me about, to walk with them. I did not know what to reply, and glanced dubiously at Mr Murdstone.

'He is at home at present,' said the latter. 'He is not being educated anywhere. I don't know what to do with him. He is a difficult subject.'

That old, double look was on me for a moment; and then his eye darkened with a frown, as it turned, in its aversion, elsewhere.

'Humph!' said Mr Quinion, looking at us both, I thought. 'Fine weather.'

Silence ensued, and I was considering how I could best disengage my shoulder from his hand, and go away, when he said: 'I suppose you are a pretty sharp fellow still? Eh, Brooks?'

'Aye! he is sharp enough,' said Mr Murdstone, impatiently. 'You had better let him go. He will not thank you for troubling him.'

On this hint, Mr Quinion released me, and I made the best of my way home. Looking back as I turned into the front garden, I saw Mr Murdstone leaning against the wicket of the church-yard, and Mr Quinion talking to him. They were both looking after me, and I felt that they were speaking of me.

Mr Quinion lay at our house that night. After breakfast, the next morning, I had put my chair away, and was going out of the room, when Mr Murdstone called me back. He then gravely repaired to another table, where his sister sat herself at her desk. Mr Quinion, with his hands in his pockets, stood looking out of window; and I stood looking at them all.

'David,' said Mr Murdstone, 'to the young this is a world for action; not for moping and droning in.'

'As you do,' added his sister.

'Jane Murdstone, leave it to me, if you please. I say, David, to the young this is a world for action, and not for moping and droning in. It is especially so for a young boy of your disposition, which requires a great deal of correcting; and to which no greater service can be done than to force it to conform to the ways of the working world, and to bend it and break it.'

'For stubbornness won't do here,' said his sister. 'What it wants is to be crushed. And crushed it must be. Shall be, too!'

He gave her a look, half in remonstrance, half in approval, and went on: 'I suppose you know, David, that I am not rich. At any rate, you know it now. You have received some considerable education already. Education is costly; and even if it were not, and I could afford it, I am of opinion that it would not be at all advantageous to you to be kept at a school. What is before you is a fight with the world; and the sooner you begin it, the better.'

I think it occurred to me that I had already begun it, in my poor way; but it occurs to me now, whether or no.

'You have heard "the counting-house" mentioned sometimes,' said Mr Murdstone.

'The counting-house, sir?' I repeated.

'Of Murdstone and Grinby, in the wine trade,' he replied.

I suppose I looked uncertain, for he went on hastily: 'You have heard the "counting-house" mentioned, or the business, or the cellars, or the wharf, or something about it.'

'I think I have heard the business mentioned, sir,' I said, remembering what I vaguely knew of his and his sister's resources. 'But I don't know when.'

'It does not matter when,' he returned. 'Mr Quinion manages that business.'

I glanced at the latter deferentially as he stood looking out of window.

'Mr Quinion suggests that it gives employment to some other boys, and that he sees no reason why it shouldn't, on the same terms, give employment to you.'

'He having,' Mr Quinion observed in a low voice, and half turning round, 'no other prospect, Murdstone.'

Mr Murdstone, with an impatient, even an angry gesture, resumed, without noticing what he had said: 'Those terms are, that you will earn enough for yourself to provide for your eating and drinking, and pocket-money. Your lodging (which I have arranged for) will be paid by me. So will your washing.'

'Which will be kept down to my estimate,' said his sister.

'Your clothes will be looked after for you, too,' said Mr Murdstone, 'as you will not be able, yet awhile, to get them for yourself. So you are now going to London, David, with Mr Quinion, to begin the world on your own account.'

'In short, you are provided for,' observed his sister, 'and will please to do your duty.'

Though I quite understood that the purpose of this announcement was to get rid of me, I have no distinct remembrance whether it pleased or frightened me. My impression is, that I was in a state of confusion about it, and, oscillating between the two points, touched neither. Nor had I much time for the clearing of my thoughts, as Mr Quinion was to go upon the morrow.

Behold me, on the morrow, in a much-worn little white hat, with a black crape round it for my mother, a black jacket, and a pair of hard, stiff, corduroy trousers – which Miss Murdstone considered the best armour for the legs in that fight with the world which was now to come off – behold me so attired, and with my little worldly all before me in a small trunk, sitting, a lone lorn child (as Mrs Gummidge might have said), in the post-chaise that was carrying Mr Quinion to the London coach at Yarmouth! See, how our house and church are lessening in the distance; how the grave beneath the tree is blotted out by intervening objects; how the spire points upward from my old playground no more, and the sky is empty!

CHAPTER 11

I Begin Life on My Own Account, and Don't Like It

I know enough of the world now, to have almost lost the capacity of being much surprised by anything; but it is matter of some surprise to me, even now, that I can have been so easily thrown away at such an age. A child of excellent abilities, and with strong powers of observation, quick, eager, delicate, and soon hurt bodily or mentally, it seems wonderful to me that nobody should have made any sign in my behalf. But none was made; and I became, at ten years old, a little labouring hind in the service of Murdstone and Grinby.

Murdstone and Grinby's warehouse was at the waterside. It was down in Blackfriars. Modern improvements have altered the place; but it was the last house at the bottom of a narrow street, curving down hill to the river, with some stairs at the end, where people took boat. It was a crazy old house with a wharf of its own, abutting on the water when the tide was in, and on the mud when the tide was out, and literally overrun with rats. Its panelled rooms, discoloured with the dirt and smoke of a hundred years, I dare say; its decaying floors and staircase; the squeaking and scuffling of the old grey rats down in the cellars; and the dirt and rottenness of the place, are things, not of many years ago, in my mind, but of the present instant. They are all before me, just as they were in the evil hour when I went among them for the first time, with my trembling hand in Mr Quinion's.

Murdstone and Grinby's trade was among a good many kinds of people, but an important branch of it was the supply of wines and spirits to certain packet ships. I forget now where they chiefly went, but I think there were some among them that made voyages both to the East and West Indies. I know that a great many empty bottles were one of the consequences of this traffic, and that certain men and boys were employed to examine them against the light, and reject those that were flawed, and to rinse and wash them. When the empty bottles ran short, there were labels to be pasted on full ones, or corks to be fitted to them, or seals to be put upon the corks, or finished bottles to be packed in casks. All this work was my work, and of the boys employed upon it I was one.

There were three or four of us, counting me. My working place was established in a corner of the warehouse, where Mr

Quinion could see me, when he chose to stand up on the bottom rail of his stool in the counting-house, and look at me through a window above the desk. Hither, on the first morning of my so auspiciously beginning life on my own account, the oldest of the regular boys was summoned to show me my business. His name was Mick Walker, and he wore a ragged apron and a paper cap. He informed me that his father was a bargeman, and walked, in a black velvet head-dress, in the Lord Mayor's Show. He also informed me that our principal associate would be another boy whom he introduced by the – to me – extraordinary name of Mealy Potatoes. I discovered, however, that this youth had not been christened by that name, but that it had been bestowed upon him in the warehouse, on account of his complexion, which was pale or mealy. Mealy's father was a waterman, who had the additional distinction of being a fireman, and was engaged as such at one of the large theatres; where some young relation of Mealy's – I think his little sister – did Imps in the Pantomimes.

No words can express the secret agony of my soul as I sunk into this companionship; compared these henceforth everyday associates with those of my happier childhood – not to say with Steerforth, Traddles, and the rest of those boys; and felt my hopes of growing up to be a learned and distinguished man crushed in my bosom. The deep remembrance of the sense I had, of being utterly without hope now; of the shame I felt in my position; of the misery it was to my young heart to believe that day by day what I had learned, and thought, and delighted in, and raised my fancy and my emulation up by, would pass away from me, little by little, never to be brought back any more, cannot be written. As often as Mick Walker went away in the course of that forenoon, I mingled my tears with the water in which I was washing the bottles; and sobbed as if there were a flaw in my own breast, and it were in danger of bursting.

The counting-house clock was at half-past twelve, and there was general preparation for going to dinner, when Mr Quinion tapped at the counting-house window, and beckoned to me to go in. I went in, and found there a stoutish, middle-aged person, in a brown surtout and black tights and shoes, with no more hair upon his head (which was a large one, and very shining) than there is upon an egg, and with a very extensive face, which he turned full upon me. His clothes were shabby, but he had an imposing shirt-collar on. He carried a jaunty sort of a stick, with a large pair of rusty tassels to it; and a quizzing-glass hung outside his coat – for ornament, I afterwards found, as he very seldom looked through it, and couldn't see anything when he did.

'This,' said Mr Quinion, in allusion to myself, 'is he.'

'This,' said the stranger, with a certain condescending roll in his voice, and a certain indescribable air of doing something genteel, which impressed me very much, 'is Master Copperfield. I hope I see you well, sir?'

I said I was very well, and hoped he was. I was sufficiently ill at ease, Heaven knows; but it was not in my nature to complain much at that time of my life, so I said I was very well, and hoped he was.

'I am,' said the stranger, 'thank Heaven, quite well. I have received a letter from Mr Murdstone, in which he mentions that he would desire me to receive into an apartment in the rear of my house, which is at present unoccupied – and is, in short, to be let as a – in short,' said the stranger, with a smile and in a burst of confidence, 'as a bedroom – the young beginner whom I have now the pleasure to – ' And the stranger waved his hand, and settled his chin in his shirt-collar.

'This is Mr Micawber,' said Mr Quinion to me.

'Ahem!' said the stranger, 'that is my name.'

'Mr Micawber,' said Mr Quinion, 'is known to Mr Murdstone. He takes orders for us on commission, when he can get any. He has been written to by Mr Murdstone, on the subject of your lodgings, and he will receive you as a lodger.'

'My address,' said Mr Micawber, 'is Windsor Terrace, City Road. I – in short,' said Mr Micawber, with the same genteel air, and in another burst of confidence – 'I live there.'

I made him a bow.

'Under the impression,' said Mr Micawber, 'that your peregrinations in this metropolis have not as yet been extensive, and that you might have some difficulty in penetrating the arcana of the Modern Babylon in the direction of the City Road – in short,' said Mr Micawber, in another burst of confidence, 'that you might lose yourself – I shall be happy to call this evening, and install you in the knowledge of the nearest way.'

I thanked him with all my heart, for it was friendly in him to offer to take that trouble.

'At what hour,' said Mr Micawber, 'shall I – '

'At about eight,' said Mr Quinion.

'At about eight,' said Mr Micawber. 'I beg to wish you good-day, Mr Quinion. I will intrude no longer.'

So he put on his hat, and went out with his cane under his arm, very upright, and humming a tune when he was clear of the counting-house.

Mr Quinion then formally engaged me to be as useful as I could in the warehouse of Murdstone and Grinby, at a salary, I think, of six shillings a week. I am not clear whether it was six or seven. I am inclined to believe, from my uncertainty on this head, that it was six at first and seven afterwards. He paid me a week down (from his own pocket, I believe), and I gave Mealy sixpence out of it to get my trunk carried to Windsor Terrace at night, it being too heavy for my strength, small as it was. I paid sixpence more for my dinner, which was a meat pie and a turn at a neighbouring pump; and passed the hour which was allowed for that meal in walking about the streets.

At the appointed time in the evening, Mr Micawber reappeared. I washed my hands and face, to do the greater honour to his gentility, and we walked to our house, as I suppose I must now call it, together; Mr Micawber impressing the names of streets, and the shapes of corner houses upon me, as we went along, that I might find my way back easily, in the morning.

Arrived at his house in Windsor Terrace (which I noticed was shabby like himself, but also, like himself, made all the show it could), he presented me to Mrs Micawber, a thin and faded lady, not at all young, who was sitting in the parlour (the first floor was altogether unfurnished, and the blinds were kept down to delude the neighbours), with a baby at her breast. This baby was one of twins; and I may remark here that I hardly ever, in all my experience of the family, saw both the twins detached from Mrs Micawber at the same time. One of them was always taking refreshment.

There were two other children; Master Micawber, aged about four, and Miss Micawber, aged about three. These, and a dark-complexioned young woman, with a habit of snorting, who was servant to the family, and informed me, before half an hour had expired, that she was 'a Orfling,' and came from St Luke's workhouse, in the neighbourhood, completed the establishment. My room was at the top of the house, at the back; a close chamber; stencilled all over with an ornament, which my young imagination represented as a blue muffin, and very scantily furnished.

'I never thought,' said Mrs Micawber when she came up, twin and all, to show me the apartment, and sat down to take breath, 'before I was married, when I lived with papa and mama, that I should ever find it necessary to take a lodger. But Mr Micawber being in difficulties, all considerations of private feeling must give way.'

I said, 'Yes, ma'am.'

'Mr Micawber's difficulties are almost overwhelming just at present,' said Mrs Micawber; 'and whether it is possible to bring him through them, I don't know. When I lived at home with papa and mama, I really should have hardly understood what the word meant, in the sense in which I now employ it, but experientia does it – as papa used to say.'

I cannot satisfy myself whether she told me that Mr Micawber had been an officer in the Marines, or whether I have imagined it. I only know that I believe to this hour that he was in the Marines once upon a time, without knowing why. He was a sort of town traveller for a number of miscellaneous houses, now, but made little or nothing of it, I am afraid.

'If Mr Micawber's creditors *will not* give him time,' said Mrs Micawber, 'they must take the consequences; and the sooner they bring it to an issue the better. Blood cannot be obtained from a stone, neither can anything on account be obtained at present (not to mention law expenses) from Mr Micawber.'

I never can quite understand whether my precocious self-dependence confused Mrs Micawber in reference to my age, or whether she was so full of the subject that she would have talked about it to the very twins if there had been nobody else to communicate with, but this was the strain in which she began, and she went on accordingly all the time I knew her.

Poor Mrs Micawber! She said she had tried to exert herself; and so, I have no doubt, she had. The centre of the street door was perfectly covered with a great brass plate, on which was engraved 'Mrs Micawber's Boarding Establishment for Young Ladies'; but I never found that any young lady had ever been to school there; or that any young lady ever came, or proposed to come; or that the least preparation was ever made to receive any young lady. The only visitors I ever saw or heard of, were creditors. They used to come at all hours, and some of them were quite ferocious. One dirty-faced man, I think he was a bootmaker, used to edge himself into the passage as early as seven o'clock in the morning, and call up the stairs to Mr Micawber: 'Come! You ain't out yet, you know. Pay us, will you? Don't hide, you know; that's mean. I wouldn't be mean if I was you. Pay us, will you? You just pay us, d' ye hear? Come!' Receiving no answer to these taunts, he would mount in his wrath to the words 'swindlers' and 'robbers'; and these being ineffectual too, would sometimes go to the extremity of crossing the street, and roaring up at the windows of the second floor, where he knew Mr Micawber was. At these times, Mr Micawber would be transported with grief and mortification, even to the length (as I was once made aware by a scream from his wife) of making motions at himself with a razor; but within half an hour afterwards, he would polish up his shoes with extraordinary pains, and go out, humming a tune with a greater air of gentility than ever. Mrs Micawber was quite as elastic. I have known her to be thrown into fainting fits by the king's taxes at three o'clock, and to eat lamb-chops, breaded, and drink warm ale (paid for with two teaspoons that had gone to the pawnbroker's) at four. On one occasion, when an execution had just been put in, coming home through some chance as early as six o'clock, I saw her lying (of course with a twin) under the grate in a swoon, with her hair all torn about her face; but I never knew her more cheerful than she was, that very same night, over a veal-cutlet before the kitchen fire, telling me stories about her papa and mama, and the company they used to keep.

In this house, and with this family, I passed my leisure time. My own exclusive breakfast of a penny loaf and a pennyworth of milk, I provided myself; I kept another small loaf, and a modicum of cheese, on a particular shelf of a particular cupboard, to make my supper on when I came back at night. This made a hole in the six or seven shillings, I know well; and I was out at the warehouse all day, and had to support myself on that money all the week. From Monday morning until Saturday night, I had no advice, no counsel, no encouragement, no consolation, no assistance, no support, of any kind, from anyone, that I can call to mind, as I hope to go to Heaven!

I was so young and childish, and so little qualified – how could I be otherwise? – to undertake the whole charge of my own existence, that often, in going to Murdstone and Grinby's, of a morning, I could not resist the stale pastry put out for sale at half price at the pastry cooks' doors, and spent in that the money I should have kept for my dinner. Then, I went without my dinner, or bought a roll or a slice of pudding. I remember two pudding-shops between which I was divided, according to my finances. One was in a court close to St Martin's Church – at the back of the church – which is now removed altogether. The pudding at that shop was made of currants, and was rather a special pudding, but was dear, two-pennyworth not being larger than a pennyworth of more ordinary pudding. A good shop for the latter was in the Strand – somewhere in that part which has been rebuilt since. It was a stout pale pudding, heavy and flabby, and with great flat raisins in it, stuck in whole at wide distances apart. It came up hot at about my time every day, and many a day did I dine off it. When I dined regularly and handsomely, I had a saveloy and a penny loaf, or a fourpenny plate of red beef from a cook's shop; or a plate of bread and cheese and a glass of beer, from a miserable old public-house opposite our place of business, called the Lion, or the Lion and something else that I have forgotten. Once, I remember carrying my own bread (which I had brought from home in the morning) under my arm, wrapped in a piece of paper, like a book, and going to a famous alamode beef-house near Drury Lane, and ordering a 'small plate' of that delicacy to eat with it. What the waiter thought of such a strange little apparition coming in all alone, I don't know; but I can see him now, staring at me as I ate my dinner, and bringing up the other waiter to look. I gave him a halfpenny for himself, and I wish he hadn't taken it.

We had half an hour, I think, for tea. When I had money enough, I used to get half a pint of ready-made coffee and a slice of bread and butter. When I had none, I used to look at a venison-shop in Fleet Street; or I have strolled, at such a time, as far as Covent Garden Market, and stared at the pineapples. I was fond of wandering about the Adelphi, because it was a mysterious place, with those dark arches. I see myself emerging one evening from some of these arches, on a little public-house close to the river, with an open space before it, where some coal-heavers were dancing; to look at whom I sat down upon a bench. I wonder what they thought of me!

I was such a child, and so little, that frequently when I went into the bar of a strange public-house for a glass of ale or porter, to moisten what I had had for dinner, they were afraid to give it me. I remember one hot evening I went into the bar of a public-house, and said to the landlord: 'What is your best – your *very best* – ale a glass?' For it was a special occasion. I don't know what. It may have been my birthday.

'Twopence-halfpenny,' says the landlord, 'is the price of the Genuine Stunning ale.'

'Then,' says I, producing the money, 'just draw me a glass of the Genuine Stunning, if you please, with a good head to it.'

The landlord looked at me in return over the bar, from head to foot, with a strange smile on his face; and instead of drawing the beer, looked round the screen and said something to his wife. She came out from behind it, with her work in her hand, and joined him in surveying me. Here we stand, all three, before me now. The landlord in his shirt-sleeves, leaning against the bar window-frame; his wife looking over the little half door; and I, in some confusion, looking up at them from outside the partition. They asked me a good many questions; as, what my name was, how old I was, where I lived, how I was employed, and how I came there. To all of which, that I might commit nobody, I invented, I am afraid, appropriate answers. They served me with the ale, though I suspect it was not the Genuine Stunning; and the landlord's wife, opening the little half door of the bar, and bending down, gave me my money back, and gave me a kiss that was half admiring, and half compassionate, but all womanly and good, I am sure.

I know I do not exaggerate, unconsciously and unintentionally, the scantiness of my resources or the difficulties of my life. I know that if a shilling were given me by Mr Quinion at any time, I spent it in a dinner or a tea. I know that I worked from morning until night, with common men and boys, a shabby child. I know that I lounged about the streets, insufficiently and unsatisfactorily fed. I know that, but for the mercy of God, I might easily have been, for any care that was taken of me, a little robber or a little vagabond.

Yet I held some station at Murdstone and Grinby's too. Besides that Mr Quinion did what a careless man so occupied, and dealing with a thing so anomalous, could, to treat me as one upon a different footing from the rest, I never said, to man or boy, how it was that I came to be there, or gave the least indication of being sorry that I was there. That I suffered in secret, and that I suffered exquisitely, no one ever knew but I. How much I suffered, it is, as I have said already, utterly beyond my power to tell. But I kept my own counsel, and I did my work. I knew from the first, that, if I could not do my work as well as any of the rest, I could not hold myself above slight and contempt. I soon became at least as expeditious and as skilful as either of the other boys. Though perfectly familiar with them, my conduct and manner were different enough from theirs to place a space between us. They and the men generally spoke of me as 'the little gent,' or 'the young Suffolker.' A certain man named Gregory, who was foreman of the packers, and another named Tipp, who was the carman, and wore a red jacket, used to address me sometimes as 'David'; but I think it was mostly when we were very confidential, and when I had made some efforts to entertain them, over our work, with some results of the old readings – which were fast perishing out of my remembrance. Mealy Potatoes uprose once, and rebelled against my being so distinguished; but Mick Walker settled him in no time.

My rescue from this kind of existence I considered quite hopeless, and abandoned, as such, altogether. I am solemnly convinced that I never for one hour was reconciled to it, or was otherwise than miserably unhappy; but I bore it; and even to Peggotty, partly for the love of her and partly for shame, never in any letter (though many passed between us) revealed the truth.

Mr Micawber's difficulties were an addition to the distressed state of my mind. In my forlorn state I became quite attached to the family, and used to walk about, busy with Mrs Micawber's calculations of ways and means, and heavy with the weight of Mr Micawber's debts. On a Saturday night, which was my grand treat – partly because it was a great thing to walk home with six or seven shillings in my pocket, looking into the shops and thinking what such a sum would buy, and partly because I went home early – Mrs Micawber would make the most heart-rending confidences to me; also on a Sunday morning, when I mixed the portion of tea or coffee I had bought overnight, in a little shaving-pot, and sat late at my breakfast. It was nothing at all unusual for Mr Micawber to sob violently at the beginning of one of these Saturday night conversations, and sing about Jack's delight being his lovely Nan, towards the end of it. I have known him come home to supper with a flood of tears, and a declaration that nothing was now left but a jail; and go to bed making a calculation of the expense of putting bow-windows to the house, 'in case anything turned up,' which was his favourite expression. And Mrs Micawber was just the same.

A curious equality of friendship, originating, I suppose, in our respective circumstances, sprung up between me and these people notwithstanding the ludicrous disparity in our years. But I never allowed myself to be prevailed upon to accept any invitation to eat and drink with them out of their stock (knowing that they got on badly with the butcher and baker, and had often not too much for themselves), until Mrs Micawber took me into her entire confidence. This she did one evening as follows: 'Master Copperfield,' said Mrs Micawber, 'I make no stranger of you, and therefore do not hesitate to say that Mr Micawber's difficulties are coming to a crisis.'

It made me very miserable to hear it, and I looked at Mrs Micawber's red eyes with the utmost sympathy.

'With the exception of the heel of a Dutch cheese – which is not adapted to the wants of a young family' – said Mrs Micawber, 'there is really not a scrap of anything in the larder. I was accustomed to speak of the larder when I lived with papa and mama, and I used the word almost unconsciously. What I mean to express is, that there is nothing to eat in the house.'

'Dear me!' I said, in great concern.

I had two or three shillings of my week's money in my pocket – from which I presume that it must have been on a Wednesday night when we held this conversation – and I hastily produced them, and with heartfelt emotion begged Mrs Micawber to accept of them as a loan. But that lady, kissing me, and making me put them back in my pocket, replied that she couldn't think of it.

My magnificent order at the public-house

'No, my dear Master Copperfield,' said she, 'far be it from my thoughts! But you have a discretion beyond your years, and can render me another kind of service, if you will; and a service I will thankfully accept of.'

I begged Mrs Micawber to name it.

'I have parted with the plate myself,' said Mrs Micawber. 'Six tea, two salt, and a pair of sugars, I have at different times borrowed money on, in secret, with my own hands. But the twins are a great tie; and to me, with my recollections of papa and mama, these transactions are very painful. There are still a few trifles that we could part with. Mr Micawber's feelings would never allow *him* to dispose of them; and Clickett' – this was the girl from the workhouse – 'being of a vulgar mind, would take painful liberties if so much confidence was reposed in her. Master Copperfield, if I might ask you – '

I understood Mrs Micawber now, and begged her to make use of me to any extent. I began to dispose of the more portable articles of property that very evening; and went out on a similar expedition almost every morning, before I went to Murdstone and Grinby's.

Mr Micawber had a few books on a little chiffonier, which he called the library; and those went first. I carried them, one after another, to a bookstall in the City Road – one part of which, near our house, was almost all bookstalls and birdshops then – and sold them for whatever they would bring. The keeper of this bookstall, who lived in a little house behind it, used to get tipsy every night, and to be violently scolded by his wife every morning. More than once, when I went there early, I had audience of him in a turn-up bedstead, with a cut in his forehead or a black eye, bearing witness to his excesses overnight (I am afraid he was quarrelsome in his drink), and he, with a shaking hand, endeavouring to find the needful shillings in one or other of the pockets of his clothes, which lay upon the floor, while his wife, with a baby in her arms and her shoes down at heel, never left off rating him. Sometimes he had lost his money, and then he would ask me to call again; but his wife had always got some – had taken his, I dare say, while he was drunk – and secretly completed the bargain on the stairs, as we went down together.

At the pawnbroker's shop, too, I began to be very well known. The principal gentleman who officiated behind the counter took a good deal of notice of me; and often got me, I recollect, to decline a Latin noun or adjective, or to conjugate a Latin verb, in his ear, while he transacted my business. After all these occasions, Mrs Micawber made a little treat, which was generally a supper; and there was a peculiar relish in these meals which I well remember.

At last Mr Micawber's difficulties came to a crisis, and he was arrested early one morning, and carried over to the King's Bench Prison in the Borough. He told me, as he went out of the house, that the God of day had now gone down upon him – and I really thought his heart was broken, and mine too. But I heard, afterwards, that he was seen to play a lively game of skittles before noon.

On the first Sunday after he was taken there, I was to go and see him, and have dinner with him. I was to ask my way to such a place, and just short of that place I should see such another place, and just short of that I should see a yard, which I was to cross, and keep straight on until I saw a turnkey. All this I did; and when at last I did see a turnkey (poor little fellow that I was!), and thought how, when Roderick Random was in a debtors' prison, there was a man there with nothing on him but an old rug, the turnkey swam before my dimmed eyes and my beating heart.

Mr Micawber was waiting for me within the gate, and we went up to his room (top storey but one), and cried very much. He solemnly conjured me, I remember, to take warning by his fate; and to observe that if a man had twenty pounds a year for his income, and spent nineteen pounds nineteen shillings and sixpence, he would be happy, but that if he spent twenty pounds one, he would be miserable. After which he borrowed a shilling off me for porter, gave me a written order on Mrs Micawber for the amount, and put away his pocket-handkerchief, and cheered up.

We sat before a little fire, with two bricks put within the rusted grate, one on each side, to prevent its burning too many coals; until another debtor, who shared the room with Mr Micawber, came in from the bakehouse with the loin of mutton which was our joint-stock repast. Then I was sent up to 'Captain Hopkins' in the room overhead, with Mr Micawber's compliments, and I was his young friend, and would Captain Hopkins lend me a knife and fork.

Captain Hopkins lent me the knife and fork, with his compliments to Mr Micawber. There was a very dirty lady in his little room, and two wan girls, his daughters, with shock heads of hair. I thought it was better to borrow Captain Hopkins's knife and fork, than Captain Hopkins's comb. The captain himself was in the last extremity of shabbiness, with large whiskers, and an old, old brown greatcoat with no other coat below it. I saw his bed rolled up in a corner; and what plates and dishes and pots he had, on a shelf; and I divined (God knows how) that though the two girls with the shock heads of hair were Captain Hopkins's children, the dirty lady was not married to Captain Hopkins. My timid station on his threshold was not occupied more than a couple of minutes at most; but I came down again with all this in my knowledge, as surely as the knife and fork were in my hand.

There was something gypsy-like and agreeable in the dinner, after all. I took back Captain Hopkins's knife and fork early in the afternoon, and went home to comfort Mrs Micawber with an account of my visit. She fainted when she saw me return, and made a little jug of egg-hot afterwards to console us while we talked it over.

I don't know how the household furniture came to be sold for the family benefit, or who sold it, except that *I* did not. Sold it was, however, and carried away in a van; except the beds, a few chairs, and the kitchen table. With these possessions we encamped, as it were, in the two parlours of the emptied house in Windsor Terrace; Mrs Micawber, the children, the Orfling, and myself; and lived in those rooms night and day. I have no idea for how long, though it seems to me for a long time. At last Mrs Micawber resolved to move into the prison, where Mr

Micawber had now secured a room to himself. So I took the key of the house to the landlord, who was very glad to get it; and the beds were sent over to the King's Bench, except mine, for which a little room was hired outside the walls in the neighbourhood of that Institution, very much to my satisfaction, since the Micawbers and I had become too used to one another, in our troubles, to part. The Orfling was likewise accommodated with an inexpensive lodging in the same neighbourhood. Mine was a quiet back garret with a sloping roof, commanding a pleasant prospect of a timber-yard; and when I took possession of it, with the reflection that Mr Micawber's troubles had come to a crisis at last, I thought it quite a paradise.

All this time I was working at Murdstone and Grinby's in the same common way, and with the same common companions, and with the same sense of unmerited degradation as at first. But I never, happily for me, no doubt, made a single acquaintance, or spoke to any of the many boys whom I saw daily in going to the warehouse, in coming from it, and in prowling about the streets at meal-times. I led the same secretly unhappy life; but I led it in the same lonely, self-reliant manner. The only changes I am conscious of are, first, that I had grown more shabby, and secondly, that I was now relieved of much of the weight of Mr and Mrs Micawber's cares; for some relatives or friends had engaged to help them at their present pass, and they lived more comfortably in the prison than they had lived for a long while out of it. I used to breakfast with them now, in virtue of some arrangement, of which I have forgotten the details. I forget, too, at what hour the gates were opened in the morning, admitting of my going in; but I know that I was often up at six o'clock, and that my favourite lounging-place in the interval was old London Bridge, where I was wont to sit in one of the stone recesses, watching the people going by, or to look over the balustrades at the sun shining in the water, and lighting up the golden flame on the top of the Monument. The Orfling met me here sometimes, to be told some astonishing fictions respecting the wharves and the Tower; of which I can say no more than that I hope I believed them myself. In the evening I used to go back to the prison, and walk up and down the parade with Mr Micawber; or play casino with Mrs Micawber, and hear reminiscences of her papa and mama. Whether Mr Murdstone knew where I was, I am unable to say. I never told them at Murdstone and Grinby's.

Mr Micawber's affairs, although past their crisis, were very much involved by reason of a certain 'Deed,' of which I used to hear a great deal, and which I suppose, now, to have been some former composition with his creditors, though I was so far from being clear about it then that I am conscious of having confounded it with those demoniacal parchments which are held to have, once upon a time, obtained to a great extent in Germany. At last this document appeared to be got out of the way, somehow; at all events, it ceased to be the rock ahead it had been; and Mrs Micawber informed me that 'her family' had decided that Mr Micawber should apply for his release under the Insolvent Debtors' Act, which would set him free, she expected, in about six weeks.

'And then,' said Mr Micawber, who was present, 'I have no

doubt I shall, please Heaven, begin to be beforehand with the world, and to live in a perfectly new manner, if – in short, if anything turns up.'

By way of going in for anything that might be on the cards, I call to mind that Mr Micawber, about this time, composed a petition to the House of Commons, praying for an alteration in the law of imprisonment for debt. I set down this remembrance here, because it is an instance to myself of the manner in which I fitted my old books to my altered life, and made stories for myself, out of the streets, and out of men and women; and how some main points in the character I shall unconsciously develop, I suppose, in writing my life, were gradually forming all this while.

There was a club in the prison, in which Mr Micawber, as a gentleman, was a great authority. Mr Micawber had stated his idea of this petition to the club, and the club had strongly approved of the same. Wherefore Mr Micawber (who was a thoroughly good-natured man, and as active a creature about everything but his own affairs as ever existed, and never so happy as when he was busy about something that could never be of any profit to him) set to work at the petition, invented it, engrossed it on an immense sheet of paper, spread it out on a table, and appointed a time for all the club, and all within the walls, if they chose, to come up to his room and sign it.

When I heard of this approaching ceremony, I was so anxious to see them all come in, one after another, though I knew the greater part of them already, and they me, that I got an hour's leave of absence from Murdstone and Grinby's, and established myself in a corner for that purpose. As many of the principal members of the club as could be got into the small room without filling it, supported Mr Micawber in front of the petition, while my old friend Captain Hopkins (who had washed himself, to do honour to so solemn an occasion) stationed himself close to it, to read it to all who were unacquainted with its contents. The door was then thrown open, and the general population began to come in, in a long file; several waiting outside, while one entered, affixed his signature, and went out. To everybody in succession, Captain Hopkins said: 'Have you read it?' – 'No.' 'Would you like to hear it read?' If he weakly showed the least disposition to hear it, Captain Hopkins, in a loud sonorous voice, gave him every word of it. The captain would have read it twenty thousand times, if twenty thousand people would have heard him, one by one. I remember a certain luscious roll he gave to such phrases as 'The people's representatives in parliament assembled,' 'Your petitioners therefore humbly approach your honourable house,' 'His gracious Majesty's unfortunate subjects,' as if the words were something real in his mouth, and delicious to taste; Mr Micawber, meanwhile, listening with a little of an author's vanity, and contemplating (not severely) the spikes on the opposite wall.

As I walked to and fro daily between Southwark and Black-friars, and lounged about at meal-times in obscure streets, the stones of which may, for anything I know, be worn at this moment by my childish feet, I wonder how many of these people were wanting in the crowd that used to come filing before me in review again, to the echo of Captain Hopkins's

voice! When my thoughts go back now to that slow agony of my youth, I wonder how much of the histories I invented for such people hangs like a mist of fancy over well-remembered facts! When I tread the old ground, I do not wonder that I seem to see and pity, going on before me, an innocent romantic boy, making his imaginative world out of such strange experiences and sordid things.

CHAPTER 12

Liking Life on My Own Account No Better,
I Form a Great Resolution

In due time Mr Micawber's petition was ripe for hearing; and that gentleman was ordered to be discharged under the Act, to my great joy. His creditors were not implacable; and Mrs Micawber informed me that even the revengeful bootmaker had declared in open court that he bore him no malice, but that when money was owing to him he liked to be paid. He said he thought it was human nature.

Mr Micawber returned to the King's Bench, when his case was over, as some fees were to be settled, and some formalities observed, before he could be actually released. The club received him with transport, and held an harmonic meeting that evening in his honour; while Mrs Micawber and I had a lamb's fry in private, surrounded by the sleeping family.

'On such an occasion I will give you, Master Copperfield,' said Mrs Micawber, 'in a little more flip,' for we had been having some already, 'the memory of my papa and mama.'

'Are they dead, ma'am?' I enquired, after drinking the toast in a wineglass.

'My mama departed this life,' said Mrs Micawber, 'before Mr Micawber's difficulties commenced, or at least before they became pressing. My papa lived to bail Mr Micawber several times, and then expired, regretted by a numerous circle.'

Mrs Micawber shook her head, and dropped a pious tear upon the twin who happened to be in hand.

As I could hardly hope for a more favourable opportunity of putting a question in which I had a near interest, I said to Mrs Micawber: 'May I ask, ma'am, what you and Mr Micawber intend to do, now that Mr Micawber is out of difficulties, and at liberty? Have you settled yet?'

'My family,' said Mrs Micawber, who always said those two words with an air, though I never could discover who came under the denomination, 'my family are of opinion that Mr Micawber should quit London, and exert his talents in the country. Mr Micawber is a man of great talent, Master Copperfield.'

I said I was sure of that.

'Of great talent,' repeated Mrs Micawber. 'My family are of opinion that, with a little interest, something might be done for a man of his ability in the Custom House. The influence of my family being local, it is their wish that Mr Micawber should go down to Plymouth. They think it indispensable that he should be upon the spot.'

'That he may be ready?' I suggested.

'Exactly,' returned Mrs Micawber. 'That he may be ready – in case of anything turning up.'

'And do you go too, ma'am?'

The events of the day, in combination with the twins, if not with the flip, had made Mrs Micawber hysterical, and she shed tears as she replied: 'I never will desert Mr Micawber. Mr Micawber may have concealed his difficulties from me in the first instance, but his sanguine temper may have led him to expect that he would overcome them. The pearl necklace and bracelets which I inherited from mama, have been disposed of for less than half their value; and the set of coral, which was the wedding gift of my papa, has been actually thrown away for nothing. But I never will desert Mr Micawber. No!' cried Mrs Micawber, more affected than before, 'I never will do it! It's of no use asking me!'

I felt quite uncomfortable – as if Mrs Micawber supposed I had asked her to do anything of the sort! – and sat looking at her in alarm.

'Mr Micawber has his faults. I do not deny that he is improvident. I do not deny that he has kept me in the dark as to his resources and his liabilities, both,' she went on, looking at the wall; 'but I never will desert Mr Micawber!'

Mrs Micawber having now raised her voice into a perfect scream, I was so frightened that I ran off to the club-room, and disturbed Mr Micawber in the act of presiding at a long table, and leading the chorus of

'Gee up, Dobbin,
Gee ho, Dobbin,
Gee up, Dobbin,
Gee up, and gee ho – o – o!'

– with the tidings that Mrs Micawber was in an alarming state, upon which he immediately burst into tears, and came away with me with his waistcoat full of the heads and tails of shrimps, of which he had been partaking.

'Emma, my angel!' cried Mr Micawber, running into the room; 'what is the matter?'

'I never will desert you, Micawber!' she exclaimed.

'My life!' said Mr Micawber, taking her in his arms, 'I am perfectly aware of it.'

'He is the parent of my children! He is the father of my twins! He is the husband of my affections,' cried Mrs Micawber, struggling; 'and I ne – ver – will – desert Mr Micawber!'

Mr Micawber was so deeply affected by this proof of her devotion (as to me, I was dissolved in tears) that he hung over her in a passionate manner, imploring her to look up, and to be calm. But the more he asked Mrs Micawber to look up, the more she fixed her eyes on nothing; and the more he asked her to compose herself, the more she wouldn't. Consequently Mr Micawber was soon so overcome that he mingled his tears with hers and mine; until he begged me to do him the favour of taking a chair on the staircase, while he got her into bed. I would have taken my leave for the night, but he would not hear of my doing that until the strangers' bell should ring. So I sat at the staircase window, until he came out with another chair and joined me.

'How is Mrs Micawber now, sir?' I said.

'Very low,' said Mr Micawber, shaking his head; 'reaction. Ah, this has been a dreadful day! We stand alone now – everything is gone from us!'

Mr Micawber pressed my hand, and groaned, and afterwards shed tears. I was greatly touched, and disappointed, too, for I had expected that we should be quite gay on this happy and long-looked-for occasion. But Mr and Mrs Micawber were so used to their old difficulties, I think, that they felt quite shipwrecked when they came to consider that they were released from them. All their elasticity was departed, and I never saw them half so wretched as on this night; insomuch that when the bell rang, and Mr Micawber walked with me to the lodge, and parted from me there with a blessing, I felt quite afraid to leave him by himself, he was so profoundly miserable.

But through all the confusion and lowness of spirits in which we had been, so unexpectedly to me, involved, I plainly discerned that Mr and Mrs Micawber and their family were going away from London, and that a parting between us was near at hand. It was in my walk home that night, and in the sleepless hours which followed when I lay in bed, that the thought first occurred to me – though I don't know how it came into my head – which afterwards shaped itself into a settled resolution.

I had grown to be so accustomed to the Micawbers, and had been so intimate with them in their distresses, and was so utterly friendless without them, that the prospect of being thrown upon some new shift for a lodging, and going once more among unknown people, was like being that moment turned adrift into my present life, with such a knowledge of it ready made as experience had given me. All the sensitive feelings it wounded so cruelly, all the shame and misery it kept alive within my breast, became more poignant as I thought of this, and I determined that the life was unendurable.

That there was no hope of escape from it, unless the escape was my own act, I knew quite well. I rarely heard from Miss Murdstone, and never from Mr Murdstone; but two or three parcels of made or mended clothes had come up for me, consigned to Mr Quinion, and in each there was a scrap of paper to the effect that J. M. trusted D. C. was applying himself to business, and devoting himself wholly to his duties – not the least hint of my ever being anything else than the common drudge into which I was fast settling down.

The very next day showed me, while my mind was in the first agitation of what it had conceived, that Mrs Micawber had not spoken of their going away without warrant. They took a lodging in the house where I lived, for a week; at the expiration of which time they were to start for Plymouth. Mr Micawber himself came down to the counting-house in the afternoon, to tell Mr Quinion that he must relinquish me on the day of his departure, and to give me a high character, which I am sure I deserved. And Mr Quinion, calling in Tipp the carman, who was a married man, and had a room to let, quartered me prospectively on him – by our mutual consent, as he had every reason to think; for I said nothing, though my resolution was now taken.

I passed my evenings with Mr and Mrs Micawber, during

the remaining term of our residence under the same roof; and I think we became fonder of one another as the time went on. On the last Sunday, they invited me to dinner; and we had a loin of pork and apple sauce, and a pudding. I had bought a spotted wooden horse overnight as a parting gift to little Wilkins Micawber – that was the boy – and a doll for little Emma. I had also bestowed a shilling on the Orfling, who was about to be disbanded.

We had a very pleasant day, though we were all in a tender state about our approaching separation.

'I shall never, Master Copperfield,' said Mrs Micawber, 'revert to the period when Mr Micawber was in difficulties, without thinking of you. Your conduct has always been of the most delicate and obliging description. You have never been a lodger. You have been a friend.'

'My dear,' said Mr Micawber; 'Copperfield,' for so he had been accustomed to call me of late, 'has a heart to feel for the distresses of his fellow-creatures when they are behind a cloud, and a head to plan, and a hand to – in short, a general ability to dispose of such available property as could be made away with.'

I expressed my sense of this commendation, and said I was very sorry we were going to lose one another.

'My dear young friend,' said Mr Micawber, 'I am older than you; a man of some experience in life, and – and of some experience, in short, in difficulties, generally speaking. At present, and until something turns up (which I am, I may say, hourly expecting), I have nothing to bestow but advice. Still my advice is so far worth taking that – in short, that I have never taken it myself, and am the' – here Mr Micawber, who had been beaming and smiling, all over his head and face, up to the present moment, checked himself and frowned – 'the miserable wretch you behold.'

'My dear Micawber!' urged his wife.

'I say,' returned Mr Micawber, quite forgetting himself, and smiling again, 'the miserable wretch you behold. My advice is, never do tomorrow what you can do today. Procrastination is the thief of time. Collar him!'

'My poor papa's maxim,' Mrs Micawber observed.

'My dear,' said Mr Micawber, 'your papa was very well in his way, and Heaven forbid that I should disparage him. Take him for all in all, we ne'er shall – in short, make the acquaintance, probably, of anybody else possessing, at his time of life, the same legs for gaiters, and able to read the same description of print, without spectacles. But he applied that maxim to our marriage, my dear; and that was so far prematurely entered into, in consequence, that I never recovered the expense.'

Mr Micawber looked aside at Mrs Micawber, and added: 'Not that I am sorry for it. Quite the contrary, my love.' After which he was grave for a minute or so.

'My other piece of advice, Copperfield,' said Mr Micawber, 'you know. Annual income, twenty pounds; annual expenditure, nineteen nineteen six; result, happiness. Annual income, twenty pounds; annual expenditure, twenty pounds ought and six; result, misery. The blossom is blighted, the leaf is withered, the God of day goes down upon the dreary scene, and – and, in short, you are for ever floored. As I am!'

To make his example the more impressive, Mr Micawber drank a glass of punch with an air of great enjoyment and satisfaction, and whistled the College Hornpipe.

I did not fail to assure him that I would store these precepts in my mind, though indeed I had no need to do so, for, at the time, they affected me visibly. Next morning I met the whole family at the coach-office, and saw them, with a desolate heart, take their places outside, at the back.

'Master Copperfield,' said Mrs Micawber, 'God bless you! I never can forget all that, you know, and I never would if I could.'

'Copperfield,' said Mr Micawber, 'farewell! Every happiness and prosperity! If, in the progress of revolving years, I could persuade myself that my blighted destiny had been a warning to you, I should feel that I had not occupied another man's place in existence altogether in vain. In case of anything turning up (of which I am rather confident), I shall be extremely happy if it should be in my power to improve your prospects.'

I think, as Mrs Micawber sat at the back of the coach, with the children, and I stood in the road looking wistfully at them, a mist cleared from her eyes, and she saw what a little creature I really was. I think so, because she beckoned to me to climb up, with quite a new and motherly expression in her face, and put her arm round my neck, and gave me just such a kiss as she might have given to her own boy. I had barely time to get down again before the coach started, and I could hardly see the family for the handkerchiefs they waved. It was gone in a minute. The Orfling and I stood looking vacantly at each other in the middle of the road, and then shook hands and said goodbye; she going back, I suppose, to St Luke's workhouse, as I went to begin my weary day at Murdstone and Grinby's.

But with no intention of passing many more weary days there. No. I had resolved to run away. To go, by some means or other, down into the country, to the only relation I had in the world, and tell my story to my aunt, Miss Betsey.

I have already observed that I don't know how this desperate idea came into my brain. But, once there, it remained there; and hardened into a purpose than which I have never entertained a more determined purpose in my life. I am far from sure that I believed there was anything hopeful in it, but my mind was thoroughly made up that it must be carried into execution.

Again, and again, and a hundred times again, since the night when the thought had first occurred to me and banished sleep, I had gone over that old story of my poor mother's about my birth, which it had been one of my great delights in the old time to hear her tell, and which I knew by heart. My aunt walked into that story, and walked out of it, a dread and awful personage; but there was one little trait in her behaviour which I liked to dwell on, and which gave me some faint shadow of encouragement. I could not forget how my mother had thought that she felt her touch her pretty hair with no ungentle hand; and though it might have been altogether my mother's fancy, and might have had no foundation whatever in fact, I made a little picture, out of it, of my terrible aunt relenting towards the girlish beauty that I recollected so well, and loved so much, which softened the whole narrative. It is very possible that it had been in my mind a long time, and had gradually engendered my determination.

As I did not even know where Miss Betsey lived, I wrote a long letter to Peggotty, and asked her, incidentally, if she remembered; pretending that I had heard of such a lady living at a certain place I named at random, and had a curiosity to know if it were the same. In the course of that letter I told Peggotty that I had a particular occasion for half a guinea; and that if she could lend me that sum until I could repay it, I should be very much obliged to her, and would tell her afterwards what I had wanted it for.

Peggotty's answer soon arrived, and was, as usual, full of affectionate devotion. She enclosed the half-guinea (I was afraid she must have had a world of trouble to get it out of Mr Barkis's box), and told me that Miss Betsey lived near Dover, but whether at Dover itself, at Hythe, Sandgate, or Folkstone, she could not say. One of our men, however, informing me on my asking him about these places, that they were all close together, I deemed this enough for my object, and resolved to set out at the end of that week.

Being a very honest little creature, and unwilling to disgrace the memory I was going to leave behind me at Murdstone and Grinby's, I considered myself bound to remain until Saturday night; and, as I had been paid a week's wages in advance when I first came there, not to present myself in the counting-house at the usual hour to receive my stipend. For this express reason, I had borrowed the half-guinea, that I might not be without a fund for my travelling expenses. Accordingly, when the Saturday night came, and we were all waiting in the warehouse to be paid, and Tipp, the carman, who always took precedence, went in first to draw his money, I shook Mick Walker by the hand; asked him when it came to his turn to be paid, to say to Mr Quinion that I had gone to move my box to Tipp's; and, bidding a last good-night to Mealy Potatoes, ran away.

My box was at my old lodging over the water, and I had written a direction for it on the back of one of our address cards that we nailed on the casks: 'Master David, to be left till called for at the coach-office, Dover.' This I had in my pocket ready to put on the box, after I should have got it out of the house; and as I went towards my lodging I looked about me for someone who would help me to carry it to the booking-office.

There was a long-legged young man with a very little empty donkey-cart, standing near the Obelisk, in the Blackfriars Road, whose eye I caught as I was going by, and who, addressing me as 'Sixpenn'orth of bad ha'pence,' hoped 'I should know him agin to swear to' – in allusion, I have no doubt, to my staring at him. I stopped to assure him that I had not done so in bad manners, but uncertain whether he might or might not like a job.

'Wot job?' said the long-legged young man.

'To move a box,' I answered.

'Wot box?' said the long-legged young man.

I told him mine, which was down that street there, and which I wanted him to take to the Dover coach-office for sixpence.

'Done with you for a tanner!' said the long-legged young

man, and directly got upon his cart, which was nothing but a large wooden tray on wheels, and rattled away at such a rate that it was as much as I could do to keep pace with the donkey.

There was a defiant manner about this young man, and particularly about the way in which he chewed straw as he spoke to me, that I did not much like; as the bargain was made, however, I took him upstairs to the room I was leaving, and we brought the box down, and put it on his cart. Now, I was unwilling to put the direction-card on there, lest any of my landlord's family should fathom what I was doing, and detain me; so I said to the young man that I would be glad if he would stop for a minute, when he came to the dead-wall of the King's Bench prison. The words were no sooner out of my mouth, than he rattled away, as if he, my box, the cart, and the donkey were all equally mad; and I was quite out of breath with running and calling after him, when I caught him at the place appointed.

Being much flushed and excited I tumbled my half-guinea out of my pocket in pulling the card out. I put it in my mouth for safety, and though my hands trembled a good deal, had just tied the card on very much to my satisfaction, when I felt myself violently chucked under the chin by the long-legged young man, and saw my half-guinea fly out of my mouth into his hand.

'Wot!' said the young man, seizing me by my jacket collar, with a frightful grin. 'This is a pollis case, is it? You're a going to bolt, are you? Come to the pollis, you young warmin, come to the pollis!'

'You give me my money back, if you please,' said I, very much frightened, 'and leave me alone.'

'Come to the pollis!' said the young man. 'You shall prove it yourn to the pollis.'

'Give me my box and money, will you!' I cried, bursting into tears.

The young man still replied: 'Come to the pollis!' and was dragging me against the donkey in a violent manner, as if there were any affinity between that animal and a magistrate, when he changed his mind, jumped into the cart, sat upon my box, and exclaiming that he would drive to the pollis straight, rattled away harder than ever.

I ran after him as fast as I could, but I had no breath to call out with, and should not have dared to call out, now, if I had. I narrowly escaped being run over, twenty times at least, in half a mile. Now I lost him, now I saw him, now I lost him, now I was cut at with a whip, now shouted at, now down in the mud, now up again, now running into somebody's arms, now running headlong at a post. At length, confused by fright and heat, and doubting whether half London might not by this time be turning out for my apprehension, I left the young man to go where he would with my box and money; and, panting and crying, but never stopping, faced about for Greenwich, which I had understood was on the Dover Road, taking very little more out of the world, towards the retreat of my aunt, Miss Betsey, than I had brought into it, on the night when my arrival gave her so much umbrage.

CHAPTER 13

The Sequel of My Resolution

For anything I know, I may have had some wild idea of running all the way to Dover, when I gave up the pursuit of the young man with the donkey-cart, and started for Greenwich. My scattered senses were soon collected as to that point, if I had; for I came to a stop in the Kent Road, at a terrace with a piece of water before it, and a great foolish image in the middle, blowing a dry shell. Here I sat down on a doorstep, quite spent and exhausted with the efforts I had already made, and with hardly breath enough to cry for the loss of my box and half-guinea.

It was by this time dark; I heard the clocks strike ten, as I sat resting. But it was a summer night fortunately, and fine weather. When I had recovered my breath, and had got rid of a stifling sensation in my throat, I rose up and went on. In the midst of my distress, I had no notion of going back. I doubt if I should have had any, though there had been a Swiss snowdrift in the Kent Road.

But my standing possessed of only three halfpence in the world (and I am sure I wonder how *they* came to be left in my pocket on a Saturday night!) troubled me none the less because I went on. I began to picture to myself, as a scrap of newspaper intelligence, my being found dead in a day or two, under some hedge; and I trudged on miserably, though as fast as I could, until I happened to pass a little shop, where it was written up that ladies' and gentlemen's wardrobes were bought, and that the best price was given for rags, bones, and kitchen-stuff. The master of this shop was sitting at the door in his shirt-sleeves, smoking; and as there were a great many coats and pairs of trousers dangling from the low ceiling, and only two feeble candles burning inside to show what they were, I fancied that he looked like a man of a revengeful disposition, who had hung all his enemies, and was enjoying himself.

My late experiences with Mr and Mrs Micawber suggested to me that here might be a means of keeping off the wolf for a little while. I went up the next by-street, took off my waistcoat, rolled it neatly under my arm, and came back to the shop door. 'If you please, sir,' I said, 'I am to sell this for a fair price.'

Mr Dolloby – Dolloby was the name over the shop door, at least – took the waistcoat, stood his pipe on its head against the doorpost, went into the shop, followed by me, snuffed the two candles with his fingers, spread the waistcoat on the counter, and looked at it there, held it up against the light, and looked at it there, and ultimately said: 'What do you call a price, now, for this here little weskit?'

'Oh! you know best, sir,' I returned modestly.

'I can't be buyer and seller too,' said Mr Dolloby. 'Put a price on this here little weskit.'

'Would eighteenpence be – ?' I hinted, after some hesitation.

Mr Dolloby rolled it up again, and gave it me back. 'I should rob my family,' he said, 'if I was to offer ninepence for it.'

This was a disagreeable way of putting the business, because it imposed upon me, a perfect stranger, the unpleasantness of asking Mr Dolloby to rob his family on my account. My circumstances being so very pressing, however, I said I would take ninepence for it, if he pleased. Mr Dolloby, not without some grumbling, gave ninepence. I wished him good-night, and walked out of the shop, the richer by that sum, and the poorer by a waistcoat. But when I buttoned my jacket, that was not much.

Indeed, I foresaw pretty clearly that my jacket would go next, and that I should have to make the best of my way to Dover in a shirt and a pair of trousers, and might deem myself lucky if I got there even in that trim. But my mind did not run so much on this as might be supposed. Beyond a general impression of the distance before me, and of the young man with the donkey-cart having used me cruelly, I think I had no very urgent sense of my difficulties when I once again set off with my ninepence in my pocket.

A plan had occurred to me for passing the night, which I was going to carry into execution. This was, to lie behind the wall at the back of my old school, in a corner where there used to be a haystack. I imagined it would be a kind of company to have the boys, and the bedroom where I used to tell the stories, so near me, although the boys would know nothing of my being there, and the bedroom would yield me no shelter.

I had had a hard day's work, and was pretty well jaded when I came climbing out, at last, upon the level of Blackheath. It cost me some trouble to find out Salem House; but I found it, and I found a haystack in the corner, and lay down by it; having first walked round the wall, and looked up at the windows, and seen that all was dark and silent within. Never shall I forget the lonely sensation of first lying down, without a roof above my head!

Sleep came upon me as it came on many other outcasts, against whom house doors were locked, and house dogs barked that night – and I dreamed of lying on my old school-bed, talking to the boys in my room; and found myself sitting upright, with Steerforth's name upon my lips, looking wildly at the stars that were glistening and glimmering above me. When I remembered where I was at that untimely hour, a feeling stole upon me that made me get up, afraid of I don't know what, and walk about. But the fainter glimmering of the stars, and the pale light in the sky where the day was coming, reassured me; and my eyes being very heavy, I lay down again and slept – though with a knowledge in my sleep that it was cold – until the warm beams of the sun, and the ringing of the getting-up bell at Salem House, awoke me. If I could have hoped that Steerforth was there, I would have lurked about until he came out alone; but I knew he must have left long since. Traddles still remained, perhaps, but it was very doubtful; and I had not sufficient confidence in his discretion or good luck, however strong my reliance was on his good-nature, to wish to trust him with my situation. So I crept away from the wall as Mr Creakle's boys were getting up, and struck into the long dusty track which I had first known to be the Dover Road when I was one of them, and when I little expected that any eyes would ever see me the wayfarer I was now, upon it.

What a different Sunday morning from the old Sunday morning at Yarmouth! In due time I heard the church bells ringing, as I plodded on; and I met people who were going to church; and I passed a church or two where the congregation were inside, and the sound of singing came out into the sunshine, while the beadle sat and cooled himself in the shade of the porch, or stood beneath the yew tree, with his hand to his forehead, glowering at me going by. But the peace and rest of the old Sunday morning were on everything, except me. That was the difference. I felt quite wicked in my dirt and dust, and with my tangled hair. But for the quiet picture I had conjured up, of my mother in her youth and beauty, weeping by the fire, and my aunt relenting to her, I hardly think I should have had courage to go on until next day. But it always went before me, and I followed.

I got, that Sunday, through three-and-twenty miles on the straight road, though not very easily, for I was new to that kind of toil. I see myself, as evening closes in, coming over the bridge at Rochester, footsore and tired, and eating bread that I had bought for supper. One or two little houses, with the notice, 'Lodgings for Travellers,' hanging out, had tempted me, but I was afraid of spending the few pence I had, and was even more afraid of the vicious looks of the trampers I had met or overtaken. I sought no shelter, therefore, but the sky; and toiling into Chatham – which, in that night's aspect, is a mere dream of chalk, and drawbridges, and mastless ships in a muddy river, roofed like Noah's arks – crept, at last, upon a sort of grass-grown battery overhanging a lane, where a sentry was walking to and fro. Here I lay down, near a cannon; and happy in the society of the sentry's footsteps, though he knew no more of my being above him than the boys at Salem House had known of my lying by the wall, slept soundly until morning.

Very stiff and sore of foot I was in the morning, and quite dazed by the beating of drums and marching of troops, which seemed to hem me in on every side when I went down towards the long narrow street. Feeling that I could go but a very little way that day, if I were to reserve any strength for getting to my journey's end, I resolved to make the sale of my jacket its principal business. Accordingly I took the jacket off, that I might learn to do without it; and carrying it under my arm, began a tour of inspection of the various slop-shops.

It was a likely place to sell a jacket in; for the dealers in second-hand clothes were numerous, and were, generally speaking, on the look-out for customers at their shop doors. But as most of them had, hanging up among their stock, an officer's coat or two, epaulettes and all, I was rendered timid by the costly nature of their dealings, and walked about for a long time without offering my merchandise to anyone.

This modesty of mine directed my attention to the marine-store shops, and such shops as Mr Dolloby's, in preference to the regular dealers. At last I found one that I thought looked promising, at the corner of a dirty lane, ending in an enclosure full of stinging nettles, against the palings of which some second-hand sailors' clothes, that seemed to have overflowed the shop, were fluttering among some cots, and rusty guns, and oilskin hats, and certain trays full of so many old rusty keys of so many sizes that they seemed various enough to open all the doors in the world.

Into this shop, which was low and small, and which was darkened rather than lighted by a little window, overhung with clothes, and was descended into by some steps, I went with a palpitating heart; which was not relieved when an ugly old man, with the lower part of his face all covered with a stubbly grey beard, rushed out of a dirty den behind it, and seized me by the hair of my head. He was a dreadful old man to look at, in a filthy flannel waistcoat, and smelling terribly of rum. His bedstead, covered with a tumbled and ragged piece of patch-work, was in the den he had come from, where another little window showed a prospect of more stinging nettles, and a lame donkey.

'Oh, what do you want?' grinned this old man, in a fierce, monotonous whine. 'Oh, my eyes and limbs, what do you want? Oh, my lungs and liver, what do you want? Oh, goroo, goroo!'

I was so much dismayed by these words, and particularly by the repetition of the last unknown one, which was a kind of rattle in his throat, that I could make no answer; hereupon the old man, still holding me by the hair, repeated: 'Oh, what do you want? Oh, my eyes and limbs, what do you want? Oh, my lungs and liver, what do you want? Oh, goroo!' which he screwed out of himself, with an energy that made his eyes start in his head.

'I wanted to know,' I said, trembling, 'if you would buy a jacket.'

'Oh, let's see the jacket!' cried the old man. 'Oh, my heart on fire, show the jacket to us! Oh, my eyes and limbs, bring the jacket out.'

With that he took his trembling hands, which were like the claws of a great bird, out of my hair; and put on a pair of spectacles, not at all ornamental to his inflamed eyes.

'Oh, how much for the jacket?' cried the old man, after examining it. 'Oh – goroo! – how much for the jacket?'

'Half a crown,' I answered, recovering myself.

'Oh, my lungs and liver,' cried the old man, 'no! Oh, my eyes, no! Oh, my limbs, no! Eighteenpence. Goroo!'

Every time he uttered this ejaculation, his eyes seemed to be in danger of starting out; and every sentence he spoke, he delivered in a sort of tune, always exactly the same, and more like a gust of wind, which begins low, mounts up high, and falls again, than any other comparison I can find for it.

'Well,' said I, glad to have closed the bargain, 'I'll take eighteenpence.'

'Oh, my liver!' cried the old man, throwing the jacket on a shelf.

'Get out of the shop! Oh, my lungs, get out of the shop! Oh, my eyes and limbs – goroo! – don't ask for money – make it an exchange.'

I never was so frightened in my life, before or since; but I told him humbly that I wanted money, and that nothing else was of any use to me, but that I would wait for it, as he desired, outside, and had no wish to hurry him. So I went outside, and sat down in the shade in a corner. And I sat there so many hours that the shade became sunlight, and the sunlight became shade again, and still I sat there waiting for the money.

There never was such another drunken madman in that line of business, I hope. That he was well known in the neighbourhood, and enjoyed the reputation of having sold himself to the devil, I soon understood from the visits he received from the boys, who continually came skirmishing about the shop, shouting that legend, and calling to him to bring out his gold. 'You ain't poor, you know, Charley, as you pretend. Bring out your gold. Bring out some of the gold you sold yourself to the devil for. Come! It's in the lining of the mattress, Charley. Rip it open, and let's have some!' This, and many offers to lend him a knife for the purpose, exasperated him to such a degree that the whole day was a succession of rushes on his part, and flights on the part of the boys. Sometimes, in his rage, he would take me for one of them, and come at me, mouthing as if he were going to tear me in pieces; then, remembering me, just in time, would dive into the shop, and lie upon his bed, as I thought from the sound of his voice, yelling in a frantic way, to his own windy tune, the Death of Nelson; with an Oh! before every line, and innumerable Goroos interspersed. As if this were not bad enough for me, the boys, connecting me with the establishment, on account of the patience and perseverance with which I sat outside, half-dressed, pelted me, and used me very ill all day.

He made many attempts to induce me to consent to an exchange; at one time coming out with a fishing rod, at another with a fiddle, at another with a cocked hat, at another with a flute. But I resisted all these overtures, and sat there in desperation; each time asking him, with tears in my eyes, for my money or my jacket. At last he began to pay me in halfpence at a time; and he was full two hours getting by easy stages to a shilling.

'Oh, my eyes and limbs!' he then cried, peeping hideously out of the shop, after a long pause, 'will you go for twopence more?'

'I can't,' I said; 'I shall be starved.'

'Oh, my lungs and liver, will you go for threepence?'

'I would go for nothing if I could,' I said, 'but I want the money badly.'

'Oh, go–roo!' (it is really impossible to express how he twisted this ejaculation out of himself, as he peeped round the doorpost at me, showing nothing but his crafty old head) 'will you go for fourpence?'

I was so faint and weary that I closed with this offer; and taking the money out of his claw, not without trembling, went away more hungry and thirsty than I had ever been, a little before sunset. But at an expense of threepence I soon refreshed myself completely; and, being in better spirits then, limped seven miles upon my road.

My bed at night was under another haystack, where I rested comfortably, after having washed my blistered feet in a stream, and dressed them as well as I was able, with some cool leaves. When I took the road again next morning, I found that it lay through a succession of hop-grounds and orchards. It was sufficiently late in the year for the orchards to be ruddy with ripe apples; and in a few places the hop-pickers were already at work. I thought it all extremely beautiful, and made up my mind to sleep among the hops that night; imagining some cheerful companionship in the long perspectives of poles, with the graceful leaves twining round them.

The trampers were worse than ever that day, and inspired me with a dread that is yet quite fresh in my mind. Some of them were most ferocious-looking ruffians, who stared at me as I went by; and stopped, perhaps, and called after me to come back and speak to them; and when I took to my heels, stoned me. I recollect one young fellow – a tinker, I suppose, from his wallet and brazier – who had a woman with him, and who faced about and stared at me thus; and then roared to me in such a tremendous voice to come back that I halted and looked round.

'Come here when you're called,' said the tinker, 'or I'll rip your young body open.'

I thought it best to go back. As I drew nearer to them, trying to propitiate the tinker by my looks, I observed that the woman had a black eye.

'Where are you going?' said the tinker, gripping the bosom of my shirt with his blackened hand.

'I am going to Dover,' I said.

'Where do you come from?' asked the tinker, giving his hand another turn in my shirt, to hold me more securely.

'I came from London,' I said.

'What lay are you upon?' asked the tinker. 'Are you a prig?'

'N–no,' I said.

'Ain't you, by G—? If you make a brag of your honesty to me,' said the tinker, 'I'll knock your brains out.'

With his disengaged hand he made a menace of striking me, and then looked at me from head to foot.

'Have you got the price of a pint of beer about you?' said the tinker. 'If you have, out with it, afore I take it away!'

I should certainly have produced it, but that I met the woman's look, and saw her very slightly shake her head, and form 'No!' with her lips.

'I am very poor,' I said, attempting to smile, 'and have got no money.'

'Why, what do you mean?' said the tinker, looking so sternly at me that I almost feared he saw the money in my pocket.

'Sir!' I stammered.

'What do you mean,' said the tinker, 'by wearing my brother's silk handkercher? Give it over here!' And he had mine off my neck in a moment, and tossed it to the woman.

The woman burst into a fit of laughter, as if she thought this a joke, and tossed it back to me, nodded once, as slightly as before, and made the word 'Go!' with her lips. Before I could obey, however, the tinker seized the handkerchief out of my hand with a roughness that threw me away like a feather, and, putting it loosely round his own neck, turned upon the woman with an oath, and knocked her down. I never shall forget seeing her fall backward on the hard road, and lie there with her bonnet tumbled off, and her hair all whitened in the dust; nor, when I looked back from a distance, seeing her sitting on the pathway, which was a bank by the roadside, wiping the blood from her face with a corner of her shawl, while he went on ahead.

This adventure frightened me so that afterwards, when I saw

any of these people coming, I turned back until I could find a hiding-place, where I remained until they had gone out of sight; which happened so often that I was very seriously delayed. But under this difficulty, as under all the other difficulties of my journey, I seemed to be sustained and led on by my fanciful picture of my mother in her youth, before I came into the world. It always kept me company. It was there, among the hops, when I lay down to sleep; it was with me on my waking in the morning; it went before me all day. I have associated it, ever since, with the sunny street of Canterbury, dozing as it were in the hot light; and with the sight of its old houses and gateways, and the stately grey Cathedral, with the rooks sailing round the towers. When I came, at last, upon the bare, wide downs near Dover, it relieved the solitary aspect of the scene with hope; and not until I reached that first great aim of my journey, and actually set foot in the town itself, on the sixth day of my flight, did it desert me. But then, strange to say, when I stood with my ragged shoes, and my dusty, sunburnt, half-clothed figure, in the place so long desired, it seemed to vanish like a dream, and to leave me helpless and dispirited.

I enquired about my aunt among the boatmen first, and received various answers. One said she lived in the South Fore-land Light, and had singed her whiskers by doing so; another, that she was made fast to the great buoy outside the harbour, and could only be visited at half tide; a third, that she was locked up in Maidstone Jail for child-stealing; a fourth, that she was seen to mount a broom, in the last high wind, and make direct for Calais. The fly-drivers, among whom I enquired next, were equally jocose and equally disrespectful; and the shopkeepers, not liking my appearance, generally replied, without hearing what I had to say, that they had got nothing for me. I felt more miserable and destitute than I had done at any period of my running away. My money was all gone; I had nothing left to dispose of; I was hungry, thirsty, and worn out; and seemed as distant from my end as if I had remained in London.

The morning had worn away in these enquiries, and I was sitting on the step of an empty shop at a street corner, near the market-place, deliberating upon wandering towards those other places which had been mentioned, when a fly-driver, coming by with his carriage, dropped a horsecloth. Something good-natured in the man's face, as I handed it up, encouraged me to ask him if he could tell me where Miss Trotwood lived; though I had asked the question so often that it almost died upon my lips.

'Trotwood,' said he. 'Let me see. I know the name, too. Old lady?'

'Yes,' I said, 'rather.'

'Pretty stiff in the back?' said he, making himself upright.

'Yes,' I said. 'I should think it very likely.'

'Carries a bag?' said he: 'bag with a good deal of room in it: is gruffish, and comes down upon you, sharp?'

My heart sank within me as I acknowledged the undoubted accuracy of this description.

'Why, then, I tell you what,' said he. 'If you go up there,' pointing with his whip towards the heights, 'and keep right on till you come to some houses facing the sea, I think you'll hear of her. My opinion is she won't stand anything, so here's a penny for you.'

I accepted the gift thankfully, and bought a loaf with it. Despatching this refreshment by the way, I went in the direction my friend had indicated, and walked on a good distance without coming to the houses he had mentioned. At length I saw some before me; and approaching them, went into a little shop (it was what we used to call a general shop, at home), and enquired if they would have the goodness to tell me where Miss Trotwood lived. I addressed myself to a man behind the counter, who was weighing some rice for a young woman; but the latter, taking the enquiry to herself, turned round quickly.

'My mistress?' she said. 'What do you want with her, boy?'

'I want,' I replied, 'to speak to her, if you please.'

'To beg of her, you mean,' retorted the damsel.

'No,' I said, 'indeed.' But suddenly remembering that in truth I came for no other purpose, I held my peace in confusion, and felt my face burn.

My aunt's handmaid, as I supposed she was from what she had said, put her rice in a little basket and walked out of the shop; telling me that I could follow her, if I wanted to know where Miss Trotwood lived. I needed no second permission; though I was by this time in such a state of consternation and agitation that my legs shook under me. I followed the young woman, and we soon came to a very neat little cottage with cheerful bow-windows; in front of it, a small, square, gravelled court or garden full of flowers, carefully tended, and smelling deliciously.

'This is Miss Trotwood's,' said the young woman. 'Now you know; and that's all I have got to say.' With which words she hurried into the house, as if to shake off the responsibility of my appearance; and left me standing at the garden gate, looking disconsolately over the top of it towards the parlour window, where a muslin curtain partly undrawn in the middle, a large, round, green screen or fan fastened on to the window-sill, a small table, and a great chair, suggested to me that my aunt might be at that moment seated in awful state.

My shoes were by this time in a woeful condition. The soles had shed themselves bit by bit and the upper leathers had broken and burst until the very shape and form of shoes had departed from them. My hat (which had served me for a nightcap, too) was so crushed and bent that no old battered handleless saucepan on a dunghill need have been ashamed to vie with it. My shirt and trousers, stained with heat, dew, grass, and the Kentish soil on which I had slept – and torn besides – might have frightened the birds from my aunt's garden, as I stood at the gate. My hair had known no comb or brush since I left London. My face, neck, and hands, from unaccustomed exposure to the air and sun, were burnt to a berry-brown. From head to foot I was powdered almost as white with chalk and dust as if I had come out of a limekiln. In this plight, and with a strong consciousness of it, I waited to introduce myself to, and make my first impression on, my formidable aunt.

The unbroken stillness of the parlour window leading me to

infer, after a while, that she was not there, I lifted up my eyes to the window above it, where I saw a florid, pleasant-looking gentleman, with a grey head, who shut up one eye in a grotesque manner, nodded his head at me several times, shook it at me as often, laughed, and went away.

I had been discomposed enough before; but I was so much the more discomposed by this unexpected behaviour that I was on the point of slinking off, to think how I had best proceed, when there came out of the house a lady with her handkerchief tied over her cap, and a pair of gardening gloves on her hands, wearing a gardening pocket like a tollman's apron, and carrying a great knife. I knew her immediately to be Miss Betsey, for she came stalking out of the house exactly as my poor mother had so often described her stalking up our garden at Blunderstone Rookery.

'Go away!' said Miss Betsey, shaking her head, and making a distant chop in the air with her knife. 'Go along! No boys here!'

I watched her, with my heart at my lips, as she marched to a corner of her garden and stooped to dig up some little root there. Then, without a scrap of courage, but with a great deal of desperation, I went softly in and stood beside her, touching her with my finger.

'If you please, ma'am,' I began.

She started and looked up.

'If you please, aunt.'

'Eh?' exclaimed Miss Betsey, in a tone of amazement I have never heard approached.

'If you please, aunt, I am your nephew.'

'Oh, Lord!' said my aunt; and sat flat down in the garden path.

'I am David Copperfield, of Blunderstone, in Suffolk – where you came, on the night when I was born, and saw my dear mama. I have been very unhappy since she died. I have been slighted, and taught nothing, and thrown upon myself, and put to work not fit for me. It made me run away to you. I was robbed at first setting out, and have walked all the way, and have never slept in a bed since I began the journey.' Here my self-support gave way all at once; and with a movement of my hands, intended to show her my ragged state, and call it to witness that I had suffered something, I broke into a passion of crying, which I suppose had been pent up within me all the week.

My aunt, with every sort of expression but wonder discharged from her countenance, sat on the gravel, staring at me, until I began to cry; when she got up in a great hurry, collared me, and took me into the parlour. Her first proceeding there was to unlock a tall press, bring out several bottles, and pour some of the contents of each into my mouth. I think they must have been taken out at random, for I am sure I tasted aniseed water, anchovy sauce, and salad dressing. When she had administered these restoratives, as I was still quite hysterical, and unable to control my sobs, she put me on the sofa, with a shawl under my head, and the handkerchief from her own head under my feet, lest I should sully the cover; and then, sitting herself down behind the green fan or screen I have already mentioned, so that I could not see her face, ejaculated at

intervals, 'Mercy on us!' letting those exclamations off like minute guns.

After a time she rang the bell. 'Janet,' said my aunt, when her servant came in, 'go upstairs, give my compliments to Mr Dick, and say I wish to speak to him.'

Janet looked a little surprised to see me lying stiffly on the sofa (I was afraid to move lest it should be displeasing to my aunt), but went on her errand. My aunt, with her hands behind her, walked up and down the room, until the gentleman who had squinted at me from the upper window came in laughing.

'Mr Dick,' said my aunt, 'don't be a fool, because nobody can be more discreet than you can, when you choose. We all know that. So don't be a fool, whatever you are.'

The gentleman was serious immediately, and looked at me, I thought, as if he would entreat me to say nothing about the window.

'Mr Dick,' said my aunt, 'you have heard me mention David Copperfield? Now don't pretend not to have a memory, because you and I know better.'

'David Copperfield?' said Mr Dick, who did not appear to me to remember much about it. '*David* Copperfield? Oh, yes, to be sure, David, certainly.'

'Well,' said my aunt, 'this is his boy – his son. He would be as like his father as it's possible to be, if he was not so like his mother, too.'

'His son?' said Mr Dick. 'David's son? Indeed!'

'Yes,' pursued my aunt, 'and he has done a pretty piece of business. He has run away. Ah! His sister, Betsey Trotwood, never would have run away.' My aunt shook her head firmly, confident in the character and behaviour of the girl who never was born.

'Oh! you think she wouldn't have run away?' said Mr Dick.

'Bless and save the man,' exclaimed my aunt sharply, 'how he talks! Don't I know she wouldn't? She would have lived with her godmother, and we should have been devoted to one another. Where, in the name of wonder, should his sister, Betsey Trotwood, have run from, or to?'

'Nowhere,' said Mr Dick.

'Well then,' returned my aunt, softened by the reply, 'how can you pretend to be wool-gathering, Dick, when you are as sharp as a surgeon's lancet? Now, here you see young David Copperfield, and the question I put to you is, what shall I do with him?'

'What shall you do with him?' said Mr Dick feebly, scratching his head. 'Oh! do with him?'

'Yes,' said my aunt, with a grave look, and her forefinger held up. 'Come! I want some very sound advice.'

'Why, if I was you,' said Mr Dick, considering, and looking vacantly at me, 'I should – ' The contemplation of me seemed to inspire him with a sudden idea, and he added briskly, 'I should wash him!'

'Janet,' said my aunt, turning round with a quiet triumph, which I did not then understand, 'Mr Dick sets us all right. Heat the bath!'

Although I was deeply interested in this dialogue, I could not help observing my aunt, Mr Dick, and Janet, while it was in progress, and completing a survey I had already been engaged in making of the room.

My aunt was a tall, hard-featured lady, but by no means ill-looking. There was an inflexibility in her face, in her voice, in her gait and carriage, amply sufficient to account for the effect she had made upon a gentle creature like my mother; but her features were rather handsome than otherwise, though unbending and austere. I particularly noticed that she had a very quick, bright eye. Her hair, which was grey, was arranged in two plain divisions, under what I believe would be called a mob-cap; I mean a cap, much more common then than now, with side-pieces fastening under the chin. Her dress was of a lavender colour, and perfectly neat; but scantily made, as if she desired to be as little encumbered as possible. I remember that I thought it, in form, more like a riding-habit with the superfluous skirt cut off, than anything else. She wore at her side a gentleman's gold watch, if I might judge from its size and make, with an appropriate chain and seals; she had some linen at her throat not unlike a shirt-collar, and things at her wrists like little shirt wristbands.

Mr Dick, as I have already said, was grey-headed and florid; I should have said all about him, in saying so, had not his head been curiously bowed – not by age; it reminded me of one of Mr Creakle's boys' heads after a beating – and his grey eyes prominent and large, with a strange kind of watery brightness in them that made me, in combination with his vacant manner,

I make myself known to my aunt

his submission to my aunt, and his childish delight when she praised him, suspect him of being a little mad, though, if he were mad, how he came to be there puzzled me extremely. He was dressed like any other ordinary gentleman, in a loose grey morning-coat and waistcoat, and white trousers; and had his watch in his fob, and his money in his pockets, which he rattled as if he were very proud of it.

Janet was a pretty blooming girl, of about nineteen or twenty, and a perfect picture of neatness. Though I made no further observation of her at the moment, I may mention here what I did not discover until afterwards, namely, that she was one of a series of protégées whom my aunt had taken into her service expressly to educate in a renouncement of mankind, and who had generally completed their abjuration by marrying the baker.

The room was as neat as Janet or my aunt. As I laid down my pen, a moment since, to think of it, the air from the sea came blowing in again, mixed with the perfume of the flowers; and I saw the old-fashioned furniture brightly rubbed and polished, my aunt's inviolable chair and table by the round green fan in the bow-window, the drugget-covered carpet, the cat, the kettle-holder, the two canaries, the old china, the punch-bowl full of dried rose leaves, the tall press guarding all sorts of bottles and pots, and, wonderfully out of keeping with the rest, my dusty self upon the sofa, taking note of everything.

Janet had gone away to get the bath ready, when my aunt, to my great alarm, became in one moment rigid with indignation, and had hardly voice to cry out, 'Janet! Donkeys!'

Upon which, Janet came running up the stairs as if the house were in flames, darted out on a little piece of green in front, and warned off two saddle-donkeys, lady ridden, that had presumed to set hoof upon it; while my aunt, rushing out of the house, seized the bridle of a third animal laden with a bestriding child, turned him, led him forth from those sacred precincts, and boxed the ears of the unlucky urchin in attendance who had dared to profane that hallowed ground.

To this hour I don't know whether my aunt had any lawful right of way over that patch of green; but she had settled it in her own mind that she had, and it was all the same to her. The one great outrage of her life, demanding to be constantly avenged, was the passage of a donkey over that immaculate spot. In whatever occupation she was engaged, however interesting to her the conversation in which she was taking part, a donkey turned the current of her ideas in a moment, and she was upon him straight. Jugs of water, and watering-pots, were kept in secret places ready to be discharged on the offending boys; sticks were laid in ambush behind the door; sallies were made at all hours; and incessant war prevailed. Perhaps this was an agreeable excitement to the donkey-boys; or perhaps the more sagacious of the donkeys, understanding how the case stood, delighted with constitutional obstinacy in coming that way. I only know that there were three alarms before the bath was ready, and that on the occasion of the last and most desperate of all, I saw my aunt engage, single-handed, with a sandy-headed lad of fifteen, and bump his sandy head against her own gate, before he seemed to comprehend what was the matter. These interruptions were the more ridiculous to me, because she was giving me broth out of a tablespoon at the time (having firmly persuaded herself that I was actually starving, and must receive nourishment at first in very small quantities), and, while my mouth was yet open to receive the spoon, she would put it back into the basin, cry 'Janet! Donkeys!' and go out to the assault.

The bath was a great comfort. For I began to be sensible of acute pains in my limbs from lying out in the fields, and was now so tired and low that I could hardly keep myself awake for five minutes together. When I had bathed, they (I mean my aunt and Janet) enrobed me in a shirt and a pair of trousers belonging to Mr Dick, and tied me up in two or three great shawls. What sort of bundle I looked like, I don't know, but I felt a very hot one. Feeling also very faint and drowsy, I soon lay down on the sofa again and fell asleep.

It might have been a dream, originating in the fancy which had occupied my mind so long, but I awoke with the impression that my aunt had come and bent over me, and had put my hair away from my face, and laid my head more comfortably, and had then stood looking at me. The words, 'Pretty fellow,' or 'Poor fellow,' seemed to be in my ears, too; but certainly there was nothing else, when I awoke, to lead me to believe that they had been uttered by my aunt, who sat in the bow-window gazing at the sea from behind the green fan, which was mounted on a kind of swivel, and turned any way.

We dined soon after I awoke, off a roast fowl and a pudding; I sitting at table, not unlike a trussed bird myself, and moving my arms with considerable difficulty. But as my aunt had swathed me up, I made no complaint of being inconvenienced. All this time, I was deeply anxious to know what she was going to do with me; but she took her dinner in profound silence, except when she occasionally fixed her eyes on me sitting opposite, and said, 'Mercy upon us!' which did not by any means relieve my anxiety.

The cloth being drawn, and some sherry put upon the table (of which I had a glass), my aunt sent up for Mr Dick again, who joined us, and looked as wise as he could when she requested him to attend to my story, which she elicited from me, gradually, by a course of questions. During my recital, she kept her eyes on Mr Dick, who I thought would have gone to sleep but for that, and who, whensoever he lapsed into a smile, was checked by a frown from my aunt.

'Whatever possessed that poor unfortunate baby, that she must go and be married again,' said my aunt, when I had finished, '*I* can't conceive.'

'Perhaps she fell in love with her second husband,' Mr Dick suggested.

'Fell in love!' repeated my aunt. 'What do you mean? What business had she to do it?'

'Perhaps,' Mr Dick simpered, after thinking a little, 'she did it for pleasure.'

'Pleasure, indeed!' replied my aunt. 'A mighty pleasure for the poor baby to fix her simple faith upon any dog of a fellow, certain to ill-use her in some way or other. What did she propose to herself, I should like to know! She had had one

husband. She had seen David Copperfield out of the world, who was always running after wax dolls from his cradle. She had got a baby – oh, there were a pair of babies when she gave birth to this child sitting here, that Friday night! – and what more did she want?'

Mr Dick secretly shook his head at me, as if he thought there was no getting over this.

'She couldn't even have a baby like anybody else,' said my aunt. 'Where was this child's sister, Betsey Trotwood! Not forthcoming. Don't tell me!'

Mr Dick seemed quite frightened.

'That little man of a doctor, with his head on one side,' said my aunt, 'Jellips, or whatever his name was, what was *he* about? All he could do, was to say to me, like a robin redbreast – as he *is* – "It's a boy." A boy! Yah, the imbecility of the whole set of 'em!'

The heartiness of the ejaculation startled Mr Dick exceedingly; and me, too, if I am to tell the truth.

'And then, as if this was not enough, and she had not stood sufficiently in the light of this child's sister, Betsey Trotwood,' said my aunt, 'she marries a second time – goes and marries a Murderer – or a man with a name like it – and stands in *this* child's light! And the natural consequence is, as anybody but a baby might have foreseen, that he prowls and wanders. He's as like Cain before he was grown up as he can be.'

Mr Dick looked hard at me, as if to identify me in this character.

'And then there's that woman with the Pagan name,' said my aunt, 'that Peggotty, *she* goes and gets married next. Because she has not seen enough of the evil attending such things, *she* goes and gets married next, as the child relates. I only hope,' said my aunt, shaking her head, 'that her husband is one of those Poker husbands who abound in the newspapers, and will beat her well with one.'

I could not bear to hear my old nurse so described, and made the subject of such a wish. I told my aunt that indeed she was mistaken. That Peggotty was the best, the truest, the most faithful, most devoted, and most self-denying friend and servant in the world; who had ever loved me dearly, who had ever loved my mother dearly; who had held my mother's dying head upon her arm, on whose face my mother had imprinted her last grateful kiss. And my remembrance of them both, choking me, I broke down as I was trying to say that her home was my home, and that all she had was mine, and that I would have gone to her for shelter, but for her humble station, which made me fear that I might bring some trouble on her – I broke down, I say, as I was trying to say so, and laid my face in my hands upon the table.

'Well, well!' said my aunt, 'the child is right to stand by those who have stood by him – Janet! Donkeys!'

I thoroughly believe that but for those unfortunate donkeys, we should have come to a good understanding; for my aunt had laid her hand on my shoulder, and the impulse was upon me, thus emboldened to embrace her and beseech her protection. But the interruption, and the disorder she was thrown into by the struggle outside, put an end to all softer ideas for the present; and kept my aunt indignantly declaiming to Mr Dick about her determination to appeal for redress to the laws of her country, and to bring actions for trespass against the whole donkey proprietorship of Dover, until tea-time.

After tea, we sat at the window – on the lookout, as I imagined, from my aunt's sharp expression of face, for more invaders – until dusk, when Janet set candles and a back-gammon-board on the table, and pulled down the blinds.

'Now Mr Dick,' said my aunt, with her grave look, and her forefinger up as before, 'I am going to ask you another question. Look at this child.'

'David's son?' said Mr Dick, with an attentive, puzzled face.

'Exactly so,' returned my aunt. 'What would you do with him, now?'

'Do with David's son?' said Mr Dick.

'Aye,' replied my aunt, 'with David's son?'

'Oh!' said Mr Dick. 'Yes. Do with – I should put him to bed.'

'Janet!' cried my aunt, with the same complacent triumph that I had remarked before. 'Mr Dick sets us all right. If the bed is ready, we'll take him up to it.'

Janet reporting it to be quite ready, I was taken up to it, kindly, but in some sort like a prisoner; my aunt going in front, and Janet bringing up the rear. The only circumstance which gave me any new hope, was my aunt's stopping on the stairs to enquire about a smell of fire that was prevalent there; and Janet replying that she had been making tinder, down in the kitchen, of my old shirt. But there were no other clothes in my room than the odd heap of things I wore; and when I was left there, with a little taper which my aunt forewarned me would burn exactly five minutes, I heard them lock my door on the outside. Turning these things over in my mind, I deemed it possible that my aunt, who could know nothing of me, might suspect that I had a habit of running away, and took precautions, on that account, to have me in safe-keeping.

The room was a pleasant one, at the top of the house, over-looking the sea, on which the moon was shining brilliantly. After I had said my prayers, and the candle had burnt out, I remember how I still sat looking at the moonlight on the water, as if I could hope to read my fortune in it, as in a bright book; or to see my mother with her child, coming from Heaven, along that shining path, to look upon me as she had looked when I last saw her sweet face. I remember how the solemn feeling, with which at length I turned my eyes away, yielded to the sensation of gratitude and rest which the sight of the white curtained bed – and how much more the lying softly down upon it, nestling in the snow-white sheets! – inspired. I remember how I thought of all the solitary places under the night sky where I had slept, and how I prayed that I never might be houseless any more, and never might forget the houseless. I remember how I seemed to float, then, down the melancholy glory of that track upon the sea, away into the world of dreams.

CHAPTER 14

My Aunt Makes Up Her Mind About Me

On going down in the morning, I found my aunt musing so profoundly over the breakfast-table, with her elbow on the tray, that the contents of the urn had overflowed the teapot and were laying the whole tablecloth under water, when my entrance put her meditations to flight. I felt sure that I had been the subject of her reflections, and was more than ever anxious to know her intentions towards me. Yet I dared not express my anxiety, lest it should give her offence.

My eyes, however, not being so much under control as my tongue, were attracted towards my aunt very often during breakfast. I never could look at her for a few moments together but I found her looking at me – in an odd, thoughtful manner, as if I were an immense way off, instead of being on the other side of the small round table. When she had finished her breakfast, my aunt very deliberately leaned back in her chair, knitted her brows, folded her arms, and contemplated me at her leisure, with such a fixedness of attention that I was quite overpowered by embarrassment. Not having as yet finished my own breakfast, I attempted to hide my confusion by proceeding with it; but my knife tumbled over my fork, my fork tripped up my knife, I chipped bits of bacon a surprising height into the air instead of cutting them for my own eating, and choked myself with my tea, which persisted in going the wrong way instead of the right one, until I gave in altogether, and sat blushing under my aunt's close scrutiny.

'Hallo!' said my aunt, after a long time.

I looked up, and met her sharp, bright glance respectfully.

'I have written to him,' said my aunt.

'To – ?'

'To your father-in-law,' said my aunt. 'I have sent him a letter that I'll trouble him to attend to, or he and I will fall out, I can tell him!'

'Does he know where I am, aunt?' I enquired, alarmed.

'I have told him,' said my aunt, with a nod.

'Shall I – be – given up to him?' I faltered.

'I don't know,' said my aunt. 'We shall see.'

'Oh! I can't think what I shall do,' I exclaimed, 'if I have to go back to Mr Murdstone!'

'I don't know anything about it,' said my aunt, shaking her head. 'I can't say, I am sure. We shall see.'

My spirits sank under these words, and I became very down-cast and heavy of heart. My aunt, without appearing to take much heed of me, put on a coarse apron with a bib, which she took out of the press; washed up the teacups with her own hands; and when everything was washed and set in the tray again, and the cloth folded and put on the top of the whole, rang for Janet to remove it. She next swept up the crumbs with a little broom (putting on a pair of gloves first), until there did not appear to be one microscopic speck left on the carpet; next dusted and arranged the room, which was dusted and arranged to a hair's breadth already. When all these tasks were performed to her satisfaction, she took off the gloves and apron, folded them up, put them in the particular corner of the press from which they had been taken, brought out her work-box to her own table in the open window, and sat down, with the green fan between her and the light, to work.

'I wish you'd go upstairs,' said my aunt, as she threaded her needle, 'and give my compliments to Mr Dick, and I'll be glad to know how he gets on with his Memorial.'

I rose with all alacrity, to acquit myself of this commission.

'I suppose,' said my aunt, eyeing me as narrowly as she had eyed the needle in threading it, 'you think Mr Dick a short name, eh?'

'I thought it was rather a short name, yesterday,' I confessed.

'You are not to suppose that he hasn't got a longer name, if he chose to use it,' said my aunt, with a loftier air. 'Babley – Mr Richard Babley – that's the gentleman's true name.'

I was going to suggest, with a modest sense of my youth and the familiarity I had already been guilty of, that I had better give him the full benefit of that name, when my aunt went on to say: 'But don't you call him by it, whatever you do. He can't bear his name. That's a peculiarity of his. Though I don't know that it's much of a peculiarity, either; for he has been ill-used enough, by some that bear it, to have a mortal antipathy for it, Heaven knows. Mr Dick is his name here, and everywhere else, now – if he ever went anywhere else, which he don't. So take care, child, you don't call him anything *but* Mr Dick.'

I promised to obey, and went upstairs with my message; thinking, as I went, that if Mr Dick had been working at his Memorial long, at the same rate as I had seen him working at it, through the open door, when I came down, he was probably getting on very well indeed. I found him still driving at it with a long pen, and his head almost laid upon the paper. He was so intent upon it that I had ample leisure to observe the large paper kite in a corner, the confusion of bundles of manuscript, the number of pens, and, above all, the quantity of ink (which he seemed to have in, in half gallon jars by the dozen), before he observed my being present.

'Ha! Phoebus!' said Mr Dick, laying down his pen. 'How does the world go? I'll tell you what,' he added, in a lower tone, 'I shouldn't wish it to be mentioned, but it's a – ' here he beckoned to me, and put his lips close to my ear – 'it's a mad world. Mad as Bedlam, boy!' said Mr Dick, taking snuff from a round box on the table, and laughing heartily.

Without presuming to give my opinion on this question, I delivered my message.

'Well,' said Mr Dick, in answer, 'my compliments to her, and I – I believe I have made a start. I think I have made a start,' said Mr Dick, passing his hand among his grey hair, and casting anything but a confident look at his manuscript. 'You have been to school?'

'Yes, sir,' I answered, 'for a short time.'

'Do you recollect the date,' said Mr Dick, looking earnestly at me, and taking up his pen to note it down, 'when King Charles the First had his head cut off?'

I said I believed it happened in the year sixteen hundred and forty-nine.

'Well,' returned Mr Dick, scratching his ear with his pen, and looking dubiously at me. 'So the books say; but I don't see how that can be. Because, if it was so long ago, how could the people about him have made that mistake of putting some of the trouble out of *his* head, after it was taken off, into *mine*?'

I was very much surprised by the enquiry; but could give no information on this point.

'It's very strange,' said Mr Dick, with a despondent look upon his papers, and with his hand among his hair again, 'that I never can get that quite right; I never can make that perfectly clear. But no matter, no matter!' he said cheerfully, and rousing himself, 'there's time enough! My compliments to Miss Trotwood, I am getting on very well indeed.'

I was going away when he directed my attention to the kite.

'What do you think of that for a kite?' he said.

I answered that it was a beautiful one. I should think it must have been as much as seven feet high.

'I made it. We'll go and fly it, you and I,' said Mr Dick. 'Do you see this?'

He showed me that it was covered with manuscript, very closely and laboriously written; but so plainly, that, as I looked along the lines, I thought I saw some allusion to King Charles the First's head again, in one or two places.

'There's plenty of string,' said Mr Dick, 'and when it flies high it takes the facts a long way. That's my manner of diffusing 'em. I don't know where they may come down. It's according to circumstances, and the wind, and so forth; but I take my chance of that.'

His face was so very mild and pleasant, and had something so reverend in it, though it was hale and hearty, that I was not sure but that he was having a good-humoured jest with me. So I laughed, and he laughed, and we parted the best friends possible.

'Well, child,' said my aunt, when I went downstairs. 'And what of Mr Dick, this morning?'

I informed her that he sent his compliments, and was getting on very well indeed.

'What do you think of him?' said my aunt.

I had some shadowy idea of endeavouring to evade the question by replying that I thought him a very nice gentleman; but my aunt was not to be so put off, for she laid her work down in her lap, and said, folding her hands upon it: 'Come! Your sister Betsey Trotwood would have told me what she thought of anyone, directly. Be as like your sister as you can, and speak out!'

'Is he – is Mr Dick – I ask because I don't know, aunt – is he at all out of his mind, then?' I stammered; for I felt I was on dangerous ground.

'Not a morsel,' said my aunt.

'Oh, indeed!' I observed faintly.

'If there is anything in the world,' said my aunt, with great decision and force of manner, 'that Mr Dick is not, it's that.'

I had nothing better to offer than another timid 'Oh, indeed!'

'He has been *called* mad,' said my aunt. 'I have a selfish pleasure in saying he has been called mad, or I should not have had the benefit of his society and advice for these last ten years and upwards – in fact, ever since your sister, Betsey Trotwood, disappointed me.'

'So long as that?' I said.

'And nice people they were, who had the audacity to call him mad,' pursued my aunt. 'Mr Dick is a sort of distant connection of mine – it doesn't matter how; I needn't enter into that. If it hadn't been for me, his own brother would have shut him up for life. That's all.'

I am afraid it was hypocritical in me, but, seeing that my aunt felt strongly on the subject, I tried to look as if I felt strongly too.

'A proud fool!' said my aunt. 'Because his brother was a little eccentric – though he is not half so eccentric as a good many people – he didn't like to have him visible about his house, and sent him away to some private asylum-place; though he had been left to his particular care by their deceased father, who thought him almost a natural. And a wise man *he* must have been to think so! Mad himself, no doubt.'

Again, as my aunt looked quite convinced, I endeavoured to look quite convinced also.

'So I stepped in,' said my aunt, 'and made him an offer. I said, "Your brother's sane – a great deal more sane than you are, or ever will be, it is to be hoped. Let him have his little income, and come and live with me. *I* am not afraid of him, *I* am not proud, *I* am ready to take care of him, and shall not ill-treat him as some people (besides the asylum-folks) have done." After a good deal of squabbling,' said my aunt, 'I got him; and he has been here ever since. He is the most friendly and amenable creature in existence; and as for advice! – But nobody knows what that man's mind is, except myself.'

My aunt smoothed her dress and shook her head, as if she smoothed defiance of the whole world out of the one, and shook it out of the other.

'He had a favourite sister,' said my aunt, 'a good creature, and very kind to him. But she did what they all do – took a husband. And *he* did what they all do – made her wretched. It had such an effect upon the mind of Mr Dick (*that's* not madness, I hope!) that, combined with his fear of his brother and his sense of his unkindness, it threw him into a fever. That was before he came to me, but the recollection of it is oppressive to him even now. Did he say anything to you about King Charles the First, child?'

'Yes, aunt.'

'Ah!' said my aunt, rubbing her nose as if she were a little vexed. 'That's his allegorical way of expressing it. He connects his illness with great disturbance and agitation, naturally, and that's the figure, or the simile, or whatever it's called, which he chooses to use. And why shouldn't he, if he thinks proper!'

I said: 'Certainly, aunt.'

'It's not a businesslike way of speaking,' said my aunt, 'nor a worldly way. I am aware of that; and that's the reason why I insist upon it that there sha'n't be a word about it in his Memorial.'

'Is it a Memorial about his own history that he is writing, aunt?'

'Yes, child,' said my aunt, rubbing her nose again. 'He is memorialising the Lord Chancellor, or the Lord Somebody or other – one of those people, at all events, who are paid to *be* memorialised – about his affairs. I suppose it will go in one of these days. He hasn't been able to draw it up yet, without introducing that mode of expressing himself; but it don't signify; it keeps him employed.'

In fact, I found out afterwards that Mr Dick had been for upwards of ten years endeavouring to keep King Charles the First out of the Memorial; but he had been constantly getting into it, and was there now.

'I say again,' said my aunt, 'nobody knows what that man's mind is except myself; and he's the most amenable and friendly creature in existence. If he likes to fly a kite sometimes, what of that! Franklin used to fly a kite. He was a Quaker, or something of that sort, if I am not mistaken. And a Quaker flying a kite is a much more ridiculous object than anybody else.'

If I could have supposed that my aunt had recounted these particulars for my especial behoof, and as a piece of confidence in me, I should have felt very much distinguished, and should have augured favourably from such a mark of her good opinion. But I could hardly help observing that she had launched into them, chiefly because the question was raised in her own mind, and with very little reference to me, though she had addressed herself to me in the absence of anybody else.

At the same time, I must say that the generosity of her championship of poor harmless Mr Dick not only inspired my young breast with some selfish hope for myself, but warmed it unselfishly towards her. I believe that I began to know that there was something about my aunt, notwithstanding her many eccentricities and odd humours, to be honoured and trusted in. Though she was just as sharp that day as on the day before, and was in and out about the donkeys just as often, and was thrown into a tremendous state of indignation, when a young man, going by, ogled Janet at a window (which was one of the gravest misdemeanours that could be committed against my aunt's dignity), she seemed to me to command more of my respect, if not less of my fear.

The anxiety I underwent, in the interval which necessarily elapsed before a reply could be received to her letter to Mr Murdstone, was extreme; but I made an endeavour to suppress it, and to be as agreeable as I could in a quiet way, both to my aunt and Mr Dick. The latter and I would have gone out to fly the great kite; but that I had still no other clothes than the anything but ornamental garments with which I had been decorated on the first day, and which confined me to the house, except for an hour after dark, when my aunt, for my health's sake, paraded me up and down on the cliff outside before going to bed. At length the reply from Mr Murdstone came, and my aunt informed me, to my infinite terror, that he was coming to speak to her himself on the next day. On the next day, still bundled up in my curious habiliments, I sat counting the time, flushed and heated by the conflict of sinking hopes and rising fears within me; and waiting to be startled by the sight of the gloomy face, whose non-arrival startled me every minute.

My aunt was a little more imperious and stern than usual, but I observed no other token of her preparing herself to receive the visitor so much dreaded by me. She sat at work in the window, and I sat by, with my thoughts running astray on all possible and impossible results of Mr Murdstone's visit, until pretty late in the afternoon. Our dinner had been indefinitely postponed; but it was growing so late that my aunt had ordered it to be got ready, when she gave a sudden alarm of donkeys, and to my consternation and amazement, I beheld Miss Murdstone, on a side-saddle, ride deliberately over the sacred piece of green, and stop in front of the house, looking about her.

'Go along with you!' cried my aunt, shaking her head and her fist at the window. 'You have no business there. How dare you trespass? Go along! Oh, you bold-faced thing!'

My aunt was so exasperated by the coolness with which Miss Murdstone looked about her that I really believe she was motionless, and unable for the moment to dart out according to custom. I seized the opportunity to inform her who it was; and that the gentleman now coming near the offender (for the way up was very steep, and he had dropped behind) was Mr Murdstone himself.

'I don't care who it is!' cried my aunt, still shaking her head, and gesticulating anything but welcome from the bow-window; 'I won't be trespassed upon. I won't allow it. Go away! Janet, turn him round. Lead him off!' and I saw, from behind my aunt, a sort of hurried battle-piece, in which the donkey stood resisting everybody, with all his four legs planted different ways, while Janet tried to pull him round by the bridle, Mr Murdstone tried to lead him on, Miss Murdstone struck at Janet with a parasol, and several boys, who had come to see the engagement, shouted vigorously. But my aunt, suddenly descrying among them the young malefactor who was the donkey's guardian, and who was one of the most inveterate offenders against her, though hardly in his teens, rushed out to the scene of action, pounced upon him, captured him, dragged him, with his jacket over his head, and his heels grinding the ground, into the garden, and, calling upon Janet to fetch the constables and justices, that he might be taken, tried, and executed on the spot, held him at bay there. This part of the business, however, did not last long; for the young rascal, being expert at a variety of feints and dodges, of which my aunt had no conception, soon went whooping away, leaving some deep impressions of his nailed boots in the flower-beds, and taking his donkey in triumph with him.

Miss Murdstone, during the latter portion of the contest, had dismounted, and was now waiting with her brother at the bottom of the steps, until my aunt should be at leisure to receive them. My aunt, a little ruffled by the combat, marched past them into the house, with great dignity, and took no notice of their presence, until they were announced by Janet.

'Shall I go away, aunt?' I asked, trembling.

'No, sir,' said my aunt. 'Certainly not!' With which she pushed me into a corner near her, and fenced me in with a chair, as if it were a prison or a bar of justice. This position I continued to occupy during the whole interview, and from it I now saw Mr and Miss Murdstone enter the room.

'Oh!' said my aunt, 'I was not aware at first to whom I had the pleasure of objecting. But I don't allow anybody to ride over that turf. I make no exceptions. I don't allow anybody to do it.'

'Your regulation is rather awkward to strangers,' said Miss Murdstone.

'Is it!' said my aunt.

Mr Murdstone seemed afraid of a renewal of hostilities, and interposing began: 'Miss Trotwood!'

'I beg your pardon,' observed my aunt, with a keen look. 'You are the Mr Murdstone who married the widow of my late nephew, David Copperfield, of Blunderstone Rookery? – Though why Rookery, *I* don't know!'

'I am,' said Mr Murdstone.

'You'll excuse my saying, sir,' returned my aunt, 'that I think it would have been a much better and happier thing if you had left that poor child alone.'

'I so far agree with what Miss Trotwood has remarked,' observed Miss Murdstone, bridling, 'that I consider our lamented Clara to have been, in all essential respects, a mere child.'

'It is a comfort to you and me, ma'am,' said my aunt, 'who are getting on in life, and are not likely to be made unhappy by our personal attractions, that nobody can say the same of us.'

'No doubt!' returned Miss Murdstone, though, I thought, not with a very ready or gracious assent. 'And it certainly might have been, as you say, a better and happier thing for my brother if he had never entered into such a marriage. I have always been of that opinion.'

'I have no doubt you have,' said my aunt. 'Janet,' ringing the bell, 'my compliments to Mr Dick, and beg him to come down.'

Until he came, my aunt sat perfectly upright and stiff, frowning at the wall. When he came my aunt performed the ceremony of introduction.

'Mr Dick – an old and intimate friend – on whose judgement,' said my aunt, with emphasis, as an admonition to Mr Dick, who was biting his forefinger, and looking rather foolish, 'I rely.'

Mr Dick took his finger out of his mouth, on this hint, and stood among the group, with a grave and attentive expression of face. My aunt inclined her head to Mr Murdstone, who went on: 'Miss Trotwood, on the receipt of your letter, I considered it an act of greater justice to myself, and perhaps of more respect to you – '

'Thank you,' said my aunt, still eyeing him keenly. 'You needn't mind me.'

'To answer it in person, however inconvenient the journey,' pursued Mr Murdstone, 'rather than by letter. This unhappy boy, who has run away from his friends and his occupation – '

'And whose appearance,' interposed his sister, directing general attention to me in my indefinable costume, 'is perfectly scandalous and disgraceful.'

'Jane Murdstone,' said her brother, 'have the goodness not to interrupt me. This unhappy boy, Miss Trotwood, has been the occasion of much domestic trouble and uneasiness; both during the lifetime of my late dear wife, and since. He has a sullen, rebellious spirit; a violent temper; and an untoward, intractable disposition. Both my sister and myself have endeavoured to correct his vices, but ineffectually. And I have felt – we both have felt, I may say; my sister being fully in my confidence – that it is right you should receive this grave and dispassionate assurance from our lips.'

'It can hardly be necessary for me to confirm anything stated by my brother,' said Miss Murdstone; 'but I beg to observe that, of all the boys in the world, I believe this is the worst boy.'

'Strong!' said my aunt shortly.

'But not at all too strong for the facts,' returned Miss Murdstone.

'Ha!' said my aunt. 'Well, sir?'

'I have my own opinions,' resumed Mr Murdstone, whose face darkened more and more, the more he and my aunt observed each other, which they did very narrowly, 'as to the best mode of bringing him up; they are founded, in part, on my knowledge of him, and in part on my knowledge of my own means and resources. I am responsible for them to myself, I act upon them, and I say no more about them. It is enough that I place this boy under the eye of a friend of my own, in a respectable business; that it does not please him; that he runs away from it; makes himself a common vagabond about the country; and comes here, in rags, to appeal to you, Miss Trotwood. I wish to set before you, honourably, the exact consequences – so far as they are within my knowledge – of your abetting him in this appeal.'

'But about the respectable business first,' said my aunt. 'If he had been your own boy you would have put him to it, just the same, I suppose?'

The momentous interview

'If he had been my brother's own boy,' returned Miss Murdstone, striking in, 'his character, I trust, would have been altogether different.'

'Or if the poor child, his mother, had been alive, he would still have gone into the respectable business, would he?' said my aunt.

'I believe,' said Mr Murdstone, with an inclination of his head, 'that Clara would have disputed nothing which myself and my sister Jane Murdstone were agreed was for the best.'

Miss Murdstone confirmed this with an audible murmur.

'Humph!' said my aunt. 'Unfortunate baby!'

Mr Dick, who had been rattling his money all this time, was rattling it so loudly now that my aunt felt it necessary to check him with a look before saying: 'The poor child's annuity died with her?'

'Died with her,' replied Mr Murdstone.

'And there was no settlement of the little property – the house and garden – the what's-its-name Rookery without any rooks in it – upon her boy?'

'It had been left to her, unconditionally, by her first husband,' Mr Murdstone began, when my aunt caught him up with the greatest irascibility and impatience.

'Good Lord, man, there's no occasion to say that. Left to her unconditionally! I think I see David Copperfield looking forward to any condition of any sort or kind, though it stared him point-blank in the face! Of course it was left to her unconditionally. But when she married again – when she took that most disastrous step of marrying you, in short,' said my aunt, 'to be plain – did no one put in a word for the boy at that time?'

'My late wife loved her second husband, madam,' said Mr Murdstone, 'and trusted implicitly in him.'

'Your late wife, sir, was a most unworldly, most unhappy, most unfortunate baby,' returned my aunt, shaking her head at him. 'That's what *she* was. And, now, what have you got to say next?'

'Merely this, Miss Trotwood,' he returned. 'I am here to take David back – to take him back unconditionally, to dispose of him as I think proper, and to deal with him as I think right. I am not here to make any promise, or give any pledge to anybody. You may possibly have some idea, Miss Trotwood, of abetting him in his running away, and in his complaints to you. Your manner, which I must say does not seem intended to propitiate, induces me to think it possible. Now I must caution you that if you abet him once, you abet him for good and all; if you step in between him and me now, you must step in, Miss Trotwood, for ever. I cannot trifle, or be trifled with. I am here, for the first and last time, to take him away. Is he ready to go? If he is not – and you tell me he is not; on any pretence, it is indifferent to me what – my doors are shut against him henceforth, and yours, I take it for granted, are open to him.'

To this address, my aunt had listened with the closest attention, sitting perfectly upright, with her hands folded on one knee, and looking grimly on the speaker. When he had finished, she turned her eyes so as to command Miss Murdstone, without otherwise disturbing her attitude, and said: 'Well, ma'am, have *you* got anything to remark?'

'Indeed, Miss Trotwood,' said Miss Murdstone, 'all that I could say has been so well said by my brother, and all that I know to be the fact has been so plainly stated by him, that I have nothing to add except my thanks for your politeness. For your very great politeness, I am sure,' said Miss Murdstone; with an irony which no more affected my aunt than it discomposed the cannon I had slept by at Chatham.

'And what does the boy say?' said my aunt. 'Are you ready to go, David?'

I answered no, and entreated her not to let me go. I said that neither Mr nor Miss Murdstone had ever liked me, or had ever been kind to me. That they had made my mama, who always loved me dearly, unhappy about me, and that I knew it well, and that Peggotty knew it. I said that I had been more miserable than I thought anybody could believe who only knew how young I was; and I begged and prayed my aunt – I forget in what terms now, but I remember that they affected me very much then – to befriend and protect me, for my father's sake.

'Mr Dick,' said my aunt, 'what shall I do with this child?'

Mr Dick considered, hesitated, brightened, and rejoined, 'Have him measured for a suit of clothes directly.'

'Mr Dick,' said my aunt triumphantly, 'give me your hand, for your common sense is invaluable.' Having shaken it with great cordiality, she pulled me towards her, and said to Mr Murdstone: 'You can go when you like; I'll take my chance with the boy. If he's all you say he is, at least I can do as much for him then, as you have done. But I don't believe a word of it.'

'Miss Trotwood,' rejoined Mr Murdstone, shrugging his shoulders as he rose, 'if you were a gentleman – '

'Bah! Stuff and nonsense!' said my aunt. 'Don't talk to me!'

'How exquisitely polite!' exclaimed Miss Murdstone, rising. 'Overpowering, really!'

'Do you think I don't know,' said my aunt, turning a deaf ear to the sister, and continuing to address the brother, and to shake her head at him with infinite expression, 'what kind of life you must have led that poor, unhappy, misdirected baby? Do you think I don't know what a woeful day it was for the soft little creature when *you* first came in her way – smirking and making great eyes at her, I'll be bound, as if you couldn't say boh! to a goose?'

'I never heard anything so elegant!' said Miss Murdstone.

'Do you think I can't understand you as well as if I had seen you,' pursued my aunt, 'now that I *do* see and hear you – which I tell you candidly is anything but a pleasure to me? Oh yes, bless us! who so smooth and silky as Mr Murdstone at first! The poor, benighted innocent had never seen such a man. He was made of sweetness. He worshipped her. He doted on her boy – tenderly doted on him! He was to be another father to him, and they were all to live together in a garden of roses, weren't they? Ugh! Get along with you, do!' said my aunt.

'I never heard anything like this person in my life!' exclaimed Miss Murdstone.

'And when you had made sure of the poor little fool,' said my aunt – 'God forgive me that I should call her so, and she gone where you won't go in a hurry – because you had not done wrong enough to her and hers, you must begin to train her, must you? begin to break her, like a poor caged bird, and wear her deluded life away, in teaching her to sing *your* notes?'

'This is either insanity or intoxication,' said Miss Murdstone, in a perfect agony at not being able to turn the current of my aunt's address towards herself; 'and my suspicion is that it's intoxication.'

Miss Betsey, without taking the least notice of the interruption, continued to address herself to Mr Murdstone, as if there had been no such thing.

'Mr Murdstone,' she said, shaking her finger at him, 'you were a tyrant to the simple baby, and you broke her heart. She was a loving baby – I know that; I knew it years before *you* ever saw her – and through the best part of her weakness, you gave her the wounds she died of. There is the truth for your comfort, however you like it. And you and your instruments may make the most of it.'

'Allow me to enquire, Miss Trotwood,' interposed Miss Murdstone, 'whom you are pleased to call, in a choice of words in which I am not experienced, my brother's instruments?'

Still stone deaf to the voice, and utterly unmoved by it, Miss Betsey pursued her discourse.

'It was clear enough, as I have told you, years before *you* ever saw her – and why, in the mysterious dispensations of Providence, you ever did see her, is more than humanity can comprehend – it was clear enough that the poor soft little thing would marry somebody, at sometime or other; but I did hope it wouldn't have been as bad as it has turned out. That was the time, Mr Murdstone, when she gave birth to her boy here,' said my aunt; 'to the poor child you sometimes tormented her through afterwards, which is a disagreeable remembrance, and makes the sight of him odious now. Aye, aye! you needn't wince!' said my aunt. 'I know it's true without that.'

He had stood by the door, all this while, observant of her with a smile upon his face, though his black eyebrows were heavily contracted. I remarked now that, though the smile was on his face still, his colour had gone in a moment, and he seemed to breathe as if he had been running.

'Good-day, sir,' said my aunt, 'and goodbye! Good-day to you, too, ma'am,' said my aunt, turning suddenly upon his sister. 'Let me see you ride a donkey over *my* green again, and as sure as you have a head upon your shoulders, I'll knock your bonnet off, and tread upon it!'

It would require a painter, and no common painter, too, to depict my aunt's face as she delivered herself of this very unexpected sentiment, and Miss Murdstone's face as she heard it. But the manner of the speech, no less than the matter, was so fiery that Miss Murdstone, without a word in answer, discreetly put her arm through her brother's, and walked haughtily out of the cottage; my aunt remaining in the window looking after them; prepared, I have no doubt, in case of the donkey's reappearance, to carry her threat into instant execution.

No attempt at defiance being made, however, her face gradually relaxed, and became so pleasant that I was emboldened to kiss and thank her; which I did with great heartiness, and with both my arms clasped round her neck. I then shook hands with Mr Dick, who shook hands with me a great many times, and hailed this happy close of the proceedings with repeated bursts of laughter.

'You'll consider yourself guardian, jointly with me, of this child, Mr Dick,' said my aunt.

'I shall be delighted,' said Mr Dick, 'to be the guardian of David's son.'

'Very good,' returned my aunt, '*that's* settled. I have been thinking, do you know, Mr Dick, that I might call him Trotwood?'

'Certainly, certainly. Call him Trotwood, certainly,' said Mr Dick. 'David's son's Trotwood.'

'Trotwood Copperfield, you mean,' returned my aunt.

'Yes, to be sure; yes; Trotwood Copperfield,' said Mr Dick, a little abashed.

My aunt took so kindly to the notion that some ready-made clothes, which were purchased for me that afternoon, were marked 'Trotwood Copperfield,' in her own handwriting, and in indelible marking-ink, before I put them on; and it was settled that all the other clothes which were ordered to be made for me (a complete outfit was bespoke that afternoon) should be marked in the same way.

Thus I began my new life, in a new name, and with everything new about me. Now that the state of doubt was over, I felt, for many days, like one in a dream. I never thought that I had a curious couple of guardians in my aunt and Mr Dick. I never thought of anything about myself, distinctly. The two things clearest in my mind were that a remoteness had come upon the old Blunderstone life – which seemed to lie in the haze of an immeasurable distance; and that a curtain had for ever fallen on my life at Murdstone and Grinby's. No one has ever raised that curtain since. I have lifted it for a moment, even in this narrative, with a reluctant hand, and dropped it gladly. The remembrance of that life is fraught with so much pain to me, with so much mental suffering and want of hope, that I have never had the courage even to examine how long I was doomed to lead it. Whether it lasted for a year, or more, or less, I do not know. I only know that it was, and ceased to be, and that I have written, and there I leave it.

CHAPTER 15

I Make Another Beginning

Mr Dick and I soon became the very best of friends, and very often, when his day's work was done, went out together to fly the great kite. Every day of his life he had a long sitting at the Memorial, which never made the least progress, however hard he laboured, for King Charles the First always strayed into it, sooner or later, and then it was thrown aside, and another one begun. The patience and hope with which he bore these perpetual disappointments, the mild perception he had that there was something wrong about King Charles the First, the feeble efforts he made to keep him out, and the certainty with which he came in, and tumbled the Memorial out of all shape, made a deep impression on me. What Mr Dick supposed

would come of the Memorial, if it were completed; where he thought it was to go, or what he thought it was to do, he knew no more than anybody else, I believe. Nor was it at all necessary that he should trouble himself with such questions, for if anything were certain under the sun, it was certain that the Memorial never would be finished.

It was quite an affecting sight, I used to think, to see him with the kite when it was up a great height in the air. What he had told me, in his room, about his belief in its disseminating the statements pasted on it, which were nothing but old leaves of abortive Memorials, might have been a fancy with him sometimes; but not when he was out, looking up at the kite in the sky, and feeling it pull and tug at his hand. He never looked so serene as he did then. I used to fancy, as I sat by him of an evening, on a green slope, and saw him watch the kite high in the quiet air, that it lifted his mind out of his confusion, and bore it (such was my boyish thought) into the skies. As he wound the string in, and it came lower and lower down out of the beautiful light, until it fluttered to the ground, and lay there like a dead thing, he seemed to wake gradually out of a dream; and I remember to have seen him take it up, and look about him in a lost way, as if they had both come down together, so that I pitied him with all my heart.

While I advanced in friendship and intimacy with Mr Dick, I did not go backward in the favour of his staunch friend, my aunt. She took so kindly to me, that, in the course of a few weeks, she shortened my adopted name of Trotwood into Trot; and even encouraged me to hope that if I went on as I had begun, I might take equal rank in her affections with my sister Betsey Trotwood.

'Trot,' said my aunt one evening, when the backgammon-board was placed as usual for herself and Mr Dick, 'we must not forget your education.'

This was my only subject of anxiety, and I felt quite delighted by her referring to it.

'Should you like to go to school at Canterbury?' said my aunt.

I replied that I should like it very much, as it was so near her.

'Good,' said my aunt. 'Should you like to go tomorrow?'

Being already no stranger to the general rapidity of my aunt's evolutions, I was not surprised by the suddenness of the proposal, and said, 'Yes.'

'Good,' said my aunt again. 'Janet, hire the grey pony and chaise tomorrow morning at ten o'clock, and pack up Master Trotwood's clothes tonight.'

I was greatly elated by these orders; but my heart smote me for my selfishness, when I witnessed their effect on Mr Dick, who was so low-spirited at the prospect of our separation, and played so ill in consequence, that my aunt, after giving him several admonitory raps on the knuckles with her dice-box, shut up the board, and declined to play with him any more. But, on hearing from my aunt that I should sometimes come over on a Saturday, and that he could sometimes come and see me on a Wednesday, he revived; and vowed to make another kite for those occasions, of proportions greatly surpassing the present one. In the morning he was down-hearted again, and would have sustained himself by giving me all the money he had in his possession, gold and silver too, if my aunt had not interposed, and limited the gift to five shillings, which, at his earnest petition, were afterwards increased to ten. We parted at the garden gate in a most affectionate manner, and Mr Dick did not go into the house until my aunt had driven me out of sight of it.

My aunt, who was perfectly indifferent to public opinion, drove the grey pony through Dover in a masterly manner; sitting high and stiff like a stage coachman, keeping a steady eye upon him wherever he went, and making a point of not letting him have his own way in any respect. When we came into the country road, she permitted him to relax a little, however; and looking at me down in a valley of cushion by her side, asked me whether I was happy.

'Very happy indeed, thank you, aunt,' I said.

She was much gratified; and both her hands being occupied, patted me on the head with her whip.

'Is it a large school, aunt?' I asked.

'Why, I don't know,' said my aunt. 'We are going to Mr Wickfield's first.'

'Does *he* keep a school?' I asked.

'No, Trot,' said my aunt. 'He keeps an office.'

I asked for no more information about Mr Wickfield, as she offered none, and we conversed on other subjects until we came to Canterbury, where, as it was market-day, my aunt had a great opportunity of insinuating the grey pony among carts, baskets, vegetables, and hucksters' goods. The hair-breadth turns and twists we made drew down upon us a variety of speeches from the people standing about, which were not always complimentary, but my aunt drove on with perfect indifference, and I dare say would have taken her own way with as much coolness through an enemy's country.

At length we stopped before a very old house bulging out over the road; a house with long, low, lattice-windows bulging out still farther, and beams with carved heads on the ends bulging out too, so that I fancied the whole house was leaning forward, trying to see who was passing on the narrow pavement below. It was quite spotless in its cleanliness. The old-fashioned brass knocker on the low arched door, ornamented with carved garlands of fruit and flowers, twinkled like a star; the two stone steps descending to the door were as white as if they had been covered with fair linen; and all the angles and corners, and carvings and mouldings, and quaint little panes of glass, and quainter little windows, though as old as the hills, were as pure as any snow that ever fell upon the hills.

When the pony-chaise stopped at the door, and my eyes were intent upon the house, I saw a cadaverous face appear at a small window on the ground floor (in a little round tower that formed one side of the house) and quickly disappear. The low arched door then opened, and the face came out. It was quite as cadaverous as it had looked in the window, though in the grain of it there was that tinge of red which is sometimes to be observed in the skins of red-haired people. It belonged to a red-haired person – a youth of fifteen, as I take it now, but looking much older – whose hair was cropped as close as the closest stubble; who had hardly any eyebrows, and no eyelashes, and eyes of a red-brown; so unsheltered and unshaded that I remember wondering how he went to sleep. He was high-shouldered and bony; dressed in decent black, with a white wisp of a neckcloth; buttoned up to the throat; and had a long, lank, skeleton hand, which particularly attracted my attention, as he stood at the pony's head, rubbing his chin with it, and looking up at us in the chaise.

'Is Mr Wickfield at home, Uriah Heep?' said my aunt.

'Mr Wickfield's at home, ma'am,' said Uriah Heep, 'if you'll please to walk in there' – pointing with his long hand to the room he meant.

We got out; and leaving him to hold the pony, went into a long low parlour looking towards the street, from the window of which I caught a glimpse, as I went in, of Uriah Heep breathing into the pony's nostrils, and immediately covering them with his hand, as if he were putting some spell upon him. Opposite to the tall old chimney-piece, were two portraits: one of a gentleman with grey hair (though not by any means an old man) and black eyebrows, who was looking over some papers tied together with red tape; the other, of a lady, with a very placid and sweet expression of face, who was looking at me.

I believe I was turning about in search of Uriah's picture, when, a door at the farther end of the room opening, a gentleman entered, at sight of whom I turned to the first-mentioned portrait again, to make quite sure that it had not come out of its frame. But it was stationary; and as the gentleman advanced into the light, I saw that he was some years older than when he had had his picture painted.

'Miss Betsey Trotwood,' said the gentleman, 'pray walk in. I was engaged for the moment, but you'll excuse my being busy. You know my motive. I have but one in life.'

Miss Betsey thanked him, and we went into his room, which was furnished as an office, with books, papers, tin boxes, and so forth. It looked into a garden, and had an iron safe let into the wall; so immediately over the mantelshelf, that I wondered, as I sat down, how the sweeps got round it when they swept the chimney.

'Well, Miss Trotwood,' said Mr Wickfield – for I soon found that it was he, and that he was a lawyer, and steward of the estates of a rich gentleman of the county – 'what wind blows you here? Not an ill wind, I hope?'

'No,' replied my aunt, 'I have not come for any law.'

'That's right, ma'am,' said Mr Wickfield. 'You had better come for anything else.'

His hair was quite white now, though his eyebrows were still black. He had a very agreeable face, and, I thought, was handsome. There was a certain richness in his complexion, which I had been long accustomed, under Peggotty's tuition, to connect with port wine; and I fancied it was in his voice too, and referred his growing corpulency to the same cause. He was very cleanly dressed, in a blue coat, striped waistcoat, and nankeen trousers; and his fine frilled shirt and cambric neckcloth looked unusually soft and white, reminding my strolling fancy (I call to mind) of the plumage on the breast of a swan.

'This is my nephew,' said my aunt.

'Wasn't aware you had one, Miss Trotwood,' said Mr Wickfield.

'My grandnephew, that is to say,' observed my aunt.

'Wasn't aware you had a grandnephew, I give you my word,' said Mr Wickfield.

'I have adopted him,' said my aunt, with a wave of her hand, importing that his knowledge and his ignorance were all one to her, 'and I have brought him here to put him to a school where he may be thoroughly well taught and well treated. Now, tell me where that school is, and what it is, and all about it.'

'Before I can advise you properly,' said Mr Wickfield – 'the old question, you know – what's your motive in this?'

'Deuce take the man!' exclaimed my aunt. 'Always fishing for motives, when they're on the surface! Why, to make the child happy and useful.'

'It must be a mixed motive, I think,' said Mr Wickfield, shaking his head and smiling incredulously.

'A mixed fiddlestick!' returned my aunt. 'You claim to have one plain motive in all you do yourself. You don't suppose, I hope, that you are the only plain dealer in the world?'

'Aye, but I have only one motive in life, Miss Trotwood,' he rejoined, smiling. 'Other people have dozens, scores, hundreds. I have only one. There's the difference. However, that's beside the question. The best school? Whatever the motive, you want the best?'

My aunt nodded assent.

'At the best we have,' said Mr Wickfield, considering, 'your nephew couldn't board just now.'

'But he could board somewhere else, I suppose?' suggested my aunt.

Mr Wickfield thought I could. After a little discussion, he proposed to take my aunt to the school, that she might see it and judge for herself; also, to take her, with the same object, to two or three houses where he thought I could be boarded. My aunt embracing the proposal, we were all three going out together, when he stopped and said: 'Our little friend here might have some motive, perhaps, for objecting to the arrangements. I think we had better leave him behind.'

My aunt seemed disposed to contest the point; but to facilitate matters I said I would gladly remain behind, if they pleased; and returned into Mr Wickfield's office, where I sat down again in the chair I had first occupied, to await their return.

It so happened that this chair was opposite a narrow passage, which ended in the little circular room where I had seen Uriah Heep's pale face looking out of the window. Uriah, having taken the pony to a neighbouring stable, was at work at a desk in this room, which had a brass frame on the top to hang papers upon, and on which the writing he was making a copy of was then hanging. Though his face was towards me, I thought, for some time, the writing being between us, that he could not see me; but looking that way more attentively, it made me uncomfortable to observe that, every now and then, his sleepless eyes would come below the writing like two red suns, and stealthily stare at me for I dare say a whole minute at

a time, during which his pen went, or pretended to go, as cleverly as ever. I made several attempts to get out of their way – such as standing on a chair to look at a map on the other side of the room, and poring over the columns of a Kentish newspaper – but they always attracted me back again; and whenever I looked towards those two red suns, I was sure to find them, either just rising or just setting.

At length, much to my relief, my aunt and Mr Wickfield came back, after a pretty long absence. They were not so successful as I could have wished; for though the advantages of the school were undeniable, my aunt had not approved of any of the boarding-houses proposed for me.

'It's very unfortunate,' said my aunt. 'I don't know what to do, Trot.'

'It *does* happen unfortunately,' said Mr Wickfield. 'But I'll tell you what you can do, Miss Trotwood.'

'What's that?' enquired my aunt.

'Leave your nephew here, for the present. He's a quiet fellow. He won't disturb me at all. It's a capital house for study. As quiet as a monastery, and almost as roomy. Leave him here.'

My aunt evidently liked the offer, though she was delicate of accepting it. So did I.

'Come, Miss Trotwood,' said Mr Wickfield. 'This is the way out of the difficulty. It's only a temporary arrangement, you know. If it don't act well, or don't quite accord with our mutual convenience, he can easily go to the right about. There will be time to find some better place for him in the meanwhile. You had better determine to leave him here for the present!'

'I am very much obliged to you,' said my aunt; 'and so is he, I see; but – '

'Come! I know what you mean,' cried Mr Wickfield. 'You shall not be oppressed by the receipt of favours, Miss Trotwood. You may pay for him if you like. We won't be hard about terms, but you shall pay if you will.'

'On that understanding,' said my aunt, 'though it doesn't lessen the real obligation, I shall be very glad to leave him.'

'Then come and see my little housekeeper,' said Mr Wickfield.

We accordingly went up a wonderful old staircase – with a balustrade so broad that we might have gone up that, almost as easily – and into a shady old drawing-room, lighted by some three or four of the quaint windows I had looked up at from the street; which had old oak seats in them, that seemed to have come of the same trees as the shining oak floor, and the great beams in the ceiling. It was a prettily furnished room, with a piano and some lively furniture in red and green, and some flowers. It seemed to be all old nooks and corners; and in every nook and corner there was some queer little table, or cupboard, or bookcase, or seat, or something or other, that made me think there was not such another good corner in the room; until I looked at the next one, and found it equal to it, if not better. On everything there was the same air of retirement and cleanliness that marked the house outside.

Mr Wickfield tapped at a door in a corner of the panelled wall, and a girl of about my own age came quickly out and kissed him. On her face, I saw immediately the placid and sweet expression of the lady whose picture had looked at me downstairs. It seemed to my imagination as if the portrait had grown womanly, and the original remained a child. Although her face was quite bright and happy, there was a tranquillity about it, and about her – a quiet, good, calm spirit – that I never have forgotten; that I never shall forget.

This was his little housekeeper, his daughter Agnes, Mr Wickfield said. When I heard how he said it, and saw how he held her hand, I guessed what the one motive of his life was.

She had a little basket-trifle hanging at her side, with keys in it; and she looked as staid and as discreet a housekeeper as the old house could have. She listened to her father as he told her about me, with a pleasant face; and when he had concluded, proposed to my aunt that we should go upstairs and see my room. We all went together; she before us. And a glorious old room it was, with more oak beams, and diamond panes, and the broad balustrade going all the way up to it.

I cannot call to mind where or when, in my childhood, I had seen a stained glass window in a church. Nor do I recollect its subject. But I know that when I saw her turn round, in the grave light of the old staircase, and wait for us, above, I thought of that window; and that I associated something of its tranquil brightness with Agnes Wickfield ever afterwards.

My aunt was as happy as I was, in the arrangement made for me; and we went down to the drawing-room again, well pleased and gratified. As she would not hear of staying to dinner, lest she should by any chance fail to arrive at home with the grey pony before dark, and as I apprehend Mr Wickfield knew her too well to argue any point with her, some lunch was provided for her there, and Agnes went back to her governess, and Mr Wickfield to his office. So we were left to take leave of one another without any restraint.

She told me that everything would be arranged for me by Mr Wickfield, and that I should want for nothing, and gave me the kindest words and the best advice.

'Trot,' said my aunt in conclusion, 'be a credit to yourself, to me, and Mr Dick, and Heaven be with you!'

I was greatly overcome, and could only thank her, again and again, and send my love to Mr Dick.

'Never,' said my aunt, 'be mean in anything; never be false; never be cruel. Avoid those three vices, Trot, and I can always be hopeful of you.'

I promised, as well as I could, that I would not abuse her kindness or forget her admonition.

'The pony's at the door,' said my aunt, 'and I am off! Stay here.'

With these words she embraced me hastily, and went out of the room, shutting the door after her. At first I was startled by so abrupt a departure, and almost feared I had displeased her; but when I looked into the street, and saw how dejectedly she got into the chaise, and drove away without looking up, I understood her better, and did not do her that injustice.

By five o'clock, which was Mr Wickfield's dinner-hour, I had mustered up my spirits again, and was ready for my knife and fork. The cloth was only laid for us two; but Agnes was waiting in the drawing-room before dinner, went down with her father, and sat opposite to him at table. I doubted whether he could have dined without her.

We did not stay there, after dinner, but came upstairs into the drawing-room again; in one snug corner of which, Agnes set glasses for her father, and a decanter of port wine. I thought he would have missed its usual flavour, if it had been put there for him by any other hands.

There he sat, taking his wine, and taking a good deal of it, for two hours; while Agnes played on the piano, worked, and talked to him and me. He was, for the most part, gay and cheerful with us; but sometimes his eyes rested on her, and he fell into a brooding state, and was silent. She always observed this quickly, as I thought, and always roused him with a question or caress. Then he came out of his meditation, and drank more wine.

Agnes made the tea, and presided over it; and the time passed away after it, as after dinner, until she went to bed; when her father took her in his arms and kissed her, and, she being gone, ordered candles in his office. Then I went to bed too.

But in the course of the evening I had rambled down to the door, and a little way along the street, that I might have another peep at the old houses, and the grey Cathedral; and might think of my coming through that old city on my journey, and of my passing the very house I lived in, without knowing it. As I came back, I saw Uriah Heep shutting up the office; and feeling friendly towards everybody, went in and spoke to him, and at parting gave him my hand. But oh, what a clammy hand his was! as ghostly to the touch as to the sight! I rubbed mine afterwards, to warm it, *and to rub his off*.

It was such an uncomfortable hand that, when I went to my room, it was still cold and wet upon my memory. Leaning out of the window, and seeing one of the faces on the beam ends looking at me sideways, I fancied it was Uriah Heep got up there somehow, and shut him out in a hurry.

CHAPTER 16

I Am a New Boy in More Senses than One

Next morning, after breakfast, I entered on school life again. I went, accompanied by Mr Wickfield, to the scene of my future studies – a grave building in a courtyard, with a learned air about it that seemed very well suited to the stray rooks and jackdaws who came down from the Cathedral towers to walk with a clerkly bearing on the grass-plot – and was introduced to my new master, Doctor Strong.

Doctor Strong looked almost as rusty, to my thinking, as the tall iron rails and gates outside the house; and almost as stiff and heavy as the great stone urns that flanked them, and were set up, on the top of the redbrick wall, at regular distances all round the court, like sublimated skittles, for Time to play at. He was in his library (I mean Doctor Strong was), with his clothes not particularly well brushed, and his hair not particularly well combed; his knee-smalls unbraced; his long black gaiters unbuttoned; and his shoes yawning like two caverns on the hearth-rug. Turning upon me a lustreless eye, that reminded me of a long-forgotten blind old horse who once used to crop the grass, and tumble over the graves in Blunderstone churchyard, he said he was glad to see me; and then he gave me his hand, which I didn't know what to do with, as it did nothing for itself.

But sitting at work, not far from Doctor Strong, was a very pretty young lady – whom he called Annie, and who was his daughter, I supposed – who got me out of my difficulty by kneeling down to put Doctor Strong's shoes on, and button his gaiters, which she did with great cheerfulness and quickness. When she had finished, and we were going out to the schoolroom, I was much surprised to hear Mr Wickfield, in bidding her good-morning, address her as 'Mrs Strong;' and I was wondering could she be Doctor Strong's son's wife, or could she be Mrs Doctor Strong, when Doctor Strong himself unconsciously enlightened me.

'By the by, Wickfield,' he said, stopping in a passage with his hand on my shoulder; 'you have not found any suitable provision for my wife's cousin yet?'

'No,' said Mr Wickfield; 'no; not yet.'

'I could wish it done as soon as it *can* be done, Wickfield,' said Doctor Strong, 'for Jack Maldon is needy and idle, and of those two bad things, worse things sometimes come. What does Doctor Watts say,' he added, looking at me, and moving his head to the time of his quotation, ' "Satan finds some mischief still for idle hands to do." '

'Egad, Doctor,' returned Mr Wickfield, 'if Doctor Watts knew mankind, he might have written, with as much truth, "Satan finds some mischief still for busy hands to do." The busy people achieve their full share of mischief in the world, you may rely upon it. What have the people been about who have been the busiest in getting money, and in getting power, this century or two? No mischief?'

'Jack Maldon will never be very busy in getting either, I expect,' said Doctor Strong, rubbing his chin thoughtfully.

'Perhaps not,' said Mr Wickfield; 'and you bring me back to the question, with an apology for digressing. No, I have not been able to dispose of Mr Jack Maldon yet. I believe,' he said this with some hesitation, 'I penetrate your motive, and it makes the thing more difficult.'

'My motive,' returned Doctor Strong, 'is to make some suitable provision for a cousin, and an old playfellow, of Annie's.'

'Yes, I know,' said Mr Wickfield; 'at home or abroad.'

'Aye!' replied the Doctor, apparently wondering why he emphasised those words so much. 'At home or abroad.'

'Your own expression, you know,' said Mr Wickfield. 'Or abroad.'

'Surely,' the Doctor answered. 'Surely. One or other.'

'One or other? Have you no choice?' asked Mr Wickfield.

'No,' returned the Doctor.

'No?' with astonishment.

'Not the least.'

'No motive,' said Mr Wickfield, 'for meaning abroad, and not at home?'

'No,' returned the Doctor.

'I am bound to believe you, and of course I do believe you,' said Mr Wickfield. 'It might have simplified my office very much, if I had known it before. But I confess I entertained another impression.'

Doctor Strong regarded him with a puzzled and doubting look, which almost immediately subsided into a smile that gave me great encouragement; for it was full of amiability and sweetness, and there was a simplicity in it, and indeed in his whole manner, when the studious, pondering frost upon it was got through, very attractive and hopeful to a young scholar like me. Repeating 'no,' and 'not the least,' and other short assurances to the same purport, Doctor Strong jogged on before us, at a queer, uneven pace; and we followed: Mr Wickfield looking grave, I observed, and shaking his head to himself, without knowing that I saw him.

The schoolroom was a pretty large hall, on the quietest side of the house, confronted by the stately stare of some half-dozen of the great urns, and commanding a peep of an old secluded garden belonging to the Doctor, where the peaches were ripening on the sunny south wall. There were two great aloes, in tubs, on the turf outside the windows; the broad hard leaves of which plant (looking as if they were made of painted tin) have ever since, by association, been symbolical to me of silence and retirement. About five-and-twenty boys were studiously engaged at their books when we went in, but they rose to give the Doctor good-morning, and remained standing when they saw Mr Wickfield and me.

'A new boy, young gentlemen,' said the Doctor; 'Trotwood Copperfield.'

One Adams, who was the head-boy, then stepped out of his place and welcomed me. He looked like a young clergyman, in his white cravat, but he was very affable and good-humoured; and he showed me my place, and presented me to the masters in a gentlemanly way that would have put me at my ease, if anything could.

It seemed to me so long, however, since I had been among such boys, or among any companions of my own age, except Mick Walker and Mealy Potatoes, that I felt as strange as ever I have done in all my life. I was so conscious of having passed through scenes of which they could have no knowledge, and of having acquired experiences foreign to my age, appearance, and condition as one of them, that I half believed it was an imposture to come there as an ordinary little schoolboy. I had become, in the Murdstone and Grinby time, however short or long it may have been, so unused to the sports and games of boys, that I knew I was awkward and inexperienced in the commonest things belonging to them. Whatever I had learnt, had so slipped away from me in the sordid cares of my life from day to night, that now, when I was examined about what I knew, I knew nothing, and was put into the lowest form of the school. But, troubled as I was, by my want of boyish skill, and of book-learning too, I was made infinitely more uncomfortable by the consideration, that, in what I did know, I was much farther removed from my companions than in what I did not. My mind ran upon what they would think, if they knew of my familiar acquaintance with the King's Bench prison? Was there anything about me which would reveal my proceedings in connection with the Micawber family – all those pawnings, and sellings, and suppers – in spite of myself? Suppose some of the boys had seen me coming through Canterbury, wayworn and ragged, and should find me out? What would they say, who made so light of money, if they could know how I scraped my halfpence together, for the purchase of my daily saveloy and beer, or my slices of pudding? How would it affect them, who were so innocent of London life, and London streets, to discover how knowing I was (and was ashamed to be) in some of the meanest phases of both? All this ran in my head so much, on that first day at Doctor Strong's, that I felt distrustful of my slightest look and gesture; shrunk within myself whensoever I was approached by one of my new schoolfellows; and hurried off the minute school was over, afraid of committing myself in my response to any friendly notice or advance.

But there was such an influence in Mr Wickfield's old house, that when I knocked at it, with my new school-books under my arm, I began to feel my uneasiness softening away. As I went up to my airy old room, the grave shadow of the staircase seemed to fall upon my doubts and fears, and to make the past more indistinct. I sat there sturdily conning my books, until dinner-time (we were out of school for good at three); and went down, hopeful of becoming a passable sort of boy yet.

Agnes was in the drawing-room, waiting for her father, who was detained by someone in his office. She met me with her pleasant smile, and asked me how I liked the school. I told her I should like it very much, I hoped; but I was a little strange to it at first.

'*You* have never been to school,' I said, 'have you?'

'Oh, yes! Every day.'

'Ah, but you mean here, at your own home?'

'Papa couldn't spare me to go anywhere else,' she answered, smiling and shaking her head. 'His housekeeper must be in his house, you know.'

'He is very fond of you, I am sure,' I said.

She nodded 'Yes,' and went to the door to listen for his coming up, that she might meet him on the stairs. But as he was not there, she came back again.

'Mama has been dead ever since I was born,' she said, in her quiet way. 'I only know her picture, downstairs. I saw you looking at it yesterday. Did you think whose it was?'

I told her yes, because it was so like herself.

'Papa says so too,' said Agnes, pleased. 'Hark! That's papa now?'

Her bright calm face lighted up with pleasure as she went to meet him, and as they came in, hand in hand. He greeted me cordially; and told me I should certainly be happy under Doctor Strong, who was one of the gentlest of men.

'There may be some, perhaps – I don't know that there are – who abuse his kindness,' said Mr Wickfield. 'Never be one of those, Trotwood, in anything. He is the least suspicious of mankind; and whether that's a merit, or whether it's a blemish, it deserves consideration in all dealings with the Doctor, great or small.'

He spoke, I thought, as if he were weary, or dissatisfied with

something; but I did not pursue the question in my mind, for dinner was just then announced, and we went down and took the same seats as before.

We had scarcely done so, when Uriah Heep put in his red head and his lank hand at the door, and said: 'Here's Mr Maldon begs the favour of a word, sir.'

'I am but this moment quit of Mr Maldon,' said his master.

'Yes, sir,' returned Uriah; 'but Mr Maldon has come back, and he begs the favour of a word.'

As he held the door open with his hand, Uriah looked at me, and looked at Agnes, and looked at the dishes, and looked at the plates, and looked at every object in the room, I thought – yet seemed to look at nothing, he made such an appearance all the while of keeping his red eyes dutifully on his master.

'I beg your pardon. It's only to say, on reflection,' observed a voice behind Uriah, as Uriah's head was pushed away, and the speaker's substituted – 'pray excuse me for this intrusion – that as it seems I have no choice in the matter, the sooner I go abroad the better. My cousin Annie did say, when we talked of it, that she liked to have her friends within reach rather than to have them banished, and the old Doctor – '

'Doctor Strong, was that?' Mr Wickfield interposed gravely.

'Doctor Strong, of course,' returned the other; 'I call him the old Doctor – it's all the same, you know.'

'I *don't* know,' returned Mr Wickfield.

'Well, Doctor Strong,' said the other. 'Doctor Strong was of the same mind, I believe. But as it appears from the course you take with me that he has changed his mind, why there's no more to be said, except that the sooner I am off the better. Therefore, I thought I'd come back and say, that the sooner I am off the better. When a plunge is to be made into the water, it's of no use lingering on the bank.'

'There shall be as little lingering as possible, in your case, Mr Maldon, you may depend upon it,' said Mr Wickfield.

'Thank'ee,' said the other. 'Much obliged. I don't want to look a gift-horse in the mouth, which is not a gracious thing to do; otherwise, I dare say, my cousin Annie could easily arrange it in her own way. I suppose Annie would only have to say to the old Doctor – '

'Meaning that Mrs Strong would only have to say to her husband – do I follow you?' said Mr Wickfield.

'Quite so,' returned the other ' – would only have to say, that she wanted such and such a thing to be so and so; and it would be so and so, as a matter of course.'

'And why as a matter of course, Mr Maldon?' asked Mr Wickfield, sedately eating his dinner.

'Why, because Annie's a charming young girl, and the old Doctor – Doctor Strong, I mean – is not quite a charming young boy,' said Mr Jack Maldon, laughing. 'No offence to anybody, Mr Wickfield. I only mean that I suppose some compensation is fair and reasonable in that sort of marriage.'

'Compensation to the lady, sir?' asked Mr Wickfield gravely.

'To the lady, sir,' Mr Jack Maldon answered, laughing. But appearing to remark that Mr Wickfield went on with his dinner in the same sedate, immovable manner, and that there was no hope of making him relax a muscle of his face, he added:

'However, I have said what I came back to say, and, with another apology for this intrusion, I may take myself off. Of course I shall observe your directions, in considering the matter as one to be arranged between you and me solely, and not to be referred to, up at the Doctor's.'

'Have you dined?' asked Mr Wickfield, with a motion of his hand towards the table.

'Thank'ee. I am going to dine,' said Mr Maldon, 'with my cousin Annie. Goodbye!'

Mr Wickfield, without rising, looked after him thoughtfully as he went out. He was rather a shallow sort of young gentleman, I thought, with a handsome face, a rapid utterance, and a confident bold air. And this was the first I ever saw of Mr Jack Maldon, whom I had not expected to see so soon, when I heard the Doctor speak of him that morning.

When we had dined, we went upstairs again, where everything went on exactly as on the previous day. Agnes set the glasses and decanters in the same corner, and Mr Wickfield sat down to drink, and drank a good deal. Agnes played the piano to him, sat by him, and worked and talked, and played some games at dominoes with me. In good time she made tea; and afterwards, when I brought down my books, looked into them, and showed me what she knew of them (which was no slight matter, though she said it was), and what was the best way to learn and understand them. I see her, with her modest, orderly, placid manner, and I hear her beautiful calm voice, as I write these words. The influence for all good, which she came to exercise over me at a later time, begins already to descend upon my breast. I love little Em'ly, and I don't love Agnes – no, not at all in that way – but I feel that there are goodness, peace, and truth, wherever Agnes is; and that the soft light of the coloured window in the church, seen long ago, falls on her always, and on me when I am near her, and on everything around.

The time having come for her withdrawal for the night, and she having left us, I gave Mr Wickfield my hand, preparatory to going away myself. But he checked me and said, 'Should you like to stay with us, Trotwood, or to go elsewhere?'

'To stay,' I answered quickly.

'You are sure?'

'If you please. If I may!'

'Why, it's but a dull life that we lead here, boy, I am afraid,' he said.

'Not more dull for me than Agnes, sir. Not dull at all!'

'Than Agnes,' he repeated, walking slowly to the great chimney-piece, and leaning against it. 'Than Agnes!'

He had drank wine that evening (or I fancied it), until his eyes were bloodshot. Not that I could see them now, for they were cast down, and shaded by his hand; but I had noticed them a little while before.

'Now I wonder,' he muttered, 'whether my Agnes tires of me. When should I ever tire of her! But that's different – that's quite different.'

He was musing – not speaking to me; so I remained quiet.

'A dull old house,' he said, 'and a monotonous life; but I must have her near me. I must keep her near me. If the thought that I may die and leave my darling, or that my darling may die and

leave me, comes, like a spectre to distress my happiest hours, and is only to be drowned in – '

He did not supply the word; but pacing slowly to the place where he had sat, and mechanically going through the action of pouring wine from the empty decanter, set it down and paced back again.

'If it is miserable to bear when she is here,' he said, 'what would it be and she away? No, no, no. I cannot try that.'

He leaned against the chimney-piece, brooding so long that I could not decide whether to run the risk of disturbing him by going, or to remain quietly where I was, until he should come out of his reverie. At length he roused himself, and looked about the room until his eyes encountered mine.

'Stay with us, Trotwood, eh?' he said in his usual manner, and as if he were answering something I had just said. 'I am glad of it. You are company to us both. It is wholesome to have you here. Wholesome for me, wholesome for Agnes, wholesome perhaps for all of us.'

'I am sure it is for me, sir,' I said. 'I am so glad to be here.'

'That's a fine fellow!' said Mr Wickfield. 'As long as you are glad to be here, you shall stay here.' He shook hands with me upon it, and clapped me on the back; and told me that when I had anything to do at night after Agnes had left us, or when I wished to read for my own pleasure, I was free to come down to his room, if he were there, and if I desired it for company's sake, and to sit with him. I thanked him for his consideration; and, as he went down soon afterwards, and I was not tired, went down too, with a book in my hand, to avail myself, for half an hour, of his permission.

But, seeing a light in the little round office, and immediately feeling myself attracted towards Uriah Heep, who had a sort of fascination for me, I went in there instead. I found Uriah reading a great fat book, with such demonstrative attention, that his lank forefinger followed up every line as he read, and made clammy tracks along the page (or so I fully believed) like a snail.

'You are working late tonight, Uriah,' says I.

'Yes, Master Copperfield,' says Uriah.

As I was getting on the stool opposite, to talk to him more conveniently, I observed that he had not such a thing as a smile about him, and that he could only widen his mouth and make two hard creases down his cheeks, one on each side, to stand for one.

'I am not doing office-work, Master Copperfield,' said Uriah.

'What work, then?' I asked.

'I am improving my legal knowledge, Master Copperfield,' said Uriah. 'I am going through *Tidd's Practice*. Oh, what a writer Mr Tidd is, Master Copperfield!'

My stool was such a tower of observation, that as I watched him reading on again, after this rapturous exclamation, and following up the lines with his forefinger, I observed that his nostrils, which were thin and pointed, with sharp dints in them, had a singular and most uncomfortable way of expanding and contracting themselves – that they seemed to twinkle instead of his eyes, which hardly ever twinkled at all.

'I suppose you are quite a great lawyer?' I said, after looking at him for some time.

'Me, Master Copperfield?' said Uriah. 'Oh, no! I'm a very 'umble person.'

It was no fancy of mine about his hands, I observed; for he frequently ground the palms against each other as if to squeeze them dry and warm, besides often wiping them, in a stealthy way, on his pocket-handkerchief.

'I am well aware that I am the 'umblest person going,' said Uriah Heep modestly, 'let the other be where he may. My mother is likewise a very 'umble person. We live in an 'umble abode, Master Copperfield, but have much to be thankful for. My father's former calling was 'umble. He was a sexton.'

'What is he now?' I asked.

'He is a partaker of glory at present, Master Copperfield,' said Uriah Heep. 'But we have much to be thankful for. How much have I to be thankful for in living with Mr Wickfield!'

I asked Uriah if he had been with Mr Wickfield long.

'I have been with him going on four year, Master Copperfield,' said Uriah, shutting up his book, after carefully marking the place where he had left off. 'Since a year after my father's death. How much have I to be thankful for, in that! How much have I to be thankful for, in Mr Wickfield's kind intention to give me my articles, which would otherwise not lay within the 'umble means of mother and self!'

'Then, when your articled time is over, you'll be a regular lawyer, I suppose?' said I.

'With the blessing of Providence, Master Copperfield,' returned Uriah.

'Perhaps you'll be a partner in Mr Wickfield's business, one of these days,' I said, to make myself agreeable; 'and it will be Wickfield and Heep, or Heep late Wickfield.'

'Oh, no, Master Copperfield,' returned Uriah, shaking his head, 'I am much too 'umble for that!'

He certainly did look uncommonly like the carved face on the beam outside my window as he sat, in his humility, eyeing me sideways, with his mouth widened, and the creases in his cheeks.

'Mr Wickfield is a most excellent man, Master Copperfield,' said Uriah. 'If you have known him long, you know it, I am sure, much better than I can inform you.'

I replied that I was certain he was; but that I had not known him long myself, though he was a friend of my aunt's.

'Oh, indeed, Master Copperfield,' said Uriah. 'Your aunt is a sweet lady, Master Copperfield!'

He had a way of writhing when he wanted to express enthusiasm, which was very ugly; and which diverted my attention from the compliment he had paid my relation to the snaky twistings of his throat and body.

'A sweet lady, Master Copperfield!' said Uriah Heep. 'She has a great admiration for Miss Agnes, Master Copperfield, I believe?'

I said, 'Yes,' boldly; not that I knew anything about it, Heaven forgive me!

'I hope you have, too, Master Copperfield,' said Uriah. 'But I am sure you must have.'

'Everybody must have,' I returned.

'Oh, thank you, Master Copperfield,' said Uriah Heep, 'for

that remark! It is so true! 'Umble as I am, I know it is so true! Oh, thank you, Master Copperfield!'

He writhed himself quite off his stool in the excitement of his feelings, and, being off, began to make arrangements for going home.

'Mother will be expecting me,' he said, referring to a pale, inexpressive-faced watch in his pocket, 'and getting uneasy; for though we are very 'umble, Master Copperfield, we are much attached to one another. If you would come and see us, any afternoon, and take a cup of tea at our lowly dwelling, mother would be as proud of your company as I should be.'

I said I should be glad to come.

'Thank you, Master Copperfield,' returned Uriah, putting his book away upon a shelf. – 'I suppose you stop here, some-time, Master Copperfield?'

I said I was going to be brought up there, I believed, as long as I remained at school.

'Oh, indeed!' exclaimed Uriah. 'I should think *you* would come into the business at last, Master Copperfield!'

I protested that I had no views of that sort, and that no such scheme was entertained in my behalf by anybody; but Uriah insisted on blandly replying to all my assurances, 'Oh, yes, Master Copperfield, I should think you would, indeed!' and, 'Oh, indeed, Master Copperfield, I should think you would, certainly!' over and over again. Being, at last, ready to leave the office for the night, he asked me if it would suit my convenience to have the light put out; and on my answering, 'Yes,' instantly extinguished it. After shaking hands with me – his hand felt like a fish, in the dark – he opened the door into the street a very little, and crept out, and shut it, leaving me to grope my way back into the house, which cost me some trouble and a fall over his stool. This was the proximate cause, I suppose, of my dreaming about him, for what appeared to me to be half the night; and dreaming, among other things, that he had launched Mr Peggotty's house on a piratical expedition, with a black flag at the mast-head, bearing the inscription, 'Tidd's Practice', under which diabolical ensign he was carrying me and little Em'ly to the Spanish Main, to be drowned.

I got a little the better of my uneasiness when I went to school next day, and a good deal the better next day, and so shook it off by degrees that in less than a fortnight I was quite at home and happy among my new companions. I was awkward enough in their games, and backward enough in their studies; but custom would improve me in the first respect, I hoped, and hard work in the second. Accordingly, I went to work very hard, both in play and in earnest, and gained great commendation; and in a very little while the Murdstone and Grinby life became so strange to me that I hardly believed in it, while my present life grew so familiar that I seemed to have been leading it a long time.

Doctor Strong's was an excellent school; as different from Mr Creakle's as good is from evil. It was very gravely and decorously ordered, and on a sound system; with an appeal, in everything, to the honour and good faith of the boys, and an avowed intention to rely on their possession of those qualities unless they proved themselves unworthy of it, which worked wonders. We all felt that we had a part in the management of the place, and in sustaining its character and dignity. Hence we soon became warmly attached to it – I am sure I did, for one, and I never knew, in all my time, of any other boy being otherwise – and learnt with a good will, desiring to do it credit. We had noble games out of hours, and plenty of liberty; but even then, as I remember, we were well spoken of in the town, and rarely did any disgrace, by our appearance or manner, to the reputation of Doctor Strong and Doctor Strong's boys.

Some of the higher scholars boarded in the Doctor's house, and through them I learned, at second hand, some particulars of the Doctor's history. As, how he had not yet been married twelve months to the beautiful young lady I had seen in the study, whom he had married for love; for she had not a sixpence and had a world of poor relations (so our fellows said) ready to swarm the Doctor out of house and home. Also, how the Doctor's cogitating manner was attributable to his being always engaged in looking out for Greek roots; which, in my innocence and ignorance, I supposed to be a botanical furor on the Doctor's part – especially as he always looked at the ground when he walked about – until I understood that they were roots of words, with a view to a new Dictionary which he had in contemplation. Adams, our head-boy, who had a turn for mathematics, had made a calculation, I was informed, of the time this Dictionary would take in completing on the Doctor's plan, and at the Doctor's rate of going. He considered that it might be done in one thousand six hundred and forty-nine years, counting from the Doctor's last, or sixty-second birthday.

But the Doctor himself was the idol of the whole school; and it must have been a badly composed school if he had been anything else, for he was the kindest of men, with a simple faith in him that might have touched the stone hearts of the very urns upon the wall. As he walked up and down that part of the courtyard which was at that side of the house, with the stray rooks and jackdaws looking after him with their heads cocked slily, as if they knew how much more knowing they were in worldly affairs than he, if any sort of vagabond could only get near enough to his creaking shoes to attract his attention to one sentence of a tale of distress, that vagabond was made for the next two days. It was so notorious in the house that the masters and head-boys took pains to cut these marauders off at angles, and to get out of windows, and turn them out of the courtyard, before they could make the Doctor aware of their presence; which was sometimes happily effected within a few yards of him, without his knowing anything of the matter, as he jogged to and fro. Outside his own domain, and unprotected, he was a very sheep for the shearers. He would have taken his gaiters off his legs to give away. In fact, there was a story current among us (I have no idea, and never had, on what authority, but I have believed it for so many years that I feel quite certain it is true) that on a frosty day, one wintertime, he actually did bestow his gaiters on a beggar-woman, who occasioned some scandal in the neighbourhood by exhibiting a fine infant from door to door, wrapped in those garments, which were universally recognised, being as well known in the vicinity as the Cathedral. The legend added that the only person who did not identify them was the Doctor himself, who, when they were shortly afterwards displayed at the door of a little second-hand shop of no very good repute, where such things were taken in exchange for gin, was more than once observed to handle them approvingly, as if admiring some curious novelty in the pattern, and considering them an improvement on his own.

It was very pleasant to see the Doctor with his pretty young wife. He had a fatherly, benignant way of showing his fondness for her, which seemed in itself to express a good man. I often saw them walking in the garden where the peaches were, and I sometimes had a nearer observation of them in the study or the parlour. She appeared to me to take great care of the Doctor, and to like him very much, though I never thought her vitally interested in the Dictionary; some cumbrous fragments of which work the Doctor always carried in his pockets, and in the lining of his hat, and generally seemed to be expounding to her as they walked about.

I saw a good deal of Mrs Strong, both because she had taken a liking for me on the morning of my introduction to the Doctor, and was always afterwards kind to me, and interested in me; and because she was very fond of Agnes, and was often backwards and forwards at our house. There was a curious constraint between her and Mr Wickfield, I thought (of whom she seemed to be afraid), that never wore off. When she came there of an evening, she always shrunk from accepting his escort home, and ran away with me instead. And sometimes, as we were running gaily across the Cathedral yard together, expecting to meet nobody, we would meet Mr Jack Maldon, who was always surprised to see us.

Mrs Strong's mama was a lady I took great delight in. Her name was Mrs Markleham; but our boys used to call her the Old Soldier, on account of her generalship, and the skill with which she marshalled great forces of relations against the Doctor. She was a little, sharp-eyed woman, who used to wear, when she was dressed, one unchangeable cap ornamented with some artificial flowers, and two artificial butterflies supposed to be hovering above the flowers. There was a superstition among us that this cap had come from France, and could only originate in the workmanship of that ingenious nation; but all I certainly know about it is that it always made its appearance of an evening, wheresoever Mrs Markleham made *her* appearance; that it was carried about to friendly meetings in a Hindu basket; that the butterflies had the gift of trembling constantly; and that they improved the shining hours at Doctor Strong's expense, like busy bees.

I observed the Old Soldier – not to adopt the name disrespectfully – to pretty good advantage, on a night which is made memorable to me by something else I shall relate. It was the night of a little party at the Doctor's, which was given on the occasion of Mr Jack Maldon's departure for India, whither he was going as a cadet, or something of that kind; Mr Wickfield having at length arranged the business. It happened to be the Doctor's birthday, too. We had had a holiday, had made presents to him in the morning, had made a speech to him through the head-boy, and had cheered him until we were hoarse, and until he had shed tears. And now, in the evening,

Mr Wickfield, Agnes, and I, went to have tea with him in his private capacity.

Mr Jack Maldon was there, before us. Mrs Strong, dressed in white, with cherry-coloured ribbons, was playing the piano, when we went in; and he was leaning over her to turn the leaves. The clear red and white of her complexion was not so blooming and flower-like as usual, I thought, when she turned round; but she looked very pretty, wonderfully pretty.

'I have forgotten, Doctor,' said Mrs Strong's mama, when we were seated, 'to pay you the compliments of the day – though they are, as you may suppose, very far from being mere compliments in my case. Allow me to wish you many happy returns.'

'I thank you, ma'am,' replied the Doctor.

'Many, many, many, happy returns,' said the Old Soldier. 'Not only for your own sake, but for Annie's, and John Maldon's, and many other people's. It seems but yesterday to me, John, when you were a little creature, a head shorter than Master Copperfield, making baby love to Annie behind the gooseberry bushes in the back garden.'

'My dear mama,' said Mrs Strong, 'never mind that now.'

'Annie, don't be absurd,' returned her mother. 'If you are to blush to hear of such things, now you are an old married woman, when are you not to blush to hear of them?'

'Old?' exclaimed Mr Jack Maldon. 'Annie? Come!'

'Yes, John,' returned the Soldier. 'Virtually an old married woman. Although not old by years – for when did you ever hear me say, or who has ever heard me say, that a girl of twenty was old by years? – your cousin *is* the wife of the Doctor, and, as such, what I have described her. It is well for you, John, that your cousin is the wife of the Doctor. You have found in him an influential and kind friend, who will be kinder yet, I venture to predict, if you deserve it. I have no false pride. I never hesitate to admit, frankly, that there are some members of our family who want a friend. You were one yourself, before your cousin's influence raised up one for you.'

The Doctor, in the goodness of his heart, waved his hand as if to make light of it, and save Mr Jack Maldon from any further reminder. But Mrs Markleham changed her chair for one next the Doctor's, and, putting her fan on his coat-sleeve, said: 'No, really, my dear Doctor, you must excuse me if I appear to dwell on this rather, because I feel so very strongly. I call it quite my monomania, it is such a subject of mine. You are a blessing to us. You really are a boon, you know.'

'Nonsense, nonsense,' said the Doctor.

'No, no, I beg your pardon,' retorted the Old Soldier. 'With nobody present but our dear and confidential friend Mr Wickfield, I cannot consent to be put down. I shall begin to assert the privileges of a mother-in-law, if you go on like that, and scold you. I am perfectly honest and outspoken. What I am saying is what I said when you first overpowered me with surprise – you remember how surprised I was? – by proposing for Annie. Not that there was anything so very much out of the way, in the mere fact of the proposal – it would be ridiculous to say that! – but because, you having known her poor father and having known her from a baby six months old, I hadn't thought of you in such a light at all, or indeed as a marrying man in any way – simply that, you know.'

'Aye, aye,' returned the Doctor good-humouredly. 'Never mind.'

'But I *do* mind,' said the Old Soldier, laying her fan upon his lips. 'I mind very much. I recall these things that I may be contradicted if I am wrong. Well! Then I spoke to Annie, and I told her what had happened. I said, "My dear, here's Doctor Strong has positively been and made you the subject of a handsome declaration and an offer." Did I press it in the least? No. I said, "Now, Annie, tell me the truth this moment; is your heart free?" "Mama," she said, crying, "I am extremely young" – which was perfectly true – "and I hardly know if I have a heart at all." "Then, my dear," I said, "you may rely upon it, it's free. At all events, my love," said I, "Doctor Strong is in an agitated state of mind, and must be answered. He cannot be kept in his present state of suspense." "Mama," said Annie, still crying, "would he be unhappy without me? If he would, I honour and respect him so much that I think I will have him." So it was settled. And then, and not till then, I said to Annie, "Annie, Doctor Strong will not only be your husband, but he will represent your late father; he will represent the head of our family, he will represent the wisdom and station, and I may say the means, of our family; and will be, in short, a Boon to it." I used the word at the time, and I have used it again, today. If I have any merit, it is consistency.'

The daughter had sat quite silent and still during this speech, with her eyes fixed on the ground; her cousin standing near her, and looking on the ground too. She now said very softly, in a trembling voice: 'Mama, I hope you have finished?'

'No, my dear Annie,' returned the Soldier, 'I have not quite finished. Since you ask me, my love, I reply that I have *not*. I complain that you really are a little unnatural towards your own family; and as it is of no use complaining to you, I mean to complain to your husband. Now, my dear Doctor, do look at that silly wife of yours.'

As the Doctor turned his kind face, with its smile of simplicity and gentleness, towards her, she drooped her head more. I noticed that Mr Wickfield looked at her steadily.

'When I happened to say to that naughty thing, the other day,' pursued her mother, shaking her head and her fan at her playfully, 'that there was a family circumstance she might mention to you – indeed, I think, was bound to mention – she said that to mention it was to ask a favour; and that, as you were too generous, and as for her to ask was always to have, she wouldn't.'

'Annie, my dear,' said the Doctor, 'that was wrong. It robbed me of a pleasure.'

'Almost the very words I said to her!' exclaimed her mother. 'Now really, another time, when I know what she would tell you but for this reason, and won't, I have a great mind, my dear Doctor, to tell you myself.'

'I shall be glad if you will,' returned the Doctor.

'Shall I?'

'Certainly.'

'Well, then, I will!' said the Old Soldier. 'That's a bargain.'

And having, I suppose, carried her point, she tapped the Doctor's hand several times with her fan (which she kissed first), and returned triumphantly to her former station.

Some more company coming in, among whom were the two masters and Adams, the talk became general; and it naturally turned on Mr Jack Maldon, and his voyage, and the country he was going to, and his various plans and prospects. He was to leave that night, after supper, in a post-chaise, for Gravesend, where the ship in which he was to make the voyage lay; and was to be gone – unless he came home on leave, or for his health – I don't know how many years. I recollect it was settled by general consent that India was quite a misrepresented country, and had nothing objectionable in it but a tiger or two, and a little heat in the warm part of the day. For my own part, I looked on Mr Jack Maldon as a modern Sinbad, and pictured him the bosom friend of all the Rajahs in the East, sitting under canopies, smoking curly golden pipes – a mile long, if they could be straightened out.

Mrs Strong was a very pretty singer, as I knew, who often heard her singing by herself. But whether she was afraid of singing before people, or was out of voice that evening, it was certain that she couldn't sing at all. She tried a duet, once, with her cousin Maldon, but could not so much as begin; and afterwards, when she tried to sing by herself, although she began sweetly, her voice died away on a sudden, and left her quite distressed, with her head hanging down over the keys. The good Doctor said she was nervous, and, to relieve her, proposed a round game at cards; of which he knew as much as of the art of playing the trombone. But I remarked that the Old Soldier took him into custody directly, for her partner; and instructed him, as the first preliminary of initiation, to give her all the silver he had in his pocket.

We had a merry game, not made the less merry by the Doctor's mistakes, of which he committed an innumerable quantity, in spite of the watchfulness of the butterflies, and to their great aggravation. Mrs Strong had declined to play, on the ground of not feeling very well; and her cousin Maldon had excused himself because he had some packing to do. When he had done it, however, he returned, and they sat together, talking, on the sofa. From time to time she came and looked over the Doctor's hand, and told him what to play. She was very pale, as she bent over him, and I thought her finger trembled as she pointed out the cards; but the Doctor was quite happy in her attention, and took no notice of this, if it were so.

At supper, we were hardly so gay. Everyone appeared to feel that a parting of that sort was an awkward thing, and that the nearer it approached, the more awkward it was. Mr Jack Maldon tried to be very talkative, but was not at his ease, and made matters worse. And they were not improved, as it appeared to me, by the Old Soldier; who continually recalled passages of Mr Jack Maldon's youth.

The Doctor, however, who felt, I am sure, that he was making everybody happy, was well pleased, and had no suspicion but that we were all at the utmost height of enjoyment.

'Annie, my dear,' said he, looking at his watch, and filling his glass, 'it is past your cousin Jack's time, and we must not detain him, since time and tide – both concerned in this case – wait for no man. Mr Jack Maldon, you have a long voyage and a strange country before you; but many men have had both, and many men will have both, to the end of time. The winds you are going to tempt have wafted thousands upon thousands to fortune, and brought thousands upon thousands happily back.'

'It's an affecting thing,' said Mrs Markleham, 'however it's viewed, it's affecting – to see a fine young man one has known from an infant going away to the other end of the world, leaving all he knows behind, and not knowing what's before him. A young man really well deserves constant support and patronage,' looking at the Doctor, 'who makes such sacrifices.'

'Time will go fast with you, Mr Jack Maldon,' pursued the Doctor, 'and fast with all of us. Some of us can hardly expect, perhaps, in the natural course of things, to greet you on your return. The next best thing is to hope to do it, and that's my case. I shall not weary you with good advice. You have long had a good model before you, in your cousin Annie. Imitate her virtues as nearly as you can.'

Mrs Markleham fanned herself, and shook her head.

'Farewell, Mr Jack,' said the Doctor, standing up; on which we all stood up. 'A prosperous voyage out, a thriving career abroad, and a happy return home!'

We all drank the toast, and all shook hands with Mr Jack Maldon, after which he hastily took leave of the ladies who were there, and hurried to the door, where he was received, as he got into the chaise, with a tremendous broadside of cheers discharged by our boys, who had assembled on the lawn for the purpose. Running in among them to swell the ranks, I was very near the chaise when it rolled away; and I had a lively impression made upon me, in the midst of the noise and dust, of having seen Mr Jack Maldon rattle past with an agitated face, and something cherry-coloured in his hand.

After another broadside for the Doctor, and another for the Doctor's wife, the boys dispersed, and I went back into the house, where I found the guests all standing in a group about the Doctor, discussing how Mr Jack Maldon had gone away, and how he had borne it, and how he had felt it, and all the rest of it. In the midst of these remarks, Mrs Markleham cried: 'Where's Annie!'

No Annie was there; and when they called to her, no Annie replied. But all pressing out of the room in a crowd, to see what was the matter, we found her lying on the hall floor. There was great alarm at first, until it was found that she was in a swoon, and that the swoon was yielding to the usual means of recovery; when the Doctor, who had lifted her head upon his knee, put her curls aside with his hand, and said, looking around: 'Poor Annie! She's so faithful and tender-hearted! It's the parting from her old playfellow and friend – her favourite cousin – that has done this. Ah! It's a pity! I am very sorry!'

When she opened her eyes, and saw where she was, and that we were all standing about her, she arose with assistance, turning her head, as she did so, to lay it on the Doctor's shoulder – or to hide it, I don't know which. We went into the drawing-room, to leave her with the Doctor and her mother; but she said, it seemed, that she was better than she had been since morning, and that she would rather be brought among us; so they brought her in, looking very white and weak, I thought, and set her on the sofa.

'Annie, my dear,' said her mother, doing something to her dress. 'See here! You have lost a bow. Will anybody be so good as find a ribbon; a cherry-coloured ribbon?'

It was the one she had worn at her bosom. We all looked for it – I myself looked everywhere, I am certain – but nobody could find it.

'Do you recollect where you had it last, Annie?' said her mother.

I wondered how I could have thought she looked white, or anything but burning red, when she answered that she had had it safe, a little while ago, she thought, but it was not worth looking for.

Nevertheless, it was looked for again, and still not found. She entreated that there might be no more searching; but it was still sought for in a desultory way, until she was quite well, and the company took their departure.

We walked very slowly home, Mr Wickfield, Agnes, and I – Agnes and I admiring the moonlight, and Mr Wickfield scarcely raising his eyes from the ground. When we, at last, reached our own door, Agnes discovered that she had left her little reticule behind. Delighted to be of any service to her, I ran back to fetch it.

I went into the supper-room where it had been left, which was deserted and dark. But a door of communication between that and the Doctor's study, where there was a light, being open, I passed on there, to say what I wanted, and to get a candle.

The Doctor was sitting in his easy-chair by the fireside, and his young wife was on a stool at his feet. The Doctor, with a complacent smile, was reading aloud some manuscript explanation or statement of a theory out of that interminable Dictionary, and she was looking up at him. But with such a face as I never saw; it was so beautiful in its form, it was so ashy pale, it was so fixed in its abstraction, it was so full of a wild, sleep-walking, dreamy horror of I don't know what. The eyes were wide open, and her brown hair fell in two rich clusters on her shoulders, and on her white dress, disordered by the want of the lost ribbon. Distinctly as I recollect her look, I cannot say of what it was expressive. I cannot even say of what it is expressive to me now, rising again before my older judgement. Penitence, humiliation, shame, pride, love, and trustfulness – I see them all; and in them all, I see that horror of I don't know what.

My entrance, and my saying what I wanted, roused her. It disturbed the Doctor, too, for, when I went back to replace the candle I had taken from the table, he was patting her head, in his fatherly way, and saying he was a merciless drone to let her tempt him into reading on; and he would have her go to bed.

But she asked him, in a rapid, urgent manner, to let her stay – to let her feel assured (I heard her murmur some broken words to this effect) that she was in his confidence that night. And as she turned again towards him, after glancing at me as I left the room and went out at the door, I saw her cross her hands upon his knee, and look up at him with the same face, something quieted, as he resumed his reading.

It made a great impression on me, and I remembered it a long time afterwards, as I shall have occasion to narrate when the time comes.

CHAPTER 17

Somebody Turns Up

It has not occurred to me to mention Peggotty since I ran away; but, of course, I wrote her a letter almost as soon as I was housed at Dover, and another and a longer letter, containing all particulars fully related, when my aunt took me formally under her protection. On my being settled at Doctor Strong's, I wrote to her again, detailing my happy condition and prospects. I never could have derived anything like the pleasure from spending the money Mr Dick had given me, that I felt in sending a gold half-guinea to Peggotty, per post, enclosed in this last letter, to discharge the sum I had borrowed of her; in which epistle, not before, I mentioned about the young man with the donkey-cart.

To these communications Peggotty replied as promptly, if not as concisely, as a merchant's clerk. Her utmost powers of expression (which were certainly not great in ink) were exhausted in the attempt to write what she felt on the subject of my journey. Four sides of incoherent and interjectional beginnings of sentences, that had no end, except blots, were inadequate to afford her any relief. But the blots were more expressive to me than the best composition; for they showed me that Peggotty had been crying all over the paper, and what could I have desired more?

I made out, without much difficulty, that she could not take quite kindly to my aunt yet. The notice was too short after so long a prepossession the other way. We never knew a person, she wrote; but to think that Miss Betsey should seem to be so different from what she had been thought to be was a Moral! That was her word. She was evidently still afraid of Miss Betsey, for she sent her grateful duty to her but timidly; and she was evidently afraid of me, too, and entertained the probability of my running away again soon; if I might judge from the repeated hints she threw out that the coach-fare to Yarmouth was always to be had of her for the asking.

She gave me one piece of intelligence which affected me very much, namely, that there had been a sale of the furniture at our old home, and that Mr and Miss Murdstone were gone away, and the house was shut up, to be let or sold. God knows I had had no part in it while they remained there, but it pained me to think of the dear old place as altogether abandoned; of the weeds growing tall in the garden, and the fallen leaves lying thick and wet upon the paths. I imagined how the winds of winter would howl round it, how the cold rain would beat upon the window-glass, how the moon would make ghosts on the walls of the empty rooms, watching their solitude all night. I thought afresh of the grave in the churchyard, underneath the tree; and it seemed as if the house were dead too, now, and all connected with my father and mother were faded away.

There was no other news in Peggotty's letters. Mr Barkis was an excellent husband, she said, though still a little near; but we all had our faults, and she had plenty (though I am sure I don't know what they were); and he sent his duty, and my little bed-room was always ready for me. Mr Peggotty was well, and Ham was well, and Mrs Gummidge was but poorly, and little Em'ly wouldn't send her love, but said that Peggotty might send it, if she liked.

All this intelligence I dutifully imparted to my aunt, only reserving to myself the mention of little Em'ly, to whom I instinctively felt that she would not very tenderly incline. While I was yet new at Doctor Strong's, she made several excursions over to Canterbury to see me, and always at unseasonable hours; with the view, I suppose, of taking me by surprise. But finding me well employed, and bearing a good character, and hearing on all hands that I rose fast in the school, she soon discontinued these visits. I saw her on a Saturday, every third or fourth week, when I went over to Dover for a treat; and I saw Mr Dick every alternate Wednesday, when he arrived by stagecoach at noon, to stay until next morning.

On these occasions Mr Dick never travelled without a leathern writing-desk, containing a supply of stationery and the Memorial; in relation to which document he had a notion that time was beginning to press now, and that it really must be got out of hand.

I return to the Doctor's after the party

Mr Dick was very partial to gingerbread. To render his visits the more agreeable, my aunt had instructed me to open a credit for him at a cake-shop, which was hampered with the stipulation that he should not be served with more than one shilling's worth in the course of any one day. This and the reference of all his little bills at the county inn where he slept, to my aunt, before they were paid, induced me to suspect that he was only allowed to rattle his money, and not to spend it. I found on further investigation that this was so, or at least there was an agreement between him and my aunt that he should account to her for all his disbursements. As he had no idea of deceiving her, and always desired to please her, he was thus made chary of launching into expense. On this point, as well as on all other possible points, Mr Dick was convinced that my aunt was the wisest and most wonderful of women; as he repeatedly told me with infinite secrecy, and always in a whisper.

'Trotwood,' said Mr Dick, with an air of mystery, after imparting this confidence to me, one Wednesday; 'who's the man that hides near our house and frightens her?'

'Frightens my aunt, sir?'

Mr Dick nodded. 'I thought nothing would have frightened her,' he said, 'for she's – ' here he whispered softly, 'don't mention it – the wisest and most wonderful of women.' Having said which, he drew back, to observe the effect which this description of her made upon me.

'The first time he came,' said Mr Dick, 'was – let me see – sixteen hundred and forty-nine was the date of King Charles's execution. I think you said sixteen hundred and forty-nine?'

'Yes, sir.'

'I don't know how it can be,' said Mr Dick, sorely puzzled, and shaking his head. 'I don't think I am as old as that.'

'Was it in that year that the man appeared, sir?' I asked.

'Why, really,' said Mr Dick, 'I don't see how it can have been in that year, Trotwood. Did you get that date out of history?'

'Yes, sir.'

'I suppose history never lies, does it?' said Mr Dick, with a gleam of hope.

'Oh, dear, no, sir!' I replied, most decisively. I was ingenuous and young, and I thought so.

'I can't make it out,' said Mr Dick, shaking his head. 'There's something wrong somewhere. However, it was very soon after the mistake was made of putting some of the trouble out of King Charles's head into my head that the man first came. I was walking out with Miss Trotwood after tea, just at dark, and there he was, close to our house.'

'Walking about?' I enquired.

'Walking about?' repeated Mr Dick. 'Let me see. I must recollect a bit. N–no, no; he was not walking about.'

I asked, as the shortest way to get at it, what he *was* doing.

'Well, he wasn't there at all,' said Mr Dick, 'until he came up behind her, and whispered. Then she turned round and fainted, and I stood still and looked at him, and he walked away; but that he should have been hiding ever since (in the ground or somewhere) is the most extraordinary thing!'

'*Has* he been hiding ever since?' I asked.

'To be sure he has,' retorted Mr Dick, nodding his head gravely. 'Never came out till last night! We were walking last night and he came up behind her again, and I knew him again.'

'And did he frighten my aunt again?'

'All of a shiver,' said Mr Dick, counterfeiting that affection and making his teeth chatter. 'Held by the palings. Cried. But, Trotwood, come here,' getting me close to him, that he might whisper very softly; 'why did she give him money, boy, in the moonlight?'

'He was a beggar, perhaps.'

Mr Dick shook his head, as utterly renouncing the suggestion; and having replied a great many times, and with great confidence, 'No beggar, no beggar, no beggar, sir!' went on to say that from his window he had afterwards, and late at night, seen my aunt give this person money outside the garden rails in the moonlight, who then slunk away – into the ground again, as he thought probable – and was seen no more; while my aunt came hurriedly and secretly back into the house, and had, even that morning, been quite different from her usual self; which preyed on Mr Dick's mind.

I had not the least belief, in the outset of this story, that the unknown was anything but a delusion of Mr Dick's, and one of the line of that ill-fated Prince who occasioned him so much difficulty; but after some reflection I began to entertain the question whether an attempt, or threat of an attempt, might have been twice made to take poor Mr Dick himself from under my aunt's protection, and whether my aunt, the strength of whose kind feeling towards him I knew from herself, might have been induced to pay a price for his peace and quiet. As I was already much attached to Mr Dick, and very solicitous for his welfare, my fears favoured this supposition; and for a long time his Wednesday hardly ever came round, without my entertaining a misgiving that he would not be on the coach-box as usual. There he always appeared, however, grey-headed, laughing, and happy; and he never had anything more to tell of the man who could frighten my aunt.

These Wednesdays were the happiest days of Mr Dick's life; they were far from being the least happy of mine. He soon became known to every boy in the school; and though he never took an active part in any game but kite-flying, was as deeply interested in all our sports as anyone among us. How often have I seen him, intent upon a match at marbles or pegtop, looking on with a face of unutterable interest, and hardly breathing at the critical times! How often, at hare and hounds, have I seen him mounted on a little knoll, cheering the whole field on to action, and waving his hat above his grey head, oblivious of King Charles the Martyr's head, and all belonging to it! How many summer hours have I known to be but blissful minutes to him in the cricket-field! How many winter days have I seen him, standing blue-nosed, in the snow and east wind, looking at the boys going down the long slide, and clapping his worsted gloves in rapture!

He was an universal favourite, and his ingenuity in little things was transcendent. He could cut oranges into such devices as none of us had an idea of. He could make a boat out of anything, from a skewer upwards. He could turn crampbones into chessmen; fashion Roman chariots from old court cards; make spoked wheels out of cotton reels, and birdcages of old wire. But he was greatest of all, perhaps, in the articles of string and straw; with which we were all persuaded he could do anything that could be done by hands.

Mr Dick's renown was not long confined to us. After a few Wednesdays, Doctor Strong himself made some enquiries of me about him, and I told him all my aunt had told me; which interested the Doctor so much that he requested, on the occasion of his next visit, to be presented to him. This ceremony I performed; and the Doctor begging Mr Dick, whensoever he should not find me at the coach-office, to come on there, and rest himself until our morning's work was over, it soon passed into a custom for Mr Dick to come on as a matter of course, and, if we were a little late, as often happened on a Wednesday, to walk about the courtyard, waiting for me. Here he made the acquaintance of the Doctor's beautiful young wife (paler than formerly, all this time; more rarely seen by me or anyone, I think; and not so gay, but not less beautiful), and so became more and more familiar by degrees, until, at last, he would come into the school and wait. He always sat in a particular corner, on a particular stool, which was called 'Dick,' after him; here he would sit, with his grey head bent forward, attentively listening to whatever might be going on, with a profound veneration for the learning he had never been able to acquire.

This veneration Mr Dick extended to the Doctor, whom he thought the most subtle and accomplished philosopher of any age. It was long before Mr Dick ever spoke to him otherwise than bareheaded; and even when he and the Doctor had struck up quite a friendship, and would walk together by the hour, on that side of the courtyard which was known among us as The Doctor's Walk, Mr Dick would pull off his hat at intervals to show his respect for wisdom and knowledge. How it ever came about that the Doctor began to read out scraps of the famous Dictionary, in these walks, I never knew; perhaps he felt it all the same, at first, as reading to himself. However, it passed into a custom, too; and Mr Dick, listening with a face shining with pride and pleasure, in his heart of hearts, believed the Dictionary to be the most delightful book in the world.

As I think of them going up and down before those school-room windows – the Doctor reading with his complacent smile, an occasional flourish of the manuscript, or grave motion of his head; and Mr Dick listening, enchained by interest, with his poor wits calmly wandering God knows where, upon the wings of hard words – I think of it as one of the pleasantest things, in a quiet way, that I have ever seen. I feel as if they might go walking to and fro for ever, and the world might somehow be the better for it – as if a thousand things it makes a noise about were not one half so good for it, or me.

Agnes was one of Mr Dick's friends, very soon; and in often coming to the house, he made acquaintance with Uriah. The friendship between himself and me increased continually, and it was maintained on this odd footing: that, while Mr Dick came professedly to look after me as my guardian, he always consulted me in any little matter of doubt that arose, and invariably guided himself by my advice; not only having a high respect for my native sagacity, but considering that I inherited a good deal from my aunt.

One Thursday morning, when I was about to walk with Mr Dick from the hotel to the coach-office before going back to school (for we had an hour's school before breakfast), I met Uriah in the street, who reminded me of the promise I had made to take tea with himself and his mother; adding, with a writhe, 'But I didn't expect you to keep it, Master Copperfield, we're so very 'umble.'

I really had not yet been able to make up my mind whether I liked Uriah or detested him; and I was very doubtful about it still, as I stood looking him in the face in the street. But I felt it quite an affront to be supposed proud, and said I only wanted to be asked.

'Oh, if that's all, Master Copperfield,' said Uriah, 'and it really isn't our 'umbleness that prevents you, will you come this evening? But if it is our 'umbleness, I hope you won't mind owning to it, Master Copperfield; for we are well aware of our condition.'

I said I would mention it to Mr Wickfield, and if he approved, as I had no doubt he would, I would come with pleasure. So, at six o'clock that evening, which was one of the early office evenings, I announced myself as ready to Uriah.

'Mother will be proud, indeed,' he said, as we walked away together. 'Or she would be proud, if it wasn't sinful, Master Copperfield.'

'Yet you didn't mind supposing *I* was proud this morning,' I returned.

'Oh, dear, no, Master Copperfield!' returned Uriah. 'Oh, believe me, no! Such a thought never came into my head! I shouldn't have deemed it at all proud if you had thought *us* too 'umble for you. Because we are so very 'umble.'

'Have you been studying much law lately?' I asked, to change the subject.

'Oh, Master Copperfield,' he said, with an air of self-denial, 'my reading is hardly to be called study. I have passed an hour or two in the evening, sometimes, with Mr Tidd.'

'Rather hard, I suppose?' said I.

'He is hard to *me* sometimes,' returned Uriah. 'But I don't know what he might be to a gifted person.'

After beating a little tune on his chin as we walked on, with the two forefingers of his skeleton right hand, he added: 'There are expressions, you see, Master Copperfield – Latin words and terms – in Mr Tidd, that are trying to a reader of my 'umble attainments.'

'Would you like to be taught Latin?' I said briskly. 'I will teach it you with pleasure, as I learn it.'

'Oh, thank you, Master Copperfield,' he answered, shaking his head. 'I am sure it's very kind of you to make the offer, but I am much too 'umble to accept it.'

'What nonsense, Uriah!'

'Oh, indeed you must excuse me, Master Copperfield! I am greatly obliged, and I should like it of all things, I assure you; but I am far too 'umble. There are people enough to tread upon me in my lowly state, without my doing outrage to their feelings by possessing learning. Learning ain't for me. A person like myself had better not aspire. If he is to get on in life, he must get on 'umbly, Master Copperfield!'

I never saw his mouth so wide, or the creases in his cheeks so deep, as when he delivered himself of these sentiments, shaking his head all the time, and writhing modestly.

'I think you are wrong, Uriah,' I said. 'I dare say there are several things that I could teach you, if you would like to learn them.'

'Oh, I don't doubt that, Master Copperfield,' he answered; 'not in the least. But not being 'umble yourself, you don't judge well, perhaps, for them that are. I won't provoke my betters with knowledge, thank you. I'm much too 'umble. Here is my 'umble dwelling, Master Copperfield!'

We entered a low, old-fashioned room, walked straight into from the street, and found there, Mrs Heep, who was the dead image of Uriah, only short. She received me with the utmost humility, and apologised to me for giving her son a kiss, observing that, lowly as they were, they had their natural affections, which they hoped would give no offence to anyone. It was a perfectly decent room, half parlour and half kitchen, but not at all a snug room. The tea-things were set upon the table, and the kettle was boiling on the hob. There was a chest of drawers with an escritoire top, for Uriah to read or write at of an evening; there was Uriah's blue bag lying down and vomiting papers; there was a company of Uriah's books commanded by Mr Tidd; there was a corner cupboard; and there were the usual articles of furniture. I don't remember that any individual object had a bare, pinched, spare look; but I do remember that the whole place had.

It was perhaps a part of Mrs Heep's humility, that she still wore weeds. Notwithstanding the lapse of time that had occurred since Mr Heep's decease, she still wore weeds. I think there was some compromise in the cap; but otherwise she was as weedy as in the early days of her mourning.

'This is a day to be remembered, my Uriah, I am sure,' said Mrs Heep, making the tea, 'when Master Copperfield pays us a visit.'

'I said you'd think so, mother,' said Uriah.

'If I could have wished father to remain among us for any reason,' said Mrs Heep, 'it would have been, that he might have known his company this afternoon.'

I felt embarrassed by these compliments; but I was sensible, too, of being entertained as an honoured guest, and I thought Mrs Heep an agreeable woman.

'My Uriah,' said Mrs Heep, 'has looked forward to this, sir, a long while. He had his fears that our 'umbleness stood in the way, and I joined in them myself. 'Umble we are, 'umble we have been, 'umble we shall ever be,' said Mrs Heep.

'I am sure you have no occasion to be so, ma'am,' I said, 'unless you like.'

'Thank you, sir,' retorted Mrs Heep. 'We know our station and are thankful in it.'

I found that Mrs Heep gradually got nearer to me, and that Uriah gradually got opposite to me, and that they respectfully plied me with the choicest of the eatables on the table. There was nothing particularly choice there, to be sure; but I took the will for the deed, and felt that they were very attentive. Presently they began to talk about aunts, and then I told them about mine; and about fathers and mothers, and then I told them about mine; and then Mrs Heep began to talk about fathers-in-law, and then I began to tell her about mine – but stopped, because my aunt had advised me to observe a silence on that subject. A tender young cork, however, would have had no more chance against a pair of corkscrews, or a tender young tooth against a pair of dentists, or a little shuttlecock against two battledores, than I had against Uriah and Mrs Heep. They did just what they liked with me; and wormed things out of me that I had no desire to tell, with a certainty I blush to think of: the more especially as, in my juvenile frankness, I took some credit to myself for being so confidential, and felt that I was quite the patron of my two respectful entertainers.

They were very fond of one another, that was certain. I take it that had its effect upon me, as a touch of nature; but the skill with which the one followed up whatever the other said was a touch of art which I was still less proof against. When there was nothing more to be got out of me about myself (for on the Murdstone and Grinby life, and on my journey, I was dumb), they began about Mr Wickfield and Agnes. Uriah threw the ball to Mrs Heep, Mrs Heep caught it and threw it back to Uriah, Uriah kept it up a little while, then sent it back to Mrs Heep, and so they went on tossing it about until I had no idea who had got it, and was quite bewildered. The ball itself was always changing too. Now it was Mr Wickfield, now Agnes, now the excellence of Mr Wickfield, now my admiration of Agnes; now the extent of Mr Wickfield's business and resources, now our domestic life after dinner; now the wine that Mr Wickfield took, the reason why he took it, and the pity that it was he took so much; now one thing, now another, then everything at once; and all the time, without appearing to speak very often, or to do anything but sometimes encourage them a little, for fear they should be overcome by their humility and the honour of my company, I found myself perpetually letting out something or other that I had no business to let out, and seeing the effect of it in the twinkling of Uriah's dinted nostrils.

I had begun to be a little uncomfortable, and to wish myself well out of the visit, when a figure coming down the street passed the door – it stood open to air the room, which was warm, the weather being close for the time of year – came back again, looked in, and walked in, exclaiming loudly, 'Copperfield! Is it possible!'

It was Mr Micawber! It was Mr Micawber, with his eyeglass, and his walking-stick, and his shirt-collar, and his genteel air, and the condescending roll in his voice, all complete!

'My dear Copperfield,' said Mr Micawber, putting out his hand, 'this is indeed a meeting which is calculated to impress the mind with a sense of the instability and uncertainty of all human – in short, it is a most extraordinary meeting. Walking along the street, reflecting upon the probability of something turning up (of which I am at present rather sanguine), I find a young but valued friend turn up, who is connected with the most eventful period of my life; I may say, with the turning point of my existence. Copperfield, my dear fellow, how do you do?'

I cannot say – I really can*not* say – that I was glad to see Mr Micawber there; but I was glad to see him too, and shook hands with him heartily, enquiring how Mrs Micawber was.

'Thank you,' said Mr Micawber, waving his hand as of old, and settling his chin in his shirt-collar. 'She is tolerably convalescent. The twins no longer derive their sustenance from Nature's founts – in short,' said Mr Micawber, in one of his bursts of confidence, 'they are weaned – and Mrs Micawber is, at present, my travelling companion. She will be rejoiced, Copperfield, to renew her acquaintance with one who has proved himself in all respects a worthy minister at the sacred altar of friendship.'

I said I should be delighted to see her.

'You are very good,' said Mr Micawber.

Mr Micawber then smiled, settled his chin again, and looked about him.

'I have discovered my friend Copperfield,' said Mr Micawber genteelly, and without addressing himself particularly to anyone, 'not in solitude, but partaking of a social meal in company with a widow lady, and one who is apparently her offspring – in short,' said Mr Micawber, in another of his bursts of confidence, 'her son. I shall esteem it an honour to be presented.'

I could do no less, under these circumstances, than make Mr Micawber known to Uriah Heep and his mother; which I accordingly did. As they abased themselves before him, Mr Micawber took a seat, and waved his hand in his most courtly manner.

'Any friend of my friend Copperfield's,' said Mr Micawber, 'has a personal claim upon myself.'

'We are too 'umble, sir,' said Mrs Heep, 'my son and me, to be the friends of Master Copperfield. He has been so good as to take his tea with us, and we are thankful to him for his company; also to you, sir, for your notice.'

'Ma'am,' returned Mr Micawber, with a blow, 'you are very obliging; and what are you doing, Copperfield? Still in the wine-trade?'

I was excessively anxious to get Mr Micawber away; and replied, with my hat in my hand, and a very red face, I have no doubt, that I was a pupil at Doctor Strong's.

'A pupil?' said Mr Micawber, raising his eyebrows, 'I am extremely happy to hear it. Although a mind like my friend Copperfield's' – to Uriah and Mrs Heep – 'does not require that cultivation which, without his knowledge of men and things, it would require, still it is rich soil teeming with latent vegetation – in short,' said Mr Micawber, smiling, in another burst of confidence, 'it is an intellect capable of getting up the classics to any extent.'

Uriah, with his long hands slowly twining over one another, made a ghastly writhe from the waist upwards, to express his concurrence in this estimation of me.

'Shall we go and see Mrs Micawber, sir?' I said, to get Mr Micawber away.

'If you will do her that favour, Copperfield,' replied Mr Micawber, rising. 'I have no scruple in saying, in the presence of our friends here, that I am a man who has, for some years, contended against the pressure of pecuniary difficulties.' I knew he was certain to say something of this kind; he always would be so boastful about his difficulties. 'Sometimes I have risen superior to my difficulties. Sometimes my difficulties have – in short, have floored me. There have been times when I have administered a succession of faces to them; there have been times when they have been too many for me, and I have given in, and said to Mrs Micawber, in the words of Cato, "Plato, thou reasonest well." It's all up now. I can show fight no more. But at no time of my life,' said Mr Micawber, 'have I enjoyed a higher degree of satisfaction than in pouring my griefs (if I may describe difficulties, chiefly arising out of warrants of attorney and promissory notes at two and four months, by that word) into the bosom of my friend Copperfield.'

Mr Micawber closed this handsome tribute by saying, 'Mr Heep! Good-evening. Mrs Heep! Your servant,' and then walking out with me in his most fashionable manner, making a good deal of noise on the pavement with his shoes, and humming a tune as we went.

It was a little inn where Mr Micawber put up, and he occupied a little room in it, partitioned off from the commercial room, and strongly flavoured with tobacco smoke. I think it was over the kitchen, because a warm, greasy smell appeared to come up through the chinks in the floor, and there was a flabby perspiration on the walls. I know it was near the bar, on account of the smell of spirits and jingling of glasses. Here, recumbent on a small sofa, underneath a picture of a racehorse, with her head close to the fire, and her feet pushing the mustard off the dumb-waiter at the other end of the room, was Mrs Micawber, to whom Mr Micawber entered first, saying, 'My dear, allow me to introduce to you a pupil of Doctor Strong's.'

I noticed, by the by, that although Mr Micawber was just as much confused as ever about my age and standing, he always remembered, as a genteel thing, that I was a pupil of Doctor Strong's.

Mrs Micawber was amazed, but very glad to see me. I was very glad to see her too, and after an affectionate greeting on both sides, sat down on the small sofa near her.

'My dear,' said Mr Micawber, 'if you will mention to Copperfield what our present position is, which I have no doubt he will like to know, I will go and look at the paper the while, and see whether anything turns up among the advertisements.'

'I thought you were at Plymouth, ma'am,' I said to Mrs Micawber, as he went out.

'My dear Master Copperfield,' she replied, 'we went to Plymouth.'

'To be on the spot,' I hinted.

'Just so,' said Mrs Micawber. 'To be on the spot. But, the truth is, talent is not wanted in the Custom House. The local influence of my family was quite unavailing to obtain any employment in that department for a man of Mr Micawber's abilities. They would rather *not* have a man of Mr Micawber's abilities. He would only show the deficiency of the others. Apart from which,' said Mrs Micawber, 'I will not disguise from you, my dear Master Copperfield, that when that branch of my family which is settled in Plymouth became aware that Mr Micawber was accompanied by myself, and by little Wilkins and his sister, and by the twins, they did not receive him with that ardour which he might have expected, being so newly released from captivity. In fact,' said Mrs Micawber, lowering her voice – 'this is between ourselves – our reception was cool.'

'Dear me!' I said.

'Yes,' said Mrs Micawber. 'It is truly painful to contemplate

Somebody turns up

mankind in such an aspect, Master Copperfield, but our reception was, decidedly, cool. There is no doubt about it. In fact, that branch of my family which is settled in Plymouth became quite personal to Mr Micawber, before we had been there a week.'

I said, and thought, that they ought to be ashamed of themselves.

'Still, so it was,' continued Mrs Micawber. 'Under such circumstances, what could a man of Mr Micawber's spirit do? But one obvious course was left. To borrow of that branch of my family the money to return to London, and to return at any sacrifice.'

'Then you all came back again, ma'am?' I said.

'We all came back again,' replied Mrs Micawber. 'Since then, I have consulted other branches of my family on the course which it is most expedient for Mr Micawber to take – for I maintain that he must take some course, Master Copperfield,' said Mrs Micawber argumentatively. 'It is clear that a family of six, not including a domestic, cannot live upon air.'

'Certainly, ma'am,' said I.

'The opinion of those other branches of my family,' pursued Mrs Micawber, 'is that Mr Micawber should immediately turn his attention to coals.'

'To what, ma'am?'

'To coals,' said Mrs Micawber. 'To the coal trade. Mr Micawber was induced to think, on enquiry, that there might be an opening for a man of his talent in the Medway Coal Trade. Then, as Mr Micawber very properly said, the first step to be taken clearly was, to come and *see* the Medway. Which we came and saw. I say "we," Master Copperfield; for I never will,' said Mrs Micawber with emotion, 'I never will desert Mr Micawber.'

I murmured my admiration and approbation.

'We came,' repeated Mrs Micawber, 'and saw the Medway. My opinion of the coal trade on that river is, that it may require talent, but that it certainly requires capital. Talent, Mr Micawber has; capital, Mr Micawber has not. We saw, I think, the greater part of the Medway; and that is my individual conclusion. Being so near here, Mr Micawber was of opinion that it would be rash not to come on, and see the Cathedral. Firstly, on account of its being so well worth seeing, and our never having seen it; and secondly, on account of the great probability of something turning up in a cathedral town. We have been here,' said Mrs Micawber, 'three days. Nothing has, as yet, turned up; and it may not surprise you, my dear Master Copperfield, so much as it would a stranger, to know that we are at present waiting for a remittance from London, to discharge our pecuniary obligations at this hotel. Until the arrival of that remittance,' said Mrs Micawber, with much feeling, 'I am cut off from my home (I allude to lodgings in Pentonville), from my boy and girl, and from my twins.'

I felt the utmost sympathy for Mr and Mrs Micawber in this anxious extremity, and said as much to Mr Micawber, who now returned; adding that I only wished I had money enough to lend them the amount they needed. Mr Micawber's answer expressed the disturbance of his mind. He said, shaking hands

with me, 'Copperfield, you are a true friend; but when the worst comes to the worst, no man is without a friend who is possessed of shaving materials.' At this dreadful hint Mrs Micawber threw her arms round Mr Micawber's neck and entreated him to be calm. He wept; but so far recovered, almost immediately, as to ring the bell for the waiter, and bespeak a hot kidney pudding and a plate of shrimps for breakfast in the morning.

When I took my leave of them, they both pressed me so much to come and dine before they went away, that I could not refuse. But, as I knew I could not come next day, when I should have a good deal to prepare in the evening, Mr Micawber arranged that he would call at Doctor Strong's in the course of the morning (having a presentiment that the remittance would arrive by that post), and propose the day after, if it would suit me better. Accordingly I was called out of school next forenoon, and found Mr Micawber in the parlour; who had called to say that the dinner would take place as proposed. When I asked him if the remittance had come, he pressed my hand and departed.

As I was looking out of the window that same evening, it surprised me, and made me rather uneasy, to see Mr Micawber and Uriah Heep walk past, arm in arm: Uriah humbly sensible of the honour that was done him, and Mr Micawber taking a bland delight in extending his patronage to Uriah. But I was still more surprised, when I went to the little hotel next day at the appointed dinner hour, which was four o'clock, to find, from what Mr Micawber said, that he had gone home with Uriah, and had drunk brandy and water at Mrs Heep's.

'And I'll tell you what, my dear Copperfield,' said Mr Micawber, 'your friend Heep is a young fellow who might be attorney-general. If I had known that young man, at the period when my difficulties came to a crisis, all I can say is, that I believe my creditors would have been a great deal better managed than they were.'

I hardly understood how this could have been, seeing that Mr Micawber had paid them nothing at all as it was; but I did not like to ask. Neither did I like to say, that I hoped he had not been too communicative to Uriah; or to enquire if they had talked much about me. I was afraid of hurting Mr Micawber's feelings, or, at all events, Mrs Micawber's, she being very sensitive; but I was uncomfortable about it, too, and often thought about it afterwards.

We had a beautiful little dinner. Quite an elegant dish of fish; the kidney-end of a loin of veal, roasted; fried sausage-meat; a partridge and a pudding. There was wine, and there was strong ale; and after dinner Mrs Micawber made us a bowl of hot punch with her own hands.

Mr Micawber was uncommonly convivial. I never saw him such good company. He made his face shine with the punch, so that it looked as if it had been varnished all over. He got cheerfully sentimental about the town, and proposed success to it; observing that Mrs Micawber and himself had been made extremely snug and comfortable there, and that he never should forget the agreeable hours they had passed in Canterbury. He proposed me afterwards; and he, and Mrs Micawber, and I, took a review of our past acquaintance, in the course of which, we sold the property all over again. Then I proposed Mrs Micawber; or, at least, said, modestly, 'If you'll allow me, Mrs Micawber, I shall now have the pleasure of drinking *your* health, ma'am.' On which Mr Micawber delivered an eulogium on Mrs Micawber's character, and said she had ever been his guide, philosopher, and friend, and that he would recommend me, when I came to a marrying time of life, to marry such another woman, if such another woman could be found.

As the punch disappeared, Mr Micawber became still more friendly and convivial. Mrs Micawber's spirits becoming elevated, too, we sang 'Auld Lang Syne'. When we came to 'Here's a hand, my trusty frere,' we all joined hands round the table; and when we declared we would 'take a right gude Willie Waught,' and hadn't the least idea what it meant, we were really affected.

In a word, I never saw anybody so thoroughly jovial as Mr Micawber was, down to the very last moment of the evening, when I took a hearty farewell of himself and his amiable wife. Consequently, I was not prepared, at seven o'clock next morning, to receive the following communication, dated half-past nine in the evening; a quarter of an hour after I had left him.

MY DEAR YOUNG FRIEND – The die is cast – all is over. Hiding the ravages of care with a sickly mask of mirth, I have not informed you, this evening, that there is no hope of the remittance! Under these circumstances, alike humiliating to endure, humiliating to contemplate, and humiliating to relate, I have discharged the pecuniary liability contracted at this establishment, by giving a note of hand, made payable fourteen days after date at my residence, Pentonville, London. When it becomes due, it will not be taken up. The result is destruction. The bolt is impending, and the tree must fall.

Let the wretched man who now addresses you, my dear Copperfield, be a beacon to you through life. He writes with that intention, and in that hope. If he could think himself of so much use, one gleam of day might, by possibility, penetrate into the cheerless dungeon of his remaining existence – though his longevity is, at present (to say the least of it), extremely problematical.

This is the last communication, my dear Copperfield, you will ever receive
From
The
Beggared Outcast,

WILKINS MICAWBER

I was so shocked by the contents of this heart-rending letter, that I ran off directly towards the little hotel with the intention of taking it on my way to Doctor Strong's, and trying to soothe Mr Micawber with a word of comfort. But, halfway there, I met the London coach with Mr and Mrs Micawber up behind; Mr Micawber, the very picture of tranquil enjoyment, smiling at Mrs Micawber's conversation, eating walnuts out of a paper bag, with a bottle sticking out of his breast pocket. As they did not see me, I thought it best, all things considered, not to see

them. So, with a great weight taken off my mind, I turned into a by-street that was the nearest way to school, and felt, upon the whole, relieved that they were gone: though I still liked them very much, nevertheless.

CHAPTER 18

A Retrospect

My school-days! The silent gliding on of my existence – the unseen, unfelt progress of my life – from childhood up to youth! Let me think, as I look back upon that flowing water, now a dry channel overgrown with leaves, whether there are any marks along its course, by which I can remember how it ran.

A moment, and I occupy my place in the Cathedral, where we all went together, every Sunday morning, assembling first at school for that purpose. The earthy smell, the sunless air, the sensation of the world being shut out, the resounding of the organ through the black and white arched galleries and aisles are wings that take me back, and hold me hovering above those days, in a half-sleeping and half-waking dream.

I am not the last boy in the school. I have risen, in a few months, over several heads. But the first boy seems to me a mighty creature, dwelling afar off, whose giddy height is un-attainable. Agnes says 'No,' but I say 'Yes,' and tell her that she little thinks what stores of knowledge have been mastered by the wonderful Being, at whose place she thinks I, even I, weak aspirant, may arrive in time. He is not my private friend and public patron, as Steerforth was, but I hold him in a reverential respect. I chiefly wonder what he'll be, when he leaves Doctor Strong's, and what mankind will do to maintain any place against him.

But who is this that breaks upon me? This is Miss Shepherd, whom I love.

Miss Shepherd is a boarder at the Misses Nettingalls' estab-lishment. I adore Miss Shepherd. She is a little girl, in a spencer, with a round face and curly flaxen hair. The Misses Nettingalls' young ladies come to the Cathedral too. I cannot look upon my book, for I must look upon Miss Shepherd. When the choristers chant, I hear Miss Shepherd. In the service I mentally insert Miss Shepherd's name – I put her in among the Royal Family. At home, in my own room, I am sometimes moved to cry out, 'Oh, Miss Shepherd!' in a transport of love.

For some time, I am doubtful of Miss Shepherd's feelings, but, at length, Fate being propitious, we meet at the dancing-school. I have Miss Shepherd for my partner. I touch Miss Shepherd's glove, and feel a thrill go up the right arm of my jacket, and come out at my hair. I say nothing tender to Miss Shepherd, but we understand each other. Miss Shepherd and myself live but to be united.

Why do I secretly give Miss Shepherd twelve Brazil nuts for a present, I wonder? They are not expressive of affection, they are difficult to pack into a parcel of any regular shape, they are hard to crack, even in room doors, and they are oily when cracked; yet I feel that they are appropriate to Miss Shepherd. Soft, seedy biscuits, also, I bestow upon Miss Shepherd; and oranges innumerable. Once, I kiss Miss Shepherd in the cloakroom. Ecstasy! What are my agony and indignation next day when I hear a flying rumour that the Misses Nettingall have stood Miss Shepherd in the stocks for turning in her toes!

Miss Shepherd being the one pervading theme and vision of my life, how do I ever come to break with her? I can't conceive. And yet a coolness grows between Miss Shepherd and myself. Whispers reach me of Miss Shepherd having said she wished I wouldn't stare so, and having avowed a preference for Master Jones – for Jones! a boy of no merit whatever! The gulf between me and Miss Shepherd widens. At last, one day, I meet the Misses Nettingalls' establishment out walking. Miss Shepherd makes a face as she goes by, and laughs to her companion. All is over. The devotion of a life – it seems a life, it is all the same – is at an end; Miss Shepherd comes out of the morning service, and the Royal Family know her no more.

I am higher in the school, and no one breaks my peace. I am not at all polite, now, to the Misses Nettingalls' young ladies, and shouldn't dote on any of them, if they were twice as many and twenty times as beautiful. I think the dancing-school a tiresome affair, and wonder why the girls can't dance by them-selves, and leave us alone. I am growing great in Latin verses, and neglect the laces of my boots. Doctor Strong refers to me in public as a promising young scholar. Mr Dick is wild with joy, and my aunt remits me a guinea by the next post.

The shade of a young butcher rises, like the apparition of an armed head in Macbeth. Who is this young butcher? He is the terror of the youth of Canterbury. There is a vague belief abroad that the beef suet with which he anoints his hair gives him unnatural strength, and that he is a match for a man. He is a broad-faced, bull-necked young butcher, with rough red cheeks, an ill-conditioned mind, and an injurious tongue. His main use of this tongue is to disparage Doctor Strong's young gentlemen. He says publicly that if they want anything he'll give it 'em. He names individuals among them (myself included), whom he could undertake to settle with one hand, and the other tied behind him. He waylays the smaller boys to punch their unprotected heads, and calls challenges after me in the open streets. For these sufficient reasons I resolve to fight the butcher.

It is a summer evening, down in a green hollow, at the corner of a wall. I meet the butcher by appointment. I am attended by a select body of our boys; the butcher, by two other butchers, a young publican, and a sweep. The preliminaries are adjusted, and the butcher and myself stand face to face. In a moment the butcher lights ten thousand candles out of my left eyebrow. In another moment, I don't know where the wall is, or where I am, or where anybody is. I hardly know which is myself and which the butcher, we are always in such a tangle and tussle, knocking about upon the trodden grass. Sometimes I see the butcher, bloody but confident; sometimes I see nothing, and sit gasping on my second's knee; sometimes I go in at the butcher madly, and cut my knuckles open against his face, without appearing to discompose him at all. At last I awake, very queer about the head, as from a giddy sleep, and see the butcher walking off, congratulated by the two other butchers and the sweep and publican, and putting on his coat as he goes; from which I augur, justly, that the victory is his.

I am taken home in a sad plight, and I have beef-steaks put to my eyes, and am rubbed with vinegar and brandy, and find a great white puffy place bursting out on my upper lip, which swells immoderately. For three or four days I remain at home, a very ill-looking subject, with a green shade over my eyes; and I should be very dull, but that Agnes is a sister to me, and condoles with me, and reads to me, and makes the time light and happy. Agnes has my confidence completely, always; I tell her all about the butcher, and the wrongs he has heaped upon me; and she thinks I couldn't have done otherwise than fight the butcher, while she shrinks and trembles at my having fought him.

Time has stolen on unobserved, for Adams is not the head-boy in the days that are come now, nor has he been this many and many a day. Adams has left the school so long that when he comes back, on a visit to Doctor Strong, there are not many there, besides myself, who know him. Adams is going to be called to the bar almost directly, and is to be an advocate, and to wear a wig. I am surprised to find him a meeker man than I had thought, and less imposing in appearance. He has not staggered the world yet, either; for it goes on (as well as I can make out) pretty much the same as if he had never joined it.

A blank, through which the warriors of poetry and history march on in stately hosts that seem to have no end – and what comes next! *I* am the head-boy, now! I look down on the line of boys below me, with a condescending interest in such of them as bring to my mind the boy I was myself, when I first came there. That little fellow seems to be no part of me; I remember him as something left behind upon the road of life – as some-thing I have passed, rather than have actually been – and almost think of him as of someone else.

And the little girl I saw on that first day at Mr Wickfield's, where is she? Gone also. In her stead, the perfect likeness of the picture, a child likeness no more, moves about the house; and Agnes – my sweet sister, as I call her in my thoughts, my counsellor and friend, the better angel of the lives of all who come within her calm, good, self-denying influence – is quite a woman.

What other changes have come upon me, besides the changes in my growth and looks, and in the knowledge I have garnered all this while? I wear a gold watch and chain, a ring upon my little finger, and a long-tailed coat; and I use a great deal of bear's grease – which, taken in conjunction with the ring, looks bad. Am I in love again? I am. I worship the eldest Miss Larkins.

The eldest Miss Larkins is not a little girl. She is a tall, dark, black-eyed, fine figure of a woman. The eldest Miss Larkins is not a chicken; for the youngest Miss Larkins is not that, and the eldest must be three or four years older. Perhaps the eldest Miss Larkins may be about thirty. My passion for her is beyond all bounds.

The eldest Miss Larkins knows officers. It is an awful thing to bear. I see them speaking to her in the street. I see them cross the way to meet her, when her bonnet (she has a bright taste in bonnets) is seen coming down the pavement, accompanied by her sister's bonnet. She laughs and talks, and seems to like it. I spend a good deal of my own spare time in walking up and down to meet her. If I can bow to her once in the day (I know her to bow to, knowing Mr Larkins), I am happier. I deserve a bow now and then. The raging agonies I suffer on the night of the Race Ball, where I know the eldest Miss Larkins will be dancing with the military, ought to have some compensation, if there be even-handed justice in the world.

My passion takes away my appetite, and makes me wear my newest silk neckerchief continually. I have no relief but in putting on my best clothes, and having my boots cleaned over and over again. I seem then to be worthier of the eldest Miss Larkins. Everything that belongs to her, or is connected with her, is precious to me. Mr Larkins (a gruff old gentleman with a double chin, and one of his eyes immovable in his head) is fraught with interest to me. When I can't meet his daughter, I go where I am likely to meet him. To say, 'How do you do, Mr Larkins? Are the young ladies and all the family quite well?' seems so pointed that I blush.

I think continually about my age. Say I am seventeen, and say that seventeen is young for the eldest Miss Larkins, what of that? Besides I shall be one-and-twenty in no time almost. I regularly take walks outside Mr Larkins's house in the evening, though it cuts me to the heart to see the officers go in, or to hear them up in the drawing-room, where the eldest Miss Larkins plays the harp. I even walk, on two or three occasions, in a sickly, spoony manner, round and round the house after the family are gone to bed, wondering which is the eldest Miss Larkins's chamber (and pitching, I dare say now, on Mr Larkins's instead); wishing that a fire would burst out; that the assembled crowd would stand appalled; that I, dashing through them with a ladder, might rear it against her window, save her in my arms, go back for something she had left behind, and perish in the flames. For I am generally disinterested in my love, and think I could be content to make a figure before Miss Larkins, and expire – generally, but not always. Sometimes brighter visions rise before me. When I dress (the occupation of two hours) for a great ball given at the Larkins's (the anticipation of three weeks), I indulge my fancy with pleasing images. I picture myself taking courage to make a declaration to Miss Larkins. I picture Miss Larkins sinking her head upon my shoulder, and saying, 'Oh, Mr Copperfield, can I believe my ears!' I picture Mr Larkins waiting on me next morning, and saying, 'My dear Copperfield, my daughter has told me all. Youth is no objection. Here are twenty thousand pounds. Be happy!' I picture my aunt relenting, and blessing us; and Mr Dick and Doctor Strong being present at the marriage ceremony. I am a sensible fellow, I believe – I believe, on looking back, I mean – and modest, I am sure; but all this goes on notwithstanding.

I repair to the enchanted house, where there are lights, chattering, music, flowers, officers (I am sorry to see), and the eldest Miss Larkins, a blaze of beauty. She is dressed in blue, with blue flowers in her hair – forget-me-nots – as if *she* had any need to wear forget-me-nots! It is the first really grown-up party that I have ever been invited to, and I am a little uncomfortable; for I appear not to belong to anybody, and nobody appears to have anything to say to me, except Mr Larkins, who asks me how my schoolfellows are, which he needn't do, as I have not come there to be insulted.

But after I have stood in the doorway for some time, and feasted my eyes upon the goddess of my heart, she approaches me – she, the eldest Miss Larkins! – and asks me pleasantly, if I dance.

I stammer, with a bow, 'With you, Miss Larkins.'

'With no one else?' enquires Miss Larkins.

'I should have no pleasure in dancing with anyone else.'

Miss Larkins laughs and blushes (or I think she blushes), and says, 'Next time but one I shall be very glad.'

The time arrives. 'It is a waltz, I think,' Miss Larkins doubtfully observes, when I present myself. 'Do you waltz? If not, Captain Bailey – '

But I do waltz (pretty well, too, as it happens), and I take Miss Larkins out. I take her sternly from the side of Captain Bailey. He is wretched, I have no doubt; but he is nothing to me. I have been wretched, too. I waltz with the eldest Miss Larkins! I don't know where, among whom, or how long. I only know that I swim about in space, with a blue angel, in a state of blissful delirium, until I find myself alone with her in a little room, resting on a sofa. She admires a flower (pink camelia japonica, price half a crown) in my buttonhole. I give it her, and say: 'I ask an inestimable price for it, Miss Larkins.'

'Indeed! What is that?' returns Miss Larkins.

'A flower of yours, that I may treasure it as a miser does gold.'

'You're a bold boy,' says Miss Larkins. 'There.'

She gives it me, not displeased; and I put it to my lips, and then into my breast. Miss Larkins, laughing, draws her hand through my arm, and says, 'Now, take me back to Captain Bailey.'

I am lost in the recollection of this delicious interview, and the waltz, when she comes to me again, with a plain elderly gentleman, who has been playing whist all night, upon her arm, and says: 'Oh! here is my bold friend! Mr Chestle wants to know you, Mr Copperfield.'

I feel at once that he is a friend of the family, and am much gratified.

'I admire your taste, sir,' says Mr Chestle. 'It does you credit. I suppose you don't take much interest in hops; but I am a pretty large grower myself; and if you ever like to come over to our neighbourhood – neighbourhood of Ashford – and take a run about our place, we shall be glad for you to stop as long as you like.'

I thank Mr Chestle warmly, and shake hands. I think I am in a happy dream. I waltz with the eldest Miss Larkins once again – she says I waltz so well! I go home in a state of unspeakable bliss, and waltz in imagination, all night long, with my arm round the blue waist of my dear divinity. For some days afterwards, I am lost in rapturous reflections; but I neither see her in the street, nor when I call. I am imperfectly consoled for this disappointment by the sacred pledge, the perished flower.

'Trotwood,' says Agnes, one day after dinner, 'who do you think is going to be married tomorrow? Someone you admire.'

'Not you, I suppose, Agnes?'

'Not me!' raising her cheerful face from the music she is copying. 'Do you hear him, Papa? – The eldest Miss Larkins.'

'To – to Captain Bailey?' I have just enough power to ask.

'No; to no captain. To Mr Chestle, a hop-grower.'

I am terribly dejected for about a week or two. I take off my ring, I wear my worst clothes, I use no bear's grease, and I frequently lament over the late Miss Larkins's faded flower. Being, by that time, rather tired of this kind of life, and having received new provocation from the butcher, I throw the flower away, go out with the butcher, and gloriously defeat him.

This, and the resumption of my ring, as well as of the bear's grease in moderation, are the last marks I can discern, now, in my progress to seventeen.

CHAPTER 19

I Look About Me, and Make a Discovery

I am doubtful whether I was at heart glad or sorry when my school-days drew to an end, and the time came for my leaving Doctor Strong's. I had been very happy there, I had a great attachment for the Doctor, and I was eminent and distinguished in that little world. For these reasons I was sorry to go; but for other reasons, unsubstantial enough, I was glad. Misty ideas of being a young man at my own disposal, of the importance attaching to a young man at his own disposal, of the wonderful things to be seen and done by that magnificent animal, and the wonderful effects he could not fail to make upon society, lured me away. So powerful were these visionary considerations in my boyish mind that I seem, according to my present way of thinking, to have left school without natural regret. The separation has not made the impression on me that other separations have. I try in vain to recall how I felt about it, and what its circumstances were; but it is not momentous in my recollection. I suppose the opening prospect confused me. I know that my juvenile experiences went for little or nothing then; and that life was more like a great fairy story, which I was just about to begin to read, than anything else.

My aunt and I had held many grave deliberations on the calling to which I should be devoted. For a year or more I had endeavoured to find a satisfactory answer to her often-repeated question, 'What I would like to be?' But I had no particular liking, that I could discover, for anything. If I could have been inspired with a knowledge of the science of navigation, taken the command of a fast-sailing expedition, and gone round the world on a triumphant voyage of discovery, I think I might have considered myself completely suited. But in the absence of any such miraculous provision, my desire was to apply myself to some pursuit that would not lie too heavily upon her purse; and to do my duty in it, whatever it might be.

Mr Dick had regularly assisted at our councils, with a meditative and sage demeanour. He never made a suggestion but once; and on that occasion (I don't know what put it in his head), he suddenly proposed that I should be 'a Brazier.' My aunt received this proposal so very ungraciously that he never ventured on a second; but ever afterwards confined himself to looking watchfully at her for her suggestions, and rattling his money.

'Trot, I tell you what, my dear,' said my aunt, one morning in the Christmas season when I left school; 'as this knotty point is still unsettled, and as we must not make a mistake in our decision if we can help it, I think we had better take a little breathing-time. In the meanwhile, you must try to look at it from a new point of view, and not as a schoolboy.'

'I will, aunt.'

'It has occurred to me,' pursued my aunt, 'that a little change, and a glimpse of life out of doors, may be useful, in helping you to know your own mind, and form a cooler judgement. Suppose you were to take a little journey now. Suppose you were to go down into the old part of the country again, for instance, and see that – that out-of-the-way woman with the savagest of names,' said my aunt, rubbing her nose, for she could never thoroughly forgive Peggotty for being so called.

'Of all things in the world, aunt, I should like it best.'

'Well,' said my aunt, 'that's lucky, for I should like it, too. But it's natural and rational that you should like it. And I am very well persuaded that whatever you do, Trot, will always be natural and rational.'

'I hope so, aunt.'

'Your sister, Betsey Trotwood,' said my aunt, 'would have been as natural and rational a girl as ever breathed. You'll be worthy of her, won't you?'

'I hope I shall be worthy of *you*, aunt. That will be enough for me.'

'It's a mercy that poor dear baby of a mother of yours didn't live,' said my aunt, looking at me approvingly, 'or she'd have been so vain of her boy by this time that her soft little head would have been completely turned, if there was anything of it left to turn.' (My aunt always excused any weakness of her own in my behalf by transferring it in this way to my poor mother.) 'Bless me, Trotwood, how you do remind me of her!'

'Pleasantly, I hope, aunt?' said I.

'He's as like her, Dick,' said my aunt emphatically, 'he's as like her, as she was that afternoon, before she began to fret – bless my heart, he's as like her, as he can look at me out of his two eyes!'

'Is he, indeed?' said Mr Dick.

'And he's like David, too,' said my aunt decisively.

'He is very like David!' said Mr Dick.

'But what I want you to be, Trot,' resumed my aunt; 'I don't mean physically, but morally; you are very well physically – is, a firm fellow. A fine firm fellow, with a will of your own. With resolution,' said my aunt, shaking her cap at me, and clenching her hand. 'With determination. With character, Trot – with strength of character that is not to be influenced, except on good reason, by anybody, or by anything. That's what I want you to be. That's what your father and mother might both have been, Heaven knows, and been the better for it.'

I intimated that I hoped I should be what she described.

'That you may begin, in a small way, to have a reliance upon yourself, and to act for yourself,' said my aunt, 'I shall send you upon your trip alone. I did think, once, of Mr Dick's going with you; but on second thoughts, I shall keep him to take care of me.'

Mr Dick, for a moment, looked a little disappointed; until the honour and dignity of having to take care of the most wonderful woman in the world, restored the sunshine to his face.

'Besides,' said my aunt, 'there's the Memorial – '

'Oh, certainly,' said Mr Dick in a hurry, 'I intend, Trotwood, to get that done immediately – it really must be done immediately! And then it will go in, you know – and then,' said Mr Dick, after checking himself, and pausing a long time, 'there'll be a pretty kettle of fish!'

In pursuance of my aunt's kind scheme, I was shortly afterwards fitted out with a handsome purse of money, and a portmanteau, and tenderly dismissed upon my expedition. At parting, my aunt gave me some good advice, and a good many kisses; and said that as her object was that I should look about me, and should think a little, she would recommend me to stay a few days in London, if I liked it, either on my way down into Suffolk, or in coming back. In a word, I was at liberty to do what I would, for three weeks or a month; and no other conditions were imposed upon my freedom than the beforementioned thinking and looking about me, and a pledge to write three times a week and faithfully report myself.

I went to Canterbury first, that I might take leave of Agnes and Mr Wickfield (my old room in whose house I had not yet relinquished), and also of the good Doctor. Agnes was very glad to see me, and told me that the house had not been like itself since I had left it.

'I am sure I am not like myself when I am away,' said I. 'I seem to want my right hand when I miss you. Though that's not saying much; for there's no head in my right hand, and no heart. Everyone who knows you consults with you, and is guided by you, Agnes.'

'Every one who knows me, spoils me, I believe,' she answered, smiling.

'No. It's because you are like no one else. You are so good and so sweet-tempered. You have such a gentle nature, and you are always right.'

'You talk,' said Agnes, breaking into a pleasant laugh, as she sat at work, 'as if I were the late Miss Larkins.'

'Come! It's not fair to abuse my confidence,' I answered, reddening at the recollection of my blue enslaver. 'But I shall confide in you, just the same, Agnes. I can never grow out of that. Whenever I fall into trouble, or fall in love, I shall always tell you, if you'll let me – even when I come to fall in love in earnest.'

'Why, you have always been in earnest!' said Agnes, laughing again.

'Oh! that was as a child, or a schoolboy,' said I, laughing in my turn, not without being a little shamefaced. 'Times are altering now, and I suppose I shall be in a terrible state of earnestness one day or other. My wonder is that you are not in earnest yourself, by this time, Agnes.'

Agnes laughed again, and shook her head.

'Oh, I know you are not!' said I, 'because if you had been, you would have told me. Or at least,' for I saw a faint blush in her face, 'you would have let me find it out for myself. But there is no one that I know of, who deserves to love *you*, Agnes. Someone of a nobler character, and more worthy altogether than anyone I have ever seen here, must rise up, before I give *my* consent. In the time to come, I shall have a wary eye on all admirers, and shall exact a great deal from the successful one, I assure you.'

We had gone on, so far, in a mixture of confidential jest and earnest, that had long grown naturally out of our familiar relations, begun as mere children. But Agnes, now suddenly lifting up her eyes to mine, and speaking in a different manner, said: 'Trotwood, there is something that I want to ask you, and that I may not have another opportunity of asking for a long time, perhaps – something I would ask, I think, of no one else. Have you observed any gradual alteration in Papa?'

I had observed it, and had often wondered whether she had too. I must have shown as much now in my face; for her eyes were in a moment cast down, and I saw tears in them.

'Tell me what it is,' she said, in a low voice.

'I think – shall I be quite plain, Agnes, liking him so much?'

'Yes,' she said.

'I think he does himself no good by the habit that has increased upon him since I first came here. He is often very nervous – or I fancy so.'

'It is not fancy,' said Agnes, shaking her head.

'His hand trembles, his speech is not plain, and his eyes look wild. I have remarked that at those times, and when he is least like himself, he is most certain to be wanted on some business.'

'By Uriah,' said Agnes.

'Yes; and the sense of being unfit for it, or of not having understood it, or of having shown his condition in spite of himself, seems to make him so uneasy that next day he is worse, and next day worse, and so he becomes jaded and haggard. Do not be alarmed by what I say, Agnes, but in this state I saw him, only the other evening, lay down his head upon his desk, and shed tears like a child.'

Her hand passed softly before my lips while I was yet speaking, and in a moment she had met her father at the door of the room, and was hanging on his shoulder. The expression of her face, as they both looked towards me, I felt to be very touching. There was such deep fondness for him, and gratitude to him for all his love and care, in her beautiful look; and there was such a fervent appeal to me to deal tenderly by him, even in my inmost thoughts, and to let no harsh construction find any place against him; she was, at once, so proud of him and devoted to him, yet so compassionate and sorry, and so reliant upon me to be so, too, that nothing she could have said would have expressed more to me, or moved me more.

We were to drink tea at the Doctor's. We went there at the usual hour, and round the study-fireside found the Doctor, and his young wife, and her mother. The Doctor, who made as much of my going away as if I were going to China, received me as an honoured guest; and called for a log of wood to be thrown on the fire, that he might see the face of his old pupil reddening in the blaze.

'I shall not see many more new faces in Trotwood's stead, Wickfield,' said the Doctor, warming his hands; 'I am getting lazy, and want ease. I shall relinquish all my young people in another six months, and lead a quieter life.'

'You have said so, any time these ten years, Doctor,' Mr Wickfield answered.

'But now I mean to do it,' returned the Doctor. 'My first master will succeed me – I am in earnest at last – so you'll soon have to arrange our contracts, and to bind us firmly to them, like a couple of knaves.'

'And to take care,' said Mr Wickfield, 'that you're not imposed on, eh? As you certainly would be, in any contract you should make for yourself. Well! I am ready. There are worse tasks than that, in my calling.'

'I shall have nothing to think of, then,' said the Doctor, with a smile, 'but my Dictionary; and this other contract-bargain – Annie.'

As Mr Wickfield glanced towards her, sitting at the tea-table by Agnes, she seemed to me to avoid his look with such unwonted hesitation and timidity, that his attention became fixed upon her, as if something were suggested to his thoughts.

'There is a post come in from India, I observe,' he said, after a short silence.

'By the by! and letters from Mr Jack Maldon!' said the Doctor.

'Indeed?'

'Poor dear Jack!' said Mrs Markleham, shaking her head. 'That trying climate! Like living, they tell me, on a sand-heap, underneath a burning-glass! He looked strong, but he wasn't. My dear Doctor, it was his spirit, not his constitution, that he ventured on so boldly. Annie, my dear, I am sure you must perfectly recollect that your cousin never was strong – not what can be called *robust*, you know,' said Mrs Markleham with emphasis, and looking round upon us generally; 'from the time when my daughter and himself were children, together, and walking about, arm in arm, the livelong day.'

Annie, thus addressed, made no reply.

'Do I gather from what you say, ma'am, that Mr Maldon is ill?' asked Mr Wickfield.

'Ill!' replied the Old Soldier. 'My dear sir, he's all sorts of things.'

'Except well?' said Mr Wickfield.

'Except well, indeed!' said the Old Soldier. 'He has had dreadful strokes of the sun, no doubt, and jungle fevers and agues, and every kind of thing you can mention. As to his liver,' said the Old Soldier resignedly, 'that, of course, he gave up altogether, when he first went out!'

'Does he say all this?' asked Mr Wickfield.

'Say? My dear sir,' returned Mrs Markleham, shaking her head and her fan, 'you little know my poor Jack Maldon when you ask that question. Say? Not he. You might drag him at the heels of four wild horses first.'

'Mama!' said Mrs Strong.

'Annie, my dear,' returned her mother, 'once for all, I must really beg that you will not interfere with me, unless it is to confirm what I say. You know as well as I do, that your cousin Maldon would be dragged at the heels of any number of wild horses – why should I confine myself to four! I *won't* confine myself to four – eight, sixteen, two-and-thirty, rather than say anything calculated to overturn the Doctor's plans.'

'Wickfield's plans,' said the Doctor, stroking his face, and looking penitently at his adviser. 'That is to say, our joint plans for him. I said myself, abroad or at home.'

'And I said,' added Mr Wickfield gravely, 'abroad. I was the means of sending him abroad. It's my responsibility.'

'Oh! Responsibility!' said the Old Soldier. 'Everything was done for the best, my dear Mr Wickfield; everything was done for the kindest and best, we know. But if the dear fellow can't live there, he can't live there. And if he can't live there, he'll die there, sooner than he'll overturn the Doctor's plans. I know him,' said the Old Soldier, fanning herself, in a sort of calm prophetic agony, 'and I know he'll die there sooner than he'll overturn the Doctor's plans.'

'Well, well, ma'am,' said the Doctor cheerfully, 'I am not bigoted to my plans, and I can overturn them myself. I can substitute some other plans. If Mr Jack Maldon comes home on account of ill-health, he must not be allowed to go back, and we must endeavour to make some more suitable and fortunate provision for him in this country.'

Mrs Markleham was so overcome by this generous speech – which, I need not say, she had not at all expected or led up to – that she could only tell the Doctor it was like himself, and go several times through that operation of kissing the sticks of her fan, and then tapping his hand with it. After which she gently chid her daughter Annie, for not being more demonstrative when such kindnesses were showered, for her sake, on her old playfellow, and entertained us with some particulars concerning other deserving members of her family, whom it was desirable to set on their deserving legs.

All this time, her daughter Annie never once spoke, or lifted up her eyes. All this time, Mr Wickfield had his glance upon her as she sat by his own daughter's side. It appeared to me that he never thought of being observed by anyone; but was so intent upon her, and upon his own thoughts in connection with her, as to be quite absorbed. He now asked what Mr Jack Maldon had actually written in reference to himself, and to whom he had written it?

'Why, here,' said Mrs Markleham, taking a letter from the chimney-piece above the Doctor's head, 'the dear fellow says to the Doctor himself – where is it? Oh! – "I am sorry to inform you that my health is suffering severely, and that I fear I may be reduced to the necessity of returning home for a time, as the only hope of restoration." That's pretty plain, poor fellow! His only hope of restoration! But Annie's letter is plainer still. Annie, show me that letter again.'

'Not now, mama,' she pleaded, in a low tone.

'My dear, you absolutely are, on some subjects, one of the most ridiculous persons in the world,' returned her mother, 'and perhaps the most unnatural to the claims of your own family. We never should have heard of the letter at all, I believe, unless I had asked for it myself. Do you call that confidence, my love, towards Doctor Strong? I am surprised. You ought to know better.'

The letter was reluctantly produced; and as I handed it to the old lady, I saw how the unwilling hand from which I took it trembled.

'Now let us see,' said Mrs Markleham, putting her glass to her eye, 'where the passage is. "The remembrance of old times, my dearest Annie" – and so forth – it's not there. "The amiable old Proctor" – who's he? Dear me, Annie, how illegibly your cousin Maldon writes, and how stupid I am! "Doctor," of course. Ah! amiable indeed!' Here she left off, to kiss her fan again, and shake it at the Doctor, who was looking at us in a state of placid satisfaction. 'Now I have found it. "You may not be surprised to hear, Annie" – no, to be sure, knowing that he never was really strong; what did I say just now? – "that I have undergone so much in this distant place, as to have decided to leave it at all hazards; on sick leave, if I can; on total resignation, if that is not to be obtained. What I have endured, and do endure here, is insupportable." And but for the promptitude of that best of creatures,' said Mrs Markleham, telegraphing the Doctor as before, and refolding the letter, 'it would be insupportable to me to think of.'

Mr Wickfield said not one word, though the old lady looked to him as if for his commentary on this intelligence, but sat severely silent, with his eyes fixed on the ground. Long after the subject was dismissed, and other topics occupied us, he remained so; seldom raising his eyes, unless to rest them for a moment, with a thoughtful frown, upon the Doctor, or his wife, or both.

The Doctor was very fond of music. Agnes sang with great sweetness and expression, and so did Mrs Strong. They sang together, and played duets together, and we had quite a little concert. But I remarked two things: first, that though Annie soon recovered her composure, and was quite herself, there was a blank between her and Mr Wickfield which separated them wholly from each other; secondly, that Mr Wickfield seemed to dislike the intimacy between her and Agnes, and to watch it with uneasiness. And now, I must confess, the recollection of what I had seen on that night when Mr Maldon went away, first began to return upon me with a meaning it had never had, and to trouble me. The innocent beauty of her face was not as innocent to me as it had been; I mistrusted the natural grace and charm of her manner; and when I looked at Agnes by her side, and thought how good and true Agnes was, suspicions arose within me that it was an ill-assorted friendship.

She was so happy in it herself, however, and the other was so happy too, that they made the evening fly away as if it were but an hour. It closed in an incident which I well remember. They were taking leave of each other, and Agnes was going to embrace and kiss her, when Mr Wickfield stepped between them, as if by accident, and drew Agnes quickly away. Then I saw, as though all the intervening time had been cancelled, and I were still standing in the doorway on the night of the departure, the expression of that night in the face of Mrs Strong, as it confronted his.

I cannot say what an impression this made upon me, or how impossible I found it, when I thought of her afterwards, to separate her from this look, and remember her face in its innocent loveliness again. It haunted me when I got home. I seemed to have left the Doctor's roof with a dark cloud lowering on it. The reverence that I had for his grey head was mingled with commiseration for his faith in those who were treacherous to him, and with resentment against those who injured him. The impending shadow of a great affliction, and a great disgrace that had no distinct form in it yet, fell like a stain upon the quiet place where I had worked and played as a boy, and did it a cruel wrong. I had no pleasure in thinking, any more, of the grave, old, broad-leaved aloe trees which remained shut up in themselves a hundred years together, and of the trim, smooth grass-plot, and the stone urns, and the Doctor's Walk, and the congenial sound of the Cathedral bell hovering above them all. It was as if the tranquil sanctuary of my boyhood had been sacked before my face, and its peace and honour given to the winds.

But morning brought with it my parting from the old house, which Agnes had filled with her influence; and that occupied my mind sufficiently. I should be there again soon, no doubt; I might sleep again – perhaps often – in my old room; but the days of my inhabiting there were gone, and the old time was past. I was heavier at heart when I packed up such of my books and clothes as still remained there, to be sent to Dover, than I cared to show to Uriah Heep, who was so officious to help me, that I uncharitably thought him mighty glad that I was going.

I got away from Agnes and her father, somehow, with an indifferent show of being very manly, and took my seat upon the box of the London coach. I was so softened and forgiving, going through the town, that I had half a mind to nod to my old enemy the butcher, and throw him five shillings to drink. But he looked such a very obdurate butcher as he stood scraping the great block in the shop, and, moreover, his appearance was so little improved by the loss of a front tooth which I had knocked out, that I thought it best to make no advances.

The main object on my mind, I remember, when we got fairly on the road, was to appear as old as possible to the coachman, and to speak extremely gruff. The latter point I achieved at great personal inconvenience; but I stuck to it, because I felt it was a grown-up sort of thing.

'You are going through, sir?' said the coachman.

'Yes, William,' I said, condescendingly (I knew him); 'I am going to London. I shall go down into Suffolk afterwards.'

'Shooting, sir?' said the coachman.

He knew as well as I did that it was just as likely, at that time of year, I was going down there whaling; but I felt complimented, too.

'I don't know,' I said, pretending to be undecided, 'whether I shall take a shot or not.'

'Birds is got wery shy, I'm told,' said William.

'So I understand,' said I.

'Is Suffolk your county, sir?' asked William.

'Yes,' I said, with some importance. 'Suffolk's my county.'

'I'm told the dumplings is uncommon fine down there,' said William.

I was not aware of it myself, but I felt it necessary to uphold the institutions of my county, and to evince a familiarity with them; so I shook my head, as much as to say, 'I believe you!'

'And the Punches,' said William. 'There's cattle! A Suffolk Punch, when he's a good 'un, is worth his weight in gold. Did you ever breed any Suffolk Punches yourself, sir?'

'N – no,' I said, 'not exactly.'

'Here's a gen'lm'n behind me, I'll pound it,' said William, 'as has bred 'em by wholesale.'

The gentleman spoken of was a gentleman with a very un-promising squint, and a prominent chin, who had a tall white hat on with a narrow flat brim, and whose close-fitting drab trousers seemed to button all the way up outside his legs from his boots to his hips. His chin was cocked over the coachman's shoulder, so near to me that his breath quite tickled the back of my head; and as I looked round at him, he leered at the leaders with the eye with which he didn't squint, in a very knowing manner.

'Ain't you?' asked William.

'Ain't I what?' said the gentleman behind.

'Bred them Suffolk Punches by wholesale?'

'I should think so,' said the gentleman. 'There ain't no sort of 'orse that I ain't bred, and no sort of dorg. 'Orses and dorgs is some men's fancy. They're wittles and drink to me – lodging, wife, and children – reading, writing, and 'rithmetic – snuff, tobacker, and sleep.'

'That ain't a sort of man to see sitting behind a coach-box, is it, though?' said William in my ear, as he handled the reins.

I construed this remark into an indication of a wish that he should have my place, so I blushingly offered to resign it.

'Well, if you don't mind, sir,' said William, 'I think it *would* be more correct.'

I have always considered this as the first fall I had in life. When I booked my place at the coach-office, I had had 'Box Seat' written against the entry, and had given the bookkeeper half a crown. I was got up in a special greatcoat and shawl, expressly to do honour to that distinguished eminence; had glorified myself upon it a good deal; and had felt that I was a credit to the coach. And here, in the very first stage, I was supplanted by a shabby man with a squint, who had no other merit than smelling like a livery-stable, and being able to walk across me, more like a fly than a human being, while the horses were at a canter!

A distrust of myself, which has often beset me in life on small occasions, when it would have been better away, was assuredly not stopped in its growth by the little incident outside the Canterbury coach. It was in vain to take refuge in gruffness of speech. I spoke from the pit of my stomach for the rest of the journey, but I felt completely extinguished, and dreadfully young.

It was curious and interesting, nevertheless, to be sitting up there, behind four horses; well educated, well dressed, and with plenty of money in my pocket; and to look out for the places where I had slept on my weary journey. I had abundant occupation for my thoughts, in every conspicuous landmark on the road. When I looked down at the trampers whom we passed, and saw that well-remembered style of face turned up, I felt as if the tinker's blackened hand were in the bosom of my shirt again. When we clattered through the narrow street of Chatham, and I caught a glimpse, in passing, of the lane where the old monster lived who had bought my jacket, I stretched my neck eagerly to look for the place where I had sat, in the sun and in the shade, waiting for my money. When we came, at last, within a stage of London, and passed the veritable Salem House where Mr Creakle had laid about him with a heavy hand, I would have given all I had for lawful permission to get down and thrash him, and let all the boys out like so many caged sparrows.

We went to the Golden Cross at Charing Cross, then a mouldy sort of establishment in a close neighbourhood. A waiter showed me into the coffee-room; and a chambermaid introduced me to my small bedchamber, which smelt like a hackney-coach, and was shut up like a family vault. I was still painfully conscious of my youth, for nobody stood in any awe of me at all; the chambermaid being utterly indifferent to my opinions on any subject, and the waiter being familiar with me, and offering advice to my inexperience.

'Well, now,' said the waiter, in a tone of confidence, 'what would you like for dinner? Young gentlemen likes poultry in general; have a fowl!'

I told him, as majestically as I could, that I wasn't in the humour for a fowl.

'Ain't you!' said the waiter. 'Young gentlemen is generally tired of beef and mutton; have a weal cutlet!'

I assented to this proposal, in default of being able to suggest anything else.

'Do you care for taters?' said the waiter, with an insinuating smile, and his head on one side. 'Young gentlemen generally has been overdosed with taters.'

I commanded him, in my deepest voice, to order a veal cutlet and potatoes, and all things fitting; and to enquire at the bar if there were any letters for Trotwood Copperfield, Esquire – which I knew there were not, and couldn't be, but thought it manly to appear to expect.

He soon came back to say that there were none (at which I was much surprised), and began to lay the cloth for my dinner in a box by the fire. While he was so engaged, he asked me what I would take with it; and on my replying, 'Half a pint of sherry,' thought it a favourable opportunity, I am afraid, to extract that measure of wine from the stale leavings at the bottoms of several small decanters. I am of this opinion, because, while I was reading the newspaper, I observed him behind a low wooden partition, which was his private apartment, very busy pouring out of a number of those vessels into one, like a chemist and druggist making up a prescription. When the wine came, too, I thought it flat; and it certainly had more English crumbs in it than were to be expected in a foreign wine in anything like a pure state; but I was bashful enough to drink it, and say nothing.

Being then in a pleasant frame of mind (from which I infer that poisoning is not always disagreeable in some stages of the process), I resolved to go to the play. It was Covent Garden Theatre that I chose; and there, from the back of a centre box, I saw *Julius Caesar* and the new Pantomime. To have all those noble Romans alive before me, and walking in and out for my entertainment, instead of being the stern taskmasters they had been at school, was a most novel and delightful effect. But the mingled reality and mystery of the whole show, the influence upon me of the poetry, the lights, the music, the company, the smooth stupendous changes of glittering and brilliant scenery, were so dazzling, and opened up such illimitable regions of delight, that when I came out into the rainy street, at twelve o'clock at night, I felt as if I had come from the clouds, where I had been leading a romantic life for ages, to a bawling, splashing, link-lighted, umbrella-struggling, hackney-coach-jostling, patten-clinking, muddy, miserable world.

I had emerged by another door, and stood in the street for a little while, as if I really were a stranger upon earth; but the unceremonious pushing and hustling that I received soon recalled me to myself, and put me in the road back to the hotel; whither I went, revolving the glorious vision all the way; and where, after some porter and oysters, I sat revolving it still, at past one o'clock, with my eyes on the coffee-room fire.

I was so filled with the play and with the past – for it was, in a manner, like a shining transparency, through which I saw my earlier life moving along – that I don't know when the figure of

My first fall in life

a handsome, well-formed young man, dressed with a tasteful, easy negligence which I have reason to remember very well, became a real presence to me. But I recollect being conscious of his company without having noticed his coming in – and my still sitting, musing, over the coffee-room fire.

At last I rose to go to bed, much to the relief of the sleepy waiter, who had got the fidgets in his legs, and was twisting them, and hitting them, and putting them through all kinds of contortions in his small pantry. In going towards the door, I passed the person who had come in, and saw him plainly. I turned directly, came back, and looked again. He did not know me, but I knew him in a moment.

At another time I might have wanted the confidence or the decision to speak to him, and might have put it off until next day, and might have lost him. But in the then condition of my mind, where the play was still running high, his former protection of me appeared so deserving of my gratitude, and my old love for him overflowed my breast so freshly and spontaneously, that I went up to him at once, with a fast-beating heart, and said: 'Steerforth! Won't you speak to me?'

He looked at me – just as he used to look, sometimes – but I saw no recognition in his face.

'You don't remember me, I am afraid,' said I.

'My God!' he suddenly exclaimed. 'It's little Copperfield!'

I grasped him by both hands, and could not let them go. But for very shame, and the fear that it might displease him, I could have held him round the neck and cried.

'I never, never, never, was so glad! My dear Steerforth, I am so overjoyed to see you!'

'And I am rejoiced to see you, too!' he said, shaking my hands heartily. 'Why, Copperfield, old boy, don't be overpowered!' And yet he was glad, too, I thought, to see how the delight I had in meeting him affected me.

I brushed away the tears that my utmost resolution had not been able to keep back, and I made a clumsy laugh of it, and we sat down together, side by side.

'Why, how do you come to be here?' said Steerforth, clapping me on the shoulder.

'I came here by the Canterbury coach, today. I have been adopted by an aunt down in that part of the country, and have just finished my education there. How do *you* come to be here, Steerforth?'

'Well, I am what they call an Oxford man,' he returned; 'that is to say, I get bored to death down there, periodically – and I am on my way now to my mother's. You're a devilish amiable-looking fellow, Copperfield. Just what you used to be, now I look at you! Not altered in the least!'

'I knew *you* immediately,' I said; 'but you are more easily remembered.'

He laughed as he ran his hand through the clustering curls of his hair, and said gaily: 'Yes, I am on an expedition of duty. My mother lives a little way out of town; and the roads being in a beastly condition, and our house tedious enough, I remained here tonight instead of going on. I have not been in town half a dozen hours, and those I have been dozing and grumbling away at the play.'

'I have been at the play, too,' said I; 'at Covent Garden. What a delightful and magnificent entertainment, Steerforth!'

Steerforth laughed heartily.

'My dear young Davy,' he said, clapping me on the shoulder again, 'you are a very Daisy. The daisy of the field, at sunrise, is not fresher than you are! I have been at Covent Garden, too, and there never was a more miserable business. Holloa, you, sir?'

This was addressed to the waiter, who had been very attentive to our recognition, at a distance, and now came forward deferentially.

'Where have you put my friend, Mr Copperfield?' said Steerforth.

'Beg your pardon, sir?'

'Where does he sleep? What's his number? You know what I mean,' said Steerforth.

'Well, sir,' said the waiter, with an apologetic air. 'Mr Copperfield is at present in forty-four, sir.'

'And what the devil do you mean,' retorted Steerforth, 'by putting Mr Copperfield into a little loft over a stable?'

'Why, you see, we wasn't aware, sir,' returned the waiter, still apologetically, 'as Mr Copperfield was anyways particular. We can give Mr Copperfield seventy-two, sir, if it would be preferred. Next you, sir.'

'Of course it would be preferred,' said Steerforth. 'And do it at once.'

The waiter immediately withdrew to make the exchange. Steerforth, very much amused at my having been put into forty-four, laughed again, and clapped me on the shoulder again, and invited me to breakfast with him next morning at ten o'clock – an invitation I was only too proud and happy to accept. It being now pretty late, we took our candles and went upstairs, where we parted with friendly heartiness at his door, and where I found my new room a great improvement on my old one, it not being at all musty, and having an immense four-post bedstead in it, which was quite a little landed estate. Here, among pillows enough for six, I soon fell asleep in a blissful condition, and dreamed of ancient Rome, Steerforth, and friendship, until the early morning coaches, rumbling out of the archway underneath, made me dream of thunder and the gods.

CHAPTER 20

Steerforth's Home

When the chambermaid tapped at my door at eight o'clock, and informed me that my shaving-water was outside, I felt severely the having no occasion for it, and blushed in my bed. The suspicion that she laughed too, when she said it, preyed upon my mind all the time I was dressing, and gave me, I was conscious, a sneaking and guilty air when I passed her on the staircase, as I was going down to breakfast. I was so sensitively aware, indeed, of being younger than I could have wished, that for some time I could not make up my mind to pass her at all, under the ignoble circumstances of the case; but, hearing

her there with a broom, stood peeping out of a window at King Charles on horseback, surrounded by a maze of hackney-coaches and looking anything but regal in a drizzling rain and a dark-brown fog, until I was admonished by the waiter that the gentleman was waiting for me.

It was not in the coffee-room that I found Steerforth expecting me, but in a snug private apartment, red-curtained and Turkey-carpeted, where the fire burnt bright, and a fine hot breakfast was set forth on a table covered with a clean cloth, and a cheerful miniature of the room, the fire, the breakfast, Steerforth, and all, was shining in the little round mirror over the sideboard. I was rather bashful at first, Steerforth being so self-possessed, and elegant, and superior to me in all respects (age included); but his easy patronage soon put that to rights, and made me quite at home. I could not enough admire the change he had wrought in the Golden Cross, or compare the dull forlorn state I had held yesterday with this morning's comfort and this morning's entertainment. As to the waiter's familiarity, it was quenched as if it had never been. He attended on us, as I may say, in sackcloth and ashes.

'Now, Copperfield,' said Steerforth, when we were alone, 'I should like to hear what you are doing, and where you are going, and all about you. I feel as if you were my property.'

Glowing with pleasure to find that he had still this interest in me, I told him how my aunt had proposed the little expedition that I had before me, and whither it tended.

'As you are in no hurry, then,' said Steerforth, 'come home with me to Highgate, and stay a day or two. You will be pleased with my mother – she is a little vain and prosy about me, but that you can forgive her – and she will be pleased with you.'

'I should like to be as sure of that as you are kind enough to say you are,' I answered smiling.

'Oh!' said Steerforth, 'everyone who likes me has a claim on her that is sure to be acknowledged.'

'Then I think I shall be a favourite,' said I.

'Good!' said Steerforth. 'Come and prove it. We will go and see the lions for an hour or two – it's something to have a fresh fellow like you to show them to, Copperfield – and then we'll journey out to Highgate by the coach.'

I could hardly believe but that I was in a dream, and that I should wake presently in number forty-four, to the solitary box in the coffee-room and the familiar waiter again. After I had written to my aunt and told her of my fortunate meeting with my admired old schoolfellow, and my acceptance of his invitation, we went out in a hackney-chariot, and saw a Panorama and some other sights, and took a walk through the Museum, where I could not help observing how much Steerforth knew, on an infinite variety of subjects, and of how little account he seemed to make his knowledge.

'You'll take a high degree at college, Steerforth,' said I, 'if you have not done so already; and they will have good reason to be proud of you.'

'*I* take a degree!' cried Steerforth. 'Not I! my dear Daisy – will you mind my calling you Daisy?'

'Not at all!' said I.

'That's a good fellow! My dear Daisy,' said Steerforth,

laughing, 'I have not the least desire or intention to distinguish myself in that way. I have done quite sufficient for my purpose. I find that I am heavy company enough for myself as I am.'

'But the fame – ' I was beginning.

'You romantic Daisy!' said Steerforth, laughing still more heartily; 'why should I trouble myself, that a parcel of heavy-headed fellows may gape and hold up their hands? Let them do it at some other man. There's fame for him, and he's welcome to it.'

I was abashed at having made so great a mistake, and was glad to change the subject. Fortunately it was not difficult to do, for Steerforth could always pass from one subject to another with a carelessness and lightness that were his own.

Lunch succeeded to our sightseeing, and the short winter day wore away so fast, that it was dusk when the stage-coach stopped with us at an old brick house at Highgate on the summit of the hill. An elderly lady, though not very far advanced in years, with a proud carriage and a handsome face, was in the doorway as we alighted; and greeting Steerforth as 'My dearest James,' folded him in her arms. To this lady he presented me as his mother, and she gave me a stately welcome.

It was a genteel old-fashioned house, very quiet and orderly. From the windows of my room I saw all London lying in the distance like a great vapour, with here and there some lights twinkling through it. I had only time, in dressing, to glance at the solid furniture, the framed pieces of work (done, I supposed, by Steerforth's mother when she was a girl), and some pictures in crayons of ladies with powdered hair and bodices, coming and going on the walls, as the newly kindled fire crackled and sputtered, when I was called to dinner.

There was a second lady in the dining-room, of a slight, short figure, dark, and not agreeable to look at, but with some appearance of good looks too, who attracted my attention: perhaps because I had not expected to see her: perhaps because I found myself sitting opposite to her: perhaps because of something really remarkable in her. She had black hair and eager black eyes, and was thin, and had a scar upon her lip. It was an old scar – I should rather call it seam, for it was not discoloured, and had healed years ago – which had once cut through her mouth, downward towards the chin, but was now barely visible across the table, except above and on her upper lip, the shape of which it had altered. I concluded in my own mind that she was about thirty years of age, and that she wished to be married. She was a little dilapidated – like a house – with having been so long to let; yet had, as I have said, an appearance of good looks. Her thinness seemed to be the effect of some wasting fire within her, which found a vent in her gaunt eyes.

She was introduced as Miss Dartle, and both Steerforth and his mother called her Rosa. I found that she lived there and had been for a long time Mrs Steerforth's companion. It appeared to me that she never said anything she wanted to say outright, but hinted it, and made a great deal more of it by this practice. For example, when Mrs Steerforth observed, more in jest than earnest, that she feared her son led but a wild life at college, Miss Dartle put in thus: 'Oh, really? You know how ignorant I am, and that I only ask for information, but isn't it always so? I thought that kind of life was on all hands understood to be – eh?'

'It is education for a very grave profession, if you mean that, Rosa,' Mrs Steerforth answered, with some coldness.

'Oh! Yes! That's very true,' returned Miss Dartle. 'But isn't it, though? – I want to be put right if I am wrong – isn't it, really?'

'Really what?' said Mrs Steerforth.

'Oh! You mean it's *not*!' returned Miss Dartle. 'Well, I'm very glad to hear it! Now, I know what to do! That's the advantage of asking. I shall never allow people to talk before me about wastefulness and profligacy, and so forth, in connection with that life, any more.'

'And you will be right,' said Mrs Steerforth. 'My son's tutor is a conscientious gentleman; and if I had not implicit reliance on my son, I should have reliance on him.'

'Should you?' said Miss Dartle. 'Dear me! Conscientious, is he? Really conscientious, now?'

'Yes, I am convinced of it,' said Mrs Steerforth.

'How very nice!' exclaimed Miss Dartle. 'What a comfort! Really conscientious? Then he's not – but of course he can't be, if he's really conscientious. Well, I shall be quite happy in my opinion of him, from this time. You can't think how it elevates him in my opinion, to know for certain that he's really conscientious!'

Her own views of every question, and her correction of everything that was said to which she was opposed, Miss Dartle insinuated in the same way; sometimes, I could not conceal from myself, with great power, though in contradiction even of Steerforth. An instance happened before dinner was done. Mrs Steerforth speaking to me about my intention of going down into Suffolk, I said at hazard how glad I should be, if Steerforth would only go there with me; and explaining to him that I was going to see my old nurse, and Mr Peggotty's family, I reminded him of the boatman whom he had seen at school.

'Oh! That bluff fellow!' said Steerforth. 'He had a son with him, hadn't he?'

'No. That was his nephew,' I replied; 'whom he adopted, though, as a son. He has a very pretty little niece, too, whom he adopted as a daughter. In short, his house (or rather his boat, for he lives in one, on dry land) is full of people who are objects of his generosity and kindness. You would be delighted to see that household.'

'Should I?' said Steerforth. 'Well, I think I should. I must see what can be done. It would be worth a journey – not to mention the pleasure of a journey with you, Daisy – to see that sort of people together, and to make one of 'em.'

My heart leaped with a new hope of pleasure. But it was in reference to the tone in which he had spoken of 'that sort of people,' that Miss Dartle, whose sparkling eyes had been watchful of us, now broke in again.

'Oh, but, really? Do tell me. Are they, though?' she said.

'Are they what? And are who what?' said Steerforth.

'That sort of people. Are they really animals and clods, and beings of another order? I want to know, *so* much.'

'Why, there's a pretty wide separation between them and us,' said Steerforth, with indifference. 'They are not to be expected to be as sensitive as we are. Their delicacy is not to be shocked, or hurt very easily. They are wonderfully virtuous, I dare say – some people contend for that, at least; and I am sure I don't want to contradict them – but they have not very fine natures, and they may be thankful that, like their coarse rough skins, they are not easily wounded.'

'Really!' said Miss Dartle. 'Well, I don't know, now, when I have been better pleased than to hear that. It's so consoling! It's such a delight to know that when they suffer they don't feel! Sometimes I have been quite uneasy for that sort of people; but now I shall just dismiss the idea of them altogether. Live and learn. I had my doubts, I confess, but now they're cleared up. I didn't know, and now I do know, and that shows the advantage of asking – don't it?'

I believed that Steerforth had said what he had, in jest, or to draw Miss Dartle out; and I expected him to say as much when she was gone, and we two were sitting before the fire. But he merely asked me what I thought of her.

'She is very clever, is she not?' I asked.

'Clever! She brings everything to a grindstone,' said Steerforth, 'and sharpens it, as she has sharpened her own face and figure these years past. She has worn herself away by constant sharpening. She is all edge.'

'What a remarkable scar that is upon her lip!' I said.

Steerforth's face fell, and he paused a moment.

'Why, the fact is,' he returned, '*I* did that.'

'By an unfortunate accident?'

'No. I was a young boy, and she exasperated me, and I threw a hammer at her. A promising young angel I must have been!'

I was deeply sorry to have touched on such a painful theme, but that was useless now.

'She has borne the mark ever since, as you see,' said Steerforth; 'and she'll bear it to her grave, if she ever rests in one – though I can hardly believe she will ever rest anywhere. She was the motherless child of a sort of cousin of my father's. He died one day. My mother, who was then a widow, brought her here to be company to her. She has a couple of thousand pounds of her own, and saves the interest of it every year, to add to the principal. There's the history of Miss Rosa Dartle for you.'

'And I have no doubt she loves you like a brother?' said I.

'Humph!' retorted Steerforth, looking at the fire. 'Some brothers are not loved over much; and some love – but, help yourself, Copperfield? We'll drink the daisies of the field, in compliment to you: and the lilies of the valley, that toil not, neither do they spin, in compliment to me – the more shame for me!' A moody smile that had overspread his features cleared off as he said this merrily, and he was his own frank, winning self again.

I could not help glancing at the scar with a painful interest when we went in to tea. It was not long before I observed that it was the most susceptible part of her face, and that, when she turned pale, that mark altered first, and became a dull lead-coloured streak, lengthening out to its full extent like a mark in invisible ink brought to the fire. There was a little altercation between her and Steerforth about a cast of the dice at back-gammon – when I thought her, for one moment, in a storm of rage; and then I saw it start forth like the old writing on the wall.

It was no matter of wonder to me to find Mrs Steerforth devoted to her son. She seemed to be able to speak or think about nothing else. She showed me his picture as an infant, in a locket, with some of his baby-hair in it; she showed me his picture as he had been when I first knew him; and she wore at her breast his picture as he was now. All the letters he had ever written to her, she kept in a cabinet near her own chair, by the fire; and she would have read me some of them, and I should have been very glad to hear them, too, if he had not interposed, and coaxed her out of the design.

'It was at Mr Creakle's, my son tells me, that you first became acquainted,' said Mrs Steerforth, as she and I were talking at one table, while they played backgammon at another. 'Indeed, I recollect his speaking, at that time, of a pupil younger than himself who had taken his fancy there; but your name, as you may suppose, has not lived in my memory.'

'He was very generous and noble to me in those days, I assure you, ma'am,' said I, 'and I stood in need of such a friend. I should have been quite crushed without him.'

'He is always generous and noble,' said Mrs Steerforth proudly.

I subscribed to this with all my heart, God knows. She knew I did; for the stateliness of her manner already abated towards me, except when she spoke in praise of him, and then her air was always lofty.

'It was not a fit school generally for my son,' said she; 'far from it; but there were particular circumstances to be considered at the time, of more importance even than that selection. My son's high spirit made it desirable that he should be placed with some man who felt its superiority, and would be content to bow himself before it; and we found such a man there.'

I knew that, knowing the fellow. And yet I did not despise him the more for it, but thought it a redeeming quality in him – if he could be allowed any grace for not resisting one so irresistible as Steerforth.

'My son's great capacity was tempted on, there, by a feeling of voluntary emulation and conscious pride,' the fond lady went on to say. 'He would have risen against all constraint; but he found himself the monarch of the place, and he haughtily determined to be worthy of his station. It was like himself.'

I echoed, with all my heart and soul, that it was like himself.

'So my son took, of his own will, and on no compulsion, to the course in which he can always, when it is his pleasure, outstrip every competitor,' she pursued. 'My son informs me, Mr Copperfield, that you were quite devoted to him, and that when you met yesterday you made yourself known to him with tears of joy. I should be an affected woman if I made any pretence of being surprised by my son's inspiring such emotions; but I cannot be indifferent to anyone who is so sensible of his merit, and I am very glad to see you here, and can assure you that he feels an unusual friendship for you, and that you may rely on his protection.'

Miss Dartle played backgammon as eagerly as she did every-thing else. If I had seen her, first, at the board, I should have fancied that her figure had got thin, and her eyes had got large, over that pursuit, and no other. But I am very much mistaken if she missed a word of this, or lost a look of mine as I received it with the utmost pleasure, and, honoured by Mrs Steerforth's confidence, felt older than I had done since I left Canterbury.

When the evening was pretty far spent, and a tray of glasses and decanters came in, Steerforth promised, over the fire, that he would seriously think of going down into the country with me. There was no hurry, he said; a week hence would do; and his mother hospitably said the same. While we were talking, he more than once called me Daisy; which brought Miss Dartle out again.

'But really, Mr Copperfield,' she asked, 'is it a nickname? And why does he give it you? Is it – eh? – because he thinks you young and innocent? I am so stupid in these things.'

I coloured in replying that I believed it was.

'Oh!' said Miss Dartle. 'Now I am glad to know that. I ask for information, and I am glad to know it. He thinks you young and innocent; and so you are his friend. Well, that's quite delightful!'

She went to bed soon after this, and Mrs Steerforth retired too. Steerforth and I, after lingering for half an hour over the fire, talking about Traddles and all the rest of them at old Salem House, went upstairs together. Steerforth's room was next to mine, and I went in to look at it. It was a picture of comfort, full of easy-chairs, cushions, and footstools, worked by his mother's hand, and with no sort of thing omitted that could help to render it complete. Finally, her handsome features looked down on her darling from a portrait on the wall, as if it were even something to her that her likeness should watch him while he slept.

I found the fire burning clear enough in my room by this time, and the curtains drawn before the windows and round the bed, giving it a very snug appearance. I sat down in a great chair upon the hearth to meditate on my happiness; and had enjoyed the contemplation of it for some time, when I found a likeness of Miss Dartle looking eagerly at me from above the chimney-piece.

It was a startling likeness, and necessarily had a startling look. The painter hadn't made the scar, but *I* made it, and there it was, coming and going; now confined to the upper lip as I had seen it at dinner, and now showing the whole extent of the wound inflicted by the hammer, as I had seen it when she was passionate.

I wondered peevishly why they couldn't put her anywhere else instead of quartering her on me. To get rid of her, I undressed quickly, extinguished my light, and went to bed. But as I fell asleep, I could not forget that she was still there looking, 'Is it really, though? I want to know;' and when I awoke in the night, I found that I was uneasily asking all sorts of people in my dreams whether it really was or not – without knowing what I meant.

CHAPTER 21

Little Em'ly

There was a servant in that house, a man who, I understood, was usually with Steerforth, and had come into his service at the University, who was in appearance a pattern of respectability. I believe there never existed in his station a more respectable-looking man. He was taciturn, soft-footed, very quiet in his manner, deferential, observant, always at hand when wanted, and never near when not wanted; but his great claim to consideration was his respectability. He had not a pliant face, he had rather a stiff neck, rather a tight smooth head with short hair clinging to it at the sides, a soft way of speaking with a peculiar habit of whispering the letter 's' so distinctly that he seemed to use it oftener than any other man; but every peculiarity that he had he made respectable. If his nose had been upside down, he would have made that respectable. He surrounded himself with an atmosphere of respectability, and walked secure in it. It would have been next to impossible to suspect him of anything wrong, he was so thoroughly respectable. Nobody could have thought of putting him in a livery, he was so highly respectable. To have imposed any derogatory work upon him would have been to inflict a wanton insult on the feelings of a most respectable man. And of this, I noticed the women-servants in the household were so intuitively conscious that they always did such work them-selves, and generally while he read the paper by the pantry fire.

Such a self-contained man I never saw. But in that quality, as in every other he possessed, he only seemed to be the more respectable. Even the fact that no one knew his Christian name seemed to form a part of his respectability. Nothing could be objected against his surname Littimer, by which he was known. Peter might have been hanged, or Tom transported; but Littimer was perfectly respectable.

It was occasioned, I suppose, by the reverend nature of respectability in the abstract, but I felt particularly young in this man's presence. How old he was himself I could not guess – and that again went to his credit on the same score; for in the calmness of respectability he might have numbered fifty years as well as thirty.

Littimer was in my room in the morning before I was up, to bring me that reproachful shaving-water, and to put out my clothes. When I undrew the curtains and looked out of bed, I saw him, in an equable temperature of respectability, unaffected by the east wind of January, and not even breathing frostily, standing my boots right and left in the first dancing position, and blowing specks of dust off my coat as he laid it down like a baby.

I gave him good-morning, and asked him what o'clock it was. He took out of his pocket the most respectable hunting-watch I ever saw, and, preventing the spring with his thumb from opening far, looked in at the face as if he were consulting an oracular oyster, shut it up again, and said, if I pleased, it was half-past eight.

'Mr Steerforth will be glad to hear how you have rested, sir.'

'Thank you,' said I; 'very well, indeed. Is Mr Steerforth quite well?'

'Thank you, sir; Mr Steerforth is tolerably well.' Another of his characteristics. No use of superlatives. A cool, calm medium always.

'Is there anything more I can have the honour of doing for you, sir? The warning-bell will ring at nine; the family take breakfast at half-past nine.'

'Nothing, I thank you.'

'I thank *you*, sir, if you please'; and with that, and with a little inclination of his head when he passed the bedside, as an apology for correcting me, he went out, shutting the door as delicately as if I had just fallen into a sweet sleep on which my life depended.

Every morning we held exactly this conversation; never any more, and never any less; and yet, invariably, however far I might have been lifted out of myself overnight, and advanced towards maturer years, by Steerforth's companionship, or Mrs Steerforth's confidence, or Miss Dartle's conversation, in the presence of this most respectable man I became, as our smaller poets sing, 'a boy again.'

He got horses for us; and Steerforth, who knew everything, gave me lessons in riding. He provided foils for us, and Steerforth gave me lessons in fencing – gloves, and I began, of the same master, to improve in boxing. It gave me no manner of concern that Steerforth should find me a novice in these sciences, but I never could bear to show my want of skill before the respectable Littimer. I had no reason to believe that Littimer understood such arts himself; he never led me to suppose anything of the kind, by so much as the vibration of one of his respectable eyelashes; yet whenever he was by, while we were practising, I felt myself the greenest and most inexperienced of mortals.

I am particular about this man, because he made a particular effect on me at that time, and because of what took place thereafter.

The week passed away in a most delightful manner. It passed rapidly, as may be supposed, to one entranced as I was; and yet it gave me so many occasions for knowing Steerforth better, and admiring him more in a thousand respects, that at its close I seemed to have been with him for a much longer time. A dashing way he had of treating me like a plaything was more agreeable to me than any behaviour he could have adopted. It reminded me of our old acquaintance; it seemed the natural sequel of it; it showed me that he was unchanged; it relieved me of any uneasiness I might have felt, in comparing my merits with his, and measuring my claims upon his friendship by any equal standard; above all, it was a familiar, unrestrained, affectionate demeanour that he used towards no one else. As he had treated me at school differently from all the rest, I joyfully believed that he treated me in life unlike any other friend he had. I believed that I was nearer to his heart than any other friend, and my own heart warmed with attachment to him.

He made up his mind to go with me into the country, and the day arrived for our departure. He had been doubtful at first whether to take Littimer or not, but decided to leave him at home. The respectable creature, satisfied with his lot whatever it was, arranged our portmanteaus on the little carriage that was to take us into London, as if they were intended to defy the shock of ages; and received my modestly proffered donation with perfect tranquillity.

We bade adieu to Mrs Steerforth and Miss Dartle, with many thanks on my part, and much kindness on the devoted mother's. The last thing I saw was Littimer's unruffled eye, fraught, as I fancied, with the silent conviction that I was very young, indeed.

What I felt, in returning so auspiciously to the old familiar places, I shall not endeavour to describe. We went down by the Mail. I was so concerned, I recollect, even for the honour of Yarmouth, that when Steerforth said, as we drove through its dark streets to the inn, that, as well as he could make out, it was a good, queer, out-of-the-way kind of hole, I was highly pleased. We went to bed on our arrival (I observed a pair of dirty shoes and gaiters in connection with my old friend the Dolphin as we passed that door), and breakfasted late in the morning. Steerforth, who was in great spirits, had been strolling about the beach before I was up, and had made acquaintance, he said, with half the boatmen in the place. Moreover, he had seen, in the distance, what he was sure must be the identical house of Mr Peggotty, with smoke coming out of the chimney; and had had a great mind, he told me, to walk in and swear he was myself grown out of knowledge.

'When do you propose to introduce me there, Daisy?' he said. 'I am at your disposal. Make your own arrangements.'

'Why, I was thinking that this evening would be a good time, Steerforth, when they are all sitting round the fire. I should like you to see it when it's snug, it's such a curious place.'

'So be it!' returned Steerforth. 'This evening.'

'I shall not give them any notice that we are here, you know,' said I, delighted. 'We must take them by surprise.'

'Oh, of course! It's no fun,' said Steerforth, 'unless we take them by surprise. Let us see the natives in their aboriginal condition.'

'Though they *are* that sort of people that you mentioned,' I returned.

'Aha! What! you recollect my skirmishes with Rosa, do you?' he exclaimed, with a quick look. 'Confound the girl, I am half afraid of her. She's like a goblin to me. But never mind her. Now what are you going to do? You are going to see your nurse, I suppose?'

'Why, yes,' I said, 'I must see Peggotty first of all.'

'Well,' replied Steerforth, looking at his watch; 'suppose I deliver you up to be cried over for a couple of hours. Is that long enough?'

I answered, laughing, that I thought we might get through it in that time, but that he must come also; for he would find that his renown had preceded him, and that he was almost as great a personage as I was.

'I'll come anywhere you like,' said Steerforth, 'or do anything you like. Tell me where to come to; and in two hours I'll produce myself in any state you please, sentimental or comical.'

I gave him minute directions for finding the residence of Mr Barkis, carrier to Blunderstone and elsewhere; and, on this understanding, went out alone. There was a sharp bracing air; the ground was dry; the sea was crisp and clear; the sun was diffusing abundance of light, if not much warmth; and everything was fresh and lively. I was so fresh and lively myself, in the pleasure of being there, that I could have stopped the people in the streets and shaken hands with them.

The streets looked small, of course. The streets that we have only seen as children always do, I believe, when we go back to them. But I had forgotten nothing in them, and found nothing changed, until I came to Mr Omer's shop. Omer and Joram was now written up, where Omer used to be; but the inscription, Draper, Tailor, Haberdasher, Funeral Furnisher, etc., remained as it was.

My footsteps seemed to tend so naturally to the shop door, after I had read these words from over the way, that I went across the road and looked in. There was a pretty woman at the back of the shop, dancing a little child in her arms, while another little fellow clung to her apron. I had no difficulty in recognising either Minnie or Minnie's children. The glass door of the parlour was not open; but in the workshop across the yard I could faintly hear the old tune playing, as if it had never left off.

'Is Mr Omer at home?' said I, entering. 'I should like to see him, for a moment, if he is.'

'Oh, yes, sir, he is at home,' said Minnie; 'this weather don't suit his asthma out of doors. Joe, call your grandfather!'

The little fellow, who was holding her apron, gave such a lusty shout that the sound of it made him bashful, and he buried his face in her skirts, to her great admiration. I heard a heavy puffing and blowing coming towards us, and soon Mr Omer, shorter-winded than of yore, but not much older looking, stood before me.

'Servant, sir,' said Mr Omer. 'What can I do for you, sir?'

'You can shake hands with me, Mr Omer, if you please,' said I, putting out my own. 'You were very good-natured to me once, when I am afraid I didn't show that I thought so.'

'Was I, though?' returned the old man. 'I'm glad to hear it, but I don't remember when. Are you sure it was me?'

'Quite.'

'I think my memory has got as short as my breath,' said Mr Omer, looking at me and shaking his head; 'for I don't remember you.'

'Don't you remember your coming to the coach to meet me, and my having breakfast here, and our riding out to Blunderstone together: you, and I, and Mrs Joram, and Mr Joram, too – who wasn't her husband then?'

'Why, Lord bless my soul!' exclaimed Mr Omer, after being thrown by his surprise into a fit of coughing, 'you don't say so! Minnie, my dear, you recollect? Dear me, yes – the party was a lady, I think?'

'My mother,' I rejoined.

'To – be – sure,' said Mr Omer, touching my waistcoat with his forefinger, 'and there was a little child, too! There was two parties. The little party was laid along with the other party. Over at Blunderstone it was, of course. Dear me! And how have you been since?'

Very well, I thanked him, as I hoped he had been, too.

'Oh! nothing to grumble at, you know,' said Mr Omer. 'I find my breath gets short, but it seldom gets longer as a man gets older. I take it as it comes, and make the most of it. That's the best way, ain't it?'

Mr Omer coughed again, in consequence of laughing, and was assisted out of his fit by his daughter, who now stood close beside us, dancing her smallest child on the counter.

'Dear me!' said Mr Omer. 'Yes, to be sure. Two parties! Why, in that very ride, if you'll believe me, the day was named for my Minnie to marry Joram. "Do name it, sir," says Joram. "Yes, do, father," says Minnie. And now he's come into the business. And look here! The youngest!'

Minnie laughed, and stroked her banded hair upon her temples, as her father put one of his fat fingers into the hand of the child she was dancing on the counter.

'Two parties, of course!' said Mr Omer, nodding his head retrospectively. 'Ex–actly so! And Joram's at work, at this minute, on a grey one with silver nails, not this measurement' – the measurement of the dancing child upon the counter – 'by a good two inches. Will you take something?'

I thanked him, but declined.

'Let me see,' said Mr Omer. 'Barkis's the carrier's wife – Peggotty's the boatman's sister – she had something to do with your family? She was in service there, sure?'

My answering in the affirmative gave him great satisfaction.

'I believe my breath will get long next, my memory's getting so much so,' said Mr Omer. 'Well, sir, we've got a young relation of hers here, under articles to us, that has as elegant a taste in the dressmaking business – I assure you, I don't believe there's a Duchess in England can touch her.'

'Not little Em'ly?' said I, involuntarily.

'Em'ly's her name,' said Mr Omer, 'and she's little, too. But if you'll believe me, she has such a face of her own that half the women in this town are mad against her.'

'Nonsense, father!' cried Minnie.

'My dear,' said Mr Omer, 'I don't say it's the case with you,' winking at me, 'but I say that half the women in Yarmouth, ah! and in five mile round, are mad against that girl.'

'Then she should have kept to her own station in life, father,' said Minnie, 'and not have given them any hold to talk about her, and then they couldn't have done it.'

'Couldn't have done it, my dear!' retorted Mr Omer. 'Couldn't have done it! Is that *your* knowledge of life? What is there that any woman couldn't do, that she shouldn't do – especially on the subject of another woman's good looks?'

I really thought it was all over with Mr Omer, after he had uttered this libellous pleasantry. He coughed to that extent, and his breath eluded all his attempts to recover it with that obstinacy, that I fully expected to see his head go down behind the counter, and his little black breeches, with the rusty little bunches of ribbons at the knees, come quivering up in a last ineffectual struggle. At length, however, he got better, though he still panted hard, and was so exhausted that he was obliged to sit on the stool of the shop-desk.

'You see,' he said, wiping his head, and breathing with difficulty, 'she hasn't taken much to any companions here; she hasn't taken kindly to any particular acquaintances and friends, not to mention sweethearts. In consequence, an ill-natured story got about that Em'ly wanted to be a lady. Now, my opinion is that it came into circulation principally on account of her some-times saying at the school that, if she was a lady, she would like to do so and so for her uncle – don't you see? – and buy him such and such fine things.'

'I assure you, Mr Omer, she has said so to me,' I returned eagerly, 'when we were both children.'

Mr Omer nodded his head and rubbed his chin. 'Just so. Then out of a very little, she could dress herself, you see, better than most others could out of a deal, and *that* made things unpleasant. Moreover, she was rather what might be called way-ward. I'll go so far as to say what I should call wayward myself,' said Mr Omer, 'didn't know her own mind quite; a little spoiled; and couldn't, at first, exactly bind herself down. No more than that was ever said against her, Minnie?'

'No, father,' said Mrs Joram. 'That's the worst, I believe.'

'So, when she got a situation,' said Mr Omer, 'to keep a fractious old lady company, they didn't very well agree, and she didn't stop. At last she came here, apprenticed for three years. Nearly two of 'em are over, and she has been as good a girl as ever was. Worth any six! Minnie, is she worth any six, now?'

'Yes, father,' replied Minnie. 'Never say *I* detracted from her!'

'Very good,' said Mr Omer. 'That's right. And so, young gentleman,' he added, after a few moments' further rubbing of his chin, 'that you may not consider me long-winded as well as short-breathed, I believe that's all about it.'

As they had spoken in a subdued tone, while speaking of Em'ly, I had no doubt that she was near. On my asking now, if that were not so, Mr Omer nodded yes, and nodded towards the door of the parlour. My hurried enquiry, if I might peep in, was answered with a free permission; and, looking through the glass, I saw her sitting at her work. I saw her, a most beautiful little creature, with the cloudless blue eyes that had looked into my childish heart turned laughingly upon another child of Minnie's who was playing near her; with enough of wilfulness in her bright face to justify what I had heard; with much of the old capricious coyness lurking in it; but with nothing in her pretty looks, I am sure, but what was meant for goodness and for happiness, and what was on a good and happy course.

The tune across the yard that seemed as if it never had left off – alas! it was the tune that never *does* leave off – was beating, softly, all the while.

'Wouldn't you like to step in,' said Mr Omer, 'and speak to her? Walk in and speak to her, sir! Make yourself at home!'

I was too bashful to do so then – I was afraid of confusing her, and I was no less afraid of confusing myself; but I informed myself of the hour at which she left of an evening, in order that our visit might be timed accordingly; and taking leave of Mr

Omer, and his pretty daughter, and her little children, went away to my dear old Peggotty's.

Here she was, in the tiled-kitchen, cooking dinner! The moment I knocked at the door she opened it, and asked me what I pleased to want. I looked at her with a smile, but she gave me no smile in return. I had never ceased to write to her, but it must have been seven years since we had met.

'Is Mr Barkis at home, ma'am?' I said, feigning to speak roughly to her.

'He's at home, sir,' returned Peggotty, 'but he's bad abed with the rheumatics.'

'Don't he go over to Blunderstone now?' I asked.

'When he's well he do,' she answered.

'Do *you* ever go there, Mrs Barkis?'

She looked at me more attentively, and I noticed a quick movement of her hands towards each other.

'Because I want to ask a question about a house there, that they call the – what is it? – the Rookery,' said I.

She took a step backward, and put out her hands in an undecided, frightened way, as if to keep me off.

'Peggotty!' I cried to her.

She cried, 'My darling boy!' and we both burst into tears, and were locked in one another's arms.

What extravagances she committed; what laughing and crying over me; what pride she showed, what joy, what sorrow that she whose pride and joy I might have been could never hold me in a fond embrace, I have not the heart to tell. I was troubled with no misgiving that it was young in me to respond to her emotions. I had never laughed and cried in all my life, I dare say – not even to her – more freely than I did that morning.

'Barkis will be so glad,' said Peggotty, wiping her eyes with her apron, 'that it'll do him more good than pints of liniment. May I go and tell him you are here? Will you come up and see him, my dear?'

Of course I would. But Peggotty could not get out of the room as easily as she meant to, for, as often as she got to the door and looked round at me, she came back again to have another laugh and another cry upon my shoulder. At last, to make the matter easier, I went upstairs with her; and having waited outside for a minute, while she said a word of preparation to Mr Barkis, presented myself before that invalid.

He received me with absolute enthusiasm. He was too rheumatic to be shaken hands with, but he begged me to shake the tassel on the top of his nightcap, which I did most cordially. When I sat down by the side of the bed, he said that it did him a world of good to feel as if he was driving me on the Blunder-stone road again. As he lay in bed, face upward, and so covered, with that exception, that he seemed to be nothing but a face – like a conventional cherubim – he looked the queerest object I ever beheld.

'What name was it as I wrote up in the cart, sir?' said Mr Barkis, with a slow rheumatic smile.

'Ah! Mr Barkis, we had some grave talks about that matter, hadn't we?'

'I was willin' a long time, sir?' said Mr Barkis.

'A long time,' said I.

'And I don't regret it,' said Mr Barkis. 'Do you remember what you told me once, about her making all the apple parsties and doing all the cooking?'

'Yes, very well,' I returned.

'It was as true,' said Mr Barkis, 'as turnips is. It was as true,' said Mr Barkis, nodding his nightcap, which was his only means of emphasis, 'as taxes is. And nothing's truer than them.'

Mr Barkis turned his eyes upon me, as if for my assent to this result of his reflections in bed; and I gave it.

'Nothing's truer than them,' repeated Mr Barkis; 'a man as poor as I am finds that out in his mind when he's laid up. I'm a very poor man, sir.'

'I am sorry to hear it, Mr Barkis.'

'A very poor man, indeed I am,' said Mr Barkis.

Here his right hand came slowly and feebly from under the bedclothes, and with a purposeless, uncertain grasp took hold of a stick which was loosely tied to the side of the bed. After some poking about with this instrument, in the course of which his face assumed a variety of distracted expressions, Mr Barkis poked it against a box, an end of which had been visible to me all the time. Then his face became composed.

'Old clothes,' said Mr Barkis.

'Oh!' said I.

'I wish it was Money, sir,' said Mr Barkis.

'I wish it was, indeed,' said I.

'But it ain't,' said Mr Barkis, opening both his eyes as wide as he possibly could.

I expressed myself quite sure of that, and Mr Barkis, turning his eyes more gently to his wife, said: 'She's the usefullest and best of women, C. P. Barkis. All the praise that anyone can give to C. P. Barkis, she deserves, and more! My dear, you'll get a dinner today, for company; something good to eat and drink, will you?'

I should have protested against this unnecessary demonstration in my honour, but that I saw Peggotty, on the opposite side of the bed, extremely anxious I should not. So I held my peace.

'I have got a trifle of money somewhere about me, my dear,' said Mr Barkis, 'but I'm a little tired. If you and Mr David will leave me for a short nap, I'll try and find it when I wake.'

We left the room in compliance with this request. When we got outside the door, Peggotty informed me that Mr Barkis, being now 'a little nearer' than he used to be, always resorted to this same device before producing a single coin from his store; and that he endured unheard-of agonies in crawling out of bed alone, and taking it from that unlucky box. In effect, we presently heard him uttering suppressed groans of the most dismal nature, as this magpie proceeding racked him in every joint; but while Peggotty's eyes were full of compassion for him, she said his generous impulse would do him good, and it was better not to check it. So he groaned on until he had got into bed again, suffering, I have no doubt, a martyrdom; and then called us in, pretending to have just woke up from a refreshing sleep, and to produce a guinea from under his pillow. His satisfaction in which happy imposition on us, and in having preserved the impenetrable secret of the box, appeared to be a sufficient compensation to him for all his tortures.

I prepared Peggotty for Steerforth's arrival, and it was not long before he came. I am persuaded she knew no difference between his having been a personal benefactor of hers and a kind friend to me, and that she would have received him with the utmost gratitude and devotion in any case. But his easy, spirited good-humour; his genial manner, his handsome looks, his natural gift of adapting himself to whomsoever he pleased, and making direct, when he cared to do it, to the main point of interest in anybody's heart, bound her to him wholly in five minutes. His manner to me, alone, would have won her. But through all these causes combined, I sincerely believe she had a kind of adoration for him before he left the house that night.

He stayed there with me to dinner – if I were to say willingly, I should not half express how readily and gaily. He went into Mr Barkis's room like light and air, brightening and refreshing it as if he were healthy weather. There was no noise, no effort, no consciousness, in anything he did; but in everything an indescribable lightness, a seeming impossibility of doing anything else, or doing anything better, which was so graceful, so natural, and agreeable, that it overcomes me, even now, in the remembrance.

We made merry in the little parlour, where the *Book of Martyrs*, unthumbed since my time, was laid out upon the desk as of old, and where I now turned over its terrific pictures, remembering the old sensations they had awakened, but not feeling them. When Peggotty spoke of what she called my room, and of its being ready for me at night, and of her hoping I would occupy it, before I could so much as look at Steerforth, hesitating, he was possessed of the whole case.

'Of course,' he said. 'You'll sleep here while we stay, and I shall sleep at the hotel.'

'But to bring you so far,' I returned, 'and to separate, seems bad companionship, Steerforth.'

'Why, in the name of Heaven, where do you naturally belong!' he said. 'What is "seems" compared to that!' It was settled at once.

He maintained all his delightful qualities to the last, until we started forth, at eight o'clock, for Mr Peggotty's boat. Indeed, they were more and more brightly exhibited as the hours went on; for I thought even then, and I have no doubt now, that the consciousness of success in his determination to please inspired him with a new delicacy of perception, and made it, subtle as it was, more easy to him. If anyone had told me, then, that all this was a brilliant game, played for the excitement of the moment, for the employment of high spirits, in the thoughtless love of superiority, in a mere wasteful careless course of winning what was worthless to him, and next minute thrown away – I say, if anyone had told me such a lie that night, I wonder in what manner of receiving it my indignation would have found a vent!

Probably only in an increase, had that been possible, of the romantic feelings of fidelity and friendship with which I walked beside him, over the dark wintry sands, towards the old boat; the wind sighing around us even more mournfully than it had sighed and moaned upon the night when I first darkened Mr Peggotty's door.

'This is a wild kind of place, Steerforth, is it not?'

'Dismal enough in the dark,' he said; 'and the sea roars as if it were hungry for us. Is that the boat, where I see a light yonder?'

'That's the boat,' said I.

'And it's the same I saw this morning,' he returned. 'I came straight to it, by instinct, I suppose.'

We said no more as we approached the light, but made softly for the door. I laid my hand upon the latch, and whispering Steerforth to keep close to me, went in.

A murmur of voices had been audible on the outside, and, at the moment of our entrance, a clapping of hands; which latter noise, I was surprised to see, proceeded from the generally disconsolate Mrs Gummidge. But Mrs Gummidge was not the only person there who was unusually excited. Mr Peggotty, his face lighted up with uncommon satisfaction, and laughing with all his might, held his rough arms wide open, as if for little Em'ly to run into them; Ham, with a mixed expression in his face of admiration, exultation, and a lumbering sort of bashfulness that sat upon him very well, held little Em'ly by the hand as if he were presenting her to Mr Peggotty; little Em'ly herself, blushing and shy, but delighted with Mr Peggotty's delight, as her joyous eyes expressed, was stopped by our entrance (for she saw us first) in the very act of springing from Ham to nestle in Mr Peggotty's embrace. In the first glimpse we had of them all, and at the moment of our passing from the dark cold night into the warm light room, this was the way in which they were all employed – Mrs Gummidge in the background, clapping her hands like a madwoman.

The little picture was so instantaneously dissolved by our going in, that one might have doubted whether it had ever been. I was in the midst of the astonished family, face to face with Mr Peggotty, and holding out my hand to him, when Ham shouted: 'Mas'r Davy! It's Mas'r Davy!'

In a moment we were all shaking hands with one another, and asking one another how we did, and telling one another how glad we were to meet, and all talking at once. Mr Peggotty was so proud and overjoyed to see us, that he did not know what to say or do, but kept over and over again shaking hands with me, and then with Steerforth, and then with me, and then ruffling his shaggy hair all over his head, and laughing with such glee and triumph, that it was a treat to see him.

'Why, that you two gen'lm'n – gen'lm'n growed – should come to this here roof tonight, of all nights in my life,' said Mr Peggotty, 'is such a thing as never happened afore, I do rightly believe! Em'ly, my darling, come here! Come here, my little witch! Theer's Mas'r Davy's friend, my dear! Theer's the gen'lm'n as you've heerd on, Em'ly. He comes to see you, along with Mas'r Davy, on the brightest night of your uncle's life as ever was or will be, Gorm the t' other one, and horroar for it!'

After delivering this speech all in a breath, and with extraordinary animation and pleasure, Mr Peggotty put one of his large hands rapturously on each side of his niece's face, and kissing it a dozen times, laid it with a gentle pride and love upon his broad chest, and patted it as if his hand had been a lady's. Then he let her go; and as she ran into the little chamber where I used to sleep, looked round upon us, quite hot and out of breath with his uncommon satisfaction.

'If you two gen'lm'n – gen'lm'n growed now, and such gen'lm'n –' said Mr Peggotty.

'So th' are, so th' are!' cried Ham. 'Well said! So th' are. Mas'r Davy bor – gen'lm'n growed – so th' are!'

'If you two gen'lm'n, gen'lm'n growed,' said Mr Peggotty, 'don't ex-cuse me for being in a state of mind, when you understand matters, I'll arks your pardon. Em'ly, my dear! – She knows I'm a going to tell,' here his delight broke out again, 'and

We arrive unexpectedly at Mr Peggotty's fireside

has made off. Would you be so good as look arter her, Mawther, for a minute?'

Mrs Gummidge nodded and disappeared.

'If this ain't,' said Mr Peggotty, sitting down among us by the fire, 'the brightest night o' my life, I'm a shellfish – biled too – and more I can't say. This here little Em'ly, sir,' in a low voice to Steerforth, ' – her as you see a blushing here just now –'

Steerforth only nodded, but with such a pleased expression of interest, and of participation in Mr Peggotty's feelings, that the latter answered him as if he had spoken.

'To be sure,' said Mr Peggotty. 'That's her, and so she is. Thankee, sir.'

Ham nodded to me several times, as if he would have said so too.

'This here little Em'ly of ours,' said Mr Peggotty, 'has been, in our house, what I suppose (I'm a ignorant man, but that's my belief) no one but a little bright-eyed creetur *can* be in a house. She ain't my child; I never had one; but I couldn't love her more. You understand! I couldn't do it!'

'I quite understand,' said Steerforth.

'I know you do, sir,' returned Mr Peggotty, 'and thankee again. Mas'r Davy, he can remember what she was; you may judge for your own self what she is; but neither of you can't fully know what she has been, is, and will be, to my loving art. I am rough, sir,' said Mr Peggotty, 'I am as rough as a Sea Porkypine; but no one, unless, mayhap, it is a woman, can know, I think, what our little Em'ly is to me. And betwixt ourselves,' sinking his voice lower yet, '*that* woman's name ain't Missis Gummidge neither, though she has a world of merits.'

Mr Peggotty ruffled his hair again with both hands, as a further preparation for what he was going to say, and went on with a hand upon each of his knees.

'There was a certain person as had knowed our Em'ly, from the time when her father was drownded; as had seen her constant; when a babby, when a young gal, when a woman. Not much of a person to look at, he warn't,' said Mr Peggotty, 'something o' my own build – rough – a good deal o' the sou'-wester in him – wery salt – but, on the whole, a honest sort of a chap, with his art in the right place.'

I thought I had never seen Ham grin to anything like the extent to which he sat grinning at us now.

'What does this here blessed tarpaulin go and do,' said Mr Peggotty, with his face one high noon of enjoyment, 'but he loses that art of his to our little Em'ly. He follers her about, he makes hisself a sort o' servant to her, he loses in a great measure his relish for his wittles, and in the long run he makes it clear to me wot's amiss. Now I could wish myself, you see, that our little Em'ly was in a fair way of being married. I could wish to see her, at all ewents, under articles to a honest man as had a right to defend her. I don't know how long I may live, or how soon I may die; but I know that if I was capsized, any night, in a gale of wind in Yarmouth Roads here, and was to see the town-lights shining for the last time over the rollers as I couldn't make no head against, I could go down quieter for thinking "There's a man ashore there, iron-true to my little Em'ly, God bless her, and no wrong can touch my Em'ly while so be as that man lives!" '

Mr Peggotty, in simple earnestness, waved his right arm, as if he were waving it at the town-lights for the last time, and then, exchanging a nod with Ham, whose eye he caught, proceeded as before.

'Well! I counsels him to speak to Em'ly. He's big enough, but he's bashfuller than a little 'un, and he don't like. So I speak. "What! *Him!*" says Em'ly. "*Him* that I've knowed so intimate so many years, and like so much! Oh, Uncle! I never can have *him*. He's such a good fellow!" I gives her a kiss, and I says no more to her than "My dear, you're right to speak out, you're to choose for yourself, you're as free as a little bird." Then I aways to him, and I says, "I wish it could have been so, but it can't. But you can both be as you was, and wot I say to you is, Be as you was with her, like a man." He says to me, a shaking of my hand, "I will!" he says. And he was – honourable and manful – for two year going on, and we was just the same at home here as afore.'

Mr Peggotty's face, which had varied in its expression with the various stages of his narrative, now resumed all its former triumphant delight, as he laid a hand upon my knee and a hand upon Steerforth's (previously wetting them both, for the greater emphasis of the action), and divided the following speech between us: 'All of a sudden, one evening – as it might be tonight – comes little Em'ly from her work, and him with her! There ain't so much in *that*, you'll say. No, because he takes care on her, like a brother, arter dark, and indeed afore dark, and at all times. But this tarpaulin chap, he takes hold of her hand, and he cries out to me, joyful, "Look here! This is to be my little wife!" And she says, half bold and half shy, and half a-laughing and half a-crying, "Yes, Uncle! If you please." – If I please!' cried Mr Peggotty, rolling his head in an ecstasy at the idea; 'Lord, as if I should do anythink else! – "If you please, I am steadier now, and I have thought better of it, and I'll be as good a little wife as I can to him, for he's a dear, good fellow!" Then Missis Gummidge, she claps her hands like a play, and you come in. There! the murder's out!' said Mr Peggotty – 'You come in! It took place this here present hour; and here's the man that'll marry her, the minute she's out of her time.'

Ham staggered, as well he might, under the blow Mr Peggotty dealt him in his unbounded joy, as a mark of confidence and friendship; but feeling called upon to say something to us, he said, with much faltering and great difficulty: 'She warn't no higher than you was, Mas'r Davy – when you first come – when I thought what she'd grow up to be. I see her grow up – gen'lm'n – like a flower. I'd lay down my life for her – Mas'r Davy – Oh! most content and cheerful! She's more to me – gen'lm'n – than – she's all to me that ever I can want, and more than ever I – than ever I could say. I – I love her true. There ain't a gen'lm'n in all the land – nor yet sailing upon all the sea – that can love his lady more than I love her, though there's many a common man – would say better – what he meant.'

I thought it affecting to see such a sturdy fellow as Ham was now, trembling in the strength of what he felt for the pretty little creature who had won his heart. I thought the simple confidence reposed in us by Mr Peggotty and by himself was, in itself, affecting. I was affected by the story altogether. How far my emotions were influenced by the recollections of my childhood, I don't know. Whether I had come there with any lingering fancy that I was still to love little Em'ly, I don't know. I know that I was filled with pleasure by all this; but at first, with an indescribably sensitive pleasure, that a very little would have changed to pain.

Therefore, if it had depended upon me to touch the prevailing chord among them with any skill, I should have made a poor hand of it. But it depended upon Steerforth; and he did it with such address that in a few minutes we were all as easy and as happy as it was possible to be.

'Mr Peggotty,' he said, 'you are a thoroughly good fellow, and deserve to be as happy as you are tonight. My hand upon it! Ham, I give you joy, my boy. My hand upon that, too! Daisy, stir the fire, and make it a brisk one! and Mr Peggotty, unless you can induce your gentle niece to come back (for whom I vacate this seat in the corner), I shall go. Any gap at your fireside on such a night – such a gap, least of all – I wouldn't make, for the wealth of the Indies!'

So Mr Peggotty went into my old room to fetch little Em'ly. At first little Em'ly didn't like to come, and then Ham went. Presently they brought her to the fireside, very much confused, and very shy – but she soon became more assured when she found how gently and respectfully Steerforth spoke to her; how skilfully he avoided anything that would embarrass her; how he talked to Mr Peggotty of boats, and ships, and tides, and fish; how he referred to me about the time when he had seen Mr Peggotty at Salem House; how delighted he was with the boat and all belonging to it; how lightly and easily he carried on, until he brought us, by degrees, into a charmed circle, and we were all talking away without any reserve.

Em'ly, indeed, said little all the evening; but she looked, and listened, and her face got animated, and she was charming. Steerforth told a story of a dismal shipwreck (which arose out of his talk with Mr Peggotty), as if he saw it all before him – and little Em'ly's eyes were fastened on him all the time, as if she saw it, too. He told us a merry adventure of his own, as a relief to that, with as much gaiety as if the narrative were as fresh to him as it was to us – and little Em'ly laughed until the boat rang with the musical sounds, and we all laughed (Steerforth, too), in irresistible sympathy with what was so pleasant and light-hearted. He got Mr Peggotty to sing, or rather to roar, 'When the stormy winds do blow, do blow, do blow;' and he sang a sailor's song himself, so pathetically and beautifully that I could have almost fancied that the real wind creeping sorrowfully round the house, and murmuring low through our unbroken silence, was there to listen.

As to Mrs Gummidge, he roused that victim of despondency with a success never attained by anyone else (so Mr Peggotty informed me), since the decease of the old one. He left her so little leisure for being miserable that she said next day she thought she must have been bewitched.

But he set up no monopoly of the general attention or the conversation. When little Em'ly grew more courageous, and talked (but still bashfully) across the fire to me, of our old wanderings upon the beach, to pick up shells and pebbles; and when I asked her if she recollected how I used to be devoted to her; and when we both laughed and reddened, casting these looks back on the pleasant old times, so unreal to look at now, he was silent and attentive, and observed us thoughtfully. She sat, at this time, and all the evening, on the old locker in her old little corner by the fire – Ham beside her, where I used to sit. I could not satisfy myself whether it was in her own little tormenting way, or in a maidenly reserve before us, that she kept quite close to the wall, and away from him; but I observed that she did so, all the evening.

As I remember, it was almost midnight when we took our leave. We had had some biscuit and dried fish for supper, and Steerforth had produced from his pocket a full flask of Hollands, which we men (I may say we men, now, without a blush) had emptied. We parted merrily; and as they all stood crowded round the door to light us as far as they could upon our road, I saw the sweet blue eyes of little Em'ly peeping after us, from behind Ham, and heard her soft voice calling to us to be careful how we went.

'A most engaging little Beauty!' said Steerforth, taking my arm. 'Well! It's a quaint place, and they are quaint company; and it's quite a new sensation to mix with them.'

'How fortunate we are, too,' I returned, 'to have arrived to witness their happiness in that intended marriage! I never saw people so happy. How delightful to see it, and to be made the sharers in their honest joy, as we have been!'

'That's rather a chuckle-headed fellow for the girl, isn't he?' said Steerforth.

He had been so hearty with him, and with them all, that I felt a shock in this unexpected and cold reply. But turning quickly upon him, and seeing a laugh in his eyes, I answered, much relieved: 'Ah, Steerforth! It's well for you to joke about the poor! You may skirmish with Miss Dartle, or try to hide your sympathies in jest from me, but I know better. When I see how perfectly you understand them, how exquisitely you can enter into happiness like this plain fisherman's, or humour a love like my old nurse's, I know that there is not a joy or sorrow, not an emotion, of such people, that can be indifferent to you. And I admire and love you for it, Steerforth, twenty times the more!'

He stopped, and, looking in my face, said, 'Daisy, I believe you are in earnest, and are good. I wish we all were!' Next moment he was gaily singing Mr Peggotty's song, as we walked at a round pace back to Yarmouth.

CHAPTER 22

Some Old Scenes, and Some New People

Steerforth and I stayed for more than a fortnight in that part of the country. We were very much together, I need not say; but occasionally we were asunder for some hours at a time. He was a good sailor, and I was but an indifferent one; and when he went out boating with Mr Peggotty, which was a favourite amusement of his, I generally remained ashore. My occupation of Peggotty's spare room put a constraint upon me, from which he was free; for, knowing how assiduously she attended on Mr Barkis all day, I did not like to remain out late at night; whereas Steerforth, lying at the inn, had nothing to consult but his own humour. Thus it came about that I heard of his making little treats for the fishermen at Mr Peggotty's house of call, 'The Willing Mind,' after I was in bed, and of his being afloat, wrapped in fisherman's clothes, whole moonlight nights, and coming back when the morning tide was at flood. By this time, however, I knew that his restless nature and bold spirit delighted to find a vent in rough toil and hard weather, as in any other means of excitement that presented itself freshly to him; so none of his proceedings surprised me.

Another cause of our being sometimes apart was that I had naturally an interest in going over to Blunderstone, and revisiting the old familiar scenes of my childhood; while Steerforth, after being there once, had naturally no great interest in going there again. Hence, on three or four days that I can at once recall, we went our several ways after an early breakfast, and met again at a late dinner. I had no idea how he employed his time in the interval, beyond a general knowledge that he was very popular in the place, and had twenty means of actively diverting himself where another man might not have found one.

For my own part, my occupation in my solitary pilgrimages was to recall every yard of the old road as I went along it, and to haunt the old spots, of which I never tired. I haunted them, as my memory had often done, and lingered among them as my younger thoughts had lingered when I was far away. The grave beneath the tree, where both my parents lay – on which I had looked out, when it was my father's only, with such curious feelings of compassion, and by which I had stood, so desolate, when it was opened to receive my pretty mother and her baby – the grave which Peggotty's own faithful care had ever since kept neat, and made a garden of, I walked near, by the hour. It lay a little off the churchyard path, in a quiet corner, not so far removed but I could read the names upon the stone as I walked to and fro, startled by the sound of the church bell when it struck the hour, for it was like a departed voice to me. My reflections at these times were always associated with the figure I was to make in life, and the distinguished things I was to do. My echoing footsteps went to no other tune, but were as constant to that as if I had come home to build my castles in the air at a living mother's side.

There were great changes in my old home. The ragged nests, so long deserted by the rooks, were gone; and the trees were lopped and topped out of their remembered shapes. The garden had run wild, and half the windows of the house were shut up. It was occupied, but only by a poor lunatic gentleman, and the people who took care of him. He was always sitting at my little window, looking out into the churchyard; and I wondered whether his rambling thoughts ever went upon any of the fancies that used to occupy mine, on the rosy mornings when I peeped out of that same little window in my night-clothes, and saw the sheep quietly feeding in the light of the rising sun.

Our old neighbours, Mr and Mrs Grayper, were gone to South America, and the rain had made its way through the roof of their empty house, and stained the outer walls. Mr Chillip was married again to a tall, raw-boned, high-nosed wife; and they had a weazen little baby, with a heavy head that it couldn't hold up, and two weak staring eyes, with which it seemed to be always wondering why it had ever been born.

It was with a singular jumble of sadness and pleasure that I used to linger about my native place, until the reddening winter sun admonished me that it was time to start on my returning walk. But when the place was left behind, and especially when Steerforth and I were happily seated over our dinner by a blazing fire, it was delicious to think of having been there. So it was, though in a softened degree, when I went to my neat room at night; and turning over the leaves of the crocodile-book (which was always there, upon a little table), remembered with a grateful heart how blessed I was in having such a friend as Steerforth, such a friend as Peggotty, and such a substitute for what I had lost as my excellent and generous aunt.

My nearest way to Yarmouth, in coming back from these long walks, was by a ferry. It landed me on the flat between the town and the sea, which I could make straight across, and so save myself a considerable circuit by the high road. Mr Peggotty's house being on that waste place, and not a hundred yards out of my track, I always looked in as I went by. Steerforth was pretty sure to be there expecting me, and we went on together through the frosty air and gathering fog towards the twinkling lights of the town.

One dark evening, when I was later than usual – for I had, that day, been making my parting visit to Blunderstone, as we were now about to return home – I found him alone in Mr Peggotty's house, sitting thoughtfully before the fire. He was so intent upon his own reflections that he was quite unconscious of my approach. This, indeed, he might easily have been if he had been less absorbed, for footsteps fell noiselessly on the sandy ground outside; but even my entrance failed to rouse him. I was standing close to him, looking at him; and still, with a heavy brow, he was lost in his meditations.

He gave such a start when I put my hand upon his shoulder that he made me start, too.

'You come upon me,' he said, almost angrily, 'like a reproachful ghost!'

'I was obliged to announce myself somehow,' I replied. 'Have I called you down from the stars?'

'No,' he answered. 'No.'

'Up from anywhere, then?' said I, taking my seat near him.

'I was looking at the pictures in the fire,' he returned.

'But you are spoiling them for me,' said I, as he stirred it quickly with a piece of burning wood, striking out of it a train of red-hot sparks that went careering up the little chimney, and roaring out into the air.

'You would not have seen them,' he returned. 'I detest this mongrel time, neither day nor night. How late you are! Where have you been?'

'I have been taking leave of my usual walk,' said I.

'And I have been sitting here,' said Steerforth, glancing round the room, 'thinking that all the people we found so glad on the night of our coming down might – to judge from the present wasted air of the place – be dispersed, or dead, or come to I don't know what harm. David, I wish to God I had had a judicious father these last twenty years!'

'My dear Steerforth, what is the matter?'

'I wish with all my soul I had been better guided!' he exclaimed. 'I wish with all my soul I could guide myself better!'

There was a passionate dejection in his manner that quite amazed me. He was more unlike himself than I could have supposed possible.

'It would be better to be this poor Peggotty, or his lout of a nephew,' he said, getting up and leaning moodily against the chimney-piece, with his face towards the fire, 'than to be myself, twenty times richer and twenty times wiser, and be the torment to myself that I have been, in this devil's bark of a boat, within the last half hour!'

I was so confounded by the alteration in him that at first I could only observe him in silence, as he stood leaning his head upon his hand, and looking gloomily down at the fire. At length I begged him, with all the earnestness I felt, to tell me what had occurred to cross him so unusually, and to let me sympathise with him, if I could not hope to advise him. Before I had well concluded, he began to laugh – fretfully at first, but soon with returning gaiety.

'Tut, it's nothing, Daisy! nothing!' he replied. 'I told you at the inn in London, I am heavy company for myself sometimes. I have been a nightmare to myself, just now – must have had one, I think. At odd dull times, nursery tales come up into the memory, unrecognised for what they are. I believe I have been confounding myself with the bad boy who "didn't care," and became food for lions – a grander kind of going to the dogs, I suppose. What old women call the horrors have been creeping over me from head to foot. I have been afraid of myself.'

'You are afraid of nothing else, I think,' said I.

'Perhaps not, and yet may have enough to be afraid of, too,' he answered. 'Well! So it goes by! I am not about to be hipped again, David; but I tell you, my good fellow, once more, that it would have been well for me (and for more than me) if I had had a steadfast and judicious father!'

His face was always full of expression, but I never saw it express such a dark kind of earnestness as when he said these words, with his glance bent on the fire.

'So much for that!' he said, making as if he tossed something light into the air, with his hand.

' "Why, being gone, I am a man again,"

like Macbeth. And now for dinner; if I have not (Macbeth-like) broken up the feast with most admired disorder, Daisy.'

'But where are they all, I wonder!' said I.

'God knows,' said Steerforth. 'After strolling to the ferry looking for you, I strolled in here and found the place deserted. That set me thinking, and you found me thinking.'

The advent of Mrs Gummidge with a basket explained how the house had happened to be empty. She had hurried out to buy something that was needed against Mr Peggotty's return with the tide; and had left the door open in the meanwhile, lest Ham and little Em'ly, with whom it was an early night, should come home while she was gone. Steerforth, after very much improving Mrs Gummidge's spirits by a cheerful salutation and a jocose embrace, took my arm, and hurried me away.

He had improved his own spirits, no less than Mrs Gummidge's, for they were again at their usual flow, and he was full of vivacious conversation as we went along.

'And so,' he said gaily, 'we abandon this buccaneer life tomorrow, do we?'

'So we agreed,' I returned. 'And our places by the coach are taken, you know.'

'Aye! there's no help for it, I suppose,' said Steerforth. 'I have almost forgotten that there is anything to do in the world but to go out tossing on the sea here. I wish there was not.'

'As long as the novelty should last,' said I, laughing.

'Like enough,' he returned; 'though there's a sarcastic meaning in that observation for an amiable piece of innocence like my young friend. Well! I dare say I am a capricious fellow, David. I know I am; but while the iron *is* hot, I can strike it vigorously, too. I could pass a reasonably good examination already, as a pilot in these waters, I think.'

'Mr Peggotty says you are a wonder,' I returned.

'A nautical phenomenon, eh?' laughed Steerforth.

'Indeed he does, and you know how truly; knowing how ardent you are in any pursuit you follow, and how easily you can master it. And that amazes me most in you, Steerforth – that you should be contented with such fitful uses of your powers.'

'Contented?' he answered merrily. 'I am never contented, except with your freshness, my gentle Daisy. As to fitfulness, I have never learnt the art of binding myself to any of the wheels on which the Ixions of these days are turning round and round. I missed it somehow in a bad apprenticeship, and now don't care about it. You know I have bought a boat down here?'

'What an extraordinary fellow you are, Steerforth!' I exclaimed, stopping – for this was the first I had heard of it. 'When you may never care to come near the place again!'

'I don't know that,' he returned. 'I have taken a fancy to the place. At all events,' walking me briskly on, 'I have bought a boat that was for sale – a clipper, Mr Peggotty says; and so she is – and Mr Peggotty will be master of her in my absence.'

'Now I understand you, Steerforth!' said I, exultingly. 'You pretend you have bought it for yourself, but you have really done so to confer a benefit on him. I might have known as much at first, knowing you. My dear kind Steerforth, how can I tell you what I think of your generosity?'

'Tush!' he answered, turning red. 'The less said, the better.'

'Didn't I know?' cried I, 'didn't I say that there was not a joy, or sorrow, or any emotion, of such honest hearts that was indifferent to you?'

'Aye, aye,' he answered, 'you told me all that. There let it rest, we have said enough!'

Afraid of offending him by pursuing the subject when he made so light of it, I only pursued it in my thoughts as we went on at even a quicker pace than before.

'She must be newly rigged,' said Steerforth, 'and I shall leave Littimer behind to see it done, that I may know she is quite complete. Did I tell you Littimer had come down?'

'No.'

'Oh, yes! came down this morning, with a letter from my mother.'

As our looks met, I observed that he was pale even to his lips, though he looked very steadily at me. I feared that some difference between him and his mother might have led to his being in the frame of mind in which I had found him at the solitary fireside. I hinted so.

'Oh, no!' he said, shaking his head, and giving a slight laugh. 'Nothing of the sort! Yes. He is come down, that man of mine.'

'The same as ever?' said I.

'The same as ever,' said Steerforth. 'Distant and quiet as the North Pole. He shall see to the boat being fresh named. She's the *Stormy Petrel* now. What does Mr Peggotty care for Stormy Petrels! I'll have her christened again.'

'By what name?' I asked.

'The *Little Em'ly*.'

As he had continued to look steadily at me, I took it as a reminder that he objected to being extolled for his consideration. I could not help showing in my face how much it pleased me, but I said little, and he resumed his usual smile, and seemed relieved.

'But, see here,' he said, looking before us, 'where the original little Em'ly comes! And that fellow with her, eh? Upon my soul, he's a true knight. He never leaves her!'

Ham was a boat-builder in these days, having improved a natural ingenuity in that handicraft, until he had become a skilled workman. He was in his working-dress, and looked rugged enough, but manly withal, and a very fit protector for the blooming little creature at his side. Indeed, there was a frankness in his face, an honesty, and an undisguised show of his pride in her, and his love for her, which were, to me, the best of good looks. I thought, as they came towards us, that they were well matched, even in that particular.

She withdrew her hand timidly from his arm as we stopped to speak to them, and blushed as she gave it to Steerforth and to me. When they passed on, after we had exchanged a few words, she did not like to replace that hand, but, still appearing timid and constrained, walked by herself. I thought all this very pretty and engaging, and Steerforth seemed to think so too, as we looked after them fading away in the light of a young moon.

Suddenly there passed us – evidently following them – a young woman whose approach we had not observed, but whose face I saw as she went by, and thought I had a faint remembrance of. She was lightly dressed, looked bold, and haggard, and flaunting, and poor; but seemed, for the time, to have given all that to the wind which was blowing, and to have nothing in her mind but going after them. As the dark distant level, absorbing their figures into itself, left but itself visible between us and the sea and clouds, her figure disappeared in like manner, still no nearer to them than before.

'That is a black shadow to be following the girl,' said Steerforth, standing still; 'what does it mean?'

He spoke in a low voice that sounded almost strange to me.

'She must have it in her mind to beg of them, I think,' said I.

'A beggar would be no novelty,' said Steerforth; 'but it is a strange thing that the beggar should take that shape tonight.'

'Why?' I asked him.

'For no better reason, truly, than because I was thinking,' he said, after a pause, 'of something like it, when it came by. Where the devil did it come from, I wonder!'

'From the shadow of this wall, I think,' said I, as we emerged upon a road on which a wall abutted.

'It's gone!' he returned, looking over his shoulder. 'And all ill go with it. Now for our dinner!'

But he looked again over his shoulder towards the sea-line glimmering afar off; and yet again. And he wondered about it, in some broken expressions, several times, in the short remainder of our walk; and only seemed to forget it when the light of fire and candle shone upon us, seated warm and merry, at table.

Littimer was there, and had his usual effect upon me. When I said to him that I hoped Mrs Steerforth and Miss Dartle were well, he answered respectfully (and of course respectably) that they were tolerably well, he thanked me, and had sent their compliments. This was all, and yet he seemed to me to say as plainly as a man could say: 'You are very young, sir; you are exceedingly young.'

We had almost finished dinner, when taking a step or two towards the table, from the corner where he kept watch upon us, or rather upon me, as I felt, he said to his master: 'I beg your pardon, sir. Miss Mowcher is down here.'

'Who?' cried Steerforth, much astonished.

'Miss Mowcher, sir.'

'Why, what on earth does *she* do here?' said Steerforth.

'It appears to be her native part of the country, sir. She informs me that she makes one of her professional visits here, every year, sir. I met her in the street this afternoon, and she wished to know if she might have the honour of waiting on you after dinner, sir.'

'Do you know the Giantess in question, Daisy?' enquired Steerforth.

I was obliged to confess – I felt ashamed, even of being at this disadvantage before Littimer – that Miss Mowcher and I were wholly unacquainted.

'Then you shall know her,' said Steerforth, 'for she is one of the seven wonders of the world. When Miss Mowcher comes, show her in.'

I felt some curiosity and excitement about this lady, especially as Steerforth burst into a fit of laughing when I referred to her, and positively refused to answer any question of which I made her the subject. I remained, therefore, in a state of considerable expectation until the cloth had been removed some half an hour, and we were sitting over our decanter of wine before the fire, when the door opened, and Littimer, with his habitual serenity quite undisturbed, announced: 'Miss Mowcher!'

I looked at the doorway and saw nothing. I was still looking at the doorway, thinking that Miss Mowcher was a long while making her appearance, when, to my infinite astonishment, there came waddling round a sofa which stood between me and it, a pursy dwarf, of about forty or forty-five, with a very large head and face, a pair of roguish grey eyes, and such extremely little arms that, to enable herself to lay a finger archly against her snub nose as she ogled Steerforth, she was obliged to meet the finger halfway, and lay her nose against it. Her chin, which was what is called a double-chin, was so fat that it entirely swallowed up the strings of her bonnet, bow and all. Throat she had none; waist she had none; legs she had none, worth mentioning; for though she was more than full-sized down to where her waist would have been, if she had had any, and though she terminated, as human beings generally do, in a pair of feet, she was so short that she stood at a common-sized chair as at a table, resting a bag she carried on the seat. This lady, dressed in an offhand, easy style, bringing her nose and her forefinger together with the difficulty I have described, standing with her head necessarily on one side, and with one of her sharp eyes shut up making an uncommonly knowing face, after ogling Steerforth for a few moments, broke into a torrent of words.

'What! My flower!' she pleasantly began, shaking her large head at him. 'You're there, are you! Oh, you naughty boy, fie for shame, what do you do so far away from home? Up to mischief, I'll be bound. Oh, you're a downy fellow, Steerforth, so you are, and I'm another, ain't I? Ha, ha, ha! You'd have betted a hundred pound to five, now, that you wouldn't have seen me here, wouldn't you? Bless you, man alive, I'm everywhere. I'm here, and there, and where not, like the conjurer's half-crown in the lady's hankercher. Talking of hankerchers – *and* talking of ladies – what a comfort you are to your blessed mother, ain't you, my dear boy, over one of my shoulders, and I don't say which!'

Miss Mowcher untied her bonnet, at this passage of her discourse, threw back the strings, and sat down, panting, on a footstool, in front of the fire – making a kind of arbour of the dining-table, which spread its mahogany shelter above her head.

'Oh, my stars and what's-their-names!' she went on, clapping a hand on each of her little knees, and glancing shrewdly at me. 'I'm of too full a habit, that's the fact, Steerforth. After a flight of stairs, it gives me as much trouble to draw every breath I want, as if it was a bucket of water. If you saw me looking out of an upper window, you'd think I was a fine woman, wouldn't you?'

'I should think that, wherever I saw you,' replied Steerforth.

'Go along, you dog, do!' cried the little creature, making a whisk at him with the handkerchief with which she was wiping her face, 'and don't be impudent! But I give you my word and honour I was at Lady Mithers's last week – *there's* a woman. How *she* wears! – and Mithers himself came into the room where I was waiting for her – *there's* a man! How *he* wears! and his wig too, for he's had it these ten years – and he went on at that rate in the complimentary line, that I began to think I should be obliged to ring the bell. Ha, ha, ha! He's a pleasant wretch, but he wants principle.'

'What were you doing for Lady Mithers?' asked Steerforth.

'That's tellings, my blessed infant,' she retorted, tapping her nose again, screwing up her face, and twinkling her eyes like an imp of supernatural intelligence. 'Never *you* mind! You'd like to know whether I stop her hair from falling off, or dye it, or touch up her complexion, or improve her eyebrows, wouldn't you? And so you shall, my darling – when I tell you! Do you know what my great-grandfather's name was?'

'No,' said Steerforth.

'It was Walker, my sweet pet,' replied Miss Mowcher, 'and he came of a long line of Walkers, that I inherit all the Hookey estates from.'

I never beheld anything approaching to Miss Mowcher's wink, except Miss Mowcher's self-possession. She had a wonderful way too, when listening to what was said to her, or when waiting for an answer to what she had said herself, of pausing with her head cunningly on one side, and one eye turned up like a magpie's. Altogether I was lost in amazement, and sat staring at her, quite oblivious, I am afraid, of the laws of politeness.

She had by this time drawn the chair to her side, and was busily engaged in producing from the bag (plunging in her short arm to the shoulder, at every dive) a number of small bottles, sponges, combs, brushes, bits of flannel, little pairs of curling irons, and other instruments, which she tumbled in a heap upon the chair. From this employment she suddenly desisted, and said to Steerforth, much to my confusion: 'Who's your friend?'

'Mr Copperfield,' said Steerforth; 'he wants to know you.'

'Well, then, he shall! I thought he looked as if he did!' returned Miss Mowcher, waddling up to me, bag in hand, and laughing on me as she came. 'Face like a peach!' standing on tiptoe to pinch my cheek as I sat. 'Quite tempting! I'm very fond of peaches. Happy to make your acquaintance, Mr Copperfield, I'm sure.'

I said that I congratulated myself on having the honour to make hers, and that the happiness was mutual.

'Oh, my goodness, how polite we are!' exclaimed Miss Mowcher, making a preposterous attempt to cover her large face with her morsel of a hand. 'What a world of gammon and spinnage it is, though, ain't it!'

This was addressed confidentially to both of us, as the morsel of a hand came away from the face, and buried itself, arm and all, in the bag again.

'What do you mean, Miss Mowcher?' said Steerforth.

'Ha, ha, ha! What a refreshing set of humbugs we are, to be sure, ain't we, my sweet child?' replied that morsel of a woman, feeling in the bag with her head on one side and her eye in the air. 'Look here!' taking something out. 'Scraps of the Russian Prince's nails! Prince Alphabet turned topsy-turvy, *I* call him, for his name's got all the letters in it, higgledy-piggledy.'

'The Russian Prince is a client of yours, is he?' said Steerforth.

'I believe you, my pet,' replied Miss Mowcher. 'I keep his nails in order for him. Twice a week! Fingers *and* toes!'

'He pays well, I hope?' said Steerforth.

'Pays as he speaks, my dear child – through the nose,' replied Miss Mowcher. 'None of your close shavers the Prince ain't. You'd say so, if you saw his moustachios. Red by nature, black by art.'

'By your art, of course,' said Steerforth.

Miss Mowcher winked assent. 'Forced to send for me. Couldn't help it. The climate affected *his* dye; it did very well in Russia, but it was no go here. You never saw such a rusty Prince in all your born days as he was. Like old iron!'

'Is that why you called him a humbug just now?' enquired Steerforth.

'Oh, you're a broth of a boy, ain't you?' returned Miss Mowcher, shaking her head violently. 'I said what a set of humbugs we were in general, and I showed you the scraps of the Prince's nails to prove it. The Prince's nails do more for me in private families of the genteel sort, than all my talents put together. I always carry 'em about. They're the best introduction. If Miss Mowcher cuts the Prince's nails, she *must* be all right. I give 'em away to the young ladies. They put 'em in albums, I believe. Ha, ha, ha! Upon my life, "the whole social system" (as the men call it when they make speeches in Parliament) is a system of Prince's nails!' said this least of women, trying to fold her short arms, and nodding her large head.

Steerforth laughed heartily, and I laughed too. Miss Mowcher continuing all the time to shake her head (which was very much on one side), and to look into the air with one eye, and to wink with the other.

'Well, well!' she said, smiting her small knees, and rising, 'this is not business. Come, Steerforth, let's explore the polar regions, and have it over.'

She then selected two or three of the little instruments, and a

I make the acquaintance of Miss Mowcher

little bottle, and asked (to my surprise) if the table would bear. On Steerforth's replying in the affirmative, she pushed a chair against it, and begging the assistance of my hand, mounted up, pretty nimbly, to the top, as if it were a stage.

'If either of you saw my ankles,' she said, when she was safely elevated, 'say so, and I'll go home and destroy myself.'

'*I* did not,' said Steerforth.

'*I* did not,' said I.

'Well, then,' cried Miss Mowcher, 'I'll consent to live. Now, ducky, ducky, ducky, come to Mrs Bond and be killed.'

This was an invocation to Steerforth to place himself under her hands; who, accordingly, sat himself down, with his back to the table, and his laughing face towards me, and submitted his head to her inspection, evidently for no other purpose than our entertainment. To see Miss Mowcher standing over him, looking at his rich profusion of brown hair through a large, round magnifying-glass, which she took out of her pocket, was a most amazing spectacle.

'*You're* a pretty fellow!' said Miss Mowcher, after a brief inspection. 'You'd be as bald as a friar on the top of your head in twelve months, but for me. Just half a minute, my young friend, and we'll give you a polishing that shall keep your curls on for the next ten years!'

With this, she tilted some of the contents of the little bottle on to one of the little bits of flannel, and, again imparting some of the virtues of that preparation to one of the little brushes, began rubbing and scraping away with both on the crown of Steerforth's head in the busiest manner I ever witnessed, talking all the time.

'There's Charley Pyegrave, the duke's son,' she said. 'You know Charley?' peeping round into his face.

'A little,' said Steerforth.

'What a man *he* is! *There's* a whisker! As to Charley's legs, if they were only a pair (which they ain't), they'd defy competition. Would you believe he tried to do without me – in the Life Guards, too!'

'Mad!' said Steerforth.

'It looks like it. However, mad or sane, he tried,' returned Miss Mowcher. 'What does he do, but, lo and behold you, he goes into a perfumer's shop, and wants to buy a bottle of the Madagascar Liquid.'

'Charley does?' said Steerforth.

'Charley does. But they haven't got any of the Madagascar Liquid.'

'What is it? Something to drink?' asked Steerforth.

'To drink?' returned Miss Mowcher, stopping to slap his cheek. 'To doctor his own moustachios with, you *know*. There was a woman in the shop – elderly female – quite a Griffin – who had never even heard of it by name. "Begging pardon, sir," said the Griffin to Charley, "it's not – not – not rouge, is it?" "Rouge," said Charley to the Griffin. "What the unmentionable to ears polite, do you think I want with rouge?" "No offence, sir," said the Griffin; "we have it asked for by so many names, I thought it might be." Now that, my child,' continued Miss Mowcher, rubbing all the time as busily as ever, 'is another instance of the refreshing humbug I was speaking of. *I* do something in that way myself – perhaps a good deal – perhaps a little – sharp's the word, my dear boy – never mind!'

'In what way do you mean? In the rouge way?' said Steerforth.

'Put this and that together, my tender pupil,' returned the wary Mowcher, touching her nose, 'work it by the rule of Secrets in all trades, and the product will give you the desired result. I say *I* do a little in that way myself. One Dowager, *she* calls it lip-salve. Another, *she* calls it gloves. Another, *she* calls it tucker-edging. Another, *she* calls it a fan. *I* call it whatever *they* call it. I supply it for 'em, but we keep up the trick so, to one another, and make believe with such a face, that they'd as soon think of laying it on, before a whole drawing-room, as before me. And when I wait upon 'em, they'll say to me sometimes – *with it on* – thick, and no mistake – "How am I looking, Mowcher? Am I pale?" Ha, ha, ha, ha! Isn't *that* refreshing, my young friend!'

I never did in my days behold anything like Mowcher as she stood upon the dining-table, intensely enjoying this refreshment, rubbing busily at Steerforth's head, and winking at me over it.

'Ah!' she said. 'Such things are not much in demand hereabouts. That sets me off again! I haven't seen a pretty woman since I've been here, Jemmy.'

'No?' said Steerforth.

'Not the ghost of one,' replied Miss Mowcher.

'We could show her the substance of one, I think?' said Steerforth, addressing his eyes to mine. 'Eh, Daisy?'

'Yes, indeed,' said I.

'Aha?' cried the little creature, glancing sharply at my face, and then peeping round at Steerforth's. 'Umph?'

The first exclamation sounded like a question put to both of us, and the second like a question put to Steerforth only. She seemed to have found no answer to either, but continued to rub, with her head on one side and her eye turned up, as if she were looking for an answer in the air, and were confident of its appearing presently.

'A sister of yours, Mr Copperfield?' she cried, after a pause, and still keeping the same lookout. 'Aye, aye?'

'No,' said Steerforth, before I could reply. 'Nothing of the sort. On the contrary, Mr Copperfield used – or I am much mistaken – to have a great admiration for her.'

'Why, hasn't he now?' returned Miss Mowcher. 'Is he fickle? oh for shame! Did he sip every flower, and change every hour, until Polly his passion requited? – Is her name Polly?'

The elfin suddenness with which she pounced upon me with this question, and a searching look, quite disconcerted me for a moment.

'No, Miss Mowcher,' I replied. 'Her name is Emily.'

'Aha?' she cried exactly as before. 'Umph? What a rattle I am! Mr Copperfield, ain't I volatile?'

Her tone and look implied something that was not agreeable to me in connection with the subject. So I said, in a graver manner than any of us had yet assumed: 'She is as virtuous as she is pretty. She is engaged to be married to a most worthy and deserving man in her own station of life. I esteem her for her good sense, as much as I admire her for her good looks.'

'Well said!' cried Steerforth. 'Hear, hear, hear! Now I'll quench the curiosity of this little Fatima, my dear Daisy, by leaving her nothing to guess at. She is at present apprenticed, Miss Mowcher, or articled, or whatever it may be, to Omer and Joram, Haberdashers, Milliners, and so forth, in this town. Do you observe? Omer and Joram. The promise of which my friend has spoken is made and entered into with her cousin; Christian name, Ham; surname, Peggotty; occupation, boat-builder; also of this town. She lives with a relative; Christian name, unknown; surname, Peggotty; occupation, seafaring; also of this town. She is the prettiest and most engaging little fairy in the world. I admire her – as my friend does – exceedingly. If it were not that I might appear to disparage her Intended, which I know my friend would not like, I would add, that to *me* she seems to be throwing herself away; that I am sure she might do better; and that I swear she was born to be a lady.'

Miss Mowcher listened to these words, which were very slowly and distinctly spoken, with her head on one side, and her eye in the air, as if she were still looking for that answer. When he ceased she became brisk again in an instant, and rattled away with surprising volubility.

'Oh! And that's all about it, is it?' she exclaimed, trimming his whiskers with a little restless pair of scissors, that went glancing round his head in all directions. 'Very well; *very* well! Quite a long story. Ought to end "and they lived happy ever afterwards;" oughtn't it? Ah! What's that game at forfeits? I love my love with an E, because she's enticing; I hate her with an E, because she's engaged. I took her to the sign of the exquisite, and treated her with an elopement, her name's Emily, and she lives in the east? Ha, ha, ha! Mr Copperfield, ain't I volatile?'

Merely looking at me with extravagant slyness, and not waiting for any reply, she continued, without drawing breath: 'There! If ever any scapegrace was trimmed and touched up to perfection, you are, Steerforth. If I understand any noddle in the world, I understand yours. Do you hear me when I tell you that, my darling? I understand yours,' peeping down into his face. 'Now you may mizzle, Jemmy (as we say at Court), and if Mr Copperfield will take the chair I'll operate on him.'

'What do you say, Daisy?' enquired Steerforth, laughing, and resigning his seat. 'Will you be improved?'

'Thank you, Miss Mowcher, not this evening.'

'Don't say no,' returned the little woman, looking at me with the aspect of a connoisseur; 'a little bit more eyebrow?'

'Thank you,' I returned, 'some other time.'

'Have it carried half a quarter of an inch towards the temple,' said Miss Mowcher. 'We can do it in a fortnight.'

'No, I thank you. Not at present.'

'Go in for a tip,' she urged. 'No? Let's get the scaffolding up, then, for a pair of whiskers. Come!'

I could not help blushing as I declined, for I felt we were on my weak point, now. But Miss Mowcher, finding that I was not at present disposed for any decoration within the range of her art, and that I was, for the time being, proof against the blandishments of the small bottle which she held up before one eye to enforce her persuasions, said we would make a beginning on an early day, and requested the aid of my hand to descend from her elevated station. Thus assisted, she skipped down with much agility, and began to tie her double-chin into her bonnet.

'The fee,' said Steerforth, 'is – '

'Five bob,' replied Miss Mowcher, 'and dirt cheap, my chicken. Ain't I volatile, Mr Copperfield?'

I replied politely, 'Not at all.' But I thought she was rather so, when she tossed up his two half-crowns like a goblin pieman, caught them, dropped them in her pocket, and gave it a loud slap.

'That's the Till!' observed Miss Mowcher, standing at the chair again, and replacing in the bag a miscellaneous collection of little objects she had emptied out of it. 'Have I got all my traps? It seems so. It won't do to be like long Ned Beadwood, when they took him to church "to marry him to somebody," as he says, and left the bride behind. Ha, ha, ha! A wicked rascal, Ned, but droll! Now, I know I'm going to break your hearts, but I am forced to leave you. You must call up all your fortitude, and try to bear it. Goodbye, Mr Copperfield! Take care of yourself, Jockey of Norfolk! How I *have* been rattling on! It's all the fault of you two wretches. *I* forgive you! "Bob swore!" – as the Englishman said for "Good-night," when he first learnt French, and thought it so like English. "Bob swore," my ducks!'

With a bag slung over her arm, and rattling as she waddled away, she waddled to the door; where she stopped to enquire if she should leave us a lock of her hair. 'Ain't I volatile?' she added, as a commentary on this offer, and, with her finger on her nose, departed.

Steerforth laughed to that degree, that it was impossible for me to help laughing too; though I am not sure I should have done so, but for this inducement. When we had had our laugh quite out, which was after some time, he told me that Miss Mowcher had quite an extensive connection, and made herself useful to a variety of people in a variety of ways. Some people trifled with her as a mere oddity, he said; but she was as shrewdly and sharply observant as anyone he knew, and as long-headed as she was short-armed. He told me that what she had said of being here, and there, and everywhere, was true enough; for she made little darts into the provinces, and seemed to pick up customers everywhere, and to know everybody. I asked him what her disposition was; whether it was at all mischievous, and if her sympathies were generally on the right side of things; but not succeeding in attracting his attention to these questions after two or three attempts, I forbore or forgot to repeat them. He told me instead, with much rapidity, a good deal about her skill, and her profits; and about her being a scientific cupper, if I should ever have occasion for her services in that capacity.

She was the principal theme of our conversation during the evening; and when we parted for the night Steerforth called after me over the banisters, 'Bob swore!' as I went downstairs.

I was surprised, when I came to Mr Barkis's house, to find Ham walking up and down in front of it, and still more surprised to learn from him that little Em'ly was inside. I naturally enquired why he was not there too, instead of pacing the streets by himself.

'Why, you see, Mas'r Davy,' he rejoined, in a hesitating manner, 'Em'ly, she's talking to some 'un in here.'

'I should have thought,' said I, smiling, 'that that was a reason for your being in here too, Ham.'

'Well, Mas'r Davy, in a general way, so 't would be,' he returned; 'but look'ee here, Mas'r Davy,' lowering his voice, and speaking very gravely. 'It's a young woman, sir – a young woman that Em'ly knowed once, and doen't ought to know no more.'

When I heard these words, a light began to fall upon the figure I had seen following them, some hours ago.

'It's a poor wurem, Mas'r Davy,' said Ham, 'as is trod under foot by all the town. Up street and down street. The mowld o' the churchyard don't hold any that the folk shrink away from, more.'

'Did I see her tonight, Ham, on the sands, after we met you?'

'Keeping us in sight?' said Ham. 'It's like you did, Mas'r Davy. Not that I knowed then, she was theer, sir, but along of her creeping soon arterwards under Em'ly's little winder, when she see the light come, and whisp'ring "Em'ly, Em'ly, for Christ's sake, have a woman's heart towards me. I was once like you!" Those was solemn words, Mas'r Davy, fur to hear!'

'They were indeed, Ham. What did Em'ly do?'

'Says Em'ly, "Martha, is it you? Oh, Martha, can it be you!" – for they had sat at work together, many a day, at Mr Omer's.'

'I recollect her now!' cried I, recalling one of the two girls I had seen when I first went there. 'I recollect her quite well!'

'Martha Endell,' said Ham. 'Two or three year older than Em'ly, but was at the school with her.'

'I never heard her name,' said I. 'I didn't mean to interrupt you.'

'For the matter o' that, Mas'r Davy,' replied Ham, 'all's told a'most in them words, "Em'ly, Em'ly, for Christ's sake, have a woman's heart towards me. I was once like you!" She wanted to speak to Em'ly. Em'ly couldn't speak to her theer, for her loving uncle was come home, and he wouldn't – no, Mas'r Davy,' said Ham, with great earnestness, 'he couldn't, kind-natur'd, tender-hearted as he is, see them two together, side by side, for all the treasures that's wrecked in the sea.'

I felt how true this was. I knew it, on the instant, quite as well as Ham.

'So Em'ly writes in pencil on a bit of paper,' he pursued, 'and gives it to her out o' window to bring here. "Show that," she says, "to my aunt, Mrs Barkis, and she'll set you down by her fire, for the love of me, till uncle is gone out, and I can come." By and by she tells me what I tell you, Mas'r Davy, and asks me to bring her. What can I do? She doen't ought to know any such, but I can't deny her, when the tears is on her face.'

He put his hand into the breast of his shaggy jacket, and took out with great care a pretty little purse.

'And if I could deny her when the tears was on her face, Mas'r Davy,' said Ham, tenderly adjusting it on the rough palm of his hand, 'how could I deny her when she give me this to carry for her – knowing what she brought it for? Such a toy as it is!' said Ham, thoughtfully looking on it. 'With such a little money in it, Em'ly my dear!'

I shook him warmly by the hand when he had put it away again – for that was more satisfactory to me than saying anything – and we walked up and down, for a minute or two, in silence. The door opened then, and Peggotty appeared, beckoning to Ham to come in. I would have kept away, but she came after me, entreating me to come in too. Even then, I would have avoided the room where they all were, but for its being the neat-tiled kitchen I have mentioned more than once. The door opening immediately into it, I found myself among them, before I considered whither I was going.

The girl – the same I had seen upon the sands – was near the fire. She was sitting on the ground, with her head and one arm lying on a chair. I fancied, from the disposition of her figure, that Em'ly had but newly risen from the chair, and that the forlorn head might perhaps have been lying on her lap. I saw but little of the girl's face, over which her hair fell loose and scattered, as if she had been disordering it with her own hands; but I saw that she was young, and of a fair complexion. Peggotty had been crying. So had little Em'ly. Not a word was spoken when we first went in; and the Dutch clock by the dresser seemed, in the silence, to tick twice as loud as usual.

Em'ly spoke first.

'Martha wants,' she said to Ham, 'to go to London.'

'Why to London?' returned Ham.

He stood between them, looking on the prostrate girl with a mixture of compassion for her, and of jealousy of her holding any companionship with her whom he loved so well, which I have always remembered distinctly. They both spoke as if she were ill; in a soft, suppressed tone that was plainly heard, although it hardly rose above a whisper.

'Better there than here,' said a third voice aloud – Martha's, though she did not move. 'No one knows me there. Everybody knows me here.'

'What will she do there?' enquired Ham.

She lifted up her head, and looked darkly round at him for a moment; then laid it down again, and curved her right arm about her neck, as a woman in a fever, or in an agony of pain from a shot, might twist herself.

'She will try to do well,' said little Em'ly. 'You don't know what she has said to us. Does he – do they – aunt?'

Peggotty shook her head compassionately.

'I'll try,' said Martha, 'if you'll help me away. I never can do worse than I have done here. I may do better. Oh!' with a dreadful shiver, 'take me out of these streets, where the whole town knows me from a child!'

As Em'ly held out her hand to Ham, I saw him put in it a little canvas bag. She took it as if she thought it were her purse, and made a step or two forward; but finding her mistake, came back to where he had retired near me, and showed it to him.

'It's all yourn, Em'ly,' I could hear him say. 'I haven't nowt in all the wureld that ain't yourn, my dear. It ain't of no delight to me, except for you!'

The tears rose freshly in her eyes, but she turned away and went to Martha. What she gave her, I don't know. I saw her

stooping over her, and putting money in her bosom. She whispered something, and asked was that enough? 'More than enough,' the other said, and took her hand and kissed it.

Then Martha arose, and gathering her shawl about her, covering her face with it, and weeping aloud, went slowly to the door. She stopped a moment before going out, as if she would have uttered something or turned back; but no word passed her lips. Making the same low, dreary, wretched moaning in her shawl, she went away.

As the door closed, little Em'ly looked at us three in a hurried manner, and then hid her face in her hands, and fell to sobbing.

'Doen't, Em'ly!' said Ham, tapping her gently on the shoulder. 'Doen't, my dear! You doen't ought to cry so, pretty!'

'Oh, Ham!' she exclaimed, still weeping pitifully, 'I am not as good a girl as I ought to be! I know I have not the thankful heart sometimes I ought to have!'

'Yes, yes, you have, I'm sure,' said Ham.

'No! no! no!' cried little Em'ly, sobbing and shaking her head. 'I am not as good a girl as I ought to be. Not near! not near!'

And still she cried as if her heart would break.

'I try your love too much. I know I do!' she sobbed. 'I'm often cross to you, and changeable with you, when I ought to be far different. You are never so to me. Why am I ever so to you, when I should think of nothing but how to be grateful, and to make you happy!'

'You always make me so,' said Ham, 'my dear! I am happy in the sight of you. I am happy, all day long, in the thoughts of you.'

'Ah! that's not enough!' she cried. 'That is because you are good; not because I am! Oh, my dear, it might have been a better fortune for you, if you had been fond of someone else – of someone steadier and much worthier than me, who was all bound up in you, and never vain and changeable like me!'

'Poor little tender-heart,' said Ham, in a low voice. 'Martha has overset her, altogether.'

'Please, aunt,' sobbed Em'ly, 'come here, and let me lay my head upon you. Oh, I am very miserable tonight, aunt! Oh, I am not as good a girl as I ought to be. I am not, I know!'

Peggotty had hastened to the chair before the fire. Em'ly, with her arms around her neck, kneeled by her, looking up most earnestly into her face.

'Oh, pray, aunt, try to help me! Ham, dear, try to help me! Mr David, for the sake of old times, do, please, try to help me! I want to be a better girl than I am. I want to feel a hundred times more thankful than I do. I want to feel more, what a blessed thing it is to be the wife of a good man, and to lead a peaceful life. Oh me, oh me! Oh, my heart, my heart!'

She dropped her face on my old nurse's breast, and, ceasing this supplication, which in its agony and grief was half a woman's, half a child's, as all her manner was (being, in that, more natural, and better suited to her beauty, as I thought, than any other manner could have been), wept silently, while my old nurse hushed her like an infant.

She got calmer by degrees, and then we soothed her; now talking encouragingly, and now jesting a little with her, until she began to raise her head and speak to us. So we got on, until she was able to smile, and then to laugh, and then to sit up, half ashamed; while Peggotty recalled her stray ringlets, dried her eyes, and made her neat again, lest her uncle should wonder, when he got home, why his darling had been crying.

I saw her do, that night, what I had never seen her do before. I saw her innocently kiss her chosen husband on the cheek, and creep close to his bluff form as if it were her best support. When they went away together, in the waning moonlight, and I looked after them, comparing their departure in my mind with Martha's, I saw that she held his arm with both her hands, and still kept close to him.

CHAPTER 23

I Corroborate Mr Dick, and Choose a Profession

When I awoke in the morning I thought very much of little Em'ly, and her emotion last night, after Martha had left. I felt as if I had come into the knowledge of those domestic weaknesses and tendernesses in a sacred confidence, and that to disclose them, even to Steerforth, would be wrong. I had no gentler feeling towards anyone than towards the pretty creature who had been my playmate, and whom I have always been persuaded, and shall always be persuaded, to my dying day, I then devotedly loved. The repetition to any ears – even to Steerforth's – of what she had been unable to repress when her heart lay open to me by an accident, I felt would be a rough deed, unworthy of myself, unworthy of the light of our pure

Martha

childhood, which I always saw encircling her head. I made a resolution, therefore, to keep it in my own breast; and there it gave her image a new grace.

While we were at breakfast, a letter was delivered to me from my aunt. As it contained matter on which I thought Steerforth could advise me as well as anyone, and on which I knew I should be delighted to consult him, I resolved to make it a subject of discussion on our journey home. For the present we had enough to do, in taking leave of all our friends. Mr Barkis was far from being the last among them, in his regret at our departure; and I believe would even have opened the box again, and sacrificed another guinea, if it would have kept us eight-and-forty hours in Yarmouth. Peggotty and all her family were full of grief at our going. The whole house of Omer and Joram turned out to bid us goodbye; and there were so many seafaring volunteers in attendance on Steerforth, when our portmanteaus went to the coach, that if we had had the baggage of a regiment with us, we should hardly have wanted porters to carry it. In a word, we departed to the regret and admiration of all concerned, and left a great many people very sorry behind us.

'Do you stay long here, Littimer?' said I, as he stood waiting to see the coach start.

'No, sir,' he replied; 'probably not very long, sir.'

'He can hardly say just now,' observed Steerforth carelessly. 'He knows what he has to do, and he'll do it.'

'That I am sure he will,' said I.

Littimer touched his hat in acknowledgment of my good opinion, and I felt about eight years old. He touched it once more, wishing us a good journey; and we left him standing on the pavement, as respectable a mystery as any pyramid in Egypt.

For some little time we held no conversation, Steerforth being unusually silent, and I being sufficiently engaged in wondering, within myself, when I should see the old places again, and what new changes might happen to me or them in the meanwhile. At length Steerforth, becoming gay and talkative in a moment, as he could become anything he liked at any moment, pulled me by the arm.

'Find a voice, David. What about the letter you were speaking of at breakfast?'

'Oh!' said I, taking it out of my pocket. 'It's from my aunt.'

'And what does she say, requiring consideration?'

'Why, she reminds me, Steerforth,' said I, 'that I came out on this expedition to look about me, and to think a little.'

'Which, of course, you have done?'

'Indeed, I can't say I have, particularly. To tell you the truth, I am afraid I had forgotten it.'

'Well! look about you now, and make up for your negligence,' said Steerforth. 'Look to the right, and you'll see a flat country, with a good deal of marsh in it; look to the left, and you'll see the same. Look to the front, and you'll find no difference; look to the rear, and there it is still.'

I laughed, and replied that I saw no suitable profession in the whole prospect; which was perhaps to be attributed to its flatness.

'What says our aunt on the subject?' enquired Steerforth, glancing at the letter in my hand. 'Does she suggest anything?'

'Why, yes,' said I. 'She asks me, here, if I think I should like to be a proctor? What do you think of it?'

'Well, I don't know,' replied Steerforth coolly. 'You may as well do that as anything else, I suppose?'

I could not help laughing again, at his balancing all callings and professions so equally; and I told him so.

'What *is* a proctor, Steerforth?' said I.

'Why, he is a sort of monkish attorney,' replied Steerforth. 'He is, to some faded courts held in Doctors' Commons – a lazy old nook near St Paul's Churchyard – what solicitors are to the courts of law and equity. He is a functionary whose existence, in the natural course of things, would have terminated about two hundred years ago. I can tell you best what he is, by telling you what Doctors' Commons is. It's a little out-of-the-way place, where they administer what is called ecclesiastical law, and play all kinds of tricks with obsolete old monsters of acts of Parliament, which three-fourths of the world know nothing about, and the other fourth supposes to have been dug up, in a fossil state, in the days of the Edwards. It's a place that has an ancient monopoly in suits about people's wills and people's marriages, and disputes among ships and boats.'

'Nonsense, Steerforth!' I exclaimed. 'You don't mean to say that there is any affinity between nautical matters and ecclesiastical matters?'

'I don't, indeed, my dear boy,' he returned; 'but I mean to say that they are managed and decided by the same set of people, down in that same Doctors' Commons. You shall go there one day, and find them blundering through half the nautical terms in Young's *Dictionary*, apropos of the *Nancy* having run down the *Sarah Jane*, or Mr Peggotty and the Yarmouth boatmen having put off in a gale of wind with an anchor and cable to the *Nelson* Indiaman in distress; and you shall go there another day, and find them deep in the evidence, pro and con, respecting a clergyman who has misbehaved himself; and you shall find the judge in the nautical case the advocate in the clergyman's case, or contrariwise. They are like actors: now a man's a judge, and now he is not a judge; now he's one thing, now he's another; now he's something else, change and change about; but it's always a very pleasant profitable little affair of private theatricals presented to an uncommonly select audience.'

'But advocates and proctors are not one and the same?' said I, a little puzzled. 'Are they?'

'No,' returned Steerforth, 'the advocates are civilians – men who have taken a doctor's degree at college – which is the first reason of my knowing anything about it. The proctors employ the advocates. Both get very comfortable fees, and altogether they make a mighty snug little party. On the whole I would recommend you to take to Doctors' Commons kindly, David. They plume themselves on their gentility there, I can tell you, if that's any satisfaction.'

I made allowance for Steerforth's light way of treating the subject, and considering it with reference to the staid air of gravity and antiquity which I associated with that 'lazy old nook near St Paul's Churchyard,' did not feel indisposed towards my aunt's suggestion; which she left to my free decision, making no scruple of telling me that it had occurred to her, on her lately visiting her own proctor in Doctors' Commons for the purpose of settling her will in my favour.

'That's a laudable proceeding on the part of our aunt, at all events,' said Steerforth, when I mentioned it; 'and one deserving of all encouragement. Daisy, my advice is that you take kindly to Doctors' Commons.'

I quite made up my mind to do so. I then told Steerforth that my aunt was in town awaiting me (as I found from her letter), and that she had taken lodgings for a week at a kind of private hotel in Lincoln's Inn Fields, where there was a stone staircase, and a convenient door in the roof; my aunt being firmly persuaded that every house in London was going to be burnt down every night.

We achieved the rest of our journey pleasantly, sometimes recurring to Doctors' Commons, and anticipating the distant days when I should be a proctor there, which Steerforth pictured in a variety of humorous and whimsical lights, that made us both merry. When we came to our journey's end, he went home, engaging to call upon me next day but one; and I drove to Lincoln's Inn Fields, where I found my aunt up, and waiting supper.

If I had been round the world since we parted, we could hardly have been better pleased to meet again. My aunt cried outright as she embraced me; and said, pretending to laugh, that if my poor mother had been alive, that silly little creature would have shed tears, she had no doubt.

'So you have left Mr Dick behind, aunt?' said I. 'I am sorry for that. Ah, Janet, how do you do?'

As Janet curtsied, hoping I was well, I observed my aunt's visage lengthen very much.

'I am sorry for it, too,' said my aunt, rubbing her nose, 'I have had no peace of mind, Trot, since I have been here.'

Before I could ask why, she told me.

'I am convinced,' said my aunt, laying her hand with melancholy firmness on the table, 'that Dick's character is not a character to keep the donkeys off. I am confident he wants strength of purpose. I ought to have left Janet at home, instead, and then my mind might perhaps have been at ease. If ever there was a donkey trespassing on my green,' said my aunt, with emphasis, 'there was one this afternoon at four o'clock. A cold feeling came over me from head to foot, and I *know* it was a donkey!'

I tried to comfort her on this point, but she rejected consolation.

'It was a donkey,' said my aunt; 'and it was the one with the stumpy tail which that Murdering sister of a woman rode, when she came to my house.' (This had been, ever since, the only name my aunt knew for Miss Murdstone.) 'If there is any donkey in Dover, whose audacity it is harder to me to bear than another's, that,' said my aunt, striking the table, 'is the animal!'

Janet ventured to suggest that my aunt might be disturbing herself unnecessarily, and that she believed the donkey in question was then engaged in the sand and gravel line of business, and was not available for purposes of trespass. But my aunt wouldn't hear of it.

Supper was comfortably served and hot, though my aunt's rooms were very high up – whether that she might have more stone stairs for her money, or might be nearer to the door in the roof, I don't know – and consisted of a roast fowl, a steak, and some vegetables, to all of which I did ample justice, and which were all excellent. But my aunt had her own ideas concerning London provision, and ate but little.

'I suppose this unfortunate fowl was born and brought up in a cellar,' said my aunt, 'and never took the air except on a hackney-coach stand. I *hope* the steak may be beef, but I don't believe it. Nothing's genuine in the place, in my opinion, but the dirt.'

'Don't you think the fowl may have come out of the country, aunt?' I hinted.

'Certainly not,' returned my aunt. 'It would be no pleasure to a London tradesman to sell anything which was what he pretended it was.'

I did not venture to controvert this opinion, but I made a good supper, which it greatly satisfied her to see me do. When the table was cleared, Janet assisted her to arrange her hair, to put on her nightcap, which was of a smarter construction than usual ('in case of fire,' my aunt said), and to fold her gown back over her knees, these being her usual preparations for warming herself before going to bed. I then made her, according to certain established regulations from which no deviation, however slight, could ever be permitted, a glass of hot white wine and water, and a slice of toast cut into long thin strips. With these accompaniments we were left alone to finish the evening, my aunt sitting opposite to me drinking her wine and water; soaking her strips of toast in it, one by one, before eating them; and looking benignly on me, from among the borders of her nightcap.

'Well, Trot,' she began, 'what do you think of the proctor plan? Or have you not begun to think about it yet?'

'I have thought a good deal about it, my dear aunt, and I have talked a good deal about it with Steerforth. I like it very much, indeed. I like it exceedingly.'

'Come!' said my aunt; 'that's cheering!'

'I have only one difficulty, aunt.'

'Say what it is, Trot,' she returned.

'Why, I want to ask, aunt, as this seems, from what I understand, to be a limited profession, whether my entrance into it would not be very expensive?'

'It will cost,' returned my aunt, 'to article you, just a thousand pounds.'

'Now, my dear aunt,' said I, drawing my chair nearer, 'I am uneasy in my mind about that. It's a large sum of money. You have expended a great deal on my education, and have always been as liberal to me in all things as it was possible to be. You have been the soul of generosity. Surely there are some ways in which I might begin life with hardly any outlay, and yet begin with a good hope of getting on by resolution and exertion. Are you sure that it would not be better to try that course? Are you

certain that you can afford to part with so much money, and that it is right that it should be so expended? I only ask you, my second mother, to consider. Are you certain?'

My aunt finished eating the piece of toast on which she was then engaged, looking me full in the face all the while; and then setting her glass on the chimney-piece, and folding her hands upon her folded skirts, replied as follows: 'Trot, my child, if I have any object in life, it is to provide for your being a good, a sensible, and a happy man. I am bent upon it – so is Dick. I should like some people that I know to hear Dick's conversation on the subject. Its sagacity is wonderful. But no one knows the resources of that man's intellect except myself!'

She stopped for a moment to take my hand between hers, and went on: 'It's in vain, Trot, to recall the past, unless it works some influence upon the present. Perhaps I might have been better friends with your poor father. Perhaps I might have been better friends with that poor child your mother, even after your sister Betsey Trotwood disappointed me. When you came to me, a little runaway boy, all dusty and way-worn, perhaps I thought so. From that time until now, Trot, you have ever been a credit to me and a pride and a pleasure. I have no other claim upon my means; at least' – here to my surprise she hesitated, and was confused – 'no, I have *no* other claim upon my means – and you are my adopted child. Only be a loving child to me in my age, and bear with my whims and fancies; and you will do more for an old woman, whose prime of life was not so happy or conciliating as it might have been, than ever that old woman did for you.'

It was the first time I had heard my aunt refer to her past history. There was a magnanimity in her quiet way of doing so, and of dismissing it, which would have exalted her in my respect and affection, if anything could.

'All is agreed and understood between us now, Trot,' said my aunt, 'and we need talk of this no more. Give me a kiss, and we'll go to the Commons after breakfast tomorrow.'

We had a long chat by the fire before we went to bed. I slept in a room on the same floor with my aunt's, and was a little disturbed in the course of the night by her knocking at my door as often as she was agitated by a distant sound of hackney-coaches, or market-carts, and enquiring, 'if I heard the engines?' But towards morning she slept better, and suffered me to do so too.

At about midday, we set out for the office of Messrs Spenlow and Jorkins in Doctors' Commons. My aunt, who had this other general opinion in reference to London, that every man she saw was a pickpocket, gave me her purse to carry for her, which had ten guineas in it and some silver.

We made a pause at the toy-shop in Fleet Street, to see the giants of St Dunstan's strike upon the bells – we had timed our going, so as to catch them at it, at twelve o'clock – and then went on towards Ludgate Hill and St Paul's Churchyard. We were crossing to the former place, when I found that my aunt greatly accelerated her speed, and looked frightened. I observed, at the same time, that a lowering, ill-dressed man, who had stopped and stared at us in passing, a little before, was coming so close after us as to brush against her.

'Trot! My dear Trot!' cried my aunt, in a terrified whisper, and pressing my arm. 'I don't know what I am to do.'

'Don't be alarmed,' said I. 'There's nothing to be afraid of. Step into a shop, and I'll soon get rid of this fellow.'

'No, no, child!' she returned. 'Don't speak to him for the world. I entreat, I order you!'

'Good Heaven, aunt!' said I. 'He is nothing but a sturdy beggar.'

'You don't know what he is!' replied my aunt. 'You don't know who he is! You don't know what you say!'

We had stopped in an empty doorway, while this was passing, and he had stopped too.

'Don't look at him!' said my aunt, as I turned my head indignantly, 'but get me a coach, my dear, and wait for me in St Paul's Churchyard.'

'Wait for you?' I repeated.

'Yes,' rejoined my aunt, 'I must go alone. I must go with him.'

'With him, aunt? This man?'

'I am in my senses,' she replied, 'and I tell you I *must*. Get me a coach!'

However much astonished I might be, I was sensible that I had no right to refuse compliance with such a peremptory command. I hurried away a few paces, and called a hackney-chariot which was passing empty. Almost before I could let down the steps, my aunt sprang in, I don't know how, and the man followed. She waved her hand to me to go away, so earnestly, that, all confounded as I was, I turned from them at once. In doing so, I heard her say to the coachman, 'Drive anywhere! Drive straight on!' and presently the chariot passed me, going up the hill.

What Mr Dick had told me, and what I had supposed to be a delusion of his, now came into my mind. I could not doubt that this person was the person of whom he had made such mysterious mention, though what the nature of his hold upon my aunt could possibly be, I was quite unable to imagine. After half an hour's cooling in the churchyard, I saw the chariot coming back. The driver stopped beside me, and my aunt was sitting in it alone.

She had not yet sufficiently recovered from her agitation to be quite prepared for the visit we had to make. She desired me to get into the chariot, and to tell the coachman to drive slowly up and down a little while. She said no more, except, 'My dear child, never ask me what it was, and don't refer to it,' until she had perfectly regained her composure, when she told me she was quite herself now, and we might get out. On her giving me her purse, to pay the driver, I found that all the guineas were gone, and only the loose silver remained.

Doctors' Commons was approached by a little low archway. Before we had taken many paces down the street beyond it, the noise of the city seemed to melt, as if by magic, into a softened distance. A few dull courts, and narrow ways, brought us to the sky-lighted offices of Spenlow and Jorkins; in the vestibule of which temple, accessible to pilgrims without the ceremony of knocking, three or four clerks were at work as copyists. One of these, a little dry man, sitting by himself, who wore a stiff brown wig that looked as if it were made of gingerbread, rose to receive my aunt, and show us into Mr Spenlow's room.

'Mr Spenlow's in Court, ma'am,' said the dry man; 'it's an Arches day; but it's close by, and I'll send for him directly.'

As we were left to look about us while Mr Spenlow was fetched, I availed myself of the opportunity. The furniture of the room was old-fashioned and dusty; and the green baize on the top of the writing-table had lost all its colour, and was as withered and pale as an old pauper. There were a great many bundles of papers on it, some endorsed as Allegations, and some (to my surprise) as Libels, and some as being in the Consistory Court, and some in the Arches Court, and some in the Prerogative Court, and some in the Admiralty Court, and some in the Delegates' Court; giving me occasion to wonder much, how many Courts there might be in the gross, and how long it would take to understand them all. Besides these, there were sundry immense manuscript Books of Evidence taken on affidavit, strongly bound, and tied together in massive sets, a set to each cause, as if every cause were a history in ten or twenty volumes. All this looked tolerably expensive, I thought, and gave me an agreeable notion of a proctor's business. I was casting my eyes with increasing complacency over these and many similar objects, when hasty footsteps were heard in the room outside, and Mr Spenlow, in a black gown trimmed with white fur, came hurrying in, taking off his hat as he came.

He was a little, light-haired gentleman, with undeniable boots, and the stiffest of white cravats and shirt-collars. He was buttoned up mighty trim and tight, and must have taken a great deal of pains with his whiskers, which were accurately curled. His gold watch-chain was so massive, that a fancy came across me, that he ought to have a sinewy golden arm, to draw it out with, like those which are put up over the gold-beaters' shops. He was got up with such care, and was so stiff, that he could hardly bend himself; being obliged, when he glanced at some papers on his desk, after sitting down in his chair, to move his whole body, from the bottom of his spine, like Punch.

I had previously been presented by my aunt, and had been courteously received. He now said: 'And so, Mr Copperfield, you think of entering into our profession? I casually mentioned to Miss Trotwood, when I had the pleasure of an interview with her the other day' – with another inclination of his body – Punch again – 'that there was a vacancy here. Miss Trotwood was good enough to mention that she had a nephew who was her peculiar care, and for whom she was seeking to provide genteelly in life. That nephew, I believe, I have now the pleasure of' – Punch again.

I bowed my acknowledgments, and said, my aunt had mentioned to me that there was that opening, and that I believed I should like it very much. That I was strongly inclined to like it, and had taken immediately to the proposal. That I could not absolutely pledge myself to like it, until I knew something more about it. That although it was little else than a matter of form, I presumed I should have an opportunity of trying how I liked it, before I bound myself to it irrevocably.

'Oh, surely! surely!' said Mr Spenlow. 'We always, in this house, propose a month – an initiatory month. I should be happy, myself, to propose two months – three – an indefinite period, in fact – but I have a partner. Mr Jorkins.'

'And the premium, sir,' I returned, 'is a thousand pounds.'

'And the premium, Stamp included, is a thousand pounds,' said Mr Spenlow. 'As I have mentioned to Miss Trotwood, I am actuated by no mercenary considerations; few men are less so, I believe; but Mr Jorkins has his opinions on these subjects, and I am bound to respect Mr Jorkins's opinions. Mr Jorkins thinks a thousand pounds too little, in short.'

'I suppose, sir,' said I, still desiring to spare my aunt, 'that it is not the custom here, if an articled clerk were particularly useful, and made himself a perfect master of his profession –' I could not help blushing, this looked so like praising myself – 'I suppose it is not the custom, in the later years of his time, to allow him any –'

Mr Spenlow, by a great effort, just lifted his head far enough out of his cravat, to shake it, and answered, anticipating the word 'salary.'

'No. I will not say what consideration I might give to that point myself, Mr Copperfield, if I were unfettered. Mr Jorkins is immovable.'

I was quite dismayed by the idea of this terrible Jorkins. But I found out afterwards that he was a mild man of a heavy temperament, whose place in the business was to keep himself in the background, and be constantly exhibited by name as the most obdurate and ruthless of men. If a clerk wanted his salary raised, Mr Jorkins wouldn't listen to such a proposition. If a client were slow to settle his bill of costs, Mr Jorkins was resolved to have it paid; and however painful these things might be (and always were) to the feelings of Mr Spenlow, Mr Jorkins would have his bond. The heart and hand of the good angel Spenlow would have been always open, but for the restraining demon Jorkins. As I have grown older, I think I have had experience of some other houses doing business on the principle of Spenlow and Jorkins!

It was settled that I should begin my month's probation as soon as I pleased, and that my aunt need neither remain in town nor return at its expiration, as the articles of agreement of which I was to be the subject could easily be sent to her at home for her signature. When we had got so far, Mr Spenlow offered to take me into Court then and there and show me what sort of place it was. As I was willing enough to know, we went out with this object, leaving my aunt behind; who would trust herself, she said, in no such place, and who, I think, regarded all Courts of Law as a sort of powder-mills that might blow up at any time.

Mr Spenlow conducted me through a paved courtyard formed of grave brick houses, which I inferred, from the Doctors' names upon the doors, to be the official abiding-places of the learned advocates of whom Steerforth had told me; and into a large, dull room, not unlike a chapel to my thinking, on the left hand. The upper part of this room was fenced off from the rest; and there, on the two sides of a raised platform of the horseshoe form, sitting on easy, old-fashioned dining-room chairs, were sundry gentlemen in red gowns and grey wigs, whom I found to be the Doctors aforesaid. Blinking over a little desk like a pulpit-desk, in the curve of the horseshoe, was an

old gentleman, whom, if I had seen him in an aviary, I should certainly have taken for an owl, but who, I learned, was the presiding judge. In the space within the horseshoe, lower than these, that is to say on about the level of the floor, were sundry other gentlemen of Mr Spenlow's rank, and dressed like him in black gowns with white fur upon them, sitting at a long green table. Their cravats were in general stiff, I thought, and their looks haughty; but in this last respect, I presently conceived I had done them an injustice, for when two or three of them had to rise and answer a question of the presiding dignitary, I never saw anything more sheepish. The public represented by a boy with a comforter, and a shabby-genteel man secretly eating crumbs out of his coat-pockets, was warming itself at a stove in the centre of the Court. The languid stillness of the place was only broken by the chirping of this fire and by the voice of one of the Doctors, who was wandering slowly through a perfect library of evidence, and stopping to put up, from time to time, at little roadside inns of argument on the journey. Altogether, I have never, on any occasion, made one at such a cosy, dozy, old-fashioned, time-forgotten, sleepy-headed little family-party in all my life; and I felt it would be quite a soothing opiate to belong to it in any character – except perhaps as a suitor.

Very well satisfied with the dreamy nature of this retreat, I informed Mr Spenlow that I had seen enough for that time, and we rejoined my aunt; in company with whom I presently departed from the Commons, feeling very young when I went out of Spenlow and Jorkins's, on account of the clerks poking one another with their pens to point me out.

We arrived at Lincoln's Inn Fields without any new adventures except encountering an unlucky donkey in a coster-monger's cart, who suggested painful associations to my aunt. We had another long talk about my plans, when we were safely housed; and as I knew she was anxious to get home, and, between fire, food, and pickpockets, could never be considered at her ease for half an hour in London, I urged her not to be uncomfortable on my account, but to leave me to take care of myself.

'I have not been here a week tomorrow, without considering that too, my dear,' she returned. 'There is a furnished little set of chambers to be let in the Adelphi, Trot, which ought to suit you to a marvel.'

With this brief introduction, she produced from her pocket an advertisement, carefully cut out of a newspaper, setting forth that in Buckingham Street in the Adelphi there was to be let furnished, with a view of the river, a singularly desirable and compact set of chambers, forming a genteel residence for a young gentleman, a member of one of the Inns of Court, or otherwise, with immediate possession. Terms moderate, and could be taken for a month only if required.

'Why, this is the very thing, aunt!' said I, flushed with the possible dignity of living in chambers.

'Then come,' replied my aunt, immediately resuming the bonnet she had a minute before laid aside. 'We'll go and look at 'em.'

Away we went. The advertisement directed us to apply to Mrs Crupp on the premises, and we rung the area bell, which we supposed to communicate with Mrs Crupp. It was not until we had rung three or four times that we could prevail on Mrs Crupp to communicate with us, but at last she appeared, being a stout lady with a flounce of flannel petticoat below a nankeen gown.

'Let us see these chambers of yours, if you please, ma'am,' said my aunt.

'For this gentleman?' said Mrs Crupp, feeling in her pocket for her keys.

'Yes, for my nephew,' said my aunt.

'And a sweet set they is for sich!' said Mrs Crupp.

So we went upstairs.

They were on the top of the house – a great point with my aunt, being near the fire-escape – and consisted of a little half-blind entry where you could see hardly anything, a little stone-blind pantry where you could see nothing at all, a sitting-room, and a bedroom. The furniture was rather faded, but quite good enough for me; and, sure enough, the river was outside the windows.

As I was delighted with the place, my aunt and Mrs Crupp withdrew into the pantry to discuss the terms, while I remained on the sitting-room sofa, hardly daring to think it possible that I could be destined to live in such a noble residence. After a single combat of some duration, they returned, and I saw, to my joy, both in Mrs Crupp's countenance and in my aunt's, that the deed was done.

'Is it the last occupant's furniture?' enquired my aunt.

'Yes, it is, ma'am,' said Mrs Crupp.

'What's become of him?' asked my aunt.

Mrs Crupp was taken with a troublesome cough, in the midst of which she articulated with much difficulty. 'He was took ill here, ma'am, and – ugh! ugh! ugh! dear me! – and he died.'

'Hey! What did he die of?' asked my aunt.

'Well, ma'am, he died of drink,' said Mrs Crupp in confidence. 'And smoke.'

'Smoke? You don't mean chimneys?' said my aunt.

'No, ma'am,' returned Mrs Crupp. 'Cigars and pipes.'

'*That's* not catching, Trot, at any rate,' remarked my aunt, turning to me.

'No, indeed,' said I.

In short, my aunt, seeing how enraptured I was with the premises, took them for a month, with leave to remain for twelve months when that time was out. Mrs Crupp was to find linen, and to cook; every other necessary was already provided; and Mrs Crupp expressly intimated that she should always yearn towards me as a son. I was to take possession the day after tomorrow, and Mrs Crupp said thank Heaven she had now found summun she could care for!

On our way back, my aunt informed me how she confidently trusted that the life I was now to lead would make me firm and self-reliant, which was all I wanted. She repeated this several times next day, in the intervals of our arranging for the transmission of my clothes and books from Mr Wickfield's; relative to which, and to all my late holiday, I wrote a long letter to Agnes, of which my aunt took charge, as she was to leave on the succeeding day. Not to lengthen these particulars, I need only

add, that she made a handsome provision for all my possible wants during my month of trial; that Steerforth, to my great disappointment, and hers too, did not make his appearance before she went away; that I saw her safely seated in the Dover coach, exulting in the coming discomfiture of the vagrant donkeys, with Janet at her side; and that when the coach was gone, I turned my face to the Adelphi, pondering on the old days when I used to roam about its subterranean arches, and on the happy changes which had brought me to the surface.

CHAPTER 24

My First Dissipation

It was a wonderfully fine thing to have that lofty castle to myself, and to feel, when I shut my outer door, like Robinson Crusoe, when he had got into his fortification, and pulled his ladder up after him. It was a wonderfully fine thing to walk about town with the key of my house in my pocket, and to know that I could ask any fellow to come home, and make quite sure of its being inconvenient to nobody, if it were not so to me. It was a wonderfully fine thing to let myself in and out, and to come and go without a word to anyone, and to ring Mrs Crupp up, gasping, from the depths of the earth, when I wanted her – and when she was disposed to come. All this, I say, was wonderfully fine; but I must say, too, that there were times when it was very dreary.

It was fine in the morning, particularly in the fine mornings. It looked a very fresh, free life, by daylight; still fresher, and more free, by sunlight. But as the day declined, the life seemed to go down too. I don't know how it was; it seldom looked well by candle-light. I wanted somebody to talk to, then. I missed Agnes. I found a tremendous blank, in the place of that smiling repository of my confidence. Mrs Crupp appeared to be a long way off. I thought about my predecessor, who had died of drink and smoke; and I could have wished he had been so good as to live, and not bother me with his decease.

After two days and nights, I felt as if I had lived there for a year, and yet I was not an hour older, but was quite as much tormented by my own youthfulness as ever.

Steerforth not yet appearing, which induced me to apprehend that he must be ill, I left the Commons early on the third day, and walked out to Highgate. Mrs Steerforth was very glad to see me, and said that he had gone away with one of his Oxford friends to see another who lived near St Alban's, but that she expected him to return tomorrow. I was so fond of him that I felt quite jealous of his Oxford friends.

As she pressed me to stay to dinner, I remained, and I believe we talked about nothing but him all day. I told her how much the people liked him at Yarmouth, and what a delightful companion he had been. Miss Dartle was full of hints and mysterious questions, but took a great interest in all our proceedings there, and said, 'was it really, though?' and so forth, so often, that she got everything out of me she wanted to know. Her appearance was exactly what I have described it, when I first saw her; but the society of the two ladies was so agreeable, and came so natural to me, that I felt myself falling a little in love with her. I could not help thinking, several times in the course of the evening, and particularly when I walked home at night, what delightful company she would be in Buckingham Street.

I was taking my coffee and roll in the morning, before going to the Commons – and I may observe in this place that it is surprising how much coffee Mrs Crupp used, and how weak it was, considering – when Steerforth himself walked in, to my unbounded joy.

'My dear Steerforth,' cried I, 'I began to think I should never see you again!'

'I was carried off, by force of arms,' said Steerforth, 'the very next morning after I got home. Why, Daisy, what a rare old bachelor you are here!'

I showed him over the establishment, not omitting the pantry, with no little pride, and he commended it highly. 'I tell you what, old boy,' he added, 'I shall make quite a town-house of this place, unless you give me notice to quit.'

This was a delightful hearing. I told him if he waited for that, he would have to wait till doomsday.

'But you shall have some breakfast!' said I, with my hand on the bell-rope; 'and Mrs Crupp shall make you some fresh coffee, and I'll toast you some bacon in a bachelor's Dutch-oven that I have got here.'

'No, no!' said Steerforth. 'Don't ring! I can't! I am going to breakfast with one of these fellows who is at the Piazza Hotel, in Covent Garden.'

'But you'll come back to dinner?' said I.

'I can't, upon my life. There's nothing I should like better, but I *must* remain with these two fellows. We are all three off together tomorrow morning.'

'Then bring them here to dinner,' I returned. 'Do you think they would come?'

'Oh! they would come fast enough,' said Steerforth; 'but we should inconvenience you. You had better come and dine with us somewhere.'

I would not by any means consent to this, for it occurred to me that I really ought to have a little housewarming, and that there never could be a better opportunity. I had a new pride in my rooms after his approval of them, and burned with a desire to develop their utmost resources. I therefore made him promise positively in the names of his two friends, and we appointed six o'clock as the dinner-hour.

When he was gone, I rang for Mrs Crupp, and acquainted her with my desperate design. Mrs Crupp said, in the first place, of course it was well known she couldn't be expected to wait, but she knew a handy young man, who she thought could be prevailed upon to do it, and whose terms would be five shillings, and what I pleased. I said, certainly we would have him. Next, Mrs Crupp said it was clear she couldn't be in two places at once (which I felt to be reasonable), and that 'a young gal' stationed in the pantry with a bedroom candle, there never to desist from washing plates, would be indispensable. I said, what would be the expense of this young female, and Mrs Crupp said she supposed eighteenpence would neither make

me nor break me. I said I supposed not; and *that* was settled. Then Mrs Crupp said, 'Now, about the dinner.'

It was a remarkable instance of want of forethought on the part of the ironmonger who had made Mrs Crupp's kitchen fireplace that it was capable of cooking nothing but chops and mashed potatoes. As to a fish-kettle, Mrs Crupp said, well! would I only come and look at the range? She couldn't say fairer than that. Would I come and look at it? As I should not have been much the wiser if I *had* looked at it, I declined, and said, 'Never mind fish.' But Mrs Crupp said, 'Don't say that; oysters was in, and why not them?' So *that* was settled. Mrs Crupp then said what she would recommend would be this: A pair of hot roast fowls – from the pastry cook's; a dish of stewed beef, with vegetables – from the pastry cook's; two little corner things, as a raised pie and a dish of kidneys – from the pastry cook's; a tart, and (if I liked) a shape of jelly – from the pastry cook's. This, Mrs Crupp said, would leave her at full liberty to concentrate her mind on the potatoes, and to serve up the cheese and celery as she could wish to see it done.

I acted on Mrs Crupp's opinion, and gave the order at the pastry cook's myself. Walking along the Strand, afterwards, and observing a hard mottled substance in the window of a ham and beef shop, which resembled marble, but was labelled 'Mock Turtle,' I went in and bought a slab of it, which I have since seen reason to believe would have sufficed for fifteen people. This preparation, Mrs Crupp, after some difficulty, consented to warm up; and it shrunk so much in a liquid state that we found it what Steerforth called 'rather a tight fit' for four.

These preparations happily completed, I bought a little dessert in Covent Garden Market, and gave a rather extensive order at a retail wine-merchant's in that vicinity. When I came home in the afternoon, and saw the bottles drawn up in a square on the pantry-floor, they looked so numerous (though there were two missing, which made Mrs Crupp very uncomfortable) that I was absolutely frightened at them.

One of Steerforth's friends was named Grainger, and the other Markham. They were both very gay and lively fellows; Grainger, something older than Steerforth; Markham, youthful-looking, and I should say not more than twenty. I observed that the latter always spoke of himself indefinitely as 'a man,' and seldom or never in the first person singular.

'A man might get on very well here, Mr Copperfield,' said Markham – meaning himself.

'It's not a bad situation,' said I, 'and the rooms are really commodious.'

'I hope you have both brought appetites with you?' said Steerforth.

'Upon my honour,' returned Markham, 'town seems to sharpen a man's appetite. A man is hungry all day long. A man is perpetually eating.'

Being a little embarrassed at first, and feeling much too young to preside, I made Steerforth take the head of the table when dinner was announced, and seated myself opposite to him. Everything was very good; we did not spare the wine; and he exerted himself so brilliantly to make the thing pass off well that there was no pause in our festivity. I was not quite such good company during dinner, as I could have wished to be, for my chair was opposite the door, and my attention was distracted by observing that the handy young man went out of the room very often, and that his shadow always presented itself, immediately afterwards, on the wall of the entry, with a bottle at his mouth. The 'young gal' likewise occasioned me some uneasiness; not so much by neglecting to wash the plates, as by breaking them. For being of an inquisitive disposition, and unable to confine herself (as her positive instructions were) to the pantry, she was constantly peering in at us, and constantly imagining herself detected; in which belief, she several times retired upon the plates (with which she had carefully paved the floor), and did a great deal of destruction.

These, however, were small drawbacks, and easily forgotten when the cloth was cleared, and the dessert put on the table; at which period of the entertainment the handy young man was discovered to be speechless. Giving him private directions to seek the society of Mrs Crupp, and to remove the 'young gal' to the basement also, I abandoned myself to enjoyment.

I began by being singularly cheerful and light-hearted; all sorts of half-forgotten things to talk about came rushing into my mind, and made me hold forth in a most unwonted manner. I laughed heartily at my own jokes, and everybody else's; called Steerforth to order for not passing the wine; made several engagements to go to Oxford; announced that I meant to have a dinner party exactly like that, once a week until further notice; and madly took so much snuff out of Grainger's box that I was obliged to go into the pantry, and have a private fit of sneezing ten minutes long.

I went on, by passing the wine faster and faster yet, and continually starting up with a corkscrew to open more wine, long before any was needed. I proposed Steerforth's health. I said he was my dearest friend, the protector of my boyhood, and the companion of my prime. I said I was delighted to propose his health. I said I owed him more obligations than I could ever repay, and held him in a higher admiration than I could ever express. I finished by saying, 'I'll give you Steerforth! God bless him! Hurrah!' We gave him three times three, and another, and a good one to finish with. I broke my glass in going round the table to shake hands with him, and I said (in two words) 'Steerforth you'retheguidingstarofmyexistence.'

I went on, by finding suddenly that somebody was in the middle of a song. Markham was the singer, and he sang, 'When the heart of a man is depressed with care.' He said, when he had sung it, he would give us 'Woman!' I took objection to that, and I couldn't allow it. I said it was not a respectful way of proposing the toast, and I would never permit that toast to be drunk in my house otherwise than as 'The Ladies!' I was very high with him, mainly, I think, because I saw Steerforth and Grainger laughing at me – or at him – or at both of us. He said a man was not to be dictated to. I said a man *was*. He said a man was not to be insulted, then. I said he was right there – never under my roof, where the Lares were sacred, and the laws of hospitality paramount. He said it was no derogation from a man's dignity to confess that I was a devilish good fellow. I instantly proposed his health.

Somebody was smoking. We were all smoking. *I* was smoking, and trying to suppress a rising tendency to shudder. Steerforth had made a speech about me, in the course of which I had been affected almost to tears. I returned thanks, and hoped the present company would dine with me tomorrow, and the day after – each day at five o'clock, that we might enjoy the pleasures of conversation and society through a long evening. I felt called upon to propose an individual. I would give them my aunt. Miss Betsey Trotwood, the best of her sex!

Somebody was leaning out of my bedroom window, refreshing his forehead against the cool stone of the parapet, and feeling the air upon his face. It was myself. I was addressing myself as 'Copperfield,' and saying, 'Why did you try to smoke? You might have known you couldn't do it.' Now, somebody was unsteadily contemplating his features in the looking-glass. That was I, too. I was very pale in the looking-glass; my eyes had a vacant appearance; and my hair – only my hair, nothing else – looked drunk.

Somebody said to me, 'Let us go to the theatre, Copperfield!' There was no bedroom before me, but again the jingling table covered with glasses; the lamp; Grainger on my right hand, Markham on my left, and Steerforth opposite – all sitting in a mist, and a long way off. The theatre? To be sure. The very thing. Come along! But they must excuse me if I saw everybody out first, and turned the lamp off – in case of fire.

Owing to some confusion in the dark, the door was gone. I was feeling for it in the window-curtains, when Steerforth, laughing, took me by the arm and led me out. We went downstairs, one behind another. Near the bottom, somebody fell, and rolled down. Somebody else said it was Copperfield. I was angry at that false report, until, finding myself on my back in the passage, I began to think there might be some foundation for it.

A very foggy night, with great rings round the lamps in the streets! There was an indistinct talk of its being wet. *I* considered it frosty. Steerforth dusted me under a lamp-post, and put my hat into shape, which somebody produced from somewhere in a most extraordinary manner, for I hadn't had it on before. Steerforth then said, 'You are all right, Copperfield, are you not?' and I told him, 'Neverberrer.'

A man, sitting in a pigeon-hole place, looked out of the fog, and took money from somebody, enquiring if I was one of the gentlemen paid for, and appearing rather doubtful (as I remember in the glimpse I had of him) whether to take the money for me or not. Shortly afterwards, we were very high up in a very hot theatre, looking down into a large pit that seemed to me to smoke; the people with whom it was crammed were so indistinct. There was a great stage, too, looking very clean and smooth after the streets; and there were people upon it, talking about something or other, but not at all intelligibly. There was an abundance of bright lights, and there was music, and there were ladies down in the boxes, and I don't know what more. The whole building looked to me as if it were learning to swim; it conducted itself in such an unaccountable manner when I tried to steady it.

On somebody's motion, we resolved to go downstairs to the

dress-boxes, where the ladies were. A gentleman lounging, full dressed, on a sofa, with an opera-glass in his hand, passed before my view, and also my own figure at full length in a glass. Then I was being ushered into one of these boxes, and found myself saying something as I sat down, and people about me crying 'Silence!' to somebody, and ladies casting indignant glances at me, and – what! yes! – Agnes, sitting on the seat before me, in the same box, with a lady and gentleman beside her whom I didn't know. I see her face now, better than I did then, I dare say, with its indelible look of regret and wonder turned upon me.

'Agnes!' I said, thickly, 'Lorblessmer! Agnes!'

'Hush! Pray!' she answered, I could not conceive why. 'You disturb the company. Look at the stage!'

I tried, on her injunction, to fix it, and to hear something of what was going on there, but quite in vain. I looked at her again by and by, and saw her shrink into her corner, and put her gloved hand to her forehead.

'Agnes!' I said. 'I'mafraidyou'renorwell.'

'Yes, yes. Do not mind me, Trotwood,' she returned. 'Listen! Are you going away soon?'

'Amigoarawaysoo?' I repeated.

'Yes.'

I had a stupid intention of replying that I was going to wait, to hand her downstairs. I suppose I expressed it somehow; for after she had looked at me attentively for a little while, she appeared to understand, and replied in a low tone: 'I know you will do as I ask you, if I tell you I am very earnest in it. Go away now, Trotwood, for my sake, and ask your friends to take you home.'

She had so far improved me, for the time, that, though I was angry with her, I felt ashamed, and with a short 'Goori!' (which I intended for 'Good-night!') got up and went away. They followed, and I stepped at once out of the box-door into my bedroom, where only Steerforth was with me, helping me to undress, and where I was by turns telling him that Agnes was my sister, and adjuring him to bring the corkscrew, that I might open another bottle of wine.

How somebody, lying in my bed, lay saying and doing all this over again, at cross purposes, in a feverish dream all night – the bed a rocking sea, that was never still! How, as that somebody slowly settled down into myself, did I begin to parch, and feel as if my outer covering of skin were a hard board; my tongue the bottom of an empty kettle, furred with long service, and burning up over a slow fire; the palms of my hands hot plates of metal which no ice could cool!

But the agony of mind, the remorse, and shame I felt when I became conscious next day! My horror of having committed a thousand offences I had forgotten, and which nothing could ever expiate – my recollection of that indelible look which Agnes had given me – the torturing impossibility of communicating with her, not knowing, beast that I was, how she came to be in London, or where she stayed – my disgust of the very sight of the room where the revel had been held – my racking head – the smell of smoke, the sight of glasses, the impossibility of going out, or even getting up! Oh, what a day it was!

Oh, what an evening, when I sat down by my fire to a basin of mutton broth, dimpled all over with fat, and thought I was going the way of my predecessor, and should succeed to his dismal story as well as to his chambers, and had half a mind to rush express to Dover and reveal all! What an evening, when Mrs Crupp, coming in to take away the broth-basin, produced one kidney on a cheese-plate as the entire remains of yesterday's feast, and I was really inclined to fall upon her nankeen breast, and say, in heartfelt penitence, 'Oh, Mrs Crupp, Mrs Crupp, never mind the broken meats! I am very miserable!' – only that I doubted, even at that pass, if Mrs Crupp were quite the sort of woman to confide in!

CHAPTER 25

Good and Bad Angels

I was going out at my door on the morning after that deplorable day of headache, sickness, and repentance, with an odd confusion in my mind relative to the date of my dinner party, as if a body of Titans had taken an enormous lever and pushed the day before yesterday some months back, when I saw a ticket-porter coming upstairs, with a letter in his hand. He was taking his time about his errand then; but when he saw me on the top of the staircase, looking at him over the banisters, he swung into a trot, and came up panting as if he had run himself into a state of exhaustion.

'T. Copperfield, Esquire,' said the ticket-porter, touching his hat with his little cane.

I could scarcely lay claim to the name; I was so disturbed by the conviction that the letter came from Agnes. However, I told him I was T. Copperfield, Esquire, and he believed it, and gave me the letter, which he said required an answer. I shut him out on the landing to wait for the answer, and went into my chambers again, in such a nervous state that I was fain to lay the letter down on my breakfast-table, and familiarise myself with the outside of it a little, before I could resolve to break the seal.

I found, when I did open it, that it was a very kind note, containing no reference to my condition at the theatre. All it said was, 'My dear Trotwood. I am staying at the house of papa's agent, Mr Waterbrook, in Ely Place, Holborn. Will you come and see me today, at any time you like to appoint? Ever yours affectionately, Agnes.'

It took me such a long time to write an answer at all to my satisfaction that I don't know what the ticket-porter can have thought, unless he thought I was learning to write. I must have written half a dozen answers at least. I began one, 'How can I ever hope, my dear Agnes, to efface from your remembrance the disgusting impression' – there I didn't like it, and then I tore it up. I began another, 'Shakespeare has observed, my dear Agnes, how strange it is that a man should put an enemy into his mouth' – that reminded me of Markham, and it got no further. I even tried poetry. I began one note, in a six syllable line, 'Oh, do not remember' – but that associated itself with the fifth of November, and became an absurdity. After many attempts, I wrote, 'My dear Agnes. Your letter is like you, and what could I say of it that would be higher praise than that? I will come at four o'clock. Affectionately and sorrowfully, T. C.' With this missive (which I was in twenty minds at once about recalling, as soon as it was out of my hands), the ticket-porter at last departed.

If the day were half as tremendous to any other professional gentleman in Doctors' Commons as it was to me, I sincerely believe he made some expiation for his share in that rotten old ecclesiastical cheese. Although I left the office at half-past three, and was prowling about the place of appointment within a few minutes afterwards, the appointed time was exceeded by a full quarter of an hour, according to the clock of St Andrew's, Holborn, before I could muster up sufficient desperation to pull the private bell-handle let into the left-hand doorpost of Mr Waterbrook's house.

The professional business of Mr Waterbrook's establishment was done on the ground-floor, and the genteel business (of which there was a good deal) in the upper part of the building. I was shown into a pretty but rather close drawing-room, and there sat Agnes, netting a purse.

She looked so quiet and good, and reminded me so strongly of my airy fresh school days at Canterbury, and the sodden, smoky, stupid wretch I had been the other night, that, nobody being by, I yielded to my self-reproach and shame, and – in short, made a fool of myself. I cannot deny that I shed tears. To this hour I am undecided whether it was upon the whole the wisest thing I could have done, or the most ridiculous.

'If it had been anyone but you, Agnes,' said I, turning away my head, 'I should not have minded it half so much. But that it should have been you who saw me! I almost wish I had been dead, first.'

She put her hand – its touch was like no other hand – upon my arm for a moment; and I felt so befriended and comforted that I could not help moving it to my lips, and gratefully kissing it.

'Sit down,' said Agnes cheerfully. 'Don't be unhappy, Trotwood. If you cannot confidently trust me, whom will you trust?'

'Ah, Agnes!' I returned. 'You are my good Angel!'

She smiled rather sadly, I thought, and shook her head.

'Yes, Agnes, my good Angel! Always my good Angel!'

'If I were, indeed, Trotwood,' she returned, 'there is one thing that I should set my heart on very much.'

I looked at her enquiringly; but already with a foreknowledge of her meaning.

'On warning you,' said Agnes, with a steady glance, 'against your bad Angel.'

'My dear Agnes,' I began, 'if you mean Steerforth – '

'I do, Trotwood,' she returned.

'Then, Agnes, you wrong him very much. He my bad Angel, or anyone's! He, anything but a guide, a support, and a friend to me! My dear Agnes! Now, is it not unjust, and unlike you, to judge him from what you saw of me the other night?'

'I do not judge him from what I saw of you the other night,' she quietly replied.

'From what, then?'

'From many things – trifles in themselves, but they do not seem to me to be so, when they are put together. I judge him, partly from your account of him, Trotwood, and your character, and the influence he has over you.'

There was always something in her modest voice that seemed to touch a chord within me, answering to that sound alone. It was always earnest; but when it was very earnest, as it was now, there was a thrill in it that quite subdued me. I sat looking at her as she cast her eyes down on her work; I sat seeming still to listen to her; and Steerforth, in spite of all my attachment to him, darkened in that tone.

'It is very bold in me,' said Agnes, looking up again, 'who have lived in such seclusion, and can know so little of the world, to give you my advice so confidently, or even to have this strong opinion. But I know in what it is engendered, Trotwood – in how true a remembrance of our having grown up together, and in how true an interest in all relating to you. It is that which makes me bold. I am certain that what I say is right. I am quite sure it is. I feel as if it were someone else speaking to you and not I, when I caution you that you have made a dangerous friend.'

Again I looked at her, again I listened to her after she was silent, and again his image, though it was still fixed in my heart, darkened.

'I am not so unreasonable as to expect,' said Agnes, resuming her usual tone, after a little while, 'that you will, or that you can, at once, change any sentiment that has become a conviction to you; least of all a sentiment that is rooted in your trusting disposition. You ought not hastily to do that. I only ask you, Trotwood, if you ever think of me – I mean,' with a quiet smile, for I was going to interrupt her, and she knew why, 'as often as you think of me – to think of what I have said. Do you forgive me for all this?'

'I will forgive you, Agnes,' I replied, 'when you come to do Steerforth justice, and to like him as well as I do.'

'Not until then?' said Agnes.

I saw a passing shadow on her face when I made this mention of him, but she returned my smile, and we were again as unreserved in our mutual confidence as of old.

'And when, Agnes,' said I, 'will you forgive me the other night?'

'When I recall it,' said Agnes.

She would have dismissed the subject so, but I was too full of it to allow that, and insisted on telling her how it happened that I had disgraced myself, and what chain of accidental circumstances had had the theatre for its final link. It was a great relief to me to do this, and to enlarge on the obligation that I owed to Steerforth for his care of me when I was unable to take care of myself.

'You must not forget,' said Agnes, calmly changing the conversation as soon as I had concluded, 'that you are always to tell me, not only when you fall into trouble, but when you fall in love. Who has succeeded to Miss Larkins, Trotwood?'

'No one, Agnes.'

'Someone, Trotwood,' said Agnes, laughing, and holding up her finger.

'No, Agnes, upon my word! There is a lady, certainly, at Mrs Steerforth's house, who is very clever, and whom I like to talk to – Miss Dartle – but I don't adore her.'

Agnes laughed again at her own penetration, and told me that if I were faithful to her in my confidence she thought she should keep a little register of my violent attachments, with the date, duration, and termination of each, like the table of the reigns of the kings and queens, in the History of England. Then she asked me if I had seen Uriah.

'Uriah Heep?' said I. 'No. Is he in London?'

'He comes to the office downstairs, every day,' returned Agnes. 'He was in London a week before me. I am afraid on disagreeable business, Trotwood.'

'On some business that makes you uneasy, Agnes, I see,' said I. 'What can that be?'

Agnes laid aside her work, and replied, folding her hands upon one another, and looking pensively at me out of those beautiful soft eyes of hers: 'I believe he is going to enter into partnership with papa.'

'What? Uriah? That mean, fawning fellow, worm himself into such promotion?' I cried indignantly. 'Have you made no remonstrance about it, Agnes? Consider what a connection it is likely to be. You must speak out. You must not allow your father to take such a mad step. You must prevent it, Agnes, while there's time.'

Still looking at me, Agnes shook her head while I was speaking, with a faint smile at my warmth, and then replied: 'You remember our last conversation about papa? It was not long after that – not more than two or three days – when he gave me the first intimation of what I tell you. It was sad to see him struggling between his desire to represent it to me as a matter of choice on his part, and his inability to conceal that it was forced upon him. I felt very sorry.'

'Forced upon him, Agnes? Who forces it upon him?'

'Uriah,' she replied, after a moment's hesitation, 'has made himself indispensable to papa. He is subtle and watchful. He has mastered papa's weaknesses, fostered them, and taken advantage of them, until – to say all that I mean in a word, Trotwood, until papa is afraid of him.'

There was more that she might have said, more that she knew, or that she suspected, I clearly saw. I could not give her pain by asking what it was, for I knew that she withheld it from me to spare her father. It had long been going on to this, I was sensible; yes, I could not but feel, on the least reflection, that it had been going on to this for a long time. I remained silent.

'His ascendancy over papa,' said Agnes, 'is very great. He professes humility and gratitude – with truth, perhaps; I hope so – but his position is really one of power, and I fear he makes a hard use of his power.'

I said he was a hound, which, at the moment, was a great satisfaction to me.

'At the time I speak of, as the time when papa spoke to me,' pursued Agnes, 'he had told papa that he was going away; that he was very sorry and unwilling to leave, but that he had better prospects. Papa was very much depressed then, and more bowed down by care than ever you or I have seen him; but he seemed

relieved by this expedient of the partnership, though at the same time he seemed hurt by it and ashamed of it.'

'And how did you receive it, Agnes?'

'I did, Trotwood,' she replied, 'what I hope was right. Feeling sure that it was necessary for papa's peace that the sacrifice should be made, I entreated him to make it. I said it would lighten the load of his life – I hope it will! – and that it would give me increased opportunities of being his companion. Oh, Trotwood!' cried Agnes, putting her hands before her face, as her tears started on it, 'I almost feel as if I had been papa's enemy, instead of his loving child. For I know how he has altered, in his devotion to me. I know how he has narrowed the circle of his sympathies and duties, in the concentration of his whole mind upon me. I know what a multitude of things he has shut out for my sake, and how his anxious thoughts of me have shadowed his life, and weakened his strength and energy, by turning them always upon one idea. If I could ever set this right! If I could ever work out his restoration, as I have so innocently been the cause of his decline!'

I had never before seen Agnes cry. I had seen tears in her eyes when I had brought new honours home from school, and I had seen them there when we last spoke about her father, and I had seen her turn her gentle head aside when we took leave of one another; but I had never seen her grieve like this. It made me so sorry that I could only say, in a foolish, helpless manner, 'Pray, Agnes, don't! Don't, my dear sister!' But Agnes was too superior to me in character and purpose, as I know well now, whatever I might know or not know then, to be long in need of my entreaties. The beautiful, calm manner, which makes her so different in my remembrance from everybody else, came back again, as if a cloud had passed from a serene sky.

'We are not likely to remain alone much longer,' said Agnes, 'and while I have an opportunity, let me earnestly entreat you, Trotwood, to be friendly to Uriah. Don't repel him. Don't resent (as I think you have a general disposition to do) what may be uncongenial to you in him. He may not deserve it, for we know no certain ill of him. In any case, think first of papa and me!'

Agnes had no time to say more, for the room door opened, and Mrs Waterbrook, who was a large lady – or who wore a large dress, I don't exactly know which, for I don't know which was dress and which was lady – came sailing in. I had a dim recollection of having seen her at the theatre, as if I had seen her in a pale magic lantern; but she appeared to remember me perfectly, and still to suspect me of being in a state of intoxication.

Finding by degrees, however, that I was sober, and (I hope) that I was a modest young gentleman, Mrs Waterbrook softened towards me considerably, and enquired, firstly, if I went much into the parks, and secondly, if I went much into society. On my replying to both these questions in the negative, it occurred to me that I fell again in her good opinion; but she concealed the fact gracefully, and invited me to dinner next day. I accepted the invitation, and took my leave; making a call on Uriah in the office as I went out, and leaving a card for him in his absence.

When I went to dinner next day, and, on the street door being opened, plunged into a vapour-bath of haunch of mutton,

I divined that I was not the only guest; for I immediately identified the ticket-porter in disguise, assisting the family servant, and waiting at the foot of the stairs to carry up my name. He looked, to the best of his ability, when he asked me for it confidentially, as if he had never seen me before; but well did I know him, and well did he know me. Conscience made cowards of us both.

I found Mr Waterbrook to be a middle-aged gentleman, with a short throat, and a good deal of shirt-collar, who only wanted a black nose to be the portrait of a pug-dog. He told me he was happy to have the honour of making my acquaintance; and when I had paid my homage to Mrs Waterbrook, presented me, with much ceremony, to a very awful lady in a black velvet dress, and a great black velvet hat, whom I remember as looking like a near relation of Hamlet's – say his aunt.

Mrs Henry Spiker was this lady's name; and her husband was there too – so cold a man, that his head, instead of being grey, seemed to be sprinkled with hoar frost. Immense deference was shown to the Henry Spikers, male and female; which Agnes told me was on account of Mr Henry Spiker being solicitor to something or to somebody, I forget what or which, remotely connected with the Treasury.

I found Uriah Heep among the company, in a suit of black, and in deep humility. He told me, when I shook hands with him, that he was proud to be noticed by me, and that he really felt obliged to me for my condescension. I could have wished he had been less obliged to me, for he hovered about me in his gratitude all the rest of the evening; and whenever I said a word to Agnes, was sure, with his shadowless eyes and cadaverous face, to be looking gauntly down upon us from behind.

There were other guests – all iced for the occasion, as it struck me, like the wine. But, there was one who attracted my attention before he came in, on account of my hearing him announced as Mr Traddles! My mind flew back to Salem House; and could it be Tommy, I thought, who used to draw the skeletons!

I looked for Mr Traddles with unusual interest. He was a sober, steady-looking young man of retiring manners, with a comic head of hair, and eyes that were rather wide open; and he got into an obscure corner so soon, that I had some difficulty in making him out. At length I had a good view of him, and either my vision deceived me, or it was the old unfortunate Tommy.

I made my way to Mr Waterbrook, and said, that I believed I had the pleasure of seeing an old schoolfellow there.

'Indeed?' said Mr Waterbrook, surprised. 'You are too young to have been at school with Mr Henry Spiker?'

'Oh, I don't mean him!' I returned. 'I mean the gentleman named Traddles.'

'Oh! Aye, aye! Indeed!' said my host, with much diminished interest. 'Possibly.'

'If it's really the same person,' said I, glancing towards him, 'it was at a place called Salem House where we were together, and he was an excellent fellow.'

'Oh, yes. Traddles is a good fellow,' returned my host, nodding his head with an air of toleration. 'Traddles is quite a good fellow.'

'It's a curious coincidence,' said I.

'It is really,' returned my host, 'quite a coincidence, that Traddles should be here at all, as Traddles was only invited this morning, when the place at table, intended to be occupied by Mrs Henry Spiker's brother, became vacant, in consequence of his indisposition. A very gentlemanly man, Mrs Henry Spiker's brother, Mr Copperfield.'

I murmured an assent, which was full of feeling, considering that I knew nothing at all about him; and I enquired what Mr Traddles was by profession.

'Traddles,' returned Mr Waterbrook, 'is a young man reading for the bar. Yes. He is quite a good fellow – nobody's enemy but his own.'

'Is he his own enemy?' said I, sorry to hear this.

'Well,' returned Mr Waterbrook, pursing up his mouth, and playing with his watch-chain, in a comfortable, prosperous sort of way. 'I should say he was one of those men who stand in their own light. Yes, I should say he would never, for example, be worth five hundred pound. Traddles was recommended to me by a professional friend. Oh, yes. Yes. He has a kind of talent for drawing briefs, and stating a case in writing, plainly. I am able to throw something in Traddles's way, in the course of the year; something – for him – considerable. Oh, yes. Yes.'

I was much impressed by the extremely comfortable and satisfied manner in which Mr Waterbrook delivered himself of this little word 'Yes,' every now and then. There was wonderful expression in it. It completely conveyed the idea of a man who had been born, not to say with a silver spoon, but with a scaling-ladder, and had gone on mounting all the heights of life one after another, until now he looked, from the top of the fortifications, with the eye of a philosopher and a patron, on the people down in the trenches.

My reflections on this theme were still in progress when dinner was announced. Mr Waterbrook went down with Hamlet's aunt. Mr Henry Spiker took Mrs Waterbrook. Agnes, whom I should have liked to take myself, was given to a simpering fellow with weak legs. Uriah, Traddles, and I, as the junior part of the company, went down last, how we could. I was not so vexed at losing Agnes as I might have been, since it gave me an opportunity of making myself known to Traddles on the stairs, who greeted me with great fervour; while Uriah writhed with such obtrusive satisfaction and self-abasement, that I could gladly have pitched him over the banisters.

Traddles and I were separated at table, being billeted in two remote corners: he, in the glare of a red velvet lady; I, in the gloom of Hamlet's aunt. The dinner was very long, and the conversation was about the Aristocracy – and Blood. Mrs Waterbrook repeatedly told us, that if she had a weakness, it was Blood.

It occurred to me several times that we should have got on better, if we had not been quite so genteel. We were so exceedingly genteel, that our scope was very limited. A Mr and Mrs Gulpidge were of the party, who had something to do at second-hand (at least, Mr Gulpidge had) with the law business of the Bank; and what with the Bank, and what with the Treasury, we were as exclusive as the Court Circular. To mend the matter, Hamlet's aunt had the family failing of indulging in soliloquy, and held forth in a desultory manner, by herself, on every topic that was introduced. These were few enough, to be sure; but as we always fell back upon Blood, she had as wide a field for abstract speculation as her nephew himself.

We might have been a party of Ogres, the conversation assumed such a sanguine complexion.

'I confess I am of Mrs Waterbrook's opinion,' said Mr Waterbrook, with his wineglass at his eye. 'Other things are all very well in their way, but give me Blood!'

'Oh! There is nothing,' observed Hamlet's aunt, 'so satisfactory to one! There is nothing that is so much one's *beau idéal* of – of all that sort of thing, speaking generally. There are some low minds (not many, I am happy to believe, but there are *some*) that would prefer to do what *I* should call bow down before idols. Positively idols! Before services, intellect, and so on. But these are intangible points. Blood is not so. We see Blood in a nose, and we know it. We meet with it in a chin, and we say, "There it is! That's Blood!" It is an actual matter of fact. We point it out. It admits of no doubt.'

The simpering fellow with the weak legs, who had taken Agnes down, stated the question more decisively yet, I thought.

'Oh, you know, deuce take it,' said this gentleman, looking round the board with an imbecile smile, 'we can't forego Blood, you know. We must have Blood, you know. Some young fellows, you know, may be a little behind their station, perhaps, in point of education and behaviour, and may go a little wrong, you know, and get themselves and other people into a variety of fixes – and all that – but deuce take it, it's delightful to reflect that they've got Blood in 'em! Myself, I'd rather at any time be knocked down by a man who had got Blood in him, than I'd be picked up by a man who hadn't!'

This sentiment, as compressing the general question into a nutshell, gave the utmost satisfaction, and brought the gentleman into great notice until the ladies retired. After that I observed that Mr Gulpidge and Mr Henry Spiker, who had hitherto been very distant, entered into a defensive alliance against us, the common enemy, and exchanged a mysterious dialogue across the table for our defeat and overthrow.

'That affair of the first bond for four thousand five hundred pounds has not taken the course that was expected, Spiker,' said Mr Gulpidge.

'Do you mean the D. of A.'s?' said Mr Spiker.

'The C. of B.'s?' said Mr Gulpidge.

Mr Spiker raised his eyebrows, and looked much concerned.

'When the question was referred to Lord — I needn't name him,' said Mr Gulpidge, checking himself – 'I understand,' said Mr Spiker, 'N.'

Mr Gulpidge darkly nodded – 'was referred to him, his answer was, "Money, or no release." '

'Lord bless my soul!' cried Mr Spiker.

' "Money, or no release," ' repeated Mr Gulpidge firmly. 'The next in reversion – you understand me?'

'K.,' said Mr Spiker, with an ominous look.

' – K. then positively refused to sign. He was attended at Newmarket for that purpose, and he pointblank refused to do it.'

Mr Spiker was so interested, that he became quite stony.

'So the matter rests at this hour,' said Mr Gulpidge, throwing himself back in his chair. 'Our friend Waterbrook will excuse me if I forbear to explain myself generally, on account of the magnitude of the interests involved.'

Mr Waterbrook was only too happy, as it appeared to me, to have such interests, and such names, even hinted at, across his table. He assumed an expression of gloomy intelligence (though I am persuaded he knew no more about the discussion than I did), and highly approved of the discretion that had been observed. Mr Spiker, after the receipt of such a confidence, naturally desired to favour his friend with a confidence of his own; therefore the foregoing dialogue was succeeded by another, in which it was Mr Gulpidge's turn to be surprised, and that by another in which the surprise came round to Mr Spiker's turn again, and so on, turn and turn about. All this time we, the outsiders, remained oppressed by the tremendous interests involved in the conversation; and our host regarded us with pride, as the victims of a salutary awe and astonishment.

I was very glad indeed to get upstairs to Agnes, and to talk with her in a corner, and to introduce Traddles to her, who was shy, but agreeable, and the same good-natured creature still. As he was obliged to leave early, on account of going away next morning for a month, I had not nearly so much conversation with him as I could have wished; but we exchanged addresses, and promised ourselves the pleasure of another meeting when he should come back to town. He was greatly interested to hear that I knew Steerforth, and spoke of him with such warmth that I made him tell Agnes what he thought of him. But Agnes only looked at me the while, and very slightly shook her head when only I observed her.

As she was not among people with whom I believed she could be very much at home, I was almost glad to hear that she was going away within a few days, though I was sorry at the prospect of parting from her again so soon. This caused me to remain until all the company were gone. Conversing with her, and hearing her sing, was such a delightful reminder to me of my happy life in the grave old house she had made so beautiful, that I could have remained there half the night; but, having no excuse for staying any longer, when the lights of Mr Waterbrook's society were all snuffed out, I took my leave very much against my inclination. I felt then, more than ever, that she was my better Angel; and if I thought of her sweet face and placid smile, as though they had shone on me from some removed being, like an Angel, I hope I thought no harm.

I have said that the company were all gone; but I ought to have excepted Uriah, whom I don't include in that denomination, and who had never ceased to hover near us. He was close behind me when I went downstairs. He was close beside me when I walked away from the house, slowly fitting his long skeleton fingers into the still longer fingers of a great Guy Fawkes pair of gloves.

It was in no disposition for Uriah's company, but in remembrance of the entreaty Agnes had made to me, that I asked him if he would come to my rooms, and have some coffee.

'Oh, really, Master Copperfield,' he rejoined – 'I beg your pardon, Mister Copperfield, but the other comes so natural – I don't like that you should put a constraint upon yourself to ask an 'umble person like me to your 'ouse.'

'There is no constraint in the case,' said I. 'Will you come?'

'I should like to, very much,' replied Uriah, with a writhe.

'Well, then, come along!' said I.

I could not help being rather short with him, but he appeared not to mind it. We went the nearest way, without conversing much upon the road; and he was so humble in respect of those scarecrow gloves, that he was still putting them on, and seemed to have made no advance in that labour, when we got to my place.

I led him up the dark stairs, to prevent his knocking his head against anything, and really his damp cold hand felt so like a frog in mine, that I was tempted to drop it and run away. Agnes and hospitality prevailed, however, and I conducted him to my fireside. When I lighted my candles, he fell into meek transports with the room that was revealed to him; and when I heated the coffee in an unassuming block-tin vessel in which Mrs Crupp delighted to prepare it (chiefly, I believe, because it was not intended for the purpose, being a shaving-pot, and because there was a patent invention of great price mouldering away in the pantry), he professed so much emotion, that I could joyfully have scalded him.

'Oh, really, Master Copperfield – I mean Mister Copperfield,' said Uriah, 'to see you waiting upon me is what I never could have expected! But, one way and another, so many things happen to me which I never could have expected, I am sure, in my 'umble station, that it seems to rain blessings on my ed. You have heard something, I des-say, of a change in my expectations, Master Copperfield, *I* should say, Mister Copperfield?'

As he sat on my sofa, with his long knees drawn up under his coffee-cup, his hat and gloves upon the ground close to him, his spoon going softly round and round, his shadowless red eyes, which looked as if they had scorched their lashes off, turned towards me without looking at me, the disagreeable dints I have formerly described in his nostrils coming and going with his breath, and a snaky undulation pervading his frame from his chin to his boots, I decided in my own mind that I disliked him intensely. It made me very uncomfortable to have him for a guest, for I was young then, and unused to disguise what I so strongly felt.

'You have heard something, I des-say, of a change in my expectations, Master Copperfield – I should say, Mister Copperfield?' observed Uriah.

'Yes,' said I, 'something.'

'Ah! I thought Miss Agnes would know of it!' he quietly returned. 'I'm glad to find Miss Agnes knows of it. Oh, thank you, Master – Mister Copperfield!'

I could have thrown my bootjack at him (it lay ready on the rug), for having entrapped me into the disclosure of anything concerning Agnes, however immaterial. But I only drank my coffee.

'What a prophet you have shown yourself, Mister Copperfield!' pursued Uriah. 'Dear me, what a prophet you have

proved yourself to be! Don't you remember saying to me once, that perhaps I should be a partner in Mr Wickfield's business, and perhaps it might be Wickfield and Heep! *You* may not recollect it; but when a person is 'umble, Master Copperfield, a person treasures such things up!'

'I recollect talking about it,' said I, 'though I certainly did not think it very likely then.'

'Oh! who *would* have thought it likely, Mister Copperfield!' returned Uriah enthusiastically; 'I am sure I didn't myself. I recollect saying with my own lips that I was much too 'umble. So I considered myself really and truly.'

He sat, with that carved grin on his face, looking at the fire, as I looked at him.

'But the 'umblest persons, Master Copperfield,' he presently resumed, 'may be the instruments of good. I am glad to think I have been the instrument of good to Mr Wickfield, and that I may be more so. Oh, what a worthy man he is, Mister Copperfield, but how imprudent he has been!'

'I am sorry to hear it,' said I. I could not help adding, rather pointedly, 'on all accounts.'

'Decidedly so, Mister Copperfield,' replied Uriah. 'On all accounts. Miss Agnes above all! You don't remember your own eloquent expressions, Master Copperfield; but *I* remember how you said one day that everybody must admire her, and how I thanked you for it? You have forgot that, I have no doubt, Master Copperfield?'

'No,' said I dryly.

'Oh, how glad I am, you have not!' exclaimed Uriah. 'To think that you should be the first to kindle the sparks of ambition in my 'umble breast, and that you've not forgot it! Oh! – Would you excuse me asking for a cup more coffee?'

Something in the emphasis he laid upon the kindling of those sparks, and something in the glance he directed at me as he said it, had made me start as if I had seen him illuminated by a blaze of light. Recalled by his request, preferred in quite another tone of voice, I did the honours of the shaving-pot; but I did them with an unsteadiness of hand, a sudden sense of being no match for him, and a perplexed suspicious anxiety as to what he might be going to say next, which I felt could not escape his observation.

He said nothing at all. He stirred his coffee round and round, he sipped it, he felt his chin softly with his grisly hand, he looked at the fire, he looked about the room, he gasped rather than smiled at me, he writhed and undulated about, in the deferential servility, he stirred and sipped again, but he left the renewal of the conversation to me.

'So Mr Wickfield,' said I, at last, 'who is worth five hundred of you – or me,' – for my life, I think, I could not have helped dividing that part of the sentence with an awkward jerk; 'has been imprudent, has he, Mr Heep?'

'Oh, very imprudent indeed, Master Copperfield,' returned Uriah, sighing modestly. 'Oh, very much so! But I wish you'd call me Uriah, if you please. It's like old times.'

'Well! Uriah,' said I, bolting it out with some difficulty.

'Thank you!' he returned with fervour. 'Thank you, Master Copperfield! It's like the blowing of old breezes or the ringing of old bellses to hear *you* say Uriah. I beg your pardon. Was I making any observation?'

'About Mr Wickfield,' I suggested.

'Oh! Yes, truly,' said Uriah. 'Ah! Great imprudence, Master Copperfield. It's a topic that I wouldn't touch upon to any soul but you. Even to you I can only touch upon it, and no more. If anyone else had been in my place during the last few years, by this time he would have had Mr Wickfield (oh, what a worthy man he is, Master Copperfield, too!) under his thumb. Un–der – his thumb,' said Uriah, very slowly, as he stretched out his cruel-looking hand above my table, and pressed his own thumb down upon it, until it shook, and shook the room.

If I had been obliged to look at him with his splay foot on Mr Wickfield's head, I think I could scarcely have hated him more.

'Oh, dear, yes, Master Copperfield,' he proceeded in a soft voice, most remarkably contrasting with the action of his thumb, which did not diminish its hard pressure in the least degree, 'there's no doubt of it. There would have been loss, disgrace, I don't know what all. Mr Wickfield knows it. I am the 'umble instrument of 'umbly serving him, and he puts me on an eminence I hardly could have hoped to reach. How thankful should I be!' With his face turned towards me as he finished, but without looking at me, he took his crooked thumb off the spot where he had planted it, and slowly and thoughtfully scraped his lank jaw with it, as if he were shaving himself.

I recollect well how indignantly my heart beat, as I saw his crafty face, with the appropriately red light of the fire upon it, preparing for something else.

'Master Copperfield,' he began – 'but am I keeping you up?'

'You are not keeping me up. I generally go to bed late.'

'Thank you, Master Copperfield! I have risen from my 'umble station since first you used to address me, it is true; but I am 'umble still. I hope I never shall be otherwise than 'umble. You will not think the worse of my 'umbleness, if I make a little confidence to you, Master Copperfield? Will you?'

'Oh, no,' said I, with an effort.

'Thank you!' He took out his pocket-handkerchief, and began wiping the palms of his hands. 'Miss Agnes, Master Copperfield –'

'Well, Uriah?'

'Oh, how pleasant to be called Uriah spontaneously!' he cried; and gave himself a jerk, like a convulsive fish. 'You thought her looking very beautiful, tonight, Master Copperfield?'

'I thought her looking as she always does – superior, in all respects, to everyone around her,' I returned.

'Oh, thank you! It's so true!' he cried. 'Oh, thank you very much for that!'

'Not at all,' I said loftily. 'There is no reason why you should thank me.'

'Why that, Master Copperfield,' said Uriah, 'is in fact the confidence that I am going to take the liberty of reposing. 'Umble as I am,' he wiped his hands harder, and looked at them and at the fire by turns, ' 'umble as my mother is, and lowly as our poor but honest roof has ever been, the image of Miss Agnes (I don't mind trusting you with my secret, Master Copperfield, for I have always overflowed towards you since the first moment I had the pleasure of beholding you in a pony-shay) has been in my breast for years. Oh, Master Copperfield, with what a pure affection do I love the ground my Agnes walks on!'

I believe I had a delirious idea of seizing the red-hot poker

Uriah persists in hovering near us at the dinner party

out of the fire, and running him through with it. It went from me with a shock, like a ball fired from a rifle; but the image of Agnes, outraged by so much as a thought of this red-headed animal's, remained in my mind (when I looked at him, sitting all awry as if his mean soul gripped his body), and made me giddy. He seemed to swell and grow before my eyes; the room seemed full of the echoes of his voice; and the strange feeling (to which, perhaps, no one is quite a stranger) that all this had occurred before, at some indefinite time, and that I knew what he was going to say next, took possession of me.

A timely observation of the sense of power that there was in his face did more to bring back to my remembrance the entreaty of Agnes, in its full force, than any effort I could have made. I asked him, with a better appearance of composure than I could have thought possible a minute before, whether he had made his feelings known to Agnes.

'Oh, no, Master Copperfield!' he returned; 'oh, dear, no! Not to anyone but you. You see I am only just emerging from my lowly station. I rest a good deal of hope on her observing how useful I am to her father (for I trust to be very useful to him, indeed, Master Copperfield), and how I smooth the way for him, and keep him straight. She's so much attached to her father, Master Copperfield (oh, what a lovely thing it is in a daughter!), that I think she may come, on his account, to be kind to me.'

I fathomed the depth of the rascal's whole scheme, and understood why he laid it bare.

'If you'll have the goodness to keep my secret, Master Copperfield,' he pursued, 'and not, in general, to go against me, I shall take it as a particular favour. You wouldn't wish to make unpleasantness. I know what a friendly heart you've got; but having only known me on my 'umble footing (on my 'umblest, I should say, for I am very 'umble still), you might, unbeknown, go against me rather, with my Agnes. I call her mine, you see, Master Copperfield. There's a song that says, "I'd crowns resign, to call her mine!" I hope to do it, one of these days.'

Dear Agnes! So much too loving and too good for anyone that I could think of, was it possible that she was reserved to be the wife of such a wretch as this!

'There's no hurry at present, you know, Master Copperfield,' Uriah proceeded in his slimy way, as I sat gazing at him, with this thought in my mind. 'My Agnes is very young still; and mother and me will have to work our way upwards, and make a good many new arrangements, before it would be quite convenient. So I shall have time gradually to make her familiar with my hopes, as opportunities offer. Oh, I'm so much obliged to you for this confidence! Oh, it's such a relief you can't think, to know that you understand our situation, and are certain (as you wouldn't wish to make unpleasantness in the family) not to go against me!'

He took the hand which I dared not withhold, and having given it a damp squeeze, referred to his pale-faced watch.

'Dear me!' he said, 'it's past one. The moments slip away so, in the confidence of old times, Master Copperfield, that it's almost half-past one!'

I answered that I had thought it was later. Not that I had really thought so, but because my conversational powers were effectually scattered.

'Dear me!' he said, considering. 'The 'ouse that I am stopping at – a sort of a private hotel and boarding 'ouse, Master Copperfield, near the New River 'ed – will have gone to bed these two hours.'

'I am sorry,' I returned, 'that there's only one bed here, and that I – '

'Oh, don't think of mentioning beds, Master Copperfield!' he rejoined ecstatically, drawing up one leg. 'But *would* you have any objections to my laying down before the fire?'

'If it comes to that,' I said, 'pray take my bed, and I'll lie down before the fire.'

His repudiation of this offer was almost shrill enough, in the excess of its surprise and humility, to have penetrated to the ears of Mrs Crupp, then sleeping, I suppose, in a distant chamber, situated at about the level of low-water mark, soothed in her slumbers by the ticking of an incorrigible clock, to which she always referred me when we had any little difference on the score of punctuality, and which was never less than three-quarters of an hour too slow, and had always been put right in the morning by the best authorities. As no arguments I could urge, in my bewildered condition, had the least effect upon his modesty in inducing him to accept my bedroom, I was obliged to make the best arrangements I could for his repose before the fire. The mattress of the sofa (which was a great deal too short for his lank figure), the sofa pillows, a blanket, the table-cover, a clean breakfast-cloth, and a greatcoat, made him a bed and covering, for which he was more than thankful. Having lent him a nightcap, which he put on at once, and in which he made such an awful figure that I have never worn one since, I left him to his rest.

I never shall forget that night. I never shall forget how I turned and tumbled; how I wearied myself with thinking about Agnes and this creature; how I considered what could I do, and what ought I to do; how I could come to no other conclusion than that the best course for her peace, was to do nothing, and to keep to myself what I had heard. If I went to sleep for a few moments, the image of Agnes with her tender eyes, and of her father looking fondly on her, as I had so often seen him look, arose before me with appealing faces, and filled me with vague terrors. When I awoke, the recollection that Uriah was lying in the next room sat heavy on me like a waking nightmare; and oppressed me with a leaden dread, as if I had had some meaner quality of devil for a lodger.

The poker got into my dozing thoughts besides, and wouldn't come out. I thought, between sleeping and waking, that it was still red-hot, and I had snatched it out of the fire, and run him through the body. I was so haunted at last by the idea, though I knew there was nothing in it, that I stole into the next room to look at him. There I saw him, lying on his back, with his legs extending to I don't know where, gurglings taking place in his throat, stoppages in his nose, and his mouth open like a post-office. He was so much worse in reality than in my distempered fancy, that afterwards I was attracted to him in very repulsion, and could not help wandering in and out every half hour or so, and taking another look at him. Still, the long, long night seemed heavy and hopeless as ever, and no promise of day was in the murky sky.

When I saw him going downstairs early in the morning (for, thank Heaven! he would not stay to breakfast), it appeared to me as if the night was going away in his person. When I went out to the Commons, I charged Mrs Crupp with particular directions to leave the windows open, that my sitting-room might be aired, and purged of his presence.

CHAPTER 26

I Fall into Captivity

I saw no more of Uriah Heep, until the day when Agnes left town. I was at the coach-office to take leave of her and see her go; and there was he, returning to Canterbury by the same conveyance. It was some small satisfaction to me to observe his spare, short-waisted, high-shouldered, mulberry-coloured greatcoat perched up, in company with an umbrella like a small tent, on the edge of the back seat on the roof, while Agnes was, of course, inside; but what I underwent in my efforts to be friendly with him, while Agnes looked on, perhaps deserved that little recompense. At the coach-window, as at the dinner-party, he hovered about us without a moment's intermission, like a great vulture; gorging himself on every syllable that I said to Agnes, or Agnes said to me.

In the state of trouble into which his disclosure by my fire had thrown me, I had thought very much of the words Agnes had used in reference to the partnership: 'I did what I hope was right. Feeling sure that it was necessary for papa's peace that the sacrifice should be made, I entreated him to make it.' A miserable foreboding that she would yield to, and sustain herself by, the same feeling in reference to any sacrifice for his sake, had oppressed me ever since. I knew how she loved him. I know what the devotion of her nature was. I knew from her own lips that she regarded herself as the innocent cause of his errors, and as owing him a great debt she ardently desired to pay. I had no consolation in seeing how different she was from this detestable Rufus with the mulberry-coloured greatcoat, for I felt that in the very difference between them, in the self-denial of her pure soul and the sordid baseness of his, the greatest danger lay. All this, doubtless, he knew thoroughly, and had, in his cunning, considered well.

Yet, I was so certain that the prospect of such a sacrifice afar off must destroy the happiness of Agnes; and I was so sure, from her manner, of its being unseen by her then, and having cast no shadow on her yet, that I could as soon have injured her, as given her any warning of what impended. Thus it was that we parted without explanation: she waving her hand and smiling farewell from the coach-window; her evil genius writhing on the roof, as if he had her in his clutches and triumphed.

I could not get over this farewell glimpse of them for a long time. When Agnes wrote to tell me of her safe arrival, I was as miserable as when I saw her going away. Whenever I fell into a thoughtful state, this subject was sure to present itself, and all my uneasiness was sure to be redoubled. Hardly a night passed without my dreaming of it. It became a part of my life, and as inseparable from my life as my own head.

I had ample leisure to refine upon my uneasiness, for Steerforth was at Oxford, as he wrote to me, and when I was not at the Commons, I was very much alone. I believe I had at this time some lurking distrust of Steerforth. I wrote to him most affectionately in reply to his, but I think I was glad, upon the whole, that he could not come to London just then. I suspect the truth to be, that the influence of Agnes was upon me, undisturbed by the sight of him; and that it was the more powerful with me, because she had so large a share in my thoughts and interest.

In the meantime, days and weeks slipped away. I was articled to Spenlow and Jorkins. I had ninety pounds a year (exclusive of my house-rent and sundry collateral matters) from my aunt. My rooms were engaged for twelve months certain; and though I still found them dreary of an evening, and the evenings long, I could settle down into a state of equable low spirits, and resign myself to coffee; which I seem, on looking back, to have taken by the gallon at about this period of my existence. At about this time, too, I made three discoveries: first, that Mrs Crupp was a martyr to a curious disorder called 'the spazzums', which was generally accompanied with inflammation of the nose, and required to be constantly treated with peppermint; secondly, that something peculiar in the temperature of my pantry made the brandy-bottles burst; thirdly, that I was alone in the world, and much given to record that circumstance in fragments of English versification.

On the day when I was articled, no festivity took place, beyond my having sandwiches and sherry into the office for the clerks, and going alone to the theatre at night. I went to see *The Stranger* as a Doctors' Commons sort of play, and was so dreadfully cut up, that I hardly knew myself in my own glass when I got home. Mr Spenlow remarked, on this occasion, when we concluded our business, that he should have been happy to have seen me at his house at Norwood to celebrate our becoming connected, but for his domestic arrangements being in some disorder, on account of the expected return of his daughter from finishing her education at Paris. But, he intimated that when she came home he should hope to have the pleasure of entertaining me. I knew that he was a widower with one daughter, and expressed my acknowledgments.

Mr Spenlow was as good as his word. In a week or two, he referred to this engagement, and said, that if I would do him the favour to come down next Saturday, and stay till Monday, he would be extremely happy. Of course I said I *would* do him the favour; and he was to drive me down in his phaeton, and to bring me back.

When the day arrived, my very carpet-bag was an object of veneration to the stipendiary clerks, to whom the house at Norwood was a sacred mystery. One of them informed me that he had heard that Mr Spenlow ate entirely off plate and china; and another hinted at champagne being constantly on draught, after the usual custom of table beer. The old clerk with the wig, whose name was Mr Tiffy, had been down on business several times in the course of his career, and had on each occasion penetrated to the breakfast-parlour. He described it as an apartment of the most sumptuous nature, and said that he had drunk brown East India sherry there, of a quality so precious as to make a man wink.

We had an adjourned cause in the Consistory that day – about excommunicating a baker who had been objecting in a vestry to a paving-rate – and as the evidence was just twice the length of Robinson Crusoe, according to a calculation I made, it was rather late in the day before we finished. However, we got him excommunicated for six weeks, and sentenced in no end of costs; and then the baker's proctor, and the judge, and the advocates on both sides (who were all nearly related), went out of town together, and Mr Spenlow and I drove away in the phaeton.

The phaeton was a very handsome affair; the horses arched their necks and lifted up their legs as if they knew they belonged to Doctors' Commons. There was a good deal of competition in the Commons on all points of display, and it turned out some very choice equipages then; though I always have considered, and always shall consider, that in my time the great article of competition there was starch; which I think was worn among the proctors to as great an extent as it is in the nature of man to bear.

We were very pleasant going down, and Mr Spenlow gave me some hints in reference to my profession. He said it was the genteelest profession in the world, and must on no account be confounded with the profession of a solicitor, being quite another sort of thing, infinitely more exclusive, less mechanical, and more profitable. We took things much more easily in the Commons than they could be taken anywhere else, he observed, and that set us, as a privileged class, apart. He said it was impossible to conceal the disagreeable fact, that we were chiefly employed by solicitors; but he gave me to understand that they were an inferior race of men, universally looked down upon by all proctors of any pretensions.

I asked Mr Spenlow what he considered the best sort of professional business? He replied, that a good case of a disputed will, where there was a neat little estate of thirty or forty thousand pounds, was, perhaps, the best of all. In such a case, he said, not only were there very pretty pickings in the way of arguments at every stage of the proceedings, and mountains upon mountains of evidence on interrogatory and counter-interrogatory (to say nothing of an appeal lying, first to the Delegates, and then to the Lords); but, the costs being pretty sure to come out of the estate at last, both sides went at it in a lively and spirited manner, and expense was no consideration. Then, he launched into a general eulogium on the Commons. What was to be particularly admired (he said) in the Commons, was its compactness. It was the most conveniently organised place in the world. It was the complete idea of snugness. It lay in a nutshell. For example: You brought a divorce case, or a restitution case, into the Consistory. Very good. You tried it in the Consistory. You made a quiet little round game of it, among a family group, and you played it out at leisure.

Suppose you were not satisfied with the Consistory, what did you do then? Why, you went into the Arches. What was the Arches? The same court, in the same room, with the same bar, and the same practitioners, but another judge, for there the Consistory judge could plead any court-day as an advocate. Well, you played your round game out again. Still you were not satisfied. Very good. What did you do then? Why, you went to the Delegates. Who were the Delegates? Why, the Ecclesiastical Delegates were the advocates without any business, who had looked on at the round game when it was playing in both courts, and had seen the cards shuffled, and cut, and played, and had talked to all the players about it, and now came fresh, as judges, to settle the matter to the satisfaction of everybody! Discontented people might talk of corruption in the Commons, closeness in the Commons, and the necessity of reforming the Commons, said Mr Spenlow solemnly, in conclusion; but when the price of wheat per bushel had been highest, the Commons had been busiest; and a man might lay his hand upon his heart, and say this to the whole world – 'Touch the Commons, and down comes the country!'

I listened to all this with attention; and though, I must say, I had my doubts whether the country was quite as much obliged to the Commons as Mr Spenlow made out, I respectfully deferred to his opinion. That about the price of wheat per bushel I modestly felt was too much for my strength, and quite settled the question. I have never, to this hour, got the better of that bushel of wheat. It has reappeared to annihilate me, all through my life, in connection with all kinds of subjects. I don't know now, exactly, what it has to do with me, or what right it has to crush me, on an infinite variety of occasions; but whenever I see my old friend the bushel brought in by the head and shoulders (as he always is, I observe), I give up a subject for lost.

This is a digression. *I* was not the man to touch the Commons, and bring down the country. I submissively expressed, by my silence, my acquiescence in all I had heard from my superior in years and knowledge; and we talked about *The Stranger* and the Drama, and the pair of horses, until we came to Mr Spenlow's gate.

There was a lovely garden to Mr Spenlow's house; and though that was not the best time of the year for seeing a garden, it was so beautifully kept, that I was quite enchanted. There was a charming lawn, there were clusters of trees, and there were perspective walks that I could just distinguish in the dark, arched over with trellis-work, on which shrubs and flowers grew in the growing season. 'Here Miss Spenlow walks by herself,' I thought. 'Dear me!'

We went into the house, which was cheerfully lighted up, and into a hall where there were all sorts of hats, caps, greatcoats, plaids, gloves, whips, and walking-sticks. 'Where is Miss Dora?' said Mr Spenlow to the servant. 'Dora!' I thought. 'What a beautiful name!'

We turned into a room near at hand (I think it was the identical breakfast-room, made memorable by the brown East India sherry), and I heard a voice say, 'Mr Copperfield, my daughter Dora, and my daughter Dora's confidential friend!' It was, no doubt, Mr Spenlow's voice, but I didn't know it, and I didn't care whose it was. All was over in a moment. I had fulfilled my destiny. I was a captive and a slave. I loved Dora Spenlow to distraction!

She was more than human to me. She was a Fairy, a Sylph, I don't know what she was – anything that no one ever saw, and everything that everybody ever wanted. I was swallowed up in an abyss of love in an instant. There was no pausing on the brink; no looking down, or looking back; I was gone, headlong, before I had sense to say a word to her.

'*I*,' observed a well-remembered voice, when I had bowed and murmured something, 'have seen Mr Copperfield before.'

The speaker was not Dora. No; the confidential friend, Miss Murdstone!

I don't think I was much astonished. To the best of my judgement, no capacity of astonishment was left in me. There was nothing worth mentioning in the material world, but Dora Spenlow, to be astonished about. I said, 'How do you do, Miss Murdstone? I hope you are well.' She answered, 'Very well.' I said, 'How is Mr Murdstone?' She replied, 'My brother is robust, I am obliged to you.'

Mr Spenlow, who, I suppose, had been surprised to see us recognise each other, then put in his word.

'I am glad to find,' he said, 'Copperfield, that you and Miss Murdstone are already acquainted.'

'Mr Copperfield and myself,' said Miss Murdstone, with severe composure, 'are connections. We were once slightly acquainted. It was in his childish days. Circumstances have separated us since. I should not have known him.'

I replied that I should have known her, anywhere. Which was true enough.

'Miss Murdstone has had the goodness,' said Mr Spenlow to me, 'to accept the office – if I may so describe it – of my daughter Dora's confidential friend. My daughter Dora having, unhappily, no mother, Miss Murdstone is obliging enough to become her companion and protector.'

A passing thought occurred to me that Miss Murdstone, like the pocket instrument called a life-preserver, was not so much designed for purposes of protection as of assault. But as I had none but passing thoughts for any subject save Dora, I glanced at her, directly afterwards, and was thinking that I saw, in her prettily pettish manner, that she was not very much inclined to be particularly confidential to her companion and protector, when a bell rang, which Mr Spenlow said was the first dinner-bell, and so carried me off to dress.

The idea of dressing one's self, or doing anything in the way of action, in that state of love, was a little too ridiculous. I could only sit down before my fire, biting the key of my carpet-bag, and think of the captivating, girlish, bright-eyed, lovely Dora. What a form she had, what a face she had, what a graceful, variable, enchanting manner!

The bell rang again so soon that I made a mere scramble of my dressing, instead of the careful operation I could have wished under the circumstances, and went downstairs. There was some company. Dora was talking to an old gentleman with a grey head. Grey as he was – and a great-grandfather into the bargain, for he said so – I was madly jealous of him.

What a state of mind I was in! I was jealous of everybody. I couldn't bear the idea of anybody knowing Mr Spenlow better than I did. It was torturing to me to hear them talk of occurrences in which I had had no share. When a most amiable person, with a highly polished bald head, asked me across the dinner-table, if that were the first occasion of my seeing the grounds, I could have done anything to him that was savage and revengeful.

I don't remember who was there, except Dora. I have not the least idea what we had for dinner, besides Dora. My impression is, that I dined off Dora entirely, and sent away half a dozen plates untouched. I sat next to her. I talked to her. She had the most delightful little voice, the gayest little laugh, the pleasantest and most fascinating little ways, that ever led a lost youth into hopeless slavery. She was rather diminutive altogether. So much the more precious, I thought.

When she went out of the room with Miss Murdstone (no other ladies were of the party), I fell into a reverie, only disturbed by the cruel apprehension that Miss Murdstone would disparage me to her. The amiable creature with the polished head told me a long story, which I think was about gardening. I think I heard him say 'my gardener' several times. I seemed to pay the deepest attention to him, but I was wandering in a garden of Eden all the while with Dora.

My apprehensions of being disparaged to the object of my engrossing affection were revived when we went into the drawing-room, by the grim and distant aspect of Miss Murdstone. But I was relieved of them in an unexpected manner.

'David Copperfield,' said Miss Murdstone, beckoning me aside into a window. 'A word.'

I confronted Miss Murdstone alone.

'David Copperfield,' said Miss Murdstone, 'I need not enlarge upon family circumstances. They are not a tempting subject.'

'Far from it, ma'am,' I returned.

'Far from it,' assented Miss Murdstone. 'I do not wish to revive the memory of past differences, or of past outrages. I have received outrages from a person – a female, I am sorry to say, for the credit of my sex – who is not to be mentioned without scorn and disgust; and therefore I would rather not mention her.'

I felt very fiery on my aunt's account, but I said it would certainly be better, if Miss Murdstone pleased, *not* to mention her. I could not hear her disrespectfully mentioned, I added, without expressing my opinion in a decided tone.

Miss Murdstone shut her eyes, and disdainfully inclined her head; then, slowly opening her eyes, resumed: 'David Copperfield, I shall not attempt to disguise the fact, that I formed an unfavourable opinion of you in your childhood. It may have been a mistaken one, or you may have ceased to justify it. That is not in question between us now. I belong to a family, remarkable, I believe, for some firmness; and I am not the creature of circumstance or change. I may have my opinion of you. You may have your opinion of me.'

I inclined my head, in my turn.

'But it is not necessary,' said Miss Murdstone, 'that these

opinions should come into collision here. Under existing circumstances, it is as well on all accounts that they should not. As the chances of life have brought us together again, and may bring us together on other occasions, I would say let us meet here as distant acquaintances. Family circumstances are a sufficient reason for our only meeting on that footing, and it is quite unnecessary that either of us should make the other the subject of remark. Do you approve of this?'

'Miss Murdstone,' I returned, 'I think you and Mr Murdstone used me very cruelly, and treated my mother with great unkindness. I shall always think so, as long as I live. But I quite agree in what you propose.'

Miss Murdstone shut her eyes again, and bent her head. Then, just touching the back of my hand with the tips of her cold stiff fingers, she walked away, arranging the little fetters on her wrists and round her neck, which seemed to be the same set, in exactly the same state, as when I had seen her last. These reminded me, in reference to Miss Murdstone's nature, of the fetters over a jail door; suggesting on the outside, to all beholders, what was to be expected within.

All I know of the rest of the evening is that I heard the empress of my heart sing enchanted ballads in the French language, generally to the effect that, whatever was the matter, we ought always to dance, Ta ra la, Ta ra la! accompanying herself on a glorified instrument, resembling a guitar; that I was lost in blissful delirium; that I refused refreshment; that my soul recoiled from punch particularly; that when Miss Murdstone took her into custody and led her away, she smiled and gave me her delicious hand; that I caught a view of myself in the mirror, looking perfectly imbecile and idiotic; that I retired to bed in a most maudlin state of mind, and got up in a crisis of feeble infatuation.

It was a fine morning and early, and I thought I would go and take a stroll down one of those wire-arched walks, and indulge my passion by dwelling on her image. On my way through the hall, I encountered her little dog, who was called Jip – short for Gypsy. I approached him tenderly, for I loved even him; but he showed his whole set of teeth, got under a chair expressly to snarl, and wouldn't hear of the least familiarity.

The garden was cool and solitary. I walked about, wondering what my feelings of happiness would be, if I could ever become engaged to this dear wonder. As to marriage, and fortune, and all that, I believe I was almost as innocently undesigning then as when I loved little Em'ly. To be allowed to call her 'Dora', to write to her, to dote upon and worship her, to have reason to think that when she was with other people she was yet mindful of me, seemed to me the summit of human ambition – I am sure it was the summit of mine. There is no doubt whatever that I was a lackadaisical young spoony; but there was a purity of heart in all this still that prevents my having quite a contemptuous recollection of it, let me laugh as I may.

I had not been walking long, when I turned a corner, and met her. I tingle again from head to foot as my recollection turns that corner, and my pen shakes in my hand.

'You – are – out early, Miss Spenlow,' said I.

'It's so stupid at home,' she replied, 'and Miss Murdstone is

so absurd! She talks such nonsense about its being necessary for the day to be aired, before I come out. Aired!' (She laughed here, in the most melodious manner.) 'On a Sunday morning, when I don't practise, I must do something. So I told papa last night I must come out. Besides, it's the brightest time of the whole day. Don't you think so?'

I hazarded a bold flight, and said (not without stammering) that it was very bright to me then, though it had been very dark to me a minute before.

'Do you mean a compliment?' said Dora; 'or that the weather has really changed?'

I stammered worse than before, in replying that I meant no compliment, but the plain truth; though I was not aware of any change having taken place in the weather. It was in the state of my own feelings, I added bashfully, to clench the explanation.

I never saw such curls – how could I, for there never were such curls! – as those she shook out to hide her blushes. As to the straw hat and blue ribbons which was on the top of the curls, if I could only have hung it up in my room in Buckingham Street, what a priceless possession it would have been!

'You have just come home from Paris,' said I.

'Yes,' said she. 'Have you ever been there?'

'No.'

'Oh! I hope you'll go soon! You would like it so much!'

Traces of deep-seated anguish appeared in my countenance. That she should hope I would go, that she should think it possible I *could* go, was insupportable. I depreciated Paris; I depreciated France. I said I wouldn't leave England, under

I fall into captivity

existing circumstances, for any earthly consideration. Nothing should induce me. In short, she was shaking the curls again, when the little dog came running along the walk to our relief.

He was mortally jealous of me, and persisted in barking at me. She took him up in her arms – oh, my goodness! – and caressed him, but he insisted upon barking still. He wouldn't let me touch him, when I tried; and then she beat him. It increased my sufferings greatly to see the pats she gave him for punishment on the bridge of his blunt nose, while he winked his eyes, and licked her hand, and still growled within himself like a little double-bass. At length he was quiet – well he might be with her dimpled chin upon his head! – and we walked away to look at a greenhouse.

'You are not very intimate with Miss Murdstone, are you?' said Dora. 'My pet.'

(The two last words were to the dog. Oh, if they had only been to me!)

'No,' I replied. 'Not at all so.'

'She is a tiresome creature,' said Dora, pouting. 'I can't think what papa can have been about, when he chose such a vexatious thing to be my companion. Who wants a protector? I am sure I don't want a protector. Jip can protect me a great deal better than Miss Murdstone – can't you, Jip, dear?'

He only winked lazily, when she kissed his ball of a head.

'Papa calls her my confidential friend, but I am sure she is no such thing – is she, Jip? We are not going to confide in such cross people, Jip and I. We mean to bestow our confidence where we like, and to find out our own friends, instead of having them found out for us – don't we, Jip?'

Jip made a comfortable noise, in answer, a little like a tea-kettle when it sings. As for me, every word was a new heap of fetters, riveted above the last.

'It is very hard, because we have not a kind mama, that we are to have, instead, a sulky, gloomy old thing like Miss Murd-stone, always following us about – isn't it, Jip? Never mind, Jip. We won't be confidential, and we'll make ourselves as happy as we can in spite of her, and we'll tease her, and not please her – won't we, Jip?'

If it had lasted any longer, I think I must have gone down on my knees on the gravel, with the probability before me of grazing them, and of being presently ejected from the premises besides. But by good fortune the greenhouse was not far off, and these words brought us to it.

It contained quite a show of beautiful geraniums. We loitered along in front of them, and Dora often stopped to admire this one or that one, and I stopped to admire the same one, and Dora, laughing, held the dog up childishly to smell the flowers; and if we were not all three in Fairyland, certainly *I* was. The scent of a geranium leaf, at this day, strikes me with a half-comical, half-serious wonder as to what change has come over me in a moment; and then I see a straw hat and blue ribbons, and a quantity of curls, and a little black dog being held up, in two slender arms, against a bank of blossoms and bright leaves.

Miss Murdstone had been looking for us. She found us here; and presented her uncongenial cheek, the little wrinkles in it

filled with hair powder, to Dora to be kissed. Then she took Dora's arm in hers, and marched us in to breakfast as if it were a soldier's funeral.

How many cups of tea I drank, because Dora made it, I don't know. But I perfectly remember that I sat swilling tea until my whole nervous system, if I had had any in those days, must have gone by the board. By and by we went to church. Miss Murdstone was between Dora and me in the pew; but I heard her sing, and the congregation vanished. A sermon was delivered – about Dora, of course – and I am afraid that is all I know of the service.

We had a quiet day. No company, a walk, a family dinner of four, and an evening of looking over books and pictures; Miss Murdstone, with a homily before her, and her eye upon us, keeping guard vigilantly. Ah! little did Mr Spenlow imagine, when he sat opposite to me after dinner that day, with his pocket-handkerchief over his head, how fervently I was embracing him, in my fancy, as his son-in-law! Little did he think, when I took leave of him at night, that he had just given his full consent to my being engaged to Dora, and that I was invoking blessings on his head!

We departed early in the morning, for we had a Salvage case coming on in the Admiralty Court, requiring a rather accurate knowledge of the whole science of navigation, in which (as we couldn't be expected to know much about those matters in the Commons) the judge had entreated two old Trinity Masters, for charity's sake, to come and help him out. Dora was at the breakfast-table to make the tea again, however; and I had the melancholy pleasure of taking off my hat to her in the phaeton, as she stood on the doorstep with Jip in her arms.

What the Admiralty was to me that day; what nonsense I made of our case in my mind, as I listened to it; how I saw 'Dora' engraved upon the blade of the silver oar which they lay upon the table, as the emblem of that high jurisdiction; and how I felt when Mr Spenlow went home without me (I had had an insane hope that he might take me back again), as if I were a mariner myself, and the ship to which I belonged had sailed away and left me on a desert island; I shall make no fruitless effort to describe. If that sleepy old court could rouse itself, and present in any visible form the day-dreams I have had in it about Dora, it would reveal my truth.

I don't mean the dreams that I dreamed on that day alone, but day after day, from week to week, and term to term. I went there, not to attend to what was going on, but to think about Dora. If ever I bestowed a thought upon the cases, as they dragged their slow length before me, it was only to wonder, in the matrimonial cases (remembering Dora), how it was that married people could ever be otherwise than happy; and, in the Prerogative cases, to consider, if the money in question had been left to me, what were the foremost steps I should immediately have taken in regard to Dora. Within the first week of my passion, I bought four sumptuous waistcoats – not for myself; *I* had no pride in them; for Dora – and took to wearing straw-coloured kid gloves in the streets, and laid the foundations of all the corns I have ever had. If the boots I wore at that period could only be produced and compared with the natural size of my feet, they would show what the state of my heart was, in a most affecting manner.

And yet, wretched cripple as I made myself by this act of homage to Dora, I walked miles upon miles daily in the hope of seeing her. Not only was I soon as well known on the Norwood Road as the postmen on that beat, but I pervaded London likewise. I walked about the streets where the best shops for ladies were, I haunted the Bazaar like an unquiet spirit, I fagged through the Park again and again, long after I was quite knocked up. Sometimes, at long intervals and on rare occasions, I saw her. Perhaps I saw her glove waved in a carriage window; perhaps I met her, walked with her and Miss Murdstone a little way, and spoke to her. In the latter case I was always very miserable afterwards, to think that I had said nothing to the purpose; or that she had no idea of the extent of my devotion, or that she cared nothing about me. I was always looking out, as may be supposed, for another invitation to Mr Spenlow's house. I was always being disappointed, for I got none.

Mrs Crupp must have been a woman of penetration; for when this attachment was but a few weeks old, and I had not had the courage to write more explicitly even to Agnes than that I had been to Mr Spenlow's house, 'whose family,' I added, 'consists of one daughter' – I say Mrs Crupp must have been a woman of penetration, for, even in that early stage, she found it out. She came up to me one evening, when I was very low, to ask (she being then afflicted with the disorder I have mentioned) if I could oblige her with a little tincture of cardamoms, mixed with rhubarb, and flavoured with seven drops of the essence of cloves, which was the best remedy for her complaint – or, if I had not such a thing by me, with a little brandy, which was the next best. It was not, she remarked, so palatable to her, but it was the next best. As I had never even heard of the first remedy, and always had the second in the closet, I gave Mrs Crupp a glass of the second, which (that I might have no suspicion of its being devoted to any improper use) she began to take in my presence.

'Cheer up, sir,' said Mrs Crupp; 'I can't abear to see you so, sir; I'm a mother myself.'

I did not quite perceive the application of this fact to myself, but I smiled on Mrs Crupp, as benignly as was in my power.

'Come, sir,' said Mrs Crupp. 'Excuse me. I know what it is, sir. There's a lady in the case.'

'Mrs Crupp?' I returned, reddening.

'Oh, bless you! Keep a good heart, sir!' said Mrs Crupp, nodding encouragement. 'Never say die, sir! If She don't smile upon you, there's a many as will. You're a young gentleman to *be* smiled on, Mr Copperfull, and you must learn your walue, sir.'

Mrs Crupp always called me Mr Copperfull; firstly, no doubt, because it was not my name; and secondly, I am inclined to think, in some indistinct association with a washing-day.

'What makes you suppose there is any young lady in the case, Mrs Crupp?' said I.

'Mr Copperfull,' said Mrs Crupp, with a great deal of feeling, 'I'm a mother myself.'

For some time Mrs Crupp could only lay her hand upon her nankeen bosom, and fortify herself against returning pain with sips of her medicine. At length she spoke again.

'When the present set were took for you by your dear aunt, Mr Copperfull,' said Mrs Crupp, 'my remark were, I had now found summun I could care for. "Thank Ev'in!" were the expression, "I have now found summun I can care for!" You don't eat enough, sir, nor yet drink.'

'Is that what you found your supposition on, Mrs Crupp?' said I.

'Sir,' said Mrs Crupp, in a tone approaching to severity, 'I've laundressed other young gentlemen besides yourself. A young gentleman may be over-careful of himself, or he may be under-careful of himself. He may brush his hair too regular, or too unregular. He may wear his boots much too large for him, or much too small. That is according as the young gentleman has his original character formed. But let him go to which extreme he may, sir, there's a young lady in both of 'em.'

Mrs Crupp shook her head in such a determined manner, that I had not an inch of vantage-ground left.

'It was but the gentleman which died here before yourself,' said Mrs Crupp, 'that fell in love – with a barmaid – and had his waistcoats took in directly, though much swelled by drinking.'

'Mrs Crupp,' said I, 'I must beg you not to connect the young lady in my case with a barmaid, or anything of that sort, if you please.'

'Mr Copperfull,' returned Mrs Crupp, 'I'm a mother myself, and not likely. I ask your pardon, sir, if I intrude. I should never wish to intrude where I were not welcome. But you are a young gentleman, Mr Copperfull, and my adwice to you is, to cheer up, sir, to keep a good heart, and to know your own walue. If you was to take to something, sir,' said Mrs Crupp, 'if you was to take to skittles, now, which is healthy, you might find it divert your mind, and do you good.'

With these words, Mrs Crupp, affecting to be very careful of the brandy – which was all gone – thanked me with a majestic curtsey, and retired. As her figure disappeared into the gloom of the entry, this counsel certainly presented itself to my mind in the light of a slight liberty on Mrs Crupp's part; but, at the same time, I was content to receive it, in another point of view, as a word to the wise, and a warning in future to keep my secret better.

CHAPTER 27

Tommy Traddles

It may have been in consequence of Mrs Crupp's advice, and perhaps, for no better reason than because there was a certain similarity in the sound of the words skittles and Traddles, that it came into my head, next day, to go and look after Traddles. The time he had mentioned was more than out, and he lived in a little street near the Veterinary College at Camden Town, which was principally tenanted, as one of our clerks who lived in that direction informed me, by gentlemen students, who bought live donkeys, and made experiments on those quadrupeds in their private apartments. Having obtained from this clerk a direction to the academic grove in question, I set out, the same afternoon, to visit my old schoolfellow.

I found that the street was not as desirable a one as I could have wished it to be, for the sake of Traddles. The inhabitants appeared to have a propensity to throw any little trifles they were not in want of, into the road; which not only made it rank and sloppy, but untidy, too, on account of the cabbage-leaves. The refuse was not wholly vegetable either, for I myself saw a shoe, a doubled-up saucepan, a black bonnet, and an umbrella, in various stages of decomposition, as I was looking out for the number I wanted.

The general air of the place reminded me forcibly of the days when I lived with Mr and Mrs Micawber. An indescribable character of faded gentility that attached to the house I sought, and made it unlike all the other houses in the street – though they were all built on one monotonous pattern, and looked like the early copies of a blundering boy who was learning to make houses, and had not yet got out of his cramped brick and mortar pothooks – reminded me still more of Mr and Mrs Micawber. Happening to arrive at the door as it was opened to the afternoon milkman, I was reminded of Mr and Mrs Micawber more forcibly yet.

'Now,' said the milkman to a very youthful servant girl, 'has that there little bill of mine been heard on?'

'Oh, master says he'll attend to it immediate,' was the reply.

'Because,' said the milkman, going on as if he had received no answer, and speaking, as I judged from his tone, rather for the edification of somebody within the house than of the youthful servant – an impression which was strengthened by his manner of glaring down the passage – 'Because that there little bill has been running so long that I begin to believe it's run away altogether, and never won't be heerd of. Now, I'm not a going to stand it, you know!' said the milkman, still throwing his voice into the house, and glaring down the passage.

As to his dealing in the mild article of milk, by the by, there never was a greater anomaly. His deportment would have been fierce in a butcher or a brandy merchant.

The voice of the youthful servant became faint, but she seemed to me, from the action of her lips, again to murmur that it would be attended to immediate.

'I tell you what,' said the milkman, looking hard at her for the first time, and taking her by the chin, 'are you fond of milk?'

'Yes, I likes it,' she replied.

'Good,' said the milkman. 'Then you won't have none tomorrow. D'ye hear? Not a fragment of milk you won't have tomorrow.'

I thought she seemed, upon the whole, relieved, by the prospect of having any today. The milkman, after shaking his head at her darkly, released her chin, and with anything rather than goodwill opened his can, and deposited the usual quantity in the family jug. This done, he went away, muttering, and uttered the cry of his trade next door, in a vindictive shriek.

'Does Mr Traddles live here?' I then enquired.

A mysterious voice from the end of the passage replied 'Yes.' Upon which the youthful servant replied 'Yes.'

'Is he at home?' said I.

Again the mysterious voice replied in the affirmative, and again the servant echoed it. Upon this, I walked in, and in pursuance of the servant's directions walked upstairs; conscious, as I passed the back parlour door, that I was surveyed by a mysterious eye, probably belonging to the mysterious voice.

When I got to the top of the stairs – the house was only a story high above the ground-floor – Traddles was on the landing to meet me. He was delighted to see me, and gave me welcome, with great heartiness, to his little room. It was in the front of the house, and extremely neat, though sparely furnished. It was his only room, I saw; for there was a sofa-bedstead in it, and his blacking-brushes and blacking were among his books – on the top shelf, behind a dictionary. His table was covered with papers, and he was hard at work in an old coat. I looked at nothing, that I know of, but I saw everything, even to the prospect of a church upon his china ink-stand, as I sat down – and this, too, was a faculty confirmed in me in the old Micawber times. Various ingenious arrangements he had made, for the disguise of his chest of drawers, and the accommodation of his boots, his shaving-glass, and so forth, particularly impressed themselves upon me, as evidences of the same Traddles, who used to make models of elephants' dens in writing-paper to put flies in; and to comfort himself under ill-usage with the memorable works of art I have so often mentioned.

In a corner of the room was something neatly covered up with a large white cloth. I could not make out what that was.

'Traddles,' said I, shaking hands with him again, after I had sat down, 'I am delighted to see you.'

'I am delighted to see *you*, Copperfield,' he returned. 'I am very glad, indeed, to see you. It was because I was thoroughly glad to see you when we met in Ely Place, and was sure you were thoroughly glad to see me, that I gave you this address instead of my address at chambers.'

'Oh! You have chambers?' said I.

'Why, I have the fourth of a room and a passage, and the fourth of a clerk,' returned Traddles. 'Three others and myself unite to have a set of chambers – to look businesslike – and we quarter the clerk, too. Half a crown a week he costs me.'

His old simple character and good temper, and something of his old unlucky fortune also, I thought, smiled at me in the smile with which he made this explanation.

'It's not because I have the least pride, Copperfield, you understand,' said Traddles, 'that I don't usually give my address here. It's only on account of those who come to me, who might not like to come here. For myself, I am fighting my way on in the world against difficulties, and it would be ridiculous if I made a pretence of doing anything else.'

'You are reading for the bar, Mr Waterbrook informed me?' said I.

'Why, yes,' said Traddles, rubbing his hands slowly over one another, 'I am reading for the bar. The fact is I have just begun to keep my terms, after rather a long delay. It's some time since I was articled, but the payment of that hundred pounds was a great pull. A great pull!' said Traddles, with a wince, as if he had had a tooth out.

'Do you know what I can't help thinking of, Traddles, as I sit here looking at you?' I asked him.

'No,' said he.

'That sky-blue suit you used to wear.'

'Lord, to be sure!' cried Traddles, laughing. 'Tight in the arms and legs, you know! Dear me! Well! Those were happy times, weren't they?'

'I think our schoolmaster might have made them happier, without doing any harm to any of us, I acknowledge,' I returned.

'Perhaps he might,' said Traddles. 'But dear me, there was a good deal of fun going on. Do you remember the nights in the bedroom? When we used to have the suppers? And when you used to tell the stories? Ha, ha, ha! And do you remember when I got caned for crying about Mr Mell? Old Creakle! I should like to see him again too!'

'He was a brute to you, Traddles,' said I indignantly; for his good-humour made me feel as if I had seen him beaten but yesterday.

'Do you think so?' returned Traddles. 'Really? Perhaps he was, rather. But it's all over, a long while. Old Creakle!'

'You were brought up by an uncle, then?' said I.

'Of course I was!' said Traddles. 'The one I was always going to write to. And always didn't, eh? Ha, ha, ha! Yes, I had an uncle then. He died soon after I left school.'

'Indeed?'

'Yes. He was a retired – what do you call it? – draper – cloth-merchant – and had made me his heir. But he didn't like me when I grew up.'

'Do you really mean that?' said I. He was so composed that I fancied he must have some other meaning.

'Oh, dear, yes, Copperfield! I mean it,' replied Traddles. 'It was an unfortunate thing, but he didn't like me at all. He said I wasn't at all what he expected, and so he married his house-keeper.'

'And what did you do?' I asked.

'I didn't do anything in particular,' said Traddles. 'I lived with them, waiting to be put out in the world, until his gout unfortunately flew to his stomach – and so he died, and so she married a young man, and so I wasn't provided for.'

'Did you get nothing, Traddles, after all?'

'Oh, dear, yes!' said Traddles. 'I got fifty pounds. I had never been brought up to any profession, and at first I was at a loss what to do for myself. However, I began, with the assistance of the son of a professional man, who had been to Salem House – Yawler, with his nose on one side. Do you recollect him?'

No. He had not been there with me; all the noses were straight in my day.

'It don't matter,' said Traddles. 'I began, by means of his assistance, to copy law writings. That didn't answer very well; and then I began to state cases for them, and make abstracts, and do that sort of work. For I am a plodding kind of fellow, Copperfield, and had learnt the way of doing such things pithily. Well! That put it in my head to enter myself as a law student; and that ran away with all that was left of the fifty

pounds. Yawler recommended me to one or two other offices, however – Mr Waterbrook's for one – and I got a good many jobs. I was fortunate enough, too, to become acquainted with a person in the publishing way, who was getting up an Encyclopaedia, and he set me to work; and, indeed' (glancing at his table), 'I am at work for him at this minute. I am not a bad compiler, Copperfield,' said Traddles, preserving the same air of cheerful confidence in all he said, 'but I have no invention at all; not a particle. I suppose there never was a young man with less originality than I have.'

As Traddles seemed to expect that I should assent to this as a matter of course, I nodded; and he went on, with the same sprightly patience – I can find no better expression – as before.

'So, by little and little, and not living high, I managed to scrape up the hundred pounds at last,' said Traddles; 'and thank Heaven that's paid – though it was – though it certainly was,' said Traddles, wincing again as if he had had another tooth out, 'a pull. I am living by the sort of work I have mentioned, still, and I hope, one of these days, to get connected with some newspaper, which would almost be the making of my fortune. Now, Copperfield, you are so exactly what you used to be, with that agreeable face, and it's so pleasant to see you, that I sha'n't conceal anything. Therefore you must know that I am engaged.'

Engaged! Oh, Dora!

'She is a curate's daughter,' said Traddles; 'one of ten, down in Devonshire. Yes!' For he saw me glance, involuntarily, at the prospect on the inkstand. 'That's the church! You come round here, to the left, out of this gate,' tracing his finger along the inkstand, 'and exactly where I hold this pen, there stands the house – facing, you understand, towards the church.'

The delight with which he entered into these particulars did not fully present itself to me until afterwards; for my selfish thoughts were making a ground-plan of Mr Spenlow's house and garden at the same moment.

'She is such a dear girl!' said Traddles. 'A little older than me, but the dearest girl! I told you I was going out of town? I have been down there. I walked there, and I walked back, and I had the most delightful time! I dare say ours is likely to be a rather long engagement, but our motto is, "Wait and hope!" We always say that. "Wait and hope," we always say. And she would wait, Copperfield, till she was sixty – any age you can mention – for me!'

Traddles rose from his chair, and, with a triumphant smile, put his hand upon the white cloth I had observed.

'However,' he said, 'it's not that we haven't made a beginning towards housekeeping. No, no; we have begun. We must get on by degrees, but we have begun. Here,' drawing the cloth off with great pride and care, 'are two pieces of furniture to commence with. This flowerpot and stand, she bought herself. You put that in a parlour window,' said Traddles, falling a little back from it to survey it with the greater admiration, 'with a plant in it, and – and there you are! This little round table with the marble top (it's two feet ten in circumference), *I* bought. You want to lay a book down, you know, or somebody comes to see you or your wife, and wants a place to stand a cup of tea upon, and – and there you are again!' said Traddles. 'It's an admirable piece of workmanship – firm as a rock!'

I praised them both highly, and Traddles replaced the covering as carefully as he had removed it.

'It's not a great deal towards the furnishing,' said Traddles, 'but it's something. The tablecloths, and pillowcases, and articles of that kind, are what discourage me most, Copperfield. So does the ironmongery – candle-boxes, and gridirons, and that sort of necessaries – because those things tell, and mount up. However, "wait and hope." And I assure you she's the dearest girl!'

'I am quite certain of it,' said I.

'In the meantime,' said Traddles, coming back to his chair, 'and this is the end of my prosing about myself, I get on as well as I can. I don't make much, but I don't spend much. In general, I board with the people downstairs, who are very agreeable people, indeed. Both Mr and Mrs Micawber have seen a good deal of life, and are excellent company.'

'My dear Traddles!' I quickly exclaimed. 'What are you talking about?'

Traddles looked at me, as if he wondered what *I* was talking about.

'Mr and Mrs Micawber!' I repeated. 'Why, I am intimately acquainted with them!'

An opportune double knock at the door, which I knew well from old experience in Windsor Terrace, and which nobody but Mr Micawber could ever have knocked at that door, resolved any doubt in my mind as to their being my old friends. I begged Traddles to ask his landlord to walk up. Traddles accordingly did so, over the bannister; and Mr Micawber, not a bit changed – his tights, his stick, his shirt-collar, and his eyeglass, all the same as ever – came into the room with a genteel and youthful air.

'I beg your pardon, Mr Traddles,' said Mr Micawber, with the old roll in his voice, as he checked himself in humming a soft tune. 'I was not aware that there was any individual, alien to this tenement, in your sanctum.'

Mr Micawber slightly bowed to me, and pulled up his shirt-collar.

'How do you do, Mr Micawber?' said I.

'Sir,' said Mr Micawber, 'you are exceedingly obliging. I am in *statu quo.*'

'And Mrs Micawber?' I pursued.

'Sir,' said Mr Micawber, 'she is also, thank God, *in statu quo.*'

'And the children, Mr Micawber?'

'Sir,' said Mr Micawber, 'I rejoice to reply that they are, likewise, in the enjoyment of salubrity.'

All this time Mr Micawber had not known me in the least, though he had stood face to face with me. But now, seeing me smile, he examined my features with more attention, fell back, cried, 'Is it possible! Have I the pleasure of again beholding Copperfield!' and shook me by both hands with the utmost fervour.

'Good Heaven, Mr Traddles!' said Mr Micawber, 'to think that I should find you acquainted with the friend of my youth, the companion of earlier days! My dear!' calling over the banisters to Mrs Micawber, while Traddles looked (with reason) not a little amazed at this description of me; 'here is a gentleman in Mr Traddles's apartment, whom he wishes to have the pleasure of presenting to you, my love!'

Mr Micawber immediately reappeared, and shook hands with me again.

'And how is our good friend the Doctor, Copperfield?' said Mr Micawber; 'and all the circle at Canterbury?'

'I have none but good accounts of them,' said I.

'I am most delighted to hear it,' said Mr Micawber. 'It was at Canterbury where we last met. Within the shadow, I may figuratively say, of that religious edifice immortalised by Chaucer, which was anciently the resort of Pilgrims from the remotest corners of – in short,' said Mr Micawber, 'in the immediate neighbourhood of the Cathedral.'

I replied that it was. Mr Micawber continued talking as volubly as he could; but not, I thought, without showing, by some marks of concern in his countenance, that he was sensible of sounds in the next room, as of Mrs Micawber washing her hands, and hurriedly opening and shutting drawers that were uneasy in their action.

'You find us, Copperfield,' said Mr Micawber, with one eye on Traddles, 'at present established on what may be designated as a small and unassuming scale; but you are aware that I have, in the course of my career, surmounted difficulties, and conquered obstacles. You are no stranger to the fact that there have been periods of my life when it has been requisite that I should pause until certain expected events should turn up; when it has been necessary that I should fall back before making what I trust I shall not be accused of presumption in terming – a spring. The present is one of those momentous stages in the life of man. You find me, fallen back, *for* a spring; and I have every reason to believe that a vigorous leap will shortly be the result.'

I was expressing my satisfaction when Mrs Micawber came in; a little more slatternly than she used to be, or so she seemed now, to my unaccustomed eyes, but still with some preparation of herself for company, and with a pair of brown gloves on.

'My dear,' said Mr Micawber, leading her towards me. 'Here is a gentleman of the name of Copperfield, who wishes to renew his acquaintance with you.'

It would have been better, as it turned out, to have led gently up to his announcement, for Mrs Micawber, being in a delicate state of health, was overcome by it, and was taken so unwell that Mr Micawber was obliged, in great trepidation, to run down to the water-butt in the back yard, and draw a basinful to lave her brow with. She presently revived, however, and was really pleased to see me. We had half an hour's talk, altogether; and I asked her about the twins, who, she said, were 'grown great creatures;' and after Master and Miss Micawber, whom she described as 'absolute giants,' but they were not produced on that occasion.

Mr Micawber was very anxious that I should stay to dinner. I should not have been averse to do so, but that I imagined I detected trouble, and calculation relative to the extent of the cold meat, in Mrs Micawber's eye. I therefore pleaded another engagement; and observing that Mrs Micawber's spirits were immediately lightened, I resisted all persuasion to forego it.

But I told Traddles, and Mr and Mrs Micawber, that, before I could think of leaving, they must appoint a day when they would come and dine with me. The occupations to which Traddles stood pledged rendered it necessary to fix a somewhat distant one; but an appointment was made for the purpose, that suited us all, and then I took my leave.

Mr Micawber, under pretence of showing me a nearer way than that by which I had come, accompanied me to the corner of the street, being anxious (he explained to me) to say a few words to an old friend, in confidence.

'My dear Copperfield,' said Mr Micawber, 'I need hardly tell you that to have beneath our roof, under existing circumstances, a mind like that which gleams – if I may be allowed the expression – which gleams – in your friend Traddles, is an unspeakable comfort. With a washerwoman, who exposes hard-bake for sale in her parlour window, dwelling next door, and a Bow Street officer residing over the way, you may imagine that his society is a source of consolation to myself and to Mrs Micawber. I am at present, my dear Copperfield, engaged in the sale of corn upon commission. It is not an avocation of a remunerative description – in other words, it does *not* pay – and some temporary embarrassments of a pecuniary nature have been the consequence. I am, however, delighted to add that I have now an immediate prospect of something turning up (I am not at liberty to say in what direction), which I trust will enable me to provide, permanently, both for myself and for your friend Traddles, in whom I have an unaffected interest. You may, perhaps, be prepared to hear that Mrs Micawber is in a state of health which renders it not wholly improbable that an addition may be ultimately made to those pledges of affection which – in short, to the infantine group. Mrs Micawber's family have been so good as to express their dissatisfaction at this state of things. I have merely to observe that I am not aware it is any business of theirs, and that I repel that exhibition of feeling with scorn, and with defiance!'

Mr Micawber then shook hands with me again, and left me.

CHAPTER 28

Mr Micawber's Gauntlet

Until the day arrived on which I was to entertain my newly found old friends, I lived principally on Dora and coffee. In my lovelorn condition, my appetite languished; and I was glad of it, for I felt as though it would have been an act of perfidy towards Dora to have a natural relish for my dinner. The quantity of walking exercise I took was not in this respect attended with its usual consequence, as the disappointment counteracted the fresh air. I have my doubts, too, founded on the acute experience acquired at this period of my life, whether a sound enjoyment of animal food can develop itself freely in any human subject who is always in torment from tight boots. I

think the extremities require to be at peace before the stomach will conduct itself with vigour.

On the occasion of this domestic little party, I did not repeat my former extensive preparations. I merely provided a pair of soles, a small leg of mutton, and a pigeon-pie. Mrs Crupp broke out into rebellion on my first bashful hint in reference to the cooking of the fish and joint, and said, with a dignified sense of injury, 'No! No, sir! You will not ask me sich a thing, for you are better acquainted with me than to suppose me capable of doing what I cannot do with ampial satisfaction to my own feelings!' But, in the end, a compromise was effected; and Mrs Crupp consented to achieve this feat, on condition that I dined from home for a fortnight afterwards.

And here I may remark that what I underwent from Mrs Crupp, in consequence of the tyranny she established over me, was dreadful. I never was so much afraid of anyone. We made a compromise of everything. If I hesitated, she was taken with that wonderful disorder which was always lying in ambush in her system, ready, at the shortest notice, to prey upon her vitals. If I rang the bell impatiently, after half a dozen unavailing modest pulls, and she appeared at last – which was not by any means to be relied upon – she would appear with a reproachful aspect, sink breathless on a chair near the door, lay her hand upon her nankeen bosom, and become so ill that I was glad, at any sacrifice of brandy or anything else, to get rid of her. If I objected to having my bed made at five o'clock in the afternoon – which I *do* still think an uncomfortable arrangement – one motion of her hand towards the same nankeen region of wounded sensibility was enough to make me falter an apology. In short, I would have done anything in an honourable way rather than give Mrs Crupp offence; and she was the terror of my life.

I bought a second-hand dumb-waiter for this dinner-party, in preference to re-engaging the handy young man, against whom I had conceived a prejudice, in consequence of meeting him in the Strand, one Sunday morning, in a waistcoat remarkably like one of mine, which had been missing since the former occasion. The 'young gal' was re-engaged; but on the stipulation that she should only bring in the dishes, and then withdraw to the landing-place, beyond the outer door; where a habit of sniffing she had contracted would be lost upon the guests, and where her retiring on the plates would be a physical impossibility.

Having laid in the materials for a bowl of punch, to be compounded by Mr Micawber; having provided a bottle of lavender-water, two wax candles, a paper of mixed pins, and a pincushion, to assist Mrs Micawber in her toilette, at my dressing-table; having also caused the fire in my bedroom to be lighted for Mrs Micawber's convenience; and having laid the cloth with my own hands, I awaited the result with composure.

At the appointed time, my three visitors arrived together. Mr Micawber with more shirt-collar than usual, and a new ribbon to his eyeglass; Mrs Micawber with her cap in a whity-brown paper parcel; Traddles carrying the parcel, and supporting Mrs Micawber on his arm. They were all delighted with my residence. When I conducted Mrs Micawber to my dressing-table, and she saw the scale on which it was prepared for her, she was in such raptures that she called Mr Micawber to come in and look.

'My dear Copperfield,' said Mr Micawber, 'this is luxurious. This is a way of life which reminds me of the period when I was myself in a state of celibacy, and Mrs Micawber had not yet been solicited to plight her faith at the Hymeneal altar.'

'He means, solicited by him, Mr Copperfield,' said Mrs Micawber archly. 'He cannot answer for others.'

'My dear,' returned Mr Micawber, with sudden seriousness, 'I have no desire to answer for others. I am too well aware that when, in the inscrutable decrees of Fate, you were reserved for me, it is possible you may have been reserved for one, destined, after a protracted struggle, at length to fall a victim to pecuniary involvements of a complicated nature. I understand your allusion, my love. I regret it, but I can bear it.'

'Micawber!' exclaimed Mrs Micawber, in tears. 'Have I deserved this! I, who never have deserted you; who never *will* desert you, Micawber!'

'My love,' said Mr Micawber, much affected, 'you will forgive, and our old and tried friend Copperfield will, I am sure, forgive, the momentary laceration of wounded spirit, made sensitive by a recent collision with the Minion of Power – in other words, with a ribald Turncock attached to the waterworks – and will pity, not condemn, its excesses.'

Mr Micawber then embraced Mrs Micawber, and pressed my hand; leaving me to infer from this broken allusion that his domestic supply of water had been cut off that afternoon, in consequence of default in the payment of the company's rates.

To divert his thoughts from this melancholy subject, I informed Mr Micawber that I relied upon him for a bowl of punch, and led him to the lemons. His recent despondency, not to say despair, was gone in a moment. I never saw a man so thoroughly enjoy himself amid the fragrance of lemon-peel and sugar, the odour of burning rum, and the steam of boiling water, as Mr Micawber did that afternoon. It was wonderful to see his face shining at us out of a thin cloud of these delicate fumes, as he stirred, and mixed, and tasted, and looked as if he were making, instead of punch, a fortune for his family down to the latest posterity. As to Mrs Micawber, I don't know whether it was the effect of the cap, or the lavender-water, or the pins, or the fire, or the wax candles, but she came out of my room, comparatively speaking, lovely. And the lark was never gayer than that excellent woman.

I suppose – I never ventured to enquire, but I suppose – that Mrs Crupp, after frying the soles, was taken ill; because we broke down at that point. The leg of mutton came up very red within, and very pale without; besides having a foreign substance of a gritty nature sprinkled over it, as if it had had a fall into the ashes of that remarkable kitchen fireplace. But we were not in a condition to judge of this fact from the appearance of the gravy, forasmuch as the 'young gal' had dropped it all upon the stairs – where it remained, by the by, in a long train, until it was worn out. The pigeon-pie was not bad, but it was a delusive pie; the crust being like a disappointing head, phrenologically speaking; full of lumps and bumps, with nothing particular underneath. In short, the banquet was such a failure that I

should have been quite unhappy – about the failure, I mean, for I was always unhappy about Dora – if I had not been relieved by the great good-humour of my company, and by a bright suggestion from Mr Micawber.

'My dear friend Copperfield,' said Mr Micawber, 'accidents will occur in the best-regulated families; and in families not regulated by that pervading influence which sanctifies while it enhances the – a – I would say, in short, by the influence of Woman, in the lofty character of Wife, they may be expected with confidence, and must be borne with philosophy. If you will allow me to take the liberty of remarking that there are few comestibles better, in their way, than a Devil, and that I believe, with a little division of labour, we could accomplish a good one if the young person in attendance could produce a gridiron, I would put it to you, that this little misfortune may be easily repaired.'

There was a gridiron in the pantry, on which my morning rasher of bacon was cooked. We had it in in a twinkling, and immediately applied ourselves to carrying Mr Micawber's idea into effect. The division of labour to which he had referred was this: Traddles cut the mutton into slices; Mr Micawber (who could do anything of this sort to perfection) covered them with pepper, mustard, salt, and cayenne; I put them on the gridiron, turned them with a fork, and took them off, under Mr Micawber's direction; and Mrs Micawber heated, and continually stirred, some mushroom ketchup in a little saucepan. When he had slices enough done to begin upon, we fell to, with our sleeves still tucked up at the wrists, more slices sputtering and blazing on the fire, and our attention divided between the mutton on our plates and the mutton then preparing.

What with the novelty of this cookery, the excellence of it, the bustle of it, the frequent starting up to look after it, the frequent sitting down to dispose of it, as the crisp slices came off the gridiron hot and hot, the being so busy, so flushed with the fire, so amused, and in the midst of such a tempting noise and savour, we reduced the leg of mutton to the bone. My own appetite came back miraculously. I am ashamed to record it, but I really believe I forgot Dora for a little while. I am satisfied that Mr and Mrs Micawber could not have enjoyed the feast more if they had sold a bed to provide it. Traddles laughed as heartily, almost the whole time, as he ate and worked. Indeed we all did, all at once; and I dare say there never was a greater success.

We were at the height of our enjoyment, and were all busily engaged, in our several departments, endeavouring to bring the last batch of slices to a state of perfection that should crown the feast, when I was aware of a strange presence in the room, and my eyes encountered those of the staid Littimer, standing hat in hand before me.

'What's the matter?' I involuntarily asked.

'I beg your pardon, sir, I was directed to come in. Is my master not here, sir?'

'No.'

'Have you not seen him, sir?'

'No; don't you come from him?'

'Not immediately so, sir.'

'Did he tell you you would find him here?'

'Not exactly so, sir. But I should think he might be here tomorrow, as he has not been here today.'

'Is he coming up from Oxford?'

'I beg, sir,' he returned respectfully, 'that you will be seated, and allow me to do this.' With which he took the fork from my unresisting hand, and bent over the gridiron, as if his whole attention were concentrated on it.

We should not have been much discomposed, I dare say, by the appearance of Steerforth himself, but we became in a moment the meekest of the meek before his respectable serving-man. Mr Micawber, humming a tune, to show that he was quite at ease, subsided into his chair, with the handle of a hastily concealed fork sticking out of the bosom of his coat, as if he had stabbed himself. Mrs Micawber put on her brown gloves, and assumed a genteel languor. Traddles ran his greasy hands through his hair, and stood it bolt upright, and stared in confusion on the tablecloth. As for me, I was a mere infant at the head of my own table; and hardly ventured to glance at the respectable phenomenon, who had come from Heaven knows where, to put my establishment to rights.

Meanwhile he took the mutton off the gridiron, and gravely handed it round. We all took some, but our appreciation of it was gone, and we merely made a show of eating it. As we severally pushed away our plates, he noiselessly removed them, and set on the cheese. He took that off, too, when it was done with; cleared the table; piled everything on the dumb-waiter; gave us our wineglasses; and, of his own accord, wheeled the dumb-waiter into the pantry. All this was done in a perfect manner, and he never raised his eyes from what he was about. Yet his very elbows, when he had his back towards me, seemed

to teem with the expression of his fixed opinion that I was extremely young.

'Can I do anything more, sir?'

I thanked him, and said, No; but would he take no dinner himself?

'None, I am obliged to you, sir.'

'Is Mr Steerforth coming from Oxford?'

'I beg your pardon, sir?'

'Is Mr Steerforth coming from Oxford?'

'I should imagine that he might be here tomorrow, sir. I rather thought he might have been here today, sir. The mistake is mine, no doubt, sir.'

'If you should see him first – ' said I.

'If you'll excuse me, sir, I don't think I shall see him first.'

'In case you do,' said I, 'pray say that I am sorry he was not here today, as an old schoolfellow of his was here.'

'Indeed, sir!' and he divided a bow between me and Traddles, with a glance at the latter.

He was moving softly to the door, when, in a forlorn hope of saying something naturally – which I never could, to this man – I said: 'Oh! Littimer!'

'Sir!'

'Did you remain long at Yarmouth, that time?'

'Not particularly so, sir.'

'You saw te boat completed?'

'Yes, sir. I remained behind on purpose to see the boat completed.'

'I know!' He raised his eyes to mine respectfully. 'Mr Steerforth has not seen it yet, I suppose?'

'I really can't say, sir. I think – but I really can't say, sir. I wish you good-night, sir.'

We are disturbed in our cookery

He comprehended everybody present, in the respectful bow with which he followed these words, and disappeared. My visitors seemed to breathe more freely when he was gone; but my own relief was very great, for besides the constraint, arising from that extraordinary sense of being at a disadvantage which I always had in this man's presence, my conscience had embarrassed me with whispers that I had mistrusted his master, and I could not repress a vague uneasy dread that he might find it out. How was it, having so little in reality to conceal, that I always *did* feel as if this man were finding me out?

Mr Micawber roused me from this reflection, which was blended with a certain remorseful apprehension of seeing Steerforth himself, by bestowing many encomiums on the absent Littimer as a most respectable fellow, and a thoroughly admirable servant. Mr Micawber, I may remark, had taken his full share of the general bow, and had received it with infinite condescension.

'But punch, my dear Copperfield,' said Mr Micawber, tasting it, 'like time and tide, waits for no man. Ah! it is at the present moment in high flavour. My love, will you give me your opinion?'

Mrs Micawber pronounced it excellent.

'Then I will drink,' said Mr Micawber, 'if my friend Copperfield will permit me to take that social liberty, to the days when my friend Copperfield and myself were younger, and fought our way in the world side by side. I may say, of myself and Copperfield, in words we have sung together before now, that

> We twa hae run about the braes
> And pu'd the gowans fine

– in a figurative point of view – on several occasions. I am not exactly aware,' said Mr Micawber, with the old roll in his voice, and the old indescribable air of saying something genteel, 'what gowans may be, but I have no doubt that Copperfield and myself would frequently have taken a pull at them, if it had been feasible.'

Mr Micawber, at the then present moment, took a pull at his punch. So we all did; Traddles evidently lost in wondering at what distant time Mr Micawber and I could have been comrades in the battle of the world.

'Ahem!' said Mr Micawber, clearing his throat, and warming with the punch and with the fire. 'My dear, another glass?'

Mrs Micawber said it must be very little, but we couldn't allow that, so it was a glassful.

'As we are quite confidential here, Mr Copperfield,' said Mrs Micawber, sipping her punch, 'Mr Traddles being a part of our domesticity, I should much like to have your opinion on Mr Micawber's prospects. For corn,' said Mrs Micawber argumentatively, 'as I have repeatedly said to Mr Micawber, may be gentlemanly, but it is not remunerative. Commission to the extent of two and ninepence in a fortnight cannot, however limited our ideas, be considered remunerative.'

We were all agreed upon that.

'Then,' said Mrs Micawber, who prided herself on taking a clear view of things, and keeping Mr Micawber straight by her woman's wisdom, when he might otherwise go a little crooked, 'then I ask myself this question. If corn is not to be relied upon, what is? Are coals to be relied upon? Not at all. We have turned our attention to that experiment, on the suggestion of my family, and we find it fallacious.'

Mr Micawber, leaning back in his chair with his hands in his pockets, eyed us aside, and nodded his head, as much as to say that the case was very clearly put.

'The articles of corn and coals,' said Mrs Micawber, still more argumentatively, 'being equally out of the question, Mr Copperfield, I naturally look round the world, and say, "What is there in which a person of Mr Micawber's talent is likely to succeed?" And I exclude the doing anything on commission, because commission is not a certainty. What is best suited to a person of Mr Micawber's peculiar temperament is, I am convinced, a certainty.'

Traddles and I both expressed, by a feeling murmur, that this great discovery was no doubt true of Mr Micawber, and that it did him much credit.

'I will not conceal from you, my dear Mr Copperfield,' said Mrs Micawber, 'that *I* have long felt the Brewing business to be particularly adapted to Mr Micawber. Look at Barclay and Perkins! Look at Truman, Hanbury, and Buxton! It is on that extensive footing that Mr Micawber, I know from my own knowledge of him, is calculated to shine; and the profits, I am told, are e-nor–mous! But if Mr Micawber cannot get into those firms – which decline to answer his letters, when he offers his services even in an inferior capacity – what is the use of dwelling upon that idea? None. I may have a conviction that Mr Micawber's manners – '

'Hem! Really, my dear,' interposed Mr Micawber.

'My love, be silent,' said Mrs Micawber, laying her brown glove on his hand. 'I may have a conviction, Mr Copperfield, that Mr Micawber's manners peculiarly qualify him for the Banking business. I may argue within myself, that if *I* had a deposit at a banking-house, the manners of Mr Micawber, as representing that banking-house, would inspire confidence, and must extend the connection. But if the various banking-houses refuse to avail themselves of Mr Micawber's abilities, or receive the offer of them with contumely, what is the use of dwelling upon *that* idea? None. As to originating a banking-business, I may know that there are members of my family who, if they chose to place their money in Mr Micawber's hands, might found an establishment of that description. But if they do *not* choose to place their money in Mr Micawber's hands – which they don't – what is the use of that? Again I contend that we are no farther advanced than we were before.'

I shook my head, and said, 'Not a bit.' Traddles also shook his head, and said, 'Not a bit.'

'What do I deduce from this?' Mrs Micawber went on to say, still with the same air of putting a case lucidly. 'What is the conclusion, my dear Mr Copperfield, to which I am irresistibly brought? Am I wrong in saying, it is clear that we must live?'

I answered, 'Not at all!' and Traddles answered, 'Not at all!' and I found myself afterwards sagely adding, alone, that a person must either live or die.

'Just so,' returned Mrs Micawber. 'It is precisely that. And the fact is, my dear Mr Copperfield, that we can *not* live without something widely different from existing circumstances shortly turning up. Now I am convinced, myself, and this I have pointed out to Mr Micawber several times of late, that things cannot be expected to turn up of themselves. We must, in a measure, assist to turn them up. I may be wrong, but I have formed that opinion.'

Both Traddles and I applauded it highly.

'Very well,' said Mrs Micawber. 'Then what do I recommend? Here is Mr Micawber with a variety of qualifications – with great talent – '

'Really, my love,' said Mr Micawber.

'Pray, my dear, allow me to conclude. Here is Mr Micawber, with a variety of qualifications, with great talent – *I* should say, with genius, but that may be the partiality of a wife – '

Traddles and I both murmured 'No.'

'And here is Mr Micawber without any suitable position or employment. Where does that responsibility rest? Clearly on society. Then I would make a fact so disgraceful known, and boldly challenge society to set it right. It appears to me, my dear Mr Copperfield,' said Mrs Micawber forcibly, 'that what Mr Micawber has to do, is to throw down the gauntlet to society, and say, in effect, "Show me who will take that up. Let the party immediately step forward." '

I ventured to ask Mrs Micawber how this was to be done.

'By advertising,' said Mrs Micawber, 'in all the papers. It appears to me, that what Mr Micawber has to do, in justice to himself, in justice to his family, and I will even go so far as to say in justice to society, by which he has been hitherto overlooked, is to advertise in all the papers; to describe himself plainly as so and so, with such and such qualifications, and to put it thus: "*Now* employ me, on remunerative terms, and address, post-paid, to *W. M.*, Post Office, Camden Town." '

'This idea of Mrs Micawber's, my dear Copperfield,' said Mr Micawber, making his shirt-collar meet in front of his chin, and glancing at me sideways, 'is, in fact, the Leap, to which I alluded, when I last had the pleasure of seeing you.'

'Advertising is rather expensive,' I remarked dubiously.

'Exactly so!' said Mrs Micawber, preserving the same logical air. 'Quite true, my dear Mr Copperfield! I have made the identical observation to Mr Micawber. It is for that reason especially, that I think Mr Micawber ought (as I have already said, in justice to himself, in justice to his family, and in justice to society) to raise a certain sum of money – on a bill.'

Mr Micawber, leaning back in his chair, trifled with his eyeglass, and cast his eyes up at the ceiling; but I thought him observant of Traddles, too, who was looking at the fire.

'If no member of my family,' said Mrs Micawber, 'is possessed of sufficient natural feeling to negotiate that bill – I believe there is a better business term to express what I mean – '

Mr Micawber, with his eyes still cast up at the ceiling, suggested: 'Discount.'

'To discount that bill,' said Mrs Micawber, 'then my opinion is, that Mr Micawber should go into the City, should take that bill into the Money Market, and should dispose of it for what he can get. If the individuals in the Money Market

oblige Mr Micawber to sustain a great sacrifice, that is between themselves and their consciences. I view it, steadily, as an investment. I recommend Mr Micawber, my dear Mr Copperfield, to do the same; to regard it as an investment which is sure of return, and to make up his mind to *any* sacrifice.'

I felt, but I am sure I don't know why, that this was self-denying and devoted in Mrs Micawber, and I uttered a murmur to that effect. Traddles, who took his tone from me, did likewise, still looking at the fire.

'I will not,' said Mrs Micawber, finishing her punch, and gathering her scarf about her shoulders, preparatory to her withdrawal to my bedroom: 'I will not protract these remarks on the subject of Mr Micawber's pecuniary affairs. At your fireside, my dear Mr Copperfield, and in the presence of Mr Traddles, who, though not so old a friend, is quite one of ourselves, I could not refrain from making you acquainted with the course *I* advised Mr Micawber to take. I feel that the time is arrived when Mr Micawber should exert himself and – I will add – assert himself, and it appears to me that these are the means. I am aware that I am merely a female, and that a masculine judgement is usually considered more competent to the discussion of such questions; still I must not forget that, when I lived at home with my papa and mama, my papa was in the habit of saying, "Emma's form is fragile, but her grasp of a subject is inferior to none." That my papa was too partial, I well know; but that he was an observer of character in some degree, my duty and my reason equally forbid me to doubt.'

With these words, and resisting our entreaties that she would grace the remaining circulation of the punch with her presence, Mrs Micawber retired to my bedroom. And really I felt that she was a noble woman – the sort of woman who might have been a Roman matron, and done all manner of heroic things, in times of public trouble.

In the fervour of this impression, I congratulated Mr Micawber on the treasure he possessed. So did Traddles. Mr Micawber extended his hand to each of us in succession, and then covered his face with his pocket-handkerchief, which I think had more snuff upon it than he was aware of. He then returned to the punch, in the highest state of exhilaration.

He was full of eloquence. He gave us to understand that in our children we lived again, and that, under the pressure of pecuniary difficulties, any accession to their number was doubly welcome. He said that Mrs Micawber had latterly had her doubts on this point, but that he had dispelled them, and reassured her. As to her family, they were totally unworthy of her, and their sentiments were utterly indifferent to him, and they might – I quote his own expression – go to the Devil.

Mr Micawber then delivered a warm eulogy on Traddles. He said Traddles's was a character, to the steady virtues of which he (Mr Micawber) could lay no claim, but which, he thanked Heaven, he could admire. He feelingly alluded to the young lady, unknown, whom Traddles had honoured with his affection, and who had reciprocated that affection by honouring and blessing Traddles with *her* affection. Mr Micawber pledged her. So did I. Traddles thanked us both, by saying, with a simplicity and honesty I had sense enough to be quite charmed with, 'I am very much obliged to you indeed. And I do assure you, she's the dearest girl! – '

Mr Micawber took an early opportunity, after that, of hinting, with the utmost delicacy and ceremony, at the state of *my* affections. Nothing but the serious assurance of his friend Copperfield to the contrary, he observed, could deprive him of the impression that his friend Copperfield loved and was beloved. After feeling very hot and uncomfortable for some time, and after a good deal of blushing, stammering, and denying, I said, having my glass in my hand, 'Well! I would give them D.!' which so excited and gratified Mr Micawber, that he ran with a glass of punch into my bedroom, in order that Mrs Micawber might drink D., who drank it with enthusiasm, crying from within, in a shrill voice, 'Hear, hear! My dear Mr Copperfield, I am delighted. Hear!' and tapping at the wall, by way of applause.

Our conversation, afterwards, took a more worldly turn; Mr Micawber telling us that he found Camden Town inconvenient, and that the first thing he contemplated doing, when the advertisement should have been the cause of something satisfactory turning up, was to move. He mentioned a terrace at the western end of Oxford Street, fronting Hyde Park, on which he had always had his eye, but which he did not expect to attain immediately, as it would require a large establishment. There would probably be an interval, he explained, in which he should content himself with the upper part of a house, over some respectable place of business – say in Piccadilly – which would be a cheerful situation for Mrs Micawber; and where, by throwing out a bow-window, or carrying up the roof another story, or making some little alteration of that sort, they might live, comfortably and reputably, for a few years. Whatever was reserved for him, he expressly said, or wherever his abode might be, we might rely on this – there would always be a room for Traddles, and a knife and fork for me. We acknowledged his kindness; and he begged us to forgive his having launched into these practical and businesslike details, and to excuse it as natural in one who was making entirely new arrangements in life.

Mrs Micawber tapping at the wall again, to know if tea were ready, broke up this particular phase of our friendly conversation. She made tea for us in a most agreeable manner; and, whenever I went near her, in handing about the teacups and bread and butter, asked me, in a whisper, whether D. was fair, or dark, or whether she was short, or tall, or something of that kind; which I think I liked. After tea, we discussed a variety of topics before the fire, and Mrs Micawber was good enough to sing us (in a small, thin, flat voice, which I remembered to have considered, when I first knew her, the very table-beer of acoustics) the favourite ballads of 'The Dashing White Serjeant', and 'Little Tafflin'. For both of these songs Mrs Micawber had been famous when she lived at home with her papa and mama. Mr Micawber told us, that when he heard her sing the first one, on the first occasion of his seeing her beneath the parental roof, she had attracted his attention in an extraordinary degree; but that when it came to

'Little Tafflin', he had resolved to win that woman or perish in the attempt.

It was between ten and eleven o'clock when Mrs Micawber rose to replace her cap in the whity-brown paper parcel, and to put on her bonnet. Mr Micawber took the opportunity of Traddles putting on his greatcoat, to slip a letter into my hand, with a whispered request that I would read it at my leisure. I also took the opportunity of my holding a candle over the banisters to light them down, when Mr Micawber was going first, leading Mrs Micawber, and Traddles was following with the cap, to detain Traddles for a moment on the top of the stairs.

'Traddles,' said I, 'Mr Micawber don't mean any harm, poor fellow; but, if I were you, I wouldn't lend him anything.'

'My dear Copperfield,' returned Traddles, smiling, 'I haven't got anything to lend.'

'You have got a name, you know,' said I.

'Oh! You call *that* something to lend?' returned Traddles, with a thoughtful look.

'Certainly.'

'Oh!' said Traddles. 'Yes, to be sure! I am very much obliged to you, Copperfield; but – I am afraid I have lent him that already.'

'For the bill that is to be a certain investment?' I enquired.

'No,' said Traddles. 'Not for that one. This is the first I have heard of that one. I have been thinking that he will most likely propose that one, on the way home. Mine's another.'

'I hope there will be nothing wrong about it,' said I.

'I hope not,' said Traddles. 'I should think not, though, because he told me only the other day, that it was provided for. That was Mr Micawber's expression, "Provided for."'

Mr Micawber looking up at this juncture to where we were standing, I had only time to repeat my caution. Traddles thanked me, and descended. But I was much afraid, when I observed the good-natured manner in which he went down with the cap in his hand, and gave Mrs Micawber his arm, that he would be carried into the Money Market neck and heels.

I returned to my fireside, and was musing, half gravely and half laughing, on the character of Mr Micawber and the old relations between us, when I heard a quick step ascending the stairs. At first, I thought it was Traddles coming back for something Mrs Micawber had left behind; but as the step approached, I knew it, and felt my heart beat high, and the blood rush to my face, for it was Steerforth's.

I was never unmindful of Agnes, and she never left that sanctuary in my thoughts – if I may call it so – where I had placed her from the first. But when he entered, and stood before me with his hand out, the darkness that had fallen on him changed to light, and I felt confounded and ashamed of having doubted one I loved so heartily. I loved her none the less; I thought of her as the same benignant, gentle angel in my life; I reproached myself, not her, with having done him an injury; and I would have made him any atonement if I had known what to make, and how to make it.

'Why, Daisy, old boy, dumbfounded?' laughed Steerforth, shaking my hand heartily, and throwing it gaily away. 'Have I detected you in another feast, you Sybarite! These Doctors'

Commons fellows are the gayest men in town, I believe, and beat us sober Oxford people all to nothing!' His bright glance went merrily round the room, as he took the seat on the sofa opposite to me, which Mrs Micawber had recently vacated, and stirred the fire into a blaze.

'I was so surprised at first,' said I, giving him welcome with all the cordiality I felt, 'that I had hardly breath to greet you with, Steerforth.'

'Well, the sight of me *is* good for sore eyes, as the Scotch say,' replied Steerforth, 'and so is the sight of you, Daisy, in full bloom. How are you, my Bacchanal?'

'I am very well,' said I; 'and not at all Bacchanalian tonight, though I confess to another party of three.'

'All of whom I met in the street, talking loud in your praise,' returned Steerforth. 'Who's our friend in the tights?'

I gave him the best idea I could, in a few words, of Mr Micawber. He laughed heartily at my feeble portrait of that gentleman, and said he was a man to know, and he must know him.

'But who do you suppose our other friend is?' said I, in my turn.

'Heaven knows,' said Steerforth. 'Not a bore, I hope? I thought he looked a little like one.'

'Traddles!' I replied triumphantly.

'Who's he?' asked Steerforth, in his careless way.

'Don't you remember Traddles? Traddles in our room at Salem House?'

'Oh! That fellow!' said Steerforth, beating a lump of coal on the top of the fire with the poker. 'Is he as soft as ever? And where the deuce did you pick *him* up?'

I extolled Traddles in reply, as highly as I could; for I felt that Steerforth rather slighted him. Steerforth, dismissing the subject with a light nod, and a smile, and the remark that he would be glad to see the old fellow too, for he had always been an odd fish, enquired if I could give him anything to eat. During most of this short dialogue, when he had not been speaking in a wild vivacious manner, he had sat idly beating on the lump of coal with the poker. I observed that he did the same thing while I was getting out the remains of the pigeon-pie, and so forth.

'Why, Daisy, here's a supper for a king!' he exclaimed, starting out of his silence with a burst, and taking his seat at the table. 'I shall do it justice, for I have come from Yarmouth.'

'I thought you came from Oxford?' I returned.

'Not I,' said Steerforth. 'I have been seafaring – better employed.'

'Littimer was here today, to enquire for you,' I remarked, 'and I understood him that you were at Oxford; though, now I think of it, he certainly did not say so.'

'Littimer is a greater fool than I thought him, to have been enquiring for me at all,' said Steerforth, jovially pouring out a glass of wine, and drinking to me. 'As to understanding him, you are a cleverer fellow than most of us, Daisy, if you can do that.'

'That's true, indeed,' said I, moving my chair to the table. 'So you have been at Yarmouth, Steerforth!' interested to know all about it. 'Have you been there long?'

'No,' he returned. 'An *escapade* of a week or so.'

'And how are they all? Of course, little Em'ly is not married yet?'

'Not yet. Going to be, I believe – in so many weeks, or months, or something or other. I have not seen much of 'em. By the by;' he laid down his knife and fork, which he had been using with great diligence, and began feeling in his pockets; 'I have a letter for you.'

'From whom?'

'Why, from your old nurse,' he returned, taking some papers out of his breast pocket. ' "J. Steerforth, Esquire, debtor, to the Willing Mind;" that's not it. Patience, and we'll find it presently. Old what's-his-name's in a bad way, and it's about that, I believe.'

'Barkis, do you mean?'

'Yes!' still feeling in his pockets, and looking over their contents; 'it's all over with poor Barkis, I am afraid. I saw a little apothecary there – surgeon, or whatever he is – who brought your worship into the world. He was mighty learned about the case, to me; but the upshot of his opinion was, that the carrier was making his last journey rather fast. Put your hand into the breast pocket of my greatcoat on the chair yonder, and I think you'll find the letter. Is it there?'

'Here it is!' said I.

'That's right!'

It was from Peggotty; something less legible than usual, and brief. It informed me of her husband's hopeless state, and hinted at his being 'a little nearer' than heretofore, and consequently more difficult to manage for his own comfort. It said nothing of her weariness and watching, and praised him highly. It was written with a plain, unaffected, homely piety that I knew to be genuine, and ended with 'my duty to my ever darling' – meaning myself.

While I deciphered it, Steerforth continued to eat and drink.

'It's a bad job,' he said, when I had done; 'but the sun sets every day, and people die every minute, and we mustn't be scared by the common lot. If we failed to hold our own, because that equal foot at all men's doors was heard knocking somewhere, every object in this world would slip from us. No! Ride on! Roughshod if need be, smooth-shod if that will do, but ride on! Ride on over all obstacles, and win the race!'

'And win what race?' said I.

'The race that one has started in,' said he. 'Ride on!'

I noticed, I remember, as he paused, looking at me with his handsome head a little thrown back, and his glass raised in his hand, that, though the freshness of the sea-wind was on his face, and it was ruddy, there were traces in it, made since I last saw it, as if he had applied himself to some habitual strain of the fervent energy which, when roused, was so passionately roused within him. I had it in my thoughts to remonstrate with him upon his desperate way of pursuing any fancy that he took – such as this buffeting of rough seas, and braving of hard weather, for example – when my mind glanced off to the immediate subject of our conversation again, and pursued that instead.

'I tell you what, Steerforth,' said I, 'if your high spirits will listen to me –'

'They are potent spirits, and will do whatever you like,' he answered, moving from the table to the fireside again.

'Then I tell you what, Steerforth. I think I will go down and see my old nurse. It is not that I can do her any good, or render her any real service; but she is so attached to me that my visit will have as much effect on her, as if I could do both. She will take it so kindly that it will be a comfort and support to her. It is no great effort to make, I am sure, for such a friend as she has been to me. Wouldn't you go a day's journey, if you were in my place?'

His face was thoughtful, and he sat considering a little before he answered, in a low voice, 'Well! Go. You can do no harm.'

'You have just come back,' said I, 'and it would be in vain to ask you to go with me?'

'Quite,' he returned. 'I am for Highgate tonight. I have not seen my mother this long time, and it lies upon my conscience, for it's something to be loved as she loves her prodigal son. – Bah! Nonsense! – You mean to go tomorrow, I suppose?' he said, holding me out at arm's length, with a hand on each of my shoulders.

'Yes, I think so.'

'Well, then, don't go till next day. I wanted you to come and stay a few days with us. Here I am, on purpose to bid you, and you fly off to Yarmouth!'

'You are a nice fellow to talk of flying off, Steerforth, who are always running wild on some unknown expedition or other!'

He looked at me for a moment without speaking, and then rejoined, still holding me as before, and giving me a shake: 'Come! say the next day, and pass as much of tomorrow as you can with us! Who knows when we may meet again, else? Come! Say the next day! I want you to stand between Rosa Dartle and me, and keep us asunder.'

'Would you love each other too much, without me?'

'Yes; or hate,' laughed Steerforth; 'no matter which. Come! Say the next day!'

I said the next day; and he put on his greatcoat and lighted his cigar, and set off to walk home. Finding him in this intention, I put on my own greatcoat (but did not light my own cigar, having had enough of that for one while), and walked with him as far as the open road; a dull road, then, at night. He was in great spirits all the way; and when we parted, and I looked after him going so gallantly and airily homeward, I thought of his saying, 'Ride on over all obstacles, and win the race!' and wished, for the first time, that he had some worthy race to run.

I was undressing in my own room, when Mr Micawber's letter tumbled on the floor. Thus reminded of it, I broke the seal and read as follows. It was dated an hour and a half before dinner. I am not sure whether I have mentioned that, when Mr Micawber was at any particularly desperate crisis, he used a sort of legal phraseology; which he seemed to think equivalent to winding up his affairs.

SIR – for I dare not say my dear Copperfield – It is expedient that I should inform you that the undersigned is Crushed. Some flickering efforts to spare you the premature knowledge of his calamitous position, you may observe in him this day; but hope has sunk beneath the horizon, and the undersigned is Crushed.

The present communication is penned within the personal range (I cannot call it the society) of an individual, in a state closely bordering on intoxication, employed by a broker. That individual is in legal possession of the premises, under a distress for rent. His inventory includes, not only the chattels and effects of every description belonging to the undersigned, as yearly tenant of this habitation, but also those appertaining to Mr Thomas Traddles, lodger, a member of the Honourable Society of the Inner Temple.

If any drop of gloom were wanting in the overflowing cup, which is now "commended" (in the language of an immortal Writer) to the lips of the undersigned, it would be found in the fact that a friendly acceptance granted to the undersigned by the before-mentioned Mr Thomas Traddles, for the sum of £23 4s. 9½d. is overdue, and is not provided for. Also, in the fact that the living responsibilities clinging to the undersigned will, in the course of nature, be increased by the sum of one more helpless victim; whose miserable appearance may be looked for – in round numbers – at the expiration of a period not exceeding six lunar months from the present date.

After premising thus much, it would be a work of supererogation to add, that dust and ashes are for ever scattered

On
The
Head
Of

WILKINS MICAWBER

Poor Traddles! I knew enough of Mr Micawber by this time to foresee that *he* might be expected to recover the blow; but my night's rest was sorely distressed by thoughts of Traddles, and of the curate's daughter, who was one of ten, down in Devonshire, and who was such a dear girl, and who would wait for Traddles (ominous praise!) until she was sixty, or any age that could be mentioned.

CHAPTER 29

I Visit Steerforth at His Home Again

I mentioned to Mr Spenlow in the morning that I wanted leave of absence for a short time; and as I was not in the receipt of any salary, and consequently was not obnoxious to the implacable Jorkins, there was no difficulty about it. I took that opportunity, with my voice sticking in my throat, and my sight failing as I uttered the words, to express my hope that Miss Spenlow was quite well; to which Mr Spenlow replied, with no more emotion than if he had been speaking of an ordinary human being, that he was much obliged to me, and she was very well.

We articled clerks, as germs of the patrician order of proctors, were treated with so much consideration that I was almost my own master at all times. As I did not care, however, to get to

Highgate before one or two o'clock in the day, and as we had another little excommunication case in court that morning, which was called 'The office of the Judge promoted by Tipkins against Bullock for his soul's correction,' I passed an hour or two in attendance on it with Mr Spenlow very agreeably. It arose out of a scuffle between two church wardens, one of whom was alleged to have pushed the other against a pump; the handle of which pump projecting into a schoolhouse, which schoolhouse was under a gable of the church roof, made the push an ecclesiastical offence. It was an amusing case; and sent me up to Highgate, on the box of the stage-coach, thinking about the Commons, and what Mr Spenlow had said about touching the Commons and bringing down the country.

Mrs Steerforth was pleased to see me, and so was Rosa Dartle. I was agreeably surprised to find that Littimer was not there, and that we were attended by a modest little parlour-maid, with blue ribbons in her cap, whose eye it was much more pleasant, and much less disconcerting, to catch by accident, than the eye of that respectable man. But what I particularly observed, before I had been half an hour in the house, was the close and attentive watch Miss Dartle kept upon me; and the lurking manner in which she seemed to compare my face with Steerforth's, and Steerforth's with mine, and to lie in wait for something to come out between the two. So surely as I looked towards her, did I see that eager visage, with its gaunt black eyes and searching brow, intent on mine; or passing suddenly from mine to Steerforth's; or comprehending both of us at once. In this lynx-like scrutiny she was so far from faltering when she saw I observed it that at such a time she only fixed her piercing look upon me with a more intent expression still. Blameless as I was, and knew that I was, in reference to any wrong she could possibly suspect me of, I shrunk before her strange eyes, quite unable to endure their hungry lustre.

All day she seemed to pervade the whole house. If I talked to Steerforth in his room, I heard her dress rustle in the little gallery outside. When he and I engaged in some of our old exercises on the lawn behind the house, I saw her face pass from window to window, like a wandering light, until it fixed itself in one and watched us. When we all four went out walking in the afternoon, she closed her thin hand on my arm like a spring, to keep me back, while Steerforth and his mother went on out of hearing; and then spoke to me.

'You have been a long time,' she said, 'without coming here. Is your profession really so engaging and interesting as to absorb your whole attention? I ask because I always want to be informed when I am ignorant. Is it really, though?'

I replied that I liked it well enough, but that I certainly could not claim so much for it.

'Oh! I am glad to know that, because I always like to be put right when I am wrong,' said Rosa Dartle. 'You mean it is a little dry, perhaps?'

Well, I replied; perhaps it *was* a little dry.

'Oh! and that's a reason why you want relief and change – excitement, and all that?' said she. 'Ah! very true! But isn't it a little – eh? – for him; I don't mean you?'

A quick glance of her eye towards the spot where Steerforth was walking, with his mother leaning on his arm, showed me whom she meant; but beyond that, I was quite lost. And I looked so, I have no doubt.

'Don't it – I don't say that it *does*, mind; I want to know – don't it rather engross him? Don't it make him, perhaps, a little more remiss than usual in his visits to his blindly doting – eh?' – with another quick glance at them, and such a glance at me as seemed to look into my innermost thoughts.

'Miss Dartle,' I returned, 'pray do not think – '

'I don't!' she said. 'Oh, dear me, don't suppose that I think anything! I am not suspicious. I only ask a question. I don't state any opinion. I want to found an opinion on what you tell me. Then, it's not so? Well! I am very glad to know it.'

'It certainly is not the fact,' said I, perplexed, 'that I am accountable for Steerforth's having been away from home longer than usual – if he has been; which I really don't know at this moment, unless I understand it from you. I have not seen him this long while, until last night.'

'No?'

'Indeed, Miss Dartle, no!'

As she looked full at me, I saw her face grow sharper and paler, and the marks of the old wound lengthen out until it cut through the disfigured lip, and deep into the nether lip, and slanted down the face. There was something positively awful to me in this, and in the brightness of her eyes, as she said, looking fixedly at me: 'What is he doing?'

I repeated the words, more to myself than her, being so amazed.

'What is he doing?' she said, with an eagerness that seemed enough to consume her like a fire. 'In what is that man assisting him, who never looks at me without an inscrutable falsehood in his eyes? If you are honourable and faithful, I don't ask you to betray your friend. I ask you only to tell me, is it anger, is it hatred, is it pride, is it restlessness, is it some wild fancy, is it love, *what is it*, that is leading him?'

'Miss Dartle,' I returned, 'how shall I tell you, so that you will believe me, that I know of nothing in Steerforth different from what there was when I first came here. I can think of nothing. I firmly believe there is nothing. I hardly understand even what you mean.'

As she still stood looking fixedly at me, a twitching or throbbing, from which I could not dissociate the idea of pain, came into that cruel mark; and lifted up the corner of her lip as if with scorn, or with a pity that despised its object. She put her hand upon it hurriedly – a hand so thin and delicate that, when I had seen her hold it up before the fire to shade her face, I had compared it in my thoughts to fine porcelain – and saying, in a quick, fierce, passionate way, 'I swear you to secrecy about this!' said not a word more.

Mrs Steerforth was particularly happy in her son's society, and Steerforth was, on this occasion, particularly attentive and respectful to her. It was very interesting to me to see them together, not only on account of their mutual affection, but because of the strong personal resemblance between them, and the manner in which what was haughty or impetuous in him was softened by age and sex, in her, to a gracious dignity. I thought, more than once, that it was well no serious cause of division had ever come between them; or two such natures – I ought rather to express it, two such shades of the same nature – might have been harder to reconcile than the two extremist opposites in creation. The idea did not originate in my own discernment, I am bound to confess, but in a speech of Rosa Dartle's.

She said at dinner: 'Oh, but do tell me, though, somebody, because I have been thinking about it all day, and I want to know.'

'You want to know what, Rosa?' returned Mrs Steerforth. 'Pray, pray, Rosa, do not be mysterious.'

'Mysterious!' she cried. 'Oh! really? Do you consider me so?'

'Do I constantly entreat you,' said Mrs Steerforth, 'to speak plainly, in your own natural manner?'

'Oh! then this is *not* my natural manner?' she rejoined. 'Now you must really bear with me, because I ask for information. We never know ourselves.'

'It has become a second nature,' said Mrs Steerforth, without any displeasure; 'but I remember – and so must you, I think – when your manner was different, Rosa; when it was not so guarded, and was more trustful.'

'I am sure you are right,' she returned; 'and so it is that bad habits grow upon one! Really? Less guarded and more trustful? How *can* I, imperceptibly, have changed, I wonder! Well, that's very odd! I must study to regain my former self.'

'I wish you would,' said Mrs Steerforth, with a smile.

'Oh! I really will, you know!' she answered. 'I will learn frankness from – let me see – from James.'

'You cannot learn frankness, Rosa,' said Mrs Steerforth quickly – for there was always some effect of sarcasm in what Rosa Dartle said, though it was said, as this was, in the most unconscious manner in the world – 'in a better school.'

'That I am sure of,' she answered, with uncommon fervour. 'If I am sure of anything, of course, you know, I am sure of that.'

Mrs Steerforth appeared to me to regret having been a little nettled; for she presently said, in a kind tone: 'Well, my dear Rosa, we have not heard what it is that you want to be satisfied about?'

'That I want to be satisfied about?' she replied, with provoking coldness. 'Oh! It was only whether people, who are like each other in their moral constitution – is that the phrase?'

'It's as good a phrase as another,' said Steerforth.

'Thank you – whether people, who are like each other in their moral constitution, are in greater danger than people not so circumstanced, supposing any serious cause of variance to arise between them, of being divided angrily and deeply?'

'I should say yes,' said Steerforth.

'Should you?' she retorted. 'Dear me! Supposing, then, for instance – any unlikely thing will do for a supposition – that you and your mother were to have a serious quarrel.'

'My dear Rosa,' interposed Mrs Steerforth, laughing good-naturedly, 'suggest some other supposition! James and I know our duty to each other better, I pray Heaven!'

'Oh!' said Miss Dartle, nodding her head thoughtfully. 'To be sure. *That* would prevent it? Why, of course it would. Exactly. Now, I am glad I have been so foolish as to put the case, for it is so very good to know that your duty to each other would prevent it! Thank you very much.'

One other little circumstance connected with Miss Dartle I must not omit; for I had reason to remember it thereafter, when all the irremediable past was rendered plain. During the whole of this day, but especially from this period of it, Steerforth exerted himself with his utmost skill, and that was with his utmost ease, to charm this singular creature into a pleasant and pleased companion. That he should succeed was no matter of surprise to me. That she should struggle against the fascinating influence of his delightful art – delightful nature I thought it then – did not surprise me either; for I knew that she was sometimes jaundiced and perverse. I saw her features and her manner slowly change; I saw her look at him with growing admiration; I saw her try, more and more faintly, but always angrily, as if she condemned a weakness in herself, to resist the captivating power that he possessed; and finally I saw her sharp glance soften, and her smile become quite gentle, and I ceased to be afraid of her as I had really been all day, and we all sat about the fire, talking and laughing together, and with as little reserve as if we had been children.

Whether it was because we had sat there so long, or because Steerforth was resolved not to lose the advantage he had gained, I do not know; but we did not remain in the dining-room more than five minutes after her departure. 'She is playing her harp,' said Steerforth softly, at the drawing-room door, 'and nobody but my mother has heard her do that, I believe, these three years.' He said it with a curious smile, which was gone directly; and we went into the room and found her alone.

'Don't get up,' said Steerforth (which she had already done), 'my dear Rosa, don't! Be kind for once, and sing us an Irish song.'

'What do you care for an Irish song?' she returned.

'Much!' said Steerforth. 'Much more than for any other. Here is Daisy, too, loves music from his soul. Sing us an Irish song, Rosa! and let me sit and listen as I used to do.'

He did not touch her, or the chair from which she had risen, but sat himself near the harp. She stood beside it for some little while, in a curious way, going through the motion of playing it with her right hand, but not sounding it. At length she sat down, and drew it to her with one sudden action, and played and sang.

I don't know what it was, in her touch or voice, that made that song the most unearthly I have ever heard in my life, or can imagine. There was something fearful in the reality of it. It was as if it had never been written, or set to music, but sprung out of the passion within her; which found imperfect utterance in the low sounds of her voice, and crouched again when all was still. I was dumb when she leaned beside the harp again, playing it, but not sounding it, with her right hand.

A minute more, and this had roused me from my trance: Steerforth had left his seat, and gone to her, and had put his arm laughingly about her, and had said, 'Come, Rosa, for the future we will love each other very much!' And she had struck him, and had thrown him off with the fury of a wild cat, and had burst out of the room.

'What is the matter with Rosa?' said Mrs Steerforth, coming in.

'She has been an angel, mother,' returned Steerforth, 'for a little while; and has run into the opposite extreme, since, by way of compensation.'

'You should be careful not to irritate her, James. Her temper has been soured, remember, and ought not to be tried.'

Rosa did not come back; and no other mention was made of her, until I went with Steerforth into his room to say good-night. Then he laughed about her, and asked me if I had ever seen such a fierce little piece of incomprehensibility.

I expressed as much of my astonishment as was then capable of expression, and asked if he could guess what it was that she had taken so much amiss, so suddenly.

'Oh, Heaven knows,' said Steerforth. 'Anything you like – or nothing! I told you she took everything, herself included, to a grindstone, and sharpened it. She is an edge-tool, and requires great care in dealing with. She is always dangerous. Good-night!'

'Good-night!' said I, 'my dear Steerforth! I shall be gone before you wake in the morning. Good-night!'

He was unwilling to let me go; and stood, holding me out, with a hand on each of my shoulders, as he had done in my own room.

'Daisy,' he said, with a smile – 'for though that's not the name your godfathers and godmothers gave you, it's the name I like best to call you by – and I wish, I wish, I wish, you could give it to me!'

'Why, so I can, if I choose,' said I.

'Daisy, if anything should ever separate us, you must think of me at my best, old boy. Come! let us make that bargain. Think of me at my best if circumstances should ever part us!'

'You have no best to me, Steerforth,' said I, 'and no worst. You are always equally loved and cherished in my heart.'

So much compunction for having ever wronged him, even by a shapeless thought, did I feel within me that the confession of having done so was rising to my lips. But for the reluctance I had to betray the confidence of Agnes, but for my uncertainty how to approach the subject with no risk of doing so, it would have reached them before he said, 'God bless you, Daisy, and good-night!' In my doubt it did *not* reach them; and we shook hands, and we parted.

I was up with the dull dawn, and, having dressed as quietly as I could, looked into his room. He was fast asleep; lying, easily, with his head upon his arm, as I had often seen him lie at school.

The time came in its season, and that was very soon, when I almost wondered that nothing troubled his repose, as I looked at him. But he slept – let me think of him so again – as I had often seen him sleep at school; and thus, in this silent hour, I left him.

Never more, oh, God forgive you, Steerforth! to touch that passive hand in love and friendship. Never, never more!

CHAPTER 30

A Loss

I got down to Yarmouth in the evening, and went to the inn. I knew that Peggotty's spare room – my room – was likely to have occupation enough in a little while, if that great Visitor, before whose presence all the living must give place, were not already in the house; so I betook myself to the inn, and dined there, and engaged my bed.

It was ten o'clock when I went out. Many of the shops were shut, and the town was dull. When I came to Omer and Joram's, I found the shutters up, but the shop door standing open. As I could obtain a perspective view of Mr Omer inside, smoking his pipe by the parlour door, I entered, and asked him how he was.

'Why, bless my life and soul!' said Mr Omer, 'how do you find yourself? Take a seat. Smoke not disagreeable, I hope?'

'By no means,' said I. 'I like it – in somebody else's pipe.'

'What, not in your own, eh?' Mr Omer returned, laughing. 'All the better, sir. Bad habit for a young man. Take a seat. I smoke, myself, for the asthma.'

Mr Omer had made room for me, and placed a chair. He now sat down again very much out of breath, gasping at his pipe as if it contained a supply of that necessary, without which he must perish.

'I am sorry to have heard bad news of Mr Barkis,' said I.

Mr Omer looked at me with a steady countenance, and shook his head.

'Do you know how he is tonight?' I asked.

'The very question I should have put to you, sir,' returned Mr Omer, 'but on account of delicacy. It's one of the drawbacks of our line of business. When a party's ill, we *can't* ask how the party is.'

The difficulty had not occurred to me; though I had had my apprehensions, too, when I went in, of hearing the old tune. On its being mentioned, I recognised it, however, and said as much.

'Yes, yes, you understand,' said Mr Omer, nodding his head. 'We dursn't do it. Bless you, it would be a shock that the generality of parties mightn't recover, to say "Omer and Joram's compliments, and how do you find yourself this morning?" – or this afternoon – as it may be.'

Mr Omer and I nodded at each other, and Mr Omer recruited his wind by the aid of his pipe.

'It's one of the things that cut the trade off from attentions they could often wish to show,' said Mr Omer. 'Take myself. If I have known Barkis a year, to move to as he went by, I have known him forty year. But *I* can't go and say, "how is he?"'

I felt it was rather hard on Mr Omer, and I told him so.

'I'm not more self-interested, I hope, than another man,' said Mr Omer. 'Look at me! My wind may fail me at any moment, and it ain't likely that, to my own knowledge, I'd be self-interested under such circumstances. I say it ain't likely, in a man who knows his wind will go, when it *does* go, as if a pair of bellows was cut open; and that man a grandfather,' said Mr Omer.

I said, 'Not at all.'

'It ain't that I complain of my line of business,' said Mr Omer; 'it ain't that. Some good and some bad goes, no doubt, to all callings. What I wish is, that parties were brought up stronger-minded.'

Mr Omer, with a very complacent and amiable face, took several puffs in silence; and then said, resuming his first point: 'Accordingly we're obleeged, in ascertaining how Barkis goes on, to limit ourselves to Em'ly. She knows what our real objects are, and she don't have any more alarms or suspicions about us than if we was so many lambs. Minnie and Joram have just stepped down to the house, in fact (she's there, after hours, helping her aunt a bit), to ask her how he is tonight; and if you was to please to wait till they come back, they'd give you full partic'lers. Will you take something? A glass of srub and water, now? I smoke on srub and water, myself,' said Mr Omer, taking up his glass, 'because it's considered softening to the passages, by which this troublesome breath of mine gets into action. But, Lord bless you,' said Mr Omer, huskily, 'it ain't the passages that's out of order! "Give me breath enough," says I to my daughter Minnie, "and *I*'ll find passages, my dear."'

He really had no breath to spare, and it was alarming to see him laugh. When he was again in a condition to be talked to, I thanked him for the proffered refreshment, which I declined, as I had just had dinner; and observing that I would wait, since he was so good as to invite me, until his daughter and his son-in-law came back, I enquired how little Em'ly was.

'Well, sir,' said Mr Omer, removing his pipe, that he might rub his chin; 'I tell you truly, I shall be glad when her marriage has taken place.'

'Why so?' I enquired.

'Well, she's unsettled at present,' said Mr Omer. 'It ain't that she's not as pretty as ever, for she's prettier – I do assure you, she is prettier. It ain't that she don't work as well as ever, for she does. She *was* worth any six, and she *is* worth any six. But somehow she wants heart. If you understand,' said Mr Omer, after rubbing his chin again, and smoking a little, 'what I mean in a general way by the expression, "A long pull, and a strong pull, and a pull altogether, my hearties, hurrah!" I should say to you that *that* was – in a general way – what I miss in Em'ly.'

Mr Omer's face and manner went for so much that I could conscientiously nod my head, as divining his meaning. My quickness of apprehension seemed to please him, and he went on: 'Now, I consider this is principally on account of her being in an unsettled state, you see. We have talked it over a good deal, her uncle and myself, and her sweetheart and myself after business; and I consider it is principally on account of her being unsettled. You must always recollect of Em'ly,' said Mr Omer, shaking his head gently, 'that she's a most extra-ordinary affectionate little thing. The proverb says, "You can't make a silk purse out of a sow's ear." Well, I don't know about that. I rather think you may, if you begin early in life. She has made a home out of that old boat, sir, that stone and marble couldn't beat.'

'I am sure she has!' said I.

'To see the clinging of that pretty little thing to her uncle,' said Mr Omer; 'to see the way she holds on to him, tighter and tighter, and closer and closer, every day, is to see a sight. Now, you know, there's a struggle going on when that's the case. Why should it be made a longer one than is needful?'

I listened attentively to the good old fellow, and acquiesced, with all my heart, in what he said.

'Therefore, I mentioned to them,' said Mr Omer, in a comfortable, easy-going tone, 'this. I said, "Now, don't consider Em'ly nailed down in point of time, at all. Make it your own time. Her services have been more valuable than was supposed; her learning has been quicker than was supposed; Omer and Joram can run their pen through what remains; and she's free when you wish. If she likes to make any little arrangement, afterwards, in the way of doing any little thing for us at home, very well. If she don't, very well still. We're no losers, anyhow." For – don't you see,' said Mr Omer, touching me with his pipe, 'it ain't likely that a man so short of breath as myself, and a grandfather, too, would go and strain points with a little bit of a blue-eyed blossom, like *her*?'

'Not at all, I am certain,' said I.

'Not at all! You're right!' said Mr Omer. 'Well, sir, her cousin – you know it's a cousin she's going to be married to?'

'Oh, yes,' I replied. 'I know him well.'

'Of course you do,' said Mr Omer. 'Well, sir! Her cousin being, as it appears, in good work, and well to do, thanked me in a very manly sort of manner for this (conducting himself altogether, I must say, in a way that gives me a high opinion of him), and went and took as comfortable a little house as you or I could wish to clap eyes on. That little house is now furnished right through, as neat and complete as a doll's parlour; and but for Barkis's illness having taken this bad turn, poor fellow, they would have been man and wife, I dare say, by this time. As it is, there's a postponement.'

'And Emily, Mr Omer?' I enquired. 'Has she become more settled?'

'Why that you know,' he returned, rubbing his double chin again, 'can't naturally be expected. The prospect of the change and separation, and all that is, as one may say, close to her and far away from her, both at once. Barkis's death needn't put it off much, but his lingering might. Anyway, it's an uncertain state of matters, you see.'

'I see,' said I.

'Consequently,' pursued Mr Omer, 'Em'ly's still a little down and a little fluttered; perhaps, upon the whole, she's more so than she was. Every day she seems to get fonder and fonder of her uncle, and more loth to part from all of us. A kind word from me brings the tears into her eyes; and if you was to see her with my daughter Minnie's little girl, you'd never forget it. Bless my heart alive!' said Mr Omer, pondering, 'how she loves that child!'

Having so favourable an opportunity, it occurred to me to ask Mr Omer, before our conversation should be interrupted by the return of his daughter and her husband, whether he knew anything of Martha.

'Ah!' he rejoined, shaking his head, and looking very much dejected. 'No good. A sad story, sir, however you come to know it. I never thought there was harm in the girl. I wouldn't wish to mention it before my daughter Minnie – for she'd take me up directly – but I never did. None of us ever did.'

Mr Omer, hearing his daughter's footstep before I heard it, touched me with his pipe and shut up one eye, as a caution. She and her husband came in immediately afterwards.

Their report was that Mr Barkis was 'as bad as bad could be'; that he was quite unconscious; and that Mr Chillip had mournfully said in the kitchen, on going away just now, that the College of Physicians, the College of Surgeons, and Apothecaries' Hall, if they were all called in together, couldn't help him. He was past both Colleges, Mr Chillip said, and the Hall could only poison him.

Hearing this, and learning that Mr Peggotty was there, I determined to go to the house at once. I bade good-night to Mr Omer, and to Mr and Mrs Joram; and directed my steps thither with a solemn feeling, which made Mr Barkis quite a new and different creature.

My low tap at the door was answered by Mr Peggotty. He was not so much surprised to see me as I had expected. I remarked this in Peggotty, too, when she came down; and I have seen it since; and I think, in the expectation of that dread surprise, all other changes and surprises dwindle into nothing.

I shook hands with Mr Peggotty, and passed into the kitchen, while he softly closed the door. Little Emily was sitting by the fire, with her hands before her face. Ham was standing near her.

We spoke in whispers; listening between whiles, for any sound in the room above. I had not thought of it on the occasion of my last visit, but how strange it was to me now, to miss Mr Barkis out of the kitchen!

'This is very kind of you, Mas'r Davy,' said Mr Peggotty.

'It is oncommon kind,' said Ham.

'Em'ly, my dear,' cried Mr Peggotty. 'See here! Here's Mas'r Davy come! What, cheer up, pretty! Not a wurrud to Mas'r Davy?'

There was a trembling upon her that I can see now. The coldness of her hand when I touched it, I can feel yet. Its only sign of animation was to shrink from mine; and then she glided from the chair, and, creeping to the other side of her uncle, bowed herself, silently and trembling still, upon his breast.

'It's such a loving art,' said Mr Peggotty, smoothing her rich hair with his great hard hand, 'that it can't abear the sorrer of this. It's nat'ral in young folk, Mas'r Davy, when they're new to these here trials, and timid, like my little bird – it's nat'ral.'

She clung the closer to him, but neither lifted up her face, nor spoke a word.

'It's getting late, my dear,' said Mr Peggotty, 'and here's Ham come fur to take you home. Theer! Go along with t' other loving art! What, Em'ly? Eh, my pretty?'

The sound of her voice had not reached me, but he bent his head as he listened to her, and then said: 'Let you stay with your uncle? Why, you don't mean to ask me that! Stay with your uncle, Moppet? When your husband that'll be so soon is

here fur to take you home? Now a person wouldn't think it, fur to see this little thing alongside a rough-weather chap like me,' said Mr Peggotty, looking round at both of us, with infinite pride; 'but the sea ain't more salt in it than she has fondness in her for her uncle – a foolish little Em'ly!'

'Em'ly's in the right in that, Mas'r Davy!' said Ham. 'Lookee here! As Em'ly wishes of it, and as she's hurried and frightened, like, besides, I'll leave her till morning. Let me stay, too!'

'No, no,' said Mr Peggotty. 'You doesn't ought – a married man like you – or what's as good – to take and hull away a day's work. And you doesn't ought to watch and work both. That won't do. You go home and turn in. You ain't aferd of Em'ly not being took good care on, *I* know.'

Ham yielded to this persuasion, and took his hat to go. Even when he kissed her – and I never saw him approach her, but I felt that nature had given him the soul of a gentleman – she seemed to cling closer to her uncle, even to the avoidance of her chosen husband. I shut the door after him, that it might cause no disturbance of the quiet that prevailed; and when I turned back, I found Mr Peggotty still talking to her.

'Now, I'm a going upstairs to tell your aunt as Mas'r Davy's here, and that'll cheer her up a bit,' he said. 'Sit ye down by the fire, the while, my dear, and warm these mortal cold hands. You doesn't need to be so fearsome, and take on so much. What? You'll go along with me? – Well! come along with me – come! If her uncle was turned out of house and home, and forced to lay down in a dyke, Mas'r Davy,' said Mr Peggotty, with no less pride than before, 'it's my belief she'd go along with him, now! But there'll be someone else, soon – someone else, soon, Em'ly!'

Afterwards, when I went upstairs, as I passed the door of my little chamber, which was dark, I had an indistinct impression of her being within it, cast down upon the floor. But whether it was really she, or whether it was a confusion of the shadows in the room, I don't know now.

I had leisure to think, before the kitchen fire, of pretty little Em'ly's dread of death – which, added to what Mr Omer had told me, I took to be the cause of her being so unlike herself – and I had leisure, before Peggotty came down, even to think more leniently of the weakness of it, as I sat counting the ticking of the clock, and deepening my sense of the solemn hush around me. Peggotty took me in her arms, and blessed and thanked me over and over again for being such a comfort to her (that was what she said) in her distress. She then entreated me to come upstairs, sobbing that Mr Barkis had always liked me and admired me; that he had often talked of me, before he fell into a stupor; and that she believed, in case of his coming to himself again, he would brighten up at sight of me, if he could brighten up at any earthly thing.

The probability of his ever doing so appeared to me, when I saw him, to be very small. He was lying with his head and shoulders out of bed, in an uncomfortable attitude, half resting on the box which had cost him so much pain and trouble. I learned that, when he was past creeping out of bed to open it, and past assuring himself of its safety by means of the divining rod I had seen him use, he had required to have it placed on the chair at the bedside, where he had ever since embraced it, night and day. His arm lay on it now. Time and the world were slipping from beneath him, but the box was there; and the last words he had uttered were (in an explanatory tone) 'Old clothes!'

'Barkis, my dear!' said Peggotty, almost cheerfully, bending over him, while her brother and I stood at the bed's foot; 'here's my dear boy – my dear boy, Master Davy, who brought us together, Barkis! That you sent messages by, you know! Won't you speak to Master Davy?'

He was as mute and senseless as the box, from which his form derived the only expression it had.

'He's a going out with the tide,' said Mr Peggotty to me, behind his hand.

My eyes were dim, and so were Mr Peggotty's; but I repeated in a whisper, 'With the tide?'

'People can't die, along the coast,' said Mr Peggotty, 'except when the tide's pretty nigh out. They can't be born, unless it's pretty nigh in – not properly born, till flood. He's a going out with the tide. It's ebb at half-arter three, slack water half an hour. If he lives till it turns, he'll hold his own till past the flood, and go out with the next tide.'

We remained there, watching him, a long time – hours. What mysterious influence my presence had upon him in that state of his senses, I shall not pretend to say; but when he at last began to wander feebly, it is certain he was muttering about driving me to school.

'He's coming to himself,' said Peggotty.

Mr Peggotty touched me, and whispered with much awe and reverence, 'They are both a going out fast.'

'Barkis, my dear!' said Peggotty.

'C. P. Barkis,' he cried faintly. 'No better woman anywhere!'

'Look! Here's Master Davy!' said Peggotty. For he now opened his eyes.

I was on the point of asking him if he knew me, when he tried to stretch out his arm, and said to me, distinctly, with a pleasant smile: 'Barkis is willin'!'

And it being low water, he went out with the tide.

CHAPTER 31

A Greater Loss

It was not difficult for me, on Peggotty's solicitation, to resolve to stay where I was, until after the remains of the poor carrier should have made their last journey to Blunderstone. She had long ago bought, out of her own savings, a little piece of ground in our old churchyard near the grave 'of her sweet girl,' as she always called my mother; and there they were to rest.

In keeping Peggotty company, and doing all I could for her (little enough at the utmost), I was as grateful, I rejoice to think, as even now I could wish myself to have been. But I am afraid I had a supreme satisfaction, of a personal and professional nature, in taking charge of Mr Barkis's will, and expounding its contents.

I may claim the merit of having originated the suggestion that the will should be looked for in the box. After some search, it was found in the box, at the bottom of a horse's nosebag; wherein (besides hay) there was discovered an old gold watch,

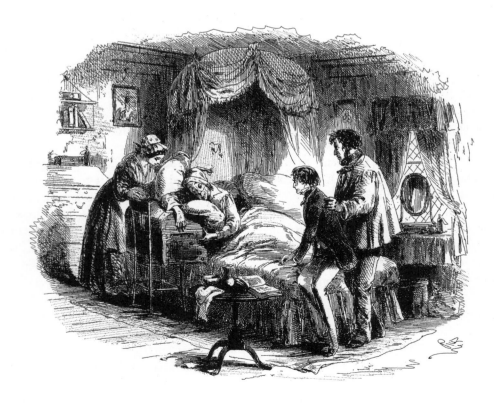

I find Mr Barkis 'going out with the tide'

with chain and seals, which Mr Barkis had worn on his wedding-day, and which had never been seen before or since; a silver tobacco-stopper, in the form of a leg; an imitation lemon, full of minute cups and saucers, which I have some idea Mr Barkis must have purchased to present to me when I was a child, and afterwards found himself unable to part with; eighty-seven guineas and a half, in guineas and half guineas; two hundred and ten pounds, in perfectly clean bank notes; certain receipts for Bank of England stock; an old horseshoe, a bad shilling, a piece of camphor, and an oyster-shell. From the circumstance of the latter article having been much polished, and displaying prismatic colours on the inside, I conclude that Mr Barkis had some general ideas about pearls, which never resolved themselves into anything definite.

For years and years, Mr Barkis had carried this box, on all his journeys, every day. That it might the better escape notice, he had invented a fiction that it belonged to 'Mr Blackboy,' and was 'to be left with Barkis till called for'; a fable he had elaborately written on the lid, in characters now scarcely legible.

He had hoarded, all these years, I found, to good purpose. His property in money amounted to nearly three thousand pounds. Of this he bequeathed the interest of one thousand to Mr Peggotty for his life; on his decease, the principal to be equally divided between Peggotty, little Emily, and me, or the survivor or survivors of us, share and share alike. All the rest he died possessed of, he bequeathed to Peggotty; whom he left residuary legatee, and sole executrix of that his last will and testament.

I felt myself quite a proctor when I read this document aloud with all possible ceremony, and set forth its provisions, any number of times, to those whom they concerned. I began to think there was more in the Commons than I had supposed. I examined the will with the deepest attention, pronounced it perfectly formal in all respects, made a pencil-mark or so in the margin, and thought it rather extraordinary that I knew so much.

In this abstruse pursuit; in making an account for Peggotty of all the property into which she had come; in arranging all the affairs in an orderly manner; and in being her referee and adviser on every point, to our joint delight, I passed the week before the funeral. I did not see little Emily in that interval, but they told me she was to be quietly married in a fortnight.

I did not attend the funeral in character, if I may venture to say so. I mean I was not dressed up in a black cloak and a streamer, to frighten the birds; but I walked over to Blunderstone early in the morning, and was in the churchyard when it came, attended only by Peggotty and her brother. The mad gentleman looked on, out of my little window; Mr Chillip's baby wagged its heavy head, and rolled its goggle eyes, at the clergyman, over its nurse's shoulder; Mr Omer breathed short in the background; no one else was there; and it was very quiet. We walked about the churchyard for an hour, after all was over; and pulled some young leaves from the tree above my mother's grave.

A dread falls on me here. A cloud is lowering on the distant town, towards which I retraced my solitary steps. I fear to approach it. I cannot bear to think of what did come, upon that

memorable night; of what must come again if I go on.

It is no worse, because I write of it. It would be no better, if I stopped my most unwilling hand. It is done. Nothing can undo it; nothing can make it otherwise than as it was.

My old nurse was to go to London with me next day, on the business of the will. Little Emily was passing that day at Mr Omer's. We were all to meet in the old boat-house that night. Ham would bring Emily at the usual hour. I would walk back at my leisure. The brother and sister would return as they had come, and be expecting us, when the day closed in, at the fireside.

I parted from them at the wicket gate, where visionary Straps had rested with Roderick Random's knapsack in the days of yore; and, instead of going straight back, walked a little distance on the road to Lowestoft. Then I turned, and walked back towards Yarmouth. I stayed to dine at a decent alehouse, some mile or two from the ferry I have mentioned before; and thus the day wore away, and it was evening when I reached it. Rain was falling heavily by that time, and it was a wild night; but there was a moon behind the clouds, and it was not dark.

I was soon within sight of Mr Peggotty's house, and of the light within it shining through the window. A little floundering across the sand, which was heavy, brought me to the door, and I went in.

It looked very comfortable, indeed. Mr Peggotty had smoked his evening pipe, and there were preparations for some supper by and by. The fire was bright, the ashes were thrown up, the locker was ready for little Emily in her old place. In her own old place sat Peggotty, once more, looking (but for her dress) as if she had never left it. She had fallen back, already, on the society of the work-box with St Paul's upon the lid, the yard-measure in the cottage, and the bit of wax candle; and there they all were, just as if they had never been disturbed. Mrs Gummidge appeared to be fretting a little, in her old corner; and consequently looked quite natural, too.

'You're first of the lot, Mas'r Davy!' said Mr Peggotty, with a happy face. 'Doen't keep in that coat, sir, if it's wet.'

'Thank you, Mr Peggotty,' said I, giving him my outer coat to hang up. 'It's quite dry.'

'So 't is!' said Mr Peggotty, feeling my shoulders. 'As a chip! Sit ye down, sir. It ain't o' no use saying welcome to you, but you're welcome, kind and hearty.'

'Thank you, Mr Peggotty, I am sure of that. Well, Peggotty!' said I, giving her a kiss. 'And how are you, old woman?'

'Ha, ha!' laughed Mr Peggotty, sitting down beside us, and rubbing his hands in his sense of relief from recent trouble, and in the genuine heartiness of his nature; 'there's not a woman in the wureld, sir – as I tell her – that need to feel more easy in her mind than her! She done her dooty by the departed, and the departed knowed it; and the departed done what was right by her, as she done what was right by the departed – and – and – and it's *all* right!'

Mrs Gummidge groaned.

'Cheer up, my pretty mawther!' said Mr Peggotty. (But he shook his head aside at us, evidently sensible of the tendency of the late occurrences to recall the memory of the old one.)

'Doen't be down! Cheer up, for your own self, on'y a little bit, and see if a good deal more doen't come nat'ral!'

'Not to me, Dan'l,' returned Mrs Gummidge. 'Nothink's nat'ral to me but to be lone and lorn.'

'No, no,' said Mr Peggotty, soothing her sorrows.

'Yes, yes, Dan'l!' said Mrs Gummidge. 'I ain't a person to live with them as has had money left. Thinks go too contrairy with me. I had better be a riddance.'

'Why, how should I ever spend it without you?' said Mr Peggotty, with an air of serious remonstrance. 'What are you a talking on? Doen't I want you more now than ever I did?'

'I knowed I was never wanted before!' cried Mrs Gummidge, with a pitiable whimper, 'and now I'm told so! How could I expect to be wanted, being so lone and lorn, and so contrairy!'

Mr Peggotty seemed very much shocked at himself for having made a speech capable of this unfeeling construction, but was prevented from replying by Peggotty's pulling his sleeve, and shaking her head. After looking at Mrs Gummidge for some moments, in sore distress of mind, he glanced at the Dutch clock, rose, snuffed the candle, and put it in the window.

'Theer!' said Mr Peggotty cheerily. 'Theer we are, Misses Gummidge!' Mrs Gummidge slightly groaned. 'Lighted up, accordin' to custom! You're a wonderin' what that's fur, sir! Well, it's fur our little Em'ly. You see, the path ain't over light or cheerful arter dark; and when I'm here at the hour as she's a comin' home, I puts the light in the winder. That, you see,' said Mr Peggotty, bending over me with great glee, 'meets two objects. She says, says Em'ly, "Theer's home!" she says. And likewise, says Em'ly, "My uncle's theer!" Fur if I ain't theer, I never have no light showed.'

'You're a baby!' said Peggotty; very fond of him for it, if she thought so.

'Well,' returned Mr Peggotty, standing with his legs pretty wide apart, and rubbing his hands up and down them in his comfortable satisfaction, as he looked alternately at us and at the fire, 'I doen't know but I am. Not you see, to look at.'

'Not azackly,' observed Peggotty.

'No,' laughed Mr Peggotty, 'not to look at, but to – to consider on, you know. *I* doen't care, bless you! Now I tell you. When I go a looking and looking about that theer pritty house of our Em'ly's, I'm – I'm Gormed,' said Mr Peggotty, with sudden emphasis – 'theer! I can't say more – if I doen't feel as if the littlest things was her, a'most. I takes 'em up and I puts 'em down, and I touches of 'em as delicate as if they was our Em'ly. So 't is with her little bonnets and that. I couldn't see one on 'em rough used a purpose – not fur the whole wureld. There's a babby for you, in the form of a great Sea Porkypine!' said Mr Peggotty, relieving his earnestness with a roar of laughter.

Peggotty and I both laughed, but not so loud.

'It's my opinion, you see,' said Mr Peggotty, with a delighted face, after some further rubbing of his legs, 'as this is along of my havin' played with her so much, and made believe as we was Turks, and French, and sharks, and every wariety of forinners – bless you, yes; and lions and whales, and I don't know what all! – when she warn't no higher than my knee. I've got into the way on it, you know. Why, this here candle, now,' said Mr Peggotty, gleefully holding out his hand towards it, '*I* know wery well that arter she's married and gone, I shall put that candle theer, just that same as now. I know wery well that when I'm here o' nights (and where else should I live, bless your arts, whatever fortun I come into!) and she ain't here, or I ain't theer, I shall put the candle in the winder, and sit afore the fire, pretending I'm expecting of her, like I'm a doing now. *There's* a babby for you,' said Mr Peggotty, with another roar, 'in the form of a Sea Porkypine! Why, at the present minute, when I see the candle sparkle up, I says to myself, "She's a looking at it! Em'ly's a coming!" *There's* a babby for you, in the form of a Sea Porkypine! Right for all that,' said Mr Peggotty, stopping in his roar, and smiting his hands together, 'fur here she is!'

It was only Ham. The night should have turned more wet since I came in, for he had a large sou'wester hat on, slouched over his face.

'Where's Em'ly?' said Mr Peggotty.

Ham made a motion with his head, as if she were outside. Mr Peggotty took the light from the window, trimmed it, put it on the table, and was busily stirring the fire, when Ham, who had not moved, said: 'Mas'r Davy, will you come out a minute, and see what Em'ly and me has got to show you?'

We went out. As I passed him at the door, I saw, to my astonishment and fright, that he was deadly pale. He pushed me hastily into the open air, and closed the door upon us. Only upon us two.

'Ham! what's the matter?'

'Mas'r Davy! – ' Oh, for his broken heart, how dreadfully he wept!

I was paralysed by the sight of such grief. I don't know what I thought, or what I dreaded. I could only look at him.

'Ham! Poor good fellow! For Heaven's sake tell me what's the matter!'

'My love, Mas'r Davy – the pride and hope of my art – her that I'd have died for, and would die for now – she's gone!'

'Gone?'

'Em'ly's run away! Oh, Mas'r Davy, think *how* she's run away, when I pray my good and gracious God to kill her (her that is so dear above all things) sooner than let her come to ruin and disgrace!'

The face he turned up to the troubled sky, the quivering of his clasped hands, the agony of his figure remain associated with that lonely waste, in my remembrance, to this hour. It is always night there, and he is the only object in the scene.

'You're a scholar,' he said hurriedly, 'and know what's right and best. What am I to say, indoors? How am I ever to break it to him, Mas'r Davy?'

I saw the door move, and instinctively tried to hold the latch on the outside, to gain a moment's time. It was too late. Mr Peggotty thrust forth his face; and never could I forget the change that came upon it when he saw us, if I were to live five hundred years.

I remember a great wail and cry, and the women hanging about him, and we all standing in the room; I with a paper in my hand, which Ham had given me; Mr Peggotty, with his vest torn open, his hair wild, his face and lips quite white, and blood trickling down his bosom (it had sprung from his mouth, I think), looking fixedly at me.

'Read it, sir,' he said, in a low, shivering voice. 'Slow, please, I doesn't know as I can understand.'

In the midst of the silence of death, I read thus, from a blotted letter:

'When you, who love me so much better than I ever have deserved, even when my mind was innocent, see this, I shall be far away.'

'I shall be fur away,' he repeated slowly. 'Stop! Em'ly fur away. Well!'

'When I leave my dear home – my dear home – oh, my dear home! – in the morning – '

the letter bore date on the previous night:

' – it will be never to come back, unless he brings me back a lady. This will be found at night, many hours after, instead of me. Oh, if you knew how my heart is torn. If even you, that I have wronged so much, that never can forgive me, could only know what I suffer! I am too wicked to write about myself. Oh, take comfort in thinking that I am so bad. Oh, for mercy's sake, tell uncle that I never loved him half so dear as now. Oh, don't remember how affectionate and kind you have all been to me – don't remember we were ever to be married – but try to think as if I died when I was little, and was buried somewhere. Pray Heaven, that I am going away from, have compassion on my uncle! Tell him that I never loved him half so dear. Be his comfort. Love some good girl, that will be what I was once to uncle, and be true to you, and worthy of you, and know no shame but me. God bless all! I'll pray for all, often, on my knees. If he don't bring me back a lady, and I don't pray for my own self, I'll pray for all. My parting love to uncle. My last tears, and my last thanks for uncle!'

That was all.

He stood, long after I had ceased to read, still looking at me. At length I ventured to take his hand, and to entreat him, as well as I could, to endeavour to get some command of himself. He replied, 'I thankee, sir, I thankee!' without moving.

Ham spoke to him. Mr Peggotty was so far sensible of *his* affliction, that he wrung his hand; but, otherwise, he remained in the same state, and no one dared to disturb him.

Slowly, at last he moved his eyes from my face, as if he were waking from a vision, and cast them round the room. Then he said, in a low voice: 'Who's the man? I want to know his name.'

Ham glanced at me, and suddenly I felt a shock that struck me back.

'There's a man suspected,' said Mr Peggotty. 'Who is it?'

'Mas'r Davy!' implored Ham. 'Go out a bit, and let me tell him what I must. You doesn't ought to hear it, sir.'

I felt the shock again. I sank down in a chair, and tried to utter some reply; but my tongue was fettered, and my sight was weak.

'I want to know his name!' I heard said, once more.

'For some time past,' Ham faltered, 'there's been a servant

about here, at odd times. There's been a gen'lm'n, too. Both of 'em belonged to one another.'

Mr Peggotty stood fixed as before, but now looking at him.

'The servant,' pursued Ham, 'was seen along with – our poor girl – last night. He's been in hiding about here, this week or over. He was thought to have gone, but he was hiding. Doen't stay, Mas'r Davy, doen't!'

I felt Peggotty's arm round my neck, but I could not have moved if the house had been about to fall upon me.

'A strange chay and hosses was outside town, this morning, on the Norwich road, a'most afore the day broke,' Ham went on. 'The servant went to it, and come from it, and went to it again. When he went to it again, Em'ly was nigh him. The t' other was inside. He's the man!'

'For the Lord's love,' said Mr Peggotty, falling back, and putting out his hand, as if to keep off what he dreaded, 'doen't tell me his name's Steerforth!'

'Mas'r Davy,' exclaimed Ham, in a broken voice, 'it ain't no fault of yourn – and I am far from laying of it to you – but his name is Steerforth, and he's a damned villain!'

Mr Peggotty uttered no cry, and shed no tear, and moved no more, until he seemed to wake again, all at once, and pulled down his rough coat from its peg in a corner.

'Bear a hand with this! I'm struck of a heap, and can't do it,' he said impatiently. 'Bear a hand and help me. Well!' when somebody had done so. 'Now give me that theer hat!'

Ham asked him whither he was going.

'I'm a going to seek my niece. I'm a going to seek my Em'ly. I'm a going, first, to stave in that theer boat, and sink it where I would have drownded *him*, as I'm a livin' soul, if I had had one thought of what was in him! As he sat afore me,' he said wildly, holding out his clenched right hand, 'as he sat afore me, face to face, strike me down dead, but I'd have drownded him, and thought it right! – I'm a going to seek my niece!'

'Where?' cried Ham, interposing himself before the door.

'Anywhere! I'm a going to seek my niece through the wureld. I'm a going to find my poor niece in her shame, and bring her back. No one stop me! I tell you I'm a going to seek my niece!'

'No, no!' cried Mrs Gummidge, coming between them, in a fit of crying. 'No, no, Dan'l, not as you are now. Seek her in a little while, my lone, lorn Dan'l, and that'll be but right! but not as you are now. Sit ye down, and give me your forgiveness for having ever been a worrit to you, Dan'l – what have *my* contrairies ever been to this! – and let us speak a word about them times when she was first an orphan, and when Ham was, too, and when I was a poor widder woman, and you took me in. It'll soften your poor heart, Dan'l,' laying her head upon his shoulder, 'and you'll bear your sorrow better; for you know the promise, Dan'l, "As you have done it unto one of the least of these, you have done it unto me"; and that can never fail under this roof, that's been our shelter for so many, many year!'

He was quite passive now; and when I heard him crying, the impulse that had been upon me to go down upon my knees, and ask their pardon for the desolation I had caused, and curse Steerforth, yielded to a better feeling. My overcharged heart found the same relief, and I cried too.

CHAPTER 32

The Beginning of a Long Journey

What is natural in me, is natural in many other men, I infer, and so I am not afraid to write that I never had loved Steerforth better than when the ties that bound me to him were broken. In the keen distress of the discovery of his unworthiness, I thought more of all that was brilliant in him, I softened more towards all that was good in him, I did more justice to the qualities that might have made him a man of a noble nature and a great name, than ever I had done in the height of my devotion to him. Deeply as I felt my own unconscious part in his pollution of an honest home, I believed that if I had been brought face to face with him, I could not have uttered one reproach. I should have loved him so well still – though he fascinated me no longer – I should have held in so much tenderness the memory of my affection for him, that I think I should have been as weak as a spirit-wounded child, in all but the entertainment of a thought that we could ever be reunited. That thought I never had. I felt, as he had felt, that all was at an end between us. What his remembrances of me were, I have never known – they were light enough, perhaps, and easily dismissed – but mine of him were as the remembrances of a cherished friend, who was dead.

Yes, Steerforth, long removed from the scenes of this poor history! My sorrow may bear involuntary witness against you at the Judgement Throne, but my angry thoughts or my reproaches never will, I know!

The news of what had happened soon spread through the town; insomuch that as I passed along the streets next morning, I overheard the people speaking of it at their doors. Many were hard upon her, some few were hard upon him, but towards her second father and her lover there was but one sentiment. Among all kinds of people a respect for them in their distress prevailed, which was full of gentleness and delicacy. The seafaring men kept apart, when those two were seen early, walking with slow steps on the beach; and stood in knots, talking compassionately among themselves.

It was on the beach, close down by the sea, that I found them. It would have been easy to perceive that they had not slept all last night, even if Peggotty had failed to tell me of their still sitting just as I left them, when it was broad day. They looked worn; and I thought Mr Peggotty's head was bowed in one night more than in all the years I had known him. But they were both as grave and steady as the sea itself, then lying beneath a dark sky, waveless – yet with a heavy roll upon it, as if it breathed in its rest – and touched, on the horizon, with a strip of silvery light from the unseen sun.

'We have had a mort of talk, sir,' said Mr Peggotty to me, when we had all three walked a little while in silence, 'of what we ought and doen't ought to do. But we see our course now.'

I happened to glance at Ham, then looking out to sea upon the distant light, and a frightful thought came into my mind – not that his face was angry, for it was not; I recall nothing but an expression of stern determination in it – that if ever he encountered Steerforth he would kill him.

'My dooty here, sir,' said Mr Peggotty, 'is done. I'm a going to seek my – ' he stopped, and went on in a firmer voice, 'I'm a going to seek her. That's my dooty evermore.'

He shook his head when I asked him where he would seek her, and enquired if I were going to London tomorrow? I told him I had not gone today, fearing to lose the chance of being of any service to him, but that I was ready to go when he would.

'I'll go along with you, sir,' he rejoined, 'if you're agreeable, tomorrow.'

We walked again, for a while, in silence.

'Ham,' he presently resumed, 'he'll hold to his present work, and go and live along with my sister. The old boat yonder – '

'Will you desert the old boat, Mr Peggotty?' I gently interposed.

'My station, Mas'r Davy,' he returned, 'ain't there no longer; and if ever a boat foundered, since there was darkness on the face of the deep, that one's gone down. But no, sir, no; I don't mean as it should be deserted. Fur from that.'

We walked again for a while, as before, until he explained: 'My wishes is, sir, as it shall look, day and night, winter and summer, as it has always looked since she first knowed it. If ever she should come a wandering back, I wouldn't have the old place seem to cast her off, you understand, but seem to tempt her to draw nigher to't, and to peep in, may be, like a ghost, out of the wind and rain, through the old winder, at the old seat by the fire. Then, may be, Mas'r Davy, seein' none but Missis Gummidge there, she might take heart to creep in, trembling; and might come to be laid down in her old bed, and rest her weary head where it was once so gay.'

I could not speak to him in reply, though I tried.

'Every night,' said Mr Peggotty, 'as reg'lar as the night comes, the candle must be stood in its old pane of glass, that if ever she should see it, it may seem to say, "Come back, my child, come back!" If ever there's a knock, Ham (partic'ler a soft knock), arter dark, at your aunt's door, doen't you go nigh it. Let it be her – not you – that sees my fallen child!'

He walked a little in front of us, and kept before us for some minutes. During this interval, I glanced at Ham again, and observing the same expression on his face, and his eyes still directed to the distant light, I touched his arm.

Twice I called him by his name, in the tone in which I might have tried to rouse a sleeper, before he heeded me. When I at last enquired on what his thoughts were so bent, he replied: 'On what's afore me, Mas'r Davy; and over yon.'

'On the life before you, do you mean?' He had pointed confusedly out to sea.

'Aye, Mas'r Davy. I doen't rightly know how 't is, but from over yon there seemed to me to come – the end of it like;' looking at me as if he were waking, but with the same determined face.

'What end?' I asked, possessed by my former fear.

'I doen't know,' he said thoughtfully; 'I was calling to mind that the beginning of it all did take place here – and then the end come. But it's gone! Mas'r Davy,' he added; answering, as I think, my look; 'you hain't no call to be afeered of me; but

I'm kiender muddled; I doen't fare to feel no matters' – which was as much as to say that he was not himself, and quite confounded.

Mr Peggotty stopping for us to join him, we did so, and said no more. The remembrance of this, in connection with my former thought, however, haunted me at intervals, even until the inexorable end came at its appointed time.

We insensibly approached the old boat, and entered. Mrs Gummidge, no longer moping in her especial corner, was busy, preparing breakfast. She took Mr Peggotty's hat, and placed his seat for him, and spoke so comfortably and softly, that I hardly knew her.

'Dan'l, my good man,' said she, 'you must eat and drink, and keep up your strength, for without it you'll do nowt. Try, that's a dear soul! And if I disturb you with my clicketen,' she meant her chattering, 'tell me so, Dan'l, and I won't.'

When she had served us all, she withdrew to the window, where she sedulously employed herself in repairing some shirts and other clothes belonging to Mr Peggotty, and neatly folding and packing them in an old oilskin bag, such as sailors carry. Meanwhile, she continued talking, in the same quiet manner: 'All times and seasons, you know, Dan'l,' said Mrs Gummidge, 'I shall be allus here, and everythink will look accordin' to your wishes. I'm a poor scholar, but I shall write to you, odd times, when you're away, and send my letters to Mas'r Davy. May be you'll write to me too, Dan'l, odd times, and tell me how you fare to feel upon your lone lorn journeys.'

'You'll be a solitary woman here, I'm afeerd!' said Mr Peggotty.

'No, no, Dan'l,' she returned, 'I shan't be that. Doen't you mind me. I shall have enough to do to keep a Beein for you' (Mrs Gummidge meant a home) 'again you come back – to keep a Beein here for any that may hap to come back, Dan'l. In the fine time, I shall set outside the door as I used to do. If any *should* come nigh, they shall see the old widder woman true to 'em, a long way off.'

What a change in Mrs Gummidge in a little time! She was another woman. She was so devoted, she had such a quick perception of what it would be well to say, and what it would be well to leave unsaid, she was so forgetful of herself, and so regardful of the sorrow about her, that I held her in a sort of veneration. The work she did that day! There were many things to be brought up from the beach and stored in the outhouse – as oars, nets, sails, cordage, spars, lobster-pots, bags of ballast, and the like; and though there was abundance of assistance rendered, there being not a pair of working hands on all that shore but would have laboured hard for Mr Peggotty, and been well paid in being asked to do it, yet she persisted, all day long, in toiling under weights that she was quite unequal to, and fagging to and fro on all sorts of unnecessary errands. As to deploring her misfortune, she appeared to have entirely lost the recollection of ever having had any. She preserved an equable cheerfulness in the midst of her sympathy, which was not the least astonishing part of the change that had come over her. Querulousness was out of the question. I did not even observe her voice to falter, or a tear to escape from her eyes, the whole day through, until twilight; when she and I and Mr Peggotty being alone together, and he having fallen asleep in perfect exhaustion, she broke into a half-suppressed fit of sobbing and crying, and taking me to the door, said, 'Ever bless you, Mas'r Davy, be a friend to him, poor dear!' Then she immediately ran out of the house to wash her face, in order that she might sit quietly beside him, and be found at work there, when he should awake. In short I left her, when I went away at night, the prop and staff of Mr Peggotty's affliction; and I could not meditate enough upon the lesson that I read in Mrs Gummidge, and the new experience she unfolded to me.

It was between nine and ten o'clock when, strolling in a melancholy manner through the town, I stopped at Mr Omer's door. Mr Omer had taken it so much to heart, his daughter told me, that he had been very low and poorly all day, and had gone to bed without his pipe.

'A deceitful, bad-hearted girl,' said Mrs Joram. 'There was no good in her, ever!'

'Don't say so,' I returned. 'You don't think so.'

'Yes, I do!' cried Mrs Joram angrily.

'No, no,' said I.

Mrs Joram tossed her head, endeavouring to be very stern and cross; but she could not command her softer self, and began to cry. I was young, to be sure, but I thought much the better of her for this sympathy, and fancied it became her, as a virtuous wife and mother, very well indeed.

'What will she ever do!' sobbed Minnie. 'Where will she go! What will become of her! Oh, how could she be so cruel, to herself and him!'

I remembered the time when Minnie was a young and pretty girl; and I was glad that she remembered it too, so feelingly.

'My little Minnie,' said Mrs Joram, 'has only just now been got to sleep. Even in her sleep she is sobbing for Em'ly. All day long, little Minnie has cried for her, and asked me, over and over again, whether Em'ly was wicked? What can I say to her, when Em'ly tied a ribbon off her own neck round little Minnie's the last night she was here, and laid her head down on the pillow beside her till she was fast asleep! The ribbon's round my little Minnie's neck now. It ought not to be, perhaps, but what can I do? Em'ly is very bad, but they were fond of one another. And the child knows nothing!'

Mrs Joram was so unhappy, that her husband came out to take care of her. Leaving them together, I went home to Peggotty's; more melancholy myself, if possible, than I had been yet.

That good creature – I mean Peggotty – all untired by her late anxieties and sleepless nights, was at her brother's, where she meant to stay till morning. An old woman, who had been employed about the house for some weeks past, while Peggotty had been unable to attend to it, was the house's only other occupant besides myself. As I had no occasion for her services, I sent her to bed, by no means against her will; and sat down before the kitchen fire a little while, to think about all this.

I was blending it with the deathbed of the late Mr Barkis, and was driving out with the tide towards the distance at which Ham had looked so singularly in the morning, when I was recalled from my wanderings by a knock at the door. There was a knocker upon the door, but it was not that which made the sound. The tap was from a hand, and low down upon the door, as if it were given by a child.

It made me start as much as if it had been the knock of a footman to a person of distinction. I opened the door; and at first looked down, to my amazement, on nothing but a great umbrella that appeared to be walking about of itself. But presently I discovered underneath it, Miss Mowcher.

I might not have been prepared to give the little creature a very kind reception, if, on her removing the umbrella, which her utmost efforts were unable to shut up, she had shown me the 'volatile' expression of face which had made so great an impression on me at our first and last meeting. But her face, as she turned it up to mine, was so earnest, and when I relieved her of the umbrella (which would have been an inconvenient one for the Irish Giant), she wrung her little hands in such an afflicted manner, that I rather inclined towards her.

'Miss Mowcher!' said I, after glancing up and down the empty street, without distinctly knowing what I expected to see besides, 'how do you come here? What is the matter?'

She motioned to me, with her short right arm, to shut the umbrella for her; and passing me hurriedly, went into the kitchen. When I had closed the door, and followed, with the umbrella in my hand, I found her sitting on the corner of the fender – it was a low iron one, with two flat bars at top to stand plates upon – in the shadow of the boiler, swaying herself backwards and forwards, and chafing her hands upon her knees like a person in pain.

Quite alarmed at being the only recipient of this untimely visit, and the only spectator of this portentous behaviour, I exclaimed again, 'Pray tell me, Miss Mowcher, what is the matter! are you ill?'

'My dear young soul,' returned Miss Mowcher, squeezing her hands upon her heart one over the other, 'I am ill here, I am very ill. To think that it should come to this, when I might have known it, and perhaps prevented it, if I hadn't been a thoughtless fool!'

Again her large bonnet (very disproportionate to her figure) went backwards and forwards, in her swaying of her little body to and fro; while a most gigantic bonnet rocked, in unison with it, upon the wall.

'I am surprised,' I began, 'to see you so distressed and serious' – when she interrupted me.

'Yes, it's always so!' she said. 'They are all surprised, these inconsiderate young people, fairly and full grown, to see any natural feeling in a little thing like me! They make a plaything of me, use me for their amusement, throw me away when they are tired, and wonder that I feel more than a toy horse or a wooden soldier! Yes, yes, that's the way. The old way!'

'It may be, with others,' I returned, 'but I do assure you it is not with me. Perhaps I ought not to be at all surprised to see you as you are now, I know so little of you. I said, without consideration, what I thought.'

'What can I do?' returned the little woman, standing up, and holding out her arms to show herself. 'See! What I am, my father was; and my sister is; and my brother is. I have worked for sister and brother these many years – hard, Mr Copperfield – all day. I must live. I do no harm. If there are people so unreflecting or so cruel as to make a jest of me, what is left for me to do but to make a jest of myself, them, and everything? If I do so, for the time, whose fault is that? Mine?'

No. Not Miss Mowcher's, I perceived.

'If I had shown myself a sensitive dwarf to your false friend,' pursued the little woman, shaking her head at me, with reproachful earnestness, 'how much of his help or goodwill do you think I should ever have had? If little Mowcher (who had no hand, young gentleman, in the making of herself) addressed herself to him, or the like of him, because of her misfortunes, when do you suppose her small voice would have been heard? Little Mowcher would have as much need to live, if she was the bitterest and dullest of pigmies; but she couldn't do it. No. She might whistle for her bread and butter till she died of Air.'

Miss Mowcher sat down on the fender again, and took out her handkerchief, and wiped her eyes.

'Be thankful for me, if you have a kind heart, as I think you have,' she said, 'that while I know well what I am, I can be cheerful and endure it all. I am thankful for myself, at any rate, that I can find my tiny way through the world, without being beholden to anyone; and that in return for all that is thrown at me, in folly or vanity, as I go along, I can throw bubbles back. If I don't brood over all I want, it is the better for me, and not the worse for anyone. If I am a plaything for you giants, be gentle with me.'

Miss Mowcher replaced her handkerchief in her pocket, looking at me with very intent expression all the while, and pursued: 'I saw you in the street just now. You may suppose I am not able to walk as fast as you, with my short legs and short breath, and I couldn't overtake you; but I guessed where you came, and came after you. I have been here before today, but the good woman wasn't at home.'

'Do you know her?' I demanded.

'I know *of* her, and about her,' she replied, 'from Omer and Joram. I was there at seven o'clock this morning. Do you remember what Steerforth said to me about this unfortunate girl, that time when I saw you both at the inn?'

The great bonnet on Miss Mowcher's head, and the greater bonnet on the wall, began to go backwards and forwards again when she asked this question.

I remembered very well what she referred to, having had it in my thoughts many times that day. I told her so.

'May the Father of all Evil confound him,' said the little woman, holding up her forefinger between me and her sparkling eyes; 'and ten times more confound that wicked servant; but I believed it was *you* who had a boyish passion for her!'

'I?' I repeated.

'Child, child! In the name of blind ill-fortune,' cried Miss Mowcher, wringing her hands impatiently, as she went to and fro again upon the fender, 'why did you praise her so, and blush, and look disturbed?'

I could not conceal from myself that I had done this, though for a reason very different from her supposition.

'What did I know?' said Miss Mowcher, taking out her

handkerchief again, and giving one little stamp on the ground whenever, at short intervals, she applied it to her eyes with both hands at once. 'He was crossing you and wheedling you, I saw; and you were soft wax in his hands, I saw. Had I left the room a minute, when his man told me that "Young Innocence" (so he called you, and you may call him "Old Guilt" all the days of your life) had set his heart upon her, and she was giddy and liked him, but his master was resolved that no harm should come of it – more for your sake than for hers – and that that was their business here? How could I *but* believe him? I saw Steerforth soothe and please you by his praise of her! You were the first to mention her name. You owned to an old admiration of her. You were hot and cold, and red and white, all at once when I spoke to you of her. What could I think – what *did* I think – but that you were a young libertine in everything but experience, and had fallen into hands that had experience enough, and could manage you (having the fancy) for your own good? Oh! oh! oh! They were afraid of my finding out the truth,' exclaimed Miss Mowcher, getting off the fender, and trotting up and down the kitchen with her two short arms distressfully lifted up, 'because I am a sharp little thing – I need be, to get through the world at all! – and they deceived me altogether, and I gave the poor unfortunate girl a letter, which I fully believe was the beginning of her ever speaking to Littimer, who was left behind on purpose!'

I stood amazed at the revelation of all this perfidy, looking at Miss Mowcher as she walked up and down the kitchen until she was out of breath, when she sat upon the fender again, and, drying her face with her handkerchief, shook her head for a long time, without otherwise moving, and without breaking silence.

'My country rounds,' she added at length, 'brought me to Norwich, Mr Copperfield, the night before last. What I happened to find out there, about their secret way of coming and going, without you – which was strange – led to my suspecting something wrong. I got into the coach from London last night, as it came through Norwich, and was here this morning. Oh, oh, oh! too late!'

Poor little Mowcher turned so chilly after all her crying and fretting, that she turned round on the fender, putting her poor little wet feet in among the ashes to warm them, and sat looking at the fire, like a large doll. I sat in a chair on the other side of the hearth, lost in unhappy reflections, and looking at the fire too, and sometimes at her.

'I must go,' she said at last, rising as she spoke. 'It's late. You don't mistrust me?'

Meeting her sharp glance, which was as sharp as ever when she asked me, I could not on that short challenge answer no, quite frankly.

'Come!' said she, accepting the offer of my hand to help her over the fender, and looking wistfully up into my face, 'you know you wouldn't mistrust me, if I was a full-sized woman!'

I felt that there was much truth in this; and I felt rather ashamed of myself.

'You are a young man,' she said, nodding. 'Take a word of advice, even from three foot nothing. Try not to associate bodily defects with mental, my good friend, except for a solid reason.'

She had got over the fender now, and I had got over my suspicion. I told her that I believed she had given me a faithful account of herself, and that we had both been hapless instruments in designing hands. She thanked me, and said I was a good fellow.

'Now, mind!' she exclaimed, turning back on her way to the door, and looking shrewdly at me, with her forefinger up again. 'I have some reason to suspect, from what I have heard – my ears are always open; I can't afford to spare what powers I have – that they are gone abroad. But if ever they return, if ever any one of them returns, while I am alive, I am more likely than another, going about as I do, to find it out soon. Whatever I know, you shall know. If ever I can do anything to serve the poor betrayed girl, I will do it faithfully, please Heaven! And Littimer had better have a bloodhound at his back, than little Mowcher!'

I placed implicit faith in this last statement, when I marked the look with which it was accompanied.

'Trust me no more, but trust me no less, than you would trust a full-sized woman,' said the little creature, touching me appealingly on the wrist. 'If ever you see me again, unlike what I am now, and like what I was when you first saw me, observe what company I am in. Call to mind that I am a very helpless and defenceless little thing. Think of me at home with my brother like myself and sister like myself, when my day's work is done. Perhaps you won't; then, be very hard upon me, or surprised if I can be distressed and serious. Good-night!'

I gave Miss Mowcher my hand, with a very different opinion of her from that which I had hitherto entertained, and opened the door to let her out. It was not a trifling business to get the great umbrella up, and properly balanced in her grasp; but at last I successfully accomplished this, and saw it go bobbing down the street through the rain, without the least appearance of having anybody underneath it, except when a heavier fall than usual from some overcharged waterspout sent it toppling over, on one side, and discovered Miss Mowcher struggling violently to get it right. After making one or two sallies to her relief, which were rendered futile by the umbrella's hopping on again, like an immense bird, before I could reach it, I came in, went to bed, and slept till morning.

In the morning I was joined by Mr Peggotty and by my old nurse, and we went at an early hour to the coach-office, where Mrs Gummidge and Ham were waiting to take leave of us.

'Mas'r Davy,' Ham whispered, drawing me aside, while Mr Peggotty was stowing his bag among the luggage, 'his life is quite broke up. He doesn't know wheer he's going; he doesn't know what's afore him; he's bound upon a voyage that'll last, on and off, all the rest of his days, take my wured for 't, unless he finds what he's a seeking of. I am sure you'll be a friend to him, Mas'r Davy?'

'Trust me, I will, indeed,' said I, shaking hands with Ham earnestly.

'Thankee. Thankee, very kind, sir. One thing furder. I'm in good employ, you know, Mas'r Davy, and I ha'n't no way now of spending what I gets. Money's of no use to me no more, except to live. If you can lay it out for him, I shall do my work with a better art. Though as to that, sir,' and he spoke very steadily and mildly, 'you're not to think but I shall work at all times, like a man, and act the best that lays in my power!'

I told him I was well convinced of it; and I hinted that I hoped the time might even come when he would cease to lead the lonely life he naturally contemplated now.

'No, sir,' he said, shaking his head, 'all that's past and over with me, sir. No one can never fill the place that's empty. But you'll bear in mind about the money, as theer's at all times some laying by for him?'

Reminding him of the fact that Mr Peggotty derived a steady, though certainly a very moderate income from the bequest of his late brother-in-law, I promised to do so. We then took leave of each other. I cannot leave him even now, without remembering with a pang, at once his modest fortitude and his great sorrow.

As to Mrs Gummidge, if I were to endeavour to describe how she ran down the street by the side of the coach, seeing nothing but Mr Peggotty on the roof, through the tears she tried to repress, and dashing herself against the people who were coming in the opposite direction, I should enter on a task of some difficulty. Therefore I had better leave her sitting on a baker's doorstep, out of breath, with no shape at all remaining in her bonnet, and one of her shoes off, lying on the pavement at a considerable distance.

When we got to our journey's end, our first pursuit was to look about for a little lodging for Peggotty, where her brother could have a bed. We were so fortunate as to find one of a very clean and cheap description, over a chandler's shop, only two streets removed from me. When we had engaged this domicile, I bought some cold meat at an eating-house, and took my fellow-travellers home to tea; a proceeding, I regret to state, which did not meet with Mrs Crupp's approval, but quite the contrary. I ought to observe, however, in explanation of that lady's state of mind that she was much offended by Peggotty's tucking up her widow's gown before she had been ten minutes in the place, and setting to work to dust my bedroom. This Mrs Crupp regarded in the light of a liberty, and a liberty, she said, was a thing she never allowed.

Mr Peggotty had made a communication to me on the way to London for which I was not unprepared. It was that he purposed first seeing Mrs Steerforth. As I felt bound to assist him in this, and also to mediate between them, with the view of sparing the mother's feelings as much as possible, I wrote to her that night. I told her as mildly as I could what his wrong was, and what my own share in his injury. I said he was a man in very common life, but of a most gentle and upright character; and that I ventured to express a hope that she would not refuse to see him in his heavy trouble. I mentioned two o'clock in the afternoon as the hour of our coming, and I sent the letter myself by the first coach in the morning.

At the appointed time, we stood at the door – the door of that house where I had been, a few days since, so happy; where my youthful confidence and warmth of heart had been yielded up so freely; which was closed against me henceforth; which was now a waste, a ruin.

No Littimer appeared. The pleasanter face which had replaced his, on the occasion of my last visit, answered to our summons, and went before us to the drawing-room. Mrs Steerforth was sitting there. Rosa Dartle glided, as we went in, from another part of the room, and stood behind her chair.

I saw, directly, in his mother's face, that she knew from himself what he had done. It was very pale, and bore the traces of deeper emotion than my letter alone, weakened by the doubts her fondness would have raised upon it, would have been likely to create. I thought her more like him than ever I had thought her; and I felt, rather than saw, that the resemblance was not lost on my companion.

She sat upright in her armchair, with a stately, immovable, passionless air, that it seemed as if nothing could disturb. She looked very steadfastly at Mr Peggotty when he stood before her; and he looked quite as steadfastly at her. Rosa Dartle's keen glance comprehended all of us. For some moments not a word was spoken. She motioned to Mr Peggotty to be seated. He said, in a low voice, 'I shouldn't feel it nat'ral, ma'am, to sit down in this house. I'd sooner stand.' And this was succeeded by another silence, which she broke thus: 'I know, with deep regret, what has brought you here. What do you want of me? What do you ask me to do?'

He put his hat under his arm, and feeling in his breast for Emily's letter, took it out, unfolded it, and gave it to her. 'Please to read that, ma'am. That's my niece's hand!'

She read it, in the same stately and impressive way – untouched by its contents, as far as I could see – and returned it to him.

' "Unless he brings me back a lady," ' said Mr Peggotty, tracing out that part with his finger. 'I come to know, ma'am, whether he will keep his wured?'

'No,' she returned.

'Why not?' said Mr Peggotty.

'It is impossible. He would disgrace himself. You cannot fail to know that she is far below him.'

'Raise her up!' said Mr Peggotty.

'She is uneducated and ignorant.'

'Maybe she's not; maybe she is,' said Mr Peggotty. '*I* think not, ma'am; but I'm no judge of them things. Teach her better!'

'Since you oblige me to speak more plainly, which I am very unwilling to do, her humble connections would render such a thing impossible, if nothing else did.'

'Hark to this, ma'am,' he returned, slowly and quietly. 'You know what it is to love your child. So do I. If she was a hundred times my child, I couldn't love her more. You doesn't know what it is to lose your child. I do. All the heaps of riches in the wureld would be nowt to me (if they was mine) to buy her back! But save her from this disgrace, and she shall never be disgraced by us. Not one of us that she's growed up among, not one of us that's lived along with her, and had her for their all in all, these many year, will ever look upon her pritty face again. We'll be content to let her be; we'll be content to think of her, far off, as if she was underneath another sun and sky; we'll be content to trust her to her husband – to her little children, p'raps – and bide the time when all of us shall be alike in quality afore our God!'

The rugged eloquence with which he spoke was not devoid of all effect. She still preserved her proud manner, but there was a touch of softness in her voice, as she answered: 'I justify nothing. I make no counter-accusations. But I am sorry to repeat, it is impossible. Such a marriage would irretrievably blight my son's career, and ruin his prospects. Nothing is more certain than that it never can take place, and never will. If there is any other compensation – '

'I am looking at the likeness of the face,' interrupted Mr Peggotty, with a steady but a kindling eye, 'that has looked at me, in my home, at my fireside, in my boat – wheer not? – smiling and friendly when it was so treacherous, that I go half wild when I think of it. If the likeness of that face doesn't turn to burning fire, at the thought of offering money to me for my child's blight and ruin, it's as bad. I doen't know, being a lady's, but what it's worse.'

She changed now, in a moment. An angry flush overspread her features; and she said, in an intolerant manner, grasping the armchair tightly with her hands: 'What compensation can you make to *me* for opening such a pit between me and my son? What is your love to mine? What is your separation to ours?'

Miss Dartle softly touched her, and bent down her head to whisper, but she would not hear a word.

'No, Rosa, not a word! Let the man listen to what I say! My son, who has been the object of my life, to whom its every thought has been devoted, whom I have gratified from a child in every wish, from whom I have had no separate existence, since his birth – to take up in a moment with a miserable girl, and avoid me! To repay my confidence with systematic deception, for her sake, and quit me for her! To set this wretched fancy against his mother's claims upon his duty, love, respect, gratitude – claims that every day and hour of his life should have strengthened into ties that nothing could be proof against! Is this no injury?'

Again Rosa Dartle tried to soothe her; again ineffectually.

'I say, Rosa, not a word! If he can stake his all upon the lightest object, I can stake my all upon a greater purpose. Let him go where he will, with the means that my love has secured to him! Does he think to reduce me by long absence? He knows his mother very little if he does. Let him put away his whim now, and he is welcome back. Let him not put her away now, and he never shall come near me, living or dying, while I can raise my hand to make a sign against it, unless, being rid of her for ever, he comes humbly to me and begs for my forgiveness. This is my right. This is the acknowledgment I *will have*. This is the separation that there is between us! And is this,' she added, looking at her visitor with the proud, intolerant air with which she had begun, 'no injury?'

While I heard and saw the mother as she said these words, I seemed to hear and see the son, defying them. All that I had ever seen in him of an unyielding, wilful spirit, I saw in her. All the understanding that I had now of his misdirected energy became an understanding of her character, too, and a perception that it was, in its strongest springs, the same.

She now observed to me, aloud, resuming her former restraint, that it was useless to hear more, or to say more, and that she begged to put an end to the interview. She rose with an air of dignity to leave the room, when Mr Peggotty signified that it was needless.

'Doen't fear me being any hindrance to you; I have no more to say, ma'am,' he remarked as he moved towards the door. 'I come heer with no hope, and I take away no hope. I have done what I thowt should be done, but I never looked fur any good to come of my stan'ning where I do. This has been too evil a house

Mr Peggotty and Mrs Steerforth

fur me and mine fur me to be in my right senses and expect it.'

With this, we departed; leaving her standing by her elbow-chair, a picture of a noble presence and a handsome face.

We had, on our way out, to cross a paved hall, with glass sides and roof, over which a vine was trained. Its leaves and shoots were green then, and the day being sunny a pair of glass doors leading to the garden were thrown open. Rosa Dartle, entering this way with a noiseless step, when we were close to them, addressed herself to me: 'You do well,' she said, 'indeed, to bring this fellow here!'

Such a concentration of rage and scorn as darkened her face, and flashed in her jet-black eyes, I could not have thought compressible even into that face. The scar made by the hammer was, as usual in this excited state of her features, strongly marked. When the throbbing I had seen before came into it as I looked at her, she absolutely lifted up her hand and struck it.

'This is a fellow,' she said, 'to champion and bring here, is he not? You are a true man!'

'Miss Dartle,' I returned, 'you are surely not so unjust as to condemn *me*!'

'Why do you bring division between these two mad creatures?' she returned. 'Don't you know that they are both mad with their own self-will and pride?'

'Is it my doing?' I returned.

'Is it your doing!' she retorted. 'Why do you bring this man here?'

'He is a deeply injured man, Miss Dartle,' I replied. 'You may not know it.'

'I know that James Steerforth,' she said, with her hand on her bosom, as if to prevent the storm that was raging there, from being loud, 'has a false, corrupt heart, and is a traitor. But what need I know or care about this fellow, and his common niece?'

'Miss Dartle,' I returned, 'you deepen the injury. It is sufficient already. I will only say, at parting, that you do him a great wrong.'

'I do him no wrong,' she returned. 'They are a depraved, worthless set. I would have her whipped!'

Mr Peggotty passed on, without a word, and went out at the door.

'Oh, shame, Miss Dartle! shame!' I said indignantly. 'How can you bear to trample on his undeserved affliction!'

'I would trample on them all,' she answered. 'I would have his house pulled down. I would have her branded on the face, dressed in rags, and cast out in the streets to starve. If I had the power to sit in judgement on her, I would see it done. See it done? I would do it! I detest her. If I ever could reproach her with her infamous condition, I would go anywhere to do so. If I could hunt her to her grave, I would. If there was any word of comfort that would be a solace to her in her dying hour, and only I possessed it, I wouldn't part with it for Life itself.'

The mere vehemence of her words can convey, I am sensible, but a weak impression of the passion by which she was possessed, and which made itself articulate in her whole figure, though her voice, instead of being raised, was lower than usual. No description I could give of her would do justice to my recollection of her, or to her entire deliverance of herself to her anger. I have seen passion in many forms, but I have never seen it in such a form as that.

When I joined Mr Peggotty, he was walking slowly and thoughtfully down the hill. He told me, as soon as I came up with him, that having now discharged his mind of what he had purposed doing in London, he meant 'to set out on his travels,' that night. I asked him where he meant to go. He only answered, 'I'm a going, sir, to seek my niece.'

We went back to the little lodging over the chandler's shop, and there I found an opportunity of repeating to Peggotty what he had said to me. She informed me, in return, that he had said the same to her that morning. She knew no more than I did, where he was going, but she thought he had some project shaped out in his mind.

I did not like to leave him, under such circumstances, and we all three dined together off a beefsteak pie – which was one of the many good things for which Peggotty was famous; and which was curiously flavoured on this occasion, I recollect well, by a miscellaneous taste of tea, coffee, butter, bacon, cheese, new loaves, firewood, candles, and walnut ketchup, continually ascending from the shop. After dinner we sat for an hour or so near the window, without talking much; and then Mr Peggotty got up, and brought his oilskin bag and his stout stick, and laid them on the table.

He accepted, from his sister's stock of ready money, a small sum on account of his legacy; barely enough, I should have thought, to keep him for a month. He promised to communicate with me, when anything befell him; and he slung his bag about him, took his hat and stick, and bade us both 'Goodbye!'

'All good attend you, dear old woman,' he said, embracing Peggotty, 'and you, too, Mas'r Davy!' shaking hands with me. 'I'm a going to seek her, fur and wide. If she should come home while I'm away – but ah, that ain't like to be! – or if I should bring her back, my meaning is that she and me shall live and die where no one can't reproach her. If any hurt should come to me, remember that the last words I left for her was, "My unchanged love is with my darling child, and I forgive her!"'

He said this solemnly, bare-headed; then, putting on his hat, he went down the stairs, and away. We followed to the door. It was a warm, dusty evening, just the time when, in the great main thoroughfare out of which that byway turned, there was a temporary lull in the eternal tread of feet upon the pavement, and a strong, red sunshine. He turned alone, at the corner of our shady street, into a glow of light, in which we lost him.

Rarely did that hour of the evening come, rarely did I wake at night, rarely did I look up at the moon, or stars, or watch the falling rain, or hear the wind, but I thought of his solitary figure toiling on, poor pilgrim, and recalled the words: 'I'm a going to seek her, fur and wide. If any hurt should come to me, remember that the last words I left for her was, "My unchanged love is with my darling child, and I forgive her!"'

CHAPTER 33

Blissful

All this time, I had gone on loving Dora, harder than ever. Her idea was my refuge in disappointment and distress, and made some amends to me, even for the loss of my friend. The more I pitied myself, or pitied others, the more I sought for consolation in the image of Dora. The greater the accumulation of deceit and trouble in the world, the brighter and the purer shone the star of Dora high above the world. I don't think I had any definite idea where Dora came from, or in what degree she was related to a higher order of beings; but I am quite sure I should have scouted the notion of her being simply human, like any other young lady, with indignation and contempt.

If I may so express it, I was steeped in Dora. I was not merely over head and ears in love with her, but I was saturated through and through. Enough love might have been wrung out of me, metaphorically speaking, to drown anybody in; and yet there would have remained enough within me, and all over me, to pervade my entire existence.

The first thing I did, on my own account, when I came back, was to take a night-walk to Norwood, and, like the subject of a venerable riddle of my childhood, to go 'round and round the house, without ever touching the house,' thinking about Dora. I believe the theme of this incomprehensible conundrum was the moon. No matter what it was, I, the moonstruck slave of Dora, perambulated round and round the house and garden for two hours, looking through crevices in the palings, getting my chin by dint of violent exertion above the rusty nails on the top, blowing kisses at the lights in the windows, and romantically calling on the night, at intervals, to shield my Dora – I don't exactly know what from, I suppose from fire. Perhaps from mice, to which she had a great objection.

My love was so much on my mind, and it was so natural to me to confide in Peggotty, when I found her again by my side of an evening with the old set of industrial implements, busily making the tour of my wardrobe, that I imparted to her, in a sufficiently roundabout way, my great secret. Peggotty was strongly interested, but I could not get her into my view of the case at all. She was audaciously prejudiced in my favour, and quite unable to understand why I should have any misgivings, or be low-spirited about it. 'The young lady might think herself well off,' she observed, 'to have such a beau. And as to her Pa,' she said, 'what *did* the gentleman expect, for gracious' sake!'

I observed, however, that Mr Spenlow's Proctorial gown and stiff cravat took Peggotty down a little, and inspired her with a greater reverence for the man who was gradually becoming more and more etherealised in my eyes every day, and about whom a reflected radiance seemed to me to beam when he sat erect in Court among his papers, like a little lighthouse in a sea of stationery. And by the by, it used to be uncommonly strange to me to consider, I remember, as I sat in Court too, how those dim old judges and doctors wouldn't have cared for Dora if they had known her; how they wouldn't have gone out of their senses with rapture, if marriage with Dora had been proposed to them; how Dora might have sung and played upon that glorified guitar, until she led *me* to the verge of madness, yet not have tempted one of those slow-goers an inch out of his road!

I despised them, to a man. Frozen-out old gardeners in the flower-beds of the heart, I took a personal offence against them all. The Bench was nothing to me but an insensible blunderer. The Bar had no more tenderness or poetry in it, than the Bar of a public-house.

Taking the management of Peggotty's affairs into my own hands, with no little pride, I proved the will, and came to a settlement with the Legacy Duty-office, and took her to the Bank, and soon got everything into an orderly train. We varied the legal character of these proceedings by going to see some perspiring Waxwork, in Fleet Street (melted, I should hope, these twenty years); and by visiting Miss Linwood's Exhibition, which I remember as a Mausoleum of needlework, favourable to self-examination and repentance; and by inspecting the Tower of London; and going to the top of St Paul's. All these wonders afforded Peggotty as much pleasure as she was able to enjoy, under existing circumstances, except, I think, St Paul's, which, from her long attachment to her work-box, became a rival of the picture on the lid, and was, in some particulars, vanquished, she considered, by that work of art.

Peggotty's business, which was what we used to call 'common-form business' in the Commons (and very light and lucrative the common-form business was), being settled, I took her down to the office one morning to pay her bill. Mr Spenlow had stepped out, old Tiffey said, to get a gentleman sworn for a marriage licence; but as I knew he would be back directly, our place lying close to the Surrogate's, and to the Vicar-General's office too, I told Peggotty to wait.

We were a little like undertakers, in the Commons, as regarded Probate transactions; generally making it a rule to look more or less cut up, when we had to deal with clients in mourning. In a similar feeling of delicacy, we were always blithe and light-hearted with the licence clients. Therefore I hinted to Peggotty that she would find Mr Spenlow much recovered from the shock of Mr Barkis's decease; and indeed he came in like a bridegroom.

But neither Peggotty nor I had eyes for him, when we saw, in company with him, Mr Murdstone. He was very little changed. His hair looked as thick, and was certainly as black, as ever; and his glance was as little to be trusted as of old.

'Ah, Copperfield,' said Mr Spenlow. 'You know this gentleman, I believe?'

I made my gentleman a distant bow, and Peggotty barely recognised him. He was, at first, somewhat disconcerted to meet us two together; but quickly decided what to do, and came up to me.

'I hope,' he said, 'that you are doing well?'

'It can hardly be interesting to you,' said I. 'Yes, if you wish to know.'

We looked at each other, and he addressed himself to Peggotty.

'And you,' said he. 'I am sorry to observe that you have lost your husband.'

'It's not the first loss I have had in my life, Mr Murdstone,' replied Peggotty, trembling from head to foot. 'I am glad to hope that there is nobody to blame for this one – nobody to answer for it.'

'Ha!' said he, 'that's a comfortable reflection. You have done your duty?'

'I have not worn anybody's life away,' said Peggotty, 'I am thankful to think! No, Mr Murdstone, I have not worrited and frightened any sweet creetur to an early grave!'

He eyed her gloomily – remorsefully I thought – for an instant; and said, turning his head towards me, but looking at my feet instead of my face: 'We are not likely to encounter soon again; a source of satisfaction to us both, no doubt, for such meetings as this can never be agreeable. I do not expect that you, who always rebelled against my just authority, exerted for your benefit and reformation, should owe me any goodwill now. There is an antipathy between us – '

'An old one, I believe?' said I, interrupting him.

He smiled, and shot as evil a glance at me as could come from his dark eyes.

'It rankled in your baby breast,' he said. 'It embittered the life of your poor mother. You are right. I hope you may do better yet; I hope you may correct yourself.'

Here he ended the dialogue, which had been carried on in a low voice, in a corner of the outer office, by passing into Mr Spenlow's room, and saying aloud, in his smoothest manner: 'Gentlemen of Mr Spenlow's profession are accustomed to family differences, and know how complicated and difficult they always are!' With that, he paid the money for his licence; and, receiving it neatly folded from Mr Spenlow, together with a shake of the hand, and a polite wish for his happiness and the lady's, went out of the office.

I might have had more difficulty in constraining myself to be silent under his words, if I had had less difficulty in impressing upon Peggotty (who was only angry on my account, good creature!) that we were not in a place for recrimination, and that I besought her to hold her peace. She was so unusually roused, that I was glad to compound for an affectionate hug, elicited by this revival in her mind of our old injuries, and to make the best I could of it, before Mr Spenlow and the clerks.

Mr Spenlow did not appear to know what the connection between Mr Murdstone and myself was; which I was glad of, for I could not bear to acknowledge him, even in my own breast, remembering what I did of the history of my poor mother. Mr Spenlow seemed to think, if he thought anything about the matter, that my aunt was the leader of the state party in our family, and that there was a rebel party commanded by somebody else – so I gathered at least from what he said, while we were waiting for Mr Tiffey to make out Peggotty's bill of costs.

'Miss Trotwood,' he remarked, 'is very firm, no doubt, and not likely to give way to opposition. I have an admiration for her character, and I may congratulate you, Copperfield, on being on the right side. Differences between relations are much

to be deplored – but they are extremely general – and the great thing is, to be on the right side,' meaning, I take it, on the side of the moneyed interest.

'Rather a good marriage this, I believe?' said Mr Spenlow.

I explained that I knew nothing about it.

'Indeed!' he said. 'Speaking from the few words Mr Murdstone dropped – as a man frequently does on these occasions – and from what Miss Murdstone let fall, I should say it was rather a good marriage.'

'Do you mean that there is money, sir?' I asked.

'Yes,' said Mr Spenlow; 'I understand there's money. Beauty too, I am told.'

'Indeed? Is his new wife young?'

'Just of age,' said Mr Spenlow. 'So lately, that I should think they had been waiting for that.'

'Lord deliver her!' said Peggotty. So very emphatically and unexpectedly, that we were all three discomposed, until Tiffey came in with the bill.

Old Tiffey soon appeared, however, and handed it to Mr Spenlow, to look over. Mr Spenlow, settling his chin in his cravat and rubbing it softly, went over the items with a deprecatory air – as if it were all Jorkins's doing – and handed it back to Tiffey with a bland sigh.

'Yes,' he said. 'That's right. Quite right. I should have been extremely happy, Copperfield, to have limited these charges to the actual expenditure out of pocket, but it is an irksome incident in my professional life that I am not at liberty to consult my own wishes. I have a partner – Mr Jorkins.'

As he said this with a gentle melancholy, which was the next thing to making no charge at all, I expressed my acknowledgments on Peggotty's behalf, and paid Tiffey in bank-notes. Peggotty then retired to her lodging, and Mr Spenlow and I went into Court, where we had a divorce-suit coming on, under an ingenious little statute (repealed now, I believe, but in virtue of which I have seen several marriages annulled), of which the merits were these. The husband, whose name was Thomas Benjamin, had taken out his marriage licence as Thomas only; suppressing the Benjamin, in case he should not find himself as comfortable as he expected. *Not* finding himself as comfortable as he expected, or being a little fatigued with his wife, poor fellow, he now came forward, by a friend, after being married a year or two, and declared that his name was Thomas Benjamin, and therefore he was not married at all. Which the Court confirmed, to his great satisfaction.

I must say that I had my doubts about the strict justice of this, and was not even frightened out of them by the bushel of wheat which reconciles all anomalies.

But Mr Spenlow argued the matter with me. He said, Look at the world, there was good and evil in that; look at the ecclesiastical law, there was good and evil in *that*. It was all part of a system. Very good. There you were!

I had not the hardihood to suggest to Dora's father that possibly we might even improve the world a little, if we got up early in the morning, and took off our coats to the work; but I confessed that I thought we might improve the Commons. Mr Spenlow replied that he would particularly advise me to dismiss that idea from my mind, as not being worthy of my gentlemanly character; but that he would be glad to hear from me of what improvement I thought the Commons susceptible?

Taking that part of the Commons which happened to be nearest to us – for our man was unmarried by this time, and we were out of Court, and strolling past the Prerogative Office – I submitted that I thought the Prerogative Office rather a queerly managed institution. Mr Spenlow enquired in what respect? I replied, with all due deference to his experience (but with more deference, I am afraid, to his being Dora's father), that perhaps it was a little nonsensical that the Registry of that Court, containing the original wills of all persons leaving effects within the immense province of Canterbury, for three whole centuries, should be an accidental building, never designed for the purpose, leased by the registrars for their own private emolument, unsafe, not even ascertained to be fireproof, choked with the important documents it held, and positively, from the roof to the basement, a mercenary speculation of the registrars, who took great fees from the public, and crammed the public's wills away anyhow and anywhere, having no other object than to get rid of them cheaply. That, perhaps, it was a little unreasonable that these registrars, in the receipt of profits amounting to eight or nine thousand pounds a year (to say nothing of the profits of the deputy registrars, and clerks of seats), should not be obliged to spend a little of that money, in finding a reasonably safe place for the important documents which all classes of people were compelled to hand over to them, whether they would or no. That, perhaps, it was a little unjust that all the great offices in this great office should be magnificent sinecures, while the unfortunate working-clerks in the cold dark room upstairs were the worst rewarded, and the least considered men, doing important services, in London. That perhaps it was a little indecent that the principal registrar of all, whose duty it was to find the public, constantly resorting to this place, all needful accommodation, should be an enormous sinecurist in virtue of that post (and might be, besides, a clergyman, a pluralist, the holder of a stall in a cathedral, and what not), while the public was put to the inconvenience of which we had a specimen every afternoon when the office was busy, and which we knew to be quite monstrous. That, perhaps, in short, this Prerogative Office of the diocese of Canterbury was altogether such a pestilent job, and such a pernicious absurdity, that but for its being squeezed away, in a corner of St Paul's Churchyard, which few people knew, it must have been turned completely inside out, and upside down, long ago.

Mr Spenlow smiled as I became modestly warm on the subject, and then argued this question with me as he had argued the other. He said, what was it after all? It was a question of feeling. If the public felt that their wills were in safekeeping, and took it for granted that the office was not to be made better, who was the worse for it? Nobody. Who was the better for it? All the sinecurists. Very well. Then the good predominated. It might not be a perfect system; nothing *was* perfect; but what he objected to, was, the insertion of the wedge. Under the Prerogative Office, the country had been glorious. Insert the wedge into the Prerogative Office, and the country would cease to be glorious. He considered it the principle of a gentleman to take things as he found them; and he had no doubt the Prerogative Office would last our time. I deferred to his opinion, though I had great doubts of it myself. I find he was right, however; for it has not only lasted to the present moment, but has done so in the teeth of a great parliamentary report made (not too willingly) eighteen years ago, when all these objections of mine were set forth in detail, and when the existing stowage for wills was described as equal to the accumulation of only two years and a half more. What they have done with them since, whether they have lost many, or whether they sell any, now and then, to the butter shops, I don't know. I am glad mine is not there, and I hope it may not go there, yet awhile.

I have set all this down, in my present blissful chapter, because here it comes into its natural place. Mr Spenlow and I falling into this conversation, prolonged it and our saunter to and fro, until we diverged into general topics. And so it came about, in the end, that Mr Spenlow told me this day week was Dora's birthday, and he would be glad if I would come down and join a little picnic on the occasion. I went out of my senses immediately; became a mere driveller next day, on receipt of a little lace-edged sheet of notepaper, 'Favoured by papa. To remind'; and passed the intervening period in a state of dotage.

I think I committed every possible absurdity, in the way of preparation for this blessed event. I turn hot when I remember the cravat I bought. My boots might be placed in any collection of instruments of torture. I provided, and sent down by the Norwood coach the night before, a delicate little hamper, amounting in itself, I thought, almost to a declaration. There were crackers in it with the tenderest mottoes that could be got for money. At six in the morning I was in Covent Garden Market, buying a bouquet for Dora. At ten I was on horseback (I hired a gallant grey for the occasion), with the bouquet in my hat, to keep it fresh, trotting down to Norwood.

I suppose that when I saw Dora in the garden and pretended not to see her, and rode past the house pretending to be anxiously looking for it, I committed two small fooleries which other young gentlemen in my circumstances might have committed – because they came so very natural to me. But oh! when I *did* find the house, and *did* dismount at the garden gate, and drag those stony-hearted boots across the lawn to Dora sitting on a garden seat under a lilac tree, what a spectacle she was, upon that beautiful morning, among the butterflies, in a white chip bonnet and a dress of celestial blue!

There was a young lady with her – comparatively stricken in years – almost twenty, I should say. Her name was Miss Mills, and Dora called her Julia. She was the bosom friend of Dora. Happy Miss Mills!

Jip was there, and Jip *would* bark at me again. When I presented my bouquet, he gnashed his teeth with jealousy. Well he might. If he had the least idea how I adored his mistress, well he might!

'Oh, thank you, Mr Copperfield! What dear flowers!' said Dora.

I had had an intention of saying (and had been studying the best form of words for three miles) that I thought them beautiful before I saw them so near *her*. But I couldn't manage it. She was too bewildering. To see her lay the flowers against her little dimpled chin, was to lose all presence of mind and power of language in feeble ecstasy. I wonder I didn't say, 'Kill me, if you have a heart, Miss Mills. Let me die here!'

Then Dora held my flowers to Jip to smell. Then Jip growled, and wouldn't smell them. Then Dora laughed, and held them a little closer to Jip, to make him. Then Jip laid hold of a bit of geranium with his teeth, and worried imaginary cats in it. Then Dora beat him, and pouted, and said, 'My poor beautiful flowers!' as compassionately, I thought, as if Jip had laid hold of me. I wished he had!

'You'll be so glad to hear, Mr Copperfield,' said Dora, 'that that cross Miss Murdstone is not here. She has gone to her brother's marriage, and will be away at least three weeks. Isn't that delightful?'

I said I was sure it must be delightful to her, and all that was delightful to her was delightful to me. Miss Mills, with an air of superior wisdom and benevolence, smiled upon us.

'She is the most disagreeable thing I ever saw,' said Dora. 'You can't believe how ill-tempered and shocking she is, Julia.'

'Yes, I can, my dear!' said Julia.

'*You* can, perhaps, love,' returned Dora, with her hand on Julia's. 'Forgive my not excepting you, my dear, at first.'

I learnt, from this, that Miss Mills had had her trials in the course of a chequered existence; and that to these, perhaps, I might refer that wise benignity of manner which I had already noticed. I found, in the course of the day, that this was the case: Miss Mills having been unhappy in a misplaced affection, and being understood to have retired from the world on her awful stock of experience, but still to take a calm interest in the unblighted hopes and loves of youth.

But now Mr Spenlow came out of the house, and Dora went to him, saying, 'Look, papa, what beautiful flowers!' And Miss Mills smiled thoughtfully, as who should say, 'Ye Mayflies enjoy your brief existence in the bright morning of life!' And we all walked from the lawn towards the carriage, which was getting ready.

I shall never have such a ride again. I have never had such another. There were only those three, their hamper, my hamper, and the guitar-case, in the phaeton; and, of course, the phaeton was open; and I rode behind it, and Dora sat with her back to the horses, looking towards me. She kept the bouquet close to her on the cushion, and wouldn't allow Jip to sit on that side of her at all, for fear he should crush it. She often carried it in her hand, often refreshed herself with its fragrance. Our eyes at those times often met; and my great astonishment is that I didn't go over the head of my gallant grey into the carriage.

There was dust, I believe. There was a good deal of dust, I believe. I have a faint impression that Mr Spenlow remonstrated with me for riding in it; but I knew of none. I was sensible of a mist of love and beauty about Dora, but of nothing else. He stood up sometimes, and asked me what I thought of the prospect. I said it was delightful, and I dare say it was; but it was all Dora to me. The sun shone Dora, and the birds sang Dora. The south wind blew Dora, and the wild flowers in the hedges were all Doras, to a bud. My comfort is, Miss Mills understood me. Miss Mills alone could enter into my feelings thoroughly.

I don't know how long we were going, and to this hour I know as little where we went. Perhaps it was near Guildford. Perhaps some Arabian-night magician opened up the place for the day, and shut it up for ever when we came away. It was a green spot, on a hill, carpeted with soft turf. There were shady trees, and heather, and, as far as the eye could see, a rich landscape.

It was a trying thing to find people here, waiting for us; and my jealousy, even of the ladies, knew no bounds. But all of my own sex – especially one impostor, three or four years my elder, with a red whisker, on which he established an amount of presumption not to be endured – were my mortal foes.

We all unpacked our baskets, and employed ourselves in getting dinner ready. Red Whisker pretended he could make a salad (which I don't believe), and obtruded himself on public notice. Some of the young ladies washed the lettuces for him, and sliced them under his directions. Dora was among these. I felt that fate had pitted me against this man, and one of us must fall.

Red Whisker made his salad (I wondered how they could eat it. Nothing should have induced *me* to touch it!) and voted himself into the charge of the wine-cellar, which he constructed, being an ingenious beast, in the hollow trunk of a tree. By and by I saw him, with the majority of a lobster on his plate, eating his dinner at the feet of Dora!

I have but an indistinct idea of what happened for some time after this baleful object presented itself to my view. I was very merry, I know; but it was hollow merriment. I attached myself to a young creature in pink, with little eyes, and flirted with her desperately. She received my attentions with favour; but whether on my account solely, or because she had any designs on Red Whisker, I can't say. Dora's health was drunk. When I drank it, I affected to interrupt my conversation for that purpose, and to resume it immediately afterwards. I caught Dora's eye as I bowed to her, and I thought it looked appealing. But it looked at me over the head of Red Whisker, and I was adamant.

The young creature in pink had a mother in green; and I rather think the latter separated us from motives of policy. Howbeit, there was a general breaking up of the party, while the remnants of the dinner were being put away; and I strolled off by myself among the trees, in a raging and remorseful state. I was debating whether I should pretend that I was not well, and fly – I don't know where – upon my gallant grey, when Dora and Miss Mills met me.

'Mr Copperfield,' said Miss Mills, 'you are dull.'

I begged her pardon. Not at all.

'And Dora,' said Miss Mills, '*you* are dull.'

Oh, dear no! Not in the least.

'Mr Copperfield and Dora,' said Miss Mills, with an almost venerable air. 'Enough of this. Do not allow a trivial misunderstanding to wither the blossoms of spring, which, once put forth and blighted, cannot be renewed. I speak,' said Miss Mills, 'from experience of the past – the remote irrevocable past. The gushing fountains which sparkle in the sun must not be stopped in mere caprice; the oasis in the desert of Sahara must not be plucked up idly.'

I hardly knew what I did, I was burning all over to that extraordinary extent; but I took Dora's little hand and kissed it – and she let me! I kissed Miss Mills's hand; and we all seemed, to my thinking, to go straight up to the seventh heaven.

We did not come down again. We stayed up there all the evening. At first we strayed to and fro among the trees – I with Dora's shy arm drawn through mine – and Heaven knows, folly as it all was, it would have been a happy fate to have been struck immortal with those foolish feelings, and have strayed among the trees for ever!

But, much too soon, we heard the others laughing and talking, and calling 'Where's Dora!' So we went back, and they wanted Dora to sing. Red Whisker would have got the guitar-case out of the carriage, but Dora told him nobody knew where it was but I. So Red Whisker was done for in a moment; and *I* got it, and *I* unlocked it, and *I* took the guitar out, and *I* sat by her, and *I* held her handkerchief and gloves, and *I* drank in every note of her dear voice, and she sang to *me* who loved her, and all the others might applaud as much as they liked, but they had nothing to do with it!

I was intoxicated with joy. I was afraid it was too happy to be real, and that I should wake in Buckingham Street presently, and hear Mrs Crupp clinking the teacups in getting breakfast ready. But Dora sang, and others sang, and Miss Mills sang – about the slumbering echoes in the caverns of Memory; as if she were a hundred years old – and the evening came on; and we had tea, with the kettle boiling gypsy-fashion; and I was still as happy as ever.

I was happier than ever when the party broke up, and the other people, defeated Red Whisker and all, went their several ways, and we went ours through the still evening and the dying light, with sweet scents rising up around us. Mr Spenlow being a little drowsy after the champagne – honour to the soil that grew the grape, to the grape that made the wine, to the sun that ripened it, and to the merchant who adulterated it! – and being fast asleep in a corner of the carriage, I rode by the side and talked to Dora. She admired my horse and patted him – oh, what a dear little hand it looked upon a horse! – and her shawl would not keep right, and now and then I drew it round her with my arm; and I even fancied that Jip began to see how it was, and to understand that he must make up his mind to be friends with me.

That sagacious Miss Mills, too; that amiable, though quite used-up, recluse; that little patriarch of something less than twenty, who had done with the world, and mustn't on any account have the slumbering echoes in the caverns of Memory awakened – what a kind thing *she* did!

'Mr Copperfield,' said Miss Mills, 'come to this side of the carriage a moment – if you can spare a moment. I want to speak to you.'

Behold me, on my gallant grey, bending at the side of Miss Mills, with my hand upon the carriage door!

'Dora is coming to stay with me. She is coming home with me the day after tomorrow. If you would like to call, I am sure papa would be happy to see you.'

What could I do but invoke a silent blessing on Miss Mills's head, and store Miss Mills's address in the securest corner of my memory! What could I do but tell Miss Mills, with grateful looks and fervent words, how much I appreciated her good offices, and what an inestimable value I set upon her friendship!

Then Miss Mills benignantly dismissed me, saying, 'Go back to Dora!' and I went; and Dora leaned out of the carriage to talk to me, and we talked all the rest of the way, and I rode my gallant grey so close to the wheel that I grazed his near foreleg against it, and 'took the bark off,' as his owner told me, 'to the tune of three pun' sivin' – which I paid, and thought extremely cheap for so much joy. What time Miss Mills sat looking at the moon, murmuring verses and recalling, I suppose, the ancient days when she and earth had anything in common.

Norwood was many miles too near, and we reached it many hours too soon; but Mr Spenlow came to himself a little short of it, and said, 'You must come in, Copperfield, and rest!' and I consenting, we had sandwiches and wine and water. In the light room, Dora blushing looked so lovely that I could not tear myself away, but sat there staring, in a dream, until the snoring of Mr Spenlow inspired me with sufficient consciousness to take my leave. So we parted; I riding all the way to London with the farewell touch of Dora's hand still light on mine, recalling every incident and word ten thousand times; lying down in my own bed at last, as enraptured a young noodle as ever was carried out of his five wits by love.

When I awoke next morning, I was resolute to declare my passion to Dora, and know my fate. Happiness or misery was now the question. There was no other question that I knew of in the world, and only Dora could give the answer to it. I passed three days in a luxury of wretchedness, torturing myself by putting every conceivable variety of discouraging construction on all that ever had taken place between Dora and me. At last, arrayed for the purpose at a vast expense, I went to Miss Mills's, fraught with a declaration.

How many times I went up and down the street, and round the square – painfully aware of being a much better answer to the old riddle than the original one – before I could persuade myself to go up the steps and knock, is no matter now. Even when, at last, I had knocked, and was waiting at the door, I had some flurried thoughts of asking if that were Mr Blackboy's (in imitation of poor Barkis), begging pardon, and retreating. But I kept my ground.

Mr Mills was not at home. I did not expect he would be. Nobody wanted *him*. Miss Mills was at home. Miss Mills would do.

I was shown into a room upstairs, where Miss Mills and Dora were. Jip was there. Miss Mills was copying music (I recollect, it was a new song, called 'Affection's Dirge'), and Dora was painting flowers. What were my feelings, when I recognised my own flowers; the identical Covent Garden Market purchase! I cannot say that they were very like, or that they particularly resembled any flowers that have ever come under my observation; but I knew from the paper round them, which was accurately copied, what the composition was.

Miss Mills was very glad to see me, and very sorry her papa was not at home; though I thought we all bore that with fortitude. Miss Mills was conversational for a few minutes, and then, laying down her pen upon 'Affection's Dirge', got up, and left the room.

I began to think I would put it off till tomorrow.

'I hope your poor horse was not tired, when he got home at night,' said Dora, lifting up her beautiful eyes. 'It was a long way for him.'

I began to think I would do it today.

'It was a long way for *him*,' said I, 'for *he* had nothing to uphold him on the journey.'

'Wasn't he fed, poor thing?' asked Dora.

I began to think I would put it off till tomorrow.

'Ye–yes,' I said, 'he was well taken care of. I mean he had not the unutterable happiness that I had in being so near you.'

Dora bent her head over her drawing, and said, after a little while – I had sat, in the interval, in a burning fever, and with my legs in a very rigid state – 'You didn't seem to be sensible of that happiness yourself, at one time of the day.'

I saw now that I was in for it, and it must be done on the spot.

'You didn't care for that happiness in the least,' said Dora, slightly raising her eyebrows, and shaking her head, 'when you were sitting by Miss Kitt.'

Kitt, I should observe, was the name of the creature in pink, with the little eyes.

'Though certainly I don't know why you should,' said Dora, 'or why you should call it a happiness at all. But of course you don't mean what you say. And I am sure no one doubts your being at liberty to do whatever you like. Jip, you naughty boy, come here!'

I don't know how I did it. I did it in a moment. I intercepted Jip. I had Dora in my arms. I was full of eloquence. I never stopped for a word. I told her how I loved her. I told her I should die without her. I told her that I idolised and worshipped her. Jip barked madly all the time.

When Dora hung her head and cried, and trembled, my eloquence increased so much the more. If she would like me to die for her, she had but to say the word, and I was ready. Life without Dora's love was not a thing to have on any terms. I couldn't bear it, and I wouldn't. I had loved her every minute, day and night, since I first saw her. I loved her at that minute to distraction. I should always love her, every minute, to distraction. Lovers had loved before, and lovers would love again; but no lover had ever loved, might, could, would, or should ever love, as I loved Dora. The more I raved, the more Jip barked. Each of us, in his own way, got more mad every moment.

Well, well! Dora and I were sitting on the sofa by and by, quiet enough, and Jip was lying in her lap, winking peacefully at me. It was off my mind. I was in a state of perfect rapture. Dora and I were engaged.

I suppose we had some notion that this was to end in marriage. We must have had some, because Dora stipulated that we were never to be married without her papa's consent. But in our youthful ecstasy, I don't think that we really looked before us or behind us; or had any aspiration beyond the ignorant present. We were to keep our secret from Mr Spenlow; but I am sure the idea never entered my head then that there was anything dishonourable in that.

Miss Mills was more than usually pensive when Dora, going to find her, brought her back – I apprehend, because there was a tendency in what had passed to awaken the slumbering echoes in the caverns of memory. But she gave us her blessing, and the assurance of her lasting friendship, and spoke to us, generally, as became a Voice from the Cloister.

What an idle time it was! What an unsubstantial, happy, foolish time it was!

When I measured Dora's finger for a ring that was to be made of forget-me-nots, and when the jeweller, to whom I took the measure, found me out, and laughed over his order-book, and charged me anything he liked for the pretty little toy, with its blue stones – so associated in my remembrance with Dora's hand, that yesterday, when I saw such another, by chance, on the finger of my own daughter, there was a momentary stirring in my heart, like pain!

When I walked about, exalted with my secret, and full of my own interest, and felt the dignity of loving Dora, and of being beloved, so much, that if I had walked the air, I could not have been more above the people not so situated, who were creeping on the earth!

When we had those meetings in the garden of the square, and sat within the dingy summer-house, so happy that I love the London sparrows to this hour for nothing else, and see the plumage of the tropics in their smoky feathers!

When we had our first great quarrel (within a week of our betrothal), and when Dora sent me back the ring, enclosed in a despairing, cocked-hat note, wherein she used the terrible expression that 'our love had begun in folly, and ended in madness!' which dreadful words occasioned me to tear my hair, and cry that all was over!

When, under cover of the night, I flew to Miss Mills, whom I saw by stealth in a back kitchen where there was a mangle, and implored Miss Mills to interpose between us and avert insanity. When Miss Mills undertook the office and returned with Dora, exhorting us, from the pulpit of her own bitter youth, to mutual concession, and the avoidance of the Desert of Sahara!

When we cried, and made it up, and were so blessed again, that the back kitchen, mangle and all, changed to Love's own temple, where we arranged a plan of correspondence through Miss Mills, always to comprehend at least one letter on each side every day!

What an idle time! What an unsubstantial, happy, foolish time! Of all the times of mine that Time has in his grip, there is none that in one retrospection I can smile at half so much, and think of half so tenderly.

CHAPTER 34

My Aunt Astonishes Me

I wrote to Agnes as soon as Dora and I were engaged. I wrote her a long letter, in which I tried to make her comprehend how blessed I was, and what a darling Dora was. I entreated Agnes not to regard this as a thoughtless passion which could ever yield to any other, or had the least resemblance to the boyish fancies that we used to joke about. I assured her that its profundity was quite unfathomable, and expressed my belief that nothing like it had ever been known.

Somehow, as I wrote to Agnes on a fine evening by my open window, and the remembrance of her clear calm eyes and gentle face came stealing over me, it shed such a peaceful influence upon the hurry and agitation in which I had been living lately, and of which my very happiness partook in some degree, that it soothed me into tears. I remember that I sat resting my head upon my hand, when the letter was half done, cherishing a general fancy as if Agnes were one of the elements of my natural home. As if, in the retirement of the house made almost sacred to me by her presence, Dora and I must be happier than anywhere. As if, in love, joy, sorrow, hope, or disappointment; in all emotions; my heart turned naturally there, and found its refuge and best friend.

Of Steerforth, I said nothing. I only told her there had been sad grief at Yarmouth, on account of Emily's flight; and that on me it made a double wound, by reason of the circumstances attending it. I knew how quick she always was to divine the truth, and that she would never be the first to breathe his name.

To this letter, I received an answer by return of post. As I read it, I seemed to hear Agnes speaking to me. It was like her cordial voice in my ears. What can I say more!

While I had been away from home lately, Traddles had called twice or thrice. Finding Peggotty within, and being informed by Peggotty (who always volunteered that information to whomsoever would receive it) that she was my old nurse, he had established a good-humoured acquaintance with her, and had stayed to have a little chat with her about me. So Peggotty said; but I am afraid the chat was all on her own side, and of immoderate length, as she was very difficult indeed to stop, God bless her! when she had me for her theme.

This reminds me, not only that I expected Traddles on a certain afternoon of his own appointing, which was now come, but that Mrs Crupp had resigned everything appertaining to her office (the salary excepted) until Peggotty should cease to present herself. Mrs Crupp, after holding divers conversations respecting Peggotty, in a very high-pitched voice, on the staircase – with some invisible Familiar it would appear, for corporeally speaking she was quite alone at those times – addressed a letter to me, developing her views. Beginning it with that statement of universal application, which fitted every occurrence of her life, namely, that she was a mother herself, she went on to inform me that she had once seen very different days, but that at all periods of her existence she had had a constitutional objection to spies, intruders, and informers. She named no names, she said; let them the cap fitted, wear it; but spies, intruders, and informers, especially in widders' weeds (this clause was underlined), she had ever accustomed herself to look down upon. If a gentleman was the victim of spies, intruders, and informers (but still naming no names), that was his own pleasure. He had a right to please himself; so let him do. All that she, Mrs Crupp, stipulated for, was, that she should not be 'brought in contract' with such persons. Therefore she begged to be excused from any further attendance on the top set, until things were as they formerly was, and as they could be wished to be; and further mentioned that her little book would be found upon the breakfast-table every Saturday morning, when she requested an immediate settlement of the same, with the benevolent view of saving trouble, 'and an ill-conwenience' to all parties.

After this, Mrs Crupp confined herself to making pitfalls on the stairs, principally with pitchers, and endeavouring to delude Peggotty into breaking her legs. I found it rather harassing to live in this state of siege, but was too much afraid of Mrs Crupp to see any way out of it.

'My dear Copperfield,' cried Traddles, punctually appearing at my door, in spite of all these obstacles, 'how do you do?'

'My dear Traddles,' said I, 'I am delighted to see you at last, and very sorry I have not been at home before. But I have been so much engaged – '

'Yes, yes, I know,' said Traddles, 'of course. Yours lives in London, I think.'

'What did you say?'

'She – excuse me – Miss D., you know,' said Traddles, colouring in his great delicacy, 'lives in London, I believe?'

'Oh, yes; near London.'

'Mine, perhaps you recollect,' said Traddles, with a serious look, 'lives down in Devonshire – one of ten. Consequently I am not so much engaged as you – in that sense.'

'I wonder you can bear,' I returned, 'to see her so seldom.'

'Ha!' said Traddles thoughtfully. 'It does seem a wonder. I suppose it is, Copperfield, because there's no help for it?'

'I suppose so,' I replied with a smile, and not without a blush. 'And because you have so much constancy and patience, Traddles.'

'Dear me,' said Traddles, considering about it, 'do I strike you in that way, Copperfield? Really I didn't know that I had. But she is such an extraordinarily dear girl herself that it's possible she may have imparted something of those virtues to me. Now you mention it, Copperfield, I shouldn't wonder at all. I assure you she is always forgetting herself, and taking care of the other nine.'

'Is she the eldest?' I enquired.

'Oh dear, no,' said Traddles. 'The eldest is a Beauty.'

He saw, I suppose, that I could not help smiling at the simplicity of this reply; and added, with a smile upon his own ingenuous face: 'Not, of course, but that my Sophy – pretty name, Copperfield, I always think?'

'Very pretty!' said I.

'Not, of course, but that Sophy is beautiful too in my eyes, and would be one of the dearest girls that ever was, in anybody's eyes (I should think). But when I say the eldest is a Beauty, I mean she really is a – ' he seemed to be describing clouds about himself, with both hands: 'splendid, you know,' said Traddles energetically.

'Indeed!' said I.

'Oh, I assure you,' said Traddles, 'something very uncommon, indeed! Then, you know, being formed for society and admiration, and not being able to enjoy much of it in consequence of their limited means, she naturally gets a little irritable and exacting sometimes. Sophy puts her in good humour!'

'Is Sophy the youngest?' I hazarded.

'Oh dear, no!' said Traddles, stroking his chin. 'The two youngest are only nine and ten. Sophy educates 'em.'

'The second daughter, perhaps?' I hazarded.

'No,' said Traddles. 'Sarah's the second. Sarah has something the matter with her spine, poor girl. The malady will wear out by and by, the doctors say, but in the mean time she has to lie down for a twelvemonth. Sophy nurses her. Sophy's the fourth.'

'Is the mother living?' I enquired.

'Oh yes,' said Traddles, 'she is alive. She is a very superior woman, indeed, but the damp country is not adapted to her constitution, and – in fact, she has lost the use of her limbs.'

'Dear me!' said I.

'Very sad, is it not?' returned Traddles. 'But in a merely domestic view it is not so bad as it might be, because Sophy takes her place. She is quite as much a mother *to* her mother, as she is to the other nine.'

I felt the greatest admiration for the virtues of this young lady; and honestly, with the view of doing my best to prevent the good-nature of Traddles from being imposed upon, to the detriment of their joint prospects in life, enquired how Mr Micawber was.

'He is quite well, Copperfield, thank you,' said Traddles. 'I am not living with him at present.'

'No?'

'No. You see the truth is,' said Traddles, in a whisper, 'he has changed his name to Mortimer, in consequence of his temporary embarrassments; and he don't come out till after dark – and then in spectacles. There was an execution put into our house for rent. Mrs Micawber was in such a dreadful state that I really couldn't resist giving my name to that second bill we spoke of here. You may imagine how delightful it was to my feelings, Copperfield, to see the matter settled with it, and Mrs Micawber recover her spirits.'

'Hum!' said I.

'Not that her happiness was of long duration,' pursued Traddles, 'for, unfortunately, within a week another execution came in. It broke up the establishment. I have been living in a furnished apartment since then, and the Mortimers have been very private, indeed. I hope you won't think it selfish, Copperfield, if I mention that the broker carried off my little round table with the marble top, and Sophy's flowerpot and stand?'

'What a hard thing!' I exclaimed indignantly.

'It was a – it was a pull,' said Traddles, with his usual wince at that expression. 'I don't mention it reproachfully, however, but with a motive. The fact is, Copperfield, I was unable to repurchase them at the time of their seizure; in the first place, because the broker, having an idea that I wanted them, ran the price up to an extravagant extent; and, in the second place, because I – hadn't any money. Now, I have kept my eye since upon the broker's shop,' said Traddles, with a great enjoyment of his mystery, 'which is up at the top of Tottenham Court Road, and, at last, today I find them put out for sale. I have only noticed them from over the way, because if the broker saw *me*, bless you, he'd ask any price for them! What has occurred to me, having now the money, is, that perhaps you wouldn't object to ask that good nurse of yours to come with me to the shop – I can show it her from round the corner of the next street – and make the best bargain for them, as if they were for herself, that she can!'

The delight with which Traddles propounded this plan to me, and the sense he had of its uncommon artfulness, are among the freshest things in my remembrance.

I told him that my old nurse would be delighted to assist him, and that we would all three take the field together, but on one condition. That condition was that he should make a solemn resolution to grant no more loans of his name, or anything else, to Mr Micawber.

'My dear Copperfield,' said Traddles, 'I have already done so, because I begin to feel that I have not only been inconsiderate, but that I have been positively unjust to Sophy. My word being passed to myself, there is no longer any apprehension; but I pledge it to you, too, with the greatest readiness. That first unlucky obligation, I have paid. I have no doubt Mr Micawber would have paid it if he could, but he could not. One thing I ought to mention, which I like very much in Mr Micawber, Copperfield. It refers to the second obligation, which is not yet due. He don't tell me that it *is* provided for, but he says it *will be*. Now, I think there is something very fair and honest about that!'

I was unwilling to damp my good friend's confidence, and therefore assented. After a little further conversation, we went round to the chandler's shop to enlist Peggotty; Traddles declining to pass the evening with me, both because he endured the liveliest apprehensions that his property would be bought by somebody else before he could repurchase it, and because it was the evening he always devoted to writing to the dearest girl in the world.

I never shall forget him peeping round the corner of the street in Tottenham Court Road, while Peggotty was bargaining for the precious articles; or his agitation when she came slowly towards us after vainly offering a price, and was hailed by the relenting broker, and went back again. The end of the negotiation was that she bought the property on tolerably easy terms, and Traddles was transported with pleasure.

'I am very much obliged to you, indeed,' said Traddles, on hearing it was to be sent to where he lived, that night. 'If I might ask one other favour, I hope you would not think it absurd, Copperfield?'

I said beforehand, certainly not.

'Then if you *would* be good enough,' said Traddles to Peggotty, 'to get the flowerpot now, I think I should like (it being Sophy's, Copperfield) to carry it home myself!'

Peggotty was glad to get it for him, and he overwhelmed her with thanks, and went his way up Tottenham Court Road, carrying the flowerpot affectionately in his arms, with one of the most delighted expressions of countenance I ever saw.

We then turned back towards my chambers. As the shops had charms for Peggotty which I never knew them possess in the same degree for anybody else, I sauntered easily along, amused by her staring in at the windows, and waiting for her as often as she chose. We were thus a good while in getting to the Adelphi.

On our way upstairs, I called her attention to the sudden disappearance of Mrs Crupp's pitfalls, and also to the prints of recent footsteps. We were both very much surprised, coming higher up, to find my outer door standing open (which I had shut), and to hear voices inside.

We looked at one another, without knowing what to make of this, and went into the sitting-room. What was my amazement to find, of all people upon earth, my aunt there, and Mr Dick! My aunt sitting on a quantity of luggage, with her two birds before her, and her cat on her knee, like a female Robinson Crusoe, drinking tea. Mr Dick leaning thoughtfully on a great kite such as we had often been out together to fly, with more luggage piled about him!

'My dear aunt!' cried I. 'Why, what an unexpected pleasure!'

We cordially embraced; and Mr Dick and I cordially shook hands; and Mrs Crupp, who was busy making tea, and could not be too attentive, cordially said she had knowed well as Mr Copperfull would have his heart in his mouth when he see his dear relations.

'Halloa!' said my aunt to Peggotty, who quailed before her awful presence. 'How are *you*?'

'You remember my aunt, Peggotty?' said I.

'For the love of goodness, child,' exclaimed my aunt, 'don't call the woman by that South Sea Island name! If she married and got rid of it, which was the best thing she could do, why don't you give her the benefit of the change? What's your name now – P.?' said my aunt, as a compromise for the obnoxious appellation.

'Barkis, ma'am,' said Peggotty, with a curtsey.

'Well! That's human,' said my aunt. 'It sounds less as if you wanted a Missionary. How d'ye do, Barkis? I hope you're well?'

Encouraged by these gracious words, and by my aunt's extending her hand, Barkis came forward, and took the hand, and curtseyed her acknowledgments.

'We are older than we were, I see,' said my aunt. 'We have only met each other once before, you know. A nice business we made of it then! Trot, my dear, another cup.'

I handed it dutifully to my aunt, who was in her usual inflexible state of figure; and ventured a remonstrance with her on the subject of her sitting on a box.

'Let me draw the sofa here, or the easy-chair, aunt,' said I. 'Why should you be so uncomfortable?'

'Thank you, Trot,' replied my aunt. 'I prefer to sit upon my property.' Here my aunt looked hard at Mrs Crupp, and observed, 'We needn't trouble you to wait, ma'am.'

'Shall I put a little more tea in the pot afore I go, ma'am?' said Mrs Crupp.

'No, I thank you, ma'am,' replied my aunt.

'Would you let me fetch another pat of butter, ma'am?' said Mrs Crupp. 'Or would you be persuaded to try a new-laid

My aunt astonishes me

hegg? or should I brile a rasher? Ain't there nothing I could do for your dear aunt, Mr Copperfull?'

'Nothing, ma'am,' returned my aunt. 'I shall do very well, I thank you.'

Mrs Crupp, who had been incessantly smiling, to express sweet temper, and incessantly holding her head on one side, to express a general feebleness of constitution, and incessantly rubbing her hands, to express a desire to be of service to all deserving objects, gradually smiled herself, one-sided herself, and rubbed herself, out of the room.

'Dick,' said my aunt. 'You know what I told you about time-servers and wealth-worshippers?'

Mr Dick – with rather a scared look, as if he had forgotten it – returned a hasty answer in the affirmative.

'Mrs Crupp is one of them,' said my aunt. 'Barkis, I'll trouble you to look after the tea, and let me have another cup, for I don't fancy that woman's pouring out!'

I knew my aunt sufficiently well to know that she had something of importance on her mind, and that there was far more matter in this arrival than a stranger might have supposed. I noticed how her eye lighted on me, when she thought my attention otherwise occupied; and what a curious process of hesitation appeared to be going on within her, while she preserved her outward stiffness and composure. I began to reflect whether I had done anything to offend her; and my conscience whispered me that I had not yet told her about Dora. Could it by any means be that, I wondered!

As I knew she would only speak in her own good time, I sat down near her, and spoke to the birds, and played with the cat, and was as easy as I could be. But I was very far from being really easy; and I should still have been so, even if Mr Dick, leaning over the great kite behind my aunt, had not taken every secret opportunity of shaking his head darkly at me, and pointing at her.

'Trot,' said my aunt at last, when she had finished her tea, and carefully smoothed down her dress, and wiped her lips – 'you needn't go, Barkis! – Trot, have you got to be firm, and self-reliant?'

'I hope so, aunt.'

'What do you think?' enquired Miss Betsey.

'I think so, aunt.'

'Then why, my love,' said my aunt, looking earnestly at me, 'why do you think I prefer to sit upon this property of mine tonight?'

I shook my head, unable to guess.

'Because,' said my aunt, 'it's all I have. Because I'm ruined, my dear!'

If the house, and every one of us, had tumbled out into the river together, I could hardly have received a greater shock.

'Dick knows it,' said my aunt, laying her hand calmly on my shoulder. 'I am ruined, my dear Trot! All I have in the world is in this room, except the cottage; and that I have left Janet to let. Barkis, I want to get a bed for this gentleman tonight. To save expense, perhaps you can make up something here for myself. Anything will do. It's only for tonight. We'll talk about this, more, tomorrow.'

I was roused from my amazement and concern for her – I am sure, for her – by her falling on my neck for a moment, and crying that she only grieved for me. In another moment she suppressed this emotion; and said with an aspect more triumphant than dejected: 'We must meet reverses boldly, and not suffer them to frighten us, my dear. We must learn to act the play out. We must live misfortune down, Trot!'

CHAPTER 35

Depression

As soon as I could recover my presence of mind, which quite deserted me in the first overpowering shock of my aunt's intelligence, I proposed to Mr Dick to come round to the chandler's shop, and take possession of the bed which Mr Peggotty had lately vacated. The chandler's shop being in Hungerford Market, and Hungerford Market being a very different place in those days, there was a low wooden colonnade before the door (not very unlike that before the house where the little man and woman used to live, in the old weather-glass), which pleased Mr Dick mightily. The glory of lodging over this structure would have compensated him, I dare say, for many inconveniences; but as there were really few to bear, beyond the compound of flavours I have already mentioned, and perhaps the want of a little more elbow-room, he was perfectly charmed with his accommodation. Mrs Crupp had indignantly assured him that there wasn't room to swing a cat there; but as Mr Dick justly observed to me, sitting down on the foot of the bed, nursing his leg, 'You know, Trotwood, I don't want to swing a cat. I never do swing a cat. Therefore, what does that signify to *me*!'

I tried to ascertain whether Mr Dick had any understanding of the causes of this sudden and great change in my aunt's affairs. As I might have expected, he had none at all. The only account he could give of it was that my aunt had said to him, the day before yesterday, 'Now, Dick, are you really and truly the philosopher I take you for?' That then he had said, Yes, he hoped so. That then my aunt had said, 'Dick, I am ruined.' That then he had said, 'Oh, indeed!' That then my aunt had praised him highly, which he was very glad of. And that then they had come to me, and had had bottled porter and sandwiches on the road.

Mr Dick was so very complacent, sitting on the foot of the bed, nursing his leg, and telling me this, with his eyes wide open and a surprised smile, that I am sorry to say I was provoked into explaining to him that ruin meant distress, want, and starvation; but I was soon bitterly reproved for this harshness by seeing his face turn pale, and tears course down his lengthened cheeks, while he fixed upon me a look of such unutterable woe that it might have softened a far harder heart than mine. I took infinitely greater pains to cheer him up again than I had taken to depress him; and I soon understood (as I ought to have known at first) that he had been so confident, merely because of his faith in the wisest and most wonderful of women, and his unbounded reliance on my intellectual resources. The latter, I believe, he considered a match for any kind of disaster not absolutely mortal.

'What can we do, Trotwood?' said Mr Dick. 'There's the Memorial –'

'To be sure there is,' said I. 'But all we can do just now, Mr Dick, is to keep a cheerful countenance, and not let my aunt see that we are thinking about it.'

He assented to this in the most earnest manner; and implored me, if I should see him wandering an inch out of the right course, to recall him by some of those superior methods which were always at my command. But I regret to state that the fright I had given him proved too much for his best attempts at concealment. All the evening his eyes wandered to my aunt's face, with an expression of the most dismal apprehension, as if he saw her growing thin on the spot. He was conscious of this, and put a constraint upon his head; but his keeping that immovable, and sitting rolling his eyes like a piece of machinery, did not mend the matter at all. I saw him look at the loaf at supper (which happened to be a small one), as if nothing else stood between us and famine; and when my aunt insisted on his making his customary repast, I detected him in the act of pocketing fragments of his bread and cheese; I have no doubt for the purpose of reviving us with those savings, when we should have reached an advanced state of attenuation.

My aunt, on the other hand, was in a composed frame of mind, which was a lesson to all of us – to me, I am sure. She was extremely gracious to Peggotty, except when I inadvertently called her by that name; and strange as I knew she felt in London, appeared quite at home. She was to have my bed, and I was to lie in the sitting-room, to keep guard over her. She made a great point of being so near the river, in case of a conflagration; and I suppose really did find some satisfaction in that circumstance.

'Trot, my dear,' said my aunt, when she saw me making preparations for compounding her usual night draught, 'no!'

'Nothing, aunt?'

'Not wine, my dear. Ale.'

'But there is wine here, aunt. And you always have it made of wine.'

'Keep that, in case of sickness,' said my aunt. 'We mustn't use it carelessly, Trot. Ale for me. Half a pint.'

I thought Mr Dick would have fallen insensible. My aunt being resolute, I went out and got the ale myself. As it was growing late, Peggotty and Mr Dick took that opportunity of repairing to the chandler's shop together. I parted from him, poor fellow, at the corner of the street, with his great kite at his back, a very monument of human misery.

My aunt was walking up and down the room when I returned, crimping the borders of her nightcap with her fingers. I warmed the ale and made the toast on the usual infallible principles. When it was ready for her, she was ready for it, with her nightcap on, and the skirt of her gown turned back on her knees.

'My dear,' said my aunt, after taking a spoonful of it, 'it's a great deal better than wine. Not half so bilious.'

I suppose I looked doubtful, for she added: 'Tut, tut, child. If nothing worse than ale happens to us, we are well off.'

'I should think so myself, aunt, I am sure,' said I.

'Well, then, why *don't* you think so?' said my aunt.

'Because you and I are very different people,' I returned.

'Stuff and nonsense, Trot,' replied my aunt.

My aunt went on with a quiet enjoyment, in which there was very little affectation, if any; drinking the warm ale with a teaspoon, and soaking her strips of toast in it.

'Trot,' said she, 'I don't care for strange faces in general, but I rather like that Barkis of yours, do you know!'

'It's better than a hundred pounds to hear you say so!' said I.

'It's a most extraordinary world,' observed my aunt, rubbing her nose; 'how that woman ever got into it with that name is unaccountable to me. It would be much more easy to be born a Jackson, or something of that sort, one would think.'

'Perhaps she thinks so, too; it's not her fault,' said I.

'I suppose not,' returned my aunt, rather grudging the admission; 'but it's very aggravating. However, she's Barkis *now*. That's some comfort. Barkis is uncommonly fond of you, Trot.'

'There is nothing she would leave undone to prove it,' said I.

'Nothing, I believe,' returned my aunt. 'Here, the poor fool has been begging and praying about handing over some of her money – because she has got too much of it! A simpleton!'

My aunt's tears of pleasure were positively trickling down into the warm ale.

'She's the most ridiculous creature that ever was born,' said my aunt. 'I knew, from the first moment when I saw her with that poor dear blessed baby of a mother of yours, that she was the most ridiculous of mortals. But there are good points in Barkis!'

Affecting to laugh, she got an opportunity of putting her hand to her eyes. Having availed herself of it, she resumed her toast and her discourse together.

'Ah! Mercy upon us!' sighed my aunt. 'I know all about it, Trot! Barkis and myself had quite a gossip while you were out with Dick. I know all about it. I don't know where these wretched girls expect to go to, for my part. I wonder they don't knock out their brains against – against mantelpieces,' said my aunt; an idea which was probably suggested to her by her contemplation of mine.

'Poor Em'ly!' said I.

'Oh, don't talk to me about poor,' returned my aunt. 'She should have thought of that, before she caused so much misery! Give me a kiss, Trot. I am sorry for your early experience.'

As I bent forward, she put her tumbler on my knee to detain me, and said: 'Oh, Trot, Trot! And so you fancy yourself in love. Do you?'

'Fancy, aunt!' I exclaimed, as red as I could be. 'I adore her with my whole soul!'

'Dora, indeed!' returned my aunt. 'And you mean to say the little thing is very fascinating, I suppose?'

'My dear aunt,' I replied, 'no one can form the least idea what she is!'

'Ah! And not silly?' said my aunt.

'Silly, aunt!'

I seriously believe it had never once entered my head for a single moment, to consider whether she was or not. I resented the idea, of course; but I was in a manner struck by it, as a new one altogether.

'Not light-headed?' said my aunt.

'Light-headed, aunt!' I could only repeat this daring speculation with the same kind of feeling with which I had repeated the preceding question.

'Well, well!' said my aunt. 'I only ask. I don't depreciate her. Poor little couple! And so you think you were formed for one another, and are to go through a party-supper-table kind of life, like two pretty pieces of confectionery, do you, Trot?'

She asked me this so kindly, and with such a gentle air, half playful and half sorrowful, that I was quite touched.

'We are young and inexperienced, aunt, I know,' I replied; 'and I dare say we say and think a good deal that is rather foolish. But we love one another truly, I am sure. If I thought Dora could ever love anybody else, or cease to love me; or that I could ever love anybody else, or cease to love her; I don't know what I should do – go out of my mind, I think!'

'Ah, Trot!' said my aunt, shaking her head, and smiling gravely; 'blind, blind, blind!'

'Someone that I know, Trot,' my aunt pursued, after a pause, 'though of a very pliant disposition, has an earnestness of affection in him that reminds me of poor Baby. Earnestness is what that Somebody must look for, to sustain him and improve him, Trot. Deep, downright, faithful earnestness.'

'If you only knew the earnestness of Dora, aunt!' I cried.

'Oh, Trot!' she said again; 'blind, blind!' and without knowing why, I felt a vague unhappy loss or want of something over-shadow me like a cloud.

'However,' said my aunt, 'I don't want to put two young creatures out of conceit with themselves, or to make them unhappy; so, though it is a girl and boy attachment, and girl and boy attachments very often – mind! I don't say always! – come to nothing, still we'll be serious about it, and hope for a prosperous issue one of these days. There's time enough for it to come to anything!'

This was not upon the whole very comforting to a rapturous lover; but I was glad to have my aunt in my confidence, and I was mindful of her being fatigued. So I thanked her ardently for this mark of her affection, and for all her other kindnesses towards me; and after a tender good-night, she took her night-cap into my bedroom.

How miserable I was, when I lay down! How I thought and thought of my being poor, in Mr Spenlow's eyes; about my not being what I thought I was, when I proposed to Dora; about the chivalrous necessity of telling Dora what my worldly condition was, and releasing her from her engagement if she thought fit; about how I should contrive to live, during the long term of my articles, when I was earning nothing; about doing something to assist my aunt, and seeing no way of doing anything; about coming down to have no money in my pocket, and to wear a shabby coat, and to be able to carry Dora no little presents, and to ride no gallant greys, and to show myself in no agreeable light! Sordid and selfish as I knew it was, and as I tortured

myself by knowing that it was, to let my mind run on my own distress so much, I was so devoted to Dora that I could not help it. I knew that it was base in me not to think more of my aunt, and less of myself; but, so far, selfishness was inseparable from Dora, and I could not put Dora on one side for any mortal creature. How exceedingly miserable I was, that night!

As to sleep, I had dreams of poverty in all sorts of shapes, but I seemed to dream without the previous ceremony of going to sleep. Now I was ragged, wanting to sell Dora matches, six bundles for a halfpenny; now I was at the office in a nightgown and boots, remonstrated with by Mr Spenlow on appearing before the clients in that airy attire; now I was hungrily picking up the crumbs that fell from old Tiffey's daily biscuit, regularly eaten when St Paul's struck one; now I was hopelessly endeavouring to get a licence to marry Dora, having nothing but one of Uriah Heep's gloves to offer in exchange, which the whole Commons rejected; and still more or less conscious of my own room, I was always tossing about like a distressed ship in a sea of bedclothes.

My aunt was restless, too, for I frequently heard her walking to and fro. Two or three times in the course of the night, attired in a long flannel wrapper in which she looked seven feet high, she appeared, like a disturbed ghost, in my room, and came to the side of the sofa on which I lay. On the first occasion I started up in alarm, to learn that she inferred from a particular light in the sky, that Westminster Abbey was on fire; and to be con-sulted in reference to the probability of its igniting Bucking-ham Street, in case the wind changed. Lying still, after that, I found that she sat down near me, whispering to herself 'Poor boy!' And then it made me twenty times more wretched, to know how unselfishly mindful she was of me, and how selfishly mindful I was of myself.

It was difficult to believe that a night so long to me could be short to anybody else. This consideration set me thinking and thinking of an imaginary party where people were dancing the hours away, until that became a dream too, and I heard the music incessantly playing one tune, and saw Dora incessantly dancing one dance, without taking the least notice of me. The man who had been playing the harp all night, was trying in vain to cover it with an ordinary-sized nightcap, when I awoke; or I should rather say, when I left off trying to go to sleep, and saw the sun shining in through the window at last.

There was an old Roman bath in those days at the bottom of one of the streets out of the Strand – it may be there still – in which I have had many a cold plunge. Dressing myself as quietly as I could, and leaving Peggotty to look after my aunt, I tumbled head-foremost into it, and then went for a walk to Hampstead. I had a hope that this brisk treatment might freshen my wits a little; and I think it did them good, for I soon came to the conclusion that the first step I ought to take was to try if my articles could be cancelled and the premium recovered. I got some breakfast on the Heath, and walked back to Doctors' Commons, along the watered roads and through a pleasant smell of summer flowers, growing in gardens and carried into town on hucksters' heads, intent on this first effort to meet our altered circumstances.

I arrived at the office so soon, after all, that I had half an hour's loitering about the Commons, before old Tiffey, who was always first, appeared with his key. Then I sat down in my shady corner, looking up at the sunlight on the opposite chimney-pots, and thinking about Dora; until Mr Spenlow came in, crisp and curly.

'How are you, Copperfield?' said he. 'Fine morning!'

'Beautiful morning, sir,' said I. 'Could I say a word to you before you go into Court?'

'By all means,' said he. 'Come into my room.'

I followed him into his room, and he began putting on his gown, and touching himself up before a little glass he had, hanging inside a closet door.

'I am sorry to say,' said I, 'that I have some rather disheartening intelligence from my aunt.'

'No!' said he. 'Dear me! Not paralysis, I hope?'

'It has no reference to her health, sir,' I replied. 'She has met with some large losses. In fact, she has very little left, indeed.'

'You astound me, Copperfield!' cried Mr Spenlow.

I shook my head. 'Indeed, sir,' said I, 'her affairs are so changed, that I wished to ask you whether it would be possible – at a sacrifice on our part of some portion of the premium, of course,' I put in this on the spur of the moment, warned by the blank expression of his face – 'to cancel my articles?'

What it cost me to make this proposal, nobody knows. It was like asking, as a favour, to be sentenced to transportation from Dora.

'To cancel your articles, Copperfield? Cancel?'

I explained with tolerable firmness, that I really did not know where my means of subsistence were to come from, unless I could earn them for myself. I had no fear for the future, I said – and I laid great emphasis on that, as if to imply that I should still be decidedly eligible for a son-in-law one of these days – but, for the present, I was thrown upon my own resources.

'I am extremely sorry to hear this, Copperfield,' said Mr Spenlow. 'Extremely sorry. It is not usual to cancel articles for any such reason. It is not a professional course of proceeding. It is not a convenient precedent at all. Far from it. At the same time – '

'You are very good, sir,' I murmured, anticipating a concession.

'Not at all. Don't mention it,' said Mr Spenlow. 'At the same time, I was going to say, if it had been my lot to have my hands unfettered – if I had not a partner – Mr Jorkins – '

My hopes were dashed in a moment, but I made another effort.

'Do you think, sir,' said I, 'if I were to mention it to Mr Jorkins – '

Mr Spenlow shook his head discouragingly. 'Heaven forbid, Copperfield,' he replied, 'that I should do any man an injustice; still less, Mr Jorkins. But I know my partner, Copperfield. Mr Jorkins is *not* a man to respond to a proposition of this peculiar nature. Mr Jorkins is very difficult to move from the beaten track. You know what he is?'

I am sure I knew nothing about him, except that he had originally been alone in the business, and now lived by himself in a house near Montagu Square, which was fearfully in want of painting; that he came very late of a day, and went away very early; that he never appeared to be consulted about anything; and that he had a dingy little black-hole of his own upstairs, where no business was ever done, and where there was a yellow old cartridge-paper pad upon his desk, unsoiled by ink, and reported to be twenty years of age.

'Would you object to my mentioning it to him, sir?' I asked.

'By no means,' said Mr Spenlow. 'But I have some experience of Mr Jorkins, Copperfield. I wish it were otherwise, for I should be happy to meet your views in any respect. I cannot have the least objection to your mentioning it to Mr Jorkins, Copperfield, if you think it worth while.'

Availing myself of this permission, which was given with a warm shake of the hand, I sat thinking about Dora, and looking at the sunlight stealing from the chimney-pots down the wall of the opposite house, until Mr Jorkins came. I then went up to Mr Jorkins's room, and evidently astonished Mr Jorkins very much by making my appearance there.

'Come in, Mr Copperfield,' said Mr Jorkins. 'Come in!'

I went in, and sat down, and stated my case to Mr Jorkins pretty much as I had stated it to Mr Spenlow. Mr Jorkins was not by any means the awful creature one might have expected, but a large, mild, smooth-faced man of sixty, who took so much snuff that there was a tradition in the Commons that he lived principally on that stimulant, having little room in his system for any other article of diet.

'You have mentioned this to Mr Spenlow, I suppose?' said Mr Jorkins, when he had heard me, very restlessly, to an end.

I answered, Yes, and told him that Mr Spenlow had introduced his name.

'He said I should object?' asked Mr Jorkins.

I was obliged to admit that Mr Spenlow had considered it probable.

'I am sorry to say, Mr Copperfield, I can't advance your object,' said Mr Jorkins nervously. 'The fact is – but I have an appointment at the Bank, if you'll have the goodness to excuse me.'

With that he rose in a great hurry, and was going out of the room, when I made bold to say that I feared, then, there was no way of arranging the matter?

'No!' said Mr Jorkins, stopping at the door to shake his head. 'Oh, no! I object, you know,' which he said very rapidly and went out. 'You must be aware, Mr Copperfield,' he added, looking restlessly in at the door again, 'if Mr Spenlow objects – '

'Personally he does not object, sir,' said I.

'Oh! Personally!' repeated Mr Jorkins in an impatient manner. 'I assure you there's an objection, Mr Copperfield. Hopeless! What you wish to be done, can't be done. I – I really have got an appointment at the Bank.' With that he fairly ran away; and to the best of my knowledge it was three days before he showed himself in the Commons again.

Being very anxious to leave no stone unturned, I waited until Mr Spenlow came in, and then described what had passed; giving him to understand that I was not hopeless of his being able to soften the adamantine Jorkins, if he would undertake the task.

'Copperfield,' returned Mr Spenlow, with a gracious smile, 'you have not known my partner, Mr Jorkins, as long as I have. Nothing is farther from my thoughts than to attribute any degree of artifice to Mr Jorkins. But Mr Jorkins has a way of stating his objections which often deceives people. No, Copperfield!' shaking his head, 'Mr Jorkins is not to be moved, believe me!'

I was completely bewildered between Mr Spenlow and Mr Jorkins, as to which of them really was the objecting partner; but I saw with sufficient clearness that there was obduracy somewhere in the firm, and that the recovery of my aunt's thousand pounds was out of the question. In a state of despondency, which I remember with anything but satisfaction, for I know it still had too much reference to myself (though always in connection with Dora), I left the office, and went homeward.

I was trying to familiarise my mind with the worst, and to present to myself the arrangements we should have to make for the future in their sternest aspect, when a hackney-chariot coming after me, and stopping at my very feet, occasioned me to look up. A fair hand was stretched forth to me from the window; and the face I had never seen without a feeling of serenity and happiness, from the moment when it first turned back on the old oak staircase with the great broad balustrade, and when I associated its softened beauty with the stained-glass window in the church, was smiling on me.

'Agnes!' I joyfully exclaimed. 'Oh, my dear Agnes, of all people in the world, what a pleasure to see you!'

'Is it, indeed?' she said, in her cordial voice.

'I want to talk to you so much!' said I. 'It's such a lightening of my heart, only to look at you! If I had had a conjurer's cap, there is no one I should have wished for but you!'

'What?' returned Agnes.

'Well! perhaps Dora first,' I admitted with a blush.

'Certainly, Dora first, I hope,' said Agnes, laughing.

'But you next!' said I. 'Where are you going?'

She was going to my rooms to see my aunt. The day being very fine, she was glad to come out of the chariot, which smelt (I had my head in it all this time) like a stable put under a cucumber-frame. I dismissed the coachman, and she took my arm, and we walked on together. She was like Hope embodied, to me. How different I felt in one short minute, having Agnes at my side!

My aunt had written her one of the odd, abrupt notes – very little longer than a bank-note – to which her epistolary efforts were usually limited. She had stated therein that she had fallen into adversity, and was leaving Dover for good, but had quite made up her mind to it, and was so well that nobody need be uncomfortable about her. Agnes had come to London to see my aunt, between whom and herself there had been a mutual liking these many years; indeed, it dated from the time of my taking up my residence in Mr Wickfield's house. She was not alone, she said. Her papa was with her – and Uriah Heep.

'And now they are partners,' said I. 'Confound him!'

'Yes,' said Agnes. 'They have some business here; and I took advantage of their coming, to come too. You must not think my visit all friendly and disinterested, Trotwood, for – I am afraid I may be cruelly prejudiced – I do not like to let papa go away alone, with him.'

'Does he exercise the same influence over Mr Wickfield still, Agnes?'

Agnes shook her head. 'There is such a change at home,' said she, 'that you would scarcely know the dear old house. They live with us now.'

'They?' said I.

'Mr Heep and his mother. He sleeps in your old room,' said Agnes, looking up into my face.

'I wish I had the ordering of his dreams,' said I. 'He wouldn't sleep there long.'

'I keep my own little room,' said Agnes, 'where I used to learn my lessons. How the time goes! You remember? The little panelled room that opens from the drawing-room?'

'Remember, Agnes? When I saw you, for the first time, coming out at the door, with your quaint little basket of keys hanging at your side?'

'It is just the same,' said Agnes, smiling. 'I am glad you think of it so pleasantly. We were very happy.'

'We were, indeed,' said I.

'I keep that room to myself still; but I cannot always desert Mrs Heep, you know. And so,' said Agnes, quietly, 'I feel obliged to bear her company, when I might prefer to be alone. But I have no other reason to complain of her. If she tires me, sometimes, by her praises of her son, it is only natural in a mother. He is a very good son to her.'

I looked at Agnes when she said these words, without detecting in her any consciousness of Uriah's design. Her mild but earnest eyes met mine with their own beautiful frankness, and there was no change in her gentle face.

'The chief evil of their presence in the house,' said Agnes, 'is that I cannot be as near papa as I could wish – Uriah Heep being so much between us – and cannot watch over him, if that is not too bold a thing to say, as closely as I would. But, if any fraud or treachery is practising against him, I hope that simple love and truth will be stronger, in the end. I hope that real love and truth are stronger in the end than any evil or misfortune in the world.'

A certain bright smile, which I never saw on any other face, died away, even while I thought how good it was, and how familiar it had once been to me; and she asked me, with a quick change of expression (we were drawing very near my street), if I knew how the reverse in my aunt's circumstances had been brought about. On my replying no, she had not told me yet, Agnes became thoughtful, and I fancied I felt her arm tremble in mine.

We found my aunt alone, in a state of some excitement. A difference of opinion had arisen between herself and Mrs Crupp, on an abstract question (the propriety of chambers being inhabited by the gentler sex); and my aunt, utterly indifferent to spasms on the part of Mrs Crupp, had cut the dispute short, by informing that lady that she smelt of my brandy, and that she would trouble her to walk out. Both of these expressions Mrs Crupp considered actionable, and had expressed her intention of bringing before a 'British Judy' – meaning, it was supposed, the bulwark of our national liberties.

My aunt, however, having had time to cool, while Peggotty was out showing Mr Dick the soldiers at the Horse Guards – and being, besides, greatly pleased to see Agnes – rather plumed herself on the affair than otherwise, and received us with unimpaired good-humour. When Agnes laid her bonnet on the table, and sat down beside her, I could not but think, looking on her mild eyes and her radiant forehead, how natural it seemed to have her there; how trustfully, although she was so young and inexperienced, my aunt confided in her; how strong she was, indeed, in simple love and truth.

We began to talk about my aunt's losses, and I told them what I had tried to do that morning.

'Which was injudicious, Trot,' said my aunt, 'but well meant. You are a generous boy – I suppose I must say, young man, now – and I am proud of you, my dear. So far so good. Now, Trot and Agnes, let us look the case of Betsey Trotwood in the face, and see how it stands.'

I observed Agnes turn pale, as she looked very attentively at my aunt. My aunt, patting her cat, looked very attentively at Agnes.

'Betsey Trotwood,' said my aunt, who had always kept her money matters to herself: ' – I don't mean your sister, Trot, my dear, but myself – had a certain property. It don't matter how much; enough to live on. More; for she had saved a little and added to it. Betsey funded her property for some time, and then, by the advice of her man of business, laid it out on landed security. That did very well, and returned very good interest, till Betsey was paid off. I am talking of Betsey as if she was a man-of-war. Well! Then, Betsey had to look about her, for a new investment. She thought she was wiser, now, than her man of business, who was not such a good man of business by this time as he used to be – I am alluding to your father, Agnes – and she took it into her head to lay it out for herself. So she took her pigs,' said my aunt, 'to a foreign market; and a very bad market it turned out to be. First, she lost in the mining way, and then she lost in the diving way – fishing up treasure, or some such Tom Tiddler nonsense,' explained my aunt, rubbing her nose; 'and then she lost in the mining way again, and, last of all, to set the thing entirely to rights, she lost in the banking way. I don't know what the bank shares were worth for a little while,' said my aunt; 'cent per cent was the lowest of it, I believe; but the bank was at the other end of the world, and tumbled into space, for what I know; anyhow, it fell to pieces, and never will and never can pay sixpence; and Betsey's sixpences were all there, and there's an end of them. Least said, soonest mended!'

My aunt concluded this philosophical summary, by fixing her eyes with a kind of triumph on Agnes, whose colour was gradually returning.

'Dear Miss Trotwood, is that all the history?' said Agnes.

'I hope it's enough, child,' said my aunt. 'If there had been more money to lose, it wouldn't have been all, I dare say. Betsey would have contrived to throw that after the rest, and make another chapter, I have little doubt. But there was no more money, and there's no more story.'

Agnes had listened at first with suspended breath. Her colour still came and went, but she breathed more freely. I thought I knew why. I thought she had had some fear that her unhappy father might be in some way to blame for what had happened. My aunt took her hand in hers, and laughed.

'Is that all?' repeated my aunt. 'Why, yes, that's all, except, "And she lived happy ever afterwards." Perhaps I may add that of Betsey yet, one of these days. Now, Agnes, you have a wise head. So have you, Trot, in some things, though I can't compliment you always'; and here my aunt shook her own at me, with an energy peculiar to herself. 'What's to be done? Here's the cottage, taking one time with another, will produce, say seventy pounds a year. I think we may safely put it down at that. Well! – That's all we've got,' said my aunt; with whom it was an idiosyncrasy, as it is with some horses, to stop very short when she appeared to be in a fair way of going on for a long while.

'Then,' said my aunt, after a rest, 'there's Dick. He's good for a hundred a year, but of course that must be expended on himself. I would sooner send him away, though I know I am the only person who appreciates him, than have him and not spend his money on himself. How can Trot and I do best, upon our means? What do you say, Agnes?'

'*I* say, aunt,' I interposed, 'that I must do something!'

'Go for a soldier, do you mean?' returned my aunt, alarmed; 'or go to sea? I won't hear of it. You are to be a proctor. We're not going to have any knockings on the head in *this* family, if you please, sir.'

I was about to explain that I was not desirous of introducing that mode of provision into the family, when Agnes enquired if my rooms were held for any long term.

'You come to the point, my dear,' said my aunt. 'They are not to be got rid of, for six months at least, unless they could be under-let, and that I don't believe. The last man died here. Five people out of six *would* die – of course – of that woman in nankeen with the flannel petticoat. I have a little ready money; and I agree with you, the best thing we can do is, to live the term out here, and get Dick a bedroom hard by.'

I thought it my duty to hint at the discomfort my aunt would sustain, from living in a continual state of guerilla warfare with Mrs Crupp; but she disposed of that objection summarily by declaring, that, on the first demonstration of hostilities, she was prepared to astonish Mrs Crupp for the whole remainder of her natural life.

'I have been thinking, Trotwood,' said Agnes, diffidently, 'that if you had time – '

'I have a good deal of time, Agnes. I am always disengaged after four or five o'clock, and I have time early in the morning. In one way and another,' said I, conscious of reddening a little as I thought of the hours and hours I had devoted to fagging about town, and to and fro upon the Norwood road, 'I have abundance of time.'

'I know you would not mind,' said Agnes, coming to me, and speaking in a low voice, so full of sweet and hopeful consideration that I hear it now, 'the duties of a secretary.'

'Mind, my dear Agnes?'

'Because,' continued Agnes, 'Doctor Strong has acted on his

intention of retiring, and has come to live in London; and he asked papa, I know, if he could recommend him one. Don't you think he would rather have his favourite old pupil near him, than anybody else?'

'Dear Agnes!' said I. 'What should I do without you! You are always my good angel. I told you so. I never think of you in any other light.'

Agnes answered with her pleasant laugh, that one good Angel (meaning Dora) was enough; and went on to remind me that the Doctor had been used to occupy himself in his study, early in the morning, and in the evening – and that probably my leisure would suit his requirements very well. I was scarcely more delighted with the prospect of earning my own bread, than with the hope of earning it under my old master; in short, acting on the advice of Agnes, I sat down and wrote a letter to the Doctor, stating my object, and appointing to call on him next day at ten in the forenoon. This I addressed to Highgate – for in that place, so memorable to me, he lived – and went and posted, myself, without losing a minute.

Wherever Agnes was, some agreeable token of her noiseless presence seemed inseparable from the place. When I came back, I found my aunt's birds hanging, just as they had hung so long in the parlour window of the cottage; and my easy-chair imitating my aunt's much easier chair in its position at the open window; and even the round green fan, which my aunt had brought away with her, screwed on to the window-sill. I knew who had done all this, by its seeming to have quietly done itself; and I should have known in a moment who had arranged my neglected books in the old order of my school-days, even if I had supposed Agnes to be miles away, instead of seeing her busy with them, and smiling at the disorder into which they had fallen.

My aunt was quite gracious on the subject of the Thames (it really did look very well with the sun upon it, though not like the sea before the cottage), but she could not relent towards the London smoke, which, she said, 'peppered everything.' A complete revolution, in which Peggotty bore a prominent part, was being effected in every corner of my rooms, in regard of this pepper; and I was looking on, thinking how little even Peggotty seemed to do with a good deal of bustle, and how much Agnes did without any bustle at all, when a knock came at the door.

'I think,' said Agnes, turning pale, 'it's papa. He promised me that he would come.'

I opened the door, and admitted, not only Mr Wickfield, but Uriah Heep. I had not seen Mr Wickfield for some time. I was prepared for a great change in him, after what I had heard from Agnes, but his appearance shocked me.

It was not that he looked many years older, though still dressed with the old scrupulous cleanliness; or that there was an unwholesome ruddiness upon his face; or that his eyes were full and bloodshot; or that there was a nervous trembling in his hand, the cause of which I knew, and had for some years seen at work. It was not that he had lost his good looks, or his old bearing of a gentleman – for that he had not – but the thing that struck me most was, that with the evidences of his native

superiority still upon him, he should submit himself to that crawling impersonation of meanness, Uriah Heep. The reversal of the two natures, in their relative positions, Uriah's of power, and Mr Wickfield's of dependence, was a sight more painful to me than I can express. If I had seen an Ape taking command of a Man, I should hardly have thought it a more degrading spectacle.

He appeared to be only too conscious of it himself. When he came in, he stood still; and with his head bowed, as if he felt it. This was only for a moment; for Agnes softly said to him, 'Papa! Here is Miss Trotwood – and Trotwood, whom you have not seen for a long while!' and then he approached, and constrainedly gave my aunt his hand, and shook hands more cordially with me. In the moment's pause I speak of, I saw Uriah's countenance form itself into a most ill-favoured smile. Agnes saw it, too, I think, for she shrank from him.

What my aunt saw, or did not see, I defy the science of physiognomy to have made out, without her own consent. I believe there never was anybody with such an imperturbable countenance when she chose. Her face might have been a dead wall on the occasion in question, for any light it threw upon her thoughts; until she broke silence with her usual abruptness.

'Well, Wickfield!' said my aunt; and he looked up at her for the first time. 'I have been telling your daughter how well I have been disposing of my money for myself, because I couldn't trust it to you, as you were growing rusty in business matters. We have been taking counsel together, and getting on very well, all things considered. Agnes is worth the whole firm, in my opinion.'

'If I may 'umbly make the remark,' said Uriah Heep, with a writhe, 'I fully agree with Miss Betsey Trotwood, and should be only too 'appy if Miss Agnes was a partner.'

'You're a partner yourself, you know,' returned my aunt, 'and that's about enough for you, I expect. How do you find your-self, sir?'

In acknowledgment of this question, addressed to him with extraordinary curtness, Mr Heep, uncomfortably clutching the blue bag he carried, replied that he was pretty well, he thanked my aunt, and hoped she was the same.

'And you, Master – I should say, Mister Copperfield,' pursued Uriah. 'I hope I see you well! I am rejoiced to see you, Mister Copperfield, even under present circumstances.' I believed that; for he seemed to relish them very much. 'Present circumstances is not what your friends would wish for you, Mister Copperfield, but it isn't money makes the man: it's – I am really unequal with my 'umble powers to express what it is,' said Uriah, with a fawning jerk, 'but it isn't money!'

Here he shook hands with me; not in the common way, but standing at a good distance from me, and lifting my hand up and down like a pump-handle, that he was a little afraid of.

'And how do you think we are looking, Master Copperfield – I should say, Mister?' fawned Uriah. 'Don't you find Mr Wick-field blooming, sir? Years don't tell much in our firm, Master Copperfield, except in raising up the 'umble, namely, mother and self – and in developing,' he added as an afterthought, 'the beautiful, namely, Miss Agnes.'

He jerked himself about, after this compliment, in such an intolerable manner, that my aunt, who had sat looking straight at him, lost all patience.

'Deuce take the man!' said my aunt sternly, 'what's he about? Don't be galvanic, sir!'

'I ask your pardon, Miss Trotwood,' returned Uriah; 'I'm aware you're nervous.'

'Go along with you, sir!' said my aunt, anything but appeased. 'Don't presume to say so! I am nothing of the sort. If you're an eel, sir, conduct yourself like one. If you're a man, control your limbs, sir! Good God!' said my aunt, with great indignation, 'I am not going to be serpentined and corkscrewed out of my senses!'

Mr Heep was rather abashed, as most people might have been, by this explosion; which derived great additional force from the indignant manner in which my aunt afterwards moved in her chair, and shook her head as if she were making snaps or bounces at him. But he said to me aside in a meek voice: 'I am well aware, Master Copperfield, that Miss Trotwood, though an excellent lady, has a quick temper (indeed, I think I had the pleasure of knowing her, when I was an 'umble clerk, before you did, Master Copperfield), and it's only natural, I am sure, that it should be made quicker by present circumstances. The wonder is that it isn't much worse! I only called to say that if there was anything we could do, in present circumstances, mother or self, or Wickfield and Heep, we should be really glad. I may go so far?' said Uriah, with a sickly smile at his partner.

'Uriah Heep,' said Mr Wickfield, in a monotonous, forced way, 'is active in the business, Trotwood. What he says, I quite concur in. You know I had an old interest in you. Apart from that, what Uriah says I quite concur in!'

'Oh, what a reward it is,' said Uriah, drawing up one leg, at the risk of bringing down upon himself another visitation from my aunt, 'to be so trusted in! But I hope I am able to do something to relieve him from the fatigues of business, Master Copperfield!'

'Uriah Heep is a great relief to me,' said Mr Wickfield, in the same dull voice. 'It's a load off my mind, Trotwood, to have such a partner.'

The red fox made him say all this, I knew, to exhibit him to me in the light he had indicated on the night when he poisoned my rest. I saw the same ill-favoured smile upon his face again, and saw how he watched me.

'You are not going, papa?' said Agnes anxiously. 'Will you not walk back with Trotwood and me?'

He would have looked to Uriah, I believe, before replying, if that worthy had not anticipated him.

'I am bespoke myself,' said Uriah, 'on business; otherwise I should have been 'appy to have kept with my friends. But I leave my partner to represent the firm. Miss Agnes, ever yours! I wish you good-day, Master Copperfield, and leave my 'umble respects for Miss Betsey Trotwood.'

With those words, he retired, kissing his great hand, and leering at us like a mask.

We sat there, talking about our pleasant old Canterbury days, an hour or two. Mr Wickfield, left to Agnes, soon became more like his former self; though there was a settled depression upon him which he never shook off. For all that, he brightened; and had an evident pleasure in hearing us recall the little incidents of our old life, many of which he remembered very well. He said it was like those times, to be alone with Agnes and me again; and he wished to Heaven they had never changed. I am

Mr Wickfield and his partner wait upon my aunt

sure there was an influence in the placid face of Agnes, and in the very touch of her hand upon his arm, that did wonders for him.

My aunt (who was busy nearly all this while with Peggotty, in the inner room), would not accompany us to the place where they were staying, but insisted on my going; and I went. We dined together. After dinner, Agnes sat beside him, as of old, and poured out his wine. He took what she gave him, and no more – like a child – and we all three sat together at a window as the evening gathered in. When it was almost dark, he lay down on a sofa, Agnes pillowing his head and bending over him a little while; and when she came back to the window, it was not so dark but I could see tears glittering in her eyes.

I pray Heaven that I never may forget the dear girl in her love and truth, at that time of my life; for if I should, I must be drawing near the end, and then I would desire to remember her best! She filled my heart with such good resolutions, strengthened my weakness so, by her example, so directed – I know not how, she was too modest and gentle to advise me in many words – the wandering ardour and unsettled purpose within me, that all the little good I have done, and all the harm I have forborne, I solemnly believe I may refer to her.

And how she spoke to me of Dora, sitting at the window in the dark; listened to my praises of her; praised again; and round the little fairy figure shed some glimpses of her own pure light, that made it yet more precious and more innocent to me! Oh, Agnes, sister of my boyhood, if I had known then, what I knew long afterwards!

There was a beggar in the street, when I went down; and as I turned my head towards the window, thinking of her calm, seraphic eyes, he made me start by muttering, as if he were an echo of the morning: 'Blind! Blind! Blind!'

CHAPTER 36

Enthusiasm

I began the next day with another dive into the Roman bath, and then started for Highgate. I was not dispirited now. I was not afraid of the shabby coat, and had no yearnings after gallant greys. My whole manner of thinking of our late misfortune was changed. What I had to do was to show my aunt that her past goodness to me had not been thrown away on an insensible, ungrateful object. What I had to do was to turn the painful discipline of my younger days to account, by going to work with a resolute and steady heart. What I had to do was to take my woodman's axe in my hand, and clear my own way through the forest of difficulty, by cutting down the trees until I came to Dora. And I went on at a mighty rate, as if it could be done by walking.

When I found myself on the familiar Highgate road, pursuing such a different errand from that old one of pleasure, with which it was associated, it seemed as if a complete change had come on my whole life. But that did not discourage me. With the new life came new purpose, new intention. Great was the labour; priceless the reward. Dora was the reward, and Dora must be won.

I got into such a transport that I felt quite sorry my coat was not a little shabby already. I wanted to be cutting at those trees in the forest of difficulty, under circumstances that should prove my strength. I had a good mind to ask an old man, in wire spectacles, who was breaking stones upon the road, to lend me his hammer for a little while, and let me begin to beat a path to Dora out of granite. I stimulated myself into such a heat, and got so out of breath, that I felt as if I had been earning I don't know how much. In this state, I went into a cottage that I saw was to let, and examined it narrowly – for I felt it necessary to be practical. It would do for me and Dora admirably; with a little front garden for Jip to run about in, and bark at the tradespeople through the railings, and a capital room upstairs for my aunt. I came out again, hotter and faster than ever, and dashed up to Highgate, at such a rate that I was there an hour too early; and, though I had not been, should have been obliged to stroll about to cool myself, before I was at all presentable.

My first care, after putting myself under this necessary course of preparation, was to find the Doctor's house. It was not in that part of Highgate where Mrs Steerforth lived, but quite on the opposite side of the little town. When I had made this discovery, I went back, in an attraction I could not resist, to a lane by Mrs Steerforth's, and looked over the corner of the garden wall. His room was shut up close. The conservatory doors were standing open, and Rosa Dartle was walking, bareheaded, with a quick, impetuous step, up and down a gravel walk on one side of the lawn. She gave me the idea of some fierce thing, that was dragging the length of its chain to and fro upon a beaten track, and wearing its heart out.

I came softly away from my place of observation, and avoiding that part of the neighbourhood, and wishing I had not gone near it, strolled about until it was ten o'clock. The church with the slender spire, that stands on the top of the hill now, was not there then to tell me the time. An old redbrick mansion, used as a school, was in its place; and a fine old house it must have been to go to school at, as I recollect it.

When I approached the Doctor's cottage – a pretty old place, on which he seemed to have expended some money, if I might judge from the embellishments and repairs that had the look of being just completed – I saw him walking in the garden at the side, gaiters and all, as if he had never left off walking since the days of my pupilage. He had his old companions about him, too; for there were plenty of high trees in the neighbourhood, and two or three rooks were on the grass, looking after him, as if they had been written to about him by the Canterbury rooks, and were observing him closely in consequence.

Knowing the utter hopelessness of attracting his attention from that distance, I made bold to open the gate, and walk after him, so as to meet him when he should turn round. When he did, and came towards me, he looked at me thoughtfully for a few moments, evidently without thinking about me at all; and then his benevolent face expressed extraordinary pleasure, and he took me by both hands.

'Why, my dear Copperfield,' said the Doctor; 'you are a man!

How do you do? I am delighted to see you. My dear Copperfield, how very much you have improved! You are quite – yes – dear me!'

I hoped he was well, and Mrs Strong, too.

'Oh, dear, yes!' said the Doctor, 'Annie's quite well, and she'll be delighted to see you. You were always her favourite. She said so, last night, when I showed her your letter. And – yes, to be sure – you recollect Mr Jack Maldon, Copperfield?'

'Perfectly, sir.'

'Of course,' said the Doctor. 'To be sure. *He's* pretty well, too.'

'Has he come home, sir?' I enquired.

'From India?' said the Doctor. 'Yes. Mr Jack Maldon couldn't bear the climate, my dear. Mrs Markleham – you have not forgotten Mrs Markleham?'

Forgotten the Old Soldier! And in that short time!

'Mrs Markleham,' said the Doctor, 'was quite vexed about him, poor thing; so we have got him at home again; and we have bought him a little Patent place, which agrees with him much better.'

I knew enough of Mr Jack Maldon to suspect from this account that it was a place where there was not much to do, and which was pretty well paid. The Doctor, walking up and down with his hand on my shoulder, and his kind face turned encouragingly to mine, went on: 'Now, my dear Copperfield, in reference to this proposal of yours. It's very gratifying and agreeable to me, I am sure; but don't you think you could do better? You achieved distinction, you know, when you were with us. You are qualified for many good things. You have laid a foundation that any edifice may be raised upon; and is it not a pity that you should devote the spring-time of your life to such a poor pursuit as I can offer?'

I became very glowing again, and, expressing myself in rhapsodical style, I am afraid, urged my request strongly; reminding the Doctor that I had already a profession.

'Well, well,' returned the Doctor, 'that's true. Certainly, your having a profession, and being actually engaged in studying it, makes a difference. But, my good young friend, what's seventy pounds a year?'

'It doubles our income, Doctor Strong,' said I.

'Dear me!' replied the Doctor. 'To think of that! Not that I mean to say it's rigidly limited to seventy pounds a year, because I have always contemplated making any young friend I might thus employ, a present, too. Undoubtedly,' said the Doctor, still walking me up and down with his hand on my shoulder, 'I have always taken an annual present into account.'

'My dear tutor,' said I (now, really, without any nonsense), 'to whom I owe more obligations already than I ever can acknowledge – '

'No, no,' interposed the Doctor. 'Pardon me!'

'If you will take such time as I have, and that is my mornings and evenings, and can think it worth seventy pounds a year, you will do me such a service as I cannot express.'

'Dear me!' said the Doctor innocently. 'To think that so little should go for so much! Dear, dear! And when you can do better, you will? On your word, now?' said the Doctor – which

he had always made a very grave appeal to the honour of us boys.

'On my word, sir!' I returned, answering in our old school manner.

'Then be it so,' said the Doctor, clapping me on the shoulder, and still keeping his hand there, as we still walked up and down.

'And I shall be twenty times happier, sir,' said I, with a little – I hope innocent – flattery, 'if my employment is to be on the Dictionary.'

The Doctor stopped, smilingly clapped me on the shoulder again, and exclaimed, with a triumph most delightful to behold, as if I had penetrated to the profoundest depths of mortal sagacity, 'My dear young friend, you have hit it. It is the Dictionary!'

How could it be anything else! His pockets were as full of it as his head. It was sticking out of him in all directions. He told me that since his retirement from scholastic life, he had been advancing with it wonderfully; and that nothing could suit him better than the proposed arrangements for morning and evening work, as it was his custom to walk about in the daytime with his considering cap on. His papers were in a little confusion, in consequence of Mr Jack Maldon having lately proffered his occasional services as an amanuensis, and not being accustomed to that occupation; but we should soon put right what was amiss, and go on swimmingly. Afterwards, when we were fairly at our work, I found Mr Jack Maldon's efforts more troublesome to me than I had expected, as he had not confined himself to making numerous mistakes, but had sketched so many soldiers, and ladies' heads, over the Doctor's manuscript, that I often became involved in labyrinths of obscurity.

The Doctor was quite happy in the prospect of our going to work together on that wonderful performance, and we settled to begin next morning at seven o'clock. We were to work two hours every morning, and two or three hours every night, except on Saturdays, when I was to rest. On Sundays, of course, I was to rest also, and I considered these very easy terms.

Our plans being thus arranged to our mutual satisfaction, the Doctor took me into the house to present me to Mrs Strong, whom we found in the Doctor's new study, dusting his books – a freedom which he never permitted anybody else to take with those sacred favourites.

They had postponed their breakfast on my account, and we sat down to table together. We had not been seated long when I saw an approaching arrival in Mrs Strong's face, before I heard any sound of it. A gentleman on horseback came to the gate, and leading his horse into the little court, with the bridle over his arm, as if he were quite at home, tied him to a ring in the empty coach-house wall, and came into the breakfast parlour, whip in hand. It was Mr Jack Maldon; and Mr Jack Maldon was not at all improved by India, I thought. I was in a state of ferocious virtue, however, as to young men who were not cutting down the trees in the forest of difficulty; and my impression must be received with due allowance.

'Mr Jack!' said the Doctor. 'Copperfield!'

Mr Jack Maldon shook hands with me; but not very warmly, I believed; and with an air of languid patronage, at which I

David Copperfield

secretly took great umbrage. But his languor altogether was quite a wonderful sight; except when he addressed himself to his cousin Annie.

'Have you breakfasted this morning, Mr Jack?' said the Doctor.

'I hardly ever take breakfast, sir,' he replied, with his head thrown back in an easy-chair. 'I find it bores me.'

'Is there any news today?' enquired the Doctor.

'Nothing at all, sir,' replied Mr Maldon. 'There's an account about the people being hungry and discontented down in the North, but they are always being hungry and discontented somewhere.'

The Doctor looked grave, and said, as though he wished to change the subject, 'Then there's no news at all; and no news, they say, is good news.'

'There's a long statement in the papers, sir, about a murder,' observed Mr Maldon. 'But somebody is always being murdered, and I didn't read it.'

A display of indifference to all the actions and passions of mankind was not supposed to be such a distinguished quality at that time, I think, as I have observed it to be considered since. I have known it very fashionable, indeed. I have seen it displayed with such success that I have encountered some fine ladies and gentlemen who might as well have been born caterpillars. Perhaps it impressed me the more then, because it was new to me, but it certainly did not tend to exalt my opinion of or to strengthen my confidence in Mr Jack Maldon.

'I came out to enquire whether Annie would like to go to the opera tonight,' said Mr Maldon, turning to her. 'It's the last good-night there will be, this season; and there's a singer there whom she really ought to hear. She is perfectly exquisite. Besides which, she is so charmingly ugly,' relapsing into languor.

The Doctor, ever pleased with what was likely to please his young wife, turned to her and said: 'You must go, Annie. You must go.'

'I would rather not,' she said to the Doctor. 'I prefer to remain at home. I would much rather remain at home.'

Without looking at her cousin, she then addressed me, and asked me about Agnes, and whether she should see her, and whether she was not likely to come that day; and was so much disturbed that I wondered how even the Doctor, buttering his toast, could be blind to what was so obvious.

But he saw nothing. He told her, good-naturedly, that she was young and ought to be amused and entertained, and must not allow herself to be made dull by a dull old fellow. Moreover, he said, he wanted to hear her sing all the new singer's songs to him; and how could she do that well, unless she went? So the Doctor persisted in making the engagement for her, and Mr Jack Maldon was to come back to dinner. This concluded, he went to his Patent place, I suppose; but at all events went away on his horse, looking very idle.

I was curious to find out next morning, whether she had been. She had not, but had sent into London to put her cousin off; and had gone out in the afternoon to see Agnes, and had prevailed upon the Doctor to go with her; and they had walked home by the fields, the Doctor told me, the evening being

delightful. I wondered then, whether she would have gone if Agnes had not been in town, and whether Agnes had some good influence over her, too!

She did not look very happy, I thought, but it was a good face, or a very false one. I often glanced at it, for she sat in the window all the time we were at work; and made our breakfast, which we took by snatches as we were employed. When I left, at nine o'clock, she was kneeling on the ground at the Doctor's feet, putting on his shoes and gaiters for him. There was a softened shade upon her face, thrown from some green leaves overhanging the open window of the low room; and I thought, all the way to Doctors' Commons, of the night when I had seen it looking at him as he read.

I was pretty busy now; up at five in the morning, and home at nine or ten at night. But I had infinite satisfaction in being so closely engaged, and never walked slowly on any account, and felt enthusiastically that the more I tired myself, the more I was doing to deserve Dora. I had not revealed myself in my altered character to Dora yet, because she was coming to see Miss Mills in a few days, and I deferred all I had to tell her until then; merely informing her in my letters (all our communications were secretly forwarded through Miss Mills), that I had much to tell her. In the meantime, I put myself on a short allowance of bear's grease, wholly abandoned scented soap and lavender water, and sold off three waistcoats at a prodigious sacrifice, as being too luxurious for my stern career.

Not satisfied with all these proceedings, but burning with impatience to do something more, I went to see Traddles, now lodging up behind the parapet of a house in Castle Street, Holborn. Mr Dick, who had been with me to Highgate twice already, and had resumed his companionship with the Doctor, I took with me.

I took Mr Dick with me, because, acutely sensitive to my aunt's reverses, and sincerely believing that no galley slave or convict worked as I did, he had begun to fret and worry himself out of spirits and appetite, as having nothing useful to do. In this condition, he felt more incapable of finishing the Memorial than ever; and the harder he worked at it, the oftener that unlucky head of King Charles the First got into it. Seriously apprehending that his malady would increase, unless we put some innocent deception upon him, and caused him to believe that he was useful, or unless we could put him in the way of being really useful (which would be better), I made up my mind to try if Traddles could help us. Before we went, I wrote Traddles a full statement of all that had happened, and Traddles wrote me back a capital answer expressive of his sympathy and friendship.

We found him hard at work with his inkstand and papers, refreshed by the sight of the flowerpot stand and the little round table in a corner of the small apartment. He received us cordially, and made friends with Mr Dick in a moment. Mr Dick professed an absolute certainty of having seen him before, and we both said, 'Very likely.'

The first subject on which I had to consult Traddles was this: I had heard that many men distinguished in various pursuits had begun life by reporting the debates in Parliament. Traddles having mentioned newspapers to me, as one of his hopes, I had put the two things together, and told Traddles in my letter that I wished to know how I could qualify myself for this pursuit. Traddles now informed me, as the result of his enquiries, that the mere mechanical acquisition necessary, except in rare cases, for thorough excellence in it, that is to say, a perfect and entire command of the mystery of shorthand writing and reading, was about equal in difficulty to the mastery of six languages; and that it might perhaps be attained, by dint of perseverance, in the course of a few years. Traddles reasonably supposed that this would settle the business; but I, only feeling that here indeed were a few tall trees to be hewn down, immediately resolved to work my way on to Dora through this thicket, axe in hand.

'I am very much obliged to you, my dear Traddles!' said I. 'I'll begin tomorrow.'

Traddles looked astonished, as he well might; but he had no notion as yet of my rapturous condition.

'I'll buy a book,' said I, 'with a good scheme of this art in it; I'll work at it at the Commons, where I haven't half enough to do; I'll take down the speeches in our court for practice – Traddles, my dear fellow, I'll master it!'

'Dear me,' said Traddles, opening his eyes, 'I had no idea you were such a determined character, Copperfield!'

I don't know how he should have had, for it was new enough to me. I passed that off, and brought Mr Dick on the carpet.

'You see,' said Mr Dick wistfully, 'if I could exert myself, Mr Traddles – if I could beat a drum – or blow anything!'

Poor fellow! I have little doubt he would have preferred such an employment in his heart to all others. Traddles, who would not have smiled for the world, replied composedly: 'But you are a very good penman, sir. You told me so, Copperfield?'

'Excellent!' said I. And indeed he was. He wrote with extraordinary neatness.

'Don't you think,' said Traddles, 'you could copy writings, sir, if I got them for you?'

Mr Dick looked doubtfully at me. 'Eh, Trotwood?'

I shook my head. Mr Dick shook his, and sighed. 'Tell him about the Memorial,' said Mr Dick.

I explained to Traddles that there was a difficulty in keeping King Charles the First out of Mr Dick's manuscripts; Mr Dick in the meanwhile looking very deferentially and seriously at Traddles, and sucking his thumb.

'But these writings, you know, that I speak of, are already drawn up and finished,' said Traddles after a little consideration. 'Mr Dick has nothing to do with them. Wouldn't that make a difference, Copperfield? At all events wouldn't it be well to try?'

This gave us new hope. Traddles and I laying our heads together apart, while Mr Dick anxiously watched us from his chair, we concocted a scheme in virtue of which we got him to work next day, with triumphant success.

On a table by the window in Buckingham Street, we set out the work Traddles procured for him – which was to make, I forget how many copies of a legal document about some right of way – and on another table we spread the last unfinished original of the great Memorial. Our instructions to Mr Dick were that he should copy exactly what he had before him, without the least departure from the original; and that when he felt it necessary to make the slightest allusion to King Charles the First, he should fly to the Memorial. We exhorted him to be resolute in this, and left my aunt to observe him. My aunt reported to us, afterwards, that, at first, he was like a man playing the kettledrums, and constantly divided his attentions between the two; but that, finding this confuse and fatigue him, and having his copy there, plainly before his eyes, he soon sat at it in an orderly businesslike manner, and postponed the Memorial to a more convenient time. In a word, although we took great care that he should have no more to do than was good for him, and although he did not begin with the beginning of a week, he earned by the following Saturday night ten shillings and ninepence; and never, while I live, shall I forget his going about to all the shops in the neighbourhood to change this treasure into sixpences, or his bringing them to my aunt arranged in the form of a heart upon a waiter, with tears of joy and pride in his eyes. He was like one under the propitious influence of a charm, from the moment of his being usefully employed; and if there were a happy man in the world, that Saturday night, it was the grateful creature who thought my aunt the most wonderful woman in existence, and me the most wonderful young man.

'No starving now, Trotwood,' said Mr Dick, shaking hands with me in a corner. 'I'll provide for her, sir!' and he flourished his ten fingers in the air, as if they were ten banks.

I hardly know which was the better pleased, Traddles or I.

'It really,' said Traddles suddenly, taking a letter out of his pocket, and giving it to me, 'put Mr Micawber quite out of my head!'

The letter (Mr Micawber never missed any possible opportunity of writing a letter) was addressed to me 'By the kindness of T. Traddles, Esquire, of the Inner Temple.' It ran thus:

MY DEAR COPPERFIELD – You may possibly not be unprepared to receive the intimation that something has turned up. I may have mentioned to you on a former occasion that I was in expectation of such an event.

I am about to establish myself in one of the provincial towns of our favoured island (where the society may be described as a happy admixture of the agricultural and the clerical), in immediate connection with one of the learned professions. Mrs Micawber and our offspring will accompany me. Our ashes, at a future period, will probably be found commingled in the cemetery attached to a venerable pile, for which the spot to which I refer has acquired a reputation, shall I say from China to Peru?

In bidding adieu to the modern Babylon, where we have undergone many vicissitudes, I trust not ignobly, Mrs Micawber and myself cannot disguise from our minds that we part, it may be for years and it may be for ever, with an individual linked by strong associations to the altar of our domestic life. If, on the eve of such a departure, you will accompany our mutual friend, Mr Thomas Traddles, to our present abode and there reciprocate the wishes natural to the occasion, you will confer a Boon

On

One

Who

Is

Ever yours,

WILKINS MICAWBER

I was glad to find that Mr Micawber had got rid of his dust and ashes, and that something really had turned up at last. Learning from Traddles that the invitation referred to the evening then wearing away, I expressed my readiness to do honour to it; and we went off together to the lodging which Mr Micawber occupied as Mr Mortimer, and which was situated near the top of the Gray's Inn Road.

The resources of this lodging were so limited, that we found the twins, now some eight or nine years old, reposing in a turn-up bedstead in the family sitting-room, where Mr Micawber had prepared, in a wash-hand-stand jug, what he called a 'Brew' of the agreeable beverage for which he was famous. I had the pleasure, on this occasion, of renewing the acquaintance of Master Micawber, whom I found a promising boy of about twelve or thirteen, very subject to that restlessness of limb which is not an unfrequent phenomenon in youths of his age. I also became once more known to his sister, Miss Micawber, in whom, as Mr Micawber told us, 'her mother renewed her youth, like the Phoenix.'

'My dear Copperfield,' said Mr Micawber, 'yourself and Mr Traddles find us on the brink of migration, and will excuse any little discomforts incidental to that position.'

Glancing round as I made a suitable reply, I observed that the family effects were already packed, and that the amount of luggage was by no means overwhelming. I congratulated Mrs Micawber on the approaching change.

'My dear Mr Copperfield,' said Mrs Micawber, 'of your friendly interest in all our affairs, I am well assured. My family may consider it banishment, if they please; but I am a wife and mother, and I never will desert Mr Micawber.'

Traddles appealed to, by Mrs Micawber's eye, feelingly acquiesced.

'That,' said Mrs Micawber, 'that, at least, is my view, my dear Mr Copperfield and Mr Traddles, of the obligation which I took upon myself when I repeated the irrevocable words, "I, Emma, take thee, Wilkins." I read the service over with a flat candle on the previous night, and the conclusion I derived from it was, that I never could desert Mr Micawber. And,' said Mrs Micawber, 'though it is possible I may be mistaken in my view of the ceremony, I never will!'

'My dear,' said Mr Micawber, a little impatiently, 'I am not conscious that you are expected to do anything of the sort.'

'I am aware, my dear Mr Copperfield,' pursued Mrs Micawber, 'that I am now about to cast my lot among strangers; and I am also aware that the various members of my family, to whom Mr Micawber has written in the most gentlemanly terms, announcing that fact, have not taken the least notice of Mr Micawber's communication. Indeed I may be superstitious,' said Mrs Micawber, 'but it appears to me that Mr Micawber is destined never to receive any answers whatever to the great majority of the communications he writes. I may augur from the silence of my family, that they object to the resolution I have taken; but I should not allow myself to be swerved from the path of duty, Mr Copperfield, even by my papa and mama, were they still living.'

I expressed my opinion that this was going in the right direction.

'It may be a sacrifice,' said Mrs Micawber, 'to immure one's self in a Cathedral town; but surely, Mr Copperfield, if it is a sacrifice in me, it is much more a sacrifice in a man of Mr Micawber's abilities.'

'Oh! You are going to a Cathedral town?' said I.

Mr Micawber, who had been helping us all, out of the wash-hand-stand jug, replied: 'To Canterbury. In fact, my dear Copperfield, I have entered into arrangements, by virtue of which I stand pledged and contracted to our friend Heep, to assist and serve him in the capacity of – and to be – his confidential clerk.'

I stared at Mr Micawber, who greatly enjoyed my surprise.

'I am bound to state to you,' he said, with an official air, 'that the business habits, and the prudent suggestions, of Mrs Micawber, have in a great measure conduced to this result. The gauntlet, to which Mrs Micawber referred upon a former occasion, being thrown down in the form of an advertisement, was taken up by my friend Heep, and led to a mutual recognition. Of my friend Heep,' said Mr Micawber, 'who is a man of remarkable shrewdness, I desire to speak with all possible respect. My friend Heep has not fixed the positive remuneration at too high a figure, but he has made a great deal, in the way of extrication from the pressure of pecuniary difficulties, contingent on the value of my services; and on the value of those services, I pin my faith. Such address and intelligence as I chance to possess,' said Mr Micawber, boastfully disparaging himself, with the old genteel air, 'will be devoted to my friend Heep's service. I have already some acquaintance with the law – as a defendant on civil process – and I shall immediately apply myself to the Commentaries of one of the most eminent and remarkable of our English Jurists. I believe it is unnecessary to add that I allude to Mr Justice Blackstone.'

These observations, and indeed the greater part of the observations made that evening, were interrupted by Mrs Micawber's discovering that Master Micawber was sitting on his boots, or holding his head on with both arms as if he felt it loose, or accidentally kicking Traddles under the table, or shuffling his feet over one another, or producing them at distances from himself apparently outrageous to nature, or lying sideways with his hair among the wineglasses, or developing his restlessness of limb in some other form incompatible with the general interests of society; and by Master Micawber's receiving those discoveries in a resentful spirit. I sat all the while, amazed by Mr Micawber's disclosure, and wondering what it meant, until Mrs Micawber resumed the thread of the discourse, and claimed my attention.

'What I particularly request Mr Micawber to be careful of, is,' said Mrs Micawber, 'that he does not, my dear Mr Copperfield, in applying himself to this subordinate branch of the law, place it out of his power to rise, ultimately, to the top of the tree. I am convinced that Mr Micawber, giving his mind to a profession so adapted to his fertile resources, and his flow of language, *must* distinguish himself. Now, for example, Mr Traddles,' said Mrs Micawber, assuming a profound air, 'a Judge, or even say a Chancellor. Does an individual place himself beyond the pale of those preferments by entering on such an office as Mr Micawber has accepted?'

'My dear,' observed Mr Micawber – but glancing inquisitively at Traddles too; 'we have time enough before us, for the consideration of those questions.'

'Micawber,' she returned, 'no! Your mistake in life is, that you do not look forward far enough. You are bound in justice to your family, if not to yourself, to take in at a comprehensive glance the extremest point in the horizon to which your abilities may lead you.'

Mr Micawber coughed, and drank his punch with an air of exceeding satisfaction – still glancing at Traddles, as if he desired to have his opinion.

'Why, the plain state of the case, Mrs Micawber,' said Traddles, mildly breaking the truth to her, 'I mean the real prosaic fact, you know – '

'Just so,' said Mrs Micawber. 'My dear Mr Traddles, I wish to be as prosaic and literal as possible on a subject of so much importance.'

' – is,' said Traddles, 'that this branch of the law, even if Mr Micawber were a regular solicitor – '

'Exactly so,' returned Mrs Micawber. ('Wilkins, you are squinting, and will not be able to get your eyes back.')

' – has nothing,' pursued Traddles, 'to do with that. Only a barrister is eligible for such preferments; and Mr Micawber could not be a barrister, without being entered at an inn of court as a student, for five years.'

'Do I follow you?' said Mrs Micawber, with her most affable air of business. 'Do I understand, my dear Mr Traddles, that, at the expiration of that period, Mr Micawber would be eligible as a Judge or Chancellor?'

'He would be *eligible*,' returned Traddles, with a strong emphasis on that word.

'Thank you,' said Mrs Micawber. 'That is quite sufficient. If such is the case, and Mr Micawber forfeits no privilege by entering on these duties, my anxiety is set at rest. I speak,' said Mrs Micawber, 'as a female, necessarily; but I have always been of opinion that Mr Micawber possesses what I have heard my papa call, when I lived at home, the judicial mind; and I hope Mr Micawber is now entering on a field where that mind will develop itself, and take a commanding station.'

I quite believe that Mr Micawber saw himself, in his judicial mind's eye, on the woolsack. He passed his hand complacently over his bald head, and said with ostentatious resignation: 'My dear, we will not anticipate the decrees of fortune. If I am reserved to wear a wig, I am at least prepared, externally,' in allusion to his baldness, 'for that distinction. I do not,' said Mr Micawber, 'regret my hair, and I may have been deprived of it for a specific purpose. I cannot say it is my intention, my dear Copperfield, to educate my son for the Church; I will not deny that I should be happy, on his account, to attain to eminence.'

'For the Church?' said I, still pondering between whiles on Uriah Heep.

'Yes,' said Mr Micawber. 'He has a remarkable head-voice, and will commence as a chorister. Our residence at Canterbury, and our local connection, will, no doubt, enable him to take advantage of any vacancy that may arise in the Cathedral corps.'

On looking at Master Micawber again, I saw that he had a certain expression of face, as if his voice were behind his eye-brows; where it presently appeared to be, on his singing us (as an alternative between that and bed) 'The Wood-Pecker Tapping.' After many compliments on this performance, we fell into some general conversation; and as I was too full of my desperate intentions to keep my altered circumstances to myself, I made them known to Mr and Mrs Micawber. I cannot express how extremely delighted they both were, by the idea of my aunt's being in difficulties, and how comfortable and friendly it made them.

When we were nearly come to the last round of the punch, I addressed myself to Traddles, and reminded him that we must not separate, without wishing our friends health, happiness, and success in their new career. I begged Mr Micawber to fill us bumpers, and proposed the toast in due form, shaking hands with him across the table, and kissing Mrs Micawber, to commemorate that eventful occasion. Traddles imitated me in the first particular, but did not consider himself a sufficiently old friend to venture on the second.

'My dear Copperfield,' said Mr Micawber, rising with one of his thumbs in each of his waistcoat pockets, 'the companion of my youth: if I may be allowed the expression – and my esteemed friend Traddles: if I may be permitted to call him so – will allow me, on the part of Mrs Micawber, myself, and our offspring, to thank them in the warmest and most uncompromising terms for their good wishes. It may be expected that on the eve of a migration which will consign us to a perfectly new existence,' Mr Micawber spoke as if they were going five hundred thousand miles, 'I should offer a few valedictory remarks to two such friends as I see before me. But all that I have to say in this way, I have said. Whatever station in society I may attain, through the medium of the learned profession of which I am about to become an unworthy member, I shall endeavour not to disgrace, and Mrs Micawber will be safe to adorn. Under the temporary pressure of pecuniary liabilities, contracted with a view to their immediate liquidation, but remaining unliquidated through a combination of circumstances, I have been under the necessity of assuming a garb from which my natural instincts recoil – I allude to spectacles – and possessing myself of a cognomen, to which I can establish no legitimate pretensions. All I have to say on that score is, that the cloud has passed from the dreary scene, and the God of Day is once more high upon the mountain tops. On Monday next, on the arrival of the four o'clock afternoon coach at Canterbury, my foot will be on my native heath – my name, Micawber!'

Mr Micawber resumed his seat on the close of these remarks, and drank two glasses of punch in grave succession. He then said with much solemnity: 'One thing more I have to do, before this separation is complete, and that is to perform an act of justice. My friend Mr Thomas Traddles has, on two several occasions, "put his name," if I may use a common expression, to bills of exchange for my accommodation. On the first occasion Mr Thomas Traddles was left – let me say, in short, in the lurch. The fulfilment of the second has not yet arrived. The amount of the first obligation,' here Mr Micawber carefully referred to papers, 'was, I believe, twenty-three, four, nine and a half; of the second, according to my entry of that transaction, eighteen, six, two. These sums, united, make a total, if my calculation is correct, amounting to forty-one, ten, eleven and a half. My friend Copperfield will perhaps do me the favour to check that total?'

I did so and found it correct.

'To leave this metropolis,' said Mr Micawber, 'and my friend Mr Thomas Traddles, without acquitting myself of the pecuniary part of this obligation, would weigh upon my mind to an insupportable extent. I have, therefore, prepared for my friend Mr Thomas Traddles, and I now hold in my hand a document, which accomplishes the desired object. I beg to hand to my friend Mr Thomas Traddles my I. O. U. for forty-one, ten, eleven and a half; and I am happy to recover my moral dignity, and to know that I can once more walk erect before my fellow-man!'

With this introduction (which greatly affected him), Mr Micawber placed his I. O. U. in the hands of Traddles, and said he wished him well in every relation of life. I am persuaded, not only that this was quite the same to Mr Micawber as paying the money, but that Traddles himself hardly knew the difference until he had had time to think about it.

Mr Micawber walked so erect before his fellow-man, on the strength of this virtuous action, that his chest looked half as broad again when he lighted us downstairs. We parted with great heartiness on both sides; and when I had seen Traddles to his own door, and was going home alone, I thought, among the other odd and contradictory things I mused upon, that, slippery as Mr Micawber was, I was probably indebted to some compassionate recollection he retained of me as his boy-lodger, for never having been asked by him for money. I certainly should not have had the moral courage to refuse it; and I have no doubt he knew that (to his credit be it written) quite as well as I did.

CHAPTER 37

A Little Cold Water

My new life had lasted for more than a week, and I was stronger than ever in those tremendous practical resolutions that I felt the crisis required. I continued to walk extremely fast, and to have a general idea that I was getting on. I made it a rule to take as much out of myself as I possibly could, in my way of doing everything to which I applied my energies. I made a perfect victim of myself. I even entertained some idea of putting myself on a vegetable diet, vaguely conceiving that, in becoming a graminivorous animal, I should sacrifice to Dora.

As yet, little Dora was quite unconscious of my desperate firmness, otherwise than as my letters darkly shadowed it forth.

Mr Micawber delivers some valedictory remarks

But, another Saturday came, and on that Saturday evening she was to be at Miss Mills's; and when Mr Mills had gone to his whist-club (telegraphed to me in the street, by a birdcage in the drawing-room middle window), I was to go there to tea.

By this time, we were quite settled down in Buckingham Street, where Mr Dick continued his copying in a state of absolute felicity. My aunt had obtained a signal victory over Mrs Crupp, by paying her off, throwing the first pitcher she planted on the stairs out of the window, and protecting in person, up and down the staircase, a supernumerary whom she engaged from the outer world. These vigorous measures struck such terror to the breast of Mrs Crupp, that she subsided into her own kitchen, under the impression that my aunt was mad. My aunt being supremely indifferent to Mrs Crupp's opinion and everybody else's, and rather favouring than discouraging the idea, Mrs Crupp, of late the bold, became within a few days so fainthearted, that rather than encounter my aunt upon the staircase, she would endeavour to hide her portly form behind doors – leaving visible, however, a wide margin of flannel petticoat – or would shrink into dark corners. This gave my aunt such unspeakable satisfaction, that I believe she took a delight in prowling up and down, with her bonnet insanely perched on the top of her head, at times when Mrs Crupp was likely to be in the way.

My aunt, being uncommonly neat and ingenious, made so many little improvements in our domestic arrangements, that I seemed to be richer instead of poorer. Among the rest, she converted the pantry into a dressing-room for me; and purchased and embellished a bedstead for my occupation, which looked as like a bookcase in the daytime as a bedstead could. I was the object of her constant solicitude; and my poor mother herself could not have loved me better, or studied more how to make me happy.

Peggotty had considered herself highly privileged in being allowed to participate in these labours; and, although she still retained something of her old sentiment of awe in reference to my aunt, had received so many marks of encouragement and confidence, that they were the best friends possible. But the time had now come (I am speaking of the Saturday when I was to take tea at Miss Mills's) when it was necessary for her to return home, and enter on the discharge of the duties she had undertaken in behalf of Ham. 'So goodbye, Barkis,' said my aunt, 'and take care of yourself! I am sure I never thought I could be sorry to lose you!'

I took Peggotty to the coach-office, and saw her off. She cried at parting, and confided her brother to my friendship as Ham had done. We had heard nothing of him since he went away, that sunny afternoon.

'And now, my own dear Davy,' said Peggotty, 'if, while you're a 'prentice, you should want any money to spend; or if, when you're out of your time, my dear, you should want any to set you up (and you must do one or other, or both, my darling), who has such a good right to ask leave to lend it you, as my sweet girl's own old stupid me!'

I was not so savagely independent as to say anything in reply, but that if ever I borrowed money of anyone, I would borrow it of her. Next to accepting a large sum on the spot, I believe this gave Peggotty more comfort than anything I could have done.

'And, my dear!' whispered Peggotty, 'tell the pretty little angel that I should so have liked to see her, only for a minute! And tell her that before she marries my boy, I'll come and make your house so beautiful for you, if you'll let me!'

I declared that nobody else should touch it; and this gave Peggotty such delight, that she went away in good spirits.

I fatigued myself as much as I possibly could in the Commons all day, by a variety of devices, and at the appointed time in the evening repaired to Mr Mills's street. Mr Mills, who was a terrible fellow to fall asleep after dinner, had not yet gone out, and there was no birdcage in the middle window.

He kept me waiting so long, that I fervently hoped the club would fine him for being late. At last he came out; and then I saw my own Dora hang up the birdcage, and peep into the balcony to look for me, and run in again when she saw I was there, while Jip remained behind, to bark injuriously at an immense butcher's dog in the street, who could have taken him like a pill.

Dora came to the drawing-room door to meet me; and Jip came scrambling out, tumbling over his own growls, under the impression that I was a Bandit; and we all three went in, as happy and loving as could be. I soon carried desolation into the bosom of our joys – not that I meant to do it, but that I was so full of the subject – by asking Dora, without the smallest preparation, if she could love a beggar?

My pretty, little startled Dora! Her only association with the word was a yellow face and a nightcap, or a pair of crutches, or a wooden leg, or a dog with a decanter-stand in his mouth, or something of that kind; and she stared at me with the most delightful wonder.

'How can you ask me anything so foolish?' pouted Dora. 'Love a beggar!'

'Dora, my own dearest!' said I. '*I* am a beggar!'

'How can you be such a silly thing,' replied Dora, slapping my hand, 'as to sit there, telling such stories? I'll make Jip bite you!'

Her childish way was the most delicious way in the world to me, but it was necessary to be explicit, and I solemnly repeated: 'Dora, my own life, I am your ruined David!'

'I declare I'll make Jip bite you!' said Dora, shaking her curls, 'if you are so ridiculous.'

But I looked so serious, that Dora left off shaking her curls, and laid her trembling little hand upon my shoulder, and first looked scared and anxious, then began to cry. That was dreadful. I fell upon my knees before the sofa, caressing her, and imploring her not to rend my heart; but for some time, poor little Dora did nothing but exclaim, Oh dear! Oh dear! And oh, she was so frightened! And where was Julia Mills! And oh, take her to Julia Mills, and go away, please! until I was almost beside myself.

At last, after an agony of supplication and protestation, I got Dora to look at me, with a horrified expression of face, which I gradually soothed until it was only loving, and her soft, pretty cheek was lying against mine. Then I told her, with my arms clasped round her, how I loved her, so dearly, and so dearly;

how I felt it right to offer to release her from her engagement, because now I was poor; how I never could bear it, or recover it, if I lost her; how I had no fears of poverty, if she had none, my arm being nerved and my heart inspired by her; how I was already working with a courage such as none but lovers knew; how I had begun to be practical, and to look into the future; how a crust well earned was sweeter far than a feast inherited; and much more to the same purpose, which I delivered in a burst of passionate eloquence quite surprising to myself, though I had been thinking about it, day and night, ever since my aunt had astonished me.

'Is your heart mine still, dear Dora?' said I rapturously, for I knew by her clinging to me that it was.

'Oh, yes!' cried Dora. 'Oh, yes, it's all yours. Oh, don't be dreadful!'

I dreadful! To Dora!

'Don't talk about being poor, and working hard!' said Dora, nestling closer to me. 'Oh, don't, don't!'

'My dearest love,' said I, 'the crust well earned – '

'Oh, yes; but I don't want to hear any more about crusts!' said Dora. 'And Jip must have a mutton-chop every day at twelve, or he'll die!'

I was charmed with her childish, winning way. I fondly explained to Dora that Jip should have his mutton-chop with his accustomed regularity. I drew a picture of our frugal home, made independent by my labour – sketching in the little house I had seen at Highgate, and my aunt in her room upstairs.

'I am not dreadful now, Dora?' said I tenderly.

'Oh, no, no!' cried Dora. 'But I hope your aunt will keep in her own room a good deal! And I hope she's not a scolding old thing!'

If it were possible for me to love Dora more than ever, I am sure I did. But I felt she was a little impracticable. It damped my newborn ardour to find that ardour so difficult of communication to her. I made another trial. When she was quite herself again, and was curling Jip's ears, as he lay upon her lap, I became grave, and said: 'My own! May I mention something?'

'Oh, please don't be practical!' said Dora coaxingly. 'Because it frightens me so!'

'Sweetheart!' I returned; 'there is nothing to alarm you in all this. I want you to think of it quite differently. I want to make it nerve you, and inspire you, Dora!'

'Oh, but that's so shocking!' cried Dora.

'My love, no. Perseverance and strength of character will enable us to bear much worse things.'

'But I haven't got any strength at all,' said Dora, shaking her curls. 'Have I, Jip? Oh, do kiss Jip, and be agreeable!'

It was impossible to resist kissing Jip, when she held him up to me for that purpose, putting her own bright, rosy little mouth into kissing form, as she directed the operation, which she insisted should be performed symmetrically, on the centre of his nose. I did as she bade me – rewarding myself afterwards for my obedience – and she charmed me out of my graver character for I don't know how long.

'But, Dora, my beloved!' said I, at last resuming it; 'I was going to mention something.'

The Judge of the Prerogative Court might have fallen in love with her, to see her fold her little hands and hold them up, begging and praying me not to be dreadful any more.

'Indeed, I am not going to be, my darling!' I assured her. 'But, Dora, my love, if you will sometimes think – not despondingly, you know; far from that! – but if you will sometimes think – just to encourage yourself – that you are engaged to a poor man – '

'Don't, don't! Pray don't!' cried Dora. 'It's so very dreadful!'

'My soul, not at all!' said I cheerfully. 'If you will sometimes think of that, and look about now and then at your papa's housekeeping, and endeavour to acquire a little habit – of accounts, for instance – '

Poor little Dora received this suggestion with something that was half a sob and half a scream.

' – it would be so useful to us afterwards,' I went on. 'And if you would promise me to read a little – a little Cookery Book that I would send you, it would be so excellent for both of us. For our path in life, my Dora,' said I, warming with the subject, 'is stony and rugged now, and it rests with us to smooth it. We must fight our way onward. We must be brave. There are obstacles to be met, and we must meet, and crush them!'

I was going on at a great rate, with a clenched hand, and a most enthusiastic countenance; but it was quite unnecessary to proceed. I had said enough. I had done it again. Oh, she was so frightened! Oh, where was Julia Mills! Oh, take her to Julia Mills, and go away, please! So that, in short, I was quite distracted, and raved about the drawing-room.

I thought I had killed her, this time. I sprinkled water on her face. I went down on my knees. I plucked at my hair. I denounced myself as a remorseless brute, and a ruthless beast. I implored her forgiveness. I besought her to look up. I ravaged Miss Mills's work-box for a smelling-bottle, and in my agony of mind applied an ivory needle-case instead, and dropped all the needles over Dora. I shook my fists at Jip, who was as frantic as myself. I did every wild extravagance that could be done, and was a long way beyond the end of my wits when Miss Mills came into the room.

'Who has done this!' exclaimed Miss Mills, succouring her friend.

I replied, '*I*, Miss Mills! *I* have done it! Behold the destroyer!' – or words to that effect – and hid my face from the light, in the sofa cushion.

At first Miss Mills thought it was a quarrel, and that we were verging on the Desert of Sahara; but she soon found out how matters stood, for my dear affectionate little Dora, embracing her, began exclaiming that I was 'a poor labourer'; and then cried for me, and embraced me, and asked me would I let her give me all her money to keep, and then fell on Miss Mills's neck, sobbing as if her tender heart were broken.

Miss Mills must have been born to be a blessing to us. She ascertained from me in a few words what it was all about, comforted Dora, and gradually convinced her that I was not a labourer – from my manner of stating the case I believe Dora concluded that I was a navigator, and went balancing myself up and down a plank all day with a wheelbarrow – and so brought us together in peace. When we were quite composed, and Dora had gone upstairs to put some rose-water to her eyes, Miss Mills rang for tea. In the ensuing interval, I told Miss Mills that she was evermore my friend, and that my heart must cease to vibrate ere I could forget her sympathy.

I then expounded to Miss Mills what I had endeavoured, so very unsuccessfully, to expound to Dora. Miss Mills replied, on general principles, that the Cottage of content was better than the Palace of cold splendour, and that where love was, all was.

I said to Miss Mills that this was very true, and who should know it better than I, who loved Dora with a love that never mortal had experienced yet. But on Miss Mills observing, with despondency, that it were well indeed for some hearts if this were so, I explained that I begged leave to restrict the observation to mortals of the masculine gender.

I then put it to Miss Mills to say whether she considered that there was or was not any practical merit in the suggestion I had been anxious to make concerning the accounts, the housekeeping, and the Cookery Book?

Miss Mills, after some consideration, thus replied: 'Mr Copperfield, I will be plain with you. Mental suffering and trial supply, in some natures, the place of years, and I will be as plain with you as if I were a Lady Abbess. No. The suggestion is not appropriate to our Dora. Our dearest Dora is a favourite child of nature. She is a thing of light, and airiness, and joy. I am free to confess that if it could be done, it might be well, but – ' And Miss Mills shook her head.

I was encouraged by this closing admission on the part of Miss Mills to ask her whether, for Dora's sake, if she had any opportunity of luring her attention to such preparations for an earnest life, she would avail herself of it. Miss Mills replied in the affirmative so readily that I further asked her if she would take charge of the Cookery Book; and if she ever could insinuate it upon Dora's acceptance, without frightening her, undertake to do me that crowning service. Miss Mills accepted this trust, too; but was not sanguine.

And Dora returned, looking such a lovely little creature that I really doubted whether she ought to be troubled with anything so ordinary. And she loved me so much, and was so captivating (particularly when she made Jip stand on his hind legs for toast, and when she pretended to hold that nose of his against the hot tea-pot for punishment because he wouldn't), that I felt like a sort of Monster who had got into a Fairy's bower, when I thought of having frightened her, and made her cry.

After tea we had the guitar; and Dora sang those same dear old French songs about the impossibility of ever on any account leaving off dancing, La ra la, La ra la, until I felt a much greater Monster than before.

We had only one check to our pleasure, and that happened a little while before I took my leave, when, Miss Mills chancing to make some allusion to tomorrow morning, I unluckily let out that, being obliged to exert myself now, I got up at five o'clock. Whether Dora had any idea that I was a Private Watchman, I am unable to say; but it made a great impression on her, and she neither played nor sang any more.

It was still on her mind when I bade her adieu; and she said to me in her pretty coaxing way – as if I were a doll, I used to think!

'Now, don't get up at five o'clock, you naughty boy. It's so nonsensical!'

'My love,' said I, 'I have work to do.'

'But don't do it!' returned Dora. 'Why should you?'

It was impossible to say to that sweet little surprised face, otherwise than lightly and playfully, that we must work to live.

'Oh! How ridiculous!' cried Dora.

'How shall we live without, Dora?' said I.

'How? Anyhow!' said Dora.

She seemed to think she had quite settled the question, and gave me such a triumphant little kiss, direct from her innocent heart, that I would hardly have put her out of conceit with her answer for a fortune.

Well! I loved her, and I went on loving her, most absorbingly, entirely, and completely. But going on, too, working pretty hard, and, busily keeping red hot all the irons I now had in the fire, I would sit sometimes of a night, opposite my aunt, thinking how I had frightened Dora that time, and how I could best make my way with a guitar-case through the forest of difficulty, until I used to fancy that my head was turning quite grey.

CHAPTER 38

A Dissolution of Partnership

I did not allow my resolution, with respect to the Parliamentary Debates, to cool. It was one of the irons I began to heat immediately, and one of the irons I kept hot, and hammered at with a perseverance I may honestly admire. I bought an approved scheme of the noble art and mystery of stenography (which cost me ten and sixpence); and plunged into a sea of perplexity that brought me in a few weeks to the confines of distraction. The changes that were rung upon dots, which in such a position meant such a thing, and in such another position something else, entirely different; the wonderful vagaries that were played by circles; the unaccountable consequences that resulted from marks like flies' legs; the tremendous effects of a curve in a wrong place; not only troubled my waking hours, but reappeared before me in my sleep. When I had groped my way, blindly, through these difficulties, and had mastered the alphabet, which was an Egyptian Temple in itself, there then appeared a procession of new horrors, called arbitrary characters; the most despotic characters I have ever known; who insisted, for instance, that a thing like the beginning of a cobweb meant 'expectation,' and that a pen and ink skyrocket stood for 'disadvantageous.' When I had fixed these wretches in my mind, I found that they had driven everything else out of it; then, beginning again, I forgot them; while I was picking them up, I dropped the other fragments of the system; in short, it was almost heart-breaking.

It might have been quite heart-breaking, but for Dora, who was the stay and anchor of my tempest-driven bark. Every

379

scratch in the scheme was a gnarled oak in the forest of difficulty, and I went on cutting them down, one after another, with such vigour that in three or four months I was in a condition to make an experiment on one of our crack speakers in the Commons. Shall I ever forget how the crack speaker walked off from me before I began, and left my imbecile pencil staggering about the paper as if it were in a fit!

This would not do, it was quite clear. I was flying too high, and should never get on, so. I resorted to Traddles for advice; who suggested that he should dictate speeches to me at a pace, and with occasional stoppages, adapted to my weakness. Very grateful for this friendly aid, I accepted the proposal; and night after night, almost every night, for a long time, we had a sort of private Parliament in Buckingham Street, after I came home from the Doctor's.

I should like to see such a Parliament anywhere else! My aunt and Mr Dick represented the Government or the Opposition (as the case might be), and Traddles, with the assistance of Enfield's Speaker or a volume of parliamentary orations, thundered astonishing invectives against them. Standing by the table, with his finger in the page to keep the place, and his right arm flourishing above his head, Traddles, as Mr Pitt, Mr Fox, Mr Sheridan, Mr Burke, Lord Castlereagh, Viscount Sidmouth, or Mr Canning, would work himself into the most violent heats, and deliver the most withering denunciations of the profligacy and corruption of my aunt and Mr Dick; while I used to sit, at a little distance, with my notebook on my knee, fagging after him with all my might and main. The inconsistency and recklessness of Traddles were not to be exceeded by any real politician. He was for any description of policy in the compass of a week; and nailed all sorts of colours to every denomination of mast. My aunt, looking very like an immovable Chancellor of the Exchequer, would occasionally throw in an interruption or two, as 'Hear!' or 'No!' or 'Oh!' when the text seemed to require it; which was always a signal to Mr Dick (a perfect country gentleman) to follow lustily with the same cry. But Mr Dick got taxed with such things in the course of his Parliamentary career, and was made responsible for such awful consequences, that he became uncomfortable in his mind sometimes. I believe he actually began to be afraid he really had been doing something tending to the annihilation of the British constitution and the ruin of the country.

Often and often we pursued these debates until the clock pointed to midnight, and the candles were burning down. The result of so much good practice was that by and by I began to keep pace with Traddles pretty well, and should have been quite triumphant if I had had the least idea what my notes were about. But as to reading them after I had got them, I might as well have copied the Chinese inscriptions on an immense collection of tea-chests, or the golden characters on all the great red and green bottles in the chemists' shops!

There was nothing for it but to turn back and begin all over again. It was very hard, but I turned back, though with a heavy heart, and began laboriously and methodically to plod over the

Traddles makes a figure in parliament and I report him

same tedious ground at a snail's pace; stopping to examine minutely every speck in the way, on all sides, and making the most desperate efforts to know these elusive characters by sight wherever I met them. I was always punctual at the office; at the Doctor's, too; and I really did work, as the common expression is, like a cart-horse.

One day, when I went to the Commons as usual, I found Mr Spenlow in the doorway looking extremely grave, and talking to himself. As he was in the habit of complaining of pains in his head – he had naturally a short throat, and I do seriously believe he overstarched himself – I was at first alarmed by the idea that he was not quite right in that direction; but he soon relieved my uneasiness.

Instead of returning my 'Good-morning' with his usual affability, he looked at me in a distant, ceremonious manner, and coldly requested me to accompany him to a certain coffee-house, which in those days had a door opening into the Commons, just within the little archway in St Paul's churchyard. I complied, in a very uncomfortable state, and with a warm shooting all over me, as if my apprehensions were breaking out into buds. When I allowed him to go on a little before, on account of the narrowness of the way, I observed that he carried his head with a lofty air that was particularly unpromising; and my mind misgave me that he had found out about my darling Dora.

If I had not guessed this, on the way to the coffee-house, I could hardly have failed to know what was the matter when I followed him into an upstairs room, and found Miss Murdstone there, supported by a background of sideboard, on which were several inverted tumblers sustaining lemons, and two of those extraordinary boxes, all corners and flutings, for sticking knives and forks in, which, happily for mankind, are now obsolete.

Miss Murdstone gave me her chilly finger-nails, and sat severely rigid. Mr Spenlow shut the door, motioned me to a chair, and stood on the hearth-rug in front of the fireplace.

'Have the goodness to show Mr Copperfield,' said Mr Spenlow, 'what you have in your reticule, Miss Murdstone.'

I believe it was the old identical steel-clasped reticule of my childhood, that shut up like a bite. Compressing her lips, in sympathy with the snap, Miss Murdstone opened it – opening her mouth a little at the same time – and produced my last letter to Dora, teeming with expressions of devoted affection.

'I believe that is your writing, Mr Copperfield?' said Mr Spenlow.

I was very hot, and the voice I heard was very unlike mine, when I said, 'It is, sir!'

'If I am not mistaken,' said Mr Spenlow, as Miss Murdstone brought a parcel of letters out of her reticule, tied round with the dearest bit of blue ribbon, 'those are also from your pen, Mr Copperfield?'

I took them from her with a most desolate sensation; and glancing at such phrases at the top as, 'My ever dearest and own Dora,', 'My best beloved angel,', 'My blessed one for ever,' and the like, blushed deeply, and inclined my head.

'No, thank you!' said Mr Spenlow coldly, as I mechanically offered them back to him. 'I will not deprive you of them. Miss Murdstone, be so good as to proceed!'

That gentle creature, after a moment's thoughtful survey of the carpet, delivered herself with much dry unction as follows: 'I must confess to having entertained my suspicions of Miss Spenlow, in reference to David Copperfield, for some time. I observed Miss Spenlow and David Copperfield when they first met; and the impression made upon me then was not agreeable. The depravity of the human heart is such – '

'You will oblige me, ma'am,' interrupted Mr Spenlow, 'by confining yourself to facts.'

Miss Murdstone cast down her eyes, shook her head as if protesting against this unseemly interruption, and with frowning dignity resumed: 'Since I am to confine myself to facts, I will state them as drily as I can. Perhaps that will be considered an acceptable source of proceeding. I have already said, sir, that I have had my suspicions of Miss Spenlow, in reference to David Copperfield, for some time. I have frequently endeavoured to find decisive corroboration of those suspicions, but without effect. I have therefore forborne to mention them to Miss Spenlow's father'; looking severely at him; 'knowing how little disposition there usually is, in such cases, to acknowledge the conscientious discharge of duty.'

Mr Spenlow seemed quite cowed by the gentlemanly sternness of Miss Murdstone's manner, and deprecated her severity with a conciliatory little wave of his hand.

'On my return to Norwood, after the period of absence occasioned by my brother's marriage,' pursued Miss Murdstone in a disdainful voice, 'and on the return of Miss Spenlow from her visit to her friend Miss Mills, I imagined that the manner of Miss Spenlow gave me greater occasion for suspicion than before. Therefore I watched Miss Spenlow closely.'

Dear, tender little Dora, so unconscious of this Dragon's eye.

'Still,' resumed Miss Murdstone, 'I found no proof until last night. It appeared to me that Miss Spenlow received too many letters from her friend Miss Mills; but Miss Mills being her friend with her father's full concurrence,' another telling blow at Mr Spenlow, 'it was not for me to interfere. If I may not be permitted to allude to the natural depravity of the human heart, at least I may – I must – be permitted, so far to refer to misplaced confidence.'

Mr Spenlow apologetically murmured his assent.

'Last evening after tea,' pursued Miss Murdstone, 'I observed the little dog starting, rolling, and growling about the drawing-room, worrying something. I said to Miss Spenlow, "Dora, what is that the dog has in his mouth? It's paper." Miss Spenlow immediately put her hand to her frock, gave a sudden cry, and ran to the dog. I interposed, and said, "Dora, my love, you must permit me."'

Oh, Jip, miserable Spaniel, this wretchedness, then, was your work!

'Miss Spenlow endeavoured,' said Miss Murdstone, 'to bribe me with kisses, work-boxes, and small articles of jewellery – that, of course, I pass over. The little dog retreated under the sofa on my approaching him, and was with great difficulty dislodged by the fire-irons. Even when dislodged, he still kept the letter in his mouth; and on my endeavouring to take it from him, at the imminent risk of being bitten, he kept it between his teeth so pertinaciously as to suffer himself to be held suspended in the air by means of the document. At length I obtained possession of it. After perusing it, I taxed Miss Spenlow with having many such letters in her possession; and ultimately obtained from her the packet which is now in David Copperfield's hand.'

Here she ceased; and snapping her reticule again, and shutting her mouth, looked as if she might be broken, but could never be bent.

'You have heard Miss Murdstone,' said Mr Spenlow, turning to me. 'I beg to ask, Mr Copperfield, if you have anything to say in reply?'

The picture I had before me, of the beautiful little treasure of my heart, sobbing and crying all night – of her being alone, frightened, and wretched, then – of her having so piteously begged and prayed that stony-hearted woman to forgive her – of her having vainly offered her those kisses, work-boxes, and trinkets – of her being in such grievous distress, and all for me – very much impaired the little dignity I had been able to muster. I am afraid I was in a tremulous state for a minute or so, though I did my best to disguise it.

'There is nothing I can say, sir,' I returned, 'except that all the blame is mine. Dora – '

'Miss Spenlow, if you please,' said her father majestically.

' – was induced and persuaded by me,' I went on, swallowing that colder designation, 'to consent to this concealment, and I bitterly regret it.'

'You are very much to blame, sir,' said Mr Spenlow, walking to and fro upon the hearth-rug, and emphasising what he said with his whole body instead of his head, on account of the stiffness of his cravat and spine. 'You have done a stealthy and unbecoming action, Mr Copperfield. When I take a gentleman to my house, no matter whether he is nineteen, twenty-nine, or ninety, I take him there in a spirit of confidence. If he abuses my confidence, he commits a dishonourable action, Mr Copperfield.'

'I feel it, sir, I assure you,' I returned. 'But I never thought so, before. Sincerely, honestly, indeed, Mr Spenlow, I never thought so, before. I love Miss Spenlow to that extent – '

'Pooh! nonsense!' said Mr Spenlow, reddening. 'Pray don't tell me to my face that you love my daughter, Mr Copperfield!'

'Could I defend my conduct if I did not, sir?' I returned, with all humility.

'Can you defend your conduct if you do, sir?' said Mr Spenlow, stopping short upon the hearth-rug. 'Have you considered your years, and my daughter's years, Mr Copperfield? Have you considered what it is to undermine the confidence that should subsist between my daughter and myself? Have you considered my daughter's station in life, the projects I may contemplate for her advancement, the testamentary intentions I may have with reference to her? Have you considered anything, Mr Copperfield?'

'Very little, sir, I am afraid,' I answered, speaking to him as respectfully and sorrowfully as I felt; 'but pray believe me, I have considered my own worldly position. When I explained it to you, we were already engaged – '

'I beg,' said Mr Spenlow, more like Punch than I had ever seen him, as he energetically struck one hand upon the other – I could not help noticing that even in my despair – 'that you will not talk to me of engagements, Mr Copperfield!'

The otherwise immovable Miss Murdstone laughed contemptuously in one short syllable.

'When I explained my altered position to you, sir,' I began again, substituting a new form of expression for what was so unpalatable to him, 'this concealment, into which I am so unhappy as to have led Miss Spenlow, had begun. Since I have been in that altered position, I have strained every nerve, I have exerted every energy, to improve it. I am sure I shall improve it in time. Will you grant me time – any length of time? We are both so young, sir – '

'You are right,' interrupted Mr Spenlow, nodding his head a great many times, and frowning very much, 'you are both very young. It's all nonsense. Let there be an end of the nonsense. Take away those letters, and throw them in the fire. Give me Miss Spenlow's letters to throw in the fire; and although our future intercourse must, you are aware, be restricted to the Commons here, we will agree to make no further mention of the past. Come, Mr Copperfield, you don't want sense; and this is the sensible course.'

No. I couldn't think of agreeing to it. I was very sorry, but there was a higher consideration than sense. Love was above all earthly considerations, and I loved Dora to idolatry, and Dora loved me. I didn't exactly say so; I softened it down as much as I could; but I implied it, and I was resolute upon it. I don't think I made myself very ridiculous, but I know I was resolute.

'Very well, Mr Copperfield,' said Mr Spenlow, 'I must try my influence with my daughter.'

Miss Murdstone, by an expressive sound, a long drawn respiration, which was neither a sigh nor a moan, but was like both, gave it as her opinion that he should have done this at first.

'I must try,' said Mr Spenlow, confirmed by this support, 'my influence with my daughter. Do you decline to take those letters, Mr Copperfield?' For I had laid them on the table.

Yes. I told him I hoped he would not think it wrong, but I couldn't possibly take them from Miss Murdstone.

'Nor from me?' said Mr Spenlow.

No, I replied with the profoundest respect; nor from him.

'Very well!' said Mr Spenlow.

A silence succeeding, I was undecided whether to go or stay. At length I was moving quietly towards the door, with the intention of saying that perhaps I should consult his feelings best by withdrawing, when he said, with his hands in his coat pockets, into which it was as much as he could do to get them, and with what I should call, upon the whole, a decidedly pious air: 'You are probably aware, Mr Copperfield, that I am not altogether destitute of worldly possessions, and that my daughter is my nearest and dearest relative?'

I hurriedly made him a reply to the effect that I hoped the error into which I had been betrayed by the desperate nature of my love did not induce him to think me mercenary, too.

'I don't allude to the matter in that light,' said Mr Spenlow. 'It would be better for yourself, and all of us, if you *were* mercenary, Mr Copperfield – I mean, if you were more discreet and less influenced by all this youthful nonsense. No. I merely say, with quite another view, you are probably aware I have some property to bequeath to my child?'

I certainly supposed so.

'And you can hardly think,' said Mr Spenlow, 'having experience of what we see, in the Commons here, every day, of the various unaccountable and negligent proceedings of men, in respect of their testamentary arrangements – of all subjects, the one on which perhaps the strangest revelations of human inconsistency are to be met with – but that mine are made?'

I inclined my head in acquiescence.

'I should not allow,' said Mr Spenlow, with an evident increase of pious sentiment, and slowly shaking his head as he poised himself upon his toes and heels alternately, 'my suitable provision for my child to be influenced by a piece of youthful folly like the present. It is mere folly; mere nonsense. In a little while, it will weigh lighter than any feather. But I might – I might – if this silly business were not completely relinquished altogether, be induced in some anxious moment to guard her from, and surround her with protections against, the consequences of any foolish step in the way of marriage. Now, Mr Copperfield, I hope that you will not render it necessary for me to open, even for a quarter of an hour, that closed page in the book of life, and unsettle, even for a quarter of an hour, grave affairs long since composed.'

There was a serenity, a tranquillity, a calm-sunset air about him, which quite affected me. He was so peaceful and resigned – clearly had his affairs in such perfect train, and so systematically wound up – that he was a man to feel touched in the contemplation of. I really think I saw tears rise to his eyes, from the depth of his own feeling of all this.

But what could I do? I could not deny Dora and my own heart. When he told me I had better take a week to consider of what he had said, how could I say I wouldn't take a week, yet how could I fail to know that no amount of weeks could influence such love as mine?

'In the meantime, confer with Miss Trotwood, or with any person with any knowledge of life,' said Mr Spenlow, adjusting his cravat with both hands. 'Take a week, Mr Copperfield.'

I submitted; and with a countenance as expressive as I was able to make it of dejected and despairing constancy, came out of the room. Miss Murdstone's heavy eyebrows followed me to the door – I say her eyebrows rather than her eyes, because they were much more important in her face – and she looked so exactly as she used to look, at about that hour of the morning, in our parlour at Blunderstone, that I could have fancied I had been breaking down in my lessons again, and that the dead weight on my mind was that horrible old spelling-book with oval woodcuts, shaped, to my youthful fancy, like the glasses out of spectacles.

When I got to the office, and, shutting out old Tiffey and the rest of them with my hands, sat at my desk, in my own particular nook, thinking of this earthquake that had taken place so unexpectedly, and in the bitterness of my spirit cursing Jip, I fell into such a state of torment about Dora that I wonder I did not take up my hat and rush insanely to Norwood. The idea of their frightening her, and making her cry, and of my not being there to comfort her, was so excruciating that it impelled me to write a wild letter to Mr Spenlow, beseeching him not to visit upon her the consequences of my awful destiny. I implored him to spare her gentle nature – not to crush a fragile flower – and addressed him generally, to the best of my remembrance, as if, instead of being her father, he had been an Ogre, or the Dragon of Wantley. This letter I sealed and laid upon his desk before he returned; and when he came in, I saw him, through the half-opened door of his room, take it up and read it.

He said nothing about it all the morning; but before he went away in the afternoon he called me in, and told me that I need not make myself at all uneasy about his daughter's happiness. He had assured her, he said, that it was all nonsense; and he had nothing more to say to her. He believed he was an indulgent father (as indeed he was), and I might spare myself any solicitude on her account.

'You may make it necessary, if you are foolish or obstinate, Mr Copperfield,' he observed, 'for me to send my daughter abroad again, for a term; but I have a better opinion of you. I hope you will be wiser than that in a few days. As to Miss Murdstone,' for I had alluded to her in the letter, 'I respect that lady's vigilance, and feel obliged to her; but she has strict charge to avoid the subject. All I desire, Mr Copperfield, is, that it should be forgotten. All you have got to do, Mr Copperfield, is, to forget it.'

All! In the note I wrote to Miss Mills, I bitterly quoted this sentiment. All I had to do, I said, with gloomy sarcasm, was to forget Dora. That was all, and what was that? I entreated Miss Mills to see me, that evening. If it could not be done with Mr Mills's sanction and concurrence, I besought a clandestine interview in the back kitchen where the Mangle was. I informed her that my reason was tottering on its throne, and only she, Miss Mills, could prevent its being deposed. I signed myself, hers distractedly; and I couldn't help feeling, when I read this composition over, before sending it by a porter, that it was something in the style of Mr Micawber.

However, I sent it. At night I repaired to Miss Mills's street, and walked up and down, until I was stealthily fetched in by Miss Mills's maid, and taken the area way to the back kitchen. I have since seen reason to believe that there was nothing on earth to prevent my going in at the front door, and being shown up into the drawing-room, except Miss Mills's love of the romantic and mysterious.

In the back kitchen I raved as became me. I went there, I suppose, to make a fool of myself, and I am quite sure I did it. Miss Mills had received a hasty note from Dora, telling her that all was discovered, and saying, 'Oh, pray come to me, Julia, do, do!' But Miss Mills, mistrusting the acceptability of her presence to the higher powers, had not yet gone; and we were all benighted in the Desert of Sahara.

Miss Mills had a wonderful flow of words, and liked to pour

them out. I could not help feeling, though she mingled her tears with mine, that she had a dreadful luxury in our afflictions. She petted them, as I may say, and made the most of them. A deep gulf, she observed, had opened between Dora and me, and Love could only span it with its rainbow. Love must suffer in this stern world; it ever had been so, it ever would be so. No matter, Miss Mills remarked. Hearts confined by cobwebs would burst at last, and then Love was avenged.

This was small consolation, but Miss Mills wouldn't encourage fallacious hopes. She made me much more wretched than I was before, and I felt (and told her with the deepest gratitude) that she was indeed a friend. We resolved that she should go to Dora the first thing in the morning, and find some means of assuring her, either by looks or words, of my devotion and misery. We parted, overwhelmed with grief; and I think Miss Mills enjoyed herself completely.

I confided all to my aunt when I got home; and in spite of all she could say to me, went to bed despairing. I got up despairing, and went out despairing. It was Saturday morning, and I went straight to the Commons.

I was surprised, when I came within sight of our office door, to see the ticket-porters standing outside talking together, and some half dozen stragglers gazing at the windows, which were shut up. I quickened my pace, and, passing among them, wondering at their looks, went hurriedly in.

The clerks were there, but nobody was doing anything. Old Tiffey, for the first time in his life I should think, was sitting on somebody else's stool, and had not hung up his hat.

'This is a dreadful calamity, Mr Copperfield,' said he, as I entered.

'What is?' I exclaimed. 'What's the matter?'

'Don't you know?' cried Tiffey, and all the rest of them, coming round me.

'No!' said I, looking from face to face.

'Mr Spenlow,' said Tiffey.

'What about him?'

'Dead!'

I thought it was the office reeling and not I, as one of the clerks caught hold of me. They sat me down in a chair, untied my neckcloth, and brought me some water. I have no idea whether this took any time.

'Dead?' said I.

'He dined in town yesterday, and drove down in the phaeton by himself,' said Tiffey, 'having sent his own groom home by the coach, as he sometimes did, you know –'

'Well?'

'The phaeton went home without him. The horses stopped at the stable gate. The man went out with a lantern. Nobody in the carriage.'

'Had they run away?'

'They were not hot,' said Tiffey, putting on his glasses, 'no hotter, I understand, than they would have been, going down at the usual pace. The reins were broken, but they had been dragging on the ground. The house was roused up directly, and three of them went out along the road. They found him a mile off.'

'More than a mile off, Mr Tiffey,' interposed a junior.

'Was it? I believe you are right,' said Tiffey, '*more* than a mile off – not far from the church – lying partly on the roadside, and partly on the path, upon his face. Whether he fell out in a fit, or got out, feeling ill before the fit came on – or even whether he was quite dead then, though there is no doubt he was quite insensible – no one appears to know. If he breathed, certainly he never spoke. Medical assistance was got as soon as possible, but it was quite useless.'

I cannot describe the state of mind into which I was thrown by this intelligence. The shock of such an event happening so suddenly, and happening to one with whom I had been in any respect at variance – the appalling vacancy in the room he had occupied so lately, where his chair and table seemed to wait for him, and his handwriting of yesterday was like a ghost – the indefinable impossibility of separating him from the place, and feeling, when the door opened, as if he might come in – the lazy hush and rest there was in the office, and the insatiable relish with which our people talked about it, and other people came in and out all day, and gorged themselves with the subject – this is easily intelligible to anyone. What I cannot describe is, how, in the innermost recesses of my own heart, I had a lurking jealousy even of Death. How I felt as if its might would push me from my ground in Dora's thoughts. How I was, in a grudging way I have no words for, envious of her grief. How it made me restless to think of her weeping to others, or being consoled by others. How I had a grasping, avaricious wish to shut out everybody from her but myself, and to be all in all to her, at that unseasonable time of all times.

In the trouble of this state of mind – not exclusively my own, I hope, but known to others – I went down to Norwood that night; and finding from one of the servants, when I made my enquiries at the door, that Miss Mills was there, got my aunt to direct a letter to her, which I wrote. I deplored the untimely death of Mr Spenlow most sincerely, and shed tears in doing so. I entreated her to tell Dora, if Dora were in a state to hear it, that he had spoken to me with the utmost kindness and consideration; and had coupled nothing but tenderness, not a single or reproachful word, with her name. I know I did this selfishly, to have my name brought before her; but I tried to believe it was an act of justice to his memory. Perhaps I did believe it.

My aunt received a few lines next day in reply; addressed, outside, to her; within, to me. Dora was overcome by grief; and when her friend had asked her should she send her love to me, had only cried, as she was always crying, 'Oh, dear papa! oh, poor papa!' But she had not said No, and that I made the most of.

Mr Jorkins, who had been at Norwood since the occurrence, came to the office a few days afterwards. He and Tiffey were closeted together for some few moments, and then Tiffey looked out at the door and beckoned me in.

'Oh!' said Mr Jorkins. 'Mr Tiffey and myself, Mr Copperfield, are about to examine the desk, the drawers, and other such repositories of the deceased, with the view of sealing up his private papers, and searching for a will. There is no trace of any, elsewhere. It may be as well for you to assist us, if you please.'

I had been in agony to obtain some knowledge of the circumstances in which my Dora would be placed – as, in whose guardianship, and so forth – and this was something towards it. We began the search at once; Mr Jorkins unlocking the drawers and desks, and we all taking out the papers. The office papers we placed on one side, and the private papers (which were not numerous) on the other. We were very grave; and when we came to a stray seal, or pencil-case, or ring, or any little article of that kind which we associated personally with him, we spoke very low.

We had sealed up several packets; and were still going on dustily and quietly, when Mr Jorkins said to us, applying exactly the same words to his late partner as his late partner had applied to him: 'Mr Spenlow was very difficult to move from the beaten track. You know what he was! I am disposed to think he had made no will.'

'Oh, I know he had!' said I.

They both stopped and looked at me.

'On the very day when I last saw him,' said I, 'he told me that he had, and that his affairs were long since settled.'

Mr Jorkins and old Tiffey shook their heads with one accord.

'That looks unpromising,' said Tiffey.

'Very unpromising,' said Mr Jorkins.

'Surely you don't doubt – ' I began.

'My good Mr Copperfield!' said Tiffey, laying his hand upon my arm, and shutting up both his eyes as he shook his head; 'if you had been in the Commons as long as I have, you would know that there is no subject on which men are so inconsistent, and so little to be trusted.'

'Why, bless my soul, he made that very remark!' I replied persistently.

'I should call that almost final,' observed Tiffey. 'My opinion is – no will.'

It appeared a wonderful thing to me, but it turned out that there *was* no will. He had never so much as thought of making one, so far as his papers afforded any evidence; for there was no kind of hint, sketch, or memorandum, of any testamentary intention whatever. What was scarcely less astonishing to me was, that his affairs were in a most disordered state. It was extremely difficult, I heard, to make out what he owed, or what he had paid, or of what he died possessed. It was considered likely that for years he could have had no clear opinion on these subjects himself. By little and little it came out that, in the competition on all points of appearance and gentility then running high in the Commons, he had spent more than his professional income, which was not a very large one, and had reduced his private means, if they ever had been great (which was exceedingly doubtful), to a very low ebb, indeed. There was a sale of the furniture and lease, at Norwood; and Tiffey told me, little thinking how interested I was in the story, that, paying all the just debts of the deceased, and deducting his share of outstanding bad and doubtful debts due to the firm, he wouldn't give a thousand pounds for all the assets remaining.

This was at the expiration of about six weeks. I had suffered

tortures all the time; and thought I really must have laid violent hands upon myself, when Miss Mills still reported to me that my broken-hearted little Dora would say nothing, when I was mentioned, but 'Oh, poor papa! Oh, dear papa!' Also, that she had no other relations than two aunts, maiden sisters of Mr Spenlow, who lived at Putney, and who had not held any other than chance communication with their brother for many years. Not that they had ever quarrelled (Miss Mills informed me); but that having been on the occasion of Dora's christening invited to tea, when they considered themselves privileged to be invited to dinner, they had expressed their opinion in writing that it was 'better for the happiness of all parties' that they should stay away; since which they had gone their road, and their brother had gone his.

These two ladies now emerged from their retirement, and proposed to take Dora to live at Putney. Dora, clinging to them both, and weeping, exclaimed, 'Oh, yes, aunts! Please take Julia Mills and me and Jip to Putney!' So they went, very soon after the funeral.

How I found time to haunt Putney, I am sure I don't know; but I contrived, by some means or other, to prowl about the neighbourhood pretty often. Miss Mills, for the more exact discharge of the duties of friendship, kept a journal; and she used to meet me sometimes, on the Common, and read it, or (if she had not time to do that) lend it to me. How I treasured up the entries, of which I subjoin a sample!

'Monday. My sweet D. still much depressed. Headache. Called attention to J. as being beautifully sleek. D. fondled J. Associations thus awakened opened floodgates of sorrow. Rush of grief admitted. (Are tears the dewdrops of the heart? J. M.)

'Tuesday. D. weak and nervous. Beautiful in pallor. (Do we not remark this in moon likewise? J. M.) D., J. M., and J. took airing in carriage. J. looking out of window, and barking violently at dustmen, occasioned smile to overspread features of D. (Of such slight links is chain of life composed! J. M.)

'Wednesday. D. comparatively cheerful. Sang to her, as congenial melody, 'Evening Bells'. Effect not soothing, but reverse. D. inexpressibly affected. Found sobbing afterwards, in own room. Quoted verses respecting self and young Gazelle. Ineffectually. Also referred to Patience on Monument. (Qy. Why on Monument? J. M.)

'Thursday. D. certainly improved. Better night. Slight tinge of damask revisiting cheek. Resolved to mention name of D. C. Introduced same, cautiously, in course of airing. D. immediately overcome. "Oh, dear, dear Julia! Oh, I have been a naughty and undutiful child!" Soothed and caressed. Drew ideal picture of D. C. on verge of tomb. D. again overcome. "Oh, what shall I do, what shall I do? Oh, take me somewhere!" Much alarmed. Fainting of D. and glass of water from public-house. (Poetical affinity. Chequered sign on doorpost; chequered human life. Alas! J. M.)

'Friday. Day of incident. Man appears in kitchen, with blue bag, "for lady's boots left out to heel." Cook replies, "No such orders." Man argues point. Cook withdraws to enquire, leaving man alone with J. On Cook's return, man still argues point, but ultimately goes. J. missing. D. distracted. Information sent to police. Man to be identified by broad nose, and legs like balustrades of bridge. Search made in every direction. No J. D. weeping bitterly, and inconsolable. Renewed reference to young Gazelle. Appropriate, but unavailing. Towards evening, strange boy calls. Brought into parlour. Broad nose, but no balustrades. Says he wants a pound, and knows a dog. Declines to explain further, though much pressed. Pound being produced by D. takes Cook to little house, where J. alone tied up to leg of table. Joy of D., who dances round J. while he eats his supper. Emboldened by this happy change, mention D. C. upstairs. D. weeps afresh, cries piteously. "Oh, don't, don't, don't. It is so wicked to think of anything but poor papa!" – embraces J. and sobs herself to sleep. (Must not D. C. confine himself to the broad pinions of Time? J. M.)'

Miss Mills and her journal were my sole consolation at this period. To see her, who had seen Dora but a little while before – to trace the initial letter of Dora's name through her sympathetic pages – to be made more and more miserable by her – were my only comforts. I felt as if I had been living in a palace of cards, which had tumbled down, leaving only Miss Mills and me among the ruins; as if some grim enchanter had drawn a magic circle round the innocent goddess of my heart, which nothing, indeed, but those same strong pinions, capable of carrying so many people over so much, would enable me to enter!

CHAPTER 39

Wickfield and Heep

My aunt beginning, I imagine, to be made seriously uncomfortable by my prolonged dejection, made a pretence of being anxious that I should go to Dover, to see that all was working well at the cottage, which was let; and to conclude an agreement, with the same tenant, for a longer term of occupation. Janet was drafted into the service of Mrs Strong, where I saw her every day. She had been undecided, on leaving Dover, whether or no to give the finishing touch to that renunciation of mankind in which she had been educated, by marrying a pilot; but she decided against that venture. Not so much for the sake of principle, I believe, as because she happened not to like him.

Although it required an effort to leave Miss Mills, I fell rather willingly into my aunt's pretence, as a means of enabling me to pass a few tranquil hours with Agnes. I consulted the good Doctor relative to an absence of three days; and the Doctor wishing me to take that relaxation – he wished me to take more; but my energy could not bear that – I made up my mind to go.

As to the Commons, I had no great occasion to be particular about my duties in that quarter. To say the truth, we were getting in no very good odour among the tip-top proctors, and were rapidly sliding down to but a doubtful position. The business had been indifferent under Mr Jorkins, before Mr Spenlow's time; and although it had been quickened by the infusion of new blood, and by the display which Mr Spenlow made, still it was not established on a sufficiently strong basis to bear, without being shaken, such a blow as the sudden loss of its active manager. It fell off very much. Mr Jorkins, notwithstanding his reputation in the firm, was an easy-going, incapable sort of man, whose reputation out of doors was not calculated to back it up. I was turned over to him now, and when I saw him take his snuff and let the business go, I regretted my aunt's thousand pounds more than ever.

But this was not the worst of it. There were a number of hangers-on and outsiders about the Commons, who, without being proctors themselves, dabbled in common-form business, and got it done by real proctors, who lent their names in consideration of a share in the spoil; – and there were a good many of these, too. As our house now wanted business on any terms, we joined this noble band; and threw out lures to the hangers-on and outsiders, to bring their business to us. Marriage licences and small probates were what we all looked for, and what paid us best; and the competition for these ran very high indeed. Kidnappers and inveiglers were planted in all the avenues or entrance to the Commons, with instructions to do their utmost to cut off all persons in mourning, and all gentlemen with anything bashful in their appearance, and entice them to the offices in which their respective employers were interested – which instructions were so well observed, that I myself, before I was known by sight, was twice hustled into the premises of our principal opponent. The conflicting interests of these touting gentlemen being of a nature to irritate their feelings, personal collisions took place; and the Commons was even scandalised by our principal inveigler (who had formerly been in the wine trade, and afterwards in the sworn brokery line) walking about for some days with a black eye. Any one of these scouts used to think nothing of politely assisting an old lady in black out of a vehicle, killing any proctor whom she enquired for, representing his employer as the lawful successor and representative of that proctor, and bearing the old lady off (sometimes greatly affected) to his employer's office. Many captives were brought to me in this way. As to marriage licences, the competition rose to such a pitch, that a shy gentleman in want of one, had nothing to do but submit himself to the first inveigler, or be fought for, and become the prey of the strongest. One of our clerks, who was an outsider, used, in the height of this contest, to sit with his hat on, that he might be ready to rush out and swear before a surrogate any victim who was brought in. The system of inveigling continues, I believe, to this day. The last time I was in the Commons, a civil able-bodied person in a white apron pounced out upon me from a doorway, and whispering the word 'Marriage-licence' in my ear, was with great difficulty prevented from taking me up in his arms and lifting me into a proctor's.

From this digression, let me proceed to Dover.

I found everything in a satisfactory state at the cottage; and was enabled to gratify my aunt exceedingly by reporting that the tenant inherited her feud, and waged incessant war against donkeys. Having settled the little business I had to transact there, and slept there one night, I walked on to Canterbury early in the morning. It was now winter again; and the fresh, cold, windy day, and the sweeping down-land, brightened up my hopes a little.

Coming into Canterbury, I loitered through the old streets with a sober pleasure that calmed my spirits, and eased my heart. There were the old signs, the old names over the shops, the old people serving in them. It appeared so long, since I had been a schoolboy there, that I wondered the place was so little changed, until I reflected how little I was changed myself. Strange to say, that quiet influence which was inseparable in my mind from Agnes, seemed to pervade even the city where she dwelt. The venerable Cathedral towers, and the old jackdaws and rooks, whose airy voices made them more retired than perfect silence would have done; the battered gateways, once stuck full with statues, long thrown down, and crumbled away, like the reverential pilgrims who had gazed upon them; the still nooks, where the ivied growth of centuries crept over gabled ends and ruined walls; the ancient houses, the pastoral landscape of field, orchard, and garden; everywhere – on everything – I felt the same serener air, the same calm, thoughtful, softening spirit.

Arrived at Mr Wickfield's house, I found, in the little lower room on the ground floor, where Uriah Heep had been of old accustomed to sit, Mr Micawber plying his pen with great assiduity. He was dressed in a legal-looking suit of black, and loomed, burly and large, in that small office.

Mr Micawber was extremely glad to see me, but a little confused, too. He would have conducted me immediately into the presence of Uriah, but I declined.

'I know the house of old, you recollect,' said I, 'and will find my way upstairs. How do you like the law, Mr Micawber?'

'My dear Copperfield,' he replied, 'to a man possessed of the higher imaginative powers, the objection to legal studies is the amount of detail which they involve. Even in our professional correspondence,' said Mr Micawber, glancing at some letters he was writing, 'the mind is not at liberty to soar to any exalted form of expression. Still it is a great pursuit. A great pursuit!'

He then told me that he had become the tenant of Uriah Heep's old house; and that Mrs Micawber would be delighted to receive me, once more, under her own roof.

'It is humble,' said Mr Micawber, 'to quote a favourite expression of my friend Heep; but it may prove the stepping-stone to more ambitious domiciliary accommodation.'

I asked him whether he had reason, so far, to be satisfied with his friend Heep's treatment of him? He got up to ascertain if the door were close shut, before he replied, in a lower voice: 'My dear Copperfield, a man who labours under the pressure of pecuniary embarrassments is, with the generality of people, at a disadvantage. That disadvantage is not diminished, when that pressure necessitates the drawing of stipendiary emoluments before those emoluments are strictly due and payable. All I can say is, that my friend Heep has responded to appeals to which I need not more particularly refer, in a manner calculated to redound equally to the honour of his head, and of his heart.'

'I should not have supposed him to be very free with his money either,' I observed.

'Pardon me!' said Mr Micawber, with an air of constraint, 'I speak of my friend Heep as I have experience.'

'I am glad your experience is so favourable,' I returned.

'You are very obliging, my dear Copperfield,' said Mr Micawber, and hummed a tune.

'Do you see much of Mr Wickfield?' I asked, to change the subject.

'Not much,' said Mr Micawber slightingly. 'Mr Wickfield is, I dare say, a man of very excellent intentions; but he is – in short, he is obsolete.'

'I am afraid his partner seeks to make him so,' said I.

'My dear Copperfield!' returned Mr Micawber, after some uneasy evolutions on his stool, 'allow me to offer a remark! I am here, in a capacity of confidence. I am here in a position of trust. The discussion of some topics, even with Mrs Micawber herself (so long the partner of my various vicissitudes, and a woman of a remarkable lucidity of intellect), is, I am led to consider, incompatible with the functions now devolving on me. I would therefore take the liberty of suggesting that in our friendly intercourse – which I trust will never be disturbed! – we draw a line. On one side of this line,' said Mr Micawber, representing it on the desk with the office ruler, 'is the whole range of the human intellect, with a trifling exception; on the other, *is* that exception; that is to say, the affairs of Messrs Wickfield and Heep, with all belonging and appertaining thereunto. I trust I give no offence to the companion of my youth, in submitting this proposition to his cooler judgement?'

Though I saw an uneasy change in Mr Micawber, which sat tightly on him, as if his new duties were a misfit, I felt I had no right to be offended. My telling him so appeared to relieve him, and he shook hands with me.

'I am charmed, Copperfield,' said Mr Micawber, 'let me assure you, with Miss Wickfield. She is a very superior young lady, of very remarkable attractions, graces, and virtues. Upon my honour,' said Mr Micawber, indefinitely kissing his hand and bowing with his genteelest air, 'I do Homage to Miss Wickfield! Hem!'

'I am glad of that, at least,' said I.

'If you had not assured us, my dear Copperfield, on the occasion of that agreeable afternoon we had the happiness of passing with you, that D. was your favourite letter,' said Mr Micawber, 'I should unquestionably have supposed that A. had been so.'

We have all some experience of a feeling, that comes over us occasionally, of what we are saying and doing having been said and done before, in a remote time – of our having been surrounded, dim ages ago, by the same faces, objects, and circumstances – of our knowing perfectly what will be said next, as if we suddenly remembered it! I never had this mysterious impression more strongly in my life, than before he uttered those words.

I took my leave of Mr Micawber, for the time, charging him with my best remembrances to all at home. As I left him, resuming his stool and his pen, and rolling his head in his stock, to get it into easier writing order, I clearly perceived that there was something interposed between him and me, since he had come into his new functions which prevented our getting at each other as we used to do, and quite altered the character of our intercourse.

There was no one in the quaint old drawing-room, though it presented tokens of Mrs Heep's whereabout. I looked into the room still belonging to Agnes, and saw her sitting by the fire, at a pretty old-fashioned desk she had, writing.

My darkening the light made her look up. What a pleasure to be the cause of that bright change in her attentive face, and the object of that sweet regard and welcome!

'Ah, Agnes!' said I, when we were sitting together, side by side, 'I have missed you so much, lately!'

'Indeed?' she replied. 'Again! And so soon?'

I shook my head.

'I don't know how it is, Agnes; I seem to want some faculty of mind that I ought to have. You were so much in the habit of thinking for me, in the happy old days here, and I came so naturally to you for counsel and support, that I really think I have missed acquiring it.'

'And what is it?' said Agnes cheerfully.

'I don't know what to call it,' I replied. 'I think I am earnest and persevering?'

'I am sure of it,' said Agnes.

'And patient, Agnes?' I enquired, with a little hesitation.

'Yes,' returned Agnes, laughing. 'Pretty well.'

'And yet,' said I, 'I get so miserable and worried, and am so unsteady and irresolute in my power of assuring myself, that I know I must want – shall I call it – reliance, of some kind?'

'Call it so, if you will,' said Agnes.

'Well!' I returned. 'See here! You come to London, I rely on you, and I have an object and a course at once. I am driven out of it, I come here, and in a moment I feel an altered person. The circumstances that distressed me are not changed since I came into this room, but an influence comes over me in that short interval that alters me, oh, how much for the better! What is it? What is your secret, Agnes?'

Her head was bent down, looking at the fire.

'It's the old story,' said I. 'Don't laugh, when I say it was always the same in little things as it is in greater ones. My old troubles were nonsense, and now they are serious; but whenever I have gone away from my adopted sister –'

Agnes looked up – with such a Heavenly face! – and gave me her hand, which I kissed.

'Whenever I have not had you, Agnes, to advise and approve in the beginning, I have seemed to go wild, and to get into all sorts of difficulty. When I have come to you, at last (as I have always done), I have come to peace and happiness. I come home now, like a tired traveller, and find such a blessed sense of rest!'

I felt so deeply what I said, it affected me so sincerely, that my voice failed, and I covered my face with my hand, and broke into tears. I write the truth. Whatever contradictions and inconsistencies there were within me, as there are within so many of us; whatever might have been so different, and so much better; whatever I had done, in which I had perversely wandered away from the voice of my own heart, I knew nothing

of. I only knew that I was fervently in earnest, when I felt the rest and peace of having Agnes near me.

In her placid, sisterly manner, with her beaming eyes, with her tender voice, and with that sweet composure, which had long ago made the house that held her quite a sacred place to me, she soon won me from this weakness, and led me on to tell all that had happened since our last meeting.

'And there is not another word to tell, Agnes,' said I, when I had made an end of my confidence. 'Now, my reliance is on you.'

'But it must not be on me, Trotwood,' returned Agnes, with a pleasant smile. 'It must be on someone else.'

'On Dora?' said I.

'Assuredly.'

'Why, I have not mentioned, Agnes,' said I, a little embarrassed, 'that Dora is rather difficult to – I would not, for the world, say, to rely upon, because she is the soul of purity and truth – but rather difficult to – I hardly know how to express it, really, Agnes. She is a timid little thing, and easily disturbed and frightened. Some time ago, before her father's death, when I thought it right to mention to her – but I'll tell you, if you will bear with me, how it was.'

Accordingly, I told Agnes about my declaration of poverty, about the cookery-book, the housekeeping accounts, and all the rest of it.

'Oh, Trotwood!' she remonstrated, with a smile. 'Just your old headlong way! You might have been in earnest in striving to get on in the world, without being so very sudden with a timid, loving, inexperienced girl. Poor Dora!'

I never heard such sweet forbearing kindness expressed in a voice as she expressed in making this reply. It was as if I had seen her admiringly and tenderly embracing Dora, and tacitly reproving me, by her considerate protection, for my hot haste in fluttering that little heart. It was as if I had seen Dora, in all her fascinating artlessness, caressing Agnes, and thanking her, and coaxingly appealing against me, and loving me with all her childish innocence.

I felt so grateful to Agnes, and admired her so! I saw those two together, in a bright perspective, such well-associated friends, each adoring the other so much!

'What ought I to do then, Agnes?' I enquired, after looking at the fire a little while. 'What would it be right to do?'

'I think,' said Agnes, 'that the honourable course to take, would be to write to those two ladies. Don't you think that any secret course is an unworthy one?'

'Yes. If *you* think so,' said I.

'I am poorly qualified to judge of such matters,' replied Agnes, with a modest hesitation, 'but I certainly feel – in short, I feel that your being secret and clandestine is not being like yourself.'

'Like myself, in the too high opinion you have of me, Agnes, I am afraid,' said I.

'Like yourself, in the candour of your nature,' she returned; 'and therefore I would write to those two ladies. I would relate, as plainly and as openly as possible, all that has taken place; and I would ask their permission to visit sometimes, at their house.

Considering that you are young, and striving for a place in life, I think it would be well to say that you would readily abide by any conditions they might impose upon you. I would entreat them not to dismiss your request, without a reference to Dora; and to discuss it with her when they should think the time suitable. I would not be too vehement,' said Agnes gently, 'or propose too much. I would trust to my fidelity and perseverance – and to Dora.'

'But if they were to frighten Dora again, Agnes, by speaking to her,' said I. 'And if Dora were to cry, and say nothing about me!'

'Is that likely?' enquired Agnes, with the same sweet consideration in her face.

'God bless her, she is as easily scared as a bird,' said I. 'It might be! Or if the two Miss Spenlows (elderly ladies of that sort are odd characters sometimes) should not be likely persons to address in that way!'

'I don't think, Trotwood,' returned Agnes, raising her soft eyes to mine, 'I would consider that. Perhaps it would be better only to consider whether it is right to do this; and, if it is, to do it.'

I had no longer any doubt on the subject. With a lightened heart, though with a profound sense of the weighty importance of my task, I devoted the whole afternoon to the composition of the draft of this letter, for which great purpose, Agnes relinquished her desk to me. But first I went downstairs to see Mr Wickfield and Uriah Heep.

I found Uriah in possession of a new, plaster-smelling office, built out in the garden; looking extraordinarily mean, in the midst of a quantity of books and papers. He received me in his usual fawning way, and pretended not to have heard of my arrival from Mr Micawber; a pretence I took the liberty of disbelieving. He accompanied me into Mr Wickfield's room, which was the shadow of its former self – having been divested of a variety of conveniences, for the accommodation of the new partner – and stood before the fire, warming his back, and shaving his chin with his bony hand, while Mr Wickfield and I exchanged greetings.

'You stay with us, Trotwood, while you remain in Canterbury?' said Mr Wickfield, not without a glance at Uriah for his approval.

'Is there room for me?' said I.

'I am sure, Master Copperfield – I should say Mister, but the other comes so natural,' said Uriah, 'I would turn out of your old room with pleasure, if it would be agreeable.'

'No, no,' said Mr Wickfield. 'Why should *you* be inconvenienced? There's another room. There's another room.'

'Oh, but you know,' returned Uriah, with a grin, 'I should really be delighted!'

To cut the matter short, I said I would have the other room, or none at all; so it was settled that I should have the other room; and, taking my leave of the firm until dinner, I went upstairs again.

I had hoped to have no other companion than Agnes. But Mrs Heep had asked permission to bring herself and her knitting near the fire, in that room; on pretence of its having an aspect more favourable for her rheumatics, as the wind then was, than the drawing-room or dining-parlour. Though I could almost have consigned her to the mercies of the wind on the topmost pinnacle of the Cathedral, without remorse, I made a virtue of necessity, and gave her a friendly salutation.

'I'm 'umbly thankful to you, sir,' said Mrs Heep, in acknowledgment of my enquiries concerning her health, 'but I'm only pretty well. I haven't much to boast of. If I could see my Uriah well settled in life, I couldn't expect much more, I think. How do you think my Ury looking, sir?'

I thought him looking as villainous as ever, and I replied that I saw no change in him.

'Oh, don't you think he's changed?' said Mrs Heep. 'There I must 'umbly beg leave to differ from you. Don't you see a thinness in him?'

'Not more than usual,' I replied.

'*Don't* you though!' said Mrs Heep. 'But you don't take notice of him with a mother's eye!'

His mother's eye was an evil eye to the rest of the world, I thought as it met mine, howsoever affectionate to him; and I believe she and her son were devoted to one another. It passed me, and went on to Agnes.

'Don't *you* see a wasting and a wearing in him, Miss Wickfield?' enquired Mrs Heep.

'No,' said Agnes, quietly pursuing the work on which she was engaged. 'You are too solicitous about him. He is very well.'

Mrs Heep, with a prodigious sniff, resumed her knitting.

She never left off, or left us for a moment. I had arrived early in the day, and we had still three or four hours before dinner; but she sat there, plying her knitting-needles as monotonously as an hourglass might have poured out its sands. She sat on one side of the fire; I sat at the desk in front of it; a little beyond me, on the other side, sat Agnes. Whensoever, slowly pondering over my letter, I lifted up my eyes, and meeting the thoughtful face of Agnes, saw it clear, and beam encouragement upon me, with its own angelic expression, I was conscious presently of the evil eye passing me, and going on to her, and coming back to me again, and dropping furtively upon the knitting. What the knitting was, I don't know, not being learned in that art; but it looked like a net; and as she worked away with those Chinese chopsticks of knitting-needles, she showed in the firelight like an ill-looking enchantress, baulked as yet by the radiant goodness opposite, but getting ready for a cast of her net by and by.

At dinner she maintained her watch, with the same unwinking eyes. After dinner, her son took his turn; and when Mr Wickfield, himself, and I were left alone together, leered at me, and writhed until I could hardly bear it. In the drawing-room, there was the mother knitting and watching again. All the time that Agnes sang and played, the mother sat at the piano. Once she asked for a particular ballad, which she said her Ury (who was yawning in a great chair) doted on; and at intervals she looked round at him, and reported to Agnes that he was in raptures with the music. But she hardly ever spoke – I question if she ever did – without making some mention of him. It was evident to me that this was the duty assigned to her.

This lasted until bedtime. To have seen the mother and son, like two great bats hanging over the whole house, and darkening it with their ugly forms, made me so uncomfortable, that I would rather have remained downstairs, knitting and all, than gone to bed. I hardly got any sleep. Next day the knitting and watching began again, and lasted all day.

I had not an opportunity of speaking to Agnes for ten minutes. I could barely show her my letter. I proposed to her to walk out with me; but Mrs Heep repeatedly complaining that she was worse, Agnes charitably remained within, to bear her company. Towards the twilight I went out by myself, musing on what I ought to do, and whether I was justified in withholding from Agnes, any longer, what Uriah Heep had told me in London; for that began to trouble me again, very much.

I had not walked out far enough to be quite clear of the town, upon the Ramsgate road, where there was a good path, when I was hailed, through the dusk, by somebody behind me. The shambling figure and the scanty greatcoat were not to be mistaken. I stopped, and Uriah Heep came up.

'Well?' said I.

'How fast you walk!' said he. 'My legs are pretty long, but you've given 'em quite a job.'

'Where are you going?' said I.

'I am coming with you, Master Copperfield, if you'll allow me the pleasure of a walk with an old acquaintance.' Saying this, with a jerk of his body, which might have been either propitiatory or derisive, he fell into step beside me.

'Uriah!' said I, as civilly as I could, after a silence.

'Master Copperfield!' said Uriah.

'To tell you the truth (at which you will not be offended), I came out to walk alone, because I have had so much company.'

He looked at me sideways, and said with his hardest grin, 'You mean mother.'

'Why yes, I do,' said I.

'Ah! But you know we're so very 'umble,' he returned. 'And having such a knowledge of our own 'umbleness, we must really take care that we're not pushed to the wall by them as isn't 'umble. All stratagems are fair in love, sir.'

Raising his great hands until they touched his chin, he rubbed them softly, and softly chuckled; looking as like a malevolent baboon, I thought, as anything human could look.

'You see,' he said, still hugging himself in that unpleasant way, and shaking his head at me, 'you're quite a dangerous rival, Master Copperfield. You always was, you know.'

'Do you set a watch upon Miss Wickfield, and make her home no home, because of me?' said I.

'Oh! Master Copperfield! Those are very 'arsh words,' he replied.

'Put my meaning into any words you like,' said I. 'You know what it is, Uriah, as well as I do.'

'Oh, no! You must put it into words,' he said. 'Oh, really! I couldn't myself.'

'Do you suppose,' said I, constraining myself to be very temperate and quiet with him, on account of Agnes, 'that I regard Miss Wickfield otherwise than as a very dear sister?'

'Well, Master Copperfield,' he replied, 'you perceive I am not bound to answer that question. You may not, you know. But then, you see, you may!'

Anything to equal the low cunning of his visage, and of his shadowless eyes without the ghost of an eyelash, I never saw.

'Come then!' said I. 'For the sake of Miss Wickfield – '

'My Agnes!' he exclaimed, with a sickly, angular contortion of himself. 'Would you be so good as call her Agnes, Master Copperfield!'

'For the sake of Agnes Wickfield – Heaven bless her!'

'Thank you for that blessing, Master Copperfield!' he interposed.

'I will tell you what I should, under any other circumstances, as soon have thought of telling to – Jack Ketch.'

'To who, sir?' said Uriah, stretching out his neck, and shading his ear with his hand.

'To the hangman,' I returned. 'The most unlikely person I could think of' – though his own face had suggested the allusion quite as a natural sequence. 'I am engaged to another young lady. I hope that contents you.'

'Upon your soul?' said Uriah.

I was about indignantly to give my assertion the confirmation he required, when he caught hold of my hand, and gave it a squeeze.

'Oh, Master Copperfield,' he said. 'If you had only had the condescension to return my confidence when I poured out the fullness of my art, the night I put you so much out of the way by sleeping before your sitting-room fire, I never should have doubted you. As it is, I'm sure I'll take off mother directly, and only too 'appy. I know you'll excuse the precautions of affection, won't you? What a pity, Master Copperfield, that you didn't condescend to return my confidence! I'm sure I gave you every opportunity. But you never have condescended to me, as much as I could have wished. I know you have never liked me, as I have liked you!'

All this time he was squeezing my hand with his damp fishy fingers, while I made every effort I decently could to get it away. But I was quite unsuccessful. He drew it under the sleeve of his mulberry-coloured greatcoat, and I walked on, almost upon compulsion, arm in arm with him.

'Shall we turn?' said Uriah, by and by wheeling me face about towards the town, on which the early moon was now shining, silvering the distant windows.

'Before we leave the subject, you ought to understand,' said I, breaking a pretty long silence, 'that I believe Agnes Wickfield to be as far above *you*, and as far removed from all *your* aspirations, as that moon herself!'

'Peaceful! Ain't she!' said Uriah. 'Very! Now confess, Master Copperfield, that you haven't liked me quite as I have liked you. All along you've thought me too 'umble now, I shouldn't wonder?'

'I am not fond of professions of humility,' I returned, 'or professions of anything else.'

'There now!' said Uriah, looking flabby and lead-coloured in the moonlight. 'Didn't I know it! But how little you think of the rightful 'umbleness of a person in my station, Master Copperfield! Father and me was both brought up at a foundation school for boys; and mother, she was likewise brought up at a public, sort of charitable, establishment. They taught us all a deal of 'umbleness – not much else that I know of, from morning to night. We was to be 'umble to this person, and 'umble to that; and to pull off our caps here, and to make bows there; and always to know our place, and abase ourselves before our betters. And we had such a lot of betters! Father got the monitor medal by being 'umble. So did I. Father got made a sexton by being 'umble. He had the character, among the gentlefolks, of being such a well-behaved man, that they were determined to bring him in. "Be 'umble, Uriah," says father to me, "and you'll get on. It was what was always being dinned into you and me at school; it's what goes down best. Be 'umble," says father, "and you'll do!" And really it ain't done bad!'

It was the first time it had ever occurred to me, that this detestable cant of false humility might have originated out of the Heep family. I had seen the harvest, but had never thought of the seed.

'When I was quite a young boy,' said Uriah, 'I got to know what 'umbleness did, and I took to it. I ate 'umble pie with an appetite. I stopped at the 'umble point of my learning, and says I, "Hold hard!" When you offered to teach me Latin, I knew better. "People like to be above you," says father, "keep yourself down." I am very 'umble to the present moment, Master Copperfield, but I've got a little power!'

And he said all this – I knew, as I saw his face in the moonlight – that I might understand he was resolved to recompense himself by using his power. I had never doubted his meanness, his craft and malice; but I fully comprehended now, for the first time, what a base, unrelenting, and revengeful spirit must have been engendered by this early, and this long suppression.

His account of himself was so far attended with an agreeable result, that it led to his withdrawing his hand in order that he might have another hug of himself under the chin. Once apart from him, I was determined to keep apart; and we walked back, side by side, saying very little more by the way.

Whether his spirits were elevated by the communication I had made to him, or by his having indulged in this retrospect, I don't know; but they were raised by some influence. He talked more at dinner than was usual with him; asked his mother (off duty from the moment of our re-entering the house), whether he was not growing too old for a bachelor; and once looked at Agnes so, that I would have given all I had for leave to knock him down.

When we three males were left alone after dinner, he got into a more adventurous state. He had taken little or no wine; and I presume it was the mere insolence of triumph that was upon him, flushed perhaps by the temptation my presence furnished to its exhibition.

I had observed yesterday, that he tried to entice Mr Wickfield to drink; and interpreting the look which Agnes had given me as she went out, had limited myself to one glass, and then proposed that we should follow her. I would have done so again today, but Uriah was too quick for me.

'We seldom see our present visitor, sir,' he said, addressing Mr Wickfield, sitting, such a contrast to him, at the end of the table, 'and I should propose to give him welcome in another glass or two of wine, if you have no objections. Mr Copperfield, your elth and 'appiness!'

I was obliged to make a show of taking the hand he stretched across to me; and then, with very different emotions, I took the hand of the broken gentleman, his partner.

'Come, fellow-partner,' said Uriah, 'if I may take the liberty – now, suppose you give us something or another appropriate to Copperfield!'

I pass over Mr Wickfield's proposing my aunt, his proposing Mr Dick, his proposing Doctors' Commons, his proposing Uriah, his drinking everything twice; his consciousness of his own weakness, the ineffectual effort that he made against it; the struggle between his shame in Uriah's deportment, and his desire to conciliate him; the manifest exultation with which Uriah twisted and turned and held him up before me. It made me sick at heart to see, and my hand recoils from writing it.

'Come, fellow-partner!' said Uriah, at last, 'I'll give you another one, and I 'umbly ask for bumpers, seeing I intend to make it the divinest of her sex.'

Her father had his empty glass in his hand. I saw him set it down, look at the picture she was so like, put his hand to his forehead, and shrink back in his elbow-chair.

'I'm an 'umble individual to give you her elth,' proceeded Uriah, 'but I admire – adore her.'

No physical pain that her father's grey head could have borne, I think, could have been more terrible to me, than the mental endurance I saw compressed now within both his hands.

'Agnes,' said Uriah, either not regarding him, or not knowing what the nature of his action was, 'Agnes Wickfield is, I am safe to say, the divinest of her sex. May I speak out, among friends? To be her father is a proud distinction, but to be her 'usband – '

Spare me from ever again hearing such a cry as that with which her father rose up from the table!

'What's the matter?' said Uriah, turning of a deadly colour. 'You are not gone mad, after all, Mr Wickfield, I hope? If I say, I've an ambition to make your Agnes my Agnes, I have as good a right to it as another man. I have a better right to it than any other man!'

I had my arms round Mr Wickfield, imploring him by everything that I could think of, oftenest of all by his love for Agnes, to calm himself a little. He was mad for the moment; tearing out his hair, beating his head, trying to force me from him and to force himself from me, not answering a word, not looking at or seeing anyone; blindly striving for he knew not what, his face all staring and distorted – a frightful spectacle.

I conjured him, incoherently, but in the most impassioned manner, not to abandon himself to this wildness, but to hear me. I besought him to think of Agnes, to connect me with Agnes, to recollect how Agnes and I had grown up together, how I honoured her and loved her, how she was his pride and joy. I tried to bring her idea before him in any form; I even reproached him with not having firmness to spare her the knowledge of such a scene as this. I may have effected something, or his wildness may have spent itself; but by degrees he struggled less, and began to look at me – strangely at first, then with recognition in his eyes. At length he said, 'I know, Trotwood! My darling child and you – I know! But look at him!'

He pointed to Uriah, pale and glowering in a corner, evidently very much out in his calculations and taken by surprise.

'Look at my torturer,' he replied. 'Before him I have step by step abandoned name and reputation, peace and quiet, house and home.'

'I have kept your name and reputation for you, and your peace and quiet, and your house and home too,' said Uriah, with a sulky, hurried, defeated air of compromise. 'Don't be foolish, Mr Wickfield. If I have gone a little beyond what you were prepared for, I can go back, I suppose? There's no harm done.'

'I looked for single motives in everyone,' said Mr Wickfield, 'and I was satisfied I had bound him to me by motives of interest. But see what he is – oh, see what he is!'

'You had better stop him, Copperfield, if you can,' cried Uriah, with his long forefinger pointing towards me. 'He'll say something presently – mind you! – he'll be sorry to have said afterwards, and you'll be sorry to have heard!'

'I'll say anything!' cried Mr Wickfield, with a desperate air. 'Why should I not be in all the world's power if I am in yours!'

'Mind! I tell you!' said Uriah, continuing to warn me. 'If you don't stop his mouth, you're not his friend! Why shouldn't you be in all the world's power, Mr Wickfield? Because you have got a daughter. You and me know what we know, don't we? Let sleeping dogs lie – who wants to rouse 'em? I don't. Can't you see I am as 'umble as I can be? I tell you, if I've gone too far, I'm sorry. What would you have, sir?'

'Oh, Trotwood, Trotwood!' exclaimed Mr Wickfield, wringing his hands. 'What I have come down to be, since I first saw you in this house! I was on my downward way then, but the dreary, dreary road I have travelled since! Weak indulgence has ruined me. Indulgence in remembrance, and indulgence in forgetfulness. My natural grief for my child's mother turned to disease; my natural love for my child turned to disease. I have infected everything I touched. I have brought misery on what I dearly love, I know – *You* know! I thought it possible that I could truly love one creature in the world, and not love the rest; I thought it possible that I could truly mourn for one creature gone out of the world, and not have some part in the grief of all who mourned. Thus the lessons of my life have been perverted! I have preyed on my own morbid coward heart, and it has preyed on me. Sordid in my grief, sordid in my love, sordid in my miserable escape from the darker side of both, oh, see the ruin I am, and hate me, shun me!'

He dropped into a chair, and weakly sobbed. The excitement into which he had been roused was leaving him. Uriah came out of his corner.

'I don't know all I have done, in my fatuity,' said Mr Wickfield, putting out his hands, as if to deprecate my condemnation. '*He* knows best,' meaning Uriah Heep, 'for he has always been at my elbow, whispering me. You see the millstone that he is about my neck. You find him in my house, you find

him in my business. You heard him but a little time ago. What need have I to say more!'

'You haven't need to say so much, nor half so much, nor anything at all,' observed Uriah, half defiant, and half fawning. 'You wouldn't have took it up so, if it hadn't been for the wine. You'll think better of it tomorrow, sir. If I have said too much, or more than I meant, what of it? I haven't stood by it!'

The door opened, and Agnes, gliding in, without a vestige of colour in her face, put her arm round his neck, and steadily said, 'Papa, you are not well. Come with me!' He laid his head upon her shoulder, as if he were oppressed with heavy shame, and went out with her. Her eyes met mine for but an instant, yet I saw how much she knew of what had passed.

'I didn't expect he'd cut up so rough, Master Copperfield,' said Uriah. 'But it's nothing. I'll be friends with him tomorrow. It's for his good. I'm 'umbly anxious for his good.'

I gave him no answer, and went upstairs into the quiet room where Agnes had so often sat beside me at my books. Nobody came near me until late at night. I took up a book and tried to read. I heard the clock strike twelve, and was still reading, without knowing what I read, when Agnes touched me.

'You will be going early in the morning, Trotwood! Let us say goodbye, now!'

She had been weeping, but her face then was so calm and beautiful!

'Heaven bless you!' she said, giving me her hand.

'Dearest Agnes!' I returned, 'I see you ask me not to speak of tonight – but is there nothing to be done?'

'There is God to trust in!' she replied.

'Can *I* do nothing – I, who come to you with *my* poor sorrows?'

'And make mine so much lighter,' she replied. 'Dear Trotwood, no.'

'Dear Agnes,' I said, 'it is presumptuous for me, who am so poor in all in which you are so rich – goodness, resolution, all noble qualities – to doubt or direct you; but you know how much I love you, and how much I owe you. You will never sacrifice yourself to a mistaken sense of duty? Agnes?'

More agitated for a moment than I had ever seen her, she took her hand from me, and moved a step back.

'Say you have no such thought, dear Agnes! Much more than sister! Think of the priceless gift of such a heart as yours, of such a love as yours!'

Oh! long, long afterwards, I saw that face rise up before me, with its momentary look, not wondering, not accusing, not regretting. Oh, long, long afterwards, I saw that look subside, as it did now, into the lovely smile, with which she told me she had no fear for herself – I need have none for her – and parted from me by the name of Brother, and was gone!

It was dark in the morning when I got upon the coach at the inn door. The day was just breaking when we were about to start, and then, as I sat thinking of her, came struggling up the coach side, through the mingled day and night, Uriah's head.

'Copperfield!' said he, in a croaking whisper, as he hung by the iron on the roof, 'I thought you'd be glad to hear before you went off, that there are no squares broke between us. I've been into his room already, and we've made it all smooth. Why, though I'm 'umble, I'm useful to him, you know, and he understands his interest when he isn't in liquor! What an agreeable man he is, after all, Master Copperfield!'

I obliged myself to say that I was glad he had made his apology.

'Oh, to be sure!' said Uriah. 'When a person's 'umble, you know, what's an apology? So easy! I say! I suppose,' with a jerk, 'you have sometimes plucked a pear before it was ripe, Master Copperfield?'

'I suppose I have,' I replied.

'*I* did that last night,' said Uriah; 'but it'll ripen yet! It only wants attending to. I can wait!'

Profuse in his farewells, he got down again as the coachman got up. For anything I know, he was eating something to keep the raw morning air out; but he made motions with his mouth as if the pear were ripe already, and he were smacking his lips over it.

CHAPTER 40

The Wanderer

We had a very serious conversation in Buckingham Street that night, about the domestic occurrences I have detailed in the last chapter. My aunt was deeply interested in them, and walked up and down the room with her arms folded, for more than two hours afterwards. Whenever she was particularly discomposed, she always performed one of these pedestrian feats; and the amount of her discomposure might always be estimated by the duration of her walk. On this occasion she was so much disturbed in mind as to find it necessary to open the bedroom door, and make a course for herself, comprising the full extent of the bedrooms from wall to wall; and while Mr Dick and I sat quietly by the fire, she kept passing in and out, along this measured track, at an unchanging pace, with the regularity of a clock-pendulum.

When my aunt and I were left to ourselves by Mr Dick's going out to bed, I sat down to write my letter to the two old ladies. By that time she was tired of walking, and sat by the fire with her dress tucked up as usual. But instead of sitting in her usual manner, holding her glass upon her knee, she suffered it to stand neglected on the chimney-piece; and, resting her left elbow on her right arm, and her chin on her left hand, looked thoughtfully at me. As often as I raised my eyes from what I was about, I met hers. 'I am in the lovingest of tempers, my dear,' she would assure me with a nod, 'but I am fidgeted and sorry!'

I had been too busy to observe, until after she was gone to bed, that she had left her night-mixture, as she always called it, untasted on the chimney-piece. She came to her door, with even more than her usual affection of manner, when I knocked to acquaint her with this discovery; but only said, 'I have not the heart to take it, Trot, tonight,' and shook her head, and went in again.

She read my letter to the two old ladies, in the morning, and

approved of it. I posted it, and had nothing to do then but wait, as patiently as I could, for the reply. I was still in this state of expectation, and had been, for nearly a week, when I left the Doctor's one snowy night, to walk home.

It had been a bitter day, and a cutting north-east wind had blown for some time. The wind had gone down with the light, and so the snow had come on. It was a heavy, settled fall, I recollect, in great flakes; and it lay thick. The noise of wheels and tread of people were as hushed as if the streets had been strewn that depth with feathers.

My shortest way home – and I naturally took the shortest way on such a night – was through St Martin's Lane. Now, the church which gives its name to the lane stood in a less free situation at that time, there being no open space before it, and the lane winding down to the Strand. As I passed the steps of the portico, I encountered, at the corner, a woman's face. It looked in mine, passed across the narrow lane, and disappeared. I knew it. I had seen it somewhere. But I could not remember where. I had some association with it, that struck upon my heart directly; but I was thinking of anything else when it came upon me, and was confused.

On the steps of the church, there was the stooping figure of a man, who had put down some burden on the smooth snow, to adjust it; my seeing the face and my seeing him were simultaneous. I don't think I had stopped in my surprise; but, in any case, as I went on, he rose, turned, and came down towards me. I stood face to face with Mr Peggotty!

Then I remembered the woman. It was Martha, to whom Emily had given the money that night in the kitchen. Martha Endell – side by side with whom, he would not have seen his dear niece, Ham had told me, for all the treasures wrecked in the sea.

We shook hands heartily. At first neither of us could speak a word.

'Mas'r Davy!' he said, gripping me tight, 'it do my art good to see you, sir. Well met, well met!'

'Well met, my dear old friend!' said I.

'I had my thowts o' coming to make enquiration for you, sir, tonight,' he said, 'but knowing as your aunt was living along wi' you – for I've been down yonder – Yarmouth way – I was afeerd it was too late. I should have come early in the morning, sir, afore going away.'

'Again?' said I.

'Yes, sir,' he replied, patiently shaking his head, 'I'm away tomorrow.'

'Where were you going now?' I asked.

'Well!' he replied, shaking the snow out of his long hair, 'I was a going to turn in somewheers.'

In those days there was a side-entrance to the stable-yard of the 'Golden Cross', the inn so memorable to me in connection with his misfortune, nearly opposite to where we stood. I pointed out the gateway, put my arm through his, and we went across. Two or three public rooms opened out of the stable-yard; and looking into one of them, and finding it empty, and a good fire burning, I took him in there.

When I saw him in the light, I observed, not only that his hair was long and ragged, but that his face was burnt dark by the sun. He was greyer, the lines in his face and forehead were deeper, and he had every appearance of having toiled and wandered through all varieties of weather; but he looked very strong, and like a man upheld by steadfastness of purpose, whom nothing could tire out. He shook the snow from his hat and clothes, and brushed it away from his face, while I was inwardly making these remarks. As he sat down opposite to me at a table, with his back to the door by which we had entered, he put out his rough hand again, and grasped mine warmly.

'I'll tell you, Mas'r Davy,' he said, 'wheer-all I've been, and what-all we've heerd. I've been fur, and we've heerd little; but I'll tell you!'

I rang the bell for something hot to drink. He would have nothing stronger than ale; and while it was being brought, and being warmed at the fire, he sat thinking. There was a fine massive gravity in his face, I did not venture to disturb.

'When she was a child,' he said, lifting up his head soon after we were left alone, 'she used to talk to me a deal about the sea, and about them coasts where the sea got to be dark blue, and to lay a shining and a shining in the sun. I thowt, odd times, as her father being drownded, made her think on it so much. I doen't know, you see, but may be she believed – or hoped – he had drifted out to them parts where the flowers is always a blowing, and the country bright.'

'It is likely to have been a childish fancy,' I replied.

'When she was – lost,' said Mr Peggotty, 'I knowed in my mind, as he would take her to them countries. I knowed in my mind, as he'd have told her wonders of 'em, and how she was to be a lady theer, and how he got her to listen to him first, along o' sech like. When we see his mother, I knowed quite well as I was right. I went across-channel to France, and landed theer, as if I'd fell down from the sky.'

I saw the door move, and the snow drift in. I saw it move a little more, and a hand softly interpose to keep it open.

'I found out an English gentleman, as was in authority,' said Mr Peggotty, 'and told him I was a going to seek my niece. He got me them papers as I wanted fur to carry me through – I doen't rightly know how they're called – and he would have give me money, but that I was thankful to have no need on. I thank him kind, for all he done, I'm sure! "I've wrote afore you," he says to me, "and I shall speak to many as will come that way, and many will know you, fur distant from here, when you're a travelling alone." I told him, best as I was able, what my gratitoode was, and went away through France.'

'Alone, and on foot?' said I.

'Mostly afoot,' he rejoined; 'sometimes in carts along with people going to market; sometimes in empty coaches. Many mile a day afoot, and often with some poor soldier or another, travelling to see his friends. I couldn't talk to him,' said Mr Peggotty, 'nor he to me; but we was company for one another, too, along the dusty roads.'

I should have known that by his friendly tone.

'When I come to any town,' he pursued, 'I found the inn, and waited about the yard till someone turned up (someone mostly did) as knowed English. Then I told how that I was on my way

to seek my niece, and they told me what manner of gentlefolks was in the house, and I waited to see any as seemed like her, going in or out. When it warn't Em'ly, I went on agen. By little and little, when I come to a new village or that, among the poor people, I found they knowed about me. They would set me down at their cottage doors, and give me what-not fur to eat and drink, and show me where to sleep; and many a woman, Mas'r Davy, as has had a daughter of about Em'ly's age, I've found a waiting for me, at Our Saviour's Cross outside the village, fur to do me sim'lar kindnesses. Some has had daughters as was dead. And God only knows how good them mothers was to me!'

It was Martha at the door. I saw her haggard, listening face distinctly. My dread was lest he should turn his head, and see her too.

'They would often put their children – partic'lar their little girls,' said Mr Peggotty, 'upon my knee; and many a time you might have seen me sitting at their doors, when night was coming on, a'most as if they'd been my Darling's children. Oh, my Darling!'

Overpowered by sudden grief, he sobbed aloud. I laid my trembling hand upon the hand he put before his face. 'Thankee, sir,' he said, 'doen't take no notice.'

In a very little while he took his hand away and put it in his breast, and went on with his story.

'They often walked with me,' he said, 'in the morning, may be a mile or two upon my road; and when we parted, and I said, "I'm very thankful to you! God bless you!" they always seemed to understand, and answered pleasant. At last I come to the sea. It warn't hard, you may suppose, for a seafaring man like me to work his way over to Italy. When I got theer, I wandered on as I had done afore. The people was just as good to me, and I should have gone from town to town, may be the country through, but that I got news of her being seen among them Swiss mountains yonder. One as knowed his sarvant see 'em theer, all three, and told me how they travelled, and wheer they was. I made for them mountains, Mas'r Davy, day and night. Ever so fur as I went, ever so fur the mountains seemed to shift away from me. But I come up with 'em, and I crossed 'em. When I got nigh the place as I had been told of, I began to think within my own self, "What shall I do when I see her?" '

The listening face, insensible to the inclement night, still drooped at the door, and the hands begged me – prayed me – not to cast it forth.

'I never doubted her,' said Mr Peggotty. 'No! Not a bit! On'y let her see my face – on'y let her hear my voice – on'y let my stanning still afore her bring to her thoughts the home she had fled away from, and the child she had been – and if she had growed to be a royal lady, she'd have fell down at my feet! I knowed it well! Many a time in my sleep had I heerd her cry out, "Uncle!" and seen her fall like death afore me. Many a time in my sleep had I raised her up, and whispered to her, "Em'ly, my dear, I am come fur to bring forgiveness, and to take you home!" '

He stopped and shook his head, and went on with a sigh.

'He was nowt to me now. Em'ly was all. I bought a country dress to put upon her; and I knowed that, once found, she would walk beside me over them stony roads, go wheer I would, and never, never, leave me more. To put that dress upon her, and to cast off what she wore – to take her on my arm again, and wander towards home – to stop sometimes upon the road, and heal her bruised feet and her worse bruised heart – was all that I thowt of now. I don't believe I should have done so much as look at him. But, Mas'r Davy, it warn't to be – not yet! I was too late, and they was gone. Wheer, I couldn't learn. Some said heer, some said theer. I travelled heer, and I travelled theer, but I found no Em'ly, and I travelled home.'

'How long ago?' I asked.

'A matter o' fower days,' said Mr Peggotty. 'I sighted the old boat arter dark, and the light a shining in the winder. When I come nigh and looked in through the glass, I see the faithful creetur Missis Gummidge sittin' by the fire, as we had fixed upon, alone. I called out, "Doen't be afeerd! It's Dan'l!" and I went in. I never could have thowt the old boat would have been so strange!'

From some pocket in his breast, he took out, with a very careful hand, a small paper bundle containing two or three letters or little packets, which he laid upon the table.

'This first one come,' he said, selecting it from the rest, 'afore I had been gone a week. A fifty pound bank note, in a sheet of paper, directed to me, and put underneath the door in the night. She tried to hide her writing, but she couldn't hide it from Me!'

He folded up the note again, with great patience and care in exactly the same form, and laid it on one side.

'This come to Missis Gummidge,' he said, opening another, 'two or three months ago.' After looking at it for some moments, he gave it to me, and added in a low voice, 'Be so good as read it, sir.'

I read as follows:

Oh, what will you feel when you see this writing, and know it comes from my wicked hand! But try, try – not for my sake, but for uncle's goodness, try to let your heart soften to me, only for a little little time! Try, pray do, to relent towards a miserable girl, and write down on a bit of paper whether he is well, and what he said about me before you left off even naming me among yourselves – and whether, of a night, when it is my old time of coming home, you ever see him look as if he thought of one he used to love so dear. Oh, my heart is breaking when I think about it! I am kneeling down to you, begging and praying you not to be as hard with me as I deserve – as I well, well know I deserve – but to be so gentle and so good as to write down something of him and to send it to me. You need not call me Little, you need not call me by the name I have disgraced; but oh, listen to my agony, and have mercy on me so far as to write me some word of uncle, never, never to be seen in this world by my eyes again!

Dear, if your heart is hard towards me – justly hard, I know – but, listen, if it is hard, dear, ask him I have wronged the most – him whose wife I was to have been – before you quite decide against my poor, poor prayer! If he should be so compassionate as to say that you might write something

for me to read – I think he would, oh, I think he would, if you would only ask him, for he always was so brave and so forgiving – tell him then (but not else) that, when I hear the wind blowing at night, I feel as if it was passing angrily from seeing him and uncle, and was going up to God against me. Tell him that if I was to die tomorrow (and oh, if I was fit, I would be so glad to die!) I would bless him and uncle with my last words, and pray for his happy home with my last breath!

Some money was enclosed in this letter also. Five pounds. It was untouched like the previous sum, and he refolded it in the same way. Detailed instructions were added relative to the address of a reply, which, although they betrayed the intervention of several hands, and made it difficult to arrive at any very probable conclusion in reference to her place of concealment, made it at least not unlikely that she had written from that spot where she was stated to have been seen.

'What answer was sent?' I enquired of Mr Peggotty.

'Missis Gummidge,' he returned, 'not being a good scholar, sir, Ham kindly drawed it out, and she made a copy on it. They told her I was gone to seek her, and what my parting words was.'

'Is that another letter in your hand?' said I.

'It's money, sir,' said Mr Peggotty, unfolding it a little way. 'Ten pound, you see. And wrote inside, "From a true friend," like the first. But the first was put underneath the door, and this come by the post, day afore yesterday. I'm going to seek her at the postmark.'

The wanderer

He showed it to me. It was a town on the Upper Rhine. He had found out, at Yarmouth, some foreign dealer, who knew that country, and they had drawn him a rude map on paper, which he could very well understand. He laid it between us on the table; and with his chin resting on one hand, tracked his course upon it with the other.

I asked him how Ham was. He shook his head.

'He works,' he said, 'as bold as a man can. His name's as good, in all that part, as any man's is, anywheres in the wureld. Anyone's hand is ready to help him, you understand, and his is ready to help them. He's never been heerd fur to complain. But my sister's belief is ('twixt ourselves) as it has cut him deep.'

'Poor fellow, I can believe it!'

'He ain't no care, Mas'r Davy,' said Mr Peggotty in a solemn whisper – 'keinder no care no-how for his life. When a man's wanted for rough service in rough weather, he's theer. When there's hard duty to be done with danger in it, he steps forward afore all his mates. And yet he's as gentle as any child. There ain't a child in Yarmouth that doesn't know him.'

He gathered up the letters thoughtfully, smoothing them with his hand; put them into their little bundle; and placed it tenderly in his breast again. The face was gone from the door. I still saw the snow drifting in; but nothing else was there.

'Well!' he said, looking to his bag, 'having seen you tonight, Mas'r Davy (and that does me good!), I shall away betimes tomorrow morning. You have seen what I've got heer;' putting his hand on where the little packet lay; 'all that troubles me is to think that any harm might come to me, afore that money was give back. If I was to die, and it was lost, or stole, or elseways made away with, and it was never knowed by him but what I'd took it, I believe t' other wureld wouldn't hold me! I believe I must come back!'

He rose, and I rose, too; we grasped each other by the hand again, before going out.

'I'd go ten thousand mile,' he said; 'I'd go till I dropped dead, to lay that money down afore him. If I do that, and find my Em'ly, I'm content. If I doen't find her, maybe she'll come to hear, sometime, as her loving uncle only ended his search for her when he ended his life; and if I know her, even that will turn her home at last!'

As we went out into the rigorous night, I saw the lonely figure flit away before us. I turned him hastily on some pretence, and held him in conversation until it was gone.

He spoke of a traveller's house on the Dover road, where he knew he could find a clean, plain lodging for the night. I went with him over Westminster Bridge, and parted from him on the Surrey shore. Everything seemed, to my imagination, to be hushed in reverence for him, as he resumed his solitary journey through the snow.

I returned to the inn yard, and, impressed by my remembrance of the face, looked awfully around for it. It was not there. The snow had covered our late footprints; my new track was the only one to be seen; and even that began to die away (it snowed so fast) as I looked back over my shoulder.

CHAPTER 41

Dora's Aunts

At last, an answer came from the two old ladies. They presented their compliments to Mr Copperfield, and informed him that they had given his letter their best consideration, 'with a view to the happiness of both parties' – which I thought rather an alarming expression, not only because of the use they had made of it in relation to the family difference before mentioned, but because I had (and have all my life) observed that conventional phrases are a sort of fireworks, easily let off, and liable to take a great variety of shapes and colours not at all suggested by their original form. The Misses Spenlow added that they begged to forbear expressing, 'through the medium of correspondence,' an opinion on the subject of Mr Copperfield's communication; but that if Mr Copperfield would do them the favour to call, upon a certain day (accompanied, if he thought proper, by a confidential friend), they would be happy to hold some conversation on the subject.

To this favour, Mr Copperfield immediately replied, with his respectful compliments, that he would have the honour of waiting on the Misses Spenlow, at the time appointed, accompanied, in accordance with their kind permission, by his friend Mr Thomas Traddles of the Inner Temple. Having despatched which missive, Mr Copperfield fell into a condition of strong nervous agitation; and so remained until the day arrived.

It was a great augmentation of my uneasiness to be bereaved, at this eventful crisis, of the inestimable services of Miss Mills. But Mr Mills, who was always doing something or other to annoy me – or I felt as if he were, which was the same thing – had brought his conduct to a climax, by taking it into his head that he would go to India. Why should he go to India, except to harass me? To be sure, he had nothing to do with any other part of the world, and had a good deal to do with that part; being entirely in the Indian trade, whatever that was (I had floating dreams myself concerning golden shawls and elephants' teeth); having been at Calcutta in his youth; and designing now to go out there again, in the capacity of resident partner. But this was nothing to me. However, it was so much to him that for India he was bound, and Julia with him; and Julia went into the country to take leave of her relations; and the house was put into a perfect suit of bills, announcing that it was to be let or sold, and that the furniture (Mangle and all) was to be taken at a valuation. So here was another earthquake of which I became the sport, before I had recovered from the shock of its predecessor!

I was in several minds how to dress myself on the important day. Being divided between my desire to appear to advantage and my apprehensions of putting on anything that might impair my severely practical character in the eyes of the Misses Spenlow, I endeavoured to hit a happy medium between these two extremes; my aunt approved the result; and Mr Dick threw one of his shoes after Traddles and me, for luck, as we went down-stairs.

Excellent fellow as I knew Traddles to be, and warmly attached to him as I was, I could not help wishing, on that delicate occasion, that he had never contracted the habit of brushing his hair so very upright. It gave him a surprised look – not to say a hearth-broomy kind of expression – which, my apprehensions whispered, might be fatal to us.

I took the liberty of mentioning it to Traddles, as we were walking to Putney; and saying that if he *would* smooth it down a little – 'My dear Copperfield,' said Traddles, lifting off his hat, and rubbing his hair all kinds of ways, 'nothing would give me greater pleasure. But it won't.'

'Won't be smoothed down?' said I.

'No,' said Traddles; 'nothing will induce it. If I was to carry a half-hundredweight upon it, all the way to Putney, it would be up again the moment the weight was taken off. You have no idea what obstinate hair mine is, Copperfield. I am quite a fretful porcupine.'

I was a little disappointed, I must confess, but thoroughly charmed by his good nature, too. I told him how I esteemed his good nature; and said that his hair must have taken all the obstinacy out of his character, for *he* had none.

'Oh!' returned Traddles laughing, 'I assure you, it's quite an old story, my unfortunate hair. My uncle's wife couldn't bear it. She said it exasperated her. It stood very much in my way, too, when I first fell in love with Sophy; very much!'

'Did she object to it?'

'*She* didn't,' rejoined Traddles; 'but her eldest sister – the one that's the Beauty – quite made game of it, I understand. In fact, all the sisters laugh at it.'

'Agreeable!' said I.

'Yes,' returned Traddles, with perfect innocence, 'it's a joke for us. They pretend that Sophy has a lock of it in her desk, and is obliged to shut it in a clasped book to keep it down. We laugh about it.'

'By the by, my dear Traddles,' said I, 'your experience may suggest something to me. When you became engaged to the young lady whom you have just mentioned, did you make a regular proposal to her family? Was there anything like – what we are going through today, for instance?' I added nervously.

'Why,' replied Traddles, on whose attentive face a thoughtful shade had stolen, 'it was rather a painful transaction, Copperfield, in my case. You see, Sophy being of so much use in the family, none of them could endure the thought of her ever being married. Indeed, they had quite settled among themselves that she never was to be married, and they called her the old maid. Accordingly, when I mentioned it, with the greatest precaution, to Mrs Crewler – '

'The mama?' said I.

'The mama,' said Traddles – 'Reverend Horace Crewler – when I mentioned it with every possible precaution to Mrs Crewler, the effect upon her was such that she gave a scream and became insensible. I couldn't approach the subject again for months.'

'You did it at last?' said I.

'Well, the Reverend Horace did,' said Traddles. 'He is an excellent man, most exemplary in every way; and he pointed out to her that she ought, as a Christian, to reconcile herself to the sacrifice (especially as it was so uncertain), and to bear no uncharitable feeling towards me. As to myself, Copperfield, I give you my word, I felt a perfect bird of prey towards the family.'

'The sisters took your part, I hope, Traddles?'

'Why, I can't say they did,' he returned. 'When we had comparatively reconciled Mrs Crewler to it, we had to break it to Sarah. You recollect my mentioning Sarah as the one that has something the matter with her spine?'

'Perfectly!'

'She clenched both her hands,' said Traddles, looking at me in dismay; 'shut her eyes; turned lead-colour; became perfectly stiff; and took nothing for two days but toast and water, administered with a teaspoon.'

'What a very unpleasant girl, Traddles!' I remarked.

'Oh, I beg your pardon, Copperfield!' said Traddles. 'She is a very charming girl, but she has a great deal of feeling. In fact, they all have. Sophy told me afterwards that the self-reproach she underwent while she was in attendance upon Sarah, no words can describe. I know it must have been severe by my own feelings, Copperfield, which were like a criminal's. After Sarah was restored, we still had to break it to the other eight; and it produced various effects upon them of a most pathetic nature. The two little ones, whom Sophy educates, have only just left off detesting me.'

'At any rate, they are all reconciled to it now, I hope?' said I.

'Ye – yes, I should say they were, on the whole, resigned to it,' said Traddles doubtfully. 'The fact is, we avoid mentioning the subject; and my unsettled prospects and indifferent circumstances are a great consolation to them. There will be a deplorable scene whenever we are married. It will be much more like a funeral than a wedding. And they'll all hate me for taking her away!'

His honest face, as he looked at me with a serio-comic shake of his head, impresses me more in the remembrance than it did in the reality, for I was by this time in a state of such excessive trepidation and wandering of mind as to be quite unable to fix my attention on anything. On our approaching the house where the Misses Spenlow lived, I was at such a discount in respect of my personal looks and presence of mind that Traddles proposed a gentle stimulant in the form of a glass of ale. This having been administered at a neighbouring public-house, he conducted me, with tottering steps, to the Misses Spenlow's door.

I had a vague sensation of being, as it were, on view, when the maid opened it; and of wavering, somehow, across a hall with a weather-glass in it, into a quiet little drawing-room on the ground-floor, commanding a neat garden. Also of sitting down here, on a sofa, and seeing Traddles's hair start up, now his hat was removed, like one of those obtrusive little figures made of springs, that fly out of fictitious snuff-boxes when the lid is taken off. Also of hearing an old-fashioned clock ticking away on the chimney-piece, and trying to make it keep time to the jerking of my heart – which it wouldn't. Also of looking round the room for any sign of Dora, and seeing none. Also of thinking that Jip once barked in the distance, and was instantly choked by somebody. Ultimately I found myself backing Traddles into the fireplace, and bowing in great confusion to two dry little elderly ladies, dressed in black, and each looking wonderfully like a preparation in chip or tan of the late Mr Spenlow.

'Pray,' said one of the two little ladies, 'be seated.'

When I had done tumbling over Traddles, and had sat upon something which was not a cat – my first seat was – I so far recovered my sight as to perceive that Mr Spenlow had evidently been the youngest of the family; that there was a disparity of six or eight years between the two sisters; and that the younger appeared to be the manager of the conference, inasmuch as she had my letter in her hand – so familiar as it looked to me, and yet so odd! – and was referring to it through an eyeglass. They were dressed alike, but this sister wore her dress with a more youthful air than the other; and perhaps had a trifle more frill, or tucker, or brooch, or bracelet, or some little thing of that kind, which made her look more lively. They were both upright in their carriage, formal, precise, composed, and quiet. The sister who had not my letter, had her arms crossed on her breast, and resting on each other, like an Idol.

'Mr Copperfield, I believe?' said the sister who had got my letter, addressing herself to Traddles.

This was a frightful beginning. Traddles had to indicate that I was Mr Copperfield, and I had to lay claim to myself, and they had to divest themselves of a preconceived opinion that Traddles was Mr Copperfield, and altogether we were in a nice condition. To improve it, we all distinctly heard Jip give two short barks, and receive another choke.

'Mr Copperfield!' said the sister with the letter.

I did something – bowed, I suppose – and was all attention, when the other sister struck in.

'My sister Lavinia,' said she, 'being conversant with matters of this nature, will state what we consider most calculated to promote the happiness of both parties.'

I discovered afterwards that Miss Lavinia was an authority in affairs of the heart, by reason of there having anciently existed a certain Mr Pidger, who played short whist, and was supposed to have been enamoured of her. My private opinion is that this was entirely a gratuitous assumption, and that Pidger was altogether innocent of any such sentiments – to which he had never given any sort of expression that I could ever hear of. Both Miss Lavinia and Miss Clarissa had a superstition, however, that he would have declared his passion, if he had not been cut short in his youth (at about sixty) by over-drinking his constitution, and overdoing an attempt to set it right again by swilling Bath water. They had a lurking suspicion even, that he died of secret love; though I must say there was a picture of him in the house with a damask nose, which concealment did not appear to have ever preyed upon.

'We will not,' said Miss Lavinia, 'enter on the past history of this matter. Our poor brother Francis's death has cancelled that.'

'We had not,' said Miss Clarissa, 'been in the habit of frequent association with our brother Francis; but there was no decided division or disunion between us. Francis took his road; we took ours. We considered it conducive to the happiness of all parties that it should be so; and it was so.'

Each of the sisters leaned a little forward to speak, shook her head after speaking, and became upright again when silent. Miss Clarissa never moved her arms. She sometimes played tunes upon them with her fingers – minuets and marches, I should think – but never moved them.

'Our niece's position, or supposed position, is much changed by our brother Francis's death,' said Miss Lavinia; 'and therefore we consider our brother's opinions as regarded her position as being changed, too. We have no reason to doubt, Mr Copperfield, that you are a young gentleman possessed of good qualities and honourable character; or that you have an affection – or are fully persuaded that you have an affection – for our niece.'

I replied, as I usually did whenever I had a chance, that nobody had ever loved anybody else as I loved Dora. Traddles came to my assistance with a confirmatory murmur.

Miss Lavinia was going on to make some rejoinder, when Miss Clarissa, who appeared to be incessantly beset by a desire to refer to her brother Francis, struck in again: 'If Dora's mama,' she said, 'when she married our brother Francis, had at once said that there was not room for the family at the dinner-table, it would have been better for the happiness of all parties.'

'Sister Clarissa,' said Miss Lavinia, 'perhaps we needn't mind that now.'

'Sister Lavinia,' said Miss Clarissa, 'it belongs to the subject.'

Traddles and I in conference with the Misses Spenlow

With your branch of the subject, on which alone you are competent to speak, I should not think of interfering. On this branch of the subject I have a voice and an opinion. It would have been better for the happiness of all parties, if Dora's mama, when she married our brother Francis, had mentioned plainly what her intentions were. We should then have known what we had to expect. We should have said, "Pray do not invite us, at any time"; and all possibility of misunderstanding would have been avoided.'

When Miss Clarissa had shaken her head, Miss Lavinia resumed; again referring to my letter through her eyeglass. They both had little, bright, round, twinkling eyes, by the way, which were like birds' eyes. They were not unlike birds, altogether; having a sharp, brisk, sudden manner, and a little short, spruce way of adjusting themselves, like canaries.

Miss Lavinia, as I have said, resumed: 'You ask permission of my sister Clarissa and myself, Mr Copperfield, to visit here, as the accepted suitor of our niece.'

'If our brother Francis,' said Miss Clarissa, breaking out again, if I may call anything so calm a breaking out, 'wished to surround himself with an atmosphere of Doctors' Commons, and of Doctors' Commons only, what right or desire had we to object? None, I am sure. We have ever been far from wishing to obtrude ourselves on anyone. But why not say so? Let our brother Francis and his wife have their society. Let my sister Lavinia and myself have our society. We can find it for ourselves, I hope!'

As this appeared to be addressed to Traddles and me, both Traddles and I made some sort of reply. Traddles was inaudible. I think I observed, myself, that it was highly creditable to all concerned. I don't in the least know what I meant.

'Sister Lavinia,' said Miss Clarissa, having now relieved her mind, 'you can go on, my dear.'

Miss Lavinia proceeded: 'Mr Copperfield, my sister Clarissa and I have been very careful, indeed, in considering this letter; and we have not considered it without finally showing it to our niece, and discussing it with our niece. We have no doubt that you think you like her very much.'

'Think, ma'am,' I rapturously began. 'Oh – '

But Miss Clarissa giving me a look (just like a sharp canary), as requesting that I would not interrupt the oracle, I begged pardon.

'Affection,' said Miss Lavinia, glancing at her sister for corroboration, which she gave in the form of a little nod to every clause, 'mature affection, homage, devotion, does not easily express itself. Its voice is low. It is modest and retiring, it lies in ambush, waits and waits. Such is the mature fruit. Sometimes a life glides away, and finds it still ripening in the shade.'

Of course I did not understand then that this was an allusion to her supposed experience of the stricken Pidger; but I saw, from the gravity with which Miss Clarissa nodded her head, that great weight was attached to these words.

'The light – for I call them, in comparison with such sentiments, the light – inclinations of very young people,' pursued Miss Lavinia, 'are dust, compared to rocks. It is owing to the difficulty of knowing whether they are likely to endure or

have any real foundation, that my sister Clarissa and myself have been very undecided how to act, Mr Copperfield, and Mr – '

'Traddles,' said my friend, finding himself looked at.

'I beg pardon. Of the Inner Temple, I believe?' said Miss Clarissa, again glancing at my letter.

Traddles said, 'Exactly so,' and became pretty red in the face.

Now, although I had not received any express encouragement as yet, I fancied that I saw in the two little sisters, and particularly in Miss Lavinia, an intensified enjoyment of this new and fruitful subject of domestic interest, a settling down to make the most of it, a disposition to pet it, in which there was a good bright ray of hope. I thought I perceived that Miss Lavinia would have uncommon satisfaction in superintending two young lovers, like Dora and me; and that Miss Clarissa would have hardly less satisfaction in seeing her superintend us, and in chiming in with her own particular department of the subject whenever that impulse was strong upon her. This gave me courage to protest most vehemently that I loved Dora better than I could tell, or anyone believe; that all my friends knew how I loved her; that my aunt, Agnes, Traddles, everyone who knew me, knew how I loved her, and how earnest my love had made me. For the truth of this, I appealed to Traddles. And Traddles, firing up as if he were plunging into a Parliamentary Debate, really did come out nobly; confirming me in good round terms, and in a plain, sensible, practical manner, that evidently made a favourable impression.

'I speak, if I may presume to say so, as one who has some little experience of such things,' said Traddles, 'being myself engaged to a young lady – one of ten, down in Devonshire – and seeing no probability, at present, of our engagement coming to a termination.'

'You may be able to confirm what I have said, Mr Traddles,' observed Miss Lavinia, evidently taking a new interest in him, 'of the affection that is modest and retiring; that waits and waits?'

'Entirely, ma'am,' said Traddles.

Miss Clarissa looked at Miss Lavinia, and shook her head gravely. Miss Lavinia looked consciously at Miss Clarissa, and heaved a little sigh.

'Sister Lavinia,' said Miss Clarissa, 'take my smelling bottle.'

Miss Lavinia revived herself with a few whiffs of aromatic-vinegar – Traddles and I looking on with great solicitude the while; and then went on to say, rather faintly: 'My sister and myself have been in great doubt, Mr Traddles, what course we ought to take in reference to the likings, or imaginary likings, of such very young people as your friend Mr Copperfield, and our niece.'

'Our brother Francis's child,' remarked Miss Clarissa. 'If our brother Francis's wife had found it convenient in her lifetime (though she had an unquestionable right to act as she thought best) to invite the family to her dinner-table, we might have known our brother Francis's child better at the present moment. Sister Lavinia, proceed.'

Miss Lavinia turned my letter, so as to bring the superscription towards herself, and referred through her eyeglass to some orderly-looking notes she had made on that part of it.

'It seems to us,' said she, 'prudent, Mr Traddles, to bring these feelings to the test of our own observation. At present we know nothing of them, and are not in a situation to judge how much reality there may be in them. Therefore, we are inclined so far to accede to Mr Copperfield's proposal as to admit his visits here.'

'I shall never, dear ladies,' I exclaimed, relieved of an immense load of apprehension, 'forget your kindness!'

'But,' pursued Miss Lavinia – 'but we would prefer to regard those visits, Mr Traddles, as made, at present, to us. We must guard ourselves from recognising any positive engagement between Mr Copperfield and our niece, until we have had an opportunity – '

'Until *you* have had an opportunity, sister Lavinia,' said Miss Clarissa.

'Be it so,' assented Miss Lavinia, with a sigh – 'until I have had an opportunity of observing them.'

'Copperfield,' said Traddles, turning to me, 'you feel, I am sure, that nothing could be more reasonable or considerate.'

'Nothing!' cried I. 'I am deeply sensible of it.'

'In this position of affairs,' said Miss Lavinia, again referring to her notes, 'and admitting his visits on this understanding only, we must require from Mr Copperfield a distinct assurance, on his word of honour, that no communication of any kind shall take place between him and our niece without our knowledge. That no project whatever shall be entertained with regard to our niece, without being first submitted to us – '

'To you, sister Lavinia,' Miss Clarissa interposed.

'Be it so, Clarissa!' assented Miss Lavinia resignedly – 'to me – and receiving our concurrence. We must make this a most express and serious stipulation, not to be broken on any account. We wished Mr Copperfield to be accompanied by some confidential friend today,' with an inclination of her head towards Traddles, who bowed, 'in order that there might be no doubt or misconception on this subject. If Mr Copperfield, or if you, Mr Traddles, feel the least scruple in giving this promise, I beg you to take time to consider it.'

I exclaimed, in a state of high ecstatic fervour, that not a moment's consideration could be necessary. I bound myself by the required promise, in a most impassioned manner; called upon Traddles to witness it; and denounced myself as the most atrocious of characters if I ever swerved from it in the least degree.

'Stay!' said Miss Lavinia, holding up her hand; 'we resolved, before we had the pleasure of receiving you two gentlemen, to leave you alone for a quarter of an hour, to consider this point. You will allow us to retire.'

It was in vain for me to say that no consideration was necessary. They persisted in withdrawing for the specified time. Accordingly, these little birds hopped out with great dignity; leaving me to receive the congratulations of Traddles, and to feel as if I were translated to regions of exquisite happiness. Exactly at the expiration of the quarter of an hour, they reappeared with no less dignity than they had disappeared. They had gone rustling away as if their little dresses were made of autumn leaves; and they came rustling back, in like manner.

I then bound myself once more to the prescribed conditions.

'Sister Clarissa,' said Miss Lavinia, 'the rest is with you.' Miss Clarissa, unfolding her arms for the first time, took the notes and glanced at them.

'We shall be happy,' said Miss Clarissa, 'to see Mr Copperfield to dinner, every Sunday, if it should suit his convenience. Our hour is three.'

I bowed.

'In the course of the week,' said Miss Clarissa, 'we shall be happy to see Mr Copperfield to tea. Our hour is half-past six.'

I bowed again.

'Twice in the week,' said Miss Clarissa, 'but, as a rule, not oftener.'

I bowed again.

'Miss Trotwood,' said Miss Clarissa, 'mentioned in Mr Copperfield's letter, will perhaps call upon us. When visiting is better for the happiness of all parties, we are glad to receive visits, and return them. When it is better for the happiness of all parties that no visiting should take place (as in the case of our brother Francis and his establishment), that is quite different.'

I intimated that my aunt would be proud and delighted to make their acquaintance; though I must say I was not quite sure of their getting on very satisfactorily together. The conditions being now closed, I expressed my acknowledgments in the warmest manner; and taking the hand, first of Miss Clarissa, and then of Miss Lavinia, pressed it, in each case, to my lips.

Miss Lavinia then arose, and, begging Mr Traddles to excuse us for a minute, requested me to follow her. I obeyed, all in a tremble, and was conducted into another room. There I found my blessed darling stopping her ears behind the door, with her dear little face against the wall; and Jip in the plate-warmer with his head tied up in a towel.

Oh! How beautiful she was in her black frock, and how she sobbed and cried at first, and wouldn't come out from behind the door! How fond we were of one another, when she did come out at last; and what a state of bliss I was in, when we took Jip out of the plate-warmer, and restored him to the light, sneezing very much, and were all three reunited!

'My dearest Dora! Now, indeed, my own for ever!'

'Oh, don't!' pleaded Dora. 'Please!

'Are you not my own for ever, Dora?'

'Oh, yes, of course I am!' cried Dora; 'but I am so frightened!'

'Frightened, my own?'

'Oh, yes! I don't like him,' said Dora. 'Why don't he go?'

'Who, my life?'

'Your friend,' said Dora. 'It isn't any business of his. What a stupid he must be!'

'My love!' (There never was anything so coaxing as her childish ways.) 'He is the best creature!'

'Oh, but we don't want any best creatures!' pouted Dora.

'My dear,' I argued, 'you will soon know him well, and like him of all things. And here is my aunt coming soon; and you'll like her of all things, too, when you know her.'

'No, please don't bring her!' said Dora, giving me a horrified little kiss, and folding her hands. 'Don't. I know she's a naughty, mischief-making old thing! Don't let her come here, Doady!' which was a corruption of David.

Remonstrance was of no use, then; so I laughed, and admired, and was very much in love and very happy; and she showed me Jip's new trick of standing on his hind legs in a corner – which he did for about the space of a flash of lightning, and then fell down; and I don't know how long I should have stayed there, oblivious of Traddles, if Miss Lavinia had not come in to take me away. Miss Lavinia was very fond of Dora (she told me Dora was exactly like what she had been herself at her age – she must have altered a good deal), and she treated Dora just as if she had been a toy. I wanted to persuade Dora to come and see Traddles, but on my proposing it she ran off to her own room, and locked herself in; so I went to Traddles without her, and walked away with him on air.

'Nothing could be more satisfactory,' said Traddles; 'and they are very agreeable old ladies, I am sure. I shouldn't be at all surprised if you were to be married years before me, Copperfield.'

'Does your Sophy play on any instrument, Traddles?' I enquired, in the pride of my heart.

'She knows enough of the piano to teach it to her little sisters,' said Traddles.

'Does she sing at all?' I asked.

'Why, she sings ballads, sometimes, to freshen up the others a little when they're out of spirits,' said Traddles. 'Nothing scientific.'

'She doesn't sing to the guitar?' said I.

'Oh, dear, no!' said Traddles.

'Paint at all?'

'Not at all,' said Traddles.

I promised Traddles that he should hear Dora sing, and see some of her flower-painting. He said he should like it very much, and we went home arm in arm in great good-humour and delight. I encouraged him to talk about Sophy, on the way; which he did with a loving reliance on her that I very much admired. I compared her in my mind with Dora, with considerable inward satisfaction; but I candidly admitted to myself that she seemed to be an excellent kind of girl for Traddles, too.

Of course my aunt was immediately made acquainted with the successful issue of the conference, and with all that had been said and done in the course of it. She was happy to see me so happy, and promised to call on Dora's aunts without loss of time. But she took such a long walk up and down our rooms that night, while I was writing to Agnes, that I began to think she meant to walk till morning.

My letter to Agnes was a fervent and grateful one, narrating all the good effects that had resulted from my following her advice. She wrote, by return of post, to me. Her letter was hopeful, earnest, and cheerful. She was always cheerful from that time.

I had my hands more full than ever, now. My daily journeys to Highgate considered, Putney was a long way off; and I naturally wanted to go there as often as I could. The proposed tea-drinkings being quite impracticable, I compounded with Miss Lavinia for permission to visit every Saturday afternoon, without detriment to my privileged Sundays. So, the close of every week was a delicious time for me; and I got through the rest of the week by looking forward to it.

I was wonderfully relieved to find that my aunt and Dora's aunts rubbed on, all things considered, much more smoothly than I could have expected. My aunt made her promised visit within a few days of the conference; and within a few more days, Dora's aunts called upon her, in due state and form. Similar but more friendly exchanges took place afterwards, usually at intervals of three or four weeks. I know that my aunt distressed Dora's aunts very much by utterly setting at naught the dignity of fly-conveyance, and walking out to Putney at extraordinary times, as shortly after breakfast or just before tea; likewise by wearing her bonnet in any manner that happened to be comfortable to her head, without at all deferring to the prejudices of civilisation on that subject. But Dora's aunts soon agreed to regard my aunt as an eccentric and somewhat masculine lady, with a strong understanding; and although my aunt occasionally ruffled the feathers of Dora's aunts by expressing heretical opinions on various points of ceremony, she loved me too well not to sacrifice some of her little peculiarities to the general harmony.

The only member of our small society who positively refused to adapt himself to circumstances was Jip. He never saw my aunt without immediately displaying every tooth in his head, retiring under a chair, and growling incessantly; with now and then a doleful howl, as if she really were too much for his feelings. All kinds of treatment were tried with him, coaxing, scolding, slapping, bringing him to Buckingham Street (where he instantly dashed at the two cats, to the terror of all beholders); but he never could prevail upon himself to bear my aunt's society. He would sometimes think he had got the better of his objection, and be amiable for a few minutes; and then would put up his snub nose, and howl to that extent that there was nothing for it but to blind him and put him in the plate-warmer. At length, Dora regularly muffled him in a towel and shut him up there, whenever my aunt was reported at the door.

One thing troubled me much, after we had fallen into this quiet train. It was that Dora seemed by one consent to be regarded like a pretty toy or plaything. My aunt, with whom she gradually became familiar, always called her Little Blossom; and the pleasure of Miss Lavinia's life was to wait upon her, curl her hair, make ornaments for her, and treat her like a pet child. What Miss Lavinia did, her sister did as a matter of course. It was very odd to me; but they all seemed to treat Dora, in her degree, much as Dora treated Jip in his.

I made up my mind to speak to Dora about this; and one day when we were out walking (for we were licensed by Miss Lavinia, after a while, to go out walking by ourselves), I said to her that I wished she could get them to behave towards her differently.

'Because, you know, my darling,' I remonstrated, 'you are not a child.'

'There!' said Dora. 'Now you're going to be cross!'

'Cross, my love?'

'I am sure they're very kind to me,' said Dora, 'and I am very happy.'

'Well! But my dearest life!' said I, 'you might be very happy, and yet be treated rationally.'

Dora gave me a reproachful look – the prettiest look! – and then began to sob, saying if I didn't like her, why had I ever wanted so much to be engaged to her? And why didn't I go away now, if I couldn't bear her?

What could I do but kiss away her tears, and tell her how I doted on her, after that!

'I am sure I am very affectionate,' said Dora; 'you oughtn't to be cruel to me, Doady!'

'Cruel, my precious love! As if I would – or could – be cruel to you, for the world!'

'Then don't find fault with me,' said Dora, making a rosebud of her mouth; 'and I'll be good.'

I was charmed by her presently asking me, of her own accord, to give her that cookery-book I had once spoken of, and to show her how to keep accounts, as I had once promised I would. I brought the volume with me on my next visit (I got it prettily bound, first, to make it look less dry and more inviting); and as we strolled about the Common, I showed her an old housekeeping-book of my aunt's, and gave her a set of tablets, and a pretty little pencil-case, and box of leads, to practise housekeeping with.

But the cookery-book made Dora's head ache, and the figures made her cry. They wouldn't add up, she said. So she rubbed them out, and drew little nosegays, and likenesses of me and Jip, all over the tablets.

Then I playfully tried verbal instruction in domestic matters, as we walked about on a Saturday afternoon. Sometimes, for example, when we passed a butcher's shop, I would say: 'Now, suppose, my pet, that we were married, and you were going to buy a shoulder of mutton for dinner, would you know how to buy it?'

My pretty little Dora's face would fall, and she would make her mouth into a bud again, as if she would very much prefer to shut mine with a kiss.

'Would you know how to buy it, my darling?' I would repeat, perhaps, if I were very inflexible.

Dora would think a little, and then reply, perhaps, with great triumph: 'Why, the butcher would know how to sell it, and what need *I* know? Oh, you silly boy!'

So, when I once asked Dora, with an eye to the cookery-book, what she would do, if we were married, and I were to say I should like a nice Irish stew, she replied that she would tell the servant to make it; and then clapped her little hands together across my arm, and laughed in such a charming manner that she was more delightful than ever.

Consequently the principal use to which the cookery-book was devoted was being put down in the corner for Jip to stand upon. But Dora was so pleased, when she had trained him to stand upon it without offering to come off, and at the same time to hold the pencil case in his mouth, that I was very glad I had bought it.

And we fell back on the guitar-case, and the flower-painting, and the songs about never leaving off dancing, Ta ra la! and were as happy as the week was long. I occasionally wished I could venture to hint to Miss Lavinia that she treated the darling of my heart a little too much like a plaything; and I sometimes awoke, as it were, wondering to find that I had fallen into the general fault, and treated her like a plaything, too – but not often.

CHAPTER 42

Mischief

I feel as if it were not for me to record, even though this manuscript is intended for no eyes but mine, how hard I worked at that tremendous shorthand, and all improvement appertaining to it, in my sense of responsibility to Dora and her aunts. I will only add to what I have already written of my perseverance at this time of my life, and of a patient and continuous energy which then began to be matured within me, and which I know to be the strong part of my character, if it have any strength at all, that there, on looking back, I find the source of my success. I have been very fortunate in worldly matters: many men have worked much harder, and not succeeded half so well; but I never could have done what I have done, without the habits of punctuality, order, and diligence, without the determination to concentrate myself on one object at a time, no matter how quickly its successor should come upon its heels, which I then formed. Heaven knows I write this in no spirit of self-laudation. The man who reviews his own life, as I do mine, in going on here, from page to page, had need to have been a good man, indeed, if he would be spared the sharp consciousness of many talents neglected, many opportunities wasted, many erratic and perverted feelings constantly at war within his breast, and defeating him. I do not hold one natural gift, I dare say, that I have not abused. My meaning simply is that, whatever I have tried to do in life, I have tried with all my heart to do well; that whatever I have devoted myself to, I have devoted myself to completely; that in great aims and in small, I have always been thoroughly in earnest. I have never believed it possible that any natural or improved ability can claim immunity from the companionship of the steady, plain, hard-working qualities, and hope to gain its end. There is no such thing as such fulfilment on this earth. Some happy talent, and some fortunate opportunity, may form the two sides of the ladder on which some men mount, but the rounds of that ladder must be made of stuff to stand wear and tear; and there is no substitute for thoroughgoing, ardent, and sincere earnestness. Never to put one hand to anything on which I could throw my whole self; and never to affect depreciation of my work, whatever it was, I find, now, to have been my golden rules.

How much of the practice I have just reduced to precept, I owe to Agnes, I will not repeat here. My narrative proceeds to Agnes, with a thankful love.

She came on a visit of a fortnight to the Doctor's. Mr

Wickfield was the Doctor's old friend, and the Doctor wished to talk with him, and do him good. It had been matter of conversation with Agnes when she was last in town, and this visit was the result. She and her father came together. I was not much surprised to hear from her that she had engaged to find a lodging in the neighbourhood for Mrs Heep, whose rheumatic complaint required change of air, and who would be charmed to have it in such company. Neither was I surprised when, on the very next day, Uriah, like a dutiful son, brought his worthy mother to take possession.

'You see, Master Copperfield,' said he, as he forced himself upon my company for a turn in the Doctor's garden, 'where a person loves, a person is a little jealous – leastways, anxious to keep an eye on the beloved one.'

'Of whom are you jealous, now?' said I.

'Thanks to you, Master Copperfield,' he returned, 'of no one in particular just at present – no male person, at least.'

'Do you mean that you are jealous of a female person?'

He gave me a sidelong glance out of his sinister red eyes, and laughed.

'Really, Master Copperfield,' he said, ' – I should say Mister, but I know you'll excuse the 'abit I've got into – you're so insinuating that you draw me like a corkscrew! Well, I don't mind telling you,' putting his fish-like hand on mine, 'I'm not a lady's man in general, sir, and I never was, with Mrs Strong.'

His eyes looked green now, as they watched mine with a rascally cunning.

'What do you mean?' said I.

'Why, though I am a lawyer, Master Copperfield,' he replied, with a dry grin, 'I mean, just at present, what I say.'

'And what do you mean by your look?' I retorted quietly.

'By my look? Dear me, Copperfield, that's sharp practice! What do I mean by my look?'

'Yes,' said I. 'By your look.'

He seemed very much amused, and laughed as heartily as it was in his nature to laugh. After some scraping of his chin with his hand, he went on to say, with his eyes cast downward – still scraping, very slowly: 'When I was but an 'umble clerk, she always looked down upon me. She was for ever having my Agnes backwards and forwards at her 'ouse, and she was for ever being a friend to you, Master Copperfield; but I was too far beneath her, myself, to be noticed.'

'Well?' said I; 'suppose you were!'

' – And beneath him, too,' pursued Uriah, very distinctly, and in a meditative tone of voice, as he continued to scrape his chin.

'Don't you know the Doctor better,' said I, 'than to suppose him conscious of your existence, when you were not before him?'

He directed his eyes at me in that sidelong glance again, and he made his face very lantern-jawed, for the greater convenience of scraping, as he answered: 'Oh, dear, I am not referring to the Doctor! Oh, no, poor man! I mean Mr Maldon!'

My heart quite died within me. All my old doubts and apprehensions on that subject, all the Doctor's happiness and peace, all the mingled possibilities of innocence and compromise, that I could not unravel, I saw, in a moment, at the mercy of this fellow's twisting.

'He never could come into the office, without ordering and shoving me about,' said Uriah. 'One of your fine gentlemen he was! I was very meek and 'umble – and I am. But I didn't like that sort of thing – and I don't!'

He left off scraping his chin, and sucked in his cheeks until they seemed to meet inside; keeping his sidelong glance upon me all the while.

'She is one of your lovely women, she is,' he pursued, when he had slowly restored his face to its natural form; 'and ready to be no friend to such as me, *I* know. She's just the person as would put my Agnes up to higher sort of game. Now, I ain't one of your lady's men, Master Copperfield; but I've had eyes in my ed, a pretty long time back. We 'umble ones have got eyes, mostly speaking – and we look out of 'em.'

I endeavoured to appear unconscious and not disquieted, but, I saw in his face, with poor success.

'Now, I'm not a going to let myself be run down, Copperfield,' he continued, raising that part of his countenance, where his red eyebrows would have been if he had had any, with malignant triumph, 'and I shall do what I can to put a stop to this friendship. I don't approve of it. I don't mind acknowledging to you that I've got rather a grudging disposition, and want to keep off all intruders. I ain't a going, if I know it, to run the risk of being plotted against.'

'You are always plotting, and delude yourself into the belief that everybody else is doing the like, I think,' said I.

'Perhaps so, Master Copperfield,' he replied. 'But I've got a motive, as my fellow-partner used to say; and I go at it tooth and nail. I mustn't be put upon, as an 'umble person, too much. I can't allow people in my way. Really, they must come out of the cart, Master Copperfield!'

'I don't understand you,' said I.

'Don't you, though?' he returned, with one of his jerks. 'I'm astonished at that, Master Copperfield, you being usually so quick! I'll try to be plainer, another time. Is that Mr Maldon a-horseback, ringing at the gate, sir?'

'It looks like him,' I replied, as carelessly as I could.

Uriah stopped short, put his hands between his great knobs of knees, and doubled himself up with laughter. With perfectly silent laughter. Not a sound escaped from him. I was so repelled by his odious behaviour, particularly by this concluding instance, that I turned away without any ceremony; and left him doubled up in the middle of the garden, like a scarecrow in want of support.

It was not on that evening, but, as I well remember, on the next evening but one, which was a Saturday, that I took Agnes to see Dora. I had arranged the visit beforehand, with Miss Lavinia; and Agnes was expected to tea.

I was in a flutter of pride and anxiety; pride in my dear little betrothed, and anxiety that Agnes should like her. All the way to Putney, Agnes being inside the stage-coach, and I outside, I pictured Dora to myself in every one of the pretty looks I knew so well; now making up my mind that I should like her to look exactly as she looked at such a time, and then doubting whether I should not prefer her looking as she looked at such another time; and almost worrying myself into a fever about it.

I was troubled by no doubt of her being very pretty, in any case; but it fell out that I had never seen her look so well. She was not in the drawing-room when I presented Agnes to her little aunts, but was shyly keeping out of the way. I knew where to look for her, now; and sure enough I found her stopping her ears again, behind the same dull old door.

At first she wouldn't come at all; and then she pleaded for five minutes by my watch. When at length she put her arm through mine, to be taken to the drawing-room, her charming little face was flushed, and had never been so pretty. But, when we went into the room, and it turned pale, she was ten thousand times prettier yet.

Dora was afraid of Agnes. She had told me that she knew Agnes was 'too clever.' But when she saw her looking at once so cheerful and so earnest, and so thoughtful, and so good, she gave a faint little cry of pleased surprise, and just put her affectionate arms round Agnes's neck, and laid her innocent cheek against her face.

I never was so happy. I never was so pleased as when I saw those two sit down together, side by side. As when I saw my little darling looking up so naturally to those cordial eyes. As when I saw the tender, beautiful regard which Agnes cast upon her.

Miss Lavinia and Miss Clarissa partook, in their way, of my joy. It was the pleasantest tea-table in the world. Miss Clarissa presided. I cut and handed the sweet seed-cake – the little sisters had a bird-like fondness for picking up seeds and pecking at sugar; Miss Lavinia looked on with benignant patronage, as if our happy love were all her work; and we were perfectly contented with ourselves and one another.

The gentle cheerfulness of Agnes went to all their hearts. Her quiet interest in everything that interested Dora; her manner of making acquaintance with Jip (who responded instantly); her pleasant way, when Dora was ashamed to come over to her usual seat by me; her modest grace and ease, eliciting a crowd of blushing little marks of confidence from Dora, seemed to make our circle quite complete.

'I am so glad,' said Dora, after tea, 'that you like me. I didn't think you would; and I want, more than ever, to be liked, now Julia Mills is gone.'

I have omitted to mention it, by the by. Miss Mills had sailed, and Dora and I had gone aboard a great East Indiaman at Gravesend to see her; and we had had preserved ginger, and guava, and other delicacies of that sort for lunch; and we had left Miss Mills weeping on a camp-stool on the quarter-deck, with a large new diary under her arm, in which the original reflections awakened by the contemplation of Ocean were to be recorded under lock and key.

Agnes said, she was afraid I must have given her an unpromising character; but Dora corrected that directly.

'Oh, no!' she said, shaking her curls at me; 'it was all praise. He thinks so much of your opinion, that I was quite afraid of it.'

'My good opinion cannot strengthen his attachment to some people whom he knows,' said Agnes, with a smile; 'it is not worth their having.'

'But please let me have it,' said Dora, in her coaxing way, 'if you can!'

We made merry about Dora's wanting to be liked, and Dora said I was a goose, and she didn't like me at any rate, and the short evening flew away on gossamer-wings. The time was at hand when the coach was to call for us. I was standing alone before the fire, when Dora came stealing softly in, to give me that usual precious little kiss before I went.

'Don't you think, if I had had her for a friend a long time ago, Doady,' said Dora, her bright eyes shining very brightly, and her little right hand idly busying itself with one of the buttons of my coat, 'I might have been more clever perhaps?'

'My love!' said I, 'what nonsense!'

'Do you think it is nonsense?' returned Dora, without looking at me. 'Are you sure it is?'

'Of course I am!'

'I have forgotten,' said Dora, still turning the button round and round, 'what relation Agnes is to you, you dear bad boy.'

'No blood-relation,' I replied; 'but we were brought up together, like brother and sister.'

'I wonder why you ever fell in love with me?' said Dora, beginning on another button of my coat.

'Perhaps because I couldn't see you, and not love you, Dora!'

'Suppose you had never seen me at all,' said Dora, going to another button.

'Suppose we had never been born!' said I gaily.

I wondered what she was thinking about, as I glanced in admiring silence at the little soft hand travelling up the row of buttons on my coat, and at the clustering hair that lay against my breast, and at the lashes of her downcast eyes, slightly rising as they followed her idle fingers. At length her eyes were lifted up to mine, and she stood on tiptoe to give me, more thoughtfully than usual, that precious little kiss – once, twice, three times – and went out of the room.

They all came back together within five minutes afterwards, and Dora's unusual thoughtfulness was quite gone then. She was laughingly resolved to put Jip through the whole of his performances before the coach came. They took some time (not so much on account of their variety, as Jip's reluctance), and were still unfinished when it was heard at the door. There was a hurried but affectionate parting between Agnes and herself; and Dora was to write to Agnes (who was not to mind her letters being foolish, she said), and Agnes was to write to Dora; and they had a second parting at the coach door, and a third when Dora, in spite of the remonstrances of Miss Lavinia, would come running out once more to remind Agnes at the coach-window about writing, and to shake her curls at me on the box.

The stage-coach was to put us down near Covent Garden, where we were to take another stage-coach for Highgate. I was impatient for the short walk in the interval, that Agnes might praise Dora to me. Ah! what praise it was! How lovingly and fervently did it commend the pretty creature I had won, with all her artless graces best displayed, to my most gentle care! How thoughtfully remind me, yet with no pretence of doing so, of the trust in which I held the orphan child!

Never, never, had I loved Dora so deeply and truly as I loved her that night. When we had again alighted, and were walking in the starlight along the quiet road that led to the Doctor's house, I told Agnes it was her doing.

'When you were sitting by her,' said I, 'you seemed to be no less *her* guardian angel than mine; and you seem so now, Agnes.'

'A poor angel,' she returned, 'but faithful.'

The clear tone of her voice going straight to my heart, made it natural to me to say: 'The cheerfulness that belongs to you, Agnes (and to no one else that ever I have seen), is so restored, I have observed today, that I have begun to hope you are happier at home?'

'I am happier in myself,' she said; 'I am quite cheerful and light-hearted.'

I glanced at the serene face looking upward, and thought it was the stars that made it seem so noble.

'There has been no change at home,' said Agnes, after a few moments.

'No fresh reference,' said I, 'to – I wouldn't distress you, Agnes, but I cannot help asking – to what we spoke of, when we parted last?'

'No, none,' she answered.

'I have thought so much about it.'

'You must think less about it. Remember that I confide in simple love and truth at last. Have no apprehensions for me, Trotwood,' she added, after a moment; 'the step you dread my taking, I shall never take.'

Although I think I had never really feared it, in any season of cool reflection, it was an unspeakable relief to me to have this assurance from her own truthful lips. I told her so earnestly.

'And when this visit is over,' said I – 'for we may not be alone another time – how long is it likely to be, my dear Agnes, before you come to London again?'

'Probably a long time,' she replied; 'I think it will be best – for papa's sake – to remain at home. We are not likely to meet often, for some time to come; but I shall be a good correspondent of Dora's, and we shall frequently hear of one another that way.'

We were now within the little courtyard of the Doctor's cottage. It was growing late. There was a light in the window of Mrs Strong's chamber, and Agnes, pointing to it, bade me good-night.

'Do not be troubled,' she said, giving me her hand, 'by our misfortunes and anxieties. I can be happier in nothing than in your happiness. If you can ever give me help, rely upon it I will ask you for it. God bless you always!'

In her beaming smile, and in these last tones of her cheerful voice, I seemed again to see and hear my little Dora in her company. I stood awhile, looking through the porch at the stars, with a heart full of love and gratitude, and then walked slowly forth. I had engaged a bed at a decent alehouse close by, and was going out at the gate, when, happening to turn my head, I saw a light in the Doctor's study. A half-reproachful fancy came into my mind, that he had been working at the Dictionary without my help. With the view of seeing if this were so, and, in any case, of bidding him good-night, if he were yet sitting among his books, I turned back, and going softly across the hall, and gently opening the door, looked in.

The first person whom I saw, to my surprise, by the sober light of the shaded lamp, was Uriah. He was standing close beside it, with one of his skeleton hands over his mouth, and the other resting on the Doctor's table. The Doctor sat in his study chair, covering his face with his hands. Mr Wickfield, sorely troubled and distressed, was leaning forward, irresolutely touching the Doctor's arm.

For an instant, I supposed that the Doctor was ill. I hastily advanced a step under that impression, when I met Uriah's eye, and saw what was the matter. I would have withdrawn, but the Doctor made a gesture to detain me, and I remained.

'At any rate,' observed Uriah, with a writhe of his ungainly person, 'we may keep the door shut. We needn't make it known to all the town.'

Saying which, he went on his toes to the door, which I had left open, and carefully closed it. He then came back, and took up his former position. There was an obtrusive show of compassionate zeal in his voice and manner, more intolerable – at least to me – than any demeanour he could have assumed.

'I have felt it incumbent upon me, Master Copperfield,' said Uriah, 'to point out to Doctor Strong what you and me have already talked about. You didn't exactly understand me, though!'

I gave him a look, but no other answer; and, going to my good old master, said a few words that I meant to be words of comfort and encouragement. He put his hand upon my shoulder, as it had been his custom to do when I was quite a little fellow, but did not lift his grey head.

'As you didn't understand me, Master Copperfield,' resumed Uriah in the same officious manner, 'I may take the liberty of 'umbly mentioning, being among friends, that I have called Doctor Strong's attention to the goings-on of Mrs Strong. It's much against the grain with me, I assure you, Copperfield, to be concerned in anything so unpleasant; but really, as it is, we're all mixing ourselves up with what oughtn't to be. That was what my meaning was, sir, when you didn't understand me.'

I wonder now, when I recall his leer, that I did not collar him, and try to shake the breath out of his body.

'I dare say I didn't make myself very clear,' he went on, 'nor you neither. Naturally, we was both of us inclined to give such a subject a wide berth. Hows'ever, at last I have made up my mind to speak plain; and I have mentioned to Doctor Strong that – did you speak, sir?'

This was to the Doctor, who had moaned. The sound might have touched any heart, I thought, but it had no effect upon Uriah's.

' – mentioned to Doctor Strong,' he proceeded, 'that anyone may see that Mr Maldon and the lovely and agreeable lady as is Doctor Strong's wife are too sweet on one another. Really the time is come (we being at present all mixing ourselves up with what oughtn't to be), when Doctor Strong must be told that this was full as plain to everybody as the sun, before Mr Maldon went to India; that Mr Maldon made excuses to come back, for nothing else; and that he's always here, for nothing else. When you come in, sir, I was just putting it to my fellow-partner,' towards whom he turned, 'to say to Doctor Strong upon his word and honour, whether he'd ever been of this opinion long ago, or not. Come, Mr Wickfield, sir! Would you be so good as tell us? Yes or no, sir? Come, partner!'

'For God's sake, my dear Doctor,' said Mr Wickfield, again laying his irresolute hand upon the Doctor's arm, 'don't attach too much weight to any suspicions I may have entertained.'

'There!' cried Uriah, shaking his head. 'What a melancholy confirmation, ain't it? Him! Such an old friend! Bless your soul, when I was nothing but a clerk in his office, Copperfield, I've seen him twenty times, if I've seen him once, quite in a taking about it – quite put out, you know (and very proper in him as a father; I'm sure *I* can't blame him), to think that Miss Agnes was mixing herself up with what oughtn't to be.'

'My dear Strong,' said Mr Wickfield, in a tremulous voice, 'my good friend, I needn't tell you that it has been my vice to look for some one master motive in everybody, and to try all actions by one narrow test. I may have fallen into such doubts as I have had, through this mistake.'

'You have had doubts, Wickfield,' said the Doctor, without lifting up his head. 'You have had doubts.'

'Speak up, fellow-partner,' urged Uriah.

'I had, at one time, certainly,' said Mr Wickfield. 'I – God forgive me – I thought *you* had.'

'No, no, no!' returned the Doctor, in a tone of most pathetic grief.

'I thought, at one time,' said Mr Wickfield, 'that you wished to send Maldon abroad to effect a desirable separation.'

'No, no, no!' returned the Doctor. 'To give Annie pleasure, by making some provision for the companion of her childhood. Nothing else.'

'So I found,' said Mr Wickfield. 'I couldn't doubt it, when you told me so. But I thought – I implore you to remember the narrow construction which has been my besetting sin – that, in a case where there was so much disparity in point of years – '

'That's the way to put it, you see, Master Copperfield!' observed Uriah, with fawning and offensive pity.

' – a lady of such youth, and such attractions, however real her respect for you, might have been influenced in marrying, by worldly considerations only. I made no allowance for innumerable feelings and circumstances that may have all tended to good. For Heaven's sake remember that!'

'How kind he puts it!' said Uriah, shaking his head.

'Always observing her from one point of view,' said Mr Wickfield; 'but by all that is dear to you, my old friend, I entreat you to consider what it was; I am forced to confess now, having no escape – '

'No! There's no way out of it, Mr Wickfield, sir,' observed Uriah, 'when it's got to this.'

' – that I did,' said Mr Wickfield, glancing helplessly and distractedly at his partner, 'that I did doubt her, and think her wanting in her duty to you; and that I did sometimes, if I must say all, feel averse to Agnes being in such a familiar relation towards her, as to see what I saw, or in my diseased theory fancied that I saw. I never mentioned this to anyone. I never meant it to be known to anyone. And though it is terrible to you to hear,' said Mr Wickfield, quite subdued, 'if you knew how terrible it is to me to tell, you would feel compassion for me!'

The Doctor, in the perfect goodness of his nature, put out his hand. Mr Wickfield held it for a little while in his, with his head bowed down.

'I am sure,' said Uriah, writhing himself into the silence like a Conger-eel, 'that this is a subject full of unpleasantness to everybody. But since we have got so far, I ought to take the liberty of mentioning that Copperfield has noticed it too.'

I turned upon him, and asked him how he dared refer to me!

'Oh! it's very kind of you, Copperfield,' returned Uriah, undulating all over, 'and we all know what an amiable character yours is; but you know that the moment I spoke to you the other night, you knew what I meant. You know you knew what I meant, Copperfield. Don't deny it! You deny it with the best intentions; but don't do it, Copperfield.'

I saw the mild eye of the good old Doctor turned upon me for a moment, and I felt that the confession of my old misgivings and remembrances was too plainly written in my face to be overlooked. It was of no use raging. I could not undo that. Say what I would, I could not unsay it.

We were silent again, and remained so, until the Doctor rose and walked twice or thrice across the room. Presently he returned to where his chair stood; and, leaning on the back of it, and occasionally putting his handkerchief to his eyes, with a simple honesty that did him more honour, to my thinking, than any disguise he could have affected, said: 'I have been much to blame. I believe I have been very much to blame. I have exposed one whom I hold in my heart, to trials and aspersions – I call them aspersions, even to have been conceived in anybody's inmost mind – of which she never, but for me, could have been the object.'

Uriah Heep gave a kind of snivel. I think to express sympathy.

'Of which my Annie,' said the Doctor, 'never, but for me, could have been the object. Gentlemen, I am old now, as you know; I do not feel, tonight, that I have much to live for. But my life – my Life – upon the truth and honour of the dear lady who has been the subject of this conversation!'

I do not think that the best embodiment of chivalry, the realisation of the handsomest and most romantic figure ever imagined by painter, could have said this with a more impressive and affecting dignity than the plain old Doctor did.

'But I am not prepared,' he went on, 'to deny – perhaps I may have been, without knowing it, in some degree prepared to admit – that I may have unwittingly ensnared that lady into an unhappy marriage. I am a man quite unaccustomed to observe; and I cannot but believe that the observation of several people, of different ages and positions, all too plainly tending in one direction (and that so natural), is better than mine!'

I have often admired, as I have elsewhere described, his benignant manner towards his youthful wife; but the respectful tenderness he manifested in every reference to her on this occasion, and the almost reverential manner in which he put away from him the lightest doubt of her integrity, exalted him, in my eyes, beyond description.

'I married that lady,' said the Doctor, 'when she was extremely young. I took her to myself when her character was scarcely formed. So far as it was developed, it had been my happiness to form it. I knew her father well. I knew her well. I had taught her what I could, for the love of all her beautiful and virtuous qualities. If I did her wrong, as I fear I did, in taking advantage (but I never meant it) of her gratitude and her affection, I ask pardon of that lady, in my heart!'

He walked across the room, and came back to the same place, holding the chair with a grasp that trembled, like his subdued voice, in his earnestness.

'I regarded myself as a refuge for her, from the dangers and vicissitudes of life. I persuaded myself that, unequal though we were in years, she would live tranquilly and contentedly with me. I did not shut out of my consideration the time when I should leave her free, and still young and still beautiful, but with her judgement more matured – no, gentlemen – upon my truth!'

His homely figure seemed to be lighted up by his fidelity and generosity. Every word he uttered had a force that no other grace could have imparted to it.

'My life with this lady has been very happy. Until tonight, I have had uninterrupted occasion to bless the day on which I did her great injustice.'

His voice, more and more faltering in the utterance of these words, stopped for a few moments; then he went on: 'Once awakened from my dream – I have been a poor dreamer, in one way or other, all my life – I see how natural it is that she should have some regretful feeling towards her old companion and her equal. That she does regard him with some innocent regret, with some blameless thoughts of what might have been, but for me, is, I fear, too true. Much that I have seen, but not noted, has come back upon me with new meaning, during this last trying hour. But, beyond this, gentlemen, the dear lady's name never must be coupled with a word, a breath, of doubt.'

For a little while, his eye kindled and his voice was firm; for a little while he was again silent. Presently, he proceeded as before: 'It only remains for me to bear the knowledge of the unhappiness I have occasioned, as submissively as I can. It is she who should reproach; not I. To save her from miscon-struction, cruel misconstruction, that even my friends have not been able to avoid, becomes my duty. The more retired we live, the better I shall discharge it. And when the time comes – may it come soon, if it be His merciful pleasure! – when my death shall release her from constraint, I shall close my eyes upon her honoured face, with unbounded confidence and love; and leave her, with no sorrow then, to happier and brighter days.'

I could not see him for the tears which his earnestness and goodness, so adorned by, and so adorning, the perfect simplicity of his manner, brought into my eyes. He had moved to the door, when he added: 'Gentlemen, I have shown you my heart. I am sure you will respect it. What we have said tonight is never to be said more. Wickfield, give me an old friend's arm upstairs!'

Mr Wickfield hastened to him. Without interchanging a word they went slowly out of the room together, Uriah looking after them.

'Well, Master Copperfield!' said Uriah, meekly turning to me. 'The thing hasn't took quite the turn that might have been expected, for the old Scholar – what an excellent man! – is as blind as a brickbat; but *this* family's out of the cart, I think!'

I needed but the sound of his voice to be so madly enraged as I never was before, and never have been since.

'You villain,' said I, 'what do you mean by entrapping me into your schemes? How dare you appeal to me just now, you false rascal, as if we had been in discussion together?'

As we stood, front to front, I saw so plainly, in the stealthy exultation of his face, what I already so plainly knew; I mean that he forced his confidence upon me, expressly to make me miserable, and had set a deliberate trap for me in this very matter; that I couldn't bear it. The whole of his lank cheek was invitingly before me, and I struck it with my open hand with that force that my fingers tingled as if I had burnt them.

He caught the hand in his, and we stood in that connection, looking at each other. We stood so, a long time; long enough for me to see the white marks of my fingers die out of the deep red of his cheek, and leave it a deeper red.

'Copperfield,' he said at length, in a breathless voice, 'have you taken leave of your senses?'

'I have taken leave of you,' said I, wresting my hand away. 'You dog, I'll know no more of you.'

'Won't you?' said he, constrained by the pain of his cheek to put his hand there. 'Perhaps you won't be able to help it. Isn't this ungrateful of you, now?'

'I have shown you often enough,' said I, 'that I despise you. I have shown you now more plainly that I do. Why should I dread your doing your worst to all about you? What else do you ever do?'

He perfectly understood this allusion to the considerations that had hitherto restrained me in my communications with him. I rather think that neither the blow, nor the allusion, would have escaped me, but for the assurance I had had from Agnes that night. It is no matter.

There was another long pause. His eyes, as he looked at me, seemed to take every shade of colour that could make eyes ugly.

'Copperfield,' he said, removing his hand from his cheek, 'you have always gone against me. I know you always used to be against me at Mr Wickfield's.'

'You may think what you like,' said I, still in a towering rage. 'If it is not true, so much the worthier you.'

'And yet I always liked you, Copperfield,' he rejoined.

I deigned to make him no reply; and, taking up my hat, was going out to bed, when he came between me and the door.

'Copperfield,' he said, 'there must be two parties to a quarrel. I won't be one.'

'You may go to the devil!' said I.

'Don't say that!' he replied. 'I know you'll be sorry afterwards. How can you make yourself so inferior to me as to show such a bad spirit? But I forgive you.'

'You forgive me!' I repeated disdainfully.

'I do, and you can't help yourself,' replied Uriah. 'To think of your going and attacking *me*, that have always been a friend to you! But there can't be a quarrel without two parties, and I won't be one. I will be a friend to you, in spite of you. So you know what you've got to expect.'

The necessity of carrying on this dialogue (his part in which was very slow; mine very quick) in a low tone, that the house might not be disturbed at an unseasonable hour, did not improve my temper, though my passion was cooling down. Merely telling him that I should expect from him what I always had expected, and had never yet been disappointed in, I opened the door upon him, as if he had been a great walnut put there to be cracked, and went out of the house. But he slept out of the house, too, at his mother's lodging, and, before I had gone many hundred yards, came up with me.

'You know, Copperfield,' he said, in my ear (I did not turn my head), 'you're in quite a wrong position'; which I felt to be true, and that made me chafe the more; 'you can't make this a brave thing, and you can't help being forgiven. I don't intend to mention it to mother, nor to any living soul. I'm determined to forgive you. But I do wonder that you should lift your hand against a person that you knew to be so 'umble!'

I felt only less mean than he. He knew me better than I knew myself. If he had retorted or openly exasperated me, it would have been a relief and a justification; but he had put me on a slow fire, on which I lay tormented half the night.

In the morning when I came out, the early church bell was ringing, and he was walking up and down with his mother. He addressed me as if nothing had happened, and I could do no less than reply. I had struck him hard enough to give him the toothache, I suppose. At all events his face was tied up in a black silk handkerchief, which, with his hat perched on the top of it, was far from improving his appearance. I heard that he went to a dentist's in London on the Monday morning, and had a tooth out. I hope it was a double one.

The Doctor gave out that he was not quite well; and he remained alone, for a considerable part of every day, during the remainder of the visit. Agnes and her father had been gone a week, before we resumed our usual work. On the day preceding its resumption, the Doctor gave me with his own hands a folded note not sealed. It was addressed to myself; and laid an injunction on me, in a few affectionate words, never to refer to the subject of that evening. I had confided it to my aunt, but to no one else. It was not a subject I could discuss with Agnes, and Agnes certainly had not the least suspicion of what had passed.

Neither, I felt convinced, had Mrs Strong then. Several weeks elapsed before I saw the least change in her. It came on slowly, like a cloud when there is no wind. At first, she seemed to wonder at the gentle compassion with which the Doctor spoke to her, and at his wish that she should have her mother with her, to relieve the dull monotony of her life. Often, when we were at work, and she was sitting by, I would see her pausing and looking at him with that memorable face. Afterwards, I sometimes observed her rise, with her eyes full of tears, and go out of the room. Gradually, an unhappy shadow fell upon her beauty, and deepened every day. Mrs Markleham was a regular inmate of the cottage then; but she talked and talked and saw nothing.

As this change stole on Annie, once like sunshine in the Doctor's house, the Doctor became older in appearance, and more grave; but the sweetness of his temper, the placid kindness of his manner, and his benevolent solicitude for her, if they were capable of any increase, were increased. I saw him once, early on the morning of her birthday, when she came to sit in the window while we were at work (which she had always done, but now began to do with a timid and uncertain air that I thought very touching), take her forehead between his hands, kiss it, and go hurriedly away, too much moved to remain. I saw her stand where he had left her, like a statue; and then bend down her head, and clasp her hands, and weep, I cannot say how sorrowfully.

Sometimes, after that, I fancied that she tried to speak, even to me, in intervals when we were left alone. But she never uttered a word. The Doctor always had some new project for her participating in amusements away from home, with her mother; and Mrs Markleham, who was very fond of amusements, and very easily dissatisfied with anything else, entered into them with great good will, and was loud in her commendations. But Annie, in a spiritless, unhappy way, only went whither she was led, and seemed to have no care for anything.

I did not know what to think. Neither did my aunt; who must have walked, at various times, a hundred miles in her uncertainty. What was strangest of all was that the only real relief which seemed to make its way into the secret region of this domestic unhappiness made its way there in the person of Mr Dick.

What his thoughts were on the subject, or what his observation was, I am as unable to explain as I dare say he would have been to assist me in the task. But as I have recorded in the narrative of my school days, his veneration for the Doctor was unbounded; and there is a subtlety of perception in real attachment, even when it is borne towards man by one of the lower animals, which leaves the highest intellect behind. To this mind of the heart, if I may call it so, in Mr Dick, some bright ray of the truth shot straight.

He had proudly resumed his privilege, in many of his spare hours, of walking up and down the garden with the Doctor; as he had been accustomed to pace up and down The Doctor's Walk at Canterbury. But matters were no sooner in this state than he devoted all his spare time (and got up earlier to make it more) to these perambulations. If he had never been so happy as when the Doctor read that marvellous performance, the Dictionary, to him, he was now quite miserable unless the Doctor pulled it out of his pocket, and began. When the Doctor and I were engaged, he now fell into the custom of walking up and down with Mrs Strong, and helping her to trim her favourite flowers, or weed the beds. I dare say he rarely spoke a dozen words in an hour; but his quiet interest, and his wistful face, found immediate response in both their breasts; each knew that the other liked him, and that he loved both; and he became what no one else could be – a link between them.

When I think of him, with his impenetrably wise face, walking up and down with the Doctor, delighted to be battered by the hard words in the Dictionary; when I think of him carrying huge watering-pots after Annie; kneeling down in very paws of gloves, at patient microscopic work among the little leaves; expressing as no philosopher could have expressed, in everything he did, a delicate desire to be her friend; showering sympathy, trustfulness, and affection out of every hole in the watering-pot; when I think of him never wandering in that better mind of his to which unhappiness addressed itself, never bringing the unfortunate King Charles into the garden, never wavering in his grateful service, never diverted from his knowledge that there was something wrong, or from his wish to set it right – I really feel almost ashamed of having known that he was not quite in his wits, taking account of the utmost I have done with mine.

'Nobody but myself, Trot, knows what that man is!' my aunt would proudly remark, when we conversed about it. 'Dick will distinguish himself yet!'

I must refer to one other topic before I close this chapter. While the visit at the Doctor's was still in progress, I observed that the postman brought two or three letters every morning for Uriah Heep, who remained at Highgate until the rest went back, it being a leisure time; and that these were always directed in a businesslike manner by Mr Micawber, who now assumed a round legal hand. I was glad to infer, from these slight premises, that Mr Micawber was doing well; and consequently was much surprised to receive, about this time, the following letter from his amiable wife:

Canterbury, Monday Evening

You will doubtless be surprised, my dear Mr Copperfield, to receive this communication. Still more so, by its contents. Still more so, by the stipulation of implicit confidence which I beg to impose. But my feelings as a wife and mother require relief; and as I do not wish to consult my family (already obnoxious to the feelings of Mr Micawber), I know no one of whom I can better ask advice than my friend and former lodger.

You may be aware, my dear Mr Copperfield, that between myself and Mr Micawber (whom I will never desert), there has always been preserved a spirit of mutual confidence. Mr Micawber may have occasionally given a bill without consulting me, or he may have misled me as to the period when that obligation would become due. This has actually happened. But in general, Mr Micawber has had no secrets from the bosom of affection – I allude to his wife – and has invariably, on our retirement to rest, recalled the events of the day.

You will picture to yourself, my dear Mr Copperfield, what the poignancy of my feelings must be, when I inform you that Mr Micawber is entirely changed. He is reserved. He is secret. His life is a mystery to the partner of his joys and sorrows – I again allude to his wife – and if I should assure you that beyond knowing that it is passed from morning till night at the office, I now know less of it than I do of the man in the south, connected with whose mouth the thoughtless children repeat an idle tale respecting cold plum porridge, I should adopt a popular fallacy to express an actual fact.

But this is not all. Mr Micawber is morose. He is severe. He is estranged from our eldest son and daughter, he has no pride in his twins, he looks with an eye of coldness even on the unoffending stranger who last became a member of our circle. The pecuniary means of meeting our expenses, kept down to the utmost farthing, are obtained from him with great difficulty, and even under fearful threats that he will Settle himself (the exact expression); and he inexorably refuses to give any explanation whatever of this distracting policy.

This is hard to bear. This is heart-breaking. If you will advise me, knowing my feeble powers such as they are, how you think it will be best to exert them in a dilemma so unwonted, you will add another friendly obligation to the many you have already rendered me. With loves from the children, and a smile from the happily-unconscious stranger, I remain, dear Mr Copperfield,

Your afflicted,

EMMA MICAWBER

I did not feel justified in giving a wife of Mrs Micawber's experience any other recommendation than that she should try to reclaim Mr Micawber by patience and kindness (as I knew she would in any case); but the letter set me thinking about him very much.

CHAPTER 43

Another Retrospect

Once again let me pause upon a memorable period of my life. Let me stand aside, to see the phantoms of those days go by me, accompanying the shadow of myself, in dim procession.

Weeks, months, seasons, pass along. They seem little more than a summer day and a winter evening. Now, the Common where I walk with Dora is all in bloom, a field of bright gold; and now the unseen heather lies in mounds and bunches underneath a covering of snow. In a breath, the river that flows through our Sunday walks is sparkling in the summer sun, is ruffled by the winter wind, or thickened with drifting heaps of ice. Faster than ever river ran towards the sea, it flashes, darkens, and rolls away.

Not a thread changes, in the house of the two little bird-like ladies. The clock ticks over the fireplace, the weather-glass hangs in the hall. Neither clock nor weather-glass is ever right; but we believe in both devoutly.

I have come legally to man's estate. I have attained the dignity of twenty-one. But this is a sort of dignity that may be thrust upon one. Let me think what I have achieved.

I have tamed that savage stenographic mystery. I make a respectable income by it. I am in high repute for my accomplishment in all pertaining to the art, and am joined with eleven others in reporting the debates in Parliament for a Morning Newspaper. Night after night, I record predictions that never come to pass, professions that are never fulfilled, explanations that are only meant to mystify. I wallow in words. Britannia, that unfortunate female, is always before me, like a trussed fowl: skewered through and through with office-pens, and bound hand and foot with red tape. I am sufficiently behind the scenes to know the worth of political life. I am quite an infidel about it, and shall never be converted.

My dear old Traddles has tried his hand at the same pursuit, but it is not in Traddles's way. He is perfectly good-humoured respecting his failure, and reminds me that he always did consider himself slow. He has occasional employment on the same newspaper, in getting up the facts of dry subjects, to be written about and embellished by more fertile minds. He is called to the bar, and with admirable industry and self-denial has scraped another hundred pounds together, to fee a conveyancer whose chambers he attends. A great deal of very hot port wine was consumed at his call; and, considering the figure, I should think the Inner Temple must have made a profit by it.

I have come out in another way. I have taken with fear and trembling to authorship. I wrote a little something, in secret, and sent it to a magazine, and it was published in the magazine. Since then, I have taken heart to write a good many trifling pieces. Now, I am regularly paid for them. Altogether, I am well off; when I tell my income on the fingers of my left hand, I pass the third finger and take in the fourth to the middle joint.

We have removed from Buckingham Street to a pleasant little cottage very near the one I looked at, when my enthusiasm first came on. My aunt, however (who has sold the house at Dover, to good advantage), is not going to remain here, but intends removing herself to a still more tiny cottage close at hand. What does this portend? My marriage? Yes!

Yes! I am going to be married to Dora! Miss Lavinia and Miss Clarissa have given their consent; and if ever canary birds were in a flutter, they are. Miss Lavinia, self-charged with the superintendence of my darling's wardrobe, is constantly cutting out brown-paper cuirasses, and differing in opinion from a highly respectable young man, with a long bundle, and a yard measure under his arm. A dressmaker, always stabbed in the breast with a needle and thread, boards and lodges in the house; and seems to me, eating, drinking, or sleeping, never to take her thimble off. They make a lay-figure of my dear. They are always sending for her to come and try something on. We can't be happy together for five minutes in the evening, but some intrusive female knocks at the door, and says, 'Oh, if you please, Miss Dora, would you step upstairs!'

Miss Clarissa and my aunt roam all over London, to find out articles of furniture for Dora and me to look at. It would be better for them to buy the goods at once, without this ceremony of inspection; for, when we go to see a kitchen fender and meat screen, Dora sees a Chinese house for Jip, with little bells on the top, and prefers that. And it takes a long time to accustom Jip to his new residence, after we have bought it; whenever he goes in or out, he makes all the little bells ring, and is horribly frightened.

Peggotty comes up to make herself useful, and falls to work immediately. Her department appears to be to clean everything over and over again. She rubs everything that can be rubbed, until it shines, like her own honest forehead, with perpetual friction. And now it is that I begin to see her solitary brother passing through the dark streets at night, and looking, as he goes, among the wandering faces. I never speak to him at such an hour. I know too well, as his grave figure passes onward, what he seeks, and what he dreads.

Why does Traddles look so important when he calls upon me this afternoon in the Commons – where I still occasionally attend, for form's sake, when I have time? The realisation of my boyish daydreams is at hand. I am going to take out the licence.

It is a little document to do so much; and Traddles contemplates it, as it lies upon my desk, half in admiration, half in awe. There are the names in the sweet old visionary connection, David Copperfield and Dora Spenlow; and there, in the corner, is that Parental Institution, the Stamp Office, which is so benignantly interested in the various transactions of human life, looking down upon our union; and there is the Archbishop of Canterbury invoking a blessing on us in print, and doing it as cheap as could possibly be expected.

Nevertheless, I am in a dream, a flustered, happy, hurried dream. I can't believe that it is going to be; and yet I can't believe but that everyone I pass in the street must have some kind of perception that I am to be married the day after tomorrow. The Surrogate knows me, when I go down to be sworn; and disposes of me easily, as if there were a Masonic understanding between us. Traddles is not at all wanted, but is in attendance as my general backer.

'I hope the next time you come here, my dear fellow,' I say to Traddles, 'it will be on the same errand for yourself. And I hope it will be soon.'

'Thank you for your good wishes, my dear Copperfield,' he replies. 'I hope so, too. It's a satisfaction to know that she'll wait for me any length of time, and that she really is the dearest girl – '

'When are you to meet her at the coach?' I ask.

'At seven,' says Traddles, looking at his plain old silver watch – the very watch he once took a wheel out of, at school, to make a water-mill. 'That is about Miss Wickfield's time, is it not?'

'A little earlier. Her time is half-past eight.'

'I assure you, my dear boy,' says Traddles, 'I am almost as pleased as if I were going to be married myself, to think that this event is coming to such a happy termination. And really the great friendship and consideration of personally associating Sophy with the joyful occasion, and inviting her to be a bridesmaid in conjunction with Miss Wickfield, demands my warmest thanks. I am extremely sensible of it.'

I hear him, and shake hands with him; and we talk, and walk, and dine, and so on; but I don't believe it. Nothing is real.

Sophy arrives at the house of Dora's aunts, in due course. She has the most agreeable of faces – not absolutely beautiful, but extraordinarily pleasant – and is one of the most genial, unaffected, frank, engaging creatures I have ever seen. Traddles presents her to us with great pride; and rubs his hands for ten minutes by the clock, with every individual hair upon his head standing on tiptoe, when I congratulate him in a corner on his choice.

I have brought Agnes from the Canterbury coach, and her cheerful and beautiful face is among us for the second time. Agnes has a great liking for Traddles, and it is capital to see them meet, and to observe the glory of Traddles as he commends the dearest girl in the world to her acquaintance.

Still I don't believe it. We have a delightful evening, and are supremely happy; but I don't believe it yet. I can't collect myself. I can't check off my happiness as it takes place. I feel in a misty and unsettled kind of state, as if I had got up very early in the morning a week or two ago, and had never been to bed since. I can't make out when yesterday was. I seem to have been carrying the licence about, in my pocket, many months.

Next day, too, when we all go in a flock to see the house – our house – Dora's and mine – I am quite unable to regard myself as its master. I seem to be there by permission of somebody else. I half expect the real master to come home presently, and say he is glad to see me. Such a beautiful little house as it is, with everything so bright and new; with the flowers on the carpets looking as if freshly gathered, and the green leaves on the paper as if they had just come out; with the spotless muslin curtains, and the blushing rose-coloured furniture, and Dora's garden hat with the blue ribbon – do I remember, now, how I loved her in such another hat when I first knew her! – already hanging on its little peg; the guitar-case quite at home on its heels in a corner; and everybody tumbling over Jip's Pagoda, which is much too big for the establishment.

Another happy evening, quite as unreal as all the rest of it, and I steal into the usual room before going away. Dora is not there. I suppose they have not done trying on yet. Miss Lavinia peeps in, and tells me mysteriously that she will not be long. She is rather long, notwithstanding; but by and by I hear a rustling at the door, and someone taps.

I say, 'Come in!' but someone taps again.

I go to the door, wondering who it is; there I meet a pair of bright eyes, and a blushing face: they are Dora's eyes and face, and Miss Lavinia has dressed her in tomorrow's dress, bonnet and all, for me to see. I take my little wife to my heart; and Miss Lavinia gives a little scream because I tumble the bonnet, and Dora laughs and cries at once, because I am so pleased; and I believe it less than ever.

'Do you think it pretty, Doady?' says Dora.

Pretty! I should rather think I did.

'And are you sure you like me very much?' says Dora.

The topic is fraught with such danger to the bonnet that Miss Lavinia gives another little scream, and begs me to understand that Dora is only to be looked at, and on no account to be touched. So Dora stands in a delightful state of confusion for a minute or two, to be admired; and then takes off her bonnet – looking so natural without it! – and runs away with it in her hand; and comes dancing down again in her old familiar dress, and asks Jip if I have got a beautiful little wife, and whether he'll forgive her for being married, and kneels down to make him stand upon the cookery-book, for the last time in her single life.

I go home, more incredulous than ever, to a lodging that I have hard by; and get up very early in the morning, to ride to the Highgate road and fetch my aunt.

I have never seen my aunt in such state. She is dressed in lavender-coloured silk, and has a white bonnet on, and is amazing. Janet has dressed her, and is there to look at me. Peggotty is ready to go to church, intending to behold the ceremony from the gallery. Mr Dick, who is to give my darling to me at the altar, has had his hair curled. Traddles, whom I have taken up by appointment at the turnpike, presents a dazzling combination of cream colour and light blue; and both he and Mr Dick have a general effect about them of being all gloves.

No doubt I see this, because I know it is so; but I am astray, and seem to see nothing. Nor do I believe anything whatever. Still, as we drive along in an open carriage, this fairy marriage is real enough to fill me with a sort of wondering pity for the unfortunate people who have no part in it, but are sweeping out the shops, and going to their daily occupations.

My aunt sits with my hand in hers all the way. When we stop a little way short of the church, to put down Peggotty, whom we have brought on the box, she gives it a squeeze, and me a kiss.

'God bless you, Trot! My own boy never could be dearer. I think of poor dear Baby this morning.'

'So do I. And of all I owe to you, dear aunt.'

'Tut, child!' says my aunt; and gives her hand in overflowing cordiality to Traddles, who then gives his to Mr Dick, who then gives his to me, who then give mine to Traddles, and then we come to the church door.

The church is calm enough, I am sure; but it might be a steam-power loom in full action, for any sedative effect it has on me. I am too far gone for that.

The rest is all a more or less incoherent dream.

A dream of their coming in with Dora; of the pew-opener arranging us, like a drill-sergeant, before the altar rails; of my wondering, even then, why pew-openers must always be the most disagreeable females procurable, and whether there is any religious dread of a disastrous infection of good-humour which renders it indispensable to set those vessels of vinegar upon the road to Heaven.

Of the clergyman and clerk appearing; of a few boatmen and some other people strolling in; of an ancient mariner behind me, strongly flavouring the church with rum; of the service beginning in a deep voice, and our all being very attentive.

Of Miss Lavinia, who acts as a semi-auxiliary bridesmaid, being the first to cry, and of her doing homage (as I take it) to the memory of Pidger, in sobs; of Miss Clarissa applying a smelling-bottle; of Agnes taking care of Dora; of my aunt endeavouring to represent herself as a model of sternness, with tears rolling down her face; of little Dora trembling very much, and making her responses in faint whispers.

Of our kneeling down together, side by side; of Dora's trembling less and less, but always clasping Agnes by the hand; of the service being got through, quietly and gravely; of our all looking at each other in an April state of smiles and tears, when it is over; of my young wife being hysterical in the vestry, and crying for her poor papa, her dear papa.

Of her soon cheering up again, and our signing the register all round. Of my going into the gallery for Peggotty to bring *her* to sign it; of Peggotty's hugging me in a corner, and telling me she saw my own dear mother married; of its being over, and our going away.

Of my walking so proudly and lovingly down the aisle with my sweet wife upon my arm, through a mist of half-seen people, pulpits, monuments, pews, fonts, organs, and church windows, in which there flutter faint airs of association with my childish church at home, so long ago.

Of their whispering, as we pass, what a youthful couple we are, and what a pretty little wife she is. Of our all being so merry and talkative in the carriage going back. Of Sophy telling us that when she saw Traddles (whom I had entrusted with the licence) asked for it, she almost fainted, having been convinced that he would contrive to lose it, or to have his pocket picked. Of Agnes laughing gaily; and of Dora being so fond of Agnes that she will not be separated from her, but still keeps her hand.

Of there being a breakfast, with abundance of things, pretty and substantial, to eat and drink, whereof I partake, as I should do in any other dream, without the least perception of their flavour; eating and drinking, as I may say, nothing but love and marriage, and no more believing in the viands than in anything else.

Of my making a speech in the same dreamy fashion, without having an idea of what I want to say, beyond such as may be comprehended in the full conviction that I haven't said it. Of our being very sociably and simply happy (always in a dream, though); and of Jip's having wedding cake, and its not agreeing with him afterwards.

Of the pair of hired post-horses being ready, and of Dora's going away to change her dress. Of my aunt and Miss Clarissa remaining with us; and our walking in the garden; and my aunt, who has made quite a speech at breakfast touching Dora's aunts, being mightily amused with herself, but a little proud of it, too.

Of Dora's being ready, and of Miss Lavinia's hovering about her, loth to lose the pretty toy that has given her so much pleasant occupation. Of Dora's making a long series of surprised discoveries that she has forgotten all sorts of little things; and of everybody's running everywhere to fetch them.

Of their all closing about Dora, when at last she begins to say goodbye, looking, with their bright colours and ribbons, like a bed of flowers. Of my darling being almost smothered among the flowers, and coming out, laughing and crying both together, to my jealous arms.

Of my wanting to carry Jip (who is to go along with us), and Dora's saying no, that she must carry him, or else he'll think she don't like him any more, now she is married, and will break his heart. Of our going, arm in arm, and Dora stopping and looking back, and saying, 'If I have ever been cross or ungrateful to anybody, don't remember it!' and bursting into tears.

Of her waving her little hand, and our going away once more. Of her once more stopping and looking back, and hurrying to Agnes, and giving Agnes, above all the others, her last kisses and farewells.

We drive away together, and I awake from the dream. I believe it at last. It is my dear, dear, little wife beside me whom I love so well!

'Are you happy now, you foolish boy?' says Dora; 'and sure you don't repent?'

I have stood aside to see the phantoms of those days go by me. They are gone, and I resume the journey of my story.

CHAPTER 44

Our Housekeeping

It was a strange condition of things, the honeymoon being over, and the bridesmaids gone home, when I found myself sitting down in my own small house with Dora; quite thrown out of employment, as I may say, in respect of the delicious old occupation of making love.

It seemed such an extraordinary thing to have Dora always there. It was so unaccountable not to be obliged to go out to see her, not to have any occasion to be tormenting myself about her, not to have to write to her, not to be scheming and devising opportunities of being alone with her. Sometimes of an evening, when I looked up from my writing, and saw her seated opposite, I would lean back in my chair, and think how queer it was that there we were, alone together as a matter of course – nobody's business any more – all the romance of our engagement put away upon a shelf, to rust – no one to please but one another – one another to please, for life.

When there was a debate, and I was kept out very late, it seemed so strange to me, as I was walking home, to think that Dora was at home! It was such a wonderful thing, at first, to have her coming softly down to talk to me as I ate my supper. It was such a stupendous thing to know for certain that she put her hair in papers. It was altogether such an astonishing event to see her do it!

I doubt whether two young birds could have known less about keeping house, than I and my pretty Dora did. We had a servant, of course. She kept house for us. I have still a latent belief that she must have been Mrs Crupp's daughter in disguise, we had such an awful time of it with Mary Anne.

Her name was Paragon. Her nature was represented to us, when we engaged her, as being feebly expressed in her name. She had a written character, as large as a proclamation; and according to this document, could do everything of a domestic nature that ever I heard of, and a great many things that I never did hear of. She was a woman in the prime of life; of a severe countenance; and subject (particularly in the arms) to a sort of perpetual measles or fiery rash. She had a cousin in the Life Guards, with such long legs that he looked like the afternoon shadow of somebody else. His shell-jacket was as much too little for him as he was too big for the premises. He made the cottage smaller than it need have been, by being so very much out of proportion to it. Besides which, the walls were not thick, and, whenever he passed the evening at our house, we always knew of it by hearing one continual growl in the kitchen.

Our treasure was warranted sober and honest. I am therefore willing to believe that she was in a fit when we found her under the boiler; and that the deficient teaspoons were attributed to the dustman.

But she preyed upon our minds dreadfully. We felt our inexperience, and were unable to help ourselves. We should have been at her mercy, if she had had any; but she was a remorseless woman, and had none. She was the cause of our first little quarrel.

'My dearest life,' I said one day to Dora, 'do you think Mary Anne has any idea of time?'

I am married

'Why, Doady?' enquired Dora, looking up, innocently, from her drawing.

'My love, because it's five, and we were to have dined at four.'

Dora glanced wistfully at the clock, and hinted that she thought it was too fast.

'On the contrary, my love,' said I, referring to my watch, 'it's a few minutes too slow.'

My little wife came and sat upon my knee, to coax me to be quiet, and drew a line with her pencil down the middle of my nose; but I couldn't dine off that, though it was very agreeable.

'Don't you think, my dear,' said I, 'it would be better for you to remonstrate with Mary Anne?'

'Oh, no, please! I couldn't, Doady!' said Dora.

'Why not, my love?' I gently asked.

'Oh, because I am such a little goose,' said Dora, 'and she knows I am.'

I thought this sentiment so incompatible with the establishment of any system of check on Mary Anne, that I frowned a little.

'Oh, what ugly wrinkles in my bad boy's forehead!' said Dora, and still being on my knee, she traced them with her pencil; putting it to her rosy lips to make it mark blacker, and working at my forehead with a quaint little mockery of being industrious, that quite delighted me in spite of myself.

'There's a good child,' said Dora, 'it makes its face so much prettier to laugh.'

'But, my love,' said I.

'No, no! please!' cried Dora, with a kiss, 'don't be a naughty Blue Beard! Don't be serious!'

'My precious wife,' said I, 'we must be serious sometimes. Come! Sit down on this chair, close beside me! Give me the pencil! There! Now let us talk sensibly. You know, dear;' what a little hand it was to hold, and what a tiny wedding-ring it was to see! 'You know, my love, it is not exactly comfortable to have to go out without one's dinner. Now, is it?'

'N–n–no!' replied Dora faintly.

'My love, how you tremble!'

'Because I know you're going to scold me,' exclaimed Dora, in a piteous voice.

'My sweet, I am only going to reason.'

'Oh, but reasoning is worse than scolding!' exclaimed Dora, in despair. 'I didn't marry to be reasoned with. If you meant to reason with such a poor little thing as I am, you ought to have told me so, you cruel boy!'

I tried to pacify Dora, but she turned away her face, and shook her curls from side to side, and said, 'You cruel, cruel boy!' so many times, that I really did not exactly know what to do; so I took a few turns up and down the room in my uncertainty, and came back again.

'Dora, my darling!'

'No, I am not your darling. Because you *must* be sorry that you married me, or else you wouldn't reason with me!' returned Dora.

I felt so injured by the inconsequential nature of this charge, that it gave me courage to be grave.

'Now, my own Dora,' said I, 'you are very childish, and are

talking nonsense. You must remember, I am sure, that I was obliged to go out yesterday when dinner was half over; and that, the day before, I was made quite unwell by being obliged to eat underdone veal in a hurry; today, I don't dine at all – and I am afraid to say how long we waited for breakfast – and *then* the water didn't boil. I don't mean to reproach you, my dear, but this is not comfortable.'

'Oh, you cruel, cruel boy, to say I am a disagreeable wife!' cried Dora.

'Now, my dear Dora, you must know that I never said that!'

'You said I wasn't comfortable!' said Dora.

'I said the housekeeping was not comfortable.'

'It's exactly the same thing!' cried Dora. And she evidently thought so, for she wept most grievously.

I took another turn across the room, full of love for my pretty wife, and distracted by self-accusatory inclinations to knock my head against the door. I sat down again, and said: 'I am not blaming you, Dora. We have both a great deal to learn. I am only trying to show you, my dear, that you must – you really must' (I was resolved not to give this up) 'accustom yourself to look after Mary Anne. Likewise to act a little for yourself and me.'

'I wonder, I do, at your making such ungrateful speeches,' sobbed Dora. 'When you know that the other day, when you said you would like a little bit of fish, I went out myself, miles and miles, and ordered it, to surprise you.'

'And it was very kind of you, my own darling,' said I. 'I felt it so much that I wouldn't on any account have even mentioned that you bought a Salmon – which was too much for two. Or that it cost one pound six – which was more than we can afford.'

'You enjoyed it very much,' sobbed Dora. 'And you said I was a Mouse.'

'And I'll say so again, my love,' I returned, 'a thousand times!'

But I had wounded Dora's soft little heart, and she was not to be comforted. She was so pathetic in her sobbing and bewailing, that I felt as if I had said I don't know what to hurt her. I was obliged to hurry away; I was kept out late; and I felt all night such pangs of remorse as made me miserable. I had the conscience of an assassin, and was haunted by a vague sense of enormous wickedness.

It was two or three hours past midnight when I got home. I found my aunt, in our house, sitting up for me.

'Is anything the matter, aunt?' said I, alarmed.

'Nothing, Trot,' she replied. 'Sit down, sit down. Little Blossom has been rather out of spirits, and I have been keeping her company. That's all.'

I leaned my head upon my hand, and felt more sorry and downcast, as I sat looking at the fire, than I could have supposed possible so soon after the fulfilment of my brightest hopes. As I sat thinking, I happened to meet my aunt's eyes, which were resting on my face. There was an anxious expression in them, but it cleared directly.

'I assure you, aunt,' said I, 'I have been quite unhappy myself all night, to think of Dora's being so. But I had no other intention than to speak to her tenderly and lovingly about our home-affairs.'

My aunt nodded encouragement.

'You must have patience, Trot,' said she.

'Of course. Heaven knows I don't mean to be unreasonable, aunt!'

'No, no,' said my aunt. 'But Little Blossom is a very tender little blossom, and the wind must be gentle with her.'

I thanked my good aunt, in my heart, for her tenderness towards my wife; and I was sure that she knew I did.

'Don't you think, aunt,' said I, after some further contemplation of the fire, 'that you could advise and counsel Dora a little, for our mutual advantage, now and then?'

'Trot,' returned my aunt, with some emotion, 'no. Don't ask me such a thing!'

Her tone was so very earnest that I raised my eyes in surprise.

'I look back on my life, child,' said my aunt, 'and I think of some who are in their graves, with whom I might have been on kinder terms. If I judged harshly of other people's mistakes in marriage, it may have been because I had bitter reason to judge harshly of my own. Let that pass. I have been a grumpy, frumpy, wayward sort of a woman, a good many years. I am still, and I always shall be. But you and I have done one another some good, Trot – at all events, you have done me good, my dear; and division must not come between us, at this time of day.'

'Division between *us*!' cried I.

'Child, child!' said my aunt, smoothing her dress, 'how soon it might come between us, or how unhappy I might make our Little Blossom, if I meddled in anything, a prophet couldn't say. I want our pet to like me, and be as gay as a butterfly. Remember your own home, in that second marriage; and never do both me and her the injury you have hinted at!'

I comprehended, at once, that my aunt was right; and I comprehended the full extent of her generous feeling towards my dear wife.

'These are early days, Trot,' she pursued, 'and Rome was not built in a day, nor in a year. You have chosen freely for yourself'; a cloud passed over her face for a moment, I thought; 'and you have chosen a very pretty and a very affectionate creature. It will be your duty, and it will be your pleasure too – of course I know that; I am not delivering a lecture – to estimate her (as you chose her) by the qualities she has, and not by the qualities she may not have. The latter you must develop in her, if you can. And if you cannot, child,' here my aunt rubbed her nose, 'you must just accustom yourself to do without 'em. But remember, my dear, your future is between you two. No one can assist you; you are to work it out for yourselves. This is marriage, Trot; and Heaven bless you both, in it, for a pair of babes in the wood as you are!'

My aunt said this in a sprightly way, and gave me a kiss to ratify the blessing.

'Now,' said she, 'light my little lantern, and see me into my band-box by the garden path'; for there was a communication between our cottages in that direction. 'Give Betsey Trotwood's love to Blossom, when you come back; and whatever you do, Trot, never dream of setting Betsey up as a scarecrow, for if I ever saw her in the glass, she's quite grim enough and gaunt enough in her private capacity!'

With this my aunt tied her head up in a handkerchief with which she was accustomed to make a bundle of it on such occasions, and I escorted her home. As she stood in her garden, holding up her little lantern to light me back, I thought her observation of me had an anxious air again; but I was too much occupied in pondering on what she had said, and too much impressed – for the first time, in reality – by the conviction that Dora and I had indeed to work out our future for ourselves, and that no one could assist us, to take much notice of it.

Dora came stealing down in her little slippers, to meet me, now that I was alone; and cried upon my shoulder, and said I had been hard-hearted and she had been naughty; and I said much the same thing in effect, I believe; and we made it up, and agreed that our first little difference was to be our last, and that we were never to have another if we lived a hundred years.

The next domestic trial we went through was the Ordeal of Servants. Mary Anne's cousin deserted into our coal-hole, and was brought out, to our great amazement, by a picket of his companions in arms, who took him away handcuffed in a procession that covered our front-garden with ignominy. This nerved me to get rid of Mary Anne, who went so mildly, on receipt of wages, that I was surprised, until I found out about the teaspoons, and also about the little sums she had borrowed in my name of the tradespeople without authority. After an interval of Mrs Kidgerbury – the oldest inhabitant of Kentish Town, I believe, who went out charing, but was too feeble to execute her conceptions of that art – we found another treasure, who was one of the most amiable of women, but who generally made a point of falling either up or down the kitchen stairs with the tray, and almost plunged into the parlour, as into a bath, with the tea-things. The ravages committed by this unfortunate rendering her dismissal necessary, she was succeeded (with intervals of Mrs Kidgerbury) by a long line of Incapables; terminating in a young person of genteel appearance, who went to Greenwich Fair in Dora's bonnet. After whom I remember nothing but an average equality of failure.

Everybody we had anything to do with seemed to cheat us. Our appearance in a shop was a signal for the damaged goods to be brought out immediately. If we bought a lobster, it was full of water. All our meat turned out to be tough, and there was hardly any crust to our loaves. In search of the principle on which joints ought to be roasted, to be roasted enough, and not too much, I myself referred to the Cookery Book, and found it there established as the allowance of a quarter of an hour to every pound, and say a quarter over. But the principle always failed us by some curious fatality, and we never could hit any medium between redness and cinders.

I had reason to believe that in accomplishing these failures we incurred a far greater expense than if we had achieved a series of triumphs. It appeared to me, on looking over the tradesmen's books, as if we might have kept the basement story paved with butter, such was the extensive scale of our consumption of that article. I don't know whether the Excise returns of the period may have exhibited any increase in the demand for pepper, but if our performances did not affect the market, I should say several families must have left off using it. And the most wonderful fact of all was, that we never had anything in the house.

As to the washerwoman pawning the clothes, and coming in a state of penitent intoxication to apologise, I suppose that might have happened several times to anybody. Also the chimney on fire, the parish engine, and perjury on the part of the Beadle. But I apprehend that we were personally unfortunate in engaging a servant with a taste for cordials, who swelled our running account for porter at the public-house by such inexplicable items as 'quartern rum shrub (Mrs C.)' 'Half-quartern gin and cloves (Mrs C.)' 'Glass rum and peppermint (Mrs C.)' – the parenthesis always referring to Dora, who was supposed, it appeared on explanation, to have imbibed the whole of these refreshments.

One of our first feats in the housekeeping way was a little dinner to Traddles. I met him in town, and asked him to walk out with me that afternoon. He readily consenting, I wrote to Dora, saying I would bring him home. It was pleasant weather, and on the road we made my domestic happiness the theme of conversation. Traddles was very full of it; and said, that, picturing himself with such a home, and Sophy waiting and preparing for him, he could think of nothing wanting to complete his bliss.

I could not have wished for a prettier little wife at the opposite end of the table, but I certainly could have wished when we sat down for a little more room. I did not know how it was, but though there were only two of us, we were at once always cramped for room, and yet had always room enough to lose everything in. I suspect it may have been because nothing had a place of its own, except Jip's pagoda, which invariably blocked up the main thoroughfare. On the present occasion, Traddles was so hemmed in by the pagoda and the guitar-case, and Dora's flower-painting, and my writing-table, that I had serious doubts of the possibility of his using his knife and fork; but he protested, with his own good-humour, 'Oceans of room, Copperfield! I assure you, Oceans!'

There was another thing I could have wished, namely, that Jip had never been encouraged to walk about the tablecloth during dinner. I began to think there was something disorderly in his being there at all, even if he had not been in the habit of putting his foot in the salt or the melted butter. On this occasion he seemed to think he was introduced expressly to keep Traddles at bay; and he barked at my old friend, and made short runs at his plate, with such undaunted pertinacity that he may be said to have engrossed the conversation.

However, as I knew how tender-hearted my dear Dora was, and how sensitive she would be to any slight upon her favourite, I hinted no objection. For similar reasons I made no allusion to the skirmishing plates upon the floor; or to the disreputable appearance of the casters, which were all at sixes and sevens, and looked drunk; or to the further blockade of Traddles by wandering vegetable dishes and jugs. I could not help wondering in my own mind, as I contemplated the boiled leg of mutton before me, previous to carving it, how it came to pass that our joints of meat were of such extraordinary shapes – and whether our butcher contracted for all the deformed sheep that came into the world; but I kept my reflections to myself.

'My love,' said I to Dora, 'what have you got in that dish?'

I could not imagine why Dora had been making tempting little faces at me, as if she wanted to kiss me.

'Oysters, dear,' said Dora timidly.

'Was that *your* thought?' said I, delighted.

'Ye–yes, Doady,' said Dora.

'There never was a happier one!' I exclaimed, laying down the carving-knife and fork. 'There is nothing Traddles likes so much!'

'Ye–yes, Doady,' said Dora, 'and so I bought a beautiful little barrel of them, and the man said they were very good. But I – I am afraid there's something the matter with them. They don't seem right.' Here Dora shook her head, and diamonds twinkled in her eyes.

'They are only opened in both shells,' said I. 'Take the top one off, my love.'

'But it won't come off,' said Dora, trying very hard, and looking very much distressed.

'Do you know, Copperfield,' said Traddles, cheerfully examining the dish, 'I think it is in consequence – they are capital oysters, but I *think* it is in consequence – of their never having been opened.'

They never had been opened; and we had no oyster-knives – and couldn't have used them if we had; so we looked at the oysters and ate the mutton. At least we ate as much of it as was done, and made up with capers. If I had permitted him, I am satisfied that Traddles would have made a perfect savage of himself, and eaten a plateful of raw meat, to express enjoyment of the repast; but I would hear of no such immolation on the altar of friendship; and we had a course of bacon instead, there happening, by good fortune, to be cold bacon in the larder.

My poor little wife was in such affliction when she thought I should be annoyed, and in such a state of joy when she found I was not, that the discomfiture I had subdued very soon vanished, and we passed a happy evening; Dora sitting with her arm on my chair while Traddles and I discussed a glass of wine, and taking every opportunity of whispering in my ear that it was so good of me not to be a cruel, cross old boy. By and by she made tea for us; which it was so pretty to see her do, as if she was busying herself with a set of doll's tea-things, that I was not particular about the quality of the beverage. Then Traddles and I played a game or two at cribbage, and Dora singing to the guitar the while, it seemed to me as if our courtship and marriage were a tender dream of mine, and the night when I first listened to her voice were not yet over.

When Traddles went away, and I came back into the parlour from seeing him out, my wife planted her chair close to mine, and sat down by my side.

'I am very sorry,' she said. 'Will you try to teach me, Doady?'

'I must teach myself first, Dora,' said I. 'I am as bad as you, love.'

'Ah! But you can learn,' she returned; 'and you are a clever, clever man!'

'Nonsense, Mouse!' said I.

'I wish,' resumed my wife, after a long silence, 'that I could have gone down into the country for a whole year, and lived with Agnes!'

Her hands were clasped upon my shoulder, and her chin rested on them, and her blue eyes looked quietly into mine.

'Why so?' I asked.

Our housekeeping

'I think she might have improved me, and I think I might have learnt from *her*,' said Dora.

'All in good time, my love. Agnes has had her father to take care of for these many years, you should remember. Even when she was quite a child, she was the Agnes whom we know,' said I.

'Will you call me a name I want you to call me?' enquired Dora, without moving.

'What is it?' I asked with a smile.

'It's a stupid name,' she said, shaking her curls for a moment. 'Child-wife.'

I laughingly asked my child-wife what her fancy was in desiring to be so called? She answered without moving, otherwise than as the arm I twined about her may have brought her blue eyes nearer to me: 'I don't mean, you silly fellow, that you should use the name, instead of Dora. I only mean that you should think of me that way. When you are going to be angry with me, say to yourself, "it's only my child-wife!" When I am very disappointing, say, "I knew, a long time ago, that she would make but a child-wife!" When you miss what I should like to be, and I think can never be, say, "still my foolish child-wife loves me!" For indeed I do.'

I had not been serious with her, having no idea, until now, that she was serious herself. But her affectionate nature was so happy in what I now said to her with my whole heart, that her face became a laughing one before her glittering eyes were dry. She was soon my child-wife indeed; sitting down on the floor outside the Chinese House, ringing all the little bells one after another, to punish Jip for his recent bad behaviour, while Jip lay blinking in the doorway with his head out, even too lazy to be teased.

This appeal of Dora's made a strong impression on me. I look back on the time I write of; I invoke the innocent figure that I dearly loved, to come out from the mists and shadows of the past, and turn its gentle head towards me once again; and I can still declare that this one little speech was constantly in my memory. I may not have used it to the best account; I was young and inexperienced; but I never turned a deaf ear to its artless pleading.

Dora told me, shortly afterwards, that she was going to be a wonderful housekeeper. Accordingly, she polished the tablets, pointed the pencil, bought an immense account-book, carefully stitched up with a needle and thread all the leaves of the Cookery Book which Jip had torn, and made quite a desperate little attempt 'to be good,' as she called it. But the figures had the old obstinate propensity – they *would not* add up. When she had entered two or three laborious items in the account-book, Jip would walk over the page, wagging his tail, and smear them all out. Her own little right-hand middle finger got steeped to the very bone in ink; and I think that was the only decided result obtained.

Sometimes, of an evening, when I was at home and at work – for I wrote a good deal now, and was beginning in a small way to be known as a writer – I would lay down my pen, and watch my child-wife trying to be good. First of all, she would bring out the immense account-book, and lay it down upon the table, with a deep sigh. Then she would open it at the place where Jip had made it illegible last night, and call Jip up to look at his misdeeds. This would occasion a diversion in Jip's favour, and some inking of his nose, perhaps, as a penalty. Then she would tell Jip to lie down on the table instantly, 'like a lion' – which was one of his tricks, though I cannot say the likeness was striking – and, if he were in an obedient humour, he would obey. Then she would take up a pen, and begin to write, and find a hair in it. Then she would take up another pen, and begin to write, and find that it spluttered. Then she would take up another pen, and begin to write, and say in a low voice, 'Oh, it's a talking pen, and will disturb Doady!' And then she would give it up as a bad job, and put the account-book away, after pretending to crush the lion with it.

Or, if she were in a very sedate and serious state of mind, she would sit down with the tablets, and a little basket of bills and other documents, which looked more like curl-papers than anything else, and endeavour to get some result out of them. After severely comparing one with another, and making entries on the tablets, and blotting them out, and counting all the fingers of her left hand over and over again, backwards and forwards, she would be so vexed and discouraged, and would look so unhappy, that it gave me pain to see her bright face clouded – and for me! – and I would go softly to her, and say: 'What's the matter, Dora?'

Dora would look up hopelessly, and reply, 'They won't come right. They make my head ache so. And they won't do anything I want!'

Then I would say, 'Now, let us try together. Let me show you, Dora.'

Then I would commence a practical demonstration, to which Dora would pay profound attention, perhaps for five minutes; when she would begin to be dreadfully tired, and would lighten the subject by curling my hair, or trying the effect of my face with my shirt-collar turned down. If I tacitly checked this playfulness, and persisted, she would look so scared and disconsolate, as she became more and more bewildered, that the remembrance of her natural gaiety when I first strayed into her path, and of her being my child-wife, would come reproachfully upon me; and I would lay the pencil down, and call for the guitar.

I had a great deal of work to do, and had many anxieties, but the same considerations made me keep them to myself. I am far from sure, now, that it was right to do this, but I did it for my child-wife's sake. I search my breast, and I commit its secrets, if I know them, without any reservation to this paper. The old unhappy loss or want of something had, I am conscious, some place in my heart; but not to the embitterment of my life. When I walked alone in the fine weather, and thought of the summer days when all the air had been filled with my boyish enchantment, I did miss something of the realisation of my dreams; but I thought it was a softened glory of the Past, which nothing could have thrown upon the present time. I did feel, sometimes, for a little while, that I could have wished my wife had been my counsellor; had had more character and purpose to sustain me and improve me by; had been endowed with power to fill up the void which somewhere seemed to be about me; but I felt as if this were an unearthly consummation of my happiness, that never had been meant to be, and never could have been.

I was a boyish husband as to years. I had known the softening influence of no other sorrows or experiences than those recorded in these leaves. If I did any wrong, as I may have done much, I did it in mistaken love, and in my want of wisdom. I write the exact truth. It would avail me nothing to extenuate it now.

Thus it was that I took upon myself the toils and cares of our life, and had no partner in them. We lived much as before, in reference to our scrambling household arrangements; but I had got used to those, and Dora I was pleased to see was seldom vexed now. She was bright and cheerful in the old childish way, loved me dearly, and was happy with her old trifles.

When the debates were heavy – I mean as to length, not quality, for in the last respect they were not often otherwise – and I went home late, Dora would never rest when she heard my footsteps, but would always come downstairs to meet me. When my evenings were unoccupied by the pursuit for which I had qualified myself with so much pains, and I was engaged in writing at home, she would sit quietly near me, however late the hour, and be so mute, that I would often think she had dropped asleep. But generally, when I raised my head, I saw her blue eyes looking at me with the quiet attention of which I have already spoken.

'Oh, what a weary boy!' said Dora one night when I met her eyes as I was shutting up my desk.

'What a weary girl!' said I. 'That's more to the purpose. You must go to bed another time, my love. It's far too late for you.'

'No, don't send me to bed!' pleaded Dora, coming to my side. 'Pray don't do that!'

'Dora!'

To my amazement she was sobbing on my neck.

'Not well, my dear! not happy!'

'Yes! quite well, and very happy!' said Dora. 'But say you'll let me stop, and see you write.'

'Why, what a sight for such bright eyes at midnight!' I replied.

'Are they bright, though?' returned Dora laughing. 'I'm so glad they're bright.'

'Little Vanity!' said I.

But it was not vanity; it was only harmless delight in my admiration. I knew that very well, before she told me so.

'If you think them pretty, say I may always stop, and see you write!' said Dora. '*Do* you think them pretty?'

'Very pretty.'

'Then let me always stop and see you write.'

'I am afraid that won't improve their brightness, Dora.'

'Yes, it will! Because, you clever boy, you'll not forget me then, while you are full of silent fancies. Will you mind it, if I say something very, very silly? – more than usual?' enquired Dora, peeping over my shoulder into my face.

'What wonderful thing is that?' said I.

'Please let me hold the pens?' said Dora. 'I want to have something to do with all those many hours when you are so industrious. May I hold the pens?'

The remembrance of her pretty joy when I said yes, brings tears into my eyes. The next time I sat down to write, and regularly afterwards, she sat in her old place, with a spare bundle of pens at her side. Her triumph in this connection with my work, and her delight when I wanted a new pen – which I very often feigned to do – suggested to me a new way of pleasing my child-wife. I occasionally made a pretence of wanting a page or two of manuscript copied. Then Dora was in her glory. The preparations she made for this great work, the aprons she put on, the bibs she borrowed from the kitchen to keep off the ink, the time she took, the innumerable stoppages she made to have a laugh with Jip as if he understood it all, her conviction that her work was incomplete unless she signed her name at the end, and the way in which she would bring it to me, like a school-copy, and then, when I praised it, clasp me round the neck, are touching recollections to me, simple as they might appear to other men.

She took possession of the keys soon after this, and went jingling about the house with the whole bunch in a little basket, tied to her slender waist. I seldom found that the places to which they belonged were locked, or that they were of any use except as a plaything for Jip – but Dora was pleased, and that pleased me. She was quite satisfied that a good deal was effected by this make-belief of housekeeping, and was as merry as if we had been keeping a baby-house, for a joke.

So we went on. Dora was hardly less affectionate to my aunt than to me, and often told her of the time when she was afraid she was 'a cross old thing.' I never saw my aunt unbend more systematically to anyone. She courted Jip, though Jip never responded; listened, day after day, to the guitar, though I am afraid she had no taste for music; never attacked the Incapables, though the temptation must have been severe; went wonderful distances on foot to purchase, as surprises, any trifles that she found out Dora wanted; and never came in by the garden, and missed her from the room, but she would call out, at the foot of the stairs, in a voice that sounded cheerfully all over the house: 'Where's Little Blossom!'

CHAPTER 45

Mr Dick Fulfils my Aunt's Predictions

It was some time now since I had left the Doctor. Living in his neighbourhood, I saw him frequently; and we all went to his house on two or three occasions to dinner or tea. The Old Soldier was in permanent quarters under the Doctor's roof. She was exactly the same as ever, and the same immortal butterflies hovered over her cap.

Like some other mothers, whom I have known in the course of my life, Mrs Markleham was far more fond of pleasure than her daughter was. She required a great deal of amusement, and, like a deep old soldier, pretended, in consulting her own inclinations, to be devoting herself to her child. The Doctor's desire that Annie should be entertained was therefore particularly acceptable to this excellent parent, who expressed unqualified approval of his discretion.

I have no doubt, indeed, that she probed the Doctor's wound without knowing it. Meaning nothing but a certain matured frivolity and selfishness, not always inseparable from full-blown years, I think she confirmed him in his fear that he was a constraint upon his young wife, and that there was no congeniality of feeling between them, by so strongly commending his design of lightening the load of her life.

'My dear soul,' she said to him one day when I was present, 'you know there is no doubt it would be a little poky for Annie to be always shut up here.'

The Doctor nodded his benevolent head.

'When she comes to her mother's age,' said Mrs Markleham, with a flourish of her fan, 'then it'll be another thing. You might put me into a Jail, with genteel society and a rubber, and I should never care to come out. But I am not Annie, you know; and Annie is not her mother.'

'Surely, surely,' said the Doctor.

'You are the best of creatures – no, I beg your pardon!' – for the Doctor made a gesture of deprecation, 'I must say before your face, as I always say behind your back, you are the best of creatures; but of course you don't – now, do you? – enter into the same pursuits and fancies as Annie?'

'No,' said the Doctor, in a sorrowful tone.

'No, of course not,' retorted the Old Soldier. 'Take your Dictionary, for example. What a useful work a Dictionary is! What a necessary work! The meanings of words! Without Doctor Johnson, or somebody of that sort, we might have been at this present moment calling an Italian-iron a bedstead. But we can't expect a Dictionary – especially when it's making – to interest Annie, can we?'

The Doctor shook his head.

'And that's why I *so* much approve,' said Mrs Markleham, tapping him on the shoulder with her shut-up fan, 'of your thoughtfulness. It shows that you don't expect, as many elderly people do expect, old heads on young shoulders. You have studied Annie's character, and you understand it. *That's* what I find so charming!'

Even the calm and patient face of Doctor Strong expressed some little sense of pain, I thought, under the infliction of these compliments.

'Therefore, my dear Doctor,' said the Soldier, giving him several affectionate taps, 'you may command me, at all times and seasons. Now, do understand that I am entirely at your service. I am ready to go with Annie to operas, concerts, exhibitions, all kinds of places; and you shall never find that I am tired. Duty, my dear Doctor, before every consideration in the universe!'

She was as good as her word. She was one of those people who can bear a great deal of pleasure, and she never flinched in her perseverance in the cause. She seldom got hold of the newspaper (which she settled herself down in the softest chair in the house to read through an eyeglass, every day, for two hours), but she found out something that she was certain Annie would like to see. It was in vain for Annie to protest that she was weary of such things. Her mother's remonstrance always was,

'Now, my dear Annie, I am sure you know better; and I must tell you, my love, that you are not making a proper return for the kindness of Doctor Strong.'

This was usually said in the Doctor's presence, and appeared to me to constitute Annie's principal inducement for withdrawing her objections when she made any. But in general she resigned herself to her mother, and went where the Old Soldier would.

It rarely happened now that Mr Maldon accompanied them. Sometimes my aunt and Dora were invited to do so, and accepted the invitation. Sometimes Dora only was asked. The time had been when I should have been uneasy in her going; but reflection on what had passed that former night in the Doctor's study, had made a change in my mistrust. I believed that the Doctor was right, and I had no worse suspicions.

My aunt rubbed her nose sometimes when she happened to be alone with me, and said she couldn't make it out; she wished they were happier; she didn't think our military friend (so she always called the Old Soldier) mended the matter at all. My aunt further expressed her opinion 'that if our military friend would cut off those butterflies, and give 'em to the chimney-sweepers for May-day, it would look like the beginning of something sensible on her part.'

But her abiding reliance was on Mr Dick. That man had evidently an idea in his head, she said; and if he could only once pen it up into a corner, which was his great difficulty, he would distinguish himself in some extraordinary manner.

Unconscious of this prediction, Mr Dick continued to occupy precisely the same ground in reference to the Doctor and to Mrs Strong. He seemed neither to advance nor to recede. He appeared to have settled into his original foundation, like a building; and I must confess that my faith in his ever moving was not much greater than if he had been a building.

But one night, when I had been married some months, Mr Dick put his head into the parlour, where I was writing alone (Dora having gone out with my aunt to take tea with the two little birds), and said, with a significant cough: 'You couldn't speak to me without inconveniencing yourself, Trotwood, I am afraid?'

'Certainly, Mr Dick,' said I; 'come in!'

'Trotwood,' said Mr Dick, laying his finger on the side of his nose, after he had shaken hands with me, 'before I sit down, I wish to make an observation. You know your aunt?'

'A little,' I replied.

'She is the most wonderful woman in the world, sir!'

After the delivery of this communication, which he shot out of himself as if he were loaded with it, Mr Dick sat down with greater gravity than usual, and looked at me.

'Now, boy,' said Mr Dick, 'I am going to put a question to you.'

'As many as you please,' said I.

'What do you consider me, sir?' asked Mr Dick, folding his arms.

'A dear old friend,' said I.

'Thank you, Trotwood,' returned Mr Dick, laughing, and reaching across in high glee to shake hands with me. 'But I mean, boy,' resuming his gravity, 'what do you consider me in this respect?' touching his forehead.

I was puzzled how to answer, but he helped me with a word. 'Weak?' said Mr Dick.

'Well,' I replied dubiously. 'Rather so.'

'Exactly!' cried Mr Dick, who seemed quite enchanted by my reply. 'That is, Trotwood, when they took some of the trouble out of you-know-who's head, and put it you know where, there was a – ' Mr Dick made his two hands revolve very fast about each other a great number of times, and then brought them into collision, and rolled them over and over one another, to express confusion. 'There was that sort of thing done to me somehow? Eh?'

I nodded at him, and he nodded back again.

'In short, boy,' said Mr Dick, dropping his voice to a whisper, 'I am simple.'

I would have qualified that conclusion, but he stopped me.

'Yes, I am! She pretends I am not. She won't hear of it; but I am. I know I am. If she hadn't stood my friend, sir, I should have been shut up, to lead a dismal life, these many years. But I'll provide for her! I never spend the copying money. I put it in a box. I have made a will. I'll leave it all to her. She shall be rich – noble!'

Mr Dick took out his pocket-handkerchief, and wiped his eyes. He then folded it up with great care, pressed it smooth between his two hands, put it in his pocket, and seemed to put my aunt away with it.

'Now, you are a scholar, Trotwood,' said Mr Dick. 'You are a fine scholar. You know what a learned man, what a great man, the Doctor is. You know what honour he has always done me. Not proud in his wisdom. Humble, humble – condescending even to poor Dick, who is simple and knows nothing. I have sent his name up, on a scrap of paper, to the kite, along the string, when it has been in the sky, among the larks. The kite has been glad to receive it, sir, and the sky has been brighter with it.'

I delighted him by saying, most heartily, that the Doctor was deserving of our best respect and highest esteem.

'And his beautiful wife is a star,' said Mr Dick. 'A shining star. I have seen her shine, sir. But,' bringing his chair nearer and laying one hand upon my knee – 'clouds, sir – clouds.'

I answered the solicitude which his face expressed, by conveying the same expression into my own, and shaking my head.

'What clouds?' said Mr Dick.

He looked so wistfully into my face, and was so anxious to understand, that I took great pains to answer him slowly and distinctly, as I might have entered on an explanation to a child.

'There is some unfortunate division between them,' I replied. 'Some unhappy cause of separation. A secret. It may be inseparable from the discrepancy in their years. It may have grown up out of almost nothing.'

Mr Dick, who told off every sentence with a thoughtful nod, paused when I had done, and sat considering, with his eyes upon my face, and his hand upon my knee.

'Doctor not angry with her, Trotwood?' he said, after some time.

'No. Devoted to her.'

'Then, I have got it, boy!' said Mr Dick.

The sudden exaltation with which he slapped me on the knee, and leaned back in his chair, with his eyebrows lifted up as high as he could possibly lift them, made me think him farther out of his wits than ever. He became as suddenly grave again, and leaning forward as before, said – first respectfully taking out his pocket-handkerchief, as if it really did represent my aunt: 'Most wonderful woman in the world, Trotwood. Why has *she* done nothing to set things right?'

'Too delicate and difficult a subject for such interference,' I replied.

'Fine scholar,' said Mr Dick, touching me with his finger. 'Why has *he* done nothing?'

'For the same reason,' I returned.

'Then I have got it, boy!' said Mr Dick. And he stood up before me, more exultingly than before, nodding his head, and striking himself repeatedly upon the breast, until one might have supposed that he had nearly nodded and struck all the breath out of his body.

'A poor fellow with a craze, sir,' said Mr Dick, 'a simpleton, a weak-minded person – present company, you know!' striking himself again, 'may do what wonderful people may not do. I'll bring them together, boy, I'll try. They'll not blame *me*. They'll not object to *me*. They'll not mind what I do, if it's wrong. I'm only Mr Dick. And who minds Dick? Dick's nobody! Whoo!' He blew a slight, contemptuous breath, as if he blew himself away.

It was fortunate he had proceeded so far with his mystery, for we heard the coach stop at the little garden gate, which brought my aunt and Dora home.

'Not a word, boy!' he pursued in a whisper; 'leave all the blame with Dick – simple Dick – mad Dick. I have been thinking, sir, for some time that I was getting it, and now I have got it. After what you have said to me, I am sure I have got it. All right!'

Not another word did Mr Dick utter on the subject; but he made a very telegraph of himself for the next half hour (to the great disturbance of my aunt's mind), to enjoin inviolable secrecy on me.

To my surprise I heard no more about it for some two or three weeks, though I was sufficiently interested in the result of his endeavours; descrying a strange gleam of good sense – I say nothing of good feeling, for that he always exhibited – in the conclusion to which he had come. At last I began to believe, that, in the flighty and unsettled state of his mind, he had either forgotten his intention or abandoned it.

One fair evening, when Dora was not inclined to go out, my aunt and I strolled up to the Doctor's cottage. It was autumn, when there were no debates to vex the evening air; and I remember how the leaves smelt like our garden at Blunderstone as we trod them under foot, and how the old, unhappy feeling seemed to go by, on the sighing wind.

It was twilight when we reached the cottage. Mrs Strong was just coming out of the garden, where Mr Dick yet lingered, busy with his knife, helping the gardener to point some stakes. The Doctor was engaged with someone in his study; but the visitor would be gone directly, Mrs Strong said, and begged us to remain and see him. We went into the drawing-room with her, and sat down by the darkening window. There was never any ceremony about the visits of such old friends and neighbours as we were.

We had not sat here many minutes when Mrs Markleham, who usually contrived to be in a fuss about something, came bustling in, with her newspaper in her hand, and said, out of breath, 'My goodness gracious, Annie, why didn't you tell me there was someone in the study!'

'My dear mama,' she quietly returned, 'how could I know that you desired the information?'

'Desired the information!' said Mrs Markleham, sinking on the sofa. 'I never had such a turn in all my life!'

'Have you been to the study, then, mama?' asked Annie.

'*Been* to the study, my dear!' she returned emphatically. 'Indeed I have! I came upon the amiable creature – if you'll imagine my feelings, Miss Trotwood and David – in the act of making his will.'

Her daughter looked round from the window quickly.

'In the act, my dear Annie,' repeated Mrs Markleham, spreading the newspaper on her lap like a tablecloth, and patting her hands upon it, 'of making his last Will and Testament. The foresight and affection of the dear! I must tell you how it was. I really must, in justice to the darling – for he is nothing less! – tell you how it was. Perhaps you know, Miss Trotwood, that there is never a candle lighted in this house, until one's eyes are literally falling out of one's head with being stretched to read the paper. And that there is not a chair in this house, in which a paper can be what I call read, except one in the study. This took me to the study, where I saw a light. I opened the door. In company with the dear Doctor were two professional people, evidently connected with the law, and they were all three standing at the table, the darling Doctor pen in hand. "This simply expresses, then," said the Doctor – Annie, my love, attend to the very words – "this simply expresses, then, gentlemen, the confidence I have in Mrs Strong, and gives her all unconditionally?" One of the professional people replied, "And gives her all unconditionally." Upon that, with the natural feelings of a mother, I said, "Good God, I beg your pardon!" fell over the doorstep, and came away through the little back passage where the pantry is.'

Mrs Strong opened the window, and went out into the verandah, where she stood leaning against a pillar.

'But now isn't it, Miss Trotwood, isn't it, David, invigorating,' said Mrs Markleham, mechanically following her with her eyes, 'to find a man at Doctor Strong's time of life, with the strength of mind to do this kind of thing? It only shows how right I was. I said to Annie, when Doctor Strong paid a very flattering visit to myself, and made her the subject of a declaration and an offer, I said, "My dear, there is no doubt whatever, in my opinion, with reference to a suitable provision for you, that Doctor Strong will do more than he binds himself to do."'

Here the bell rang, and we heard the sound of the visitors' feet as they went out.

'It's all over, no doubt,' said the Old Soldier, after listening; 'the dear creature has signed, sealed, and delivered, and his mind's at rest. Well it may be! What a mind! Annie, my love, I am going to the study with my paper, for I am a poor creature without news. Miss Trotwood, David, pray come and see the Doctor.'

I was conscious of Mr Dick's standing in the shadow of the room, shutting up his knife, when we accompanied her to the study; and of my aunt's rubbing her nose violently, by the way, as a mild vent for her intolerance of our military friend; but who got first into the study, or how Mrs Markleham settled herself in a moment in her easy-chair, or how my aunt and I came to be left together near the door (unless her eyes were quicker than mine, and she held me back), I have forgotten if I ever knew. But this I know – that we saw the Doctor before he saw us, sitting at his table, among the folio volumes in which he delighted, resting his head calmly on his hand. That, in the same moment, we saw Mrs Strong glide in, pale and trembling. That Mr Dick supported her on his arm. That he laid his other hand upon the Doctor's arm, causing him to look up with an abstracted air. That, as the Doctor moved his head, his wife dropped down on one knee at his feet, and, with her hands imploringly lifted, fixed upon his face the memorable look I had never forgotten. That at this sight Mrs Markleham dropped the newspaper, and stared more like a figure-head intended for a ship to be called The Astonishment, than anything else I can think of.

The gentleness of the Doctor's manner and surprise, the dignity that mingled with the supplicating attitude of his wife, the amiable concern of Mr Dick, and the earnestness with which my aunt said to herself, '*That* man mad!' (triumphantly expressive of the misery from which she had saved him), I see and hear, rather than remember, as I write about it.

'Doctor!' said Mr Dick. 'What is it that's amiss? Look here!'

'Annie!' cried the Doctor. 'Not at my feet, my dear!'

'Yes!' she said. 'I beg and pray that no one will leave the room! Oh, my husband and father, break this long silence. Let us both know what it is that has come between us!'

Mrs Markleham, by this time recovering the power of speech, and seeming to swell with family pride and motherly indignation, here exclaimed, 'Annie, get up immediately, and don't disgrace everybody belonging to you by humbling yourself like that, unless you wish to see me go out of my mind on the spot!'

'Mama!' returned Annie. 'Waste no words on me, for my appeal is to my husband, and even you are nothing here.'

'Nothing!' exclaimed Mrs Markleham. 'Me, nothing! The child has taken leave of her senses. Please to get me a glass of water!'

I was too attentive to the Doctor and his wife to give any heed to this request, and it made no impression on anybody else; so Mrs Markleham panted, stared, and fanned herself.

'Annie!' said the Doctor, tenderly taking her in his hands. 'My dear! If any unavoidable change has come, in the sequence of time, upon our married life, you are not to blame. The fault is mine, and only mine. There is no change in my affection, admiration, and respect. I wish to make you happy. I truly love and honour you. Rise, Annie, pray!'

But she did not rise. After looking at him for a little while, she sank down closer to him, laid her arm across his knee, and dropping her head upon it, said: 'If I have any friend here, who can speak one word for me, or for my husband in this matter; if I have any friend here, who can give a voice to any suspicion that my heart has sometimes whispered to me; if I have any friend here, who honours my husband, or has ever cared for me, and has anything within his knowledge, no matter what it is, that may help to mediate between us, I implore that friend to speak!'

There was a profound silence. After a few moments of painful hesitation, I broke the silence.

'Mrs Strong,' I said, 'there is something within my knowledge, which I have been earnestly entreated by Doctor Strong to conceal, and have concealed until tonight. But I believe the time has come when it would be mistaken faith and delicacy to conceal it any longer, and when your appeal absolves me from his injunction.'

She turned her face towards me for a moment, and I knew that I was right. I could not have resisted its entreaty, if the assurance that it gave me had been less convincing.

'Our future peace,' she said, 'may be in your hands. I trust it confidently to your not suppressing anything. I know beforehand that nothing you, or anyone, can tell me, will show my husband's noble heart in any other light than one. Howsoever it may seem to you to touch me, disregard that. I will speak for myself, before him, and before God, afterwards.'

Thus earnestly besought, I made no reference to the Doctor for his permission, but, without any other compromise of the truth than a little softening of the coarseness of Uriah Heep, related plainly what had passed in that same room that night.

The staring of Mrs Markleham during the whole narration and the shrill, sharp interjections with which she occasionally interrupted it defy description.

When I had finished, Annie remained, for some few moments, silent, with her head bent down as I have described. Then, she took the Doctor's hand (he was sitting in the same attitude as when we had entered the room), and pressed it to her breast, and kissed it. Mr Dick softly raised her; and she stood, when she began to speak, leaning on him, and looking down upon her husband – from whom she never turned her eyes.

'All that has ever been in my mind since I was married,' she said, in a low, submissive, tender voice, 'I will lay bare before you. I could not live and have one reservation, knowing what I know now.'

'Nay, Annie,' said the Doctor mildly, 'I have never doubted you, my child. There is no need; indeed there is no need, my dear.'

'There is great need,' she answered, in the same way, 'that I should open my whole heart before the soul of generosity and truth, whom, year by year, and day by day, I have loved and venerated more and more, as Heaven knows!'

'Really,' interrupted Mrs Markleham, 'if I have any discretion at all – '

('Which you haven't, you Marplot,' observed my aunt, in an indignant whisper.)

' – I must be permitted to observe that it cannot be requisite to enter into these details.'

'No one but my husband can judge of that, mama,' said Annie, without removing her eyes from his face, 'and he will hear me. If I say anything to give you pain, mama, forgive me. I have borne pain first, often and long, myself.'

Mr Dick fulfils my aunt's prediction

'Upon my word!' gasped Mrs Markleham.

'When I was very young,' said Annie, 'quite a little child, my first associations with knowledge of any kind were inseparable from a patient friend and teacher – the friend of my dead father – who was always dear to me. I can remember nothing that I know without remembering him. He stored my mind with its first treasures, and stamped his character upon them all. They never could have been, I think, as good as they have been to me, if I had taken them from any other hands.'

'Makes her mother nothing!' exclaimed Mrs Markleham.

'Not so, mama,' said Annie; 'but I make him what he was. I must do that. As I grew up, he occupied the same place still. I was proud of his interest – deeply, fondly, gratefully attached to him. I looked up to him, I can hardly describe how – as a father, as a guide, as one whose praise was different from all other praise, as one in whom I could have trusted and confided, if I had doubted all the world. You know, mama, how young and inexperienced I was, when you presented him before me, of a sudden, as a lover.'

'I have mentioned the fact, fifty times at least, to everybody here!' said Mrs Markleham.

('Then hold your tongue, for the Lord's sake, and don't mention it any more!' muttered my aunt.)

'It was so great a change, so great a loss, I felt it at first,' said Annie, still preserving the same look and tone, 'that I was agitated and distressed. I was but a girl; and when so great change came in the character in which I had so long looked up to him, I think I was sorry. But nothing could have made him what he used to be again – and I was proud that he should think me so worthy, and we were married.'

' – At St Alphage, Canterbury,' observed Mrs Markleham.

('Confound the woman!' said my aunt, 'she *won't* be quiet!')

'I never thought,' proceeded Annie, with a heightened colour, 'of any worldly gain that my husband would bring to me. My young heart had no room in its homage for any such poor reference. Mama, forgive me when I say that it was *you* who first presented to my mind the thought that anyone could wrong me, and wrong him, by such a cruel suspicion.'

'Me!' cried Mrs Markleham.

('Ah! You, to be sure!' observed my aunt, 'and you can't fan it away, my military friend!')

'It was the first unhappiness of my new life,' said Annie. 'It was the first occasion of every unhappy moment I have known. Those moments have been more, of late, than I can count; but not – my generous husband! – not for the reason you suppose; for in my heart there is not a thought, a recollection, or a hope, that any power could separate from you.'

She raised her eyes, and clasped her hands, and looked as beautiful and true, I thought, as any Spirit. The Doctor looked on her, henceforth, as steadfastly as she on him.

'Mama is blameless,' she went on, 'of having ever urged you for herself, and she is blameless in intention every way, I am sure – but when I saw how many importunate claims that were no claims were pressed upon you in my name; how you were traded on in my name; how generous you were, and how Mr Wickfield, who had your welfare very much at heart, resented it; the first sense of my exposure to the mean suspicion that my tenderness was bought – and sold to you, of all men, on earth – fell upon me like unmerited disgrace, in which I forced you to participate. I cannot tell you what it was – mama cannot imagine what it was – to have this dread and trouble always on my mind, yet know in my own soul that on my marriage-day I crowned the love and honour of my life.'

'A specimen of the thanks one gets,' cried Mrs Markleham, in tears, 'for taking care of one's family! I wish I was a Turk!'

('I wish you were, with all my heart – and in your native country!' said my aunt.)

'It was at that time that mama was most solicitous about my Cousin Maldon. I had liked him,' she spoke softly, but without any hesitation, 'very much. We had been little lovers once. If circumstances had not happened otherwise, I might have come to persuade myself that I really loved him, and might have married him, and been most wretched. There can be no disparity in marriage like unsuitability of mind and purpose.'

I pondered on those words, even while I was studiously attending to what followed, as if they had some particular interest, or some strange application that I could not divine. 'There can be no disparity in marriage like unsuitability of mind and purpose' – 'no disparity in marriage like unsuitability of mind and purpose.'

'There is nothing,' said Annie, 'that we have in common. I have long found that there is nothing. If I were thankful to my husband for no more, instead of for so much, I should be thankful to him for having saved me from the first mistaken impulse of my undisciplined heart.'

She stood quite still, before the Doctor, and spoke with an earnestness that thrilled me. Yet her voice was just as quiet as before.

'When he was waiting to be the object of your munificence, so freely bestowed for my sake, and when I was unhappy in the mercenary shape I was made to wear, I thought it would have become him better to have worked his own way on. I thought that if I had been he, I would have tried to do it, at the cost of almost any hardship. But I thought no worse of him, until the night of his departure for India. That night I knew he had a false and thankless heart. I saw a double meaning, then, in Mr Wickfield's scrutiny of me. I perceived, for the first time, the dark suspicion that shadowed my life.'

'Suspicion, Annie!' said the Doctor. 'No, no, no!'

'In your mind there was none, I know, my husband!' she returned. 'And when I came to you, that night, to lay down all my load of shame and grief, and knew that I had to tell, that, underneath your roof, one of my own kindred, to whom you had been a benefactor, for the love of me, had spoken to me words that should have found no utterance, even if I had been the weak and mercenary wretch he thought me – my mind revolted from the taint the very tale conveyed. It died upon my lips, and from that hour till now has never passed them.'

Mrs Markleham, with a short groan, leaned back in her easy-chair; and retired behind her fan, as if she were never coming out any more.

'I have never, but in your presence, interchanged a word

with him from that time; then, only when it has been necessary for the avoidance of this explanation. Years have passed since he knew from me what his situation here was. The kindnesses you have secretly done for his advancement, and then disclosed to me, for my surprise and pleasure, have been, you will believe, but aggravations of the unhappiness and burden of my secret.'

She sunk down gently at the Doctor's feet, though he did his utmost to prevent her; and said, looking up, tearfully, into his face: 'Do not speak to me yet! Let me say a little more! Right or wrong, if this were to be done again, I think I should do just the same. You never can know what it was to be devoted to you, with those old associations; to find that anyone could be so hard as to suppose that the truth of my heart was bartered away, and to be surrounded by appearances confirming that belief. I was very young, and had no adviser. Between mama and me, in all relating to you, there was a wide division. If I shrunk into myself, hiding the disrespect I had undergone, it was because I honoured you so much, and so much wished that you should honour me!'

'Annie, my pure heart!' said the Doctor, 'my dear girl!'

'A little more! a very few words more! I used to think there were so many whom you might have married, who would not have brought such charge and trouble on you, and who would have made your home a worthier home. I used to be afraid that I had better have remained your pupil, and almost your child. I used to fear that I was so unsuited to your learning and wisdom. If all this made me shrink within myself (as indeed it did), when I had that to tell, it was still because I honoured you so much, and hoped that you might one day honour me.'

'That day has shone this long time, Annie,' said the Doctor, 'and can have but one long night, my dear.'

'Another word! I afterwards meant – steadfastly meant, and purposed to myself – to bear the whole weight of knowing the unworthiness of one to whom you had been so good. And now a last word, dearest and best of friends! The cause of the late change in you, which I have seen with so much pain and sorrow, and have sometimes referred to my old apprehension – at other times to lingering suppositions nearer to the truth – has been made clear tonight; and by an accident I have also come to know, tonight, the full measure of your noble trust in me, even under that mistake. I do not hope that any love and duty I may render in return, will ever make me worthy of your priceless confidence; but with all this knowledge fresh upon me, I can lift my eyes to this dear face, revered as a father's, loved as a husband's, sacred to me in my childhood as a friend's, and solemnly declare that in my lightest thought I have never wronged you; never wavered in the love and the fidelity I owe you!'

She had her arms around the Doctor's neck, and he leant his head down over her, mingling his grey hair with her dark brown tresses.

'Oh, hold me to your heart, my husband! Never cast me out! Do not think or speak of disparity between us, for there is none, except in all my many imperfections. Every succeeding year I have known this better, as I have esteemed you more and more.

Oh, take me to your heart, my husband, for my love was founded on a rock, and it endures!'

In the silence that ensued, my aunt walked gravely up to Mr Dick, without at all hurrying herself, and gave him a hug and a sounding kiss. And it was very fortunate, with a view to his credit, that she did so; for I am confident that I detected him at that moment in the act of making preparations to stand on one leg, as an appropriate expression of delight.

'You are a very remarkable man, Dick!' said my aunt, with an air of unqualified approbation; 'and never pretend to be anything else, for I know better!'

With that, my aunt pulled him by the sleeve, and nodded to me; and we three stole quietly out of the room, and came away.

'That's a settler for our military friend, at any rate,' said my aunt, on the way home. 'I should sleep the better for that, if there was nothing else to be glad of!'

'She was quite overcome, I am afraid,' said Mr Dick, with great commiseration.

'What! Did you ever see a crocodile overcome?' enquired my aunt.

'I don't think I ever saw a crocodile,' returned Mr Dick mildly.

'There never would have been anything the matter, if it hadn't been for that old Animal,' said my aunt, with strong emphasis. 'It's very much to be wished that some mothers would leave their daughters alone after marriage, and not be so violently affectionate. They seem to think the only return that can be made them for bringing an unfortunate young woman into the world – God bless my soul, as if she asked to be brought, or wanted to come! – is full liberty to worry her out of it again. What are you thinking of, Trot?'

I was thinking of all that had been said. My mind was still running on some of the expressions used. 'There can be no disparity in marriage like unsuitability of mind and purpose.' 'The first mistaken impulse of an undisciplined heart.' 'My love was founded on a rock.' But we were at home; and the trodden leaves were lying underfoot, and the autumn wind was blowing.

CHAPTER 46

Intelligence

I must have been married, if I may trust to my imperfect memory for dates, about a year or so, when one evening, as I was returning from a solitary walk, thinking of the book I was then writing – for my success had steadily increased with my steady application, and I was engaged at that time upon my first work of fiction – I came past Mrs Steerforth's house. I had often passed it before, during my residence in that neighbourhood, though never when I could choose another road. Howbeit, it did sometimes happen that it was not easy to find another, without making a long circuit; and so I had passed that way, upon the whole, pretty often.

I had never done more than glance at the house, as I went by with a quickened step. It had been uniformly gloomy and dull.

None of the best rooms abutted on the road; and the narrow, heavily framed, old-fashioned windows, never cheerful under any circumstances, looked very dismal, close shut, and with their blinds always drawn down. There was a covered way across a little paved court, to an entrance that was never used; and there was one round staircase window, at odds with all the rest, and the only one unshaded by a blind, which had the same unoccupied, blank look. I do not remember that I ever saw a light in all the house. If I had been a casual passer-by, I should have probably supposed that some childless person lay dead in it. If I had happily possessed no knowledge of the place, and had seen it often in that changeless state, I should have pleased my fancy with many ingenious speculations, I dare say.

As it was, I thought as little of it as I might. But my mind could not go by it and leave it, as my body did; and it usually awakened a long train of meditations. Coming before me on this particular evening that I mention, mingled with the childish recollections and later fancies, the ghosts of half-formed hopes, the broken shadows of disappointments dimly seen and understood, the blending of experience and imagination, incidental to the occupation with which my thoughts had been busy, it was more than commonly suggestive. I fell into a brown study as I walked on, and a voice at my side made me start.

It was a woman's voice, too. I was not long in recollecting Mrs Steerforth's little parlour-maid, who had formerly worn blue ribbons in her cap. She had taken them out now, to adapt herself, I suppose, to the altered character of the house; and wore but one or two disconsolate bows of sober brown.

'If you please, sir, would you have the goodness to walk in, and speak to Miss Dartle?'

'Has Miss Dartle sent you for me?' I enquired.

'Not tonight, sir, but it's just the same. Miss Dartle saw you pass a night or two ago; and I was to sit at work on the staircase, and, when I saw you pass again, to ask you to step in and speak to her.'

I turned back, and enquired of my conductor, as we went along, how Mrs Steerforth was. She said her lady was but poorly, and kept her own room a good deal.

When we arrived at the house, I was directed to Miss Dartle in the garden, and left to make my presence known to her myself. She was sitting on a seat at one end of a kind of terrace, overlooking the great city. It was a sombre evening, with a lurid light in the sky; and as I saw the prospect scowling in the distance, with here and there some larger object starting up into the sullen glare, I fancied it was no inapt companion to the memory of this fierce woman.

She saw me as I advanced, and rose for a moment to receive me. I thought her, then, still more colourless and thin than when I had seen her last; the flashing eyes still brighter, and the scar still plainer.

Our meeting was not cordial. We had parted angrily on the last occasion; and there was an air of disdain about her, which she took no pains to conceal.

'I am told you wish to speak to me, Miss Dartle,' said I, standing near her, with my hand upon the back of the seat, and declining her gesture of invitation to sit down.

'If you please,' said she. 'Pray has this girl been found?'

'No.'

'And yet she has run away!'

I saw her thin lips working while she looked at me, as if they were eager to load her with reproaches.

'Run away?' I repeated.

'Yes! From him,' she said with a laugh. 'If she is not found, perhaps she never will be found. She may be dead!'

The vaunting cruelty with which she met my glance, I never saw expressed in any other face that ever I have seen.

'To wish her dead,' said I, 'may be the kindest wish that one of her own sex could bestow upon her. I am glad that time has softened you so much, Miss Dartle.'

She condescended to make no reply, but, turning on me with another scornful laugh, said: 'The friends of this excellent and much-injured young lady are friends of yours. You are their champion, and assert their rights. Do you wish to know what is known of her?'

'Yes,' said I.

She rose with an ill-favoured smile, and taking a few steps towards a wall of holly that was near at hand, dividing the lawn from a kitchen-garden, said, in a louder voice, 'Come here!' – as if she were calling to some unclean beast.

'You will restrain any demonstrative championship or vengeance in this place, of course, Mr Copperfield?' said she, looking over her shoulder at me with the same expression.

I inclined my head, without knowing what she meant; and she said, 'Come here!' again; and returned, followed by the respectable Mr Littimer, who, with undiminished respectability, made me a bow, and took up his position behind her. The air of wicked grace, of triumph, in which, strange to say, there was yet something feminine and alluring, with which she reclined upon the seat between us, and looked at me, was worthy of a cruel Princess in a Legend.

'Now,' said she imperiously, without glancing at him, and touching the old wound as it throbbed, perhaps, in this instance, with pleasure rather than pain, 'tell Mr Copperfield about the flight.'

'Mr James and myself, ma'am – '

'Don't address yourself to me!' she interrupted, with a frown.

'Mr James and myself, sir – '

'Nor to me, if you please,' said I.

Mr Littimer, without being at all discomposed, signified by a slight obeisance that anything that was most agreeable to us was most agreeable to him; and began again: 'Mr James and myself have been abroad with the young woman, ever since she left Yarmouth under Mr James's protection. We have been in a variety of places, and seen a deal of foreign country. We have been in France, Switzerland, Italy, in fact, almost all parts.'

He looked at the back of the seat, as if he were addressing himself to that; and softly played upon it with his hands, as if he were striking chords upon a dumb piano.

'Mr James took quite uncommonly to the young woman; and was more settled, for a length of time, than I have known him to be since I have been in his service. The young woman was very improvable, and spoke the languages; and wouldn't have been known for the same country person. I noticed that she was much admired wherever we went.'

Miss Dartle put her hand upon her side. I saw him steal a glance at her, and slightly smile to himself.

'Very much admired, indeed, the young woman was. What with her dress; what with the – ; what with being made so much of; what with this, that, and the other; her merits really attracted general notice.'

He made a short pause. Her eyes wandered restlessly over the distant prospect, and she bit her nether lip to stop that busy mouth.

Taking his hands from the seat, and placing one of them within the other, as he settled himself on one leg, Mr Littimer proceeded, with his eyes cast down, and his respectable head a little advanced, and a little on one side: 'The young woman went on in this manner for some time, being occasionally low in her spirits, until I think she began to weary Mr James by giving way to her low spirits and tempers of that kind; and things were not so comfortable. Mr James he began to be restless again. The more restless he got, the worse she got; and I must say, for myself, that I had a very difficult time of it indeed between the two. Still matters were patched up here, and made good there, over and over again; and altogether lasted, I am sure, for a longer time than anybody could have expected.'

Recalling her eyes from the distance, she looked at me again now, with her former air. Mr Littimer, clearing his throat behind his hand with a respectable short cough, changed legs, and went on: 'At last, when there had been, upon the whole, a good many words and reproaches, Mr James he set off one morning from the neighbourhood of Naples, where we had a villa (the young woman being very partial to the sea), and, under pretence of coming back in a day or so, left it in charge with me to break it out, that, for the general happiness of all concerned, he was' – here an interruption of the short cough – 'gone. But Mr James, I must say, certainly did behave extremely honourable; for he proposed that the young woman should marry a very respectable person, who was fully prepared to overlook the past, and who was, at least, as good as anybody the young woman could have aspired to in a regular way: her connections being very common.'

He changed legs again, and wetted his lips. I was convinced that the scoundrel spoke of himself, and I saw my conviction reflected in Miss Dartle's face.

'This I also had it in charge to communicate. I was willing to do anything to relieve Mr James from his difficulty, and to restore harmony between himself and an affectionate parent, who has undergone so much on his account. Therefore I undertook the commission. The young woman's violence when she came to, after I broke the fact of his departure, was beyond all expectations. She was quite mad, and had to be held by force; or if she couldn't have got to a knife, or got to the sea, she'd have beaten her head against the marble floor.'

Miss Dartle, leaning back upon the seat, with a light of exultation in her face, seemed almost to caress the sounds this fellow had uttered.

'But when I came to the second part of what had been entrusted to me,' said Mr Littimer, rubbing his hands, uneasily, 'which anybody might have supposed would have been, at all events, appreciated as a kind intention, then the young woman came out in her true colours. A more outrageous person I never did see. Her conduct was surprisingly bad. She had no more gratitude, no more feeling, no more patience, no more reason in her, than a stock or a stone. If I hadn't been upon my guard, I am convinced she would have had my blood.'

'I think the better of her for it,' said I indignantly.

Mr Littimer bent his head, as much as to say, 'Indeed, sir? But you're young!' and resumed his narrative.

'It was necessary, in short, for a time, to take away everything nigh her, that she could do herself, or anybody else, an injury with, and to shut her up close. Notwithstanding which, she got out in the night; forced the lattice of a window that I had nailed up myself; dropped on a vine that was trailed below; and never has been seen or heard of, to my knowledge, since.'

'She is dead, perhaps,' said Miss Dartle, with a smile, as if she could have spurned the body of the ruined girl.

'She may have drowned herself, miss,' returned Mr Littimer, catching at an excuse for addressing himself to somebody. 'It's very possible. Or she may have had assistance from the boatmen, and the boatmen's wives and children. Being given to low company, she was very much in the habit of talking to them on the beach, Miss Dartle, and sitting by their boats. I have known her to do it, when Mr James has been away, whole days. Mr James was far from pleased to find out once, that she had told the children she was a boatman's daughter, and that in her own country, long ago, she had roamed about the beach, like them.'

Oh, Emily! Unhappy beauty! What a picture rose before me of her sitting on the far-off shore, among the children like herself when she was innocent, listening to little voices such as might have called her Mother had she been a poor man's wife; and to the great voice of the sea, with its eternal 'Never more!'

'When it was clear that nothing could be done, Miss Dartle –'

'Did I tell you not to speak to me?' she said, with stern contempt.

'You spoke to me, miss,' he replied. 'I beg your pardon. But it's my service to obey.'

'Do your service,' she returned. 'Finish your story, and go!'

'When it was clear,' he said, with infinite respectability and an obedient bow, 'that she was not to be found, I went to Mr James, at the place where it had been agreed that I should write to him, and informed him of what had occurred. Words passed between us in consequence, and I felt it due to my character to leave him. I could bear, and I have borne, a great deal from Mr James; but he insulted me too far. He hurt me. Knowing the unfortunate difference between himself and his mother, and what her anxiety of mind was likely to be, I took the liberty of coming home to England, and relating –'

'For money which I paid him,' said Miss Dartle to me.

'Just so, ma'am – and relating what I knew. I am not aware,' said Mr Littimer, after a moment's reflection, 'that there is anything else. I am at present out of employment, and should be happy to meet with a respectable situation.'

Miss Dartle glanced at me, as though she would enquire if there were anything that I desired to ask. As there was something which had occurred to my mind, I said in reply: 'I could wish to know from this – creature,' I could not bring myself to utter any more conciliatory word, 'whether they intercepted a letter that was written to her from home, or whether he supposes that she received it.'

He remained calm and silent, with his eyes fixed on the ground, and the tip of every finger of his right hand delicately poised against the tip of every finger of his left.

Miss Dartle turned her head disdainfully towards him.

'I beg your pardon, miss,' he said, awakening from his abstraction, 'but, however submissive to you, I have my position, though a servant. Mr Copperfield and you, miss, are different people. If Mr Copperfield wishes to know anything from me, I take the liberty of reminding Mr Copperfield that he can put a question to me. I have a character to maintain.'

After a momentary struggle with myself, I turned my eyes upon him, and said, 'You have heard my question. Consider it addressed to yourself, if you choose. What answer do you make?'

'Sir,' he rejoined, with an occasional separation and reunion of those delicate tips, 'my answer must be qualified; because, to betray Mr James's confidence to his mother, and to betray it to you, are two different actions. It is not probable, I consider, that Mr James would encourage the receipt of letters likely to increase low spirits and unpleasantness, but further than that, sir, I should wish to avoid going.'

'Is that all?' enquired Miss Dartle of me.

I indicated that I had nothing more to say. 'Except,' I added, as I saw him moving off, 'that I understand this fellow's part in the wicked story, and that, as I shall make it known to the honest man who has been her father from her childhood, I would recommend him to avoid going too much into public.'

He had stopped the moment I began, and had listened with his usual repose of manner.

'Thank you, sir. But you'll excuse me if I say, sir, that there are neither slaves nor slave-drivers in this country, and that people are not allowed to take the law into their own hands. If they do, it is more to their own peril, I believe, than to other people's. Consequently speaking, I am not at all afraid of going wherever I may wish, sir.'

With that, he made a polite bow; and, with another to Miss Dartle, went away through the arch in the wall of holly by which he had come. Miss Dartle and I regarded each other for a little while in silence; her manner being exactly what it was when she had produced the man.

'He says, besides,' she observed, with a slow curling of her lip, 'that his master, as he hears, is coasting Spain; and this done, is away to gratify his seafaring tastes till he is weary. But that is of no interest to you. Between these two proud persons, mother and son, there is a wider breach than before, and little hope of its healing, for they are one at heart, and time makes each more obstinate and imperious. Neither is this of any interest to you; but it introduces what I wish to say. This devil whom you make an angel of, I mean this low girl whom he picked out of the tide-mud,' with her black eyes full upon me,

and her passionate finger up, 'may be alive – for I believe some common things are hard to die. If she is, you will desire to have a pearl of such price found and taken care of. We desire that, too; that he may not by any chance be made her prey again. So far, we are united in one interest; and that is why I, who would do her any mischief that so coarse a wretch is capable of feeling, have sent for you to hear what you have heard.'

I saw, by the change in her face, that someone was advancing behind me. It was Mrs Steerforth, who gave me her hand more coldly than of yore, and with an augmentation of her former stateliness of manner; but still I perceived – and I was touched by it – with an ineffaceable remembrance of my old love for her son. She was greatly altered. Her fine figure was far less upright, her handsome face was deeply marked, and her hair was almost white. But when she sat down on the seat, she was a handsome lady still; and well I knew the bright eye with its lofty look, that had been a light in my very dreams at school.

'Is Mr Copperfield informed of everything, Rosa?'

'Yes.'

'And has he heard Littimer himself?'

'Yes; I have told him why you wished it.'

'You are a good girl. I have had some slight correspondence with your former friend, sir,' addressing me, 'but it has not restored his sense of duty or natural obligation. Therefore I have no other object in this than what Rosa has mentioned. If, by the course which may relieve the mind of the decent man you brought here (for whom I am sorry – I can say no more), my son may be saved from again falling into the snares of a designing enemy, well!'

She drew herself up, and sat looking straight before her, far away.

'Madam,' I said respectfully, 'I understand. I assure you I am in no danger of putting any strained construction on your motives. But I must say, even to you, having known this injured family from childhood, that if you suppose the girl, so deeply wronged, has not been cruelly deluded, and would not rather die a hundred deaths than take a cup of water from your son's hand now, you cherish a terrible mistake.'

'Well, Rosa, well!' said Mrs Steerforth, as the other was about to interpose, 'it is no matter. Let it be. You are married, sir, I am told?'

I answered that I had been some time married.

'And are doing well? I hear little in the quiet life I lead, but I understand you are beginning to be famous.'

'I have been very fortunate,' I said, 'and find my name connected with some praise.'

'You have no mother?' – in a softened voice.

'No.'

'It is a pity,' she returned. 'She would have been proud of you. Good-night!'

I took the hand she held out with a dignified, unbending air, and it was as calm in mine as if her breast had been in peace. Her pride could still its very pulses, it appeared, and draw the placid veil before her face, through which she sat looking straight before her on the far distance.

As I moved away from them along the terrace, I could not

help observing how steadily they both sat gazing on the prospect, and how it thickened and closed around them. Here and there, some early lamps were seen to twinkle in the distant city; and in the eastern quarter of the sky the lurid light still hovered. But from the greater part of the broad valley interposed, a mist was rising like a sea, which, mingling with the darkness, made it seem as if the gathering waters would encompass them. I have reason to remember this, and think of it with awe; for before I looked upon those two again, a stormy sea had risen to their feet.

Reflecting on what had been thus told me, I felt it right that it should be communicated to Mr Peggotty. On the following evening I went into London in quest of him. He was always wandering about from place to place, with his one object of recovering his niece before him; but was more in London than elsewhere. Often and often, now, had I seen him in the dead of night passing along the streets, searching, among the few who loitered out of doors at those untimely hours, for what he dreaded to find.

He kept a lodging over the little chandler's shop in Hungerford Market, which I have had occasion to mention more than once, and from which he first went forth upon his errand of mercy. Hither I directed my walk. On making enquiry for him, I learned from the people of the house that he had not gone out yet, and I should find him in his room upstairs.

He was sitting reading by a window in which he kept a few plants.

The room was very neat and orderly. I saw in a moment that it was always kept prepared for her reception, and that he never went out but he thought it possible he might bring her home. He had not heard my tap at the door, and only raised his eyes when I laid my hand upon his shoulder.

'Mas'r Davy! Thankee, sir! thankee hearty, for this visit! Sit ye down. You're kindly welcome, sir.'

'Mr Peggotty,' said I, taking the chair he handed me, 'don't expect much! I have heard some news.'

'Of Em'ly!'

He put his hand, in a nervous manner, on his mouth, and turned pale, as he fixed his eyes on mine.

'It gives no clue to where she is; but she is not with him.'

He sat down, looking intently at me, and listened in profound silence to all I had to tell. I well remember the sense of dignity, beauty even, with which the patient gravity of his face impressed me, when, having gradually removed his eyes from mine, he sat looking downward, leaning his forehead on his hand. He offered no interruption, but remained throughout perfectly still. He seemed to pursue her figure through the narrative, and to let every other shape go by him, as if it were nothing.

When I had done, he shaded his face, and continued silent. I looked out of the window for a little while, and occupied myself with the plants.

'How do you fare to feel about it, Mas'r Davy?' he enquired at length.

'I think that she is living,' I replied.

'I doen't know. Maybe the first shock was too rough, and in

the wildness of her art – ! That there blue water as she used to speak on. Could she have thowt o' that so many year, because it was to be her grave!'

He said this, musing, in a low, frightened voice; and walked across the little room.

'And yet,' he added, 'Mas'r Davy, I have felt so sure as she was living – I have knowed, awake and sleeping, as it was so trew that I should find her – I have been so led on by it, and held up by it – that I doen't believe I can have been deceived. No! Em'ly's alive!'

He put his hand down firmly on the table, and set his sunburnt face into a resolute expression.

'My niece, Em'ly, is alive, sir!' he said steadfastly. 'I doen't know wheer it comes from, or how 't is, but *I am told* as she's alive!'

He looked almost like a man inspired, as he said it. I waited for a few moments, until he could give me his undivided attention; and then proceeded to explain the precaution, that, it had occurred to me last night, it would be wise to take.

'Now, my dear friend – ' I began.

'Thankee, thankee, kind sir,' he said, grasping my hand in both of his.

'If she should make her way to London, which is likely – for where could she lose herself so readily as in this vast city; and what would she wish to do, but lose and hide herself, if she does not go home? – '

'And she won't go home,' he interposed, shaking his head mournfully. 'If she had left of her own accord, she might; not as 't was, sir.'

'If she should come here,' said I, 'I believe there is one person, here, more likely to discover her than any other in the world. Do you remember – hear what I say, with fortitude – think of your great object! – do you remember Martha?'

'Of our town?'

I needed no other answer than his face.

'Do you know that she is in London?'

'I have seen her in the streets,' he answered with a shiver.

'But you don't know,' said I, 'that Emily was charitable to her, with Ham's help, long before she fled from home. Nor that, when we met one night, and spoke together in the room yonder, over the way, she listened at the door.'

'Mas'r Davy?' he replied in astonishment. 'That night when it snew so hard?'

'That night. I have never seen her since. I went back, after parting from you, to speak to her, but she was gone. I was unwilling to mention her to you then, and I am now; but she is the person of whom I speak, and with whom I think we should communicate. Do you understand?'

'Too well, sir,' he replied. We had sunk our voices, almost to a whisper, and continued to speak in that tone.

'You say you have seen her. Do you think that you could find her? I could only hope to do so by chance.'

'I think, Mas'r Davy, I know wheer to look.'

'It is dark. Being together, shall we go out now, and try to find her tonight?'

He assented, and prepared to accompany me. Without

appearing to observe what he was doing, I saw how carefully he adjusted the little room, put a candle ready and the means of lighting it, arranged the bed, and finally took out of a drawer one of her dresses (I remember to have seen her wear it), neatly folded with some other garments, and a bonnet, which he placed upon a chair. He made no allusion to these clothes, neither did I. There they had been waiting for her, many and many a night, no doubt.

'The time was, Mas'r Davy,' he said, as we came downstairs, 'when I thowt this girl, Martha, a'most like the dirt underneath my Em'ly's feet. God forgive me, there's a difference now!'

As we went along, partly to hold him in conversation, and partly to satisfy myself, I asked him about Ham. He said, almost in the same words as formerly, that Ham was just the same, 'wearing away his life with kiender no care nohow for 't; but never murmuring, and liked by all.'

I asked him what he thought Ham's state of mind was, in reference to the cause of their misfortunes? Whether he believed it was dangerous? What he supposed, for example, Ham would do, if he and Steerforth ever should encounter?

'I doen't know, sir,' he replied. 'I have thowt of it oftentimes, but I can't arrise myself of it, no matters.'

I recalled to his remembrance the morning after her departure, when we were all three on the beach. 'Do you recollect,' said I, 'a certain wild way in which he looked out to sea, and spoke about "the end of it"?'

'Sure I do!' said he.

'What do you suppose he meant?'

'Mas'r Davy,' he replied, 'I've put the question to myself a mort o' times, and never found no answer. And theer's one curious thing – that, though he is so pleasant, I wouldn't fare to feel comfortable to try and get his mind upon 't. He never said a wured to me as warn't as dootiful as dootiful could be, and it ain't likely as he'd begin to speak any other ways now; but it's fur from being fleet water in his mind, wheer them thowts lays. It's deep, sir, and I can't see down.'

'You are right,' said I, 'and that has sometimes made me anxious.'

'And me, too, Mas'r Davy,' he rejoined. 'Even more so, I do assure you, than his ventersome ways, though both belongs to the alteration in him. I doen't know as he'd do violence under any circumstances, but I hope as them two may be kep' asunders.'

We had come, through Temple Bar, into the city. Conversing no more now, and walking at my side, he yielded himself up to the one aim of his devoted life, and went on, with that hushed concentration of his faculties which would have made his figure solitary in a multitude. We were not far from Blackfriars Bridge, when he turned his head and pointed to a solitary female figure flitting along the opposite side of the street. I knew it, readily, to be the figure that we sought.

We crossed the road, and were pressing on towards her, when it occurred to me that she might be more disposed to feel a woman's interest in the lost girl, if we spoke to her in a quieter place, aloof from the crowd, and where we should be less observed. I advised my companion, therefore, that we should

not address her yet, but follow her; consulting in this, likewise, an indistinct desire I had to know where she went.

He acquiescing, we followed at a distance: never losing sight of her, but never caring to come very near, as she frequently looked about. Once, she stopped to listen to a band of music; and then we stopped, too.

She went on a long way. Still we went on. It was evident, from the manner in which she held her course, that she was going to some fixed destination; and this, and her keeping in the busy streets, and, I suppose, the strange fascination in the secrecy and mystery of so following anyone, made me adhere to my first purpose. At length she turned into a dull, dark street, where the noise and crowd were lost; and I said, 'We may speak to her now'; and, mending our pace, we went after her.

CHAPTER 47

Martha

We were now down in Westminster. We had turned back to follow her, having encountered her coming towards us; and Westminster Abbey was the point at which she passed from the lights and noise of the leading streets. She proceeded so quickly, when she got free of the two currents of passengers setting towards and from the bridge, that, between this and the advance she had of us when she struck off, we were in the narrow waterside street by Millbank before we came up with her. At that moment she crossed the road, as if to avoid the footsteps that she heard so close behind; and, without looking back, passed on even more rapidly.

A glimpse of the river through a dull gateway, where some wagons were housed for the night, seemed to arrest my feet. I touched my companion without speaking, and we both forbore to cross after her, and both followed on that opposite side of the way; keeping as quietly as we could in the shadow of the houses, but keeping very near her.

There was, and is when I write, at the end of the low-lying street, a dilapidated little wooden building, probably an obsolete old ferry-house. Its position is just at that point where the street ceases, and the road begins to lie between a row of houses and the river. As soon as she came here, and saw the water, she stopped as if she had come to her destination; and presently went slowly along by the brink of the river, looking intently at it.

All the way here, I had supposed that she was going to some house; indeed, I had vaguely entertained the hope that the house might be in some way associated with the lost girl. But that one dark glimpse of the river, through the gateway, had instinctively prepared me for her going no farther.

The neighbourhood was a dreary one at that time; as oppressive, sad, and solitary by night, as any about London. There were neither wharves nor houses on the melancholy waste of road near the great blank Prison. A sluggish ditch deposited its mud at the prison walls. Coarse grass and rank weeds straggled over all the marshy land in the vicinity. In one part, carcases of houses, inauspiciously begun and never finished, rotted away. In another, the ground was cumbered with rusty iron monsters of steam-boilers, wheels, cranks, pipes, furnaces, paddles, anchors, diving-bells, windmill-sails, and I know not what strange objects, accumulated by some speculator, and grovelling in the dust, underneath which – having sunk into the soil of their own weight in wet weather – they had the appearance of vainly trying to hide themselves. The clash and glare of sundry fiery Works upon the riverside, arose by night to disturb everything except the heavy and unbroken smoke that poured out of their chimneys. Slimy gaps and causeways, winding among old wooden piles, with a sickly substance clinging to the latter, like green hair, and the rags of last year's handbills offering rewards for drowned men fluttering above high-water mark, led down through the ooze and slush to the ebb tide. There was a story that one of the pits dug for the dead in the time of the Great Plague was here-about; and a blighting influence seemed to have proceeded from it over the whole place. Or else it looked as if it had gradually decomposed into that nightmare condition, out of the overflowings of the polluted stream.

As if she were a part of the refuse it had cast out, and left to corruption and decay, the girl we had followed strayed down to the river's brink, and stood in the midst of this night-picture, lonely and still, looking at the water.

There were some boats and barges astrand in the mud, and these enabled us to come within a few yards of her without being seen. I then signed to Mr Peggotty to remain where he was, and emerged from their shade to speak to her. I did not approach her solitary figure without trembling; for this gloomy end to her determined walk, and the way in which she stood, almost within the cavernous shadow of the iron bridge, looking at the lights crookedly reflected in the strong tide, inspired a dread within me.

I think she was talking to herself. I am sure, although absorbed in gazing at the water, that her shawl was off her shoulders, and that she was muffling her hands in it, in an unsettled and bewildered way, more like the action of a sleepwalker than a waking person. I know, and never can forget, that there was that in her wild manner which gave me no assurance but that she would sink before my eyes, until I had her arm within my grasp.

At the same moment I said, 'Martha!'

She uttered a terrified scream, and struggled with me with such strength that I doubt if I could have held her alone. But a stronger hand than mine was laid upon her; and when she raised her frightened eyes and saw whose it was, she made but one more effort and dropped down between us. We carried her away from the water to where there were some dry stones, and there laid her down, crying and moaning. In a little while she sat among the stones, holding her wretched head with both her hands.

'Oh, the river!' she cried passionately. 'Oh, the river!'

'Hush, hush!' said I. 'Calm yourself.'

But she still repeated the same words, continually exclaiming, 'Oh, the river!' over and over again.

'I know it's like me!' she exclaimed. 'I know that I belong to it. I know that it's the natural company of such as I am! It comes from country places, where there was once no harm in it – and it creeps through the dismal streets, defiled and miserable – and it goes away, like my life, to a great sea, that is always troubled – and I feel that I must go with it!'

I have never known what despair was, except in the tone of those words.

'I can't keep away from it. I can't forget it. It haunts me day and night. It's the only thing in all the world that I am fit for, or that's fit for me. Oh, the dreadful river!'

The thought passed through my mind that in the face of my companion, as he looked upon her without speech or motion, I might have read his niece's history, if I had known nothing of it. I never saw, in any painting or reality, horror and compassion so impressively blended. He shook as if he would have fallen; and his hand – I touched it with my own, for his appearance alarmed me – was deadly cold.

'She is in a state of frenzy,' I whispered to him. 'She will speak differently in a little time.'

I don't know what he would have said in answer. He made some motion with his mouth, and seemed to think he had spoken; but he had only pointed to her with his outstretched hand.

A new burst of crying came upon her now, in which she once more hid her face among the stones, and lay before us, a prostrate image of humiliation and ruin. Knowing that this state must pass, before we could speak to her with any hope, I ventured to restrain him when he would have raised her, and we stood by in silence until she became more tranquil.

'Martha,' said I then, leaning down, and helping her to rise – she seemed to want to rise as if with the intention of going away, but she was weak, and leaned against a boat. 'Do you know who this is, who is with me?'

She said faintly, 'Yes.'

'Do you know that we have followed you a long way tonight?'

She shook her head. She looked neither at him nor at me, but stood in a humbled attitude, holding her bonnet and shawl in one hand, without appearing conscious of them, and pressing the other, clenched, against her forehead.

'Are you composed enough,' said I, 'to speak on the subject which so interested you – I hope Heaven may remember it! – that snowy night?'

Her sobs broke out afresh, and she murmured some inarticulate thanks to me for not having driven her away from the door.

'I want to say nothing for myself,' she said, after a few moments. 'I am bad, I am lost. I have no hope at all. But tell him, sir,' she had shrunk away from him, 'if you don't feel too hard to me to do it, that I never was in any way the cause of his misfortune.'

'It has never been attributed to you,' I returned, earnestly responding to her earnestness.

'It was you, if I don't deceive myself,' she said, in a broken voice, 'that came into the kitchen, the night she took such pity on me; was so gentle to me; didn't shrink away from me like all the rest, and gave me such kind help! Was it you, sir?'

'It was,' said I.

'I should have been in the river long ago,' she said, glancing at it with a terrible expression, 'if any wrong to her had been upon my mind. I never could have kept out of it a single winter's night, if I had not been free of any share in that!'

'The cause of her flight is too well understood,' I said. 'You are innocent of any part in it, we thoroughly believe, we know.'

'Oh, I might have been much the better for her, if I had had a better heart!' exclaimed the girl, with most forlorn regret; 'for she was always good to me! She never spoke a word to me but what was pleasant and right. Is it likely I would try to make her what I am myself, knowing what I am myself, so well! When I lost everything that makes life dear, the worst of all my thoughts was that I was parted for ever from her!'

Mr Peggotty, standing with one hand on the gunwale of the boat, and his eyes cast down, put his disengaged hand before his face.

'And when I heard what had happened before that snowy night, from some belonging to our town,' cried Martha, 'the bitterest thought in all my mind was that the people would remember she once kept company with me, and would say I had corrupted her! When, Heaven knows, I would have died to have brought back her good name!'

Long unused to any self-control, the piercing agony of her remorse and grief was terrible.

'To have died, would not have been much – what can I say? – I would have lived!' she cried. 'I would have lived to be old, in the wretched streets – and to wander about, avoided, in the dark – and to see the day break on the ghastly line of houses, and remember how the same sun used to shine into my room, and wake me once – I would have done even that to save her!'

Sinking on the stones, she took some in each hand, and clenched them up, as if she would have ground them. She writhed into some new posture constantly, stiffening her arms, twisting them before her face, as though to shut out from her eyes the little light there was, and drooping her head, as if it were heavy with insupportable recollections.

'What shall I ever do!' she said, fighting thus with her despair. 'How can I go on as I am, a solitary curse to myself, a living disgrace to everyone I come near!' Suddenly she turned to my companion. 'Stamp upon me, kill me! When she was your pride, you would have thought I had done her harm if I had brushed against her in the street. You can't believe – why should you? – a syllable that comes out of my lips. It would be a burning shame upon you, even now, if she and I exchanged a word. I don't complain. I don't say she and I are alike – I know there is a long, long way between us. I only say, with all my guilt and wretchedness upon my head, that I am grateful to her from my soul, and love her. Oh, don't think that all the power I had of loving anything is quite worn out! Throw me away, as all the world does. Kill me for being what I am, and having ever known her; but don't think that of me!'

He looked upon her, while she made this supplication, in a wild, distracted manner; and, when she was silent, gently raised her.

'Martha,' said Mr Peggotty, 'God forbid as I should judge you. Forbid as I, of all men, should do that, my girl! You doesn't know half the change that's come, in course of time, upon me, when you think it likely. Well!' he paused a moment, then went on. 'You doesn't understand how 't is that this here gentleman and me has wished to speak to you. You doesn't understand what 't is we has afore us. Listen, now!'

The river

His influence upon her was complete. She stood, shrinkingly, before him, as if she were afraid to meet his eyes; but her passionate sorrow was quite hushed and mute.

'If you heerd,' said Mr Peggotty, 'owt of what passed between Mas'r Davy and me, th' night when it snew so hard, you know as I have been – wheer not – fur to seek my dear niece. My dear niece,' he repeated steadily. 'Fur she's more dear to me now, Martha, than ever she was dear afore.'

She put her hands before her face; but otherwise remained quiet.

'I have heerd her tell,' said Mr Peggotty, 'as you was early left fatherless and motherless, with no friend fur to take, in a rough seafaring way, their place. Maybe you can guess that, if you'd had such a friend, you'd have got into a way of being fond of him in course of time, and that my niece was kiender daughter-like to me.'

As she was silently trembling, he put her shawl carefully about her, taking it up from the ground for that purpose.

'Whereby,' said he, 'I know, both as she would go to the wureld's furdest end with me, if she could once see me again; and that she would fly to the wureld's furdest end to keep off seeing me. For though she ain't no call to doubt my love, and doen't – and doen't,' he repeated, with a quiet assurance of the truth of what he said, 'there's shame steps in, and keeps betwixt us.'

I read, in every word of his plain impressive way of delivering himself, new evidence of his having thought of this one topic, in every feature it presented.

'According to our reckoning,' he proceeded, 'Mas'r Davy's here, and mine, she is like, one day, to make her own poor solitary course to London. We believe – Mas'r Davy, me, and all of us – that you are as innocent of everything that has befell her, as the unborn child. You've spoke of her being pleasant, kind, and gentle to you. Bless her, I knew she was! I knew she always was, to all. You're thankful to her, and you love her. Help us all you can to find her, and may Heaven reward you!'

She looked at him hastily, and for the first time, as if she were doubtful of what he had said.

'Will you trust me?' she asked, in a low voice of astonishment.

'Full and free!' said Mr Peggotty.

'To speak to her, if I should ever find her; shelter her, if I have any shelter to divide with her; and then, without her knowledge, come to you, and bring you to her?' she asked hurriedly.

We both replied together, 'Yes!'

She lifted up her eyes, and solemnly declared that she would devote herself to this task, fervently and faithfully. That she would never waver in it, never be diverted from it, never relinquish it while there was any chance of hope. If she were not true to it, might the object she now had in life, which bound her to something devoid of evil, in its passing away from her, leave her more forlorn and more despairing, if that were possible, than she had been upon the river's brink that night; and then might all help, human and Divine, renounce her evermore!

She did not raise her voice above her breath, or address us, but said this to the night sky; then stood profoundly quiet, looking at the gloomy water.

We judged it expedient, now, to tell her all we knew, which I recounted at length. She listened with great attention, and with a face that often changed, but had the same purpose in all its varying expressions. Her eyes occasionally filled with tears, but those she repressed. It seemed as if her spirit were quite altered, and she could not be too quiet.

She asked, when all was told, where we were to be communicated with, if occasion should arise. Under a dull lamp in the road, I wrote our two addresses on a leaf of my pocket-book, which I tore out and gave to her, and which she put in her poor bosom. I asked her where she lived herself. She said, after a pause, in no place long. It were better not to know.

Mr Peggotty suggesting to me, in a whisper, what had already occurred to myself, I took out my purse; but I could not prevail upon her to accept any money, nor could I exact any promise from her that she would do so at another time. I represented to her that Mr Peggotty could not be called, for one in his condition, poor; and that the idea of her engaging in this search, while depending on her own resources, shocked us both. She continued steadfast. In this particular, his influence upon her was equally powerless with mine. She gratefully thanked him, but remained inexorable.

'There may be work to be got,' she said. 'I'll try.'

'At least take some assistance,' I returned, 'until you have tried.'

'I could not do what I have promised for money,' she replied. 'I could not take it if I was starving. To give me money would be to take away your trust, to take away the object that you have given me, to take away the only certain thing that saves me from the river.'

'In the name of the great Judge,' said I, 'before whom you and all of us must stand at his dread time, dismiss that terrible idea! We can all do some good, if we will.'

She trembled, and her lip shook, and her face was paler, as she answered: 'It has been put into your hearts, perhaps, to save a wretched creature for repentance. I am afraid to think so; it seems too bold. If any good should come of me, I might begin to hope; for nothing but harm has ever come of my deeds yet. I am to be trusted, for the first time in a long while, with my miserable life, on account of what you have given me to try for. I know no more, and I can say no more.'

Again she repressed the tears that had begun to flow; and, putting out her trembling hand, and touching Mr Peggotty, as if there was some healing virtue in him, went away along the desolate road. She had been ill, probably, for a long time. I observed, upon that closer opportunity of observation, that she was worn and haggard, and that her sunken eyes expressed privation and endurance.

We followed her at a short distance, our way lying in the same direction, until we came back into the lighted and populous streets. I had such implicit confidence in her declaration that I then put it to Mr Peggotty, whether it would not seem, in the onset, like distrusting her, to follow her any further. He being of the same mind, and equally reliant on her, we suffered her to take her own road, and took ours, which was towards Highgate. He accompanied me a good part of the way; and when we parted, with a prayer for the success of this fresh effort, there was a new and thoughtful compassion in him that I was at no loss to interpret.

It was midnight when I arrived at home. I had reached my own gate, and was standing listening for the deep bell of St Paul's, the sound of which I thought had been borne towards me among the multitude of striking clocks, when I was rather surprised to see that the door of my aunt's cottage was open, and that a faint light in the entry was shining out across the road.

Thinking that my aunt might have relapsed into one of her old alarms, and might be watching the progress of some imaginary conflagration in the distance, I went to speak to her. It was with very great surprise that I saw a man standing in her little garden.

He had a glass and bottle in his hand, and was in the act of drinking. I stopped short among the thick foliage outside, for the moon was up now, though obscured; and I recognised the man whom I had once supposed to be a delusion of Mr Dick's, and had once encountered with my aunt in the streets of the city.

He was eating as well as drinking, and seemed to eat with a hungry appetite. He seemed curious regarding the cottage, too, as if it were the first time he had seen it. After stooping to put the bottle on the ground, he looked up at the windows and looked about; though with a covert and impatient air, as if he was anxious to be gone.

The light in the passage was obscured for a moment, and my aunt came out. She was agitated, and told some money into his hand. I heard it chink.

'What's the use of this?' he demanded.

'I can spare no more,' returned my aunt.

'Then I can't go,' said he. 'Here! You may take it back!'

'You bad man,' returned my aunt, with great emotion; 'how can you use me so? But why do I ask? It is because you know how weak I am! What have I to do, to free myself for ever of your visits, but to abandon you to your deserts?'

'And why don't you abandon me to my deserts?' said he.

'*You* ask me why!' returned my aunt. 'What a heart you must have!'

He stood moodily rattling the money, and shaking his head, until at length he said: 'Is this all you mean to give me, then?'

'It is all I *can* give you,' said my aunt. 'You know I have had losses, and am poorer than I used to be. I have told you so. Having got it, why do you give me the pain of looking at you for another moment, and seeing what you have become?'

'I have become shabby enough, if you mean that,' he said. 'I lead the life of an owl.'

'You stripped me of the greater part of all I ever had,' said my aunt. 'You closed my heart against the whole world, years and years. You treated me falsely, ungratefully, and cruelly. Go, and repent of it. Don't add new injuries to the long, long list of injuries you have done me!'

'Aye!' he returned. 'It's all very fine! – Well! I must do the best I can, for the present, I suppose.'

In spite of himself, he appeared abashed by my aunt's indignant tears, and came slouching out of the garden. Taking two or three quick steps, as if I had just come up, I met him at the gate, and went in as he came out. We eyed one another narrowly in passing, and with no favour.

'Aunt,' said I hurriedly. 'This man alarming you again! Let me speak to him. Who is he?'

'Child,' returned my aunt, taking my arm, 'come in, and don't speak to me for ten minutes.'

We sat down in her little parlour. My aunt retired behind the round green fan of former days, which was screwed on the back of a chair, and occasionally wiped her eyes, for about a quarter of an hour. Then she came out, and took a seat beside me.

'Trot,' said my aunt calmly, 'it's my husband.'

'Your husband, aunt? I thought he had been dead!'

'Dead to me,' returned my aunt, 'but living.'

I sat in silent amazement.

'Betsey Trotwood don't look a likely subject for the tender passion,' said my aunt composedly, 'but the time was, Trot, when she believed in that man most entirely. When she loved him, Trot, right well. When there was no proof of attachment and affection that she would not have given him. He repaid her by breaking her fortune, and nearly breaking her heart. So she put all that sort of sentiment once and for ever in a grave, and filled it up, and flattened it down.'

'My dear, good aunt!'

'I left him,' my aunt proceeded, laying her hand as usual on the back of mine, 'generously. I may say at this distance of time, Trot, that I left him generously. He had been so cruel to me, that I might have effected a separation on easy terms for myself; but I did not. He soon made ducks and drakes of what I gave him, sank lower and lower, married another woman, I believe, became an adventurer, a gambler, and a cheat. What he is now, you see. But he was a fine-looking man when I married him,' said my aunt, with an echo of her old pride and admiration in her tone; 'and I believed him – I was a fool! – to be the soul of honour!'

She gave my hand a squeeze, and shook her head.

'He is nothing to me now, Trot, less than nothing. But, sooner than have him punished for his offences (as he would be if he prowled about in this country), I give him more money than I can afford, at intervals when he reappears, to go away. I was a fool when I married him; and I am so far an incurable fool on that subject, that, for the sake of what I once believed him to be, I wouldn't have even this shadow of my idle fancy hardly dealt with. For I was in earnest, Trot, if ever a woman was.'

My aunt dismissed the matter with a heavy sigh, and smoothed her dress.

'There, my dear!' she said. 'Now, you know the beginning, middle, and end, and all about it. We won't mention the subject to one another any more; neither, of course, will you mention it to anybody else. This is my grumpy, frumpy story, and we'll keep it to ourselves, Trot!'

CHAPTER 48

Domestic

I laboured hard at my book, without allowing it to interfere with the punctual discharge of my newspaper duties; and it came out and was very successful. I was not stunned by the praise which sounded in my ears, notwithstanding that I was keenly alive to it, and thought better of my own performance, I have little doubt, than anybody else did. It has always been in my observation of human nature, that a man who has any good reason to believe in himself never flourishes himself before the faces of other people in order that they may believe in him. For this reason, I retained my modesty in very self-respect; and the more praise I got, the more I tried to deserve.

It is not my purpose, in this record, though in all other essentials it is my written memory, to pursue the history of my own fictions. They express themselves, and I leave them to themselves. When I refer to them, incidentally, it is only as a part of my progress.

Having some foundation for believing, by this time, that nature and accident had made me an author, I pursued my vocation with confidence. Without such assurance I should certainly have left it alone, and bestowed my energy on some other endeavour. I should have tried to find out what nature and accident really had made me, and to be that, and nothing else.

I had been writing, in the newspaper and elsewhere, so prosperously, that when my new success was achieved, I considered myself reasonably entitled to escape from the dreary debates. One joyful night, therefore, I noted down the music of the parliamentary bagpipes for the last time, and I have never heard it since; though I still recognise the old drone in the newspapers, without any substantial variation (except, perhaps, that there is more of it) all the livelong session.

I now write of the time when I had been married, I suppose, about a year and a half. After several varieties of experiment, we had given up the housekeeping as a bad job. The house kept itself, and we kept a page. The principal function of this retainer was to quarrel with the cook; in which respect he was a perfect Whittington, without his cat, or the remotest chance of being made Lord Mayor.

He appears to me to have lived in a hail of saucepan-lids. His whole existence was a scuffle. He would shriek for help on the most improper occasions – as when we had a little dinner party, or a few friends in the evening – and would come tumbling out of the kitchen, with iron missiles flying after him. We wanted to get rid of him, but he was very much attached to us, and wouldn't go. He was a tearful boy, and broke into such deplorable lamentations, when a cessation of our connection was hinted at, that we were obliged to keep him. He had no mother – no anything in the way of a relative, that I could discover, except a sister, who fled to America the moment we had taken him off her hands; and he became quartered on us

like a horrible young changeling. He had a lively perception of his own unfortunate state, and was always rubbing his eyes with the sleeve of his jacket, or stooping to blow his nose on the extreme corner of a little pocket-handkerchief, which he never *would* take completely out of his pocket, but always economised and secreted.

This unlucky page, engaged in an evil hour at six pounds ten per annum, was a source of continual trouble to me. I watched him as he grew – and he grew like scarlet beans – with painful apprehensions of the time when he would begin to shave; even of the days when he would be bald or grey. I saw no prospect of ever getting rid of him; and, projecting myself into the future, used to think what an inconvenience he would be when he was an old man.

I never expected anything less, than this unfortunate's manner of getting me out of my difficulty. He stole Dora's watch, which, like everything else belonging to us, had no particular place of its own; and, converting it into money, spent the produce (he was always a weak-minded boy) in incessantly riding up and down between London and Uxbridge outside the coach. He was taken to Bow Street, as well as I remember, on the completion of his fifteenth journey; when four-and-sixpence and a second-hand fife which he couldn't play were found upon his person.

The surprise and its consequences would have been much less disagreeable to me if he had not been penitent. But he was very penitent indeed, and in a peculiar way – not in the lump, but by instalments. For example: the day after that on which I was obliged to appear against him, he made certain revelations touching a hamper in the cellar, which we believed to be full of wine, but which had nothing in it except bottles and corks. We supposed he had now eased his mind, and told the worst he knew of the cook; but, a day or two afterwards, his conscience sustained a new twinge, and he disclosed how she had a little girl, who, early every morning, took away our bread; and also how he himself had been suborned to maintain the milkman in coals. In two or three days more, I was informed by the authorities of his having led to the discovery of sirloins of beef among the kitchen-stuff, and sheets in the rag-bag. A little while afterwards, he broke out in an entirely new direction, and confessed to a knowledge of burglarious intentions as to our premises, on the part of the pot-boy, who was immediately taken up. I got to be so ashamed of being such a victim, that I would have given him any money to hold his tongue, or would have offered a round bribe for his being permitted to run away. It was an aggravating circumstance in the case that he had no idea of this, but conceived that he was making me amends in every new discovery, not to say, heaping obligations on my head.

At last I ran away myself, whenever I saw an emissary of the police approaching with some new intelligence; and lived a stealthy life until he was tried and ordered to be transported. Even then he couldn't be quiet, but was always writing us letters; and wanted so much to see Dora before he went away, that Dora went to visit him, and fainted when she found herself inside the iron bars. In short, I had no peace of my life until he was expatriated, and made (as I afterwards heard) a shepherd of, 'up the country' somewhere; I have no geographical idea where.

All this led me into some serious reflections, and presented our mistakes in a new aspect, as I could not help communicating to Dora one evening, in spite of my tenderness for her.

'My love,' said I, 'it is very painful to me to think that our want of system and management involves not only ourselves (which we have got used to), but other people.'

'You have been silent for a long time, and now you are going to be cross!' said Dora.

'No, my dear, indeed! Let me explain to you what I mean.'

'I think I don't want to know,' said Dora.

'But I want you to know, my love. Put Jip down.'

Dora put his nose to mine, and said 'Boh!' to drive my seriousness away; but, not succeeding, ordered him into his pagoda, and sat looking at me, with her hands folded, and a most resigned little expression of countenance.

'The fact is, my dear,' I began, 'there is contagion in us. We infect everyone about us.'

I might have gone on in this figurative manner, if Dora's face had not admonished me that she was wondering with all her might whether I was going to propose any new kind of vaccination, or other medical remedy, for this unwholesome state of ours. Therefore I checked myself and made my meaning plainer.

'It is not merely, my pet,' said I, 'that we lose money and comfort, and even temper sometimes, by not learning to be more careful; but that we incur the serious responsibility of spoiling everyone who comes into our service, or has any dealings with us. I begin to be afraid that the fault is not entirely on one side, but that these people all turn out ill because we don't turn out very well ourselves.'

'Oh, what an accusation,' exclaimed Dora, opening her eyes wide, 'to say that you ever saw me take gold watches! Oh!'

'My dearest,' I remonstrated, 'don't talk preposterous nonsense! Who has made the least allusion to gold watches?'

'You did,' returned Dora. 'You know you did. You said I hadn't turned out well, and compared me to him.'

'To whom?' I asked.

'To the page,' sobbed Dora. 'Oh, you cruel fellow, to compare your affectionate wife to a transported page! Why didn't you tell me your opinion of me before we were married? Why didn't you say, you hard-hearted thing, that you were convinced I was worse than a transported page? Oh, what a dreadful opinion to have of me! Oh, my goodness!'

'Now, Dora, my love,' I returned, gently trying to remove the handkerchief she pressed to her eyes, 'this is not only very ridiculous of you, but very wrong. In the first place, it's not true.'

'You always said he was a story-teller,' sobbed Dora. 'And now you say the same of me! Oh, what shall I do! What shall I do!'

'My darling girl,' I retorted, 'I really must entreat you to be reasonable, and listen to what I did say, and do say. My dear

Dora, unless we learn to do our duty to those whom we employ, they will never learn to do their duty to us. I am afraid we present opportunities to people to do wrong, that never ought to be presented. Even if we were as lax as we are, in all our arrangements, by choice – which we are not – even if we liked it, and found it agreeable to be so – which we don't – I am persuaded we should have no right to go on in this way. We are positively corrupting people. We are bound to think of that. I can't help thinking of it, Dora. It is a reflection I am unable to dismiss, and it sometimes makes me very uneasy. There, dear, that's all. Come now. Don't be foolish!'

Dora would not allow me, for a long time, to remove the handkerchief. She sat sobbing and murmuring behind it, that, if I was uneasy, why had I ever been married? Why hadn't I said, even the day before we went to church, that I knew I should be uneasy, and I would rather not? If I couldn't bear her, why didn't I send her away to her aunts at Putney, or to Julia Mills in India? Julia would be glad to see her, and would not call her a transported page; Julia never had called her anything of the sort. In short, Dora was so afflicted, and so afflicted me by being in that condition, that I felt it was of no use repeating this kind of effort, though never so mildly, and I must take some other course.

What other course was left to take! To 'form her mind!' This was a common phrase of words which had a fair and promising sound, and I resolved to form Dora's mind.

I began immediately. When Dora was very childish, and I would have infinitely preferred to humour her, I tried to be grave – and disconcerted her and myself too. I talked to her on the subjects which occupied my thoughts; and I read Shakespeare to her – and fatigued her to the last degree. I accustomed myself to giving her, as it were quite casually, little scraps of useful information, or sound opinion – and she started from them when I let them off, as if they had been crackers. No matter how incidentally or naturally I endeavoured to form my little wife's mind, I could not help seeing that she always had an instinctive perception of what I was about, and became a prey to the keenest apprehensions. In particular it was clear to me, that she thought Shakespeare a terrible fellow. The formation went on very slowly.

I pressed Traddles into the service without his knowledge; and whenever he came to see us, exploded my mines upon him for the edification of Dora at second hand. The amount of practical wisdom I bestowed upon Traddles in this manner was immense, and of the best quality; but it had no other effect upon Dora than to depress her spirits, and make her always nervous with the dread that it would be her turn next. I found myself in the condition of a schoolmaster, a trap, a pitfall; of always playing spider to Dora's fly, and always pouncing out of my hole to her infinite disturbance.

Still, looking forward through this intermediate stage, to the time when there should be a perfect sympathy between Dora and me, and when I should have 'formed her mind' to my entire satisfaction, I persevered, even for months. Finding at last, however, that, although I had been all this time a very porcupine or hedgehog, bristling all over with determination, I had effected nothing, it began to occur to me that perhaps Dora's mind was already formed.

On further consideration this appeared so likely, that I abandoned my scheme, which had had a more promising appearance in words than in action; resolving henceforth to be satisfied with my child-wife, and to try to change her into nothing else by any process. I was heartily tired of being sagacious and prudent by myself, and of seeing my darling under restraint; so I bought a pretty pair of ear-rings for her, and a collar for Jip, and went home one day to make myself agreeable.

Dora was delighted with the little presents, and kissed me joyfully; but there was a shadow between us, however slight, and I had made up my mind that it should not be there. If there must be such a shadow anywhere, I would keep it for the future in my own breast.

I sat down by my wife on the sofa, and put the ear-rings in her ears; and then I told her that I feared we had not been quite as good company lately as we used to be, and that the fault was mine. Which I sincerely felt, and which indeed it was.

'The truth is, Dora, my life,' I said, 'I have been trying to be wise.'

'And to make me wise, too,' said Dora timidly. 'Haven't you, Doady?'

I nodded assent to the pretty enquiry of the raised eyebrows, and kissed the parted lips.

'It's of not a bit of use,' said Dora, shaking her head, until the ear-rings rang again. 'You know what a little thing I am, and what I wanted you to call me from the first. If you can't do so, I'm afraid you'll never like me. Are you sure you don't think, sometimes, it would have been better to have – '

'Done what, my dear?' For she made no effort to proceed.

'Nothing,' said Dora.

'Nothing?' I repeated.

She put her arms round my neck, and laughed, and called herself by her favourite name of a goose, and hid her face on my shoulder in such a profusion of curls that it was quite a task to clear them away and see it.

'Don't I think it would have been better to have done nothing, than to have tried to form my little wife's mind?' said I, laughing at myself. 'Is that the question? Yes, indeed, I do.'

'Is that what you have been trying?' cried Dora. 'Oh, what a shocking boy!'

'But I shall never try any more,' said I. 'For I love her dearly as she is.'

'Without a story – really?' enquired Dora, creeping closer to me.

'Why should I seek to change,' said I, 'what has been so precious to me for so long! You never can show better than as your own natural self, my sweet Dora; and we'll try no conceited experiments, but go back to our old way, and be happy.'

'And be happy!' returned Dora. 'Yes! All day. And you won't mind things going a tiny morsel wrong, sometimes?'

'No, no,' said I. 'We must do the best we can.'

'And you won't tell me, any more, that we make other people bad,' coaxed Dora, 'will you? Because you know it's so dreadfully cross!'

'No, no,' said I.

'It's better for me to be stupid than uncomfortable, isn't it?' said Dora.

'Better to be naturally Dora than anything else in the world.'

'In the world! Ah Doady, it's a large place!'

She shook her head, turned her delighted bright eyes up to mine, kissed me, broke into a merry laugh, and sprang away to put on Jip's new collar.

So ended my last attempt to make any change in Dora. I had been unhappy in trying it; I could not endure my own solitary wisdom; I could not reconcile it with her former appeal to me as my child-wife. I resolved to do what I could, in a quiet way, to improve our proceedings myself; but I foresaw that my utmost would be very little, or I must degenerate into the spider again, and be for ever lying in wait.

And the shadow I have mentioned, that was not to be between us any more, but was to rest wholly on my own heart? How did that fall?

The old unhappy feeling pervaded my life. It was deepened, if it were changed at all; but it was as undefined as ever, and addressed me like a strain of sorrowful music faintly heard in the night. I loved my wife dearly, and I was happy; but the happiness I had vaguely anticipated, once, was not the happiness I enjoyed, and there was always something wanting.

In fulfilment of the compact I have made with myself, to reflect my mind on this paper, I again examine it, closely, and bring its secrets to the light. What I missed, I still regarded – I always regarded – as something that had been a dream of my youthful fancy; that was incapable of realisation; that I was now discovering to be so, with some natural pain, as all men did. But, that it would have been better for me if my wife could have helped me more, and shared the many thoughts in which I had no partner; and that this might have been, I knew.

Between these two irreconcilable conclusions – the one, that what I felt was general and unavoidable; the other, that it was particular to me, and might have been different – I balanced curiously, with no distinct sense of their opposition to each other. When I thought of the airy dreams of youth that are incapable of realisation, I thought of the better state preceding manhood that I had outgrown; and then the contented days with Agnes, in the dear old house, arose before me, like spectres of the dead, that might have some renewal in another world, but never, never more could be reanimated here.

Sometimes, the speculation came into my thoughts, What might have happened, or what would have happened, if Dora and I had never known each other? But she was so incorporated with my existence, that it was the idlest of all fancies, and would soon rise out of my reach and sight, like gossamer floating in the air.

I always loved her. What I am describing slumbered, and half awoke, and slept again, in the innermost recesses of my mind. There was no evidence of it in me; I know of no influence it had in anything I said or did. I bore the weight of all our little cares, and all my projects; Dora held the pens; and we both felt that our shares were adjusted as the case required. She was truly fond of me, and proud of me; and when Agnes wrote a few earnest words in her letters to Dora, of the pride and interest with which my old friends heard of my growing reputation, and read my book as if they heard me speaking its contents, Dora read them out to me with tears of joy in her bright eyes, and said I was a dear old clever, famous boy.

'The first mistaken impulse of an undisciplined heart.' These words of Mrs Strong's were constantly recurring to me, at this time; were almost always present to my mind. I awoke with them, often, in the night; I remember to have even read them, in dreams, inscribed upon the walls of houses. For I knew, now, that my own heart was undisciplined when it first loved Dora; and that if it had been disciplined, it never could have felt, when we were married, what it had felt in its secret experience.

'There can be no disparity in marriage like unsuitability of mind and purpose.' Those words I remembered too. I had endeavoured to adapt Dora to myself, and found it impracticable. It remained for me to adapt myself to Dora; to share with her what I could, and be happy; to bear on my own shoulders what I must, and be happy still. This was the discipline to which I tried to bring my heart, when I began to think. It made my second year much happier than my first; and, what was better still, made Dora's life all sunshine.

But, as that year wore on, Dora was not strong. I had hoped that lighter hands than mine would help to mould her character, and that a baby-smile upon her breast might change my child-wife to a woman. It was not to be. The spirit fluttered for a moment on the threshold of its little prison, and, unconscious of captivity, took wing.

'When I can run about again, as I used to do, aunt,' said Dora, 'I shall make Jip race. He is getting quite slow and lazy.'

'I suspect, my dear,' said my aunt, quietly working by her side, 'he has a worse disorder than that. Age, Dora.'

'Do you think he is old?' said Dora, astonished. 'Oh, how strange it seems that Jip should be old!'

'It's a complaint we are all liable to, Little One, as we get on in life,' said my aunt cheerfully; 'I don't feel more free from it than I used to be, I assure you.'

'But Jip,' said Dora, looking at him with compassion, 'even little Jip! Oh, poor fellow!'

'I dare say he'll last a long time yet, Blossom,' said my aunt, patting Dora on the cheek, as she leaned out of her couch to look at Jip, who responded by standing on his hind legs, and baulking himself in various asthmatic attempts to scramble up by the head and shoulders. 'He must have a piece of flannel in his house this winter, and I shouldn't wonder if he came out quite fresh again, with the flowers in the spring. Bless the little dog!' exclaimed my aunt, 'if he had as many lives as a cat, and was on the point of losing 'em all, he'd bark at me with his last breath, I believe!'

Dora had helped him up on the sofa; where he really was defying my aunt to such a furious extent, that he couldn't keep straight, but barked himself sideways. The more my aunt looked at him, the more he reproached her; for she had lately

taken to spectacles, and for some inscrutable reason he considered the glasses personal.

Dora made him lie down by her, with a good deal of persuasion; and when he was quiet, drew one of his long ears through and through her hand, repeating thoughtfully, 'Even little Jip! Oh, poor fellow!'

'His lungs are good enough,' said my aunt gaily, 'and his dislikes are not at all feeble. He has a good many years before him, no doubt. But if you want a dog to race with, Little Blossom, he has lived too well for that, and I'll give you one.'

'Thank you, aunt,' said Dora faintly. 'But don't, please!'

'No?' said my aunt, taking off her spectacles.

'I couldn't have any other dog but Jip,' said Dora. 'It would be so unkind to Jip! Besides, I couldn't be such friends with any other dog but Jip; because he wouldn't have known me before I was married, and wouldn't have barked at Doady when he first came to our house. I couldn't care for any other dog but Jip, I am afraid, aunt.'

'To be sure!' said my aunt, patting her cheek again. 'You are right.'

'You are not offended,' said Dora. 'Are you?'

'Why, what a sensitive pet it is!' cried my aunt, bending over her affectionately. 'To think that I could be offended!'

'No, no, I didn't really think so,' returned Dora; 'but I am a little tired, and it made me silly for a moment – I am always a silly little thing, you know; but it made me more silly – to talk about Jip. He has known me in all that has happened to me, haven't you, Jip? And I couldn't bear to slight him, because he was a little altered – could I, Jip?'

Jip nestled closer to his mistress, and lazily licked her hand.

'You are not so old, Jip, are you, that you'll leave your mistress yet,' said Dora. 'We may keep one another company, a little longer!'

My pretty Dora! When she came down to dinner on the ensuing Sunday, and was so glad to see old Traddles (who always dined with us on Sunday), we thought she would be 'running about as she used to do,' in a few days. But they said, wait a few days more; and then, wait a few days more; and still she neither ran nor walked. She looked very pretty, and was very merry; but the little feet that used to be so nimble when they danced round Jip were dull and motionless.

I began to carry her downstairs every morning, and upstairs every night. She would clasp me round the neck and laugh, the while, as if I did it for a wager. Jip would bark and caper round us, and go on before, and look back on the landing, breathing short, to see that we were coming. My aunt, the best and most cheerful of nurses, would trudge after us, a moving mass of shawls and pillows. Mr Dick would not have relinquished his post of candle-bearer to anyone alive. Traddles would be often at the bottom of the staircase, looking on, and taking charge of sportive messages from Dora to the dearest girl in the world. We made quite a gay procession of it, and my child-wife was the gayest there.

But, sometimes, when I took her up, and felt that she was lighter in my arms, a dead blank feeling came upon me, as if I were approaching to some frozen region yet unseen, that numbed my life. I avoided the recognition of this feeling by any name, or by any communing with myself; until one night, when it was very strong upon me, and my aunt had left her with a parting cry of 'Good-night, Little Blossom,' I sat down at my desk alone, and cried to think, oh, what a fatal name it was, and how the blossom withered in its bloom upon the tree!

CHAPTER 49

I Am Involved in Mystery

I received one morning by the post the following letter, dated Canterbury, and addressed to me at Doctors' Commons, which I read with some surprise:

MY DEAR SIR – Circumstances beyond my individual control have, for a considerable lapse of time, effected a severance of that intimacy which, in the limited opportunities conceded to me in the midst of my professional duties, of contemplating the scenes and events of the past, tinged by the prismatic hues of memory, has ever afforded me, as it ever must continue to afford, gratifying emotions of no common description. This fact, my dear sir, combined with the distinguished elevation to which your talents have raised you, deters me from presuming to aspire to the liberty of addressing the companion of my youth, by the familiar appellation of Copperfield! It is sufficient to know that the name to which I do myself the honour to refer, will ever be treasured among the muniments of our house (I allude to the archives connected with our former lodgers, preserved by Mrs Micawber), with sentiments of personal esteem amounting to affection.

It is not for one situated, through his original errors and a fortuitous combination of unpropitious events, as is the foundered Bark (if he may be allowed to assume so maritime a denomination), who now takes up the pen to address you – it is not, I repeat, for one so circumstanced, to adopt the language of compliment, or of congratulation. That, he leaves to abler and to purer hands.

If your more important avocations should admit of your ever tracing these imperfect characters thus far – which may be, or may not be, as circumstances arise – you will naturally enquire by what object am I influenced, then, in inditing the present missive? Allow me to say that I fully defer to the reasonable character of that enquiry, and proceed to develop it; premising that it is *not* an object of a pecuniary nature.

Without more directly referring to any latent ability that may possibly exist, on my part, of wielding the thunderbolt, or directing the devouring and avenging flame in any quarter, I may be permitted to observe, in passing, that my brightest visions are for ever dispelled – that my peace is shattered and my power of enjoyment destroyed – that my heart is no longer in the right place – and that I no more walk erect before my fellow-man. The canker is in the flower. The cup is bitter to the brim. The worm is at his

work, and will soon dispose of his victim. The sooner the better. But I will not digress.

Placed in a mental position of peculiar painfulness, beyond the assuaging reach even of Mrs Micawber's influence, though exercised in the tripartite character of woman, wife, and mother, it is my intention to fly from myself for a short period, and devote a respite of eight-and-forty hours to revisiting some metropolitan scenes of past enjoyment. Among other havens of domestic tranquillity and peace of mind, my feet will naturally tend towards the King's Bench Prison. In stating that I shall be (D. V.) on the outside of the south wall of that place of incarceration on civil process, the day after tomorrow, at seven in the evening, precisely, my object in this epistolary communication is accomplished.

I do not feel warranted in soliciting my former friend Mr Copperfield, or my former friend Mr Thomas Traddles of the Inner Temple, if that gentleman is still existent and forthcoming, to condescend to meet me, and renew (so far as may be) our past relations of the olden time. I confine myself to throwing out the observation that, at the hour and place I have indicated, may be found such ruined vestiges as yet

Remain,

Of

A

Fallen Tower,

WILKINS MICAWBER

P. S. It may be advisable to superadd to the above, the statement that Mrs Micawber is *not* in confidential possession of my intentions.'

I read the letter over several times. Making due allowance for Mr Micawber's lofty style of composition, and for the extraordinary relish with which he sat down and wrote long letters on all possible and impossible occasions, I still believed that something important lay hidden at the bottom of this roundabout communication. I put it down, to think about it; and took it up again, to read it once more; and was still pursuing it, when Traddles found me in the height of my perplexity.

'My dear fellow,' said I, 'I never was better pleased to see you. You come to give me the benefit of your sober judgement at a most opportune time. I have received a very singular letter, Traddles, from Mr Micawber.'

'No?' cried Traddles. 'You don't say so? And I have received one from Mrs Micawber!'

With that, Traddles, who was flushed with walking, and whose hair, under the combined effects of exercise and excitement, stood on end as if he saw a cheerful ghost, produced his letter and made an exchange with me. I watched him into the heart of Mr Micawber's letter, and returned the elevation of eyebrows with which he said ' "Wielding the thunderbolt, or directing the devouring and avenging flame!" Bless me, Copperfield!' – and then entered on the perusal of Mrs Micawber's epistle.

It ran thus:

My best regards to Mr Thomas Traddles, and if he should still remember one who formerly had the happiness of being well acquainted with him, may I beg a few moments of his leisure time? I assure Mr T. T. that I would not intrude upon his kindness, were I in any other position than on the confines of distraction.

Though harrowing to myself to mention, the alienation of Mr Micawber (formerly so domesticated) from his wife and family is the cause of my addressing my unhappy appeal to Mr Traddles, and soliciting his best indulgence. Mr T. can form no adequate idea of the change in Mr Micawber's conduct, of his wildness, of his violence. It has gradually augmented, until it assumes the appearance of aberration of intellect. Scarcely a day passes, I assure Mr Traddles, on which some paroxysm does not take place. Mr T. will not require me to depict my feelings, when I inform him that I have become accustomed to hear Mr Micawber assert that he has sold himself to the D. Mystery and secrecy have long been his principal characteristic, have long replaced unlimited confidence. The slightest provocation, even being asked if there is anything he would prefer for dinner, causes him to express a wish for a separation. Last night on being childishly solicited for twopence, to buy 'lemon-stunners' – a local sweetmeat – he presented an oyster-knife at the twins!

I entreat Mr Traddles to bear with me in entering into these details. Without them, Mr T. would indeed find it difficult to form the faintest conception of my heart-rending situation.

May I now venture to confide to Mr T. the purport of my letter? Will he now allow me to throw myself on his friendly consideration? Oh, yes, for I know his heart!

The quick eye of affection is not easily blinded, when of the female sex. Mr Micawber is going to London. Though he studiously concealed his hand, this morning before breakfast, in writing the direction-card which he attached to the little brown valise of happier days, the eagle-glance of matrimonial anxiety detected d, o, n, distinctly traced. The West-End destination of the coach is the Golden Cross. Dare I fervently implore Mr T. to see my misguided husband, and to reason with him? Dare I ask Mr T. to endeavour to step in between Mr Micawber and his agonised family? Oh, no, for that would be too much!

If Mr Copperfield should yet remember one unknown to fame, will Mr T. take charge of my unalterable regards and similar entreaties? In any case, he will have the benevolence *to consider this communication strictly private, and on no account whatever to be alluded to, however distantly, in the presence of Mr Micawber*. If Mr T. should ever reply to it (which I cannot but feel to be *most* improbable), a letter addressed to M. E., Post Office, Canterbury, will be fraught with less painful consequences than any addressed immediately to one, who subscribes herself, in extreme distress,

Mr Thomas Traddles's respectful friend and suppliant,

EMMA MICAWBER

'What do you think of that letter?' said Traddles, casting his eyes upon me, when I had read it twice.

'What do you think of the other?' said I. For he was still reading it with knitted brows.

'I think that the two together, Copperfield,' replied Traddles, 'mean more than Mr and Mrs Micawber usually mean in their correspondence – but I don't know what. They are both written in good faith, I have no doubt, and without any collusion. Poor thing!' he was now alluding to Mrs Micawber's letter, and we were standing side by side comparing the two; 'it will be a charity to write to her, at all events, and tell her that we will not fail to see Mr Micawber.'

I acceded to this, the more readily, because I now reproached myself with having treated her former letter rather lightly. It had set me thinking a good deal at the time, as I have mentioned in its place; but my absorption in my own affairs, my experience of the family, and my hearing nothing more, had gradually ended in my dismissing the subject. I had often thought of the Micawbers, but chiefly to wonder what 'pecuniary liabilities' they were establishing in Canterbury, and to recall how shy Mr Micawber was of me when he became clerk to Uriah Heep.

However, I now wrote a comforting letter to Mrs Micawber, in our joint names, and we both signed it. As we walked into town to post it, Traddles and I held a long conference, and launched into a number of speculations, which I need not repeat. We took my aunt into our counsels in the afternoon; but our only decided conclusion was that we would be very punctual in keeping Mr Micawber's appointment.

Although we appeared at the stipulated place a quarter of an hour before the time, we found Mr Micawber already there. He was standing with his arms folded, over against the wall, looking at the spikes on the top, with a sentimental expression, as if they were the interlacing boughs of trees that had shaded him in his youth.

When we accosted him, his manner was something more confused, and something less genteel than of yore. He had relinquished his legal suit of black for the purposes of this excursion, and wore the old surtout and tights, but not quite with the old air. He gradually picked up more and more of it as we conversed with him; but his very eyeglass seemed to hang less easily, and his shirt-collar, though still of the old formidable dimensions, rather drooped.

'Gentlemen!' said Mr Micawber, after the first salutations, 'you are friends in need, and friends indeed. Allow me to offer my enquiries with reference to the physical welfare of Mrs Copperfield *in esse*, and Mrs Traddles *in posse* – presuming, that is to say, that my friend Mr Traddles is not yet united to the object of his affections, for weal and for woe.'

We acknowledged his politeness, and made suitable replies. He then directed our attention to the wall, and was beginning 'I assure you, gentlemen,' when I ventured to object to that ceremonious form of address, and to beg that he would speak to us in the old way.

'My dear Copperfield,' he returned, pressing my hand, 'your cordiality overpowers me. This reception of a shattered fragment of the Temple once called Man – if I may be permitted so to express myself – bespeaks a heart that is an honour to our common nature. I was about to observe that I again behold the serene spot where some of the happiest hours of my existence fleeted by.'

'Made so, I am sure, by Mrs Micawber,' said I. 'I hope she is well?'

'Thank you,' returned Mr Micawber, whose face clouded at this reference, 'she is but so-so. And this,' said Mr Micawber, nodding his head sorrowfully, 'is the Bench! Where, for the first time in many revolving years, the overwhelming pressure of pecuniary liabilities was not proclaimed, from day to day, by importunate voices declining to vacate the passage; where there was no knocker on the door for any creditor to appeal to; where personal service of process was not required, and detainers were merely lodged at the gate! Gentlemen,' said Mr Micawber, 'when the shadow of that ironwork on the summit of the brick structure has been reflected on the gravel of the Parade, I have seen my children thread the mazes of the intricate pattern, avoiding the dark marks. I have been familiar with every stone in the place. If I betray weakness, you will know how to excuse me.'

'We have all got on in life since then, Mr Micawber,' said I.

'Mr Copperfield,' returned Mr Micawber bitterly, 'when I was an inmate of that retreat I could look my fellow-man in the face, and punch his head if he offended me. My fellow-man and myself are no longer on those glorious terms!'

Turning from the building in a downcast manner, Mr Micawber accepted my proffered arm on one side, and the proffered arm of Traddles on the other, and walked away between us.

'There are some landmarks,' observed Mr Micawber, looking fondly back over his shoulder, 'on the road to the tomb, which, but for the impiety of the aspiration, a man would wish never to have passed. Such is the Bench in my chequered career.'

'Oh, you are in low spirits, Mr Micawber,' said Traddles.

'I am, sir,' interposed Mr Micawber.

'I hope,' said Traddles, 'it is not because you have conceived a dislike to the law – for I am a lawyer myself, you know.'

Mr Micawber answered not a word.

'How is our friend Heep, Mr Micawber,' said I, after a silence.

'My dear Copperfield,' returned Mr Micawber, bursting into a state of much excitement, and turning pale, 'if you ask after my employer as *your* friend, I am sorry for it; if you ask after him as my friend, I sardonically smile at it. In whatever capacity you ask after my employer, I beg, without offence to you, to limit my reply to this – that whatever his state of health may be, his appearance is foxy, not to say diabolical. You will allow me, as a private individual, to decline pursuing a subject which has lashed me to the utmost verge of desperation in my professional capacity.'

I expressed my regret for having innocently touched upon a theme that roused him so much. 'May I ask,' said I, 'without any hazard of repeating the mistake, how my old friends Mr and Miss Wickfield are?'

'Miss Wickfield,' said Mr Micawber, now turning red, 'is, as she always is, a pattern, and a bright example. My dear Copperfield, she is the only starry spot in a miserable existence. My respect for that young lady, my admiration of her character, my devotion to her for her love, and truth, and goodness! – Take me,' said Mr Micawber, 'down a turning, for, upon my soul, in my present state of mind, I am not equal to this!'

We wheeled him off into a narrow street, where he took out his pocket-handkerchief, and stood with his back to a wall. If I looked as gravely at him as Traddles did, he must have found our company by no means inspiriting.

'It is my fate,' said Mr Micawber, unfeignedly sobbing, but doing even that with a shadow of the old expression of doing something genteel; 'it is my fate, gentlemen, that the finer feelings of our nature have become reproaches to me. My homage to Miss Wickfield is a flight of arrows in my bosom. You had better leave me, if you please, to walk the earth as a vagabond. The worm will settle *my* business in double-quick time.'

Without attending to this invocation, we stood by until he put up his pocket-handkerchief, pulled up his shirt-collar, and, to delude any person in the neighbourhood who might have been observing him, hummed a tune with his hat very much on one side. I then mentioned – not knowing what might be lost if we lost sight of him yet – that it would give me great pleasure to introduce him to my aunt, if he would ride out to Highgate, where a bed was at his service.

'You shall make us a glass of your own punch, Mr Micawber,' said I, 'and forget whatever you have on your mind, in pleasanter reminiscences.'

'Or, if confiding anything to friends will be more likely to relieve you, you shall impart it to us, Mr Micawber,' said Traddles prudently.

'Gentlemen,' returned Mr Micawber, 'do with me as you will! I am a straw upon the surface of the deep, and am tossed in all directions by the elephants – I beg your pardon; I should have said the elements.'

We walked on, arm in arm, again; found the coach in the act of starting; and arrived at Highgate without encountering any difficulties by the way. I was very uneasy and very uncertain in my mind what to say or do for the best – so was Traddles, evidently. Mr Micawber was for the most part plunged into deep gloom. He occasionally made an attempt to smarten himself, and hum the fag-end of a tune; but his relapses into profound melancholy were only made the more impressive by the mockery of a hat exceedingly on one side, and a shirt-collar pulled up to his eyes.

We went to my aunt's house rather than to mine, because of Dora's not being well. My aunt presented herself on being sent for, and welcomed Mr Micawber with gracious cordiality. Mr Micawber kissed her hand, retired to the window, and, pulling out his pocket-handkerchief, had a mental wrestle with himself.

Mr Dick was at home. He was by nature so exceedingly compassionate of anyone who seemed to be ill at ease, and was so quick to find any such person out, that he shook hands with

Mr Micawber at least half a dozen times in five minutes. To Mr Micawber, in his trouble, this warmth, on the part of a stranger, was so extremely touching that he could only say, on the occasion of each successive shake, 'My dear sir, you overpower me!' Which gratified Mr Dick so much that he went at it again with greater vigour than before.

'The friendliness of this gentleman,' said Mr Micawber to my aunt, 'if you will allow me, ma'am, to cull a figure of speech from the vocabulary of our coarser national sports – floors me. To a man, who is struggling with a complicated burden of perplexity and disquiet, such a reception is trying, I assure you.'

'My friend Mr Dick,' replied my aunt proudly, 'is not a common man.'

'That I am convinced of,' said Mr Micawber. 'My dear sir!' for Mr Dick was shaking hands with him again; 'I am deeply sensible of your cordiality!'

'How do you find yourself?' said Mr Dick, with an anxious look.

'Indifferent, my dear sir,' returned Mr Micawber, sighing.

'You must keep up your spirits,' said Mr Dick, 'and make yourself as comfortable as possible.'

Mr Micawber was quite overcome by these friendly words, and by finding Mr Dick's hand again within his own. 'It has been my lot,' he observed, 'to meet, in the diversified panorama of human existence, with an occasional oasis, but never with one so green, so gushing, as the present!'

At another time I should have been amused by this; but I felt that we were all constrained and uneasy, and I watched Mr Micawber so anxiously, in his vacillations between an evident disposition to reveal something and a counter-disposition to reveal nothing, that I was in a perfect fever. Traddles, sitting on the edge of his chair, with his eyes wide open, and his hair more emphatically erect than ever, stared by turns at the ground and at Mr Micawber, without so much as attempting to put in a word. My aunt, though I saw that her shrewdest observation was concentrated on her new guest, had more useful possession of her wits than either of us; for she held him in conversation, and made it necessary for him to talk, whether he liked it or not.

'You are a very old friend of my nephew's, Mr Micawber,' said my aunt. 'I wish I had had the pleasure of seeing you before.'

'Madam,' returned Mr Micawber, 'I wish I had had the honour of knowing you at an earlier period. I was not always the wreck you at present behold.'

'I hope Mrs Micawber and your family are well, sir,' said my aunt.

Mr Micawber inclined his head. 'They are as well, ma'am,' he desperately observed, after a pause, 'as Aliens and Outcasts can ever hope to be.'

'Lord bless you, sir!' exclaimed my aunt in her abrupt way. 'What are you talking about?'

'The subsistence of my family, ma'am,' returned Mr Micawber, 'trembles in the balance. My employer –'

Here Mr Micawber provokingly left off; and began to peel

the lemons that had been under my directions set before him, together with all the other appliances he used in making punch.

'Your employer, you know,' said Mr Dick, jogging his arm as a gentle reminder.

'My good sir,' returned Mr Micawber, 'you recall me. I am obliged to you.' They shook hands again. 'My employer, ma'am – Mr Heep – once did me the favour to observe to me that, if I were not in the receipt of the stipendiary emoluments appertaining to my engagement with him, I should probably be a mountebank about the country swallowing a sword-blade, and eating the devouring element. For anything that I can perceive to the contrary, it is still probable that my children may be reduced to seek a livelihood by personal contortion, while Mrs Micawber abets their unnatural feats, by playing the barrel-organ.'

Mr Micawber, with a random but expressive flourish of his knife, signified that these performances might be expected to take place after he was no more; then resumed his peeling with a desperate air.

My aunt leaned her elbow on the little round table that she usually kept beside her, and eyed him attentively. Notwithstanding the aversion with which I regarded the idea of entrapping him into any disclosure he was not prepared to make voluntarily, I should have taken him up at this point, but for the strange proceedings in which I saw him engaged; whereof his putting the lemon-peel into the kettle, the sugar into the snuffer-tray, the spirit into the empty jug, and confidently attempting to pour boiling water out of a candlestick, were among the most remarkable. I saw that a crisis was at hand, and it came. He clattered all his means and implements together, rose from his chair, pulled out his pocket-handkerchief, and burst into tears.

'My dear Copperfield,' said Mr Micawber, behind his handkerchief, 'this is an occupation, of all others, requiring an untroubled mind, and self-respect. I cannot perform it. It is out of the question.'

'Mr Micawber,' said I, 'what is the matter? Pray speak out. You are among friends.'

'Among friends, sir!' repeated Mr Micawber; and all he had reserved came breaking out of him. 'Good heavens, it is principally because I *am* among friends that my state of mind is what it is. What is the matter, gentlemen? What is *not* the matter? Villainy is the matter; baseness is the matter; deception, fraud, conspiracy, are the matter; and the name of the whole atrocious mass is – Heep!'

My aunt clapped her hands, and we all started up as if we were possessed.

'The struggle is over!' said Mr Micawber, violently gesticulating with his pocket-handkerchief, and fairly striking out from time to time with both arms, as if he were swimming under superhuman difficulties. 'I will lead this life no longer. I am a wretched being, cut off from everything that makes life tolerable. I have been under a Taboo in that infernal scoundrel's service. Give me back my wife, give me back my family, substitute Micawber for the petty wretch who walks about in the boots at present on my feet, and call upon me to swallow a sword tomorrow, and I'll do it. With an appetite!'

I never saw a man so hot in my life. I tried to calm him, that we might come to something rational; but he got hotter and hotter, and wouldn't hear a word.

'I'll put my hand in no man's hand,' said Mr Micawber, gasping, puffing, and sobbing, to that degree that he was like a man fighting with cold water, 'until I have – blown to fragments – the – a – detestable – serpent – Heep! I'll partake of no one's hospitality, until I have – a – moved Mount Vesuvius – to eruption – on – a – the abandoned rascal – Heep! Refreshment – a – underneath this roof – particularly punch – would – a – choke me – unless – I had – previously – choked the eyes – out of the head – a – of – interminable cheat, and liar – Heep! I – a – I'll know nobody – and – a – say nothing – and – a – live nowhere – until I have crushed – to – a – undiscoverable atoms – the – transcendent and immortal hypocrite and perjurer – Heep!'

I really had some fear of Mr Micawber's dying on the spot. The manner in which he struggled through these inarticulate sentences, and, whenever he found himself getting near the name of Heep, fought his way on to it, dashed at it in a fainting state, and brought it out with a vehemence little less than marvellous, was frightful; but now, when he sank into a chair, steaming, and looked at us, with every possible colour in his face that had no business there, and an endless procession of lumps following one another in hot haste up his throat, whence they seemed to shoot into his forehead, he had the appearance of being in the last extremity. I would have gone to his assistance, but he waved me off, and wouldn't hear a word.

'No, Copperfield! – No communication – a – until – Miss Wickfield – a – redress from wrongs inflicted by consummate scoundrel – Heep!' (I am quite convinced he could not have uttered three words, but for the amazing energy with which this word inspired him when he felt it coming.) 'Inviolable secret – a – from the whole world – a – no exceptions – this day week – a – at breakfast time – a – everybody present – including aunt – a – and extremely friendly gentleman – to be at the hotel at Canterbury – a – where – Mrs Micawber and myself – Auld Lang Syne in chorus – and – a – will expose intolerable ruffian – Heep! No more to say – a – or listen to persuasion – go immediately – not capable – a – bear society – upon the track of devoted and doomed traitor – Heep!'

With this last repetition of the magic word that had kept him going at all, and in which he surpassed all his previous efforts, Mr Micawber rushed out of the house; leaving us in a state of excitement, hope, and wonder, that reduced us to a condition little better than his own. But even there his passion for writing letters was too strong to be resisted; for while we were yet in the height of our excitement, hope, and wonder, the following pastoral note was brought to me from a neighbouring tavern, at which he had called to write it:

Most secret and confidential

MY DEAR SIR – I beg to be allowed to convey, through you, my apologies to your excellent aunt for my late excitement. An explosion of a smouldering volcano, long suppressed,

was the result of an internal contest more easily conceived than described.

I trust I rendered tolerably intelligible my appointment for the morning of this day week, at the house of public entertainment at Canterbury, where Mrs Micawber and myself had once the honour of uniting our voices to yours, in the well-known strain of the Immortal exciseman nurtured beyond the Tweed.

The duty done, an act of reparation performed, which can alone enable me to contemplate my fellow-mortal, I shall be known no more. I shall simply require to be deposited in that place of universal resort, where

> Each in his narrow cell for ever laid,
> The rude forefathers of the hamlet sleep,

– With the plain Inscription,

WILKINS MICAWBER

CHAPTER 50

Mr Peggotty's Dream Comes True

By this time, some months had passed since our interview on the bank of the river with Martha. I had never seen her since, but she had communicated with Mr Peggotty on several occasions. Nothing had come of her zealous intervention; nor could I infer, from what he told me, that any clue had ever been obtained, for a moment, to Emily's fate. I confess that I began to despair of her recovery, and gradually to sink deeper and deeper into the belief that she was dead.

His conviction remained unchanged. So far as I know – and I believe his honest heart was transparent to me – he never wavered again, in his solemn certainty of finding her. His patience never tired. And although I trembled for the agony it might one day be to him to have his strong assurance shivered at a blow, there was something so religious in it, so affectingly expressive of its anchor being in the purest depths of his fine nature, that the respect and honour in which I held him were exalted every day.

His was not a lazy trustfulness that hoped, and did no more. He had been a man of sturdy action all his life, and he knew that in all things wherein he wanted help he must do his own part faithfully, and help himself. I have known him set out in the night, on a misgiving that the light might not be, by some accident, in the window of the old boat, and walk to Yarmouth. I have known him, on reading something in the newspaper, that might apply to her, take up his stick, and go forth on a journey of three or four score miles. He made his way by sea to Naples, and back, after hearing the narrative to which Miss Dartle had assisted me. All his journeys were ruggedly performed; for he was always steadfast in a purpose of saving money for Emily's sake, when she should be found. In all this long pursuit, I never heard him repine; I never heard him say he was fatigued, or out of heart.

Dora had often seen him since our marriage, and was quite

fond of him. I fancy his figure before me now, standing near her sofa, with his rough cap in his hand, and the blue eyes of my child-wife raised, with a timid wonder, to his face. Sometimes of an evening, about twilight, when he came to talk with me, I would induce him to smoke his pipe in the garden, as we slowly paced to and fro together; and then the picture of his deserted home, and the comfortable air it used to have in my childish eyes of an evening when the fire was burning, and the wind moaning round it, came most vividly into my mind.

One evening, at this hour, he told me that he had found Martha waiting near his lodging on the preceding night when he came out, and that she had asked him not to leave London on any account until he should have seen her again.

'Did she tell you why?' I enquired.

'I asked her, Mas'r Davy,' he replied, 'but it is but few words as she ever says, and she on'y got my promise and so went away.'

'Did she say when you might expect to see her again?' I demanded.

'No, Mas'r Davy,' he returned, drawing his hand thoughtfully down his face. 'I asked that, too; but it was more (she said) than she could tell.'

As I had long forborne to encourage him with hopes that hung on threads, I made no other comment on this information than that I supposed he would see her soon. Such speculations as it engendered within me I kept to myself, and those were faint enough.

I was walking alone in the garden one evening, about a fortnight afterwards. I remember that evening well. It was the second in Mr Micawber's week of suspense. There had been rain all day, and there was a damp feeling in the air. The leaves were thick upon the trees, and heavy with wet; but the rain had ceased, though the sky was still dark; and the hopeful birds were singing cheerfully. As I walked to and fro in the garden, and the twilight began to close around me, their little voices were hushed; and that peculiar silence which belongs to such an evening in the country when the lightest trees are quite still, save for the occasional droppings from their boughs, prevailed.

There was a little green perspective of trellis-work and ivy at the side of our cottage, through which I could see, from the garden where I was walking, into the road before the house. I happened to turn my eyes towards this place, as I was thinking of many things, and I saw a figure beyond, dressed in a plain cloak. It was bending eagerly towards me, and beckoning.

'Martha!' said I, going to it.

'Can you come with me?' she enquired, in an agitated whisper. 'I have been to him, and he is not at home. I wrote down where he was to come, and left it on his table with my own hand. They said he would not be out long. I have tidings for him. Can you come directly?'

My answer was to pass out at the gate immediately. She made a hasty gesture with her hand, as if to entreat my patience and my silence, and turned towards London, whence, as her dress betokened, she had come expeditiously on foot.

I asked her if that were not our destination? On her motioning Yes, with the same hasty gesture as before, I stopped an empty coach that was coming by, and we got into it. When I asked her where the coachman was to drive, she answered 'Anywhere near Golden Square! And quick!' – then shrunk into a corner, with one trembling hand before her face, and the other making the former gesture, as if she could not bear a voice.

Now much disturbed, and dazzled with conflicting gleams of hope and dread, I looked at her for some explanation. But seeing how strongly she desired to remain quiet, and feeling that it was my own natural inclination, too, at such a time, I did not attempt to break the silence. We proceeded without a word being spoken. Sometimes she glanced out of the window, as though she thought we were going slowly, though, indeed, we were going fast; but otherwise remained exactly as at first.

We alighted at one of the entrances to the Square she had mentioned, where I directed the coach to wait, not knowing but that we might have some occasion for it. She laid her hand on my arm, and hurried me on to one of the sombre streets, of which there are several in that part, where the houses were once fair dwellings, in the occupation of single families, but have, and had, long degenerated into poor lodgings let off in rooms. Entering at the open door of one of these, and releasing my arm, she beckoned me to follow her up the common staircase, which was like a tributary channel to the street.

The house swarmed with inmates. As we went up, doors of rooms were opened and people's heads put out; and we passed other people on the stairs, who were coming down. In glancing up from the outside, before we entered, I had seen women and children lolling at the windows over flowerpots; and we seemed to have attracted their curiosity, for these were principally the observers who looked out of their doors. It was a broad panelled staircase, with massive balustrades of some dark wood; cornices above the doors, ornamented with carved fruit and flowers; and broad seats in the windows. But all these tokens of past grandeur were miserably decayed and dirty; rot, damp, and age had weakened the flooring, which in many places was unsound and even unsafe. Some attempts had been made, I noticed, to infuse new blood into this dwindling frame, by repairing the costly old woodwork here and there with common deal; but it was like the marriage of a reduced old noble to a plebeian pauper, and each party to the ill-assorted union shrunk away from the other. Several of the back windows on the staircase had been darkened, or wholly blocked up. In those that remained, there was scarcely any glass; and through the crumbling frames by which the bad air seemed always to come in, and never to go out, I saw, through other glassless windows, into other houses in a similar condition, and looked giddily down into a wretched yard, which was the common dust-heap of the mansion.

We proceeded to the top story of the house. Two or three times, by the way, I thought I observed in the indistinct light the skirts of a female figure going up before us. As we turned to ascend the last flight of stairs between us and the roof, we caught a full view of this figure pausing for a moment at a door. Then it turned the handle, and went in.

'What's this!' said Martha, in a whisper. 'She has gone into my room. I don't know her!'

I knew her. I had recognised her with amazement, for Miss Dartle. I said something to the effect that it was a lady whom I had seen before, in a few words, to my conductress; and had scarcely done so when we heard her voice in the room, though not, from where we stood, what she was saying. Martha, with an astonished look, repeated her former action, and softly led me up the stairs; and then, by a little back door which seemed to have no lock, and which she pushed open with a touch, into a small empty garret with a low sloping roof, little better than a cupboard. Between this and the room she had called hers there was a small door of communication, standing partly open. Here we stopped, breathless with our ascent, and she placed her hand lightly on my lips. I could only see, of the room beyond, that it was pretty large; that there was a bed in it; and that there were some common pictures of ships upon the walls. I could not see Miss Dartle, or the person whom we had heard her address. Certainly, my companion could not, for my position was the best.

A dead silence prevailed for some moments. Martha kept one hand on my lips, and raised the other in a listening attitude.

'It matters little to me her not being at home,' said Rosa Dartle haughtily, 'I know nothing of her. It is you I come to see.'

'Me?' replied a soft voice.

At the sound of it a thrill went through my frame. For it was Emily's!

'Yes,' returned Miss Dartle, 'I have come to look at you. What! You are not ashamed of the face that has done so much?'

The resolute and unrelenting hatred of her tone, its cold stern sharpness, and its mastered rage, presented her before me, as if I had seen her standing in the light. I saw the flashing black eyes, and the passion-wasted figure; and I saw the scar, with its white track cutting through her lips, quivering and throbbing as she spoke.

'I have come to see,' she said, 'James Steerforth's fancy; the girl who ran away with him, and is the town-talk of the commonest people of her native place; the bold, flaunting, practised companion of persons like James Steerforth. I want to know what such a thing is like.'

There was a rustle, as if the unhappy girl, on whom she heaped these taunts, ran towards the door, and the speaker swiftly interposed herself before it. It was succeeded by a moment's pause.

When Miss Dartle spoke again, it was through her set teeth, and with a stamp upon the ground.

'Stay there!' she said, 'or I'll proclaim you to the house, and the whole street! If you try to evade *me* I'll stop you, if it's by the hair, and raise the very stones against you!'

A frightened murmur was the only reply that reached my ears. A silence succeeded. I did not know what to do. Much as I desired to put an end to the interview, I felt that I had no right to present myself; that it was for Mr Peggotty alone to see her and recover her. Would he never come? I thought impatiently.

'So!' said Rosa Dartle, with a contemptuous laugh, 'I see her

at last! Why, he was a poor creature to be taken by that delicate mock-modesty, and that hanging head!'

'Oh, for Heaven's sake, spare me!' exclaimed Emily. 'Whoever you are, you know my pitiable story, and for Heaven's sake, spare me, if you would be spared yourself!'

'If *I* would be spared!' returned the other fiercely; 'what is there in common between *us*, do you think?'

'Nothing but our sex,' said Emily, with a burst of tears.

'And that,' said Rosa Dartle, 'is so strong a claim, preferred by one so infamous, that if I had any feeling in my breast but scorn and abhorrence of you, it would freeze it up. Our sex! You are an honour to our sex!'

'I have deserved this,' cried Emily, 'but it's dreadful! Dear, dear lady, think what I have suffered, and how I am fallen! Oh, Martha, come back! Oh, home, home.'

Miss Dartle placed herself in a chair, within view of the door, and looked downward, as if Emily were crouching on the floor before her. Being now between me and the light, I could see her curled lip, and her cruel eyes intently fixed on one place, with a greedy triumph.

'Listen to what I say!' she said; 'and reserve your false arts for your dupes. Do you hope to move *me* by your tears? No more than you could charm me by your smiles, you purchased slave.'

'Oh, have some mercy on me!' cried Emily. 'Show me some compassion, or I shall die mad!'

'It would be no great penance,' said Rosa Dartle, 'for your crimes. Do you know what you have done? Do you ever think of the home you have laid waste?'

'Oh, is there ever night or day, when I don't think of it!' cried Emily; and now I could just see her, on her knees, with her head thrown back, her pale face looking upward, her hands wildly clasped and held out, and her hair streaming about her. 'Has there ever been a single minute, waking or sleeping, when it hasn't been before me, just as it used to be in the lost days when I turned my back upon it for ever and for ever! Oh, home, home! Oh, dear, dear uncle, if you ever could have known the agony your love would cause me when I fell away from good, you never would have shown it to me so constant, much as you felt it; but would have been angry to me, at least once in my life, that I might have had some comfort! I have none, none, no comfort upon earth, for all of them were always fond of me!' She dropped on her face, before the imperious figure in the chair, with an imploring effort to clasp the skirt of her dress.

Rosa Dartle sat looking down upon her, as inflexible as a figure of brass. Her lips were tightly compressed, as if she knew that she must keep a strong constraint upon herself – I write what I sincerely believe – or she would be tempted to strike the beautiful form with her foot. I saw her, distinctly, and the whole power of her face and character seemed forced into that expression. Would he never come!

'The miserable vanity of these earthworms!' she said, when she had so far controlled the angry heavings of her breast that she could trust herself to speak. '*Your* home! Do you imagine that I bestow a thought on it, or suppose you could do any harm to that low place, which money would not pay for, and handsomely? *Your* home! You were a part of the trade of your home, and were bought and sold like any other vendible thing your people dealt in.'

'Oh, not that!' cried Emily. 'Say anything of me; but don't visit my disgrace and shame, more than I have done, on folks who are as honourable as you! Have some respect for them, as you are a lady, if you have no mercy for me.'

'I speak,' she said, not deigning to take any heed of this appeal, and drawing away her dress from the contamination of Emily's touch, 'I speak of *his* home – where I live. Here,' she said, stretching out her hand with her contemptuous laugh, and looking down upon the prostrate girl, 'is a worthy cause of division between lady-mother and gentleman-son; of grief in a house where she wouldn't have been admitted as a kitchen-girl; of anger, and repining, and reproach. This piece of pollution, picked up from the waterside, to be made much of for an hour, and then tossed back to her original place!'

'No! no!' cried Emily, clasping her hands together. 'When he first came into my way – that the day had never dawned upon me, and he had met me being carried to my grave! – I had been brought up as virtuous as you or any lady, and was going to be the wife of as good a man as you or any lady in the world can ever marry. If you live in his home and know him, you know, perhaps, what his power with a weak, vain girl might be. I don't defend myself, but I know well, and he knows well, or he will know when he comes to die, and his mind is troubled with it, that he used all his power to deceive me, and that I believed him, trusted him, and loved him!'

Rosa Dartle sprang up from her seat; recoiled; and in recoiling struck at her, with a face of such malignity, so darkened and disfigured by passion, that I had almost thrown myself between them. The blow, which had no aim, fell upon the air. As she now stood panting, looking at her with the utmost detestation that she was capable of expressing, and trembling from head to foot with rage and scorn, I thought I had never seen such a sight, and never could see such another.

'*You* love him? *You?*' she cried, with her clenched hand quivering as if it only wanted a weapon to stab the object of her wrath.

Emily had shrunk out of my view. There was no reply.

'And tell that to *me*,' she added, 'with your shameful lips? Why don't they whip these creatures! If I could order it to be done, I would have this girl whipped to death.'

And so she would, I have no doubt. I would not have trusted her with the rack itself, while that furious look lasted.

She slowly, very slowly, broke into a laugh, and pointed at Emily with her hand, as if she were a sight of shame for gods and men.

'*She* love!' she said. 'That carrion! And he ever cared for her, she'd tell me? Ha, ha! The liars that these traders are!'

Her mockery was worse than her undisguised rage. Of the two, I would have much preferred to be the object of the latter. But when she suffered it to break loose, it was only for a moment. She had chained it up again, and, however it might tear her within, she subdued it to herself.

'I came here, you pure fountain of love,' she said, 'to see – as

I began by telling you – what such a thing as you was like. I was curious. I am satisfied. Also to tell you that you had best seek that home of yours, with all speed, and hide your head among those excellent people who are expecting you, and whom your money will console. When it's all gone, you can believe, and trust, and love again, you know! I thought you a broken toy that had lasted its time; a worthless spangle that was tarnished, and thrown away. But finding you true gold, a very lady, and an ill-used innocent, with a fresh heart full of love and trustfulness – which you look like, and is quite consistent with your story! – I have something more to say. Attend to it; for what I say I'll do. Do you hear me, you fairy spirit? What I say, I mean to do!'

Her rage got the better of her again, for a moment; but it passed over her face like a spasm, and left her smiling.

'Hide yourself,' she pursued, 'if not at home, somewhere. Let it be somewhere beyond reach; in some obscure life – or, better still, in some obscure death. I wonder, if your loving heart will not break, you have found no way of helping it to be still! I have heard of such means sometimes. I believe they may be easily found.'

A low crying on the part of Emily interrupted her here. She stopped, and listened to it as if it were music.

'I am of a strange nature, perhaps,' Rosa Dartle went on; 'but I can't breathe freely in the air you breathe. I find it sickly. Therefore, I will have it cleared; I will have it purified of you. If you live here tomorrow, I'll have your story and your character proclaimed on the common stair. There are decent women in the house, I am told; and it is a pity such a light as you should be among them, and concealed. If, leaving here, you seek any refuge in this town in any character but your true one (which you are welcome to bear, without molestation from me), the same service shall be done you, if I hear of your retreat. Being assisted by a gentleman who not long ago aspired to the favour of your hand, I am sanguine as to that.'

Would he never, never come? How long was I to bear this? How long could I bear it?

'Oh me, oh me!' exclaimed the wretched Emily, in a tone that might have touched the hardest heart, I should have thought; but there was no relenting in Rosa Dartle's smile.

'What, what, shall I do!'

'Do?' returned the other. 'Live happy in your own reflections! Consecrate your existence to the recollection of James Steerforth's tenderness – he would have made you his serving-man's wife, would he not? – or to feeling grateful to the upright and deserving creature who would have taken you as his gift. Or, if those proud remembrances, and the consciousness of your own virtues, and the honourable position to which they have raised you in the eyes of everything that wears the human shape, will not sustain you, marry that good man, and be happy in his condescension. If this will not do either, die! There are door-ways and dust-heaps for such deaths, and such despair – find one, and take your flight to Heaven!'

I heard a distant foot upon the stairs. I knew it, I was certain. It was his, thank God!

She moved slowly from before the door when she said this,

and passed out of my sight.

'But, mark!' she added, slowly and sternly, opening the other door to go away, 'I am resolved, for reasons that I have and hatreds that I entertain, to cast you out, unless you withdraw from my reach altogether, or drop your pretty mask. This is what I had to say; and what I say, I mean to do!'

The foot upon the stairs came nearer – nearer – passed her as she went down – rushed into the room!

'Uncle!'

A fearful cry followed the word. I paused a moment, and, looking in, saw him supporting her insensible figure in his arms. He gazed for a few seconds in the face; then stooped to kiss it – oh, how tenderly! – and drew a handkerchief before it.

'Mas'r Davy,' he said, in a low tremulous voice, when it was covered, 'I thank my Heav'nly Father as my dream's come true! I thank Him hearty for having guided of me, in His own ways, to my darling!'

With those words he took her up in his arms; and with the veiled face lying on his bosom, and addressed towards his own, carried her, motionless and unconscious, down the stairs.

CHAPTER 51

The Beginning of a Longer Journey

It was yet early in the morning of the following day, when, as I was walking in my garden with my aunt (who took little other exercise now, being so much in attendance on my dear Dora), I was told that Mr Peggotty desired to speak with me. He came into the garden to meet me halfway, on my going towards the gate; and bared his head as it was always his custom to do when he saw my aunt, for whom he had a high respect. I had been telling her all that had happened overnight. Without saying a word, she walked up with a cordial face, shook hands with him, and patted him on the arm. It was so expressively done that she had no need to say a word. Mr Peggotty understood her quite as well as if she had said a thousand.

'I'll go in now, Trot,' said my aunt, 'and look after Little Blossom, who will be getting up presently.'

'Not along of my being heer, ma'am, I hope?' said Mr Peggotty. 'Unless my wits is gone a bahd's neezing' – by which Mr Peggotty meant to say, bird's nesting – 'this morning, 't is along of me as you're a going to quit us?'

'You have something to say, my good friend,' returned my aunt, 'and will do better without me.'

'By your leave, ma'am,' returned Mr Peggotty, 'I should take it kind, pervising you don't mind my clicketten, if you'd bide heer.'

'Would you?' said my aunt, with short good-nature. 'Then I am sure I will!'

So she drew her arm through Mr Peggotty's, and walked with him to a leafy little summer-house there was at the bottom of the garden, where she sat down on a bench, and I beside her. There was a seat for Mr Peggotty, too, but he preferred to stand, leaning his hand on the small rustic table. As he stood looking at his cap for a little while before beginning to speak, I could not help observing what power and force of character his sinewy hand expressed, and what a good and trusty companion it was to his honest brow and iron-grey hair.

'I took my dear child away last night,' Mr Peggotty began, as he raised his eyes to ours, 'to my lodging, wheer I have a long time been expecting of her and preparing fur her. It was hours afore she knowed me right; and when she did, she kneeled down at my feet, and kiender said to me, as if it was her prayers, how it all come to be. You may believe me, when I heerd her voice, as I had heerd at home so playful – and see her humbled, as it might be, in the dust our Saviour wrote in with his blessed hand – I felt a wownd go to my 'art in the midst of all its thankfulness.'

He drew his sleeve across his face, without any pretence of concealing why; and then cleared his voice.

'It warn't for long as I felt that; for she was found. I had on'y to think as she was found and it was gone. I doen't know why I do so much as mention of it now, I'm sure. I didn't have it in my mind a minute ago to say a word about myself; but it come up so nat'ral, that I yielded to it afore I was aweer.'

'You are a self-denying soul,' said my aunt, 'and will have your reward.'

Mr Peggotty, with the shadows of the leaves playing athwart his face, made a surprised inclination of the head towards my aunt, as an acknowledgment of her good opinion; then took up the thread he had relinquished.

'When my Em'ly took flight,' he said, in stern wrath for the moment, 'from the house wheer she was made a pris'ner by that theer spotted snake as Mas'r Davy see – and his story's trew, and may God confound him! – she took flight in the night. It was a dark night, with a many stars a shining. She was wild. She ran along the sea beach, believing the old boat was theer; and calling out to us to turn away our faces, for she was a coming by. She heerd herself a crying out, like as if it was another person; and cut herself on them sharp-pinted stones and rocks, and felt it no more than if she had been rock herself. Ever so fur she run, and there was fire afore her eyes and roarings in her ears. Of a sudden – or so she thowt, you unner-stand – the day broke, wet and windy, and she was lying b'low a heap of stone upon the shore, and a woman was a speaking to her, saying, in the language of that country, what was it as had gone so much amiss?'

He saw everything he related. It passed before him, as he spoke, so vividly, that, in the intensity of his earnestness, he presented what he described to me with greater distinctness than I can express. I can hardly believe, writing now, long after-wards, but that I was actually present in these scenes, they are impressed upon me with such an astonishing air of fidelity.

'As Em'ly's eyes – which was heavy – see this woman better,' Mr Peggotty went on, 'she knowed as she was one of them as she had often talked to on the beach. Fur, though she had run (as I have said) ever so fur in the night, she had oftentimes wandered long ways, partly afoot, partly in boats and carriages, and knowed all that country, 'long the coast, miles and miles. She hadn't no children of her own, this woman, being a young wife; but she was a looking to have one afore long. And may my prayers go up to Heaven that 't will be a happ'ness to her, and a comfort, and a honour, all her life! May it love her, and be dootiful to her, in her old age; helpful of her at the last; a Angel to her heer, and heerafter!'

'Amen!' said my aunt.

'She had been summat timorous and down,' said Mr Peggotty, 'and had sat, at first, a little way off, at her spinning, or such work as it was, when Em'ly talked to the children. But Em'ly had took notice of her, and had gone and spoke to her; and as the young woman was partial to the children herself, they had soon made friends. Sermuchser, that when Em'ly went that way, she always giv Em'ly flowers. This was her as now asked what it was that had gone so much amiss. Em'ly told her, and she – took her home. She did indeed. She took her home,' said Mr Peggotty, covering his face.

He was more affected by this act of kindness, than I had ever seen him affected by anything since the night she went away. My aunt and I did not attempt to disturb him.

'It was a little cottage, you may suppose,' he said, presently, 'but she found space for Em'ly in it – her husband was away at sea – and she kep' it secret, and prevailed upon such neighbours as she had (they was not many near) to keep it secret, too. Em'ly was took bad with fever, and what is very strange to me is – may be 't is not so strange to scholars – the language of that country went out of her head, and she could only speak her own, that no one unnerstood. She recollects, as if she had dreamed it, that she lay there, always a talking her own tongue, always believing as the old boat was round the next pint in the bay, and begging and imploring of 'em to send theer and tell how she was dying, and bring back a message of forgiveness if it was on'y a wured. A'most the whole time she thowt – now, that him as I made mention on just now was lurking for her unnerneath the winder, now that him as had brought her to this was in the room – and cried to the good young woman not to give her up, and knowed at the same time that she couldn't unnerstand, and dreaded that she must be took away. Likewise the fire was afore her eyes, and the roarings in her ears; and there was no today, nor yesterday, nor yet tomorrow; but everything in her life as ever had been, or as ever could be, and everything as never had been, and as never could be, was a crowding on her all at once, and nothing clear nor welcome, and yet she sang and laughed about it! How long this lasted, I doen't know; but then there come a sleep; and in that sleep, from being a many times stronger than her own self, she fell into the weakness of the littlest child.'

Here he stopped, as if for relief from the terrors of his own description. After being silent for a few moments, he pursued his story.

'It was a pleasant arternoon when she awoke; and so quiet, that there warn't a sound but the rippling of that blue sea without a tide, upon the shore. It was her belief, at first, that she was at home upon a Sunday morning; but, the vine leaves as she see at the winder, and the hills beyond, warn't home, and contradicted of her. Then come in her friend, to watch alongside of her bed; and then she knowed as the old boat warn't round that next pint in the bay no more, but was fur off; and knowed where she was, and why; and broke out a crying on that good young woman's bosom, wheer I hope her baby is a lying now, a cheering of her with its pretty eyes!'

Mr Peggotty's dream comes true

He could not speak of this good friend of Emily's without a flow of tears. It was in vain to try. He broke down again, endeavouring to bless her!

'That done my Em'ly good,' he resumed, after such emotion as I could not behold without sharing in; and as to my aunt, she wept with all her heart; 'that done Em'ly good, and she begun to mend. But the language of that country was quite gone from her, and she was forced to make signs. So she went on, getting better from day to day, slow, but sure, and trying to learn the names of common things – names as she seemed never to have heerd in all her life – till one evening come, when she was a setting at her window, looking at a little girl at play upon the beach. And of a sudden this child held out her hand, and said, what would be in English, "Fisherman's daughter, here's a shell!" – for you are to unnerstand that they used at first to call her "Pretty lady," as the general way in that country is, and that she had taught 'em to call her "Fisherman's daughter" instead. The child says of a sudden, "Fisherman's daughter, here's a shell!" Then Em'ly unnerstands her; and she answers, bursting out a crying; and it all comes back!

'When Em'ly got strong again,' said Mr Peggotty, after another short interval of silence, 'she cast about to leave that good young creetur, and get to her own country. The husband was come home, then; and the two together put her aboard a small trader bound to Leghorn, and from that to France. She had a little money, but it was less than little as they would take for all they done. I'm a'most glad on it, though they was so poor! What they done, is laid up wheer neither moth nor rust doth corrupt, and wheer thieves do not break through nor steal. Mas'r Davy, it'll outlast all the treasure in the wureld.

'Em'ly got to France, and took service to wait on travelling ladies at a inn in the port. Theer, theer come, one day, that snake. – Let him never come nigh me. I doen't know what hurt I might do him! – Soon as she see him, without him seeing her, all her fear and wildness returned upon her, and she fled afore the very breath he drawed. She come to England, and was set ashore at Dover.

'I doen't know,' said Mr Peggotty, 'for sure, when her 'art begun to fail her; but all the way to England she had thowt to come to her dear home. Soon as she got to England she turned her face tow'rds it. But fear of not being forgiv, fear of being pinted at, fear of some of us being dead along of her, fear of many things, turned her from it, kiender by force, upon the road: "Uncle, uncle," she says to me, "the fear of not being worthy to do, what my torn and bleeding breast so longed to do, was the most fright'ning fear of all! I turned back, when my 'art was full of prayers, that I might crawl to the old doorstep, in the night, kiss it, lay my wicked face upon it, and theer be found dead in the morning."

'She come,' said Mr Peggotty, dropping his voice to an awe-stricken whisper, 'to London. She – as had never seen it in her life – alone – without a penny – young – so pretty – come to London. A'most the moment as she lighted heer, all so desolate, she found (as she believed) a friend; a decent woman as spoke to her about the needlework as she had been brought up to do, about finding plenty of it fur her, about a lodging fur the night, and making secret enquiration concerning of me and all at home, tomorrow. When my child,' he said aloud, and with an energy of gratitude that shook him from head to foot, 'stood upon the brink of more than I can say or think on – Martha, trew to her promise, saved her!'

I could not repress a cry of joy.

'Mas'r Davy!' he said, gripping my hand in that strong hand of his, 'it was you as first made mention of her to me. I thankee, sir! She was arnest. She had knowed of her bitter knowledge wheer to watch and what to do. She had done it. And the Lord was above all! She come, white and hurried, upon Em'ly in her sleep. She says to her, "Rise up from worse than death, and come with me!" Them belonging to the house would have stopped her, but they might as soon have stopped the sea. "Stand away from me," she says, "I am a ghost that calls her from beside her open grave!" She told Em'ly she had seen me, and knowed I loved her, and forgiv her. She wrapped her, hasty, in her clothes. She took her, faint and trembling, on her arm. She heeded no more what they said than if she had had no ears. She walked among 'em with my child, minding only her; and brought her safe out, in the dead of the night, from that black pit of ruin!

'She attended on Em'ly,' said Mr Peggotty, who had released my hand, and put his own hand on his heaving chest; 'she attended to my Em'ly, lying wearied out, and wandering betwixt whiles, till late next day. Then she went in search of me; then in search of you, Mas'r Davy. She didn't tell Em'ly what she come out fur, lest her 'art should fail, and she should think of hiding of herself. How the cruel lady knowed of her being theer, I can't say. Whether him as I have spoke so much of chanced to see 'em going theer, or whether (which is most like, to my thinking) he had heerd it from the woman, I doen't greatly ask myself. My niece is found.'

'All night long,' said Mr Peggotty, 'we have been together, Em'ly and me. 'Tis little (considering the time) as she has said, in wureds, through them broken-hearted tears; 'tis less as I have seen of her dear face, as growed into a woman's at my hearth. But all night long, her arms has been about my neck; and her head was laid heer; and we knows full well as we can put our trust in one another ever more.'

He ceased to speak, and his hand upon the table rested there in perfect repose, with a resolution in it that might have conquered lions.

'It was a gleam of light upon me, Trot,' said my aunt, drying her eyes, 'when I formed the resolution of being godmother to your sister Betsey Trotwood, who disappointed me; but, next to that, hardly anything would have given me greater pleasure, than to be godmother to that good young creature's baby!'

Mr Peggotty nodded his understanding of my aunt's feelings, but could not trust himself with any verbal reference to the subject of her commendation. We all remained silent, and occupied with our own reflections (my aunt drying her eyes, and now sobbing convulsively, and now laughing and calling herself a fool), until I spoke.

'You have quite made up your mind,' said I to Mr Peggotty, 'as to the future, good friend? I need scarcely ask you.'

'Quite, Mas'r Davy,' he returned; 'and told Em'ly. Theer's mighty countries, fur from heer. Our future life lays over the sea.'

'They will emigrate together, aunt,' said I.

'Yes,' said Mr Peggotty, with a hopeful smile. 'No one can't reproach my darling in Australia. We will begin a new life over theer!'

I asked him if he yet proposed to himself any time for going away.

'I was down at the Docks early this morning, sir,' he returned, 'to get information concerning of them ships. In about six weeks or two months from now, there'll be one sailing – I see her this morning – went aboard – and we shall take our passage in her.'

'Quite alone?' I asked.

'Aye, Mas'r Davy!' he returned. 'My sister, you see, she's that fond of you and yourn, and that accustomed to think on'y of her own country, that it wouldn't be hardly fair to let her go. Besides which, theer's one she has in charge, Mas'r Davy, as doesn't ought to be forgot.'

'Poor Ham!' said I.

'My good sister takes care of his house, you see, ma'am, and he takes kiendly to her,' Mr Peggotty explained for my aunt's better information. 'He'll set and talk to her, with a calm spirit, wen it's like he couldn't bring himself to open his lips to another. Poor fellow!' said Mr Peggotty, shaking his head, 'theer's not so much left him that he could spare the little as he has!'

'And Mrs Gummidge?' said I.

'Well, I've had a mort of consideration, I do tell you,' returned Mr Peggotty, with a perplexed look which gradually cleared as he went on, 'concerning of Missis Gummidge. You see, wen Missis Gummidge falls a thinking of the old 'un, she ain't what you may call good company. Betwixt you and me, Mas'r Davy – and you, ma'am – wen Missis Gummidge takes to wimicking,' – our old county word for crying – 'she's liable to be considered to be, by them as didn't know the old 'un, peevish-like. Now I *did* know the old 'un,' said Mr Peggotty, 'and I knowed his merits, so I unnerstan' her; but 't ain't entirely so, you see, with others – nat'rally can't be!'

My aunt and I both acquiesced.

'Wheerby,' said Mr Peggotty, 'my sister might – I don't say she would, but might – find Missis Gummidge give her a leetle trouble now and again. Theerfur 't ain't my intentions to moor Missis Gummidge 'long with them, but to find a beein' fur her wheer she can fisherate fur herself.' (A beein' signifies, in that dialect, a home, and to fisherate is to provide.) 'Fur which purpose,' said Mr Peggotty, 'I means to make her a 'lowance afore I go, as'll leave her pretty comfort'ble. She's the faith-fullest of creeturs. 'T ain't to be expected, of course, at her time of life, and being lone and lorn, as the good old Mawther is to be knocked about aboardship, and in the woods and wilds of a new and fur-away country. So that's what I'm going to do with *her*.'

He forgot nobody. He thought of everybody's claims and strivings, but his own.

'Em'ly,' he continued, 'will keep along with me – poor child, she's sore in need of peace and rest! – until such time as we goes upon our voyage. She'll work at them clothes, as must be made; and I hope her troubles will begin to seem longer ago than they was, wen she finds herself once more by her rough but loving uncle.'

My aunt nodded confirmation of this hope, and imparted great satisfaction to Mr Peggotty.

'Theer's one thing furder, Mas'r Davy,' said he, putting his hand in his breast pocket, and gravely taking out the little paper bundle I had seen before, which he unrolled on the table. 'Theer's these heer bank-notes – fifty pound, and ten. To them I wish to add the money as she come away with. I've asked her about that (but not saying why), and have added of it up. I ain't a scholar. Would you be so kind as see how 't is?'

He handed me, apologetically for his scholarship, a piece of paper, and observed me while I looked it over. It was quite right.

'Thankee, sir,' he said, taking it back. 'This money, if you don't see objections, Mas'r Davy, I shall put up jest afore I go, in a cover d'rected to him; and put that up in another d'rected to his mother. I shall tell her, in no more wureds than I speak to you, what it's the price on; and that I'm gone, and past receiving of it back.'

I told him that I thought it would be right to do so – that I was thoroughly convinced it would be, since he felt it to be right.

'I said that theer was on'y one thing furder,' he proceeded with a grave smile, when he had made up his little bundle again, and put it in his pocket; 'but theer was two. I warn't sure in my mind, wen I come out this morning, as I could go and break to Ham, of my own self, what had so thankfully happened. So I writ a letter while I was out, and put it in the post-office, telling of 'em how all was as 't is; and that I should come down tomorrow to unload my mind of what little needs a doing of down theer, and, mostlike take my farewell leave of Yarmouth.'

'And do you wish me to go with you?' said I, seeing that he left something unsaid.

'If you could do me that kind favour, Mas'r Davy,' he replied, 'I know the sight on you would cheer 'em up a bit.'

My little Dora being in good spirits, and very desirous that I should go – as I found on talking it over with her – I readily pledged myself to accompany him in accordance with his wish. Next morning, consequently, we were on the Yarmouth coach, and again travelling over the old ground.

As we passed along the familiar street at night – Mr Peggotty, in despite of all my remonstrances, carrying my bag – I glanced into Omer and Joram's shop, and saw my old friend Mr Omer there, smoking his pipe. I felt reluctant to be present when Mr Peggotty first met his sister and Ham, and made Mr Omer my excuse for lingering behind.

'How is Mr Omer after this long time?' said I, going in.

He fanned away the smoke of his pipe, that he might get a better view of me, and soon recognised me with great delight.

'I should get up, sir, to acknowledge such an honour as this visit,' said he, 'only my limbs are rather out of sorts, and I am

449

wheeled about. With the exception of my limbs and my breath, hows'ever, I am as hearty as a man can be, I'm thankful to say.'

I congratulated him on his contented looks and his good spirits, and saw, now, that his easy-chair went on wheels.

'It's an ingenious thing, ain't it?' he enquired, following the direction of my glance, and polishing the elbow with his arm. 'It runs as light as a feather, and tracks as true as a mail-coach. Bless you, my little Minnie – my granddaughter you know, Minnie's child – puts her little strength against the back, gives it a shove, and away we go, as clever and merry as ever you see anything! And I tell you what – it's a most uncommon chair to smoke a pipe in.'

I never saw such a good old fellow to make the best of a thing, and find out the enjoyment of it, as Mr Omer. He was as radiant as if his chair, his asthma, and the failure of his limbs were the various branches of a great invention for enhancing the luxury of a pipe.

'I see more of the world, I can assure you,' said Mr Omer, 'in this chair, than ever I see out of it. You'd be surprised at the number of people that looks in of a day to have a chat. You really would! There's twice as much in the newspaper, since I've taken to this chair, as there used to be. As to general reading, dear me, what a lot of it I do get through! That's what I feel so strong, you know! If it had been my eyes, what should I have done? If it had been my ears, what should I have done? Being my limbs, what does it signify? Why, my limbs only made my breath shorter when I used 'em. And now, if I want to go out into the street or down to the sands, I've only got to call Dick, Joram's youngest 'prentice, and away I go in my own carriage, like the Lord Mayor of London.'

He half suffocated himself with laughing here.

'Lord bless you!' said Mr Omer, resuming his pipe, 'a man must take the fat with the lean; that's what he must make up his mind to in this life. Joram does a fine business. Excellent business!'

'I am very glad to hear it,' said I.

'I knew you would be,' said Mr Omer. 'And Joram and Minnie are like valentines. What more can a man expect? What's his limbs to *that*!'

His supreme contempt for his own limbs, as he sat smoking, was one of the pleasantest oddities I have ever encountered.

'And since I've took to general reading, you've took to general writing, eh, sir?' said Mr Omer, surveying me admiringly. 'What a lovely work that was of yours! What expressions in it! I read it every word – every word. And as to feeling sleepy! Not at all!'

I laughingly expressed my satisfaction, but I must confess that I thought this association of ideas significant.

'I give you my word and honour, sir,' said Mr Omer, 'that when I lay that book upon the table, and look at it outside, compact in three separate and indiwidual wollumes – one, two, three, I am as proud as Punch to think that I once had the honour of being connected with your family. And dear me, it's a long time ago, now, ain't it? Over at Blunderstone. With a pretty little party laid along with the other party. And you quite a small party then, yourself. Dear, dear!'

I changed the subject by referring to Emily. After assuring him that I did not forget how interested he had always been in her, and how kindly he had always treated her, I gave him a general account of her restoration to her uncle by the aid of Martha, which I knew would please the old man. He listened with the utmost attention, and said, feelingly, when I had done: 'I am rejoiced at it, sir! It's the best news I have heard for many a day. Dear, dear, dear! And what's going to be undertook for that unfortunate young woman, Martha, now?'

'You touch a point that my thoughts have been dwelling on since yesterday,' said I, 'but on which I can give you no information yet, Mr Omer. Mr Peggotty has not alluded to it, and I have a delicacy in doing so. I am sure he has not forgotten it. He forgets nothing that is disinterested and good.'

'Because you know,' said Mr Omer, taking himself up, where he had left off, 'whatever *is* done, I should wish to be a member of. Put me down for anything you may consider right, and let me know. I never could think the girl all bad, and I am glad to find she's not. So will my daughter Minnie be. Young women are contradictory creatures in some things – her mother was just the same as her – but their hearts are soft and kind. It's all show with Minnie, about Martha. Why she should consider it necessary to make any show, I don't undertake to tell you. But it's all show, bless you. She'd do her any kindness in private. So, put me down for whatever you may consider right, will you be so good? and drop me a line where to forward it. Dear me!' said Mr Omer, 'when a man is drawing on to a time of life where the two ends of life meet; when he finds himself, however hearty he is, being wheeled about for the second time in a speeches of go-cart, he should be over-rejoiced to do a kindness if he can. He wants plenty. And I don't speak of myself, particular,' said Mr Omer, 'because, sir, the way I look at it is, that we are all drawing on to the bottom of the hill, whatever age we are, on account of time never standing still for a single moment. So let us always do a kindness, and be over-rejoiced. To be sure!'

He knocked the ashes out of his pipe, and put it on a ledge in the back of his chair, expressly made for its reception.

'There's Em'ly's cousin, him that she was to have been married to,' said Mr Omer, rubbing his hands feebly, 'as fine a fellow as there is in Yarmouth! He'll come and talk or read to me, in the evening, for an hour together sometimes. That's a kindness, I should call it! All his life's a kindness.'

'I am going to see him now,' said I.

'Are you?' said Mr Omer. 'Tell him I was hearty, and sent my respects. Minnie and Joram's at a ball. They would be as proud to see you as I am, if they was at home. Minnie won't hardly go out at all, you see, "on account of father," as she says. So I swore tonight, that if she didn't go, I'd go to bed at six. In consequence of which,' Mr Omer shook himself and his chair with laughter at the success of his device, 'she and Joram's at a ball.'

I shook hands with him, and wished him good-night.

'Half a minute, sir,' said Mr Omer. 'If you was to go without seeing my little elephant, you'd lose the best of sights. You never see such a sight! Minnie!'

A musical little voice answered, from somewhere upstairs, 'I am coming, grandfather!' and a pretty little girl with long, flaxen, curling hair, soon came running into the shop.

'This is my little elephant, sir,' said Mr Omer, fondling the child. 'Siamese breed, sir. Now, little elephant!'

The little elephant set the door of the parlour open, enabling me to see that, in these latter days, it was converted into a bedroom for Mr Omer, who could not be easily conveyed upstairs; and then hid her pretty forehead, and tumbled her long hair against the back of Mr Omer's chair.

'The elephant butts, you know, sir,' said Mr Omer, winking, 'when he goes at a object. Once, elephant. Twice. Three times!'

At this signal, the little elephant, with a dexterity that was next to marvellous in so small an animal, whisked the chair round with Mr Omer in it, and rattled it off, pell-mell, into the parlour, without touching the doorpost, Mr Omer indescribably enjoying the performance, and looking back at me on the road as if it were the triumphant issue of his life's exertions.

After a stroll about the town, I went to Ham's house. Peggotty had now removed here for good; and had let her own house to the successor of Mr Barkis in the carrying business, who had paid her very well for the goodwill, cart, and horse. I believe the very same slow horse that Mr Barkis drove was still at work.

I found them in the neat kitchen, accompanied by Mrs Gummidge, who had been fetched from the old boat by Mr Peggotty himself. I doubt if she could have been induced to desert her post by anyone else. He had evidently told them all. Both Peggotty and Mrs Gummidge had their aprons to their eyes, and Ham had just stepped out 'to take a turn on the beach.' He presently came home, very glad to see me; and I hope they were all the better for my being there. We spoke, with some approach to cheerfulness, of Mr Peggotty's growing rich in a new country, and of the wonders he would describe in his letters. We said nothing of Emily by name, but distantly referred to her more than once. Ham was the serenest of the party.

But Peggotty told me, when she lighted me to a little chamber where the Crocodile Book was lying ready for me on the table, that he always was the same. She believed (she told me, crying) that he was broken-hearted though he was as full of courage as of sweetness, and worked harder and better than any boat-builder in any yard in all that part. There were times, she said, of an evening, when he talked of their old life in the boathouse; and then he mentioned Emily as a child. But he never mentioned her as a woman.

I thought I had read in his face that he would like to speak to me alone. I therefore resolved to put myself in his way next evening, as he came home from his work. Having settled this with myself, I fell asleep. That night, for the first time in all those many nights, the candle was taken out of the window, Mr Peggotty swung in his old hammock in the old boat, and the wind murmured with the old sound round his head.

All next day, he was occupied in disposing of his fishing-boat and tackle; in packing up, and sending to London by wagon, such of his little domestic possessions as he thought would be useful to him; and in parting with the rest, or bestowing them on Mrs Gummidge. She was with him all day. As I had a sorrowful wish to see the old place once more, before it was locked up, I engaged to meet them there in the evening. But I so arranged it as that I should meet Ham first.

It was easy to come in his way, as I knew where he worked. I met him at a retired part of the sands which I knew he would cross, and turned back with him, that he might have leisure to speak to me if he really wished. I had not mistaken the expression of his face. We had walked but a little way together, when he said, without looking at me: 'Mas'r Davy, have you seen her?'

'Only for a moment, when she was in a swoon,' I softly answered.

We walked a little farther, and he said: 'Mas'r Davy, shall you see her, d'ye think?'

'It would be too painful to her, perhaps,' said I.

'I have thowt of that,' he replied. 'So 't would, sir, so 't would.'

'But, Ham,' said I gently, 'if there is anything that I could write to her, for you, in case I could not tell it; if there is anything you would wish to make known to her through me; I should consider it a sacred trust.'

'I am sure on 't. I thankee, sir, most kind! I think theer is something I could wish said or wrote.'

'What is it?'

We walked a little farther in silence, and then he spoke.

''Tain't that I forgive her. 'Tain't that so much. 'Tis more as I beg of her to forgive me, for having pressed my affections upon her. Odd times, I think that if I hadn't had her promise fur to marry me, sir, she was that trustful of me, in a friendly way, that she'd have told me what was struggling in her mind, and would have counselled with me, and I might have saved her.'

I pressed his hand. 'Is that all?'

'Theer's yet a something else,' he returned, 'if I can say it, Mas'r Davy.'

We walked on, farther than we had walked yet, before he spoke again. He was not crying when he made the pauses I shall express by lines. He was merely collecting himself to speak very plainly.

'I loved her – and I love the mem'ry of her – too deep – to be able to lead her to believe of my own self as I'm a happy man. I could only be happy – by forgetting of her – and I'm afeerd I couldn't hardly bear as she should be told I done that. But if you, being so full of learning, Mas'r Davy, could think of anything to say as might bring her to believe I wasn't greatly hurt, still loving of her, and mourning for her – anything as might bring her to believe as I was not tired of my life, and yet was hoping fur to see her without blame, wheer the wicked cease from troubling and the weary are at rest – anything as would ease her sorrowful mind, and yet not make her think as I could ever marry, or as 't was possible that anyone could ever be to me what she was – I should ask of you to say that – with my prayers for her – that was so dear.'

I pressed his manly hand again, and told him I would charge myself to do this as well as I could.

'I thankee, sir,' he answered. ''Twas kind of you to meet me. 'Twas kind of you to bear him company down. Mas'r Davy, I unnerstan' very well, though my aunt will come to Lon'on afore they sail, and they'll unite once more, that I am not like to see him agen. I fare to feel sure on 't. We don't say so, but so 't will be, and better so. The last you see on him – the very last – will you give him the lovingest duty and thanks of the orphan, as he was ever more than a father to?'

This I also promised, faithfully.

'I thankee again, sir,' he said, heartily shaking hands. 'I know wheer you're a going. Goodbye!'

With a slight wave of his hand, as though to explain to me that he could not enter the old place, he turned away. As I looked after his figure, crossing the waste in the moonlight, I saw him turn his face towards a strip of silvery light upon the sea, and pass on, looking at it, until he was a shadow in the distance.

The door of the boat-house stood open when I approached; and, on entering, I found it emptied of all its furniture, saving one of the old lockers, on which Mrs Gummidge, with a basket on her knee, was seated, looking at Mr Peggotty. He leaned his elbow on the rough chimney-piece, and gazed upon a few expiring embers in the grate; but he raised his head, hopefully, on my coming in, and spoke in a cheery manner.

'Come, according to promise, to bid farewell to 't, eh, Mas'r Davy!' he said, taking up the candle. 'Bare enough, now, ain't it?'

'Indeed, you have made good use of the time,' said I.

'Why we have not been idle, sir. Missis Gummidge has worked like a – I don't know what Missis Gummidge ain't worked like,' said Mr Peggotty, looking at her, at a loss for a sufficiently approving simile.

Mrs Gummidge, leaning on her basket, made no observation.

'Theer's the very locker that you used to sit on, 'long with Em'ly!' said Mr Peggotty, in a whisper. 'I'm a going to carry it away with me, last of all. And heer's your old little bedroom, see, Mas'r Davy? A'most as bleak tonight as 'art could wish!'

In truth, the wind, though it was low, had a solemn sound, and crept around the deserted house with a whispered wailing that was very mournful. Everything was gone, down to the little mirror with the oyster-shell frame. I thought of myself lying here, when that first great change was being wrought at home. I thought of the blue-eyed child who had enchanted me; I thought of Steerforth; and a foolish, fearful fancy came upon me of his being near at hand, and liable to be met at any turn.

' 'Tis like to be long,' said Mr Peggotty, in a low voice, 'afore the boat finds new tenants. They look upon 't down heer as being unfort'nate now!'

'Does it belong to anybody in the neighbourhood?' I asked.

'To a mast-maker up town,' said Mr Peggotty. 'I'm a going to give the key to him tonight.'

We looked into the other little room, and came back to Mrs Gummidge, sitting on the locker, whom Mr Peggotty, putting the light on the chimney-piece, requested to rise, that he might carry it outside the door before extinguishing the candle.

'Dan'l,' said Mrs Gummidge, suddenly deserting her basket, and clinging to his arm, 'my dear Dan'l, the parting words I speak in this house is, I mustn't be left behind. Doen't ye think of leaving me behind, Dan'l! Oh, doen't ye ever do it!'

Mr Peggotty, taken aback, looked from Mrs Gummidge to me, and from me to Mrs Gummidge, as if he had been awakened from a sleep.

'Doen't ye, dearest Dan'l, doen't ye!' cried Mrs Gummidge fervently. 'Take me 'long with you, Dan'l, take me 'long with you and Em'ly! I'll be your servant, constant and trew. If there's slaves in them parts where you're a going, I'll be bound to you for one, and happy; but doen't ye leave me behind, Dan'l, that's a deary dear!'

'My good soul,' said Mr Peggotty, shaking his head, 'you doen't know what a long voyage and what a hard life 't is!'

'Yes I do, Dan'l; I can guess!' cried Mrs Gummidge. 'But my parting words under this roof is, I shall go into the house and die, if I am not took. I can dig, Dan'l. I can work. I can live hard. I can be loving and patient now – more than you think, Dan'l, if you'll on'y try me. I wouldn't touch the 'lowance, not if I was dying of want, Dan'l Peggotty; but I'll go with you and Em'ly, if you'll on'y let me, to the world's end! I know how 't is; I know you think that I am lone and lorn; but, deary love, 't ain't so no more! I ain't sat here, so long, a watching, and a thinking of your trials, without some good being done me. Mas'r Davy, speak to him for me; I knows his ways, and Em'ly's, and I knows their sorrows, and can be a comfort to 'em, some odd times, and labour for 'em allus! Dan'l, deary Dan'l, let me go 'long with you!'

And Mrs Gummidge took his hand, and kissed it with a homely pathos and affection, in a homely rapture of devotion and gratitude, that he well deserved.

We brought the locker out, extinguished the candle, fastened the door on the outside, and left the old boat close shut up, a dark speck in the cloudy night. Next day, when we were returning to London outside the coach, Mrs Gummidge and her basket were on the seat behind, and Mrs Gummidge was happy.

CHAPTER 52

I Assist at an Explosion

When the time Mr Micawber had appointed so mysteriously was within four-and-twenty hours of being come, my aunt and I consulted how we should proceed; for my aunt was very unwilling to leave Dora. Ah! how easily I carried Dora up and down stairs, now!

We were disposed, notwithstanding Mr Micawber's stipulation for my aunt's attendance, to arrange that she should stay at home, and be represented by Mr Dick and me. In short, we had resolved to take this course, when Dora again unsettled us by declaring that she never would forgive herself, and never would forgive her bad boy, if my aunt remained behind on any pretence.

'I won't speak to you,' said Dora, shaking her curls at my aunt. 'I'll be disagreeable! I'll make Jip bark at you all day. I shall be sure that you really are a cross old thing, if you don't go!'

'Tut, Blossom!' laughed my aunt. 'You know you can't do without me!'

'Yes, I can,' said Dora. 'You are no use to me at all. You never run up and down stairs for me, all day long. You never sit and tell me stories about Doady, when his shoes were worn out, and he was covered with dust – oh, what a poor little mite of a fellow! You never do anything at all to please me, do you, dear?' Dora made haste to kiss my aunt, and say, 'Yes, you do! I'm only joking!' – lest my aunt should think she really meant it.

'But, aunt,' said Dora coaxingly, 'now, listen. You must go. I shall tease you till you let me have my own way about it. I shall lead my naughty boy *such* a life, if he don't make you go. I shall make myself *so* disagreeable – and so will Jip! You'll wish you had gone like a good thing, for ever and ever so long, if you don't go. Besides,' said Dora, putting back her hair, and looking wonderingly at my aunt and me, 'why shouldn't you both go? I am not very ill, indeed. Am I?'

'Why, what a question!' cried my aunt.

'What a fancy!' said I.

'Yes! I know I am a silly little thing!' said Dora, slowly looking from one of us to the other, and then putting up her pretty lips to kiss us as she lay upon her couch. 'Well, then, you must both go, or I shall not believe you; and then I shall cry!'

I saw in my aunt's face that she began to give way now, and Dora brightened again, as she saw it, too.

'You'll come back with so much to tell me that it'll take at least a week to make me understand!' said Dora. 'Because I *know* I sha'n't understand, for a length of time, if there's any business in it. And there's sure to be some business in it! If there's anything to add up, besides, I don't know when I shall make it out; and my bad boy will look *so* miserable all the time. There! Now you'll go, won't you? You'll only be gone one night, and Jip will take care of me while you are gone. Doady will carry me upstairs before you go, and I won't come down again till you come back; and you shall take Agnes a dreadfully scolding letter from me because she has never been to see us!'

We agreed, without any more consultation, that we would both go, and that Dora was a little Impostor, who feigned to be rather unwell because she liked to be petted. She was greatly pleased, and very merry; and we four, that is to say, my aunt, Mr Dick, Traddles, and I, went down to Canterbury by the Dover mail that night.

At the hotel, where Mr Micawber had requested us to await him, which we got into, with some trouble, in the middle of the night, I found a letter, importing that he would appear in the morning punctually at half-past nine. After which, we went shivering, at that uncomfortable hour, to our respective beds, through various close passages; which smelt as if they had been steeped, for ages, in a solution of soup and stables.

Early in the morning, I sauntered through the dear old tranquil streets, and again mingled with the shadows of the venerable gateways and churches. The rooks were sailing about the Cathedral towers; and the towers themselves, overlooking many a long, unaltered mile of the rich country and its pleasant streams, were cutting the bright morning air, as if there were no such thing as change on earth. Yet the bells when they sounded told me sorrowfully of change in everything; told me of their own age, and my pretty Dora's youth; and of the many, never old, who had lived and loved and died, while the reverberations of the bells had hummed through the rusty armour of the Black Prince hanging up within, and, motes upon the deep of Time, had lost themselves in air, as circles do in water.

I looked at the old house from the corner of the street, but did not go nearer to it, lest, being observed, I might unwittingly do any harm to the design I had come to aid. The early sun was striking edgewise on its gables and lattice-windows, touching them with gold; and some beams of its old peace seemed to touch my heart.

I strolled into the country for an hour or so, and then returned by the main street, which in the interval had shaken off its last night's sleep. Among those who were stirring in the shops, I saw my ancient enemy, the butcher, now advanced to top-boots and a baby, and in business for himself. He was nursing the baby, and appeared to be a benignant member of society.

We all became very anxious and impatient, when we sat down to breakfast. As it approached nearer and nearer to half-past nine o'clock, our restless expectation of Mr Micawber increased. At last we made no more pretence of attending to the meal, which, except with Mr Dick, had been a mere form from the first; but my aunt walked up and down the room, Traddles sat upon the sofa affecting to read the paper, with his eyes on the ceiling; and I looked out of the window to give early notice of Mr Micawber's coming. Nor had I long to watch, for, at the first chime of the half hour, he appeared in the street.

'Here he is,' said I, 'and not in his legal attire!'

My aunt tied the strings of her bonnet (she had come down to breakfast in it), and put on her shawl, as if she were ready for anything that was resolute and uncompromising. Traddles buttoned his coat with a determined air. Mr Dick, disturbed by these formidable appearances, but feeling it necessary to imitate them, pulled his hat, with both hands, as firmly over his ears as he possibly could; and instantly took it off again, to welcome Mr Micawber.

'Gentlemen, and madam,' said Mr Micawber, 'good-morning! My dear sir,' to Mr Dick, who shook hands with him violently, 'you are extremely good.'

'Have you breakfasted?' said Mr Dick. 'Have a chop!'

'Not for the world, my good sir!' cried Mr Micawber, stopping him on his way to the bell; 'appetite and myself, Mr Dickson, have long been strangers.'

Mr Dickson was so well pleased with his new name, and appeared to think it so very obliging in Mr Micawber to confer it upon him, that he shook hands with him again, and laughed rather childishly.

'Dick,' said my aunt, 'attention!'

Mr Dick recovered himself, with a blush.

'Now, sir,' said my aunt to Mr Micawber, as she put on her gloves, 'we are ready for Mount Vesuvius, or anything else, as soon as *you* please.'

'Madam,' returned Mr Micawber, 'I trust you will shortly witness an eruption. Mr Traddles, I have your permission, I

David Copperfield

believe, to mention here that we have been in communication together?'

'It is undoubtedly the fact, Copperfield,' said Traddles, to whom I looked in surprise. 'Mr Micawber has consulted me, in reference to what he has in contemplation; and I have advised him to the best of my judgement.'

'Unless I deceive myself, Mr Traddles,' pursued Mr Micawber, 'what I contemplate is a disclosure of an important nature.'

'Highly so,' said Traddles.

'Perhaps, under such circumstances, madam and gentlemen,' said Mr Micawber, 'you will do me the favour to submit yourselves, for the moment, to the direction of one, who, however unworthy to be regarded in any other light but as a Waif and Stray upon the shore of human nature, is still your fellow-man, though crushed out of his original form by individual errors, and the accumulative force of a combination of circumstances?'

'We have perfect confidence in you, Mr Micawber,' said I, 'and will do what you please.'

'Mr Copperfield,' returned Mr Micawber, 'your confidence is not, at the existing juncture, ill-bestowed. I would beg to be allowed a start of five minutes by the clock; and then to receive the present company, enquiring for Miss Wickfield, at the office of Wickfield and Heep, whose Stipendiary I am.'

My aunt and I looked at Traddles, who nodded his approval.

'I have no more,' observed Mr Micawber, 'to say at present.'

With which, to my infinite surprise, he included us all in a comprehensive bow, and disappeared; his manner being extremely distant, and his face extremely pale.

Traddles only smiled, and shook his head (with his hair standing upright on the top of it), when I looked to him for an explanation; so I took out my watch, and, as a last resource, counted off the five minutes. My aunt with her own watch in her hand did the like. When the time was expired, Traddles gave her his arm; and we all went out together to the old house, without saying one word on the way. We found Mr Micawber at his desk, in the turret office on the ground-floor, either writing, or pretending to write, hard. The large office-ruler was stuck into his waistcoat, and was not so well concealed but that a foot or more of that instrument protruded from his bosom, like a new kind of shirt-frill.

As it appeared to me that I was expected to speak, I said aloud: 'How do you do, Mr Micawber?'

'Mr Copperfield,' said Mr Micawber gravely, 'I hope I see you well?'

'Is Miss Wickfield at home?' said I.

'Mr Wickfield is unwell in bed, sir, of a rheumatic fever,' he returned; 'but Miss Wickfield, I have no doubt, will be happy to see old friends. Will you walk in, sir?'

He preceded us to the dining-room – the first room I had entered in that house – and flinging open the door of Mr Wickfield's former office, said, in a sonorous voice: 'Miss Trotwood, Mr David Copperfield, Mr Thomas Traddles, and Mr Dixon!'

I had not seen Uriah Heep since the time of the blow. Our visit astonished him, evidently; not the less, I dare say, because it astonished ourselves. He did not gather his eyebrows together, for he had none worth mentioning; but he frowned to that degree that he almost closed his small eyes, while the hurried raising of his gristly hand to his chin betrayed some trepidation or surprise. This was only when we were in the act of entering his room, and when I caught a glance at him over my aunt's shoulder. A moment afterwards, he was as fawning and as humble as ever.

'Well, I am sure,' he said. 'This is indeed an unexpected pleasure! To have, as I may say, all friends round St Paul's, at once, is a treat unlooked for! Mr Copperfield, I hope I see you well, and – if I may 'umbly express self so – friendly towards them as is ever your friends, whether or not. Mrs Copperfield, sir, I hope she's getting on. We have been made quite uneasy by the poor accounts we have had of her state, lately, I do assure you.'

I felt ashamed to let him take my hand, but I did not know yet what else to do.

'Things are changed in this office, Miss Trotwood, since I was an 'umble clerk, and held your pony, ain't they?' said Uriah, with his sickliest smile. 'But I am not changed, Miss Trotwood.'

'Well, sir,' returned my aunt, 'to tell you the truth, I think you are pretty constant to the promise of your youth, if that's any satisfaction to you.'

'Thank you, Miss Trotwood,' said Uriah, writhing in his ungainly manner, 'for your good opinion! Micawber, tell 'em to let Miss Agnes know – and mother. Mother will be quite in a state, when she sees the present company!' said Uriah, setting chairs.

'You are not busy, Mr Heep?' said Traddles, whose eye the cunning red eye accidentally caught, as it at once scrutinised and evaded us.

'No, Mr Traddles,' replied Uriah, resuming his official seat, and squeezing his bony hands, laid palm to palm between his bony knees. 'Not so much as I could wish. But lawyers, sharks, and leeches are not easily satisfied, you know! Not but what myself and Micawber have our hands pretty full in general, on account of Mr Wickfield's being hardly fit for any occupation, sir. But it's a pleasure as well as a duty, I am sure, to work for *him*. You've not been intimate with Mr Wickfield, I think, Mr Traddles? I believe I've only had the honour of seeing you once myself?'

'No, I have not been intimate with Mr Wickfield,' returned Traddles, 'or I might perhaps have waited on you long ago, Mr Heep.'

There was something in the tone of this reply which made Uriah look at the speaker again, with a very sinister and suspicious expression. But, seeing only Traddles, with his good-natured face, simple manner, and hair on end, he dismissed it as he replied, with a jerk of his whole body, but especially his throat: 'I am sorry for that, Mr Traddles. You would have admired him as much as we all do. His little failings would only have endeared him to you the more. But if you would like to hear my fellow-partner eloquently spoken of, I should refer you to Copperfield. The family is a subject he's very strong upon, if you never heard him.'

I was prevented from disclaiming the compliment (if I should have done so, in any case) by the entrance of Agnes, now ushered in by Mr Micawber. She was not quite so self-possessed as usual, I thought, and had evidently undergone anxiety and fatigue. But her earnest cordiality, and her quiet beauty, shone with the gentler lustre for it.

I saw Uriah watch her while she greeted us; and he reminded me of an ugly and rebellious genie watching a good spirit. In the meanwhile, some slight sign passed between Mr Micawber and Traddles; and Traddles, unobserved except by me, went out.

'Don't wait, Micawber,' said Uriah.

Mr Micawber, with his hand upon the ruler in his breast, stood erect before the door, most unmistakably contemplating one of his fellow-men, and that man his employer.

'What are you waiting for?' said Uriah. 'Micawber! did you hear me tell you not to wait?'

'Yes!' replied the immovable Mr Micawber.

'Then why *do* you wait?' said Uriah.

'Because I – in short choose,' replied Mr Micawber, with a burst.

Uriah's cheeks lost colour, and an unwholesome paleness, still faintly tinged by his pervading red, overspread them. He looked at Mr Micawber attentively, with his whole face breathing short and quick in every feature.

'You are a dissipated fellow, as all the world knows,' he said, with an effort at a smile, 'and I am afraid you'll oblige me to get rid of you. Go along! I'll talk to you presently.'

'If there is a scoundrel on this earth,' said Mr Micawber, suddenly breaking out again with the utmost vehemence, 'with whom I have already talked too much, that scoundrel's name is – Heep!'

Uriah fell back, as if he had been struck or stung. Looking slowly round upon us with the darkest and wickedest expression that his face could wear, he said, in a lower voice: 'Oho! This is a conspiracy! You have met here, by appointment! You are playing Booty with my clerk, are you, Copperfield? Now, take care. You'll make nothing of this. We understand each other, you and me. There's no love between us. You were always a puppy with a proud stomach, from your first coming here; and you envy me my rise, do you? None of your plots against me; I'll counterplot you! Micawber, you be off. I'll talk to you presently.'

'Mr Micawber,' said I, 'there is a sudden change in this fellow, in more respects than the extraordinary one of his speaking the truth in one particular, which assures me that he is brought to bay. Deal with him as he deserves!'

'You are a precious set of people, ain't you?' said Uriah, in the same low voice, and breaking out into a clammy heat, which he wiped from his forehead with his long lean hand, 'to buy over my clerk, who is the very scum of society – as you yourself were, Copperfield, you know it, before anyone had charity on you – to defame me with his lies? Miss Trotwood, you had better stop this; or I'll stop your husband shorter than will be pleasant to you. I won't know your story professionally, for nothing, old lady! Miss Wickfield, if you have any love for your father, you had better not join that gang. I'll ruin him, if you do. Now, come! I have got some of you under the harrow. Think twice, before it goes over you. Think twice, you, Micawber, if you don't want to be crushed. I recommend you to take yourself off, and be talked to presently, you fool! while there's time to retreat. Where's mother!' he said, suddenly appearing to notice, with alarm, the absence of Traddles, and pulling down the bell-rope. 'Fine doings in a person's own house!'

'Mrs Heep is here, sir,' said Traddles, returning with that worthy mother of a worthy son. 'I have taken the liberty of making myself known to her.'

'Who are you to make yourself known?' retorted Uriah. 'And what do you want here?'

'I am the agent and friend of Mr Wickfield, sir,' said Traddles, in a composed, businesslike way. 'And I have a power of attorney from him in my pocket, to act for him in all matters.'

'The old ass has drunk himself into a state of dotage,' said Uriah, turning uglier than before, 'and it has been got from him by fraud!'

'Something has been got from him by fraud, I know,' returned Traddles quietly; 'and so do you, Mr Heep. We will refer that question, if you please, to Mr Micawber.'

'Ury –!' Mrs Heep began, with an anxious gesture.

'You hold your tongue, mother,' he returned; 'least said, soonest mended.'

'But, my Ury –'

'Will you hold your tongue, mother, and leave it to me?'

Though I had long known that his servility was false, and all his pretences knavish and hollow, I had had no adequate conception of the extent of his hypocrisy until I now saw him with his mask off. The suddenness with which he dropped it, when he perceived that it was useless to him; the malice, insolence, and hatred he revealed; the leer with which he exulted, even at this moment, in the evil he had done – all this time being desperate, too, and at his wits' end for the means of getting the better of us – though perfectly consistent with the experience I had of him, at first took even me by surprise, who had known him so long, and disliked him so heartily.

I say nothing of the look he conferred on me, as he stood eyeing us, one after another; for I had always understood that he hated me, and I remembered the marks of my hand upon his cheek. But when his eyes passed on to Agnes, and I saw the rage with which he felt his power over her slipping away, and the exhibition, in their disappointment, of the odious passions that had led him to aspire to one whose virtues he could never appreciate or care for, I was shocked by the mere thought of her having lived, an hour, within sight of such a man.

After some rubbing of the lower part of his face, and some looking at us with those bad eyes, over his gristly fingers, he made one more address to me, half whining, and half abusive.

'You think it justifiable, do you, Copperfield, you who pride yourself so much on your honour and all the rest of it, to sneak about my place, eavesdropping with my clerk? If it had been *me*, I shouldn't have wondered; for I don't make myself out a gentleman (though I never was in the streets either, as you were, according to Micawber), but being *you*! – And you're not afraid of doing this, either? You don't think at all of what I shall do, in return; or of getting yourself into trouble for conspiracy and so forth? Very well. We shall see! Mr What's-your-name, you were going to refer some question to Micawber. There's your referee. Why don't you make him speak? He has learnt his lesson, I see.'

Seeing that what he said had no effect on me or any of us, he sat on the edge of his table with his hands in his pockets, and one of his splay feet twisted round the other leg, waiting doggedly for what might follow.

Mr Micawber, whose impetuosity I had restrained thus far with the greatest difficulty, and who had repeatedly interposed with the first syllable of Scoun-drel! without getting to the second, now burst forward, drew the ruler from his breast (apparently as a defensive weapon), and produced from his pocket a foolscap document, folded in the form of a large letter. Opening this packet, with his old flourish, and glancing at the contents, as if he cherished an artistic admiration of their style of composition, he began to read as follows: ' "Dear Miss Trot-wood and gentlemen – " '

'Bless and save the man!' exclaimed my aunt, in a low voice. 'He'd write letters by the ream, if it was a capital offence!'

Mr Micawber, without hearing her, went on.

' "In appearing before you to denounce probably the most consummate Villain that has ever existed," ' Mr Micawber, without looking off the letter, pointed the ruler, like a ghostly truncheon, at Uriah Heep, ' "I ask no consideration for myself. The victim, from my cradle, of pecuniary liabilities to which I have been unable to respond, I have ever been the sport and toy of debasing circumstances. Ignominy, Want, Despair, and Madness, have, collectively or separately, been the attendants of my career." '

The relish with which Mr Micawber described himself, as a prey to these dismal calamities, was only to be equalled by the emphasis with which he read his letter; and the kind of homage he rendered to it with a roll of his head, when he thought he had hit a sentence very hard indeed.

' "In an accumulation of Ignominy, Want, Despair, and Madness, I entered the office – or, as our lively neighbour the Gaul would term it, the Bureau – of the Firm, nominally conducted under the appellation of Wickfield and – Heep, but, in reality, wielded by – Heep, alone. Heep, and only Heep, is the main-spring of that machine. Heep, and only Heep, is the Forger and the Cheat." '

Uriah, more blue than white at these words, made a dart at the letter, as if to tear it in pieces. Mr Micawber, with a perfect miracle of dexterity or luck, caught his advancing knuckles with the ruler, and disabled his right hand. It dropped at the wrist, as if it were broken. The blow sounded as if it had fallen on wood.

'The Devil take you!' said Uriah, writhing in a new way with pain. 'I'll be even with you.'

'Approach me again you – you – you Heep of infamy,' gasped Mr Micawber, 'and if your head is human, I'll break it. Come on, come on!'

I think I never saw anything more ridiculous – I was sensible of it, even at the time – than Mr Micawber making broadsword guards with the ruler, and crying, 'Come on!' while Traddles

and I pushed him back into a corner, from which, as often as we got him into it, he persisted in emerging again.

His enemy, muttering to himself, after wringing his wounded hand for some time, slowly drew off his neckerchief and bound it up; then, held it in his other hand, and sat upon his table with his sullen face looking down.

Mr Micawber, when he was sufficiently cool, proceeded with his letter.

' "The stipendiary emoluments in consideration of which I entered into the service of – Heep," ' always pausing before that word, and uttering it with astonishing vigour, ' "were not defined beyond the pittance of twenty-two shillings and six per week. The rest was left contingent on the value of my professional exertions; in other and more expressive words, on the baseness of my nature, the cupidity of my motives, the poverty of my family, the general moral (or rather immoral) resemblance between myself and – Heep. Need I say that it soon became necessary for me to solicit from – Heep – pecuniary advances towards the support of Mrs Micawber, and our blighted but rising family! Need I say that this necessity had been foreseen by – Heep? That those advances were secured by I. O. U.s and other similar acknowledgments, known to the legal institutions of this country. And that I thus became immeshed in the web he had spun for my reception?" '

Mr Micawber's enjoyment of his epistolary powers, in describing this unfortunate state of things, really seemed to outweigh any pain or anxiety that the reality could have caused him. He read on: ' "Then it was that – Heep – began to favour me with just so much of his confidence as was necessary to the discharge of his infernal business. Then it was that I began, if I may so Shakespearianly express myself, to dwindle, peak, and pine. I found that my services were constantly called into requisition for the falsification of business and the mystification of an individual whom I will designate as Mr W. That Mr W. was imposed upon, kept in ignorance, and deluded, in every possible way; yet, that all this while, the ruffian – Heep – was professing unbounded gratitude to, and unbounded friendship for, that much abused gentleman. This was bad enough; but, as the philosophic Dane observes, with that universal applicability which distinguishes the illustrious ornament of the Elizabethan Era, worse remains behind!" '

Mr Micawber was so very much struck by this happy rounding off with a quotation, that he indulged himself, and us, with a second reading of the sentence, under pretence of having lost his place.

' "It is not my intention," he continued, reading on, ' "to enter on a detailed list, within the compass of the present epistle (though it is ready elsewhere), of the various mal-practices of a minor nature, affecting the individual whom I have denominated Mr W., to which I have been a tacitly consenting party. My object, when the contest within myself between stipend and no stipend, baker and no baker, existence and non-existence, ceased, was to take advantage of my opportunities to discover and expose the major malpractices committed, to that gentleman's grievous wrong and injury, by – Heep. Stimulated by the silent monitor within, and by a no less touching and appealing monitor without – to whom I will briefly refer as Miss W. – I entered on a not unlaborious task of clandestine investigation, protracted now, to the best of my knowledge, information, and belief, over a period exceeding twelve calendar months." '

He read this passage as if it were from an Act of Parliament, and appeared majestically refreshed by the sound of the words.

' "My charges against – Heep," he read on, glancing at him, and drawing the ruler into a convenient position under his left arm, in case of need, ' "are as follows:" '

We all held our breath, I think. I am sure Uriah held his.

' "First," ' said Mr Micawber. ' "When Mr W.'s faculties and memory for business became, through causes into which it is not necessary or expedient for me to enter, weakened and confused – Heep – designedly perplexed and complicated the whole of the official transactions. When Mr W. was least fit to enter on business – Heep was always at hand to force him to enter on it. He obtained Mr W.'s signature under such circumstances to documents of importance, representing them to be other documents of no importance. He induced Mr W. to empower him to draw out, thus, one particular sum of trust-money, amounting to twelve six fourteen, two and nine, and employed it to meet pretended business charges and deficiencies which were either already provided for, or had never really existed. He gave this proceeding, throughout, the appearance of having originated in Mr W.'s own dishonest intention, and of having been accomplished by Mr W.'s own dishonest act; and has used it, ever since, to torture and constrain him." '

'You shall prove this, you Copperfield!' said Uriah, with a threatening shake of the head. 'All in good time!'

'Ask – Heep – Mr Traddles, who lived in his house after him,' said Mr Micawber, breaking off from the letter; 'will you?'

'The fool himself – and lives there now,' said Uriah disdainfully.

'Ask – Heep – if he ever kept a pocket-book in that house,' said Mr Micawber; 'will you?'

I saw Uriah's lank hand stop, involuntarily, in the scraping of his chin.

'Or ask him,' said Mr Micawber, 'if he ever burnt one there? If he says yes, and asks you where the ashes are, refer him to Wilkins Micawber, and he will hear of something not at all to his advantage!'

The triumphant flourish with which Mr Micawber delivered himself of these words had a powerful effect in alarming the mother, who cried out in much agitation: 'Ury, Ury! Be 'umble, and make terms, my dear!'

'Mother!' he retorted, 'will you keep quiet? You're in a fright, and don't know what you say or mean. 'Umble!' he repeated, looking at me, with a snarl; 'I've 'umbled some of 'em for a pretty long time back, 'umble as I was!'

Mr Micawber, genteelly adjusting his chin in his cravat, presently proceeded with his composition.

' "Second. Heep has, on several occasions, to the best of my knowledge, information, and belief – "

'But *that* won't do,' muttered Uriah, relieved. 'Mother, you keep quiet.'

'We will endeavour to provide something that WILL do, and do for you finally, sir, very shortly,' replied Mr Micawber.

' "Second. Heep has, on several occasions, to the best of my knowledge, information, and belief, systematically forged, to various entries, books, and documents, the signature of Mr W.; and has distinctly done so in one instance, capable of proof by me. To wit, in manner following, that is to say:" '

Again, Mr Micawber had a relish in this formal piling up of words, which, however ludicrously displayed in his case, was, I must say, not at all peculiar to him. I have observed it, in the course of my life, in numbers of men. It seems to me to be a general rule. In the taking of legal oaths, for instance, deponents seem to enjoy themselves mightily when they come to several good words in succession, for the expression of one idea; as, that they utterly detest, abominate, and abjure, or so forth; and the old anathemas were made relishing on the same principle. We talk about the tyranny of words, but we like to tyrannise over them too; we are fond of having a large superfluous establishment of words to wait upon us on great occasions; we think it looks important, and sounds well. As we are not particular about the meaning of our liveries on state occasions, if they be but fine and numerous enough, so the meaning or necessity of our words is a secondary consideration, if there be but a great parade of them. And as individuals get into trouble by making too great a show of liveries, or as slaves when they are too numerous rise against their masters, so I think I could mention a nation that has got into many great difficulties, and will get into many greater, from maintaining too large a retinue of words.

Mr Micawber read on, almost smacking his lips: ' "To wit, in manner following, that is to say. Mr W. being infirm, and it being within the bounds of probability that his decease might lead to some discoveries, and to the downfall of – Heep's – power over the W. family – as I, Wilkins Micawber, the undersigned, assume – unless the filial affection of his daughter could be secretly influenced from allowing any investigation of the partnership affairs to be ever made, the said – Heep – deemed it expedient to have a bond ready by him, as from Mr W., for the before-mentioned sum of twelve six fourteen, two and nine, with interest, stated therein to have been advanced by – Heep – to Mr W. to save Mr W. from dishonour; though really the sum was never advanced by him, and has long been replaced. The signatures to this instrument, purporting to be executed by Mr W. and attested by Wilkins Micawber, are forgeries by – Heep. I have, in my possession, in his hand and pocket-book, several similar imitations of Mr W.'s signature, here and there defaced by fire, but legible to anyone. I never attested any such document. And I have the document itself, in my possession." '

Uriah Heep, with a start, took out of his pocket a bunch of keys, and opened a certain drawer; then suddenly bethought himself of what he was about, and turned again toward us, without looking in it.

' "And I have the document," ' Mr Micawber read again,

looking about as if it were the text of a sermon, ' "in my possession," – that is to say, I had, early this morning, when this was written, but have since relinquished it to Mr Traddles.'

'It is quite true,' assented Traddles.

'Ury, Ury!' cried the mother, 'be 'umble and make terms. I know my son will be 'umble, gentlemen, if you'll give him time to think. Mr Copperfield, I'm sure you know that he was always very 'umble, sir!'

It was singular to see how the mother still held to the old trick, when the son had abandoned it as useless.

'Mother,' he said, with an impatient bite at the handkerchief in which his hand was wrapped, 'you had better take and fire a loaded gun at me.'

'But I love you, Ury,' cried Mrs Heep. And I have no doubt she did; or that he loved her, however strange it may appear; though, to be sure, they were a congenial couple. 'And I can't bear to hear you provoking the gentleman, and endangering of yourself more. I told the gentleman at first, when he told me upstairs it was come to light, that I would answer for your being 'umble, and making amends. Oh, see how 'umble *I* am, gentlemen, and don't mind him!'

'Why, there's Copperfield, mother,' he angrily retorted, pointing his lean finger at me, against whom all his animosity was levelled, as the prime mover in the discovery, and I did not undeceive him – 'there's Copperfield would have given you a hundred pound to say less than you've blurted out!'

'I can't help it, Ury,' cried his mother. 'I can't see you running into danger, through carrying your head so high. Better be 'umble, as you always was.'

He remained for a little, biting the handkerchief, and then said to me with a scowl: 'What more have you got to bring forward? If anything, go on with it. What do you look at me for?'

Mr Micawber promptly resumed his letter, only too glad to revert to a performance with which he was so highly satisfied.

' "Third – and last. I am now in a condition to show, by – Heep's – false books, and – Heep's – real memoranda, beginning with the partially destroyed pocket-book (which I was unable to comprehend, at the time of its accidental discovery by Mrs Micawber, on our taking possession of our present abode, in the locker or bin devoted to the reception of the ashes calcined on our domestic hearth), that the weaknesses, the faults, the very virtues, the parental affections, and the sense of honour, of the unhappy Mr W. have been for years acted on by, and warped to the base purposes of – Heep. That Mr W. has been for years deluded and plundered, in every conceivable manner, to the pecuniary aggrandisement of the avaricious, false, and grasping – Heep. That the engrossing object of – Heep – was, next to gain, to subdue Mr and Miss W. (of his ulterior views in reference to the latter I say nothing) entirely to himself. That his last act, completed but a few months since, was to induce Mr W. to execute a relinquishment of his share in the partnership, and even a bill of sale on the very furniture of his house, in consideration of a certain annuity, to be well and truly paid by – Heep – on the four common quarter-days in each and every year. That these meshes, beginning with alarming and falsified accounts of the estate of which Mr W. is the receiver, at a period when Mr W. had launched into imprudent and ill-judged speculations, and may not have had the money, for which he was morally and legally responsible, in hand; going on with pretended borrowings of money at enormous interest, really coming from – Heep – and by – Heep – fraudulently obtained or withheld from Mr W. himself, on pretence of such speculations or otherwise; perpetuated by a miscellaneous catalogue of unscrupulous chicaneries – gradually thickened until the unhappy Mr W. could see no world beyond. Bankrupt, as he believed, alike in circumstances, in all other hope, and in honour, his sole reliance was upon the monster in the garb of man" ' – Mr Micawber made a good deal of this, as a new turn of expression – ' "who, by making himself necessary to him, had achieved his destruction. All this I undertake to show. Probably much more!" '

I whispered a few words to Agnes, who was weeping, half joyfully, half sorrowfully, at my side; and there was a movement among us, as if Mr Micawber had finished. He said, with exceeding gravity, 'Pardon me,' and proceeded, with a mixture of the lowest spirits and the most intense enjoyment, to the peroration of his letter.

' "I have now concluded. It merely remains for me to substantiate these accusations; and then, with my ill-starred family, to disappear from the landscape on which we appear to be an encumbrance. That is soon done. It may be reasonably inferred that our baby will first expire of inanition, as being the frailest member of our circle; and that our twins will follow next in order. So be it! For myself, my Canterbury Pilgrimage has done much; imprisonment on civil process, and want, will soon do more. I trust that the labour and hazard of an investigation – of which the smallest results have been slowly pieced together, in the pressure of arduous avocations, under grinding penurious apprehensions, at rise of morn, at dewy eve, in the shadows of night, under the watchful eye of one whom it were superfluous to call Demon – combined with the struggle of parental Poverty to turn it, when completed, to the right account – may be as the sprinkling of a few drops of sweet water on my funereal pyre. I ask no more. Let it be, in justice, merely said of me, as of a gallant and eminent naval Hero, with whom I have no pretensions to cope, that what I have done, I did, in despite of mercenary and selfish objects, 'For England, Home, and Beauty.' Remaining always, etc., etc., Wilkins Micawber." '

Much affected, but still intensely enjoying himself, Mr Micawber folded up his letter, and handed it with a bow to my aunt, as something she might like to keep.

There was, as I had noticed on my first visit long ago, an iron safe in the room. The key was in it. A hasty suspicion seemed to strike Uriah; and with a glance at Mr Micawber, he went to it, and threw the doors clanking open. It was empty.

'Where are the books!' he cried, with a frightful face. 'Some thief has stolen the books!'

Mr Micawber tapped himself with the ruler. '*I* did, when I got the key from you as usual – but a little earlier – and opened it this morning.'

'Don't be uneasy,' said Traddles. 'They have come into my possession. I will take care of them, under the authority I mentioned.'

'You receive stolen goods, do you?' cried Uriah.

'Under such circumstances,' answered Traddles, 'yes.'

What was my astonishment when I beheld my aunt, who had been profoundly quiet and attentive, make a dart at Uriah Heep, and seize him by the collar with both hands!

'You know what *I* want?' said my aunt.

'A strait-waistcoat,' said he.

'No. My property!' returned my aunt. 'Agnes, my dear, as long as I believed it had been really made away with by your father, I wouldn't – and, my dear, I didn't, even to Trot, as he knows – breathe a syllable of its having been placed here for investment. But now I know this fellow's answerable for it, and I'll have it! Trot, come and take it away from him!'

Whether my aunt supposed, for the moment, that he kept her property in his neckerchief, I am sure I don't know, but she certainly pulled at it as if she thought so. I hastened to put myself between them, and to assure her that we would all take care that he should make the utmost restitution of everything he had wrongly got. This, and a few moments' reflection, pacified her; but she was not at all disconcerted by what she had done (though I cannot say as much for her bonnet) and resumed her seat composedly.

During the last few minutes, Mrs Heep had been clamouring to her son to be ''umble'; and had been going down on her knees to all of us in succession, and making the wildest promises. Her son sat her down in his chair; and standing sulkily by her, holding her arm with his hand, but not rudely, said to me, with a ferocious look: 'What do you want done?'

'I will tell you what must be done,' said Traddles.

'Has that Copperfield no tongue?' muttered Uriah. 'I would do a good deal for you if you could tell me, without lying, that somebody had cut it out.'

'My Uriah means to be 'umble!' cried his mother. 'Don't mind what he says, good gentlemen!'

'What must be done,' said Traddles, 'is this. First, the deed of relinquishment, that we have heard of, must be given over to me now – here.'

'Suppose I haven't got it,' he interrupted.

'But you have,' said Traddles; 'therefore, you know, we won't suppose so.' And I cannot help avowing that this was the first occasion on which I really did justice to the clear head, and the plain, patient, practical good sense of my old schoolfellow. 'Then,' said Traddles, 'you must prepare to disgorge all that your rapacity has become possessed of, and to make restoration to the last farthing. All the partnership books and papers must remain in our possession; all your books and papers; all money accounts and securities, of both kinds. In short, everything here.'

'Must it? I don't know that,' said Uriah. 'I must have time to think about that.'

'Certainly,' replied Traddles; 'but, in the meanwhile, and until everything is done to our satisfaction, we shall maintain possession of these things; and beg you – in short, compel you – to keep your own room, and hold no communication with anyone.'

'I won't do it!' said Uriah, with an oath.

'Maidstone Jail is a safer place of detention,' observed Traddles; 'and though the law may be longer in righting us, and may not be able to right us so completely as you can, there is no doubt of its punishing *you*. Dear me, you know that quite as well as I! Copperfield, will you go round to the Guildhall, and bring a couple of officers?'

Here, Mrs Heep broke out again, crying on her knees to Agnes to interfere in their behalf, exclaiming that he was very humble, and it was all true, and, if he didn't do what we wanted, she would, and much more to the same purpose; being half frantic with fears for her darling. To enquire what he might have done, if he had had any boldness, would be like enquiring what a mongrel cur might do, if it had the spirit of a tiger. He was a coward, from head to foot; and showed his dastardly nature, through his sullenness and mortification, as much as at any time of his mean life.

'Stop!' he growled to me; and wiped his hot face with his hand. 'Mother, hold your noise. Well! Let 'em have that deed. Go and fetch it!'

'Do you help her, Mr Dick,' said Traddles, 'if you please.'

Proud of his commission, and understanding it, Mr Dick accompanied her as a shepherd's dog might accompany a sheep. But Mrs Heep gave him little trouble; for she not only returned with the deed, but with the box in which it was, where we found a banker's book and some other papers that were afterwards serviceable.

'Good!' said Traddles, when this was brought. 'Now, Mr Heep, you can retire to think; particularly observing, if you please, that I declare to you, on the part of all present, that there is only one thing to be done; that it is what I have explained; and that it must be done without delay.'

Uriah, without lifting his eyes from the ground, shuffled across the room with his hand to his chin, and, pausing at the door, said: 'Copperfield, I have always hated you. You've always been an upstart, and you've always been against me.'

'As I think I told you once before,' said I, 'it is you who have been, in your greed and cunning, against all the world. It may be profitable to you to reflect, in future, that there never were greed and cunning in the world yet, that did not do too much, and overreach themselves. It is as certain as death.'

'Or as certain as they used to teach at school (the same school where I picked up so much 'umbleness), from nine o'clock to eleven, that labour was a curse; and from eleven o'clock to one, that it was a blessing and a cheerfulness, and a dignity, and I don't know what all, eh?' said he with a sneer. 'You preach about as consistent as they did. Won't 'umbleness go down? I shouldn't have got round my gentleman fellow-partner with-out it, I think. – Micawber, you old bully, I'll pay *you*!'

Mr Micawber, supremely defiant of him and his extended finger, and making a great deal of his chest until he had slunk out at the door, then addressed himself to me, and proffered me the satisfaction of 'witnessing the re-establishment of mutual confidence between himself and Mrs Micawber.' After which he invited the company generally to the contemplation of that affecting spectacle.

'The veil that has long been interposed between Mrs Micawber and myself is now withdrawn,' said Mr Micawber; 'and my children and the Author of their Being can once more come in contact on equal terms.'

As we were all very grateful to him, and all desirous to show that we were, as well as the hurry and disorder of our spirits would permit, I dare say we should all have gone, but that it was necessary for Agnes to return to her father, as yet unable to bear more than the dawn of hope; and for someone else to hold Uriah in safe keeping. So Traddles remained for the latter purpose, to be presently relieved by Mr Dick; and Mr Dick, my aunt, and I went home with Mr Micawber. As I parted hurriedly from the dear girl to whom I owed so much, and thought from what she had been saved, perhaps, that morning – her better resolution notwithstanding – I felt devoutly thankful for the miseries of my younger days which had brought me to the knowledge of Mr Micawber.

His house was not far off; and as the street door opened into the sitting-room, and he bolted in with a precipitation quite his own, we found ourselves at once in the bosom of the family. Mr Micawber, exclaiming, 'Emma! my life!' rushed into Mrs Micawber's arms. Mrs Micawber shrieked, and folded Mr Micawber in her embrace. Miss Micawber, nursing the unconscious stranger of Mrs Micawber's last letter to me, was sensibly affected. The stranger leaped. The twins testified their joy by several inconvenient but innocent demonstrations. Master Micawber, whose disposition appeared to have been soured by early disappointment, and whose aspect had become morose, yielded to his better feelings, and blubbered.

'Emma!' said Mr Micawber. 'The cloud is past from my mind. Mutual confidence, so long preserved between us once, is restored, to know no further interruption. Now, welcome poverty!' cried Mr Micawber, shedding tears. 'Welcome misery, welcome houselessness, welcome hunger, rags, tempest, and beggary! Mutual confidence will sustain us to the end!'

With these expressions, Mr Micawber placed Mrs Micawber in a chair, and embraced the family all round; welcoming a variety of bleak prospects, which appeared, to the best of my judgement, to be anything but welcome to them; and calling upon them to come out into Canterbury and sing a chorus, as nothing else was left for their support.

But Mrs Micawber having, in the strength of her emotions, fainted away, the first thing to be done, even before the chorus could be considered complete, was to recover her. This my aunt and Mr Micawber did; and then my aunt was introduced, and Mrs Micawber recognised me.

'Excuse me, dear Mr Copperfield,' said the poor lady, giving me her hand, 'but I am not strong; and the removal of the late misunderstanding between Mr Micawber and myself was at first too much for me.'

'Is this all your family, ma'am?' said my aunt.

'There are no more at present,' returned Mrs Micawber.

'Good gracious, I didn't mean that, ma'am,' said my aunt. 'I mean are all these yours?'

'Madam,' replied Mr Micawber, 'it is a true bill.'

'And that eldest young gentleman, now,' said my aunt, musing; 'what has *he* been brought up to?'

'It was my hope when I came here,' said Mr Micawber, 'to have got Wilkins into the Church; or perhaps I shall express my meaning more strictly, if I say the Choir. But there was no vacancy for a tenor in the venerable Pile for which this city is so justly eminent; and he has – in short, he has contracted a habit of singing in public-houses, rather than in sacred edifices.'

'But he means well,' said Mrs Micawber tenderly.

'I dare say, my love,' rejoined Mr Micawber, 'that he means particularly well; but I have not yet found that he carries out his meaning, in any given direction whatsoever.'

Master Micawber's moroseness of aspect returned upon him again, and he demanded, with some temper, what he was to do? Whether he had been born a carpenter, or a coach painter, any more than he had been born a bird? Whether he could go into the next street, and open a chemist's shop? Whether he could rush to the next assizes, and proclaim himself a lawyer? Whether he could come out by force at the opera, and succeed by violence? Whether he could do anything, without being brought up to something?

My aunt mused a little while, and then said: 'Mr Micawber, I wonder you have never turned your thoughts to emigration.'

'Madam,' returned Mr Micawber, 'it was the dream of my youth, and the fallacious aspiration of my riper years.' I am thoroughly persuaded, by the by, that he had never thought of it in his life.

'Aye?' said my aunt, with a glance at me. 'Why, what a thing it would be for yourselves and your family, Mr and Mrs Micawber, if you were to emigrate now.'

'Capital, madam, capital,' urged Mr Micawber gloomily.

'That is the principal, I may say the only difficulty, my dear Mr Copperfield,' assented his wife.

'Capital?' cried my aunt. 'But you are doing us a great service – have done us a great service, I may say, for surely much will come out of the fire – and what could we do for you, that would be half so good as to find the capital?'

'I could not receive it as a gift,' said Mr Micawber, full of fire and animation, 'but if a sufficient sum could be advanced, say at five per cent interest per annum, upon my personal liability – say my notes of hand, at twelve, eighteen, and twenty-four months, respectively, to allow time for something to turn up –'

'Could be? Can be and shall be, on your own terms,' returned my aunt, 'if you say the word. Think of this now, both of you. Here are some people David knows, going out to Australia shortly. If you decide to go, why shouldn't you go in the same ship? You may help each other. Think of this now, Mr and Mrs Micawber. Take your time, and weigh it well.'

'There is but one question, my dear ma'am, I could wish to ask,' said Mrs Micawber. 'The climate, I believe, is healthy.'

'Finest in the world!' said my aunt.

'Just so,' returned Mrs Micawber. 'Then my question arises. Now, *are* the circumstances of the country such that a man of Mr Micawber's abilities would have a fair chance of rising in the social scale? I will not say, at present, might he aspire to be Governor, or anything of that sort; but would there be a reasonable opening for his talents to develop themselves – that would be amply sufficient – and find their own expansion?'

'No better opening anywhere,' said my aunt, 'for a man who conducts himself well, and is industrious.'

'For a man who conducts himself well,' repeated Mrs Micawber, with her clearest business manner, 'and is industrious. Precisely. It is evident to me that Australia is the legitimate sphere of action for Mr Micawber!'

'I entertain the conviction, my dear madam,' said Mr Micawber, 'that it is, under existing circumstances, the land, the only land, for myself and family; and that something of an extraordinary nature will turn up on that shore. It is no distance – comparatively speaking; and though consideration is due to the kindness of your proposal, I assure you that is a mere matter of form.'

Shall I ever forget how, in a moment, he was the most sanguine of men, looking on to fortune; or how Mrs Micawber presently discoursed about the habits of the kangaroo! Shall I ever recall that street of Canterbury on a market day, without recalling him, as he walked back with us; expressing, in the hardy roving manner he assumed, the unsettled habits of a temporary sojourner in the land; and looking at the bullocks, as they came by, with the eye of an Australian farmer!

CHAPTER 53

Another Retrospect

I must pause yet once again. Oh, my child-wife, there is a figure in the moving crowd before my memory, quiet and still, saying in its innocent love and childish beauty, Stop to think of me – turn to look upon the Little Blossom, as it flutters to the ground!

I do. All else grows dim, and fades away. I am again with Dora, in our cottage. I do not know how long she has been ill. I am so used to it in feeling that I cannot count the time. It is not really long, in weeks or months; but, in my usage and experience, it is a weary, weary while.

They have left off telling me to 'wait a few days more.' I have begun to fear, remotely, that the day may never shine, when I shall see my child-wife running in the sunlight with her old friend Jip.

He is, as it were suddenly, grown very old. It may be that he misses in his mistress something that enlivened him and made him younger; but he mopes, and his sight is weak, and his limbs are feeble, and my aunt is sorry that he objects to her no more, but creeps near her as he lies on Dora's bed – she sitting at the bedside – and mildly licks her hand.

Restoration of mutual confidence between Mr and Mrs Micawber

Dora lies smiling on us, and is beautiful, and utters no hasty or complaining word. She says that we are very good to her; that her dear old careful boy is tiring himself out, she knows; that my aunt has no sleep, yet is always wakeful, active, and kind. Sometimes, the little bird-like ladies come to see her; and then we talk about our wedding-day, and all that happy time.

What a strange rest and pause in my life there seems to be – and in all life, within doors and without – when I sit in the quiet, shaded, orderly room, with the blue eyes of my child-wife turned towards me, and her little fingers twining round my hand! Many and many an hour I sit thus; but of all those times, three times come the freshest on my mind.

It is morning; and Dora, made so trim by my aunt's hands, shows me how her pretty hair *will* curl upon the pillow yet, and how long and bright it is, and how she likes to have it loosely gathered in that net she wears.

'Not that I am vain of it, now, you mocking boy,' she says, when I smile; 'but because you used to say you thought it so beautiful; and because, when I first began to think about you, I used to peep in the glass, and wonder whether you would like very much to have a lock of it. Oh, what a foolish fellow you were, Doady, when I gave you one!'

'That was on the day when you were painting the flowers I had given you, Dora, and when I told you how much in love I was.'

'Ah! but I didn't like to tell *you*,' says Dora, '*then*, how I had cried over them, because I believed you really liked me! When I can run about again as I used to do, Doady, let us go and see those places where we were such a silly couple, shall we? And take some of the old walks? And not forget poor papa?'

'Yes, we will, and have some happy days. So you must make haste to get well, my dear.'

'Oh, I shall soon do that! I am so much better, you don't know!'

It is evening; and I sit in the same chair, by the same bed, with the same face turned towards me. We have been silent, and there is a smile upon her face. I have ceased to carry my light burden up and down stairs now. She lies here all the day.

'Doady!'

'My dear Dora!'

'You won't think what I am going to say unreasonable after what you told me, such a little while ago, of Mr Wickfield's not being well? I want to see Agnes. Very much, I want to see her.'

'I will write to her, my dear.'

'Will you?'

'Directly.'

'What a good, kind boy! Doady, take me on your arm. Indeed, my dear, it's not a whim. It's not a foolish fancy. I want very much, indeed, to see her!'

'I am certain of it. I have only to tell her so, and she is sure to come.'

'You are very lonely when you go downstairs now?' Dora whispers, with her arm about my neck.

'How can I be otherwise, my own love, when I see your empty chair?'

'My empty chair!' She clings to me for a little while, in silence. 'And you really miss me, Doady?' looking up, and brightly smiling. 'Even poor, giddy, stupid me?'

'My heart, who is there upon earth that I could miss so much?'

'Oh, husband! I am so glad, yet so sorry!' creeping closer to me, and folding me in both her arms. She laughs and sobs, and then is quiet, and quite happy.

'Quite!' she says. 'Only give Agnes my dear love, and tell her that I want very, very much to see her; and I have nothing left to wish for.'

'Except to get well again, Dora.'

'Ah, Doady! Sometimes I think – you know I always was a silly little thing! – that that will never be!'

'Don't say so, Dora! Dearest love, don't think so!'

'I won't, if I can help it, Doady. But I am very happy; though my dear boy is so lonely by himself, before his child-wife's empty chair!'

It is night; and I am with her still. Agnes has arrived; has been among us for a whole day and an evening. She, my aunt, and I have sat with Dora since the morning, all together. We have not talked much, but Dora has been perfectly contented and cheerful. We are now alone.

Do I know, now, that my child-wife will soon leave me? They have told me so; they have told me nothing new to my thoughts; but I am far from sure that I have taken that truth to heart. I cannot master it. I have withdrawn by myself, many times today, to weep. I have remembered Who wept for a parting between the living and the dead. I have bethought me of all that gracious and compassionate history. I have tried to resign myself, and to console myself; and that, I hope, I may have done imperfectly; but what I cannot firmly settle in my mind is that the end will absolutely come. I hold her hand in mine, I hold her heart in mine, I see her love for me, alive in all its strength. I cannot shut out a pale lingering shadow of belief that she will be spared.

'I am going to speak to you, Doady. I am going to say something I have often thought of saying, lately. You won't mind?' with a gentle look.

'Mind, my darling?'

'Because I don't know what you will think or what you may have thought sometimes. Perhaps you have often thought the same. Doady, dear, I am afraid I was too young.'

I lay my face upon the pillow by her, and she looks into my eyes, and speaks very softly. Gradually, as she goes on, I feel with a stricken heart that she is speaking of herself as past.

'I am afraid, dear, I was too young. I don't mean in years only, but in experience, and thoughts, and everything. I was such a silly little creature! I am afraid it would have been better, if we had only loved each other as a boy and girl, and forgotten it. I have begun to think I was not fit to be a wife.'

I try to stay my tears, and to reply, 'Oh, Dora, love, as fit as I to be a husband!'

'I don't know,' with the old shake of her curls. 'Perhaps! But if I had been more fit to be married, I might have made you more so, too. Besides, you are very clever, and I never was.'

'We have been very happy, my sweet Dora.'

'I was very happy, very. But as years went on, my dear boy would have wearied of his child-wife. She would have been less and less a companion for him. He would have been more and more sensible of what was wanting in his home. She wouldn't have improved. It is better as it is.'

'Oh, Dora, dearest, dearest, do not speak to me so. Every word seems a reproach!'

'No, not a syllable!' she answers, kissing me. 'Oh, my dear, you never deserved it, and I loved you far too well, to say a reproachful word to you, in earnest – it was all the merit I had, except being pretty – or you thought me so. Is it lonely downstairs, Doady?'

'Very! Very!'

'Don't cry! Is my chair there?'

'In its old place.'

'Oh, how my poor boy cries! Hush, hush! Now, make me one promise. I want to speak to Agnes. When you go downstairs, tell Agnes so, and send her up to me; and while I speak to her, let no one come – not even aunt. I want to speak to Agnes by herself. I want to speak to Agnes, quite alone.'

I promise that she shall, immediately; but I cannot leave her, for my grief.

'I said that it was better as it is!' she whispers, as she holds me in her arms. 'Oh, Doady, after more years, you never could have loved your child-wife better than you do; and after more years, she would so have tried and disappointed you that you might not have been able to love her half so well! I know I was too young and foolish. It is much better as it is!'

Agnes is downstairs, when I go into the parlour; and I give her the message. She disappears, leaving me alone with Jip.

His Chinese house is by the fire; and he lies within it, on his bed of flannel, querulously trying to sleep. The bright moon is high and clear. As I look out on the night, my tears fall fast, and my undisciplined heart is chastened heavily – heavily.

I sit down by the fire, thinking with a blind remorse of all those secret feelings I have nourished since my marriage. I think of every little trifle between me and Dora, and feel the truth, that trifles make the sum of life. Ever rising from the sea of my remembrance is the image of the dear child as I knew her first, graced by my young love, and by her own, with every fascination wherein such love is rich. Would it, indeed, have been better if we had loved each other as a boy and girl, and forgotten it? Undisciplined heart, reply!

How the time wears, I know not; until I am recalled by my child-wife's old companion. More restless than he was, he crawls out of his house, and looks at me, and wanders to the door, and whines to go upstairs.

'Not tonight, Jip! Not tonight!'

He comes very slowly back to me, licks my hand, and lifts his dim eyes to my face. 'Oh, Jip! It may be, never again!'

He lies down at my feet, stretches himself out as if to sleep, and, with a plaintive cry, is dead.

'Oh, Agnes! Look, look here!'

That face, so full of pity, and of grief, that rain of tears, that awful mute appeal to me, that solemn hand upraised towards Heaven!

'Agnes?'

It is over. Darkness comes before my eyes; and for a time all things are blotted out of my remembrance.

CHAPTER 54

Mr Micawber's Transactions

This is not the time at which I am to enter on the state of my mind beneath its load of sorrow. I came to think that the Future was walled up before me, that the energy and action of my life were at an end, that I never could find any refuge but in the grave. I came to think so, I say, but not in the first shock of my grief. It slowly grew to that. If the events I go on to relate had not thickened around me, in the beginning to confuse, and in the end to augment, my affliction, it is possible (though I think not probable) that I might have fallen at once into this condition. As it was, an interval occurred before I fully knew my own distress; an interval, in which I even supposed that its sharpest pangs were past; and when my mind could soothe itself by resting on all that was most innocent and beautiful, in the tender story that was closed for ever.

When it was first proposed that I should go abroad, or how it came to be agreed among us that I was to seek the restoration of my peace in change and travel, I do not, even now, distinctly know. The spirit of Agnes so pervaded all we thought, and said, and did, in that time of sorrow, that I assume I may refer the project to her influence. But her influence was so quiet that I know no more.

And now, indeed, I began to think that in my old association of her with the stained-glass window in the church, a prophetic foreshadowing of what she would be to me, in the calamity that was to happen in the fullness of time, had found a way into my mind. In all that sorrow, from the moment, never to be forgotten, when she stood before me with her upraised hand, she was like a sacred presence in my lonely house. When the Angel of Death alighted there, my child-wife fell asleep – they told me so when I could bear to hear it – on her bosom, with a smile. From my swoon, I first awoke to a consciousness of her compassionate tears, her words of hope and peace, her gentle face bending down, as from a purer region nearer Heaven, over my undisciplined heart, and softening its pain.

Let me go on.

I was to go abroad. That seemed to have been determined among us from the first. The ground now covering all that could perish of my departed wife, I waited only for what Mr Micawber called the 'final pulverisation of Heep,' and for the departure of the emigrants.

At the request of Traddles, most affectionate and devoted of friends in my trouble, we returned to Canterbury: I mean my aunt, Agnes, and I. We proceeded by appointment straight to Mr Micawber's house; where, and at Mr Wickfield's, my friend had been labouring ever since our explosive meeting. When poor Mrs Micawber saw me come in, in my black clothes, she was sensibly affected. There was a great deal of good in Mrs Micawber's heart, which had not been dunned out of it in all those many years.

'Well, Mr and Mrs Micawber,' was my aunt's first salutation after we were seated. 'Pray, have you thought about that emigration proposal of mine?'

'My dear madam,' returned Mr Micawber, 'perhaps I cannot better express the conclusion at which Mrs Micawber, your humble servant, and I may add our children, have jointly and severally arrived, than by borrowing the language of an illustrious poet, to reply that our Boat is on the shore, and our Bark is on the sea.'

'That's right,' said my aunt. 'I augur all sorts of good from your sensible decision.'

'Madam, you do us a great deal of honour,' he rejoined. He then referred to a memorandum. 'With respect to the pecuniary assistance enabling us to launch our frail canoe on the ocean of enterprise, I have reconsidered that important business point; and would beg to propose my notes of hand – drawn, it is needless to stipulate, on stamps of the amounts respectively required by the various Acts of Parliament applying to such securities – at eighteen, twenty-four, and

My child-wife's old companion

thirty months. The proposition I originally submitted was twelve, eighteen, and twenty-four; but I am apprehensive that such an arrangement might not allow sufficient time for the requisite amount of – Something – to turn up. We might not,' said Mr Micawber, looking round the room as if it represented several hundred acres of highly cultivated land, 'on the first responsibility becoming due, have been successful in our harvest, or we might not have got our harvest in. Labour, I believe, is sometimes difficult to obtain in that portion of our colonial possessions where it will be our lot to combat with the teeming soil.'

'Arrange it in any way you please, sir,' said my aunt.

'Madam,' he replied, 'Mrs Micawber and myself are deeply sensible of the very considerate kindness of our friends and patrons. What I wish is, to be perfectly businesslike, and perfectly punctual. Turning over, as we are about to turn over, an entirely new leaf; and falling back, as we are now in the act of falling back, for a Spring of no common magnitude; it is important to my sense of self-respect, besides being an example to my son, that these arrangements should be concluded as between man and man.'

I don't know that Mr Micawber attached any meaning to this last phrase; I don't know that anybody ever does, or did; but he appeared to relish it uncommonly, and repeated, with an impressive cough, 'as between man and man.'

'I propose,' said Mr Micawber, 'Bills – a convenience to the mercantile world, for which, I believe, we are originally indebted to the Jews, who appear to me to have had a devilish deal too much to do with them ever since – because they are negotiable. But if a Bond, or any other description of security, would be preferred, I should be happy to execute any such instrument. As between man and man.'

My aunt observed, that in a case where both parties were willing to agree to anything, she took it for granted there would be no difficulty in settling this point. Mr Micawber was of her opinion.

'In reference to our domestic preparations, madam,' said Mr Micawber, with some pride, 'for meeting the destiny to which we are now understood to be self-devoted, I beg to report them. My eldest daughter attends at five every morning in a neighbouring establishment, to acquire the process – if process it may be called – of milking cows. My younger children are instructed to observe, as closely as circumstances will permit, the habits of the pigs and poultry maintained in the poorer parts of this city; a pursuit from which they have, on two occasions, been brought home, within an inch of being run over. I have myself directed some attention, during the past week, to the art of baking; and my son Wilkins has issued forth with a walking-stick and driven cattle, when permitted, by the rugged hirelings who had them in charge, to render any voluntary service in that direction – which I regret to say, for the credit of our nature, was not often, he being generally warned, with imprecations, to desist.'

'All very right, indeed,' said my aunt encouragingly. 'Mrs Micawber has been busy, too, I have no doubt.'

'My dear madam,' returned Mrs Micawber, with her

businesslike air, 'I am free to confess, that I have not been actively engaged in pursuits immediately connected with cultivation or with stock, though well aware that both will claim my attention on a foreign shore. Such opportunities as I have been enabled to alienate from my domestic duties, I have devoted to corresponding at some length with my family. For I own it seems to me, my dear Mr Copperfield,' said Mrs Micawber, who always fell back on me, I suppose from old habit, to whomsoever else she might address her discourse at starting, 'that the time is come when the past should be buried in oblivion; when my family should take Mr Micawber by the hand, and Mr Micawber should take my family by the hand; when the lion should lie down with the lamb, and my family be on terms with Mr Micawber.'

I said I thought so too.

'This, at least, is the light, my dear Mr Copperfield,' pursued Mrs Micawber, 'in which *I* view the subject. When I lived at home with my papa and mama, my papa was accustomed to ask, when any point was under discussion in our limited circle, "In what light does my Emma view the subject?" That my papa was too partial, I know; still, on such a point as the frigid coldness which has ever subsisted between Mr Micawber and my family, I necessarily have formed an opinion, delusive though it may be.'

'No doubt. Of course you have, ma'am,' said my aunt.

'Precisely so,' assented Mrs Micawber. 'Now, I may be wrong in my conclusions; it is very likely that I am; but my individual impression is, that the gulf between my family and Mr Micawber may be traced to an apprehension, on the part of my family, that Mr Micawber would require pecuniary accommodation. I cannot help thinking,' said Mrs Micawber, with an air of deep sagacity, 'that there are members of my family who have been apprehensive that Mr Micawber would solicit them for their names. I do not mean to be conferred in Baptism upon our children, but to be inscribed on Bills of Exchange, and negotiated in the Money Market.'

The look of penetration with which Mrs Micawber announced this discovery, as if no one had ever thought of it before, seemed rather to astonish my aunt, who abruptly replied, 'Well, ma'am, upon the whole, I shouldn't wonder if you were right!'

'Mr Micawber being now on the eve of casting off the pecuniary shackles that have so long enthralled him,' said Mrs Micawber, 'and of commencing a new career in a country where there is sufficient range for his abilities – which, in my opinion, is exceedingly important; Mr Micawber's abilities peculiarly requiring space – it seems to me that my family should signalise the occasion by coming forward. What I could wish to see, would be a meeting between Mr Micawber and my family at a festive entertainment, to be given at my family's expense; where Mr Micawber's health and prosperity being proposed, by some leading member of my family, Mr Micawber might have an opportunity of developing his views.'

'My dear,' said Mr Micawber, with some heat, 'it may be better for me to state distinctly, at once, that if I were to develop my views to that assembled group, they would possibly be found of an offensive nature; my impression being that your family are, in the aggregate, impertinent Snobs; and, in detail, unmitigated Ruffians.'

'Micawber,' said Mrs Micawber, shaking her head, 'no! You have never understood them, and they have never understood you.'

Mr Micawber coughed.

'They have never understood you, Micawber,' said his wife. 'They may be incapable of it. If so, that is their misfortune. I can pity their misfortune.'

'I am extremely sorry, my dear Emma,' said Mr Micawber, relenting, 'to have been betrayed into any expressions that might, even remotely, have the appearance of being strong expressions. All I would say is, that I can go abroad without your family coming forward to favour me – in short, with a parting Shove of their cold shoulders; and that, upon the whole, I would rather leave England with such impetus as I possess, than derive any acceleration of it from that quarter. At the same time, my dear, if they should condescend to reply to your communications – which our joint experience renders most improbable – far be it from me to be a barrier to your wishes.'

The matter being thus amicably settled, Mr Micawber gave Mrs Micawber his arm, and, glancing at the heap of books and papers lying before Traddles on the table, said they would leave us to ourselves; which they ceremoniously did.

'My dear Copperfield,' said Traddles, leaning back in his chair when they were gone, and looking at me with an affection that made his eyes red, and his hair all kinds of shapes, 'I don't make any excuse for troubling you with business, because I know you are deeply interested in it, and it may divert your thoughts. My dear boy, I hope you are not worn out?'

'I am quite myself,' said I, after a pause. 'We have more cause to think of my aunt than of anyone. You know how much she has done.'

'Surely, surely,' answered Traddles. 'Who can forget it!'

'But even that is not all,' said I. 'During the last fortnight, some new trouble has vexed her; and she has been in and out of London every day. Several times she has gone out early, and been absent until evening. Last night, Traddles, with this journey before her, it was almost midnight before she came home. You know what her consideration for others is. She will not tell me what has happened to distress her.'

My aunt, very pale, and with deep lines in her face, sat immovable until I had finished; when some stray tears found their way to her cheeks, and she put her hand on mine.

'It's nothing, Trot; it's nothing. There will be no more of it. You shall know by and by. Now, Agnes, my dear, let us attend to these affairs.'

'I must do Mr Micawber the justice to say,' Traddles began, 'that, although he would appear not to have worked to any good account for himself, he is a most untiring man when he works for other people. I never saw such a fellow. If he always goes on in the same way, he must be, virtually, about two hundred years old, at present. The heat into which he has been continually putting himself; and the distracted and impetuous manner in which he has been diving, day and night, among papers and books; to say nothing of the immense number of letters he has written me between this house and Mr Wickfield's, and often across the table when he has been sitting opposite, and might much more easily have spoken, is quite extraordinary.'

'Letters!' cried my aunt. 'I believe he dreams in letters!'

'There's Mr Dick, too,' said Traddles, 'has been doing wonders! As soon as he was released from overlooking Uriah Heep, whom he kept in such charge as *I* never saw exceeded, he began to devote himself to Mr Wickfield. And really his anxiety to be of use in the investigations we have been making, and his real usefulness in extracting, and copying, and fetching, and carrying, have been quite stimulating to us.'

'Dick is a very remarkable man,' exclaimed my aunt; 'and I always said he was. Trot, you know it!'

'I am happy to say, Miss Wickfield,' pursued Traddles, at once with great delicacy and with great earnestness, 'that in your absence Mr Wickfield has considerably improved. Relieved of the incubus that had fastened upon him for so long a time, and of the dreadful apprehensions under which he had lived, he is hardly the same person. At times, even his impaired power of concentrating his memory and attention on particular points of business has recovered itself very much; and he has been able to assist us in making some things clear, that we should have found very difficult, indeed, if not hopeless, without him. But what I have to do is to come to results, which are short enough; not to gossip on all the hopeful circumstances I have observed, or I shall never have done.'

His natural manner and agreeable simplicity made it transparent that he said this to put us in good heart, and to enable Agnes to hear her father mentioned with greater confidence; but it was not the less pleasant for that.

'Now, let me see,' said Traddles, looking among the papers on the table. 'Having counted our funds, and reduced to order a great mass of unintentional confusion in the first place, and of wilful confusion and falsification in the second, we take it to be clear that Mr Wickfield might now wind up his business, and his agency-trust, and exhibit no deficiency or defalcation whatever.'

'Oh, thank Heaven!' cried Agnes fervently.

'But,' said Traddles, 'the surplus that would be left as his means of support – and I suppose the house to be sold, even in saying this – would be so small, not exceeding in all probability some hundreds of pounds, that, perhaps, Miss Wickfield, it would be best to consider whether he might not retain his agency of the estate to which he has so long been receiver. His friends might advise him, you know; now he is free. You yourself, Miss Wickfield – Copperfield – I – '

'I have considered it, Trotwood,' said Agnes, looking to me, 'and I feel that it ought not to be, and must not be; even on the recommendation of a friend to whom I am so grateful, and owe so much.'

'I will not say that I recommend it,' observed Traddles. 'I think it right to suggest it; no more.'

'I am happy to hear you say so,' answered Agnes steadily, 'for it gives me hope, almost assurance, that we think alike. Dear Mr Traddles and dear Trotwood, papa once free with honour, what could I wish for! I have always aspired, if I could have released him from the toils in which he was held, to render back some little portion of the love and care I owe him, and to devote my life to him. It has been, for years, the utmost height of my hopes. To take our future on myself will be the next great happiness – the next to his release from all trust and responsibility – that I can know.'

'Have you thought how, Agnes?'

'Often! I am not afraid, dear Trotwood. I am certain of success. So many people know me here, and think kindly of me, that I am certain. Don't mistrust me. Our wants are not many. If I rent the dear old house and keep a school, I shall be useful and happy.'

The calm fervour of her cheerful voice brought back so vividly, first the dear old house itself, and then my solitary home, that my heart was too full for speech. Traddles pretended for a little while to be busily looking among the papers.

'Next, Miss Trotwood,' said Traddles, 'that property of yours.'

'Well, sir,' sighed my aunt. 'All I have got to say about it is that if it's gone, I can bear it; and if it's not gone, I shall be glad to get it back.'

'It was originally, I think, eight thousand pounds, Consols?' said Traddles.

'Right!' replied my aunt.

'I can't account for more than five,' said Traddles, with an air of perplexity.

' – thousand, do you mean?' enquired my aunt, with uncommon composure, 'or pounds?'

'Five thousand pounds,' said Traddles.

'It was all there was,' returned my aunt. 'I sold three, myself. One, I paid for your articles, Trot, my dear; and the other two I have by me. When I lost the rest, I thought it wise to say nothing about that sum, but to keep it secretly for a rainy day. I wanted to see how you would come out of the trial, Trot; and you came out nobly – persevering, self-reliant, self-denying! So did Dick. Don't speak to me, for I find my nerves a little shaken!'

Nobody would have thought so, to see her sitting upright, with her arms folded; but she had wonderful self-command.

'Then I am delighted to say,' cried Traddles, beaming with joy, 'that we have recovered the whole money!'

'Don't congratulate me, anybody!' exclaimed my aunt. 'How so, sir?'

'You believed it had been misappropriated by Mr Wickfield?' said Traddles.

'Of course I did,' said my aunt, 'and was therefore easily silenced. Agnes, not a word!'

'And indeed,' said Traddles, 'it was sold, by virtue of the power of management he held from you; but I needn't say by whom sold, or on whose actual signature. It was afterwards pretended to Mr Wickfield, by that rascal – and proved, too, by figures – that he had possessed himself of the money (on general instructions, *he* said) to keep other deficiencies and difficulties from the light. Mr Wickfield, being so weak and helpless in his hands as to pay you, afterwards, several sums of interest on a pretended principal which he knew did not exist, made himself, unhappily, a party to the fraud.'

'And at last took the blame upon himself,' added my aunt, 'and wrote me a mad letter, charging himself with robbery, and wrong unheard of. Upon which I paid him a visit early one morning, called for a candle, burnt the letter, and told him if he ever could right me and himself, to do it; and if he couldn't, to keep his own counsel for his daughter's sake. – If anybody speaks to me, I'll leave the house!'

We all remained quiet; Agnes covering her face.

'Well, my dear friend,' said my aunt, after a pause, 'and you have really extorted the money back from him?'

'Why, the fact is,' returned Traddles, 'Mr Micawber had so completely hemmed him in, and was always ready with so many new points if an old one failed, that he could not escape from us. A most remarkable circumstance is, that I really don't think he grasped this sum even so much for the gratification of his avarice, which was inordinate, as in the hatred he felt for Copperfield. He said so to me, plainly. He said he would even have spent as much to baulk or injure Copperfield.'

'Ha!' said my aunt, knitting her brows thoughtfully, and glancing at Agnes. 'And what's become of him?'

'I don't know. He left here,' said Traddles, 'with his mother, who had been clamouring, and beseeching, and disclosing, the whole time. They went away by one of the London night coaches, and I know no more about him; except that his malevolence to me at parting was audacious. He seemed to consider himself hardly less indebted to me, than to Mr Micawber; which I consider (as I told him) quite a compliment.'

'Do you suppose he has any money, Traddles?' I asked.

'Oh, dear, yes, I should think so,' he replied, shaking his head seriously. 'I should say he must have pocketed a good deal, in one way or other. But I think you would find, Copperfield, if you had an opportunity of observing his course, that money would never keep that man out of mischief. He is such an incarnate hypocrite, that whatever object he pursues, he must pursue crookedly. It's his only compensation for the outward restraints he puts upon himself. Always creeping along the ground to some small end or other, he will always magnify every object in the way; and consequently will hate and suspect everybody that comes, in the most innocent manner, between him and it. So, the crooked courses will become crookeder, at any moment, for the least reason or for none. It's only necessary to consider his history here,' said Traddles, 'to know that.'

'He's a monster of meanness!' said my aunt.

'Really I don't know about that,' observed Traddles, thoughtfully. 'Many people can be very mean, when they give their minds to it.'

'And now, touching Mr Micawber,' said my aunt.

'Well, really,' said Traddles cheerfully, 'I must, once more, give Mr Micawber high praise. But for his having been so patient and persevering for so long a time, we never could have hoped to do anything worth speaking of. And I think we ought to consider that Mr Micawber did right, for right's sake, when

we reflect what terms he might have made with Uriah Heep himself, for his silence.'

'I think so too,' said I.

'Now, what would you give him?' enquired my aunt.

'Oh! Before you come to that,' said Traddles, a little disconcerted, 'I am afraid I thought it discreet to omit (not being able to carry everything before me) two points, in making this lawless adjustment – for it's perfectly lawless from beginning to end – of a difficult affair. Those I. O. U.s, and so forth, which Mr Micawber gave him for the advances he had – '

'Well! They must be paid,' said my aunt.

'Yes, but I don't know when they may be proceeded on, or where they are,' rejoined Traddles, opening his eyes; 'and I anticipate, that, between this time and his departure, Mr Micawber will be constantly arrested, or taken in execution.'

'Then he must be constantly set free again, and taken out of execution,' said my aunt. 'What's the amount altogether?'

'Why, Mr Micawber has entered the transactions – he calls them transactions – with great form, in a book,' rejoined Traddles, smiling; 'and he makes the amount a hundred and three pounds, five.'

'Now, what shall we give him, that sum included?' said my aunt. 'Agnes, my dear, you and I can talk about division of it afterwards. What shall it be? Five hundred pounds?'

Upon this, Traddles and I both struck in at once. We both recommended a small sum in money, and the payment, without stipulation to Mr Micawber, of the Uriah claims as they came in. We proposed that the family should have their passage and their outfit, and a hundred pounds; and that Mr Micawber's arrangement for the repayment of the advances should be gravely entered into, as it might be wholesome for him to suppose himself under that responsibility. To this, I added the suggestion, that I should give some explanation of his character and history to Mr Peggotty, who I knew could be relied on; and that to Mr Peggotty should be quietly entrusted the discretion of advancing another hundred. I further proposed to interest Mr Micawber in Mr Peggotty, by confiding so much of Mr Peggotty's story to him as I might feel justified in relating, or might think expedient; and to endeavour to bring each of them to bear upon the other, for the common advantage. We all entered warmly into these views; and I may mention at once, that the principals themselves did so, shortly afterwards, with perfect goodwill and harmony.

Seeing that Traddles now glanced anxiously at my aunt again, I reminded him of the second and last point to which he had adverted.

'You and your aunt will excuse me, Copperfield, if I touch upon a painful theme, as I greatly fear I shall,' said Traddles, hesitating; 'but I think it necessary to bring it to your recollection. On the day of Mr Micawber's memorable denunciation, a threatening allusion was made by Uriah Heep to your aunt's – husband.'

My aunt, retaining her stiff position, and apparent composure, assented, with a nod.

'Perhaps,' observed Traddles, 'it was mere purposeless impertinence?'

'No,' returned my aunt.

'There was – pardon me – really such a person, and at all in his power?' hinted Traddles.

'Yes, my good friend,' said my aunt.

Traddles, with a perceptible lengthening of his face, explained that he had not been able to approach this subject; that it had shared the fate of Mr Micawber's liabilities, in not being comprehended in the terms he had made; that we were no longer of any authority with Uriah Heep; and that if he could do us, or any of us, any injury or annoyance, no doubt he would.

My aunt remained quiet; until again some stray tears found their way to her cheeks.

'You are quite right,' she said. 'It was very thoughtful to mention it.'

'Can I – or Copperfield – do anything?' asked Traddles gently.

'Nothing,' said my aunt. 'I thank you many times. Trot, my dear, a vain threat! Let us have Mr and Mrs Micawber back. And don't any of you speak to me!' With that she smoothed her dress, and sat, with her upright carriage, looking at the door.

'Well, Mr and Mrs Micawber!' said my aunt, when they entered. 'We have been discussing your emigration, with many apologies to you for keeping you out of the room so long, and I'll tell you what arrangements we propose.'

These she explained to the unbounded satisfaction of the family – children and all being then present – and so much to the awakening of Mr Micawber's punctual habits in the opening stage of all bill transactions, that he could not be dissuaded from immediately rushing out, in the highest spirits, to buy the stamps for his notes of hand. But his joy received a sudden check; for within five minutes, he returned in the custody of a sheriff's officer, informing us, in a flood of tears, that all was lost. We, being quite prepared for this event, which was of course a proceeding of Uriah Heep's, soon paid the money; and in five minutes more Mr Micawber was seated at the table, filling up the stamps with an expression of perfect joy, which only that congenial employment, or the making of punch, could impart in full completeness to his shining face. To see him at work on the stamps, with the relish of an artist, touching them like pictures, looking at them sideways, taking weighty notes of dates and amounts in his pocket-book, and contemplating them when finished, with a high sense of their precious value, was a sight indeed.

'Now, the best thing you can do, sir, if you'll allow me to advise you,' said my aunt, after silently observing him, 'is to abjure that occupation for ever more.'

'Madam,' replied Mr Micawber, 'it is my intention to register such a vow on the virgin page of the future. Mrs Micawber will attest it. I trust,' said Mr Micawber solemnly, 'that my son Wilkins will ever bear in mind, that he had infinitely better put his fist in the fire, than use it to handle the serpents that have poisoned the lifeblood of his unhappy parent!' Deeply affected, and changed in a moment to the image of despair, Mr Micawber regarded the serpents with a look of gloomy abhorrence (in which his late admiration of them was not quite subdued), folded them up, and put them in his pocket.

This closed the proceedings of the evening. We were weary with sorrow and fatigue, and my aunt and I were to return to London on the morrow. It was arranged that the Micawbers should follow us, after effecting a sale of their goods to a broker; that Mr Wickfield's affairs should be brought to a settlement, with all convenient speed, under the direction of Traddles; and that Agnes should also come to London, pending those arrangements. We passed the night at the old house, which, freed from the presence of the Heeps, seemed purged of a disease; and I lay in my old room, like a shipwrecked wanderer come home.

We went back next day to my aunt's house – not to mine; and when she and I sat alone, as of old, before going to bed, she said: 'Trot, do you really wish to know what I have had upon my mind lately?'

'Indeed I do, aunt. If there ever was a time when I felt unwilling that you should have a sorrow or anxiety which I could not share, it is now.'

'You have had sorrow enough, child,' said my aunt affectionately, 'without the addition of *my* little miseries. I could have no other motive, Trot, in keeping anything from you.'

'I know that well,' said I. 'But tell me now.'

'Would you ride with me a little way tomorrow morning?' asked my aunt.

'Of course.'

'At nine,' said she. 'I'll tell you then, my dear.'

At nine, accordingly, we went out in a little chariot, and drove to London. We drove a long way through the streets until we came to one of the large hospitals. Standing hard by the building was a plain hearse. The driver recognised my aunt, and in obedience to a motion of her hand at the window, drove slowly off, we following.

'You understand it now, Trot,' said my aunt. 'He is gone!'

'Did he die in the hospital?'

'Yes.'

She sat immovable beside me; but, again I saw the stray tears on her face.

'He was there once before,' said my aunt presently. 'He was ailing a long time – a shattered, broken man, these many years. When he knew his state in this last illness, he asked them to send for me. He was sorry then. Very sorry.'

'You went, I know, aunt.'

'I went. I was with him a good deal afterwards.'

'He died the night before we went to Canterbury?' said I.

My aunt nodded. 'No one can harm him now,' she said. 'It was a vain threat.'

We drove away, out of town, to the churchyard at Hornsey. 'Better here than in the streets,' said my aunt. 'He was born here.'

We alighted; and followed the plain coffin to a corner I remember well, where the service was read, consigning it to the dust.

'Six-and-thirty years ago, this day, my dear,' said my aunt, as we walked back to the chariot, 'I was married. God forgive us all!'

We took our seats in silence; and so she sat beside me for a long time, holding my hand. At length she suddenly burst into tears, and said: 'He was a fine-looking man when I married him, Trot – and he was sadly changed!'

It did not last long. After the relief of tears, she soon became composed, and even cheerful. Her nerves were a little shaken, she said, or she would not have given way to it. God forgive us all!

So we rode back to her little cottage at Highgate, where we found the following short note, which had arrived by that morning's post, from Mr Micawber:

Canterbury, Friday

MY DEAR MADAM, AND COPPERFIELD – The fair land of promise lately looming on the horizon is again enveloped in impenetrable mists, and for ever withdrawn from the eyes of a drifting wretch whose Doom is sealed!

Another writ has been issued (in His Majesty's High Court of King's Bench at Westminster), in another cause of Heep *v.* Micawber, and the defendant in that cause is the prey of the sheriff having legal jurisdiction in this bailiwick.

Now's the day, and now's the hour,
See the front of battle lower,
See approach proud Edward's power –
Chains and slavery!

Consigned to which, and to a speedy end (for mental torture is not supportable beyond a certain point, and that point I feel I have attained), my course is run. Bless you, bless you! Some future traveller, visiting, from motives of curiosity, not unmingled, let us hope, with sympathy, the place of confinement allotted to debtors in this city, may, and I trust will, Ponder, as he traces on its wall, inscribed with a rusty nail,

The obscure initials,

W. M.

P. S. I reopen this to say that our common friend, Mr Thomas Traddles (who has not yet left us, and is looking extremely well), has paid the debt and costs, in the noble name of Miss Trotwood; and that myself and family are at the height of earthly bliss.'

CHAPTER 55

Tempest

I now approach an event in my life, so indelible, so awful, so bound by an infinite variety of ties to all that has preceded it, in these pages, that, from the beginning of my narrative, I have seen it growing larger and larger as I advanced, like a great tower in a plain, and throwing its forecast shadow even on the incidents of my childish days.

For years after it occurred, I dreamed of it often. I have started up so vividly impressed by it that its fury has yet seemed raging in my quiet room, in the still night. I dream of it sometimes, though at lengthened and uncertain intervals, to this hour. I have an association between it and a stormy wind, or the lightest mention of a sea-shore, as strong as any of which my mind is conscious. As plainly as I behold what happened, I will try to write it down. I do not recall it, but see it done; for it happens again before me.

The time drawing on rapidly for the sailing of the emigrant ship, my good old nurse (almost broken-hearted for me, when we first met) came up to London. I was constantly with her, and her brother, and the Micawbers (they being very much together); but Emily I never saw.

One evening when the time was close at hand, I was alone with Peggotty and her brother. Our conversation turned on Ham. She described to us how tenderly he had taken leave of her, and how manfully and quietly he had borne himself; most of all, of late, when she believed he was most tried. It was a subject of which the affectionate creature never tired; and our interest in hearing the many examples which she, who was so much with him, had to relate, was equal to hers in relating them.

My aunt and I were at that time vacating the two cottages at Highgate; I intending to go abroad, and she to return to her house at Dover. We had a temporary lodging in Covent Garden. As I walked home to it, after this evening's conversation, reflecting on what had passed between Ham and myself when I was last at Yarmouth, I wavered in the original purpose I had formed, of leaving a letter for Emily when I should take leave of her uncle on board the ship, and thought it would be better to write to her now. She might desire, I thought, after receiving my communication, to send some parting word by me to her unhappy lover. I ought to give her the opportunity.

I therefore sat down in my room, before going to bed, and wrote to her. I told her that I had seen him, and that he had requested me to tell her what I have already written in its place in these sheets. I faithfully repeated it. I had no need to enlarge upon it, if I had had the right. Its deep fidelity and goodness were not to be adorned by me or any man. I left it out, to be sent round in the morning; with a line to Mr Peggotty, requesting him to give it to her; and went to bed at daybreak.

I was weaker than I knew then; and, not falling asleep until the sun was up, lay late, and unrefreshed, next day. I was roused by the silent presence of my aunt at my bedside. I felt it in my sleep, as I suppose we all do feel such things.

'Trot, my dear,' she said, when I opened my eyes, 'I couldn't make up my mind to disturb you. Mr Peggotty is here; shall he come up?'

I replied yes, and he soon appeared.

'Mas'r Davy,' he said, when we had shaken hands, 'I giv' Em'ly your letter, sir, and she writ this heer; and begged of me fur to ask you to read it, and, if you see no hurt in 't, to be so kind as to take charge on 't.'

'Have you read it?' said I.

He nodded sorrowfully. I opened it, and read as follows:

I have got your message. Oh, what can I write, to thank you for your good and blessed kindness to me!

I have put the words close to my heart. I shall keep them

till I die. They are sharp thorns, but they are such comfort. I have prayed over them, oh, I have prayed so much. When I find what you are, and what uncle is, I think what God must be, and can cry to him.

Goodbye for ever. Now, my dear, my friend, goodbye for ever in this world. In another world, if I am forgiven, I may wake a child, and come to you. All thanks and blessings. Farewell, evermore.

This, blotted with tears, was the letter.

'May I tell her as you don't see no hurt in 't, and as you'll be so kiend as take charge on 't, Mas'r Davy?' said Mr Peggotty, when I had read it.

'Unquestionably,' said I; 'but I am thinking – '

'Yes, Mas'r Davy?'

'I am thinking,' said I, 'that I'll go down again to Yarmouth. There's time, and to spare, for me to go and come back before the ship sails. My mind is constantly running on him, in his solitude; to put this letter of her writing in his hand at this time, and to enable you to tell her, in the moment of parting, that he has got it, will be a kindness to both of them. I solemnly accepted his commission, dear good fellow, and cannot discharge it too completely. The journey is nothing to me. I am restless, and shall be better in motion. I'll go down tonight.'

Though he anxiously endeavoured to dissuade me, I saw that he was of my mind; and this, if I had required to be confirmed in my intention, would have had the effect. He went round to the coach-office, at my request, and took the box-seat for me on the mail. In the evening I started, by that conveyance, down the road I had traversed under so many vicissitudes.

'Don't you think that,' I asked the coachman, in the first stage out of London, 'a very remarkable sky? I don't remember to have seen one like it.'

'Nor I – not equal to it,' he replied. 'That's wind, sir. There'll be mischief done at sea, I expect, before long.'

It was a murky confusion – here and there blotted with a colour like the colour of the smoke from damp fuel – of flying clouds tossed up into most remarkable heaps, suggesting greater heights in the clouds than there were depths below them to the bottom of the deepest hollows in the earth, through which the wild moon seemed to plunge headlong, as if, in a dread disturbance of the laws of nature, she had lost her way, and were frightened. There had been a wind all day; and it was rising then, with an extraordinary great sound. In another hour it had much increased, and the sky was more overcast, and it blew hard.

But as the night advanced, the clouds closing in and densely over-spreading the whole sky, then very dark, it came on to blow, harder and harder. It still increased, until our horses could scarcely face the wind. Many times, in the dark part of the night (it was then late in September, when the nights were not short), the leaders turned about, or came to a dead stop; and we were often in serious apprehension that the coach would be blown over. Sweeping gusts of rain came up before this storm like showers of steel; and at those times, when there was any shelter of trees or lee walls to be got, we were fain to stop, in a sheer impossibility of continuing the struggle.

When the day broke, it blew harder and harder. I had been in Yarmouth when the seamen said it blew great guns, but I had never known the like of this, or anything approaching to it. We came to Ipswich – very late, having had to fight every inch of ground since we were ten miles out of London; and found a cluster of people in the market-place, who had risen from their beds in the night, fearful of falling chimneys. Some of these, congregating about the inn-yard while we changed horses, told us of great sheets of lead having been ripped off a high church tower, and flung into a by-street, which they then blocked up. Others had to tell of country people, coming in from neighbouring villages, who had seen great trees lying torn out of the earth, and whole ricks scattered about the roads and fields. Still there was no abatement in the storm, but it blew harder.

As we struggled on, nearer and nearer to the sea, from which this mighty wind was blowing dead on shore, its force became more and more terrific. Long before we saw the sea, its spray was on our lips, and showered salt rain upon us. The water was out, over miles and miles of the flat country adjacent to Yarmouth; and every sheet and puddle lashed its banks, and had its stress of little breakers setting heavily towards us. When we came within sight of the sea, the waves on the horizon, caught at intervals above the rolling abyss, were like glimpses of another shore with towers and buildings. When at last we got into the town, the people came out to their doors, all aslant, and with streaming hair, making a wonder of the mail that had come through such a night.

I put up at the old inn, and went down to look at the sea; staggering along the street, which was strewn with sand and seaweed, and with flying blotches of sea-foam; afraid of falling slates and tiles; and holding by people I met at angry corners. Coming near the beach, I saw, not only the boatmen, but half the people of the town, lurking behind buildings; some now and then braving the fury of the storm to look away to sea, and blown sheer out of their course in trying to get zigzag back.

Joining these groups, I found bewailing women whose husbands were away in herring or oyster boats, which there was too much reason to think might have foundered before they could run in anywhere for safety. Grizzled old sailors were among the people, shaking their heads as they looked from water to sky, and muttering to one another; ship-owners, excited and uneasy; children huddling together, and peering into older faces; even stout mariners, disturbed and anxious, levelling their glasses at the sea from behind places of shelter, as if they were surveying an enemy.

The tremendous sea itself, when I could find sufficient pause to look at it, in the agitation of the blinding wind, the flying stones and sand, and the awful noise, confounded me. As the high watery walls came rolling in, and, at their highest, tumbled into surf, they looked as if the least would engulf the town. As the receding wave swept back with a hoarse roar, it seemed to scoop out deep caves in the beach, as if its purpose were to undermine the earth. When some white-headed billows thundered on, and dashed themselves to pieces before they reached the land, every fragment of the late whole seemed possessed by the full might of its wrath, rushing to be gathered to the composition of another monster. Undulating hills were changed to valleys, undulating valleys (with a solitary storm-bird sometimes skimming through them) were lifted up to hills; masses of water shivered and shook the beach with a booming sound; every shape tumultuously rolled on, as soon as made, to change its shape and place, and beat another shape and place away; the ideal shore on the horizon, with its towers and buildings, rose and fell; the clouds flew fast and thick; I seemed to see a rending and upheaving of all nature.

Not finding Ham among the people whom this memorable wind – for it is still remembered down there as the greatest ever known to blow upon that coast – had brought together, I made my way to his house. It was shut; and as no one answered to my knocking, I went by back ways and by-lanes, to the yard where he worked. I learned, there, that he had gone to Lowestoft, to meet some sudden exigency of ship-repairing in which his skill was required; but that he would be back tomorrow morning, in good time.

I went back to the inn; and when I had washed and dressed, and tried to sleep, but in vain, it was five o'clock in the afternoon. I had not sat five minutes by the coffee-room fire, when the waiter coming to stir it, as an excuse for talking, told me that two colliers had gone down, with all hands, a few miles away; and that some other ships had been seen labouring hard in the Roads, and trying, in great distress, to keep off shore. Mercy on them, and on all poor sailors, said he, if we had another night like the last!

I was very much depressed in spirits; very solitary; and felt an uneasiness in Ham's not being there, disproportionate to the occasion. I was seriously affected, without knowing how much, by late events; and my long exposure to the fierce wind had confused me. There was that jumble in my thoughts and recollections that I had lost the clear arrangement of time and distance. Thus, if I had gone out into the town, I should not have been surprised, I think, to encounter someone who I knew must be then in London. So to speak, there was in these respects a curious inattention in my mind. Yet it was busy, too, with all the remembrances the place naturally awakened; and they were particularly distinct and vivid.

In this state the waiter's dismal intelligence about the ships immediately connected itself, without any effort of my volition, with my uneasiness about Ham. I was persuaded that I had an apprehension of his returning from Lowestoft by sea, and being lost. This grew so strong with me that I resolved to go back to the yard before I took my dinner, and ask the boat-builder if he thought his attempting to return by sea at all likely? If he gave me the least reason to think so, I would go over to Lowestoft and prevent it by bringing him with me.

I hastily ordered my dinner, and went back to the yard. I was none too soon; for the boat-builder, with a lantern in his hand, was locking the yard gate. He quite laughed, when I asked him the question, and said there was no fear; no man in his senses, or out of them, would put off in such a gale of wind, least of all Ham Peggotty, who had been born to seafaring.

So sensible of this beforehand that I had really felt ashamed of doing what I was nevertheless impelled to do, I went back to

the inn. If such a wind could rise, I think it was rising. The howl and roar, the rattling of the doors and windows, the rumbling in the chimneys, the apparent rocking of the very house that sheltered me, and the prodigious tumult of the sea, were more fearful than in the morning. But there was now a great darkness besides; and that invested the storm with new terrors, real and fanciful.

I could not eat, I could not sit still, I could not continue steadfast to anything. Something within me, faintly answering to the storm without, tossed up the depths of my memory, and made a tumult in them. Yet, in all the hurry of my thoughts, wild running with the thundering sea – the storm and my uneasiness regarding Ham were always in the foreground.

My dinner went away almost untasted, and I tried to refresh myself with a glass or two of wine. In vain. I fell into a dull slumber before the fire, without losing my consciousness, either of the uproar out of doors, or of the place in which I was. Both became overshadowed by a new and indefinable horror; and when I awoke – or rather when I shook off the lethargy that bound me in my chair – my whole frame thrilled with objectless and unintelligible fear.

I walked to and fro, tried to read an old gazetteer, listened to the awful noises; looked at faces, scenes, and figures in the fire. At length, the steady ticking of the undisturbed clock on the wall tormented me to that degree that I resolved to go to bed.

It was reassuring, on such a night, to be told that some of the inn-servants had agreed together to sit up until morning. I went to bed, exceedingly weary and heavy; but on my lying down, all such sensations vanished, as if by magic, and I was broad awake, with every sense refined.

For hours I lay there, listening to the wind and water; imagining, now, that I heard shrieks out at sea; now, that I distinctly heard the firing of signal guns; and now, the fall of houses in the town. I got up, several times, and looked out; but could see nothing, except the reflection in the window-panes of the faint candle I had left burning, and of my own haggard face looking in at me from the black void.

At length, my restlessness attained to such a pitch that I hurried on my clothes, and went downstairs. In the large kitchen, where I dimly saw bacon and ropes of onions hanging from the beams, the watchers were clustered together, in various attitudes, about a table, purposely moved away from the great chimney, and brought near the door. A pretty girl, who had her ears stopped with her apron, and her eyes upon the door, screamed when I appeared, supposing me to be a spirit; but the others had more presence of mind, and were glad of an addition to their company. One man, referring to the topic they had been discussing, asked me whether I thought the souls of the collier-crews who had gone down were out in the storm?

I remained there, I dare say, two hours. Once, I opened the yard gate, and looked into the empty street. The sand, the seaweed, and the flakes of foam were driving by, and I was obliged to call for assistance before I could shut the gate again, and make it fast against the wind.

There was a dark gloom in my solitary chamber, when I at

length returned to it; but I was tired now, and getting into bed again, fell – off a tower and down a precipice – into the depths of sleep. I have an impression that for a long time, though I dreamed of being elsewhere and in a variety of scenes, it was always blowing in my dream. At length, I lost that feeble hold upon reality, and was engaged with two dear friends, but who they were I don't know, at the siege of some town in a roar of cannonading.

The thunder of the cannon was so loud and incessant, that I could not hear something I much desired to hear, until I made a great exertion and awoke. It was broad day – eight or nine o'clock; the storm raging, in lieu of the batteries; and someone knocking and calling at my door.

'What is the matter?' I cried.

'A wreck! Close by!'

I sprung out of bed, and asked what wreck?

'A schooner, from Spain or Portugal, laden with fruit and wine. Make haste, sir, if you want to see her! It's thought, down on the beach, she'll go to pieces every moment.'

The excited voice went clamouring along the staircase; and I wrapped myself in my clothes as quickly as I could, and ran into the street.

Numbers of people were there before me, all running in one direction, to the beach. I ran the same way, outstripping a good many, and soon came facing the wild sea.

The wind might by this time have lulled a little, though not more sensibly than if the cannonading I had dreamed of had been diminished by the silencing of half a dozen guns out of hundreds. But the sea, having upon it the additional agitation of the whole night, was infinitely more terrific than when I had seen it last. Every appearance it had then presented bore the expression of being *swelled*; and the height to which the breakers rose, and, looking over one another, bore one another down, and rolled in, in interminable hosts, was most appalling.

In the difficulty of hearing anything but wind and waves, and in the crowd, and the unspeakable confusion, and my first breathless efforts to stand against the weather, I was so confused that I looked out to sea for the wreck, and saw nothing but the foaming heads of the great waves. A half-dressed boatman, standing next me, pointed with his bare arm (a tattooed arrow on it, pointing in the same direction) to the left. Then, O great Heaven, I saw it, close in upon us!

One mast was broken short off, six or eight feet from the deck, and lay over the side, entangled in a maze of sail and rigging; and all that ruin, as the ship rolled and beat – which she did without a moment's pause, and with a violence quite inconceivable – beat the side as if it would stave it in. Some efforts were even then being made to cut this portion of the wreck away; for, as the ship, which was broadside on, turned towards us in her rolling, I plainly descried her people at work with axes, especially one active figure with long curling hair, conspicuous among the rest. But a great cry, which was audible even above the wind and water, rose from the shore at this moment; the sea, sweeping over the rolling wreck, made a clean breach, and carried men, spars, casks, planks, bulwarks, heaps of such toys, into the boiling surge.

The second mast was yet standing, with the rags of a rent sail, and a wild confusion of broken cordage flapping to and fro. The ship had struck once, the same boatman hoarsely said in my ear, and then lifted in and struck again. I understood him to add that she was parting amidships, and I could readily suppose so, for the rolling and beating were too tremendous for any human work to suffer long. As he spoke, there was another great cry of pity from the beach; four men arose with the wreck out of the deep, clinging to the rigging of the remaining mast; uppermost, the active figure with the curling hair.

There was a bell on board; and as the ship rolled and dashed, like a desperate creature driven mad, now showing us the whole sweep of her deck, as she turned on her beam-ends towards the shore, now nothing but her keel, as she sprung wildly over and turned towards the sea, the bell rang; and its sound, the knell of those unhappy men, was borne towards us on the wind. Again we lost her, and again she rose. Two men were gone. The agony on shore increased. Men groaned, and clasped their hands; women shrieked, and turned away their faces. Some ran wildly up and down along the beach, crying for help where no help could be. I found myself one of these, frantically imploring a knot of sailors whom I knew, not to let those two lost creatures perish before our eyes.

They were making out to me, in an agitated way – I don't know how, for the little I could hear I was scarcely composed enough to understand – that the lifeboat had been bravely manned an hour ago, and could do nothing; and that as no man would be so desperate as to attempt to wade off with a rope, and establish a communication with the shore, there was nothing left to try, when I noticed that some new sensation moved the people on the beach, and saw them part, and Ham come breaking through them to the front.

I ran to him – as well as I know, to repeat my appeal for help. But, distracted though I was, by a sight so new to me and terrible, the determination in his face, and his look, out to sea – exactly the same look as I remembered in connection with the morning after Emily's flight – awoke me to a knowledge of his danger. I held him back with both arms; and implored the men with whom I had been speaking, not to listen to him, not to do murder, not to let him stir from off that sand!

Another cry arose on shore; and looking to the wreck, we saw the cruel sail, with blow on blow, beat off the lower of the two men, and fly up in triumph round the active figure left alone upon the mast.

Against such a sight, and against such determination as that of the calmly desperate man who was already accustomed to lead half the people present, I might as hopefully have entreated the wind. 'Mas'r Davy,' he said, cheerily grasping me by both hands, 'if my time is come, 't is come. If 't ain't, I'll bide it. Lord above bless you, and bless all! Mates, make me ready! I'm a going off!'

I was swept away, but not unkindly, to some distance, where the people around me made me stay; urging, as I confusedly perceived, that he was bent on going, with help or without, and that I should endanger the precautions for his safety by troubling those with whom they rested. I don't know what I answered, or what they rejoined; but I saw hurry on the beach, and men running with ropes from a capstan that was there, and penetrating into a circle of figures that hid him from me. Then I saw him standing alone, in a seaman's frock and trousers, a rope in his hand or slung to his wrist, another round his body, and several of the best men holding, at a little distance, to the latter, which he laid out himself, slack upon the shore, at his feet.

The wreck, even to my unpractised eye, was breaking up. I saw that she was parting in the middle, and that the life of the solitary man upon the mast hung by a thread. Still, he clung to it. He had a singular red cap on, not like a sailor's cap, but of a finer colour; and as the few yielding planks between him and destruction rolled and bulged, and his anticipative death-knell rung, he was seen by all of us to wave it. I saw him do it now, and thought I was going distracted, when his action brought an old remembrance to my mind of a once dear friend.

Ham watched the sea, standing alone, with the silence of suspended breath behind him, and the storm before, until there was a great retiring wave, when, with a backward glance at those who held the rope which was made fast round his body, he dashed in after it, and in a moment was buffeting with the water; rising with the hills, falling with the valleys, lost beneath the foam; then drawn again to land. They hauled in hastily.

He was hurt. I saw blood on his face, from where I stood; but he took no thought of that. He seemed hurriedly to give them some directions for leaving him more free – or so I judged from the motion of his arm – and was gone as before.

And now he made for the wreck, rising with the hills, falling with the valleys, lost beneath the rugged foam, borne in towards the shore, borne on towards the ship, striving hard and valiantly. The distance was nothing, but the power of the sea and wind made the strife deadly. At length he neared the wreck. He was so near, that with one more of his vigorous strokes he would be clinging to it – when, a high, green, vast hillside of water, moving on shoreward, from beyond the ship, he seemed to leap up into it with a mighty bound, and the ship was gone!

Some eddying fragments I saw in the sea, as if a mere cask had been broken, in running to the spot where they were hauling in. Consternation was in every face. They drew him to my very feet – insensible – dead. He was carried to the nearest house; and, no one preventing me now, I remained near him, busy, while every means of restoration were tried; but he had been beaten to death by the great wave, and his generous heart was stilled for ever.

As I sat beside the bed, when hope was abandoned and all was done, a fisherman, who had known me when Emily and I were children, and ever since, whispered my name at the door.

'Sir,' said he, with tears starting to his weather-beaten face, which, with his trembling lips, was ashy pale, 'will you come over yonder?'

The old remembrance that had been recalled to me was in his look. I asked him, terror-stricken, leaning on the arm he held out to support me: 'Has a body come ashore?'

He said, 'Yes.'

'Do I know it?' I asked then.

He answered nothing.

But he led me to the shore. And on that part of it where she and I had looked for shells, two children – on that part of it where some lighter fragments of the old boat, blown down last night, had been scattered by the wind – among the ruins of the home he had wronged – I saw him lying with his head upon his arm, as I had often seen him lie at school.

CHAPTER 56

The New Wound, and the Old

No need, O Steerforth, to have said, when we last spoke together, in that hour which I so little deemed to be our parting hour – no need to have said, 'Think of me at my best!' I had done that ever; and could I change now, looking on this sight!

They brought a hand-bier, and laid him on it, and covered him with a flag, and took him up and bore him on towards the houses. All the men who carried him had known him, and gone sailing with him, and seen him merry and bold. They carried him through the wild roar, a hush in the midst of all the tumult; and took him to the cottage where Death was already.

But when they set their bier down on the threshold, they looked at one another, and at me, and whispered. I knew why. They felt as if it were not right to lay him down in the same quiet room.

We went into the town, and took our burden to the inn. So soon as I could at all collect my thoughts, I sent for Joram, and begged him to provide me a conveyance in which it could be got to London in the night. I knew that the care of it, and the hard duty of preparing his mother to receive it, could only rest with me, and I was anxious to discharge that duty as faithfully as I could.

I chose the night for the journey, that there might be less curiosity when I left the town. But although it was nearly midnight when I came out of the yard in a chaise, followed by what I had in charge, there were many people waiting. At intervals, along the town, and even a little way out upon the road, I saw more; but at length only the bleak night and the open country were around me, and the ashes of my youthful friendship.

Upon a mellow autumn day, about noon, when the ground was perfumed by fallen leaves, and many more, in beautiful tints of yellow, red, and brown, yet hung upon the trees, through which the sun was shining, I arrived at Highgate. I walked the last mile, thinking as I went along of what I had to do; and left the carriage that had followed me all through the night, awaiting orders to advance.

The house, when I came up to it, looked just the same. Not a blind was raised; no sign of life was in the dull paved court, with its covered way leading to the disused door. The wind had quite gone down, and nothing moved.

I had not, at first, the courage to ring at the gate; and when I did ring, my errand seemed to me to be expressed in the very sound of the bell. The little parlour-maid came out, with the key in her hand; and looking earnestly at me as she unlocked the gate, said: 'I beg your pardon, sir. Are you ill?'

'I have been much agitated, and am fatigued.'

'Is anything the matter, sir? – Mr James? – '

'Hush!' said I. 'Yes, something has happened, that I have to break to Mrs Steerforth. She is at home?'

The girl anxiously replied that her mistress was very seldom out now, even in a carriage; that she kept her room; that she saw no company, but would see me. Her mistress was up, she said, and Miss Dartle was with her. What message should she take upstairs?

Giving her a strict charge to be careful of her manner, and only to carry in my card and say I waited, I sat down in the drawing-room (which we had now reached) until she should come back. Its former pleasant air of occupation was gone, and the shutters were half closed. The harp had not been used for many and many a day. His picture, as a boy, was there. The cabinet in which his mother had kept his letters was there. I wondered if she ever read them now; if she would ever read them more!

The house was so still, that I heard the girl's light step upstairs. On her return, she brought a message, to the effect that Mrs Steerforth was an invalid and could not come down; but that if I would excuse her being in her chamber, she would be glad to see me. In a few moments I stood before her.

She was in his room; not in her own. I felt, of course, that she had taken to occupy it, in remembrance of him; and that the many tokens of his old sports and accomplishments, by which she was surrounded, remained there, just as he had left them, for the same reason. She murmured, however, even in her reception of me, that she was out of her own chamber because its aspect was unsuited to her infirmity; and with her stately look repelled the least suspicion of the truth.

At her chair, as usual, was Rosa Dartle. From the first moment of her dark eyes resting on me, I saw she knew I was the bearer of evil tidings. The scar sprung into view that instant. She withdrew herself a step behind the chair, to keep her own face out of Mrs Steerforth's observation; and scrutinised me with a piercing gaze that never faltered, never shrunk.

'I am sorry to observe you are in mourning, sir,' said Mrs Steerforth.

'I am unhappily a widower,' said I.

'You are very young to know so great a loss,' she returned. 'I am grieved to hear it. I am grieved to hear it. I hope Time will be good to you.'

'I hope Time,' said I, looking at her, 'will be good to all of us. Dear Mrs Steerforth, we must all trust to that, in our heaviest misfortunes.'

The earnestness of my manner, and the tears in my eyes, alarmed her. The whole course of her thoughts appeared to stop, and change.

I tried to command my voice in gently saying his name, but it trembled. She repeated it to herself, two or three times, in a low tone. Then, addressing me, she said, with enforced calmness: 'My son is ill.'

'Very ill.'

'You have seen him?'

'I have.'

'Are you reconciled?'

I could not say Yes, I could not say No. She slightly turned her head towards the spot where Rosa Dartle had been standing at her elbow, and in that moment I said, by the motion of my lips, to Rosa, 'Dead!'

That Mrs Steerforth might not be induced to look behind her, and read, plainly written, what she was not yet prepared to know, I met her look quickly, but I had seen Rosa Dartle throw her hands up in the air with vehemence of despair and horror, and then clasp them on her face.

The handsome lady – so like, oh, so like! – regarded me with a fixed look, and put her hand to her forehead. I besought her to be calm, and prepare herself to bear what I had to tell; but I should rather have entreated her to weep, for she sat like a stone figure.

'When I was last here,' I faltered, 'Miss Dartle told me he was sailing here and there. The night before last was a dreadful one at sea. If he were at sea that night, and near a dangerous coast, as it is said he was; and if the vessel that was seen should really be the ship which – '

'Rosa!' said Mrs Steerforth, 'come to me!'

She came, but with no sympathy or gentleness. Her eyes gleamed like fire as she confronted his mother, and broke into a frightful laugh.

'Now,' she said, 'is your pride appeased, you madwoman? *Now* has he made atonement to you – with his life! Do you hear? – His life!'

Mrs Steerforth, fallen back stiffly in her chair, and making no sound but a moan, cast her eyes upon her with a wide stare.

'Aye!' cried Rosa, smiting herself passionately on the breast, 'look at me! Moan, and groan, and look at me! Look here!' striking the scar, 'at your dead child's handiwork!'

The moan the mother uttered, from time to time, went to my heart. Always the same. Always inarticulate and stifled. Always accompanied with an incapable motion of the head, but with no change of face. Always proceeding from a rigid mouth and closed teeth, as if the jaw were locked and the face frozen up in pain.

'Do you remember when he did this?' she proceeded. 'Do you remember when, in his inheritance of your nature, and in your pampering of his pride and passion, he did this, and disfigured me for life? Look at me, marked until I die with his high displeasure; and moan and groan for what you made him!'

'Miss Dartle,' I entreated her. 'For Heaven's sake – '

'I *will* speak!' she said, turning on me with her lightning eyes. 'Be silent, you! Look at me, I say, proud mother of a proud false son! Moan for your nurture of him, moan for your corruption of him, moan for your loss of him, moan for mine!'

She clenched her hand, and trembled through her spare worn figure, as if her passion were killing her by inches.

'You resent his self-will!' she exclaimed. 'You, injured by his haughty temper! You, who opposed to both, when your hair was grey, the qualities which made both when you gave him birth! You, who from his cradle reared him to be what he was, and stunted what he should have been! Are you rewarded, *now*, for your years of trouble?'

'Oh, Miss Dartle, shame! oh, cruel!'

'I tell you,' she returned, 'I *will* speak to her. No power on earth should stop me, while I was standing here! Have I been silent all these years, and shall I not speak now? I loved him better than you ever loved him!' turning on her fiercely. 'I could have loved him, and asked no return. If I had been his wife, I could have been the slave of his caprices for a word of love a year. I should have been. Who knows it better than I? You were exacting, proud, punctilious, selfish. My love would have been devoted – would have trod your paltry whimpering under foot!'

With flashing eyes, she stamped upon the ground as if she actually did it.

'Look here!' she said, striking the scar again, with a relentless hand. 'When he grew into the better understanding of what he had done, he saw it, and repented of it! I could sing to him, and talk to him, and show the ardour that I felt in all he did, and attain with labour to such knowledge as most interested him; and I attracted him. When he was freshest and truest, he loved *me*. Yes, he did! Many a time, when you were put off with a slight word, he has taken Me to his heart!'

She said it with a taunting pride in the midst of her frenzy – for it was little less – yet with an eager remembrance of it, in which the smouldering embers of a gentler feeling kindled for the moment.

'I descended – as I might have known I should, but that he fascinated me with his boyish courtship – into a doll, a trifle for

I am the bearer of evil tidings

the occupation of an idle hour, to be dropped, and taken up, and trifled with, as the inconstant humour took him. When he grew weary, I grew weary. As his fancy died out, I would no more have tried to strengthen any power I had than I would have married him on his being forced to take me for his wife. We fell away from one another without a word. Perhaps you saw it, and were not sorry. Since then, I have been a mere disfigured piece of furniture between you both; having no eyes, no ears, no feelings, no remembrances. Moan? Moan for what you made him; not for your love. I tell you that the time was when I loved him better than you ever did!'

She stood with her bright angry eyes confronting the wide stare, and the set face; and softened no more, when the moaning was repeated, than if the face had been a picture.

'Miss Dartle,' said I, 'if you can be so obdurate as not to feel for this afflicted mother – '

'Who feels for me?' she sharply retorted. 'She has sown this. Let her moan for the harvest that she reaps today!'

'And if his faults – ' I began.

'Faults!' she cried, bursting into passionate tears. 'Who dares malign him? He had a soul worth millions of the friends to whom he stooped!'

'No one can have loved him better, no one can hold him in dearer remembrance than I,' I replied. 'I meant to say, if you have no compassion for his mother; or if his faults – you have been bitter on them – '

'It's false,' she cried, tearing her black hair; 'I loved him!'

' – if his faults cannot,' I went on, 'be banished from your remembrance, in such an hour; look at that figure, even as one you have never seen before, and render it some help!'

All this time, the figure was unchanged, and looked un-changeable. Motionless, rigid, staring; moaning in the same dumb way from time to time, with the same helpless motion of the head; but giving no other sign of life. Miss Dartle suddenly kneeled down before it, and began to loosen the dress.

'A curse upon you!' she said, looking round at me, with a mingled expression of rage and grief. 'It was in an evil hour that you ever came here! A curse upon you! Go!'

After passing out of the room, I hurried back to ring the bell, the sooner to alarm the servants. She had then taken the impassive figure in her arms, and, still, upon her knees, was weeping over it, kissing it, calling to it, rocking it to and fro upon her bosom like a child, and trying every tender means to rouse the dormant senses. No longer afraid of leaving her, I noiselessly turned back again; and alarmed the house as I went out.

Later in the day, I returned, and we laid him in his mother's room. She was just the same, they told me; Miss Dartle never left her; doctors were in attendance; many things had been tried; but she lay like a statue, except for the low sound now and then.

I went through the dreary house, and darkened the windows. The windows of the chamber where he lay, I darkened last. I lifted up the leaden hand, and held it to my heart; and all the world seemed death and silence, broken only by his mother's moaning.

475

CHAPTER 57

The Emigrants

One thing more I had to do, before yielding myself to the shock of these emotions. It was to conceal what had occurred from those who were going away; and to dismiss them on their voyage in happy ignorance. In this, no time was to be lost.

I took Mr Micawber aside that same night, and confided to him the task of standing between Mr Peggotty and intelligence of the late catastrophe. He zealously undertook to do so, and to intercept any newspaper through which it might, without such precautions, reach him.

'If it penetrates to him, sir,' said Mr Micawber, striking himself on the breast, 'it shall first pass through this body!'

Mr Micawber, I must observe, in his adaptation of himself to a new state of society, had acquired a bold buccaneering air, not absolutely lawless, but defensive and prompt. One might have supposed him a child of the wilderness, long accustomed to live out of the confines of civilisation, and about to return to his native wilds.

He had provided himself, among other things, with a complete suit of oilskin, and a straw hat with a very low crown, pitched or caulked on the outside. In this rough clothing, with a common mariner's telescope under his arm, and a shrewd trick of casting up his eye at the sky as looking out for dirty weather, he was far more nautical, after his manner, than Mr Peggotty. His whole family, if I may so express it, were cleared for action. I found Mrs Micawber in the closest and most uncompromising of bonnets, made fast under the chin; and in a shawl which tied her up (as I had been tied up, when my aunt first received me) like a bundle, and was secured behind at the waist, in a strong knot. Miss Micawber I found made snug for stormy weather, in the same manner; with nothing superfluous about her. Master Micawber was hardly visible in a Guernsey shirt, and the shaggiest suit of slops I ever saw; and the children were done up, like preserved meats, in impervious cases. Both Mr Micawber and his eldest son wore their sleeves loosely turned back at the wrists, as being ready to lend a hand in any direction, and to 'tumble up,' or sing out, 'Yeo – Heave – Yeo!' on the shortest notice.

Thus Traddles and I found them at nightfall, assembled on the wooden steps, at that time known as Hungerford Stairs, watching the departure of a boat with some of their property on board. I had told Traddles of the terrible event, and it had greatly shocked him; but there could be no doubt of the kindness of keeping it a secret, and he had come to help me in this last service. It was here that I took Mr Micawber aside, and received his promise.

The Micawber family were lodged in a little, dirty, tumbledown public-house, which in those days was close to the stairs, and whose protruding wooden rooms overhung the river. The family, as emigrants, being objects of some interest in and about Hungerford, attracted so many beholders that we were glad to take refuge in their room. It was one of the wooden chambers upstairs, with the tide flowing underneath. My aunt and Agnes were there, busily making some little extra comforts, in the way of dress, for the children. Peggotty was quietly assisting, with the old insensible work-box, yard-measure, and bit of wax candle before her, that had now outlived so much.

It was not easy to answer her enquiries; still less to whisper to Mr Peggotty, when Mr Micawber brought him in, that I had given the letter, and all was well. But I did both, and made them happy. If I showed any trace of what I felt, my own sorrows were sufficient to account for it.

'And when does the ship sail, Mr Micawber?' asked my aunt.

Mr Micawber considered it necessary to prepare either my aunt or his wife, by degrees, and said, sooner than he had expected yesterday.

'The boat brought you word, I suppose?' said my aunt.

'It did, ma'am,' he returned.

'Well?' said my aunt. 'And she sails – '

'Madam,' he replied, 'I am informed that we must positively be on board before seven tomorrow morning.'

'Heyday!' said my aunt, 'that's soon. Is it a seagoing fact, Mr Peggotty?'

''Tis so, ma'am. She'll drop down the river with that theer tide. If Mas'r Davy and my sister comes aboard at Gravesen', arternoon o' next day, they'll see the last on us.'

'And that we shall do,' said I, 'be sure!'

'Until then, and until we are at sea,' observed Mr Micawber, with a glance of intelligence at me, 'Mr Peggotty and myself will constantly keep a double look-out together, on our goods and chattels. Emma, my love,' said Mr Micawber, clearing his throat in his magnificent way, 'my friend Mr Thomas Traddles is so obliging as to solicit, in my ear, that he should have the privilege of ordering the ingredients necessary to the composition of a moderate portion of that Beverage which is peculiarly associated, in our minds, with the Roast Beef of Old England. I allude to – in short, Punch. Under ordinary circumstances, I should scruple to entreat the indulgence of Miss Trotwood and Miss Wickfield, but – '

'I can only say for myself,' said my aunt, 'that I will drink all happiness and success to you, Mr Micawber, with the utmost pleasure.'

'And I, too!' said Agnes, with a smile.

Mr Micawber immediately descended to the bar, where he appeared to be quite at home; and in due time returned with a steaming jug. I could not but observe that he had been peeling the lemons with his own clasp-knife, which, as became the knife of a practical settler, was about a foot long; and which he wiped, not wholly without ostentation, on the sleeve of his coat. Mrs Micawber and the two elder members of the family I now found to be provided with similar formidable instruments, while every child had its own wooden spoon attached to its body by a strong line. In a similar anticipation of life afloat, and in the Bush, Mr Micawber, instead of helping Mrs Micawber and his eldest son and daughter to punch, in wineglasses, which he might easily have done, for there was a shelf-full in the room, served it out to them in a series of villainous little tin pots; and I never saw him enjoy anything so much as drinking out of his own particular pint pot, and putting it in his pocket at the close of the evening.

'The luxuries of the old country,' said Mr Micawber, with an intense satisfaction in their renouncement, 'we abandon. The denizens of the forest cannot, of course, expect to participate in the refinements of the land of the Free.'

Here a boy came in to say that Mr Micawber was wanted downstairs.

'I have a presentiment,' said Mrs Micawber, setting down her tin pot, 'that it is a member of my family!'

'If so, my dear,' observed Mr Micawber, with his usual suddenness of warmth on that subject, 'as the member of your family – whoever he, she, or it may be – has kept *us* waiting for a considerable period, perhaps the Member may now wait *my* convenience.'

'Micawber,' said his wife in a low tone, 'at such a time as this – '

' "It is not meet," ' said Mr Micawber, rising, ' "that every nice offence should bear its comment!" Emma, I stand reproved.'

'The loss, Micawber,' observed his wife, 'has been my family's, not yours. If my family are at length sensible of the deprivation to which their own conduct has, in the past, exposed them, and now desire to extend the hand of fellowship, let it not be repulsed.'

'My dear,' he returned, 'so be it!'

'If not for their sakes, for mine, Micawber,' said his wife.

'Emma,' he returned, 'that view of the question is, at such a moment, irresistible. I cannot, even now, distinctly pledge myself to fall upon your family's neck; but the member of your family, who is now in attendance, shall have no genial warmth frozen by me.'

Mr Micawber withdrew, and was absent some little time; in the course of which Mrs Micawber was not wholly free from an apprehension that words might have arisen between him and the Member. At length the same boy reappeared, and presented me with a note written in pencil, and headed, in a legal manner, 'Heep v. Micawber.' From this document, I learned that Mr Micawber, being again arrested, was in a final paroxysm of despair; and that he begged me to send him his knife and pint pot, by bearer, as they might prove serviceable during the brief remainder of his existence, in jail. He also requested, as a last act of friendship, that I would see his family to the Parish Workhouse, and forget that such a Being ever lived.

Of course I answered this note by going down with the boy to pay the money, where I found Mr Micawber sitting in a corner, looking darkly at the Sheriff's Officer who had effected the capture. On his release, he embraced me with the utmost fervour; and made an entry of the transaction in his pocket-book – being very particular, I recollect, about a halfpenny I inadvertently omitted from my statement of the total.

This momentous pocket-book was a timely reminder to him of another transaction. On our return to the room upstairs (where he accounted for his absence by saying that it had been occasioned by circumstances over which he had no control), he took out of it a large sheet of paper, folded small, and quite covered with long sums, carefully worked. From the glimpse I had of them, I should say that I never saw such sums out of a school ciphering-book. These, it seemed, were calculations of compound interest on what he called 'the principal amount of forty-one, ten, eleven and a half,' for various periods. After a careful consideration of these, and an elaborate estimate of his resources, he had come to the conclusion to select that sum which represented the amount with compound interest to two years, fifteen calendar months, and fourteen days, from that date. For this he had drawn a note of hand with great neatness, which he handed over to Traddles on the spot, a discharge of his debt in full (as between man and man), with many acknowledgments.

'I have still a presentiment,' said Mrs Micawber, pensively shaking her head, 'that my family will appear on board, before we finally depart.'

Mr Micawber evidently had his presentiment on the subject too, but he put it in his tin pot and swallowed it.

'If you have any opportunity of sending letters home, on your passage, Mrs Micawber,' said my aunt, 'you must let us hear from you, you know.'

'My dear Miss Trotwood,' she replied, 'I shall only be too happy to think that anyone expects to hear from us. I shall not fail to correspond. Mr Copperfield, I trust, as an old and familiar friend, will not object to receive occasional intelligence, himself, from one who knew him when the twins were yet unconscious?'

I said that I should hope to hear, whenever she had an opportunity of writing.

'Please Heaven, there will be many such opportunities,' said Mr Micawber. 'The ocean, in these times, is a perfect fleet of ships; and we can hardly fail to encounter many, in running over. It is merely crossing,' said Mr Micawber, trifling with his eyeglass, 'merely crossing. The distance is quite imaginary.'

I think, now, how odd it was, but how wonderfully like Mr Micawber, that, when he went from London to Canterbury, he should have talked as if he were going to the farthest limits of the earth; and when he went from England to Australia, as if he were going for a little trip across the channel.

'On the voyage, I shall endeavour,' said Mr Micawber, 'occasionally to spin them a yarn; and the melody of my son Wilkins will, I trust, be acceptable at the galley-fire. When Mrs Micawber has her sea-legs on – an expression in which I hope there is no conventional impropriety – she will give them, I dare say, 'Little Tafflin'. Porpoises and dolphins, I believe, will be frequently observed athwart our Bows, and, either on the Starboard or the Larboard Quarter, objects of interest will be continually descried. In short,' said Mr Micawber, with the old genteel air, 'the probability is, all will be found so exciting, alow and aloft, that when the look-out stationed in the main-top cries Land-ho! we shall be very considerably astonished!'

With that he flourished off the contents of his little tin pot, as if he had made the voyage, and had passed a first-class examination before the highest naval authorities.

'What *I* chiefly hope, my dear Mr Copperfield,' said Mrs Micawber, 'is, that in some branches of our family we may live again in the old country. Do not frown, Micawber! I do not now refer to my own family, but to our children's children. However vigorous the sapling,' said Mrs Micawber, shaking her head, 'I cannot forget the parent-tree; and when our race attains to eminence and fortune, I own I should wish that fortune to flow into the coffers of Britannia.'

'My dear,' said Mr Micawber, 'Britannia must take her chance. I am bound to say that she has never done much for me, and that I have no particular wish upon the subject.'

'Micawber,' returned Mrs Micawber, 'there you are wrong. You are going out, Micawber, to this distant clime, to strengthen, not to weaken, the connection between yourself and Albion.'

'The connection in question, my love,' rejoined Mr Micawber, 'has not laid me, I repeat, under that load of personal obligation, that I am at all sensitive as to the formation of another connection.'

'Micawber,' returned Mrs Micawber, 'there, I again say, you are wrong. You do not know your power, Micawber. It is that which will strengthen, even in this step you are about to take, the connection between yourself and Albion.'

Mr Micawber sat in his elbow-chair, with his eyebrows raised; half receiving and half repudiating Mrs Micawber's views as they were stated, but very sensible of their foresight.

'My dear Mr Copperfield,' said Mrs Micawber, 'I wish Mr Micawber to feel his position. It appears to me highly important that Mr Micawber should, from the hour of his embarkation, feel his position. Your old knowledge of me, my dear Mr Copperfield, will have told you that I have not the sanguine disposition of Mr Micawber. My disposition is, if I may say so, eminently practical. I know that this is a long voyage. I know that it will involve many privations and inconveniences. I cannot shut my eyes to those facts. But I also know what Mr Micawber is. I know the latent power of Mr Micawber. And therefore I consider it vitally important that Mr Micawber should feel his position.'

'My love,' he observed, 'perhaps you will allow me to remark that it is barely possible that I *do* feel my position at the present moment.'

'I think not, Micawber,' she rejoined. 'Not fully. My dear Mr Copperfield, Mr Micawber's is not a common case. Mr Micawber is going to a distant country, expressly in order that he may be fully understood and appreciated for the first time. I wish Mr Micawber to take his stand upon that vessel's prow, and firmly say, "This country I am come to conquer! Have you honours? Have you riches? Have you posts of profitable pecuniary emolument? Let them be brought forward. They are mine!" '

Mr Micawber, glancing at us all, seemed to think there was a good deal in this idea.

'I wish Mr Micawber, if I make myself understood,' said Mrs Micawber, in her argumentative tone, 'to be the Caesar of his own fortunes. That, my dear Mr Copperfield, appears to me to be his true position. From the first moment of this voyage, I wish Mr Micawber to stand upon that vessel's prow and say, "Enough of delay, enough of disappointment, enough of limited means. That was in the old country. This is the new. Produce your reparation. Bring it forward!" '

Mr Micawber folded his arms in a resolute manner, as if he were then stationed on the figure-head.

'And doing that,' said Mrs Micawber, ' – feeling his position – am I not right in saying that Mr Micawber will strengthen, and not weaken, his connection with Britain? An important public character arising in that hemisphere, shall I be told that its influence will not be felt at home? Can I be so weak as to imagine that Mr Micawber, wielding the rod of talent and of power in Australia, will be nothing in England? I am but a woman; but I should be unworthy of myself, and of my papa, if I were guilty of such absurd weakness.'

Mrs Micawber's conviction that her arguments were unanswerable gave a moral elevation to her tone which I think I had never heard in it before.

'And therefore it is,' said Mrs Micawber, 'that I the more wish, that, at a future period, we may live again on the parent soil. Mr Micawber may be – I cannot disguise from myself that the probability is Mr Micawber will be – a page of History; and he ought then to be represented in the country which gave him birth and did *not* give him employment!'

'My love,' observed Mr Micawber, 'it is impossible for me not to be touched by your affection. I am always willing to defer to your good sense. What will be – will be. Heaven forbid that I should grudge my native country any portion of the wealth that may be accumulated by our descendants!'

'That's well,' said my aunt, nodding towards Mr Peggotty, 'and I drink my love to you all, and every blessing and success attend you!'

Mr Peggotty put down the two children he had been nursing, one on each knee, to join Mr and Mrs Micawber in drinking to all of us in return; and when he and the Micawbers cordially shook hands as comrades, and his brown face brightened with a smile, I felt that he would make his way, establish a good name, and be beloved, go where he would.

Even the children were instructed, each to dip a wooden spoon into Mr Micawber's pot, and pledge us in its contents. When this was done, my aunt and Agnes rose, and parted from the emigrants. It was a sorrowful farewell. They were all crying; the children hung about Agnes to the last; and we left poor Mrs Micawber in a very distressed condition, sobbing and weeping by a dim candle, that must have made the room look, from the river, like a miserable lighthouse.

I went down again next morning to see that they were away. They had departed, in a boat, as early as five o'clock. It was a wonderful instance to me of the gap such partings make, that although my association of them with the tumbledown public-house and the wooden stairs dated only from last night, both seemed dreary and deserted, now that they were gone.

In the afternoon of the next day, my old nurse and I went down to Gravesend. We found the ship in the river, surrounded by a crowd of boats; a favourable wind blowing; the signal for sailing at her masthead. I hired a boat directly, and we put off to her; and getting through the little vortex of confusion of which she was the centre, went on board.

Mr Peggotty was waiting for us on deck. He told me that Mr Micawber had just now been arrested again (and for the last time) at the suit of Heep, and that, in compliance with a request I had made to him, he had paid the money, which I repaid him. He then took us down between decks, and there, any lingering fears I had of his having heard any rumours of what had happened were dispelled by Mr Micawber's coming out of the gloom, taking his arm with an air of friendship and protection, and telling me that they had scarcely been asunder for a moment since the night before last.

It was such a strange scene to me, and so confined and dark, that, at first, I could make out hardly anything; but, by degrees, it cleared, as my eyes became more accustomed to the gloom, and I seemed to stand in a picture by Ostade. Among the great beams, bulks, and ringbolts of the ship, and the emigrant-berths, and chests, and bundles, and barrels, and heaps of miscellaneous baggage – lighted up, here and there, by dangling lanterns; and elsewhere by the yellow daylight straying down a windsail or a hatchway – were crowded groups of people, making new friendships, taking leave of one another, talking, laughing, crying, eating, and drinking; some, already settled down into the possession of their few feet of space, with their little households arranged, and tiny children established on stools, or in dwarf elbow-chairs; others, despairing of a resting-place, and wandering disconsolately. From babies who had but a week or two of life behind them, to crooked old men and women who seemed to have but a week or two of life before them; and from

ploughmen bodily carrying out soil of England on their boots, to smiths taking away samples of its soot and smoke upon their skins; every age and occupation appeared to be crammed into the narrow compass of the 'tween-decks.

As my eye glanced round this place, I thought I saw sitting, by an open port, with one of the Micawber children near her, a figure like Emily's; it first attracted my attention, by another figure parting from it with a kiss; and as it glided calmly away through the disorder, reminding me of – Agnes! But in the rapid motion and confusion, and in the unsettlement of my own thoughts, I lost it again; and only knew that the time was come when all visitors were being warned to leave the ship; that my nurse was crying on a chest beside me; and that Mrs Gummidge, assisted by some younger stooping woman in black, was busily arranging Mr Peggotty's goods.

'Is there any last wured, Mas'r Davy?' said he. 'Is there anyone forgotten thing afore we part?'

'One thing!' said I. 'Martha!'

He touched the younger woman I have mentioned on the shoulder, and Martha stood before me.

'Heaven bless you, you good man!' cried I. 'You take her with you!'

She answered for him, with a burst of tears. I could speak no more, at that time, but I wrung his hand; and if ever I have loved and honoured any man, I loved and honoured that man in my soul.

The ship was clearing fast of strangers. The greatest trial that I had, remained. I told him what the noble spirit that was gone had given me in charge to say at parting. It moved him deeply.

The emigrants

But when he charged me, in return, with many messages of affection and regret for those deaf ears, he moved me more.

The time was come. I embraced him, took my weeping nurse upon my arm, and hurried away. On deck, I took leave of poor Mrs Micawber. She was looking distractedly about for her family, even then; and her last words to me were, that she never would desert Mr Micawber.

We went over the side into our boat, and lay at a little distance to see the ship wafted on her course. It was then calm, radiant sunset. She lay between us and the red light; and every taper line and spar was visible against the glow. A sight at once so beautiful, so mournful, and so hopeful, as the glorious ship, lying, still, on the flushed water, with all the life on board her crowded at the bulwarks, and there clustering, for a moment, bare-headed and silent, I never saw.

Silent, only for a moment. As the sails rose to the wind, and the ship began to move, there broke from all the boats three resounding cheers, which those on board took up, and echoed back, and which were echoed and re-echoed. My heart burst out when I heard the sound, and beheld the waving of the hats and handkerchiefs – and then I saw her!

Then, I saw her, at her uncle's side, and trembling on his shoulder. He pointed to us with an eager hand; and she saw us, and waved her last goodbye to me. Aye, Emily, beautiful and drooping, cling to him with the utmost trust of thy bruised heart; for he has clung to thee, with all the might of his great love!

Surrounded by the rosy light, and standing high upon the deck, apart together, she clinging to him, and he holding her, they solemnly passed away. The night had fallen on the Kentish hills when we were rowed ashore – and fallen darkly upon me.

CHAPTER 58

Absence

It was a long and gloomy night that gathered on me, haunted by the ghosts of many hopes, of many dear remembrances, many errors, many unavailing sorrows and regrets.

I went away from England; not knowing, even then, how great the shock was that I had to bear. I left all who were dear to me, and went away; and believed that I had borne it, and it was past. As a man upon a field of battle will receive a mortal hurt, and scarcely know that he is struck, so I, when I was left alone with my undisciplined heart, had no conception of the wound with which it had to strive.

The knowledge came upon me, not quickly, but little by little, and grain by grain. The desolate feeling with which I went abroad, deepened and widened hourly. At first it was a heavy sense of loss and sorrow, wherein I could distinguish little else. By imperceptible degrees, it became a hopeless consciousness of all that I had lost – love, friendship, interest; of all that had been shattered – my first trust, my first affection, the whole airy castle of my life; of all that remained – a ruined blank and waste, lying wide around me, unbroken, to the dark horizon.

If my grief were selfish, I did not know it to be so. I mourned for my child-wife, taken from her blooming world, so young. I mourned for him who might have won the love and admiration of thousands, as he had won mine long ago. I mourned for the broken heart that had found rest in the stormy sea; and for the wandering remnants of the simple home, where I had heard the night-wind blowing, when I was a child.

From the accumulated sadness into which I fell, I had at length no hope of ever issuing again. I roamed from place to place, carrying my burden with me everywhere. I felt its whole weight now; and I drooped beneath it, and I said in my heart that it could never be lightened.

When this despondency was at its worst, I believed that I should die. Sometimes, I thought that I would like to die at home; and actually turned back on my road, that I might get there soon. At other times, I passed on farther away, from city to city, seeking I know not what, and trying to leave I know not what behind.

It is not in my power to retrace, one by one, all the weary phases of distress of mind through which I passed. There are some dreams that can only be imperfectly and vaguely described; and when I oblige myself to look back on this time of my life, I seem to be recalling such a dream. I see myself passing on among the novelties of foreign towns, palaces, cathedrals, temples, pictures, castles, tombs, fantastic streets – the old abiding places of History and Fancy – as a dreamer might; bearing my painful load through all, and hardly conscious of the objects as they fade before me. Listlessness to everything, but brooding sorrow, was the night that fell on my undisciplined heart. Let me look up from it – as at last I did, thank Heaven! – and from its long, sad, wretched dream, to dawn.

For many months I travelled with this ever-darkening cloud upon my mind. Some blind reasons that I had for not returning home – reasons then struggling within me, vainly, for more distinct expression – kept me on my pilgrimage. Sometimes, I had proceeded restlessly from place to place, stopping nowhere; sometimes, I had lingered long in one spot. I had had no purpose, no sustaining soul within me, anywhere.

I was in Switzerland. I had come out of Italy, over one of the great passes of the Alps, and had since wandered with a guide among the byways of the mountains. If those awful solitudes had spoken to my heart, I did not know it. I had found sublimity and wonder in the dread heights and precipices, in the roaring torrents, and the wastes of ice and snow; but as yet, they had taught me nothing else.

I came, one evening before sunset, down into a valley, where I was to rest. In the course of my descent to it, by the winding track along the mountainside, from which I saw it shining far below, I think some long unwonted sense of beauty and tranquillity, some softening influence awakened by its peace, moved faintly in my breast. I remember pausing once, with a kind of sorrow that was not all oppressive, not quite despairing. I remember almost hoping that some better change was possible within me.

I came into the valley, as the evening sun was shining on the remote heights of snow, that closed it in, like eternal clouds. The bases of the mountains, forming the gorge in which the little village lay, were richly green; and high above this gentler vegetation grew forests of dark fir, cleaving the wintry snow-drift, wedge-like, and stemming the avalanche. Above these were range upon range of craggy steeps, grey rock, bright ice, and smooth verdure-specks of pasture, all gradually blending with the crowning snow. Dotted here and there on the mountain's side, each tiny dot a home, were lonely wooden cottages, so dwarfed by the towering heights that they appeared too small for toys. So did even the clustered village in the valley, with its wooden bridge across the stream, where the stream tumbled over broken rocks, and roared away among the trees. In the quiet air there was a sound of distant singing – shepherd voices; but, as one bright evening cloud floated midway along the mountain's side, I could almost have believed it came from there, and was not earthly music. All at once, in this serenity, great Nature spoke to me; and soothed me to lay down my weary head upon the grass, and weep as I had not wept yet, since Dora died!

I had found a packet of letters awaiting me but a few minutes before, and had strolled out of the village to read them while my supper was making ready. Other packets had missed me, and I had received none for a long time. Beyond a line or two, to say that I was well, and had arrived at such a place, I had not had fortitude or constancy to write a letter since I left home.

The packet was in my hand. I opened it, and read the writing of Agnes.

She was happy and useful, was prospering as she had hoped. That was all she told me of herself. The rest referred to me.

She gave me no advice; she urged no duty on me; she only told me, in her own fervent manner, what her trust in me was. She knew (she said) how such a nature as mine would turn affliction to good. She knew how trial and emotion would exalt and strengthen it. She was sure that in my every purpose I should gain a firmer and a higher tendency, through the grief I had undergone. She, who so gloried in my fame, and so looked forward to its augmentation, well knew that I would labour on. She knew that in me, sorrow could not be weakness, but must be strength. As the endurance of my childish days had done its part to make me what I was, so greater calamities would nerve me on, to be yet better than I was; and so, as they had taught me, would I teach others. She commended me to God, who had taken my innocent darling to His rest; and in her sisterly affection cherished me always, and was always at my side go where I would; proud of what I had done, but infinitely prouder yet of what I was reserved to do.

I put the letter in my breast, and thought what had I been an hour ago! When I heard the voices die away, and saw the quiet evening cloud grow dim, and all the colours in the valley fade, and the golden snow upon the mountain tops become a remote part of the pale night sky, yet felt that the night was passing from my mind, and all its shadows clearing, there was no name for the love I bore her, dearer to me, henceforward, than ever until then.

I read her letter many times. I wrote to her before I slept. I told her that I had been in sore need of her help; that without her I was not, and I never had been, what she thought me; but that she inspired me to be that, and I would try.

I did try. In three months more, a year would have passed since the beginning of my sorrow. I determined to make no resolutions until the expiration of those three months, but to try. I lived in that valley, and its neighbourhood, all the time.

The three months gone, I resolved to remain away from home for some time longer; to settle myself for the present in Switzerland, which was growing dear to me in the remembrance of that evening; to resume my pen; to work.

I resorted humbly whither Agnes had commended me; I sought out Nature, never sought in vain; and I admitted to my breast the human interest I had lately shrunk from. It was not long before I had almost as many friends in the valley as in Yarmouth; and when I left it, before the winter set in, for Geneva, and came back in the spring, their cordial greetings had a homely sound to me, although they were not conveyed in English words.

I worked early and late, patiently and hard. I wrote a Story, with a purpose growing, not remotely, out of my experience, and sent it to Traddles, and he arranged for its publication very advantageously for me; and the tidings of my growing reputation began to reach me from travellers whom I encountered by chance. After some rest and change I fell to work, in my old ardent way, on a new fancy, which took strong possession of me. As I advanced in the execution of this task, I felt it more and more, and roused my utmost energies to do it well. This was my third work of fiction. It was not half written, when, in an interval of rest, I thought of returning home.

For a long time, though studying and working patiently, I had accustomed myself to robust exercise. My health, severely impaired when I left England, was quite restored. I had seen much. I had been in many countries, and I hope I had improved my store of knowledge.

I have now recalled all that I think it needful to recall here, of this term of absence – with one reservation. I have made it, thus far, with no purpose of suppressing any of my thoughts; for, as I have elsewhere said, this narrative is my written memory. I have desired to keep the most secret current of my mind apart, and to the last. I enter on it now.

I cannot so completely penetrate the mystery of my own heart, as to know when I began to think that I might have set its earliest and brightest hopes on Agnes. I cannot say at what stage of my grief it first became associated with the reflection, that, in my wayward boyhood, I had thrown away the treasure of her love. I believe I may have heard some whisper of that distant thought, in the old unhappy loss or want of something never to be realised, of which I had been sensible. But the thought came into my mind as a new reproach and new regret, when I was left so sad and lonely in the world.

If, at that time, I had been much with her, I should, in the weakness of my desolation, have betrayed this. It was what I remotely dreaded when I was first impelled to stay away from England. I could not have borne to lose the smallest portion of her sisterly affection; yet, in that betrayal, I should have set a constraint between us hitherto unknown.

I could not forget that the feeling with which she now regarded me had grown up in my own free choice and course. That if she had ever loved me with another love – and I sometimes thought the time was when she might have done so – I had cast it away. It was nothing, now, that I had accustomed myself to think of her, when we were both mere children, as one who was far removed from my wild fancies. I had bestowed my passionate tenderness upon another object; and what I might have done, I had not done; and what Agnes was to me, I and her own noble heart had made her.

In the beginning of the change that gradually worked in me, when I tried to get a better understanding of myself and be a better man, I did glance, through some indefinite probation, to a period when I might possibly hope to cancel the mistaken past, and to be so blessed as to marry her. But, as time wore on, this shadowy prospect faded, and departed from me. If she had ever loved me, then, I should hold her the more sacred, remembering the confidences I had reposed in her, her knowledge of my errant heart, the sacrifice she must have made to be my friend and sister, and the victory she had won. If she had never loved me, could I believe that she would love me now?

I had always felt my weakness, in comparison with her constancy and fortitude; and now I felt it more and more. Whatever I might have been to her, or she to me, if I had been more worthy of her long ago, I was not now, and she was not. The time was past. I had let it go by, and had deservedly lost her.

That I suffered much in these contentions, that they filled me with unhappiness and remorse, and yet that I had a sustaining sense that it was required of me, in right and honour, to keep away from myself, with shame, the thought of turning to the dear girl in the withering of my hopes, from whom I had frivolously turned when they were bright and fresh – which consideration was at the root of every thought I had concerning her – is all equally true. I made no effort to conceal from myself, now, that I loved her, that I was devoted to her; but I brought the assurance home to myself, that it was now too late, and that our long-subsisting relation must be undisturbed.

I had thought, much and often, of my Dora's shadowing out to me what might have happened, in those years that were destined not to try us. I had considered how the things that never happen are often as much realities to us, in their effects, as those that are accomplished. The very years she spoke of were realities now, for my correction; and would have been, one day, a little later perhaps, though we had parted in our earliest folly. I endeavoured to convert what might have been between myself and Agnes into a means of making me more self-denying, more resolved, more conscious of myself, and my defects and errors. Thus, through the reflection that it might have been, I arrived at the conviction that it could never be.

These, with their perplexities and inconsistencies, were the shifting quicksands of my mind, from the time of my departure to the time of my return home, three years afterwards. Three years had elapsed since the sailing of the emigrant ship, when, at that same hour of sunset, and in the same place, I stood on the deck of the packet vessel that brought me home, looking on the rosy water where I had seen the image of that ship reflected.

Three years. Long in the aggregate, though short as they went by. And home was very dear to me, and Agnes too – but she was not mine – she was never to be mine. She might have been, but that was past!

CHAPTER 59

Return

I landed in London on a wintry autumn evening. It was dark and raining, and I saw more fog and mud in a minute than I had seen in a year. I walked from the Custom House to the Monument before I found a coach; and although the very house-fronts, looking on the swollen gutters, were like old friends to me, I could not but admit that they were very dingy friends.

I have often remarked – I suppose everybody has – that one's going away from a familiar place would seem to be the signal for change in it. As I looked out of the coach-window, and observed that an old house on Fish-street Hill, which had stood untouched by painter, carpenter, or bricklayer, for a century, had been pulled down in my absence; and that a neighbouring street, of time-honoured insalubrity and inconvenience, was being drained and widened; I half expected to find St Paul's Cathedral looking older.

For some changes in the fortunes of my friends, I was prepared. My aunt had long been re-established at Dover, and Traddles had begun to get into some little practice at the Bar, in the very first term after my departure. He had chambers in Gray's Inn, now; and had told me, in his last letters, that he was not without hopes of being soon united to the dearest girl in the world.

They expected me home before Christmas; but had no idea of my returning so soon. I had purposely misled them, that I might have the pleasure of taking them by surprise. And yet, I was perverse enough to feel a chill and disappointment in receiving no welcome, and rattling, alone and silent, through the misty streets.

The well-known shops, however, with their cheerful lights, did something for me; and when I alighted at the door of the Gray's Inn Coffee-house, I had recovered my spirits. It recalled, at first, that so different time when I had put up at the 'Golden Cross', and reminded me of the changes that had come to pass since then; but that was natural.

'Do you know where Mr Traddles lives in the Inn?' I asked the waiter, as I warmed myself by the coffee-room fire.

'Holborn Court, sir. Number two.'

'Mr Traddles has a rising reputation among the lawyers, I believe?' said I.

'Well, sir,' returned the waiter, 'probably he has, sir; but I am not aware of it myself.'

This waiter, who was middle-aged and spare, looked for help to a waiter of more authority – a stout, potential old man, with a double-chin, in black breeches and stockings, who came out of a place like a churchwarden's pew, at the end of the coffee-room, where he kept company with a cash-box, a Directory, a Law-list, and other books and papers.

'Mr Traddles,' said the spare waiter. 'Number two in the Court.'

The potential waiter waved him away, and turned, gravely, to me.

'I was enquiring,' said I, 'whether Mr Traddles at number two in the Court has not a rising reputation among the lawyers?'

'Never heard his name,' said the waiter, in a rich, husky voice.

I felt quite apologetic for Traddles.

'He's a young man, sure?' said the portentous waiter, fixing his eyes severely on me. 'How long has he been in the Inn?'

'Not above three years,' said I.

The waiter, who I supposed had lived in his churchwarden's pew for forty years, could not pursue such an insignificant subject. He asked me what I would have for dinner?

I felt I was in England again, and really was quite cast down on Traddles's account. There seemed to be no hope for him. I meekly ordered a bit of fish and a steak, and stood before the fire musing on his obscurity.

As I followed the chief waiter with my eyes, I could not help thinking that the garden in which he had gradually blown to be the flower he was, was an arduous place to rise in. It had such a prescriptive, stiff-necked, long-established, solemn, elderly air. I glanced about the room, which had had its sanded floor sanded, no doubt, in exactly the same manner when the chief waiter was a boy – if he ever was a boy, which appeared improbable; and at the shining tables, where I saw myself reflected, in unruffled depths of old mahogany; and at the lamps, without a flaw in their trimming or cleaning; and at the comfortable green curtains, with their pure brass rods, snugly enclosing the boxes; and at the two large coal fires, brightly burning; and at the rows of decanters, burly as if with the consciousness of pipes of expensive old port wine below; and both England and the law appeared to me to be very difficult indeed to be taken by storm. I went up to my bedroom to change my wet clothes; and the vast extent of that old wainscoted apartment (which was over the archway leading to the Inn, I remember), and the sedate immensity of the four-post bedstead, and the indomitable gravity of the chests of drawers, all seemed to unite in sternly frowning on the fortunes of Traddles, or on any such daring youth. I came down again to my dinner; and even the slow comfort of the meal and the orderly silence of the place – which was bare of guests, the Long Vacation not yet being over – were eloquent on the audacity of Traddles, and his small hopes of a livelihood for twenty years to come.

I had seen nothing like this since I went away, and it quite dashed my hopes for my friend. The chief waiter had had enough of me. He came near me no more, but devoted himself to an old gentleman in long gaiters, to meet whom a pint of special port seemed to come out of the cellar of its own accord, for he gave no order. The second waiter informed me, in a whisper, that this old gentleman was a retired conveyancer living in the Square, and worth a mint of money, which it was expected he would leave to his laundress's daughter; likewise that it was rumoured that he had a service of plate in a bureau, all tarnished with lying by, though more than one spoon and a fork had never yet been beheld in his chambers by mortal vision. By this time, I quite gave Traddles up for lost; and settled in my own mind that there was no hope for him.

Being very anxious to see the dear old fellow, nevertheless, I despatched my dinner, in a manner not at all calculated to raise me in the opinion of the chief waiter, and hurried out by the back way. Number two in the Court was soon reached; and an inscription on the doorpost informing me that Mr Traddles occupied a set of chambers on the top story, I ascended the staircase. A crazy old staircase I found it to be, feebly lighted on each landing by a club-headed little oil wick, dying away in a little dungeon of dirty glass.

In the course of my stumbling upstairs, I fancied I heard a pleasant sound of laughter; and not the laughter of an attorney or barrister, or attorney's clerk or barrister's clerk, but of two or three merry girls. Happening, however, as I stopped to listen, to put my foot in a hole where the Honourable Society of Gray's Inn had left a plank deficient, I fell down with some noise, and when I recovered my footing all was silent.

Groping my way more carefully, for the rest of the journey, my heart beat high when I found the outer door, which had Mr Traddles painted on it, open. I knocked. A considerable scuffling within ensued, but nothing else. I therefore knocked again.

A small, sharp-looking lad, half-footboy and half-clerk, who was very much out of breath, but who looked at me as if he defied me to prove it legally, presented himself.

'Is Mr Traddles within?' I said.

'Yes, sir, but he's engaged.'

'I want to see him.'

After a moment's survey of me, the sharp-looking lad decided to let me in; and opening the door wider for that purpose, admitted me, first, into a little closet of a hall, and next into a little sitting-room; where I came into the presence of my old friend (also out of breath), seated at a table, and bending over papers.

'Good God!' cried Traddles, looking up. 'It's Copperfield!' and rushed into my arms, where I held him tight.

'All well, my dear Traddles?'

'All well, my dear, dear Copperfield, and nothing but good news!'

We cried with pleasure, both of us.

'My dear fellow,' said Traddles, rumpling his hair in his excitement, which was a most unnecessary operation, 'my dearest Copperfield, my long-lost and most welcome friend, how glad I am to see you! How brown you are! How glad I am! Upon my life and honour, I never was so rejoiced, my beloved Copperfield, never.'

I was equally at a loss to express my emotions. I was quite unable to speak, at first.

'My dear fellow!' said Traddles. 'And grown so famous! My glorious Copperfield! Good gracious me, *when* did you come, *where* have you come from, *what* have you been doing?'

Never pausing for an answer to anything he said, Traddles, who had clapped me into an easy-chair by the fire, all this time impetuously stirred the fire with one hand, and pulled at my neckerchief with the other, under some wild delusion that it was a greatcoat. Without putting down the poker, he now hugged me again; and I hugged him; and, both laughing, and both wiping our eyes, we both sat down, and shook hands across the hearth.

'To think,' said Traddles, 'that you should have been so nearly coming home as you must have been, my dear old boy, and not at the ceremony!'

'What ceremony, my dear Traddles?'

'Good gracious me!' cried Traddles, opening his eyes in his old way. 'Didn't you get my last letter?'

'Certainly not, if it referred to any ceremony.'

'Why, my dear Copperfield,' said Traddles, sticking his hair upright with both hands, and then putting his hands on his knees, 'I am married!'

'Married!' I cried joyfully.

'Lord bless me, yes!' said Traddles – 'by the Reverend Horace – to Sophy – down in Devonshire. Why, my dear boy, she's behind the window curtain! Look here!'

To my amazement the dearest girl in the world came at that same instant, laughing and blushing, from her place of concealment. And a more cheerful, amiable, honest, happy, bright-looking bride, I believe (as I could not help saying on the spot) the world never saw. I kissed her as an old acquaintance should, and wished them joy with all my might of heart.

'Dear me,' said Traddles, 'what a delightful reunion this is! You are so extremely brown, my dear Copperfield! God bless my soul, how happy I am!'

'And so am I,' said I.

'And I am sure I am!' said the blushing and laughing Sophy.

'We are all as happy as possible!' said Traddles. 'Even the girls are happy. Dear me, I declare I forgot them!'

'Forgot?' said I.

'The girls,' said Traddles. 'Sophy's sisters. They are staying with us. They have come to have a peep at London. The fact is, when – was it you that tumbled upstairs, Copperfield?'

'It was,' said I, laughing.

'Well, then, when you tumbled upstairs,' said Traddles, 'I was romping with the girls. In point of fact, we were playing at Puss in the Corner. But as that wouldn't do in Westminster Hall, and as it wouldn't look quite professional if they were seen by a client, they decamped. And they are now – listening, I have no doubt,' said Traddles, glancing at the door of another room.

'I am sorry,' said I, laughing afresh, 'to have occasioned such a dispersion.'

'Upon my word,' rejoined Traddles, greatly delighted, 'if you had seen them running away, and running back again, after you had knocked, to pick up the combs they had dropped out of their hair, and going on in the maddest manner, you wouldn't have said so. My love, will you fetch the girls?'

Sophy tripped away, and we heard her received in the adjoining room with a peal of laughter.

'Really musical, isn't it, my dear Copperfield?' said Traddles. 'It's very agreeable to hear. It quite lights up these old rooms. To an unfortunate bachelor of a fellow who has lived alone all his life, you know, it's positively delicious. It's charming. Poor things, they have had a great loss in Sophy – who, I do assure you, Copperfield, is, and ever was, the dearest girl! – and it gratifies me beyond expression to find them in such good spirits. The society of girls is a very delightful thing, Copperfield. It's not professional, but it's very delightful.'

Observing that he slightly faltered, and comprehending that in the goodness of his heart he was fearful of giving me some pain by what he had said, I expressed my concurrence with a heartiness that evidently relieved and pleased him greatly.

'But then,' said Traddles, 'our domestic arrangements are, to say the truth, quite unprofessional altogether, my dear Copperfield. Even Sophy's being here is unprofessional. And we have no other place of abode. We have put to sea in a cockboat, but we are quite prepared to rough it. And Sophy's an extraordinary manager! You'll be surprised how those girls are stowed away. I am sure I hardly know how it's done.'

'Are many of the young ladies with you?' I enquired.

'The eldest, the Beauty, is here,' said Traddles, in a low confidential voice, 'Caroline. And Sarah's here – the one I mentioned to you as having something the matter with her spine, you know. Immensely better! And the two youngest that Sophy educated are with us. And Louisa's here.'

'Indeed!' cried I.

'Yes,' said Traddles. 'Now the whole set – I mean the chambers – is only three rooms; but Sophy arranges for the girls in the most wonderful way, and they sleep as comfortably as possible. Three in that room,' said Traddles, pointing. 'Two in that.'

I could not help glancing round, in search of the accommodation remaining for Mr and Mrs Traddles. Traddles understood me.

'Well!' said Traddles, 'we are prepared to rough it, as I said just now, and we *did* improvise a bed last week, upon the floor here. But there's a little room in the roof – a very nice room, when you're up there – which Sophy papered herself, to surprise me; and that's our room at present. It's a capital little gypsy sort of place. There's quite a view from it.'

'And you are happily married at last, my dear Traddles,' said I. 'How rejoiced I am!'

'Thank you, my dear Copperfield,' said Traddles, as we shook hands once more. 'Yes, I am as happy as it's possible to be. There's your old friend, you see,' said Traddles, nodding triumphantly at the flowerpot and stand; 'and there's the table with the marble top! All the other furniture is plain and serviceable, you perceive. And as to plate, Lord bless you, we haven't so much as a teaspoon.'

'All to be earned?' said I cheerfully.

'Exactly so,' replied Traddles, 'all to be earned. Of course we have something in the shape of teaspoons, because we stir our tea. But they're Britannia metal.'

'The silver will be the brighter when it comes,' said I.

'The very thing we say!' cried Traddles. 'You see, my dear

Copperfield,' falling again into the low confidential tone, 'after I had delivered my argument in Doe *dem.* Jipes *versus* Wigzell, which did me great service with the profession, I went down into Devonshire, and had some serious conversation in private with the Reverend Horace. I dwelt upon the fact that Sophy – who I do assure you, Copperfield, is the dearest girl! – '

'I am certain she is!' said I.

'She is, indeed!' rejoined Traddles. 'But I am afraid I am wandering from the subject. Did I mention the Reverend Horace?'

'You said that you dwelt upon the fact – '

'True! Upon the fact that Sophy and I had been engaged f or a long period, and that Sophy, with the permission of her parents, was more than content to take me – in short,' said Traddles, with his old frank smile, 'on our present Britannia-metal footing. Very well. I then proposed to the Reverend Horace – who is a most excellent clergyman, Copperfield, and ought to be a Bishop; or at least ought to have enough to live upon, without pinching himself – that if I could turn the corner, say of two hundred and fifty pounds, in one year; and could see my way pretty clearly to that, or something better, next year; and could plainly furnish a little place like this, besides; then, and in that case, Sophy and I should be united. I took the liberty of representing that we had been patient for a good many years; and that the circumstance of Sophy's being extraordinarily useful at home, ought not to operate with her affectionate parents against her establishment in life – don't you see?'

'Certainly it ought not,' said I.

'I am glad you think so, Copperfield,' rejoined Traddles, 'because, without any imputation on the Reverend Horace, I do think, parents, and brothers, and so forth, are sometimes rather selfish in such cases. Well! I also pointed out, that my most earnest desire was, to be useful to the family; and that if I got on in the world, and anything should happen to him – I refer to the Reverend Horace – '

'I understand,' said I.

' – or to Mrs Crewler – it would be the utmost gratification of my wishes to be a parent to the girls. He replied in a most admirable manner, exceedingly flattering to my feelings, and undertook to obtain the consent of Mrs Crewler to this arrangement. They had a dreadful time of it with her. It mounted from her legs into her chest, and then into her head – '

'What mounted?' I asked.

'Her grief,' replied Traddles, with a serious look. 'Her feelings generally. As I mentioned on a former occasion, she is a very superior woman, but has lost the use of her limbs. Whatever occurs to harass her, usually settles in her legs; but on this occasion it mounted to the chest, and then to the head, and, in short, pervaded the whole system in a most alarming manner. However, they brought her through it by unremitting and affectionate attention; and we were married yesterday six weeks. You have no idea what a Monster I felt, Copperfield, when I saw the whole family crying and fainting away in every direction! Mrs Crewler couldn't see me before we left – couldn't forgive me, then, for depriving her of her child – but

she is a good creature, and has done so since. I had a delightful letter from her, only this morning.'

'And in short, my dear friend,' said I, 'you feel as blest as you deserve to feel!'

'Oh! That's your partiality!' laughed Traddles. 'But, indeed, I am in a most enviable state. I work hard, and read Law insatiably. I get up at five every morning, and don't mind it at all. I hide the girls in the daytime, and make merry with them in the evening. And I assure you I am quite sorry that they are going home on Tuesday, which is the day before the first day of Michaelmas Term. But here,' said Traddles, breaking off in his confidence, and speaking aloud, '*are* the girls! Mr Copperfield, Miss Crewler – Miss Sarah – Miss Louisa – Margaret and Lucy!'

They were a perfect nest of roses; they looked so wholesome and fresh. They were all pretty, and Miss Caroline was very handsome; but there was a loving, cheerful, fireside quality in Sophy's bright looks, which was better than that, and which assured me that my friend had chosen well. We all sat round the fire; while the sharp boy, who I now divined had lost his breath in putting the papers out, cleared them away again, and produced the tea-things. After that, he retired for the night, shutting the outer door upon us with a bang. Mrs Traddles, with perfect pleasure and composure beaming from her house-hold eyes, having made the tea, then quietly made the toast as she sat in a corner by the fire.

She had seen Agnes, she told me while she was toasting. 'Tom' had taken her down into Kent for a wedding trip, and there she had seen my aunt, too; and both my aunt and Agnes were well, and they had all talked of nothing but me. 'Tom' had never had me out of his thoughts, she really believed, all the time I had been away. 'Tom' was the authority for everything. 'Tom' was evidently the idol of her life; never to be shaken from his pedestal by any commotion; always to be believed in, and done homage to with the whole faith of her heart, come what might.

The deference which both she and Traddles showed towards the Beauty pleased me very much. I don't know that I thought it very reasonable; but I thought it very delightful, and essentially a part of their character. If Traddles ever for an instant missed the teaspoons that were still to be won, I have no doubt it was when he handed the Beauty her tea. If his sweet-tempered wife could have got up any self-assertion against anyone, I am satisfied it could only have been because she was the Beauty's sister. A few slight indications of a rather petted and capricious manner, which I observed in the Beauty, were manifestly considered by Traddles and his wife as her birthright and natural endowment. If she had been born a Queen Bee, and they labouring Bees, they could not have been more satisfied of that.

But their self-forgetfulness charmed me. Their pride in these girls, and their submission of themselves to all their whims, was the pleasantest little testimony to their own worth I could have desired to see. If Traddles were addressed as 'a darling' once in the course of that evening, and besought to bring something here, or carry something there, or take something up, or put something down, or find something, or fetch something, he was so addressed, by one or other of his sisters-in-law, at least twelve times in an hour. Neither could they do anything without Sophy. Somebody's hair fell down, and nobody but Sophy could put it up. Somebody forgot how a particular tune went, and nobody but Sophy could hum that tune right. Somebody wanted to recall the name of a place in Devonshire, and only Sophy knew it. Something was wanted to be written home, and Sophy alone could be trusted to write before breakfast in the morning. Somebody broke down in a piece of knitting, and no one but Sophy was able to put the defaulter in the right direction. They were entire mistresses of the place, and Sophy and Traddles waited on them. How many children Sophy could have taken care of in her time, I can't imagine; but she seemed to be famous for knowing every sort of song that ever was addressed to a child in the English tongue; and she sang dozens to order with the clearest little voice in the world, one after another (every sister issuing directions for a different tune, and the Beauty generally striking in last), so that I was quite fascinated. The best of all was that, in the midst of their exactions, all the sisters had a great tenderness and respect both for Sophy and Traddles. I am sure, when I took my leave, and Traddles was coming out to walk with me to the coffee-house, I thought I had never seen an obstinate head of hair, or any other head of hair, rolling about in such a shower of kisses.

Altogether, it was a scene I could not help dwelling on with pleasure, for a long time after I got back and had wished Traddles good-night. If I had beheld a thousand roses blowing in a top set of chambers, in that withered Gray's Inn, they could not have brightened it half so much. The idea of those Devonshire girls, among the dry law-stationers and the attorneys' offices; and of the tea and toast, and children's songs, in that grim atmosphere of pounce and parchment, red-tape, dusty wafers, ink-jars, brief and draft paper, law reports, writs, declarations, and bills of costs, seemed almost as pleasantly fanciful as if I had dreamed that the Sultan's famous family had been admitted on the roll of attorneys, and had brought the talking-bird, the singing-tree, and the golden water into Gray's Inn Hall. Somehow, I found that I had taken leave of Traddles for the night, and come back to the coffee-house, with a great change in my despondency about him. I began to think he would get on, in spite of all the many orders of chief waiters in England.

Drawing a chair before one of the coffee-room fires to think about him at my leisure, I gradually fell from the consideration of his happiness to tracing prospects in the live coals, and to thinking, as they broke and changed, of the principal vicissitudes and separations that had marked my life. I had not seen a coal fire since I left England three years ago; though many a wood fire had I watched, as it crumbled into hoary ashes, and mingled with the feathery heap upon the hearth, which not inaptly figured to me, in my despondency, my own dead hopes.

I could think of the past now, gravely, but not bitterly; and could contemplate the future in a brave spirit. Home, in its best sense, was for me no more. She in whom I might have inspired a dearer love, I had taught to be my sister. She would marry, and would have new claimants on her tenderness; and in doing it, would never know the love for her that had grown up in my heart. It was right that I should pay the forfeit of my headlong passion. What I reaped, I had sown.

I was thinking, and had I truly disciplined my heart to this, and could I resolutely bear it, and calmly hold the place in her home which she had calmly held in mine – when I found my eyes resting on a countenance that might have arisen out of the fire, in its association with my early remembrances.

Little Mr Chillip the Doctor, to whose good offices I was indebted in the very first chapter of this history, sat reading a newspaper in the shadow of an opposite corner. He was tolerably stricken in years by this time; but, being a mild, meek, calm little man, had worn so easily, that I thought he looked at that moment just as he might have looked when he sat in our parlour, waiting for me to be born.

Mr Chillip had left Blunderstone six or seven years ago, and I had never seen him since. He sat placidly perusing the newspaper, with his little head on one side, and a glass of warm sherry negus at his elbow. He was so extremely conciliatory in his manner that he seemed to apologise to the very newspaper for taking the liberty of reading it.

I walked up to where he was sitting, and said, 'How do you do, Mr Chillip?'

He was greatly fluttered by this unexpected address from a stranger, and replied, in his slow way, 'I thank you, sir, you are very good. Thank you, sir. I hope *you* are well.'

'You don't remember me?' said I.

'Well, sir,' returned Mr Chillip, smiling very meekly, and shaking his head as he surveyed me, 'I have a kind of an impression that something in your countenance is familiar to me, sir; but I couldn't lay my hand upon your name, really.'

'And yet you knew it long before I knew it myself,' I returned.

'Did I indeed, sir?' said Mr Chillip. 'Is it possible that I had the honour, sir, of officiating when – '

'Yes,' said I.

'Dear me!' cried Mr Chillip. 'But no doubt you are a good deal changed since then, sir?'

'Probably,' said I.

'Well, sir,' observed Mr Chillip, 'I hope you'll excuse me, if I am compelled to ask the favour of your name.'

On my telling him my name, he was really moved. He quite shook hands with me – which was a violent proceeding for him, his usual course being to slide a tepid little fish-slice, an inch or two in advance of his hip, and evince the greatest discomposure when anybody grappled with it. Even now, he put his hand in his coat-pocket as soon as he could disengage it, and seemed relieved when he had got it safe back.

'Dear me, sir!' said Mr Chillip, surveying me with his head on one side. 'And it's Mr Copperfield, is it? Well, sir, I think I should have known you, if I had taken the liberty of looking more closely at you. There's a strong resemblance between you and your poor father, sir.'

'I never had the happiness of seeing my father,' I observed.

'Very true, sir,' said Mr Chillip, in a soothing tone. 'And very much to be deplored it was, on all accounts! We are not ignorant, sir,' said Mr Chillip, slowly shaking his little head again, 'down in our part of the country, of your fame. There must be great excitement here, sir,' said Mr Chillip, tapping himself on the forehead with his forefinger. 'You must find it a trying occupation, sir!'

'What is your part of the country now?' I asked, seating myself near him.

'I am established within a few miles of Bury St Edmunds, sir,' said Mr Chillip. 'Mrs Chillip coming into a little property in that neighbourhood, under her father's will, I bought a practice down there, in which you will be glad to hear I am doing well. My daughter is growing quite a tall lass now, sir,' said Mr Chillip, giving his little head another little shake. 'Her mother let down two tucks in her frocks only last week. Such is time, you see, sir!'

As the little man put his now empty glass to his lips when he made this reflection, I proposed to him to have it refilled, and I would keep him company with another. 'Well, sir,' he returned, in his slow way, 'it's more than I am accustomed to; but I can't deny myself the pleasure of your conversation. It seems but yesterday that I had the honour of attending you in the measles. You came through them charmingly, sir!'

I acknowledged this compliment, and ordered the negus, which was soon produced. 'Quite an uncommon dissipation!' said Mr Chillip, stirring it, 'but I can't resist so extraordinary an occasion. You have no family, sir?'

I shook my head.

'I was aware that you sustained a bereavement, sir, some time ago,' said Mr Chillip. 'I heard it from your father-in-law's sister. Very decided character there, sir?'

'Why, yes,' said I, 'decided enough. Where did you see her, Mr Chillip?'

'Are you not aware, sir,' returned Mr Chillip, with his placidest smile, 'that your father-in-law is again a neighbour of mine?'

'No,' said I.

'He is indeed, sir!' said Mr Chillip. 'Married a young lady of that part, with a very good little property, poor thing. – And this action of the brain now, sir? Don't you find it fatigues you?' said Mr Chillip, looking at me like an admiring Robin.

I waived that question, and returned to the Murdstones. 'I was aware of his being married again. Do you attend the family?' I asked.

'Not regularly. I have been called in,' he replied. 'Strong phrenological development of the organ of firmness, in Mr Murdstone and his sister, sir.'

I replied with such an expressive look, that Mr Chillip was emboldened by that, and the negus together, to give his head several short shakes, and thoughtfully exclaim, 'Ah, dear me! We remember old times, Mr Copperfield!'

'And the brother and sister are pursuing their old course, are they?' said I.

'Well, sir,' replied Mr Chillip, 'a medical man, being so much in families, ought to have neither eyes nor ears for anything but his profession. Still, I must say, they are very severe, sir – both as to this life and the next.'

'The next will be regulated without much reference to them, I dare say,' I returned; 'what are they doing as to this?'

Mr Chillip shook his head, stirred his negus, and sipped it.

'She was a charming woman, sir!' he observed in a plaintive manner.

'The present Mrs Murdstone?'

'A charming woman indeed, sir,' said Mr Chillip; 'as amiable, I am sure, as it was possible to be! Mrs Chillip's opinion is, that her spirit has been entirely broken since her marriage, and that she is all but melancholy mad. And the ladies,' observed Mr Chillip, timorously, 'are great observers, sir.'

'I suppose she was to be subdued and broken to their detestable mould, Heaven help her!' said I. 'And she has been.'

'Well, sir, there were violent quarrels at first, I assure you,' said Mr Chillip; 'but she is quite a shadow now. Would it be considered forward if I was to say to you, sir, in confidence, that since the sister came to help, the brother and sister between them have nearly reduced her to a state of imbecility.'

I told him I could easily believe it.

'I have no hesitation in saying,' said Mr Chillip, fortifying himself with another sip of negus, 'between you and me, sir, that her mother died of it – or that tyranny, gloom, and worry have made Mrs Murdstone nearly imbecile. She was a lively young woman, sir, before marriage, and their gloom and austerity destroyed her. They go about with her, now, more like her keepers than her husband and sister-in-law. That was Mrs Chillip's remark to me, only last week. And I assure you, sir, the ladies are great observers. Mrs Chillip herself is a *great* observer!'

'Does he gloomily profess to be (I am ashamed to use the word in such association) religious still?' I enquired.

'You anticipate, sir,' said Mr Chillip, his eyelids getting quite red with the unwonted stimulus in which he was indulging. 'One of Mrs Chillip's most impressive remarks. Mrs Chillip,' he proceeded, in the calmest and slowest manner, 'quite electrified me, by pointing out that Mr Murdstone sets up an image of himself, and calls it the Divine Nature. You might have knocked me down on the flat of my back, sir, with the feather of a pen, I assure you, when Mrs Chillip said so. The ladies are great observers, sir?'

'Intuitively,' said I, to his extreme delight.

'I am very happy to receive such support in my opinion, sir,' he rejoined. 'It is not often that I venture to give a non-medical opinion, I assure you. Mr Murdstone delivers public addresses sometimes, and it is said – in short, sir, it is said by Mrs Chillip – that the darker tyrant he has lately been, the more ferocious is his doctrine.'

'I believe Mrs Chillip to be perfectly right,' said I.

'Mrs Chillip does go so far as to say,' pursued the meekest of little men, much encouraged, 'that what such people miscall their religion, is a vent for their bad humours and arrogance. And do you know I must say, sir,' he continued, mildly laying his head on one side, 'that I *don't* find authority for Mr and Miss Murdstone in the New Testament?'

'I never found it either!' said I.

'In the meantime, sir,' said Mr Chillip, 'they are much disliked; and as they are very free in consigning everybody who dislikes them to perdition, we really have a good deal of perdition going on in our neighbourhood! However, as Mrs Chillip says, sir, they undergo a continual punishment; for they are turned inward to feed upon their own hearts, and their own hearts are very bad feeding. Now, sir, about that brain of yours, if you'll excuse my returning to it. Don't you expose it to a good deal of excitement, sir?'

I found it not difficult, in the excitement of Mr Chillip's own brain, under his potations of negus, to divert his attention from this topic to his own affairs, on which, for the next half hour, he was quite loquacious; giving me to understand, among other pieces of information, that he was then at the Gray's Inn Coffee-house to lay his professional evidence before a Commission of Lunacy, touching the state of mind of a patient who had become deranged from excessive drinking.

'And I assure you, sir,' he said, 'I am extremely nervous on such occasions. I could not support being what is called bullied, sir. It would quite unman me. Do you know it was some time before I recovered the conduct of that alarming lady, on the night of your birth, Mr Copperfield?'

I told him that I was going down to my aunt, the Dragon of that night, early in the morning; and that she was one of the most tenderhearted and excellent of women, as he would know full well if he knew her better. The mere notion of the possibility of his ever seeing her again appeared to terrify him. He replied, with a small pale smile, 'Is she so, indeed, sir? Really?' and almost immediately called for a candle, and went to bed, as if he were not quite safe anywhere else. He did not actually stagger under the negus; but I should think his placid little pulse must have made two or three more beats in a minute, than it had done since the great night of my aunt's disappointment, when she struck at him with her bonnet.

Thoroughly tired, I went to bed too, at midnight; passed the next day on the Dover coach; burst safe and sound into my aunt's old parlour while she was at tea (she wore spectacles now); and was received by her, and Mr Dick, and dear old Peggotty, who acted as housekeeper, with open arms and tears of joy. My aunt was mightily amused, when we began to talk composedly, by my account of my meeting with Mr Chillip, and of his holding her in such dread remembrance; and both she and Peggotty had a great deal to say about my poor mother's second husband, and 'that murdering woman of a sister' – on whom I think no pain or penalty would have induced my aunt to bestow any Christian or Proper Name, or any other designation.

CHAPTER 60

Agnes

My aunt and I, when we were left alone, talked far into the night. How the emigrants never wrote home, otherwise than cheerfully and hopefully; how Mr Micawber had actually remitted divers small sums of money, on account of those 'pecuniary liabilities,' in reference to which he had been so businesslike as between man and man; how Janet, returning into my aunt's service when she came back to Dover, had finally carried out her renunciation of mankind by entering into wedlock with a thriving tavern-keeper; and how my aunt had finally set *her* seal on the same great principle, by aiding and abetting the bride, and crowning the marriage-ceremony with her presence, were among our topics – already more or less familiar to me through the letters I had had. Mr Dick, as usual, was not forgotten. My aunt informed me how he incessantly occupied himself in copying everything he could lay his hands on, and kept King Charles the First at a respectful distance by that semblance of employment; how it was one of the main joys and rewards of her life that he was free and happy, instead of pining in monotonous restraint; and how (as a novel general conclusion) nobody but she could ever fully know what he was.

'And when, Trot,' said my aunt, patting the back of my hand, as we sat in our old way before the fire, 'when are you going over to Canterbury?'

'I shall get a horse, and ride over tomorrow morning, aunt, unless you will go with me?'

'No!' said my aunt, in her short abrupt way. 'I mean to stay where I am.'

Then, I should ride, I said. I could not have come through Canterbury today without stopping, if I had been coming to anyone but her.

She was pleased, but answered, 'Tut, Trot; *my* old bones would have kept till tomorrow!' and softly patted my hand again, as I sat looking thoughtfully at the fire.

Thoughtfully, for I could not be here once more, and so near Agnes, without the revival of those regrets with which I had so long been occupied. Softened regrets they might be, teaching me what I had failed to learn when my younger life was all before me, but not the less regrets. 'Oh, Trot,' I seemed to hear my aunt say once more; and I understood her better now – 'Blind, blind, blind!'

We both kept silence for some minutes. When I raised my eyes, I found that she was steadily observant of me. Perhaps she had followed the current of my mind; for it seemed to me an easy one to track now, wilful as it had been once.

'You will find her father a white-haired old man,' said my aunt, 'though a better man in all other respects – a reclaimed man. Neither will you find him measuring all human interests, and joys, and sorrows, with his one poor little inch-rule now. Trust me, child, such things must shrink very much, before they can be measured off in *that* way.'

'Indeed they must,' said I.

'You will find her,' pursued my aunt, 'as good, as beautiful, as earnest, as disinterested, as she has always been. If I knew higher praise, Trot, I would bestow it on her.'

There was no higher praise for her; no higher reproach for me. Oh, how had I strayed so far away!

'If she trains the young girls whom she has about her to be like herself,' said my aunt, earnest even to the filling of her eyes with tears, 'Heaven knows, her life will be well employed! Useful and happy, as she said that day! How could she be otherwise than useful and happy!'

'Has Agnes any – ' I was thinking aloud, rather than speaking.

'Well? Hey? Any what?' said my aunt sharply.

'Any lover,' said I.

'A score,' cried my aunt, with a kind of indignant pride. 'She might have married twenty times, my dear, since you have been gone!'

'No doubt,' said I. 'No doubt. But has she any lover who is worthy of her? Agnes could care for no other.'

My aunt sat musing for a little while, with her chin upon her hand. Slowly raising her eyes to mine, she said: 'I suspect she has an attachment, Trot.'

'A prosperous one?' said I.

'Trot,' returned my aunt gravely, 'I can't say. I have no right to tell you even so much. She has never confided it to me, but I suspect it.'

She looked so attentively and anxiously at me (I even saw her tremble), that I felt now, more than ever, that she had followed my late thoughts. I summoned all the resolutions I had made, in all those many days and nights, and all those many conflicts of my heart.

'If it should be so,' I began, 'and I hope it is – '

'I don't know that it is,' said my aunt curtly. 'You must not be ruled by my suspicions. You must keep them secret. They are very slight, perhaps. I have no right to speak.'

'If it should be so,' I repeated, 'Agnes will tell me at her own good time. A sister to whom I have confided so much, aunt, will not be reluctant to confide in me.'

My aunt withdrew her eyes from mine, as slowly as she had turned them upon me; and covered them thoughtfully with her hand. By and by she put her other hand on my shoulder; and so we both sat looking into the past, without saying another word, until we parted for the night.

I rode away, early in the morning, for the scene of my old school-days. I cannot say that I was yet quite happy, in the hope that I was gaining a victory over myself; even in the prospect of so soon looking on her face again.

The well-remembered ground was soon traversed, and I came into the quiet streets, where every stone was a boy's book to me. I went on foot to the old house, and went away with a heart too full to enter. I returned; and looking, as I passed, through the low window of the turret-room where first Uriah Heep, and afterwards Mr Micawber, had been wont to sit, saw that it was a little parlour now, and that there was no office. Otherwise the staid old house was, as to its cleanliness and order, still just as it had been when I first saw it. I requested the new maid who admitted me, to tell Miss Wickfield that a gentleman who waited on her from a friend abroad was there; and I was shown up the grave old staircase (cautioned of the steps I knew so well), into the unchanged drawing-room. The books that Agnes and I had read together were on their shelves, and the desk where I had laboured at my lessons, many a night, stood yet at the same old corner of the table. All the little changes that had crept in when the Heeps were there were changed again. Everything was as it used to be, in the happy time.

I stood in a window, and looked across the ancient street at the opposite houses, recalling how I had watched them on wet afternoons, when I first came there; and how I had used to speculate about the people who appeared at any of the windows, and had followed them with my eyes up and down stairs, while women went clinking along the pavement in pattens, and the dull rain fell in slanting lines, and poured out of the waterspout yonder, and flowed into the road. The feeling with which I used to watch the tramps, as they came into the town on those wet evenings, at dusk, and limped past, with their bundles drooping over their shoulders at the ends of sticks, came freshly back to me; fraught, as then, with the smell of damp earth, and wet leaves and briar, and the sensation of the very airs that blew upon me in my own toilsome journey.

The opening of the little door in the panelled wall made me start and turn. Her beautiful serene eyes met mine as she came towards me. She stopped, and laid her hand upon her bosom, and I caught her in my arms.

'Agnes! my dear girl! I have come too suddenly upon you.'

'No, no! I am so rejoiced to see you, Trotwood!'

'Dear Agnes, the happiness it is to me, to see you once again!'

I folded her to my heart, and for a little while we were both silent. Presently we sat down, side by side; and her angel-face was turned upon me with the welcome I had dreamed of, waking and sleeping, for whole years.

She was so true, she was so beautiful, she was so good – I owed her so much gratitude, she was so dear to me, that I could find no utterance for what I felt. I tried to bless her, tried to thank her, tried to tell her (as I had often done in letters) what an influence she had upon me; but all my efforts were in vain. My love and joy were dumb.

With her own sweet tranquillity she calmed my agitation, led me back to the time of our parting; spoke to me of Emily, whom she had visited, in secret, many times; spoke to me tenderly of Dora's grave. With the unerring instinct of her noble heart, she touched the chords of my memory so softly and harmoniously, that not one jarred within me; I could listen to the sorrowful, distant music, and desire to shrink from nothing it awoke. How could I, when, blended with it all, was her dear self, the better angel of my life.

'And you, Agnes,' I said, by and by. 'Tell me of yourself. You have hardly ever told me of your own life in all this lapse of time!'

'What should I tell?' she answered, with her radiant smile. 'Papa is well. You see us here, quiet in our own home; our anxieties set at rest, our home restored to us; and knowing that, dear Trotwood, you know all.'

'All, Agnes?' said I.

She looked at me, with some fluttering wonder in her face.

'Is there nothing else, Sister?' I said.

Her colour, which had just now faded, returned, and faded again. She smiled, with a quiet sadness, I thought, and shook her head.

I had sought to lead her to what my aunt had hinted at; for, sharply painful to me as it must be to receive that confidence, I was to discipline my heart, and do my duty to her. I saw, however, that she was uneasy, and I let it pass.

'You have much to do, dear Agnes?'

'With my school?' said she, looking up again, in all her bright composure.

'Yes. It is laborious, is it not?'

'The labour is so pleasant,' she returned, 'that it is scarcely grateful in me to call it by that name.'

'Nothing good is difficult to you,' said I.

Her colour came and went once more; and once more, as she bent her head, I saw the same sad smile.

'You will wait and see papa,' said Agnes cheerfully, 'and pass the day with us? Perhaps you will sleep in your own room? We always call it yours.'

I could not do that, having promised to ride back to my aunt's, at night; but I would pass the day there, joyfully.

'I must be a prisoner for a little while,' said Agnes, 'but here are the old books, Trotwood, and the old music.'

'Even the old flowers are here,' said I, looking round; 'or the old kinds.'

'I have found a pleasure,' returned Agnes, smiling, 'while you have been absent, in keeping everything as it used to be when we were children. For we were very happy then, I think.'

'Heaven knows we were!' said I.

'And every little thing that has reminded me of my brother,' said Agnes, with her cordial eyes turned cheerfully upon me, 'has been a welcome companion. Even this,' showing me the basket-trifle, full of keys, still hanging at her side, 'seems to jingle a kind of old tune!'

She smiled again, and went out at the door by which she had come.

It was for me to guard this sisterly affection with religious care. It was all that I had left myself, and it was a treasure. If I once shook the foundations of the sacred confidence and usage, in virtue of which it was given to me, it was lost, and could never be recovered. I set this steadily before myself. The better I loved her, the more it behoved me never to forget it.

I walked through the streets; and, once more seeing my old adversary the butcher – now a constable, with his staff hanging up in the shop – went down to look at the place where I had fought him; and there meditated on Miss Shepherd and the eldest Miss Larkins, and all the idle loves and likings, and dislikings, of that time. Nothing seemed to have survived that time but Agnes; and she, ever a star above me, was brighter and higher.

When I returned, Mr Wickfield had come home, from a garden he had, a couple of miles or so out of the town, where he now employed himself almost every day. I found him as my aunt had described him. We sat down to dinner, with some half-dozen little girls; and he seemed but the shadow of his handsome picture on the wall.

The tranquillity and peace belonging, of old, to that quiet ground in my memory pervaded it again. When dinner was done, Mr Wickfield taking no wine, and I desiring none, we went upstairs, where Agnes and her little charges sang and played and worked. After tea the children left us; and we three sat together, talking of the bygone days.

'My part in them,' said Mr Wickfield, shaking his white head, 'has much matter for regret – for deep regret, and deep contrition, Trotwood, you well know. But I would not cancel it, if it were in my power.'

I could readily believe that, looking at the face beside him.

'I should cancel with it,' he pursued, 'such patience and devotion, such fidelity, such a child's love, as I must not forget, no! even to forget myself.'

'I understand you, sir,' I softly said. 'I hold it – I have always held it – in veneration.'

'But no one knows, not even you,' he returned, 'how much she has done, how much she has undergone, how hard she has striven. Dear Agnes!'

She had put her hand entreatingly on his arm, to stop him; and was very, very pale.

'Well, well!' he said with a sigh, dismissing, as I then saw, some trial she had borne, or was yet to bear, in connection with what my aunt had told me. 'Well! I have never told you, Trotwood, of her mother. Has anyone?'

'Never, sir.'

'It's not much – though it was much to suffer. She married me in opposition to her father's wish, and he renounced her. She prayed him to forgive her, before my Agnes came into this world. He was a very hard man, and her mother had long been dead. He repulsed her. He broke her heart.'

Agnes leaned upon his shoulder, and stole her arm about his neck.

'She had an affectionate and gentle heart,' he said; 'and it was broken. I knew its tender nature very well. No one could, if I did not. She loved me dearly, but was never happy. She was always labouring, in secret, under this distress; and being delicate and downcast at the time of his last repulse – for it was not the first, by many – pined away and died. She left me Agnes, two weeks old; and the grey hair that you recollect me with, when you first came.'

He kissed Agnes on her cheek.

'My love for my dear child was a diseased love, but my mind was all unhealthy then. I say no more of that. I am not speaking of myself, Trotwood, but of her mother, and of her. If I give you any clue to what I am, or to what I have been, you will unravel it, I know. What Agnes is, I need not say. I have always read something of her poor mother's story, in her character; and so I tell it you tonight, when we three are again together, after such great changes. I have told it all.'

His bowed head, and her angel-face and filial duty, derived a more pathetic meaning from it than they had had before. If I had wanted anything by which to mark this night of our reunion, I should have found it in this.

Agnes rose up from her father's side, before long; and going softly to her piano, played some of the old airs to which we had often listened in that place.

'Have you any intention of going away again?' Agnes asked me, as I was standing by.

'What does my sister say to that?'

'I hope not.'

'Then I have no such intention, Agnes.'

'I think you ought not, Trotwood, since you ask me,' she said mildly. 'Your growing reputation and success enlarge your power of doing good; and if *I* could spare my brother,' with her eyes upon me, 'perhaps the time could not.'

'What I am, you have made me, Agnes. You should know best.'

'*I* made you, Trotwood?'

'Yes! Agnes, my dear girl!' I said, bending over her. 'I tried to tell you, when we met today, something that has been in my thoughts since Dora died. You remember, when you came down to me in our little room – pointing upward, Agnes?'

'Oh, Trotwood!' she returned, her eyes filled with tears. 'So loving, so confiding, and so young! Can I ever forget?'

'As you were then, my sister, I have often thought since, you have ever been to me. Ever pointing upward, Agnes; ever leading me to something better; ever directing me to higher things!'

She only shook her head; through her tears I saw the same sad quiet smile.

'And I am so grateful to you for it, Agnes, so bound to you, that there is no name for the affection of my heart. I want you to know, yet don't know how to tell you, that all my life long I shall look up to you, and be guided by you, as I have been through the darkness that is past. Whatever betides, whatever new ties you may form, whatever changes may come between us, I shall always look to you, and love you, as I do now, and have always done. You will always be my solace and my resource as you have always been. Until I die, my dearest sister, I shall see you always before me, pointing upward! '

She put her hand in mine, and told me she was proud of me, and of what I said; although I praised her very far beyond her worth. Then she went on softly playing, but without removing her eyes from me.

'Do you know, what I have heard tonight, Agnes,' said I, 'strangely seems to be a part of the feeling with which I regarded you when I saw you first – with which I sat beside you in my rough school-days.'

'You knew I had no mother,' she replied with a smile, 'and felt kindly towards me.'

'More than that, Agnes, I knew, almost as if I had known this story, that there was something inexplicably gentle and softened, surrounding you; something that might have been sorrowful in someone else (as I can now understand it was), but was not so in you.'

She softly played on, looking at me still.

'Will you laugh at my cherishing such fancies, Agnes?'

'No!'

'Or at my saying that I really believe I felt, even then, that you could be faithfully affectionate against all discouragement, and never cease to be so, until you cease to live? – Will you laugh at such a dream?'

'Oh, no! Oh, no!'

For an instant, a distressful shadow crossed her face; but, even in the start it gave me, it was gone; and she was playing on, and looking at me with her own calm smile.

As I rode back in the lonely night, the wind going by me like a restless memory, I thought of this, and feared she was not happy. *I* was not happy; but, thus far, I had faithfully set the seal upon the past, and, thinking of her pointing upward, thought of her as pointing to that sky above me, where, in the mystery to come, I might yet love her with a love unknown on earth, and tell her what the strife had been within me when I loved her here.

CHAPTER 61

I Am Shown Two Interesting Penitents

For a time – at all events until my book should be completed, which would be the work of several months – I took up my abode in my aunt's house at Dover; and there, sitting in the window from which I had looked out at the moon upon the sea, when that roof first gave me shelter, I quietly pursued my task.

In pursuance of my intention of referring to my own fictions only when their course should incidentally connect itself with the progress of my story, I do not enter on the aspirations, the delights, anxieties, and triumphs of my art. That I truly devoted myself to it with my strongest earnestness, and bestowed upon it every energy of my soul, I have already said. If the books I have written be of any worth, they will supply the rest. I shall otherwise have written to poor purpose, and the rest will be of interest to no one.

Occasionally I went to London; to lose myself in the swarm of life there, or to consult with Traddles on some business point. He had managed for me, in my absence, with the soundest judgement; and my worldly affairs were prospering. As my notoriety began to bring upon me an enormous quantity of letters from people of whom I had no knowledge – chiefly about nothing, and extremely difficult to answer – I agreed with Traddles to have my name painted up on his door. There, the devoted postman on that beat delivered bushels of letters for me; and there, at intervals, I laboured through them, like a Home Secretary of State without the salary.

Among this correspondence, there dropped in, every now and then, an obliging proposal from one of the numerous out-siders always lurking about the Commons, to practise under cover of my name (if I would take the necessary steps remaining to make a proctor of myself), and pay me a percentage on the profits. But I declined these offers; being already aware that there were plenty of such covert practitioners in existence, and considering the Commons quite bad enough, without my doing anything to make it worse.

The girls had gone home, when my name burst into bloom

on Traddles's door; and the sharp boy looked, all day, as if he had never heard of Sophy, shut up in a back room, glancing down from her work into a sooty little strip of garden with a pump in it. But there I always found her, the same bright housewife; often humming her Devonshire ballads when no strange foot was coming up the stairs, and blunting the sharp boy in his official closet with melody.

I wondered, at first, why I so often found Sophy writing in a copy-book; and why she always shut it up when I appeared, and hurried it into the table-drawer. But the secret soon came out. One day, Traddles (who had just come home through the drizzling sleet from Court) took a paper out of his desk, and asked me what I thought of that handwriting?

'Oh, *don't*, Tom!' cried Sophy, who was warming his slippers before the fire.

'My dear,' returned Tom, in a delighted state, 'why not? What do you say to that writing, Copperfield?'

'It's extraordinary legal and formal,' said I. 'I don't think I ever saw such a stiff hand.'

'Not like a lady's hand, is it?' said Traddles.

'A lady's!' I repeated. 'Bricks and mortar are more like a lady's hand!'

Traddles broke into a rapturous laugh, and informed me that it was Sophy's writing; that Sophy had vowed and declared he would need a copying-clerk soon, and she would be that clerk; that she had acquired this hand from a pattern; and that she could throw off – I forget how many folios an hour. Sophy was very much confused by my being told all this, and said that when 'Tom' was made a judge he wouldn't be so ready to proclaim it. Which 'Tom' denied; averring that he should always be equally proud of it, under all circumstances.

'What a thoroughly good and charming wife she is, my dear Traddles!' said I, when she had gone away, laughing.

'My dear Copperfield,' returned Traddles, 'she is, without any exception, the dearest girl! The way she manages this place; her punctuality, domestic knowledge, economy, and order; her cheerfulness, Copperfield!'

'Indeed, you have reason to commend her!' I returned. 'You are a happy fellow. I believe you make yourselves, and each other, two of the happiest people in the world.'

'I am sure we *are* two of the happiest people,' returned Traddles. 'I admit that, at all events. Bless my soul, when I see her getting up by candle-light on these dark mornings, busying herself in the day's arrangements, going out to market before the clerks come into the Inn, caring for no weather, devising the most capital little dinners out of the plainest materials, making puddings and pies, keeping everything in its right place, always so neat and ornamental herself, sitting up at night with me if it's ever so late, sweet-tempered and encouraging always, and all for me, I positively sometimes can't believe it, Copperfield!'

He was tender of the very slippers she had been warming, as he put them on, and stretched his feet enjoying upon the fender.

'I positively sometimes can't believe it,' said Traddles. 'Then, our pleasures! Dear me, they are inexpensive, but they are quite wonderful! When we are at home here, of an evening, and

shut the outer door, and draw those curtains – which she made – where could we be more snug? When it's fine, and we go out for a walk in the evening, the streets abound in enjoyment for us. We look into the glittering windows of the jewellers' shops; and I show Sophy which of the diamond-eyed serpents, coiled up on white satin rising grounds, I would give her if I could afford it; and Sophy shows me which of the gold watches that are capped and jewelled and engine-turned, and possessed of the horizontal lever-escape-movement, and all sorts of things, she would buy for me if *she* could afford it; and we pick out the spoons and forks, fish-slices, butter-knives, and sugar-tongs, we should both prefer if we could both afford it; and really we go away as if we had got them! Then, when we stroll into the squares, and great streets, and see a house to let, sometimes we look up at it, and say, how would *that* do, if I was made a judge? And we parcel it out – such a room for us, such rooms for the girls, and so forth; until we settle to our satisfaction that it would do, or it wouldn't do, as the case may be. Sometimes, we go at half price to the pit of the theatre – the very smell of which is cheap, in my opinion, at the money – and there we thoroughly enjoy the play; which Sophy believes every word of, and so do I. In walking home, perhaps we buy a little bit of something at a cook's-shop, or a little lobster at the fish-monger's, and bring it here, and make a splendid supper, chatting about what we have seen. Now, you know, Copperfield, if I was Lord Chancellor, we couldn't do this!'

'You would do something, whatever you were, my dear Traddles,' thought I, 'that would be pleasant and amiable! And by the way,' I said aloud, 'I suppose you never draw any skeletons now?'

'Really,' replied Traddles, laughing and reddening, 'I can't wholly deny that I do, my dear Copperfield. For, being in one of the back rows of the King's Bench the other day, with a pen in hand, the fancy came into my head to try how I had preserved that accomplishment. And I am afraid there's a skeleton – in a wig – on the ledge of the desk.'

After we had both laughed heartily, Traddles wound up by looking with a smile at the fire, and saying, in his forgiving way, 'Old Creakle!'

'I have a letter from that old – Rascal here,' said I. For I never was less disposed to forgive him the way he used to batter Traddles than when I saw Traddles so ready to forgive him himself.

'From Creakle the schoolmaster?' exclaimed Traddles. 'No!'

'Among the persons who are attracted to me in my rising fame and fortune,' said I, looking over my letters, 'and who discover that they were always much attached to me, is the selfsame Creakle. He is not a schoolmaster now, Traddles. He is retired. He is a Middlesex Magistrate.'

I thought Traddles might be surprised to hear it, but he was not so at all.

'How do you suppose he comes to be a Middlesex Magistrate?' said I.

'Oh, dear me!' replied Traddles, 'it would be very difficult to answer that question. Perhaps he voted for somebody, or lent money to somebody, or bought something of somebody, or otherwise obliged somebody, or jobbed for somebody, who knew somebody who got the lieutenant of the county to nominate him for the commission.'

'On the commission he is, at any rate,' said I. 'And he writes to me here that he will be glad to show me, in operation, the only true system of prison discipline; the only unchallengeable way of making sincere and lasting converts and penitents – which, you know, is by solitary confinement. What do you say?'

'To the system?' enquired Traddles, looking grave.

'No. To my accepting the offer, and your going with me?'

'I don't object,' said Traddles.

'Then I'll write to say so. You remember (to say nothing of our treatment) this same Creakle turning his son out of doors, I suppose, and the life he used to lead his wife and daughter?'

'Perfectly,' said Traddles.

'Yet, if you'll read his letter, you'll find he is the tenderest of men to prisoners convicted of the whole calendar of felonies,' said I; 'though I can't find that his tenderness extends to any other class of created beings.'

Traddles shrugged his shoulders, and was not at all surprised. I had not expected him to be, and was not surprised myself; or my observation of similar practical satires would have been but scanty. We arranged the time of our visit, and I wrote accordingly to Mr Creakle that evening.

On the appointed day – I think it was the next day, but no matter – Traddles and I repaired to the prison where Mr Creakle was powerful. It was an immense and solid building, erected at a vast expense. I could not help thinking, as we approached the gate, what an uproar would have been made in the country, if any deluded man had proposed to spend one half the money it had cost, on the erection of an industrial school for the young, or a house of refuge for the deserving old.

In an office that might have been on the ground-floor of the Tower of Babel, it was so massively constructed, we were presented to our old schoolmaster; who was one of a group, composed of two or three of the busier sort of magistrates, and some visitors they had brought. He received me, like a man who had formed my mind in bygone years, and had always loved me tenderly. On my introducing Traddles, Mr Creakle expressed, in like manner, but in an inferior degree, that he had always been Traddles's guide, philosopher, and friend. Our venerable instructor was a great deal older, and not improved in appearance. His face was as fiery as ever; his eyes were as small, and rather deeper set. The scanty, wet-looking grey hair, by which I remembered him, was almost gone; and the thick veins in his bald head were none the more agreeable to look at.

After some conversation among these gentlemen, from which I might have supposed that there was nothing in the world to be legitimately taken into account but the supreme comfort of prisoners, at any expense, and nothing on the wide earth to be done outside prison doors, we began our inspection. It being then just dinner-time, we went, first, into the great kitchen, where every prisoner's dinner was in course of being set out separately (to be handed to him in his cell), with the regularity and precision of clockwork. I said aside, to Traddles, that I wondered whether it occurred to anybody that there was a striking contrast between these plentiful repasts of choice quality and the dinners, not to say of paupers, but of soldiers, sailors, labourers, the great bulk of the honest, working community; of whom not one man in five hundred ever dined half so well. But I learned that the 'system' required high living; and, in short, to dispose of the system, once for all, I found that on that head and on all others, 'the system' put an end to all doubts, and disposed of all anomalies. Nobody appeared to have the least idea that there was any other system but *the* system to be considered.

As we were going through some of the magnificent passages, I enquired of Mr Creakle and his friends what were supposed to be the main advantages of this all-governing and universally overriding system? I found them to be the perfect isolation of prisoners – so that no one man in confinement there knew anything about another; and the reduction of prisoners to a wholesome state of mind, leading to sincere contrition and repentance.

Now, it struck me, when we began to visit individuals in their cells, and to traverse the passages in which those cells were, and to have the manner of the going to chapel and so forth explained to us, that there was a strong probability of the prisoners knowing a good deal about each other, and of their carrying on a pretty complete system of intercourse. This, at the time I write, has been proved, I believe, to be the case; but as it would have been flat blasphemy against the system to have hinted such a doubt then, I looked out for the penitence as diligently as I could.

And here again, I had great misgivings. I found as prevalent a fashion in the form of the penitence, as I had left outside in the forms of the coats and waistcoats in the windows of the tailors' shops. I found a vast amount of profession, varying very little in character: varying very little (which I thought exceedingly suspicious), even in words. I found a great many foxes, disparaging whole vineyards of inaccessible grapes; but I found very few foxes whom I would have trusted within reach of a bunch. Above all, I found that the most professing men were the greatest objects of interest; and that their conceit, their vanity, their want of excitement, and their love of deception (which many of them possessed to an almost incredible extent, as their histories showed), all prompted to these professions, and were all gratified by them.

However, I heard so repeatedly, in the course of our goings to and fro, of a certain Number Twenty-Seven, who was the Favourite, and who really appeared to be a Model Prisoner, that I resolved to suspend my judgement until I should see Twenty-Seven. Twenty-Eight, I understood, was also a bright particular star; but it was his misfortune to have his glory a little dimmed by the extraordinary lustre of Twenty-Seven. I heard so much of Twenty-Seven, of his pious admonitions to everybody around him, and of the beautiful letters he constantly wrote to his mother (whom he seemed to consider in a very bad way), that I became quite impatient to see him.

I had to restrain my impatience for some time, on account of Twenty-Seven being reserved for a concluding effect. But, at last, we came to the door of his cell; and Mr Creakle, looking

493

through a little hole in it, reported to us, in a state of the greatest admiration, that he was reading a Hymn Book.

There was such a rush of heads immediately to see Number Twenty-Seven reading his Hymn Book that the little hole was blocked up, six or seven heads deep. To remedy this inconvenience, and give us an opportunity of conversing with Twenty-Seven in all his purity, Mr Creakle directed the door of the cell to be unlocked, and Twenty-Seven to be invited out into the passage. This was done; and whom should Traddles and I then behold, to our amazement, in this converted Number Twenty-Seven, but Uriah Heep!

He knew us directly; and said, as he came out – with the old writhe: 'How do you do, Mr Copperfield? How do you do, Mr Traddles?'

This recognition caused a general admiration in the party. I rather thought that everyone was struck by his not being proud, and taking notice of us.

'Well, Twenty-Seven,' said Mr Creakle, mournfully admiring him. 'How do you find yourself today?'

'I am very 'umble, sir!' replied Uriah Heep.

'You are always so, Twenty-Seven,' said Mr Creakle.

Here another gentleman asked, with extreme anxiety: 'Are you quite comfortable?'

'Yes, I thank you, sir!' said Uriah Heep, looking in that direction. 'Far more comfortable here than ever I was outside. I see my follies now, sir. That's what makes me comfortable.'

Several gentlemen were much affected; and a third questioner, forcing himself to the front, enquired with extreme feeling: 'How do you find the beef?'

'Thank you, sir,' replied Uriah, glancing in the new direction of this voice, 'it was tougher yesterday than I could wish; but it's my duty to bear. I have committed follies, gentlemen,' said Uriah, looking round with a meek smile, 'and I ought to bear the consequences without repining.'

A murmur, partly of gratification at Twenty-Seven's celestial state of mind, and partly of indignation against the contractor who had given him any cause of complaint (a note of which was immediately made by Mr Creakle), having subsided, Twenty-Seven stood in the midst of us, as if he felt himself the principal object of merit in a highly meritorious museum. That we, the neophytes, might have an excess of light shining upon us all at once, orders were given to let out Twenty-Eight.

I had been so much astonished already that I only felt a kind of resigned wonder when Mr Littimer walked forth, reading a good book!

'Twenty-Eight,' said a gentleman in spectacles, who had not yet spoken, 'you complained last week, my good fellow, of the cocoa. How has it been since?'

'I thank you, sir,' said Mr Littimer, 'it has been better made. If I might take the liberty of saying so, sir, I don't think the milk which is boiled with it is quite genuine; but I am aware, sir, that there is great adulteration of milk, in London, and that the article in a pure state is difficult to be obtained.'

It appeared to me that the gentleman in spectacles backed his Twenty-Eight against Mr Creakle's Twenty-Seven, for each of them took his own man in hand.

'What is your state of mind, Twenty-Eight?' said the questioner in spectacles.

'I thank you, sir,' returned Mr Littimer; 'I see my follies now, sir. I am a good deal troubled when I think of the sins of my former companions, sir; but I trust they may find forgiveness.'

'You are quite happy yourself?' said the questioner, nodding encouragement.

'I am much obliged to you, sir,' returned Mr Littimer; 'perfectly so.'

'Is there anything at all on your mind, now?' said the questioner. 'If so, mention it, Twenty-Eight.'

'Sir,' said Mr Littimer, without looking up, 'if my eyes have not deceived me, there is a gentleman present who was acquainted with me in my former life. It may be profitable to that gentleman to know, sir, that I attribute my past follies entirely to having lived a thoughtless life in the service of young men; and to having allowed myself to be led by them into weaknesses, which I had not the strength to resist. I hope that gentleman will take warning, sir, and will not be offended at my freedom. It is for his good. I am conscious of my own past follies. I hope he may repent of all the wickedness and sin to which he has been a party.'

I observed that several gentlemen were shading their eyes, each, with one hand, as if they had just come into church.

'This does you credit, Twenty-Eight,' returned the questioner. 'I should have expected it of you. Is there anything else?'

'Sir,' returned Mr Littimer, slightly lifting up his eyebrows, but not his eyes, 'there was a young woman who fell into dissolute courses, that I endeavoured to save, sir, but could not rescue. I beg that gentleman, if he has it in his power, to inform that young woman from me that I forgive her her bad conduct towards myself; and that I call her to repentance – if he will be so good.'

'I have no doubt, Twenty-Eight,' returned the questioner, 'that the gentleman you refer to feels very strongly – as we all must – what you have so properly said. We will not detain you.'

'I thank you, sir,' said Mr Littimer. 'Gentlemen, I wish you a good-day, and hoping you and your families will also see your wickedness, and amend!'

With this, Number Twenty-Eight retired, after a glance between him and Uriah, as if they were not altogether unknown to each other, through some medium of communication; and a murmur went round the group, as his door shut upon him, that he was a most respectable man, and a beautiful case.

'Now, Twenty-Seven,' said Mr Creakle, entering on a clear stage with *his* man, 'is there anything that anyone can do for you? If so, mention it.'

'I would 'umbly ask, sir,' returned Uriah, with a jerk of his malevolent head, 'for leave to write again to mother.'

'It shall certainly be granted,' said Mr Creakle.

'Thank you, sir! I am anxious about mother. I am afraid she ain't safe.'

Somebody incautiously asked, what from? But there was a scandalised whisper of 'Hush!'

'Immortally safe, sir,' returned Uriah, writhing in the

direction of the voice. 'I should wish mother to be got into my state. I never should have been got into my present state if I hadn't come here. I wish mother had come here. It would be better for everybody, if they got took up, and was brought here.'

This sentiment gave unbounded satisfaction – greater satisfaction, I think, than anything that had passed yet.

'Before I come here,' said Uriah, stealing a look at us, as if he would have blighted the outer world to which we belonged, if he could, 'I was given to follies; but now I am sensible of my follies. There's a deal of sin outside. There's a deal of sin in mother. There's nothing but sin everywhere – except here.'

'You are quite changed?' said Mr Creakle.

'Oh, dear, yes, sir!' cried this hopeful penitent.

'You wouldn't relapse, if you were going out?' asked somebody else.

'Oh, de-ar, no, sir!'

'Well!' said Mr Creakle, 'this is very gratifying. You have addressed Mr Copperfield, Twenty-Seven. Do you wish to say anything further to him?'

'You knew me a long time before I came here and was changed, Mr Copperfield,' said Uriah, looking at me; and a more villainous look I never saw, even on his visage. 'You knew me when, in spite of my follies, I was 'umble among them that was proud, and meek among them that was violent – you was violent to me yourself, Mr Copperfield. Once, you struck me a blow in the face, you know.'

General commiseration. Several indignant glances directed at me.

'But I forgive you, Mr Copperfield,' said Uriah, making his forgiving nature the subject of a most impious and awful parallel, which I shall not record. 'I forgive everybody. It would ill become me to bear malice. I freely forgive you, and I hope you'll curb your passions in future. I hope Mr W. will repent, and Miss W., and all of that sinful lot. You've been visited with affliction, and I hope it may do you good; but you'd better have come here. Mr W. had better have come here, and Miss W., too. The best wish I could give you, Mr Copperfield, and give all of you gentlemen, is, that you could be took up and brought here. When I think of my past follies, and my present state, I am sure it would be best for you. I pity all who ain't brought here!'

He sneaked back into his cell, amidst a little chorus of approbation; and both Traddles and I experienced a great relief when he was locked in.

It was a characteristic feature in this repentance that I was fain to ask what these two men had done, to be there at all. That appeared to be the last thing about which they had anything to say. I addressed myself to one of the two warders, who, I suspected, from certain latent indications in their faces, knew pretty well what all this stir was worth. 'Do you know,' said I, as we walked along the passage, 'what felony was Number Twenty-Seven's last "folly"?'

The answer was that it was a Bank case.

'A fraud on the Bank of England?' I asked.

'Yes, sir. Fraud, forgery, and conspiracy – he and some others – he set the others on. It was a deep plot for a large sum. Sentence, transportation for life. Twenty-Seven was the

I am shown two interesting penitents

knowingest bird of the lot, and had very nearly kept himself safe; but not quite. The Bank was just able to put salt upon his tail – and only just.'

'Do you know Twenty-Eight's offence?'

'Twenty-Eight,' returned my informant, speaking throughout in a low tone, and looking over his shoulder as we walked along the passage, to guard himself from being overheard, in such an unlawful reference to these Immaculates, by Creakle and the rest; 'Twenty-Eight (also transportation) got a place, and robbed a young master of a matter of two hundred and fifty pounds in money and valuables, the night before they were going abroad. I particularly recollect his case from his being took by a dwarf.'

'A what?'

'A little woman. I have forgot her name.'

'Not Mowcher?'

'That's it! He had eluded pursuit, and was going to America in a flaxen wig and whiskers, and such a complete disguise as never you see in all your born days, when the little woman, being in Southampton, met him walking along the street – picked him out with her sharp eye in a moment – ran betwixt his legs to upset him – and held on to him like grim Death.'

'Excellent Miss Mowcher!' cried I.

'You'd have said so, if you had seen her, standing on a chair in the witness-box at his trial, as I did,' said my friend. 'He cut her face right open, and pounded her in the most brutal manner, when she took him; but she never loosed her hold till he was locked up. She held so tight to him, in fact, that the officers were obliged to take 'em both together. She gave her evidence in the gamest way, and was highly complimented by the Bench, and cheered right home to her lodgings. She said in court that she'd have took him single-handed (on account of what she knew concerning him) if he had been Samson. And it's my belief she would!'

It was mine, too, and I highly respected Miss Mowcher for it.

We had now seen all there was to see. It would have been in vain to represent to such a man as the Worshipful Mr Creakle that Twenty-Seven and Twenty-Eight were perfectly consistent and unchanged; that exactly what they were then, they had always been; that the hypocritical knaves were just the subjects to make that sort of profession in such a place; that they knew its market value at least as well as we did, in the immediate service it would do them when they were expatriated; in a word, that it was a rotten, hollow, painfully suggestive piece of business altogether. We left them to their system and themselves, and went home wondering.

'Perhaps it's a good thing, Traddles,' said I, 'to have an unsound Hobby ridden hard; for it's the sooner ridden to death.'

'I hope so,' replied Traddles.

CHAPTER 62

A Light Shines on My Way

The year came round to Christmas-time, and I had been at home above two months. I had seen Agnes frequently. However loud the general voice might be in giving me encouragement, and however fervent the emotions and endeavours to which it roused me, I heard her lightest word of praise as I heard nothing else.

At least once a week, and sometimes oftener, I rode over there, and passed the evening. I usually rode back at night; for the old unhappy sense was always hovering about me now – most sorrowfully when I left her – and I was glad to be up and out, rather than wandering over the past in weary wakefulness or miserable dreams. I wore away the longest part of many wild sad nights in those rides; reviving, as I went, the thoughts that had occupied me in my long absence.

Or, if I were to say rather that I listened to the echoes of those thoughts, I should better express the truth. They spoke to me from afar off. I had put them at a distance, and accepted my inevitable place. When I read to Agnes what I wrote; when I saw her listening face; moved her to smiles or tears; and heard her cordial voice so earnest on the shadowy events of that imaginative world in which I lived; I thought what a fate mine might have been – but only thought so, as I had thought after I was married to Dora, what I could have wished my wife to be.

My duty to Agnes, who loved me with a love, which, if I disquieted, I wronged most selfishly and poorly, and could never restore; my matured assurance that I, who had worked out my own destiny, and won what I had impetuously set my heart on, had no right to murmur, and must bear; comprised what I felt and what I had learned. But I loved her; and now it even became some consolation to me, vaguely to conceive a distant day when I might blamelessly avow it; when all this should be over; when I could say, 'Agnes, so it was when I came home; and now I am old, and I never have loved since!'

She did not once show me any change in herself. What she always had been to me, she still was – wholly unaltered.

Between my aunt and me there had been something, in this connection, since the night of my return, which I cannot call a restraint, or an avoidance of the subject, so much as an implied understanding that we thought of it together, but did not shape our thoughts into words. When, according to our old custom, we sat before the fire at night, we often fell into this train; as naturally, and as consciously to each other, as if we had unreservedly said so. But we preserved an unbroken silence. I believed that she had read, or partly read, my thoughts that night; and that she fully comprehended why I gave mine no more distinct expression.

This Christmas-time being come, and Agnes having reposed no new confidence in me, a doubt that had several times arisen in my mind – whether she could have that perception of the true state of my breast, which restrained her with the apprehension of giving me pain – began to oppress me heavily. If that were so, my sacrifice was nothing; my plainest obligation to her unfulfilled; and every poor action I had shrunk from, I was hourly doing. I resolved to set this right beyond all doubt; – if such a barrier were between us, to break it down at once with a determined hand.

It was – what lasting reason have I to remember it! – a cold, harsh, winter day. There had been snow, some hours before; and it lay, not deep, but hard-frozen on the ground. Out at sea, beyond my window, the wind blew ruggedly from the north. I had been thinking of it, sweeping over those mountain wastes of snow in Switzerland, then inaccessible to any human foot; and had been speculating which was the lonelier, those solitary regions, or a deserted ocean.

'Riding today, Trot?' said my aunt, putting her head in at the door.

'Yes,' said I, 'I am going over to Canterbury. It's a good day for a ride.'

'I hope your horse may think so, too,' said my aunt, 'but at present he is holding down his head and his ears, standing before the door there, as if he thought his stable preferable.'

My aunt, I may observe, allowed my horse on the forbidden ground, but had not at all relented towards the donkeys.

'He will be fresh enough presently!' said I.

'The ride will do his master good, at all events,' observed my aunt, glancing at the papers on my table. 'Ah, child, you pass a good many hours here! I never thought, when I used to read books, what work it was to write them.'

'It's work enough to read them, sometimes,' I returned. 'As to the writing, it has its own charms, aunt.'

'Ah! I see!' said my aunt. 'Ambition, love of approbation, sympathy, and much more, I suppose? Well: go along with you!'

'Do you know anything more,' said I, standing composedly before her – she had patted me on the shoulder, and sat down in my chair, 'of that attachment of Agnes?'

She looked up in my face a little while before replying: 'I think I do, Trot.'

'Are you confirmed in your impression?' I enquired.

'I think I am, Trot.'

She looked so steadfastly at me, with a kind of doubt, or pity, or suspense in her affection, that I summoned the stronger determination to show her a perfectly cheerful face.

'And what is more, Trot – ' said my aunt.

'Yes?'

' – I think Agnes is going to be married.'

'God bless her!' said I cheerfully.

'God bless her!' said my aunt; 'and her husband, too!'

I echoed it, parted from my aunt, went lightly downstairs, mounted, and rode away. There was greater reason than before to do what I had resolved to do.

How well I recollect the wintry ride! The frozen particles of ice, brushed from the blades of grass by the wind, and borne across my face; the hard clatter of the horse's hoofs, beating a tune upon the ground; the stiff-tilled soil; the snow-drift, lightly eddying in the chalk-pit as the breeze ruffled it; the smoking team with the wagon of old hay, stopping to breathe on the hilltop, and shaking their bells musically; the whitened slopes and sweeps of Down-land lying against the dark sky, as if they were drawn on a huge slate.

I found Agnes alone. The little girls had gone to their own homes now, and she was alone by the fire, reading. She put down her book on seeing me come in; and having welcomed me as usual, took her work-basket and sat in one of the old-fashioned windows.

I sat beside her on the window-seat, and we talked of what I was doing, and when it would be done, and of the progress I had made since my last visit. Agnes was very cheerful, and laughingly predicted that I should soon become too famous to be talked to on such subjects.

'So I make the most of the present time, you see,' said Agnes, 'and talk to you while I may.'

As I looked at her beautiful face, observant of her work, she raised her mild, clear eyes, and saw that I was looking at her.

'You are thoughtful today, Trotwood!'

'Agnes, shall I tell you what about? I came to tell you.'

She put aside her work, as she was used to do when we were seriously discussing anything, and gave me her whole attention.

'My dear Agnes, do you doubt my being true to you?'

'No!' she answered, with a look of astonishment.

'Do you doubt my being what I always have been to you?'

'No!' she answered, as before.

'Do you remember that I tried to tell you, when I came home, what a debt of gratitude I owed you, dearest Agnes, and how fervently I felt towards you?'

'I remember it,' she said gently, 'very well.'

'You have a secret,' said I. 'Let me share it, Agnes.'

She cast down her eyes, and trembled.

'I could hardly fail to know, even if I had not heard – but from other lips than yours, Agnes, which seems strange – that there is someone upon whom you have bestowed the treasure of your love. Do not shut me out of what concerns your happiness so nearly! If you can trust me as you say you can, and as I know you may, let me be your friend, your brother, in this matter, of all others!'

With an appealing, almost a reproachful glance, she rose from the window; and hurrying across the room as if without knowing where, put her hands before her face, and burst into such tears as smote me to the heart.

And yet they awakened something in me, bringing promise to my heart. Without my knowing why, these tears allied themselves with the quietly sad smile which was so fixed in my remembrance, and shook me more with hope than fear or sorrow.

'Agnes! Sister! Dearest! What have I done!'

'Let me go away, Trotwood. I am not well. I am not myself. I will speak to you by and by – another time. I will write to you. Don't speak to me now. Don't! don't!'

I sought to recollect what she had said, when I had spoken to her on that former night, of her affection needing no return. It seemed a very world that I must search through in a moment.

'Agnes, I cannot bear to see you so, and think that I have been the cause. My dearest girl, dearer to me than anything in life, if you are unhappy, let me share your unhappiness. If you are in need of help or counsel, let me try to give it to you. If you have indeed a burden on your heart, let me try to lighten it. For whom do I live now, Agnes, if it is not for you!'

'Oh, spare me! I am not myself! Another time!' was all I could distinguish.

Was it a selfish error that was leading me away? Or, having once a clue to hope, was there something opening to me that I had not dared to think of?

'I must say more. I cannot let you leave me so! For Heaven's sake, Agnes, let us not mistake each other after all these years, and all that has come and gone with them! I must speak plainly. If you have any lingering thought that I could envy the happiness you will confer; that I could not resign you to a dearer protector, of your own choosing; that I could not, from my removed place, be a contented witness of your joy; dismiss it, for I don't deserve it! I have not suffered quite in vain. You have not taught me quite in vain. There is no alloy of self in what I feel for you.'

She was quiet now. In a little time, she turned her pale face towards me, and said in a low voice, broken here and there, but very clear: 'I owe it to your pure friendship for me, Trotwood – which, indeed, I do not doubt – to tell you you are mistaken. I can do no more. If I have sometimes, in the course of years, wanted help and counsel, they have come to me. If I have sometimes been unhappy, the feeling has passed away. If I have ever had a burden on my heart, it has been lightened for me. If I have any secret, it is – no new one; and is – not what you suppose. I cannot reveal it, or divide it. It has long been mine, and must remain mine.'

'Agnes! Stay! A moment!'

She was going away, but I detained her. I clasped my arm about her waist. 'In the course of years!' 'It is not a new one!' New thoughts and hopes were whirling through my mind, and all the colours of my life were changing.

'Dearest Agnes! Whom I so respect and honour – whom I so devotedly love! When I came here today, I thought that nothing could have wrested this confession from me. I thought I could have kept it in my bosom all our lives, till we were old. But, Agnes, if I have indeed any new-born hope that I may ever call you something more than Sister, widely different from Sister! – '

Her tears fell fast, but they were not like those she had lately shed, and I saw my hope brighten in them.

'Agnes! Ever my guide, and best support! If you had been more mindful of yourself, and less of me, when we grew up here together, I think my heedless fancy never would have wandered from you. But you were so much better than I, so necessary to me in every boyish hope and disappointment, that to have you to confide in, and rely upon in everything, became a second nature, supplanting for the time the first and greater one of loving you as I do!'

Still weeping, but not sadly – joyfully! And clasped in my arms as she had never been, as I had thought she never was to be!

'When I loved Dora – fondly, Agnes, as you know – '

'Yes!' she cried earnestly. 'I am glad to know it!'

'When I loved her – even then, my love would have been incomplete, without your sympathy. I had it, and it was perfected. And when I lost her, Agnes, what should I have been without you, still!'

Closer in my arms, nearer to my heart, her trembling hand upon my shoulder, her sweet eyes, shining through her tears, on mine!

'I went away, dear Agnes, loving you. I stayed away, loving you. I returned home, loving you!'

And now, I tried to tell her of the struggle I had had, and the conclusion I had come to. I tried to lay my mind before her, truly, and entirely. I tried to show her how I had hoped I had come into the better knowledge of myself and of her; how I had resigned myself to what that better knowledge brought; and how I had come there, even that day, in my fidelity to this. If she did so love me (I said) that she could take me for her husband, she could do so on no deserving of mine, except upon the truth of my love for her, and the trouble in which it had ripened to be what it was; and hence it was that I revealed it. And O Agnes, even out of thy true eyes, in that same time, the spirit of my child-wife looked upon me, saying it was well; and winning me, through thee, to tenderest recollections of the Blossom that had withered in its bloom!

'I am so blest, Trotwood – my heart is so overcharged – but there is one thing I must say.'

'Dearest, what?'

She laid her gentle hands upon my shoulders, and looked calmly in my face.

'Do you know, yet, what it is?'

'I am afraid to speculate on what it is. Tell me, my dear.'

'I have loved you all my life!'

Oh, we were happy, we were happy! Our tears were not for the trials (hers so much the greater) through which we had come to be thus, but for the rapture of being thus, never to be divided more!

We walked, that winter evening, in the fields together; and the blessed calm within us seemed to be partaken by the frosty air. The early stars began to shine while we were lingering on, and looking up to them we thanked our God for having guided us to this tranquillity.

We stood together in the same old-fashioned window at night, when the moon was shining; Agnes with her quiet eyes raised up to it; I following her glance. Long miles of road then opened out before my mind; and, toiling on, I saw a ragged, way-worn boy forsaken and neglected, who should come to call even the heart now beating against mine, his own.

It was nearly dinner-time next day when we appeared before my aunt. She was up in my study, Peggotty said, which it was her pride to keep in readiness and order for me. We found her, in her spectacles, sitting by the fire.

'Goodness me!' said my aunt, peering through the dusk, 'who's this you're bringing home?'

'Agnes,' said I.

As we had arranged to say nothing at first, my aunt was not a little discomfited. She darted a hopeful glance at me, when I said 'Agnes'; but seeing that I looked as usual, she took off her spectacles in despair, and rubbed her nose with them.

She greeted Agnes heartily, nevertheless; and we were soon in the lighted parlour downstairs, at dinner. My aunt put on her spectacles twice or thrice, to take another look at me, but as often took them off again, disappointed, and rubbed her nose with them. Much to the discomfiture of Mr Dick, who knew this to be a bad symptom.

'By the by, aunt,' said I, after dinner, 'I have been speaking to Agnes about what you told me.'

'Then, Trot,' said my aunt, turning scarlet, 'you did wrong, and broke your promise.'

'You are not angry, aunt, I trust? I am sure you won't be, when you learn that Agnes is not unhappy in any attachment.'

'Stuff and nonsense!' said my aunt.

As my aunt appeared to be annoyed, I thought the best way was to cut her annoyance short. I took Agnes in my arm to the back of her chair, and we both leaned over her. My aunt with one clap of her hands, and one look through her spectacles, immediately went into hysterics, for the first and only time in all my knowledge of her.

The hysterics called up Peggotty. The moment my aunt was restored, she flew at Peggotty, and calling her a silly old creature, hugged her with all her might. After that, she hugged Mr Dick (who was highly honoured, but a good deal surprised); and after that, told them why. Then we were all happy together.

I could not discover whether my aunt, in her last short conversation with me, had fallen on a pious fraud, or had really mistaken the state of my mind. It was quite enough, she said, that she had told me Agnes was going to be married; and that I now knew better than anyone how true it was.

We were married within a fortnight. Traddles and Sophy, and Doctor and Mrs Strong, were the only guests at our quiet wedding. We left them full of joy; and drove away together. Clasped in my embrace, I held the source of every worthy aspiration I had ever had; the centre of myself, the circle of my life, my own, my wife; my love of whom was founded on a rock!

'Dearest husband!' said Agnes. 'Now that I may call you by that name, I have one thing more to tell you.'

'Let me hear it, love.'

'It grows out of the night when Dora died. She sent you for me.'

'She did.'

'She told me that she left me something. Can you think what it was?'

I believed I could. I drew the wife who had so long loved me closer to my side.

'She told me that she made a last request to me, and left me a last charge.'

'And it was – '

'That only I would occupy this vacant place.'

And Agnes laid her head upon my breast, and wept; and I wept with her, though we were so happy.

CHAPTER 63

A Visitor

What I have purposed to record is nearly finished; but there is yet an incident conspicuous in my memory, on which it often rests with delight, and without which one thread in the web I have spun would have a ravelled end.

I had advanced in fame and fortune, my domestic joy was perfect, I had been married ten happy years. Agnes and I were sitting by the fire, in our house in London, one night in spring, and three of our children were playing in the room, when I was told that a stranger wished to see me.

He had been asked if he came on business, and had answered No; he had come for the pleasure of seeing me, and had come a long way. He was an old man, my servant said, and looked like a farmer.

As this sounded mysterious to the children, and moreover was like the beginning of a favourite story Agnes used to tell them, introductory to the arrival of a wicked old Fairy in a cloak, who hated everybody, it produced some commotion. One of our boys laid his head in his mother's lap to be out of harm's way, and little Agnes (our eldest child) left her doll in a chair to represent her, and thrust out her little heap of golden curls from between the window-curtains, to see what happened next.

'Let him come in here!' said I.

There soon appeared, pausing in the dark doorway as he entered, a hale, grey-haired old man. Little Agnes, attracted by his looks, had run to bring him in, and I had not yet clearly seen his face, when my wife, starting up, cried out to me, in a pleased and agitated voice, that it was Mr Peggotty!

It *was* Mr Peggotty. An old man now, but in a ruddy, hearty, strong old age. When our first emotion was over, and he sat before the fire with the children on his knees, and the blaze shining on his face, he looked, to me, as vigorous and robust, withal as handsome, an old man as ever I had seen.

'Mas'r Davy,' said he. And the old name in the old tone fell so naturally on my ear! 'Mas'r Davy, 't is a joyful hour as I see you, once more 'long with your own trew wife!'

'A joyful hour indeed, old friend!' cried I.

'And these heer pretty ones,' said Mr Peggotty. 'To look at these heer flowers! Why, Mas'r Davy, you was but the height of the littlest of these, when I first see you! When Em'ly warn't no bigger, and our poor lad were *but* a lad!'

'Time has changed me more than it has changed you since then,' said I. 'But let these dear rogues go to bed; and as no house in England but this must hold you, tell me where to send for your luggage (is the old black bag among it, that went so far, I wonder!), and then, over a glass of Yarmouth grog, we will have the tidings of ten years!'

'Are you alone?' asked Agnes.

'Yes, ma'am,' he said, kissing her hand, 'quite alone.'

We sat him between us, not knowing how to give him welcome

enough; and as I began to listen to his old familiar voice, I could have fancied he was still pursuing his long journey in search of his darling niece.

'It's a mort of water,' said Mr Peggotty, 'fur to come across, and on'y stay a matter of fower weeks. But water (specially when 't is salt) comes nat'ral to me; and friends is dear, and I am heer. Which is verse,' said Mr Peggotty, surprised to find it out, 'though I hadn't such intentions.'

'Are you going back those many thousand miles, so soon?' asked Agnes.

'Yes, ma'am,' he returned. 'I giv the promise to Em'ly, afore I come away. You see, I doen't grow younger as the years comes round, and if I hadn't sailed as 't was, most like I shouldn't never have done 't. And it's allus been on my mind, as I *must* come and see Mas'r Davy and your own sweet blooming self, in your wedded happiness, afore I got to be too old.'

He looked at us as if he could never feast his eyes on us sufficiently. Agnes laughingly put back some scattered locks of his grey hair, that he might see us better.

'And now tell us,' said I, 'everything relating to your fortunes.'

'Our fortuns, Mas'r Davy,' he rejoined, 'is soon told. We haven't fared nohows, but fared to thrive. We've allus thrived. We've worked as we ought to 't, and may be we lived a leetle hard at first or so, but we have allus thrived. What with sheep-farming, and what with stock-farming, and what with one thing and what with t' other, we are as well to do, as well could be. Theer's been kiender a blessing fell upon us,' said Mr Peggotty, reverentially inclining his head, 'and we've done nowt but prosper. That is, in the long run. If not yesterday, why then today. If not today, why then tomorrow.'

'And Emily?' said Agnes and I, both together.

'Em'ly,' said he, 'arter you left her, ma'am – and I never heerd her saying of her prayers at night, t' other side the canvas screen, when we was settled in the Bush, but what I heerd your name – and arter she and me lost sight of Mas'r Davy, that theer shining sundown – was that low, at first, that, if she had knowed then what Mas'r Davy kep' from us so kind and thowtful, 't is my opinion she'd have drooped away. But theer was some poor folks aboard as had illness among 'em, and she took care of *them;* and theer was the children in our company, and she took care of *them;* and so she got to be busy, and to be doing good, and that helped her.'

'When did she first hear of it?' I asked.

'I kep' it from her arter I heerd on 't,' said Mr Peggotty, 'going on nigh a year. We was living then in a solitary place, but among the beautifullest trees, and with the roses a covering our Beein to the roof. Theer come along one day, when I was out a working on the land, a traveller from our own Norfolk or Suffolk in England (I doen't rightly mind which), and of course we took him in, and giv him to eat and drink, and made him welcome. We all do that, all the colony over. He'd got an old newspaper with him, and some other account in print of the storm. That's how she knowed it. When I come home at night, I found she knowed it.'

He dropped his voice as he said these words, and the gravity I so well remembered overspread his face.

'Did it change her much?' we asked.

'Aye, for a good long time,' he said, shaking his head, 'if not to this present hour. But I think the solitoode done her good. And she had a deal to mind in the way of poultry and the

A stranger calls to see me

like, and minded of it, and come through. I wonder,' he said thoughtfully, 'if you could see my Em'ly now, Mas'r Davy, whether you'd know her!'

'Is she so altered?' I enquired.

'I doen't know. I see her ev'ry day, and doen't know; but, odd-times, I have thowt so. A slight figure,' said Mr Peggotty, looking at the fire, 'kiender worn; soft, sorrowful, blue eyes; a delicate face; a pritty head, leaning a little down; a quiet voice and way – timid a'most. That's Em'ly!'

We silently observed him as he sat, still looking at the fire.

'Some thinks,' he said, 'as her affection was ill-bestowed; some, as her marriage was broke off by death. No one knows how 't is. She might have married well a mort of times, "but, uncle," she says to me, "that's gone for ever." Cheerful along with me; retired when others is by; fond of going any distance fur to teach a child, or fur to tend a sick person, or fur to do some kindness tow'rds a young girl's wedding (and she's done a many, but has never seen one); fondly loving of her uncle; patient; liked by young and old; sowt out by all that has any trouble. That's Em'ly!'

He drew his hand across his face, and with a half-suppressed sigh looked up from the fire.

'Is Martha with you yet?' I asked.

'Martha,' he replied, 'got married, Mas'r Davy, in the second year. A young man, a farm-labourer, as come by us on his way to market with his mas'r's drays – a journey of over five hundred mile theer, and back – made offers fur to take her fur his wife (wives is very scarce theer), and then to set up fur their two selves in the Bush. She spoke to me fur to tell him her trew story. I did. They was married, and they live fower hundred mile away from any voices but their own and the singing birds.'

'Mrs Gummidge?' I suggested.

It was a pleasant key to touch, for Mr Peggotty suddenly burst into a roar of laughter, and rubbed his hands up and down his legs, as he had been accustomed to do when he enjoyed himself in the long-shipwrecked boat.

'Would you believe it!' he said. 'Why, someun even made offers fur to marry *her!* If a ship's cook that was turning settler, Mas'r Davy, didn't make offers fur to marry Missis Gummidge, I'm Gormed – and I can't say no fairer than that!'

I never saw Agnes laugh so. This sudden ecstasy on the part of Mr Peggotty was so delightful to her, that she could not leave off laughing; and the more she laughed the more she made me laugh, and the greater Mr Peggotty's ecstasy became, and the more he rubbed his legs.

'And what did Mrs Gummidge say?' I asked, when I was grave enough.

'If you'll believe me,' returned Mr Peggotty, 'Missis Gummidge, 'stead of saying "thank you, I'm much obleeged to you, I ain't a going fur to change my condition at my time of life," up'd with a bucket as was standing by, and laid it over that theer ship's cook's head till he sung out fur help, and I went in and reskied of him.'

Mr Peggotty burst into a great roar of laughter, and Agnes and I both kept him company.

'But I must say this for the good creetur,' he resumed, wiping his face when we were quite exhausted; 'she has been all she said she'd be to us, and more. She's the willingest, the trewest, the honestest-helping woman, Mas'r Davy, as ever drawed the breath of life. I have never knowed her to be lone and lorn for a single minute, not even when the colony was all afore us, and we was new to it. And thinking of the old 'un is a thing she never done, I do assure you, since she left England!'

'Now, last, not least, Mr Micawber,' said I. 'He has paid off every obligation he incurred here – even to Traddles's bill, you remember, my dear Agnes – and therefore we may take it for granted that he is doing well. But what is the latest news of him?'

Mr Peggotty, with a smile, put his hand in his breast pocket, and produced a flat-folded, paper parcel, from which he took out, with much care, a little odd-looking newspaper.

'You are to unnerstan', Mas'r Davy,' said he, 'as we have left the Bush now, being so well to do; and have gone right away round to Port Middlebay Harbor, wheer theer's what *we* call a town.'

'Mr Micawber was in the Bush near you?' said I.

'Bless you, yes,' said Mr Peggotty, 'and turned to, with a will. I never wish to meet a better gen'lm'n for turning to, with a will. I've seen that theer bald head of his a-perspiring in the sun, Mas'r Davy, till I a'most thowt it would have melted away. And now he's a magistrate.'

'A magistrate, eh?' said I.

Mr Peggotty pointed to a certain paragraph in the newspaper, where I read aloud as follows, from the *Port Middlebay Times*:

'The public dinner to our distinguished fellow-colonist and townsman, Wilkins Micawber Esquire, Port Middlebay District Magistrate, came off yesterday in the large room of the Hotel, which was crowded to suffocation. It is estimated that not fewer than forty-seven persons must have been accommodated with dinner at one time, exclusive of the company in the passage and on the stairs. The beauty, fashion, and exclusiveness of Port Middlebay, flocked to do honour to one so deservedly esteemed, so highly talented, and so widely popular. Doctor Mell (of Colonial Salem-House Grammar School, Port Middlebay) presided, and on his right sat the distinguished guest. After the removal of the cloth, and the singing of Non Nobis (beautifully executed, and in which we were at no loss to distinguish the bell-like notes of that gifted amateur, Wilkins Micawber, Esquire, Junior), the usual loyal and patriotic toasts were severally given and rapturously received. Doctor Mell, in a speech replete with feeling, then proposed "Our distinguished Guest, the ornament of our town. May he never leave us but to better himself, and may his success among us be such as to render his bettering himself impossible!" The cheering with which the toast was received defies description. Again and again it rose and fell, like the waves of ocean. At length all was hushed, and Wilkins Micawber, Esquire, presented himself to return thanks. Far be it from us, in the present comparatively imperfect state of the resources of our establishment, to endeavour to follow our distinguished townsman through the smoothly flowing periods of his polished and highly ornate address! Suffice it to observe, that it was a masterpiece of eloquence; and that those passages in which he more particularly traced his own successful career to its source, and warned the younger portion of his auditory from the shoals of ever incurring pecuniary liabilities which they were unable to liquidate, brought a tear into the manliest eye present. The remaining toasts were Doctor Mell; Mrs Micawber (who gracefully bowed her acknowledgments from the side door where a galaxy of beauty was elevated on chairs, at once to witness and adorn the gratifying scene); Mrs Ridger Begs (late Miss Micawber), Mrs Mell; Wilkins Micawber, Esquire, Junior (who convulsed the assembly by humorously remarking that he found himself unable to return thanks in a speech, but would do so, with their permission, in a song); Mrs Micawber's Family (well known, it is needless to remark, in the mother country), &c. &c. &c. At the conclusion of the proceedings the tables were cleared as if by art-magic for dancing. Among the votaries of Terpsichore, who disported themselves until Sol gave warning for departure, Wilkins Micawber, Esquire, Junior, and the lovely and accomplished Miss Helena, fourth daughter of Doctor Mell, were particularly remarkable.'

I was looking back to the name of Doctor Mell, pleased to have discovered, in these happier circumstances, Mr Mell, formerly poor pinched usher to my Middlesex magistrate, when Mr Peggotty pointing to another part of the paper, my eyes rested on my own name, and I read thus:

To David Copperfield, Esquire,
the eminent author.

My dear Sir – Years have elapsed since I had an opportunity of ocularly perusing the lineaments now familiar to the imaginations of a considerable portion of the civilised world.

But, my dear sir, though estranged (by the force of circumstances over which I have had no control) from the personal society of the friend and companion of my youth, I have not been unmindful of his soaring flight. Nor have I been debarred,

Though seas between us braid ha' roared,

(Burns) from participating in the intellectual feasts he has spread before us.

I cannot, therefore, allow of the departure from this place of an individual whom we mutually respect and esteem, without, my dear sir, taking this public opportunity of thanking you, on my own behalf, and, I may undertake to add, on that of the whole of the Inhabitants of Port Middlebay for the gratification of which you are the ministering agent.

Go on, my dear sir! You are not unknown here, you are not unappreciated. Though "remote", we are neither "unfriended", "melancholy", nor (I may add) "slow". Go on, my dear sir, in your Eagle course! The inhabitants of Port Middlebay may at least aspire to watch it, with delight, with entertainment, with instruction!

Among the eyes elevated towards you from this portion of the globe, will ever be found, while it has light and life,
The
Eye
Appertaining to

Wilkins Micawber,
Magistrate

I found, on glancing at the remaining contents of the newspaper, that Mr Micawber was a diligent and esteemed correspondent of that Journal. There was another letter from him in the same paper, touching a bridge; there was an advertisement of a collection of similar letters by him, to be shortly republished, in a neat volume, 'with considerable additions;' and, unless I am very much mistaken, the Leading Article was his also.

We talked much of Mr Micawber, on many other evenings while Mr Peggotty remained with us. He lived with us during the whole term of his stay – which, I think, was something less than a month – and his sister and my aunt came to London to see him. Agnes and I parted from him aboard-ship, when he sailed; and we shall never part from him more, on earth.

But before he left, he went with me to Yarmouth, to see a little tablet I had put up in the churchyard to the memory of Ham. While I was copying the plain inscription for him at his request, I saw him stoop, and gather a tuft of grass from the grave, and a little earth.

'For Em'ly,' he said, as he put it in his breast. 'I promised, Mas'r Davy.'

CHAPTER 64

A Last Retrospect

And now my written story ends. I look back, once more – for the last time – before I close these leaves.

I see myself, with Agnes at my side, journeying along the road of life. I see our children and our friends around us; and I hear the roar of many voices, not indifferent to me as I travel on.

What faces are the most distinct to me in the fleeting crowd? Lo, these; all turning to me as I ask my thoughts the question!

Here is my aunt, in stronger spectacles, an old woman of fourscore years and more, but upright yet, and a steady walker of six miles at a stretch in winter weather.

Always with her, here comes Peggotty, my good old nurse, likewise in spectacles, accustomed to do needlework at night very close to the lamp, but never sitting down to it without a bit of wax candle, a yard measure in a little house, and a work-box with a picture of St Paul's upon the lid.

The cheeks and arms of Peggotty, so hard and red in my childish days, when I wondered why the birds didn't peck her in preference to apples, are shrivelled now; and her eyes, that used to darken their whole neighbourhood in her face, are fainter (though they glitter still); but her rough forefinger, which I once associated with a pocket nutmeg-grater, is just the same, and when I see my least child catching at it as it totters from my aunt to her, I think of our little parlour at home, when I could scarcely walk. My aunt's old disappointment is set right, now. She is godmother to a real living Betsey Trotwood; and Dora (the next in order) says she spoils her.

There is something bulky in Peggotty's pocket. It is nothing smaller than the Crocodile Book, which is in rather a dilapidated condition by this time, with divers of the leaves torn and stitched across, but which Peggotty exhibits to the children as a precious relic. I find it very curious to see my own infant face looking up at me from the Crocodile stories; and to be reminded by it of my old acquaintance Brooks of Sheffield.

Among my boys, this summer holiday-time, I see an old man making giant kites, and gazing at them in the air, with a delight for which there are no words. He greets me rapturously, and whispers, with many nods and winks, 'Trotwood, you will be glad to hear that I shall finish the Memorial when I have nothing else to do, and that your aunt's the most extraordinary woman in the world, sir!'

Who is this bent lady, supporting herself by a stick, and showing me a countenance in which there are some traces of old pride and beauty, feebly contending with a querulous, imbecile, fretful wandering of the mind? She is in a garden; and near her stands a sharp, dark, withered woman, with a white scar on her lip. Let me hear what they say.

'Rosa, I have forgotten this gentleman's name.'

Rosa bends over her, and calls to her, 'Mr Copperfield.'

'I am glad to see you, sir. I am sorry to observe you are in mourning. I hope Time will be good to you.'

Her impatient attendant scolds her, tells her I am not in mourning, bids her look again, tries to rouse her.

'You have seen my son, sir,' says the elder lady. 'Are you reconciled?'

Looking fixedly at me, she puts her hand to her forehead, and moans. Suddenly, she cries, in a terrible voice, 'Rosa, come to me. He is dead!' Rosa, kneeling at her feet, by turns caresses her, and quarrels with her; now fiercely telling her, 'I loved him better than you ever did!' – now soothing her to sleep on her breast, like a sick child. Thus I leave them; thus I always find them; thus they wear their time away from year to year.

What ship comes sailing home from India, and what English lady is this, married to a growling old Scotch Croesus with great flaps of ears. Can this be Julia Mills?

Indeed, it is Julia Mills, peevish and fine, with a black man to carry cards and letters to her on a golden salver, and a copper-coloured woman in linen, with a bright handkerchief round her head, to serve her Tiffin in her dressing-room. But Julia keeps no diary in these days; never sings 'Affection's Dirge'; eternally quarrels with the old Scotch Croesus, who is a sort of yellow bear with a tanned hide. Julia is steeped in money to the throat, and talks and thinks of nothing else. I liked her better in the Desert of Sahara.

Or perhaps this *is* the Desert of Sahara! For, though Julia has a stately house, and mighty company, and sumptuous dinners every day, I see no green growth near her; nothing that can ever come to fruit or flower. What Julia calls 'society', I see; among it Mr Jack Maldon, from his Patent Place, sneering at the hand that gave it him, and speaking to me of the Doctor, as 'so charmingly antique.' But when society is the name for such hollow gentlemen and ladies, Julia, and when its breeding is professed indifference to everything that can advance or can retard mankind, I think we must have lost ourselves in that same Desert of Sahara, and had better find the way out.

And lo, the Doctor, always our good friend, labouring at his Dictionary (somewhere about the letter D), and happy in his home and wife. Also the Old Soldier, on a considerably reduced footing, and by no means so influential as in days of yore!

Working at his chambers in the Temple, with a busy aspect, and his hair (where he is not bald) made more rebellious than ever by the constant friction of his lawyer's wig, I come, in a later time, upon my dear old Traddles. His table is covered with thick piles of papers; and I say, as I look around me: 'If Sophy were your clerk, now, Traddles, she would have enough to do!'

'You may say that, my dear Copperfield! But those were capital days, too, in Holborn Court! Were they not?'

'When she told you you would be a judge? But it was not the town talk *then*!'

'At all events,' says Traddles, 'if I ever am one – '

'Why, you know you will be.'

'Well, my dear Copperfield, *when* I am one, I shall tell the story, as I said I would.'

We walk away, arm in arm. I am going to have a family dinner with Traddles. It is Sophy's birthday; and, on our road, Traddles discourses to me of the good fortune he has enjoyed.

'I really have been able, my dear Copperfield, to do all that I had most at heart. There's the Reverend Horace promoted to that living at four hundred and fifty pounds a year; there are our two boys receiving the very best education, and distinguishing themselves as steady scholars and good fellows; there are three of the girls married very comfortably; there are three more living with us; there are three more keeping house for the Reverend Horace since Mrs Crewler's decease; and all of them happy.'

'Except – ' I suggest.

'Except the Beauty,' says Traddles. 'Yes. It was very unfortunate that she should marry such a vagabond. But there was a certain dash and glare about him that caught her. However, now we have got her safe at our house, and got rid of him, we must cheer her up again.'

Traddles's house is one of the very houses – or it easily may have been – which he and Sophy used to parcel out, in their evening walks. It is a large house; but Traddles keeps his papers in his dressing-room, and his boots with his papers; and he and Sophy squeeze themselves into upper rooms, reserving the best bedrooms for the Beauty and the girls. There is no room to spare in the house; for more of 'the girls' are here, and always are here, by some accident or other, than I know how to count. Here, when we go in, is a crowd of them, running down to the door, and handing Traddles about to be kissed, until he is out of breath. Here, established in perpetuity, is the poor Beauty, a widow with a little girl; here, at dinner on Sophy's birthday, are the three married girls with their three husbands, and one of the husband's brothers, and another husband's cousin, and another husband's sister, who appears to me to be engaged to the cousin. Traddles, exactly the same simple, unaffected fellow as he ever was, sits at the foot of the large table like a Patriarch; and Sophy beams upon him, from the head, across a cheerful space that is certainly not glittering with Britannia metal.

And now, as I close my task, subduing my desire to linger yet, these faces fade away. But one face, shining on me like a heavenly light, by which I see all other objects, is above them and beyond them all. And that remains.

I turn my head, and see it, in its beautiful serenity, beside me. My lamp burns low, and I have written far into the night; but the dear presence, without which I were nothing, bears me company.

O Agnes, O my soul, so may thy face be by me when I close my life indeed; so may I, when realities are melting from me like the shadows which I now dismiss, still find thee near me, pointing upward!

Oliver Twist

CHAPTER I

Treats of the place where Oliver Twist was born; and of the circumstances attending his birth

Among other public buildings in a certain town, which for many reasons it will be prudent to refrain from mentioning, and to which I will assign no fictitious name, there is one anciently common to most towns, great or small – to wit, a workhouse and in this workhouse was born, on a day and date which I need not trouble myself to repeat, inasmuch as it can be of no possible consequence to the reader, in this stage of the business at all events, the item of mortality whose name is prefixed to the head of this chapter.

For a long time after it was ushered into this world of sorrow and trouble, by the parish surgeon, it remained a matter of considerable doubt whether the child would survive to bear any name at all: in which case it is somewhat more than probable that these memoirs would never have appeared; or if they had, that being comprised within a couple of pages, they would have possessed the inestimable merit of being the most concise and faithful specimen of biography extant in the literature of any age or country.

Although I am not disposed to maintain that the being born in a workhouse is in itself the most fortunate and enviable circumstance that can possibly befall a human being, I do mean to say that in this particular instance it was the best thing for Oliver Twist that could by possibility have occurred. The fact is, that there was considerable difficulty in inducing Oliver to take upon himself the office of respiration – a troublesome practice, but one which custom has rendered necessary to our easy existence; and for some time he lay gasping on a little flock mattress, rather unequally poised between this world and the next: the balance being decidedly in favour of the latter. Now, if during this brief period Oliver had been surrounded by careful grandmothers, anxious aunts, experienced nurses, and doctors of profound wisdom, he would most inevitably and indubitably have been killed in no time. There being nobody by, however, but a pauper old woman, who was rendered rather misty by an unwonted allowance of beer; and a parish surgeon, who did such matters by contract; Oliver and Nature fought out the point between them. The result was that, after a few struggles, Oliver breathed, sneezed, and proceeded to advertise to the inmates of the workhouse the fact of a new burden having been imposed upon the parish, by setting up as loud a cry as could reasonably have been expected from a male infant who had not been possessed of that very useful appendage, a voice, for a much longer space of time than three minutes and a quarter.

As Oliver gave this first proof of the free and proper action of his lungs, the patchwork coverlet, which was carelessly flung over the iron bedstead, rustled; the pale face of a young woman was raised feebly from the pillow; and a faint voice imperfectly articulated the words, 'Let me see the child and die.'

The surgeon had been sitting with his face turned towards the fire, giving the palms of his hands a warm and a rub alternately. As the young woman spoke, he rose, and advancing to the bed's head, said, with more kindness than might have been expected of him, 'Oh, you must not talk about dying yet.'

'Lor bless her dear heart, no!' interposed the nurse, hastily depositing in her pocket a green glass bottle, the contents of which she had been tasting in a corner with evident satisfaction. 'Lor bless her dear heart, when she has lived as long as I have, sir, and had thirteen children of her own, and all on 'em dead except two, and them in the wurkus with me, she'll know better than to take on in that way, bless her dear heart! Think what it is to be a mother, there's a dear young lamb, do.'

Apparently this consolatory perspective of a mother's prospects failed in producing its due effect. The patient shook her head, and stretched out her hand towards the child.

The surgeon deposited it in her arms. She imprinted her cold white lips passionately on its forehead; passed her hands over her face; gazed wildly round; shuddered; fell back – and died. They chafed her breast, hands, and temples; but the blood had stopped for ever. They talked of hope and comfort. They had been strangers too long.

'It's all over, Mrs Thingummy!' said the surgeon at last.

'Ah, poor dear, so it is!' said the nurse, picking up the cork of the green bottle, which had fallen out on the pillow, as she stooped to take up the child. 'Poor dear!'

'You needn't mind sending up to me, if the child cries, nurse,' said the surgeon, putting on his gloves with great deliberation. 'It's very likely it *will* be troublesome. Give it a little gruel if it is.' He put on his hat, and, pausing by the bedside on his way to the door, added, 'She was a good-looking girl, too; where did she come from?'

'She was brought here last night,' replied the old woman, 'by the overseer's order. She was found lying in the street. She had walked some distance, for her shoes were worn to pieces; but where she came from, or where she was going to, nobody knows.'

The surgeon leaned over the body, and raised the left hand. 'The old story,' he said, shaking his head; 'no wedding-ring, I see. Ah! Good-night!'

The medical gentleman walked away to dinner; and the nurse, having once more applied herself to the green bottle, sat down on a low chair before the fire, and proceeded to dress the infant.

What an excellent example of the power of dress young Oliver Twist was! Wrapped in the blanket which had hitherto formed his only covering, he might have been the child of a nobleman or a beggar; it would have been hard for the haughtiest stranger to have assigned him his proper station in society. But now that he was enveloped in the old calico robes which had grown yellow in the same service, he was badged and ticketed, and fell into his place at once – a parish child – the orphan of a workhouse – the humble, half-starved drudge – to be cuffed and buffeted through the world – despised by all and pitied by none. Oliver cried lustily. If he could have known that he was an orphan, left to the tender mercies of churchwardens and overseers, perhaps he would have cried the louder.

CHAPTER 2

Treats of Oliver Twist's growth, education, and board

For the next eight or ten months, Oliver was the victim of a systematic course of treachery and deception. He was brought up by the hand. The hungry and destitute situation of the infant orphan was duly reported by the workhouse authorities to the parish authorities. The parish authorities enquired with dignity of the workhouse authorities, whether there was no female then domiciled in 'the house' who was in a situation to impart to Oliver Twist the consolation and nourishment of which he stood in need. The workhouse authorities replied with humility, that there was not. Upon this the parish authorities magnanimously and humanely resolved, that Oliver should be 'farmed,' or, in other words, that he should be dispatched to a branch-workhouse some three miles off, where twenty or thirty other juvenile offenders against the poor-laws rolled about the floor all day, without the inconvenience of too much food or too much clothing, under the parental superintendence of an elderly female, who received the culprits at and for the consideration of sevenpence-halfpenny per small head per week. Sevenpence-halfpenny's worth per week is a good round diet for a child; a great deal may be got for seven-pence-halfpenny: quite enough to overload its stomach, and make it uncomfortable. The elderly female was a woman of wisdom and experience; she knew what was good for children: and she had a very accurate perception of what was good for herself. So, she appropriated the greater part of the weekly stipend to her own use, and consigned the rising parochial generation to even a shorter allowance than was originally provided for them: thereby finding in the lowest depth a deeper still; and proving herself a very great experimental philosopher.

Everybody knows the story of another experimental philosopher, who had a great theory about a horse being able to live without eating, and who demonstrated it so well, that he got his own horse down to a straw a day, and would most unquestionably have rendered him a very spirited and rampacious animal on nothing at all, if he had not died, just four-and-twenty hours before he was to have had his first comfortable bait of air. Unfortunately for the experimental philosophy of the female to whose protecting care Oliver Twist was delivered over, a similar result usually attended the operation of *her* system; for at the very moment when a child

had contrived to exist upon the smallest possible portion of the weakest possible food, it did perversely happen in eight and a half cases out of ten, either that it sickened from want and cold, or fell into the fire from neglect, or got half-smothered by accident; in any one of which cases, the miserable little being was usually summoned into another world, and there gathered to the fathers which it had never known in this.

Occasionally, when there was some more than usually interesting inquest upon a parish child who had been overlooked in turning up a bedstead, or inadvertently scalded to death when there happened to be a washing – though the latter accident was very scarce, anything approaching to a washing being of rare occurrence in the farm – the jury would take it into their heads to ask troublesome questions, or the parishioners would rebelliously affix their signatures to a remonstrance. But these impertinences were speedily checked by the evidence of the surgeon, and the testimony of the beadle; the former of whom had always opened the body and found nothing inside (which was very probable indeed), and the latter of whom invariably swore whatever the parish wanted (which was very self-devotional). Besides, the board made periodical pilgrimages to the farm, and always sent the beadle the day before, to say they were going. The children were neat and clean to behold when *they* went; and what more would the people have.

It cannot be expected that this system of farming would produce any very extraordinary or luxuriant crop. Oliver Twist's ninth birthday found him a pale thin child, somewhat diminutive in stature, and decidedly small in circumference. But nature or inheritance had implanted a good sturdy spirit in Oliver's breast. It had had plenty of room to expand, thanks to the spare diet of the establishment; and perhaps to this circumstance may be attributed his having any ninth birthday at all. Be this as it may, however, it *was* his ninth birthday, and he was keeping it in the coal-cellar with a select party of two other young gentlemen, who, after participating with him in a sound thrashing, had been locked up therein for atrociously presuming to be hungry, when Mrs Mann, the good lady of the house, was unexpectedly startled by the apparition of Mr Bumble, the beadle, striving to undo the wicket of the garden-gate.

'Goodness gracious! is that you, Mr Bumble, sir?' said Mrs Mann, thrusting her head out of the window in well-affected ecstasies of joy. '(Susan, take Oliver and them two brats upstairs, and wash 'em directly.) – My heart alive! Mr Bumble, how glad I am to see you, surely!'

Now, Mr Bumble was a fat man, and a choleric; so instead of responding to this open-hearted salutation in a kindred spirit, he gave the little wicket a tremendous shake, and then bestowed upon it a kick which could have emanated from no leg but a beadle's.

'Lor, only think,' said Mrs Mann, running out – for the three boys had been removed by this time – 'only think of that! That I should have forgotten that the gate was bolted on the inside, on account of them dear children. Walk in, sir, walk in, pray, Mr Bumble, do, sir.'

Although this invitation was accompanied with a curtsy that

might have softened the heart of a churchwarden, it by no means mollified the beadle.

'Do you think this respectful or proper conduct, Mrs Mann,' enquired Mr Bumble, grasping his cane, 'to keep the parish officers a-waiting at your garden-gate, when they come here upon porochial business connected with the porochial orphans? Are you aweer, Mrs Mann, that you are, as I may say, a porochial delegate, and a stipendiary?'

'I'm sure, Mr Bumble, that I was only a-telling one or two of the dear children as is so fond of you, that it was you a-coming,' replied Mrs Mann, with great humility.

Mr Bumble had a great idea of his oratorical powers and his importance. He had displayed the one, and vindicated the other. He relaxed.

'Well, well, Mrs Mann,' he replied, in a calmer tone, 'it may be as you say; it may be. Lead the way in, Mrs Mann, for I come on business, and have something to say.'

Mrs Mann ushered the beadle into a small parlour with a brick floor; placed a seat for him; and officiously deposited his cocked hat and cane on the table before him. Mr Bumble wiped from his forehead the perspiration which his walk had engendered; glanced complacently at the cocked hat; and smiled. Yes, he smiled. Beadles are but men; and Mr Bumble smiled.

'Now don't you be offended at what I'm a-going to say,' observed Mrs Mann, with captivating sweetness. 'You've had a long walk, you know, or I wouldn't mention it. Now, will you take a little drop of something, Mr Bumble?'

'Not a drop. Not a drop,' said Mr Bumble, waving his right hand in a dignified, but placid manner.

'I think you will,' said Mrs Mann, who had noticed the tone of the refusal, and the gesture that had accompanied it. 'Just a little drop, with a little cold water, and a lump of sugar.'

Mr Bumble coughed.

'Now, just a leetle drop,' said Mrs Mann, persuasively.

'What is it?' enquired the beadle.

'Why, it's what I'm obliged to keep a little of in the house, to put into the blessed infants' Daffy, when they ain't well, Mr Bumble,' replied Mrs Mann, as she opened a corner cupboard, and took down a bottle and glass. 'It's gin. I'll not deceive you, Mr B. It's gin.'

'Do you give the children Daffy, Mrs Mann?' enquired Bumble, following with his eyes the interesting process of mixing.

'Ah, bless 'em, that I do, dear as it is,' replied the nurse. 'I couldn't see 'em suffer before my very eyes, you know, sir.'

'No,' said Mr Bumble approvingly; 'no, you could not. You are a humane woman, Mrs Mann.' (Here she set down the glass.) 'I shall take a early opportunity of mentioning it to the board, Mrs Mann.' (He drew it towards him.) 'You feel as a mother, Mrs Mann.' (He stirred the gin-and-water.) 'I – I drink your health with cheerfulness, Mrs Mann;' and he swallowed half of it.

'And now about business,' said the beadle, taking out a leathern pocket-book. 'The child that was half-baptised Oliver Twist is nine year old today.'

'Bless him!' interposed Mrs Mann, inflaming her left eye with the corner of her apron.

'And notwithstanding a offered reward of ten pound, which was afterwards increased to twenty pound – notwithstanding the most superlative, and, I may say, supernat'ral exertions on the part of this parish,' said Bumble, 'we have never been able to discover who is his father, or what was his mother's settlement, name, or condition.'

Mrs Mann raised her hands in astonishment; but added, after a moment's reflection, 'How comes he to have any name at all, then?'

The beadle drew himself up with great pride, and said, 'I inwented it.'

'You, Mr Bumble!'

'I, Mrs Mann. We name our fondlings in alphabetical order. The last was an S – Swubble, I named him. This was a T – Twist, I named *him*. The next one as comes will be Unwin, and the next Vilkins. I have got names ready made to the end of the alphabet, and all the way through it again, when we come to Z.'

'Why, you're quite a literary character, sir!' said Mrs Mann.

'Well, well,' said the beadle, evidently gratified with the compliment; 'perhaps I may be. Perhaps I may be, Mrs Mann.' He finished the gin-and-water, and added, 'Oliver being now too old to remain here, the board have determined to have him back into the house. I have come out myself to take him there. So let me see him at once.'

'I'll fetch him directly,' said Mrs Mann, leaving the room for that purpose. Oliver having had by this time as much of the outer coat of dirt, which encrusted his face and hands, removed as could be scrubbed off in one washing, was led into the room by his benevolent protectress.

'Make a bow to the gentleman, Oliver,' said Mrs Mann.

Oliver made a bow, which was divided between the beadle on the chair and the cocked hat on the table.

'Will you go along with me, Oliver?' said Mr Bumble, in a majestic voice.

Oliver was about to say that he would go along with anybody with great readiness, when, glancing upwards, he caught sight of Mrs Mann, who had got behind the beadle's chair, and was shaking her fist at him with a furious countenance. He took the hint at once, for the fist had been too often impressed upon his body not to be deeply impressed upon his recollection.

'Will *she* go with me?' enquired poor Oliver.

'No, she can't,' replied Mr Bumble. 'But she'll come and see you sometimes.'

This was no very great consolation to the child. Young as he was, however, he had sense enough to make a feint of feeling great regret at going away. It was no very difficult matter for the boy to call the tears into his eyes. Hunger and recent ill-usage are great assistants if you want to cry; and Oliver cried very naturally indeed. Mrs Mann gave him a thousand embraces, and, what Oliver wanted a great deal more, a piece of bread and butter, lest he should seem too hungry when he got to the workhouse. With the slice of bread in his hand, and the little brown-cloth parish cap on his head, Oliver was then led away by Mr Bumble from the wretched home where one kind word or look had never lighted the gloom of his infant years. And yet he burst into an agony of childish grief as the cottage-gate closed after him.

Wretched as were the little companions in misery he was leaving behind, they were the only friends he had ever known; and a sense of his loneliness in the great wide world sank into the child's heart for the first time.

Mr Bumble walked on with long strides; little Oliver, firmly grasping his gold-laced cuff, trotted beside him – enquiring at the end of every quarter of a mile whether they were 'nearly there.' To these interrogations, Mr Bumble returned very brief and snappish replies; for the temporary blandness which gin-and-water awakens in some bosoms had by this time evaporated, and he was once again a beadle.

Oliver had not been within the walls of the workhouse a quarter of an hour, and had scarcely completed the demolition of a second slice of bread, when Mr Bumble, who had handed him over to the care of an old woman, returned; and, telling him it was a board night, informed him that the board had said he was to appear before it forthwith.

Not having a very clearly defined notion of what a live board was, Oliver was rather astounded by this intelligence, and was not quite certain whether he ought to laugh or cry. He had no time to think about the matter, however; for Mr Bumble gave him a tap on the head, with his cane, to wake him up, and another on the back to make him lively; and bidding him follow, conducted him into a large whitewashed room, where eight or ten fat gentlemen were sitting round a table. At the top of the table, seated in an armchair rather higher than the rest, was a particularly fat gentleman with a very round, red face.

'Bow to the board,' said Bumble. Oliver brushed away two or three tears that were lingering in his eyes, and seeing no board but the table, fortunately bowed to that.

'What's your name, boy?' said the gentleman in the high chair.

Oliver was frightened at the sight of so many gentlemen, which made him tremble; and the beadle gave him another tap behind, which made him cry: and these two causes made him answer in a very low and hesitating voice; whereupon a gentleman in a white waistcoat said he was a fool. Which was a capital way of raising his spirits, and putting him quite at his ease.

'Boy,' said the gentleman in the high chair, 'listen to me. You know you're an orphan, I suppose?'

'What's that, sir?' enquired poor Oliver.

'The boy *is* a fool – I thought he was,' said the gentleman in the white waistcoat.

'Hush!' said the gentleman who had spoken first. 'You know you've got no father or mother, and that you were brought up by the parish, don't you?'

'Yes, sir,' replied Oliver, weeping bitterly.

'What are you crying for?' enquired the gentleman in the white waistcoat. And to be sure it was very extraordinary. What *could* the boy be crying for?

'I hope you say your prayers every night,' said another gentleman in a gruff voice; 'and pray for the people who feed you, and take care of you – like a Christian.'

'Yes, sir,' stammered the boy. The gentleman who spoke last was unconsciously right. It would have been *very* like a Christian, and a marvellously good Christian, too, if Oliver had prayed for the people who fed and took care of *him*. But he hadn't, because nobody had taught him.

'Well! You have come here to be educated and taught a useful trade,' said the red-faced gentleman in the high chair.

'So you'll begin to pick oakum tomorrow morning at six o'clock,' added the surly one in the white waistcoat.

For the combination of both these blessings in the one simple process of picking oakum, Oliver bowed low by the direction of the beadle, and was then hurried away to a large ward, where, on a rough hard bed, he sobbed himself to sleep. What a noble illustration of the tender laws of England! They let the paupers go to sleep!

Poor Oliver! He little thought, as he lay sleeping in happy unconsciousness of all around him, that the board had that very day arrived at a decision which would exercise the most material influence over all his future fortunes. But they had. And this was it:

The members of this board were very sage, deep, philosophical men; and when they came to turn their attention to the workhouse, they found out at once what ordinary folks would never have discovered – the poor people like it! It was a regular place of public entertainment for the poorer classes; a tavern where there was nothing to pay; a public breakfast, dinner, tea, and supper all the year round; a brick and mortar elysium, where it was all play and no work. 'Oho!' said the board, looking very knowing, 'we are the fellows to set this to rights; we'll stop it all, in no time.' So they established the rule, that all poor people should have the alternative (for they would compel nobody, not they) of being starved by a gradual process in the house, or by a quick one out of it. With this view, they contracted with the waterworks to lay on an unlimited supply of water; and with a corn-factor to supply periodically small quantities of oatmeal; and issued three meals of thin gruel a day, with an onion twice a week, and half a roll on Sundays. They made a great many other wise and humane regulations, having reference to the ladies, which it is not necessary to repeat; kindly undertook to divorce poor married people, in consequence of the great expense of a suit in Doctors' Commons; and, instead of compelling a man to support his family, as they had heretofore done, took his family away from him, and made him a bachelor! There is no saying how many applicants for relief, under these two last heads, might have started up in all classes of society, if it had not been coupled with the workhouse; but the board were long-headed men, and had provided for this difficulty. The relief was inseparable from the workhouse and the gruel; and that frightened people.

For the first six months after Oliver Twist was removed the system was in full operation. It was rather expensive at first, in consequence of the increase in the undertaker's bill, and the necessity of taking in the clothes of all the paupers, which fluttered loosely on their wasted, shrunken forms, after a week or two's gruel. But the number of workhouse inmates got thin as well as the paupers; and the board were in ecstasies.

The room in which the boys were fed was a large stone hall,

with a copper at one end; out of which the master, dressed in an apron for the purpose, and assisted by one or two women, ladled the gruel at meal-times. Of this festive composition each boy had one porringer, and no more – except on occasions of great public rejoicing, when he had two ounces and a quarter of bread besides. The bowls never wanted washing. The boys polished them with their spoons till they shone again; and when they had performed this operation (which never took very long, the spoons being nearly as large as the bowls), they would sit staring at the copper, with such eager eyes, as if they could have devoured the very bricks of which it was composed; employing themselves, meanwhile, in sucking their fingers most assiduously, with the view of catching up any stray splashes of gruel that might have been cast thereon. Boys have generally excellent appetites. Oliver Twist and his companions suffered the tortures of slow starvation for three months. At last they got so voracious and wild with hunger, that one boy who was tall for his age, and hadn't been used to that sort of thing (for his father had kept a small cook's shop), hinted darkly to his companions, that unless he had another basin of gruel *per diem*, he was afraid he might some night happen to eat the boy who slept next him, who happened to be a weakly youth of tender age. He had a wild, hungry eye; and they implicitly believed him. A council was held; lots were cast who should walk up to the master after supper that evening and ask for more; and it fell to Oliver Twist.

The evening arrived, the boys took their places. The master, in his cook's uniform, stationed himself at the copper; his pauper assistants ranged themselves behind him; the gruel was served out; and a long grace was said over the short commons. The gruel disappeared; the boys whispered to each other, and winked at Oliver; while his next neighbours nudged him. Child as he was, he was desperate with hunger, and reckless with misery. He rose from the table; and advancing to the master, basin and spoon in hand, said, somewhat alarmed at his own temerity, 'Please, sir, I want some more.'

The master was a fat, healthy man; but he turned very pale. He gazed in stupefied astonishment on the small rebel for some seconds; and then clung for support to the copper. The assistants were paralysed with wonder, the boys with fear.

'What!' said the master at length, in a faint voice.

'Please, sir,' replied Oliver, 'I want some more.'

The master aimed a blow at Oliver's head with the ladle, pinioned him in his arms, and shrieked aloud for the beadle.

The board were sitting in solemn conclave, when Mr Bumble rushed into the room in great excitement, and addressing the gentleman in the high chair, said, 'Mr Limbkins, I beg your pardon, sir! Oliver Twist has asked for more.'

There was a general start. Horror was depicted on every countenance.

'For *more!*' said Mr Limbkins. 'Compose yourself, Bumble, and answer me distinctly. Do I understand that he asked for more, after he had eaten the supper allotted by the dietary?'

'He did, sir,' replied Bumble.

'That boy will be hung,' said the gentleman in the white waistcoat. 'I know that boy will be hung.'

Nobody controverted the prophetic gentleman's opinion. An animated discussion took place. Oliver was ordered into instant confinement; and a bill was next morning pasted on the outside of the gate, offering a reward of five pounds to anybody who would take Oliver Twist off the hands of the parish. In other words, five pounds and Oliver Twist were offered to any man or woman who wanted an apprentice to any trade, business, or calling.

'I never was more convinced of anything in my life,' said the gentleman in the white waistcoat, as he knocked at the gate and read the bill next morning – 'I never was more convinced of anything in my life, than I am that that boy will come to be hung.'

As I purpose to show in the sequel whether the white waistcoated gentleman was right or not, I should perhaps mar the interest of this narrative (supposing it to possess any at all), if I ventured to hint, just yet, whether the life of Oliver Twist had this violent termination or no.

CHAPTER 3

Relates how Oliver Twist was very near getting a place, which would not have been a sinecure

For a week after the commission of the impious and profane offence of asking for more, Oliver remained a close prisoner in the dark and solitary room to which he had been consigned by the wisdom and mercy of the board. It appears at first sight not

Oliver asking for more

unreasonable to suppose that, if he had entertained a becoming feeling of respect for the prediction of the gentleman in the white waistcoat, he would have established that sage individual's prophetic character, once and for ever, by tying one end of his pocket-handkerchief to a hook in the wall, and attaching himself to the other. To the performance of this feat, however, there was one obstacle: namely, that pocket-handkerchiefs, being decided articles of luxury, had been, for all future times and ages, removed from the noses of paupers by the express order of the board, in council assembled, solemnly given and pronounced under their hands and seals. There was a still greater obstacle in Oliver's youth and childishness. He only cried bitterly all day; and when the long dismal night came on, he spread his little hands before his eyes to shut out the darkness, and crouching in the corner, tried to sleep; ever and anon waking with a start and tremble, and drawing himself closer and closer to the wall, as if to feel even its cold hard surface were a protection in the gloom and loneliness which surrounded him.

Let it not be supposed by the enemies of the 'system,' that during the period of his solitary incarceration, Oliver was denied the benefit of exercise, the pleasure of society, or the advantages of religious consolation. As for exercise, it was nice cold weather, and he was allowed to perform his ablutions every morning under the pump, in a stone yard, in the presence of Mr Bumble, who prevented his catching cold, and caused a tingling sensation to pervade his frame, by repeated applications of the cane. As for society, he was carried every other day into the hall where the boys dined, and there sociably flogged as a public warning and example. And so far from being denied the advantages of religious consolation, he was kicked into the same apartment every evening at prayer-time and there permitted to listen to, and console his mind with, a general supplication of the boys, containing a special clause, therein inserted by authority of the board, in which they entreated to be made good, virtuous, contented, and obedient, and to be guarded from the sins and vices of Oliver Twist: whom the supplication distinctly set forth to be under the exclusive patronage and protection of the powers of wickedness, and an article direct from the manufactory of the very Devil himself.

It chanced one morning, while Oliver's affairs were in this auspicious and comfortable state, that Mr Gamfield, chimney-sweeper, was wending his way adown the High Street, deeply cogitating in his mind his ways and means of paying certain arrears of rent, for which his landlord had become rather pressing. Mr Gamfield's most sanguine estimate of his finances could not raise them within full five pounds of the desired amount; and, in a species of arithmetical desperation, he was alternately cudgelling his brains and his donkey, when, passing the workhouse, his eyes encountered the bill on the gate.

'Wo – o!' said Mr Gamfield to the donkey.

The donkey was in a state of profound abstraction; wondering, probably, whether he was destined to be regaled with a cabbage-stalk or two when he had disposed of the two sacks of soot with which the little cart was laden; so, without noticing the word of command, he jogged onward.

Mr Gamfield growled a fierce imprecation on the donkey generally, but more particularly on his eyes; and, running after him, bestowed a blow on his head, which would inevitably have beaten in any skull but a donkey's. Then, catching hold of the bridle, he gave his jaw a sharp wrench, by way of gentle reminder that he was not his own master; and by these means turned him round. He then gave him another blow on the head, just to stun him till he came back again. Having completed these arrangements, he walked up to the gate to read the bill.

The gentleman with the white waistcoat was standing at the gate with his hands behind him, after having delivered himself of some profound sentiments in the boardroom. Having witnessed the little dispute between Mr Gamfield and the donkey, he smiled joyously when that person came up to read the bill, for he saw at once that Mr Gamfield was exactly the sort of master Oliver Twist wanted. Mr Gamfield smiled, too, as he perused the document; for five pounds was just the sum he had been wishing for; and, as to the boy with which it was encumbered, Mr Gamfield, knowing what the dietary of the workhouse was, well knew he would be a nice small pattern, just the very thing for register stoves. So, he spelt the bill through again, from beginning to end; and then touching his fur cap in token of humility, accosted the gentleman in the white waistcoat.

'This here boy, sir, wot the parish wants to 'prentis,' said Mr Gamfield.

'Ay, my man,' said the gentleman in the white waistcoat, with a condescending smile. 'What of him?'

'If the parish would like him to learn a light pleasant trade, in a good 'spectable chimbley-sweepin' business,' said Mr Gamfield, 'I wants a 'prentis, and I'm ready to take him.'

'Walk in,' said the gentleman in the white waistcoat. Mr Gamfield having lingered behind, to give the donkey another blow on the head, and another wrench of the jaw as a caution not to run away in his absence, followed the gentleman with the white waistcoat into the room where Oliver had first seen him.

'It's a nasty trade,' said Mr Limbkins, when Gamfield had again stated his wish.

'Young boys have been smothered in chimneys before now,' said another gentleman.

'That's acause they damped the straw afore they lit it in the chimbley to make 'em come down agin,' said Gamfield; 'that's all smoke, and no blaze; vereas smoke ain't o' no use at all in makin' a boy come down, for it only sinds him to sleep, and that's wot he likes. Boys is very obstinite, and very lazy, gen'lmen, and there's nothink like a good hot blaze to make 'em come down vith a run. It's humane, too, gen'lmen, acause, even if they've stuck in the chimbley, roasting their feet makes 'em struggle to hextricate theirselves.'

The gentleman in the white waistcoat appeared very much amused by this explanation; but his mirth was speedily checked by a look from Mr Limbkins. The board then proceeded to converse among themselves for a few minutes, but in so low a tone that the words 'saving of expenditure,' 'looked well in the accounts,' 'have a printed report published,' were alone audible. These only chanced to be heard, indeed, on account of their being very frequently repeated with great emphasis.

At length the whispering ceased; and the members of the board having resumed their seats and their solemnity, Mr Limbkins said, 'We have considered your proposition, and we don't approve of it.'

'Not at all,' said the gentleman in the white waistcoat.

'Decidedly not,' added the other members.

As Mr Gamfield did happen to labour under the slight imputation of having bruised three or four boys to death already, it occurred to him that the board had, perhaps, in some unaccountable freak, taken it into their heads that this extraneous circumstance ought to influence their proceedings. It was very unlike their general mode of doing business, if they had; but still, as he had no particular wish to revive the rumour; he twisted his cap in his hands, and walked slowly from the table.

'So you won't let me have him, gen'lmen?' said Mr Gamfield, pausing near the door.

'No,' replied Mr Limbkins; 'at least, as it's a nasty business, we think you ought to take something less than the premium we offered.'

Mr Gamfield's countenance brightened, as, with a quick step, he returned to the table, and said, 'What'll you give, gen'lmen? Come! Don't be too hard on a poor man. What'll you give?'

'I should say three pound ten was plenty,' said Mr Limbkins.

'Ten shillings too much,' said the gentleman in the white waistcoat.

'Come!' said Gamfield; 'say four pound, gen'lmen. Say four pound, and you've got rid on him for good and all. There.'

'Three pound ten,' repeated Mr Limbkins, firmly.

'Come! I'll split the difference, gen'lmen,' urged Gamfield. 'Three pound fifteen.'

'Not a farthing more,' was the firm reply of Mr Limbkins.

'You're desperate hard upon me, gen'lmen,' said Gamfield, wavering.

'Pooh! pooh! nonsense!' said the gentleman in the white waistcoat. 'He'd be cheap with nothing at all as a premium. Take him, you silly fellow! He's just the boy for you. He wants the stick now and then; it'll do him good; and his board needn't come very expensive, for he hasn't been overfed since he was born. Ha! ha! ha!'

Mr Gamfield gave an arch look at the faces round the table, and, observing a smile on all of them, gradually broke into a smile himself. The bargain was made. Mr Bumble was at once instructed that Oliver Twist and his indentures were to be conveyed before the magistrate for signature and approval that very afternoon.

In pursuance of this determination, little Oliver, to his excessive astonishment, was released from bondage, and ordered to put himself into a clean shirt. He had hardly achieved this very unusual gymnastic performance, when Mr Bumble brought him, with his own hands, a basin of gruel, and the holiday allowance of two ounces and a quarter of bread. At this tremendous sight Oliver began to cry very piteously: thinking, not unnaturally, that the board must have determined to kill him for some useful purpose, or they never would have begun to fatten him up in that way.

'Don't make your eyes red, Oliver, but eat your food and be thankful,' said Mr Bumble, in a tone of impressive pomposity. 'You're a-going to be made a 'prentice of, Oliver.'

'A 'prentice, sir!' said the child, trembling.

'Yes, Oliver,' said Mr Bumble. 'The kind and blessed gentlemen which is so many parents to you, Oliver, when you have none of your own, are a-going to 'prentice you; and to set you up in life, and make a man of you; although the expense to the parish is three pound ten! – three pound ten, Oliver! seventy shillin's – one hundred and forty sixpences! – and all for a naughty orphan which nobody can't love.'

As Mr Bumble paused to take breath, after delivering this address in an awful voice, the tears rolled down the poor child's face, and he sobbed bitterly.

'Come,' said Mr Bumble, somewhat less pompously, for it was gratifying to his feelings to observe the effect his eloquence had produced; 'come, Oliver! Wipe your eyes with the cuffs of your jacket, and don't cry into your gruel; that's a very foolish action, Oliver.' It certainly was, for there was quite enough water in it already.

On their way to the magistrate, Mr Bumble instructed Oliver that all he would have to do would be to look very happy, and say, when the gentleman asked him if he wanted to be apprenticed, that he should like it very much indeed; both of which injunctions Oliver promised to obey: the rather as Mr Bumble threw in a gentle hint, that if he failed in either particular, there was no telling what would be done to him. When they arrived at the office, he was shut up in a little room by himself, and admonished by Mr Bumble to stay there until he came back to fetch him.

There the boy remained, with a palpitating heart, for half an hour. At the expiration of which time Mr Bumble thrust in his head, unadorned with the cocked hat, and said aloud, 'Now, Oliver, my dear, come to the gentleman.' As Mr Bumble said this, he put on a grim and threatening look, and added, in a low voice, 'Mind what I told you, you young rascal!'

Oliver stared innocently in Mr Bumble's face at this somewhat contradictory style of address; but that gentleman prevented his offering any remark thereupon, by leading him at once into an adjoining room, the door of which was open. It was a large room, with a great window. Behind a desk sat two old gentlemen with powdered heads, one of whom was reading the newspaper, while the other was perusing, with the aid of a pair of tortoiseshell spectacles, a small piece of parchment which lay before him. Mr Limbkins was standing in front of the desk on one side, and Mr Gamfield, with a partially washed face, on the other; while two or three bluff-looking men, in top-boots, were lounging about.

The old gentleman with the spectacles gradually dozed off, over the little bit of parchment; and there was a short pause, after Oliver had been stationed by Mr Bumble in front of the desk.

'This is the boy, your worship,' said Mr Bumble.

The old gentleman who was reading the newspaper raised his head for a moment, and pulled the other old gentleman by the sleeve; whereupon the last-mentioned old gentleman woke up.

'Oh, is this the boy?' said the old gentleman.

'This is him, sir,' replied Mr Bumble. 'Bow to the magistrate, my dear.'

Oliver roused himself, and made his best obeisance. He had been wondering, with his eyes fixed on the magistrates' powder, whether all boards were born with that white stuff on their heads, and were boards from thenceforth on that account.

'Well,' said the old gentleman. 'I suppose he is fond of chimney-sweeping?'

'He dotes on it, your worship,' replied Bumble, giving Oliver a sly pinch to intimate that he had better not say he didn't.

'And he *will* be a sweep, will he?' enquired the old gentleman.

'If we was to bind him to any other trade tomorrow he'd run away simultaneous, your worship,' replied Bumble.

'And this man that's to be his master – you, sir – you'll treat him well, and feed him, and do all that sort of thing – will you?' said the old gentleman.

'When I says I will, I means I will,' replied Mr Gamfield, doggedly.

'You're a rough speaker, my friend, but you look an honest, open-hearted man,' said the old gentleman, turning his spectacles in the direction of the candidate for Oliver's premium, whose villainous countenance was a regular stamped receipt for cruelty. But the magistrate was half-blind and half-childish, so he couldn't reasonably be expected to discern what other people did.

'I hope I am, sir,' said Mr Gamfield, with an ugly leer.

'I have no doubt you are, my friend,' replied the old gentleman, fixing his spectacles more firmly on his nose, and looking about him for the inkstand.

It was the critical moment of Oliver's fate. If the inkstand had been where the old gentleman thought it was, he would have dipped his pen into it and signed the indentures; and Oliver would have been straight-way hurried off. But, as it chanced to be immediately under his nose, it followed, as a matter of course, that he looked all over his desk for it, without finding it; and happening in the course of his search to look straight before him, his gaze encountered the pale and terrified face of Oliver Twist, who, despite all the admonitory looks and pinches of Bumble, was regarding the repulsive countenance of his future master with a mingled expression of horror and fear, too palpable to be mistaken even by a half-blind magistrate.

The old gentleman stopped, laid down his pen, and looked from Oliver to Mr Limbkins, who attempted to take snuff with a cheerful and unconcerned aspect.

'My boy!' said the old gentleman, leaning over the desk. Oliver started at the sound. He might be excused for doing so; for the words were kindly said, and strange sounds frighten one. He trembled violently, and burst into tears.

'My boy!' said the old gentleman, 'you look pale and alarmed. What is the matter?'

'Stand a little away from him, Beadle,' said the other magistrate, laying aside the paper, and leaning forward with an expression of interest. 'Now, boy, tell us what's the matter; don't be afraid.'

Oliver fell on his knees, and clasping his hands together, prayed that they would order him back to the dark room – that they would starve him – beat him – kill him if they pleased – rather than send him away with that dreadful man.

'Well!' said Mr Bumble, raising his hands and eyes with most impressive solemnity – 'well! of all the artful and designing orphans that ever I see, Oliver, you are one of the most bare-facedst.'

'Hold your tongue, Beadle,' said the second old gentleman, when Mr Bumble had given vent to this compound adjective.

'I beg your worship's pardon,' said Mr Bumble, incredulous of his having heard aright. 'Did your worship speak to me?'

'Yes. Hold your tongue.'

Mr Bumble was stupefied with astonishment. A beadle ordered to hold his tongue! A moral revolution!

The old gentleman in the tortoiseshell spectacles looked at his companion; he nodded significantly.

'We refuse to sanction these indentures,' said the old gentleman, tossing aside the piece of parchment as he spoke.

'I hope,' stammered Mr Limbkins – 'I hope the magistrates will not form the opinion that the authorities have been guilty of any improper conduct, on the unsupported testimony of a mere child.'

'The magistrates are not called upon to pronounce any opinion on the matter,' said the second old gentleman sharply. 'Take the boy back to the workhouse, and treat him kindly. He seems to want it.'

That same evening the gentleman in the white waistcoat most positively and decidedly affirmed, not only that Oliver

Oliver escapes being bound apprentice to the sweep

would be hung, but that he would be drawn and quartered into the bargain. Mr Bumble shook his head with gloomy mystery, and said he wished he might come to good; whereunto Mr Gamfield replied, that he wished he might come to him; which, although he agreed with the beadle in most matters, would seem to be a wish of a totally opposite description.

The next morning the public were once more informed that Oliver Twist was again To Let, and that five pounds would be paid to anybody who would take possession of him.

CHAPTER 4

Oliver, being offered another place, makes his first entry into public life

In great families, when an advantageous place cannot be obtained, either in possession, reversion, remainder, or expectancy, for the young man who is growing up, it is a very general custom to send him to sea. The board, in imitation of so wise and salutary an example, took counsel together on the expediency of shipping off Oliver Twist in some small trading vessel bound to a good unhealthy port; which suggested itself as the very best thing that could possibly be done with him; the probability being that the skipper would flog him to death, in a playful mood, someday after dinner, or would knock his brains out with an iron bar; both pastimes being, as is pretty generally known, very favourite and common recreations among gentlemen of that class. The more the case presented itself to the board, in this point of view, the more manifold the advantages of the step appeared; so they came to the conclusion that the only way of providing for Oliver effectually was to send him to sea without delay.

Mr Bumble had been dispatched to make various preliminary enquiries, with the view of finding out some captain or other who wanted a cabin-boy without any friends; and was returning to the workhouse to communicate the result of his mission, when he encountered, just at the gate, no less a person than Mr Sowerberry, the parochial undertaker.

Mr Sowerberry was a tall, gaunt, large-jointed man, attired in a suit of threadbare black, with darned cotton-stockings of the same colour, and shoes to answer. His features were not naturally intended to wear a smiling aspect, but he was in general rather given to professional jocosity. His step was elastic, and his face betokened inward pleasantry, as he advanced to Mr Bumble and shook him cordially by the hand.

'I have taken the measure of the two women that died last night, Mr Bumble,' said the undertaker.

'You'll make your fortune, Mr Sowerberry,' said the beadle, as he thrust his thumb and forefinger into the proffered snuff-box of the undertaker; which was an ingenious little model of a patent coffin. 'I say you'll make your fortune, Mr Sowerberry,' repeated Mr Bumble, tapping the undertaker on the shoulder, in a friendly manner, with his cane.

'Think so?' said the undertaker in a tone which half admitted and half disputed the probability of the event. 'The prices allowed by the board are very small, Mr Bumble.'

'So are the coffins,' replied the beadle, with precisely as near an approach to a laugh as a great official ought to indulge in.

Mr Sowerberry was much tickled at this – as of course he ought to be – and laughed a long time without cessation. 'Well, well, Mr Bumble,' he said at length, 'there's no denying that, since the new system of feeding has come in, the coffins are somewhat narrower and more shallow than they used to be; but we must have some profit, Mr Bumble. Well-seasoned timber is an expensive article, sir; and all the iron handles come by canal from Birmingham.'

'Well, well,' said Mr Bumble, 'every trade has its drawbacks. A fair profit is, of course, allowable.'

'Of course, of course,' replied the undertaker; 'and if I don't get a profit upon this or that particular article, why, I make it up in the long-run, you see – he! he! he!'

'Just so,' said Mr Bumble.

'Though I must say,' continued the undertaker, resuming the current of observations which the beadle had interrupted – 'though I must say, Mr Bumble, that I have to contend against one very great disadvantage – which is, that all the stout people go off the quickest. The people who have been better off, and have paid rates for many years, are the first to sink when they come into the house. And let me tell you, Mr Bumble, that three or four inches over one's calculation makes a great hole in one's profits; especially when one has a family to provide for, sir.'

As Mr Sowerberry said this with the becoming indignation of an ill-used man, and as Mr Bumble felt that it rather tended to convey a reflection on the honour of the parish, the latter gentleman thought it advisable to change the subject. Oliver Twist being uppermost in his mind, he made him his theme.

'By the by,' said Mr Bumble, 'you don't know anybody who wants a boy, do you? A porochial 'prentice, who is at present a dead-weight – a millstone, as I may say, round the porochial throat? Liberal terms, Mr Sowerberry, liberal terms!' As Mr Bumble spoke, he raised his cane to the bill above him, and gave three distinct raps upon the words 'five pounds;' which were printed thereon in Roman capitals of gigantic size.

'Gadso!' said the undertaker, taking Mr Bumble by the gilt-edged lapel of his official coat; 'that's just the very thing I wanted to speak to you about. You know – dear me, what a very elegant button this is, Mr Bumble! I never noticed it before.'

'Yes, I think it is rather pretty,' said the beadle, glancing proudly downwards at the large brass buttons which embellished his coat. 'The die is the same as the porochial seal – the Good Samaritan healing the sick and bruised man. The board presented it to me on New Year's morning, Mr Sowerberry. I put it on, I remember, for the first time, to attend the inquest on that reduced tradesman who died in a doorway at midnight.'

'I recollect,' said the undertaker. 'The jury brought in, "Died from exposure to the cold, and want of the common necessaries of life," didn't they?'

Mr Bumble nodded.

'And they made it a special verdict, I think,' said the

undertaker, 'by adding some words to the effect, that if the relieving officer had – '

'Tush! Foolery!' interposed the beadle. 'If the board attended to all the nonsense that ignorant jurymen talk, they'd have enough to do.'

'Very true,' said the undertaker; 'they would indeed.'

'Juries,' said Mr Bumble, grasping his cane tightly, as was his wont when working into a passion – 'juries is ineddicated, vulgar, grovelling wretches.'

'So they are,' said the undertaker.

'They haven't no more philosophy nor political economy about 'em than that,' said the beadle, snapping his fingers contemptuously.

'No more they have,' acquiesced the undertaker.

'I despise 'em,' said the beadle, growing very red in the face.

'So do I,' rejoined the undertaker.

'And I only wish we'd a jury of the independent sort in the house for a week or two,' said the beadle; 'the rules and regulations of the board would soon bring their spirit down for 'em.'

'Let 'em alone for that,' replied the undertaker. So saying, he smiled approvingly; to calm the rising wrath of the indignant parish officer.

Mr Bumble lifted off his cocked hat, took a handkerchief from the inside of the crown, wiped from his forehead the perspiration which his rage had engendered, fixed the cocked hat on again, and, turning to the undertaker, said in a calmer voice, 'Well, what about the boy?'

'Oh!' replied the undertaker; 'why, you know, Mr Bumble, I pay a good deal towards the poor's rates.'

'Hem!' said Mr Bumble. 'Well?'

'Well,' replied the undertaker, 'I was thinking that if I pay so much towards 'em, I've a right to get as much out of 'em as I can, Mr Bumble; and so – and so – I think I'll take the boy myself.'

Mr Bumble grasped the undertaker by the arm and led him into the building. Mr Sowerberry was closeted with the board for five minutes; and it was arranged that Oliver should go to him that evening 'upon liking,' – a phrase which means, in the case of a parish apprentice, that if the master finds, upon a short trial, that he can get enough work out of a boy without putting too much food into him, he shall have him for a term of years to do what he likes with.

When little Oliver was taken before 'the gentlemen' that evening, and informed that he was to go, that night, as general house-lad to a coffin-maker's; and that if he complained of his situation, or ever came back to the parish again, he would be sent to sea, there to be drowned, or knocked on the head, as the case might be, he evinced so little emotion, that they, by common consent, pronounced him a hardened young rascal, and ordered Mr Bumble to remove him forthwith.

Now, although it was very natural that the board, of all people in the world, should feel in a great state of virtuous astonishment and horror at the smallest tokens of want of feeling on the part of anybody, they were rather out in this particular instance. The simple fact was, that Oliver, instead of possessing too little feeling, possessed rather too much; and was in a fair way of being reduced, for life, to a state of brutal stupidity and sullenness by the ill-usage he had received. He heard the news of his destination in perfect silence; and, having had his luggage put into his hand – which was not very difficult to carry, inasmuch as it was all comprised within the limits of a brown paper parcel, about half a foot square by three inches deep – he pulled his cap over his eyes; and once more attaching himself to Mr Bumble's coat cuff, was led away by that dignitary to a new scene of suffering.

For some time Mr Bumble drew Oliver along without notice or remark; for the beadle carried his head very erect, as a beadle always should, and, it being a windy day, little Oliver was completely enshrouded by the skirts of Mr Bumble's coat as they blew open, and disclosed to great advantage his flapped waist-coat and drab plush knee-breeches. As they drew near to their destination, however, Mr Bumble thought it expedient to look down, and see that the boy was in good order for inspection by his new master, which he accordingly did, with a fit and becoming air of gracious patronage.

'Oliver!' said Mr Bumble.

'Yes, sir,' replied Oliver, in a low, tremulous voice.

'Pull that cap off your eyes, and hold up your head,

Although Oliver did as he was desired at once, and passed the back of his unoccupied hand briskly across his eyes, he left a tear in them when he looked up at his conductor. As Mr Bumble gazed sternly upon him, it rolled down his cheek. It was followed by another and another. The child made a strong effort, but it was an unsuccessful one. Withdrawing his other hand from Mr Bumble's, he covered his face with both, and wept until the tears sprung out from between his thin and bony fingers.

'Well!' exclaimed Mr Bumble, stopping short, and darting at his little charge a look of intense malignity – 'well! Of *all* the ungratefullest, and worst-disposed boys as ever I see, Oliver, you are the – '

'No, no, sir,' sobbed Oliver, clinging to the hand which held the well-known cane; 'no, no, sir: I will be good indeed; indeed, indeed I will, sir! I am a very little boy, sir; and it is so – so – '

'So what?' enquired Mr Bumble in amazement.

'So lonely, sir! So very lonely!' cried the child. 'Everybody hates me. Oh! sir, don't, don't pray be cross to me!' The child beat his hand upon his heart; and looked in his companion's face with tears of real agony.

Mr Bumble regarded Oliver's piteous and helpless look with some astonishment for a few seconds; hemmed three or four times in a husky manner; and after muttering something about 'that troublesome cough,' bid Oliver dry his eyes and be a good boy. Then, once more taking his hand, he walked on with him in silence.

The undertaker, who had just put up the shutters of his shop, was making some entries in his day-book by the light of a most appropriately dismal candle, when Mr Bumble entered.

'Aha!' said the undertaker, looking up from the book, and pausing in the middle of a word; 'is that you, Bumble?'

'No one else, Mr Sowerberry,' replied the beadle. 'Here, I've brought the boy.' Oliver made bow.

'Oh! that's the boy, is it?' said the undertaker, raising the candle above his head, to get a better view of Oliver. 'Mrs Sowerberry! will you have the goodness to come here a moment, my dear?'

Mrs Sowerberry emerged from a little room behind the shop, and presented the form of a short, thin, squeezed-up woman, with a vixenish countenance.

'My dear,' said Mr Sowerberry, deferentially, 'this is the boy from the workhouse that I told you of.' Oliver bowed again.

'Dear me!' said the undertaker's wife, 'he's very small.'

'Why, he *is* rather small,' replied Mr Bumble, looking at Oliver as if it were his fault that he was no bigger; 'he *is* small. There's no denying it. But he'll grow, Mrs Sowerberry – he'll grow.'

'Ah! I dare say he will,' replied the lady pettishly, 'on our victuals and our drink. I see no saving in parish children, not I; for they always cost more to keep than they're worth. However, men always think they know best. There! Get downstairs, little bag o' bones.' With this the undertaker's wife opened a side door, and pushed Oliver down a steep flight of stairs into a stone cell, damp and dark, forming the ante-room to the coal-cellar, and denominated 'the kitchen;' wherein sat a slatternly girl, in shoes down at heel, and blue worsted stockings very much out of repair.

'Here, Charlotte,' said Mrs Sowerberry, who had followed Oliver down, 'give this boy some of the cold bits that were put by for Trip. He hasn't come home since the morning, so he may go without 'em. I dare say the boy isn't too dainty to eat 'em – are you, boy?'

Oliver, whose eyes had glistened at the mention of meat, and who was trembling with eagerness to devour it, replied in the negative; and a plateful of coarse broken victuals was set before him.

I wish some well-fed philosopher, whose meat and drink turn to gall within him, whose blood is ice, whose heart is iron, could have seen Oliver Twist clutching at the dainty viands that the dog had neglected. I wish he could have witnessed the horrible avidity with which Oliver tore the bits asunder with all the ferocity of famine. There is only one thing I should like better – and that would be to see the philosopher making the same sort of meal himself, with the same relish.

'Well,' said the undertaker's wife, when Oliver had finished his supper – which she had regarded in silent horror, and with fearful auguries of his future appetite – 'have you done?'

There being nothing eatable within his reach, Oliver replied in the affirmative.

'Then come with me,' said Mrs Sowerberry, taking up a dim and dirty lamp, and leading the way upstairs; 'your bed's under the counter. You don't mind sleeping among the coffins, I suppose? But it doesn't much matter whether you do or don't, for you can't sleep anywhere else. Come – don't keep me here all night!'

Oliver lingered no longer, but meekly followed his new mistress.

CHAPTER 5

Oliver mingles with new associates.
Going to a funeral for the first time, he forms an
unfavourable notion of his master's business

Oliver, being left to himself in the undertaker's shop, set the lamp down on a workman's bench, and gazed timidly about him with a feeling of awe and dread which many people a good deal older than he will be at no loss to understand. An unfinished coffin on black trestles, which stood in the middle of the shop, looked so gloomy and deathlike that a cold tremble came over him every time his eyes wandered in the direction of the dismal object – from which he almost expected to see some frightful form slowly rear its head to drive him mad with terror. Against the wall were arranged, in regular array, a long row of elm boards cut into the same shape; looking, in the dim light, like high-shouldered ghosts with their hands in their breeches-pockets. Coffin-plates, elm-chips, bright-headed nails, and shreds of black cloth, lay scattered on the floor; and the wall behind the counter was ornamented with a lively representation of two mutes in very stiff neck-cloths, on duty at a large private door, with a hearse drawn by four black steeds approaching in the distance. The shop was close and hot, and the atmosphere seemed tainted with the smell of coffins. The recess beneath the counter in which his flock mattress was thrust looked like a grave.

Nor were these the only dismal feelings which depressed Oliver. He was alone in a strange place; and we all know how chilled and desolate the best of us will sometimes feel in such a situation. The boy had no friends to care for, or to care for him. The regret of no recent separation was fresh in his mind; the absence of no loved and well-remembered face sunk heavily into his heart. But his heart *was* heavy, notwithstanding; and he wished, as he crept into his narrow bed, that that were his coffin, and that he could be laid in a calm and lasting sleep in the churchyard ground, with the tall grass waving gently above his head, and the sound of the old deep bell to soothe him in his sleep.

Oliver was awakened in the morning by a loud kicking at the outside of the shop-door; which, before he could huddle on his clothes, was repeated, in an angry and impetuous manner, about twenty-five times. When he began to undo the chain, the legs desisted, and a voice began.

'Open the door, will yer?' cried the voice which belonged to the legs which had kicked at the door.

'I will directly, sir,' replied Oliver, undoing the chain, and turning the key.

'I suppose yer the new boy, a'n't yer?' said the voice through the keyhole.

'Yes, sir,' replied Oliver.

'How old are yer?' enquired the voice.

'Ten, sir,' replied Oliver.

'Then I'll whop yer when I get in,' said the voice; 'you just see if I don't, that's all, my work'us brat!' and having made this obliging promise, the voice began to whistle.

Oliver had been too often subjected to the process to which the very expressive monosyllable just recorded bears reference, to entertain the smallest doubt that the owner of the voice, whoever he might be, would redeem his pledge most honourably. He drew back the bolts with a trembling hand, and opened the door.

For a second or two, Oliver glanced up the street, and down the street, and over the way, impressed with the belief that the unknown, who had addressed him through the keyhole, had walked a few paces off, to warm himself; for nobody did he see but a big charity-boy, sitting on a post in front of the house, eating a slice of bread and butter, which he cut into wedges, the size of his mouth, with a clasp-knife, and then consumed with great dexterity.

'I beg your pardon, sir,' said Oliver, at length, seeing that no other visitor made his appearance; 'did you knock?'

'I kicked,' replied the charity-boy.

'Did you want a coffin, sir?' enquired Oliver innocently.

At this the charity-boy looked monstrous fierce, and said that Oliver would want one before long if he cut jokes with his superiors in that way.

'Yer don't know who I am, I suppose, Work'us?' said the charity-boy, in continuation, descending from the top of the post, meanwhile, with edifying gravity.

'No, sir,' rejoined Oliver.

'I'm Mister Noah Claypole,' said the charity-boy, 'and you're under me. Take down the shutters, yer idle young ruffian!'

With this, Mr Claypole administered a kick to Oliver, and entered the shop with a dignified air, which did him great credit. It is difficult for a large-headed, small-eyed youth, of lumbering make and heavy countenance, to look dignified under any circumstances; but it is more especially so, when superadded to these personal attractions are a red nose and yellow smalls.

Oliver, having taken down the shutters, and broken a pane of glass in his efforts to stagger away beneath the weight of the first one to a small court at the side of the house in which they were kept during the day, was graciously assisted by Noah; who, having consoled him with the assurance that 'he'd catch it,' condescended to help him. Mr Sowerberry came down soon after. Shortly afterwards, Mrs Sowerberry appeared; and Oliver having 'caught it', in fulfilment of Noah's prediction, followed that young gentleman downstairs to breakfast.

'Come near the fire, Noah,' said Charlotte. 'I saved a nice little bit of bacon for you from master's breakfast. Oliver, shut that door at Mister Noah's back, and take them bits that I've put out on the cover of the bread-pan. There's your tea; take it away to that box, and drink it there, and make haste, for they'll want you to mind the shop. D'ye hear?'

'D'ye hear, Work'us?' said Noah Claypole.

'Lor, Noah!' said Charlotte, 'what a rum creature you are! Why don't you let the boy alone?'

'Let him alone!' said Noah. 'Why, everybody lets him alone enough, for the matter of that. Neither his father nor his mother will ever interfere with him. All his relations let him have his own way pretty well. Eh, Charlotte? He! he! he!'

'Oh, you queer soul!' said Charlotte, bursting into a hearty laugh, in which she was joined by Noah; after which, they both looked scornfully at poor Oliver Twist, as he sat shivering on the box in the coldest corner of the room, and ate the stale pieces which had been specially reserved for him.

Noah was a charity-boy, but not a workhouse orphan. No chance-child was he, for he could trace his genealogy all the way back to his parents, who lived hard by; his mother being a washerwoman, and his father a drunken soldier, discharged with a wooden leg, and a diurnal pension of twopence-half-penny and an unstatable fraction. The shop-boys in the neighbourhood had long been in the habit of branding Noah, in the public streets, with the ignominious epithets of 'leathers,' 'charity,' and the like; and Noah had borne them without reply. But now that fortune had cast in his way a nameless orphan, at whom even the meanest could point the finger of scorn, he retorted on him with interest. This affords charming food for contemplation. It shows us what a beautiful thing human nature sometimes is, and how impartially the same amiable qualities are developed in the finest lord and the dirtiest charity-boy.

Oliver had been sojourning at the undertaker's some three weeks or a month. Mr and Mrs Sowerberry – the shop being shut up – were taking their supper in the little back-parlour, when Mr Sowerberry, after several deferential glances at his wife, said, 'My dear – ' He was going to say more; but Mrs Sowerberry looking up, with a peculiarly unpropitious aspect, he stopped short.

'Well,' said Mrs Sowerberry, sharply.

'Nothing, my dear, nothing,' said Mr Sowerberry.

'Ugh, you brute!' said Mrs Sowerberry.

'Not at all, my dear,' said Mr Sowerberry, humbly. 'I thought you didn't want to hear, my dear. I was only going to say – '

'Oh, don't tell me what you were going to say,' interposed Mrs Sowerberry. 'I am nobody; don't consult me, pray. I don't want to intrude upon your secrets.' As Mrs Sowerberry said this, she gave a hysterical laugh, which threatened violent consequences.

'But, my dear,' said Mr Sowerberry, 'I want to ask your advice.'

'No, no, don't ask mine,' replied Mrs Sowerberry, in an affecting manner; 'ask somebody else's.' Here there was another hysterical laugh, which frightened Mr Sowerberry very much. This is a very common and much-approved matrimonial course of treatment, which is often very effective. It at once reduced Mr Sowerberry to begging as a special favour to be allowed to say what Mrs Sowerberry was most curious to hear. After a short altercation of less than three quarters of an hour's duration, the permission was most graciously conceded.

'It's only about young Twist, my dear,' said Mr Sowerberry. 'A very good-looking boy, that, my dear.'

'He need be, for he eats enough,' observed the lady.

'There's an expression of melancholy in his face, my dear,' resumed Mr Sowerberry, 'which is very interesting. He would make a delightful mute, my love.'

Mrs Sowerberry looked up with an expression of considerable

wonderment. Mr Sowerberry remarked it, and without allowing time for any observation on the good lady's part, proceeded: 'I don't mean a regular mute to attend grown-up people, my dear, but only for children's practice. It would be very new to have a mute in proportion, my dear. You may depend upon it, it would have a most superb effect.'

Mrs Sowerberry, who had a good deal of taste in the undertaking way, was much struck by the novelty of this idea; but, as it would have been compromising her dignity to have said so under existing circumstances, she merely enquired, with much sharpness, why such an obvious suggestion had not presented itself to her husband's mind before? Mr Sowerberry rightly construed this as an acquiescence in his proposition. It was speedily determined, therefore, that Oliver should be at once initiated into the mysteries of the trade; and with this view, that he should accompany his master on the very next occasion of his services being required.

The occasion was not long in coming. Half an hour after breakfast next morning, Mr Bumble entered the shop; and supporting his cane against the counter, drew forth his large leathern pocket-book, from which he selected a small scrap of paper, which he handed over to Sowerberry.

'Aha!' said the undertaker, glancing over it with a lively countenance; 'an order for a coffin, eh?'

'For a coffin first, and a porochial funeral afterwards,' replied Mr Bumble, fastening the strap of the leathern pocket-book, which, like himself, was very corpulent.

'Bayton,' said the undertaker, looking from the scrap of paper to Mr Bumble. 'I never heard the name before.'

Bumble shook his head, as he replied, 'Obstinate people, Mr Sowerberry; very obstinate. Proud, too, I'm afraid, sir.'

'Proud, eh!' exclaimed Mr Sowerberry, with a sneer. 'Come, that's too much.'

'Oh, it's sickening,' replied the beadle. 'Antimonial, Mr Sowerberry!'

'So it is,' acquiesced the undertaker.

'We only heard of the family the night before last,' said the beadle; 'and we shouldn't have known anything about them then, only a woman who lodges in the same house made an application to the parochial committee for them to send the parochial surgeon to see a woman as was very bad. He had gone out to dinner; but his 'prentice (which is a very clever lad) sent 'em some medicine in a blacking-bottle, offhand.'

'Ah, there's promptness,' said the undertaker.

'Promptness, indeed!' replied the beadle. 'But what's the consequence; what's the ungrateful behaviour of these rebels, sir? Why, the husband sends back word that the medicine won't suit his wife's complaint, and so she shan't take it – says she shan't take it, sir! Good, strong, wholesome medicine, as was given with great success to two Irish labourers, and a coalheaver, only a week before – sent 'em for nothing with a blacking-bottle in – and he sends back word that she shan't take it, sir!'

As the atrocity presented itself to Mr Bumble's mind in full force, he struck the counter sharply with his cane, and became flushed with indignation.

'Well,' said the undertaker, 'I ne – ver – did – '

'Never did, sir!' ejaculated the beadle. 'No, nor nobody never did. But, now she's dead, we've got to bury her; and that's the direction; and the sooner it's done the better.'

Thus saying, Mr Bumble put on his cocked hat wrong side first, in a fever of parochial excitement, and flounced out of the shop.

'Why, he was so angry, Oliver, that he forgot even to ask after you!' said Mr Sowerberry, looking after the beadle as he strode down the street.

'Yes, sir,' replied Oliver, who had carefully kept himself out of sight during the interview, and who was shaking from head to foot at the mere recollection of the sound of Mr Bumble's voice. He needn't have taken the trouble to shrink from Mr Bumble's glance, however; for that functionary, on whom the prediction of the gentleman in the white waistcoat had made a very strong impression, thought that now the undertaker had got Oliver upon trial the subject was better avoided, until such time as he should be firmly bound for seven years, and all danger of his being returned upon the hands of the parish should be thus effectually and legally overcome.

'Well,' said Mr Sowerberry, taking up his hat, 'the sooner this job is done the better. Noah, look after the shop. Oliver, put on your cap, and come with me.' Oliver obeyed, and followed his master on his professional mission.

They walked on for some time, through the most crowded and densely inhabited part of the town; and then, striking down a narrow street more dirty and miserable than any they had yet passed through, paused to look for the house which was the object of their search. The houses on either side were high and large, but very old, and tenanted by people of the poorest class: as their neglected appearance would have sufficiently denoted, without the concurrent testimony afforded by the squalid looks of the few men and women who, with folded arms and bodies half-doubled, occasionally skulked along. A great many of the tenements had shop fronts; but these were fast closed, and mouldering away, only the upper rooms being inhabited. Some houses which had become insecure from age and decay were prevented from falling into the street, by huge beams of wood reared against the walls, and firmly planted in the road; but even these crazy dens seemed to have been selected as the nightly haunts of some houseless wretches, for many of the rough boards, which supplied the place of door and window, were wrenched from their positions, to afford an aperture wide enough for the passage of a human body. The kennel was stagnant and filthy. The very rats, which here and there lay putrefying in its rottenness, were hideous with famine.

There was neither knocker nor bell-handle at the open door where Oliver and his master stopped; so, groping his way cautiously through the dark passage, and bidding Oliver keep close to him and not be afraid, the undertaker mounted to the top of the first flight of stairs. Stumbling against a door on the landing, he rapped at it with his knuckles.

It was opened by a young girl of thirteen or fourteen. The undertaker at once saw enough of what the room contained to know it was the apartment to which he had been directed. He stepped in, and Oliver followed him.

There was no fire in the room; but a man was crouching, mechanically, over the empty stove. An old woman, too, had drawn a low stool to the cold hearth, and was sitting beside him. There were some ragged children in another corner; and in a small recess, opposite the door, there lay upon the ground something covered with an old blanket. Oliver shuddered as he cast his eyes towards the place, and crept involuntarily close to his master; for though it was covered up, the boy felt that it was a corpse.

The man's face was thin and very pale; his hair and beard were grizzly; and his eyes were bloodshot. The old woman's face was wrinkled; her two remaining teeth protruded over her under lip; and her eyes were bright and piercing. Oliver was afraid to look at either her or the man. They seemed so like the rats he had seen outside.

'Nobody shall go near her,' said the man, starting fiercely up, as the undertaker approached the recess. 'Keep back! damn you, keep back, if you've a life to lose!'

'Nonsense, my good man,' said the undertaker, who was pretty well used to misery in all its shapes. 'Nonsense!'

'I tell you,' said the man, clenching his hands, and stamping furiously on the floor – 'I tell you I won't have her put into the ground. She couldn't rest there. The worms would worry her – not eat her – she is so worn away.'

The undertaker offered no reply to this raving; but, producing a tape from his pocket, knelt down for a moment by the side of the body.

'Ah!' said the man, bursting into tears, and sinking on his knees at the feet of the dead woman; 'kneel down, kneel down, kneel round her, every one of you, and mark my words! I say she was starved to death. I never knew how bad she was till the fever came upon her; and then her bones were starting through the skin. There was neither fire nor candle; she died in the dark – in the dark! She couldn't even see her children's faces, though we heard her gasping out their names. I begged for her in the streets; and they sent me to prison. When I came back, she was dying; and all the blood in my heart has dried up, for they starved her to death. I swear it before the God that saw it. They starved her!' He twined his hands in his hair, and, with a loud scream, rolled grovelling upon the floor, his eyes fixed, and the foam gushing from his lips.

The terrified children cried bitterly; but the old woman, who had hitherto remained as quiet as if she had been wholly deaf to all that passed, menaced them into silence. Having unloosed the cravat of the man, who still remained extended on the ground, she tottered towards the undertaker.

'She was my daughter,' said the old woman, nodding her head in the direction of the corpse; and speaking with an idiotic leer, more ghastly than even the presence of death in such a place. 'Lord, Lord! Well, it *is* strange that I who gave birth to her, and was a woman then, should be alive and merry now, and she lying there, so cold and stiff! Lord, Lord! – to think of it; it's as good as a play – as good as a play!' As the wretched creature mumbled and chuckled in her hideous merriment, the undertaker turned to go away.

'Stop, stop!' said the old woman in a loud whisper, 'Will she be buried tomorrow, or next day, or tonight? I laid her out; and I must walk, you know. Send me a large cloak – a good warm one, for it is bitter cold. We should have cake and wine, too, before we go! Never mind; send some bread – only a loaf of bread and a cup of water. Shall we have some bread, dear?' she said eagerly, catching at the undertaker's coat, as he once more moved towards the door.

'Yes, yes,' said the undertaker, 'of course. Anything, everything.' He disengaged himself from the old woman's grasp, and, drawing Oliver after him, hurried away.

The next day (the family having been meanwhile relieved with a half-quartern loaf and a piece of cheese, left with them by Mr Bumble himself) Oliver and his master returned to the miserable abode, where Mr Bumble had already arrived, accompanied by four men from the workhouse, who were to act as bearers. An old black cloak had been thrown over the rags of the old woman and the man; and the bare coffin, having been screwed down, was hoisted on the shoulders of the bearers and carried into the street.

'Now, you must put your best leg foremost, old lady!' whispered Sowerberry in the old woman's ear; 'we are rather late, and it won't do to keep the clergyman waiting. Move on, my men – as quick as you like!'

Thus directed, the bearers trotted on under their light burden; and the two mourners kept as near them as they could. Mr Bumble and Sowerberry walked at a good smart pace in front; and Oliver, whose legs were not so long as his master's, ran by the side.

There was not so great a necessity for hurrying as Mr Sowerberry had anticipated, however; for when they had reached the obscure corner of the churchyard in which the nettles grew, and where the parish graves were made, the clergyman had not arrived; and the clerk, who was sitting by the vestry-room fire, seemed to think it by no means improbable that it might be an hour or so before he came. So they put the bier on the brink of the grave; and the two mourners waited patiently in the damp clay, with a cold rain drizzling down, while the ragged boys, whom the spectacle had attracted into the churchyard, played a noisy game at hide-and-seek among the tombstones, or varied their amusements by jumping backwards and forwards over the coffin. Mr Sowerberry and Bumble, being personal friends of the clerk, sat by the fire with him, and read the paper.

At length, after the lapse of something more than an hour, Mr Bumble, and Sowerberry, and the clerk, were seen running towards the grave. Immediately afterwards the clergyman appeared, putting on his surplice as he came along. Mr Bumble then thrashed a boy or two, to keep up appearances; and the reverend gentleman, having read as much of the burial service as could be compressed into four minutes, gave his surplice to the clerk, and walked away again.

'Now, Bill!' said Sowerberry to the grave-digger, 'fill up!'

It was no very difficult task, for the grave was so full that the uppermost coffin was within a few feet of the surface. The grave-digger shovelled in the earth; stamped it loosely down with his feet; shouldered his spade; and walked off, followed by the boys, who murmured very loud complaints at the fun being over so soon.

'Come, my good fellow!' said Bumble, tapping the man on the back. 'They want to shut up the yard.'

The man, who had never once moved since he had taken his station by the graveside, started, raised his head, stared at the person who had addressed him, walked forward for a few paces, and fell down in a swoon. The crazy old woman was too much occupied in bewailing the loss of her cloak (which the undertaker had taken off) to pay him any attention, so they threw a can of cold water over him, and when he came to, saw him safely out of the churchyard, locked the gate, and departed on their different ways.

'Well, Oliver,' said Sowerberry, as they walked home, 'how do you like it?'

'Pretty well, thank you, sir,' replied Oliver, with considerable hesitation. 'Not very much, sir.'

'Ah, you'll get used to it in time, Oliver,' said Sowerberry. 'Nothing when you *are* used to it, my boy.'

Oliver wondered, in his own mind, whether it had taken a very long time to get Mr Sowerberry used to it. But he thought it better not to ask the question; and walked back to the shop, thinking over all he had seen and heard.

CHAPTER 6

Oliver, being goaded by the taunts of Noah, rouses into action and rather astonishes him

The month's trial over, Oliver was formally apprenticed. It was a nice sickly season just at this time. In commercial phrase, coffins were looking up; and in the course of a few weeks, Oliver had acquired a great deal of experience. The success of Mr Sowerberry's ingenious speculation exceeded even his most sanguine hopes. The oldest inhabitants recollected no period at which measles had been so prevalent, or so fatal to infant existence; and many were the mournful processions which little Oliver headed, in a hat-band reaching down to his knees, to the indescribable admiration and emotion of all the mothers in the town. As Oliver accompanied his master in most of his adult expeditions, too, in order that he might acquire that equanimity of demeanour and full command of nerve which are so essential to a finished undertaker, he had many opportunities of observing the beautiful resignation and fortitude with which some strong-minded people bear their trials and losses.

For instance: when Sowerberry had an order for the burial of some rich old lady or gentleman, who was surrounded by a great number of nephews and nieces, who had been perfectly inconsolable during the previous illness, and whose grief had been wholly irrepressible even on the most public occasions, they would be as happy among themselves as need be – quite cheerful and contented; conversing together with as much freedom and gaiety as if nothing whatever had happened to disturb them. Husbands, too, bore the loss of their wives with the most heroic calmness. Wives, again, put on weeds for their husbands, as if, so far from grieving in the garb of sorrow, they had made up their minds to render it as becoming and attractive as possible. It was observable, too, that ladies and gentlemen who were in passions of anguish during the ceremony of interment, recovered almost as soon as they reached home, and became quite composed before the tea-drinking was over. All this was very pleasant and improving to see; and Oliver beheld it with great admiration.

That Oliver Twist was moved to resignation by the example of these good people, I cannot, although I am his biographer, undertake to affirm with any degree of confidence; but I can most distinctly say, that for many months he continued meekly to submit to the domination and ill-treatment of Noah Claypole, who used him far worse than before, now that his jealousy was roused by seeing the new boy promoted to the black stick and hat-band, while he, the old one, remained stationary in the muffin-cap and leathers. Charlotte treated him badly, because Noah did; and Mrs Sowerberry was his decided enemy because Mr Sowerberry was disposed to be his friend; so, between these three on one side, and a glut of funerals on the other, Oliver was not altogether as comfortable as the hungry pig was, when he was shut up, by mistake, in the grain department of a brewery.

And now I come to a very important passage in Oliver's history; for I have to record an act, slight and unimportant perhaps in appearance, but which indirectly produced a most material change in all his future prospects and proceedings.

One day Oliver and Noah had descended into the kitchen at the usual dinner-hour, to banquet upon a small joint of mutton – a pound and a half of the worst end of the neck – when Charlotte being called out of the way, there ensued a brief interval of time, which Noah Claypole, being hungry and vicious, considered he could not possibly devote to a worthier purpose than aggravating and tantalising young Oliver Twist.

Intent upon this innocent amusement, Noah put his feet on the tablecloth; and pulled Oliver's hair; and twitched his ears; and expressed his opinion that he was a 'sneak;' and furthermore announced his intention of coming to see him hanged, whenever that desirable event should take place; and entered upon various other topics of petty annoyance, like a malicious and ill-conditioned charity-boy as he was. But, none of these taunts producing the desired effect of making Oliver cry, Noah attempted to be more facetious still; and in this attempt did what many small wits, with far greater reputations than Noah, sometimes do to this day, when they want to be funny – he got rather personal.

'Work'us,' said Noah, 'how's your mother?'

'She's dead,' replied Oliver; 'don't you say anything about her to me!'

Oliver's colour rose as he said this; he breathed quickly; and there was a curious working of the mouth and nostrils, which Mr Claypole thought must be the immediate precursor of a violent fit of crying. Under this impression he returned to the charge.

'What did she die of, Work'us?' said Noah.

'Of a broken heart, some of our old nurses told me,' replied Oliver, more as if he were talking to himself than answering Noah. 'I think I know what it must be to die of that!'

'Tol de rol lol lol, right fol lairy, Work'us,' said Noah, as a tear rolled down Oliver's cheek. 'What's set you a snivelling now?'

'Not *you*,' replied Oliver, hastily brushing the tear away. 'Don't think it.'

'Oh, not me, eh?' sneered Noah.

'No, not you,' replied Oliver, sharply. 'There; that's enough. Don't say anything more to me about her; you'd better not!'

'Better not!' exclaimed Noah. 'Well! Better not! Work'us, don't be impudent. *Your* mother, too! She was a nice 'un, she was. Oh, Lor!' And here Noah nodded his head expressively, and curled up as much of his small red nose as muscular action could collect together for the occasion.

'Yer know, Work'us,' continued Noah, emboldened by Oliver's silence, and speaking in a jeering tone of affected pity – of all tones the most annoying – 'yer know, Work'us, it can't be helped now; and of course yer couldn't help it then: and I'm very sorry for it; and I'm sure we all are, and pity yer very much. But yer must know, Work'us, yer mother was a regular right-down bad 'un.'

'What did you say?' enquired Oliver, looking up very quickly.

'A regular right-down bad 'un, Work'us,' replied Noah, coolly. 'And it's a great deal better, Work'us, that she died when she did, or else she'd have been hard labouring in Bridewell, or transported, or hung; which is more likely than either, isn't it?'

Crimson with fury, Oliver started up; overthrew the chair and table; seized Noah by the throat; shook him in the violence of his rage, till his teeth chattered in his head; and, collecting his whole force into one heavy blow, felled him to the ground.

A minute ago the boy had looked the quiet, mild, dejected creature that harsh treatment had made him. But his spirit was roused at last; the cruel insult to his dead mother had set his blood on fire. His breast heaved; his attitude was erect; his eye bright and vivid; his whole person changed, as he stood glaring over the cowardly tormentor who now lay crouching at his feet, and defied him with an energy he had never known before.

'He'll murder me!' blubbered Noah. 'Charlotte! missis! Here's the new boy a-murdering of me! Help! help! Oliver's gone mad! Charlotte!'

Noah's shouts were responded to by a loud scream from Charlotte, and a louder from Mrs Sowerberry; the former of whom rushed into the kitchen by a side door, while the latter paused on the staircase till she was quite certain that it was consistent with the preservation of human life to come farther down.

'Oh, you little wretch!' screamed Charlotte, seizing Oliver with her utmost force, which was about equal to that of a moderately strong man in particularly good training. 'Oh, you little un-grate-ful, mur-de-rous, hor-rid vil-lain!' And between every syllable, Charlotte gave Oliver a blow with all her might, accompanying it with a scream, for the benefit of society.

Charlotte's fist was by no means a light one; but, lest it should not be effectual in calming Oliver's wrath, Mrs Sowerberry plunged into the kitchen, and assisted to hold him with one hand while she scratched his face with the other. In this favourable position of affairs Noah rose from the ground and pommelled him behind.

This was rather too violent exercise to last long. When they were all three wearied out, and could tear and beat no longer, they dragged Oliver, struggling and shouting but nothing daunted, into the dust-cellar, and there locked him up. This being done, Mrs Sowerberry sunk into a chair and burst into tears.

'Bless her, she's going off!' said Charlotte. 'A glass of water, Noah, dear. Make haste!'

'Oh, Charlotte,' said Mrs Sowerberry, speaking as well as she could, through a deficiency of breath, and a sufficiency of cold water, which Noah had poured over her head and shoulders. 'Oh! Charlotte, what a mercy we have not all been murdered in our beds!'

'Ah! mercy indeed, ma'am,' was the reply. 'I only hope this'll teach master not to have any more of these dreadful creatures, that are born to be murderers and robbers from their very cradle. Poor Noah! He was all but killed, ma'am, when I came in.'

'Poor fellow!' said Mrs Sowerberry, looking piteously on the charity-boy.

Noah, whose top waistcoat-button might have been somewhere on a level with the crown of Oliver's head, rubbed his eyes with the inside of his wrists while this commiseration was bestowed upon him, and performed some affecting tears and sniffs.

'What's to be done?' exclaimed Mrs Sowerberry. 'Your master's not at home; there's not a man in the house; and he'll kick that door down in ten minutes.' Oliver's vigorous plunges against the bit of timber in question rendered this occurrence highly probable.

Oliver plucks up a spirit

'Dear, dear! I don't know, ma'am,' said Charlotte, 'unless we send for the police-officers.'

'Or the millingtary,' suggested Mr Claypole.

'No, no,' said Mrs Sowerberry, bethinking herself of Oliver's old friend. 'Run to Mr Bumble, Noah, and tell him to come here directly, and not to lose a minute; never mind your cap! Make haste! You can hold a knife to that black eye as you run along, and it'll keep the swelling down.'

Noah stopped to make no reply, but started off at his fullest speed; and very much it astonished the people who were out walking, to see the charity-boy tearing through the streets pell-mell, with no cap on his head, and a clasp-knife at his eye.

CHAPTER 7

Oliver continues refractory

Noah Claypole ran along the streets at his swiftest pace, and paused not once for breath, until he reached the workhouse gate. Having rested here for a minute or so, to collect a good burst of sobs and an imposing show of tears and terror, he knocked loudly at the wicket; and presented such a rueful face to the aged pauper who opened it, that even he, who saw nothing but rueful faces about him at the best of times, started back in astonishment.

'Why, what's the matter with the boy?' said the old pauper.

'Mr Bumble! Mr Bumble!' cried Noah, with well-affected dismay, and in tones so loud and agitated that they not only caught the ear of Mr Bumble himself, who happened to be hard by, but alarmed him so much that he rushed into the yard without his cocked hat – which is a very curious and remarkable circumstance, as showing that even a beadle, acted upon by a sudden and powerful impulse, may be afflicted with a momentary visitation of loss of self-possession and forgetfulness of personal dignity.

'Oh, Mr Bumble, sir!' said Noah, 'Oliver, sir – Oliver has – '

'What? What?' interposed Mr Bumble, with a gleam of pleasure in his metallic eyes. 'Not run away; he hasn't run away, has he, Noah?'

'No, sir, no. Not run away, sir, but he's turned wicious,' replied Noah. 'He tried to murder me, sir; and then he tried to murder Charlotte; and then missis. Oh! what dreadful pain it is! Such agony, please, sir!' And here Noah writhed and twisted his body into an extensive variety of eel-like positions; thereby giving Mr Bumble to understand that, from the violent and sanguinary onset of Oliver Twist, he had sustained severe internal injury and damage, from which he was, at that moment, suffering the acutest torture.

When Noah saw that the intelligence he communicated perfectly paralysed Mr Bumble, he imparted additional effect thereunto by bewailing his dreadful wounds ten times louder than before; and, when he observed a gentleman in a white waistcoat crossing the yard, he was more tragic in his lamentations than ever, rightly conceiving it highly expedient to attract the notice and rouse the indignation of the gentleman aforesaid.

The gentleman's notice was very soon attracted; for he had not walked three paces, when he turned angrily round, and enquired what that young cur was howling for, and why Mr Bumble did not favour him with something which would render the series of vocular exclamations so designated, an involuntary process.

'It's a poor boy from the free-school, sir,' replied Mr Bumble, 'who has been nearly murdered – all but murdered, sir – by young Twist.'

'By Jove!' exclaimed the gentleman in the white waistcoat, stopping short. 'I knew it! I felt a strange presentiment for the very first, that that audacious young savage would come to be hung!'

'He has likewise attempted, sir, to murder the female servant,' said Mr Bumble, with a face of ashy paleness.

'And his missis,' interposed Mr Claypole.

'And his master, too, I think you said, Noah?' added Mr Bumble.

'No; he's out, or he would have murdered him,' replied Noah. 'He said he wanted to.'

'Ah! Said he wanted to: did he, my boy?' enquired the gentleman in the white waistcoat.

'Yes, sir,' replied Noah. 'And please, sir, missis wants to know whether Mr Bumble can spare time to step up there, directly, and flog him – 'cause master's out.'

'Certainly, my boy; certainly,' said the gentleman in the white waistcoat, smiling benignly, and patting Noah's head, which was about three inches higher than his own. 'You're a good boy – a very good boy. Here's a penny for you. Bumble, just step up to Sowerberry's with your cane, and see what's best to be done. Don't spare him, Bumble.'

'No, I will not, sir,' replied the beadle, adjusting the wax-end which was twisted round the bottom of his cane for purposes of parochial flagellation.

'Tell Sowerberry not to spare him either. They'll never do anything with him without stripes and bruises,' said the gentleman in the white waistcoat.

'I'll take care, sir,' replied the beadle. And the cocked hat and cane having been by this time adjusted to their owner's satisfaction, Mr Bumble and Noah Claypole betook themselves with all speed to the undertaker's shop.

Here the position of affairs had not at all improved, as Sowerberry had not yet returned, and Oliver continued to kick, with undiminished vigour, at the cellar-door. The accounts of his ferocity, as related by Mrs Sowerberry and Charlotte, were of so startling a nature, that Mr Bumble judged it prudent to parley before opening the door. With this view he gave a kick at the outside, by way of prelude; and then applying his mouth to the keyhole, said, in a deep and impressive tone, 'Oliver!'

'Come; you let me out!' replied Oliver from the inside.

'Do you know this here voice, Oliver?' said Mr Bumble.

'Yes,' replied Oliver.

'Ain't you afraid of it, sir? Ain't you a-trembling while I speak, sir?' said Mr Bumble.

'No!' replied Oliver, boldly.

An answer so different from the one he had expected to elicit, and was in the habit of receiving, staggered Mr Bumble not a little. He stepped back from the keyhole; drew himself up to his full height; and looked from one to another of the three bystanders, in mute astonishment.

'Oh, you know, Mr Bumble, he must be mad,' said Mrs Sowerberry. 'No boy in half his senses could venture to speak so to you.'

'It's not madness, ma'am,' replied Mr Bumble, after a few moments of deep meditation. 'It's meat.'

'What?' exclaimed Mrs Sowerberry.

'Meat, ma'am, meat,' replied Bumble, with stern emphasis. 'You've overfed him, ma'am. You've raised a artificial soul and spirit in him, ma'am, unbecoming a person of his condition; as the board, Mrs Sowerberry, who are practical philosophers, will tell you. What have paupers to do with soul or spirit? It's quite enough that we let 'em have live bodies. If you had kept the boy on gruel, ma'am, this would never have happened.'

'Dear, dear!' ejaculated Mrs Sowerberry, piously raising her eyes to the kitchen ceiling, 'this comes of being liberal!'

The liberality of Mrs Sowerberry to Oliver had consisted in a profuse bestowal upon him of all the dirty odds and ends which nobody else would eat; so there was a great deal of meekness and self-devotion in her voluntary remaining under Mr Bumble's heavy accusation, of which, to do her justice, she was wholly innocent, in thought, word or deed.

'Ah!' said Mr Bumble, when the lady brought her eyes down to earth again, 'the only thing that can be done now, that I know of, is to leave him in the cellar for a day or so till he's a little starved down; and then to take him out, and keep him on gruel all through his apprenticeship. He comes of a bad family. Excitable natures, Mrs Sowerberry! Both the nurse and doctor said that that mother of his made her way here against difficulties and pain that would have killed any well-disposed woman weeks before.'

At this point of Mr Bumble's discourse, Oliver, just hearing enough to know that some further allusion was being made to his mother, recommenced kicking with a violence that rendered every other sound inaudible. Sowerberry returned at this juncture; and Oliver's offence having been explained to him, with such exaggerations as the ladies thought best calculated to rouse his ire, he unlocked the cellar-door in a twinkling, and dragged his rebellious apprentice out by the collar.

Oliver's clothes had been torn in the beating he had received; his face was bruised and scratched; and his hair scattered over his forehead. The angry flush had not disappeared, however, and when he was pulled out of his prison, he scowled boldly on Noah, and looked quite undismayed.

'Now, you are a nice young fellow, ain't you?' said Sowerberry, giving Oliver a shake, and a box on the ear.

'He called my mother names,' replied Oliver.

'Well, and what if he did, you little ungrateful wretch?' said Mrs Sowerberry. 'She deserved what he said, and worse.'

'She didn't,' said Oliver.

'She did,' said Mrs Sowerberry.

'It's a lie!' said Oliver.

Mrs Sowerberry burst into a flood of tears.

This flood of tears left Mr Sowerberry no alternative. If he had hesitated for one instant to punish Oliver most severely, it must be quite clear to every experienced reader that he would have been, according to all precedents in disputes of matrimony established, a brute, an unnatural husband, an insulting creature, a base imitation of a man, and various other agreeable characters too numerous for recital within the limits of this chapter. To do him justice, he was, as far as his power went – it was not very extensive – kindly disposed towards the boy; perhaps because it was his interest to be so, perhaps because his wife disliked him. The flood of tears, however, left him no resource; so he at once gave him a drubbing, which satisfied even Mrs Sowerberry herself, and rendered Mr Bumble's subsequent application of the parochial cane rather unnecessary. For the rest of the day he was shut up in the back kitchen, in company with a pump and a slice of bread; and, at night, Mrs Sowerberry, after making various remarks outside the door, by no means complimentary to the memory of his mother, looked into the room, and, amidst the jeers and pointings of Noah and Charlotte, ordered him upstairs to his dismal bed.

It was not until he was left alone in the silence and stillness of the gloomy workshop of the undertaker that Oliver gave way to the feelings which the day's treatment may be supposed likely to have awakened in a mere child. He had listened to their taunts with a look of contempt; he had borne the lash without a cry: for he felt that pride swelling in his heart which would have kept down a shriek to the last, though they had roasted him alive. But now, when there were none to see or hear him, he fell upon his knees on the floor, and, hiding his face in his hands, wept such tears as, God send for the credit of our nature, few so young may ever have cause to pour out before Him!

For a long time Oliver remained motionless in this attitude. The candle was burning low in the socket when he rose to his feet. Having gazed cautiously round him, and listened intently, he gently undid the fastenings of the door and looked abroad.

It was a cold, dark night. The stars seemed, to the boy's eyes, farther from the earth than he had ever seen them before; there was no wind; and the sombre shadows thrown by the trees upon the ground looked sepulchral and death-like, from being so still. He softly reclosed the door; and having availed himself of the expiring light of the candle to tie up in a handkerchief the few articles of wearing apparel he had, sat himself down upon a bench to wait for morning.

With the first ray of light that struggled through the crevices in the shutters, Oliver rose, and again unbarred the door. One timid look around – one moment's pause of hesitation – he had closed it behind him, and was in the open street.

He looked to the right and to the left, uncertain whither to fly. He remembered to have seen the wagons, as they went out, toiling up the hill. He took the same route; and arriving at the footpath across the fields, which he knew, after some distance, led out again into the road, struck into it, and walked quickly on.

Along this same footpath Oliver well remembered he had trotted beside Mr Bumble, when he first carried him to the workhouse from the farm. His way lay directly in front of the cottage. His heart beat quickly when he bethought himself of this, and he half resolved to turn back. He had come a long way though, and should lose a great deal of time by doing so. Besides, it was so early that there was very little fear of his being seen; so he walked on.

He reached the house. There was no appearance of its inmates stirring at that early hour. Oliver stopped, and peeped into the garden. A child was weeding one of the little beds; and as he stopped, he raised his pale face, and disclosed the features of one of his former companions. Oliver felt glad to see him before he went; for, though younger than himself, he had been his little friend and playmate. They had been beaten and starved, and shut up together, many and many a time.

'Hush, Dick!' said Oliver, as the boy ran to the gate and thrust his thin arm between the rails to greet him. 'Is anyone up?'

'Nobody but me,' replied the child.

'You mustn't say you saw me, Dick,' said Oliver. 'I am running away. They beat and ill-use me, Dick; and I am going to seek my fortune some long way off. I don't know where. How pale you are!'

'I heard the doctor tell them I was dying,' replied the child, with a faint smile. 'I am very glad to see you, dear; but don't stop, don't stop!'

'Yes, yes, I will, to say goodbye to you,' replied Oliver. 'I shall see you again, Dick. I know I shall. You will be well and happy.'

'I hope so,' replied the child. 'After I am dead, but not before. I know the doctor must be right, Oliver, because I dream so much of Heaven, and Angels, and kind faces that I never see when I am awake. Kiss me,' said the child, climbing up the low gate, and flinging his little arms round Oliver's neck. 'Goodbye, dear! God bless you!'

The blessing was from a young child's lips, but it was the first that Oliver had ever heard invoked upon his head; and through all the struggles and sufferings, and troubles and changes, of his after life, he never once forgot it.

CHAPTER 8

Oliver walks to London. He encounters on the road a strange sort of young gentleman

Oliver reached the stile at which the footpath terminated, and once more gained the highroad. It was eight o'clock now. Though he was nearly five miles away from the town, he ran and hid behind hedges, by turns, till noon, fearing that he might be pursued and overtaken. Then he sat down to rest by the side of a milestone, and began to think, for the first time, where he had better go and try to live.

The stone by which he was seated bore, in large characters, an intimation that it was just seventy miles from that spot to London. The name awakened a new train of ideas in the boy's mind. London! – that great large place! – nobody, not even Mr Bumble, could ever find him there. He had often heard the old

men in the workhouse, too, say that no lad of spirit need want in London; and that there were ways of living in that vast city which those who had been bred up in country parts had no idea of. It was the very place for a homeless boy, who must die in the streets unless someone helped him. As these things passed through his thoughts, he jumped upon his feet, and again walked forward.

He had diminished the distance between himself and London by full four miles more, before he recollected how much he must undergo ere he could hope to reach his place of destination. As this consideration forced itself upon him, he slackened his pace a little, and meditated upon his means of getting there. He had a crust of bread, a coarse shirt, and two pairs of stockings in his bundle. He had a penny too – a gift of Sowerberry's, after some funeral in which he had acquitted himself more than ordinarily well – in his pocket. 'A clean shirt,' thought Oliver, 'is a very comfortable thing, very; and so are two pairs of darned stockings; and so is a penny: but they are small helps to a sixty-five miles' walk in winter time.' But Oliver's thoughts, like those of most other people, although they were extremely ready and active to point out his difficulties, were wholly at a loss to suggest any feasible mode of surmounting them; so after a good deal of thinking to no particular purpose, he changed his little bundle over to the other shoulder, and trudged on.

Oliver walked twenty miles that day, and all that time tasted nothing but the crust of dry bread, and a few draughts of water which he begged at the cottage-doors by the roadside. When the night came he turned into a meadow, and, creeping close under a hayrick, determined to lie there till morning. He felt frightened at first; for the wind moaned dismally over the empty fields, and he was cold and hungry, and more alone than he had ever felt before. Being very tired with his walk, however, he soon fell asleep, and forgot his troubles.

He felt cold and stiff when he got up next morning, and so hungry that he was obliged to exchange the penny for a small loaf, in the very first village through which he passed. He had walked no more than twelve miles when night closed in again; for his feet were sore, and his legs so weak that they trembled beneath him. Another night passed in the bleak damp air made him worse, and when he set forward on his journey next morning he could hardly crawl along.

He waited at the bottom of a steep hill till a stage-coach came up, and then begged of the outside passengers. But there were very few who took any notice of him; and even those told him to wait till they got to the top of the hill, and then let them see how far he could run for a halfpenny. Poor Oliver tried to keep up with the coach a little way, but was unable to do it, by reason of his fatigue and sore feet. When the outsides saw this, they put their halfpence back into their pockets again, declaring that he was an idle young dog, and didn't deserve anything; and the coach rattled away, and left only a cloud of dust behind.

In some villages large painted boards were fixed up, warning all persons who begged within the district that they would be sent to jail. This frightened Oliver very much, and made him glad to get out of them with all possible expedition. In others, he would stand about the inn-yards, and look mournfully at everyone who passed; a proceeding which generally terminated in the landlady's ordering one of the post-boys who were lounging about to drive that strange boy out of the place, for she was sure he had come to steal something. If he begged at a farmer's house, ten to one but they threatened to set the dog on him; and when he showed his nose in a shop, they talked about the beadle, which brought Oliver's heart into his mouth – very often the only thing he had there for many hours together.

In fact, if it had not been for a good-hearted turnpike-man, and a benevolent old lady, Oliver's troubles would have been shortened by the very same process which put an end to his mother's: in other words, he would most assuredly have fallen dead upon the king's highway. But the turnpike-man gave him a meal of bread and cheese; and the old lady, who had a ship-wrecked grandson wandering barefooted in some distant part of the earth, took pity upon the poor orphan, and gave him what little she could afford – and more – with such kind and gentle words, and such tears of sympathy and compassion, that they sank deeper into Oliver's soul than all the sufferings he had ever undergone.

Early on the seventh morning after he had left his native place, Oliver limped slowly into the little town of Barnet. The window-shutters were closed; the street was empty; not a soul had awakened to the business of the day. The sun was rising in all its splendid beauty; but the light only served to show the boy his own lonesomeness and desolation, as he sat, with bleeding feet and covered with dust, upon a cold doorstep.

By degrees the shutters were opened; the window-blinds were drawn up; and people began passing to and fro. Some few stopped to gaze at Oliver for a moment or two, or turned round to stare at him as they hurried by; but none relieved him, or troubled themselves to enquire how he came there. He had no heart to beg. And there he sat.

He had been crouching on the step for some time, wondering at the great number of public-houses (every other house in Barnet was a tavern, large or small); gazing listlessly at the coaches as they passed through, and thinking how strange it seemed that they could do, with ease, in a few hours, what it had taken him a whole week of courage and determination beyond his years to accomplish; when he was roused by observing that a boy, who had passed him carelessly some minutes before, had returned, and was now surveying him most earnestly from the opposite side of the way. He took little heed of this at first; but the boy remained in the same attitude of close observation so long, that Oliver raised his head, and returned his steady look. Upon this, the boy crossed over, and, walking close up to Oliver, said, 'Hallo! my covey, what's the row?'

The boy who addressed this enquiry to the young wayfarer was about his own age, but one of the queerest-looking boys that Oliver had ever seen. He was a snub-nosed, flat-browed, common-faced boy enough, and as dirty a juvenile as one would wish to see; but he had about him all the airs and manners of a man. He was short of his age, with rather bow-legs, and little, sharp, ugly eyes. His hat was stuck on the top of his head so lightly, that it threatened to fall off every moment –

and would have done so very often, if the wearer had not had a knack of every now and then giving his head a sudden twitch, which brought it back to its old place again. He wore a man's coat, which reached nearly to his heels. He had turned the cuffs back, half way up his arm, to get his hands out of the sleeves, apparently with the ultimate view of thrusting them into the pockets of his corduroy trousers, for there he kept them. He was, altogether, as roistering and swaggering a young gentleman as ever stood four feet six, or something less, in his bluchers.

'Hallo, my covey, what's the row?' said this strange young gentleman to Oliver.

'I am very hungry and tired,' replied Oliver, the tears standing in his eyes as he spoke. 'I have walked a long way. I have been walking these seven days.'

'Walking for sivin days!' said the young gentleman. 'Oh, I see. Beak's order, eh? But,' he added, noticing Oliver's look of surprise, 'I suppose you don't know what a beak is, my flash com–pan–i–on.'

Oliver mildly replied that he had always heard a bird's mouth described by the term in question.

'My eyes, how green!' exclaimed the young gentleman. 'Why, a beak's a madgst'rate; and when you walk by a beak's order, it's not straight forerd, but always a-going up, and nivir a-coming down agin. Was you never on the mill?'

'What mill?' enquired Oliver.

'What mill! – why, *the* mill – the mill as takes up so little room that it'll work inside a Stone Jug; and always goes better when the wind's low with people than when it's high, acos then they can't get workmen. But come,' said the young gentleman; 'you want grub, and you shall have it. I'm at low-water-mark myself – only one bob and a magpie; but *as far as* it goes, I'll fork out and stump. Up with you on your pins. There! Now then! Morrice!'

Assisting Oliver to rise, the young gentleman took him to an adjacent chandler's shop, where he purchased a sufficiency of ready-dressed ham and a half-quartern loaf, or as he himself expressed it, 'a four-penny bran'; the ham being kept clean and preserved from dust by the ingenious expedient of making a hole in the loaf by pulling out a portion of the crumb, and stuffing it therein. Taking the bread under his arm, the young gentleman turned into a small public-house, and led the way to a tap-room in the rear of the premises. Here a pot of beer was brought in, by direction of the mysterious youth; and Oliver, falling to, at his new friend's bidding, made a long and hearty meal, during the progress of which the strange boy eyed him from time to time with great attention.

'Going to London?' said the strange boy, when Oliver had at length concluded.

'Yes.'

'Got any lodgings?'

'No.'

'Money?'

'No.'

The strange boy whistled; and put his arms into his pockets, as far as the big coat sleeves would let them go.

'Do you live in London?' enquired Oliver.

'Yes. I do, when I'm at home,' replied the boy. 'I suppose you want some place to sleep in tonight, don't you?'

'I do indeed,' answered Oliver. 'I have not slept under a roof since I left the country.'

'Don't fret your eyelids on that score,' said the young gentleman. 'I've got to be in London tonight; and I knows a 'spectable old genelman as lives there, wot'll give you lodgings for nothink, and never ask for the change – that is, if any genelman he knows interduces you. And don't he know me? Oh, no! Not in the least! By no means. Certainly not '

The young gentleman smiled, as if to intimate that the latter fragments of discourse were playfully ironical; and finished the beer as he did so.

This unexpected offer of shelter was too tempting to be resisted, especially as it was immediately followed up by the assurance that the old gentleman already referred to would doubtless provide Oliver with a comfortable place, without loss of time.

This led to a more friendly and confidential dialogue; from which Oliver discovered that his friend's name was Jack Dawkins, and that he was a peculiar pet and *protégé* of the elderly gentleman before mentioned.

Mr Dawkins's appearance did not say a vast deal in favour of the comforts which his patron's interest obtained for those whom he took under his protection; but, as he had a rather flighty and dissolute mode of conversing, and furthermore avowed that among his intimate friends he was better known by the *sobriquet* of 'The Artful Dodger,' Oliver concluded that, being of a dissipated and careless turn, the moral precepts of his benefactor had hitherto been thrown away upon him. Under this impression, he secretly resolved to cultivate the good opinion of the old gentleman as quickly as possible; and, if he found the Dodger incorrigible, as he more than half suspected he should, to decline the honour of his further acquaintance.

As John Dawkins objected to their entering London before nightfall, it was nearly eleven o'clock when they reached the turnpike at Islington. They crossed from the Angel into St John's Road, struck down the small street which terminates at Sadler's Wells Theatre; through Exmouth Street and Coppice Row; down the little court by the side of the workhouse; across the classic ground which once bore the name of Hockley-in-the-Hole; thence into Little Saffron Hill; and so into Saffron Hill the Great, along which the Dodger scudded at a rapid pace, directing Oliver to follow close at his heels.

Although Oliver had enough to occupy his attention in keeping sight of his leader, he could not help bestowing a few hasty glances on either side of the way as he passed along. A dirtier or more wretched place he had never seen. The street was very narrow and muddy, and the air was impregnated with filthy odours. There were a good many small shops; but the only stock in trade appeared to be heaps of children, who, even at that time of night, were crawling in and out at the doors, or screaming from the inside. The sole places that seemed to prosper, amid the general blight of the place, were the public-houses; and in them the lowest orders of Irish were wrangling with might and main. Covered ways and yards, which here and there diverged from the main street, disclosed little knots of houses, where drunken men and women were positively wallowing in the filth; and from several of the doorways great ill-looking fellows were cautiously emerging, bound, to all appearance, on no very well-disposed or harmless errands.

Oliver was just considering whether he hadn't better run away when they reached the bottom of the hill. His conductor, catching him by the arm, pushed open the door of a house near Field Lane, and drawing him into the passage, closed it behind them.

'Now, then!' cried a voice from below, in reply to a whistle from the Dodger.

'Plummy and slam!' was the reply.

This seemed to be some watchword or signal that all was right; for the light of a feeble candle gleamed on the wall at the remote end of the passage, and a man's face peeped out from where a balustrade of the old kitchen staircase had been broken away.

'There's two on you,' said the man, thrusting the candle farther out, and shading his eyes with his hand. 'Who's the t'other one?'

'A new pal,' replied Jack Dawkins, pulling Oliver forward.

'Where did he come from?'

'Greenland. Is Fagin upstairs?'

'Yes, he's a-sortin' the wipes. Up with you!' The candle was drawn back, and the face disappeared.

Oliver, groping his way with one hand, and having the other firmly grasped by his companion, ascended with much difficulty the dark and broken stairs, which his conductor mounted with an ease and expedition that showed he was well acquainted with them. He threw open the door of a back-room, and drew Oliver in after him.

The walls and ceiling of the room were perfectly black with age and dirt. There was a deal table before the fire; upon which were a candle, stuck in a ginger-beer bottle, two or three pewter pots, a loaf and butter, and a plate. In a frying-pan, which was on the fire, and which was secured to the mantelshelf by a string, some sausages were cooking; and standing over them, with a toasting-fork in his hand, was a very old shrivelled Jew, whose villainous-looking and repulsive face was obscured by a quantity of matted red hair. He was dressed in a greasy flannel gown, with his throat bare; and seemed to be dividing his attention between the frying-pan and a clothes-horse, over which a great number of silk handkerchiefs were hanging. Several rough beds, made of old sacks, were huddled side by side on the floor; and seated round the table were four or five boys, none older than the Dodger, smoking long clay pipes, and drinking spirits with the air of middle-aged men. These all crowded about their associate as he whispered a few words to the Jew, and then turned round and grinned at Oliver; as did the Jew himself, toasting-fork in hand.

'This is him, Fagin,' said Jack Dawkins; 'my friend, Oliver Twist.'

The Jew grinned, and, making a low obeisance to Oliver, took him by the hand, and hoped he should have the honour of his intimate acquaintance. Upon this the young gentlemen with the pipes came round him, and shook both his hands very hard, especially the one in which he held his little bundle. One young gentleman was very anxious to hang up his cap for him; and another was so obliging as to put his hands in his pockets, in order that, as he was very tired, he might not have the trouble of emptying them himself when he went to bed. These civilities would probably have been extended much further, but for a liberal exercise of the Jew's toasting-fork on the heads and shoulders of the affectionate youths who offered them.

'We are very glad to see you, Oliver – very,' said the Jew. 'Dodger, take off the sausages, and draw a tub near the fire for Oliver. Ah, you're a-staring at the pocket-handkerchiefs! eh, my dear? There are a good many of 'em, ain't there? We've just looked 'em out, ready for the wash; that's all, Oliver – that's all. Ha! ha! ha!'

The latter part of this speech was hailed by a boisterous shout from all the hopeful pupils of the merry old gentleman. In the midst of which they went to supper.

Oliver ate his share, and the Jew then mixed him a glass of hot gin and water; telling him he must drink it off directly, because another gentleman wanted the tumbler. Oliver did as he was desired. Immediately afterwards he felt himself gently lifted on to one of the sacks, and then he sank into a deep sleep.

Oliver introduced to the respectable old gentleman

CHAPTER 9

Containing further particulars concerning the pleasant old gentleman and his hopeful pupils

It was late next morning when Oliver awoke from a sound long sleep. There was no other person in the room but the old Jew, who was boiling some coffee in a saucepan for breakfast, and whistling softly to himself as he stirred it round and round with an iron spoon. He would stop every now and then to listen, when there was the least noise below; and, when he had satisfied himself, he would go on, whistling and stirring again, as before.

Although Oliver had roused himself from sleep, he was not thoroughly awake. There is a drowsy state, between sleeping and waking, when you dream more in five minutes with your eyes half open, and yourself half conscious of everything that is passing around you, than you would in five nights with your eyes fast closed, and your senses wrapt in perfect unconsciousness. At such times, a mortal knows just enough of what his mind is doing to form some glimmering conception of its mighty powers, its bounding from earth and spurning time and space, when freed from the restraint of its corporeal associate.

Oliver was precisely in this condition. He saw the Jew with his half-closed eyes, heard his low whistling, and recognised the sound of the spoon grating against the saucepan's sides; and yet the selfsame senses were mentally engaged, at the same time, in busy action with almost everybody he had ever known.

When the coffee was done, the Jew drew the saucepan to the hob; and, standing in an irresolute attitude for a few minutes, as if he did not well know how to employ himself, turned round and looked at Oliver, and called him by his name. He did not answer, and was to all appearance asleep.

After satisfying himself upon this head, the Jew stepped gently to the door, which he fastened. He then drew forth, as it seemed to Oliver, from some trap in the floor, a small box, which he placed carefully on the table. His eyes glistened as he raised the lid and looked in. Dragging an old chair to the table, he sat down, and took from it a magnificent gold watch, sparkling with jewels.

'Aha!' said the Jew, shrugging up his shoulders, and distorting every feature with a hideous grin. 'Clever dogs! clever dogs! Stanch to the last! Never told the old parson where they were. Never peached upon old Fagin! And why should they? It wouldn't have loosened the knot, or kept the drop up a minute longer. No, no, no! Fine fellows! Fine fellows!'

With these, and other muttered reflections of the like nature, the Jew once more deposited the watch in its place of safety. At least half a dozen more were severally drawn forth from the same box and surveyed with equal pleasure; besides rings, brooches, bracelets, and other articles of jewellery, of such magnificent materials and costly workmanship, that Oliver had no idea even of their names.

Having replaced these trinkets, the Jew took out another, so small that it lay in the palm of his hand. There seemed to be some very minute inscription on it; for the Jew laid it flat upon the table, and shading it with his hand, pored over it long and earnestly. At length he put it down, as if despairing of success; and leaning back in his chair, muttered, 'What a fine thing capital punishment is! Dead men never repent; dead men never bring awkward stories to light. Ah, it's a fine thing for the trade! Five of 'em strung up in a row, and none left to play booty, or turn white-livered!'

As the Jew uttered these words, his bright dark eyes, which had been staring vacantly before him, fell on Oliver's face. The boy's eyes were fixed on his in mute curiosity; and, although the recognition was only for an instant – for the briefest space of time that can possibly be conceived – it was enough to show the old man that he had been observed. He closed the lid of the box with a loud crash; and, laying his hand on a bread-knife which was on the table, started furiously up. He trembled very much, though; for, even in his terror, Oliver could see that the knife quivered in the air.

'What's that?' said the Jew. 'What do you watch me for? Why are you awake? What have you seen? Speak out, boy! – Quick – quick! for your life!'

'I wasn't able to sleep any longer, sir,' replied Oliver, meekly. 'I am very sorry if I have disturbed you, sir.'

'You were not awake an hour ago?' said the Jew, scowling fiercely on the boy.

'No – no, indeed,' replied Oliver.

'Are you sure?' cried the Jew, with a still fiercer look than before, and a threatening attitude.

'Upon my word I was not, sir,' replied Oliver, earnestly. 'I was not, indeed, sir.'

'Tush, tush, my dear!' said the Jew, abruptly resuming his old manner, and playing with the knife a little, before he laid it down, as if to induce the belief that he had caught it up in mere sport. 'Of course I know that, my dear. I only tried to frighten you. You're a brave boy. Ha! ha! you're a brave boy, Oliver!' The Jew rubbed his hands with a chuckle, but glanced uneasily at the box notwithstanding.

'Did you see any of these pretty things, my dear?' said the Jew, laying his hand upon it after a short pause.

'Yes, sir,' replied Oliver.

'Ah!' said the Jew, turning rather pale. 'They – they're mine, Oliver; my little property. All I have to live upon in my old age. The folks call me a miser, my dear – only a miser, that's all.'

Oliver thought the old gentleman must be a decided miser to live in such a dirty place, with so many watches; but, thinking that perhaps his fondness for the Dodger and the other boys cost him a good deal of money, he only cast a deferential look at the Jew, and asked if he might get up.

'Certainly, my dear – certainly,' replied the old gentleman. 'Stay. There's a pitcher of water in the corner by the door. Bring it here; and I'll give you a basin to wash in, my dear.'

Oliver got up, walked across the room, and stooped for one instant to raise the pitcher. When he turned his head the box was gone.

He had scarcely washed himself, and made everything tidy, by emptying the basin out of the window, agreeably to the Jew's directions, when the Dodger returned, accompanied by a very sprightly young friend, whom Oliver had seen smoking on the previous night, and who was now formally introduced to him as Charley Bates. The four sat down to breakfast on the coffee, and some hot rolls and ham, which the Dodger had brought home in the crown of his hat.

'Well,' said the Jew, glancing slyly at Oliver, and addressing himself to the Dodger, 'I hope you've been at work this morning, my dears?'

'Hard,' replied the Dodger.

'As Nails,' added Charley Bates.

'Good boys, good boys!' said the Jew. 'What have *you* got, Dodger?'

'A couple of pocket-books,' replied that young gentleman.

'Lined?' enquired the Jew, with eagerness.

'Pretty well,' replied the Dodger, producing two pocket-books, one green and the other red.

'Not so heavy as they might be,' said the Jew, after looking at the insides carefully; 'but very neat and nicely made. Ingenious workman, ain't he, Oliver?'

'Very, indeed, sir,' said Oliver. At which Mr Charles Bates laughed uproariously; very much to the amazement of Oliver, who saw nothing to laugh at in anything that had passed.

'And what have you got, my dear?' said Fagin to Charley Bates.

'Wipes,' replied Master Bates, at the same time producing four pocket-handkerchiefs.

'Well,' said the Jew, inspecting them closely, 'they're very good ones – very. You haven't marked them well, though, Charley; so the marks shall be picked out with a needle, and we'll teach Oliver how to do it. Shall us, Oliver, eh? Ha! ha! ha!'

'If you please, sir,' said Oliver.

'You'd like to be able to make pocket-handkerchiefs as easy as Charley Bates, wouldn't you, my dear?' said the Jew.

'Very much indeed, if you'll teach me, sir,' replied Oliver.

Master Bates saw something so exquisitely ludicrous in this reply that he burst into another laugh, which laugh, meeting the coffee he was drinking, and carrying it down some wrong channel, very nearly terminated in his premature suffocation.

'He is so jolly green!' said Charley when he recovered, as an apology to the company for his unpolite behaviour.

The Dodger said nothing, but he smoothed Oliver's hair down over his eyes, and said he'd know better by and by; upon which the old gentleman, observing Oliver's colour mounting, changed the subject by asking whether there had been much of a crowd at the execution that morning. This made him wonder more and more; for it was plain from the replies of the two boys that they had both been there, and Oliver naturally wondered how they could possibly have found time to be so very industrious.

When the breakfast was cleared away, the merry old gentleman and the two boys played at a very curious and uncommon game, which was performed in this way. The merry old gentleman, placing a snuff-box in one pocket of his trousers, a note-case in the other, and a watch in his waistcoat pocket, with a guard chain round his neck, and sticking a mock diamond pin in his shirt, buttoned his coat tight round him, and putting his spectacle-case and handkerchief in his pockets, trotted up and down the room with a stick, in imitation of the manner in which old gentlemen walk about the streets any hour of the day. Sometimes he stopped at the fireplace, and sometimes at the door, making believe that he was staring with all his might into shop windows. At such times he would look constantly round him, for fear of thieves, and keep slapping all his pockets in turn, to see that he hadn't lost anything, in such a very funny and natural manner that Oliver laughed till the tears ran down his face. All this time the two boys followed him closely about; getting out of his sight so nimbly, every time he turned round, that it was impossible to follow their motions. At last the Dodger trod upon his toes, or ran upon his boot accidentally, while Charley Bates stumbled up against him behind; and in that one moment they took from him, with the most extraordinary rapidity, snuff-box, note-case, watch-guard, chain, shirt-pin, pocket-handkerchief – even the spectacle-case. If the old gentleman felt a hand in any one of his pockets, he cried out where it was; and then the game began all over again.

When this game had been played a great many times, a couple of young ladies called to see the young gentlemen; one of whom was named Bet, and the other Nancy. They wore a good deal of hair, not very neatly turned up behind, and were rather untidy about the shoes and stockings. They were not exactly pretty, perhaps; but they had a great deal of colour in their faces, and looked quite stout and hearty. Being remarkably free and agreeable in their manners, Oliver thought them very nice girls indeed. As there is no doubt they were.

These visitors stopped a long time. Spirits were produced, in consequence of one of the young ladies complaining of a coldness in her inside; and the conversation took a very convivial and improving turn. At length Charley Bates expressed his opinion that it was time to pad the hoof. This, it occurred to Oliver, must be French for going out; for directly afterwards, the Dodger, and Charley, and the two young ladies, went away together, having been kindly furnished by the amiable old Jew with money to spend.

'There, my dear,' said Fagin, 'that's a pleasant life, isn't it? They have gone out for the day.'

'Have they done work, sir?' enquired Oliver.

'Yes,' said the Jew; 'that is, unless they should unexpectedly come across any when they are out; and they won't neglect it, if they do, my dear – depend upon it.

'Make 'em your models, my dear – make 'em your models,' said the Jew, tapping the fire-shovel on the hearth to add force to his words; 'do everything they bid you, and take their advice in all matters – especially the Dodger's, my dear. He'll be a great man himself, and will make you one too, if you take pattern by him. – Is my handkerchief hanging out of my pocket, my dear?' said the Jew, stopping short.

'Yes, Sir,' said Oliver.

'See if you can take it out without my feeling it, as you saw them do when we were at play this morning.'

Oliver held up the bottom of the pocket with one hand, as he

had seen the Dodger hold it, and drew the handkerchief lightly out of it with the other.

'Is it gone?' cried the Jew.

'Here it is, sir,' said Oliver, showing it in his hand.

'You're a clever boy, my dear,' said the playful old gentleman, patting Oliver on the head approvingly. 'I never saw a sharper lad. Here's a shilling for you. If you go on in this way, you'll be the greatest man of the time. And now come here, and I'll show you how to take the marks out of the handkerchiefs.'

Oliver wondered what picking the old gentleman's pocket in play had to do with his chances of being a great man. But, thinking that the Jew, being so much his senior, must know best, he followed him quietly to the table, and was soon deeply involved in his new study.

CHAPTER 10

Oliver becomes better acquainted with the characters of his new associates; and purchases experience at a high price. Being a short but very important chapter in this history

For many days Oliver remained in the Jew's room, picking the marks out of the pocket-handkerchiefs (of which a great number were brought home), and sometimes taking part in the game already described, which the two boys and the Jew played regularly every morning. At length he began to languish for the fresh air, and took many occasions of earnestly entreating the old gentleman to allow him to go out to work with his two companions.

Oliver was rendered the more anxious to be actively employed, by what he had seen of the stern morality of the old gentleman's character. Whenever the Dodger or Charley Bates came home at night empty handed, he would expatiate with great vehemence on the misery of idle and lazy habits, and would enforce upon them the necessity of an active life by sending them supperless to bed. On one occasion, indeed, he even went so far as to knock them both down a flight of stairs; but this was carrying out his virtuous precepts to an unusual extent.

At length one morning Oliver obtained the permission he had so eagerly sought. There had been no handkerchiefs to work upon for two or three days, and the dinners had been rather meagre. Perhaps these were the reasons for the old gentleman's giving his assent; but, whether they were or no, he told Oliver he might go, and placed him under the joint guardianship of Charley Bates and his friend the Dodger.

The three boys sallied out; the Dodger with his coat sleeves tucked up, and his hat cocked, as usual; Master Bates sauntering along with his hands in his pockets; and Oliver between them, wondering where they were going, and what branch of manufacture he would be instructed in first.

The pace at which they went was such a very lazy, ill-looking saunter, that Oliver soon began to think his companions were going to deceive the old gentleman, by not going to work at all. The Dodger had a vicious propensity, too, of pulling the caps from the heads of small boys and tossing them down areas; while Charley Bates exhibited some very loose notions concerning the rights of property, by pilfering divers apples and onions from the stalls at the kennel sides, and thrusting them into pockets which were so surprisingly capacious that they seemed to undermine his whole suit of clothes in every direction. These things looked so bad, that Oliver was on the point of declaring his intention of seeking his way back, in the best way he could, when his thoughts were suddenly directed into another channel by a very mysterious change of behaviour on the part of the Dodger.

They were just emerging from a narrow court not far from the open square in Clerkenwell, which is yet called, by some strange perversion of terms, 'The Green,' when the Dodger made a sudden stop, and, laying his finger on his lip, drew his companions back again, with the greatest caution and circumspection.

'What's the matter?' demanded Oliver.

'Hush!' replied the Dodger. 'Do you see that old cove at the bookstall?'

'The old gentleman over the way?' said Oliver. 'Yes, I see him.'

'He'll do,' said the Dodger.

'A prime plant,' observed Master Charley Bates.

Oliver looked from one to the other with the greatest surprise; but he was not permitted to make any enquiries, for the two boys walked stealthily across the road, and slunk close behind the old gentleman towards whom his attention had been directed. Oliver walked a few paces after them, and, not knowing whether to advance or retire, stood looking on in silent amazement.

The old gentleman was a very respectable looking personage, with a powdered head and gold spectacles. He was dressed in a bottle-green coat with a black velvet collar, wore white trousers, and carried a smart bamboo cane under his arm. He had taken up a book from the stall, and there he stood, reading away as hard as if he were in his elbow-chair in his own study. It is very possible that he fancied himself there, indeed; for it was plain, from his utter abstraction, that he saw not the bookstall, nor the street, nor the boys, nor, in short, anything but the book itself, which he was reading straight through, turning over the leaf when he got to the bottom of a page, beginning at the top line of the next one, and going regularly on, with the greatest interest and eagerness.

What was Oliver's horror and alarm as he stood a few paces off, looking on with his eyelids as wide open as they would possibly go, to see the Dodger plunge his hand into the old gentleman's pocket, and draw from thence a handkerchief; to see him hand the same to Charley Bates; and finally to behold them both running away round the corner at full speed!

In an instant the whole mystery of the handkerchiefs, and the watches, and the jewels, and the Jew, rushed upon the boy's mind. He stood for a moment, with the blood so tingling through all his veins from terror, that he felt as if he were in a burning fire; then, confused and frightened, he took to his heels, and, not knowing what he did, made off as fast as he could lay his feet to the ground.

This was all done in a minute's space. In the very instant when Oliver began to run, the old gentleman, putting his hand to his pocket, and missing his handkerchief, turned sharp round. Seeing the boy scudding away at such a rapid pace, he very naturally concluded him to be the depredator; and, shouting 'Stop thief!' with all his might, made off after him, book in hand.

But the old gentleman was not the only person who raised the hue-and-cry. The Dodger and Master Bates, unwilling to attract public attention by running down the open street, had merely retired into the very first doorway round the corner. They no sooner heard the cry, and saw Oliver running, than, guessing exactly how the matter stood, they issued forth with great promptitude, and shouting 'Stop thief!' too, joined in the pursuit like good citizens.

Although Oliver had been brought up by philosophers, he was not theoretically acquainted with the beautiful axiom that self-preservation is the first law of nature. If he had been, perhaps he would have been prepared for this. Not being prepared, however, it alarmed him the more; so away he went like the wind, with the old gentleman and the two boys roaring and shouting behind him.

'Stop thief ! Stop thief !' There is a magic in the sound. The tradesman leaves his counter, and the carman his wagon; the butcher throws down his tray, the baker his basket, the

Oliver amazed at the Dodger's mode of 'going to work'

milkman his pail, the errand-boy his parcels, the schoolboy his marbles, the pavior his pickaxe, the child his battledore. Away they run, pell-mell, helter-skelter, slapdash; tearing, yelling, and screaming; knocking down the passengers as they turn the corners, rousing up the dogs, and astonishing the fowls; and streets, squares, and courts re-echo with the sound.

'Stop thief! Stop thief!' The cry is taken up by a hundred voices, and the crowd accumulate at every turning. Away they fly, splashing through the mud, and rattling along the pavements. Up go the windows, out run the people, onward bear the mob, a whole audience desert Punch in the very thickest of the plot, and, joining the rushing throng, swell the shout, and lend fresh vigour to the cry, 'Stop thief! Stop thief!'

'Stop thief! Stop thief!' There is a passion *for hunting something* deeply implanted in the human breast. One wretched breathless child, panting with exhaustion, terror in his looks, agony in his eye, large drops of perspiration streaming down his face, strains every nerve to make head upon his pursuers; and as they follow on his track, and gain upon him every instant, they hail his decreasing strength with still louder shouts, and whoop and scream with joy. 'Stop thief!' Ay, stop him, for God's sake, were it only in mercy!

Stopped at last! A clever blow! He is down upon the pavement; and the crowd eagerly gather round him, each newcomer jostling and struggling with the others to catch a glimpse. 'Stand aside!' 'Give him a little air!' 'Nonsense! he don't deserve it.' 'Where's the gentleman?' 'Here he is, coming down the street.' 'Make room there for the gentleman!' 'Is this the boy, sir?'

'Yes.'

Oliver lay, covered with mud and dust, and bleeding from the mouth, looking wildly round upon the heap of faces that surrounded him, when the old gentleman was officiously dragged and pushed into the circle by the foremost of the pursuers.

'Yes,' said the gentleman, 'I am afraid it is the boy.'

'Afraid!' murmured the crowd. 'That's a good 'un.'

'Poor fellow!' said the gentleman. 'He has hurt himself.'

'*I* did that, sir,' said a great lubberly fellow, stepping forward; 'and preciously I cut my knuckle agin' his mouth. *I* stopped him, sir.'

The fellow touched his hat with a grin expecting something for his pains; but the old gentleman, eyeing him with an expression of dislike, looked anxiously round, as if he contemplated running away himself, which it is very possible he might have attempted to do, and thus afforded another chase, had not a police officer (who is generally the last person to arrive in such cases) at that moment made his way through the crowd, and seized Oliver by the collar.

'Come, get up,' said the man, roughly.

'It wasn't me, indeed, sir. Indeed, indeed, it was two other boys,' said Oliver, clasping his hands passionately, and looking round.

'They are here somewhere.'

'Oh, no, they ain't,' said the officer. He meant this to be ironical, but it was true besides, for the Dodger and Charley Bates had filed off down the first convenient court they came to. 'Come, get up!

'Don't hurt him,' said the old gentleman, compassionately.

'Oh, no, I won't hurt him,' replied the officer, tearing his jacket half off his back in proof thereof. 'Come, I know you; it won't do. Will you stand upon your legs, you young devil?'

Oliver, who could hardly stand, made a shift to raise himself on his feet, and was at once lugged along the streets by the jacket-collar at a rapid pace. The gentleman walked on with them by the officer's side; and as many of the crowd as could achieve the feat got a little ahead, and stared back at Oliver from time to time. The boys shouted in triumph; and on they went.

CHAPTER II

Treats of Mr Fang, the police magistrate; and furnishes a slight specimen of his mode of administering justice

The offence had been committed within the district, and indeed in the immediate neighbourhood, of a very notorious metropolitan police office. The crowd had only the satisfaction of accompanying Oliver through two or three streets, and down a place called Mutton-hill, when he was led beneath a low archway, and up a dirty court, into this dispensary of summary justice, by the back way. It was a small paved yard into which they turned; and here they encountered a stout man with a bunch of whiskers on his face and a bunch of keys in his hand.

'What's the matter now?' said the man carelessly.

'A young fogle-hunter,' replied the man who had Oliver in charge.

'Are you the party that's been robbed, sir?' enquired the man with the keys.

'Yes, I am,' replied the old gentleman; 'but I am not sure that this boy actually took the handkerchief. I – I would rather not press the case.'

'Must go before the magistrate now, sir,' replied the man. 'His worship will be disengaged in half a minute. Now, young gallows.'

This was an invitation for Oliver to enter through a door which he unlocked as he spoke, and which led into a stone cell. Here he was searched, and nothing being found upon him, locked up.

This cell was in shape and size something like an area cellar, only not so light. It was most intolerably dirty; for it was Monday morning, and it had been tenanted by six drunken people, who had been locked up, elsewhere, since Saturday night. But this is little. In our station-houses men and women are every night confined on the most trivial *charges* – the word is worth noting – in dungeons, compared with which those in Newgate, occupied by the most atrocious felons, tried, found guilty, and under sentence of death, are palaces. Let any man who doubts this compare the two.

The old gentleman looked almost as rueful as Oliver when

the key grated in the lock. He turned with a sigh to the book which had been the innocent cause of all this disturbance.

'There is something in that boy's face,' said the old gentleman to himself as he walked slowly away, tapping his chin with the cover of the book in a thoughtful manner – 'something that touches and interests me. *Can* he be innocent? He looked like. – By the by,' exclaimed the old gentleman, halting very abruptly and staring up into the sky. – 'Bless my soul! – where have I seen something like that look before?'

After musing for some minutes, the old gentleman walked, with the same meditative face, into a back ante-room opening from the yard; and there, retiring into a corner, called up before his mind's eye a vast amphitheatre of faces over which a dusky curtain had hung for many years. 'No,' said the old gentleman, shaking his head; 'it must be imagination.'

He wandered over them again. He had called them into view, and it was not easy to replace the shroud that had so long concealed them. There were the faces of friends and foes, and of many that had been almost strangers, peering intrusively from the crowd; there were the faces of young and blooming girls that were now old women; there were faces that the grave had changed and closed upon, but which the mind, superior to its power, still dressed in their old freshness and beauty, calling back the lustre of the eyes, the brightness of the smile, the beaming of the soul through its mask of clay, and whispering of beauty beyond the tomb, changed but to be heightened, and taken from earth only to be set up as a light to shed a soft and gentle glow upon the path to Heaven.

But the old gentleman could recall no one countenance of which Oliver's features bore a trace. So he heaved a sigh over the recollections he had awakened; and being, happily for himself, an absent old gentleman, buried them again in the pages of the musty book.

He was roused by a touch on the shoulder, and a request from the man with the keys to follow him into the office. He closed his book hastily, and was at once ushered into the imposing presence of the renowned Mr Fang.

The office was a front parlour, with a panelled wall. Mr Fang sat behind a bar, at the upper end; and on one side of the door was a sort of wooden pen, in which poor little Oliver was already deposited, trembling very much at the awfulness of the scene.

Mr Fang was a lean, long-backed, stiff-necked, middle-sized man, with no great quantity of hair and what he had growing on the back and sides of his head. His face was stern and much flushed. If he were not really in the habit of drinking rather more than was exactly good for him, he might have brought an action against his countenance for libel, and have recovered heavy damages.

The old gentleman bowed respectfully, and advancing to the magistrate's desk, said, suiting the action to the word, 'That is my name and address, sir.' He then withdrew a pace or two, and with another polite and gentlemanly inclination of the head waited to be questioned.

Now, it so happened that Mr Fang was at that moment perusing a leading article in the newspaper of the morning, adverting to some recent decision of his, and commending him, for the three hundred and fiftieth time, to the special and particular notice of the Secretary of State for the Home Department. He was out of temper, and he looked up with an angry scowl.

'Who are you?' said Mr Fang.

The old gentleman pointed with some surprise to his card.

'Officers!' said Mr Fang, tossing the card contemptuously away with the newspaper, 'who is this fellow?'

'My name, sir,' said the old gentleman, speaking like a gentleman, 'my name, sir, is Brownlow. Permit me to enquire the name of the magistrate who offers a gratuitous and unprovoked insult to a respectable person, under the protection of the bench.' Saying this, Mr Brownlow looked round the office as if in search of some person who would afford him the required information.

'Officer!' said Mr Fang, throwing the paper on one side, 'what's this fellow charged with?'

'He's not charged at all, your worship,' replied the officer. 'He appears against the boy, your worship.'

His worship knew this perfectly well, but it was a good annoyance, and a safe one.

'Appears against the boy, does he?' said Fang, surveying Mr Brownlow contemptuously from head to foot. 'Swear him!'

'Before I am sworn, I must beg to say one word,' said Mr Brownlow, 'and that is, that I really never, without actual experience, could have believed – '

'Hold your tongue, sir!' said Mr Fang peremptorily.

'I will not, sir!' replied the old gentleman.

'Hold your tongue this instant, or I'll have you turned out of the office!' said Mr Fang. 'You're an insolent, impertinent fellow. How dare you bully a magistrate?'

'What!' exclaimed the old gentleman, reddening.

'Swear this person!' said Fang to the clerk. 'I'll not hear another word. Swear him.'

Mr Brownlow's indignation was greatly roused, but, reflecting perhaps that he might only injure the boy by giving vent to it, he suppressed his feelings, and submitted to be sworn at once.

'Now,' said Fang, 'what's the charge against this boy? What have you got to say, sir?'

'I was standing at a bookstall – ' Mr Brownlow began.

'Hold your tongue, sir!' said Mr Fang. 'Policeman! Where's the policeman? Here, swear this policeman. Now, policeman, what is this?'

The policeman, with becoming humility, related how he had taken the charge; how he had searched Oliver, and found nothing on his person; and how that was all he knew about it.

'Are there any witnesses?' enquired Mr Fang.

'None, your worship,' replied the policeman.

Mr Fang sat silent for some minutes, and then turning round to the prosecutor, said in a towering passion, 'Do you mean to state what your complaint against this boy is, fellow, or do you not? You have been sworn. Now if you stand there refusing to give evidence, I'll punish you for disrespect to the bench; I will, by – '

By what, or by whom, nobody knows; for the clerk and jailer

coughed very loud, just at the right moment, and the former dropped a heavy book upon the floor, thus preventing the word from being heard – accidentally, of course.

With many interruptions, and repeated insults, Mr Brownlow contrived to state his case; observing that, in the surprise of the moment, he had run after the boy because he saw him running away; and expressing his hope that, if the magistrate should believe him, although not actually the thief, to be connected with thieves, he would deal as leniently with him as justice would allow.

'He has been hurt already,' said the old gentleman in conclusion. 'And I fear,' he added with great energy, looking towards the bar, 'I really fear that he is very ill.'

'Oh, yes; I dare say!' said Mr Fang, with a sneer. – 'Come, none of your tricks here, you young vagabond; they won't do. What's your name?'

Oliver tried to reply, but his tongue failed him. He was deadly pale, and the whole place seemed turning round and round.

'What's your name, you hardened scoundrel?' demanded Mr Fang. 'Officer, what's his name?'

This was addressed to a bluff old fellow, in a striped waistcoat, who was standing by the bar. He bent over Oliver, and repeated the enquiry; but finding him really incapable of understanding the question, and knowing that his not replying would only infuriate the magistrate the more, and add to the severity of his sentence, he hazarded a guess.

'He says his name's Tom White, your worship,' said this kind-hearted thief-taker.

'Oh, he won't speak out, won't he?' said Fang. 'Very well, very well. Where does he live?'

'Where he can, your worship,' replied the officer, again pretending to receive Oliver's answer.

'Has he any parents?' enquired Mr Fang.

'He says they died in his infancy, your worship,' replied the officer, hazarding the usual reply.

At this point of the enquiry Oliver raised his head, and looking round with imploring eyes, murmured a feeble prayer for a draught of water.

'Stuff and nonsense!' said Mr Fang; 'don't try to make a fool of me.'

'I think he really is ill, your worship,' remonstrated the officer.

'I know better,' said Mr Fang.

'Take care of him, officer,' said the old gentleman, raising his hands instinctively; 'he'll fall down.'

'Stand away, officer,' cried Fang; 'let him, if he likes.'

Oliver availed himself of the kind permission, and fell heavily to the floor in a fainting fit. The men in the office looked at each other, but no one dared to stir.

'I knew he was shamming,' said Fang, as if this were incontestable proof of the fact. 'Let him lie there; he'll soon be tired of that.'

'How do you propose to deal with the case, sir?' enquired the clerk in a low voice.

'Summarily,' replied Mr Fang. 'He stands committed for three months – hard labour, of course. Clear the office.'

The door was opened for this purpose, and a couple of men were preparing to carry the insensible boy to his cell, when an elderly man of decent but poor appearance, clad in an old suit of black, rushed hastily into the office and advanced towards the bench.

'Stop, stop! Don't take him away! For Heaven's sake, stop a moment!' cried the newcomer, breathless with haste.

Although the presiding Genii in such an office as this exercise a summary and arbitrary power over the liberties, the good name, the character, almost of the lives of Her Majesty's subjects, especially of the poorer class; and although, within such walls, enough fantastic tricks are daily played to make the angels blind with weeping; they are closed to the public, save through the medium of the daily press. Mr Fang was consequently not a little indignant to see an unbidden guest enter in such irreverent disorder.

'What is this? Who is this? Turn this man out. Clear the office!' cried Mr Fang.

'I will speak,' cried the man; 'I will not be turned out. I saw it all. I keep the bookstall. I demand to be sworn. I will not be put down. Mr Fang, you must hear me. You must not refuse, sir.'

The man was right. His manner was bold and determined; and the matter was growing rather too serious to be hushed up.

'Swear the fellow,' growled Fang, with a very ill grace. 'Now, man, what have you got to say?'

'This,' said the man: 'I saw three boys – two others and the prisoner here – loitering on the opposite side of the way, when this gentleman was reading. The robbery was committed by another boy. I saw it done; and I saw that this boy was perfectly amazed and stupefied by it.' Having by this time recovered a little breath, the worthy bookstall keeper proceeded to relate, in a more coherent manner, the exact circumstances of the robbery.

'Why didn't you come here before?' said Fang, after a pause.

'I hadn't a soul to mind the shop,' replied the man. 'Everybody who could have helped me had joined in the pursuit. I could get nobody till five minutes ago; and I've run here all the way.'

'The prosecutor was reading, was he?' enquired Fang, after another pause.

'Yes,' replied the man. 'The very book he has in his hand.'

'Oh, that book, eh?' said Fang. 'Is it paid for?'

'No, it is not,' replied the man, with a smile.

'Dear me, I forgot all about it!' exclaimed the absent old gentleman, innocently.

'A nice person to prefer a charge against a poor boy!' said Fang, with a comical effort to look humane. 'I consider, sir, that you have obtained possession of that book under very suspicious and disreputable circumstances; and you may think yourself very fortunate that the owner of the property declines to prosecute. Let this be a lesson to you, my man, or the law will overtake you yet. The boy is discharged. Clear the office.'

'Damn me!' cried the old gentleman, bursting out with the rage he had kept down so long, 'damn me! I'll – '

'Clear the office!' said the magistrate. 'Officers, do you hear! Clear the office!'

The mandate was obeyed, and the indignant Mr Brownlow was conveyed out, with the book in one hand and the bamboo cane in the other, in a perfect frenzy of rage and defiance. He reached the yard, and it vanished in a moment. Little Oliver Twist lay on his back on the pavement, with his shirt unbuttoned, and his temples bathed with water; his face a deadly white, and a cold tremble convulsing his whole frame.

'Poor boy, poor boy!' said Mr Brownlow, bending over him. 'Call a coach, somebody, pray, directly.'

A coach was obtained, and Oliver, having been carefully laid on one seat, the old gentleman got in and sat himself on the other.

'May I accompany you?' said the bookstall keeper, looking in.

'Bless me, yes, my dear friend,' said Mr Brownlow quickly. 'I forgot you. Dear, dear! I have this unhappy book still! Jump in. Poor fellow! there's no time to lose.'

The bookstall keeper got into the coach, and away they drove.

CHAPTER 12

In which Oliver is taken better care of than he ever was before. And in which the narrative reverts to the merry old gentleman and his youthful friends

The coach rattled away, down Mount Pleasant and up Exmouth Street, over nearly the same ground as that which Oliver had traversed when he first entered London in company with the Dodger and, turning a different way when it reached the Angel at Islington, stopped at length before a neat house, in a quiet shady street near Pentonville. Here a bed was prepared without loss of time, in which Mr Brownlow saw his young charge carefully and comfortably deposited; and here he was tended with a kindness and solicitude that knew no bounds.

But, for many days, Oliver remained insensible to all the goodness of his new friends. The sun rose and sunk, and rose and sunk again, and many times after that, and still the boy lay stretched on his uneasy bed, dwindling away beneath the dry and wasting heat of fever. The worm does not his work more surely on the dead body than does this slow creeping fire upon the living frame.

Weak, and thin, and pallid, he awoke at last from what seemed to have been a long and troubled dream. Feebly raising himself in the bed, with his head resting on his trembling arm, he looked anxiously round.

'What room is this? Where have I been brought to?' said Oliver. 'This is not the place l went to sleep in.'

He uttered these words in a feeble voice; being very faint and weak, but they were overheard at once for the curtain at the bed's head was hastily drawn back, and a motherly old lady, very neatly and precisely dressed, rose as she withdrew it from an armchair close by, in which she had been sitting at needlework.

'Hush, my dear,' said the old lady softly. 'You must be very quiet, or you will be ill again; and you have been very bad – as

bad as bad could be, pretty nigh. Lie down again; there's a dear!' With these words, the old lady very gently placed Oliver's head upon the pillow, and, smoothing back his hair from his forehead, looked so kindly and lovingly in his face, that he could not help placing his little withered hand in hers, and drawing it round his neck.

'Save us!' said the old lady, with tears in her eyes, 'what a grateful little dear it is! Pretty creature! What would his mother feel if she had sat by him as I have, and could see him now?'

'Perhaps she does see me,' whispered Oliver, folding his hands together; 'perhaps she has sat by me. I almost feel as if she had.'

'That was the fever, my dear,' said the old lady mildly.

'I suppose it was,' replied Oliver; 'because Heaven is a long way off, and they are too happy there to come down to the bedside of a poor boy. But if she knew I was ill she must have pitied me, even there; for she was very ill herself before she died. She can't know anything about me though,' added Oliver, after a moment's silence. 'If she had seen me hurt, it would have made her sorrowful; and her face has always looked sweet and happy when I have dreamed of her.'

The old lady made no reply to this, but wiping her eyes first, and her spectacles, which lay on the counterpane, afterwards, as if they were part and parcel of those features, brought some cool stuff for Oliver to drink; and then, patting him on the cheek, told him he must lie very quiet, or he would be ill again.

So Oliver kept very still; partly because he was anxious to obey the kind old lady in all things, and partly, to tell the truth, because he was completely exhausted with what he had already said. He soon fell into a gentle doze, from which he was awakened by the light of a candle, which, being brought near the bed, showed him a gentleman, with a very large and loud-ticking gold watch in his hand, who felt his pulse, and said he was a great deal better.

'You *are* a great deal better, are you not, my dear?' said the gentleman.

'Yes, thank you, sir,' replied Oliver.

'Yes, I know you are,' said the gentleman. 'You're hungry, too, ain't you?'

'No, sir,' answered Oliver.

'Hem!' said the gentleman. 'No, I know you're not. He is not hungry, Mrs Bedwin,' said the gentleman, looking very wise.

The old lady made a respectful inclination of the head, which seemed to say that she thought the doctor was a very clever man. The doctor appeared very much of the same opinion himself.

'You feel sleepy, don't you, my dear?' said the doctor.

'No, sir,' replied Oliver.

'No,' said the doctor, with a very shrewd and satisfied look, 'you're not sleepy. Nor thirsty are you?'

'Yes, sir, rather thirsty,' answered Oliver.

'Just as I expected, Mrs Bedwin,' said the doctor. 'It's very natural that he should be thirsty. You may give him a little tea, ma'am, and some dry toast without any butter. Don't keep him too warm, ma'am; but be careful that you don't let him be too cold – will you have the goodness?'

The old lady dropped a curtsy. The doctor, after tasting the cold stuff, and expressing a qualified approval thereof, hurried away, his boots creaking in a very important and wealthy manner as he went downstairs.

Oliver dozed off again soon after this, and when he awoke it was nearly twelve o'clock. The old lady tenderly bade him good-night shortly afterwards, and left him in charge of a fat old woman, who had just come; bringing with her, in a little bundle, a small Prayer Book and a large nightcap. Putting the latter on her head and the former on the table, the old woman, after telling Oliver that she had come to sit up with him, drew her chair close to the fire and went off into a series of short naps, chequered at frequent intervals with sundry tumblings forward, and divers moans and chokings, which, however, had no worse effect than causing her to rub her nose very hard, and then fall asleep again.

And thus the night crept slowly on. Oliver lay awake for some time, counting the little circles of light which the reflection of the rushlight-shade threw upon the ceiling, or tracing with his languid eyes the intricate pattern of the paper on the wall. The darkness and deep stillness of the room were very solemn; and as they brought into the boy's mind the thought that death had been hovering there for many days and nights, and might yet fill it with the gloom and dread of his awful presence, he turned his face upon the pillow and fervently prayed to Heaven.

Gradually he fell into that deep tranquil sleep which ease from recent suffering alone imparts, that calm and peaceful rest which it is pain to wake from. Who, if this were death, would be roused again to all the struggles and turmoils of life; to all its cares for the present, its anxieties for the future; more than all, its weary recollections of the past!

It had been bright day for hours when Oliver opened his eyes; and when he did so he felt cheerful and happy. The crisis of the disease was safely past. He belonged to the world again.

In three days' time he was able to sit in an easy-chair, well propped up with pillows; and, as he was still too weak to walk, Mrs Bedwin had him carried downstairs into the little house-keeper's room which belonged to her, where, having sat him up by the fireside, the good old lady sat herself down too, and being in a state of considerable delight at seeing him so much better, forthwith began to cry most violently.

'Never mind me, my dear,' said the old lady. 'I'm only having a regular good cry. There; it's all over now, and I'm quite comfortable.'

'You're very, very kind to me, ma'am,' said Oliver.

'Well, never you mind that, my dear,' said the old lady; 'that's got nothing to do with your broth, and it's full time you had it. For the doctor says Mr Brownlow may come in to see you this morning; and we must get up our best looks, because the better we look the more he'll be pleased.' And with this, the old lady applied herself to warming up in a little saucepan a basinful of broth, strong enough to furnish an ample dinner, when reduced to the regulation strength, for three hundred and fifty paupers, at the very lowest computation.

'Are you fond of pictures, dear?' enquired the old lady, seeing that Oliver had fixed his eyes, most intently, on a portrait which hung against the wall, just opposite his chair.

'I don't quite know, ma'am,' said Oliver, without taking his eyes from the canvas; 'I have seen so few that I hardly know. What a beautiful mild face that lady's is!'

'Ah!' said the old lady, 'painters always make ladies out prettier than they are, or they wouldn't get any custom, child. The man that invented the machine for taking likenesses might have known *that* would never succeed; it's a deal too honest. A deal,' said the old lady, laughing very heartily at her own acuteness.

'Is – is that a likeness, ma'am?' said Oliver.

'Yes,' said the old lady, looking up for a moment from the broth; 'that's a portrait.'

'Whose, ma'am?' asked Oliver eagerly.

'Why, really, my dear, I don't know,' answered the old lady in a good-humoured manner. 'It's not a likeness of anybody that you or I know, I expect. It seems to strike your fancy, dear.'

'It is so very pretty,' replied Oliver.

'Why, sure you're not afraid of it?' said the old lady, observing, in great surprise, the look of awe with which the child regarded the painting.

'Oh, no, no,' returned Oliver quickly; 'but the eyes look so sorrowful, and where I sit they seem fixed upon me. It makes my heart beat,' added Oliver, in a low voice, 'as if it was alive, and wanted to speak to me, but couldn't.'

'Lord save us!' exclaimed the old lady, starting; 'don't talk in that way, child. You're weak and nervous after your illness. Let me wheel your chair round to the other side, and then you won't see it. There!' said the old lady, suiting the action to the word; 'you don't see it now, at all events.'

Oliver *did* see it in his mind's eye as distinctly as if he had not altered his position; but he thought it better not to worry the kind old lady, so he smiled gently when she looked at him, and Mrs Bedwin, satisfied that he felt more comfortable, salted and broke bits of toasted bread into the broth, with all the bustle befitting so solemn a preparation. Oliver got through it with extraordinary expedition, and had scarcely swallowed the last spoonful when there came a soft tap at the door. 'Come in,' said the old lady; and in walked Mr Brownlow.

Now, the old gentleman came in as brisk as need be; but he had no sooner raised his spectacles on his forehead, and thrust his hands behind the skirts of his dressing-gown, to take a good long look at Oliver, than his countenance underwent a very great variety of odd contortions. Oliver looked very worn and shadowy from sickness, and made an ineffectual attempt to stand up, out of respect to his benefactor, which terminated in his sinking back into the chair again; and the fact is, if the truth must be told, that Mr Brownlow's heart, being large enough for any six ordinary old gentlemen of humane disposition, forced a supply of tears into his eyes, by some hydraulic process which we are not sufficiently philosophical to be in a condition to explain.

'Poor boy, poor boy!' said Mr Brownlow, clearing his throat. 'I'm rather hoarse this morning, Mrs Bedwin. I'm afraid I have caught cold.'

'I hope not, sir,' said Mrs Bedwin. 'Everything you have had has been well aired, sir.'

'I don't know, Bedwin. I don't know,' said Mr Brownlow; 'I rather think I had a damp napkin at dinner-time yesterday; but never mind that. How do you feel, my dear?'

'Very happy, sir,' replied Oliver. 'And very grateful indeed, sir, for your goodness to me.'

'Good boy,' said Mr Brownlow, stoutly. 'Have you given him any nourishment, Bedwin? Any slops, eh?'

'He has just had a basin of beautiful strong broth, sir,' replied Mrs Bedwin, drawing herself up slightly and laying a strong emphasis on the last word, to intimate that between slops, and broth well compounded, there existed no affinity or connection whatsoever.

'Ugh!' said Mr Brownlow, with a slight shudder; 'a couple of glasses of port wine would have done him a great deal more good. Wouldn't they, Tom White, eh?'

'My name is Oliver, sir,' replied the little invalid, with a look of great astonishment.

'Oliver!' said Mr Brownlow – 'Oliver what? Oliver White, eh?'

'No, sir; Twist – Oliver Twist.'

'Queer name!' said the old gentleman. 'What made you tell the magistrate your name was White?'

'I never told him so, sir,' returned Oliver in amazement.

This sounded so like a falsehood that the old gentleman looked somewhat sternly in Oliver's face. It was impossible to doubt him; there was truth in every one of its thin and sharpened lineaments.

'Some mistake,' said Mr Brownlow. But, although his motive for looking steadily at Oliver no longer existed, the old idea of the resemblance between his features and some familiar face came upon him so strongly that he could not withdraw his gaze.

Oliver recovering from the fever

'I hope you are not angry with me, sir?' said Oliver, raising his eyes beseechingly.

'No, no,' replied the old gentleman. – 'Why! what's this? Bedwin, look here!'

As he spoke, he pointed hastily to the picture above Oliver's head, and then to the boy's face. There was its living copy. The eyes, the head, the mouth – every feature was the same. The expression was, for the instant, so precisely alike, that the minutest line seemed copied with a startling accuracy!

Oliver knew not the cause of this sudden exclamation, for, not being strong enough to bear the start it gave him, he fainted away. A weakness on his part which affords the narrative an opportunity of relieving the reader from suspense in behalf of the two young pupils of the Merry Old Gentleman, and of recording –

That when the Dodger and his accomplished friend Master Bates joined in the hue-and-cry which was raised at Oliver's heels in consequence of their executing an illegal conveyance of Mr Brownlow's personal property, as has been already described, they were actuated by a very laudable and becoming regard for themselves; and forasmuch as the freedom of the subject and the liberty of the individual are among the first and proudest boasts of a true-hearted Englishman, so I need hardly beg the reader to observe that this action should tend to exalt them in the opinion of all public and patriotic men, in almost as great a degree as this strong proof of their anxiety for their own preservation and safety goes to corroborate and confirm the little code of laws which certain profound and sound-judging philosophers have laid down as the mainsprings of all Nature's deeds and actions: the said philosophers very wisely reducing the good lady's proceedings to matters of maxim and theory, and, by a very neat and pretty compliment to her exalted wisdom and understanding, putting entirely out of sight any considerations of heart or generous impulse and feeling. For these are matters totally beneath a female who is acknowledged by universal admission to be far above the numerous little foibles and weaknesses of her sex.

If I wanted any further proof of the strictly philosophical nature of the conduct of these young gentlemen in their very delicate predicament, I should at once find it in the fact (also recorded in the foregoing part of this narrative) of their quitting the pursuit when the general attention was fixed upon Oliver, and making immediately for their home by the shortest possible cut. For although I do not mean to assert that it is usually the practice of renowned and learned sages to shorten the road to any great conclusion – their course indeed being rather to lengthen the distance by various circumlocutions and discursive staggerings like unto those in which drunken men, under the pressure of a too mighty flow of ideas, are prone to indulge – still I do mean to say, and do say distinctly, that it is the invariable practice of many mighty philosophers, in carrying out their theories, to evince great wisdom and foresight in providing against every possible contingency which can be supposed at all likely to affect themselves. Thus to do a great right, you may do a little wrong; and you may take any means which the end to be attained will justify, the amount of the right, or the amount of the wrong, or indeed the distinction between the two, being left entirely to the philosopher concerned, to be settled and determined by his clear, comprehensive, and impartial view of his own particular case.

It was not until the two boys had scoured, with great rapidity, through a most intricate maze of narrow streets and courts, that they ventured to halt, by one consent, beneath a low and dark archway. Having remained silent here just long enough to recover breath to speak, Master Bates uttered an exclamation of amusement and delight, and, bursting into an uncontrollable fit of laughter, flung himself upon a doorstep, and rolled thereon in a transport of mirth.

'What's the matter?' enquired the Dodger.

'Ha! ha! ha!' roared Charley Bates.

'Hold your noise,' remonstrated the Dodger, looking cautiously around. 'Do you want to be grabbed, stupid?'

'I can't help it,' said Charley – 'I can't help it. To see him splitting away at that pace, and cutting round the corners, and knocking up against the posts, and starting on again as if he was made of iron as well as them, and me, with the wipe in my pocket, singing out arter him – oh, my eye!' The vivid imagination of Master Bates presented the scene before him in too strong colours. As he arrived at this apostrophe, he again rolled upon the doorstep, and laughed louder than before.

'What'll Fagin say?' enquired the Dodger, taking advantage of the next interval of breathlessness on the part of his friend to propound the question.

'What?' repeated Charley Bates.

'Ah, what?' said the Dodger.

'Why, what should he say?' enquired Charley, stopping rather suddenly in his merriment; for the Dodger's manner was impressive. 'What should he say?'

Mr Dawkins whistled for a couple of minutes; then, taking off his hat, scratched his head, and nodded thrice.

'What do you mean?' said Charley.

'Toor rul lol loo, gammon and spinnage, the frog he wouldn't, and high cockolorum,' said the Dodger, with a slight sneer on his intellectual countenance.

This was explanatory, but not satisfactory. Master Bates felt it so, and again said, 'What do you mean?'

The Dodger made no reply; but putting his hat on again, and gathering the skirts of his long-tailed coat under his arm, thrust his tongue into his cheek, slapped the bridge of his nose some half-dozen times in a familiar but expressive manner, and turning on his heel, slunk down the court. Master Bates followed, with a thoughtful countenance.

The noise of footsteps on the creaking stairs, a few minutes after the occurrence of this conversation, roused the merry old gentleman as he sat over the fire with a saveloy and a small loaf in his left hand, a pocket-knife in his right, and a pewter pot on the trivet. There was a rascally smile on his white face as he turned round, and, looking sharply out from under his thick red eyebrows, bent his ear towards the door and listened intently.

'Why, how's this?' muttered the Jew, changing countenance; 'only two of 'em? Where's the third? They can't have got into trouble. Hark!'

The footsteps approached nearer; they reached the landing. The door slowly opened, and the Dodger and Charley Bates entered, closing it behind them.

CHAPTER 13

Some new acquaintances are introduced to the intelligent reader; connected with whom various pleasant matters are related appertaining to this history

'Where's Oliver?' said the furious Jew, rising with a menacing look. 'Where's the boy?'

The young thieves eyed their preceptor as if they were alarmed at his violence, and looked uneasily at each other. But they made no reply.

'What's become of the boy?' said the Jew, seizing the Dodger tightly by the collar, and threatening him with horrid imprecations. 'Speak out, or I'll throttle you!'

Mr Fagin looked so very much in earnest that Charley Bates, who deemed it prudent in all cases to be on the safe side, and who conceived it by no means improbable that it might be his turn to be throttled second, dropped upon his knees, and raised a loud, well-sustained, and continuous roar – something between a mad bull and a speaking trumpet.

'Will you speak?' thundered the Jew, shaking the Dodger so much that his keeping in the big coat at all seemed perfectly miraculous.

'Why, the traps have got him, and that's all about it,' said the Dodger, sullenly. 'Come, let go o' me, will you!' And, swinging himself, at one jerk, clean out of the big coat, which he left in the Jew's hands, the Dodger snatched up the toasting-fork, and made a pass at the merry old gentleman's waistcoat, which, if it had taken effect, would have let a little more merriment out than could have been easily replaced in a month or two.

The Jew stepped back, in this emergency, with more agility than could have been anticipated in a man of his apparent decrepitude, and seizing up the pot, prepared to hurl it at his assailant's head. But Charley Bates, at this moment, calling his attention by a perfectly terrific howl, he suddenly altered its destination, and flung it full at that young gentleman.

'Why, what the blazes is in the wind now?' growled a deep voice. 'Who pitched that 'ere at me? It's well it's the beer, and not the pot, as hit me, or I'd have settled somebody. I might have know'd as nobody but an infernal, rich, plundering, thundering old Jew could afford to throw away any drink but water – and not that, unless he done the River Company every quarter. Wot's it all about, Fagin? Damn me, if my neckankercher ain't lined with beer! Come in, you sneaking warmint; wot are you stopping outside for, as if you was ashamed of your master? Come in!'

The man who growled out these words was a stoutly-built fellow of about five-and-thirty, in a black velveteen coat, very soiled drab breeches, lace-up half-boots, and grey cotton stockings, which enclosed a very bulky pair of legs, with large swelling calves – the kind of legs that, in such costume, always look in an unfinished and incomplete state without a set of fetters to garnish them. He had a brown hat on his head, and a dirty belcher handkerchief round his neck, with the long frayed ends of which he smeared the beer from his face as he spoke. He disclosed, when he had done so, a broad heavy countenance with a beard of three days' growth, and two scowling eyes, one of which displayed various parti-coloured symptoms of having been recently damaged by a blow.

'Come in – d'ye hear?' growled this engaging ruffian.

A white shaggy dog, with his face scratched and torn in twenty different places, skulked into the room.

'Why didn't you come in afore?' said the man. 'You're getting too proud to own me afore company, are you? Lie down.'

This command was accompanied with a kick which sent the animal to the other end of the room. He appeared well used to it, however; for he coiled himself up in a corner very quietly, without uttering a sound, and, winking his very ill-looking eyes about twenty times in a minute, appeared to occupy himself in taking a survey of the apartment.

'What are you up to? – ill-treating the boys, you covetous, avaricious, in-sa-ti-a-ble old fence?' said the man, seating himself deliberately. 'I wonder they don't murder you! *I* would, if I was them. If I'd been your 'prentice, I'd have done it long ago; and – no, I couldn't have sold you afterwards, though, for you're fit for nothing but keeping as a curiosity of ugliness in a glass bottle, and I suppose they don't blow glass bottles large enough.'

'Hush! hush! Mr Sikes,' said the Jew, trembling; 'don't speak so loud.'

'None of your mistering,' replied the ruffian; 'you always mean mischief when you come that. You know my name; out with it! I shan't disgrace it when the time comes.'

'Well, well, then – Bill Sikes,' said the Jew, with abject humility. 'You seem out of humour, Bill.'

'Perhaps I am,' replied Sikes; 'I should think *you* was rather out of sorts too, unless you mean as little harm when you throw pewter pots about as you do when you blab and – '

'Are you mad?' said the Jew, catching the man by the sleeve, and pointing towards the boys.

Mr Sikes contented himself with tying an imaginary knot under his left ear, and jerking his head over on the right shoulder – a piece of dumb show which the Jew appeared to understand perfectly. He then, in cant terms, with which his whole conversation was plentifully besprinkled, but which would be quite unintelligible if they were recorded here, demanded a glass of liquor.

'And mind you don't poison it,' said Mr Sikes, laying his hat upon the table.

This was said in jest; but if the speaker could have seen the evil leer with which the Jew bit his pale lip as he turned round to the cupboard, he might have thought the caution not wholly unnecessary, or the wish (at all events) to improve upon the distiller's ingenuity not very far from the old gentleman's merry heart.

After swallowing two or three glasses of spirits, Mr Sikes condescended to take some notice of the young gentlemen; which gracious act led to a conversation, in which the cause and manner of Oliver's capture were circumstantially detailed, with such alterations and improvements on the truth as to the Dodger appeared most advisable under the circumstances.

'I'm afraid,' said the Jew, 'that he may say something which will get us into trouble.'

'That's very likely,' returned Sikes, with a malicious grin. 'You're blowed upon, Fagin.'

'And I'm afraid, you see,' added the Jew, speaking as if he had not noticed the interruption, and regarding the other closely as he did so – 'I'm afraid that, if the game was up with us, it might be up with a good many more, and that it would come out rather worse for you than it would for me, my dear.'

The man started, and turned fiercely round upon the Jew. But the old gentleman's shoulders were shrugged up to his ears, and his eyes were vacantly staring on the opposite wall.

There was a long pause. Every member of the respectable coterie appeared plunged in his own reflections, not excepting the dog, who, by a certain malicious licking of his lips, seemed to be meditating an attack upon the legs of the first gentleman or lady he might encounter in the streets when he went out.

'Somebody must find out wot's been done at the office,' said Mr Sikes in a much lower tone than he had taken since he came in.

The Jew nodded assent.

'If he hasn't peached, and is committed, there's no fear till he comes out again,' said Mr Sikes; 'and then he must be taken care on. You must get hold of him somehow.'

Again the Jew nodded.

The prudence of this line of action, indeed, was obvious; but, unfortunately, there was one very strong objection to its being adopted – and this was, that the Dodger, and Charley Bates, and Fagin, and Mr William Sikes, happened, one and all, to entertain a most violent and deeply-rooted antipathy to going near a police-office on any ground or pretext whatever.

How long they might have sat and looked at each other in a state of uncertainty not the most pleasant of its kind, it is difficult to say. It is not necessary to make any guesses on the subject, however; for the sudden entrance of the two young ladies whom Oliver had seen on a former occasion, caused the conversation to flow afresh.

'The very thing!' said the Jew. 'Bet will go; won't you, my dear?'

'Where?' enquired the young lady.

'Only just up to the office, my dear,' said the Jew coaxingly.

It is due to the young lady to say that she did not positively affirm that she would not, but that she merely expressed an emphatic and earnest desire to be 'blessed' if she would; a polite and delicate evasion of the request, which shows the young lady to have been possessed of that natural good breeding which cannot bear to inflict upon a fellow-creature the pain of a direct and pointed refusal.

The Jew's countenance fell; and he turned from this young lady, who was gaily, not to say gorgeously attired, in a red gown, green boots, and yellow curl-papers, to the other female.

'Nancy, my dear,' said the Jew in a soothing manner, 'what do *you* say?'

'That it won't do; so it's no use a-trying it on, Fagin,' replied Nancy.

'What do you mean by that?' said Mr Sikes, looking up in a surly manner.

'What I say, Bill,' replied the lady collectedly.

'Why, you're just the very person for it,' reasoned Mr Sikes; 'nobody about here knows anything of you.'

'And as I don't want 'em to, neither,' replied Nancy in the same composed manner, 'it's rather more no than yes with me, Bill.'

'She'll go, Fagin,' said Sikes.

'No, she won't, Fagin,' said Nancy.

'Yes, she will, Fagin,' said Sikes.

And Mr Sikes was right. By dint of alternate threats, promises, and bribes, the lady in question was ultimately prevailed upon to undertake the commission. She was not, indeed, withheld by the same considerations as her agreeable friend; for having very recently removed into the neighbourhood of Field Lane from the remote but genteel suburb of Ratcliffe, she was not under the same apprehension of being recognised by any of her numerous acquaintances.

Accordingly, with a clean white apron tied over her gown, and her curl-papers tucked up under a straw bonnet – both articles of dress being provided from the Jew's inexhaustible stock – Miss Nancy prepared to issue forth on her errand.

'Stop a minute, my dear,' said the Jew, producing a little covered basket. 'Carry that in one hand; it looks more respectable, my dear.'

'Give her a door-key to carry in her t'other one, Fagin,' said Sikes; 'it looks real and geniuine like.'

'Yes, yes, my dear, so it does,' said the Jew, hanging a large street-door key on the forefinger of the young lady's right hand. 'There; very good! very good indeed, my dear!' said the Jew, rubbing his hands.

'Oh, my brother! My poor, dear, sweet, innocent little brother!' exclaimed Nancy, bursting into tears, and wringing the little basket and the street-door key in an agony of distress. 'What has become of him? Where have they taken him to? Oh, do have pity and tell me what's been done with the dear boy, gentlemen; do, gentlemen, if you please, gentlemen!'

Having uttered these words in a most lamentable and heart-broken tone, to the immeasurable delight of her hearers, Miss Nancy paused, winked to the company, nodded smilingly round, and disappeared.

'Ah! she's a clever girl, my dears,' said the Jew, turning round to his young friends, and shaking his head gravely, as if in mute admonition to them to follow the bright example they had just beheld.

'She's a honour to her sex,' said Mr Sikes, filling his glass, and smiting the table with his enormous fist. 'Here's her health, and wishing they was all like her!'

While these, and many other encomiums, were being passed on the accomplished Nancy, that young lady made the best of her way to the police-office, whither, notwithstanding a little natural timidity consequent upon walking through the streets alone and unprotected, she arrived in perfect safety shortly afterwards.

Entering by the back way, she tapped softly with the key at one of the cell-doors, and listened. There was no sound within; so she coughed and listened again. Still there was no reply; so she spoke.

'Nolly, dear?' murmured Nancy in a gentle voice: 'Nolly?'

There was nobody inside but a miserable shoeless criminal, who had been taken up for playing the flute, and who, the offence against society having been clearly proved, had been very properly committed by Mr Fang to the House of Correction for one month, with the appropriate and amusing remark that since he had so much breath to spare, it would be much more wholesomely expended on the treadmill than in a musical instrument. He made no answer, being occupied in mentally bewailing the loss of the flute, which had been confiscated for the use of the county; so Nancy passed on to the next cell, and knocked there.

'Well!' cried a faint and feeble voice.

'Is there a little boy here?' enquired Nancy, with a preliminary sob.

'No,' replied the voice; 'God forbid!'

This was a vagrant of sixty-five, who was going to prison for *not* playing the flute – or in other words, for begging in the streets, and doing nothing for his livelihood. In the next cell was another man, who was going to the same prison for hawking tin saucepans without a licence; thereby doing something for his living, in defiance of the Stamp Office.

But, as neither of these criminals answered to the name of Oliver, or knew anything about him, Nancy made straight up to the bluff officer in the striped waistcoat, and with the most piteous wailings and lamentations, rendered more piteous by a prompt and efficient use of the street-door key and the little basket, demanded her own dear brother.

'*I* haven't got him, my dear,' said the old man.

'Where is he?' screamed Nancy, in a distracted manner.

'Why, the gentleman's got him,' replied the officer.

'What gentleman? Oh, gracious heavens! what gentleman?' exclaimed Nancy.

In reply to this incoherent questioning, the old man informed the deeply-affected sister that Oliver had been taken ill in the office, and discharged in consequence of a witness having proved the robbery to have been committed by another boy, not in custody; and that the prosecutor had carried him away in an insensible condition to his own residence, of and concerning which all the informant knew was, that it was somewhere at Pentonville, he having heard that word mentioned in the directions to the coachman.

In a dreadful state of doubt and uncertainty the agonised young woman staggered to the gate, and then, exchanging her faltering walk for a good, swift, steady run, returned by the most devious and complicated route she could think of to the domicile of the Jew.

Mr Bill Sikes no sooner heard the account of the expedition delivered than he very hastily called up the white dog, and putting on his hat, expeditiously departed, without devoting any time to the formality of wishing the company good-morning.

'We must know where he is, my dears; he must be found,' said the Jew, greatly excited. 'Charley, do nothing but skulk about till you bring home some news of him. Nancy, my dear, I must have him found. I trust to you, my dear – to you and the Artful, for everything! Stay, stay,' added the Jew, unlocking a drawer with a shaking hand; 'there's money, my dears. I shall shut up this shop tonight. You'll know where to find me. Don't stop here a minute – not an instant, my dears!'

With these words he pushed them from the room; and carefully double-locking and barring the door behind them, drew from its place of concealment the box which he had unintentionally disclosed to Oliver. Then he hastily proceeded to dispose the watches and jewellery beneath his clothing.

A rap at the door started him in this occupation. 'Who's there?' he cried in a shrill tone.

'Me!' replied the voice of the Dodger through the keyhole.

'What now?' cried the Jew impatiently.

'Is he to be kidnapped to the other ken, Nancy says?' enquired the Dodger.

'Yes,' replied the Jew, 'wherever she lays hands on him. Find him, find him out, that's all! I shall know what to do next; never fear.'

The boy murmured a reply of intelligence, and hurried downstairs after his companions.

'He has not peached so far,' said the Jew as he pursued his occupation. 'If he means to blab us among his new friends, we may stop his mouth yet.'

CHAPTER 14

Comprising further particulars of Oliver's stay at Mr Brownlow's, with the remarkable prediction which one Mr Grimwig uttered concerning him when he went out on an errand

Oliver soon recovered from the fainting fit into which Mr Brownlow's abrupt exclamation had thrown him; and the subject of the picture was carefully avoided, both by the old gentleman and Mrs Bedwin, in the conversation that ensued, which indeed bore no reference to Oliver's history or prospects, but was confined to such topics as might amuse without exciting him. He was still too weak to get up to breakfast; but, when he came down into the housekeeper's room next day, his first act was to cast an eager glance at the wall, in the hope of again looking on the face of the beautiful lady. His expectations were disappointed however, for the picture had been removed.

'Ah!' said the housekeeper, watching the direction of Oliver's eyes. 'It is gone, you see.'

'I see it is, ma'am,' replied Oliver with a sigh. 'Why have they taken it away?'

'It has been taken down, child, because Mr Brownlow said

that, as it seemed to worry you, perhaps it might prevent your getting well, you know,' rejoined the old lady.

'Oh, no, indeed. It didn't worry me, ma'am,' said Oliver. 'I liked to see it. I quite loved it.'

'Well, well!' said the old lady, good-humouredly; 'you get well as fast as ever you can, dear, and it shall be hung up again. There! I promise you that. Now, let us talk about something else.'

This was all the information Oliver could obtain about the picture at that time. As the old lady had been so kind to him in his illness, he endeavoured to think no more of the subject just then; so he listened attentively to a great many stories she told him, about an amiable and handsome daughter of hers, who was married to an amiable and handsome man, and lived in the country; and about a son, who was clerk to a merchant in the West Indies, and who was also such a good young man, and wrote such dutiful letters home four times a year, that it brought the tears into her eyes to talk about them. When the old lady had expatiated a long time on the excellences of her children, and the merits of her kind good husband besides, who had been dead and gone, poor dear soul! just six-and-twenty years, it was time to have tea; and after tea she began to teach Oliver cribbage, which he learned as quickly as she could teach, and at which game they played, with great interest and gravity, until it was time for the invalid to have some warm wine and water, with a slice of dry toast, and then to go cosily to bed.

They were happy days those of Oliver's recovery. Everything was so quiet, and neat, and orderly, everybody so kind and gentle, that after the noise and turbulence in the midst of which he had always lived, it seemed like heaven itself. He was no sooner strong enough to put his clothes on properly, than Mr Brownlow caused a complete new suit, and a new cap, and a new pair of shoes, to be provided for him. As Oliver was told that he might do what he liked with the old clothes, he gave them to a servant who had been very kind to him, and asked her to sell them to a Jew and keep the money for herself. This she very readily did; and, as Oliver looked out of the parlour window, and saw the Jew roll them up in his bag and walk away, he felt quite delighted to think that they were safely gone, and that there was now no possible danger of his ever being able to wear them again. They were sad rags, to tell the truth; and Oliver had never had a new suit before.

One evening about a week later after the affair of the picture, as he was sitting talking to Mrs Bedwin, there came a message down from Mr Brownlow, that if Oliver Twist felt pretty well, he should like to see him in his study, and talk to him a little while.

'Bless us, and save us! Wash your hands, and let me part your hair nicely for you, child,' said Mrs Bedwin. 'Dear heart alive! If we had known he would have asked for you, we would have put you a clean collar on, and made you as smart as sixpence!'

Oliver did as the old lady bade him; and although she lamented grievously, meanwhile, that there was not even time to crimp the little frill that bordered his shirt collar, he looked so delicate and handsome, despite that important personal advantage, that she went so far as to say, looking at him with great complacency from head to foot, that she really didn't think it would have been possible, on the longest notice, to have made much difference in him for the better.

Thus encouraged, Oliver tapped at the study door. On Mr Brownlow calling to him to come in, he found himself in a little back room quite full of books, with a window looking into some pleasant little gardens, There was a table drawn up before the window, at which Mr Brownlow was seated reading. When he saw Oliver he pushed the book away from him, and told him to come near the table and sit down. Oliver complied, marvelling where the people could be found to read such a great number of books as seemed to be written to make the world wiser. Which is still a marvel to more experienced people than Oliver Twist, every day of their lives.

'There are a good many books, are there not, my boy?' said Mr Brownlow, observing the curiosity with which Oliver surveyed the shelves that reached from the floor to the ceiling.

'A great number, sir,' replied Oliver. 'I never saw so many.'
'You shall read them, if you behave well,' said the old gentleman kindly; 'and you will like that better than looking at the outsides – that is, in some cases, because there *are* books of which the backs and covers are by far the best parts.'

'I suppose they are those heavy ones, sir,' said Oliver, pointing to some large quartos, with a good deal of gilding about the binding.

'Not always those,' said the old gentleman, patting Oliver on the head, and smiling as he did so; 'there are other equally heavy ones, though of a much smaller size. How should you like to grow up a clever man, and write books, eh?'

'I think I would rather read them, sir,' replied Oliver.

'What! wouldn't you like to be a bookwriter?' said the old gentleman.

Oliver considered a little while, and at last said he should think it would be a much better thing to be a bookseller; upon which the old gentleman laughed heartily, and declared he had said a very good thing. Which Oliver felt glad to have done, though he by no means knew what it was.

'Well, well,' said the old gentleman, composing his features, 'don't be afraid! We won't make an author of you while there's an honest trade to be learnt, or brickmaking to turn to.'

'Thank you, sir,' said Oliver. At the earnest manner of his reply, the old gentleman laughed again, and said something about a curious instinct, which Oliver, not understanding, paid no very great attention to.

'Now,' said Mr Brownlow, speaking if possible in a kinder, but at the same time in a much more serious manner than Oliver had ever known him assume yet, 'I want you to pay great attention, my boy, to what I am going to say. I shall talk to you without any reserve, because I am sure you are as well able to understand me as many older persons would be.'

'Oh, don't tell me you are going to send me away, sir, pray!' exclaimed Oliver, alarmed at the serious tone of the old gentleman's commencement. 'Don't turn me out of doors to wander in the streets again. Let me stay here and be a servant. Don't send me back to the wretched place I came from. Have mercy upon a poor boy, sir!'

'My dear child,' said the old gentleman, moved by the warmth of Oliver's sudden appeal, 'you need not be afraid of my deserting you, unless you give me cause.'

'I never, never will, sir,' interposed Oliver.

'I hope not,' rejoined the old gentleman. 'I do not think you ever will. I have been deceived, before, in the objects whom I have endeavoured to benefit; but I feel strongly disposed to trust you, nevertheless; and I am more interested in your behalf than I can well account for, even to myself. The persons on whom I have bestowed my dearest love lie deep in their graves; but, although the happiness and delight of my life lie buried there too, I have not made a coffin of my heart, and sealed it up, for ever, on my best affections. Deep affliction has but strengthened and refined them.'

As the old gentleman said this in a low voice, more to himself than to his companion, and as he remained silent for a short time afterwards, Oliver sat quite still.

'Well, well!' said the old gentleman at length, in a more cheerful tone, 'I only say this because you have a young heart; and knowing that I have suffered great pain and sorrow, you will be more careful, perhaps, not to wound me again. You say you are an orphan, without a friend in the world; all the enquiries I have been able to make confirm the statement. Let me hear your story – where you came from, who brought you up, and how you got into the company in which I found you. Speak the truth, and you shall not be friendless while I live.'

Oliver's sobs checked his utterance for some minutes. When he was on the point of beginning to relate how he had been brought up at the farm, and carried to the workhouse by Mr Bumble, a peculiarly impatient little double-knock was heard at the street door, and the servant, running upstairs, announced Mr Grimwig.

'Is he coming up?' enquired Mr Brownlow.

'Yes, sir,' replied the servant. 'He asked if there were any muffins in the house; and when I told him yes, he said he had come to tea.'

Mr Brownlow smiled; and, turning to Oliver, said that Mr Grimwig was an old friend of his, and he must not mind his being a little rough in his manners, for he was a worthy creature at bottom, as he had reason to know.

'Shall I go downstairs, sir?' enquired Oliver.

'No,' replied Mr Brownlow, 'I would rather you remained here.'

At this moment there walked into the room, supporting himself by a thick stick, a stout old gentleman, rather lame in one leg, who was dressed in a blue coat, striped waistcoat, nankeen breeches and gaiters, and a broad-brimmed white hat, with the sides turned up with green. A very small-plaited shirt-frill stuck out from his waistcoat; and a very long steel watch-chain, with nothing but a key at the end, dangled loosely below it. The ends of his white neckerchief were twisted into a ball about the size of an orange. The variety of shapes into which his countenance was twisted defy description. He had a manner of screwing his head on one side when he spoke, and of looking out of the corners of his eyes at the same time, which irresistibly reminded the beholder of a parrot. In this attitude he fixed himself the moment he made his appearance, and, holding out a small piece of orange peel at arm's length, exclaimed, in a growling, discontented voice, 'Look here! do you see this? Isn't it a most wonderful and extraordinary thing that I can't call at a man's house but I find a piece of this poor surgeon's friend on the staircase? I've been lamed with orange peel once, and I know orange peel will be my death at last. It will, sir; orange peel will be my death, or I'll be content to eat my own head, sir!'

This was the handsome offer with which Mr Grimwig backed and confirmed nearly every assertion he made; and it was the more singular in his case, because, even admitting, for the sake of argument, the possibility of scientific improvements being ever brought to that pass which will enable a gentleman to eat his own head in the event of his being so disposed, Mr Grimwig's head was such a particularly large one, that the most sanguine man alive could hardly entertain a hope of being able to get through it at a sitting – to put entirely out of the question a very thick coating of powder.

'I'll eat my head, sir,' repeated Mr Grimwig, striking his stick upon the ground. – 'Hallo! what's that?' looking at Oliver, and retreating a pace or two.

'This is young Oliver Twist, whom we were speaking about,' said Mr Brownlow.

Oliver bowed.

'You don't mean to say that's the boy who had the fever, I hope?' said Mr Grimwig, recoiling a little more. 'Wait a minute! Don't speak! Stop!' continued Mr Grimwig, abruptly losing all dread of the fever in his triumph at the discovery; 'that's the boy who had the orange! If that's not the boy, sir, who had the orange, and threw this bit of peel upon the staircase, I'll eat my head and his too.'

'No, no, he has not had one,' said Mr Brownlow, laughing. 'Come! put down your hat, and speak to my young friend.'

'I feel strongly on this subject, sir,' said the irritable old gentleman, drawing off his gloves. 'There's always more or less orange peel on the pavement in our street, and I *know* it's put there by the surgeon's boy at the corner. A young woman stumbled over a bit last night, and fell against my garden railings. Directly she got up I saw her look towards his infernal red lamp with the pantomime light. "Don't go to him," I called out of the window, "he's an assassin! a man-trap!" ' So he is. If he is not – ' Here the irascible old gentleman gave a great knock on the ground with his stick; which was always understood, by his friends, to imply the customary offer, whenever it was not expressed in words. Then, still keeping his stick in his hand, he sat down, and opening a double eyeglass, which he wore attached to a broad black ribbon, took a view of Oliver, who, seeing that he was the object of inspection, coloured, and bowed again.

'That's the boy, is it?' said Mr Grimwig, at length.

'That is the boy,' replied Mr Brownlow.

'How are you, boy?' said Mr Grimwig.

'A great deal better, thank you, sir,' replied Oliver.

Mr Brownlow, seeming to apprehend that his singular friend was about to say something disagreeable, asked Oliver to step downstairs and tell Mrs Bedwin they were ready for tea; which, as he did not half like the visitor's manner, he was very happy to do.

'He is a nice-looking boy, is he not?' enquired Mr Brownlow.

'I don't know,' replied Mr Grimwig, pettishly.

'Don't know?'

'No; I don't know. I never see any difference in boys. I only know two sorts of boys – mealy boys and beef-faced boys.'

'And which is Oliver?'

'Mealy. I know a friend who has a beef-faced boy – a fine boy, they call him – with a round head and red cheeks and glaring eyes; a horrid boy; with a body and limbs that appear to be swelling out of the seams of his blue clothes; with the voice of a pilot and the appetite of a wolf. I know him! The wretch!'

'Come,' said Mr Brownlow, 'these are not the characteristics of young Oliver Twist; so he needn't excite your wrath.'

'They are not,' replied Mr Grimwig. 'He may have worse.'

Here Mr Brownlow coughed impatiently, which appeared to afford Mr Grimwig the most exquisite delight.

'He may have worse, I say,' repeated Mr Grimwig. 'Where does he come from? Who is he? What is he? He has had a fever. What of that? Fevers are not peculiar to good people; are they? Bad people have fever sometimes; haven't they, eh? I knew a man who was hung in Jamaica for murdering his master. He had had a fever six times: he wasn't recommended to mercy on that account. Pooh! nonsense!'

Now, the fact was that, in the inmost recesses of his own heart, Mr Grimwig was strongly disposed to admit that Oliver's appearance and manner were unusually prepossessing. But he had a strong appetite for contradiction, sharpened on this occasion by the finding of the orange peel; and inwardly determining that no man should dictate to him whether a boy was well-looking or not, he had resolved, from the first, to oppose his friend. When Mr Brownlow admitted that on no one point of enquiry could he yet return a satisfactory answer, and that he had postponed any investigation into Oliver's previous history until he thought the boy was strong enough to bear it, Mr Grimwig chuckled maliciously. And he demanded, with a sneer, whether the housekeeper was in the habit of counting the plate at night; because, if she didn't find a tablespoon or two missing some sunshiny morning, why, he would be content to – and so forth.

All this, Mr Brownlow, although himself somewhat of an impetuous gentleman, knowing his friend's peculiarities, bore with great good-humour. As Mr Grimwig, at tea, was graciously pleased to express his entire approval of the muffins, matters went on very smoothly; and Oliver, who made one of the party, began to feel more at his ease than he had yet done in the fierce old gentleman's presence.

'And when are you going to hear a full, true, and particular account of the life and adventures of Oliver Twist?' asked Grimwig of Mr Brownlow, at the conclusion of the meal, looking sideways at Oliver, as he resumed the subject.

'Tomorrow morning,' replied Mr Brownlow. 'I would rather he was alone with me at the time. Come up to me tomorrow morning at ten o'clock, my dear.'

'Yes, sir,' replied Oliver. He answered with some hesitation, because he was confused by Mr Grimwig's looking so hard at him.

'I'll tell you what,' whispered that gentleman to Mr Brownlow; 'he won't come up to you tomorrow morning. I saw him hesitate. He is deceiving you, my good friend.'

'I'll swear he is not,' replied Mr Brownlow warmly.

'If he is not,' said Mr Grimwig, 'I'll – ' and down went the stick.

'I'll answer for that boy's truth with my life!' said Mr Brownlow, knocking the table.

'And I for his falsehood with my head!' rejoined Mr Grimwig, knocking the table also.

'We shall see,' said Mr Brownlow, checking his rising anger.

'We will,' replied Mr Grimwig, with a provoking smile; 'we will.'

As fate would have it, Mrs Bedwin chanced to bring in at this moment a small parcel of books which Mr Brownlow had that morning purchased of the identical bookstall keeper who has already figured in this history. Having laid them on the table, she prepared to leave the room.

'Stop the boy, Mrs Bedwin!' said Mr Brownlow; 'there is something to go back.'

'He has gone, sir,' replied Mrs Bedwin.

'Call after him,' said Mr Brownlow; 'it's particular. He is a poor man, and they are not paid for. There are some books to be taken back, too.'

The street door was opened. Oliver ran one way, and the girl ran another, and Mrs Bedwin stood on the step and screamed for the boy; but there was no boy in sight. Oliver and the girl returned, in a breathless state, to report that there were no tidings of him.

'Dear me, I am very sorry for that,' exclaimed Mr Brownlow; 'I particularly wished those books to be returned tonight.'

'Send Oliver with them,' said Mr Grimwig, with an ironical smile; 'he will be sure to deliver them safely, you know.'

'Yes, do let me take them, if you please, sir,' said Oliver. 'I'll run all the way, sir.'

The old gentleman was just going to say that Oliver should not go out on any account, when a most malicious cough from Mr Grimwig determined him that he should; and that by his prompt discharge of the commission, he should prove to him the injustice of his suspicions, on this head at least, at once.

'You *shall* go, my dear,' said the old gentleman. 'The books are on a chair by my table. Fetch them down.'

Oliver, delighted to be of use, brought down the books under his arm in a great bustle, and waited, cap in hand, to hear what message he was to take.

'You are to say,' said Mr Brownlow, glancing steadily at Grimwig – 'you are to say that you have brought those books back; and that you have come to pay the four pound ten I owe him. This is a five-pound note, so you will have to bring me back ten shillings change.'

'I won't be ten minutes, sir,' replied Oliver eagerly. Having buttoned up the bank-note in his jacket pocket, and placed the books carefully under his arm, he made a respectful bow, and left the room. Mrs Bedwin followed him to the street-door, giving him many directions about the nearest way, and the name of the bookseller, and the name of the street, all of which Oliver said he clearly understood; and having superadded many injunctions to be sure and not take cold, the old lady at length permitted him to depart.

'Bless his sweet face!' said the old lady, looking after him. 'I can't bear, somehow, to let him go out of my sight.'

At this moment Oliver looked gaily round, and nodded before he turned the corner. The old lady smilingly returned his salutation, and, closing the door, went back to her own room.

'Let me see: he'll be back in twenty minutes at the longest,' said Mr Brownlow, pulling out his watch, and placing it on the table. 'It will be dark by that time.'

'Oh! you really expect him to come back, do you?' enquired Mr Grimwig.

'Don't you?' asked Mr Brownlow, smiling.

The spirit of contradiction was strong in Mr Grimwig's breast at the moment, and it was rendered stronger by his friend's confident smile.

'No,' he said, smiting the table with his fist, 'I do not. The boy has a new suit of clothes on his back, a set of valuable books under his arm, and a five-pound note in his pocket. He'll join his old friends the thieves, and laugh at you. If ever that boy returns to this house, sir, I'll eat my head.'

With these words he drew his chair closer to the table; and there the two friends sat, in silent expectation, with the watch between them.

It is worthy of remark, as illustrating the importance we attach to our own judgements, and the pride with which we put forth our most rash and hasty conclusions, that, although Mr Grimwig was not by any means a bad-hearted man, and though he would have been unfeignedly sorry to see his respected friend duped and deceived, he really did, most earnestly and strongly, hope at that moment that Oliver Twist might not come back.

It grew so dark that the figures on the dial-plate were scarcely discernible; but there the two old gentlemen continued to sit, in silence, with the watch between them.

CHAPTER 15

Showing how very fond of Oliver Twist the merry old Jew and Miss Nancy were

In the obscure parlour of a low public-house, situated in the filthiest part of Little Saffron Hill – a dark and gloomy den, where a flaring gaslight burnt all day in the winter-time, and where no ray of sun ever shone in the summer – there sat brooding over a little pewter measure and a small glass, strongly impregnated with the smell of liquor, a man in a velveteen coat, drab shorts, half-boots and stockings, whom, even by that dim light, no experienced agent of police would have hesitated for one instant to recognise as Mr William Sikes. At his feet sat a white-coated, red-eyed dog, who occupied himself, alternately, in winking at his master with both eyes at the same time, and in licking a large fresh cut on one side of his mouth which appeared to be the result of some recent conflict.

'Keep quiet, you warmint! keep quiet!' said Mr Sikes, suddenly breaking silence. Whether his meditations were so intense as to be disturbed by the dog's winking, or whether his feelings were so wrought upon by his reflections that they required all the relief derivable from kicking an unoffending animal to allay them, is matter for argument and consideration. Whatever was the cause, the effect was a kick and a curse bestowed upon the dog simultaneously.

Dogs are not generally apt to revenge injuries inflicted upon them by their masters; but Mr Sikes's dog, having faults of temper in common with his owner, and labouring, perhaps, at this moment, under a powerful sense of injury, made no more ado but at once fixed his teeth in one of the half-boots. Having given it a hearty shake, he retired, growling, under a form; thereby just escaping the pewter measure which Mr Sikes levelled at his head.

'You would, would you?' said Sikes, seizing the poker in one hand, and deliberately opening with the other a large clasp-knife, which he drew from his pocket. 'Come here, you born devil! Come here. D'ye hear?'

The dog no doubt heard, because Mr Sikes spoke in the very harshest key of a very harsh voice; but appearing to entertain some unaccountable objection to having his throat cut, he remained where he was, and growled more fiercely than before, at the same time grasping the end of the poker between his teeth and biting at it like a wild beast.

This resistance only infuriated Mr Sikes the more, who, dropping on his knees, began to assail the animal most furiously. The dog jumped from right to left, and from left to right, snapping, growling, and barking; the man thrust and swore, and struck and blasphemed; and the struggle was reaching a most critical point for one or other, when, the door suddenly opening, the dog darted out, leaving Bill Sikes with the poker and the clasp-knife in his hands.

There must always be two parties to a quarrel, says the old adage. Mr Sikes being disappointed of the dog's participation, at once transferred his share in the quarrel to the newcomer.

'What the devil do you come in between me and my dog for?' said Sikes, with a fierce gesture.

'I didn't know, my dear, I didn't know,' replied Fagin, humbly – for the Jew was the newcomer.

'Didn't know, you white-livered thief!' growled Sikes. 'Couldn't you hear the noise?'

'Not a sound of it, as I'm a living man, Bill,' replied the Jew.

'Oh, no! You hear nothing, you don't,' retorted Sikes with a fierce sneer. 'Sneaking in and out, so as nobody hears how you come or go! I wish you had been the dog, Fagin, half a minute ago.'

'Why?' enquired the Jew with a forced smile.

' 'Cause the Government, as cares for the lives of such men as you, as haven't half the pluck of curs, lets a man kill a dog how he likes,' replied Sikes, shutting up the knife with a very expressive look; 'that's why.'

The Jew rubbed his hands, and, sitting down at the table, affected to laugh at the pleasantry of his friend. He was obviously very ill at ease, however.

'Grin away,' said Sikes, replacing the poker, and surveying him with savage contempt – 'grin away. You'll never have the laugh at me, though, unless it's behind a nightcap. I've got the upper hand over you, Fagin; and damn me, I'll keep it. There! if I go, you go; so take care of me.'

'Well, well, my dear,' said the Jew, 'I know all that; we – we – have a mutual interest, Bill – a mutual interest.'

'Humph,' said Sikes, as if he thought the interest lay rather more on the Jew's side than on his. 'Well, what have you got to say to me?'

'It's all passed safe through the melting-pot,' replied Fagin; 'and this is your share. It's rather more than it ought to be, my dear; but as I know you'll do me a good turn another time, and – '

'Stow that gammon,' interposed the robber, impatiently. 'Where is it? Hand over!'

'Yes, yes, Bill; give me time, give me time,' replied the Jew, soothingly. 'Here it is! All safe!' As he spoke he drew forth an old cotton handkerchief from his breast, and, untying a large knot in one corner, produced a small brown-paper packet. Sikes, snatching it from him, hastily opened it, and proceeded to count the sovereigns it contained.

'Is this all?' enquired Sikes.

'All,' replied the Jew.

'You haven't opened the parcel and swallowed one or two as you come along, have you?' enquired Sikes suspiciously. 'Don't put on an injured look at the question; you've done it many a time. Jerk the tinkler.'

These words, in plain English, conveyed an injunction to ring the bell. It was answered by another Jew – younger than Fagin, but nearly as vile and repulsive in appearance.

Bill Sikes merely pointed to the empty measure. The Jew, perfectly understanding the hint, retired to fill it – previously exchanging a remarkable look with Fagin, who raised his eyes for an instant as if in expectation of it, and shook his head in reply so slightly that the action would have been almost imperceptible to an observant third person. It was lost upon Sikes, who was stooping at the moment to tie the bootlace which the dog had torn. Possibly, if he had observed the brief interchange of signals, he might have thought that it boded no good to him.

'Is anybody here, Barney?' enquired Fagin, speaking, now that Sikes was looking on, without raising his eyes from the ground.

'Dot a shoul,' replied Barney, whose words, whether they came from the heart or not, made their way through the nose.

'Nobody?' enquired Fagin, in a tone of surprise, which perhaps might mean that Barney was at liberty to tell the truth.

'Dobody but Biss Dadsy,' replied Barney.

'Nancy!' exclaimed Sikes. 'Where? Strike me blind, if I don't honour that 'ere girl for her native talents.'

'She's bid havid a plate of boiled beef id the bar,' replied Barney.

'Send her here,' said Sikes, pouring out a glass of liquor. 'Send her here.'

Barney looked timidly at Fagin, as if for permission. The Jew remaining silent, and not lifting his eyes from the ground, he retired, and presently returned, ushering in Nancy, who was decorated with the bonnet, apron, basket, and street-door key complete.

'You are on the scent, are you, Nancy?' enquired Sikes, proffering the glass.

'Yes, I am, Bill,' replied the young lady, disposing of its contents; 'and tired enough of it I am, too. The young brat's been ill, and confined to the crib; and – '

'Ah, Nancy, dear!' said Fagin, looking up.

Now, whether a peculiar contraction of the Jew's red eye-brows, and a half-closing of his deeply-set eyes, warned Miss Nancy that she was disposed to be too communicative, is not a matter of much importance. The fact is all we need care for here; and the fact is, that she suddenly checked herself, and, with several gracious smiles upon Mr Sikes, turned the conversation to other matters. In about ten minutes' time Mr Fagin was seized with a fit of coughing; upon which Nancy pulled her shawl over her shoulders and declared it was time to go. Mr Sikes, finding that he was walking a short part of her way himself, expressed his intention of accompanying her; and they went away together, followed, at a little distance, by the dog, who slunk out of a back-yard as soon as his master was out of sight.

The Jew thrust his head out of the room door when Sikes had left it, looked after him as he walked up the dark passage, shook his clenched fist, muttered a deep curse, and then, with a horrible grin, reseated himself at the table, where he was soon deeply absorbed in the interesting pages of *The Hue-and-Cry.*

Meanwhile, Oliver Twist, little dreaming that he was within so very short a distance of the merry old gentleman, was on his way to the bookstall. When he got into Clerkenwell, he accidentally turned down a by-street which was not exactly in his way; but not discovering his mistake until he had got half-way down it, and knowing it must lead in the right direction, he did not think it worth while to turn back, and so marched on, as quickly as he could, with the books under his arm.

He was walking along, thinking how happy and contented he ought to feel, and how much he would give for only one look at poor little Dick – who, starved and beaten, might be weeping bitterly at that very moment – when he was startled by a young woman screaming out very loud, 'Oh, my dear brother!' and he had hardly looked up to see what the matter was, when he was stopped by having a pair of arms thrown tight round his neck.

'Don't,' cried Oliver, struggling. 'Let go of me. Who is it? What are you stopping me for?'

The only reply to this was a great number of loud lamentations from the young woman who had embraced him, and who had a little basket and a street-door key in her hand.

'Oh my gracious!' said the young woman, 'I've found him! Oh Oliver! Oliver! Oh, you naughty boy, to make me suffer such distress on your account! Come home, dear – come. Oh, I've found him! Thank gracious goodness heavens, I've found

him!' With these incoherent exclamations the young woman burst into another fit of crying, and got so dreadfully hysterical that a couple of women who came up at the moment asked a butcher's boy with a shiny head of hair, anointed with suet, who was also looking on, whether he didn't think he had better run for the doctor. To which the butcher's boy, who appeared of a lounging, not to say indolent disposition, replied that he thought not.

'Oh, no, no; never mind,' said the young woman, grasping Oliver's hand – 'I'm better now. Come home directly, you cruel boy! Come!'

'What's the matter, ma'am?' enquired one of the women.

'Oh, ma'am,' replied the young woman, 'he ran away, near a month ago, from his parents, who are hard-working and respectable people, and went and joined a set of thieves and bad characters, and almost broke his mother's heart.'

'Young wretch!' said one woman.

'Go home – do, you little brute!' said the other.

'I'm not,' replied Oliver, greatly alarmed. 'I don't know her. I haven't any sister, or father and mother either. I'm an orphan; I live at Pentonville.'

'Oh, only hear him, how he braves it out!' cried the young woman.

'Why, it's Nancy!' exclaimed Oliver, who now saw her face for the first time, and started back in irrepressible astonishment.

'You see he knows me!' cried Nancy, appealing to the bystanders. 'He can't help himself. Make him come home, there's good people, or he'll kill his dear mother and father, and break my heart!'

'What the devil's this?' said a man, bursting out of a beer-shop, with a white dog at his heels; 'young Oliver! Come home to your poor mother, you young dog. Come home directly.'

'I don't belong to them. I don't know them. Help! help!' cried Oliver, struggling in the man's powerful grasp.

'Help!' repeated the man. 'Yes; I'll help you, you young rascal! What books are these? You've been a-stealing 'em, have you? Give 'em here.' With these words the man tore the volumes from his grasp, and struck him on the head.

'That's right!' cried a looker-on, from a garret window. 'That's the only way of bringing him to his senses!'

'To be sure!' cried a sleepy-faced carpenter, casting an approving look at the garret window.

'It'll do him good!' said the two women.

'And he shall have it, too!' rejoined the man, administering another blow, and seizing Oliver by the collar. 'Come on, you young villain! Here, Bull's-eye! mind him, boy! Mind him!'

Weak with recent illness, stupefied by the blows and the suddenness of the attack, terrified by the fierce growling of the dog and the brutality of the man, and overpowered by the conviction of the bystanders that he really was the hardened little wretch he was described to be – what could one poor child do? Darkness had set in; it was a low neighbourhood; no help was near; resistance was useless. In another moment he was dragged into a labyrinth of dark narrow courts, and forced along them at a pace which rendered the few cries he dared to give utterance to wholly unintelligible. It was of little moment, indeed, whether they were intelligible or no, for there was nobody to care for them, had they been ever so plain.

The gas-lamps were lighted; Mrs Bedwin was waiting anxiously at the open door; the servant had run up the street twenty times, to see if there were any traces of Oliver; and still the two old gentlemen sat perseveringly in the dark parlour, with the watch between them.

CHAPTER 16

Relates what became of Oliver Twist, after he had been claimed by Nancy

The narrow streets and courts at length terminated in a large open space, scattered about which were pens for beasts, and other indications of a cattle-market. Sikes slackened his pace when they reached this spot, the girl being quite unable to support any longer the rapid rate at which they had hitherto walked. Turning to Oliver, he roughly commanded him to take hold of Nancy's hand.

'Do you hear?' growled Sikes, as Oliver hesitated and looked round.

They were in a dark corner, quite out of the track of passengers. Oliver saw, but too plainly, that resistance would be of no avail. He held out his hand, which Nancy clasped tight in hers.

'Give me the other,' said Sikes, seizing Oliver's unoccupied hand. 'Here, Bull's-eye!'

The dog looked up and growled.

'See here, boy!' said Sikes, putting his other hand to Oliver's

Oliver claimed by his affectionate friends

throat; 'if he speaks ever so soft a word, hold him! D'ye mind?'

The dog growled again, and licking his lips, eyed Oliver as if he were anxious to attach himself to his windpipe without delay.

'He's as willing as a Christian, strike me blind if he isn't!' said Sikes, regarding the animal with a kind of grim and ferocious approval. 'Now you know what you've got to expect, master, so call away as quick as you like; the dog will soon stop that game. Get on, young 'un!'

Bull's-eye wagged his tail in acknowledgment of this unusually endearing form of speech, and giving vent to another admonitory growl for the benefit of Oliver, led the way onward.

It was Smithfield that they were crossing, although it might have been Grosvenor Square for anything Oliver knew to the contrary. The night was dark and foggy. The lights in the shops could scarcely struggle through the heavy mist, which thickened every moment and shrouded the streets and houses in gloom, rendering the strange place still stranger in Oliver's eyes, and making his uncertainty the more dismal and depressing.

They had hurried on a few paces, when a deep church-bell struck the hour. With its first stroke, his two conductors stopped, and turned their heads in the direction whence the sound proceeded.

'Eight o'clock, Bill,' said Nancy, when the bell ceased.

'What's the good of telling me that? I can hear it, can't I?' replied Sikes.

'I wonder whether *they* can hear it,' said Nancy.

'Of course they can,' replied Sikes. 'It was Bartlemy time when I was shopped; and there warn't a penny trumpet in the fair as I couldn't hear the squeaking on. Arter I was locked up for the night, the row and din outside made the thundering old jail so silent, that I could almost have beat my head out against the iron plates of the door.'

'Poor fellows!' said Nancy, who still had her face turned towards the quarter in which the bell had sounded. 'Oh, Bill, such fine young chaps as them!'

'Yes; that's all you women think of,' answered Sikes. 'Fine young chaps! Well, they're as good as dead, so it don't much matter.'

With this consolation, Mr Sikes appeared to repress a rising tendency to jealousy; and clasping Oliver's wrist more firmly, told him to step out again.

'Wait a minute!' said the girl. 'I wouldn't hurry by, if it was you that was coming out to be hung the next time eight o'clock struck, Bill. I'd walk round and round the place till I dropped, if the snow was on the ground, and I hadn't a shawl to cover me.'

'And what good would that do?' enquired the unsentimental Mr Sikes. 'Unless you could pitch over a file and twenty yards of good stout rope, you might as well be walking fifty mile off, or not walking at all, for all the good it would do me. Come on, will you, and don't stand preaching there.'

The girl burst into a laugh, drew her shawl more closely round her, and they walked away. But Oliver felt her hand tremble, and looking up in her face as they passed a gas-lamp, saw that it had turned a deadly white.

They walked on, by little-frequented and dirty ways for a full half-hour – meeting very few people, and those appearing, from their looks, to hold much the same position in society as Mr Sikes himself. At length they turned into a very filthy narrow street nearly full of old-clothes shops. The dog running forward, as if conscious that there was no further occasion for his keeping on guard, stopped before the door of a shop that was closed and apparently untenanted. The house was in a ruinous condition; and on the door was nailed a board intimating that it was to let, which looked as if it had hung there for many years.

'All right,' cried Sikes, glancing cautiously about.

Nancy stopped below the shutters, and Oliver heard the sound of a bell. They crossed to the opposite side of the street, and stood for a few moments under a lamp. A noise, as if a sash window were gently raised, was heard, and soon afterwards the door softly opened. Mr Sikes then seized the terrified boy by the collar with very little ceremony, and all three were quickly inside the house.

The passage was perfectly dark. They waited while the person who had let them in chained and barred the door.

'Anybody here?' enquired Sikes.

'No,' replied a voice, which Oliver thought he had heard before.

'Is the old 'un here?' asked the robber.

'Yes,' replied the voice; 'and precious down in the mouth he has been. Won't he be glad to see you? Oh, no!'

The style of this reply, as well as the voice which delivered it, seemed familiar to Oliver's ears; but it was impossible to distinguish even the form of the speaker in the darkness.

'Let's have a glim,' said Sikes, 'or we shall go breaking our necks, or treading on the dog. Look after your legs if you do! That's all.'

'Stand still a moment, and I'll get you one,' replied the voice. The receding footsteps of the speaker were heard; and in another minute the form of Mr John Dawkins, otherwise the Artful Dodger, appeared. He bore in his right hand a tallow candle stuck in the end of a cleft stick.

The young gentleman did not stop to bestow any other mark of recognition upon Oliver than a humorous grin, but, turning away, beckoned the visitors to follow him down a flight of stairs. They crossed an empty kitchen; and, opening the door of a low earthy-smelling room, which seemed to have been built in a small backyard, were received with a shout of laughter.

'Oh, my wig, my wig!' cried Master Charles Bates, from whose lungs the laughter had proceeded; 'here he is! oh, cry, here he is! Oh, Fagin, look at him; Fagin, do look at him! I can't bear it; it is such a jolly game, I can't bear it. Hold me, somebody, while I laugh it out.'

With this irrepressible ebullition of mirth, Master Bates laid himself flat on the floor, and kicked convulsively for five minutes in an ecstasy of facetious joy. Then jumping to his feet, he snatched the cleft stick from the Dodger, and, advancing to Oliver, viewed him round and round; while the Jew, taking off

his nightcap, made a great number of low bows to the bewildered boy. The Artful, meantime, who was of a rather saturnine disposition, and seldom gave way to merriment when it interfered with business, rifled Oliver's pockets with steady assiduity.

'Look at his togs, Fagin!' said Charley, putting the light so close to his new jacket as nearly to set him on fire. 'Look at his togs – superfine cloth, and the heavy-swell cut! Oh, my eye, what a game! And his books, too; nothing but a gentleman, Fagin!'

'Delighted to see you looking so well, my dear,' said the Jew, bowing with mock humility. 'The Artful shall give you another suit, my dear, for fear you should spoil that Sunday one. Why didn't you write, my dear, and say you were coming? We'd have got something warm for supper.'

At this Master Bates roared again – so loud that Fagin himself relaxed, and even the Dodger smiled; but as the Artful drew forth the five-pound note at that instant, it is doubtful whether the sally or the discovery awakened his merriment.

'Hallo! what's that?' enquired Sikes, stepping forward as the Jew seized the note. 'That's mine, Fagin.'

'No, no, my dear,' said the Jew. 'Mine, Bill, mine. You shall have the books.'

'If that ain't mine,' said Bill Sikes, putting on his hat with a determined air – 'mine and Nancy's, that is, I'll take the boy back again.'

The Jew started. Oliver started too, though from a very different cause, for he hoped that the dispute might really end in his being taken back.

'Come! Hand over, will you?' said Sikes.

'This is hardly fair, Bill – hardly fair, is it, Nancy?' enquired the Jew.

'Fair, or not fair,' retorted Sikes, 'hand over, I tell you! Do you think Nancy and me has got nothing else to do with our precious time but to spend it in scouting arter, and kidnapping, every young boy as gets grabbed through you? Give it here, you avaricious old skeleton; give it here!'

With this gentle remonstrance Mr Sikes plucked the note from between the Jew's finger and thumb; and looking the old man coolly in the face, folded it up small, and tied it in his neckerchief.

'That's for our share of the trouble,' said Sikes; 'and not half enough, neither. You may keep the books, if you're fond of reading. If you ain't, sell 'em.'

'They're very pretty,' said Charley Bates, who, with sundry grimaces, had been affecting to read one of the volumes in question; 'beautiful writing, isn't it, Oliver?' At sight of the dismayed look with which Oliver regarded his tormentors, Master Bates, who was blessed with a lively sense of the ludicrous, fell into another ecstasy, more boisterous than the first.

'They belong to the old gentleman,' said Oliver, wringing his hands, 'to the good, kind, old gentleman who took me into his house, and had me nursed, when I was near dying of the fever. Oh, pray send them back – send him back the books and money! Keep me here all my life long; but pray, pray, send them back. He'll think I stole them; the old lady, all of them who were so kind to me, will think I stole them. Oh, do have mercy upon me, and send them back!'

With these words, which were uttered with all the energy of passionate grief, Oliver fell upon his knees at the Jew's feet, and beat his hands together in perfect desperation.

'The boy's right,' remarked Fagin, looking covertly round, and knitting his shaggy eyebrows into a hard knot. 'You're right, Oliver, you're right; they *will* think you have stolen 'em. Ha! ha!' chuckled the Jew, rubbing his hands; 'it couldn't have happened better if we had chosen our time!'

'Of course it couldn't,' replied Sikes; 'I know'd that directly I see him coming through Clerkenwell, with the books under his arm. It's all right enough. They're soft-hearted psalm-singers, or they wouldn't have taken him in at all; and they'll ask no questions after him, fear they should be obliged to prosecute, and so get him lagged. He's safe enough.'

Oliver had looked from one to the other while these words were being spoken, as if he were bewildered and could scarcely understand what passed; but when Bill Sikes concluded, he jumped suddenly to his feet, and tore wildly from the room, uttering shrieks for help, which made the bare old house echo to the roof.

'Keep back the dog, Bill!' cried Nancy, springing before the door, and closing it, as the Jew and his two pupils darted out in pursuit – 'keep back the dog; he'll tear the boy to pieces.'

'Serve him right!' cried Sikes, struggling to disengage himself from the girl's grasp. 'Stand off from me, or I'll split your head against the wall.'

'I don't care for that, Bill; I don't care for that,' screamed the girl, struggling violently with the man; 'the child shan't be torn down by the dog, unless you kill me first.'

'Shan't he!' said Sikes, setting his teeth fiercely. 'I'll soon do that, if you don't keep off.'

The housebreaker flung the girl from him to the farther end of the room, just as the Jew and the two boys returned, dragging Oliver among them.

'What's the matter here?' said Fagin, looking round.

'The girl's gone mad, I think,' replied Sikes savagely.

'No, she hasn't,' said Nancy, pale and breathless from the scuffle – 'no, she hasn't, Fagin; don't think it.'

'Then keep quiet, will you?' said the Jew, with a threatening look.

'No, I won't do that neither,' replied Nancy, speaking very loud. 'Come! what do you think of that?'

Mr Fagin was sufficiently well acquainted with the manners and customs of that particular species of humanity to which Nancy belonged to feel tolerably certain that it would be rather unsafe to prolong any conversation with her at present. With the view of diverting the attention of the company, he turned to Oliver.

'So you wanted to get away, my dear, did you?' said the Jew, taking up a jagged and knotted club which lay in a corner of the fireplace; 'eh?'

Oliver made no reply. But he watched the Jew's motions, and breathed quickly.

'Wanted to get assistance; called for the police, did you?' sneered the Jew, catching the boy by the arm. 'We'll cure you of that, my young master.'

The Jew inflicted a smart blow on Oliver's shoulder with the club, and was raising it for a second when the girl, rushing forward, wrested it from his hand. She flung it into the fire with a force that brought some of the glowing coals whirling out into the room.

'I won't stand by and see it done, Fagin!' cried the girl. 'You've got the boy, and what more would you have? Let him be – let him be, or I shall put that mark on some of you that will bring me to the gallows before my time.'

The girl stamped her foot violently on the floor as she vented this threat; and with her lips compressed, and her hands clenched, looked alternately at the Jew and the other robber, her face quite colourless from the passion of rage into which she had gradually worked herself.

'Why, Nancy!' said the Jew, in a soothing tone, after a pause, during which he and Mr Sikes had stared at one another in a disconcerted manner, 'you – you're more clever than ever tonight. Ha! ha! my dear, you are acting beautifully.'

'Am I?' said the girl. 'Take care I don't overdo it. You will be the worse for it, Fagin, if I do; and so I tell you in good time to keep clear of me.'

There is something about a roused woman, especially if she add to all her other strong passions the fierce impulses of recklessness and despair, which few men like to provoke. The Jew saw that it would be hopeless to affect any further mistake regarding the reality of Miss Nancy's rage; and shrinking involuntarily back a few paces, cast a glance, half-imploring and

Oliver's reception by Fagin and the boys

half-cowardly, at Sikes, as if to hint that he was the fittest person to pursue the dialogue.

Mr Sikes, thus mutely appealed to, and possibly feeling his personal pride and influence interested in the immediate reduction of Miss Nancy to reason, gave utterance to about a couple of score of curses and threats, the rapid production of which reflected great credit on the fertility of his invention. As they produced no visible effect on the object against whom they were discharged, however, he resorted to more tangible arguments.

'What do you mean by this?' said Sikes, backing the enquiry with a very common imprecation concerning the most beautiful of human features, which, if it were heard above only once out of every fifty thousand times that it is uttered below, would render blindness as common a disorder as measles – 'what do you mean by it? Burn my body! Do you know who you are, and what you are?'

'Oh, yes, I know all about it,' replied the girl, laughing hysterically, and shaking her head from side to side, with a poor assumption of indifference.

'Well, then, keep quiet,' rejoined Sikes, with a growl like that he was accustomed to use when addressing his dog, 'or I'll quiet you for a good long time to come.'

The girl laughed again, even less composedly than before; and darting a hasty look at Sikes, turned her face aside, and bit her lip till the blood came.

'You're a nice one,' added Sikes, as he surveyed her with a contemptuous air, 'to take up the humane and genteel side! A pretty subject for the child, as you call him, to make a friend of!'

'God Almighty help me, I am!' cried the girl passionately; 'and I wish I had been struck dead in the street, or had changed places with them we passed so near tonight, before I had lent a hand in bringing him here. He's a thief, a liar, a devil! all that's bad, from this night forth. Isn't that enough for the old wretch without blows?'

'Come, come, Sikes,' said the Jew, appealing to him in a remonstratory tone, and motioning towards the boys, who were eagerly attentive to all that passed; 'we must have civil words – civil words, Bill.'

'Civil words!' cried the girl, whose passion was frightful to see. 'Civil words, you villain! Yes; you deserve 'em from me. I thieved for you when I was a child not half as old as this!' pointing to Oliver. 'I have been in the same trade and in the same service for twelve years since. Don't you know it? Speak out! don't you know it?'

'Well, well,' replied the Jew, with an attempt at pacification; 'and, if you have, it's your living!'

'Ay, it is!' returned the girl, not speaking but pouring out the words in one continuous and vehement stream. 'It is my living; and the cold, wet, dirty streets are my home; and you are the wretch that drove me to them long ago, and that'll keep me there, day and night, day and night, till I die!'

'I shall do you a mischief,' interposed the Jew, goaded by these reproaches – 'a mischief worse than that, if you say much more!'

The girl said nothing more; but tearing her hair and dress in a transport of frenzy, made such a rush at the Jew as would probably have left signal marks of her revenge upon him, had not her wrists been seized by Sikes at the right moment, upon which she made a few ineffectual struggles, and fainted.

'She's all right now,' said Sikes, laying her down in a corner. 'She's uncommon strong in the arms when she's up in this way.'

The Jew wiped his forehead, and smiled, as if it were a relief to have the disturbance over; but neither he, nor Sikes, nor the dog, nor the boys, seemed to consider it in any other light than a common occurrence incidental to business.

'It's the worst of having to do with women,' said the Jew, replacing his club; 'but they're clever, and we can't get on, in our line, without 'em. Charley, show Oliver to bed.'

'I suppose he'd better not wear his best clothes tomorrow, Fagin, had he?' enquired Charley Bates.

'Certainly not,' replied the Jew, reciprocating the grin with which Charley put the question.

Master Bates, apparently much delighted with his commission, took the cleft stick, and led Oliver into an adjacent kitchen where there were two or three of the beds on which he had slept before; and here, with many uncontrollable bursts of laughter, he produced the identical old suit of clothes which Oliver had so much congratulated himself upon leaving off at Mr Brownlow's, and the accidental display of which, to Fagin, by the Jew who purchased them, had been the very first clue received of his whereabouts.

'Pull off the smart ones,' said Charley, 'and I'll give 'em to Fagin to take care of. What fun it is!'

Poor Oliver unwillingly complied. Master Bates, rolling up the new clothes under his arm, departed from the room, leaving Oliver in the dark, and locking the door behind him.

The noise of Charley's laughter, and the voice of Miss Betsy, who opportunely arrived to throw water over her friend, and perform other feminine offices for the promotion of her recovery, might have kept many people awake under more happy circumstances than those in which Oliver was placed. But he was sick and weary, and he soon fell sound asleep.

CHAPTER 17

*Oliver's destiny, continuing unpropitious, brings a
great man to London to injure his reputation*

It is the custom on the stage, in all good murderous melodramas, to present the tragic and the comic scenes in as regular alternation as the layers of red and white in a side of streaky, well-cured bacon. The hero sinks upon his straw bed, weighed down by fetters and misfortunes; and, in the next scene, his faithful but unconscious squire regales the audience with a comic song. We behold, with throbbing bosoms, the heroine in the grasp of a proud and ruthless baron, her virtue and her life alike in danger, drawing forth her dagger to preserve the one at the cost of the other; and, just as our expectations are wrought up to the highest pitch, a whistle is heard, and we are straightway transported to the great hall of the castle, where a grey-headed seneschal sings a funny chorus with a funnier body of vassals, who are free of all sorts of places from church vaults to palaces, and roam about in company, carolling perpetually.

Such changes appear absurd; but they are not so unnatural as they would seem at first sight. The transitions in real life from well-spread boards to deathbeds, and from mourning weeds to holiday garments, are not a whit less startling; only, there, we are busy actors, instead of passive lookers-on, which makes a vast difference. The actors in the mimic life of the theatre are blind to violent transitions and abrupt impulses of passion or feeling, which, presented before the eyes of mere spectators, are at once condemned as outrageous and preposterous.

As sudden shiftings of the scene, and rapid changes of time and place, are not only sanctioned in books by long usage, but are by many considered as the great art of authorship – an author's skill in his craft being, by such critics, chiefly estimated with relation to the dilemmas in which he leaves his characters at the end of every chapter – this brief introduction to the present one may perhaps be deemed unnecessary. If so, let it be considered a delicate intimation on the part of the historian that he is going back, directly, to the town in which Oliver Twist was born; the reader taking it for granted that there are good and substantial reasons for making the journey, or he would not be invited to proceed upon such an expedition on any account.

Mr Bumble emerged at early morning from the workhouse gate, and walked, with portly carriage and commanding steps, up the High Street. He was in the full bloom and pride of beadlehood; his cocked hat and coat were dazzling in the morning sun, and he clutched his cane with the vigorous tenacity of health and power. Mr Bumble always carried his head high; but this morning it was higher than usual. There was an abstraction in his eye, an elevation in his air, which might have warned an observant stranger that thoughts were passing in the beadle's mind too great for utterance.

Mr Bumble stopped not to converse with the small shop-keepers and others who spoke to him, deferentially, as he passed along. He merely returned their salutations with a wave of his hand, and relaxed not in his dignified pace until he reached the farm where Mrs Mann tended the infant paupers with parochial care.

'Drat that beadle!' said Mrs Mann, hearing the well-known shaking at the garden gate, 'if it isn't him at this time in the morning! – Lauk, Mr Bumble, only think of its being you! Well, dear me, it *is* a pleasure, that is! Come into the parlour, sir, please.'

The first sentence was addressed to Susan; and the exclamations of delight were uttered to Mr Bumble, as the good lady unlocked the garden gate, and showed him, with great attention and respect, into the house.

'Mrs Mann,' said Mr Bumble, not sitting upon, or dropping himself into a seat, as any common jackanapes would, but letting himself gradually and slowly down into a chair; 'Mrs Mann, ma'am, good-morning.'

'Well, and good-morning to you, sir,' replied Mrs Mann, with many smiles; 'and hoping you find yourself well, sir!'

'So-so, Mrs Mann,' replied the beadle. 'A porochial life is not a bed of roses, Mrs Mann.'

'Ah, that it isn't, indeed, Mr Bumble,' rejoined the lady. And all the infant paupers might have chorused the rejoinder with great propriety, if they had heard it.

'A porochial life, ma'am,' continued Mr Bumble, striking the table with his cane, 'is a life of worrit, and vexation, and hardihood; but all public characters, as I may say, must suffer prosecution.'

Mrs Mann, not very well knowing what the beadle meant, raised her hands with a look of sympathy, and sighed.

'Ah! you may well sigh, Mrs Mann!' said the beadle.

Finding she had done right, Mrs Mann sighed again; evidently to the satisfaction of the public character, who, repressing a complacent smile by looking sternly at his cocked hat, said, 'Mrs Mann, I am a-going to London.'

'Lauk, Mr Bumble!' cried Mrs Mann, starting back.

'To London, ma'am,' resumed the inflexible beadle, 'by coach – I and two paupers, Mrs Mann. A legal action is a-coming on, about a settlement, and the board has appointed me – me, Mrs Mann – to depose to the matter before the quarter-sessions at Clerkinwell. And I very much question,' added Mr Bumble, drawing himself up, 'whether the Clerkin-well Sessions will not find themselves in the wrong box before they have done with me.'

'Oh! you mustn't be too hard upon them, sir,' said Mrs Mann, coaxingly.

'The Clerkinwell Sessions have brought it upon themselves, ma'am,' replied Mr Bumble; 'and if the Clerkinwell Sessions find that they come off rather worse than they expected, the Clerkinwell Sessions have only themselves to thank.'

There was so much determination and depth of purpose about the menacing manner in which Mr Bumble delivered himself of these words that Mrs Mann appeared quite awed by them. At length she said, 'You're going by coach, sir? I thought it was always usual to send them paupers in carts.'

'That's when they're ill, Mrs Mann,' said the beadle. 'We put the sick paupers into open carts in the rainy weather, to prevent their taking cold.'

'Oh!' said Mrs Mann.

'The opposition coach contracts for these two, and takes them cheap,' said Mr Bumble. 'They are both in a very low state, and we find it would come two pound cheaper to move 'em than to bury 'em – that is if we can throw 'em upon another parish, which I think we shall be able to do, if they don't die upon the road to spite us. Ha! ha! ha!'

When Mr Bumble had laughed a little while, his eyes again encountered the cocked hat, and he became grave.

'We are forgetting business, ma'am,' said the beadle; 'here is your porochial stipend for the month.'

Mr Bumble produced some silver money, rolled up in paper, from his pocket-book; and requested a receipt, which Mrs Mann wrote.

'It's very much blotted, sir,' said the farmer of infants; 'but it's formal enough, I dare say. Thank you, Mr Bumble, sir; I am very much obliged to you, I'm sure.'

Mr Bumble nodded blandly, in acknowledgment of Mrs Mann's curtsy, and enquired who the children were.

'Bless their dear little hearts!' said Mrs Mann, with emotion, 'they're as well as can be, the dears! Of course, except the two that died last week. And little Dick.'

'Isn't that boy no better?' enquired Mr Bumble.

Mrs Mann shook her head.

'He's a ill-conditioned, wicious, bad-disposed porochial child that,' said Mr Bumble, angrily. 'Where is he?'

'I'll bring him to you in one minute, sir,' replied Mrs Mann. 'Here, you, Dick!'

After some calling, Dick was discovered. Having had his face put under the pump, and dried upon Mrs Mann's gown, he was led into the awful presence of Mr Bumble the beadle.

The child was pale and thin, his cheeks were sunken, and his eyes large and bright. The scanty parish dress – the livery of his misery – hung loosely on his feeble body; and his young limbs had wasted away, like those of an old man.

Such was the little being who stood trembling beneath Mr Bumble's glance, not daring to lift his eyes from the floor, and dreading even to hear the beadle's voice.

'Can't you look at the gentleman, you obstinate boy?' said Mrs Mann.

The child meekly raised his eyes, and encountered those of Mr Bumble.

'What's the matter with you, porochial Dick?' enquired Mr Bumble with well-timed jocularity.

'Nothing, sir,' replied the child faintly.

'I should think not,' said Mrs Mann, who had of course laughed very much at Mr Bumble's humour. 'You want for nothing, I'm sure.'

'I should like – ' faltered the child.

'Hey-day!' interposed Mrs Mann, 'I suppose you're going to say that you *do* want for something, now? Why, you little wretch – '

'Stop, Mrs Mann, stop!' said the beadle, raising his hand with a show of authority. 'Like what, sir – eh?'

'I should like,' faltered the child, 'if somebody that can write would put a few words down for me on a piece of paper; and fold it up and seal it; and keep it for me, after I am laid in the ground.'

'Why, what does the boy mean?' exclaimed Mr Bumble, on whom the earnest manner and wan aspect of the child had made some impression, accustomed as he was to such things. 'What do you mean, sir?'

'I should like,' said the child, 'to leave my dear love to poor Oliver Twist; and to let him know how often I have sat by myself and cried to think of his wandering about in the dark nights with nobody to help him. And I should like to tell him,' said the child, pressing his small hands together, and speaking with great fervour, 'that I was glad to die when I was very young; for, perhaps, if I had lived to be a man, and had grown old, my little sister, who is in heaven, might forget me, or be unlike me; and it would be so much happier if we were both children there together.'

Mr Bumble surveyed the little speaker from head to foot with indescribable astonishment, and, turning to his companion, said, 'They're all in one story, Mrs Mann. That outdacious Oliver has demogalised them all!'

'I couldn't have believed it, sir!' said Mrs Mann, holding up her hands, and looking malignantly at Dick. 'I never see such a hardened little wretch!'

'Take him away, ma'am!' said Mr Bumble imperiously. 'This must be stated to the board, Mrs Mann.'

'I hope the gentlemen will understand that it isn't my fault, sir?' said Mrs Mann, whimpering pathetically.

'They shall understand that, ma'am; they shall be acquainted with the true state of the case,' said Mr Bumble. 'There, take him away. I can't bear the sight on him.'

Dick was immediately taken away, and locked up in the coal-cellar. Mr Bumble shortly afterwards took himself off, to prepare for his journey.

At six o'clock next morning, Mr Bumble, having exchanged his cocked hat for a round one, and encased his person in a blue greatcoat with a cape to it, took his place on the outside of the coach, accompanied by the criminals whose settlement was disputed; with whom, in due course of time, he arrived in London. He experienced no other crosses on the way than those which originated in the perverse behaviour of the two paupers, who persisted in shivering, and complaining of the cold, in a manner which Mr Bumble declared caused his teeth to chatter in his head, and made him feel quite uncomfortable, although he had a greatcoat on.

Having disposed of these evil-minded persons for the night, Mr Bumble sat himself down in the house at which the coach stopped, and took a temperate dinner of steaks, oyster sauce, and porter. Putting a glass of hot gin-and-water on the chimney-piece, he drew his chair to the fire; and, with sundry moral reflections on the too-prevalent sin of discontent and complaining, composed himself to read the paper.

The very first paragraph upon which Mr Bumble's eyes rested was the following advertisement:

FIVE GUINEAS REWARD

Whereas a young boy, named Oliver Twist, absconded, or was enticed, on Thursday evening last, from his home, at Pentonville; and has not since been heard of. The above reward will be paid to any person who will give such information as will lead to the discovery of the said Oliver Twist, or tend to throw any light upon his previous history, in which the advertiser is, for many reasons, warmly interested.

And then followed a full description of Oliver's dress, person, appearance, and disappearance, with the name and address of Mr Brownlow at full length.

Mr Bumble opened his eyes; read the advertisement, slowly and carefully, three several times; and in something more than five minutes was on his way to Pentonville, having actually, in his excitement, left the glass of hot gin-and-water untasted.

'Is Mr Brownlow at home?' enquired Mr Bumble of the girl who opened the door.

To this enquiry the girl returned the not uncommon but rather evasive reply of 'I don't know. Where do you come from?'

Mr Bumble no sooner uttered Oliver's name in explanation of his errand, than Mrs Bedwin, who had been listening at the parlour door, hastened into the passage in a breathless state.

'Come in – come in' said the old lady; 'I knew we should hear of him. Poor dear! I knew we should! I was certain of it. Bless his heart! I said so all along.'

Having said this, the worthy old lady hurried back into the parlour again, and, seating herself on a sofa, burst into tears. The girl, who was not quite so susceptible, had run upstairs meanwhile, and now returned with a request that Mr Bumble would follow her immediately, which he did.

He was shown into the little back study, where sat Mr Brownlow and his friend Mr Grimwig, with decanters and glasses before them. The latter gentleman at once burst into the exclamation, 'A beadle! A parish beadle, or I'll eat my head.'

'Pray don't interrupt just now,' said Mr Brownlow. 'Take a seat, will you?'

Mr Bumble sat himself down, quite confounded by the oddity of Mr Grimwig's manner. Mr Brownlow moved the lamp, so as to obtain an uninterrupted view of the beadle's countenance, and said, with a little impatience, 'Now, sir, you come in consequence of having seen the advertisement?'

'Yes, sir,' said Mr Bumble.

'And you *are* a beadle, are you not?' enquired Mr Grimwig.

'I am a porochial beadle, gentlemen,' rejoined Mr Bumble proudly.

'Of course,' observed Mr Grimwig aside to his friend, 'I knew he was. A beadle all over!'

Mr Brownlow gently shook his head to impose silence on his friend, and resumed, 'Do you know where this poor boy is now?'

'No more than nobody,' replied Mr Bumble.

'Well, what *do* you know of him?' enquired the old gentleman. 'Speak out, my friend, if you have anything to say. What *do* you know of him?'

'You don't happen to know any good of him, do you?' said Mr Grimwig caustically, after an attentive perusal of Mr Bumble's features.

Mr Bumble, catching at the enquiry very quickly, shook his head with portentous solemnity.

'You see?' said Mr Grimwig, looking triumphantly at Mr Brownlow.

Mr Brownlow looked apprehensively at Mr Bumble's pursed-up countenance, and requested him to communicate what he knew regarding Oliver in as few words as possible.

Mr Bumble put down his hat, unbuttoned his coat, folded his arms, inclined his head in a retrospective manner, and, after a few moments' reflection, commenced his story.

It would be tedious if given in the beadle's words, occupying, as it did, some twenty minutes in the telling; but the sum and substance of it was, that Oliver was a foundling, born of low and vicious parents; that he had, from his birth, displayed no better qualities than treachery, ingratitude, and malice; that he had terminated his brief career in the place of his birth by making a sanguinary and cowardly attack on an unoffending lad, and running away in the night-time from his master's house. In proof of his really being the person he represented himself, Mr Bumble laid upon the table the papers he had brought to town; and folding his arms again, awaited Mr Brownlow's observations.

'I fear it is all too true,' said the old gentleman sorrowfully, after looking over the papers. 'This is not much for your intelligence; but I would gladly have given you treble the money if it had been favourable to the boy.'

It is not at all improbable that if Mr Bumble had been possessed of this information at an earlier period of the interview, he might have imparted a very different colouring to his little history. It was too late to do it now, however; so he shook his head gravely, and, pocketing the five guineas, withdrew.

Mr Brownlow paced the room to and fro for some minutes, evidently so much disturbed by the beadle's tale that even Mr Grimwig forbore to vex him further.

At length he stopped and rang the bell violently.

'Mrs Bedwin,' said Mr Brownlow, when the housekeeper appeared, 'that boy Oliver is an impostor.'

'It can't be, sir. It cannot be,' said the old lady energetically.

'I tell you he is,' retorted the old gentleman. 'What do you mean he can't be? We have just heard a full account of him from his birth, and he has been a thorough-paced little villain all his life.'

'I never will believe it, sir,' replied the old lady firmly. 'Never!'

'You old women never believe anything but quack-doctors and lying story-books,' growled Mr Grimwig. 'I knew it all along. Why didn't you take my advice in the beginning? You would, if he hadn't had a fever, I suppose, eh? He was interesting, wasn't he? Interesting! bah!' And Mr Grimwig poked the fire with a flourish.

'He was a dear, grateful, gentle child, sir,' retorted Mrs Bedwin, indignantly. 'I know what children are, sir, and have done these forty years; and people who can't say the same, shouldn't say anything about them. That's my opinion!'

This was a hard hit at Mr Grimwig, who was a bachelor. As it extorted nothing from that gentleman but a smile, the old lady tossed her head, and smoothed down her apron preparatory to another speech, when she was stopped by Mr Brownlow.

'Silence!' said the old gentleman, feigning an anger he was far from feeling. 'Never let me hear the boy's name again. I rang to tell you that. Never – never, on any pretence, mind! You may leave the room, Mrs Bedwin. Remember I am in earnest.'

There were sad hearts at Mr Brownlow's that night.

Oliver's heart sank within him when he thought of his good kind friends; it was well for him that he could not know what they had heard, or it might have broken outright.

CHAPTER 18

How Oliver passed his time in the improving society of his reputable friends

About noon next day, when the Dodger and Master Bates had gone out to pursue their customary avocations, Mr Fagin took the opportunity of reading Oliver a long lecture on the crying sin of ingratitude, of which he clearly demonstrated he had been guilty, to no ordinary extent, in wilfully absenting himself from the society of his anxious friends; and, still more, in endeavouring to escape from them after so much trouble and expense had been incurred in his recovery. Mr Fagin laid great stress on the fact of his having taken Oliver in, and cherished him, when, without his timely aid, he might have perished with hunger; and he related the dismal and affecting history of a young lad whom, in his philanthropy he had succoured under parallel circumstances, but who, proving unworthy of his confidence, and evincing a desire to communicate with the police, had unfortunately come to be hanged at the Old Bailey one morning. Mr Fagin did not seek to conceal his share in the catastrophe, but lamented with tears in his eyes that the wrong-headed and treacherous behaviour of the young person in question had rendered it necessary that he should become the victim of certain evidence for the crown, which, if it were not precisely true, was indispensably necessary for the safety of him (Mr Fagin) and a few select friends. Mr Fagin concluded by drawing a rather disagreeable picture of the discomforts of hanging; and, with great friendliness and politeness of manner, expressed his anxious hopes that he might never be obliged to submit Oliver Twist to that unpleasant operation.

Little Oliver's blood ran cold as he listened to the Jew's words, and imperfectly comprehended the dark threats conveyed in them. That it was possible even for justice itself to confound the innocent with the guilty, when they were in accidental companionship, he knew already; and that deeply-laid plans for the destruction of inconveniently knowing or over-communicative persons had been really devised and carried out by the old Jew on more occasions than one, he thought by no means unlikely, when he recollected the general nature of the altercations between that gentleman and Mr Sikes, which seemed to bear reference to some foregone conspiracy of the kind. As he glanced timidly up, and met the Jew's searching look, he felt that his pale face and trembling limbs were neither unnoticed, nor unrelished by, that wary old gentleman.

The Jew smiled hideously; and, patting Oliver on the head, said, that if he kept himself quiet, and applied himself to business, he saw they would be very good friends yet. Then, taking his hat, and covering himself with an old patched greatcoat, he went out, and locked the room door behind him.

And so Oliver remained all that day, and for the greater part of many subsequent days – seeing nobody between early morning and midnight; and left, during the long hours, to commune with his own thoughts, which, never failing to revert to his kind friends, and the opinion they must long ago have formed of him, were sad indeed.

After the lapse of a week or so, the Jew left the room door unlocked, and he was at liberty to wander about the house.

It was a very dirty place. The rooms upstairs had great high wooden chimney-pieces and large doors, with panelled walls and cornices to the ceilings, which, although they were black with neglect and dust, were ornamented in various ways; from all of which tokens Oliver concluded that a long time ago, before the old Jew was born, it had belonged to better people, and had perhaps been quite gay and handsome, dismal and dreary as it looked now.

Spiders had built their webs in the angles of the walls and ceilings; and sometimes, when Oliver walked softly into a room, the mice would scamper across the floor, and run back terrified to their holes. With these exceptions, there was neither sight nor sound of any living thing; and often, when it grew dark, and he was tired of wandering from room to room, he would crouch in the corner of the passage by the street door, to be as near living people as he could; and would remain there, listening and counting the hours, until the Jew or the boys returned.

In all the rooms the mouldering shutters were fast closed, and the bars which held them were screwed tight into the wood; the only light which was admitted, stealing its way through round holes at the top, which made the rooms more gloomy, and filled them with strange shadows. There was a back garret-window, with rusty bars outside, which had no shutter: and out of this Oliver often gazed with a melancholy face for hours together. But nothing was to be descried from it but a confused and crowded mass of house-tops, blackened chimneys, and gable-ends. Sometimes, indeed, a ragged grizzly head might be seen peering over the parapet-wall of a distant house; but it was quickly withdrawn again; and as the window of Oliver's observatory was nailed down, and dimmed with the rain and smoke of years, it was as much as he could do to make out the forms of the different objects beyond, without making any attempt to be seen or heard – which he had as much chance of being as if he had lived inside the ball of St Paul's Cathedral.

One afternoon, the Dodger and Master Bates being engaged out that evening, the first-named young gentleman took it into his head to evince some anxiety regarding the decoration of his person (which, to do him justice, was by no means an habitual weakness with him); and, with this end and aim, he condescendingly commanded Oliver to assist him in his toilet, straightway.

Oliver was but too glad to make himself useful, too happy to have some faces, however bad, to look upon, and too desirous to conciliate those about him when he could honestly do so, to throw any objection in the way of this proposal. So he at once expressed his readiness; and, kneeling on the floor, while the Dodger sat upon the table so that he could take his foot in his lap, he applied himself to a process which Mr Dawkins designated as 'jepanning his trotter-cases'. Which phrase, rendered into plain English, signifieth, cleaning his boots.

Whether it was the sense of freedom and independence

which a rational animal may be supposed to feel when he sits on a table in an easy attitude, smoking a pipe, swinging one leg carelessly to and fro, and having his boots cleaned all the time, without even the past trouble of having taken them off, or the prospective misery of putting them on to disturb his reflections; or whether it was the goodness of the tobacco that soothed the feelings of the Dodger, or the mildness of the beer that mollified his thoughts, he was evidently tinctured, for the nonce, with a spice of romance and enthusiasm foreign to his general nature. He looked down on Oliver with a thoughtful countenance, for brief space; and then raising his head, and heaving a gentle sigh, said, half in abstraction, and half to Master Bates, 'What a pity it is he isn't a prig.'

'Ah!' said Master Charles Bates, 'he don't know what's good for him.'

The Dodger sighed again, and resumed his pipe; as did Charley Bates. They both smoked, for some seconds, in silence.

'I suppose you don't even know what a prig is?' said the Dodger, mournfully.

'I think I know that,' replied Oliver, looking up. 'It's a th –; you're one, are you not?' enquired Oliver, checking himself.

'I am,' replied the Dodger. 'I'd scorn to be anythink else.' Mr Dawkins gave his hat a ferocious cock after delivering this sentiment, and looked at Master Bates, as if to denote that he would feel obliged by his saying anything to the contrary.

'I am,' repeated the Dodger. 'So's Charley. So's Fagin. So's Sikes. So's Nancy. So's Bet. So we all are, down to the dog. And he's the downiest one of the lot!'

'And the least given to peaching,' added Charley Bates.

'He wouldn't so much as bark in a witness-box for fear of committing himself – no, not if you tied him up in one, and left him there without wittles for a fortnight,' said the Dodger.

'Not a bit of it,' observed Charley.

'He's a rum dog. Don't he look fierce at any strange cove that laughs or sings when he's in company?' pursued the Dodger. 'Won't he growl at all, when he hears a fiddle playing? And don't he hate other dogs as ain't of his breed? – Oh, no!'

'He's an out-and-out Christian,' said Charley.

This was merely intended as a tribute to the animal's abilities, but it was an appropriate remark in another sense, if Master Bates had only known it; for there are a great many ladies and gentlemen, claiming to be out-and-out Christians, between whom and Mr Sikes's dog there exists very strong and singular points of resemblance.

'Well, well,' said the Dodger, recurring to the point from which they had strayed, with that mindfulness of his profession which influenced all his proceedings, 'this hasn't got anything to do with young Green here.'

'No more it has,' said Charley. 'Why don't you put yourself under Fagin, Oliver?'

'And make your fortun' out of hand?' added the Dodger, with a grin.

'And so be able to retire on your property, and do the genteel; as I mean to, in the very next leap-year but four that ever comes, and the forty-second Tuesday in Trinity-week,' said Charley Bates.

'I don't like it,' rejoined Oliver, timidly; 'I wish they would let me go. I – I – would rather go.'

'And Fagin would *rather* not!' rejoined Charley.

Oliver knew this too well; but thinking it might be dangerous to express his feelings more openly, he only sighed, and went on with his boot-cleaning.

'Go!' exclaimed the Dodger. 'Why, where's your spirit? Don't you take any pride out of yourself? Would you go and be dependent on your friends?'

'Oh, blow that!' said Master Bates, drawing two or three silk handkerchiefs from his pocket, and tossing them into a cupboard, 'that's too mean, that is.'

'*I* couldn't do it,' said the Dodger, with an air of haughty disgust.

'You can leave your friends, though,' said Oliver, with a half-smile, 'and let them be punished for what you did.'

'That,' rejoined the Dodger, with a wave of his pipe, 'that was all out of consideration for Fagin, 'cause the traps know that we work together, and he might have got into trouble if we hadn't made our lucky – that was the move, wasn't it, Charley?'

Master Bates nodded assent, and would have spoken; but the recollection of Oliver's flight came so suddenly upon him that the smoke he was inhaling got entangled with a laugh, and went up into his head and down into his throat, and brought on a fit of coughing and stamping about five minutes long.

'Look here,' said the Dodger, drawing forth a handful of shillings and halfpence. 'Here's a jolly life! What's the odds where it comes from? Here, catch hold; there's plenty more where they were took from. You won't, won't you? Oh, you precious flat!'

'It's naughty, ain't it, Oliver?' enquired Charley Bates. 'He'll come to be scragged, won't he?'

'I don't know what that means,' replied Oliver.

'Something in this way, old feller,' said Charley. As he said it, Master Bates caught up an end of his neckerchief, and holding it erect in the air, dropped his head on his shoulder, and jerked a curious sound through his teeth; thereby indicating, by a lively pantomimic representation, that scragging and hanging were one and the same thing.

'That's what it means,' said Charley. 'Look how he stares, Jack! I never did see such prime company as that 'ere boy; he'll be the death of me, I know he will.' Master Charles Bates having laughed heartily again, resumed his pipe with tears in his eyes.

'You've been brought up bad,' said the Dodger, surveying his boots with much satisfaction when Oliver had polished them. 'Fagin will make something of you, though, or you'll be the first he ever had that turned out unprofitable. You'd better begin at once; for you'll come to the trade long before you think of it, and you're only losing time, Oliver.'

Master Bates backed this advice with sundry moral admonitions of his own; which, being exhausted, he and his friend Mr Dawkins launched into a glowing description of the numerous pleasures incidental to the life they led, interspersed with a variety of hints to Oliver that the best thing he could do would be to secure Fagin's favour without more delay, by the means which they themselves had employed to gain it.

'And always put this in your pipe, Nolly,' said the Dodger, as the Jew was heard unlocking the door above, 'if you don't take fogles and tickers –'

'What's the good of talking in that way?' interposed Master Bates; 'he don't know what you mean.'

'If you don't take pocket hankechers and watches,' said the Dodger, reducing his conversation to the level of Oliver's capacity, 'some other cove will; so that the coves that lose 'em will be all the worse, and you'll be all the worse too, and nobody half a ha'p'orth the better, except the chaps wot gets them – and you have just as good a right to them as they have.'

'To be sure, to be sure!' said the Jew, who had entered unseen by Oliver. 'It all lies in a nutshell, my dear – in a nutshell; take the Dodger's word for it. Ha! ha! He understands the catechism of his trade.'

The old man rubbed his hands gleefully together as he corroborated the Dodger's reasoning in these terms, and chuckled with delight at his pupil's proficiency. The conversation proceeded no further at this time, for the Jew had returned home accompanied by Miss Betsy, and a gentleman whom Oliver had never seen before, but who was accosted by the Dodger as Tom Chitling; and who, having lingered on the stairs to exchange a few gallantries with the lady, now made his appearance.

Mr Chitling was older in years than the Dodger, having perhaps numbered eighteen winters; but there was a degree of deference in his deportment towards that young gentleman which seemed to indicate that he felt himself conscious of a slight inferiority in point of genius and professional acquirements. He had small twinkling eyes, and a pock-marked face;

Master Bates explains a professional technicality

wore a fur cap, a dark corduroy jacket, greasy fustian trousers, and an apron. His wardrobe was, in truth, rather out of repair; but he excused himself to the company by stating that his 'time' was only out an hour before, and that, in consequence of having worn the regimentals for six weeks past, he had not been able to bestow any attention on his private clothes. Mr Chitling added, with strong marks of irritation, that the new way of fumigating clothes up yonder was infernal unconstitutional, for it burnt holes in them and there was no remedy against the county. The same remark he considered to apply to the regulation mode of cutting the hair; which he held to be decidedly unlawful. Mr Chitling wound up his observations by stating that he had not touched a drop of anything for forty-two mortal long hard-working days; and that he 'wished he might be busted if he warn't as dry as a lime-basket.'

'Where do you think the gentleman has come from, Oliver?' enquired the Jew, with a grin, as the other boys put a bottle of spirits on the table.

'I – I – don't know, sir,' replied Oliver.

'Who's that?' enquired Tom Chitling, casting a contemptuous look at Oliver.

'A young friend of mine, my dear,' replied the Jew. 'He's in luck then,' said the young man, with a meaning look at Fagin. 'Never mind where I came from, young 'un; you'll find your way there soon enough, I'll bet a crown!'

At this sally the boys laughed. After some more jokes on the same subject, they exchanged a few short whispers with Fagin and withdrew.

After some words apart between the last comer and Fagin, they drew their chairs towards the fire; and the Jew, telling Oliver to come and sit by him, led the conversation to the topics most calculated to interest his hearers. These were the great advantages of the trade, the proficiency of the Dodger, the amiability of Charley Bates, and the liberality of the Jew himself. At length these subjects displayed signs of being thoroughly exhausted; and Mr Chitling did the same, for the House of Correction becomes fatiguing after a week or two. Miss Betsy accordingly withdrew, and left the party to their repose.

From this day Oliver was seldom left alone, but was placed in almost constant communication with the two boys, who played the old game with the Jew every day – whether for their own improvement or Oliver's, Mr Fagin best knew. At other times the old man would tell them stories of robberies he had committed in his younger days, mixed up with so much that was droll and curious that Oliver could not help laughing heartily, and showing that he was amused in spite of all his better feelings.

In short, the wily old Jew had the boy in his toils; and, having prepared his mind, by solitude and gloom, to prefer any society to the companionship of his own sad thoughts in such a dreary place, was now slowly instilling into his soul the poison which he hoped would blacken it, and change its hue for ever.

CHAPTER 19

In which a notable plan is discussed and determined on

It was a chill, damp, windy night, when the Jew, buttoning his greatcoat tight round his shrivelled body, and pulling the collar up over his ears so as completely to obscure the lower part of his face, emerged from his den. He paused on the step as the door was locked and chained behind him; and having listened while the boys made all secure, and until their retreating footsteps were no longer audible, slunk down the street as quickly as he could.

The house to which Oliver had been conveyed was in the neighbourhood of Whitechapel. The Jew stopped for an instant at the corner of the street, and, glancing suspiciously round, crossed the road and struck off in the direction of Spitalfields.

The mud lay thick upon the stones, and a black mist hung over the streets; the rain fell sluggishly down; and everything felt cold and clammy to the touch. It seemed just the night when it befitted such a being as the Jew to be abroad. As he glided stealthily along, creeping beneath the shelter of the walls and doorways, the hideous old man seemed like some loathsome reptile, engendered in the slime and darkness through which he moved, crawling forth by night in search of some rich offal for a meal.

He kept on his course, through many winding and narrow ways, until he reached Bethnal Green; then, turning suddenly off to the left, he soon became involved in the maze of the mean and dirty streets which abound in that close and densely-populated quarter.

The Jew was evidently too familiar with the ground he traversed, however, to be at all bewildered, either by the darkness of the night or by the intricacies of the way. He hurried through several alleys and streets; and at length turned into one, lighted only by a single lamp at the farther end. At the door of a house in this street he knocked; and having exchanged a few muttered words with the person who opened it, walked upstairs.

A dog growled as he touched the handle of a room-door, and a man's voice demanded who was there.

'Only me, Bill; only me, my dear,' said the Jew, looking in.

'Bring in your body then,' said Sikes. 'Lie down, you stupid brute! Don't you know the devil when he's got a greatcoat on?'

Apparently the dog had been somewhat deceived by Mr Fagin's outer garment; for as the Jew unbuttoned it, and threw it over the back of a chair, he retired to the corner from which he had risen, wagging his tail as he went, to show that he was as well satisfied as it was in his nature to be.

'Well!' said Sikes.

'Well, my dear,' replied the Jew. 'Ah! Nancy.'

The latter recognition was uttered with just enough of embarrassment to imply a doubt of its reception; for Mr Fagin and his young friend had not met since she had interfered in behalf of Oliver. All doubts upon the subject, if he had any, were speedily removed by the young lady's behaviour. She took her feet off the fender, pushed back her chair, and bade Fagin draw up his, without saying more about it; for it was a cold night, and no mistake.

'It *is* cold, Nancy dear,' said the Jew, as he warmed his skinny hands over the fire. 'It seems to go right through one,' added the old man, touching his side.

'It must be a piercer if it finds its way through *your* heart,' said Mr Sikes. 'Give him something to drink, Nancy. Burn my body, make haste! It's enough to turn a man ill to see his lean old carcass shivering in that way, like a ugly ghost just rose from the grave.'

Nancy quickly brought a bottle from a cupboard, in which there were many, which, to judge from the diversity of their appearance, were filled with several kinds of liquids. Sikes, pouring out a glass of brandy, bade the Jew drink it off.

'Quite enough, quite, thankye, Bill,' replied the Jew, putting down the glass, after just setting his lips to it.

'What! you're afraid of our getting the better of you, are you?' enquired Sikes, fixing his eyes on the Jew. 'Ugh!'

With a hoarse grunt of contempt, Mr Sikes seized the glass, and threw the remainder of its contents into the ashes – as a preparatory ceremony to filling it again for himself, which he did at once.

The Jew glanced round the room, as his companion tossed down the second glassful; not in curiosity, for he had seen it often before, but in a restless and suspicious manner which was habitual to him. It was a meanly-furnished apartment, with nothing but the contents of the closet to induce the belief that its occupier was anything but a working man; and with no more suspicious articles displayed to view than two or three heavy bludgeons which stood in a corner, and a 'life-preserver' that hung over the chimney-piece.

'There,' said Sikes, smacking his lips, 'now I'm ready.'

'For business?' enquired the Jew.

'For business,' replied Sikes; 'so say what you've got to say.'

'About the crib at Chertsey, Bill?' said the Jew, drawing his chair forward, and speaking in a very low voice.

'Yes. Wot about it?' enquired Sikes.

'Ah! you know what I mean, my dear,' said the Jew. 'He knows what I mean, Nancy; don't he?'

'No, he don't,' sneered Mr Sikes. 'Or he won't; and that's the same thing. Speak out and call things by their right names; don't sit there, winking and blinking, and talking to me in hints, as if you warn't the very first that thought about the robbery. What d'ye mean?'

'Hush, Bill, hush!' said the Jew, who had in vain attempted to stop this burst of indignation; 'somebody will hear us, my dear – somebody will hear us.'

'Let 'em hear,' said Sikes; 'I don't care.' But as Mr Sikes *did* care, upon reflection, he dropped his voice as he said the words, and grew calmer.

'There, there,' said the Jew, coaxingly. 'It was only my caution – nothing more. Now, my dear, about that crib at Chertsey; when is it to be done, Bill, eh? – when is it to be done? Such plate, my dear, such plate!' said the Jew, rubbing his hands, and elevating his eyebrows in a rapture of anticipation.

'Not at all,' replied Sikes, coldly.

'Not to be done at all!' echoed the Jew, leaning back in his chair.

'No, not at all,' rejoined Sikes. 'At least it can't be a put-up job, as we expected.'

'Then it hasn't been properly gone about,' said the Jew, turning pale with anger. 'Don't tell me.'

'But I will tell you,' retorted Sikes. 'Who are you that's not to be told? I tell you that Toby Crackit has been hanging about the place for a fortnight, and he can't get one of the servants into a line.'

'Do you mean to tell me, Bill,' said the Jew, softening as the other grew heated, 'that neither of the two men in the house can be got over?'

'Yes, I do mean to tell you so,' replied Sikes. 'The old lady has had 'em these twenty year, and if you were to give 'em five hundred pound, they wouldn't be in it.'

'But do you mean to say, my dear,' remonstrated the Jew, 'that the women can't be got over.'

'Not a bit of it,' replied Sikes.

'Not by flash Toby Crackit?' said the Jew incredulously. 'Think what women are, Bill.'

'No; not even by flash Toby Crackit,' replied Sikes. 'He says he's worn sham whiskers, and a canary waistcoat, the whole blessed time he's been loitering down there; and it's all of no use.'

'He should have tried mustachios and a pair of military trousers, my dear,' said the Jew.

'So he did,' rejoined Sikes, 'and they warn't of no more use than the other plant.'

The Jew looked very blank at this information. After ruminating for some minutes with his chin sunk on his breast, he raised his head, and said, with a deep sigh, that if flash Toby Crackit reported aright, he feared the game was up.

'And yet,' said the old man, dropping his hands on his knees, 'it's a sad thing, my dear, to lose so much when we had set our hearts upon it.'

'So it is,' said Mr Sikes. 'Worse luck!'

A long silence ensued, during which the Jew was plunged in deep thought, with his face wrinkled into an expression of villainy perfectly demoniacal. Sikes eyed him furtively from time to time. Nancy, apparently fearful of irritating the house-breaker, sat with her eyes fixed upon the fire, as if she had been deaf to all that passed.

'Fagin,' said Sikes, abruptly breaking the stillness that prevailed, 'is it worth fifty shiners extra, if it's safely done from the outside?'

'Yes,' said the Jew, as suddenly rousing himself.

'Is it a bargain?' enquired Sikes.

'Yes, my dear, yes,' rejoined the Jew, his eyes glistening, and every muscle in his face working, with the excitement that the enquiry had awakened.

'Then,' said Sikes, thrusting aside the Jew's hand with some disdain, 'let it come off as soon as you like. Toby and I were over the garden-wall the night afore last, sounding the panels of the door and shutters. The crib's barred up at night like a jail; but there's one part we can crack, safe and softly.'

'Which is that, Bill?' asked the Jew eagerly.

'Why,' whispered Sikes, 'as you cross the lawn – '

'Yes, yes,' said the Jew, bending his head forward, with his eyes almost starting out of it.

'Umph!' cried Sikes, stopping short, as the girl, scarcely moving her head, looked suddenly round, and pointed for an instant to the Jew's face. 'Never mind which part it is. You can't do it without me, I know; but it's best to be on the safe side when one deals with you.'

'As you like, my dear, as you like,' replied the Jew. 'Is there no help wanted but yours and Toby's?'

'None,' said Sikes. ' 'Cept a centre-bit and a boy. The first we've both got; the second you must find us.'

'A boy,' exclaimed the Jew. 'Oh! then it's a panel, eh?'

'Never mind wot it is!' replied Sikes. 'I want a boy; and he mustn't be a big 'un. Lord!' said Mr Sikes, reflectively, 'if I'd only got that young boy of Ned, the chimbley-sweeper's! He kept him small on purpose, and let him out by the job. But the father gets lagged; and then the Juvenile Delinquent Society comes, and takes the boy away from a trade where he was arning money, teaches him to read and write, and in time makes a 'prentice of him. And so they go on,' said Mr Sikes, his wrath rising with the recollection of his wrongs, 'so they go on; and, if they'd got money enough (which it's a Providence they have not) we shouldn't have half a dozen boys left in the whole trade in a year or two.'

'No more we should,' acquiesced the Jew, who had been considering during this speech, and had only caught the last sentence. 'Bill!'

'What now?' enquired Sikes.

The Jew nodded his head towards Nancy, who was still gazing at the fire, and intimated, by a sign, that he would have her told to leave the room. Sikes shrugged his shoulders impatiently, as if he thought the precaution unnecessary; but complied, nevertheless, by requesting Miss Nancy to fetch him a jug of beer.

'You don't want any beer,' said Nancy, folding her arms, and retaining her seat very composedly.

'I tell you I do!' replied Sikes.

'Nonsense,' rejoined the girl, coolly. 'Go on, Fagin. I know what he's going to say, Bill; he needn't mind me.'

The Jew still hesitated. Sikes looked from one to the other in some surprise.

'Why, you don't mind the old girl, do you, Fagin?' he asked at length. 'You've known her long enough to trust her, or the devil's in it. She ain't one to blab. Are you, Nancy?'

'*I* should think not!' replied the young lady, drawing her chair up to the table, and putting her elbows upon it.

'No, no, my dear, I know you're not,' said the Jew; 'but – ' and again the old man paused.

'But wot?' enquired Sikes.

'I didn't know whether she mightn't p'r'aps be out of sorts, you know, my dear, as she was the other night,' replied the Jew.

At this confession Miss Nancy burst into a loud laugh; and swallowing a glass of brandy, shook her head with an air of defiance, and burst into sundry exclamations of 'Keep the game a-going!' 'Never say die!' and the like. These seemed at once to have the effect of reassuring both gentlemen; for the Jew nodded his head with a satisfied air, and resumed his seat, as did Mr Sikes likewise.

'Now, Fagin,' said Nancy with a laugh, 'tell Bill at once about Oliver!'

'Ha! you're a clever one, my dear; the sharpest girl I ever saw!' said the Jew, patting her on the neck. 'It *was* about Oliver I was going to speak, sure enough. Ha! ha! ha!'

'What about him?' demanded Sikes.

'He's the boy for you, my dear,' replied the Jew in a hoarse whisper, laying his finger on the side of his nose, and grinning frightfully.

'He!' exclaimed Sikes.

'Have him, Bill!' said Nancy. 'I would, if I was in your place. He mayn't be so much up as any of the others; but that's not what you want, if he's only to open a door for you. Depend upon it he's a safe one, Bill.'

'I know he is,' rejoined Fagin. 'He's been in good training these last few weeks; and it's time he began to work for his bread. Besides, the others are all too big.'

'Well, he is just the size I want,' said Mr Sikes, ruminating.

'And will do everything you want, Bill, my dear,' interposed the Jew; 'he can't help himself – that is, if you frighten him enough.'

'Frighten him?' echoed Sikes. 'It'll be no sham frightening, mind you. If there's anything queer about him when we once get into the work, in for a penny, in for a pound. You won't see him alive again, Fagin. Think of that before you send him. Mark my words!' said the robber, poising a crowbar which he had drawn from under the bedstead.

'I've thought of it all,' said the Jew with energy. 'I've – I've had my eye upon him, my dears, close – close. Once let him feel that he is one of us – once fill his mind with the idea that he has been a thief – and he's ours! Ours for his life. Oho! It couldn't have come about better!' The old man crossed his arms upon his breast, and drawing his head and shoulders into a heap, literally hugged himself for joy.

'Ours?' said Sikes. 'Yours, you mean.'

'Perhaps I do, my dear,' said the Jew, with a shrill chuckle. 'Mine, if you like, Bill.'

'And wot,' said Sikes, scowling fiercely on his agreeable friend, 'wot makes you take so much pains about one chalk-faced kid, when you know there are fifty boys snoozing about Common Garden every night as you might pick and choose from?'

'Because they're of no use to me, my dear,' replied the Jew, with some confusion, 'not worth the taking. Their looks convict 'em when they get into trouble, and I lose 'em all. With this boy properly managed, my dears, I could do what I couldn't with twenty of them. Besides,' said the Jew, recovering his self-possession, 'he has us now if he could only give us leg-bail again; and he *must* be in the same boat with us. Never mind how he came there; it's quite enough for my power over him that he was in a robbery – that's all I want. Now, how much better this is than being obliged to put the poor leetle boy out of the way, which would be dangerous; and we should lose by it besides.'

'When is it to be done?' asked Nancy, stopping some turbulent exclamation on the part of Mr Sikes, expressive of the disgust with which he received Fagin's affectation of humanity.

'Ah, to be sure,' said the Jew. 'When is it to be done, Bill?'

'I planned, with Toby, the night arter tomorrow,' rejoined Sikes in a surly voice, 'if he heerd nothing from me to the contrary.'

'Good,' said the Jew; 'there's no moon.'

'No,' rejoined Sikes.

'It's all arranged about bringing off the swag, is it?' asked the Jew.

Sikes nodded.

'And about – '

'Oh, ah, it's all planned,' rejoined Sikes, interrupting him. 'Never mind particulars. You'd better bring the boy here tomorrow night; I shall get off the stones an hour arter daybreak. Then you hold your tongue, and keep the melting-pot ready; and that's all you'll have to do.'

After some discussion, in which all three took an active part, it was decided that Nancy should repair to the Jew's next evening when the night had set in, and bring Oliver away with her; Fagin craftily observing that, if he evinced any disinclination to the task, he would be more willing to accompany the girl who had so recently interfered in his behalf than anybody else. It was also solemnly arranged that poor Oliver should, for the purposes of the contemplated expedition, be unreservedly consigned to the care and custody of Mr William Sikes; and further, that the said Sikes should deal with him as he thought fit, and should not be held responsible by the Jew for any mischance or evil that might befall the boy, or any punishment with which it might be necessary to visit him: it being understood that, to render the compact in this respect binding, any representations made by Mr Sikes on his return should be required to be confirmed and corroborated, in all important particulars, by the testimony of flash Toby Crackit.

These preliminaries adjusted, Mr Sikes proceeded to drink brandy at a furious rate, and to flourish the crowbar in an alarming manner; yelling forth, at the same time, most un-musical snatches of song, mingled with wild execrations. At length, in a fit of professional enthusiasm, he insisted upon producing his box of housebreaking tools; which he had no sooner stumbled in with, and opened for the purpose of explaining the nature and properties of the various implements it contained, and the peculiar beauties of their construction, than he fell over it upon the floor, and went to sleep where he fell.

'Good-night, Nancy,' said the Jew, muffling himself up as before.

'Good-night.'

Their eyes met, and the Jew scrutinised her narrowly. There was no flinching about the girl. She was as true and earnest in the matter as Toby Crackit himself could be.

The Jew again bade her good-night; and bestowing a sly kick upon the prostrate form of Mr Sikes, while her back was turned, groped downstairs.

'Always the way!' muttered the Jew to himself as he turned

homewards. 'The worst of these women is, that a very little thing serves to call up some long-forgotten feeling; and the best of them is, that it never lasts. Ha! ha! the man against the child, for a bag of gold!'

Beguiling the time with these pleasant reflections, Mr Fagin wended his way, through mud and mire, to his gloomy abode, where the Dodger was sitting up impatiently awaiting his return.

'Is Oliver a-bed? I want to speak to him,' was his first remark as they descended the stairs.

'Hours ago,' replied the Dodger, throwing open a door. 'Here he is!'

The boy was lying, fast asleep, on a rude bed upon the floor, so pale with anxiety, and sadness, and the closeness of his prison, that he looked like death; not death as it shows in shroud and coffin, but in the guise it wears when life has just departed – when a young and gentle spirit has but an instant fled to Heaven, and the gross air of the world has not had time to breathe upon the changing dust it hallowed.

'Not now,' said the Jew, turning softly away. 'Tomorrow. Tomorrow.'

CHAPTER 20

Wherein Oliver is delivered over to Mr William Sikes

When Oliver awoke in the morning, he was a good deal surprised to find that a new pair of shoes, with strong thick soles, had been placed at his bedside, and that his old ones had been removed. At first he was pleased with the discovery, hoping that it might be the forerunner of his release; but such thoughts were quickly dispelled on his sitting down to breakfast along with the Jew, who told him, in a tone and manner which increased his alarm, that he was to be taken to the residence of Bill Sikes that night.

'To – to – stop there, sir?' asked Oliver anxiously.

'No, no, my dear; not to stop there,' replied the Jew. 'We shouldn't like to lose you. Don't be afraid, Oliver, you shall come back to us again. Ha! ha! ha! We won't be so cruel as to send you away, my dear. Oh, no, no!'

The old man, who was stooping over the fire toasting a piece of bread, looked round as he bantered Oliver thus, and chuckled, as if to show that he knew he would still be very glad to get away if he could.

'I suppose,' said the Jew, fixing his eyes on Oliver, 'you want to know what you're going to Bill's for – eh, my dear?'

Oliver coloured, involuntarily, to find that the old thief had been reading his thoughts; but boldly said, Yes, he did want to know.

'Why, do you think?' enquired Fagin, parrying the question.

'Indeed I don't know, sir,' replied Oliver.

'Bah!' said the Jew, turning away with a disappointed countenance from a close perusal of the boy's face. 'Wait till Bill tells you, then.'

The Jew seemed much vexed by Oliver's not expressing any greater curiosity on the subject; but the truth is, that although he felt very anxious, he was too much confused by the earnest cunning of Fagin's looks, and his own speculations, to make any further enquiries just then. He had no other opportunity; for the Jew remained very surly and silent till night, when he prepared to go abroad.

'You may burn a candle,' said the Jew, putting one upon the table. 'And here's a book for you to read, till they come to fetch you. Good-night.'

'Good-night!' replied Oliver softly.

The Jew walked to the door, looking over his shoulder at the boy as he went. Suddenly stopping, he called him by his name.

Oliver looked up, and the Jew, pointing to the candle, motioned him to light it. He did so; and as he placed the candlestick upon the table, saw that the Jew was gazing fixedly at him, with lowering and contracted brows, from the dark end of the room.

'Take heed, Oliver, take heed!' said the old man, shaking his right hand before him in a warning manner. 'He's a rough man, and thinks nothing of blood when his own is up. Whatever falls out, say nothing; and do what he bids you. Mind!' Placing a strong emphasis on the last word, he suffered his features gradually to resolve themselves into a ghastly grin, and, nodding his head, left the room.

Oliver leaned his head upon his hand when the old man disappeared, and pondered, with a trembling heart, on the words he had just heard. The more he thought of the Jew's admonition, the more he was at a loss to divine its real purpose and meaning. He could think of no bad object to be attained by sending him to Sikes, which would not be equally well answered by his remaining with Fagin; and after meditating for a long time, concluded that he had been selected to perform some ordinary menial offices for the housebreaker, until another boy, better suited for his purpose, could be engaged. He was too well accustomed to suffering, and had suffered too much where he was, to bewail the prospect of change very severely. He remained lost in thought for some minutes; and then, with a heavy sigh, snuffed the candle, and taking up the book which the Jew had left with him, began to read.

He turned over the leaves – carelessly at first; but, lighting on a passage which attracted his attention, he soon became intent upon the volume. It was a history of the lives and trials of great criminals, and the pages were soiled and thumbed with use. Here he read of dreadful crimes that made the blood run cold – of secret murders that had been committed by the lonely wayside, and bodies hidden from the eye of man in deep pits and wells, which would not keep them down, deep as they were, but had yielded them up at last, after many years, and so maddened the murderers with the sight that in their horror they had confessed their guilt, and yelled for the gibbet to end their agony. Here, too, he read of men who, lying in their beds at dead of night, had been tempted (as they said) and led on, by their own bad thoughts, to such dreadful bloodshed as it made the flesh creep and the limbs quail to think of. The terrible descriptions were so real and vivid that the sallow pages seemed to turn red with gore, and the words upon them to be sounded in his ears as if they were whispered, in hollow murmurs, by the spirits of the dead.

In a paroxysm of fear the boy closed the book, and thrust it from him. Then, falling upon his knees, he prayed Heaven to spare him from such deeds, and rather to will that he should die at once than be reserved for crimes so fearful and appalling. By degrees he grew more calm, and besought, in a low and broken voice, that he might be rescued from his present dangers; and that if any aid were to be raised up for a poor outcast boy, who had never known the love of friends or kindred, it might come to him now, when, desolate and deserted, he stood alone in the midst of wickedness and guilt.

He had concluded his prayer, but still remained with his head buried in his hands, when a rustling noise aroused him.

'What's that?' he cried, starting up, and catching sight of a figure standing by the door. 'Who's there?'

'Me – only me,' replied a tremulous voice.

Oliver raised the candle above his head, and looked towards the door. It was Nancy.

'Put down the light,' said the girl, turning away her head. 'It hurts my eyes.'

Oliver saw that she was very pale, and gently enquired if she were ill. The girl threw herself into a chair, with her back towards him, and wrung her hands, but made no reply.

'God forgive me!' she cried after a while; 'I never thought of this.'

'Has anything happened?' asked Oliver. 'Can I help you? I will if I can. I will, indeed.'

She rocked herself to and fro, caught her throat, and, uttering a gurgling sound, struggled and gasped for breath.

'Nancy!' cried Oliver, 'what is it?'

The girl beat her hands upon her knees, and her feet upon the ground, and, suddenly stopping, drew her shawl close around her, and shivered with cold.

Oliver stirred the fire. Drawing her chair close to it, she sat there, for a little time, without speaking; but at length she raised her head, and looked round.

'I don't know what comes over me sometimes,' said she, affecting to busy herself in arranging her dress; 'it's this damp, dirty room, I think. Now, Nolly, dear, are you ready?'

'Am I to go with you?' asked Oliver.

'Yes; I have come from Bill,' replied the girl. 'You are to go with me.'

'What for?' said Oliver, recoiling.

'What for?' echoed the girl, raising her eyes, and averting them again the moment they encountered the boy's face. 'Oh, for no harm.'

'I don't believe it,' said Oliver, who had watched her closely.

'Have it your own way,' rejoined the girl, affecting to laugh. 'For no good then.'

Oliver could see that he had some power over the girl's better feelings, and, for an instant, thought of appealing to her compassion for his helpless state. But then, the thought darted across his mind that it was barely eleven o'clock, and that many people were still in the streets, of whom surely some might be found to give credence to his tale. As the reflection occurred to

him, he stepped forward and said, somewhat hastily, that he was ready.

Neither his brief consideration, nor its purport, was lost on his companion. She eyed him narrowly while he spoke, and cast upon him a look of intelligence which sufficiently showed that she guessed what had been passing in his thoughts.

'Hush!' said the girl, stooping over him, and pointing to the door as she looked cautiously round. 'You can't help yourself. I have tried hard for you, but all to no purpose. You are hedged round and round; and if ever you are to get loose from here, this is not the time.'

Struck by the energy of her manner, Oliver looked up in her face with great surprise. She seemed to speak the truth; her countenance was white and agitated, and she trembled with very earnestness.

'I have saved you from being ill-used once, and I will again, and I do now,' continued the girl aloud; 'for those who would have fetched you, if I had not, would have been far more rough than me. I have promised for your being quiet and silent: if you are not, you will only do harm to yourself and me too; and perhaps be my death. See here! I have borne all this for you already, as true as God sees me show it.'

She pointed, hastily, to some livid bruises on her neck and arms, and continued with great rapidity: 'Remember this! and don't let me suffer more for you just now. If I could help you, I would; but I have not the power. They don't mean to harm you; and whatever they make you do is no fault of yours. Hush! every word from you is a blow for me. Give me your hand. Make haste! Your hand!'

She caught the hand which Oliver instinctively placed in hers, and, blowing out the light, drew him after her up the stairs. The door was opened quickly by someone shrouded in the darkness, and was as quickly closed when they had passed out. A hackney cabriolet was in waiting. With the same vehemence which she had exhibited in addressing Oliver, the girl pulled him in with her, and drew the curtains close. The driver wanted no directions, but lashed his horse into full speed without the delay of an instant.

The girl still held Oliver fast by the hand, and continued to pour into his ear the warnings and assurances she had already imparted. All was so quick and hurried that he had scarcely time to recollect where he was, or how he came there, when the carriage stopped at the house to which the Jew's steps had been directed on the previous evening.

For one brief moment Oliver cast a hurried glance along the empty street, and a cry for help hung upon his lips. But the girl's voice was in his ear, beseeching him in such tones of agony to remember her, that he had not the heart to utter it. While he hesitated, the opportunity was gone, for he was already in the house, and the door was shut.

'This way,' said the girl, releasing her hold for the first time. 'Bill!'

'Hallo!' replied Sikes, appearing at the head of the stairs with a candle. 'Oh! that's the time of day. Come on!'

This was a very strong expression of approbation, an uncommonly hearty welcome, from a person of Mr Sikes's temperament. Nancy, appearing much gratified thereby, saluted him cordially.

'Bull's-eye's gone home with Tom,' observed Sikes, as he lighted them up. 'He'd have been in the way.'

'That's right,' rejoined Nancy.

'So you've got the kid,' said Sikes, when they had all reached the room, closing the door as he spoke.

'Yes; here he is,' replied Nancy.

'Did he come quiet?' enquired Sikes.

'Like a lamb,' rejoined Nancy.

'I'm glad to hear it,' said Sikes, looking grimly at Oliver; 'for the sake of his young carcass, as would otherways have suffered for it. Come here, young 'un; and let me read you a lectur', which is as well got over at once.'

Thus addressing his new pupil, Mr Sikes pulled off Oliver's cap and threw it into a corner; and then, taking him by the shoulder, sat himself down by the table, and stood the boy in front of him.

'Now, first; do you know wot this is?' enquired Sikes, taking up a pocket-pistol which lay on the table.

Oliver replied in the affirmative.

'Well, then, look here,' continued Sikes. 'This is powder, that ere's a bullet, and this is a little bit of a old hat for waddin'.'

Oliver murmured his comprehension of the different bodies referred to; and Mr Sikes proceeded to load the pistol, with great nicety and deliberation.

'Now it's loaded,' said Mr Sikes, when he had finished.

'Yes, I see it is, sir,' replied Oliver.

'Well,' said the robber, grasping Oliver's wrist tightly, and putting the barrel so close to his temple that they touched; at which moment the boy could not repress a start – 'if you speak a word when you're out o' doors with me, except when I speak to you, that loading will be in your head without notice. So, if you *do* make up your mind to speak without leave, say your prayers first.'

Having bestowed a scowl upon the object of this warning, to increase its effect, Mr Sikes continued: 'As near as I know, there isn't anybody as would be asking very partickler arter you, if you *was* disposed of; so I needn't take this devil-and-all of trouble to explain matters to you, if it warn't for your own good. D'ye hear me?'

'The short and the long of what you mean,' said Nancy, speaking very emphatically, and slightly frowning at Oliver, as if to bespeak his serious attention to her words, 'is, that if you're crossed by him in this job you have on hand, you'll prevent his ever telling tales afterwards by shooting him through the head; and will take your chance of swinging for it, as you do for a great many other things in the way of business, every month of your life.'

'That's it!' observed Mr Sikes, approvingly; 'women can always put things in fewest words. Except when it's a-blowing up; and then they lengthens it out. And now that he's thoroughly up to it, let's have some supper, and get a snooze before starting.'

In pursuance of this request, Nancy quickly laid the cloth, and, disappearing for a few minutes, presently returned with a pot of porter and a dish of sheep's heads; which gave occasion to several pleasant witticisms on the part of Mr Sikes, founded upon the singular coincidence of 'jemmies' being a cant name common to them, and also to an ingenious implement much used in his profession. Indeed, the worthy gentleman, stimulated perhaps by the immediate prospect of being in active service, was in great spirits and good-humour; in proof whereof it may be here remarked that he humorously drank all the beer at a draught, and did not utter, on a rough calculation, more than fourscore oaths during the whole progress of the meal.

Supper being ended – it may be easily conceived that Oliver had no great appetite for it – Mr Sikes disposed of a couple of glasses of spirits and water, and threw himself upon the bed, ordering Nancy, with many imprecations in case of failure, to call him at five precisely. Oliver stretched himself in his clothes by command of the same authority on a mattress upon the floor; and the girl, mending the fire, sat before it, in readiness to rouse them at the appointed time.

For a long time Oliver lay awake, thinking it not impossible that Nancy might seek that opportunity of whispering some further advice; but the girl sat brooding over the fire, without moving, save now and then to trim the light. Weary with watching and anxiety, he at length fell asleep.

When he awoke the table was covered with tea things, and Sikes was thrusting various articles into the pockets of his great-coat, which hung over the back of a chair; while Nancy was busily engaged in preparing breakfast. It was not yet daylight, for the candle was still burning, and it was quite dark outside. A sharp rain, too, was beating against the window panes, and the sky looked black and cloudy.

'Now then!' growled Sikes, as Oliver started up; 'half-past five! Look sharp, or you'll get no breakfast, for it's late as it is.'

Oliver was not long in making his toilet; and, having taken some breakfast, replied to a surly enquiry from Sikes, by saying that he was quite ready.

Nancy, scarcely looking at the boy, threw him a handkerchief to tie round his throat; and Sikes gave him a large rough cape to button over his shoulders. Thus attired, he gave his hand to the robber, who, merely pausing to show him, with a menacing gesture, that he had the pistol in a side-pocket of his greatcoat, clasped it firmly in his, and, exchanging a farewell with Nancy, led him away.

Oliver turned, for an instant, when they reached the door, in the hope of meeting a look from the girl. But she had resumed her old seat in front of the fire, and sat perfectly motionless before it.

CHAPTER 21

The expedition

It was a cheerless morning when they got into the street – blowing and raining hard, and the clouds looking dull and stormy. The night had been very wet, for large pools of water had collected in the road, and the kennels were overflowing.

There was a faint glimmering of the coming day in the sky; but it rather aggravated than relieved the gloom of the scene, the sombre light only serving to pale that which the street lamps afforded, without shedding any warmer or brighter tints upon the wet housetops and dreary streets. There appeared to be nobody stirring in that quarter of the town; for the windows of the houses were all closely shut, and the streets through which they passed were noiseless and empty.

By the time they had turned into the Bethnal Green Road the day had fairly begun to break. Many of the lamps were already extinguished; a few country wagons were slowly toiling on towards London; and now and then a stage-coach, covered with mud, rattled briskly by, the driver bestowing, as he passed, an admonitory lash upon the heavy wagoner, who, by keeping on the wrong side of the road, had endangered his arriving at the office a quarter of a minute after his time. The public-houses, with gaslights burning inside, were already open. By degrees other shops began to be unclosed; and a few scattered people were met with. Then came straggling groups of labourers going to their work; then men and women with fish-baskets on their heads, donkey-carts laden with vegetables, chaise-carts filled with live stock or whole carcasses of meat, milk-women with pails, and an unbroken concourse of people trudging out with various supplies to the eastern suburbs of the town. As they approached the City, the noise and traffic gradually increased; and when they threaded the streets between Shoreditch and Smithfield it had swelled into a roar of sound and bustle. It was as light as it was likely to be till night came on again, and the busy morning of half the London population had begun.

Turning down Sun Street and Crown Street, and crossing Finsbury Square, Mr Sikes struck, by way of Chiswell Street, into Barbican; thence into Long Lane; and so into Smithfield, from which latter place arose a tumult of discordant sounds that filled Oliver Twist with surprise and amazement.

It was market-morning. The ground was covered, nearly ankle-deep, with filth and mire; and a thick steam, perpetually rising from the reeking bodies of the cattle, and mingling with the fog, which seemed to rest upon the chimney-tops, hung heavily above. All the pens in the centre of the large area, and as many temporary ones as could be crowded into the vacant space, were filled with sheep; tied up to posts by the gutter-side were long lines of beasts and oxen, three or four deep. Countrymen, butchers, drovers, hawkers, boys, thieves, idlers, and vagabonds of every low grade, were mingled together in a dense mass. The whistling of drovers, the barking of dogs, the bellowing and plunging of oxen, the bleating of sheep, the grunting and squeaking of pigs; the cries of hawkers, the shouts, oaths, and quarrelling on all sides; the ringing of bells and the roar of voices that issued from every public-house; the crowding, pushing, driving, beating, whooping, and yelling; the hideous and discordant din that resounded from every corner of the market; and the unwashed, unshaven, squalid, and dirty figures constantly running to and fro, and bursting in and out of the throng, rendered it a stunning and bewildering scene, which quite confounded the senses.

Mr Sikes, dragging Oliver after him, elbowed his way through the thickest of the crowd, and bestowed very little attention on the numerous sights and sounds which so astonished the boy. He nodded, twice or thrice, to a passing friend; and, resisting as many invitations to take a morning dram, pressed steadily onward, until they were clear of the turmoil, and had made their way through Hosier Lane into Holborn.

'Now, young 'un,' said Sikes, looking up at the clock of St Andrew's Church, 'hard upon seven! you must step out. Come, don't lag behind already, Lazy-legs!'

Mr Sikes accompanied this speech with a jerk at his little companion's wrist. Oliver, quickening his pace into a kind of trot, between a fast walk and a run, kept up with the rapid strides of the housebreaker as well as he could.

They held their course at this rate until they had passed Hyde Park Corner, and were on their way to Kensington, when Sikes relaxed his pace, until an empty cart, which was at some little distance behind, came up. Seeing 'Hounslow' written on it, he asked the driver, with as much civility as he could assume, if he would give them a lift as far as Isleworth.

'Jump up,' said the man. 'Is that your boy?'

'Yes; he's my boy,' replied Sikes, looking hard at Oliver, and putting his hand abstractedly into the pocket where the pistol was.

'Your father walks rather too quick for you, don't he, my man?' enquired the driver, seeing that Oliver was out of breath.

'Not a bit of it,' replied Sikes, interposing. 'He's used to it. Here, take hold of my hand, Ned. In with you!'

Thus addressing Oliver, he helped him into the cart; and the driver, pointing to a heap of sacks, told him to lie down there and rest himself.

As they passed the different milestones Oliver wondered, more and more, where his companion meant to take him. Kensington, Hammersmith, Chiswick, Kew Bridge, Brentford, were all passed; and yet they went on as steadily as if they had only just begun their journey. At length they came to a public-house called the Coach and Horses, a little way beyond which another road appeared to turn off. And here the cart stopped.

Sikes dismounted with great precipitation, holding Oliver by the hand all the while; and lifting him down directly, bestowed a furious look upon him, and rapped the side-pocket with his fist in a very significant manner.

'Goodbye, boy,' said the man.

'He's sulky,' replied Sikes, giving him a shake – 'he's sulky. A young dog! Don't mind him.'

'Not I!' rejoined the other, getting into his cart. 'It's a fine day, after all.' And he drove away.

Sikes waited until he had fairly gone, and then, telling Oliver he might look about him if he wanted, once again led him forward on his journey.

They turned round to the left, a short way past the public-house; and then, taking a right-hand road, walked on for a long time, passing many large gardens and gentlemen's houses on both sides of the way, and stopping for nothing but a little beer until they reached a town. Here, against the wall of a house, Oliver saw written up in pretty large letters, 'Hampton.' They lingered about in the fields for some hours. At length they came back into the town, and turning into an old public-house with a defaced sign-board, ordered some dinner by the kitchen fire.

The kitchen was an old, low-roofed room, with a great beam across the middle of the ceiling; and benches, with high backs to them, by the fire, on which were seated several rough men in smock-frocks, drinking and smoking. They took no notice of Oliver, and very little of Sikes; and as Sikes took very little notice of them, he and his young comrade sat in a corner by themselves without being much troubled by their company.

They had some cold meat for dinner; and sat here so long after it, while Mr Sikes indulged himself with three or four pipes, that Oliver began to feel quite certain they were not going any farther. Being much tired with the walk, and getting up so early, he dozed a little at first; and then, quite overpowered by fatigue and the fumes of the tobacco, fell asleep.

It was quite dark when he was awakened by a push from Sikes. Rousing himself sufficiently to sit up and look about him, he found that worthy in close fellowship and communication with a labouring man, over a pint of ale.

'So, you're going on to Lower Halliford, are you?' enquired Sikes.

'Yes, I am,' replied the man, who seemed a little the worse – or better, as the case might be – for drinking; 'and not slow about it neither. My horse hasn't got a load behind him going back, as he had coming up in the mornin'; and he won't be long a-doing of it. Here's luck to him! Ecod! he's a good 'un!'

'Could you give my boy and me a lift as far as there?' demanded Sikes, pushing the ale towards his new friend.

'If you're going directly, I can,' replied the man, looking out of the pot. 'Are you going to Halliford?'

'Going on to Shepperton,' replied Sikes.

'I'm you're man as far as I go,' replied the other. 'Is all paid, Becky?'

'Yes, the other gentleman's paid,' replied the girl.

'I say,' said the man, with tipsy gravity, 'that won't do, you know.'

'Why not?' rejoined Sikes. 'You're a-going to accommodate us; and wot's to prevent my standing treat for a pint or so in return!'

The stranger reflected upon this argument with a very profound face; and, having done so, seized Sikes by the hand, and declared he was a real good fellow. To which Mr Sikes replied he was joking; as, if he had been sober, there would have been strong reason to suppose he was.

After the exchange of a few more compliments they bade the company good-night, and went out, the girl gathering up the pots and glasses as they did so, and lounging out to the door with her hands full to see the party start.

The horse, whose health had been drunk in his absence, was standing outside, ready harnessed to the cart. Oliver and Sikes got in without any further ceremony; and the man to whom he belonged, having lingered for a minute or two 'to bear him up,' and to defy the hostler and the world to produce his equal, mounted also. Then the hostler was told to give the horse his head; and his head being given him, he made a very unpleasant use of it, tossing it into the air with great disdain, and running

into the parlour windows over the way. After performing these feats, and supporting himself for a short time on his hind legs, he started off at great speed, and rattled out of the town right gallantly.

The night was very dark. A damp mist rose from the river and the marshy ground about, and spread itself over the dreary fields. It was piercing cold too: all was gloomy and black. Not a word was spoken, for the driver had grown sleepy, and Sikes was in no mood to lead him into conversation. Oliver sat huddled together in a corner of the cart, bewildered with alarm and apprehension, and figuring strange objects in the gaunt trees, whose branches waved grimly to and fro, as if in some fantastic joy at the desolation of the scene.

As they passed Sunbury Church the clock struck seven. There was a light in the ferry-house window opposite, which streamed across the road, and threw into more sombre shadow a dark yew tree with graves beneath it. There was a dull sound of falling water not far off; and the leaves of the old tree stirred gently in the night wind. It seemed like quiet music for the repose of the dead.

Sunbury was passed through, and they came again into the lonely road. Two or three miles more, and the cart stopped. Sikes alighted; and taking Oliver by the hand, they once again walked on.

They turned into no house at Shepperton, as the weary boy had expected; but still kept walking on, in mud and darkness, through gloomy lanes and over cold open wastes, until they came within sight of the lights of a town at no great distance. On looking intently forward Oliver saw that the water was just below them, and that they were coming to the foot of a bridge.

Sikes kept straight on until they were close upon the bridge, and then turned suddenly down a bank upon the left.

'The water!' thought Oliver, turning sick with fear. 'He has brought me to this lonely place to murder me!'

He was about to throw himself on the ground and make one struggle for his young life, when he saw that they stood before a solitary house, all ruinous and decayed. There was a window on each side of the dilapidated entrance, and one story above; but no light was visible. It was dark, dismantled, and, to all appearance, uninhabited.

Sikes, with Oliver's hand still in his, softly approached the low porch, and raised the latch. The door yielded to the pressure, and they passed in together.

CHAPTER 22

The burglary

'Hallo!' cried a loud, hoarse voice, directly they had set foot in the passage.

'Don't make such a row,' said Sikes, bolting the door. 'Show a glim, Toby.'

'Aha, my pal,' cried the same voice – 'a glim, Barney, a glim! Show the gentleman in, Barney; and wake up first, if convenient.'

The speaker appeared to throw a boot-jack, or some such article, at the person he addressed, to arouse him from his slumbers; for the noise of a wooden body, falling violently, was heard, and then an indistinct muttering, as of a man between asleep and awake.

'Do you hear?' cried the same voice. 'There's Bill Sikes in the passage with nobody to do the civil to him; and you sleeping there, as if you took laudanum with your meals, and nothing stronger. Are you any fresher now, or do you want the iron candlestick to wake you thoroughly?'

A pair of slipshod feet shuffled, hastily, across the bare floor of the room as this interrogatory was put; and there issued, from the door on the right hand, first, a feeble candle, and next the form of the same individual who has been heretofore described as labouring under the infirmity of speaking through his nose, and officiating as waiter at the public-house on Saffron Hill.

'Bister Sikes!' exclaimed Barney, with real or counterfeit joy; 'cub id, sir; cub id.'

'Here! you get on first,' said Sikes, putting Oliver in front of him. 'Quicker! or I shall tread upon your heels.'

Muttering a curse upon his tardiness, Sikes pushed Oliver before him, and they entered a low dark room with a smoky fire, two or three broken chairs, a table, and a very old couch; on which, with his legs much higher than his head, a man was reposing at full length, smoking a long clay pipe. He was dressed in a smartly-cut snuff-coloured coat, with large brass buttons, an orange neckerchief, a coarse, staring, shawl-pattern waistcoat, and drab breeches. Mr Crackit (for he it was) had no very great quantity of hair, either upon his head or face, but what he had was of a reddish dye, and tortured into long cork-screw curls, through which he occasionally thrust some very dirty fingers ornamented with large common rings. He was a trifle above the middle size, and apparently rather weak in the legs; but this circumstance by no means detracted from his own admiration of his top-boots, which he contemplated, in their elevated situation, with lively satisfaction.

'Bill, my boy!' said this figure, turning his head towards the door, 'I'm glad to see you. I was almost afraid you'd given it up, in which case I should have made a personal wentur. Hallo!'

Uttering this exclamation in a tone of great surprise, as his eye rested on Oliver, Mr Toby Crackit brought himself into a sitting posture, and demanded who that was.

'The boy. Only the boy!' replied Sikes, drawing a chair towards the fire.

'Wud of Bister Fagid's lads,' exclaimed Barney, with a grin.

'Fagin's, eh?' exclaimed Toby, looking at Oliver. 'Wot an inwalable boy that'll make for the old ladies' pockets in chapels. His mug is a fortun' to him.'

'There – there's enough of that,' interposed Sikes, impatiently, and stooping over his recumbent friend, he whispered a few words in his ear; at which Mr Crackit laughed immensely, and honoured Oliver with a long stare of astonishment.

'Now,' said Sikes, as he resumed his seat, 'if you'll give us something to eat and drink while we're waiting, you'll put some heart in us, or in me, at all events. Sit down by the fire, younker, and rest yourself; for you'll have to go out with us again tonight, though not very far off.'

Oliver looked at Sikes in mute and timid wonder; and drawing a stool to the fire, sat with his aching head upon his hands, scarcely knowing where he was, or what was passing around him.

'Here,' said Toby, as the young Jew placed some fragments of food and a bottle upon the table, 'Success to the crack!' He rose to honour the toast; and carefully depositing his empty pipe in a corner, advanced to the table, filled a glass with spirits, and drank off its contents. Mr Sikes did the same.

'A drain for the boy,' said Toby, half-filling a wineglass. 'Down with it, innocence.'

'Indeed,' said Oliver, looking piteously up into the man's face; 'indeed, I –'

'Down with it!' echoed Toby. 'Do you think I don't know what's good for you? Tell him to drink it, Bill.'

'He had better!' said Sikes, clapping his hand upon his pocket. 'Burn my body, if he isn't more trouble than a whole family of Dodgers. Drink it, you perwerse imp! drink it!'

Frightened by the menacing gestures of the two men, Oliver hastily swallowed the contents of the glass, and immediately fell into a violent fit of coughing, which delighted Toby Crackit and Barney, and even drew a smile from the surly Mr Sikes.

This done, and Sikes having satisfied his appetite (Oliver could eat nothing but a small crust of bread which they made him swallow), the two men laid themselves down on chairs for a short nap. Oliver retained his stool by the fire, and Barney, wrapped in a blanket, stretched himself on the floor, close outside the fender.

They slept, or appeared to sleep, for some time; nobody stirring but Barney, who rose once or twice to throw coals upon the fire. Oliver fell into a heavy doze – imagining himself straying along through the gloomy lanes, or wandering about the dark churchyard, or retracing some one or other of the scenes of the past day, when he was roused by Toby Crackit jumping up and declaring it was half-past one.

In an instant the other two were on their legs, and all were actively engaged in busy preparation. Sikes and his companion enveloped their necks and chins in large dark shawls, and drew on their greatcoats; while Barney, opening a cupboard, brought forth several articles, which he hastily crammed into the pockets.

'Barkers for me, Barney,' said Toby Crackit.

'Here they are,' replied Barney, producing a pair of pistols. 'You loaded them yourself.'

'All right!' replied Toby, stowing them away. 'The persuaders?'

'I've got 'em,' replied Sikes.

'Crape, keys, centre-bits, darkies – nothing forgotten?' enquired Toby, fastening a small crowbar to a loop inside the skirt of his coat.

'All right,' rejoined his companion. 'Bring them bits of timber, Barney. That's the time of day.'

With these words, he took a thick stick from Barney's hands, who, having delivered another to Toby, busied himself in fastening on Oliver's cape.

'Now, then!' said Sikes, holding out his hand.

Oliver, who was completely stupefied by the unwonted exercise, and the air, and the drink which had been forced upon him, put his hand mechanically into that which Sikes extended for the purpose.

'Take his other hand, Toby,' said Sikes. 'Look out, Barney.'

The man went to the door, and returned to announce that all was quiet. The two robbers issued forth with Oliver between them. Barney having made all fast, rolled himself up as before, and was soon asleep again.

It was now intensely dark. The fog was much heavier than it had been in the early part of the night, and the atmosphere was so damp that, although no rain fell, Oliver's hair and eyebrows, within a few minutes after leaving the house, had become stiff with the half-frozen moisture that was floating about. They crossed the bridge, and kept on towards the lights which he had seen before. They were at no great distance off; and, as they walked pretty briskly, they soon arrived at Chertsey.

'Slap through the town,' whispered Sikes; 'there'll be nobody in the way tonight to see us.'

Toby acquiesced; and they hurried through the main street of the little town, which at that late hour was wholly deserted. A dim light shone at intervals from some bedroom window, and the hoarse barking of dogs occasionally broke the silence of the night. But there was nobody abroad, and they had cleared the town as the church-bell struck two.

Quickening their pace, they turned up a road upon the left hand. After walking about a quarter of a mile, they stopped before a detached house surrounded by a wall, to the top of which Toby Crackit, scarcely pausing to take breath, climbed in a twinkling.

'The boy next,' said Toby, 'Hoist him up; I'll catch hold of him.'

Before Oliver had time to look round, Sikes had caught him under the arms, and in three or four seconds he and Toby were lying on the grass on the other side. Sikes followed directly. And they stole cautiously towards the house.

And now, for the first time, Oliver, wellnigh mad with grief and terror, saw that housebreaking and robbery, if not murder, were the objects of the expedition. He clasped his hands together and involuntarily uttered a subdued exclamation of horror. A mist came before his eyes, the cold sweat stood upon his ashy face, his limbs failed him, and he sunk upon his knees.

'Get up!' murmured Sikes, trembling with rage, and drawing the pistol from his pocket; 'get up, or I'll strew your brains upon the grass.'

'Oh! for God's sake, let me go!' cried Oliver; 'let me run away and die in the fields. I will never come near London – never, never! Oh! pray have mercy on me, and do not make me steal. For the love of all the bright Angels that rest in heaven, have mercy upon me!'

The man to whom this appeal was made swore a dreadful oath, and had cocked the pistol, when Toby, striking it from his grasp, placed his hand upon the boy's mouth and dragged him to the house.

'Hush!' cried the man, 'it won't answer here. Say another word, and I'll do your business myself with a crack on the head. That makes no noise; and is quite as certain, and more genteel. Here, Bill, wrench the shutter open. He's game enough now, I'll engage. I've seen older hands of his age took the same way, for a minute or two, on a cold night.'

Sikes, invoking terrific imprecations upon Fagin's head for sending Oliver on such an errand, plied the crowbar vigorously, but with little noise. After some delay, and some assistance from Toby, the shutter to which he had referred swung open on its hinges.

It was a little lattice-window, about five feet and a half above the ground, at the back of the house, which belonged to a scullery, or small brewing-place, at the end of the passage. The aperture was so small that the inmates had probably not thought it worth while to defend it more securely; but it was large enough to admit a boy of Oliver's size, nevertheless. A very brief exercise of Mr Sikes's art sufficed to overcome the fastening of the lattice, and it soon stood wide open also.

'Now listen, you young limb,' whispered Sikes, drawing a dark lantern from his pocket, and throwing the glare full on Oliver's face; 'I'm a-going to put you through there. Take this light; go softly up the steps straight afore you, and along the little hall to the street door; unfasten it, and let us in.'

'There's a bolt at the top you won't be able to reach,' interposed Toby. 'Stand upon one of the hall chairs. There are three there, Bill, with a jolly large blue unicorn and a gold pitchfork on 'em, which is the old lady's arms.'

'Keep quiet, can't you?' replied Sikes, with a threatening look. 'The room door is open, is it?'

'Wide,' replied Toby, after peeping in to satisfy himself. 'The game of that is, that they always leave it open with a catch, so that the dog, who's got a bed in here, may walk up and down the passage when he feels wakeful. Ha! ha! Barney 'ticed him away tonight. So neat!'

Although Mr Crackit spoke in a scarcely audible whisper, and laughed without noise, Sikes imperiously commanded him to be silent, and to get to work. Toby complied, by first producing his lantern, and placing it on the ground; and then by planting himself firmly with his head against the wall beneath the window, and his hands upon his knees, so as to make a step of his back. This was no sooner done than Sikes, mounting upon him, put Oliver gently through the window with his feet first, and, without leaving hold of his collar, planted him safely on the floor inside.

'Take this lantern,' said Sikes, looking into the room. 'You see the stairs afore you?'

Oliver, more dead than alive, gasped out, 'Yes.' Sikes, pointing to the street-door with the pistol-barrel, briefly advised him to take notice that he was within shot all the way, and that if he faltered, he would fall dead that instant.

'It's done in a minute,' said Sikes, in the same low whisper. 'Directly I leave go of you, do your work. Hark!'

'What's that?' whispered the other man.

They listened intently.

'Nothing,' said Sikes, releasing his hold of Oliver. 'Now!'

In the short time he had had to collect his senses the boy had firmly resolved that, whether he died in the attempt or not, he would make one effort to dart upstairs from the hall and alarm the family. Filled with this idea, he advanced at once, but stealthily.

'Come back!' suddenly cried Sikes aloud. 'Back! back!'

Scared by the sudden breaking of the dead stillness of the place, and by a loud cry which followed it, Oliver let his lantern fall, and knew not whether to advance or fly.

The cry was repeated – a light appeared – a vision of two terrified, half-dressed men at the top of the stairs swam before his eyes – a flash – a loud noise – a smoke – a crash somewhere, but where, he knew not – and he staggered back.

Sikes had disappeared for an instant; but he was up again, and had him by the collar before the smoke had cleared away. He fired his own pistol after the men, who were already retreating, and dragged the boy up.

'Clasp your arm tighter,' said Sikes, as he drew him through the window. 'Give me a shawl here. They've hit him. Quick! Damnation, how the boy bleeds!'

Then came the loud ringing of a bell, mingled with the noise of firearms, and the shouts of men, and the sensation of being carried over uneven ground at a rapid pace. And then the noises grew confused in the distance, and a cold deadly feeling crept over the boy's heart; and he saw or heard no more.

CHAPTER 23

Which contains the substance of a pleasant conversation between Mr Bumble and a lady; and shows that even a beadle may be susceptible on some points

The night was bitter cold. The snow lay on the ground, frozen into a hard thick crust, so that only the heaps that had drifted into byways and corners were affected by the sharp wind that howled abroad; which, as if expending increased fury on such prey as it found, caught it savagely up in clouds, and, whirling it into a thousand misty eddies, scattered it in air. Bleak, dark, and piercing cold, it was a night for the well housed and fed to draw round the bright fire and thank God they were at home; and for the homeless starving wretch to lay him down and die. Many hunger-worn outcasts close their eyes in our bare streets, at such times, who, let their crimes have been what they may, can hardly open them in a more bitter world.

Such was the aspect of out-of-doors affairs, when Mrs Corney, the matron of the workhouse to which our readers have been already introduced as the birthplace of Oliver Twist, sat herself down before a cheerful fire in her own little room, and glanced with no small degree of complacency at a small round table, on which stood a tray of corresponding size, furnished with all necessary materials for the most grateful meal that matrons enjoy. In fact, Mrs Corney was about to solace herself with a cup of tea. As she glanced from the table to the fireplace, where the smallest of all possible kettles was

singing a small song in a small voice, her inward satisfaction evidently increased – so much so, indeed, that Mrs Corney smiled.

'Well!' said the matron, leaning her elbow on the table, and looking reflectively at the fire, 'I'm sure we have all on us a great deal to be grateful for! A great deal, if we did but know it. Ah!'

Mrs Corney shook her head mournfully, as if deploring the mental blindness of those paupers who did not know it; and thrusting a silver spoon (private property) into the inmost recesses of a two-ounce tin tea-caddy, proceeded to make the tea.

How slight a thing will disturb the equanimity of our frail minds! The black teapot, being very small and easily filled, ran over while Mrs Corney was moralising, and the water slightly scalded Mrs Corney's hand.

'Drat the pot!' said the worthy matron, setting it down very hastily on the hob; 'a little stupid thing, that only holds a couple of cups! What use is it of, to anybody? Except,' said Mrs Corney, pausing, 'except to a poor desolate creature like me. Oh dear!'

With these words the matron dropped into her chair, and, once more resting her elbow on the table, thought of her solitary fate. The small teapot, and the single cup, had awakened in her mind sad recollections of Mr Corney (who had not been dead more than five-and-twenty years); and she was overpowered.

'I shall never get another!' said Mrs Corney, pettishly; 'I shall never get another – like him.'

Whether this remark bore reference to the husband, or the teapot, is uncertain. It might have been the latter, for Mrs Corney looked at it as she spoke, and took it up afterwards. She had just tasted her first cup when she was disturbed by a soft tap at the room door.

The burglary

'Oh, come in with you!' said Mrs Corney, sharply. 'Some of the old women dying, I suppose. They always die when I'm at meals. Don't stand there letting the cold air in, don't. What's amiss now, eh?'

'Nothing, ma'am, nothing,' replied a man's voice.

'Dear me!' exclaimed the matron, in a much sweeter tone, 'is that Mr Bumble?'

'At your service, ma'am,' said Mr Bumble, who had been stopping outside to rub his shoes clean and to shake the snow off his coat, and who now made his appearance, bearing the cocked hat in one hand and a bundle in the other. 'Shall I shut the door, ma'am?'

The lady modestly hesitated to reply, lest there should be any impropriety in holding an interview with Mr Bumble with closed doors. Mr Bumble, taking advantage of the hesitation, and being very cold himself, shut it without further permission.

'Hard weather, Mr Bumble,' said the matron.

'Hard, indeed, ma'am,' replied the beadle. 'Antiporochial weather this, ma'am. We have given away, Mrs Corney, we have given away a matter of twenty quartern loaves, and a cheese and a half, this very blessed afternoon; and yet them paupers are not contented.'

'Of course not. When would they be, Mr Bumble?' said the matron, sipping her tea.

'When, indeed, ma'am!' rejoined Mr Bumble. 'Why, here's one man that, in consideration of his wife and large family, has a quartern loaf and a good pound of cheese, full weight. Is he grateful, ma'am? is he grateful? Not a copper farthing's worth of it! What does he do, ma'am, but ask for a few coals; if it's only a pocket-handkerchief full, he says! Coals! What would he do with coals? Toast his cheese with 'em, and then come back for more. That's the way with these people, ma'am: give 'em a apron full of coals today, and they'll come back for another the day after tomorrow as brazen as alabaster.'

The matron expressed her entire concurrence in this intelligible simile; and the beadle went on.

'I never,' said Mr Bumble, 'see anything like the pitch it's got to. The day afore yesterday, a man – you have been a married woman, ma'am, and I may mention it to you – a man, with hardly a rag upon his back (here Mrs Corney looked at the floor), goes to our overseer's door when he has got company coming to dinner, and says he must be relieved, Mrs Corney. As he wouldn't go away, and shocked the company very much, our overseer sent him out a pound of potatoes and half a pint of oatmeal. "My heart!" says the ungrateful villain, "what's the *use* of this to me? You might as well give me a pair of iron spectacles!" "Very good," says our overseer, taking 'em away again, "you won't get anything else here." "Then I'll die in the streets!" says the vagrant. "Oh, no, you won't," says our overseer.'

'Ha! ha! That was very good! So like Mr Grannet, wasn't it?' interposed the matron. 'Well, Mr Bumble?'

'Well, ma'am,' rejoined the beadle, 'he went away, and he *did* die in the streets. There's a obstinate pauper for you!'

'It beats anything I could have believed,' observed the matron, emphatically. 'But don't you think out-of-door relief a very bad thing, anyway, Mr Bumble? You're a gentleman of experience, and ought to know. Come.'

'Mrs Corney,' said the beadle, smiling as men smile who are conscious of superior information, 'out-of-door relief, properly managed – properly managed, ma'am – is the porochial safeguard. The great principle of out-of-door relief is, to give the paupers exactly what they don't want; and then they get tired of coming.'

'Dear me!' exclaimed Mrs Corney. 'Well, that is a good one, too!'

'Yes. Betwixt you and me, ma'am,' returned Mr Bumble, 'that's the great principle; and that's the reason why, if you look at any cases that get into them owdacious newspapers, you'll always observe that sick families have been relieved with slices of cheese. That's the rule now, Mrs Corney, all over the country. But, however,' said the beadle, stooping to unpack his bundle, 'these are official secrets, ma'am; not to be spoken of, except, as I may say, among the porochial officers, such as ourselves. This is the port wine, ma'am, that the board ordered for the infirmary – real, fresh, genuine port wine; only out of the cask this forenoon, clear as a bell, and no sediment!'

Having held the first bottle up to the light, and shaken it well to test its excellence, Mr Bumble placed them both on the top of a chest of drawers; folded the handkerchief in which they had been wrapped; put it carefully in his pocket, and took up his hat as if to go.

'You'll have a very cold walk, Mr Bumble,' said the matron.

'It blows, ma'am,' replied Mr Bumble, turning up his coat-collar, 'enough to cut one's ears off.'

The matron looked from the little kettle to the beadle, who was moving towards the door; and as the beadle coughed preparatory to bidding her good-night, bashfully enquired whether – whether he wouldn't take a cup of tea?

Mr Bumble instantly turned back his collar again, laid his hat and stick upon a chair, and drew another chair up to the table. As he slowly seated himself he looked at the lady. She fixed her eyes upon the little teapot. Mr Bumble coughed again, and slightly smiled.

Mrs Corney rose to get another cup and saucer from the closet. As she sat down, her eyes once again encountered those of the gallant beadle; she coloured, and applied herself to the task of making his tea. Again Mr Bumble coughed – louder this time than he had coughed yet.

'Sweet? Mr Bumble,' enquired the matron, taking up the sugar-basin.

'Very sweet, indeed, ma'am,' replied Mr Bumble. He fixed his eyes on Mrs Corney as he said this; and if ever a beadle looked tender, Mr Bumble was that beadle at that moment.

The tea was made, and handed in silence. Mr Bumble, having spread a handkerchief over his knees to prevent the crumbs from sullying the splendour of his shorts, began to eat and drink; varying these amusements, occasionally, by fetching a deep sigh, which, however, had no injurious effect upon his appetite, but, on the contrary, rather seemed to facilitate his operations in the tea and toast department.

'You have a cat, ma'am, I see,' said Mr Bumble, glancing at

one, who, in the centre of her family, was basking before the fire; 'and kittens, too, I declare!'

'I am so fond of them, Mr Bumble, you can't think,' replied the matron. 'They're *so* happy, *so* frolicsome, and *so* cheerful, that they are quite companions for me.'

'Very nice animals, ma'am,' replied Mr Bumble, approvingly; 'so very domestic.'

'Oh, yes!' rejoined the matron, with enthusiasm; 'so fond of their home, too, that it's quite a pleasure, I'm sure.'

'Mrs Corney, ma'am,' said Mr Bumble, slowly, and marking the time with his teaspoon, 'I mean to say this, ma'am – that any cat, or kitten, that could live with you, ma'am, and *not* be fond of its home, must be a ass, ma'am.'

'Oh, Mr Bumble!' remonstrated Mrs Corney.

'It's of no use disguising facts, ma'am,' said Mr Bumble, slowly flourishing the teaspoon with a kind of amorous dignity which made him doubly impressive; 'I would drown it myself, with pleasure.'

'Then you're a cruel man,' said the matron vivaciously, as she held out her hand for the beadle's cup; 'and a very hard-hearted man besides.'

'Hard-hearted, ma'am,' said Mr Bumble, 'hard!' Mr Bumble resigned his cup without another word, squeezed Mrs Corney's little finger as she took it, and inflicting two open-handed slaps upon his laced waistcoat, gave a mighty sigh, and hitched his chair a very little morsel farther from the fire.

It was a round table; and as Mrs Corney and Mr Bumble had been sitting opposite each other, with no great space between them, and fronting the fire, it will be seen that Mr Bumble, in receding from the fire, and still keeping at the table, increased the distance between himself and Mrs Corney; which pro-

Mr Bumble and Mrs Corney taking tea

ceeding some prudent readers will doubtless be disposed to admire, and to consider an act of great heroism on Mr Bumble's part, he being in some sort tempted by time, place, and opportunity, to give utterance to certain soft nothings, which, however well they may become the lips of the light and thoughtless, do seem immeasurably beneath the dignity of the judges of the land, members of parliament, ministers of state, lord mayors, and other great public functionaries, but more particularly beneath the stateliness and gravity of a beadle, who (as is well known) should be the sternest and most inflexible among them all.

Whatever were Mr Bumble's intentions, however – and no doubt they were of the best – it unfortunately happened, as has been twice before remarked, that the table was a round one; consequently Mr Bumble, moving his chair by little and little, soon began to diminish the distance between himself and the matron, and, continuing to travel round the outer edge of the circle, brought his chair in time close to that in which the matron was seated. Indeed, the two chairs touched; and when they did so, Mr Bumble stopped.

Now, if the matron had moved her chair to the right, she would have been scorched by the fire; and if to the left, she must have fallen into Mr Bumble's arms; so (being a discreet matron, and no doubt foreseeing these consequences at a glance) she remained where she was, and handed Mr Bumble another cup of tea.

'Hard-hearted, Mrs Corney?' said Mr Bumble, stirring his tea, and looking up into the matron's face; 'are *you* hard-hearted, Mrs Corney?'

'Dear me!' exclaimed the matron, 'what a very curious question from a single man! What can you want to know for, Mr Bumble?'

The beadle drank his tea to the last drop, finished a piece of toast, whisked the crumbs off his knees, wiped his lips, and deliberately kissed the matron.

'Mr Bumble,' cried that discreet lady in a whisper; for the fright was so great that she had quite lost her voice – 'Mr Bumble, I shall scream!' Mr Bumble made no reply, but in a slow and dignified manner put his arm round the matron's waist.

As the lady had stated her intention of screaming, of course she would have screamed at this additional boldness, but that the exertion was rendered unnecessary by a hasty knocking at the door; which was no sooner heard than Mr Bumble darted, with much agility, to the wine-bottles, and began dusting them with great violence, while the matron sharply demanded who was there. It is worthy of remark, as a curious physical instance of the efficacy of a sudden surprise in counteracting the effects of extreme fear, that her voice had quite recovered all its official asperity.

'If you please, mistress,' said a withered old female pauper, hideously ugly, putting her head in at the door, 'Old Sally is a-going fast.'

'Well, what's that to me?' angrily demanded the matron. 'I can't keep her alive, can I?'

'No, no, mistress,' replied the old woman, 'nobody can; she's far beyond the reach of help. I've seen a many people die – little babes and great strong men – and I know when death's a-coming, well enough. But she's troubled in her mind; and when the fits are not on her – and that's not often, for she is dying very hard – she says she has got something to tell, which you must hear. She'll never die quiet till you come, mistress.'

At this intelligence the worthy Mrs Corney muttered a variety of invectives against old women who couldn't even die without purposely annoying their betters; and muffling herself in a thick shawl which she hastily caught up, briefly requested Mr Bumble to stay till she came back, lest anything particular should occur, and bidding the messenger walk fast, and not be all night hobbling up the stairs, followed her from the room with a very ill grace, scolding all the way.

Mr Bumble's conduct, on being left to himself, was rather inexplicable. He opened the closet, counted the teaspoons, weighed the sugar-tongs, closely inspected a silver milk-pot to ascertain that it was of the genuine metal; and, having satisfied his curiosity on these points, put on his cocked-hat corner-wise, and danced with much gravity four distinct times round the table. Having gone through this very extraordinary performance, he took off the cocked-hat again; and, spreading himself before the fire with his back towards it, seemed to be mentally engaged in taking an exact inventory of the furniture.

CHAPTER 24

Treats of a very poor subject. But is a short one; and may be found of some importance in this history

It was no unfit messenger of death that had disturbed the quiet of the matron's room. Her body was bent by age, her limbs trembled with palsy, and her face, distorted into a mumbling leer, resembled more the grotesque shaping of some wild pencil than the work of Nature's hand.

Alas! how few of Nature's faces are left to gladden us with their beauty. The cares and sorrows and hungerings of the world change them as they change hearts; and it is only when those passions sleep, and have lost their hold for ever, that the troubled clouds pass off, and leave Heaven's surface clear. It is a common thing for the countenances of the dead, even in that fixed and rigid state, to subside into the long-forgotten expression of sleeping infancy, and settle into the very look of early life; so calm, so peaceful do they grow again, that those who knew them in their happy childhood kneel by the coffin's side in awe, and see the Angel even upon earth.

The old crone tottered along the passages, and up the stairs, muttering some indistinct answers to the chidings of her companion; and being at length compelled to pause for breath, gave the light into her hand, and remained behind to follow as she might, while the more nimble superior made her way to the room where the sick woman lay.

It was a bare garret-room, with a dim light burning at the farther end. There was another old woman watching by the bed; and the parish apothecary's apprentice was standing by the fire, making a toothpick out of a quill.

'Cold night, Mrs Corney,' said this young gentleman, as the matron entered.

'Very cold indeed, sir,' replied the mistress in her most civil tones, and dropping a curtsy as she spoke.

'You should get better coals out of your contractors,' said the apothecary's deputy, breaking a lump on the top of the fire with the rusty poker; 'these are not at all the sort of thing for a cold night.'

'They're the board's choosing, sir,' returned the matron. 'The least they could do would be to keep us pretty warm, for our places are hard enough.'

The conversation was here interrupted by a moan from the sick woman.

'Oh!' said the young man, turning his face towards the bed, as if he had previously quite forgotten the patient, 'it's all U.P. there, Mrs Corney.'

'It is, is it, sir?' asked the matron.

'If she lasts a couple of hours, I shall be surprised,' said the apothecary's apprentice, intent upon the toothpick's point. 'It's a break-up of the system altogether. Is she dozing, old lady?'

The attendant stooped over the bed to ascertain, and nodded in the affirmative.

'Then perhaps she'll go off in that way, if you don't make a row,' said the young man. 'Put the light on the floor – she won't see it there.'

The attendant did as she was told, shaking her head meanwhile, to intimate that the woman would not die so easily. Having done so, she resumed her seat by the side of the other nurse, who had by this time returned. The mistress, with an expression of impatience, wrapped herself in her shawl, and sat at the foot of the bed.

The apothecary's apprentice, having completed the manufacture of the toothpick, planted himself in front of the fire, and made good use of it for ten minutes or so, when, apparently growing rather dull, he wished Mrs Corney joy of her job, and took himself off on tip-toe.

When they had sat in silence for some time, the two old women rose from the bed, and crouching over the fire, held out their withered hands to catch the heat. The flame threw a ghastly light on their shrivelled faces, and made their ugliness appear perfectly terrible, as, in this position, they began to converse in a low voice.

'Did she say any more, Anny, dear, while I was gone?' enquired the messenger.

'Not a word,' replied the other. 'She plucked and tore at her arms for a little time; but I held her hands, and she soon dropped off. She hasn't much strength in her, so I easily kept her quiet. I ain't so weak for an old woman, although I am on parish allowance; no, no!'

'Did she drink the hot wine the doctor said she was to have?' demanded the first.

'I tried to get it down,' rejoined the other; 'but her teeth were tightly set, and she clenched the mug so hard that it was as much as I could do to get it back again. So *I* drank it; and it did me good!'

Looking cautiously round, to ascertain that they were not overheard, the two hags cowered nearer to the fire, and chuckled heartily.

'I mind the time,' said the first speaker, 'when she would have done the same, and made rare fun of it afterwards.'

'Ay, that she would,' rejoined the other; 'she had a merry heart. A many, many beautiful corpses she laid out, as nice and neat as waxwork. My old eyes have seen them – ay, and these old hands touched them, too; for I have helped her scores of times.'

Stretching forth her trembling fingers as she spoke, the old creature shook them exultingly before her face; and fumbling in her pocket, brought out an old time-discoloured tin snuff-box, from which she shook a few grains into the outstretched palm of her companion, and a few more into her own. While they were thus employed, the matron, who had been impatiently watching until the dying woman should awaken from her stupor, joined them by the fire, and sharply asked how long she was to wait.

'Not long, mistress,' replied the second woman, looking up into her face. 'We have none of us long to wait for Death. Patience, patience! He'll be here soon enough for us all.'

'Hold your tongue, you doting idiot!' said the matron sternly. 'You, Martha, tell me – has she been in this way before?'

'Often,' answered the first woman.

'But will never be again,' added the second one; 'that is, she'll never wake again but once – and mind, mistress, that won't be for long.'

'Long or short,' said the matron snappishly, 'she won't find me here when she does wake. And take care, both of you, how you worry me again for nothing. It's no part of my duty to see all the old women in the house die; and I won't – that's more. Mind that, you impudent old harridans. If you make a fool of me again, I'll soon cure you, I warrant you!'

She was bouncing away, when a cry from the two women, who had turned towards the bed, caused her to look round. The patient had raised herself upright, and was stretching her arms towards them.

'Who's that?' she cried in a hollow voice.

'Hush, hush!' said one of the women, stooping over her. 'Lie down, lie down!'

'I'll never lie down again alive!' said the woman, struggling. 'I *will* tell her! Come here! Nearer! Let me whisper in your ear.'

She clutched the matron by the arm, and forcing her into a chair by the bedside, was about to speak, when, looking round, she caught sight of the two old women bending forward in the attitude of eager listeners.

'Turn them away,' said the woman drowsily. 'Make haste! make haste!'

The two old crones, chiming in together, began pouring out many piteous lamentations that the poor dear was too far gone to know her best friends, and were uttering sundry protestations that they would never leave her, when the superior pushed them from the room, closed the door and returned to the bedside. On

being excluded, the old ladies changed their tones, and cried through the keyhole that old Sally was drunk – which, indeed, was not unlikely, since, in addition to a moderate dose of opium prescribed by the apothecary, she was labouring under the effects of a final taste of gin-and-water which had been privately administered, in the openness of their hearts, by the worthy old ladies themselves.

'Now listen to me,' said the dying woman aloud as if making a great effort to revive one latent spark of energy. 'In this very room – in this very bed – I once nursed a pretty young creetur' that was brought into the house with her feet cut and bruised with walking, and all soiled with dust and blood. She gave birth to a boy, and died. Let me think – what was the year again?'

'Never mind the year,' said the impatient auditor; 'what about her?'

'Ay,' murmured the sick woman, relapsing into her former drowsy state, 'what about her – what about – I know!' she cried, jumping fiercely up, her face flushed, and her eyes starting from her head – 'I robbed her, so I did! She wasn't cold – I tell you she wasn't cold when I stole it!'

'Stole what, for God's sake?' cried the matron, with a gesture as if she could call for help.

'*It!*' replied the woman, laying her hand over the other's mouth – 'the only thing she had. She wanted clothes to keep her warm, and food to eat; but she had kept it safe, and had it in her bosom. It was gold, I tell you! – rich gold, that might have saved her life!'

'Gold!' echoed the matron, bending eagerly over the woman as she fell back. 'Go on, go on – yes – what of it? Who was the mother? When was it?'

'She charged me to keep it safe,' replied the woman, with a groan, 'and trusted me as the only woman about her. I stole it in my heart when she first showed it me hanging round her neck; and the child's death, perhaps, is on me besides! They would have treated him better if they had known it all!'

'Known what?' asked the other. 'Speak!'

'The boy grew so like his mother,' said the woman, rambling on, and not heeding the question, 'that I could never forget it when I saw his face. Poor girl! poor girl! She was so young, too! such a gentle lamb! Wait; there's more to tell. I have not told you all, have I?'

'No, no,' replied the matron, inclining her head to catch the words as they came more faintly from the dying woman. 'Be quick, or it may be too late!'

'The mother,' said the woman, making a more violent effort than before – 'the mother, when the pains of death first came upon her, whispered in my ear that if her baby was born alive, and thrived, the day might come when it would not feel so much disgraced to hear its poor young mother named. "And oh, kind Heaven!" she said, folding her thin hands together, "whether it be boy or girl, raise up some friends for it in this troubled world, and take pity upon a lonely, desolate child, abandoned to its mercy!" '

'The boy's name?' demanded the matron.

'They *called* him Oliver,' replied the woman feebly. 'The gold I stole was –'

'Yes, yes – what?'

She was bending eagerly over the woman to hear her reply; but drew back instinctively as she once again rose, slowly and stiffly, into a sitting posture, then clutching the coverlet with both hands, muttered some indistinct sound in her throat, and fell lifeless on the bed.

'Stone dead!' said one of the old women, hurrying in as soon as the door was opened.

'And nothing to tell, after all,' rejoined the matron, walking carelessly away.

The two crones, to all appearance, too busily occupied in the preparations for their dreadful duties to make any reply, were left alone, hovering about the body.

CHAPTER 25

Wherein this history refers to Mr Fagin and company

While these things were passing in the country workhouse, Mr Fagin sat in the old den – the same from which Oliver had been removed by the girl – brooding over a dull, smoky fire. He held a pair of bellows upon his knee, with which he had apparently been endeavouring to rouse it into more cheerful action; but he had fallen into deep thought, and with his arms folded on them, and his chin resting on his thumbs, fixed his eyes abstractedly on the rusty bars.

At a table behind behind sat the Artful Dodger, Master Charles Bates, and Mr Chitling, all intent upon a game of whist; the Artful taking dummy against Master Bates and Mr Chitling. The countenance of the first-named gentleman, peculiarly intelligent at all times, acquired great additional interest from his close observance of the game, and his attentive perusal of Mr Chitling's hand; upon which, from time to time, as occasion served, he bestowed a variety of earnest glances, wisely regulating his own play by the result of his observations upon his neighbour's cards. It being a cold night, the Dodger wore his hat, as indeed was often his custom within doors. He also sustained a clay pipe between his teeth, which he only removed for a brief space when he deemed it necessary to apply for refreshment to a quart-pot upon the table, which stood ready filled with gin-and-water for the accommodation of the company.

Master Bates was also attentive to the play; but being of a more excitable nature than his accomplished friend, it was observable that he more frequently applied himself to the gin-and-water, and moreover indulged in many jests and irrelevant remarks, all highly unbecoming a scientific rubber. Indeed, the Artful, presuming upon their close attachment, more than once took occasion to reason gravely with his companion upon these improprieties; all of which remonstrances Master Bates received in extremely good part, merely requesting his friend to be 'blowed', or to insert his head in a sack, or replying with some other neatly-turned witticism of a similar kind, the happy application of which excited considerable admiration in the mind of Mr Chitling. It was remarkable that the latter gentleman and his partner invariably lost; and that the circumstance, so far from angering Master Bates, appeared to afford him the highest amusement, inasmuch as he laughed most uproariously at the end of every deal, and protested that he had never seen such a jolly game in all his born days.

'That's two doubles and the rub,' said Mr Chitling, with a very long face, as he drew half a crown from his waistcoat pocket. 'I never see such a feller as you, Jack; you win everything. Even when we've good cards, Charley and I can't make nothing of 'em.'

Either the matter or the manner of this remark, which was made very ruefully, delighted Charley Bates so much, that his consequent shout of laughter roused the Jew from his reverie, and induced him to enquire what was the matter.

'Matter, Fagin!' cried Charley. 'I wish you had watched the play. Tommy Chitling hasn't won a point; and I went partners with him against the Artful and dum.'

'Ay, ay,' said the Jew, with a grin, which sufficiently demonstrated that he was at no loss to understand the reason. 'Try 'em again, Tom; try 'em again.'

'No more of it for me, thankee, Fagin,' replied Mr Chitling; 'I've had enough. That 'ere Dodger has such a run of luck that there's no standin' again him.'

'Ha! ha! my dear,' replied the Jew, 'you must get up very early in the morning to win against the Dodger.'

'Morning!' said Charley Bates; 'you must put your boots on overnight, and have a telescope at each eye, and an opera-glass between your shoulders, if you want to come over him.'

Mr Dawkins received these handsome compliments with much philosophy, and offered to cut any gentleman in company for the first picture-card, at a shilling a time. Nobody accepting the challenge, and his pipe being by this time smoked out, he proceeded to amuse himself by sketching a ground-plan of Newgate on the table with the piece of chalk which had served him in lieu of counters, whistling, meantime, with peculiar shrillness.

'How precious dull you are, Tommy!' said the Dodger, stopping short when there had been a long silence, and addressing Mr Chitling. 'What do you think he's thinking of, Fagin?'

'How should I know, my dear?' replied the Jew, looking round as he plied the bellows. 'About his losses may be; or the little retirement in the country that he's just left, eh? Ha! ha! Is that it, my dear?'

'Not a bit of it,' replied the Dodger, stopping the subject of discourse as Mr Chitling was about to reply. 'What do *you* say, Charley?'

'*I* should say,' replied Master Bates, with a grin, 'that he was uncommon sweet upon Betsy. See how he's a-blushing! Oh, my eye! here's a merry-go-rounder! Tommy Chitling's in love! Oh, Fagin! Fagin! what a spree!'

Thoroughly overpowered with the notion of Mr Chitling being the victim of the tender passion, Master Bates threw himself back in his chair with such violence that he lost his balance and pitched over upon the floor, where (the accident abating nothing of his merriment) he lay at full length until his laugh was over, when he resumed his former position, and began another.

'Never mind him, my dear,' said the Jew, winking at Mr Dawkins, and giving Master Bates a reproving tap with the nozzle of the bellows. 'Betsy's a fine girl. Stick up to her, Tom. Stick up to her.'

'What I mean to say, Fagin,' replied Mr Chitling, very red in the face, 'is, that that isn't anything to anybody here.'

'No more it is,' replied the Jew; 'Charley will talk. Don't mind him, my dear; don't mind him. Betsy's a fine girl. Do as she bids you, Tom, and you will make your fortune.'

'So I *do* do as she bids me,' replied Mr Chitling: 'I shouldn't have been milled if it hadn't been for her advice. But it turned out a good job for you; didn't it, Fagin? And what's six weeks of it? It must come sometime or another; and why not in the winter time, when you don't want to go out a-walking so much – eh, Fagin?'

'Ah, to be sure, my dear,' replied the Jew.

'You wouldn't mind it again, Tom, would you,' asked the Dodger, winking upon Charley and the Jew, 'if Bet was all right?'

'I mean to say that I shouldn't,' replied Tom, angrily. 'There, now. Ah! Who'll say as much as that, I should like to know; eh, Fagin?'

'Nobody, my dear,' replied the Jew; 'not a soul, Tom. I don't know one of 'em that would do it besides you; not one of 'em, my dear.'

'I might have got clear off if I'd split upon her; mightn't I, Fagin?' angrily pursued the poor half-witted dupe. 'A word from me would have done it; wouldn't it, Fagin?'

'To be sure, it would, my dear,' replied the Jew.

'But I didn't blab it; did I, Fagin?' demanded Tom, pouring question upon question with great volubility.

'No, no, to be sure,' replied the Jew; 'you were too stout-hearted for that – a deal too stout, my dear!'

'Perhaps I was,' rejoined Tom, looking round; 'and if I was, what's to laugh at in that, eh, Fagin?'

The Jew, perceiving that Mr Chitling was considerably roused, hastened to assure him that nobody was laughing; and to prove the gravity of the company, appealed to Master Bates, the principal offender. But, unfortunately, Charley, in opening his mouth to reply that he was never more serious in his life, was unable to prevent the escape of such a violent roar that the abused Mr Chitling, without any preliminary ceremonies, rushed across the room and aimed a blow at the offender, who, being skilful in evading pursuit, ducked to avoid it, and chose his time so well that it lighted on the chest of the Merry Old Gentleman, and caused him to stagger to the wall where he stood panting for breath, while Mr Chitling looked on in intense dismay.

'Hark!' cried the Dodger at this moment, 'I heard the tinkler.' Catching up the light he crept softly upstairs.

The bell was rung again, with some impatience, while the party were in darkness. After a short pause, the Dodger reappeared, and whispered to Fagin mysteriously.

'What!' cried the Jew, 'alone?'

The Dodger nodded in the affirmative; and shading the flame of the candle with his hand, gave Charley Bates a private intimation, in dumb show, that he had better not be funny just then. Having performed this friendly office, he fixed his eyes on the Jew's face, and awaited his directions.

The old man bit his yellow fingers, and meditated for some seconds, his face working with agitation the while, as if he dreaded something, and feared to know the worst. At length he raised his head.

'Where is he?' he asked.

The Dodger pointed to the floor above, and made a gesture as if to leave the room.

'Yes,' said the Jew, answering the mute enquiry; 'bring him down. Hush! Quiet, Charley. Gently, Tom. Scarce, scarce!'

This brief direction to Charley Bates and his recent antagonist was softly and immediately obeyed. There was no sound of their whereabouts, when the Dodger descended the stairs, bearing the light in his hand, and followed by a man in a coarse smock-frock, who, after casting a hurried glance round the room, pulled off a large wrapper which had concealed the lower portion of his face, and disclosed – all haggard, unwashed, and unshorn – the features of flash Toby Crackit.

'How are you, Fagey?' said this worthy, nodding to the Jew. 'Pop that shawl away in my castor, Dodger, so that I may know where to find it when I cut; that's the time of day! You'll be a fine young cracksman afore the old file now.'

With these words he pulled up the smock-frock, and, winding it round his middle, drew a chair to the fire, and placed his feet upon the hob.

'See there, Fagey,' he said, pointing disconsolately to his top-boots; 'not a drop of Day and Martin since you know when – not a bubble of blacking, by – ! But don't look at me in that way, man. All in good time. I can't talk about business till I've eat and drank; so produce the sustenance, and let's have a quiet fill-out for the first time these three days!'

The Jew motioned to the Dodger to place what eatables there were upon the table, and, seating himself opposite the house-breaker, waited his leisure.

To judge from appearances, Toby was by no means in a hurry to open the conversation. At first, the Jew contented himself with patiently watching his countenance, as if to gain from its expression some clue to the intelligence he brought; but in vain. He looked tired and worn, but there was the same complacent repose upon his features that they always wore, and through dirt, and beard, and whisker there still shone, unimpaired, the self-satisfied smirk of flash Toby Crackit. Then the Jew, in an agony of impatience, watched every morsel he put into his mouth, pacing up and down the room, meanwhile, in irrepressible excitement. It was all of no use. Toby continued to eat with the utmost outward indifference, until he could eat no more; then, ordering the Dodger out, he closed the door, mixed a glass of spirits and water, and composed himself for talking.

'First and foremost, Fagey,' said Toby.

'Yes, yes!' interposed the Jew, drawing up his chair.

Mr Crackit stopped to take a draught of spirits and water, and to declare that the gin was excellent, and then, placing his feet against the low mantelpiece, so as to bring his boots to about the level of his eye, quietly resumed.

'First and foremost, Fagey,' said the housebreaker, 'how's Bill?'

'What!' screamed the Jew, starting from his seat.

'Why, you don't mean to say –' began Toby, turning pale.

'Mean!' cried the Jew, stamping furiously on the ground. 'Where are they? Sikes and the boy! Where are they? Where have they been? Where are they hiding? Why have they not been here?'

'The crack failed,' said Toby, faintly.

'I know it,' replied the Jew, tearing a newspaper from his pocket and pointing to it. 'What more?'

'They fired and hit the boy. We cut over the fields at the back with him between us – straight as the crow flies – through hedge and ditch. They gave chase. Damn me! the whole country was awake, and the dogs upon us.'

'The boy!' gasped the Jew.

'Bill had him on his back, and scudded like the wind. We stopped to take him between us; his head hung down, and he was cold. They were close upon our heels; every man for himself and each from the gallows! We parted company, and left the youngster lying in a ditch – alive or dead, that's all I know about him.'

The Jew stopped to hear no more, but uttering a loud yell, and twining his hands in his hair, rushed from the room, and from the house.

CHAPTER 26

In which a mysterious character appears upon the scene; and many things, inseparable from this history, are done and performed

The old man had gained the street corner before he began to recover the effect of Toby Crackit's intelligence. He had relaxed nothing of his unusual speed, but was still pressing onward in the same wild and disordered manner, when the sudden dashing past of a carriage, and a boisterous cry from the foot-passengers, who saw his danger, drove him back upon the pavement. Avoiding, as much as possible, all the main streets, and skulking only through the byways and alleys, he at length emerged on Snow Hill. Here he walked even faster than before; nor did he linger until he had again turned into a court, when, as if conscious that he was now in his proper element, he fell into his usual shuffling pace, and seemed to breathe more freely.

Near to the spot on which Snow Hill and Holborn Hill meet there opens, upon the right hand as you come out of the City, a narrow and dismal alley leading to Saffron Hill. In its filthy shops are exposed for sale huge bunches of second-hand silk handkerchiefs, of all sizes and patterns; for here reside the traders who purchase them from pickpockets. Hundreds of these handkerchiefs hang dangling from pegs outside the windows or flaunting from the doorpost; and the shelves, within, are piled with them. Confined as the limits of Field Lane are, it has its barber, its coffee-shop, its beer-shop, and its fried fish warehouse. It is a commercial colony of itself – the emporium of petty larceny; visited at early morning and setting-in of dusk by silent merchants, who traffic in dark back-parlours, and who go as strangely as they come. Here the clothesman, the shoe-vamper, and the rag-merchant display their goods, as sign-boards to the petty thief; here stores of old iron and bones, and heaps of mildewy fragments of woollen stuff and linen, rust and rot in the grimy cellars.

It was into this place that the Jew turned. He was well known to the sallow denizens of the lane, for such of them as were on the look-out to buy or sell nodded familiarly as he passed along. He replied to their salutations in the same way; but bestowed no closer recognition until he reached the farther end of the alley, when he stopped to address a salesman of small stature, who had squeezed as much of his person into a child's chair as the chair would hold, and was smoking a pipe at his warehouse door.

'Why, the sight of you, Mr Fagin, would cure the hoptalmy!' said this respectable trader, in acknowledgment of the Jew's enquiry after his health.

'The neighbourhood was a little too hot, Lively,' said Fagin, elevating his eyebrows, and crossing his hands upon his shoulders.

'Well, I've heerd that complaint of it once or twice before,' replied the trader; 'but it soon cools down again. Don't you find it so?'

Fagin nodded in the affirmative. Pointing in the direction of Saffron Hill, he enquired whether anyone was up yonder tonight.

'At the Cripples?' enquired the man.

The Jew nodded.

'Let me see,' pursued the merchant, reflecting. 'Yes, there's some half-dozen of 'em gone in, that I knows. I don't think your friend's there.'

'Sikes is not, I suppose?' enquired the Jew, with a disappointed countenance.

'*Non istwentus*, as the lawyers say,' replied the little man, shaking his head, and looking amazingly sly. 'Have you got anything in my line tonight?'

'Nothing tonight,' said the Jew, turning away.

'Are you going up to the Cripples, Fagin?' cried the little man, calling after him. 'Stop! I don't mind if I have a drop there with you!'

But as the Jew, looking back, waved his hand to intimate that he preferred being alone, and, moreover, as the little man could not very easily disengage himself from the chair, the sign of the Cripples was for a time bereft of the advantage of Mr Lively's presence. By the time he had got upon his legs the Jew had disappeared; so Mr Lively, after ineffectually standing on tip-toe, in the hope of catching sight of him, again forced himself into the little chair, and, exchanging a shake of the head with a lady in the opposite shop, in which doubt and mistrust were plainly mingled, resumed his pipe with a grave demeanour.

The Three Cripples, or rather the Cripples, which was the sign by which the establishment was familiarly known to its patrons, was the same public-house in which Mr Sikes and his dog have already figured. Merely making a sign to a man at the bar, Fagin walked straight upstairs, and opening the door of a room, and softly insinuating himself into the chamber, looked anxiously about, shading his eyes with his hand, as if in search of some particular person.

The room was illuminated by two gaslights, the glare of which was prevented, by the barred shutters and closely-drawn curtains of faded red, from being visible outside. The ceiling was blackened, to prevent its colour from being injured by the flaring of the lamps; and the place was so full of dense tobacco smoke, that at first it was scarcely possible to discern anything more. By degrees, however, as some of it cleared away through the open door, an assemblage of heads, as confused as the noises that greeted the ear, might be made out; and as the eye grew more accustomed to the scene, the spectator gradually became aware of the presence of a numerous company, male and female, crowded round a long table, at the upper end of which sat a chairman with a hammer of office in his hand, while a professional gentleman, with a bluish nose, and his face tied up for the benefit of the toothache, presided at a jingling piano in a remote corner.

As Fagin stepped softly in, the professional gentleman, running over the keys by way of prelude, occasioned a general cry of order for a song; which having subsided, a young lady proceeded to entertain the company with a ballad in four verses, between each of which the accompanist played the melody, all through, as loud as he could. When this was over, the chairman gave a sentiment; after which the professional gentlemen on the chairman's right and left volunteered a duet, and sang it with great applause.

It was curious to observe some faces which stood out prominently from among the group. There was the chairman himself (the landlord of the house), a coarse, rough, heavy-built fellow, who, while the songs were proceeding, rolled his eyes hither and thither, and, seeming to give himself up to joviality, had an eye for everything that was done, and an ear for everything that was said – and sharp ones, too. Near him were the singers, receiving with professional indifference the compliments of the company, and applying themselves in turn to a dozen proffered glasses of spirits and water, tendered by their more boisterous admirers, whose countenances, expressive of almost every vice in almost every grade, irresistibly attracted the attention by their very repulsiveness. Cunning, ferocity, and drunkenness in all its stages were there, in their strongest aspects; and women – some with the last lingering tinge of their early freshness almost fading as you looked; others with every mark and stamp of their sex utterly beaten out, and presenting but one loathsome blank of profligacy and crime; some mere girls, others but young women, and none past the prime of life – formed the darkest and saddest portion of this dreary picture.

Fagin, troubled by no grave emotions, looked eagerly from face to face while these proceedings were in progress, but apparently without meeting that of which he was in search. Succeeding, at length, in catching the eye of the man who occupied the chair, he beckoned to him slightly, and left the room as quietly as he had entered it.

'What can I do for you, Mr Fagin?' enquired the man, as he followed him out to the landing. 'Won't you join us? They'll be delighted, every one of 'em.'

The Jew shook his head impatiently, and said in a whisper, 'Is *he* here?'

'No,' replied the man.

'And no news of Barney?' enquired Fagin.

'None,' replied the landlord of the Cripples, for it was he. 'He won't stir till it's all safe. Depend on it, they're on the scent down there; and that, if he moved, he'd blow upon the thing at once. He's all right enough, Barney is, else I should have heard of him. I'll pound it that Barney's managing properly. Let him alone for that.'

'Will *he* be here tonight?' asked the Jew, laying the same emphasis on the pronoun as before.

'Monks, do you mean?' enquired the landlord, hesitating.

'Hush!' said the Jew. 'Yes.'

'Certain,' replied the man, drawing a gold watch from his fob. 'I expected him here before now. If you'll wait ten minutes, he'll be – '

'No, no,' said the Jew, hastily, as though, however desirous he might be to see the person in question, he was nevertheless relieved by his absence. 'Tell him I came here to see him, and that he must come to me tonight. No, say tomorrow. As he is not here, tomorrow will be time enough.'

'Good!' said the man. 'Nothing more?'

'Not a word now,' said the Jew, descending the stairs.

'I say,' said the other, looking over the rails, and speaking in a hoarse whisper, 'what a time this would be for a sell! I've got Phil Barker here, so drunk that a boy might take him.'

'Aha! But it's not Phil Barker's time,' said the Jew, looking up. 'Phil has something more to do before we can afford to part with him; so go back to the company, my dear, and tell them to lead merry lives – *while they last*. Ha! ha! ha!'

The landlord reciprocated the old man's laugh, and returned to his guests. The Jew was no sooner alone than his countenance resumed its former expression of anxiety and thought. After a brief reflection, he called a hack-cabriolet, and bade the man drive towards Bethnal Green. He dismissed him within some quarter of a mile of Mr Sikes's residence, and performed the short remainder of the distance on foot.

'Now,' muttered the Jew, as he knocked at the door, 'if there is any deep play here, I shall have it out of you, my girl, cunning as you are.'

She was in her room, the woman said. Fagin crept softly upstairs, and entered it without any previous ceremony. The girl was alone, lying with her head upon the table, and her hair straggling over it.

'She has been drinking,' thought the Jew, coolly, 'or perhaps she is only miserable.'

The old man turned to close the door, as he made this reflection, and the noise thus occasioned roused the girl. She eyed his crafty face narrowly, as she enquired whether there was any news, and listened to his recital of Toby Crackit's story. When it was concluded, she sank into her former attitude, but spoke not a word. She pushed the candle impatiently away, and once or twice, as she feverishly changed her position, shuffled her feet upon the ground; but this was all.

During this silence the Jew looked restlessly about the room, as if to assure himself that there were no appearances of Sikes having covertly returned. Apparently satisfied with his inspection, he coughed twice or thrice, and made as many efforts to open a conversation; but the girl heeded him no more than if he had been made of stone. At length he made another attempt, and, rubbing his hands together, said in his most conciliatory tone, 'And where should you think Bill was now, my dear?'

The girl moaned out some half intelligible reply, that she could not tell, and seemed, from the smothered noise that escaped her, to be crying.

'And the boy, too?' said the Jew, straining his eyes to catch a glimpse of her face. 'Poor leetle child! Left in a ditch, Nance; only think!'

'The child,' said the girl, suddenly looking up, 'is better where he is than among us; and if no harm comes to Bill from it, I hope he lies dead in the ditch, and that his young bones may rot there.'

'What!' cried the Jew in amazement.

'Ay, I do,' returned the girl, meeting his gaze. 'I shall be glad to have him away from my eyes, and to know that the worst is over. I can't bear to have him about me. The sight of him turns me against myself, and all of you.'

'Pooh!' said the Jew, scornfully. 'You're drunk.'

'Am I?' said the girl bitterly. 'It's no fault of yours if I am not! You'd never have me anything else, if you had your will, except now; – the humour doesn't suit you, doesn't it?'

'No!' rejoined the Jew, furiously. 'It does not.'

'Change it, then!' responded the girl, with a laugh.

'Change it!' exclaimed the Jew, exasperated beyond all bounds by his companion's unexpected obstinacy and the vexation of the night, 'I will change it! Listen to me, you drab. Listen to me, who, with six words, can strangle Sikes as surely as if I had his bull's throat between my fingers now. If he comes back, and leaves that boy behind him – if he gets off free, and, dead or alive, fails to restore him to me – murder him yourself if you would have him escape Jack Ketch; and do it the moment he sets foot in this room, or, mind me, it will be too late!'

'What is all this?' cried the girl, involuntarily.

'What is it?' pursued Fagin, mad with rage. 'When the boy's worth hundreds of pounds to me, am I to lose what chance threw me in the way of getting safely, through the whims of a drunken gang that I could whistle away the lives of ! And me bound, too, to a born devil that only wants the will, and has the power to, to –'

Panting for breath, the old man stammered for a word, and in that instant checked the torrent of his wrath, and changed his whole demeanour. A moment before his clenched hands had grasped the air, his eyes had dilated, and his face grown livid with passion; but now he shrunk into a chair, and, cowering together, trembled with the apprehension of having himself disclosed some hidden villainy. After a short silence, he ventured to look round at his companion. He appeared somewhat reassured, on beholding her in the same listless attitude from which he had first roused her.

'Nancy, dear!' croaked the Jew, in his usual voice. 'Did you mind me, dear?'

'Don't worry me now, Fagin!' replied the girl, raising her head languidly. 'If Bill has not done it this time, he will another. He has done many a good job for you, and will do many more when he can; and when he can't, he won't; so no more about that.'

'Regarding this boy, my dear?' said the Jew, rubbing the palms of his hands nervously together.

'The boy must take his chance with the rest,' interrupted Nancy hastily; 'and I say again, I hope he is dead, and out of harm's way, and out of yours – that is, if Bill comes to no harm. And if Toby got clear off, he's pretty sure to be safe; for he's worth two of him any time.'

'And about what I was saying, my dear?' observed the Jew, keeping his glistening eye steadily upon her.

'You must say it all over again, if it's anything you want me to do,' rejoined Nancy; 'and if it is, you had better wait till tomorrow. You put me up for a minute, but now I'm stupid again.'

Fagin put several other questions, all with the same drift of ascertaining whether the girl had profited by his unguarded hints; but she answered them so readily, and was withal so utterly unmoved by his searching looks, that his original impression of her being more than a trifle in liquor was fully confirmed. Nancy, indeed, was not exempt from a failing which was very common among the Jew's female pupils, and in which, in their tenderer years, they were rather encouraged than checked. Her disordered appearance, and a wholesale perfume of Geneva which pervaded the apartment, afforded strong confirmatory evidence of the justice of the Jew's supposition; and when, after indulging in the temporary display of violence above described, she subsided, first into dullness, and afterwards into a compound of feelings, under the influence of which she shed tears one minute, and in the next gave utterance to various exclamations of 'Never say die!' and divers calculations as to what might be the amount of the odds so long as a lady or gentleman was happy, Mr Fagin, who had had considerable experience of such matters in his time, saw, with great satisfaction, that she was very far gone indeed.

Having eased his mind by this discovery, and having accomplished his twofold object of imparting to the girl what he had that night heard, and of ascertaining, with his own eyes, that Sikes had not returned, Mr Fagin again turned his face homeward, leaving his young friend asleep, with her head upon the table.

It was within an hour of midnight, and the weather being dark, and piercing cold, he had no great temptation to loiter. The sharp wind that scoured the streets seemed to have cleared them of passengers, as of dust and mud; for few people were abroad, and they were to all appearance hastening fast home. It blew from the right quarter for the Jew, however, and straight before it he went, trembling and shivering, as every fresh gust drove him rudely on his way.

He had reached the corner of his own street, and was already fumbling in his pocket for the door-key, when a dark figure emerged from a projecting entrance which lay in deep shadow, and, crossing the road, glided up to him unperceived.

'Fagin!' whispered a voice close to his ear.

'Ah!' said the Jew, turning quickly round, 'is that – '

'Yes!' interrupted the stranger harshly. 'I have been lingering here these two hours. Where the devil have you been?'

'On your business, my dear,' replied the Jew, glancing uneasily at his companion, and slackening his pace as he spoke. 'On your business all night.'

'Oh, of course!' said the stranger, with a sneer. 'Well, and what's come of it?'

'Nothing good,' said the Jew.

'Nothing bad, I hope?' said the stranger stopping short, and turning a startled look on his companion.

The Jew shook his head, and was about to reply, when the stranger, interrupting him, motioned to the house, before which they had by this time arrived, remarking that he had better say what he had got to say under cover, for his blood was chilled with standing about so long, and the wind blew through him.

Fagin looked as if he could have willingly excused himself from taking home a visitor at that unseasonable hour, and, indeed, muttered something about having no fire; but his companion repeating his request in a peremptory manner, he unlocked the door, and requested him to close it softly, while he got a light.

'It's as dark as the grave,' said the man, groping forward a few steps. 'Make haste!'

'Shut the door,' whispered Fagin from the end of the passage. As he spoke, it closed with a loud noise.

'That wasn't my doing,' said the other man, feeling his way. 'The wind blew it to, or it shut of its own accord – one or the other. Look sharp with the light, or I shall knock my brains out against something in this confounded hole.'

Fagin stealthily descended the kitchen stairs. After a short absence, he returned with a lighted candle, and the intelligence that Toby Crackit was asleep in the back room below, and the boys in the front one. Beckoning the man to follow him, he led the way upstairs.

'We can say the few words we've got to say in here, my dear,' said the Jew, throwing open a door on the first floor; 'and as there are holes in the shutters, and we never show lights to our neighbours, we'll set the candle on the stairs. There!'

With these words the Jew, stooping down, placed the candle on an upper flight of stairs, exactly opposite to the room door. This done, he led the way into the apartment, which was destitute of all movables save a broken armchair, and an old couch or sofa without covering, which stood behind the door. Upon this piece of furniture the stranger flung himself with the air of a weary man; and the Jew drawing up the armchair opposite, they sat face to face. It was not quite dark; for the door was partially open, and the candle outside threw a feeble reflection on the opposite wall.

They conversed for some time in whispers. Though nothing of the conversation was distinguishable beyond a few disjointed words here and there, a listener might easily have perceived that Fagin appeared to be defending himself against some remarks of the stranger, and that the latter was in a state of considerable irritation. They might have been talking thus for a quarter of an hour or more, when Monks – by which name the Jew had designated the strange man several times in the course of their colloquy – said, raising his voice a little, 'I tell you again it was badly planned. Why not have kept him here among the rest, and made a sneaking, snivelling pickpocket of him at once?'

'Only hear him!' exclaimed the Jew, shrugging his shoulders.

'Why, do you mean to say you couldn't have done it, if you had chosen?' demanded Monks sternly, 'Haven't you done it with other boys scores of times? If you had had patience for a twelvemonth, at most, couldn't you have got him convicted, and sent safely out of the kingdom, perhaps for life?'

'Whose turn would that have served, my dear?' enquired the Jew humbly.

'Mine,' replied Monks.

'But not mine,' said the Jew submissively. 'He might have become of use to me. When there are two parties to a bargain, it is only reasonable that the interests of both should be consulted; is it, my good friend?'

'What then?' demanded Monks sulkily.

'I saw it was not easy to train him to the business,' replied the Jew; 'he was not like other boys in the same circumstances.'

'Curse him, no!' muttered the man, 'or he would have been a thief long ago.'

'I had no hold upon him to make him worse,' pursued the Jew, anxiously watching the countenance of his companion. 'His hand was not in. I had nothing to frighten him with; which we always must have in the beginning, or we labour in vain. What could I do? Send him out with the Dodger and Charley? We had enough of that, at first, my dear; I trembled for us all.'

'*That* was not my doing,' observed Monks.

'No, no, my dear!' renewed the Jew. 'And I don't quarrel with it, now; because, if it had never happened, you might never have clapped eyes upon the boy to notice him, and so led to the discovery that it was him you were looking for. Well! I got him back for you by means of the girl; and then *she* begins to favour him.

'Throttle the girl!' said Monks impatiently.

'Why, we can't afford to do that just now, my dear,' replied the Jew, smiling; 'and, besides, that sort of thing is not in our way, or, one of these days, I might be glad to have it done. I know what these girls are, Monks, well. As soon as the boy begins to harden, she'll care no more for him than for a block of wood. You want him made a thief. If he is alive, I can make him one from this time; and if – if – ' said the Jew, drawing nearer to the other – 'it's not likely, mind – but if the worst comes to the worst, and he is dead – '

Oliver Twist

'It's no fault of mine if he is!' interposed the other man, with a look of terror, and clasping the Jew's arm with trembling hands. 'Mind that, Fagin! I had no hand in it. Anything but his death, I told you from the first. I won't shed blood; it's always found out, and haunts a man, besides. If they shot him dead, I was not the cause; do you hear me? Fire this infernal den! What's that?'

'What?' cried the Jew, grasping the coward round the body with both arms, as he sprung to his feet. 'Where?'

'Yonder!' replied the man, glaring at the opposite wall. 'The shadow! I saw the shadow of a woman, in a cloak and bonnet, pass along the wainscot like a breath!'

The Jew released his hold, and they rushed tumultuously from the room. The candle, wasted by the draught, was standing where it had been placed. It showed them only the empty staircase and their own white faces. They listened intently; but a profound silence reigned throughout the house.

'It's your fancy,' said the Jew, taking up the light, and turning to his companion.

'I'll swear I saw it!' replied Monks, trembling. 'It was bending forward when I saw it first; and when I spoke it darted away.'

The Jew glanced, contemptuously, at the pale face of his associate, and, telling him he could follow if he pleased, ascended the stairs. They looked into all the rooms: they were cold, bare, and empty. They descended into the passage, and thence into the cellars below. The green damp hung upon the low walls, and the tracks of the snail and slug glistened in the light of the candle; but all was still as death.

'What do you think now?' said the Jew, when they had regained the passage. 'Besides ourselves, there's not a creature in the house except Toby and the boys; and they're safe enough. See here!'

As a proof of the fact, the Jew drew forth two keys from his pocket, and explained that when he first went downstairs he had locked them in, to prevent any intrusion on the conference.

This accumulated testimony effectually staggered Mr Monks. His protestations had gradually become less and less vehement as they proceeded in their search without making any discovery; and now he gave vent to several very grim laughs, and confessed it could only have been his excited imagination. He declined any renewal of the conversation, however, for that night, suddenly remembering that it was past one o'clock. And so the amiable couple parted.

CHAPTER 27

Atones for the unpoliteness of a former chapter; which deserted a lady most unceremoniously

As it would be by no means seemly in a humble author to keep so mighty a personage as a beadle waiting, with his back to the fire, and the skirts of his coat gathered up under his arms, until such time as it might suit his pleasure to relieve him; and as it would still less become his station, or his gallantry, to involve in the same neglect a lady on whom that beadle had looked with an eye of tenderness and affection, and in whose ear he had whispered sweet words, which, coming from such a quarter, might well thrill the bosom of maid or matron of whatsoever degree: the historian whose pen traces these words – trusting that he knows his place, and that he entertains a becoming reverence for those upon earth to whom high and important authority is delegated – hastens to pay them that respect which their position demands, and to treat them with all that duteous ceremony which their exalted rank, and (by consequence) great virtues, imperatively claim at his hands. Towards this end, indeed, he had purposed to introduce, in this place, a dissertation touching the divine right of beadles, and elucidative of the position that a beadle can do no wrong, which could not fail to have been both pleasurable and profitable to the right-handed reader, but which he is unfortunately compelled, by want of time and space, to postpone to some more convenient and fitting opportunity; on the arrival of which he will be prepared to show, that a beadle properly constituted – that is to say, a parochial beadle, attached to a parochial workhouse, and attending in his official capacity the parochial church – is, in right and virtue of his office, possessed of all the excellences and best qualities of humanity; and that to none of those excellences can mere companies' beadles, or court-of-law beadles, or even chapel-of-ease beadles (save the last, and they in a very lowly and inferior degree), lay the remotest sustainable claim.

Mr Bumble had recounted the teaspoons, reweighed the sugar-tongs, made a closer inspection of the milk-pot, and ascertained to a nicety the exact condition of the furniture, down to the very horsehair seats of the chairs, and had repeated each process full half a dozen times, before he began to think that it was time for Mrs Corney to return. Thinking begets thinking; and, as there were no sounds of Mrs Corney's approach, it occurred to Mr Bumble that it would be an innocent and virtuous way of spending the time, if he were further to allay his curiosity by a cursory glance at the interior of Mrs Corney's chest of drawers.

Having listened at the keyhole, to assure himself that nobody was approaching the chamber, Mr Bumble, beginning at the bottom, proceeded to make himself acquainted with the contents of the three long drawers; which, being filled with various garments of good fashion and texture, carefully preserved between two layers of old newspapers, speckled with dried lavender, seemed to yield him exceeding satisfaction. Arriving, in course of time, at the right-hand corner drawer (in which was the key), and beholding therein a small padlocked box, which, being shaken gave forth a pleasant sound, as of the chinking of coin, Mr Bumble returned with a stately walk to the fireplace, and, resuming his old attitude, said, with a grave and determined air, 'I'll do it!' He followed up this remarkable declaration by shaking his head in a waggish manner for ten minutes, as though he were remonstrating with himself for being such a pleasant dog; and then he took a view of his legs in profile, with much seeming pleasure and interest.

He was still placidly engaged in this latter survey, when Mrs

Corney, hurrying into the room, threw herself, in a breathless state, on a chair by the fireside, and covering her eyes with one hand, placed the other over her heart, and gasped for breath.

'Mrs Corney,' said Mr Bumble, stooping over the matron, 'what is this, ma'am? has anything happened, ma'am? Pray answer me; I'm on – on – ' Mr Bumble, in his alarm, could not immediately think of the word 'tenterhooks', so he said, 'broken bottles.'

'Oh, Mr Bumble' cried the lady, 'I've been so dreadfully put out!'

'Put out, ma'am!' exclaimed Mr Bumble; 'who has dared to – ? I know!' said Mr Bumble, checking himself with native majesty, 'this is them wicious paupers!'

'It's dreadful to think of,' said the lady, shuddering.

'Then *don't* think of it, ma'am,' rejoined Mr Bumble.

'I can't help it,' whimpered the lady.

'Then take something, ma'am,' said Mr Bumble, soothingly. 'A little of the wine?'

'Not for the world!' replied Mrs Corney. 'I couldn't – oh! The top shelf in the right-hand corner – oh!' Uttering these words, the good lady pointed distractedly to the cupboard and underwent a convulsion from internal spasms. Mr Bumble rushed to the closet, and snatching a pint green-glass bottle from the shelf thus incoherently indicated, filled a teacup with its contents, and held it to the lady's lips.

'I'm better now,' said Mrs Corney, falling back after drinking half of it.

Mr Bumble raised his eyes piously to the ceiling in thankfulness, and bringing them down again to the brim of the cup, lifted it to his nose.

'Peppermint,' exclaimed Mrs Corney, in a faint voice, smiling gently on the beadle as she spoke. 'Try it! There's a little – a little something else in it.'

Mr Bumble tasted the medicine with a doubtful look, smacked his lips, took another taste, and put the cup down empty.

'It's very comforting,' said Mrs Corney.

'Very much so indeed, ma'am,' said the beadle. As he spoke, he drew a chair beside the matron, and tenderly enquired what had happened to distress her.

'Nothing,' replied Mrs Corney. 'I am a foolish, excitable, weak creetur.'

'Not weak, ma'am,' retorted Mr Bumble, drawing his chair a little closer. 'Are you a weak creetur, Mrs Corney?'

'We are all weak creeturs,' said Mrs Corney, laying down a general principle.

'So we are,' said the beadle.

Nothing was said on either side for a minute or two afterwards. By the expiration of that time Mr Bumble had illustrated the position by removing his left arm from the back of Mrs Corney's chair, where it had previously rested, to Mrs Corney's apron-string, round which it gradually became entwined.

'We are all weak creeturs,' said Mr Bumble.

Mrs Corney sighed.

'Don't sigh, Mrs Corney,' said Mr Bumble.

'I can't help it,' said Mrs Corney. And she sighed again.

'This is a very comfortable room, ma'am,' said Mr Bumble, looking round. 'Another room and this, ma'am, would be a complete thing.'

'It would be too much for one,' murmured the lady.

'But not for two, ma'am,' rejoined Mr Bumble, in soft accents. 'Eh, Mrs Corney?'

Mrs Corney drooped her head, when the beadle said this. The beadle drooped his, to get a view of Mrs Corney's face. Mrs Corney, with great propriety, turned her head away, and released her hand to get at her pocket-handkerchief; but insensibly replaced it in that of Mr Bumble.

'The board allow you coals, don't they, Mrs Corney?' enquired the beadle, affectionately pressing her hand.

'And candles,' replied Mrs Corney, slightly returning the pressure.

'Coals, candles, and house-rent free,' said Mr Bumble. 'Oh, Mrs Corney, what a Angel you are!'

The lady was not proof against this burst of feeling. She sank into Mr Bumble's arms; and that gentleman, in his agitation, imprinted a passionate kiss upon her chaste nose.

'Such porochial perfection!' exclaimed Mr Bumble rapturously. 'You know that Mr Slout is worse tonight, my fascinator?'

'Yes,' replied Mrs Corney bashfully.

'He can't live a week, the doctor says,' pursued Mr Bumble. 'He is the master of this establishment; his death will cause a wacancy; that wacancy must be filled up. Oh, Mrs Corney, what a prospect this opens! What a opportunity for a joining of hearts and housekeepings!'

Mrs Corney sobbed.

'The little word?' said Mr Bumble, bending over the bashful beauty. 'The one little, little, little word, my blessed Corney?'

'Ye – ye – yes!' sighed out the matron.

'One more,' pursued the beadle; 'compose your darling feelings for only one more. When is it to come off?'

Mrs Corney twice essayed to speak, and twice failed. At length, summoning up courage, she threw her arms round Mr Bumble's neck, and said it might be as soon as ever he pleased, and that he was 'a irresistible duck.'

Matters being thus amicably and satisfactorily arranged, the contract was solemnly ratified in another teacupful of the peppermint mixture, which was rendered the more necessary by the flutter and agitation of the lady's spirits. While it was being disposed of, she acquainted Mr Bumble with the old woman's decease.

'Very good,' said that gentleman, sipping his peppermint. 'I'll call at Sowerberry's as I go home, and tell him to send tomorrow morning. Was it that as frightened you, love?'

'It wasn't anything particular, dear,' said the lady evasively.

'It must have been something, love,' urged Mr Bumble. 'Won't you tell your own B.?'

'Not now,' rejoined the lady; 'one of these days. After we're married, dear.'

'After we're married!' exclaimed Mr Bumble. 'It wasn't any impudence from any of them male paupers as – '

'No, no, love!' interposed the lady hastily.

'If I thought it was,' continued Mr Bumble – 'if I thought as any one of 'em had dared to lift his wulgar eyes to that lovely countenance – '

'They wouldn't have dared to do it, love,' responded the lady.

'They had better not!' said Mr Bumble, clenching his fist. 'Let me see any man, porochial or extraporochial, as would presume to do it, and I can tell him that he wouldn't do it a second time!'

Unembellished by any violence of gesticulation, this might have seemed no very high compliment to the lady's charms; but as Mr Bumble accompanied the threat with many warlike gestures, she was much touched with this proof of his devotion, and protested, with great admiration, that he was indeed a dove.

The dove then turned up his coat-collar, and put on his cocked hat; and, having exchanged a long and affectionate embrace with his future partner, once again braved the cold wind of the night, merely pausing for a few minutes, in the male paupers' ward, to abuse them a little with a view of satisfying himself that he could fill the office of workhouse-master with needful acerbity. Assured of his qualifications, Mr Bumble left the building with a light heart, and bright visions of his future promotion, which served to occupy his mind until he reached the shop of the undertaker.

Now, Mr and Mrs Sowerberry having gone out to tea and supper, and Noah Claypole not being at any time disposed to take upon himself a greater amount of physical exertion than is necessary to a convenient performance of the two functions of eating and drinking, the shop was not closed, although it was past the usual hour of shutting up. Mr Bumble tapped with his cane on the counter several times; but, attracting no attention, and beholding a light shining through the glass window of the little parlour at the back of the shop, he made bold to peep in and see what was going forward; and when he saw what *was* going forward, he was not a little surprised.

The cloth was laid for supper, and the table was covered with bread and butter, plates and glasses, a porter-pot, and a wine-bottle. At the upper end of the table Mr Noah Claypole lolled negligently in an easy-chair, with his legs thrown over one of the arms, an open clasp-knife in one hand, and a mass of buttered bread in the other. Close beside him stood Charlotte, opening oysters from a barrel, which Mr Claypole con-descended to swallow with remarkable avidity. A more than ordinary redness in the region of the young gentleman's nose, and a kind of fixed wink in his right eye, denoted that he was in a slight degree intoxicated; and these symptoms were con-firmed by the intense relish with which he took his oysters, for which nothing but a strong appreciation of their cooling properties, in cases of internal fever, could have sufficiently accounted.

'Here's a delicious fat one, Noah, dear!' said Charlotte; 'try him, do; only this one.'

'What a delicious thing is a oyster!' remarked Mr Claypole, after he had swallowed it. 'What a pity it is a number of 'em should ever make you feel uncomfortable; isn't it, Charlotte?'

'It's quite a cruelty,' said Charlotte.

'So it is,' acquiesced Mr Claypole. 'An't yer fond of oysters?'

'Not overmuch,' replied Charlotte. 'I like to see you eat 'em, Noah, dear, better than eating 'em myself.'

'Lor!' said Noah reflectively; 'how queer!'

'Have another,' said Charlotte. 'Here's one with such a beautiful delicate beard!'

'I can't manage any more,' said Noah; 'I'm very sorry. Come here, Charlotte, and I'll kiss yer.'

'What!' said Mr Bumble, bursting into the room. 'Say that again, sir.'

Charlotte uttered a scream, and hid her face in her apron. Mr Claypole, without making any further change in his position than suffering his legs to reach the ground, gazed at the beadle in drunken terror.

'Say it again, you wile, owdacious fellow!' said Mr Bumble. 'How dare you mention such a thing, sir? And how dare you encourage him, you insolent minx? Kiss her!' exclaimed Mr Bumble, in strong indignation. 'Faugh!'

'I didn't mean to do it!' said Noah, blubbering. 'She's always a-kissing of me, whether I like it or not.'

'Oh, Noah,' cried Charlotte reproachfully.

'Yer are; yer know yer are!' retorted Noah. 'She's always a-doing of it, Mr Bumble, sir; she chucks me under the chin, please, sir, and makes all manner of love!'

'Silence!' cried Mr Bumble sternly. 'Take yourself down-stairs, ma'am. Noah, you shut up the shop; say another word till your master comes home at your peril; and when he does come home, tell him that Mr Bumble said he was to send an old woman's shell after breakfast tomorrow morning. Do you hear, sir? Kissing!' cried Mr Bumble, holding up his hands. 'The sin and wickedness of the lower orders in this porochial district is frightful. If parliament don't take their abominable courses under consideration, this country's ruined, and the character of the peasantry gone for ever!' With these words, the beadle strode, with a lofty and gloomy air, from the under-taker's premises.

Mr Claypole as he appeared when his master was out

And now that we have accompanied him so far on his road home, and have made all necessary preparations for the old woman's funeral, let us set on foot a few enquiries after young Oliver Twist, and ascertain whether he be still lying in the ditch where Toby Crackit left him.

CHAPTER 28

Looks after Oliver, and proceeds with his adventures

'Wolves tear your throats!' muttered Sikes, grinding his teeth. 'I wish I was among some of you; you'd howl the hoarser for it.'

As Sikes growled forth this imprecation, with the most desperate ferocity that his desperate nature was capable of, he rested the body of the wounded boy across his bended knee, and turned his head for an instant to look back at his pursuers.

There was little to be made out in the mist and darkness; but the loud shouting of men vibrated through the air, and the barking of the neighbouring dogs, roused by the sound of the alarm-bell, resounded in every direction.

'Stop, you white-livered hound!' cried the robber, shouting after Toby Crackit, who, making the best use of his long legs, was already ahead. 'Stop!'

The repetition of the word brought Toby to a dead standstill. For he was not quite satisfied that he was beyond the range of pistol-shot, and Sikes was in no mood to be played with.

'Bear a hand with the boy,' roared Sikes, beckoning furiously to his confederate. 'Come back!'

Toby made a show of returning; but ventured, in a low voice, broken for want of breath, to intimate considerable reluctance as he came slowly along.

'Quicker!' cried Sikes, laying the boy in a dry ditch at his feet, and drawing a pistol from his pocket. 'Don't play booty with me.'

At this moment the noise grew louder. Sikes, again looking round, could discern that the men who had given chase were already climbing the gate of the field in which he stood, and that a couple of dogs were some paces in advance of them.

'It's all up, Bill!' cried Toby; 'drop the kid, and show 'em your heels.' With this parting advice, Mr Crackit, preferring the chance of being shot by his friend to the certainty of being taken by his enemies, fairly turned tail, and darted off at full speed. Sikes clenched his teeth; took one look round; threw over the prostrate form of Oliver the cape in which he had been hurriedly muffled; ran along the front of the hedge, as if to distract the attention of those behind from the spot where the boy lay; paused, for a second, before another hedge which met it at right angles; and whirling his pistol high into the air, cleared it at a bound, and was gone.

'Ho, ho, there!' cried a tremulous voice in the rear. 'Pincher! Neptune! Come here, come here!'

The dogs, who, in common with their masters, seemed to have no particular relish for the sport in which they were engaged, readily answered to the command; and three men, who had by this time advanced some distance into the field, stopped to take counsel together.

'My advice, or, leastways, I should say, my *orders* is,' said the fattest man of the party, 'that we 'mediately go home again.'

'I am agreeable to anything which is agreeable to Mr Giles,' said a shorter man, who was by no means of a slim figure, and who was very pale in the face, and very polite, as frightened men frequently are.

'I shouldn't wish to appear ill-mannered, gentlemen,' said the third, who had called the dogs back; 'Mr Giles ought to know.'

'Certainly,' replied the shorter man; 'and whatever Mr Giles says, it isn't our place to contradict him. No, no, I know my sitivation! Thank my stars, I know my sitivation.' To tell the truth, the little man *did* seem to know his situation, and to know perfectly well that it was by no means a desirable one, for his teeth chattered in his head as he spoke.

'You are afraid, Brittles,' said Mr Giles.

'I ain't,' said Brittles.

'You are,' said Giles.

'You're a falsehood, Mr Giles,' said Brittles.

'You're a lie, Brittles,' said Mr Giles.

Now, these four retorts arose from Mr Giles's taunt; and Mr Giles's taunt had arisen from his indignation at having the responsibility of going home again imposed upon himself under cover of a compliment. The third man brought the dispute to a close, most philosophically.

'I'll tell you what it is, gentleman,' said he, 'we're all afraid.'

'Speak for yourself, sir,' said Mr Giles, who was the palest of the party.

'So I do,' replied the man. 'It's natural and proper to be afraid under such circumstances. *I* am.'

'So am I,' said Brittles; 'only there's no call to tell a man he is, so bounceably.'

These frank admissions softened Mr Giles, who at once owned that *he* was afraid; upon which, they all three faced about, and ran back again with the completest unanimity, until Mr Giles (who had the shortest wind of the party, and was encumbered with a pitchfork) most handsomely insisted on stopping, to make an apology for his hastiness of speech.

'But it's wonderful,' said Mr Giles, when he had explained, 'what a man will do when his blood is up. I should have committed murder – I know I should – if we'd caught one of the rascals.'

As the other two were impressed with a similar presentiment, and as their blood, like his, had all gone down again, some speculation ensued upon the cause of this sudden change in their temperament.

'I know what it was,' said Mr Giles; 'it was the gate.'

'I shouldn't wonder if it was,' exclaimed Brittles, catching at the idea.

'You may depend upon it,' said Giles, 'that that gate stopped the flow of the excitement. I felt all mine suddenly going away as I was climbing over it.'

By a remarkable coincidence, the other two had been visited with the same unpleasant sensation at that precise moment. It was quite obvious, therefore, that it was the gate; especially as there was no doubt regarding the time at which the change had taken place, because all three remembered that they had come in sight of the robbers at the very instant of its occurrence.

This dialogue was held between the two men who had surprised the burglars, and a travelling tinker, who had been sleeping in an outhouse, and who had been roused, together with his two mongrel curs, to join in the pursuit. Mr Giles acted in the double capacity of butler and steward to the old lady of the mansion; and Brittles was a lad-of-all-work, who, having entered her service a mere child, was treated as a promising young boy still, though he was something past thirty.

Encouraging each other with such converse as this, but keeping very close together, notwithstanding, and looking apprehensively round whenever a fresh gust rattled through the boughs, the three men hurried back to a tree, behind which they had left their lantern, lest its light should inform the thieves in what direction to fire. Catching up the light, they made the best of their way home at a good round trot; and long after their dusky forms had ceased to be discernible, it might have been seen twinkling and dancing in the distance, like some exhalation of the damp and gloomy atmosphere through which it was swiftly borne.

The air grew colder as day came slowly on, and the mist rolled along the ground like a dense cloud of smoke. The grass was wet, the pathways and low places were all mire and water, and the damp breath of an unwholesome wind went languidly by with a hollow moaning. Still, Oliver lay motionless and insensible on the spot where Sikes had left him.

Morning drew on apace. The air became more sharp and piercing, as its first dull hue – the death of night rather than the birth of day – glimmered faintly in the sky. The objects which had looked dim and terrible in the darkness grew more and more defined, and gradually resolved into their familiar shapes. The rain came down thick and fast, and pattered, noisily, among the leafless bushes. But Oliver felt it not as it beat against him; for he still lay stretched, helpless and unconscious, on his bed of clay.

At length a low cry of pain broke the stillness that prevailed; and uttering it, the boy awoke. His left arm, rudely bandaged in a shawl, hung heavy and useless at his side; and the bandage was saturated with blood. He was so weak that he could scarcely raise himself into a sitting posture; and when he had done so, he looked feebly round for help, and groaned with pain. Trembling in every joint, from cold and exhaustion, he made an effort to stand upright; but, shuddering from head to foot, fell prostrate on the ground.

After a short return of the stupor in which he had been so long plunged, Oliver, urged by a creeping sickness at his heart which seemed to warn him that if he lay there he must surely die, got upon his feet and essayed to walk. His head was dizzy, and he staggered to and fro like a drunken man. But he kept up, nevertheless, and, with his head drooping languidly on his breast, went stumbling onward, he knew not whither.

And now hosts of bewildering and confused ideas came crowding on his mind. He seemed to be still walking between Sikes and Crackit, who were angrily disputing, for the very words they said sounded in his ears; and when he caught his own attention, as it were, by making some violent effort to save himself from falling, he found that he was talking to them.

Then he was alone with Sikes, plodding on as they had done the previous day; and as shadowy people passed them, he felt the robber's grasp upon his wrist. Suddenly, he started back at the report of firearms; and there rose into the air loud cries and shouts, lights gleamed before his eyes, and all was noise and tumult, as some unseen hand bore him hurriedly away. Through all these rapid visions there ran an undefined, uneasy consciousness of pain, which wearied and tormented him incessantly.

Thus he staggered on, creeping, almost mechanically, between the bars of gates, or through hedge-gaps, as they came in his way, until he reached a road. Here the rain began to fall so heavily that it roused him.

He looked about, and saw that at no great distance there was a house, which perhaps he could reach. Pitying his condition, they might have compassion on him; and if they did not, it would be better, he thought, to die near human beings than in the lonely, open fields. He summoned up all his strength for one last trial, and bent his faltering steps towards it.

As he drew nearer to this house, a feeling came over him that he had seen it before. He remembered nothing of its details, but the shape and aspect of the building seemed familiar to him.

That garden wall! On the grass inside he had fallen on his knees last night and prayed the two men's mercy. It was the very same house they had attempted to rob.

Oliver felt such fear come over him when he recognised the place that, for the instant, he forgot the agony of his wound, and thought only of flight. Flight! he could scarcely stand; and if he were in full possession of all the best powers of his slight and youthful frame, whither could he fly? He pushed against the garden-gate; it was unlocked, and swung open on its hinges. He tottered across the lawn, climbed the steps, knocked faintly at the door, and, his whole strength failing him, sunk down against one of the pillars of the little portico.

It happened that about this time Mr Giles, Brittles, and the tinker, were recruiting themselves, after the fatigues and terrors of the night, with tea and sundries, in the kitchen. Not that it was Mr Giles's habit to admit to too great familiarity with the humbler servants, towards whom it was rather his wont to deport himself with a lofty affability, which, while it gratified, could not fail to remind them of his superior position in society. But death, fires, and burglary make all men equals; so Mr Giles sat with his legs stretched out before the kitchen fender, leaning his left arm on the table, while with his right he illustrated a circumstantial and minute account of the robbery, to which his hearers (but especially the cook and housemaid, who were of the party) listened with breathless interest.

'It was about half-past two,' said Mr Giles, 'or I wouldn't swear that it mightn't have been a little nearer three, when I woke up, and, turning round in my bed, as it might be so (here Mr Giles turned round in his chair, and pulled the corner of the tablecloth over him to imitate bedclothes), I fancied I heerd a noise.'

At this point of the narrative the cook turned pale, and asked the housemaid to shut the door, who asked Brittles, who asked the tinker, who pretended not to hear.

' – Heerd a noise,' continued Mr Giles. 'I says, at first, "This is illusion;" and was composing myself off to sleep, when I heerd the noise again distinct.'

'What sort of a noise?' asked the cook.

'A kind of a busting noise,' replied Mr Giles, looking round him.

'More like the noise of powdering an iron bar on a nutmeg-grater,' suggested Brittles.

'It was when *you* heerd, sir,' rejoined Mr Giles: 'but at this time it had a busting sound. I turned down the clothes,' continued Mr Giles, rolling back the tablecloth, 'sat up in bed, and listened.'

The cook and housemaid simultaneously ejaculated 'Lor!' and drew their chairs closer together.

'I heerd it now, quite apparent,' resumed Mr Giles. ' "Somebody," I says, "is forcing off a door, or window; what's to be done? I'll call up that poor lad, Brittles, and save him from being murdered in his bed, or his throat," I says, "may be cut from his right ear to his left without his ever knowing it." '

Here all eyes were turned upon Brittles, who fixed his upon the speaker, and stared at him with his mouth wide open, and his face expressive of the most unmitigated horror.

'I tossed off the clothes,' said Giles, throwing away the tablecloth, and looking very hard at the cook and housemaid, 'got softly out of bed, drew on a pair of – '

'Ladies present, Mr Giles,' murmured the tinker.

Oliver Twist at Mrs Maylie's door

' – Of *shoes*, sir,' said Giles, turning upon him, and laying great emphasis on the word; 'seized the loaded pistol that always goes upstairs with the plate-basket, and walked on tip-toes to his room. "Brittles," I says, when I had woke him, "don't be frightened!" '

'So you did,' observed Brittles, in a low voice.

' " We're dead men, I think, Brittles," I says,' continued Giles; ' " but don't be frightened." '

Was he frightened?' asked the cook.

'Not a bit of it,' replied Mr Giles. 'He was as firm – ah! pretty near as firm as I was.'

'I should have died at once, I'm sure, if it had been me,' observed the housemaid.

'You're a woman,' retorted Brittles, plucking up a little.

'Brittles is right,' said Mr Giles, nodding his head approvingly; 'from a woman, nothing else was to be expected. We, being men, took a dark lantern that was standing on Brittles's hob, and groped our way downstairs in the pitch dark – as it might be so.'

Mr Giles had risen from his seat, and taken two steps with his eyes shut, to accompany his description with appropriate action, when he started violently, in common with the rest of the company, and hurried back to his chair. The cook and housemaid screamed.

'It was a knock,' said Mr Giles, assuming perfect serenity. 'Open the door, somebody.'

Nobody moved.

'It seems a strange sort of thing, a knock coming at such a time in the morning,' said Mr Giles, surveying the pale faces which surrounded him, and looking very blank himself; 'but the door must be opened. Do you hear, somebody?'

Mr Giles, as he spoke, looked at Brittles; but that young man, being naturally modest, probably considered himself nobody, and so held that the enquiry could not have any application to him; at all events, he tendered no reply. Mr Giles directed an appealing glance at the tinker; but he had suddenly fallen asleep. The women were out of the question.

'If Brittles would rather open the door in presence of witnesses,' said Mr Giles, after a short silence, 'I am ready to make one.'

'So am I,' said the tinker, waking up as suddenly as he had fallen asleep.

Brittles capitulated on these terms; and the party being somewhat reassured by the discovery (made on throwing open the shutters) that it was now broad day, took their way upstairs, with the dogs in front, and the two women, who were afraid to stay below, bringing up the rear. By the advice of Mr Giles, they all talked very loud, to warn any evil-disposed person outside that they were strong in numbers; and by a master-stroke of policy, originating in the brain of the same ingenious gentleman, the dogs' tails were well pinched, in the hall, to make them bark savagely.

These precautions having been taken, Mr Giles held on fast by the tinker's arm (to prevent his running away, as he pleasantly said), and gave the word of command to open the door. Brittles obeyed; and the group, peering timorously over each other's shoulders, beheld no more formidable object than poor little Oliver Twist, speechless and exhausted, who raised his heavy eyes, and mutely solicited their compassion.

'A boy,' exclaimed Mr Giles, valiantly pushing the tinker into the background. 'What's the matter with the – eh? – why – Brittles – look here – don't you know?'

Brittles, who had got behind the door to open it, no sooner saw Oliver than he uttered a loud cry. Mr Giles, seizing the boy by one leg and one arm (fortunately not the broken limb), lugged him straight into the hall, and deposited him at full length on the floor thereof.

'Here he is!' bawled Giles, calling in a state of great excitement up the staircase; 'here's one of the thieves, ma'am! Here's a thief, miss! Wounded, miss! I shot him, miss; and Brittles held the light.'

' – In a lantern, miss,' cried Brittles, applying one hand to the side of his mouth, so that his voice might travel the better.

The two women-servants ran upstairs to carry the intelligence that Mr Giles had captured a robber; and the tinker busied himself in endeavouring to restore Oliver, lest he should die before he could be hanged. In the midst of all this noise and commotion there was heard a sweet female voice, which quelled it in an instant.

'Giles!' whispered the voice from the stairhead.

'I'm here, miss,' replied Mr Giles. 'Don't be frightened, miss; I ain't much injured. He didn't make a very desperate resistance, miss. I was soon too many for him.'

'Hush!' replied the young lady, 'you frighten my aunt as much as the thieves did. Is the poor creature much hurt?'

'Wounded desperate, miss,' replied Giles, with indescribable complacency.

'He looks as if he was a-going, miss,' bawled Brittles, in the same manner as before. 'Wouldn't you like to come and look at him, miss, in case he should?'

'Hush, pray; there's a good man!' rejoined the young lady. 'Wait quietly one instant, while I speak to aunt.'

With a footstep as soft and gentle as the voice the speaker tripped away; and soon returned, with the direction that the wounded person was to be carried, carefully, upstairs to Mr Giles's room; and that Brittles was to saddle the pony and betake himself instantly to Chertsey, from which place he was to dispatch, with all speed, a constable and a doctor.

'But won't you take one look at him first, miss?' asked Mr Giles, with as much pride as if Oliver were some bird of rare plumage that he had skilfully brought down. 'Not one little peep, miss?'

'Not now for the world,' replied the young lady. 'Poor fellow! Oh! treat him kindly, Giles, for my sake!'

The old servant looked up at the speaker, as she turned away, with a glance as proud and admiring as if she had been his own child. Then, bending over Oliver, he helped to carry him upstairs, with the care and solicitude of a woman.

CHAPTER 29

Has an introductory account of the inmates of the house to which Oliver resorted

In a handsome room – though its furniture had rather the air of old-fashioned comfort than of modern elegance – there sat two ladies at a well-spread breakfast-table. Mr Giles, dressed with scrupulous care in a full suit of black, was in attendance upon them. He had taken his station some halfway between the sideboard and the breakfast-table, and, with his body drawn up to its full height, his head thrown back, and inclined the merest trifle on one side, his left leg advanced, and his right hand thrust into his waistcoat, while his left hung down by his side, grasping a waiter, looked like one who laboured under a very agreeable sense of his own merits and importance.

Of the two ladies, one was well advanced in years; but the high-backed oaken chair in which she sat was not more upright than she. Dressed with the utmost nicety and precision, in a quaint mixture of bygone costume, with some slight concessions to the prevailing taste, which rather served to point the old style pleasantly than to impair its effect, she sat, in a stately manner, with her hands folded on the table before her. Her eyes (and age had dimmed but little of their brightness) were attentively fixed upon her young companion.

The younger lady was in the lovely bloom and spring-time of womanhood; at that age, when, if ever angels be for God's good purposes enthroned in mortal forms, they may be, without impiety, supposed to abide in such as hers.

She was not past seventeen. Cast in so slight and exquisite a mould, so mild and gentle, so pure and beautiful, that earth seemed not her element, nor its rough creatures her fit companions. The very intelligence that shone in her deep blue eye, and was stamped upon her noble head, seemed scarcely of her age or of the world; and yet the changing expression of sweetness and good-humour, the thousand lights that played about the face and left no shadow there, above all, the smile, the cheerful, happy smile, were made for Home, for fireside peace and happiness.

She was busily engaged in the little offices of the table. Chancing to raise her eyes as the elder lady was regarding her, she playfully put back her hair, which was simply braided on her forehead, and threw into one beaming look such a gush of affection and artless loveliness, that blessed spirits might have smiled to look upon her.

'And Brittles has been gone upwards of an hour, has he?' asked the old lady, after a pause.

'An hour and twelve minutes, ma'am,' replied Mr Giles, referring to a silver watch, which he drew forth by a black ribbon.'

'He is always slow,' remarked the old lady.

'Brittles always was a slow boy, ma'am,' replied the attendant. And seeing, by the by, that Brittles had been a slow boy for upwards of thirty years, there appeared no great probability of his ever being a fast one.

'He gets worse instead of better, I think,' said the elder lady.

'It is very inexcusable in him if he stops to play with any other boys,' said the young lady, smiling.

Mr Giles was apparently considering the propriety of indulging in a respectful smile himself, when a gig drove up to the garden-gate, out of which there jumped a fat gentleman, who ran straight up to the door, and who, getting quickly into the house, by some mysterious process, burst into the room, and nearly overturned Mr Giles and the breakfast-table together.

'I never heard of such a thing!' exclaimed the fat gentleman. 'My dear Mrs Maylie – bless my soul – in the silence of night, too – I *never* heard of such a thing!'

With these expressions of condolence, the fat gentleman shook hands with both ladies, and drawing up a chair, enquired how they found themselves.

'You ought to be dead, positively dead with the fright,' said the fat gentleman. 'Why didn't you send? Bless me, my man should have come in a minute; and so would I; and my assistant would have been delighted; or anybody, I'm sure, under such circumstances. Dear, dear! So unexpected! In the silence of night, too!'

The doctor seemed especially troubled by the fact of the robbery having been unexpected, and attempted in the night time, as if it were the established custom of gentlemen in the housebreaking way to transact business at noon, and to make an appointment, by the twopenny post, a day or two previous.

'And you, Miss Rose,' said the doctor, turning to the young lady, 'I –'

'Oh! very much so, indeed,' said Rose, interrupting him; 'but there is a poor creature upstairs whom aunt wishes you to see.'

'Ah! to be sure,' replied the doctor, 'so there is. That was your handiwork, Giles, I understand.'

Mr Giles, who had been feverishly putting the teacups to rights, blushed very red, and said that he had had that honour.

'Honour, eh?' said the doctor. 'Well, I don't know; perhaps it's as honourable to hit a thief in a back kitchen as to hit your man at twelve paces. Fancy that he fired in the air, and you've fought a duel, Giles.'

Mr Giles, who thought this light treatment of the matter an unjust attempt at diminishing his glory, answered respectfully that it was not for the like of him to judge about that; but he rather thought it was no joke to the opposite party.

'Gad, that's true!' said the doctor. 'Where is he? Show me the way. I'll look in again, as I come down, Mrs Maylie. That's the little window that he got in at, eh? Well, I couldn't have believed it!'

Talking all the way, he followed Mr Giles upstairs; and while he is going upstairs the reader may be informed that Mr Losberne, a surgeon in the neighbourhood, known through a circuit of ten miles round as 'the doctor,' had grown fat, more from good-humour than from good living, and was as kind and hearty, and withal as eccentric, an old bachelor, as will be found in five times that space by any explorer alive.

The doctor was absent much longer than either he or the ladies had anticipated. A large flat box was fetched out of the gig; and a bedroom bell was rung very often; and the servants ran up and down stairs perpetually: from which tokens it was justly concluded that something important was going on above. At length he returned, and in reply to an anxious enquiry after his patient, looked very mysterious, and closed the door carefully.

'This is a very extraordinary thing, Mrs Maylie,' said the doctor, standing with his back to the door, as if to keep it shut.

'He is not in danger, I hope?' said the old lady.

'Why, that would *not* be an extraordinary thing, under the circumstances,' replied the doctor; 'though I don't think he is. Have you seen this thief?'

'No,' rejoined the old lady.

'Nor heard anything about him?'

'No.'

'I beg your pardon, ma'am,' interposed Mr Giles, 'but I was going to tell you about him when Doctor Losberne came in.'

The fact was, that Mr Giles had not, at first, been able to bring his mind to the avowal that he had only shot a boy. Such commendations had been bestowed upon his bravery that he could not, for the life of him, help postponing the explanation for a few delicious minutes, during which he had flourished in the very zenith of a brief reputation for undaunted courage.

'Rose wished to see the man,' said Mrs Maylie, 'but I wouldn't hear of it.'

'Humph!' rejoined the doctor; 'there is nothing very alarming in his appearance. Have you any objection to see him in my presence?'

'If it be necessary,' replied the old lady, 'certainly not.'

'Then I think it is necessary,' said the doctor; 'at all events, I am quite sure that you would deeply regret not having done so, if you postponed it. He is perfectly quiet and comfortable now. Allow me – Miss Rose, will you permit me? Not the slightest fear, I pledge you my honour!'

CHAPTER 30

Relates what Oliver's new visitors thought of him

With many loquacious assurances that they would be agreeably surprised in the aspect of the criminal, the doctor drew the young lady's arm through one of his, and offering his disengaged hand to Mrs Maylie, led them, with much ceremony and stateliness, upstairs.

'Now,' said the doctor in a whisper, as he softly turned the handle of a bedroom door, 'let us hear what you think of him. He has not been shaved very recently, but he don't look at all ferocious notwithstanding. Stop, though! Let me first see that he is in visiting order.'

Stepping before them, he looked into the room. Motioning them to advance, he closed the door when they had entered, and gently drew back the curtains of the bed. Upon it, in lieu of the dogged, black-visaged ruffian they had expected to behold, there lay a mere child, worn with pain and exhaustion, and sunk into a deep sleep. His wounded arm, bound and splintered up, was crossed upon his breast; his head reclined upon the other arm, which was half-hidden by his long hair as it streamed over the pillow.

The honest gentleman held the curtain in his hand, and looked on for a minute or so in silence. Whilst he was watching the patient thus, the younger lady glided softly past, and seating herself in a chair by the bedside, gathered Oliver's hair from his face. As she stooped over him her tears fell upon his forehead.

The boy stirred and smiled in his sleep, as though these marks of pity and compassion had awakened some pleasant dream of a love and affection he had never known; as a strain of gentle music, or the rippling of water in a silent place, or the odour of a flower, or even the mention of a familiar word, will sometimes call up sudden dim remembrances of scenes that never were in this life, which vanish like a breath, and which some brief memory of a happier existence, long gone by, would seem to have awakened, for no voluntary exertion of the mind can ever recall them.

'What can this mean?' exclaimed the elder lady. 'This poor child can never have been the pupil of robbers!'

'Vice,' sighed the surgeon, replacing the curtain, 'takes up her abode in many temples, and who can say that a fair outside shall not enshrine her?'

'But at so early an age!' urged Rose.

'My dear young lady,' rejoined the surgeon, mournfully shaking his head, 'crime, like death, is not confined to the old and withered alone. The youngest and fairest are too often its chosen victims.'

'But can you – oh, sir! can you really believe that this delicate boy has been the voluntary associate of the worst outcasts of society?' said Rose.

The surgeon shook his head in a manner which intimated that he feared it was very possible; and observing that they might disturb the patient, led the way into an adjoining apartment.

'But even if he has been wicked,' pursued Rose, 'think how young he is; think that he may never have known a mother's love, or the comfort of a home, and that ill-usage and blows, or the want of bread, may have driven him to herd with men who have forced him to guilt. Aunt, dear aunt, for mercy's sake, think of this before you let them drag this sick child to a prison, which in any case must be the grave of all his chances of amendment. Oh! as you love me, and know that I have never felt the want of parents in your goodness and affection, but that I might have done so, and might have been equally helpless and unprotected with this poor child, have pity upon him before it is too late!'

'My dear love,' said the elder lady, as she folded the weeping girl to her bosom, 'do you think I would harm a hair of his head?'

'Oh, no!' replied Rose eagerly.

'No,' said the old lady, with a trembling lip. 'My days are drawing to their close; and may mercy be shown to me as I show it to others! What can I do to save him, sir?'

'Let me think, ma'am,' said the doctor; 'let me think.'

Mr Losberne thrust his hands into his pockets, and took several turns up and down the room; often stopping and balancing himself on his toes, and frowning frightfully. After various exclamations of 'I've got it now,' and 'No, I haven't,' and as many renewals of the walking and frowning, he at length made a dead halt, and spoke as follows: 'I think if you give me a full and unlimited commission to bully Giles, and that little boy, Brittles, I can manage it. He is a faithful fellow, and an old servant, I know; but you can make it up to him in a thousand ways, and reward him for being such a good shot besides. You don't object to that?'

'Unless there is some other way of preserving the child,' replied Mrs Maylie.

'There is no other,' said the doctor – 'no other, take my word for it.'

'Then my aunt invests you with full power,' said Rose, smiling through her tears; 'but pray don't be harder upon the poor fellows than is indispensably necessary.'

'You seem to think,' retorted the doctor, 'that everybody is disposed to be hard-hearted today except yourself, Miss Rose. I only hope, for the sake of the rising male sex generally, that you may be found in as vulnerable and soft-hearted a mood by the first eligible young fellow who appeals to your compassion; and I wish I were a young fellow who appeals to your compassion; and I wish I were a young fellow, that I might avail myself, on the spot, of such a favourable opportunity for doing so as the present.'

'You are as great a boy as poor Brittles himself,' returned Rose, blushing.

'Well,' said the doctor, laughing heartily, 'that is no very difficult matter. But to return to this boy. The great point of our agreement is yet to come. He will wake in an hour or so, I dare say; and although I have told that thick-headed constable fellow downstairs that he mustn't be moved or spoken to, on peril of his life, I think we may converse with him without danger. Now, I make this stipulation – that I shall examine him in your presence, and that if, from what he says, we judge, and I can show to the satisfaction of your cool reason, that he is a real and thorough bad one (which is more than possible), he shall be left to his fate, without any further interference on my part, at all events.'

'Oh, no, aunt!' entreated Rose.

'Oh, yes, aunt!' said the doctor. 'Is it a bargain?'

'He cannot be hardened in vice,' said Rose, 'it is impossible!'

'Very good,' retorted the doctor; 'then so much the more reason for acceding to my proposition.'

Finally, the treaty was entered into; and the parties thereunto sat down to wait, with some impatience, until Oliver should awake.

The patience of the two ladies was destined to undergo a longer trial than Mr Losberne had led them to expect, for hour after hour passed on, and still Oliver slumbered heavily. It was evening, indeed, before the kind-hearted doctor brought them the intelligence that he was at length sufficiently restored to be spoken to. The boy was very ill, he said, and weak from the loss of blood; but his mind was so troubled with anxiety to disclose something, that he deemed it better to give him the opportunity, than to insist upon his remaining quiet until next morning, which he should otherwise have done.

The conference was a long one, for Oliver told them all his

simple history, and was often compelled to stop by pain and want of strength. It was a solemn thing to hear, in the darkened room, the feeble voice of the sick child recounting a weary catalogue of evils and calamities which hard men had brought upon him. Oh! if, when we oppress and grind our fellow-creatures, we bestowed but one thought on the dark evidences of human error, which, like dense and heavy clouds, are rising, slowly it is true, but not less surely, to Heaven, to pour their after-vengeance on our heads; if we heard, but one instant, in imagination, the deep testimony of dead men's voices, which no power can stifle and no pride shut out; where would be the injury and injustice, the suffering, misery, cruelty, and wrong, that each day's life brings with it!

Oliver's pillow was smoothed by gentle hands that night, and loveliness and virtue watched him as he slept. He felt calm and happy, and could have died without a murmur.

The momentous interview was no sooner concluded, and Oliver composed to rest again, than the doctor, after wiping his eyes, and condemning them for being weak all at once, betook himself downstairs to open upon Mr Giles. And finding nobody about the parlours, it occurred to him that he could perhaps originate the proceedings with better effect in the kitchen; so into the kitchen he went.

There were assembled, in that lower house of the domestic parliament, the women-servants, Mr Brittles, Mr Giles, the tinker (who had received a special invitation to regale himself for the remainder of the day, in consideration of his services), and the constable. The latter gentleman had a large staff, a large head, large features, and large half-boots, and looked as if he had been taking a proportionate allowance of ale – as indeed he had.

The adventures of the previous night were still under discussion; for Mr Giles was expatiating upon his presence of mind when the doctor entered, and Mr Brittles, with a mug of ale in his hand, was corroborating everything, before his superior said it.

'Sit still,' said the doctor, waving his hand.

'Thank you, sir,' said Mr Giles. 'Misses wished some ale to be given out, sir; and as I felt noways inclined for my own little room, sir, and was disposed for company, I am taking mine among 'em here.'

Brittles headed a low murmur, by which the ladies and gentlemen generally were understood to express the gratification they derived from Mr Giles's condescension. Mr Giles looked round with a patronising air, as much as to say, that so long as they behaved properly he would never desert them.

'How is the patient tonight, sir?' asked Giles.

'So-so,' returned the doctor. 'I am afraid you have got yourself into a scrape there, Mr Giles.'

'I hope you don't mean to say, sir,' said Mr Giles, trembling, 'that he's going to die. If I thought it, I should never be happy again. I wouldn't cut a boy off – no, not even Brittles here – not for all the plate in the country, sir.'

'That's not the point,' said the doctor, mysteriously. 'Mr Giles, are you a Protestant?'

'Yes, sir, I hope so,' faltered Mr Giles, who had turned very pale.

'And what are you, boy?' said the doctor, turning sharply upon Brittles.

'Lord bless me, sir!' replied Brittles, starting violently; 'I'm – the same as Mr Giles, sir.'

'Then tell me this,' said the doctor, 'both of you – both of you! Are you going to take upon yourselves to swear that that boy upstairs is the boy that was put through the little window last night? Out with it! Come! We are prepared for you!'

The doctor, who was universally considered one of the best-tempered creatures on earth, made this demand in such a dreadful tone of anger, that Giles and Brittles, who were considerably muddled by ale and excitement, stared at each other in a state of stupefaction.

'Pay attention to the reply, constable, will you?' said the doctor, shaking his forefinger with great solemnity of manner, and tapping the bridge of his nose with it, to bespeak the exercise of that worthy's utmost acuteness. 'Something may come of this before long.'

The constable looked as wise as he could, and took up his staff of office, which had been reclining indolently in the chimney-corner.

'It's a simple question of identity, you will observe,' said the doctor.

'That's what it is, sir,' replied the constable, coughing with great violence; for he had finished his ale in a hurry, and some of it had gone the wrong way.

'Here's a house broken into,' said the doctor, 'and a couple of men catch one moment's glimpse of a boy, in the midst of gunpowder-smoke, and in all the distraction of alarm and darkness. Here's a boy comes to that very same house, next morning, and because he happens to have his arm tied up, these men lay violent hands upon him; by doing which they place his life in great danger, and swear he is the thief. Now, the question is, whether these men are justified by the fact; and if not, in what situation do they place themselves?'

The constable nodded profoundly. He said, if that wasn't law, he would be glad to know what was.

'I ask you again,' thundered the doctor, 'are you, on your solemn oaths, able to identify that boy?'

Brittles looked doubtfully at Mr Giles; Mr Giles looked doubtfully at Brittles; the constable put his hand behind his ear, to catch the reply; the two women and the tinker leaned forward to listen; and the doctor glanced keenly round; when a ring was heard at the gate, and at the same moment the sound of wheels.

'It's the runners!' cried Brittles, to all appearance much relieved.

'The what!' exclaimed the doctor, aghast in his turn.

'The Bow Street officers, sir,' replied Brittles, taking up a candle; 'me and Mr Giles sent for 'em this morning.'

'What!' cried the doctor.

'Yes,' replied Brittles; 'I sent a message up by the coachman, and I only wonder they weren't here before, sir.'

'You did, did you? Then confound your – slow coaches down here; that's all,' said the doctor, walking away.

CHAPTER 31

Involves a critical position

'Who's that?' enquired Brittles, opening the door a little way, with the chain up, and peeping out, shading the candle with his hand.

'Open the door,' replied a man outside; 'it's the officers from Bow Street, as was sent to today.'

Much comforted by this assurance, Brittles opened the door to its full width, and confronted a portly man, in a greatcoat, who walked in, without saying anything more, and wiped his shoes on the mat as coolly as if he lived there.

'Just send somebody out to relieve my mate, will you, young man,' said the officer; 'he's in the gig, minding the prad. Have you got a coach'us here, that you could put it up in for five or ten minutes?'

Brittles replied in the affirmative, and pointing out the building, the portly man stepped back to the garden-gate, and helped his companion to put up the gig, while Brittles lighted them, in a state of great admiration. This done, they returned to the house; and, being shown into a parlour, took off their greatcoats and hats, and showed what they were like.

The man who had knocked at the door was a stout personage of middle height, aged about fifty, with shiny black hair cropped pretty close, half-whiskers, a round face, and sharp eyes. The other was a red-headed, bony man, in top-boots, with a rather ill-favoured countenance, and a turned-up, sinister-looking nose.

'Tell your governor that Blathers and Duff is here, will you?' said the stouter man, smoothing down his hair, and laying a pair of handcuffs on the table.

'Oh! good-evening, master. Can I have a word or two with you in private, if you please?'

This was addressed to Mr Losberne, who now made his appearance. That gentleman, motioning Brittles to retire, brought in the two ladies, and shut the door.

'This is the lady of the house,' said Mr Losberne, motioning towards Mrs Maylie.

Mr Blathers made a bow. Being desired to sit down, he put his hat upon the floor, and taking a chair, motioned Duff to do the same. The latter gentleman, who did not appear quite so much accustomed to good society, or quite so much at his ease in it – one of the two – seated himself, after undergoing several muscular affections of the limbs, and forced the head of his stick into his mouth, with some embarrassment.

'Now, with regard to this here robbery, master,' said Blathers. 'What are the circumstances?'

Mr Losberne, who appeared desirous of gaining time, recounted them at great length, and with much circumlocution. Messrs Blathers and Duff looked very knowing meanwhile, and occasionally exchanged a nod.

'I can't say, for certain, till I see the place, of course,' said Blathers; 'but my opinion at once is – I don't mind committing myself to that extent – that this wasn't done by a yokel; eh, Duff?'

'Certainly not,' replied Duff.

'And translating the word yokel for the benefit of the ladies, I apprehend your meaning to be, that this attempt was not made by a countryman?' said Mr Losberne, with a smile.

'That's it, master,' replied Blathers. 'This is all about the robbery, is it?'

'All,' replied the doctor.

'Now, what is this about this here boy that the servants are talking on?' said Blathers.

'Nothing at all,' replied the doctor. 'One of the frightened servants chose to take it into his head that he had something to do with this attempt to break into the house; but it's nonsense – sheer absurdity.'

'Wery easy disposed of, if it is,' remarked Duff.

'What he says is quite correct,' observed Blathers, nodding his head in a confirmatory way, and playing carelessly with the handcuffs, as if they were a pair of castanets. 'Who is the boy? What account does he give of himself? Where did he come from? He didn't drop out of the clouds, did he, master?'

'Of course not,' replied the doctor, with a nervous glance at the two ladies. 'I know his whole history; but we can talk about that presently. You would like, first, to see the place where the thieves made their attempt, I suppose?'

'Certainly,' rejoined Mr Blathers. 'We had better inspect the premises first, and examine the servants arterwards. That's the usual way of doing business.'

Lights were then procured, and Messrs Blathers and Duff, attended by the native constable, Brittles, Giles, and everybody else in short, went into the little room at the end of the passage and looked out at the window; and afterwards went round by way of the lawn and looked in at the window; and after that, had a candle handed out to inspect the shutter with; and after that, a lantern to trace the footsteps with; and after that, a pitchfork to poke the bushes with. This done, amidst the breathless interest of all beholders, they came in again; and Mr Giles and Brittles were put through a melodramatic representation of their share in the previous night's adventures, which they performed some six times over, contradicting each other in not more than one important respect the first time, and in not more than a dozen the last. This consummation being arrived at, Blathers and Duff cleared the room, and held a long counsel together, compared with which, for secrecy and solemnity, a consultation of great doctors on the knottiest point in medicine would be mere child's play.

Meanwhile, the doctor walked up and down the next room in a very uneasy state; and Mrs Maylie and Rose looked on, with anxious faces.

'Upon my word,' he said, making a halt, after a great number of very rapid turns, 'I hardly know what to do.'

'Surely,' said Rose, 'the poor child's story, faithfully repeated to these men, will be sufficient to exonerate him.'

'I doubt it, my dear young lady,' said the doctor, shaking his head. 'I don't think it would exonerate him, either with them or with legal functionaries of a higher grade. What is he, after all, they would say? A runaway. Judged by mere worldly considerations and probabilities, his story is a very doubtful one.'

'You believe it, surely?' interrupted Rose.

'*I* believe it, strange as it is; and perhaps I may be an old fool for doing so,' rejoined the doctor. 'But I don't think it is exactly the tale for a practised police officer, nevertheless.'

'Why not?' demanded Rose.

'Because, my pretty cross-examiner,' replied the doctor – 'because, viewed with their eyes, there are many ugly points about it; he can only prove the parts that look ill, and none of those that look well. Confound the fellows, they *will* have the why and the wherefore, and will take nothing for granted. On his own showing, you see, he has been the companion of thieves for some time past; he has been carried to a police office on a charge of picking a gentleman's pocket; he has been taken away, forcibly, from that gentleman's house, to a place which he cannot describe or point out, and of the situation of which he has not the remotest idea. He is brought down to Chertsey by men who seem to have taken a violent fancy to him, whether he will or no, and is put through a window to rob a house; and then, just at the very moment when he is going to alarm the inmates, and so do the very thing that would set him all to rights, there rushes into the way a blundering dog of a half-bred butler, and shoots him – as if on purpose to prevent his doing any good for himself ! Don't you see all this?'

'I see it, of course,' replied Rose, smiling at the doctor's impetuosity; 'but still, I do not see anything in it to criminate the poor child.'

'No,' replied the doctor; 'of course not! Bless the bright eyes of your sex! They never see, whether for good or bad, more than one side of any question; and that is, always, the one which first presents itself to them.'

Having given vent to this result of experience, the doctor put his hands into his pockets, and walked up and down the room with even greater rapidity than before.

'The more I think of it,' said the doctor, 'the more I see that it will occasion endless trouble and difficulty if we put these men in possession of the boy's real story. I am certain it will not be believed; and even if they can do nothing to him in the end, still the dragging it forward, and giving publicity to all the doubts that will be cast upon it, must interfere materially with your benevolent plan of rescuing him from misery.'

'Oh! what is to be done?' cried Rose. 'Dear, dear! why did they send for these people?'

'Why, indeed?' exclaimed Mrs Maylie. 'I would not have had them here for the world.'

'All I know is,' said Mr Losberne at last, sitting down with a kind of desperate calmness, 'that we must try and carry it off with a bold face; that's all. The object is a good one, and that must be the excuse. The boy has strong symptoms of fever upon him, and is in no condition to be talked to any more; that's one comfort. We must make the best of it; and if bad be the best, it is no fault of ours. Come in!'

'Well, master,' said Blathers, entering the room, followed by his colleague, and making the door fast before he said any more. 'This warn't a put-up thing.'

'And what the devil's a put-up thing?' demanded the doctor impatiently.

'We call it a put-up robbery, ladies,' said Blathers, turning to them, as if he pitied their ignorance, but had a contempt for the doctor's, 'when the servants is in it.'

'Nobody suspected them in this case,' said Mrs Maylie.

'Wery likely not, ma'am,' replied Blathers; 'but they might have been in it, for all that.'

'More likely on that wery account,' said Duff.

'We find it was a town hand,' said Blathers, continuing his report, 'for the style of work is first-rate.'

'Wery pretty, indeed it is,' remarked Duff, in an undertone.

'There was two of 'em in it,' continued Blathers; 'and they had a boy with 'em; that's plain from the size of the window. That's all to be said at present. We'll see this lad that you've got upstairs at once, if you please.'

'Perhaps they will take something to drink first, Mrs Maylie?' said the doctor, his face brightening, as if some new thought had occurred to him.

'Oh, to be sure!' exclaimed Rose, eagerly. 'You shall have it immediately, if you will.'

'Why, thank you, miss!' said Blathers, drawing his coat-sleeve across his mouth; 'it's dry work, this sort of duty. Anything that's handy, miss; don't put yourself out of the way on our accounts.'

'What shall it be?' asked the doctor, following the young lady to the sideboard.

'A little drop of spirits, master, if it's all the same,' replied Blathers. 'It's a cold ride from London, ma'am; and I always find that spirits comes home warmer to the feelings.'

This interesting communication was addressed to Mrs Maylie, who received it very graciously. While it was being conveyed to her, the doctor slipped out of the room.

'Ah!' said Mr Blathers, not holding his wineglass by the stem, but grasping the bottom between the thumb and forefinger of his left hand, and placing it in front of his chest; 'I have seen a good many pieces of business like this, in my time, ladies.'

'That crack down in the back lane at Edmonton, Blathers,' said Mr Duff, assisting his colleague's memory.

'That was something in this way, warn't it?' rejoined Mr Blathers; 'that was done by Conkey Chickweed, that was.'

'You always gave that to him,' replied Duff. 'It was the Family Pet, I tell you. Conkey hadn't any more to do with it than I had.'

'Get out!' retorted Mr Blathers; 'I know better. Do you mind that time when Conkey was robbed of his money, though? What a start that was! Better than any novel-book *I* ever see!'

'What was that?' enquired Rose, anxious to encourage any symptoms of good-humour in the unwelcome visitors.

'It was a robbery, miss, that hardly anybody would have been down upon,' said Blathers. 'This here Conkey Chickweed – '

'Conkey means Nosey, ma'am,' interposed Duff.

'Of course the lady knows that, don't she?' demanded Mr Blathers. 'Always interrupting, you are, partner! This here Conkey Chickweed, miss, kept a public-house over Battle-bridge way, and had a cellar, where a good many young lords went to see cock-fighting, and badger-drawing, and that; and a wery intellectual manner the sports was conducted in, for I've seen 'em off'en. He warn't one of the family at that time; and one night he was robbed of three hundred and twenty-seven guineas in a canvas bag, that was stole out of his bedroom in the dead of night, by a tall man with a black patch over his eye, who had concealed himself under the bed, and, after committing the robbery, jumped slap out of the window which was only a story high. He was wery quick about it. But Conkey was quick, too; for he was woke by the noise, and darting out of bed, he fired a blunderbuss arter him, and roused the neighbourhood. They set up a hue-and-cry directly, and when they came to look about 'em, found that Conkey had hit the robber; for there were traces of blood all the way to some palings a good distance off, and there they lost 'em. However, he had made off with the blunt; and, consequently, the name of Mr Chickweed, licensed witler, appeared in the *Gazette* among other bankrupts; and all manner of benefits and subscriptions, and I don't know what all, was got up for the poor man, who was in a wery low state of mind about his loss, and went up and down the streets, for three or four days, pulling his hair off in such a desperate manner that many people was afraid he might be going to make away with himself. One day he come up to the office, all in a hurry, and had a private interview with the magistrate, who, after a deal of talk, rings the bell, and orders Jem Spyers in (Jem was a active officer), and tells him to go and assist Mr Chickweed in apprehending the man as robbed his house. "I see him, Spyers," said Chickweed, "pass my house yesterday morning." "Why didn't you up and collar him?" says Spyers. "I was so struck all of a heap that you might have fractured my skull with a toothpick," said the poor man; "but we're sure to have him, for between ten and eleven o'clock at night he passed again." Spyers no sooner heard this than he put some clean linen and a comb in his pocket, in case he should have to stop a day or two; and away he goes, and sets himself down at one of the public-house windows, behind the little red curtain, with his hat on, all ready to bolt out at a moment's notice. He was smoking his pipe here, late at night, when all of a sudden Chickweed roars out "Here he is! Stop thief! Murder!" Jem Spyers dashes out; and there he sees Chickweed tearing down the street full cry. Away goes Spyers; on goes Chickweed; round turns the people; everybody roars out, "Thieves!" and Chickweed himself keeps on shouting, all the time, like mad. Spyers loses sight of him a minute as he turns a corner; shoots round; sees a little crowd; dives in: "Which is the man?" "Damn me!" says Chickweed, "I've lost him again." It was a remarkable occurrence; but he warn't to be seen nowhere, so they went back to the public-house, and next morning Spyers took his old place, and looked out, from behind the curtain, for a tall man with a black patch over his eye, till his own two eyes ached again. At last he couldn't help shutting 'em, to ease 'em a minute; and the wery moment he did so, he hears Chickweed roaring out, "Here he is!" Off he starts once more, with Chickweed halfway down the street ahead of him; and after twice as long a run as the yesterday's one, the man's lost again! This was done once or twice more, till one-half the neighbours gave out that Mr Chickweed had been robbed by the devil, who was playing tricks with him arterwards; and the other half, that poor Mr Chickweed had gone mad with grief.'

'What did Jem Spyers say?' enquired the doctor, who had returned to the room shortly after the commencement of the story.

'Jem Spyers,' resumed the officer, 'for a long time said nothing at all, and listened to everything without seeming to, which showed he understood his business. But one morning he walked into the bar, and taking out his snuff-box, said, "Chickweed, I've found out who's done this here robbery." "Have you?" said Chickweed. "Oh, my dear Spyers, only let me have wengeance, and I shall die contented! Oh, my dear Spyers, where is the villain?" "Come!" said Spyers, offering him a pinch of snuff, "none of that gammon! You did it yourself." So he had; and a good bit of money he had made by it, too; and nobody would ever have found it out, if he hadn't been so precious anxious to keep up appearances – that's more!' said Mr Blathers, putting down his wineglass, and clinking the handcuffs together.

'Very curious, indeed,' observed the doctor. 'Now, if you please, you can walk upstairs.'

'If *you* please, sir,' returned Mr Blathers; and closely following Mr Losberne, the two officers ascended to Oliver's bedroom, Mr Giles preceding the party with a lighted candle.

Oliver had been dozing, but looked worse, and was more feverish than he had appeared yet. Being assisted by the doctor, he managed to sit up in bed for a minute or so, and looked at the strangers without at all understanding what was going forward – in fact, without seeming to recollect where he was, or what had been passing.

'This,' said Mr Losberne, speaking softly, but with great vehemence notwithstanding, 'this is the lad who, being accidentally wounded by a spring-gun in some boyish trespass on Mr What-d'ye-call-him's grounds at the back here, comes to the house for assistance this morning, and is immediately laid hold of and maltreated by that ingenious gentleman with the candle in his hand, who has placed his life in considerable danger, as I can professionally certify.'

Messrs Blathers and Duff looked at Mr Giles, as he was thus recommended to their notice. The bewildered butler gazed from them towards Oliver, and from Oliver towards Mr Losberne, with a most ludicrous mixture of fear and perplexity.

'You don't mean to deny that, I suppose?' said the doctor, laying Oliver gently down again.

'It was all done for the – for the best, sir!' answered Giles. 'I am sure I thought it was the boy, or I wouldn't have meddled with him. I am not of an inhuman disposition, sir.'

'Thought it was what boy?' enquired the senior officer.

'The housebreakers' boy, sir!' replied Giles. 'They – they certainly had a boy.'

'Well! do you think so now?' enquired Blathers.

'Think what, now?' replied Giles, looking vacantly at his questioner.

'Think it's the same boy, Stupid-head?' rejoined Mr Blathers, impatiently.

'I don't know; I really don't know,' said Giles, with a rueful countenance. 'I couldn't swear to him.'

'What do you think?' said Mr Blathers.

'I don't know what to think,' replied poor Giles. 'I don't think it is the boy; indeed, I'm almost certain that it isn't. You know it can't be.'

'Has this man been a-drinking, sir?' enquired Blathers, turning to the doctor.

'What a precious muddle-headed chap you are!' said Duff, addressing Mr Giles with supreme contempt.

Mr Losberne had been feeling the patient's pulse during this short dialogue; but he now rose from the chair by the bedside, and remarked, that if the officers had any doubts upon the subject, they would perhaps like to step into the next room and have Brittles before them.

Acting upon this suggestion, they adjourned to a neighbouring apartment, where Mr Brittles, being called in, involved himself and his respected superior in such a wonderful maze of fresh contradictions and impossibilities as tended to throw no particular light on anything but the fact of his own strong mystification; except, indeed, his declarations that he shouldn't know the real boy if he were put before him that instant; that he had only taken Oliver to be he because Mr Giles had said he was; and that Mr Giles had, five minutes previously admitted in the kitchen that he began to be very much afraid he had been a little too hasty.

Among other ingenious surmises, the question was then raised whether Mr Giles had really hit anybody; and upon examination of the fellow-pistol to that which he had fired, it turned out to have no more destructive loading than gunpowder and brown paper; a discovery which made a considerable impression on everybody but the doctor, who had drawn the ball about ten minutes before. Upon no one, however, did it make a greater impression than on Mr Giles himself, who, after labouring for some hours under the fear of having mortally wounded a fellow-creature, eagerly caught at this new idea, and favoured it to the utmost. Finally, the officers, without troubling themselves very much about Oliver, left the Chertsey constable in the house, and took up their rest for that night in the town, promising to return next morning.

With the next morning there came a rumour that two men and a boy were in the cage at Kingston, who had been apprehended overnight under suspicious circumstances; and to Kingston Messrs Blathers and Duff journeyed accordingly. The suspicious circumstances, however, resolving themselves, on investigation, into the one fact that they had been discovered sleeping under a haystack; which, although a great crime, is only punishable by imprisonment, and is, in the merciful eye of the English law, and its comprehensive love of all the king's subjects, held to be no satisfactory proof, in the absence of all other evidence, that the sleeper, or sleepers, have committed burglary accompanied with violence, and have therefore rendered themselves liable to the punishment of death, Messrs Blathers and Duff came back again, as wise as they went.

In short, after some more examination, and a great deal more conversation, a neighbouring magistrate was readily induced to take the joint-bail of Mrs Maylie and Mr Losberne for Oliver's

appearance if he should ever be called upon; and Blathers and Duff, being rewarded with a couple of guineas, returned to town with divided opinions on the subject of their expedition: the latter gentleman, on a mature consideration of all the circumstances, inclining to the belief that the burglarious attempt had originated with the Family Pet; and the former being equally disposed to concede the full merit of it to the great Mr Conkey Chickweed.

Meanwhile, Oliver gradually throve and prospered under the united care of Mrs Maylie, Rose, and the kind-hearted Mr Losberne. If fervent prayers, gushing from hearts overcharged with gratitude, be heard in heaven – and if they be not, what prayers are! – the blessings which the orphan child called down upon them sunk into their souls, diffusing peace and happiness.

CHAPTER 32

Of the happy life Oliver began to lead with his kind friends

Oliver's ailings were neither slight nor few. In addition to the pain and delay attendant on a broken limb, his exposure to the wet and cold had brought on fever and ague; which hung about him for many weeks, and reduced him sadly. But at length he began, by slow degrees, to get better, and to be able to say sometimes, in a few tearful words, how deeply he felt the

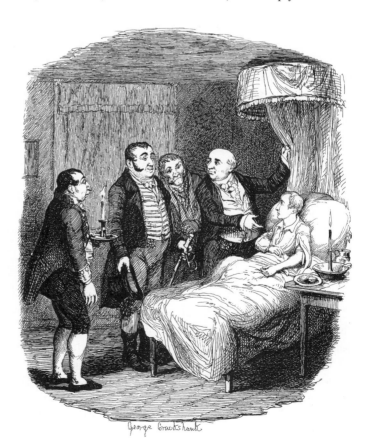

Oliver waited on by Bow Street Runners

goodness of the two sweet ladies, and how ardently he hoped that, when he grew strong and well again, he could do something to show his gratitude – only something which would let them see the love and duty with which his breast was full – something, however slight, which would prove to them that their gentle kindness had not been cast away, but that the poor boy whom their charity had rescued from misery, or death, was eager to serve them with his whole heart and soul.

'Poor fellow!' said Rose, when Oliver had been one day feebly endeavouring to utter the words of thankfulness that rose to his pale lips, 'you shall have many opportunities of serving us, if you will. We are going into the country, and my aunt intends that you shall accompany us. The quiet place, the pure air, and all the pleasures and beauties of spring, will restore you in a few days; and we will employ you in a hundred ways when you can bear the trouble.'

'The trouble!' cried Oliver. 'Oh! dear lady, if I could but work for you; if I could only give you pleasure by watering your flowers, or watching your birds, or running up and down the whole day long to make you happy; what would I give to do it!'

'You shall give nothing at all,' said Miss Maylie, smiling; 'for, as I told you before, we shall employ you in a hundred ways; and if you only take half the trouble to please us that you promise now, you will make me very happy indeed.'

'Happy, ma'am!' cried Oliver; 'how kind of you to say so!'

'You will make me happier than I can tell you,' replied the young lady. 'To think that my dear good aunt should have been the means of rescuing anyone from such sad misery as you have described to us would be an unspeakable pleasure to me; but to know that the object of her goodness and compassion was sincerely grateful and attached, in consequence, would delight me more than you can well imagine. Do you understand me?' she enquired, watching Oliver's thoughtful face.

'Oh, yes, ma'am, yes!' replied Oliver, eagerly; 'but I was thinking that I am ungrateful now.'

'To whom?' enquired the young lady.

'To the kind gentleman, and the dear old nurse, who took so much care of me before,' rejoined Oliver. 'If they knew how happy I am, they would be pleased, I am sure.'

'I am sure they would,' rejoined Oliver's benefactress; 'and Mr Losberne has already been kind enough to promise that, when you are well enough to bear the journey, he will carry you to see them.'

'Has he, ma'am?' cried Oliver, his face brightening with pleasure. 'I don't know what I shall do for joy when I see their kind faces once again!'

In a short time Oliver was sufficiently recovered to undergo the fatigue of this expedition, and one morning he and Mr Losberne set out accordingly, in a little carriage which belonged to Mrs Maylie. When they came to Chertsey Bridge, Oliver turned very pale, and uttered a loud exclamation.

'What's the matter with the boy?' cried the doctor, as usual, all in a bustle. 'Do you see anything – hear anything – feel anything – eh?'

'That, sir,' cried Oliver, pointing out of the carriage window. 'That house!'

'Yes; well, what of it? – Stop, coachman. Pull up here,' cried the doctor. – 'What of the house, my man; eh?'

'The thieves; the house they took me to,' whispered Oliver.

'The devil it is!' cried the doctor. 'Hallo, there! let me out!'

But before the coachman could dismount from his box, he had tumbled out of the coach by some means or other, and running down to the deserted tenement, began kicking at the door like a madman.

'Hallo!' said a little, ugly, humpbacked man, opening the door so suddenly that the doctor, from the very impetus of his last kick, nearly fell forward into the passage. 'What's the matter here?'

'Matter!' exclaimed the other, collaring him without a moment's reflection. 'A good deal. Robbery is the matter.'

'There'll be murder the matter, too,' replied the humpbacked man, coolly, 'if you don't take your hands off. Do you hear me?'

'I hear you,' said the doctor, giving his captive a hearty shake. 'Where's – confound the fellow, what's his rascally name – Sikes; that's it. Where's Sikes, you thief?'

The humpbacked man stared, as if in excess of amazement and indignation; and twisting himself, dexterously, from the doctor's grasp, growled forth a volley of horrid oaths, and retired into the house. Before he could shut the door, however, the doctor had passed into the parlour, without a word of parley. He looked anxiously round: not an article of furniture, not a vestige of anything animate or inanimate, not even the position of the cupboards, answered Oliver's description!

'Now!' said the humpbacked man, who had watched him keenly, 'what do you mean by coming into my house in this violent way? Do you want to rob me, or to murder me? Which is it?'

'Did you ever know a man come out to do either in a chariot and pair, you ridiculous old vampire?' said the irritable doctor.

'What do you want, then?' demanded the hunchback. 'Will you take yourself off, before I do you a mischief? Curse you!'

'As soon as I think proper,' said Mr Losberne, looking into the other parlour, which, like the first, bore no resemblance whatever to Oliver's account of it. 'I shall find you out, some-day, my friend.'

'Will you?' sneered the ill-favoured cripple. 'If you ever want me, I'm here. I haven't lived here mad, and all alone, for five-and-twenty years, to be scared by you. You shall pay for this; you shall pay for this.' And so saying, the misshapen little demon set up a hideous yell, and danced upon the ground, as if frantic with rage.

'Stupid enough, this,' muttered the doctor to himself; 'the boy must have made a mistake. Here! Put that in your pocket, and shut yourself up again.' With these words he flung the hunchback a piece of money, and returned to the carriage.

The man followed to the chariot door, uttering the wildest imprecations and curses all the way; but as Mr Losberne turned to speak to the driver, he looked into the carriage, and eyed Oliver for an instant with a glance so sharp and fierce, and at the same time so furious and vindictive, that, waking or sleeping, he could not forget it for months afterwards. He continued to utter the most fearful imprecations until the driver had resumed his seat; and when they were once more on their way, they could see him some distance behind beating his feet upon the ground, and tearing his hair in transports of frenzied rage.

'I am an ass!' said the doctor, after a long silence. 'Did you know that before, Oliver?'

'No, sir.'

'Then don't forget it another time.'

'An ass,' said the doctor again, after a further silence of some minutes. 'Even if it had been the right place, and the right fellows had been there, what could I have done single-handed? And if I had had assistance, I see no good that I should have done, except leading to my own exposure, and an unavoidable statement of the manner in which I have hushed up this business. That would have served me right, though. I am always involving myself in some scrape or other by acting on impulse; and it might have done me good.'

Now, the fact was that the excellent doctor had never acted upon anything else but impulse all through his life; and it was no bad compliment to the nature of the impulses which governed him, that so far from being involved in any peculiar troubles or misfortunes, he had the warmest respect and esteem of all who knew him. If the truth must be told, he was a little out of temper, for a minute or two, at being disappointed in procuring corroborative evidence of Oliver's story, on the very first occasion on which he had a chance of obtaining any. He soon came round again, however; and finding that Oliver's replies to his questions were still as straightforward and consistent, and still delivered with as much apparent sincerity and truth, as they had ever been, he made up his mind to attach full credence to them from that time forth.

As Oliver knew the name of the street in which Mr Brownlow resided, they were enabled to drive straight thither. When the coach turned into it, his heart beat so violently that he could scarcely draw his breath.

'Now, my boy, which house is it?' enquired Mr Losberne.

'That! that!' replied Oliver, pointing eagerly out of the window. 'The white house. Oh! make haste! Pray, make haste! I feel as if I should die; it makes me tremble so.'

'Come, come!' said the good doctor, patting him on the shoulder. 'You will see them directly, and they will be overjoyed to find you safe and well.'

'Oh! I hope so! cried Oliver. 'They were so good to me – so very, very good to me.'

The coach rolled on. It stopped. No; that was the wrong house – the next door. It went on a few paces, and stopped again. Oliver looked up at the windows, with tears of happy expectation coursing down his face.

Alas! the white house was empty, and there was a bill in the window, 'To let.'

'Knock at the next door,' cried Mr Losberne taking Oliver's arm in his. – 'What has become of Mr Brownlow, who used to live in the adjoining house, do you know?'

The servant did not know, but would go and enquire. She presently returned, and said that Mr Brownlow had sold off his goods, and gone to the West Indies, six weeks before. Oliver clasped his hands and sank feebly backwards.

'Has his housekeeper gone, too?' enquired Mr Losberne, after a moment's pause.

'Yes, sir,' replied the servant. 'The old gentleman, the house-keeper, and a gentleman who was a friend of Mr Brownlow's, all went together.'

'Then turn towards home again,' said Mr Losberne to the driver; 'and don't stop to bait the horses till you get out of this confounded London.'

'The bookstall keeper, sir!' said Oliver. 'I know the way there. See him, pray, sir! Do see him!'

'My poor boy, this is disappointment enough for one day,' said the doctor. 'Quite enough for both of us. If we go to the bookstall keeper's, we shall certainly find that he is dead, or has set his house on fire, or run away. No; home again straight!' And, in obedience to the doctor's impulse, home they went.

This bitter disappointment caused Oliver much sorrow and grief, even in the midst of his happiness; for he had pleased himself, many times during his illness, with thinking of all that Mr Brownlow and Mrs Bedwin would say to him, and what delight it would be to tell them how many long days and nights he had passed in reflecting on what they had done for him, and in bewailing his cruel separation from them. The hope of eventually clearing himself with them, too, and explaining how he had been forced away, had buoyed him up and sustained him under many of his recent trials; and now the idea that they should have gone so far, and carried with them the belief that he was an impostor and a robber – a belief which might remain uncontradicted to his dying day – was almost more than he could bear.

The circumstance occasioned no alteration, however, in the behaviour of his benefactors. After another fortnight, when the fine warm weather had fairly begun, and every tree and flower was putting forth its young leaves and rich blossoms, they made preparations for quitting the house at Chertsey for some months. Sending the plate, which had so excited the Jew's cupidity, to the bankers, and leaving Giles and another servant in care of the house, they departed to a cottage at some distance in the country, and took Oliver with them.

Who can describe the pleasure and delight, the peace of mind and soft tranquillity, the sickly boy felt in the balmy air and among the green hills and rich woods of an inland village! Who can tell how scenes of peace and quietude sink into the minds of pain-worn dwellers in close and noisy places, and carry their own freshness deep into their jaded hearts! Men who have lived in crowded, pent-up streets, through lives of toil, and never wished for change; men, to whom custom has indeed become second nature, and who have come almost to love each brick and stone that formed the narrow boundaries of their daily walks; even they, with the hand of death upon them, have been known to yearn at last for one short glimpse of Nature's face; and, carried far from the scenes of their old pains and pleasures, have seemed to pass at once into a new state of being, and crawling forth from day to day to some green sunny spot, have had such memories wakened up within them by the mere sight of sky, and hill, and plain, and glistening water, that a foretaste of heaven itself has soothed their quick decline, and they have sunk into their tombs as peacefully as the sun, whose setting they watched from their lonely chamber window but a few hours before, faded from their dim and feeble sight! The memories which peaceful country scenes call up are not of this world, nor its thoughts and hopes. Their gentle influence may teach us how to weave fresh garlands for the graves of those we loved; may purify our thoughts, and bear down before it old enmity and hatred; but beneath all this there lingers, in the least reflective mind, a vague and half-formed consciousness of having held such feelings long before, in some remote and distant time, which calls up solemn thoughts of distant times to come, and bends down pride and worldliness beneath it.

It was a lovely spot to which they repaired. Oliver, whose days had been spent among squalid crowds, and in the midst of noise and brawling, seemed to enter on a new existence there. The rose and honeysuckle clung to the cottage walls, the ivy crept round the trunks of the trees, and the garden flowers perfumed the air with delicious odours. Hard by was a little churchyard, not crowded with tall unsightly gravestones, but full of humble mounds, covered with fresh turf and moss, beneath which the old people of the village lay at rest. Oliver often wandered here, and, thinking of the wretched grave in which his mother lay, would sometimes sit him down and sob unseen; but when he raised his eyes to the deep sky overhead, he would cease to think of her as lying in the ground, and would weep for her, sadly, but without pain.

It was a happy time. The days were peaceful and serene; the nights brought with them neither fear nor care – no languishing in a wretched prison, or associating with wretched men – nothing but pleasant and happy thoughts. Every morning he went to a whiteheaded old gentleman who lived near the little church, who taught him to read better, and to write; and spoke so kindly, and took such pains, that Oliver could never try enough to please him. Then he would walk with Mrs Maylie and Rose, and hear them talk of books; or perhaps sit near them in some shady place, and listen whilst the young lady read, which he could have done until it grew too dark to see the letters. Then he had his own lessons for the next day to prepare, and at this he would work hard, in a little room which looked into the garden, till evening came slowly on, when the ladies would walk out again, and he with them; listening with such pleasure to all they said, and so happy if they wanted a flower that he could climb to reach, or had forgotten anything he could run to fetch, that he could never be quick enough about it. When it became quite dark, and they returned home, the young lady would sit down to the piano, and play some pleasant air, or sing, in a low and gentle voice, some old song which it pleased her aunt to hear. There would be no candles lighted at such times as these; and Oliver would sit by one of the windows, listening to the sweet music, in a perfect rapture.

And when Sunday came, how differently the day was spent from any way in which he had ever spent it yet! and how happily, too; like all the other days in that most happy time. There was the little church in the morning, with the green leaves fluttering at the windows, the birds singing without, and the sweet-smelling air stealing in at the low porch, and filling the homely building with fragrance. The poor people were so neat and clean, and knelt so reverently in prayer, that it seemed a pleasure, not a tedious duty, their assembling there together; and though the singing might be rude, it was real, and sounded more musical (to Oliver's ears at least) than any he had ever heard in church before. Then there were the walks as usual, and many calls at the clean houses of the labouring men; and at night Oliver read a chapter or two from the Bible, which he had been studying all the week, and in the performance of which duty he felt more proud and pleased than if he had been the clergyman himself.

In the morning, Oliver would be afoot by six o'clock, roaming the fields, and plundering the hedges, far and wide, for nosegays of wild flowers, with which he would return laden home, and which he took great care and consideration to arrange to the best advantage for the embellishment of the breakfast-table. There was fresh groundsel, too, for Miss Maylie's birds, with which Oliver, who had been studying the subject under the able tuition of the village clerk, would decorate the cages in the most approved taste. When the birds were made all spruce and smart for the day, there was usually some little commission of charity to execute in the village; or, failing that, there was rare cricket-playing sometimes on the green; or, failing that, there was always something to do in the garden, or about the plants, to which Oliver (who had studied this science also, under the same master, who was a gardener by trade) applied himself with hearty goodwill, until Miss Rose made her appearance, when there were a thousand commendations to be bestowed on all he had done.

So three months glided away; three months which, in the life of the most blessed and favoured of mortals, might have been unmingled happiness, and which, in Oliver's, were true felicity indeed. With the purest and most amiable generosity on one side, and the truest, warmest, soul-felt gratitude on the other, it is no wonder that, by the end of that short time, Oliver Twist had become completely domesticated with the old lady and her niece, and that the fervent attachment of his young and sensitive heart was repaid by their pride in, and attachment to, himself.

CHAPTER 33

Wherein the happiness of Oliver and his friends experiences a sudden check

Spring flew swiftly by, and summer came; and if the village had been beautiful at first, it was now in the full glow and luxuriance of its richness. The great trees which had looked shrunken and bare in the earlier months had now burst into strong life and health, and stretching forth their green arms over the thirsty ground, converted open and naked spots into choice nooks, where was a deep and pleasant shade from which to look upon the wide prospect, steeped in sunshine, which lay stretched out beyond. The earth had donned her mantle of brightest green, and shed her richest perfumes abroad. It was the prime and vigour of the year; all things were glad and flourishing.

Still the same quiet life went on at the little cottage, and the same cheerful serenity prevailed among its inmates. Oliver had long since grown stout and healthy; but health or sickness made no difference in his warm feelings to those about him, though they do in the feelings of a great many people. He was still the same gentle, attached, affectionate creature that he had been when pain and suffering had wasted his strength, and when he was dependent for every slight attention and comfort on those who tended him.

One beautiful night they had taken a longer walk than was customary with them; for the day had been unusually warm, and there was a brilliant moon, and a light wind had sprung up which was unusually refreshing. Rose had been in high spirits, too, and they had walked on in merry conversation, until they had far exceeded their ordinary bounds. Mrs Maylie being fatigued, they returned more slowly home. The young lady, merely throwing off her simple bonnet, sat down to the piano as usual. After running abstractedly over the keys for a few minutes, she fell into a low and very solemn air; and, as she played it, they heard her sob, as if she were weeping.

'Rose, my dear!' said the elder lady.

Rose made no reply, but played a little quicker, as though the words had roused her from some painful thoughts.

'Rose, my love!' cried Mrs Maylie, rising hastily, and bending over her. 'What is this? In tears? My dear child, what distresses you?'

'Nothing, aunt; nothing,' replied the young lady. 'I don't know what it is – I can't describe it – but I feel –'

'Not ill, my love?' interposed Mrs Maylie.

'No, no! Oh, not ill,' replied Rose, shuddering, as though some deadly chillness were passing over her while she spoke; 'I shall be better presently. Close the window, pray!'

Oliver hastened to comply with her request. The young lady, making an effort to recover her cheerfulness, strove to play some livelier tune; but her fingers dropped powerless on the keys, and covering her face with her hands, she sank upon a sofa, and gave vent to the tears which she was now unable to repress.

'My child!' said the elderly lady, folding her arms about her, 'I never saw you thus before.'

'I would not alarm you if I could avoid it,' rejoined Rose; 'but indeed I have tried very hard, and cannot help this. I fear I *am* ill, aunt.'

She was, indeed, for when candles were brought they saw that, in the very short time which had elapsed since their return home, the hue of her countenance had changed to a marble whiteness. Its expression had lost nothing of its beauty; but it was changed, and there was an anxious, haggard look about the gentle face which it had never worn before. Another minute, and it was suffused with a crimson flush, and a heavy wildness came over the soft blue eye. Again this disappeared, like the shadow thrown by a passing cloud, and she was once more deadly pale.

Oliver, who watched the old lady anxiously, observed that she was alarmed by these appearances; and so, in truth, was he, but, seeing that she affected to make light of them, he endeavoured to do the same, and they so far succeeded that when Rose was persuaded by her aunt to retire for the night, she was in better spirits, and appeared even in better health, assuring them that she felt certain she should rise in the morning quite well.

'I hope,' said Oliver, when Mrs Maylie returned, 'that nothing is the matter. She don't look well tonight, but –'

The old lady motioned to him not to speak, and, sitting herself down in a dark corner of the room, remained silent for some time. At length she said, in a trembling voice, 'I hope not, Oliver. I have been very happy with her for some years – too happy, perhaps. It may be time that I should meet with some misfortune; but I hope it is not this.'

'What?' enquired Oliver.

'The heavy blow,' said the old lady, 'of losing the dear girl who has so long been my comfort and happiness.'

'Oh! God forbid!' exclaimed Oliver, hastily.

'Amen to that, my child!' said the old lady, wringing her hands.

'Surely there is no danger of anything so dreadful,' said Oliver. 'Two hours ago she was quite well.'

'She is very ill now,' rejoined Mrs Maylie; 'and will be worse, I am sure. My dear, dear Rose! Oh, what should I do without her!'

She gave way to such great grief that Oliver, suppressing his own emotion, ventured to remonstrate with her, and to beg earnestly that, for the sake of the dear young lady herself, she would be more calm.

'And consider, ma'am,' said Oliver, as the tears forced themselves into his eyes, despite his efforts to the contrary – 'oh! consider how young and good she is, and what pleasure and comfort she gives to all about her. I am sure – certain – quite certain – that, for your sake, who are so good yourself, and for her own, and for the sake of all she makes so happy, she will not die. Heaven will never let her die so young.'

'Hush!' said Mrs Maylie, laying her hand on Oliver's head. 'You think like a child, poor boy! But you teach me my duty, notwithstanding. I had forgotten it for a moment, Oliver; but I hope I may be pardoned, for I am old, and have seen enough of illness and death to know the agony of separation from the objects of our love. I have seen enough, too, to know that it is not always the youngest and best who are spared to those that love them. But this should give us comfort in our sorrow; for Heaven is just, and such things teach us, impressively, that there is a brighter world than this, and that the passage to it is speedy. God's will be done! I love her; and He knows how well.'

Oliver was surprised to see that, as Mrs Maylie said these words, she checked her lamentations as though by one struggle, and drawing herself up as she spoke, became composed and firm. He was still more astonished to find that this firmness lasted, and that, under all the care and watching which ensued, Mrs Maylie was ever ready and collected, performing all the duties which devolved upon her steadily, and, to all external appearance, even cheerfully. But he was young, and did not know what strong minds are capable of under trying circumstances. How should he, when their possessors so seldom know themselves?

An anxious night ensued. When morning came, Mrs Maylie's predictions were but too well verified: Rose was in the first stage of a high and dangerous fever.

'We must be active, Oliver, and not give way to useless grief,' said Mrs Maylie, laying her finger on her lip, as she looked steadily into his face; 'this letter must be sent, with all possible expedition, to Mr Losberne. It must be carried to the market-town – which is not more than four miles off, by the footpath across the fields – and thence dispatched, by an express on horseback, straight to Chertsey. The people at the inn will undertake to do this; and I can trust to you to see it done, I know.'

Oliver could make no reply, but looked his anxiety to be gone at once.

'Here is another letter,' said Mrs Maylie, pausing to reflect; 'but whether to send it now, or wait until I see how Rose goes on, I scarcely know. I would not forward it unless I feared the worst.'

'Is it for Chertsey, too, ma'am?' enquired Oliver, impatient to execute his commission, and holding out his trembling hand for the letter.

'No,' replied the old lady, giving it to him mechanically. Oliver glanced at it, and saw that it was directed to Harry Maylie, Esquire, at some great lord's house in the country; where, he could not make out.

'Shall it go, ma'am?' asked Oliver, looking up, impatiently.

'I think not,' replied Mrs Maylie, taking it back. 'I will wait until tomorrow.'

With these words she gave Oliver her purse, and he started off, without more delay, at the greatest speed he could muster.

Swiftly he ran across the fields, and down the little lanes which sometimes divided them, now almost hidden by the high corn on either side, and now emerging in an open field, where the mowers and haymakers were busy at their work; nor did he stop once, save now and then for a few seconds, to recover breath until he came, in a great heat, and covered with dust, on the little market-place of the market-town.

Here he paused, and looked about for the inn. There was a white bank, and a red brewery, and a yellow town-hall; and in one corner there was a large house, with all the wood about it painted green, before which was the sign of 'The George.' To this he hastened as soon as it caught his eye.

He spoke to a postboy who was dozing under the gateway, and who, after hearing what he wanted, referred him to the hostler; who, after hearing all he had to say again, referred him to the landlord; who was a tall gentleman in a blue neckcloth, a white hat, drab breeches, and boots with tops to match, leaning against a pump by the stable-door, picking his teeth with a silver toothpick.

This gentleman walked with much deliberation into the bar to make out the bill, which took a long time making out; and after it was ready, and paid, a horse had to be saddled, and a man to be dressed, which took up ten good minutes more. Meanwhile Oliver was in such a desperate state of impatience and anxiety, that he felt as if he could have jumped upon the horse and galloped away, full tear, to the next stage. At length all was ready; and the little parcel having been handed up, with many injunctions and entreaties for its speedy delivery, the man set spurs to his horse, and rattling over the uneven paving of the market-place, was out of the town, and galloping along the turnpike road, in a couple of minutes.

It was something to feel certain that assistance was sent for, and that no time had been lost. Oliver hurried up the inn-yard with a somewhat lighter heart, and was turning out of the gateway when he accidentally stumbled against a tall man wrapped in a cloak, who was at that moment coming out of the inn door.

'Ha!' cried the man, fixing his eyes on Oliver, and suddenly recoiling. 'What the devil's this?'

'I beg you pardon, sir,' said Oliver; 'I was in a great hurry to get home, and didn't see you were coming.'

'Death!' muttered the man to himself, glaring at the boy with his large dark eyes. 'Who would have thought it? Grind him to ashes! He'd start up from a marble coffin to come in my way!'

'I am sorry,' stammered Oliver, confused by the strange man's wild look. 'I hope I have not hurt you!'

'Rot his bones!' murmured the man, in a horrible passion, between his clenched teeth; 'if I had only had the courage to say the word, I might have been free of him in a night. Curses on your head, and black death on your heart, you imp! What are you doing here?'

The man shook his fist and gnashed his teeth as he uttered these words incoherently. He advanced towards Oliver, as if with the intention of aiming a blow at him, but fell violently on the ground, writhing and foaming in a fit.

Oliver gazed for a moment at the struggles of the madman (for such he supposed him to be), and then darted into the house for help. Having seen him safely carried into the hotel, he turned his face homewards, running as fast as he could to make up for lost time, and recalling, with a great deal of astonishment and some fear, the extraordinary behaviour of the person from whom he had just parted.

The circumstance did not dwell long in his recollection, however; for when he reached the cottage there was enough to occupy his mind, and to drive all considerations of self completely from his memory.

Rose Maylie had rapidly grown worse, and before midnight was delirious. A medical practitioner, who resided on the spot, was in constant attendance upon her; and after first seeing the patient, he had taken Mrs Maylie aside, and pronounced her disorder to be one of a most alarming nature. 'In fact,' he said, 'it would be little short of a miracle if she recovered.'

How often did Oliver start from his bed that night, and stealing out, with noiseless footstep, to the staircase, listen for the slightest sound from the sick chamber! How often did a tremble shake his frame, and cold drops of terror start upon his brow, when a sudden trampling of feet caused him to fear that something too dreadful to think of had even then occurred! And what had been the fervency of all the prayers he had ever uttered, compared with those he poured forth now, in the agony and passion of his supplication for the health and life of the gentle creature who was tottering on the deep grave's verge!

The suspense, the fearful, acute suspense, of standing idly by while the life of one we dearly love is trembling in the balance; the racking thoughts that crowd upon the mind, and make the heart beat violently, and the breath come thick, by the force of the images they conjure up before it; the desperate anxiety *to be doing something* to relieve the pain, or lessen the danger which we have no power to alleviate; the sinking of soul and spirit, which the sad remembrance of our helplessness produces; – what tortures can equal these; what reflections or endeavours can, in the full tide and fever of the time, allay them?

Morning came, and the little cottage was lonely and still. People spoke in whispers; anxious faces appeared at the gate, from time to time; and women and children went away in tears. All the livelong day, and for hours after it had grown dark, Oliver paced softly up and down the garden, raising his eyes every instant to the sick chamber, and shuddering to see the darkened window, looking as if death lay stretched inside. Late at night, Mr Losberne arrived. 'It is hard,' said the good doctor, turning away as he spoke; 'so young, so much beloved, but there is very little hope.'

Another morning. The sun shone brightly – as brightly as if it looked upon no misery or care; and, with every leaf and flower in full bloom about her, with life, and health, and sounds and sights of joy, surrounding her on every side, the fair young creature lay wasting fast. Oliver crept away to the old church-yard, and, sitting down on one of the green mounds, wept and prayed for her in silence.

There was such peace and beauty in the scene, so much of brightness and mirth in the sunny landscape, such blithesome music in the songs of the summer birds, such freedom in the rapid flight of the rook careering overhead, so much of life and joyousness in all, that when the boy raised his aching eyes and looked about, the thought instinctively occurred to him that this was not a time for death – that Rose could surely never die when humbler things were all so glad and gay – that graves were for cold and cheerless winter, not for sunlight and fragrance. He almost thought that shrouds were for the old and shrunken, and that they never wrapped the young and graceful form within their ghastly folds.

A knell from the church bell broke harshly on those youthful thoughts. Another! Again! It was tolling for the funeral service. A group of humble mourners entered the gate wearing white favours, for the corpse was young. They stood uncovered by a grave; and there was a mother – a mother once – among the weeping train. But the sun shone brightly, and the birds sang on.

Oliver turned homewards, thinking on the many kindnesses he had received from the young lady, and wishing that the time could come over again, that he might never cease showing her how grateful and attached he was. He had no cause for self-reproach on the score of neglect, or want of thought, for he had been devoted to her service; and yet a hundred little occasions rose up before him, on which he fancied he might have been more zealous and more earnest, and wished he had been. We need be careful how we deal with those about us, when every death carries to some small circle of survivors thoughts of so much omitted, and so little done – of so many things forgotten, and so many more which might have been repaired! There is no remorse so deep as that which is unavailing; if we would be spared its tortures, let us remember this in time.

When he reached home Mrs Maylie was sitting in the little parlour. Oliver's heart sank at sight of her; for she had never left the bedside of her niece, and he trembled to think what change could have driven her away. He learnt that she had fallen into a deep sleep, from which she would waken, either to recovery and life, or to bid them farewell and die.

They sat, listening, and afraid to speak for hours. The untasted meal was removed; and with looks which showed that their thoughts were elsewhere, they watched the sun as he sank lower and lower, and, at length, cast over sky and earth those brilliant hues which herald his departure. Their quick ears caught the sound of an approaching footstep, and they both involuntarily darted to the door as Mr Losberne entered.

'What of Rose?' cried the old lady. 'Tell me at once! I can bear it – anything but suspense! Oh, tell me, in the name of Heaven.'

'You must compose yourself,' said the doctor, supporting her. 'Be calm, my dear ma'am, pray.'

'Let me go, in God's name! My dear child! She is dead – she is dying!'

'No!' cried the doctor, passionately. 'As He is good and merciful, she will live to bless us all for years to come.'

The lady fell upon her knees, and tried to fold her hands together; but the energy which had supported her so long fled up to Heaven with her first thanksgiving, and she sank into the friendly arms which were extended to receive her.

CHAPTER 34

Contains some introductory particulars relative to a young gentleman who now arrives upon the scene; and a new adventure which happened to Oliver

It was almost too much happiness to bear. Oliver felt stunned and stupefied by the unexpected intelligence; he could not weep, or speak, or rest. He had scarcely the power of understanding anything that had passed, until, after a long ramble in the quiet evening air, a burst of tears came to his relief, and he seemed to awaken, all at once, to a full sense of the joyful change that had occurred, and the almost insupportable load of anguish which had been taken from his breast.

The night was fast closing in when he returned homewards laden with flowers which he had culled, with peculiar care, for the adornment of the sick chamber. As he walked briskly along the road, he heard behind him the noise of some vehicle approaching at a furious pace. Looking round, he saw that it was a post-chaise, driven at great speed; and as the horses were galloping, and the road was narrow, he stood leaning against a gate until it should have passed him.

As he dashed on, Oliver caught a glimpse of a man in a white nightcap, whose face seemed familiar to him, although his view was so brief that he could not identify the person. In another second or two the nightcap was thrust out of the chaise-window, and a stentorian voice bellowed to the driver to stop, which he did, as soon as he could pull up his horses. Then the nightcap once again appeared, and the same voice called Oliver by his name.

'Here!' cried the voice. 'Master Oliver, what's the news? Miss Rose! Master O–li–ver!'

'Is it you, Giles?' cried Oliver, running up to the chaise-door.

Giles popped out his nightcap again, preparatory to making some reply, when he was suddenly pulled back by a young gentleman who occupied the other corner of the chaise, and who eagerly demanded what was the news.

'In a word!' cried the gentleman, 'better or worse?'

'Better, much better!' replied Oliver, hastily.

'Thank Heaven!' exclaimed the gentleman. 'You are sure?'

'Quite, sir,' replied Oliver. 'The change took place only a few hours ago; and Mr Losberne says that all danger is at an end.'

The gentleman said not another word, but opening the chaise door, leaped out, and taking Oliver hurriedly by the arm, led him aside.

'You are quite certain? There is no possibility of any mistake on your part, my boy, is there?' demanded the gentleman in a tremulous voice. 'Pray do not deceive me by awakening any hopes that are not to be fulfilled.'

'I would not for the world, sir,' replied Oliver. 'Indeed, you may believe me. Mr Losberne's words were that she would live to bless us all for many years to come. I heard him say so.'

The tears stood in Oliver's eyes as he recalled the scene which was the beginning of so much happiness; and the gentleman turned his face away, and remained silent for some minutes. Oliver thought he heard him sob more than once; but he feared to interrupt him by any further remark – for he could well guess what his feelings were – and so stood apart, feigning to be occupied with his nosegay.

All this time Mr Giles, with the white nightcap on, had been sitting upon the steps of the chaise, supporting an elbow on each knee, and wiping his eyes with a blue cotton pocket-hand-kerchief dotted with white spots. That the honest fellow had not been feigning emotion was abundantly demonstrated by the very red eyes with which he regarded the young gentleman, when he turned round and addressed him.

'I think you had better go on to my mother's in the chaise, Giles,' said he. 'I would rather walk slowly on, so as to gain a little time before I see her. You can say I am coming.'

'I beg your pardon, Mr Harry,' said Giles, giving a final polish to his ruffled countenance with the handkerchief, 'but if you would leave the postboy to say that, I should be very much obliged to you. It wouldn't be proper for the maids to see me in this state, sir; I should never have any more authority with them if they did.'

'Well,' rejoined Harry Maylie, smiling, 'you can do as you like. Let him go on with the luggage, if you wish it, and do you follow with us. Only first exchange that nightcap for some more appropriate covering, or we shall be taken for madmen.'

Mr Giles, reminded of his unbecoming costume, snatched off and pocketed his nightcap, and substituted a hat of grave and sober shape, which he took out of the chaise. This done, the postboy drove off, and Giles, Mr Maylie, and Oliver, followed at their leisure.

As they walked along, Oliver glanced from time to time with much interest and curiosity at the newcomer. He seemed about five-and-twenty years of age, and was of the middle height; his countenance was frank and handsome; and his demeanour singularly easy and prepossessing. Notwithstanding the difference between youth and age, he bore so strong a likeness to the old lady, that Oliver would have had no great difficulty in imagining their relationship, even if he had not already spoken of her as his mother.

Mrs Maylie was anxiously waiting to receive her son when he reached the cottage, and the meeting did not take place without great emotion on both sides.

'Mother!' whispered the young man, 'why did you not write before?'

'I did,' replied Mrs Maylie; 'but on reflection, I determined to keep back the letter until I had heard Mr Losberne's opinion.'

'But why,' said the young man, 'why run the chance of that occurring which so nearly happened? If Rose had – I cannot utter that word now – if this illness had terminated differently, how could you ever have forgiven yourself? How could I ever had known happiness again?'

'If that *had* been the case, Harry,' said Mrs Maylie, 'I fear your happiness would have been effectually blighted; and that your arrival here, a day sooner or a day later, would have been of very, very little import.'

'And who can wonder if it be so, mother?' rejoined the young man; 'or why should I say, *if*? It is – it is – you know it, mother – you must know it!'

'I know that she deserves the best and purest love the heart of man can offer,' said Mrs Maylie; 'I know that the devotion and affection of her nature require no ordinary return, but one that shall be deep and lasting. If I did not feel this, and know, besides, that a changed behaviour in one she loved would break her heart, I should not feel my task so difficult of performance, or have to encounter so many struggles in my own bosom, when I take what seems to me to be the strict line of duty.'

'This is unkind, mother,' said Harry. 'Do you still suppose that I am a boy, ignorant of my own mind, and mistaking the impulses of my own soul?'

'I think, my dear son,' returned Mrs Maylie, laying her hand upon his shoulder, 'that youth has many generous impulses which do not last; and that among them are some, which, being gratified, become only the more fleeting. Above all, I think,' said the lady, fixing her eyes on her son's face, 'that if an enthusiastic, ardent, and ambitious man marry a wife on whose name there is a stain, which, though it originate in no fault of hers, may be visited by cold and sordid people upon her, and upon his children also, and, in exact proportion to his success in the world, be cast in his teeth, and made the subject of sneers against him, he may, no matter how generous and good his nature, one day repent of the connection he formed in early life. And she may have the pain and torture of knowing that he does so.'

'Mother,' said the young man impatiently, 'he would be a selfish brute, unworthy alike of the name of man and of the woman you describe, who acted thus.'

'You think so now, Harry,' replied his mother.

'And ever will!' said the young man. 'The mental agony I have suffered, during the last two days, wrings from me the undisguised avowal to you of a passion which, as you well know, is not one of yesterday, nor one I have lightly formed. On Rose, sweet, gentle girl! my heart is set, as firmly as ever heart of man was set on woman. I have no thought, no view, no hope in life, beyond her; and if you oppose me in this great stake, you take my peace and happiness in your hands, and cast them to the wind. Mother, think better of this, and of me, and do not disregard the happiness of which you seem to think so little.'

'Harry,' said Mrs Maylie, 'it is because I think so much of warm and sensitive hearts, that I would spare them from being wounded. But we have said enough, and more than enough, on this matter just now.'

'Let it rest with Rose, then,' interposed Harry. 'You will not press these overstrained opinions of yours, so far as to throw any obstacle in my way?'

'I will not,' rejoined Mrs Maylie; 'but I would have you consider – '

'I *have* considered!' was the impatient reply. 'Mother, I have considered years and years. I have considered ever since I have been capable of serious reflection. My feelings remain unchanged, as they ever will; and why should I suffer the pain of a delay in giving them vent, which can be productive of no earthly good? No! Before I leave this place Rose shall hear me.'

'She shall,' said Mrs Maylie.

'There is something in your manner which would almost imply that she will hear me coldly, mother,' said the young man.

'Not coldly,' rejoined the old lady; 'far from it.'

'How then?' urged the young man. 'She has formed no other attachment?'

'No, indeed,' replied his mother; 'you have, or I mistake, too strong a hold on her affections already. What I would say,' resumed the old lady, stopping her son as he was about to speak, 'is this. Before you stake your all on this chance, before you suffer yourself to be carried to the highest point of hope, reflect for a few moments, my dear child, on Rose's history, and consider what effect the knowledge of her doubtful birth may have on her decision – devoted as she is to us, with all the intensity of her noble mind, and with that perfect sacrifice of self which, in all matters, great or trifling, has always been her characteristic.'

'What do you mean?'

'That I leave you to discover,' replied Mrs Maylie. 'I must go back to her. God bless you!'

'I shall see you again tonight?' said the young man eagerly.

'By and by,' replied the lady, 'when I leave Rose.'

'You will tell her I am here?' said Harry.

'Of course,' replied Mrs Maylie.

'And say how anxious I have been, and how much I have suffered, and how I long to see her. You will not refuse to do this, mother?'

'No,' said the old lady; 'I will tell her all.' And pressing her son's hand affectionately, she hastened from the room.

Mr Losberne and Oliver had remained at another end of the apartment while this hurried conversation was proceeding. The former now held out his hand to Harry Maylie, and hearty salutations were exchanged between them. The doctor then communicated, in reply to multifarious questions from his young friend, a precise account of his patient's situation, which was quite as consolatory and full of promise as Oliver's statement had encouraged him to hope, and to the whole of which, Mr Giles, who affected to be busy about the luggage, listened with greedy ears.

'Have you shot anything particular, lately, Giles?' enquired the doctor, when he had concluded.

'Nothing particular, sir,' replied Mr Giles, colouring up to the eyes.

'Nor catching any thieves, nor identifying any housebreakers?' said the doctor.

'None at all, sir,' replied Mr Giles, with much gravity.

'Well,' said the doctor, 'I am sorry to hear it, because you do that sort of thing so admirably. Pray how is Brittles?'

'The boy is very well, sir,' said Mr Giles, recovering his usual tone of patronage, 'and sends his respectful duty, sir.'

'That's well,' said the doctor. 'Seeing you here reminds me, Mr Giles, that on the day before that on which I was called away so hurriedly, I executed, at the request of your good mistress, a small commission in your favour. Just step into this corner a moment, will you?'

Mr Giles walked into the corner with much importance, and some wonder, and was honoured with a short whispering conference with the doctor, on the termination of which he made a great many bows, and retired with steps of unusual stateliness. The subject-matter of this conference was not disclosed in the parlour, but the kitchen was speedily enlightened concerning it; for Mr Giles walked straight thither, and having called for a mug of ale, announced, with an air of majesty which was highly effective, that it had pleased his mistress, in consideration of his gallant behaviour on the occasion of that attempted robbery, to deposit, in the local savings bank, the sum of five-and-twenty pounds for his sole use and benefit. At this, the two women-servants lifted up their hands and eyes, and supposed that Mr Giles would begin to be quite proud now, whereunto Mr Giles, pulling out his shirt-frill, replied, 'No, no'; and that if they observed that he was at all haughty to his inferiors, he would thank them to tell him so. And then he made a great many other remarks, no less illustrative of his humility, which were received with equal favour and applause, and were withal as original, and as much to the purpose, as the remarks of great men commonly are.

Above stairs, the remainder of the evening passed cheerfully away; for the doctor was in high spirits, and however fatigued or thoughtful Harry Maylie might have been at first, he was not proof against the worthy gentleman's good-humour, which displayed itself in a great variety of sallies and professional recollections, and an abundance of small jokes, which struck Oliver as being the drollest things he had ever heard, and caused him to laugh proportionately – to the evident satisfaction of the doctor, who laughed immoderately at himself, and made Harry laugh almost as heartily, by the very force of sympathy. So they were as pleasant a party as, under the circumstances, they could well have been; and it was late before they retired, with light and thankful hearts, to take that rest of which, after the doubt and suspense they had recently undergone, they stood so much in need.

Oliver rose next morning in better heart, and went about his usual early occupations with more hope and pleasure than he had known for many days. The birds were once more hung out to sing in their old places, and the sweetest wild flowers that could be found were once more gathered to gladden Rose with their beauty and fragrance. The melancholy which had seemed to the sad eyes of the anxious boy to hang, for days past, over every object, beautiful as all were, was dispelled by magic. The dew seemed to sparkle more brightly on the green leaves, the air to rustle among them with a sweeter music, and the sky itself to look more blue and bright. Such is the influence which the condition of our own thoughts exercises even over the appearance of external objects. Men who look on nature, and their fellow-men, and cry that all is dark and gloomy, are in the right; but the sombre colours are reflections from their own jaundiced eyes and hearts. The real hues are delicate, and need a clearer vision.

It is worthy of remark, and Oliver did not fail to note it at the time, that his morning expeditions were no longer made alone. Harry Maylie, after the very first morning when he met Oliver coming laden home, was seized with such a passion for flowers, and displayed such a taste in their arrangement, as left his young companion far behind. If Oliver were behindhand in these respects, however, he knew where the best were to be found; and morning after morning they scoured the country together, and brought home the fairest that blossomed. The window of the young lady's chamber was opened now, for she loved to feel the rich summer air stream in and revive her with its freshness; but there always stood in water, just inside the lattice, one particular little bunch, which was made up with great care every morning. Oliver could not help noticing that the withered flowers were never thrown away, although the little vase was regularly replenished; nor could he help observing, that whenever the doctor came into the garden, he invariably cast his eyes up to that particular corner, and nodded his head most expressively, as he set forth on his morning's walk. Pending these observations, the days were flying by, and Rose was rapidly recovering.

Nor did Oliver's time hang heavy on his hands, although the young lady had not yet left her chamber, and there were no evening walks, save now and then, for a short distance, with Mrs

Maylie. He applied himself, with redoubled assiduity, to the instructions of the white-headed old gentleman, and laboured so hard that his quick progress surprised even himself. It was while he was engaged in this pursuit that he was greatly startled and distressed by a most unexpected occurrence.

The little room in which he was accustomed to sit, when busy at his books, was on the ground-floor, at the back of the house. It was quite a cottage room, with a lattice window; around which were clusters of jessamine and honeysuckle, that crept over the casement, and filled the place with their delicious perfume. It looked into a garden, whence a wicket-gate opened into a small paddock; all beyond was fine meadowland and wood. There was no other dwelling near in that direction, and the prospect it commanded was very extensive.

One beautiful evening, when the first shades of twilight were beginning to settle upon the earth, Oliver sat at this window, intent upon his books. He had been poring over them for some time; and as the day had been uncommonly sultry, and he had exerted himself a great deal, it is no disparagement to the authors, whoever they may have been, to say that gradually, and by slow degrees, he fell asleep.

There is a kind of sleep that steals upon us sometimes, which, while it holds the body prisoner, does not free the mind from a sense of things about it, and enable it to ramble at its pleasure. So far as an overpowering heaviness, a prostration of strength and an utter inability to control our thoughts or power of motion, can be called sleep, this is it; and yet we have a consciousness of all that is going on about us, and if we dream at such a time, words which are really spoken, or sounds which really exist at the moment, accommodate themselves with surprising readiness to our visions, until reality and imagination become so strangely blended that it is afterwards almost a matter of impossibility to separate the two. Nor is this the most striking phenomenon incidental to such a state. It is an undoubted fact, that although our senses of touch and sight be for the time dead, yet our sleeping thoughts, and the visionary scenes that pass before us, will be influenced, and materially influenced, by the *mere silent presence* of some external object, which may not have been near us when we closed our eyes, and of whose vicinity we have had no waking consciousness.

Oliver knew perfectly well that he was in his own little room; that his books were lying on the table before him; and that the sweet air was stirring among the creeping plants outside. And yet he was asleep. Suddenly, the scene changed; the air became close and confined; and he thought, with a glow of terror, that he was in the Jew's house again. There sat the hideous old man, in his accustomed corner, pointing at him and whispering to another man, with his face averted, who sat beside him.

'Hush, my dear!' he thought he heard the Jew say; 'it is he, sure enough. Come away.'

'He!' the other man seemed to answer; 'could I mistake him, think you? If a crowd of devils were to put themselves into his exact shape, and he stood amongst them, there is something that would tell me how to point him out. If you buried him fifty feet deep, and took me across his grave, I should know, if there wasn't a mark above it, that he lay buried there, I should!'

The man seemed to say this with such dreadful hatred that Oliver awoke with the fear, and started up.

Good Heaven! what was that which sent the blood tingling to his heart, and deprived him of his voice and of power to move? There – there – at the window – close before him – so close that he could have almost touched him before he started back; with his eyes peering into the room, and meeting his – there stood the Jew! and beside him, white with rage or fear, or both, were the scowling features of the very man who had accosted him at the inn-yard!

It was but an instant, a glance, a flash, before his eyes; and they were gone. But they had recognised him, and he them; and their look was as firmly impressed upon his memory as if it had been deeply carved in stone, and set before him from his birth. He stood transfixed for a moment, and then, leaping from the window into the garden, called loudly for help.

CHAPTER 35

Containing the unsatisfactory result of Oliver's adventure; and a conversation of some importance between Harry Maylie and Rose

When the inmates of the house, attracted by Oliver's cries, hurried to the spot from which they proceeded, they found him pale and agitated, pointing in the direction of the meadows behind the house, and scarcely able to articulate the words, 'The Jew! the Jew!'

Monks and the Jew

Mr Giles was at a loss to comprehend what this outcry meant; but Harry Maylie, whose perceptions were something quicker, and who had heard Oliver's history from his mother, understood it at once.

'What direction did he take?' he asked, catching up a heavy stick which was standing in a corner.

'That,' replied Oliver, pointing out the course the men had taken, 'I missed them in an instant.'

'Then they are in the ditch,' said Harry. 'Follow, and keep as near me as you can.' So saying, he sprang over the hedge, and darted off with a speed which rendered it a matter of exceeding difficulty for the others to keep near him.

Giles followed as well as he could, and Oliver followed too; and in the course of a minute or two Mr Losberne, who had been out walking, and just then returned, tumbled over the hedge after them, and picking himself up with more agility than he could have been supposed to possess, struck into the same course at no contemptible speed, shouting all the while, most prodigiously, to know what was the matter.

On they all went; nor stopped they once to breathe, until the leader, striking off into an angle of the field indicated by Oliver, began to search narrowly the ditch and hedge adjoining, which afforded time for the remainder of the party to come up, and for Oliver to communicate to Mr Losberne the circumstances that had led to so vigorous a pursuit.

The search was all in vain; there were not even the traces of recent footsteps to be seen. They stood, now, on the summit of a little hill, commanding the open fields in every direction for three or four miles. There was the village in the hollow on the left; but, in order to gain that, after pursuing the track Oliver had pointed out, the men must have made a circuit of open ground, which it was impossible they could have accomplished in so short a time. A thick wood skirted the meadow land in another direction; but they could not have gained that covert for the same reason.

'It must have been a dream, Oliver,' said Harry Maylie.

'Oh, no, indeed, sir,' replied Oliver, shuddering at the very recollection of the old wretch's countenance; 'I saw him too plainly for that. I saw them both, as plainly as I see you now.'

'Who was the other?' enquired Harry and Mr Losberne together.

'The very same man I told you of who came so suddenly upon me at the inn,' said Oliver. 'We had our eyes fixed full upon each other, and I could swear to him.'

'They took this way?' demanded Harry; 'are you sure?'

'As I am that the men were at the window,' replied Oliver, pointing down, as he spoke, to the hedge which divided the cottage-garden from the meadow. 'The tall man leaped over just there; and the Jew, running a few paces to the right, crept through that gap.'

The two gentlemen watched Oliver's earnest face as he spoke, and looking from him to each other, seemed to feel satisfied of the accuracy of what he said. Still, in no direction were there any appearances of the trampling of men in hurried flight. The grass was long; but it was trodden down nowhere, save where their own feet had crushed it. The sides and brinks of the ditches were of damp clay; but in no one place could they discern the print of men's shoes, or the slightest mark which would indicate that any feet had pressed the ground for hours before.

'This is strange!' said Harry.

'Strange!' echoed the doctor. 'Blathers and Duff themselves could make nothing of it.'

Notwithstanding the evidently useless nature of their search, they did not desist until the coming on of night rendered its further prosecution hopeless; and, even then, they gave it up with reluctance. Giles was dispatched to the different ale-houses in the village, furnished with the best description Oliver could give of the appearance and dress of the strangers. Of these, the Jew was, at all events, sufficiently remarkable to be remembered, supposing he had been seen drinking or loitering about; but Giles returned without any intelligence calculated to dispel or lessen the mystery.

On the next day further search was made, and the enquiries renewed; but with no better success. On the following day, Oliver and Mr Maylie repaired to the market-town, in the hope of seeing or hearing something of the men there; but this effort was equally fruitless, and after a few days the affair began to be forgotten, as most affairs are, when wonder, having no fresh food to support it, dies away of itself.

Meanwhile Rose was rapidly recovering. She had left her room, was able to go out, and mixing once more with the family, carried joy into the hearts of all.

But, although this happy change had a visible effect on the little circle, and although cheerful voices and merry laughter were once more heard in the cottage, there was at times an unwonted restraint upon some there, even upon Rose herself, which Oliver could not fail to remark. Mrs Maylie and her son were often closeted together for a long time; and more than once Rose appeared with traces of tears upon her face. After Mr Losberne had fixed a day for his departure to Chertsey, these symptoms increased; and it became evident that something was in progress which affected the peace of the young lady, and of somebody else besides.

At length, one morning, when Rose was alone in the break-fast-parlour, Harry Maylie entered, and with some hesitation begged permission to speak with her for a few moments.

'A few – a very few – will suffice, Rose,' said the young man, drawing his chair towards her. 'What I shall have to say has already presented itself to your mind; the most cherished hopes of my heart are not unknown to you, though from my lips you have not yet heard them stated.'

Rose had been very pale from the moment of his entrance; but that might have been the effect of her recent illness. She merely bowed, and bending over some plants that stood near, waited in silence for him to proceed.

'I – I – ought to have left here before,' said Harry. 'You should, indeed,' replied Rose. 'Forgive me for saying so, but I wish you had.'

'I was brought here by the most dreadful and agonising of all apprehensions,' said the young man – 'the fear of losing the one dear being on whom my every wish and hope are fixed. You had

been dying – trembling between earth and heaven. We know that when the young, the beautiful and good, are visited with sickness, their pure spirits insensibly turn towards their bright home of lasting rest; we know, Heaven help us! that the best and fairest of our kind too often fade in blooming.'

There were tears in the eyes of the gentle girl as these words were spoken; and when one fell upon the flower over which she bent, and glistened brightly in its cup, making it more beautiful, it seemed as though the outpouring of her fresh young heart claimed kindred with the loveliest things in nature.

'An angel,' continued the young man passionately, 'a creature as fair and innocent of guile as one of God's own angels, fluttered between life and death. Oh! who could hope, when the distant world to which she was akin half opened to her view, that she would return to the sorrow and calamity of this! Rose, Rose, to know that you were passing away like some soft shadow which a light from above cast upon the earth; to have no hope that you would be spared to those who linger here; to know no reason why you should be; to feel that you belonged to that bright sphere whither so many of the fairest and the best have winged their early flight; and yet to pray, amid all these consolations, that you might be restored to those who loved you – these were distractions almost too great to bear. They were mine, by day and night; and with them came such a rushing torrent of fears and apprehensions, and selfish regrets lest you should die and never know how devotedly I loved you, as almost bore down sense and reason in its course. You recovered. Day by day, and almost hour by hour, some drop of health came back, and mingling with the spent and feeble stream of life which circulated languidly within you, swelled it again to a high and rushing tide. I have watched you change almost from death to life, with eyes that moistened with their eagerness and deep affection. Do not tell me that you wish I had lost this, for it has softened my heart to all mankind.'

'I did not mean that,' said Rose, weeping; 'I only wish you had left here, that you might have turned to high and noble pursuits again – to pursuits well worthy of you.'

'There is no pursuit more worthy of me, more worthy of the highest nature that exists, than the struggle to win such a heart as yours,' said the young man, taking her hand. 'Rose, my own dear Rose! for years – for years – I have loved you; hoping to win my way to fame, and then come proudly home and tell you it had been pursued only for you to share; thinking, in my day-dreams, how I would remind you, in that happy moment, of the many silent tokens I had given of a boy's attachment; and claim your hand, as in redemption of some old mute contract that had been sealed between us! That time has not arrived; but here, with no fame won, and no young vision realised, I give to you the heart so long your own, and stake my all upon the words with which you greet the offer.'

'Your behaviour has ever been kind and noble,' said Rose, mastering the emotions by which she was agitated. 'As you believe that I am not insensible or ungrateful, so hear my answer.'

'It is, that I may endeavour to deserve you; it is, dear Rose?'

'It is,' replied Rose, 'that you must endeavour to forget me;

not as your old and dearly-attached companion, for that would wound me deeply, but as the object of your love. Look into the world; think how many hearts you would be proud to gain are there. Confide some other passion to me, if you will, and I will be the truest, warmest, and most faithful friend you have.'

There was a pause, during which Rose, who had covered her face with one hand, gave free vent to her tears. Harry still retained the other.

'And your reasons, Rose,' he said at length, in a low voice – 'your reasons for this decision?'

'You have a right to know them,' rejoined Rose. 'You can say nothing to alter my resolution. It is a duty that I must perform. I owe it, alike to others and to myself.'

'To yourself?'

'Yes, Harry. I owe it to myself, that I, a friendless, portionless girl, with a blight upon my name, should not give your friends reason to suspect that I had sordidly yielded to your first passion, and fastened myself, a clog, on all your hopes and projects. I owe it to you and yours, to prevent you from opposing, in the warmth of your generous nature, this great obstacle to your progress in the world.'

'If your inclinations chime with your sense of duty – ' Harry began.

'They do not,' replied Rose, colouring deeply.

'Then you return my love?' said Harry. 'Say but that, dear Rose – say but that, and soften the bitterness of this hard disappointment.'

'If I could have done so, without doing heavy wrong to him I loved,' rejoined Rose, 'I could have – '

'Have received this declaration very differently?' said Harry. 'Do not conceal that from me, at least, Rose.'

'I could,' said Rose. 'Stay!' she added, disengaging her hand, 'why should we prolong this painful interview? Most painful to me, and yet productive of lasting happiness notwithstanding; for it *will* be happiness to know that I once held the high place in your regard which I now occupy; and every triumph you achieve in life will animate me with new fortitude and firmness. Farewell, Harry! As we have met today, we meet no more; but in other relations than those in which this conversation would have placed us, may we be long and happily entwined; and may every blessing that the prayers of a true and earnest heart can call down from the source of all truth and sincerity cheer and prosper you!'

'Another word, Rose,' said Harry. 'Your reason in your own words. From your own lips let me hear it!'

'The prospect before you,' answered Rose, firmly, 'is a brilliant one. All the honours to which great talents and powerful connections can help men in public life are in store for you. But those connections are proud; and I will neither mingle with such as hold in scorn the mother who gave me life, nor bring disgrace or failure on the son of her who has so well supplied that mother's place. In a word,' said the young lady, turning away, as her temporary firmness forsook her, 'there is a stain upon my name which the world visits on innocent heads. I will carry it into no blood but my own, and the reproach shall rest alone on me.'

'One word more, Rose. Dearest Rose! one more!' cried Harry, throwing himself before her. 'If I had been less – less fortunate, the world would call it – if some obscure and peaceful life had been my destiny – if I had been poor, sick, helpless – would you have turned from me then? Or has my probable advancement to riches and honour given this scruple birth?'

'Do not press me to reply,' answered Rose. 'The question does not arise, and never will. It is unfair, unkind, to urge it.'

'If your answer be what I almost dare to hope it is,' retorted Harry, 'it will shed a gleam of happiness upon my lonely way, and light the dreary path before me. It is not an idle thing to do so much, by the utterance of a few brief words, for one who loves you beyond all else. O Rose! in the name of my ardent and enduring attachment, in the name of all I have suffered for you, and all you doom me to undergo, answer me this one question!'

'Then, if your lot had been differently cast,' rejoined Rose – 'if you had been even a little, but not so far, above me – if I could have been a help and comfort to you in some humble scene of peace and retirement, and not a blot and drawback in ambitious and distinguished crowds, I should have been spared this trial. I have every reason to be happy, very happy, now; but then, Harry, I own I should have been happier.'

Busy recollections of old hopes, cherished, as a girl, long ago, crowded into the mind of Rose while making this avowal; but they brought tears with them, as old hopes will when they come back withered, and they relieved her.

'I cannot help this weakness, and it makes my purpose stronger,' said Rose, extending her hand. 'I must leave you now, indeed.'

'I ask one promise,' said Harry. 'Once, and only once more – say within a year, but it may be much sooner – let me speak to you again on this subject, for the last time.'

'Not to press me to alter my right determination,' replied Rose, with a melancholy smile; 'it will be useless.'

'No,' said Harry; 'to hear you repeat it, if you will – finally repeat it! I will lay at your feet whatever of station or fortune I may possess; and if you still adhere to your present resolution, will not seek, by word or act, to change it.'

'Then let it be so,' rejoined Rose, 'it is but one pang the more, and by that time I may be enabled to bear it better.'

She extended her hand again. But the young man caught her to his bosom, and imprinting one kiss on her beautiful forehead, hurried from the room.

CHAPTER 36

Is a very short one, and may appear of no great importance in its place. But it should be read, notwithstanding, as a sequel to the last, and a key to one that will follow when its time arrives

'And so you are resolved to be my travelling companion this morning, eh?' said the doctor, as Harry Maylie joined him and Oliver at the breakfast-table. 'Why, you are not in the same mind or intention two half-hours together!'

'You will tell me a different tale one of these days,' said Harry, colouring without any perceptible reason.

'I hope I may have good cause to do so,' replied Mr Losberne, 'though I confess I don't think I shall. But yesterday morning you had made up your mind in a great hurry to stay here, and to accompany your mother, like a dutiful son, to the seaside. Before noon, you announce that you are going to do me the honour of accompanying me as far as I go, on your road to London. And at night you urge me, with great mystery, to start before the ladies are stirring; the consequence of which is, that young Oliver here is pinned down to his breakfast when he ought to be ranging the meadows after botanical phenomena of all kinds. Too bad, isn't it, Oliver?'

'I should have been very sorry not to have been at home when you and Mr Maylie went away, sir,' rejoined Oliver.

'That's a fine fellow,' said the doctor; 'you shall come and see me when you return. But to speak seriously, Harry; has any communication from the great nobs produced this sudden anxiety on your part to be gone?'

'The great nobs,' replied Harry – 'under which designation, I presume, you include my most stately uncle – have not communicated with me at all since I have been here; nor, at this time of the year, is it likely that anything would occur to render necessary my immediate attendance among them.'

'Well,' said the doctor, 'you are a queer fellow. But of course they will get you into parliament at the election before Christmas, and these sudden shiftings and changes are no bad preparation for political life. There's something in that. Good training is always desirable, whether the race be for place, cup, or sweepstakes.'

Harry Maylie looked as if he could have followed up this short dialogue by one or two remarks that would have staggered the doctor not a little; but he contented himself with saying, 'We shall see,' and pursued the subject no further. The post-chaise drove up to the door shortly afterwards, and Giles coming in for the luggage, the good doctor bustled out to see it packed.

'Oliver,' said Harry Maylie, in a low voice, 'let me speak a word with you.'

Oliver walked into the window-recess to which Mr Maylie beckoned him, much surprised at the mixture of sadness and boisterous spirits which his whole behaviour displayed.

'You can write well now?' said Harry, laying his hand upon his arm.

'I hope so, sir,' replied Oliver.

'I shall not be at home again, perhaps, for some time. I wish you would write to me – say once a fortnight, every alternate Monday – to the General Post Office in London. Will you?'

'Oh! certainly, sir; I shall be proud to do it,' exclaimed Oliver, greatly delighted with the commission.

'I should like to know how – how my mother and Miss Maylie are,' said the young man; 'and you can fill up a sheet by telling me what walks you take, and what you talk about, and whether she – they, I mean – seem happy and quite well. You understand me?'

'Oh! quite, sir, quite,' replied Oliver.

'I would rather you did not mention it to them,' said Harry, hurrying over these words; 'because it might make my mother anxious to write to me oftener, and it is a trouble and worry to her. Let it be a secret between you and me; and mind you tell me everything! I depend upon you.'

Oliver, quite elated and honoured by a sense of his importance, faithfully promised to be secret and explicit in his communications; and Mr Maylie took leave of him, with many warm assurances of his regard and protection.

The doctor was in the chaise; Giles (who, it had been arranged, should be left behind) held the door open in his hand; and the women-servants were in the garden, looking on. Harry cast one slight glance at the latticed window, and jumped into the carriage.

'Drive on!' he cried, 'hard, fast, full gallop! Nothing short of flying will keep pace with me today.'

'Hallo!' cried the doctor, letting down the front glass in a great hurry, and shouting to the postilion; 'something very short of flying will keep pace with me. Do you hear?'

Jingling and clattering, till distance rendered its noise inaudible, and its rapid progress only perceptible to the eye, the vehicle wound its way along the road, almost hidden in a cloud of dust, now wholly disappearing, and now becoming visible again, as intervening objects, or the intricacies of the way, permitted. It was not until even the dusty cloud was no longer to be seen that the gazers dispersed.

And there was one looker-on, who remained with eyes fixed upon the spot where the carriage had disappeared, long after it was many miles away; for, behind the white curtain which had shrouded her from view when Harry raised his eyes towards the window, sat Rose herself.

'He seems in high spirits and happy,' she said, at length. 'I feared for a time he might be otherwise. I was mistaken. I am very, very glad.'

Tears are signs of gladness as well as of grief; but those which coursed down Rose's face, as she sat pensively at the window, still gazing in the same direction, seemed to tell more of sorrow than of joy.

CHAPTER 37

In which the reader may perceive a contrast, not uncommon in matrimonial cases

Mr Bumble sat in the workhouse parlour, with his eyes moodily fixed on the cheerless grate, whence, as it was summer time, no brighter gleam proceeded than the reflection of certain sickly rays of the sun which were sent back from its cold and shining surface. A paper fly-cage dangled from the ceiling, to which he occasionally raised his eyes in gloomy thought; and, as the heedless insects hovered round the gaudy network, Mr Bumble would heave a deep sigh, while a more gloomy shadow overspread his countenance. Mr Bumble was meditating, and it might be that the insects brought to mind some painful passage in his own past life.

Nor was Mr Bumble's gloom the only thing calculated to awaken a pleasing melancholy in the bosom of a spectator. There were not wanting other appearances, and those closely connected with his own person, which announced that a great change had taken place in the position of his affairs. The laced coat, and the cocked hat, where were they? He still wore knee-breeches, and dark cotton stockings on his nether limbs; but they were not *the* breeches. The coat was wide-skirted, and in that respect like *the* coat; but, oh, how different! The mighty cocked-hat was replaced by a modest round one. Mr Bumble was no longer a beadle.

There are some promotions in life, which, independent of the more substantial rewards they offer, acquire peculiar value and dignity from the coats and waistcoats connected with them. A field-marshal has his uniform, a bishop his silk apron, a councillor his silk gown, a beadle his cocked-hat. Strip the bishop of his apron, or the beadle of his hat and lace; what are they? Men. Mere men. Dignity, and even holiness, too, sometimes, are more questions of coat and waistcoat than some people imagine.

Mr Bumble had married Mrs Corney, and was master of the workhouse. Another beadle had come into power, and on him the cocked-hat, gold-laced coat, and staff had all three descended.

'And tomorrow two months it was done!' said Mr Bumble, with a sigh. 'It seems a age.'

Mr Bumble might have meant that he had concentrated a whole existence of happiness into the short space of eight weeks; but the sigh – there was a vast deal of meaning in the sigh.

'I sold myself,' said Mr Bumble, pursuing the same train of reflection, 'for six teaspoons, a pair of sugar-tongs, and a milk-pot; with a small quantity of second-hand furniture, and twenty pound in money. I went very reasonable. Cheap, dirt cheap!'

'Cheap!' cried a shrill voice in Mr Bumble's ear; 'you would have been dear at any price; and dear enough I paid for you, Lord above knows that!'

Mr Bumble turned, and encountered the face of his interesting consort, who, imperfectly comprehending the few words she had overheard of his complaint, had hazarded the foregoing remark at a venture.

'Mrs Bumble, ma'am!' said Mr Bumble, with sentimental sternness.

'Well?' cried the lady.

'Have the goodness to look at me,' said Mr Bumble, fixing his eyes upon her.

'If she stands such a eye as that,' said Mr Bumble to himself, 'she can stand anything. It is a eye I never knew to fail with paupers; and if it fails with her, my power is gone.

Whether an exceedingly small expansion of eye be sufficient to quell paupers, who, being lightly fed, are in no very high condition, or whether the late Mrs Corney was particularly proof against eagle glances, are matters of opinion. The matter of fact is that the matron was in no way overpowered by Mr Bumble's scowl, but, on the contrary, treated it with great disdain, and even raised a laugh thereat, which sounded as though it were genuine.

On hearing this most unexpected sound, Mr Bumble looked first incredulous, and afterwards amazed. He then relapsed into his former state; nor did he rouse himself until his attention was again awakened by the voice of his partner.

'Are you going to sit snoring there all day?' enquired Mrs Bumble.

'I am going to sit here as long as I think proper, ma'am,' rejoined Mr Bumble; 'and although I was *not* snoring, I shall snore, gape, sneeze, laugh, or cry, as the humour strikes me, such being my prerogative.'

'Your prerogative!' sneered Mrs Bumble, with ineffable contempt.

'I said the word, ma'am,' observed Mr Bumble. 'The prerogative of a man is to command.'

'And what's the prerogative of a woman, in the name of goodness?' cried the relict of Mr Corney deceased.

'To obey, ma'am,' thundered Mr Bumble. 'Your late unfort'-nate husband should have taught it you; and then, perhaps, he might have been alive now. I wish he was, poor man!'

Mrs Bumble, seeing at a glance that the decisive moment had now arrived, and that a blow struck for the mastership, on one side or other, must necessarily be final and conclusive, no sooner heard this allusion to the dead and gone than she dropped into a chair, and with a loud scream that Mr Bumble was a hard-hearted brute, fell into a paroxysm of tears.

But tears were not the things to find their way to Mr Bumble's soul; his heart was waterproof. Like washable beaver hats that improve with rain, his nerves were rendered stouter and more vigorous by showers of tears, which, being tokens of weakness, and so far tacit admissions of his own power, pleased and exalted him. He eyed his good lady with looks of great satisfaction, and begged, in an encouraging manner, that she should cry her hardest; the exercise being looked upon, by the faculty, as strongly conducive to health.

'It opens the lungs, washes the countenance, exercises the eyes, and softens down the temper,' said Mr Bumble. 'So cry away!'

As he discharged himself of this pleasantry, Mr Bumble took

his hat from a peg, and putting it on, rather rakishly, on one side, as a man might who felt he had asserted his superiority in a becoming manner, thrust his hands into his pockets, and sauntered towards the door, with much ease and waggishness depicted on his whole appearance.

Now, Mrs Corney that was had tried the tears because they were less troublesome than a manual assault; but she was quite prepared to make trial of the latter mode of proceeding, as Mr Bumble was not long in discovering.

The first proof he experienced of the fact was conveyed in a hollow sound, immediately succeeded by the sudden flying off of his hat to the opposite end of the room. This preliminary proceeding laying bare his head, the expert lady, clasping him tightly round the throat with one hand, inflicted a shower of blows (dealt with singular vigour and dexterity) upon it with the other. This done, she created a little variety by scratching his face and tearing his hair off; and having, by this time, inflicted as much punishment as she deemed necessary for the offence, she pushed him over a chair, which was luckily well situated for the purpose; and defied him to talk about his prerogative again, if he dared.

'Get up!' said Mrs Bumble, in a voice of command, 'and take yourself away from here, unless you want me to do something desperate.'

Mr Bumble rose with a very rueful countenance, wondering much what something desperate might be; and picking up his hat, looked towards the door.

'Are you going?' demanded Mrs Bumble.

'Certainly, my dear, certainly,' rejoined Mr Bumble, making a quicker motion towards the door. 'I didn't intend to – I'm going, my dear! You are so very violent that really I – '

At this instant Mrs Bumble stepped hastily forward to replace the carpet, which had been kicked up in the scuffle. Mr Bumble immediately darted out of the room, without bestowing another thought on his unfinished sentence, leaving the late Mrs Corney in full possession of the field.

Mr Bumble was fairly taken by surprise, and fairly beaten. He had a decided propensity for bullying; derived no inconsiderable pleasure from the exercise of petty cruelty; and, consequently, was (it is needless to say) a coward. This is by no means a disparagement to his character; for many official personages, who are held in high respect and admiration, are the victims of similar infirmities. The remark is made, indeed, rather in his favour than otherwise, and with a view of impressing the reader with a just sense of his qualifications for office.

But the measure of his degradation was not yet full. After making a tour of the house, and thinking for the first time that the poor-laws really were too hard on people, and that men who ran away from their wives, leaving them chargeable to the parish, ought, in justice, to be visited with no punishment at all, but rather rewarded as meritorious individuals who had suffered much, Mr Bumble came to a room where some of the female paupers were usually employed in washing the parish linen, and whence the sound of voices in conversation now proceeded.

'Hem!' said Mr Bumble, summoning up all his native dignity.

'These women at least shall continue to respect the prerogative. – Hallo! hallo there! What do you mean by this noise, you hussies?'

With these words Mr Bumble opened the door, and walked in with a very fierce and angry manner; which was at once exchanged for a most humiliated and cowering air, as his eyes unexpectedly rested on the form of his lady wife.

'My dear,' said Mr Bumble, 'I didn't know you were here.'

'Didn't know I was here!' repeated Mrs Bumble. 'What do *you* do here?'

'I thought they were talking rather too much to be doing their work properly, my dear,' replied Mr Bumble, glancing distractedly at a couple of old women at the wash-tub, who were comparing notes of admiration at the workhouse-master's humility.

'*You* thought they were talking too much?' said Mrs Bumble. 'What business is it of yours?'

'Why, my dear – ' urged Mr Bumble submissively.

'What business is it of yours?' demanded Mrs Bumble again.

'It's very true, you're matron here, my dear,' submitted Mr Bumble; 'but I thought you mightn't be in the way just then.'

'I'll tell you what, Mr Bumble,' returned his lady, 'we don't want any of your interference. You're a great deal too fond of poking your nose into things that don't concern you, making everybody in the house laugh the moment your back is turned, and making yourself look like a fool every hour in the day. Be off! come!'

Mr Bumble, seeing with excruciating feelings the delight of the two old paupers, who were tittering together most rapturously, hesitated for an instant. Mrs Bumble, whose patience brooked no delay, caught up a bowl of soapsuds, and motioning him towards the door, ordered him instantly to depart, on pain of receiving the contents upon his portly person.

What could Mr Bumble do? He looked dejectedly round, and slunk away, and as he reached the door, the titterings of the paupers broke into a shrill chuckle of irrepressible delight. It wanted but this. He was degraded in their eyes; he had lost caste and station before the very paupers; he had fallen from all the height and pomp of beadleship to the lowest depth of the most snubbed henpeckery.

'All in two months!' said Mr Bumble, filled with dismal thoughts. 'Two months! No more than two months ago I was not only my own master, but everybody else's, so far as the porochial workhouse was concerned, and now – '

It was too much. Mr Bumble boxed the ears of the boy who opened the gate for him (for he had reached the portal in his reverie), and walked distractedly into the street.

He walked up one street, and down another, until exercise had abated the first passion of his grief; and then the revulsion of feeling made him thirsty. He passed a great many public-houses, and at length paused before one in a byway, whose parlour, as he gathered from a hasty peep over the blinds, was deserted, save by one solitary customer. It began to rain heavily at the moment. This determined him. Mr Bumble stepped in, and ordering something to drink as he passed the bar, entered the apartment into which he had looked from the street.

The man who was seated there was tall and dark, and wore a large cloak. He had the air of a stranger, and seemed, by a certain haggardness in his look, as well as by the dusty soils on his dress, to have travelled some distance. He eyed Bumble askance as he entered, but scarcely deigned to nod his head in acknowledgment of his salutation.

Mr Bumble had quite dignity enough for two - supposing even that the stranger had been more familiar – so he drank his gin-and-water in silence, and read the paper with great show of pomp and circumstance.

It so happened, however – as it will happen very often, when men fall into company under such circumstances – that Mr Bumble felt, every now and then, a powerful inducement, which he could not resist, to steal a look at the stranger; and that whenever he did so, he withdrew his eyes, in some confusion, to find that the stranger was at that moment stealing a look at him. Mr Bumble's awkwardness was enhanced by the very remarkable expression of the stranger's eye, which was keen and bright, but shadowed by a scowl of distrust and suspicion, unlike anything he had ever observed before, and most repulsive to behold.

When they had encountered each other's glance several times in this way, the stranger, in a harsh, deep voice, broke silence.

'Were you looking for me,' he said, 'when you peered in at the window?'

'Not that I am aware of, unless you're Mr – ' Here Mr Bumble stopped short, for he was curious to know the stranger's name, and thought, in his impatience, he might supply the blank.

'I see you were not,' said the stranger, an expression of quiet sarcasm playing about his mouth, 'or you would have known

Mr Bumble degraded in the eyes of the paupers

my name. You don't know it. I would recommend you not to enquire.'

'I meant no harm, young man,' observed Mr Bumble, majestically.

'And have done none,' said the stranger.

Another silence succeeded this short dialogue, which was again broken by the stranger.

'I have seen you before, I think,' said he. 'You were differently dressed at that time, and I only passed you in the street, but I should know you again. You were beadle here once; were you not?'

'I was,' said Mr Bumble, in some surprise; 'porochial beadle.'

'Just so,' rejoined the other, nodding his head. 'It was in that character I saw you. What are you now?'

'Master of the workhouse,' rejoined Mr Bumble, slowly and impressively, to check any undue familiarity the stranger might otherwise assume. 'Master of the workhouse, young man!'

'You have the same eye to your own interest that you always had, I doubt not!' resumed the stranger, looking keenly into Mr Bumble's eyes, as he raised them in astonishment at the question. 'Don't scruple to answer freely, man. I know you pretty well, you see.'

'I suppose a married man,' replied Mr Bumble, shading his eyes with his hand, and surveying the stranger from head to foot, in evident perplexity, 'is not more averse to turning an honest penny when he can than a single one. Porochial officers are not so well paid that they can afford to refuse any little extra fee when it comes to them in a civil and proper manner.'

The stranger smiled, and nodded his head again, as much as to say he had not mistaken his man; then rang the bell.

'Fill this glass again,' he said, handing Mr Bumble's empty tumbler to the landlord. 'Let it be strong and hot. You like it so, I suppose?'

'Not too strong,' replied Mr Bumble, with a delicate cough.

'You understand what that means, landlord!' said the stranger dryly.

The host smiled, disappeared, and shortly afterwards returned with a steaming jorum, of which the first gulp brought the water into Mr Bumble's eyes.

'Now listen to me,' said the stranger, after closing the door and window. 'I came down to this place today to find you out, and by one of those chances which the devil throws in the way of his friends sometimes, you walked into the very room I was sitting in while you were uppermost in my mind. I want some information from you. I don't ask you to give it for nothing, slight as it is. Put up that to begin with.'

As he spoke he pushed a couple of sovereigns across the table to his companion carefully, as though unwilling that the chinking of money should be heard without. When Mr Bumble had scrupulously examined the coins, to see that they were genuine, and had put them up, with much satisfaction, in his waistcoat pocket, he went on: 'Carry your memory back – let me see – twelve years, last winter.'

'It's a long time,' said Mr Bumble. 'Very good. I've done it.'

'The scene, the workhouse.'

'Good!'

'And the time, night.'

'Yes.'

'And the place, the crazy hole, wherever it was, in which miserable drabs brought forth the life and health so often denied to themselves – gave birth to puling children for the parish to rear; and hid their shame, rot 'em, in the grave!'

'The lying-in room, I suppose?' said Mr Bumble, not quite following the stranger's excited description.

'Yes,' said the stranger. 'A boy was born there.'

'A many boys,' observed Mr Bumble, shaking his head, despondingly.

'A murrain on the young devils!' cried the stranger. 'I speak of one; a meek-looking, pale-faced hound, who was apprenticed down here to a coffin-maker – I wish he had made his coffin, and screwed his body in it – and who afterwards ran away to London, as it was supposed.'

'Why, you mean Oliver! – young Twist!' said Mr Bumble; 'I remember him, of course. There wasn't a obstinater young rascal –'

'It's not of him I want to hear; I've heard enough of him,' said the stranger, stopping Mr Bumble in the very outset of a tirade on the subject of poor Oliver's vices. 'It's of a woman; the hag that nursed his mother. Where is she?'

'Where is she?' said Mr Bumble, whom the gin-and-water had rendered facetious. 'It would be hard to tell. There's no midwifery there, whichever place she's gone to; so I suppose she's out of employment, any way.'

'What do you mean?' demanded the stranger, sternly.

'That she died last winter,' rejoined Mr Bumble.

The man looked fixedly at him when he had given this information, and although he did not withdraw his eyes for some time afterwards, his gaze gradually became vacant and abstracted, and he seemed lost in thought. For some time he appeared doubtful whether he ought to be relieved or disappointed by the intelligence; but at length he breathed more freely, and withdrawing his eyes, observed that it was no great matter. With that he rose as if to depart.

But Mr Bumble was cunning enough, and he at once saw that an opportunity was open for the lucrative disposal of some secret in the possession of his better-half. He well remembered the night of old Sally's death, which the occurrences of that day had given him good reason to recollect as the occasion on which he had proposed to Mrs Corney; and although that lady had never confided to him the disclosure of which she had been the solitary witness, he had heard enough to know that it related to something that had occurred in the old woman's attendance, as workhouse nurse, upon the young mother of Oliver Twist. Hastily calling this circumstance to mind, he informed the stranger, with an air of mystery, that one woman had been closeted with the old harridan shortly before she died, and that she could, as he had reason to believe, throw some light on the subject of his enquiry.

'How can I find her?' said the stranger, thrown off his guard, and plainly showing that all his fears (whatever they were) were aroused afresh by the intelligence.

'Only through me,' rejoined Mr Bumble.

'When?' cried the stranger hastily.

'Tomorrow,' rejoined Bumble.

'At nine in the evening,' said the stranger, producing a scrap of paper, and writing down upon it an obscure address by the waterside, in characters that betrayed his agitation; 'at nine in the evening bring her to me there. I needn't tell you to be secret. It's your interest.'

With these words he led the way to the door, after stopping to pay for the liquor that had been drunk; and shortly remarking that their roads were different, departed, without more ceremony than an emphatic repetition of the hour of appointment for the following night.

On glancing at the address, the parochial functionary observed that it contained no name. The stranger had not gone far, so he made after him to ask it.

'What do you want?' cried the man, turning quickly round, as Bumble touched him on the arm – 'following me!'

'Only to ask a question,' said the other, pointing to the scrap of paper. 'What name am I to ask for?'

'Monks!' rejoined the man, and strode hastily away.

CHAPTER 38

Containing an account of what passed between Mr and Mrs Bumble, and Monks, at their nocturnal interview

It was a dull, close, overcast summer evening, and the clouds, which had been threatening all day, spread out in a dense and sluggish mass of vapour, already yielded large drops of rain, and seemed to presage a violent thunderstorm, when Mr and Mrs Bumble, turning out of the main street of the town, directed their course towards a scattered little colony of ruinous houses, distant from it some mile and a half, or thereabouts, and erected on a low unwholesome swamp bordering upon the river.

They were both wrapped in old and shabby outer garments, which might, perhaps, serve the double purpose of protecting their persons from the rain and sheltering them from observation. The husband carried a lantern, from which, however, no light yet shone; and trudged on, a few paces in front, as though – the way being dirty – to give his wife the benefit of treading in his heavy footprints. They went on in profound silence. Every now and then Mr Bumble relaxed his pace, and turned his head as if to make sure that his helpmate was following; then, discovering that she was close at his heels, he mended his rate of walking, and proceeded, at a considerable increase of speed, towards their place of destination.

This was far from being a place of doubtful character; for it had long been known as the residence of none but low and desperate ruffians, who, under various pretences of living by their labour, subsisted chiefly on plunder and crime. It was a collection of mere hovels – some, hastily built with loose bricks; others, of old worm-eaten ship timber – jumbled together without any attempt at order or arrangement, and planted, for the most part, within a few feet of the river's bank. A few leaky boats drawn up on the mud, and made fast to the dwarf-wall which skirted it, and here and there an oar or coil of rope, appeared, at first, to indicate that the inhabitants of these miserable cottages pursued some avocation on the river; but a glance at the shattered and useless condition of the articles thus displayed would have led a passer-by, without much difficulty, to the conjecture that they were disposed there rather for the preservation of appearances than with any view to their being actually employed.

In the heart of this cluster of huts, and skirting the river, which its upper stories overhung, stood a large building, formerly used as a manufactory of some kind, and which had, in its day, probably furnished employment to the inhabitants of the surrounding tenements. But it had long since gone to ruin. The rat, the worm, and the action of the damp, had weakened and rotted the piles on which it stood, and a considerable portion of the building had already sunk down into the water beneath; while the remainder, tottering and bending over the dark stream, seemed to wait a favourable opportunity of following its old companion, and involving itself in the same fate.

It was before this ruinous building that the worthy couple paused, as the first peal of distant thunder reverberated in the air, and the rain commenced pouring violently down.

'The place should be somewhere here,' said Bumble, consulting a scrap of paper he held in his hand.

'Hallo there!' cried a voice from above.

Following the sound, Mr Bumble raised his head, and descried a man looking out of a door, breast-high, on the second story.

'Stand still a minute,' cried the voice; 'I'll be with you directly.' With which the head disappeared, and the door closed.

'Is that the man?' asked Mr Bumble's good lady.

Mr Bumble nodded in the affirmative.

'Then, mind what I told you,' said the matron, 'and be careful to say as little as you can, or you'll betray us at once.'

Mr Bumble, who had eyed the building with very rueful looks, was apparently about to express some doubts relative to the advisability of proceeding any further with the enterprise just then, when he was prevented by the appearance of Monks, who opened a small door, near which they stood, and beckoned them inwards.

'Come!' he cried impatiently, stamping his foot upon the ground, 'don't keep me here!'

The woman, who had hesitated at first, walked boldly in, without any further invitation. Mr Bumble, who was ashamed or afraid to lag behind, followed, obviously very ill at ease, and with scarcely any of that remarkable dignity which was usually his chief characteristic

'What the devil made you stand lingering there in the wet?' said Monks, turning round, and addressing Bumble, after he had bolted the door behind them.

'We – we were only cooling ourselves,' stammered Bumble, looking apprehensively about him.

'Cooling yourselves!' retorted Monks. 'Not all the rain that ever fell, or ever will fall, will put as much of hell's fire out as a man can carry about with him. You won't cool yourself so easily; don't think it!'

With this agreeable speech, Monks turned short upon the matron and bent his fierce gaze upon her, till even she, who was not easily cowed, was fain to withdraw her eyes, and turn them towards the ground.

'This is the woman, is it?' demanded Monks.

'Hem! That is the woman,' replied Mr Bumble, mindful of his wife's caution.

'You think women never can keep secrets, I suppose?' s aid the matron, interposing, and returning, as she spoke, the searching look of Monks.

'I know they will always keep *one* till it's found out,' said Monks contemptuously.

'And what may that be?' asked the matron in the same tone.

'The loss of their own good name,' replied Monks. 'So by the same rule, if a woman's a party to a secret that might hang or transport her, I'm not afraid of her telling it to anybody; not I! Do you understand me?'

'No,' rejoined the matron, slightly colouring as she spoke.

'Of course you don't!' said Monks. 'How should you?'

Bestowing something halfway between a smile and a scowl upon his two companions, and again beckoning them to follow him, the man hastened across the apartment, which was of considerable extent, but low in the roof. He was preparing to ascend a steep staircase, or rather ladder, leading to another floor of warehouses above, when a bright flash of lightning streamed down the aperture, and a peal of thunder followed, which shook the crazy building to its centre.

'Hear it!' he cried, shrinking back – 'hear it! Rolling and crashing on as if it echoed through a thousand caverns where the devils were hiding from it. I hate the sound!'

He remained silent for a few moments, and then, removing his hands suddenly from his face, showed, to the unspeakable discomposure of Mr Bumble, that it was much distorted and discoloured.

'These fits come over me now and then,' said Monks, observing his alarm; 'and thunder sometimes brings them on. Don't mind me now; it's all over for this once.'

Thus speaking, he led the way up the ladder, and hastily closing the window-shutter of the room into which it led, lowered a lantern which hung at the end of a rope and pulley passed through one of the heavy beams in the ceiling, and which cast a dim light upon an old table and three chairs that were placed beneath it.

'Now,' said Monks, when they had all three seated themselves, 'the sooner we come to our business the better for all. The woman knows what it is; does she?'

The question was addressed to Bumble; but his wife anticipated the reply, by intimating that she was perfectly acquainted with it.

'He is right in saying that you were with this hag the night she died, and that she told you something –'

'About the mother of the boy you named,' replied the matron, interrupting him. 'Yes.'

'The first question is, of what nature was her communication?' said Monks.

'That's the second,' observed the woman, with much deliberation. 'The first is, what may the communication be worth?'

'Who the devil can tell that without knowing of what kind it is?' asked Monks.

'Nobody better than you, I am persuaded,' answered Mrs Bumble, who did not want for spirit, as her yokefellow could abundantly testify.

'Humph!' said Monks significantly, and with a look of eager enquiry; 'there may be money's worth to get, eh?'

'Perhaps there may,' was the composed reply.

'Something that was taken from her,' said Monks. 'Something that she wore – something that –'

'You had better bid,' interrupted Mrs Bumble. 'I have heard enough, already, to assure me that you are the man I ought to talk to.'

Mr Bumble, who had not yet been admitted by his better-half into any greater share of the secret than he had originally possessed, listened to this dialogue with outstretched neck and distended eyes, which he directed towards his wife and Monks, by turns, in undisguised astonishment; increased, if possible, when the latter sternly demanded what sum was required for the disclosure.

'What's it worth to you?' asked the woman, as collectedly as before.

'It may be nothing; it may be twenty pounds,' replied Monks. 'Speak out, and let me know which.'

'Add five pounds to the sum you have named. Give me five-and-twenty pounds in gold,' said the woman, 'and I'll tell you all I know. Not before.'

'Five-and-twenty pounds!' exclaimed Monks, drawing back.

'I spoke as plainly as I could,' replied Mrs Bumble. 'It's not a large sum either.'

'Not a large sum for a paltry secret, that may be nothing when it's told!' cried Monks impatiently, 'and which has been lying dead for twelve years past or more!'

'Such matters keep well, and, like good wine, often double their value in course of time,' answered the matron, still preserving the resolute indifference she had assumed. 'As to lying dead, there are those who will lie dead for twelve thousand years to come, or twelve million, for anything you or I know, who will tell strange tales at last!'

'What if I pay it for nothing?' asked Monks, hesitating.

'You can easily take it away again,' replied the matron. 'I am but a woman – alone here, and unprotected.'

'Not alone, my dear, nor unprotected neither,' submitted Mr Bumble, in a voice tremulous with fear; '*I* am here, my dear. And besides,' said Mr Bumble, his teeth chattering as he spoke, 'Mr Monks is too much of a gentleman to attempt any violence on porochial persons. Mr Monks is aware that I am not a young man, my dear, and also that I am a little run to seed, as I may say; but he had heerd – I say I have no doubt Mr Monks has heerd, my dear, that I am a very determined officer, with very uncommon strength, if I'm once roused. I only want a little rousing; that's all.'

As Mr Bumble spoke, he made a melancholy feint of grasping his lantern with fierce determination, and plainly showed, by the alarmed expression of every feature, that he *did* want a little rousing, and not a little, prior to making any very warlike demonstration – unless, indeed, against paupers, or other person or persons trained down for the purpose.

'You are a fool,' said Mrs Bumble in reply, 'and had better hold your tongue.'

'He had better have cut it out before he came if he can't speak in a lower tone,' said Monks grimly. 'So! he's your husband, eh?'

'He my husband!' tittered the matron, parrying the question.

'I thought as much when you came in,' rejoined Monks, marking the angry glance which the lady darted at her spouse as she spoke. 'So much the better; I have less hesitation in dealing with two people, when I find that there's only one will between them. I'm in earnest. See here!'

He thrust his hand into a side-pocket, and producing a canvas bag, told out twenty-five sovereigns on the table, and pushed them over to the woman.

'Now,' he said, 'gather them up; and when this cursed peal of thunder, which I feel is coming up to break over the house-top, is gone, let's hear your story.'

The thunder – which seemed in fact much nearer, and to shiver and break almost over their heads – having subsided, Monks, raising his face from the table, bent forward to listen to what the woman should say. The faces of the three nearly touched, as the two men leant over the small table in their eagerness to hear, and the woman also leant forward to render her whisper audible. The sickly rays of the suspended lantern, falling directly upon them, aggravated the paleness and anxiety of their countenances, which, encircled by the deepest gloom and darkness, looked ghastly in the extreme.

'When this woman, that we called old Sally, died,' the matron began, 'she and I were alone.'

'Was there no one by?' asked Monks, in the same hollow whisper – 'no sick wretch or idiot in some other bed? No one who could hear, and might, by possibility, understand?'

'Not a soul,' replied the woman; 'we were alone. *I* stood alone beside the body when death came over it.'

'Good,' said Monks, regarding her attentively. 'Go on.'

'She spoke of a young creature,' resumed the matron, 'who had brought a child into the world some years before, not merely in the same room, but in the same bed in which she then lay dying.'

'Ay?' said Monks, with quivering lip, and glancing over his shoulder. 'Blood! How things come about!'

'The child was the one you named to him last night,' said the matron, nodding carelessly towards her husband; 'the mother this nurse had robbed.'

'In life?' asked Monks.

'In death,' replied the woman, with something like a shudder. 'She stole from the corpse, when it had hardly turned to one, that which the dead mother had prayed her, with her last breath, to keep for the infant's sake.'

'She sold it?' cried Monks, with desperate eagerness; 'did she sell it? Where? When? To whom? How long before?'

'As she told me, with great difficulty, that she had done this,' said the matron, 'she fell back and died.'

'Without saying more?' cried Monks, in a voice which, from its very suppression, seemed only the more furious, 'It's a lie! I'll not be played with. She said more. I'll tear the life out of you both, but I'll know what it was.'

'She didn't utter another word,' said the woman, to all appearance unmoved (as Mr Bumble was very far from being) by the strange man's violence; 'but she clutched my gown violently with one hand, which was partly closed; and when I saw that she was dead, and so removed the hand by force, I found it clasped a scrap of dirty paper.'

'Which contained –' interposed Monks, stretching forward.

'Nothing,' replied the woman; 'it was a pawnbroker's duplicate.'

'For what?' demanded Monks.

'In good time I'll tell you,' said the woman. 'I judge that she had kept the trinket for some time, in the hope of turning it to better account; and then had pawned it, and had saved or scraped together money to pay the pawnbroker's interest year by year, and prevent its running out, so that if anything came of it, it could still be redeemed. Nothing had come of it; and, as I tell you, she died with the scrap of paper, all worn and tattered, in her hand. The time was out in two days. I thought something might one day come of it, too, and so redeemed the pledge.'

'Where is it now?' asked Monks, quickly.

'*There!*' replied the woman. And, as if glad to be relieved of it, she hastily threw upon the table a small kid bag, scarcely large enough for a French watch, which Monks pouncing upon, tore open with trembling hands. It contained a little gold locket, in which were two locks of hair, and a plain gold wedding-ring.

'It has the word "Agnes" engraved on the inside,' said the woman. 'There is a blank left for the surname; and then follows the date, which is within a year before the child was born. I found out that.'

'And this is all,' said Monks, after a close and eager scrutiny of the contents of the little packet.

'All,' replied the woman.

Mr Bumble drew a long breath, as if he were glad to find that the story was over, and no mention made of taking the five-and-twenty pounds back again; and now he took courage to wipe off the perspiration, which had been trickling over his nose unchecked during the whole of the previous dialogue.

'I know nothing of the story beyond what I can guess at,' said his wife, addressing Monks, after a short silence; 'and I want to know nothing, for it's safer not. But I may ask you two questions, may I?'

'You may ask,' said Monks, with some show of surprise; 'but whether I answer or not is another question.'

' – Which makes three,' observed Mr Bumble, essaying a stroke of facetiousness.

'Is that what you expected to get from me?' demanded the matron.

'It is,' replied Monks. 'The other question?'

'What you propose to do with it? Can it be used against me?'

'Never,' rejoined Monks; 'nor against me either. See here! But don't move a step forward, or your life's not worth a bulrush!'

With these words he suddenly wheeled the table aside, and pulling an iron ring in the boarding, threw back a large trap-door, which opened close at Mr Bumble's feet, and caused that gentleman to retire several paces backward with great precipitation.

'Look down,' said Monks, lowering the lantern into the gulf. 'Don't fear me. I could have let you down, quietly enough, when you were seated over it, if that had been my game.'

Thus encouraged, the matron drew near to the brink; and even Mr Bumble himself, impelled by curiosity, ventured to do the same. The turbid water, swollen by the heavy rain, was rushing rapidly on below; and all other sounds were lost in the noise of its plashing and eddying against the green and slimy piles. There had once been a water-mill beneath; and the tide, foaming and chafing round the few rotten stakes and fragments of machinery that yet remained, seemed to dart onward with a new impulse when freed from the obstacles which had unavailingly attempted to stem its headlong course.

'If you flung a man's body down there, where would it be tomorrow morning?' said Monks, swinging the lantern to and fro in the dark well.

'Twelve miles down the river, and cut to pieces besides,' replied Bumble, recoiling at the very thought.

Monks drew the little packet from his breast, where he had hurriedly thrust it, and tying it to a leaden weight, which had formed a part of some pulley, and was lying on the floor, dropped it into the stream. It fell straight and true as a die, clove the water with a scarcely audible splash, and was gone.

The three, looking into each other's faces, seemed to breathe more freely.

'There!' said Monks, closing the trap-door, which fell heavily back into its former position. 'If the sea ever gives up its dead, as books say it will, it will keep its gold and silver to itself, and that trash among it. We have nothing more to say, and may break up our pleasant party.'

'By all means,' observed Mr Bumble, with great alacrity.

'You'll keep a quiet tongue in your head; will you?' said Monks, with a threatening look. 'I am not afraid of your wife.'

'You may depend upon me, young man,' answered Mr Bumble, bowing himself gradually towards the ladder, with excessive politeness. 'On everybody's account, young man; on my own, you know, Mr Monks.'

'I am glad, for your sake, to hear it,' remarked Monks. 'Light your lantern, and get away from here as fast as you can.'

It was fortunate that the conversation terminated at this point, or Mr Bumble, who had bowed himself to within six inches of the ladder, would infallibly have pitched headlong into the room below. He lighted his lantern from that which Mr Monks had detached from the rope, and now carried in his hand; and making no effort to prolong the discourse, descended in silence, followed by his wife. Monks brought up the rear, after pausing on the steps to satisfy himself that there were no other sounds to be heard than the beating of the rain without and the rushing of the water.

They traversed the lower room, slowly, and with caution, for Monks started at every shadow; and Mr Bumble, holding his lantern a foot above the ground, walked not only with remarkable care, but a marvellously light step for a gentleman of his figure, looking nervously about him for hidden trap-doors. The gate at which they had entered was softly unfastened and opened by Monks; and, merely exchanging a nod with their mysterious acquaintance, the married couple emerged into the wet and darkness outside.

They were no sooner gone than Monks, who appeared to entertain invincible repugnance to being left alone, called to a boy who had been hidden somewhere below; and bidding him go first, and bear the light, returned to the chamber he had just quitted.

CHAPTER 39

Introduces some respectable characters with whom the reader is already acquainted, and shows how Monks and the Jew laid their worthy heads together

On the evening following that upon which the three worthies mentioned in the last chapter disposed of their little matter of business as therein narrated, Mr William Sikes, awakening from a nap, drowsily growled forth an enquiry what time of night it was.

The room in which Mr Sikes propounded this question was not one of those he had tenanted previous to the Chertsey

The evidence destroyed

expedition, although it was in the same quarter of the town, and was situated at no great distance from his former lodgings. It was not, in appearance, so desirable a habitation as his old quarters, being a mean and badly-furnished apartment, of very limited size, lighted only by one small window in the shelving roof, and abutting on a close and dirty lane. Nor were there wanting other indications of the good gentleman's having gone down in the world of late; for a great scarcity of furniture, and total absence of comfort, together with the disappearance of all such small movables as spare clothes and linen, bespoke a state of extreme poverty; while the meagre and attenuated condition of Mr Sikes himself would have fully confirmed these symptoms, if they had stood in any need of corroboration.

The housebreaker was lying on the bed, wrapped in his white greatcoat, by way of dressing-gown, and displaying a set of features in no degree improved by the cadaverous hue of illness and the addition of a soiled nightcap, and a stiff black beard of a week's growth. The dog sat at the bedside; now eyeing his master with a wistful look and now pricking his ears and uttering a low growl as some noise in the street, or in the lower part of the house, attracted his attention. Seated by the window, busily engaged in patching an old waistcoat, which formed a portion of the robber's ordinary dress, was a female, so pale and reduced with watching and privation, that there would have been considerable difficulty in recognising her as the same Nancy who has already figured in this tale, but for the voice in which she replied to Mr Sikes's question.'

'Not long gone seven,' said the girl. 'How do you feel tonight, Bill?'

'As weak as water,' replied Mr Sikes, with an imprecation on his eyes and limbs. 'Here; lend us a hand, and let me get off this thundering bed anyhow.'

Illness had not improved Mr Sikes's temper; for, as the girl raised him up, and led him to a chair, he muttered various curses on her awkwardness, and struck her.

'Whining, are you?' said Sikes. 'Come! Don't stand snivelling there. If you can't do anything better than that, cut off altogether. D'ye hear me?'

'I hear you,' replied the girl, turning her face aside and forcing a laugh. 'What fancy have you got into your head now?'

'Oh! you've thought better of it, have you?' growled Sikes, marking the tears which trembled in her eye. 'All the better for you, you have.'

'Why, you don't mean to say you'd be hard upon me tonight, Bill?' said the girl, laying her hand upon his shoulder.

'No!' cried Mr Sikes. 'Why not?'

'Such a number of nights,' said the girl, with a touch of woman's tenderness, which communicated something like sweetness of tone even to her voice – 'such a number of nights as I've been patient with you, nursing and caring for you, as if you had been a child; and this the first that I've seen you like yourself: you wouldn't have served me as you did just now if you'd thought of that, would you? Come, come; say you wouldn't.'

'Well, then,' rejoined Mr Sikes, 'I wouldn't. Why, damn me, now, the girl's whining again!'

'It's nothing,' said the girl, throwing herself into a chair. 'Don't you seem to mind me. It'll soon be over.'

'What'll be over?' demanded Mr Sikes in a savage voice. 'What foolery are you up to now, again? Get up, and bustle about, and don't come over me with your woman's nonsense.'

At any other time this remonstrance, and the tone in which it was delivered, would have had the desired effect; but the girl, being really weak and exhausted, dropped her head over the back of the chair, and fainted, before Mr Sikes could get out a few of the appropriate oaths with which, on similar occasions, he was accustomed to garnish his threats. Not knowing, very well, what to do in this uncommon emergency – for Miss Nancy's hysterics were usually of that violent kind which the patient fights and struggles out of without much assistance – Mr Sikes tried a little blasphemy; and finding that mode of treatment wholly ineffectual, called for assistance.

'What's the matter here, my dear?' said the Jew, looking in.

'Lend a hand to the girl, can't you?' replied Sikes, impatiently. 'Don't stand chattering and grinning at me!'

With an exclamation of surprise, Fagin hastened to the girl's assistance, while Mr John Dawkins (otherwise the Artful Dodger), who had followed his venerable friend into the room, hastily deposited on the floor a bundle with which he was laden, and snatching a bottle from the grasp of Master Charles Bates, who came close at his heels, uncorked it in a twinkling with his teeth, and poured a portion of its contents down the patient's throat, previously taking a taste himself to prevent mistakes.

'Give her a whiff of fresh air with the bellows, Charley,' said Mr Dawkins; 'and you slap her hands, Fagin, while Bill undoes the petticuts.'

These united restoratives, administered with great energy, especially that department consigned to Master Bates, who appeared to consider his share in the proceedings a piece of unexampled pleasantry, were not long in producing the desired effect. The girl gradually recovered her senses; and, staggering to a chair by the bedside, hid her face upon the pillow, leaving Mr Sikes to confront the newcomers, in some astonishment at their unlooked-for appearance.

'Why, what evil wind has blowed you here?' he asked of Fagin.

'No evil wind at all, my dear,' replied the Jew; 'for evil winds blow nobody any good, and I've brought something good with me that you'll be glad to see. Dodger, my dear, open the bundle, and give Bill the little trifles that we spent all our money on this morning.'

In compliance with Mr Fagin's request, the Artful untied his bundle, which was of large size, and formed of an old table-cloth; and handed the articles it contained, one by one, to Charley Bates, who placed them on the table with various encomiums on their rarity and excellence.

'Sitch a rabbit pie, Bill,' exclaimed that young gentleman, disclosing to view a huge pasty; 'sitch delicate creeturs, with sitch tender limbs, Bill, that the wery bones melt in your mouth, and there's no occasion to pick 'em; half a pound of seven-and-sixpenny green, so precious strong that if you mix it with biling water, it'll go nigh to blow the lid of the teapot off; a pound and a half of moist sugar that the niggers didn't work at all at, afore they got it up to sitch a pitch of goodness – oh, no! Two half-quartern brans; pound of best fresh; piece of double Glo'ster; and, to wind up all, some of the richest sort you ever lushed!'

Uttering this last panegyric, Master Bates produced, from one of his extensive pockets, a full-sized wine-bottle, carefully corked; while Mr Dawkins, at the same instant, poured out a wine-glassful of raw spirits from the bottle he carried, which the invalid tossed down his throat without a moment's hesitation.

'Ah!' said the Jew, rubbing his hands with great satisfaction, 'you'll do, Bill; you'll do now.'

'Do!' exclaimed Mr Sikes; 'I might have been done for twenty times over afore you'd have done anything to help me. What do you mean by leaving a man in this state three weeks and more, you false-hearted wagabond?'

'Only hear him, boys!' said the Jew, shrugging his shoulders. 'And us come to bring him all these beau-ti-ful things.'

'The things is well enough in their way,' observed Mr Sikes, a little soothed as he glanced over the table; 'but what have you got to say for yourself, why you should leave me here, down in the mouth, health, blunt, and everything else, and take no more notice of me, all this mortal time, than if I was that 'ere dog. – Drive him down, Charley!'

'I never see such a jolly dog as that,' cried Master Bates, doing as he was desired. 'Smelling the grub like an old lady a-going to market! He'd make his fortun' on the stage, that dog would, and revive the drayma besides.'

Mr Fagin and his pupil recovering Nancy

'Hold your din,' cried Sikes, as the dog retreated under the bed, still growling angrily. 'What have you got to say for yourself, you withered old fence, eh?'

'I was away from London a week and more, my dear, on a plant,' replied the Jew.

'And what about the other fortnight?' demanded Sikes. 'What about the other fortnight that you've left me lying here, like a sick rat in his hole?'

'I couldn't help it, Bill,' replied the Jew. 'I can't go into a long explanation before company; but I couldn't help it, upon my honour.'

'Upon your what?' growled Sikes, with excessive disgust. 'Here! Cut me off a piece of that pie, one of you boys, to take the taste of that out of my mouth, or it'll choke me dead.'

'Don't be out of temper, my dear,' urged the Jew, submissively. 'I have never forgot you, Bill – never once.'

'No? I'll pound it that you ha'n't,' replied Sikes, with a bitter grin. 'You've been scheming and plotting away, every hour that I have laid shivering and burning here; and Bill was to do this, and Bill was to do that, and Bill was to do it all, dirt cheap, as soon as he got well, and was quite poor enough for your work! If it hadn't been for the girl I might have died.'

'There now, Bill,' remonstrated the Jew, eagerly catching at the word. 'If it hadn't been for the girl! Who but poor ould Fagin was the means of your having such a handy girl about you?'

'He says true enough there!' said Nancy, coming hastily forward. 'Let him be; let him be.'

Nancy's appearance gave a new turn to the conversation. For the boys, receiving a sly wink from the wary old Jew, began to ply her with liquor – of which, however, she partook very sparingly; while Fagin, assuming an unusual flow of spirits, gradually brought Mr Sikes, into a better temper, by affecting to regard his threats as a little pleasant banter, and, moreover, by laughing very heartily at one or two rough jokes, which, after repeated applications to the spirit bottle, he condescended to make.

'It's all very well,' said Mr Sikes, 'but I must have some blunt from you tonight.'

'I haven't a piece of coin about me,' replied the Jew.

'Then you've got lots at home,' retorted Sikes; 'and I must have some from there.'

'Lots!' cried the Jew, holding up his hands. 'I haven't so much as would – '

'I don't know how much you've got, and I dare say you hardly know yourself, as it would take a pretty long time to count it,' said Sikes; 'but I must have some tonight, and that's flat.'

'Well, well,' said the Jew, with a sigh, 'I'll send the Artful round presently.'

'You won't do nothing of the kind,' rejoined Mr Sikes. 'The Artful's a deal too artful, and would forget to come, or lose his way, or get dodged by traps, and so be perwented, or anything for an excuse, if you put him up to it. Nancy shall go to the ken and fetch it, to make all sure; and I'll lie down and have a snooze while she's gone.'

After a great deal of haggling and squabbling, the Jew beat down the amount of the required advance from five pounds to three pounds four and sixpence, protesting with many solemn asseverations that that would only leave him eighteenpence to keep house with; Mr Sikes sullenly remarking that if he couldn't get any more he must be content with that. Nancy prepared to accompany him home; while the Dodger and Master Bates put the eatables in the cupboard. The Jew then, taking leave of his affectionate friend, returned homewards, attended by Nancy and the boys; Mr Sikes, meanwhile, flinging himself on the bed, and composing himself to sleep away the time until the young lady's return.

In due course they arrived at the Jew's abode, where they found Toby Crackit and Mr Chitling intent upon their fifteenth game at cribbage which it is scarcely necessary to say the latter gentleman lost, and with it his fifteenth and last sixpence, much to the amusement of his young friends. Mr Crackit, apparently somewhat ashamed at being found relaxing himself with a gentleman so much his inferior in station and mental endowments, yawned, and enquiring after Sikes, took up his hat to go.

'Has nobody been, Toby?' asked the Jew.

'Not a living leg,' answered Mr Crackit, pulling up his collar; 'it's been as dull as swipes. You ought to stand something handsome, Fagin, to recompense me for keeping house so long. Damme, I'm as flat as a juryman; and should have gone to sleep as fast as Newgate, if I hadn't had the good natur' to amuse this youngster. Horrid dull, I'm blessed if I ain't!'

With these and other ejaculations of the same kind, Mr Toby Crackit swept up his winnings, and crammed them into his waistcoat pocket with a haughty air, as though such small pieces of silver were wholly beneath the consideration of a man of his figure. This done, he swaggered out of the room with so much elegance and gentility, that Mr Chitling, bestowing numerous admiring glances on his legs and boots till they were out of sight, assured the company that he considered his acquaintance cheap at fifteen sixpences an interview, and that he didn't value his losses the snap of his little finger.

'Wot a rum chap you are, Tom!' said Master Bates, highly amused by this declaration.

'Not a bit of it,' replied Mr Chitling. 'Am I, Fagin?'

'A very clever fellow, my dear,' said the Jew, patting him on the shoulder, and winking to his other pupils.

'And Mr Crackit *is* a heavy swell; ain't he, Fagin?' asked Tom.

'No doubt at all of that, my dear,' replied the Jew.

'And it *is* a creditable thing to have his acquaintance; ain't it, Fagin?' pursued Tom.

'Very much so, indeed, my dear,' replied the Jew. 'They're only jealous, Tom, because he won't give it to them.'

'Ah!' cried Tom, triumphantly, 'that's where it is! He has cleaned me out. But I can go and earn some more when I like; can't I, Fagin?'

'To be sure you can,' replied the Jew; 'and the sooner you go the better, Tom; so make up your loss at once, and don't lose any more time. Dodger! Charley! it's time you were on the lay. Come! It's near ten, and nothing done yet.'

In obedience to this hint, the boys, nodding to Nancy, took up their hats and left the room, the Dodger and his vivacious friend indulging, as they went, in many witticisms at the expense of Mr Chitling; in whose conduct, it is but justice to say, there was nothing very conspicuous or peculiar, inasmuch as there was a great number of spirited young bloods upon town who pay a much higher price than Mr Chitling for being seen in good society, and a great number of fine gentlemen (composing the good society aforesaid) who establish their reputation upon very much the same footing as flash Toby Crackit.

'Now,' said the Jew, when they had left the room, 'I'll go and get you that cash, Nancy. This is only the key of a little cupboard where I keep a few odd things the boys get, my dear. I never lock up my money, for I've got none to lock up, my dear – ha! ha! ha! none to lock up. It's a poor trade, Nancy, and no thanks; but I'm fond of seeing the young people about me, and I bear it all – I bear it all. Hush!' he said, hastily concealing the key in his breast; 'who's that? Listen!'

The girl, who was sitting at the table with her arms folded, appeared in no way interested in the arrival, or to care whether the person, whoever he was, came or went, until the murmur of a man's voice reached her ears. The instant she caught the sound she tore off her bonnet and shawl with the rapidity of lightning, and thrust them under the table. The Jew turning round immediately afterwards, she muttered a complaint of the heat, in a tone of languor that contrasted very remarkably with the extreme haste and violence of this action, which, however, had been unobserved by Fagin, who had his back towards her at the time.

'Bah!' whispered the Jew, as though nettled by the interruption; 'it's the man I expected before; he's coming downstairs. Not a word about the money while he's here, Nance. He won't stop long – not ten minutes, my dear.'

Laying his skinny forefinger upon his lip, the Jew carried a candle to the door, as a man's step was heard upon the stairs without. He reached it at the same moment as the visitor, who, coming hastily into the room, was close upon the girl before he observed her.

It was Monks.

'Only one of my young people,' said the Jew, observing that Monks drew back on beholding a stranger. 'Don't move, Nancy.'

The girl drew closer to the table, and glancing at Monks with an air of careless levity, withdrew her eyes; but as he turned his towards the Jew, she stole another look, so keen and searching, and full of purpose, that if there had been any bystander to observe the change, he could hardly have believed the two looks to have proceeded from the same person.

'Any news?' enquired the Jew.

'Great.'

'And – and – good?' asked the Jew, hesitating as though he feared to vex the other man by being too sanguine.

'Not bad, any way,' replied Monks, with a smile. 'I have been prompt enough this time. Let me have a word with you.'

The girl drew closer to the table, and made no offer to leave the room, although she could see that Monks was pointing to her. The Jew, perhaps fearing that she might say something aloud about the money if he endeavoured to get rid of her, pointed upwards, and took Monks out of the room.

'Not that infernal hole we were in before,' she could hear the man say as they went upstairs. The Jew laughed, and making some reply which did not reach her, seemed, by the creaking of the boards, to lead his companion to the second story.

Before the sound of their footsteps had ceased to echo through the house, the girl had slipped off her shoes, and drawing her gown loosely over her head, and muffling her arms in it, stood at the door listening with breathless interest. The moment the noise ceased she glided from the room, ascended the stairs with incredible softness and silence, and was lost in the gloom above.

The room remained deserted for a quarter of an hour or more; the girl glided back with the same unearthly tread; and immediately afterwards the two men were heard descending. Monks went at once into the street, and the Jew crawled upstairs again for the money. When he returned, the girl was adjusting her shawl and bonnet, as if preparing to be gone.

'Why, Nance,' exclaimed the Jew, starting back as he put down the candle, 'how pale you are!'

'Pale!' echoed the girl, shading her eyes with her hands, as if to look steadily at him.

'Quite horrible,' said the Jew. 'What have you been doing to yourself?'

'Nothing that I know of, except sitting in this close place for I don't know how long and all,' replied the girl carelessly. 'Come! Let me get back; that's a dear.'

With a sigh for every piece of money, Fagin told the amount into her hand. They parted without more conversation, merely interchanging a 'good-night.'

When the girl got into the open street she sat down upon a doorstep, and seemed, for a few moments, wholly bewildered and unable to pursue her way. Suddenly, she arose, and hurrying on, in a direction quite opposite to that in which Sikes was awaiting her return, quickened her pace, until it gradually resolved into a violent run. After completely exhausting herself, she stopped to take breath; and, as if suddenly recollecting herself, and deploring her inability to do something she was bent upon, wrung her hands, and burst into tears.

It might be that her tears relieved her, or that she felt the full hopelessness of her condition, but she turned back, and hurrying with nearly as great rapidity in the contrary direction, partly to recover lost time, and partly to keep pace with the violent current of her own thoughts, soon reached the dwelling where she had left the housebreaker.

If she betrayed any agitation, when she presented herself to Mr Sikes, he did not observe it; for merely enquiring if she had brought the money, and receiving a reply in the affirmative, he uttered a growl of satisfaction, and replacing his head upon the pillow, resumed the slumbers which her arrival had interrupted.

It was fortunate for her that the possession of money occasioned him so much employment next day in the way of eating and drinking, and withal had so beneficial an effect in smoothing down the asperities of his temper, that he had neither time nor inclination to be very critical upon her behaviour and deportment. That she had all the abstracted and nervous manner of one who is on the eve of some bold and hazardous step, which it has required no common struggle to resolve upon, would have been obvious to the lynx-eyed Jew, who would most probably have taken the alarm at once; but Mr Sikes, lacking the niceties of discrimination, and being troubled with no more subtle misgivings than those which resolve themselves into a dogged roughness of behaviour towards everybody, and being, furthermore, in an unusually amiable condition, as has been already observed, saw nothing unusual in her demeanour, and, indeed, troubled himself s o little about her, that had her agitation been far more perceptible than it was, it would have been very unlikely to have awakened his suspicions.

As that day closed in, the girl's excitement increased; and when night came on, and she sat by, watching until the house-breaker should drink himself asleep, there was an unusual paleness in her cheek, and a fire in her eye, that even Sikes observed with astonishment.

Mr Sikes, being weak from the fever, was lying in bed, taking hot water with his gin to render it less inflammatory, and had pushed his glass towards Nancy to be replenished for the third or fourth time, when these symptoms first struck him.

'Why, burn my body!' said the man, raising himself on his hands, as he stared the girl in the face. 'You look like a corpse come to life again. What's the matter?'

'Matter!' replied the girl. 'Nothing. What do you look at me so hard for?'

'What foolery is this?' demanded Sikes, grasping her by the arm, and shaking her roughly. 'What is it? What do you mean? What are you thinking of?'

'Of many things, Bill,' replied the girl, shivering, and as she did so, pressing her hands upon her eyes. 'But, Lord! what odds in that?'

The tone of forced gaiety in which the last words were spoken seemed to produce a deeper impression on Sikes than the wild and rigid look which had preceded them.

'I tell you wot it is,' said Sikes, 'if you haven't caught the fever, and got it comin' on now, there's something more than usual in the wind, and something dangerous, too. You're not a-going to – No, damn me! you wouldn't do that!'

'Do what?' asked the girl.

'There ain't,' said Sikes, fixing his eyes upon her, and muttering the words to himself, 'there ain't a stauncher-hearted gal going, or I'd have cut her throat three months ago. She's got the fever coming on; that's it.'

Fortifying himself with this assurance, Sikes drained the glass to the bottom, and then, with many grumbling oaths, called for his physic. The girl jumped up with great alacrity, poured it quickly out, but with her back towards him, and held the vessel to his lips while he drank off the contents.

'Now,' said the robber, 'come and sit aside of me, and put on your own face; or I'll alter it so that you won't know it again when you *do* want it.'

The girl obeyed. Sikes, locking her hand in his, fell back upon the pillow, turning his eyes upon her face. They closed; opened again; closed once more; again opened. He shifted his position restlessly; and, after dozing again, and again, for two or three minutes, and as often springing up with a look of terror, and gazing vacantly about him, was suddenly stricken, as it were, while in the very attitude of rising, into a deep and heavy sleep. The grasp of his hand relaxed; the upraised arm fell languidly by his side; and he lay like one in a profound trance.

'The laudanum has taken effect at last,' murmured the girl, as she rose from the bedside. 'I may be too late, even now.'

She hastily dressed herself in her bonnet and shawl, looking fearfully round, from time to time, as if, despite the sleeping draught, she expected every moment to feel the pressure of Sikes's heavy hand upon her shoulder; then, stooping softly over the bed, she kissed the robber's lips, and then opening and closing the room-door with noiseless touch, hurried from the house.

A watchman was crying half-past nine down a dark passage, through which she had to pass in gaining the main thorough-fare.

'Has it long gone the half-hour?' asked the girl.

'It'll strike the hour in another quarter,' said the man, raising his lantern to her face.

'And I cannot get there in less than an hour or more,' muttered Nancy, brushing swiftly past him, and gliding rapidly down the street.

Many of the shops were already closing in the back lanes and avenues through which she tracked her way in making from Spitalfields towards the West-end of London. The clock struck ten, increasing her impatience. She tore along the narrow pavement, elbowing the passengers from side to side, and, darting almost under the horses' heads, crossed crowded streets, where clusters of persons were eagerly watching their opportunity to do the like.

'The woman is mad!' said the people, turning to look after her as she rushed away.

When she reached the more wealthy quarter of the town the streets were comparatively deserted; and here her headlong progress excited a still greater curiosity in the stragglers whom she hurried past. Some quickened their pace behind, as though to see whither she was hastening at such an unusual rate; and a few made head upon her, and looked back, surprised at her undiminished speed; but they fell off one by one, and when she neared her place of destination she was alone.

It was a family hotel in a quiet but handsome street near Hyde Park. As the brilliant light of the lamp which burnt before its door guided her to the spot, the clock struck eleven. She had loitered for a few paces as though irresolute, and making up her mind to advance; but the sound determined her, and she stepped into the hall. The porter's seat was vacant. She looked round with an air of incertitude, and advanced toward the stairs.

'Now, young woman!' said a smartly-dressed female, looking out from a door behind her, 'who do you want here?'

'A lady who is stopping in this house,' answered the girl.

'A lady!' was the reply, accompanied with a scornful look. 'What lady?'

'Miss Maylie,' said Nancy.

The young woman, who had, by this time, noted her appearance, replied only by a look of virtuous disdain, and summoned a man to answer her. To him Nancy repeated her request.

'What name am I to say?' asked the waiter.

'It's of no use saying any,' replied Nancy.

'Nor business?' said the man.

'No, nor that neither,' rejoined the girl. 'I must see the lady.'

'Come!' said the man, pushing her towards the door. 'None of this! Take yourself off.'

'I shall be carried out if I go!' said the girl, violently; 'and I can make that a job that two of you won't like to do. Isn't there anybody here?' she said, looking round, 'that will see a simple message carried for a poor wretch like me?'

This appeal produced an effect on a good-tempered faced man-cook, who with some other of the servants was looking on, and who stepped forward to interfere.

'Take it up for her, Joe; can't you?' said this person.

'What's the good?' replied the man. 'You don't suppose the young lady will see such as her; do you?'

This allusion to Nancy's doubtful character raised a vast quantity of chaste wrath in the bosoms of four housemaids, who remarked, with great fervour, that the creature was a disgrace to her sex, and strongly advocated her being thrown, ruthlessly, into the kennel.

'Do what you like with me,' said the girl, turning to the men again, 'but do what I ask you first, and I ask you to give this message, for God Almighty's sake.'

The soft-hearted cook added his intercession, and the result was that the man who at first appeared undertook its delivery.

'What's it to be?' said the man, with one foot on the stairs.

'That a young woman earnestly asks to speak to Miss Maylie alone,' said Nancy; 'and that if the lady will only hear the first word she has to say, she will know whether to hear her business or to have her turned out of doors as an impostor.'

'I say,' said the man, 'you're coming it strong!'

'You give the message,' said the girl, firmly; 'and let me hear the answer.'

The man ran upstairs. Nancy remained, pale and almost breathless, listening with quivering lip to the very audible expressions of scorn, of which the chaste housemaids were very prolific, and of which they became still more so when the man returned, and said the young woman was to walk upstairs.

'It's no good being proper in this world,' said the first housemaid.

'Brass can do better than the gold what has stood the fire,' said the second.

The third contented herself with wondering 'what ladies was made of;' and the fourth took the first in a quartette of 'Shameful!' with which the Dianas concluded.

Regardless of all this, for she had weightier matters at heart, Nancy followed the man, with trembling limbs, to a small antechamber, lighted by a lamp from the ceiling. Here he left her, and retired.

CHAPTER 40

A strange interview, which is a sequel to
the last chapter

The girl's life had been squandered in the streets and among the most noisome of the stews and dens of London, but there was something of the woman's original nature left in her still; and when she heard a light step approaching the door opposite to that by which she had entered, and thought of the wide contrast which the small room would in another moment contain, she felt burdened with the sense of her own deep shame, and shrunk as though she could scarcely bear the presence of her with whom she had sought this interview.

But struggling with these better feelings was pride – the vice of the lowest and most debased creatures no less than of the high and self-assured. The miserable companion of thieves and ruffians, the fallen outcast of low haunts, the associate of the scourings of the jails and hulks, living within the shadow of the gallows itself – even this degraded being felt too proud to betray a feeble gleam of the womanly feeling which she thought a weakness, but which alone connected her with that humanity of which her wasting life had obliterated so many, many traces when a very child.

She raised her eyes sufficiently to observe that the figure which presented itself was that of a slight and beautiful girl; and then, bending them on the ground, tossed her head with affected carelessness as she said, 'It's a hard matter to get to see you, lady. If I had taken offence, and gone away, as many would have done, you'd have been sorry for it one day, and not without reason, either.'

'I am very sorry if anyone has behaved harshly to you,' replied Rose. 'Do not think of that. Tell me why you wished to see me. I am the person you enquired for.'

The kind tone of this answer, the sweet voice, the gentle manner, the absence of any accent of haughtiness or displeasure, took the girl completely by surprise, and she burst into tears.

'Oh, lady, lady!' she said, clasping her hands passionately before her face, 'if there was more like you, there would be fewer like me – there would, there would!'

'Sit down,' said Rose earnestly; 'you distress me. If you are in poverty or affliction, I shall be truly glad to relieve you if I can – I shall, indeed. Sit down.'

'Let me stand, lady,' said the girl, still weeping, 'and do not speak to me so kindly till you know me better. It is growing late. Is – is – that door shut?'

'Yes,' said Rose, recoiling a few steps, as if to be nearer assistance in case she should require it. 'Why?'

'Because,' said the girl, 'I am about to put my life, and the lives of others, in your hands. I am the girl that dragged little Oliver back to old Fagin's, the Jew's, on the night he went out from the house in Pentonville.'

'You!' said Rose Maylie.

'I, lady,' replied the girl; 'I am the infamous creature you have heard of that lives among the thieves, and that never from the first moment I can recollect my eyes and senses opening on London streets have known any better life, or kinder words than they have given me, so help me God! Do not mind shrinking openly from me, lady. I am younger than you would think, to look at me, but I am well used to it. The poorest women fall back as I make my way along the crowded pavement.'

'What dreadful things are these!' said Rose, involuntarily falling from her strange companion.

'Thank Heaven upon your knees, dear lady,' cried the girl, 'that you had friends to care for and keep you in your childhood, and that you were never in the midst of cold and hunger, and riot and drunkenness, and – and something worse than all – as I have been from my cradle. I may use the word, for the alley and the gutter were mine, as they will be my deathbed.'

'I pity you!' said Rose in a broken voice. 'It wrings my heart to hear you!'

'Heaven bless you for your goodness!' rejoined the girl. 'If you knew what I am sometimes, you would pity me indeed. But I have stolen away from those who would surely murder me if they knew I had been here, to tell you what I have overheard. Do you know a man named Monks?'

'No,' said Rose.

'He knows you,' replied the girl; 'and knew you were here, for it was by hearing him tell the place that I found you out.'

'I never heard the name,' said Rose.

'Then he goes by some other amongst us,' rejoined the girl, 'which I more than thought before. Some time ago, and soon after Oliver was put into your house on the night of the robbery, I – suspecting this man – listened to a conversation held between him and Fagin in the dark. I found out, from what I heard, that Monks – the man I asked you about, you know – '

'Yes,' said Rose 'I understand.'

' – That Monks,' pursued the girl, 'had seen him accidentally with two of our boys on the day we first lost him, and had known him directly to be the same child that he was watching for, though I couldn't make out why. A bargain was struck with Fagin, that if Oliver was got back he should have a certain sum; and he was to have more for making him a thief, which this Monks wanted for some purpose of his own.'

'For what purpose?' asked Rose.

'He caught sight of my shadow on the wall as I listened, in the hope of finding out,' said the girl; 'and there are not many people besides me that could have got out of their way in time to escape discovery. But I did; and I saw him no more till last night.'

'And what occurred then?'

'I'll tell you, lady. Last night he came again. Again they went upstairs, and I, wrapping myself up so that my shadow should not betray me, again listened at the door. The first words I heard Monks say were these: "So the only proofs of the boy's identity lie at the bottom of the river, and the old hag that received them from the mother is rotting in her coffin." They laughed, and talked of his success in doing this; and Monks, talking on about the boy, and getting very wild, said, that though he had got the young devil's money safely now, he'd rather have had it the other way; for what a game it would have been to have brought down the boast of the father's will, by driving him through every jail in town, and then hauling him up for some capital felony which Fagin could easily manage, after having made a good profit of him besides.'

'What is all this?' said Rose.

'The truth, lady, though it comes from my lips,' replied the girl. 'Then he said, with oaths common enough in my ears, but strange to yours, that if he could gratify his hatred by taking the boy's life without bringing his own neck in danger, he would; but, as he couldn't, he'd be upon the watch to meet him at every turn in life, and if he took advantage of his birth and history, he might harm him yet. "In short, Fagin," he says, "Jew as you are, you never laid such snares as I'll contrive for my young brother Oliver." '

'His brother!' exclaimed Rose.

'Those were his words,' said Nancy, glancing uneasily round, as she had scarcely ceased to do since she began to speak, for a vision of Sikes haunted her perpetually. 'And more. When he spoke of you and the other lady, and said it seemed contrived by Heaven, or the devil, against him, that Oliver should come into your hands, he laughed, and said there was some comfort in that too, for how many thousands and hundreds of thousands of pounds would you not give, if you had them, to know who your two-legged spaniel was.'

'You do not mean,' said Rose, turning very pale, 'to tell me that this was said in earnest?'

'He spoke in hard and angry earnest, if a man ever did,' replied the girl, shaking her head. 'He is an earnest man when his hatred is up. I know many who do worse things, but I'd rather listen to them all a dozen times than to that Monks once. It is growing late, and I have to reach home without suspicion of having been on such an errand as this. I must get back quickly.'

'But what can I do?' said Rose. 'To what use can I turn this communication without you? Back! Why do you wish to return to companions you paint in such terrible colours? If you repeat this information to a gentleman whom I can summon in an instant from the next room, you can be consigned to some place of safety without half an hour's delay.'

'I wish to go back,' said the girl. 'I must go back, because – how can I tell such things to an innocent lady like you? – because among the men I have told you of, there is one, the most desperate among them all, that I can't leave; no, not even to be saved from the life I am leading now.'

'Your having interfered in this dear boy's behalf before,' said Rose; 'your coming here, at so great a risk, to tell me what you have heard; your manner, which convinces me of the truth of what you say; your evident contrition and sense of shame, all lead me to believe that you might be yet reclaimed. Oh!' said the earnest girl, folding her hands as the tears coursed down her face, 'do not turn a deaf ear to the entreaties of one of your own sex; the first – the first, I do believe, who ever appealed to you in the voice of pity and compassion. Do hear my words, and let me save you yet for better things.'

'Lady,' cried the girl, sinking on her knees, 'dear, sweet, angel lady, you *are* the first that ever blessed me with such words as these; and if I had heard them years ago they might have turned me from a life of sin and sorrow; but it is too late – it is too late!'

'It is never too late,' said Rose, 'for penitence and atonement.'

'It is,' cried the girl, writhing in the agony of her mind; 'I cannot leave him now! I could not be his death!'

'Why should you be?' asked Rose.

'Nothing could save him,' cried the girl. 'If I told others what I have told you, and led to their being taken, he would be sure to die. He is the boldest, and has been so cruel!'

'Is it possible,' cried Rose, 'that for such a man as this you can resign every future hope, and the certainty of immediate rescue? It is madness.'

'I don't know what it is,' answered the girl; 'I only know that it is so, and not with me alone, but with hundreds of others as bad and wretched as myself. I must go back. Whether it is God's wrath for the wrong I have done, I do not know; but I am drawn back to him through every suffering and ill-usage, and should be, I believe, if I knew that I was to die by his hand at last.'

'What am I to do?' said Rose. 'I should not let you depart from me thus.'

'You should, lady, and I know you will,' rejoined the girl, rising. 'You will not stop my going because I have trusted in your goodness, and forced no promise from you as I might have done.'

'Of what use, then, is the communication you have made?' said Rose. 'This mystery must be investigated, or how will its disclosure to me benefit Oliver, whom you are anxious to serve?'

'You must have some kind gentleman about you that will hear it as a secret, and advise you what to do,' rejoined the girl.

'But where can I find you again when it is necessary?' asked Rose. 'I do not seek to know where these dreadful people live, but where will you be walking or passing at any settled period from this time?'

'Will you promise me that you will have my secret strictly kept, and come alone, or with the only other person that knows it; and that I shall not be watched or followed?' asked the girl.

'I promise you solemnly,' answered Rose.

'Every Sunday night, from eleven until the clock strikes twelve,' said the girl, without hesitation, 'I will walk on London Bridge, if I am alive.'

'Stay another moment,' interposed Rose as the girl moved hurriedly towards the door. 'Think once again on your own condition, and the opportunity you have of escaping from it. You have a claim on me; not only as the voluntary bearer of this intelligence, but as a woman lost almost beyond redemption. Will you return to this gang of robbers, and to this man, when a word can save you? What fascination is it that can take you back, and make you cling to wickedness and misery? Oh! is there no chord in your heart that I can touch! Is there nothing left to which I can appeal against this terrible infatuation!'

'When ladies as young, and good, and beautiful as you are,' replied the girl, steadily, 'give away your hearts, love will carry you all lengths – even such as you, who have home, friends,

other admirers, everything to fill them. When such as I, who have no certain roof but the coffin-lid, and no friend in sickness or death but the hospital nurse, set our rotten hearts on any man, and let him fill the place that has been a blank through all our wretched lives, who can hope to cure us? Pity us, lady – pity us for having only one feeling of the woman left, and for having that turned, by a heavy judgement, from a comfort and a pride, into a new means of violence and suffering.'

'You will,' said Rose, after a pause, 'take some money from me, which may enable you to live without dishonesty – at all events, until we meet again?'

'Not a penny,' replied the girl, waving her hand.

'Do not close your heart against all my efforts to help you,' said Rose, stepping gently forward. 'I wish to serve you indeed.'

'You would serve me best, lady,' replied the girl, wringing her hands, 'if you could take my life at once; for I have felt more grief to think of what I am, tonight, than I ever did before, and it would be something not to die in the same hell in which I have lived. God bless you, sweet lady, and send as much happiness on your head as I have brought shame on mine!'

Thus speaking, and sobbing aloud, the unhappy creature turned away; while Rose Maylie, overpowered by this extraordinary interview, which had more the semblance of a rapid dream than an actual occurrence, sank into a chair, and endeavoured to collect her wandering thoughts.

CHAPTER 41

Containing fresh discoveries, and showing that surprises, like misfortunes, seldom come alone

Her situation was, indeed, one of no common trial and difficulty. While she felt the most eager and burning desire to penetrate the mystery in which Oliver's history was enveloped, she could not but hold sacred the confidence which the miserable woman with whom she had just conversed had reposed in her, as a young and guileless girl. Her words and manner had touched Rose Maylie's heart; and mingled with her love for her young charge, and scarcely less intense in its truth and fervour, was her fond wish to win the outcast back to repentance and hope.

They only proposed remaining in London three days, prior to departing for some weeks to a distant part of the coast. It was now midnight of the first day. What course of action could she determine upon, which could be adopted in eight-and-forty hours? Or how could she postpone the journey without exciting suspicion?

Mr Losberne was with them, and would be for the next two days; but Rose was too well acquainted with the excellent gentleman's impetuosity, and foresaw too clearly the wrath with which, in the first explosion of his indignation, he would regard the instrument of Oliver's recapture, to trust him with the secret, when her representations in the girl's behalf could be seconded by no experienced person. These were all reasons for the greatest caution and most circumspect behaviour in communicating it to Mrs Maylie, whose first impulse would infallibly be to hold a conference with the worthy doctor on the subject. As to resorting to any legal adviser, even if she had known how to do so, it was scarcely to be thought of, for the same reasons. Once the thought occurred to her of seeking assistance from Harry; but this awakened the recollection of their last parting, and it seemed unworthy of her to call him back, when – the tears rose to her eyes as she pursued this train of reflection – he might have by this time learned to forget her, and to be happier away.

Disturbed by these different reflections – inclining now to one course and then to another, and again recoiling from all, as each successive consideration presented itself to her mind – Rose passed a sleepless and anxious night. After more communing with herself next day, she arrived at the desperate conclusion of consulting Harry.

'If it be painful to him,' she thought, 'to come back here, how painful will it be to me! But perhaps he will not come – he may write; or he may come himself, and studiously abstain from meeting me. He did when he went away. I hardly thought he would; but it was better for us both.' And here Rose dropped her pen, and turned away, as though the very paper which was to be her messenger should not see her weep.

She had taken up the same pen, and laid it down again fifty times, and had considered and reconsidered the first line of her letter without writing the first word, when Oliver, who had been walking in the streets, with Mr Giles for a bodyguard, entered the room in such breathless haste and violent agitation as seemed to betoken some new cause of alarm.

'What makes you look so flurried?' asked Rose, advancing to meet him.

'I hardly know how; I feel as if I should be choked,' replied the boy. 'Oh dear! to think that I should see him at last, and you should be able to know that I have told you all the truth!'

'I never thought you had told us anything but the truth,' said Rose, soothing him. 'But what is this? – of whom do you speak?'

'I have seen the gentleman,' replied Oliver, scarcely able to articulate, 'the gentleman who was so good to me – Mr Brownlow, that we have so often talked about.'

'Where?' asked Rose.

'Getting out of a coach,' replied Oliver, shedding tears of delight, 'and going into a house. I didn't speak to him – I couldn't speak to him, for he didn't see me, and I trembled so that I was not able to go up to him. But Giles asked, for me, whether he lived there, and they said he did. Look here,' said Oliver, opening a scrap of paper, 'here it is; here's where he lives – I'm going there directly! Oh, dear me, dear me! what shall I do when I come to see him and hear him speak again?'

With her attention not a little distracted by these and a great many other incoherent exclamations of joy, Rose read the address, which was Craven Street, in the Strand, and very soon determined upon turning the discovery to account.

'Quick!' she said, 'tell them to fetch a hackney-coach, and be ready to go with me. I will take you there directly, without a minute's loss of time. I will only tell my aunt that we are going out for an hour, and be ready as soon as you are.'

Oliver needed no prompting to dispatch, and in little more than five minutes they were on their way to Craven Street. When they arrived there, Rose left Oliver in the coach, under pretence of preparing the old gentleman to receive him; and sending up her card by the servant, requested to see Mr Brownlow on very pressing business. The servant soon returned, to beg that she would walk upstairs; and following him into an upper room, Miss Maylie was presented to an elderly gentleman of benevolent appearance, in a bottle-green coat. At no great distance from whom was seated another old gentleman, in nankeen breeches and gaiters; who did not look particularly benevolent, and who was sitting with his hands clasped on the top of a thick stick, and his chin propped thereupon.

'Dear me,' said the gentleman in the bottle-green coat, hastily rising with great politeness, 'I beg your pardon, young lady; I imagined it was some importunate person who – I beg you will excuse me. Be seated, pray.'

'Mr Brownlow, I believe, sir?' said Rose, glancing from the other gentleman to the one who had spoken.

'That is my name,' said the old gentleman. 'This is my friend, Mr Grimwig. Grimwig, will you leave us for a few minutes?'

'I believe,' interposed Miss Maylie, 'that at this period of our interview I need not give that gentleman the trouble of going away. If I am correctly informed, he is cognisant of the business on which I wish to speak to you.'

Mr Brownlow inclined his head. Mr Grimwig, who had made one very stiff bow, and risen from his chair, made another very stiff bow, and dropped into it again.

'I shall surprise you very much, I have no doubt,' said Rose, naturally embarrassed; 'but you once showed great benevolence and goodness to a very dear young friend of mine, and I am sure you will take an interest in hearing of him again.'

'Indeed!' said Mr Brownlow.

'Oliver Twist you knew him as,' replied Rose.

The words no sooner escaped her lips than Mr Grimwig, who had been affecting to dip into a large book that lay on the table, upset it with a great crash, and, falling back in his chair, discharged from his features every expression but one of the most unmitigated wonder, and indulged in a prolonged and vacant stare; then, as if ashamed of having betrayed so much emotion, he jerked himself, as it were, by a convulsion into his former attitude, and looking out straight before him, emitted a long, deep whistle, seemed, at last, not to be discharged on empty air, but to die away in the innermost recesses of his stomach.

Mr Brownlow was no less surprised, although his astonishment was not expressed in the same eccentric manner. He drew his chair nearer to Miss Maylie's, and said, 'Do me the favour, my dear young lady, to leave entirely out of the question that goodness and benevolence of which you speak, and of which nobody else knows anything, and if you have it in your power to produce any evidence which will alter the unfavourable opinion I was once induced to entertain of that poor child, in Heaven's name put me in possession of it.'

'A bad one! I'll eat my head if he is not a bad one,' growled Mr Grimwig, speaking by some ventriloquial power, without moving a muscle of his face.

'He is a child of a noble nature and a warm heart,' said Rose, colouring; 'and that Power which has thought fit to try him beyond his years, has planted in his breast affections and feelings which would do honour to many who have numbered his days six times over.'

'I'm only sixty-one,' said Mr Grimwig, with the same rigid face; 'and, as the devil's in it, if this Oliver is not twelve years old at least, I don't see the application of that remark.'

'Do not heed my friend, Miss Maylie,' said Mr Brownlow; 'he does not mean what he says.'

'Yes, he does,' growled Mr Grimwig.

'No, he does not,' said Mr Brownlow, obviously rising in wrath as he spoke.

'He'll eat his head, if he doesn't,' growled Mr Grimwig.

'He would deserve to have it knocked off, if he does,' said Mr Brownlow.

'And he'd uncommonly like to see any man offer to do it,' responded Mr Grimwig, knocking his stick upon the floor.

Having gone thus far, the two old gentlemen severally took snuff, and afterwards shook hands, according to their invariable custom.

'Now, Miss Maylie,' said Mr Brownlow, 'to return to the subject in which your humanity is so much interested. Will you let me know what intelligence you have of this poor child? allowing me to premise that I exhausted every means in my power of discovering him; and that since I have been absent from this country, my first impression that he had imposed upon me, and had been persuaded by his former associates to rob me, has been considerably shaken.'

Rose, who had had time to collect her thoughts, at once related, in a few natural words, all that had befallen Oliver since he left Mr Brownlow's house – reserving Nancy's information for that gentleman's private ear – and concluding with the assurance that his only sorrow, for some months past, had been the not being able to meet with his former benefactor and friend.

'Thank God!' said the old gentleman. 'This is great happiness to me – great happiness. But you have not told me where he is now, Miss Maylie. You must pardon my finding fault with you – but why not have brought him?'

'He is waiting in a coach at the door,' replied Rose.

'At this door!' cried the old gentleman. With which he hurried out of the room, down the stairs, up the coach-steps, and into the coach, without another word.

When the room-door closed behind him, Mr Grimwig lifted up his head, and converting one of the hind legs of his chair into a pivot, described three distinct circles, with the assistance of his stick and the table, sitting in it all the time. After performing this evolution, he rose and limped as fast as he could up and down the room at least a dozen times, and then stopping suddenly before Rose, kissed her without the slightest preface.

'Hush!' he said, as the young lady rose in some alarm at this unusual proceeding. 'Don't be afraid. I'm old enough to be your grandfather. You're a sweet girl; I like you. Here they are!'

In fact, as he threw himself at one dexterous dive into his former seat, Mr Brownlow returned, accompanied by Oliver, whom Mr Grimwig received very graciously; and if the gratification of that moment had been the only reward for all her anxiety and care in Oliver's behalf, Rose Maylie would have been well repaid.

'There is somebody else who should not be forgotten, by the by,' said Mr Brownlow, ringing the bell. 'Send Mrs Bedwin here, if you please.'

The old housekeeper answered the summons with all dispatch, and dropping a curtsy at the door, waited for orders.

'Why, you get blinder every day, Bedwin,' said Mr Brownlow rather testily.

'Well, that I do, sir,' replied the old lady. 'People's eyes, at my time of life, don't improve with age, sir.'

'I could have told you that,' rejoined Mr Brownlow. 'But put on your glasses, and see if you can't find out what you were wanted for, will you?'

The old lady began to rummage in her pocket for her spectacles. But Oliver's patience was not proof against this new trial, and yielding to his first impulse, he sprang into her arms.

'God be good to me!' cried the old lady, embracing him, 'it is my innocent boy!'

'My dear old nurse!' cried Oliver.

'He would come back – I knew he would,' said the old lady, holding him in her arms. 'How well he looks, and how like a gentleman's son he is dressed again! Where have you been this long, long while? Ah! the same sweet face, but not so pale; the same soft eye, but not so sad. I never have forgot them or his quiet smile, but have seen them every day, side by side with those of my own dear children, dead and gone since I was a lightsome young creature.' Running on thus, and now holding Oliver from her to mark how he had grown, now clasping him to her and passing her fingers fondly through his hair, the good soul laughed and wept upon his neck by turns.

Leaving her and Oliver to compare notes at leisure, Mr Brownlow led the way into another room, and there heard from Rose a full narration of her interview with Nancy, which occasioned him no little surprise and perplexity. Rose also explained her reasons for not making a confidant of her friend Mr Losberne in the first instance. The old gentleman considered that she had acted prudently, and readily undertook to hold solemn conference with the worthy doctor himself. To afford him an early opportunity for the execution of this design, it was arranged that he should call at the hotel at eight o'clock that evening, and that in the meantime Mrs Maylie should be cautiously informed of all that had occurred. These preliminaries adjusted, Rose and Oliver returned home.

Rose had by no means overrated the measure of the good doctor's wrath. Nancy's history was no sooner unfolded to him than he poured forth a shower of mingled threats and execrations – threatened to make her the first victim of the combined ingenuity of Messrs Blathers and Duff; and actually put on his hat preparatory to sallying forth immediately to obtain the assistance of those worthies. And doubtless he would, in this first outbreak, have carried the intention into effect without a moment's consideration of the consequences, if he had not been restrained, in part, by corresponding violence on the side of Mr Brownlow, who was himself of an irascible temperament, and partly by such arguments and representations as seemed best calculated to dissuade him from his hot-brained purpose.

'Then what the devil is to be done?' said the impetuous doctor, when they had rejoined the two ladies. 'Are we to pass a vote of thanks to all these vagabonds, male and female, and beg them to accept a hundred pounds or so apiece, as a trifling mark of our esteem, and some slight acknowledgment of their kindness to Oliver?'

'Not exactly that,' rejoined Mr Brownlow, laughing; 'but we must proceed gently and with great care.'

'Gentleness and care!' exclaimed the doctor. 'I'd send them one and all to – '

'Never mind where,' interposed Mr Brownlow. 'But reflect whether sending them anywhere is likely to attain the object we have in view.'

'What object?' asked the doctor.

'Simply the discovery of Oliver's parentage, and regaining for him the inheritance of which, if this story be true, he has been fraudulently deprived.'

'Ah!' said Mr Losberne, cooling himself with his pocket-handkerchief, 'I almost forgot that.'

'You see,' pursued Mr Brownlow; 'placing this poor girl entirely out of the question and supposing it were possible to bring these scoundrels to justice without compromising her safety, what good should we bring about?'

'Hanging a few of them at least, in all probability,' suggested the doctor, 'and transporting the rest.'

'Very good,' replied Mr Brownlow, smiling; 'but no doubt they will bring that about for themselves in the fullness of time; and if we step in to forestall them, it seems to me that we shall be performing a very Quixotic act, in direct opposition to our own interest – or at least to Oliver's, which is the same thing.'

'Now?' enquired the doctor.

'Thus. It is quite clear that we shall have extreme difficulty in getting to the bottom of this mystery, unless we can bring this man Monks upon his knees. That can only be done by stratagem, and by catching him when he is not surrounded by these people. For, suppose he were apprehended, we have no proof against him. He is not even (so far as we know, or as the facts appear to us) concerned with the gang in any of their robberies. If he were not discharged, it is very unlikely that he could receive any further punishment than being committed to prison as a rogue and vagabond; and of course ever afterwards his mouth is so obstinately closed that he might as well, for our purposes, be deaf, dumb, blind, and an idiot.'

'Then,' said the doctor impetuously, 'I put it to you again, whether you think it reasonable that this promise to the girl should be considered binding – a promise made with the best and kindest intentions, but really – '

'Do not discuss the point, my dear young lady, pray,' said Mr Brownlow, interrupting Rose as she was about to speak. 'The promise shall be kept. I don't think it will, in the slightest degree, interfere with our proceedings. But before we can resolve upon any precise course of action, it will be necessary to see the girl, to ascertain from her whether she will point out this Monks, on the understanding that he is to be dealt with by us, and not by the law; or if she will not or cannot do that, to procure from her such an account of his haunts and description of his person as will enable us to identify him. She cannot be seen until next Sunday night; this is Tuesday. I would suggest that in the meantime we remain perfectly quiet, and keep these matters secret even from Oliver himself.'

Although Mr Losberne received with many wry faces a proposal involving a delay of five whole days, he was fain to admit that no better course occurred to him just then; and as both Rose and Mrs Maylie sided very strongly with Mr Brownlow, that gentleman's proposition was carried unanimously.

'I should like,' he said, 'to call in the aid of my friend Grimwig. He is a strange creature, but a shrewd one, and might prove of material assistance to us. I should say that he was bred a lawyer, and quitted the bar in disgust because he had only one brief and a motion of course in twenty years, though whether that is a recommendation or not, you must determine for yourselves.'

'I have no objection to your calling in your friend if I may call in mine,' said the doctor.

'We must put it to the vote,' replied Mr Brownlow; 'who may he be?'

'That lady's son, and this young lady's – very old friend,' said the doctor, motioning towards Mrs Maylie, and concluding with an expressive glance at her niece.

Rose blushed deeply, but she did not make any audible objection to this motion (possibly she felt in a hopeless minority); and Harry Maylie and Mr Grimwig were accordingly added to the committee.

'We stay in town, of course,' said Mrs Maylie, 'while there remains the slightest prospect of prosecuting this enquiry with a chance of success. I will spare neither trouble nor expense in behalf of the object in which we are all so deeply interested, and I am content to remain here, if it be for twelve months, so long as you assure me that any hope remains.'

'Good!' rejoined Mr Brownlow. 'And as I see on the faces about me a disposition to enquire how it happened that I was not in the way to corroborate Oliver's tale, and had so suddenly left the kingdom, let me stipulate that I shall be asked no questions until such time as I may deem it expedient to forestall them by telling my own story. Believe me, I make this request with good reason, for I might otherwise excite hopes destined never to be realised, and only increase difficulties and disappointments already quite numerous enough. Come! Supper has been announced, and young Oliver, who is all alone in the next room, will have begun to think, by this time, that we have wearied of his company, and entered into some dark conspiracy to thrust him forth upon the world.'

With these words the old gentleman gave his hand to Mrs Maylie, and escorted her into the supper-room. Mr Losberne followed, leading Rose; and the council was, for the present, effectually broken up.

CHAPTER 42

An old acquaintance of Oliver's, exhibiting decided marks of genius, becomes a public character in the metropolis

Upon the very same night when Nancy, having lulled Mr Sikes to sleep, hurried on her self-imposed mission to Rose Maylie, there advanced towards London, by the Great North Road, two persons, upon whom it is expedient that this history should bestow some attention.

They were a man and a woman – or perhaps they would be better described as a male and female; for the former was one of those long-limbed, knock-kneed, shambling, bony people, to whom it is difficult to assign any precise age – looking as they do, when they are yet boys, like undergrown men, and when they are almost men, like overgrown boys. The woman was young, but of a robust and hardy make, as she need have been to bear the weight of the heavy bundle which was strapped to her back. Her companion was not encumbered with much luggage, as there merely dangled from a stick, which he carried over his shoulder, a small parcel wrapped in a common handkerchief, and apparently light enough. This circumstance, added to the length of his legs, which were of unusual extent, enabled him with much ease to keep some half-dozen paces in advance of his companion, to whom he occasionally turned with an impatient jerk of the head, as if reproaching her tardiness, and urging her to greater exertion.

Thus they toiled along the dusty road, taking little heed of any object within sight, save when they stepped aside to allow a wider passage for the mail-coaches which were whirling out of town, until they passed through Highgate archway, when the foremost traveller stopped, and called impatiently to his companion, 'Come on, can't yer? What a lazybones yer are, Charlotte.'

'It's a heavy load, I can tell you,' said the female, coming up, almost breathless with fatigue.

'Heavy! What are yer talking about? What are yer made for?' rejoined the male traveller, changing his own little bundle as he spoke to the other shoulder. 'Oh, there yer are, resting again! Well, if yer ain't enough to tire anybody's patience out, I don't know what is!'

'Is it much farther?' asked the woman, resting herself against a bank, and looking up with the perspiration streaming from her face.

'Much farther! Yer as good as there,' said the long-legged tramper, pointing out before him. 'Look there! Those are the lights of London.'

'They're a good two mile off, at least,' said the woman despondingly.

'Never mind whether they're two mile off or twenty,' said Noah Claypole, for he it was; 'but get up and come on, or I'll kick yer, and so I give yer notice.'

As Noah's red nose grew redder with anger, and as he crossed the road while speaking, as if fully prepared to put this threat into execution, the woman rose without any further remark, and trudged onward by his side.

'Where do you mean to stop for the night, Noah?' she asked, after they had walked a few hundred yards.

'How should I know?' replied Noah, whose temper had been considerably impaired by walking.

'Near, I hope,' said Charlotte.

'No, not near,' replied Mr Claypole. 'There! Not near; so don't think it.'

'Why not?'

'When I tell yer that I don't mean to do a thing, that's enough, without any why or because either,' replied Mr Claypole with dignity.

'Well, you needn't be so cross,' said his companion.

'A pretty thing it would be, wouldn't it, to go and stop at the very first public-house outside the town, so that Sowerberry, if he come up after us, might poke in his old nose, and have us taken back in a cart with handcuffs on,' said Mr Claypole in a jeering tone. 'No! I shall go and lose myself among the narrowest streets I can find, and not stop till we come to the very out-of-the-wayest house I can set eyes on. 'Cod, yer may thank yer stars I've got a head; for if we hadn't gone at first the wrong road a purpose, and come back across country, yer'd have been locked up hard and fast a week ago, my lady. And serve yer right for being a fool.'

'I know I ain't as cunning as you are,' replied Charlotte; 'but don't put all the blame on me, and say *I* should have been locked up. You would have been if I had been, any way.'

'Yer took the money from the till, yer know yer did,' said Mr Claypole.

'I took it for you, Noah, dear,' rejoined Charlotte.

'Did I keep it?' asked Mr Claypole.

'No; you trusted in me, and let me carry it, like a dear, and so you are,' said the lady, chucking him under the chin, and drawing her arm through his.

This was indeed the case, but as it was not Mr Claypole's habit to repose a blind and foolish confidence in anybody, it should be observed, in justice to that gentleman, that he had trusted Charlotte to this extent, in order that, if they were pursued, the money might be found on her, which would leave him an opportunity of asserting his utter innocence of any theft, and would greatly facilitate his chances of escape. Of course he entered at this juncture into no explanation of his motives, and they walked on very lovingly together.

In pursuance of this cautious plan, Mr Claypole went on without halting until he arrived at the Angel at Islington, where he wisely judged, from the crowd of passengers and number of vehicles, that London began in earnest. Just pausing to observe which appeared the most crowded streets, and consequently the most to be avoided, he crossed into Saint John's Road, and was soon deep in the obscurity of the intricate and dirty ways which, lying between Gray's Inn Lane and Smithfield, render that part of the town one of the lowest and worst that improvement has left in the midst of London.

Through these streets Noah Claypole walked, dragging Charlotte after him; now stepping into the kennel to embrace at a glance the whole external character of some small public-house, and now jogging on again, as some fancied appearance induced him to believe it too public for his purpose. At length he stopped in front of one, more humble in appearance and more dirty than any he had yet seen; and, having crossed over and surveyed it from the opposite pavement, graciously announced his intention of putting up there for the night.

'So give us the bundle,' said Noah, unstrapping it from the woman's shoulders, and slinging it over his own; 'and don't yer speak except when yer spoke to. What's the name of the house – t–h–r – three what?'

'Cripples,' said Charlotte.

'Three Cripples,' repeated Noah, 'and a very good sign too. Now then! Keep close at my heels, and come along.' With these injunctions, he pushed the rattling door with his shoulder, and entered the house, followed by his companion.

There was nobody in the bar but a young Jew, who, with his two elbows on the counter, was reading a dirty newspaper. He stared very hard at Noah, and Noah stared very hard at him.

If Noah had been attired in his charity boy's dress there might have been some reason for the Jew opening his eyes so wide; but as he had discarded the coat and badge, and wore a short smock-frock over his leathers, there seemed no particular reason for his appearance exciting so much attention in a public-house.

'Is this the Three Cripples?' asked Noah.

'That is the dabe of this 'ouse,' replied the Jew.

'A gentleman we met on the road, coming up from the country, recommended us here,' said Noah, nudging Charlotte, perhaps to call her attention to this most ingenious device for attracting respect, and perhaps to warn her to betray no surprise. 'We want to sleep here tonight.'

'I'b dot certaid you cad,' said Barney, who was the attendant sprite; 'but I'll idquire.'

'Show us the tap, and give us a bit of cold meat and a drop of beer while yer enquiring, will yer?' said Noah.

Barney complied by ushering them into a small back-room, and setting the required viands before them; having done which, he informed the travellers that they could be lodged that night, and left the amiable couple to their refreshment.

Now, this back-room was immediately behind the bar, and some steps lower, so that any person connected with the house undrawing a small curtain which concealed a single pane of glass fixed in the wall of the last-named apartment, about five feet from its flooring, could not only look down upon any guests in the back-room without any great hazard of being observed (the glass being in a dark angle of the wall, between which and a large upright beam the observer had to thrust himself), but could, by applying his ear to the partition, ascertain with tolerable distinctness their subject of conversation. The landlord of the house had not withdrawn his eye from this place of espial for five minutes, and Barney had only just returned from making the communication above related, when Fagin, in the course of his evening's business, came into the bar to enquire after some of his young pupils.

'Hush!' said Barney; 'stradegers id the next roob.'

'Strangers!' repeated the old man in a whisper.

'Aye! Ad rub uds too,' added Barney. 'Frob the cuttry, but subthig in your way, or I'b bistaked.'

Fagin appeared to receive this communication with great interest. Mounting on a stool, he cautiously applied his eye to the pane of glass, from which secret post he could see Mr Claypole taking cold beef from the dish, and porter from the pot, and administering homœopathic doses of both to Charlotte, who sat patiently by, eating and drinking at his pleasure.

'Aha!' whispered the Jew, looking round to Barney. 'I like that fellow's looks. He'd be of use to us; he knows how to train the girl already. Don't make as much noise as a mouse, my dear, and let me hear 'em talk – let me hear 'em.'

The Jew again applied his eye to the glass, and turning his ear to the partition, listened attentively, with a subtle and eager look upon his face that might have appertained to some old goblin.

'So I mean to be a gentleman,' said Mr Claypole, kicking out his legs, and continuing a conversation, the commencement of which Fagin had arrived too late to hear. 'No more jolly old coffins, Charlotte but a gentleman's life for me; and if yer like yer shall be a lady.'

'I should like that well enough, dear,' replied Charlotte; 'but tills ain't to be emptied every day, and people to get clear off after it.'

'Tills, be blowed!' said Mr Claypole; 'there's more things besides tills to be emptied.'

'What do you mean?' asked his companion.

'Pockets, women's ridicules, houses, mail-coaches, banks!' said Mr Claypole, rising with the porter.

'But you can't do all that, dear,' said Charlotte.

'I shall look out to get into company with them as can,' replied Noah. 'They'll be able to make us useful some way or another. Why, you yourself are worth fifty women; I never see such a precious sly and deceitful creetur as yer can be when I let yer.'

'Lor, how nice it is to hear you say so!' exclaimed Charlotte, imprinting a kiss upon his ugly face.

'There, that'll do; don't yer be too affectionate, in case I'm cross with yer,' said Noah, disengaging himself with great gravity. 'I should like to be the captain of some band, and have the whopping of 'em, and follering 'em about, unbeknown to themselves. That would suit me, if there was good profit; and if we could only get in with some gentlemen of this sort, I say it would be cheap at that twenty-pound note you've got – especially as we don't very well know how to get rid of it ourselves.'

After expressing this opinion, Mr Claypole looked into the porter-pot with an aspect of deep wisdom; and having well shaken its contents, nodded condescendingly to Charlotte, and took a draught, wherewith he appeared greatly refreshed. He was meditating another, when the sudden opening of the door, and the appearance of a stranger, interrupted him.

The stranger was Mr Fagin. And very amiable he looked, and a very low bow he made, as he advanced, and setting himself down at the nearest table, ordered something to drink of the grinning Barney.

'A pleasant night, sir, but cool for the time of the year,' said Fagin, rubbing his hands. 'From the country, I see, sir?'

'How do yer see that?' asked Noah Claypole.

'We have not so much dust as that in London,' replied the Jew, pointing from Noah's shoes to those of his companion, and from them to the two bundles.

'Yer a sharp feller,' said Noah. 'Ha! ha! only hear that, Charlotte.'

'Why, one need be sharp in this town, my dear,' replied the Jew, sinking his voice to a confidential whisper; 'and that's the truth.'

The Jew followed up this remark by striking the side of his nose with his right forefinger – a gesture which Noah attempted to imitate, though not with complete success, in consequence of his own nose not being large enough for the purpose. However, Mr Fagin seemed to interpret the endeavour as expressing a perfect coincidence with his opinion, and put about the liquor which Barney reappeared with in a very friendly manner.

'Good stuff that,' observed Mr Claypole, smacking his lips.

'Dear!' said Fagin. 'A man need be always emptying a till, or a pocket, or a woman's reticule, or a house, or a mail-coach, or a bank, if he drinks it regularly.'

Mr Claypole no sooner heard this extract from his own remarks than he fell back in his chair, and looked from the Jew to Charlotte with a countenance of ashy paleness and excessive terror.

'Don't mind me, my dear,' said Fagin, drawing his chair closer. 'Ha! ha! it was lucky it was only me that heard you by chance; it was very lucky it was only me.'

'I didn't take it,' stammered Noah, no longer stretching out his legs like an independent gentleman, but coiling them up as well as he could under his chair. 'It was all her doing. Yer've got it now, Charlotte, yer know yer have.'

'No matter who's got it, or who did it, my dear!' replied Fagin, glancing, nevertheless, with a hawk's eye at the girl and the two bundles. 'I'm in that way myself, and I like you for it.'

'In what way?' asked Mr Claypole, a little recovering.

'In that way of business,' rejoined Fagin; 'and so are the people of the house. You've hit the right nail upon the head, and are as safe here as you could be. There is not a safer place in all this town than is the Cripples – that is, when I like to make it so; and I've taken a fancy to you and the young woman; so I've said the word, and you may make your minds easy.'

Noah Claypole's mind might have been at ease after this assurance, but his body certainly was not; for he shuffled and writhed about into various uncouth positions, eyeing his new friend meanwhile with mingled fear and suspicion.

'I'll tell you more,' said the Jew, after he had reassured the girl, by dint of friendly nods and muttered encouragements. 'I have got a friend that I think can gratify your darling wish, and put you in the right way, where you can take whatever department of the business you think will suit you best at first, and be taught all the others.'

'Yer speak as if yer were in earnest,' replied Noah.

'What advantage would it be to me to be anything else?' enquired the Jew, shrugging his shoulders. 'Here! let me have a word with you outside.'

'There's no occasion to trouble ourselves to move,' said Noah, getting his legs by gradual degrees abroad again. 'She'll take the luggage upstairs the while. Charlotte, see to them bundles!'

This mandate, which had been delivered with great majesty, was obeyed without the slightest demur; and Charlotte made the best of her way off with the packages, while Noah held the door open and watched her out.

'She's kept tolerably well under, ain't she?' he asked as he resumed his seat, in the tone of a keeper who has tamed some wild animal.

'Quite perfect,' rejoined Fagin, clapping him on the shoulder. 'You're a genius, my dear.'

'Why, I suppose if I wasn't I shouldn't be here,' replied Noah. 'But, I say, she'll be back if yer lose time.'

'Now, what do you think?' said the Jew. 'If you was to like my friend, could you do better than join him?'

'Is he in a good way of business? that's where it is,' responded Noah, winking one of his little eyes.

'The top of the tree,' said the Jew; 'employs a power of hands; and has the very best society in the profession.'

'Regular town-maders?' asked Mr Claypole.

'Not a countryman among 'em; and I don't think he'd take you, even on my recommendation, if he didn't run rather short of assistants just now,' replied the Jew.

'Should I have to hand over?' said Noah, slapping his breeches-pocket.

The Jew and Morris Bolter both begin to understand each other

'It couldn't possibly be done without,' replied Fagin, in a most decided manner.

'Twenty pound, though – it's a lot of money!'

'Not when it's in a note you can't get rid of,' retorted Fagin. 'Number and date taken, I suppose? Payment stopped at the Bank? Ah! It's not worth much to him. It'll have to go abroad, and he couldn't sell it for a great deal in the market.'

'When could I see him?' asked Noah, doubtfully,

'Tomorrow morning,' replied the Jew.

'Where?'

'Here.'

'Um!' said Noah. 'What's the wages?'

'Live like a gentleman – board and lodging, pipes and spirits, free – half of all you earn, and half of all the young woman earns,' replied Mr Fagin.

Whether Noah Claypole, whose rapacity was none of the least comprehensive, would have acceded, even to these glowing terms, had he been a perfectly free agent, is very doubtful; but as he recollected that, in the event of his refusal, it was in the power of his new acquaintance to give him up to justice immediately (and more unlikely things had come to pass), he gradually relented, and said he thought that would suit him.

'But yer see,' observed Noah, 'as she will be able to do a good deal, I should like to take something very light.'

'A little fancy work?' suggested Fagin.

'Ah! something of that sort,' replied Noah. 'What do you think would suit me now? Something not too trying for the strength, and not very dangerous, you know. That's the sort of thing!'

'I heard you talk of something in the spy way upon the others, my dear,' said the Jew. 'My friend wants somebody who would do that well, very much.'

'Why, I did mention that, and I shouldn't mind turning my hand to it sometimes,' rejoined Mr Claypole slowly, 'but it wouldn't pay by itself, you know.'

'That's true,' observed the Jew, ruminating, or pretending to ruminate. 'No, it might not.'

'What do you think, then?' asked Noah, anxiously regarding him. 'Something in the sneaking way, where it was pretty sure work, and not much more risk than being at home.'

'What do you think of the old ladies?' asked the Jew. 'There's a good deal of money made in snatching their bags and parcels, and running round the corner.'

'Don't they holler out a good deal, and scratch sometimes?' asked Noah, shaking his head. 'I don't think that would answer my purpose. Ain't there any other line open?'

'Stop!' said the Jew, laying his hand on Noah's knee. 'The kinchin lay.'

'What's that?' demanded Mr Claypole.

'The kinchins, my dear,' said the Jew, 'is the young children that's sent on errands by their mothers, with sixpences and shillings; and the lay is just to take their money away – they've always got it ready in their hands – and then knock 'em into the kennel, and walk off very slow, as if there was nothing else the matter but a child fallen down and hurt itself. Ha! ha! ha!'

'Ha! ha!' roared Mr Claypole, kicking up his legs in an ecstasy. 'Lord, that's the very thing!'

'To be sure it is,' replied Fagin; 'and you can have a few good beats chalked out in Camden-town, and Battlebridge, and neighbourhoods like that, where they're always going errands, and you can upset as many kinchins as you want any hour in the day. Ha! ha! ha!'

With this, Fagin poked Mr Claypole in the side, and they joined in a burst of laughter both long and loud.

'Well, that's all right!' said Noah, when he had recovered himself, and Charlotte had returned. 'What time tomorrow shall we say?'

'Will ten do?' asked the Jew, adding, as Mr Claypole nodded assent, 'What name shall I tell my good friend?'

'Mr Bolter,' replied Noah, who had prepared himself for such an emergency – ' Mr Morris Bolter. This is Mrs Bolter.'

'Mrs Bolter's humble servant,' said Fagin, bowing with grotesque politeness. 'I hope I shall know her better very shortly.'

'Do you hear the gentleman, Charlotte?' thundered Mr Claypole.

'Yes, Noah, dear,' replied Mrs Bolter, extending her hand.

'She calls me Noah, as a sort of fond way of talking,' said Mr Morris Bolter, late Claypole, turning to the Jew. 'You understand?'

'Oh, yes, I understand – perfectly,' replied Fagin, telling the truth for once. 'Good-night! Good-night!'

With many adieus and good wishes, Mr Fagin went his way. Noah Claypole, bespeaking his good lady's attention, proceeded to enlighten her relative to the arrangement he had made, with all that haughtiness and air of superiority becoming not only a member of the sterner sex, but a gentleman who appreciated the dignity of a special appointment on the kinchin lay in London and its vicinity.

CHAPTER 43

Wherein is shown how the Artful Dodger got into trouble

'And so it was you that was your own friend, was it?' asked Mr Claypole, otherwise Bolter, when, by virtue of the compact entered into between them, he had removed the next day to the Jew's house. ' 'Cod, I thought as much last night!'

'Every man's his own friend, my dear,' replied Fagin, with his most insinuating grin. 'He hasn't as good a one as himself, anywhere.'

'Except sometimes,' replied Morris Bolter, assuming the air of a man of the world. 'Some people are nobody's enemies but their own, yer know.'

'Don't believe that!' said the Jew. 'When a man's his own enemy, it's only because he's too much his own friend; not because he's careful for everybody but himself. Pooh! pooh! There ain't such a thing in nature.'

'There oughtn't to be, if there is,' replied Mr Bolter.

'That stands to reason,' said the Jew. 'Some conjurers say that number three is the magic number, and some say number seven. It's neither, my friend, neither – it's number one.'

'Ha! ha!' cried Mr Bolter. 'Number one for ever.'

'In a little community like ours, my dear,' said the Jew, who felt it necessary to qualify this position, 'we have a general number one – that is, you can't consider yourself as number one without considering me too as the same, and all the other young people.'

'Oh, the devil!' exclaimed Mr Bolter.

'You see,' pursued the Jew, affecting to disregard this interruption, 'we are so mixed up together, and identified in our interests, that it must be so. For instance, it's your object to take care of number one – meaning yourself.'

'Certainly,' replied Mr Bolter. 'Yer about right there.'

'Well! You can't take care of yourself, number one, without taking care of me, number one.'

'Number two, you mean,' said Mr Bolter, who was largely endowed with the quality of selfishness.

'No, I don't!' retorted the Jew. 'I'm of the same importance to you as you are to yourself.'

'I say,' interrupted Mr Bolter, 'yer a very nice man, and I'm very fond of yer; but we ain't quite so thick together as all that comes to.'

'Only think,' said the Jew, shrugging his shoulders, and stretching out his hands; 'only consider. You've done what's a very pretty thing, and what I love you for doing, but what at the same time would put the cravat round your throat, that's so very easily tied and so very difficult to unloose – in plain English, the halter!'

Mr Bolter put his hand to his neckerchief, as if he felt it inconveniently tight, and murmured an assent, qualified in tone but not in substance.

'The gallows,' continued Fagin, 'the gallows, my dear, is an ugly finger-post, which points out a very short and sharp turning that has stopped many a bold fellow's career on the broad highway. To keep in the easy road, and keep it at a distance, is object number one with you.'

'Of course it is,' replied Mr Bolter. 'What do yer talk about such things for?'

'Only to show you my meaning clearly,' said the Jew, raising his eyebrows. 'To be able to do that, you depend upon me. To keep my little business all snug, I depend upon you. The first is your number one, the second my number one. The more you value your number one, the more careful you must be of mine; so we come at last to what I told you at first – that a regard for number one holds us all together, and must do so, unless we would all go to pieces in company.'

'That's true,' rejoined Mr Bolter, thoughtfully. 'Oh! yer a cunning old codger!'

Mr Fagin saw, with delight, that this tribute to his powers was no mere compliment, but that he had really impressed his recruit with a sense of his wily genius, which it was most important that he should entertain in the outset of their acquaintance. To strengthen an impression so desirable and useful, he followed up the blow by acquainting him, in some detail, with the magnitude and extent of his operations – blending truth and fiction together, as best served his purpose, and bringing both to bear, with so much art, that Mr Bolter's respect visibly increased, and became tempered, at the same time, with a degree of wholesome fear, which it was highly desirable to awaken.

'It's this mutual trust we have in each other that consoles me under heavy losses,' said the Jew. 'My best hand was taken from me yesterday morning.'

'Yer don't mean to say he died?' cried Mr Bolter.

'No, no,' replied Fagin, 'not so bad as that – not quite so bad.'

'What! I suppose he was – '

'Wanted,' interposed the Jew. 'Yes, he was wanted.'

'Very particular?' enquired Mr Bolter.

'No,' replied the Jew, 'not very. He was charged with attempting to pick a pocket, and they found a silver snuff-box on him – his own, my dear, his own, for he took snuff himself, and was very fond of it. They remanded him till today, for they thought they knew the owner. Ah! he was worth fifty boxes, and I'd give the price of as many to have him back. You should have known the Dodger, my dear; you should have known the Dodger.'

'Well, but I shall know him, I hope; don't yer think so?' said Mr Bolter.

'I'm doubtful about it,' replied the Jew with a sigh. 'If they don't get any fresh evidence, it'll only be a summary conviction, and we shall have him back again after six weeks or so; but if they do, it's a case of lagging. They know what a clever lad he is; he'll be a lifer. They'll make the Artful nothing less than a lifer.'

'What do yer mean by lagging and a lifer?' demanded Mr Bolter. 'What's the good of talking in that way to me; why don't yer speak so as I can understand yer?'

Fagin was about to translate these mysterious expressions into the vulgar tongue – and, being interpreted, Mr Bolter would have been informed that they represented that combination of words, 'transportation for life' – when the dialogue was cut short by the entry of Master Bates, with his hands in his breeches pockets, and his face twisted into a look of semi-comical woe.

'It's all up, Fagin,' said Charley, when he and his new companion had been made known to each other

'What do you mean?' asked the Jew, with trembling lips.

'They've found the gentleman as owns the box; two or three more's a-coming to 'dentify him; and the Artful's booked for a passage out,' replied Master Bates. 'I must have a full suit of mourning, Fagin, and a hatband, to wisit him in, afore he sets out upon his travels. To think of Jack Dawkins – lummy Jack – the Dodger – the Artful Dodger – going abroad for a common twopenny-halfpenny sneeze-box! I never thought he'd a done it under a gold watch, chain and seals, at the lowest. Oh, why didn't he rob some rich old gentleman of all his walables, and go out *as* a gentleman, and not like a common prig, without no honour nor glory!'

With this expression of feeling for his unfortunate friend, Master Bates sat himself on the nearest chair with an aspect of chagrin and despondency.

'What do you talk about his having neither honour nor glory for!' exclaimed Fagin, darting an angry look at his pupil. 'Wasn't he always top-sawyer among you all? Is there one of you that could touch him, or come near him on any scent? Eh?'

'Not one,' replied Master Bates, in a voice rendered husky by regret; 'not one.'

'Then what do you talk of?' replied the Jew angrily; 'what are you blubbering for?'

' 'Cause it isn't on the rec-ord, is it?' said Charley, chafed into perfect defiance of his venerable friend by the current of his regrets; ' 'cause it can't come out in the 'dictment; 'cause nobody will never know half of what he was. How will he stand in the Newgate Calendar? P'raps not be there at all. Oh, my eye, my eye, wot a blow it is!'

'Ha! ha!' cried the Jew, extending his right hand, and turning to Mr Bolter in a fit of chuckling which shook him as though he had the palsy; 'see what a pride they take in their profession, my dear. Ain't it beautiful?'

Mr Bolter nodded assent; and the Jew, after contemplating the grief of Charley Bates for some seconds with evident satisfaction, stepped up to that young gentleman and patted him on the shoulder.

'Never mind, Charley,' said Fagin, soothingly; 'it'll come out, it'll be sure to come out. They'll all know what a clever fellow he was; he'll show it himself, and not disgrace his old pals and teachers. Think how young he is, too! What a distinction, Charley, to be lagged at his time of life!'

'Well, it is a honour, that is!' said Charley, a little consoled.

'He shall have all he wants,' continued the Jew. 'He shall be kept in the Stone Jug, Charley, like a gentleman – like a gentleman! with his beer every day, and money in his pocket to pitch and toss with, if he can't spend it.'

'No! shall he, though?' cried Charley Bates.

'Ay, that he shall,' replied the Jew; 'and we'll have a big-wig, Charley, one that's got the greatest gift of the gab, to carry on his defence; and he shall make a speech for himself too, if he likes; and we'll read it all in the papers – "Artful Dodger – shrieks of laughter – here the court was convulsed" – eh, Charley, eh?'

'Ha! ha!' laughed Master Bates, 'what a lark that would be, wouldn't it, Fagin? I say, how the Artful would bother 'em, wouldn't he?'

'Would!' cried the Jew. 'He shall – he will!'

'Ah, to be sure, so he will,' repeated Charley, rubbing his hands.

'I think I see him now!' cried the Jew, bending his eyes upon his pupil.

'So do I!' cried Charley Bates. 'Ha! ha! ha! so do I. I see it all afore me – upon my soul I do, Fagin. What a game! What a regular game! All the big-wigs trying to look solemn, and Jack Dawkins addressing of 'em as intimate and comfortable as if he was the judge's own son making speech arter dinner – ha! ha! ha!'

In fact, the Jew had so well humoured his young friend's eccentric disposition, that Master Bates, who had at first been disposed to consider the imprisoned Dodger rather in the light of a victim, now looked upon him as the chief actor in a scene of most uncommon and exquisite humour, and felt quite impatient for the arrival of the time when his old companion should have so favourable an opportunity of displaying his abilities.

'We must know how he gets on today, by some handy means or other,' said Fagin. 'Let me think.'

'Shall I go?' asked Charley.

'Not for the world,' replied the Jew. 'Are you mad, my dear, stark mad, that you'd walk into the very place where – No, Charley, no. One is enough to lose at a time.'

'You don't mean to go yourself, I suppose?' said Charley, with a humorous leer.

'That wouldn't quite fit,' replied Fagin, shaking his head.

'Then why don't you send this new cove?' asked Master Bates, laying his hand on Noah's arm. 'Nobody knows him.'

'Why, if he didn't mind –' observed the Jew.

'Mind,' interposed Charley. 'What should *he* have to mind?'

'Really nothing, my dear,' said Fagin, turning to Mr Bolter, 'really nothing.'

'Oh, I dare say about that, yer know,' observed Noah, backing towards the door, and shaking his head with a kind of sober alarm. 'No, no – none of that. It's not in my department, that ain't.'

'Wot department has he got, Fagin?' enquired Master Bates, surveying Noah's lank form with much disgust. 'The cutting away when there's anything wrong, and the eating all the wittles when there's everything right; is that his branch?'

'Never mind,' retorted Mr Bolter 'and don't yer take liberties with yer superiors, little boy, or yer'll find yerself in the wrong shop.'

Master Bates laughed so vehemently at this magnificent threat, that it was some time before Fagin could interpose, and represent to Mr Bolter that he incurred no possible danger in visiting the police-office; that inasmuch as no account of the little affair in which he had been engaged, nor any description of his person, had yet been forwarded to the metropolis, it was very probable that he was not even suspected of having resorted to it for shelter; and that if he were properly disguised, it would be as safe a spot for him to visit as any in London, inasmuch as it would be, of all places, the very last to which he could be supposed likely to resort of his own free will.

Persuaded, in part, by these representations, but overborne in a much greater degree by his fear of the Jew, Mr Bolter at length consented, with a very bad grace, to undertake the expedition. By Fagin's directions, he immediately substituted for his own attire a wagoner's frock, velveteen breeches, and leather leggings, all of which articles the Jew had at hand. He was likewise furnished with a felt hat well garnished with turnpike tickets, and a carter's whip. Thus equipped, he was to saunter into the office, as some country fellow from Covent Garden market might be supposed to do for the gratification of his curiosity; and as he was as awkward, ungainly, and rawboned a fellow as need be, Mr Fagin had no fear but that he would look the part to perfection.

These arrangements completed, he was informed of the

necessary signs and tokens by which to recognise the Artful Dodger, and was conveyed by Master Bates through dark and winding ways to within a very short distance of Bow Street. Having described the precise situation of the office, and accompanied it with copious directions how he was to walk straight up the passage, and when he got into the yard take the door up the steps on the right-hand side, and pull off his hat as he went into the room, Charley Bates bade him hurry on alone, and promised to bide his return on the spot of their parting.

Noah Claypole, or Morris Bolter, as the reader pleases, punctiliously followed the directions he had received, which – Master Bates being pretty well acquainted with the locality – were so exact that he was enabled to gain the magisterial presence without asking any question, or meeting with any interruption by the way. He found himself jostled among a crowd of people, chiefly women, who were huddled together in a dirty frowzy room, at the upper end of which was a raised platform railed off from the rest, with a dock for the prisoners on the left hand against the wall, a box for the witnesses in the middle, and a desk for the magistrates on the right; the awful locality last named being screened off by a partition which concealed the bench from the common gaze, and left the vulgar to imagine (if they could) the full majesty of justice.

There were only a couple of women in the dock, who were nodding to their admiring friends, while the clerk read some depositions to a couple of policemen and a man in plain clothes who leant over the table. A jailer stood reclining against the dock-rail, tapping his nose listlessly with a large key, except when he repressed an undue tendency to conversation among the idlers, by proclaiming silence; or looked sternly up to bid some woman 'Take that baby out,' when the gravity of justice was disturbed by feeble cries, half-smothered in the mother's shawl, from some meagre infant. The room smelt close and unwholesome, the walls were dirt-discoloured, and the ceiling blackened. There was an old smoky bust over the mantelshelf, and a dusty clock above the dock – the only thing present that seemed to go on as it ought; for depravity, or poverty, or a habitual acquaintance with both, had left a taint on all the animate matter, hardly less unpleasant than the thick greasy scum on every inanimate object that frowned upon it.

Noah looked eagerly about him for the Dodger; but although there were several women who would have done very well for that distinguished character's mother or sister, and more than one man who might be supposed to bear a strong resemblance to his father, nobody at all answering the description given him of Mr Dawkins was to be seen. He waited in a state of much suspense and uncertainty until the women, being committed for trial, went flaunting out; and then was quickly relieved by the appearance of another prisoner, who he felt at once could be no other than the object of his visit.

It was indeed Mr Dawkins, who, shuffling into the office with the big coat-sleeves tucked up as usual, his left hand in his pocket, and his hat in his right hand, preceded the jailer, with a rolling gait altogether indescribable, and, taking his place in the dock, requested in an audible voice to know what he was placed in that 'ere disgraceful situation for.

'Hold your tongue, will you?' said the jailer.

'I'm an Englishman, ain't I?' rejoined the Dodger; 'where are my priwileges?'

'You'll get your privileges soon enough,' retorted the jailer, 'and pepper with 'em.'

'We'll see wot the Secretary of State for the Home Affairs has got to say to the beaks, if I don't,' replied Mr Dawkins. 'Now then! Wot is this here business? I shall thank the madg'strates to dispose of this here little affair, and not to keep me while they read the paper, for I've got an appointment with a genelman in the city, and as I'm a man of my word and wery punctual in business matters, he'll go away if I ain't there to my time, and then pr'aps there won't be an action for damage against them as kept me away. On, no, certainly not!'

At this point the Dodger, with a show of being very particular with a view to proceedings to be had thereafter, desired the jailer to communicate 'the names of them two files as was on the bench,' which so tickled the spectators, that they laughed almost as heartily as Master Bates could have done if he had heard the request.

'Silence there!' cried the jailer.

'What is this?' enquired one of the magistrates.

'A pick-pocketing case, your worship.'

'Has the boy ever been here before?'

'He ought to have been, a many times,' replied the jailer. 'He has been pretty well everywhere else. *I* know him well, your worship.'

'Oh! you know me, do you?' cried the Artful, making a note of the statement. 'Wery good. That's a case of deformation of character anyway.'

Here there was another laugh, and another cry of silence.

'Now then, where are the witnesses?' said the clerk.

'Ah! that's right,' added the Dodger. 'Where are they? I should like to see 'em.'

This wish was immediately gratified, for a policeman stepped forward who had seen the prisoner attempt the pocket of an unknown gentleman in a crowd, and indeed take a handkerchief therefrom which, being a very old one, he deliberately put back again, after trying it on his own countenance. For this reason, he took the Dodger into custody as soon as he could get near him, and the said Dodger being searched, had upon his person a silver snuff-box with the owner's name engraved upon the lid. This gentleman had been discovered on reference to the Court Guide, and being then and there present, swore that the snuff-box was his, and that he had missed it on the previous day, the moment he had disengaged himself from the crowd before referred to. He had also remarked a young gentleman in the throng particularly active in making his way about, and that young gentleman was the prisoner before him.

'Have you anything to ask this witness, boy?' said the magistrate.

'I wouldn't abase myself by descending to hold no conversation with him,' replied the Dodger.

'Have you anything to say at all?'

'Do you hear his worship ask if you have anything to say?' enquired the jailer, nudging the silent Dodger with his elbow.

'I beg your pardon,' said the Dodger, looking up with an air of abstraction. 'Did you redress yourself to me, my man?'

'I never see such an out-and-out young wagabond, your worship,' observed the officer with a grin. 'Do you mean to say anything, you young shaver?'

'No,' replied the Dodger, 'not here, for this ain't the shop for justice; besides which, my attorney is a-breakfasting this morning with the Wice-President of the House of Commons; but I shall have something to say elsewhere, and so will he, and so will a wery numerous and 'spectable circle of acquaintance as'll make them beaks wish they'd never been born, or that they'd got their footmen to hang 'em up to their own hat-pegs afore they let 'em come out this morning to try it on upon me. I'll –'

'There! He's fully committed!' interposed the clerk. 'Take him away.'

'Come on,' said the jailer.

'Oh, ah! I'll come on,' replied the Dodger, brushing his hat with the palm of his hand. 'Ah! (to the Bench) it's no use your looking frightened; I won't show you no mercy, not a ha'porth of it. *You'll* pay for this, my fine fellers. I wouldn't be you for something! I wouldn't go free, now, if you was to fall down on your knees and ask me. Here, carry me off to prison! Take me away!'

With these last words the Dodger suffered himself to be led off by the collar, threatening, till he got into the yard, to make a parliamentary business of it; and then grinning in the officer's face with great glee and self-approval.

Having seen him locked up by himself in a little cell, Noah made the best of his way back to where he had left Master Bates. After waiting here some time, he was joined by that young gentleman, who had prudently abstained from showing himself until he had looked carefully abroad from a snug retreat, and ascertained that his new friend had not been followed by any impertinent person.

The two hastened back together, to bear to Mr Fagin the animating news that the Dodger was doing full justice to his bringing-up, and establishing for himself a glorious reputation.

CHAPTER 44

The time arrives for Nancy to redeem
her pledge to Rose Maylie. She fails

Adept as she was in all the arts of cunning and dissimulation, the girl Nancy could not wholly conceal the effect which the knowledge of the step she had taken worked upon her mind. She remembered that both the crafty Jew and the brutal Sikes had confided to her schemes which had been hidden from all others, in the full confidence that she was trustworthy and beyond the reach of their suspicion. Vile as those schemes were, desperate as were their originators, and bitter as were her feelings towards the Jew, who had led her, step by step, deeper and deeper down into an abyss of crime and misery whence

was no escape, still there were times when, even towards him, she felt some relenting, lest her disclosure should bring him within the iron grasp he had so long eluded, and he should fall at last – richly as he merited such a fate – by her hand.

But these were the mere wanderings of a mind unable wholly to detach itself from old companions and associations, though enabled to fix itself steadily on one object, and resolved not to be turned aside by any consideration. Her fears for Sikes would have been more powerful inducements to recoil while there was yet time; but she had stipulated that her secret should be rigidly kept, she had dropped no clue which could lead to his discovery, she had refused even, for his sake, a refuge from all the guilt and wretchedness that encompassed her – and what more could she do? She was resolved.

Though all her mental struggles terminated in this conclusion, they forced themselves upon her again and again, and left their traces too. She grew pale and thin, even within a few days. At times she took no heed of what was passing before her, or no part in conversations where once she would have been the loudest. At other times she laughed without merriment, and was noisy without cause or meaning. At others – often within a moment afterwards – she sat silent and dejected, brooding with her head upon her hands; while the very effort by which she roused herself told more forcibly than even these indications that she was ill at ease, and that her thoughts were occupied with matters very different and distant from those in course of discussion by her companions.

It was Sunday night, and the bell of the nearest church struck the hour. Sikes and the Jew were talking, but they paused to listen. The girl looked up from the low seat on which she crouched, and listened too. Eleven.

'An hour this side of midnight,' said Sikes, raising the blind to look out, and returning to his seat. 'Dark and heavy it is too. A good night for business this.'

'Ah!' replied the Jew. 'What a pity, Bill, my dear, that there's none quite ready to be done!'

'You're right for once,' replied Sikes gruffly. 'It is a pity, for I'm in the humour too.'

The Jew sighed, and shook his head despondingly.

'We must make up for lost time when we've got things in a good train. That's all I know,' said Sikes.

'That's the way to talk, my dear,' replied the Jew, venturing to pat him on the shoulder. 'It does me good to hear you.'

'Does you good, does it?' cried Sikes. 'Well, so be it.'

'Ha! ha! ha!' laughed the Jew, as if he were relieved by even this concession. 'You're like yourself tonight, Bill – quite like yourself.'

'I don't feel like myself when you lay that withered old claw on my shoulder, so take it away,' said Sikes, casting off the Jew's hand.

'It makes you nervous, Bill – reminds you of being nabbed, does it?' said the Jew, determined not to be offended.

'Reminds me of being nabbed by the devil,' returned Sikes. 'There never was another man with such a face as yours, unless it was your father, and I suppose *he* is singeing his grizzled red beard by this time, unless you came straight from the old un without any father at all betwixt you; which I shouldn't wonder at a bit.'

Fagin offered no reply to this compliment, but pulling Sikes by the sleeve, pointed his finger towards Nancy, who had taken advantage of the foregoing conversation to put on her bonnet, and was now leaving the room.

'Hallo!' cried Sikes. 'Nance! Where's the girl going to at this time of night?'

'Not far.'

'What answer's that?' returned Sikes. 'Where are you going?'

'I say, not far.'

'And I say where?' retorted Sikes. 'Do you hear me?'

'I don't know where,' replied the girl.

'Then I do,' said Sikes, more in the spirit of obstinacy than because he had any real objection to the girl going where she liked. 'Nowhere. Sit down.'

'I'm not well. I told you that before,' rejoined the girl. 'I want a breath of air.'

'Put your head out of the winder,' replied Sikes.

'There's not enough there,' said the girl. 'I want it in the street.'

'Then you won't have it,' replied Sikes. With which assurance he rose, locked the door, took the key out, and pulling her bonnet from her head, flung it up to the top of an old press. 'There,' said the robber. 'Now stop quietly where you are, will you?'

'It's not such a matter as a bonnet would keep me,' said the girl, turning very pale. 'What do you mean, Bill? Do you know what you're doing?'

'Know what I'm – Oh!' cried Sikes, turning to Fagin, 'she's out of her senses, you know, or she daren't talk to me in that way.'

'You'll drive me on to something desperate,' muttered the girl, placing both hands upon her breast, as though to keep down by force some violent outbreak. 'Let me go, will you – this minute – this instant – '

'No!' said Sikes.

'Tell him to let me go, Fagin. He had better. It'll be better for him. Do you hear me?' cried Nancy, stamping her foot upon the ground.

'Hear you!' repeated Sikes, turning round in his chair to confront her. 'Ay! And if I hear you for half a minute longer, the dog shall have such a grip on your throat as'll tear some of that screaming voice out. Wot has come over you, you jade? Wot is it?'

'Let me go,' said the girl, with great earnestness; then sitting herself down on the floor, before the door, she said, 'Bill, let me go; you don't know what you're doing. You don't indeed. For only one hour – do – do!'

'Cut my limbs off one by one!' cried Sikes, seizing her roughly by the arm, 'if I don't think the gal's stark raving mad. Get up.'

'Not till you let me go – not till you let me go – never – never!' screamed the girl. Sikes looked on for a minute, watching his opportunity, and suddenly pinioning her hands, dragged her, struggling and wrestling with him by the way, into a small room adjoining, where he sat himself on a bench, and thrusting

her into a chair, held her down by force. She struggled and implored by turns until twelve o'clock had struck, and then, wearied and exhausted, ceased to contest the point any further. With a caution, backed by many oaths, to make no more efforts to go out that night, Sikes left her to recover at leisure, and rejoined the Jew.

'Whew!' said the housebreaker, wiping the perspiration from his face. 'Wot a precious strange gal that is!'

'You may say that, Bill,' replied the Jew thoughtfully. 'You may say that.'

'Wot did she take it into her head to go out tonight for, do you think?' asked Sikes. 'Come; you should know her better than me. Wot does it mean?'

'Obstinacy! woman's obstinacy, I suppose, my dear,' replied the Jew, shrugging his shoulders.

'Well, I suppose it is,' growled Sikes. 'I thought I had tamed her, but she's as bad as ever.'

'Worse,' said the Jew thoughtfully. 'I never knew her like this, for such a little cause.'

'Nor I,' said Sikes. 'I think she's got a touch of that fever in her blood yet, and it won't come out – eh?'

'Like enough,' replied the Jew.

'I'll let her a little blood, without troubling the doctor, if she's took that way again,' said Sikes.

The Jew nodded an expressive approval of this mode of treatment.

'She was hanging about me all day, and night too, when I was stretched on my back, and you, like a black-hearted wolf as you are, kept yourself aloof,' said Sikes. 'We was very poor, too, all the time, and I think, one way or other, it's worried and fretted her; and that being shut up here so long has made her restless – eh?'

'That's it, my dear,' replied the Jew in a whisper. 'Hush!'

As he uttered these words, the girl herself appeared and resumed her former seat. Her eyes were swollen and red; she rocked herself to and fro, tossed her head, and after a little time burst out laughing.

'Why, now she's on the other tack!' exclaimed Sikes, turning a look of excessive surprise on his companion.

The Jew nodded to him to take no further notice just then; and, in a few minutes, the girl subsided into her accustomed demeanour. Whispering to Sikes that there was no fear of her relapsing, Fagin took up his hat and bade him good-night. He paused when he reached the room-door, and looking round, asked if somebody would light him down the dark stairs.

'Light him down,' said Sikes, who was filling his pipe. 'It's a pity he should break his neck himself, and disappoint the sightseers. Show him a light.'

Nancy followed the old man downstairs, with a candle. When they reached the passage, he laid his finger on his lip, and drawing close to the girl, said in a whisper, 'What is it, Nancy, dear?'

'What do you mean?' replied the girl, in the same tone.

'The reason of all this,' replied Fagin. 'If *he* ' – he pointed with his skinny forefinger up the stairs – 'is so hard with you (he's a brute, Nancy, a brute beast), why don't you – '

'Well?' said the girl, as Fagin paused, with his mouth almost touching her ear, and his eyes looking into hers.

'No matter just now,' said the Jew, 'we'll talk of this again. You have a friend in me, Nancy – a stanch friend. I have the means at hand, quiet and close. If you want revenge on those that treat you like a dog – like a dog! worse than a dog, for he humours him sometimes – come to me. I say, come to me. He is the mere hound of a day; but you know me of old, Nance.'

'I know you well,' replied the girl, without manifesting the least emotion. 'Good-night.'

She shrunk back as Fagin offered to lay his hand on hers, but said good-night again, in a steady voice, and answering his parting look with a nod of intelligence, closed the door between them.

Fagin walked towards his own home, intent upon the thoughts that were working within his brain. He had conceived the idea – not from what had just passed, though that had tended to confirm him, but slowly and by degrees – that Nancy, wearied of the housebreaker's brutality, had conceived an attachment for some new friend. Her altered manner, her repeated absences from home alone, her comparative indifference to the interests of the gang for which she had once been so zealous, and, added to these, her desperate impatience to leave home that night at a particular hour, all favoured the supposition, and rendered it, to him at least, almost a matter of certainty. The object of this new liking was not among his myrmidons. He would be a valuable acquisition with such an assistant as Nancy, and must (thus Fagin argued) be secured without delay.

There was another and a darker object to be gained. Sikes knew too much and his ruffian taunts had not galled the Jew the less because the wounds were hidden. The girl must know well that if she shook him off, she could never be safe from his fury, and that it would be surely wreaked – to the maiming of limbs, or perhaps the loss of life – on the object of her more recent fancy. 'With a little persuasion,' thought Fagin, 'what more likely than that she would consent to poison him? Women have done such things, and worse, to secure the same object before now. There would be the dangerous villain – the man I hate – gone; another secured in his place; and my influence over the girl, with a knowledge of this crime to back it, unlimited.'

These things passed through the mind of Fagin, during the short time he sat alone, in the housebreaker's room; and with them uppermost in his thoughts, he had taken the opportunity afterwards afforded him of sounding the girl in the broken hints he threw out at parting. There was no expression of surprise, no assumption of an inability to understand his meaning. The girl clearly comprehended it. Her glance at parting showed *that*.

But perhaps she would recoil from a plot to take the life of Sikes, and that was one of the chief ends to be attained. 'How,' thought the Jew, as he crept homewards, 'can I increase my influence with her? what new power can I acquire?'

Such brains are fertile in expedients. If, without extracting a confession from herself, he laid a watch, discovered the object of her altered regard, and threatened to reveal the whole history to Sikes (of whom she stood in no common fear) unless she entered into his designs, could he not secure her compliance?

'I can,' said Fagin, almost aloud. 'She durst not refuse me then. Not for her life! not for her life! I have it all. The means are ready, and shall be set to work. I shall have you yet!'

He cast back a dark look, and a threatening motion of the hand, towards the spot where he had left the bolder villain, and went on his way, busying his bony hands in the folds of his tattered garment, which he wrenched tightly in his grasp, as though there were a hated enemy crushed with every motion of his fingers.

CHAPTER 45

Noah Claypole is employed by Fagin on a secret mission

The old man was up betimes next morning, and waited impatiently for the appearance of his new associate, who, after a delay that seemed interminable, at length presented himself, and commenced a voracious assault on the breakfast.

'Bolter,' said the Jew, drawing up a chair and seating himself opposite Morris Bolter.

'Well, here I am,' returned Noah. 'What's the matter? Don't yer ask me to do anything till I have done eating. That's a great fault in this place. Yer never get time enough over yer meals.'

'You can talk as you eat, can't you?' said Fagin, cursing his dear young friend's greediness from the very bottom of his heart.

'Oh, yes, I can talk. I get on better when I talk,' said Noah, cutting a monstrous slice of bread. 'Where's Charlotte?'

'Out,' said Fagin. 'I sent her out this morning with the other young woman, because I wanted us to be alone.'

'Oh!' said Noah. 'I wish yer'd ordered her to make some buttered toast first. Well. Talk away. Yer won't interrupt me.'

There seemed, indeed, no great fear of anything interrupting him, as he had evidently sat down with a determination to do a great deal of business.

'You did well yesterday, my dear,' said the Jew. 'Beautiful. Six shillings and ninepence halfpenny on the very first day. The kinchin lay will be a fortune to you.'

'Don't yer forget to add three pint-pots and a milk-can,' said Mr Bolter.

'No, no, my dear,' replied the Jew. 'The pint-pots were great strokes of genius, but the milk-can was a perfect masterpiece.'

'Pretty well, I think, for a beginner,' remarked Mr Bolter complacently. 'The pots I took off airy railings, and the milk-can was standing by itself outside a public-house. I thought it might get rusty with the rain, or catch cold, yer know. Eh? Ha! ha! ha!'

The Jew affected to laugh very heartily; and Mr Bolter, having had his laugh out, took a series of large bites, which finished his first hunk of bread and butter, and assisted himself to a second.

'I want you, Bolter,' said Fagin, leaning over the table, 'to do a piece of work for me, my dear, that needs great care and caution.'

'I say,' rejoined Bolter, 'don't yer go shoving me into danger, or sending me to any more o' yer police-offices. That don't suit me, that don't; and so I tell yer.'

'There's not the smallest danger in it – not the very smallest,' said the Jew; 'it's only to dodge a woman.'

'An old woman?' demanded Mr Bolter.

'A young one,' replied Fagin.

'I can do that pretty well, I know,' said Bolter. 'I was a regular cunning sneak when I was at school. What am I to dodge her for? Not to – '

'Not to do anything,' interrupted the Jew, 'but to tell me where she goes, who she sees, and, if possible, what she says; to remember the street, if it is a street, or the house, if it is a house; and to bring me back all the information you can.'

'What'll yer give me?' asked Noah, setting down his cup, and looking his employer eagerly in the face.

'If you do it well, a pound, my dear. One pound,' said Fagin, wishing to interest him in the scent as much as possible. 'And that's what I never gave yet for any job of work where there wasn't valuable consideration to be gained.'

'Who is she?' enquired Noah.

'One of us.'

'Oh, Lor!' cried Noah, curling up his nose. 'Yer doubtful of her, are yer?'

'She has found out some new friends, my dear, and I must know who they are,' replied the Jew.

'I see,' said Noah. 'Just to have the pleasure of knowing them, if they're respectable people, eh? Ha! ha! ha! I'm your man.'

'I knew you would be,' cried Fagin, elated by the success of his proposal.

'Of course, of course,' replied Noah. 'Where is she? Where am I to wait for her? When am I to go?'

'All that, my dear, you shall hear from me. I'll point her out at the proper time,' said Fagin. 'You keep ready, and leave the rest to me.'

That night, and the next, and the next again, the spy sat booted and equipped in his carter's dress, ready to turn out at a word from Fagin. Six nights passed – six long weary nights – and on each Fagin came home with a disappointed face, and briefly intimated that it was not yet time. On the seventh, he returned earlier, and with an exultation he could not conceal. It was Sunday.

'She goes abroad tonight,' said Fagin, 'and on the right errand, I'm sure; for she has been alone all day, and the man she is afraid of will not be back much before daybreak. Come with me. Quick!'

Noah started up without saying a word, for the Jew was in a state of such intense excitement that it infected him. They left the house stealthily, and, hurrying through a labyrinth of streets, arrived at length before a public-house, which Noah recognised as the same in which he had slept on the night of his arrival in London.

It was past eleven o'clock, and the door was closed. It opened softly on its hinges as the Jew gave a low whistle. They entered, without noise; and the door was closed behind them.

Scarcely venturing to whisper, but substituting dumb show for words, Fagin and the young Jew who had admitted them pointed out the pane of glass to Noah, and signed to him to climb up and observe the person in the adjoining room.

'Is that the woman?' he asked, scarcely above his breath.

The Jew nodded yes.

'I can't see her face well,' whispered Noah. 'She is looking down, and the candle is behind her.'

'Stay there,' whispered Fagin. He signed to Barney, who withdrew. In an instant, the lad entered the room adjoining, and, under pretence of snuffing the candle, moved it into the required position, and, speaking to the girl, caused her to raise her face.

'I see her now!' cried the spy.

'Plainly?' asked the Jew.

'I should know her among a thousand.'

He hastily descended, as the room-door opened, and the girl came out. Fagin drew him behind a small partition which was curtained off, and they held their breaths as she passed within a few feet of their place of concealment, and emerged by the door at which they had entered.

'Hist!' cried the lad who held the door. 'Dow.' Noah exchanged a look with Fagin, and darted out.

'To the left,' whispered the lad; 'take the left had, and keep od the other side.'

He did so; and, by the light of the lamps, saw the girl's retreating figure, already at some distance before him. He advanced as near as he considered prudent, and kept on the opposite side of the street, the better to observe her motions. She looked nervously round, twice or thrice, and once stopped to let two men who were following close behind her pass on. She seemed to gather courage as she advanced, and to walk with a steadier and firmer step. The spy preserved the same relative distance between them, and followed, with his eye upon her.

CHAPTER 46

The appointment kept

The church clock chimed three-quarters past eleven as two figures emerged on London Bridge. One, which advanced with a swift and rapid step, was that of a woman, who looked eagerly about her, as though in quest of some expected object; the other figure was that of a man, who slunk along in the deepest shadow he could find, and, at some distance, accommodated his pace to hers, stopping when she stopped, and as she moved again, creeping stealthily on, but never allowing himself, in the ardour of his pursuit, to gain upon her footsteps. Thus they crossed the bridge, from the Middlesex to the Surrey shore, when the woman, apparently disappointed in her anxious scrutiny of the foot-passengers, turned back. The movement was sudden; but he who watched her was not thrown off his guard by it, for, shrinking into one of the recesses which surmount the piers of the bridge, and leaning over the parapet the better to conceal his figure, he suffered her to pass by on the opposite pavement. When she was about the same distance in advance as she had been before, he slipped quietly down, and followed her again. At nearly the centre of the bridge she stopped. The man stopped too.

It was a very dark night. The day had been unfavourable, and at that hour and place there were few people stirring. Such as there were hurried quickly past, very possibly without seeing, but certainly without noticing, either the woman or the man who kept her in view. Their appearance was not calculated to attract the importunate regard of such of London's destitute population as chanced to make their way over the bridge that night in search of some cold arch or doorless hovel wherein to lay their heads: they stood there in silence, neither speaking nor spoken to by anyone who passed.

A mist hung over the river, deepening the red glare of the fires that burnt upon the small craft moored off the different wharfs, and rendering darker and more indistinct the mirky buildings on the banks. The old smoke-stained storehouses on either side rose heavy and dull from the dense mass of roofs and gables, and frowned sternly upon water too black to reflect even their lumbering shapes. The tower of old Saint Saviour's church and the spire of Saint Magnus, so long the giant-warders of the ancient bridge, were visible in the gloom, but the forest of shipping below the bridge, and the thickly scattered spires of churches above, were nearly all hidden from the sight.

The girl had taken a few restless turns to and fro – closely watched meanwhile by her hidden observer – when the heavy bell of St Paul's tolled for the death of another day. Midnight had come upon the crowded city. The palace, the night-cellar, the jail, the madhouse; the chambers of birth and death, of health and sickness; the rigid face of the corpse and the calm sleep of the child – midnight was upon them all.

The hour had not struck two minutes, when a young lady, accompanied by a grey-haired gentleman, alighted from a hackney-carriage within a short distance of the bridge, and having dismissed the vehicle, walked straight towards it. They had scarcely set foot upon its pavement, when the girl started, and immediately made towards them.

They walked onward, looking about them with the air of persons who entertained some very slight expectation which had little chance of being realised, when they were suddenly joined by this new associate. They halted, with an exclamation of surprise, but suppressed it immediately; for a man in the garments of a countryman came close up – brushed against them, indeed – at that precise moment.

'Not here,' said Nancy hurriedly; 'I am afraid to speak to you here. Come away – out of the public road – down the steps yonder.'

As she uttered these words, and indicated, with her hand, the direction in which she wished them to proceed, the countryman looked round, and roughly asking what they took up the whole pavement for, passed on.

The steps to which the girl had pointed were those which, on the Surrey bank, and on the same side of the bridge as Saint Saviour's church, form a landing-stairs from the river. To this spot the man bearing the appearance of a countryman hastened, unobserved; and after a moment's survey of the place, he began to descend.

These stairs are a part of the bridge; they consist of three flights. Just below the end of the second, going down, the stone wall on the left terminates in an ornamental pilaster facing towards the Thames. At this point the lower steps widen, so that a person turning that angle of the wall is necessarily unseen by any others on the stairs who chance to be above him, if only a step. The countryman looked hastily round when he reached this point; and as there seemed no better place of concealment, and, the tide being out, there was plenty of room, he slipped aside, with his back to the pilaster, and there waited, pretty certain that they would come no lower, and that even if he could not hear what was said, he could follow them again with safety.

So tardily stole the time in this lonely place, and so eager was the spy to penetrate the motives of an interview so different from what he had been led to expect, that he more than once gave the matter up for lost, and persuaded himself either that they had stopped far above, or had resorted to some entirely different spot to hold their mysterious conversation. He was on the very point of emerging from his hiding-place, and regaining the road above, when he heard the sound of footsteps, and directly afterwards of voices almost close at his ear.

He drew himself straight upright against the wall, and, scarcely breathing, listened attentively.

'This is far enough,' said a voice, which was evidently that of the gentleman. 'I will not suffer the young lady to go any farther. Many people would have distrusted you too much to have come even so far, but you see I am willing to humour you.'

'To humour me!' cried the voice of the girl whom he had followed. 'You're considerate, indeed, sir. To humour me! Well, well, it's no matter.'

'Why, for what,' said the gentleman, in a kinder tone, 'for what purpose can you have brought us to this strange place? Why not have let me speak to you above there where it is light, and there is something stirring, instead of bringing us to this dark and dismal hole?'

'I told you before,' replied Nancy, 'that I was afraid to speak to you there. I don't know why it is,' said the girl, shuddering, 'but I have such a fear and dread upon me tonight that I can hardly stand.'

'A fear of what?' asked the gentleman, who seemed to pity her.

'I scarcely know of what,' replied the girl. 'I wish I did. Horrible thoughts of death, and shrouds with blood upon them, and a fear that has made me burn, as if I was on fire, have been upon me all day. I was reading a book tonight, to wile the time away, and the same things came into the print.'

'Imagination,' said the gentleman, soothing her.

'No imagination,' replied the girl, in a hoarse voice. 'I'll swear I saw "coffin" written in every page of the book in large black letters – ay, and they carried one close to me in the streets tonight.'

'There is nothing unusual in that,' said the gentleman. 'They have passed me often.'

'*Real ones*,' rejoined the girl. 'This was not.'

There was something so uncommon in her manner, that the flesh of the concealed listener crept as he heard the girl utter these words, and the blood chilled within him. He had never experienced a greater relief than in hearing the sweet voice of the young lady as she begged her to be calm, and not allow herself to become the prey of such fearful fancies.

'Speak to her kindly,' said the young lady to her companion. 'Poor creature! she seems to need it.'

'Your haughty religious people would have held their heads up to see me as I am tonight, and preached of flames and vengeance,' cried the girl. 'Oh, dear lady, why aren't those who claim to be God's own folks as gentle and as kind to us poor wretches as you, who, having youth, and beauty, and all that they have lost, might be a little proud instead of so much humbler?'

'Ah!' said the gentleman. 'A Turk turns his face, after washing it well, to the East, when he says his prayers; these good people, after giving their faces such a rub against the World as to take the smiles off, turn, with no less regularity, to the darkest side of Heaven. Between the Mussulman and the Pharisee, commend me to the first!'

These words appeared to be addressed to the young lady, and were perhaps uttered with the view of affording Nancy time to recover herself. The gentleman, shortly afterwards, addressed himself to her.

'You were not here last Sunday night,' he said.

'I couldn't come,' replied Nancy; 'I was kept by force.'

'By whom?'

'Him that I told the young lady of before.'

'You were not suspected of holding any communication with anybody on the subject which has brought us here tonight, I hope?' asked the old gentleman.

'No,' replied the girl, shaking her head. 'It's not very easy for me to leave him unless he knows why; I couldn't have seen the lady when I did, but that I gave him a drink of laudanum before I came away.'

'Did he awake before you returned?' enquired the gentleman.

'No; and neither he nor any of them suspect me.'

'Good,' said the gentleman. 'Now listen to me.'

'I am ready,' replied the girl, as he paused for a moment.

'This young lady,' the gentleman began, 'has communicated to me, and to some other friends who can be safely trusted, what you told her nearly a fortnight since. I confess to you that I had doubts, at first, whether you were to be implicitly relied upon, but now I firmly believe you are.'

'I am,' said the girl earnestly.

'I repeat that I firmly believe it. To prove to you that I am disposed to trust you, I tell you without reserve that we propose to extort the secret, whatever it may be, from the fears of this man Monks. But if – if,' said the gentleman, 'he cannot be secured, or, if secured, cannot be acted upon as we wish, you must deliver up the Jew.'

'Fagin!' cried the girl, recoiling.

'That man must be delivered up by you,' said the gentleman.

'I will not do it! I will never do it!' replied the girl. 'Devil that he is, and worse than devil as he has been to me, I will never do that.'

'You will not?' said the gentleman, who seemed fully prepared for this answer.

'Never!' returned the girl.

'Tell me why.'

'For one reason,' rejoined the girl firmly – 'for one reason, that the lady knows and will stand by me in. I know she will, for I have her promise; and for this other reason, besides, that, bad life as he has led, I have led a bad life too. There are many of us who have kept the same courses together, and I'll not turn upon them, who might – any of them – have turned upon me, but didn't, bad as they are.'

'Then,' said the gentleman quickly, as if this had been the point he had been aiming to attain, 'put Monks into my hands, and leave him to me to deal with.'

'What if he turns against the others?'

'I promise you that in that case, if the truth is forced from him, there the matter will rest. There must be circumstances in Oliver's little history which it would be painful to drag before the public eye; and if the truth is once elicited, they shall go scot free.'

'And if it is not?' suggested the girl.

'Then,' pursued the gentleman, 'this Jew shall not be brought to justice without your consent. In such a case I could show you reasons, I think, which would induce you to yield it.'

The meeting

'Have I the lady's promise for that?' asked the girl.

'You have,' replied Rose – 'my true and faithful pledge.'

'Monks would never learn how you knew what you do?' said the girl, after a short pause.

'Never,' replied the gentleman. 'The intelligence should be so brought to bear upon him that he could never even guess.'

'I have been a liar, and among liars from a little child,' said the girl, after another interval of silence, 'but I will take your words.'

After receiving an assurance from both that she might safely do so, she proceeded, in a voice so low that it was often difficult for the listener to discover even the purport of what she said, to describe, by name and situation, the public-house whence she had been followed that night. From the manner in which she occasionally paused, it appeared as if the gentleman were making some hasty notes of the information she communicated. When she had thoroughly explained the localities of the place, the best position from which to watch it without exciting observation, and the night and hour on which Monks was most in the habit of frequenting it, she seemed to consider for a few moments, for the purpose of recalling his features and appearance more forcibly to her recollection.

'He is tall,' said the girl, 'and a strongly made man, but not stout. He has a lurking walk; and as he walks, constantly looks over his shoulder, first on one side and then on the other. Don't forget that, for his eyes are sunk in his head so much deeper than any other man's, that you might almost tell him by that alone. His face is dark, like his hair and eyes; and, although he can't be more than six- or eight-and-twenty, withered and haggard. His lips are often discoloured and disfigured with the marks of teeth; for he has desperate fits, and sometimes even bites his hands and covers them with wounds – why did you start?' said the girl, stopping suddenly.

The gentleman replied, in a hurried manner, that he was not conscious of having done so, and begged her to proceed.

'Part of this,' said the girl, 'I've drawn out from other people at the house I tell you of, for I have only seen him twice, and both times he was covered up in a large cloak. I think that's all I can give you to know him by. Stay, though,' she added. 'Upon his throat, so high that you can see a part of it below his neckerchief when he turns his face, there is – '

'A broad red mark, like a burn or scald!' cried the gentleman.

'How's this!' said the girl. 'You know him!'

The young lady uttered a cry of surprise, and for a few moments they were so still that the listener could distinctly hear them breathe.

'I think I do,' said the gentleman, breaking silence. 'I should, by your description. We shall see. Many people are singularly like each other. It may not be the same.'

As he expressed himself to this effect, with assumed carelessness, he took a step or two nearer the concealed spy, as the latter could tell from the distinctness with which he heard him mutter, 'It must be he!'

'Now,' he said, returning – so it seemed by the sound – to the spot where he had stood before, 'you have given us most valuable assistance, young woman, and I wish you to be the better for it. What can I do to serve you?'

'Nothing,' replied Nancy.

'You will not persist in saying that,' rejoined the gentleman, with a voice and emphasis of kindness that might have touched a much harder and more obdurate heart. 'Think now. Tell me.'

'Nothing, sir,' rejoined the girl, weeping. 'You can do nothing to help me. I am past all hope, indeed.'

'You put yourself beyond its pale,' said the gentleman. 'The past has been a dreary waste with you, of youthful energies misspent, and such priceless treasures lavished, as the Creator bestows but once and never grants again; but, for the future, you may hope. I do not say that it is in our power to offer you peace of heart and mind, for that must come as you seek it; but a quiet asylum, either in England, or, if you fear to remain here, in some foreign country, it is not only within the compass of our ability, but our most anxious wish to secure you. Before the dawn of morning, before this river wakes to the first glimpse of daylight, you shall be placed as entirely beyond the reach of your former associates, and leave as utter an absence of all trace behind you, as if you were to disappear from the earth this moment. Come! I would not have you go back to exchange one word with any old companion, or take one look at any old haunt, or breathe the very air which is pestilence and death to you. Quit them all, while there is time and opportunity!'

'She will be persuaded now!' cried the young lady. 'She hesitates, I am sure.'

'I fear not, my dear,' said the gentleman.

'No, sir, I do not,' replied the girl, after a short struggle. 'I am chained to my old life. I loathe and hate it now, but I cannot leave it. I must have gone too far to turn back – and yet I don't know, for if you had spoken to me so, some time ago, I should have laughed it off. But,' she said, looking hastily round, 'this fear comes over me again. I must go home.'

'Home!' repeated the young lady, with great stress upon the word.

'Home, lady,' rejoined the girl – 'to such a home as I have raised for myself with the work of my whole life. Let us part. I shall be watched or seen. Go! go! If I have done you any service, all I ask is, that you leave me, and let me go my way alone.'

'It is useless,' said the gentleman with a sigh. 'We compromise her safety, perhaps, by staying here. We may have detained her longer than she expected already.'

'Yes, yes,' urged the girl. 'You have.'

'What,' cried the young lady, 'can be the end of this poor creature's life?'

'What?' repeated the girl. 'Look before you, lady. Look at that dark water. How many times do you read of such as I who spring into the tide, and leave no living thing to care for or bewail them! It may be years hence, or it may be only months, but I shall come to that at last.'

'Do not speak thus, pray,' returned the young lady, sobbing.

'It will never reach your ears, dear lady; and God forbid such horrors should!' replied the girl. 'Good-night, good-night!'

The gentleman turned away.

'This purse,' cried the young lady; 'take it for my sake, that you may have some resource in an hour of need and trouble.'

'No!' replied the girl. 'I have not done this for money. Let me have that to think of. And yet – give me something that you have worn. I should like to have something – no, no, not a ring – your gloves or handkerchief – anything that I can keep, as having belonged to you, sweet lady. There. Bless you! God bless you! Good-night, good-night!'

The violent agitation of the girl, and the apprehension of some discovery which would subject her to ill-usage and violence, seemed to determine the gentleman to leave her, as she requested. The sound of retreating footsteps were audible, and the voices ceased.

The two figures of the young lady and her companion soon afterwards appeared upon the bridge. They stopped at the summit of the stairs.

'Hark!' cried the young lady, listening. 'Did she call? I thought I heard her voice.'

'No, my love,' replied Mr Brownlow, looking sadly back. 'She has not moved, and will not till we are gone.'

Rose Maylie lingered, but the old gentleman drew her arm through his, and led her, with gentle force, away. As they disappeared, the girl sunk down nearly at her full length upon one of the stone stairs, and vented the anguish of her heart in bitter tears.

After a time she arose, and with feeble and tottering steps ascended to the street. The astonished listener remained motionless at his post for some minutes afterwards, and having ascertained, with many cautious glances round him, that he was again alone, crept slowly from his hiding-place, and returned stealthily and in the shade of the wall, in the same manner as he had descended.

Peeping out, more than once, when he reached the top, to make sure that he was unobserved, Noah Claypole darted away at his utmost speed, and made for the Jew's house as fast as his legs could carry him.

CHAPTER 47

Fatal consequences

It was nearly two hours before daybreak – that time which, in the autumn of the year, may be truly called the dead of night, when the streets are silent and deserted, when even sound appears to slumber, and profligacy and riot have staggered home to dream – it was at this still and silent hour that the Jew sat watching in his old lair, with face so distorted and pale, and eyes so red and bloodshot, that he looked less like a man than like some hideous phantom, moist from the grave, and worried by an evil spirit.

He sat crouching over a cold hearth, wrapped in an old torn coverlet, with his face turned towards a wasting candle that stood upon a table by his side. His right hand was raised to his lips; and as, absorbed in thought, he bit his long black nails, he disclosed among his toothless gums a few such fangs as should have been a dog's or rat's.

Stretched upon a mattress on the floor lay Noah Claypole, fast asleep. Towards him the old man sometimes directed his

eyes for an instant, and then brought them back again to the candle; which, with long-burnt wick drooping almost double, and hot grease falling down in clots upon the table, plainly showed that his thoughts were busy elsewhere.

Indeed they were. Mortification at the overthrow of his notable scheme; hatred of the girl who had dared to palter with strangers; an utter distrust of the sincerity of her refusal to yield him up; bitter disappointment at the loss of his revenge on Sikes; the fear of detection, and ruin, and death; and a fierce and deadly rage kindled by all – these were the passionate considerations which, following close upon each other with rapid and ceaseless whirl, shot through the brain of Fagin, as every evil thought and blackest purpose lay working at his heart.

He sat without changing his attitude in the least, or appearing to take the smallest heed of time, until his quick ear seemed to be attracted by a footstep in the street.

'At last,' muttered the Jew, wiping his dry and fevered mouth. 'At last!'

The bell rang gently as he spoke. He crept upstairs to the door, and presently returned accompanied by a man muffled to the chin, who carried a bundle under one arm. Sitting down and throwing back his outer coat, the man displayed the burly frame of Sikes.

'There!' he said, laying the bundle on the table. 'Take care of that, and do the most you can with it. It's been trouble enough to get. I thought I should have been here three hours ago.'

Fagin laid his hand upon the bundle, and locking it in the cupboard, sat down again without speaking. But he did not take his eyes off the robber for an instant during this action; and now that they sat over against each other, face to face, he looked fixedly at him, with his lips quivering so violently, and his face so altered by the emotions which had mastered him, that the housebreaker involuntarily drew back his chair, and surveyed him with a look of real affright.

'Wot now?' cried Sikes. 'Wot do you look at a man so for?'

The Jew raised his right hand, and shook his trembling forefinger in the air; but his passion was so great that the power of speech was for the moment gone.

'Damn me!' said Sikes, feeling in his breast with a look of alarm. 'He's gone mad. I must look to myself here.'

'No, no,' rejoined Fagin, finding his voice. 'It's not – you're not the person, Bill. I have no – no fault to find with you.'

'Oh, you haven't, haven't you?' said Sikes, looking sternly at him, and ostentatiously passing a pistol into a more convenient pocket. 'That's lucky – for one of us. Which one that is, don't matter.'

'I've got that to tell you, Bill,' said the Jew, drawing his chair nearer, 'will make you worse than me.'

'Ay?' returned the robber, with an incredulous air. 'Tell away! Look sharp, or Nance will think I'm lost.'

'Lost!' cried Fagin. 'She's pretty well settled that, in her own mind, already.'

Sikes looked with an aspect of great perplexity into the Jew's face, and reading no satisfactory explanation of the riddle there, clenched his coat collar in his huge hand and shook him soundly.

'Speak, will you!' he said; 'or if you don't, it shall be for want of breath. Open your mouth and say what you've got to say in plain words. Out with it, you thundering old cur, out with it!'

'Suppose that lad that's lying there – ' Fagin began.

Sikes turned round to where Noah was sleeping, as if he had not previously observed him. 'Well?' he said, resuming his former position.

'Suppose that lad,' pursued the Jew, 'was to peach – to blow upon us all – first seeking out the right folks for the purpose, and then having a meeting with 'em in the street to paint our likenesses, describe every mark that they might know us by, and the crib where we might be most easily taken. Suppose he was to do all this, and besides to blow upon a plant we've all been in, more or less – of his own fancy; not grabbed, trapped, tried, earwigged by the parson, and brought to it on bread and water – but of his own fancy, to please his own taste; stealing out at nights to find those most interested against us, and peaching to them. Do you hear me?' cried the Jew, his eyes flashing with rage. 'Suppose he did all this, what then?'

'What then?' replied Sikes, with a tremendous oath. 'If he was left alive till I came, I'd grind his skull under the iron heel of my boot into as many grains as there are hairs upon his head.'

'What if *I* did it?' cried the Jew, almost in a yell. '*I*, that know so much, and could hang so many besides myself!'

'I don't know,' replied Sikes, clenching his teeth and turning white at the mere suggestion. 'I'd do something in the jail that 'ud get me put in irons; and if I was tried along with you, I'd fall upon you with them in the open court, and beat your brains out afore the people. I should have such strength,' muttered the robber, poising his brawny arm, 'that I could smash your head as if a loaded wagon had gone over it.'

'You would!'

'Would I?' said the housebreaker. 'Try me.'

'If it was Charley, or the Dodger, or Bet, or – '

'I don't care who,' replied Sikes impatiently. 'Whoever it was, I'd serve them the same.'

Fagin again looked hard at the robber; and motioning him to be silent, stooped over the bed upon the floor, and shook the sleeper to rouse him. Sikes leaned forward in his chair, looking on with his hands upon his knees, as if wondering much what all this questioning and preparation was to end in.

'Bolter, Bolter! – Poor lad!' said Fagin, looking up with an expression of devilish anticipation, and speaking slowly and with marked emphasis, 'he's tired – tired with watching for *her* so long – watching for *her*, Bill.'

'Wot d'ye mean?' asked Sikes, drawing back.

The Jew made no answer, but bending over the sleeper again, hauled him into a sitting posture. When his assumed name had been repeated several times, Noah rubbed his eyes, and, giving a heavy yawn, looked sleepily about him.

'Tell me that again – once again, just for him to hear,' said the Jew, pointing to Sikes as he spoke.

'Tell yer what?' asked the sleepy Noah, shaking himself pettishly.

'That about – Nancy,' said the Jew, clutching Sikes by the wrist, as if to prevent his leaving the house before he had heard enough. 'You followed her?'

'Yes.'

'To London Bridge?'

'Yes.'

'Where she met two people?'

'So she did.'

'A gentleman, and a lady that she had gone to of her own accord before, who asked her to give up all her pals, and Monks first, which she did – and to describe him, which she did – and to tell her what house it was that we meet at, and go to, which she did – and where it could be best watched from, which she did – and what time the people went there, which she did. She did all this. She told it all, every word, without a threat, without a murmur – she did – did she not?' cried the Jew, half mad with fury.

'All right,' replied Noah, scratching his head. 'That's just what it was!'

'What did they say about last Sunday?' demanded the Jew.

'About last Sunday!' replied Noah, considering. 'Why, I told yer that before.'

'Again; tell it again!' cried Fagin, tightening his grasp on Sikes, and brandishing his other hand aloft, as the foam flew from his lips.

'They asked her,' said Noah, who, as he grew more wakeful, seemed to have a dawning perception who Sikes was, 'they asked her why she didn't come last Sunday, as she promised. She said she couldn't.'

'Why – why?', interrupted the Jew, triumphantly. 'Tell him that.'

'Because she was forcibly kept at home by Bill, the man she had told them of before,' replied Noah.

'What more of him?' cried the Jew. 'What more of the man she had told them of before? Tell him that, tell him that.'

'Why, that she couldn't very easily get out of doors unless he knew where she was going to,' said Noah; 'and so the first time she went to see the lady, she – ha! ha! ha! it made me laugh when she said it, that it did – she gave him a drink of laudanum.'

'Hell's fire!' cried Sikes, breaking fiercely from the Jew. 'Let me go!'

Flinging the old man from him, he rushed from the room, and darted, wildly and furiously, up the stairs.

'Bill! Bill!' cried the Jew, following him hastily. 'A word. Only a word.'

The word would not have been exchanged, but that the house-breaker was unable to open the door; on which he was expending fruitless oaths and violence, when the Jew came panting up.

'Let me out,' said Sikes. 'Don't speak to me! it's not safe. Let me out, I say.'

'Hear me speak a word,' rejoined the Jew, laying his hand upon the lock. 'You won't be – '

'Well?' replied the other.

'You won't be – too – violent, Bill?' whined the Jew.

The day was breaking, and there was light enough for the men to see each other's faces. They exchanged one brief glance:

there was a fire in the eyes of both which could not be mistaken.

'I mean,' said Fagin, showing that he felt all disguise was now useless, 'not too violent for safety. Be crafty, Bill, and not too bold.'

Sikes made no reply, but, pulling open the door, of which the Jew had turned the lock, dashed into the silent streets.

Without one pause or moment's consideration; without once turning his head to the right or left, or raising his eyes to the sky or lowering them to the ground, but looking straight before him with savage resolution – his teeth so tightly compressed that the strained jaw seemed starting through his skin – the robber held on his headlong course, nor muttered a word, nor relaxed a muscle, until he reached his own door. He opened it softly with a key; strode lightly up the stairs; and entering his own room, double-locked the door, and lifting a heavy table against it, drew back the curtain of the bed.

The girl was lying half-dressed upon it. He had roused her from her sleep, for she raised herself with a hurried and startled look.

'Get up!' said the man.

'It *is* you, Bill!' said the girl, with an expression of pleasure at his return.

'It is,' was the reply. 'Get up.'

There was a candle burning, but the man hastily drew it from the candlestick, and hurled it under the grate. Seeing the faint light of early day without, the girl rose to undraw the curtain.

'Let it be,' said Sikes, thrusting his hand before her. 'There's light enough for wot I've got to do.'

'Bill,' said the girl, in a low voice of alarm, 'why do you look like that at me?'

The robber sat regarding her, for a few seconds, with dilated nostrils and heaving breast; and then, grasping her by the head and throat, dragged her into the middle of the room, and looking once towards the door, placed his heavy hand upon her mouth.

'Bill, Bill!' gasped the girl, wrestling with the strength of mortal fear – 'I – I won't scream or cry – not once – hear me – speak to me – tell me what I have done!'

'You know, you she-devil!' returned the robber, suppressing his breath. 'You were watched tonight; every word you said was heard.'

'Then spare my life for the love of Heaven, as I spared yours,' rejoined the girl, clinging to him. 'Bill, dear Bill, you cannot have the heart to kill me. Oh! think of all I have given up, only this one night, for you. You *shall* have time to think, and save yourself this crime. I will not loose my hold; you cannot throw me off. Bill, Bill, for dear God's sake, for your own, for mine, stop before you spill my blood! I have been true to you, upon my guilty soul I have!'

The man struggled violently to release his arms; but those of the girl were clasped round his, and tear her as he would, he could not tear them away.

'Bill,' cried the girl, striving to lay her head upon his breast, 'the gentleman, and that dear lady, told me tonight of a home in some foreign country where I could end my days in solitude and peace. Let me see them again, and beg them, on my knees,

to show the same mercy and goodness to you; and let us both leave this dreadful place, and far apart lead better lives, and forget how we have lived, except in prayers, and never see each other more. It is never too late to repent. They told me so – I feel it now – but we must have time – a little, little time!'

The housebreaker freed one arm, and grasped his pistol. The certainty of immediate detection if he fired flashed across his mind even in the midst of his fury; and he beat it twice, with all the force he could summon, upon the upturned face that almost touched his own.

She staggered and fell, nearly blinded with the blood that rained down from a deep gash in her forehead; but raising herself, with difficulty, on her knees, drew from her bosom a white handkerchief – Rose Maylie's own – and holding it up in her folded hands, as high towards heaven as her feeble strength would allow, breathed one prayer for mercy to her Maker.

It was a ghastly figure to look upon. The murderer, staggering backwards to the wall, and shutting out the sight with his hand, seized a heavy club and struck her down.

CHAPTER 48

The flight of Sikes

Of all bad deeds that, under cover of the darkness, had been committed within wide London's bounds since night hung over it, that was the worst. Of all the horrors that rose with an ill scent upon the morning air, that was the foulest and most cruel.

The sun – the bright sun, that brings back, not light alone, but new life, and hope, and freshness to man – burst upon the crowded city in clear and radiant glory. Through costly coloured glass and paper-mended window, through cathedral dome and rotten crevice, it shed its equal ray. It lighted up the room where the murdered woman lay. It did. He tried to shut it out, but it would stream in. If the sight had been a ghastly one in the dull morning, what was it now, in all that brilliant light!

He had not moved; he had been afraid to stir. There had been a moan and a motion of the hand; and, with terror added to rage, he had struck and struck again. Once he threw a rug over it; but it was worse to fancy the eyes, and imagine them moving towards him, than to see them glaring upward, as if watching the reflection of the pool of gore that quivered and danced in the sunlight on the ceiling. He had plucked it off again. And there was the body – mere flesh and blood, no more – but such flesh, and so much blood!

He struck a light, kindled a fire, and thrust the club into it. There was hair upon the end, which blazed and shrunk into a light cinder, and, caught by the air, whirled up the chimney. Even that frightened him, sturdy as he was; but he held the weapon till it broke, and then piled it on the coals to burn away, and smoulder into ashes. He washed himself, and rubbed his clothes: there were spots that would not be removed, but he cut the pieces out and burnt them. How those stains were dispersed about the room! The very feet of the dog were bloody.

All this time he had, never once, turned his back upon the corpse – no, not for a moment. Such preparations completed, he moved, backward, towards the door: dragging the dog with him, lest he should soil his feet anew and carry out new evidences of the crime into the streets. He shut the door softly, locked it, took the key, and left the house.

He crossed over and glanced up at the window, to be sure that nothing was visible from the outside. There was the curtain still drawn, which she would have opened to admit the light she never saw again. It lay nearly under there. *He* knew that. God, how the sun poured down upon the very spot!

The glance was instantaneous. It was a relief to have got free of the room. He whistled on the dog, and walked rapidly away.

He went through Islington; strode up the hill at Highgate on which stands the stone in honour of Whittington; turned down to Highgate Hill, unsteady of purpose, and uncertain where to go; struck off to the right again, almost as soon as he began to descend it, and taking the footpath across the fields, skirted Caen Wood, and so came out on Hampstead Heath. Traversing the hollow by the Vale of Health, he mounted the opposite bank, and crossing the road which joins the villages of Hampstead and Highgate, made along the remaining portion of the Heath to the fields at North End, in one of which he laid himself down under a hedge and slept.

Soon he was up again and away – not far into the country, but back towards London by the highroad – then back again – then over another part of the same ground as he had already traversed – then wandering up and down in fields, and lying on ditches' brinks to rest, and starting up to make for some other spot, and do the same, and ramble on again.

Where could he go, that was near and not too public, to get some meat and drink? Hendon. That was a good place, not far off, and out of most people's way. Thither he directed his steps – running sometimes, and sometimes, with a strange perversity, loitering at a snail's pace, or stopping altogether and idly breaking the hedges with his stick. But when he got there, all the people he met – the very children at the doors – seemed to view him with suspicion. Back he turned again, without the courage to purchase bit or drop, though he had tasted no food for many hours; and once more he lingered on the Heath, uncertain where to go.

He wandered over miles and miles of ground, and still came back to the old place. Morning and noon had passed, and the day was on the wane, and still he rambled to and fro, and up and down, and round and round, and still lingered about the same spot. At last he got away, and shaped his course for Hatfield.

It was nine o'clock at night when the man, quite tired out, and the dog limping and lame from the unaccustomed exercise, turned down the hill by the church of the quiet village, and plodding along the little street, crept into a small public-house, whose scanty light had guided him to the spot. There was a fire in the tap-room, and some country labourers were drinking before it. They made room for the stranger; but he sat down in the farthest corner, and ate and drank alone, or rather with his dog, to whom he cast a morsel of food from time to time.

The conversation of the men assembled here turned upon the neighbouring land and farmers; and when those topics were exhausted, upon the age of some old man who had been buried on the previous Sunday – the young men present considering him very old, and the old men present declaring him to have been quite young – not older, one white-haired grandfather said, than he was, with ten or fifteen year of life in him at least, if he had taken care – if he had taken care.

There was nothing to attract attention or excite alarm in this. The robber, after paying his reckoning, sat silent and unnoticed in his corner, and had almost dropped asleep, when he was half-wakened by the noisy entrance of a newcomer.

This was an antic fellow, half-pedlar and half-mountebank, who travelled about the country on foot, to vend hones, strops, razors, washballs, harness-paste, medicine for dogs and horses, cheap perfumery, cosmetics, and suchlike wares, which he carried in a case slung to his back. His entrance was the signal for various homely jokes with the countrymen, which slackened not until he had made his supper, and opened his box of treasures, when he ingeniously contrived to unite business with amusement.

'And what be that stoof? Good to eat, Harry?' asked a grinning countryman, pointing to some composition cakes in one corner.

'This,' said the fellow, producing one, 'this is the infallible and invaluable composition for removing all sorts of stain, rust, dirt, mildew, spick, speck, spot, or spatter, from silk, satin, linen, cambric, cloth, crape, stuff, carpet, merino, muslin, bombazeen, or woollen stuff. Wine-stains, fruit-stains, beer-stains, water-stains, paint-stains, pitch-stains, any stains, all come out at one rub with the infallible and invaluable composition. If a lady stains her honour, she has only need to swallow one cake, and she's cured at once – for it's poison. If a gentleman wants to prove his, he has only need to bolt one little square, and he has put it beyond question – for it's quite as satisfactory as a pistol bullet, and a great deal nastier in the flavour, consequently the more credit in taking it. One penny a square! With all these virtues, one penny a square.'

There were two buyers directly, and more of the listeners plainly hesitated. The vendor observing this, increased in loquacity.

'It's all bought up as fast as it can be made,' said the fellow. 'There are fourteen water-mills, six steam-engines, and a galvanic battery always a-working upon it; and they can't make it fast enough, though the men work so hard that they die off, and the widows is pensioned directly, with twenty pound a year for each of the children, and a premium of fifty for twins. – One penny a square! Two halfpence is all the same, and four farthings is received with joy. One penny a square! Wine-stains, fruit-stains, beer-stains, water-stains, paint-stains, pitch-stains, mud-stains, blood-stains! Here is a stain upon the hat of a gentleman in company that I'll take clean out before he can order me a pint of ale.'

'Hah!' cried Sikes, starting up. 'Give that back.'

'I'll take it clean out, sir,' replied the man, winking to the company, 'before you can come across the room to get it.

Gentlemen all, observe the dark stain upon this gentleman's hat, no wider than a shilling but thicker than a half-crown. Whether it is a wine-stain, fruit-stain, beer-stain, water-stain, paint-stain, pitch-stain, mud-stain, or blood-stain – '

The man got no further, for Sikes, with a hideous imprecation, overthrew the table, and tearing the hat from him, burst out of the house.

With the same perversity of feeling and irresolution that had fastened upon him, despite himself, all day the murderer, finding that he was not followed, and that they most probably considered him some drunken sullen fellow, turned back up the town, and getting out of the glare of the lamps of a stage-coach that was standing in the street, was walking past, when he recognised the mail from London, and saw that it was standing at a little post-office. He almost knew what was to come; but he crossed over and listened.

The guard was standing at the door, waiting for the letter-bag. A man, dressed like a gamekeeper, came up at the moment, and he handed him a basket which lay ready on the pavement.

'That's for your people,' said the guard. 'Now, look alive in there, will you? Damn that 'ere bag, it warn't ready night afore last. This won't do, you know!'

'Anything new up in town, Ben?' asked the gamekeeper, drawing back to the window-shutters, the better to admire the horses.

'No, nothing that I knows on,' replied the man, pulling on his gloves. 'Corn's up a little. I heerd talk of a murder, too, down Spitalfields way, but I don't reckon much upon it.'

'Oh, that's quite true,' said a gentleman inside, who was looking out of the window. 'And a dreadful murder it was.'

'Was it, sir?' rejoined the guard, touching his hat. 'Man or woman, pray, sir?'

'A woman,' replied the gentleman. 'It is supposed – '

'Now, Ben,' cried the coachman, impatiently.

'Damn that 'ere bag,' said the guard; 'are you going to sleep in there?'

'Coming!' cried the office-keeper, running out.

'Coming,' growled the guard. 'Ah, and so's the young 'ooman of property that's going to take a fancy to me, but I don't know when. Here, give hold. All ri – ight!'

The horn sounded a few cheerful notes, and the coach was gone.

Sikes remained standing in the street, apparently unmoved by what he had just heard, and agitated by no stronger feeling than a doubt where to go. At length he went back again, and took the road which leads from Hatfield to St Albans.

He went on doggedly; but as he left the town behind him, and plunged into the solitude and darkness of the road, he felt a dread and awe creeping upon him which shook him to the core. Every object before him, substance or shadow, still or moving, took the semblance of some fearful thing; but these fears were nothing compared to the sense that haunted him of that morning's ghastly figure following at his heels. He could trace its shadow in the gloom, supply the smallest item of the outline, and note how stiff and solemn it seemed to stalk along. He could hear its garments rustling in the leaves, and every

breath of wind came laden with that last low cry. If he stopped, it did the same. If he ran, it followed; not running too – that would have been a relief – but like a corpse endowed with the mere machinery of life, and borne on one slow melancholy wind that never rose or fell.

At times he turned with desperate determination, resolved to beat this phantom off, though it should look him dead; but the hair rose on his head, and his blood stood still, for it had turned with him, and was behind him then. He had kept it before him that morning; but it was behind him now – always. He leaned his back against a bank, and felt that it stood above him, visibly out against the cold night sky. He threw himself upon the road – on his back upon the road. At his head it stood, silent, erect, and still – a living gravestone, with its epitaph in blood.

Let no man talk of murderers escaping justice, and hint that Providence must sleep. There were twenty score of violent deaths in one long minute of that agony of fear.

There was a shed in a field he passed that offered shelter for the night. Before the door were three tall poplar trees, which made it very dark within; and the wind moaned through them with a dismal wail. He *could not* walk on till daylight came again; and here he stretched himself close to the wall – to undergo new torture.

For now, a vision came before him, as constant and more terrible than that from which he had escaped. Those widely staring eyes, so lustreless and so glassy, that he had better borne to see them than think upon them, appeared in the midst of the darkness – light in themselves, but giving light to nothing. There were but two, but they were everywhere. If he shut out the sight, there came the room with every well-known object – some, indeed, that he would have forgotten, if he had gone over its contents from memory – each in its accustomed place. The body was in *its* place, and its eyes were as he saw them when he stole away. He got up and rushed into the field without. The figure was behind him. He re-entered the shed, and shrunk down once more. The eyes were there before he had lain him-self along.

And here he remained, in such terror as none but he can know, trembling in every limb, and the cold sweat starting from every pore, when suddenly there arose upon the night-wind the noise of distant shouting, and the roar of voices mingled in alarm and wonder. Any sound of men in that lonely place, even though it conveyed a real cause of alarm, was something to him. He regained his strength and energy at the prospect of personal danger, and, springing to his feet, rushed into the open air.

The broad sky seemed on fire. Rising into the air with showers of sparks, and rolling one above the other, were sheets of flame, lighting the atmosphere for miles round, and driving clouds of smoke in the direction where he stood. The shouts grew louder as new voices swelled the roar, and he could hear the cry of Fire! mingled with the ringing of an alarm-bell, the fall of heavy bodies, and the crackling of flames as they twined round some new obstacle, and shot aloft as though refreshed by food. The noise increased as he looked. There were people there – men and women – light, bustle. It was like new life to him. He darted onward – straight, headlong – dashing through brier and brake, and leaping gate and fence as madly as the dog, who careered with loud and sounding bark before him.

He came upon the spot. There were half-dressed figures tearing to and fro, some endeavouring to drag the frightened horses from the stables, others driving the cattle from the yard and outhouses, and others coming laden from the burning pile, amidst a shower of falling sparks and the tumbling down of red-hot beams. The apertures, where doors and windows stood an hour ago, disclosed a mass of raging fire; walls rocked and crumbled into the burning well; the molten lead and iron poured down, white hot, upon the ground. Women and children shrieked, and men encouraged each other with noisy shouts and cheers. The clanking of the engine-pumps, and the spirting and hissing of the water as it fell upon the blazing wood, added to the tremendous roar. He shouted, too, till he was hoarse, and flying from memory and himself, plunged into the thickest of the throng.

Hither and thither he dived that night; now working at the pumps, and now hurrying through the smoke and flame, but never ceasing to engage himself wherever noise and men were thickest. Up and down the ladders, upon the roofs of buildings, over floors that quaked and trembled with his weight, under the lee of falling bricks and stones, in every part of that great fire was he; but he bore a charmed life, and had neither scratch nor bruise, nor weariness, nor thought, till morning dawned again, and only smoke and blackened ruins remained.

This mad excitement over, there returned, with tenfold force, the dreadful consciousness of his crime. He looked suspiciously about him, for the men were conversing in groups, and he feared to be the subject of their talk. The dog obeyed the significant beck of his finger, and they drew off stealthily together. He passed near an engine where some men were seated, and they called to him to share in their refreshment. He took some bread and meat; and as he drank a draught of beer, heard the firemen, who were from London, talking about the murder. 'He has gone to Birmingham, they say,' said one: 'but they'll have him yet, for the scouts are out, and by tomorrow night there'll be a cry all through the country.'

He hurried off, and walked till he almost dropped upon the ground; then lay down in a lane, and had a long, but broken and uneasy sleep. He wandered on again, irresolute and undecided and oppressed with the fear of another solitary night.

Suddenly, he took the desperate resolution of going back to London.

'There's somebody to speak to there, at all events,' he thought. 'A good hiding-place, too. They'll never expect to nab me there, after this country scent. Why can't I lay by for a week or so, and, forcing blunt from Fagin, get abroad to France? Damn me, I'll risk it.'

He acted upon this impulse without delay, and choosing the least frequented roads, began his journey back, resolved to lie concealed within a short distance of the metropolis, and, entering it at dusk by a circuitous route, to proceed straight to that part of it which he had fixed on for his destination.

The dog, though – if any descriptions of him were out, it would not be forgotten that the dog was missing, and had probably gone with him. This might lead to his apprehension as he passed along the streets. He resolved to drown him, and walked on, looking about for a pond, picking up a heavy stone and tying it to his handkerchief as he went.

The animal looked up into his master's face while these preparations were making; and, whether his instinct apprehended something of their purpose, or the robber's sidelong look at him was sterner than ordinary, skulked a little farther in the rear than usual, and cowered as he came more slowly along.

When his master halted at the brink of a pool, and looked round to call him, he stopped outright.

'Do you hear me call? Come here!' cried Sikes.

The animal came up from the very force of habit; but as Sikes stooped to attach the handkerchief to his throat, he uttered a low growl and started back.

'Come back!' said the robber, stamping on the ground.

The dog wagged his tail, but moved not. Sikes made a running noose, and called him again.

The dog advanced, retreated, paused an instant, turned, and scoured away at his hardest speed.

The man whistled again and again, and sat down and waited in the expectation that he would return. But no dog appeared, and at length he resumed his journey.

CHAPTER 49

Monks and Mr Brownlow at length meet. Their conversation, and the intelligence that interrupts it

The twilight was beginning to close in when Mr Brownlow alighted from a hackney-coach at his own door, and knocked softly. The door being opened, a sturdy man got out of the coach and stationed himself on one side of the steps, while another man, who had been seated on the box, dismounted too, and stood upon the other side. At a sign from Mr Brownlow they helped out a third man, and taking him between them, hurried him into the house. This man was Monks.

They walked in the same manner up the stairs without speaking, and Mr Brownlow, preceding them, led the way into a back room. At the door of this apartment Monks, who had ascended with evident reluctance, stopped. The two men looked to the old gentleman as if for instructions.

'He knows the alternative,' said Mr Brownlow. 'If he hesitates or moves a finger but as you bid him, drag him into the street, call for the aid of the police, and impeach him as a felon in my name.'

'How dare you say this of me?' asked Monks.

'How dare you urge me to it, young man?' replied Mr Brownlow, confronting him with a steady look. 'Are you mad enough to leave this house? Unhand him. There, sir. You are free to go, and we to follow. But I warn you, by all I hold most solemn and most sacred, that the instant you set foot in the street, that instant will I have you apprehended on a charge of fraud and robbery. I am resolute and immovable. If you are determined to be the same, your blood be upon your own head!'

'By what authority am I kidnapped in the street, and brought here by these dogs?' asked Monks, looking from one to the other of the men who stood beside him.

'By mine,' replied Mr Brownlow. 'Those persons are indemnified by me. If you complain of being deprived of your liberty – you had power and opportunity to retrieve it as you came along, but you deemed it advisable to remain quiet – I say again, throw yourself for protection on the law. I will appeal to the law too; but when you have gone too far to recede, do not sue to me for leniency, when the power will have passed into other hands, and do not say I plunged you down the gulf into which you rushed yourself.'

Monks was plainly disconcerted, and alarmed besides. He hesitated.

'You will decide quickly,' said Mr Brownlow, with perfect firmness and composure. 'If you wish me to prefer my charges publicly, and consign you to a punishment the extent of which, although I can with a shudder foresee, I cannot control – once more I say you know the way. If not, and you appeal to my forbearance, and the mercy of those you have deeply injured, seat yourself, without a word, in that chair. It has waited for you two whole days.'

Monks muttered some unintelligible words, but wavered still.

'You will be prompt,' said Mr Brownlow. 'A word from me, and the alternative has gone for ever.'

Still the man hesitated.

'I have not the inclination to parley,' said Mr Brownlow; 'and, as I advocate the dearest interests of others, I have not the right.'

Sikes attempting to destroy his dog

'Is there,' demanded Monks, with a faltering tongue, 'is there no middle course?'

'None.'

Monks looked at the old gentleman with an anxious eye; but reading in his countenance nothing but severity and determination, walked into the room, and, shrugging his shoulders, sat down.

'Lock the door on the outside,' said Mr Brownlow to the attendants, 'and come when I ring.'

The men obeyed, and the two were left alone together.

'This is pretty treatment, sir,' said Monks, throwing down his hat and cloak, 'from my father's oldest friend.'

'It is because I was your father's oldest friend, young man,' returned Mr Brownlow; 'it is because the hopes and wishes of young and happy years were bound up with him and that fair creature of his blood and kindred who rejoined her God in youth, and left me here a solitary, lonely man; it is because he knelt with me beside his only sister's deathbed when he was yet a boy, on the morning that would – but Heaven willed otherwise – have made her my young wife; it is because my seared heart clung to him, from that time forth, through all his trials and errors, till he died; it is because old recollections and associations fill my heart, and even the sight of you brings with it old thoughts of him; – it is because of all these things that I am moved to treat you gently now – yes, Edward Leeford, even now – and blush for your unworthiness who bear the name.'

'What has the name to do with it?' asked the other, after contemplating, half in silence and half in dogged wonder, the agitation of his companion. 'What is the name to me?'

'Nothing,' replied Mr Brownlow, 'nothing to you. But it was *hers*, and even at this distance of time brings back to me, an old man, the glow and thrill which I once felt, only to hear it repeated by a stranger. I am very glad you have changed it – very – very.'

'This is all mighty fine,' said Monks (to retain his assumed designation) after a long silence, during which he had jerked himself in sullen defiance to and fro, and Mr Brownlow had sat, shading his face with his hand. 'But what do you want with me?'

'You have a brother,' said Mr Brownlow, rousing himself – 'a brother, the whisper of whose name in your ear when I came behind you in the street, was, in itself, almost enough to make you accompany me hither in wonder and alarm.'

'I have no brother,' replied Monks. 'You know I was an only child. Why do you talk to me of brothers? You know that as well as I.'

'Attend to what I do know, and you may not,' said Mr Brownlow. 'I shall interest you by and by. I know that of the wretched marriage, into which family pride, and the most sordid and narrowest of all ambition, forced your unhappy father when a mere boy, you were the sole and most unnatural issue.'

'I don't care for hard names,' interrupted Monks, with a jeering laugh. 'You know the fact, and that's enough for me.'

'But I also know,' pursued the old gentleman, 'the misery, the slow torture, the protracted anguish of that ill-assorted union. I know how listlessly and wearily each of that wretched pair dragged on their heavy chain through a world that was poisoned to them both. I know how cold formalities were succeeded by open taunts; how indifference gave place to dislike, dislike to hate, and hate to loathing, until at last they wrenched the clanking bond asunder, and retiring a wide space apart, carried each a galling fragment, of which nothing but death could break the rivets, to hide it in new society beneath the gayest looks they could assume. Your mother succeeded; she forgot it soon. But it rusted and cankered at your father's heart for years.'

'Well, they were separated,' said Monks, 'and what of that?'

'When they had been separated for some time,' returned Mr Brownlow, 'and your mother, wholly given up to continental frivolities, had utterly forgotten the young husband ten good years her junior, who, with prospects blighted, lingered on at home, he fell among new friends. *This* circumstance at least you know already.'

'Not I,' said Monks, turning away his eyes and beating his foot upon the ground, as a man who is determined to deny everything. 'Not I.'

'Your manner, no less than your actions, assures me that you have never forgotten it, or ceased to think of it with bitterness,' returned Mr Brownlow. 'I speak of fifteen years ago, when you were not more than eleven years old, and your father but one-and-thirty, for he was, I repeat, a boy when *his* father ordered him to marry. Must I go back to events which cast a shade upon the memory of your parent, or will you spare it, and disclose to me the truth?'

'I have nothing to disclose,' rejoined Monks. 'You must talk on if you will.'

'These new friends, then,' said Mr Brownlow, 'were a naval officer retired from active service, whose wife had died some half a year before, and left him with two children: there had been more, but of all their family, happily but two survived. They were both daughters; one a beautiful creature of nineteen, and the other a mere child of two or three years old.'

'What's this to me?' asked Monks.

'They resided,' said Mr Brownlow, without seeming to hear the interruption, 'in a part of the country to which your father in his wandering had repaired, and where he had taken up his abode. Acquaintance, intimacy, friendship, fast followed on each other. Your father was gifted as few men are. He had his sister's soul and person. As the old officer knew him more and more, he grew to love him. I would that it had ended there. His daughter did the same.'

The old gentleman paused. Monks was biting his lips, with his eyes fixed upon the floor; seeing this, he immediately resumed: 'The end of a year found him contracted, solemnly contracted, to that daughter; the object of the first, true, ardent, only passion of a guileless untried girl.'

'Your tale is of the longest,' observed Monks, moving restlessly in his chair.

'It is a true tale of grief, and trial, and sorrow, young man,' returned Mr Brownlow, 'and such tales usually are. If it were one of unmixed joy and happiness, it would be very brief. At length one of those rich relations, to strengthen whose interest and importance your father had been sacrificed, as others are

often – it is no uncommon case – died, and to repair the misery he had been instrumental in occasioning, left him *his* panacea for all griefs – Money. It was necessary that he should immediately repair to Rome, whither this man had sped for health, and where he had died, leaving his affairs in great confusion. He went; was seized with mortal illness there; was followed, the moment the intelligence reached Paris, by your mother, who carried you with her; he died the day after her arrival, leaving no will – *no will* – so that the whole property fell to her and you.'

At this part of the recital Monks held his breath, and listened with a face of intense eagerness, though his eyes were not directed towards the speaker. As Mr Brownlow paused, he changed his position with the air of one who has experienced a sudden relief, and wiped his hot face and hands.

'Before he went abroad, and as he passed through London on his way,' said Mr Brownlow, slowly, and fixing his eyes upon the other's face, 'he came to me.'

'I never heard of that,' interrupted Monks, in a tone intended to appear incredulous, but savouring more of disagreeable surprise.

'He came to me, and left with me, among some other things, a picture – a portrait painted by himself – a likeness of this poor girl – which he did not wish to leave behind, and could not carry forward on his hasty journey. He was worn by anxiety and remorse almost to a shadow; talked, in a wild, distracted way, of ruin and dishonour worked by him; confided to me his intention to convert his whole property at any loss into money, and, having settled on his wife and you a portion of his recent acquisition, to fly the country – I guessed too well he would not fly alone – and never see it more. Even from me, his old and early friend, whose strong attachment had taken root in the earth that covered one most dear to both – even from me he withheld any more particular confession, promising to write and tell me all, and after that to see me once again for the last time on earth. Alas! *that* was the last time. I had no letter, and I never saw him more.

'I went,' said Mr Brownlow, after a short pause – 'I went, when all was over, to the scene of his – I will use the term the world would freely use, for worldly harshness or favour are now alike to him – of his guilty love, resolved that, if my fears were realised, that erring child should find one heart and home to shelter and compassionate her. The family had left that part a week before; they had called in such trifling debts as were outstanding, discharged them, and left the place by night. Why, or whither, none can tell.'

Monks drew his breath yet more freely, and looked round with a smile of triumph.

'When your brother,' said Mr Brownlow, drawing nearer to the other's chair – 'when your brother – a feeble, ragged, neglected child – was cast in my way by a stronger hand than chance, and rescued by me from a life of vice and infamy – '

'What?' cried Monks.

'By me,' said Mr Brownlow. 'I told you I should interest you before long. I say by me. I see that your cunning associate suppressed my name, although, for aught he knew, it would be quite strange to your ears. When he was rescued by me, then, and lay recovering from sickness in my house, his strong resemblance to this picture I have spoken of struck me with astonishment. Even when I first saw him, in all his dirt and misery, there was a lingering expression in his face that came upon me like a glimpse of some old friend flashing on one in a vivid dream. I need not tell you he was snared away before I knew his history –'

'Why not?' asked Monks hastily.

'Because you know it well.'

'I!'

'Denial to me is vain,' replied Mr Brownlow. 'I shall show you that I know more than that.'

'You – you – can't prove anything against me,' stammered Monks. 'I defy you to do it!'

'We shall see,' returned the old gentleman, with a searching glance. 'I lost the boy, and no efforts of mine could recover him. Your mother being dead, I knew that you alone could solve the mystery if anybody could; and as, when I had last heard of you, you were on your own estate in the West Indies – whither, as you well know, you retired upon your mother's death to escape the consequences of vicious courses here – I made the voyage. You had left it, months before, and were supposed to be in London, but no one could tell where. I returned. Your agents had no clue to your residence. You came and went, they said, as strangely as you had ever done – sometimes for days together and sometimes not for months – keeping, to all appearance, the same low haunts and mingling with the same infamous herd who had been your associates when a fierce ungovernable boy. I wearied them with new applications. I paced the streets by night and day, but until two hours ago all my efforts were fruitless, and I never saw you for an instant.'

'And now you do see me,' said Monks, rising boldly, 'what then? Fraud and robbery are high-sounding words – justified, you think, by a fancied resemblance in some young imp to an idle daub of a dead man's. Brother! You don't even know that a child was born of this maudlin pair; you don't even know that.'

'I *did not*,' replied Mr Brownlow, rising too; 'but within the last fortnight I have learnt it all. You have a brother; you know it, and him. There was a will, which your mother destroyed, leaving the secret and the gain to you at her own death. It contained a reference to some child likely to be the result of this sad connection, which child was born, and accidentally encountered by you, when your suspicions were first awakened by his resemblance to his father. You repaired to the place of his birth. There existed proofs – proofs long suppressed – of his birth and parentage. Those proofs were destroyed by you, and now, in your own words to your accomplice the Jew, "*the only proofs of the boy's identity lie at the bottom of the river, and the old hag that received them from the mother is rotting in her coffin.*" Unworthy son, coward, liar – you, who hold your councils with thieves and murderers in dark rooms at night – you, whose plots and wiles have brought a violent death upon the head of one worth millions such as you – you, who from your cradle were gall and bitterness to your own father's heart, and in

whom all evil passions, vice, and profligacy festered, till they found a vent in a hideous disease which has made your face an index even to your mind – you, Edward Leeford, do you still brave me?'

'No, no, no!' returned the coward, overwhelmed by these accumulated charges.

'Every word,' cried the old gentleman, 'every word that has passed between you and this detested villain is known to me! Shadows on the wall have caught your whispers, and brought them to my ear; the sight of the persecuted child has turned vice itself, and given it the courage and almost the attributes of virtue. Murder has been done, to which you were morally if not really a party.'

'No, no,' interposed Monks. 'I – I – know nothing of that. I was going to enquire the truth of the story when you overtook me. I didn't know the cause. I thought it was a common quarrel.'

'It was the partial disclosure of your secrets,' replied Mr Brownlow. 'Will you disclose the whole?'

'Yes, I will.'

'Set your hand to a statement of truth and facts, and repeat it before witnesses?'

'That I promise, too.'

'Remain quietly here until such a document is drawn up, and proceed with me to such a place as I may deem most advisable, for the purpose of attesting it?'

'If you insist upon that, I'll do that also,' replied Monks.

'You must do more than that,' said Mr Brownlow. 'Make restitution to an innocent and unoffending child, for such he is, although the offspring of a guilty and most miserable love. You have not forgotten the provisions of the will. Carry them into execution so far as your brother is concerned, and then go where you please. In this world you need meet no more.'

While Monks was pacing up and down, meditating with dark and evil looks on this proposal, and the possibilities of evading it – torn by his fears on the one hand and his hatred on the other – the door was hurriedly unlocked, and a gentleman (Mr Losberne) entered the room in violent agitation.

'The man will be taken!' he cried. 'He will be taken tonight!'

'The murderer?' asked Mr Brownlow.

'Yes, yes,' replied the other. 'His dog has been seen lurking about some old haunt, and there seems little doubt that his master either is or will be there under cover of the darkness. Spies are hovering about in every direction. I have spoken to the men who are charged with his capture, and they tell me he can never escape. A reward of a hundred pounds is proclaimed by Government tonight.'

'I will give fifty more,' said Mr Brownlow, 'and proclaim it with my own lips upon the spot, if I can reach it. Where is Mr Maylie?'

'Harry? As soon as he had seen your friend here safe in a coach with you, he hurried off to where he heard this,' replied the doctor, 'and mounting his horse sallied forth to join the first party at some place in the outskirts agreed upon between them.'

'The Jew,' said Mr Brownlow, 'what of him?'

'When I last heard he had not been taken, but he will be, or is by this time. They're sure of him.'

'Have you made up your mind?' asked Mr Brownlow, in a low voice, of Monks.

'Yes,' he replied. 'You – you – will be secret with me?'

'I will. Remain here till I return. It is your only hope of safety.'

They left the room, and the door was again locked.

'What have you done?' asked the doctor in a whisper.

'All that I could hope to do, and even more. Coupling the poor girl's intelligence with my previous knowledge, and the result of our good friend's enquiries on the spot, I left him no loophole of escape, and laid bare the whole villainy which by these lights became plain as day. Write and appoint the evening after tomorrow, at seven, for the meeting. We shall be down there a few hours before, but shall require rest; especially the young lady, who *may* have greater need of firmness than either you or I can quite foresee just now. But my blood boils to avenge this poor murdered creature. Which way have they taken?'

'Drive straight to the office and you will be in time,' replied Mr Losberne. 'I will remain here.'

The two gentlemen hastily separated, each in a fever of excitement wholly uncontrollable.

CHAPTER 50

The pursuit and escape

Near to that part of the Thames on which the church at Rotherhithe abuts, where the buildings on the banks are dirtiest and the vessels on the river blackest with the dust of colliers and the smoke of close-built low-roofed houses, there exists, at the present day, the filthiest, the strangest, the most extraordinary of the many localities that are hidden in London, wholly unknown, even by name, to the great mass of its inhabitants.

To reach this place, the visitor has to penetrate through a maze of close, narrow, and muddy streets, thronged by the roughest and poorest of waterside people, and devoted to the traffic they may be supposed to occasion. The cheapest and least delicate provisions are heaped in the shops; the coarsest and commonest articles of wearing apparel dangle at the salesman's door, and stream from the house-parapet and windows. Jostling with unemployed labourers of the lowest class, ballast-heavers, coal-whippers, brazen women, ragged children, and the very raff and refuse of the river, he makes his way with difficulty along, assailed by offensive sights and smells from the narrow alleys which branch off on the right and left, and deafened by the clash of ponderous wagons that bear great piles of merchandise from the stacks of warehouses that rise from every corner. Arriving at length in streets remoter and less frequented than those through which he has passed, he walks beneath tottering house-fronts projecting over the pavement, dismantled walls that seem to totter as he passes, chimneys half crushed, half hesitating to fall, windows guarded by rusty iron bars that time and dirt have almost eaten away, and every imaginable sign of desolation and neglect.

In such a neighbourhood, beyond Dockhead, in the Borough of Southwark, stands Jacob's Island, surrounded by a muddy ditch six or eight feet deep and fifteen or twenty wide when the tide is in, once called Mill Pond, but known in these days as Folly Ditch. It is a creek or inlet from the Thames, and can always be filled at high water by opening the sluices at the Lead Mills from which it took its old name. At such times a stranger, looking from one of the wooden bridges thrown across it at Mill Lane, will see the inhabitants of the houses on either side lowering, from their back doors and windows, buckets, pails, domestic utensils of all kinds, in which to haul the water up; and when his eye is turned from these operations to the houses themselves, his utmost astonishment will be excited by the scene before him. Crazy wooden galleries common to the backs of half a dozen houses, with holes from which to look upon the slime beneath; windows broken and patched, with poles thrust out on which to dry the linen that is never there; rooms so small, so filthy, so confined, that the air would seem too tainted even for the dirt and squalor which they shelter; wooden chambers thrusting themselves out above the mud, and threatening to fall into it, as some have done; dirt-besmeared walls and decaying foundations; every repulsive lineament of poverty, every loathsome indication of filth, rot, and garbage; – all these ornament the banks of Folly Ditch.

In Jacob's Island the warehouses are roofless and empty; the walls are crumbling down; the windows are windows no more; the doors are falling into the streets; the chimneys are blackened, but they yield no smoke. Thirty or forty years ago, before losses and chancery suits came upon it, it was a thriving place; but now it is a desolate island indeed. The houses have no owners; they are broken open, and entered upon by those who have the courage; and there they live, and there they die. They must have powerful motives for a secret residence, or be reduced to a destitute condition indeed, who seek a refuge in Jacob's Island.

In an upper room of one of these houses – a detached house of fair size, ruinous in other respects, but strongly defended at door and window, of which house the back commanded the ditch in manner already described – there were assembled three men, who, regarding each other every now and then with looks expressive of perplexity and expectation, sat for some time in profound and gloomy silence. One of these was Toby Crackit, another Mr Chitling, and the third a robber of fifty years, whose nose had been almost beaten in, in some old scuffle, and whose face bore a frightful scar which might probably be traced to the same occasion. This man was a returned transport, and his name was Kags.

'I wish,' said Toby, turning to Mr Chitling, 'that you had picked out some other crib, when the two old ones got too warm, and had not come here, my fine feller.'

'Why didn't you, blunder-head?' said Kags.

'Well, I thought you'd have been a little more glad to see me than this,' replied Mr Chitling, with a melancholy air.

'Why, look'e, young gentleman,' said Toby, 'when a man keeps himself so very exclusive as I have done, and by that means has a snug house over his head with nobody prying or smelling about it, it's rather a startling thing to have the honour of a wisit from a young gentleman (however respectable and pleasant a person he may be to play cards with at conweniency) circumstanced as you are.'

'Expecially when the exclusive young man has got a friend stopping with him, that's arrived sooner than was expected from foreign parts, and is too modest to want to be presented to the Judges on his return,' added Mr Kags.

There was a short silence, after which Toby Crackit, seeming to abandon as hopeless any further effort to maintain his usual devil-may-care swagger, turned to Chitling and said: 'When was Fagin took, then?'

'Just at dinner-time – two o'clock this afternoon. Charley and I made our lucky up the wash'us chimney, and Bolter got into the empty water-butt, head downwards; but his legs were so precious long that they stuck out at the top, and so they took him too.'

'And Bet?'

'Poor Bet! She went to see the body, to speak to who it was,' replied Chitling, his countenance falling more and more, 'and went off mad, screaming and raving, and beating her head against the boards; so they put a strait-weskut on her and took her to the hospital – and there she is.'

'Wot's come of young Bates?' demanded Kags.

'He hung about, not to come over here afore dark, but he'll be here soon,' replied Chitling. 'There's nowhere else to go to now, for the people at the Cripples are all in custody, and the bar of the ken – I went up there and see it with my own eyes – is filled with traps.'

'This is a smash,' observed Toby, biting his lips. 'There's more than one will go with this.'

'The sessions are on,' said Kags; 'if they get the inquest over, and Bolter turns King's evidence – as of course he will, from what he's said already – they can prove Fagin an accessory before the fact, and get the trial on, on Friday, and he'll swing in six days from this, by God !'

'You should have heard the people groan,' said Chitling; 'the officers fought like devils, or they'd have torn him away. He was down once, but they made a ring round him, and fought their way along. You should have seen how he looked about him, all muddy and bleeding, and clung to them as if they were his dearest friends. I can see 'em now, not able to stand upright with the pressing of the mob, and dragging him along amongst 'em; I can see the people jumping up, one behind another, and snarling with their teeth, and making at him like wild beasts; I can see the blood upon his hair and beard, and hear the cries with which the women worked themselves into the centre of the crowd at the street corner, and swore they'd tear his heart out!'

The horror-stricken witness of this scene pressed his hands upon his ears, and with his eyes closed got up and paced violently to and fro, like one distracted.

Whilst he was thus engaged, and the two men sat by in silence with their eyes fixed upon the floor, a pattering noise was heard upon the stairs, and Sikes's dog bounded into the room. They ran to the window, downstairs, and into the street. The dog had jumped in at an open window; he made no attempt to follow them, nor was his master to be seen.

'What's the meaning of this?' said Toby, when they had returned. 'He can't be coming here. I – I – hope not.'

'If he was coming here he'd have come with the dog,' said Kags, stooping down to examine the animal, who lay panting on the floor. 'Here! Give us some water for him; he has run himself faint.'

'He's drunk it all up, every drop,' said Chitling, after watching the dog some time in silence. 'Covered with mud – lame – half-blind, he must have come a long way.'

'Where can he have come from?' exclaimed Toby. 'He's been to the other kens of course, and finding them filled with strangers, come on here, where he's been many a time and often. But where can he have come from first, and how comes he here alone without the other?'

'He' (none of them called the murderer by his old name) – 'he can't have made away with himself. What do you think?' said Chitling.

Toby shook his head.

'If he had,' said Kags, 'the dog 'ud want to lead us away to where he did it. No. I think he's got out of the country, and left the dog behind. He must have given him the slip somehow, or he wouldn't be so easy.'

This solution appearing the most probable one, was adopted as the right; and the dog, creeping under a chair, coiled himself up to sleep, without more notice from anybody.

It being now dark the shutter was closed, and a candle lighted and placed upon the table. The terrible events of the last two days had made a deep impression on all three, increased by the danger and uncertainty of their own position. They drew their chairs closer together, starting at every sound. They spoke little, and that in whispers, and were as silent and awestricken as if the remains of the murdered woman lay in the next room.

They had sat thus some time, when suddenly was heard a hurried knocking at the door below.

'Young Bates,' said Kags, looking angrily round, to check the fear he felt himself.

The knocking came again. No, it wasn't he. He never knocked like that.

Crackit went to the window, and shaking all over, drew in his head. There was no need to tell them who it was; his pale face was enough. The dog too was on the alert in an instant, and ran whining to the door.

'We must let him in,' he said, taking up the candle.

'Isn't there any help for it?' asked the other man in a hoarse voice.

'None. He *must* come in.'

'Don't leave us in the dark,' said Kags, taking down a candle from the chimney-piece, and lighting it, with such a trembling hand that the knocking was twice repeated before he had finished.

Crackit went down to the door, and returned, followed by a man with the lower part of his face buried in a handkerchief, and another tied over his head under his hat. He drew them slowly off. Blanched face, sunken eyes, hollow cheeks, beard of three days' growth, wasted flesh, short thick breath – it was the very ghost of Sikes.

He laid his hand upon a chair which stood in the middle of the room, but shuddering as he was about to drop into it, and seeming to glance over his shoulder, dragged it back close to the wall – as close as it would go – ground it against it – and sat down.

Not a word had been exchanged. He looked from one to another in silence. If an eye were furtively raised and met his, it was instantly averted. When his hollow voice broke silence, they all three started. They seemed never to have heard its tones before.

'How came that dog here?' he asked.

'Alone. Three hours ago.'

'Tonight's paper says that Fagin's taken. Is it true, or a lie?'

'True.'

They were silent again.

'Damn you all,' said Sikes, passing his hand across his forehead. 'Have you nothing to say to me?'

There was an uneasy movement among them, but nobody spoke.

'You that keep this house,' said Sikes, turning his face to Crackit, 'do you mean to sell me, or to let me lie here till this hunt is over?'

'You may stop here, if you think it safe,' returned the person addressed, after some hesitation.

Sikes carried his eyes slowly up the wall behind him – rather trying to turn his head than actually doing it – and said, 'Is – it – the body – is it buried?'

They shook their heads.

'Why isn't it?' he retorted, with the same glance behind him. 'Wot do they keep such ugly things above the ground for? – Who's that knocking?'

Crackit intimated, by a motion of his hand as he left the room, that there was nothing to fear; and directly came back with Charley Bates behind him. Sikes sat opposite the door, so that the moment the boy entered the room he encountered his figure.

'Toby,' said the boy, falling back, as Sikes turned his eyes towards him, 'why didn't you tell me this downstairs?'

There had been something so tremendous in the shrinking off of the three, that the wretched man was willing to propitiate even this lad. Accordingly he nodded, and made as though he would shake hands with him.

'Let me go into some other room,' said the boy, retreating still farther.

'Charley!' said Sikes, stepping forward, 'don't you – don't you know me?'

'Don't come nearer me,' answered the boy, still retreating, and looking, with horror in his eyes, upon the murderer's face. 'You monster!'

The man stopped halfway, and they looked at each other; but Sikes's eyes sunk gradually to the ground.

'Witness you three,' cried the boy, shaking his clenched fist, and becoming more and more excited as he spoke – 'witness you three – I'm not afraid of him – if they come here after him, I'll give him up; I will. I tell you out at once. He may kill me for it if he likes, or if he dares, but if I'm here I'll give him up. I'd

give him up if he was to be boiled alive. Murder! Help! If there's the pluck of a man among you three, you'll help me. Murder! Help! Down with him!'

Pouring out these cries, and accompanying them with violent gesticulation, the boy actually threw himself, single-handed, upon the strong man, and in the intensity of his energy, and the suddenness of his surprise, brought him heavily to the ground.

The three spectators seemed quite stupefied. They offered no interference, and the boy and man rolled on the ground together; the former, heedless of the blows that showered upon him, wrenching his hands tighter and tighter in the garments about the murderer's breast, and never ceasing to call for help with all his might.

The contest, however, was too unequal to last long. Sikes had him down, and his knee was on his throat, when Crackit pulled him back with a look of alarm, and pointed to the window. There were lights gleaming below, voices in loud and earnest conversation, the tramp of hurried footsteps – endless they seemed in number – crossing the nearest wooden bridge. One man on horseback seemed to be among the crowd, for there was the noise of hoofs rattling on the uneven pavement. The gleam of lights increased; the footsteps came more thickly and noisily on. Then came a loud knocking at the door, and then a hoarse murmur from such a multitude of angry voices as would have made the boldest quail.

'Help!' shrieked the boy in a voice that rent the air. 'He's here! Break down the door!'

'In the King's name,' cried the voices without; and the hoarse cry rose again, but louder.

'Break down the door!' screamed the boy. 'I tell you they'll never open it. Run straight to the room where the light is. Break down the door!'

Strokes, thick and heavy, rattled upon the door and lower window-shutters as he ceased to speak, and a loud huzzah burst from the crowd, giving the listener, for the first time, some adequate idea of its immense extent.

'Open the door of some place where I can lock this screeching Hell-babe,' cried Sikes fiercely, running to and fro, and dragging the boy now as easily as if he were an empty sack. 'That door. Quick.' He flung him in, bolted it, and turned the key. 'Is the downstairs door fast?'

'Double-locked and chained,' replied Crackit, who with the other two men still remained quite helpless and bewildered.

'The panels – are they strong?'

'Lined with sheet-iron.'

'And the windows too?'

'Yes, and the windows.'

'Damn you!' cried the desperate ruffian, throwing up the sash and menacing the crowd. 'Do your worst! I'll cheat you yet!'

Of all the terrific yells that ever fell on mortal ears, none could exceed the cry of the infuriated throng. Some shouted to those who were nearest to set the house on fire; others roared to the officers to shoot him dead. Among them all none showed such fury as the man on horseback, who, throwing himself out of the saddle, and bursting through the crowd as if he were parting water, cried, beneath the window, in a voice that rose above all others, 'Twenty guineas to the man who brings a ladder!'

The nearest voices took up the cry, and hundreds echoed it. Some called for ladders, some for sledgehammers; some ran with torches to and fro as if to seek them, and still came back and roared again; some spent their breath in impotent curses and execrations; some pressed forward with the ecstasy of madmen, and thus impeded the progress of those below; some among the boldest attempted to climb up by the waterspout and crevices in the wall; and all waved to and fro in the darkness beneath like a field of corn moved by an angry wind, and joined from time to time in one loud furious roar.

'The tide,' cried the murderer, as he staggered back into the room, and shut the faces out, 'the tide was in as I came up. Give me a rope, a long rope. They're all in front. I may drop into the Folly Ditch and clear off that way. Give me a rope, or I shall do three more murders and kill myself at last.'

The panic-stricken men pointed to where such articles were kept. The murderer, hastily selecting the longest and strongest cord, hurried up to the house-top.

All the windows in the rear of the house had been long ago bricked up, except one small trap in the room where the boy was locked, and that was too small even for the passage of his body. But from this aperture he had never ceased to call on those without to guard the back; and thus when the murderer emerged at last on the house-top by the door in the roof, a loud shout proclaimed the fact to those in front, who immediately began to pour round, pressing upon each other in one unbroken stream.

He planted a board, which he had carried up with him for the purpose, so firmly against the door that it must be a matter of great difficulty to open it from the inside; and creeping over the tiles, looked over the low parapet.

The water was out, and the ditch a bed of mud.

The crowd had been hushed during these few moments, watching his motions, and doubtful of his purpose; but the instant they perceived it, and knew it was defeated, they raised a cry of triumphant execration to which all their previous shouting had been whispers. Again and again it rose. Those who were at too great a distance to know its meaning, took up the sound; it echoed and re-echoed; it seemed as though the whole city had poured its population out to curse him.

On pressed the people from the front – on, on, on, in a strong struggling current of angry faces, with here and there a glaring torch to light them up, and show them out in all their wrath and passion. The houses on the opposite side of the ditch had been entered by the mob; sashes were thrown up, or torn bodily out; there were tiers and tiers of faces in every window, and cluster upon cluster of people clinging to every house-top. Each little bridge (and there were three in sight) bent beneath the weight of the crowd upon it. Still the current poured on to find some nook or hole from which to vent their shouts, and only for an instant to see the wretch.

'They have him now,' cried a man on the nearest bridge. 'Hurrah!'

The crowd grew light with uncovered heads; and again the shout uprose.

'I promise fifty pounds,' cried an old gentleman from the same quarter, 'fifty pounds to the man who takes him alive. I will remain here till he comes to ask me for it.'

There was another roar. At this moment the word was passed among the crowd that the door was forced at last, and that he who had first called for the ladder had mounted into the room. The stream abruptly turned, as this intelligence ran from mouth to mouth, and the people at the windows, seeing those upon the bridges pouring back, quitted their stations, and, running into the street, joined the concourse that now thronged pell-mell to the spot they had left; each man crushing and striving with his neighbour, and all panting with impatience to get near the door, and look upon the criminal as the officers brought him out. The cries and shrieks of those who were pressed almost to suffocation, or trampled down and trodden under foot in the confusion, were dreadful; the narrow ways were completely blocked up; and at this time, between the rush of some to regain the space in front of the house, and the unavailing struggles of others to extricate themselves from the mass, the immediate attention was distracted from the murderer, although the universal eagerness for his capture was, if possible, increased.

The man had shrunk down, thoroughly quelled by the ferocity of the crowd, and the impossibility of escape; but seeing this sudden change with no less rapidity than it had occurred, he sprung upon his feet, determined to make one last effort for his life by dropping into the ditch, and, at the risk of being stifled, endeavouring to creep away in the darkness and confusion.

Roused into new strength and energy, and stimulated by the noise within the house which announced that an entrance had really been effected, he set his foot against the stack of chimneys, fastened one end of the rope tightly and firmly round it, and with the other made a strong running noose by the aid of his hands and teeth almost in a second. He could let himself down by the cord to within a less distance of the ground than his own height, and had his knife ready in his hand to cut it then and drop.

At the very instant when he brought the loop over his head previous to slipping it beneath his armpits, and when the old gentleman before-mentioned (who had clung so tight to the railing of the bridge as to resist the force of the crowd, and retain his position) earnestly warned those about him that the man was about to lower himself down – at that very instant the murderer, looking behind him on the roof, threw his arms above his head, and uttered a yell of terror.

'The eyes again!' he cried, in an unearthly screech.

Staggering as if struck by lightning, he lost his balance and tumbled over the parapet. The noose was at his neck. It ran up with his weight, tight as a bowstring, and swift as the arrow it speeds. He fell for five-and-thirty feet. There was a sudden jerk, a terrific convulsion of the limbs; and there he hung, with the open knife clenched in his stiffening hand.

The old chimney quivered with the shock, but stood it

bravely. The murderer swung lifeless against the wall; and the boy, thrusting aside the dangling body which obscured his view, called to the people to come and take him out for God's sake.

A dog which had lain concealed till now, ran backwards and forwards on the parapet with a dismal howl, and collecting himself for a spring, jumped for the dead man's shoulders. Missing his aim, he fell into the ditch, turning completely over as he went, and striking his head against a stone, dashed out his brains.

CHAPTER 51

Affording an explanation of more mysteries than one, and comprehending a proposal of marriage, with no word of settlement or pin-money

The events narrated in the last chapter were yet but two days old, when Oliver found himself, at three o'clock in the afternoon, in a travelling-carriage rolling fast towards his native town. Mrs Maylie and Rose, and Mrs Bedwin, and the good doctor, were with him; and Mr Brownlow followed in a post-chaise, accompanied by one other person whose name had not been mentioned.

They had not talked much upon the way; for Oliver was in a flutter of agitation and uncertainty, which deprived him of the power of collecting his thoughts, and almost of speech, and appeared to have scarcely less effect on his companions, who shared it in at least an equal degree. He and the two ladies had been very carefully made acquainted by Mr Brownlow with the nature of the admissions which had been forced from

The last chance

Monks; and although they knew that the object of their present journey was to complete the work which had been so well begun, still the whole matter was enveloped in enough of doubt and mystery to leave them in endurance of the most intense suspense.

The same kind friend had, with Mr Losberne's assistance, cautiously stopped all channels of communication through which they could receive intelligence of the dreadful occurrences that had so recently taken place. 'It is quite true,' he said, 'that they must know them before long; but it might be at a better time than the present, and it could not be at a worse.' So they travelled on in silence, each busied with reflections on the object which had brought them together, and no one disposed to give utterance to the thoughts which crowded upon all.

But if Oliver, under these influences, had remained silent while they journeyed towards his birthplace by a road he had never seen, how the whole current of his recollections ran back to old times, and what a crowd of emotions were wakened up in his breast, when they turned into that which he had traversed on foot, a poor, houseless, wandering boy, without a friend to help him, or a roof to shelter his head.

'See there, there!' cried Oliver, eagerly clasping the hand of Rose, and pointing out at the carriage window; 'that's the stile I came over; there are the hedges I crept behind for fear anyone should overtake me and force me back! Yonder is the path across the fields, leading to the old house where I was a little child. Oh, Dick, Dick, my dear old friend, if I could only see you now!'

'You will see him soon,' replied Rose, gently taking his folded hands between her own. 'You shall tell him how happy you are, and how rich you have grown, and that in all your happiness you have none so great as the coming back to make him happy too.'

'Yes, yes,' said Oliver, 'and we'll – we'll take him away from here, and have him clothed and taught, and send him to some quiet country place where he may grow strong and well – shall we?'

Rose nodded 'yes,' for the boy was smiling through such happy tears that she could not speak.

'You will be kind and good to him, for you are to everyone,' said Oliver. 'It will make you cry, I know, to hear what he can tell; but never mind, never mind, it will be all over, and you will smile again – I know that too – to think how changed he is: you did the same with me. He said "God bless you!" to me when I ran away,' cried the boy with a burst of affectionate emotion, 'and I will say "God bless *you*!" now, and show him how I love him for it!'

As they approached the town, and at length drove through its narrow streets, it became matter of no small difficulty to restrain the boy within reasonable bounds. There was Sowerberry's the undertaker's just as it used to be, only smaller and less imposing in appearance than he remembered it; there were all the well-known shops and houses, with almost every one of which he had some slight incident connected; there was Gamfield's cart, the very cart he used to have, standing at the old public-house door; there was the workhouse, the dreary prison of his youthful days, with its dismal windows frowning on the street; there was the same lean porter standing at the gate, at sight of whom Oliver involuntarily shrunk back, and then laughed at himself for being so foolish, then cried, then laughed again; there were scores of faces at the doors and windows that he knew quite well; there was nearly everything as if he had left it but yesterday, and all his recent life had been but a happy dream.

But it was pure, earnest, joyful reality. They drove straight to the door of the chief hotel (which Oliver used to stare up at with awe, and think a mighty palace, but which had somehow fallen off in grandeur and size); and here was Mr Grimwig all ready to receive them, kissing the young lady, and the old one too, when they got out of the coach, as if he were the grand-father of the whole party, all smiles and kindness, and not offering to eat his head – no, not once; not even when he contradicted a very old postboy about the nearest road to London, and maintained he knew it best, though he had only come that way once, and that time fast asleep. There was dinner prepared, and there were bedrooms ready, and every-thing was arranged as if by magic.

Notwithstanding all this, when the hurry of the first half-hour was over, the same silence and constraint prevailed that had marked their journey down. Mr Brownlow did not join them at dinner, but remained in a separate room. The two other gentlemen hurried in and out with anxious faces, and, during the short intervals when they were present, conversed apart. Once, Mrs Maylie was called away, and after being absent for nearly an hour, returned with eyes swollen with weeping. All these things made Rose and Oliver, who were not in any new secrets, nervous and uncomfortable. They sat wondering in silence; or if they exchanged a few words, spoke in whispers, as if they were afraid to hear the sound of their own voices.

At length, when nine o'clock had come, and they began to think they were to hear no more that night, Mr Losberne and Mr Grimwig entered the room, followed by Mr Brownlow and a man whom Oliver almost shrieked with surprise to see; for they told him it was his brother, and it was the same man he had met at the market-town, and seen looking in with Fagin at the window of his little room. Monks cast a look of hate, which, even then, he could not dissemble, at the astonished boy, and sat down near the door. Mr Brownlow, who had papers in his hand walked to a table, near which Rose and Oliver were seated.

'This is a painful task,' said he, 'but these declarations, which have been signed in London before many gentlemen, must be in substance repeated here. I would have spared you the degradation, but we must hear them from your own lips before we part, and you know why.'

'Go on,' said the person addressed, turning away his face. 'Quick. I have almost done enough, I think. Don't keep me here.'

'This child,' said Mr Brownlow, drawing Oliver to him, and laying his hand upon his head, 'is your half-brother; the illegitimate son of your father, my dear friend Edwin Leeford, by poor young Agnes Fleming, who died in giving him birth.'

'Yes,' said Monks, scowling at the trembling boy, the beating of whose heart he might have heard. 'That is their bastard child.'

'The term you use,' said Mr Brownlow sternly, 'is a reproach to those who long since passed beyond the feeble censure of the world. It reflects disgrace on no one living, except you who use it. Let that pass. He was born in this town?'

'In the workhouse of this town,' was the sullen reply. 'You have the story there.' He pointed impatiently to the papers as he spoke.

'I must have it here, too,' said Mr Brownlow, looking round upon the listeners.

'Listen then! You!' returned Monks. 'His father being taken ill at Rome, was joined by his wife, my mother, from whom he had been long separated, who went from Paris and took me with her – to look after his property for what I know, for she had no great affection for him, nor he for her. He knew nothing of us, for his senses were gone, and he slumbered on till next day, when he died. Among the papers in his desk were two, dated on the night his illness first came on, directed to your-self ' – he addressed himself to Mr Brownlow – 'and enclosed in a few short lines to you, with an intimation on the cover of the package that it was not to be forwarded till after he was dead. One of these papers was a letter to this girl Agnes; the other a will.'

'What of the letter?' asked Mr Brownlow.

'The letter? – a sheet of paper, crossed and crossed again, with a penitent confession, and prayers to God to help her. He had palmed a tale on the girl that some secret mystery – to be explained one day – prevented his marrying her just then; and so she had gone on trusting patiently to him, until she trusted too far, and lost what none could ever give her back. She was, at that time, within a few months of her confinement. He told her all he had meant to do, to hide her shame, if he had lived; and prayed her, if he died, not to curse his memory, or think the consequences of their sin would be visited on her or their young child, for all the guilt was his. He reminded her of the day he had given her the little locket and the ring with her Christian name engraved upon it, and a blank left for that which he hoped one day to have bestowed upon her – prayed her yet to keep it, and wear it next her heart, as she had done before – and then ran on, wildly, in the same words, over and over again, as if he had gone distracted. I believe he had.'

'The will,' said Mr Brownlow, as Oliver's tears fell fast.

Monks was silent.

'The will,' said Mr Brownlow, speaking for him, 'was in the same spirit as the letter. He talked of miseries which his wife had brought upon him; of the rebellious disposition, vice, malice, and premature bad passions of you, his only son, who had been trained to hate him; and left you and your mother each an annuity of eight hundred pounds. The bulk of his property he divided into two equal portions – one for Agnes Fleming, and the other for their child, if it should be born alive and ever come of age. If it were a girl, it was to inherit the money unconditionally; but if a boy, only on the stipulation that in his minority he should never have stained his name with any public act of dishonour, meanness, cowardice, or wrong. He did this, he said, to mark his confidence in the mother, and his conviction – only strengthened by approaching death – that the child would share her gentle heart and noble nature. If he were disappointed in this expectation, then the money was to come to you; for then, and not till then, when both children were equal, would he recognise your prior claim upon his purse, who had none upon his heart, but had from an infant, repulsed him with coldness and aversion.'

'My mother,' said Monks, in a louder tone, 'did what a woman should have done – she burnt this will. The letter never reached its destination; but that, and other proofs, she kept, in case they ever tried to lie away the blot. The girl's father had the truth from her with every aggravation that her violent hate – I love her for it now – could add. Goaded by shame and dishonour, he fled with his children into a remote corner of Wales, changing his very name, that his friends might never know of his retreat; and here, no great while afterwards, he was found dead in his bed. The girl had left her home, in secret, some weeks before; he had searched for her, on foot, in every town and village near; and it was on the night when he returned home, assured that she had destroyed herself, to hide her shame and his, that his old heart broke.'

There was a short silence here, until Mr Brownlow took up the thread of the narrative.

'Years after this,' he said, 'this man's – Edward Leeford's – mother came to me. He had left her, when only eighteen; robbed her of jewels and money; gambled, squandered, forged, and fled to London where for two years he had associated with the lowest outcasts. She was sinking under a painful and incurable disease, and wished to recover him before she died. Enquiries were set on foot, and strict searches made. They were unavailing for a long time, but ultimately successful; and he went back with her to France.'

'There she died,' said Monks, 'after a lingering illness; and on her deathbed, she bequeathed these secrets to me, together with her unquenchable and deadly hatred of all whom they involved – though she need not have left me that, for I had inherited it long before. She would not believe that the girl had destroyed herself, and the child too, but was filled with the impression that a male child had been born, and was alive. I swore to her, if ever it crossed my path, to hunt it down; never to let it rest; to pursue it with the bitterest and most unrelenting animosity; to vent upon it the hatred that I deeply felt, and to spit upon the empty vaunt of that insulting will by dragging it, if I could, to the very gallows-foot. She was right. He came in my way at last. I began well, and, but for babbling drabs, I would have finished as I began!'

As the villain folded his arms tight together, and muttered curses on himself in the impotence of baffled malice, Mr Brownlow turned to the terrified group beside him, and explained that the Jew, who had been his old accomplice and confidant, had a large reward for keeping Oliver ensnared, of which some part was to be given up in the event of his being rescued; and that a dispute on this head had led to their visit to the country house for the purpose of identifying him.

'The locket and ring?' said Mr Brownlow, turning to Monks.

'I bought them from the man and woman I told you of, who stole them from the nurse, who stole them from the corpse,' answered Monks, without raising his eyes. 'You know what became of them.'

Mr Brownlow merely nodded to Mr Grimwig, who, disappearing with great alacrity, shortly returned, pushing in Mrs Bumble, and dragging her unwilling consort after him.

'Do my hi's deceive me!' cried Mr Bumble, with ill-feigned enthusiasm, 'or is that little Oliver? Oh O–li–ver, if you know'd how I've been a-grieving for you – '

'Hold your tongue, fool,' murmured Mrs Bumble.

'Isn't natur natur, Mrs Bumble?' remonstrated the workhouse master. 'Can't I be supposed to feel – *I* as brought him up porochially – when I see him a-setting here among ladies and gentlemen of the very affablest description? I always loved that boy as if he'd been my – my – my own grandfather,' said Mr Bumble, halting for an appropriate comparison. 'Master Oliver, my dear, you remember the blessed gentleman in the white waistcoat? Ah! he went to heaven last week, in a oak coffin with plated handles, Oliver.'

'Come, sir,' said Mr Grimwig tartly; 'suppress your feelings.'

'I will do my endeavours, sir,' replied Mr Bumble. 'How do you do, sir? I hope you are very well.'

This salutation was addressed to Mr Brownlow, who had stepped up to within a short distance of the respectable couple. He enquired, as he pointed to Monks, 'Do you know that person?'

'No,' replied Mrs Bumble flatly.

'Perhaps *you* don't?' said Mr Brownlow, addressing her spouse.

'I never saw him in all my life,' said Mr Bumble.

'Nor sold him anything, perhaps?'

'No,' replied Mrs Bumble.

'You never had, perhaps, a certain gold locket and ring?' said Mr Brownlow.

'Certainly not,' replied the matron. 'Why are we brought here to answer to such nonsense as this?'

Again Mr Brownlow nodded to Mr Grimwig, and again that gentleman limped away with extraordinary readiness. But not again did he return with a stout man and wife; for, this time, he led in two palsied women, who shook and tottered as they walked.

'You shut the door the night old Sally died,' said the foremost one, raising her shrivelled hand, 'but you couldn't shut out the sound, nor stop the chinks.'

'No, no,' said the other, looking round her, and wagging her toothless jaws. 'No, no, no.'

'We heard her try to tell you what she'd done, and saw you take a paper from her hand, and watched you, too, next day to the pawnbroker's shop,' said the first.

'Yes,' added the second, 'and it was a "locket and gold ring." We found out that, and saw it given you. We were by. Oh! we were by.'

'And we know more than that,' resumed the first, 'for she told us often, long ago, that the young mother had told her that, feeling she should never get over it, she was on her way, at the time that she was taken ill, to die near the grave of the father of the child.'

'Would you like to see the pawnbroker himself?' asked Mr Grimwig, with a motion towards the door.

'No,' replied the woman; 'if he ' – she pointed to Monks – 'has been coward enough to confess, as I see he has, and you have sounded all these hags till you found the right ones, I have nothing more to say. I *did* sell them, and they're where you'll never get them. What then?'

'Nothing,' replied Mr Brownlow, 'except that it remains for us to take care that you are neither of you employed in a situation of trust again. You may leave the room.'

'I hope,' said Mr Bumble, looking about him with great ruefulness, as Mr Grimwig disappeared with the two old women, 'I hope that this unfortunate little circumstance will not deprive me of my porochial office?'

'Indeed it will,' replied Mr Brownlow. 'You may make up your mind to that, and think yourself well off besides.'

'It was all Mrs Bumble. She *would* do it,' urged Mr Bumble, first looking round certain that his partner had left the room.

'That is no excuse,' replied Mr Brownlow. 'You were present on the occasion of the destruction of these trinkets, and, indeed, are the more guilty of the two, in the eye of the law; for the law supposes that your wife acts under your direction.'

'If the law supposes that,' said Mr Bumble, squeezing his hat emphatically in both hands, 'the law is a ass – a idiot. If that's the eye of the law, the law's a bachelor; and the worst I wish the law is, that his eye may be opened by experience – by experience.'

Laying great stress on the repetition of these two words, Mr Bumble fixed his hat on very tight, and, putting his hands in his pockets, followed his helpmate downstairs.

'Young lady,' said Mr Brownlow, turning to Rose, 'give me your hand. Do not tremble. You need not fear to hear the few remaining words we have to say.'

'If they have – I do not know how they can, but if they have – any reference to me,' said Rose, 'pray let me hear them at some other time. I have not strength or spirits now.'

'Nay,' returned the old gentleman, drawing her arm through his; 'you have more fortitude than this, I am sure. Do you know this young lady, sir?'

'Yes,' replied Monks.

'I never saw you before,' said Rose faintly.

'I have seen you often,' returned Monks.

'The father of the unhappy Agnes had *two* daughters,' said Mr Brownlow. 'What was the fate of the other – the child?'

'The child,' replied Monks, 'when her father died in a strange place, in a strange name, without a letter, book, or scrap of paper that yielded the faintest clue by which his friends or relatives could be traced – the child was taken by some wretched cottagers, who reared it as their own.'

'Go on,' said Mr Brownlow, signing to Mrs Maylie to approach. 'Go on!'

'You couldn't find the spot to which these people had repaired,' said Monks, 'but where friendship fails, hatred will often force a way. My mother found it, after a year of cunning search – ay, and found the child.'

'She took it, did she?'

'No. The people were poor, and began to sicken – at least the man did – of their fine humanity; so she left it with them, giving them a small present of money which would not last long, and promising more, which she never meant to send. She didn't quite rely, however, on their discontent and poverty for the child's unhappiness, but told the history of the sister's shame, with such alterations as suited her; bade them take good heed of the child, for she came of bad blood; and told them she was illegitimate, and sure to go wrong at one time or other. The circumstances countenanced all this; the people believed it; and there the child dragged on an existence, miserable enough even to satisfy us, until a widow lady, residing then at Chester, saw the girl by chance, pitied her, and took her home. There was some cursed spell, I think, against us; for in spite of all our efforts she remained there and was happy. I lost sight of her two or three years ago, and saw her no more until a few months back.'

'Do you see her now?'

'Yes. Leaning on your arm.'

'But not the less my niece,' cried Mrs Maylie, folding the fainting girl in her arms – 'not the less my dearest child. I would not lose her now for all the treasures of the world. My sweet companion, my own dear girl!'

'The only friend I ever had,' cried Rose, clinging to her. 'The kindest, best of friends. My heart will burst. I cannot – cannot bear all this.'

'You have borne more, and have been, through all, the best and gentlest creature that ever shed happiness on everyone she knew,' said Mrs Maylie, embracing her tenderly. 'Come, come, my love, remember who this is who waits to clasp you in his arms, poor child! See here – look, look, my dear!'

'Not aunt,' cried Oliver, throwing his arms about her neck; 'I'll never call her aunt – sister, my own dear sister, that something taught my heart to love so dearly from the first! Rose, dear, darling Rose!'

Let the tears which fell, and the broken words which were exchanged in the long close embrace between the orphans, be sacred. A father, sister, and mother were gained, and lost, in that one moment. Joy and grief were mingled in the cup. But there were no bitter tears; for even grief itself arose so softened, and clothed in such sweet and tender recollections, that it became a solemn pleasure, and lost all character of pain.

They were a long, long time alone. A soft tap at the door at length announced that someone was without. Oliver opened it, glided away, and gave place to Harry Maylie.

'I know it all,' he said, taking a seat beside the lovely girl. 'Dear Rose, I know it all.'

'I am not here by accident,' he added, after a lengthened silence; 'nor have I heard all this tonight, for I knew it yesterday – only yesterday. Do you guess that I have come to remind you of a promise?'

'Stay,' said Rose. 'You *do* know all?'

'All. You gave me leave, at any time within a year, to renew the subject of our last discourse.'

'I did.'

'Not to press you to alter your determination,' pursued the young man, 'but to hear you repeat it, if you would. I was to lay whatever of station or fortune I might possess at your feet, and if you still adhered to your former determination, I pledged myself, by no word or act, to seek to change it.'

'The same reasons which influenced me then will influence me now,' said Rose, firmly. 'If I ever owed a strict and rigid duty to her, whose goodness saved me from a life of indigence and suffering, when should I ever feel it as I should tonight? It is a struggle,' said Rose, 'but one I am proud to make; it is a pang, but one my heart shall bear.'

'The disclosure of tonight –' Harry began.

'The disclosure of tonight,' replied Rose, softly, 'leaves me in the same position, with reference to you, as that in which I stood before.'

'You harden your heart against me, Rose,' urged her lover.

'Oh, Harry, Harry,' said the young lady, bursting into tears, 'I wish I could, and spare myself this pain.'

'Then why inflict it on yourself?' said Harry, taking her hand. 'Think, dear Rose, think what you have heard tonight.'

'And what have I heard? What have I heard?' cried Rose. 'That a sense of his deep disgrace so worked upon my own father that he shunned all – there, we have said enough, Harry, we have said enough.'

'Not yet, not yet,' said the young man, detaining her as she rose. 'My hopes, my wishes, prospects, feeling, every thought in life except my love for you, have undergone a change. I offer you, now, no distinction among a bustling crowd; no mingling with a world of malice and detraction, where the blood is called into honest cheeks by aught but real disgrace and shame; but a home – a heart and home – yes, dearest Rose, and those, and those alone, are all I have to offer.'

'What do you mean?' she faltered.

'I mean but this – that when I left you last, I left you with a firm determination to level all fancied barriers between yourself and me; resolved that if my world could not be yours, I would make yours mine; that no pride of birth should curl the lip at you, for I would turn from it. This I have done. Those who have shrunk from me because of this, have shrunk from you, and proved you so far right. Such power and patronage, such relatives of influence and rank, as smiled upon me then, look coldly now; but there are smiling fields and waving trees in England's richest county, and by one village church – mine, Rose, my own! – there stands a rustic dwelling which you can make me prouder of than all the hopes I have renounced, measured a thousand-fold. This is *my* rank and station now, and here I lay it down!'

'It's a trying thing waiting supper for lovers,' said Mr Grimwig, waking up, and pulling his pocket-handkerchief from over his head.

Truth to tell, the supper had been waiting a most unreasonable time. Neither Mrs Maylie, nor Harry, nor Rose (who all came in together) could offer a word in extenuation.

'I had serious thoughts of eating my head tonight,' said Mr Grimwig, 'for I began to think I should get nothing else. I'll take the liberty, if you'll allow me, of saluting the bride that is to be.'

Mr Grimwig lost no time in carrying this notice into effect upon the blushing girl; and the example, being contagious, was followed both by the doctor and Mr Brownlow. Some people affirm that Harry Maylie had been observed to set it, originally, in a dark room adjoining; but the best authorities consider this downright scandal, he being young and a clergyman.

'Oliver, my child,' said Mrs Maylie, 'where have you been, and why do you look so sad? There are tears stealing down your face at this moment. What is the matter?'

It is a world of disappointment – often to the hopes we most cherish, and hopes that do our nature the greatest honour.

Poor Dick was dead!

CHAPTER 52

The Jew's last night alive

The court was paved, from floor to roof, with human faces. Inquisitive and eager eyes peered from every inch of space. From the rail before the dock, away into the sharpest angle of the smallest corner of the galleries, all looks were fixed upon one man – the Jew. Before him and behind – above, below, on the right and on the left – he seemed to stand surrounded by a firmament all bright with gleaming eyes.

He stood there, in all this glare of living light, with one hand resting on the wooden slab before him, the other held to his ear, and his head thrust forward to enable him to catch with greater distinctness every word that fell from the presiding judge, who was delivering his charge to the jury. At times, he turned his eyes sharply upon them to observe the effect of the slightest featherweight in his favour; and when the points against him were stated with terrible distinctness, looked towards his counsel in mute appeal, that he would, even then, urge something in his behalf. Beyond these manifestations of anxiety, he stirred not hand or foot. He had scarcely moved since the trial began; and now that the judge ceased to speak, he still remained in the same strained attitude of close attention, with his gaze bent on him, as though he listened still.

A slight bustle in the court recalled him to himself. Looking round, he saw that the jurymen had turned together, to consider their verdict. As his eyes wandered to the gallery, he could see the people rising above each other to see his face – some hastily applying their glasses to their eyes, and others whispering their neighbours with looks expressive of abhorrence. A few there were who seemed unmindful of him, and looked only to the jury, in impatient wonder how they could delay. But in no one face – not even among the women, of whom there were many there – could he read the faintest sympathy with himself, or any feeling but one of all-absorbing interest that he should be condemned.

As he saw all this in one bewildered glance, the death-like

stillness came again, and looking back, he saw that the jurymen had turned towards the judge. Hush!

They only sought permission to retire.

He looked, wistfully, into their faces, one by one, when they passed out, as though to see which way the greater number leaned; but that was fruitless. The jailer touched him on the shoulder. He followed mechanically to the end of the dock, and sat down on a chair. The man pointed it out, or he would not have seen it.

He looked up into the gallery again. Some of the people were eating, and some fanning themselves with handkerchiefs; for the crowded place was very hot. There was one young man sketching his face in a little notebook. He wondered whether it was like, and looked on when the artist broke his pencil-point, and made another with his knife, as any idle spectator might have done.

In the same way, when he turned his eyes towards the judge, his mind began to busy itself with the fashion of his dress, and what it cost, and how he put it on. There was an old fat gentleman on the bench, too, who had gone out, some half an hour before, and now come back. He wondered within himself whether this man had been to get his dinner, what he had had, and where he had had it; and pursued this train of careless thought until some new object caught his eye and roused another.

Not that, all this time, his mind was for an instant free from one oppressive overwhelming sense of the grave that opened at his feet; it was ever present to him, but in a vague and general way, and he could not fix his thoughts upon it. Thus, even while he trembled, and turned burning hot at the idea of speedy death, he fell to counting the iron spikes before him, and wondering how the head of one had been broken off, and whether they would mend it, or leave it as it was. Then he thought of all the horrors of the gallows and the scaffold, and stopped to watch a man sprinkling the floor to cool it; and then went on to think again.

At length there was a cry of silence, and a breathless look from all towards the door. The jury returned, and passed him close. He could glean nothing from their faces; they might as well have been of stone. Perfect stillness ensued – not a rustle – not a breath – Guilty!

The building rang with a tremendous shout, and another and another, and then it echoed deep loud groans, that gathered strength as they swelled out like angry thunder. It was a peal of joy from the populace outside, greeting the news that he would die on Monday.

The noise subsided, and he was asked if he had anything to say why sentence of death should not be passed upon him. He had resumed his listening attitude, and looked intently at his questioner while the demand was made; but it was twice repeated before he seemed to hear it, and then he only muttered that he was an old man – an old man – an old man – and so dropping into a whisper, was silent again.

The judge assumed the black cap, and the prisoner still stood with the same air and gesture. A woman in the gallery uttered some exclamation, called forth by this dread solemnity; he looked hastily up, as if angry at the interruption, and bent

forward yet more attentively. The address was solemn and impressive; the sentence fearful to hear. But he stood like a marble figure, without the motion of a nerve. His haggard face was still thrust forward, his underjaw hanging down, and his eyes staring out before him, when the jailer put his hand upon his arm, and beckoned him away. He gazed stupidly about him for an instant, and obeyed.

They led him through a paved room under the court, where some prisoners were waiting till their turns came, and others were talking to their friends, who crowded round a grate which looked into the open yard. There was nobody there to speak to *him*; but, as he passed, the prisoners fell back to render him more visible to the people who were clinging to the bars, and they assailed him with opprobrious names, and screeched and hissed. He shook his fist, and would have spat upon them; but his conductors hurried him on through a gloomy passage lighted by a few dim lamps, into the interior of the prison.

Here he was searched, that he might not have about him the means of anticipating the law; this ceremony performed, they led him to one of the condemned cells, and left him there – alone.

He sat down on a stone bench opposite the door, which served for seat and bedstead, and casting his bloodshot eyes upon the ground, tried to collect his thoughts. After a while he began to remember a few disjointed fragments of what the judge had said, though it had seemed to him, at the time, that he could not hear a word. These gradually fell into their proper places, and by degrees suggested more; so that in a little time he had the whole almost as it was delivered. To be hanged by the neck till he was dead – that was the end – to be hanged by the neck till he was dead!

As it came on very dark, he began to think of all the men he had known who had died upon the scaffold, some of them through his means. They rose up in such quick succession that he could hardly count them. He had seen some of them die – and had joked too, because they died with prayers upon their lips. With what a rattling noise the drop went down, and how suddenly they changed, from strong and vigorous men to dangling heaps of clothes!

Some of them might have inhabited that very cell – sat upon that very spot. It was very dark: why didn't they bring a light? The cell had been built for many years. Scores of men must have passed their last hours there. It was like sitting in a vault strewn with dead bodies – the cap, the noose, the pinioned arms, the faces that he knew, even beneath that hideous veil. Light, light!

At length, when his hands were raw with beating against the heavy door and walls, two men appeared – one bearing a candle, which he thrust into an iron candlestick fixed against the wall; the other dragging in a mattress on which to pass the night, for the prisoner was to be left alone no more.

Then came night – dark, dismal, silent night. Other watchers are glad to hear the church clock strike, for they tell of life and coming day. To the Jew they brought despair. The boom of every iron bell came laden with the one, deep, hollow sound – Death! What availed the noise and bustle of cheerful morning which penetrated even there to him? It was another form of knell, with mockery added to the warning.

The day passed off. Day? There was no day. It was gone as soon as come; and night came on again – night so long, and yet so short; long in its dreadful silence, and short in its fleeting hours. At one time he raved and blasphemed, and at another howled and tore his hair. Venerable men of his own persuasion had come to pray beside him, but he had driven them away with curses. They renewed their charitable efforts, and he beat them off.

Saturday night. He had only one night more to live. And as he thought of this, the day broke – Sunday.

It was not until the night of this last awful day, that a withering sense of his helpless, desperate state came in its full intensity upon his blighted soul; not that he had ever held any defined or positive hope of mercy, but that he had never been able to consider more than the dim probability of dying so soon. He had spoken little to either of the two men, who relieved each other in their attendance upon him; and they, for their parts, made no effort to rouse his attention. He had sat there awake, but dreaming. Now, he started up every minute, and with gasping mouth and burning skin, hurried to and fro in such a paroxysm of fear and wrath that even they – used to such sights – recoiled from him with horror. He grew so terrible, at last, in all the tortures of his evil conscience, that one man could not bear to sit there, eyeing him alone, and so the two kept watch together.

He cowered down upon his stone bed, and thought of the past. He had been wounded with some missiles from the crowd on the day of his capture, and his head was bandaged with a linen cloth. His red hair hung down upon his bloodless face; his beard was torn, and twisted into knots; his eyes shone with a terrible light; his unwashed flesh crackled with the fever that burnt him up. Eight – nine – ten. If it was not a trick to frighten him, and those were the real hours treading on each other's heels, where would he be, when they came round again? Eleven! Another struck, before the voice of the previous hour had ceased to vibrate. At eight, he would be the only mourner in his own funeral train; at eleven –

Those dreadful walls of Newgate, which have hidden so much misery and such unspeakable anguish, not only from the eyes, but, too often and too long, from the thoughts of men, never held so dread a spectacle as that. The few who lingered as they passed, and wondered what the man was doing who was to be hung tomorrow, would have slept but ill that night if they could have seen him.

From early in the evening until nearly midnight, little groups of two and three presented themselves at the lodge-gate, and enquired, with anxious faces, whether any reprieve had been received. These being answered in the negative, communicated the welcome intelligence to clusters in the street, who pointed out to one another the door from which he must come out, and showed where the scaffold would be built, and walking with unwilling steps away, turned back to conjure up the scene. By degrees they fell off, one by one; and, for an hour in the dead of night, the street was left to solitude and darkness.

The space before the prison was cleared, and a few strong barriers, painted black, had been already thrown across the road to break the pressure of the expected crowd, when Mr Brownlow and Oliver appeared at the wicket, and presented an order of admission to the prisoner, signed by one of the sheriffs. They were immediately admitted into the lodge.

'Is the young gentleman to come too, sir?' said the man whose duty it was to conduct them. 'It's not a sight for children, sir.'

'It is not indeed, my friend,' rejoined Mr Brownlow; 'but my business with this man is intimately connected with him; and as this child has seen him in the full career of his success and villainy, I think it well – even at the cost of some pain and fear – that he should see him now.'

These few words had been said apart, so as to be inaudible to Oliver. The man touched his hat; and glancing at Oliver with some curiosity, opened another gate, opposite to that by which they had entered, and led them on, through dark and winding ways, towards the cells.

'This,' said the man, stopping in a gloomy passage where a couple of workmen were making some preparations in profound silence – 'this is the place he passes through. If you step this way, you can see the door he goes out at.'

He led them into a stone kitchen, fitted with coppers for dressing the prison food, and pointed to a door. There was an open grating above it, through which came the sound of men's voices, mingled with the noise of hammering and the throwing down of boards. They were putting up the scaffold.

From this place they passed through several strong gates, opened by other turnkeys from the inner side; and, having entered an open yard, ascended a flight of narrow steps, and came into a passage with a row of strong doors on the left hand. Motioning them to remain where they were, the turnkey knocked at one of these with his bunch of keys. The two attendants, after a little whispering, came out into the passage, stretching themselves as if glad of a temporary relief, and motioned the visitors to follow the jailer into the cell. They did so.

The condemned criminal was seated on his bed, rocking himself from side to side, with a countenance more like that of a snared beast than the face of a man. His mind was evidently wandering to his old life, for he continued to mutter, without appearing conscious of their presence otherwise than as a part of his vision.

'Good boy, Charley – well done – ' he mumbled – 'Oliver, too, ha! ha! ha! Oliver, too – quite the gentleman now - quite the – take that boy away to bed!'

The jailer took the disengaged hand of Oliver, and whispering him not to be alarmed, looked on without speaking.

'Take him away to bed!' cried the Jew. 'Do you hear me, some of you? He has been the – the – somehow the cause of all this. It's worth the money to bring him up to it – Bolter's throat, Bill; never mind the girl – Bolter's throat, as deep as you can cut. Saw his head off!'

'Fagin,' said the jailer.

'That's me!' cried the Jew, falling instantly into the attitude of listening he had assumed upon his trial. 'An old man, my lord; a very old, old man!'

'Here,' said the turnkey, laying his hand upon his breast to keep him down – 'here's somebody wants to see you – to ask you some questions, I suppose. Fagin, Fagin! Are you a man?'

'I shan't be one long,' replied the Jew, looking up with a face retaining no human expression but rage and terror. 'Strike them all dead! what right have they to butcher me?'

As he spoke he caught sight of Oliver and Mr Brownlow. Shrinking to the farthest corner of the seat, he demanded to know what they wanted there.

'Steady,' said the turnkey, still holding him down. 'Now, sir, tell him what you want – quick, if you please, for he grows worse as the time gets on.'

'You have some papers,' said Mr Brownlow, advancing, 'which were placed in your hands for better security by a man called Monks.'

'It's all a lie together,' replied the Jew. 'I haven't one – not one.'

'For the love of God,' said Mr Brownlow solemnly, 'do not say that now, upon the very verge of death, but tell me where they are. You know that Sikes is dead, that Monks has confessed, that there is no hope of any further gain. Where are those papers?'

'Oliver,' cried the Jew, beckoning to him. 'Here, here! Let me whisper to you.'

'I am not afraid,' said Oliver in a low voice, as he relinquished Mr Brownlow's hand.

'The papers,' said the Jew, drawing him towards him, 'are in a canvas bag, in a hole a little way up the chimney in the top front room. I want to talk to you, my dear; I want to talk to you.'

'Yes, yes,' returned Oliver. 'Let us say a prayer. Do! Let me say one prayer – say only one, upon your knees with me, and we will talk till morning.'

'Outside, outside,' replied the Jew, pushing the boy before him towards the door, and looking vacantly over his head. 'Say I've gone to sleep – they'll believe *you*. You can get me out, if you take me so. Now then, now then!'

'Oh! God forgive this wretched man!' cried the boy, with a burst of tears.

'That's right, that's right,' said the Jew; 'that'll help us on. This door first. If I shake and tremble as we pass the gallows, don't you mind, but hurry on. Now, now, now!'

'Have you nothing else to ask him, sir?' enquired the turnkey.

'No other question,' replied Mr Brownlow. 'If I hoped we could recall him to a sense of his position – '

'Nothing will do that, sir,' replied the man, shaking his head. 'You had better leave him.'

The door of the cell opened, and the attendants returned.

'Press on, press on,' cried the Jew. 'Softly, but not so slow. Faster, faster!'

The men laid hands upon him, and disengaging Oliver from his grasp, held him back. He struggled with the power of desperation for an instant, and then sent up cry upon cry that penetrated even those massive walls, and rang in their ears until they reached the open yard.

It was some time before they left the prison. Oliver nearly swooned after this frightful scene, and was so weak that for an hour or more he had not strength to walk.

Day was dawning when they again emerged. A great multitude had already assembled; the windows were filled with people, smoking and playing cards to beguile the time; the crowd were pushing, quarrelling and joking. Everything told of life and animation but one dark cluster of objects in the very centre of all – the black stage, the cross-beam, the rope, and all the hideous apparatus of death.

CHAPTER 53

And last

The fortunes of those who have figured in this tale are nearly closed. The little that remains to their historian to relate is told in few and simple words.

Before three months had passed, Rose Fleming and Harry Maylie were married in the village church which was henceforth to be the scene of the young clergyman's labours; on the same day they entered into possession of their new and happy home.

Mrs Maylie took up her abode with her son and daughter-in-law, to enjoy, during the tranquil remainder of her days, the greatest felicity that age and worth can know – the contemplation of the happiness of those on whom the warmest affections and tenderest cares of a well-spent life have been unceasingly bestowed.

It appeared, on full and careful investigation, that if the wreck of property remaining in the custody of Monks (which

Fagin in the condemned cell

had never prospered either in his hands or in those of his mother) were equally divided between himself and Oliver, it would yield, to each, little more than three thousand pounds. By the provisions of his father's will, Oliver would have been entitled to the whole; but Mr Brownlow, unwilling to deprive the elder son of the opportunity of retrieving his former vices, and pursuing an honest career, proposed this mode of distribution, to which his young charge joyfully acceded.

Monks, still bearing that assumed name, retired with his portion, to a distant part of the New World, where, having quickly squandered it, he once more fell into his old courses, and, after undergoing a long confinement for some fresh act of fraud and knavery, at length sank under an attack of his old disorder, and died in prison. As far from home, died the chief remaining members of his friend Fagin's gang.

Mr Brownlow adopted Oliver as his own son. Removing with him and the old housekeeper to within a mile of the parsonage-house, where his dear friends resided, he gratified the only remaining wish of Oliver's warm and earnest heart, and thus linked together a little society, whose condition approached as nearly to one of perfect happiness as can ever be known in this changing world.

Soon after the marriage of the young people, the worthy doctor returned to Chertsey, where, bereft of the presence of his old friends, he would have been discontented if his temperament had admitted of such a feeling, and would have turned quite peevish if he had known how. For two or three months he contented himself with hinting that he feared the air began to disagree with him; then, finding that the place really was, to him, no longer what it had been before, he settled his business on his assistant, took a bachelor's cottage just outside the village of which his young friend was pastor, and instantaneously recovered. Here he took to gardening, planting, fishing, carpentering, and various other pursuits of a similar kind – all undertaken with his characteristic impetuosity; and in each and all he has since become famous throughout the neighbourhood as a most profound authority.

Before his removal he had managed to contract a strong friendship for Mr Grimwig, which that eccentric gentleman cordially reciprocated. He is accordingly visited by him a great many times in the course of the year. On all such occasions Mr Grimwig plants, fishes, and carpenters with great ardour; doing everything in a very singular and unprecedented manner, but always maintaining, with his favourite asseveration, that his mode is the right one. On Sundays he never fails to criticise the sermon to the young clergyman's face; always informing Mr Losberne, in strict confidence afterwards, that he considers it an excellent performance, but deems it as well not to say so. It is a standing and very favourite joke for Mr Brownlow to rally him on his old prophecy concerning Oliver, and to remind him of the night on which they sat with the watch between them, waiting his return; but Mr Grimwig contends that he was right in the main, and, in proof thereof, remarks that Oliver *did not come back* after all, which always calls forth a laugh on his side, and increases his good-humour.

Mr Noah Claypole, receiving a free pardon from the Crown in consequence of being admitted approver against the Jew, and considering his profession not altogether as safe a one as he could wish, was, for some little time, at a loss for the means of a livelihood, not burdened with too much work. After some consideration, he went into business as an Informer, in which calling he realises a genteel subsistence. His plan is to walk out once a week during church time attended by Charlotte in respectable attire. The lady faints away at the doors of charitable publicans, and the gentleman being accommodated with three-pennyworth of brandy to restore her, lays an information next day, and pockets half the penalty. Sometimes Mr Claypole faints himself, but the result is the same.

Mr and Mrs Bumble, deprived of their situations, were gradually reduced to great indigence and misery, and finally became paupers in that very same workhouse in which they had once lorded it over others. Mr Bumble has been heard to say, that in this reverse and degradation, he has not even spirits to be thankful for being separated from his wife.

As to Mr Giles and Brittles, they still remain in their old posts, although the former is bald, and the last-named boy quite grey. They sleep at the parsonage, but divide their attentions so equally among its inmates, and Oliver, and Mr Brownlow, and Mr Losberne, that to this day the villagers have never been able to discover to which establishment they properly belong.

Master Charles Bates, appalled by Sikes's crime, fell into a train of reflection whether an honest life was not, after all, the

Rose Maylie and Oliver

best. Arriving at the conclusion that it certainly was, he turned his back upon the scenes of the past, resolved to amend it in some new sphere of action. He struggled hard, and suffered much for some time; but, having a contented disposition, and a good purpose, succeeded in the end, and, from being a farmer's drudge, and a carrier's lad, is now the merriest young grazier in all Northamptonshire.

And now the hand that traces these words falters as it approaches the conclusion of its task, and would weave, for a little longer space, the thread of these adventures.

I would fain linger yet with a few of those among whom I have so long moved, and share their happiness by endeavouring to depict it. I would show Rose Maylie, in all the bloom and grace of early womanhood, shedding on her secluded path in life such soft and gentle light as fell on all who trod it with her, and shone into their hearts. I would paint her the life and joy of the fireside circle and the lively summer group; I would follow her through the sultry fields at noon, and hear the low tones of her sweet voice in the moonlight evening walk; I would watch her in all her goodness and charity abroad, and the smiling untiring discharge of domestic duties at home; I would paint her and her dead sister's child happy in their mutual love, and passing whole hours together in picturing the friends whom they had so sadly lost; I would summon before me, once again, those joyous little faces that clustered round her knee, and listen to their merry prattle; I would recall the tones of that clear laugh, and conjure up the sympathising tear that glistened in the soft blue eye. These, and a thousand looks and smiles, and turns of thought and speech – I would fain recall them every one.

How Mr Brownlow went on, from day to day, filling the mind of his adopted child with stores of knowledge, and becoming attached to him more and more, as his nature developed itself, and showed the thriving seeds of all he wished him to become – how he traced in him new traits of his early friend, that awakened in his own bosom old remembrances, melancholy and yet sweet and soothing – how the two orphans, tried by adversity, remembered its lessons in mercy to others, and mutual love and fervent thanks to Him who had protected and preserved them – these are all matters which need not to be told. I have said that they were truly happy; and without strong affection, and humanity of heart, and gratitude to that Being whose code is Mercy, and whose great attribute is Benevolence to all things that breathe, true happiness can never be attained.

Within the altar of the old village church there stands a white marble tablet, which bears as yet but one word – 'Agnes!' There is no coffin in that tomb; and may it be many, many years, before another name is placed above it! But, if the spirits of the dead ever come back to earth to visit spots hallowed by the love – the love beyond the grave – of those whom they knew in life, I believe that the shade of Agnes sometimes hovers round that solemn nook. I believe it none the less because that nook is in a church, and she was weak and erring.

A Christmas Carol

Marley's Ghost

Marley was dead: to begin with. There is no doubt whatever about that. The register of his burial was signed by the clergyman, the clerk, the undertaker, and the chief mourner. Scrooge signed it. And Scrooge's name was good upon 'change, for anything he chose to put his hand to. Old Marley was as dead as a doornail.

Mind! I don't mean to say that I know, of my own knowledge, what there is particularly dead about a doornail. I might have been inclined, myself, to regard a coffin-nail as the deadest piece of ironmongery in the trade. But the wisdom of our ancestors is in the simile; and my unhallowed hands shall not disturb it, or the country's done for. You will therefore permit me to repeat, emphatically, that Marley was as dead as a doornail.

Scrooge knew he was dead? Of course he did. How could it be otherwise? Scrooge and he were partners for I don't know how many years. Scrooge was his sole executor, his sole administrator, his sole assign, his sole residuary legatee, his sole friend, and sole mourner. And even Scrooge was not so dreadfully cut up by the sad event, but that he was an excellent man of business on the very day of the funeral, and solemnised it with an undoubted bargain.

The mention of Marley's funeral brings me back to the point I started from. There is no doubt that Marley was dead. This must be distinctly understood, or nothing wonderful can come of the story I am going to relate. If we were not perfectly convinced that Hamlet's father died before the play began, there would be nothing more remarkable in his taking a stroll at night, in an easterly wind, upon his own ramparts, than there would be in any other middle-aged gentleman rashly turning out after dark in a breezy spot – say St Paul's churchyard for instance – literally to astonish his son's weak mind.

Scrooge never painted out Old Marley's name. There it stood, years afterwards, above the warehouse door: Scrooge and Marley. The firm was known as Scrooge and Marley. Sometimes people new to the business called Scrooge Scrooge, and sometimes Marley, but he answered to both names. It was all the same to him.

Oh! But he was a tight-fisted hand at the grindstone, Scrooge! a squeezing, wrenching, grasping, scraping, clutching, covetous, old sinner! Hard and sharp as flint, from which no steel had ever struck out generous fire; secret, and self-contained, and solitary as an oyster. The cold within him froze his old features, nipped his pointed nose, shrivelled his cheek, stiffened his gait; made his eyes red, his thin lips blue; and spoke out shrewdly in his grating voice. A frosty rime was on his head, and on his eyebrows, and his wiry chin. He carried his own low temperature always about with him; he iced his office in the dog days; and didn't thaw it one degree at Christmas.

External heat and cold had little influence on Scrooge. No warmth could warm, no wintry weather chill him. No wind that blew was bitterer than he, no falling snow was more intent upon its purpose, no pelting rain less open to entreaty. Foul weather didn't know where to have him. The heaviest rain, and snow, and hail, and sleet, could boast of the advantage over him in only one respect. They often 'came down' handsomely, and Scrooge never did.

Nobody ever stopped him in the street to say, with gladsome looks, 'My dear Scrooge, how are you? When will you come to see me?' No beggars implored him to bestow a trifle, no children asked him what it was o'clock, no man or woman ever once in all his life enquired the way to such and such a place, of Scrooge. Even the blind men's dogs appeared to know him; and when they saw him coming on, would tug their owners into doorways and up courts; and then would wag their tails as though they said, 'No eye at all is better than an evil eye, dark master!'

But what did Scrooge care! It was the very thing he liked. To edge his way along the crowded paths of life, warning all human sympathy to keep its distance, was what the knowing ones call 'nuts' to Scrooge.

Once upon a time – of all the good days in the year, on Christmas Eve – old Scrooge sat busy in his counting-house. It was cold, bleak, biting weather: foggy withal: and he could hear the people in the court outside, go wheezing up and down, beating their hands upon their breasts, and stamping their feet upon the pavement stones to warm them. The city clocks had only just gone three, but it was quite dark already – it had not been light all day – and candles were flaring in the windows of the neighbouring offices, like ruddy smears upon the palpable brown air. The fog came pouring in at every chink and keyhole, and was so dense without, that although the court was of the narrowest, the houses opposite were mere phantoms. To see the dingy cloud come drooping down, obscuring everything, one might have thought that Nature lived hard by, and was brewing on a large scale.

The door of Scrooge's counting-house was open that he might keep his eye upon his clerk, who in a dismal little cell beyond, a sort of tank, was copying letters. Scrooge had a very small fire, but the clerk's fire was so very much smaller that it looked like one coal. But he couldn't replenish it, for Scrooge kept the coal-box in his own room; and so surely as the clerk came in with the shovel, the master predicted that it would be necessary for them to part. Wherefore the clerk put on his white comforter, and tried to warm himself at the candle; in which effort, not being a man of a strong imagination, he failed.

'A merry Christmas, uncle! God save you!' cried a cheerful voice. It was the voice of Scrooge's nephew, who came upon him so quickly that this was the first intimation he had of his approach.

'Bah!' said Scrooge, 'Humbug!'

He had so heated himself with rapid walking in the fog and frost, this nephew of Scrooge's, that he was all in a glow; his face was ruddy and handsome; his eyes sparkled, and his breath smoked again.

'Christmas a humbug, uncle!' said Scrooge's nephew. 'You don't mean that, I am sure.'

'I do,' said Scrooge. 'Merry Christmas! What right have you to be merry? What reason have you to be merry? You're poor enough.'

'Come, then,' returned the nephew gaily. 'What right have you to be dismal? What reason have you to be morose? You're rich enough.'

Scrooge having no better answer ready on the spur of the moment, said 'Bah!' again; and followed it up with 'Humbug.'

'Don't be cross, uncle!' said the nephew.

'What else can I be,' returned the uncle, 'when I live in such a world of fools as this? Merry Christmas! Out upon merry Christmas! What's Christmas time to you but a time for paying bills without money; a time for finding yourself a year older, but not an hour richer; a time for balancing your books and having every item in 'em through a round dozen of months presented dead against you? If I could work my will,' said Scrooge indignantly, 'every idiot who goes about with "Merry Christmas" on his lips, should be boiled with his own pudding, and buried with a stake of holly through his heart. He should!'

'Uncle!' pleaded the nephew.

'Nephew!' returned the uncle sternly, 'Keep Christmas in your own way, and let me keep it in mine.'

'Keep it!' repeated Scrooge's nephew. 'But you don't keep it.'

'Let me leave it alone, then,' said Scrooge. 'Much good may it do you! Much good it has ever done you!'

'There are many things from which I might have derived good, by which I have not profited, I dare say,' returned the nephew. 'Christmas among the rest. But I am sure I have always thought of Christmas time, when it has come round – apart from the veneration due to its sacred name and origin, if anything belonging to it can be apart from that – as a good time; a kind, forgiving, charitable, pleasant time: the only time I know of, in the long calendar of the year, when men and women seem by one consent to open their shut-up hearts freely, and to think of people below them as if they really were fellow-passengers to the grave, and not another race of creatures bound on other journeys. And therefore, uncle, though it has never put a scrap of gold or silver in my pocket, I believe that it *has* done me good, and *will* do me good; and I say, God bless it!'

The clerk in the tank involuntarily applauded. Becoming immediately sensible of the impropriety, he poked the fire, and extinguished the last frail spark for ever.

'Let me hear another sound from *you*,' said Scrooge, 'and you'll keep your Christmas by losing your situation! You're quite a powerful speaker, sir,' he added, turning to his nephew. 'I wonder you don't go into Parliament.'

'Don't be angry, uncle. Come! Dine with us tomorrow.'

Scrooge said that he would see him – yes, indeed he did. He went the whole length of the expression, and said that he would see him in that extremity first.

'But why?' cried Scrooge's nephew. 'Why?'

'Why did you get married?' said Scrooge.

'Because I fell in love.'

'Because you fell in love!' growled Scrooge, as if that were the only one thing in the world more ridiculous than a merry Christmas. 'Good-afternoon!'

'Nay, uncle, but you never came to see me before that happened. Why give it as a reason for not coming now?'

'Good-afternoon,' said Scrooge.

'I want nothing from you; I ask nothing of you; why cannot we be friends?'

'Good-afternoon,' said Scrooge.

'I am sorry, with all my heart, to find you so resolute. We have never had any quarrel, to which I have been a party. But I have made the trial in homage to Christmas, and I'll keep my Christmas humour to the last. So a Merry Christmas, uncle!'

'Good-afternoon,' said Scrooge.

'And a Happy New Year!'

'Good-afternoon,' said Scrooge.

His nephew left the room without an angry word, notwithstanding. He stopped at the outer door to bestow the greetings of the season on the clerk, who cold as he was, was warmer than Scrooge; for he returned them cordially.

'There's another fellow,' muttered Scrooge; who overheard him: 'my clerk, with fifteen shillings a week, and a wife and family, talking about a merry Christmas. I'll retire to Bedlam.'

This lunatic, in letting Scrooge's nephew out, had let two other people in. They were portly gentlemen, pleasant to behold, and now stood, with their hats off, in Scrooge's office. They had books and papers in their hands, and bowed to him.

'Scrooge and Marley's, I believe,' said one of the gentlemen, referring to his list. 'Have I the pleasure of addressing Mr Scrooge, or Mr Marley?'

'Mr Marley has been dead these seven years,' Scrooge replied. 'He died seven years ago, this very night.'

'We have no doubt his liberality is well represented by his surviving partner,' said the gentleman, presenting his credentials.

It certainly was; for they had been two kindred spirits. At the ominous word 'liberality', Scrooge frowned, and shook his head, and handed the credentials back.

'At this festive season of the year, Mr Scrooge,' said the gentleman, taking up a pen, 'it is more than usually desirable that we should make some slight provision for the poor and destitute, who suffer greatly at the present time. Many thousands are in want of common necessaries; hundreds of thousands are in want of common comforts, sir.'

'Are there no prisons?' asked Scrooge.

'Plenty of prisons,' said the gentleman, laying down the pen again.

'And the Union workhouses?' demanded Scrooge. 'Are they still in operation?'

'They are. Still,' returned the gentleman, 'I wish I could say they were not.'

'The treadmill and the Poor Law are in full vigour, then?' said Scrooge.

'Both very busy, sir.'

'Oh! I was afraid, from what you said at first, that something had occurred to stop them in their useful course,' said Scrooge. 'I'm very glad to hear it.'

'Under the impression that they scarcely furnish Christian cheer of mind or body to the multitude,' returned the gentleman, 'a few of us are endeavouring to raise a fund to buy the poor some meat and drink, and means of warmth. We choose this time, because it is a time, of all others, when Want is keenly felt, and Abundance rejoices. What shall I put you down for?'

'Nothing!' Scrooge replied.

'You wish to be anonymous?'

'I wish to be left alone,' said Scrooge. 'Since you ask me what I wish, gentlemen, that is my answer. I don't make merry myself at Christmas and I can't afford to make idle people merry. I help to support the establishments I have mentioned – they cost enough; and those who are badly off must go there.'

'Many can't go there; and many would rather die.'

'If they would rather die,' said Scrooge, 'they had better do it, and decrease the surplus population. Besides – excuse me – I don't know that.'

'But you might know it,' observed the gentleman.

'It's not my business,' Scrooge returned. 'It's enough for a man to understand his own business, and not to interfere with other people's. Mine occupies me constantly. Good-afternoon, gentlemen!'

Seeing clearly that it would be useless to pursue their point, the gentlemen withdrew. Scrooge resumed his labours with an improved opinion of himself, and in a more facetious temper than was usual with him.

Meanwhile the fog and darkness thickened so that people ran about with flaring links, proffering their services to go before horses in carriages, and conduct them on their way. The ancient tower of a church, whose gruff old bell was always peeping slily down at Scrooge out of a Gothic window in the wall, became invisible, and struck the hours and quarters in the clouds, with tremulous vibrations afterwards as if its teeth were chattering in its frozen head up there. The cold became intense. In the main street at the corner of the court, some labourers were repairing the gas-pipes, and had lighted a great fire in a brazier, round which a party of ragged men and boys were gathered: warming their hands and winking their eyes before the blaze in rapture. The water-plug being left in solitude, its overflowings sullenly congealed, and turned to misanthropic ice. The brightness of the shops where holly sprigs and berries crackled in the lamp heat of the windows, made pale faces ruddy as they passed. Poulterers' and grocers' trades became a splendid joke; a glorious pageant, with which

it was next to impossible to believe that such dull principles as bargain and sale had anything to do. The Lord Mayor, in the stronghold of the mighty Mansion House, gave orders to his fifty cooks and butlers to keep Christmas as a Lord Mayor's household should; and even the little tailor, whom he had fined five shillings on the previous Monday for being drunk and bloodthirsty in the streets, stirred up tomorrow's pudding in his garret, while his lean wife and the baby sallied out to buy the beef.

Foggier yet, and colder! Piercing, searching, biting cold. If the good St Dunstan had but nipped the evil spirit's nose with a touch of such weather as that, instead of using his familiar weapons, then indeed he would have roared to lusty purpose. The owner of one scant young nose, gnawed and mumbled by the hungry cold as bones are gnawed by dogs, stooped down at Scrooge's keyhole to regale him with a Christmas carol: but at the first sound of: 'God bless you, merry gentlemen! May nothing you dismay!' Scrooge seized the ruler with such energy of action that the singer fled in terror, leaving the keyhole to the fog and even more congenial frost.

At length the hour of shutting up the counting-house arrived. With an ill-will Scrooge dismounted from his stool, and tacitly admitted the fact to the expectant clerk in the tank, who instantly snuffed his candle out, and put on his hat.

'You'll want all day tomorrow, I suppose?' said Scrooge.

'If quite convenient, sir.'

'It's not convenient,' said Scrooge, 'and it's not fair. If I was to stop you half a crown for it, you'd think yourself ill-used, I'll be bound?'

The clerk smiled faintly.

'And yet,' said Scrooge, 'you don't think *me* ill-used, when I pay a day's wages for no work.'

The clerk observed that it was only once a year.

'A poor excuse for picking a man's pocket every twenty-fifth of December!' said Scrooge, buttoning his greatcoat to the chin. 'But I suppose you must have the whole day. Be here all the earlier next morning.'

The clerk promised that he would; and Scrooge walked out with a growl. The office was closed in a twinkling, and the clerk, with the long ends of his white comforter dangling below his waist (for he boasted no greatcoat), went down a slide on Cornhill, at the end of a line of boys, twenty times, in honour of its being Christmas Eve, and then ran home to Camden Town as hard as he could pelt, to play at blind man's buff.

Scrooge took his melancholy dinner in his usual melancholy tavern; and having read all the newspapers, and beguiled the rest of the evening with his banker's book, went home to bed. He lived in chambers which had once belonged to his deceased partner. They were a gloomy suite of rooms, in a lowering pile of a building up a yard, where it had so little business to be, that one could scarcely help fancying it must have run there when it was a young house, playing at hide-and-seek with other houses, and forgotten the way out again. It was old enough now, and dreary enough, for nobody lived in it but Scrooge, the other rooms being all let out as offices. The yard was so dark that even Scrooge, who knew its every stone, was fain to grope with his hands. The fog and frost so hung about the black old gateway of the house, that it seemed as if the Genius of the Weather sat in mournful meditation on the threshold.

Now, it is a fact that there was nothing at all particular about the knocker on the door, except that it was very large. It is also a fact that Scrooge had seen it, night and morning, during his whole residence in that place; also that Scrooge had as little of what is called fancy about him as any man in the city of London, even including – which is a bold word – the corporation, aldermen, and livery. Let it also be borne in mind that Scrooge had not bestowed one thought on Marley, since his last mention of his seven years' dead partner that afternoon. And then let any man explain to me, if he can, how it happened that Scrooge, having his key in the lock of the door, saw in the knocker, without its undergoing any intermediate process of change – not a knocker, but Marley's face.

Marley's face. It was not in impenetrable shadow as the other objects in the yard were, but had a dismal light about it, like a bad lobster in a dark cellar. It was not angry or ferocious, but looked at Scrooge as Marley used to look: with ghostly spectacles turned up on its ghostly forehead. The hair was curiously stirred, as if by breath or hot air; and, though the eyes were wide open, they were perfectly motionless. That, and its livid colour, made it horrible; but its horror seemed to be in spite of the face and beyond its control, rather than a part of its own expression.

As Scrooge looked fixedly at this phenomenon, it was a knocker again.

To say that he was not startled, or that his blood was not conscious of a terrible sensation to which it had been a stranger from infancy, would be untrue. But he put his hand upon the key he had relinquished, turned it sturdily, walked in, and lighted his candle.

He *did* pause, with a moment's irresolution, before he shut the door; and he *did* look cautiously behind it first, as if he half-expected to be terrified with the sight of Marley's pigtail sticking out into the hall. But there was nothing on the back of the door, except the screws and nuts that held the knocker on, so he said 'Pooh, pooh!' and closed it with a bang.

The sound resounded through the house like thunder. Every room above, and every cask in the wine-merchant's cellars below, appeared to have a separate peal of echoes of its own. Scrooge was not a man to be frightened by echoes. He fastened the door, and walked across the hall, and up the stairs; slowly too: trimming his candle as he went.

You may talk vaguely about driving a coach-and-six up a good old flight of stairs, or through a bad young Act of Parliament; but I mean to say you might have got a hearse up that staircase, and taken it broadwise, with the splinter-bar towards the wall and the door towards the balustrades: and done it easy. There was plenty of width for that, and room to spare; which is perhaps the reason why Scrooge thought he saw a locomotive hearse going on before him in the gloom. Half a dozen gas-lamps out of the street wouldn't have lighted the entry too well, so you may suppose that it was pretty dark with Scrooge's dip.

Up Scrooge went, not caring a button for that. Darkness is

cheap, and Scrooge liked it. But before he shut his heavy door, he walked through his rooms to see that all was right. He had just enough recollection of the face to desire to do that.

Sitting-room, bedroom, lumber-room. All as they should be. Nobody under the table, nobody under the sofa; a small fire in the grate; spoon and basin ready; and the little saucepan of gruel (Scrooge had a cold in his head) upon the hob. Nobody under the bed; nobody in the closet; nobody in his dressing-gown, which was hanging up in a suspicious attitude against the wall. Lumber-room as usual. Old fire-guards, old shoes, two fish-baskets, washing-stand on three legs, and a poker.

Quite satisfied, he closed his door, and locked himself in; double-locked himself in, which was not his custom. Thus secured against surprise, he took off his cravat; put on his dressing-gown and slippers, and his nightcap; and sat down before the fire to take his gruel.

It was a very low fire indeed; nothing on such a bitter night. He was obliged to sit close to it, and brood over it, before he could extract the least sensation of warmth from such a handful of fuel. The fireplace was an old one, built by some Dutch merchant long ago, and paved all round with quaint Dutch tiles, designed to illustrate the Scriptures. There were Cains and Abels, pharaohs' daughters; queens of Sheba, angelic messengers descending through the air on clouds like feather beds, Abrahams, Belshazzars, apostles putting off to sea in butter-boats, hundreds of figures to attract his thoughts – and yet that face of Marley, seven years dead, came like the ancient prophet's rod, and swallowed up the whole. If each smooth tile had been a blank at first, with power to shape some picture on its surface from the disjointed fragments of his thoughts, there would have been a copy of old Marley's head on every one.

'Humbug!' said Scrooge; and walked across the room.

After several turns, he sat down again. As he threw his head back in the chair, his glance happened to rest upon a bell, a disused bell, that hung in the room, and communicated for some purpose now forgotten with a chamber in the highest storey of the building. It was with great astonishment, and with a strange, inexplicable dread, that as he looked, he saw this bell begin to swing. It swung so softly in the outset that it scarcely made a sound; but soon it rang out loudly, and so did every bell in the house.

This might have lasted half a minute, or a minute, but it seemed an hour. The bells ceased as they had begun, together. They were succeeded by a clanking noise, deep down below; as if some person were dragging a heavy chain over the casks in the wine-merchant's cellar. Scrooge then remembered to have heard that ghosts in haunted houses were described as dragging chains.

The cellar-door flew open with a booming sound, and then he heard the noise much louder, on the floors below; then coming up the stairs; then coming straight towards his door.

'It's humbug still!' said Scrooge. 'I won't believe it.'

His colour changed though, when, without a pause, it came on through the heavy door, and passed into the room before his eyes. Upon its coming in, the dying flame leaped up, as though it cried 'I know him! Marley's Ghost!' and fell again.

The same face: the very same. Marley in his pigtail, usual waistcoat, tights and boots; the tassels on the latter bristling, like his pigtail, and his coat-skirts, and the hair upon his head. The chain he drew was clasped about his middle. It was long, and wound about him like a tail; and it was made (for Scrooge observed it closely) of cash boxes, keys, padlocks, ledgers, deeds, and heavy purses wrought in steel. His body was transparent; so that Scrooge, observing him, and looking through his waistcoat, could see the two buttons on his coat behind.

Scrooge had often heard it said that Marley had no bowels, but he had never believed it until now.

No, nor did he believe it even now. Though he looked the phantom through and through, and saw it standing before him; though he felt the chilling influence of its death-cold eyes; and marked the very texture of the folded kerchief bound about its head and chin, which wrapper he had not observed before; he was still incredulous, and fought against his senses.

'How now!' said Scrooge, caustic and cold as ever. 'What do you want with me?'

'Much!' – Marley's voice, no doubt about it.

'Who are you?'

'Ask me who I *was*.'

'Who *were* you then?' said Scrooge, raising his voice. 'You're particular, for a shade.' He was going to say '*to* a shade,' but substituted this, as more appropriate.

Marley's Ghost

'In life I was your partner, Jacob Marley.'

'Can you – can you sit down?' asked Scrooge, looking doubtfully at him.

'I can.'

'Do it, then.'

Scrooge asked the question, because he didn't know whether a ghost so transparent might find himself in a condition to take a chair; and felt that in the event of its being impossible, it might involve the necessity of an embarrassing explanation. But the ghost sat down on the opposite side of the fireplace, as if he were quite used to it.

'You don't believe in me,' observed the ghost.

'I don't,' said Scrooge.

'What evidence would you have of my reality beyond that of your senses?'

'I don't know,' said Scrooge.

'Why do you doubt your senses?'

'Because,' said Scrooge, 'a little thing affects them. A slight disorder of the stomach makes them cheats. You may be an undigested bit of beef, a blot of mustard, a crumb of cheese, a fragment of an underdone potato. There's more of gravy than of grave about you, whatever you are!'

Scrooge was not much in the habit of cracking jokes, nor did he feel, in his heart, by any means waggish then. The truth is, that he tried to be smart, as a means of distracting his own attention, and keeping down his terror; for the spectre's voice disturbed the very marrow in his bones.

To sit, staring at those fixed glazed eyes, in silence for a moment, would play, Scrooge felt, the very deuce with him. There was something very awful, too, in the spectre's being provided with an infernal atmosphere of its own. Scrooge could not feel it himself, but this was clearly the case; for though the ghost sat perfectly motionless, its hair, and skirts, and tassels, were still agitated as by the hot vapour from an oven.

'You see this toothpick?' said Scrooge, returning quickly to the charge, for the reason just assigned; and wishing, though it were only for a second, to divert the vision's stony gaze from himself.

'I do,' replied the ghost.

'You are not looking at it,' said Scrooge.

'But I see it,' said the ghost, 'notwithstanding.'

'Well!' returned Scrooge, 'I have but to swallow this, and be for the rest of my days persecuted by a legion of goblins, all of my own creation. Humbug, I tell you! humbug!'

At this the spirit raised a frightful cry, and shook its chain with such a dismal and appalling noise, that Scrooge held on tight to his chair, to save himself from falling in a swoon. But how much greater was his horror, when the phantom taking off the bandage round its head, as if it were too warm to wear indoors, its lower jaw dropped down upon its breast!

Scrooge fell upon his knees, and clasped his hands before his face.

'Mercy!' he said. 'Dreadful apparition, why do you trouble me?'

'Man of the worldly mind!' replied the ghost, 'do you believe in me or not?'

'I do,' said Scrooge. 'I must. But why do spirits walk the earth, and why do they come to me?'

'It is required of every man,' the ghost returned, 'that the spirit within him should walk abroad among his fellow men, and travel far and wide; and if that spirit goes not forth in life, it is condemned to do so after death. It is doomed to wander through the world – oh, woe is me! – and witness what it cannot share, but might have shared on earth, and turned to happiness!'

Again the spectre raised a cry, and shook its chain and wrung its shadowy hands.

'You are fettered,' said Scrooge, trembling. 'Tell me why?'

'I wear the chain I forged in life,' replied the ghost. 'I made it link by link, and yard by yard; I girded it on of my own free will, and of my own free will I wore it. Is its pattern strange to *you*?'

Scrooge trembled more and more.

'Or would you know,' pursued the ghost, 'the weight and length of the strong coil you bear yourself? It was full as heavy and as long as this, seven Christmas Eves ago. You have laboured on it, since. It is a ponderous chain!'

Scrooge glanced about him on the floor, in the expectation of finding himself surrounded by some fifty or sixty fathoms of iron cable: but he could see nothing.

'Jacob,' he said, imploringly. 'Old Jacob Marley, tell me more. Speak comfort to me, Jacob!'

'I have none to give,' the ghost replied. 'It comes from other regions, Ebenezer Scrooge, and is conveyed by other ministers, to other kinds of men. Nor can I tell you what I would. A very little more, is all permitted to me. I cannot rest, I cannot stay, I cannot linger anywhere. My spirit never walked beyond our counting-house – mark me! – in life my spirit never roved beyond the narrow limits of our money-changing hole; and weary journeys lie before me!'

It was a habit with Scrooge, whenever he became thoughtful, to put his hands in his breeches pockets. Pondering on what the ghost had said, he did so now, but without lifting up his eyes, or getting off his knees.

'You must have been very slow about it, Jacob,' Scrooge observed, in a businesslike manner, though with humility and deference.

'Slow!' the ghost repeated.

'Seven years dead,' mused Scrooge. 'And travelling all the time!'

'The whole time,' said the ghost. 'No rest, no peace. Incessant torture of remorse.'

'You travel fast?' said Scrooge.

'On the wings of the wind,' replied the ghost.

'You might have got over a great quantity of ground in seven years,' said Scrooge.

The ghost, on hearing this, set up another cry, and clanked its chain so hideously in the dead silence of the night, that the ward would have been justified in indicting it for a nuisance.

'Oh! captive, bound, and double-ironed,' cried the phantom, 'not to know that ages of incessant labour, by immortal creatures, for this earth must pass into eternity before the good of which it is susceptible is all developed. Not to know that any Christian spirit working kindly in its little sphere, whatever it may be, will find its mortal life too short for its vast means of usefulness. Not to know that no space of regret can make amends for one life's opportunity misused! Yet such was I! Oh! such was I!'

'But you were always a good man of business, Jacob,' faltered Scrooge, who now began to apply this to himself.

'Business!' cried the ghost, wringing its hands again. 'Mankind was my business. The common welfare was my business; charity, mercy, forbearance, and benevolence, were, all, my business. The dealings of my trade were but a drop of water in the comprehensive ocean of my business!'

It held up its chain at arm's length, as if that were the cause of all its unavailing grief, and flung it heavily upon the ground again.

'At this time of the rolling year,' the spectre said, 'I suffer most. Why did I walk through crowds of fellow-beings with my eyes turned down, and never raise them to that blessed star which led the wise men to a poor abode! Were there no poor homes to which its light would have conducted *me*?'

Scrooge was very much dismayed to hear the spectre going on at this rate, and began to quake exceedingly.

'Hear me!' cried the ghost. 'My time is nearly gone.'

'I will,' said Scrooge. 'But don't be hard upon me! Don't be flowery, Jacob! Pray!'

'How it is that I appear before you in a shape that you can see, I may not tell. I have sat invisible beside you many and many a day.'

It was not an agreeable idea. Scrooge shivered, and wiped the perspiration from his brow.

'That is no light part of my penance,' pursued the ghost. 'I am here tonight to warn you, that you have yet a chance and hope of escaping my fate. A chance and hope of my procuring, Ebenezer.'

'You were always a good friend to me,' said Scrooge. 'Thank 'ee!'

'You will be haunted,' resumed the ghost, 'by three spirits.'

Scrooge's countenance fell almost as low as the ghost's had done.

'Is that the chance and hope you mentioned, Jacob?' he demanded, in a faltering voice.

'It is.'

'I – I think I'd rather not,' said Scrooge.

'Without their visits,' said the ghost, 'you cannot hope to shun the path I tread. Expect the first tomorrow, when the bell tolls one.'

'Couldn't I take 'em all at once, and have it over, Jacob?' hinted Scrooge.

'Expect the second on the next night at the same hour. The third upon the next night when the last stroke of twelve has ceased to vibrate. Look to see me no more; and look that, for your own sake, you remember what has passed between us!'

When it had said these words, the spectre took its wrapper from the table, and bound it round its head, as before. Scrooge knew this, by the smart sound its teeth made, when the jaws were brought together by the bandage. He ventured to raise his eyes again, and found his supernatural visitor confronting him in an erect attitude, with its chain wound over and about its arm.

The apparition walked backward from him; and at every step it took, the window raised itself a little, so that when the spectre reached it, it was wide open. It beckoned Scrooge to approach, which he did. When they were within two paces of each other, Marley's Ghost held up its hand, warning him to come no nearer. Scrooge stopped.

Not so much in obedience, as in surprise and fear: for on the raising of the hand, he became sensible of confused noises in the air; incoherent sounds of lamentation and regret; wailings inexpressibly sorrowful and self-accusatory. The spectre, after listening for a moment, joined in the mournful dirge; and floated out upon the bleak, dark night.

Scrooge followed to the window: desperate in his curiosity. He looked out.

The air was filled with phantoms, wandering hither and thither in restless haste, and moaning as they went. Every one of them wore chains like Marley's Ghost; some few (they might be guilty governments) were linked together; none were free. Many had been personally known to Scrooge in their lives. He had been quite familiar with one old ghost, in a white waistcoat, with a monstrous iron safe attached to its ankle, who cried piteously at being unable to assist a wretched woman with an infant, whom it saw below, upon a doorstep. The misery with them all was, clearly, that they sought to interfere, for good, in human matters, and had lost the power for ever.

Whether these creatures faded into mist, or mist enshrouded them, he could not tell. But they and their spirit voices faded together; and the night became as it had been when he walked home.

The air was filled with phantoms

Scrooge closed the window, and examined the door by which the ghost had entered. It was double-locked, as he had locked it with his own hands, and the bolts were undisturbed. He tried to say 'Humbug!' but stopped at the first syllable. And being, from the emotion he had undergone, or the fatigues of the day, or his glimpse of the invisible world, or the dull conversation of the ghost, or the lateness of the hour, much in need of repose; went straight to bed, without undressing, and fell asleep upon the instant.

STAVE 2

The First of the Three Spirits

When Scrooge awoke, it was so dark, that looking out of bed, he could scarcely distinguish the transparent window from the opaque walls of his chamber. He was endeavouring to pierce the darkness with his ferret eyes, when the chimes of a neighbouring church struck the four quarters. So he listened for the hour.

To his great astonishment the heavy bell went on from six to seven, and from seven to eight, and regularly up to twelve; then stopped. Twelve. It was past two when he went to bed. The clock was wrong. An icicle must have got into the works. Twelve.

He touched the spring of his repeater, to correct this most preposterous clock. Its rapid little pulse beat twelve: and stopped.

'Why, it isn't possible,' said Scrooge, 'that I can have slept through a whole day and far into another night. It isn't possible that anything has happened to the sun, and this is twelve at noon.'

The idea being an alarming one, he scrambled out of bed, and groped his way to the window. He was obliged to rub the frost off with the sleeve of his dressing-gown before he could see anything; and could see very little then. All he could make out was, that it was still very foggy and extremely cold, and that there was no noise of people running to and fro, and making a great stir, as there unquestionably would have been if night had beaten off bright day, and taken possession of the world. This was a great relief, because, 'Three days after sight of this first of exchange pay to Mr Ebenezer Scrooge on his order', and so forth, would have become a mere United States security if there were no days to count by.

Scrooge went to bed again, and thought, and thought, and thought it over and over, and could make nothing of it. The more he thought, the more perplexed he was; and, the more he endeavoured not to think, the more he thought.

Marley's Ghost bothered him exceedingly. Every time he resolved within himself, after mature enquiry, that it was all a dream, his mind flew back again, like a strong spring released, to its first position, and presented the same problem to be worked all through, 'Was it a dream or not?'

Scrooge lay in this state until the chime had gone three quarters more, when he remembered, on a sudden, that the ghost had warned him of a visitation when the bell tolled one.

He resolved to lie awake until the hour was passed; and, considering that he could no more go to sleep than go to heaven, this was, perhaps, the wisest resolution in his power.

The quarter was so long, that he was more than once convinced he must have sunk into a doze unconsciously, and missed the clock. At length it broke upon his listening ear.

'Ding, dong!'

'A quarter past,' said Scrooge, counting.

'Ding, dong!'

'Half past,' said Scrooge.

'Ding, dong!'

'A quarter to it,' said Scrooge.

'Ding, dong!'

'The hour itself,' said Scrooge triumphantly, 'and nothing else!'

He spoke before the hour bell sounded, which it now did with a deep, dull, hollow, melancholy one. Light flashed up in the room upon the instant, and the curtains of his bed were drawn.

The curtains of his bed were drawn aside, I tell you, by a hand. Not the curtains at his feet, nor the curtains at his back, but those to which his face was addressed. The curtains of his bed were drawn aside; and Scrooge, starting up into a half-recumbent attitude, found himself face to face with the unearthly visitor who drew them: as close to it as I am now to you, and I am standing in the spirit at your elbow.

It was a strange figure – like a child: yet not so like a child as like an old man, viewed through some supernatural medium, which gave him the appearance of having receded from the view, and being diminished to a child's proportions. Its hair, which hung about its neck and down its back, was white as if with age; and yet the face had not a wrinkle in it, and the tenderest bloom was on the skin. The arms were very long and muscular; the hands the same, as if its hold were of uncommon strength. Its legs and feet, most delicately formed, were, like those upper members, bare. It wore a tunic of the purest white, and round its waist was bound a lustrous belt, the sheen of which was beautiful. It held a branch of fresh green holly in its hand; and, in singular contradiction of that wintry emblem, had its dress trimmed with summer flowers. But the strangest thing about it was, that from the crown of its head there sprung a bright clear jet of light, by which all this was visible; and which was doubtless the occasion of its using, in its duller moments, a great extinguisher for a cap, which it now held under its arm.

Even this, though, when Scrooge looked at it with increasing steadiness, was *not* its strangest quality. For as its belt sparkled and glittered now in one part and now in another, and what was light one instant, at another time was dark, so the figure itself fluctuated in its distinctness: being now a thing with one arm, now with one leg, now with twenty legs, now a pair of legs without a head, now a head without a body: of which dissolving parts, no outline would be visible in the dense gloom wherein they melted away. And in the very wonder of this, it would be itself again; distinct and clear as ever.

'Are you the spirit, sir, whose coming was foretold to me?' asked Scrooge.

'I am.'

The voice was soft and gentle. Singularly low, as if instead of being so close beside him, it were at a distance.

'Who, and what are you?' Scrooge demanded.

'I am the Ghost of Christmas Past.'

'Long past?' enquired Scrooge: observant of its dwarfish stature.

'No. Your past.'

Perhaps, Scrooge could not have told anybody why, if anybody could have asked him; but he had a special desire to see the spirit in his cap; and begged him to be covered.

'What!' exclaimed the ghost, 'would you so soon put out, with worldly hands, the light I give? Is it not enough that you are one of those whose passions made this cap, and force me through whole trains of years to wear it low upon my brow?'

Scrooge reverently disclaimed all intention to offend or any knowledge of having wilfully bonneted the spirit at any period of his life. He then made bold to enquire what business brought him there.

'Your welfare,' said the ghost.

Scrooge expressed himself much obliged, but could not help thinking that a night of unbroken rest would have been more conducive to that end. The spirit must have heard him thinking, for it said immediately: 'Your reclamation, then. Take heed.'

It put out its strong hand as it spoke, and clasped him gently by the arm.

'Rise, and walk with me.'

It would have been in vain for Scrooge to plead that the weather and the hour were not adapted to pedestrian purposes; that bed was warm, and the thermometer a long way below freezing; that he was clad but lightly in his slippers, dressing-gown, and nightcap; and that he had a cold upon him at that time. The grasp, though gentle as a woman's hand, was not to be resisted. He rose: but finding that the spirit made towards the window, clasped his robe in supplication.

'I am mortal,' Scrooge remonstrated, 'and liable to fall.'

'Bear but a touch of my hand *there*,' said the spirit, laying it upon his heart, 'and you shall be upheld in more than this.'

As the words were spoken, they passed through the wall, and stood upon an open country road, with fields on either hand. The city had entirely vanished. Not a vestige of it was to be seen. The darkness and the mist had vanished with it, for it was a clear, cold, winter day, with snow upon the ground.

'Good Heaven!' said Scrooge, clasping his hands together, as he looked about him. 'I was bred in this place. I was a boy here.'

The spirit gazed upon him mildly. Its gentle touch, though it had been light and instantaneous, appeared still present to the old man's sense of feeling. He was conscious of a thousand odours floating in the air, each one connected with a thousand thoughts, and hopes, and joys, and cares long, long, forgotten.

'Your lip is trembling,' said the ghost. 'And what is that upon your cheek?'

Scrooge muttered, with an unusual catching in his voice, that it was a pimple; and begged the ghost to lead him where he would.

'You recollect the way?' enquired the spirit.

'Remember it!' cried Scrooge with fervour; 'I could walk it blindfold.'

'Strange to have forgotten it for so many years,' observed the ghost. 'Let us go on.'

They walked along the road, Scrooge recognising every gate, and post, and tree; until a little market-town appeared in the distance, with its bridge, its church, and winding river. Some shaggy ponies now were seen trotting towards them with boys upon their backs, who called to other boys in country gigs and carts, driven by farmers. All these boys were in great spirits, and shouted to each other, until the broad fields were so full of merry music, that the crisp air laughed to hear it.

'These are but shadows of the things that have been,' said the ghost. 'They have no consciousness of us.'

The jocund travellers came on; and as they came, Scrooge knew and named them every one. Why was he rejoiced beyond all bounds to see them? Why did his cold eye glisten, and his heart leap up as they went past? Why was he filled with gladness when he heard them give each other 'Merry Christmas', as they parted at crossroads and byways, for their several homes? What was merry Christmas to Scrooge? Out upon merry Christmas! What good had it ever done to him?

'The school is not quite deserted,' said the ghost. 'A solitary child, neglected by his friends, is left there still.'

Scrooge said he knew it. And he sobbed.

They left the highroad, by a well-remembered lane, and soon approached a mansion of dull red brick, with a little weathercock-surmounted cupola on the roof, and a bell hanging in it. It was a large house, but one of broken fortunes; for the spacious offices were little used, their walls were damp and mossy, their windows broken, and their gates decayed. Fowls clucked and strutted in the stables; and the coach-houses and sheds were overrun with grass. Nor was it more retentive of its ancient state within; for entering the dreary hall, and glancing through the open doors of many rooms, they found them poorly furnished, cold, and vast. There was an earthy savour in the air, a chilly bareness in the place, which associated itself somehow with too much getting up by candle-light, and not too much to eat.

They went, the ghost and Scrooge, across the hall, to a door at the back of the house. It opened before them, and disclosed a long, bare, melancholy room, made barer still by lines of plain deal forms and desks. At one of these a lonely boy was reading near a feeble fire; and Scrooge sat down upon a form, and wept to see his poor forgotten self as he used to be.

Not a latent echo in the house, not a squeak and scuffle from the mice behind the panelling, not a drip from the half-thawed waterspout in the dull yard behind, not a sigh among the leafless boughs of one despondent poplar, not the idle swinging of an empty storehouse door, no, not a clicking in the fire, but fell upon the heart of Scrooge with a softening influence, and gave a freer passage to his tears.

The spirit touched him on the arm, and pointed to his younger self, intent upon his reading. Suddenly a man in foreign garments, wonderfully real and distinct to look at, stood outside the window, with an axe stuck in his belt, and leading by the bridle an ass laden with wood.

'Why, it's Ali Baba!' Scrooge exclaimed in ecstasy. 'It's dear old honest Ali Baba. Yes, yes, I know. One Christmas time, when yonder solitary child was left here all alone, he *did* come, for the first time, just like that. Poor boy. And Valentine,' said Scrooge, 'and his wild brother, Orson; there they go. And what's his name, who was put down in his drawers, asleep, at the gate of Damascus; don't you see him. And the Sultan's groom turned upside down by the Genii; there he is upon his head. Serve him right! I'm glad of it. What business had *he* to be married to the princess?'

To hear Scrooge expending all the earnestness of his nature on such subjects, in a most extraordinary voice between laughing and crying; and to see his heightened and excited face would have been a surprise to his business friends in the city, indeed.

'There's the parrot!' cried Scrooge. 'Green body and yellow tail, with a thing like a lettuce growing out of the top of his head; there he is. Poor Robin Crusoe, he called him, when he came home again after sailing round the island. "Poor Robin Crusoe, where have you been, Robin Crusoe." The man thought he was dreaming, but he wasn't. It was the parrot, you know. There goes Friday, running for his life to the little creek. Halloa! Hoop! Halloo!'

Then, with a rapidity of transition very foreign to his usual character, he said, in pity for his former self, 'Poor boy!' and cried again.

'I wish,' Scrooge muttered, putting his hand in his pocket, and looking about him, after drying his eyes with his cuff: 'but it's too late now.'

'What is the matter?' asked the spirit.

'Nothing,' said Scrooge. 'Nothing. There was a boy singing a Christmas Carol at my door last night. I should like to have given him something: that's all.'

The ghost smiled thoughtfully, and waved its hand: saying as it did so, 'Let us see another Christmas.'

Scrooge's former self grew larger at the words, and the room became a little darker and more dirty. The panels shrunk, the windows cracked; fragments of plaster fell out of the ceiling, and the naked laths were shown instead; but how all this was brought about, Scrooge knew no more than you do. He only knew that it was quite correct; that everything had happened so; that there he was, alone again, when all the other boys had gone home for the jolly holidays.

He was not reading now, but walking up and down despairingly.

Scrooge looked at the ghost, and with a mournful shaking of his head, glanced anxiously towards the door.

It opened; and a little girl, much younger than the boy, came darting in, and putting her arms about his neck, and often kissing him, addressed him as her 'Dear, dear brother!'

'I have come to bring you home, dear brother!' said the child, clapping her tiny hands, and bending down to laugh. 'To bring you home, home, home!'

'Home, little Fan?' returned the boy.

'Yes,' said the child, brimful of glee. 'Home, for good and all! Home, for ever and ever. Father is so much kinder than he used to be, that home's like Heaven. He spoke so gently to me one dear night when I was going to bed, that I was not afraid to ask him once more if you might come home; and he said Yes, you should; and sent me in a coach to bring you. And you're to be a man!' said the child, opening her eyes, 'and are never to come back here; but first, we're to be together all the Christmas long, and have the merriest time in all the world!'

'You are quite a woman, little Fan!' exclaimed the boy.

She clapped her hands and laughed, and tried to touch his head; but being too little, laughed again, and stood on tiptoe to embrace him. Then she began to drag him, in her childish eagerness, towards the door; and he, nothing loth to go, accompanied her.

A terrible voice in the hall cried. 'Bring down Master Scrooge's box, there!' and in the hall appeared the school-master himself, who glared on Master Scrooge with a ferocious condescension, and threw him into a dreadful state of mind by shaking hands with him. He then conveyed him and his sister into the veriest old well of a shivering best parlour that ever was seen, where the maps upon the wall, and the celestial and terrestrial globes in the windows, were waxy with cold. Here he produced a decanter of curiously light wine, and a block of curiously heavy cake, and administered instalments of those dainties to the young people: at the same time, sending out a meagre servant to offer a glass of something to the postboy, who answered that he thanked the gentleman, but if it was the same tap as he had tasted before, he had rather not. Master Scrooge's trunk being by this time tied on to the top of the chaise, the children bade the schoolmaster goodbye right willingly; and getting into it, drove gaily down the garden-sweep: the quick wheels dashing the hoar-frost and snow from off the dark leaves of the evergreens like spray.

'Always a delicate creature, whom a breath might have withered,' said the ghost. 'But she had a large heart.'

'So she had,' cried Scrooge. 'You're right. I will not gainsay it, Spirit. God forbid.'

'She died a woman,' said the ghost, 'and had, as I think, children.'

'One child,' Scrooge returned.

'True,' said the ghost. 'Your nephew.'

Scrooge seemed uneasy in his mind; and answered briefly, 'Yes.'

Although they had but that moment left the school behind them, they were now in the busy thoroughfares of a city, where shadowy passengers passed and repassed; where shadowy carts and coaches battled for the way, and all the strife and tumult of a real city were. It was made plain enough, by the dressing of the shops, that here too it was Christmas time again; but it was evening, and the streets were lighted up.

The ghost stopped at a certain warehouse door, and asked Scrooge if he knew it.

'Know it?' said Scrooge. 'I was apprenticed here!'

They went in. At sight of an old gentleman in a Welsh wig, sitting behind such a high desk, that if he had been two inches taller he must have knocked his head against the ceiling, Scrooge cried in great excitement: 'Why, it's old Fezziwig! Bless his heart; it's Fezziwig alive again.'

Old Fezziwig laid down his pen, and looked up at the clock, which pointed to the hour of seven. He rubbed his hands; adjusted his capacious waistcoat; laughed all over himself, from his shoes to his organ of benevolence; and called out in a comfortable, oily, rich, fat, jovial voice: 'Yo ho, there! Ebenezer! Dick!'

Scrooge's former self, now grown a young man, came briskly in, accompanied by his fellow 'prentice.

'Dick Wilkins, to be sure!' said Scrooge to the ghost. 'Bless me, yes. There he is. He was very much attached to me, was Dick. Poor Dick. Dear, dear.'

'Yo ho, my boys,' said Fezziwig. 'No more work tonight! Christmas Eve, Dick. Christmas, Ebenezer. Let's have the shutters up,' cried old Fezziwig, with a sharp clap of his hands, 'before a man can say Jack Robinson.'

You wouldn't believe how those two fellows went at it. They charged into the street with the shutters – one, two, three – had them up in their places – four, five, six – barred them and pinned them – seven, eight, nine – and came back before you could have got to twelve, panting like racehorses.

'Hilli-ho!' cried old Fezziwig, skipping down from the high desk, with wonderful agility. 'Clear away, my lads, and let's have lots of room here. Hilli-ho, Dick. Chirrup, Ebenezer.'

Clear away. There was nothing they wouldn't have cleared away, or couldn't have cleared away, with old Fezziwig looking on. It was done in a minute. Every movable was packed off, as if it were dismissed from public life for evermore; the floor was swept and watered, the lamps were trimmed, fuel was heaped upon the fire; and the warehouse was as snug, and warm, and dry, and bright a ballroom, as you would desire to see upon a winter's night.

In came a fiddler with a music-book, and went up to the lofty desk, and made an orchestra of it, and tuned like fifty stomach-aches. In came Mrs Fezziwig, one vast substantial smile. In came the three Miss Fezziwigs, beaming and lovable. In came the six young followers whose hearts they broke. In came all the young men and women employed in the business. In came the housemaid, with her cousin, the baker. In came the cook, with her brother's particular friend, the milkman. In came the boy from over the way, who was suspected of not having board enough from his master; trying to hide himself behind the girl from next door but one, who was proved to have had her ears pulled by her mistress. In they all came, one after another; some shyly, some boldly, some gracefully, some awkwardly, some pushing, some pulling; in they all came, anyhow and everyhow. Away they all went, twenty couples at once; hands half round and back again the other way; down the middle and up again; round and round in various stages of affectionate grouping; old top couple always turning up in the wrong place; new top couple starting off again, as soon as they got there; all top couples at last, and not a bottom one to help them. When this result was brought about, old Fezziwig, clapping his hands to stop the dance, cried out, 'Well done!' and the fiddler plunged his hot face into a pot of porter, especially provided for that purpose. But scorning rest, upon his reappearance, he instantly began again, though there were no dancers yet, as if the other fiddler had been carried home, exhausted, on a shutter, and he were a bran-new man resolved to beat him out of sight, or perish.

There were more dances, and there were forfeits, and more dances, and there was cake, and there was negus, and there was a great piece of cold roast, and there was a great piece of cold boiled, and there were mince pies, and plenty of beer. But the great effect of the evening came after the roast and boiled, when the fiddler (an artful dog, mind. The sort of man who knew his business better than you or I could have told it him!) struck up 'Sir Roger de Coverley'. Then old Fezziwig stood out to dance with Mrs Fezziwig. Top couple, too; with a good stiff piece of work cut out for them; three or four and twenty pairs of partners; people who were not to be trifled with; people who would dance, and had no notion of walking.

But if they had been twice as many – ah, four times – old Fezziwig would have been a match for them, and so would Mrs Fezziwig. As to *her*, she was worthy to be his partner in every sense of the term. If that's not high praise, tell me higher, and I'll use it. A positive light appeared to issue from Fezziwig's calves. They shone in every part of the dance like moons. You couldn't have predicted, at any given time, what would have become of them next. And when old Fezziwig and Mrs Fezziwig had gone all through the dance; advance and retire, both hands to your partner, bow and curtsey, corkscrew, thread-the-needle, and back again to your place; Fezziwig cut – cut so deftly, that he appeared to wink with his legs, and came upon his feet again without a stagger.

Mr Fezziwig's ball

When the clock struck eleven, this domestic ball broke up. Mr and Mrs Fezziwig took their stations, one on either side of the door, and shaking hands with every person individually as he or she went out, wished him or her a merry Christmas. When everybody had retired but the two 'prentices, they did the same to them; and thus the cheerful voices died away, and the lads were left to their beds; which were under a counter in the back-shop.

During the whole of this time, Scrooge had acted like a man out of his wits. His heart and soul were in the scene, and with his former self. He corroborated everything, remembered everything, enjoyed everything, and underwent the strangest agitation. It was not until now, when the bright faces of his former self and Dick were turned from them, that he remembered the ghost, and became conscious that it was looking full upon him, while the light upon its head burnt very clear.

'A small matter,' said the ghost, 'to make these silly folks so full of gratitude.'

'Small,' echoed Scrooge.

The spirit signed to him to listen to the two apprentices, who were pouring out their hearts in praise of Fezziwig: and when he had done so, said,

'Why? Is it not? He has spent but a few pounds of your mortal money: three or four perhaps. Is that so much that he deserves this praise?'

'It isn't that,' said Scrooge, heated by the remark, and speaking unconsciously like his former, not his latter, self. 'It isn't that, Spirit. He has the power to render us happy or unhappy; to make our service light or burdensome; a pleasure or a toil. Say that his power lies in words and looks; in things so slight and insignificant that it is impossible to add and count them up: what then? The happiness he gives, is quite as great as if it cost a fortune.'

He felt the spirit's glance, and stopped.

'What is the matter?' asked the ghost.

'Nothing in particular,' said Scrooge.

'Something, I think,' the ghost insisted.

'No,' said Scrooge, 'No. I should like to be able to say a word or two to my clerk just now. That's all.'

His former self turned down the lamps as he gave utterance to the wish; and Scrooge and the ghost again stood side by side in the open air.

'My time grows short,' observed the spirit. 'Quick.'

This was not addressed to Scrooge, or to anyone whom he could see, but it produced an immediate effect. For again Scrooge saw himself. He was older now; a man in the prime of life. His face had not the harsh and rigid lines of later years; but it had begun to wear the signs of care and avarice. There was an eager, greedy, restless motion in the eye, which showed the passion that had taken root, and where the shadow of the growing tree would fall.

He was not alone, but sat by the side of a fair young girl in a mourning-dress: in whose eyes there were tears, which sparkled in the light that shone out of the Ghost of Christmas Past.

'It matters little,' she said, softly. 'To you, very little. Another idol has displaced me; and if it can cheer and comfort you in time to come, as I would have tried to do, I have no just cause to grieve.'

'What idol has displaced you?' he rejoined.

'A golden one.'

'This is the even-handed dealing of the world,' he said. 'There is nothing on which it is so hard as poverty; and there is nothing it professes to condemn with such severity as the pursuit of wealth.'

'You fear the world too much,' she answered, gently. 'All your other hopes have merged into the hope of being beyond the chance of its sordid reproach. I have seen your nobler aspirations fall off one by one, until the master-passion, gain, engrosses you. Have I not?'

'What then?' he retorted. 'Even if I have grown so much wiser, what then? I am not changed towards you.'

She shook her head.

'Am I?'

'Our contract is an old one. It was made when we were both poor and content to be so, until, in good season, we could improve our worldly fortune by our patient industry. You *are* changed. When it was made, you were another man.'

'I was a boy,' he said impatiently.

'Your own feeling tells you that you were not what you are,' she returned. 'I am. That which promised happiness when we were one in heart, is fraught with misery now that we are two. How often and how keenly I have thought of this, I will not say. It is enough that I *have* thought of it, and can release you.'

'Have I ever sought release?'

'In words? No. Never.'

'In what, then?'

'In a changed nature; in an altered spirit; in another atmosphere of life; another hope as its great end. In everything that made my love of any worth or value in your sight. If this had never been between us,' said the girl, looking mildly, but with steadiness, upon him; 'tell me, would you seek me out and try to win me now? Ah, no.'

He seemed to yield to the justice of this supposition, in spite of himself. But he said with a struggle, 'You think not?'

'I would gladly think otherwise if I could,' she answered, 'Heaven knows. When *I* have learned a Truth like this, I know how strong and irresistible it must be. But if you were free today, tomorrow, yesterday, can even I believe that you would choose a dowerless girl – you who, in your very confidence with her, weigh everything by gain: or, choosing her, if for a moment you were false enough to your one guiding principle to do so, do I not know that your repentance and regret would surely follow. I do; and I release you. With a full heart, for the love of him you once were.'

He was about to speak; but with her head turned from him, she resumed.

'You may – the memory of what is past half makes me hope you will – have pain in this. A very, very brief time, and you will dismiss the recollection of it, gladly, as an unprofitable dream, from which it happened well that you awoke. May you be happy in the life you have chosen.'

She left him, and they parted.

'Spirit,' said Scrooge, 'show me no more. Conduct me home. Why do you delight to torture me?'

'One shadow more,' exclaimed the ghost.

'No more!' cried Scrooge. 'No more, I don't wish to see it. Show me no more.'

But the relentless ghost pinioned him in both his arms, and forced him to observe what happened next.

They were in another scene and place; a room, not very large or handsome, but full of comfort. Near to the winter fire sat a beautiful young girl, so like that last that Scrooge believed it was the same, until he saw *her*, now a comely matron, sitting opposite her daughter. The noise in this room was perfectly tumultuous, for there were more children there, than Scrooge in his agitated state of mind could count; and, unlike the celebrated herd in the poem, they were not forty children conducting themselves like one, but every child was conducting itself like forty. The consequences were uproarious beyond belief; but no one seemed to care; on the contrary, the mother and daughter laughed heartily, and enjoyed it very much; and the latter, soon beginning to mingle in the sports, got pillaged by the young brigands most ruthlessly. What would I not have given to be one of them! Though I never could have been so rude, no, no. I wouldn't for the wealth of all the world have crushed that braided hair, and torn it down; and for the precious little shoe, I wouldn't have plucked it off, God bless my soul! to save my life. As to measuring her waist in sport, as they did, bold young brood, I couldn't have done it; I should have expected my arm to have grown round it for a punishment, and never come straight again. And yet I should have dearly liked, I own, to have touched her lips; to have questioned her, that she might have opened them; to have looked upon the lashes of her downcast eyes, and never raised a blush; to have let loose waves of hair, an inch of which would be a keepsake beyond price: in short, I should have liked, I do confess, to have had the lightest licence of a child, and yet to have been man enough to know its value.

But now a knocking at the door was heard, and such a rush immediately ensued that she with laughing face and plundered dress was borne towards it the centre of a flushed and boisterous group, just in time to greet the father, who came home attended by a man laden with Christmas toys and presents. Then the shouting and the struggling, and the on-slaught that was made on the defenceless porter! The scaling him with chairs for ladders to dive into his pockets, despoil him of brown-paper parcels, hold on tight by his cravat, hug him round his neck, pommel his back, and kick his legs in irrepressible affection! The shouts of wonder and delight with which the development of every package was received! The terrible announcement that the baby had been taken in the act of putting a doll's frying-pan into his mouth, and was more than suspected of having swallowed a fictitious turkey, glued on a wooden platter! The immense relief of finding this a false alarm! The joy, and gratitude, and ecstasy! They are all in-describable alike. It is enough that by degrees the children and their emotions got out of the parlour, and by one stair at a time, up to the top of the house; where they went to bed, and so subsided.

And now Scrooge looked on more attentively than ever, when the master of the house, having his daughter leaning fondly on him, sat down with her and her mother at his own fireside; and when he thought that such another creature, quite as graceful and as full of promise, might have called him father, and been a spring-time in the haggard winter of his life, his sight grew very dim indeed.

'Belle,' said the husband, turning to his wife with a smile, 'I saw an old friend of yours this afternoon.'

'Who was it?'

'Guess!'

'How can I? Tut, don't I know,' she added in the same breath, laughing as he laughed. 'Mr Scrooge.'

'Mr Scrooge it was. I passed his office window; and as it was not shut up, and he had a candle inside, I could scarcely help seeing him. His partner lies upon the point of death, I hear; and there he sat alone. Quite alone in the world, I do believe.'

'Spirit,' said Scrooge in a broken voice, 'remove me from this place.'

'I told you these were shadows of the things that have been,' said the ghost. 'That they are what they are, do not blame me.'

'Remove me,' Scrooge exclaimed, 'I cannot bear it.'

He turned upon the ghost, and seeing that it looked upon him with a face, in which in some strange way there were fragments of all the faces it had shown him, wrestled with it.

'Leave me! Take me back! Haunt me no longer!'

In the struggle, if that can be called a struggle in which the ghost with no visible resistance on its own part was undisturbed by any effort of its adversary, Scrooge observed that its light was burning high and bright; and dimly connecting that with its influence over him, he seized the extinguisher-cap, and by a sudden action pressed it down upon its head.

Though Scrooge pressed it down with all his force, he could not hide the light

The spirit dropped beneath it, so that the extinguisher covered its whole form; but though Scrooge pressed it down with all his force, he could not hide the light, which streamed from under it, in an unbroken flood upon the ground.

He was conscious of being exhausted, and overcome by an irresistible drowsiness; and, further, of being in his own bed-room. He gave the cap a parting squeeze, in which his hand relaxed; and had barely time to reel to bed, before he sank into a heavy sleep.

STAVE 3

The Second of the Three Spirits

Awaking in the middle of a prodigiously tough snore, and sitting up in bed to get his thoughts together, Scrooge had no occasion to be told that the bell was again upon the stroke of one. He felt that he was restored to consciousness in the right nick of time, for the especial purpose of holding a conference with the second messenger despatched to him through Jacob Marley's intervention. But, finding that he turned uncomfortably cold when he began to wonder which of his curtains this new spectre would draw back, he put them every one aside with his own hands, and lying down again, established a sharp lookout all round the bed. For he wished to challenge the spirit on the moment of its appearance, and did not wish to be taken by surprise, and made nervous.

Gentlemen of the free-and-easy sort, who plume themselves on being acquainted with a move or two, and being usually equal to the time of day, express the wide range of their capacity for adventure by observing that they are good for anything from pitch-and-toss to manslaughter; between which opposite extremes, no doubt, there lies a tolerably wide and comprehensive range of subjects. Without venturing for Scrooge quite as hardily as this, I don't mind calling on you to believe that he was ready for a good broad field of strange appearances, and that nothing between a baby and rhinoceros would have astonished him very much.

Now, being prepared for almost anything, he was not by any means prepared for nothing; and, consequently, when the bell struck one, and no shape appeared, he was taken with a violent fit of trembling. Five minutes, ten minutes, a quarter of an hour went by, yet nothing came. All this time, he lay upon his bed, the very core and centre of a blaze of ruddy light, which streamed upon it when the clock proclaimed the hour; and which, being only light, was more alarming than a dozen ghosts, as he was powerless to make out what it meant, or would be at; and was sometimes apprehensive that he might be at that very moment an interesting case of spontaneous combustion, without having the consolation of knowing it. At last, however, he began to think – as you or I would have thought at first; for it is always the person not in the predicament who knows what ought to have been done in it, and would unquestionably have done it too – at last, I say, he began to think that the source and secret of this ghostly light might be in the adjoining room, from whence, on further tracing it, it seemed to shine. This idea taking full possession of his mind, he got up softly and shuffled in his slippers to the door.

The moment Scrooge's hand was on the lock, a strange voice called him by his name, and bade him enter. He obeyed.

It was his own room. There was no doubt about that. But it had undergone a surprising transformation. The walls and ceiling were so hung with living green, that it looked a perfect grove; from every part of which, bright gleaming berries glistened. The crisp leaves of holly, mistletoe, and ivy reflected back the light, as if so many little mirrors had been scattered there; and such a mighty blaze went roaring up the chimney, as that dull petrification of a hearth had never known in Scrooge's time, or Marley's, or for many and many a winter season gone. Heaped up on the floor, to form a kind of throne, were turkeys, geese, game, poultry, brawn, great joints of meat, sucking-pigs, long wreaths of sausages, mince pies, plum puddings, barrels of oysters, red-hot chestnuts, cherry-cheeked apples, juicy oranges, luscious pears, immense twelfth-cakes, and seething bowls of punch, that made the chamber dim with their delicious steam. In easy state upon this couch, there sat a jolly giant, glorious to see, who bore a glowing torch, in shape not

Scrooge's third visitor

unlike Plenty's horn, and held it up, high up, to shed its light on Scrooge, as he came peeping round the door.

'Come in!' exclaimed the ghost. 'Come in, and know me better, man.'

Scrooge entered timidly, and hung his head before this spirit. He was not the dogged Scrooge he had been; and though the spirit's eyes were clear and kind, he did not like to meet them.

'I am the Ghost of Christmas Present,' said the spirit. 'Look upon me.'

Scrooge reverently did so. It was clothed in one simple green robe, or mantle, bordered with white fur. This garment hung so loosely on the figure, that its capacious breast was bare, as if disdaining to be warded or concealed by any artifice. Its feet, observable beneath the ample folds of the garment, were also bare; and on its head it wore no other covering than a holly wreath, set here and there with shining icicles. Its dark brown curls were long and free; free as its genial face, its sparkling eye, its open hand, its cheery voice, its unconstrained demeanour, and its joyful air. Girded round its middle was an antique scabbard; but no sword was in it, and the ancient sheath was eaten up with rust.

'You have never seen the like of me before?' exclaimed the spirit.

'Never,' Scrooge made answer to it.

'Have never walked forth with the younger members of my family; meaning (for I am very young) my elder brothers born in these later years?' pursued the phantom.

'I don't think I have,' said Scrooge. 'I am afraid I have not. Have you had many brothers, Spirit?'

'More than eighteen hundred,' said the ghost.

'A tremendous family to provide for,' muttered Scrooge.

The Ghost of Christmas Present rose.

'Spirit,' said Scrooge submissively, 'conduct me where you will. I went forth last night on compulsion, and I learnt a lesson which is working now. Tonight, if you have aught to teach me, let me profit by it.'

'Touch my robe.'

Scrooge did as he was told, and held it fast.

Holly, mistletoe, red berries, ivy, turkeys, geese, game, poultry, brawn, meat, pigs, sausages, oysters, pies, puddings, fruit, and punch, all vanished instantly. So did the room, the fire, the ruddy glow, the hour of night, and they stood in the city streets on Christmas morning, where (for the weather was severe) the people made a rough, but brisk and not unpleasant kind of music, in scraping the snow from the pavement in front of their dwellings, and from the tops of their houses, whence it was mad delight to the boys to see it come plumping down into the road below, and splitting into artificial little snowstorms.

The house fronts looked black enough, and the windows blacker, contrasting with the smooth white sheet of snow upon the roofs, and with the dirtier snow upon the ground; which last deposit had been ploughed up in deep furrows by the heavy wheels of carts and waggons; furrows that crossed and recrossed each other hundreds of times where the great streets branched off; and made intricate channels, hard to trace in the thick yellow mud and icy water. The sky was gloomy, and the shortest streets were choked up with a dingy mist, half thawed, half frozen, whose heavier particles descended in a shower of sooty atoms, as if all the chimneys in Great Britain had, by one consent, caught fire, and were blazing away to their dear hearts' content. There was nothing very cheerful in the climate or the town, and yet was there an air of cheerfulness abroad that the clearest summer air and brightest summer sun might have endeavoured to diffuse in vain.

For, the people who were shovelling away on the housetops were jovial and full of glee; calling out to one another from the parapets, and now and then exchanging a facetious snowball – better-natured missile far than many a wordy jest – laughing heartily if it went right and not less heartily if it went wrong. The poulterers' shops were still half open, and the fruiterers' were radiant in their glory. There were great, round, pot-bellied baskets of chestnuts, shaped like the waistcoats of jolly old gentlemen, lolling at the doors, and tumbling out into the street in their apoplectic opulence. There were ruddy, brown-faced, broad-girthed Spanish onions, shining in the fatness of their growth like Spanish friars, and winking from their shelves in wanton slyness at the girls as they went by, and glanced demurely at the hung-up mistletoe. There were pears and apples, clustered high in blooming pyramids; there were bunches of grapes, made, in the shopkeepers' benevolence, to dangle from conspicuous hooks, that people's mouths might water gratis as they passed; there were piles of filberts, mossy and brown, recalling, in their fragrance, ancient walks among the woods, and pleasant shufflings ankle deep through withered leaves; there were Norfolk biffins, squat and swarthy, setting off the yellow of the oranges and lemons, and, in the great compactness of their juicy persons, urgently entreating and beseeching to be carried home in paper bags and eaten after dinner. The very gold and silver fish, set forth among these choice fruits in a bowl, though members of a dull and stagnant-blooded race, appeared to know that there was something going on; and, to a fish, went gasping round and round their little world in slow and passionless excitement.

The grocers'! oh, the grocers'! nearly closed, with perhaps two shutters down, or one; but through those gaps such glimpses! It was not alone that the scales descending on the counter made a merry sound, or that the twine and roller parted company so briskly, or that the canisters were rattled up and down like juggling tricks, or even that the blended scents of tea and coffee were so grateful to the nose, or even that the raisins were so plentiful and rare, the almonds so extremely white, the sticks of cinnamon so long and straight, the other spices so delicious, the candied fruits so caked and spotted with molten sugar as to make the coldest lookers–on feel faint and subsequently bilious. Nor was it that the figs were moist and pulpy, or that the French plums blushed in modest tartness from their highly-decorated boxes, or that everything was good to eat and in its Christmas dress; but the customers were all so hurried and so eager in the hopeful promise of the day, that they tumbled up against each other at the door, crashing their wicker baskets wildly, and left their purchases upon the counter, and came running back to fetch them, and committed hundreds of the like mistakes, in the best humour possible; while the grocer and his people were so frank and fresh that the polished hearts with which they fastened their aprons behind might have been their own, worn outside for general inspection, and for Christmas daws to peck at if they chose.

But soon the steeples called good people all, to church and chapel, and away they came, flocking through the streets in their best clothes, and with their gayest faces. And at the same time there emerged from scores of by-streets, lanes, and name-less turnings, innumerable people, carrying their dinners to the bakers' shops. The sight of these poor revellers appeared to interest the spirit very much, for he stood with Scrooge beside him in a baker's doorway, and taking off the covers as their bearers passed, sprinkled incense on their dinners from his torch. And it was a very uncommon kind of torch, for once or twice when there were angry words between some dinner-carriers who had jostled each other, he shed a few drops of water on them from it, and their good humour was restored directly. For they said, it was a shame to quarrel upon Christmas Day. And so it was. God love it, so it was.

In time the bells ceased, and the bakers' were shut up; and yet there was a genial shadowing forth of all these dinners and the progress of their cooking, in the thawed blotch of wet above each baker's oven; where the pavement smoked as if its stones were cooking too.

'Is there a peculiar flavour in what you sprinkle from your torch?' asked Scrooge.

'There is. My own.'

'Would it apply to any kind of dinner on this day?' asked Scrooge.

'To any kindly given. To a poor one most.'

'Why to a poor one most?' asked Scrooge.

'Because it needs it most.'

'Spirit,' said Scrooge, after a moment's thought, 'I wonder you, of all the beings in the many worlds about us, should desire to cramp these people's opportunities of innocent enjoyment.'

'I?' cried the spirit.

'You would deprive them of their means of dining every seventh day, often the only day on which they can be said to dine at all,' said Scrooge. 'Wouldn't you?'

'I?' cried the spirit.

'You seek to close these places on the seventh day,' said Scrooge. 'And it comes to the same thing!'

'I seek?' exclaimed the spirit.

'Forgive me if I am wrong. It has been done in your name, or at least in that of your family,' said Scrooge.

'There are some upon this earth of yours,' returned the spirit, 'who lay claim to know us, and who do their deeds of passion, pride, ill–will, hatred, envy, bigotry, and selfishness in our name, who are as strange to us and all our kith and kin, as if they had never lived. Remember that, and charge their doings on themselves, not us.'

Scrooge promised that he would; and they went on, invisible, as they had been before, into the suburbs of the town. It was a remarkable quality of the ghost (which Scrooge had observed at the baker's), that notwithstanding his gigantic size, he could accommodate himself to any place with ease; and that he stood beneath a low roof quite as gracefully and like a supernatural creature, as it was possible he could have done in any lofty hall.

And perhaps it was the pleasure the good spirit had in showing off this power of his, or else it was his own kind, generous, hearty nature, and his sympathy with all poor men, that led him straight to Scrooge's clerk's; for there he went, and took Scrooge with him, holding to his robe; and on the threshold of the door the spirit smiled, and stopped to bless Bob Cratchit's dwelling with the sprinkling of his torch. Think of that. Bob had but fifteen 'bob' a week himself; he pocketed on Saturdays but fifteen copies of his Christian name; and yet the Ghost of Christmas Present blessed his four-roomed house.

Then up rose Mrs Cratchit, Cratchit's wife, dressed out but poorly in a twice-turned gown, but brave in ribbons, which are cheap and make a goodly show for sixpence; and she laid the cloth, assisted by Belinda Cratchit, second of her daughters, also brave in ribbons; while Master Peter Cratchit plunged a fork into the saucepan of potatoes, and getting the corners of his monstrous shirt collar (Bob's private property, conferred upon his son and heir in honour of the day) into his mouth, rejoiced to find himself so gallantly attired, and yearned to show his linen in the fashionable parks. And now two smaller Cratchits, boy and girl, came tearing in, screaming that outside the baker's they had smelt the goose, and known it for their own; and basking in luxurious thoughts of sage and onion, these young Cratchits danced about the table, and exalted Master Peter Cratchit to the skies, while he (not proud, although his collars nearly choked him) blew the fire, until the slow potatoes bubbling up, knocked loudly at the saucepan-lid to be let out and peeled.

'What has ever got your precious father then?' said Mrs Cratchit. 'And your brother, Tiny Tim. And Martha warn't as late last Christmas Day by half an hour.'

'Here's Martha, mother,' said a girl, appearing as she spoke.

'Here's Martha, mother!' cried the two young Cratchits. 'Hurrah! There's *such* a goose, Martha!'

'Why, bless your heart alive, my dear, how late you are!' said Mrs Cratchit, kissing her a dozen times, and taking off her shawl and bonnet for her with officious zeal.

'We'd a deal of work to finish up last night,' replied the girl, 'and had to clear away this morning, mother.'

'Well! Never mind so long as you are come,' said Mrs Cratchit. 'Sit ye down before the fire, my dear, and have a warm, Lord bless ye.'

'No, no. There's father coming,' cried the two young Cratchits, who were everywhere at once. 'Hide, Martha, hide!'

So Martha hid herself, and in came little Bob, the father, with at least three feet of comforter exclusive of the fringe, hanging down before him; and his threadbare clothes darned up and brushed, to look seasonable; and Tiny Tim upon his shoulder. Alas for Tiny Tim, he bore a little crutch, and had his limbs supported by an iron frame.

'Why, where's our Martha?' cried Bob Cratchit, looking round.

'Not coming,' said Mrs Cratchit.

'Not coming!' said Bob, with a sudden declension in his high spirits; for he had been Tim's blood horse all the way from church, and had come home rampant. 'Not coming upon Christmas Day?'

Martha didn't like to see him disappointed, if it were only in joke; so she came out prematurely from behind the closet door, and ran into his arms, while the two young Cratchits hustled Tiny Tim, and bore him off into the wash-house, that he might hear the pudding singing in the copper.

'And how did little Tim behave?' asked Mrs Cratchit, when she had rallied Bob on his credulity, and Bob had hugged his daughter to his heart's content.

'As good as gold,' said Bob, 'and better. Somehow he gets thoughtful, sitting by himself so much, and thinks the strangest things you ever heard. He told me, coming home, that he hoped the people saw him in the church, because he was a cripple, and it might be pleasant to them to remember upon Christmas Day, who made lame beggars walk, and blind men see.'

Bob's voice was tremulous when he told them this, and trembled more when he said that Tiny Tim was growing strong and hearty.

His active little crutch was heard upon the floor, and back came Tiny Tim before another word was spoken, escorted by his brother and sister to his stool before the fire; and while Bob, turning up his cuffs – as if, poor fellow, they were capable of being made more shabby – compounded some hot mixture in a jug with gin and lemons, and stirred it round and round and put it on the hob to simmer; Master Peter, and the two ubiquitous young Cratchits went to fetch the goose, with which they soon returned in high procession.

Such a bustle ensued that you might have thought a goose the rarest of all birds; a feathered phenomenon, to which a black swan was a matter of course – and in truth it was something very like it in that house. Mrs Cratchit made the gravy (ready beforehand in a little saucepan) hissing hot; Master Peter mashed the potatoes with incredible vigour; Miss Belinda sweetened up the apple sauce; Martha dusted the hot plates; Bob took Tiny Tim beside him in a tiny corner at the table; the two young Cratchits set chairs for everybody, not forgetting themselves, and mounting guard upon their posts, crammed spoons into their mouths, lest they should shriek for goose before their turn came to be helped. At last the dishes were set on, and grace was said. It was succeeded by a breathless pause, as Mrs Cratchit, looking slowly all along the carving-knife, prepared to plunge it in the breast; but when she did, and when the long expected gush of stuffing issued forth, one murmur of delight arose all round the board, and even Tiny Tim, excited by the two young Cratchits, beat on the table with the handle of his knife, and feebly cried Hurrah!

There never was such a goose. Bob said he didn't believe there ever was such a goose cooked. Its tenderness and flavour, size and cheapness, were the themes of universal admiration. Eked out by apple sauce and mashed potatoes, it was a sufficient dinner for the whole family; indeed, as Mrs Cratchit said with great delight (surveying one small atom of a bone upon the dish), they hadn't ate it all at last. Yet everyone had

had enough, and the youngest Cratchits in particular, were steeped in sage and onion to the eyebrows. But now, the plates being changed by Miss Belinda, Mrs Cratchit left the room alone – too nervous to bear witnesses – to take the pudding up and bring it in.

Suppose it should not be done enough? Suppose it should break in turning out? Suppose somebody should have got over the wall of the back yard, and stolen it, while they were merry with the goose – a supposition at which the two young Cratchits became livid. All sorts of horrors were supposed.

Hallo! A great deal of steam. The pudding was out of the copper. A smell like a washing-day! That was the cloth. A smell like an eating-house and a pastry-cook's next door to each other, with a laundress's next door to that! That was the pudding. In half a minute Mrs Cratchit entered – flushed, but smiling proudly – with the pudding, like a speckled cannonball, so hard and firm, blazing in half of half a quartern of ignited brandy, and bedight with Christmas holly stuck into the top.

Oh, a wonderful pudding! Bob Cratchit said, and calmly too, that he regarded it as the greatest success achieved by Mrs Cratchit since their marriage. Mrs Cratchit said that now the weight was off her mind, she would confess she had had her doubts about the quantity of flour. Everybody had something to say about it, but nobody said or thought it was at all a small pudding for a large family. It would have been flat heresy to do so. Any Cratchit would have blushed to hint at such a thing.

At last the dinner was all done, the cloth was cleared, the hearth swept, and the fire made up. The compound in the jug being tasted, and considered perfect, apples and oranges were put upon the table, and a shovelful of chestnuts on the fire. Then all the Cratchit family drew round the hearth, in what Bob Cratchit called a circle, meaning half a one; and at Bob Cratchit's elbow stood the family display of glass. Two tumblers, and a custard-cup without a handle.

These held the hot stuff from the jug, however, as well as golden goblets would have done; and Bob served it out with beaming looks, while the chestnuts on the fire sputtered and cracked noisily. Then Bob proposed: 'A merry Christmas to us all, my dears! God bless us!'

Which all the family re-echoed.

'God bless us everyone!' said Tiny Tim, the last of all.

He sat very close to his father's side upon his little stool. Bob held his withered little hand in his, as if he loved the child, and wished to keep him by his side, and dreaded that he might be taken from him.

'Spirit,' said Scrooge, with an interest he had never felt before, 'tell me if Tiny Tim will live.'

'I see a vacant seat,' replied the ghost, 'in the poor chimney-corner, and a crutch without an owner, carefully preserved. If these shadows remain unaltered by the Future, the child will die.'

'No, no,' said Scrooge. 'Oh, no, kind spirit! say he will be spared!'

'If these shadows remain unaltered by the Future, none other of my race,' returned the ghost, 'will find him here.

What then? If he be like to die, he had better do it, and decrease the surplus population.'

Scrooge hung his head to hear his own words quoted by the spirit, and was overcome with penitence and grief. 'Man,' said the ghost, 'if man you be in heart, not adamant, forbear that wicked cant until you have discovered what the surplus is, and where it is. Will you decide what men shall live, what men shall die? It may be, that in the sight of Heaven, you are more worthless and less fit to live than millions like this poor man's child. Oh God, to hear the insect on the leaf pronouncing on the too much life among his hungry brothers in the dust.'

Scrooge bent before the ghost's rebuke, and trembling cast his eyes upon the ground. But he raised them speedily, on hearing his own name.

'Mr Scrooge,' said Bob; 'I'll give you Mr Scrooge, the Founder of the Feast.'

'The Founder of the Feast indeed!' cried Mrs Cratchit, reddening. 'I wish I had him here! I'd give him a piece of my mind to feast upon, and I hope he'd have a good appetite for it!'

'My dear,' said Bob, 'the children! Christmas Day!'

'It should be Christmas Day, I am sure,' said she, 'on which one drinks the health of such an odious, stingy, hard, unfeeling man as Mr Scrooge! You know he is, Robert. Nobody knows it better than you do, poor fellow.'

'My dear,' was Bob's mild answer, 'Christmas Day!'

'I'll drink his health for your sake and the Day's,' said Mrs Cratchit, 'not for his. Long life to him. A merry Christmas and a happy new year. He'll be very merry and very happy, I have no doubt!'

The children drank the toast after her. It was the first of their proceedings which had no heartiness. Tiny Tim drank it last of all, but he didn't care twopence for it. Scrooge was the ogre of the family. The mention of his name cast a dark shadow on the party, which was not dispelled for full five minutes.

After it had passed away, they were ten times merrier than before, from the mere relief of Scrooge the Baleful being done with. Bob Cratchit told them how he had a situation in his eye for Master Peter, which would bring in, if obtained, full five-and-sixpence weekly. The two young Cratchits laughed tremendously at the idea of Peter's being a man of business; and Peter himself looked thoughtfully at the fire from between his collars, as if he were deliberating what particular investments he should favour when he came into the receipt of that bewildering income. Martha, who was a poor apprentice at a milliner's, then told them what kind of work she had to do, and how many hours she worked at a stretch, and how she meant to lie abed tomorrow morning for a good long rest; tomorrow being a holiday she passed at home. Also how she had seen a countess and a lord some days before, and how the lord was much about as tall as Peter; at which Peter pulled up his collars so high that you couldn't have seen his head if you had been there. All this time the chestnuts and the jug went round and round; and by and by they had a song, about a lost child travelling in the snow, from Tiny Tim, who had a plaintive little voice, and sang it very well indeed.

There was nothing of high mark in this. They were not a

handsome family; they were not well dressed; their shoes were far from being waterproof; their clothes were scanty; and Peter might have known, and very likely did, the inside of a pawnbroker's. But, they were happy, grateful, pleased with one another, and contented with the time; and when they faded, and looked happier yet in the bright sprinklings of the spirit's torch at parting, Scrooge had his eye upon them, and especially on Tiny Tim, until the last.

By this time it was getting dark, and snowing pretty heavily; and as Scrooge and the spirit went along the streets, the brightness of the roaring fires in kitchens, parlours, and all sorts of rooms, was wonderful. Here, the flickering of the blaze showed preparations for a cosy dinner, with hot plates baking through and through before the fire, and deep red curtains, ready to be drawn to shut out cold and darkness. There all the children of the house were running out into the snow to meet their married sisters, brothers, cousins, uncles, aunts, and be the first to greet them. Here, again, were shadows on the window-blind of guests assembling; and there a group of handsome girls, all hooded and fur-booted, and all chattering at once, tripped lightly off to some near neighbour's house; where, woe upon the single man who saw them enter – artful witches, well they knew it – in a glow.

But, if you had judged from the numbers of people on their way to friendly gatherings, you might have thought that no one was at home to give them welcome when they got there, instead of every house expecting company, and piling up its fires half-chimney high. Blessings on it, how the ghost exulted. How it bared its breadth of breast, and opened its capacious palm, and floated on, outpouring, with a generous hand, its bright and harmless mirth on everything within its reach! The very lamp-lighter, who ran on before, dotting the dusky street with specks of light, and who was dressed to spend the evening somewhere, laughed out loudly as the spirit passed, though little kenned the lamplighter that he had any company but Christmas.

And now, without a word of warning from the ghost, they stood upon a bleak and desert moor, where monstrous masses of rude stone were cast about, as though it were the burial-place of giants; and water spread itself wheresoever it listed, or would have done so, but for the frost that held it prisoner; and nothing grew but moss and furze, and coarse rank grass. Down in the west the setting sun had left a streak of fiery red, which glared upon the desolation for an instant, like a sullen eye, and frowning lower, lower, lower yet, was lost in the thick gloom of darkest night.

'What place is this?' asked Scrooge.

'A place where miners live, who labour in the bowels of the earth,' returned the spirit. 'But they know me. See!'

A light shone from the window of a hut, and swiftly they advanced towards it. Passing through the wall of mud and stone, they found a cheerful company assembled round a glowing fire. An old, old man and woman, with their children and their children's children, and another generation beyond that, all decked out gaily in their holiday attire. The old man, in a voice that seldom rose above the howling of the wind upon the barren waste, was singing them a Christmas song –

it had been a very old song when he was a boy – and from time to time they all joined in the chorus. So surely as they raised their voices, the old man got quite blithe and loud; and so surely as they stopped, his vigour sank again.

The spirit did not tarry here, but bade Scrooge hold his robe, and passing on above the moor, sped – whither? Not to sea. To sea! To Scrooge's horror, looking back, he saw the last of the land, a frightful range of rocks, behind them; and his ears were deafened by the thundering of water, as it rolled and roared, and raged among the dreadful caverns it had worn, and fiercely tried to undermine the earth.

Built upon a dismal reef of sunken rocks, some league or so from shore, on which the waters chafed and dashed, the wild year through, there stood a solitary lighthouse. Great heaps of seaweed clung to its base, and storm-birds – born of the wind one might suppose, as seaweed of the water – rose and fell about it, like the waves they skimmed.

But even here, two men who watched the light had made a fire, that through the loophole in the thick stone wall shed out a ray of brightness on the awful sea. Joining their horny hands over the rough table at which they sat, they wished each other merry Christmas in their can of grog; and one of them: the elder, too, with his face all damaged and scarred with hard weather, as the figurehead of an old ship might be: struck up a sturdy song that was like a gale in itself.

Again the ghost sped on, above the black and heaving sea – on, on – until, being far away, as he told Scrooge, from any shore, they lighted on a ship. They stood beside the helmsman at the wheel, the lookout in the bow, the officers who had the watch; dark, ghostly figures in their several stations; but every man among them hummed a Christmas tune, or had a Christmas thought, or spoke below his breath to his companion of some bygone Christmas Day, with homeward hopes belonging to it. And every man on board, waking or sleeping, good or bad, had had a kinder word for another on that day than on any day in the year; and had shared to some extent in its festivities; and had remembered those he cared for at a distance, and had known that they delighted to remember him.

It was a great surprise to Scrooge, while listening to the moaning of the wind, and thinking what a solemn thing it was to move on through the lonely darkness over an unknown abyss, whose depths were secrets as profound as death: it was a great surprise to Scrooge, while thus engaged, to hear a hearty laugh. It was a much greater surprise to Scrooge to recognise it as his own nephew's and to find himself in a bright, dry, gleaming room, with the spirit standing smiling by his side, and looking at that same nephew with approving affability.

'Ha, ha!' laughed Scrooge's nephew. 'Ha, ha, ha!'

If you should happen, by any unlikely chance, to know a man more blest in a laugh than Scrooge's nephew, all I can say is, I should like to know him too. Introduce him to me, and I'll cultivate his acquaintance.

It is a fair, even-handed, noble adjustment of things, that while there is infection in disease and sorrow, there is nothing in the world so irresistibly contagious as laughter and good-humour. When Scrooge's nephew laughed in this way: holding his sides, rolling his head, and twisting his face into the most extravagant contortions: Scrooge's niece, by marriage, laughed as heartily as he. And their assembled friends being not a bit behindhand, roared out lustily.

'Ha, ha! Ha, ha, ha, ha!'

'He said that Christmas was a humbug, as I live!' cried Scrooge's nephew. 'He believed it too!'

'More shame for him, Fred,' said Scrooge's niece, indignantly. Bless those women; they never do anything by halves. They are always in earnest.

She was very pretty: exceedingly pretty. With a dimpled, surprised-looking, capital face; a ripe little mouth, that seemed made to be kissed – as no doubt it was; all kinds of good little dots about her chin, that melted into one another when she laughed; and the sunniest pair of eyes you ever saw in any little creature's head. Altogether she was what you would have called provoking, you know; but satisfactory.

'He's a comical old fellow,' said Scrooge's nephew, 'that's the truth: and not so pleasant as he might be. However, his offences carry their own punishment, and I have nothing to say against him.'

'I'm sure he is very rich, Fred,' hinted Scrooge's niece. 'At least you always tell *me* so.'

'What of that, my dear?' said Scrooge's nephew. 'His wealth is of no use to him! He don't do any good with it. He don't make himself comfortable with it. He hasn't the satisfaction of thinking – ha, ha, ha! – that he is ever going to benefit us with it!'

'I have no patience with him,' observed Scrooge's niece. Scrooge's niece's sisters, and all the other ladies, expressed the same opinion.

'Oh, I have,' said Scrooge's nephew. 'I am sorry for him; I couldn't be angry with him if I tried. Who suffers by his ill whims? Himself, always. Here, he takes it into his head to dislike us, and he won't come and dine with us. What's the consequence? He don't lose much of a dinner!'

'Indeed, I think he loses a very good dinner,' interrupted Scrooge's niece. Everybody else said the same, and they must be allowed to have been competent judges, because they had just had dinner; and, with the dessert upon the table, were clustered round the fire, by lamplight.

'Well, I'm very glad to hear it,' said Scrooge's nephew, 'because I haven't great faith in these young housekeepers. What do *you* say, Topper?'

Topper had clearly got his eye upon one of Scrooge's niece's sisters, for he answered that a bachelor was a wretched outcast, who had no right to express an opinion on the subject. Whereat Scrooge's niece's sister – the plump one with the lace tucker: not the one with the roses – blushed.

'Do go on, Fred,' said Scrooge's niece, clapping her hands. 'He never finishes what he begins to say. He is such a ridiculous fellow!'

Scrooge's nephew revelled in another laugh, and as it was impossible to keep the infection off; though the plump sister tried hard to do it with aromatic vinegar; his example was unanimously followed.

'I was only going to say,' said Scrooge's nephew, 'that the consequence of his taking a dislike to us, and not making merry with us, is, as I think, that he loses some pleasant moments, which could do him no harm. I am sure he loses pleasanter companions than he can find in his own thoughts, either in his mouldy old office, or his dusty chambers. I mean to give him the same chance every year, whether he likes it or not, for I pity him. He may rail at Christmas till he dies, but he can't help thinking better of it – I defy him – if he finds me going there, in good temper, year after year, and saying Uncle Scrooge, how are you. If it only puts him in the vein to leave his poor clerk fifty pounds, *that's* something; and I think I shook him yesterday.'

It was their turn to laugh now at the notion of his shaking Scrooge. But being thoroughly good-natured, and not much caring what they laughed at, so that they laughed at any rate, he encouraged them in their merriment, and passed the bottle joyously.

After tea, they had some music. For they were a musical family, and knew what they were about, when they sung a glee or catch, I can assure you: especially Topper, who could growl away in the bass like a good one, and never swell the large veins in his forehead, or get red in the face over it. Scrooge's niece played well upon the harp; and played among other tunes a simple little air (a mere nothing: you might learn to whistle it in two minutes), which had been familiar to the child who fetched Scrooge from the boarding-school, as he had been reminded by the Ghost of Christmas Past. When this strain of music sounded, all the things that Ghost had shown him, came upon his mind; he softened more and more; and thought that if he could have listened to it often, years ago, he might have cultivated the kindnesses of life for his own happiness with his own hands, without resorting to the sexton's spade that buried Jacob Marley.

But they didn't devote the whole evening to music. After a while they played at forfeits; for it is good to be children sometimes, and never better than at Christmas, when its mighty Founder was a child himself. Stop! There was first a game at blind man's buff. Of course there was. And I no more believe Topper was really blind than I believe he had eyes in his boots. My opinion is, that it was a done thing between him and Scrooge's nephew; and that the Ghost of Christmas Present knew it. The way he went after that plump sister in the lace tucker, was an outrage on the credulity of human nature. Knocking down the fire-irons, tumbling over the chairs, bumping against the piano, smothering himself among the curtains, wherever she went, there went he. He always knew where the plump sister was. He wouldn't catch anybody else! If you had fallen up against him (as some of them did), on purpose, he would have made a feint of endeavouring to seize you, which would have been an affront to your understanding, and would instantly have sidled off in the direction of the plump sister. She often cried out that it wasn't fair; and it really was not. But when at last, he caught her; when, in spite of all her silken rustlings, and her rapid flutterings past him, he got her into a corner whence there was no escape; then his conduct was the most execrable. For his pretending not to know her; his pretending that it was necessary to touch her headdress, and further to assure himself of her identity by pressing a certain ring upon her finger, and a certain chain about her neck; was vile, monstrous. No doubt she told him her opinion of it, when, another blind man being in office, they were so very confidential together, behind the curtains.

Scrooge's niece was not one of the blind man's buff party, but was made comfortable with a large chair and a footstool, in a snug corner, where the ghost and Scrooge were close behind her. But she joined in the forfeits, and loved her love to admiration with all the letters of the alphabet. Likewise at the game of 'how, when, and where', she was very great, and to the secret joy of Scrooge's nephew, beat her sisters hollow: though they were sharp girls too, as I could have told you. There might have been twenty people there, young and old, but they all played, and so did Scrooge, for, wholly forgetting the interest he had in what was going on, that his voice made no sound in their ears, he sometimes came out with his guess quite loud, and very often guessed quite right, too; for the sharpest needle, best Whitechapel, warranted not to cut in the eye, was not sharper than Scrooge; blunt as he took it in his head to be.

The ghost was greatly pleased to find him in this mood, and looked upon him with such favour, that he begged like a boy to be allowed to stay until the guests departed. But this the spirit said could not be done.

'Here is a new game,' said Scrooge. 'One half hour, spirit, only one!'

It was a game called Yes and No, where Scrooge's nephew had to think of something, and the rest must find out what; he only answering to their questions yes or no, as the case was. The brisk fire of questioning to which he was exposed, elicited from him that he was thinking of an animal, a live animal, rather a disagreeable animal, a savage animal, an animal that growled and grunted sometimes, and talked sometimes, and lived in London, and walked about the streets, and wasn't made a show of, and wasn't led by anybody, and didn't live in a menagerie, and was never killed in a market, and was not a horse, or an ass, or a cow, or a bull, or a tiger, or a dog, or a pig, or a cat, or a bear. At every fresh question that was put to him, this nephew burst into a fresh roar of laughter; and was so inexpressibly tickled, that he was obliged to get up off the sofa and stamp. At last the plump sister, falling into a similar state, cried out: 'I have found it out! I know what it is, Fred! I know what it is!'

'What is it?' cried Fred.

'It's your Uncle Scrooge!'

Which it certainly was. Admiration was the universal sentiment, though some objected that the reply to 'Is it a bear?' ought to have been 'Yes'; inasmuch as an answer in the negative was sufficient to have diverted their thoughts from Mr Scrooge, supposing they had ever had any tendency that way.

'He has given us plenty of merriment, I am sure,' said Fred, 'and it would be ungrateful not to drink his health. Here is a glass of mulled wine ready to our hand at the moment; and I say, "Uncle Scrooge!" '

'Well! Uncle Scrooge!' they cried.

'A merry Christmas and a happy New Year to the old man, whatever he is!' said Scrooge's nephew. 'He wouldn't take it from me, but may he have it, nevertheless. Uncle Scrooge.'

Uncle Scrooge had imperceptibly become so gay and light of heart, that he would have pledged the unconscious company in return, and thanked them in an inaudible speech, if the ghost had given him time. But the whole scene passed off in the breath of the last word spoken by his nephew; and he and the spirit were again upon their travels.

Much they saw, and far they went, and many homes they visited, but always with a happy end. The spirit stood beside sick beds, and they were cheerful; on foreign lands, and they were close at home; by struggling men, and they were patient in their greater hope; by poverty, and it was rich. In almshouse, hospital, and jail, in misery's every refuge, where vain man in his little brief authority had not made fast the door and barred the spirit out, he left his blessing, and taught Scrooge his precepts.

It was a long night, if it were only a night; but Scrooge had his doubts of this, because the Christmas holidays appeared to be condensed into the space of time they passed together. It was strange, too, that while Scrooge remained unaltered in his outward form, the ghost grew older, clearly older. Scrooge had observed this change, but never spoke of it, until they left a children's Twelfth Night party, when, looking at the spirit as they stood together in an open place, he noticed that its hair was grey.

'Are spirits' lives so short?' asked Scrooge.

'My life upon this globe is very brief,' replied the ghost. 'It ends tonight.'

This boy is Ignorance. This girl is Want

'Tonight!' cried Scrooge.

'Tonight at midnight. Hark! The time is drawing near.'

The chimes were ringing the three quarters past eleven at that moment.

'Forgive me if I am not justified in what I ask,' said Scrooge, looking intently at the spirit's robe, 'but I see something strange, and not belonging to yourself, protruding from your skirts. Is it a foot or a claw?'

'It might be a claw, for the flesh there is upon it,' was the spirit's sorrowful reply. 'Look here!'

From the foldings of its robe, it brought two children; wretched, abject, frightful, hideous, miserable. They knelt down at its feet, and clung upon the outside of its garment.

'Oh, Man, look here! Look, look, down here!' exclaimed the ghost.

They were a boy and a girl. Yellow, meagre, ragged, scowling, wolfish; but prostrate, too, in their humility. Where graceful youth should have filled their features out, and touched them with its freshest tints, a stale and shrivelled hand, like that of age, had pinched, and twisted them, and pulled them into shreds. Where angels might have sat enthroned, devils lurked, and glared out menacing. No change, no degradation, no perversion of humanity, in any grade, through all the mysteries of wonderful creation, has monsters half so horrible and dread.

Scrooge started back, appalled. Having them shown to him in this way, he tried to say they were fine children, but the words choked themselves, rather than be parties to a lie of such enormous magnitude.

'Spirit, are they yours?' Scrooge could say no more.

'They are Man's,' said the spirit, looking down upon them. 'And they cling to me, appealing from their fathers. This boy is Ignorance. This girl is Want. Beware them both, and all of their degree, but most of all beware this boy, for on his brow I see that written which is doom, unless the writing be erased. Deny it!' cried the spirit, stretching out its hand towards the city. 'Slander those who tell it ye! Admit it for your factious purposes, and make it worse. And bide the end.'

'Have they no refuge or resource?' cried Scrooge.

'Are there no prisons?' said the spirit, turning on him for the last time with his own words. 'Are there no workhouses?'

The bell struck twelve.

Scrooge looked about him for the ghost, and saw it not. As the last stroke ceased to vibrate, he remembered the prediction of old Jacob Marley, and lifting up his eyes, beheld a solemn phantom, draped and hooded, coming, like a mist along the ground, towards him.

The Last of the Spirits

The phantom slowly, gravely, silently approached. When it came, Scrooge bent down upon his knee; for in the very air through which this spirit moved it seemed to scatter gloom and mystery.

It was shrouded in a deep black garment, which concealed its head, its face, its form, and left nothing of it visible save one outstretched hand. But for this it would have been difficult to detach its figure from the night, and separate it from the darkness by which it was surrounded.

He felt that it was tall and stately when it came beside him, and that its mysterious presence filled him with a solemn dread. He knew no more, for the spirit neither spoke nor moved.

'Am I in the presence of the Ghost of Christmas Yet to Come?' said Scrooge.

The spirit answered not, but pointed onward with its hand.

'You are about to show me shadows of the things that have not happened, but will happen in the time before us,' Scrooge pursued. 'Is that so, Spirit?'

The upper portion of the garment was contracted for an instant in its folds, as if the spirit had inclined its head. That was the only answer he received.

Although well used to ghostly company by this time, Scrooge feared the silent shape so much that his legs trembled

The last of the spirits

beneath him, and he found that he could hardly stand when he prepared to follow it. The spirit paused a moment, as observing his condition, and giving him time to recover.

But Scrooge was all the worse for this. It thrilled him with a vague uncertain horror, to know that behind the dusky shroud there were ghostly eyes intently fixed upon him, while he, though he stretched his own to the utmost, could see nothing but a spectral hand and one great heap of black.

'Ghost of the Future!' he exclaimed, 'I fear you more than any spectre I have seen. But as I know your purpose is to do me good, and as I hope to live to be another man from what I was, I am prepared to bear you company, and do it with a thankful heart. Will you not speak to me?'

It gave him no reply. The hand was pointed straight before them.

'Lead on,' said Scrooge. 'Lead on. The night is waning fast, and it is precious time to me, I know. Lead on, Spirit!'

The phantom moved away as it had come towards him. Scrooge followed in the shadow of its dress, which bore him up, he thought, and carried him along.

They scarcely seemed to enter the city; for the city rather seemed to spring up about them, and encompass them of its own act. But there they were, in the heart of it; on 'Change, amongst the merchants who hurried up and down, and chinked the money in their pockets, and conversed in groups, and looked at their watches, and trifled thoughtfully with their great gold seals; and so forth, as Scrooge had seen them often.

The spirit stopped beside one little knot of business men. Observing that the hand was pointed to them, Scrooge advanced to listen to their talk.

'No,' said a great fat man with a monstrous chin, 'I don't know much about it, either way. I only know he's dead.'

'When did he die?' enquired another.

'Last night, I believe.'

'Why, what was the matter with him?' asked a third, taking a vast quantity of snuff out of a very large snuff box. 'I thought he'd never die.'

'God knows,' said the first, with a yawn.

'What has he done with his money?' asked a red-faced gentleman with a pendulous excrescence on the end of his nose, that shook like the gills of a turkey-cock.

'I haven't heard,' said the man with the large chin, yawning again. 'Left it to his company, perhaps. He hasn't left it to *me*. That's all I know.'

This pleasantry was received with a general laugh.

'It's likely to be a very cheap funeral,' said the same speaker; 'for upon my life I don't know of anybody to go to it. Suppose we make up a party and volunteer?'

'I don't mind going if a lunch is provided,' observed the gentleman with the excrescence on his nose. 'But I must be fed, if I make one!'

Another laugh.

'Well, I am the most disinterested among you, after all,' said the first speaker, 'for I never wear black gloves, and I never eat lunch. But I'll offer to go, if anybody else will. When I come to think of it, I'm not at all sure that I wasn't his most particular

friend; for we used to stop and speak whenever we met. Bye-bye.'

Speakers and listeners strolled away, and mixed with other groups. Scrooge knew the men, and looked towards the spirit for an explanation.

The phantom glided on into a street. Its finger pointed to two persons meeting. Scrooge listened again, thinking that the explanation might lie here.

He knew these men, also, perfectly. They were men of business: very wealthy, and of great importance. He had made a point always of standing well in their esteem: in a business point of view, that is; strictly in a business point of view.

'How are you?' said one.

'How are you?' returned the other.

'Well,' said the first. 'Old Scratch has got his own at last, hey?'

'So I am told,' returned the second. 'Cold, isn't it?'

'Seasonable for Christmas time. You're not a skater, I suppose?'

'No. No. Something else to think of. Good-morning!'

Not another word. That was their meeting, their conversation, and their parting.

Scrooge was at first inclined to be surprised that the spirit should attach importance to conversations apparently so trivial; but feeling assured that they must have some hidden purpose, he set himself to consider what it was likely to be. They could scarcely be supposed to have any bearing on the death of Jacob, his old partner, for that was past, and this ghost's province was the future. Nor could he think of anyone immediately connected with himself to whom he could apply them. But nothing doubting that to whomsoever they applied they had some latent moral for his own improvement, he resolved to treasure up every word he heard, and everything he saw; and especially to observe the shadow of himself when it appeared. For he had an expectation that the conduct of his future self would give him the clue he missed, and would render the solution of these riddles easy.

He looked about in that very place for his own image; but another man stood in his accustomed corner, and though the clock pointed to his usual time of day for being there, he saw no likeness of himself among the multitudes that poured in through the porch. It gave him little surprise, however; for he had been revolving in his mind a change of life, and thought and hoped he saw his newborn resolutions carried out in this.

Quiet and dark, beside him stood the phantom, with its outstretched hand. When he roused himself from his thoughtful quest, he fancied from the turn of the hand, and its situation in reference to himself, that the unseen eyes were looking at him keenly. It made him shudder, and feel very cold.

They left the busy scene, and went into an obscure part of the town where Scrooge had never penetrated before, although he recognised its situation, and its bad repute. The ways were foul and narrow; the shops and houses wretched; the people half-naked, drunken, slipshod, ugly. Alleys and archways, like so many cesspools, disgorged their offences of smell, and dirt, and life, upon the straggling streets; and the whole quarter reeked with crime, with filth, and misery.

Far in this den of infamous resort, there was a low-browed, beetling shop, below a penthouse roof, where iron, old rags, bottles, bones, and greasy offal, were bought. Upon the floor within, were piled up heaps of rusty keys, nails, chains, hinges, files, scales, weights, and refuse iron of all kinds. Secrets that few would like to scrutinise were bred and hidden in mountains of unseemly rags, masses of corrupted fat, and sepulchres of bones. Sitting in among the wares he dealt in, by a charcoal stove, made of old bricks, was a grey-haired rascal, nearly seventy years of age; who had screened himself from the cold air without, by a frousy curtaining of miscellaneous tatters, hung upon a line; and smoked his pipe in all the luxury of calm retirement.

Scrooge and the phantom came into the presence of this man, just as a woman with a heavy bundle slunk into the shop. But she had scarcely entered, when another woman, similarly laden, came in too; and she was closely followed by a man in faded black, who was no less startled by the sight of them, than they had been upon the recognition of each other. After a short period of blank astonishment, in which the old man with the pipe had joined them, they all three burst into a laugh.

'Let the charwoman alone to be the first!' cried she who had entered first. 'Let the laundress alone to be the second; and let the undertaker's man alone to be the third! Look here, old Joe, here's a chance. If we haven't all three met here without meaning it.'

'You couldn't have met in a better place,' said old Joe, removing his pipe from his mouth. 'Come into the parlour. You were made free of it long ago, you know; and the other two an't strangers. Stop till I shut the door of the shop. Ah! How it skreeks. There an't such a rusty bit of metal in the place as its own hinges, I believe; and I'm sure there's no such old bones here, as mine. Ha, ha! We're all suitable to our calling, we're well matched. Come into the parlour. Come into the parlour.'

The parlour was the space behind the screen of rags. The old man raked the fire together with an old stair-rod, and having trimmed his smoky lamp (for it was night), with the stem of his pipe, put it in his mouth again.

While he did this, the woman who had already spoken threw her bundle on the floor, and sat down in a flaunting manner on a stool; crossing her elbows on her knees, and looking with a bold defiance at the other two.

'What odds then? What odds, Mrs Dilber?' said the woman. 'Every person has a right to take care of themselves. *He* always did.'

'That's true, indeed,' said the laundress. 'No man more so.'

'Why then, don't stand staring as if you was afraid, woman; who's the wiser? We're not going to pick holes in each other's coats, I suppose!'

'No, indeed!' said Mrs Dilber and the man together. 'We should hope not.'

'Very well, then!' cried the woman. 'That's enough. Who's the worse for the loss of a few things like these? Not a dead man, I suppose!'

'No, indeed,' said Mrs Dilber, laughing.

'If he wanted to keep 'em after he was dead, a wicked old

screw,' pursued the woman, 'why wasn't he natural in his lifetime? If he had been, he'd have had somebody to look after him when he was struck with death, instead of lying gasping out his last there, alone by himself.'

'It's the truest word that ever was spoke,' said Mrs Dilber. 'It's a judgement on him!'

'I wish it was a little heavier judgement,' replied the woman; 'and it should have been, you may depend upon it, if I could have laid my hands on anything else. Open that bundle, old Joe, and let me know the value of it. Speak out plain. I'm not afraid to be the first, nor afraid for them to see it! We know pretty well that we were helping ourselves, before we met here, I believe. It's no sin. Open the bundle, Joe.'

But the gallantry of her friends would not allow of this; and the man in faded black, mounting the breach first, produced *his* plunder. It was not extensive. A seal or two, a pencil-case, a pair of sleeve-buttons, and a brooch of no great value, were all. They were severally examined and appraised by old Joe, who chalked the sums he was disposed to give for each, upon the wall, and added them up into a total when he found there was nothing more to come.

'That's your account,' said Joe, 'and I wouldn't give another sixpence, if I was to be boiled for not doing it. Who's next?'

Mrs Dilber was next. Sheets and towels, a little wearing apparel, two old-fashioned silver teaspoons, a pair of sugar-tongs, and a few boots. Her account was stated on the wall in the same manner.

'I always give too much to ladies. It's a weakness of mine, and that's the way I ruin myself,' said old Joe. 'That's your account. If you asked me for another penny, and made it an open question, I'd repent of being so liberal and knock off half a crown.'

'And now undo *my* bundle, Joe,' said the first woman.

Joe went down on his knees for the greater convenience of opening it, and having unfastened a great many knots, dragged out a large and heavy roll of some dark stuff.

'What do you call this?' said Joe. 'Bed-curtains?'

'Ah!' returned the woman, laughing and leaning forward on her crossed arms. 'Bed-curtains!'

'You don't mean to say you took them down, rings and all, with him lying there?' said Joe.

'Yes I do,' replied the woman. 'Why not?'

'You were born to make your fortune,' said Joe, 'and you'll certainly do it!'

'I certainly shan't hold my hand, when I can get anything in it by reaching it out, for the sake of such a man as he was, I promise you, Joe,' returned the woman coolly. 'Don't drop that oil upon the blankets, now.'

'His blankets?' asked Joe.

'Whose else's do you think?' replied the woman. 'He isn't likely to take cold without them, I dare say.'

'I hope he didn't die of anything catching! Eh?' said old Joe, stopping in his work, and looking up.

'Don't you be afraid of that,' returned the woman. 'I an't so fond of his company that I'd loiter about him for such things, if he did. Ah! you may look through that shirt till your eyes ache;

but you won't find a hole in it, nor a threadbare place. It's the best he had, and a fine one too. They'd have wasted it, if it hadn't been for me.'

'What do you call wasting of it?' asked old Joe.

'Putting it on him to be buried in, to be sure,' replied the woman with a laugh. 'Somebody was fool enough to do it, but I took it off again. If calico an't good enough for such a purpose, it isn't good enough for anything. It's quite as becoming to the body. He can't look uglier than he did in that one.'

Scrooge listened to this dialogue in horror. As they sat grouped about their spoil, in the scanty light afforded by the old man's lamp, he viewed them with a detestation and disgust, which could hardly have been greater, though they had been obscene demons, marketing the corpse itself.

'Ha, ha!' laughed the same woman, when old Joe, producing a flannel bag with money in it, told out their several gains upon the ground. 'This is the end of it, you see. He frightened every-one away from him when he was alive, to profit us when he was dead! Ha, ha, ha!'

'Spirit,' said Scrooge, shuddering from head to foot. 'I see, I see. The case of this unhappy man might be my own. My life tends that way, now. Merciful heaven, what is this?'

He recoiled in terror, for the scene had changed, and now he almost touched a bed: a bare, uncurtained bed: on which, beneath a ragged sheet, there lay a something covered up, which, though it was dumb, announced itself in awful language.

The room was very dark, too dark to be observed with any accuracy, though Scrooge glanced round it in obedience to a secret impulse, anxious to know what kind of room it was. A pale light, rising in the outer air, fell straight upon the bed; and on it, plundered and bereft, unwatched, unwept, uncared for, was the body of this man.

Scrooge glanced towards the phantom. Its steady hand was pointed to the head. The cover was so carelessly adjusted that the slightest raising of it, the motion of a finger upon Scrooge's part, would have disclosed the face. He thought of it, felt how easy it would be to do, and longed to do it; but had no more power to withdraw the veil than to dismiss the spectre at his side.

Oh cold, cold, rigid, dreadful death, set up thine altar here, and dress it with such terrors as thou hast at thy command: for this is thy dominion. But of the loved, revered, and honoured head, thou canst not turn one hair to thy dread purposes, or make one feature odious. It is not that the hand is heavy and will fall down when released; it is not that the heart and pulse are still; but that the hand *was* open, generous, and true; the heart brave, warm, and tender; and the pulse a man's. Strike, Shadow, strike! And see his good deeds springing from the wound, to sow the world with life immortal!

No voice pronounced these words in Scrooge's ears, and yet he heard them when he looked upon the bed. He thought, if this man could be raised up now, what would be his foremost thoughts? Avarice, hard dealing, griping cares? They have brought him to a rich end, truly.

He lay, in the dark empty house, with not a man, a woman, or a child, to say that he was kind to me in this or that, and for the memory of one kind word I will be kind to him. A cat was tearing at the door, and there was a sound of gnawing rats beneath the hearthstone. What *they* wanted in the room of death, and why they were so restless and disturbed, Scrooge did not dare to think.

'Spirit,' he said, 'this is a fearful place. In leaving it, I shall not leave its lesson, trust me. Let us go.'

Still the ghost pointed with an unmoved finger to the head.

'I understand you,' Scrooge returned, 'and I would do it, if I could. But I have not the power, Spirit. I have not the power.'

Again it seemed to look upon him.

'If there is any person in the town, who feels emotion caused by this man's death,' said Scrooge quite agonised, 'show that person to me, Spirit, I beseech you.'

The phantom spread its dark robe before him for a moment, like a wing; and withdrawing it, revealed a room by daylight, where a mother and her children were.

She was expecting someone, and with anxious eagerness; for she walked up and down the room; started at every sound; looked out from the window; glanced at the clock; tried, but in vain, to work with her needle; and could hardly bear the voices of the children in their play.

At length the long-expected knock was heard. She hurried to the door, and met her husband; a man whose face was careworn and depressed, though he was young. There was a remarkable expression in it now; a kind of serious delight of which he felt ashamed, and which he struggled to repress.

He sat down to the dinner that had been hoarding for him by the fire; and when she asked him faintly what news (which was not until after a long silence), he appeared embarrassed how to answer.

'Is it good?' she said, 'or bad?' – to help him.

'Bad,' he answered.

'We are quite ruined!'

'No. There is hope yet, Caroline.'

'If *he* relents,' she said, amazed, 'there is. Nothing is past hope, if such a miracle has happened!'

'He is past relenting,' said her husband. 'He is dead.'

She was a mild and patient creature if her face spoke truth; but she was thankful in her soul to hear it, and she said so, with clasped hands. She prayed forgiveness the next moment, and was sorry; but the first was the emotion of her heart.

'What the half-drunken woman whom I told you of last night, said to me, when I tried to see him and obtain a week's delay; and what I thought was a mere excuse to avoid me; turns out to have been quite true. He was not only very ill, but dying, then.'

'To whom will our debt be transferred?'

'I don't know. But before that time we shall be ready with the money; and even though we were not, it would be a bad fortune indeed to find so merciless a creditor in his successor. We may sleep tonight with light hearts, Caroline.'

Yes. Soften it as they would, their hearts were lighter. The children's faces, hushed and clustered round to hear what they so little understood, were brighter; and it was a happier house for this man's death. The only emotion that the ghost could show him, caused by the event, was one of pleasure.

'Let me see some tenderness connected with a death,' said Scrooge, 'or that dark chamber, Spirit, which we left just now, will be for ever present to me.'

The ghost conducted him through several streets familiar to his feet; and as they went along, Scrooge looked here and there to find himself, but nowhere was he to be seen. They entered poor Bob Cratchit's house; the dwelling he had visited before; and found the mother and the children seated round the fire.

Quiet. Very quiet. The noisy little Cratchits were as still as statues in one corner, and sat looking up at Peter, who had a book before him. The mother and her daughters were engaged in sewing. But surely they were very quiet.

'And he took a child, and set him in the midst of them.'

Where had Scrooge heard those words? He had not dreamed them. The boy must have read them out, as he and the spirit crossed the threshold. Why did he not go on?

The mother laid her work upon the table, and put her hand up to her face.

'The colour hurts my eyes,' she said.

The colour! Ah, poor Tiny Tim.

'They're better now again,' said Cratchit's wife. 'It makes them weak by candlelight; and I wouldn't show weak eyes to your father when he comes home, for the world. It must be near his time.'

'Past it rather,' Peter answered, shutting up his book. 'But I think he has walked a little slower than he used, these few last evenings, mother.'

They were very quiet again. At last she said, and in a steady, cheerful voice, that only faltered once: 'I have known him walk with – I have known him walk with Tiny Tim upon his shoulder, very fast indeed.'

'And so have I,' cried Peter. 'Often.'

'And so have I,' exclaimed another. So had all.

'But he was very light to carry,' she resumed, intent upon her work, 'and his father loved him so, that it was no trouble: no trouble. And there is your father at the door.'

She hurried out to meet him; and little Bob in his comforter – he had need of it, poor fellow – came in. His tea was ready for him on the hob, and they all tried who should help him to it most. Then the two young Cratchits got upon his knees and laid, each child a little cheek, against his face, as if they said, 'Don't mind it, father. Don't be grieved.'

Bob was very cheerful with them, and spoke pleasantly to all the family. He looked at the work upon the table, and praised the industry and speed of Mrs Cratchit and the girls. They would be done long before Sunday, he said.

'Sunday! You went today, then, Robert?' said his wife.

'Yes, my dear,' returned Bob. 'I wish you could have gone. It would have done you good to see how green a place it is. But you'll see it often. I promised him that I would walk there on a Sunday. My little, little child!' cried Bob. 'My little child!'

He broke down all at once. He couldn't help it. If he could have helped it, he and his child would have been farther apart perhaps than they were.

He left the room, and went upstairs into the room above, which was lighted cheerfully, and hung with Christmas. There was a chair set close beside the child, and there were signs of someone having been there, lately. Poor Bob sat down in it, and when he had thought a little and composed himself, he kissed the little face. He was reconciled to what had happened, and went down again quite happy.

They drew about the fire, and talked; the girls and mother working still. Bob told them of the extraordinary kindness of Mr Scrooge's nephew, whom he had scarcely seen but once, and who, meeting him in the street that day, and seeing that he looked a little – 'just a little down you know,' said Bob, enquired what had happened to distress him. 'On which,' said Bob, 'for he is the pleasantest-spoken gentleman you ever heard, I told him. "I am heartily sorry for it, Mr Cratchit," he said, "and heartily sorry for your good wife." By the by, how he ever knew *that*, I don't know.'

'Knew what, my dear?'

'Why, that you were a good wife,' replied Bob.

'Everybody knows that,' said Peter.

'Very well observed, my boy!' cried Bob. 'I hope they do. "Heartily sorry," he said, "for your good wife. If I can be of service to you in any way," he said, giving me his card, "that's where I live. Pray come to me." Now, it wasn't,' cried Bob, 'for the sake of anything he might be able to do for us, so much as for his kind way, that this was quite delightful. It really seemed as if he had known our Tiny Tim, and felt with us.'

'I'm sure he's a good soul,' said Mrs Cratchit.

'You would be surer of it, my dear,' returned Bob, 'if you saw and spoke to him. I shouldn't be at all surprised – mark what I say – if he got Peter a better situation.'

'Only hear that, Peter,' said Mrs Cratchit.

'And then,' cried one of the girls, 'Peter will be keeping company with someone, and setting up for himself.'

'Get along with you,' retorted Peter, grinning.

'It's just as likely as not,' said Bob, 'one of these days; though there's plenty of time for that, my dear. But however and when-ever we part from one another, I am sure we shall none of us forget poor Tiny Tim – shall we – or this first parting that there was among us.'

'Never, father!' cried they all.

'And I know,' said Bob, 'I know, my dears, that when we recollect how patient and how mild he was; although he was a little, little child; we shall not quarrel easily among ourselves, and forget poor Tiny Tim in doing it.'

'No, never, father!' they all cried again.

'I am very happy,' said little Bob, 'I am very happy.'

Mrs Cratchit kissed him, his daughters kissed him, the two young Cratchits kissed him, and Peter and himself shook hands. Spirit of Tiny Tim, thy childish essence was from God.

'Spectre,' said Scrooge, 'something informs me that our parting moment is at hand. I know it, but I know not how. Tell me what man that was whom we saw lying dead.'

The Ghost of Christmas Yet to Come conveyed him, as before – though at a different time, he thought: indeed, there seemed no order in these latter visions, save that they were in the future – into the resorts of business men, but showed him not himself. Indeed, the spirit did not stay for anything, but went straight on, as to the end just now desired, until besought by Scrooge to tarry for a moment.

'This court,' said Scrooge, 'through which we hurry now, is where my place of occupation is, and has been for a length of time. I see the house. Let me behold what I shall be, in days to come.'

The spirit stopped; the hand was pointed elsewhere.

'The house is yonder,' Scrooge exclaimed. 'Why do you point away?'

The inexorable finger underwent no change.

Scrooge hastened to the window of his office, and looked in. It was an office still, but not his. The furniture was not the same, and the figure in the chair was not himself. The phantom pointed as before.

He joined it once again, and wondering why and whither he had gone, accompanied it until they reached an iron gate. He paused to look round before entering.

A churchyard. Here, then, the wretched man whose name he had now to learn, lay underneath the ground. It was a worthy place. Walled in by houses; overrun by grass and weeds, the growth of vegetation's death, not life; choked up with too much burying; fat with repleted appetite. A worthy place.

The spirit stood among the graves, and pointed down to one. He advanced towards it trembling. The phantom was exactly as it had been, but he dreaded that he saw new meaning in its solemn shape.

'Before I draw nearer to that stone to which you point,' said Scrooge, 'answer me one question. Are these the shadows of the things that Will be, or are they shadows of things that May be, only?'

Still the ghost pointed downward to the grave by which it stood.

'Men's courses will foreshadow certain ends, to which, if persevered in, they must lead,' said Scrooge. 'But if the courses be departed from, the ends will change. Say it is thus with what you show me!'

The spirit was immovable as ever.

Scrooge crept towards it, trembling as he went; and following the finger, read upon the stone of the neglected grave his own name:

EBENEZER SCROOGE.

'Am *I* that man who lay upon the bed?' he cried, upon his knees.

The finger pointed from the grave to him, and back again.

'No, Spirit. Oh no, no!'

The finger still was there.

'Spirit!' he cried, tight clutching at its robe, 'hear me. I am not the man I was! I will not be the man I must have been but for this intercourse! Why show me this, if I am past all hope?'

For the first time the hand appeared to shake.

'Good Spirit!' he pursued, as down upon the ground he fell before it: 'Your nature intercedes for me, and pities me. Assure me that I yet may change these shadows you have shown me, by an altered life!'

The kind hand trembled.

'I will honour Christmas in my heart, and try to keep it all the year. I will live in the past, the present, and the future. The spirits of all three shall strive within me. I will not shut out the lessons that they teach. Oh, tell me I may sponge away the writing on this stone!'

In his agony, he caught the spectral hand. It sought to free itself, but he was strong in his entreaty, and detained it. The spirit, stronger yet, repulsed him.

Holding up his hands in a last prayer to have his fate reversed, he saw an alteration in the phantom's hood and dress. It shrank, collapsed, and dwindled down into a bedpost.

STAVE 5

The End of It

Yes! and the bedpost was his own. The bed was his own, the room was his own. Best and happiest of all, the time before him was his own, to make amends in!

'I will live in the past, the present, and the future!' Scrooge repeated, as he scrambled out of bed. 'The spirits of all three shall strive within me. Oh, Jacob Marley, Heaven, and the Christmastime be praised for this. I say it on my knees, old Jacob, on my knees.'

He was so fluttered and so glowing with his good intentions, that his broken voice would scarcely answer to his call. He had been sobbing violently in his conflict with the spirit, and his face was wet with tears.

'They are not torn down!' cried Scrooge, folding one of his bed-curtains in his arms, 'they are not torn down, rings and all. They are here – I am here – the shadows of the things that would have been, may be dispelled. They will be! I know they will.'

His hands were busy with his garments all this time; turning them inside out, putting them on upside down, tearing them, mislaying them, making them parties to every kind of extravagance.

'I don't know what to do!' cried Scrooge, laughing and crying in the same breath; and making a perfect Laocoön of himself with his stockings. 'I am as light as a feather, I am as happy as an angel, I am as merry as a schoolboy! I am as giddy as a drunken man! A merry Christmas to everybody! A happy New Year to all the world! Hallo here! Whoop! Hallo!'

He had frisked into the sitting-room, and was now standing there: perfectly winded.

'There's the saucepan that the gruel was in,' cried Scrooge, starting off again, and going round the fireplace. 'There's the door, by which the ghost of Jacob Marley entered. There's the corner where the Ghost of Christmas Present sat. There's the window where I saw the wandering spirits. It's all right, it's all true, it all happened! Ha, ha, ha!'

Really, for a man who had been out of practice for so many years, it was a splendid laugh, a most illustrious laugh. The father of a long, long line of brilliant laughs.

'I don't know what day of the month it is,' said Scrooge. 'I don't know how long I've been among the spirits. I don't know anything. I'm quite a baby! Never mind. I don't care. I'd rather be a baby! Hallo! Whoop! Hallo here!'

He was checked in his transports by the churches ringing out the lustiest peals he had ever heard. Clash, clang, hammer; ding, dong, bell! Bell, dong, ding; hammer, clang, clash. Oh, glorious, glorious!

Running to the window, he opened it, and put out his head. No fog, no mist; clear, bright, jovial, stirring, cold; cold, piping for the blood to dance to; golden sunlight; heavenly sky; sweet fresh air; merry bells. Oh, glorious. Glorious!

'What's today?' cried Scrooge, calling downward to a boy in Sunday clothes, who perhaps had loitered in to look about him.

'Eh?' returned the boy, with all his might of wonder.

'What's today, my fine fellow?' said Scrooge.

'Today?' replied the boy. 'Why, Christmas Day!'

'It's Christmas Day!' said Scrooge to himself. 'I haven't missed it! The spirits have done it all in one night. They can do anything they like. Of course they can. Of course they can. Hallo, my fine fellow!'

'Hallo!' returned the boy.

'Do you know the poulterer's, in the next street but one, at the corner?' Scrooge enquired.

'I should hope I did,' replied the lad.

'An intelligent boy!' said Scrooge. 'A remarkable boy. Do you know whether they've sold the prize turkey that was hanging up there – Not the little prize turkey: the big one?'

'What, the one as big as me?' returned the boy.

'What a delightful boy!' said Scrooge. 'It's a pleasure to talk to him. Yes, my buck!'

'It's hanging there now,' replied the boy.

'Is it!' said Scrooge. 'Go and buy it!'

'Walk–er!' exclaimed the boy.

'No, no,' said Scrooge, 'I am in earnest. Go and buy it, and tell them to bring it here, that I may give them the direction where to take it. Come back with the man, and I'll give you a shilling. Come back with him in less than five minutes and I'll give you half a crown!'

The boy was off like a shot. He must have had a steady hand at a trigger who could have got a shot off half so fast.

'I'll send it to Bob Cratchit's,' whispered Scrooge, rubbing his hands, and splitting with a laugh. 'He shan't know who sent it. It's twice the size of Tiny Tim. Joe Miller never made such a joke as sending it to Bob's will be.'

The hand in which he wrote the address was not a steady one, but write it he did, somehow, and went downstairs to open the street door, ready for the coming of the poulterer's man. As he stood there, waiting his arrival, the knocker caught his eye.

'I shall love it, as long as I live,' cried Scrooge, patting it with his hand. 'I scarcely ever looked at it before. What an honest expression it has in its face! It's a wonderful knocker! – Here's the turkey! Hallo! Whoop! How are you? Merry Christmas!'

It *was* a turkey. He never could have stood upon his legs, that bird. He would have snapped them short off in a minute, like sticks of sealing-wax.

'Why, it's impossible to carry that to Camden Town,' said Scrooge. 'You must have a cab.'

The chuckle with which he said this, and the chuckle with which he paid for the turkey, and the chuckle with which he paid for the cab, and the chuckle with which he recompensed the boy, were only to be exceeded by the chuckle with which he sat down breathless in his chair again, and chuckled till he cried.

Shaving was not an easy task, for his hand continued to shake very much; and shaving requires attention, even when you don't dance while you are at it. But if he had cut the end of his nose off, he would have put a piece of sticking-plaster over it, and been quite satisfied.

He dressed himself all in his best, and at last got out into the streets. The people were by this time pouring forth, as he had seen them with the Ghost of Christmas Present; and walking with his hands behind him, Scrooge regarded everyone with a delighted smile. He looked so irresistibly pleasant, in a word, that three or four good-humoured fellows said, 'Good-morning, sir. A merry Christmas to you!' And Scrooge said often afterwards, that of all the blithe sounds he had ever heard, those were the blithest in his ears.

He had not gone far, when coming on towards him he beheld the portly gentleman, who had walked into his counting-house the day before, and said, 'Scrooge and Marley's, I believe.' It sent a pang across his heart to think how this old gentleman would look upon him when they met; but he knew what path lay straight before him, and he took it.

'My dear sir,' said Scrooge, quickening his pace, and taking the old gentleman by both his hands. 'How do you do? I hope you succeeded yesterday. It was very kind of you. A merry Christmas to you, sir.'

'Mr Scrooge?'

'Yes,' said Scrooge. 'That is my name, and I fear it may not be pleasant to you. Allow me to ask your pardon. And will you have the goodness' – here Scrooge whispered in his ear.

'Lord bless me!' cried the gentleman, as if his breath were taken away. 'My dear Mr Scrooge, are you serious?'

'If you please,' said Scrooge. 'Not a farthing less. A great many back-payments are included in it, I assure you. Will you do me that favour?'

'My dear sir,' said the other, shaking hands with him. 'I don't know what to say to such munificence.'

'Don't say anything, please,' retorted Scrooge. 'Come and see me. Will you come and see me?'

'I will!' cried the old gentleman. And it was clear he meant to do it.

'Thank you,' said Scrooge. 'I am much obliged to you. I thank you fifty times. Bless you!'

He went to church, and walked about the streets, and watched the people hurrying to and fro, and patted children on the head, and questioned beggars, and looked down into the kitchens of houses, and up to the windows, and found that everything could yield him pleasure. He had never dreamed that any walk – that anything – could give him so much happiness. In the afternoon he turned his steps towards his nephew's house.

He passed the door a dozen times, before he had the courage to go up and knock. But he made a dash, and did it: 'Is your master at home, my dear?' said Scrooge to the girl. Nice girl. Very.

'Yes, sir.'

'Where is he, my love?' said Scrooge.

'He's in the dining-room, sir, along with mistress. I'll show you upstairs, if you please.'

'Thank you. He knows me,' said Scrooge, with his hand already on the dining-room lock. 'I'll go in here, my dear.'

He turned it gently, and sidled his face in, round the door. They were looking at the table (which was spread out in great array); for these young housekeepers are always nervous on such points, and like to see that everything is right.

'Fred,' said Scrooge.

Dear heart alive, how his niece by marriage started. Scrooge had forgotten, for the moment, about her sitting in the corner with the footstool, or he wouldn't have done it, on any account.

'Why bless my soul!' cried Fred, 'Who's that?'

'It's I. Your uncle Scrooge. I have come to dinner. Will you let me in, Fred?'

Let him in! It is a mercy he didn't shake his arm off! He was at home in five minutes. Nothing could be heartier. His niece looked just the same. So did Topper when *he* came. So did the plump sister when *she* came. So did everyone when *they* came. Wonderful party, wonderful games, wonderful unanimity, won--der–ful happiness.

But he was early at the office next morning. Oh, he was early there. If he could only be there first, and catch Bob Cratchit coming late. That was the thing he had set his heart upon.

And he did it; yes, he did. The clock struck nine. No Bob. A quarter past. No Bob. He was full eighteen minutes and a half behind his time. Scrooge sat with his door wide open, that he might see him come into the tank.

His hat was off, before he opened the door; his comforter too. He was on his stool in a jiffy; driving away with his pen, as if he were trying to overtake nine o'clock.

'Hallo!' growled Scrooge, in his accustomed voice, as near as he could feign it. 'What do you mean by coming here at this time of day?'

'I am very sorry, sir,' said Bob. 'I *am* behind my time.'

'You are,' repeated Scrooge. 'Yes. I think you are. Step this way, sir, if you please.'

'It's only once a year, sir,' pleaded Bob, appearing from the tank. 'It shall not be repeated. I was making rather merry yesterday, sir.'

'Now, I'll tell you what, my friend,' said Scrooge, 'I am not going to stand this sort of thing any longer. And therefore,' he continued, leaping from his stool, and giving Bob such a dig in the waistcoat that he staggered back into the tank again: 'and therefore I am about to raise your salary.'

Bob trembled, and got a little nearer to the ruler. He had a momentary idea of knocking Scrooge down with it, holding him, and calling to the people in the court for help and a strait-waistcoat.

'A merry Christmas, Bob,' said Scrooge, with an earnestness that could not be mistaken, as he clapped him on the back. 'A merrier Christmas, Bob, my good fellow, than I have given you for many a year! I'll raise your salary, and endeavour to assist your struggling family, and we will discuss your affairs this very afternoon, over a Christmas bowl of smoking bishop, Bob. Make up the fires, and buy another coal-scuttle before you dot another i, Bob Cratchit.'

Scrooge was better than his word. He did it all, and infinitely more; and to Tiny Tim, who did not die, he was a second father. He became as good a friend, as good a master, and as good a man, as the good old city knew, or any other good old city, town, or borough, in the good old world. Some people laughed to see the alteration in him, but he let them laugh, and little heeded them; for he was wise enough to know that nothing ever happened on this globe, for good, at which some people did not have their fill of laughter in the outset; and knowing that such as these would be blind anyway, he thought it quite as well that they should wrinkle up their eyes in grins, as have the malady in less attractive forms. His own heart laughed: and that was quite enough for him.

He had no further intercourse with spirits, but lived upon the total abstinence principle, ever afterwards; and it was always said of him, that he knew how to keep Christmas well, if any man alive possessed the knowledge. May that be truly said of us, and all of us! And so, as Tiny Tim observed, God bless us, everyone!